175°

For Bill
with best wishes
for David

The Faber Book of
Twentieth-Century Scottish Poetry

The Faber Book of
TWENTIETH-CENTURY
SCOTTISH POETRY

Edited by DOUGLAS DUNN

faber and faber

LONDON · BOSTON

First published in Great Britain in 1992
by Faber and Faber Limited
3 Queen Square London WC1N 3AU

Photoset by Wilmaset Ltd, Wirral
Printed in England by Clays Ltd, St Ives plc

The publisher acknowledges a subsidy from the Scottish Arts
Council towards the publication of this volume.

A CIP record for this book
is available from the British Library

ISBN 0-571-15431-X

Contents

Language and Liberty   Douglas Dunn, xvii

JOHN DAVIDSON (1857–1909)
  Snow, 3

VIOLET JACOB (1863–1946)
  The Baltic, 6

MARION ANGUS (1866–1946)
  Alas! Poor Queen, 7

LEWIS SPENCE (1874–1955)
  The Prows O' Reekie, 9
  The Carse, 9
  Great Tay of the Waves, 10
  The Stown Bairn, 10

RACHEL ANNAND TAYLOR (1876–1960)
  The Princess of Scotland, 12

SIR ALEXANDER GRAY (1882–1967)
  Scotland, 13

ANDREW YOUNG (1885–1971)
  On the Pilgrims' Road, 15
  The Stockdoves, 15
  A Heap of Faggots, 16
  A Prehistoric Camp, 16
  Passing the Graveyard, 17
  Sudden Thaw, 17
  The Shepherd's Hut, 18

HELEN B. CRUICKSHANK (1886–1975)
  The Ponnage Pool, 19

EDWIN MUIR (1887–1959)
  Childhood, 21
  The Town Betrayed, 21
  Scotland 1941, 23
  The Ring, 24
  The Castle, 25

The Labyrinth, 26
The Combat, 28
One Foot in Eden, 29
To Franz Kafka, 30
The Difficult Land, 31
The Horses, 32

HUGH MACDIARMID (Christopher Murray Grieve)
(1892–1978)
The Bonnie Broukit Bairn, 35
The Watergaw, 35
The Eemis Stane, 35
Scunner, 36
Empty Vessel, 36
from A Drunk Man Looks at the Thistle, 37
    Man and the Infinite, 38
    O Wha's the Bride?, 39
    Repetition Complex, 40
    The Problem Child, 41
    The Thistle's Characteristics, 41
    A Stick-Nest in Ygdrasil, 42
    Farewell to Dostoevsky, 45
    The Great Wheel, 46
First Hymn to Lenin, 49
Water Music, 51
Ho, My Little Sparrow, 55
On a Raised Beach, 56
Harry Semen, 68

WILLIAM SOUTAR (1898–1943)
The Tryst, 71
The Guns, 71
The Hungry Mauchs, 72
Song, 73
The Makar, 73

WILLIAM MONTGOMERIE (b. 1904)
The Edge of the War, 74

NORMAN CAMERON (1905–53)
She and I, 77
Forgive Me, Sire, 77

A Visit to the Dead, 77
Green, Green, is El Aghir, 78

ROBERT GARIOCH (Robert Garioch Sutherland)
(1909–81)
  Embro to the Ploy, 80
  To Robert Fergusson, 84
  The Wire, 92
  Property, 97
  Glisk of the Great, 98
  Heard in the Cougate, 99
  At Robert Fergusson's Grave, 99
  Elegy, 100
  In Princes Street Gairdens, 101
  Merulius Lacrymans, 101

NORMAN MACCAIG (b. 1910)
  Summer Farm, 103
  Drifter, 103
  Crofter's Kitchen, Evening, 104
  Half-built Boat in a Hayfield, 105
  Explicit Snow, 105
  Celtic Cross, 106
  Feeding Ducks, 107
  Things in Each Other, 107
  The Shore Road, 108
  Byre, 109
  Loch Sionascaig, 109
  July Evening, 110
  Porpoises, 110
  Looking Down on Glen Canisp, 111
  Blue Tit on a String of Peanuts, 112
  Old Edinburgh, 112
  Basking Shark, 113
  Intruder in a Set Scene, 113
  No Interims in History, 114

SOMHAIRLE MACGILL-EAIN/SORLEY MACLEAN
(b. 1911)
  Gaoir na h-Eòrpa/The Cry of Europe, 115/116
  Am Bata Dubh/The Black Boat, 117/117

Ban-Ghàidheal/*A Highland Woman*, 118/119
Calbharaigh/*Calvary* and *My Een Are Nae on
    Calvary*, 120/120 and 120
Clann Ghill-Eain/*The Clan MacLean*, 121/121
Dol an Iar/*Going Westwards*, 122/123
Glac a' Bhàis/*Death Valley*, 125/126
Curaidhean/*Heroes*, 127/128
Hallaig/*Hallaig*, 129/131

SYDNEY TREMAYNE (1912–86)
  Legend, 134
  A Burial, 135
  Wanting News, 136

DOUGLAS YOUNG (1913–73)
  For a Wife in Jizzen, 137
  Sainless, 137
  The Shepherd's Dochter, 138

RUTHVEN TODD (1914–78)
  Trout Flies, 140
  Of Moulds and Mushrooms, 141

G. S. FRASER (1914–80)
  Lean Street, 144
  Home Town Elegy, 144

SYDNEY GOODSIR SMITH (1915–75)
  from Armageddon in Albyn, 146
    I El Alamein, 146
    II The Mither's Lament, 146
    VII The War in Fife, 147
  The Grace of God and the Meth-Drinker, 148
  Time Be Brief, 149
  Omens, 150
  Aa My Life, 151
  from Under the Eildon Tree, 152
    V Slugabed, 152

DEORSA CAIMBEUL HAY/GEORGE CAMPBELL HAY
(1915–84)
  Bisearta/*Bizerta*, 154/155
  Atman/*Atman*, 156/157

To a Loch Fyne Fisherman, 159

W. S. GRAHAM (1918–86)
The Children of Greenock, 160
from Seven Letters – II and VI, 161 and 164
Baldy Bane, 164
Malcolm Mooney's Land, 170
The Lying Dear, 174
The Night City, 175
Johann Joachim Quantz's Five Lessons, 176
The Stepping Stones, 179

TOM SCOTT (b. 1918)
The Mankind Toun, 180

MURIEL SPARK (b. 1918)
Going up to Sotheby's, 182
Against the Transcendentalists, 184
Elegy in a Kensington Churchyard, 185
Litany of Time Past, 186

ELMA MITCHELL (b. 1919)
Thoughts after Ruskin, 187

HAMISH HENDERSON (b. 1919)
Seventh Elegy, 189
Seven Good Germans, 189

ALEXANDER SCOTT (1920–89)
Coronach, 193

EDWIN MORGAN (b. 1920)
The Starlings in George Square, 195
The Second Life, 197
Glasgow Sonnets, 199
The First Men on Mercury, 203
Cinquevalli, 205
The Dowser, 207
from Sonnets from Scotland, 208
Pilate at Fortingall, 208
De Quincey in Glasgow, 209
Post-Referendum, 209
After a Death, 209

The Coin, 210

RUARAIDH MACTHOMAIS/DERICK THOMSON
(b. 1921)
   Dà Thaibhse/*Two Ghosts*, 211/211
   An Tobar/*The Well*, 212/213
   Srath Nabhair/*Strathnaver*, 214/214
   Eilean Chaluim Chille, an Loch Eiriosort, Leòdhas/
      St Columba's Isle, Loch Erisort, Lewis, 215/216
   Clann-Nighean an Sgadain/*The Herring Girls*,
      216/217
   Dùn Nan Gall/*Donegal*, 218/219
   Cisteachan-Laighe/*Coffins*, 219/220
   An Dàrna Eilean/*The Second Island*, 221/222

GEORGE MACKAY BROWN (b. 1921)
   The Funeral of Ally Flett, 223
   Old Fisherman with Guitar, 224
   Trout Fisher, 225
   Hamnavoe Market, 226
   The Five Voyages of Arnor, 227
   Kirkyard, 228
   Taxman, 229
   from Runes from a Holy Island, 229
   Beachcomber, 230
   Island School, 231

WILLIAM NEILL (b. 1922)
   Map Makers, 232
   De A Thug Ort Sgriobhadh Ghaidhlig?/*What
      Compelled You to Write in Gaelic?*, 232/234

IVOR CUTLER (b. 1923)
   The Purposeful Culinary Implements, 237
   The Darkness, 238
   The Railway Sleepers, 238

G. F. DUTTON (b. 1924)
   street, 240
   clach eanchainn, 240

ALASTAIR MACKIE (b. 1925)
   from Back-Green Odyssey, 242

ALASTAIR REID (b. 1926)
  A Lesson for Beautiful Women, 245
  Scotland, 246
  Isle of Arran, 246
  James Bottle's Year, 247

ALASDAIR MACLEAN (b. 1926)
  Death of an Old Woman, 249
  Home Thoughts from Home, 249
  Waking the Dead, 250
  The Rain, 251

IAIN CRICHTON SMITH (b. 1928)
  The Clearances, 252
  Highlanders, 252
  Poem in March, 253
  The Law and the Grace, 253
  from By the Sea, 254
  from The White Air of March, 257
  Gaelic Stories, 260
  Shall Gaelic Die?, 262
  Gaelic Songs, 264
  Christmas 1971, 265
  The Glass of Water, 265
  How Often I Feel Like You, 266
  Chinese Poem, 267
  from A Life, 269
  Listen, 273

BURNS SINGER (1928–64)
  A Sort of Language, 274
  Peterhead in May, 274
  For Josef Herman, 275
  SOS Lifescene, 276

ALASTAIR FOWLER (b. 1930)
  Catacomb Suburb, 279
  Relative, 280

GEORGE MACBETH (1932–92)
  An Ode to English Food, 282
  The Renewal, 284

Draft for an Ancestor, 286

ALASDAIR GRAY (b. 1934)
Awakening, 288

CHRISTOPHER SALVESEN (b. 1935)
Ninian Winyet, 289
History of Strathclyde, 290
Among the Goths, 291

KENNETH WHITE (b. 1936)
The House at the Head of the Tide, 293
from Late August on the Coast, 296
A Short Introduction to White Poetics, 296

STEWART CONN (b. 1936)
Todd, 299
On Craigie Hill, 299
The Yard, 300
Summer Afternoon, 301
To My Father, 302
Under the Ice, 303

WILLIAM MCILVANNEY (b. 1936)
Bless This House, 304
The Song Mickey Heard at the Bottom of his Pint
in the Zodiac Bar, 305
Passing Through Petra, 305

ROBIN FULTON (b. 1937)
Remembering an Island, 307
Travelling Alone, 307
Museums and Journeys, 308
Stopping by Shadows, 308
Resolutions, 309
Remembering Walls, 309

D. M. BLACK (b. 1941)
From the Privy Council, 311
Kew Gardens, 312

AONGHAS MACNEACAIL (b. 1942)
dol dhachaigh – 2/*going home* – 2, 314/314
gleann fadamach/*glen remote*, 315/316

from an cathadh mor/from *the great snowbattle*,
316/318

ALAN BOLD (b. 1943)
June 1967 at Buchenwald, 320
Grass, 323
A Special Theory of Relativity, 323
Love-Lowe, 324
The Auld Symie, 325

ALISON FELL (b. 1944)
Desire, 326
Pushing Forty, 327
Freeze-frame, 327

IAN ABBOT (1944–89)
The Mechanisms of the Gin, 329
A Body of Work, 329

TOM LEONARD (b. 1944)
Six Glasgow Poems, 331
The Good Thief, 331
Simple Simon, 331
Cold, isn't it, 332
A Scream, 332
The Miracle of the Burd and the Fishes, 333
Good Style, 333
Poetry, 333
Just ti Let Yi No, 334
Paroakial, 334
Feed Ma Lamz, 335
from Unrelated Incidents, 336
from Ghostie Men, 339
Fathers and Sons, 340

VERONICA FORREST-THOMSON (1947–75)
Strike, 341

LIZ LOCHHEAD (b. 1947)
Dreaming Frankenstein, 344
Heartbreak Hotel, 345
Mirror's Song, 347
The Grim Sisters, 348

from The Furies
  1: Harridan, 350
  My Mother's Suitors, 351

VALERIE GILLIES (b. 1948)
  Fellow Passenger, 353
  The Piano-tuner, 353
  Young Harper, 354
  The Ericstane Brooch, 355

RON BUTLIN (b. 1949)
  This Evening, 357
  Night-life, 357
  Inheritance, 357
  Claiming My Inheritance, 358

RAYMOND VETTESE (b. 1950)
  Prologue, 360
  My Carrion Words, 362
  The Vieve Cry, 363

TOM POW (b. 1950)
  from The Gift of Sight
    Saint Medan, 364

BRIAN MCCABE (b. 1951)
  Spring's Witch, 367
  The Blind, 367
  This is Thursday, 368

GERALD MANGAN (b. 1951)
  Glasgow 1956, 370
  Heraclitus at Glasgow Cross, 370
  Nights in Black Valley, 372

ANDREW GREIG (b. 1951)
  In the Tool-shed, 373
  The Winter Climbing, 374
  The Maid & I, 374

FRANK KUPPNER (b. 1951)
  Passing Through Doorways, 376

ANGUS MARTIN (b. 1952)
Malcolm MacKerral, 385
Forest, 386

JOHN GLENDAY (b. 1952)
The Apple Ghost, 388

DILYS ROSE (b. 1954)
Figurehead, 390
Fetish, 390

JOHN BURNSIDE (b. 1955)
Out of Exile, 392
Vallejo, 392

CAROL ANN DUFFY (b. 1955)
Politico, 394
Plainsong, 394
In Your Mind, 395

MICK IMLAH (b. 1956)
Goldilocks, 397

ROBERT CRAWFORD (b. 1959)
Scotland in the 1890s, 401
Rain, 401
The Herr-Knit Bunnet, 402

W. N. HERBERT (b. 1961)
Coco-de-Mer, 405
The Derelict Birth, 405
Cormundum, 405

KATHLEEN JAMIE (b. 1962)
Black Spiders, 408
Aunt Janet's Museum, 408
The Way We Live, 409

Acknowledgements, 411
Index of Poets, 417
Index of Titles, 419

Language and Liberty

The first part of the history of Scottish literature is part of the history of English literature when English was several dialects; the second part is part of the history of English literature when English was two dialects – English and Scots; the third part is something quite different – it is the history of a provincial literature. And finally, there is no longer any tenable distinction to be drawn for the present day between the two literatures. (T. S. ELIOT, 'Was There a Scottish Literature?' *The Atheneum*, 1 August 1919)

Seldom can Max Weinreich's famous aphorism – 'a language is a dialect with an army and a navy' – have found such a classy illustration. Were they to appear now, Eliot's crudely potted history and questionable philology would look calculated to offend. However, in 1919, Eliot reflected the status quo of his day in politics and literature. Few Scottish readers would have felt irked, as if by a snub, while the book he was reviewing, G. Gregory Smith's *Scottish Literature: Character and Influence*,* went some way towards encouraging Eliot's decisions. Smith interpreted the vernacular Scots poetry of Ramsay, Fergusson and Burns as the last kick of a vividly indigenous Scottish poetry. Indeed, many Scottish readers would have supported Eliot's defensively British (or English) post-war anxiety before the threat of European cultural disintegration.

At almost exactly the same time as Eliot deliberated on Scottish literature as a meaningless phrase, Christopher Murray Grieve (better known as Hugh Mac-Diarmid, the pseudonym he adopted in 1922) was demobbed from the Royal Army Medical Corps when not far off his twenty-seventh birthday. Although in the kindliest of military corps, Grieve had participated in a World War, fought, or so it was believed, for the rights of small nations, and, in the process, grown aware of his own country. An articulate, political (as opposed to sentimental) Scottish nationalism still lay a few years in the future. Grieve's national awareness was first of all one of a country in a state of cultural stagnation and contented provincialism. Grieve (b. 1892) and Edwin Muir (b. 1889) were contemporaneous with modernism's early adventures. Deplorable as the local literary condition was – things were more interesting in painting and architecture – neither Grieve nor Muir was insulated from European literature and ideas.

We Moderns,† Muir's collection of aphorisms (published under the pseudonym Edward Moore), could be hailed as the first publication in modern Scottish literature after the death of Scotland's proto-modernist, John Davidson, in 1909.

* Macmillan, 1919.
† George Allen & Unwin, 1918.

That is, if the book deserved it in anything other than a bibliographical sense. Muir was to disown it as 'pinchbeck Nietzschean prose peppered with exclamation marks'. It is easy to see why. Equality and humility, for example, were dismissed as 'great fosterers of the mediocre'. It was to be around these and similar qualities that Muir would later form his personality and work. Grieve, however, was to cultivate Nietzschean cerebral solitude and super-élitism as a platform for the lofty intellectual superstructure of his alter ego, Hugh MacDiarmid. It is tempting to think that Muir and Grieve parted company in advance of meeting.

Weariness of immediate resources and lack of predecessors are suggested by the sort of thing Grieve was writing in April 1918:

> The ancient chorus of the rich blue flood,
>   The mystic sundance of the Middle Seas,
> What have you in your heart, Scots Borderman,
>   Prithee, that can compare with these?

If he had been reading John Davidson's later poetry (and it is almost certain he had), then it made little impact on Grieve's own until some time later.

In his 1919 review Eliot wrote that:

The historian of literature must count with as shifting and massive forces as the historian of politics. In the modern world the struggle of capitals of civilization is apparent on a large scale. A powerful literature, with a powerful capital, tends to attract and absorb all the drifting shreds of force about it. Up to a certain limit of dissimilarity, this fusion is of very great value. English and Scottish, probably English and Irish (if not prevented by political friction), are cognate enough for the union to be of value. The basis for one literature is one language.

That finely crafted detail – 'Up to a certain limit of dissimilarity' – expresses perfectly the established attitude that MacDiarmid determined to contest. Scottish culture had become provincial because a nation had allowed itself to become a province. A return to Scottish principles of poetry and thought was therefore understood by MacDiarmid to be necessary. After a few attempts at poetry in the Scots vernacular – at first, MacDiarmid thought little could come of these experiments – he realized that the language of his poetry should externalize the Scottishness of his mind and imagination. Dissimilarity was, therefore, to be cultivated in a language that would take him beyond conventional Scottish wisdom as expressed in Stevenson's phrase, 'a strong Scotch accent of the mind'. Eliot sketched Scottish literature in four phases, the last being its assimilation into English literature. For several productive years, marked with fiery self-awareness, Grieve/MacDiarmid set himself to create what, in Eliot's terms, amounts to a *fifth* phase. As well as a loathing of the provincial, an even more remarkable instinct lies at the heart of MacDiarmid's struggle. It is nothing less than the recovery of a distinctive Scottish psyche and its true objectives and concerns from the slow sundering initiated by the Union of 1707. It is hard to see how such a feat of psychological archaeology was supposed to have been feasible. Clearly, though, in MacDiarmid's poetry in Scots, and in the work of the poets he inspired, it was the ideal that mattered. The desire to reconstruct a national identity was never matched by an accurate expression of what that identity might be outside of poetry and philosophy. *Political* nationalism turned out to be a phenomenon of more recent times.

Sangschaw, MacDiarmid's firt collection of lyrics, appeared in 1925. *A Drunk Man Looks at the Thistle* and *Penny Wheep* came out the following year. Other poets were also writing in Scots and had appeared in *The Scottish Chapbook*,* which Grieve founded and edited and where he began to proselytize the vernacular cause. But none of them wrote with anything like MacDiarmid's intuitive philology or campaigning critical ardour. Perhaps the most remarkable aspect of MacDiarmid's first three major books (at least, with hindsight) is that his poetry remained undamaged by the extensive prose suburbs that grew around it. The same can hardly be said of his later poetry, which was invaded by prose (some of it not even his own), purposive clamour, and political extremism – although that had existed from the beginning.

MacDiarmid's poetry in Scots is different from his contemporaries', although Lewis Spence was a forerunner, and poets like Violet Jacob and Marion Angus at least helped to keep the Scots language alive. Nor is it like Stevenson's verse in Scots, Burns's, Fergusson's, Ross's or Ramsay's; and it is unlike the poetry of the Makars, William Dunbar, Robert Henryson and Gavin Douglas, whose artistry and accomplishment MacDiarmid held up as exemplary. It was not an art of simple rediscovery so much as one of transformation in the crucible of modern sensibility. Diction and cadence combine to suggest that a lapsed phonology has been restored to the Lowland Scottish voice. In MacDiarmid's best lyrics – 'The Eemis Stane' is a good example – the poetry depends on a daring, speculative image. In that poem, it is the world seen as a loose gravestone, or an unsteady boulder on which words have been inscribed, now buried beneath the moss and fame of history. The poem seems to withhold its meaning. It could evoke a poet glimpsing posterity, perhaps his own, and the vanity of having believed this

---

*Fifteen issues were published between August 1922 and November/December 1923. William Soutar, Edwin Muir and Neil Gunn were among its contributors. In retrospect, however, it looks more like a remarkable one-man show, serving to present MacDiarmid's poetry in Scots, and C. M. Grieve' s editorials.

possible. It could be the world seen as a stone book in which its written chronicles fade into the half-forgotten and incomplete. What the poet might glimpse in the sky is a vision of the human record. It is the poem's mysteriousness that is exact, not its meaning. It is a poem that persists in a state of permanent unfamiliarity.

Equally remarkable is that a stunningly modern image should be conveyed in a language that had been interrupted by history. 'The Eemis Stane' is not only a fine poem; it is a gesture through which the reader witnesses a lapsed language modifying itself in order to engage with a new aesthetic. MacDiarmid's essays and comment in *Scottish Chapbook* leave you in no doubt that he intended Scots (or the Vernacular, as he called it then) to serve a double function: modernity, and the reconstruction of a national identity fitted to inhabit the Scottish republic of which he dreamt – but no, he was not a dreamer: he was a visionary exclaimer, an urger of extremes and upheavals. In October 1922 he rediscovered in the Scots language 'unrealized qualities which correspond to "unconscious" elements of distinctively Scottish psychology.' In March 1923 he wrote that

we base our belief in the possibility of a great Scottish literary Renaissance, deriving its strength from the resources that lie latent and almost unsuspected in the Vernacular, upon the fact that the genius of our Vernacular enables us to secure with comparative ease the very effects and swift transitions which other literatures are for the most part unsuccessfully endeavouring to cultivate in languages that have a very different and inferior bias.

He also noticed a 'strong moral resemblance' between Jamieson's *Etymological Dictionary of the Scottish Language** and James Joyce's *Ulysses*.

A *vis comica* that has not yet been liberated lies bound by desuetude and misappreciation in the recesses of the Doric [Scots]; and its potential uprising would be no less prodigious, uncontrollable, and utterly at variance with conventional morality than was Joyce's tremendous outpouring.

Passionate modernism and a low opinion of the English language and its literature were united in MacDiarmid's excitable advocacy:

The Vernacular is a vast unutilized mass of lapsed observation made by minds whose attitudes to experience and whose speculative and imaginative tendencies were quite different from any possible to Englishmen and Anglicized Scots today. It is an inchoate Marcel Proust – a Dostoevskian debris of ideas – an inexhaustible quarry of subtle and significant sound.

MacDiarmid went far beyond the customary critical risk of trying to create the taste in which a new poetry could be appreciated. He leapt from his own

---

* 1808; the revised, expanded edition of 1879–82, in four volumes, is the one on the reference shelves of most Scottish libraries. There is also an abridgement in one volume ed. W. Metcalfe, 1912.

unpredictable inspiration towards the would-be deliverance of a nation-language. His action can be seen as extraordinarily generous; or it can be seen as an attempt to externalize an interior bigotry, a great heave of will, or a charge against history's facts and fences. By 'minds', 'attitudes to experience', and 'speculative and imaginative tendencies', he meant that the poet was obliged to remake Scottish poetry on the basis of a pre-1707 mentality. That is, write *as if history had never happened*; or write in such a way that history would be rewritten, and unknitted, in the work. Both, I think, are involved. But the first is a forlorn choice, and the second, to say the least, a challenge. In terms of modernism, though, it can be seen as MacDiarmid's Scottish equivalent of Pound's eccentric scholarship, Eliot's literary erudition and concern with civilization and its values, or William Carlos Williams's belief in the American Grain.

The difference is that MacDiarmid was trying to make a nation as well as poetry. He did so with a language that through disuse had become the victim of an inbuilt preterite. Vernacular, Doric, Braid Scots, Scots, Synthetic Scots, Plastic Scots, Aggrandized Scots, or Lallans, were and are (but, by and large, they are all one) instruments with which to cleanse the Scottish psyche of generations of English influence. It was for decades, and remains, a language unexposed to actual contact with changing intellectual and domestic life. It is a language with very few, if any, new words. Indeed, it is a language in which old words are used in poetry with the force of neologisms, the shock of the unfamiliar.

Synthetic Scots is a language devised to enrich its vernacular foundation through the culling of words and expressions from the dialects of the several districts of Lowland Scotland. MacDiarmid *made a language* as he wrote – not just 'an individual voice', but a language. Spontaneity might seem hampered by principles of composition that rely clearly on the patient or inspired rediscovery of apt terms from dictionaries, old poetry, field work, and childhood memory. MacDiarmid rationalized his methods in *Lucky Poet* (1943), where he stated that the act of poetry is 'the reverse of what it is usually thought to be; not an idea gradually shaping itself in words, but deriving entirely from words.' His experience of writing in synthetic Scots could have encouraged that dogmatic overstatement. It can also be associated with his beliefs about the imagination, for these, too, run counter to the usual convictions. Here he quotes P. D. Ouspensky:

. . . one of the barriers preventing us from waking up is our imagination, which intrudes constantly into our thought. Imagination runs away with our thoughts and leads a thoroughly destructive life within us. We are only able to think beyond a certain point, and this point is very soon reached. Our thoughts are then taken over by our imagination, which runs amuck with them, without direction, aim, or control. We can only stop the wasteful chase of our imagination by being attentive. The moment we are attentive the activities of our imagination cease, and thought can come into action. Imagination is a very violent destructor of energy; mental effort on the other hand stores energy.

Later in *Lucky Poet* he discloses what he held to be the imagination's more positive function. This time he quotes Kierkegaard:

The imagination is what providence uses in order to get men into reality, into existence, to get them far enough out, or in, or down in existence. And when imagination has helped them as far out as they are meant to go – that is where reality, properly speaking, begins.

By 'reality' MacDiarmid meant the place 'where the unknowable ends'.

Although *Lucky Poet* appeared after he had given up writing in synthetic Scots, an eclectic intellectualism was always massively present in MacDiarmid's mind.* It was probably that cerebral poetic passion that enabled his work in Scots to surpass its antiquarian, lexicographical trappings, with which it was always in danger of being burdened. However, it can hardly be denied that the idiom he explored is one that asks to be absolved from the usual contingencies to which languages are tied, especially that of living, quotidian usage. It is – above all – a Scottish language; but it is also devised and artificial. On the evidence of the poetry that has been written in it, it seems to resist the forms and techniques of the modernity which it was created to exploit. In terms of psychology, MacDiarmid was probably right; in terms of form (the essential modernist wager), technique, and contemporaneity of expression, he could hardly have been more wrong so far as wider usage was concerned, if not for his own poetic practice.

MacDiarmid's poetry has tended to identify his synthesized use of Scots with his notions of nationalism and politics, some of which are curious, eccentric, cruel, wilfully extreme, or poses which exploit eccentricity, cruelty and extremism. A founder member of the first nationalist party, he was later expelled for being a communist. In due course the Communist Party found his nationalism inappropriate, and he was dismissed, re-joining after the Soviet invasion of Hungary. While these knee-jerk reactions among the political parties disclose their own pathos, they say something about MacDiarmid, too. His nationalism coexisted with hard-core Stalinism, which itself had been preceded by a brief but tantalizing affair with Nazism (in the 'Blutesgefühl' section of his essay, 'The Caledonian Antisyzygy and the Gaelic Ideal').† A decade's interest in Mussolini's fascism probably prepared MacDiarmid's own nationalism for one totalitarian

---

*Part II of George Elder Davie's *The Crisis of the Democratic Intellect*, Polygon, 1986, describes MacDiarmid's poetry in terms of philosophy, especially Scottish thought.
†Reprinted in *Selected Essays of Hugh MacDiarmid*; ed. D. Glen, Jonathan Cape, 1969.

escapade after another. Whatever its turbulence, or sheer ill will, it seems safe to conclude that his political mind had little use for democracy.

'Dissimilarity' was not enough for MacDiarmid: he wanted synthetic Scots to achieve a complete break from its near-sorority with English. 'Quite untranslatable Scots', he wrote in *Lucky Poet*, was what he aimed for when he rose to 'the height of my theme'. 'Water Music' should give some idea of the lexical density of which synthetic Scots is capable; the poem is contrived from sheer love of the language it uses, a devotion to its exuberance and peculiarity. Its word-gathering, its felt philology, is far removed from Burns's Scots. Rarely, if ever, do individual words in Burns's poems draw attention to themselves as lexical splendours. Some of them may have been unusual to Burns, but they were insured by the experience of speech, and introduced on a balanced, colloquial metre, and on a voice that insists on the demotic integrity of its idiom. 'Water Music' revels in as many words associated with streams and rivers as MacDiarmid could manage to get in. Here, too, as in his criticism, as in many of his poems, a modernist concern is announced, in this case in the opening lines:

> *Wheesht, wheesht, Joyce, and let me hear*
> *Nae Anna Livvy's lilt,*
> *But Wauchope, Esk, and Ewes again,*
> *Each wi' its ain rhythms till't.*

Joyce's famous passage is being passed over in favour of the waters native to MacDiarmid. A Scottish assertion is undoubtedly present in the poem, but, in playfully silencing Joyce, MacDiarmid draws attention to himself as *another* modernist, albeit a lonelier one, stranded proudly in Scotland with his aboriginal, urgent concerns, and dedicated as well, to the language that he believed could solve them. But it is also a poem of remembering; it is a poem in which garnered Scottish words are made to adhere to memory. As Alan Bold suggests in his admirable biography of MacDiarmid,* it was the *personally* regressive ingredient in Scots that contributed to MacDiarmid's transition from Scots to English. It might also be suggested that he could have written one lexical rhapsody too many, or gone a 'divertissement philologique' (as he sub-titled 'Stony Limits') too far, and left himself facing the closed doors of the language that he had himself opened in the first place. If that is true, it hardly detracts from his linguistic audacity; it might even reveal it more clearly. Acumen and recklessness, an intuitive poetic scholarship, abundant energy, and national passion, could have led him to exhaust the idiom that to a large extent he invented, at least for his own

---

* *MacDiarmid. Christopher Murray Grieve. A Critical Biography*, John Murray, 1988; Paladin/ Grafton Books, 1990.

poetry. He continued to support other poets who wrote in Scots, and I doubt if he 'would have deplored the procedures of three contemporary poets, Raymond Vettese, Robert Crawford and W. N. Herbert, who, in their different ways, demonstrate that MacDiarmid's philological verve is far from dead.

Places and times matter in appreciating the use of Scots in poetry. William Soutar's language, for example, stems from his native Perth, and, while enriched by his reading, relies less on the synthesizing impulses necessary to MacDiarmid's conception of a new poetry in Scots. Soutar's best lyrics, like 'The Tryst', are more regular and less 'modern' than MacDiarmid's (which could be why 'The Tryst' appeared in Cecil Day Lewis's update of *The Golden Treasury*). MacDiarmid's lyrics characteristically set two or three uncommon or well-retrieved words, so as to make them appear not just out of the common way, but as having arrived from out of this world. Soutar's instinctive goal seems to have been a lyrical but local timelessness. It is the voice of an individual poet; but it is just as much the voice of a people's poetry. MacDiarmid's lyrics often create the same startling effect. Although at a higher, more intense, and more intellectual level of poetry, MacDiarmid's lyrics can sound as if they have emerged from a language and its community as much as an individual writer, a point that is worth stressing: it is, after all, unique in the poetry of modernism. In MacDiarmid's *A Drunk Man Looks at the Thistle*, however, long passages are clearly self-centred, the result of the poem's real and imaginary occasions, and of a 'thinner' Scots diction, at times little more than the notation of accent. Scots loses much of its poetic power when stripped of words and expressions rediscovered in 'the recesses of the Doric'. Its strength could lie largely in the meaningful past which it embodies, and which it thrusts, either joltingly or melismatically, against a frustrated present.

The language of Lowland Scotland was known as 'Inglis' until the late fifteenth and early sixteenth centuries, and only after that as 'Scottis'. English and Scots are both dialects of the same original language stock. Gaelic and Norse are additional etymological sources, as are Brythonic Welsh and Pictish, especially as far as place names are concerned, which form an important part of any country's linguistic atmosphere. Geographical, climatic and other domestic and historical forces contributed to its distinctive vocabulary, the extent of which is recorded in *Dictionary of the Older Scottish Tongue** and *The Scottish National Dictionary*.† Latin is another presence, intellectually more than linguistically, but powerful enough for all that, especially in the educated mind. Modern Scottish poetry is reminded of it through Robert Garioch's verse translations from the Latin of George Buchanan and Arthur Johnstone.

*In progress, 7 vols. so far: A – Sanct.
†10 vols. 1931–76.

Characteristic or traditional stanzas are associated with Scottish poetry, the best known being Standard Habbie (or Burns's Stanza). MacDiarmid left these well alone. A form like Burns's Stanza, closely identified with the eighteenth century (although it is considerably older), would have looked far from a modernist ploy. In the new climate that MacDiarmid was attempting to create it would have risked establishing the wrong loyalties and pieties. Imitated Burns provided much of the worst poetry in the century after his death (and the travesty is not yet over and done with). MacDiarmid also believed that Burns sold short the revival of the Scots language. It was left to Robert Garioch to renegotiate the terms on which the stanzaic verse of Burns, and, especially, Robert Fergusson (1750–74) could re-enter the living stream of Scottish poetry without fudging contemporary subjects and attitudes to them. In other words, the revival of writing in Scots that was instigated by MacDiarmid in the early 1920s was modified by other talents. MacDiarmid's work was important to Garioch, but he tired of the older poet's worst dogmatic habits so far as to refer to them as 'pulpit objurgations'. Garioch's poetic personality is self-consciously wry and sensible. Behind his poetry the persona is often that of an Edinburgh Everyman. Powerfully, and often wittily direct, his work is crafted on a metrical pulse and these older stanzaic shapes which pull back into Scottish poetry the eighteenth-century tempos of Fergusson and Burns (see 'To Robert Fergusson') and of earlier fifteenth- and sixteenth-century verse forms that influenced them (see 'Embro to the Ploy').

Garioch's 'The Wire' is one of the finest poems of the Second World War. Its mood, its almost panoptic view of a prisoner-of-war camp (in Silesia), and the eeriness with which tetrameter metricality enforces the poem's Scots diction, all contribute to what seems a virtually mediaeval poetic atmosphere. Time seems as displaced as those incarcerated on

> . . . this dour mechanistic muir
> wi nae land's end, and endless day,
> whaur nae thing thraws a shadow, here
> the truth is clear, and it is wae.

Garioch's poetry is almost always direct and candid, drawn from life and experience. MacDiarmid's 'Water Music' can sound like word-fantasy, and, despite its passionate evocation of streams and rivers, it seems diminished when compared with the harrowing fortitude, despair and indignant energy of Garioch's 'The Wire'. Synthetic Scots, lavishly employed for its own sake, is a creative tactic largely limited to MacDiarmid. Narrative, lyric and other pressures enforced on writers younger than him a more tactful, perhaps a more experienced distribution of wondrous or otherwise exceptional diction. Passages in Garioch's writing are often lexically massy, but usually appear on a more colloquial pulse. Some sections of *A Drunk Man Looks at the Thistle*, though, could hardly be more demotic or colloquial, or more metaphysical. Poetry in Scots can seem like a search for a convincing balance between stupendous Scots vocabulary and commoner terms in Scots and Scots-English. Garioch's poetry achieves that harmony through its spokenness, personality, humour and direct-ness. His work diverges from MacDiarmid's example while at the same time drawing from the energy created by it. Indeed, given MacDiarmid's 'pulpit objurgations' on poetry and politics, it can seem remarkable that individual talents not only survived their friendship with his ideas, but took strength from them. On the evidence of Alan Bold's biography and the testimony of several writers, MacDiarmid's personality in print may have been considerably more severe than in his companionship. From MacDiarmid's criticism, for example, you would expect him to have had little time for Sydney Goodsir Smith's highly personalized poems, or much of their language. Again, Smith's poetic tempera-ment is strikingly different, for his poetry courts a kind of Scottish neo-classicism infected with a late-romantic self-loathing, or a willingness to exploit bad behaviour for lyrical or humorous poetic ends. Garioch, too, dabbled in native neo-classicism, as in his Scots translation from Arthur Johnstone (1587–1641), who wrote in Latin. Garioch especially, and Smith, too (only in Smith's poetry it is more superficial) possessed a sense of the Scots language of the fifteenth, sixteenth and seventeenth centuries. Echoic resonances sound through their poetry when read in the available collected editions.

'Sorley MacLean, a Scottish poet second only to MacDiarmid, writes in our third language – Gaelic', Norman MacCaig once declared, 'and thereby restricts his intelligent audience to a mere handful. Nobody does that except for the deepest and most compulsive reasons.'

Conventional opinion invites us to believe that a poet can write in only one language – the language of a life's lengths and affections, experience, memory, and dreams. Conventional belief may well be right, but only for those born and brought up in a rigidly monoglot environment, which, in the British Isles, is likely to mean a middle-class background and notional RP from birth. Poets drawn to write in Scots do so on a basis of childhood acquaintance with its residual, colloquial forms, or what, for practical purposes, might best be described as a strong Scottish accent of one kind or another. An awareness of accent, together with curiosity directed at a few Scottish words spoken since childhood, can convince young Scottish poets that their authenticity lies in the dictionaries and poetry from which a complete native poetic idiom can be reconstructed. With Scots, it is not a case of bilingualism as it might be with French-and-English or

English-and-Russian, or English-and-Gaelic. What it shows is an urge to insist on Scots as a language worthy of the poetry that can be written in it, as a language separate and of-itself in relationship to the English language. It is when this urge is involuntary that Scots becomes the medium of poetry, as in MacDiarmid's lyrics, or in the best work of Soutar, Garioch, Goodsir Smith, Douglas Young, Tom Scott, Alexander Scott, Alasdair Mackie and the younger poets who work with the forms that Scots can take. Although applied to poetry in Gaelic, MacCaig's pointer to 'the deepest and most compulsive reasons' is very apt when directed at poetry in Scots. It is when the language of poetry arises from decision rather than instinctive need that it risks artificiality and fraudulence. By its nature, poetry in Scots risks a confrontation of real feeling with unreal or archaeological diction. Faked emotion could also be encouraged by a national overview of language and poetry. That is, priorities other than those of poetry could come higher up the list then they should.

Before attempting to discuss poetry in Gaelic (for which I have to depend on translations) this might be the moment to say something about what is a common feeling among Scottish poets and readers, no matter their preferred or necessary language. Despite the survival of poetry in three languages (and it was far from guaranteed) there seems a hunger for unity, not through a single language, but through one nationality that sanctions a tripled linguistic and poetic experience. An introduction to an anthology of poetry might seem an improper occasion on which to introduce the topic of nationalism; but it can hardly be avoided without tampering with the record. Scottish poetry has been steeped in politics ever since MacDiarmid's instigatory drum-beating back in the early 1920s. By 1943, however, in *Lucky Poet*, he could say 'The language element, the Scottish national character of my poetry, is not the most important thing about it.' A little later in the same book he expounded Scots as an anti-English stop-gap on the way to achieving a 'Gaelic Scotland', and he described poetry in Scots as 'a temporary fighting literature'. By this time his overviews of culture and politics had gone awry. They were summed up by his vision of a Celtic Union of Soviet Republics – Brittany, Cornwall, Wales, Ireland, Man and Scotland. MacDiarmid's satisfaction in that kind of make-believe map-making is difficult to detach from racism of a fairly crude sort. However, despite his extremism, and to some extent because of his kinder, personal influence, Scottish poetry has moved gradually into its liberty. For those 'deepest and most compulsive reasons' it has managed to resolve the more petty of its inner controversies; it is more and more the poetry in three languages of one nationality.

A passable attempt could be made at writing a poem in Scots after two or three days of leafing through a dictionary. Developing an ability to 'think' in Scots would take considerably longer. To learn to think in Gaelic would take a very long time indeed. Those 'deepest and most compulsive reasons' would seem to apply to writers who grew up speaking Gaelic, or whose family backgrounds included the language – perhaps not much, but some – and for whom loyalty's tug is not to be denied. Sorley MacLean's family was not only Gaelic-speaking but included bearers of traditional song, an important element in Gaelic culture, and in Scotland as a whole. Yet while Gaelic traditions are crucial to MacLean, he was able to introduce to them such ostensibly divergent influences as Yeats and Eliot. MacLean has also testified to the importance of MacDiarmid's lyrics where his earlier work is concerned, as well as to that of personal contact with MacDiarmid himself.

His first collection was *Dàin do Eimhir* (*Songs to Eimhir*) in 1943. Passionate lyrics, sometimes in an adjectival Gaelic manner, their intensity and incantatory pitch survive in the poet's own translation:

> Girl of the yellow heavy-yellow gold-yellow hair,
> the song of your mouth and Europe's shivering cry,
> fair, heavy-haired, spirited, beautiful girl,
> the disgrace of our day would not be bitter in your kiss.

'Small-scale, face-to-face rural societies, with a strong emphasis on communality, seldom set a high premium' on 'cool analysis of life', D. J. MacLeod writes in his essay 'Gaelic: the Dynamics of a Renaissance'.* Irony plays little part in the work of Gaelic poetry, the exception being Rob Donn (d. 1778). Interestingly, MacLean describes Donn's poetry as 'humanist sermo-pedestrian verse', and while he praises its 'courageous sense of honour', he asks, 'how can such relaxed poetry be great?' Large-scale urban societies, placing a strong emphasis on mass organization and individual privacy, rely on irony as a defensive, sometimes critically explosive, cultural device. In earlier Gaelic poetry, it was simply out of place, which is not to say that the ironies of history are allowed to go undetected.

MacLean's reputation was deserved long before his work was more widely distributed; a general awareness of his importance dates from the 1970s. Around 80,000 people speak Gaelic (the population of Scotland is not much more than 5 million). Within its own cultural boundaries, then, Gaelic's demographic pool is small enough to suggest its vulnerability – a language not only on the edge of Europe, but on the edge of time. Sorley MacLean accepts the threatened existence of Gaelic with a characteristic lack of passivity:

It is natural for a poet to love his own language if it is the language of his ancestors, and dying, even if it were a poor defective thing. Gaelic is not a poor language, in art at any rate. Though it had only its ineffable songs, which cannot be put in other words, it would

---

* In *Gaelic and Scotland*; ed. W. Gillies, Edinburgh University Press, 1989.

still be a priceless medium of expression. Therefore the Gaelic writer must be 'political', and in our day the teaching of the language is the prime business of its 'politics'.*

Love of a native language is a powerful force in poetry, especially in countries where it can be subjected to political pressures (for example, the Highland post-Jacobite period clearly exemplifies this, but it has happened in more subtle ways since) or frustrated, or diminished by depopulation and emigration, or the tendency of modern life with all its blandishments to change the social structures which language and poetry reflect. Against such a background Gaelic might be expected to look like a fallen language, exhausted, miniaturized, and relegated to scholarly sub-departments dedicated to pathos. It is not what has happened. Gaelic poets, who have been prominent in Scottish poetry as a whole, have contributed in a major way to halting the decline of a language poised, for more than a century, before the prospect of extinction. Derick Thomson, for instance, founded the magazine and publishing imprint, *Gairm*, and the Gaelic Books Council. His *Introduction to Gaelic Poetry*† is an indispensable guide for readers who want to know more of the subject. Gaelic poets, however, can seem surprised by their renascent surge, or coincidence of talents:

Can there have emerged from such a small area, with its declining Gaelic population, against all contemporary pressures, a modern Gaelic literature? Is it possible that such an extraordinary thing could have happened? Is it possible too that against anaemic ceilidhs, primitive breast-beating, the backward look, there should have come into existence a truly contemporary Gaelic literature? The answer to this is that strangely enough such a literature has emerged.‡

MacLean's passionate directness, his quality of spoken singing, is less pronounced in Derick Thomson's writing, or Smith's poetry in Gaelic. Much of their work is drawn from a burdened, rueful awareness of a dispiriting cultural present, and the past from which it emerges. Thomson's 'Coffins', for example, contains the line 'I did not understand that my race was dying'. Both its dilemma and directness run counter to the English poetry of Thomson's lifetime; but the point is worth making only because of the distance between English and Gaelic poetry, as well as the disregard and complacency which identify as expendable traditions which are not native to the official State. 'Gaelic poetry must be judged within the culture itself': Iain Crichton Smith's opinion is probably true, but it tends to block what might be valuable for non-Gaelic speaking readers, that dissimilarity to poetry in English which has been found fruitful and exciting over

---

*Sorley MacLean, *Ris a' bhruthaich: criticism and prose writings*; ed. W. Gillies, Acair, 1985
†Gollancz, 1974; Edinburgh University Press, 1989.
‡Iain Crichton Smith, 'Modern Gaelic Poetry', in *Towards the Human*, Macdonald Publishers, 1986.

the past few decades. Poetry from other languages, and other national traditions in English, have exerted a considerable influence on the poetry of the British Isles. There seems no good reason to insulate Gaelic poetry, even when it laments its own history, as in Thomson's fine poem 'Strathnaver', with its bitterly exalted portrayal of the Highland Clearances; or 'The Well', where the source of his people's culture is seen as almost-lost, hidden, but still available:

> 'Nobody goes to that well now,'
> said the old woman, 'as we once went,
> when we were young,
> though its water is lovely and white.'
> And when I looked in her eyes through the bracken
> I saw the sparkle of that water
> that makes whole every hurt
> till the hurt of the heart.

Iain Crichton Smith places a quite different emphasis on Rob Donn than does Sorley MacLean. 'One of our most important poets, in many ways our most important', Smith writes of Rob Donn in 'A Note on Gaelic Criticism', an article in which he finds Gaelic adjectival listing 'a menace to the development of good poetry', and where he praises Donn's intelligence and irony. Smith's 'Gaelic Stories'* is drawn, at least to an extent, from exactly the kind of 'relaxation' that MacLean found questionable in Donn. It is a divergence of opinion that does not prevent Smith from acknowledging MacLean as the 'Gaelic master'. That it should exist, however, suggests that Gaelic poetry's struggle with modernity is one in which traditional expectations could be resistant to ideas of 'good poetry' when these have been taken in some measure from languages other than Gaelic itself.

By the time of *Stony Limits* (1934) MacDiarmid's creative engagement with Scots began to weaken. Poems in colloquial and synthetic Scots appear in the collection, but it is his newer work in English, such as 'On a Raised Beach', which suggests that a combination of philosophical, meditative and temperamental pressures forced him into a more extensive language. While that language is English, it is hard to appreciate it as the language of English poetry. It is English in its guise of a world-auxiliary language; it is an idiom that MacDiarmid also bent to his will as part of the gesture that extended poetry into scientific and philosophical knowledge.

---

*Smith prints his Gaelic poems in translation only in his *Selected Poems*, and some other volumes, although they appear in Gaelic collections first. Accordingly, his Gaelic writing is represented by his translations without a parallel text.

Edwin Muir's *Scott and Scotland* came out two years later.* MacDiarmid promptly opened fire on arguments which seemed to undermine everything for which his Scottish Renaissance movement stood. Not only was his own poetry in Scots challenged, but so was the direction he insisted Scottish poetry should take, as well as the Scottishness of mind, character and nationhood which he had expounded, and, in the process, fantasticated. Expertly vituperative – he fingered Muir as the leader of 'the white mouse faction' in Scottish letters – MacDiarmid's counter attack is usually regarded as having won the day. However, *Scott and Scotland* can be seen as other than treasonable. Only in recent years has its insistence on English as the only authentic language of Scottish poetry been proved mistaken through developments which have brought about a healing in the controversy that used to be described as 'the language question'. Much of what Muir says is still of interest. His admittedly tentative emphasis on Sir Walter Scott highlights the very curious neglect of 'the greatest creative force in Scottish literature as well as one of the greatest in English'. Some of the reasons for avoiding Scott are social and political. Like Stevenson, or Buchan, he was born on the wrong side of the tracks. All three were Tories, and more or less High. Each has become a casualty of nationalism's rush as well as of its simplifications.

In spite of its variousness, its disproportionately high count of achievements in the arts and sciences, Scotland *is* a small country. Genuine critical debate tends to be discouraged by the intimacy of the cultural atmosphere. Back-slapping and other exaggerated forms of courtesy can turn the critical process into little more than flag-waving. On the other hand, the consequences of an opposed view can be immediate. There are some famous silences in Scottish poetry. There are also celebrated enmities. That of Muir and MacDiarmid is the most disagreeable. Not only did it separate the two most gifted writers of their generation, it introduced conspicuous side-taking and the exploitation of controversy.

Muir's extended essay provides a contrary view, a series of arguments with which poets who use either Scots or English have had to contend, just as they are obliged to come to a workable decision regarding MacDiarmid's poetry and the convictions from which it was made. I shall quote it at some length:

The riddle which confronted me in approaching Scott himself, by far the greatest creative force in Scottish literature as well as one of the greatest in English, was to account for a very curious emptiness which I felt behind the wealth of his imagination. Many critics have acknowledged this blemish in Scott's work, but have either made no attempt to account for it, or else have put it down to a defect in Scott's mind and character. Yet men of Scott's enormous genius have rarely Scott's faults; they may have others but not these particular ones; and so I was forced to account for the hiatus in Scott's endowment by considering the environment in which he lived, by invoking the fact – if the reader will agree it is one –

* George Routledge & Sons, 1936; Polygon Books, 1982.

that he spent most of his days in a hiatus, in a country, that is to say, which was neither a nation nor a province, and had, instead of a centre, a blank, an Edinburgh, in the middle of it. But this Nothing in which Scott wrote was not merely a spatial one; it was a temporal Nothing as well, dotted with a few disconnected figures arranged at abrupt intervals: Henryson, Dunbar, Allan Ramsay, Burns, with a rude buttress of ballads and folk songs to shore them up and keep them from falling. Scott, in other words, lived in a community which was not a community, and set himself to carry on a tradition which was not a tradition; and the result was that his work was an exact reflection of his predicament. His picture of life had no centre, because the environment in which he lived had no centre. What traditional virtue his work possessed was at second hand, and derived mainly from English literature, which he knew intimately but which was a semi-foreign literature to him. Scotland did not have enough life of its own to nourish a writer of his scope; it had neither a real community to foster him nor a tradition to direct him; for the anonymous ballad tradition was not sufficient for his genius. . . .

So that my inquiry into what Scotland did for Scott came down finally to what it did not do for Scott. What it did not do, or what it could not do. Considered historically these alternatives are difficult to separate.

Having traced Scott's greatest fault to his geographical and historical position as a writer, I began to wonder what he might have been, given his genius, if he had been born into a genuine organic society such as England, or even into a small self-subsistent state like Weimar. Could he possibly have left his picture of life in such a tentative state, half flesh and blood and half pasteboard, unreal where he dealt with highly civilized people, and real where he dealt with peasants, adventurers and beggars? Would he not have been forced to give it unity? or rather, would not a sociological unity at least have been there without his having to make a specific effort to achieve it? . . .

But behind this problem of the Scottish writer there is another which, if not for the individual author, for Scotland itself is of crucial importance. This is the problem of Scottish literature, and it is clearly a question for the Scottish people as a whole, not for the individual Scottish writer; for only a people can create a literature. The practical present-day problem may be put somewhat as follows: that a Scottish writer who wishes to achieve some approximation to completeness has no choice except to absorb the English tradition, and that if he thoroughly does so his work belongs not merely to Scottish literature but to English literature as well. On the other hand, if he wishes to add to an indigenous Scottish literature, and roots himself deliberately in Scotland, he will find there, no matter how long he may search, neither an organic community to round off his conceptions, nor a major literary tradition to support him, nor even a faith among the people themselves that a Scottish literature is possible or desirable, nor any opportunity, finally, of making a livelihood by his work. All these things are part of a single problem which can only be understood by considering Scottish literature historically, and the qualities in the Scottish people which have made them what they are; it cannot be solved by writing poems in Scots, or by looking forward to some hypothetical Scotland in the future . . .

Every genuine literature, in other words, requires as its condition a means of expression capable of dealing with everything the mind can think or the imagination conceive. It must be a language for criticism as well as poetry, for abstract speculation as well as fact, and since we live in a scientific age, it must be a language for science as well. A language which can serve for one or two of those purposes but not for the others is, considered as a vehicle for literature, merely an anachronism. Scots has survived to our time as a language for simple poetry and the simpler kind of short story, such as *Thrawn Janet*; all its other uses have lapsed, and it expresses therefore only a fragment of the Scottish mind. One can go further than this, however, and assert that its very use is a proof that the Scottish consciousness is divided. For, reduced to it simplest terms, this linguistic division means that Scotsmen feel in one language and think in another; that their emotions turn to the Scottish tongue, with all its associations of local sentiment, and their minds to a standard English which for them is almost bare of associations other than those of the classroom. If Henryson and Dunbar had written prose they would have written in the same language as they used for poetry, for their minds were still whole; but Burns never thought of doing so, nor did Scott, nor did Stevenson, nor has any Scottish writer since. In an organic literature poetry is always influencing prose, and prose poetry; and their interaction energizes them both. Scottish poetry exists in a vacuum; it neither acts on the rest of literature nor reacts to it; and consequently it has shrunk to the level of anonymous folk-song. Hugh MacDiarmid has recently tried to revive it by impregnating it with all the contemporary influences of Europe one after another, and thus galvanize it into life by a series of violent shocks. In carrying out this experiment he has written some remarkable poetry; but he has left Scottish verse very much where it was before. For the major forms of poetry rise from a collision between emotion and intellect on a plane where both meet on equal terms; and it can never come into existence where the poet feels in one language and thinks in another, even though he should subsequently translate his thoughts into the language of his feelings. Scots poetry can only be revived, that is to say, when Scotsmen begin to think *naturally* in Scots. The curse of Scottish literature is the lack of a whole language, which finally means the lack of a whole mind.

MacDiarmid's basic premiss was that discontinuity in literature and national-ity could be repaired simply by taking vigorous action. It was probably MacDiarmid whom Muir had in mind when he wrote that the problems of Scottish literature could not be solved by individual writers – 'only a people can create a literature'. Over the last two or three decades, however, Muir's major reservations have decreased in pertinence. Scotland has revealed itself to be a more 'organic community' than was suspected. Its literary traditions have become clearer as the result of scholarly and critical work. Readers, or, if you like, 'the people themselves', have demonstrated that a Scottish literature is desirable. A poet in Scotland is no more likely to make a living from his or her work than a poet anywhere else, but fellowships, bursaries, literary journalism and public performances extend a system of support – if always fragile – which is superior to anything enjoyed by Muir or MacDiarmid.

In a letter in 1940, Muir wrote: 'It seems to me, looking at Scottish life, that discouragement is everywhere in it'. That is no longer anything like as true as it undoubtedly was, even if contemporary conditions are far from perfect in whatever sphere of life you care to investigate. Muir and MacDiarmid wrote from circumstances of near-penury. Neither MacDiarmid's productivity, which was ferocious, nor Muir's, which was considerable, could support life and family on its own. MacDiarmid's self-imposed exile on Whalsay in the Shetland Islands (where he wrote 'On a Raised Beach'), his nervous breakdown, wartime industrial conscription, and service as a crewman on an Admiralty tender in the Clyde naval anchorages suggest some of the disappointments and humiliations which he had to endure. Muir's background as a boy displaced from the Orkney Islands to industrial Glasgow created the foundations of heartbreaking inner turmoil. His work in a boneyard, in Lobnitz's shipyard in Renfrew, and, by 1940, in the Food Office in Dundee, illustrate what Muir was up against.

Scotland was neglectful of its poets and artists, chiefly, it would seem, because as a non-nation it was scarcely aware of possessing any. With a disliked status quo to react against, writers tended to be identified as outspoken and 'colourful', but embarrassing in their contrariness. National caricatures were preferred to realities, truth and aspiration. It can hardly be denied that an element of that persists. Most poetry in the twentieth century has been oppositional in its relations with society and the political scene at large. Scottish poetry, however, in some of its major figures, has been peculiarly hostile to standard assumptions. MacDiarmid, Muir (earlier in his career), MacLean, Goodsir Smith, Thomson and a number of others have been either on the Left and/or explicitly nationalist. Others have been less conspicuously political; but in their relish of language, or their directness, or breadth of outlook, they have identified their nationality in other ways.

Scottish poetry in this century has been far from a tragic scenario; but an undoubted awkwardness has been the relatively limited object lesson communicated by two of its major figures to subsequent writers for whom the available, common language is the obvious and natural one to use. MacDiarmid's English is too much of a special case, while Muir's, although appropriate to the timelessness of the stories he tells, would look archaic in any other context.

Neither was a formative influence on Norman MacCaig, for instance, whose first two collections, which he disowns, were deeply coloured by the rhetoric of the Apocalypse School, in which Scottish poets were prominent. Having rejected that – a friend, apparently, asked: 'When are you publishing the answers?' – MacCaig then began the long haul back to lucidity. A poet like Andrew Young may have been of more help than either MacDiarmid or Muir. *Riding Lights* (1955) established MacCaig as an important presence, while since MacDiarmid's death in 1978 his work has looked like the major body of poetry that it is.

Until around the mid-1960s MacCaig's poetry appeared in elegant English, often with intricate stanzas in which his metrical artfulness and rhymes surpass recent Scottish averages in those aspects of versification. Lightness of touch, intellectual playfulness, conceited figures, melismatic smoothness, a highly *polished* English – these were, and still are, unusual in Scottish poetry. But it would be mistaken to think of MacCaig's idiom as one of English-English. Muir was surely wrong to talk of 'English', pure and simple, as if English were one language. Although 1936 could have been too early for the wider ramifications of the English language to have been explored in confident detail, Muir's detailed knowledge of American and Irish writing should have led him to notice the particularity of the case with which he was dealing. Not much about Scottish poetry in English is likely to be appreciated at the highest aesthetic level without its intonations being taken into account. Muir's mistake was to ignore how accent represents the phonology of a previous way of speaking – a Scottish accent could be described as Scots stripped of its diction. Nor did MacDiarmid appear to think it worthy of consideration that the English written by Scottish poets is to varying degrees English repossessed by the voice of the Scots vernacular, or, as in MacCaig's case, modified by proximity to a Gaelic inheritance if not by Gaelic itself. No one seems to have paid much attention to the natural phenomenon of language in Scotland as dictated by history. Most of the attention swings to the glamorous, fateful and possibly luckless last-ditch stands of Scots and Gaelic. Between the three languages of Scotland, however, writers have managed to negotiate a climate of opinion which allows the freedom to write in the tongue in which a poet feels most at home. That obvious liberty was not one always to be taken for granted. Despite the excellence of the poetry that was being written, the justifications surrounding it could give the impression that a romantically inferiorist insularity was preferred. It was a failure of criticism, a flaw in the literary atmosphere, and it helped to make Scottish poetry as a whole look like a subject best left to its participants and native readers to squabble over.

One consequence of that state of affairs was the postponement of criticism in favour of the puffery that supports a 'reputation', or the malice, or silence, that destroys or prevents it. Only in recent years have MacLean, MacCaig, Edwin Morgan and W. S. Graham been written about intelligently or at any length,* while proper studies of Soutar, Goodsir Smith and Garioch† do not exist.

---

* Raymond J. Ross and Joy Hendry eds. *Sorley MacLean: Critical Essays*, Scottish Academic Press, 1986; Joy Hendry and Raymond J. Ross eds. *Norman MacCaig: Critical Essays*, Edinburgh University Press, 1990; Robert Crawford and Hamish Whyte, *About Edwin Morgan*, Edinburgh University Press, 1990; Tony Lopez, *The Poetry of W. S. Graham*, Edinburgh University Press, 1989.
† A collection of critical essays on Robert Garioch is in preparation, edited by Joy Hendry and Raymond J. Ross, for Edinburgh University Press, due 1992.

MacCaig's *Collected Poems* (1985; new edition 1990) encouraged a belated attention to his work, and more detailed examination than it had hitherto received. As a body of poetry made up for the most part of short lyrics, brief discursive narratives and satires, it can seem to resist identification as the work of a major writer. However, what finally marks it as such is the importance of its themes, and the extent to which poem after poem seeks to define and clarify the individual's relationship to existence. It is a poetry of detailed resemblances that cumulate into a glimpse of 'the whole world's shape'. 'Summer Farm' and 'Byre' should illustrate MacCaig's figurative habits of mind and feeling. Perception itself is explored and investigated in many of his poems, while others put history, topicality and politics firmly in their place (see 'No Interims in History'). Between 'Summer Farm' and 'Intruder in a Set Scene' the change in style is measurable: MacCaig has moved from precise verse to a freer idiom. As a result, his later poetry feels less 'literary'. It is also more open to achieving a direct form of address to reader or listener.

A good deal of Scottish poetry is close to its potential audience. The poet as Everyman/woman is a cherished persona, or fact of poetic identity, as might be expected in a country where Robert Burns is a figure of national importance. G. Gregory Smith's image of the grinning gargoyle beside the kneeling saint pictorializes the happy coexistence of the vulgar and the holy, the cruel and the kind, the low and the high, the demotic and the artistic, the anarchic and the ordered, the simple and the elaborate, which seem characteristic of Scottish psychologies, or of what criticism makes of them.

A poet like W. S. Graham, for example, addressed his often difficult subject of communication in a language that is rarely very far from an accented and demotic spokenness. 'Baldy Bane' might even suggest that a balladic momentum is an aspect of literary Scottishness that many poets have been unable or unwilling to get away from entirely. As Graham wrote in 'The Dark Dialogues',

> . . . always language
> Is where the people are.

Hart Crane, Joyce, Marianne Moore, Dylan Thomas and Beckett might have been among Graham's sources. So, too, were Scottish ballads, and there was room left for a native, perhaps even specifically Greenockian bias to the language of a poet otherwise instinctively preoccupied with modernity and far from prone to placing his nationality in a poem's foreground.

Graham has been less influential than a poet of his importance would at first lead you to believe. His style is eccentric, or individual, close to being a special case, like MacDiarmid's poetry in English, or Muir's. It begins to become clearer that it is characteristic of the best Scottish poets that their work contains an instinctively inimitable quality, or an audible signature.

Other, more disagreeable reasons, help to explain why Graham has been neglected in Scotland. Those antithetical 'characteristics' could tend to exclude poetry which illustrates them less obviously than an insecure taste might prefer. 'Scottishness' is a quality open to crass exaggeration as well as more subtle forms of garbled excess. Graham's appetite for language and poetry – surely the best 'characteristic' of the Scottish poetic gift – is visible on just about every page of his *Collected Poems*. Scottish people and places are quite clearly implicated in his struggle with 'seeing new' (as he called it), or with 'the jungle of mistakes of communication'. However, he lived furth of Scotland for most of his adult life, and loved Cornwall. His relative neglect is due to more than the quirk of having been not-quite-obviously-Scottish-enough; he had the cheek to live somewhere else. Andrew Young, Edwin Muir, and several others, have been treated to petty discriminations of a similar kind.

Graham published young, in 1942, but fifteen years were to elapse between *The Nightfishing* (1955) – the same year as MacDiarmid's *In Memoriam James Joyce* – and *Malcolm Mooney's Land* (1970). *Riding Lights* (1955), which announced Norman MacCaig's first mature style, appeared when he was in his mid-forties. Edwin Morgan was around the same age when he re-invented his talent by writing the poems that appeared in *The Second Life* (1968). Bearing in mind Sorley MacLean's delayed reputation, and Robert Garioch's, and Derick Thomson's – outside a handful of readers – the career pattern that seems to be revealed suggests that Scottish poetry underwent a difficult mid-century phase which subsequent success has tended to obscure. No doubt publishing was part of the trouble. Scottish imprints no longer represented the proud industry of former years – Nelson, Blackie, Collins, Blackwoods, Chambers, Oliver & Boyd. Whatever else they were doing, the support of native talent was not a priority. MacDiarmid was issuing his books from Castle Wynd Printers, for the most part work written years earlier: the impression is that he was exhausted by his efforts of the 1930s, and experiences of the 1940s. Garioch's poetry, and Goodsir Smith's, was not easy to come by. Nor, for that matter, was MacDiarmid's. It was a period of *cognoscenti*, adepts and coteries. In retrospect it seems remarkable that poetic society should have been so enclosed when much of its work was robust. For the best part of twenty years Scottish literary culture showed all the symptoms of provincial decline, even when, as far as writing itself was concerned, it was far from moribund. It indicates the undeserved slump into which the poetry of a small country can fall when its housekeeping is in bad order.

Prior to 1968 Edwin Morgan's work was well-known in literary circles, but chiefly on the strength of magazine appearances and small press publications. In all likelihood he was less known as a poet than as a reviewer and translator (especially of *Beowulf*). Critics have found it hard to pin him down. Wisely, they have stopped trying, and admitted that his various kinds of poetry not only resist theme-spotting but represent the fluid, transformational wagers which are of its essence. Much of his importance – and, like MacCaig, he has been generally influential – stems from his obvious up-to-dateness. After that momentary torpor of the 1950s Morgan's internationalism and experimental verve (concrete poetry, sound poetry etc.) were needed as much as MacCaig's perfected intellectual lyrics and Garioch's hearty Scots. Morgan, however, uses formal versification when it suits him (as in his many sonnets) as well as free verse. He has been a vigorous translator* and essayist. Openness to change, humour and liveliness have made his work attractive to younger readers, especially in Glasgow. His urban *joie de vivre* provides a balance to MacCaig's predilection for more rural and natural settings and celebrations.

Scottish literature has not always been the city's friend. Gaelic culture expressed a distinctive civilization, but it did not create a city, nor could it have done so without contradicting its essential spirit. Until well into the twentieth century, Scottish cities were depicted as stone wildernesses into which rural Lowlanders, displaced Highlanders and immigrant Irish families drifted in search of a livelihood, becoming industrial fodder. Slums, squalor and urban hardships tended and still tend to be depicted in Scottish poetry and fiction, if only because their obviousness invites them. Few countries are as afflicted as Scotland with stark contrasts of urban scale and rural extensiveness within a relatively small but extremely various territory. It is part of the drama of modern Scottish literature. MacDiarmid, for instance, loathed Glasgow as a recalcitrant hotbed of the social conditions that produced just about everything except the energy required for its revolutionary redemption. In what might be his shortest poem, the unpleasant 'Placenta Previa; or, the Case of Glasgow', he wrote:

> It'll be no easy matter to keep the dirt in its place
> And get the Future out alive in *this* case!

For all his cerebral, intellectual reach and pretensions, MacDiarmid was as prime an example of Scottish small-town and village man as you could have found in his day. It took Garioch's eighteenth-century, Fergussonian Edinburgh sensibility to

---

*See especially his Scots versions of Mayakovksy, *Wi the Haill Voice*, Carcanet Press, 1972. His translations are collected in *Rites of Passage*, Carcanet Press, 1976. I have excluded translations from the anthology as the subject is taken care of elsewhere. A useful measure of the demotic vigour of Scots, however, can be acquired by comparing Morgan's Mayakovsky, or Garioch's Belli, with English versions.

re-introduce to Scottish poetry a critical urbanity rooted in a real city and the present tense. Many of MacCaig's poems, however, are set in Edinburgh, while Goodsir Smith's are stamped with Edinburgh citizenship.

Although one of the best-known cities of the world, to Scots Edinburgh can feel like a lapsed capital, a city of history riddled with picturesque and turbulent resonances, the architectural digest of historical tomes in three volumes. Despite its ancient beauty, 'hie-heapit' as Lewis Spence evoked it in a memorable phrase, or its ordered, Georgian neo-classical loveliness, much of Edinburgh is low-down, dark and shadowy; it can feel like the dungeons of Scottish time. Alastair Reid has noticed – accurately, it seems to me – that the Castle Rock looks suspiciously like the chip on Scotland's shoulder. An easy city to poeticize in general, it is a hard one about which to be poetically specific. Glasgow is, too, but for different reasons. Its past is one of Atlantic trade, and the industrial revolution (which was to a large extent a creation of Scottish technology). Only since Edwin Morgan's poetry of the 1960s has Glasgow been imagined in a significantly modern way. Once known as Juteopolis, or the City of Dreadful Knights, Dundee delivers its own harsh industrial, imperial and working-class heartbreak. Relaxed, aesthetic approaches to poetry are far from impossible in Scottish writing, but the effort required in order to clear the necessary imaginative space is considerable when you bear in mind what might have to be left out of the poetic reckoning. As the city of the North East, 'The Silver City', Aberdeen's long-lived business with the North Sea, the Baltic, and a large agricultural hinterland, have brought about yet another distinctive city. All four are water-cities (with Leith the port for Edinburgh). All four, too, prospered on international contacts. Scotland might seem remote, but its artistic and intellectual character is founded on the opposite of the insularity that its history might seem to invite. Internal linguistic complexity might even have predisposed scholars to lexicography and linguistics in general, and its writers to translation.

At the other extreme, George Mackay Brown's work – Brown has seldom left his native Orkney Islands – could be the outstanding example in recent poetry in the British Isles of an extended chronicle of remote place and a traditional way of life. As with Edwin Muir, for whose poetry and personality Brown maintains a strong affection, the nationality is Orcadian and Norse more than Scottish. A Catholic religious faith is part of his poetry's confidence, which is unusual in a country where a poetic religious impulse tends to be stifled in infancy. Otherwise much of Brown's energy is drawn from a refusal of deracination. Modern life is portrayed as the bestower of unwanted changes on traditional communities whose contentments were sustained by harmonious if also hazardous transactions with the land and the sea. He is an unashamed storyteller, a poet who has taken the risk of assuming his people's lore, legends, character and destiny. As a result, the time-scale of his poetry runs from the dawn of time to the present era of pollution. Brown's poetry is a brave gesture of time and place, a heave of the allegedly remote up against the distempers of modernity. Within Scottish or any other poetry there could hardly be a greater contrast between Brown's inspiration and Edwin Morgan's. Brown's beliefs are all on the side of traditional values, the natural round of the seasons, the organic community; Morgan's convictions relate to the city, science, technology, and the future. Both have imagined Armageddon. In Brown's case it takes the form of a Black Pentecost, which returns the traditional world to its first principles (much as in Muir's poem, 'The Horses'). Morgan envisages a post-Apocalypse Glasgow as Clyde-grad, perhaps a riskily optimistic echo of MacDiarmid's communist hopes.

A rural and island inspiration is continued by Iain Crichton Smith whose poetry and fiction have appeared in both Gaelic and English. 'Law' and 'grace', to use Smith's terms, indicate the tensions which he exploited in his earlier work but which survive, too, in his more recent writing. By 'law' he means the authoritarian Christianity of the United Free Church as well as secular systems designed to inhibit individual freedom. 'Grace' signifies the world of art, love, human choice, beauty, philosophy, poetry, and the glamorous self-confidence of those who seize opportunity unhindered by inherited restrictions. His contemporary instances are often set against the heroes and heroines of Rome and Greece or the classics of English literature and found wanting. In a section of his sequence 'At the Sea', for example, denizens of a public park are re-modelled as Helen and Achilles, while 'a fat loud Ajax's waddling up to bowl'. Larkin's presence can be detected gloomily in the shadows behind some of Smith's writing in that vein, in his powers of observation and the emphasis put on them if not in Smith's lavish use of the 'myth-kitty'. In the same sequence the US naval base at the Holy Loch is said to be defending

> the clattering tills, the taxis, thin pale girls
> who wear at evening their Woolworth pearls
> and from the dewed railings gaze at the world's end.

He can also be humorously satirical (see 'The White Air of March'), while in 'Chinese Poem' a native Gaelic dilemma is wittily transposed into the manner of another culture.

Smith has been hospitable to many influences, especially from recent poetry. George Mackay Brown is less eclectic – his sources include the sagas, ballads, Catholic liturgy, Hopkins (in Brown's earlier work) and Edwin Muir, whose poetry is often close to balladic narrative modified by allegory or the mythology and symbolism which bespeak poetry as an eternal craft. Contemporaneity can be an awkward issue in a country where history and national identity are partly unresolved. Writers can be drawn back into time in an effort to overwhelm what Smith calls the 'impenetrable dullness' of an ingrained philistinism, a repressive religiosity, a love of the couthy, the homely, and an infatuation with the second-rate. Significantly, though, Smith mounts his challenge in a passage about the dreaded McGonagall. Poetic contempt is directed, not at the worst poet in the world, but at the hypocritical mentality that reserves a place for 'poetic gems'. In laughing at McGonagall, the Scottish habit is to mock the idea of poetry itself, not just an obvious example of its pathetic delusions.

For many Scots, Burns is not only the National Poet; he is The Only Poet, a conviction which is often expressed with much whisky-o-lated jauntiness but not a lot of reading. Burns is still read by men and women with little or no pretension to cultivated literary taste, read closely, and memorized, as he should be. Edwin Muir was probably right when he remarked that Burns is an 'object-lesson in what poetic popularity really means – the prime object-lesson in the poetry of the world, perhaps the unique instance'. Serious consequences for Scottish poetry, some good, others dismal, have followed in the train of Burns's enduring prestige in the popular mind. MacDiarmid, for example, was probably right in the justification which underlay his slogan – 'Not Burns – Dunbar!' It was the calculated misunderstanding of Burns which irritated MacDiarmid, and which, in its turn, was used to denigrate other kinds of poetry. Literatures sometimes stand in need of punishing reassessment, and what MacDiarmid attempted was the redirection of Scottish taste to Dunbar's more cultivated and comprehensive artistry. Unfortunately, he also intended by it the need to reconstruct that pre-1707 Scottish psyche, which, as I've suggested already, smacks of an intellectually conceived regression on a heroic scale and may anyway be impossible. Perhaps all it amounts to is a dismissal of Englishness. He also underrated Burns's artistry, an aspect of the national poet which has been appreciated only in relatively recent times.

Much of Burns's democratic and egalitarian spirit is continued by Scottish writing in both verse and prose. After all, Burns came from the common people, not from a privileged section of society, as, too, did MacDiarmid, and as have many Scottish writers since. Most Scottish poetry, when compared with its English counterpart, stands in a closer relationship to its potential audience. A natural, uncourted ease of popularity is self-evident, to those who have experienced it, in MacCaig, MacLean (and, possibly, poetry by native speakers of Gaelic in general), Morgan, Smith, and some younger writers like Tom Leonard and Liz Lochhead. Garioch enjoyed it, as did Goodsir Smith and Douglas Young. But by *A Drunk Man Looks at the Thistle* MacDiarmid was set on a course plotted to avoid vulgar repute.

It is too soon to be sure of what Scottish poetry (or any other) might be like in even a decade's time; but there are good grounds for believing that it will continue to merge demotic with more aesthetic approaches. Robin Fulton, Kenneth White and Stewart Conn occupy what Europeans call 'the middle generation'. Of the three I've mentioned Conn is closest to the examples of his predecessors, while Fulton and White have founded most of their work on eclectic resources. Fulton lives in Scandinavia; in addition to his own poetry he is the translator of Tomas Tranströmer and other Swedish writers. Kenneth White lives and works in France, and is widely travelled, an experience which has helped him to form his idea of 'geo-poetics', or what Norman Douglas called 'intellectual nomadism'. His work was re-introduced to British readers as recently as 1989, although it had been appearing consistently in France in bilingual editions. There was nothing new about the postponement of White's reputation in Scotland. What was surprising was, and perhaps still is, his importance in France, in contrast to his (relative) neglect at home. His work shows a more modernist style as well as a more spiritual and philosophical bias than most Scottish poetry of his time. Equally interesting is that he counts MacDiarmid's poetry in English among his other influences.

Another version of vernacular Scots, urban Glaswegian speech, has been released by Tom Leonard. His concern with langwij ('the langwij a thi guhtr') contests political and other forms of condescension with a humour that emphasizes rather than disguises his indignation. He could have been assisted in this liberating act of local discovery by the climate of experiment and self-confidence established by Edwin Morgan. Other sources of energy, however, include William Carlos Williams, the guidance provided by socio-linguistics and the support of a growing number of writers in Glasgow, of both verse and prose. Political as Leonard's poetry is, it opens up the wider issues of indigenous speech. 'Fathers and Sons' exposes class shame and general pressures on personal and poetic identity more damaging than the use of phonetic urban dialect which he is questioned about at a poetry reading:

> I remember being ashamed of my father
> when he whispered the words out loud
> reading the newspaper.

In a country where the majority of writers are born to non-literary families, the subsequent distance which education can put between them and their origins is often painfully vivid. Accent is an audible yardstick for gauging social origins throughout the British Isles; but in Scotland it can seem as if the social controllers have turned up the volume. Leonard's poetry has contributed towards an improved equanimity in a society which used to be more than vulnerable to condescension and discouragement.

As with James Kelman's novels and stories it could come to be regarded as a major innovation in recent Scottish writing. If so, it was one which could hardly have been predicted, in the light of what preceded it – MacDiarmid's imperiously intellectual perspectives on just-about-everything; the use of a Scots diction rooted in the past and remote from modern city life; the rural associations of MacCaig, Smith, Brown and the Gaelic poets.

However, there is a connection between Leonard's Glaswegian idiom and Scots language in general. When Lord Cockburn described the speech of the ruthless judge Lord Braxfield (d. 1799) as one of a 'cherished coarseness', he pointed to an aspect of the Scots vernacular of which readers and writers have since proved themselves shy. As well as a sonorous dignity, it has a bias towards a raspingly reductive indignation and low humour. Perhaps that is true of most languages; but it seems peculiar to Scotland that it should be enjoyed, the evidence being the extent to which it seeps across class barriers while remaining identified with one class. In his Glaswegian poems, Leonard writes through that single class, the Glasgow working class, relishing the degree to which he exposes himself to charges of impropriety as he proceeds, and showing these accusations as vulnerable, class-informed assumptions.

Leonard's style is a difficult one for younger writers to emulate without at the same time announcing where it was found. Once again it is the distinctiveness of the best Scottish poets that asserts itself; it is as if an intuitive, anti-canonical urge runs through a major part of Scottish poetry in this century, which, if true, suggests the extent to which an anxious seriousness lies just beneath the surface of a good deal of the poetry that has appeared, or even an obligation to contribute to a culture worthy of a writer's best redemptive effort. The value of Leonard's work lies in how it castigates social shame and the encumbrances of inferiorist points of view directed at poetry in either English, Scots or Gaelic. It adds to the voice's confidence. Time-dishonoured customs locate the Glasgow voice and its idiom in low comedy or brutalized social circumstances; it is a voice which convention steeps in shame, squalor, crime, frustration and violence. Leonard's poetry takes these predictable attitudes and stands them on their heads. As in W. S. Graham's very different poetry, the energy flows from an intuitive emphasis on everything suggested by 'always language / Is where the people are;' or, as Leonard says, perhaps tongue-in-cheekily, 'all living language is sacred' – an easy piety to utter, but a more difficult one to demonstrate in poetry. Leonard's work tries to show that a demotic urban dialect is as fitted for poetry as more predictable forms of language.

Equally colloquial in its reliance on accent and an actual speaking voice (or voices), Liz Lochhead's poetry appears to have drawn its justifications from the poetry-reading performance as much as from anything in print that has gone into its making. In her work, freer, if punchily rhythmical passages of writing tend to evolve into snappily metrical and rhyming clusters. Her verve is that of a story-teller. Live listeners seem taken for granted, as if the poet was quite unafraid of her audience, whether her purpose is to entertain or deliver more critical perspectives on her feminine subjects. Even if they describe accurately what has been written in the past, the so-called characteristics of a country's poetry may end up inhibiting new work, and it could be wise to be wary of them.* Directness, immediacy of address, the sense of an audience, combine, however, into what does seem to be a permanent feature of much if not all Scottish poetry, a distinctive part of *praefervidum ingenium Scotorum.*

Earlier in the century women poets were prominent – Rachel Annand Taylor, Violet Jacob, Marion Angus and H. B. Cruickshank being the best known. Until the 1960s, however, literary women might have been discouraged by a conspicuously male-centred poetic country. Liz Lochhead, Valerie Gillies, Kathleen Jamie and a number of others have corrected that imbalance, a development which could be as important as the banishing of stigma from the Scottish voice.

'Did I ever hear him mention Scotland?' Geoffrey Grigson wrote of Norman Cameron in his *Recollections*:†

It was himself he insisted on, not a Scotch self; a human self. I knew vaguely he had been at school at Fettes, which was no more than a name to me. Otherwise he seemed as much a Southern Englishman, as much a user of the English language as any of us. Partition or a cultural sub-nationalism would have seemed to him pointless, even ridiculous. His English, the English he spoke, the English he wrote, had no trace of Scotch accent or Scotch peculiarity.

Relatively few Scottish writers would care to deserve the kind of compliment that Grigson paid his friend. What Grigson reveals is a wrinkled eighteenth-century distrust of too much dissimilarity; it emanates from a state of mind foreshadowed in Boswell's *Life of Johnson*, where, as Boswell makes clear, nervousness at differences in accent and vocabulary constituted a powerful fear among Scots for whom Scotland was too small for their ambitions. Advancement in England and the Empire was understood to demand a transformation of self and language. 'Scotticisms' were dreaded as tell-tale signs of social and intellectual inferiority. Merely to mention that most Scottish poets did not attend Fettes or any other public school can sound like labouring the point. Grigson's attitude would seem

---

*Such multiple 'characteristics' can be encountered in Kurt Wittig's *The Scottish Tradition in Literature*, Oliver & Boyd, 1958.
†Chatto & Windus, 1985.

to suggest that Scottish writing ought not to be taken seriously unless its language is as much that of a Southern Englishman as his own and that of others of his milieu. 'Scotch self' and 'Scotch peculiarity' give him away as having been misled by social class and nationality – his own. At the other extreme, it can hardly be denied that in this war of the accents the Scots are well capable of returning the insult with the same mindless prejudice. Over-strenuous insistences on a 'Scotch self' can result in the staging of highly unpleasant caricatures. Nationality, and its chum, patriotism, encourage unedifying hyperbole. In a country like Scotland, where nationalism is an active political force, and not just in the Scottish National Party, the temptation is that Scottish subjects should be foregrounded explicitly and at the expense of poetry's inclusiveness.

Younger writers have succeeded in circumventing the cruder embarrassments (to poetry) of what at times can appear to be a depressing political scene. In the relatively recent past, Scottish poetry tended to look like too much of a special case. It suffered from its own introverted publicity. Poets like Stewart Conn and Robin Fulton can seem unusual in the Scottish context in that they have been content to write what they write. Liz Lochhead and poets younger than her have shown a similar lack of embarrassment with their own subjects. Andrew Greig, Gerald Mangan and Frank Kuppner reflect a local personality, but there is rarely any sense of their having gone out of their way to get it into a poem. If anything explains the unclenched nationalism, or refusal of any kind of nationalism on a poem's surface, it is the eclectic reading and wider range of influences to which younger writers have exposed themselves. Greig, for example, admits John Berryman among his formative sources. Robert Crawford's work is usually very Scottish in subject matter, but its panache derives chiefly from the treatment of Scottish incidents and personalities with a newer confidence. A wide frame of literary experience is self-evident in MacCaig, Smith and Morgan, but it has taken some time for it to percolate through to the general advantage of younger generations of writers. It seems narrower and more aboriginal in the work of Scots-writing poets like Garioch and Goodsir Smith, despite their translating. While Raymond Vettese's poetry in Scots sometimes ruminates about the language he uses and whether the struggle is worth the sweat, there are signs of a newer kind of formal engagement in his work, as there is in W. N. Herbert's.

Whatever else it might be, a poetry that includes MacDiarmid, Muir, MacLean, MacCaig, Soutar, Garioch, Goodsir Smith, Morgan, Graham, Brown, Thomson and Iain Crichton Smith, is not weak or lacking in variety. In this century Scottish poetry has come a long way indeed from those 'analphabetic versifiers of post-Burnsian Scotland' whose ghosts were hunted down by MacDiarmid. 'Myopic toe-the-line all-in patrioteering' has been shut away in the Caledonian cupboard, too, where, however, it hangs in the shape of a skeleton.

Poetry in Scots has survived its worst history; since MacDiarmid, it has been less prone to sound like the affectation of the national stammer. That poetry in Gaelic should not only have survived, but enjoyed a renascence, is little short of miraculous. At one time a Scottish poet writing in English could be bullied into believing that his or her language was not a native tongue. Similarly, the translating-back-in-time feeling of the Scots language, with its sometimes extruded diction, could generate unsettling questions about the authenticity of what seemed an archaizing mode. Hectoring issues such as these now appear to have been settled, and the liberty of three languages established. To continue to use Eliot's outline, contemporary poetry in Scotland amounts to a *sixth* phase in its history. It is one which enjoys enough self-confidence to be able to reject historical summaries such as Eliot's; and it can accommodate individual acceptances or rejections of the positions taken by its major figures. It is markedly open to the stimulus of poetry from beyond the British Isles. It might even have developed an easier relationship with English poetry, while, at the same time, maintaining that the differences between Scottish and English literature are obvious, in whatever language. It speaks for itself that Eliot's fourth phase of Scottish literature should have been erased (it was always doubtful, in any case), and replaced with another, with yet another growing from it. It has been a hectic century for Scottish poetry, one filled with thrilling turbulence, and in which the stakes have been high – the survival of a national identity.

Douglas Dunn, Ferry-port-on-Craig, April 1992

Twentieth-Century Scottish Poetry

JOHN DAVIDSON (1857–1909)

Snow

I

'Who affirms that crystals are alive?'
    I affirm it, let who will deny: –
Crystals are engendered, wax and thrive,
    Wane and wither; I have seen them die.

Trust me, masters, crystals have their day,
    Eager to attain the perfect norm,
Lit with purpose, potent to display
    Facet, angle, colour, beauty, form.

II

Water-crystals need for flower and root
    Sixty clear degrees, no less, no more;
Snow, so fickle, still in this acute
    Angle thinks, and learns no other lore:

Such its life, and such its pleasure is,
    Such its art and traffic, such its gain,
Evermore in new conjunctions this
    Admirable angle to maintain.

Crystalcraft in every flower and flake
    Snow exhibits, of the welkin free:
Crystalline are crystals for the sake,
    All and singular, of crystalry.

Yet does every crystal of the snow
    Individualize, a seedling sown
Broadcast, but instinct with power to grow
    Beautiful in beauty of its own.

Every flake with all its prongs and dints
  Burns ecstatic as a new-lit star:
Men are not more diverse, finger-prints
  More dissimilar than snow-flakes are.

Worlds of men and snow endure, increase,
  Woven of power and passion to defy
Time and travail: only races cease,
  Individual men and crystals die.

III

Jewelled shapes of snow whose feathery showers,
  Fallen or falling wither at a breath,
All afraid are they, and loth as flowers
  Beasts and men to tread the way to death.

Once I saw upon an object-glass,
  Martyred underneath a microscope,
One elaborate snow-flake slowly pass,
  Dying hard, beyond the reach of hope.

Still from shape to shape the crystal changed,
  Writhing in its agony; and still,
Less and less elaborate, arranged
  Potently the angle of its will.

Tortured to a simple final form,
  Angles six and six divergent beams,
Lo, in death it touched the perfect norm
  Verifying all its crystal dreams!

IV

Such the noble tragedy of one
  Martyred snow-flake. Who can tell the fate
Heinous and uncouth of showers undone,
  Fallen in cities! – showers that expiate

Errant lives from polar worlds adrift
    Where the great millennial snows abide;
Castaways from mountain-chains that lift
    Snowy summits in perennial pride;

Nomad snows, or snows in evil day
    Born to urban ruin, to be tossed,
Trampled, shovelled, ploughed and swept away
    Down the seething sewers: all the frost

Flowers of heaven melted up with lees,
    Offal, recrement, but every flake
Showing to the last in fixed degrees
    Perfect crystals for the crystal's sake.

    V

Usefulness of snow is but a chance
    Here in temperate climes with winter sent,
Sheltering earth's prolonged hibernal trance:
    All utility is accident.

Sixty clear degrees the joyful snow,
    Practising economy of means,
Fashions endless beauty in, and so
    Glorifies the universe with scenes

Arctic and antarctic: stainless shrouds,
    Ermine woven in silvery frost, attire
Peaks in every land among the clouds
    Crowned with snows to catch the morning's fire.

VIOLET JACOB (1863–1946)

The Baltic

'Whaur are ye gaen sae fast, my bairn,
    It's no tae the schule ye'll win?'
'Doon tae the shore at the fit o' the toon
    Tae bide till the brigs come in.'

'Awa' noo wi' ye and turn ye hame,
    Ye'll no hae the time tae bide;
It's twa lang months or the brigs come back
    On the lift o' a risin' tide.'

'I'll sit me doon at the water's mou'
    Till there's niver a blink o' licht,
For my feyther bad' me tae tryst wi' him
    In the dairkness o' yesternicht.

' "Rise ye an' rin tae the shore", says he,
    "At the cheep o' the waukin' bird,
And I'll bring ye a tale o' a foreign land
    The like that ye niver heard."'

'Oh, haud yer havers, ye feckless wean,
    It was but a dream ye saw,
For he's far, far north wi' the Baltic men
    I' the hurl o' the Baltic snaw;

And what did he ca' yon foreign land?'
    'He tell'tna its name tae me,
But I doot it's no by the Baltic shore,
    For he said there was nae mair sea.'

Margin glosses:
beam of light — (line 2, stanza 3)
stop your nonsense — (stanza 5)
violent fall — (stanza 5)

MARION ANGUS (1866–1946)

Alas! Poor Queen

She was skilled in music and the dance
And the old arts of love
At the court of the poisoned rose
And the perfumed glove,
And gave her beautiful hand
To the pale Dauphin
A triple crown to win –
And she loved little dogs
    And parrots
   And red-legged partridges
And the golden fishes of the Duc de Guise
And a pigeon with a blue ruff
She had from Monsieur d'Elbœuf.

Master John Knox was no friend to her;
She spoke him soft and kind,
Her honeyed words were Satan's lure
The unwary soul to bind
'Good sir, doth a lissome shape
And a comely face
Offend your God His Grace
Whose Wisdom maketh these
Golden fishes of the Duc de Guise?'

She rode through Liddesdale with a song;
'Ye streams sae wondrous strang,
Oh, mak' me a wrack as I come back
But spare me as I gang,'
While a hill-bird cried and cried
Like a spirit lost
By the grey storm-wind tost.

Consider the way she had to go.
Think of the hungry snare,
The net she herself had woven,

Aware or unaware,
Of the dancing feet grown still,
The blinded eyes –
Queens should be cold and wise,
And she loved little things,
    Parrots
  And red-legged partridges
And the golden fishes of the Duc de Guise
And the pigeon with the blue ruff
She had from Monsieur d'Elbœuf.

LEWIS SPENCE (1874–1955)

The Prows O' Reekie

*ne

O wad this braw hie-heapit toun
Sail aff like an enchanted ship,
Drift owre the warld's seas up and doun,
And kiss wi' Venice lip to lip,
Or anchor into Naples' Bay
A misty island far astray
Or set her rock to Athens' wa',
Pillar to pillar, stane to stane,
The cruikit spell o' her backbane,
Yon shadow-mile o' spire and vane,
would surpass them all
Wad ding them a', wad ding them a'!
ose
Cadiz wad tine the admiralty
merald
O' yonder emerod fair sea,
Gibraltar frown for frown exchange
lbow
Wi' Nigel's crags at elbuck-range,
The rose-red banks o' Lisbon make
Mair room in Tagus for her sake.

A hoose is but a puppet-box
To keep life's images frae knocks,
crape
But mannikins scrieve oot their sauls
tepped gables
Upon its craw-steps and its walls;
Whaur hae they writ them mair sublime
Than on yon gable-ends o' time?

The Carse

It is a thousand sunsets since I lay
In many-birded Gowrie,* and did know
Its shadow for my soul, that passionate Tay
Out of my heart did flow.

Carse of Gowrie low-lying river-land

The immortal hour the hate of time defies.
Men of my loins a million years away
Shall have the gloom of Gowrie in their eyes,
And in their blood the Tay.

Great Tay of the Waves

O that yon river micht nae mair
   Rin through the channels o' my sleep;
too sorely   My bluid has felt its tides owre sair,
   Its waves hae drooned my dreams owre deep.

O why should Tay be a' my day
   And Buddon links be a' my nicht,
The warld o' a' my walks be gray
   Wi' yon far sands' unwarldly licht?

sea mists   As haars the windless waters find
   The unguarded instant falls a prey
innocent   To sakeless shadows o' the mind,
   And a' my life rins back to Tay.

Deep in the saul the early scene –
   Ah, let him play wi' suns wha can,
The cradle's pented on the een,
quarter   The native airt resolves the man!

stolen ## The Stown Bairn

O dinna ye spy yon castel braw
beyond/crests   Ayont the gress-green riggs o'sea,
inside it There's a tower intil't and a bower intil't
   And a louping lyon has power intil't
Rampin' amang the win's that thraw
rowdily   Yon banner bousteouslie.
mother O whaten a castel is yon, ma minnie,

compels

fate

magic

barren and gorse-choked

sea mist

then a stronghold

besides

swims

exclusively

fond

That harles the hert's bluid oot o' me
And beckons me owre a warld o' watters
   To seek its weird or dee?

You castel braw, ma bonny bit hinny,
   It is the Scottis Glamourie;
There's a spell intil't and a well intil't
   And the sang o' a siller bell intil't,
But the braes abune it are dowf and whinny,
   And the bracken buries the lea.
It's noo a ship wi' the haar for sail,
   And syne a strength, as ye may see,
Forbye it's a hill wi' a hollow ha',
   Whaur the fludes sough eerilie.

O minnie, see yon mune-white steed
   That sowms sae soople owre the sea;
Wi' a horn on his heid, he mak's sic speid
   As alanerlie the clan o' the deid,
And I ken he's fain o' me.
   O whaur are ye, ma gentle bairn
This moment was upon ma knee?
   I cuddled ye i' the cruik o' ma airm,
And noo ye're awa frae me!

RACHEL ANNAND TAYLOR (1876–1960)

The Princess of Scotland

'Who are you that so strangely woke,
  And raised a fine hand?'
Poverty wears a scarlet cloke
      In my land.

'Duchies of dreamland, emerald, rose
  Lie at your command?'
Poverty like a princess goes
      In my land.

'Wherefore the mask of silken lace
  Tied with a golden band?'
Poverty walks with wanton grace
      In my land.

'Why do you softly, richly speak
  Rhythm so sweetly-scanned?'
Poverty hath the Gaelic and Greek
      In my land.

'There's a far-off scent about you seems
  Born in Samarkand.'
Poverty hath luxurious dreams
      In my land.

'You have wounds that like passion-flowers you hide:
  I cannot understand.'
Poverty hath one name with Pride
      In my land.

'Oh! Will you draw your last sad breath
  'Mid bitter bent and sand?'
Poverty begs from none but Death
      In my land.

SIR ALEXANDER GRAY (1882–1967)

Scotland

Here in the uplands
The soil is ungrateful;
The fields, red with sorrel,
Are stony and bare.
A few trees, wind-twisted –
Or are they but bushes? –
Stand stubbornly guarding
A home here and there.

Scooped out like a saucer,
The land lies before me,
The waters, once scattered,
Flow orderly now
Through fields where the ghosts
Of the marsh and the moorland
Still ride the old marches,
Despising the plough.

The marsh and the moorland
Are not to be banished;
The bracken and heather,
The glory of broom,
Usurp all the balks
And the field's broken fringes,
And claim from the sower
Their portion of room.

This is my country,
The land that begat me.
These windy spaces
Are surely my own.
And those who here toil
In the sweat of their faces
Are flesh of my flesh
And bone of my bone.

Hard is the day's task –
Scotland, stern Mother! –
Wherewith at all times
Thy sons have been faced –
Labour by day,
And scant rest in the gloaming
With want an attendant
Not lightly outpaced.

Yet do thy children
Honour and love thee,
Harsh is thy schooling
Yet great is the gain.
True hearts and strong limbs,
The beauty of faces
Kissed by the wind
And caressed by the rain.

ANDREW YOUNG (1885–1971)

On the Pilgrims' Road

That I had hit the Road
  I partly knew
From a great Roman snail
  And sombre yew;
But that my steps went from
  And not towards
The shrine of good St Thomas,
  I thought of afterwards.

So I adored today
  No, not his ghost,
But the saints in Westwell window,
  And her the most
Who knelt there with no head
  But was so very
Adorable a saint
  In dress of crushed strawberry.

The Stockdoves

They rose up in a twinkling cloud
And wheeled about and bowed
To settle on the trees
Perching like small clay images.

Then with a noise of sudden rain
They clattered off again
And over Ballard Down
They circled like a flying town.

Though one could sooner blast a rock
Than scatter that dense flock
That through the winter weather
Some iron rule has held together,

Yet in another month from now
Love like a spark will blow
Those birds the country over
To drop in trees, lover by lover.

A Heap of Faggots

Faggots of ash, elm, oak
That dark loose snowflakes touch and soak,
An unlit fire they lie
With cold inhospitality.

Nothing will light them now,
Sticks that with only lichen glow
And crumble to touchwood
Soft and unfit for fire's food.

And with wren, finch and tit
And all the silent birds that sit
In this snow-travelled wood
I warm myself at my own blood.

A Prehistoric Camp

It was the time of year
  Pale lambs leap with thick leggings on
Over small hills that are not there,
  That I climbed Eggardon.

The hedgerows still were bare,
  None ever knew so late a year;
Birds built their nests in the open air,
  Love conquering their fear.

But there on the hill-crest,
  Where only larks or stars look down,
Earthworks exposed a vaster nest,
  Its race of men long flown.

Passing the Graveyard

I see you did not try to save
The bouquet of white flowers I gave;
So fast they wither on your grave.

Why does it hurt the heart to think
Of that most bitter abrupt brink
Where the low-shouldered coffins sink?

These living bodies that we wear
So change by every seventh year
That in a new dress we appear;

Limbs, spongy brain and slogging heart,
No part remains the selfsame part;
Like streams they stay and still depart.

You slipped slow bodies in the past;
Then why should we be so aghast
You flung off the whole flesh at last?

Let him who loves you think instead
That like a woman who has wed
You undressed first and went to bed.

Sudden Thaw

When day dawned with unusual light,
Hedges in snow stood half their height
And in the white-paved village street
Children were walking without feet.

But now by their own breath kept warm
Muck-heaps are naked at the farm
And even through the shrinking snow
Dead bents and thistles start to grow.

The Shepherd's Hut

The smear of blue peat smoke
That staggered on the wind and broke,
The only sign of life,
Where was the shepherd's wife,
Who left those flapping clothes to dry,
Taking no thought for her family?
For, as they bellied out
And limbs took shape and waved about,
I thought, She little knows
That ghosts are trying on her children's clothes.

HELEN B. CRUICKSHANK (1886–1975)

The Ponnage Pool

'. . . Sing
Some simple silly sang
O' willows or o' mimulus
A river's banks alang.'
  Hugh MacDiarmid

remember

[place name]

I mind o' the Ponnage Pule,
The reid brae risin',
Morphie Lade,
An' the saumon that louped the dam,
A tree i' Martin's Den
Wi' names carved on it;
But I ken na wha I am.

one

Ane o' the names was mine,
An' still I own it.
Naething it kens
O' a' that mak's up me.
Less I ken o' mysel'
Than the saumon wherefore
It rins up Esk frae the sea.

I am the deep o' the pule,
The fish, the fisher,
The river in spate,
The broon o' the far peat-moss,
The shingle bricht wi' the flooer
O' the yallow mim'lus,
The martin fleein' across.

I mind o' the Ponnage Pule
On a shinin' mornin',
The saumon fishers
Nettin' the bonny brutes –
I' the slithery dark o' the boddom
O' Charon's Coble
one   Ae day I'll faddom my doobts.

EDWIN MUIR (1887–1959)

Childhood

Long time he lay upon the sunny hill,
  To his father's house below securely bound.
Far off the silent, changing sound was still,
  With the black islands lying thick around.

He saw each separate height, each vaguer hue,
  Where the massed islands rolled in mist away,
And though all ran together in his view
  He knew that unseen straits between them lay.

Often he wondered what new shores were there.
  In thought he saw the still light on the sand,
The shallow water clear in tranquil air,
  And walked through it in joy from strand to
                               strand.

Over the sound a ship so slow would pass
  That in the black hill's gloom it seemed to lie.
The evening sound was smooth like sunken glass,
  And time seemed finished ere the ship passed by.

Grey tiny rocks slept round him where he lay,
  Moveless as they, more still as evening came,
The grasses threw straight shadows far away,
  And from the house his mother called his name.

The Town Betrayed

Our homes are eaten out by time,
  Our lawns strewn with our listless sons,
Our harlot daughters lean and watch
  The ships crammed down with shells and guns.

Like painted prows far out they lean:
  A world behind, a world before.
The leaves are covering up our hills,
  Neptune has locked the shore.

Our yellow harvests lie forlorn
  And there we wander like the blind,
Returning from the golden field
  With famine in our mind.

Far inland now the glittering swords
  In order rise, in order fall,
In order on the dubious field
  The dubious trumpets call.

Yet here there is no word, no sign
  But quiet murder in the street.
Our leaf-light lives are spared or taken
  By men obsessed and neat.

We stand beside our windows, see
  In order dark disorder come,
And prentice killers duped by death
  Bring and not know our doom.

Our cattle wander at their will.
  To-day a horse pranced proudly by.
The dogs run wild. Vultures and kites
  Wait in the towers for us to die.

At evening on the parapet
  We sit and watch the sun go down,
Reading the landscape of the dead,
  The sea, the hills, the town.

There our ancestral ghosts are gathered.
  Fierce Agamemnon's form I see,
Watching as if his tents were time
  And Troy eternity.

We must take order, bar our gates,
   Fight off these phantoms. Inland now
Achilles, Siegfried, Lancelot
   Have sworn to bring us low.

Scotland 1941

We were a tribe, a family, a people.
Wallace and Bruce guard now a painted field,
And all may read the folio of our fable,
Peruse the sword, the sceptre and the shield.
A simple sky roofed in that rustic day,
The busy corn-fields and the haunted holms,
The green road winding up the ferny brae.
But Knox and Melville clapped their preaching palms
And bundled all the harvesters away,
Hoodicrow Peden in the blighted corn
Hacked with his rusty beak the starving haulms.
Out of that desolation we were born.

Courage beyond the point and obdurate pride
Made us a nation, robbed us of a nation.
Defiance absolute and myriad-eyed
That could not pluck the palm plucked our
                                        damnation.
We with such courage and the bitter wit
To fell the ancient oak of loyalty,
And strip the peopled hill and the altar bare,
And crush the poet with an iron text,
How could we read our souls and learn to be?
Here a dull drove of faces harsh and vexed,
We watch our cities burning in their pit,
To salve our souls grinding dull lucre out,
We, fanatics of the frustrate and the half,
Who once set Purgatory Hill in doubt.
Now smoke and dearth and money everywhere,
Mean heirlooms of each fainter generation,
And mummied housegods in their musty niches,
Burns and Scott, sham bards of a sham nation,

And spiritual defeat wrapped warm in riches,
No pride but pride of pelf. Long since the young
Fought in great bloody battles to carve out
This towering pulpit of the Golden Calf,
Montrose, Mackail, Argyle, perverse and brave,
Twisted the stream, unhooped the ancestral hill.
Never had Dee or Don or Yarrow or Till
Huddled such thriftless honour in a grave.

Such wasted bravery idle as a song,
Such hard-won ill might prove Time's verdict wrong,
And melt to pity the annalist's iron tongue.

The Ring

Long since we were a family, a people,
The legends say; an old kind-hearted king
Was our foster father, and our life a fable.

Nature in wrath broke through the grassy ring
Where all our gathered treasures lay in sleep –
Many a rich and many a childish thing.

She filled with hoofs and horns the quiet keep.
Her herds beat down the turf and nosed the shrine
In bestial wonder, bull and adder and ape,

Lion and fox, all dressed by fancy fine
In human flesh and armed with arrows and spears;
But on the brow of each a secret sign

That haughtily put aside the sorrowful years
Or struck them down in stationary rage;
Yet they had tears that were not like our tears,

And new, all new, for Nature knows no age.
Fatherless, sonless, homeless haunters, they
Had never known the vow and the pilgrimage,

Poured from one fount into the faithless day.
We are their sons, but long ago we heard
Our fathers or our fathers' fathers say

Out of their dream the long-forgotten word
That rounded again the ring where sleeping lay
Our treasures, still unrusted and unmarred.

The Castle

All through that summer at ease we lay,
And daily from the turret wall
We watched the mowers in the hay
And the enemy half a mile away.
They seemed no threat to us at all.

For what, we thought, had we to fear
With our arms and provender, load on load,
Our towering battlements, tier on tier,
And friendly allies drawing near
On every leafy summer road.

Our gates were strong, our walls were thick,
So smooth and high, no man could win
A foothold there, no clever trick
Could take us, have us dead or quick.
Only a bird could have got in.

What could they offer us for bait?
Our captain was brave and we were true . . .
There was a little private gate,
A little wicked wicket gate.
The wizened warder let them through.

Oh then our maze of tunnelled stone
Grew thin and treacherous as air.
The cause was lost without a groan,
The famous citadel overthrown,
And all its secret galleries bare.

How can this shameful tale be told?
I will maintain until my death
We could do nothing, being sold;
Our only enemy was gold,
And we had no arms to fight it with.

The Labyrinth

Since I emerged that day from the labyrinth,
Dazed with the tall and echoing passages,
The swift recoils, so many I almost feared
I'd meet myself returning at some smooth corner,
Myself or my ghost, for all there was unreal
After the straw ceased rustling and the bull
Lay dead upon the straw and I remained,
Blood-splashed, if dead or alive I could not tell
In the twilight nothingness (I might have been
A spirit seeking his body through the roads
Of intricate Hades) – ever since I came out
To the world, the still fields swift with flowers, the
                            trees
All bright with blossom, the little green hills, the sea,
The sky and all in movement under it,
Shepherds and flocks and birds and the young and
                            old,
(I stared in wonder at the young and the old,
For in the maze time had not been with me;
I had strayed, it seemed, past sun and season and
                           change,
Past rest and motion, for I could not tell
At last if I moved or stayed; the maze itself
Revolved around me on its hidden axis
And swept me smoothly to its enemy,
The lovely world) – since I came out that day,
There have been times when I have heard my
                           footsteps
Still echoing in the maze, and all the roads
That run through the noisy world, deceiving streets
That meet and part and meet, and rooms that open

Into each other – and never a final room –
Stairways and corridors and antechambers
That vacantly wait for some great audience,
The smooth sea-tracks that open and close again,
Tracks undiscoverable, indecipherable,
Paths on the earth and tunnels underground,
And bird-tracks in the air – all seemed a part
Of the great labyrinth. And then I'd stumble
In sudden blindness, hasten, almost run,
As if the maze itself were after me
And soon must catch me up. But taking thought,
I'd tell myself, 'You need not hurry. This
Is the firm good earth. All roads lie free before you.'
But my bad spirit would sneer, 'No, do not hurry.
No need to hurry. Haste and delay are equal
In this one world, for there's no exit, none,
No place to come to, and you'll end where you are,
Deep in the centre of the endless maze.'

I could not live if this were not illusion.
It is a world, perhaps; but there's another.
For once in a dream or trance I saw the gods
Each sitting on the top of his mountain-isle,
While down below the little ships sailed by,
Toy multitudes swarmed in the habours, shepherds
                                                    drove
Their tiny flocks to the pastures, marriage feasts
Went on below, small birthdays and holidays,
Ploughing and harvesting and life and death,
And all permissible, all acceptable,
Clear and secure as in a limpid dream.
But they, the gods, as large and bright as clouds,
Conversed across the sounds in tranquil voices
High in the sky above the untroubled sea,
And their eternal dialogue was peace
Where all these things were woven, and this our life
Was as a chord deep in that dialogue,
As easy utterance of harmonious words,
Spontaneous syllables bodying forth a world.

That was the real world; I have touched it once,
And now shall know it always. But the lie,
The maze, the wild-wood waste of falsehood, roads
That run and run and never reach an end,
Embowered in error – I'd be prisoned there
But that my soul has birdwings to fly free.

Oh these deceits are strong almost as life.
Last night I dreamt I was in the labyrinth,
And woke far on. I did not know the place.

The Combat

It was not meant for human eyes,
That combat on the shabby patch
Of clods and trampled turf that lies
Somewhere beneath the sodden skies
For eye of toad or adder to catch.

And having seen it I accuse
The crested animal in his pride,
Arrayed in all the royal hues
Which hide the claws he well can use
To tear the heart out of the side.

Body of leopard, eagle's head
And whetted beak, and lion's mane,
And frost-grey hedge of feathers spread
Behind – he seemed of all things bred.
I shall not see his like again.

As for his enemy, there came in
A soft round beast as brown as clay;
All rent and patched his wretched skin;
A battered bag he might have been,
Some old used thing to throw away.

Yet he awaited face to face
The furious beast and the swift attack.

Soon over and done. That was no place
Or time for chivalry or for grace.
The fury had him on his back.

And two small paws like hands flew out
To right and left as the trees stood by.
One would have said beyond a doubt
This was the very end of the bout,
But that the creature would not die.

For ere the death-stroke he was gone,
Writhed, whirled, huddled into his den,
Safe somehow there. The fight was done,
And he had lost who had all but won.
But oh his deadly fury then.

A while the place lay blank, forlorn,
Drowsing as in relief from pain.
The cricket chirped, the grating thorn
Stirred, and a little sound was born.
The champions took their posts again.

And all began. The stealthy paw
Slashed out and in. Cold nothing save
These rags and tatters from the claw?
Nothing. And yet I never saw
A beast so helpless and so brave.

And now, while the trees stand watching, still
The unequal battle rages there.
The killing beast that cannot kill
Swells and swells in his fury till
You'd almost think it was despair.

One Foot in Eden

One foot in Eden still, I stand
And look across the other land.
The world's great day is growing late,

Yet strange these fields that we have planted
So long with crops of love and hate.
Time's handiworks by time are haunted,
And nothing now can separate
The corn and tares compactly grown.
The armorial weed in stillness bound
About the stalk; these are our own.
Evil and good stand thick around
In the fields of charity and sin
Where we shall lead our harvest in.

Yet still from Eden springs the root
As clean as on the starting day.
Time takes the foliage and the fruit
And burns the archetypal leaf
To shapes of terror and of grief
Scattered along the winter way.
But famished field and blackened tree
Bear flowers in Eden never known.
Blossoms of grief and charity
Bloom in these darkened fields alone.
What had Eden ever to say
Of hope and faith and pity and love
Until was buried all its day
And memory found its treasure trove?
Strange blessings never in Paradise
Fall from these beclouded skies.

To Franz Kafka

If we, the proximate damned, presumptive blest,
Were called one day to some high consultation
With the authentic ones, the worst and best
Picked from all time, how mean would be our
                                                    station.
Oh we could never bear the standing shame,
Equivocal ignominy of non-election;
We who will hardly answer to our name,
And on the road direct ignore direction.

But you, dear Franz, sad champion of the drab
And half, would watch the tell-tale shames drift in
(As if they were troves of treasure) not aloof,
But with a famishing passion quick to grab
Meaning, and read on all the leaves of sin
Eternity's secret script, the saving proof.

The Difficult Land

This is a difficult land. Here things miscarry
Whether we care, or do not care enough.
The grain may pine, the harlot weed grow haughty,
Sun, rain, and frost alike conspire against us:
You'd think there was malice in the very air.
And the spring floods and summer droughts: our
                                                    fields
Mile after mile of soft and useless dust.
On dull delusive days presaging rain
We yoke the oxen, go out harrowing,
Walk in the middle of an ochre cloud,
Dust rising before us and falling again behind us,
Slowly and gently settling where it lay.
These days the earth itself looks sad and senseless.
And when next day the sun mounts hot and lusty
We shake our fists and kick the ground in anger.
We have strange dreams: as that, in the early
                                                    morning
We stand and watch the silver drift of stars
Turn suddenly to a flock of black-birds flying.
And once in a lifetime men from over the border,
In early summer, the season of fresh campaigns,
Come trampling down the corn, and kill our cattle.
These things we know and by good luck or guidance
Either frustrate or, if we must, endure.
We are a people; race and speech support us,
Ancestral rite and custom, roof and tree,
Our songs that tell of our triumphs and disasters
(Fleeting alike), continuance of fold and hearth,
Our names and callings, work and rest and sleep,

And something that, defeated, still endures –
These things sustain us. Yet there are times
When name, identity, and our very hands,
Senselessly labouring, grow most hateful to us,
And we would gladly rid us of these burdens,
Enter our darkness through the doors of wheat
And the light veil of grass (leaving behind
Name, body, country, speech, vocation, faith)
And gather into the secrecy of the earth
Furrowed by broken ploughs lost deep in time.

We have such hours, but are drawn back again
By faces of goodness, faithful masks of sorrow,
Honesty, kindness, courage, fidelity,
The love that lasts a life's time. And the fields,
Homestead and stall and barn, springtime and
                                          autumn.
(For we can love even the wandering seasons
In their inhuman circuit.) And the dead
Who lodge in us so strangely, unremembered,
Yet in their place. For how can we reject
The long last look on the ever-dying face
Turned backward from the other side of time?
And how offend the dead and shame the living
By these despairs? And how refrain from love?
This is a difficult country, and our home.

The Horses

Barely a twelvemonth after
The seven days war that put the world to sleep,
Late in the evening the strange horses came.
By then we had made our covenant with silence,
But in the first few days it was so still
We listened to our breathing and were afraid.
On the second day
The radios failed; we turned the knobs; no answer.
On the third day a warship passed us, heading north,
Dead bodies piled on the deck. On the sixth day

A plane plunged over us into the sea. Thereafter
Nothing. The radios dumb;
And still they stand in corners of our kitchens,
And stand, perhaps, turned on, in a million rooms
All over the world. But now if they should speak,
If on a sudden they should speak again,
If on the stroke of noon a voice should speak,
We would not listen, we would not let it bring
That old bad world that swallowed its children quick
At one great gulp. We would not have it again.
Sometimes we think of the nations lying asleep,
Curled blindly in impenetrable sorrow,
And then the thought confounds us with its
                                        strangeness.

The tractors lie about our fields; at evening
They look like dank sea-monsters couched and
                                        waiting.
We leave them where they are and let them rust:
'They'll moulder away and be like other loam'.
We make our oxen drag our rusty ploughs,
Long laid aside. We have gone back
Far past our fathers' land.
                          And then, that evening
Late in the summer the strange horses came.
We heard a distant tapping on the road,
A deepening drumming; it stopped, went on again
And at the corner changed to hollow thunder.
We saw the heads
Like a wild wave charging and were afraid.
We had sold our horses in our fathers' time
To buy new tractors. Now they were strange to us
As fabulous steeds set on an ancient shield
Or illustrations in a book of knights.
We did not dare go near them. Yet they waited,
Stubborn and shy, as if they had been sent
By an old command to find our whereabouts
And that long-lost archaic companionship.
In the first moment we had never a thought
That they were creatures to be owned and used.

Among them were some half-a-dozen colts
Dropped in some wilderness of the broken world,
Yet new as if they had come from their own Eden.
Since then they have pulled our ploughs and borne
                                              our loads
But that free servitude still can pierce our hearts.
Our life is changed; their coming our beginning.

HUGH MACDIARMID (Christopher Murray Grieve) (1892–1978)

The Bonnie Broukit Bairn

For Peggy

fine in crimson

Mars is braw in crammasy,
Venus in a green silk goun,
The auld mune shak's her gowden feathers,

a bit of nonsense

Their starry talk's a wheen o' blethers,
Nane for thee a thochtie sparin',

neglected child

Earth, thou bonnie broukit bairn!

but weep
the whole of worthless
humanity

– *But greet, an' in your tears ye'll droun*
The haill clanjamfrie!

The Watergaw

one wet dusk in the ewe-
*tremble**

A e weet forenicht i' the yow-trummle

rare

I saw yon antrin thing,

a broken rainbow

A watergaw wi' its chitterin' licht

beyond the downpour

Ayont the on-ding;
An' I thocht o' the last wild look ye gied
Afore ye deed!

no quarrel in the lark's house

There was nae reek i' the laverock's hoose
That nicht – an' nane i' mine;
But I hae thocht o' that foolish licht

since then

Ever sin' syne;
An' I think that mebbe at last I ken
What your look meant then.

The Eemis Stane

unsteady

at the very heart/harvest

I' the how-dumb-deid o' the cauld hairst nicht
The warl' like an eemis stane

in the sky

Wags i' the lift;

* *yow-trummle* a cold spell in summer after sheep-shearing

An' my eerie memories fa'
snow blown in the air   Like a yowdendrift.

Like a yowdendrift so's I couldna read
The words cut oot i' the stane
moss   Had the fug o' fame
lichen   An' history's hazelraw
buried   No' yirdit thaim.

disgust

Scunner

hides   Your body derns
In its graces again
dreary earth As dreich grun' does
In the gowden grain,
And oot o' the daith
O' pride you rise
Wi' beauty yet
· For a hauf-disguise.

sparkling   The skinklan' stars
Are but distant dirt.
very close   Tho' fer owre near
sometimes   You are still – whiles – girt
Wi' the bonnie licht
you should have lost You bood ha'e tint
– And I lo'e Love
Wi' a scunner in't.

Empty Vessel

beyond the hillock I met ayont the cairney
unkempt   A lass wi' tousie hair
Singin' till a bairnie
That was nae langer there.

winds   Wunds wi' warlds to swing
Dinna sing sae sweet,

The licht that bends owre a' thing
Is less ta'en up wi't.

from A Drunk Man Looks at the Thistle

lines 101–44

if she's not here   *Jean! Jean!* Gin *she's* no' here it's no' *oor* bed,
            Or else I'm dreamin' deep and canna wauken,
very   But it's a fell queer dream if this is no'
            A real hillside – and thae things thistles and bracken!

holding   It's hard wark haud'n by a thocht worth ha'en'
every man   And harder speakin't, and no' for ilka man;
            Maist Thocht's like whisky – a thoosan' under proof,
            And a sair price is pitten on't even than.

            As Kirks wi' Christianity ha'e dune,
            Burns Clubs wi' Burns – wi' a'thing it's the same,
anything   The core o' ocht is only for the few,
busy   Scorned by the mony, thrang wi'ts empty name.

            And a' the names in History mean nocht
            To maist folk but 'ideas o' their ain,'
            The vera opposite o' onything
            The Deid 'ud awn gin they cam' back again.

            A greater Christ, a greater Burns, may come.
            The maist they'll dae is to gi'e bigger pegs
            To folly and conceit to hank their rubbish on.
truly!   They'll cheenge folks' talk but no' their natures, fegs!

            I maun feed frae the common trough ana'
            Whaur a' the lees o' hope are jumbled up;
            While centuries like pigs are slorpin' owre't
            Sall my wee 'oor by cryin': 'Let pass this cup'?

pig's snout   In wi' your gruntle then, puir wheengin' saul,
cattle-piss/the rest   Lap up the ugsome aidle wi' the lave,

What gin it's your ain vomit that you swill
yawning   And frae Life's gantin' and unfaddomed grave?

very much   I doot I'm geylies mixed, like Life itsel',
But I was never ane that thocht to pit
pint-pot*   An ocean in a mutchkin. As the haill's
Mair than the pairt sae I than reason yet.

I dinna haud the warld's end in my heid
As maist folk think they dae; nor filter truth
In fishy gills through which its tides may poor
For ony *animalcula* forsooth.

laugh   I lauch to see my crazy little brain
      – And ither folks' – tak'n' itsel' seriously,
blaze   And in a sudden lowe o' fun my saul
dazed   Blinks dozent as the owl I ken't to be.

I'll ha'e nae hauf-way hoose, but aye be whaur
Extremes meet – it's the only way I ken
To dodge the curst conceit o' bein' richt
That damns the vast majority o' men.

lines 477–512

[MAN AND THE INFINITE]

throbs   Nerves in stounds o' delight,
Muscles in pride o' power,
arrayed   Bluid as wi' roses dight
prominent   Life's toppin' pinnacles owre,
The thistle yet'll unite
Man and the Infinite!

nimble and swift with vigour   Swippert and swith wi' virr
hollows   In the howes o' man's hert
great   Forever its muckle roots stir
astir   Like a Leviathan astert,
Till'ts coils like a thistle's leafs

---

*mutchkin quarter of a Scottish pint (i.e. three-quarters of an imperial pint) *lightning*   Sweep space wi' levin sheafs.

lowest   Frae laichest deeps o' the ocean
                       It rises in flight upon flight,
                       And yont its uttermaist motion
                       Can still set roses alight,
                       As else unreachable height
                       Fa's under its triumphin' sight.

                       Here is the root that feeds
stalk*   The shank wi' the blindin' wings
dwindling overhead to sparks*   Dwinin' abundheid to gleids
nimbuses*   Like stars in their keethin' rings,
                       And blooms in sunrise and sunset
gate   Inowre Eternity's yett.

                       Lay haud o' my hert and feel
stars   Fountains ootloupin' the starns
                       Or see the Universe reel
ardent brains   Set gaen' by my eident harns,
shoulder   Or test the strength o' my spauld
weight   The wecht o' a' thing to hauld!

                       – The howes o' Man's hert are bare,
                       The Dragon's left them for good,
                       There's nocht but naethingness there,
                       The hole whaur the Thistle stood,
                       That rootless and radiant flies
                       A Phoenix in Paradise! . . .

                       lines 612–35

                       [O WHA'S THE BRIDE?]

                       O wha's the bride that cairries the bunch
glimmering   O' thistles blinterin' white?
suspects   Her cuckold bridegroom little dreids
                       What he sall ken this nicht.

---

*shank also, a salmon after spawning (see keethin'); *gleids* or, something glimpsed through having been forced to squint (?); *keethin'* turbulence in water made by fish

husband   For closer than gudeman can come
                 And closer to'r than hersel',
                 Wha didna need her maidenheid
                 Has wrocht his purpose fell.

                 O wha's been here afore me, lass,
                 And hoo did he get in?
                   – A man that deed or I was born
                   This evil thing has din.

                 And left, as it were on a corpse,
                 Your maidenheid to me?
                   – Nae lass, gudeman, sin' Time began
has had   *'S hed ony mair to gi'e.*

                 But I can gi'e ye kindness, lad,
                 And a pair o' willin' hands,
                 And you sall ha'e my briests like stars,
                 My limb like willow wands,

                 And on my lips ye'll heed nae mair,
                 And in my hair forget,
                 The seed o' a' the men that in
                 My virgin womb ha'e met . . .

                 lines 636–43

                 [REPETITION COMPLEX]

                 Millions o' wimmen bring forth in pain
                 Millions o' bairns that are no' worth ha'en.

                 Wull ever a wumman be big again
                 Wi's muckle's a Christ? Yech, there's nae sayin'.

                 Gin that's the best that you ha'e comin',
faith   Fegs but I'm sorry for you, wumman!

Yet a'e thing's certain. — Your faith is great.

hy

Whatever happens, you'll no' be blate! . . .

lines 644–51

[THE PROBLEM CHILD]

hildbed

Mary lay in jizzen
As it were claith o' gowd.

ags

But it's in orra duds

very other birth* is wrapped

Ilka ither bairntime's row'd.

Christ had never toothick,
Christ was never seeck,

roublesome

But Man's a fiky bairn

olic, diarrhoea and toothache

Wi' bellythraw, ripples, and worm-i'-the-cheek! . . .

lines 1219–30

[THE THISTLE'S CHARACTERISTICS]

The language that but sparely flooers
And maistly gangs to weed;
The thocht o' Christ and Calvary

oing backwards and forwards

Aye liddenin' in my heid;
And a' the dour provincial thocht
That merks the Scottish breed
— These are the thistle's characters,

rgue

To argie there's nae need.
Hoo weel my verse embodies
The thistle you can read!
— But will a Scotsman never
Frae this vile growth be freed? . . .

lines 1334–60

A black leaf owre a white leaf twirls,

utters

A grey leaf flauchters in atween,
Sae ply my thochts aboot the stem

---

* *bairntime* 'a woman's breeding time' (MacDiarmid); labour or lying-in

coagulated   O' loppert slime frae which they spring.
The thistle like a snawstorm drives,
Or like a flicht o' swallows lifts,
Or like a swarm o'_midges hings,
A plague o' moths, a starry sky,
But's naething but a thistle yet,
And still the puzzle stands unsolved.
Beauty and ugliness alike,
And life and daith and God and man,
Are aspects o't but nane can tell
The secret that I'd fain find oot
O' this bricht hive, this sorry weed,
The tree that fills the universe,
like a dried herring shrinks   Or like a reistit herrin' crines.

if   Gin I was sober I micht think
It was like something drunk men see!

The necromancy in my bluid
Through a' the gamut cheenges me
O' dwarf and giant, foul and fair,
But winna let me be mysel'
— My mither's womb that reins me still
test for occult authenticity   Until I tae can prick the witch
And 'Wumman' cry wi' Christ at last,
'Then what hast thou to do wi' me?'

lines 1451–1548

[*part of* A STICK-NEST IN YGDRASIL*]

in every direction   Thou art the facts in ilka airt
force a way through   That breenge into infinity.
Criss-crossed wi' coontless ither facts
Nae man can follow, and o' which
He is himsel' a helpless pairt.
Held in their tangle as he were
A stick-nest in Ygdrasil!

* *stick-nest* probably MacDiarmid's poetic compound imaging a nest like a magpie's, in *Ygdrasil*, the world ash tree of ancient Norse myth

The less man sees the mair he is
Content wi't, but the mair he sees
The mair he kens hoo little o'
A' that there is he'll ever see,
And hoo it mak's confusion aye
The waur confoondit till at last
His brain inside his heid is like
bobbin   Ariadne wi' an empty pirn,
spinning   Or like a birlin' reel frae which
A whale has rived the line awa'.

abandoned   What better's a forhooied nest
loose straw Than shasloch scattered owre the grun'?

O hard it is for man to ken
He's no creation's goal nor yet
A benefitter by't at last –
A means to ends he'll never ken,
And as to michtier elements
The slauchtered brutes he eats to him
Or forms o' life owre sma' to see
Wi' which his heedless body swarms,
And a' man's thocht nae mair to them
spider's web Than ony moosewob to a man,
glittering   His Heaven to them the blinterin' o'
shithoose   A snail-trail on their closet wa'!

For what's an atom o' a twig
That tak's a billion to an inch
abundance To a' the routh o' shoots that mak'
The bygrowth o' the Earth aboot
The michty trunk o' Space that spreids
small branches Ramel o' licht that ha'e nae end,
– The trunk wi' centuries for rings,
Comets for fruit, November shooers
For leafs that in its Autumns fa'
such   – And Man at maist o' sic a twig
Ane o' the coontless atoms is!

sinews	My sinnens and my veins are but
much	As muckle o' a single shoot
unweave	Wha's fibre I can ne'er unwaft
	O' my wife's flesh and mither's flesh
	And a' the flesh o' humankind,
ravelled threads	And revelled thrums o' beasts and plants
	As gangs to mak' twixt birth and daith
	A'e sliver for a microscope;
	And a' the life o' Earth to be
	Can never lift frae underneath
	The shank o' which oor destiny's pairt
as high as/facing	As heich's to stand forenenst the trunk
straw*	Stupendous as a windlestrae!

	I'm under nae delusions, fegs!
whopping sucker	The whuppin' sooker at wha's tip
	Oor little point o' view appears,
honeycomb	A midget coom o' continents
blobs	Wi' blebs o' oceans set, sends up
	The braith o' daith as weel as life,
and we must sprout	And we maun braird anither tip
	Oot owre us ere we wither tae,
wooden*	And join the sentrice skeleton
build	As coral insects big their reefs.

	What is the tree? As fer as Man's
	Concerned it disna maitter
	Gin but a giant thistle 'tis
	That spreids eternal mischief there,
	As I'm inclined to think.
	Ruthless its sends its solid growth
	Through mair than he can e'er conceive,
asunder	And braks his warlds abreid and rives
	His Heavens to tatters on its horns.

	The nature or the purpose o't
bother to ask	He needna fash to spier, for he

*windlestrae withered grass, anything weak or slender, worthless; *sentrice* timbers used to support an arch in the process of building

Is destined to be sune owre grown
And hidden wi' the parent wud
cover   The spreidin' boughs in darkness hap,
And a' its future life'll be
Ootwith'm as he's ootwith his banes.

Juist as man's skeleton has left
behind   Its ancient ape-like shape ahint,
Sae states o' mind in turn gi'e way
To different states, and quickly seem
Impossible to later men.
And Man's mind in its final shape
Or lang'll seem a monkey's spook,
very   And, strewth, to me the vera thocht
extreme   O Thocht already's fell like that!
Yet still the cracklin' thorns persist
In fitba' match and peepy show;
To antic hay a dog-fecht's mair
Than Jacob *v.* the Angel;
And through a cylinder o' wombs,
puddle   A star reflected in a dub,
brains   I see as 'twere my ain wild harns
intestines   The ripple o' Eve's moniplies.

lines 2216–35

[FAREWELL TO DOSTOEVSKI]

over us   *The wan leafs shak' atour us like the snaw.*
heavy snowfall/lost   *Here is the cavaburd in which Earth's tint.*
There's naebody but Oblivion and us,
vagrants   *Puir gangrel buddies, wanderin' hameless in't.*

remains   *The stars are larochs o' auld cottages,*
blinding snow   *And a' Time's glen is fu' o' blinnin stew.*
window glimmers   *Nae freen'ly lozen skimmers: and the wund*
*Rises and separates even me and you.**

* Dostoevski

I ken nae Russian and you ken nae Scots.
We canna tell oor voices frae the wund.
The snaw is seekin' everywhere: oor herts
hearths   *At last like roofless ingles it has f'und,*

And gethers there in drift on endless drift,
Oor broken herts that it can never fill;
And still – its leafs like snaw, its growth like wund –
The thistle rises and forever will! . . .

The thistle rises and forever will,
Getherin' the generations under't.
This is the monument o' a' they were,
And a' they hoped and wondered.

lines 2482–2529

[*part of* THE GREAT WHEEL]

whit   Nae verse is worth a ha'et until
It can join issue wi' the Will
That raised the Wheel and spins it still,

But a' the music that mankind
'S made yet is to the Earth confined,
Poo'erless to reach the general mind,

next   Poo'erless to reach the neist star e'en,
That as a pairt o'ts sel' is seen,
And only men can tell between.

Yet I exult oor sang has yet
To grow wings that'll cairry it
beyond   Ayont its native speck o' grit,

And I exult to find me
The thocht that this can ever be,
A hope still for humanity.

if the sum

For gin the sun and mune at last
Are as a neebor's lintel passed,

lose

The wheel'll tine its stature fast,

spin

And birl in time inside oor heids

sparks

Till we can thraw oot conscious gleids
That draw an answer to oor needs,

Or if nae answer still we find
Brichten till a' thing is defined
In the huge licht-beams o' oor kind,

And if we still can find nae trace

behind

Ahint the Wheel o' ony Face,
There'll be a glory in the place,

perhaps

And we may aiblins swing content
Upon the wheel in which we're pent
In adequate enlightenment.

Nae ither thocht can mitigate
The horror o' the endless Fate
A'thing's whirled in predestinate.

O whiles I'd fain be blin' to it,
As men wha through the ages sit,

off the one spot

And never move frae aff the bit,

Wha hear a Burns or Shakespeare sing,

their own little jingles

Yet still their ain bit jingles string,
As they were worth the fashioning.

Whatever Scotland is to me,
Be it aye pairt o' a' men see
O' Earth and o' Eternity

Wha winna hide their heids in't till
It seems the haill o' Space to fill,
As 'twere an unsurmounted hill.

He canna Scotland see wha yet
Canna see the Infinite,
And Scotland in true scale to it.

lines 2614–46

[*part of* THE GREAT WHEEL]

endure

nondescript

hush

'Mercy o' Gode, I canna thole
Wi' sic an orra mob to roll.'
— 'Wheesht! It's for the guid o' your soul.'

'But what's the meanin', what's the sense?'
— *'Men shift but by experience.*
'Twixt Scots there is nae difference.

They canna learn, sae canna move,
But stick for aye to their auld groove
— The only race in History who've

Bidden in the same category
Frae stert to present o' their story,
And deem their ignorance their glory.

capsize

The mair they differ, mair the same.
The wheel can whummle a' but them,
— They ca' their obstinacy "Hame",

And "Puir Auld Scotland" bleat wi' pride,
And wi' their minds made up to bide
A thorn in a' the wide world's side.

who have had

There ha'e been Scots wha ha'e ha'en thochts.
They're strewn through maist o' the various lots
— Sic traitors are nae langer Scots!'

'But in this huge ineducable
Heterogeneous hotch and rabble,
Why am *I* condemned to squabble?'

'A Scottish poet maun assume
The burden o' his people's doom,
And dee to brak' their livin' tomb.

Mony ha'e tried, but a' ha'e failed.
Their sacrifice has nocht availed.
Upon the thistle they're impaled.

You maun choose but gin ye'd see
Anither category ye
Maun tine your nationality.'

must lose

First Hymn to Lenin

To Prince D. S. Mirsky

Few even o' the criminals, cravens, and fools
Wha's voices vilify a man they ken
They've cause to fear and are unfit to judge
As they're to stem his influence again
But in the hollows where their herts should be
    Foresee your victory.

Churchills, Locker-Lampsons, Beaverbrooks'll be
In history's perspective less to you
(And them!) than the Centurions to Christ
Of whom, as you, at least this muckle's true
– 'Tho' pairtly wrang he cam' to richt amang's
    Faur greater wrangs.'

Christ's cited no' by chance or juist because
You mark the greatest turnin'-point since him
But that your main redress has lain where he's
Least use – fulfillin' his sayin' lang kept dim
That whasae followed him things o' like natur'
    'Ud dae – and greater!

Certes nae ither, if no' you's dune this.
It maitters little. What you've dune's the thing,
No' hoo't compares, corrects, or complements

The work of Christ that's taen owre lang to bring
Sic a successor to keep the reference back
    Natural to mak'.

Great things ha'e aye ta'en great men in the past
In some proportion to the work they did,
But you alane to what you've dune are nocht
Even as the poo'ers to greater ends are hid
In what's ca'd God, or in the common man,
    Withoot your plan.

Descendant o' the unkent Bards wha made
Sangs peerless through a' post-anonymous days
I glimpse again in you that mightier poo'er
troubles   Than fashes wi' the laurels and the bays
But kens that it is shared by ilka man
    Since time began.

Great things, great men — but at faur greater's cost!
If first things first had had their rightfu' sway
Life and Thocht's misused poo'er might ha' been ane
For a' men's benefit — as still they may
Noo that through you this mair than elemental force
    Has f'und a clearer course.

Christ said: 'Save ye become as bairns again.'
common run   Bairnly eneuch the feck o' us ha' been!
Your work needs men; and its worst foes are juist
The traitors wha through a' history ha' gi'en
compelled   The dope that's gar'd the mass o' folk pay heed
    And bide bairns indeed.

As necessary, and insignificant, as death
Wi' a' its agonies in the cosmos still
The Cheka's horrors are in their degree;
And'll end suner! What maitters 't wha we kill
To lessen that foulest murder that deprives
    Maist men o' real lives?

For now in the flower and iron of the truth
To you we turn; and turn in vain nae mair,
Ilka fool has folly eneuch for sadness
But at last we are wise and wi' laughter tear
The veil of being, and are face to face
   Wi' the human race.

Here lies your secret, O Lenin, – yours and oors,
No' in the majority will that accepts the result
But in the real will that bides its time and kens
inmost   The benmaist resolve is the poo'er in which we exult
Since naebody's willingly deprived o' the good;
crowd   And, least o' a', the crood!

Water Music

To William and Flora Johnstone

hush   *Wheesht, wheesht, Joyce, and let me hear*
   Nae Anna Livvy's lilt.
But Wauchope, Esk, and Ewes again,
with its own rhythms to it   *Each wi' its ain rhythms till't.*

I

flowing smoothly here and   Archin' here and arrachin there,
tumultuous there
volatile or orderly   Allevolie or allemand,
sometimes compliant, sometimes Whiles appliable, whiles areird,
troublesome
   The polysemous poem's planned.

downcast, between, between   Lively, louch, atweesh, atween,
reduced to a thread or in full   Auchimuty or aspate,
flood
through the heather stems   Threidin' through the averins
ample in the outcome   Or bightsom in the aftergait.

wanton or perverse   Or barmybrained or barritchfu',
like a spider   Or rinnin' like an attercap,
like a coin*   Or shinin' like an Atchison,
with a cry or with a surge   Wi' a blare or wi' a blawp.

* *Atchison* old copper coin washed with silver

all that opens and shuts

> They ken a' that opens and steeks,
>   Frae Fiddleton Bar to Callister Ha',
> And roon aboot for twenty miles,

make rings, bubble and make waves

>   They bead and bell and swaw.

straight or circuitous or crooked

> Brent on or boutgate or beshacht

hesitant or headlong

>   Bellwaverin' or borne-heid,

they pose and pout,* or cry and cringe

> They mimp and primp, or bick and birr,
>   Dilly-dally or show speed.

impulsive or slovenly, ruffted, smooth*
outrageous or austere

> Brade-up or sclafferin', rouchled, sleek,
>   Abstraklous or austerne,

in whirlpools below the banks*

> In belths below the brae-hags

and carousals* in the fern

>   And bebbles in the fern.

> Bracken, blaeberries, and heather

know their babble and chatter

>   Ken their amplefeysts and toves,

here goes one with spangles*

> Here gangs ane wi' aiglets jinglin',

another struggles through a gorge

>   Through a gowl anither goves.

> Lint in the bell whiles hardly vies

with one the wind disturbs

>   Wi' ane the wind amows,

down eroded steeps decorated with gold another pours

> While blithely doon abradit linns
>   Wi' gowd begane anither jows.

hacking, hawking, choking and croaking
flattery in one another's throats

> Cougher, blocher, boich and croichle,
>   Fraise in ane anither's witters,

with vortexes, currents, side-channels
light brown or bluish

> Wi' backthraws, births, by-rinnin's,
>   Beggar's-broon or blae – the critters!

or brown, holly green, dark green, mottled*

> Or burnet, holine, watchet, chauve,
>   Or wi' a' the colours dyed

of the sky above

> O' the lift abune and plants and trees
>   That grow on either side.

---

*mimp speak or act affectedly; *primp* behave prudishly or affectedly; *bick* sob or cry, *birr* move energetically or be in turmoil, *bick and birr* (trad.) to imitate the cry of a grouse; *sleek* smoothly, with cunning (as a noun it can mean ooze on a river bed); *brae-hags* wooded overhanging banks of a stream; *bebbles* sips, drinks, tipples; *aiglets* points (i.e. metal tips or ornaments on the ends of laces or cords); *chauve* having white and black hair more or less equally (used of cattle)

pitted	Or coinyelled wi' the midges,
	Or swallows a'aboot,
	The shadow o' an eagle,
the splash of a trout	The aiker o' a troot.
distorting	Toukin' ootrageous face
winding stair	The turn-gree o' your mood,
climbed	I've climmed until I'm lost
	Like the sun ahint a clood.
a pop-gun from the elder	*But a tow-gun frae the boon-tree,*
	A whistle frae the elm,
	A spout-gun frae the hemlock,
	And, back in this auld realm,
colt's-foot	*Dry leafs o' dishielogie*
'crab's claw'*	*To smoke in a 'partan's tae'!*
	And you've me in your creel again,
dull or bright	Brim or shallow, bauch or bricht,
	Singin' in the mornin',
murmuring	Corrieneuchin' a' the nicht.

II

on the turf	Lappin' on the shirrel,
bursting down the glen	Or breengin' doon the cleuch,
chequerboard*	Slide-thrift for stars and shadows,
come to grief over the crag*	Or sun-'couped owre the heuch'.
	Wi' the slughorn o' a folk,
lookouts*	Sightsmen for a thoosand years,
in spate or serene*	In fluther or at shire
	O' the Border burns' careers,
let them bubble, let them purl	Let them popple, let them pirl,
	Plish-plash and plunk and plop and ploot,
in risky quagmire* or fish sanctuary	In quakin' quaw or fish-currie
	I ken a' they're aboot.

*'*partan's tae*' a short, stubby pipe (or 'cutty-clay'); *slide-thrift* the game of 'first off the board' at draughts; *heuch* crag, cliff, hollow, or deep glen; *sight(s)men* fishermen posted as lookouts for salmon; *at shire* clear, not muddy; *quaw* also a hole from which peats have been cut

caper

dance

And 'twixt the pavvy o' the Wauchope,
   And the paspey o' the Ewes,
And the pavane o' Esk itsel',
   It's no' for me to choose.

lively

like striped satin or cream*

a toy mill*

make all the country toil

Be they querty, be they quiet,
   Flow like railya or lamoo,
Only turn a rashmill or
   Gar a' the country tew,

snowing*
or pours pipestems and chimney cowls
so Waich Water flashes and swarms*

romps, and ruptures and rages

As it's froggin' in the hills,
   Or poors pipestapples and auld wives,
Sae Waich Water glents and scrows,
   Reels and ratches and rives.

Some day they say the Bigly Burn

will jump out from its scrub and overwhelm the lovely birch wood

all to wrack and ruin

   'll loup oot frae its scrabs and thistles,
And ding the bonnie birken shaw
   A' to pigs and whistles.

And there's yon beck – I winna name't –
   That hauds the fish that aince was hookit

a century ago

and abandoned all his gear

A century syne – the fisher saw't,
   And flew, and a' his graith forsookit.

And as for Unthank Water,

reeds and rushes*

it's still up to thieving*

the golden-eye duck's eggs

   That seeps through miles o' reeds and seggs,
It's aye at pilliewinkie syne
   Wi' the gowdnie's eggs.

than you yourself could piss

yet famous and I still see them sprouting*

Nae mair than you could stroan yoursel'
   The biggest o' them you may say,
Yet lood and still I see them stoan
   To oceans and the heaven's sway.

---

* *lamoo* anything easily swallowed; *rashmill* toy mill made of rushes; *froggin'* snowing or sleeting at intervals; *scrows* or, possibly, tears apart *seggs* various plants with sword-shaped leaves – yellow iris, etc. *pilliewinkie* children's cruel pastime of raiding birds' nests for eggs and younglings; *stoan* send out shoots, tendrils, suckers – here 'tributaries'

Fleetin' owre the meadows,
   Or cleitchin' in the glaur,

falling [?] in the mud

The haill world answers to them,

the furthest star

   And they rein the faurest star.

Humboldt, Howard, Maury,
   Hildebrandsson, Hann, and Symons,
A digest o' a' their work's

in these stubborn drops

   In these dour draps or diamonds.

And weel I ken the air's wild rush
   As it comes owre the seas,
Clims up and whistles 'twixt the hills,
   Wi' a' the weather gi'es

O' snaw and rain and thunder,
   Is a single circle spun
By the sun's bricht heat and guided by

of the ground

   Earth's spin and the shapes o' the grun'.

Lappin' on the shirrel,
   Or breengin' doon the cleuch,
I can listen to the waters
   Lang – and no' lang – eneuch.

Wheesht, wheesht, Joyce, and let me hear
   No' Anna Livvy's lilt,
But Wauchope, Esk, and Ewes again,
   Each wi' its ain rhythms till't.

Ho, My Little Sparrow

Ho, my little sparrow! For well I know
The profound and subtle soft lights in your eyes
Mean no more than two grains of wheat
In a basin full of water. And so
   I call you my little sparrow,
   For so a sparrow's wings go.

Ho, my little sparrow! Sparrows are common
Yet who can describe their thousand and one changes
Of colour as they quiver in the sun
Like thoughts of old rainbows? But what omen
    Is this? – All the live arc at home in
    Your look again, woman!

On a Raised Beach

To James H. Whyte

All is lithogenesis – or lochia,
Carpolite fruit of the forbidden tree,
Stones blacker than any in the Caaba,
Cream-coloured caen-stone, chatoyant pieces,
Celadon and corbeau, bistre and beige,
Glaucous, hoar, enfouldered, cyathiform,
Making mere faculae of the sun and moon
I study you glout and gloss, but have
No cadrans to adjust you with, and turn again
From optik to haptik and like a blind man run
My fingers over you, arris by arris, burr by burr,
Slickensides, truité, rugas, foveoles,
Bringing my aesthesis in vain to bear,
An angle-titch to all your corrugations and coigns,
Hatched foraminous cavo-relievo of the world,
Deictic, fiducial stones. Chiliad by chiliad
What bricole piled you here, stupendous cairn?
What artist poses the Earth écorché thus,
Pillar of creation engouled in me?
What eburnation augments you with men's bones,
Every energumen an Endymion yet?
All the other stones are in this haecceity it seems,
But where is the Christophanic rock that moved?
What Cabirian song from this catasta comes?

Deep conviction or preference can seldom
Find direct terms in which to express itself.
Today on this shingle shelf
I understand this pensive reluctance so well,

This not discommendable obstinacy,
These contrivances of an inexpressive critical feeling,
These stones with their resolve that Creation shall
                             not be
Injured by iconoclasts and quacks. Nothing has
                             stirred
Since I lay down this morning an eternity ago
But one bird. The widest open door is the least liable
                         to intrusion,
Ubiquitous as the sunlight, unfrequented as the sun.
The inward gates of a bird are always open.
It does not know how to shut them.
That is the secret of its song,
But whether any man's are ajar is doubtful.
I look at these stones and know little about them.
But I know their gates are open too,
Always open, far longer open, than any bird's can be,
That every one of them has had its gates wide open
                         `far longer
Than all birds put together, let alone humanity,
Though through them no man can see,
No man nor anything more recently born than
                         themselves
And that is everything else on the Earth.
I too lying here have dismissed all else.
Bread from stones is my sole and desperate dearth,
From stones, which are to the Earth as to the sunlight
Is the naked sun which is for no man's sight.
I would scorn to cry to any easier audience
Or, having cried, to lack patience to await the
                         response.
I am no more indifferent or ill-disposed to life than
                         death is;
I would fain accept it all completely as the soil does;
Already I feel all that can perish perishing in me
As so much has perished and all will yet perish in
                       these stones.
I must begin with these stones as the world began.

Shall I come to a bird quicker than the world's course
                                               ran?
        To a bird, and to myself, a man?
        And what if I do, and further?
I shall only have gone a little way to go back again
And be like a fleeting deceit of development,
Iconoclasts, quacks. So these stones have dismissed
All but all of evolution, unmoved by it,
(Is there anything to come they will not likewise
                                           dismiss?)
As the essential life of mankind in the mass
Is the same as their earliest ancestors yet.

Actual physical conflict or psychological warfare
        Incidental to love or food
Brings out animal life's bolder and more brilliant
                                            patterns
        Concealed as a rule in habitude.
        There is a sudden revelation of colour,
        The protrusion of a crest,
        The expansion of an ornament,
– But no general principle can be guessed
From these flashing fragments we are seeing,
These foam-bells on the hidden currents of being.
The bodies of animals are visible substances
And must therefore have colour and shape, in the
                                          first place
Depending on chemical composition, physical
                         structure, mode of growth,
Psychological rhythms and other factors in the case,
But their purposive function is another question.
Brilliant-hued animals hide away in the ocean deeps;
The mole has a rich sexual colouring in due season
Under the ground; nearly every beast keeps
Brighter colours inside it than outside.
What the seen shows is never anything to what it's
                                       designed to hide,
The red blood which makes the beauty of a maiden's
                                             cheek
Is as red under a gorilla's pigmented and hairy face.

Varied forms and functions though life may seem to
                                                    have shown
They all come back to the likeness of stone,
So to the intervening stages we can best find a clue
In what we all came from and return to.
There are no twirly bits in this ground bass.

We must be humble. We are so easily baffled by
                                                    appearances
And do not realise that these stones are one with the
                                                    stars.
It makes no difference to them whether they are high
                                                    or low,
Mountain peak or ocean floor, palace, or pigsty.
There are plenty of ruined buildings in the world but
                                                    no ruined stones.
No visitor comes from the stars
But is the same as they are.
– Nay, it is easy to find a spontaneity here,
An adjustment to life, an ability
To ride it easily, akin to 'the buoyant
Prelapsarian naturalness of a country girl
Laughing in the sun, not passion-rent,
But sensing in the bound of her breasts vigours to
                                                    come
Powered to make her one with the stream of earthlife
                                                    round her,'
But not yet as my Muse is, with this ampler scope,
This more divine rhythm, wholly at one
With the earth, riding the Heavens with it, as the
                                                    stones do
And all soon must.
But it is wrong to indulge in these illustrations
Instead of just accepting the stones.
It is a paltry business to try to drag down
The arduus furor of the stones to the futile
                                                    imaginings of men,
To all that fears to grow roots into the common
                                                    earth,
As it soon must, lest it be chilled to the core,

As it will be – and none the worse for that.
Impatience is a poor qualification for immortality.
Hot blood is of no use in dealing with eternity.
It is seldom that promises or even realisations
Can sustain a clear and searching gaze.
But an emotion chilled is an emotion controlled;
This is the road leading to certainty,
Reasoned planning for the time when reason can no
                                longer avail.
It is essential to know the chill of all the objections
That come creeping into the mind, the battle between
                                opposing ideas
Which gives the victory to the strongest and most
                                universal
Over all others, and to wage it to the end
With increasing freedom, precision, and detachment
A detachment that shocks our instincts and ridicules
                                our desires.
All else in the world cancels out, equal, capable
Of being replaced by other things (even as all the
                                ideas
That madden men now must lose their potency in a
                                few years
And be replaced by others – even as all the religions,
All the material sacrifices and moral restraints,
That in twenty thousand years have brought us no
                                nearer to God
Are irrelevant to the ordered adjustments
Out of reach of perceptive understanding
Forever taking place on the Earth and in the
                                unthinkable regions around it;
This cat's cradle of life; this reality volatile yet
                                determined;
This intense vibration in the stones
That makes them seem immobile to us)
But the world cannot dispense with the stones.

They alone are not redundant. Nothing can replace
                                                          them
Except a new creation of God.

I must get into this stone world now.
Ratchel, striae, relationships of tesserae,
    Innumerable shades of grey,
    Innumerable shapes,
And beneath them all a stupendous unity,
Infinite movement visibly defending itself
Against all the assaults of weather and water,
Simultaneously mobilised at full strength
At every point of the universal front,
    Always at the pitch of its powers,
    The foundation and end of all life.
I try them with the old Norn words – hraun
Duss, rønis, queedaruns, kollyarum:
They hvarf from me in all directions
Over the hurdifell – klett, millya, hellya, hellyina
                                                          bretta,
Hellyina wheeda, hellyina grø, bakka, ayre, –
    And lay my world in kolgref.

This is no heap of broken images.
Let men find the faith that builds mountains
Before they seek the faith that moves them. Men
                                                          cannot hope
To survive the fall of the mountains
Which they will no more see than they saw their rise
Unless they are more concentrated and determined,
Truer to themselves and with more to be true to,
Than these stones, and as inerrable as they are.
Their sole concern is that what can be shaken
Shall be shaken and disappear
And only the unshakable be left.
What hardihood in any man has part or parcel in the
                                                          latter?
It is necessary to make a stand and maintain it
                                                          forever.

These stones go through Man, straight to God, if
there is one.
What have they not gone through already?
Empires, civilisations, aeons. Only in them
If in anything, can His creation confront Him.
They came so far out of the water and halted forever.
That larking dallier, the sun, has only been able to
play
With superficial by-products since;
The moon moves the waters backwards and
forwards,
But the stones cannot be lured an inch farther
Either on this side of eternity or the other.
Who thinks God is easier to know than they are?
Trying to reach men any more, any otherwise, than
they are?
These stones will reach us long before we reach them.
Cold, undistracted, eternal and sublime.
They will stem all the torrents of vicissitude forever
With a more than Roman peace.
Death is a physical horror to me no more.
I am prepared with everything else to share
Sunshine and darkness and wind and rain
And life and death bare as these rocks though it be
In whatever order nature may decree,
But, not indifferent to the struggle yet
Nor to the ataraxia I might get
By fatalism, a deeper issue see
Than these, or suicide, here confronting me.
It is reality that is at stake.
Being and non-being with equal weapons here
Confront each other for it, non-being unseen
But always on the point, it seems, of showing clear,
Though its reserved contagion may breed
This fancy too in my still susceptible head
And then by its own hidden movement lead
Me as by aesthetic vision to the supposed
Point where by death's logic everything is
recomposed,
Object and image one, from their severance freed,

As I sometimes, still wrongly, feel 'twixt this storm
                                        beach and me.
What happens to us
Is irrelevant to the world's geology
But what happens to the world's geology
Is not irrelevant to us.
We must reconcile ourselves to the stones,
Not the stones to us.
Here a man must shed the encumbrances that muffle
Contact with elemental things, the subtleties
That seem inseparable from a humane life, and go
                                        apart
Into a simple and sterner, more beautiful and more
                                        oppressive world,
Austerely intoxicating; the first draught is
                                        overpowering;
Few survive it. It fills me with a sense of perfect form,
The end seen from the beginning, as in a song.
It is no song that conveys the feeling
That there is no reason why it should ever stop,
But the kindred form I am conscious of here
Is the beginning and end of the world,
The unsearchable masterpiece, the music of the
                                        spheres,
Alpha and Omega, the Omnific Word.
These stones have the silence of supreme creative
                                        power,
The direct and undisturbed way of working
Which alone leads to greatness.
What experience has any man crystallised,
What weight of conviction accumulated,
What depth of life suddenly seen entire
In some nigh supernatural moment
And made a symbol and lived up to
With such resolution, such Spartan impassivity?
It is a frenzied and chaotic age,
Like a growth of weeds on the site of a demolished
                                        building.
How shall we set ourselves against it,

Imperturbable, inscrutable, in the world and yet not
>in it,
>>Silent under the torments it inflicts upon us,
>>>With a constant centre,
>With a single inspiration, foundations firm and
>>>>invariable;
>>By what immense exercise of will,
Inconceivable discipline, courage, and endurance,
>>Self-purification and anti-humanity,
>>>Be ourselves without interruption,
>>>>Adamantine and inexorable?
It will be ever increasingly necessary to find
In the interests of all mankind
Men capable of rejecting all that all other men
>>Think, as a stone remains
Essential to the world, inseparable from it,
>>And rejects all other life yet.
Great work cannot be combined with surrender to
>>>the crowd.
>>– Nay, the truth we seek is as free
From all yet thought as a stone from humanity.
Here where there is neither haze nor hesitation
Something at least of the necessary power has entered
>>>into me.
I have still to see any manifestation of the human
>>>spirit
That is worthy of a moment's longer exemption than
>>>it gets
From petrifaction again – to get out if it can.
All is lithogenesis – or lochia;
And I can desire nothing better,
An immense familiarity with other men's imaginings
Convinces me that they cannot either
(If they could, it would instantly be granted
– The present order must continue till then)
Though, of course, I still keep an open mind,
A mind as open as the grave.
You may say that the truth cannot be crushed out,
That the weight of the whole world may be tumbled
>>>on it,

And yet, in puny, distorted, phantasmal shapes albeit,
It will braird again; it will force its way up
Through unexpectable fissures? look over this beach.
What ruderal and rupestrine growth is here?
What crop confirming any credulities?
Conjure a fescue to teach me with from this
And I will listen to you, but until then
Listen to me – Truth is not crushed;
It crushes, gorgonises all else into itself.
The trouble is to know it when you see it?
You will have no trouble with it when you do.
Do not argue with me. Argue with these stones.
Truth has no trouble in knowing itself.
This is it. The hard fact. The inoppugnable reality,
Here is something for you to digest.
Eat this and we'll see what appetite you have left
For a world hereafter.
I pledge you in the first and last crusta,
The rocks rattling in the bead-proof seas.

O we of little faith,
As romanticists viewed the philistinism of their days
As final and were prone to set over against it
Infinite longing rather than manly will –
Nay, as all thinkers and writers find
The indifference of the masses of mankind, –
So are most men with any stone yet,
Even those who juggle with lapidary's, mason's,
                                        geologist's words
        And all their knowledge of stones in vain,
Tho' these stones have far more differences in colour,
                                        shape and size
        Than most men to my eyes –
Even those who develop precise conceptions to
                                        immense distances
        Out of these bleak surfaces.
All human culture is a Goliath to fall
To the least of these pebbles withal.
A certain weight will be added yet
To the arguments of even the most foolish

And all who speak glibly may rest assured
That to better their oratory they will have the whole
                                                earth
For a Demosthenean pebble to roll in their mouths.

I am enamoured of the desert at last,
The abode of supreme serenity is necessarily a desert.
My disposition is towards spiritual issues
Made inhumanly clear; I will have nothing interposed
Between my sensitiveness and the barren but
                                    beautiful reality;
The deadly clarity of this 'seeing of a hungry man'
Only traces of a fever passing over my vision
Will vary, troubling it indeed, but troubling it only
In such a way that it becomes for a moment
Superhumanly, menacingly clear – the reflection
Of a brightness through a burning crystal.
A culture demands leisure and leisure presupposes
A self-determined rhythm of life; the capacity for
                                            solitude
Is its test; by that the desert knows us.
It is not a question of escaping from life
But the reverse – a question of acquiring the power
To exercise the loneliness, the independence, of
                                            stones,
And that only comes from knowing that our function
                                            remains
However isolated we seem fundamental to life as
                                            theirs.
        We have lost the grounds of our being,
        We have not built on rock.
Thinking of all the higher zones
Confronting the spirit of man I know they are bare
Of all so-called culture as any stone here;
Not so much of all literature survives
As any wisp of scriota that thrives
On a rock – (interesting though it may seem to be
As de Bary's and Schwendener's discovery
Of the dual nature of lichens, the partnership,
Symbiosis, of a particular fungus and particular alga).

These bare stones bring me straight back to reality.
     I grasp one of them and I have in my grip
The beginning and the end of the world,
My own self, and as before I never saw
The empty hand of my brother man,
The humanity no culture has reached, the mob.
Intelligentsia, our impossible and imperative job!

'Ah!' you say, 'if only one of these stones would
                           move
— Were it only an inch — of its own accord.
     This is the resurrection we await,
— The stone rolled away from the tomb of the Lord.
     I know there is no weight in infinite space,
       No impermeability in infinite time,
But it is as difficult to understand and have patience
                       here
      As to know that the sublime
Is theirs no less than ours, no less confined
To men than men's to a few men, the stars of their
                      kind.'
     (The masses too have begged bread from stones,
       From human stones, including themselves,
     And only got it, not from their fellow-men,
      But from stones such as these here — if then.)
Detached intellectuals, not one stone will move,
Not the least of them, not a fraction of an inch. It is
                       not
     The reality of life that is hard to know.
It is nearest of all and easiest to grasp,
But you must participate in it to proclaim it.
— I lift a stone; it is the meaning of life I clasp
Which is death, for that is the meaning of death;
How else does any man yet participate
     In the life of a stone,
How else can any man yet become
Sufficiently at one with creation, sufficiently alone,
Till as the stone that covers him he lies dumb
And the stone at the mouth of his grave is not
                    overthrown?

– Each of these stones on this raised beach,
    Every stone in the world,
Covers infinite death, beyond the reach
Of the dead it hides; and cannot be hurled
Aside yet to let any of them come forth, as love
    Once made a stone move
  (Though I do not depend on that
    My case to prove).
So let us beware of death; the stones will have
Their revenge; we have lost all approach to them,
But soon we shall become as those we have betrayed,
And they will seal us fast in our graves
As our indifference and ignorance seals them;
    But let us not be afraid to die.
No heavier and colder and quieter then,
No more motionless, do stones lie
    In death than in life to all men.
It is not more difficult in death than here
– Though slow as the stones the powers develop
To rise from the grave – to get a life worth having;
And in death – unlike life – we lose nothing that is
                  truly ours.

Diallage of the world's debate, end of the long
                  auxesis,
Although no ébrillade of Pegasus can here avail,
I prefer your enchorial characters – the futhorc of the
                  future –
To the hieroglyphics of all the other forms of Nature.
Song, your apprentice encrinite, seems to sweep
The Heavens with a last entrochal movement;
And, with the same word that began it, closes
Earth's vast epanadiplosis.

Harry Semen

I ken these islands each inhabited
Forever by a single man
Livin' in his separate world as only

In dreams yet maist folk can.

dogfish

Mine's like the moonwhite belly o' a hoo
Seen in the water as a fisher draws in his line.
I canna land it nor can it ever brak awa'.
It never moves, yet seems a' movement in the brine;
A movin' picture o' the spasm frae which I was born,
It writhes again, and back to it I'm willy-nilly torn.
A' men are similarly fixt; and the difference 'twixt
    The sae-ca'd sane and insane
Is that the latter whiles ha'e glimpses o't
    And the former nane.

Particle frae particle'll brak asunder,

each one/next

Ilk ane o' them mair livid than the neist.
A separate life? – incredible war o' equal lichts,
Nane o' them wi' ocht in common in the least.
Nae threid o' a' the fabric o' my thocht
Is left alangside anither; a pack

mangling

O' leprous scuts o' weasels riddlin' a plaid

loose ends

    Sic thrums could never mak'.

went

Hoo mony shades o' white gaed curvin' owre

bluish

To yon blae centre o' her belly's flower?

Scottish bluebell

Milk-white, and dove-grey, wi' harebell veins.

one

Ae scar in fair hair like the sun in sunlicht lay,
And pelvic experience in a thin shadow line;

such soft

Thocht canna mairry thocht as sic saft shadows dae.

Grey ghastly commentaries on my puir life,
A' the sperm that's gane for naething rises up to
                                    damn
In sick-white onanism the single seed
Frae which in sheer irrelevance I cam.
What were the odds against me? Let me coont.
What worth am I to a' that micht ha'e been?
To a' the wasted slime I'm capable o'
Appeals this lurid emission, whirlin' lint-white and
                                    green.

Am I alane richt, solidified to life,
Disjoined frae a' this searin' like a white-het knife,

And vauntin' my alien accretions here,
Boastin' sanctions, purpose, sense the endless tide
I cam frae lacks – the tide I still sae often feed?
O bitter glitter; wet sheet and flowin' sea – and what
                                    beside?

festering

in all directions

Sae the bealin' continents lie upon the seas,
    Sprawlin' in shapeless shapes a' airts,
Like ony splash that ony man can mak'
    Frae his nose or throat or ither pairts,
Fantastic as ink through blottin' paper rins.

wild cherry

But this is white, white like a flooerin' gean,
Passin' frae white to purer shades o' white,
Ivory, crystal, diamond, till nae difference is seen
Between its fairest blossoms and the stars
Or the clear sun they melt into,
And the wind mixes them amang each ither
Forever, hue upon still mair dazzlin' hue.

Sae Joseph may ha'e pondered; sae a snawstorm
Comes whirlin' in grey sheets frae the shadowy sky
And only in a sma' circle are the separate flakes seen.
White, whiter, they cross and recross as capricious
                              they fly,
Mak' patterns on the grund and weave into wreaths,
Load the bare boughs, and find lodgments in corners
                               frae
The scourin' wind that sends a snawstorm up frae the
                               earth
To meet that frae the sky, till which is which nae
                         man can say.
They melt in the waters. They fill the valleys. They
                      scale the peaks.
There's a tinkle o' icicles. The topmaist summit
                      shines oot.
Sae Joseph may ha'e pondered on the coiled fire in
                      his seed,
The transformation in Mary, and seen Jesus tak' root.

WILLIAM SOUTAR (1898–1943)

The Tryst

softly   O luely, luely cam she in
                 And luely she lay doun:
cool   I kent her be her caller lips
                 And her breists sae sma' and roun'.

                 A' thru the nicht we spak nae word
parted bone from bone   Nor sinder'd bane frae bane:
                 A' thru the nicht I heard her hert
                 Gang soundin' wi' my ain.

wakeful   It was about the waukrife hour
                 Whan cocks begin to craw
slipped away   That she smool'd saftly thru the mirk
                 Afore the day wud daw.

                 Sae luely, luely, cam she in
                 Sae luely was she gaen
                 And wi' her a' my simmer days
                 Like they had never been.

The Guns

Now, on the moors where the guns bring down
The predestinated birds,
Shrill, wavering cries pass
Like the words of an international peace;
And I would that these cries were heard in every
                                   town,
Astounding the roar of the wheel
And the lying mouth of the news:
And I would that these cries might more and more
                                   increase

Until the machine stood still;
And men, despairing in the deathly queues,

Heard their own heart-beats
Shouting aloud, in the silence of the streets:
'Are we not also hand-fed in a wilderness:
What are we waiting for?'

The Hungry Mauchs

a sickly, mother maggot There was a moupit, mither mauch
Wha hadna onie meat;
always quick to laugh And a' her bairns, aye gleg to lauch,
to weep Were gether'd round to greet.

who was that 'O mither, mither, wha was yon
That breisted on through bluid:
who broke crowns and wrecked towns Wha crackit crouns, and wrackit touns,
And was our faithers' pride?

'O mither, mither, wha was yon
bold That was sae frack and fell?'
'My loves, it was Napoleon
in ruins But he's sma' brok himsel'.'

bow low 'Noo lat us a' lowt on our knees,'
The spunkiest shaver said:
'And prig upon the Lord to gie's
Napoleon frae the dead.'

The mither mauch began to lauch:
fuss or complain 'Ye needna fash nor wurn:
pressed down and covered over He's clappit doun, and happit roun',
iron chest And in a kist o' airn.'

'O whaur, O whaur's my faither gaen?'
smallest The peeriest bairn outspak.
'Wheesht, wheesht, ye wee bit loonickin,
wonder He'll fetch a ferlie back.'

'Will he bring hame Napoleon's head

make my stomach better To cockle up my kite?'
hothead 'He'll bring ye hame the wuff o' bluid
That's reid and rinnin yet.'

Song

bridge Whaur you broken brig hings owre;
Whaur yon water maks nae soun';
in dust Babylon blaws by in stour:
go down Gang doun wi' a sang, gang doun.

for any Deep, owre deep, for onie drouth:
gloomy Wan eneuch an ye wud droun:
salty or pleasant Saut, or seelfu', for the mouth;
Gang doun wi' a sang, gang doun.

Babylon blaws by in stour
Whaur yon water maks nae soun':
Darkness is your only door;
Gang doun wi' a sang, gang doun.

The Makar

the poet

Nae man wha loves the lawland tongue
wrestles But warsles wi' the thocht –
There are mair sangs that bide unsung
Nor a' that hae been wrocht.

below the wastefulness Ablow the wastrey o' the years,
shackle The thorter o' himsel',
Deep buried in his bluid he hears
loyal A music that is leal.

And wi' this lealness gangs his ain;
And there's nae ither gait
all his comrades were foreign Though a' his feres were fremmit men
Wha cry: *Owre late, owre late.*

WILLIAM MONTGOMERIE (b. 1904)

The Edge of the War (1939–)

On the esplanade
the deck-chair hirer
watches his summer
shovelled into sandbags
till at high tide
the beach is flooded to the Promenade

Our submarines like five alligators
pass
always at dusk
to the North Sea
where a German plane has sown surface mines

One mine circles the harbour slowly
missing the pier
again and again and again
until defused by a simple twist of the wrist

The whelk-seller leaves his bag and barrow
to pull a mine up the beach
and dies
'Stretchers! Stretchers here!'
they shout from the Castle

A policeman arrests one mine on the shore
and drags it halfway to the police-station
his tombstone a cottage gable-end
pocked with holes packed with red putty

Casks of brandy butter and ham
float on to the beach
from a mined ship

A grocer's van parks at dusk
by the Castle railings

Sergeant MacPherson pins on his notice-board
'Flotsam butter from the beach
must be left immediately
at the police-station'

For days the streets are sweet
with the smell of shortbread

Blue-mould butter
is dumped on the counter
or thrown at night
over the wall of the station
where greased door-handles will not turn

A German plane
following the wrong railway
dumps his bombs on an up-country farm

A plane from the North-Sea sunrise
machine-gunning our little fishing fleet
brushes a wing against a mast
and ditches

'Hilfe! Hilfe!'

'Take your time lads!'
shouts a skipper
to a drifter turning toward the sinking plane

'One of our planes
has sunk a German U-boat
off Montrose'

A war-rumour

The submarine
one of ours
dented
is in dry-dock
in Dundee

Bennet from Stratford-on-Avon
one of the crew
cycles to our house
with no lights
sings to us
of Boughton's Lordly Ones
from *The Immortal Hour*
talks of his wife in Stratford
and of the night they watched Birmingham burning

After late supper
he returns to the night
having left his ration of pipe-tobacco
on the piano

If his submarine sinks
he knows how to escape
and is found afloat
on the Pacific Ocean
drowned

On Tents Muir
across the Tay estuary
parachutes are falling
from war planes

We talk of the Second Front

One parachute does not open

Broughty Ferry

NORMAN CAMERON (1905–53)

She and I

She and I, we thought and fought
And each of us won by the other's defeat;
She and I, we danced and pranced
And lost by neglect the use of our feet;
She and I caught ills and chills
And were cured or dead before we could cough;
She and I, we walked and talked
Half an hour after our heads were cut off.

Forgive Me, Sire

Forgive me, Sire, for cheating your intent,
That I, who should command a regiment,
Do amble amiably here, O God,
One of the neat ones in your awkward squad.

A Visit to the Dead

I bought (I was too wealthy for my age)
A passage to the dead ones' habitat,
And learnt, under their tutelage,
To twitter like a bat

In imitation of their dialect.
Crudely I aped their subtle practices;
By instinct knew how to respect
Their strict observances.

The regions of the dead are small and pent,
Their movements faint, sparing of energy.
Yet, like an exiled Government,
With so much jealousy

As were the issue a campaign or Crown,
They hold debates, wage Cabinet intrigues,
Move token forces up and down,
Turn inches into leagues.

Long I was caught up in their twilit strife.
Almost they got me, almost had me weaned
From all my memory of life.
But laughter supervened:

Laughter, like sunlight in the cucumber,
The innermost resource, that does not fail.
I, Marco Polo, traveller,
Am back, with what a tale!

Green, Green is El Aghir

Sprawled on the crates and sacks in the rear of the
truck,
I was gummy-mouthed from the sun and the dust of
the track.
And the two Arab soldiers I'd taken on as hitch-
hikers
At a torrid petrol-dump, had been there on their
hunkers
Since early morning. I said, in a kind of French
'On m'a dit, qu'il y a une belle source d'eau fraîche.
Plus loin, à El Aghir' . . .

It was eighty more kilometres
Until round a corner we heard a splashing of waters,
And there, in a green, dark street, was a fountain
with two faces
Discharging both ways, from full-throated faucets
Into basins, thence into troughs and thence into
brooks.
Our negro corporal driver slammed his brakes,
And we yelped and leapt from the truck and went at
the double

To fill our bidons and bottles and drink and dabble.
Then, swollen with water, we went to an inn for
                                                wine.
The Arabs came, too, though their faith might have
                                        stood between.
'After all,' they said, 'it's a boisson,' without
                                        contrition.

Green, green is El Aghir. It has a railway-station,
And the wealth of its soil has borne many another
                                                fruit,
A mairie, a school and an elegant Salle de Fêtes.
Such blessings, as I remarked, in effect, to the waiter,
Are added unto them that have plenty of water.

ROBERT GARIOCH (Robert Garioch Sutherland) (1909–81)

Edinburgh to the frolic*	**Embro to the Ploy**
	In simmer, whan aa sorts foregether
	in Embro to the ploy,
people/chinwag	fowk seek out friens to hae a blether,
enemies	or faes they'd fain annoy;
smothered/smoke	smorit wi British Railways' reek
	frae Glesca or Glen Roy
	or Wick, they come to hae a week
	of cultivatit joy,
	or three,
	in Embro to the ploy.
plenty	Americans wi routh of dollars,
	wha drink our whisky neat,
	wi Sasunachs and Oxford Scholars
eager	are eydent for the treat
	of music sedulously high-tie
	at thirty-bob a seat;
	Wop opera performed in Eytie
	to them's richt up their street,
	they say,
	in Embro to the ploy.
expatriate	Furthgangan Embro folk come hame
	for three weeks in the year,
	and find Auld Reekie no the same,
in a frenzy	fu sturrit in a steir.
buildings	The stane-faced biggins whaur they froze
took in poorhouse learning yesterday's staple culture, reheated	and suppit puirshous leir
	of cultural cauld-kale and brose
antics disconcerting	see cantraips unco queer
	thae days
	in Embro to the ploy.

* i.e. the Edinburgh Festival

trade/laugh	The tartan tred wad gar ye lauch;
too difficult	nae problem is owre teuch.
	Your surname needna end in -*och*;
hook you up to the high places	they'll cleik ye up the cleuch.
few	A puckle dollar bills will aye
prove	prieve Hiram Teufelsdrockh
	a septary of Clan McKay,
	it's maybe richt eneuch,
	verfluch!
	in Embro to the ploy.

blow	The auld High Schule, whaur monie a skelp
	of triple-tonguit tawse
	has gien a hyst-up and a help
	towards Doctorates of Laws,
cheerful	nou hears, for Ramsay's cantie rhyme,
palm-strokes	loud pawmies of applause
	frae folk that pey a pund a time
	to sit on wudden raws
very	gey hard
	in Embro to the ploy.

	The haly kirk's Assembly-haa
makes a mess of it	nou fairly coups the creel
fine	wi Lindsay's Three Estaitis, braw
	devices of the Deil.
bounces	About our heids the satire stots
	like hailstanes till we reel;
jokes/old-fashioned	the bawrs are in auld-farrant Scots,
	it's maybe jist as weill,
	imphm,
	in Embro to the ploy.

	The Epworth Haa wi wunner did
quarrel	behold a piper's bicker;
	wi *hadarid* and *hindarid*
	the air gat thick and thicker.
	Cumha na Cloinne pleyed on strings
	torments a piper quicker
	to get his dander up, by jings,

than thirty u.p. liquor,
         hooch aye!
in Embro to the ploy.

The Northern British Embro Whigs
that stayed in Charlotte Square,
lost   they fairly wad hae tined their wigs
to see the Stuarts there,
bleeding/everyone else   the bleidan Earl of Moray and aa
well-painted/very   weill-pentit and gey bare;
beautifully adorned Our Queen and Princess, buskit braw,
enjoyed the hale affair
        (see Press)
in Embro to the ploy.

Whan day's anomalies are cled
in decent shades of nicht,
the Castle is transmogrified
by braw electric licht.
shelters   The toure that bields the Bruce's croun
presents an unco sicht
kin   mair sib to Wardour Street nor Scone,
wae's me for Scotland's micht,
        says I
in Embro to the ploy.

prank   A happening, incident, or splore
affrontit them that saw
a thing they'd never seen afore –
in the McEwan Haa:
a lassie in a wheelie-chair
wi naething on at aa,
jist like my luck! I wasna there,
at all   it's no the thing ava,
        tut-tut,
in Embro to the ploy.

The Café Royal and Abbotsford
sundry   are filled wi orra folk
written whaes stock-in trade's the scrievit word,

or twicet-scrievit joke.
Brains, weak or strang, in heavy beer,
or ordinary, soak.

said one/ale   Quo yin: This yill is aafie dear,

coins in purse   I hae nae clinks in poke,
                 nor fauldan-money,
in Embro to the ploy.

The auld Assembly-rooms, whaur Scott

comrades   foregethert wi his fiers,

eye-catching   nou see a gey kenspeckle lot
ablow the chandeliers.

to Edinburgh thirsts (or drunks)   Til Embro drouths the Festival Club
a richt godsend appears;
it's something new to find a pub
that gaes on sairvan beers
                 eftir hours
in Embro to the ploy.

ejected/drunken   Jist pitten-out, the drucken mobs

taverns   frae howffs in Potterraw,
fleean, to hob-nob wi the Nobs,
ran to this Music Haa,
Register Rachel, Cougait Kate,

nose-less   Nae-neb Nellie and aa

staggered   stauchert about amang the Great,
what fun! I never saw
                 the like,
in Embro to the ploy.

They toddle hame doun lit-up streets
filled wi synthetic joy;

oh well/such   aweill, the year brings few sic treats

much   and muckle to annoy.

many spirited   There's monie hartsom braw high-jinks
mixed up in this alloy
in simmer, whan aa sorts foregether
in Embro to the ploy.

To Robert Fergusson

Fergusson, tho twa-hunder year
awa, your image is mair clear
than many things   nor monie things that nou appear
       in braid daylicht.
makes   What gars perspective turn sae queer?
       What ails my sicht?

Pairtlie, nae dout, because your een
so very   gey clearlie saw the Embro scene
young woman   in times when Embro was a quean
       sae weill worth seein
few   that life wi her still had a wheen
sampling   guid things worth preein.

homely
whose life was stirring, hot and   A hameil, Scottish place eneuch,
rough   whas life was steiran, het and reuch
plough   whilst yet the fairmer wi his pleuch
       turned owre the sod
    whar classie Queen Street and Drumsheugh
trim   nou stand sae snod.

But what a pairtner for your life!
cheerful   Gey like a weill-bred, cantie wife
chilly   wha wears an apron, no cauldrife
false   wi fause gentilitie,
    wi mind keen-edgit as a knife,
       used wi civilitie.

each   In ae gret tenement or land,*
big building   a muckle rubble biggin, planned
save/found   to hain grund-rent, folk wad be fand
jumbled together   aa mixter-maxter —
    lordies and lawyers, no owre grand
baker   to ken a baxter

* *land* building, let out in tenements

or Ramsay wi his curlin-tangs,
guid makar baith of wigs and sangs,
or, Fergusson, yoursel; sae lang's

shy   ye werena blate,
shocks   they were your friens, whatever bangs
served up   were sair'd by fate.

a lawyer's hack by trade   Altho to tred a lawyer's hack
paid by the tuppence or the   peyed by the bodle or the plack
penny
writing   for scrievin till your wrist wad crack,
early   baith ear and late,
                 yet of guid friens ye had nae lack
at every level   in ilk estait.

the Cape [Club]'s   The 'Cape's' self-knichted cavaliers
suchlike   'Sir Scrape-Greystiel' and siclike fiers,
chose/above   they waled ye weill abune their peers
                      for cannie capers
                 whan ye'd got throu, wi nae arrears,
stint   your stent of papers.

sprightly   Hou gleglie they'd kick owre the traces
                in the Daft Days* or at Leith Races,
                wi trips to Fife or siccan places
cram   to stech their leisor
alcoholic pranks/pimply faces   wi drouthie ploys, while plookie faces
scorched   birslit wi pleisor.

                And what a knack ye had of scrievin
in fresh verse/abundance of living in caller verse yon rowth of levin,
stone world, fighting   your wee stane warld, fechtin, thievin,
working   drinkin and swinkin,
lots of fun and little grieving wi muckle fun and puckle grievin
plenty   and fowth of thinkin.

                In praise of Wilkie* ye declared
                his verses wad be aye revered

---

* *Daft Days* period of festivity at Christmas and New Year; *Wilkie* William Wilkie (1721–72) professor, poet and farmer

oxen

while slaw-gaun owsen turned the swaird;
      nou ither factors
hae shown the doctor gey ill-sair'd –
      we dae't wi tractors.

But this I'll say: while there's a still

ale
in Scotland, or a pint of yill,

weak
houever washie, fit to swill
      atween the tide
at Leith Port and the Blackford Hill,
      your fame sall byde.

hooked
Whan Daith raxed out his airm and cleikit

gate was shut
Ramsay, folk thocht the yett was steekit,

poet's right to citizenship
yet sune your makar's burgess-ticket
      gied ye the freedom

joined
of Scottish verse, in whilk were eikit

heart and spirit
      baith hert and smeddum.

For ye had at your fingernebbs

living
real levan words to weave your webs

frowns
of sound and sense, of smiles and slebs,

young men
      whilst Embro callants

turn up their noses
ne'er thocht to runkle up their nebs
      at guid braid Lallans.

with perfect certainty
And yet, owre surelie did ye ken

guid Scots wad mak bad Englishmen

they looked too deeply into England
whan owre faur South they keekit ben
      and sune were smitten,
tho barelie three-score years and ten
      had seen Great Britain.

squint-eyed
South-keekan Scots gaed skellie-ee'd

silly head
and tuke it in their tawpie-heid
to hae their bairns anglified

force
      and gar their stiff tongues

language
transmogrifie their Lallan leid
      frae vowels to diphthongs.

Of Heriot's or Watson's* ghaist
which   or yours, I wonder whilk is maist
dumbfounert, dozent and bumbazed
         wi indignation
to see our modern Embro taste
         in education.

guess/bones
complain the most with grisly   We may jalouse George Watson's banes
moans   will gowl the maist wi grieslie maens
poverty's children   nou that his schule for puirtith's weans,
         foundit sae weill,
chairges sic fees and taks sic pains
         to be genteel.

No that I'd hae a body think
the worse for being clean   our toun's the waur of bein perjink
in some weys; Embro's famous stink
         is banish'd nou;
forced you to dodge   gane are the shouts, that garred ye jink,
         of 'Gardyloo!'*

our filth's poisoned   Our fulyie's pusionit the Firth
and caused, I dout, an unco dearth
oysters of great size   of thae Pandores of muckle girth
         ye thocht sae fair;
what wad ye think our gain was worth?
         I'm no that shair.

Auld Reekie's bigger, nou, what's mair,
and folk wha hae the greater share
of warldlie gear may tak the air
         in Morningside,
climb   and needna sclim the turnpike stair
         whar ye wad byde.

comfortable   But truth it is, our couthie city
curdled   has cruddit in twa pairts a bittie

---

*founders of Edinburgh schools; warning call that slops were about to be thrown from a window into the street: French 'gardez (vous de) l'eau'

and speaks twa tongues, ane coorse and grittie,
   heard in the Cougait,
the tither copied, mair's the pitie,
   frae Wast of Newgate.

which   Whilk is the crudd and whilk the whey
hard pushed   I wad be kinna sweirt to say,
        but this I ken, that of the twae
          the corrupt twang
        of Cougait is the nearer tae
language   the leid ye sang.

these   Thir days, whan cities seem unreal
conscience   to makars, inwit gars us feel
        fause as the hauf-inch marble peel
          in Princes Street
        whaur new shop-fronts wad shame the Deil
          wi their deceit.

on the other hand   A conter, we've some rotten riggin
rat-infested tenements in
Cowgate   of ratton-eaten Cougait biggin
long ago the skilled rhythms that heard langsyne the skeelie jiggin
          of your new verse.
I chose this direction Hard-pressed, I wale yon airt to dig in
          and micht dae worse.

ghost-haunted   Our life's a bogle-hauntit dream
too full of terrors   owre thrang wi wirrikows to seem
lightning   quite real; our fun a fireflaucht-gleam
sliced   whang'd throu a nicht
unforeseen evils/furious of gurliewhirkies huge and breme,
clotted with fright   loppert wi fricht.

        Ye gaed about in guid braid claith
with never a thought/harm wi fient a thocht of want or skaith,
loath   in howffs at hy-jinks never laith
         to blaw your chanter,
[an Edinburgh madhouse] syne in cursed Darien's bedlam, Daith
wrought your misfortune wrocht your mishanter.

what made you   What gart ye break throu reason's ice?
sane   Compared wi ye, we're no sae wyce.
used to   Maybe we're yaised wi madness; vice
              and lust for pouer
         bring furth some hellish new device
every other   ilk ither hour.

         Was it the dreidit mental state
earthly   in whilk things yerdlie, smaa and great,
         become irrelevant, and Fate
              dauntin the Kirk,
from the far side of   glowres at a man frae ben Hell's gate
gloom   throu endless mirk?

         Syne even poetrie becomes
remnants   a naething, an affair of thrums
booms   of words, words, a noise that jumms
lying verbosity   wi leean skreed,
lost   the purport tint, man's sperit numbs —
              as weill be deid.

         The flicker-pictur on the screen
         bursts as by boomb-blast, and is gane;
last night   What was sae firm and good yestreen
              seems foul indeed.
then a man bums his books forthwith   Syne a man brenns his buiks bedeen,
              afore he's deid.

trouble yourself   Ye didna hae to fash your thoombs
         wi hydrogen or atom boombs,
swims   nor monie a nesty thocht that soums
              aye in our heid
scares   and flegs us in our flimsie rooms,
              and yet, ye're deid.

oh well/a very long time ago   Aweill, ye're deid, gey lang sinsyne —
         the Scottish elegiac line
         I'll spare ye, tho, as ye ken fine,
              ye scrievit monie

lively/lose   crouse stanzas whan ye'd cam to tine
                           some decent cronie.

My ain toun's makar, monie an airt
formed us in common, faur apairt
extremely alike   in time, but fell alike in hert;
                      I whiles forget
mud   that ye ligg there ablow the clart
                       of Canogait.

great daring   Like me, nae dout, wi muckle darin,
tasted   ye pree'd grim joys at Muschat's cairn*
gruesome   and grugous thochts of Effie's bairn,*
                       or, as a laddie,
slid/scratches   ye skliddert doun, for scarts no caring,
                       the Guttit Haddie.*

The auld High Schule (gane Royal syne)
your Alma Mater was and mine,
and whar ye construed, line by line,
                     the Gallic Weirs
we ken the airt, doun by the Wynd
                     of the Black Friars.*

The wind that blaws frae Nor to South,
shrieking   skirlan frae ilka close's* mouth,
chilled both of us   has nithert baith o's in our youth
upended   and coupt us, whiles,
slaked thirst   as we gaed hame wi slockent drouth
                     doun by Sanct Giles'.

But aye we'd rise wi little hairm
and cleik ilk ither by the airm,
singan in unison to chairm

Muschat's cairn a memorial in Holyrood Park to Nichol Muschat who murdered his wife in 1702 after failing to obtain a divorce; *Effie's bairn* Effie Dean's son, known as The Whistler (see Sir Walter Scott's *The Heart of Midlothian*); *Guttit Haddie* exposed rock on Arthur's Seat said to have been caused by a waterspout in 1744; *Wynd of the Black Friars* was on the south side of the Cowgate; *close* common entry to a tenement

harm
then seek some antic, happy-go-lucky

loath

                    awa the skaith,
syne seek some cantraip, harum-skarum
              and naething laith.

            Ye stickit minister,* young Rab,

keep your defiant talk   ye wadnae hain your giff-gaff gab
a schoolmaster or bore   frae me, a dominie or crab
forever disputing it   aye stickan it,
begrudge/thief   nor gruch your brain, nor cry me scab
               for pickin it.

           To Warld's End Close frae Ramsay Lane*

batter/spine   we'd ding Auld Reekie's black rigg-bane.
Nethergate   Whan Ne'er-gate's ten-hour bell had gane
            that wadnae daunt us;
accompany you all the way home   I'd gie scotch-convoy back again
            to Dawnie Douglas.

           Ye'd quote frae Ramsay, I frae Grieve;

I'd fill your belly   wi Happy Days your wame I'd steeve
           and aye the mair ye'd hae me prieve
             your aqua vitae,
deafen   syne we wad rair out sangs to deave
the city breathing loudly in sleep   the swuffan citie.

up went every window with lots of shrieking

           Up gaed ilk sash wi feck of skriekan,
peeping   frae the wee windaes heids were keekan;
complaining   the Embro folk gied owre their gleekin
             for very joy;
bright fire-glow/basking   in ae bricht lowe we aa were beekan —
            wow! what a ploy!

           But ach! the nippie-tongue of morn

puts all such enchantment   pits aa sic glaumerie to scorn;
foolish   I stand here, glaikit and forlorn
             in Canogait,

---

* *stickit minister* minister of the Church of Scotland who never gets a pastoral charge; *stickit* unfinished; i.e. to the end of the High Street from Edinburgh Castle

*determined, yet afraid to beg
by force*

ettlesome, yet feart to sorn
        on your estait.

*my way is steep, not sensible at
all*

Robert, fareweill; I maun awa.
My gait is stey, no wyce ava,
by Jacob's Ladder,* Burns's smaa
        Greek pepperpat,*
Sanct Andrew's Hous* an' aa an' aa –
        nae mair of that!

panting/language

calm

living/lie dead

Pechan, I turn, whilst aye your leid
of lowan Scots sounds in my heid
wi levan braith, tho ye ligg deid;
        I glowre faur doun

woeful wreck

and see the waesome wrak outspreid
        of your auld toun.

*then struggling up the slope once
more*

Syne trauchlan up the brae yince mair,
frae Canogait, I leave ye there,
whar wee white roses scent the air
        about your grave,

and to

go with the rest of them

and til some suburb new and bare
        gang wi the lave.

The Wire

moor

This day I saw ane endless muir
wi sad horizon, like the sea
around some uncouth landless globe

where/flicker

whaur waters flauchter endlessly.

bilberry

Heather bell and blaeberry
grow on this muir; reid burns rin

sky

in clear daylicht; the luift is free

mist

frae haar, and yet there is nae sun.

Jacob's Ladder steep path, including steps, on Calton Hill; *Burns's smaa Greek pepperpat* on Calton Hill, monument to Robert Burns raised in 1830, and a copy of the monument of Lysicrates in Athens; *Sanct Andrew's Hous* St Andrew's House, HQ of the Scottish Office, a sort of cut-price Kremlin

everywhere Gossamers glint in aa the airts,
flower-heads criss-cross about the lang flure-heids
grass and thistles of girss and thristles here, and there
 amang the purpie willow-weeds.

 Bog-myrtle scent is in the air
honey heavy wi hinnie-sap and peat
mixed whiles mellit like uneasy thochts
excrement or sweat wi something human, shairn or sweit.

powder smoke Nou guns gaun aff, and pouther-reik
dogs and yappin packs of foetid dugs,
red/blisters and blobs of cramosie, like blebs
 of bluid squeezed frae vanilla bugs

knock violently pash suddenlike intill the licht
that beats that dings on this unshadowed muir
from every direction, and then are gone frae ilka airt, and syne are gane
whirlwinds/dust like tourbillions of twisted stour.

 The criss-cross gossamers, the while,
tight twang owre the heather, ticht and real;
slender I ken, houever jimp they seem,
 that they are spun frae strands of steel.

 And they are barbed wi twisted spikes
 wi scant a handsbreidth space atween,
iron and reinforced wi airn rods
 and hung about wi bits of tin

 that hing in pairs alang the Wire,
each one ilkane three-cornered like a fang:
 clashin thegither at a touch
unnaturally into the lark's song they break aukwart the lairick's sang.

high Heich in their sentry-posts, the guairds
who dare not wha daurna sleep, on pain of daith,
 watch throu the graticules of guns,
 cruel and persecuted, baith.

<table>
<tr><td>crowded</td><td>This endless muir is thrang wi folk</td></tr>
</table>

crowded
limp in all directions at once
This endless muir is thrang wi folk
that hirple aye aa airts at aince
wi neither purport nor content
restless
nor rest, in fidgan impotence.

They gae in danger of the Wire
but stagger
but staucher on anither mile
frae line to line of spider steel
to leap
to loup anither deidlie stile.

A man trips up; the Wire gaes ding,
tins clash, the guaird lifts up his heid;
very slowly
fu slaw he traverses his gun
and blatters at him till he's deid.

tearing
The dugs loup on him, reivan flesh,
bones/wood
crunchin the bane as they were wud;
swiftly
swith they come and swith are gane,
syne nocht is left but pools of bluid.

blood dripping
Bluid dreipan doun amang the roots
is sucked
is soukit up the vampire stem
cruel flowers
and suin the gaudy felloun flures
cheat and mock
begowk the man that nourished them.

Some pairts the Wires close in and leave
go
smaa space whaur men may freely gang,
and ilka step is taen in dreid;
there flures and men maist thickly thrang.

entangled
A man gets taiglit on a barb,
the length of his stomach
endlang his wame the cauld fear creeps;
he daurna muve, the hert beats hard,
but beats awa. The sentry sleeps.

energy
Aye! his virr comes back in spate,
sly
as some auld trout this man is slee;
he hauds himsel still as a stane,
back comes his ain self-maistery.

Cannily he sets to wark,
warp by warp his sleeve is free,
it hings nou by a single threid:
loud clash the tins and bullets flee.

forward   Forrit and back and in and out
woeful   they darn in waesome figure-dance;
staying/endure   bydin still they canna thole
and each man works   and ilk man warks his ain mischance.

                       They see the Wire, and weill they ken
which   whilk wey it warks. In middle-air
                       the glintan guns are clear in sicht,
who   tho nae man kens wha set them there.

                       Impersonal in uniform,
                       the guairds are neither friens nor faes;
none tries   nane ettles to propitiate
upsets   nor fashes them wi bribes or praise.

                       Efficient and predictable,
immediately   they cairry out their orders stricht;
                       here naething happens unforeseen;
                       it is jist sae, no wrang nor richt.

                       On this dour mechanistic muir
                       wi nae land's end, and endless day,
                       whaur nae thing thraws a shadow, here
sorrowful   the truth is clear, and it is wae.

                       The crouds that thrang the danger-spots
                       weill ken what wey their warld's wrocht,
struggle on   but aye the mair they pauchle on
                       to win release frae nigglin thocht.

                       Some pairts the pattern of the Wire
                       leaves clear for fifty yairds and mair
dried up/dust   whaur soil has crined to desert stuir
with stunted shrubs wi scroggie bussels puir and bare.

more sensible than the rest
given to taking fright

Here some folk wycer nor the lave
or maybe suiner gien to skar
tether theirsels wi chains to stakes,
sae they may gang, but no owre far.

spinning
must endure

Birlan in wretchedness aroun
their safe lives' centre, they maun dree
temptation sair to break their chains
for aye they ettle to gang free.

saunter aimlessly their patch
ponies
mettle

Some stark and strang stravaig their yird
like shelties that hae never taen
the bit; mere smeddum drives them on,
their lives are short, but are their ain.

some in odd, ill-favoured
directions

A wheen in orra ill-faur'd airts
on barren streitches of the muir

to soak the wearisome
unmoistened dust

gae whaur nae bluid is ever shed
to drouk the dreich unslockent stour.

Within a pentagon of wire
they gang alane, or twae by twae,

endure

thole the condition of their life

and suffer what happens

and dree the weird as best they may.

in all that alien
slow-going/eyes
as if
reflected marvels

Alane in thon hale fremmit globe
thae slaw-gaun folk hae in their een
some sapience, as gin their looks
refleckit ferlies they hae seen

revealed

in their ain thochts, the nucleus
of man himsel is keethit there.
Expressed in terms of happiness
are premises of pure despair.

unusually small

faded away

Thae guidlie folk are nae great men;
the best of men are unco smaa
whan in the autumn of despair
irrelevance has dwined awa.

then the leaf
shrink

Their syllogisms widdershins
wither the petal; syne the leaf
and stem crine in as life gaes doun
intill a corm of prime belief.

mighty thought

Wi utmaist pouer of forcy thocht
they crine their life within its core,
and what they ken wi certainty

known beside

is kent inby the bracken-spore.

vexation
that cruel/eyes
blaze

And aye alane or twae by twae
they gang unhurt amang the noy
of thon fell planet, and their een
lowe wi the licht of inwart joy.

save for

vibrating

Outwartly they seem at rest,
binna the glint of hidden fires.
Their warld shaks, but they bide still
as nodal points on dirlan wires.

In ither airts, whaur folk are thrang,
the Wire vibrates, clash gae the tins,
flures blume frae bluidie marl, dugs
yowl throu the blatter of the guns.

spin

dust

I saw thon planet slawlie birl;
I saw it as ane endless muir
in daylicht, and I saw a few
guid men bide still amang the stour.

Property

A man should have no thought for property,
he said, and drank down his pint.
Mirage is found in the Desert and elswhere.
Later, in Libya (sand & scrub,
the sun two weeks to midsummer)
he carried all his property over the sand:
socks, knife and spoon, a dixie,

toilet kit, the Works of Shakespeare,
blanket, groundsheet, greatcoat,
and a water-bottle holding no more water.
He walked with other scorched men
in the dryness of this littoral waste land,
a raised beach without even sea water
with a much damned escarpment
unchanged throughout a day's truck-bumping
or a lifetime of walking without water,
confirming our worst fears of eternity.
Two men only went on whistling,
skidding on a beat-frequency.
Tenderness to music's dissonances,
and much experience of distress in art
was distressed, this time, in life.
A hot dry wind rose, moving the sand,
the sand-shifting Khamsin, rustling over
the land, whistling through hardy sandy
scrub, where sand-snails' brittle
shells on the sand, things in themselves,
roll for ever. Suffusing the sand in the
air, the sun burned in darkness.
No man now whistled, only the sandy wind.
The greatcoat first, then blanket discarded
and the other property lay absurd on the Desert,
but he kept his water-bottle.
In February, in a cold wet climate,
he has permanent damp in his bones
for lack of that groundsheet.
He has a different notion of the values of things.

Glisk of the Great

   I saw him comin out the N.B. Grill,
creashy and winey, wi his famous voice
crackin some comic bawr to please three choice
notorious bailies, lauchan fit to kill.

glimpse

greasy
joke
magistrates, laughing

then the four merry cronies
climbed into   Syne thae fowre crousie cronies clam intill
a great big   a muckle big municipal Rolls-Royce,
                    and disappeared, aye lauchan, wi a noise
                    that droont the traffic, towards the Calton Hill.

                    As they rade by, it seemed the sun was shinin
cheerful   brichter nor usual roun thae cantie three
that well-known magnifico that wi thon weill-kent Heid-yin had been dinin.

                    Nou that's the kinna thing I like to see;
                    tho ye and I look on and canna jyne in,
                    it gies our toun some tone, ye'll aa agree.

Heard in the Cougate

'Whu's aa thae fflagpoles ffur in Princes Street?
Chwoich! Ptt! Hechyuch! Ab-boannie cairry-on.
Seez-owre the wa'er. Whu' the deevil's thon
inaidie, heh?' 'The Queen's t'meet

The King o Norway wi his royal suite.'
'His royal wh'?' 'The hale jing-bang. It's aw in
the papur. Whaur's ma speck-sh? Aye they're gaun
t'day-cor-ate the toun. It's a fair treat,

something ye dinnae see jist ivry day,
foun'uns in the Gairdens, muckle spates
dancing t'music, an thir's t'be nae

chairge t'gi'in, it aw gaes on the Rates.'
'Ah ddae-ken whu' the pplace is comin tae
wi aw thae, hechyuch! fforeign po'entates.'

At Robert Fergusson's Grave

October 1962

                    Canongait kirkyaird in the failing year
rose bushes   is auld and grey, the wee roseirs are bare,

gleam

five gulls leam white agin the dirty air:
why are they here? There's naething for them here.

Why are we here oursels? We gaither near
the grave. Fergusons mainly, quite a fair
turn-out, respectfu, ill at ease, we stare
at daith – there's an address – I canna hear.

oh well/mist

went back to the pool

mud

Aweill, we staund bareheidit in the haar,
murnin a man that gaed back til the pool
twa-hunner year afore our time. The glaur

that covers his bones

sorrow

tugs/disparage this if you dare

earth (on a grave)

that haps his banes glowres back. Strang, present
                                                    dool
ruggs at my hairt. Lichtlie this gin ye daur:
here Robert Burns knelt and kissed the mool.

Elegy

They are lang deid, folk that I used to ken,

all mouldering and awry

their firm-set lips aa mowdert and agley,
sherp-tempert een rusty amang the cley:

sensible, pleasant

they are baith deid, thae wycelike, bienlie men,

heidmaisters, that had been in pouer for ten

entangling

or twenty year afore fate's taiglie wey

well-educated, shy and fated

just-hatched schoolmaster

brocht me, a young, weill-harnit, blate and fey
new-cleckit dominie, intill their den.

one told me

Ane tellt me it was time I learnt to write –
round-haund, he meant – and saw about my hair:

I remember him well/paunch

I mind of him, beld-heidit, wi a kyte.

Ane sneerit quarterly – I cuidna square
my savings bank – and sniftert in his spite.

if they aren't dead

Weill, gin they arena deid, it's time they were.

In Princes Street Gairdens

barrow

     Doun by the baundstaund, by the ice-cream barrie,
there is a sait that says, Wilma is Fab.

give me your talk
a pigeon

Sit doun aside me here and gieze your gab,
jist you and me, a dou, and a wee cock-sparrie.

     Up in the street, shop-folk sairve and harrie;

prosperous
lay slates and paint and cobble

weill-daean tredsmen sclate and pent and snab

take notice

and jyne and plaister. We never let dab

dodge

sae lang as we can jink the strait-and-narrie.

     A sculptured growp, classical and symbolic,
staunds by the path, maist beautiful to see:
National Savings, out for a bit frolic,

to

     peys echt per cent til Thrift and Industry,
but dour Inflatioun, a diabolic
dou, has owrecam, and duin Thrift in the ee.

Merulius Lacrymans*

make you snort

     My name is dreidfu. Did it garr ye snirk?
I cam in wi your braith, syne. Whan I'm seen

mad-red
suit/gloom

I'm growin, wud-reid, nae Bolshevik, green
jist wadnae sair me; I bide in the mirk,

dark
corner/you're not keen
to look into/glows between
fine plaster and cracked joist

     nae chlorophyll in me. But in some dirk
neuk of your property ye arena keen
to keek intill, my floure-heid lowes atween
braw plaister and crackt jeest, in hous or kirk.

moisten
suck/under

     Onie bit weakness whaur the rain may flow
or slocken, even, and it's aa the same,
I'll souk the guid dry timmer frae ablow

*dry rot

your feet, and lay my water-warks. My name?
In France they used to cry me Collabo;
I'm Greitan Muriel whan I'm at hame.

Summer Farm

Straws like tame lightnings lie about the grass
And hang zigzag on hedges. Green as glass
The water in the horse-trough shines.
Nine ducks go wobbling by in two straight lines.

A hen stares at nothing with one eye,
Then picks it up. Out of an empty sky
A swallow falls and, flickering through
The barn, dives up again into the dizzy blue.

I lie, not thinking, in the cool, soft grass,
Afraid of where a thought might take me – as
This grasshopper with plated face
Unfolds his legs and finds himself in space.

Self under self, a pile of selves I stand
Threaded on time, and with metaphysic hand
Lift the farm like a lid and see
Farm within farm, and in the centre, me.

Drifter

The long net, tasselled with corpses, came
Burning through the water, flowing up.
Dogfish following it to the surface
Turned away slowly to the deep.

The *Daffodil* squatted, slid ahead
Through the red kyle with thirty crans
Of throttled silver in her belly.
Her anchor snored amid its chains.

And memory gathered tarry splinters,
Put shadowy sparkles in her bag,

Slid up her sleeve the hills of Harris
And stole Orion and the Dog.

I sat with that kind thief inside me;
I sat with years I did not know
Heaped on my knees. With these two treasures
I sailed home through the Gaelic sea.

Crofter's Kitchen, Evening

A man's boots with a woman in them
Clatter across the floor. A hand
Long careless of the lives it kills
Comes down and thwacks on newspapers
A long black fish with bloody gills.

The kettle's at her singsong — minor
Prophetess in her sooty cave.
A kitten climbs the bundled net
On the bench, and, curled up like a cowpat,
Purrs on the *Stornoway Gazette*.

The six hooks of a Mackerel Dandy
Climb their thin rope — an exclamation
By the curled question of a gaff.
Three rubber eels cling like a crayfish
On top of an old photograph.

Peats fur themselves in gray. The door
Bursts open, chairs creak, hands reach out
For spectacles, a lamp flairs high . . .
The collie underneath the table
Slumps with a world-rejecting sigh.

Half-built Boat in a Hayfield

A cradle, at a distance, of a kind:
Or, making midget its neat pastoral scene,
A carcass rotted and its bones picked clean.

Rye-grass was silk and sea, whose rippling was
Too suave to rock it. Solid in the sun,
Its stiff ribs ached for voyages not begun.

The gathering word was not completed yet.
The litter of its own genesis lay around,
Sunk in the bearded sea, or on the ground.

As though evolving brilliances could show
In their first utterances what would end as one
Continuous proclamation of a sun.

Only when these clawed timbers could enclose
Their own completing darkness would they be
Phoenixed from It and phoenixed into She.

And fit then, as such noticing reveals,
To split her first wave open and explore
The many ways that all lead to one shore.

Explicit Snow

First snow is never all the snows there were
Come back again, but novel in the sun
As though a newness had but just begun.

It does not fall as rain does from nowhere
Or from that cloud spinnakered on the blue,
But from a place we feel we could go to.

As a great actor steps, not from the wings,
But from the play's extension – all he does
Is move to the seen from the mysterious –

And his performance is the first of all –
The snow falls from its implications and
Stages pure newness on the uncurtained land.

And the hill we've looked out of existence comes
Vivid in its own language; and this tree
Stands self-explained, its own soliloquy.

Celtic Cross

The implicated generations made
This symbol of their lives, a stone made light
By what is carved on it.
                              The plaiting masks,
But not with involutions of a shade,
What a stone says and what a stone cross asks.

Something that is not mirrored by nor trapped
In webs of water or bag-nets of cloud;
The tangled mesh of weed
                              lets it go by.
Only men's minds could ever have unmapped
Into abstraction such a territory.

No green bay going yellow over sand
Is written on by winds to tell a tale
Of death-dishevelled gull
                              or heron, stiff
As a cruel clerk with gaunt writs in his hand
– Or even of light, that makes its depths a cliff.

Singing responses order otherwise.
The tangled generations ravelled out
In links of song whose sweet
                              strong choruses

Are these stone involutions to the eyes
Given to the ear in abstract vocables.

The stone remains, and the cross, to let us know
Their unjust, hard demands, as symbols do.
But on them twine and grow
                  beneath the dove
Serpents of wisdom whose cool statements show
Such understanding that it seems like love.

Feeding Ducks

One duck stood on my toes.
The others made watery rushes after bread
Thrown by my momentary hand; instead,
She stood duck-still and got far more than those.

An invisible drone boomed by
With a beetle in it; the neighbour's yearning bull
Bugled across five fields. And an evening full
Of other evenings quietly began to die.

And my everlasting hand
Dropped on my hypocrite duck her grace of bread.
And I thought, 'The first to be fattened, the first to be
                                            dead',
Till my gestures enlarged, wide over the darkening
                                            land.

Things in Each Other

To fake green strokes in water, light fidgets,
A niggling fidget, and the green is there,
Born of a blue and marrying into blue
With clouds blushed pink on it from the upper air.

And water breathing upwards from itself
Sketches an island with blurred pencillings,

A phase of space, a melting out of space:
Mind does this, too, with the pure shapes of things.

Or the mind fidgets and a thought, grown green,
Born of nowhere and marrying nowhere,
Fakes a creation, that is one and goes
Into the world and makes its difference there.

A thing to be regarded: whose pure shape
Blurs in the quality of the noticing mind
And is blushed pink and makes the hard jump from
Created to creator, like human kind.

The Shore Road

The sea pursued
Its beastlike amours, rolling in its sweat
And beautiful under the moon; and a leaf was
A lively architecture in the light.

The space between
Was full, to splitting point, of presences
So oilily adjustable a walking man
Pushed through and trailed behind no turbulence.

The walking man
With octaves in his guts was a quartertone
In octaves of octaves that climbed up and down
Beyond his hearing, to back parts of the moon.

As though things were
Perpetual chronologies of themselves,
He sounded his small history, to make complete
The interval of leaf and rutting waves.

Or so he thought,
And heard his hard shoes scrunching in the grit,
Smelt salt and iodine in the wind and knew
The door was near, the supper, the small lamplight.

Byre

The thatched roof rings like heaven where mice
Squeak small hosannahs all night long,
Scratching its golden pavements, skirting
The gutter's crystal river-song.

Wild kittens in the world below
Glare with one flaming eye through cracks,
Spurt in the straw, are tawny brooches
Splayed on the chests of drunken sacks.

The dimness becomes darkness as
Vast presences come mincing in,
Swagbellied Aphrodites, swinging
A silver slaver from each chin.

And all is milky, secret, female.
Angels are hushed and plain straws shine.
And kittens miaow in circles, stalking
With tail and hindleg one straight line.

Loch Sionascaig

Hard to remember how the water went
Shaking the light,
Until it shook like peas in a riddling plate.

Or how the islands snored into the wind,
Or seemed to, round
Stiff, plunging headlands that they never cleared.

Or how a trout hung high its drizzling bow
For a count of three –
Heraldic figure on a shield of spray.

Yet clear the footprint in the puddled sand
That slowly filled
And rounded out and smoothed and disappeared.

July Evening

A bird's voice chinks and tinkles
Alone in the gaunt reedbed –
    Tiny silversmith
Working late in the evening.

I sit and listen. The rooftop
With a quill of smoke stuck in it
    Wavers against the sky
In the dreamy heat of summer.

Flowers' closing time: bee lurches
Across the hayfield, singing
    And feeling its drunken way
Round the air's invisible corners.

And grass is grace. And charlock
Is gold of its own bounty.
    The broken chair by the wall
Is one with immortal landscapes.

Something has been completed
That everything is part of,
    Something that will go on
Being completed forever.

Porpoises

In twos and threes and fives
they made a circus-ring of the Minch,
wheeling over, and leaving behind them in the air
two puffs, three puffs, five puffs –
audible plumes.

One looked to see on their backs
or in the carved car they might well be pulling
some plump mythical boy
or sea-green sea-nymph
or Arion himself, twangling from his lyre
audible spray.

But not
these days.

All the same, I myself
(in a mythical sort of way)
have been drawn over metaphorical waters
by these curving backs, till,
filled with an elation
I don't want to have explained to me,
I lifted a pagan face and shouted
audible nonsense.

Looking Down on Glen Canisp

The summer air is thick, is wads
that muffle the hill burn's voice
and stifle colours
to their cloudier selves – and
bright enough: the little loch
is the one clear pane
in a stained-glass window.

The scent of thyme and bog myrtle
is so thick
one listens for it, as though it might be
a drowsy honey-hum
in the heavy air.

Even the ravens
have sunk into the sandstone cliffs
of Suilven, that are dazed blue
and fuzz into the air around them –

as my mind does, till I hear
a thin far clatter and
look down to where two stags
canter across the ford, splashing up before them
antlers of water.

Blue Tit on a String of Peanuts

A cubic inch of some stars
weighs a hundred tons – Blue tit,
who could measure the power
of your tiny spark of energy? Your hair-thin legs
(one north-east, one due west) support
a scrap of volcano, four inches
of hurricane: and, seeing me, you make the sound
of a grain of sawdust being sawn
by the minutest of saws.

Old Edinburgh

Down the Canongate
down the Cowgate
go vermilion dreams
snake's tongues of bannerets
trumpets with words from their mouths
saying *Praise me, praise me.*

Up the Cowgate
up the Canongate
lice on the march
tar on the amputated stump
Hell speaking with the tongue of Heaven
a woman tied to the tail of a cart.

And history leans by a dark entry
with words from his mouth
that say *Pity me, pity me
but never forgive.*

Basking Shark

To stub an oar on a rock where none should be,
To have it rise with a slounge out of the sea
Is a thing that happened once (too often) to me.

But not too often – though enough. I count as gain
That once I met, on a sea tin-tacked with rain,
That roomsized monster with a matchbox brain.

He displaced more than water. He shoggled me
Centuries back – this decadent townee
Shook on a wrong branch of his family tree.

Swish up the dirt and, when it settles, a spring
Is all the clearer. I saw me, in one fling,
Emerging from the slime of everything.

So who's the monster? The thought made me grow
                                                    pale
For twenty seconds while, sail after sail,
The tall fin slid away and then the tail.

Intruder in a Set Scene

The way the water goes is blink blink blink.
That heap of trash was once
a swan's throne. The swans now lean their chests
against the waves that spill on Benbecula.
On the towpath a little girl
peers over the handle of the pram she's pushing.
Her mother follows her, reading a letter.

Everything is winter, everything
is a letter from another place, measuring
absence. Everything laments
the swan, drifting and dazzling on a western sealoch.

– But the little girl, five years of self-importance,
walks in her own season, not noticing
the stop-go's of water, the mouldering swan-throne,
the tears turning cold in the eyes of her mother.

No Interims in History

Barbarians! growled Attila
as the pile of skulls mounted higher.
What fun! squealed Robespierre,
shaking the gloved hand of Monsieur Guillotin.
The sword of the Lord! roared Cromwell
while the church and the people in it
became a stack of fire.

It would be good to think
that Attila felt a headache coming on,
that Monsieur Guillotin fingered the crick in his neck,
that Cromwell had a grey taste on his tongue

– while, as now, the dove
flew wildly over the world
finding nowhere to land,
growing weaker and weaker.

SOMHAIRLE MACGILL-EAIN/SORLEY MACLEAN (b. 1911)

Gaoir na h-Eòrpa

A nighean a' chùil bhuidhe, throm-bhuidh òr-bhuidh,
fonn do bheòil-sa 's gaoir na h-Eòrpa,
a nighean gheal chasurlach aighearach bhòidheach
cha bhiodh masladh ar latha-ne searbh 'nad phòig-sa.

An tugadh t' fhonn no t' àilleachd ghlòrmhor
bhuam-sa gràinealachd mharbh nan dòigh seo,
a' bhrùid 's am meàirleach air ceann na h-Eòrpa
's do bhial-sa uaill-dhearg 'san t-seann òran?

An tugadh corp geal is clàr gréine
bhuam-sa cealgaireachd dhubh na bréine,
nimh bhùirdeasach is puinnsean créide
is dìblidheachd ar n-Albann éitigh?

An cuireadh bòidhchead is ceòl suaimhneach
bhuam-sa breòiteachd an aobhair bhuain seo,
am mèinear Spàinnteach a' leum ri cruadal
is' anam mórail dol sìos gun bhruaillean?

Dé bhiodh pòg do bheòil uaibhrich
mar ris gach braon de 'n fhuil luachmhoir
a thuit air raointean reòta fuara
nam beann Spàinnteach bho fhòirne cruadhach?

Dé gach cuach de d' chual òr-bhuidh
ris gach bochdainn, àmhghar 's dórainn
a thig 's a thàinig air sluagh na h-Eòrpa
bho Long nan Daoine gu daors' a' mhór-shluaigh?

The Cry of Europe

Girl of the yellow, heavy-yellow, gold-yellow hair,
the song of your mouth and Europe's shivering cry,
fair, heavy-haired, spirited, beautiful girl,
the disgrace of our day would not be bitter in your
                                                            kiss.

Would your song and splendid beauty take
from me the dead loathsomeness of these ways,
the brute and the brigand at the head of Europe
and your mouth red and proud with the old song?

Would white body and forehead's sun take
from me the foul black treachery,
spite of the bourgeois and poison of their creed
and the feebleness of our dismal Scotland?

Would beauty and serene music put
from me the sore frailty of this lasting cause,
the Spanish miner leaping in the face of horror
and his great spirit going down untroubled?

What would the kiss of your proud mouth be
compared with each drop of the precious blood
that fell on the cold frozen uplands
of Spanish mountains from a column of steel?

What every lock of your gold-yellow head
to all the poverty, anguish and grief
that will come and have come on Europe's people
from the Slave Ship to the slavery of the whole
                                                            people?

Am Bata Dubh

A bhàta dhuibh, a Ghreugaich choimhlionta,
cluas siùil, balg siùil làn is geal,
agus tu fhéin gu foirfeach ealanta,
sàmhach uallach gun ghiamh gun ghais;
do chùrsa réidh gun bhròn gun fhaireachadh;
cha b' iadsan luingis dhubha b' ealanta
a sheòl Odysseus a nall á Itaca
no Mac Mhic Ailein a nall á Uidhist,
cuid air muir fìon-dhorcha
's cuid air sàl uaine-ghlas.

The Black Boat

Black boat, perfect Greek,
sail tack, sail belly full and white,
and you yourself complete in craft,
silent, spirited, flawless;
your course smooth, sorrowless, unfeeling;
they were no more skilled black ships
that Odysseus sailed over from Ithaca,
or Clanranald over from Uist,
those on a wine-dark sea,
these on a grey-green brine.

Ban-Ghàidheal

Am faca Tu i, Iùdhaich mhóir,
ri 'n abrar Aon Mhac Dhé?
Am fac' thu 'coltas air Do thriall
ri strì an fhìon-lios chéin?

An cuallach mhiosan air a druim,
fallus searbh air mala is gruaidh;
's a' mhios chreadha trom air cùl
a cinn chrùibte bhochd thruaigh.

Chan fhaca Tu i, Mhic an t-saoir,
ri 'n abrar Rìgh na Glòir,
a miosg nan cladach carrach siar,
fo fhallus cliabh a lòin.

An t-earrach so agus so chaidh
's gach fichead earrach bho 'n an tùs
tharruing ise 'n fheamainn fhuar
chum biadh a cloinne 's duais an tùir.

'S gach fichead foghar tha air triall
chaill i samhradh buidh nam blàth;
is threabh an dubh-chosnadh an clais
tarsuinn mìnead ghil a clàir.

Agus labhair T' eaglais chaomh
mu staid chaillte a h-anama thruaigh;
agus leag an cosnadh dian
a corp gu sàmhchair dhuibh an uaigh.

Is thriall a tìm mar shnighe dubh
a' drùdhadh tughaidh fàrdaich bochd;
mheal ise an dubh-chosnadh cruaidh;
is glas a cadal suain an nochd.

A Highland Woman

Hast Thou seen her, great Jew,
who art called the One Son of God?
Hast Thou seen on Thy way the like of her
labouring in the distant vineyard?

The load of fruits on her back,
a bitter sweat on brow and cheek,
and the clay basin heavy on the back
of her bent poor wretched head.

Thou hast not seen her, Son of the carpenter,
who art called the King of Glory,
among the rugged western shores
in the sweat of her food's creel.

This Spring and last Spring
and every twenty Springs from the beginning,
she has carried the cold seaweed
for her children's food and the castle's reward.

And every twenty Autumns gone
she has lost the golden summer of her bloom,
and the Black Labour has ploughed the furrow
across the white smoothness of her forehead.

And Thy gentle church has spoken
about the lost state of her miserable soul,
and the unremitting toil has lowered
her body to a black peace in a grave.

And her time has gone like a black sludge
seeping through the thatch of a poor dwelling:
the hard Black Labour was her inheritance;
grey is her sleep to-night.

Calbharaigh

Chan eil mo shùil air Calbharaigh
no air Betlehem an àigh
ach air cùil ghrod an Glaschu
far bheil an lobhadh fàis,
agus air seòmar an Dùn-éideann,
seòmar bochdainn 's cràidh,
far a bheil an naoidhean creuchdach
ri aonagraich gu bhàs.

Calvary

My eye is not on Calvary
nor on Bethlehem the Blessed,
but on a foul-smelling backland in Glasgow,
where life rots as it grows;
and on a room in Edinburgh,
a room of poverty and pain,
where the diseased infant
writhes and wallows till death.

My Een Are Nae on Calvary

Frae the Gaelic o Sorley MacLean

My een are nae on Calvary
or the Bethlehem they praise,
but on the shitten back-lands in Glesga toun
whaur growan life decays,
and a stairheid room in an Embro land,
a chalmer o puirtith and skaith,
whaur monie a shilpet bairnikie
gaes smoorit doun til daith.

trans. Douglas Young

Clann Ghill-Eain

Chan e iadsan a bhàsaich
an àrdan Inbhir-chéitein
dh'aindeoin gaisge is uabhair
ceann uachdrach ar sgeula;
ach esan bha 'n Glaschu,
ursann-chatha nam feumach,
Iain mór MacGill-Eain,
ceann is fèitheam ar sgeula.

The Clan MacLean

Not they who died
in the hauteur of Inverkeithing
in spite of valour and pride
the high head of our story;
but he who was in Glasgow
the battle-post of the poor,
great John MacLean,
the top and hem of our story.

Dol an Iar

Tha mi dol an iar 'san Fhàsaich
is mo thàmailt air mo ghuaillean,
gun d' rinneadh a' chuis-bhùrta dhiom
on a bha mi mar bu dual dhomh.

An gaol 's an t-iomrall bu mhotha
an onair mheallta mo mhilleadh,
le sgleò na laige air mo léirsinn,
claonadh an éiginn a' chinne.

'S fhada bhuam-sa an t-Eilean
is gealach ag éirigh air Catàra,
's fhada bhuam an Aird Ghiuthais
is rudhadh maidne air an Fhàsaich.

Tha Camus Alba fada bhuam
agus daorsa na Roinn-Eòrpa.
fada bhuam 'san Aird an Iarthuath
na sùilean glas-ghorma 's bòidhche.

'S fhada bhuam-sa an t-Eilean
agus gach ìomhaigh ghaoil an Alba,
tha gainmheach choigreach anns an Eachdraidh
a' milleadh innealan na h-eanchainn.

'S fhada bhuam Belsen's Dachau
Rotterdam is Cluaidh is Pràga
is Dimitrov air bialaibh cùirte
a' bualadh eagail le ghlag gàire.

Tha Guernica fhéin glé fhada
bho chuirp neoichiontach nan Nàsach
a tha 'nan laighe ann an greibheal
's an gainmhich lachduinn na Fàsaich.

Chan eil gamhlas 'na mo chridhe
ri saighdearan calma 'n Nàmhaid
ach an càirdeas a tha eadar
fir am prìosan air sgeir-thràghad,

a' fuireach ris a' mhuir a' lìonadh
's a' fuarachadh na creige blàithe,
agus fuaralachd na beatha
ann an gréin theth na Fàsaich.

Ach 's e seo an spàirn nach seachnar,
éiginn ghoirt a' chinne-daonna,
's ged nach fuath liom armailt Roimeil
tha sùil na h-eanchainn gun chlaonadh.

Agus biodh na bha mar bhà e,
tha mi de dh'fhir mhór' a' Bhràighe,
de Chloinn Mhic Ghille Chaluim threubhaich,
de Mhathanaich Loch Aills nan geurlann,
agus fir m' ainme – có bu tréine
nuair dh' fhàdadh uabhar an léirchreach?

Going Westwards

I go westwards in the Desert
with my shame on my shoulders,
that I was made a laughing-stock
since I was as my people were.

Love and the greater error,
deceiving honour spoiled me,
with a film of weakness on my vision,
squinting at mankind's extremity.

Far from me the Island
when the moon rises on Quattara,
far from me the Pine Headland
when the morning ruddiness is on the Desert.

Camus Alba is far from me
and so is the bondage of Europe,
far from me in the North-West
the most beautiful grey-blue eyes.

Far from me the Island
and every loved image in Scotland,
there is a foreign sand in History
spoiling the machines of the mind.

Far from me Belsen and Dachau,
Rotterdam, the Clyde and Prague,
and Dimitrov before a court
hitting fear with the thump of his laugh.

Guernica itself is very far
from the innocent corpses of the Nazis
who are lying in the gravel
and in the khaki sand of the Desert.

There is no rancour in my heart
against the hardy soldiers of the Enemy,
but the kinship that there is among
men in prison on a tidal rock

waiting for the sea flowing
and making cold the warm stone;
and the coldness of life
in the hot sun of the Desert.

But this is the struggle not to be avoided,
the sore extreme of human-kind,
and though I do not hate Rommel's army
the brain's eye is not squinting.

And be what was as it was,
I am of the big men of Braes,
of the heroic Raasay MacLeods,
of the sharp-sword Mathesons of Lochalsh;

and the men of my name – who were braver
when their ruinous pride was kindled?

Glac a' Bhàis

Thubhairt Nàsach air choireigin gun tug am Furair air ais do fhir
na Gearmailte 'a' chòir agus an sonas bàs fhaotainn anns an
àraich'

'Na shuidhe marbh an 'Glaic a' Bhàis'
fo Dhruim Ruidhìseit,
gill' òg 's a logan sìos m' a ghruaidh
's a thuar grìsionn.

Smaoinich mi air a' chòir's an àgh
a fhuair e bho Fhurair,
bhith tuiteam ann an raon an àir
gun éirigh tuilleadh;

air a' ghreadhnachas's air a' chliù
nach d' fhuair e 'na aonar,
ged b' esan bu bhrònaiche snuadh
ann an glaic air laomadh

le cuileagan mu chuirp ghlas'
air gainmhich lachduinn
's i salach-bhuidhe 's làn de raip
's de sprùidhlich catha.

An robh an gille air an dream
a mhàb na h-Iùdhaich
's na Comunnaich , no air an dream
bu mhotha, dhiùbh-san

a threòraicheadh bho thoiseach àl
gun deòin gu buaireadh
agus bruaillean cuthaich gach blàir
air sgàth uachdaran?

Ge b'e a dheòin-san no a chàs,
a neoichiontas no mhìorun,
cha do nochd e toileachadh 'na bhàs
fo Dhruim Ruidhìseit.

Death Valley

*Some Nazi or other has said that the Fuehrer had restored to
German manhood the 'right and joy of dying in battle'*

Sitting dead in 'Death Valley'
below the Ruweisat Ridge
a boy with his forelock down about his cheek
and his face slate-grey;

I thought of the right and the joy
that he got from his Fuehrer,
of falling in the field of slaughter
to rise no more;

of the pomp and the fame
that he had, not alone,
though he was the most piteous to see
in a valley gone to seed

with flies about grey corpses
on a dun sand
dirty yellow and full of the rubbish
and fragments of battle.

Was the boy of the band
who abused the Jews
and Communists, or of the greater
band of those

led, from the beginning of generations,
unwillingly to the trial
and mad delirium of every war
for the sake of rulers?

Whatever his desire or mishap,
his innocence or malignity,
he showed no pleasure in his death
below the Ruweisat Ridge.

Curaidhean

Chan fhaca mi Lannes aig Ratasbon
no MacGill-Fhinnein aig Allt Eire
no Gill-Iosa aig Cuil-Lodair,
ach chunnaic mi Sasunnach 'san Eiphit.

Fear beag truagh le gruaidhean pluiceach
is glùinean a' bleith a chéile,
aodann guireanach gun tlachd ann –
còmhdach an spioraid bu tréine.

Cha robh buaidh air " 'san tigh-òsda
'n àm nan dòrn a bhith 'gan dùnadh",
ach leóghann e ri uchd a' chatha,
anns na frasan guineach mùgach.

Thàinig uair-san leis na sligean,
leis na spealgan-iaruinn beàrnach,
anns an toit is anns an lasair,
ann an crith is maoim na h-àraich.

Thàinig fios dha 'san fhrois pheileir
e bhith gu spreigearra 'na dhiùlnach:
is b'e sin e fhad 's a mhair e,
ach cha b' fhada fhuair e dh' ùine.

Chum e ghunnachan ris na tancan,
a' bocail le sgriach shracaidh stàirnich
gus an d' fhuair e fhéin mu 'n stamaig
an deannal ud a chuir ri làr e,
bial sìos an gainmhich 's an greabhal,
gun diog o ghuth caol grànnda.

Cha do chuireadh crois no meadal
ri uchd no ainm no g' a chàirdean:
cha robh a bheag dhe fhòirne maireann,
's nan robh cha bhiodh am facal làidir;
's có dhiubh, ma sheasas ursann-chatha
leagar móran air a shàilleabh
gun dùil ri cliù, nach iarr am meadal
no cop 'sam bith á bial na h-àraich.

Chunnaic mi gaisgeach mór á Sasuinn,
fearachan bochd nach laigheadh sùil air;
cha b' Alasdair á Gleanna Garadh –
is thug e gal beag air mo shùilean.

Heroes

I did not see Lannes at Ratisbon
nor MacLennan at Auldearn
nor Gillies MacBain at Culloden,
but I saw an Englishman in Egypt.

A poor little chap with chubby cheeks
and knees grinding each other,
pimply unattractive face –
garment of the bravest spirit.

He was not a hit 'in the pub
in the time of the fists being closed',
but a lion against the breast of battle,
in the morose wounding showers.

His hour came with the shells,
with the notched iron splinters,
in the smoke and flame,
in the shaking and terror of the battlefield.

Word came to him in the bullet shower
that he should be a hero briskly,

and he was that while he lasted
but it wasn't much time he got.

He kept his guns to the tanks,
bucking with tearing crashing screech,
until he himself got, about the stomach,
that biff that put him to the ground,
mouth down in sand and gravel,
without a chirp from his ugly high-pitched voice.

No cross or medal was put to his
chest or to his name or to his family;
there were not many of his troop alive,
and if there were their word would not be strong.
And at any rate, if a battle post stands
many are knocked down because of him,
not expecting fame, not wanting a medal
or any froth from the mouth of the field of slaughter.

I saw a great warrior of England,
a poor manikin on whom no eye would rest;
no Alasdair of Glen Garry;
and he took a little weeping to my eyes.

Hallaig

'Tha tìm, am fiadh, an coille Hallaig'

Tha bùird is tàirnean air an uinneig
troimh 'm faca mi an Aird an Iar
's tha mo ghaol aig Allt Hallaig
'na craoibh bheithe, 's bha i riamh

eadar an t-Inbhir 's Poll a' Bhainne,
thall 's a bhos mu Bhaile-Chùirn:
tha i 'na beithe, 'na calltuinn,
'na caorunn dhìreach sheang ùir.

Ann an Screapadal mo chinnidh,
far robh Tarmad 's Eachunn Mór,

tha 'n nigheanan 's am mic 'nan coille
ag gabhail suas ri taobh an lóin.

Uaibhreach a nochd na coilich ghiuthais
ag gairm air mullach Cnoc an Rà,
dìreach an druim ris a' ghealaich –
chan iadsan coille mo ghràidh.

Fuirichidh mi ris a' bheithe
gus an tig i mach an Càrn,
gus am bi am bearradh uile
o Bheinn na Lice f' a sgàil.

Mura tig 's ann theàrnas mi a Hallaig
a dh'ionnsaigh sàbaid nam marbh,
far a bheil an sluagh a' tathaich,
gach aon ghinealach a dh' fhalbh.

Tha iad fhathast ann a Hallaig,
Clann Ghill-Eain's Clann MhicLeòid,
na bh' ann ri linn Mhic Ghille-Chaluim:
Chunnacas na mairbh beò.

Na fir 'nan laighe air an lianaig
aig ceann gach taighe a bh' ann,
na h-igheanan 'nan coille bheithe,
direach an druim, crom an ceann.

Eadar an Leac is na Feàrnaibh
tha 'n rathad mór fo chóinnich chiùin,
's na h-igheanan 'nam badan sàmhach
s' dol a Chlachan mar o thùs.

Agus a' tilleadh as a' Chlachan,
á Suidhisnis 's á tir nam beò;
a chuile té òg uallach
gun bhristeadh cridhe an sgeòil.

O Allt na Feàrnaibh gus an fhaoilinn
tha soilleir an dìomhaireachd nam beann

chan eil ach coimhthional nan nighean
ag cumail na coiseachd gun cheann.

A' tilleadh a Hallaig anns an fheasgar,
anns a' chamhanaich bhalbh bheò'
a' lìonadh nan leathadan casa,
an gàireachdaich 'nam chluais 'na ceò,

's am bòidhche 'na sgleò air mo chridhe
mun tig an ciaradh air na caoil,
's nuair theàrnas grian air cùl Dhùn Cana
thig peileir dian á gunna Ghaoil;

's buailear am fiadh a tha 'na thuaineal
a' snòtach nan làraichean feòir;
thig reothadh air a shùil 'sa' choille:
chan fhaighear lorg air fhuil ri m' bheò.

Hallaig

'Time, the deer, is in the wood of Hallaig'

The window is nailed and boarded
through which I saw the West
and my love is at the Burn of Hallaig,
a birch tree, and she has always been

between Inver and Milk Hollow,
here and there about Baile-chuirn:
she is a birch, a hazel,
a straight, slender young rowan.

In Screapadal of my people
where Norman and Big Hector were,
their daughters and their sons are a wood
going up beside the stream.

Proud tonight the pine cocks
crowing on the top of Cnoc an Ra,

straight their backs in the moonlight –
they are not the wood I love.

I will wait for the birch wood
until it comes up by the cairn,
until the whole ridge from Beinn na Lice
will be under its shade.

If it does not, I will go down to Hallaig,
to the Sabbath of the dead,
where the people are frequenting,
every single generation gone.

They are still in Hallaig,
MacLeans and MacLeods,
all who were there in the time of Mac Gille Chaluim
the dead have been seen alive.

The men lying on the green
at the end of every house that was,
the girls a wood of birches,
straight their backs, bent their heads.

Between the Leac and Fearns
the road is under mild moss
and the girls in silent bands
go to Clachan as in the beginning,

and return from Clachan,
from Suisnish and the land of the living;
each one young and light-stepping,
without the heartbreak of the tale.

From the Burn of Fearns to the raised beach
that is clear in the mystery of the hills,
there is only the congregation of the girls
keeping up the endless walk,

coming back to Hallaig in the evening,
in the dumb living twilight,

filling the steep slopes,
their laughter a mist in my ears,

and their beauty a film on my heart
before the dimness comes on the kyles,
and when the sun goes down behind Dun Cana
a vehement bullet will come from the gun of Love;

and will strike the deer that goes dizzily,
sniffing at the grass-grown ruined homes;
his eye will freeze in the wood,
his blood will not be traced while I live.

SYDNEY TREMAYNE (1912–86)

Legend

When I grew strong to climb
Over the high stone wall,
First needling through the cushat wood,
Led by a cushat's call,
I reached the slope of a black hill
That wore a cloud for shawl.

I saw the sun prick through the cloud,
I heard the water run
Under the roots of the long grass
That hid the chuckling stone.
I cupped some water in my hands
And raised them to the sun.

The world and both my shining hands
Brightened my mouth to sing.
The little chipping birds as well
Went skipping on the wing
And donkey thistles kicked their heels,
Mocking the highland fling.

Never I guessed I was alone
Until the sun went in
And with a whistling wind there stooped
A dark bird from the rain.
The ground rushed by me as I swung
From talons cold as chain.

So long ago, so far from here
The rainbird let me fall
I have been trudging through the world
To find that high stone wall:
Restlessly turning round and round,
A beetle in a bowl.

Here is the wall, you wandering man;
Never this side you'll climb.
Look, there the dandelions grow
Unchanging since the game
When you were three feet low, and blew
Their white heads for the time.

And there's the black bull-shouldered hill
With all its trees cut down,
But through the roots of the long grass
You'll hear the water run.
Go catch the water in your hands,
And lift them to the sun.

A Burial

Of one who was much to me,
Nothing to anyone else,
I shall have least to say,
For silence is not false.
Once when I walked in iron
Through dead formalities,
I wished that I need not summon
The barbarous preaching voice.
So simple an act as death
Needs no pomp to excuse,
Nor any expense of breath
To magnify what is.
The sun shot the red apples,
Flies swung on summer air,
The world swam in green ripples
As a slow sea might stir.
There is no more to do
But to turn and go away,
Turn and finally go
From one who was much to me,
Nothing to anyone else.
Often it must be so
And always words be false.

Child, do you blame what is?
Child, do you blame what was?

Wanting News

Crystals of fog have frozen on the thorns,
Black trees stand coated in a web of white
As though a snow had fallen overnight
But missed the red field where the bracken burns.

A ridge of rime bevels all spiky things,
Barbed wire and holly, brambles, the one pine,
And wind out of the north makes a low whine,
A thin glissando played on icy strings.

Across the stoneless landscape of long hills
Midwinter daylight has no sun to shed:
All last year's nettle stalks are touched instead
Into unsparkling lightness, stiff as quills.

My house is hard to find, green lichen stains
The wooden box for letters. Far from roads
The wintry silence grips the rigid woods
Against mind's fidgetting, discordant strains,

Waiting for words to fall into the box
And ice to drop from hedges, wanting news.
Missing your voice, cold stillness builds unease:
The eye looks round for movement, like a fox.

DOUGLAS YOUNG (1913–73)

For a Wife in Jizzen

in childbed

Lassie, can ye say
　　whaur ye ha been,
whaur ye ha come frae,
marvels　　whatna ferlies seen?

Eftir the bluid and swyte,
struggling　　the warsslin o yestreen,
exhausted　ye ligg forfochten, whyte,
than　　prouder nor onie Queen.

although　Albeid ye hardly see me
　　I read it i your een,
sae saft blue and dreamy,
remembering　　mindan whaur ye've been.

only　Anerly wives ken
the roots of joy and grief　　the ruits o joy and tene,
　　　the march o daith and birth,
　　　the tryst o love and strife
midnight sunshine　i the howedumbdeidsuinsheen,
　　fire, air, water, yirth
mixing　　mellan to mak new life,
laughing and weeping, passionate lauchan and greetan, feiman and serene.

hide from all men　Dern frae aa men
　　the ferlies ye ha seen.

Sainless

incurable [and, unblessed]

quiet　I hae stuid an hour o the lown midsimmer nicht
twelve o'clock
magic light   livelong　til twal o the knock i the leelang glamarie-licht
looking all round　by the cherry-tree at the midden, luikan aa round.
over by the farm buildings　There's never a steer owreby at the ferm-toun,

smoke/in the sky/soft

the reek gangs straucht i the luift, that's lither and
                                                  gray,

occasional patch of gold

wi an auntran gair o gowd i the North by the Tay.
The whyte muin owre Drumcarro, the Lomond
                                          shawan

lone curlew calling

purpie i the West, and a lane whaup caaan.

active
vibrating

The ither birds are duin, but thon whaup's aye busy,
wi the dirlan bubble-note that maks ye dizzy,
the daft cratur's in luve, tho it's late i the year,

unusual fuss
a few bullocks

aa round Lucklaw he's fleean wi an unco steer.
There's a wheen stots owre i the park by the
                                          mansion-hous,

shambling/sleepy and gentle

skemblan about whiles, dozent and douce,
and a rabbit nibbles amang our raspberry canes

and the rest

for aa our wire and our traps and the lave o our
                                          pains.

most/gaped
over there
colt

But the feck o the hour I hae gowpit owre the dyke,
taen up wi a sicht thonder that I dinna like,
a day-auld cowt liggan doun i the gress
and the Clydesdale mear standan there motionless.
The hale hour she has made never a steer,
but stuid wi her heid forrit, rigid wi fear,
it's a wonder onie beast can haud sae still.

suspects
healed/ask if

The fermer douts the cowt has the joint-ill,
that canna be sained. Ye'd speir gin his mither kens?
Ay, beasts hae their tragedies as sair as men's.

The Shepherd's Dochter

Written on the occasion described in Fife in 1949

gaping

Lay her and lea her here i the gantan grund,
    the blythest, bonniest lass o the countryside,

shrunk in a timber shift, covered

    crined in a timber sark, hapt wi the pride
o hothous flouers, the dearest that could be fund.

Her faither and brithers stand, as suddentlie stunned

weight of sorrow; gentle

    wi the wecht o dule; douce neebours side by side

wrench and fidget askance –
looking, reluctant to stay
performing and his passionate
words

wriest and fidge, sclent-luikan, sweirt tae bide
while the Minister's duin and his threep gane wi the
wind.

scatter

[graveyard] earth

dance/solidly

labour

The murners skail, thankfu tae lea thon place
   whar the blythest, bonniest lass liggs i the mouls,
      Lent lilies lowp and cypresses stand stieve.
Time tae gae back tae the darg, machines and tools
   and beasts and seeds, the things men uis tae live,
and lea the puir lass there in her state o Grace.

RUTHVEN TODD (1914–1978)

Trout Flies

for J.K.M.

Ten years of age and intent upon a tea-brown burn
Across a moor in Lanarkshire, brass reel and
                                  greenheart
Rod, my first, I tried them out and came to learn
These magic names, from which I now can never
                                   part.

The insignificant ones were best, so ran the story
Of the old man who slowly taught me how to cast:
Dark Snipe, perhaps, Cow Dung, or favourite
                               Greenwell's Glory,
Would attract the sleek trout that moved so fast

To attack and suck the right and only fly.
Gaudy Partridge & Orange could be used, he said,
By those who fished on lochs, *his* fish would shy
From bright Butcher, Cardinal, or Teal & Red.

Now, on a clear day, a Wickham's Fancy might
Deceive a hungry trout, or even a Red Spinner,
But Coch-y-Bondu, or March Brown, in failing light,
Were more certain to bring home the dinner.

Watching the dull fly settle gently on the water
I would await the tug and make my strike,
While these names became a permanent mortar
Between my memories, names that I like

And tongue familiarly, Black Midge and August Dun,
Blue Upright, Cinnamon Sedge, Coachman and
                               Pheasant Tail,
Red Ant, Red Hackle, Furnace Palmer, and Yellow
                               Sally, in the sun,
Ghost, Green Midge, Half Stone and, sometimes,
                               Never Fail.

Of Moulds and Mushrooms

Agrippina, well aware of Claudius' greed
For Caesar's mushroom, knew also that it looked
Like death-cap or destroying angel, so a god
Made room on earth for Nero, whose joke,
'Food of the gods', allowed for deadly poison.

Some still, with unreasoning fear, disgust,
Kick or switch down the mushrooms by their path.
Leaving the amanita rudely shattered, gills
Like fallen feathers scattered, veil and volva
Broken, and all this symmetry destroyed.

The lack of chlorophyll suggests the parasite
Which guilty man so readily despises.
These are strange fruit of the thin mycellium,
That webs this world beneath the surface,
And which can persist in its invisibility

Breaking down discard of leaves and timber,
Which otherwise would overtop the wood
Extinguishing everything, so that the seed
May sprout to nourishment, and the cycle
Of death, decay and rebirth still go on.

And I, aesthetic and somewhat botanical,
Would note and praise the diversity
Of shapes, variety of colours of the fungi,
Ball, club, shelf, parasol, cup and horn,
And the suave velvet of the different moulds.

I would recall the fungi in their settings:
Fly-agaric, scarlet with wrinkled creamy warts,
In birch woods of Dumbartonshire, but lemon-
Yellow in New England, toxic they said to flies,
But intoxicant for the Kamchatka tribesman.

Near Selkirk once I found a monstrous puff ball,
Far bigger than my younger brother's head,
A gleaming baldpate beckoning me across the field
To find and greet poor Yorick's vegetable skull,
Solitary underneath the well-clipped hazel hedge.

Where anciently the monks had had their abbey,
Beside my Essex farmhouse, clustered blewits
Were palely violet below the dark-fruited sloes,
And the old gnarled oaks within the woods
Were sometimes richly shelved with beefsteaks;

And I, in a strictly rationed world,
Welcomed and ate these, and others that I found,
Spongy cèpe, chanterelle and honeycombed morel,
Grey oyster-mushroom and tall dignified parasol,
Which I again met later on a Chilmark lawn.

Brown-purple trumpets of the cornucopia
Stand clear against the brilliance of the moss
Under a clump of beech-trees at Gay Head,
While vast fairy-rings, some centuries of age,
Manacle the cropped grass of the South Downs.

The wooden ships of England knew dry-rot,
Pepys gathering toadstools bigger than his fists,
So that ten oaks were cut for each one used,
And the white-rimmed tawniness rioted again
Among the bombed buildings that I sometime knew.

Fungi have made their share of history:
St Anthony's fire, from ergot in the rye,
Swept savagely through medieval France,
Rotting potatoes drove the Irishman abroad,
And French grapes grown on North American stock.

A mouldering cantaloup from a Peoria supermarket
Supplanted the culture Fleming kept for years,
And others now sample soil, remove and scan
The moulds that, in their destructiveness,
Aid ailing man by driving out his enemies.

But I, walking in fields or through the woods,
Welcome the vermilion russula, the sulphur
Polyporus, or inky shaggy-cap upon a heap of dung,
Without questioning their usefulness to me.
The ecology of my appreciation seems to need

Clavaria's coral branches on a damp dark bank,
Odorous stink-horns prodding through the grass,
And petalled dry geasters studding a sandy road.
These many-fangled fruits make bright
My sundry places where no flowers can bloom.

G. S. FRASER (1914–80)

Lean Street

Here, where the baby paddles in the gutter,
    Here in the slaty greyness and the gas,
Here where the women wear dark shawls and mutter
    A hasty word as other women pass,

Telling the secret, telling, clucking and tutting,
    Sighing, or saying that it served her right,
The bitch! – the words and weather both are cutting
    In Causewayend, on this November night.

At pavement's end and in the slaty weather
    I stare with glazing eyes at meagre stone,
Rain and the gas are sputtering together
    A dreary tune! O leave my heart alone,

O leave my heart alone, I tell my sorrows,
    For I will soothe you in a softer bed
And I will numb your grief with fat to-morrows
    Who break your milk teeth on this stony bread!

They do not hear. Thought stings me like an adder,
    A doorway's sagging plumb-line squints at me,
The fat sky gurgles like a swollen bladder
    With the foul rain than rains on poverty.

Home Town Elegy

For Aberdeen in Spring

Glitter of mica at the windy corners,
Tar in the nostrils, under blue lamps budding
Like bubbles of glass the blue buds of a tree,
Night-shining shopfronts, or the sleek sun flooding
The broad abundant dying sprawl of the Dee:
For these and for their like my thoughts are mourners

That yet shall stand, though I come home no more,
Gas-works, white ballroom, and the red brick baths
And salmon nets along a mile of shore,
Or beyond the municipal golf-course, the moorland
                                                      paths
And the country lying quiet and full of farms.
This is the shape of a land that outlasts a strategy
And is not to be taken with rhetoric or arms.
Or my own room, with a dozen books on the bed
(Too late, still musing what I mused, I lie
And read too lovingly what I have read),
Brantôme, Spinoza, Yeats, the bawdy and wise,
Continuing their interminable debate,
With no conclusion, they conclude too late,
When their wisdom has fallen like a grey pall on my
                                                      eyes.

Syne we maun part, their sall be nane remeid –
Unless my country is my pride, indeed,
Or I can make my town that homely fame
That Byron has, from boys in Carden Place,
Struggling home with books to midday dinner,
For whom he is not the romantic sinner,
The careless writer, the tormented face,
The hectoring bully or the noble fool,
But, just like Gordon or like Keith, a name:
A tall, proud statue at the Grammar School.

SYDNEY GOODSIR SMITH (1915–75)

from Armageddon in Albyn

I EL ALAMEIN

O, dearlie they deed
St Valery's vengers
kites — The gleds dine weel
In the Libyan desert —
Dearlie they deed,
Aa the winds furthtell it.

Around El Alamein
Ranks o carrion
Faur frae their hame
lie stark Ligg sterk in the sun,
In the rutted sand
Whaur the tanks has run.

burning dawn Yon burnan daw
dead of night Than dumb-deid blacker,
Whiter than snaw
bones Will the bricht banes glitter;
Scotland That this was for Alba
must we make sure Maun we mak siccar!

It wasna for thraldom
Ye ligg there deid,
if Gin we should fail ye
The rocks wad bleed!
— O, the gleds foregaither
Roun Alba's deid.

II THE MITHER'S LAMENT

Whit care I for the leagues o sand,
The prisoners an the gear theyve won?

Ma darlin liggs amang the dunes
Wi mony a mither's son.

Doutless he deed for Scotland's life;
do not lie Doutless the statesmen dinna lee;
lamented But och tis sair begrutten pride
sour An wersh the wine o victorie!

VII THE WAR IN FIFE

storm-growling/cold Gurlie an gray the snell Fife shore,
mist Frae the peat-green sea the cauld haar drives,
The weet wind sings on the wire, and war
Looks faur frae the land o Fife.

in every house tarnished In ilka house tashed by the faem
empty Tuim beds tell o anither life,
The windae's blind wi the scuddan rain,
While war taks toll o the land o Fife.

By the 'Crusoe', backs tae the rain-straikit waa,
Auld jersied men staun hauf the day,
The fishing killt by trawlers, nou
They drink the rents the tourists pay.

But anither race has come, the pits
a headstrong folk no trick Breed a raucle fowk nae geck beguiles,
beguiles Deep in the yerth nae haar affects
earth The second war in the land o Fife.

Thae are the banded future; here
waste away Dwine the auld defeated race;
Unseen throu the cauld an seepan haar
Destroyers slip at a snail's pace.

across A foghorn booms athort the Forth,
troubled Drumlie lament for a sundered life,
The root an flouer that aince were kith
Made strangers in the land o Fife.

to the shore	The haar is chill, near in til the shore,
gulls/over the yellow firth	Nae maws screich owre the yalla freith,
swinging	The wireless frae a sweyan door
	Ennobles horror, fire, an daith.
	The foreign war tuims mony a bed
	But yet seems faur awa –
	Twa hunner years o Union's bled
than any war	The veins mair white nor ony war.
old man and lad	A third war cracks; lyart an loon
plunder	Thegither curse the lang stouthrife,
gloom	Mirk ower Scotland hings its rule
bitter cold	Like the snell haar hings ower Fife.

The Grace of God and the Meth-Drinker

go	There ye gang, ye daft
raving half-wit	And doitit dotterel, ye saft
outcast* vagabond soul	Crazed outland skalrag saul
big-holed* clothes	In your bits and ends o winnockie duds
fouled and musty rags	Your fyled and fozie-fousome clouts
triple-plastered	As fou's a fish, crackt and craftie-drunk
	Wi bleerit reid-rimmed
whingeing mouth	Ee and slaveran crozie mou
staggering over the street	Dwaiblan owre the causie like a ship
	Storm-toss't i' the Bay of Biscay O
	At-sea indeed and hauf-seas-owre
uvula	Up-til-the-thrapple's-pap
	Or up-til-the-crosstrees-sunk –
cares	*Wha kens? Wha racks?*
hither-and-thither tottering in a stupefied daydream	Hidderie-hetterie stouteran in a dozie dwaum
fiery red-biddy*	O' ramsh reid-biddie – Christ!
	The stink
	O' jake ahint him, a mephitic
reek/unusually exotic	Rouk o miserie, like some unco exotic
put up with	Perfume o the Orient no juist sae easilie tholit

* *outland* lit., landless; *winnockie* i.e., 'windowed'; *reid-biddie* red wine spliced with methylated spirits or other alcohol, prob. Irish – 'biddie' = diminutive of 'Bridget'

By the bleak barbarians o the Wast

penetrating the nostrils But subtil, acrid, jaggan the nebstrous

supremely horrible stench Wi 'n owrehailan ugsome guff, maist delicat,

the piss of a ruffian tomcat Like in scent til the streel o a randie gib . . .

O-hone-a-ree!

red His toothless gums, his lips, bricht cramasie

very-bright A schere-bricht slash o bluid

a beauty [?] like the shining fire A schene like the leaman gleid o rubies

Throu the gray-white stibble

unshaven cheeks O' his blank unrazit chafts, a hangman's

Heid, droolie wi gob, the bricht een

unseeing, cautious, indifferent and sly Sichtless, cannie, blythe, and slee –

unknowing Unkennan.

Ay,

poor outcast Puir gangrel!

There

incomprehensible – But for the undeemous glorie and grace

O' a mercifu omnipotent majestic God

Superne eterne and sceptred in the firmament

where to/of the faithful Whartil the praises o the leal rise

Like incense aye about Your throne,

everlasting Ayebydan, thochtless, and eternallie hauf-drunk

Wi nectar, Athole-brose,* ambrosia – nae jake for

You –

God there! –

the aforementioned But for the 'bunesaid unsocht grace, unprayed-for,

Undeserved

Gangs,

Unregenerate,

Me.

Time Be Brief

Time be brief
My fair luve far –
Time be brief

* *Athole-brose* whisky, with honey and/or oatmeal

partings's hurtful

Our twynin's sair
This wearie week
I wad be whar
Titania sleeps
Amang her hair.

Time be brief
My witch is far
these   Lang thir nichts
And langer mair
The wearie days
everywhere   Her face aawhar
Her voice that speaks
In aa I hear.

Time be brief
The hert is sair
quick   Days be rathe
Nichts, draw her near —
swift   Time time be swith
My constant prayer
This wearie week
lacking   Wantan my dear.

Time be brief
My true-luve far
Rin on auld week
And bring me whar
She bydes for me
And I for her —
Time be brief
My true-luve far.

Omens

The lane hills and the mune
at night   (Nichtertale in Yarrow
Under the Gray Mear's Tail)*

* *Gray Mear's Tail* a waterfall near Moffat, NE Dumfriesshire

lament   — By me the white coronach
roaring waterfall O' rairan linn
mountain torrent   Skriddan and cataract
White i the wan
Licht o the sickle mune.

Throu the blae gulph
and gloom   O' mune and mirk
across   Athort my vision suddenlie
lone   A lane white bird
— The screich o the linn
At my back, and abune
The far and numenous mune —
Silent, the bird, and was gane.

O, my hert, and I kent nocht
The gods' intent
Nor kent their omens'
Truth or this
if I had   — But what gin I had then
knowledge   The kennin I hae nou?
— Maybe's as weill our een
See little, and far less
Can understand.

Aa My Life

all

lover   Aa my life, my leman said,
livelong   Aa my life leelang
Thou sall be my luve alane
   Aa my life leelang.

And sae sall be, my dearest luve,
   I'll nane but thee belang,
Till daith sall see us beddit doun
   As in life leelang.

Aa my life, my leman said,
   This be our ainlie sang —

We'se gie auld Dis a kyndlie kiss
   When time it is to gang.

love

But here we've aa our life to loe
   Aa our life leelang
— We'se sleep hereafter, lou me nou
   And aa my life leelang
                  Leelang —
   Aa my life leelang.

from Under the Eildon Tree

V SLUGABED

here I lie
and poet

alone
gaping/mist

smoking

ash/pillow

elegy

Here I ligg, Sydney Slugabed Godless Smith,
The Smith, the Faber, ποιητής and Makar,
And Oblomov has nocht to learn me,
Auld Oblomov has nocht on me
Liggan my lane in bed at nune
Gantan at gray December haar,
A cauld, scummie, hauf-drunk cup o' tea
   At my bed-side,
     Luntan Virginian fags
— The New World thus I haud in fief
And levie kyndlie tribute. Black men slave
Aneath a distant sun to mak for me
Cheroots at hauf-a-croun the box.
   Wi ase on the sheets, ase on the cod,
And crumbs of toast under my bum,
Scrievan the last great coronach
O' the westren flickeran bourgeois world.
   Eheu fugaces!
                Lacrimæ rerum!
Nil nisi et cætera ex cathedra
            Requiescat up your jumper.

O, michtie Stalin in the Aist!
Could ye but see me nou,

The type, endpynt and final blume
servitude O' decadent capitalistical thirldom
     – It took five hunder year to produce me –
Och, could ye but see me nou
What a sermon could ye gie
     Further frae the Hailie Kremlin
bustling Bummlan and thunderan owre the Steppes,
humming Athort the mountains o' Europe humman
Till Swack! at my front door, the great *Schloss*
                               Schmidt

That's *Numéro Cinquante* (ПЯТЬДЕСЯТ* ye ken)
former In the umquhile pairk o' Craigmillar House
complexion Whar Marie Stewart o the snawie blee
Aince plantit ane o' a thousand treen.
     Losh, what a sermon yon wad be!
For Knox has nocht on Uncle Joe
And Oblomov has nocht on Smith
     And sae we come by a route maist devious
     Til the far-famed Aist-West Synthesis!
     Beluved by Hugh that's beluved by me
love/whisky And the baith o' us loe the barley-bree –
But wha can afford to drink the stuff?
     Certies no auld Oblomov!
     – And yet he does! Whiles!
not as much But no as muckle as Uncle Joe – I've smaa dout!
НА ЗГОРОВЬЕ* then, auld Muscovite!

Thus are the michtie faaen,
Thus the end o' a michtie line,
Dunbar til Smith the Slugabed
whose love burns no less bright Whas luve burns brichter nor them aa
than anyone's
And whas dounfaain is nae less,
fall from respectability
     Deid for a ducat deid
By the crueltie o' his ain maistress.

---

* *piat' desiat* fifty; *Na zdorovye* good health

DEORSA CAIMBEUL HAY/GEORGE CAMPBELL HAY (1915–84)

Bisearta

Chi mi rè geàrd na h-oidhche
dreòs air chrith 'na fhroidhneas thall air fàire,
a' clapail le a sgiathaibh,
a' sgapadh 's a' ciaradh rionnagan na h-àird' ud.

Shaoileadh tu gun cluinnte,
ge cian, o 'bhuillsgein ochanaich no caoineadh,
ràn corruich no gàir fuatha,
comhart chon cuthaich uaidh no ulfhairt fhaolchon,
gun ruigeadh drannd an fhòirneirt
o'n fhùirneis òmair iomall fhéin an t-saoghail;
ach sud a' dol an leud e
ri oir an speur an tosdachd olc is aognaidh.

C' ainm nochd a th' orra,
na sràidean bochda anns an sgeith gach uinneag
a lasraichean 's a deatach,
a sradagan is sgreadail a luchd thuinidh,
is taigh air thaigh 'ga reubadh
am broinn a chéile am brùchdadh toit a' tuiteam?
Is có an nochd tha 'g atach
am Bàs a theachd gu grad 'nan cainntibh uile,
no a' spàirn measg chlach is shailthean
air bhàinidh a' gairm air cobhair, is nach cluinnear?
Cò an nochd a phàidheas
sean chìs àbhaisteach na fala cumant?

Uair dearg mar lod na h-àraich,
uair bàn mar ghile thràighte an eagail éitigh,
a' dìreadh 's uair a' teàrnadh,
a' sìneadh le sitheadh àrd 's a' call a mheudachd,
a' fannachadh car aitil
's ag at mar anail dhiabhail air dhéinead,
an t-Olc 'na chridhe 's 'na chuisle,
chì mi 'na bhuillean a' sìoladh 's a' leum e.

Tha 'n dreòs 'na oillt air fàire,
'na fhàinne ròis is òir am bun nan speuran,
a' breugnachadh 's ag àicheadh
le shoillse sèimhe àrsaidh àrd nan reultan.

Bizerta

I see during the night guard
a blaze flickering, fringing the skyline over yonder,
beating with its wings
and scattering and dimming the stars of that airt.

You would think that there would be heard
from its midst, though far away, wailing and
lamentation,
the roar of rage and the yell of hate,
the barking of the dogs from it or the howling of
wolves,
that the snarl of violence would reach
from yon amber furnace the very edge of the world;
but yonder it spreads
along the rim of the sky in evil ghastly silence.

What is their name tonight,
the poor streets where every window spews
its flame and smoke,
its sparks and the screaming of its inmates,
while house upon house is rent
and collapses in a gust of smoke?
And who tonight are beseeching
Death to come quickly in all their tongues,
or are struggling among stones and beams,
crying in frenzy for help, and are not heard?
Who tonight is paying
the old accustomed tax of common blood?

Now red like a battlefield puddle,
now pale like the drained whiteness of foul fear,
climbing and sinking,

reaching and darting up and shrinking in size,
growing faint for a moment
and swelling like the breath of a devil in intensity,
I see Evil as a pulse
and a heart declining and leaping in throbs.
The blaze, a horror on the skyline,
a ring of rose and gold at the foot of the sky,
belies and denies
with its light the ancient high tranquillity of the stars.

Atman

Rinn thu goid 'nad éiginn,
dh'fheuch thu breug gu faotainn as;
dhìt iad, chàin is chuip iad thu,
is chuir iad thu fo ghlais.

Bha 'm beul onorach a dhìt thu
pladach, bìdeach 'sa ghnùis ghlais;
bha Ceartas sreamshùileach o sgrùdadh
a leabhar cunntais 's iad sìor phailt.

Ach am beul a dhearbhadh breugach,
bha e modhail, éibhinn, binn;
fhuair mi eirmseachd is sgeòil uaith
's gun e ro eòlach air tràth bìdh.

Thogte do shùil o'n obair
á cruth an t-saoghail a dheoghal tlachd;
mhol thu Debel Iussuf dhomh,
a cumadh is a dath.

Is aithne dhomh thu, Atmain,
bean do thaighe 's do chóignear òg,
do bhaidnein ghobhar is t' asail,
do ghoirtein seagail is do bhó.

Is aithne dhomh thu, Atmain:
is fear thu 's tha thu beò,

dà nì nach eil am breitheamh,
's a chaill e 'chothrom gu bhith fòs.

Chan ainmig t' fhallus 'na do shùilean;
is eòl duit sùgradh agus fearg;
bhlais is bhlais thu'n difir
eadar milis agus searbh.

Dh'fheuch thu gràin is bròn is gàire;
dh'fheuch thu ànradh agus grian;
dh'fhairich thu a' bheatha
is cha do mheath thu roimpe riamh.

Na'n robh thu beairteach, is do chaolan
garbh le caoile t' airein sgìth,
cha bhiodh tu 'chuideachd air na mìolan
an dubh phrìosan Mhondovì.

Nuair gheibh breitheamh còir na cùirte
làn a shùla de mo dhruim,
thig mi a thaobh gu d'fhàilteachadh
trasd an t-sràid ma chì mi thu.

Sidna Aissa, chaidh a cheusadh
mar ri mèirlich air bàrr sléibh,
is b'e 'n toibheum, Atmain, àicheadh
gur bràthair dhomh thu fhéin.

Atman

You thieved in your need,
and you tried a lie to get off;
they condemned you, reviled you and whipped you,
and they put you under lock and key.

The honourable mouth that condemned you
was blubberish and tiny in the grey face;
and Justice was blear-eyed from scrutinising
its account-books, that ever showed abundance.

But the mouth which was found lying
was mannerly, cheerful and melodious;
I got sharp repartee and tales from it,
though it was not too well acquainted with a meal.

Your eye would be raised from your work
to draw pleasure from the shape of the world;
you praised Jebel Yussuf to me,
its form and its colour.

I know you, Atman,
the woman of your house and your five youngsters,
your little clump of goats and your ass,
your plot of rye and your cow.

I know you, Atman:
you are a man, and you are alive;
two things the judge is not,
and that he has lost his chance of being ever.

Your sweat is not seldom in your eyes;
you know what sporting and anger are;
you have tasted and tasted the difference
between sweet and bitter.

You have tried hatred and grief and laughter;
you have tried tempest and sun;
you have experienced life
and never shrunk before it.

Had you been wealthy, and your gut
thick with the leanness of your tired ploughmen,
you would not be keeping company with the lice
in the black prison of Mondovi.

When the decent judge of the court
gets the fill of his eye of my back,
I will come aside to welcome you
across the street if I see you.

Our Lord Jesus was crucified
along with thieves on the top of a hill,
and it would be blasphemy, Atman, to deny
that you are a brother of mine.

To a Loch Fyne Fisherman

yonder

Calum thonder, long's the night to your thinking,
night long till dawn and the sun set at the tiller,
age and the cares of four and a boat to keep you
high in the stern, alone for the winds to weary.

A pillar set in the shifting moss, a beacon
fixed on the wandering seas and changing waters,
bright on the midnight waves and the hidden terrors;
the ancient yew of the glen, not heeding the ages.

Set among men that waver like leaves on the
                                    branches,
still among minds that flicker like light on the water.
Those are the shadows of clouds, the speckled and
                                    fleeting;
you are the hill that stands through shadow and
                                    sunlight.

Little you heed, or care to change with changes,
to go like a broken branch in the grip of a torrent;
you are your judge and master, your sentence
                                    unshaken,
a man with a boat of his own and a mind to guide
                                    her.

W. S. GRAHAM (1918–86)

The Children of Greenock

Local I'll bright my tale on, how
She rose up white on a Greenock day
Like the one first-of-all morning
On earth, and heard children singing.

She in a listening shape stood still
In a high tenement at Spring's sill
Over the street and chalked lawland
hopscotched*   Peevered and lined and fancymanned

On a pavement shouting games and faces.
She saw them children of all cries
With everyone's name against them bled
In already the helpless world's bed.

Already above the early town
The smoky government was blown
To cover April. The local orient's
Donkeymen, winches and steel giants

Wound on the sugar docks. Clydeside,
Webbed in its foundries and loud blood,
Binds up the children's cries alive.
Her own red door kept its young native.

Her own window by several sights
Wept and became the shouting streets.
And her window by several sights
Adored the even louder seedbeats.

She leaned at the bright mantle brass
Fairly a mirror of surrounding sorrows,

**peever the stone used in the game

The sown outcome of always war
Against the wordperfect, public tear.

Brighter drifted upon her the sweet sun
High already over all the children
So chained and happy in Cartsburn Street
Barefoot on authority's alphabet.

Her window watched the woven care
Hang webbed within the branched and heavy
Body. It watched the blind unborn
Copy book after book of sudden

Elements within the morning of her
Own man-locked womb. It saw the neighbour
Fear them housed in her walls of blood.
It saw two towns, but a common brood.

Her window watched the shipyards sail
Their men away. The sparrow sill
Bent grey over the struck town clocks
Striking two towns, and fed its flocks.

from Seven Letters

LETTER II

Burned in this element
To the bare bone, I am
Trusted on the language.
I am to walk to you
Through the night and through
Each word you make between
Each word I burn bright in
On this wide reach. And you,
Within what arms you lie,
Hear my burning ways
Across these darknesses

That move and merge like foam.
Lie in the world's room,
My dear, and contribute
Here where all dialogues write.

Younger in the towered
Tenement of night he heard
The shipyards with nightshifts
Of lathes turning their shafts.
His voice was a humble ear
Hardly turned to her.
Then in a welding flash
He found his poetry arm
And turned the coat of his trade.
From where I am I hear
Clearly his heart beat over
Clydeside's far hammers
And the nightshipping firth.
What's he to me? Only
Myself I died from into
These present words that move.
In that high tenement
I got a great grave.

Tonight in sadly need
Of you I move inhuman
Across this space of dread
And silence in my mind.
I walk the dead water
Burning language towards
You where you lie in the dark
Ascension of all words.
Yet where? Where do you lie
Lost to my cry and hidden
Away from the world's downfall?
O offer some way tonight
To make your love take place
In every word. Reply.
Time's branches burn to hear.
Take heed. Reply. Here

I am driven burning on
This loneliest element. Break
Break me out of this night,
This silence where you are not,
Nor any within earshot.
Break break me from this high
Helmet of idiocy.

　Water water wallflower
　Growing up so high
　We are all children
　We all must die.
　Except Willie Graham
　The fairest of them all.
　He can dance and he can sing
　And he can turn his face to the wall.
　Fie, fie, fie for shame
　Turn your face to the wall again.

Yes laugh then cloudily laugh
Though he sat there as deaf
And worn to a stop
As the word had given him up.
Stay still. That was the sounding
Sea he moved on burning
His still unending cry.
That night hammered and waved
Its starry shipyard arms,
And it came to inherit
His death where these words merge.
This is his night writ large.
In Greenock the bright breath
Of night's array shone forth
On the nightshifting town.
Thus younger burning in
The best of his puny gear
He early set out
To write him to his death
And to that great breath
Taking of the sea,

The graith of Poetry.
My musing love lie down
Within his arms. He dies
Word by each word into

Myself now at this last
Word I die in. This last.

LETTER VI

A day the wind was hardly
Shaking the youngest frond
Of April I went on
The high moor we know.
I put my childhood out
Into a cocked hat
And you moving the myrtle
Walked slowly over.
A sweet clearness became.
The Clyde sleeved in its firth
Reached and dazzled me.
I moved and caught the sweet
Courtesy of your mouth.
My breath to your breath.
And as you lay fondly
In the crushed smell of the moor
The courageous and just sun
Opened its door.
And there we lay halfway
Your body and my body
On the high moor. Without
A word then we went
Our ways. I heard the moor
Curling its cries far
Across the still loch.

The great verbs of the sea
Come down on us in a roar.
What shall I answer for?

Baldy Bane

Shrill the fife, kettle the drum,
　　My Queens my Sluts my Beauties
Show me your rich attention
　　Among the shower of empties.
And quiet be as it was once
　　It fell on a night late
The muse has felled me in this bed
　　That in the wall is set.
Lie over to me from the wall or else
　　Get up and clean the grate.

On such a night as this behind
　　McKellar's Tanworks' wall
It seems I put my hand in hers
　　As we played at the ball.
So began a folly that
　　I hope will linger late,
Though I am of the kitchen bed
　　And of the flannel sheet.
Lie over to me from the wall or else
　　Get up and clean the grate.

Now pay her no attention now,
　　Nor that we keep our bed.
It is yon hoodie on the gate
　　Would speak me to the dead.
And though I am embedded here
　　The creature to forget
I ask you one and all to come.
　　Let us communicate.
Lie over to me from the wall or else
　　Get up and clean the grate.

Make yourself at home here.
　　My words you move within.
I made them all by hand for you
　　To use as your own.

hooded crow

Yet I'll not have it said that they
    Leave my intention out,
Else I, an old man, I will up
    And at that yella-yite.*
Lie over to me from the wall or else
    Get up and clean the grate.

You're free to jig your fiddle or let
    It dally on the bow.
Who's he that bums his chat there,
    Drunk as a wheelbarrow?
Hey, you who visit an old man
    That a young wife has got,
Mind your brain on the beam there
    And watch the lentil pot.
Lie over to me from the wall or else
    Get up and clean the grate.

Now pay her no attention.
    I am the big bowbender.
These words shall lie the way I want
    Or she'll blacklead the fender.

[i.e. shilp] pale, sickly girl No shallop she, her length and depth
    Is Clyde and clinker built.
When I have that one shafted I
    Allow my best to out.
Lie over to me from the wall or else
    Get up and clean the grate.

Full as a whelk, full as a whelk
    And sad when all is done.
The children cry me Baldy Bane
    And the great catches are gone.
But do you know my mother's tune,
    For it is very sweet?
I split my thumb upon the barb
    The last time I heard it.

---

* yella-yite yellow-hammer, but here probably rhyming slang meaning excrement personified, a worthless person

Lie over to me from the wall or else
   Get up and clean the grate.

Squeeze the box upon the tune
   They call Kate Dalrymple O.
Cock your ears upon it and
   To cock your legs is simple O.
Full as a whelk, full as a whelk
   And all my hooks to bait.
Is that the nightshift knocking off?
   I hear men in the street.
Lie over to me from the wall or else
   Get up and clean the grate.

twirl

Move to me as you birl, Meg.
   Your mother was a great whore.
I have not seen such pas de bas
   Since up in Kirriemuir.
I waded in your shallows once,
   Now drink up to that.
It makes the blood go up and down

latch

   And lifts the sneck a bit.
Lie over to me from the wall or else
   Get up and clean the grate.

Through the word and through the word,
   And all is sad and done,
Who are you that these words
   Make this fall upon?
Fair's fair, upon my word,
   And that you shall admit, .
Or I will blow your face in glass
   And then I'll shatter it.
Lie over to me from the wall or else
   Get up and clean the grate.

If there's a joke between us
   Let it lie where it fell.
The exact word escapes me
   And that's just as well.

I always have the tune by ear.
    You are an afterthought.
But when the joke and the grief strike
    Your heart beats on the note.
Lie over to me from the wall or else
    Get up and clean the grate.

Full as a whelk, full as a whelk
    My brain is blanketstitched.
It is the drink has floored us
    And Meg lies unlatched.
Lie over to me, my own muse.
    The bed is our estate.
Here's a drink to caulk your seams
    Against the birling spate.
Lie over to me from the wall or else
    Get up and clean the grate.

Now pay her no attention, you.
    Your gears do not engage.
By and large it's meet you should
    Keep to your gelded cage.
My ooze, my merry-making muse,
    You're nothing to look at.
But prow is proud and rudder rude
    Is the long and short of that.
Lie over to me from the wall or else
    Get up and clean the grate.

Think of a word and double it.
    Admit my metaphor.
But leave the muscle in the verse,
    It is the Skerry Vore.
Can you wash a sailor's shirt
    And can you wash it white?
O can you wash a sailor's shirt
    The whitest in the fleet?
Lie over to me from the wall or else
    Get up and clean the grate.

Full as a whelk and ending,
  Surprise me to my lot.
The glint of the great catches
  Shall not again be caught.
But the window is catching
  The slow mend of light.
Who crossed these words before me
  Crossed my meaning out.
Lie over to me from the wall or else
  Get up and clean the grate.

Cry me Baldy Bane but cry
  The hoodie off the gate,
And before you turn away
  Turn to her last estate.
She lies to fell me on the field
  Of silence I wrote.
By whose endeavour do we fare?
  By the word in her throat.
Lie over to me from the wall or else
  Get up and clean the grate.

She lies to fell me on the field
  That is between us here.
I have but to lift the sneck
  With a few words more.
Take kindly to Baldy Bane, then
  And go your ways about.
Tell it in the Causewayside
  And in Cartsburn Street,
Lie over to me from the wall or else
  Get up and clean the grate.

Love me near, love me far.
  Lie over from the wall.
You have had the best of me
  Since we played at the ball.
I cross the Fingal of my stride
  With you at beauty heat.
And I burn my words behind me.

Silence is shouted out.
Lie over to me from the wall or else
Get up and clean the grate.

Malcolm Mooney's Land

1

Today, Tuesday, I decided to move on
Although the wind was veering. Better to move
Than have them at my heels, poor friends
I buried earlier under the printed snow.
From wherever it is I urge these words
To find their subtle vents, the northern dazzle
Of silence cranes to watch. Footprint on foot
Print, word on word and each on a fool's errand.
Malcolm Mooney's Land. Elizabeth
Was in my thoughts all morning and the boy.
Wherever I speak from or in what particular
Voice, this is always a record of me in you.
I can record at least out there to the west
The grinding bergs and, listen, further off
Where we are going, the glacier calves
Making its sudden momentary thunder.
This is as good a night, a place as any.

2

From the rimed bag of sleep, Wednesday,
My words crackle in the early air.
Thistles of ice about my chin,
My dreams, my breath a ruff of crystals.
The new ice falls from canvas walls.
O benign creature with the small ear-hole,
Submerger under silence, lead
Me where the unblubbered monster goes
Listening and makes his play.
Make my impediment mean no ill
And be itself a way.

A fox was here last night (Maybe Nansen's,
Reading my instruments.) the prints
All round the tent and not a sound.
Not that I'd have him call my name.
Anyhow how should he know? Enough
Voices are with me here and more
The further I go. Yesterday
I heard the telephone ringing deep
Down in a blue crevasse.
I did not answer it and could
Hardly bear to pass.

Landlice, always my good bedfellows,
Ride with me in my sweaty seams.
Come bonny friendly beasts, brother
To the grammarsow and the word-louse,
Bite me your presence, keep me awake
In the cold with work to do, to remember
To put down something to take back.
I have reached the edge of earshot here
And by the laws of distance
My words go through the smoking air
Changing their tune on silence.

  3

    My friend who loves owls
    Has been with me all day
    Walking at my ear
    And speaking of old summers
    When to speak was easy.
    His eyes are almost gone
    Which made him hear well.
    Under our feet the great
    Glacier drove its keel.
    What is to read there
    Scored out in the dark?
    Later the north-west distance
    Thickened towards us.
    The blizzard grew and proved

Too filled with other voices
High and desperate
For me to hear him more.
I turned to see him go
Becoming shapeless into
The shrill swerving snow.

4

Today, Friday, holds the white
Paper up too close to see
Me here in a white-out in this tent of a place
And why is it there has to be
Some place to find, however momentarily
To speak from, some distance to listen to?

Out at the far-off edge I hear
Colliding voices, drifted, yes
To find me through the slowly opening leads.
Tomorrow I'll try the rafted ice.
Have I not been trying to use the obstacle
Of language well? It freezes round us all.

5

Why did you choose this place
For us to meet? Sit
With me between this word
And this, my furry queen.
Yet not mistake this
For the real thing. Here
In Malcolm Mooney's Land
I have heard many
Approachers in the distance
Shouting. Early hunters
Skittering across the ice
Full of enthusiasm
And making fly and,
Within the ear, the yelling
Spear steepening to

The real prey, the right
Prey of the moment.
The honking choir in fear
Leave the tilting floe
And enter the sliding water.
Above the bergs the foolish
Voices are lighting lamps
And all their sounds make
This diary of a place
Writing us both in.

Come and sit. Or is
It right to stay here
While, outside the tent
The bearded blinded go
Calming their children
Into the ovens of frost?
And what's the news? What
Brought you here through
The spring leads opening?

Elizabeth, you and the boy
Have been with me often
Especially on those last
Stages. Tell him a story.
Tell him I came across
An old sulphur bear
Sawing his log of sleep
Loud beneath the snow.
He puffed the powdered light
Up on to this page
And here his reek fell
In splinters among
These words. He snored well.
Elizabeth, my furry
Pelted queen of Malcolm
Mooney's Land, I made
You here beside me
For a moment out
Of the correct fatigue.

I have made myself alone now.
Outside the tent endless
Drifting hummock crests.
Words drifting on words.
The real unabstract snow.

The Lying Dear

At entrance cried out but not
For me (Should I have needed it?)
Her bitching eyes under
My pressing down shoulder
Looked up to meet the face
In cracks on the flaking ceiling
Descending. The map of damp
Behind me, up, formed
Itself to catch the look
Under the closed (now)
Lids of my lying dear.

Under my pinning arm
I suddenly saw between
The acting flutters, a look
Catch on some image not me.

With a hand across her eyes
I changed my weight of all
Knowledge of her before.
And like a belly sledge
I steered us on the run
Mounting the curves to almost
The high verge. Her breath
Flew out like smoke. Her beauty
Twisted into another
Beauty and we went down
Into the little village
Of a new language.

The Night City

Unmet at Euston in a dream
Of London under Turner's steam
Misting the iron gantries, I
Found myself running away
From Scotland into the golden city.

I ran down Gray's Inn Road and ran
Till I was under a black bridge.
This was me at nineteen
Late at night arriving between
The buildings of the City of London.

And then I (O I have fallen down)
Fell in my dream beside the Bank
Of England's wall to bed, me
With my money belt of Northern ice.
I found Eliot and he said yes

And sprang into a Holmes cab.
Boswell passed me in the fog
Going to visit Whistler who
Was with John Donne who had just seen
Paul Potts shouting on Soho Green.

Midnight. I hear the moon
Light chiming on St Paul's.

The City is empty. Night
Watchmen are drinking their tea.

The Fire had burnt out.
The Plague's pits had closed
And gone into literature.

Between the big buildings
I sat like a flea crouched
In the stopped works of a watch.

Johann Joachim Quantz's Five Lessons

THE FIRST LESSON

So that each person may quickly find that
Which particularly concerns him, certain metaphors
Convenient to us within the compass of this
Lesson are to be allowed. It is best I sit
Here where I am to speak on the other side
Of language. You, of course, in your own time
And incident (I speak in the small hours.)
Will listen from your side. I am very pleased
We have sought us out. No doubt you have read
My Flute Book. Come. The Guild clock's iron men
Are striking out their few deserted hours
And here from my high window Brueghel's winter
Locks the canal below. I blow my fingers.

THE SECOND LESSON

Good morning, Karl. Sit down. I have been thinking
About your progress and my progress as one
Who teaches you, a young man with talent
And the rarer gift of application. I think
You must now be becoming a musician
Of a certain calibre. It is right maybe
That in our lessons now I should expect
Slight and very polite impatiences
To show in you. Karl, I think it is true,
You are now nearly able to play the flute.

Now we must try higher, aware of the terrible
Shapes of silence sitting outside your ear
Anxious to define you and really love you.
Remember silence is curious about its opposite
Element which you shall learn to represent.

Enough of that. Now stand in the correct position
So that the wood of the floor will come up through
                                                    you.

Stand, but not too stiff. Keep your elbows down.
Now take a simple breath and make me a shape
Of clear unchained started and finished tones.
Karl, as well as you are able, stop
Your fingers into the breathing apertures
And speak and make the cylinder delight us.

THE THIRD LESSON

Karl, you are late. The traverse flute is not
A study to take lightly. I am cold waiting.
Put one piece of coal in the stove. This lesson
Shall not be prolonged. Right. Stand in your place.

Ready? Blow me a little ladder of sound
From a good stance so that you feel the heavy
Press of the floor coming up through you and
Keeping your pitch and tone in character.

Now that is something, Karl. You are getting on.
Unswell your head. One more piece of coal.
Go on now but remember it must be always
Easy and flowing. Light and shadow must
Be varied but be varied in your mind
Before you hear the eventual return sound.

Play me the dance you made for the barge-master.
Stop stop Karl. Play it as you first thought
Of it in the hot boat-kitchen. That is a pleasure
For me. I can see I am making you good.
Keep the stove red. Hand me the matches. Now
We can see better. Give me a shot at the pipe.
Karl, I can still put on a good flute-mouth
And show you in this high cold room something
You will be famous to have said you heard.

THE FOURTH LESSON

You are early this morning. What we have to do
Today is think of you as a little creator
After the big creator. And it can be argued
You are as necessary, even a composer
Composing in the flesh an attitude
To slay the ears of the gentry. Karl,
I know you find great joy in the great
Composers. But now you can put your lips to
The messages and blow them into sound
And enter and be there as well. You must
Be faithful to who you are speaking from
And yet it is all right. You will be there.

Take your coat off. Sit down. A glass of Bols
Will help us both. I think you are good enough
To not need me anymore. I think you know
You are not only an interpreter.
What you will do is always something else
And they will hear you simultaneously with
The Art you have been given to read. Karl,

I think the Spring is really coming at last.
I see the canal boys working. I realise
I have not asked you to play the flute today.
Come and look. Are the barges not moving?
You must forgive me. I am not myself today.
Be here on Thursday. When you come, bring
Me five herrings. Watch your fingers. Spring
Is apparent but it is still chilblain weather.

THE LAST LESSON

Dear Karl, this morning is our last lesson.
I have been given the opportunity to
Live in a certain person's house and tutor
Him and his daughters on the traverse flute.
Karl, you will be all right. In those recent
Lessons my heart lifted to your playing.

I know. I see you doing well, invited
In a great chamber in front of the gentry. I
Can see them with their dresses settling in
And bored mouths beneath moustaches sizing
You up as you are, a lout from the canal
With big ears but an angel's tread on the flute.

But you will be all right. Stand in your place
Before them. Remember Johann. Begin with good
Nerve and decision. Do not intrude too much
Into the message you carry and put out.

One last thing, Karl, remember when you enter
The joy of those quick high archipelagoes,
To make to keep your finger-stops as light
As feathers but definite. What can I say more?
Do not be sentimental or in your Art.
I will miss you. Do not expect applause.

The Stepping Stones

I have my yellow boots on to walk
Across the shires where I hide
Away from my true people and all
I can't put easily into my life.

So you will see I am stepping on
The stones between the runnels getting
Nowhere nowhere. It is almost
Embarrassing to be alive alone.

Take my hand and pull me over from
The last stone on to the moss and
The three celandines. Now my dear
Let us go home across the shires.

TOM SCOTT (b. 1918)

The Mankind Toun

For Shirley Bridges

Hou lang we've socht
I dinna ken
For a toun that micht
Be fit for men.
Ten thousant year
Or mair or less
But yond or here
Wi smaa success.

We've fled mirk Thebes
Wi Ikhnaton,
startled   Fleggit the grebes
By Babylon
And sat in quorum,
Man til man
In Karakorum
Wi Jenghis Khan.

Seen Nineveh,
Byzantium,
Sidon, Troy,
Cartaga, Rome;
Corinth, wi its
Wreathit touers,
Damascan streets
Wi Asterte's whures;
Been amang the tents
Round Samarkan
bent-grass   And alang the bents
By Trebizon.

Frae Nippur, Tyre,
Jerusalem,
Athens, Palmyra,

Pergamum
Til Florence, Venice,
The toun on Thames,
Imperial Vienna's
Waltzan dames,
Braw touns we've seen,
And will again,
But nane that hes been
Fit for men.

Shall we never find
The toun whaur love
Rules mankind?
Whaur the hawk, the dove,
owl And houlet form
A trinitie
That keeps frae hairm
each Ilk chimney tree?
Whaur first is laist
And ilk and ane
Gie free their best
Til brither-men?

Whiles it seems
It canna be,
unless Binna in dreams;
Or till we see
The minarets,
The spires that rise
above the gates Abuin the yetts
O paradise.

But na, we'll find
Midnicht or noon,
journey's Our vaigin's end,
The mankind toun:
Yet bidan true
Til the Sender's aims
Seek further new
Jerusalems.

MURIEL SPARK (b. 1918)

Going up to Sotheby's

This was the wine. It stained the top of the page
when she knocked over the glass accidentally. A pity,
                                            she said,
to lose that drop. For the wine was a treat.
Here's a coffee-cup ring, and another. He preferred
                                            coffee to tea.
Some pages re-written entirely, scored through,
                                    cancelled over and over
on this, his most important manuscript.

That winter they took a croft in Perthshire,
living on oats and rabbits bought for a few pence
                                            from the madman.
The children thrived, and she got them to school
                                    daily, mostly by trudge.
He was glad to get the children out of the way, but
                                            always felt cold
while working on his book. This
is his most important manuscript, completed 1929.
'Children, go and play outside. Your father's trying
                                            to work.
But keep away from the madman's house.'
He looked up from his book. 'There's nothing
wrong with the madman.' Which was true.

She typed out the chapters in the afternoons. He
                                    looked happily at her.
He worked best late at night.
'Aren't you ever coming to bed? I often wonder,
are you married to me or to your bloody book?'
A smudge on the page, still sticky after all these
                                                    years.
Something greasy on the last page.
This is that manuscript, finished in the late spring,
crossed-out, dog-eared; this, the original,

passed through several literary hands while
the pages she had typed were at the publishers'.
One personage has marked a passage with red ink,
has written in the margin, 'Are you *sure*?'

Five publishers rejected it in spite of
                                        recommendations.
The sixth decided to risk his pounds sterling down
                                                the drain
for the sake of prestige. The author was a difficult
                                        customer. However,
they got the book published at last.
Her parents looked after the children while the
                                        couple went to France
for a short trip. This bundle of paper, the original
                                                manuscript,
went into a fibre trunk, got damp into it, got mouldy
                                                and furled.
It took fifteen more years for him to make his
                                                reputation,
by which time the children had grown up, Agnes as a
secretary at the BBC, Leo as a teacher.

The author died in '48, his wife in '68.
Agnes and Leo married and begat.
And now the grandchildren are selling the
                                                manuscript.
Bound and proud, documented and glossed
by scholars of the land, smoothed out
and precious, these leaves of paper
are going up to Sotheby's. The wine-stained,
stew-stained and mould-smelly papers are
going up to Sotheby's. They occupy the front seat
of the Renault, beside the driver.
They are a national event. They are going up
to make their fortune at last,
which once were so humble, tattered, and so truly
                                                working class.

Against the Transcendentalists

There are more visionaries
Than poets and less
Poets than missionaries,
Poets are a meagre species.

There is more vanity, more charity,
There is more of everything than poetry
Which, for personal purposes,
I wish may preserve
Identity from any other commodity
Also from Delphic insanity,
Drunkenness and discrepancy
Of which there's already a great plenty.
And so I reserve
The right not to try to
Fulfil the wilderness or fly to
Empyreal vacuity with an eye to
Publication, for what am I to
Byzantium or Byzantium
To me? I live in Kensington
And walk about, and work in Kensington
And do not foresee departing from Kensington.
So if there's no law in Kensington
Adaptable to verse without contravening
The letter to prove
The law, I'll make one.

The first text is
The word. The next is
(Since morals prevent quarrels
And writers make poor fighters)
Love your neighbour, meaning
Your neighbour, let him love
His neighbour, and he his.
Who is Everyman, what is he
That he should stand in lieu of
A poem? What is Truth true of?

And what good's a God's-eye-view of
Anyone to anyone
But God? In the Abstraction
Many angels make sweet moan
But never write a stanza down.
Poets are few and they are better
Equipped to love and animate the letter.

I therefore resign
The seven-league line
In footwear of super-cosmic design
To the global hops
Of wizards and wops;
Hoping that if Byzantium
Should appear in Kensington
The city will fit the size
Of the perimeter of my eyes
And of the span of my hand:
Hands and eyes that understand
This law of which the third
Text is the thing defined,
The flesh made word.

Elegy in a Kensington Churchyard

Lady who lies beneath this stone,
Pupil of Time pragmatical,
Though in a lifetime's cultivation
You did not blossom, summer shall.

The fierce activity of grass
Assaults a century's constraint.
Vigour survives the vigorous,
Meek as you were, or proud as paint.

And bares its fist for insurrection
Clenched in the bud; lady who lies
Those leaves will spend in disaffection
Your fond estate and purposes.

Death's a contagion: spring's a bright
Green fit; the blight will overcome
The plague that overcame the blight
That laid this lady low and dumb,

And laid a parish on its back
So soon amazed, so long enticed
Into an earthy almanack,
And musters now the spring attack;
Which render passive, latent Christ.

Litany of Time Past

What's today?
  Hoops today.
What's yesterday?
  Tops yesterday.
What's tomorrow?
  Diabolo.

Moons and planets come out to play,
The Bear bowled, the Sun spun.
See the Devil-on-sticks run
Today, tomorrow, and yesterday.

What's Hope?
  Skipping rope.
What's Clarity?
  Salty peppery.
What's Faith?
  Edinburgh, Leith,
  Portobello, Musselburgh,
  and Dalkeith.

Out you are.
  In you are.
Mustard.
  Vinegar.

ELMA MITCHELL (b. 1919)

Thoughts after Ruskin

Women reminded him of lilies and roses.
Me they remind rather of blood and soap,
Armed with a warm rag, assaulting noses,
Ears, neck, mouth and all the secret places:

Armed with a sharp knife, cutting up liver,
Holding hearts to bleed under a running tap,
Gutting and stuffing, pickling and preserving,
Scalding, blanching, broiling, pulverising,
– All the terrible chemistry of their kitchens.

Their distant husbands lean across mahogany
And delicately manipulate the market,
While safe at home, the tender and the gentle
Are killing tiny mice, dead snap by the neck,
Asphyxiating flies, evicting spiders,
Scrubbing, scouring aloud, disturbing cupboards,
Committing things to dustbins, twisting, wringing,
Wrists red and knuckles white and fingers puckered,
Pulpy, tepid. Steering screaming cleaners
Around the snags of furniture, they straighten
And haul out sheets from under the incontinent
And heavy old, stoop to importunate young,
Tugging, folding, tucking, zipping, buttoning,
Spooning in food, encouraging excretion,
Mopping up vomit, stabbing cloth with needles,
Contorting wool around their knitting needles,
Creating snug and comfy on their needles.

Their huge hands! their everywhere eyes! their voices
Raised to convey across the hullabaloo,
Their massive thighs and breasts dispensing comfort,
Their bloody passages and hairy crannies,
Their wombs that pocket a man upside down!

And when all's over, off with overalls,
Quickly consulting clocks, they go upstairs,
Sit and sigh a little, brushing hair,
And somehow find, in mirrors, colours, odours,
Their essences of lilies and of roses.

HAMISH HENDERSON (b. 1919)

Seventh Elegy

SEVEN GOOD GERMANS

The track running between Mekili and Tmimi was at one time a
kind of no-man's-land. British patrolling was energetic, and there
were numerous brushes with German and Italian elements. El
Eleba lies about half-way along this track.

> Of the swaddies
> who came to the desert with Rommel
> there were few who had heard (or would hear) of El
>   Eleba.
> They recce'd,
>   or acted as medical orderlies
> or patched up their tanks in the camouflaged
>   workshops
> and never gave a thought to a place like El Eleba.

> To get there, you drive into the blue, take a bearing
> and head for damn-all. Then you're there. And where
>   are you?

> — Still, of some few who did cross our path at El
>   Eleba
> there are seven who bide under their standing crosses.

> The first a Lieutenant.
>   When the medicos passed him
> for service overseas, he had jotted in a note-book
> *to the day and the hour   keep me steadfast   there*
> *is only the decision and the will*
>   *the rest has no importance*

The second a Corporal.
                        He had been in the Legion
and had got one more chance to redeem his lost
                                            honour.
What he said was
Listen here, I'm fed up with your griping –
If you want extra rations, go get 'em from Tommy!
You're green, that's your trouble. Dodge the column,
                                    pass the buck
and scrounge all you can – that's our law in the
                                        Legion.
You know Tommy's got 'em. . . . He's got mineral
                                        waters,
and beer, and fresh fruit in that white crinkly paper
and God knows what all! Well, what's holding you
                                        back?
Are you windy or what?
                        Christ, you 'old Afrikaners'!
If you're wanting the eats, go and get 'em from
                                        Tommy!

The third had been a farm-hand in the March of
                                        Silesia
and had come to the desert as fresh fodder for
                                    machine guns.
His dates are inscribed on the files, and on the cross-
                                        piece.

The fourth was a lance-jack.
                        He had trusted in Adolf
while working as a chemist in the suburb of Spandau.
His loves were his 'cello, and the woman who had
                                        borne him
two daughters and a son. He had faith in the
                                        Endsieg.
THAT THE NEW REICH MAY LIVE prayed the flyleaf
                                    of his Bible.

The fifth a mechanic.

         All the honour and glory,
the siege of Tobruk and the conquest of Cairo
meant as much to that Boche as the Synod of

               Whitby.
Being wise to all this, he had one single headache,
which was, how to get back to his sweetheart (called

               Ilse).
— He had said

Can't the Tommy wake up and get

           weaving?
If he tried, he could put our whole Corps in the bag.
May God damn this Libya and both of its palm-trees!

The sixth was a Pole

         — or to you, a Volksdeutscher —
who had put off his nation to serve in the

             Wehrmacht.
He siegheiled, and talked of 'the dirty Polacken,'
and said what he'd do if let loose among Russkis.
His mates thought that, though 'just a polnischer

             Schweinhund',
he was not a bad bloke.

         On the morning concerned
he was driving a truck with mail, petrol and rations.
The MP on duty shouted five words of warning.
He nodded

     laughed

       revved

         and drove straight for El

           Eleba
not having quite got the chap's Styrian lingo.

The seventh a young swaddy.

         Riding cramped in a lorry
to death along the road which winds eastward to

             Halfaya
he had written three verses in appeal against his

             sentence
which soften for an hour the anger of Lenin.

Seven poor bastards
dead in African deadland
(tawny tousled hair under the issue blanket)
wie einst Lili
dead in African deadland
einst Lili Marlene

ALEXANDER SCOTT (1920–89)

Coronach

For the dead of the 5/7th Battalion, The Gordon Highlanders

lament

lament

one of the remainder
stayed
trouble my spiritless

from the fighting's fear

back to my books

longing

endured our fates
remain behind
beyond/haven

brittle broken bone

dull speech

must disperse
poet's

to the world we loved
lied

Waement the deid
I never did,
Owre gled I was ane o the lave
That somewey baid alive
To trauchle my thowless hert
Wi ithers' hurt.

But nou that I'm far
Frae the fechtin's fear,
Nou I hae won awa frae aa thon pain
Back til my beuks and my pen,
They croud aroun me out o the grave
Whaur love and langourie sae lanesome grieve.

Cryan the cauld words:
'We hae dree'd our weirds,
But you that byde ahin,
Ayont our awesome hyne,
You are the flesh we aince had been,
We that are bruckle brokken bane.'

Cryan a drumlie speak:
'You hae the words we spak,
You hae the sang
We canna sing,
Sen death maun skail
The makar's skill.

'Makar, frae nou ye maun
Be singan for us deid men,
Sing til the warld we loo'd
(For aa that its brichtness lee'd)

And tell hou the sudden nicht
nothing
Cam doun and made us nocht.'

Waement the deid
I never did,
But nou I am safe awa
I hear their wae
weeping/dawn
Greetan greetan dark and daw,
their death yesterday my work
today
Their death the-streen my darg the-day.

EDWIN MORGAN (b. 1920)

The Starlings in George Square

I

Sundown on the high stonefields!
The darkening roofscape stirs –
thick – alive with starlings
gathered singing in the square –
like a shower of arrows they cross
the flash of a western window,
they bead the wires with jet,
they nestle preening by the lamps
and shine, sidling by the lamps
and sing, shining, they stir
the homeward hurrying crowds.
A man looks up and points
smiling to his son beside him
wide-eyed at the clamour on those cliffs –
it sinks, shrills out in waves,
levels to a happy murmur,
scatters in swooping arcs,
a stab of confused sweetness
that pierces the boy like a story,
a story more than a song.
He will never forget that evening,
the silhouette of the roofs,
the starlings by the lamps.

II

The City Chambers are hopping mad.
Councillors with rubber plugs in their ears!
Secretaries closing windows!
Window-cleaners want protection and danger money.
The Lord Provost can't hear herself think, man.
What's that?
Lord Provost, can't hear herself think.

At the General Post Office
the clerks write Three Pounds Starling in the savings-
                                                    books.

Each telephone-booth is like an aviary.
I tried to send a parcel to County Kerry but –
tangled   The cables to Cairo got fankled, sir.
What's that?
I said the cables to Cairo got fankled.

And as for the City Information Bureau –
I'm sorry I can't quite chirrup did you twit –
No I wanted to twee but perhaps you can't cheep –
Would you try once again, that's better, I – sweet –
When's the last boat to Milngavie? Tweet?
What's that?
I said when's the last boat to Milngavie?

III

There is nothing for it now but scaffolding:
clamp it together, send for the bird-men,
Scarecrow Strip for the window-ledge landings,
Cameron's Repellent on the overhead wires.
Armour our pediments against eavesdroppers.
This is a human outpost. Save our statues.
Send back the jungle. And think of the joke:
as it says in the papers, It is very comical
to watch them alight on the plastic rollers
and take a tumble. So it doesn't kill them?
All right, so who's complaining? This isn't Peking
where they shoot the sparrows for hygiene and cash.
So we're all humanitarians, locked in our cliff-
                                                    dwellings
encased in our repellent, guano-free and guilt-free.
The Lord Provost sings in her marble hacienda.
The Postmaster-General licks an audible stamp.
Sir Walter is vexed that his column's deserted.
I wonder if we really deserve starlings?
There is something to be said for these joyous
                                                    messengers

that we repel in our indignant orderliness.
They lift up the eyes, they lighten the heart,
and some day we'll decipher that sweet frenzied

> whistling

as they wheel and settle along our hard roofs
and take those grey buttresses for home.
One thing we know they say, after their fashion.
They like the warm cliffs of man.

The Second Life

But does every man feel like this at forty —
I mean it's like Thomas Wolfe's New York, his
heady light, the stunning plunging canyons, beauty —
pale stars winking hazy downtown quitting-time,
and the winter moon flooding the skyscrapers,

> northern —

an aspiring place, glory of the bridges, foghorns
are enormous messages, a looming mastery
that lays its hand on the young man's bowels
until he feels in that air, that rising spirit
all things are possible, he rises with it
until he feels that he can never die —
Can it be like this, and is this what it means
in Glasgow now, writing as the aircraft roar
over building sites, in this warm west light
by the daffodil banks that were never so crowded and

> lavish —

green May, and the slow great blocks rising
under yellow tower cranes, concrete and glass and

> steel

out of a dour rubble it was and barefoot children

> gone —

Is it only the slow stirring, a city's renewed life
that stirs me, could it stir me so deeply
as May, but could May have stirred
what I feel of desire and strength
like an arm saluting a sun?

All January, all February the skaters
enjoyed Bingham's pond, the crisp cold evenings,
they swung and flashed among car headlights,
the drivers parked round the unlit pond
to watch them, and give them light, what laughter
and pleasure rose in the rare lulls
of the yards-away stream of wheels along Great
                                    Western Road!
The ice broke up, but the boats came out.
The painted boats are ready for pleasure.
The long light needs no headlamps.

Black oar cuts a glitter: it is heaven on earth.

Is it true that we come alive
not once, but many times?
We are drawn back to the image
of the seed in darkness, or the greying skin
of the snake that hides a shining one –
it will push that used-up matter off
and even the film of the eye is sloughed –
That the world may be the same, and we are not
and so the world is not the same,
the second eye is making again
this place, these waters and these towers,
they are rising again
as the eye stands up to the sun,
as the eye salutes the sun.

Many things are unspoken
in the life of a man, and with a place
there is an unspoken love also
in undercurrents, drifting, waiting its time.
A great place and its people are not renewed lightly.
The caked layers of grime
grow warm, like homely coats.
But yet they will be dislodged
and men will still be warm.
The old coats are discarded.

The old ice is loosed.
The old seeds are awake.

Slip out of darkness, it is time.

Glasgow Sonnets

I

A mean wind wanders through the backcourt trash.
Hackles on puddles rise, old mattresses
puff briefly and subside. Play-fortresses
of brick and bric-a-brac spill out some ash.
Four storeys have no windows left to smash,
but in the fifth a chipped sill buttresses
mother and daughter the last mistresses
of that black block condemned to stand, not crash.
Around them the cracks deepen, the rats crawl.
The kettle whimpers on a crazy hob.
Roses of mould grow from ceiling to wall.
The man lies late since he has lost his job,
smokes on one elbow, letting his coughs fall
thinly into an air too poor to rob.

II

puny

A shilpit dog fucks grimly by the close.
Late shadows lengthen slowly, slogans fade.
The YY PARTICK TOI grins from its shade
like the last strains of some lost *libera nos
a malo*. No deliverer ever rose
from these stone tombs to get the hell they made

children

unmade. The same weans never make the grade.
The same grey street sends back the ball it throws.
Under the darkness of a twisted pram
a cat's eyes glitter. Glittering stars press
between the silent chimney-cowls and cram
the higher spaces with their SOS.

Don't shine a torch on the ragwoman's dram.
Coats keep the evil cold out less and less.

III

'See a tenement due for demolition?
I can get ye rooms in it, two, okay?
Seven hundred and nothin legal to pay
for it's no legal, see? That's my proposition,
ye can take it or leave it but. The position
is simple, you want a hoose, I say
for eight hundred pounds it's yours.' And they,
trailing five bairns, accepted his omission
of the foul crumbling stairwell, windows wired
not glazed, the damp from the canal, the cooker
without pipes, packs of rats that never tired –
any more than the vandals bored with snooker
who stripped the neighbouring houses, howled, and
                                                    fired
their aerosols – of squeaking 'Filthy lucre!'

IV

Down by the brickworks you get warm at least.
Surely soup-kitchens have gone out? It's not
the Thirties now. Hugh MacDiarmid forgot
in 'Glasgow 1960' that the feast
of reason and the flow of soul have ceased
to matter to the long unfinished plot
of heating frozen hands. We never got
an abstruse song that charmed the raging beast.
So you have nothing to lose but your chains,
dear Seventies. Dalmarnock, Maryhill,
Blackhill and Govan, better sticks and stanes
should break your banes, for poets' words are ill
to hurt ye. On the wrecker's ball the rains
weeping   of greeting cities drop and drink their fill.

V

'Let them eat cake' made no bones about it.
But we say let them eat the hope deferred
and that will sicken them. We have preferred
silent slipways to the riveters' wit.
And don't deny it – that's the ugly bit.
Ministers' tears might well have launched a herd
of bucking tankers if they'd been transferred
from Whitehall to the Clyde. And smiles don't fit
either. 'There'll be no bevvying' said Reid
at the work-in. But all the dignity you muster
can only give you back a mouth to feed
and rent to pay if what you lose in bluster
is no more than win patience with 'I need'
while distant blackboards use you as their duster.

VI

The North Sea oil-strike tilts east Scotland up,
and the great sick Clyde shivers in its bed.
But elegists can't hang themselves on fled-
from trees or poison a recycled cup –
If only a less faint, shaky sunup
glimmered through the skeletal shop and shed
and men washed round the piers like gold and spread
golder in soul than Mitsubishi or Krupp –
The images are ageless but the thing
is now. Without my images the men
ration their cigarettes, their children cling
to broken toys, their women wonder when
the doors will bang on laughter and a wing
over the firth be simply joy again.

VII

Environmentalists, ecologists
and conservationists are fine no doubt.
Pedestrianization will come out
fighting, riverside walks march off the lists,

pigeons and starlings be somnambulists
in far-off suburbs, the sandblaster's grout
multiply pink piebald facades to pout
at sticky-fingered mock-Venetianists.
Prop up's the motto. Splint the dying age.
Never displease the watchers from the grave.
Great when fake architecture was the rage,
but greater still to see what you can save.
The gutted double fake meets the adage:
a wig's the thing to beat both beard and shave.

VIII

Meanwhile the flyovers breed loops of light
in curves that would have ravished tragic Toshy —
clean and unpompous, nothing wishy-washy.
Vistas swim out from the bulldozer's bite
by day, and banks of earthbound stars at night
begin. In Madame Emé's Sauchie Haugh, she
could never gain in leaves or larks or sploshy
lanes what's lost in a dead boarded site —
the life that overspill is overkill to.
Less is not more, and garden cities are
the flimsiest oxymoron to distil to.
And who wants to distil? Let bus and car
and hurrying umbrellas keep their skill to
feed ukiyo-e beyond Lochnagar.

IX

It groans and shakes, contracts and grows again.
Its giant broken shoulders shrug off rain.
shuffling   It digs its pits to a shauchling refrain.
bold   Roadworks and graveyards like their gallus men.
It fattens fires and murders in a pen
and lets them out in flaps and squalls of pain.
It sometimes tears its smoky counterpane
to hoist a bleary fist at nothing, then
at everything, you never know. The west
could still be laid with no one's tears like dust

and barricaded windows be the best
to see from till the shops, the ships, the trust
return like thunder. Give the Clyde the rest.
Man and the sea make cities as they must.

    x

From thirtieth floor windows at Red Road
he can see choughs and samphires, dreadful trade –
the schoolboy reading *Lear* has that scene made.
A multi is a sonnet stretched to ode
and some say that's no joke. The gentle load
of souls in clouds, vertiginously stayed
above the windy courts, is probed and weighed.
Each monolith stands patient, ah'd and oh'd.
And stalled lifts generating high-rise blues
can be set loose. But stalled lives never budge.
They linger in the single-ends that use
their spirit to the bone, and when they trudge
from closemouth to laundrette their steady shoes
carry a world that weighs us like a judge.

The First Men on Mercury

– We come in peace from the third planet.
Would you take us to your leader?

– Bawr stretter! Bawr. Bawr. Stretterhawl?

– This is a little plastic model
of the solar system, with working parts.
You are here and we are there and we
are now here with you, is this clear?

– Gawl horrop. Bawr. Abawrhannahanna!

– Where we come from is blue and white
with brown, you see we call the brown
here 'land', the blue is 'sea', and the white

is 'clouds' over land and sea, we live
on the surface of the brown land,
all round is sea and clouds. We are 'men'.
Men come —

— Glawp men! Gawrbenner menko. Menhawl?

— Men come in peace from the third planet
which we call 'earth'. We are earthmen.
Take us earthmen to your leader.

— Thmen? Thmen? Bawr. Bawrhossop.
Yuleeda tan hanna. Harrabost yuleeda.

— I am the yuleeda. You see my hands,
we carry no benner, we come in peace.
The spaceways are all stretterhawn.

— Glawn peacemen all horrabhanna tantko!
Tan come at'mstrossop. Glawp yuleeda!

— Atoms are peacegawl in our harraban.
Menbat worrabost from tan hannahanna.

— You men we know bawrhossoptant. Bawr.
We know yuleeda. Go strawg backspetter quick.

— We cantantabawr, tantingko backspetter now!

— Banghapper now! Yes, third planet back.
Yuleeda will go back blue, white, brown
nowhanna! There is no more talk.

— Gawl han fasthapper?

— No. You must go back to your planet.
Go back in peace, take what you have gained
but quickly.

— Stretterworra gawl, gawl . . .

– Of course, but nothing is ever the same,
now is it? You'll remember Mercury.

Cinquevalli

Cinquevalli is falling, falling.
The shining trapeze kicks and flirts free,
solo performer at last.
The sawdust puffs up with a thump,
settles on a tangle of broken limbs.
St Petersburg screams and leans.
His pulse flickers with the gas-jets. He lives.

Cinquevalli has a therapy.
In his hospital bed, in his hospital chair
he holds a ball, lightly, lets it roll round his hand,
or grips it tight, gauging its weight and resistance,
begins to balance it, to feel its life attached to his
by will and knowledge, invisible strings
that only he can see. He throws it
from hand to hand, always different,
always the same, always
different, always the
same.
His muscles learn to think, his arms grow very
                                                    strong.

Cinquevalli in sepia
looks at me from an old postcard: bundle of enigmas.
Half faun, half military man; almond eyes, curly hair,
conventional moustache; tights, and a tunic loaded
with embroideries, tassels, chains, fringes; hand on
                                                    hip
with a large signet-ring winking at the camera
but a bull neck and shoulders and a cannon-ball
at his elbow as he stands by the posing pedestal;
half reluctant, half truculent,
half handsome, half absurd,
but let me see you forget him: not to be done.

Cinquevalli is a juggler.
In a thousand theatres, in every continent,
he is the best, the greatest. After eight years
                                        perfecting
he can balance one billiard ball on another billiard
                                        ball
on top of a cue on top of a third billiard ball
in a wine-glass held in his mouth. To those
who say the balls are waxed, or flattened,
he patiently explains the trick will only work
because the spheres are absolutely true.
There is no deception in him. He is true.

Cinquevalli is juggling with a bowler,
a walking-stick, a cigar, and a coin.
Who foresees? How to please.
The last time round, the bowler
flies to his head, the stick sticks in his hand,
the cigar jumps into his mouth, the coin
lands on his foot – ah, but
is kicked into his eye
and held there as the miraculous monocle
without which the portrait would be incomplete.

Cinquevalli is practising.
He sits in his dressing-room talking to some friends,
at the same time writing a letter with one hand
and with the other juggling four balls.
His friends think of demons, but
'You could do all this,' he says,
sealing the letter with a billiard ball.

Cinquevalli is on the high wire in Odessa.
The roof cracks, he is falling, falling
into the audience, a woman breaks his fall,
he cracks her like a flea, but lives.

Cinquevalli broods in his armchair in Brixton Road.
He reads in the paper about the shells whining
at Passchendaele, imagines the mud and the dead.

He goes to the window and wonders through that
                                    dark evening
what is happening in Poland where he was born.
His neighbours call him a German spy.
'Kestner, Paul Kestner, that's his name!'
'Keep Kestner out of the British music-hall!'
He frowns; it is cold; his fingers seem stiff and old.

Cinquevalli tosses up a plate of soup
and twirls it on his forefinger; not a drop spills.
He laughs, and well may he laugh
who can do that. The astonished table
breathe again, laugh too, think the world
a spinning thing that spills, for a moment, no drop.

Cinquevalli's coffin sways through Brixton
only a few months before the Armistice.
Like some trick they cannot get off the ground
it seems to burden the shuffling bearers, all their arms
cross-juggle that displaced person, that man
of balance, of strength, of delights and marvels,
in his unsteady box at last into the earth.

The Dowser

With my forked branch of Lebanese cedar
I quarter the dunes like downs and guide
an invisible plough far over the sand.
But how to quarter such shifting acres
when the wind melts their shapes, and shadows
mass where all was bright before,
and landmarks walk like wraiths at noon?
All I know is that underneath,
how many miles no one can say,
an unbroken water-table waits
like a lake; it has seen no bird or sail
in its long darkness, and no man;
not even pharaohs dug so far
for all their thirst, or thirst of glory,

or thrust-power of ten thousand slaves.
I tell you I can smell it though,
that water. I am old and black
and I know the manners of the sun
which makes me bend, not break. I lose
my ghostly footprints without complaint.
I put every mirage in its place.
I watch the lizard make its lace.
Like one not quite blind I go
feeling for the sunken face.
So hot the days, the nights so cold,
I gather my white rags and sigh
but sighing step so steadily
that any vibrance in so deep
a lake would never fail to rise
towards the snowy cedar's bait.
Great desert, let your sweetness wake.

from Sonnets from Scotland

PILATE AT FORTINGALL

A Latin harsh with Aramaicisms
poured from his lips incessantly; it made
no sense, for surely he was mad. The glade
of birches shamed his rags, in paroxysms
he stumbled, toga'd, furred, blear, brittle, grey.
They told us he sat here beneath the yew
even in downpours; ate dog-scraps. Crows flew
from prehistoric stone to stone all day.
'See him now.' He crawled to the cattle-trough
at dusk, jumbled the water till it sloshed
and spilled into the hoof-mush in blue strands,
slapped with useless despair each sodden cuff,
and washed his hands, and watched his hands, and
                                                      washed
his hands, and watched his hands, and washed his
                                                      hands.

DE QUINCEY IN GLASGOW

Twelve thousand drops of laudanum a day
kept him from shrieking. Wrapped in a duffle
buttoned to the neck, he made his shuffle,
door, table, window, table, door, bed, lay
on bed, sighed, groaned, jumped from bed, sat and
wrote

till the table was white with pages, rang
for his landlady, ordered mutton, sang
to himself with pharmacies in his throat.
When afternoons grew late, he feared and longed
for dusk. In that high room in Rottenrow
he looks out east to the Necropolis.
Its crowded tombs rise jostling, living, thronged
with shadows, and the granite-bloodying glow
flares on the dripping bronze of a used kris.

POST-REFERENDUM

'No no, it will not do, it will not be.
I tell you you must leave your land alone.
Who do you think is poised to ring the phone?
Fish your straitjacket packet from the sea
you threw it in, get your headphones mended.
You don't want the world now, do you? Come on,
you're pegged out on your heathery futon,
take the matches from your lids, it's ended.'
We watched the strong sick dirkless Angel groan,
shiver, half-rise, batter with a shrunk wing
the space the Tempter was no longer in.
He tried to hear feet, calls, car-doors, shouts, drone
of engines, hooters, hear a meeting sing.
A coin clattered at the end of its spin.

AFTER A DEATH

A writer needs nothing but a table.
His pencil races, pauses, crosses out.

Five years ago he lost his friend, without
him he struggles through a different fable.
The one who died, he is the better one.
The other one is selfish, ruthless, he
uses people, floats in an obscure sea
of passions, half-drowns as the livid sun
goes down, calls out for help he will not give.
Examine yourself! He is afraid to.
But that is not quite true, I saw him look
into that terrible place, let him live
at least with what is eternally due
to love that lies in earth in cold Carluke.

THE COIN

We brushed the dirt off, held it to the light.
The obverse showed us *Scotland*, and the head
of a red deer; the antler-glint had fled
but the fine cut could still be felt. All right:
we turned it over, read easily *One Pound*,
but then the shock of Latin, like a gloss,
Respublica Scotorum, sent across
such ages as we guessed but never found
at the worn edge where once the date had been
and where as many fingers had gripped hard
as hopes their silent race had lost or gained.
The marshy scurf crept up to our machine,
sucked at our boots. Yet nothing seemed ill-starred.
And least of all the realm the coin contained.

RUARAIDH MACTHOMAIS/DERICK THOMSON (b. 1921)

Dà Thaibhse

Anns an dìg dhomhainn aig ceann na buaile,
bhiodh na cailleachan ag ràdh chaidh murt a
dhèanamh;
bu tric a chunncas taibhse a' gluasad
air oir an rathaid, ri fèath 's ri siantan.

Is iomadh feasgar a ghabh mi seachad
air oir na h-iomagain is mi 'nam bhalach,
eadar coiseachd 's ruith, air eagal sealladh
fhaotainn a chaoidh den taibhs' gun anail.

'S ged ruiginn ceann na buaile an dràsda
tha fhios gu bheil tannasg truagh a' tàmh ann,
ach dhèanainn an diugh am barrachd dàlach
ri taibhse a' bhalaich a chaidh a bhàthadh.

Two Ghosts

In the deep ditch at the field end
the old women said there had been a murder;
often a ghost was seen moving
at the edge of the road, in calm or storm.

Many an evening I passed the place,
on edge and anxious when I was a boy,
half running, for fear of catching
a glimpse of the ghost with no breath in its body.

Though I were to reach the field-end now
I'm sure there's a poor ghost staying there,
but today I'd wait a little longer
for the ghost of the boy who has been drowned.

An Tobar

Tha tobar beag am meadhon a' bhaile
's am feur ga fhalach,
am feur gorm sùghor ga dhlùth thughadh,
fhuair mi brath air bho sheann chaillich,
ach thuirt i, 'Tha 'm frith-rathad fo raineach
far am minig a choisich mi le'm chogan,
's tha'n cogan fhèin air dèabhadh.'
Nuair sheall mi 'na h-aodann preasach
chunnaic mi 'n raineach a' fàs mu thobar a sùilean
's ga fhalach bho shireadh 's bho rùintean,
's ga dhùnadh 's ga dhùnadh.

'Cha teid duine an diugh don tobar tha sin'
thuirt a' chailleach, 'mar a chaidh sinne
nuair a bha sinn òg,
ged tha 'm bùrn ann cho brèagh 's cho geal.'
'S nuair sheall mi troimhn raineach 'na sùilean
chunnaic mi lainnir a' bhùirn ud
a ni slàn gach ciùrradh
gu ruig ciùrradh cridhe.

'Is feuch an tadhail thu dhòmhsa,'
thuirt a' chailleach, 'ga b'ann le meòirean,
's thoir thugam boinne den uisge chruaidh sin
a bheir rudhadh gu m' ghruaidhean.'
Lorg mi an tobar air èiginn
's ged nach b'ise bu mhotha feum air
'sann thuice a thug mi 'n eudail.

Dh' fhaodadh nach eil anns an tobar
ach nì a chunnaic mi 'm bruadar,
oir nuair chaidh mi an diugh ga shireadh
cha d'fhuair mi ach raineach is luachair,
's tha sùilean na caillich dùinte
's tha lì air tighinn air an luathghair.

The Well

Right in the village there's a little well
and the grass hides it,
green grass in sap closely thatching it.
I heard of it from an old woman
but she said: 'The path is overgrown with bracken
pail   where I often walked with my cogie,
and the cogie itself is warped.'
When I looked in her lined face
I saw the bracken growing round the well of her
                                                 eyes,
and hiding it from seeking and from desires,
and closing it, closing it.

'Nobody goes to that well now,'
said the old woman, 'as we once went,
when we were young,
though its water is lovely and white.'
And when I looked in her eyes through the bracken
I saw the sparkle of that water
that makes whole every hurt
till the hurt of the heart.

'And will you go there for me,'
said the old woman, 'even with a thimble,
and bring me a drop of that hard water
that will bring colour to my cheeks.'
I found the well at last,
and though her need was not the greatest
it was to her I brought the treasure.

It may be that the well
is something I saw in a dream,
for today when I went to seek it
I found only bracken and rushes,
and the old woman's eyes are closed
and a film has come over their merriment.

Srath Nabhair

Anns an adhar dhubh-ghorm ud,
àirde na sìorraidheachd os ar cionn,
bha rionnag a' priobadh ruinn
's i freagairt mireadh an teine
ann an cabair taigh m' athar
a' bhlianna thugh sinn an taigh le bleideagan
sneachda.

Agus siud a' bhlianna cuideachd
a shlaod iad a' chailleach don t-sitig,
a shealltainn cho eòlach 's a bha iad air an Fhìrinn,
oir bha nid aig eunlaith an adhair
(agus cròthan aig na caoraich)
ged nach robh àit aice-se anns an cuireadh i a ceann
fòidhpe.

A Shrath Nabhair 's a Shrath Chill Donnain,
is beag an t-iongnadh ged a chinneadh am fraoch
àlainn oirbh,
a' falach nan lotan a dh' fhàg Pàdraig Sellar 's a
sheòrsa,
mar a chunnaic mi uair is uair boireannach cràbhaidh
a dh' fhiosraich dòrainn an t-saoghail-sa
is sìth Dhè 'na sùilean.

Strathnaver

In that blue-black sky,
as high above us as eternity,
a star was winking at us,
answering the leaping flames of fire
in the rafters of my father's house,
that year we thatched the house with snowflakes.

And that too was the year
they hauled the old woman out on to the dung-heap,

to demonstrate how knowledgeable they were in
                                                    Scripture,
for the birds of the air had nests
(and the sheep had folds)
though she had no place in which to lay down her
                                                    head.

O Strathnaver and Strath of Kildonan,
it is little wonder that the heather should bloom on
                                                    your slopes,
hiding the wounds that Patrick Sellar, and such as he,
                                                    made,
just as time and time again I have seen a pious
                                                    woman
who has suffered the sorrow of this world,
with the peace of God shining from her eyes.

Eilean Chaluim Chille an Loch Eiriosort, Leòdhas

Chaidh sinn air chuairt don eilean air là samhraidh, an 1955, là
teth bruthainneach, is na pèileagan a' cluiche anns an loch, far am
minig a dh' fhairich Murchadh Mòr Mac Mhic Mhurchaidh
'sadadh nan tonn' mu sh ròin na Làir Dhuinn

Fàs, fàs an grian-shruth bruthainneach trath-nòin,
sliosan do chnuic dathte le raineach 's fraoch,
còinteach is riasg do ghleannain, feur do lòin,
gort agus iodhlann shaidhbhir gheal nan naomh.

'S torrach an deanntag mu do chlachan lom,
i frasadh sìol as t-fhoghar thar nan leac;
far an robh gillean dìreach thogadh fonn
tha 'n seileasdair gun lùbadh nise streap.

Mhùch gnùsdaich chaorach seirm nan salm o chian,
tha guth na fìdhle balbh 's am bogha brist,
tha fodair na *Làir Dhuinn* am brù nan sian,
is Murchadh Mòr aig neoni anns a' chist.

Bho abhal-ghort gu goirt, bho ghorm gu bàn,
fàsach ath-nuadhaicht' far 'n robh ionad Dhè,
bu leis an fhaoileig thu aig toiseach tràth'
's tha 'n fhaoileag fhathast crochte air a' sgèith.

St Columba's Isle, Loch Erisort, Lewis

Deserted in the noon-time's shimmering, pouring sun,
your hillsides stained with heather and with fern,
the moss and peat-mould of your glen, your meadow
                                              grass,
the rich bright field and corn-yard of the saints.

The nettles multiply beside your rain-washed stones,
showering their autumn seeds over the slabs;
where once upstanding lads joined in the song,
the never-bending iris now grows tall.

The grunting sheep have drowned the chanted psalms
long since; the fiddle's still, broken its bow;
chest [coffin]   *the Brown Mare's fodder eaten by the winds,*
and Murchadh Mòr* a cypher in his kist.

The orchard starved, the green field fallow now,
a re-created desert in God's place,
you were the seagull's land when time began,
and still the seagull hangs from its own wings.

Clann-Nighean an Sgadain

An gàire mar chraiteachan salainn
ga fhroiseadh bho 'm beul,
an sàl 's am picil air an teanga,
's na miaran cruinne, goirid a dheanadh giullachd,

---

* *Murchadh Mòr, or Murdoch Mackenzie, seventeenth century Factor to the Earl of Seaforth in Lewis, chief of the Mackenzies of Achilty, and poet, lived on St Columba's Isle. He composed a poem entitled* An Làir Dhonn, *'The Brown Mare'. He thinks of his own boat as a mare that needs no feeding other than the thudding of the waves against her prow.*

no a thogadh leanabh gu socair, cuimir,
seasgair, fallain,
gun mhearachd,
's na sùilean cho domhainn ri fèath.

B'e bun-os-cionn na h-eachdraidh a dh' fhàg iad
'nan tràillean aig ciùrairean cutach,
thall 's a-bhos air Galldachd 's an Sasainn.
Bu shaillte an duais a thàrr iad
ás na mìltean bharaillean ud,
gaoth na mara geur air an craiceann,
is eallach a' bhochdainn 'nan ciste,
is mara b'e an gàire
shaoileadh tu gu robh an teud briste.

Ach bha craiteachan uaille air an cridhe,
ga chumail fallain,
is bheireadh cutag an teanga
slisinn á fanaid nan Gall –
agus bha obair rompa fhathast
nuair gheibheadh iad dhachaigh,
ged nach biodh maoin ac':
air oidhche robach gheamhraidh,
ma bha siud an dàn dhaibh,
dheanadh iad daoine.

The Herring Girls

Their laughter like a sprinkling of salt
showered from their lips,
brine and pickle on their tongues,
and the stubby short fingers that could handle fish,
or lift a child gently, neatly,
safely, wholesomely,
unerringly,
and the eyes that were as deep as a calm.

The topsy-turvy of history had made them
slaves to short-arsed curers,

here and there in the Lowlands, in England.
Salt the reward they won
from those thousands of barrels,
the sea-wind sharp on their skins,
and the burden of poverty in their kists,
and were it not for their laughter
you might think the harp-string was broken.

But there was a sprinkling of pride on their hearts,
keeping them sound,
and their tongues' gutting-knife
would tear a strip from the Lowlanders' mockery —
and there was work awaiting them
when they got home,
though they had no wealth:
on a wild winter's night,
if that were their lot,
they would make men.

Dun Nan Gall

Far a bheil a' Ghàidhlig sgrìobht air na creagan
an sin dh' fhan i,
is pàisdean luideagach ga caitheamh,
a stiallan sgaoilte air na rubhachan an iar,
os cionn na mara
far a bheil grian na h-Eireann a' dol sìos,
is grian Ameireagaidh ag èirigh le èigheachd 's
                                  caithream.

Cha bheathaich feur a' chànain seo,
chan fhàs i sultmhor an guirt no 'n iodhlainn;
fòghnaidh dhi beagan coirce 's eòrna,
cuirear grad fhuadachadh oirr' leis a' chruithneachd;
chan iarr i ach, cleas nan gobhar, a bhith sporghail
os cionn muir gorm, air na bideanan biorach.

Gus an tog a' chlann luideagach leoth' i
air bàta-smùid a Shasainn,

no a Ghlaschu, far a faigh i bàs,
an achlais a peathar –
Gàidhlig rìoghail na h-Albann 's na h-Eireann
'na h-ìobairt-rèite air altair beairteis.

Donegal

Where Gaelic is written on the rocks
there it has lived,
and ragged children use it;
its shreds are scattered on the western headlands,
above the sea,
where the sun of Ireland goes down
and the sun of America rises with exultant clamour.

Grass does not nourish this language,
it does not grow fat in fields or cornyards;
a little oats and barley suffices it,
wheat quickly frightens it away;
all it asks is to clamber, like the goats,
on sharp rocky pinnacles, above the blue sea,

Until the ragged children carry it away with them
on the steamer to England,
or to Glasgow, where it dies
in its sister's arms –
the royal language of Scotland and of Ireland
become a sacrifice of atonement on the altar of
                                              riches.

Cisteachan-Laighe

Duin' àrd, tana
's fiasag bheag air,
's locair 'na làimh:
gach uair theid mi seachad
air bùth-shaoirsneachd sa' bhaile,
's a thig gu mo chuinnlean fàileadh na min-sàibh,

thig gu mo chuimhne cuimhne an àit ud,
le na cisteachan-laighe,
na h-ùird 's na tairgean,
na sàibh 's na sgeilbean,
is mo sheanair crom,
is sliseag bho shliseag ga locradh
bhon bhòrd thana lom.

Mus robh fhios agam dè bh' ann bàs;
beachd, bloigh fios, boillsgeadh
den dorchadas, fathann den t-sàmhchair.
'S nuair a sheas mi aig uaigh,
là fuar Earraich, cha dainig smuain
thugam air na cisteachan-laighe
a rinn esan do chàch:
'sann a bha mi 'g iarraidh dhachaigh,
far am biodh còmhradh, is tea, is blàths.

Is anns an sgoil eile cuideachd,
san robh saoir na h-inntinn a' locradh,
cha tug mi 'n aire do na cisteachan-laighe,
ged a bha iad 'nan suidhe mun cuairt orm;
cha do dh' aithnich mi 'm brèid Beurla,
an lìomh Gallda bha dol air an fhiodh,
cha do leugh mi na facail air a' phràis,
cha do thuig mi gu robh mo chinneadh a' dol bàs.
Gus an dainig gaoth fhuar an Earraich-sa
a locradh a' chridhe;
gus na dh' fhairich mi na tairgean a' dol tromham,
's cha shlànaich tea no còmhradh an cràdh.

Coffins

A tall thin man
with a short beard,
and a plane in his hand:
whenever I pass
a joiner's shop in the city,
and the scent of sawdust comes to my nostrils,

memories return of that place,
with the coffins,
the hammers and nails,
saws and chisels,
and my grandfather, bent,
planing shavings
from a thin, bare plank.

Before I knew what death was;
or had any notion, a glimmering
of the darkness, a whisper of the stillness.
And when I stood at his grave,
on a cold Spring day, not a thought
came to me of the coffins
he made for others:
I merely wanted home
where there would be talk, and tea, and warmth.

And in the other school also,
where the joiners of the mind were planing,
I never noticed the coffins,
though they were sitting all round me;
I did not recognise the English braid,
the Lowland varnish being applied to the wood,
I did not read the words on the brass,
I did not understand that my race was dying.
Until the cold wind of this Spring came
to plane the heart;
until I felt the nails piercing me,
and neither tea nor talk will heal the pain.

An Dàrna Eilean

Nuair a ràinig sinn an t-eilean
bha feasgar ann
's bha sinn aig fois,
a' ghrian a' dol a laighe
fo chuibhrig cuain
's am bruadar a' tòiseachadh ás ùr.

Ach anns a' mhadainn
shad sinn dhinn a' chuibhrig
's anns an t-solas gheal sin
chunnaic sinn loch anns an eilean
is eilean anns an loch,
is chunnaic sinn
gun do theich am bruadar pìos eile bhuainn.

Tha an staran cugallach
chon an dàrna eilein,
tha a' chlach air uideil
tha a' dion nan dearcag,
tha chraobh chaorainn a' crìonadh,
fàileadh na h-iadhshlait a' faileachdainn oirnn a-nis.

The Second Island

When we reached the island
it was evening
and we were at peace,
the sun lying down
under the sea's quilt
and the dream beginning anew.

But in the morning
we tossed the cover aside
and in that white light
saw a loch in the island,
and an island in the loch,
and we recognised
that the dream had moved away from us again.

The stepping-stones are chancy
to the second island,
the stone totters
that guards the berries,
the rowan withers,
we have lost now the scent of the honeysuckle.

GEORGE MACKAY BROWN (b. 1921)

The Funeral of Ally Flett

Because of his long pilgrimage
   From pub to alehouse
      And all the liquor laws he'd flout,
Being under age
      And wringing peatbog spirit from a clout
Into a secret kettle,
      And making every Sabbath a carouse,
Mansie brought a twelve-year bottle.

Because his shy foot turned aside
   From Merran's door,
      And Olga's coat with the red button
And Inga's side
      Naked as snow or swan or wild bog cotton
Made him laugh loud
      And after, spit with scunner on the floor,
Marget sewed a long chaste shroud.

disgust

Because the scythe was in the oats
   When he lay flat,
      And Jean Macdonald's best March ale
Cooled the long throats
      (At noon the reapers drank from the common
                       pail)
And Sanders said
   'Corn enough here for every tramp and rat',
Sigrid baked her lightest bread.

Although the fleet from Hamnavoe
   Drew heavy nets
      Off Noup Head, in a squall of rain,
Turning in slow
      Gull-haunted circles near the three-mile line,
And mouthing cod

Went iced and salted into slippery crates,
One skipper heard and bowed his head.

Because at Dounby and the fair
   Twelve tearaways
      Brought every copper in the islands
Round their uproar
      And this one made a sweet and sudden silence
Like that white bird
   That broke the tempest with a twig of praise,
The preacher spoke the holy word.

Because the hour of grass is brief
   And the red rose
      Is a bare thorn in the east wind
And a strong life
      Runs out and spends itself like barren sand
And the dove dies
   And every loveliest lilt must have a close,
Old Betsy came with bitter cries.

Because his dance was gathered now
   And parish feet
      Went blundering their separate roads
After the plough
      And after net and peat and harvest loads,
Yet from the cradle
   Their fated steps with a fixed passion beat,
Tammas brought his Swedish fiddle.

Old Fisherman with Guitar

A formal exercise for withered fingers.
   The head is bent,
      The eyes half closed, the tune
Lingers
      And beats, a gentle wing the west had thrown
      Against his breakwater wall with salt savage
                              lament.

So fierce and sweet the song on the plucked string,
　　Know now for truth
　　　Those hands have cut from the net
The strong
　　　Crag-eaten corpse of Jock washed from a boat
　　One old winter, and gathered the mouth of Thora
　　　　　　　　　　　　　　　　　　to his mouth.

Trout Fisher

Semphill, his hat stuck full of hooks
　　Sits drinking ale
　　　Among the English fishing visitors,
　　Probes in detail
　　　　Their faults in casting, reeling, selection of
　　　　　　　　　　　　　　　　　　　　flies.
'Never', he urges, 'do what it says in the books'.
　　　Then they, obscurely wise,
　　　Abandon by the loch their dripping oars
And hang their throttled tarnish on the scale.

'Forgive me, every speckled trout',
　　Says Semphill then,
　　　'And every swan and eider on these waters.
　　Certain strange men
　　　Taking advantage of my poverty
Have wheedled all my subtle loch-craft out
　　　So that their butchery
　　　Seem fine technique in the ear of wives and
　　　　　　　　　　　　　　　　　　　daughters.
　　And I betray the loch for a white coin.'

Hamnavoe Market

They drove to the Market with ringing pockets.

Folster found a girl
Who put wounds on his face and throat,
Small and diagonal, like red doves.

Johnston stood beside the barrel.
All day he stood there.
He woke in a ditch, his mouth full of ashes.

Grieve bought a balloon and a goldfish.
He swung through the air.
He fired shotguns, rolled pennies, ate sweet fog from
                                               a stick.

Heddle was at the Market also.
I know nothing of his activities.
He is and always was a quiet man.

Garson fought three rounds with a negro boxer,
And received thirty shillings,
Much applause, and an eye loaded with thunder.

Where did they find Flett?
They found him in a brazen circle,
All flame and blood, a new Salvationist.

A gypsy saw in the hand of Halcro
Great strolling herds, harvests, a proud woman.
He wintered in the poorhouse.

They drove home from the Market under the stars
Except for Johnston
Who lay in a ditch, his mouth full of dying fires.

The Five Voyages of Arnor

I, Arnor the red poet, made
Four voyages out of Orkney.

The first was to Ireland.
That was a viking cruise.
Thorleif came home with one leg.
We left Guthorm in Ulster,
His blood growing cold by the saint's well.
Rounding Cape Wrath, I made my first poem.

Norway hung fogs about me.
I won the girl Ragnhild
From Paul her brother, after
I beat him at draughts, three games to two.
Out of Bergen, the waves made her sick.
She was uglier than I expected, still
I made five poems about her
That men sing round the benches at Yule.
She filled my quiet house with words.

'The cousin Sweyn is howe-laid in Iceland
After his man-slaying' . . .
They put an axe in my hand, the edge turned north.
Women in black stood all about me.
We sailed no further than Unst in Shetland.
We bade there a month.
We drank the ale and discussed new metres.
For the women, I reddened the axe at a whale
                                    wound.

I went the blue road to Jerusalem
With fifteen ships in a brawling company
Of poets, warriors, and holy men.
A hundred swords were broken that voyage.
Prayer on a hundred white wings
Rose every morning. The Mediterranean
Was richer by a hundred love songs.

We saw the hills where God walked
And the last hill where his feet were broken.
At Rome, the earl left us. His hooves beat north.

Three Fridays sick of the black cough
Tomorrow I make my last voyage.
I should have endured this thing,
A bright sword in the storm of swords,
At Dublin, Micklegarth, Narbonne.
But here, at Hamnavoe, a pillow is under my head.
May all things be done in order.
The priest has given me oil and bread, a sweet cargo.
Ragnhild my daughter will cross my hands.
The boy Ljot must ring the bell.
I have said to Erling Saltfingers, *Drop my harp*
Through a green wave, off Yesnaby,
Next time you row to the lobsters.

Kirkyard

A silent conquering army,
The island dead,
Column on column, each with a stone banner
Raised over his head.

A green wave full of fish
Drifted far
In wavering westering ebb-drawn shoals beyond
Sinker or star.

A labyrinth of celled
And waxen pain.
Yet I come to the honeycomb often, to sip the
                                                    finished
Fragrance of men.

Taxman

Seven scythes leaned at the wall.
Beard upon golden beard
The last barley load
Swayed through the yard.
The girls uncorked the ale.
Fiddle and feet moved together.
Then between stubble and heather
A horseman rode.

from Runes from a Holy Island

Press-Gang
  A man-of-war enchanted
  Three boys away.
  Pinleg, Windbag, Lord Rum returned.

Hierarchy
  A claret laird,
  Seven fishermen with ploughs,
  Women, beasts, corn, fish, stones.

Harpoonist
  He once riveted boat to whale.
  Frail-fingered now
  He weaves crab prisons.

Books
  No more ballads in Eynhallow.
  The schoolmaster
  Opens a box of grammars.

Ruined Chapel
  Among scattered Christ stones
  Devoutly leave
  Torn nets, toothache, winter wombs.

Saint
      A starved island, Cormack
      With crossed hands,
      Stones become haddock and loaf.

Fish and Corn
      Our isle is oyster-gray,
      That patched coat
      Is the Island of Horses.

Beachcomber

Monday I found a boot —
Rust and salt leather.
I gave it back to the sea, to dance in.

Tuesday a spar of timber worth thirty bob.
Next winter
It will be a chair, a coffin, a bed.

Wednesday a half can of Swedish spirits.
I tilted my head.
The shore was cold with mermaids and angels.

Thursday I got nothing, seaweed,
A whale bone,
Wet feet and a bad cough.

Friday I held a seaman's skull,
Sand spilling from it
The way time is told on kirkyard stones.

Saturday a barrel of sodden oranges.
A Spanish ship
Was wrecked last month at The Kame.

Sunday, for fear of the elders,
I smoke on the stone.
What's heaven? A sea chest with a thousand gold
coins.

Island School

A boy leaves a small house
   Of sea light. He leaves
      The sea smells, creel
      And limpet and cod.

The boy walks between steep
   Stone houses, echoing
      Gull cries, the all-around
      Choirs of the sea,

Ship noises, shop noises, clamours
   Of bellman and milkcart.
      The boy comes at last
      To a tower with a tall desk

And a globe and a blackboard
   And a stern chalk-
      smelling lady. A bell
      Nods and summons.

A girl comes, cornlight
   In the eyes, smelling
      Of peat and cows
      And the rich midden.

Running she comes, late,
   Reeling in under the last
      Bronze brimmings. She sits
      Among twenty whispers.

WILLIAM NEILL (b. 1922)

Map Makers

When Irongray grew out of *Earran Reidh*
the culture could not stand on level ground.
schoolmasters   Grey dominies of unmalleable will
invented newer legends of their own
to satisfy the blacksmith and his children.

After *Cill Osbran* closed up to Closeburn
more books were shut than Osbran's psalter.
Seeking to baptize the new born name
the pedants hurried to the nearest water
which wasn't even warm.

When *Seann Bhaile* swelled to Shambelly
the old steading became a glutton's belch.
Every tourist pointed a magic finger
padding lean Fingal to a flabby Falstaff.

The cold men in the city
who circumscribe all latitude
wiped their bullseye glasses
laid down the stabbing pens
that had dealt the mortal wounds
slaying the history of a thousand years
in the hour between lunch and catching the evening
         train.

De A Thug Ort Sgriobhadh Ghaidhlig?

Theirinn gum bu dual domh sin . . .
docha Bhaltair Mòr is coireach,

---

* *Earran Reidh*, the level ground; *Cill Osbran*, the Church of Osbran (or Osbern); *Seann Bhaile*, the Old Steading. These are all Gaelic place names in south-west Scotland, where Gaelic survived until c.1700. (See Journal of Scottish Studies Vol 17.) Our modern map makers have anglicized and bastardized these, and many others. W.N.

sgeadaichte gu leir 'sa bhreacan:
ged nach spiocach e mu bhriogais
b'e gluntow wi giltin hippis,
ag eubhadh 'Suas leis a'Ghàidhlig'
mus robh An Comann idir againn
's a'Bheurla Mhòr a tighinn 'san fhasan
sa Chathair cheòthach mhòir Dhuneideinn,
bu chaomh an àite sin le Uilleam
is e ag radh *ane lawland ers*
wad mak a better noyis, ma tha.

Greitand doun in Gallowa
mar bu dual don *gallow breid*
a' dranndail is ag cainntearachd
le *my trechour tung,* gun teagamh
that *hes tane ane heland strynd.*

A' siùbhal dùthaich Chinneide
bho 'Carrick tae the Cruives o Cree'
mur eil luchd-labhairt eile ann
o horo nach bithinn sùgrach
bruidhinn ris gach craobh a th'innte.

Nach b'fheàrrde mi mo neart a chur
gu sgriobhadh Beurla Lunnainn slàn,
gu faighinn leabhar bàrdachd beag
is e le còmhdach cruaidh glan
na bhithinn a' toirt *the Carrick clay*
to Edinburgh Cors a' ghràidh.

Chan abrainn gu robh daoin' agam
cho uasal ris na Cinneadaich,
ach luchd-na-speàla an Culshian
Moireasdan, Ceallach, Nèill, is Odhar
a' glaodh gu h-àrd nam chuislean-sa
b'e *hungert helant ghaists a bh'annta;*
mus robh Albais nar measg-ne
Gàidhlig aig gach fear is tè dhiubh,
is mairg gun do dh'fhairtlich sin
air Raibeart san aon dùthaich seo.

O horo nach mi tha bàigheil
bhith nam fhuigheal nan Gaidheal deasaich;
Gaidhlig bhlasda Bhaltair Cinneide
eadar Rachrainn agus Manainn
eadar Dalruigh is Cinntire,
is Creag Ealasaid mar usgar
chnapa 'r thargaid dùthaich Ualraig,
Bruis is Aonghais is na Dughallaich,
dùthaich Bhluchbard agus Cian,
Rabbie is The Helant Captain,
is ma bhios feadhainn a' gearann
gun do sgriobh mi cùs 'sa Ghàidhlig,
b'e Cinneide a nochd an ròd dhomh;
le *sic eloquence*, mo thruaighe,
as they in Erschry use, mo thogair
is set my thraward appetyte.

Ro-fhadalach a nis bhith toinneadh
teanga borb gu bhlaschainnt Lunnainn,
but blabberand wi my Carrick lippis
Ersche and brybour I maun bide,
sawsy in saffron back and side.

What Compelled You to Write in Gaelic?

I would say that was my right,
probably Walter Mor's to blame
dressed up in the Gaelic fashion;
though not mean about the breeches
he went bare-kneed with saffron hippings
shouting 'Up with the Gaelic'
before An Comann was with us at all,
and posh English coming into fashion
in the big smoky city of Edinburgh
a place that William (Dunbar) much liked
and he saying that one lowland arse
would make a better noise, indeed.

Grumbling down in Galloway
the habit of yon gallows breed,
muttering and deedling (like a piper)
with my traitor tongue; doubtless,
that has taken a Highland twist.

Travelling in Kennedy's country
from 'Carrick to the Cruives o Cree'
if I find no other speakers (of Gaelic)
o horo won't I be joyful
speaking to each tree that's there.

Would it not have been better to spend my powers
writing faultless London English,
so I could get a little poetry book
with clean hard covers on it,
than that I should bring the Carrick clay
to Edinburgh Cross, my dear.

I would not say I came from people
as lordly as the Kennedies,
but farmhands in Culzean
Morrison, Kellie, Neill and Orr
crying aloud in my veins,
hungry highland ghosts they were,
before braid Scots came in among us
every man and woman had Gaelic
a pity that it was denied
to Robert (Burns) in that same country.

O horo am I not joyful
to be a relic of the Southern Gaels;
warm Gaelic of Walter Kennedy
between Rathlinn and the Isle of Man
between (St John's Town of) Dalry and Kintyre,
and Ailsa Craig like the jewel
on the boss of the shield of the land of Kennedy
of Bruce, of Angus (of Islay) and of the MacDowalls,
the land of the Bluchbard and Cian
Rabbie and the Highland Captain,

and if some should complain
that I write too much in Gaelic
it was Kennedy that pointed the way;
with some eloquence, (Gaelic exclamation)
as Gaelic poets use, (Gaelic exclamation)
is set my capricious (literary) taste.

Too late now to be twisting
a rough tongue to the accents of London,
but blabbering with my Carrick lips
Gaelic and villain I must bide,
impudent in saffron back and side.

IVOR CUTLER (b. 1923)

The Purposeful Culinary Implements

Open,
You patent-leather canteen!
Lift your
Fresh-cheeked faces,
Electro-plated nickle silver cutlery!
Run twinkling to the
Damask tablecover
And lay down flat
Into a pattern
To stimulate
My salivaries.
Complement the chinaware,
The fresh sausage rolls,
Crisply succulent,
The roundels of boiled beetroot
Each a crimson chariot-wheel
Fit to speed Mars,
The God of War.
Green lettuce leaves
Stroked with white
With,
Coyly esconced in their troughs,
Boiled shrimps,
Pink as cherubs.

O knives
Forks
And spoons!
Fulfil yourselves.
Then lay
In the washing-up bowl,
To emerge
Radiant
And be set
By a soft loving hand

Back in your
Patent-leather canteen
To sleep
And drowsily wait
Another purposeful waking.

The Darkness

The darkness
is in the tunnel.
When you walk through
you are dark.
As you near the exit
your front lightens,
the dark fades off.
And when you are out,
all the darkness is
back in the tunnel.
Just at the exit,
a faint shadow sits gently
on your shoulders
before sliding
away regretfully.

Now, at night —

The Railway Sleepers

The railway sleepers
heavy and dry
from old workingwomen's bones.

Trains press over like stout husbands.

Jacket vest and trousers
smelling of cloth and husband
lay black on a chair
not responding to light.

My nose on the pillow.
Breath flows along the cotton hollows.

A bare bulb
yellow in the signal box.

The heavy sleepers lie dark.
Creak under the frost.

A starving bush
perched on the verge
shrieks at dense air out the tunnel
tearing its twigs.
Ends of roots
suck cinders for organic compounds.

The signalman
is noticing his painted tea-flask
on the sill.
He picks his nose without knowing.
Snot drops about his feet.

Dawn
gleams like mercury
afraid to come up.

G. F. DUTTON (b. 1924)

street

this is a street,
paved and flat, saying
it leads somewhere.

I shall take it
but not seriously.
it will lose itself

in courts, piazzas
a haggle
of other streets, will end

in some smoking crater.
I shall take it
as if at my pleasure

as if I could choose
Kirkton Cross
or Ballymet

or Gorton Feus,
with this map in my head
this blood in my shoes.

clach eanchainn

that great stone
the shape of a brain
twisted and left there

out on the moor,
crystals and fire
fisted within it,

often has seen
forests go down
their soil squandered,

seeds blown in
blown out again,
ashes and iron

beneath it surrendered.
it was begun
with the first star

is now a stone
sheltering foxes
out on the moor.

often have men
marched through the dawn
to give it a name.

ALASTAIR MACKIE (b. 1925)

from Back-Green Odyssey

1

ablaze	The sun's oot. I sit, my pipe alunt and puff.
	The claes-line's pegged wi washin. They could be
reach and thresh	sails. (Let them) Hou they rax and thraw, and yet
drive nothing forward	caa naething forrit. Gress growes on my deck.

Thro the wheep-cracks o my sails the blue
wine o the sea is blinkin to the bouwl rim
o the horizon whaur my classic tap
the Berwick Law hides oor nothrin Athens.

Nae watters for an odyssey ye'll think
whaur jist tankers, coasters, seine-netters ply.
Still ablow this blue roof and burst o sun

	my mind moves amon islands. Ulysses –
master/moorings rope	dominie, I cast aff the tether-tow
backside	and steer my boat sittin on my doup-end.

2

The central belt unbuckles on the sands.
The only reek here is the cloods; the croods

waves	are swaws that brakkin, skyte quicksiller baas.
	The view is bigger nor Glesga toun.

throwing down	The air is cowpin pints and nips for free;
than	the sun's a bargain, cheaper nor Majorca.
pallid	Fowks swap a peely-wally white for broun,
	like chips, wi troosers or bikinis on.

	They tak a dander oot at nichts, or jig
	on the Folly; hing aff the pier for fish;
odds and ends	sheet at targets for Hongkong trok. But still

thudding

fowk hae a duty to enjoy theirsels.
Aulder nor the thrum o the transistors
the sea is duntin cymbals to the moon.

3

woman/as if

I saw ye Penelope hingin oot claes;
a lang deem, lookin as gin ye didna
ken ye were lookt at; your brou frouned runkles
and your mou set like a dour horizon

far away
eyes
simmering

like the times ye tell me I'm hyne awa.
Then, naething steers me to the stars o your een
and the silence is hotterin wi the bile
o auld wars (twice as lang as dung doun Troy)

home to

intense darkness

You are the lang island I come hame till
in the beddit dark when I see your een,
the only starns the pit-mirk hisna dowsed.

breath

The herbour crooks its airms. Tethert I lie
at last. I listen. The soond o the sea!
I smell its tides forgaither in your souch.

4

prow

My main deck is a green. Near the foreheid
the kitchen plot. I am weel stockit wi
vittles. On the starboard gunnels, flouers

wrangle

and bushes whaur the birds tulzie and skriech.

sun-scorched
day-dreaming
scribble
voyage

I sit here, the captain and the haill crew
and keep my sun-birsled watches dwaumin.
Whiles I scour the sky-line, whiles I scart a line
in the log-book o my tethert vaigin;

whines

the sea has a blue doze; a raggit skirlin
o bairns rises frae the beach; a sea gull
peenges like a wean and oars air back.

I canna read my Homer in this sun.
I feel the reid meat of my body plot.
a dozing off   My odyssey is jist a doverin.

*

7

stretched out behind   Streekit ahint the winbreak I let
pricks my eyes   Homer drap. The print jobs my een. Instead
I watch a sma green-like beastie craalin
snowstorm   owre the blindrift of summer sun on the page,
that sang o him blattered by Poseidon

lightning   owre the levin and whirlypeels o the sea.
I watch this sudden drappin frae the air on till
the hexameters. Whaur was his Ithaca?

earth-shaker   I felt like the yird-shakker himsel then,
non-entity   heich abeen this nochtie o a cratur.
I let him streetch his pins a bit. A god

choose   can byde his time and wyle it tae, whit's mair.
itchy   Atween ennui and yokey fingers
sent him flying/then   I skytit him aff the page. Yaawned syne.

ALASTAIR REID (b. 1926)

A Lesson for Beautiful Women

Gazing and gazing in the glass,
she might have noticed slow cotillions pass
and might have seen
a blur of others in the antique green.
Transfixed instead,
she learned the inclinations of her neat small head
and, startling her own surprise,
wondered at the wonder in her jewelled eyes.

Gardens of rainbow and russet might have caught her
but, leaning over goldfish water,
she watched the red carp emphasise her mouth,
saw underneath
the long green weeds lace in
through a transparency of face and skin,
smiled at herself smiling reflectively,
lending a new complexion to the sky.

In service to her beauty
long mornings lengthened to a duty
patiently served before the triple mirror
whose six eyes sent her many a time in terror
to hide in rows of whispering dresses;
but her glass soul her own three goddesses
pursued, and if she turned away,
the same three mouths would breathe 'Obey, obey!'

And in procession, young men princely came,
ambassadors to her cool perfect kingdom.
Set at a distance by their praise,
she watched their unspeaking eyes adore her face.
Inside, her still self waited. Nothing moved.
Finally, by three husbands richly loved
(none of them young), she drifted into death,
the glass clouding with her last moist breath.

Changed into legend, she was given rest;
and, left alone at last,
the small mim servant shuttered in her being
peeped mousily out; and seeing
the imperious mirrors glazed and still,
whimpered forlornly down the dark hall
'Oh, grieve for my body, who would not let me be.
She, not I, was a most beautiful lady.'

Scotland

It was a day peculiar to this piece of the planet,
when larks rose on long thin strings of singing
and the air shifted with the shimmer of actual angels.
Greenness entered the body. The grasses
shivered with presences, and sunlight
stayed like a halo on hair and heather and hills.
Walking into town, I saw, in a radiant raincoat,
the woman from the fish-shop. 'What a day it is!'
cried I, like a sunstruck madman.
And what did she have to say for it?
Her brow grew bleak, her ancestors raged in their
graves
as she spoke with their ancient misery:
'We'll pay for it, we'll pay for it, we'll pay for it!'

Isle of Arran

Where no one was was where my world was stilled
into hills that hung behind the lasting water,
a quiet quilt of heather where bees slept,
and a single slow bird in circles winding
round the axis of my head.

Any wind being only my breath, the weather
stopped, and a woollen cloud smothered the sun.
Rust and a mist hung over the clock of the day.

A mountain dreamed in the light of the dark
and marsh mallows were yellow for ever.

Still as a fish in the secret loch alone
I was held in the water where my feet found ground
and the air where my head ended,
all thought a prisoner of the still sense —
till a butterfly drunkenly began the world.

James Bottle's Year

December finds him
outside, looking skyward.
The year gets a swearword.

His rage is never permanent.
By January he's out,
silent and plough-bent.

All white February,
he's in a fury
of wind-grief and ground-worry.

By March, he's back
scouring the ground for luck,
for rabbit-run and deer-track.

April is all sounds and smiles.
The hill is soft with animals.
His arms describe miles.

The local girls say
he's honeyed and bee-headed
at haytime in May.

In June,
he'll stay up late, he'll moon
and talk to children.

No one sees him in July.
At dawn, he'll ride away
with distance in his eye.

In August, you'd assume
yourself to be almost welcome.
He keeps open time.

But, on one September morning,
you'll see cloud-worries form.
His eyes flash storm warnings.

October is difficult.
He tries to puzzle out
if it's his or the season's fault.

In November, he keeps still
through hail and snowfall,
thinking through it all.

What's causing the odd weather?
Himself, or the capricious air?
Or the two together?

December, breathing hard,
he's back outside, hurling skyward
his same swearword.

ALASDAIR MACLEAN (b. 1926)

Death of an Old Woman

She lived too much alone to be aware of it,
in a cottage on a stretch of moor,
built before the distant road was built
and shunned by everything built since.
Her croft had faded through the years
for lack of drainage and proper food,
bled of its green until the eye
could hardly tell where it began or ended.
Her house had a hole in the thatch
to let the smoke out – when there was any –
and the rain in, and three small openings
in the walls, two for light and one for charity,
and all about the size she was accustomed to.
The man who found her dead was drawn
in that direction by the movement.
That was the door of her empty henhouse
flapping in the wind, a nerve continuing to twitch.
She herself was lying in her bed,
causing a slight ripple in the blankets.
She had an English Bible in her hands,
upside down. The doctor who examined her
stated that her mouth was full of raw potato.

Home Thoughts from Home

No doubt I'm spoiled. One's soon accustomed to
being plied with spoonfuls of the best of jam.
It's only when at home that I forgo
the luxury of knowing who I am.

And to decide with some exactness what
my status is would be a lifetime's labour,
though not perhaps of love. I am not brother
to my brothers quite, more next-door neighbour.

My parents, too, have faded from my sight,
lost in a wondering air of 'Well, I never!'
There's no way back. I've lost the knack of them.
I've been away too long and grown too clever.

Well, I suppose each rescues what he needs
from time and mounts it under pin and label.
It's something, that. But oh! those glances
that avoid my glance, that politesse at table.

If you're a peasant who writes poetry
and bear the stamp of it on all you say
your family are those you visit most
and home is how they live when you're away.

Waking the Dead

The dead man lay quietly,
beamed back by candles at his head and feet
but tired, dead tired, after travelling.
He wore his Sunday suit for us
and on his face a mild surprise
as if at last he half believed we loved him.
How we fixed him with our eyes!
But if he meant to go or stay,
to satisfy the new house or the old,
he dared not for the life of him
to either family say.
And so we sat
and gave those others glare for glare
and I sat too.
With us it was not Irish lack of care
despite the whisky going from hand to hand
and the little plates of cold ham tripping after.
This was the harder land
and not a farewell or a giving up the ghost
but a presbyterian stare and business.
I leaned over him.
The air was colder and more hollow there

as if I leaned above a well
and when I dropped my stone I saw him flinch,
or I did, as it passed through.
But what the distance was between us
never never would he tell.
How many years is it since childhood now?
Yet I remember well:
'Stay, Donald, stay!' my mother said
but I said 'Donald, go to hell!'

The Rain

In April now I think upon the rain.
It makes its way down through the loosened earth.
In ooze not honest drops it penetrates
the wooden roof of she who gave me birth.

She is insensible, you say, being dead,
to the passing of the seasons, how they wheel?
Indeed you miss the point, my friend. It does
not matter if she feels or not; I feel.

IAIN CRICHTON SMITH (b. 1928)

The Clearances

The thistles climb the thatch. Forever
this sharp scale in our poems,
as also the waste music of the sea.

The stars shine over Sutherland
in a cold ceilidh of their own,
as, in the morning, the silver cane

cropped among corn. We will remember this.
Though hate is evil we cannot
but hope your courtier's heels in hell

are burning: that to hear
the thatch sizzling in tanged smoke
your hot ears slowly learn.

Highlanders

They sailed away into the coloured prints
of Balaclava, or at tall Quebec
you'll see them climbing almost native rock
in search of French and not of cormorants.

Abroad, they fought the silks and bright coats
while to their homes the prancing dandies came
on horses like Napoleon's, in the calm
(but clouds of snuff) of all their ruined boats,

them high on Nelson's topmasts looking over
a coloured sea at evening coming up
with complex tackle and harmonious rope
from pictured oceans and a roaring fire.

Poem in March

Old cans sparkle. Tie slaps at the chin.
The mind puts on its sword.
This is the country of the daffodil
and the new flannels, radiant and belled.

The drawn cheeks and the spiky knees
are suddenly tulips, roses,
an England and the Low Countries.
A map of shadows passes

out on the sixteenth century sea,
Raleigh to sail and Drake
beyond the monks of eternity
reading a winter book.

The Law and the Grace

It's law they ask of me and not grace.
'Conform,' they say, 'your works are not enough.
Be what we say you should be,' even if
graceful hypocrisy obscures my face.

'We know no angels. If you say you do
that's blasphemy and devilry.' Yet I have
known some bright angels, of spontaneous love.
Should I deny them, be to falsehood true,

the squeeze of law which has invented torture
to bring the grace to a malignant head?
Do you want me, angels, to be wholly dead?
Do you need, black devils, steadfastly to cure

life of itself? And you to stand beside
the stone you set on me? No, I have angels. Mine
are free and perfect. They have no design
on anyone else, but only on my pride,

my insufficiency, imperfect works.
They often leave me but they sometimes come
to judge me to the core, till I am dumb.
Is this not law enough, you patriarchs?

from By the Sea

I

Sitting here by the foreshore day after day
on the Bed and Breakfast routine

I cower in green shelters, watch the sea
bubble in brown sea-pools, watch the sea

climb to the horizon and fall back
rich with its silver coins, its glittering.

Warmly scarfed, I almost remember how
beggars were, and in the thirties men

jumped from the wheel. I lock my will
on the National Health Service, will not fall

too deep for rescue but for the mind, the mind.
Two clouds loom together and are joined

as are two lovers in their nylon wings,
a yellow flutter on cramped bench. Thick rings

of routine save us, rings like marriage rings.
The yachts seem free in their majestic goings

and the great ships at rest. Helmeted girls
emerge from salons with their golden curls.

4

IN THE CAFE

The leaf-fringed fountain
with the grey Scots cherub
arches water
over the waterlogged pennies.

Mouths and moustaches move.
The sad-eyed waitress
hides her unringed hand.
Umbrellas stand at ease.

Outside, rain drips
soupily, 'the soup of the day.'
The sauce bottles are filled with old blood
above the off-white linen.

('Not that I didn't have
suitors', said the Edinburgh lady
seated in the shelter like a queen,
gloved hands on her worn sceptre.)

But the waitress meltingly watches
that white-haired three-year-old,
a huge bubble with wicked teeth,
combing his hair with his knife.

5

Milk jugs, cups,
pastries with pink ice,
menus rotating through one meal.
Most of what we do is refuel
then head for stations, lost in driving rain.

Waitresses with frilly aprons,
I can tell you
how the teeth rot under the pink ice,

and the sky-blue ashtrays contain
a little fire with lipstick, a little fire.

So few are beautiful,
so few outwear the rainy
sag of a dull air, so few ride
naturally as in woodland, the dream
of the eternally cantering proud horses.

Everything drips, drips, drips.
The water, blood, adulterated milk.
The stalls advertise 'Condensed Books'.
All week I have fed on cheap paper
turning like logged swing doors.

10

DUNOON AND THE HOLY LOCH

The huge sea widens from us, mile on mile.
Kenneth MacKellar sings from the domed pier.
A tinker piper plays a ragged tune
on ragged pipes. He tramps under a moon
which rises like the dollar. Think how here

missiles like sugar rocks are all incised
with Alabaman Homer. These defend
the clattering tills, the taxis, thin pale girls
who wear at evening their Woolworth pearls
and from dewed railings gaze at the world's end.

12

IN THE PARK

Over the shoes in pebbles I sit here.
Behind me, the silent bells of those red flowers.
Under that winged structure Greeks might wander,
retired Achilles in the varying shade

drifted from the Home, telling of wars,
and Helen's mouth open like that soft bloom
which turns to the sun softly in the dew
and busy orbit of the striped wasp.

On the smooth lawn a cat pursues a bird,
great Disney fool. The bird looks at him, flies,
lands and flies and this time doesn't stop.
The cat slouches back among the trees.

A lot of marble, messages in flowers –
this is Barnardo's Year – the door is open
to orphans ejected from our Welfare State,
that cosy bubble with few images.

The marble and carnations of Elysium.
Columns of lilies drink at the warm water.
All day the furious sun scans the lawns
and fat loud Ajax's waddling up to bowl.

from The White Air of March

I

This is the land God gave to Andy Stewart –
           we have our inheritance.
There shall be no ardour, there shall be indifference.
There shall not be excellence, there shall be the
                          average.
We shall be the intrepid hunters of golf balls.
Have you not known, have you not heard, has it not
                       been reported
that Mrs Macdonald has given an hour-long lecture
                       on Islay
and at the conclusion was presented with a bouquet
                       of flowers
by Marjory, aged five?
               Have you not noted
the photograph of the whist drive, skeleton hands,

rings on skeleton fingers?
                              Have you not seen
the glossy weddings in the glossy pages,
champagne and a 'shared joke'.
                         Do you not see
the Music Hall's still alive here in the North? and on
                                              the stage
the yellow gorse is growing.
                  'Tragedy,' said Walpole, 'for those who feel.
For those who think, it's comic.'
                         Pity then those who feel
and, as for the Scottish Soldier, off to the wars!
The Cuillins stand and will forever stand.
Their streams scream in the moonlight.

     2

The Cuillins tower
clear and white.
In the crevices the Gaelic bluebells flower.

(Eastward
Culloden
where the sun shone
on the feeding raven.
Let it be forgotten!)

The Cuillins tower
scale on scale.
The music of the imagination must be restored,
upward.

(The little Highland dancer
in white shirt green kilt
regards her toe
arms akimbo.
Avoids the swords.)

To avoid the sword
is death.
      To walk the ward
of Dettol, loss of will,
where old men watch the wall,
eyes in a black wheel,
and the nurse in a starched dress
changes the air.

The Cuillins tower
tall and white.
March breeds white sails.

The eagle soars.
On the highest peaks
The sharpest axe.

8

The exiles have departed,
                    leaving old houses.
The Wind wanders like an old man who has lost his
                         mind.
'What do you want?' asks the wind. 'Why are you
                        crying?
Are those your tears or the rain?'
I do not know. I touch my cheek. It is wet.
I think it must be the rain.

It is bitter
to be an exile in one's own land.
It is bitter
to walk among strangers
when the strangers are in one's own land.

It is bitter
to dip a pen in continuous water
to write poems of exile
in a verse without honour or style.

Gaelic Stories

Translated from Gaelic by the author

1

A fisherman in wellingtons
and his sweetheart
and his mother.

2

A story
about an old man
and a seal.

3

A woman
reading a Bible for seven years
waiting for a sailor.

4

A melodeon.
A peat stack.
An owl.

5

A croft.
Two brothers.
A plate with potatoes.

6

A girl from Glasgow
wearing a mini
in church.

7

The sea
and a drifter,
the Golden Rose.

8

A man who was in Australia
coming home
on a wedding night.

9

A romance
between cheese
and milk.

10

Glasgow
in a world of nylons
and of neon.

11

Two women
talking
in a black house.

12

A monster
rising from the sea,
'Will you take tea?'

13

A comedy
in a kitchen,
with jerseys.

14

A conversation
between a loaf and
cheese.

15

A conversation
between a wellington
and a herring.

16

A conversation
between fresh butter
and a cup.

17

A conversation
between Yarmouth
and Garrabost.

18

A moon
hard and high
above a marsh.

Shall Gaelic Die?

Translated by the author

1

A picture has no grammar. It has neither evil nor
good. It has only colour, say orange or mauve.
Can Picasso change a minister? Did he make a
sermon to a bull?

Did heaven rise from his brush? Who saw a church
that is orange?
In a world like a picture, a world without language,
would your mind go astray, lost among objects?

2

Advertisements in neon, lighting and going out, 'Shall
it . . . shall it . . . Shall Gaelic . . . shall it . . . shall
Gaelic . . . die?'

3

Words rise out of the country. They are around us. In
every month in the year we are surrounded by words.
Spring has its own dictionary, its leaves are turning in
the sharp wind of March, which opens the shops.
Autumn has its own dictionary, the brown words
lying on the bottom of the loch, asleep for a season.
Winter has its own dictionary, the words are a
blizzard building a tower of Babel. Its grammar is
like snow.
Between the words the wild-cat looks sharply across
a No-Man's-Land, artillery of the Imagination.

4

They built a house with stones. They put windows in
the house, and doors. They filled the room with
furniture and the beards of thistles.
They looked out of the house on a Highland world,
the flowers, the glens, distant Glasgow on fire.
They built a barometer of history.
Inch after inch, they suffered the stings of suffering.
Strangers entered the house, and they left.
But now, who is looking out with an altered gaze?
What does he see?
What has he got in his hands? A string of words.

5

He who loses his language loses his world. The
Highlander who loses his language loses his world.
The space ship that goes astray among planets loses
the world.
In an orange world how would you know orange? In
a world without evil how would you know good?
Wittgenstein is in the middle of his world. He is like
a spider.

sea and wood

The flies come to him. 'Cuan' and 'coill' rising.
When Wittgenstein dies, his world dies.
The thistle bends to the earth. The earth is tired of it.

6

I came with a 'sobhrach' in my mouth. He came with
a 'primrose'.
A 'primrose by the river's brim'. Between the two
languages, the word 'sobhrach' turned to 'primrose'.
Behind the two words, a Roman said 'prima rosa'.
The 'sobhrach' or the 'primrose' was in our hands. Its
reasons belonged to us.

Gaelic Songs

I listen to these songs
from a city studio.
They belong to a different country,
to a barer sky,
to a district of heather and stone.
They belong to the sailors
who kept their course
through nostalgia and moonlight.
They belong to the maidens
who carried the milk in pails
home in the twilight.
They belong to the barking of dogs,
to the midnight of stars,

to the sea's terrible force,
exile past the equator.
They belong to the sparse grass,
to the wrinkled faces,
to the houses sunk in the valleys,
to the mirrors
brought home from the fishing.

Now they are made of crystal
taking just a moment
between two programmes
elbowing them fiercely
between two darknesses.

Christmas 1971

There's no snow this Christmas . . . there was snow
when we received the small horses and small cart,
brothers together all those years ago.
There were small watches made of liquorice
surrealist as time hung over chairs.
I think perhaps that when we left the door
of the white cottage with its fraudulent icing
we were quite fixed as to our different ways.
Someone is waving with black liquorice hands
at the squashed windows as the soundless bells
and the soundless whips lash our dwarf horses
                                             forward.
We diverge at the road-end in the whirling snow
never to meet but singing, pulling gloves
over and over our disappearing hands.

The Glass of Water

My hand is blazing on the cold tumbler.
My eye looks through it to the other side.
If it were what is real, if it were heaven
how I corrupt it with my worn flesh.

How its neutrality is aggrandised
by fever and by empire. I constrain
and grasp this parish which is pastoral.

To be pure is not difficult, it's impossible.
How could the saint work to this poverty,
this unassumingness, this transparency?
How could his levels be so wholly calm?
The fact of water is unteachable.
It's less and more than honour standing up
invulnerable in its vulnerable glass.

How Often I Feel Like You

Ah, you Russians, how often I feel like you
full of ennui, hearing the cry of wolves
on frontiers of green glass.
In the evening
one dreams of white birches and of bears.
There are picnics in bright glades and someone
                                        talking
endlessly of verse as if mowing grass,
endlessly of philosophy round and round
like a red fair with figures of red soldiers
spinning forever at their 'Present Arms'.
How long it takes for a letter to arrive.
Postmen slog heavily over the steppes
and drop their dynamite through the letter-box.
For something is happening everywhere but here.
Here there are Hamlets and old generals.
Everyone sighs and says 'Ekh' and in the stream
a girl is swimming naked among gnats.
This space is far too much for us like time.
Even the clocks have asthma. There is honey,
herring and jam and an old samovar.
Help us, let something happen, even death.
God has forgotten us. We are like fishers
with leather leggings dreaming in a stream.

Chinese Poem

I

To Seumas Macdonald,
                    now resident in Edinburgh –
I am alone here, sacked from the Department
for alcoholic practices and disrespect.
A cold wind blows from Ben Cruachan.
There is nothing here but sheep and large boulders.
Do you remember the nights with *Reliquae Celticae*
and those odd translations by Calder?
Buzzards rest on the wires. There are many seagulls.
My trousers grow used to the dung.
What news from the frontier? Is Donald still
                                        Colonel?
Are there more pupils than teachers in Scotland?
I send you this by a small boy with a pointed head.
Don't trust him. He is a Campbell.

2

The dog brought your letter today
from the red postbox on the stone gate
two miles away and a bit.
I read it carefully with tears in my eyes.
At night the moon is high over Cladach
and the big mansions of prosperous Englishmen.
I drank a half bottle thinking of Meg
and the involved affairs of Scotland.
When shall we two meet again
in thunder, lightning or in rain?
The carrots and turnips are healthy,
the *Farmers' Weekly* garrulous.
Please send me a *Radio Times* and a book
on cracking codes. I have much sorrow.
Mrs Macleod has a blue lion on her pants.
They make a queenly swish in a high wind.

3

There is a man here who has been building a house
for twenty years and a day.
He has a barrow in which he carries large stones.
He wears a canvas jacket.
I think I am going out of my mind.
When shall I see the city again,
its high towers and insurance offices,
its glare of unprincipled glass?
The hens peck at the grain.
The wind brings me pictures of exiles,
ghosts in tackety boots, lies,
adulteries in cornfields and draughty cottages.
I hear Donald is a brigadier now
and that there is fighting on the frontier.
The newspapers arrive late with strange signs on
                                              them.
I go out and watch the road.

4

Today I read five books.
I watched Macleod weaving a fence
to keep the eagles from his potatoes.
A dull horse is cobwebbed in rain.
When shall our land consider itself safe
from the assurance of the third rate mind?
We lack I think nervous intelligence.
Tell them I shall serve in any capacity,
a field officer, even a private,
so long as I can see the future
through uncracked field glasses.

5

A woman arrived today
in a brown coat and a brown muff.
She says we are losing the war,
that the Emperor's troops are everywhere
in their blue armour and blue gloves.

She says there are men in a stupor
in the ditches among the marigolds
crying 'Alas, alas.'
I refuse to believe her.
She is, I think, an agent provocateur.
She pretends to breed thistles.

from A Life

LEWIS 1928–45

3

Our landmark is the island, complex thing.
A rock, a death, a house in which were made
our narrow global seaward-going wings,
the rings of blue, the cloth both fine and frayed.
It sails within us, as one poet said,
its empty shelves are resonant. A scant
religion drives us to our vague tremens.
We drag it at our heels, as iron chains.
A winsome boyhood among glens and bens
casts, later, double images and shades.
And ceilidhs in the cities are the lens
through which we see ourselves, unmade, remade,
by music and by grief. The island sails
within us and around us. Startled we
see it in Glasgow, hulk of the humming dead,
and of the girls in cornfields disarrayed.

10

Roses, I think there is salt on you,
and on the headland I hear the exiles' songs.

The thatched roofs, woven by dead hands,
are sunk among the superannuated school buses,

in a field of daisies and lush grasses.
The buzzard slants over the untilled ground.

Varying perfumes taunt me. In church I saw
the fifty-year-old girl I used to know,

her face curdled and gaunt. Bibles
are open in the churchyards, marbly white,

and the sea sighs towards the gravestones.
On the moors

the heather is wine-red and the lochs
teem with unhunted fish. The sky

is an eternal blue and God drowses
momently from his justice. Singing,

the drunk sways among poppies, missing
the rusty unused scythe. The boats are

a frieze on the far horizon, smoking gently,
and almost motionless. The cornfields were

a nest of snaky legs: and now it is
the butterfly that wafts there. This is not

a haunt of angels. The devils kneel at night
offering whisky in a bottle to

those who despise church windows in their reds.
Gaunt girl I walked with in the long ago,

sleep gently in the beams of the red moon,
whose claws are crablike in your drained breast.

OBAN 1955–82

I

Oban in autumn, and reflective Mull
cast on the water. How the snowy gull

pecks at waste herring bones on the scaly quay.
The central glitter of the boundless sea.

Like pots that boil on Sundays, engines find
their drumming destination, and the mind

its fixed direction. By tall cliffs I see
the jackdaws playing. On green benches the

tourists repose at evening, while the tide
whispers and chuckles. O I see you, bride,

Gaelic, mysterious: and this radiance is
the extravagant presence of the sea's abyss

extending to Iona and its graves.
The very stones are green. The sea is sheaves

of endless blue on blue and lucid crowns
of jellyfish drift lazily. No one drowns

in this amazing light. The War Memorial burns.
One soldier helps another through the stone.

2

A Roman rector, measured gravitas,
a Gaelic scholar too. He knows each child.
Our own names honour us and each one salutes

us from his sparkling bicycle. The school hums,
directed engine. Black-winged he comes
along the shiny corridors. In the hall

appointing prefects he quotes from Paul.
The race is to the kind, not to the smart,
to Brutus not to Antony. The clear art

of human Homer is our constant aim:
whatever's comely. Casually he says,
'It was Housman taught me in my Cambridge days.'

And behind him Macintyre and William Ross.
Where's Eliot and Auden? Horace glows,
each marble phrase, the clarity of prose.

'Transposing Greek to Gaelic is no toil.
They had their clans, their sea terms. And the style
of the great *Odyssey* is what Gaelic knows.'

Easily he chats to the crofting man
who sucks a straw: as easily as he scans
those vast hexameters or the pibroch.

                    Does
what's comely and what's right by natural rule,
by Roman cheerfulness and harmonious Greek.
Propounds a human yet a rigorous school.

3

For Donalda

So I come home to you
as the one I didn't leave behind
as the quick diligent
drawer back of curtains,

lest the house should be seen
as too much slept in
when there is so much wind
among the sunlight:

so many rainbows
trembling among news
of the daft old glasses
twinkling together:

so many owls
sucking to their eyes
the moon-struck mice
in the leafy classroom,

and the world a skirt
turning a corner
altering pleat by pleat
its breezy sculpture.

Listen

Listen, I have flown through darkness towards joy,
I have put the mossy stones away from me,
and the thorns, the thistles, the brambles.
I have swum upward like a fish

through the black wet earth, the ancient roots
which insanely fight with each other
in a grave which creates a treasure house
of light upward-springing leaves.

Such joy, such joy! Such airy drama
the clouds compose in the heavens,
such interchange of comedies,
disguises, rhymes, denouements.

I had not believed that the stony heads
would change to actors and actresses,
and that the grooved armour of statues
would rise and walk away

into a resurrection of villages,
townspeople, citizens, dead exiles,
who sing with the salt in their mouths,
winged nightingales of brine.

BURNS SINGER (1928–64)

A Sort of Language

Who, when night nears, would answer for the
                                         patterns
Words will take on? emerging huge, far, shiny,
What unfrequented systems? Or like clouds
Unseen and hiding brightness, bringing rain,
Progressions that the wind drives on, drives after,
Who will say? I who have seen, seen many,
Imagining I scattered them abroad,
Starlight for Calvary and the immense equations
That drew to unity two who knew not either,
As to a hill at midnight, I have seen words,
Seen them with thanks too, shivering, become
Fragile and useless, pale as the steel sparks
Tramcars make waifs of when they round a corner.

Peterhead in May

Small lights pirouette
Among these brisk little boats.
A beam, cool as a butler,
Steps from the lighthouse.

Wheelroom windows are dark.
Reflections of light quickly
Skip over them tipsily like
A girl in silk.

One knows there is new paint
And somehow an intense
Suggestion of ornament
Comes into mind.

Imagine elephants here.
They'd settle, clumsily sure

Of themselves and of us and of four
Square meals and of water.

Then you will have it. This
Though a grey and quiet place
Finds nothing much amiss.
It keeps its stillness.

There is no wind. A thin
Mist fumbles above it and,
Doing its best to be gone,
Obscures the position.

This place is quiet or,
Better, impersonal. There
Now you have it. No verdict
Is asked for, no answer.

Yet nets will lie all morning,
Limp like stage scenery,
Unused but significant
Of something to come.

For Josef Herman

Nothing, nothing, nothing
Can never ever happen
To this man who sits here
Some distance from the river.

His plump and portly hands
Conjure the daylight out
Of the pits' blackness and
Absorb the sun of Spain.

The Hebrides are his,
The ghetto and the city.
His loneliness is such
That children love to share it.

Companionship is his
And wise frivolities.
I wonder, if you could look
Quietly into his eyes

And they laughed as confidently
As the humming wings of flies,
If it would seem to you
That you had never died.

SOS Lifescene

That plunging mast, nailed to a whirligig gale,
Shows its three sheer signs of drowning. Those
                              crewed wet boards
Drag at the spray. Oceans drip backwards and forth
From that tall steel prow, those seamen, crouched
                                   that sail.

Crouched to climb: cling of the white wetnesses.
Heave of the sea's deep sheets, wheezing like twenty
Conferences stacked round tables, pressing
Processions, quarrel of kingdoms: pitch salt centre.

Out of it, down from it, hangs the electric shout,
Nine gooseflesh sparks breathing white out on the
                                   rabble
Of sweaty and swaggering gales. Held hard to the
                                   squabbling
Waters, to Save Our Souls the sounds fade out.

Yet steered, here steered, and over the sea's salt dregs
Set climbing forth, is crewed by the conscious and
                                   steered.
Wheeled in two knotted hands through the callous
                               but prayer-
Breasting, heart-wresting hour, is ruddered with rags.

For the men, backed out to the bone, catch up on the
                                                            past
In a straight line, like winter . . . the trees. Burn back
The barren courses, confront the naked mistake,
The embezzled hours accounted, the fake blot erased.

Talk yourself out of it! Out of it! Talk yourself! Talk!
And a death's click closes those offices foaming with
                                                           grins.
That stoke-black lascar, damp and salt with work,
Looks through a lurch at the red wreck under his
                                                            skin.

That engineer who's thistle-eyed for sleep
Circles the clock through goaded hoops and trances
To where she departs . . . to where she hurries . . .
                                        she dances . . .
The damp cellar and whisky . . . the heart in a
                                         heap . . .

SOS it repeats, repeats, told, retold.
Small white far cry for help as they kindle close
Together or blaze in a curse. For the storm grows
To death for the captain and the boy blown blue by
                                             the cold.

Corked nets and clinging baits, those sodden boards
Muscled about by their men, drag deep at the shoals
And their hooked catchings draw blood. But bite to
                                           the core!
There are nine white pips crying 'help' in a black
                                           bowl.

Seeds of the storm, quick fish, the intense alone
Of their human cry, where the storm bleats down like
                                            a ram
And the waves whinny away; where the smooth sky's
                                            brown
Blacks out, and the stars are dead and don't matter a
                                            damn.

What matters is the cry, the cry like a screw,
Sharp-oiled to turning, clean-cutting fish-silver
through
And through the teak air,
A makeshift repetitive batter to riveting prayer.

Like stitching sails this windfall patches men,
Question to answer, push and heave and tug,
Thick-fibred needlework, an electric plug,
Nine cock-crows savage the air and cry us all home.

ALASTAIR FOWLER (b. 1930)

Catacomb Suburb

Other burial places console more.
Torcello's reeds moan, blur in the wind,
Palliate: its green air steeps
And clarifies marble, immersed apostles merging
With reawakened stone. San Michele's door
Gives on water. Country headstones thrust
Lichen out, art's distracting slips.

But here nothing mitigates or changes.
Not the dull grids of cypress avenues;
Not guide-stops where we chose to queue
For the least alien Dante to underworlds
Down San Callisto's broken steps. Worn,
Sudden steps. Jokes about being found
Lost in the catacombs fixed our jaws.

Below, what waits beneath is not below,
But all about, not to be missed. Our guide
Goes with the torch to find why the power failed.
We are posted in darknesses that I clench
Avoiding others in close-tiered *niches*.
A Giant of cells condemned for miles around,
Crumbled, decayed, will bring conviction in,

At last. Lights and friends are nothing now.
Numbers have no safety in them, even,
In this close corridor, odd slice
Of tufa cake. I used to think the name
'Fly cemeteries' meant they both were black.
But five tiers of graves, a hundred miles,
Is what can swallow thought. *In pace; in pace;*

In pace; in pace; mansionem in pace.
Everywhere the signs of believers,
Who came here, first of dying men,

Against the law, all law and fear, to live.
Not to hide, rather set out in witness
These adverse cases. They laid out quite openly
That Severa lived nine days eleven hours.

Yet here resolve enlarges beyond surprise.
I think of working powers: fathers of later
Unsepulchral cities trying claims
Of love and space: housing priorities raised
With the dead. 'My dear Crome, as to your last,
We must make common cause in finding ways
Through time's mansions to keep the loved in phase.'

Relative

No Rembrandt's mother's face,
It changed in its possession.
I didn't want to sit in her dark, hated
Going to hear the blurring cataract
And see the same stories told again.
But the last times of all
She was too home-trained to blame neglect.
Gentled. She had a migratory look,
All steep eyes and fine glass bone.
Her knuckle tugged and clung to make quite sure:
Tell me I'm not to die.
(The old promise to stay young was broken.)
If you'd seen you would have wanted to keep her
                                                going
In spite of age: age that I might have kept
Coming some time more slowly. She was lucid,
                                                though.
To think that that could disconcert.
The senses fade and seem to leave quiet;
So that we feel relief when the fluttering stops.
Then a flame I thought was out blazed up
Again, like the bedroom fire she used to light
To make the harmless shadows, when I was ill.
Tell me I'm not to die.

Oh she is wonderful, they said, considering.
Only considering; not remembering, like me
(But unlike her), her former judgement. Have parts
Of all living been mislaid as far?
Knowing less of herself she similarly clung
To sameness. Her mind remained.
Then something much more fugitive would stray
Along old bridle-paths long overgrown,
Until the words were lost, and then their sound;
Even the stories. Visits anthologized
Only the most familiar recensions.
In longer episodes I might have told her
Apart from the tale. Tell me I still may.

GEORGE MACBETH (1932–92)

An Ode to English Food

O English Food! How I adore looking forward
to you, Scotch trifle at the North British Hotel,
Princes Street, Edinburgh. Yes, it is good, very good,
the best in Scotland.

Once I ate a large helping at your sister
establishment, the Carlton Hotel on Waverley Bridge
overlooking the cemetery on Carlton Hill. It was rich,
very rich and pleasant. O, duck, though,

roast, succulent duck of the Barque and Bite,
served with orange sauce, mouth-meltingly delicious!
You I salute. Fresh, tender and unbelievable English
duck. Such

luscious morsels of you! Heap high the
groaning platter with pink fillets, sucking pig and
thick gammon, celestial chef. Be generous with the
crackling. Let your hand slip with the gravy trough,
dispensing plenty. Yes, gravy, I give you your due,
too. O savoury and delightsome gravy, toothsome
over

the white soft backs of my English potatoes,
fragrant with steam. Brave King Edwards, rough-
backed in your dry scrubbed excellence, or with
butter, salty. Sweet

potatoes! Dear new knobbly ones, beside the
oiled sides of meaty carrots. Yes, carrots. Even you,
dumplings,

with indigestible honey, treacle-streaky things.
You tongue-burners. You stodgy darlings. Tumbled
out of the Marks and Spencer's tin or Mr Kipling

silver paper wrapper, warm and ready except in
summer. Cold strawberry sauce, cream and
raspberries. O sour gooseberry pie, dissemble
nothing, squeezed essence

      of good juice. Joy in lieu of jelly at children's
parties, cow-heel that gives the horn a man seeing my
twelve-year-old buttocks oiled in hospital by a nurse
assured me, dirty

      old bugger. I eat my six chosen slices of bread,
well buttered, remembering you and your successor
the tramp who stole a book for me. Cracked

      coffee cup of the lucky day, betokening
mother-love, nostalgic. Fill with Nescafé and milk for
me. It is all great, sick-making allure of old food,
sentiment of the belly. I fill with aniseed's

      parboiled scagliola, porphyry of the balls.
With, O with, licorice, thin straws of it in sherbert,
sucked up, nose-bursting explosives of white
powders! Yes,

      montage of pre-European Turkish delights
obtained under the counter in wartime, or during
periods of crisis, and

      O the English sickness of it. Food, I adore you.
Pink-faced and randy! Come to me, mutton chops.
Whiskers of raw chicken-bones, wishes

      and plastic cups. Unpourable Tizer. Take me
before I salivate. I require your exotic fineness, taste

      of the English people, sweep me off my feet
into whiteness, a new experience. With beer. And
with blue twists of salt in the chip packets. Grease of
newspaper. Vinegar of the winter nights holding
hands in lanes after *The Way to the Stars*. It

is all there. Such past and reticence! O such
untranslatable grief and growing pains of the delicate
halibut. The heavy cod, solid as gumboots. And the
wet haddock, North Sea lumber of a long Tuesday's
lunch. Fish and sauce. Nibbles and nutshells. Gulps
of draught ale, Guinness or cider made with steaks.
English food, you are all we have. Long may you
reign!

The Renewal

The need to find a place always returns.
In Richmond, where my eighteenth-century bricks
Fashioned an avenue to stable skin,

I built a proper house. At Holland Park,
That fleece and leather took their comfort from,
I tried another, in another way.

Both worked. And what the simple martyrdom
Of wanting some position broke for sticks,
And set in place, held back the creeping dark.

I turned there, in my darkness, on my beds.
In tiny rooms, alone, and with my wives,
Or girls who passed for wives. And all my burns

From being lonely, and unsatisfied,
Flared in the silence, like a sheen from tin.
I waited, and, while waiting, something died.

Then, in the heat of Norfolk, I found you.
You brought the sun, through darkness, to my hives,
The bolted iron to my crumbling sheds,

You changed the whole world's shape. Your power
                                              grew
And I, in feeling that, wanted some place
More generous for it than those gentle homes.

I needed somewhere with a flirt of grace
To match your fervour for long acreage.
I found it, here at Oby. Naked space

Over the cornfields, and the next-door farm,
Contracts to an oasis with great trees
That north-east winds can ravage in their rage

And leave still rooted and serene. In these
I feel the sweep of beech-wood, like an arm,
And something deeper, in our copper beech.

That brings a birthright in its massive reach,
A sense of giant time. Seeing it blaze
In widespread feathering, I feel the past,

The creak of longships on the Caister shore,
The swing of mills beside the easy broads,
And something closer, groping slow, at last,

The pleasant rectors, knocking croquet balls.
I take their heritage, and what it pays,
And vow today to make its profits pour

Through founded channels, in my well-kept grounds,
As growth, and preservation. Nothing falls
Or sings, in this wide garden, but its sounds

Calm me, and make our full liaison rich.
So my dream-Scotland grief was noble in
Will drag its graves beneath these grounded urns,

And stake its base in watered Norfolk clay,
And Kinburn be reborn, as what it was,
And my grandfather, and our Springer bitch,

Both live, in their own way, and like it here,
And feel the rain and sunlight on their skin,
And no one tell apart, which one is which,

The dream of former grandeur, and the firm
Everyday presence of our daily lives.
This is my hope, and what these lines affirm.

Draft for an Ancestor

When I was young, and wrote about him first,
My Uncle Hugh was easier to hold.
            Now, in my age, at worst
            I take him by some outer fold
Of what was his. His Humber, by the door.
            That, at the least, if nothing more

Creates an image of his prosperous time
And thumbs in waistcoats to suggest their power.
            I hear tall glasses chime
            And clocks from walnut sound the hour
As they drive to Derby, where their horse will lose.
            At last, it seems, men have to choose

What traits in relatives they will to raise
To the height of models, awkward, fey, or strong,
            And there arrange as praise
            For the unhooked soul, keen to belong
To its family, some tree of love and grace
            In which there blossoms no mean face.

I feel this drive. As years go by, it grows
And I want an ancestry of heroic mould
            Fit for a world that knows
            How to accept the subtly bold
Who grasp at shields and leaves with a sprig of wit
            And honours their effrontery with it.

So Uncle Hugh, that self-made, stubborn man
I see in photographs, and hear in my head,
        Provides a flash of élan
    To the ranks of my more sombre dead
And, startling, floods their quarters with his brash
    And flighty Scottish kind of dash.

ALASDAIR GRAY (b. 1934)

Awakening

I woke to find pain laid on a bare bed with me,
so near, his head, cut in pale stone, was my head,
his brain my brain,
and I could not resign my thoughts to that proximity.
He was so close a company he felt like loneliness.

I tried at length to know a door to make him leave
                  by,
           a bribe to make him go,
but oh my dear, he grins
from everywhere I look, at everything I do.
I meet his image where I once met you.
He feeds at every meal, beckons down every street
and yet could not withstand
one pressure of your hand.

Come back to me soon. I am changing without you.
My mind turns cold and luminous like a moon.
Keys, coins, receipts accumulate in my pockets.
I grow calm and brutal on beer and thick meat.

CHRISTOPHER SALVESEN (b. 1935)

Ninian Winyet*

Ninian am I? Why, this is none of I . . .
My little dog is barking. What door is this,
Which gates have I gone through? Rain and the dark
Have soaked me – searched me, drawn me out and
                                                                           home:
Linlithgow my kindly town, where I taught
And, teaching, learnt to fasten in my mind
The restless gulls, the wildfowl on the loch.
Passand to the sea, when I tuik that name –
builder   The bringer – biggar of a bricht white cell –
Lytle I thocht on the onset and meaning
Of *nox*, my self to be banissit, deth
In a strangearis land. Luik, in yonder manger –
halls   Yule was aye the feast: the haas nou are bare,
The wintry fields excludit fra the warmth,
The palace, the haly palace, subvertit
To a stabil, levelling a fause wey out.
bones dashed violently   They cry it 'casting doun' – banes wappit furth
Of their sepulture, fruit-trees pluckit up
By the ruits, altars and images smashed
To the singing of psalms. Whattin a Scotland
much too close   Survives? Ower-near was it to the groves
hissing   Of Baal, bizzand in the beautie of summer –
Paradise lives its past thir present dayis.
gates   I knaw about yettis – expellit, shot out
from teaching   Fra teching schule; on til a soldier, catcht
on to be a soldier caught
in the fight   In the fecht: 'Och for mair papir or pennyis':
Exiled, wryting *in Germania res Scoticas*,
Orisons, epistilis, in Latin tongue.
Our auld plain Scottis, with Sotheron unacquaint,
Maks speech in me and music still fra hame –
locked   But aa for nocht, thae yettis are steikit fast.

*Ninian Winzet (or Winyet, as it would have been pronounced) wrote and spoke against John Knox and the Reformation in Scotland. He was appointed Abbot of the Benedictine Monastery of St James (a twelfth-century Scottish foundation) in Ratisbon (Regensburg) in 1577. He died 21 September 1592, aged 75. C.S.

away from my beginning
to a narrow street where

Driven furth of my setting-out, I carry
Back to a wynd whaur there's nae gaun back. *Janua*
Mordax, the door whaur the dog is chained, turns me
Awa to my business, with inward bite.
Banisht, dimmed – but furth of Europe, nae: nor
Furth of my unhurried citie, Hierusalem.
The pilgrims pass as years back once they did;
Voices lodge in cloisters their fathers founded,
Ruins I minister to and restore.
Others remain like rookeries, ancient, disbanded:
'The sure way to banish the rooks, pull down their
                                        nests' –
Those bundles of sticks, those notes in the living
                                        branches.
They will bury me here, a Scot; the gates
Of the motherland open through the night.
When I win back home to the glinting loch
My nation works abroad – who says I'm allowed it,
Dreams of ruin to come, rats' bones, a town in rain.

History of Strathclyde

How earth was made, I might have had it sung,
How life began – hushed rocking of the tide
Lapping the sleepy margins of the world.

But – searching back into almost unsearchable
Time (and yet, the waters have always stirred) –
Footprints tell a different order of fact:
Three-toed, Batrachian, printed in the rocks,
In the flaggy sandstone of Euchan Water
In the upper reaches of Nithsdale – early
Exploratory steps as the moment passed;
Petrified, along with suncracks and ripples,
Like those of any casual hen or dog
On a wet concrete path – the same sun shone.

Ah but the earth, this grassy land, has changed.
These pitted marks I long to think are raindrops

More properly interpreted as sea-spray:
No fossil bones or plants remain to help us
But — carcasses and all organic debris
Devoured by scavengers and scouring tides —
It was a coast, the glaring salty shore
Where bushy banks run now and the rowans sway.

A kingdom in the history of man,
A Dark Age kingdom and in that well named —
So little known of family and fighting,
Thus easily guessed at but so hard to grasp —
It was a border, and a middle ground,
As the power of Rome withdrew: other tides,
Less tied to the moon's control, carried on
The moves of life, washed over them as well.

Today in the bright afternoon I saw,
As I walked a drove-road towards the north,
The black-faced ewes cropping the heathery hills,
One, by the track, seeming asleep: except —
A neat dark-red pit in the bony face —
The crows had pecked its eyes out: for a moment,
As the sun went on with its mindless work,
In that wool hulk, a history of Strathclyde.

Among the Goths

Who *is* there to listen, who hears me? The wind
                                while I walk
On the shore blows steadily colder, the cloud
All-covering shifts in itself, a white
Inhospitable sky, the sea — how I hate
The sea: if it tells me of rhythm, the beginning of life,
With equal insistence it tells me of no return,
Of the daytime of life unadapted to the unlit depths.
And yet, when I look to the dusty freezing plain
The lack of escape is what chills me even more.
Somewhere in summer on quiet days I can hear,
Enrolled in the landmass, music, an inland voice:

Theodora is dozing, the corn gathers the sun;
The cattle are sleek, the smell of the farm is health,
The bees are at work, later the village will dance.
Will I get there ever? What could a visitor give?
Confined to this strand I can wait for community,
                                                wait
Just as well for the wings to carry me, soaring, alone,
To words of the upper air and the traveller's view.
How far that Forest, its Gothic cold how far
From blooming like the Golden world: and yet —
                                         where else?
That imperial island — remembered there: will it root,
Be held, my laurel buried, by this Pontic shore?
Illyrian, a castle — Princess, allow me place
By the swarming waves alone, all winter long
A prisoner of elegy, work, the denial of home:
But granted nevertheless unfettered time,
No terminus to strain for, nor any need
Save singing, spelling out the syllables of exile and
                                              love.
Withdrawn, that dream: returned to barbarity, wild
Wind-cropped grass, where I dwell on my words and
                                              fate,
Where I lie in longing, examined with diffident stare,
Approached with gifts and rough unmanageable
                                          tongue.
I feel the frontier pressing towards an end —
A stone could be planted, those miles from the city's
                                          heart;
But the land goes on, over the brackish lake,
To where mountains mass, and the clouds, and the
                                     blue beyond
Shows through: not understood, and captive, on the
                                          edge,
Though I never get back, there is more to come, there
                                       is room.

KENNETH WHITE (b. 1936)

The House at the Head of the Tide

Five miles out of town
you come to a place called
the White Field

two wings and a whiteness
(ideogram for 'perseverance')

moorland, a rocky coast
and a hundred islands
the sea often green, gurly green
but every now and then
a sharp, breath-catching blue
with always breakers

peace, peace in the breakers

a place, this, of darkness and of light
darknesses and lights
in quick succession
the sun reveals, cloud conceals
and always a music
of wind on moor, tide on shore
and a silence

a fifth quartet

'we must be still
and still moving
for a further union
a deeper communion
through the dark cold
and the empty desolation
the wave cry, the wind cry
the vast waters
of the petrel and the porpoise'

a country lane lined with gorse
this house of stone
lined with a thousand books
that speak of ideas, islands
according to an order
as yet only dimly apprehended
vaguely sensed

chaoticism

where are we?
where are we going?
one who has thought his way
through the thicket
says it is a question of
moving into a new place
a clearing
we speak here in terms of
atlantica
a breathing and a breadth

pelagian space:
what was left out and behind
when the roads were built
and the codes of command
crammed into the mind
what was left out
becoming more and more
faintly articulate

still there in the gull cry
the wave clash
those darknesses, those lights
(but who hears? who sees?
who can say?)

another mindscape

moving out then
into the landscape

walking
in the white of the morning

walking and watching
listening

yellow flowers
tossing in the wind
a crow on a branch
caw-cawing
the rivulet
reflecting the sky
in blue-grey ripples
white beach, wrack
the high gait and snootiness
of oyster-catchers
a blue crab groping in a pool
bright shell

the notes accumulate

towards a writing
that has more in view
than the art of making verse
out of blunt generalities
and personal complaining

atlantic archipelago
and a sense of something
to be gathered in

the mind gropes
like a blue crab in a pool
tosses in the wind
reflects the sky in ripples
flies high
leaves signs in the sand
lies recklessly strewn
at the edge of the tide

comes back to the books
the many manuscripts

scriptorium
in candida casa
altus prosator

binoculars focused also
on the red-roofed
abandoned sardine-factory
at the tip of the promontory –
some kind of homology

a place to work from
(to work it all out)
a place in which to
house a strangeness

this strange activity
(philosophy? poetry?
practice? theory?)

from an accumulation of data
to the plural poem

beyond the generality

from Late August on the Coast

A SHORT INTRODUCTION TO WHITE POETICS

Consider first the Canada Goose
brown body, whitish breast
black head, long black neck
with a white patch from throat to cheek
bill and legs black
flies in regular chevron or line formation
flight note: *aa-honk*
(that's the one old Walt heard on Long Island)

Then there's the Barnacle Goose
black and white plumage
white face and forehead
(in German, it's *Weisswangengans*)
flight in close ragged packs
flight note
a rapidly repeated *gnuk:*
gnuk gnuk gnuk gnuk gnuk gnuk gnuk
(like an ecstatic Eskimo)

Look now at the Brent Goose
small and dark
black head, neck and breast
brillant white arse
more sea-going than other geese
feeds along the coast
by day or by night
rapid flight
seldom in formation
irregularly changing flocks
her cry:
a soft, throaty gut-bucket *rronk*

The Red-Breasted Goose
has a combination of
black, white and chestnut plumage
legs and bill blackish
quick and agile, this beauty
seldom flies in regular formation
cry:
a shrill *kee-kwa kee-kwa*
(who, what? who, what?)

The Greylag
pale grey forewings
thick orange bill
lives near the coastline
flies to grazing grounds at dawn
usually in regular formation
cry: *aahng ung-ung*

(like a Chinese poet
exiled in Mongolia)

As to the Bean Goose
she has a dark forewing
and a long black bill
talks a lot less than other geese
just a low, rich, laconic *ung-unk*

The Snow Goose
has a pure white plumage
with blacktipped wings
dark pink bill and legs
(in North America turns blue
a dusky blue-grey)
in Europe you might take her for a swan
or maybe a gannet
till she lets you know abruptly
with one harsh *kaank*
she's all goose

so
there they go
through the wind, the rain, the snow

wild spirits
knowing what they know

STEWART CONN (b. 1936)

Todd

My father's white uncle became
  Arthritic and testamental in
  Lyrical stages. He held cardinal sin
Was misuse of horses, then any game

Won on the sabbath. A Clydesdale
  To him was not bells and sugar or declension
  From paddock, but primal extension
Of rock and soil. Thundered nail

Turned to sacred bolt. And each night
  In the stable he would slaver and slave
  At-cracked hooves, or else save
Bowls of porridge for just the right

Beast. I remember I lied
  To him once, about oats: then I felt
  The brand of his loving tongue, the belt
Of his own horsey breath. But he died,

When the mechanised tractor came to pass.
  Now I think of him neighing to some saint
  In a simple heaven or, beyond complaint,
Leaning across a fence and munching grass.

On Craigie Hill

The farmhouse seems centuries ago,
The steadings slouched under a sifting of snow
For weeks on end, lamps hissing, logs stacked
Like drums in the shed, the ice having to be cracked
To let the shaggy cats drink. Or
Back from the mart through steaming pastures
Men would come riding – their best

Boots gleaming, rough tweeds pressed
To a knife-edge, pockets stuffed with notes.

Before that even, I could visualise (from coloured
Prints) traps rattling, wheels spinning; furred
Figures posing like sepia dolls
In a waxen world of weddings and funerals.
When Todd died, last of the old-stagers,
Friends of seventy years followed the hearse.
Soon the farm went out of the family; the Cochranes
Going to earth or, like their cousins,
Deciding it was time to hit town.

The last link broken, the farm-buildings stand
In a clutter below the quarry. The land
Retains its richness – but in other hands.
Kilmarnock has encroached. It is hard to look
Back with any sense of belonging.
Too much has changed, is still changing.
This blustery afternoon on Craigie Hill
I regard remotely the muddy track
My father used to trudge along, to school.

The Yard

The yard is littered with scrap, with axles
And tyres, buckled hoops and springs, all rusting.
The wreckage of cars that have been dumped.

The hut is still there. In the doorway
Two men talk horses – but not as he did
In the days when the Clydesdales came

To be shod, the milk-wagons for repair.
The din of iron on iron brings it all back:
Rob beating the anvil, to a blue flame.

The beast straining, the bit biting in,
Horn burning, the sour tang of iron,
The sizzling, the perfect fit of the shoe.

In his mind's eye, the whole yard is teeming
With horses, ducking blackthorn, tails
Swishing, the gates behind them clanging . . .

The men have started to strip an old van.
In passing he takes a kick at the wing. No one
Notices. The dead metal does not ring at all.

Summer Afternoon

She spends the afternoon in a deckchair,
Not moving, a handkerchief over
Her head. From the end of the garden
Her eyes look gouged. The children stare,
Then return to their game. She used to take
Them on country walks, or swimming in the lake.
These days are gone, and will not come again.

Dazzling slats of sunlight on the lawn
Make her seem so vulnerable; her bombazine
Costume fading with each drifting beam.
As the children squall, she imagines
Other generations: Is that you, Tom,
Or Ian, is it? – forgetting one was blown
To bits at Ypres, the other on the Somme.

Momentarily in pain, she tightens
Her lips into something like a grin.
There comes the first rustle of rain.
Carrying her in, you avoid my eye
For fear of interception, as who should say
Shall we, nearing extremity,
Be equal objects of distaste and pity?

Yet desperate in the meantime to forbear
For the sake of the love this poor
Creature bore us, who was once so dear.

To My Father

One of my earliest memories (remember
Those Capone hats, the polka-dot ties)
Is of the late thirties: posing
With yourself and grandfather before
The park railings; me dribbling
Ice cream, you so spick and smiling
The congregation never imagined
How little you made. Three generations,
In the palm of a hand. A year later
Grandfather died. War was declared.

In '42 we motored to Kilmarnock
In Alec Martin's Terraplane Hudson.
We found a pond, and six goldfish
Blurred under ice. They survived
That winter, but a gull got them in the end.
Each year we picnicked on the lawn;
Mother crooking her finger
As she sipped her lime. When
They carried you out on a stretcher
She knew you'd never preach again.

Since you retired, we've seen more
Of each other. Yet I spend this forenoon
Typing, to bring you closer – when
We could have been together. Part of what
I dread is that clear mind nodding
Before its flickering screen. If we come over
Tonight, there will be the added irony
Of proving my visit isn't out of duty
When, to myself, I doubt the dignity
Of a love comprising so much guilt and pity.

Under the Ice

Like Coleridge, I waltz
on ice. And watch my shadow
on the water below. Knowing that
if the ice were not there
I'd drown. Half willing it.

In my cord jacket
and neat cravat, I keep
returning to the one spot.
How long, to cut
a perfect circle out?

Something in me
rejects the notion.
The arc is never complete.
My figures-of-eight
almost, not quite, meet.

Was Raeburn's skating parson
a man of God, poised
impeccably on the brink;
or his bland stare
no more than a decorous front?

If I could keep my cool
like that. Gazing straight ahead,
not at my feet. Giving
no sign of knowing
how deep the water, how thin the ice.

Behind that, the other
question: whether the real you
pirouettes in space,
or beckons from under the ice
for me to come through.

WILLIAM MCILVANNEY (b. 1936)

Bless This House

A sampler for Glasgow bedsits

Bless this house, wherever it is,
This house and this and this and this

Pitched shaky as small nomad tents
Within Victorian permanence,

Where no names stay long, no families meet
In Observatory Road and Clouston Street

Where Harry and Sally who want to be 'free'
And Morag who works in the BBC

And Andy the Artist and Mhairi and Fran
(Whose father will never understand)

And John from Kilmarnock and Jean from the Isles
And Michael who jogs every day for miles

And Elspeth are passing through this year:
Bless them the short time they are here.

Bless the cup left for a month or more
On the dust of the window-ledge, the door

That won't quite shut, the broken fan,
The snowscape of fat in the frying pan.

Bless each burnt chop, each unseen smile
That they may nourish their hopes a while.

Bless the persistence of their faith,
The gentle incense of their breath.

Bless the wild dreams that are seeded here,
The lover to come, the amazing career.

Bless such small truths as they may find
By the lonely night-light of the mind.

Bless these who camp out in the loss of the past
And scavenge their own from what others have lost,

Who have courage to reach for what they cannot see
And have gambled what was for what may never be.

So turn up the hi-fi, Michael and John.
What is to come may be already gone.

And pull up the covers, Jean and Mhairi.
The island is far and you've missed the ferry.

The Song Mickey Heard at the Bottom of his Pint in the Zodiac Bar

I am the man whose back you see
In any crowded bar.
The future never reaches me
Though they say it isn't far.

The mirror stores my quiet smiles,
The pillow hoards my sighs.
Nations have watched for centuries
And never seen my eyes.

Who baked the bread in Babylon?
Who swept the streets in Rome?
Who held the reins that held the horse
That brought the great men home?

Passing Through Petra

Places persist, time stays
Beyond the uses of itself,
The small insistent residue,
Ubiquity in nowhere,
Buttercup pollen on our shoes as children.

The wall the sunlight softened for no reason.
The room in sudden stasis,
The body-moulded jacket on a chair,
The heel of bread, a table and some dust.
The Maltese girl,
The way a hand touched forehead,
Half-lost face.

And this not for regretting
Nor forcibly retained. But just admitted.
An intractable,
A part of us beyond our purposes.

Places we have to go, need things to do,
Arrive, it seems, past our own destinations.

Always in each of us
The part that stays
Where nothing has a use beyond endurance,
Becalmed in ancient sunlight of our own,
Touching a braille of stone, sunk just in being,
Flowering in old clefts of our lives,
Passing through Petra.

ROBIN FULTON (b. 1937)

Remembering an Island

'Island
what shall I say of you, your peat-bogs,
your lochs, your moors and berries?' Strange words
to remember on a Stockholm street-crossing – it's like
a dream where you find a door in a solid wall.

North-east, east and south-east
a top-heavy pile of thunderclouds,
west over Kungsholmen a glassy fire:
between, the city is a Dutch masterpiece,
still-life with evening traffic-flow.

And not a dream. I know where the walls end
and begin again. I touch doors on time.
The highland roads in my mind have been
                                        redeveloped –
a few old curves still visible, like
the creases in my birth-certificate from the thirties.

Travelling Alone

The countless forests we pass hour after hour,
they are anonymous with such grace.
Would we feel safer
if all the dead came back and stood waiting?

The north train and the south train pass.
Sitting in one I see myself in the other.
Without much grace
I keep crossing my own invisible path.

A film suddenly stopping in a crowd-scene:
black holes in space, where the people were.
Each has stepped into
the outer darkness of his own company.

Museums and Journeys

An exhibition: a hundred years of Edinburgh life.
Coming out I move as heavily as a diver
on the ocean floor: one step, one breath
against the weight of the invisible dead. So many
yet the air is clear. And they've no time for me,
their view of the future blocked by giant headlines.

A journey: one I didn't want to take but took
shutting my eyes – a child again hoping the needle
wouldn't hurt. Lakes and forests, lakes and forests
pass with the weightless ease of delirium. So many.
My view of the past stays clear but hard to read
like a radio-map of a secret corner in the night sky.

Museums and journeys. We meet as strangers do
at the end of long ellipses over continents.
We exchange histories. Our view of the present is
                                                    clear
but the landscapes go on sliding past. So many
memories, I try to say 'One at a time!'
They keep piling up like urgent unanswered letters.

Stopping by Shadows

High up, birches have a homely aspect,
small, like things we discover and recognise,
returning after an absence of many years.
Closer, they're almost transparent in the snow
and above, boulders big as cathedrals poise
– on the edge since prehistory.

Midday. I stop at the edge of the shadow
that has filled this space all winter,
the sun a white breath at the cliff-top,
a brief flame in the ice of a remote tree.
I turn and watch my own shadow dissolving
slowly in the luminous dark air

then take a cold step back to life,
skis hiss-hiss on snow-crystals
that spent all night quietly hardening.
Across the valley red and yellow figures
on a brilliant field jump into focus
like true events under a microscope.

Resolutions

All day the air got harder and harder.
I woke in the small hours, rooftops

frozen seas of tranquillity, while far
below the first flakes fell on the street.

The air of another planet come down to earth,
we breathe harshly between familiar stones.

No place for flesh. Spirit and bone
at odds, the nerves caught between, singing:

'Must it be?' It must be must be must be
bouncing like a ball in a small room without
                                                                    windows.

Remembering Walls

I once wanted these walls
to turn magically clear
as air and let me walk through.

Now that strangers have moved in
strange furniture I want
the house stone-solid and dour,

resisting the dank strath winds
and to the dry pine-descant
adding a worn ground-bass

angular, melancholy.
It follows me from winter to
winter. Safe in its lulls

voices that cannot last long,
that did not always please me,
will last as long as I shall.

No one watches the wet slates
dry and glisten again and dry.
My private music remembers me.

D. M. BLACK (b. 1941)

From the Privy Council

Delicacy was never enormously
My style. All my favourite girls
Walked at five miles an hour or ate haggis,
Or swam like punts. I myself,
Though not of primeval clumsiness, would often
Crack tumblers in my attention to their content
Or bruise with my embrace some tittering nymph.
It was accidental only – I have little
Sadistic enthusiasm – yet when the time came
And they sent me to the Consultant on Careers,
Executioner was the immediate decision.
My nature is a quiet, conforming thing,
I like to be advised, and am not arrogant:
I agreed:
They stripped me of my suit, shored off my hair
And shaved a gleaming scalp onto my skull;
Clad me in fitting hides,
Hid my poignant features with a black mask,
And led me the very first day to the public platform.
I had to assist only: the carriage of carcasses
Is a heavy job, and not for a spent headsman.
Later they let me handle the small hatchet
For cutting off hands and so forth – what is called
                                        hackwork
Merely; but I earned the prize for proficiency
And the end of my first year brought total
                                        promotion:
Hangman and headsman for the metropolitan burgh
Of Aberfinley. I had a black band
Printed on all my note-paper. Every morning
I hectored my hatchetmen into a spruce turn-out,
Insisted on a keen edge to all their axes.
My jurisdiction spilled
Over the county border – half Scotland's assassins
Dragged their victims into the benign realm

Where I held sway;
And the trade was gripped in the rigours of
                                        unemployment
Outside my scope. There was one solution:
The London parliament passed an urgent Act
Creating a new sinecure: Hangman
And headsman in the Royal Chamber – the post
To be of Cabinet rank, and in the Privy Council.
How many lepers and foundling-hospitals
Have cause to bless me now! On the Privy Council
My stately head is much admired, and the opulent
                                                grace
With which I swing my kindly turnip watch.
And here you will find the origin of the tired joke
About passing from executive to admin.

Kew Gardens

In memory of Ian A. Black, died January 1971

Distinguished scientist, to whom I greatly defer
(old man, moreover, whom I dearly love),
I walk today in Kew Gardens, in sunlight the colour
                                        of honey
which flows from the cold autumnal blue of the
                        heavens to light these tans and golds,
these ripe corn and leather and sunset colours of the
                                East Asian liriodendrons,
of the beeches and maples and plum-trees and the
                stubborn green banks of the holly hedges –
and you walk always beside me, you with your
                                knowledge of names
and your clairvoyant gaze, in what for me is sheer
                                                panorama
seeing the net or web of connectedness. But today it
                                        is I who speak
(and you are long dead, but it is to you I say it):

'The leaves are green in summer because of
                                        chlorophyll

and the flowers are bright to lure the pollinators,
and without remainder (so you have often told me)
these marvellous things that shock the heart the head
                              can account for;
but I want to sing an excess which is not so simply
                              explainable,
to say that the beauty of the autumn is a redundant
                              beauty,
that the sky had no need to be this particular shade
                              of blue,
nor the maple to die in flames of this particular
                              yellow,
nor the heart to respond with an ecstasy that does
                              not beget children.
I want to say that I do not believe your science
although I believe every word of it, and intend to
                              understand it
that although I rate that unwavering gaze higher than
                              almost everything
there is another sense, a hearing, to which I more
                              deeply attend.
Thus I withstand and contradict you, I, your child,
who have inherited from you the passion which
                              causes me to oppose you.'

AONGHAS MACNEACAIL (b. 1942)

dol dhachaigh – 2

seall na geòidh
a' siubhal 's
na gobhlain-gaoithe

's fhad' o dh'fhalbh a' chuthag

seall na duilleagan dearg ag
éirigh air
sgiath sgairt-ghaoith
ag éirigh 's a' siubhal

tha'm bradan sgrìob mhór a-mach
air a shlighe

ghrian a' dol 'na sìneadh
ghealach ag éirigh
          'nam parabolathan caochlaideach eòlach

samhradh a' siubhal
foghar air a dhruim
          cleòc mór a' sgaoileadh as a dhéidh

null 's a-nall air cala
          fògarrach a-null 's a-nall
null 's a-nall
          null 's a-nall

going home – 2

see the geese
journeying and
the swallows

long since the cuckoo went

see the red leaves
rising on
the wing of a gust
rising and travelling

the salmon is a great way out
on his journey

the sun reclining
moon rising
            in their familiar changing parabolas

summer journeying
autumn on his back
            a great cloak spreading behind

back and forward on the wharf
            an exile back and forward
back and forward
            back and forward

gleann fadamach

plèan a' dol tarsainn
cho àrd 's nach cluinnear i
long a' dol sìos an cuan
ach fada mach air fàire

cuid dhen t-saoghal
a' siubhal 's a' siubhal

sa bhaile seo
chan eileas a' siubhal ach an aon uair
's na clachan a rinn ballaichean
a' dol 'nan càirn

glen remote

plane crossing
so high it can't be heard
ship going down the ocean
far out on the horizon

a part of the world
travelling travelling

in this village
people only travel once
and the stones that made walls
become cairns

from an cathadh mor

3

mìorbhail an t-sneachda
gach criostal àraid
gach criostal gun chàraid
meanbh-chlachaireachd
gach lóineag a' tàthadh
saoghal fo chidhis

sneachda fìorghlan
     (ìocshlaint nan galair
     fras chalman air iteal
     mealltach mesmearach)
sneachda gun lochd
     (cléireach ag ùrnaigh
     an cille stàilinn
     ghlas a chreideimh
     cléireach a' guidhe
     fhradharc 'na bhoisean
     ag àicheadh a bhruadar)

sneachda lainnireach
  (leanabh a' ruidhleadh aig uinneig
  sùilean a' dealradh)
sneachda grioglannach
  (speuran brùite dùinte)
sneachda brìodalach
   snàigeach sniagach
sneachda lìonmhorachadh
   sàmhach sàmhach
sneachda càrnach
sneachda fillteach
sneachda casgrach

 6

sìneadh a h-éididh air
cathair caisteal clachan

sgaoileadh a còt' air
gach buaile gach bealach
gach sgurr is gach rubha
h-uile sràid anns gach baile
geal geal geal

plangaid air saoghal
brat-sìth do threubhan domhain

an gilead gealltanach gluasadach

 8

chan fhaic an t-iasgair ach cobhar
sgorran is sgeirean fo chobhar
sgaothan a' gluasad
     thar a' chala
     thar an raoin
     thar an t-sléibh
cha dhearc a shùil air cuan air cala
chan fhaic e ach cobhar nan sgaoth
a' traoghadh air raointean

an eathar 'na taibhse air teadhair
a lìn nan greasain gheal bhreòiteach
oillsginn gun anam a' crochadh is
　　bòtainnean laighe mar chuirp

sluaghan a' chuain do-ruigsinn

from *the great snowbattle*

3

marvel of snow
every crystal unique
every crystal without peer
micro-masonry
every flake cementing
a world beneath its mask

virginal snow
　　(balm for plagues
　　flurry of flying doves
　　deceptive, deadening)
faultless snow
　　(a cleric prays
　　in the steel cell
　　of his credo
　　cleric beseeches,
　　his sight in his palms
　　denying his dreams)

brilliant snow
　　(child dancing at window
　　eyes reflect glitter)
constellated snow
　　(the skies are bruised　　enclosed)
cajoling snow
　　snaking sneaking
multiplying snow
　　silent silent

mounding snow
pleating snow
slaughtering snow

6

stretching her raiment on
city   castle   clachan

spreading her coat on
each meadow   each pass
each peak and each reef
all the streets in each town
white   white   white

a blanket on the world
a flag of truce for
all the tribes in a universe

the whiteness promising   shifting

8

the fisher sees nothing but foam
summits and skerries are under the spray
shoals are moving
                              over harbours
                              across fields
                              across the moors
his eye cannot see ocean, anchorage
he sees only foaming shoals
subsiding on meadows

the boat is a tethered ghost
his nets white friable webs
his oilskins hang soulless while
      boots are outstretched corpses

ocean's multitudes are out of reach

ALAN BOLD (b. 1943)

June 1967 at Buchenwald

*The stillness of death all around the camp was uncanny and
intolerable.*
BRUNO APITZ, *Naked Among Wolves*

This is the way in. The words
Wrought in iron on the gate:
JEDEM DAS SEINE. Everybody
Gets what he deserves.

The bare drab rubble of the place.
The dull damp stone. The rain.
The emptiness. The human lack.
JEDEM DAS SEINE. JEDEM DAS SEINE.
Everybody gets what he deserves.

It all forms itself
Into one word: Buchenwald.
And those who know and those
Born after that war but living
In its shadow, shiver at the words.
Everybody gets what he deserves.

It is so quiet now. So
Still that it makes an absence.
At the silence of the metal loads
We can almost hear again the voices,
The moaning of the cattle that were men.
Ahead, acres of abandoned gravel.
Everybody gets what he deserves.

Wood, beech wood, song
Of birds. The sky, the usual sky.
A stretch of trees. A sumptuous sheet
Of colours dragging through the raindrops.
Drizzle loosening the small stones
We stand on. Stone buildings. Doors. Dark.

A dead tree leaning in the rain.
Everybody gets what he deserves.

Cold, numb cold. Despair
And no despair. The very worst
Of men against the very best.
A joy in brutality from lack
Of feeling for the other. The greatest
Evil, racialism. A man, the greatest good.
Much more than a biological beast.
An aggregate of atoms. Much more.
Everybody gets what he deserves.

And it could happen again
And they could hang like broken carcasses
And they could scream in terror without light
And they could count the strokes that split their skin
And they could smoulder under cigarettes
And they could suffer and bear every blow
And they could starve and live for death
And they could live for hope alone
And it could happen again.
Everybody gets what he deserves.

We must condemn our arrogant
Assumption that we are immune as well
As apathetic. We let it happen.
History is always more comfortable
Than the implications of the present.
We outrage our own advance as beings
By being merely men. The miracle
Is the miracle of matter. Mind
Knows this but sordid, cruel and ignorant
Tradition makes the world a verbal shell.
Everybody gets what he deserves.

Words are fallible. They cannot do
More than hint at torment. Let us
Do justice to words. No premiss is ever
Absolute; so certain that enormous wreckage

Of flesh follows it syllogistically
In the name of mere consistency. In the end
All means stand condemned. In a cosmic
Context human life is short. The future
Is not made, but waits to be created.
Everybody gets what he deserves.

There is the viciously vicarious in us
All. The pleasure in chance misfortune
That lets us patronise or helps to lose
Our limitations for an instant.
It is that, that struggle for survival
I accuse. Let us not forget
Buchenwald is not a word. Its
Meaning is defined with every day.
Everybody gets what he deserves.

Now it is newsprint and heavy headlines
And looking with a camera's eyes.
Now for many it is only irritating
While for others it is absolutely deadly.
No one is free while some are not free.
While the world is ruled by precedent
It remains a monstrous chance irrelevance.
Everybody gets what he deserves.

We turn away. We always do.
It's what we turn into that matters.
From the invisible barracks of Buchenwald
Where only an unsteady horizon
Remains. The dead cannot complain.
They never do. But we, we live.
Everybody gets what he deserves.

That which once united man
Now drives him apart. We are not helpless
Creatures crashing onwards irresistibly to doom.
There is time for everything and time to choose
For everything. We are that time, that choice.
Everybody gets what he deserves.

This happened near the core
Of a world's culture. This
Occurred among higher things.
This was a philosophical conclusion.
Everybody gets what he deserves.

The bare drab rubble of the place.
The dull damp stone. The rain.
The emptiness. The human lack.

Grass

Grass basks greedily in the sun
As light penetrates each vein
Saturating the stem in the sheath.

Grass contains every gradation of green:
Loves both fiery sun and drenching rain;
Tugs the watcher downwards, underneath

Grass to crushing earth and stone.
Still the watcher comes to watch again,
To see the grass caress the gravel path.

A Special Theory of Relativity

According to Einstein
There's no still centre of the universe:
Everything is moving
Relative to something else.
My love, I move myself towards you,
Measure my motion
In relation to yours.

According to Einstein
The mass of a moving body
Exceeds its mass
When standing still.

My love, in moving
Through you
I feel my mass increase.

According to Einstein
The length of a moving body
Diminishes
As speed increases.
My love, after accelerating
Inside you
I spectacularly shrink.

According to Einstein
Time slows down
As we approach
The speed of light.
My love, as we approach
The speed of light
Time is standing still.

Love-Lowe

fireside   Yer glowin' gowden by the guschach
                 Tho' the flames are red.
[fish] churning   Like water thresh'd wi' keethin'-sight
                 Ye mak me feel guid.

ill-gotten property   As a thief wi' glender-gear
                 I keep ye close
passing sunbeam   Ye gae through me as the sun-glaff glides
                 Straight through ma gless.

shine/brightly   Aye, ye gleet an' glitter glegly
small boat   A saft sunblink on a scow.
blundering   I'm aye blowthirin', but, lassie,
love-flame   It's the richt love-lowe,
                 The richt love-lowe.

The Auld Symie

raw-cold

Winter is deasie
   An' ootside the snaw
Churns like a salmon
   In its deid-thraw.

death-throe

White gettin' mair white
   Piled on the stanes
Folk look stark naked
   Clad in their banes.

bones

devil

But still the auld symie
   Wi' bent kipper-nose
Maks for the kirk where
   God alane goes.

hook-nose

ALISON FELL (b. 1944)

Desire

The wind is strong enough to move wasps.
This blowing branch is mine,
silvery thing, all mine,
my teethmarks swarm over it:
what sweet sap and small beetles racing.

Mother warns me I will get worms
from this zest
for chewing and digesting
fur buds and the satin
leaves of beech, from all this
testing and possessing.
'Stop that,' she says.
'Stop this minute. See the
wee eggs you'll swallow!'

My needle-bright eye is rash
and scans greedily,
sees pine-cones lose pollen
in yellow gusts;
the loch's rim has a
curd of it, the face of
the middle deeps is
skimmed with dust and wrinkles.

The birch trunk wears a
sleeve of paper, clear-layered,
like sunburned skin – a wrap.
It streams from my thumbnail
till the wind snatches it.

Pushing Forty

Just before winter
we see the trees show
their true colours:
the mad yellow of chestnuts
two maples like blood sisters
the orange beech
braver than lipstick

Pushing forty, we vow
that when the time comes
rather than wither
ladylike and white
we will henna our hair
like Colette, we too
will be gold and red
and go out
in a last wild blaze

Freeze-frame

*On my bedroom wall there's an old black-and-white snapshot of
two sisters in a snow-crusted garden. The wee one is caught in the
act of smashing a snowball at the big one, who stands knock-
kneed, unprotesting.*

1947. That winter they talk of.
A winter like fists or wizards,

one or the other. The frozen lawn
pitted with porridge and scraps,

soup-bone fat with marrow
that the crows brawl over,

big sister buttoned up
with her puppet gloves dangling.

For background, there's the gable
where old Jessie lived,

a black wedge, and her
the witch of a hundred cats,

reading
your mind's eye, your bad eye.

1947. Small birds dumb as dolls
on the winter wire. I saw

their hearts like peas
and pitied them

that they were never born with tongues
to tell us things. I emptied

my wishes up chimneys, insisted
on reindeer.

Click of the camera fixes
my mittened hand to a blur:

the snowball's invisible as anger
shuttered in the nick of time.

My sister is too patient,
with her face like Petrouchka

and her snow-drifted smile.
She has no tongue, she says

nothing, thinks of Jessie
with the soot under her skirts

and the cats
wicked on the wall.

IAN ABBOT (1944–89)

The Mechanisms of the Gin

Sixteen teeth, set
in a lurid, iron smile.
Chained to the earth, anchored
into black soil, nonetheless
its everyday, simple grin sustains itself.

Its mouth spills feathers.
White bones tumble from it
one upon another: numberless
but laid like runes across the ground.
The great jaw of the badger, skull of the grouse,
an endless filigree of weasels. Yearly
it raises cairns that honour
no more than its own eternal memory.

You tend it with utmost care. Intimately prime as
                                        your father did
its double jagged sickles and its tight-sprung mouth,
                                        arrange
its hidden ribbon of links. Then turn for home,
                                        moving
heavily downward into sleep.
Only to dream of iron laughter shouting in the
                                        wood
and the spare, insatiable gaze
that will see your own flesh folded in the earth
and then will sit back patient, waiting;
grinning till the wandered, bone-white stars begin to
                                        fall.

A Body of Work

Do you not see, finally,
how the earth is moving to inhabit me?

My teeth
are the white stones of the river-bed;
throughout the day
an otter dozes in the dank holt of my mouth.
The sinews of my legs
go down into the earth like roots, and knots of
                                        shifting clay
compose the muscles of my face.
My hair, my sex becoming
clumps of hoary winter grass.

Seasons are manifest in me:
I know their white, their green, their turning yellow.
Laughing, my voice is the fever of stags; the pure
transparency of leaves is in my speech. Constellations
sift their burning atoms through my veins.

But in singing, weeping,
waking in the night and crying out,
my language is a deer dismembered under pines,
bloody and netted with shadows.
An intricate labyrinth of entrails,
lit from within
and patiently transfigured to the lightning grin of
                                        bones.

TOM LEONARD (b. 1944)

Six Glasgow Poems

1

THE GOOD THIEF

heh jimmy
yawright ih
stull wayiz urryi
ih

heh jimmy
ma right insane yirra pape
ma right insane yirwanny us jimmy
see it nyir eyes
wanny uz

heh

heh jimmy
lookslik wirgonny miss thi gemm
gonny miss thi GEMM jimmy
nearly three a cloke thinoo

dork init
good jobe theyve gote thi lights

2

SIMPLE SIMON

thurteen bluddy years wi thim ih
no even a day aff
jiss gee im thi fuckin heave
weeks noatiss nur nuthin
gee im thi heave
thats aw

ahll tellyi sun
see if ah wiz Scot Symon
ahd tell him wherrty stuff thir team
thi hole fuckin lota thim
thats right

a bluddy skandal thats whit it iz
a bluddy skandal

sicken yi

3
COLD, ISN'T IT

wirraw init thigithir missyz
geezyir kross

4
A SCREAM

yi mist yirsell so yi did
we aw skiptwirr ferz njumptaffit thi lights
YIZIR AW PINE THEY FERZ THIMORRA
o it wizza scream
thaht big shite wiz dayniz nut

tellnyi jean
we wirraw shoutn backit im
rrose shoutit shi widny puhllit furra penshin
o yi shooda seeniz face
hi didny no wherrty look

thing iz tay
thirz nay skool thimorra
thi daft kunt wullny even getiz bluddy ferz

5

THE MIRACLE OF THE BURD AND THE FISHES

ach sun
jiss keepyir chin up
dizny day gonabootlika hawf shut knife
inaw jiss cozzy a burd

luvur day yi
ach well
gee it a wee while sun
thirz a loat merr fish in thi sea

6

GOOD STYLE

helluva hard tay read theez init
stull
if yi canny unnirston thim jiss clear aff then
gawn
get tay fuck ootma road

ahmaz goodiz thi lota yiz so ah um
ah no whit ahm dayn
tellnyi
jiss try enny a yir fly patir wi me
stick thi bootnyi good style
so ah wull

Poetry

the pee as in pulchritude,
oh pronounced ough
as in bough

the ee rather poised
(pronounced ih as in wit)
then a languid high tea . . .

pause: then the coda –
ray pronounced rih
with the left eyebrow raised
– what a gracious bouquet!

Poetry.
Poughit. rih.

That was my education
– and nothing to do with me.

Jist ti Let Yi No

from the American of Carlos Williams

ahv drank
thi speshlz
that wurrin
thi frij

n thit
yiwurr probbli
hodn back
furthi pahrti

awright
they wur great
thaht stroang
thaht cawld

Paroakial

thahts no whurrits aht
thahts no cool man
jiss paroakial

aw theez sporran heads
tahty scoan vibes
thi haggis trip

bad buzz man
dead seen

goahty learna new langwij
sumhm ihnturnashnl
Noah Glasgow hangup
bunnit husslin

gitinty elektroniks man
really blow yir mine
real good blast
no whuhta mean

mawn
turn yirself awn

Feed Ma Lamz

Amyir gaffirz Gaffir. Hark.

    nay fornirz ur communists
    nay langwij
    nay lip
    nay laffn ina sunday
    nay g.b.h. (septina wawr)
    nay nooky huntn
    nay tea-leaven
    nay chanty rasslin
    nay nooky huntn nix doar
    nur kuvitn their ox

Oaky doaky. Stick way it
— rahl burn thi lohta yiz.

from Unrelated Incidents

I

its thi lang-
wij a thi
guhtr thaht hi
said its thi
langwij a
thi guhtr

awright fur
funny stuff
ur
Stanley Bax-
ter ur but
luv n science
n thaht naw

thi langwij
a thi
intillect hi
said thi lang-
wij a thi intill-
ects Inglish

then whin thi
doors slid
oapn hi raised
his hat geen
mi a fare-
well nod flung
oot his right

fit boldly n
fell eight
storeys
doon thi

empty
lift-shaft

   2

ifyi stull
huvny
wurkt oot
thi diff-
rince tween
yir eyes
n
yir ears;
– geez peace.
pal!

fyi stull
huvny
thoata lang-
wij izza
sound-system:
fyi huvny
hudda thingk
aboot thi dif-
frince tween
sound
n object n
symbol; well,
ma innocent
wee
friend – iz
god said ti
adam:

a doant kerr
fyi caw it
an apple
ur
an aippl –

jist leeit
alane!

3

this is thi
six a clock
news thi
man said n
thi reason
a talk wia
BBC accent
iz coz yi
widny wahnt
mi ti talk
aboot thi
trooth wia
voice lik
wanna yoo
scruff. if
a toktaboot
thi trooth
lik wanna yoo
scruff yi
widny thingk
it wuz troo.
jist wanna yoo
scruff tokn.
thirza right
way ti spell
ana right way
ti tok it. this
is me tokn yir
right way a
spellin. this
is ma trooth.
yooz doant no
thi trooth
yirsellz cawz
yi canny talk

right. this is
the six a clock
nyooz. belt up.

from Ghostie Men

right inuff
ma language is disgraceful

ma maw tellt mi
ma teacher tellt mi
thi doactir tellt mi
thi priest tellt mi

ma boss tellt mi
ma landlady in carrington street tellt mi
thi lassie ah tried tay get aff way in 1969 tellt mi
sum wee smout thit thoat ah hudny read chomsky
                                              tellt mi
a calvinistic communist thit thoat ah wuz revisionist
                                              tellt mi

po-faced literati grimly kerryin thi burden a thi past
                                              tellt mi
po-faced literati grimly kerryin thi burden a thi future
                                              tellt mi
ma wife tellt mi jist-tay-get-inty-this-poem tellt mi
ma wainz came hame fray school an tellt mi
jist aboot ivry book ah oapnd tellt mi
even thi introduction tay thi Scottish National
                                    Dictionary tellt mi

ach well
all livin language is sacred
fuck thi lohta thim

Fathers and Sons

I remember being ashamed of my father
when he whispered the words out loud
reading the newspaper.

'Don't you find
the use of phonetic urban dialect
rather constrictive?'
asks a member of the audience.

The poetry reading is over.
I will go home to my children.

VERONICA FORREST-THOMSON (1947–75)

Strike

For Bonnie, my first horse

I

Hail to thee, blithe horse, bird thou never wert!
And, breaking into a canter, I set off on the long road
                                south
Which was to take me to so many strange places,
That room in Cambridge, that room in Cambridge,
                        that room in Cambridge,
That room in Cambridge, this room in Cambridge,
The top of a castle in Provence and an aeroplane in
                              mid-Atlantic.
Strange people, that lover, that lover, that lover, that
                                  lover.
Eyes that last I saw in lecture-rooms
Or in the Reading Room of The British Museum
                         reading, writing,
Reeling, writhing, and typing all night (it's cheaper
                        than getting drunk),
Doing tour en diagonale in ballet class (that's cheaper
                     than getting drunk too).
But first I should describe my mount. His strange
                              colour;
He was lilac with deep purple points (he was really a
                         siamese cat).
His strange toss and whinny which turned my
                              stomach
And nearly threw me out of the saddle. His eyes
His eyes his eyes his eyes his eyes
Eyes that last I saw in lecture rooms
His eyes were hazel brown and deceptively
                           disingenuous.
I got to know those eyes very well.
Our journey through England was not made easier by
                              the fact

That he would eat only strawberries and cream (at
             any season).
And he wanted a lot of that.
Nevertheless I got here and the first time I ever set
             foot in the place
I knew it was my home. The trouble was to convince
             the authorities.
Jobs were scarce and someone with a purple-point
             siamese to keep
In strawberries and cream has a certain standard of
             living.
When I sold my rings and stopped buying clothes I
             knew
It was the end. When I cut down on food it was clear
I was on some sort of quest.
There was an I-have-been-here-before kind of feeling
             about it.
That hateful cripple with the twisted grin. But
Dauntless the slughorn to my ear I set.

II

How many miles to Babylon?
Threescore and ten.
Can I get there by candlelight?
Yes. But back again?
From perfect leaf there need not be
Petals or even rosemary.
One thing then burnt rests on the tree:
The woodspurge has a cup of three,
One for you, and one for me,
And one for the one we cannot see.

III

What there is now to celebrate:
The only art where failure is renowned.
A local loss
Across and off the platform-ticket found
For the one journey we can tolerate:

To withered fantasy
From stale reality. Father, I cannot tell a lie;
I haven't got the time.
Mirth cannot move a soul in agony.
Stainless steel sintered and disowned;
Stars in the brittle distance just on loan.
The timetables of our anxiety glitter, grow
One in the alone. The cosmic ozones know
Our lease is running out.
Deserted now the house of fiction stands
Exams within and driving tests without,
Shading the purpose from the promised lands
No milk our honey.
And the train we catch can't take us yet
To the blind corner where he waits
Between the milk and honey gates:
The god we have not met.

LIZ LOCHHEAD (b. 1947)

Dreaming Frankenstein

For Lys Hansen, Jacki Parry and June Redfern

She said she
woke up with him in
her head, in her bed.
Her mother-tongue clung to her mouth's roof
in terror, dumbing her, and he came with a name
that was none of her making.

No maidservant ever
in her narrow attic, combing
out her hair in the midnight mirror
on Hallowe'en (having eaten
that egg with its yolk hollowed out
then filled with salt)
— oh never one had such success as this
she had not courted.
The amazed flesh of her
neck and shoulders nettled
at his apparition.

Later, stark staring awake to everything
(the room, the dark parquet, the white high Alps
                                        beyond)
all normal in the moonlight
and him gone, save a ton-weight sensation,
the marks fading visibly where
his buttons had bit into her and
the rough serge of his suiting had chafed her sex,
she knew — oh that was not how —
but he'd entered her utterly.

This was the penetration
of seven swallowed apple pips.
Or else he'd slipped like a silver dagger
between her ribs and healed her up secretly

again. Anyway
he was inside her
and getting him out again
would be agony fit to quarter her,
unstitching everything.

Eyes on those high peaks
in the reasonable sun of the morning,
she dressed in damped muslin
and sat down to quill and ink
and icy paper.

Heartbreak Hotel

Honeymooning alone
oh the food's
quite good (but it all needs salting).
Breadsticks admonish,
brittle fingers among formality – bishops' hats,
stiff skirts, white linen, silver implements.

This dining room
is all set for a funeral,
an anatomy lesson,
a celebration of communion
or a conjuring trick – maybe someone
will be sawn in half,
or a napkin could crumple
to an amazing dove.
Except
it's all empty
though I eat my helping
under a notice that says This Place
is Licensed for Singing and Dancing.

Go to your room.
What more lovely than to be alone
with a Teasmade a radio and a telephone?
Loose end? Well, this is what you find

when you take the time off to unwind.
Empty twinbeds
and the space all hanging heavy
above your neat spare shoes
in your wall-to-wall wardrobe
underneath the jangling wires.

Honeymooning alone
can't get to sleep without the lights on,
can't swallow all that darkness on my own.
Syrup from the radio's
synthetically soothing late night show
oh remember, remember
then I reach to pop one of those press-stud pills
I keep under the pillow so
my system will still tick next week
on the blink
a little crazily for you.
I can't sleep –
it's as livid as a scar
the white neon striplight
above my vanity bar.

Mirror, Mirror on the wall
does he love me enough,
does he love me at all?
Should I go back
with that celebrated shout?
Did my eyebrows offend you?
Well I've plucked them out.
Oh me and my mudpack,
I can't smile
my face will crack.
I'll come clean.
I've made good new resolutions
re my skincare routine.
Every day
there's a basket of blossomheads,
crumpled kleenex to throw away.
As if I found it easy to discard.

Think hard.
I've got a week to think it over
a shelf full of creams, sweet lotions
I can cover,
smother all my darkness in, smooth it over.
Oh it'll take more than this aerosol
to fix it all, to fix it all.

Mirror's Song

For Sally Potter

Smash me looking-glass glass
coffin, the one
that keeps your best black self on ice.
Smash me, she'll smash back –
without you she can't lift a finger.
Smash me she'll whirl out like Kali,
trashing the alligator mantrap handbags
with her righteous karate.
The ashcan for the stubbed lipsticks
and the lipsticked butts,
the wet lettuce of fivers.
She'll spill the Kleenex blossoms,
the tissues of lies, the matted
nests of hair from the brushes'
hedgehog spikes, she'll junk
the dead mice and the tampons
the twinking single eyes
of winkled out diamanté, the hatpins
the whalebone and lycra,
the appleblossom and the underwires,
the chafing iron that kept them maiden,
the Valium and initialled hankies,
the lovepulps and the Librium,
the permanents and panstick and
Coty and Tangee Indelible,
Thalidomide and junk jewellery.

Smash me for your daughters and dead
mothers, for the widowed
spinsters of the first and every war
let her
rip up the appointment cards for the
terrible clinics,
the Greenham summonses, that date
they've handed us. Let her rip.
She'll crumple all the
tracts and the adverts, shred
all the wedding dresses, snap
all the spike-heel icicles
in the cave she will claw out of –
a woman giving birth to herself.

The Grim Sisters

And for special things
(weddings, school-
concerts) the grown up girls next door
would do my hair.

Luxembourg announced *Amami Night*.

I sat at peace passing bobbipins
from a marshmallow pink cosmetic purse
embossed with jazzmen,
girls with pony tails and a November
topaz lucky birthstone.
They doused my cow's-lick, rollered
and skewered tightly.
I expected that to be lovely
would be worth the hurt.

They read my Stars,
tied chiffon scarves to doorhandles, tried
to teach me tight dancesteps
you'd no guarantee

any partner you might find would ever be able to
keep up with as far as I could see.

There were always things to burn
before the men came in.

For each disaster
you were meant to know the handy hint.
Soap at a pinch
but better nailvarnish (clear) for ladders.
For kisscurls, spit.
Those days womanhood was quite a sticky thing
and that was what these grim sisters came to mean.

'You'll know all about it soon enough.'
But when the clock struck they
stood still, stopped dead.
And they were left there
out in the cold with the wrong skirtlength
and bouffant hair,
dressed to kill,

who'd been
all the rage in fifty-eight,
a swish of Persianelle
a slosh of perfume.
In those big black mantrap handbags
they snapped shut at any hint of *that*
were hedgehog hairbrushes
cottonwool mice and barbed combs to tease.
Their heels spiked bubblegum, dead leaves.

Wasp waist and cone breast, I see them yet.
I hope, I hope
there's been a change of more than silhouette.

from The Furies

I: HARRIDAN

Mad Meg on my mantelpiece,
Dulle Griet by Brueghel, a Flemish masterpiece
in anybody's eyes. 'Well worth historical
                                    consideration'
was how I looked at it. The surrealist tradition
from Bosch to Magritte is such a Flemish thing!
Oh a work of great power, most interesting . . .
I chose it for my History of Art essay, took pains
to enumerate the monsters, reduce it all to picture
                                              planes.
I was scholarly, drew parallels
between Hieronymus Bosch's and Pieter Brueghel's
                                              Hells;
Compared and contrasted
Symbolism and Realism in the Flemish School;
discussed: Was Meg 'mad' or more the
                              Shakespearean Fool?

The fool I was! Mad Meg, Sour-Tongued Margot,
maddened slut in this mass of misery, a Virago,
at her wit's end, running past Hell's Mouth, all
                                        reason gone,
she has one mailed glove, one battered breastplate
                                                on.
Oh that kitchen knife, that helmet, that silent shout,
I know Meg from the inside out.
All she owns in one arm, that lost look in her eyes.
These days I more than sympathise.

Oh I am wild-eyed, unkempt, hellbent, a harridan.
My sharp tongue will shrivel any man.
Should our paths cross
I'll embarrass you with public tears, accuse you with
                                              my loss.

My Mother's Suitors

have come to court me
have come to call oh
yes with their wonderful world
war two moustaches their long
stem roses their cultivated
accents (they're English aren't they
at very least they're
educated-Scots).
They are absolutely
au fait with menu-French
they know the language of flowers
& oh they'd die
rather than send a dozen yellow
they always get them right & red.
Their handwriting on the florist's card
slants neither too much to the left or right.

They are good sorts.
They have the profile for it – note
the not too much nose
the plenty chin. The
stockings they bring have no strings
& their square
capable hands are forever
lifting your hair and gently
pushing your head away from them
to fumble endearingly at your nape
with the clasp of the pretty heirloom
little necklace they know their
grandmother would have wanted
you to have.
(Never opals – they know
that pearls mean tears).

They have come to call & we'll all
go walking under the black sky's
droning big bombers

among the ratatat of ack-ack.
We'll go dancing & tonight
shall I wear the lilac, or the
scarlet, or the white?

VALERIE GILLIES (b. 1948)

Fellow Passenger

Mister B. Rajan, diamond buyer,
crystallises from this travelling companion.
He goes by rail, it seems, by criss
and cross, Hyderabad to Bangalore
to Madras, Madras, Madras,
seeking the industrial diamond.

He brings new orient gems from hiding.
Himself, he wears goldwealthy rings
of ruby, and, for fortune,
another of God Venkateswaran.
His smile is a drillpoint diamond's,
incisive his kindness.

Sparrowboned, he walks unstable passageways,
living on boiled eggs and lady's-fingers
with noggins of whisky to follow.
He dreams of his house, the shrineroom picture
of Sai Baba, corkscrew-haired young saint.
And he has at home beautiful hidden daughters.

The Piano-tuner

Two hundred miles, he had come
        to tune one piano, the last hereabouts.
Both of them were relics of imperial time:
        the Anglo-Indian and the old upright
                                        knockabout.

He peered, and peered again
        into its monsoon-warped bowels.
From the flats of dead sound he'd beckon
        a tune on the bones out to damp vowels.

His own sounds were pidgin.
        The shapeliness of his forearms
lent his body an English configuration,
        but still, sallow as any snakecharmer

he was altogether piebald.
        Far down the bridge of his nose
perched roundrimmed tortoiseshell spectacles;
        his hair, a salt-and-pepper, white foreclosed.

But he rings in the ear yet,
        his interminable tapping of jarring notes:
and, before he left,
        he gave point to those hours of discord.

With a smile heavenly
        because so out of place, cut off from any home
                                                    there,
he sat down quietly
        to play soft music: that tune of 'Beautiful
                                                    Dreamer',

a melody seized from yellowed ivories
        and rotting wood. A damper
muffled the pedal point of lost birthright. We eaves-
        dropped on an extinct creature.

Young Harper

Above Tweed Green levels
Maeve first raises the harp.

Prosper her hand that plucks
then clenches fist like a jockey.

Grip inside thighs
the colt with a cropped mane.

Turn blades on the curved neck
bristling with spigots.

Out from the rosewood forest
came this foal of strung nerve.

Stand in your grainy coat,
let her lift elbows over you.

Keep her thumbs bent
and fingers hard to do the playing.

Eight summers made them, clarsach,
I freely give you my elder daughter.

The Ericstane Brooch

The gold cross-bow brooch,
The Emperors' gift to an officer,
Was lost on the upland moor.
The pierced work and the inscription
Lay far from human habitation.

It worked on time and space
And they were at work on it.
What could withstand them?
But it was waiting for the human,
To address itself to a man or woman.

In the wilderness it meant nothing.
The great spaces dissolved its image,
Time obliterated its meaning.
Without being brought in,
It was less than the simplest safety-pin.

Now the brooch is transporting the past
To the present, the far to the near.
Between the two, its maker and wearer

And watcher live mysteriously.
Who is this who values it so seriously?

It exists, it has been seen by him.
If it speaks, it can only say
'He lost me.' And we reply, 'Who?
For he can also be our loss,
This moment floating face-down in the moss.'

Dumb replica: the original is in Los Angeles.
How is it, the man once destroyed,
His brooch continues boundlessly?
Our very existence is what it defies:
We no longer see what once we scrutinized.

RON BUTLIN (b. 1949)

This Evening

You placed yellow roses by the window, then,
leaning forwards, began combing your red hair;
perhaps you were crying.
To make the distance less I turned away
and faced you across the earth's circumference.

The window-pane turns black:
across its flawed glass suddenly your image
runs on mine.
I stare at the vase until yellow
is no longer a colour, nor the roses flowers.

Night-life

My nerves are stretched tight above the city:
a night-map of neon and sodium.

Hours earlier you wore darkness as love itself:
moonlight you ground more finely with each kiss,
starlight you scattered out of reach.

And now, what burning inside me?
what light trapped in a clenched sky?

Inheritance

Although there are nettles here, and thorns,
you will not be stung. Trust me. I've something
to show you made from twigs, bird-spittle, down
and journeyings in all weathers.
See how easily your hand covers
the nest and its eggs. How weightless they are.
Your fingernail, so very much smaller than mine,

can trace the delicate shell's blue veins
until they crack apart, letting silence
spill into your hand. There is a sense
of separation almost too great to bear
– and suddenly you long to crush all colour
from these pale blue eggs, for in their brief
fragility you recognise as grief
the overwhelming tenderness you feel.
    This is your inheritance:
your fist clenched on yolk and broken shell,
on fragments of an unfamiliar tense.

Claiming My Inheritance

I paused, then briefly tried to clear the mess
of yolk-slime and albumen. My distress
was private: I could not explain
what made me run home faster than
I ever ran before.

                    Since then I've taken pains
to learn the language of what's done and said
(in restaurants, in stations, on the beach, in bed)
to friends (observing gender, number, business/
                                            social),
my fellow-guests and God. For interpersonal
dynamics read *non-verbal empathy*: offence
or reinforcement at a glance. I'm quick to sense
unhappiness in others – that reassuring smile
(too well-timed), that altered tone of voice. My skill
at recognising joy is rather minimal,
however – seeming to suggest
the world is one vast Rorschach test.
I've learnt the words for things and feelings: how and
                                            when
to use them. In making conversation,
love and enemies I take especial care
no accent-lapse, no unfamiliar
tense construction, clumsy phrase

or hesitation (worst of all) betrays
I am a foreigner.

After I had crushed the eggs. A pause:

as if the colours of the earth and sky –

as if all laws affirming spontaneity –

As if the present tense were happening too soon
the fence I stood beside became a wooden thing,
the gate was iron-lengths – heated, hammered, bent
and riveted in place years earlier. I leant
against it. I struck it, but could not animate the dead
place to suffer for me. Instead,
the emptiness that stained
the empty sky above me blue,
gave definition to
my isolation.
Only this completed world remained.

The older I become the more
I am aware of exile, of longing for –

I clench my fist on nothing and hold on.

RAYMOND VETTESE (b. 1950)

Prologue

Ae nicht I sat by mysel at the fire
except   and thocht. Nae soond in the street forbyes
the wun blawin thro the telephone wire.
stars   A quarter-muin gied but sma licht, starns,
in clood, barely shone: a dour compromise
'twixt soond, silence, dairk, licht –
brains   the ootward cast o the state o my harns,
caught in a whirl, sometimes sure   catched in a swither, whiles shair o the richt,
wrung/troubled   whiles thrawed wi doot . . . this maitter's fasht me
                                   lang,
th' uprisin o Scots, och, I micht be wrang.

all this could but waste   Mebbe aa this cuid but connach braith.
many a fool pursued a choice   There's monie a gow gaed aifter a wile,
certain of it, yet found, dejected,
sore death   fu-shair o't, yet fun', disjaskit, sair daith,
pledge   no hecht o life. Ay, and sae it micht be
my trifling flowery style   wi mysel, and my foot'rin phraisie style:
petulant/worn-out   snashgab, nocht mair, a silly dashelt screed,
bummlin aboot, barmy on words, skinkin orra bree* –
ach, the thocht o the waste is whit I maist dreid,
a lifetime pursuing   waste o span hundin a deein cause,
my thick bluid dreepin clause by clause.

doubtful*   Whit's the point in this dootsum endeavour
tae bring back whit's lang gane, whit purpose?
Mebbe the fowk wha say it's gane forever
are richt, and mèbbe I should turn awa
bound to this   frae sic daft notions. Yet I'm thirlt til this,
I canna gie it owre, it's stuck in me
beyond reason.   like faith, ayont reason. It's my weird's caa,
destiny's summons
boast   or sae I blaw, tae shaw whit it micht be,
this language, used/whim   this leid, yased aricht. That's mebbe a fraik
challenge/path   but's the brag that sets me oot on this raik.

---

* *skinkin orra bree* pouring leftover liquor from one dish to another; *dootsum* also formidable

I hae a vision o Scotland set free

is one

and freedom and language tae me is ane.
I hae a vision that Scotland micht be
itsel again, its present and its past

united

souderet for the future's sake, tho the pain
o Freedom's no easy nor wantin doot
and whiles I dae nocht but staun aghast

seeping

from assurance/half-night

at the thocht o't, feel the strength sypin oot
frae sickerness, as I dae this hauf-nicht
fu o gloamin unease, an' dootsum licht.

nimble feet stamp in the empty
street beyond

The toon is quiet, only noo and then
swippert feet dunt in the tuim street ayont.
I sit and think on the likely again,

question

final/a downfall not lit

with a last flicker/dreary drizzle

lively hope

on such a night when
I must rise above the mire* of
disquiet
flounder/woe-scooping
an idle fool

speir the chances o mendin, the chances
o hinmaist decline, a doonfaa no alunt
wi ae laist leam, but dairk wi dreich smirr
o lichtless silence. Nae gleg hope dances
on sic a nicht whaun nae sunk life can stir,
yet I maun rise abuin the lair o wanrufe
or slutter in't, wae-gowpin, a slottery coof.

strange [foreign] direction

search/star

weary thoughts/strike out

released

perhaps/floundering

haven/must be

I set my compass tae a fremmit airt,
reenge aifter yon driven starn, let it lead
whaur it will, ayont stoundin fearfu hairt;
fling aff my trauchelt thochts and stramp oot
on the lang traik til the truth in my heid
that winna be lowsed save in words like these.
It's aiblins daft, this ploiter o pursuit
owre bitter acres whaur the braith micht freeze,
but it's the ae gait, I doot, for me.
Somewhaur the bield and the green maun be.

* *lair* also lore, learning

My Carrion Words

In deep
o dairk sleep
I dreamt my words
gaithert like stairvin birds
on a bare tree
and skreiched owre me
cough   wi carrion hoast:
Lost! Lost!

and then   And syne
would lose   I ran, wad tine
sobbing   that greetin
forsaken   o things forleeten
intense darkness   i the muckle dairk,
anxiety   but aye the cark
murmured in the background   souched ahent:
beware!   Tak tent! Tent!

Whaun I woke
the day spoke
wi anither voice
purred pleasant choice   that croodled douce choice:
give up this nonsense,
this pretence;
what's gone is gone, here's
English for contemporary ears.

But ach, I doot
I'm no cut oot
for sic mense
weakened language   (that's dowit leid for 'common sense');
the auld coorse Scotland's in me,
an' the bare tree
an' the stairvin birds:
frae sic as them, frae yon, my carrion words.

The Vieve Cry

Gloss	
living	
sullenly	Dour-hunched in a drizzle
wearisome	o dreich November
enveloped in mist	or smoort in haar
	frae bitter North Sea
forlorn	this toon's forlane.
	Yet I've seen
	yon steeple-vane
shine above [and in good fettle]	skyre abuin
as if unafraid of anything it would crow	as gin unfleggit o ocht it wad craw
brazen-faced on everything	braisant on aa!
	In dourest season
near-extinct	o near-tint sun
cheerfulness	that crouseness vaunts
shadows	oot o shaddas,
chill wind-blasted narrow alleys	oot a snell-wun narra wynds,
beyond/into	an' ayont, intil nicht,
barren	whaur hirsty fields
	streetch cauld
embrace in toil [or darkness?]	yet hause in dairk
power	the starry maucht o seed.
sad [and infertile]	In dowf season,
dismal	dowie, deid still,
above	abuin frozen braith,
	I hear it:
death-grip distorts	the vieve cry nae daith-grupp thraws.

TOM POW (b. 1950)

part two of The Gift of Sight

SAINT MEDAN

That Medan was beautiful,
  there was no doubt.
Wherever she went,
  hearts were routed.

But, to her, these looks
  were but a costume
she couldn't cast off.
  She saw her fortune

not in the fancy
  of romantic play –
it was in inner things
  her interests lay.

Medan took a vow
  of chastity; her life
she bound to Christ.
  It was a sharp knife

in the hearts of men.
  But one noble knight
did not believe her.
  To quit his sight

she left Ireland
  for green Galloway.
To the Rhinns she came,
  to live in poverty.

The knight followed.
  He would die or wed

his heart's crusade.
    Pure Medan now fled

to a rock in the sea.
    With prayer, the rock
became a boat;
    the boat she took

thirty miles away.
    Still, he followed;
blindly obeying
    what the hollow

in his heart called for.
    He'd have been lost,
but a crowing cock –
    to both their costs –

told him the house
    where Medan lay.
Shaken, she climbed
    and she prayed

as she climbed
    into a thorn tree.
From there, she asked,
    'What do you see

in me to excite
    your passion?' 'Your face
and eyes,' he replied.
    She sighed, 'In which case . . .'

then impaled her eyes
    on two sharp thorns
and flung them at him.
    Desire was torn

forever from that knight.
    He looked at his feet,

where the eyes had rolled –
    lustrous jade, now meat

for ants. Horror-struck,
    he left – a penitent.
Medan washed her face,
    for a spring – heaven-sent –

gurgled from the dry earth.
    The rest of her days
were lived in poverty
    and sanctity. (*Praise*

the Lord, sang Ninian.)
    The proud cock half-lived,
but crowed no more.
    And sight became the gift

Saint Medan gave,
    so that all could suffer
in equal measure,
    beauty and terror.

BRIAN MCCABE (b. 1951)

Spring's Witch

I wait out winter plagued by your ghost –
impatient rains whisper, winds rumour you,
caressing the skins of my windows,
speaking into the ears of my chimneys:

She's coming, say the rains.
As before, wind says.

And you do, one dark March day:
loud and chaotic, incanting your 'ohs',
no prim Primavera, no flowers-in-toes,
but cackling as you cast off your clothes.

She's here, say the rains.
As before, wind says.

Your black hair is treacled by the rain.
You raise the wand and you conjure again
whatever love I have for living
from this world's rebirth in spring.

She's leaving, say the rains.
Gone, gone, wind says.

The Blind

The blind old men who come arm in arm
On good-smelling days to the park,
Grateful to the girl who brings them
Since they seldom have the chance
Of a slow, recollective game of bowls.
The sun that signs their faces
With smudge-like marks where eyes were
Suggests to their memories a notion

Of green, and summer days ago.
Taking pleasure from the silence of grass
And the weight of the wood in the hand,
They engross themselves in the game
They play by sound intuition:
The girl is young, sighted.
She stands at the far end of darkness
And claps her hands – once, twice –
And then the first bowler stoops,
As if about to kneel and be blessed,
Then throws to her clapping hands.
As the dark wood is travelling the green
She waits, motionless, and waits
As if by any slight move she might alter
The swing and slowing of the bowl.
When it halts, she bows, she measures,
Then calls its distance, its 'time':
'*Seven feet, at four o'clock.*'
Again she claps her hands.
Another player stoops, lets go . . .
This time it comes closer, close enough
To enter the young girl's shadow.
When it kisses the jack, there's a 'cloc'.

The old men smile.

This is Thursday

The key argues with the lock
before the ward door is opened
and a male nurse orders me in.
I note the military manner,
the clipped moustache, explain
I'm an old friend of hers
come to visit on impulse.
He nods, inspects my appearance
and suggests that I wait here.
'Here' is a windowless room
where television tells the news

to a range of empty chairs.
A chalked blackboard declares
that this is Thursday.
I wish it wasn't, aware
of the custard-yellow walls
and someone's hand over there —
waving to me, and to no one.
A pale plant starved of light
wilts in its own dim corner.
I ask myself: How could anyone
leap from a tenement window
and land in this dark asylum?
And I wait. Wait for the present
to step out of the past. Then,
across a wasteland of years,
through a fog of sedation,
my old friend looks at me again
with her violated eyes.

GERALD MANGAN (b. 1951)

Glasgow 1956

There's always a headscarf stooped
into a pram, nodding in time
with a plastic rattle, outside a shop
advertising a sale of wallpaper.

There's a queue facing another queue
like chessmen across the street;
a hearse standing at a petrol-pump
as the chauffeur tests the tyres,

the undertaker brushes ash off
his morning paper, and my mother,
looking down at me looking up,
is telling me not to point.

The background is a level site
where we recreate the war.
Calder Street is Calder Street,
level as far as the Clyde.

Without a tree to denote it,
the season is moot. That faint
thunder is the Cathcart tram,
and the sky is white as a trousseau

posed against blackened bricks.
A grey posy in her hands,
the bride stands smiling there
for decades, waiting for the click.

Heraclitus at Glasgow Cross

Where Gallowgate meets London Road
    and the world walks out with his wife,

umbrellas sail in long flotillas
  through streets you can't cross twice.

The old home town looks just the same
  when you step down off the Sixty-Three.
The jukebox music takes you back
  to the green, green grass of Polmadie.

drizzle   Everything swarms and eddies in smirr.
                  Wine flows out from the Saracen's Head.
                Mascara runs, like soot from a guttering.
                  Day-glo signs glow green on red.

Something for Everyone. Nothing for Nothing.
  Social Security Estimates Free.
It's Scotland's Friendliest Market-Place.
  Watch Your Handbags, Ladies, Please.

Watch the Do-nuts fry in grease,
  the tailgate-auctioneers compete
with the broken-winded squeezebox player,
  wheezing through his leaking pleats.

Or under Clyde Street's railway arches,
  see the stubbled dossers soak
like debris snagged in shallows, blowing
  old Virginia up in smoke.

Down where the fishwives trade in rags,
  they curl like snails in paper shells:
lips of sponge, skins of mould,
  eyes like cinders doused in hell.

They're watching concrete fill the docks,
  the bollards rust on the graving-quays.
The green green grass grows overhead,
  on gantries still as gallows-trees.

Where Gorbals faces Broomielaw,
  the river's black and still as ice.

When the ferryman takes the fare, he says
You can cross this river twice.

Nights in Black Valley

Hours when nothing but the rumours
of the mountain fill your ears:
the vixen wailing, or the whisper of rain
as a cloud caresses the roof.

Hours when nothing moves in the house
but the spider and its thread,
the candle spilling its tallow
when the draught disturbs it,

or the grubs worming from the log,
shrivelling into the flame.
The eye of the dog is entranced,
and his shadow is a behemoth.

In the morning when the light breaks up
the conspiracy of mists,
and the flock flows down to the water
like a liquid finding its level,

the time comes round to choose
what to leave and what to take
back to the electricity.
And I memorise the silence:

the moon sliding on the lough,
as the stars endure their space.
And the hawk stropping his beak,
like an axe dreaming of wood.

ANDREW GREIG (b. 1951)

In the Tool-shed

'Hummingbirds' he said, and spat. Winged tongues
hovered in the half-light of their names;
cat, cobra, cockatoo rose hissing from the juice.
Piece-time in Africa, amid the terrapins
and jerrycans! Steam swirled above the Congo
of his cup, mangrove-rooted fingers plugged the air –
'Baboons? Make sure you look them in eyes.' Birds
of paradise! Parrots, paraffin, parakeets
flashed blue and raucous through
thickets of swoe, scythe, riddle, adze.
He sat bow-backed and slack in the dark
heart of his kingdom – creator, guide
in that jungle of sounds, boxes, cloches, canes,
twine, twill, galoshes, jumbled all
across, over, through and into one another
from floor to roof, prowled by fabled carnivores,
the jaguar! the secateurs! Words poke
wet muzzles through reeds of sound
grown enormous overnight. Twin depths
of pitch and pitcher! Elephants lean
patiently upon their ponderous names.
They come in clutches: azaleas, zebras, zambesi.
Orchids, oranges, oran-utangs hang
from their common mouth. Lemming, gorilla, lynx
slink nose to tail through mango groves,
drenched in this sibilant monsoon: moonstone,
                                                    machetes,
peacocks, paw-paws, lepers, leopards – the walls
are creaking but hold them all, swaying, sweating,
in that dark continent between the ears.
Easy, easy genesis! Old witchdoctor, gardener,
deity of the shed, I grew that garden
from his words, caught the fever
pitch of his Niagara; I follow still
the Orinoco of his blue forearm veins

that beat among the talking drums
of all my childhood afternoons.

The Winter Climbing

(For Marj)

It is late January and at last the snow.
I lie back dreaming about Glencoe
as fluent, hungry, dressed in red,
you climb up and over me. That passion
claimed the darkest, useless months
for risk and play. You rise
up on me, I rise through you . . .

The shadowed face of Aonach Dubh
where Mal first took me climbing
and as we clanked exhausted, happy,
downwards through the dark, I asked
'What route was that?' 'Call it
what you want – it's new.'

You reach the top and exit out;
from way above, your cry comes down.
The rope pulls tight. What shall we call
this new thing we're about?
These days we live in taking
care and chances. Why name it?
My heart is in my mouth as I shout *Climbing* . . .

The Maid & I

'At this stage, I work most closely with the Maid.'
                    New York composer of film scores

It's nothing personal when she slips in
at half-dawn, half-dusk, any drifting
time of day, to make mere solitude complete.
That's how come we get on
so well, so long. You smile, you picture

black seamed stockings, white muslin crown
on hair that's poised to be let down? No,
she is not Naughty Lola –
nor Mrs Mopp! With us it is
importunate to talk or stare;
touch is right out. This fortunate
proximity is all we share.

She has arrived.
You are in the backroom,
by the Steinway, fiddling with the Blues.
You hear her humming as she moves
among the papers and abandoned meals, clearing up
the ashtrays, scripts and coffee cups,
the litter of aloneness. Redeeming fingers touch
your old scores lightly, as if it were yourself
she dusts and settles on the shelf. Praise the maid
who sets out flowers and white clouds
where you might see them and be glad!
The shambles would be total were it not for her.

Now she is singing an old refrain
you can't quite . . . The sky
is pale, washed clean by rain,
hung up against the evening.
As you attend, a melody floats
through apartment walls so intimately
it is as though you quote yourself –
debris is sorted, order
is invented or restored.
Now she is done. You will work on alone
but that's all right. Grace must have its means.
She flicks the light on as she leaves.

FRANK KUPPNER (b. 1951)

Passing Through Doorways

I

i

I can no longer remain in this building,
Not after this latest turn of events;
After I have shut the door, my watch says 9.26;
I walk down those few stairs again, determined,
                      above all, to pass time.

ii

Having spent all my life not merely in one city,
But in a tightly circumscribed part of one city,
I find that most of the significant doors in my life
Opened and shut within a few minutes of each other.

iii

A leisurely evening walk could unite the four of
                            them;
Have I really never gone on such a walk before?
It is autumn, and again the sky is completely dark;
It is the wrong time of the evening to have crowds on
                            the streets.

II

iv

After twenty minutes, and hardly more than four
                            roads,
I am once again in the street where I was born;
Closer with every footstep to the very house;
I hurry guiltily up the steps into the tenement close.

v

I climbed those steps countless times in the 1950s;
I descended those steps countless times in the 1960s;
In the 1970s I visited the place, I think, once;
And this is my first visit of the 1980s.

vi

The names on the doors were mostly those they had
                                        always been;
I crept by them, hand caressing the banister,
Unhappy at the apparent shortage of steps,
By their narrowness, by how deeply worn they were.

vii

For, in all the many times I climbed those stairs,
Hundred upon differentiated hundred,
Perhaps still warehoused within the memory,
Sufficient to erode from it the width of a skin,

viii

From my first, stumbling, partly aided steps,
Wearing small spectacles and a very round face,
Followed by a mother, or preceded by a larger sister,
Who now has two effortlessly walking sons in a
                                        house on the coast

ix

To the routine exhaustion of yet another evening,
Dragging my way round the corners of the banister,
Sunlight through the windows upon me and a grimy
                                        football,
As I climbed towards my mother's call, and cold
                                water gulped too quickly,

x

And the insecure rushing of an adolescent,
Propelled by the moment's enthusiasm to a record
                                                shop,
Now obliterated, to a park, to a tv programme,
To an illustrated dictionary of medical terms,

xi

I doubt if it ever once occurred to me,
That 50, 70 and 30 years before,
Equivalent breath was expelled from roughly equal
                                                lungs,
In other people's passages of the same stairway.

xii

Now, I am fascinated by such, as it were, pauses in
                                                life,
As being closer to what life normally is
Than the supreme events which documents tend to
                                                fill with,
As if only spectacular oceans are deep.

xiii

My door has changed beyond recognition;
The least recognisable part of an unrecognisable
                                                place;
Reinforced blocks of wood over the lock
Show where some people have tried to force their
                                                way in.

xiv

When, in my dreams I pass through that door so
                                                often,
Why does seeing it with real eyes not seem like a
                                                homecoming?
What door is it then that I pass through in my
                                                dreams?

I return down the dark stairway, too tall for that
                                                building.

xv

And down even to the stairway to the back-court;
Ill-lit, a place of fear to me as a child;
When, carrying down ashes at an untimely hour,
The sight of such a man as I am now,

xvi

Standing, for obscure purposes, at the entrance to the
                                                back garden,
Feeling the high wall of a garage too oppressively
                                                near,
Puzzled by the widespread, moonlit vegetation,
Would have terrified me into immediate retreat;

xvii

The enormously heavy bucket resting against my leg,
As I half-carried, half-levered it along,
The heat of a dead fire still burning at its sides;
Stopping in silence at the turns, to rest my hands.

xviii

So I walked up, from that implausible moonlight,
Into the implausible lamplight of the stairs;
For a second or two, in the turn at the top of the
                                                flight,
Being in the same time in my dreams and in my
                                                childhood;

xix

And continued down a shrunken corridor,
Onto a street abandoned for at most five minutes,
Which would take me off to other destinations,
Unsuspected through the previous 4,001 such exits.

III

xx

As I walk, some minutes later, into the other
                                            building,
It seems even less probable that I have done so
                                            before;
How often was it? A dozen? Two dozen times?
I have made so little impression on this stonework.

xxi

And yet, it is exactly the correct size;
The windows still retain their appropriate views;
I simply did not visit it often enough,
During the years she used to live here with him.

xxii

On what stair did I stop her from the back,
Lean forward over her newly-washed hair,
And inhale its unparalleled perfume, while she stood,
Motionless, in unusual docility?

xxiii

It seems to me I did not really live through those
                                            days;
As it seemed, at the time, so utterly improbable
That, at the top of those curving ordinary stairs,
I could knock at a door and have her answer it.

xxiv

I did not understand then, and do not understand
                                            now,
How such a banal building could contain her;
How her tears could be deadened by such walls;
How these same graceless stairs could daily accept
                                            her feet.

xxv

I do not yet know into what fragments
That particular star exploded when it did explode;
But that some sort of displacement has occurred
At some time during my consecutive years of absence

xxvi

Became obvious as soon as I reached the point
At the very top, when the door became visible:
A heavy chair was propped against its exterior;
The well-remembered nameplate had been removed;

xxvii

And so, knowing that such things were happening
                                    beyond me,
Whether they involved me in the slightest or not,
I picked my way hurriedly back down the stairway,
Hoping, above all else, to meet no-one quite yet.

IV

xxviii

In less than three minutes, another building received
                                            me,
Where she had lived when first I got to know her;
A wider, more spacious stairway than the others,
Leading to a door that opened for me scarcely ten
                                            times.

xxix

As I stood here, looking at a list of names,
On which, for some reason, her own did not appear,
A vague suggestion of noise behind it unnerved me,
And I hurried away before I had intended to.

xxx

Before I had had time to remember such moments
As her padding barefoot behind me to the door,
Asking me to tell her what was wrong:
Something is wrong, isn't it, something is wrong?

xxxi

And I said to her, no, nothing is wrong;
And hurried down the stairway as quickly as this;
Hearing her close the door above me after a longish
                                                    pause,
And reaching the street, in acute misery.

V

xxxii

Half an hour later, I reach the fourth doorway,
The one I am most recently aware of,
Utterly unconnected with the others,
Behind which, I now feel, lies future happiness.

xxxiii

Like the doorway I started out from, it too is on the
                                                ground floor;
And so far, the only unhappiness I have known there
Is the unhappiness of having to leave too early;
No doubt other unhappinesses will arrive in time.

xxxiv

But ah, what hopes I have of the fair occupant!
There will come an evening of stunning buoyancy,
When our nerves and our cautiousness will cancel
                                                each other out,
And love will turn that surprised air to liquid gold.

XXXV

But, at the moment, I am still a semi-stranger,
And must behave as such an oddity should;
Carefully stopping to listen outside her door,
Trying to hear her words, or the silence that is hers.

xxxvi

And then, leaning forward to the nameplate,
Delighted at the precision with which the lettering
Makes an unequivocal public reference to her,
Perhaps (surely not) the only such reference in the
                                                city,

xxxvii

Delicately placing a lingering kiss on the nameplate,
And, even as I did so, feeling oddly proud
At being the author of that sublimated gesture,
Ridiculously immature for a man of my age.

xxxviii

There is still enough time, I hope, for the mature
                                              gesture;
I have wasted almost an hour and half, all told,
And require from here scarcely ten minutes for home.
Still there are very few people in the streets.

xxxix

And, although the city lies open to the public,
Can anyone else, in the course of a single day,
Have strung precisely those four buildings together?
A doctor, perhaps; or policemen; or only myself.

xl

Surely, even in the complexity of autobiography,
Those four doors have not opened on anyone else's
                                                life?

And those wandering restlessly along the streets
Are going to different places, in different orders.

xli

I open and shut the door of my own house;
I hurry across the common corridor,
Trying not to hear voices in other rooms,
Reach my own room, and close the door behind me.

ANGUS MARTIN (b. 1952)

Malcolm MacKerral

MacKerral, that was one hard winter.
Your father died on the moor road,
his bag of meal buried under snows.
Death relieved him of his load.

Raking wilks with freezing fingers,
your little sisters crawled the shore,
scourged by gusting showers
until their knees were raw and sore.

Your few black cattle, thin and famished,
lay and died at the far end
of the draughty common dwelling.
There was little else you owned.

In the factor's oaken-panelled room
that the shafting sunlight glossed
you looked for your reflection:
you had become a ghost.

That month a stranger entered
the green cleft of the glen.
You watched him coming, from a hill,
and stabbed the earth again.

When he returned he brought the sheep.
At the house where you were born
you closed a door behind you.
Two hundred years had gone.

There was no end to the known land.
You looked, and there were names
on every shape around you.
The language had its homes.

Words had their lives in rivers;
they coursed them to the sea.
Words were great birds on mountains,
crying down on history.

Words were stones that waited
in the silence of the fields
for the voices of the people
whose tenures there had failed.

You knew those names, MacKerral;
your father placed them in your mouth
when language had no tragic power
and you ran in your youth.

You ran in the house of the word
and pressed your face upon the glass
and watched the mute processions
of your grave ancestors pass.

Look back on what you cannot alter.
Not a stone of it is yours to turn.
All that you leave with now:
lost words for the unborn.

Forest

For Sid Gallagher

Since I lately came to live
in an old house with a fire in it,
wood has got into my vision.

I put my saw to wood
and glance a nick, and then I cut
wood into bits that please me.

Weight and form may please me,
and I am pleased to own
what at last I have to burn.

I am a Scottish wood-collector;
I belong to a great tradition
of bleeding hands and thick coats.

Wood accumulates about me;
I build it into piles,
I bag it and I lug it.

I love the look of wood:
its surfaces are maps and pictures,
and staring eyes and voiceless mouths.

Wood to the end is unresisting:
it lets me lift and drag it
far from the place that it lay down.

Wood will never fight
the blade's truncating stroke
or scream when fire consumes it.

But I had dreams of wood.
I was alone in a high forest,
sun and seasons banished.

The trees bent down their silent heads
and closed their branches round about
and I was gathered into air.

I burn in my dreams of wood,
a melting torch suspended
in the dark heart of a silent forest.

JOHN GLENDAY (b. 1952)

The Apple Ghost

A musty smell of dampness filled the room
Where wrinkled green and yellow apples lay
On folded pages from an August newspaper.

She said:
'*My husband brought them in, you understand,*
Only a week or two before he died.
He never had much truck with waste, and
I can't bring myself to throw them out.
He passed away so soon . . .'

I understood then how the wonky kitchen door,
And the old Austin, settling upon its
Softened tyres in the wooden shed,
Were paying homage to the absence of his quiet
                                                    hands.

In the late afternoon, I opened
Shallow cupboards where the sunlight leaned on
Shelf over shelf of apples, weightless with decay.
Beneath them, sheets of faded wallpaper
Showed ponies prancing through a summer field.
This must have been the only daughter's room
Before she left for good.

I did not sleep well.

The old woman told me over breakfast
How the boards were sprung in that upper hall;
But I knew I had heard his footsteps in the night,
As he dragged his wasted body to the attic room
Where the angles of the roof slide through the walls,
And the fruit lay blighted by his helpless gaze.

I knew besides that, had I crossed to the window
On the rug of moonlight,
I would have seem him down in the frosted garden,
Trying to hang the fruit back on the tree.

DILYS ROSE (b. 1954)

Figurehead

The fog thickens.
I see no ships.
The gulls left days ago

Ebbing into the wake
Like friends grown tired
Of chasing failure.

I miss their uncouth snatch and grab
Their loud insatiable hunger.
I see nothing but fog.

Before my ever-open eyes
The horizon has closed in
The world's end dissolved.

I lumber on, grudging my status –
I'm purpose-built to dip and toss
My cleavage, crudely carved

To split waves
My hair caked with salt
My face flaking off.

Fetish

Whisper if you must
But the walls absorb all confession
    – I've run through this ritual so often
    If he insists, I make a confession
    Kid on his demand has me truly enthralled
    If that's not sufficient try *deeply appalled.*

Your wish, for the moment, is my command
I'm mistress of every disguise
Is it rubber fur leather or silk I've to use
To pull the wool over your eyes?
Watch me concoct your burning obsession
Spell out your lust, own up to your passion.

So that's all it was that you wanted
A secret so paltry – I'd never have guessed
It could send a man scouring the town.
A scrap of mock silk – I'm no longer impressed.
You looked like the type who'd know I don't tout
My quality goods. See yourself out.

JOHN BURNSIDE (b. 1955)

Out of Exile

When we are driving through the border towns
we talk of houses, empty after years
of tea and conversation;
of afternoons marooned against a clock
and silences elected out of fear,
of lives endured for what we disbelieved.

We recognise the shop fronts and the names,
the rushing trees and streets into the dark;
we recognise a pattern in the sky:
blackness flapping like a broken tent,
shadow foxes running in the stars.
But what we recognise is what we bring.

Driving, early, through the border towns,
the dark stone houses clanging at our wheels,
and we invent things as they might have been:
a light switched on, some night, against the cold,
and children at the door, with bags and coats,
telling stories, laughing, coming home.

Vallejo

Me moriré en París con aguacero

I dreamed of you in Paris:

you opened a door and stepped in from the rain
and you were standing in the hallway of
the eternal Thursday where all the dead
wait in their rented rooms;

you smelled the wax and burning vegetables
and the stale rain in your winter coat

as you climbed the stairs of
the eternal Thursday; ten francs

paid in advance to lie down
in your cold suit of hunger
beside mother and brothers and tortured bulls
in the long bed of the eternal Thursday

in the Paris of dreams where bleeding angels
hover like flies in the drapery of rain.

CAROL ANN DUFFY (b. 1955)

Politico

Corner of Thistle Street, two slack shillings jangled
in his pocket. Wee Frank. Politico. A word in the
right ear
got things moving. *A free beer for they dockers
and the guns will come through in the morning. No*
bother.

Bread rolls and Heavy came up the rope to the
window
where he and McShane were making a stand.
Someone
sent up a megaphone, for Christ's sake. Occupation.
Aye. And the soldiers below just biding their time.

loathesome person   Blacklisted. Bar L.* *That scunner, Churchill.* The
Clyde
where men cheered theirselves out of work as
champagne
butted a new ship. Spikes at the back of the toilet
seat.
Alls I'm doing is fighting for wur dignity. Away.

*Smoke-filled rooms? Wait till I tell you . . . Listen,
I'm ten years dead and turning in my urn. Socialism?
These days?* There's the tree that never grew. *Och,
a shower of shites.* There's the bird that never flew.

Plainsong

Stop. Along this path, in phrases of light,
trees sing their leaves. No Midas touch
has turned the wood to gold, late in the year

* Bar L. Barlinnie Prison

when you pass by, suddenly sad, straining
to remember something you're sure you knew.

Listening. The words you have for things die
in your heart, but grasses are plainsong,
patiently chanting the circles you cannot repeat
or understand. This is your homeland,
Lost One, Stranger who speaks with tears.

It is almost impossible to be here and yet
you kneel, no one's child, absolved by late sun
through the branches of a wood, distantly
the evening bell reminding you, *Home, Home,
Home*, and the stone in your palm telling the time.

In Your Mind

The other country, is it anticipated or half-
                                      remembered?
Its language is muffled by the rain which falls all
                                      afternoon
one autumn in England, and in your mind
you put aside your work and head for the airport
with a credit card and a warm coat you will leave
on the plane. The past fades like newsprint in the
                                      sun.

You know people there. Their faces are photographs
on the wrong side of your eyes. A beautiful boy
in the bar on the harbour serves you a drink –
                                    what? –
asks you if men could possibly land on the moon.
A moon like an orange drawn by a child. No.
Never. You watch it peel itself into the sea.

Sleep. The rasp of carpentry wakes you. On the wall,
a painting lost for thirty years renders the room
                                    yours.

Of course. You go to your job, right at the old hotel,
                                                  left,
then left again. You love this job. Apt sounds
mark the passing of the hours. Seagulls. Bells. A flute
practising scales. You swap a coin for a fish on the
                                          way home.

Then suddenly you are lost but not lost, dawdling
on the blue bridge, watching six swans vanish
under your feet. The certainty of place turns on the
                                            lights
all over town, turns up the scent on the air. For a
                                          moment
you are there, in the other country, knowing its
                                            name.
And then a desk. A newspaper. A window. English
                                            rain.

MICK IMLAH (b. 1956)

Goldilocks

This is a story about the possession of beds.
It begins at the foot of a staircase in Oxford, one
                                        midnight,
When (since my flat in the suburbs of London
                                        entailed
A fiancée whose claims I did not have the nerve to
                                        evict)

I found myself grateful for climbing alone on a spiral
To sleep I could call with assurance exclusively mine,
For there was the name on the oak that the Lodge
                                        had assigned
Till the morning to me (how everything tends to its
                                        place!)

And flushed with the pleasing (if not unexpected)
                                        success
Of the paper on 'Systems of Adult-to-Infant
                                        Regression'
With which the Young Fireball had earlier baffled his
                                        betters
At the Annual Excuse for Genetics to let down its
                                        ringlets,

I'd just sniggered slightly (pushing the unlocked door
Of the room where I thought there was nothing of
                                        mine to protect)
To observe that my theory, so impudent in its
                                        address
To the Masters of Foetal Design and their perfect
                                        disciples,

Was rubbish – and leant to unfasten the window a
                                        notch, –

When I suddenly grasped with aversion before I
could
                                           see it
The fact that the bed in the corner directly behind me
Had somebody in it. A little ginger chap,

Of the sort anthropologists group in the genus of
                                       tramp,
Was swaddled, as though with an eye to the state of
                                   the sheets,
With half of his horrible self in the pouch of the
                                   bedspread
And half (both his raggled and poisonous trouser-
                                 legs) out;

Whose snore, like the rattle of bronchial stones in a
                                 bucket,
Resounded the length and the depth and the breadth
                              of the problem
Of how to establish in safety a climate conducive
To kicking him out – till at last I could suffer no
                                 longer

The sight of his bundle of curls on my pillow, the
                                 proof
That even the worst of us look in our sleep like the
                                 angels
Except for a few. I closed to within a yard
And woke him, with a curt hurrahing sound.

And he reared in horror, like somebody late for work
Or a debutante subtly apprised of a welcome
                                 outstayed,
To demand (not of me, but more of the dreary
                                 familiar
Who exercised in its different styles the world's

Habit of persecution, and prodded him now)
Phit time is it? – so you'd think that it made any
                                 difference –

So you'd think after all that the berth had a rota
                                        attached
And Ginger was wise to some cynical act of
                                        encroachment;

But when, with a plausible echo of fatherly firmness,
I answered, 'It's bedtime' – he popped out and stood
                                        in a shiver,
And the released smell of his timid existence swirled
Like bracing coffee between our dissimilar stances.

Was there a dim recollection of tenement stairways
And jam and the Rangers possessed him, and
                                        sounded a moment
In creaks of remorse? 'Ah'm sorry, son – Ah
                                        couldnae tell
They'd hae a wee boy sleepin here – ye know?'

(And I saw what a file of degradations queued
In his brown past, to explain how Jocky there
Could make me out to be innocent and wee:
As if to be wee was not to be dying of drink;

As if to be innocent meant that you still belonged
Where beds were made for one in particular.)
Still, the lifespan of sociable feelings is shortest of all
In the breast of the migrant Clydesider; and soon he
                                        relapsed

Into patterns of favourite self-pitying sentiments.
                                        'Son –
Ah'm warse than – Ah cannae, ye know? Ah'm off
                                        tae ma dandy!
Ah've done a wee josie – aye, wheesh! – it's warse
                                        what Ah'm gettin –
Aye – warse!' And again the appeal to heredity –
                                        'Son.'

(In the course of his speech, the impostor had
                                        gradually settled

Back on the bed, and extended as visual aids
His knocked-about knuckles; tattooed with indelible
                                          foresight
On one set of these was the purple imperative SAVE.)

Now I'm keen for us all to be just as much worse as
                                          we want,
In our own time and space – but not, after midnight,
                                          in my bed;
And to keep his inertia at bay, I went for the parasite,
Scuttling him off with a shout and the push of a boot

That reminded his ribs I suppose of a Maryhill
                                          barman's,
Until I had driven him out of the door and his cough
Could be heard to deteriorate under a clock in the
                                          landing.
(Och, if he'd known *I* was Scottish! Then I'd have
                                          got it.)

ROBERT CRAWFORD (b. 1959)

Scotland in the 1890s

'I came across these facts which, mixed with
                                   others. . .'
Thinking of Helensburgh, J. G. Frazer
Revises flayings and human sacrifice;
Abo of the Celtic Twilight, St Andrew Lang
Posts him a ten-page note on totemism
And a coloured fairy book – an Oxford man
From Selkirk, he translates Homer in his sleep.

'When you've lived here, even for a short time,
Samoa's a bit like Scotland – there's the sea . . .
Back in Auld Reekie with a pen that sputtered
I wrote my ballad, "Ticonderoga" or
"A Legend of the West Highlands", then returned
To King Kalakaua's beach and torches –
You know my grandfather lit Lismore's south end?'

Mr Carnegie has bought Skibo Castle.
His Union Jack's sewn to the stars and stripes.
James Murray combs the dialect from his beard
And files slips for his massive *Dictionary*.
Closing a fine biography of mother,
Remembering Dumfries, and liking boys,
James Barrie, caught in pregnant London silence,
Begins to conceive the Never Never Land.

Rain

A motorbike breaks down near Sanna in torrential
                                   rain,
Pouring loud enough to perforate limousines, long
                                   enough
To wash us to Belize. Partick's

Fish-scaled with wetness. Drips shower from foliage,
                                    cobbles, tourists
From New York and Dusseldorf at the tideline
smeared with mud   Shoes lost in bogs, soaked in potholes, clarted with
                                    glaur.
An old woman is splashed by a bus. A gash
In cloud. Indians
Arrived this week to join their families and who do
                                    not feel
Scottish one inch push onwards into a drizzle
That gets heavy and vertical. Golf umbrellas
Come up like orchids on fast-forward film; exotic
Cagoules fluoresce nowhere, speckling a hillside, and
                                    plump.

Off dykes and gutters, overflowing
Ditches, a granary of water drenches the shoulders
Of Goatfell and Schiehallion. Maps under perspex go
                                    bleary,
Spectacles clog, Strathclyde, Tayside, Dundee
Catch it, fingers spilling with water, oil-stained
As it comes down in sheets, blows
Where there are no trees, snow-wet, without thought
                                    of the morrow.
Weddings, prunes, abattoirs, strippers, Glen Nevis,
                                    snails
Blur in its democracy, down your back, on your
                                    breasts.
In Kilmarnock a child walks naked. A woman laughs.
In cars, in Tiree bedrooms, in caravans and
                                    tenements,
Couples sleeved in love, the gibbous Govan rain.

The Herr-Knit Bunnet

Ah glaum lik a clood amang Munros, turnin thi
                                    dwang
O Scoatlan: gramlochness, thrawnness, granate
                                    plotcocks, saving-trees

Ar jist scaffie tae Goad, but it's noo we need
Yon pronyeand scuddin-stanes tae shak us free
An hair butter a naishun. 'Proochie, baist, proochie!'
Ah'd scraich tae thi future – an nae tae a moartcloath
Fur haigs an snibbed haingles tae mak tairensie
                                                    owre –
But a kinna hainch tae rase thi laun oot
O bein swiffed in midsimmer an tae tak it doon
Laughin thru thi snaa wi a sairin sae yi'd ken aa its
                                                    nocks
Vieve again, thi cunt o thi yird.

Ah tell yi Ah huv seen thi herr-knit bunnet,
Nae Scoatlan's powcap o Orkneys an Arctic
But a het teuchter's bunnet purled fae human herr
Dour lik thi greek o stanes. Yon punk's
Mohican flambé, cockendy-bill-bricht, an yon
Jillet's blak strand ur menkit thegither. Ae jink
Micht skerr it awa. It's plattit oot
O thi scalps o this laun, an Ah've seen it lie
Tiree-naikit–Ah've seen ye, Scoatlan!
If yince yi wur tint Ah'd plowter owre
Yon glumshy Atlantic rubbit wi trais o gowd.
But (Goad!) lik yi ar, yir skerrs aye tappit
Wi locks o thi deid an thi manky blawn herr o thi
                                                    vivual,
Ah am in luve wi yir skaab-dark bunnet,
Douce Aranda clood-tip, moosewob atwen thi bens'
                                                    shanks
Electric wi threids o herr.

Ah've tuik tae masel thi herr-knit bunnet
Lik a poaridge spune drapt intae cream.

Author's Translation

*I grope in the dark like a cloud among high mountains,
attempting the trial of strength in trying to raise the
heavy caber of Scotland: utter worldliness, stubborn-
ness, ingrained devils, abortionists' plants that kill the
foetus in the womb are just severe passing showers as
far as God is concerned, but it's now we need those
piercing stones skimming the surface of the water to
shake us free and cleanse a nation of impurities.
'Approach, beast, approach!' I'd cry out to the future –
and not to a coffin-drape for tale-telling women and
gelded louts to make evil fury over – but a kind of
sudden throw to pluck the land out of being blown over
by sad winds in midsummer, and to take it down
laughing through the snow with a knowledge of satisfaction so that you would see its beautiful small hills
clear again, the vagina of the earth.*

*I tell you I have seen the hair-knit beret, not Scotland's
cap of Orkneys and Arctic but a hot unsophisticated
Highlander's beret stocking-stiched from human hair
grimly stubborn as the grain of stones. That punk's
Mohican flambé, bright as a puffin's bill, and that
pubertal girl's black strand are mixed together. One
elusive turn might scare it away. It is pleated out of the
scalps of this land, and I have seen it lie naked as Tiree –
I've seen you, Scotland! If once you were lost I would
wade as in a bog over the almost weeping Atlantic
rubbed with gold lace. But (God!) as you are, your bare
precipices always topped with locks of the dead and the
disgusting, woolly blown hair of the living, I am in love
with your beret dark as the bottom of the sea, gently
respectable Aranda cloud-tip, spiderweb between the
legs of the mountains electric with threads of hair.*

*I have taken to myself the hair-knit beret like a porridge
spoon dropped into cream.*

W. N. HERBERT (b. 1961)

Coco-de-Mer

don't bother with the age and unsteadiness of our loins — Dinna bathir wi thi braiggil o wir lends
surfeit — that maks a cothaman o gravy
cowering hearts — i thi cot, but famine in wir crullit herts —
sea-swell* — let gae oan thi dumbswaul, be
dolled up/float — brankie i thi breakirs, an flocht,
flocht lyk thi crospunk* intae Lewis —
hands/moor — thi lucky-bean tae thi haunds o thi misk.

The Derelict Birth

what/childbirth — Fit barnie fur yir bairnie-haein?
— Therr's nane
i thi Inane
wi thi mune fur a midwife,
bricks fur a crib.

portent* — Nae meddum kent o frankincense.
Th'Immense
gentle* — maun hud thi mense,
but thi mune's yir midwife,
ash his bib

Cormundum

confession

Create in me a clean heart, O God; and renew
a right spirit within me. Psalms LI, 10

unendingly releasing, only to lose the drift of it — Onendanly leasin, tae anely loss
I confess my fault — thi lease o ut, Eh creh cormundum, Eh lat

---

* *dumbswaul* a long, noiseless sea-swell in calm, windless weather (W.N.H.); *crospunk* the Molucca bean, drifted to the shores of some of the Western Islands (W.N.H.); *meddum* tickle in the nose, portending a visitor (W.N.H.); *mense* usually means common sense

	a rivir gae, as tho
drain	ma nostrils werr a cundie, but
	sae relucktantly, aa thi Carse* Eh gee awa,
Sidlaw Hills	Seedlies lyk snot, Balmarino's solitude o wreckage,
all a decoration* I'm drawn to	aa a graith Eh'm draan tae, but
must leave	maun laive; aa thi *grana creshentia** o
	ma birthin-lands, thi verra stanes
	emergin fae thir wintir snoods,
	Pictland's buttirflehs o ridirs, z-rods, tunan
	foarks an fans o Abernethy.* Eh gee thum up lyk
my guts	ma thairms flang i thi air
abdomen [Japanese]	ma hara i thi haar an
in the mist	becumman clood –
	Eh tell a leh;
	Eh widna gee a smell o ut awa,
layer* of beer	thi cotonar o beer that lines thi Seagate,
[seaweed]	dulse an whulks aa clingan til
Hilltown's	
all the edible seaweed's	thi Hulltoon's shitey pipe; aa thi tangil's reek o ut,
fish-bright/face	thi fush-bricht ignorance oan ivry fiss,
	thi Cox's Stack* o hung Dundee, game fur
	ivry cheap hate o thi urbin, thi wurkir turnin oan
	thi wurkir lyk
	a cannibal turbine, let alane merry Inglan (aye –
	lat well alane) –
	Eh cudna gee
crab's shell	a cartie o ut awa, a
crab's	mussil's shell, a partin's fart: this
	is Scoatlan's braith draggin lyk a serpint owre
cobblestoned road	thi causie o ma spine: exhale thi haill

Carse low-lying river-lands, e.g. Carse of Gowrie, etc.; *graith* appropriate tools or decorations for a task or ceremony (w.n.h.); *grana creshentia* a rent in corn, here metaphorically a birth-right (w.n.h.); *ridirs, z-rods, tunan foarks an fans o Abernethy* all representations, shapes or symbols on Pictish carved stones; *cotonar* a piece of some small fur, used for lining (w.n.h.); *Cox's Stack* was Dundee's highest jute chimney, in Lochee (w.n.h.)

*collection**   bagdalin oot, inhale

whirlpools   thi bullirs o'ut,

                                 this Disnaeland, this

                 Brokendoon, Eh breath ut,

breath   aynd withoot end, Eh am

              thi coontircheck* that cuts thi groove

on which our severed head and
glass arse   oan whilk oor severt heid an erse o gless

of nothing, the stars   sall open til thir celsitudes o noth, thi stern.

---

* *bagdalin* anything used to line the hold of a ship before putting the cargo in (w.n.h.); *coontircheck* tool for cutting
the groove that unites two sashes of a window (w.n.h)

KATHLEEN JAMIE (b. 1962)

Black Spiders

He looked up to the convent
she'd gone to. She answered no questions
but he knew by the way she'd turned away
that morning.
He felt like swimming to the caves.

*

The nuns have retreated. The eldest still
peals the bell in glee, although no one comes
from the ruins. All their praying was done
when they first saw the ships and the Turks'
swords reflecting the sun.

In the convent the cistern is dry,
the collection boxes empty – cleft skulls
severed and bleached,
are kept in a shrine, and stare to the East.

*

She caught sight of him later, below, brushing salt
from the hair of his nipples. She wanted them
to tickle; black spiders on her lips.

Aunt Janet's Museum

What can be gained by rushing these things?
Huddle in from the rain, compose ourselves, let
a forefinger rest on the bell button which
requests kindly 'p   s'. We wait, listening
to bus tyres on rain say 'hush' and 'west'.
People hurry behind us, we wait,
for shuffling inside the door,
tumbling locks, and admission to dark.

One after the other we make up the stair.
No one looks back, we know what's there,
fear what lies ahead may disappear. Could we
forget these ritual sounds, or alter their order?
Scuffle of feet on the narrow stair,
the alcove, the turn where
pallid light faints through the glass of the doors.

Let it be right. She takes the handle, still
softly exclaiming over our height, and lets her weight
drop it. The click of the latch. She pushes the door
till the shop bell above gives a delicate ting.
Sounds of inside step forward. The faraway drill
of bells warning the kitchen, and the fallible clock.

The Way We Live

Pass the tambourine, let me bash out praises
to the Lord God of movement, to Absolute
non-friction, flight, and the scary side:
death by avalanche, birth by failed contraception.
Of chicken tandoori and reggae, loud, from
                                        tenements,
commitment, driving fast and unswerving
friendship. Of tee-shirts on pulleys, giros and
                                        Bombay,
barmen, dreaming waitresses with many fake-gold
bangles. Of airports, impulse, and waking to
                                        uncertainty,
to strip-lights, motorways, or that pantheon –
the mountains. To overdrafts and grafting

and the fit slow pulse of wipers as you're
creeping over Rannoch, while the God of moorland
walks abroad with his entourage of freezing fog,
his bodyguard of snow.
Of endless gloaming in the North, of Asiatic swelter,
to launderettes, anecdotes, passions and exhaustion,
Final Demands and dead men, the skeletal grip

of government. To misery and elation; mixed,
the sod and caprice of landlords.
To the way it fits, the way it is, the way it seems
to be: let me bash out praises – pass the tambourine.

Acknowledgements

For permission to reprint copyright material the publishers gratefully acknowledge the following:

IAN ABBOT: 'The Mechanisms of the Gin' and 'A Body of Work' from *Avoiding the Gods* (Chapman, 1988) by permission of Chapman

MARION ANGUS: 'Alas! Poor Queen' from *Selected Poems* (Serif Books, 1950) by permission of Faber and Faber Limited

D. M. BLACK: 'From the Privy Council' and 'Kew Gardens' from *Collected Poems 1964–87* (Polygon, 1991) by permission of Polygon

ALAN BOLD: 'June 1967 at Buchenwald', 'Grass', 'A Special Theory of Relativity', 'Love-Lowe' and 'The Auld Symie' by permission of the author

GEORGE MACKAY BROWN: 'The Funeral of Ally Flett' and 'Hamnavoe Market' from *Poems New and Selected* (The Hogarth Press, 1971), 'Island School' from *The Wreck of the Archangel* (John Murray, 1989), and 'Old Fisherman with Guitar', 'Trout Fisher', 'The Five Voyages of Arnor', 'Kirkyard', 'Taxman' *from* 'Runes from a Holy Island', and 'Beachcomber' from *Selected Poems 1954–1983* (John Murray, 1991) by permission of John Murray (Publishers) Ltd

JOHN BURNSIDE: 'Out of Exile' and 'Vallejo' from *The Hoop* (Carcanet Press, 1988) by permission of Carcanet Press Limited

RON BUTLIN: 'This Evening', 'Night-life', 'Inheritance' and 'Claiming My Inheritance' from *Ragtime in Unfamiliar Bars* (Secker & Warburg, 1985) © Ron Butlin, 1985, by permission of Martin Secker and Warburg Limited

NORMAN CAMERON: 'She and I', 'Forgive Me, Sire', 'A Visit to the Dead' and 'Green, Green, is El Aghir' from *Collected Poems*, edited by W. Hope and J. Barker (Anvil Press, 1989) by permission of Anvil Press Poetry Ltd

STEWART CONN: 'Todd', 'On Craigie Hill', 'The Yard', 'Summer Afternoon', 'To My Father' and 'Under the Ice' from *In the Kibble Palace: New and Selected Poems* (Bloodaxe Books, 1987) by permission of Bloodaxe Books Ltd

ROBERT CRAWFORD: 'Scotland in the 1890s' and 'Rain' from *A Scottish Assembly* (Chatto & Windus, 1990) by permission of Random Century Group, and 'The Herr-Knit Bunnet' from *Sharawaggi* (Polygon, 1990) by permission of Polygon

HELEN B. CRUICKSHANK: 'The Ponnage Pool' from *Collected Poems* (Reprographia, 1971) by permission of A. C. Hunter

IVOR CUTLER: 'The Purposeful Culinary Instruments' from *Many Flies Have Feathers* (Trigram Press, 1973), and 'The Darkness' and 'The Railway Sleepers' from *A Flat Man* (Trigram Press, 1977) by permission of the author

JOHN DAVIDSON: 'Snow' from *The Poems of John Davidson*, edited by Andrew Turnbull, 2 vols. (Scottish Academic Press, 1973) by permission of Scottish Academic Press Limited

CAROL ANN DUFFY: 'Politico' and 'Plainsong' from *Selling Manhattan* (Anvil Press,

1987), and 'In Your Mind' from *The Other Country* (Anvil Press, 1990) by permission of Anvil Press Poetry Ltd

G. F. DUTTON: 'street' and 'clach eanchainn' from *Squaring the Waves* (Bloodaxe Books, 1986) by permission of Bloodaxe Books Ltd

ALISON FELL: 'Desire' and 'Pushing Forty' from *Kisses for Mayakovsky* (Virago Press, 1984) by permission of Peake Associates, and 'Freeze-frame' from *The Crystal Owl* (Methuen, 1988) © 1988 by Alison Fell, by permission of Methuen, London and Peake Associates

VERONICA FORREST-THOMSON: 'Strike' from *Collected Poems and Translations* (London, Lewes, Berkeley: Allardyce, Barnett, Publishers, 1990) Copyright © Jonathan Culler and The Estate of Veronica Forrest-Thomson 1990. Editorial matter Copyright © Anthony Barnett 1990. First printed in Veronica Forrest-Thomson, *Cordelia: or 'A Poem Should Not Mean, but Be'*. Copyright © Veronica Forrest-Thomson 1974; reprinted in Veronica Forrest-Thomson, *On the Periphery*. Copyright © Jonathan Culler 1976, by permission of Allardyce, Barnett, Publishers

ALASTAIR FOWLER: 'Catacomb Suburb' from *Catacomb Suburb* (Edinburgh University Press, 1976) by permission of Edinburgh University Press, and 'Relative' from *From the Domain of Arnheim* (Secker & Warburg, 1982). © Alastair Fowler, 1982, by permission of Martin Secker and Warburg Limited

ROBIN FULTON: 'Remembering an Island' and 'Travelling Alone' from *Selected Poems 1963–1978* (Macdonald Publishers, 1980) by permission of The Saltire Society, and 'Museums and Journeys', 'Stopping by Shadows', 'Resolutions' and 'Remembering Walls' from *Fields of Focus* (Anvil Press, 1982) by permission of Anvil Press Poetry Ltd

ROBERT GARIOCH: 'Embro to the Ploy', 'To Robert Fergusson', 'The Wire', 'Property', 'Glisk of the Great', 'Heard in the Cougate', 'At Robert Fergusson's Grave', 'Elegy', 'In Princes Street Gairdens' and 'Merulius Lacrymans' from *Complete Poetical Works* (Macdonald Publishers, 1983) by permission of The Saltire Society

VALERIE GILLIES: 'Fellow Passenger' and 'The Piano-tuner' from *Each Bright Eye* (Canongate, 1977), and 'Young Harper' and 'The Ericstane Brooch' from *The Chanter's Tune* (Canongate, 1990) by permission of Canongate Press Plc

JOHN GLENDAY: 'The Apple Ghost' from *The Apple Ghost* (Peterloo Poets, 1989) by permission of Peterloo Poets

W. S. GRAHAM: 'The Children of Greenock', *from* 'Seven Letters – II and VI', 'Baldy Bane', 'Malcolm Mooney's Land', 'The Lying Dear', 'The Night City', 'Johann Joachim Quantz's Five Lessons' and 'The Stepping Stones' from *Collected Poems 1942–1977* (Faber, 1979) by permission of Mrs W. S. Graham

ALASDAIR GRAY: 'Awakening' from *Old Negatives* (Jonathan Cape, 1989) by permission of Random Century Group

SIR ALEXANDER GRAY: 'Scotland' from *Selected Poems* (William MacLellan, n.d.) by permission of Stuart Titles Ltd

ANDREW GREIG: 'In the Tool-shed' from *Surviving Passages* (Canongate, 1982) by permission of Canongate Press Plc, and 'The Winter Climbing' and 'The Maid & I' from *The Order of the Day* (Bloodaxe Books, 1990) by permission of Bloodaxe Books Ltd

CHRISTOPHER MURRAY GRIEVE — see HUGH MacDIARMID

GEORGE CAMPBELL HAY: 'Bisearta'/'Bizerta' and 'Atman'/'Atman' from *Modern Scottish Gaelic Poems*, edited by D. Macaulay (Southside, 1976) by permission of Canongate Press Plc

HAMISH HENDERSON: 'Seven Good Germans' from *Elegies for the Dead in Cyrenaica* (Polygon, 1990) by permission of Polygon

W. N. HERBERT: 'Coco-de-Mer', 'The Derelict Birth' and 'Cormundum' from *Sharawaggi* (Polygon, 1990) by permission of Polygon

MICK IMLAH: 'Goldilocks' from *Birthmarks* (Chatto & Windus, 1988) by permission of Random Century Group

KATHLEEN JAMIE: 'Black Spiders', 'Aunt Janet's Museum' and 'The Way We Live' from *The Way We Live* (Bloodaxe Books, 1987) by permission of Bloodaxe Books Ltd

FRANK KUPPNER: 'Passing Through Doorways' from *The Intelligent Observation of Naked Women* (Carcanet Press, 1987) by permission of Carcanet Press Limited

TOM LEONARD: 'Six Glasgow Poems', 'Poetry', 'Jist ti Let Yi No', 'Paroakial', 'Feed Ma Lamz', *from* 'Unrelated Incidents', *from* 'Ghostie Men' and 'Fathers and Sons' from *Intimate Voices: Selected Work 1965–1983* (Galloping Dog Press, 1984) by permission of the author

LIZ LOCHHEAD: 'Dreaming Frankenstein', 'Heartbreak Hotel', 'Mirror's Song', 'The Grim Sisters', *from* 'The Furies' and 'My Mother's Suitors' from *Dreaming Frankenstein and Collected Poems* (Polygon, 1984) by permission of Polygon

GEORGE MACBETH: 'An Ode to English Food', 'The Renewal' and 'Draft for an Ancestor' from *Collected Poems 1958–1982* (Hutchinson, 1989) Copyright © George MacBeth, 1989, by permission of Sheil Land Associates Ltd

BRIAN MCCABE: 'Spring's Witch' from *Spring's Witch* (Mariscat, 1984) by permission of Mariscat Publishers, and 'The Blind' and 'This is Thursday' from *One Atom to Another* (Polygon, 1987) by permission of Polygon

NORMAN MACCAIG: 'Summer Farm', 'Drifter', 'Crofter's Kitchen, Evening', 'Half-built Boat in a Hayfield', 'Explicit Snow', 'Celtic Cross', 'Feeding Ducks', 'Things in Each Other', 'The Shore Road', 'Byre', 'Loch Sionascaig', 'July Evening', 'Porpoises', 'Looking Down on Glen Canisp', 'Blue Tit on a String of Peanuts', 'Old Edinburgh', 'Basking Shark', 'Intruder in a Set Scene' and 'No Interims in History' from *Collected Poems* (Chatto & Windus, 1990) by permission of Random Century Group

HUGH MACDIARMID (Christopher Murray Grieve): 'The Bonnie Broukit Bairn', 'The Watergaw', 'The Eemis Stane', 'Scunner', 'Empty Vessel', *from* 'A Drunk Man Looks at the Thistle', 'First Hymn to Lenin', 'Water Music', 'Ho, My Little Sparrow', 'On a Raised Beach' and 'Harry Semen' from *Selected Poetry of Hugh MacDiarmid* (to be published by Carcanet Press, August 1992) by permission of Carcanet Press Limited

WILLIAM MCILVANNEY: 'Bless This House', 'The Song Mickey Heard at the Bottom of his Pint in the Zodiac Bar' and 'Passing Through Petra' from *In Through the Head* (Mainstream Publishing, 1988) by permission of Mainstream Publishing Co. (Edinburgh) Ltd

ALASTAIR MACKIE: *from* 'Back-Green Odyssey' from *Ingaitherins. Selected Poems* (Aberdeen University Press, 1987) by permission of Aberdeen University Press

ALASDAIR MACLEAN: 'Death of an Old Woman' and 'Home Thoughts from Home' from *From the Wilderness* (Gollancz, 1973) by permission of Victor Gollancz Ltd, and 'Waking the Dead' and 'The Rain' from *Waking the Dead* (Gollancz, 1976) by permission of David Higham Associates Limited

SORLEY MACLEAN: 'Gaoir na h-Eòrpa'/'The Cry of Europe', 'Am Bata Dubh'/'The Black Boar', 'Ban-Ghàidheal'/'A Highland Woman', 'Calbharaigh'/'Calvary', 'Clann Ghill-Eain'/'The Clan MacLean', 'Dol an Iar'/'Going Westwards', 'Glac a' Bhàis'/ 'Death Valley', 'Curaidhean'/'Heroes' and 'Hallaig'/'Hallaig' from *From Wood to Ridge: Collected Poems in Gaelic and English* (Carcanet Press, 1989) by permission of Carcanet Press Limited

AONGHAS MACNEACAIL: 'dol dhachaigh – 2'/'going home – 2', 'gleann fademach'/ 'glen remote' and *from* 'an cathadh mor'/*from* 'the great snowbattle' from *an seachnadh agus dain eile. The avoiding and other poems* (Macdonald Publishers, 1986) by permission of The Saltire Society

GERALD MANGAN: 'Glasgow 1956', 'Heraclitus at Glasgow Cross' and 'Nights in Black Valley' from *Waiting for the Storm* (Bloodaxe Books, 1990) by permission of Bloodaxe Books Ltd

ANGUS MARTIN: 'Malcolm MacKerral' and 'Forest' from *The Larch Plantation* (Macdonald Publishers, 1990) by permission of The Saltire Society

ELMA MITCHELL: 'Thoughts after Ruskin' from *People Etcetera: Poems New & Selected* (Peterloo Poets, 1987) by permission of Peterloo Poets

WILLIAM MONTGOMERIE: 'The Edge of the War' from *From Time to Time* (Canongate, 1985) by permission of Canongate Press Plc

EDWIN MORGAN: 'The Starlings in George Square', 'The Second Life', 'Glasgow Sonnets', 'The First Men on Mercury', 'Cinquevalli', 'The Dowser' and *from* 'Sonnets from Scotland: "Pilate at Fortingall", "De Quincey in Glasgow", "Post-Referendum", "After a Death" and "The Coin" ' from *Collected Poems* (Carcanet Press, 1990) by permission of Carcanet Press Limited

EDWIN MUIR: 'Childhood', 'The Town Betrayed', 'Scotland 1941', 'The Ring', 'The Castle', 'The Labyrinth', 'The Combat', 'One Foot in Eden', 'To Franz Kafka', 'The Difficult Land' and 'The Horses' from *Collected Poems* (Faber, 1960) by permission of Faber and Faber Limited

WILLIAM NEILL: 'Map Makers' from *Wild Places* (Luath Press, 1985), and 'De A Thug Ort Sgriobhadh Ghaidhlig?'/'What Compelled You to Write in Gaelic?' from *Making Tracks* (Gordon Wright Publishing Ltd, 1988) by permission of the author

TOM POW: 'Saint Medan' from *The Moth Trap* (Canongate, 1990) by permission of Canongate Press Plc

ALASTAIR REID: 'A Lesson for Beautiful Women', 'Scotland', 'Isle of Arran' and

'James Bottle's Year' from *Weathering* (Canongate, 1978) by permission of Canongate Press Plc

DILYS ROSE: 'Figurehead' and 'Fetish' from *Madame Doubtfire's Dilemma* (Chapman, 1989) by permission of Chapman

CHRISTOPHER SALVESEN: 'Ninian Winyet', 'History of Strathclyde' and 'Among the Goths' from *Among the Goths* (Mariscat, 1986) by permission of Mariscat Publishers

TOM SCOTT: 'The Mankind Toun' from *The Ship, and Ither Poems* (OUP, 1963) by permission of the author

BURNS SINGER: 'A Sort of Language', 'Peterhead in May', 'For Josef Herman' and 'SOS Lifescene' from *Selected Poems*, edited by A. Cluysenaar (Carcanet Press, 1977) by permission of Carcanet Press Limited

IAN CRICHTON SMITH: 'Highlanders' and 'Poem in March' from *The Law and the Grace* (Eyre & Spottiswoode, 1965) © 1965 by Ian Crichton Smith, by permission of the author, extracts from 'By the Sea' from *Selected Poems* (Gollancz, 1970) by permission of Victor Gollancz Ltd, 'The Clearances' and 'Gaelic Stories' from *Selected Poems 1955–1980* (Macdonald Publishers, 1981) by permission of The Saltire Society, 'The Law and the Grace', *from* 'The White Air of March', 'Shall Gaelic Die?', 'Gaelic Songs', 'Christmas 1971', 'The Glass of Water', 'How Often I Feel Like You' and 'Chinese Poem' from *Selected Poems* (Carcanet Press, 1985), three extracts from *A Life* (Carcanet Press, 1986), and 'Listen' from *The Village* (Carcanet Press, 1989) by permission of Carcanet Press Limited

SYDNEY GOODSIR SMITH: *from* 'Armageddon in Albyn', 'The Grace of God and the Meth-Drinker', 'Time Be Brief', 'Omens', 'As My Life' and *from* 'Under The Eidon Tree – V: Slugabed' from *Collected Poems* (John Calder, 1975) Copyright © John Calder (Publishers) Ltd 1975. By permission of Calder Publications Ltd

WILLIAM SOUTAR: 'The Tryst', 'The Guns', 'The Hungry Mauchs', 'Song' and 'The Makar' from *The Poems of William Soutar* edited by W. R. Aitken (Scottish Academic Press, 1988) by permission of The Trustees of The National Library of Scotland

MURIEL SPARK: 'Going up to Sotheby's', 'Against the Transcendentalists', 'Elegy in a Kensington Churchyard' and 'Litany of Time Past' from *Going Up to Sotheby's, and Other Poems* (Granada Publishing, 1982) by permission of David Higham Associates Limited

DERICK THOMSON: 'Dà Thaibhse'/'Two Ghosts', 'An Tobar'/'The Well', 'Srath Nabhair'/'Strathnaver', 'Eilean Chaluim Chille, an Loch Eiriosort, Leòdhas'/'St Columba's Isle, Loch Erisort, Lewis', 'Clann-Nighean an Sgadain'/'The Herring Girls', 'Dùn Nan Gall'/'Donegal', 'Cisteachan-Laighe'/'Coffins' and 'An Dàrna Eilean'/'The Second Island' from *Creachadh na clarsaich . . . : Plundering the Harp. Collected Poems 1940–1980* (Macdonald Publishers, 1982) by permission of The Saltire Society

RUTHVEN TODD: 'Trout Flies' and 'Of Moulds and Mushrooms' from *Garland for the Winter Solstice* (Dent, 1961) by permission of David Higham Associates Limited

SYDNEY TREMAYNE: 'Legend', 'A Burial' and 'Wanting News' from *Selected and New Poems* (Chatto & Windus, 1973) Copyright © Sydney Tremayne, 1973, by permission of Sheil Land Associates Ltd

RAYMOND VETESSE: 'Prologue', 'My Carrion Words' and 'The Vieve Cry' from *The Richt Noise* (Macdonald Publishers, 1988) by permission of The Saltire Society

KENNETH WHITE: 'The House at the Head of the Tide', and *from* 'Late August on the Coast' from *The Bird Path: Collected Longer Poems* (Mainstream Publishing, 1989) by permission of Mainstream Publishing Co. (Edinburgh) Ltd

ANDREW YOUNG: 'On the Pilgrim's Road', 'The Stockdoves', 'A Heap of Faggots', 'A Prehistoric Camp', 'Passing the Graveyard', 'Sudden Thaw' and 'The Shepherd's Hut' from *The Poetical Works* (Secker & Warburg, 1985) by permission of The Estate of Andrew Young

DOUGLAS YOUNG: 'For a Wife in Jizzen', 'Sainless' and 'The Shepherd's Dochter' from *A Clear Voice: Douglas Young, Poet and Polymath*, edited by C. Young and D. Murison (Macdonald Publishers, 1976) by permission of The Saltire Society

Faber and Faber Limited apologize for any errors or omissions in the above list and would be grateful to be notified of any corrections that should be incorporated in the next edition or reprint of this volume.

Index of Poets

Abbot, Ian, 329–30
Angus, Marion, 7–8

Black, D. M., 311–13
Bold, Alan, 320–25
Brown, George Mackay, 223–31
Burnside, John, 392–3
Butlin, Ron, 357–9

Cameron, Norman, 77–9
Conn, Stewart, 299–303
Crawford, Robert, 401–4
Cruickshank, Helen B., 19–20
Cutler, Ivor, 237–8

Davidson, John, 3–5
Duffy, Carol Ann, 394–6
Dutton, G. F., 240–41

Fell, Alison, 326–8
Forrest-Thomson, Veronica, 341–3
Fowler, Alastair, 279–81
Fraser, G. S., 144–5
Fulton, Robin, 307–10

Garioch, Robert, 80–102
Gillies, Valerie, 353–6
Glenday, John, 388–9
Goodsir Smith, Sydney, 146–53
Graham, W. S., 160–79
Gray, Alasdair, 288
Gray, Sir Alexander, 13–14
Greig, Andrew, 373–5
Grieve, Christopher Murray *see* MacDiarmid, Hugh Murray

Hay, Deorsa Caimbeul, 154–9
Hay, George Campbell *see* Hay, Deorsa Caimbeul
Henderson, Hamish, 189–92
Herbert, W. N., 405–7

Imlah, Mick, 397–400

Jacob, Violet, 6
Jamie, Kathleen, 408–10

Kuppner, Frank, 376–84

Leonard, Tom, 331–40
Lochhead, Liz, 344–52

MacBeth, George, 282–7
McCabe, Brian, 367–9
MacCaig, Norman, 103–14

MacDiarmid, Hugh Murray, 35–70
Macgill-Eain, Somhairle, 115–33
McIlvanney, William, 304–6
Mackie, Alastair, 242–4
Maclean, Alasdair, 249–51
Maclean, Sorley *see* Somhairle Macgill-Eain
Macneacail, Aonghas, 314–19
MacThomais, Ruaraidh, 211–22
Mangan, Gerald, 370–72
Martin, Angus, 385–7
Mitchell, Elma, 187–8
Montgomerie, William, 74–6
Morgan, Edwin, 195–210
Muir, Edwin, 21–34

Neill, William, 232–6

Pow, Tom, 364–6

Reid, Alastair, 245–8
Rose, Dilys, 390–91

Salvesen, Christopher, 289–92
Scott, Alexander, 193–4
Scott, Tom, 180–81
Singer, Burns, 274–8
Smith, Iain Crichton, 252–73
Soutar, William, 71–3
Spark, Muriel, 182–6
Spence, Lewis, 9–11
Sutherland, Robert Garioch *see* Garioch, Robert

Taylor, Rachel Annand, 12
Thomson, Derick *see* MacThomais, Ruaraidh
Todd, Ruthven, 140–43
Tremayne, Sydney, 134–6

Vettese, Raymond, 360–63

White, Kenneth, 293–8

Young, Andrew, 15–18
Young, Douglas, 137–9

Index of Titles

A Body of (Abbot), 329–30
A Burial (Tremayne), 135–6
A Drunk Man Looks at the Thistle (MacDiarmid), 37–49
A Heap of Faggots (Young), 16
A Highland Woman (Macgill-Eain), 119
A Lesson for Beautiful Women (Reid), 245–6
A Life (Smith), 269–73
A Prehistoric Camp (Young), 16
A Sort of Language (Singer), 274
A Special Theory of Relativity (Bold), 323–4
A Visit to the Dead (Cameron), 77–8
Aa My Life (Smith), 151–2
Against the Transcendentalists (Spark), 184–5
Alas! Poor Queen (Angus), 7–8
Am Bata Dubh (Macgill-Eain), 117
Among the Goths (Salvesen), 291–2
an cathadh mor (Macneacail), 316–18
An Darna Eilean (MacThomais), 221–2
An Ode to English Food (MacBeth), 282–4
An Tobar (MacThomais), 212
Armageddon in Albyn (Smith), 146–8
At Robert Fergusson's Grave (Garioch), 99–100
Atman (English) (Hay), 157–9
Atman (Gaelic) (Hay), 156–7
Aunt Janet's Museum (Jamie), 408–9
Awakening (Gray), 288

Back-Green Odyssey (Mackie), 242–4
Baldy Bane (Graham), 164–9
Ban-Ghàidheal (Macgill-Eain), 118
Basking Shark (MacCaig), 113
Beachcomber (Brown), 230–31
Bisearta (Hay), 154–5
Bizerta (Hay), 155–6
Black Spiders (Jamie), 408
Bless This House (McIlvanney), 304–5
Blue Tit on a String of Peanuts (MacCaig), 112
By the Sea (Smith), 254–7
Byre (MacCaig), 109

Calbharaigh (Macgill-Eain), 120
Calvary (Macgill-Eain), 120
Catacomb Suburb (Fowler), 279–80
Celtic Cross (MacCaig), 106–7
Childhood (Muir), 21
Chinese Poem (Smith), 267–9
Christmas 1971 (Smith), 265
Cinquevalli (Morgan), 205–7
Cisteachan-Laighe (MacThomais), 219–20
clach eanchainn (Dutton), 240–41
Claiming My Inheritance (Butlin), 358–9
Clann Ghill-Eain (Macgill-Eain), 121
Clann-Nighean an Sgadain (MacThomais), 216–17

Coco-de-Mer (Herbert), 405
Coffins (MacThomais), 220–21
Cormundum (Herbert), 405–7
Coronach (Scott), 193–4
Crofter's Kitchen, Evening (MacCaig), 104
Curaidhean (Macgill-Eain), 127–8

Dà Thaibhse (MacThomais), 211
De A Thug Ort Sgriobhadh Ghaidhlig? (Neill), 232–4
Death of an Old Woman (Maclean), 249
Death Valley (Macgill-Eain), 126–7
Desire (Fell), 326
Dol an Iar (Macgill-Eain), 122–3
dol dhachaigh – 2 (Macneacail), 314
Donegal (MacThomais), 219
Draft for an Ancestor (MacBeth), 286–7
Dreaming Frankenstein (Lochhead), 344–5
Drifter (MacCaig), 103–4
Dun Nan Gall (MacThomais), 218–19

Eilean Chaluim Chille an Loch Eiriosort, Leòdhas (MacThomais),
    215–16
Elegy (Garioch), 100
Elegy in a Kensington Churchyard (Spark), 185–6
Embro to the Ploy (Garioch), 80–83
Empty Vessel (MacDiarmid), 36–7
Explicit Show (MacCaig), 105–6

Fathers and Sons (Leonard), 340
Feed Ma Lamz (Leonard), 335
Feeding Ducks (MacCaig), 107
Fellow Passenger (Gillies), 353
Fetish (Rose), 390–91
Figurehead (Rose), 390
First Hymn to Lenin (MacDiarmid), 49–51
For a Wife in Jizzen (Young), 137
For Josef Herman (Singer), 275–6
Forest (Martin), 386–7
Forgive Me, Sire (Cameron), 77
Freeze-Frame (Fell), 327–8
From the Privy Council (Black), 311–12

Gaelic Songs (Smith), 264–5
Gaelic Stories (Smith), 260–62
Gaoir na h-Eòrpa (Macgill-Eain), 115
Ghostie Men (Leonard), 339
Glac a' Bhàis (Macgill-Eain), 125–6
Glasgow 1956 (Mangan), 370
Glasgow Sonnets (Morgan), 199–203
gleann fadamach (Macneacail), 315
glen remote (Macneacail), 316
Glisk of the Great (Garioch), 98–9
going home – 2 (Macneacail), 314–15
Going up to Sotheby's (Spark), 182–3
Going Westwards (Macgill-Eain), 123–5
Goldilocks (Imlah), 397–400
Grass (Bold), 323

Great Tay of the Waves (Spence), 10
Green, Green is El Aghir (Cameron), 78–9

Half-built Boat in a Hayfield (MacCaig), 105
Hallaig (English) (Macgill-Eain), 131–3
Hallaig (Gaelic) (Macgill-Eain), 129–31
Hamnavoe Market (Brown), 226
Harry Semen (MacDiarmid), 68–70
Heard in the Cougate (Garioch), 99
Heartbreak Hotel (Lochhead), 345–7
Heraclitus at Glasgow Cross (Mangan), 370–72
Heroes (Macgill-Eain), 128–9
Highlanders (Smith), 252
History of Strathclyde (Salvesen), 290–91
Ho, My Little Sparrow (MacDiarmid), 56–7
Home Thoughts from Home (MacLean), 249–50
Home Town Elegy (Fraser), 144–5
How Often I Feel Like You (Smith), 266

In Princes Street Gairdens (Garioch), 101
In the Tool-shed (Greig), 373–4
Inheritance (Butlin), 357–8
Intruder in a Set Scene (MacCaig), 113–14
Island School (Brown), 231
Isle of Arran (Reid), 246–7

James Bottle's Year (Reid), 247–8
Jist ti Let Yi No (Leonard), 334
Johann Joachim Quantz's Five Lessons (Graham), 176–9
July Evening (MacCaig), 110
June 1967 at Buchenwald (Bold), 320–23

Kew Gardens (Black), 312–13
Kirkyard (Brown), 228

Late August on the Coast (White), 296–8
Lean Street (Fraser), 144
Legend (Tremayne), 134–5
Listen (Smith), 273
Litany of Time Past (Spark), 186
Loch Sionascaig (MacCaig), 109
Looking down on Glen Canisp (MacCaig), 111–12
Love-Lowe (Bold), 324

Malcolm MacKerral (Martin), 385–6
Malcolm Mooney's Land (Graham), 170–74
Map Makers (Neill), 232
Merulius Lacrymans (Garioch), 101–2
Mirror's Song (Lochhead), 347–8
Museums and Journeys (Fulton), 308
My Carrion Words (Vettese), 362
My Een Are Nae on Calvary (Macgill-Eain), 120
My Mother's Suitors (Lochhead), 351–2

Night-life (Butlin), 357
Nights in Black Valley (Mangan), 372
Ninian Winyet (Salvesen), 289–90
No Interims in History (MacCaig), 114

Of Moulds and Mushrooms (Todd), 141–3
Old Edinburgh (MacCaig), 112
Old Fisherman with Guitar (Brown), 224–5
Omens (Smith), 150–51
On a Raised Beach (MacDiarmid), 56–68
On Craigie Hill (Conn), 299–300
On the Pilgrim's Road (Young), 15
One Foot in Eden (Muir), 29–30
Out of Exile (Burnside), 392

Paroakial (Leonard), 334–5
Passing the Graveyard (Young), 17
Passing through Doorways (Kuppner), 376–84
Passing through Petra (McIlvanney), 305–6
Peterhead in May (Singer), 274–5
Plainsong (Duffy), 394–5
Poem in March (Smith), 253
Poetry (Leonard), 333–4
Politico (Duffy), 394
Porpoises (MacCaig), 110–11
Prologue (Vettese), 360–61
Property (Garioch), 97–8
Pushing Forty (Fell), 327

Rain (Crawford), 401–2
Relative (Fowler), 280–81
Remembering an Island (Fulton), 307
Remembering Walls (Fulton), 309–10
Resolutions (Fulton), 309
Runes from a Holy Island (Brown), 229–30

Sainless (Young), 137–8
St Columba's Isle, Loch Erisort, Lewis (MacThomais), 216
Scotland (Gray), 13–14
Scotland (Reid), 246
Scotland 1941 (Muir), 23–4
Scotland in the 1890s (Crawford), 401
Scunner (MacDiarmid), 36
Seven Letters (Graham), 161–4
Seventh Elegy (Henderson), 189–92
Shall Gaelic Die (Smith), 262–4
She and I (Cameron), 77
Six Glasgow Poems (Leonard), 331–3
Snow (Davidson), 3–5
Song (Soutar), 73
Sonnets from Scotland (Morgan), 208–10
SOS Lifescene (Singer), 276–8
Spring's Witch (McCabe), 367
Srath Nabhair (MacThomais), 214
Starlings in George Square, The (Morgan), 195–7
Stopping by Shadows (Fulton), 308–9
Strathnaver (MacThomais), 214–15
Street (Dutton), 240
Strike (Forrest-Thomson), 341–3
Sudden Thaw (Young), 17
Summer Afternoon (Conn), 301–2
Summer Farm (MacCaig), 103

Taxman (Brown), 229
The Apple Ghost (Glenday), 388–9
The Auld Symie (Bold), 325
The Baltic (Jacob), 6
The Black Boat (Macgill-Eain), 117
The Blind (McCabe), 367–8
The Bonnie Broukit Bairn (MacDiarmid), 35
The Carse (Spence), 9–10
The Castle (Muir), 25–6
The Children of Greenock (Graham), 160–61
The Clan MacLean (Macgill-Eain), 21
The Clearances (Smith), 252
The Combat (Muir), 28–9
The Cry of Europe (Macgill-Eain), 116
The Darkness (Cutler), 238
The Derelict Birth (Herbert), 405
The Difficult Land (Muir), 31–2
The Dowser (Morgan), 207–8
The Edge of the War (Montgomerie), 74–6
The Eemis Stane (MacDiarmid), 35–6
The Ericstane Brooch (Gillies), 355–6
The First Men on Mercury (Morgan), 203–5
The Five Voyages of Arnor (Brown), 227–8
The Funeral of Ally Flett (Brown), 223–4
The Furies (Lochhead), 350
The Gift of Sight (Pow), 364–6
The Glass of Water (Smith), 265–6
The Grace of God and the Meth-Drinker (Smith), 148–9
the great snowbattle (Macneacail), 318–19
The Grim Sisters (Lochhead), 348–9
The Guns (Soutar), 71–2
The Herr-Knit Bunnet (Crawford), 402–3 (author's translation
    404)
The Herring Girls (MacThomais), 217–18
The Horses (Muir), 32–4
The House at the Head of the Tide (White), 293–6
The Hungry Mauchs (Soutar), 72–3
The Labyrinth (Muir), 26–8
The Law and the Grace (Smith), 253–4
The Lying Dear (Graham), 174
The Makar (Soutar), 73
The Mankind Town (Scott), 180–81
The Mechanisms of the Gin (Abbot), 329
The Night City (Graham), 175
The Piano-tuner (Gillies), 353–4
The Ponnage Pool (Cruickshank), 19–20
The Princess of Scotland (Taylor), 12
The Prows O'Reekie (Spence), 9
The Purposed Culinary Implements (Cutler), 237–8
The Railway Sleepers (Cutler), 238–9
The Rain (Maclean), 251
The Renewal (MacBeth), 284–6
The Ring (Muir), 24–5
The Second Island (MacThomais), 222
The Second Life (Morgan), 197–9
The Shepherd's Dochter (Young), 138–9
The Shepherd's Hut (Young), 18

The Shore Road (MacCaig), 108
The Song Mickey Heard at the Bottom of his Pint in the Zodiac
    Bar (McIlvanney), 305
The Stepping Stones (Graham), 179
The Stockdoves (Young), 15–16
The Stown Bairn (Spence), 10–11
The Town Betrayed (Muir), 21–3
The Tryst (Soutar), 71
The Vieve Cry (Vettese), 363
The Watergaw (MacDiarmid), 35
The Way We Live (Jamie), 409–10
The Well (MacThomais), 213
The White Air of March (Smith), 257–60
The Winter Climbing (Greig), 374
The Wire (Garioch), 92–7
The Yard (Conn), 300–301
Things in Each Other (MacCaig), 107–8
This Evening (Butlin), 357
This is Thursday (McCabe), 368–9
Thoughts after Ruskin (Mitchell), 187–8
Time Be Brief (Smith), 149–50
To Franz Kafka (Muir), 30–31
To a Loch Fyne Fisherman (Hay), 159
To My Father (Conn), 302
To Robert Fergusson (Garioch), 84–92
Todd (Conn), 299
Travelling Alone (Fulton), 307–8
Trout Fisher (Brown), 225
Trout Flies (Todd), 140
Two Ghosts (MacThomais), 211

Under the Eildon Tree (Smith), 152–3
Under the Ice (Conn), 303
Unrelated Incidents (Leonard), 336–9

Vallejo (Burnside), 392–3

Waking the Dead (Maclean), 250–51
Wanting News (Tremayne), 136
Water Music (MacDiarmid), 51–5
What Compelled You to Write in Gaelic? (Neill), 234–6

Young Harper (Gillies), 354–5

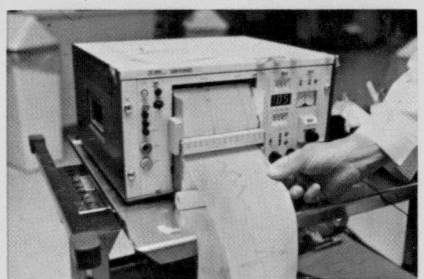

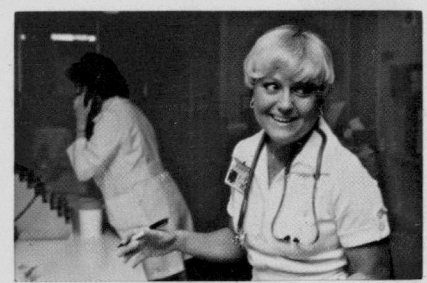

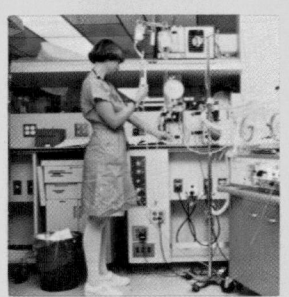

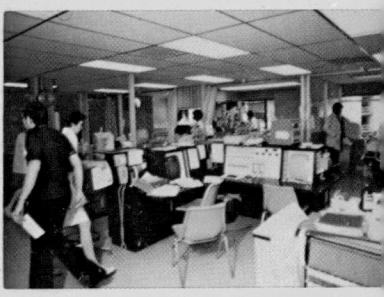

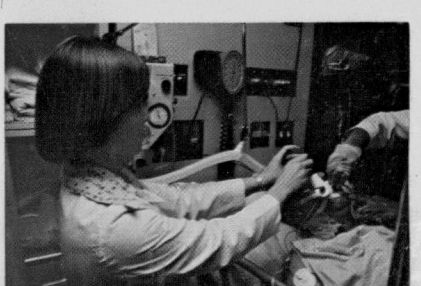

AACN'S CLINICAL REFERENCE FOR CRITICAL-CARE NURSING

AACN'S CLINICAL REFERENCE FOR CRITICAL-CARE NURSING

EDITOR-IN-CHIEF

Marguerite Rodgers Kinney, R.N., D.N.Sc.
Professor of Nursing
University of Alabama School of Nursing
Birmingham, Alabama

EDITORS

Cynthia Boyd Dear, R.N., M.S.
Staff Nurse, Coronary Care Unit
St. Luke's Episcopal Hospital, Houston, Texas

Donna Rogers Packa, R.N., M.S.N.
Assistant Professor of Nursing
University of Alabama School of Nursing
Birmingham, Alabama

Dorothy M. Nagelhout Voorman, R.N., B.S.N., CCRN, C.E.N.
Assistant Director of Nursing, Critical-Care Division
Montefiore Hospital and Medical Center, Bronx, New York

McGRAW-HILL BOOK COMPANY

New York St. Louis San Francisco Auckland Bogotá Guatemala Hamburg
Johannesburg Lisbon London Madrid Mexico Montreal New Delhi Panama
Paris San Juan São Paulo Singapore Sydney Tokyo Toronto

AACN'S CLINICAL REFERENCE FOR CRITICAL-CARE NURSING

Copyright © 1981 by McGraw-Hill, Inc. All rights reserved. Printed in the United States of America. No part of this publication may be reproduced, stored in a retrieval system, or transmitted, in any form or by any means, electronic, mechanical, photocopying, recording, or otherwise, without the prior written permission of the publisher.

234567890 RMRM 8987654321

This book was set in Helvetica Light by Monotype Composition Company, Inc. The editors were Orville W. Haberman, Jr., Stuart D. Boynton, Henry C. De Leo, and John J. Fitzpatrick; the production supervisor was Jeanne Skahan. The designer was Elliot Epstein. The drawings were done by ANCO/Boston.
Rand McNally & Company was printer and binder.

Color Photo credits: James de Leon, Jr. (opposite inside front cover), Kathleen J. Mikan, Marie L. O'Koren, and Christopher Bryan-Brown.

Library of Congress Cataloging in Publication Data
Main entry under title:

AACN's clinical reference for critical-care
    nursing.

    Includes bibliographical references and index
    1. Intensive care nursing. I. Kinney,
Marguerite Rodgers. II. American Association of
Critical-Care Nurses. [DNLM: 1. Critical
care—Nursing texts. WY154 A112]
RT120.I5A18   610.73'61   80-11722
ISBN 0-07-001133-8

To Bob, Meredith, Dorothy, and Wilson   *M.R.K.*

To Clydene, Robert, Wayne, Jim, and Jess   *C.B.D.*

To Joe, Loris, Haydon, Mae, and Nell   *D.R.P.*

To the memory of Jacob R. Siegers and to Honoré   *D.M.N.V.*

For love, patience, encouragement, and confidence.

CONTENTS

List of Contributors		xi
Foreword by Hans Selye		xv
Preface		xvii

PART 1
CONCEPTUAL
FOUNDATIONS

1. Critical-Care Nursing: An Art, a Science, and a Spirit   3
Dorothy M. Nagelhout Voorman

2. The Holistic Approach to the Care of the Critically Ill   9
Marguerite Rodgers Kinney

PART 2
THE PHYSIOLOGIC
BASIS OF
CRITICAL-CARE
NURSING

3. The Pulmonary System   15
Mary Webb Waldron and Laura McHenry Fray

4. Cardiovascular Physiology   33
Lin C. Weeks

5. The Hematopoietic System   79
Dorothy Gosnell Moses

6. The Nervous System   101
Marilyn M. Ricci

7. The Endocrine System   125
Sarah J. Sanford

8. The Renal System   151
LaNelle E. Geddes

9. The Gastrointestinal Tract and the Liver   179
Gail L. Bongiovanni

10. The Integumentary System   211
Vera M. Harmon

11. Physiology of the Musculoskeletal System   221
Helen F. Ptak

12. The Reproductive Systems   237
Ann Daly

PART 3
PHYSICAL
ASSESSMENT

13. Concepts of Physical Assessment in Critical-Care Nursing   253
Betty Henderson and Gayle T. Ferguson

14. Application of Physical Assessment Techniques Appropriate to Patient Status   309
Betty Henderson and Gayle T. Ferguson

vii

PART 4

**THE PSYCHOSOCIAL
BASIS OF
CRITICAL-CARE
NURSING**

15. Anxiety, Stress, and Crisis   323
Doris S. Greiner

16. Psychological Equilibrium   331
Sharon L. Roberts

17. The Critical-Care Milieu   343
Susan B. Biddle

18. Psychosocial Assessment of the Patient and Family   349
Carol J. Dashiff and Susan B. Biddle

PART 5

**THE DYNAMIC
INTERRELATIONSHIP
OF SYSTEMS:
PRIORITIES
IN PROBLEM
SOLVING**

19. Adequate Oxygenation   363
Scott M. Nadel

**20. Regulation and Assessment of Water and Electrolyte
Balance**   389
Charold Lee Baer

21. Maintenance of Nonspecific and Immunologic Defenses   437
Sister Mary Rebecca Fidler

22. Dynamics of Interpersonal Relationships   471
Sharon L. Roberts

PART 6

**PATIENT CARE
MANAGEMENT:
SELECTED PROBLEMS**

23. Respiratory Disorders   485
Sheila A. Glennon, Vickie White Matus, and Christopher W. Bryan-Brown

**24. Cardiovascular Evaluation and Therapy of Unstable
Patients**   543
John A. Mantle, William J. Rogers, Silvio Papapietro, Richard O. Russell, Jr.,
and Charles E. Rackley

25. Hematopoietic Disorders   579
Jerome B. Bart and Cynthia Boyd Dear

26. Neurologic Disorders   599
Pamela H. Mitchell

27. Endocrine Disorders   641
Madeline Musante Wake

**28. Management of Patients with Critical Renal and
Genitourinary Disorders**   657
RENAL DISORDERS   Cleo J. Richard
GENITOURINARY DISORDERS   Michael J. Moran

29. Gastrointestinal Disorders   697
Debra C. Broadwell and William C. McGarity

30. Burn Care   741
Claudella Archambeault-Jones and Irving Feller

31. The Management of Trauma   795
A. Crane Charters and Nancy Stewart

32. Sepsis 821
Robert F. Wilson and Jacqueline A. Wilson

33. Perinatal Crisis 851
Carole Ann Miller McKenzie and Katherine Wheeler Vestal

34. Pediatric Crises 879
Gladys M. Scipien and Susan D. Foster

PART 7
**PRINCIPLES
OF SPECIAL
PROCEDURES
AND THERAPIES**

35. Advanced Life Support 913
Shannon Champion and John M. Packard

36. Circulatory Assistance 925
Penny J. Ford and Mortimer J. Buckley

37. Extracorporeal Circulation 949
Billy M. Hightower and Marguerite Rodgers Kinney

38. Mechanical Support of Ventilation 957
Joanne Lagerson

39. Dialysis Therapy 971
Charold Lee Baer

40. Parenteral Nutrition 981
Jeanne M. Wilson and M. Theresa Holland

41. Hypothermia 991
Sister Maurita Soukup

PART 8
**THE CRITICAL-CARE
ENVIRONMENT**

42. The Critical-Care Environment: Instrumentation 999
Richard A. de Asla and Rae Nadine Smith

43. The Critical-Care Environment: Safety 1037
Elizabeth A. Trought

PART 9
**ISSUES IN
CRITICAL-CARE**

44. Issues in Critical Care: Contemporary Opinions 1051
THE ROLE OF CONSENT   Marvin S. Fish
SOME MEDICAL, ETHICAL, AND LEGAL ISSUES   Mark H. Elovitz
SPIRITUAL CONCERNS OF THE CRITICALLY ILL   Robert D. Wheelock
TWO QUESTIONS ABOUT SHARED RESPONSIBILITY   Jeanne Quint-Benoliel

PART 10
**PATIENT TEACHING
AND REHABILITATION**

**45. Principles of Teaching and Learning Applied to Critical
Care** 1071
Andrea M. Nassen

PART 11
APPENDIXES

A. Dysrhythmias 1103
Carolyn B. Chalkley

B. Drugs 1137
Joseph A. Albanese

Index 1181

LIST OF CONTRIBUTORS

Joseph A. Albanese, R.Ph., Ph.D.
Associate Professor of Biological Sciences
College of Staten Island
Staten Island, New York

Claudella Archambeault-Jones, R.N.
Director of Education
National Institute for Burn Medicine
Ann Arbor, Michigan

Charold Lee Baer, R.N., Ph.D.
Professor and Chairperson
Department of Medical-Surgical Nursing
School of Nursing
University of Oregon Health Services Center
Portland, Oregon

Jerome B. Bart, M.D., F.A.C.P.
Clinical Hematologist
Kelsey-Seybold Clinic
Houston, Texas

Susan B. Biddle, R.N., M.S.N.
Instructor of Nursing
University of Alabama School of Nursing
Birmingham, Alabama

Gail L. Bongiovanni, M.D.
Department of Medicine
Massachusetts General Hospital
Boston, Massachusetts

Debra C. Broadwell, R.N., M.N., E.T.
Curriculum Director
Enterostomal Therapy Educational Program
Emory University
Atlanta, Georgia

Christopher W. Bryan-Brown, M.D.
Professor of Clinical Anesthesiology
Mount Sinai Medical School
City University of New York;
Director, Surgical-Respiratory Intensive Care Unit
Mount Sinai Medical Center
New York, New York

Mortimer J. Buckley, M.D.
Professor of Surgery
Harvard Medical School;
Chief, Cardiac Surgical Unit
Massachusetts General Hospital
Boston, Massachusetts

Carolyn B. Chalkley, R.N., M.S.N.
Director, Cardiovascular Nursing
Brookwood Medical Center
Birmingham, Alabama

Shannon Champion, R.N.
Member, Emergency Cardiac Care Committee
Alabama Affiliate
American Heart Association
Birmingham, Alabama

A. Crane Charters, M.D.
Associate Professor of Surgery
Stanford University School of Medicine;
Chairman, Department of Surgery
Santa Clara Valley Medical Center
San Jose, California

Ann Daly, R.N., B.S.
Assistant Administrator–Nursing Service
Community Hospital of Brazosport
Freeport, Texas

Carol J. Dashiff, R.N., Ph.D.
Associate Professor of Nursing
University of Alabama School of Nursing
Birmingham, Alabama

Cynthia Boyd Dear, R.N., M.S.
Staff Nurse, Coronary Care Unit
St. Luke's Episcopal Hospital
Houston, Texas

Richard A. de Asla, B.A.
Bioengineering Coordinator
Division of Cardiothoracic Surgery
Mount Sinai Hospital
New York, New York

Mark H. Elovitz, Ph.D., J.D.
Attorney, Denaburg, Schoel, Meyerson & Ogle;
President, Birmingham Area
Legal Services Corporation
Birmingham, Alabama

Irving Feller, M.D.
Director, Michigan Burn Center
Ann Arbor, Michigan

Gayle T. Ferguson, R.N., M.N.
Assistant Professor
College of Nursing
Texas Woman's University
Houston, Texas

Sister Mary Rebecca Fidler, Ph.D.
Associate Professor of Nursing
University of Iowa
Cedar Rapids, Iowa

Marvin S. Fish, B.S., J.D.
Attorney, Slavitt, Fish and Cowen;.
College of Nursing
Seton Hall University;
New Jersey College of Medicine and Dentistry
Newark, New Jersey

Penny J. Ford, R.N., M.S.
Cardiac Clinician
Massachusetts General Hospital
Boston, Massachusetts

Susan D. Foster, R.N., M.S.
Pediatric Nursing Coordinator
Grady Memorial Hospital
Atlanta, Georgia

Laura McHenry Fray, R.N., M.S.N., C.C.R.N.
Clinical Resource Nurse
Surgical/Respiratory ICU
Mt. Sinai Medical Center
New York, New York

LaNelle E. Geddes, R.N., Ph.D.
Professor
Department of Nursing
Purdue University
West Lafayette, Indiana

Sheila A. Glennon, R.N., M.A., C.C.R.N.
Clinical Instructor, Critical Care Division
Montefiore Hospital and Medical Center
Bronx, New York

Doris S. Greiner, R.N., M.S.N.
Associate Professor of Nursing
University of Alabama School of Nursing
Birmingham, Alabama

Vera M. Harmon, R.N., M.S.
Assistant Professor
College of Nursing
Texas Woman's University
Houston, Texas

Betty Henderson, R.N., M.N.
Assistant Professor
College of Nursing
Texas Woman's University
Houston, Texas

Billy M. Hightower, M.D.
Associate Professor of Surgery
University of South Alabama Medical Center
Mobile, Alabama

M. Theresa Holland, R.N., B.A.
Hyperalimentation Nurse Clinician
Nutritional Support Unit
Massachusetts General Hospital
Boston, Massachusetts

Marguerite Rodgers Kinney, R.N., D.N.Sc.
Professor of Nursing
University of Alabama School of Nursing
Birmingham, Alabama

Joanne Lagerson, R.N., R.R.T., Ph.D.
Assistant Professor of Pulmonary Nursing
School of Nursing;

Director, Pulmonary Rehabilitation
Department of Pulmonary Medicine
Vanderbilt University
Nashville, Tennessee

John A. Mantle, M.D.
Associate Professor, Department of Medicine
University of Alabama Medical School;
Director of Cardiac Care Unit
University of Alabama Hospitals
Birmingham, Alabama

Vickie White Matus, R.N., M.S.N., C.C.R.N.
Head Nurse, Surgical Intensive Care Unit
Jackson Memorial Hospital
University of Miami Medical Center
Miami, Florida

William C. McGarity, M.D.
Professor of Surgery
Emory University Medical School;
Chief of Surgery, Emory University Hospital;
Director, Enterostomal Therapy Educational Program
Atlanta, Georgia

Carole Ann Miller McKenzie, R.N., C.N.M., M.S.N.
Associate Professor of Nursing
Chairperson, Graduate Maternity Nursing
Medical University of South Carolina
Charleston, South Carolina

Pamela H. Mitchell, R.N., M.S.
Associate Professor
Department of Physiological Nursing;
Neurological Nurse Specialist
Division of Neurology
University of Washington
Seattle, Washington

Michael J. Moran, M.D.
Instructor of Urology
Loyola University of Chicago
Stritch School of Medicine;
Senior Resident in Urology
Hines Veterans Administration Hospital
Hines, Illinois

Dorothy Gosnell Moses, R.N., M.S.N., C.C.R.N.
Assistant Professor
Graduate Program, Medical-Surgical Nursing
School of Nursing
University of Texas Health Science Center
San Antonio, Texas

Scott M. Nadel, M.D.
Fellow in Pulmonary Diseases
Department of Medicine
University of Alabama
Birmingham, Alabama

Andrea M. Nassen, R.N., M.S.N.
Assistant Clinical Professor
College of Nursing
Texas Woman's University;
Cardiovascular Clinical Specialist
St. Paul Hospital, Dallas Cardiac Institute
Dallas, Texas

Donna Rogers Packa, R.N., M.S.N.
Assistant Professor of Nursing
University of Alabama School of Nursing
Birmingham, Alabama

John M. Packard, M.D.
Director of Medical Education
Clinical Professor of Medicine
University of Alabama School of Medicine
Birmingham, Alabama;
National Faculty, Advanced Cardiac Life Support
American Heart Association

Silvio Papapietro, M.D.
Instructor of Medicine
Department of Medicine
University of Alabama Medical School
Birmingham, Alabama

Helen F. Ptak, R.N., Ph.D.
Assistant Dean
School of Nursing
Associate Director, Nursing Service
University of Texas Medical Branch
Galveston, Texas

Jeanne Quint-Benoliel, R.N., D.N.Sc.
Professor of Nursing
Community Health Care Systems Department
Affiliate, Center for Health Services Research
University of Washington
Seattle, Washington

Charles E. Rackley, M.D.
Professor of Medicine
Department of Medicine
University of Alabama Medical School;
Director, Myocardial Infarction Research Unit
University of Alabama Hospitals
Birmingham, Alabama

Marilyn M. Ricci, R.N., M.S., C.N.R.N.
Clinical Nurse Specialist
Barrow Neurological Institute
St. Joseph's Hospital and Medical Center
Phoenix, Arizona

Cleo J. Richard, R.N., M.S.N.
Practitioner-Teacher, Department of Medical Nursing
Rush-Presbyterian-St. Luke's Medical Center;
Instructor, College of Nursing, Rush University;
Instructor, Medical-Surgical Nursing
College of Nursing
University of Illinois
Chicago, Illinois

Sharon L. Roberts, R.N., M.S.
Associate Professor of Nursing
California State University
Long Beach, California

William J. Rogers, M.D.
Professor of Medicine
Department of Medicine
University of Alabama Medical School
Birmingham, Alabama

Richard O. Russell, Jr., M.D.
Professor of Medicine
Department of Medicine
University of Alabama Medical School
Birmingham, Alabama

Sarah J. Sanford, R.N., M.A.
Head Nurse, Critical Care
Overlake Memorial Hospital
Bellevue, Washington

Gladys M. Scipien, R.N., M.S.
Associate Professor
School of Nursing
Boston University
Boston, Massachusetts

Rae Nadine Smith, R.N., M.S.
Clinical Nursing Specialist
Sorenson Research Company
Salt Lake City, Utah

Sister Maurita Soukup, R.N., M.S.N.
Critical Care Clinical Nurse Specialist
St. Luke's Hospital
Cedar Rapids, Iowa

Nancy Stewart, R.N., M.S.N.
Intensive Care Unit Coordinator
University Hospital of California
San Diego, California

Elizabeth A. Trought, R.N., M.S.
Administrator for Nursing
Pitt County Memorial Hospital
Greenville, North Carolina

Katherine Wheeler Vestal, R.N., M.S.
Assistant Professor of Nursing
School of Nursing
University of Texas
Health Science Center at Houston
Houston, Texas

Dorothy M. Nagelhout Voorman, R.N., B.S.N., CCRN, C.E.N.
Assistant Director of Nursing
Critical-Care Division
Montefiore Hospital and Medical Center
Bronx, New York

Madeline Musante Wake, R.N., M.S.N.
Assistant Professor
College of Nursing
Director, Continuing Education in Nursing
Marquette University
Milwaukee, Wisconsin

Mary Webb Waldron, R.N., M.S.N.
Burn Clinical Specialist
Burn Center
Westchester County Medical Center
Valhalla, New York

Lin C. Weeks, R.N., M.S.
Director, Medical Nursing
Hermann Hospital
University of Texas Medical School
Houston, Texas

Robert D. Wheelock, O.P.M., Cap., D. Min.
Campus Minister
Assistant Professor of Medicine and Religion
St. Louis University Medical Center
St. Louis, Missouri

Jacqueline A. Wilson, R.N., M.S.N.
Detroit, Michigan

Jeanne M. Wilson, R.N., B.S.
Hyperalimentation Nurse Clinician
Nutritional Support Unit

Massachusetts General Hospital
Boston, Massachusetts

Robert F. Wilson, M.D.
Professor
Department of Surgery
School of Medicine
Wayne State University
Detroit, Michigan

FOREWORD

When I first encountered "the syndrome of just being sick" in 1936, I gave little thought to its psychological or sociological implications, for I saw stress as a purely physiological and medical phenomenon. The growing interest in this field, however, evidenced by the tremendous response of the general public to some of my nontechnical books, has made me realize that a knowledge of stress can benefit everyone, regardless of educational background or profession.

To my mind, the most important task facing today's nursing profession is to better comprehend what became particularly evident in my work on stress, that psychological factors can often be the decisive influence both in the causation of disease and in the course taken by an established disorder. Critical-care nurses, by virtue of their very direct control of such variables, can make a special contribution toward applying this understanding. It would be an error, however, to think that a clear distinction can always be made between physical and mental causes of stress; for example, anticipation of physical trauma can be a psychic stressor, as anyone who has ever required surgery will understand. What is really needed are principles for the management of *stress as such*, that would ensure our homeostasis on all levels.

The goal of modern medicine should be to understand the patient as a person, to establish the circumstances that precipitated the illness, the underlying conflicts, hostilities, griefs—in short, the bruised nature of the patient's emotional state. The modern physician ought to know as much about emotions and thoughts as about disease symptoms and drugs. This approach would appear to hold more promise of cure than anything that medicine has given humanity to date.

The field of stress has much to offer in this regard. The degree to which homeostasis, the basic determinant of health, is an issue of the total organism—of consciousness as well as physical existence—becomes quite apparent when one considers the following facts that emerge from stress theory: (a) that the aspects of life requiring adaptation, i.e., calling forth the organic stress reaction and initiating the general adaptation syndrome, are not merely composed of matter, but often can be grasped only in terms of concepts (e.g., one's "life situation"); (b) that these nonmaterial demands can disrupt homeostasis in two ways, either by being simply beyond our power of adaptability or by causing diseases of adaptation because there is a particularly "weak link" in the structure of our organism.

Medical science has far too frequently concentrated merely on individual interactions between pathogens and human beings, rather than in the patient's entire spectrum of other relationships, including those with spouse, employer, children, neighbors, and spiritual or medical advisers. Too much consideration has been directed toward specific pathogens and specific disease models, and not enough toward the patient and how he or she developed his or her particular disease. Only when we shift our focus from diseased parts to the whole integrated being, can we learn more about what activates the adaptation syndrome at all levels within the organism, and fully understand why stress affects people in different ways.

The concept of health as a question of body, mind, and spirit is receiving wide public recognition and importance. This holistic approach aims at enhancing our total well-being, in part through self-awareness. By learning to gauge our own innate energy, potential weaknesses, and strengths, we can all benefit from this approach. True, it requires a great deal of self-discipline and willpower, but we must not lose sight of the vital awareness that each of us is responsible for his or her own health and well-being. Otherwise, no matter what new treatments are developed, we will continue to be plagued by stress diseases.

Throughout history, innumerable great thinkers have approached the problem of health from the points of view of theology, psychology, sociology, and particularly medicine. But whatever the approach or technique they favored, the focus has always been specialized. Only now are we really beginning to look upon health as an interdisciplinary problem. After all, we are thinking of the health of the most complex species known, and we will never arrive at a satisfactory solution if all of us take different and reductionist points of view. Of course, we have been very successful in improving health by research limited to molecular biology, electron microscopy, pharmacology, behavioral philosophy (including religious codes), sociology, politics, economics, or any of the other specialized disciplines; but each of us must avoid looking upon our particular field of expertise as the only, all-encompassing solution to human troubles and the only road to happiness. There is no point in understanding and repairing isolated parts of the human machine if the person considered as a total organism is deteriorating for lack of integration.

I believe that new findings in medical science will provide many answers to humankind's everyday psychosocial problems. I do know that my own experience with health and disease has helped me to develop a very satisfactory code of conduct.

In essence, my code encourages people to lead purposeful lives, but to strive only for aims attainable to them as individuals. In this manner they satisfy nature's requirement that our adaptation energy and its machinery be used without, however, destroying it through overwork. The code is designed to achieve the pleasant stress of fulfillment, *eustress,* without the harmful consequences of damaging stress, *distress.*

The point of the code is not to abolish stress but to master it. It is a matter of choosing, not an undemanding lifestyle, but a eustressfully rather than distressfully demanding one.

I am proud to have been asked to write a foreword for AACN's Clinical Reference for Critical-Care Nursing, the first comprehensive reference book for critical-care nurses. The diverse nature of the administration and management of the critically ill demands a team effort of educated, dedicated, highly motivated professionals.

Assistance must be given, however, to health professionals to make a transition to holistic health. The AACN recognizes the need to promote a high standard of care for all patients. The text, by incorporating holistic methods into the regular healing practice, encourages the practitioner to become aware of the root of disease, through direct contact with the patient.

Hans Selye, C.C., M.D., Ph.D., D.Sc.
President, International Institute of Stress
Hans Selye Foundation

Editor's note: For further reading on Hans Selye's theory of stress, the reader is referred to his following works:
"Coping with Stress in 1979," *Information Please Almanac 1979,* Information Please Publishing, Inc., New York, 1979; *The Stress of Life,* McGraw-Hill, New York, 1976; *Stress Without Distress,* Lippincott, Philadelphia, 1974; "A Syndrome Produced by Diverse Nocuous Agents," *Nature* (London), 138:32, 1936.

PREFACE

Care of the critically ill person demands the attention of educated, dedicated, and highly motivated professionals. The American Association of Critical-Care Nurses recognizes the complexity of the nursing management of these patients and strives to meet the educational needs of critical-care nurses in order to ensure a high standard of care for all patients.

This volume represents another innovation in the promotion of competence in critical-care nursing practice. The competent critical-care nurse is one who has requisite knowledge and is adept in the skills of critical-care nursing. Requisite knowledge is outlined in the *AACN Core Curriculum for Critical-Care Nursing,* and this knowledge is measured by the AACN Certification Board in a program established to certify nurses in critical-care nursing (CCRN), thereby promoting a standard of excellence in the care of patients.

Providing a comprehensive reference for the practice of critical-care nursing, this book will serve to broaden and enhance the knowledge and skills of experienced nurses as they prepare for board certification. We highly recommend that it be included as a resource for critical-care unit libraries. Certain basic knowledge must be assumed. If supplements are required, the reader is encouraged to refer to references at the end of each chapter. This book is further recommended as a resource for the new graduate who enters practice. Its use is strongly encouraged in basic nursing educational programs and represents the AACN's support of the inclusion of critical-care nursing content and practice on the undergraduate level.

This collaborative multidiscipline work supports AACN's belief in and commitment to the team approach to the care of the critically ill. It focuses primarily on the adult patient and presents an original, integrated, and comprehensive study of serious illnesses as they involve and affect body systems. The contributors have attempted to avoid detailed descriptions of techniques and management of care that might be largely regional in nature.

Part 1 presents an overview of the conceptual foundation for critical-care nursing, including historical and philosophical considerations. Part 2 describes the physiology of body systems, the understanding of which serves as a basis for nursing practice. In Part 3 the reader will encounter a systems approach to physical assessment of the critically ill patient, including appropriate integration of historical data and consideration of patient status relative to application of examination techniques. The psychosocial aspects of critical-care nursing including psychosocial assessment of a critically ill person and his or her family are presented in Part 4. The interrelationship of systems in the assessment of clinical problems is featured in Part 5 with problems presented according to the degree to which they threaten life and well-being. Selective problems in patient care management are identified and discussed in Part 6 with special sections included on the management of patients with burns, multiple trauma, sepsis, and pediatric and perinatal crises. Realizing that criteria for and implementation of special procedures and therapies are varied, the purpose of Part 7 is to describe the rationale for their use and related nursing interventions. Part 8 is concerned with the critical-care environment. Instrumentation yielding important data is described, as are environmental hazards and mechanisms designed to enhance environmental safety. A divergent approach has been utilized in the presentation of Part 9—Issues in Critical–Care. A panel of experts provides insight and review by responding to questions dealing with current practice, legal, ethical, and spiritual considerations in the care of the critically ill. Part 10 focuses on the learning needs of the critically ill person and his family. Assessment of the need for an organized program of patient teaching as well as implementation of such a program is described. Principles of teaching and learning, as utilized by the critical-care nurse, are discussed. In the appendixes two subjects are presented in table format—dysrhythmias and pharmacology. A thorough review of these two topics is needed since they are common threads throughout all parts of the reference text.

The future of critical-care nursing and the quality of care of the critically ill patient will be determined by those who study these pages. The American Association of Critical-Care Nurses is pleased to initiate another means for the dissemination of information to our colleagues.

A volume such as this attests to the contributions of many and the indebtedness of the editors is great. Primary acknowledgment is given to the Board of Directors and National Office Staff of AACN, including the late Warren F. Stevens, for initial and continuing support of this endeavor.

The consistent guidance of the staff at McGraw-Hill Book Company is appreciated, particularly Orville Haberman, Stuart Boynton, Bob Leap, Hank De Leo, Carol Swain and Jeanne Skahan. In the early days McGraw-Hill was represented by Cathy Somer, Joseph J. Brehm, and Sally J. Barhydt, and we remember with fondness their wise counsel and humor.

Invaluable assistance was provided by the following individuals: Ellen Adkins and Ann Severson for typing and manuscript preparation; J. Stanley Conner, M.D., Wayne E. Dear, M.D., Sara Sanford, R.N., Sandra Dunbar, R.N., and Carolyn Sue Dery, R.N., for review and critique of selected manuscripts; Paula Bernal, for assistance in ways too numerous to mention.

The editors are grateful to the following individuals for providing the endpaper color photographs: Christopher Bryan-Brown, M.D., Director, Surgical-Respiratory Intensive Care Unit, Mount Sinai Medical Center, New York City; James de Leon, Jr., Technical Director, Medical Photography and Illustrations, St. Luke's Episcopal Hospital, Houston, Texas; Kathleen J. Mikan, R.N., Ph.D., Director, Learning Resource Center, University of Alabama School of Nursing, Birmingham, Alabama; and Marie L. O'Koren, R.N., Ed.D., Dean, University of Alabama School of Nursing, Birmingham. Alabama.

Special acknowledgment is given to Carolyn House Ehrlich for her valuable contributions provided in the early stages of this project. Her enthusiasm and vision have meant a great deal to the editors.

Finally, we wish to acknowledge our contributors whose expertise they so willingly shared. Fond memories will continue of new associations formed as a result of this volume.

Marguerite Rodgers Kinney
Cynthia Boyd Dear
Donna Rogers Packa
Dorothy M. Nagelhout Voorman

PART 1

CONCEPTUAL FOUNDATIONS

THE ART

In the last two decades the concept of critical care has marked the beginning of a new dimension in nursing, that of focusing on the whole patient as a one-body system. Critical-care nursing offers a challenge to those nurses who are attracted to frontiers of patient care. The critical-care nurse fulfills a complex role in bedside nursing which involves expert assessment of the clinical status of the patient in the hope of prompt diagnosis, detection of the earliest signs of complications, and initiation of and participation in a program of treatment.

A successful organizational structure recognizes the primacy of the nurse. The increased diagnostic and therapeutic responsibility of the nurse is the most important component of the structure of any critical-care unit.

In the early 1960s some of us may have been frightened by our awesome responsibility, mortal privileges, and undefined scope of practice. We were fed a great deal of knowledge by superb minds, our physician mentors. The advent of critical care, or "intensive care," as it was formerly known, required individuals who were innovative—individuals who made an impact and had influence on the prevailing norms and values of the time. These individuals were often labeled "supernurses" or "junior doctors." The inference, many times, was a deviant personality. In reality, they were simply providers of optimal nursing care and highly motivated, intelligent, skilled, and caring individuals.

Cardiovascular Critical Care

Nursing needs of patients became more complex as cardiopulmonary bypass and open-heart surgery evolved in the 1950s. In the early 1960s cardiopulmonary resuscitation, electrical defibrillation, hemodialysis, and cardiac pacemakers came into routine use. Dedicated patient surveillance with monitoring of the electrocardiogram, central venous pressure, intra-arterial pressure, and intra-aortic balloon counterpulsation was implemented in critical care units.

The intensive coronary care unit (CCU) dates back to 1962. The appearance of the CCU was made possible by advances in closed-chest resuscitation, proliferation of continuous electronic monitoring techniques, and the development of defibrillation and synchronized cardioversion. The early units relied on these approaches to achieve the limited objective of responding to acute catastrophic disturbances which

1

CRITICAL-CARE NURSING: AN ART, A SCIENCE, AND A SPIRIT

Dorothy M. Nagelhout Voorman

THE ART
Cardiovascular Critical Care
Pulmonary Critical Care
Neurological-Neurosurgical Critical Care
Renal Critical Care
Medical-Surgical Critical Care
Burn Care
Pediatric Critical Care
Newborn Critical Care
Obstetrical Care
Future Directions

THE SCIENCE
Assessment of Competence
An Educational Barrier
Continuing Education

THE SPIRIT
The Separation of Nursing Education and Nursing Practice
Image of Nursing
Technical versus Professional Preparation for Practice
Fragmentation of Care
Technology and Lifesaving Techniques
Death by Chance or by Choice?
Nurse-Physician Relationships

FORECASTS FOR THE FUTURE
The Team Approach
Research
The Critical-Care Nurse

REFERENCES

often proved fatal in patients with myocardial infarction. As a result, the mortality rate from acute myocardial infarction has been reduced from 30 or 35 percent of hospitalized patients to 10 or 15 percent.

Evolution and change have characterized the CCU since its inception. These units have become the place to prevent rather than react to catastrophe. As a result, the role of the nurse is constantly changing.

More recently, automated dysrhythmia detection, the use of flow-directed pulmonary artery catheters, the measurement of cardiac output, and the use of the left ventricular assist devices have rapidly moved to the forefront. Radiographic techniques have made possible the emergency diagnosis of life-threatening defects involving the coronary, aortic, cerebral, pulmonary, renal, and mesenteric circulations. The most difficult and unresolved problem continues to be satisfactory therapy of the power failure syndrome, which is still responsible for 80 to 90 percent of deaths.

Dysrhythmias are controlled with numerous drugs, pacemakers, synchronized cardioversion, and defibrillators. The ruptured septum, torn papillary muscle, and ventricular aneurysms are now surgically correctable. Diseased coronary arteries are successfully bypassed with venous and arterial grafts. We look forward to the day when uncontrolled dysrhythmias, cardiogenic shock, and intractable heart failure will prove amenable to therapy.

Pulmonary Critical Care

Endotracheal intubation and mechanical ventilation have come into routine use within the last 10 years. The field of pulmonary care has mushroomed in the last decade and is now considered a distinct clinical discipline. With this growth, the level of competence of the nurse, as well as that of the entire team, has been raised considerably. The immediate availability of repetitive blood-gas analysis as a guide to respiratory and metabolic management has become routine during the last 10 years.

Positive end-expiratory pressure (PEEP) has been used increasingly during the last decade to improve oxygenation with a lower FI_{O_2}. Newer developments aiding nursing care include smaller, quieter ventilators with alarm systems, low-pressure endotracheal tubes, weaning protocols, and intermittent mandatory ventilation. Extracorporeal membrane oxygenation has been studied and determined useful only in highly specific instances.

It has been predicted that the future will reveal the following: acute respiratory distress syndrome (ARDS) will have more iatrogenic causes than suspected at this time; yoga and breathing techniques will be used in clinical practice; selective treatment and ventilation of affected lung segments will be possible; the concept of humidification for patients with artificial airways will be altered radically; iron lungs will see increased service; and a group of antibiotic-resistant organisims will choose the lungs as the ideal medium.

The pulmonary nurse specialist, because of preparation, experience, ongoing education, and participation in research is uniquely prepared to coordinate the efforts of all pulmonary team members.

Neurological-Neurosurgical Critical Care

The twentieth century has brought with it an unprecedented era of technical and scientific discovery which has had a profound effect on neurological-neurosurgical nursing. Craniotomies for brain tumor, abscess, hematoma, and aneurysm are routine. Spinal surgery for herniated disk, spinal cord tumor, and vascular malformations of the cord are performed successfully. Increased numbers and complexity of neurosurgical procedures have produced a need for a large number of specialized nurses. As a routine, these individuals must work closely with many other specialists, such as the neurosurgeon, the social worker, respiratory therapist, physical therapist, psychiatric nurse clinician, community health nurse, and often the oncology nurse clinician.

Advances in the area of intracranial pressure monitoring have been made and continue to develop and improve.

Advances made in pulmonary care have contributed significantly to the safe and effective care of the neurological-neurosurgical patient who is critically ill. Advances in the field of microneurosurgery are continually being made. Microscopic anastomosis and transplantation of peripheral, cranial, and spinal nerves are in the early stages of development.

All these advances have demanded sophisticated nursing knowledge and practice in highly stressful life-and-death situations.

Renal Critical Care

One of the major scientific advances in medicine of the last 25 years has been the development of the artificial kidney, the first time a physical device has been able to substitute for the function of a human internal organ. Although in theory hemodialysis might appear to be a simple procedure, in practice it is a complex operation requiring a closely integrated team approach for its successful completion.

The introduction of scientific and technological advances has increased the number of patients amenable to peritoneal dialysis, hemodialysis, and renal transplantation. New discoveries have contributed to earlier diagnosis and prolonged survival of individuals with renal dysfunction.

The evolution of nephrology nursing practice has been an exciting process. However, progress to date seems minimal in comparison to the potential for future growth. Nephrology nursing is now in a stage of dynamic activism.

Medical-Surgical Critical Care

Medical-surgical critical-care units were developed in the early 1960s for the care of patients with medical and surgical emergencies and/or extensive or complicated surgery. Patients undergoing hemodialysis are often found in these units. Care is also provided for patients with multisystem failure, metabolic disorders, blood dyscrasias, hepatic dysfunction, and a host of other serious disorders. The complexity and the variety of the patient population in these units creates a complex task in terms of organization and management.

Burn Care

Burn units were established to provide a safe environment for the resuscitation of patients with serious burns. The nurse plays a major role in facilitating the patient's acceptance of a new body image and adaptation to numerous stressors. The burn nurse must integrate the knowledge of physiology, pathophysiology, microbiology, nutrition, psychology, and sociology.

Pediatric Critical Care

Pediatric units were designed in order to separate children with acute diseases or injuries from the adult population. The needs of children are obviously so specialized that this is now a specialty unto itself.

Newborn Critical Care

Neonatal units are a more recent addition to the system. Newborns of low birth weight and with severe illness requiring life support demand highly special-

ized care delivered by a team separate and distinct from all other specialties.

Obstetrical Care

Obstetrical units have been created to provide optimal care for the woman at high risk during labor and delivery. In general, both the mother and the neonate can be expected to benefit from specialized care and facilities prior to delivery.

Future Directions

There are many unknowns regarding the future of critical-care nursing and its many subspecialties. Nurses have played a major role in advancing patient care to date, and they will continue to be among the leaders of the health care team in the future.

We must continue to address the numerous problems affecting all types of units. These include our leadership structure, infection control, pain control, nutritional management, as well as psychosocial and ethical issues.

Care of the critically ill patient encompasses all aspects of nursing, and therefore it is the ultimate nursing role.

THE SCIENCE

Competence in one's chosen field is generally accepted as a basic characteristic of all professions. In order to be accountable for competence, the nurse must be cognizant of accepted standards of nursing practice. What particular clinical knowledge and skills are necessary to practice effectively within one's specific area of professional nursing? What avenues are open to the nurse who seeks to grow professionally? The nurse's daily experience in caring for acutely ill patients is a dimension of education which cannot be achieved in any other manner. Critical-care nurses have not been content to wait for others to define their role. Indeed, who can question the integrity and professionalism of nurses who care enough to develop and maintain methods for their own professional growth in their chosen specialty?

Assessment of Competence

All of us begin as professionals. What we do beyond that has been more or less left up to the individual. The biggest advantage of critical-care nursing practice is that one can develop a significant knowledge base without leaving the bedside for an extended period of time.

Critical-care nursing practice demands that the individual practitioner assume the responsibility for identification of personal needs for continuing education. As Hammerschmidt (1973) has pointed out, this evaluation is not entirely an internal one, for the individual functions as a member of a group. How do other disciplines represented in the health care team see the nurse's contribution to patient care? How does the employing agency view a nurse's level of competence? How do patients respond to the level of nursing care provided them? The sum of this information provides the individual with the assessment upon which continuing education can be carried out.

The very existence of a profession implies the need for constant updating, constant refinement, and constant growth. In the writings of Florence Nightingale there appears the following statement:

> Nursing is a progressive art, In which to stand still is to go back. A woman who thinks to herself, Now I am a full nurse, a skilled nurse, I have learnt all there is to be learnt. Take my word for it, she does not know What a nurse is, and never will know, She is gone back already. Progress can never end but with a nurse's life.

An Educational Barrier

One of the barriers to close collaboration of physicians and nurses has been the huge knowledge gap that lay between them. With increasing numbers of nurses being educated in university schools and with more interest in clinical graduate programs, continuing education, and certification, the knowledge bases of physician and nurse have taken on a similar structure. This does not mean that nurses will encroach on medical practice or that physicians will pass on to nurses unwanted tasks. It does mean that the care of patients will be more certain and of higher quality.

Continuing Education

Continuing education for professions has rapidly increased in importance in recent years. With increased sophistication of monitoring techniques and increased scrutiny of health care delivery by consumers, the professional nurse needs more opportunities for continuing education in order to meet the stresses and demands in caring for the critically ill. The passage of mandatory continuing education requirements for relicensure in many states reflects the consumers' demand for current and proficient delivery of health care. Continuing education and certification programs are vital to the nurse who wants to meet the challenges of critical-care nursing.

THE SPIRIT

The practice of critical-care nursing has played a major role in the evolution of nursing as a true profession. As we strive to continue our focus on the whole patient, the client, and the public, this evolution will continue.

Our practice as critical-care professionals is confronted by many far-reaching issues destined to affect the lives and careers of all of us. Issues to be addressed and resolved are discussed below.

The Separation of Nursing Education and Nursing Practice

American nursing has actively worked to make changes and improve content in nursing education. Certainly, astute individuals in nursing perceive that not all the results have been positive nor has a totality of solutions been secured. Barriers remain for many nurses attempting to secure the next step in the educational ladder. Some nurses have overcome this barrier, but through much effort, expense, and negotiation in terms of family and life-style.

Image of Nursing

Our function is still viewed by much of society as nurturing, and patients will continue to expect our nurturance; but increasing numbers of patients will demand deliberative, competent nursing practice and will give less support to the inadequate medical and nursing practice of others.

Technical versus Professional Preparation for Practice

In the past, nurses have been charged with conforming to existing patterns that are task-oriented or technically oriented. Critical-care nursing practitioners continue to bridge the gap between nursing theory and practice. If theory becomes practice, both the patient and the nursing profession will experience satisfaction. The care of seriously ill people demands competent and dedicated professionals who espouse the philosophy that education is a process to be continued—not a task to be completed.

Fragmentation of Care

All members of the critical-care team are vital and necessary, but all physician-directed care must remain coordinated by the registered professional nurse. This responsibility must not be diluted. The contribution of other team members is not to be minimized. Their presence is desired and essential and they should provide service in our units, but we must not allow independent function or authority of these individuals where the patient's total integrity is essential to survival.

Technology and Lifesaving Techniques

For all of us, death is inevitable. In critical care we sometimes deny this natural phenomenon. Advanced technology has provided the means to maintain biological life and also to prolong the process of dying. Is this what we want for our patients, our loved ones, and even for ourselves?

Death by Chance or by Choice?

The burden of guilt compounded by prolonging the life of hopeless cases through costly and complex treatments is very real. Must it continue until euthanasia engenders sufficient support for acceptable alternatives? Must we allow patients to determine their own destiny by the use of a "living will" so that health professionals will not incur liability?

Our society tends to ignore death as an integral part of the life cycle. Many of us are often offended by the lengths to which we go to prolong the dying individual's suffering, thus denying a person's human right to a dignified and natural death.

Nurse-Physician Relationships

Important as well-engineered hardware is, the success of a system for the care of the critically ill depends upon the critical-care team. The physicians and nurses which make up this team must continually interact and grow. Performance evaluation must be ongoing as physiologic data are translated into improved patient care.

The unit that adheres to the traditional nurse-physician roles is, at best, mediocre. The historic dependent relationship between physician and nurse is being replaced by one of interdependence. Instead of functioning almost exclusively on physician dictate, nurses are now more willing to act on their own

observations and are responsible for the consequences of their decisions. As physicians and nurses work together under this format of care, new relationships are springing forth. Desires, demands, and wishes of both groups are laid aside, so that the total care structure is built upon a scientific assessment of the patients' clinical needs.

Clinical competence is the chief status symbol. These changes have demanded courage and candor, but the professional excitement and quality of patient care make the investment of time and effort in the endeavor seem more than worthwhile.

FORECASTS FOR THE FUTURE

Basic physiologic concepts will probably change very little, but therapeutic methods may change as unpredictably as women's hemlines.

As critical-care nurses we will be faced with ever-increasing automation and computerization. An important challenge will be to prevent dehumanization in patient care.

One area of vital importance in the overall management of the patient will not change. The one consistent need expressed by patients and families is for emotional support. Perhaps the need for humanism is the most dramatic, yet the most intangible, since it involves people-to-people relationships. This indescribable concern for the well-being of the patient who is seriously ill somehow enhances the effectiveness of medical, nursing, and technological skills.

The Team Approach

Care of the critically ill will continue to demand educated, dedicated, and highly motivated professionals. The respect and trust developed as a team of physicians and nurses works together to assist the patient adds immeasurably to the quality of care afforded that patient. The team approach to patient care, more than any other single factor—more than specially designed rooms or sophisticated equipment—is the justification for our commitment to the critical-care concept.

Research

The possibilities are endless when contemplating the future of critical-care nursing and the role of the nurse. Research-based nursing practice will be the "common" practice. Nursing's unique body of knowledge and right to independent practice are being evidenced through research. Standards of care, such as those developed by the American Association of Critical-Care Nurses (AACN), are another important form of research assuring quality of care.

The Critical-Care Nurse

One forecast would seem a certainty: Professional nurses responsible for the care of critically ill patients must be selected on the basis of competence as well as certain personality characteristics. The competent nurse is one who has the requisite knowledge and who is adept in the skills of critical-care nursing. Requisite knowledge is outlined in "AACN's Core Curriculum for Critical-Care Nursing," and this knowledge is measured by the AACN Certification Board in a program established to certify nurses in critical-care nursing (CCRN) and thereby promote excellence in the care of patients.

In a quotation from Otis Maxwell, the criteria used in the selection of National Aeronautics and Space Administration personnel fittingly describes the personality necessary for high-stress critical-care nursing:

A capacity and quality for self acceptance,
The ability to function in the face of Ambiguity,
A minimum of No-no,
A maximum of Yes-yes,
A vocabulary of enthusiasm
and a capacity for mutuality.

REFERENCES

AACN Position Paper: Prevention of fragmentation of patient care: The coordinative role of the critical-care nurse, *Heart & Lung* 5(5):693, 1976.

Adler, D. C.: Pulmonary nursing, 1900–1979, and future projections, *Heart & Lung* 8(5):882, 1979.

Baer, C.: The growth and development of nephrology nursing practice, *Heart & Lung* 8(5): 896, 1979.

Hammerschmidt, R.: President's message, *Heart & Lung* 2(3):330, 1973.

Larson, C.: Where are you . . . in the process of becoming? *Heart & Lung* 2(4):480, 1973.

Simpson, L.: CEUs-CERPs and CCRN: The future of critical care nursing, *Heart & Lung* 5(2): 201, 1976.

Stevens, W.: Expanded roles of critical care nurses, *Heart & Lung* 4(5):673, 1975.

Willie, R.: Neurosurgical nursing: Past, present, and future, *Heart & Lung* 8(5):891, 1979.

Man is a multiple amphibian living in many worlds at once; he lives in the world of the individual and the world of society; he lives in the world of symbols and in the world of given heredity and of acquired cultural values; and everything that happens to so complex a human being must necessarily have multiple causes.

Aldous Huxley

The focus of the nurse engaged in care of the critically ill is the individual with all of the human complexities. Our understanding of human beings and their behavior is quite incomplete, and yet the critical-care nurse is faced with the responsibility of dealing not only with the patient's response to the illness or injury but with the response to treatment as well. The definition of critical-care nursing practice adopted by the American Association of Critical-Care Nurses identifies as part of the bases for practice a recognition and appreciation of one's wholeness, uniqueness, and significant social and environmental relationships.

What is meant by wholeness and uniqueness, and how are they to be recognized? What is meant by social and environmental relationships, and what are their dimensions? These questions must be addressed if a holistic approach to the care of the critically ill is to be identified.

Holism is a philosophical theory according to which wholes are not reducible to the sum of their parts. Fundamental to the concept of holism is the generalization that certain attributes which are not present, or at least not evident, become evident as components are added together. For example, springs and wheels and a variety of moving parts put together in a certain way may form a clock which is distinct from any of the separate parts. An understanding of how a clock works cannot be obtained from study of any of the separate parts. Understanding can come only from study of both the components and the functional whole. Muller (1943) has stated that even though parts and processes may be isolated for purposes of analysis, they cannot be understood except in the context of a dynamic unified whole that is more than their sum.

The concept of holistic man is expanded by Whitehead (1964), who presents an ecological view of the individual in saying that the body is continuous with the rest of the world. What dimensions are added to the concept of holistic man by this ecological view?

Ecology is derived from the Greek word *oikos,* meaning "house," and refers to the study of the totality of human beings and environment, or to the whole "environmental house." Ecology has been combined

2
THE HOLISTIC APPROACH TO THE CARE OF THE CRITICALLY ILL

Marguerite Rodgers Kinney

with the term *system* to form a new term, *ecosystem.* System, defined as regularly interacting and interdependent components forming a unified whole, provides regularity and interdependence to a concept of individuals and their relationship with the environment. Considering the individual within the context of the ecosystem enlarges the view beyond the person, encompassing social and environmental relationships.

The ecosystem of an individual undergoes rapid and drastic alteration with the onset of a critical illness. Obier and Haywood (1973) describe the critically ill as being in a desperate situation. Many are catapulted into the critical-care unit with no time for preparation, resulting in a psychosocial as well as physiologic crisis. The environment exists as an obstacle to the patient who is attempting to adjust to the situation. Typically there is separation from family and the usual support systems, strange and unusual sights and sounds, repetitive routines, numerous unfamiliar personnel, lack of privacy or quiet, and a variety of machines and equipment surrounding the bedside. In discussing the advances which have occurred in the care of the critically ill, Weinberg (1973) concluded that scientific excellence was inadequate if it is accompanied by a failure to recognize the patient and the person attached to the disease.

A holistic conception offered by Spring (1969) delineates three subsystems within the individual, namely, physical, intellectual, and emotional. Each of these subsystems is influenced by and strongly influences the others. Spring's conception takes into account the individual's interaction with the environment even though the environmental subsystems are not specified and described.

The physical subsystem is seen to be important in that the individual is a biological being. There are physiologic limits within which the physical subsystem optimally operates. Complex monitoring and feedback systems serve to maintain the physiologic variables within rather narrow ranges. Taxation of these systems beyond their capabilities evokes compensatory mechanisms which serve to optimize physiologic functioning but, generally speaking, with temporal limitations.

The intellectual subsystem is described as an extension of the physical subsystem and is characterized by the ordering of information, dependence upon the environment, and adaptability to additional information. Important to consider is the patient's perception of the situation and interpretation of what is happening. Behavioral responses will not be related to the overt reality of the situation but to the individual's own perception of the situation. A myriad of variables interplay to color this perception of what is taking place. According to Kiely (1973), the patient's age, intelligence, characteristic personality style, belief systems, emotional state, and cognitive capacity all contribute to the illness experience and determine the patient's reaction to that experience.

The emotional subsystem encompasses feelings or responses to internal and external stimuli and the capacity for response is intimately related to both the physical and intellectual subsystems. Emotional responses to sudden, serious alterations in health have been equated with responses to other types of loss. These patterned responses have been labeled the "grieving process," with nonpathologic as well as pathologic behaviors described. Initially, in the process of coming to grips with the situation, the individual attempts to alter reality through such behaviors as denial, striking out in anger, or stoicism. Gradually the person begins to acknowledge the loss and works through depression and mourning to resolution of the grief process. Abnormally long periods of denial, anger, or depression are pathologic and require intervention.

The conception of subsystems which are strongly interrelated allows for attention to be focused within one subsystem with recognition of the influence of and on the other two. However, the primary merit of this conception is seen to be that inattention to or ignoring of other subsystems and their potential influences is not allowed. For example, during a cardiopulmonary arrest, attention to the physical subsystem is mandatory, but successful resuscitation is followed by assessment of the needs within the intellectual and emotional subsystems with appropriate interventions. To practice otherwise would be to ignore the intimate relationships between and among the three subsystems and would therefore be contrary to a holistic approach to care.

What implications for nursing can be derived from a holistic conception? Attention to the physical subsystem by critical-care nurses is unsurpassed by any other subgroup within the profession. Utilizing sophisticated instrumentation and biomedical devices, the critical-care nurse collects data related to the physical subsystem and, through complex cognitive processes, makes judgments about the physical status of the patient. Subtle alterations in status and/or responses to therapy can be detected early before they become profound. The tenuous reliance upon intuition has been replaced by the confident collection and use of reliable data. Additionally, the critical-care nurse attends to the physical subsystem by supporting the physical level of functioning and promoting the development of physical resources. Patients in critical-care units are particularly susceptible to diminishing physical levels of functioning. Catabolic states and immobility compound the problems of illness and injury. Nursing interventions designed to minimize energy requirements and passively mobilize the extremities support the present physical level of functioning and diminish susceptibility to a reduced level of functioning.

Attention to the intellectual subsystem by the critical-care nurse includes replacing haphazard patient contacts with purposeful, informed communication. According to Obier and Haywood (1973) some of the deleterious effects of the critical-care environment can be minimized or alleviated by simple, direct, and sensitive communication with the patient. Sharing information with the patient is reassuring and supports the patient's adjustment to the situation. Because pain, anxiety, fear, and fatigue alter comprehension and retention, simple and brief explanations should be offered and should be repeated and reinforced at intervals.

The emotional subsystem may suffer more inattention by the critical-care nurse than the other two subsystems. Kiely (1973) underscores the importance of appraising and evaluating the attitudes, feelings, and responses of the sick person. He concludes that even though treatment of disease or injury may be highly impersonal and technical, the care of the patient must be highly personal if the so-called "intensive-care syndrome" is to be avoided. Attention to the emotional subsystem by the critical-care nurse is reflected in the purposeful collection of data related to the emotional response of the patient to the illness or injury and to the treatment being given. Further, the development of a plan of care which supports adaptive behavior or intervenes in maladaptive responses is seen as an essential component of nursing care.

At the first glance the subsystem conception proposed by Spring (1969) appears to emphasize the similarities which exist among human beings. However, with more detailed study, one can easily identify that it is the differences in physical components and functioning, in thoughts and ideas, and in feelings and responses which make each individual unique. Unique is derived from the Latin word *unicus*, meaning "one." As defined by Webster the word means being the only one. Inasmuch as variables particular to the

individual contribute to the illness experience, it is readily apparent that the individual's reaction to the experience will be unique. Humanizing critical care means recognizing the uniqueness of each patient without placing a value on the variables which account for the uniqueness.

Levine (1971) has identified the goal of all nursing care as the promotion of wholeness and offers the reminder that for each individual promotion of wholeness requires a unique and separate cluster of activities. Spring (1969) says that nurses have been and are in an advantageous position to interact with persons who for a circumscribed time are patients, and she reminds us that coupled to this advantage is the responsibility to interact with human beings rather than attend to organs or systems. She warns that this advantage is not a permanent opportunity and must not be taken for granted. The alternative to a holistic approach is fragmented care which will be resisted by individuals who see themselves not as a collection of parts but as whole beings. They will recognize such an approach as dehumanizing, an outcome described as intolerable by Griffith (1973), who identified attention to the human needs of the critically ill as a goal of highest priority. Weinberg (1973) has admonished health care professionals to make progress in the humane aspects of critical care as they keep pace with technical and scientific advances.

Progress in the humane aspects of critical care can be made through planning interventions that are essentially a "keeping together" or conservation of the wholeness of the individual patient. Levine (1971) identifies four major areas of care in which nurses can fulfill a conservation function: energy, structural integrity, personal integrity, and social integrity. Energy conservation requires attention to both the input of elements necessary for production and the proper disbursement of energy. Parameters indicative of the individual's capabilities, safety, and comfort have not been empirically tested and verified and are a fruitful area for clinical research.

Conservation of structural integrity is seen in those interventions which serve to defend the patient from extension of disease or injury to unaffected parts, from bacterial invasion, and from bodily injury.

Personal integrity can be conserved by first recognizing that the patient brings to the critical-care unit those patterns of behavior which have been developed over a lifetime. Levine suggests that the first step in the holistic appraisal of the patient must always be the identification of the patterns of response to the predicament followed by mutual planning toward the goal of renewed well-being.

Finally, conservation of social integrity means consideration of the patient within the context of cultural, ethnic, religious, and family relationships. Levine says that the holistic view of the individual must include the close, personal ties the patient has with life beyond the predicament of illness itself. Visiting policies in many critical-care units foster the interruption of social relationships and augment the "desperate situation" in which the critical-care patient finds himself. If such policies must remain, the critical-

care nurse can serve as an intermediary between the patient and significant others. Frequent reminders that those close to the patient are nearby, are inquiring about the patient's well-being, and are being kept informed of all progress may be helpful in conserving the patient's social integrity.

As increasing dehumanization accompanies automated technology and scientific advances, a holistic approach to care of the critically ill offers an alternative to fragmented, dehumanized interactions with persons who for a period of time happen to be patients.

REFERENCES

Encyclopaedia Britannica, Chicago, 1975, 6:2816.

Gentry, William Doyle, and Redford B. Williams (eds.): *Psychological Aspects of Myocardial Infarction and Coronary Care,* St. Louis: Mosby, 1975.

Griffith, George C.: The human needs of the critically ill, *Heart and Lung* 2(1):47–48, 1973.

Kiely, William F.: Critical-care psychiatric syndromes, *Heart and Lung* 2(1):54–57, 1973.

Levine, Myra E.: Holistic nursing, *Nurs Clin North Am* 6:253–264, June 1971.

Muller, H. J.: *Science and Criticism,* New Haven: Yale University Press, 1943.

Obier, Kathleen, and L. Julian Haywood: Enhancing therapeutic communication with acutely ill patients, *Heart and Lung* 2(1):49–53, 1973.

Spring, Faye E.: Man: A holistic conception for nursing; Final report of pilot project, Frances Payne Bolton School of Nursing, Case Western Reserve University, Cleveland, 1969.

Webster's Third New International Dictionary, Springfield, Mass.: Merriam, 1961.

Weinberg, Sylvan Lee: Toward humane care for the critically ill, *Heart and Lung* 2(1):43–44, 1973.

Whitehead, Alfred North: *Adventures of Ideas,* New York: Mentor, 1964.

PART 2

THE PHYSIOLOGIC BASIS OF CRITICAL-CARE NURSING

Often much time is spent in the pursuit of understanding in great detail the various phases of respiration. However it must be remembered that the ultimate goal of respiration is to provide the cells with oxygen for their efficient and effective use. The goal is not merely to have an acyanotic patient with a Pa_{O_2} of 95 mmHg, but to have a patient whose cells are receiving and using oxygen. Otherwise, despite an excellent Pa_{O_2} and good coloring, the patient will die.

REVIEW OF GAS LAWS

It is necessary to review the gas laws that are the principles by which the respiratory gases are obtained and eliminated.

The *ideal gas law* states that pressure, volume, and temperature have fixed relationships. An ideal gas is an abstract entity of chemistry and physics. The gases discussed here are real gases which behave differently at extreme temperatures and pressures. However, within the normal temperatures and pressures of the earth, they closely mimic ideal gases. Therefore, we will equate them. According to the ideal gas law, if one of the three—temperature, pressure, or volume—changes and a second remains unchanged, then the third will change in a predictable manner.

Boyle's Law

$$T(temperature) = P(pressure) \times V(volume)$$

When temperature remains constant, the pressure of a gas varies inversely to the volume. Hence, if the volume decreases, the pressure will increase, and if the volume increases, the pressure will decrease.

Charles's Law

$$P = T/V$$

When pressure remains constant, the volume and temperature vary proportionately. Thus, if the temperature rises, so does the volume and vice versa.

Gay LuSaac's Law

$$V = T/P$$

When the volume remains constant, the temperature and pressure vary proportionately. Again, if the temperature rises, so does the pressure and vice versa. Remember this when storing oxygen tanks or any gas sealed under pressure.

3
THE PULMONARY SYSTEM
Mary Webb Waldron
Laura McHenry Fray

REVIEW OF GAS LAWS
Boyle's Law
Charles's Law
Gay-LuSaac's Law
Dalton's Law of Partial Pressure
Henry's Law

VENTILATION
Sources of Resistance in Ventilation
Gas Distribution

DIFFUSION OF RESPIRATORY GASES
Partial Pressures
Effects of Gas Concentration Changes

PERFUSION OF BLOOD
Determinants of Pulmonary Resistance
Pressure Variations in the Lung

TRANSPORTATION OF RESPIRATORY GASES
Dissolved Oxygen
Oxygen Bound to Hemoglobin
Carbon Dioxide

NERVOUS SYSTEM CONTROL OF BLOOD GASES
Location and Function of Centers
Chemoreceptors
Secondary Receptors Within the Lungs
Secondary Receptors Outside the Lungs

ABNORMALITIES OF VENTILATION/PERFUSION RATIO

HYPOXEMIA AND HYPOXIA

REFERENCES

Dalton's Law of Partial Pressure

This law states that, in a gas mixture, the total pressure of that volume equals the sum of the pressures that each individual gas exerts. Each gas exerts a pressure according to the percentage of the total volume it occupies. This fact remains regardless of which gases are making up the mixture. An obvious example of this is room air. Room air at sea level of 1 atm has a total pressure of 760 mmHg. Since it is a gas mixture, it is made up of multiple gases, among which are nitrogen, water vapor, oxygen, and carbon dioxide. Thus, in order to determine the pressure exerted by oxygen, one needs to know that approximately 21 percent of room air is oxygen. This is approximately 158 mmHg. Thus the *partial pressure* (P_{O_2}) of oxygen in room air is 158 mmHg. *Tension* is, another word for partial pressure.

Henry's Law

When a gas is over a liquid, some molecules from that gas move into that liquid and they will exert a pressure within the liquid, as long as they do not combine chemically with substances within the liquid. (See Fig. 3-1.) The amount of gas that enters depends on the pressure of the gas over the liquid and the solubility of the particular gas in the particular liquid. The movement of the gas into and out of the liquid occurs in order to achieve equilibrium. It is this pressure exerted by oxygen or carbon dioxide in the blood plasma that is measured when an arterial blood gas analysis is done. The results are written as Pa_{O_2} for the arterial partial pressure of oxygen and Pa_{CO_2} for that of carbon dioxide.

VENTILATION

Ventilation, the first phase of respiration, is the process of getting gas into and out of the lungs. The flow of gas into the lungs occurs by the process of diffusion. Diffusion states that a gas flows from an area of higher pressure or concentration to one of lower pressure or concentration. Here Boyle's law is seen at work. The diaphragm contracts downward and the intercostals contract upward. These two actions together increase the area (volume) of the thoracic cavity; thus, the intrapulmonary pressures decrease. Air then enters the lung. Normal, quiet expiration is a passive process resulting from the recoil of the diaphragm and the elastic properties of the lung itself. This decreases

the area of the lung which increases the pressure within the lung over that of the atmosphere; hence air exits the lung.

The negative pressure of inspiration not only brings air into the lungs, but by its transmission throughout the thoracic cavity, aids venous return to the right heart. When this normal negative pressure is lost, as in the use of mechanical ventilation, cardiac output can be reduced because of decreased venous return.

It is important to know that the diaphragm is innervated by the phrenic nerves which originate from the spinal cord at the sixth cervical vertebra. The diaphragm is the chief inspiratory muscle, without which no respiration takes place. This is not so for the intercostals, which are supplied by the intercostal nerves. The intercostal nerves arise from the sixth cervical vertebra. What this means is that it is the higher cervical injuries, C5 and above, that will cause respiratory paralysis.

The amount of air inhaled or exhaled is known as the *tidal volume* (VT). It is normally 10 to 15 mL per kg of body weight. Not all the tidal volume is involved in gas exchange. Some of it does not reach the alveoli and bronchioles where gas exchange with the pulmonary capillaries takes place. This air remains in the conduction tubes of the respiratory system at the end of inspiration: the nose, mouth, pharnyx, larynx, trachea, and large bronchi. This amount is normally approximately one-third of the tidal volume and is termed *anatomical dead space*. Anatomical dead space is reduced when a tracheostomy is used for ventilation and increased when a long endotracheal tube is used. A general definition for all types of dead space is that it is wasted ventilation (because it is not involved in gas exchange).

Alveolar dead space is air that reaches alveoli that are not perfused with blood. An example of this is a pulmonary embolus occluding a portion of the pulmonary vasculature. The total amount of dead space (VD) equals the sum of anatomical and alveolar dead space. More attention will be given to this topic later in the chapter.

The volume of air that is directly involved in gas exchange is known as *alveolar ventilation*. It is equal to VT−VD. The carbon dioxide tension of systemic arterial blood (Pa_{CO_2}) is an accurate indicator of alveolar ventilation. As alveolar ventilation increases, the removal of CO_2 increases linearly. Therefore, the Pa_{CO_2} decreases. The opposite also holds true. This reciprocal relationship is not true for the Pa_{O_2}. Arterial oxygen tensions are determined by multiple factors of which alveolar ventilation is only one.

Sources of Resistance in Ventilation

Inspiration is an active process and expiration is normally a passive one. There are forces opposing inspiration that are termed *resistance*. The types of resistance found in the pulmonary system are (1) elastic resistance, (2) nonelastic, or viscous, resistance, and (3) airflow resistance.

Elastic Resistance

The lung deflates during expiration because of the recoil due to its elastic tissue.

The relative rigidity of the thorax counterbalances the recoil of the lung and thus prevents a total collapse with each expiration. Lung and chest wall work together as a unit. Surface tension of the pleural fluid contributes to this smooth-working relationship. Surface tension is the force of attraction exerted by fluid molecules on one another. The pleural fluid forms a thin layer between the visceral pleura embracing the lung and the parietal pleura adhering to the chest wall. Pleural fluid surface tension causes the lung to follow the chest wall in insaration and hence is responsible for expansion of the lung.

The chest is rigid yet has spring to it, as long as the pleura is intact. When the pleura is interrupted, for example, by an external puncture or the rupture of a bleb, this counterbalancing force is lost and the lung collapses, causing what is known as *pneumothorax*. Any time a sudden increase in resistance is noted, a pneumothorax should be suspected.

Nonelastic, or Viscous, Resistance

This type of resistance is exerted by the diaphragm and the abdominal contents. Their force decreases the volume or size of the thorax. Usually this resistance is not excessive when the weight of the abdominal contents are not great and when the body is in an upright position. However, obesity, abdominal distention, ascites, and late-term pregnancy can cause increased viscous resistance and make the work of breathing more difficult.

Airflow Resistance

Factors that affect airflow resistance are the following:

Airway size—As the radius of the airway decreases by half, the resistance to flow increases by sixteenfold. Examples of this can be seen in bronchospasm,

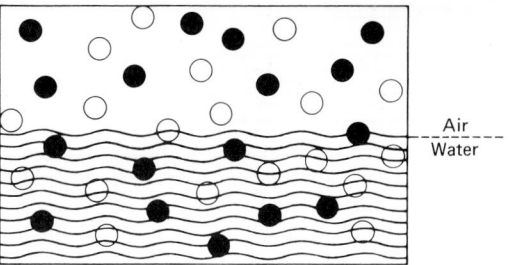

FIGURE 3-1

Equilibrium between air and water (Henry's law). Water is exposed to air, which contains various molecules (black and white circles). Some of the molecules collide with the surface of the water and enter the water, i.e., some of the gas is dissolved. The gas molecules that enter the water still have motion: they disperse throughout the water and may even leave the water and re-enter the air. Eventually the number of gas molecules in the air will equal the number in the water; this is called *equilibrium*. As many molecules enter as leave the water, because the gas pressures are equal on both sides. There are as many circles in the air as in the water, and the distribution of black and white circles is equal. Thus, at equilibrium the atmospheric pressure equals the dissolved gas pressures, and the various partial pressures will equal each other in air and water. (*From Barry Shapiro, Clinical Application of Blood Gases, Yearbook, Chicago, 1979.*)

narrowing of the airway lumen by secretions, or even the narrowing of ventilator tubings by water condensation.

Airway length—Airway length is directly proportional to airway resistance. As the length of the airway doubles, so does the resistance. This can occur in the use of an excessively long endotracheal tube and is why the length of ventilator tubings is strictly limited.

Type of flow—Laminar flow is a linear type of flow, where there is little interaction between gas molecules (Fig. 3-2). This kind of flow offers little resistance. Turbulent flow is characterized by much bombardment and interaction between gas molecules. Resistance is greater, and thus greater energy is required. Laminar flow is then preferable and in the body is encouraged by the smooth angles in the bronchial tree. The connections in ventilator tubings are designed to mimic these smooth angles. Edema, increased secretions, excess humidity in tubings, and bronchoconstriction all promote turbulent flow and should be prevented in patient care. High flow rates also cause turbulent flow, and thus higher flow rates require higher pressures to deliver the same tidal volume. In the patient on a volume ventilator, in-

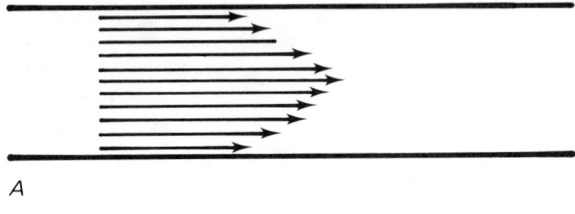

A

B

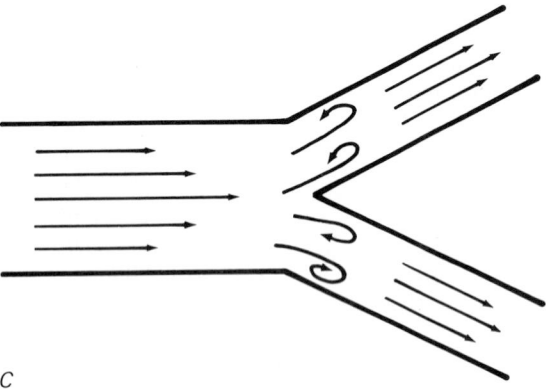

C

FIGURE 3-2

Patterns of airflow. (*A*) Laminar flow, found in small airways. (*B*) Turbulent flow, found in the trachea and the largest bronchi. (*C*) Transitional flow, found in larger airways, especially at branch points. (*From Murray D. Altose, Pulmonary mechanics, in Alfred P. Fishman (ed.), Pulmonary Diseases and Disorders, McGraw-Hill, New York, 1980. Used by permission of the publisher.*)

creased peak pressures will be seen in such cases and the results will be an uneven distribution of inspired air. The effect of uneven distribution will be discussed later in this chapter.

Compliance is the relative ease of lung inflation. Compliance is the reciprocal of resistance. Thus, as resistance increases, compliance decreases, and as resistance decreases, compliance increases. There are two types of compliance: static and dynamic. Static compliance is determined by dividing the tidal volume by the pressure required to deliver it. Thus the change in volume for every cmH_2O pressure

increase is determined. When a patient is on a volume ventilator, such as Bennett's MA I, this pressure can be observed on the system pressure gauge. The normal static compliance is 0.05 to 0.04 L/cmH_2O pressure; 0.03 L/cmH_2O and below signifies a stiff, noncompliant lung. Dynamic compliance is the volume after which an increase in pressure will not increase the volume of gas delivered. Obviously this is not a practical measurement to determine in patients. Anything that affects resistance affects compliance.

Gas Distribution

Distribution of inspired gas for the most part follows local changes in transpulmonary pressures. *Transpulmonary pressure* is the pressure difference between the mouth and intrapleural space. Also affecting distribution are (1) decreased elasticity of lung tissue, (2) airway obstruction, (3) closing volumes, and (4) decreased supply of surfactant.[1]

In general, the alveoli in the bases of the upright lung are better ventilated than those in the apices. However, the alveoli in the apices tend to be larger in size and are ventilated more rapidly. Perfusion of the apices is less than in the bases, causing a ventilation-perfusion inequality.

At the end of inspiration all alveoli are normally open. But as expiration occurs, some of the smaller alveoli tend to close, trapping air within. The amount of gas in the alveoli when this occurs is known as the *closing volume*. These smaller alveoli then are the slower ones to open during inspiration. Slower flow rates are required then to avoid inspiration ending before these alveoli have opened. In general, slower inspiration and expiration promotes more even gas distribution to the lung areas. Whenever the functional residual volume (the amount of air left in lungs after a normal expiration) is decreased, as in the supine position, the anesthetized patient, and the obese, closing volumes are increased. Thus, the semi-Fowler's rather than the supine position is more beneficial to the patient with respiratory problems.

DIFFUSION OF RESPIRATORY GASES

When the inspired gas finally reaches the alveoli, the next stage of respiration, diffusion, begins.

---

[1] *Surfactant* is a lipoprotein secreted by cells of the alveoli. It serves to reduce surface tension within the film of water that coats alveoli. Low surfactant levels thus increase the difficulty of lung expansion.

The diffusion of most interest here is that of carbon dioxide and oxygen across the alveolar capillary membrane. In order for appreciable amounts of a particular gas to cross, there must be a gradient, across the two sides. The transfer of oxygen from the alveoli to the pulmonary capillary is a function of the gradient across the capillary membrane. Carbon dioxide diffuses out in the opposite direction. The solubility of the gas in blood determines the amount of gradient required and the rapidity of the diffusion process. Carbon dioxide is much more diffusible and soluble than oxygen. Thus in conditions where the alveolar capillary membrane is increased in area, for example in pulmonary edema, carbon dioxide may still be excreted, maintaining a normal tension in systemic blood; but oxygen will have difficulty crossing the membrane and its P_{O_2} will fall.

Partial Pressures

In order to visualize diffusion gradients in action, it is necessary to know the normal partial pressures in the alveoli and in pulmonary venous blood (Fig. 3-3).

Recall first Dalton's law of partial pressures, which states that in a gas mixture the pressure exerted by each gas is proportionate to the percentage of the total mixture that particular gas occupies.

As mentioned earlier, inspired air at sea level has a total pressure of 760 mmHg. Oxygen, approximately 21 percent of air, exerts a pressure of about 158 mmHg. Carbon dioxide is a very small part of inspired air, with a pressure of about 0.3 mmHg. Nitrogen occupies a large part, a little less than 80 percent, with a pressure of 596 mmHg. The normal water pressure is 5.7 mmHg. Once the air is inspired, it is warmed and humidified by the upper respiratory tract and the water vapor pressure increases to 47 mmHg (at normal body temperature). Because the total pressure of the gas mixture remains at 760 mmHg, the other gas's partial pressures must fall. Before this inspired air enters the alveoli, it mixes with the gas that was not exhaled. (Remember that not all air is exhaled with expiration.) The gas that is left has a higher P_{CO_2} and lower P_{O_2} than that of the air entering. So once again the pressures change. The partial pressures that are around the norm for the alveoli are:

O₂, 100 mmHg
CO₂, 40 mmHg
H₂O, 47 mmHg
N₂, 573 mmHg

Blood from the right ventricle is normally deoxygenated with P_{O_2} of 40 mmHg and P_{CO_2} of 47 mmHg. Nitrogen and water vapor are at the same pressure as in alveoli; there is no gradient. The steepest gradient across the membrane is for oxygen:

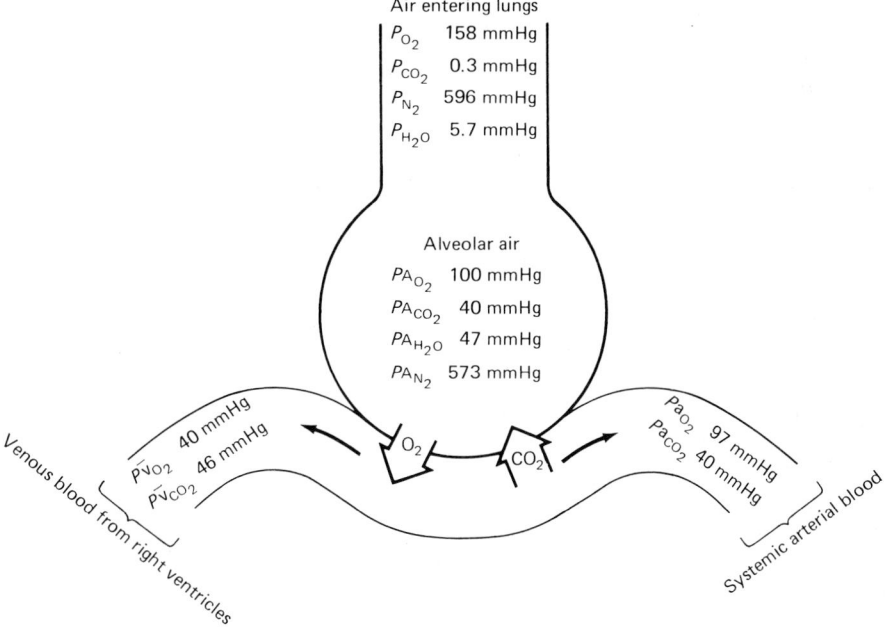

FIGURE 3-3

Partial pressures of respiratory gases in normal respiration. $P\bar{v}$ refers to mixed venous blood (combining blood from inferior and superior venae cavae).

	Venous blood	Alveolus
P_{O_2}	40 mmHg	100 mmHg
P_{CO_2}	47 mmHg	40 mmHg

Understand that venous blood here refers to blood from the right ventricle; it reaches alveoli through the pulmonary artery and its branches. After exposure of blood to the alveoli, carbon dioxide remains unchanged but oxygen assumes a new value in systemic arterial blood because of the normal anatomical shunt:

	Arterial blood	Alveolus	Venous blood
P_{O_2}	95 mmHg	100 mmHg	40 mmHg
P_{CO_2}	40 mmHg	40 mmHg	47 mmHg

If pulmonary capillary blood could be sampled, the oxygen tension would be identical with that in the alveoli. But the blood in the systemic arteries has been mixed already with blood from the thebesian and bronchial veins, which empty directly into the left heart, bypassing the lungs. There is consequently an oxygen gradient between the alveoli and arterial blood, normally no greater than 10 mmHg.

Effects of Gas Concentration Changes

By varying the concentration of a particular gas in inhaled air, the gradient can be changed, leading to a change in the arterial partial pressure of the gas, if diffusion remains normal (Fig. 3-4). The following are examples of this approach.

Increased Alveolar P_{CO_2}

If for some reason the carbon dioxide in alveoli is not being exhaled, the partial pressure will rise. In order to accommodate this increase, the oxygen partial pressure falls. The end result is a decreased gradient for oxygen between alveoli and the pulmonary capillaries. Less oxygen diffuses into the blood. What will be seen in blood gas analysis of systemic arteries is a rise in P_{CO_2} and a fall in P_{O_2}.

Nitrogen Washout

If a person is placed on 100% oxygen, there will still be an alveolar P_{CO_2}, since the gas will continue to diffuse across the capillary membrane. There will still be a water vapor partial pressure, since air is warmed and humidified in the respiratory tract. However, alveolar P_{N_2} will drop to zero. The place of the nitrogen is taken by the oxygen, and the alveolar P_{O_2} becomes 673 mmHg. If the diffusion of oxygen is normal, this will be reflected in a large rise in systemic arterial P_{O_2}. The normal gradient across the pulmonary capillary membrane for a person receiving 100% oxygen should not exceed 100 mmHg. Very high concentrations of oxygen are harmful to the alveolar membrane; smaller, carefully selected increments in the fraction of inspired air devoted to oxygen can be used to increase the gradient and aid oxygen diffusion (Fig. 3-4).

PERFUSION OF BLOOD

It is obvious that the alveoli must be perfused with blood in order for oxygen and carbon dioxide diffusion to take place.

The pulmonary circulation begins in the main pulmonary artery, which receives venous blood from the right ventricle. The pulmonary artery then branches and follows the airway system down to the terminal bronchioles. The capillary beds in the walls of the alveoli are thereby supplied with blood. Oxygenated blood is collected from the capillary bed and returned to the left atrium via the pulmonary veins.

The classic feature of the normal pulmonary circulation is that the pressure remains low throughout. The pulmonary artery pressure is approximately 25 mmHg systolic and 8 mmHg diastolic, with a mean of 15 mmHg. Unlike systemic arteries, which must direct and redirect blood flow to various body organs, the pulmonary arteries need only supply the lungs. Thus, pulmonary artery pressure remains low while still being able to perfuse all the way to the apices of the lungs. The walls of the pulmonary artery and its branches are thin, containing little smooth muscle. Because of this low-pressure system the heart expends less energy perfusing the lungs than supplying the systemic circulation. The pressure in the pulmonary capillaries themselves is uncertain but may be somewhere between the pulmonary arterial and venous pressures. This pressure will vary throughout the lung because of hydrostatic effects.

Determinants of Pulmonary Resistance

The caliber of the pulmonary vessels largely depends on the difference in pressure within the vessel and that surrounding it. Because the pulmonary vasculature is thin and very compliant, the small capillaries surrounding the alveoli are greatly affected by the intra-alveolar pressure. A large increase in such pressure, for example, in excessive sighing and use of high tidal volumes on a volume ventilator, can compress or even collapse these small vessels.

On the other hand, the caliber of arteries and veins located in the lung parenchyma are affected by the lung volumes, which determine the pull of the parenchyma on the vessel walls. The large vessels near the hilum are truly outside the lung and are influenced chiefly by the intrapleural pressure.

Although the pulmonary vascular resistance is low, it can be increased and decreased despite the lack of muscular arterioles in the pulmonary circulatory system. Two mechanisms are responsible. Normally some capillaries of the pulmonary circulation are not receiving blood flow. As the pressure increases, these vessels begin to conduct blood and therefore decrease overall resistance. This is termed *recruitment*. It is the most important mechanism for decreasing pulmonary vascular resistance in the event of increasing pulmonary artery pressure. The second mechanism is *capillary distention*. A distended capillary offers less resistance to blood flow. The thin membrane between the alveolar space and the capillary facilitates capillary distention.

Because the caliber of the extra-alveolar vessels is influenced by lung volumes, so is their resistance. As the lung expands, the vessels are made to enlarge in caliber, thereby lowering resistance. The vessel walls contain smooth muscle and elastic tissue which resists expansion. If normal lung volume is diminished, there will be an increase in resistance. In the event of total lung collapse, the muscle tone in the extra-alveolar vessels would make it necessary to raise the pulmonary artery pressure several centimeters of water pressure above that of the pulmonary vein to allow flow. This pressure is termed the *critical opening pressure*.

As the blood pressure of pulmonary capillaries is uncertain, so is the normal vascular resistance. It is possible to see what factors can affect resistance. For example, if the alveolar pressure were to increase, the vessels will collapse and resistance will increase. If a large lung volume is used in inspiration, the caliber of the capillary will decrease, again increasing resistance. In addition, hypoxia causes vasoconstriction of pulmonary vasculature, which increases resistance. Some humoral agents also cause vasoconstriction, such as epinephrine, norepinephrine, angiotensin, and histamine. Bradykinin and acetylcholine cause vasodilatation.

Pressure Variations in the Lung

Understanding distribution of blood and the factors that affect it is very important since it is best for blood flow to match ventilation. Even under normal condi-

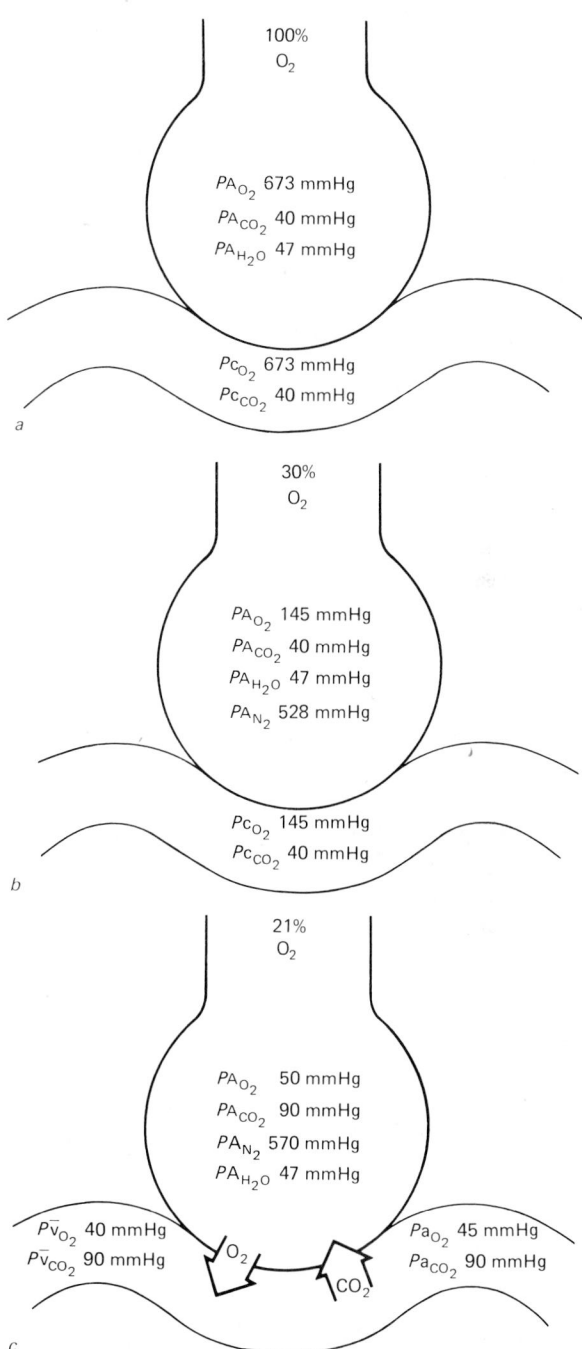

FIGURE 3-4

(a) Respiratory gases during breathing of 100% oxygen. Pc refers to the partial pressure of a gas in the pulmonary end capillary blood. (b) Oxygen fraction of inspired air is 30%. (c) Oxygen fraction of inspired air is 21%. (*Adapted from Barry Shapiro, Clinical Application of Blood Gases, Yearbook, Chicago, 1976.*)

tions this is not the case. The blood flow in the normal lung is affected by posture and exercise. In an upright lung, the blood flow is decreased in a linear fashion from bottom to top (Fig. 3-5). If the position is altered to the supine, the apical flow will increase and the basal flow will be virtually unchanged, but flow to the posterior regions will increase and flow to the anterior regions will decrease. The effect of exercise is one of decreasing these regional differences and increasing flow.

The distribution of blood flow is best explained by the hydrostatic pressure differences in the blood vessels. The low pressure of the pulmonary circulation cannot enforce even blood flow against large pressure differences (Fig. 3-6).

In order to examine distribution in a more systematic way, the lung has been divided into three areas or zones—top, center, and bottom.

In the apices or top region of the lung in an upright subject, the pulmonary artery pressure has the task of raising the blood to the highest part of the lung, against gravity. If arterial pressure falls below alveolar pressure, then the capillaries collapse and flow ceases. The same occurs if the alveolar pressure is increased over capillary pressure, as for example, in positive pressure ventilation. Areas which may be ventilated but not perfused become nonfunctional for gas exchange. Recall that this is termed *alveolar dead space.*

In the center region of the lung, pulmonary artery pressure is greater than alveolar pressure. However, venous pressure is still less than alveolar pressure. Blood flow is determined by the difference between arterial and alveolar pressures. In order for venous pressure to influence flow, it must exceed the alveolar pressure.

Arterial pressure continues to increase as one moves toward the lung bases, but alveolar pressure remains unchanged. This is the bottom region of the lung and has the largest amount of blood flow. In this region venous pressure exceeds alveolar pressure so that the determination of blood flow is the arterial-venous pressure difference. The most important factor which contributes to the increase of flow here is thought to be the distention of the capillaries. The internal pressure of the capillaries rises, whereas alveolar pressure is unchanged.

To make all this now applicable to the clinical setting, it can be seen that persons receiving large tidal volumes on ventilators, or continuous positive airway pressure (CPAP) and positive end-expiratory pressure (PEEP), must be well hydrated and have optimal hemodynamic pressures.

Pulmonary vascular resistance may also be affected by various forms of obstruction. Occlusion of the lumen by emboli or obstruction of the outflow tract, as seen in mitral stenosis, will increase resistance. Similarly, there can be obstruction from outside

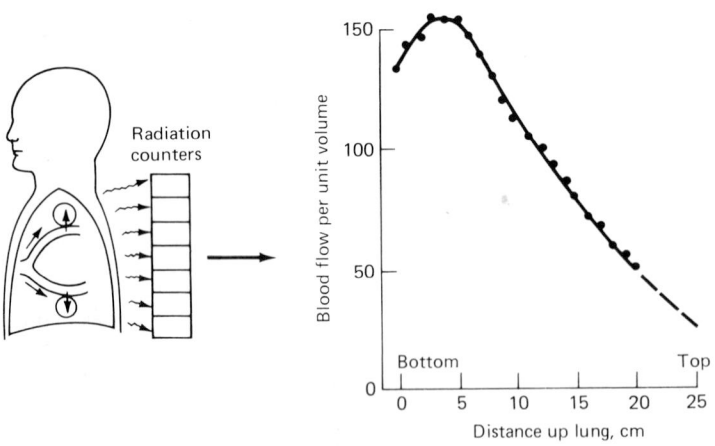

FIGURE 3-5

Measurement of the distribution of blood flow in the upright human lung using radioactive xenon. Note the small flow at the apex. (*From John West, Respiratory Physiology, the Essentials, Williams & Wilkins, Baltimore, 1979.*)

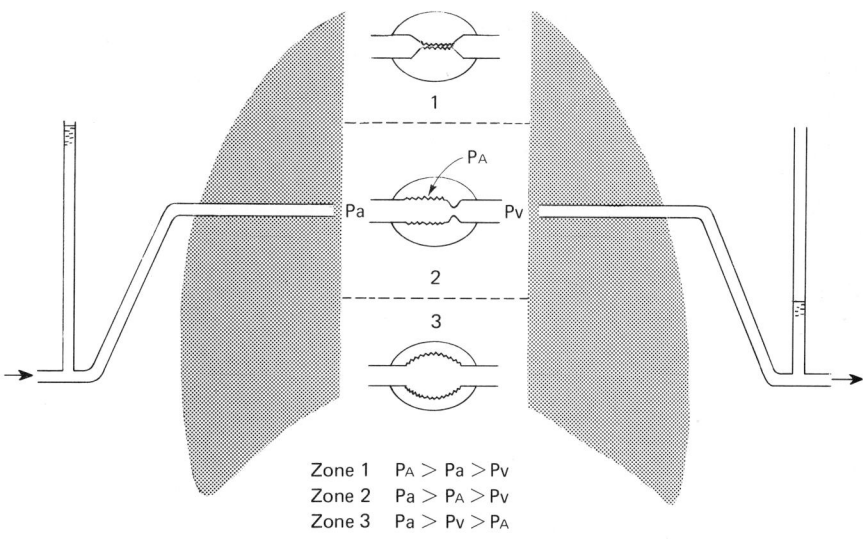

Zone 1 $P_A > P_a > P_v$
Zone 2 $P_a > P_A > P_v$
Zone 3 $P_a > P_v > P_A$

FIGURE 3-6

Model to explain the distribution of pulmonary blood flow based on pressures affecting the capillaries. The lung is divided into three zones depending on the magnitude of the pulmonary arterial, alveolar, and venous pressures. The lines separating the zones are not topographically precise. (*From John B. West, The use of radioactive materials in the study of lung function, in Alfred P. Fishman (ed.), Pulmonary Diseases and Disorders, McGraw-Hill, New York, 1980. Used by permission of the publisher.*)

the capillary wall. Inflammatory conditions may increase resistance as a result of destruction of the total pulmonary vascular bed.

TRANSPORTATION OF RESPIRATORY GASES

Once the lung is ventilated and diffusion has occurred, the gases are transported to their final destination in the tissues. Oxygen is carried in two forms: that dissolved in plasma and that carried by hemoglobin.

Dissolved Oxygen

The amount carried in plasma is governed by Henry's law. Recall that this law states that the amount of a gas dissolved in a liquid is directly related to the pressure of that gas over that liquid; as the pressure increases, the amount dissolved increases by a constant amount (Fig. 3-7). This constant is determined by the solubility of the gas in that liquid. Oxygen is not very soluble in plasma. For every millimeter of mercury of arterial oxygen tension only 0.003 mL of oxygen is dissolved in every 100 mL of plasma. Thus, at an ideal Pa_{O_2} of 100 mmHg, only 0.3 mL of oxygen

is carried per 100 mL of plasma. If this were the body's only source of oxygen, a resting cardiac output of nearly 120 L/min would be required to sustain life. The normal resting cardiac output is 5 L/min.

Oxygen Bound to Hemoglobin

Hemoglobin is the other more efficient method of oxygen transport. Hemoglobin is a protein complex which combines with oxygen quickly and loosely to form oxyhemoglobin (HbO_2). One molecule of hemoglobin combines with two oxygen molecules (four atoms). Normally, when exposed to the low P_{O_2} of the tissues, it swiftly releases the oxygen it carries.

It is the iron sites of the hemoglobin that attract the oxygen. Hemoglobin must be in a ferrous (Fe^{2+}) state to do this. Certain chemicals, such as nitrites, can change these sites from ferrous to ferric (Fe^{3+}), which is known as *methemoglobin*. Such a hemoglobin molecule cannot combine with oxygen.

The percentage of the hemoglobin molecule combined with oxygen is termed *hemoglobin saturation* (S_{O_2}). Hemoglobin is 100 percent saturated when each gram is combined with 1.39 mL of oxygen. The degree of saturation varies according to the plasma P_{O_2}.

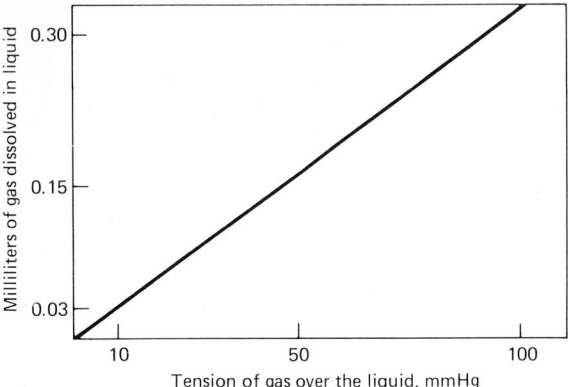

FIGURE 3-7

Henry's law. Henry's law states that the solubility of a gas in a liquid is proportional to the tension of the gas over the liquid. But O_2 is not very soluble in plasma, so only a small amount is dissolved in the blood. [*From Mary W. Waldron, Oxygen transport, Amer J Nurs 9(2): 272–275, 1979.*]

Remember, the P_{O_2} of the plasma is a function of the P_{O_2} in the alveoli and the diffusion rate.

When hemoglobin is near 100 percent saturation, it becomes a bright red color; this is the color identified with healthy arterial blood. Desaturated hemoglobin, also termed *reduced hemoglobin,* is purple in color. It is this color as seen in the capillaries through the skin that causes the bluish hue of cyanosis.

Cyanosis is an unreliable detector of hypoxemia. It is not appreciable until at least 5 g of hemoglobin is reduced. The clinical significance of cyanosis depends on the total amount of a patient's hemoglobin. Five grams of reduced hemoglobin is far more serious when the hemoglobin total is an anemic 8 g than when it is a polycythemic 20 g.

Hemoglobin also has the ability to carry carbon dioxide at the same time it carries oxygen. This is not the case, however, for carbon monoxide. Hemoglobin cannot carry carbon monoxide and oxygen at the same time, and since carbon monoxide is about 240 times more attractive to hemoglobin, the oxygen loses. An extremely low fraction of carbon monoxide in inspired air is enough to cause death. The amount of oxygen exerting pressure in the plasma will be the same in such a case. Thus the Pa_{O_2} will be normal if not high. The hemoglobin still has a bright, almost cherry-red color when saturated with carbon monoxide. However, because little oxygen is delivered to the tissues, the person will die of hypoxia.

Measuring Total Oxygen Content

To determine the total amount of oxygen carried by the blood, one simply adds the amount carried in plasma to that carried by hemoglobin. This sum is the *oxygen content* and is abbreviated Ca_{O_2} when speaking of the arterial blood. The equation is thus:

$$Ca_{O_2}/100\,mL\ blood = (Pa_{O_2} \times 0.003\,mL) + (Hb \times 1.39\,mL \times Sa_{O_2})$$

where Sa_{O_2} stands for hemoglobin saturation of arterial blood. If a sample other than arterial blood is used, the appropriate substitutions of values are made.

The difference between arterial and venous oxygen content of a specific organ is an indicator of that organ's oxygen consumption. If a mixed venous blood sample from a pulmonary artery catheter is used, the entire body's oxygen consumption can be estimated. A modification of this technique is used to estimate cardiac output. The difference between arterial and mixed venous oxygen contents is inversely proportional to the cardiac output. Thus, in states of decreased cardiac output the arterial-venous difference is greater than normal and in increased cardiac output states the arterial-venous difference is decreased.

Measuring Oxygen-Hemoglobin Affinity

A total understanding of hemoglobin's ability to carry oxygen requires knowledge of the oxygen-hemoglobin dissociation curve. This curve relates the Pa_{O_2} to the percentage of hemoglobin saturated (Fig. 3-8). In the illustration it can be seen that this curve is S-shaped. There is a plateau which signifies that the hemoglobin saturation does not increase indefinitely as the Pa_{O_2} rises. This is the fact for the oxygen dissolved in the plasma, since there is a direct linear relationship (Fig. 3-7). For hemoglobin, there is a clear limit to the amount of oxygen it can carry despite increases of Pa_{O_2}.

The flat portion of the curve normally begins at about a saturation of 80 percent and a P_{O_2} of 50 mmHg. Increasing the P_{O_2} after this point does not appreciably increase the hemoglobin saturation. This plateau functions to protect the body against the systemic effects of hyperoxia, since hemoglobin can only accept a limited amount of oxygen (Fig. 3-8).

The flat portion of the curve shows that even if a small decrease in Pa_{O_2} does occur, the Sa_{O_2} will not be greatly reduced; thus oxygen content will be maintained.

The middle portion of the curve of the normal functioning man is the normal range of the body for arterial and mixed venous blood.

The steep portion of the curve lies within the low Pa_{O_2} ranges. Here, for even a small increase in Pa_{O_2}, the saturation can double and even triple. This is the body's protection against hypoxia.

Shifts in Oxygen-Hemoglobin Affinity

The curve discussed so far is a normal curve. The position of the curve, that is, the ability of hemoglobin to pick up and deliver oxygen, can be altered by certain physical factors. The results of such alterations are shifts in the position of the curve.

In the normal curve the 50 percent saturation, called the P_{50}, occurs at a P_{O_2} of 27 mmHg. When the curve is shifted to the right, the P_{50} becomes greater than 27 mmHg (Fig. 3-9). Thus, for a given P_{O_2} the saturation is less. This may seem undesirable, but it must be remembered that although the hemoglobin and oxygen do not combine as readily, when the time comes for hemoglobin to release the oxygen at the cell, the separation is far quicker. This is advantageous, for the cell is the ultimate destination for oxygen. Circumstances that cause a shift to the right are those that indicate an increase in oxygen consumption. Among such factors are hyperthermia, acidosis, and the presence of certain organic phosphates.

2,3-Diphosphoglycerate (2,3-DPG) is by far the most important of these organic phosphates. Its role has only in the past decade been more fully appreciated and understood. An increase in serum 2,3-DPG shifts the curve to the right, enhancing oxygen release. Persons residing at high altitudes have increased levels of 2,3-DPG as well as some element of polycythemia to compensate for the low fraction of oxygen in the air they inspire at that altitude. This is also seen in persons with chronic hypoxemia, such as the chronic lung patient.

Stored preserved whole blood and red blood cells are not only devoid of coagulation factors but of 2,3-DPG. Usually within one-half hour of the transfusion the body has restored this; but in a patient receiving massive rapid transfusions of stored blood, a decreased oxygen release must be anticipated.

A shift of the oxygen-hemoglobin dissociation curve to the left results in a P_{50} at a P_{O_2} below 27 mmHg. The oxygen and hemoglobin are more attracted to each other, but at the tissue site they do not want to be separated. Alkalosis, hypothermia, and a

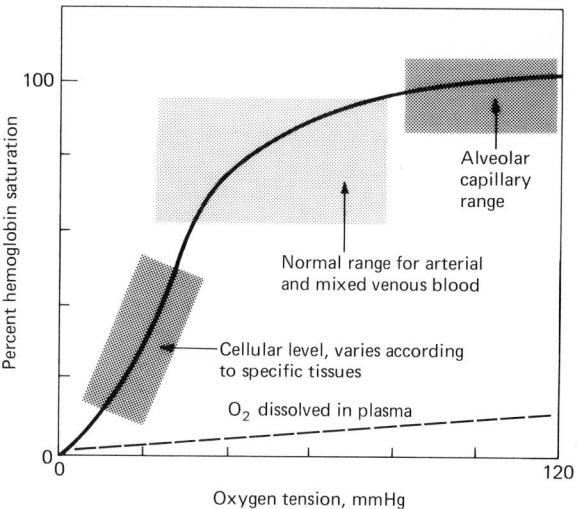

FIGURE 3-8

The oxygen-hemoglobin relationship exerts a protective effect. When need is greatest, at low O_2 tensions, saturation increases quickly, protecting against hypoxia. At high O_2 tensions, little increase is seen, protecting against O_2 toxicity. [*From Mary W. Waldron, Oxygen transport, Amer J Nurs 9(2):272–275, 1979.*]

decreased 2,3-DPG are among factors that shift the curve to the left.

Thus, as it has been explained, the calculation of oxygen-hemoglobin saturation is influenced by such factors as temperature and pH. It is important that such factors be noted and taken into consideration when interpreting arterial blood gas results.

Carbon Dioxide

Carbon dioxide is carried in the blood in three ways. The first way is directly dissolved in plasma (Fig. 3-10). Only 5 percent of the carbon dioxide is carried this way. Some of this CO_2 exerts a pressure which is measured in a blood gas analysis, and the rest interacts with water to form carbonic acid ($CO_2 + H_2O \rightleftharpoons H_2CO_3$). This is a very slow process. Carbonic acid can further dissociate to form hydrogen and bicarbonate ions ($H_2CO_3 \rightleftharpoons H^+ + HCO_3^-$). Both of these equations are reversible.

Some 65 percent of the CO_2 is carried in the red blood cell as carbonic acid. This reaction occurs swiftly because of the presence of an enzyme, carbonic anhydrase. Again the carbonic acid dissociates and bicarbonate and hydrogen ions are formed. The bicarbonate ions can diffuse easily out of the red cell

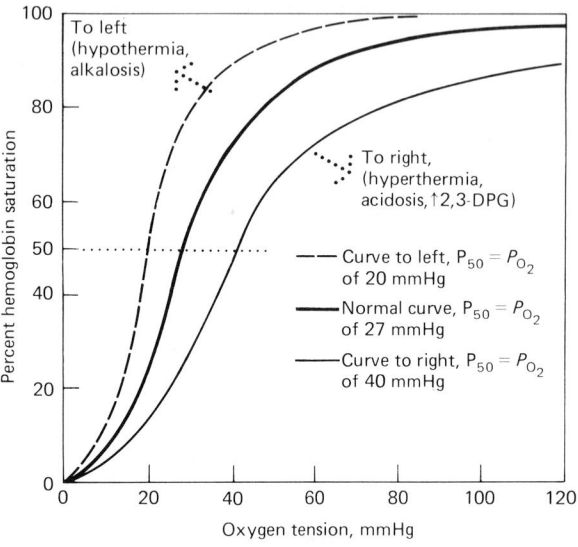

FIGURE 3-9

Normal hemoglobin-oxygen saturation curve (middle), shift to left (top), shift to right (bottom). A curve is considered normal if hemoglobin is 50 percent saturated at a Pa_{O_2} of 27 mmHg. With shift to the left, oxygen-hemoglobin bonding occurs more readily than normal, and 50 percent saturation is seen at a lower O_2 tension; however, hemoglobin does not release oxygen to tissues as readily. Shift to right causes opposite effect. [*From Mary W. Waldron, Oxygen transport, Amer J Nurs 9(2): 272–275, 1975.*]

into the plasma. This is not the case for the hydrogen ions. This is done when there is an excess of bicarbonate in the cell. When the bicarbonate diffuses out,

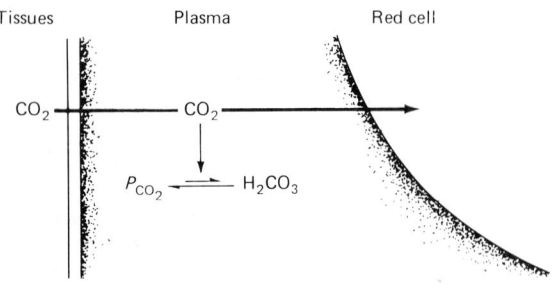

FIGURE 3-10

Carbon dioxide–carbonic acid relationship in plasma; 5 percent of the CO_2 entering the blood remains in plasma. Most of this exists as dissolved CO_2 since the chemical reaction $H_2O + CO_2 \rightarrow H_2CO_3$ is very slow; therefore, measuring P_{CO_2} is equivalent to measuring H_2CO_3 concentration. (*From Barry Shapiro, Clinical Application of Blood Gases, Yearbook, Chicago, 1979.*)

chloride (Cl^-) ions diffuse into the cell; this is known as the *chloride shift*. In this way the cell remains electrically neutral.

The third way in which CO_2 is carried is as *carbaminohemoglobin*, a compound of hemoglobin and carbon dioxide. This accounts for approximately 30 percent of the CO_2 carried.

Once the blood enters the pulmonary capillaries via the right heart, all the reversible chemical equations reverse. The CO_2 is once again formed, hemoglobin releases its load of CO_2, and this CO_2 diffuses across the capillary-alveolar membrane into the alveoli for expiration.

The role of CO_2 in acid-base balance can be seen by the chemical equation already discussed, $CO_2 + H_2O \rightarrow H_2CO_3 \rightarrow H^{\pm} + HCO_3^-$. An acid is a substance that donates hydrogen ions, and a base is a substance that accepts hydrogen ions. In order for the normal pH of the body to be maintained around 7.4, the body needs a ratio of hydrogen ions to bicarbonate ions of 1:20.

Carbon dioxide in the plasma is directly responsible for the amount of carbonic acid made. As the Pa_{CO_2} rises, so does the amount of carbonic acid. And as the carbonic acid level rises, so does the hydrogen ion concentration. Remember that hydrogen ion concentration and pH are inversely related. To sum up then, as the Pa_{CO_2} rises, the pH falls. This would cause a respiratory acidosis. The converse holds true also. If the Pa_{CO_2} falls, the pH rises. This is known as a respiratory alkalosis. The lungs can change the pH of the blood in this manner in just minutes. The lungs can be the cause of an acid-base imbalance or an aid to the body in compensating for a metabolic acid-base imbalance.

The bicarbonate ion concentration is predominantly a product of kidney functioning. An increase in the bicarbonate to hydrogen ratio can tip the acid-base balance to the base side, increasing the pH. On the other side, a deficit of hydrogen ion can tip the balance to the other side, decreasing the pH. This kind of imbalance is termed metabolic, either acidosis or alkalosis.

The Henderson-Hasselbach equation illustrates the hydrogen ion and bicarbonate buffer system relationship best (Table 3-1).

NERVOUS SYSTEM CONTROL OF BLOOD GASES

The functioning of the lungs in maintaining proper levels of CO_2 is the responsibility of ventilation, which is controlled by the various centers and receptors of the nervous system. The regulation of gas exchange is made possible by the control of the rate and depth of ventilation. Spontaneous respiration depends on a rhythmic discharge from the respiratory center (Fig. 3-11).

Location and Function of Centers

Voluntary centers are in the motor cortex of the forebrain and the limbic cerebral area. Automatic control employs afferents from the glossopharyngeal and vagus nerves, peripheral chemoreceptors, and the proprioceptors. Efferents are the phrenic nerve to the diaphragm and the ventral and lateral columns of the upper thoracic spinal cord to the intercostal muscles.

The respiratory center is a poorly defined group of neurons. There is a diffuse grouping of cell bodies in the reticular formation of the caudal medulla. There are tracts which are ascending and descending, excitatory and inhibitory.

There are three main divisions of the respiratory center.

The *medullary respiratory center* anatomically is two poorly delineated groups of neurons. There is an interaction between cells associated with inspiration and cells associated with expiration. The inherent rhythm of respiration results from this interaction. The inspiratory component neurons are dominant at a ratio of 2:1, and their stimulation causes an inspiratory effort for as long as they are stimulated. Stimulation

| **TABLE 3-1** |
| Calculation of Blood pH |

$$pH = pK^* + \log \frac{base}{acid}$$

$$(1)\frac{HCO_3}{H_2CO_3} = \frac{25.4\ meq/L}{1.27\ meq/L} = \frac{20}{1}$$

(2) Blood pK at BTPS = 6.1

$$pH = 6.1 + \log \frac{20}{1}$$

$$pH = 6.1 + 1.3 = 7.4$$

* The pK is the pH at which the substance is half dissociated and half undissociated.
Source: Shapiro, B.: *Clinical Application of Blood Gases,* Chicago: Yearbook, 1979.

of the expiratory component causes a temporary expiratory effort and a temporary inhibition of the inspiratory component. As reciprocal inhibition occurs, rhythmicity is maintained in breathing.

The *apneustic center* is located in the lower pons at the level of the area vestibularis. It exerts a strong regulating action on the medullary center. The effect is to stimulate inspiration. The apneustic center is regulated by vagal afferent impulses from receptors in the lung and pneumotaxic center. If the spinal cord is transected at the level of the inferior portion of the pons, then the inspiratory neurons will continuously discharge, causing sustained inspiration or, as it is called, *apneusis.* Pulmonary stretch receptors serve

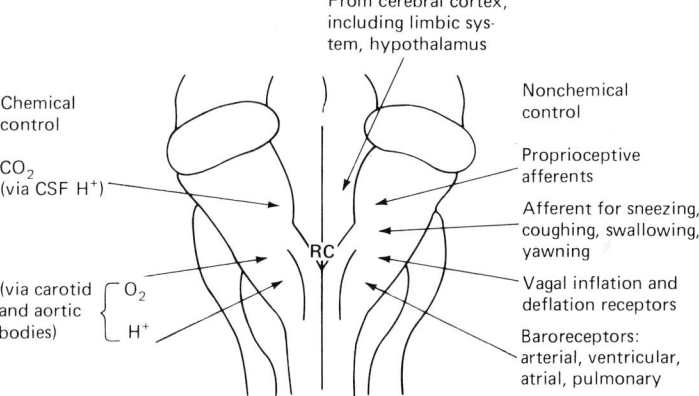

FIGURE 3-11

The chemical and nonchemical stimuli which affect the respiratory center in regulation of respiration. (*From William Ganong, Review of Medical Physiology, Lange, Los Altos, Calif., 1971.*)

to decrease the drive of the center and cause expiration.

The *pneumotaxic center* is located in the upper anterior pons. This center serves to inhibit the inspiratory activity of subordinate centers and thereby regulate rate. Under unusual circumstances, the pneumotaxic center takes over to maintain respiratory rhythm. It may cyclically inhibit the apneustic center and directly inhibit the inspiratory center neurons. Respiratory rhythm is achieved by periodic impulses from the medullary apneustic centers.

It is also worth mentioning that the cerebral cortex may modify the breathing pattern. This constitutes conscious control of respiration and may be effective but only to a limit.

Chemoreceptors

Chemoreceptors make an important contribution to these mechanisms. A chemoreceptor responds to changes in the chemical composition of the blood or of the fluid around it.

Central Chemoreceptors

The most important chemoreceptors in the human, the *central chemoreceptors,* are located on the ventral surface of the medulla in the vicinity of the exit of the ninth and tenth nerves.

These central chemoreceptors are exposed to cerebrospinal fluid. They respond to changes in the level of hydrogen ion concentration. An increase in hydrogen ion concentration stimulates ventilation and a decrease depresses ventilation. This action is analogous to the peripheral chemoreceptors, the aortic and carotid bodies. The composition of the extracellular fluid is governed by the cerebrospinal fluid, the local blood flow, and the local metabolism.

Carbon dioxide freely diffuses across the blood-brain barrier into the cerebrospinal fluid, while the barrier is relatively impermeable to hydrogen ions and bicarbonate ions. This means that when blood P_{CO_2} rises, the CO_2 diffuses into the cerebrospinal fluid readily from the cerebral blood vessels. This causes release of hydrogen ions, which stimulates the chemoreceptors (Selkurt, 1975).

Therefore, it can be said that carbon dioxide regulates ventilation by its effect on the pH of the cerebrospinal fluid. The cerebral vasodilatation which accompanies an increase in Pa_{CO_2} also enhances the diffusion of CO_2 into the cerebrospinal fluid.

The cerebrospinal fluid is not as buffered as the blood because it has smaller amounts of protein. Therefore, any change in cerebrospinal fluid pH will be greater than that in the blood. This means that hydrogen ions will accumulate faster and stimulate respiration. If the change in cerebrospinal fluid pH occurs over a long period, then compensatory changes in the bicarbonate ion will occur. The cerebrospinal pH is restored faster and more completely than that of the arterial blood (Fig. 3-12).

The central chemoreceptors are not stimulated by hypoxia; rather, hypoxia depresses central respiratory neurons.

Peripheral Chemoreceptors

The most significant of the peripheral chemoreceptors are the carotid bodies. The carotid bodies are located at the bifurcation of the common carotid arteries within the walls of the vessels. These receptors are sensitive to both hypoxia and increases in P_{CO_2} and H^+ (Fig. 3-13). In hypoxia, the blood flow to the carotid bodies is greatly increased, which allows oxygen requirements to be met by dissolved oxygen alone. The receptors are also thus prevented from being stimulated by anemia or carbon monoxide poisoning. In these conditions the amount of dissolved oxygen is usually normal (Ganong, 1973).

Since there is little arterial-venous oxygen difference due to the high blood flow, the carotid bodies do not respond to arterial changes. If the peripheral chemoreceptors did not exist, severe hypoxemia would result, since they are responsible for all increases in ventilation in response to arterial hypoxemia. Hypoxemia stimulates impulses which are then generated in the afferent terminals of the carotid sinus nerve. They are sensitive to a decrease in arterial P_{O_2} due to venous stasis, or to drugs which prevent the release of oxygen at the tissue site, e.g., in cyanide or nicotine poisoning. In patients who have bilateral carotid body resection, a complete absence of the hypoxic drive is seen.

The aortic bodies are two or more small groups of cells located above and below the arch, whose afferents ascend to the medulla via the vagi. The importance of these structures is not fully understood, but they appear to respond in a less significant way than the carotid bodies to decreases in Pa_{O_2} and increases in Pa_{CO_2}. They do not respond to decreases in pH.

The response of all the peripheral chemoreceptors to P_{CO_2} levels is of much less importance than the response of the central chemoreceptors to Pa_{CO_2}. Their response is more rapid than the central chemoreceptors and may aid in matching ventilation to rapid alterations in P_{CO_2}.

Secondary Receptors Within the Lungs

There are other receptors and reflexes whose roles are not clear in the regulation of ventilation. They will be briefly described here. There are two basic types of receptors in this category. Slowly adapting receptors are excited by small increases in lung volume. They are inhibitory to inspiration and form the basis of the inhibito-inspiratory reflex. Stimulation of these receptors causes prolonged expiration.

Rapidly adapting receptors are excited by lung deflation. These are active for under 1 second.

Among these rapidly adapting receptors are the *pulmonary stretch receptors,* located in the airways' smooth muscles. They discharge in response to lung distention, and their impulses travel via the vagus nerve. The Hering-Breuer inflation reflex employs these stretch receptors. When they are stimulated, expiratory time is increased and respiration therefore slowed. The reflex is felt to be of little significance in the adult, unless the tidal volume is over 1 L.

Irritant receptors, also rapidly adapting receptors, are between the airway epithelial cells and are stimulated by noxious gases, dusts, and cold air. Impulses travel via the vagus, causing bronchoconstriction and hyperpnea. These receptors respond to released histamine and so may play a role in the symptoms of asthma.

J receptors are *juxtacapillary receptors,* named so because of their believed position in the alveolar walls. These receptors appear to respond to pulmonary capillary distention or chemicals which enter into the pulmonary circulation, such as inhalation anesthetics. Impulses travel up the vagus and cause rapid shallow breathing or even apnea. The dyspnea of left heart failure or interstitial lung disease may be related to these receptors, as is the ventilatory response to pulmonary emboli and exercise (Nunn, 1977, and West, 1979).

Secondary Receptors Outside the Lungs

Gamma system receptors are spindles within the intercostal muscles and the diaphragm. They sense the elongation of these muscles. The strength of contraction is controlled by this reflex. The gamma

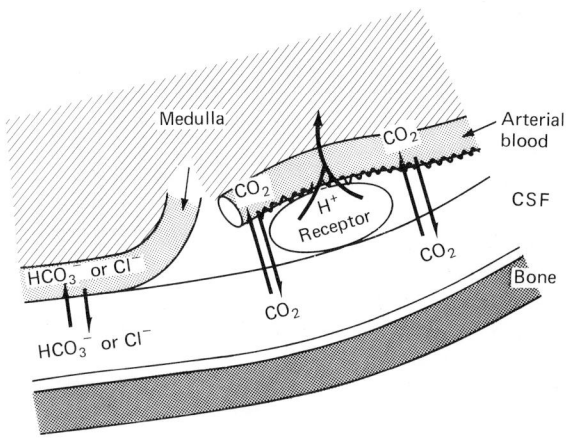

FIGURE 3-12

The central H^+ receptors are on or near the ventral and lateral surfaces of the upper medulla. They are influenced by the H^+ and P_{CO_2} of cerebrospinal fluid (CSF) and by arterial P_{CO_2}. CO_2 molecules diffuse readily across the walls of the brain capillaries, but there is a barrier to other molecules. A segment of a capillary perfused by the arterial blood supply vessel is shown at the right, with CO_2 readily diffusing into the cerebrospinal fluid bathing the cells of the chemoreceptor site (H^+ receptor). These cells, in turn, very directly influence the neurons of the respiratory centers (inspiratory, apneustic?). Conversion of CO_2 to H^+ follows the equation: $CO_2 + H_2O \rightleftharpoons H_2CO_3^- \rightleftharpoons H^+ + HCO_3$. The capillary segment at the left of the figure illustrates outward diffusion of HCO_3^- or Cl^- into the CSF (which helps in buffering the cerebrospinal fluid). [*From Ewald Selkurt* (ed.), *Basic Physiology for the Health Sciences, Little Brown, Boston, 1975.*]

system may be involved in sensing large efforts to move the chest wall.

Joint and muscle receptors receive impulses from movement of the extremities. These impulses are felt to contribute to regulation of the ventilation during exercise.

The nose, nasopharynx, larynx, and trachea all contain receptors. These receptors respond to both chemical and mechanical irritation with a sneeze, cough, laryngeal spasm, or bronchoconstriction, respectively.

Arterial baroreceptors are located in the carotid sinus and around the aortic arch. The pathway of these receptors is still unclear. They are concerned mostly with circulation regulation, however. Thus an increase in blood pressure can cause a reflex hypoventilation or apnea. Conversely, a decrease in blood pressure may cause hyperventilation (Nunn, 1977, and West, 1979).

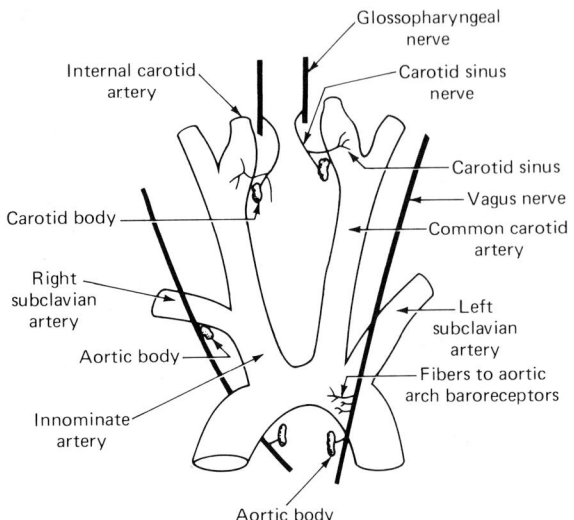

FIGURE 3-13

The location and innervation of the carotid and aortic bodies. [*From Ewald Selkurt (ed.), Basic Physiology for the Health Sciences, Little, Brown, Boston, 1975.*]

ABNORMALITIES OF VENTILATION/PERFUSION RATIO

The normal lung does not have alveoli that are equally ventilated and perfused. In reality, the alveolar ventilation is about 4 L/min, whereas the cardiac output is about 5 L/min (Selkurt, 1975). This results in a $\dot{V}/\dot{Q}$

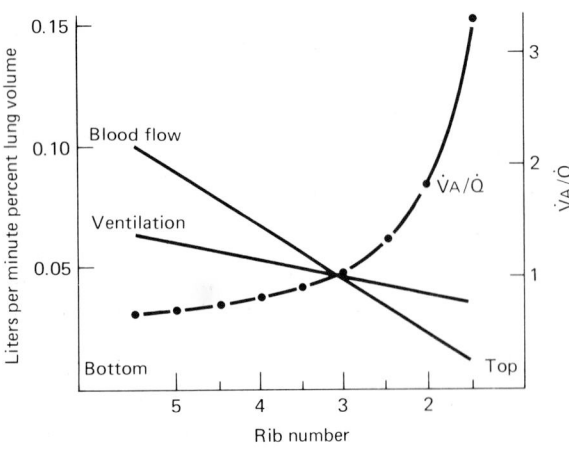

FIGURE 3-14

Distribution of ventilation, blood flow, and ventilation/perfusion ratio up the normal upright lung. (*From John West, Ventilation/Blood Flow and Gas Exchange, Blackwell, London, 1977.*)

ratio of 4:5 or 0.8. The additional factor here is that the alveoli at the base of the lung are overperfused in relation to ventilation with a ratio of about 0.6 and the alveoli at the apex are underperfused in relation to ventilation, yielding a ratio of about 3.0 (Selkurt, 1975). The determinant of gas exchange in any lung region is the $\dot{V}/\dot{Q}$ ratio (Fig. 3-14).

If the lung were examined in slices, the volume of lung would be less near the apex than at the base. Ventilation is faster at the apex and therefore is greater than perfusion. As one travels down the lung, this relation reverses itself. Therefore the $\dot{V}/\dot{Q}$ ratio increases. This causes alteration in gas exchange.

The alteration in P_{O_2} from the apex to the base is over 40 mmHg; the P_{CO_2} change is much less. The uptake of oxygen by the apex is low because of the decreased blood flow; this uptake will increase with exercise. pH differences between apex and base reflect the P_{CO_2} difference between apex and base. Carbon dioxide output, which is closely related to ventilation, does not show as great a difference between the apex and the base (Fig. 3-15).

An alteration in the ventilation component of the $\dot{V}/\dot{Q}$ ratio will change this ratio. The alveolus may become partially or completely unventilated while capillary blood flow continues. For example, this occurs in atelectasis and severe obstruction as in bronchospasm. The result is a shunt unit which allows blood to travel from the right heart to the left heart without any gas exchange. A simpler definition for all types of shunts is blood that does not see oxygen (see Fig. 3-15). Recall the normal anatomical shunt of 2 percent.

If the patient who has a pulmonary shunt is administered 100% oxygen, the Pa_{O_2} will not increase appreciably as one might expect. The shunted blood, whose oxygen content may approximate mixed venous blood, will mix with the unshunted blood and the Pa_{O_2} will only marginally rise. This is explained by the flat portion of the oxygen-hemoglobin dissociation curve. The Pa_{CO_2} will usually not rise because of the stimulation of the central chemoreceptors and the hypoxic stimulation to ventilation. Ventilation effort will increase and the Pa_{CO_2} will usually be normal or low.

The concept of a physiologic shunt includes the portion of the cardiac output which does not undergo gas exchange. The physiologic shunt can be split into anatomic and capillary shunts. The anatomic shunt includes blood which goes from the right to left side of the heart without alveolar gas exchange. This has already been discussed. A capillary shunt or pulmonary shunt is pathological. This shunt includes blood which has the opportunity for exchange with alveolar gas but it does not occur. It is said to be a true capillary shunt if ventilation is zero and perfusion is infinite. It is said to have a venous admixture if there is some alteration in the $\dot{V}/\dot{Q}$ ratio (Shapiro, 1977). This can be appreciated by large variations in the gradient between alveoli and pulmonary capillaries.

Nunn (1977) gives this calculation of a physiologic shunt:

$$\frac{\dot{Q}s}{\dot{Q}t} = \frac{Cc_{O_2} - Ca_{O_2}}{Cc_{O_2} - C\bar{v}_{O_2}}$$

where
$\dot{Q}s$ = flow of blood through the shunt
$\dot{Q}t$ = the entire blood flow
Ca_{O_2} = the content of oxygen in the arterial blood
Cc_{O_2} = the content of oxygen in the pulmonary end capillary blood
$C\bar{v}_{O_2}$ = the content of oxygen in the mixed venous blood.

When perfusion through the normal lung unit is interrupted but ventilation continues, a physiologic dead space unit is created. In such a unit there is no gas exchange. Dead space units may be subdivided. Anatomic dead space refers to the portion of ventilation which is in the tracheobronchial tree. The normal amount of anatomic dead space is usually 1 mL per pound of ideal body weight. Alveolar dead space is ventilation which enters the alveoli but is not exposed to blood flow. There is opportunity for gas exchange here, but none occurs because of decreased or absent pulmonary blood flow (Fig. 19-7b).

To calculate the amount of physiologic dead space, West (1979) gives the following formula:

$$\frac{V_D}{V_T} = \frac{(Pa_{CO_2} - PE_{CO_2})}{Pa_{CO_2}}$$

where V_D/V_T = the dead space to tidal volume ratio
PE_{CO_2} = the P_{CO_2} in the mixed expired air

When the ventilation/perfusion ratio is disturbed, an impairment of all gas exchange will occur. On a continuum: the perfused but unventilated lung has a V/Q ratio of zero and the alveolar P_{O_2} and P_{CO_2} will become equal to that of mixed venous blood. If there is ventilation but no perfusion, then the V/Q ratio increases to infinity and the alveolar gases will equal the inspired gas but will never leave the lung unit.

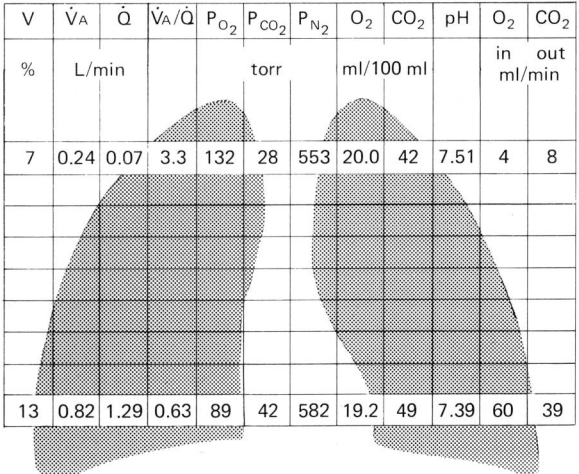

V	$\dot{V}_A$	$\dot{Q}$	$\dot{V}_A/\dot{Q}$	P_{O_2}	P_{CO_2}	P_{N_2}	O_2	CO_2	pH	O_2	CO_2
%	L/min				torr		ml/100 ml			in out ml/min	
7	0.24	0.07	3.3	132	28	553	20.0	42	7.51	4	8
13	0.82	1.29	0.63	89	42	582	19.2	49	7.39	60	39

FIGURE 3-15

Regional differences in gas exchange down the normal lung. Only the apical and basal values are shown for clarity. [*From John West, The use of radioactive materials in the study of lung function, in Alfred P. Fishman (ed.), Pulmonary Diseases and Disorders, McGraw-Hill, New York, 1980. Used by permission of the publisher.*]

If the condition should exist where there is no perfusion and no ventilation to a lung unit, then the unit is described as silent. There is no gas exchange taking place in a silent unit.

HYPOXEMIA AND HYPOXIA

Before ending this chapter on pulmonary physiology, it is essential to make a special point of differentiating hypoxemia and hypoxia.

Hypoxia refers to a decrease in oxygen concentration which occurs at any point from inspiration of gas to the tissue metabolism. If the P_{O_2} of the mitochondria falls, then anaerobic metabolism must occur in order to supply the energy requirements of the cell. The mechanisms of hypoxia are varied because the delivery of oxygen to the tissues is dependent on the oxygen capacity of the blood. The cardiac output and the blood flow to the periphery also affect the delivery of oxygen. Varied mechanisms were recognized as early as 1920, when Joseph Barcroft described "anoxaemia" as anoxic, anemic, and stagnant. The classifications commonly used now are not far altered from Barcroft's 1920 description.

1. *Hypoxic hypoxia* occurs when the Pa_{O_2} decreases; it is treated with oxygen therapy.

2. *Anemic hypoxia* occurs when the blood decreases its ability to carry oxygen.

3. *Circulatory hypoxia* is seen in generalized shock or with local obstruction when the blood flow to the tissue is decreased.

4. *Histotoxic hypoxia* results from the interference of a toxic substance in the ability of the tissues to utilize the available oxygen.

In anemic, circulatory, and histotoxic hypoxia, oxygen therapy alone will not be sufficient to correct the oxygen deficit at the tissue level.

The term *hypoxemia* refers to the Pa_{O_2}. The mechanisms of hypoxemia have been discussed throughout the chapter and include hypoventilation, diffusion impairment, shunt, and $\dot{V}/\dot{Q}$ inequality. Hypoxemia does not always mean hypoxia is present. The definitive treatment of hypoxemia will depend on the underlying cause.

REFERENCES

Altose, M.: Clinical Symposia: *The Physiological Basis of Pulmonary Function Testing*, CIBA, 1979.

Barcroft, J.: Anoxemia, *Lancet* 485–489, 1920.

Burton, G., G. Gee, and J. Hodgkins: *Respiratory Care—Guide to Clinical Practice*, Philadelphia: Lippincott, 1977.

Ganong, W. F.: *Review of Medical Physiology*, Los Altos, Calif.: Lange, 1973.

Nunn, J. F.: *Applied Respiratory Physiology*, Boston: Butterworth, 1977.

Selkurt, E. E. (ed.): *Basic Physiology for the Health Sciences*, Boston: Little Brown, 1975.

Shapiro, B.: *Clinical Applications of Blood Gases*, Chicago: Yearbook, 1979.

————, R. Harrison, and C. Trout: *Clinical Application of Respiratory Care*, Chicago: Yearbook, 1975.

Slonim-Balfour, N., and L. H. Hamilton: *Respiratory Physiology*, St. Louis: Mosby, 1971.

West, J. B.: *Ventilation/Blood Flow and Gas Exchange*, London: Blackwell, 1977a.

————: *Pulmonary Pathophysiology—The Essentials*, Baltimore: Williams & Wilkins, 1977b.

————: *Respiratory Physiology—The Essentials*, Baltimore: Williams & Wilkins, 1979.

INTRODUCTION

When considering the breadth and scope of human physiology, it is helpful to begin with a sense of awe. That perspective must be maintained in order to appreciate the vast areas of theory, conjecture, and educated guesswork regarding even the most basic functional elements. Consider the most basic functional element—the cell. It is the cell which ultimately determines the regulatory mechanisms necessary within the circulation; survival is dependent upon meeting metabolic logistics through provision of oxygen and nutrients and elimination of waste products. Lewis Thomas in his *The Lives of a Cell* comments eloquently, and with humility, about our current state of knowledge:

> I have been trying to think of the earth as a kind of organism, but it is no go. I cannot think of it this way. It is too big, too complex, with too many working parts lacking visible connections. The other night, driving through a hilly, wooded part of southern New England, I wondered about this. If not like an organism, what is it like, what is it *most* like? Then, satisfactorily for that moment, it came to me: it is *most* like a single cell.

The cardiovascular circuit, then, is charged with two fundamental tasks: circulation of blood without interruption in order to supply oxygen and nutrients to, and remove waste products from, the billions of cells within the body; and to be able to adjust the volume of blood flow upon demand. It is a truly staggering undertaking which becomes all the more so as one begins to realize the precision with which the regulatory mechanisms govern blood flow to the various vascular beds within the body, with the heart normally playing only a passive role. The circulatory system is most basically a transport system composed of two subsystems. The pulmonary circuit provides oxygenation, while the systemic circuit provides the transport mechanism. Simplistically, the transport mechanism is pulsatile flow, the energy for which is provided by the heart. Thus the first concept to be explored within the contents of this chapter is the genesis of the cardiac contraction.

ELECTROPHYSIOLOGY

Transmembrane Potential

Within intracellular and extracellular fluids are concentrations of electrolytes normally totaling about 155 meq per liter of positively charged ions (cations) and negatively charged ions (anions). Usually, excess numbers of cations accumulate along the outside

4
CARDIOVASCULAR PHYSIOLOGY
Lin C. Weeks

INTRODUCTION

ELECTROPHYSIOLOGY
Transmembrane Potential
Propagation of the Action Potential
Normal Electrical Conduction
Electrocardiography
The Vectorcardiogram

THE CARDIOVASCULAR SYSTEM AS A CIRCUIT
Hemodynamics of the Circulation

THE SYSTEMIC CIRCULATION
Functional Characteristics
Capillary Dynamics
Venous System

PULMONARY CIRCULATION
Functional Anatomy

THE CARDIAC PUMP
Functional Anatomy
Coronary Circulation
Structure of the Normal Myocardium
The Cardiac Cycle
Heart Sounds

PERIPHERAL CIRCULATION
The Vascular Tree
Intrinsic Regulation
Control Mechanisms of Specific Vascular Systems
Regulation of Blood and Extracellular Fluid Volumes
Extrinsic Regulation

ARTERIAL PRESSURE REGULATION
Factors Determining Arterial Pressure
Control of Arterial Pressure

CONTROL OF CARDIAC OUTPUT
Measurement of Cardiac Output
Control of Heart Rate
Ventricular Distensibility
Ventricular Contractility
Summary

REFERENCES

BIBLIOGRAPHY

surface of the membrane, while excess numbers of anions accumulate along the inside of the membrane, resulting in a transmembrane potential. If the internal environment of the cell were electrically measured, it would be found to have an internal charge of −90 mV with respect to the outside. The cell is said to be *polarized,* or at resting potential, when the internal environment is negative with respect to the outside.

Development of Potential

The two electrolytes most involved in the physics of transmembrane potentials are sodium and potassium. The intracellular concentration of potassium is approximately 140 meq/L, while the extracellular concentration normally ranges between 3.5 and 4.5 meq/L. Conversely, the intracellular sodium concentration is approximately 10 meq/L; the extracellular sodium concentration is about 140 meq/L. The concentration gradient for potassium favors movement from the inside to the outside of the cell. Sodium is favored to move intracellularly along its concentration gradient.

The calculation of the resting transmembrane potential is based on the potential for diffusion across the cell membrane as a result of concentration and electrical gradients. As potassium diffuses out of the cell along its concentration gradient, it leaves behind large numbers of negatively charged proteins, organic phosphates, and other anions which are too large to diffuse through the cell membrane. The internal concentration of nondiffusible anions is approximately 150 meq/L; the external concentration is approximately 5 meq/L. Thus the internal environment of the cell becomes increasingly negative, while the outside of the membrane becomes increasingly positive. The positive charges line up outside the cell membrane, attracted by the internal negativity. A balance is reached when the concentration gradient for potassium efflux is equalized by the internal attraction of the negative ions for those remaining positive ions. The actual calculation of −90 mV is based upon the Nernst equation, which states that a cation gradient favoring outward movement causes internal negativity, while an anion gradient in the reverse direction also causes internal electronegativity.

If the extracellular potassium concentration increases, the resting transmembrane potential can become more negative. The electrical gradient would remain unchanged, but the concentration gradient for potassium would diminish; therefore, the transmem-

brane potential could exceed the normal negativity of −90 mV (hyperpolarization).

Maintenance of the resting potential is clearly dependent upon potassium. However, sodium has a concentration gradient favoring movement inward. During the resting state the membrane is 50 to 100 times less permeable to sodium than to potassium. Even so, some sodium does leak into the cell during the resting state. Were the sodium allowed to build up within the cell, resting potential would soon be dissipated. The sodium pump is in constant operation in order to actively transport sodium back to the extracellular fluid against its concentration gradient. An active transport pump also functions to bring potassium back into the cell against its concentration gradient. The sodium and potassium pumps require energy in order to function and can become inhibited by medication such as digitalis and perhaps also by ischemia. The effect of inhibition of the potassium pump is the same as inhibition of the sodium active transport mechanism: loss of internal electronegativity.

The role of other ions in the development of transmembrane potential is a relatively passive one. The next most abundant anion is chloride, which has an extracellular concentration of approximately 100 meq/L and intracellular concentration of about 4 meq/L. This distribution is maintained by the electrical gradient within the cell which repels the negative chloride ion. Magnesium, a cation with an intracellular concentration of 58 meq/L and a very low extracellular concentration, follows a diffusion pattern similar to that of potassium, while calcium has a relatively low concentration both intra- and extracellularly. The major role of calcium and magnesium appears to be in alteration of membrane permeability to other ions.

The Action Potential

Any stimulus which increases the permeability of the membrane to sodium so that a critical threshold is reached will generate an action potential (Fig. 4-1). Once the internal negativity decreases from its resting potential of approximately −90 mV to −60 mV or the threshold point (*TP* in Fig. 4-1), a very rapid loss of negativity and positive overshoot to about 30 mV occurs and the fiber is depolarized (phase 0 in Fig. 4-1).

The basis for the very rapid change in the permeability of the membrane is unknown. Guyton postulates that certain channels or pores exist for the passage of sodium which during resting potential, are obstructed through calcium binding to proteins in the membrane. Since calcium is a cation, sodium is repelled and cannot pass through. Following excitation of the membrane, the calcium ions are somehow dislodged from their binding sites and sodium rapidly diffuses inside the cell. Others theorize the existence of actual activation gates which open to allow sodium passage during phase 0 of the action potential, and inactivation gates which inhibit the fast sodium current later on in the depolarization of the muscle fiber.

The resting membrane potential is a critical determinant in depolarization. A low (less negative) resting potential can lead to inexcitability of the fiber even if the concentration for sodium is normal. The inactivation process for the sodium channels, then, is extremely important because the fast sodium channels do not appear to function properly unless the membrane is returned to resting potential. Membrane permeability to sodium is the basis for the absolute refractory period; once an action potential has been generated, the fast sodium channels cannot be activated until the membrane has been returned to phase 4 or resting potential, thus preventing sustained muscle contraction.

Once the peak of the positive overshoot occurs within the membrane, the rapid sodium influx has diminished considerably. This happens for at least two reasons: (1) The increase in positivity inside the membrane begins to repel further inrush of sodium. (2) The inactivation process blocks the fast sodium channels perhaps through binding with calcium or by means of the inactivation gates.

The Plateau

In cardiac cells there is a period of sustained contraction known as the *plateau* (phase 2). There seems to be a slow inward sodium current which is different from the rapid phase 0 influx of sodium. In addition, there is a slow calcium inward current which is instrumental in myocardial contractility; the augmentation of contractility produced by norepinephrine and epinephrine is probably related to their ability to increase the calcium and sodium slow inward currents. Apparently, both ions are carried by the same inward channel.

The concentration gradient is unchanged for potassium, thereby promoting an outward current of potassium which would bring about rapid repolarization of the fiber. During phase 2, however, the permeability of the membrane for potassium de-

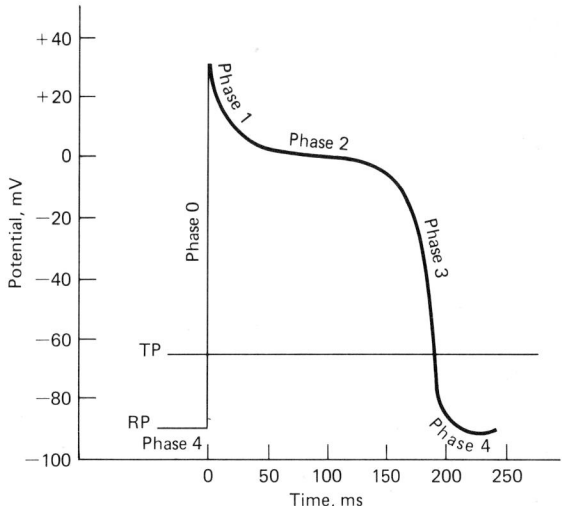

FIGURE 4-1

Transmembrane potential from ordinary myocardial muscle fiber. See text for discussion. (*From J. Willis Hurst, The Heart, Arteries, and Veins, 4th ed., McGraw-Hill, New York, 1978. Used by permission of the publisher.*)

creases, thereby decreasing potassium conductance (anomalous rectification). Consequently the fiber is able to sustain contraction.

Repolarization

Return of the membrane to resting potential in phase 3 (repolarization) is accomplished almost entirely by potassium efflux along its concentration gradient. Also, the slow inward currents of sodium and potassium are inactivated. With the rapid outward movement of potassium, the cell becomes increasingly negative until resting potential is restored. The sodium pump functions during phase 4 to return excess sodium to the extracellular fluid.

Automaticity

Certain specialized fibers within the myocardium are capable of the property of automaticity, that is, attaining threshold in the absence of any external stimulus. These pacemaker cells lie primarily within the sinoatrial node, the atrioventricular node, and the Purkinje network of the cardiac conduction system. A comparison of the action potential of the automatic myocardial fiber (Fig. 4-2) with that of the normal myocardial fiber (Fig. 4-1) shows the following: The resting potential of the sinus node automatic cells can

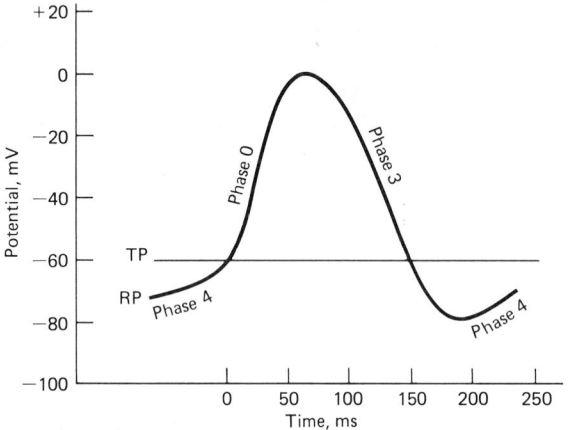

FIGURE 4-2

Transmembrane potential from myocardial cells capable of automaticity. Here the action potential of the sinus node is represented. See text for discussion. (*From J. Willis Hurst, The Heart, Arteries, and Veins, 4th ed., McGraw-Hill, New York, 1978. Used by permission of the publisher.*)

be seen to be much lower and less negative; the phase 0 upstroke is more sluggish; and the amplitude of the action potential is not as great as that of normal myocardial fibers—there is little or no positive overshoot within the action potential of the automatic cell. In addition, the automatic cell is capable of diastolic depolarization. During phase 4 of the SA node fiber, the membrane does not maintain a constant resting potential as do normal myocardial fibers, and diastolic depolarization brings the membrane to threshold, eliciting an action potential. Normally, diastolic depolarization of automatic fibers is modified by the autonomic nervous system. Generally these properties are limited to automatic cells; however, under certain conditions such as ischemia, the action potential of normal cells may shift to assume some of the properties of the pacemaker or "slow" action potential by a rise in threshold potential from −90 mV to levels of approximately −60 mV. It is apparent that conduction in tissue responding with a "slow" action potential would be characterized by a decreased conduction velocity, a property which can increase the potential for conduction block.

The ionic basis of the slow-response action potential parallels phase 2 of the normal myocardial fiber or fast response. The positive overshoot does not occur within the slow response, presumably because there is no rapid influx of sodium. For all practical purposes, then, there is no corollary of phase 1 or phase 2 within the slow response; the slow inward currents for sodium and calcium account for the slow positive spike of phase 0 in Fig. 4-2.

Propagation of the Action Potential

Since the myocardium is surrounded by intracellular and extracellular fluids which are replete with electrolytes, the myocardial fibers are surrounded by excellent conductors of electricity. With stimulation of the fiber, the positive charges flow inward, thus attracting negative ions to the external surface. Since current flows from higher to lower potential, the external flow will be in the direction of right to left (from positive to negative), while intracellularly it will flow from left to right (Fig. 4-3). At any given point in the process of activation there is a boundary which separates the depolarized and polarized zones. It is these differences in potential which are measured by the lead systems of the electrocardiogram. During the period in which depolarization has been completed and the muscle sustains activation, there is no difference in electrical potential and therefore no current to be measured by the electrocardiogram.

The velocity of the conduction across the muscle is dependent upon the difference in potential between the activated and resting muscle. The greater the magnitude of the action potential and the faster the positive overshoot occurs, the more rapidly conduction occurs. Should the resting potential become more positive such as in ischemic tissue or in premature beats, the velocity of conduction will diminish.

The impulse, once initiated, will be propagated in all directions until depolarization of the entire myocardium has been effected. Known as the "all-or-nothing law," the impulse will spread from one muscle fiber to the next with no additional stimulation unless the wave of excitation reaches a point where there is sufficient voltage to obtain threshold potential. The heart behaves as a single cell, a functional syncytium.

Automatic pacemaker cells, or those cells which are characterized by the slow response, possess a much slower speed of conduction. The greater vulnerability of the slow-response fibers to block has already been mentioned. In addition, these fibers are unable to conduct at rapid rates. The velocity of conduction may differ according to the direction of conduction (whether antegrade or retrograde) in the slow-response fibers. The basis of reentry exists in the frequency with which a slow-response fiber can conduct an impulse in one direction but block it in the opposite direction.

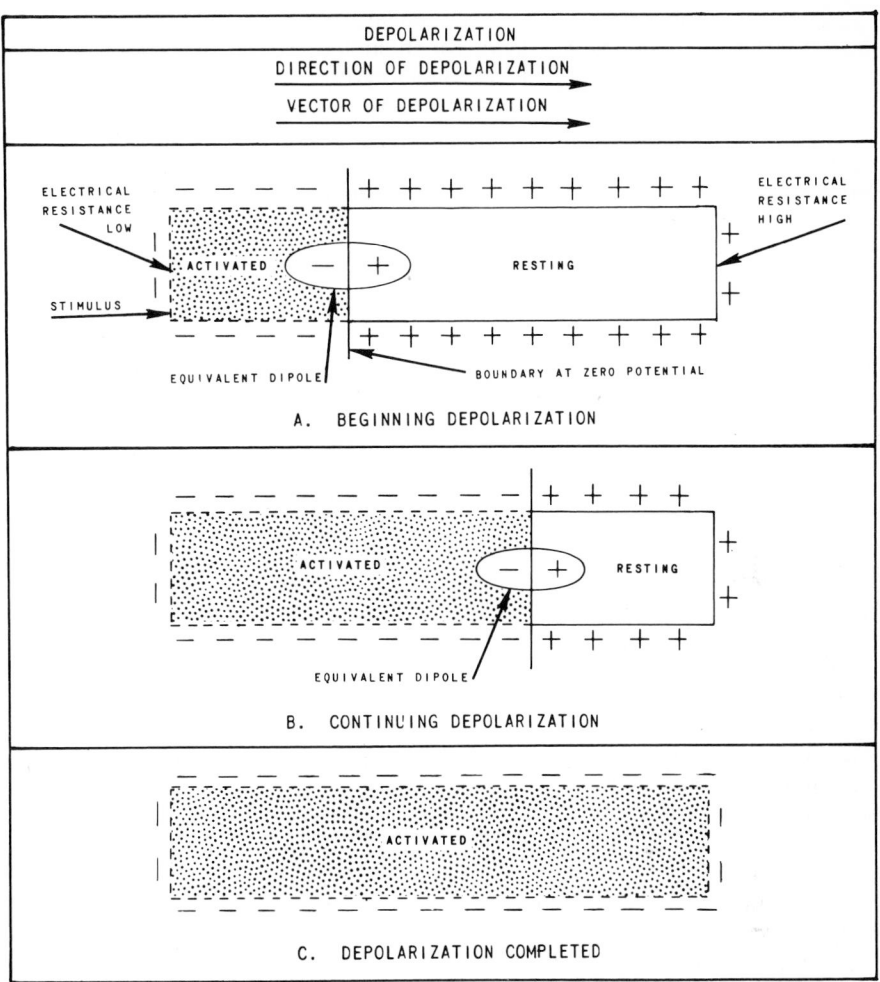

FIGURE 4-3

Depolarization of the muscle fiber. See text for description. (*From H. Harold Friedman, Diagnostic Electrocardiography and Vectorcardiography, 2d ed., McGraw-Hill, New York, 1976. Used by permission of the publisher.*)

Refractory Period

During the period in which a depolarized fiber is recovering from excitation, it is refractory to another stimulus and cannot generate an action potential. The duration of the refractory period varies according to the type of action potential, whether a fast or slow response, and probably according to other factors as well. The concept of cardiac excitability is assuming an increasingly important role in uncovering the genesis as well as the treatment of certain cardiac arrhythmias.

The absolute or effective refractory period begins at phase 0 and continues to the approximate midpoint of phase 3. The period from the midpoint of phase 3 extending to phase 4 (Fig. 4-1) is known as the *relative refractory period*. The fiber is capable of generating an action potential, but only if the stimulus is stronger than that which would be required during phase 4. The later in phase 3 that stimulation occurs, the greater the amplitude and velocity of conduction. The basis for the refractory periods probably resides with the inactivation of the fast sodium currents occurring in repolarization; thus, the closer the membrane is to resting potential when excited, the more fast sodium channels will be reactivated.

In cells characterized by the slow response, the effective refractory periods are longer than in the normal myocardial fiber. The absolute refractory period can continue well beyond phase 3, and the relative refractory period continues into phase 4. Impulses which arrive somewhat early in phase 4 are conducted very slowly, even though the membrane is at resting potential and fully repolarized.

Normal Electrical Conduction

The SA Node

Located at the junction of the superior vena cava and the right atrium lies the normal pacemaker of the heart, the sinoatrial node (SA node). The node is approximately 10 to 20 mm long, 3 to 4 mm wide, and 2 mm thick. It would appear that the functional organization of the sinus node is such that several groups of sinus node cells undergo pacemaker activity simultaneously and without interference from each other. The obvious benefit is that in the event of failure in the excitation of one group of cells, another would be available with little change in rate. Pathology involving the SA node is frequently a result of its anatomic position or blood supply. Since the node is superficial, lying scarcely a millimeter beneath the pericardium, it is subject to diseases affecting the superficial tissues, for example, pericarditis.

Since the major function of the SA node is to serve as pacemaker of the heart, its action potential is typical of a slow response (Fig. 4-2). The property which determines its role as pacemaker is that of diastolic depolarization. In addition, the SA node has a low resting membrane potential in comparison to other myocardial fibers. The cause of the low resting potential appears to be a very high sodium conductance within the sinus membranes. Inactivation of the potassium current during phase 4, together with early opening of the slow sodium and calcium channels, presumably is the basis of diastolic depolarization.

Effect of Nervous System

The frequency of discharge of the SA node is ordinarily determined through control of the sympathetic and parasympathetic nervous systems. With an increase in sympathetic stimulation, norepinephrine is released from the nerve endings to increase the heart rate, as well as increase cardiac excitability and contractility. Apparently the effect of norepinephrine lies in its ability to increase membrane permeability to sodium which, in the sinus node, causes an increase in the velocity of reduction in membrane potential to threshold, thus increasing the heart rate. Stimulation of the parasympathetic system causes release of acetylcholine at the vagal nerve endings. Acetylcholine has just the opposite effect on the heart: It decreases the rate of discharge at the SA node and decreases the rate of conduction of the impulse from the atria to the ventricles. When stimulated by acetylcholine, the cardiac fibers become extremely permeable to potassium so that very rapid efflux of potassium occurs within the cell. This results in hyperpolarization of the fiber, since its resting potential is more negative than normal and therefore less excitable.

Another effect of vagal stimulation upon the SA node, resulting from the decrease in rate, can be escape beats from lower pacemakers within the conduction system; if the reduction in sinus discharge continues, the lower pacemaker takes over at a slower rate than that of the sinus node. Normally the intrinsic rate of sinus discharge is between 60 and 100 beats per minute, with a minimum range of 40 to 50 and a maximum of 200 beats per minute.

Atrial Conduction

From the SA node, the impulse is immediately conducted through the atria and to the AV node via the internodal pathways. The sinus node fibers are continuous with the atrial fibers; thus the impulse spreads in a wavelike pattern in all directions, reaching the distal portions of the atria in about 0.08 s. The internodal pathways are comprised of a combination of ordinary myocardial fibers and fibers which are functionally similar to the Purkinje fibers within the ventricles. The internodal pathways consist of the anterior, middle, and posterior branches. Bachmann's bundle, or the first portion of the anterior internodal pathway, is primarily responsible for rapid propagation of the impulse to the left atrium. The remainder of the anteronodal branch conducts impulses to the AV node. The middle branch or Wenckebach's tract, crosses to the interatrial septum and to the AV node. The posterior pathway (Thorel's) is easily seen and has been demonstrated as the major pathway connecting the two nodes. The atrial action potential is demonstrated in Fig. 4-4. It is difficult to differentiate phase 2 from phase 3; repolarization (phase 3) is also prolonged.

AV Conduction

The atrioventricular (AV) node is anatomically similar to the SA node, but is shorter and thicker. It is located in the right atrium, directly above the tricuspid valve

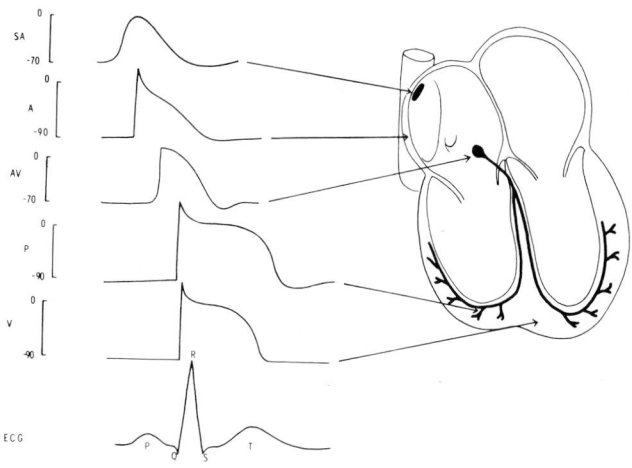

FIGURE 4-4

Comparison of action potentials in differing myocardial tissue. Sinoatrial (*SA*) pacemaker cells possess phase 4 spontaneous depolarization, a slow upstroke in phase 0, poorly differentiated phases 1 and 2, and a well-developed repolarization in phase 3. Atrial muscle cells (*A*) are characterized by a rapid upstroke in phase 1, with a well-developed positive overshoot and a relatively long phase 3. Phases 2 and 3 are difficult to differentiate. Atrioventricular cells (*AV*) may possess a period of hyperpolarization at the end of phase 3 and do not appear to possess true phase 4 diastolic depolarization. The Purkinje cells (*P*) possess an extremely rapid upstroke in phase 1 and a lengthy phase 2, and they appear to demonstrate phase 4 depolarization. Ventricular cells (*V*) have a much shorter repolarization phase (phase 2) than Purkinje cells and do not possess diastolic depolarization. (*From J. Willis Hurst, The Heart, Arteries, and Veins, 4th ed., McGraw-Hill, New York, 1978. Used by permission of the publisher.*)

and anterior to the coronary sinus. The most common pathology within the AV node occurs from ischemia resulting from occlusion of the main artery supplying the AV nodal branch of the coronary artery, frequently seen in posterior myocardial infarction.

Functionally, the node can be divided into three separate areas: (1) the A-N division, the distal atrial and proximal nodal areas; (2) the N area, the midpoint of the node; and (3) the N-H area, the transitional area where the nodal fibers combine with the bundle of His. In the N region, the major delay between atrial and ventricular contractions occurs so that atrial contraction can augment ventricular diastolic volume; electrocardiographically the delay is depicted as the P-R interval (Fig. 4-4).

The action potential within the N region is similar to that of the SA node (Fig. 4-4). The resting potential is less than in the ordinary myocardial fiber, and the refractory period extends beyond phase 4. There may be a period of hyperpolarization at the end of phase 3, followed by a return to a stable resting potential. Cells within this area do not appear to demonstrate true diastolic depolarization. The AV node exhibits the property of decremental conduction; i.e., impulses are blocked that would be conducted in other areas of the heart, and should the atria depolarize at a high rate, only a portion of the impulses are normally conducted through the AV node. The major goal of decremental conduction is to prevent the ventricles from contracting before adequate filling occurs.

The effects of norepinephrine and sympathetic stimulation upon the AV node is one of increasing excitability within the potential pacemakers of the AV junction as well as increasing conduction time. Parasympathetic stimulation, as previously mentioned, can either simply lengthen conduction time from the node to the ventricle, or cause partial or even complete blockage of atrial impulses within the node and result in junctional escape rhythms. The intrinsic rate within the junction is approximately 40 to 60 impulses per minute.

Transmission Through Purkinje System

The bundle of His divides almost immediately into the right and left bundle branches. The right bundle, a single, slender group of fibers, descends the right side of the interventricular septum. The left bundle is much thicker than the right and originates at a sharp angle from the His bundle as it penetrates the interventricular septum to descend the left side of the ventricular septum. After 20 to 30 mm the left bundle divides to form two direct pathways to the anterior and posterior papillary muscles. The bundle branches subdivide into the many small fibers of the Purkinje network once they reach the ventricular apex. The Purkinje fibers enter the ventricular muscle from the endocardium and terminate within the ventricular myocardium.

The Purkinje system has the major task of rapidly and synchronously conducting the wave of excitation to the ventricular myocardial fibers. In Fig. 4-4, the

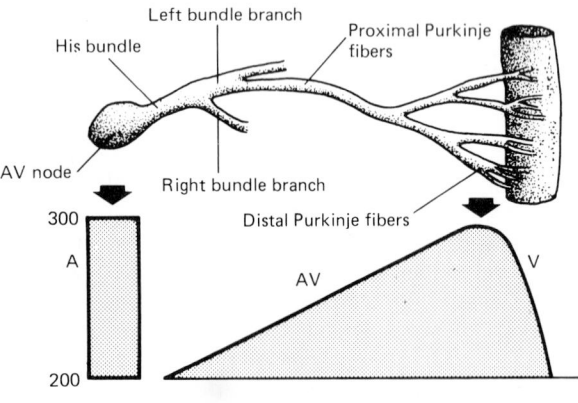

FIGURE 4-5

Refractory periods within the heart. Represented in the upper diagram is the conduction system: the AV node, His bundle, left and right bundle branches, and the conduction tissue connecting junctional and ventricular conducting tissue, which is divided into the proximal Purkinje fibers and distal Purkinje fibers. The shaded areas are representative of refractory periods, the ordinate being 200 to 300 ms. The arrows emphasize peak refractory periods in the AV node and distal Purkinje network. See text for further details.

action potential of the Purkinje fiber has a very rapid upstroke as well as a prolonged repolarization phase (a lengthy phase 2). In addition, the Purkinje action potential demonstrates spontaneous diastolic depolarization.

In addition to its primary function as an extremely rapid conductor of the atrial impulse to the ventricles, the Purkinje system has two other fundamental properties. The first relates to the very long repolarization phase mentioned above. Figure 4-5 compares the refractory periods of the specialized conducting system. The shaded areas at the bottom represent refractory periods; it is apparent that the areas with the greatest refractory periods are the AV node and the distal Purkinje fibers (DPF). The distal Purkinje fibers are also called *gate cells* in deference to their role in protecting the ventricles from premature beats which may be conducted by the AV node but are blocked by the gate cells because of their long refractory period. This mechanism is especially effective at slow heart rates. As the heart rate increases, the refractory period within the gate cells decreases. Within the AV node, however, the absolute refractory period remains unchanged and can even increase with very rapid rates; thus the AV node assumes the role of the Purkinje gate cells in tachycardia.

The second function of the Purkinje system is that of pacemaker. Though the action potential does not exhibit the classic slow response of the other automatic cells, the pacemaker function of the Purkinje fibers is evident through diastolic depolarization and can become manifest through escape rhythms or in assumption of the role of pacemaker of the heart in severe conduction disturbances, as in complete heart block. The intrinsic rate of the Purkinje system is less than 40 impulses per minute.

Electrocardiography

Purpose

The electrocardiogram gives essential information regarding variations in rate and rhythm of the heart, effects of altered electrolyte concentrations, the electrical orientation of the heart as influenced by anatomic factors, and the influence of some drugs such as digitalis. The electrocardiogram gives no direct information regarding the contractile state or mechanical performance of the heart.

Basis of Lead System

An electrocardiograph is essentially a modification of the galvanometer, in that there are two terminals:

one connected to a positive electrode and one connected to a negative electrode. When the two electrodes are placed at different points in an electrical field, a lead is formed; the axis of that lead is described by joining the two sites with a hypothetical line.

Bipolar leads record the potential between a positive and negative electrode which are placed within the area of electrical potential. The unipolar lead gives information about the variations in potential taking place underneath a single exploring electrode. It records the difference between an indifferent negative electrode (which is at zero potential) and the exploring electrode (positive).

Figure 4-6 represents a ventricular muscle strip which is connected to a unipolar lead. Exploring electrodes, which are attached to a recorder, are placed at three points on the muscle strip: on the endocardium, on the epicardium, and at the midportion of the strip. The direction of depolarization in the normal ventricle extends from endocardium to epicardium; the reverse is true for the direction of repolarization.

In the polarized or resting state, depicted in section *A* of Fig. 4-6, there is no difference in potential and therefore no activity to be measured. With excitation, the epicardial lead begins to inscribe an upstroke, since it faces the positive side of the advancing electric charge. As the wave of depolarization arrives at the electrode, depicted in sections *C* and *D*, the peak of the deflection occurs and the muscle strip is completely depolarized; the deflection then returns very suddenly to baseline. The conventional description of the first positive deflection in ventricular activation is the *R wave*. Briefly following the R wave is a short period in which the muscle remains activated

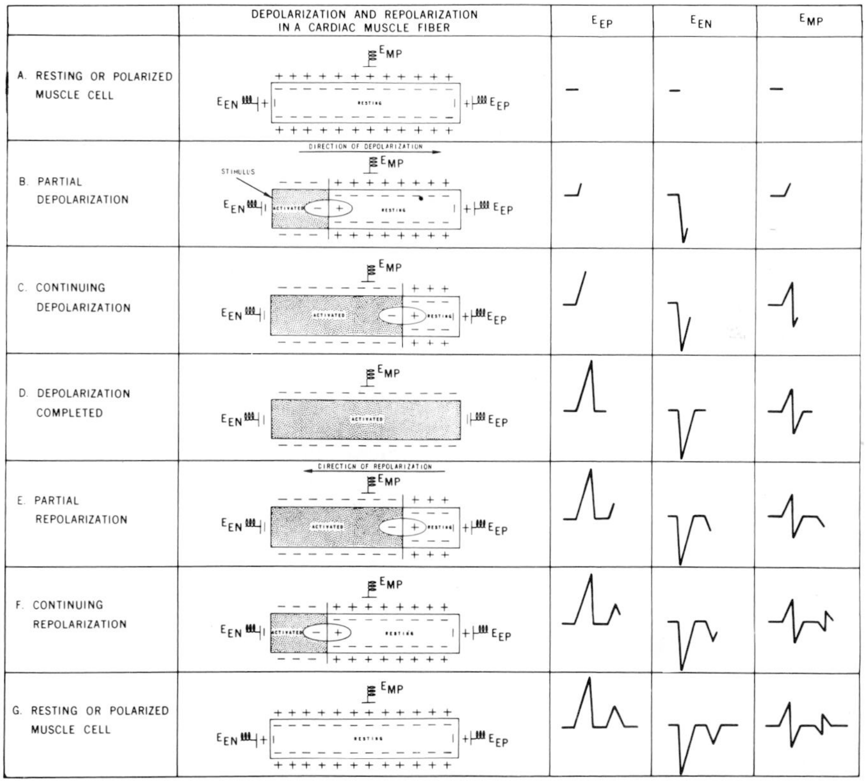

FIGURE 4-6

The electrical potentials resulting from three unipolar leads recording depolarization and repolarization of a cardiac muscle fiber: from an epicardial lead (*Eep*), an endocardial lead (*Ee$_n$*), and a lead placed in the middle of the muscle (*Emp*). See text for further description. (*From H. Harold Friedman, Outline of Electrocardiography, McGraw-Hill, New York, 1963. Used by permission of the publisher.*)

and at the same potential. This period in which no change in potential occurs (isoelectric period) is called the *S-T segment.* With repolarization, the negative charge precedes the positive and travels to the endocardial end of the muscle. Since the positive charge faces the positive exploring electrode, an upright deflection is inscribed, the *T wave.* As long as polarization and depolarization take place in opposite directions, the R and T waves are recorded in the same direction.

In the endocardial lead, the electrode faces the negative side of pair of charges; therefore a negative deflection, the *Q wave,* is inscribed. The peak of the activation occurs rapidly and closer to the beginning of the wave of current where the electrode is closest to the negative charge. As the wave moves away from the electrode to complete activation of the muscle, the deflection returns gradually to baseline. This ventricular deflection is termed the *QS complex.* Since repolarization occurs in the reverse direction and the negative charge faces the electrode, an inverted T wave is recorded.

When the exploring electrode is equidistant from the ends of the muscle, first a positive deflection occurs; as the wave of excitation passes the electrode (Fig. 4-6*C*), maximum amplitude is reached and the deflection becomes negative as the charge moves away from the electrode. A biphasic complex is recorded which is termed an *RS waveform.* The T wave also is biphasic.

Summary of Relationship between Lead Axis and Amplitude

The magnitude of the waveform is greatest when the direction of electrical forces (vector) lies parallel with the lead axis. As the angle decreases, the deflection also diminishes. Finally, if the vector is perpendicular to the lead axis, a small or indistinguishable waveform is inscribed.

Stimulation of the muscle in an abnormal direction can cause alteration in the direction of depolarization and repolarization. Repolarization can be altered independently of a change in direction of depolarization through factors such as ischemia, drugs, electrolytes, and change in temperature. The effect of ischemia is such that the duration of epicardial activation (normally very short) lengthens, causing a reversal in the direction of repolarization so that repolarization occurs in the same direction as depolarization (Fig. 4-7). The epicardial electrode records a normal R wave (depolarization is unaffected)

and an inverted T wave. The endocardial recording is just the reverse.

Einthoven's Triangle

The basis of modern electrocardiography resides in the system devised by William Einthoven. His hypothesis assumes that the heart lies in the center of an equilateral triangle, the apices of which are the right and left shoulders and pubic region; and that the body fluids act as a volume conductor so that the standard limb leads can record differences in potential between the apices of the triangle. The conventional limb leads are (1) lead I, recording the differences in potential between the negative right (RA) and positive left (LA) arms; (2) lead II, recording the differences between the negative RA and positive left leg (LL); and (3) lead III, measuring the variations between the left leg (positive) and left arm (negative). The standard limb leads are such that in most persons the three leads are positive.

Unipolar leads recorded from the right arm (VR), left arm (VL), and left leg (VF) are based on the theory that the indifferent electrode located at the central terminal maintains zero potential throughout the cardiac cycle. By comparing the potential of an exploring electrode with that of the central terminal, it is evident that only the variation of potential under the exploring electrode is recorded. Since the deflections which are measured are very small, augmentation of their amplitude is performed so that these leads are designated as aVR, aVL, and aVF. These leads, in addition to the six unipolar precordial leads, form the basis of the 12-lead electrocardiogram.

The Vectorcardiogram

The vectorcardiogram displays the electrical activity of the heart in the three planes of the body. A vector has three qualities: magnitude, direction, and polarity, which may be displayed in one or all three planes. The vector represents the magnitude of a force through its length, the relationship between the force and planes of the body by its direction, and its polarity through the location of the arrowhead, as can be seen in Fig. 4-8 (the arrowhead represents positivity; the tail represents negativity).

Ventricular Excitation

The papillary muscles and interventricular septum are activated first, except for a small section near the

VENTRICULAR DEPOLARIZATION IN THE NORMAL HEART

SEQUENCE OF VENTRICULAR ACTIVATION

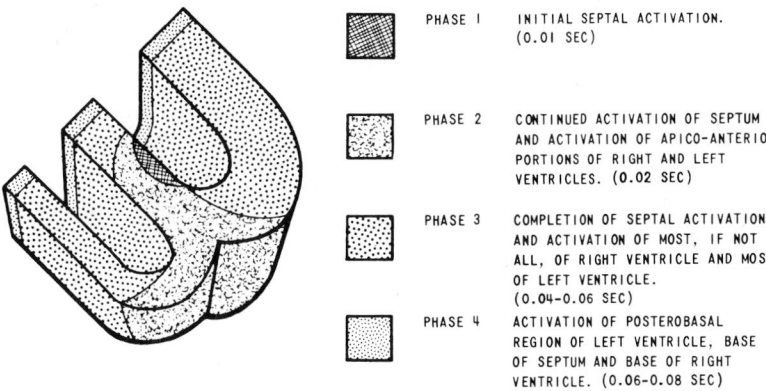

	PHASE 1	INITIAL SEPTAL ACTIVATION. (0.01 SEC)
	PHASE 2	CONTINUED ACTIVATION OF SEPTUM AND ACTIVATION OF APICO-ANTERIOR PORTIONS OF RIGHT AND LEFT VENTRICLES. (0.02 SEC)
	PHASE 3	COMPLETION OF SEPTAL ACTIVATION AND ACTIVATION OF MOST, IF NOT ALL, OF RIGHT VENTRICLE AND MOST OF LEFT VENTRICLE. (0.04-0.06 SEC)
	PHASE 4	ACTIVATION OF POSTEROBASAL REGION OF LEFT VENTRICLE, BASE OF SEPTUM AND BASE OF RIGHT VENTRICLE. (0.06-0.08 SEC)

VENTRICULAR ACTIVATION VECTORS IN THE TRANSVERSE PLANE

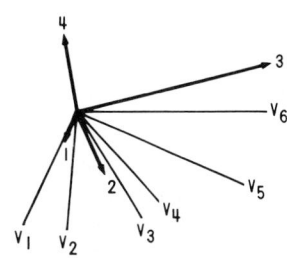

QRS COMPLEXES IN THE PRECORDIAL LEADS

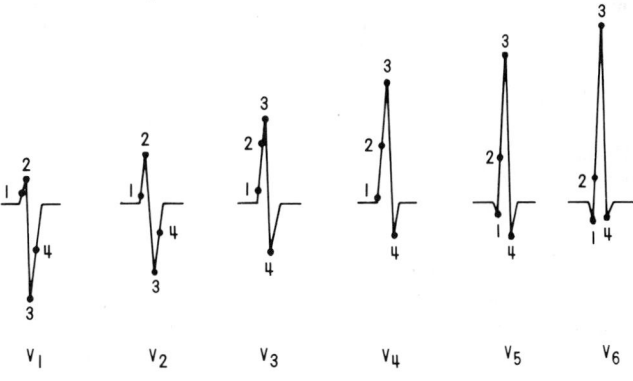

FIGURE 4-7

Normal ventricular depolarization. See text for description. (*From H. Harold Friedman, Outline of Electrocardiography, McGraw-Hill, New York, 1963. Used by permission of the publisher.*)

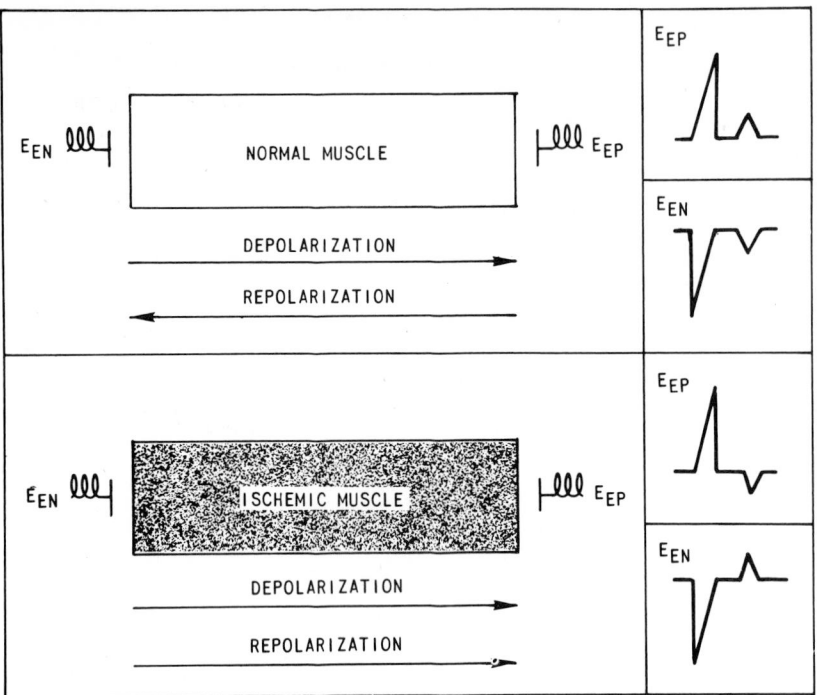

FIGURE 4-8

Effects of ischemia in cardiac muscle. See text for discussion. (*From H. Harold Friedman, Outline of Electrocardiography, McGraw-Hill, New York, 1963. Used by permission of the publisher.*)

base of the septum (Fig. 4-7). Since the initial vector is oriented to the right and superiorly, an R wave is recorded in the right precordial leads (V_1 and V_2) and a small Q wave is recorded on the left precordium (V_5 and V_6). The early septal activation results in the septum becoming quite rigid so that it can function as a fulcrum for the remaining ventricular contraction. Similarly, early contraction of the papillary muscles prevents eversion of the atrioventricular valves during contraction.

The activation spreads from endocardium to epicardium and spreads over both right and left ventricles. Since the left ventricular waveform has greater potential, it determines the QRS vector as anterior and leftward and inscribes a positive R wave. During the third phase, most of both ventricles are depolarized and again overpower the right ventricular waveforms. Since this phase has considerable amplitude, a deep S wave is recorded in the right precordial leads, while tall R waves are recorded in the portions of both ventricles; generally, the left ventricular vector is dominant. The waveform is oriented leftward and

posteriorly, thus recording the downstroke of the R wave; a small S wave may be inscribed in the left precordial leads.

THE CARDIOVASCULAR SYSTEM AS A CIRCUIT

The most salient feature of the cardiovascular system is that it is a continuous circuit. If a portion of the blood volume is displaced from one portion of the circuit, another segment must accommodate the additional volume through expansion unless it is lost from the circulation.

In Fig. 4-9, the circulation is subdivided schematically into the pulmonary and systemic circuits—respectively, the distensible and resistive segments of the cardiovascular system. In the lower portion of the diagram, the resistive arterial circulation is represented by a single slightly distensible chamber, while an even greater distensible chamber represents all the veins, the venous reservoir.

The principal determinants of blood flow are pressure and resistance. In the large vessels of the circulation, blood flows with little impedance; it is in the arterioles, the "valves" of the circulation, where considerable resistance is met. In order to overcome arteriolar resistance, the ventricles must pump blood into the arteries at a high pressure, about 120 mmHg in the systemic circuit and about 22 mmHg in the pulmonary circulation.

Hemodynamics of the Circulation

An important determinant of blood flow is viscosity. There are several factors which influence the viscosity of blood; principal among them are the hematocrit and the internal diameter of the vessel. An increase in the percentage of cells within the blood, the hematocrit, from the normal of 40 to 70 or 80, can triple the viscosity and seriously impair blood flow.

Within the small vessels, blood flow decreases markedly. Because of the decrease in velocity of flow, blood viscosity can increase tenfold. Following division of an artery or vein, the cross-sectional area of the branches taken together exceeds that of the vessel of origin. Since the volumes of blood moving through each segment of the circulation are equal, changes in a cross-sectional area necessarily influence the velocity of blood flow. In the aorta, blood travels very rapidly, slows significantly within the capillaries (large cross-sectional area), and accelerates in the veins, where the cross-sectional area once again is smaller. The relatively slow capillary blood flow provides sufficient time for exchange of oxygen and nutrients through the capillary walls.

Determinants of Blood Flow

Blood flow is directly proportional to the pressure difference between two ends of a vessel and inversely proportional to the resistance imposed by characteristics within the vessel. The relationship is expressed in Fig. 4-10, where any vessel within the circulation is depicted. Were there no difference or gradient between P_1 and P_2, there could be no blood flow. The resistance, which includes any factor which serves to impede flow, can be calculated from measurements of blood flow and pressure gradients within the vessel.

In a resting individual, blood flow within the circulation occurs at a rate of approximately 100 mL/s. The normal arterial to venous pressure gradient within the total circulation is around 100 mmHg. The resistance within the circulation (total peripheral resist-

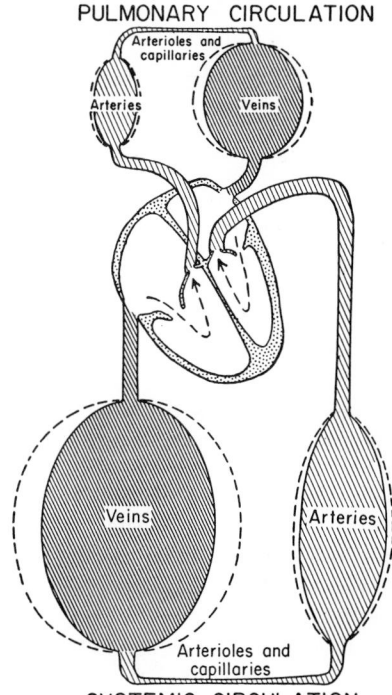

PULMONARY CIRCULATION

SYSTEMIC CIRCULATION

FIGURE 4-9

Representation of the major subdivisions of the cardiovascular circulation, demonstrating the distensibility and resistance of the systemic and pulmonary circulations. (*From Arthur C. Guyton, Textbook of Medical Physiology, Saunders, Philadelphia, 1970. Used by permission of the publisher.*)

ance), then, is 100 to 100, or one peripheral resistance unit (PRU). Another method for measurement of total peripheral resistance is obtained by relating the cardiac output and arterial pressure. An individual with a cardiac output of 5000 mL/min and arterial pressure of 100 mmHg would have a calculated peripheral resistance of 0.02 PRU. The systemic resistance will vary considerably when vasoconstriction or vasodilatation occurs, increasing with the former and dropping as vascular capacity is increased through vessel dilatation.

The effect of vessel diameter upon blood flow is graphically demonstrated in Fig. 4-11. In Fig. 4-11A, increasing the vessel diameter by four-fold results in an increase in blood flow by 256-fold with no change in pressure gradient. The basis behind such marked changes in flow with relatively small changes in

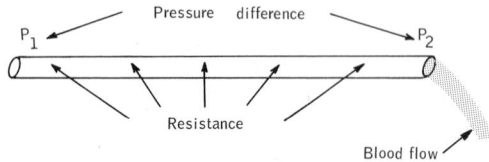

FIGURE 4-10

Factors influencing blood flow: pressure resistance and pressure gradient (P_1 and P_2). (*From Arthur C. Guyton, Textbook of Medical Physiology, Saunders, Philadelphia, 1970. Used by permission of the publisher.*)

vessel diameter is explained in Fig. 4-11*B*. Blood flows within a vessel in layers; the layers closest to the vessel wall experience the greatest "drag" and move very slowly, while the layers farther away from the vessel wall move with increasing velocity. The phenomenon is known as *streamlining,* or *laminar flow.* The greater the internal diameter of the vessel, the more layers can form, thereby increasing flow.

The major factors influencing blood flow are often expressed through the Poiseuille equation, *Poiseuille's law,* which states that the flow (Q) of fluid through a tube is directly proportional to the pressure gradient ($P_1 - P_2$) across the tube, to the fourth power of the radius of the tube (r^4), and inversely proportional

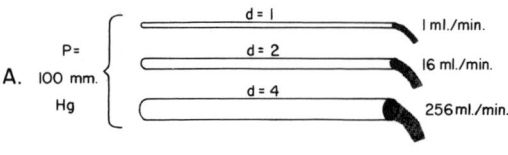

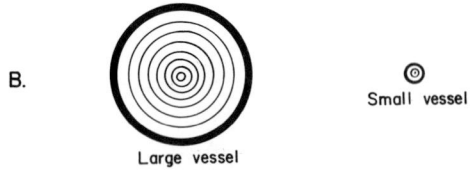

FIGURE 4-11

Effect of increasing vessel diameter on blood flow. (*A*) Demonstration of increasing velocity of blood flow with formation of layers of blood flowing at varying velocity; the farther away from the vessel wall, the more rapid the flow (*B*). (*From Arthur C. Guyton, Textbook of Medical Physiology, Saunders, Philadelphia, 1970. Used by permission of the publisher.*)

to the length of the tube (L) and the viscosity (n) of the fluid:

$$\frac{Q(P_1 - P_2)r^4}{Ln} \cdot \frac{\pi}{8}$$

with $\pi/8$ serving as a geometric proportional value. Resistance, then, increases in direct proportion to the viscosity and length of the vessel, but decreases in direct proportion to the vessel diameter (the fourth power of the radius of the vessel) and pressure gradient.

Although the relationships of Poiseuille's law are helpful in isolating the dynamics of blood flow, there are several factors which hinder a qualitative application. The formula is based upon a system of rigid tubes which, unlike distensible blood vessels, cannot increase in both length and diameter; in addition, there are other factors unique to the fluid characteristics of blood which are not considered in the Poiseuille relationship.

The caliber of blood vessels is unquestionably significant in determining pressure gradients and flow through various segments of the circulation. Approximately 80 percent of the pressure drop occurs in the terminal arteries and arterioles (Fig. 4-12). The resistance imposed by the arteriolar circulation must, in addition, be related to the cross-sectional area. Since the different types of vessels lie in a series arrangement with one another and the various vascular beds are parallel, it is apparent that the total flow is a sum of the individual flows through each vascular bed (Fig. 4-12*A*). Since resistance is increased both by an increase in cross-sectional area and by a reduction in vessel diameter, it follows that the resistance of each individual resistance bed exceeds the total systemic resistance. The resistance of the renal circulation, for instance, will exceed that of the total peripheral circulation, since far greater volumes of blood will flow through the total circulation than through the renal vasculature.

THE SYSTEMIC CIRCULATION

Functional Characteristics

The walls of the systemic arteries are extremely thick and tough. Functionally they serve to transport blood under high pressure to the tissues through their role as a pressure reservoir. With left ventricular ejection, the walls within the aortic arch distend and the arterial pressure rises, resulting in transmission of a pressure pulse down the aorta and on into the arteries. When the ventricular contraction ceases, the arterial pressure gradually falls, but sufficient tension remains within the walls to drive blood through the capillaries to the tissues and overcome peripheral resistance. By so doing, the systemic arterial pressure fluctuates above and below a mean pressure of approximately 90 mmHg and maintains forward flow, as demonstrated in Fig. 4-13.

Between the arteries and veins lie the capillaries, whose walls are composed only of endothelial cells. The thin capillary walls are essential in permitting rapid diffusion of substances between the blood and tissue. Because of their very small caliber they can support pressures of up to 100 mmHg in the lower extremities during standing. At heart level, the capillary pressure is normally between 20 and 30 mmHg.

The veins are very thin and normally are under very low pressure with very little fluctuation. Contrasted with the arterial circulation, in which even small increases in volume can induce large pressure fluctuations, the principal function of the venous system as a low-pressure variable-volume reservoir becomes apparent. In fact, almost three-quarters of the systemic circulation is stored within the venous circulation (Fig. 4-12*B*). Note the very small amount of blood within the capillaries, where the most important function of the cardiovascular system occurs.

Capillary Dynamics

The most important method for exchange of substances through the capillary wall is diffusion. Though there are many factors which affect the rate at which a substance diffuses across the capillary wall, the chief influence is derived from the concentration gradient between the two sides of the membrane. The greater the difference between the concentrations of any substance, the more rapidly will it diffuse across the cell membrane. Tiny passageways connect the interior of the capillary with the exterior. Substances which are insoluble in the lipid capillary membrane can diffuse only through these capillary "pores."

Starling Equilibrium

Maintenance of fluid within the vascular system is the very basis of capillary dynamics. According to the Starling equilibrium or law of the capillaries, filtration or reabsorption of fluid across the capillary wall depends on the interrelation of four forces. Figure 4-14 depicts the four major factors involved in fluid transfer: (1) capillary pressure, which tends to filter

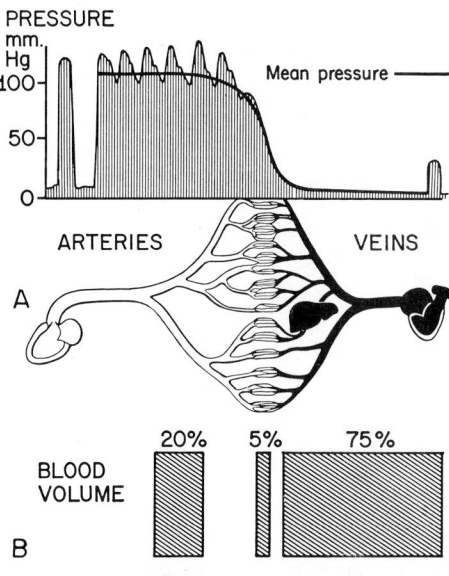

FIGURE 4-12

(*A*) Resistance and resulting loss of pressure within the circulation. Arterial pressure diminishes very rapidly in the small resistance vessels of the circulation. In the venous vessels the pressure gradient is very low. (*B*) The volume of blood stored in the distensible venous circulation is between 60 and 75 percent and can change dramatically. Arterial volume, however, remains at about 20 percent of total blood volume and does not vary significantly. (*From Robert Rushmer, Cardiovascular Dynamics, Saunders, Philadelphia, 1970. Used by permission of the publisher.*)

fluid out of the capillary membrane to the tissues; (2) interstitial fluid pressure, which maintains a negative value, tending to draw fluid back into the interstitium; (3) plasma colloid osmotic pressure (oncotic pressure), which promotes absorption of fluid through osmotic attraction back into the capillary; and (4) interstitial fluid colloid osmotic pressure, which osmotically attracts fluid into the interstitium (tissue space).

The hydrostatic pressure (blood pressure) within the capillaries cannot be directly measured. It is not a constant value since it is dependent upon the arterial and venous pressures and the pre- and postcapillary resistance. The capillary pressure is assumed to be somewhere between 25 and 32 mmHg at the arterial end. Guyton approximates the normal functional mean capillary pressure to be about 17

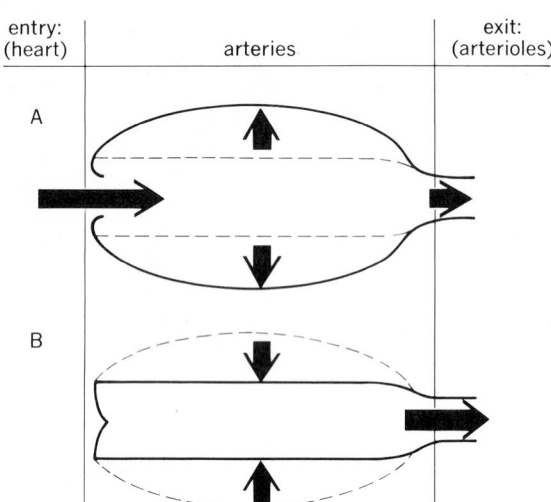

FIGURE 4-13

During systole much of the blood is stored in the elastic arteries, although some forward flow does occur. In diastole the stored tension within the walls, or elastic recoil, is instrumental in modifying pulsatile flow into constant flow throughout the cardiac cycle. (*From Robert M. Berne and Matthew N. Levy, Cardiovascular Physiology, 3d ed., Mosby, St. Louis, 1977. Used by permission of the publisher.*)

mmHg and the average pressure at the venous end to be about 10 mmHg.

The tissue pressure is also difficult to measure directly but is thought to be approximately −7 mmHg, a partial vacuum since it is less than atmospheric pressure. The tissue pressure should not be considered without relation to the lymphatic system, since the latter appears to maintain negativity of the interstitium.

Strategic factors in preventing the fluid loss from the capillaries are the plasma proteins. The major determinant in the maintenance of the colloidal osmotic pressure is the protein albumin. Since the protein molecule is so large, it cannot diffuse readily into the tissue space; the few molecules that do diffuse into the interstitium are removed by the lymph system. In addition, a phenomenon known as the *Gibbs-Donnan equilibrium* enhances the osmotic attraction of proteins. Since proteins are anions, they attract an equal number of cations, predominantly sodium, in order to achieve electrical balance. This increases the osmotic attraction of proteins by about 50 percent. In addition, the Donnan effect increases in proportion to increasing concentrations of proteins. In other words, additional grams of protein over the first few have much greater oncotic attraction than do

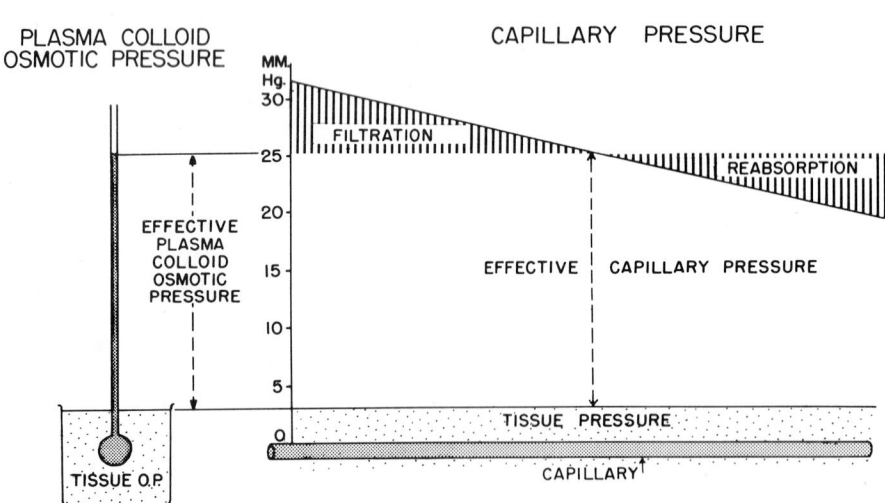

FIGURE 4-14

Capillary fluid exchange. Factors favoring filtration occur at the arterial end of the capillary and reabsorption at the venous end. The determination is the result of a balance between four pressures: (1) arterial and venous capillary mean pressures, (2) plasma colloidal pressure, (3) tissue colloidal osmotic pressure, and (4) interstitial fluid pressure. The lymphatic system is involved in maintenance of normal capillary dynamics. See text for further explanation. (*From Robert Rushmer, Cardiovascular Dynamics, Saunders, Philadelphia, 1970. Used by permission of the publisher.*)

the original few grams, a fact which makes hypoalbuminemia increasingly significant. The oncotic pressure is estimated to be about 28 mmHg. Within the interstitium, the oncotic pressure is approximately 4.5 mmHg.

The pressures, when combined, favor filtration, or movement outward, at the arterial end of the capillary. The low hydrostatic pressure at the venous end of the capillary reverses the balance. There the oncotic pressure exceeds the filtration (outward) force, and reabsorption into the venule occurs. The Starling equilibrium states that in a steady state, the positive filtration forces favoring diffusion outward at the arterial end of the capillary are equal to the forces favoring reabsorption at the venous end. The total amount of fluid leaving the circulation is almost equal to the amount of fluid being reabsorbed in the venous end. The small amount of excess fluid and protein which accumulates within the interstitial space is removed by the lymphatic drainage system.

Causes of Edema

It is immediately evident that a significant increase in capillary pressure, which causes an imbalance of filtration and reabsorptive forces, can result in an accumulation of fluid within the tissue. Similarly, edema can result from a reduction of oncotic pressure, or an increase in the permeability of the capillary such that excessive protein is lost from the plasma, causing reduction of oncotic pressure within the plasma, and from an increase in colloid osmotic pressure within the tissue spaces. There are two major protective mechanisms against the development of edema within the pulmonary vasculature: (1) The pulmonary capillary pressure is substantially lower, about 7 mmHg, and (2) the negative interstitial pressure is thought to be approximately −17 mmHg, both of which favor absorption from the alveolus into the interstitial fluid spaces.

Exchange Across Capillary Membrane

The permeability of the capillaries is not consistent in all tissues. Lymph flow can be used to determine capillary permeability, and the lymph flow from the heart, lungs, intestines, and kidneys reveal a higher concentration of protein than does that from the skin and connective tissues. The liver capillary system is far more permeable than the others, which results in a protein concentration within the lymph flow almost equal to that of plasma.

Other factors affecting the rate of exchange of substances across the capillary are (1) the area of capillary available for filtration, (2) thickness of the capillary wall, (3) viscosity of the filtrate, and (4) the sum of the hydrostatic and osmotic pressures, as discussed earlier.

Although filtration and absorption are critically important in the maintenance of normal capillary dynamics, they play a relatively minor role in the normal exchange of substances. It is diffusion which provides the governing factor in the exchange of water, gases, waste products, and substrates across the capillary membranes. Since the principal limiting factors of diffusion are concentration gradient, molecular size, and lipid solubility, small molecules like water and glucose diffuse with little restriction.

Lymphatic System

The lymphatic vessels are the principal routes by which protein and other large particulate matter can be removed from the interstitium. It is fundamentally a drainage system. The distribution of the lymphatics parallels that of the venous system in that they both have extensive superficial and deep collecting systems. Only cartilage, epithelium, and tissues of the central nervous system lack lymph supply. In addition to returning fluid and protein to the circulation, the lymphatic system removes debris such as bacteria, toxins, and degenerating tissues.

The major factor which determines the rate of lymph flow is the interstitial fluid pressure. A rise in tissue pressure, which can result from a rise in capillary pressure, reduction in oncotic pressure, increase in capillary permeability, or increase in tissue oncotic pressure, will accelerate lymph flow.

As in the veins, lymphatic vessels are liberally supplied with one-way valves which prevent backflow and contribute to the lymphatic pump. Contraction of the muscles, passive movements of parts of the body such as respiration or abdominal movement, arterial pulsations, and external compression of the tissues all stimulate the lymphatic pump. In addition, there is evidence that certain lymphatics possess independent contractility which performs similarly to a type of peristalsis. About 120 mL of lymph flows through the thoracic system of a resting adult per hour. Although it is a very small volume in comparison to total capillary exchange, were protein not removed by the lymph vessels, it would significantly increase tissue oncotic pressure and cause severe edema.

Venous System

The veins function not only as conduits for blood flow, but as a variable-volume reservoir, thereby helping to regulate cardiac output. Marked changes in venous capacity can occur without a significant effect on venous pressure. Thus the veins are a *capacitance* system. Capacitance, as defined by Berne, is the increment of volume accommodated per unit change of pressure. Assuming normal arterial and venous pressures, a 1-mmHg increase in venous pressure would accommodate 20 times more blood within the venous system than within the arterial system for the same pressure change.

Since the pressure at the point of outflow from a series of tubes to a large extent determines the pressure gradient, an understanding of the right atrial pressure and its role as the central venous pressure (CVP) is important. Three factors contribute to the regulation of the CVP: (1) capacitance of the venous system (C), (2) total blood volume (V), and (3) the pumping ability of the heart (P). Normally the right atrial pressure, or CVP, is about equal to the atmospheric pressure around the body—zero. With hypervolemia or ventricular failure resulting from a reduction in contractility or pumping ability, the CVP can rise to very high levels. The effect within the peripheral veins is a backing up of blood, resulting in distention. Usually, many of the large veins which lie adjacent to the ribs and abdominal organs are almost totally collapsed, therefore offering considerable resistance to venous flow. Normally the pressure gradient between peripheral venous pressure and right atrial pressure is approximately 6 to 10 mmHg. As right atrial pressure climbs above its norm, blood begins to distend the large veins, correspondingly decreasing resistance; elevated peripheral venous pressure is therefore not seen until the later stages of failure, or until all the collapsed veins have opened. This is usually seen when right atrial pressure exceeds 4 to 6 mmHg.

Effects of Hydrostatic Pressure

The pressure resulting from the weight of water within a chamber is called *hydrostatic pressure*; at the surface of the fluid, the pressure equals atmospheric, but for each 13.6-mm distance under the surface, pressure increases 1 mmHg. In a standing, immobile person with a normal right atrial pressure (zero), venous pressure within the feet will be 90 mmHg. The same relationship exists within the arterial system.

Were the arterial pressure within the same individual 100 mmHg, arterial pressure at the feet would approximate 190 mmHg. It is only at the phlebostatic axis—the level of the tricuspid valve—that venous pressures are not significantly affected by hydrostatic influence. The external references for that point are approximately two-thirds of thickness of the anterior-posterior chest, the approximate midline, and one-fourth of the distance above the lower end of the sternum. Regardless of the position of the body, the pressure will not vary more than about 1 mmHg.

The venous pump and the valves enable the standing individual to overcome hydrostatic pressure as long as muscle compression occurs. As in the lymphatic vessels, the veins are supplied with unidirectional valves so that muscle compression causes blood to flow back toward the heart. In the quietly standing individual, of course, the venous pump cannot function, and extravasation of fluid from the capillaries into the tissue can occur fairly rapidly, causing edema and possibly significant loss of volume from the vascular space.

Although the resistance imposed by the veins and venules does not approach that of the arterioles, it is important to note that constriction and dilation of the postcapillary venous vessels can cause marked changes in blood volume. Constriction of the venule will produce an increase in capillary pressure and result in enhanced filtration of fluid from the capillary. Dilation, along with precapillary constriction, can result in expansion of blood volume and dehydration of the tissue.

PULMONARY CIRCULATION

Although the systemic and pulmonary circulations together form the cardiovascular circuit, there are very important differences between the two circuits (Fig. 4-15). The pulmonary circulation is a low-pressure, low-resistance system which has a limited perfusion area. The high-pressure, high-resistance systemic circulation, on the other hand, must supply the variable requirements within the entire body, thus requiring many controls and adaptation to a great variety of vascular conditions.

Functional Anatomy

The significant differences between the two circuits are graphically demonstrated by the anatomic configuration of their two pumps. In Fig. 4-16, the relatively thin-walled crescent-shaped right ventricle is con-

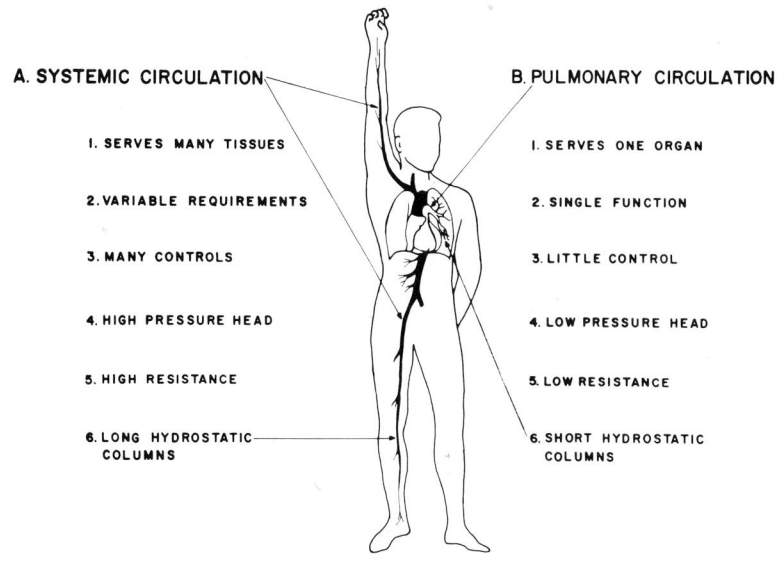

A. SYSTEMIC CIRCULATION

1. SERVES MANY TISSUES

2. VARIABLE REQUIREMENTS

3. MANY CONTROLS

4. HIGH PRESSURE HEAD

5. HIGH RESISTANCE

6. LONG HYDROSTATIC COLUMNS

B. PULMONARY CIRCULATION

1. SERVES ONE ORGAN

2. SINGLE FUNCTION

3. LITTLE CONTROL

4. LOW PRESSURE HEAD

5. LOW RESISTANCE

6. SHORT HYDROSTATIC COLUMNS

FIGURE 4-15

Functional differences between pulmonary and systemic circuits. (*From Robert Rushmer, Cardiovascular Dynamics, Saunders, Philadelphia, 1970. Used by permission of the publisher.*)

trasted with the muscular, cylindrical left ventricle, obviously well-suited for pumping against high resistance. The ventricular septum forms the medial wall of both chambers, although functionally it seems to serve the left ventricle.

Similarly, the pulmonary vasculature is thin-walled and distensible, with relatively short branches. Since the pulmonary branches have much larger internal diameters than do the systemic arteries, the distensible pulmonary vasculature accommodates the same stroke volume as the systemic arterial circuit.

The pulmonary artery extends approximately 4 cm beyond the right ventricle before dividing into the right and left arteries. The four pulmonary veins have similar compliance to the veins of the systemic circuit. Oxygenation of the lungs themselves is performed by the bronchial vessels, which arise from the aorta and drain into the left atrium via the pulmonary veins to contribute a slight mixing of venous with arterial blood—approximately 1 to 2 percent of the cardiac output.

Resistance to Flow

There is no corollary to the arteriole within the pulmonary circuit. That fact, in addition to the factors previously mentioned which contribute to the com-

pliance of the pulmonary vessels (large internal diameter of the vessels and the enormous cross-sectional area of the pulmonary vasculature), results in a resistance imposed on the right ventricle which is about one-eighth that imposed on the left ventricle.

Atrial contraction occurs just prior to right ventricular contraction and contributes a small amount of blood as well as a slight rise in diastolic pressure within the right ventricle. Immediately following atrial contraction, the pressure within the right ventricle continues to rise, closing the tricuspid valve, until the pressure is equal to pulmonary pressure (22 mmHg) and can open the pulmonary valve. With the opening of the valve, right ventricular and pulmonary pressures are essentially the same, and blood flows into the pulmonary artery. During right ventricular relaxation, the right ventricular pressure falls, the pulmonary valve shuts, and the normal diastolic pressure of around zero resumes within the ventricle. Following systole, pressure within the pulmonary artery drops to about 8 mmHg.

The pulmonary veins, like the peripheral veins, are collapsed at low pressures; with distention, they open up, thereby offering negligible resistance to flow. It is for this reason that as much as a 7-mm change in pressure within the left atrium, the point of outflow for the pulmonary veins, will have little effect upon pul-

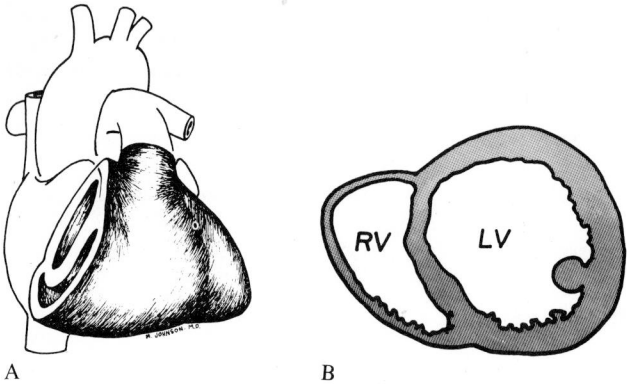

A   B

FIGURE 4-16

The striking structural difference between the left and right ventricular chambers. The interventricular septum protrudes into the right ventricle, causing a crescent shape which is in marked contrast to the circular left ventricle. [*From J. Willis Hurst (ed.), The Heart, Arteries, and Veins, 4th ed., McGraw-Hill, New York, 1974.*]

monary arterial pressure. If the left atrial pressure exceeds about 7 mmHg, however, the pulmonary system begins to assume the characteristics of a system of almost rigid tubes, thereby causing retrograde transmission of pressure to the pulmonary artery and right ventricle. Normally the right ventricle can sustain an increase in systolic pressure of 10 to 20 mmHg. Above a systolic pressure of 40 mmHg, however, the increased resistance causes an increase in right atrial pressure and resulting signs and symptoms of right ventricular failure.

Functions of the Pulmonary Circuit

In addition to its major function in diffusion of oxygen and carbon dioxide, the pulmonary circuit can function as a variable-volume reservoir. Normally about 12 percent (600 mL) of the circulation is contained within the pulmonary vasculature at any one time. When the supine position is assumed, a considerable amount of blood can be displaced into the pulmonary vasculature. There appears to be a volume of blood which can be contained within the lungs and can be displaced as necessary without significantly increasing pulmonary pressure.

The cardiac output can increase to 3 or 4 times normal before causing an elevation in pulmonary pressures. The sole purpose, of course, of circulation through the lungs is oxygenation; it is important that the blood circulate without elevating the energy de-

mands on the heart. An increase in pulmonary pressure imposes just such an increase in metabolic demand.

Lastly, the lungs are well adapted for filtration of emboli, foreign bodies, air bubbles, and other particles because of their extensive dual blood supply, which is a result of the bronchial arterial supply running parallel to the pulmonary vessels.

THE CARDIAC PUMP

The purpose of contraction is to provide energy to the circulation; potential energy is added through an increase in pressure, kinetic energy through the pulsatile flow of blood. Since the moment-to-moment metabolic demands of the peripheral tissues are so variable, the heart must be able to adjust its output with precision and speed.

Normally the myocardium develops sufficient force to raise the pressure within the chamber such that it exceeds that of the outflow chamber. At the point that the valve opens into the next chamber, the muscle holds its pressure and begins to shorten and eject its contents. There are two basic properties which influence myocardial contractility: force and shortening. In order to supply the demands of the peripheral circulation, the heart has three major methods through which it can increase its output: (1) increasing the length of the myocardial fiber prior to contraction, (2) increasing the rate at which it contracts, and (3) increasing myocardial contractility or the strength of the contraction.

Functional Anatomy

The Atria

The left and right atria are volume reservoirs. During ventricular systole they normally accept large amounts of blood from the pulmonary veins and venae cavae. During filling there is very little resistance: normal right atrial pressure is about zero during filling, and left atrial pressure is generally 2 to 3 mmHg. With filling, both pressures rise to a high during atrial contraction of about 5 mmHg on the right and 7 to 8 mmHg on the left. Assuming normal ventricular filling pressures, the majority of ventricular filling occurs prior to atrial contraction; atrial contraction normally contributes only about 20 to 30 percent of the total ventricular diastolic volume.

Sympathetic activity, resulting in increased atrial filling, will increase atrial contractility. During conditions of exercise or drug-induced hypersympathetic activity, the atria can significantly contribute to ventricular filling, a phenomenon often referred to as "atrial kick." Under normal resting conditions, the loss of atrial contraction goes unnoticed; however, with increased metabolic activity or in a heart with a compromised cardiac reserve, loss of the atrial contribution to ventricular filling can cause severe reduction of cardiac output.

The Valves

Three functional properties of the cardiac valves are the following: (1) prevention of regurgitation of blood from one chamber to another, (2) permitting rapid antegrade flow without imposing resistance on that flow, and (3) the ability to withstand high-pressure loads. Though medical science has been attempting for over three decades to prosthetically mimic these functions, our most sophisticated technology has resulted in a very poor second to the engineering marvels of the atrioventricular and semilunar valves (Fig. 4-17).

The AV valves are structurally the more complex of the two sets of valves. Situated between the atria and ventricles, the *tricuspid valve* on the right and *mitral valve* on the left are functionally very similar. Each has two large primary cusps which are opposite one another and connected via chordae tendineae, which descend as if from an inverted parachute to the papillary muscles. Note that the chordae tendineae

arise from the large anterior and posterior cusps of the mitral valve and individually insert into two sets of papillary muscles. The tricuspid has a third intermediate cusp which inserts with the anterior and posterior cusps, into a total of three sets of papillary muscles.

The total area of the AV cusps is almost double that of the orifice which they occlude. During ventricular filling, the valves serve as a funnel as they transfer blood from the atria to the ventricles (Fig. 4-17). With ventricular contraction, the papillary muscles exert tension on the chordae; this tension tends to allow the valve leaflets to balloon upward and draw together. Should the chordae tendineae rupture or the papillary muscle suffer acute ischemia, the result can be severe valvular regurgitation or insufficiency.

The semilunar valves each consist of three cuplike cusps which are symmetrical. Structurally they are very dissimilar to the AV valves; since a much greater pressure load is imposed on these valves, their design is much simpler. Following termination of ventricular systole, the high pressure within the pulmonary artery and aorta drops, causing retrograde flow of blood back toward the ventricles, thus filling the aortic and pulmonary cusps with blood and snapping them shut. The event can be seen on the normal arterial waveform and is known as the *dicrotic notch*.

The *sinuses of Valsalva* are two outpouchings immediately behind the semilunar cusps. In the aorta they serve to prevent obstruction of the coronary ostia by the valve cusps.

The Ventricles

The ventricular walls are composed of sheets of fibers which apparently arise from the base of the heart; through a complex series of twisting and winding, these sheets of fibers form the endocardial and papillary muscles. The result of such a complex musculature is that ventricular ejection is accomplished through a reduction in circumference as well as a decrease in external length of the chamber.

The right ventricle is normally the more anterior and lies immediately underneath the sternum. It can be divided into an inflow and outflow tract. The former, consisting of the trabecular muscles within the anterior and inferior walls and the tricuspid valve, directs incoming blood toward the infundibulum, or outflow tract. The infundibulum forms the superior aspect of the chamber. It is divided from the inflow tract by a band of muscle, the crista supraventricularis, which joins other constrictor muscles from the outflow tract

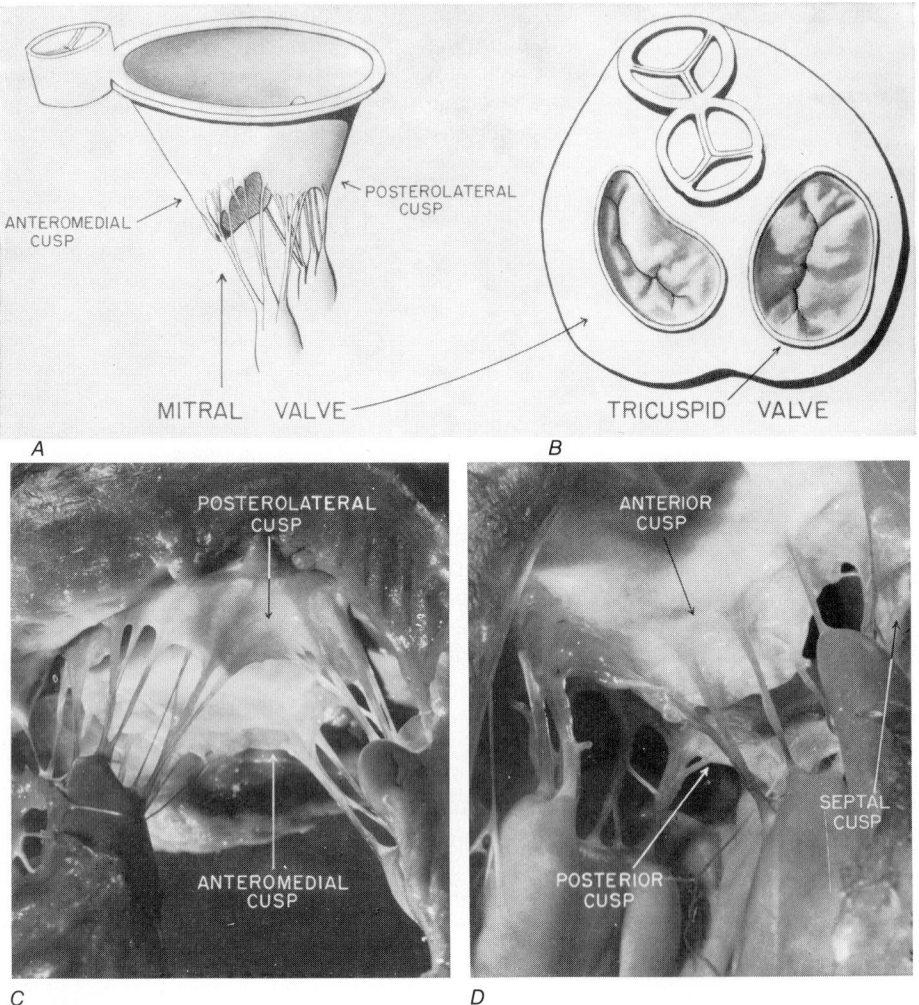

FIGURE 4-17

Anatomical structure of atrioventricular valves. (*A*) The funnel-shaped mitral valve is schematically demonstrated on the left, with the two cusps attaching via chordae tendineae to individual sets of papillary muscles. (*B*) Schematic representation of the closed mitral and tricuspid valves. Though very similar structurally, the tricuspid has a larger intermediate cusp which attaches to a third set of papillary muscles. (*After W. Spalteholz, Hand Atlas of Human Anatomy, Lippincott, Philadelphia, 1933.*) (*C*) Excision of a normal left ventricle to demonstrate the cusps of the mitral valve and attachment to papillary muscles. (*D*) View of the tricuspid valve from within the right ventricular chamber. (*From Robert Rushmer, Cardiovascular Dynamics, Saunders, Philadelphia, 1970. Used by permission of the publisher.*)

to direct blood toward the pulmonary artery during ventricular contraction. Early activation and contraction of the ventricular apex, in addition to the muscular design, effectively propel blood toward the infundibulum.

The left ventricle is somewhat bullet-shaped, with the tip directed anteriorly, inferiorly, and leftward where, along with the lower interventricular septum, it forms the cardiac apex. The septum is entirely muscular save for a small superior portion which is membranous. The muscles of the septum, as well as the ventricular wall, are jutted with the trabeculae carnae muscles. The wall, exclusive of the septum, is frequently called the *ventricular free wall*.

The funnel-shaped inflow tract, formed by the mitral ring or annulus, along with the curtainlike mitral leaflets and their chordae tendineae, directs blood toward the apex. Apical depolarization occurs early and hence blood is oriented upward and outward by the septum, free wall, and anterior mitral cusp (outflow tract).

The Pericardium

There are two surfaces which make up the pericardial sac. The *visceral pericardium,* or epicardium, closely embraces the surface of the heart and a small portion of cavae and aorta; it then reflects back to form the *parietal pericardium.* The two surfaces are normally lubricated by about 10 to 20 mL of serous pericardial fluid. The compliance of the pericardium is limited, and since it resists stretching, it is involved in prevention of acute cardiac overdistention.

Coronary Circulation

Anatomy

The right and left coronary arteries arise from the coronary ostia in the aortic root. The left coronary artery almost always emerges from a single ostium in the coronary sinus of the aorta, while the right coronary sinus sometimes gives rise to two ostia, the smaller of which becomes the conus artery (Fig. 4-18a).

The left coronary artery is of variable length but divides, usually within a few centimeters, into the left anterior descending artery and left circumflex artery. The branches of the main vessel take a diagonal route over the left ventricular free wall and are frequently referred to as the *diagonal left ventricular branches.* They are generally situated between the anterior descending and circumflex arteries (Fig. 4-18b). The anterior descending supplies the ventricular free wall, the septum, and portions of the right ventricle. In addition, it usually supplies the anterior as well as portions of the posterior apex. The circumflex usually emerges at a 90° angle from the main left coronary and courses toward the lateral left ventricle and apex. Branches from the circumflex supply the posterior and lateral walls of the left ventricle. In about 10 percent of persons, it gives rise to the AV nodal artery; in such cases the left coronary and its branches supply the entire left ventricle and septum.

If the conus does not originate directly from the aorta, it is the first branch of the right coronary artery. The sinus node artery emerges from the right coronary

in approximately 50 percent of persons; in the remainder it emerges from the circumflex. In the majority of cases the right coronary supplies the right atrium and right ventricle and gives rise to branches supplying the posterior surface of the left ventricle. The determination of right or left coronary artery dominance is made by comparison of the respective lengths of the right coronary and circumflex in the posterior left ventricle. If the right coronary is longer, as is the case in 90 percent of persons, the heart is said to have right coronary dominance; the AV nodal artery arises from the right coronary in right-sided dominance.

Coronary venous drainage is accomplished via the thebesian veins on the right atrium and ventricle and the anterior cardiac veins, which course over the anterior right ventricular wall. Left ventricular venous drainage occurs mainly through the coronary sinus and its branches.

Regulation of Coronary Flow

In the resting state, coronary flow is about 5 percent of the cardiac output (100 to 150 mL/min). As metabolic demands increase, blood flow can increase to more than 4 to 5 times resting value. The myocardial oxygen extraction remains fixed at 65 to 70 percent, regardless of physiologic conditions, which leaves an arterial P_{O_2} of 18 to 20 mmHg and a venous oxygen saturation of about 30 percent. That is the lowest value for venous oxygen saturation in the body. The heart functions exclusively on aerobic metabolism and cannot sustain an oxygen debt as can skeletal muscle. The most basic regulator, then, of coronary flow is the degree of oxygen need. Since oxygen extraction is maximal, the sole mechanism for meeting increased oxygen demand is an increase in coronary flow.

Coronary blood flow is intermittent; it is dependent upon phasic aortic pressure and faces significant resistance within the myocardium. External compression during systole causes severe reduction of flow within the left ventricle. Although the right ventricle is subjected to the same factors, the lower right ventricular pressures result in relatively mild changes in coronary flow. The left ventricular coronary flow, however, occurs almost exclusively during ventricular diastole. In addition, the thickness of the left ventricular wall results in some variance in flow from endocardium to epicardium. Normally, however, the endocardium is compensated during diastole for the increased systolic epicardial flow. With pathologic

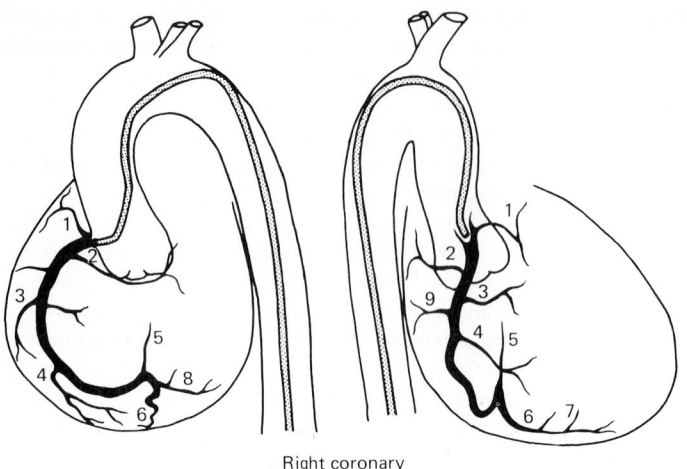

Right coronary

a

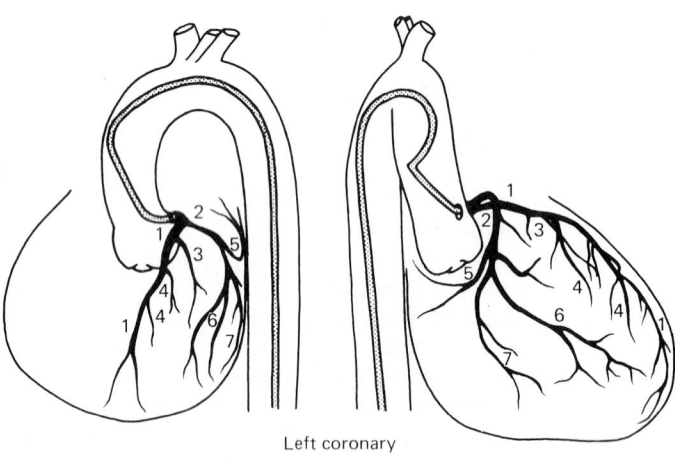

Left coronary

b

FIGURE 4-18

Normal coronary anatomy from right and left posterior oblique positions. (*a*) Right artery: (1) conus branch, (2) sinus node artery, (3) muscular branches to right ventricle, (4) artery of acute margins, (5) AV nodal artery, (6) posterior descending, (7) posterior septal, (8) posterolateral branches, (9) arterial branch. (*b*) Left coronary artery: (1) anterior descending, (2) circumflex, (3) diagonal branches, (4) septal branches, (5) atrial circumflex, (6) marginal artery, (7) posterolateral branches. (*Adapted from Stephen Ayres and V. Gianelli, Cardiology: A Clinicophysiologic Approach,* courtesy of *Appleton Century Crofts,* New York, 1971.)

conditions such as severe atherosclerosis, severe reduction of flow can occur within the endocardium.

Since the major regulator of coronary flow is oxygen deficiency, it is believed that hypoxia causes coronary arteriolar dilation, whether directly or from the release of neurotransmitters is unclear. The primary method appears to be automatic regulation of flow through arteriolar constriction and dilation. Influence of the sympathetic nervous system or of the catecholamines (norepinephrine and epinephrine) is complex; coronary blood flow increases either through dilation or from increased heart rate and perfusion pressure.

Factors which can contribute to increased myocardial oxygen consumption are the following: (1) increased heart rate, (2) rise in arterial pressure, (3) increased contractility, and (4) increased fiber tension. The last of these, myocardial tension, plays an extremely important role in determining oxygen consumption, particularly in the event of ventricular decompensation. The Laplace relationship states that a dilated ventricle will utilize increased tension to maintain adequate stroke volumes, even against a normal arterial pressure. That phenomenon, coupled with coronary atherosclerosis, can have a malignant effect on cardiac efficiency in the failing heart.

Collateral circulation within the vasculature is apparently present from infancy in the form of arterial anastomoses. They are particularly plentiful within the ventricular septum, apex, right ventricular anterior surface, and in the atria. Epicardial anastomoses exist between all three major coronary vessels of the left ventricle. The crucial determinant for success of the anastomoses is the rapidity with which occlusion occurs; the anastomotic connections become functional only when there is a need for increased flow. Other determining factors in the development of adequate collateral circulation are the location of the anastomosis to the occluded artery and the amount of disease in adjacent vessels.

Garlin summarizes the following properties which characterize the coronary circulation and dramatize its unique regulatory mechanisms.

1. Flow to the chamber of the heart with the greatest energy demand (the left ventricle) occurs almost solely during its relaxation phase, diastole.

2. Coronary oxygen extraction is extremely high with a relatively low flow.

3. Oxygen supply and energy demands can be simultaneously affected, often in opposing directions, by one variable.

4. Blood flow is intensely responsive to changing metabolic demands.

Structure of the Normal Myocardium

The heart is composed of three major types of cardiac muscle: (1) the specialized conduction fibers discussed earlier, (2) the atrial muscle fibers, and (3) fibers of the ventricles. The contractile properties of the heart are contained within the latter two types of fibers. Cardiac muscle is often compared to skeletal muscle because of its striated appearance and color, as well as some of its functional characteristics. It should be remembered, however, that myocardial muscle shares many similarities with certain types of visceral smooth muscle such as the ureter, uterus, and gastrointestinal tract. These muscles appear to have inherent rhythmicity and to be able to conduct a wave of excitation in a manner similar to that of the myocardium.

During the previous discussion of electrophysiology, mention was made of the fact that the heart behaves functionally as a syncytium—as a single cell. The structures which separate the cells end to end are called *intercalated disks*. These structures are a form of membrane known as a *"tight junction."* Such junctions are believed to impose 400 times less electrical resistance than does the sarcolemma, the fiber which encases the myocardial fibers. Since the electrical resistance is so low, the heart behaves as if there were no differentiation into separate cells. Indeed, recent histologic work indicates there may be small "pipeline" connections across such tight junctions.

Within the sarcolemma are a number of rodlike structures called *myofibrils,* which run the length of the fiber and are composed of a repeating unit, the sarcomere.

Next to the sarcomeres are the mitochondria, which are vitally important in cardiac metabolism. These bodies are the source of high-energy compounds such as ATP (adenosine triphosphate) for conversion into chemical energy for myocardial contraction as well as synthesis of nutrients. The prodigious oxygen demands of the heart can be appreciated by noting that between 30 and 50 percent of the myocardium is occupied by mitochondria. When ischemia exists within the heart, the balance between energy supply and demand can become most precarious. There is some suggestion that a deficiency of ATP may be an important factor in the determinant of infarct size and in the development of cardiac failure.

The contractile properties of the heart are the result of a complicated interaction of at least four protein molecules that are included within the myofibrils of the muscle cell. The myofibril divides into sarcomeres, the functional units of contraction, which extend from one Z band to the next (Fig. 4-19). Extending from each Z band toward the middle of the sarcomere can be seen the thin filament, which is predominantly composed of the protein actin. The thick filaments of myosin are found in the middle of the sarcomere, the A band, where they overlap with the thin actin filaments. The central light area, or H zone, is occupied only by the thicker filaments, while the I band contains

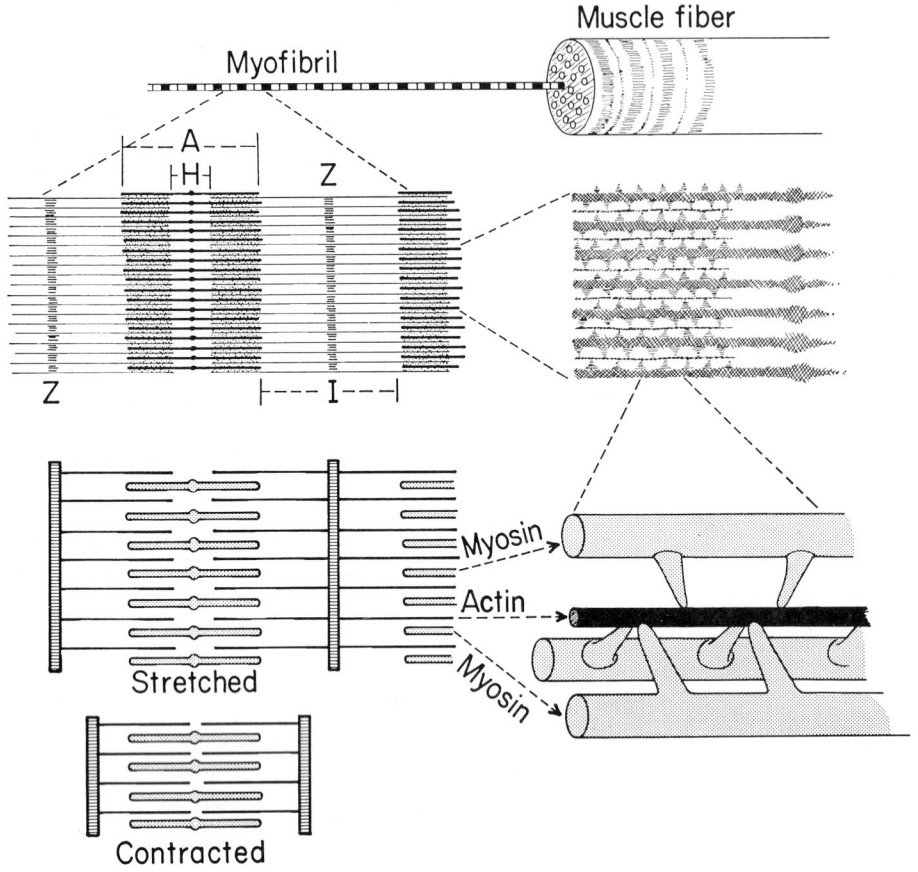

FIGURE 4-19

Structural components of myocardial muscle fiber. The myofibrils are composed of thick myosin and thin actin filaments. Many cross bridges may be seen periodically between the two filaments which are activated during contraction so that the myosin filaments are able to draw the actin filaments, resulting in much greater interdigitation of actin and myosin. (*From Robert Rushmer, Cardiovascular Dynamics, Saunders, Philadelphia, 1970. Used by permission of the publisher.*)

only the thin actin filaments. It is postulated that cross bridges protrude from the myosin filaments at regular intervals, and it is these cross bridges which, during contraction, cause lateral movement of the actin and myosin filaments so that they slide past one another, bringing about the development of tension and shortening within the muscle. During contraction it appears that the widths of the I band and H band shrink as the actin is drawn past the myosin and the Z bands draw closer together, while the A bands remain of one length both during stretching and contraction of the fiber.

Excitation-Contraction Coupling

The method by which the electrical wave of depolarization at the cell membrane produces the mechanical contraction is known as *excitation-contraction coupling*. The major pathological alterations in myocardial contractility have their basis in the degeneration of this very complex and intricate mechanism.

Calcium seems to have a dual role in cardiac contraction: as a trigger for initiation of contraction and as a regulating factor for the contractile process. The method for release of calcium from its storage place in the sarcoplasmic reticulum to the sarcomere is poorly understood; the method, however, apparently employs a system of intracellular tubules existing within the myofibrils. At the Z lines, the sarcolemma plunges deeply into the sarcomere to form the transverse (T) system. When the wave of depolarization initiates the release of calcium from its storage sites, the ion activates myosin to interdigitate with actin. There is evidence that calcium enters the cell during phase 1 and phase 2 of the action potential.

Interdigitation of the actin and myosin filaments depends upon two more proteins which are present with actin within the thin filaments: troponin and tropomyosin. During relaxation these two proteins appear to inhibit activation of the myosin cross bridges. When calcium is released during excitation, however, the inhibition is reversed and calcium is bound to troponin so that the myosin cross bridge is activated to draw the thin filament toward itself. It appears that the amount of calcium available to bind with troponin has a direct bearing on the strength of the cardiac contraction.

During repolarization of the muscle, relaxation occurs by pumping calcium back into the reticulum until its concentration is insufficient to utilize ATP and cross bridges can no longer be formed. Complete recovery of the cells coincides with the return of calcium to its storage sites.

Other potential influences on cardiac contractility are those caused by abnormal extracellular concentrations of electrolytes, specifically calcium and potassium. Increased concentrations of potassium can cause hyperpolarization of the resting membrane and result in cardiac arrest. Hypercalcemia can induce systolic arrest of the heart, while a decrease in serum calcium can have deleterious effects on contractility.

The Frank-Starling Phenomenon

Similar to that of the skeletal muscle fiber, the force of myocardial contraction is a function of the initial muscle length. The classic studies by Frank in 1895 demonstrated that the myocardial fiber responds with a more forceful contraction when it is stretched. Also referred to as the *length-tension relationship,* the results of Frank's work further demonstrated that there are physiologic limits to the relationship; excessive stretch of the muscle fiber results in development of less tension, resulting in a decrease in contractility.

Maximal force is developed at a length of 2.2 μm. It is at that length in which the actin and myosin filaments are able to provide the greatest number of cross bridges, or force-generating sites. When stretch exceeds a length of 2.4 μm, less interdigitation of thick and thin filaments occurs and fewer contractile sites are activated. Wiggers, and later Starling, continued Frank's work by studying the heart in an isolated heart-lung preparation and demonstrated that the length-tension relationship for the sarcomere can be applied graphically within the heart by substitution of ventricular filling pressure for tension and end-diastolic volume for fiber length.

The normal ventricle is very compliant. Initially the ventricle can accept large increases in volume without a significant increase in pressure. Physiologic limits operate here as well, however; should increases in ventricular end-diastolic volume cause an elevated filling pressure within the ventricle, further increases in diastolic filling will result in a decrease in ventricular performance, the so-called descending limb of the Starling curve. In the normal heart, optimal tension is achieved at a filling pressure of about 10 to 12 mmHg, which corresponds to a fiber length of 2.2 μm. Usually, end-diastolic pressure is approximately 0 to 7 mmHg and myocardial length about 2 μm, resulting in normal ventricular performance on the ascending limb of the curve.

The Cardiac Cycle

In order to comprehend cardiac physiology, it is essential that the sequential relationships between the electrical and mechanical events be understood. Figure 4-20 concisely demonstrates the interrelation of those events along with the resulting pressure and volume changes within the cardiac chambers.

Correlation of Electrical and Mechanical Activity

With generation of an action potential within the sinus node and corresponding movement of calcium into the cells, atrial depolarization occurs and a P wave is recorded on the electrocardiogram. Atrial pressure rises immediately thereafter and atrial contraction occurs, adding an additional increment of blood to ventricular diastolic filling volume. The resulting waveform causes the "a" wave demonstrated in Fig. 4-20. Within 0.2 s following atrial depolarization, the wave of excitation activates the ventricles, resulting in the ventricular action potential and the inscription of the QRS complex, and generating ventricular contraction and the resulting rapid rise in ventricular pressure. The QRS complex, then, precedes ventric-

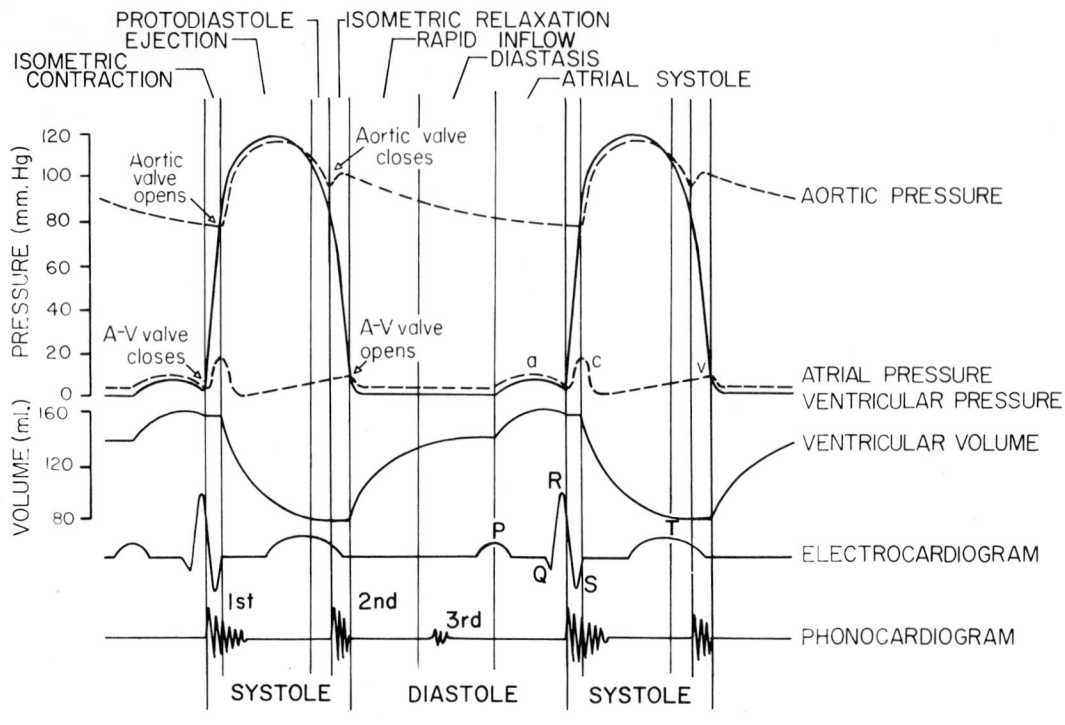

FIGURE 4-20

Coordination of the electrical and mechanical events in the cardiac cycle. Demonstrated as well are the heart sounds and intraventricular volume. (*From Arthur C. Guyton, Textbook of Medical Physiology, Saunders, Philadelphia, 1970. Used by permission of the publisher.*)

ular systole very slightly. The contraction of the ventricles causes two additional waveforms within the atria: the "c" wave occurs early and probably results from a combination of factors which include bulging of the AV valves retrogradely into the atria: the "v" wave is seen later, following ventricular systole, and results from atrial filling and the reflection of the increase in atrial pressure on the closed AV valves.

The T wave signals the beginning of ventricular repolarization (atrial repolarization cannot be measured) and the resulting ventricular relaxation. Hence ventricular diastole follows the T wave.

Ventricular Systole

The initial portion of ventricular contraction is directed at raising pressure within the chamber. As described previously, the sharp rise in pressure is caused by contraction of the papillary muscles which exerts pressure on the chordae tendineae so that the leaflets of the AV valves are drawn closer together. The resulting pressure increase closes them tightly. The early component of ventricular contraction is called *isovolumic* or *isovolumetric*. Since all four valves are closed, the contracting muscles elevate ventricular pressure without a change in volume. Since this period includes lengthening of some as well as shortening of other ventricular muscle fibers, it is termed *isovolumetric*, meaning "maintenance of a constant volume."

At the point that intraventricular pressure exceeds the diastolic pressure within the outflow tract, approximately 80 mmHg in the aorta (Fig. 4-20) and 8 mmHg in the pulmonary artery, the semilunar valves are opened and ejection begins. In the initial portion of ventricular ejection, left ventricular pressure rises above that of the aorta, producing a very rapid flow. Later in ejection, ventricular pressure drops below aortic, resulting in a diminished velocity of outflow. The amount of blood ejected from each ventricle under resting conditions, the stroke volume, is about 70 to 80 mL

Right Ventricular Ejection

The geometric differences between the two ventricles were mentioned earlier (Fig. 4-16). The right ventricular ejection performance resembles that of a bellows; since the surface area of the two walls is large in relation to the area contained between them, very slight movement from the free wall toward the septum is quite effective in accomplishing systolic ejection. Shortening of the length of the right ventricle occurs as well, but this is not as effective as the bellows action.

It is apparent that the right ventricular structure is suited for performance as a high-volume, low-resistance pump; severely deleterious effects can occur from an acute pressure load upon the right ventricle, such as a massive pulmonary embolism. Currently under much investigation is the effect of right ventricular ischemia and infarct upon cardiac performance.

Left Ventricular Ejection

Contraction within the left ventricle receives most of its power and efficiency through the reduction of its circumference. In contrast to the right ventricle, the left chamber has a small surface area in relation to its volume. The law of Laplace ($P = T/R$) states that the muscle tension (T) necessary to maintain a level of pressure (P) is reduced as the radius (R) is decreased. In other words, a chronically dilated, hypertrophied ventricular chamber requires greater muscle tension, and therefore a greater energy supply, to sustain a given ventricular pressure, thus the value of digoxin in reduction of left ventricular work load through reduction of chamber size. Since the left ventricle, with each ejection, must overcome a pressure gradient of over 90 mmHg, it is structurally designed as a high-pressure pump. When subjected to excessive volume loads, however, the resulting ventricular dilatation can cause severe compromise of left ventricular efficiency.

With cessation of ventricular contraction and the resulting pressure drop within the arteries, closure of the semilunar valves occurs and systolic ejection ceases. Under resting conditions the ejected stroke volume equals approximately 50 to 60 percent of ventricular diastolic volume. The residual volume is influenced by many factors; among them are contractility, outflow resistance, and heart rate.

Similar to the early ejection period, the initial period of ventricular diastole is called the *isovolumic* or *isovolumetric relaxation*. Here a precipitous drop in ventricular pressure occurs without a change in volume. Because of increased accumulation of blood within the atrial chambers during ventricular systole, atrial pressures rise significantly. With reduction of diastolic pressures to levels less than those within the atria, the AV valves open and the rapid filling phase begins. Phenomena such as diastolic recoil or diastolic suction significantly affect the rapid filling phase, during which ventricular volume apparently increases without a significant elevation of filling pressure. Rushmer emphasizes the importance of diastolic recoil in explanation for the more complete systolic ejection which occurs in tachycardia. Rushmer postulates that a portion of the contractile tension occurring during systole is stored within the walls of the left ventricle; with sudden diastolic relaxation, the ventricular walls appear to spring outward during early ventricular filling. This diastolic recoil causes a drop in diastolic filling pressure thus greatly augmenting filling. During tachycardia, when filling time is very brief, this phenomenon becomes even more important in accomplishing a rise in cardiac output.

Atrial Systole

Following the period of early ventricular filling, blood flow diminishes and effectively ceases. This phase is known as the period of diastasis and occurs only if the ventricular diastolic period is sufficiently long. Since there is no blood flow and the AV valves are open, the pressures within the atria and ventricles are equal during the period of diastasis. With atrial excitation, atrial contraction occurs. The amount of blood entering the ventricle during atrial contraction is variable and is influenced by the following factors: (1) duration of the P-R interval, (2) heart rate, and (3) chamber filling pressures. Blood flow resulting from atrial contraction will follow the path of least resistance, forward into the left ventricle or retrogradely into the great veins.

The atrial contraction is not essential for adequate cardiac performance. During exercise or any increase in metabolic demand resulting in tachycardia, however, the atrial contribution can be significant, particularly if the heart rate becomes so rapid that it affects the rapid filling phase.

Heart Sounds

The exact cause of the heart sounds is unknown. They appear to be a result of the sudden acceleration and deceleration of blood within the ventricular chamber as a result of valvular closure and muscular contraction. Normally only two of the four sounds are audible; the first and second heart sounds are auscultated, while scrutiny of the third and fourth sounds require phonocardiography.

First Heart Sound

Simultaneous with closure of the AV valves, the first heart sound, or S1, is heard. Signaling the beginning of ventricular systole, S1 is best auscultated at the fifth intercostal space in the midclavicular line. The sound is composed of two components, mitral and tricuspid valvular closure; the mitral sound is best heard in the apical area, while the tricuspid sound is best heard at the fifth intercostal space at the left sternal border. Usually only one sound is heard, although conditions such as right bundle branch block can produce a split first heart sound resulting from late closure of the tricuspid valve. The intensity of the first sound is influenced by the condition of the valve and the strength of the contraction as well as by the P-R interval.

Second Heart Sound

The second sound, S2, occurs simultaneous with closure of the aortic and pulmonary valves and the end of ventricular ejection. The pulmonary component is best heard at the second intercostal space to the left of the sternum. The aortic component is loudest at the second intercostal space to the right of the sternum. Normally the aortic and pulmonary components are split during inspiration because of a slight delay in pulmonary valvular closure which is caused by a prolongation of right ventricular ejection time. During inspiration, intrathoracic pressure falls, causing an increase in venous return to the right side of the heart and thus augmenting right ventricular stroke volume. During expiration, the split disappears or is diminished. In pathologic conditions such as right bundle branch block, the interval between the two components is significantly increased and does not vary with respiration.

Gallop Rhythm

The likening of the audible appearance of the third and/or fourth heart sound to the sound of a galloping horse was a phenomenon described almost 100 years ago. The gallop is a diastolic event and usually indicates pathology.

The ventricular or the protodiastolic gallop, the third heart sound, S3, is the classic sign of ventricular failure. Heard in children or young adults with thin chests, however, it is usually physiologic and therefore not indicative of any pathology. The third sound is best heard at the apical area with the patient lying on the left side.

The fourth sound, S4, is also called the *atrial* or *presystolic gallop* and may be heard with or without clinical signs of ventricular failure. It is commonly heard in patients who have sustained a myocardial infarction, particularly within the first 24 h following the infarct.

Not infrequently, both atrial and ventricular gallops may be heard, in which case a *summation gallop* is said to exist. Obviously, gallop rhythms are more easily distinguished at slower heart rates; with significant tachycardias, it may be extremely difficult to determine whether a gallop is atrial, ventricular, or summation.

PERIPHERAL CIRCULATION

The fundamental requirements of the cardiovascular circulation, that is, blood flow without interruption and adjustment of that circulation to meet the variable metabolic needs of the tissues, are staggering when one considers that there are literally billions of cells, all organized into specific functional units and supplied by capillaries which are about 0.017 mm in diameter and extend approximately 60,000 miles in length. Rushmer utilizes Krogh's account to enhance one's appreciation of the magnitude of the microcirculation.

> It requires some mental effort to conceive how there can be room (on an area no larger than the cross section of an ordinary pin) for about 700 parallel tubes carrying blood, in addition to about 200 (skeletal) muscle fibers.

It will be remembered that the blood flow is proportional to the pressure gradient between the point of inflow and outflow of a vessel, in this case from the arteries to the veins, and the resistance imposed through vessel caliber as well as other factors which were reviewed earlier in this chapter.

The Vascular Tree

We know that the major resistance within the peripheral circulation is exerted by the extremely muscular arterioles and their precapillary sphincters. The distension properties of the venae cavae and of the aorta are exemplified by a comparison of the relative diameter, wall thickness, and proportion of elastic tissue with those of the arteriole and sphincter (Fig. 4-21). It is through constriction and dilation of these resistance vessels, thereby changing their internal diameters, that blood flow is distributed to the tissues. Note that the capillary walls contain only endothelial tissue, a structural composition which is highly appropriate for rapid diffusion. Although much of the arterial pressure head is dissipated prior to reaching the capillary bed, the capillaries must be able to withstand significant pressure in order to effect a sufficient pressure gradient for maintenance of blood flow.

The law of Laplace, which was used earlier to explain the relationship between cardiac dilation and resulting increase in oxygen consumption, is operative as well within the vascular system. The relationship as applied to blood vessels states that the tension sustained by the wall of a cylinder is directly proportional to the product of the pressure within the cylinder and its radius. In other words, the smaller a blood vessel, the less the amount of tension required to maintain a given pressure; at normal aortic and capillary pressures, the tension necessary to support the pressure exerted upon the wall of the aorta is over 10,000 times as great as that in the capillary.

Vascular Smooth Muscle

Vascular smooth muscle shares some characteristics of cardiac and skeletal muscle. The contractile process basically operates in a similar manner, since it is contingent upon the action of the proteins actin, myosin, and troponin-tropomyosin. In addition, the ability of certain of the smooth muscles to exhibit automaticity has already been reviewed. Since it is very difficult to separate the structural components of smooth muscle, no consistent pattern of myofibril organization has been observed. The actual mechanism behind vascular smooth muscle shortening is unknown, since the relationship of the actin and myosin filaments during contraction and the mechanism for calcium release can only be inferred. The relationship between stimulation and contraction seems to vary, although the contractile time of smooth muscle is generally much more prolonged than that of cardiac and skeletal muscle. Neural and hormonal stimuli (epinephrine, angiotensin) usually elicit a contractile response.

The sympathetic nervous system innervates a majority of the arterial and venous circulation. Arterioles apparently have a relatively greater concentration of neuromuscular connections, which is in keeping with their role as resistance vessels. It is this property of relative contraction or relaxation which determines

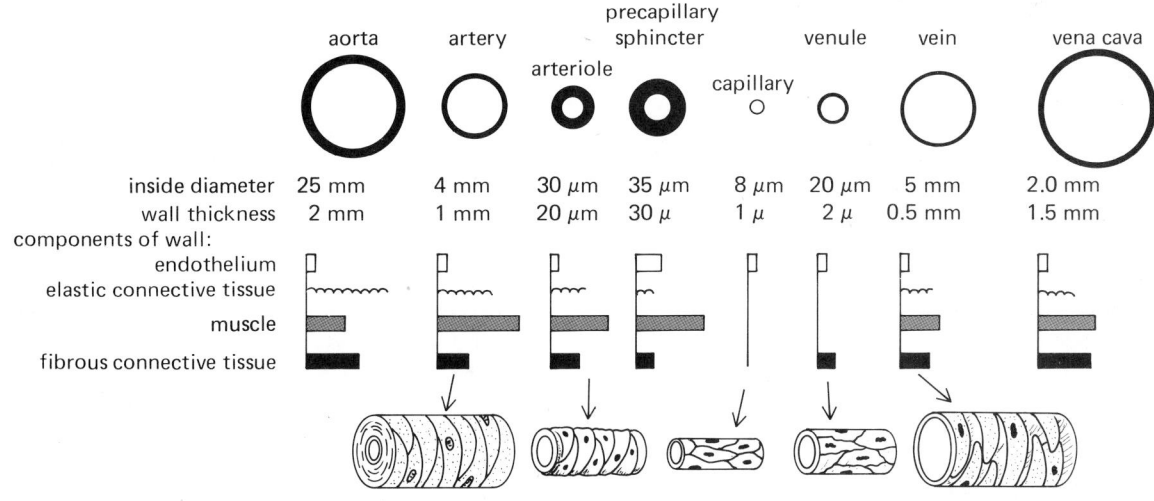

	aorta	artery	arteriole	precapillary sphincter	capillary	venule	vein	vena cava
inside diameter	25 mm	4 mm	30 μm	35 μm	8 μm	20 μm	5 mm	2.0 mm
wall thickness	2 mm	1 mm	20 μm	30 μ	1 μ	2 μ	0.5 mm	1.5 mm

components of wall:
endothelium
elastic connective tissue
muscle
fibrous connective tissue

FIGURE 4-21

Schematic representation of anatomy of circulatory vasculature. Comparisons of internal diameters, musculature, wall thickness, and vascular components. (*From D. Luciano, A. J. Vander, and J. H. Sherman, Human Function and Structure, McGraw-Hill, New York, 1978; adapted from A. C. Burton; Physiol Rev 34:619, 1954.*)

the tone of vascular smooth muscle. Although sympathetic control is very important, it is crucial to understand that the routine control of the peripheral circulation is independent of extrinsic mechanisms.

Intrinsic Regulation

Normally the regulation of blood through the vast capillary network is controlled very precisely. An exact amount of blood is provided to the tissue in accordance with its metabolic demands. Blood flows continuously through the arterioles and then into metarterioles through the precapillary sphincter and on into the capillary. Two types of capillaries can be seen in Fig. 4-22: thoroughfare channels (TC), which serve as a direct channel from the arteriole to the venule, and the true capillaries (C). By reviewing Fig. 4-22, it will be recalled that the capillaries are not invested with muscle, while the thoroughfare channels are supplied with smooth muscle which is more pronounced at the arterial end.

Through dilation and constriction of the precapillary sphincters, thoroughfare channels, and the arterioles, blood flow is controlled according to the specific needs of a group of cells. Since the process involves rhythmic movement of the vessels, it is also called *vasomotion*. With dilation of these vessels, a steeper pressure gradient occurs and therefore an increase in blood flow. With constriction, the arterial pressure gradient is decreased, resulting in either reduction or cessation of blood flow.

Specific Circulation Requirements

Generally, when one considers the circulation of the body, it is the cardiac output which comes to mind—that 5000 mL or so of blood which is pumped from the heart each minute in a resting individual of average size. It is important to remember that circulation also takes place at the capillary membranes throughout all body tissues. The Starling law of the capillaries states that the amount of fluid which is filtered at the arterial end of the capillary (about 14 mL/min) is almost equal to the amount of fluid reabsorbed into the venous capillary blood (11 mL/min). The remainder (3 mL/min) is returned to the circulation via the lymph vessels.

Far more effective and important to the circulation within the cells is the process of diffusion. It has been estimated that the rate at which water diffuses in and out of the capillary is about 40 times the speed with which the plasma can flow along the capillary. The total amount of water exchanged in this manner is unknown, but it far exceeds the cardiac output.

Tissues with variable or very high metabolic demands are provided with very dense capillary networks so that the cells are closely adjacent to the capillaries. The reason for this is apparent: The oxygen tension decreases as the capillary blood approaches venous so that the cells immediately surrounding the arterial capillary benefit from the steep pressure gradients necessary for rapid diffusion of oxygen. In tissues such as skeletal muscle, brain, and liver, steep oxygen gradients are maintained through such increased vascularity.

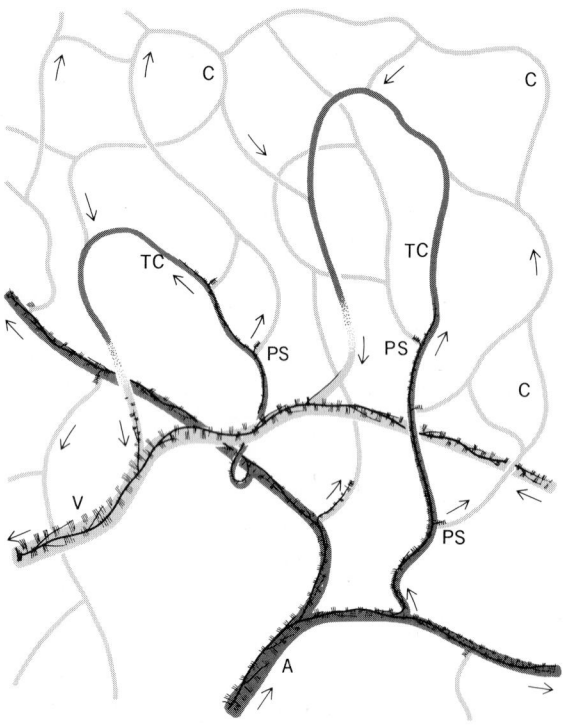

A = arteriole   C = capillaries
V = venule   PS = precapillary
TC = thoroughfare channel   sphincter

FIGURE 4-22

Schematic representation of the microcirculation. The arrows indicate blood flow direction. Circular structures on arteriole and venule indicate smooth muscle fibers, and branching solid lines are indicative of sympathetic nervous innervation. (*From A. H. Vander, J. H. Sherman, and D. S. Luciano, Human Physiology, 2d ed., McGraw-Hill, New York, 1975. Adapted from B. W. Zweifach, Fed Proc 24: 1074, 1965. Used by permission of the publisher.*)

The success of the circulatory system in providing nutrients to the tissue is contingent upon two basic factors: transport of the blood to the microcirculation and the adequacy of diffusion gradients for rapid transfer of substances.

Oxygen Distribution

Oxygen consumption varies widely from tissue to tissue. In the heart, brain, and liver, blood flow is apportioned to their metabolic needs; these organs extract a large proportion of the oxygen presented to them. Resting skeletal muscle utilizes only about 30 percent of the oxygen it receives and is supplied with 30 percent of the cardiac output. During heavy exercise the blood flow can increase many times over and oxygen extraction can triple. Both the blood flow and the difference between arterial and venous oxygen concentrations (AV oxygen difference) are variable from tissue to tissue. The average AV oxygen difference is about 5 mL per 100 mL of mixed venous blood.

Mechanisms of Control

The actual method by which each local tissue is able to regulate its blood flow is unknown. Several theories seek to explain it. Since a decrease in the available oxygen supply or increase in the metabolic activity of tissue causes an immediate increase in blood flow, it is postulated that hypoxia is a stimulant for the phasic opening and closing of the precapillary sphincters. Another possibility is that an unknown vasodilator substance accumulates within the tissue as a result of increased metabolic activity. Vasodilators which have been proposed as substances are carbon dioxide, adenosine, and hydrogen.

Autoregulation

A phenomenon which has received considerable attention is the ability of the vessels to maintain blood flow in the face of marked changes in arterial pressure. Changing arterial pressure from a low of 80 mmHg to 175 mmHg has remarkably little effect. The principles previously discussed are able to obviate the effects of acute changes in pressure.

Another example of a type of autoregulation is known as reactive hyperemia. Occlusion of arterial flow to a specific organ or vascular bed will result in a quadrupling of flow to the affected area following removal of the occlusion. This phenomenon may be observed in an extremity following occlusion via a tourniquet; the arm may be seen to redden considerably, and dilation of blood vessels is observed.

If the change in arterial pressure persists for an indefinite period of time or if the metabolic demands of a tissue increase chronically, a system of long-term autoregulation develops over a period of days and weeks. An example of this type of chronic local autoregulation probably occurs with coarctation of the aorta. *Coarctation* is a congenital condition in which an area of partial occlusion occurs within the aorta and causes an extremely high pressure above the occlusion and a lower than normal pressure below it. Despite the enormous pressure gradient, blood flow to the upper and lower body appears to be equal within several weeks.

Earlier in this section, an almost linear correlation was made between the vascularity of the tissue and its metabolic demands: the higher the activity, the more vascular the tissue. It appears that this increase in vascularity may develop on demand. For an example, consider coarctation once more. Should the arterial pressure below the coarctation drop to 80 mmHg, the number of vessels probably increases, so that blood flow is not compromised. In the upper extremities, however, where the arterial pressure may be 220 mmHg, the reverse situation occurs; the vessels decrease both in number and in size. The rate at which the tissue can adjust its vasculature undoubtedly relates to many factors, not the least of which is age.

Collateral circulation can be considered as a mechanism of chronic long-term autoregulation. In the discussion relating to the coronary circulation, the observation was made that the anastamotic connections were assumed to be present from early life but that their use as channels for blood flow only occurred following occlusion or insufficiency within a vessel. The same pattern for utilization of collateral vessels appears to exist in most vascular systems.

Control Mechanisms of Specific Vascular Systems

The fact that the response of the vascular bed for each tissue is extremely variable has been stressed repeatedly. Prior to an exploration of the extrinsic control mechanisms, which are largely those imposed by the sympathetic nervous system, an understanding of the special requirements of certain organ systems is necessary.

Cerebral Vessels

Although it has not been established that sympathetic innervation does exist within the brain, there is little evidence of any effect on cerebral circulation by the autonomic nervous system. Cerebral flow is remarkable in its consistent blood flow and in its resistance to any change in that flow. In addition, drugs appear to have very little effect. The most potent stimulant within the cerebral vasculature appears to be carbon dioxide, which does elicit vasodilation.

Pulmonary Vessels

The characteristic quality of the pulmonary system is its low resistance to extremely high flow rates which it appears to achieve through the distensibility of the blood vessels. The autonomic system or other extrinsic controls appear to have as negligible an effect within the pulmonary circuit as within the cerebral circulation.

Hypoxia, in addition to acidosis, appears to be the most potent stimulant within the pulmonary vessels; contrary to other vascular systems, a response of vasoconstriction is elicited rather than the expected dilation. The vasoconstrictive response within the lung very functionally results in the diversion or shunting of blood from poorly ventilated and/or perfused areas to those where effective diffusion of gases can take place.

Portal Circulation

The liver, too, is apparently relatively unresponsive to external controls. The majority of the portal circulation is venous, therefore low pressure; only about 20 percent of total portal flow is arterial. Sympathetic innervation does exist within the arterial and venous vessels, but the vasoconstrictive response of sympathetic stimulation is apparently quite mild.

Renal Vessels

The rate of blood flow through the renal blood vessels is much greater than its metabolic activity would warrant. This is evident through a measurement of renal AV oxygen difference. Normally, renal venous oxygen is only slightly less than arterial, resulting in a very high tolerance within the kidney for hypoxia and maintenance of renal flow in the face of low oxygen availability.

The rationale for the disproportionate flow is, of course, maintenance of adequate filtration pressure for the formation of glomerular filtrate. Blood flow through the renal vessels is also markedly resistant to arterial pressure variations, although changes in arterial pressure can have major influence upon the volume of urine produced by the tubules. Both an increase in sodium load and an increase in the concentration of metabolic end products can increase renal blood flow significantly.

Regulation of Blood and Extracellular Fluid Volumes

A review of the intrinsic control mechanisms within the circulation would be imcomplete without at least brief attention to the integral role of the blood and extracellular fluid volumes upon circulatory control, and of the key role of the kidney in maintaining fluid balance. Proper function of the intrinsic vascular mechanisms in maintenance of adequate tissue perfusion is dependent upon sufficient blood volume and an adequate pressure gradient (arterial pressure) to move blood through the circulatory system.

Simplistically, extracellular fluid volume is maintained through daily ingestion of fluid and sodium. With increases in the extracellular fluid volume, proportionate amounts will remain in the plasma as increased blood volume until the point at which capillary balance is lost and fluid extravasates into the tissues, resulting in edema.

As blood volume increases, venous return to the heart is increased, causing a rise in both cardiac output and arterial pressure. With an increase in arterial pressure, the rate of urine production correspondingly increases in order to restore plasma and extracellular fluid volumes to their normal levels. For example, the rate of glomerular filtrate formed within the kidneys at a normal arterial pressure of 100 mmHg is approximately 1 mL/min. Elevating the arterial pressure to 150 mmHg will increase the rate of filtrate production to about 4 mL/min.

Extrinsic Regulation

The sympathetic branch of the autonomic nervous system seems to have a coordinative role in adjustment of cardiac output to meet the demands of the circulatory system as a whole without compromise to essential circulations such as those of the heart and the brain, and can override intrinsic vascular controls in order to do so. Just as with the intrinsic controls, it is important to recall that the response of specific vascular systems to neural control can be quite variable. Several examples of vascular beds which are relatively insensitive to nervous regulation were discussed earlier. Generally, the neural regulatory mechanisms are the more potent of the two types of extrinsic control mechanisms; the other major external control being exerted by the hormones will be reviewed later. The salient feature of nervous regulation is the rapidity with which the sympathetic system can respond, usually within seconds.

The Vasomotor System

Located within the medulla and a portion of the pons is the vasomotor center, depicted in Fig. 4-23. From the vasoconstrictor portion of the vasomotor center, sympathetic fibers descend to synapse in the thoracolumbar region of the spinal cord and to innervate all major blood vessels except the capillaries. Through this massive innervation of the entire vasculature, sympathetic stimulation results in alteration of arterial and venous resistance.

The vasomotor center is able to maintain sympathetic vasoconstrictor tone through continual transmission of impulses, the frequency of which is increased or decreased in relation to stimulation received from the cardiovascular reflexes and hormones. This continual activity of the vasomotor center causes release of the sympathetic hormone norepinephrine from the nerve endings, and elicits through its alpha-adrenergic effect upon the blood vessels a partial state of contraction, or tone.

Within the vasomotor center, near the vasoconstrictor center, lies a depressor or inhibitory portion. Its function is, at intervals, to inhibit impulse transmission from the vasoconstrictor center, thus permitting vasodilation.

The major effect of neural control is demonstrated within the microcirculation. Though innervation exists in all major vessels, it is through constriction of the resistance vessels that localized reduction in blood flow is effected, and through constriction in the venous or capacitance vessels that circulating blood volume is increased. In response to any increase in metabolic demand, whether exercise or shock, circulating blood volume is increased and cardiac contractility enhanced through an elevation in venous return to the right side of the heart. Arterial pressure, in addition, is augmented by arterial and venous vasoconstriction.

Control of the vasomotor center can be exercised by other higher nervous centers. Areas within the diencephalon, mesencephalon, and pons can have either a stimulative or suppressive effect. The hypothalamus as well can have powerful influence upon neural control of the vasculature. Many coordinative

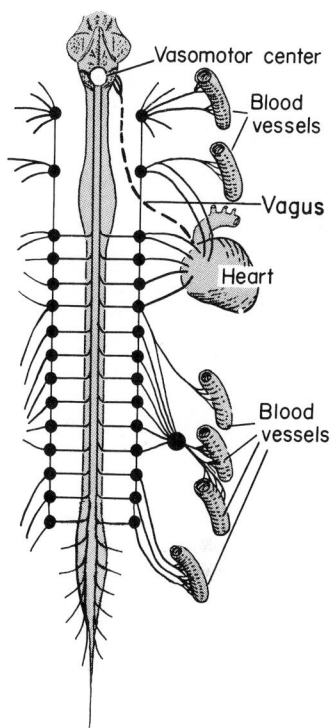

FIGURE 4-23

Neural control of the circulatory system through sympathetic and vagal nervous innervation. (*From A. C. Guyton, Textbook of Medical Physiology, Saunders, Philadelphia, 1970. Used by permission of the publisher.*)

responses which involve the circulatory system are known to center within the hypothalamus: temperature control, osmotic regulation of circulating plasma through water balance, and cardiovascular responses to exercise. Experimental excitation of the hypothalamus is known to produce vast alterations in arterial pressure, heart rate, and cardiac contractility. Lastly, vasomotor control can be affected to some extent by the cerebral cortex, as investigation of areas such as biofeedback and relaxation therapy have demonstrated.

Sympathetic Vasodilatation

The sympathetic vasodilator fibers emerge from the motor cortex and hypothalamus. Upon excitation, these fibers release acetylcholine from their nerve endings, thus their name as sympathetic cholinergic fibers. Normally this system probably plays a relatively insignificant role in circulatory control; however, if the normal vasoconstrictor response is blocked by a pharmacologic blocking agent or the customary stores of norepinephrine are reduced by reserpine, sympathetic stimulation can result in active vasodilatation.

The existence of beta-adrenergic receptors within the vascular smooth muscles of skeletal muscle has been confirmed using isoproterenol; stimulation of beta receptors produces vasodilatation (Berne, 1977). In addition, epinephrine under certain circumstances can cause vasodilatation within skeletal and cardiac vasculature (Guyton, 1976). Since the two effects can be elicited, the terms *alpha* and *beta receptors* were proposed to name the binding sites within vascular smooth muscle controlling each. Neural control of the beta-receptor system is undetermined; it appears doubtful, however, that the circulating catecholamines (epinephrine and norepinephrine) have a significant role in the everyday neural control of peripheral blood flow.

Parasympathetic Nervous System

Vascular innervation by the parasympathetic nervous system exists only in the head, viscera, bladder, and genitalia; within the skin and the majority of the muscles, there are no parasympathetic nervous connections. Thus the vasodilatation evoked by acetylcholine, the neurohumor of the parasympathetic system, while potent, is limited to certain vascular beds. It is possible that the vasodilatation which accompanies sweating and follows parasympathetic stimulation of the salivary glands may be caused partially by acetylcholine, by the production of the enzyme bradykinin (which produces vasodilatation), or by a combination of both.

Circulatory Reflexes

The most important of the cardiovascular reflexes are the baroreceptors, or stretch receptors. Although baroreceptors are situated within the walls of most large thoracic and neck arteries, the highest concentrations are within the carotid sinus, which is located in the internal carotid artery slightly above the bifurcation of the external and internal carotids. With a rise in arterial pressure, the baroreceptors respond extremely rapidly through inhibition of the vasomotor center in the medulla and stimulation of the vagal center (Fig. 4-23). The vagal center functions primarily

as a countercheck on the heart in that excitation produces bradycardia, while inhibition results in tachycardia. The overall effects of the baroreceptors are vasodilatation due to suppression of the vasomotor center, and reduction of heart rate and contractility, which results in a decrease in arterial pressure. Conversely, arterial pressure is augmented through opposite effects of the baroreceptors—should there be a drop in arterial pressure. Since these neural receptors mitigate increases and decreases in arterial pressure, they are called *buffer nerves* and the baroreceptors a *buffer system*.

The baroreceptor response can be obviated if the hypertension or hypotension persists for a protracted length of time. The major effect of the circulatory reflexes exists in acute changes; over a longer time period, the baroreceptors simply adapt by decreasing their rate of excitation to normal, although the blood pressure remains very high or very low.

Other Types of Cardiovascular Reflexes

The chemoreceptors, which are located at the bifurcation of the internal and external carotids and within the aortic arch, are sensitive to hypoxia and hypercapnia, which causes stimulation of the vasomotor center and results in elevation of arterial blood pressure.

The atrial baroreceptors appear to include two types of receptors. The A receptors are synchronous with the a wave of atrial contraction, while the B receptors appear to be stimulated by the v wave occurring during atrial filling. The actual effects and the significance of this reflex are somewhat controversial; it appears that stimulation can cause an increase in urinary flow, either a decrease or increase in heart rate, and reduction of arterial pressure, at least experimentally.

Spinal cord receptors become evident following cervical spinal cord transection. Initially following the trauma, arterial pressure drops but can eventually return to near-normal levels, probably through local sympathetic vasoconstriction.

Other potential reflexes occur within the pulmonary vasculature. Distention of the pulmonary vessels can cause reduction in both heart rate and arterial pressure. Distention of the abdominal viscera may elicit a depressor response. Lastly, pain can cause either vasoconstriction or vasodilatation; usually, however, pain elicits a sympathetic response.

The cardiac and respiratory reflexes are very closely related. It can be safely surmised that anything affecting the respiratory center will also stimulate the vasomotor center. Elevations of P_{CO_2} and reduction of pH produce vasoconstriction. Conversely, vasodilatation results from a drop in P_{CO_2} or rise in pH.

Hormonal Influences

The most important of the humoral or hormonal substances is *aldosterone*. Secreted by the cortex of the adrenal gland, aldosterone is important in regulation of blood volume through its control over sodium and water concentrations within the extracellular fluid. Stimulated by a decrease in cardiac output, total body volume, or reduction in sodium concentration, aldosterone promotes increased renal tubular reabsorption of sodium and, indirectly, chloride and water. The end result is an increase in plasma and extracellular fluid volume.

Epinephrine, norepinephrine, and *acetylcholine* exert their major influence when released at sympathetic and parasympathetic nerve endings. Stimulation of sympathetic nerves also prompts the adrenal medulla to secrete epinephrine and norepinephrine as circulating catecholamines. The major vascular effects of these neurohumors were reviewed earlier.

Vasodilator substances known as *kinins* can be identified within the blood following obstruction of flow or decrease in oxygen. Little is known about kinins other than their very potent vasodilator effect. *Bradykinin* and *kallikrein* are two kinins which can be activated with relative ease and appear to function throughout the circulation.

Angiotensin is formed through the release of renin from the kidney. When renin acts on another substance to produce angiotensin I, an activating enzyme converts angiotensin I to angiotensin. The mechanism for renin release is uncertain, but it is believed to be governed by variations in arterial pressure; increased renin secretion follows hypotension. Renal vascular constriction and low serum sodium also appear to influence the rate of renin production. Angiotensin has very powerful vasoconstrictive effects on the arterioles; there is apparently little or no significant influence on the venous system. The renin mechanism has, in addition, an important role in raising aldosterone secretion in response to hypotension and reducing it in response to elevations in arterial pressure.

Vasopressin (*Pitressin*) Similar to angiotensin, *vasopressin* is a potent vasoconstrictor which acts primarily on the arterioles. It is produced in the neurohypophysis and is secreted by the posterior pituitary gland. Its influence upon the peripheral circulation appears to be relatively minor. The primary function of this hormone is in controlling the volume of water reabsorbed across the renal tubule.

Serotonin Serotonin is concentrated predominantly in the intestinal and other abdominal tissue as well as within platelets. It can have very powerful vasodilator as well as vasoconstrictor effects. The role of serotonin within control of the peripheral circulation is obscure.

Histamine Histamine is probably not involved in normal circulatory control. Almost every tissue within the body releases histamine in response to injury. The result is local vasoconstriction, surrounding vasodilatation, and edema. Histamine causes intense dilation of the arterioles and constriction within the venous system, a combination which produces edema. The hormone is involved with allergic responses and tissue injury such as burns in addition to trauma.

ARTERIAL PRESSURE REGULATION

The essential feature of the arterial circulation is its function as a pressure reservoir in order to convert the intermittent ventricular ejection into relatively constant flow. In Fig. 4-13, the intrinsic properties of normal arteries which permit such a function were reviewed. The fact that the arteries are capable of storing a portion of energy received from the heart during systolic contraction within their elastic walls is critically important in maintaining flow to the tissues in a pulsatile circulation. The greater the distensibility or compliance of the arterial circulation, the more constant is blood flow during diastole and systole. In addition, the arterial circulation has an important influence upon the work load imposed on the heart. Since the phasic pumping of the heart requires much more energy expenditure from the heart than would be demanded for steady flow, the capability for the normal arterial circulation to transmit pressure throughout the diastolic phase of the heart results in a decrease in cardiac work load. On the other hand, loss of the property of elastic recoil within the arterial circulation can profoundly increase cardiac work.

Factors Determining Arterial Pressure

The basic control of arterial pressure was reviewed earlier in the section exploring hemodynamics of the circulation. Pressure is controlled by the product of flow, in this case cardiac output, and resistance, here the total peripheral resistance (TPR), which is the sum of the resistance in all vascular systems. Anything that results in an elevation or reduction of either cardiac output or of the total peripheral resistance will influence arterial pressure.

Systolic Pressure

The normal left ventricle ejects the majority of its stroke volume during the early period of ventricular systole, the rapid ejection phase. As was described earlier in this chapter, the left ventricular pressure momentarily exceeds aortic pressure (Fig. 4-20). Following the rapid ejection phase, the peak systolic pressure is reached; it is determined by the volume of ventricular volume, the rate of ejection, and the compliance of the arterial vessels. A relatively small stroke volume injected into a distensible aorta will produce a small increase in aortic pressure, while a very rapid ventricular ejection into a rigid arteriosclerotic vessel will produce significant elevations in arterial pressure.

Diastolic Pressure

In the absence of ventricular systole, arterial pressure falls to a low level just prior to the next contraction. The rate of pressure drop is influenced by many factors; among them are the systolic pressure, the rate of flow through the periphery (peripheral runoff), and the length of diastole. End-diastolic pressure is determined mainly by total peripheral resistance and heart rate.

Mean Arterial Pressure

The average pressure throughout the phasic cardiac cycle is known as the *mean pressure*. It can be measured by recording the area under the curve of an arterial pressure tracing and dividing the area by the concurrent time period. Normally, the mean is slightly less than the average of the systolic and diastolic pressures; it can be grossly approximated by adding one-third of the pulse pressure (difference between the systolic and diastolic pressures) to the diastolic pressure. The average adult with a normal systolic pressure of 120 mmHg and diastolic pressure of 80 mmHg has a mean arterial pressure of 96 mmHg.

The mean pressure will vary directly with systolic and diastolic fluctuations. In the newborn it is normally about 70 mmHg; it remains approximately 100 to 110 mmHg in the adult. With arteriosclerosis the arterial mean pressure can rise to 140 mmHg. Since the mean arterial pressure is the average pressure responsible for the arterial to venous pressure gradient, it has very important influence on tissue flow.

Pulse Pressure

Since the major factors influencing arterial pressure are cardiac output and total peripheral resistance, the complexity of arterial pressure regulation should be self-evident. Many factors are involved in alteration of either variable. Control of the cardiac output will be explored in more detail later in this chapter; it is, however, ultimately determined by the product of the heart rate and stroke volume.

The pulse pressure, according to Berne, can be utilized to assess both arterial capacitance and stroke volume. Normally the pulse pressure is approximately 40 mmHg. Factors which alter either stroke volume or arterial capacitance can cause variations in the pulse pressure. If a reduction in arterial compliance occurs, for example, in arteriosclerosis, a greater pulse pressure will result than if the arterial wall were normally distensible, thus causing increased left ventricular work and energy requirements. Increases in total peripheral resistance resulting from conditions such as hypertension will obviously increase arterial pressure if the same volume is to be maintained.

Heart rate, then, will change the pulse pressure according to the degree by which stroke volume and compliance of the arterial tree are changed. If a tachycardia and the resulting normal increase in arterial pressure are accompanied by a drop in arterial compliance, pulse pressure will be increased, assuming stroke volume is constant. Conversely, if the volume of blood ejected from the left ventricle is reduced without a change in arterial compliance, the pulse pressure will usually decrease. In summary, factors which tend to increase systolic pressure and/or cause a drop in diastolic pressure will tend to augment the pulse pressure.

Transmission of the Arterial Pulse Wave

Since the left ventricular stroke volume is ejected with such force and velocity, it tends to accumulate in the aortic root (the first portion of the aorta), causing stretching and increased tension within the aortic wall. The transmission of the stretching and development of tension into each adjacent section of the aorta and arterial vasculature results in a measurable pressure waveform and palpable pulse within the peripheral arterial circulation. The rate at which the pressure waveform is transmitted depends upon arterial compliance.

The shape of the arterial waveform changes as the pressure pulse reaches the more peripheral segments of the arterial tree. The systolic peak becomes significantly higher, as much as 20 mmHg higher within the brachial and femoral arteries than in the central aorta. The dicrotic notch (point of closure of the aortic valve) becomes increasingly more distorted and eventually disappears. In addition, a hump is often seen on the diastolic portion of the peripheral arterial waveform. The changes in morphology of the transmitted aortic waveform decrease with age, and in older individuals with severe arteriosclerosis there may be relatively little difference between central and peripheral waveforms.

Control of Arterial Pressure

Everyday control of variations in arterial pressure is exercised mainly by the circulatory reflexes. Were it not for this vital integrative role, arterial pressure and thereby vital cerebral and cardiac perfusion could be dangerously compromised by changes in position, or by extreme localized demand for increased flow. When simply assuming the erect position from the supine, the tendency is for cerebral arterial pressure to drop precipitously; through excitation of the circulatory reflexes, increased sympathetic tone through vasoconstriction maintains cerebral flow.

Circulatory Reflexes

The principal reflexes involved in maintaining normal arterial pressure are the baroreceptors and chemoreceptors. The baroreceptors (reviewed earlier in this chapter) can correct for up to two-thirds of a fall in pressure. According to Guyton, the baroreceptors can moderate a 60-mm fall in arterial pressure to a 20-mm fall; what would be a drop from 120 to 60 mmHg becomes instead a drop of 120 to 100 mmHg.

The chemoreceptor reflex appears to function at a lower range of pressure. While the baroreceptors function in the pressure range of 60 to 200 mmHg, the chemoreceptors are operative in the range of 40 to 100 mmHg.

Guyton also includes the central nervous system (CNS) ischemic response in the reflexes responsible for control of pressure variations. Calling this reflex the "last ditch" effort to prevent lethal hypotension, Guyton maintains that it is not activated until arterial pressure has dropped to 50 mmHg or less. Excitation of the ischemic response elicits profound sympathetic vasoconstriction, perhaps more powerful than that evoked by any other of the cardiovascular reflexes.

Other cardiovascular reflexes involved in arterial pressure control were reviewed in the section concerned with peripheral circulation. It is important to recall that the reflexes are extremely effective for acute changes because they can be fully effective within minutes; if the elevation or reduction in pressure persists for a period of time, however, the reflexes adapt. For long-term regulation, then, the reflexes do not appear to be effective.

Intrinsic Control

Through variations in capillary pressure which are a direct result of changes in arterial pressure, changes in vascular volume via capillary-to-tissue fluid shifts can effectively participate in arterial pressure control. Although capillary fluid shift takes longer than the cardiovascular reflexes to become fully effective (about 1 h), this system can be twice as effective as the baroreceptors in restoring normal ranges of arterial pressure. The reader is referred to the previous discussion on capillary dynamics for a review of normal fluid balance.

Long-Term Regulation

The crucial role of the kidney in long-term regulation of arterial pressure cannot be overemphasized. It is estimated that an increase in arterial pressure from 100 mmHg to 200 mmHg can increase water and sodium excretion approximately sixfold. Hypotension, of course, has the opposite effect of increasing reabsorption of water and salt, thus augmenting blood volume and therefore pressure. The importance of aldosterone in selective water and salt reabsorption or excretion was reviewed earlier.

The kidneys can begin to respond to an acute situation within a few hours; for complete effect, though, several days are necessary.

CONTROL OF CARDIAC OUTPUT

When quantifying cardiac output, the pulmonary and systemic circuits are maintained as functional units. Cardiac output is defined as that amount of blood which is pumped from the left ventricle into the aorta per minute. Although the right ventricle ejects an equivalent amount of blood into the pulmonary artery, it is not included in measurement of total cardiac output. Venous return is considered as the amount of blood which is returned to the right atrium. Venous return may differ from the cardiac output for short periods of time because blood can be stored in some areas of the circulation; the cardiac output and venous return are eventually equivalent amounts and are inextricably related to one another.

The normal value for cardiac output is about 5600 mL/min or 5.6 L in the average male. Since the cardiac output varies considerably in accordance with body size, the *cardiac index* is utilized to achieve an accurate estimate of blood flow in proportion to body surface area. The average 70-kg male has an estimated standard cardiac index of approximately 3 L/min.

Cardiac output is defined as the product of the heart rate and the amount of blood ejected from the left ventricle with each contraction—stroke volume. The control of cardiac output resides in the ability of the heart to alter either its frequency of beating or the

stroke volume. Alteration of heart rate is chiefly controlled through innervation of the autonomic nervous system, while alteration of the stroke volume involves a much more complex group of control mechanisms (Fig. 4-24).

The stroke volume is defined as the difference between the diastolic volume within the left ventricle and the residual volume of blood within the ventricle following systole. The major factors which influence stroke volume are diastolic filling and systolic ejection. As depicted in Fig. 4-24, diastolic filling is dependent upon normal filling pressures and the compliance, or distensibility, of the ventricular chamber. Systolic ejection is the result of the interaction of the many factors which influence contractility: the quality of tension developed within the ventricle, its rate, and its duration; and the resistance imposed by arterial pressure.

Cardiac output, then, is dependent upon the interrelationships developed between (1) heart rate, (2) ventricular compliance (distensibility), (3) diastolic filling pressure, (4) myocardial contractility, and (5) arterial pressure.

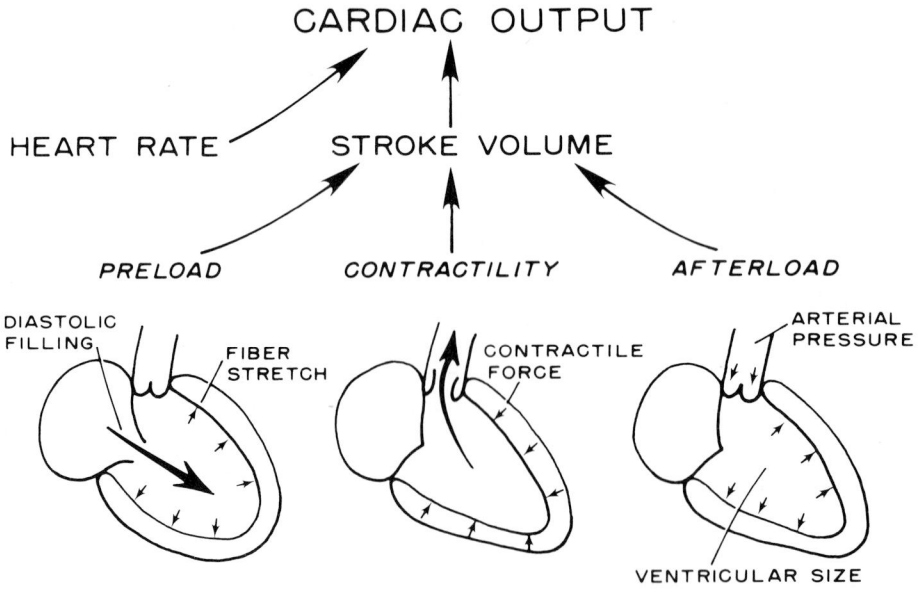

FIGURE 4-24

Factors influencing cardiac output. Among the complex variables which affect cardiac output are changes in heart rate and four factors which influence stroke volume : (1) diastolic filling pressure, (2) ventricular distensibility, (3) arterial pressure, and (4) myocardial contractility. (*From S. Price and L. Wilson, Pathophysiology, McGraw-Hill, New York, 1978. Used by permission of the publisher.*)

Measurement of Cardiac Output

The classical method for measurement of cardiac output is obtained via the Fick principle, which requires simultaneous enumeration of total oxygen consumption and the arteriovenous oxygen difference (AV O_2 difference). To obtain an AV oxygen difference, the mean oxygen concentration of venous and arterial blood must be measured; for venous blood it is necessary to obtain a sample of mixed venous blood from either the right ventricle or pulmonary artery. Oxygen content of venous blood differs from one vein to another, since the oxygen extraction of one organ system can vary considerably from that of others in the body. Arterial oxygen content can be measured at any artery within the body.

The oxygen consumption is measured by collecting exhaled air in order to measure oxygen utilization per minute. By dividing the oxygen consumption per minute by the arteriovenous oxygen difference, the cardiac output is calculated as follows:

$$\text{Cardiac output} = \frac{O_2 \text{ consumption}}{\text{AV } O_2 \text{ difference}}$$

For example, if an individual has a normal AV oxygen difference, 5 mL of oxygen per 100 mL blood, and has an oxygen consumption of 250 mL/min, that individual has a cardiac output of 5000 mL (250 ÷ 5 = 50 × 100 mL = 5000).

The indicator dilution technique of measurement of cardiac output is based upon the injection of a predetermined amount of indicator, in this case a dye, into the venous system. When sufficient time is allowed for mixing and a sample of blood is analyzed for concentration of dye, the cardiac output can be obtained. While the dye is instilled into the venous circulation, arterial blood is simultaneously sampled for dye concentration. The time in which the dye appears and increases to peak concentration within arterial blood becomes a time concentration curve for estimation of cardiac output. The formula for measurement of the cardiac output is based upon the relationship between the total amount of dye which is injected, the average concentration of the dye within the blood, and the duration of the curve.

Thermodilution is probably the most popular method for measurement of cardiac output. Its popularity is based upon several advantages: (1) It is a relatively simple procedure to perform. (2) Arterial samples are unnecessary. (3) The indicator utilized is harmless and inexpensive (usually cold saline).

(4) Results are extremely rapid and may be obtained repeatedly.

A small amount of cold saline is injected into a specialized pulmonary arterial catheter which is equipped with a thermistor at its distal tip. The temperature variations within the blood are monitored by the thermistor and recorded as a temperature time curve. The cardiac output is then calculated within a computer from the temperature curve.

Control of Heart Rate

The normal adult heart beats at a frequency of between 60 and 80 beats per minute. Although the principal regulators of cardiac rate are the nerves of the parasympathetic and sympathetic nervous systems, it is important to review the intrinsic control mechanism within the heart, namely the property of automaticity.

Specialized cardiac myofibrils can drive the denervated heart. There have even been reports of implantation of pacemaker cells which have been successful in controlling the heart. Usually the denervated heart beats at a rate somewhat slower than when under the influence of the nervous system. The heart rate does not increase in response to exercise or stress until influenced by the circulating catecholamines (norepinephrine and epinephrine, which are secreted from the adrenal medulla). Clinically, the heart may mimic denervation in a variety of circumstances: (1) cardiac transplantation, (2) vagolytic effects produced by atropine and beta-blocking effects of propranolol, (3) depletion of the normal stores of norepinephrine through antihypertensives such as reserpine, and (4) depletion of norepinephrine resulting from cardiac pathology such as chronic ventricular failure. The latter two conditions exhibit their effect through mitigation of the sympathetic effect resulting from a reduction in norepinephrine release from the sympathetic nerve endings.

The function of the extrinsic neural and humoral controls is generally integrative; they increase the functional effectiveness of the heart as well as acting as a higher control center, and one therefore capable of more specialized action.

The divisions of the automatic nervous system exhibit tonic influence upon the heart rate. Increased parasympathetic stimulation along with reciprocal decrease in sympathetic activity results in a drop in rate. Acceleration of the heart rate is produced by the opposite action of the two divisions of the nervous system.

The parasympathetic cardiac fibers originate in the medulla and have their innervation primarily within the atria. Animal experimentation has revealed that the right vagus nerve affects the sinoatrial node predominantly, and that the left vagus has its greatest effect upon atrioventricular (AV) conduction tissue. Some ventricular innervation occurs at the base of the ventricles near the conduction tissue. However, ventricular muscle is relatively unresponsive to acetylcholine and thus the parasympathetic effect upon the ventricles is presumed to be insignificant.

The effect of vagal stimuli is transient since the acetylcholine is rapidly dissipated by the enzyme cholinesterase, of which the SA and AV nodes have abundant stores.

The sympathetic nerve fibers arise from the thoracic spinal cord and penetrate the myocardium in a manner similar to the parasympathetic nerve fibers; i.e., left and right fibers appear to be functionally specific. Under experimental conditions, the left sympathetic fibers appear to augment cardiac contractility more than they accelerate the heart rate. The right sympathetic fibers selectively increase heart rate with relatively little effect upon contractility. In addition, fibers from the right primarily innervate the SA node and atria, while those from the left have their predominant influence within the ventricles.

In contrast to acetylcholine, norepinephrine remains active following release from the nerve endings; relatively little undergoes degradation within the tissues. Most of the remaining norepinephrine is taken up again by the nerve terminals. Norepinephrine acts on the beta receptors within the myocardium (most of the adrenergic receptors within the nodal regions and myocardium are beta receptors) and on the alpha receptors within the coronary arteries.

The antagonistic interaction between acetylcholine and the catecholamines is very complex and poorly understood. Normally, in the resting heart, the parasympathetic system predominates in controlling the SA node.

Cardioregulatory Center

Impulses from the cerebral cortex can have a substantial effect upon the heart rate; fear, excitement, and anger can all induce significant acceleration in rate. Areas within the hypothalamus can also effect changes in the heart rate. Experiments have demonstrated that sympathetic fibers descending from the medulla can be separated into accelerator and augmentor fibers, and further, that the augmentor sites are more prevalent on the left, the accelerator on the right. A cardioregulatory center is frequently assumed to exist and carry out upper nervous control of cardiac function.

Baroreceptor Reflex

An elevation in right atrial pressure sufficient to cause distention causes a reflex acceleration of heart rate. Bainbridge hypothesized that the tachycardia resulted from a vagal reflex. The effect of the *Bainbridge reflex* is somewhat controversial, but recent study has supported the existence of "accelerator" receptors located in both atria which excite the nervous system and elicit diuresis.

Stretch receptors within the ventricles have been identified within the epicardium and deep within the myocardium. A potent stimulus can induce bradycardia, hypotension, and a drop in the respiratory rate.

The reciprocal relationship between arterial pressure and heart rate has been called *Marey's law of the heart*. The stretch receptors within the carotid sinus and aortic arch respond to an increase in arterial pressure with a reflex bradycardia. The pulmonary vasculature responds to distention with a reflex reduction in rate. The well-known carotid sinus reflex, similar to occipital pressure, can produce a bradycardia and can frequently convert tachyarrhythmia to normal sinus rhythm. The carotid sinus reflex is so sensitive in some individuals that tight collars or sudden movement of the head can cause syncope through induction of bradycardia and hypotension. Such syncopal reactions can be produced by many other types of stimuli. Called a *vasovagal response,* the reaction can be elicited by stimulation of the upper respiratory tract during endotracheal suctioning and during intubation of the trachea and the esophagus. Since the gastrointestinal tract has afferent fibers leading to the medulla, nausea and vomiting in addition to rectal stimulation can be associated with a reflex bradycardia. Generally, stimulation of visceral pain fibers can cause a marked bradycardia. Pressure on the eyeball, in addition to painful stimulation of skeletal muscle, may elicit a significant reduction of heart rate. Conversely, somatic pain in the skin frequently produces tachycardia.

The close relationship between the cardiac and respiratory responses has already been mentioned. The phenomenon of phasic acceleration and deceleration in heart rate simultaneous with inspiration and expiration occurs frequently and is known as *sinus arrhythmia.* Since intrathoracic pressure drops during inspiration, resulting in an increase in venous return, sinus arrhythmia has been attributed to stimulation of the Bainbridge reflex, causing increased heart rate. With the corresponding increase in left ventricular output and resulting rise in arterial pressure, a decrease in heart rate occurs through excitation of the aortic baroreceptors. Pulmonary stretch receptors may be operative as well in the bradycardia associated with sinus arrhythmia.

Control of Stroke Volume

The fundamental control mechanism for the stroke volume is the Frank-Starling law of the heart. Though the experiments done by Starling were in isolated hearts on heart-lung machines and many complex variables exist within the intact animal and human heart, the basic qualitative relationships regarding ventricular performance can be extrapolated and applied to ventricular function.

When the Starling mechanism was mentioned earlier in this chapter, it was referred to as an intrinsic method for autoregulation of cardiac performance. Its most basic effect is to guarantee equal stroke volumes from the right and left ventricles. Should there be a momentary increase in venous return to the right ventricle, the normal left ventricle will automatically increase its stroke volume, thus the term *autoregulation.* The mechanism through which the heart can automatically respond is one it shares with all striated muscle: the length-tension relationship. Increasing the length of the ventricular fiber, in practice, measured as filling pressure (Fig. 4-25), will shift the curve to the left, augmenting ventricular contractility.

The normal left ventricle is extremely distensible and accepts increases in diastolic volume, or preload, without significant increase in ventricular filling pressure (end-diastolic pressure). Generally, peak contractility occurs at a fiber length of 2.2 μm or 12 mmHg. Further increases in filling pressure beyond the physiologic limits of the length-tension relationship will result in a reduction in effective ventricular performance. Once fiber length reaches 4 to 4.5 μm corresponding to a filling pressure of 14 or 15 mmHg, the rate of rise in ventricular end-diastolic pressure occurs very rapidly.

In the noncompliant, stiff ventricle, the situation is very different. A higher filling pressure results for the same fiber length, which results in a shift in the performance curve to the right, as shown in Fig. 4-25. The end result, then, is a reduction in ventricular

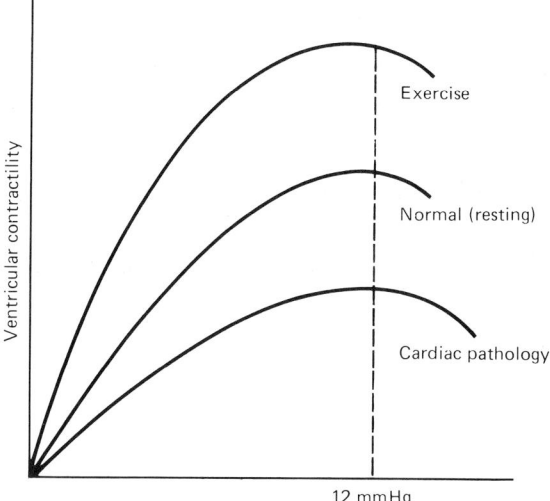

FIGURE 4-25

Schematic drawing of the Frank-Starling law of the heart. Stretching of the myocardial fiber will within physiologic limits produce an augmentation of ventricular contraction. Since myocardial fiber length cannot be measured, left ventricular end-diastolic filling pressure (LVEDP) is utilized to assess ventricular ejection. Peak ventricular ejection generally occurs at a ventricular filling pressure of 12 mmHg, represented by the dashed line. Sympathetic effects can shift the curve to the left, resulting in more rapid increase of ventricular ejection; pathology can shift the curve to the right causing greater filling pressures for the same or lesser ventricular ejection volume. Thus greater filling pressures than 12 mmHg are generally required in the diseased heart for optimal performance.

performance while simultaneously causing higher filling pressures.

There are many other types of function curves which more definitively assess ventricular performance. Cardiac function curves, such as those which measure the stroke work index, are utilized to gain more specific information regarding left ventricular function.

There is evidence that other types of autoregulation can occur within the heart which are not related to an increase in ventricular fiber length. Afterload, or increased peripheral resistance (aortic), may result in ventricular adaptation by augmenting ventricular contractility (Anrep effect). Other examples of the augmentation of ventricular contractility can be seen in tachycardia and with premature beats. Berne theorizes that the increased contractility seen with elevation of heart rate is based upon increases in intracellular calcium (Treppe phenomenon). Similarly, the phenomenon known as "postextrasystolic potentiation" may be the result of elevated intracellular calcium. It is well known that a premature beat generally produces a feeble contraction, which probably relates to low concentrations of calcium. The fact that the beat following the premature (extrasystolic) beat is usually much stronger relates not only to the increased time for diastolic filling during the long pause following the premature beat, but according to Berne, may be potentiated by increased concentrations of intracellular calcium as well.

Ventricular Distensibility

The factors which determine ventricular distension or compliance are extremely complex. Among them are characteristics which were mentioned earlier. The structural configuration of the ventricular musculature, the size of the ventricles, and factors such as diastolic recoil as well as the presence or lack of conditioning of the heart—all these directly affect ventricular compliance. It is known that less myocardial shortening is required to eject a large stroke volume than is required for a small stroke volume, since the initial fiber length is extended (Starling relationship). The existence of pathology will also bear a direct influence on ventricular compliance.

Ventricular Contractility

Rushmer points out that the factors which cannot be ascribed to the length-tension relationship are usually combined to mean contractility, a fact which confuses the meaning of the word. Rushmer groups the following variables under the concept of contractility: (1) the degree of systolic emptying, (2) rate of muscle shortening, (3) rate of tension development, (4) ejection velocity, (5) inotropic effects, (6) vigor of contraction, and (7) rate of myocardial shortening. In addition, the ratio of pressure development and resulting myocardial tension (dP/dT) is frequently utilized as a determinant of contractility.

Nervous Control

Sympathetic Sympathetic innervation has already been reviewed with respect to control of the heart rate. The atria are liberally supplied with both para-sympathetic and sympathetic nerves, while the ventricles are mainly supplied by sympathetic nerves. Generally, the sympathetics are effective in augmentation of contractility; the parasympathetics function to diminish the strength of ventricular contraction.

The amount of sympathetic activity can be estimated by comparing the quantity of norepinephrine within the atria, in the SA and AV nodes, and within the ventricles; ventricular concentration of norepinephrine is triple that in the atria and nodes.

Sympathetic stimulation within the heart is inotropic; within the atria, stimulation can cause a 20 to 30 percent increase in atrial contractility. The effect of sympathetic activity within the ventricle is, of course, more complicated and is dependent upon the relationship of the factors listed earlier which influence contractility in addition to heart rate. The stroke volume may or may not increase; the primary benefit from the inotropic effect of sympathetic activity appears to be the increased rate and velocity of pressure change, ventricular outflow, and change in ventricular dimensions. The net result is ejection of the same or slightly higher stroke volume in a much shorter period of time, and more frequently per minute, thereby increasing cardiac output. The results of sympathetic effects upon cardiac function are summarized in Fig. 4-26.

Parasympathetic The vagal inhibitory effect on the nodes and other conduction tissue within the atria and AV junction are very potent. Recently the existence of parasympathetic influence within the ventricle has been demonstrated. Its effect is the reverse of sympathetic: Left ventricular pressure falls, as does the maximum rate of pressure development.

Effect of Electrolyte Imbalance

Hyperkalemia can result in extreme cardiac dilation and bradycardia. If extreme hyperpolarization is caused by the increased extracellular potassium concentration, no action potential will be generated and asystole will ensue. An acute increase in serum potassium to 8 meq is sufficient to cause death through this mechanism.

Hypercalcemia results in tetany, probably resulting from the excitatory effects of calcium upon the contractile process. Clinically this is rarely seen, since the tetany would more likely result in respiratory arrest prior to exhibition of significant effects from hypercalcemia.

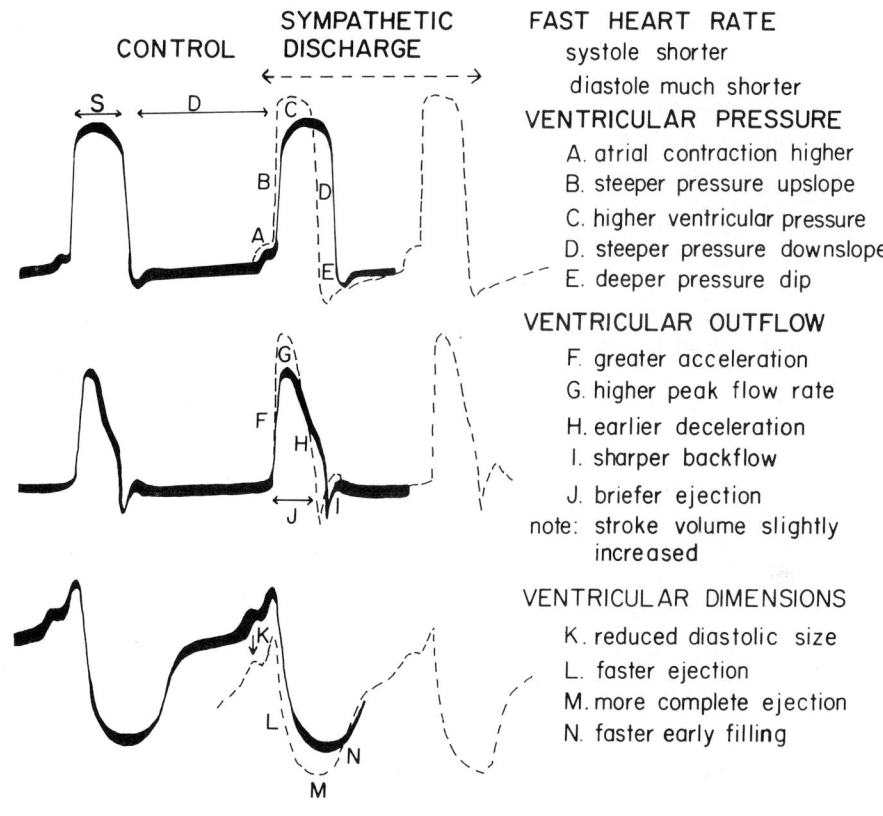

CONTROL   SYMPATHETIC DISCHARGE

FAST HEART RATE
systole shorter
diastole much shorter

VENTRICULAR PRESSURE
A. atrial contraction higher
B. steeper pressure upslope
C. higher ventricular pressure
D. steeper pressure downslope
E. deeper pressure dip

VENTRICULAR OUTFLOW
F. greater acceleration
G. higher peak flow rate
H. earlier deceleration
I. sharper backflow
J. briefer ejection
note: stroke volume slightly increased

VENTRICULAR DIMENSIONS
K. reduced diastolic size
L. faster ejection
M. more complete ejection
N. faster early filling

FIGURE 4-26

Summary of sympathetic effect upon cardiac performance. The major results of sympathetic discharge is in increasing the following: (1) functioning, (2) heart rate, (3) pressure rise and fall within ventricle, (4) ejection velocity. (5) change in velocity (acceleration), (6) deceleration, and (7) change in ventricular dimensions. (*From Robert Rushmer, Cardiovascular Dynamics, Saunders, Philadelphia, 1970. Used by permission of the publisher.*)

Peripheral Circulation: Venous Return

The vital role of the peripheral circulation in maintenance of cardiac output cannot be overemphasized. Cardiac output and venous return are, in the broad sense, inseparable. The heart can obviously pump no more blood than it receives from the peripheral circulation; therefore, venous return and cardiac output must eventually be equal, although temporary differences can exist.

Guyton describes the role of the heart as permissive in its regulation of cardiac output. Up to a physiologic limit of 13 to 15 L/min, the heart will pump the amount of blood that returns to the right atrium. If venous return exceeds that amount, sympathetic stimulation is required. The normal resting venous return is approximately 5 L/min; therefore, the normal cardiac output is also 5 L/min.

With sympathetic stimulation, the cardiac output can more than double by utilizing the systolic and diastolic reserve capacities. The normal resting cardiac output is achieved through the product of a resting stroke volume of 80 mL and a resting heart rate of 70 beats per minute. The heart rate can increase to an effective rate of 180 beats per minute while the ventricles respond to the inotropic sympathetic effects.

Summary

The basic determinants of cardiac output are heart rate and stroke volume. Normally the rate of the SA node is determined by an antagonistic relationship between the two main divisions of the autonomic nervous system. If only the rate of the SA node is increased by electrical stimulation or specific localized sympathetic excitation upon the SA node, without generalized peripheral effects, cardiac output will probably not increase.

Afterload or wall tension during ventricular ejection is determined primarily by arterial pressure but is influenced by other factors influencing resistance as well: aortic distensibility, peripheral vascular resistance, and characteristics of the blood itself. The effect of increasing afterload on the normal ventricle is possibly augmentation of contractility. Within the diseased heart, however, severely deleterious effects may result from the resistance imposed by normal aortic impedance (afterload).

Diastolic filling (preload) is dependent upon total blood volume and peripheral circulatory regulation. Atrial contraction can augment diastolic filling by as much as 35 percent. Increase in stroke volume is effected by the length-tension relationship of the Frank-Starling mechanism within physiologic limits. The effects are augmented through the inotropic effects of the sympathetic nervous system. Ventricular contractility is determined by a very complex relationship between many factors involved in ventricular structure and dimensions. Cardiac dilation impedes effective contractility because of the Laplace relationship.

REFERENCES

Ayres, S., and V. Gianelli: *Cardiology: A Clinicophysiologic Approach,* New York: Appleton Century Crofts, 1971.

Berne, R. M., and M. N. Levy: *Cardiovascular Physiology,* St. Louis: Mosby, 1977.

Friedman, H. H.: *Outline of Electrocardiography,* New York: McGraw-Hill, 1963.

Guyton, A.C.: *Textbook of Medical Physiology,* 5th ed., Philadelphia: Saunders, 1976.

Hurst, J. W.: *The Heart, Arteries, and Veins,* 4th ed., New York: McGraw-Hill, 1978.

Rushmer, R. F.: *Cardiovascular Dynamics,* 4th ed., Philadelphia: Saunders, 1976.

Thomas, L.: *The Lives of a Cell,* New York: Viking, 1974.

Vassalee, M. (ed.): *Cardiac Physiology for the Clinician,* New York: Academic, 1976.

BIBLIOGRAPHY

Guyton, A. C.: *Circulatory Physiology: Cardiac Output and Its Regulation,* Philadelphia: Saunders, 1973.

————: *Circulatory Physiology II,* Philadelphia: Saunders, 1975.

Mirsky, I., and D. Ghista: *Cardiac Mechanics: Physiologic Clinical and Mathematical Considerations,* New York: Wiley, 1975.

Rushmer, R. F.: *Organ Physiology: Structure and Function of the Cardiovascular System,* Philadelphia: Saunders, 1976.

As multicellular organisms evolved, cells lost their direct contact with the external environment. A means of transporting nutrients and wastes between the interior and exterior environments gradually took form. The pump and conduits are the heart and blood vessels; the medium for carrying nutrients and wastes is, of course, the blood, consisting of a fluid in which cells and other substances are suspended. This *blood circulatory system* restores a kind of interface between the external and internal environments for essential functions.

The *hematopoietic system* includes blood-forming organs as well as blood-circulating organs. The blood-forming organs consist of the bone marrow, liver, spleen, thymus gland, and lymph nodes. During the years of early childhood, all the bones are filled with red marrow, whereas in the adult the major centers for erythropoietic (red cell) and granulopoietic (white cell) activity are the marrow of the ribs, the sternum, and the bodies of the vertebrae.

This chapter will focus on the physiological characteristics and unique contributions of the various constituents of the hematopoietic system to homeostasis.

FUNCTIONS OF THE HEMATOPOIETIC SYSTEM

The primary physiologic functions of the hematopoietic system are respiration, nutrition, and excretion. Blood carries the respiratory gases (oxygen and carbon dioxide), nutrients, and wastes, providing transport among the hematopoietic tissues, the connective tissues, and other tissues and organs of the body. In its travels it distributes heat and it flows through specialized sensors which selectively react to such variables as osmotic pressure, pH, temperature, and the level of certain hormones. These other functions in which blood participates are temperature regulation and fluid and acid-base balance, respectively. The hematopoietic system also participates in defense. The blood contains cells and substances that attack infectious organisms and other foreign antigens. Through the process of hemostasis, blood participates in a mechanism which controls escape of the blood from the vascular compartment.

BLOOD: COMPOSITION AND CHARACTERISTICS

Blood is actually a fluid "connective tissue" containing circulating cells and liquid intercellular substances.

5
THE HEMATOPOIETIC SYSTEM
Dorothy Gosnell Moses

FUNCTIONS OF THE HEMATOPOIETIC SYSTEM

BLOOD: COMPOSITION AND CHARACTERISTICS
Color, Specific Gravity, Osmotic Pressure, and pH Reaction
Blood Volume

PLASMA
Site of Plasma Protein Synthesis
The Plasma Proteins

HEMATOPOIESIS
Blood Cell Origins and Development
Erythropoiesis

BLOOD CELLS
Erythrocytes: Red Blood Cells
Leukocytes: White Blood Cells
Platelets

COAGULATION AND COAGULATION FACTORS
Nomenclature
Intrinsic and Extrinsic System of Coagulation
Coagulation Factors

MECHANISM OF COAGULATION
System Antagonists
Hemostasis

REFERENCES

79

This pale yellow liquid, called *plasma,* constitutes approximately 55 percent of the total blood volume. Plasma represents part of the extracellular fluid of the body. The 45 percent of the blood volume remaining consists of the solid suspended particles, cells being the majority of this solid material. The ratio of red blood cells to blood plasma is expressed as the *hematocrit.* The normal hematocrit is approximately 40 percent for the adult female and 45 percent for the adult male. These values have a wide range and can be influenced by many factors. The hematocrit can serve as a valuable guide, useful in the assessment of the patient's hydration status. For example, it can be used in the monitoring of the patient response to aggressive fluid replacement in the event of an acute burn. As with most lab studies, it is best used in conjunction with other tests so that several parameters are being monitored and compared in a comprehensive and serial manner.

Color, Specific Gravity, Osmotic Pressure, and pH Reaction

Color

The color of normal blood varies with the state of hemoglobin oxygenation. Arterial blood is normally bright red, reflecting the high oxygen saturation of the hemoglobin molecule contained within the red blood cells. Venous blood is a darker red because much of the oxygen has been removed from the hemoglobin and given up to the tissues.

Specific Gravity

Blood normally has a *specific gravity* that ranges between 1.048 and 1.066, averaging about 1.055. Specific gravity is the ratio of the weight of a certain volume of a substance to the weight of an equal volume of water. The specific gravity of blood depends largely on the number of red blood cells present. Blood is also three to four times more viscous than water. The viscosity of a liquid is due to the mutual attraction of its molecules, the molecules thereby tending to offer resistance to blood flow. The degree of viscosity is of clinical consideration because the greater the viscosity, the more slowly blood flows through blood vessels and the greater is the force required to propel it through the circulatory system. Conditions which increase the viscosity of the blood, such as dehydration and polycythemia (increase in the number of red blood cells), decrease blood flow and can actually make circulation quite sluggish.

Osmotic Pressure

Osmotic pressure of the blood averages about 5100 mmHg or 6.7 atm. It is due primarily to the presence of the various salts, waste products, glucose, and other crystalloids dissolved in the plasma. Plasma proteins also contribute to osmotic pressure, in particular the plasma protein albumin. Because the composition of the blood undergoes continual change, although small, the osmotic pressure varies slightly. The change in composition is due to the passage of water and dissolved nutrients and various waste products which continually pass in and out of the blood. The osmotic pressure is maintained within physiological limits by the kidneys.

pH: Hydrogen Ion Concentration

The pH of the blood is of great importance to homeostasis and can facilitate or retard the action of the many enzyme systems within the body. Optimum activity of enzymes requires that the pH of the blood remain within a relatively narrow range. In health this normal range is approximately 7.35 to 7.40, which is slightly alkaline in reaction. Various mechanisms which are related to the buffering capacity of the blood are involved in maintaining the constancy of the range within acceptable limits.

Blood Volume

The quantity of blood in the human body represents approximately 8 percent of the body weight. (The blood and the tissue fluid constitute almost 20 percent of the total body weight.) It is estimated that there are about 5 L of blood in the adult male and 3.5 to 4.5 L in the adult female. Normal increases occur in the pregnant state. Assuming normal renal function, this amount is relatively constant and is not increased or decreased markedly or for any length of time by drinking fluid, by injections, or by hemorrhage. When an individual drinks a large quantity of water, the water is rather rapidly removed from the blood by the tissues or is eliminated by the kidneys. Keeping the amount of blood in the vascular compartment constant is of great importance since, without a minimum amount, adequate circulation is impaired and life is endangered.

Distribution of Blood

Approximately 1300 mL of the blood volume is present within the pulmonary circulation, of which about 32 percent (400 mL) is in the arteries, 4 percent (60 mL) is in the capillaries, and 64 percent (840 mL) is in the veins and venules. Of the 3000 mL present within the systemic circuit, about 18 percent (550 mL) is in the arteries and 10 percent (300 mL) is in the capillaries. The remaining 72 percent (about 2150 mL) is within the venules and veins. Veins are considered the body's capacitance or reservoir system. They have the ability to accommodate a large extra volume of blood, with minimal increase in intravascular venous pressure.

Effects of Acute Blood Loss

For a period of time after an acute blood loss, hemoglobin values and plasma protein concentrations may remain normal. But because of the protective process known as *autotransfusion,* a decrease in intravascular pressure allows protein-free fluid to enter the circulation from the interstitial space. Initially, arteriolar vasoconstriction produces a change in the capillary filtration pressure, reducing the positive pushing force of blood under normal arterial pressure. After 2 or 3 h, sufficient amounts of interstitial fluid enter the vascular compartment to dilute the blood, so that both the hemoglobin value and the plasma protein value fall. Over the next 24 h, as the circulating blood volume is restored, the decline in the plasma protein and hemoglobin values continues. Should this sequence of events occur without fluid replacement, a state of relative interstitial and intracellular dehydration will result.

Between 2 to 4 days after the blood loss, normal plasma protein concentration is restored. Hemoglobin values become normalized much more slowly, depending upon the quantity of blood lost and upon the availability of the body's iron stores, which are requisite to hemoglobin synthesis. In a healthy adult it is estimated that approximately 20 days are required for hemoglobin levels to become normal after a blood loss of 200 mL.

The clinical implication of this information resides in the fact that hemoglobin and hematocrit values obtained soon after a hemorrhage may not yet reflect the severity of the blood loss. After autotransfusion has begun, however, the lowering of the two values will reflect the movement of the interstitial fluid into the vascular compartment, or the quantity of infused intravenous crystalloids and colloids. All these variables must be considered in relation to the time of the hemorrhage for accurate evaluation of the hemoglobin and hematocrit values.

PLASMA

Plasma constitutes 55 percent of the blood volume. It is composed of *serum* and fibrinogen. If whole blood is withdrawn into a test tube and allowed to clot, after a period of time the clot will withdraw from the sides of the tube. The fluid expressed from the clot is called *serum.* Serum is primarily plasma minus the plasma protein fibrinogen.

Blood plasma is an extremely complex fluid containing large quantities of organic and inorganic substances. The yellowish color of plasma is due to the presence of bile pigments. The solutes which make up the largest percent of total plasma weight are the plasma proteins. With the exception of hepatic failure or prolonged malnutrition, plasma proteins tend to be the most constant constituent of blood.

Site of Plasma Protein Synthesis

The parenchymal liver cell, the *hepatocyte,* is the main site of protein synthesis, with the exception of immunoglobulins and plasminogen. (Immunoglobulins are synthesized by lymphocytes and plasminogen is synthesized by eosinophil granulocytes.) The hepatocyte is also the site of synthesis of the trace proteins in the plasma which constitute the coagulation factors essential to clot formation.

The Plasma Proteins

Approximately 6 to 8 percent of the plasma weight is made up of protein substances: albumin, serum globulins, fibrinogen, prothrombin, and plasminogen.

Serum Albumin

Serum albumin, the largest of the plasma proteins, plays an important part in the regulation of intravascular plasma volume. Since very little protein escapes from blood vessels, there is far more inside than outside the interstitial space. This difference in protein concentration sets up an osmotic pressure, tending to bring fluid in from the interstitial space. At the arteriolar end of a capillary bed this pressure is successfully opposed by blood pressure so that there is a net movement of fluid out of blood vessels. With the drop in blood pressure at the venous end of the capillary bed, the net movement of fluid is no longer outward but inward in accord with the osmotic pressure created by the plasma proteins.

If this dynamic relationship is deranged as a result of a decrease in plasma proteins, for instance, in hypoalbuminemia, more fluid leaves the vessel at the arterial end than reenters at the venous end and the result is interstitial edema.

Pathological conditions associated with abnormally low serum protein levels include liver disorders in which protein decline is the result of inadequate synthesis, and the nephrotic syndrome, in which the problem is the loss of large quantities of plasma proteins through the kidney.

Serum Globulins

Serum globulins can be subdivided into alpha, beta, and gamma fractions. The alpha fraction is associated with the transport of steroids, lipids, and bilirubin. The beta fraction is associated with iron and copper transport. Gamma globulin will be discussed in the section dealing with the immune response. Fibrinogen, prothrombin, and plasminogen will be discussed in the section dealing with coagulation factors.

HEMATOPOIESIS

Hematopoiesis is a process of self-renewal. It involves the production and maintenance of physiologic levels of the blood and bone marrow cells. The process includes cellular proliferation, division of immature hematopoietic stem cells, and ultimately, the differentiation of the stem cells into mature cell types. Cells produced by the organs of the hematopoietic system include erythrocytes (red blood cells), neutrophils, lymphocytes, monocytes, eosinophils, basophils (white blood cells), platelets and plasma cells. Most of these cell types are illustrated in Fig. 5-1, and their normal values are listed in Table 5-1.

Blood Cell Origins and Development

In postnatal life in man, erythrocytes, granular leukocytes, and monocytes, in addition to platelet precursors and megakaryocytes, are produced in the bone marrow or myeloid tissue. However, the lymphocytes are produced in lymphoid tissue as well as in the bone marrow and thymus gland. Although there is general agreement that all blood cells originate from *stem cells,* there is considerable controversy over whether all blood cells originate from a single polyvalent cell known as the *hemocytoblast.* (A stem cell is defined as a hematopoietic cell capable of both reproducing itself and, through the process of mitotic division, giving rise to more differentiated cells.) One school of thought regarding stem cells

proposes that all cells originate from the hemocytoblast, which is capable of differentiating into any type of blood cell. Another school of thought proposes that there is a separate type of stem cell for each of the blood cell types. Still another group believes that a primitive white blood cell produces the granulocytes, lymphocytes, and monocytes, whereas the erythrocytes and platelets arise from distinctly different types of cells. The essence of the controversy associated with this last group's proposal is predicated upon whether or not lymphocytes can differentiate.

Stem cells are what is considered a dormant reserve; they are present in small numbers in blood and bone marrow. Normally they have a slow turnover, depending upon the needs of the body. Indirect evidence suggests that the structure of the stem cell is quite similar to that of lymphocytes. The parent cell is described as resembling a large lymphocyte which contains a large nucleus with one or more nucleoli and with considerable basophilic cytoplasm.

Research with experimental animals has demonstrated the presence of multipotential stem cells. Evidence in humans for such a cell is derived from certain myeloproliferative disorders such as polycythemia vera, myelofibrosis with myeloid metaplasia, and chronic myelogenous leukemia. With respect to these abnormal conditions, it has been shown that one precursor cell gives rise to the abnormal erythrocytes, granulocytes, and platelets, but not to lymphocytes, marrow fibroblasts, and other cell lines.

Hematopoietic Principle

The factors that control the development and production of erythrocytes, leukocytes, and platelets are quite diverse. Not much is known or clearly understood regarding this process. In general, it is thought that hematopoiesis is maintained in a steady state in which mature cell production equals mature cell loss. A feedback mechanism of control is hypothesized in which increased demand for cells creates a situation in which increased cell production results. In erythropoiesis (red blood cell production) the marrow responds according to its own inherent capacity for production and as influenced by susceptibility to hypoxia and antibodies of various types. Leukopoiesis, however, is thought to be influenced by chemicals resulting from dead or dying granulocytes and bacteria through the stimulus of chemotaxis. Leukopoiesis is thought to have both direct and indirect marrow and peripheral blood relationships to infection, foreign substances, antibodies, and blood

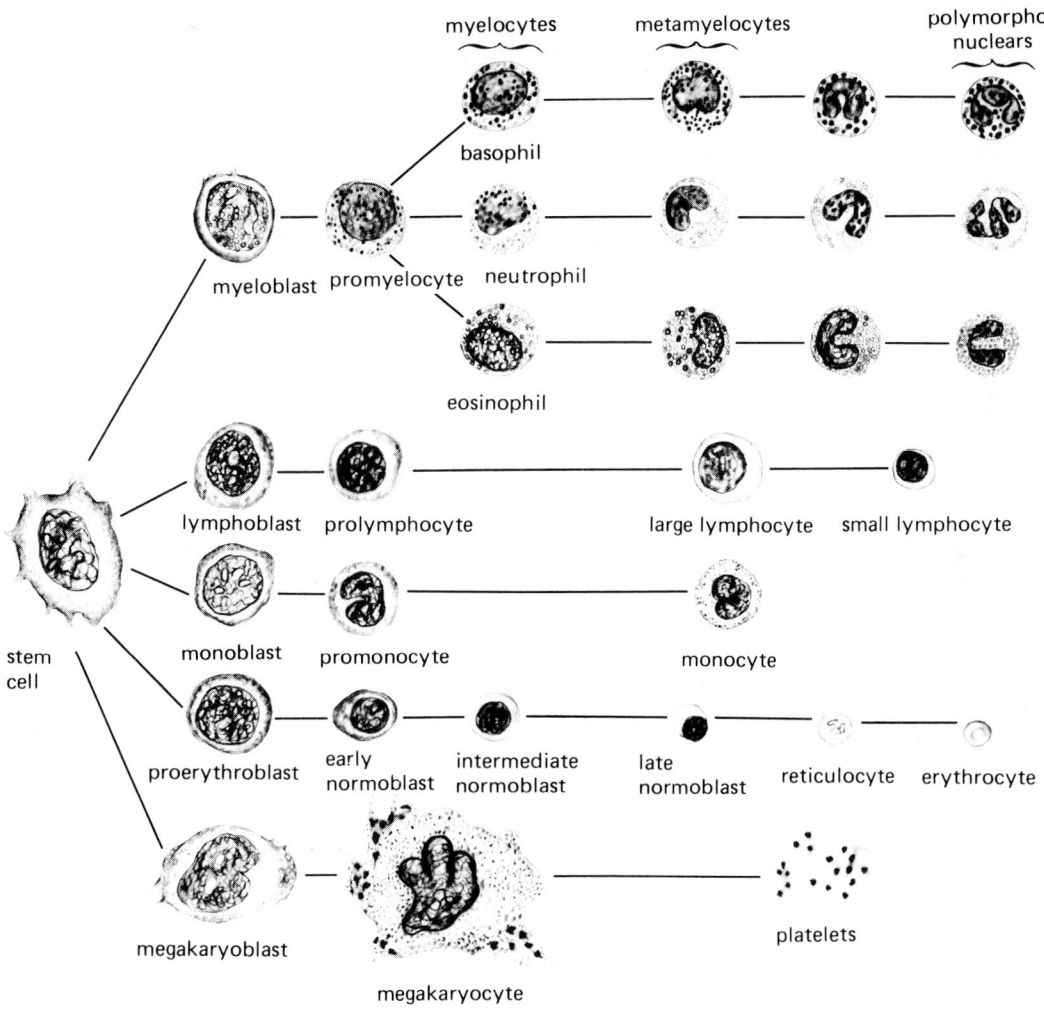

FIGURE 5-1

Development of the formed elements of the blood from bone marrow cells. (*From D. Luciano, A. Vander, and J. Sherman, Human Function and Structure, McGraw-Hill, New York, 1978. Used with permission of the publisher. Redrawn from Whitby and Britton.*)

loss into body spaces. Androgen hormones are also reported to influence leukopoiesis. Thrombopoiesis (platelet production) is thought to be regulated by the number of circulating platelets, with this regulation being mediated by a humoral factor, thrombopoietin.

Erythropoiesis

Under physiological conditions the level of circulating red cells remains relatively constant. This equilibrium between red blood cell formation and removal is necessary to provide for tissue oxygenation and to prevent the viscosity of blood from becoming so high that it interferes with blood flow. Excessive production of red blood cells, known as *polycythemia,* is reflected in an abnormally high hematocrit value. "Secondary" polycythemia is the result of a preexisting condition versus a disease of a primary etiology.

Regulation of Erythrocyte Production

Red blood cell production is thought to be mediated by a hormone called *erythropoietin.* Research has demonstrated the presence of this circulating factor

TABLE 5-1
The Average Range of Normal
Blood Values Measured at Different Ages

Component	Premature	Full term	7 days	2 months	6 months	1 year	8–12 years	Adult male	Adult female
Hemoglobulin, g/dL	13–18	13.7–20	19.6	13.3	10.5–14	11–12.2	11–19	14–18	12–16
RBC/mm³, in millions	5–6	5–6	5.3	4.5	4.6	4.6–4.7	4.8–5.1	5.4	4.8
Nucleated RBC, %	5–15	1–5	0*						
Hematocrit, g/dL	45–55	43–65	52.7	38.9	33–42	32–40	39–47	42–52	37–47
WBC/mm³, in thousands	15	9–38	5–21	5–21	1–15	4.5–13.5	8	5–10	5–10
Neutrophils, %	40–80	40–80	40	36–40	30–45	40–50	55–60	35–70	35–70
Eosinophils, %	2–3	2–3	5					2–3	2–3
Lymphocytes, %	30–31	30–31	20	48–53	48–60	48–53	30–38	30–35	30–35
Monocytes, %	6–12	6–12	15	8–9	5	5	5–8	5–8	5–8
Immature WBC, %	Over 10	3–10	0*						
Platelets/mm³, in thousands	50–300	100–350	400	300–400	250–350†			250–350	250–350
Reticulocytes, %	Up to 10	4–6	3	0.5–1.6†				0.5–1.6	0.5–1.6

* Not normally found in the circulating blood after this age.

† Remains approximately the same for succeeding age levels.

Source: Greene, P., and L. Cooper: *Comprehensive Pediatric Nursing,* G. Scipien et al. (eds.), New York: McGraw-Hill, 1975, pp. 600–601.

in the bloodstream and suggests that one possible site of production is the kidney. Although it is believed that the kidney is the primary production site, it is considered to be a coproducer. Extrarenal sites of production are suspected because erythropoietin can be found in the bloodstream after bilateral nephrectomy and also in end-stage renal disease when there is little, if any, functioning renal tissue. Also, red blood cell production does not completely cease in either of these situations.

Another theory proposes that the kidney actually produces an enzyme which influences activation of an erythropoietin factor. Some researchers claim to have isolated this hormone in the glomeruli of the kidney but not in the renal tubules. Those that dispute this site of synthesis claim that erythropoietin is in the glomeruli as a result of plasma clearance rather than because it actually is being produced at this location.

In general, much research needs to be done to establish the precise location(s) of synthesis and mechanism of action. The site of action, the bone marrow, is known. No red cell production in the bone marrow is possible without the presence of the hormone erythropoietin, regardless of where it is produced.

One more interesting observation is the relation-ship between erythropoietin and renal ischemia. In both experimental animals and in individuals experiencing renal ischemia due to some type of pathology, an increase in the level of erythropoietin and a secondary polycythemia has occasionally been observed to occur. This mechanism, renal ischemia, is proposed to be operant in the similar effects associated with cases of renal transplant rejection.

BLOOD CELLS

Erythrocytes: Red Blood Cells

The erythrocyte is a vehicle for the transport of hemoglobin, which is produced in the precursor cells of the erythrocytes. The function of hemoglobin is the transport of oxygen and carbon dioxide. It is believed that certain microenvironmental influences induce the multipotential stem cell to become the precursor cell of the erythrocyte, responsive to the influence of erythropoietin. In response to erythropoietin, the "committed" precursor in the bone marrow undergoes mitosis and enters into the erythroid maturation.

Normal human erythrocytes are extremely flexible and elastic biconcave disks without nuclei. Red blood cells (RBCs) are capable of traveling at high speeds and under increasing pressure, and can bend and twist as they pass through the tiny capillaries. This ability to assume an elongated shape exposes more surface area for the exchange of oxygen and carbon dioxide.

Although RBCs contain no nucleus, they are capable of maintaining hemoglobin in the functional state but are unable to maintain their structural integrity or to reproduce. Despite the fact that they are not true cells, since they are without a nucleus, they are metabolically quite active. It is estimated that erythrocytes consume 1.5 to 2.2 mmol of glucose per liter of blood per hour. This metabolic activity is required to pump out sodium and to pump in potassium against an electrochemical gradient, and to reduce the methemoglobin to hemoglobin.

Transport of Oxygen: DPG Activity

The main function of the erythrocytes in respiration. This process is accomplished by the unique presence of the hemoglobin pigment in the RBC. This iron-containing protein, hemoglobin, binds with oxygen as it transports it from the lungs to the tissue. Hemoglobin is a simple protein which is attached to heme, the iron-containing pigment.

Normally there is about 15 g of hemoglobin per 100 mL of blood. In general, it is thought that the hemoglobin level is adjusted according to the delivery of oxygen to the tissues. This is modified by the affinity of the hemoglobin molecule for oxygen, and this affinity is thought to be influenced by certain phosphates in the erythrocyte. Intracellular phosphates combine with hemoglobin which has given up its oxygen; the hemoglobin then has less affinity for oxygen. It is referred to as *reduced*. The main intracellular phosphate compound of interest is 2,3-diphosphoglycerate (2,3-DPG). In areas of tissue hypoxia, as the oxygen leaves the hemoglobin compound, the amount of reduced hemoglobin in the red cell increases, which binds more 2,3-DPG in the process. As this process proceeds, 2,3-DPG is depleted in the red cell, the result of which is increased glycolysis with the production of more 2,3-DPG. As this occurs, more hemoglobin is bound and its oxygen affinity is further reduced, the end result of which is more oxygen delivered to the tissue.

Life Span and Removal of Erythrocytes

Erythrocyte formation is one of the most active anabolic processes in the body. In the adult about 2×10^{11} of these cells are replaced by the bone marrow every 24 h. Each milliliter of blood contains approximately 5 billion erythrocytes, and since the average life span is normally about 120 days, $\frac{1}{120}$ of the circulating cells (about 25 g) must be removed every day from the circulation. This 120-day life span represents the interval between a cell's delivery from the bone marrow and its ultimate destruction. The process of elimination results in almost 1 percent of the total RBCs in the body being destroyed daily.

Clinical Consideration of Red Blood Cell Maturity

When bone marrow produces RBCs at a very rapid rate in response to body demands, many of the released cells are not mature. The degree of immaturity and the number of cells present in the bloodstream at any one time reflect the stress that is being placed upon the system. When demands for production are great, the percentage of circulating reticulocytes may rise as much as 30 to 50 percent above normal. Should the demand continue or increase, a cell type which is even more immature, the *normoblast,* may appear in large numbers. In some of the serious anemias the number of normoblasts may be as high as 5 to 20 percent of all circulating RBCs. Cells of even greater immaturity, the erythrocyte precursors such as *proerythroblasts,* may also appear in the circulating blood. This information has diagnostic significance in the determination of the various types of anemias. In general, there are classic abnormalities associated with specific types of anemias. See Table 5-1 for normal RBC values at various ages. Figure 5-1 depicts the various erythrocyte precursors.

Leukocytes: White Blood Cells

The leukocytes are the body's primary defense against infectious and parasitic organisms and they function in the immune response. Leukocytes are larger than red blood cells and are nucleated. The different types of white blood cells (WBCs) are classified on the basis of their unique structure and the affinity of each cell type for a certain dye (Fig. 5-1). Polymorphonuclear granulocytes (PMNs) include those WBCs which have a granular appearance because of the presence of various cytoplasmic granules. Occasionally these are referred to as "polys." Granulocytes are of three types: neutrophils, eosinophils, and basophils. Nongranular leukocytes are of two types: monocytes and lymphocytes. Table 5-1 shows the normal values for each type of WBC at various ages and for male and female adults.

Although the leukocytes are less numerous than RBCs, this group of blood cells contains a variety of cells which are specialized for different functions. As mentioned, the primary function of the WBCs is to provide the required humoral and cellular response to invading infectious organisms and foreign antigens. This function is accomplished in part by a process called *phagocytosis*. Through this process the neutrophils and monocytes ingest and destroy invading organisms and foreign particles. Although the leukocytes are transported via the circulating blood to all parts of the body, phagocytosis actually occurs within the interstitial fluid.

Neutrophils

Neutrophils are the most numerous of the granulocytes. They make up 60 to 70 percent of the total number of WBCs in the peripheral blood of adults and 18 to 40 percent in infants.

The nuclei of neutrophils stain deeply with neutral dye. The nuclei are irregular and often have shapes which look like the letters *E, Z,* and *S.* Delicate filaments separate segments of the cell, making it appear that there are several nuclei. Such filaments have length but no breadth. A *segmented* neutrophil has at least two of its lobes separated by such filaments. A *band* neutrophil has either a strand of nuclear material that is thicker than one of these filaments connecting the lobes, or a U-shaped nucleus of uniform thickness. The number of lobes in normal neutrophils ranges from two to five. This description is given as a basis for a later discussion of various findings in different clinical situations.

Segmented neutrophils average 56 percent of leukocytes, whereas band neutrophils average 3 percent. A *shift to the left* occurs when there is an increased number of bands and less mature neutrophils in the blood, as well as a lower than average number of lobes in segmented cells.

Neutrophilia

Neutrophilia is defined as an increase in the number of circulating neutrophils and is associated with any inflammatory process. Neutrophils are attracted to areas of inflammation and bacterial proliferation by *chemotaxis*. Chemotaxis occurs in response to the liberation of serum chemicals called *chemotaxins*. This reaction is quite complex, and it is suggested that there is participation by the complement system and the blood coagulation system, as well as interaction with agents such as kallikrein and plasminogen activator. In fact, neutrophils themselves may release chemotaxic substances. (See Chap. 25 for further discussion.)

Neutrophilia can be expected to occur in association with any activity or process which increases the level of norephinephrine in the bloodstream. Such diverse conditions as foreign protein injection, extreme exercise, blood loss, and excessive fatigue all result in an increase in circulating neutrophils. The vasodilatory effects of norepinephrine and the resultant increase in blood flow through capillary beds flush out sequestered leukocytes. Rapid blood flow through the capillaries mobilizes these granular leukocytes, making them available for response to any insulted body tissue.

Eosinophils

The mature eosinophil comprises 2 to 4 percent of the total number of leukocytes in the adult peripheral circulation. The cell is slightly larger than the mature neutrophil, and the nucleus occupies a relatively smaller volume of the cell. The function of eosinophils is thought to be detoxification of foreign proteins, but this is still under investigation. During an allergic attack the total number of circulating eosinophils increases, collecting at the site of antigen-antibody reaction. Eosinophils are thought to be responsible for the removal of the antigen-antibody complex from the bloodstream upon completion of the immune response. Eosinophils are present in large numbers in the mucosa of the intestinal tract and also in the tissues of the lungs. Both of these locations are points of entry of foreign protein into the body.

Eosinophils are also thought to participate in the digestion of fibrin clots. These WBCs migrate into blood clots where they secrete an enzyme, *plasmin,* which is responsible for clot digestion. This function is considered important in the removal of old clots from the bloodstream.

With respect to their phagocytic activity, eosinophils are referred to as *microphages.* These WBCs are thought to be active in the phagocytosis of the causative organism of trichinosis, the trichinae parasite. The suggested function of the eosinophil is the detoxification of the protein substances secreted by these organisms.

Basophils

A third type of leukocyte with specific granules is the basophil. The basophil is not a phagocytic cell per se, but basophils are similar to mast cells, which are located outside many of the body's capillaries. Mast cells liberate heparin into the bloodstream. Endogenously secreted heparin is considered important in preventing blood clot formation or growth, and also active in accelerating the removal of fat particles from the bloodstream after a fatty meal. Basophils have a high content of heparin and histamine and play an important role in acute systemic allergic reactions. When the basophil undergoes degranulation during an anaphylactic reaction, it liberates heparin and histamine in the process.

Although normally the total number of basophils is relatively low, this number may increase during asthma as well as in association with myeloproliferative disorders such as tuberculosis, estrogen administration, carcinoma, postsplenectomy, inflammatory bowel disease, and hypothyroidism. A slight elevation is maintained in states of chronic inflammation. Inflammation has a coagulant effect upon RBCs and it is theorized that the increase in basophils is in response to the body's need for more heparin to prevent RBC loss in coagulation.

Monocytes

Monocytes are regarded as mobile components of the reticuloendothelial system (RES). Most of the RES is composed of fixed cells lining sinusoids in the lymph nodes, liver, and bone marrow. Mature monocytes are released into the circulation and are carried to their sites of function.

Monocytes are the largest of the nongranular leukocytes, but they have relatively few cytoplasmic granules. Upon release into the bloodstream, they are transformed into mature forms known as *macrophages*. Macrophages are capable of phagocytizing large foreign particles and cell fragments. They even have the capacity to engulf whole red blood cells and the malarial parasite. An important function of the macrophage is to phagocytize necrotic tissue in chronic infections.

Both the microphage (eosinophil) and macrophage contain large quantities of lysosomal enzymes which are both proteolytic and lipolytic. In addition, these phagocytes contain substances which are bactericidal; that is, they are capable of destroying bacteria before they can multiply and destroy the phagocytic cell.

In the process of combatting infection and clearing necrotic debris, the phagocytes themselves eventually die. The accumulation of the dead phagocytes and varying composition of necrotic tissue result in the production of material commonly known as *pus*.

The body's ability to contain the infectious process and prevent its dissemination is a vital component of the defense function of these cells.

Monocytes have demonstrated a unique sensitivity in in vitro studies with corticosteroids. After brief exposure to low concentrations of hydrocortisone, monocytes show impaired random movement, chemotaxis, and bactericidal activity.

Leukocytosis, Significance of Cell Type and Age

The term *leukocytosis* refers to an absolute increase in the concentration of white blood cells in the peripheral blood. No reference is made to the degree of immaturity or cell type with this definition, and both of these are important considerations. The normal range for the WBC is 5000 to 10,000 per mm³. In the healthy adult, leukocytosis is present whenever the total white blood cell count is above 10,000 to 12,000 per mm³. *Granulocytosis* refers to an increase in the number of circulating granulocytes and is calculated as the product of the total leukocyte count and the percent of the cell type in the differential. The upper limit of normal for the absolute number of neutrophils is 8000 per mm³.

Various types of nonpathologic stimuli such as exercise, sudden emotional surges, or administration of epinephrine may produce an increase in the circulating granulocytes as much as two to three times normal. These acute reactions result from the release of the granulocytes from maturation-storage pools in the bone marrow.

Pathologic stimuli which produce neutrophilic leukocytosis include infections, inflammation, invasive tumors, and myeloproliferative disease. The mechanism producing the increase in granulocytes may be increased proliferation, prolongation of survival time, shift of this type of WBC from storage to the circulating pool, or any combination of these factors. The observed response in terms of cell type tends to be quite specific to the inciting stimuli. In certain granulomatous disorders, monocytes respond; in allergic and parasitic conditions, however, it is the eosinophils which respond by increasing. Basophilic leukocytes are associated with hypersensitivity reactions. If the stimuli or stress on the system continues over a period of time, immature forms of these cell types may be seen, and this is diagnostic of the magnitude of the disorder.

Neutrophilia: Shift to the Left; Shift to the Right

Pyogenic bacteria in particular induce neutrophilia, or neutrophilic leukocytosis (an increase in the absolute count of neutrophils). Typically this type of infection is a localized process such as appendicitis, salpingitis, and otitis media. In general, it is believed that the more pathogenic the agent, the higher the resulting neutrophil count. In fact, the height of the leukocytosis is frequently used as an index of the individual's resistance potential. A *shift to the left* refers to a neutrophilic leukocytosis in which there is an increase in young or immature forms and in segmented forms of neutrophils. The greater the shift to the left, the more severe the infection. As mentioned previously, there is also an increase in the number of bands as well as a lower average number of lobes in the segmented cells.

A *shift to the right* refers to an increase in the mature hypersegmented polymorphonuclear leukocytes. This type of shift, in contrast to the infectious etiology of the shift to the left, is associated with pernicious anemia and chronic morphine addiction. It has been reported that in early chronic granulocytic leukemia, it is possible to occasionally see both types of shifts simultaneously, i.e., a right and a left shift.

Immunocytes, Lymphocytes and Plasma Cells

The immunocytes work synergistically with the phagocytes to maintain the integrity of the whole organism against invading organisms. Immunocytes are classified morphologically as lymphocytes, plasma cells, and their precursor cells. Lymphocytes are mononuclear leukocytes which originate and first differentiate in the primary lymphoid structures of the bone marrow and the thymus gland and then are distributed to the secondary lymphoid tissue of the lymph nodes, spleen, Peyer's patches in the liver, and the intestines.

Lymphocytes have a relatively large nucleus and scanty nongranular cytoplasm. These cells make up about 20 to 35 percent of the total leukocytes in the normal adult and approximately 40 to 70 percent of the leukocytes in infants.

As mentioned in the discussion of the hematoblast and stem cells, there is some controversy with regard to the exact participant(s) in the sequence of development of precursor cells. In general, the precursor of the lymphocyte is believed to be the multipotential, primitive stem cell that also gives rise to the common progenitor cell of the myeloid, erythroid, and megakaryocytic cell lines. Lymphoid precursor cells travel to specific sites and then differentiate into cells capable of either expressing cell-mediated immune responses or secreting immunoglobulins. The influence for the former type of differentiation in man is

the thymus gland. The resulting cell type is defined as a *thymus-dependent lymphocyte,* or *T cell.* The site of formation of lymphocytes with the potential to differentiate into antibody-producing cells (plasma cells) has not been definitively identified. In chickens it is the bursa of Fabricius, and for this reason lymphocytes from the "bursa-equivalent" organ in human beings are called *B cells.* These lymphocytes are thought to originate from central and peripheral lymphoid tissue, which includes the thymus, bone marrow, lymph nodes, and spleen.

Lymphocytes participate in the process of immunity in several unique ways. It is this cell type that gives specificity to the attack by phagocytes upon foreign antigenic material. Memory of such specificity is also a responsibility of these immunocytes, so that future defenses against a known antigenic agent are more rapidly mobilized. The immune response is described in detail in Chap. 25.

Traditionally the concept of immunity was almost synonymous with infectious disease. If an individual was fortunate enough to have survived an actue infection, that person was then considered to have developed an immunity, i.e., a resistance against future episodes of that particular infection.

The concept of immunity has broadened in recent years to include other than infectious agents. Through this process an individual organizes an immune attack against a foreign protein or tissue, but not against his or her own or genetically identical tissue. The immune system is extremely sensitive in its ability to recognize even slight differences between what is "self" or native to the organism and what is foreign or "nonself."

Plasma Cells

Plasma cells are free cells and nonnuclear, and are found primarily in lymphatic tissue, lymph nodes, the spleen, and also in the connective tissues throughout the body. They are the primary producers of antibody (gamma globulin). There is a close relationship between lymphocytes and plasma cells. Following appropriate antigenic stimulation, the bone marrow–dependent B lymphocytes have the capacity to differentiate into antibody-producing plasma cells. In fact, B lymphocytes are considered plasma cell precursors. This conversion is highly specific, since only those antigens which chemically and physically fit with the already produced immunoglobulin can trigger the reaction. The role of the antigen is very specific. It stimulates the differentiation of the B lymphocyte cell and induces a high level of antibody formation.

Abnormal malignant proliferation of plasma cells produces a condition known as *multiple myeloma*. Individuals with this disease have an increased susceptibility to infections which is believed to be the result of the disturbed antibody formation resulting from the plasma cell abnormalities.

Platelets

Platelets are the smallest of the formed elements of the blood. They are minute biconvex disks about 2 to 3 μm in diameter. Platelets are formed by the cytoplasmic division of *megakaryoctyes*. Megakaryocytes are extremely large cells of the hematopoietic series present in the adult in the bone marrow, lung, and spleen. The separation of the individual platelets from the parent cell is an orderly process involving the formation and fusion of small cytoplasmic vesicles to form the platelet membrane. It is estimated that each megakaryocyte is capable of producing more than a thousand platelets. Figure 5-1 depicts platelet precursors.

Platelets normally have a life span of 7 to 14 days. Approximately 10 to 15 percent of circulating platelets are continually being consumed in normal ongoing intravascular clot formation. Previously it was thought that platelets also were consumed or utilized in the maintenance of normal vascular integrity. However, there is now evidence against this theory, since electron microscopy has failed to demonstrate this phenomenon in normal animals. Currently the more acceptable theory is that platelets are used to repair small vascular injuries but not to support or maintain normal endothelium.

The platelet count for a normal adult ranges from 150,000 to 400,000 per mm³, with slightly higher levels being found in arterial blood. In general there is no sex-linked difference in platelet counts, although variation in the normal range is associated with the menstrual cycle and with pregnancy. A slight increase in platelet count is reported to occur at the time of ovulation, followed by a progressive decrease in the 14 days preceding menstruation. A second rapid increase occurs after the onset of menses. During pregnancy there is a slight progressive decline in the platelet count which may evidence an even further decrease in the first stage of labor. Later in the puerperium the platelet count reflects a moderate thrombocytosis.

Variables Affecting Quantity and Quality of Platelets

The rate of platelet production and the level of circulating platelets are believed to be controlled by two factors: the actual number of platelets which are circulating and a humoral factor called *thrombopoietin* or thrombopoietic stimulating factor. It has been demonstrated that chronic thrombocytopenia may very well be the result of the deficiency of a factor which is normally present in the plasma and which is necessary for the maturation of megakaryocytes and therefore normal platelet production. Relatedly, it is now believed that the clinical value of using fresh whole blood in correcting platelet deficiencies is predicated upon the fact that the transfusion provides the thrombopoietin versus providing platelet replacement or supplement.

The level of circulating catecholamines has been documented to have a profound effect on platelet levels. Administration of adrenalin produces an immediate 20 to 50 percent increase in the platelet count. This response is thought to be the result of platelet mobilization from the splenic pool. However, since an increase in the platelet count, which is normally associated with exercise, has been demonstrated to occur in patients after a splenectomy, it is now believed that the lung also releases platelets into the circulation. Regardless of the type of stimulus, i.e., exercise or catecholamines, the platelet count will return to normal within 30 min after the initial rise. The biochemical effects of exercise are reported to be associated with adenosine-diphosphate (ADP)-induced platelet aggregation and platelet adhesion. Platelets effect most of their hemostatic function by *aggregation* and *adhesion*. Aggregation refers to platelets attaching to one another. Adhesion is the attachment of platelets to nonplatelet surfaces, e.g., blood vessel wall or foreign surfaces.

Other variables are known to influence the quantity and quality of circulating platelets. Altitude, hypoxia, and smoking may influence both the number and the characteristics of platelets. A significant increase in platelet number is produced by high altitudes, and in animal studies even short-term hypoxia produces thrombocytosis. Studies have suggested that smoking may not only shorten the life of platelets but also may produce the hyperaggregability of these cell fragments. A large number of disease states as well as various drugs are also associated with adverse effects upon platelet number and function.

Platelets in Hemostasis

Platelets are often referred to as *thrombocytes* because of the primary role which platelets play in hemostasis. Platelets contribute to hemostasis in two distinct ways. They participate in the hemostatic mechanism physically by occluding rents and tears in small vessels by the formation of platelet plugs. They are also involved in the coagulation process by their biochemical activities.

During the process of coagulation the platelets respond to thrombin in an all-or-none fashion. This response of platelets is referred to as the *release reaction*. During the release reaction the platelets release intracellular constituents into the surrounding plasma, e.g., ADP, adenosine triphosphate (ATP), serotonin, catecholamines, potassium, calcium, and platelet factor 4. This is not a passive process but is energy-dependent and is accomplished by the cell's contractile mechanism. The release reaction is considered to be a secretory function which resembles secretory processes observed in other cell systems, such as in the adrenal gland. The functioning of platelets in hemostasis is measured in the standard tests summarized in Table 5-2.

Relative and Absolute Thrombocytopenia

Platelets must be both qualitatively or functionally adequate in addition to being present in adequate numbers. An artificial thrombocytopenia, a clinical state in which lab values reflect normal or near normal platelet levels, may exist if the platelets are functionally abnormal. This possibility must always be considered should unexplained bleeding (oozing) or petechiae occur in the presence of normal platelet levels.

Characteristics of Platelets

The mature platelet is a complex structure and is quite active metabolically, although like the erythrocyte, it contains no nucleus. Protein comprises about 52 to 60 percent of the dry weight of thrombocytes and approximately 10 percent of their net weight. Some of the protein is bound in the form of enzymes, while the remainder is incorporated in structural components of the cell. A number of different platelet proteins have been identified. Two of these are of particular importance in hemostasis. Fibrinogen, normally considered to be only a plasma protein, represents between 10 and 13 percent of the soluble protein fraction present in platelets. Fibrinogen, as will be discussed later, undergoes physical and chemical changes to form the fibrin threads of the clot. With respect to platelet function, fibrinogen is an essential cofactor for ADP-induced platelet aggregation besides being involved in other platelet activities.

Another platelet protein active in hemostasis and having unique contractile properties is called *thrombostenin*. Platelets have occasionally been referred to as *muscle cells*. Thrombostenin is believed to be active in the consolidation phase of the hemostatic plug formation, which is characterized by active contraction of the platelet mass. Ninety percent of the total amount of platelet thrombostenin is contained in the cytoplasm, while the remainder is located on the surface of the platelet.

TABLE 5-2
Tests of Hemostatic Function: Platelets

Test	Function tested	Normal value
Platelet count	Number of platelets	Approximately 1 platelet per 20 RBC (assuming normal RBC count)
		150,000–400,000/mm³ (150–400 × 10⁹/L)
Bleeding time	Platelet plug formation	Earlobe: 1–3 min Forearm: 5–7 min
Clot retraction	Ability of platelets to support retraction of a clot	50% retraction within 1 h Compare to normal value
Platelet aggregation	Ability of platelets to aggregate	Compare to normal control
Platelet phospholipid (factor 3) availability	Availability of platelet phospholipid for coagulation	Compare to normal control

Source: Zieve, P. D., and L. Levin: *Disorders of Hemostasis,* Philadelphia: Saunders, 1976, p. 10. Used with permission.

Coagulation Factor XIII

Coagulation factor XIII is an intracellular constituent of platelets. Platelets contain approximately 30 to 50 percent of the total amount of this factor.

Platelet Coagulation Factors

Platelets contain other substances which are active in blood coagulation and which are unique to thrombocytes. These are indicated in the literature by arabic numbers rather than by the roman numerals which are used to indicate the plasma coagulation factors. There are four platelet factors, factors 1 through 4.

Platelet factor 1 is also plasma coagulation factor V, which is contained within the platelets.

Platelet factor 2 is a protein known as *fibrinogen-activating factor*. It accelerates the clotting of fibrinogen by thrombin: thrombin-catalyzed fibrinogen→fibrin monomer. It has been suggested that platelet factor 2 acts as a specific proteolytic enzyme rendering fibrinogen more sensitive as a substrate for thrombin activation.

Platelet factor 3 is a phospholipid-like activity present in platelets which becomes evident when platelets aggregate. This activity can develop even when the release reaction does not occur. Although not sufficient to initiate clotting, platelet factor 3's presence is necessary for clotting in the intrinsic system.

Platelet factor 4 is also known for its heparin-neutralizing activity. It is a glycoprotein which is released from platelets which have been aggregated. Several procoagulant activities are associated with this factor, and it is suggested that it is an extremely potent and specific triggering agent in vivo, in addition to being active in platelet aggregation and in coagulation.

Bleeding Associated with Platelets

Thrombocytopenia, quantitative platelet deficiency, is one of the most common causes of hemorrhagic diatheses. This condition is characterized clinically by petechiae and ecchymoses of the skin and mucous membranes. Bleeding produced by platelet deficiency differs from that observed in disorders of plasma coagulation factors in that platelet-associated bleeding results in petechiae of the skin and mucous membranes and a tendency to internal (cerebral and gastrointestinal), menorrhagic, epistaxis, gingival, and tongue bleeding. The petechiae are more numerous over dependent areas of the body because of increased venous pressure. If these grow and become confluent, large ecchymoses will occur, but petechiae still tend to be present at the margins. Coagulopathies of nonplatelet etiology tend to involve hemorrhages into skin, muscle, and joints in contrast to the more superficial areas of petechial involvement. A general tendency toward bleeding occurs with or without petechiae when platelet levels fall below 100,000 per mm^3.

COAGULATION AND COAGULATION FACTORS

The process of visible coagulation and fibrin clot formation represents the end result of a very intricate series of reactions that involve a number of different factors present in the blood and tissues. These substances influence the clotting mechanism either by promoting clotting with *procoagulants,* or by retarding or inhibiting clotting with *anticoagulants;* some even function in the removal of the clot once it is formed. Coagulation function can be measured by the standard tests reviewed in Table 5-3.

Nomenclature

Within the circulating blood there are certain trace proteins known collectively as *clotting factors.* These proteins or *procoagulants* directly participate in the coagulation process. Over the years considerable misunderstanding and confusion has developed related to their identification and description. During one era, descriptive names such as *fibrinogen, thrombin,* and *prothrombin* were used. Later functional names such as *labile* and *stable factors* were adopted to describe these proteins. Then there was a period of time during which the surnames of the kindreds in which the hereditary defects were initially observed were used to identify the clotting factors, such as Hageman, Stuart, Fletcher, and so on. To compound the problem, not infrequently several names were being used simultaneously to describe the same substance.

In an attempt to remedy the problem, an international committee established a nomenclature of blood clotting factors. Roman numerals are now used to identify the various factors in the order of their discovery. (This numerical sequence in no way suggests their order of reaction and participation in the coagulation process.) In addition to the roman numerals, a shorthand abbreviation, a subscript letter *a,* is used

TABLE 5-3
Tests of Hemostatic Function: Coagulation

Test	Function tested	Normal value
Clotting time of whole blood	Intrinsic and common pathways	5–10 min to clot 50% retraction within 1 h
Partial thromboplastin time (PTT)	Intrinsic and common pathways	Unactivated: 60–90 s Activated: 30–60 s
Prothrombin time	Extrinsic and common pathways	Varies according to source thromboplastin Compare to normal control (usually 12–15 s)
Thrombin time	Fibrinogen concentration: structure of fibrinogen; presence of inhibitors	Varies according to concentration of thrombin: Compare to normal value
Specific factor assay	Concentration of functional factor in plasma	50–150% of activity in pooled normal plasma

Source: Zieve, P. D., and L. Levin: *Disorders of Hemostasis,* Philadelphia: Saunders, 1976, p. 12. Used with permission.

to indicate the active forms of each factor. For example, conversion of factor X to its active form is written $X------X_a$. It is worth mentioning again that the platelet factors which are active in clotting are indicated by arabic numerals to distinguish them from the coagulation factors. (See Table 5-4.)

Intrinsic and Extrinsic System of Coagulation

Two chains or cascades have been used to describe the interaction of the coagulation factors which evolve to a final common pathway of clot formation. In effect, each are alternate modes of activating factor X. In the *intrinsic* pathway, all the procoagulants necessary for clot formation are contained within the circulating blood. This system is activated when factor XII contacts an abnormal surface. In turn, factors XI, IX, VIII, X, II, and I are activated. In contrast, the *extrinsic* system requires the release of tissue factor from the endothelial cells or other tissue extracts before activation can occur. The extrinsic system is activated when the tissue factor contacts factor VII, producing sequential activation of factors X, V, II, and I.

Whether the inciting stimulus occurs when the blood comes in contact with an abnormal surface (the intrinsic system) or when tissue thromboplastin gains access to the bloodstream (the extrinsic system), the final result is the same—the production of large amounts of thrombin followed by the transformation of fibrinogen to fibrin. Figure 5-2 depicts this sequential reaction.

Coagulation Factors

Factor I (Fibrinogen)

Fibrinogen is the protein converted into fibrin by the action of the proteolytic enzyme, thrombin. The resulting fibrin strands form the microstructure of the hemostatic plug. When fibrin is mixed with thrombin, two peptides are split off, resulting in a fibrin monomer which then undergoes continuous polymerization and depolymerization in the bloodstream. The rapid turnover of fibrinogen in the bloodstream suggests that this process of polymerization and depolymerization occurs normally and continually in the bloodstream in addition to that which may be taking place at the endothelial surface of traumatized blood vessels.

Fibrinogen is a relatively insoluble glycoprotein synthesized by the parenchymal cells in the liver. It is normally found in the bloodstream, in the lymph, and in many tissues. Approximately 75 percent of the total body pool is present in the circulating blood. This clotting factor is thought to be essential in normal platelet function and in the process of wound healing.

In health, the concentration of fibrinogen in the blood remains relatively constant. Normal values of fibrinogen range from 200 to 400 mg per 100 mL of blood. It is produced by the liver and catabolized at about the same rate. The overall mechanism of fibrinogen catabolism is still under study.

Various disease states may increase fibrinogen metabolism. These include conditions such as cirrhosis, multiple myeloma, and nephrosis. In fact, virtually any disorder associated with stress, inflammation, or tissue necrosis may produce hyperfibrin-

TABLE 5-4
Coagulation Proteins of the Blood

Factor	Synonym	Non-pregnant, mg/mL	Pregnant, Mg/dL
I	Fibrinogen	200–400	300–700
II	Prothrombin	100	92
III	Thromboplastin		
IV	Calcium		
V	Proaccelerin	75–125	200–400
VII	Proconvertin	72–125	
VIII	Antihemophilic globulin (AHG)	75–150	200–600
IX	Christmas factor or plasma thromboplastin, component (PTC)	75–150	200–600
X	Stuart-Prower factor	75–125	200–400
XI	Plasma thromboplastin antecedent (PTA)	70–130	
XII	Hageman factor	70–130	
XIII	Fibrin stabilizing factor (FSF)	9.4 U	4.6 U
Platelet		175,000–400,000	

Source: Coopland, A. T.: The hemostatic mechanism and its disturbances in pregnancy," in *Perinatal Medicine,* Baltimore: Williams & Wilkins, 1976, p. 449. Used with permission.

ogenemia. This response develops within a matter of hours and is the major factor leading to acceleration of the erythrocyte sedimentation rate (ESR, or sed rate). Normal increases in fibrinogen are associated with pregnancy as well as with the administration of anovulatory drugs, in addition to elevations associated with hypermetabolic states.

Depressed fibrinogen levels are associated with hypothyroidism. Large amounts of circulating tissue thromboplastin may produce a severe depression of fibrinogen. As will be discussed later, tissue thromboplastin is a procoagulant material which interacts with fibrinogen to form the microstructure of the fibrin clot. *Fibrinogenopenia,* also known as *hypofibrinogenemia* or *defibrination,* is associated with the entry into the bloodstream of fragments of various body tissues which are particularly rich in tissue thromboplastin. These areas include the lungs and prostatic and cerebral tissues, in addition to fragments of placenta which happen to gain access to the maternal circulation. Regardless of the source, when such

tissue enters the circulation, large quantities of fibrinogen are consumed in the formation of fibrin clots. A consumption coagulopathy is produced, since platelets and other clotting factors are also depleted in the process of disseminated intravascular clotting. The magnitude of the coagulation response is directly related to the quantity of the entering tissue thromboplastin and also to the ability of the reticuloendothelial system to cope with imposed stress.

The production of fibrinogen is known to increase under various experimental conditions, and there is now evidence that suggests that fibrinogen degradation products (fibrin split products) may constitute the major regulator of the synthesis rate of fibrinogen. Relatedly, recent research has demonstrated that free fatty acids increase fibrinogen synthesis by human liver slices. This could have clinical implications because of the association of the release of free fatty acids with long-bone fractures and the possible adverse effect that this might have on enhanced clotting or thrombus formation.

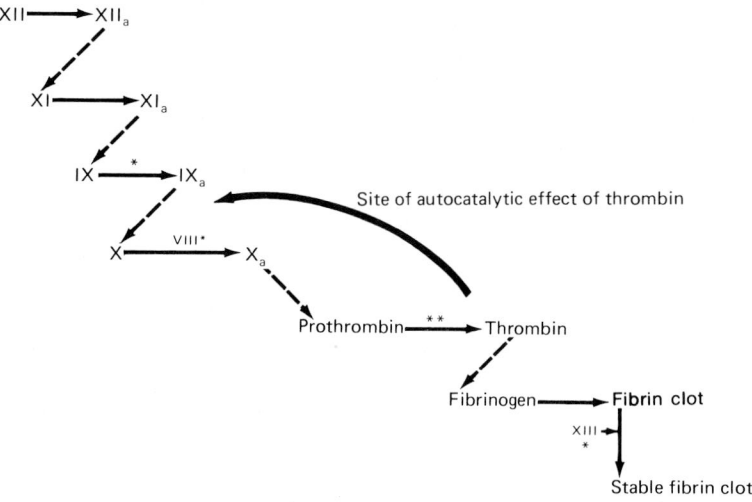

* Reaction requires calcium ions
** Reaction requires calcium and platelet phospholipid

FIGURE 5-2

The coagulation sequence. [*Adapted from C. Hudak, B. Gallo, and T. Lohr,* (eds.), *Critical Care Nursing, Lippincott, Philadelphia, 1973.*]

Factor II (Prothrombin)

Prothrombin, the inactive precursor of thrombin, is constantly present in the blood in excess of clotting requirements. Even with a 50 percent reduction in the blood volume, blood can clot normally.

Prothrombin is one of four vitamin K–dependent factors; that is, the hepatocyte requires the presence of vitamin K for prothrombin synthesis. (The other three factors which are dependent upon the presence of vitamin K are factors VII, IX, and X, with some reports that factor XI may also be vitamin K–dependent. These will be discussed later.) It is suggested that vitamin K acts as a rate regulator for the assembly of the prothrombin molecule and may be responsible for the calcium binding sites. When vitamin K is deficient, regardless of the cause, a marked decrease in prothrombin occurs.

Vitamin K is not stored in the body but is synthesized by bacteria which are part of the normal intestinal flora. Should this flora be disturbed, as when certain antibiotics are given, a decrease in prothrombin will result. Since vitamin K is a fat-soluble vitamin, bile salts produced by the liver are required for its absorption from the intestinal tract. Diseases which interfere with fat absorption, such as obstructive jaundice and steatorrhea, may produce impaired vitamin K absorption.

Severe liver disease may also produce the same type of deficiency as vitamin K deficiency because the liver cells, in this case, are unable to utilize vitamin K sufficiently to make prothrombin in adequate quantities. Coumarin-type anticoagulants, when present in therapeutic blood levels, may also alter the level of circulating prothrombin.

Congenital hemorrhagic diseases of the newborn were previously attributed to a maternal diet deficient in vitamin K. This line of reasoning leads to the practice of prophylactic administration of vitamin K to the pregnant mother prior to delivery and to the neonate. Vitamin K is no longer thought to be routinely necessary to be administered to the normal neonate. In fact, large doses of vitamin K are contraindicated because these tend to produce even more hemolysis and thus increase the extent of jaundice.

Catabolism of prothrombin is increased by fever and hyperthyroidism, whereas hypothyroidism decreases it.

Factor III (Tissue Thromboplastin)

Homogenates of normal tissues are known to markedly accelerate blood coagulation. Tissue thromboplastin functions by interacting with factor VII in the extrinsic pathway. The active principle or its biochemistry has not been definitively described.

Although factor III is thought to arise from virtually any body tissue, the brain, lung, prostate, and placental tissue are particularly rich sources of tissue thromboplastin.

Factor IV (Calcium)

Factor IV, calcium, is found in the blood in normal concentrations of 9 to 11 mg/mL. Approximately 50 percent is present in the ionized state (Ca^{2+}). Only very small quantities of Ca^{2+} are required for normal functioning of the coagulation mechanism; therefore, calcium deficiency as a cause of a coagulopathy is quite rare. The coagulopathy which is an occasional exception to this statement is that associated with a large quantity of blood replacement therapy after a severe hemorrhage. The numerous transfusions with the citrated blood produce a relative hypocalcemia as a result of the combination of the ionized calcium with ethylenediaminetetraacetic acid (EDTA), oxalate, citrate, fluoride, and ion-exchange resins. These are irreversible reactions which make calcium unavailable for participation in the coagulation mechanism.

Hyperglobulinemia and Dysglobulinemia

Hyperglobulinemia and dysglobulinemia associated with sarcoidosis and myeloma may also result in abnormal binding of calcium. In these situations the calcium binds to the abnormal globulins, resulting in a hemostatic defect. The point to be emphasized in both of these conditions is that they produce a relative calcium deficiency in the presence of lab reports which reflect a normal calcium level or even hypercalcemia. Despite the normalcy of the clinical laboratory studies, calcium is not available for the coagulation process.

Factor V (Labile Factor, Ac Globulin, Proaccelerin)

Factor V occurs in the plasma of all normal persons. It is synthesized in the liver and is a labile, water-soluble globulin. Factor V is totally consumed in the process of coagulation and is not found in serum. Factor V is essential in the formation of prothrombin in the common pathway (Fig. 5-2). The extrinsic and intrinsic thromboplastic products appear to react with factor V in the presence of calcium (Ca^{2+}).

The fact that factor V is quite labile has made purification and thorough study of its biochemical role difficult. Its exact contribution in the process of coagulation remains unclear.

A congenital deficiency of factor V results from an autosomal recessive trait that is not sex-linked but which is manifested when the trait is inherited from both parents. The deficiency is characterized by parahemophilia, in which there is a tendency for excessive bleeding from vascular areas of the body, e.g., mucous membranes and from such occurrences as epistaxis and menorrhagia.

Acquired factor V deficiency may occur in severe liver disease (hepatocellular) or from circulating anticoagulants. Increased fibrinolysis (lysis of fibrin clots) may also produce factor V deficiency.

Factor VI

Factor VI is now known as *activated factor V.*

Factor VII (Stable Factor, Proconvertin)

Factor VII is related to prothrombin and is capable of being converted to prothrombin by the liver. It is subjected to the influences of vitamin K just as prothrombin is. Factor VII is active only in the presence of factor III.

In contrast to factor V, factor VII is quite stable. Stored serum is a useful source of factor VII; however, it decreases during the administration of bishydroxycoumarin and related drugs.

Factor VIII (Antihemophilic Factor)

Factor VIII, the antihemophilic factor, is a trace protein that is involved in the intrinsic pathway of coagulation. It is important because of the association of its molecular abnormality with hemophilia, in addition to the important role which it plays in the evolution of plasma thromboplastin.

Despite extensive study, the production site of this factor has yet to be established. Most investigation has involved study of the role of the liver, spleen, and reticuloendothelial system. The available data suggest that factor VIII originates in a system of cells that may be found in various organs. The primary source of factor VIII appears to be the liver, whereas the spleen is considered to be a major storage site. The most likely explanation is that there is involvement of two or more cellular or organ systems.

Factor VIII exhibits three distinct characteristics: procoagulant activity, antisera properties, and a portion which normally reacts with a specific reactor site on platelets, the von Willebrand factor.

Factor VIII is normally present in excess of need. Although it is required for thromboplastin generation, it has been determined that this process can proceed even when factor VIII is present at 40 percent of normal concentrations. Significant impairment of the coagulation mechanism does not occur until the concentration has dropped to between 10 and 20 percent of normal.

Circulating levels of factor VIII are reported to increase after vigorous exercise, following epinephrine administration, and in certain metabolic states.

Factor IX (Plasma Thromboplastin Component)

Factor IX, plasma thromboplastin, is also known as Christmas factor, antihemophilic factor B, and plasma thromboplastin component (PTC). This factor plays an essential role in the intrinsic pathway of coagulation. It is present in both serum and plasma. Plasma levels of factor IX are depressed by the pharmacologic activity of coumarin drugs although not as significantly as those of factors VII and X.

Clinically, abnormalities of factor IX are associated with the sex-linked recessive condition of hemophilia B, or Christmas disease. Like factor VII, it is also associated with hemorrhagic disease of the newborn.

Factor IX is associated with vitamin K deficiency, advanced hepatocellular disease, and with prolonged anti-vitamin K therapy.

Factor X (Stuart-Prower Factor)

Factor X is also known as Stuart-Prower factor or *autoprothrombin*. It is a glycoprotein which is found both in the plasma and in the serum. Factor X is required for intrinsic thromboplastin formation and for prothrombin conversion, although the exact nature or location of this clotting factor is not known.

The activity of factor X in the final common pathway It appears that factor X forms the final common pathway through which the products of both the extrinsic and intrinsic thromboplastin generating system proceed as they form the terminal thromboplastic substances necessary for the conversion of prothrombin to thrombin. This reaction requires the presence of Ca^{2+} and factor VI.

Deficiency of factor X is primarily seen as a hereditary disorder produced by an incompletely recessive autosomal trait. An acquired deficiency is seen in liver disease and vitamin K deficiency.

Factor XI (Plasma Thromboplastin Antecedent)

Factor XI, plasma thromboplastin antecedent (PTA), or antihemophilic factor, also appears to be essential in the intrinsic pathway. A deficiency of this factor is probably inherited as a simple autosomal dominant trait that leads to a mild hemophilia-like state following trauma or surgery. This disorder is referred to as *hemophilia C*. Plasma levels of this factor are frequently diminished in liver disease, despite the fact that proof of hepatic biosynthesis of this protein has yet to be established.

Factor XII (Hageman Factor)

Factor XII, also known as *Hageman factor,* is maintained in an inactive state in normal blood by the action of coagulation inhibitors. Factor XII reacts with factor XI to form an active prothromboplastic substance initiating the intrinsic pathway of coagulation. A deficiency of factor XII does not usually produce a hemorrhagic state, but it is associated with a prolonged venous clotting time, a long partial thromboplastin time, and an abnormal thromboplastin generation test. Clinically it is transmitted as an autosomal recessive trait.

There is evidence to suggest that activated factor XII (XIII_a) serves as a surface-sensitive trigger mechanism that translates the stimuli of injury into diverse physiologic process associated with hemostasis and fibrinolysis, humoral and cellular defense, and inflammation and wound healing.

Factor XIII (Fibrin Stabilizing Factor)

Fibrin stabilizing factor is a glycoprotein with as much as 50 percent of the amount present in the blood being associated with platelets. Clinical evidence suggests that the quantity that is associated with the platelets is actually synthesized by the megakaryocyte rather than being adsorbed from the plasma. Factor XIII acts in the common pathway of coagulation where it forms a stabilizing covalent bond within fibrin strands.

Although deficiency of factor XIII occurs in many patients with liver disease, direct evidence for biosynthesis is lacking. Explanation for this observation suggests that factor XIII may be activated by the liver or that the liver may produce an inhibitor of the factor. Hereditary deficiencies of factor XIII (and fibrinogen) are frequently associated with abnormal scar formation, wound dehiscence, postcircumcision bleeding, and bleeding from the umbilical stump.

MECHANISM OF COAGULATION

Over the years the sequence of reactions resulting in blood coagulation was considered to be of the nature of an enzyme-substrate reaction. According to this theory, each clotting factor functions as an enzyme which, upon activation, proceeds in a stepwise fashion in amplifying the reaction by activation of many times its own weight in substrate. In the process of activation, there is a net gain response in which a single molecule of an activated enzyme (clotting factor) converts not only one, but perhaps thousands of specific substrate molecules into active enzymes. A chain reaction, in a cascade or waterfall effect, occurs whereby activation of a single proenzyme molecule may lead to the explosive generation of the entire clotting mechanism. Figure 5-2 depicts this reaction.

This explanation of the coagulation mechanism is still proposed but with minor alteration. It has been reported that at least three of the reactions do not appear to follow the typical enzyme-substrate format. The following reactions are believed to result in the formation of a complex in contrast to the serial activation of a single enzyme substrate: the reaction involving factor III (tissue factor) and factor VII and calcium; the reaction involving activated factor IX, factor VIII, phospholipid, and calcium; and the reaction involving activated factor X, factor V, phospholipid, and calcium. In the formation of a complex, the product of the reaction is a mixture of several of the reactants. The current concept of the coagulation mechanism consists of both enzymatic conversion of the protein clotting factors and the formation of complexes (physical combination of reactants).

Positive Feedback

In addition to acting upon their primary substrate, some of the clotting factors are capable of activating other inactive clotting factors. For example, thrombin, in addition to acting upon fibrinogen, has the ability to activate factors V and VIII. Thrombin may also act upon and destroy platelets. Because of this ability to act upon these other factors, including platelets, as soon as a small amount of thrombin is formed, the clotting mechanism becomes autocatalytic (self-activating). A large amount of thrombin once formed can then rapidly activate even more platelets, degrading even more of the clotting factors, V and VIII, ultimately producing even more fibrin. Freely circulating thrombin can have a significant influence on the acceleration of the coagulation process because of this multiple activity.

Kallikrein, a substance which results from the activity of activated factor XII, and plasmin both have multiple effects on the coagulation mechanism. Plasmin will be considered under the topic of fibrinolysis. See Fig. 5-2 for cascade sequence and feedback effects.

Implications of the Cascade Theory

The theoretical basis for the cascade theory of coagulation is based upon the enzymatic activation of the various inactive clotting factors and the biological amplifier effect of this process. Although subscribed to for a number of years, the theoretical basis for this hypothesis has largely been based upon in vitro studies. Considerable research has yet to be done to establish the precise in vivo mechanism(s). The reader is encouraged to keep this point in mind and to evaluate future research in terms of whether the design was based on in vitro or in vivo study. Until disproved or qualified by new research findings, the cascade theory deserves mention and consideration in relation to its physiologic implications.

System Antagonists

The delicate balance that exists in health between clot formation and clot lysis is maintained by a number of factors and forces. Homeostasis of the hemostatic mechanism is maintained by a system of naturally occurring anticoagulant forces and factors, procoagulant activity of thrombin, and the lysis of formed clots by the fibrinolytic system. In fact, when one considers the proposed biological amplifier effect of enzyme activation and the positive feedback or autocatalytic effects of thrombin outlined in Fig. 5-2, one might well ask why episodes of exaggerated clotting do not occur. It is the precise interaction of these forces that maintains a system of checks and balances.

Coagulant Force

Thrombin is the most powerful coagulant force in the body. It has been reported that there is enough prothrombin in 10 mL of blood to clot 2500 mL of plasma in 15 s. Considering that the average adult male typically has about 5 L of blood within the circulatory system, the significance of these figures can be appreciated. This being the case, the factors and forces in the body which prevent abnormal clotting must be very effective.

Anticoagulant Forces

The anticoagulant forces normally present and active in the body include the following factors which serve as a system of checks and balances against the powerful procoagulant force of thrombin.

1. Smoothness of normal vascular endothelium

2. A monomolecular layer of negatively charged proteins which are described as repelling the positively charged clotting factors

3. Blood flow velocity which promotes dispersion of activated clotting factors which fail to be contained within the clot

4. Fibrin threads of the clot which are thought to absorb 85 to 90 percent of all activated thrombin, containing it within the clot

5. Antithrombin,[1] a plasma protein which is believed to inactivate that thrombin which fails to be contained within or absorbed to the clot

6. Heparin, produced by mast cells located primarily in the lungs and the liver, in addition to that produced by basophils; normally produced in minute quantities, but considered important in the ongoing maintenance of homeostasis

7. The functional capacity of the liver to both produce and filter activated clotting factors which fail to be contained within the clot

In addition to those specific factors and forces mentioned above, there are natural inhibitors of coagulation thought to be present and effective against every step in the process of coagulation. For example, there is a lipid inhibitor, antithromboplastin, normally present in the blood, which retards the formation of plasma thromboplastin (intrinsic system) or neutralizes plasma thromboplastin after it is formed. The basis for this activity is believed to be the binding of factor VIII and probably also factor IX, making them unavailable for thromboplastin generation. Dissociation of this lipid inhibitor occurs when platelet factor III is made available by platelet lysis or as a result of plasma dilution. Other natural inhibitors occur in women during or following pregnancy. In some disease states, such as lupus and cirrhosis, chelating of normal clotting factors can occur which make them unavailable for participation in the coagulation process.

Fibrinolytic Forces; Plasmin

Plasma contains two complex enzyme systems which function in hemostasis. In addition to the coagulation

---

[1] This substance is attracting increasing interest and study as an important anticoagulant.

system, there is a system that is responsible for the removal of the clot after its function has been accomplished and the integrity of the blood vessel has been restored. Once the vessel has been repaired, loss of blood no longer being a threat, restoration of distal blood flow is critical.

The fibrinolytic system is one of the most important defense mechanisms of the body. The activity of this system is mediated by the enzyme plasmin, which is capable of digesting fibrinogen and fibrin, in addition to two of the plasma coagulation factors, factors V and VIII. Plasmin also has the capacity to hydrolyze several other body proteins including ACTH, the growth hormone, and components of the complement system.

The specific effect of the fibrin lysis is the production of fibrin split products (FSP), also known as *fibrin degradation products* (FDP). Determination of the presence of FSP is a very sensitive lab test which can be used to monitor the abnormal activity of the fibrinolytic system (Table 5-5). Normally FSP should not be present in the circulation.

Plasminogen is normally present in the plasma but is kept in check by a system of activators and inhibitors. Plasma plasminogen activators can be found in trace amounts in all body fluids, in urine, and in most tissues. In body cells, the activators are proteolytic enzymes found in lysosomes, whereas in blood vessels the activator tends to be located in the endothelial lining. In general, the activators are a heterogenous group of proteins which react with plasminogen to produce plasmin. The activator concentrated in the endothelial lining of blood vessels is readily soluble and diffusible, and is available for release in response to a variety of vasoactive stimuli, especially vasodilation. It is this mechanism that provides for local concentration of the activator at the site of trauma or inflammation in time of need.

The activity of plasmin, called *fibrinolysis,* is considerably greater at all times within the microcirculation. It assumed that it is this high level of activity, as compared with that of the systemic circulation, that maintains patency of the capillary beds. The larger vessels, since they contain a lower concentration of endothelial cells, therefore contain a lower concentration of plasminogen activator. This situation would tend to suggest that the larger vessels are not as well prepared to deal effectively with fibrin deposition and thrombi formation. In fact, this lower level of fibrinolytic activity may be considered to somewhat predispose the larger vessels to the growth of clots, once formed.

Normally, when clots are formed, there is a certain amount of plasminogen and plasminogen activator

	TABLE 5-5 Tests of Hemostatic Function: Fibrinolysis		
Test	**Function tested**	**Normal value**	
Euglobulin lysis time	Fibrinolytic activity of plasma	90 min	
Assay of fibrinogen or fibrin degradation products (FSP)	Presence of FDP (FSP) in serum	1:8: 10 mg/mL* 1:4: 0–8 mg/mL*	

* Highest dilution of serum that is positive; or concentration, dependent upon assay.

Source: Zieve, P. D., and L. Levin: *Disorders of Hemostasis, Philadelphia: Saunders, 1976, p. 14. Used with permission.*

incorporated within the clot. It is also assumed that some plasminogen activator diffuses into the formed clot, providing an opportunity for the larger vessels to benefit from the circulating plasminogen activator. Whether the presence of the activator within the clot is due to the process of diffusion, absorption, or incorporation, once inside, plasmin activity mediates the progressive lysis of the clot.

Certain physiologic states are associated with transient increases of plasminogen activator above basal levels. These include intense exercise, sudden fright, and procedures such as electroshock and pneumoencephalography. Levels of plasma plasminogen, on the other hand, are increased by hypoglycemia, after administration of insulin and anabolic steroids, and following extensive surgery on the heart and lungs. Certain diseases such as prostatic malignancy and cirrhosis of the liver and various infections are also associated with elevated levels of plasminogen.

Plasma contains a large amount of antiplasmin activity. In fact it is estimated that there is a sufficient quantity of these substances to inactivate 10 times all the available plasmin in the plasma. This activity is believed to reside in the activity of two α-globulin components. Platelets are also known to contain some antiplasmin activity.

Anticoagulant Effects of Plasmin Activity

Fibrinolysis and coagulation are both normal components of the hemostatic response to vascular injury. Although both thrombin and plasmin have the capacity to act on fibrinogen, they act on different sites. The digestion of fibrinogen by plasmin produces fragments which are potent anticoagulants. They function in several ways: one fragment (X) may be acted upon by thrombin to form a fragile fibrin clot. This reaction occurs slowly, delaying the formation of a clot. Other fragments (Y, D, and E) do not form a clot, but the fragments inhibit fibrin polymerization and inhibit thrombin activity. Normally the situation described above is not problematic, but in situations of excessive clotting and clot lysis, these events aggravate a consumption coagulopathy. Figure 5-3 illustrates the action of plasmin and generation of plasmin split products.

Hemostasis

Normally, blood is in a liquid state circulating throughout the vascular compartment. Whenever a blood vessel loses its integrity and allows the escape of the liquid blood, clotting is initiated. Blood changes from its liquid state to a solid gel. The events in hemostasis include:

1. Vascular spasm

2. Sticking of the endothelial surfaces

3. Formation of the platelet plug

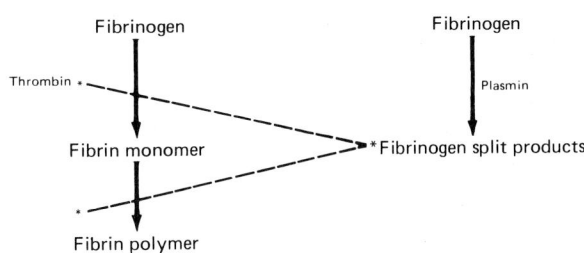

FIGURE 5-3

The action of plasmin in anticoagulation. (*The initial fibrin split products impair fibrin monomer formation, whereas late fibrin split products impair fibrin monomer polymerization.)

4. Formation of the blood clot (coagulation of plasma coagulation factors)

5. Clot retraction

6. Fibrous repair of the injured vessel wall

7. Clot lysis

Several of the events listed above are closely interrelated functionally and are simultaneous, whereas others occur in a sequential fashion.

Coagulation Process in Small Blood Vessels

A few seconds after the blood vessel is injured and integrity is lost, platelets adhere to the margin and stick to the exposed subendothelial fibers, usually collagen, forming a loose mesh. This mechanism, in addition to vasospasm, reduces blood loss. Platelets release potent chemicals which facilitate the process and which also attract more platelets. One of these chemicals is a thromboplastic substance essential to the coagulation mechanism. In the process the platelets extrude a contractile protein which draws together the threads of fibrin, producing retraction of the clot. Platelets and red blood cells are trapped within the clot as are plasminogen and plasminogen activator, substances which will ultimately produce plasmin, which lyses the clot. Within 30 to 60 min serum is expressed from the clot; it is estimated that after a few hours fibroblasts begin to invade the clot, initiating a fibrous organization. Complete fibrous organization of the clot into fibrous tissue requires approximately 7 to 10 days. This very effective mechanism prevents blood loss in arterioles, venules, and the capillaries of the microcirculation, but immediate mechanical action, e.g., pressure or a ligature, is required to stop blood loss in medium- to large-sized arteries and veins.

REFERENCES

Esnof, M. P.: Biochemistry of blood coagulation, *Br Med Bull,* 33:213–218, 1977.

Henry, J. B.: *Clinical Diagnosis and Management by Laboratory Methods,* vol. I, 16th ed., Philadelphia: Saunders, 1979.

Platt, W. R.: *Color Atlas and Textbook of Hematology,* 2d ed., Philadelphia: Lippincott, 1979.

Vander, A. J., S. Sherman, and D. Luciano: *Human Physiology—The Mechanisms of Body Functions,* 2d ed., New York: McGraw-Hill, 1975.

Weiss, H. J.: Platelet physiology and abnormalities of platelet function, *N Engl J Med,* 293: 531–540, 1975.

Williams, W. J., E. Beutler, A. J. Erslev, and R. W. Rundles (eds.), *Hematology,* 2d ed., New York: McGraw-Hill, 1977.

INTRODUCTION

A comprehensive approach to neuroanatomy and neurophysiology must include an understanding of the associated supportive, protective, and nutritional structures as well as the gross and microscopic anatomical and functional divisions of the nervous system. The structures which support, protect, and nourish the nervous system include the skull, vertebrae, meningeal layers, ventricular system,· and the cerebral vasculature.

The gross anatomical divisions of the nervous system are the *central nervous system* and the *peripheral nervous system.* The central nervous system (CNS) is composed of the brain, brainstem, and spinal cord. The peripheral nervous system comprises cranial and spinal nerves. The autonomic nervous system, which is frequently considered separately, is composed of part of the central and peripheral nervous systems.

Microscopically, the nervous system is composed of support structures called *neuroglial* cells, and the basic nerve cell, or *neuron.* The glial cells, which serve to support, protect, and nourish the neurons, include astrocytes, oligodendroglia, microglia, and ependymal cells. The astrocytes are located between the blood vessels and neurons, restricting the passage of substances into the central nervous system. The oligodendroglia synthesize and maintain myelin. The microglia serve as phagocytes. The ependymal cells, which line the ventricular system and the central canal of the spinal cord, play a major role in cerebrospinal fluid production. The peripheral neuroglia are found in ganglia and along nerve trunks.

The *neuron* is the structural, genetic, and functional unit of the nervous system. The neuron is composed of a cell body, dendrites, and axons. The *cell bodies,* or gray matter, are located in layers on the surface of the brain, or *cortex,* and in groups deeper within the brain; cell bodies are also found in the brainstem and spinal cord, and certain other locations.

Dendrites are short receptor fibers which receive impulses and conduct them to the cell body. *Axons* are the myelinated long fibers which transmit impulses away from the cell body. Within the central nervous system, the axons form the white matter. The *myelin sheath* is a semifluid protein and lipid substance surrounding the axon and providing insulation. *Schwann cells* form a delicate membrane which surrounds the myelin sheath of the peripheral nerve fibers (Fig. 6-1). Within the central nervous system, groups of axons with a common origin that travel alongside each other constitute a *tract.*

6
THE NERVOUS SYSTEM
Marilyn M. Ricci

INTRODUCTION

SUPPORT STRUCTURES OF THE CENTRAL NERVOUS SYSTEM
Skull
Vertebral Column
Meninges
Ventricular System
Cerebrospinal Fluid
Brain Barrier System
Vascular System

GROSS ANATOMY OF THE NERVOUS SYSTEM
The Brain
Cranial Nerves
Spinal Cord and Spinal Nerves
Autonomic Nervous System

PHYSIOLOGY OF THE NERVOUS SYSTEM
Sensory Integration
Motor Integration
Autonomic Nervous System
Reflex Activities

REFERENCES

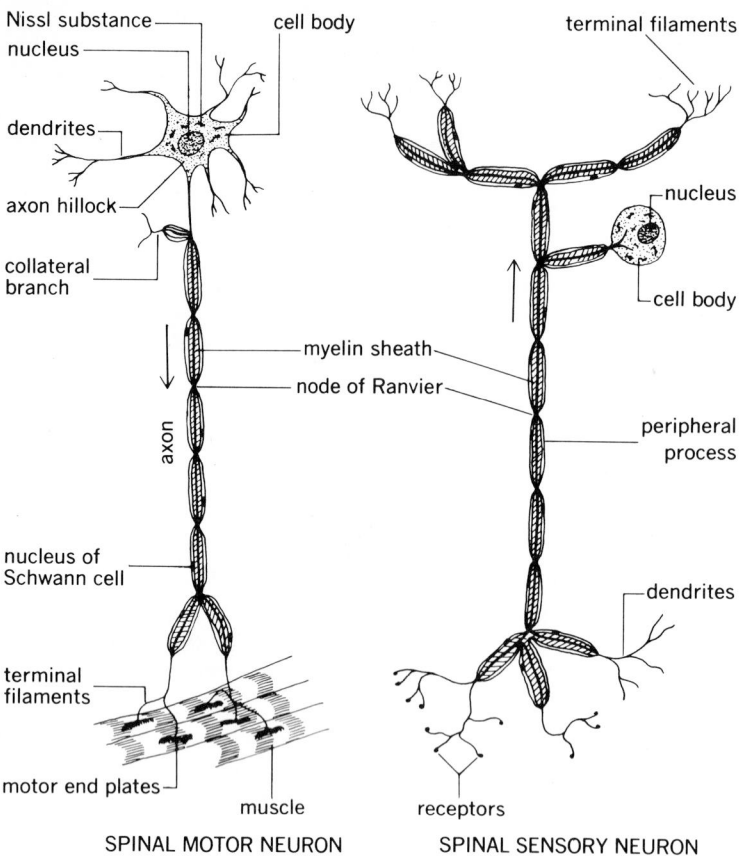

SPINAL MOTOR NEURON   SPINAL SENSORY NEURON

FIGURE 6-1

Two common types of neurons, motor and sensory. (*From R. M. DeCoursey, The Human Organism, 4th ed., McGraw-Hill, New York, 1974. Used by permission of the publisher.*)

Functionally, the nervous system is subdivided into (1) sensory or receptor mechanisms; (2) data processing, that is, integrative and interpretive, mechanisms; and (3) motor or effector mechanisms. The sensory input to the CNS is transmitted along *afferent* fibers, beginning in the peripheral nervous system. The information is integrated and interpreted by the central nervous system. Motor responses are transmitted by *efferent* fibers from the central nervous system to peripheral structures. Cells of the motor cortex and their descending motor pathways within the central nervous system are called *upper motor neurons*. The anterior horn cells of the spinal cord and the motor cranial nerve nuclei with their axons which extend peripherally are called *lower motor neurons*.

SUPPORT STRUCTURES OF THE CENTRAL NERVOUS SYSTEM

The structures which encase, support, and protect the delicate, semisolid central nervous system include the bones of the skull and vertebral column, the three meningeal layers, the ventricular system, and the cerebrospinal fluid. The nutritional needs of the central nervous system are met by the cerebrospinal fluid and the vascular system.

Skull

The roof of the cranial cavity, or *calvaria,* covers the superior aspects of the brain. The calvaria is composed of the frontal, the occipital, and the paired parietal and temporal bones which are fused at suture lines. The floor of the cranial cavity consists of a group of bony structures which have many ridges and grooves (Fig. 6-2). The floor conforms to the shape of the base of the brain and is divided into three compartments: the anterior, the middle, and the posterior fossae. The anterior fossa contains the frontal lobes. The middle fossa contains parts of the temporal lobes, the upper brainstem, and the pituitary gland. The posterior fossa contains the brainstem and the cerebellar hemispheres. A number of small openings, or *foramina,* are located in the base of the skull to permit paired blood vessels and cranial nerves to enter and leave the intracranial cavity. There is also a large opening, the *foramen magnum,* where the brainstem connects to the upper cervical spinal cord (Fig. 6-2).

The bones which form the cranial cavity are composed of three layers: the outer solid layer (outer table), the middle spongy layer (diploë), and the inner solid layer (inner table) (see Fig. 6-4). The construction

of the skull provides for greater strength with economy of weight and insulation. The thickest parts of the skull are the midfrontal and midoccipital bones. The thinnest parts of the skull are the temporal bones. The inner table, which lies over the convexity of the brain, is very smooth and contains grooves in which the branches of the middle meningeal arteries are located. The viability of the skull is maintained by thin layers of periosteum which are attached to the inner and outer tables.

Vertebral Column

The vertebral column consists of 7 cervical, 12 thoracic, 5 lumbar, 5 sacral, and 4 fused coccygeal vertebrae (Fig. 6-3). The vertebrae are joined together by multiple ligaments and intervening disks which provide flexibility and stability. The vertebral column supports the skull, forms a spinal canal which surrounds the spinal cord, and provides protection for the spinal cord, spinal nerves, and the underlying

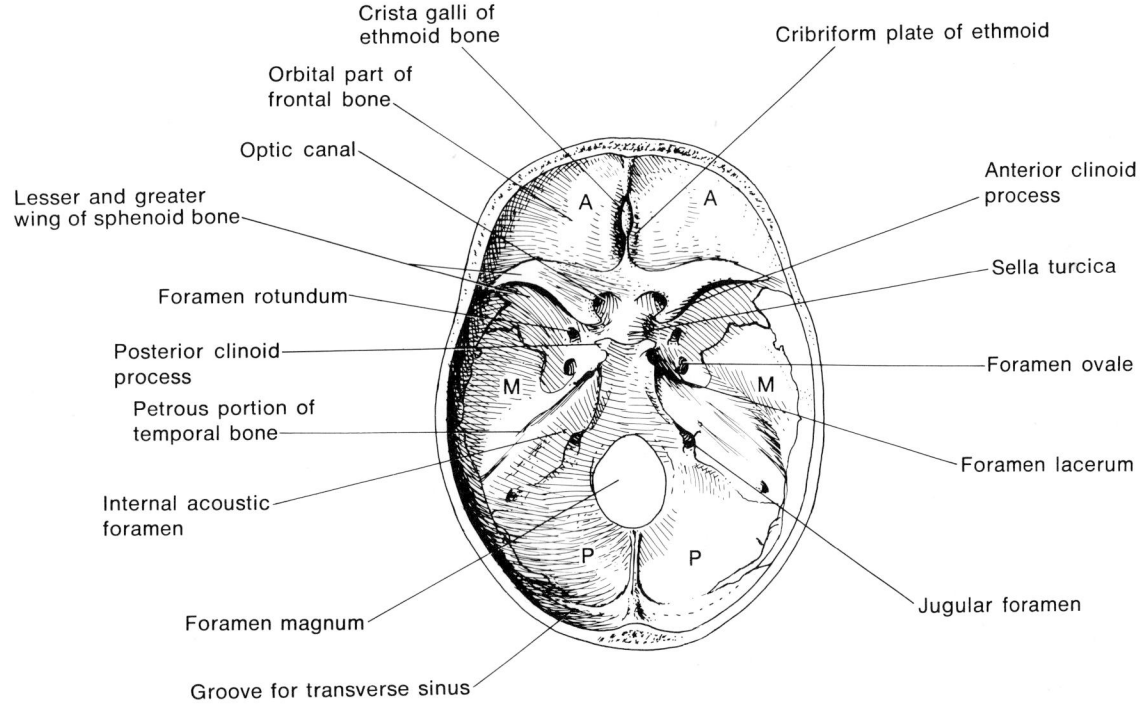

Crista galli of ethmoid bone

Orbital part of frontal bone

Optic canal

Lesser and greater wing of sphenoid bone

Foramen rotundum

Posterior clinoid process

Petrous portion of temporal bone

Internal acoustic foramen

Foramen magnum

Groove for transverse sinus

Cribriform plate of ethmoid

Anterior clinoid process

Sella turcica

Foramen ovale

Foramen lacerum

Jugular foramen

A = ANTERIOR CRANIAL FOSSA   M = MIDDLE CRANIAL FOSSA   P = POSTERIOR CRANIAL FOSSA

FIGURE 6-2

The floor of the cranial cavity. (*From L. Elson, It's Your Body, McGraw-Hill, New York, 1975. Used by permission of the publisher.*)

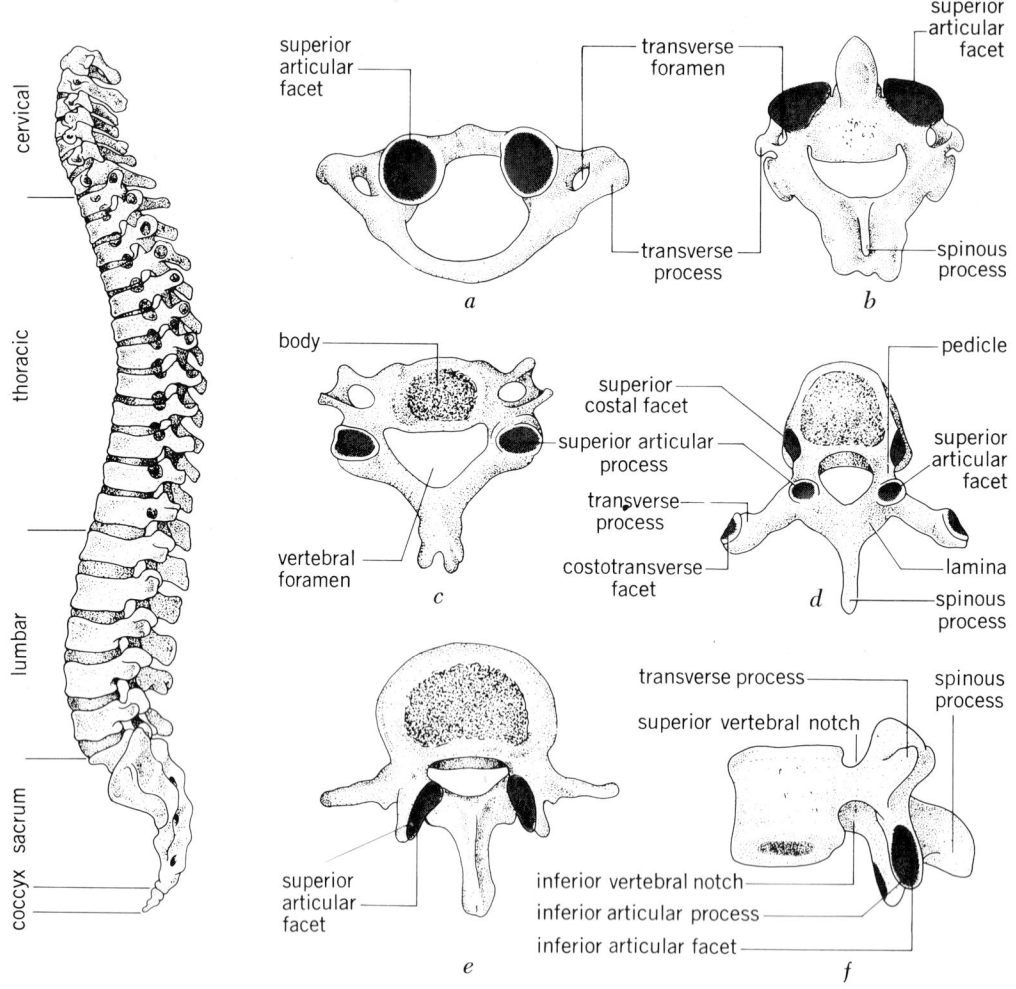

FIGURE 6-3

The vertebral column, with individual vertebra: (*a*) atlas; (*b*) axis; (*c*) 4th cervical; (*d*) 6th thoracic; (*e*) 3d lumbar, superior view; (*f*) 3d lumbar, lateral view. (*From R. M. DeCoursey, The Human Organism, 4th ed., McGraw-Hill, New York, 1974. Used by permission of the publisher.*)

structures. The spinal canal extends for the length of the vertebral column and conforms to the various spinal curvatures and to the variations in the size of the spinal cord. The vertebrae are progressively larger down to the sacrum and then become smaller. The diameter of the spinal canal is largest in the cervical region.

The first and second cervical vertebrae are very specialized. The first cervical vertebra, or *atlas,* is joined to the base of the skull. The second cervical vertebra, or *axis,* forms a pivot around which the atlas rotates the skull. The remaining cervical, thoracic,

and lumbar vertebrae have typical characteristics. Each vertebra consists of a body, a vertebral arch, and several processes for muscular and articular attachments. The vertebral body is located anteriorly and consists of a spongy bone which gives strength and supports weight. The vertebral arch is located posterior to the body and completes the formation of the spinal canal. The arch is composed of pedicles and lamina. A spinous process projects posteriorly and transverse processes project laterally from the vertebral arch.

Each vertebral arch has several articulating processes which permit motion between adjacent vertebrae. The vertebral notches in each pedicle form an intervertebral foramen which permits passage of the spinal nerves and associated blood vessels. The transverse processes of the cervical vertebrae have foramen which form a passageway for the vertebral arteries, veins, and sympathetic nerves.

An intervertebral disk, which acts as a cushion, separates the adjacent vertebral bodies. The disk is composed of a central cartilaginous core, the *nucleus pulposus,* which is surrounded by a fibrous capsule, the *anulus fibrosus.* A series of strong, fibrous, overlapping ligaments connect the vertebrae with each other and with the cranium. The ligaments allow safe, smooth movement of the head; protection from trauma; and stability and motion at the articulating processes. Additional support of the thoracic vertebrae is provided by the rib attachments.

Meninges

The brain and spinal cord are protected, supported, and surrounded by three layers of meninges (Fig. 6-4). The outer layer, or *dura mater,* consists of thick, tough connective tissue. The cranial dura forms an envelope which lines the inside and is firmly attached to the skull, serving as a periosteum. Folds of dura divide the intracranial cavity into four compartments. The horizontal dural fold which forms the roof over the posterior fossa is known as the *tentorium.* The occipital and posterior temporal lobes are located directly above the tentorium. The cerebellar hemispheres are located under the tentorium in the *infratentorial* compartment. The dural fold which separates the cerebellar hemispheres is called the *falx cerebelli.* The supratentorial compartment is divided by a midline dural fold, the *falx cerebri,* which separates the cerebral hemispheres. The cranial dural layers separate to form large venous sinuses at the junction of the dural folds.

The spinal dura is a continuation of the cranial dura. The dura surrounds the spinal cord from the foramen magnum to the level of the second sacral vertebra where it terminates as the dural sac. The spinal dura is not attached to the vertebrae. Extensions of the dura surround the spinal nerve roots, forming dural root sleeves.

The *pia mater* is the inner vascular membrane which adheres to the surface of the brain and spinal cord. Folds of pia form part of the choroid plexus, support the superficial blood vessels which penetrate the central nervous system, and provide support for the spinal cord. Tissue bands, the *dentate ligaments,* which attach the spinal cord to the dura, are formed by the pia. At the end of the cord, the pia forms the *filum terminale,* which merges with the dura and is attached to the coccyx.

The *arachnoid* is the delicate, spiderweblike membrane between the dural and pial layers. The arachnoid surrounds the surface of the brain without following its contour, surrounds the spinal cord, and extends along the roots of the cranial and spinal nerves. The combined pial and arachnoid membranes are referred to as the *leptomeninges.*

There is a potential space between the dura and the arachnoid, the *subdural space.* Vessels cross this area with very little support. The space between the arachnoid and the pia mater, the *subarachnoid space,* is filled with cerebrospinal fluid. The depth of the subarachnoid space varies. The space is narrow over the convexity of the cerebral hemispheres. At the base of the brain and around the brainstem the space widens to form large cisterns. The largest cistern, the *cisterna magna,* is located between the medulla and the inferior surface of the cerebellum. A lumbar cistern is located at the end of the spinal cord and contains sacral nerve roots.

Tiny projections of meninges, *arachnoid granulations,* protrude into the large venous sinuses formed by the dural layers, e.g., the *superior sagittal sinus* (Fig. 6-4). The cerebrospinal fluid which is contained in the subarachnoid space is transferred into the venous sinuses as a result of hydrostatic pressure. The arachnoid granulations are very permeable and permit one-way flow of cerebrospinal fluid, plasma proteins, and serum albumin into the venous blood.

Ventricular System

The ventricular system is located within the brain substance. It is composed of four communicating compartments: two lateral ventricles and a third and a fourth ventricle (Fig. 6-5). Each of the lateral ventricles is a cavity within the cerebral hemispheres which communicates with the third ventricle by intraventricular foramen, *foramen of Monro.* Each lateral ventricle consists of a body and the anterior (frontal), inferior (temporal), and posterior (occipital) horns.

The third ventricle is a thin, centrally located cavity which is surrounded by the thalamic structures. The third ventricle is connected to the fourth ventricle by a narrow channel, the *aqueduct of Sylvius,* which is located in the midbrain. The fourth ventricle is an angular cavity which is located posterior to the pons

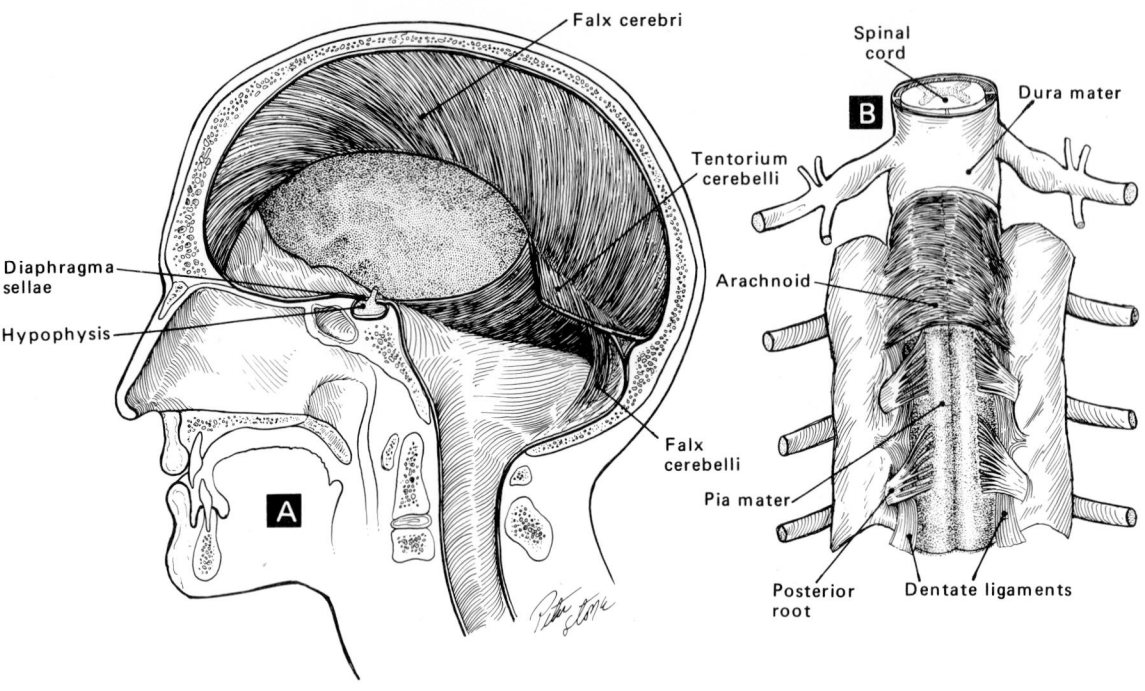

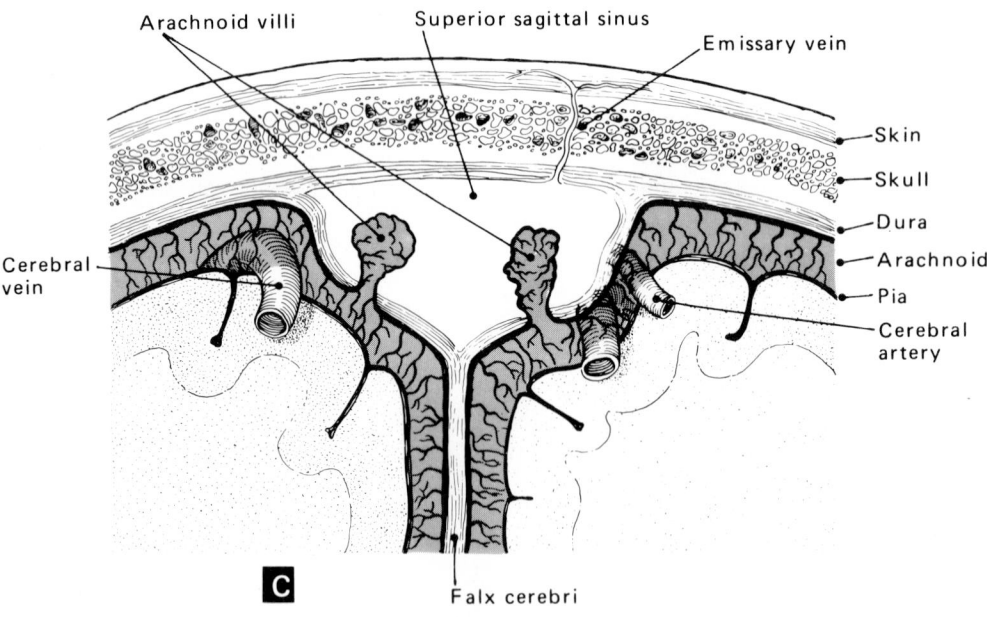

FIGURE 6-4

The meninges: (*A*) Extensions of the dura mater in the cranial cavity, sagittal view. (*B*) The dura and arachnoid sheath the spinal nerves at their origin. The dentate ligament separates dorsal from ventral roots and adheres to the dura. (*C*) Coronal section through the superior sagittal sinus. (*From L. L. Langley, I. R. Telford, and J.B. Christensen, Dynamic Anatomy and Physiology, 5th ed., McGraw-Hill, New York, 1980. Used by permission of the publisher.*)

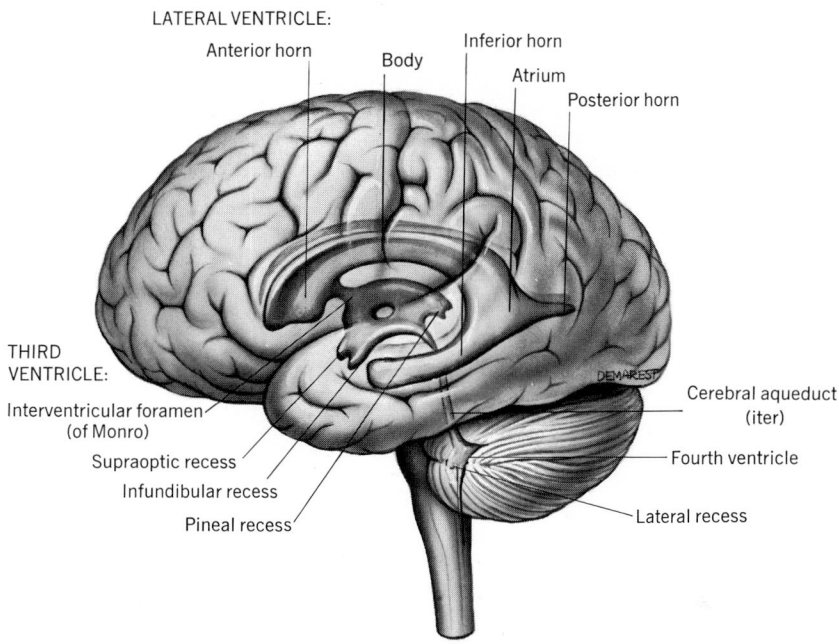

LATERAL VENTRICLE:
Anterior horn
Body
Inferior horn
Atrium
Posterior horn

THIRD VENTRICLE:
Interventricular foramen (of Monro)
Supraoptic recess
Infundibular recess
Pineal recess

Cerebral aqueduct (iter)
Fourth ventricle
Lateral recess

FIGURE 6-5
Lateral view of the ventricles of the brain. (*From C. R. Noback and R. J. Demarest, The Human Nervous System, 2d ed., McGraw-Hill, New York, 1975.*)

and medulla, anterior to the cerebellum, and extends to the central canal of the upper cervical cord. Three foramina connect the fourth ventricle with the subarachnoid spaces.

Cerebrospinal Fluid

Cerebrospinal fluid (CSF) is a clear, colorless liquid which contains a small amount of protein, glucose, and cells and a large amount of sodium chloride. CSF provides the central nervous system with support, cushion against trauma, and nutrition; assists in the removal of the waste products of neuronal metabolism; and assists in maintaining a relatively constant intracranial pressure. The pressure of the CSF at the lumbar cistern is 100 to 150 mmH$_2$O in the recumbent position.

The formation of CSF occurs principally in the lateral and third ventricles by a network of capillaries, the *choroid plexus*. CSF is produced as a result of active transport mechanisms, the expenditure of energy, and osmotic pressure. The rate of CSF formation is estimated at 500 to 600 mL/day. The CSF circulates from the lateral ventricles through the foramen of Monro into the third ventricle, through the aqueduct

of Sylvius into the fourth ventricle, and into the cranial and spinal subarachnoid spaces where it is returned to the venous system. The total volume of CSF in the ventricular system and the subarachnoid spaces at any given time is approximately 140 mL.

Brain Barrier System

The activity of the central nervous system is dependent upon the physical and chemical environment. The brain barrier system is a complex network of structures which provide a stable environment by regulating the transport of chemical substances between the plasma, the cerebrospinal fluid, and the brain. A barrier exists between the bloodstream and the brain, between the bloodstream and CSF, and between CSF and the brain. The barrier system includes the capillary endothelium, the pial-glial membrane, astrocytes, ependymal cells, the choroid plexus, and the arachnoid membrane.

Vascular System

The metabolic demands of the central nervous system for oxygen and glucose are very high in comparison to other body organs. The brain consumes approximately 20 percent of the total body oxygen requirements. The oxygen is utilized for the oxidation of glucose, which is the major source of energy. The constant delivery of oxygen and glucose via the bloodstream is maintained by a complex network of arteries.

Cerebral Circulation

The brain receives its blood from the paired carotid and vertebral arteries which fill from the aortic arch. The carotid arteries supply 80 percent of the total cerebral flow, with the vertebral arteries supplying the remaining 20 percent. The internal carotid arteries supply the anterior and middle parts of the cerebral hemispheres. The vertebral arteries join to form the basilar artery. The vertebral-basilar arteries supply the posterior parts of the cerebral hemispheres, the brainstem, and the cerebellum. Blood flows from the internal carotid and vertebral-basilar arteries into a ring of anastomotic vessels, the *circle of Willis*, which is located at the base of the brain (Fig. 6-6). The circle of Willis is composed of an anterior communicating artery and the paired anterior cerebral, internal carotid, the posterior communicating, and posterior

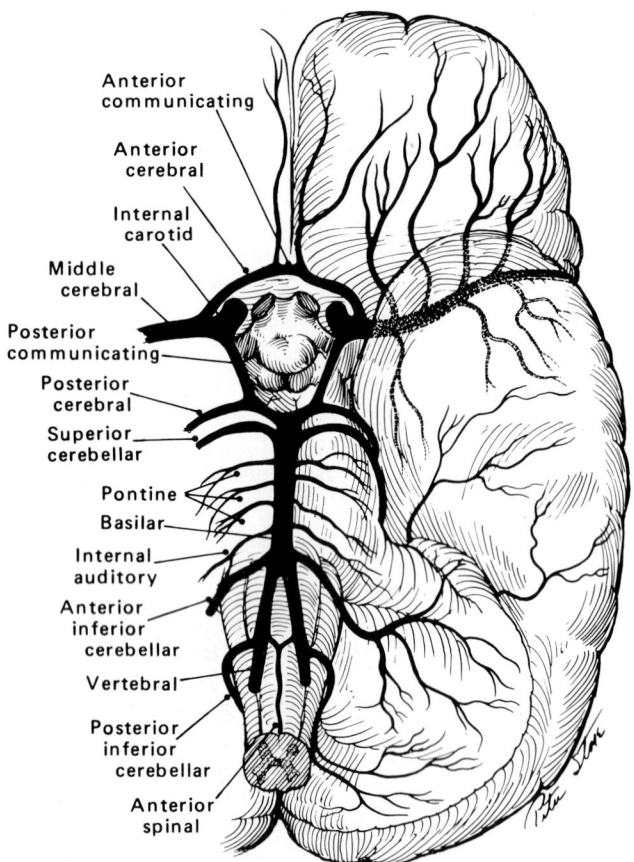

Anterior communicating

Anterior cerebral

Internal carotid

Middle cerebral

Posterior communicating

Posterior cerebral

Superior cerebellar

Pontine

Basilar

Internal auditory

Anterior inferior cerebellar

Vertebral

Posterior inferior cerebellar

Anterior spinal

FIGURE 6-6

Arteries of the brain. The circle of Willis, at the center, joins branches of the basilar and internal carotid arteries. The vertebral arteries provide the main supply of blood to the spinal cord. (*From L. L. Langley, I. R. Telford, and J. B. Christensen, Dynamic Anatomy and Physiology, 5th ed., McGraw-Hill, New York, 1980. Used by permission of the publisher.*)

cerebral arteries. The posterior arteries are the major branches of the basilar artery.

Each cerebral artery supplies a very specific region of the brain. The anterior cerebral arteries supply the medial surface of the frontal and parietal lobes. The middle cerebral arteries supply the lateral surfaces of the cerebral hemispheres and provide penetrating arteries to supply the deeper structures, e.g., the internal capsule, basal ganglia, and thalamic nuclei. The posterior cerebral arteries supply the medial and inferior surfaces of the occipital and temporal lobes (Fig. 6-7).

The venous drainage of the brain is composed of a network of fine veins which drain into superficial and deep veins. The superficial veins pass over the surface of the brain, pass through the subarachnoid space, and empty into the venous sinuses in the margins of the dura. The paired deep cerebral veins also drain into the venous sinuses. Blood then drains into the superior and inferior sagittal sinuses, into the cavernous sinuses, through the transverse sinuses, and into the jugular veins. The venous sinuses are usually distended and do not collapse. Cerebral veins and sinuses do not have valves.

Spinal Cord Circulation

The spinal cord receives its blood supply from descending branches of the vertebral arteries and multiple radicular arteries. The vertebral arteries give rise to the anterior spinal artery and the posterior spinal arteries (Fig. 6-6). The radicular arteries enter the spinal canal through intervertebral foramen and divide into anterior and posterior radicular arteries. The anterior spinal arteries join to form a single midline vessel which is joined by anterior radicular arteries to supply the anterior and lateral parts of the spinal cord. The pair of posterior spinal arteries descend the posterior surface of the spinal cord and receive blood from the posterior radicular arteries to supply the posterior third of the spinal cord. The cervical cord segments are supplied primarily by branches of the vertebral arteries. The radicular arteries are the major source of blood supply to the thoracic and lumbar spinal cord segments.

A complex network of intradural and extradural veins provides for the venous return from the spinal cord. The distribution of the spinal veins is similar to that of the spinal arteries. Since the spinal veins have no valves, venous blood may flow directly into the systemic venous system.

GROSS ANATOMY OF THE NERVOUS SYSTEM

The Brain

The brain consists of three basic subdivisions: the cerebral hemispheres, the brainstem structures, and the cerebellum.

Cerebral Hemispheres

The cerebral hemispheres are paired structures which are mirror images. Each hemisphere consists of gray matter (cerebral cortex and basal ganglia) and white

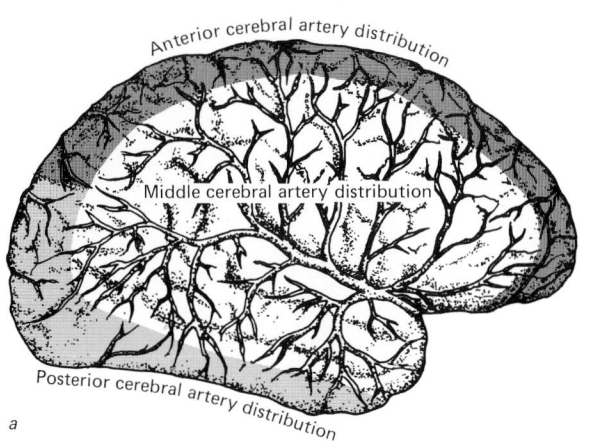

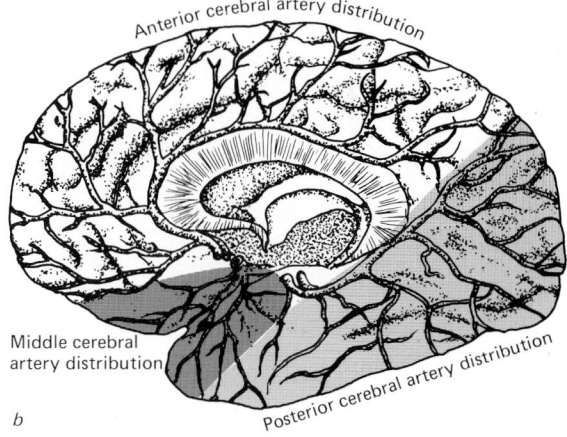

FIGURE 6-7
Distribution of the major cerebral arteries. (*a*) Lateral view. (*b*) Medial view.

matter (fiber tracts) which connect adjacent and distant areas. Association fibers connect adjacent and distant areas within the same hemisphere. Transverse (commissural) fibers connect symmetrical areas of the two hemispheres. Projection fibers connect the cerebral cortex with the deeper brain structures, brainstem, and spinal cord. A compact bundle of projection fibers near the upper brainstem is known as the *internal capsule*. The *corpus callosum* is a major commissural fiber tract which connects the two hemispheres.

The cerebral hemispheres are separated by the longitudinal fissure, which contains the falx cerebri. The surfaces of the cerebral hemispheres contain grooves known as *fissures* and *sulci* (Fig. 6-8). The convolutions of the brain between the sulci are known as *gyri*. Each hemisphere is subdivided into lobes which are separated by deep sulci or fissures. The major lobes of the brain are the frontal, parietal, temporal, occipital, and limbic lobes. The central sulcus (fissure of Rolando) separates the frontal and parietal lobes. The fissure of Sylvius separates the temporal from the parietal and frontal lobes. The parieto-occipital fissure separates the occipital from the parietal and temporal lobes. The limbic lobe is

composed of large cortical convolutions surrounding the upper brainstem and interhemispheric connections. The structures which are included in the limbic system are the cingulate gyrus, the hippocampal gyrus, olfactory connections, and amygdala.

The *basal ganglia* are paired subcortical gray structures which are located adjacent to the internal capsule (Fig. 6-9). The structures which compose the basal ganglia include the caudate nucleus, the putamen, the globus pallidus, and the amygdala.

Brainstem

The brainstem is composed of the diencephalon, the midbrain, the pons, and the medulla oblongata (Fig. 6-9). The diencephalon is overlapped by the lateral and posterior surfaces of the cerebral hemispheres and the cerebellum. The superior portion of the diencephalon or thalamus is located on either side of the third ventricle. The anterior portion of the diencephalon or hypothalamus is connected to the pituitary gland or hypophysis by the pituitary stalk. The hypothalamic nuclei, the pituitary stalk, and the posterior pituitary are known as the *neurohypophysis*.

The midbrain is composed of fibers which connect

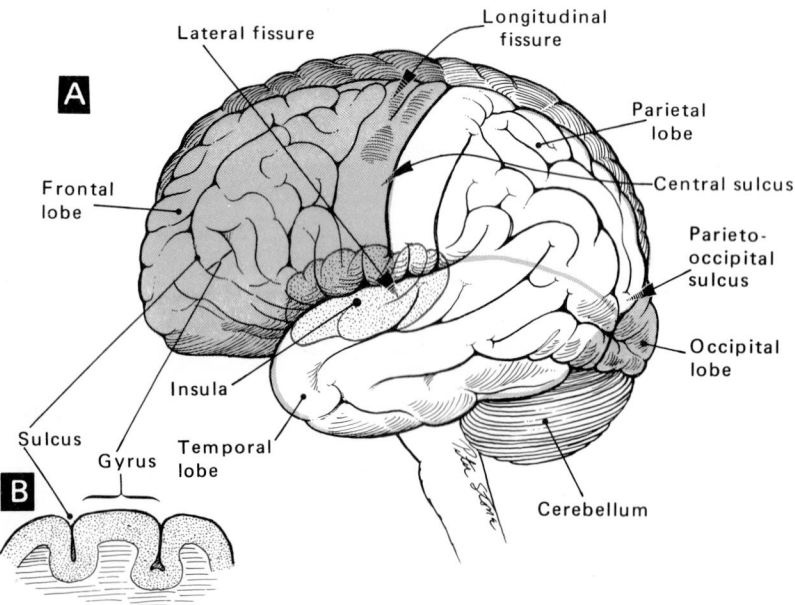

FIGURE 6-8

(*A*) Lateral view of the cerebrum. (*B*) A portion of the cortex in cross section. (*From L. L. Langley, I. R. Telford, and J. B. Christensen, Dynamic Anatomy and Physiology, 5th ed., McGraw-Hill, New York, 1980. Used by permission of the publisher.*)

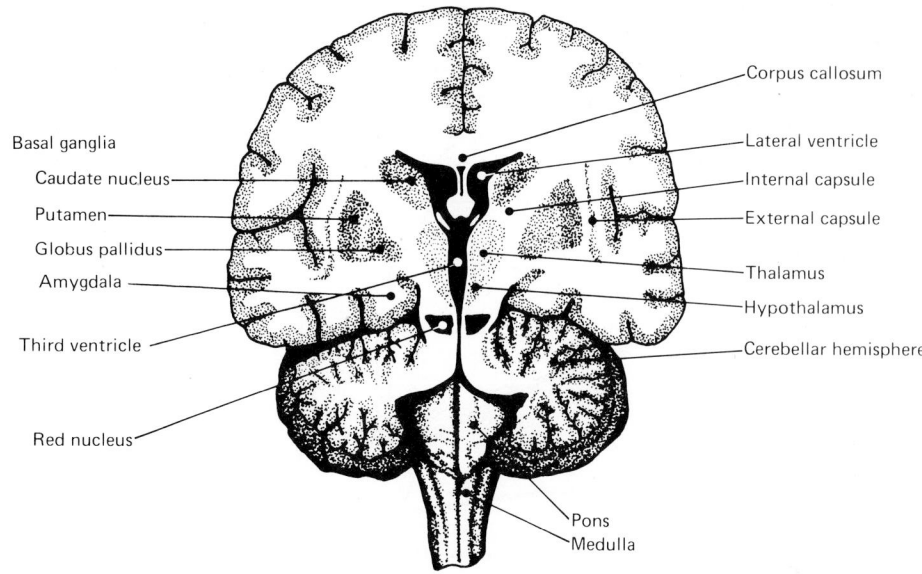

FIGURE 6-9
Coronal section of the cerebrum with basal ganglia, cerebellum and posterior view of brainstem.

the diencephalon with the lower brainstem and cerebellum. The substantia nigra and the red nucleus are located in the midbrain. The nuclei of cranial nerves III (oculomotor) and IV (trochlear) are located in the midbrain. The midbrain is located in the tentorial notch.

The pons lies in the front of the cerebellum. Fibers which connect to the underlying spinal cord pathways pass through the pons. The nuclei of cranial nerves V (trigeminal), VI (abducens), VII (facial), and VIII (acoustic) are located in the pontine area.

The medulla oblongata is a pyramid-shaped structure which connects the pons with the spinal cord at the level of the foramen magnum. Tracts which connect the cerebral cortical areas with the spinal pathways cross in the medulla. The nuclei of cranial nerves IX (glossopharyngeal), X (vagus), XI (spinal accessory), and XII (hypoglossal) are located in the medulla.

Cerebellum

The cerebellum consists of a midline portion, the *vermis,* and two lobes or hemispheres. Each cerebellar hemisphere contains an outer cortex of gray matter, a core of white fibers, and central nuclei. It is located directly below the occipital lobes and is covered by the tentorium.

Cranial Nerves

The cranial nerves are considered part of the peripheral nervous system. There are 12 pairs of cranial nerves (Fig. 6-10). Cranial nerves I (olfactory) and II (optic) are not typical of the remaining cranial nerves. Cranial nerves I and II extend to become tracts which connect with various structures within the cerebral hemispheres. Cranial nerves III through XII originate from the nuclei which are located either superficially or deep within the brainstem structures.

Cranial nerve I (olfactory) arises from the olfactory bulb and extends under the frontal lobes to penetrate the frontal and temporal lobes where it becomes part of the limbic system.

Cranial nerve II (optic) arises from the inner retinal layer of the eye and extends posteriorly to enter the intracranial cavity. The optic nerves join at the optic chiasm which lies above the pituitary gland. The optic tracts and radiations then extend posteriorly to areas of the occipital lobe.

Cranial nerves III (oculomotor), IV (trochlear), V (trigeminal), VI (abducens), VII (facial), VIII (acoustic), IX (glossopharyngeal), X (vagus), and XII (hypoglossal) extend peripherally to the eye muscles, face, ear, and pharynx. Cranial nerve X (vagus) extends down the neck into the thorax and the abdomen. Cranial nerve XI (spinal accessory) extends to the pharynx,

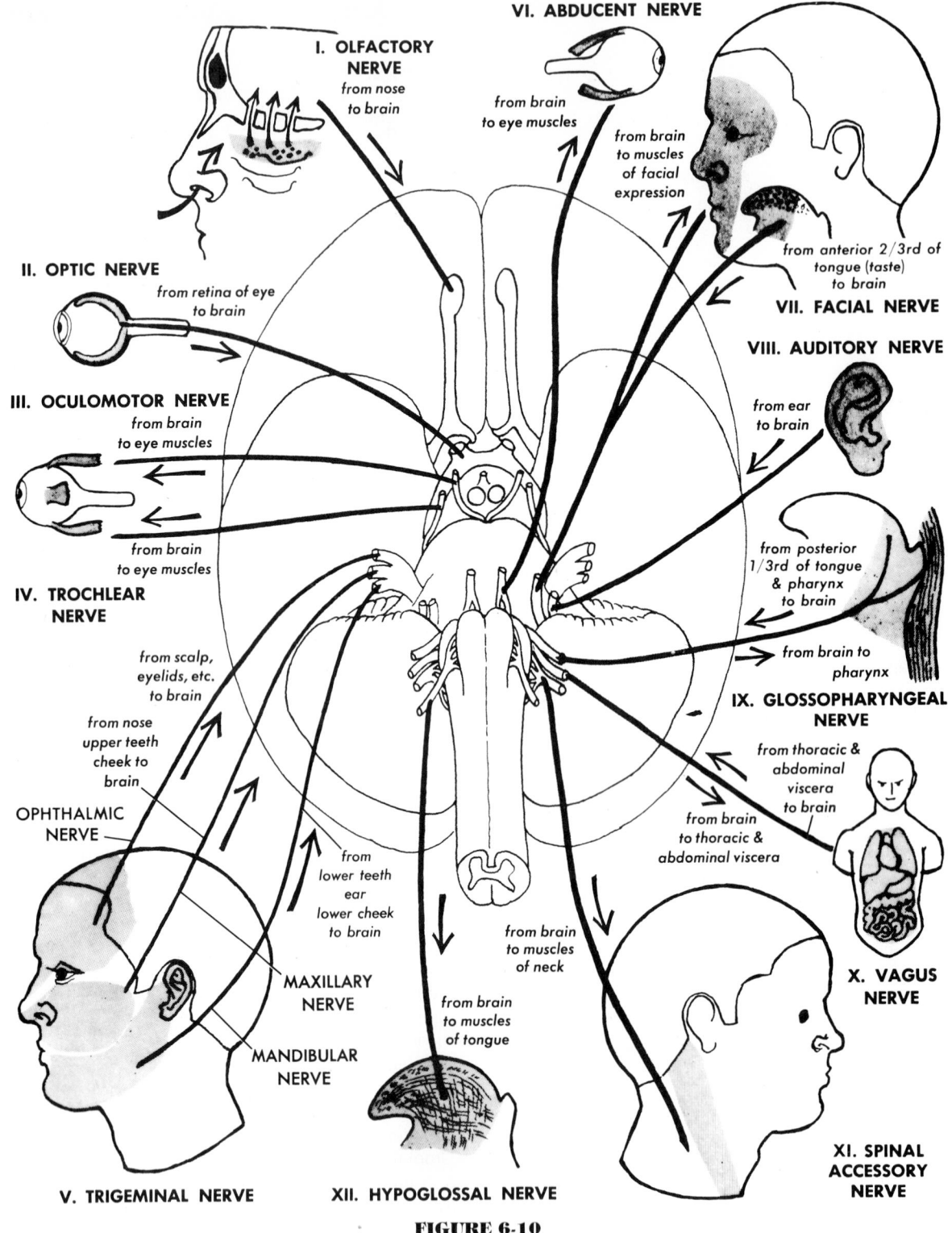

FIGURE 6-10

The cranial nerves. (*From E. J. Reith, B. Breidenbach, and M. Lorenc, Textbook of Anatomy and Physiology, 2d ed., McGraw-Hill, New York, 1978. Used by permission of the publisher.*)

larynx, and muscles of the neck and shoulders (Table 6-1). Parasympathetic fibers of the autonomic nervous system extend peripherally with the oculomotor, facial, glossopharyngeal, and vagus cranial nerves.

Spinal Cord and Spinal Nerves

The spinal cord is a cylindrical structure which joins the brainstem at the level of the foramen magnum and ends at the L_1–L_2 vertebral level as the *conus medullaris*. The upper cervical cord segments correspond to the same vertebral level, whereas cord segments from C_8 and below correspond to the vertebral level above each segment. For example, the C_3 cord segment lies opposite vertebra C_3, but the T_1 cord segment lies above vertebra T_1 (Fig. 6-11).

There are 31 pairs of spinal nerves which are distributed along the spinal cord: 8 cervical, 12 thoracic, 5 lumbar, 5 sacral, and 1 coccygeal. Each

TABLE 6-1
Summary of Cranial Nerves

Number	Name	Brain-stem level	Type	Major functions
I	Olfactory	None	Sensory	Sense of smell
II	Optic	None	Sensory	Central and peripheral vision
III	Oculomotor	Midbrain	Motor	Eye movement, elevation of upper eyelid
			Parasympathetic	Pupil constriction
IV	Trochlear	Midbrain	Motor	Downward and inward eye movement
V	Trigeminal	Pons to cervical cord	Sensory	Touch, pain, temperature Jaw and eye muscle proprioception
			Motor	Mastication
VI	Abducens	Pons	Motor	Abduction of the eye
VII	Facial	Pons	Motor	Close eyelid, muscles of facial expression
			Parasympathetic	Secretion by glands of mouth and eyes
			Sensory	Taste (anterior two-thirds of tongue)
VIII	Acoustic	Pons and medulla	Sensory	
	Vestibular branch			Equilibrium
	Cochlear branch			Hearing
IX	Glossopharyn-geal	Medulla	Motor Parasympathetic Sensory	Movement of pharyngeal muscles Secretion by parotid glands Pharyngeal and posterior tongue sensation
X	Vagus	Medulla	Motor Parasympathetic Sensory	Pharyngeal and laryngeal movement Visceral activities Pharyngeal and laryngeal sensation, taste
XI	Spinal accessory	Medulla	Motor	Pharyngeal, sternocleidomastoid, and trapezius movement
XII	Hypoglossal	Medulla	Motor	Tongue movement

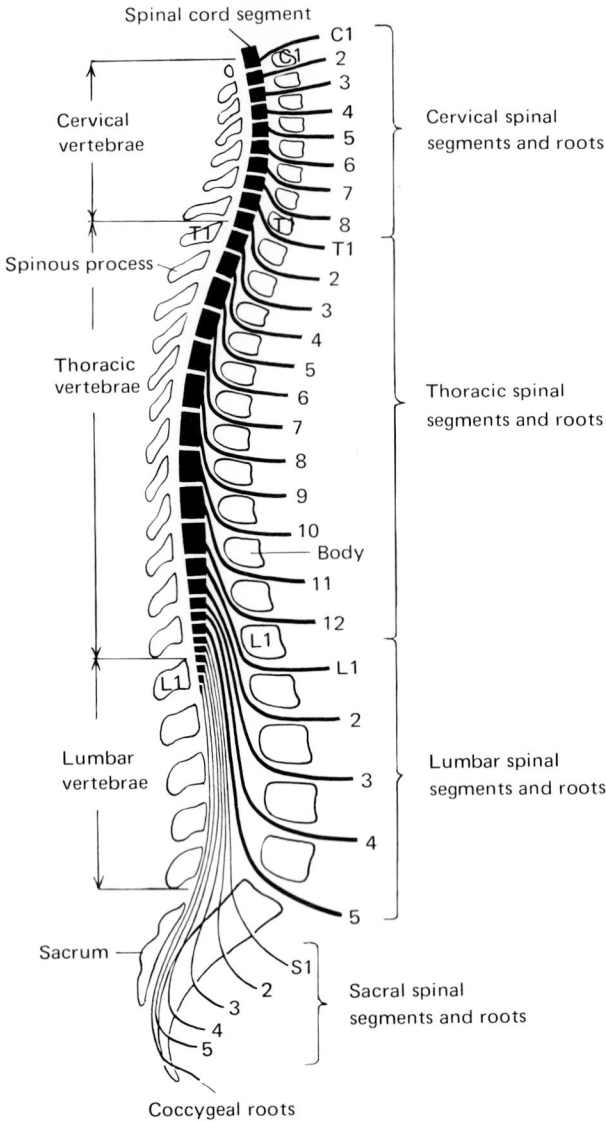

FIGURE 6-11

The relation of the spinal cord segments and spinal nerves to the vertebral column. (*From C. R. Noback and R. J. Demarest, The Human Nervous System, 2d ed., McGraw-Hill, New York, 1975. Used by permission of the publisher.*)

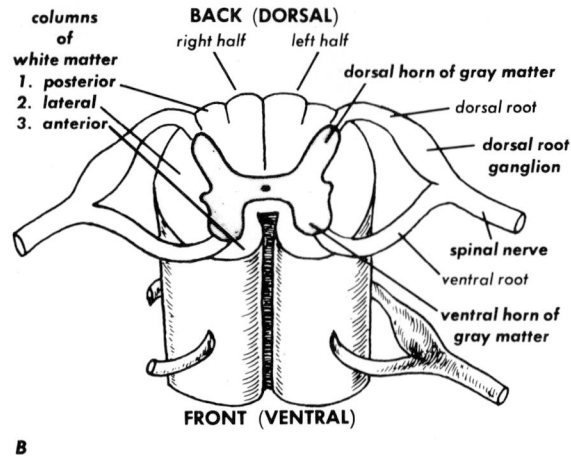

FIGURE 6-12

A segment of the thoracic spinal cord seen in cross section. (*From E. J. Reith, B. Breidenbach, and M. Lorenc, Textbook of Anatomy and Physiology, 2d ed., McGraw-Hill, New York, 1978. Used by permission of the publisher.*)

the corresponding vertebral level. All other spinal nerves exit one or two vertebral levels below the vertebra having the same number. The spinal nerves join peripherally to form plexuses. The cervical and brachial plexuses supply the upper extremities. The lumbar and sacral plexuses supply the lower extremities. The plexuses subdivide to form the various peripheral nerves.

The spinal cord consists of central gray horns which form an H-shape (Fig. 6-12). The gray matter is surrounded by columns of white matter which are fiber tracts. The size and shape of the spinal cord and the relative proportion of gray and white matter with the configuration of the gray matter varies according to the segmental level. The cervical cord is the largest in diameter. The cervical and lumbar segments contain a greater proportion of gray than white matter because of the larger number of neurons used to control the upper and lower extremities. The spinal cord is divided into left and right halves by a posterior sulcus and an anterior fissure. The halves are connected by commissures of gray and white matter.

The anterior, or *ventral,* horn contains the cell bodies of anterior (motor) nerve roots. The posterior, or *dorsal,* horn, contains cells on which posterior (sensory) nerve roots terminate. The lateral horn of gray matter in the thoracolumbar area contains cells which give rise to the sympathetic fibers of the

segment of the spinal cord has posterior (dorsal) nerve roots with ganglia and anterior (ventral) nerve roots (Fig. 6-12) which exit the vertebrae through the intervertebral foramina and join to form the spinal nerves. The large bundle of lumbosacral nerve roots which descend from the end of the cord are referred to as the *cauda equina.* The cervical nerves exit at

autonomic nervous system. Gray matter in the sacral cord, segments 2 through 4, give rise to parasympathetic fibers.

The white matter is subdivided into groups of tracts which ascend and descend the spinal cord. The major tracts are located posteriorly and anteriorly. The posterior tracts (*dorsal columns*) and the lateral spinothalamic tracts conduct sensory impulses to the thalamus and the cerebral cortex. The lateral (corticospinal, pyramidal) tracts conduct motor impulses to anterior horn cells.

Autonomic Nervous System

The autonomic nervous system consists of the hypothalamus, descending pathways within the brainstem and spinal cord, a series of ganglia, and small nerve fibers. The hypothalamus receives axons from the anterior and inferior portions of the frontal lobes. Fibers leave the hypothalamus and descend to groups of cells in the brainstem and spinal cord. The autonomic fibers are distributed with the cranial and spinal peripheral nerves to the visceral organs (Fig. 6-13).

The autonomic nervous system consists of the parasympathetic and sympathetic divisions. Each division differs anatomically, functionally, and pharmacologically. The peripheral autonomic fibers which originate in the cranial and sacral areas make up the parasympathetic division. Peripheral sympathetic fibers originate in the thoracic and lumbar areas (Fig. 6-13). Each visceral organ controlled by the autonomic nervous system has both parasympathetic and sympathetic innervation.

All autonomic fibers extend to synapses in ganglia after leaving their points of origin in the central nervous system. The sympathetic preganglionic fibers extend to a chain of paired ganglia which are located along the vertebral column. The presynaptic fiber tends to be short. The postsynaptic fiber must travel the remaining distance to the organ it innervates and tends to be long. Sympathetic fibers are distributed to the head, neck, thorax, abdomen, and pelvic areas in conjunction with thoracolumbar spinal nerves.

Parasympathetic fibers extend to ganglia located adjacent to the organs they innervate. Thus the presynaptic fibers are long and the postsynaptic fibers short. Parasympathetic fibers are not as widely distributed as the sympathetic fibers.

The adrenal medulla, unlike other viscera, is innervated directly by presynaptic fibers. The cells of the adrenal medulla are derived from nerve tissue and constitute a modified sympathetic ganglion.

PHYSIOLOGY OF THE NERVOUS SYSTEM

Functionally the neurons of the nervous system receive sensory stimuli, perceive the environment, interpret at various reflex and conscious levels, maintain communication between body parts, transmit motor responses, and integrate all body activities. The sensory stimulus which may be transmitted by the peripheral nerves may be mechanical, chemical, thermal, and electrical. Interpretation and integration take place by a variety of very complex mechanisms within the central nervous system. Appropriate motor responses are then transmitted from the central nervous system via the peripheral nerves.

Neuronal impulse transmission is unidirectional. Impulses are transmitted toward the central nervous system by afferent (sensory) neurons. Efferent (motor) neurons conduct impulses away from the central nervous system.

Transmission of impulses within each neuron is a result of a complex electrochemical process in which the cell membrane permeability to sodium and potassium changes. The action potential or ability for repolarization and depolarization results in impulse conduction (Fig. 6-14).

Transmission of impulses from one neuron to another at the synapse is a chemical process. As an impulse reaches the synapse, a neurotransmitter is released. It crosses the gap to the postsynaptic neuron and triggers an impulse there. The major neurotransmitters in the brain include acetylcholine, gamma aminobutyric acid (GABA), serotonin, dopamine, and norepinephrine. Norepinephrine is secreted by sympathetic postganglionic fibers (adrenergic neurons). Acetylcholine is secreted by the parasympathetic postganglionic fibers (cholinergic neurons) and at the myoneural junction. Acetylcholine esterase (cholinesterase) is found within parasympathetic motor nerve fibers and at nerve endings (e.g., myoneural junction). It readily inactivates acetylcholine, thereby controlling the synaptic activity mediated by the acetylcholine.

Sensory Integration

The sensory system is composed of afferent peripheral nerves; the spinothalamic tracts and dorsal columns of the spinal cord; tracts within the brainstem; the thalamus; and the frontal, parietal, temporal, occipital, and limbic lobes.

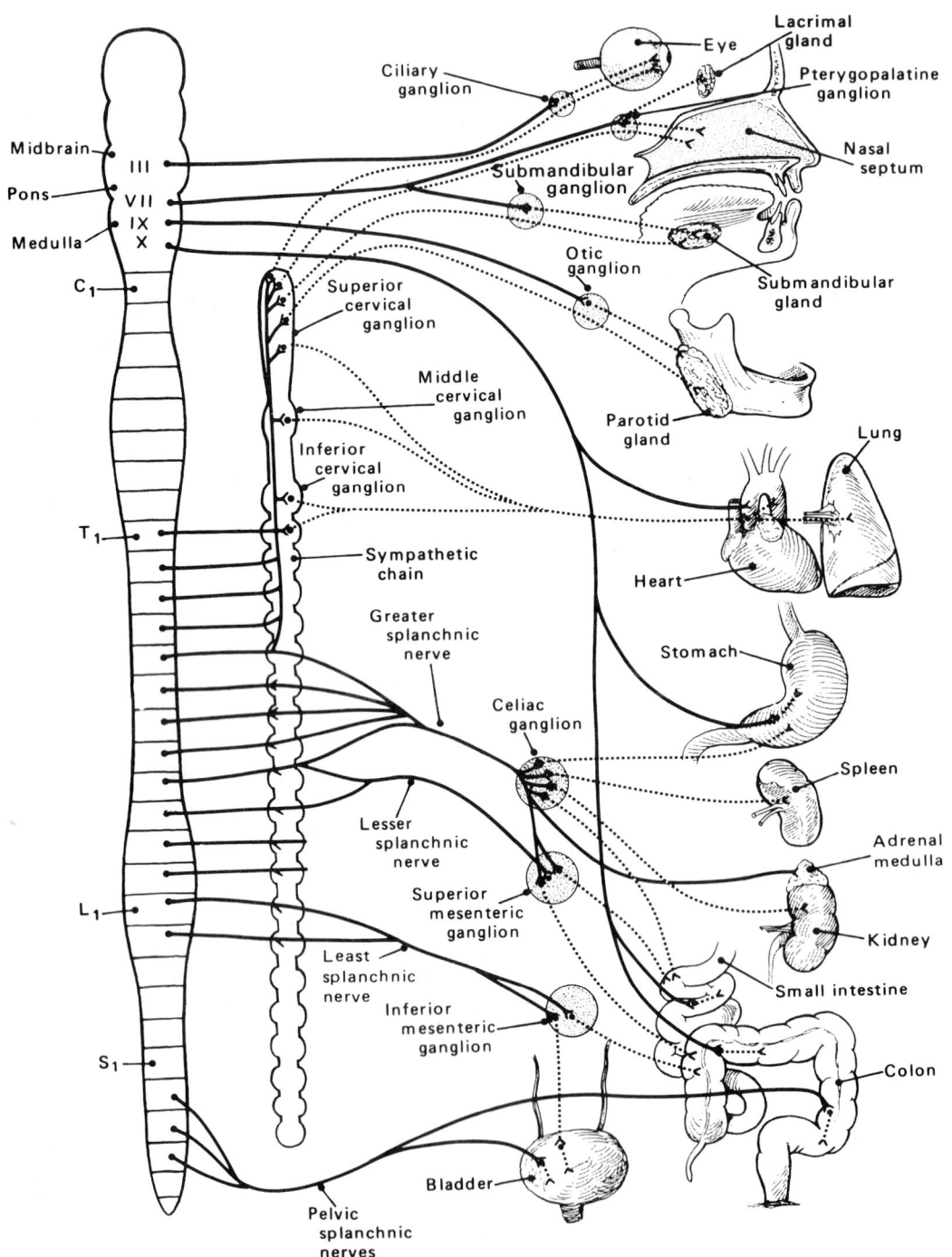

FIGURE 6-13

The autonomic nervous system, schematic drawing. Only one of the two sympathetic chain ganglia is shown. (*From L. L. Langley, I. R. Telford, and J. B. Christensen, Dynamic Anatomy and Physiology, 5th ed., McGraw-Hill, New York, 1980. Used by permission of the publisher.*)

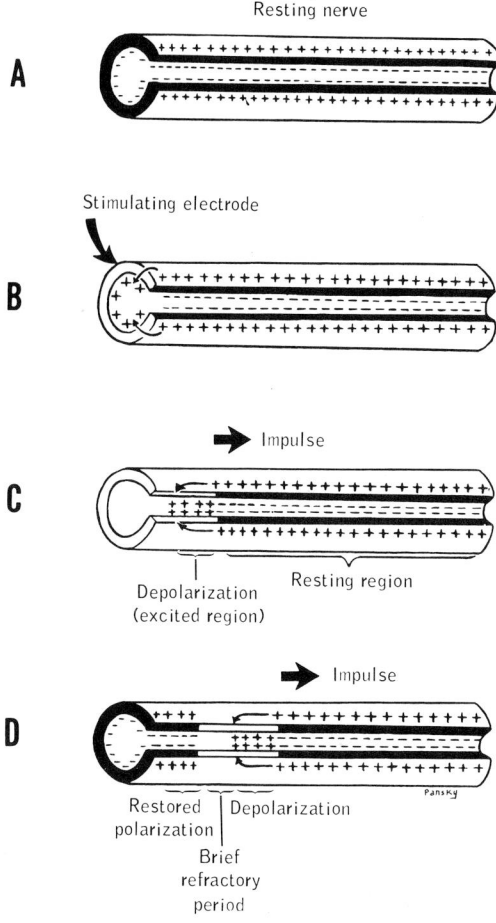

A

Resting nerve

B

Stimulating electrode

C

Impulse

Depolarization
(excited region)

Resting region

D

Impulse

Restored
polarization

Depolarization

Brief
refractory
period

FIGURE 6-14

The membrane theory of nerve conduction. Stimulation changes the axon membrane's barrier characteristics so that, at that point, sodium is allowed to rush in and potassium to rush out. For an instant this reverses the normal balance of electric charges across the membrane. Each point on the membrane destabilizes the adjacent point so that it, in turn, becomes depolarized. In this way the impulse moves along the axon to its end. (*From E. L. House, B. Pansky, and A. Siegel, A Systematic Approach to Neuroscience, 3d ed., McGraw-Hill, New York, 1979. Used by permission of the publisher.*)

The cranial nerves transmit highly specialized sensations to the central nervous system. The olfactory nerves transmit the sense of smell. Optic nerves receive and transmit visual input. The acoustic nerves transmit sound by the cochlear branch and the sense of equilibrium by the vestibular branch. Taste is transmitted by the glossopharyngeal and facial nerves.

The superficial sensations of crude touch, pain, and temperature of the eye and face are transmitted by the trigeminal, facial, and vagus nerves into the brainstem. The cutaneous receptors for the superficial sensations of the body are located in specific anatomical areas known as *dermatomes,* which correspond to the peripheral distribution of the sensory spinal nerve fibers (see Fig. 26-9). The superficial sensations are transmitted to the spinal cord by the posterior spinal nerve roots where they synapse, pass immediately to the contralateral spinothalamic tract, and are transmitted to the thalamus and cerebral cortex.

The deep, more complex sensations of pressure, position (proprioception), vibration, fine touch, and deep pain are transmitted by the posterior spinal nerve roots to the dorsal column to ascend to the level of the medulla oblongata where the fibers cross to the opposite side and extend to the thalamus and cerebral cortex (Fig. 6-15).

A network of fibers and cells known as the *reticular formation* lies in the brainstem. All sensory input is received in this area prior to going to higher levels. The stimulation of the reticular formation in the upper brainstem produces impulses which result in cortical arousal and contribute to conscious awareness.

All the lobes of the cerebral hemispheres have specific areas which receive sensory impulses and other areas which integrate this information and enable it to be understood (Fig. 6-16). The frontal lobe functions include the reception of the sense of smell, storage of information for memory, abstract thought processes, judgment, and other higher intellectual functions.

The activities of the parietal lobes consist primarily of sensory discrimination and bodily awareness for the opposite side of the body. Awareness of size, shape, and texture of objects; the relationship of body parts; two-point discrimination; and localization of other sensations are parietal lobe functions. The sensory speech center is located in the parietal lobe.

The occipital lobes are primary visual receiving and understanding areas. The temporal lobes are primarily auditory and olfactory reception areas; however, the hippocampal gyrus receives the sensory input associated with memory and bodily awareness. The limbic structures process and sort information as well as supply information for storage; therefore, learning and memory for recent events are under the influence of the limbic system.

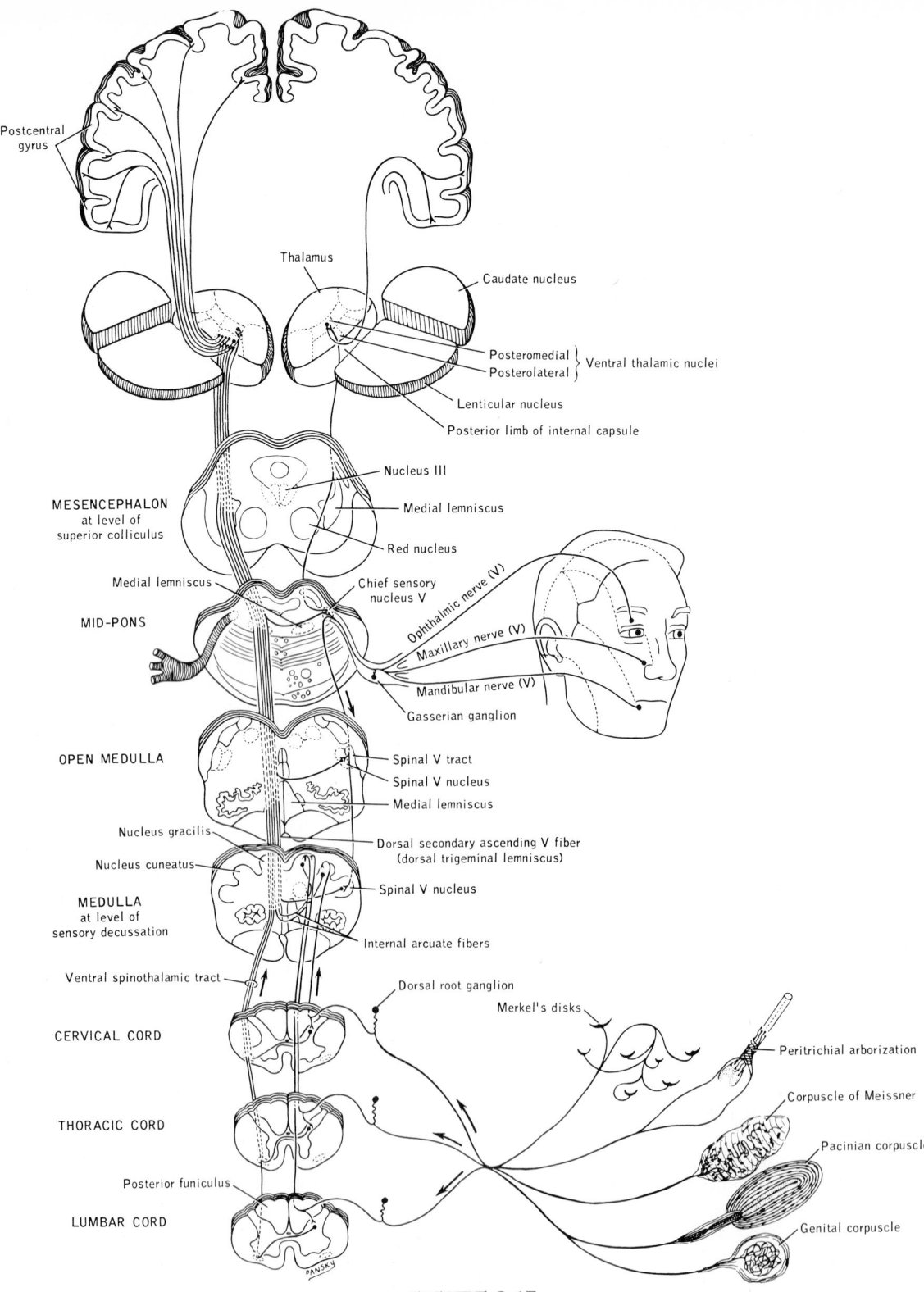

FIGURE 6-15

Transmission of sensations of light touch follow the pathways shown. (*From E. L. House, B. Pansky, and A. Siegel, A Systematic Approach to Neuroscience, 3d ed., McGraw-Hill, New York, 1979. Used by permission of the publisher.*)

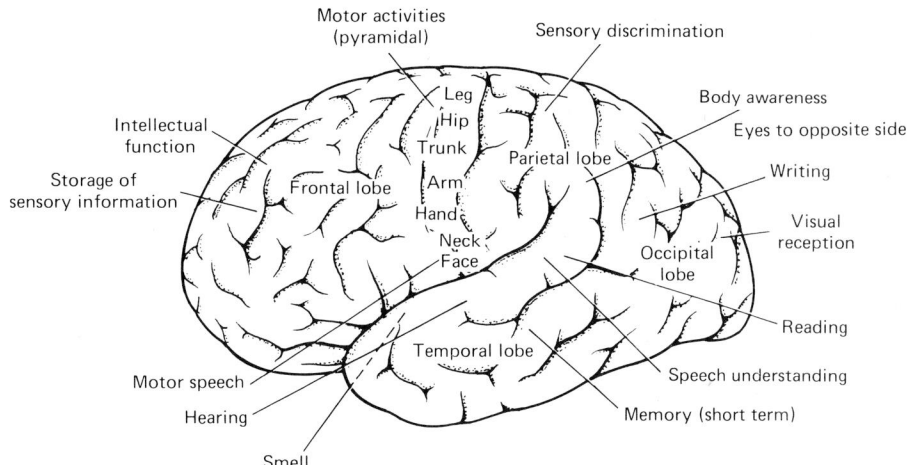

FIGURE 6-16

Localized functional areas of the cerebral cortex.

Motor Integration

The motor system is subdivided into two systems, the pyramidal and extrapyramidal systems. The pyramidal system is composed of the cells of the precentral gyrus of the frontal lobes and several tracts which descend through the internal capsule to the brainstem and spinal cord. It is the system serving voluntary muscle movement. The corticomesencephalic tract terminates in the brainstem at the motor nuclei of the oculomotor (III), trochlear (IV), and abducens (VI) cranial nerves. The corticobulbar tract terminates at the motor nuclei of the trigeminal (V), facial (VII), glossopharyngeal (IX), vagus (X), spinal accessory (XI), and hypoglossal (XII) cranial nerves. Fibers forming the corticospinal tract arise from each hemisphere, pass through the posterior limb of the internal capsule, descend through the brainstem, and the majority cross over (decussate) to the opposite side of the medulla to form the lateral corticospinal tract (Fig. 6-17). These fibers terminate at the various spinal cord segments and synapse with the anterior horn cells. The fibers which do not cross descend as the anterior corticospinal tract and synapse directly with neurons in the spinal cord.

Motor impulses, which originate in the prefrontal gyrus, are transmitted by the corticospinal tract to the efferent cranial and spinal fibers and so to the periphery. The pyramidal system primarily regulates skilled motor activities of the distal extremities and the skeletal musculature of the head and neck. The cerebral cortex has several *suppressor areas* which inhibit movements of the musculature when they are stimulated. Eye movements are influenced by suppressor areas in the frontal and occipital lobes. The motor speech area is located in the posterior-inferior aspect of the frontal lobe, with the main language center being located in the left hemisphere. Motor speech is also influenced by the facial (VII), glossopharyngeal (IX), vagus (X), and hypoglossal (XII) nerves.

The extrapyramidal system is composed of the basal ganglia and a complex network of tracts which connect the cerebral cortex, basal ganglia, the cerebellum, the brainstem, and the spinal cord. There are many circuits and feedback loops within and between each of the structures, providing the interaction and constant influence over the parts of the cerebral cortex which give rise to the descending motor tracts, both pyramidal and extrapyramidal. The activity of the lower motor neurons of the peripheral nervous system are under the influence of the extrapyramidal system.

The extrapyramidal spinal tract either facilitates or inhibits flexor and extensor activities. The net result of extrapyramidal activity is the maintenance of muscle tone; control of gross skeletal muscle activities; control of rhythmic movements, e.g., running and walking; and control of head and trunk movements related to maintaining an upright position.

The cerebellum and the related fibers which provide connections with the basal ganglia and the reticular formation coordinate muscle activities and time muscle contractions to facilitate smoothness and

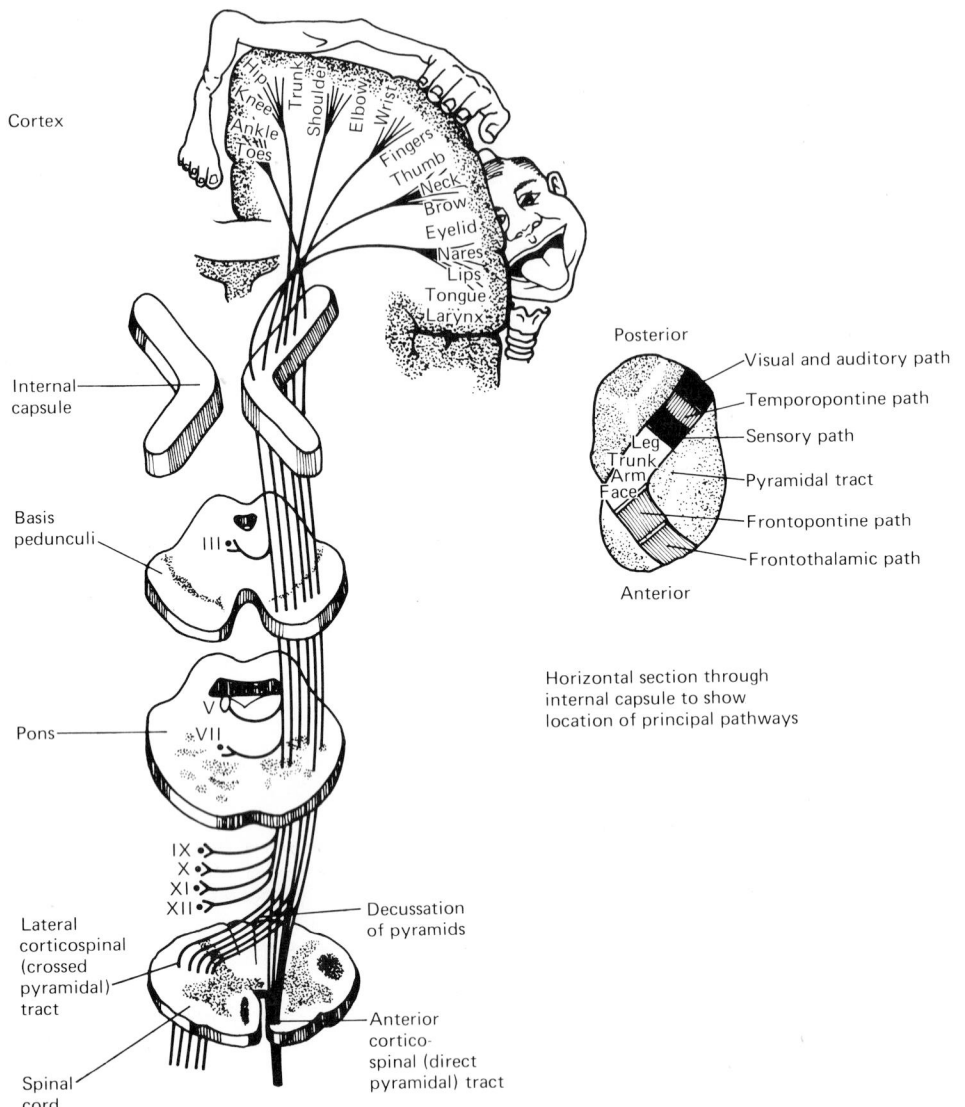

FIGURE 6-17

Corticospinal (pyramidal) tract. The figure drawn at the edge of the cerebral hemisphere depicts the amount of surface area on the cortex assigned to the motor function of each body part. (*From J. G. Chusid, Correlative Neuroanatomy and Functional Neurology, 17th ed., Lange, Los Altos, 1979.*)

accuracy (synergy). Intent and performance are correlated, providing for error control. The cerebellum also provides a "braking" or damping function to enable movements to be stopped where intended. The cerebellum receives sensory input from a number of afferent fibers which assist in maintaining equilibrium and the control of spinal reflex movements (Fig. 6-18).

Impulses from visual, auditory, vestibular tactile and proprioceptive stimuli, as well as input from the cerebral cortex, reach the cerebellum where rapid correlation and integration take place. The cerebellum then transmits impulses which modify motor commands to voluntary muscles.

Impulses from the basal ganglia and cerebellum are first transmitted to the thalamus where modification

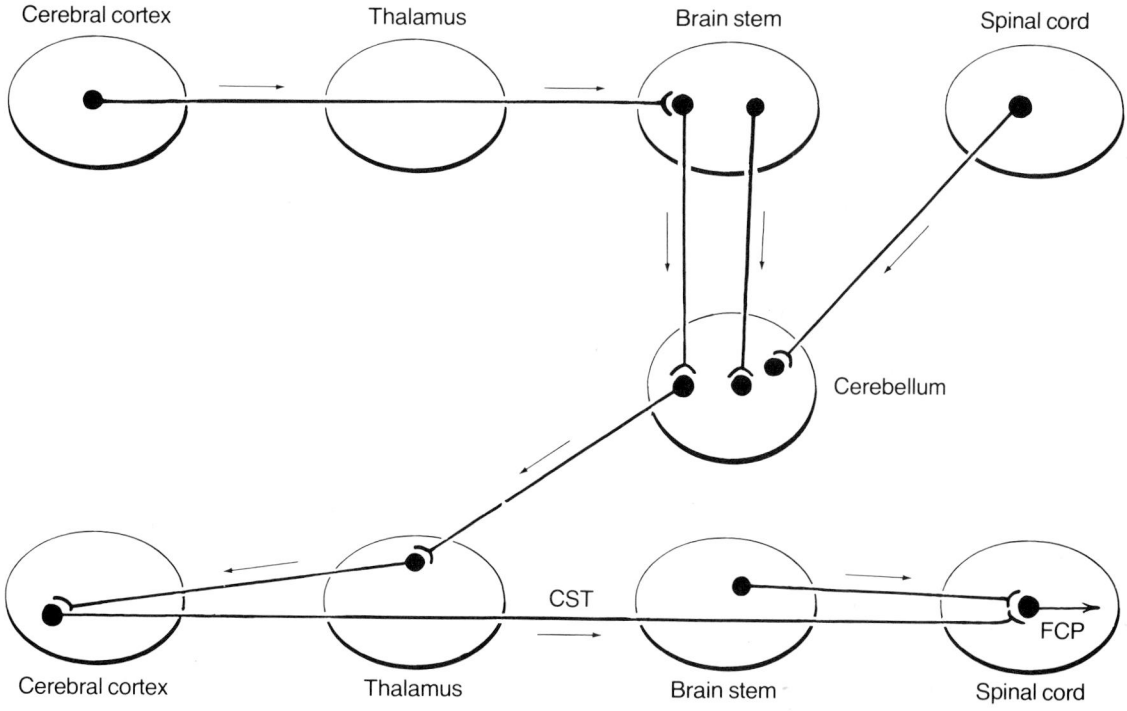

FIGURE 6-18.

Some of the relations between the cerebellum and other structures active in motor functions. The final common path (FCP) refers to the anterior horn cells, which receive influences from the corticospinal tract (CST) and cells of the brainstem. Each of the regions which influence the ventral horn cells appear to maintain either direct or indirect reciprocal connections with the cerebellum. (*From E. L. House, B. Pansky, and A. Siegel, A Systematic Approach to Neuroscience, 3d ed., McGraw-Hill, New York, 1979. Used by permission of the publisher.*)

and integration occurs prior to transmission to the cerebral cortex. Impulses from the facilatory and inhibitory reticular nuclei are transmitted by the reticulospinal tracts to the anterior horn motor nuclei. When facilatory impulses are transmitted to extensor muscles, reciprocal impulses are transmitted to inhibit flexor muscle activity, with the effect being extensor facilitation and flexor inhibition. When inhibitory impulses predominate, lower motor neurons transmit impulses to inhibit muscle activity. There is normally a balance of facilatory and inhibitory impulses at the lower neuron level so that muscle tone is maintained.

Autonomic Nervous System

The highly integrated activities of the autonomic nervous system are regulated by several complex mechanisms. The activities of the hypothalamus, reticular formation, limbic structures, and possibly the cerebellum influence autonomic function. Reflex arcs at the brainstem and spinal cord level reflect autonomic activities. The limbic lobes appear to modulate autonomic activity and provide the integration with somatic motor activities to produce and control complex emotional behavior. Parasympathetic activities conserve energy, whereas sympathetic activities typically consume energy.

The rostral portion of the hypothalamus excites parasympathetic activity, causing sweating, vasodilatation, a decrease in the rate and force of cardiac contractions, and pupil constriction. The caudal portion of the hypothalamus excites sympathetic activity, causing vasoconstriction, increased rate and force of cardiac contractions, increased respirations, pupil dilatation, and inhibition of peristalsis (Table 6-2). The physical expression of emotion, which includes accelerated heart rate, elevated blood pressure, flushing or pallor of the skin, sweating, gooseflesh, dry

TABLE 6-2
Summary of Functional and
Pharmacological Autonomic Activities

Organ	Sympathetic function (response to adrenergic impulses)	Parasympathetic function (response to cholinergic impulses)
Eye	Pupil dilatation (mydriasis)	Pupil constriction (miosis)
Heart	Increase in heart rate and contractility	Decrease in heart rate and contractility
Blood vessels	Dilates coronary and skeletal muscle vessels Constricts vessels of skin and visceral organs	
Lungs	Dilates bronchial tree	Constricts bronchial tree Stimulates bronchial gland secretion
Glands	Increased secretion	Decreased secretion
Gastrointestinal tract	Inhibits motility Inhibits secretion Sphincter contraction	Stimulates motility Stimulates secretion Sphincter relaxation
Gallbladder	Relaxation	Contraction
Spleen	Contraction	
Adrenal medulla	Secretion of epinephrine and norepinephrine	
Urinary bladder	Sphincter contraction	Sphincter relaxation
Male sex organs	Ejaculation	Erection
Skin	Gooseflesh	Generalized sweating

mouth, and gastrointestinal disturbances, are a reflection of autonomic activities which are modulated by the hypothalamus.

The hypothalamic nuclei regulate body temperature. The parasympathetic activities of sweating and vasodilatation result in lowering the body temperature. Shivering and vasoconstriction, which are sympathetic activities, result in the elevation of body temperature. The regulation of eating, drinking, emptying the urinary bladder, defecation, and sexual activity is under the influence of the hypothalamic structures and the sympathetic and parasympathetic fibers (Table 6-2).

The supraoptic nuclei of the hypothalamus and its neuronal connections with the posterior pituitary are referred to as the *neurohypophysis* (see Chap. 7). The neurohypophysis regulates body water metabolism as a result of its production, storage, and release of antidiuretic hormone (ADH). ADH is produced by the hypothalamic nuclei and transferred to the posterior pituitary for storage. The network of capillaries in the supraoptic nuclei monitor the osmolality of the blood. The secretion of ADH by the posterior pituitary is either stimulated or inhibited on the basis of the existing osmolality. Increased osmolality of the body fluids and a reduction of extracellular volume which stimulates the pressure receptors in the hypothalamus result in the secretion of ADH by the posterior pituitary. The presence of ADH in the blood promotes increased water reabsorption from the distal convoluted tubules of the kidney, thereby limiting the volume of water loss in the urine. The return to normal osmolality is further assisted by the hypothalamic structures since the stimulation of the hypothalamus by a state of increased osmolality brings with it a feeling of thirst.

Reflex Activities

The reflex arc is the basic functional unit of neural activity. Reflex pathways are found in the cranial, spinal, and autonomic fibers of the peripheral nervous system. The majority of reflexes occur in simple neural pathways, although some reflexes involve complex pathways to the brain. The reflex arc is composed of a sense organ or receptor, an afferent neuron, one or more synapses in a central integrating station, an efferent neuron, and an effector (e.g., muscle, gland). The stimulation of specific afferent neurons which have synaptic connections with specific efferent neurons results in a relatively stereotyped action or reflex. Reflex activities are the muscle contractions or glandular secretions which result from sensory input. Reflexes are integrated into all motor activities but are involuntary in nature. Some of the basic reflex activities may be altered and/or suppressed on a conscious level.

There are three major types of reflexes: the superficial, the deep, and the visceral. The superficial reflexes are responses to mucous membrane and cutaneous stimulation. The deep reflexes are known as deep tendon or stretch reflexes which are basic spinal cord activities. Visceral reflexes are conducted by cranial nerve and autonomic fibers, resulting in alterations in the activities of visceral organs.

The superficial reflexes which have their pathways within the cranial nerves and brainstem structures include the corneal and pharyngeal (gag, swallow) reflexes. The afferent limb of the corneal reflex arc is the trigeminal (V) nerve and the efferent limb is the facial (VII) nerve. The pathways for the pharyngeal reflexes are found in the cranial nerves in the afferent fibers of the glossopharyngeal (IX) and the efferent fibers of the vagus (X). Cutaneous stimulation of specific dermatomes results in transmission of impulses by spinal nerves to their spinal cord segments with the appropriate reflex motor response. The abdominal reflex is transmitted at the thoracic spinal segments 7 through 12. The cremasteric reflex response to stimulation of the inner aspect of the thigh is transmitted at the lumbar spinal segments 1 and 2. The plantar reflex response to stimulating the sole of the foot is transmitted at the lumbar 4th and 5th

and sacral 1st and 2d, spinal segments. The anal reflex is transmitted at the sacral 4th and 5th spinal segments.

The deep tendon or stretch reflexes are monosynaptic reflexes. The muscle spindle is the sensory organ. Stretching of the muscle is the sensory stimulus which is transmitted to the posterior horn cells of the spinal cord where they synapse directly with the anterior horn cells of the motor neurons which supply the same muscle. The motor response is contraction of the corresponding muscle. The major deep tendon reflexes include the biceps, triceps, brachioradialis, quadriceps, and Achilles tendon. The cervical spinal segments 5 and 6 form the biceps and brachioradialis reflex pathways. The cervical spinal segments 7 and 8 form the triceps reflex pathway. The quadriceps reflex pathway is at the lumbar 2d, 3d, and 4th spinal segment. The pathways for the Achilles tendon reflex are the sacral 1st and 2d spinal segments.

The visceral reflex pathways are found within the cranial and autonomic nerve fibers. There are several pupillary reflexes, the blink reflex, cardiovascular reflexes, bladder, and rectal reflexes. There are four distinct pupillary reflexes and two major cardiovascular reflexes.

The pupillary reflexes include the direct and consensual light reflex, the accommodation reflex, and the ciliospinal reflex. When light is transmitted by the optic nerve (II) to the Edinger-Westphal nucleus in the midbrain, the pupil constricts in the same eye (direct light reflex) and in the opposite eye (consensual reflex). When the visual stimulation of looking at near objects with eye convergence is transmitted by the optic nerve (II) and tracts to the occipital cortex, constriction of the pupil occurs (accommodation reflex). Pupillary constriction is the response to transmission of impulses by the parasympathetic fibers of the oculomotor nerve (III). When the afferent fibers of the thoracic spinal nerves at T_1 and T_2 are stimulated, the pupil on the same side dilates as a result of cervical sympathetic activity (ciliospinal reflex).

The blink reflex is a visceral reflex. The afferent limb of the reflex pathway is the optic nerve (II) or the trigeminal nerve (V); the efferent limb is the facial nerve (VII). Additional reflex pathways which are located in the cranial nerves and brainstem include the oculocephalic (doll's eye) and oculovestibular (caloric) reflexes. The stimulation of the vestibular nuclei of the acoustic nerve (VIII) results in conjugate eye movements which are stimulated by the efferent fibers of the oculomotor (III), trochlear (IV), and abducens (VI) nerves. Eye movements also require complex and integrated efforts of the cerebral cortex, cerebellum, and reticular formation.

The cardiovascular reflexes include the oculocardiac reflex and the carotid sinus reflex. The afferent limb of the oculocardiac reflex is the trigeminal nerve (V), and the efferent limb is the vagus (X) nerve. The carotid sinus reflex response is the slowing of the heart rate in response to a rise in blood pressure due to stimulation of the baroreceptors. The afferent limb carried via the glossopharyngeal nerve (IX) is stimulated when the baroreceptors respond to stretch such as in elevation of the blood pressure. Slowing of the heart rate occurs in response to the application of pressure on the eyeball.

The reflexes which involve genitourinary and rectal activities include the bulbocavernosus, the voiding, rectal, and mass reflexes. Cutaneous stimulation of the glans penis is transmitted to the sacral 2d, 3d, and 4th spinal segments, with the resultant reflex contraction of the bulbocavernosus muscle via pelvic autonomic fibers. The normal bladder and rectal sphincter control is under the influence of the sacral 2d, 3d, and 4th spinal segments and the reflex responses of the autonomic fibers. Reflex emptying of the bowel and bladder, flexion of the lower extremities, and sweating may occur unless they are under the control of higher cortical centers.

There are a variety of postural reflex pathways which assist in maintaining the body in an upright balanced position and provide the constant adjustments necessary to maintain a stable posture for voluntary activity. The sensory input from muscle stretch, proprioception, pressure, and visual cues is received and integrated at spinal cord, medulla, midbrain, and cerebral cortical centers. The response, which is primarily transmitted by extrapyramidal pathways, results in muscle contractions, extension and flexion patterns, righting of the head and body, and maintaining the limbs in position to support the body.

REFERENCES

Carpenter, M. B.: *Core Text of Neuroanatomy,* 2d ed., Baltimore: Williams & Wilkins, 1978.

Chusid, J. G.: *Correlative Neuroanatomy and Functional Neurology,* 17th ed., Los Altos: Lange, 1979.

Clark, R. G.: *Essentials of Clinical Neuroanatomy and Neurophysiology,* 5th ed., Philadelphia: Davis, 1975.

Ganong, W. F.: *Review of Medical Physiology,* 6th ed., Los Altos: Lange, 1973.

Goss, C. M. (ed.): *Gray's Anatomy of the Body,* 29th ed., Philadelphia: Lea & Febiger, 1973.

Guyton, A. C.: *Textbook of Medical Physiology,* 5th ed., Philadelphia: Saunders, 1976.

Netter, F. H.: *The Ciba Collection of Medical Illustrations,* vol. 1, *The Nervous System,* Summit, N.J.: Ciba Corporation, 1972.

Walton, J. H. (ed.): *The Pathophysiology of Head Injury,* Summit, N.J.: Ciba Corporation, 1966.

Willis, W. D., and R. G. Grossman: *Medical Neurobiology,* 2d ed., St. Louis: Mosby, 1977.

Functional integrity of the human organism requires that activities of all body systems are adjusted to correlate with changes in demands posed by the external and internal environments. Delicate physiologic balance must be achieved and maintained, and complex processes must be precisely regulated. The endocrine system, closely interacting with the nervous system, is responsible for many vital adjustments in physiologic integration. Mechanisms in that integration overlap; those of the nervous system are discussed in Chap. 6. Integration by the endocrine system is effected through secretion of hormones into the circulation to be carried to the various body tissues.

In this chapter structural and functional categories of hormones as well as mechanisms by which they exert their effect are discussed as background for discussion of the anatomy and physiology of the various glands of the endocrine system. A list of the glands and their locations can be found in Table 7-1.

Exaggeration of the importance of the endocrine glands is almost impossible. Each of the glands is capable of exerting a specific effect, and at times this effect is profound with regard to physiologic influence upon body tissues. As an interacting system, the endocrine glands are responsible for the regulation of complex processes including growth and development, reproduction, metabolism, and the stress response. In addition, they play vital roles in the establishment and maintenance of fluid and electrolyte, acid-base, and energy balance. The nature of their regulation and maintenance of homeostasis is multifaceted and widespread.

HORMONES: THE PHYSIOLOGIC EFFECTORS

It is through hormones that the endocrine system performs its vital functions.

Structural Categories

Hormones fall into one of the following four structural categories: amines, steroids, polypeptides, and prostaglandins.

Amines

The amines include the catecholamines norepinephrine and epinephrine. Norepinephrine is formed by hydroxylation and decarboxylation of the amino acids phenylalanine and tyrosine. Enzymes necessary for

7
THE ENDOCRINE SYSTEM
Sarah J. Sanford

HORMONES: THE PHYSIOLOGIC EFFECTORS
Structural Categories
Mechanisms of Hormone Action
Functional Categories of Hormones

PITUITARY GLAND (HYPOPHYSIS)
Anterior Pituitary (Adenohypophysis)
Posterior Pituitary (Neurohypophysis)
Intermediate Pituitary (Pars Intermedia)

THYROID
Thyroxine (Tetraiodothyronine, T_4) and
Triiodothyronine (T_3)
Thyrocalcitonin (Calcitonin)

PARATHYROIDS
Parathormone (PTH)

ADRENALS
Adrenal Cortex
Adrenal Medulla

ENDOCRINE PANCREAS
Insulin
Glucagon

GONADS
Testes
Ovaries

PINEAL
Melatonin

THYMUS
Thymosin

REFERENCES

TABLE 7-1
Names and Locations of the Endocrine Glands

Name	Location
Pituitary gland (hypophysis) Anterior lobe (adenohypophysis) Posterior lobe (neurohypophysis) Intermediate lobe (pars intermedia)	Cranial cavity (pituitary fossa)
Thyroid gland	Neck—either side of trachea
Parathyroid glands	Neck—embedded in thyroid
Adrenal glands	Kidneys—upper poles (retroperitoneal space)
Adrenal cortex	Outer layer of gland
Adrenal medulla	Interior portion of gland
Endocrine pancreas (islets of Langerhans)	Abdomen—pancreas
Gonads	
Testes	Scrotum
Ovaries	Pelvis
Pineal gland	Cranial cavity (below third ventricle)
Thymus	Mediastinum

the conversion of the amino acids to norepinephrine are present in adrenergic nerve endings. However, conversion of norepinephrine to epinephrine involves methylation of the former by enzymes found only in the adrenal medulla. Release of norepinephrine occurs at adrenergic nerve endings, while both epinephrine and norepinephrine, but predominantly epinephrine, are released from the adrenal medulla.

Steroids

Steroid hormones include the glucocorticoids, mineralocorticoids, and sex hormones (androgens and estrogens). They are synthesized and secreted by both the adrenal cortex and the gonads. All steroid hormones are derivatives of cholesterol. The cells in which synthesis occurs as well as the biochemical pathways employed are similar. The actual structure formed is determined by sequential action of catalytic enzyme systems present in each of the respective glands. Deficiencies of any of these enzyme systems can result in the production of abnormally high quantities of other, similar structures that are not subject to the normal physiologic control mechanisms. Such deficiencies therefore produce manifestations of a wide variety, all of which are attributable to aberrant steroid activity. In the adrenal cortex, enzymes result in the synthesis of physiologically significant amounts of two glucocorticoids (cortisol and corticosterone), one mineralocorticoid (aldosterone), and one androgen. Small amounts of several androgens, estrogens, and other structurally similar sex hormones are also secreted. The gonads, testes in the male and ovaries in the female, contain enzyme systems capable of synthesis of androgens, and in the ovary, androgens are further acted upon to become estrogens.

Polypeptides

Polypeptide hormones include those secreted by the endocrine pancreas, the thyroid, and the anterior pituitary. These hormones have in common varying numbers and combinations of amino acids arranged in chainlike structures. All are synthesized within the cells of the gland which secrete them under the direction of messenger ribonucleic acid (mRNA). In the case of the thyroid hormones, tetraiodothyronine and triiodothyronine, iodine molecules are also incorporated.

Prostaglandins

Unlike the other three structural categories just discussed, these hormones are not primarily synthesized or secreted by a specific structure. Rather, they are synthesized by a wide variety of tissues and are frequently referred to as *tissue hormones.* Tissues in which prostaglandins are synthesized include the seminal vesicles, kidneys, lungs, iris, brain, and thymus. They are composed of a series of closely related unsaturated fatty acids containing a cyclopentane ring. Three categories of prostaglandins have been established on the basis of the configuration of that (cyclopentane) ring. They are group A prostaglandins (PGA), group E prostaglandins (PGE), and group F prostaglandins (PGF). Although they are similar to other hormones in that they enter the bloodstream, they do so in miniscule amounts and probably exert their major effects by diffusing to cells adjacent to those from which they are secreted.

This group of hormones has diverse physiologic effects, generally of an extremely potent nature. Group A prostaglandins are thought to result in relaxation of smooth muscle fibers in the walls of arteries and arterioles. They therefore produce an immediate decrease in blood pressure with simultaneous increases in the blood flow of the regions in close proximity to the cells from which they are released, one of these regions being the kidney. Prostaglandins in the E group have been implicated as mediators of hematopoietic, inflammatory, and gastrointestinal processes including platelet aggregation, fever, and the regulation of hydrochloric acid secretion. Group F prostaglandins apparently affect contraction of smooth muscle in the uterus and bowel. Compounds in this group have been found to induce labor and accelerate delivery as well as play an essential role in the maintenance of normal peristalsis.

Mechanisms of Hormone Action

Once secreted, hormones enter the circulation and exert their influence upon *target organ tissues,* or tisues that contain specific receptors capable of reacting with the particular structure of the hormone involved. Upon reaction of a target cell receptor with a hormone, one of two mechanisms is initiated.

cAMP Activation: The "Second Messenger"

The "second messenger" mechanism of hormonal action involves formation of adenosine 3',5'-monophosphate, *cyclic AMP (cAMP),* from intracellular adenosine triphosphate (ATP). Conversion of ATP is possible because the combination of the hormone with the target-cell receptor liberates a catalytic enzyme, *adenyl cyclase.* Adenyl cyclase then converts ATP to cAMP. Once formed, cAMP directs the target cell to perform its specialized function. In this mechanism, the hormone serves as the first messenger, ostensibly delivering a biochemical message from the endocrine gland to the target organ. The second message is then delivered by cAMP, which is the one responsible for the actual response on the part of the cell. Recent research indicates that adenyl cyclase activation may be effected by the prostaglandins. They are known to both facilitate and antagonize activation of adenyl cyclase in tissue cells. Through selective adenyl cyclase activation they are believed to play a role in the regulation of cellular cAMP content and thus mediate the cellular response to hormones acting by this mechanism.

Three hormones that affect cellular function via the second messenger mechanism include epinephrine, glucagon, and parathormone. Activation of cAMP in the cells of bronchiolar smooth muscle, hepatic cells, and the cells of bones results in relaxation and bronchiolar dilatation, breakdown of hepatic glycogen (and an elevation in blood glucose), and release of ionized calcium from bones, respectively. Characteristic of this mechanism is a rapid tissue response, due in part to the fact that hormone receptors are located on or within the target cell membranes and thus are readily exposed to circulating hormones. Hormones activating cAMP also tend to exert a profound impact on target cells.

Some pharmacologic agents are known to exert their effect by alteration of the second messenger mechanism of hormone response. One of these is aminophylline. This substance prolongs epinephrine-induced bronchiolar dilatation by inhibiting phosphodiesterase, the enzyme that normally results in breakdown of cAMP. A second agent is aspirin. Current research indicates that the anti-inflammatory and anticoagulant properties of aspirin probably occur at least in part due to prevention of group E prostaglandin synthesis. As a result of decreased PGE, alteration of cellular cAMP content occurs, presumably limiting cellular responsiveness.

Intracellular Mechanism

The second mechanism of hormone action is the intracellular mechanism. Hormones exerting their effect via this mechanism must be lipid-soluble and able to transverse cell membranes, because receptors are located within cellular boundaries. Once within the cell, the hormone is transferred to the cell nucleus where the hormone-receptor complex directs alterations in the synthesis of mRNA and subsequently, in specific proteins. Both transversing cellular membranes and altering mRNA synthesis requires a longer time frame than that required for cAMP activation. Therefore, while no less profound in impact, hormones acting via the intracellular mechanism require days to weeks not only to reach peak effect but to subside. Steroid and thyroid hormones are examples of hormones exerting their impact by this mechanism. Schematic representations of both of these mechanisms are presented in Fig. 7-1.

Functional Categories of Hormones

Placing the endocrine hormones into functional categories facilitates their organization.

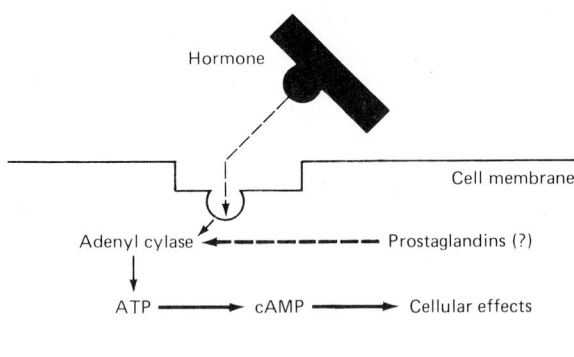

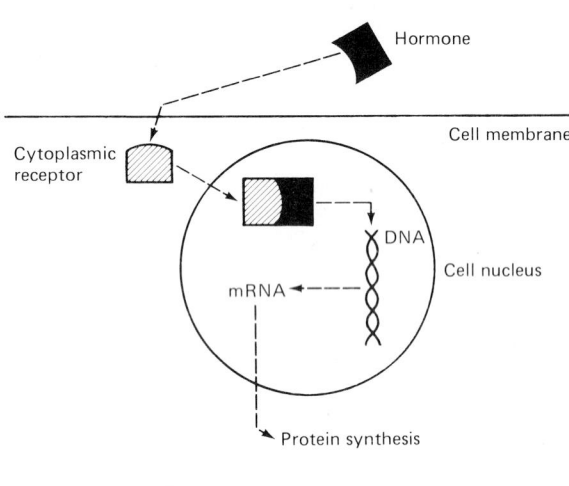

FIGURE 7-1

Mechanisms of hormone action. (*a*) The "second messenger," cAMP activation. (*b*) Intracellular mechanism.

Releasing and Inhibiting Hormones

The releasing and inhibiting hormones are a group of hormones that are synthesized by the hypothalamus. They differ from all but the posterior pituitary hormones in that their synthesis occurs within the central nervous system, as opposed to synthesis in the gland from which they are secreted. Their only target is the anterior pituitary. For each of the hormones secreted by the anterior pituitary there is thought to be both a releasing and inhibiting hormone secreted by the hypothalamus; however, only eight have been identified:

1. Corticotropin releasing hormone (CRH)

2. Thyrotropin releasing hormone (TRH)

3. Growth hormone releasing hormone (GRH)

4. Growth hormone inhibiting hormone (GIH)

5. Follicle-stimulating hormone releasing hormone (FRH)

6. Luteinizing hormone releasing hormone (LRH)

7. Prolactin releasing hormone (PRH)

8. Prolactin inhibiting hormone (PIH).

As their names imply, these hormones either stimulate or inhibit the secretion of the hormones of the anterior pituitary. Each is discussed in conjunction with the hormone it directly affects in the section that follows. Secretion of the releasing and inhibiting hormones is regulated by diffuse interaction within the central nervous system and also by the condition of the blood perfusing the hypothalamus through the negative feedback mechanism described below.

Tropic Hormones

By definition, tropic hormones increase the size and secretion rates of other endocrine glands. These hormones are secreted only by the anterior pituitary. From there they enter the general circulation to be carried to target endocrine glands. Control of their secretion is directly influenced by hypothalamic secretion of releasing and inhibiting hormones. It is also affected by blood levels of hormones secreted by their target glands. As the blood level of a target gland hormone increases, the secretion rate of the anterior pituitary tropic hormones decreases; thus target gland hormones exert *negative feedback* upon further tropic hormone release. Negative feedback also operates at the hypothalamic level with regard to secretion of releasing hormones. Each of the tropic hormones is discussed in detail in the section dealing with the anterior pituitary that follows.

Peripheral Hormones

The category of hormones with which we are most familiar are those that act directly upon peripheral tissues. With the exception of the two hormones secreted by the posterior pituitary, peripheral hormones are gland-specific in origin in that they are secreted by the gland in which their synthesis occurs. Their targets are perfused by the general circulation and are defined by the presence of receptors capable of responding to their particular structure.

Control over their secretion rates is twofold. Nervous system influence is prominent. The autonomic nervous system directly affects release of some peripheral hormones (e.g., catecholamines); the hypothalamus directly affects release of others (e.g., oxytocin and antidiuretic hormone) and indirectly affects release of still others via secretion of releasing hormones (e.g., prolactin, growth hormone, and all the pituitary tropic hormones, which then increase the secretion of target glands). In addition, blood-borne or humoral conditions directly stimulate release of still other peripheral hormones. Insulin and glucagon are two examples, and these are secreted in response to elevations or insufficient levels of blood glucose, respectively. A summary of the hormonal relationships between the hypothalamus, pituitary, and periphery is presented in Table 7-2.

PITUITARY GLAND (HYPOPHYSIS)

The pituitary gland is an almond-sized organ located deep in the cranium in the pituitary fossa of the sella turcica. It is protected not only by virtue of the surrounding bone but also by a layer of dura known as the *pituitary diaphragm.* Off the upper aspect there is a cylindrical projection, the *pituitary stalk,* that joins the gland to the hypothalamus.

Because of the wide variety and profound influence exerted by hormones secreted by the pituitary, it is frequently referred to as the "master" gland. It is composed of three lobes (the anterior, intermediate, and posterior), each of which functions independently with regard to hormones secreted.

The anterior and intermediate lobes microscopically resemble other endocrine tissue. Functionally, they are connected to the hypothalamus by a portal capillary network (*portal-hypophyseal tract*) in the pituitary stalk. Axons from hypothalamic secretory cells terminate closely adjacent to the origin of this network, and it is into these capillaries that hypothalamic releasing and inhibiting hormones are released to be transported to the anterior pituitary.

The posterior lobe of the pituitary microscopically resembles nervous system tissue. In contrast to the circulatory network between the hypothalamus and the anterior and intermediate lobes, the posterior lobe is functionally linked to the hypothalamus by a tract of nerve fibers. Transmission of neural impulses down

TABLE 7-2
Hormonal Relationships Between the Hypothalamus, Pituitary, and Periphery

Hypothalamic Hormones		Pituitary tropic hormone	Peripheral hormone
Releasing	Inhibiting		
Growth hormone releasing hormone (GRH)	Growth hormone inhibiting hormone (GIF)	—	Growth hormone
Prolactin releasing hormone (PRH)	Prolactin inhibiting hormone (PIH)	—	Prolactin
Corticotropin releasing hormone (CRF)	—	Adrenocorticotropic hormone (ACTH)	Adrenal steroids
Follicle-stimulating hormone releasing hormone (FRH)	—	Follicle-stimulating hormone	Gonadal steroids
Luteinizing hormone releasing hormone (LRF)	—	Luteinizing hormone (LH)	Gonadal steroids
Thyrotropin releasing hormone (TRH)	—	Thyroid-stimulating hormone (TSH)	Thyroid hormones
—	—	—	Oxytocin
—	—	—	Antidiuretic hormone (ADH)
—	—	—	Melanotropins (melanocyte-stimulating hormones, MSHs)

this tract is the mechanism by which secretion of posterior pituitary hormones is influenced by the hypothalamus. An illustration of the anatomical hypothalamic-pituitary relationship is presented in Fig. 7-2.

Anterior Pituitary (Adenohypophysis)

Histologically, the anterior pituitary is composed of three types of granular secretory cells as well as connective tissue and a dense vascular network. Named for their reaction to dyes, the secretory cells consist of acidophils, or those whose granules readily stain with acid dyes; basophils, or those whose granules readily stain with basic dyes; and chromophobes, those which do not readily stain with either type of dye (from the Greek *chroma*, meaning "color," and the Latin *phobia*, meaning "fear of"). Acidophils secrete the two anterior pituitary peripheral hormones prolactin and growth hormone, and basophils secrete the four anterior pituitary tropic hormones. Chromophobes are probably "burned out" acidophils or basophils and no longer function in a secretory capacity.

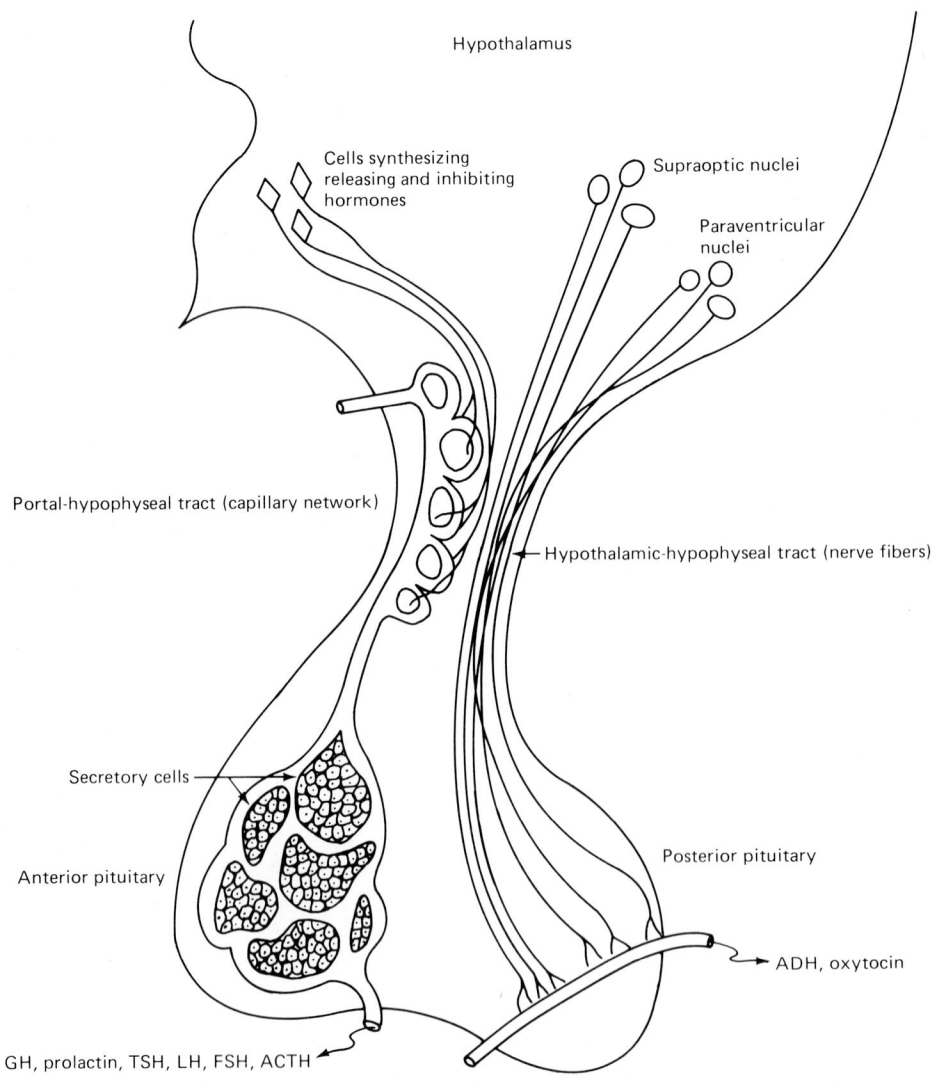

FIGURE 7-2

Anatomical basis of hypothalamic-pituitary relationships.

The vascular network of the anterior pituitary enters the gland as a continuation of the portal capillary network in the pituitary stalk. After extensive winding between the secretory cells, it empties into the general circulation. The dense circulatory nature of the anterior pituitary provides the anatomical basis for the high degree of interaction that exists between the hypothalamus and the anterior pituitary. Functionally, it not only allows a means of bathing the anterior pituitary secretory cells in blood which contains releasing and inhibiting hormones from the hypothalamus, but it also provides a readily accessible means of delivering anterior pituitary hormones to the general circulation.

Anterior Pituitary Tropic Hormones

Four of the six hormones secreted by the anterior pituitary are tropic hormones. They are thyroid-stimulating hormone (TSH); adrenocorticotropic hormone (ACTH); and the gonadotropins, follicle-stimulating hormone (FSH) and luteinizing hormone (LH), also called interstitial cell–stimulating hormone (ICSH) in males. Prolactin is no longer considered a gonadotropin and is discussed under peripheral tissue hormones of the anterior pituitary in the section that follows.

Thyroid-stimulating hormone (TSH) is necessary for appropriate thyroid gland function. Without it the thyroid gland atrophies. If it is present in excessive quantities, gland enlargement or *goiter* formation occurs.

Neural influences regulate TSH secretion via thyrotropin releasing hormone (TRH) from the hypothalamus. In addition, negative feedback upon both the anterior pituitary and hypothalamus produced by high circulating blood levels of thyroid hormones regulates TSH secretion. Changes in the internal and external environment can therefore produce appropriate adjustments in the rate of thyroid secretion.

The function of the adrenal cortex is dependent upon *adrenocorticotropic hormone (ACTH)*. Without this anterior pituitary tropic hormone, the adrenal gland atrophies and becomes incapable of synthesizing and secreting adequate quantities of both glucocorticoids and mineralocorticoids. In addition, insufficient ACTH also results in a progressive decline in adrenal responsiveness to the tropic hormone, a situation which requires repeated exposure to ACTH to restore normal responsiveness.

Neither basal adrenal cortical secretion of glucocorticoids nor the increased secretion necessary in stress situations can occur in the absence of ACTH.

Basal output of glucocorticoids is dependent upon a diurnal pattern of ACTH secretion. Peak secretion occurs consistently during one part of the day, most commonly in the morning, while lowest secretion levels occur 12 h before (and after) each peak. While the time clock mechanism directing this pattern is not fully understood, it is known to be dictated by the hypothalamus via release of corticotropin releasing hormone (CRH). Stress in the form of physical, chemical, or emotional trauma superimposes bursts of ACTH secretion upon the underlying diurnal pattern of secretion. These bursts are also effected by hypothalamic release of CRH.

Negative feedback at both the hypothalamus and anterior pituitary is produced by high circulating levels of glucocorticoids. It matters not whether the source of these glucocorticoids is internal or external. Significant danger exists when prolonged therapeutic doses of glucocorticoids are abruptly stopped. Decreased ACTH secretion induced by negative feedback has resulted in both adrenal atrophy and decreased responsiveness to ACTH. Because return of responsiveness requires prolonged periods, adequate levels of glucocorticoids can not be synthesized or secreted by the adrenal cortex during this period. Gradual withdrawal of exogenous glucocorticoids is therefore necessary to provide the time needed for normal adrenal gland function and responsiveness to return.

The two remaining tropic hormones secreted by the anterior pituitary are the gonadotropins *follicle-stimulating hormone (FSH)*, and *luteinizing hormone (LH)*. Both these hormones are necessary to prevent atrophy of the gonads, ovaries in the female and testes in the male. Reproductive capability is dependent upon their secretion as well. FSH is necessary for the maintenance of spermatogenic capability by the cells of the testes and is responsible for the early growth of the ovarian follicles in the ovary. LH is responsible for maintaining the synthesis and secretory capacity of testicular Leydig cells with regard to testosterone. In females LH directs the final maturation of ovarian follicles, including development of their capability for estrogen secretion. In addition, possibly interacting with FSH, LH is necessary for ovulation, formation and maintenance of the corpus luteum, and subsequent synthesis and secretion of progesterone. (See "Gonads," below.)

Secretion patterns of the gonadotropins are influenced by hypothalamic secretion of follicle-stimulating hormone releasing hormone (FRH) and luteinizing hormone releasing hormone (LRH) and involves cyclic sequences. Complete discussion of these sequences with regard to gonadotropin secretion is beyond the scope of this chapter and the reader is referred to the literature. Further discussion is presented in Chap. 12. Negative feedback is exerted at the level of the hypothalamus by high circulating levels of the target gland hormones, namely estrogen and testosterone, leading to inhibition of anterior pituitary secretion of FSH and LH, respectively.

Peripheral Hormones of the Anterior Pituitary

Two hormones that exert their effect directly upon peripheral tissues are secreted by the acidophils of the anterior pituitary. These are prolactin and growth hormone (GH). *Prolactin* has been categorized as a gonadotropin and has been referred to as *luteotropic hormone* (LTH) because it has been found to maintain the corpus luteum of many laboratory animals, specifically rodents. However, LH, *not* prolactin, performs this function in mammals, including humans. Thus classification of prolactin as a gonadotropin is misleading, since its primary target is not an endocrine gland but rather the alveolar cells of the breasts.

Prolactin is a lactogenic hormone; that is, it prepares milk and effects its synthesis by the mammary alveolar cells. However, this requires prior estrogen and progesterone preparation, or "priming." The function of prolactin in males is unknown.

Except during pregnancy, secretion of prolactin is tonically suppressed by prolactin-inhibiting hormone (PIH) from the hypothalamus. When pregnancy occurs, hypothalamic secretion of prolactin releasing hormone (PRH) exceeds that of PIH, and as a result prolactin secretion increases. Peak prolactin secretion occurs at delivery and then falls to nonpregnant levels roughly 8 days later. While suckling produces increases in its secretion rate, the degree of increase progressively declines in females nursing for more than 3 months.

Growth hormone (GH) is a peripheral tissue hormone with widespread physiologic activity. It is a protein anabolic hormone; that is, it promotes tissue synthesis and is thus essential for healing and repair. Mechanisms by which it exerts its anabolic effects include acceleration of intracellular amino acid transport, stimulation of intracellular mRNA-mediated amino acid synthesis, and stimulation of production of peptide substance known as *somatomedin* in the liver and kidneys. Somatomedin facilitates chondrogenesis, or cartilage formation, and plasma levels of this substance have been found to correlate more closely to tissue synthesis rates than plasma growth hormone levels.

Tissues particularly high in protein content, such as cartilage and muscle, are profoundly influenced by GH. Bones are also affected and, like muscle and cartilage, increase in mass under the influence of growth hormone. Linear growth of long bones occurs between epiphyseal growth plates at each end. There, chondrogenesis produces a matrix structure that later serves as the site of bony calcification. Growth hormone facilitates chondrogenesis and thus promotes long-bone lengthening until fusion or closure of epiphyseal plates occurs. This closure roughly corresponds to the termination of puberty, at which time total stature has been achieved.

Insufficient quantities of growth hormone result in decreased linear growth, or *dwarfism,* if it occurs prior to puberty. In contrast, increased quantities of growth hormone during this same time result in excessive stature, or *gigantism.* Following epiphyseal closure, linear growth is physiologically impossible and only flat bones or those without growth plates can continue to increase mass. Such bones include the frontal portion of the cranium, mandible, and maxilla. Excess growth hormone secretion in adults thus produces deformities of flat bones and cartilagenous soft tissue and is referred to as *acromegaly.* Characteristically, it involves enlargement of the forehead, cheeks, jaws, and nose, and facial features generally become coarse and heavy.

Growth hormone also affects carbohydrate and fat metabolism. It has been referred to as a *diabetogenic hormone* because it produces hyperglycemia and tends to promote ketogenesis by shifting cellular energy pathways to reliance upon free fatty acids. GH produces hyperglycemia by increasing hepatic glucose output at the same time it exerts an anti-insulin effect upon cellular glucose uptake. Cells unable to use glucose for energy need a replacement source of fuel. Growth hormone supplies that replacement by breaking down adipose tissue and releasing free fatty acids. Individuals suffering from acromegaly or gigantism are thus highly susceptible to the development of diabetes, and to make matters worse, it is frequently of a somewhat insulin-resistant nature.

Secretion of GH occurs as a result of hypothalamic secretion of growth hormone releasing hormone (GRH). Similar to that of ACTH, it follows a diurnal pattern of fluctuation that is determined by a hypothalamic time clock. This time clock produces periods in which GRH secretion predominates, alternating with periods in which growth hormone inhibiting hormone (GIH) is dominant. Peak GH secretion is usually at night and is associated with both the onset and occurrences of non–rapid eye movement (non-REM) sleep.

Superimposed upon the diurnal GH secretion pattern are wide fluctuations. These fluctuations are also a function of the hypothalamus. Stimuli responsible for some of these include conditions in which there is an insufficient availability of substances capable of supplying cellular energy such as fasting, hypoglycemia, or strenuous exercise. Conditions where high levels of amino acids are circulating, such as following a large (especially protein-rich) meal, also result in GH secretion. Physiologically these stimuli are appropriate in that growth hormone secretion mobilizes free fatty acids and thus creates a readily available energy pool to reverse any insufficiency. At the same time, it facilitates amino acid transport into cells to be used for tissue synthesis rather than fuel and in effect protects, or "spares," amino acids from undergoing hepatic gluconeogenesis. Other stimuli for the secretion of growth hormone include stress and the presence of glucagon. The latter will be

discussed in detail in the section concerning the endocrine pancreas that follows. A schematic representation of the hypothalamic-anterior pituitary hormonal interrelationships is presented in Fig. 7-3.

Posterior Pituitary (Neurohypophysis)

The posterior pituitary is composed of modified nervous system cells incapable of synthesis of the two hormones secreted by this gland. Both these hormones, oxytocin and antidiuretic hormone (ADH), are synthesized within cell bodies of the hypothalamus, specifically in the supraoptic and paraventricular nuclei. Axons of these cells combine and form the *hypothalamic-hypophyseal nerve tract* that functionally connects the hypothalamus to the posterior pituitary (Fig. 7-2). Once synthesized, the hormones are bound into small pouches or vesicles which are transported down the axons (axoplasm transport) to the posterior pituitary. Secretion of these hormones occurs in response to neural impulses from the hypothalamus. Both oxytocin and ADH are peripheral hormones.

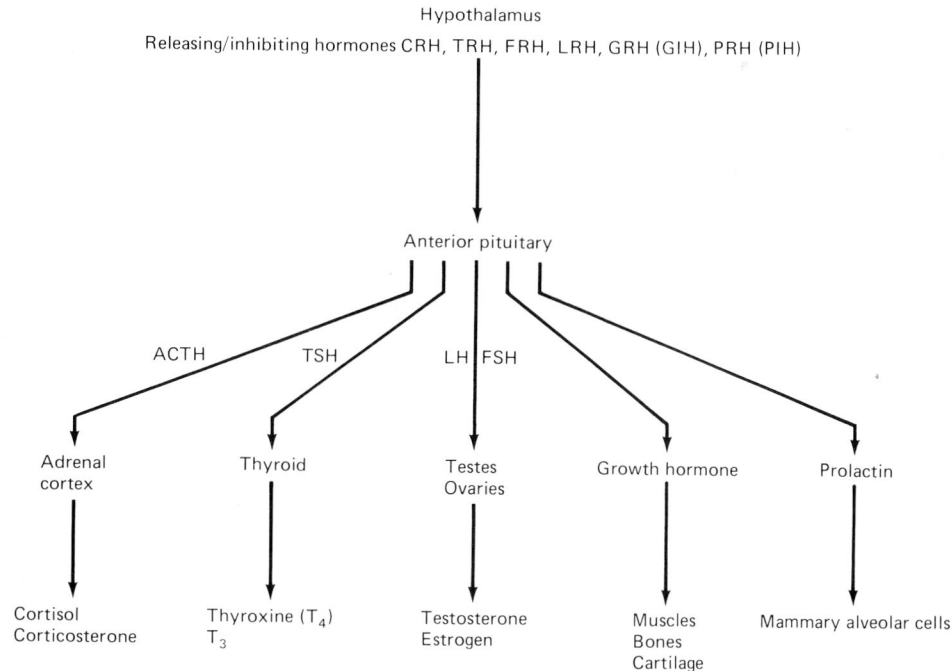

FIGURE 7-3

Hormonal interrelationships between the hypothalamus and anterior pituitary.

Oxytocin

The major physiologic effect of oxytocin is milk ejection from the secretory ducts of the breast. It does not influence milk synthesis, which instead is dependent upon the actions of estrogen, progesterone, and prolactin. Milk ejection occurs as a reflex and is initiated by stimulation of touch receptors around the nipple. As a result of nipple stimulation, impulses are generated which are then transmitted to the supraoptic and paraventricular nuclei of the hypothalamus. The posterior pituitary is stimulated and oxytocin is released. The milk-ejection reflex can also be initiated by genital stimulation and strong emotions.

Oxytocin also causes contraction of uterine smooth muscle. It is secreted during labor as a result of transmission of impulses generated by touch receptors in the birth canal. As in the milk-ejection reflex, these impulses reach the hypothalamus and effect oxytocin release. It may also play a role in the initiation of labor; however, this process involves many complex mechanisms, and the precise role of oxytocin has yet to be defined.

Antidiuretic Hormone (ADH)

Antidiuretic hormone is also known as *vasopressin* and *arginine vasopressin*. Its principal action is to conserve or retain free water or effect an "antidiuresis." It acts upon the distal tubules and collecting ducts of the kidney where it produces an increase in permeability, thus allowing water to freely follow the osmotic gradient out of the tubules into the surrounding hypertonic interstitium. As water leaves the collecting tubules, less urine volume remains, urine concentration increases, and since water is retained in excess of solute, the osmotic tonicity or pressure of the body fluids decreases (e.g., becomes more dilute). When ADH secretion is low, collecting tubule permeability does not allow water to leave the tubular lumen; therefore, urine volume increases while concentration decreases. In this situation, urine is hypotonic in comparison to the body fluids, a net loss of water occurs, and the osmotic pressure of the body fluids is increased. In large amounts, ADH also constricts arteriolar smooth muscle and consequently elevates arterial blood pressure, although this is a minor effect compared with its effect upon body free water balance.

Secretion of ADH is dictated by the hypothalamus. There, receptor cells alter their rate of both impulse generation and transmission to the posterior pituitary in the face of changes in body fluid tonicity or osmolarity. These cells, known as *osmoreceptors*, shrink when body fluid tonicity is increased or hyperosmolarity exists, because of intracellular water loss to the surrounding (abnormally) hypertonic interstitium. The result is secretion of ADH, maximal retention of water, and a decrease in osmolarity. Thus, in hyperosmolar states, ADH secretion results in the production of low volumes of highly concentrated urine. In contrast, situations in which excess free water is present cause osmoreceptor cells to swell because of water influx from a hypotonic environment. As a result, impulse transmission to the posterior pituitary decreases, affecting suppression of ADH secretion. Water is unable to escape the tubular lumen and therefore contributes to the production of large volumes of dilute urine.

In addition to the osmotic feedback regulatory mechanism just described, regulation of ADH is also affected by the status of the extracellular fluid (ECF) volume. Stretch receptors within the vascular system, specifically in the atria and pulmonary vasculature, respond to ECF volume changes by altering their rate of impulse transmission to the hypothalamus. When ECF volume is decreased, ADH secretion is increased. The opposite occurs in the case of ECF volume overload. These receptors provide the prime volume-based mediation of ADH secretion and are extremely sensitive. They are known to produce an increase in ADH secretion in response to a mere change in body position from recumbent to upright. Presumably this occurs because an overall decrease in ECF volume is perceived when actually the only thing that has happened is a decreased venous return due to blood pooling in the lower extremities. In situations in which a loss of ECF volume is of sufficient magnitude to produce a decrease in blood pressure, other volume receptors become involved in the regulation of ADH secretion. These receptors in the aortic arch and carotid sinuses, then, also produce an increase in ADH.

Multiple stimuli other than osmolarity and ECF volume increase ADH secretion. These include pain, emotional or physiologic stress, sympathetic nervous system activation, and a variety of pharmacological agents including anesthetic agents, morphine, and barbiturates in large doses. Alcohol, on the other hand, decreases ADH secretion. A schematic depiction of stimuli affecting ADH secretion is presented in Fig. 7-4.

Clinically, altered secretion and regulation of ADH can produce a variety of problems. Water retention and hyponatremia can appear postoperatively because of the use of anesthetic agents and the fact that surgery subjects the body to stress. In congestive

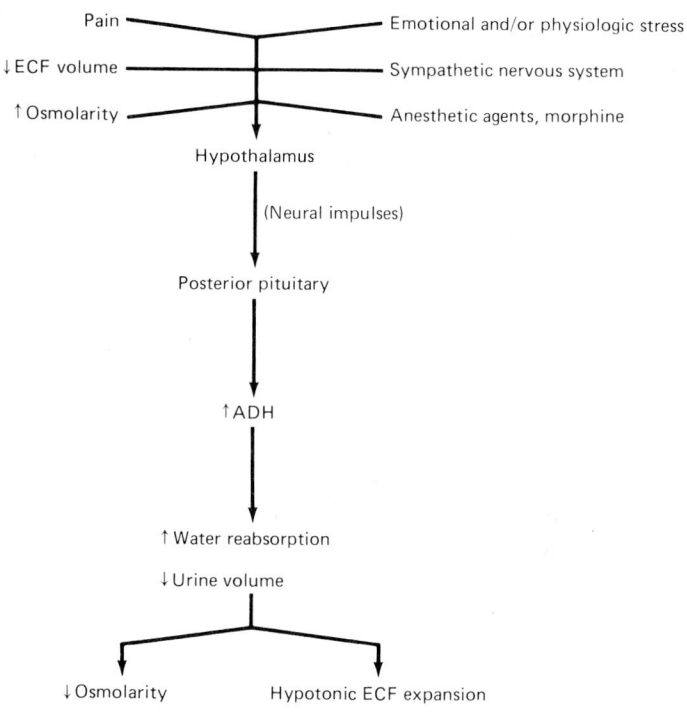

FIGURE 7-4
Stimuli affecting ADH secretion.

heart failure, cirrhosis of the liver, and nephrosis, interstitial sodium shifts and edema may be compounded by water retention. While prolongation of the half-life of ADH due to diminished metabolism and excretion by the liver and kidneys probably plays a role, a normally functioning osmoreceptor mechanism should be capable of correcting the (excess) water-induced decrease in osmolarity. The fact that it does not consistently do so has resulted in speculation that the volume-sensing mechanism has been "fooled" and is overriding osmotic regulation. In all these states, overall ECF volume may be perceived as being decreased when, in actuality, the basis of pathology is poor cardiac efficacy and third space and/or peritoneal fluid shifting. In these situations, ADH secretion is "inappropriate" and its secretion exaggerates and complicates the initial pathology.

Cerebral and pulmonary disease may also promote inappropriate secretion of ADH. Intracranial lesions are thought to produce this effect by one of three possible mechanisms: (1) by allowing "escape" of the hormone because of structural damage of the posterior pituitary; (2) by producing an irritated focus that stimulates the posterior pituitary to release ADH; and/or (3) by stimulation of the sympathetic nervous

system due to cerebral hypoxia. Intrathoracic lesions may interfere with neural pathways that normally translate and transmit the message of increased volume to the hypothalamus to suppress ADH secretion. As a result of increased ADH, water ingested or supplied is not excreted and produces hypotonic expansion of body fluids. Glomerular filtration is increased and promotes sodium excretion with a subsequent progressive decline in body sodium. The result is absolute sodium depletion, water retention, and consequently, a marked decrease in the serum sodium. Clinically these situations have been labeled *cerebral salt wasting, pulmonary salt wasting,* and *syndrome of inappropriate ADH (SIADH)*.

Insufficient ADH can also produce clinical problems. *Diabetes insipidus* is the condition in which ADH is inadequately secreted because of inflammatory cerebral edema or direct damage to the hypothalamus, the hypothalamic-hypophyseal tract, or the posterior pituitary. Pathological mechanisms include errant sensing of water overload by edematous cells, and in these situations, inability to generate or transmit impulses to the posterior pituitary. ADH secretion is thus diminished. Clinically the syndrome presents as *polyuria* with excessive loss of large volumes of hypotonic urine. Excessive free water loss increases body osmolarity and is the basis for thirst and *polydipsia* in those capable of responding. Those unable to respond to thirst or those in whom perception of thirst is diminished are extremely vulnerable to development of dangerous and potentially lethal hyperosmolarity. Acute traumatic head injuries, craniotomies, and cerebral infarcts are pathologies that can produce diabetes insipidus.

In the presence of a decreased ability to perceive or respond to thirst, another related clinical problem may develop. Because depressed levels of consciousness are frequent in this group, tube feedings and parenteral hyperalimentation are often instituted to meet nutritional needs. The majority of these solutions are extremely hypertonic, and development of severe hyperosmolarity is possible. Hypertonic enteric preparations produce a net flow of water into the gastrointestinal tract. The result is gastrointestinal distension, one of the most powerful stimuli to increased motility. Diarrhea is likely, and with it, a net free water loss and increase in osmolarity occur. In the case of parenteral hyperalimentation solutions, a large glucose load is delivered to the blood and hyperglycemia occurs. If the renal threshold for glucose reabsorption is exceeded, glucose spills into the urine, initiating an osmotic diuresis. Large volumes of urine are produced and result in loss of sodium and water but proportionately more water. If allowed to progress, overall ECF volume depletion and net free water loss compound the initial hyperosmolarity due to hyperglycemia. Despite ADH secretion and maximal collecting tubule permeability, free water availability is decreased and the water that is present follows the strongest osmotic gradient. The presence of continued high quantities of tubular glucose results in physiologic competition for water between the tubular and interstitial spaces. In these situations, water intake is dependent upon its administration by those providing care, and vulnerability to hyperosmolarity must be decreased by vigilant monitoring of osmolarity and supplying extra water as necessary. Noting the adequacy of urine volume as an indicator of water status is misleading at best because urine output may be maintained at the expense of body water balance.

Intermediate Pituitary (Pars Intermedia)

The intermediate lobe of the pituitary is normally quiescent in humans. Although some basophils are present, the majority of the cells composing it are agranular and nonsecreting. In the basophils two peripheral hormones are synthesized. Both are *melanotropins* or *melanocyte-stimulating hormones* (MSH). They are so named because they disperse melanin (pigment) granules known as *melanocytes* in the cells of the skin. The function of MSHs in humans is uncertain, but pituitary tumors can produce hyperpigmentation presumably because increased MSHs excessively stimulate melanocytes.

Structurally MSHs are similar to estrogen, progesterone, and ACTH. In pregnancy, high circulating levels of estrogen and progesterone are thought to be responsible for the hyperpigmentation commonly seen around the nipples and, less commonly, on the face. Hyperpigmentation also occurs in the presence of ACTH-secreting tumors. In the presence of symptoms of insufficient adrenal glucocorticoids (a strong stimulus to ACTH secretion), that hyperpigmentation is often the basis for the diagnosis of primary adrenal pathology. In contrast, pallor is a classic manifestation of hypopituitarism and presumably occurs because of decreased secretion of ACTH.

THYROID

The thyroid gland is composed of two lobes located on either side of the upper trachea. Connecting these lobes is an isthmus or bridge that lies anterior to the larnyx. Microscopically it is composed of follicles or small, closed sacs defining central cavities, parafollicular cells distributed on the outer aspects of the follicles, and a rich vascular network. The follicles are responsible for the synthesis of iodine-containing thyroid hormones, actually two hormones with similar structures known as thyroxine or tetraiodothyronine (T_4), which contains four iodine molecules, and triiodothyronine (T_3), which contains three iodine molecules. These hormones are responsible for metabolic regulation of body tissues at levels necessary for optimum performance of normal function. Parafollicular cells synthesize a hormone known as thyrocalcitonin or calcitonin, a hormone that plays a role in serum calcium level regulation and produces a calcium-lowering effect. The high degree of vascularity of the thyroid is responsible for a rate of blood flow among the highest of all the organs in the body on a gram-for-gram basis. This large blood flow is necessary for synthesis of thyroxine and T_3. Plasma iodine levels are generally low (about 0.3 μg per 100 mL). Normal rates of thyroid hormone synthesis require that the gland pick up 120 μg each day; therefore, blood flow through the gland must be high if hormone synthesis is to occur at normal rates.

Thyroxine (Tetraiodothyronine, T_4) and Triiodothyronine (T_3)

Both T_4 and T_3 act by the intracellular mechanism of hormone action. They are calorigenic in that they increase metabolic rate and stimulate oxygen consumption by most of the cells of the body. In addition, they have an effect upon carbohydrate and lipid metabolism in that they increase the rate of carbohydrate absorption from the gastrointestinal tract and stimulate cholesterol synthesis. Thyroid hormones also play a vital role in growth and maturation by increasing the metabolic rate to levels necessary to promote tissue synthesis. They are also necessary for the secretion of growth hormone to occur. Finally, thyroid hormones are necessary for the development and maintenance of the nervous system. In the peripheral nerves, thyroid hormone regulates the reaction time of reflexes. In the central nervous system, thyroid hormones are necessary for functional development and maintenance. Their precise role in this regard is not known, but apparently thyroid hormones have a unique relationship with the catecholamines. They are synergistic with each other, and thyroid hormones potentiate catecholamine effects. Since catecholamines are neurotransmitters, this thyroid-catecholamine relationship may be one of the mechanisms involved in thyroid-dependent nervous system maturation and function.

Thyroid hormone–induced increases in metabolic rate may promote development of a negative nitrogen balance because of catabolism of fat and protein to meet increased energy needs. This occurs in conditions associated with hypersecretion of the thyroid hormones. One such condition is *Graves' disease,* which is believed to occur as a result of production of antibodies to thyroid tissue. The mechanism by which these antibodies are produced is not understood. Their effect is to cause thyroid inflammation and result in diffuse enlargement and hyperplasia of the gland or *exophthalmic goiter.* Characteristics of Graves' disease include weight loss and heat intolerance due to an increased metabolic rate. *Exophthalmos,* or bulging of the ocular orbits, is also thought to occur as a result of antibody action but has yet to be precisely explained.

If severe, hyperthyroidism is classified as *thyrotoxicosis,* which is characterized by nervousness and tremors, warm pink skin, hyperthermia, and increased pulse pressure and urine output. Potentiation of catecholamines with regard to neurotransmission and increased excitability of peripheral reflexes is the basis of the nervousness and tremors. Warm pink skin reflects activation of heat-dissipating mechanisms (vasodilatation) necessary because the increased metabolic rate has produced hyperthermia. Pulse pressure and urine output elevations reflect a compensatory increase in cardiac output and thus glomerular filtration. Since heart failure is present whenever the cardiac output (regardless of actual volume) is unable to maintain adequate tissue perfusion, *high-output cardiac failure* may occur if compensatory increases in cardiac output are inadequate. Thyrotoxic individuals are vulnerable to the development of liver failure because of chronic depletion of liver glycogen which results from an attempt to meet the increased metabolic needs. Such glycogen depletion increases susceptibility to hepatic injury and degeneration.

Hypothyroidism is manifested by signs of decreased metabolic rate. Weight gain and intolerance to cold are two of the classic findings. Reflexes and mentation are frequently slowed. Accumulations of protein-polysaccharide compounds and water occur in the skin because of slow cutaneous metabolism and protein synthesis. A puffy appearance of the skin is the basis for referring to adult hypothyroidism as *myxedema.*

Children who are hypothyroid from birth display mental retardation and small stature, presumably due to decreased thyroid effects upon the developing nervous system and overall decreased tissue synthesis. Children so affected are known as *cretins.* Once established, the syndrome is irreversible; however, it can be greatly alleviated by prompt thyroid replacement soon after birth.

Thyroid hormone secretion is under the influence of the hypothalamus via thyrotropin-releasing hormone (TRH) and subsequent alteration of the secretion rate of TSH. Day-to-day control of thyroid hormone secretion is primarily a function of negative feedback exerted upon TSH and to a lesser extent TRH secretion in the presence of high circulating levels of T_4 and T_3. A drop in body temperature or exposure to cold as perceived by the hypothalamus increases thyroid secretion, although not markedly. Certain hormones, namely catecholamines and ADH, exert a direct stimulatory effect upon the thyroid and therefore increase the release of thyroxine and T_3. A schematic depiction of control of thyroid secretion is presented in Fig. 7-5.

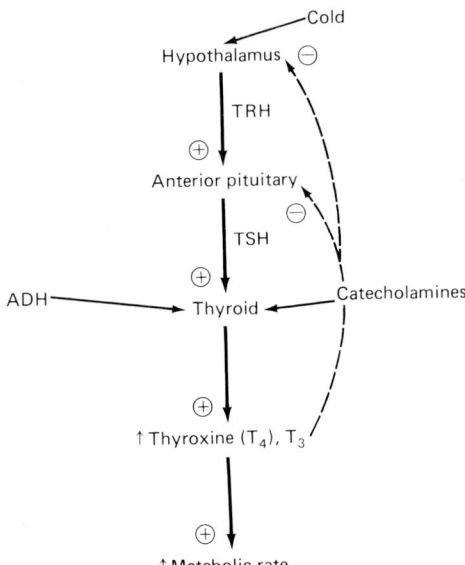

FIGURE 7-5

Stimuli affecting thyroid hormone secretion.

Thyrocalcitonin (Calcitonin)

The exact physiologic role of thyrocalcitonin is unknown, and it may be relatively inactive in adult humans. The serum ionized calcium level is lowered under its influence because it inhibits bone breakdown (resorption) and decreases formation of the active form of vitamin D (1,25-dihydroxycholecalciferol), which is necessary for calcium absorption from the intestine. Secretion of thyrocalcitonin occurs in response to elevations in serum concentrations of ionized calcium; a direct effect on the gland is postulated because thyrocalcitonin secretion is unaffected by TSH. However, adequate ionized calcium is vital in many important physiologic processes, and regulation of its concentration is dominated by the action of parathormone from the parathyroid, which acts to increase serum levels.

PARATHYROIDS

Parathyroid function is accomplished by anywhere from two to six parathyroid glands, each with identical function. They can be found in many locations but most commonly are embedded in the posterior aspect of the thyroid gland. The secretory cells of the parathyroids are known as *chief cells* and they secrete parathormone (PTH), a hormone whose action is essential for survival.

Parathormone (PTH)

This hormone acts to increase the serum level of ionized calcium, a vital mineral which must be in adequate supply if blood coagulation, normal contraction by cardiac and skeletal muscle, and the maintenance of nerve excitability are to be assured. Parathormone secretion occurs when the blood perfusing the parathyroid glands contains insufficient levels of ionized calcium and involves a direct stimulatory effect upon the gland. Parathormone then increases ionized calcium by exerting a direct resorptive or mobilizing influence on bones and affecting active transport of calcium into the ECF. In addition, it stimulates both renal reabsorption of calcium and renal production of *1,25-dihydroxycholecalciferol,* or *active vitamin D,* that is necessary for calcium absorption from the intestines. A general reciprocal relationship exists between ionized calcium and phosphate ions, and parathormone tends to decrease serum phosphate levels by increasing their excretion by the kidney.

Insufficient quantities of parathormone may have lethal effects. Without it, serum ionized calcium falls, producing neuromuscular hyperexcitability. This hyperexcitability can progress to a state of *tetany* or muscle twitching and spasm that prevents effective contraction. Ineffective function of the muscles involved in respiratory function is the terminal event in severe hypocalcemia. The most common clinical situation in which this potential exists is in thyroid surgery with inadvertent parathyroidectomy.

Excessive quantities of parathormone can occur in the presence of a secreting parathyroid tumor. Increased parathormone leads to progressive demineralization of bones, increased renal phosphate excretion, and hypercalcemia. Because the renal threshold for calcium reabsorption is exceeded, calcium is lost in the urine despite parathormone. As a result of the presence of both calcium and phosphate ions in the urine, stone formation is facilitated, and if this occurs to any more than a minimal degree, renal damage results. Severe or prolonged hypercalcemia also alters myocardial conduction, producing a prolongation of the Q-T interval on the electrocardiogram. Peripheral neuromuscular hypotonia and hyporeflexia also occur. In the presence of hypercalcemia, thyrocalcitonin is secreted from the thyroid but is ineffective in correcting serum calcium levels because it is less potent than parathormone and antagonizes only two of the four actions of the parathyroid hormone.

ADRENALS

There are two adrenal glands, each of which contains two distinct and independently functioning portions. The outer layer is the adrenal cortex; it surrounds the adrenal medulla, which composes the gland's interior. The adrenal glands are located at the upper poles of each of the kidneys in the retroperitoneal space.

Adrenal Cortex

The adrenal cortex secretes three steroids: (1) glucocorticoids, steroids which produce effects on the metabolism as well as playing a role in a multitude of other important functions; (2) a mineralocorticoid, which is essential to the maintenance of sodium balance and therefore the ECF volume; and (3) sex hormones, predominantly androgens, which exert minor effects on secondary sex characteristics. All three steroids synthesized by the adrenal cortex are structurally similar. Even though the secretion of these steroids in physiologic amounts produces distinct effects, when secreted in abnormally elevated amounts, their effects may overlap.

Glucocorticoids

Two glucocorticoids, *cortisol* and *corticosterone,* are secreted by the adrenal cortex. Direct metabolic effects of these hormones include increased protein breakdown in all but hepatic cells, impaired peripheral tissue utilization of insulin and thus glucose, and increased hepatic glucose output by increasing gluconeogenesis and glycogenesis simultaneously with increasing production of glucose 6-phosphatase, an enzyme which rapidly converts glycogen to glucose. The result of these actions is hyperglycemia, catabolism, and a pronounced tendency for development of a negative nitrogen balance. The glucocorticoids also increase plasma lipids and in the presence of insufficient insulin produce ketone body formation. (See "Insulin," below.) Needless to say, diabetes is more pronounced in the presence of these hormones.

Glucocorticoids exert a multitude of *permissive actions;* that is, they must be present for many other physiologic events to occur. The effectiveness of glucagon in hypoglycemic states depends upon their presence, as does the metabolic response to catecholamines. (See "Adrenal Medulla," and "Glucagon" below.) The action of norepinephrine on vascular smooth muscle and of ADH upon the collecting tubules of the kidney also requires the presence of glucocorticoids. The glucocorticoids also have permissive effects on the maintenance of normal excitability in the central nervous system as well as in the myocardium.

The secretion of glucocorticoids in the presence of stress is critical. Apart from their permissive role with regard to catecholamines, the mechanism by which they produce physiologic resistance to stress is unclear. However, adrenalectomized animals which have been supplied with maintenance levels of glucocorticoids, but are unable to secrete increased levels when exposed to stress, die when exposed to even minor insults. That they are essential for survival under stress is unquestioned.

Glucocorticoids also produce an anti-inflammatory effect when supplied in doses greater than those normally secreted. They inhibit the release of histamine and other kinins and thus limit the physiologic cascade of events involved in the inflammatory response. They increase splenic sequestration of two types of leukocytes, the eosinophils and basophils, and thus decrease their levels in the circulating blood. They may also exert a protective effect against bacterial toxins by a mechanism that involves stabilization of the membranes containing lysosomes (autolytic enzymes) within all body cells. Since toxins are known to affect release of these enzymes and in that way promote cellular autolysis, this action facilitates the maintenance of cellular integrity. However, glucocorticoids can mask symptoms of potentially serious or fatal bacterial invasion, so their use is not without significant danger.

Both basal secretion of glucocorticoids and the increased secretion provoked by stress are dependent upon ACTH from the anterior pituitary and thus CRH from the hypothalamus. The reader is referred to the detailed discussion of ACTH within the section dealing with the anterior pituitary. A schematic representation of the hypothalamic-pituitary-adrenal relationship or "axis" with regard to glucocorticoid secretion is presented in Fig. 7-6.

Excess glucocorticoids produce a characteristic set of manifestations known as *Cushing's syndrome.* Exogenous administration of large doses of glucocorticoids, hypersecretion of ACTH from the pituitary or CHR from the hypothalamus, and glucocorticoid-producing tumors can all produce this syndrome. Effects include excessive protein catabolism and consequent depletion of these substances in skin, subcutaneous tissues, muscles, and bones. Because

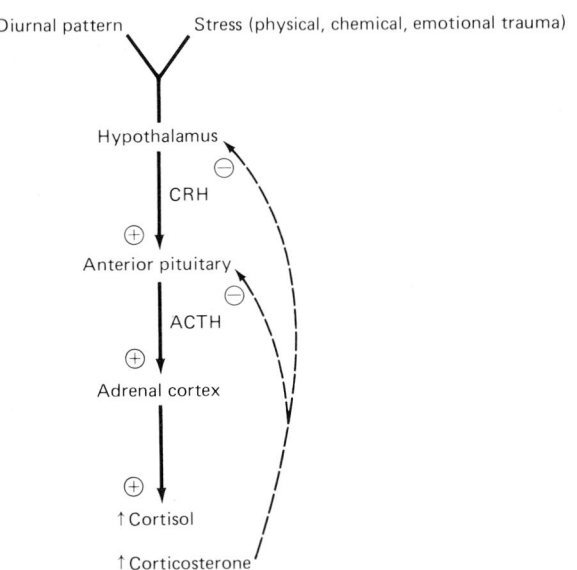

FIGURE 7-6

Hypothalamic-pituitary-adrenal cortical axis in glucocorticoid secretion.

excessive glucocorticoid use inhibits new bone formation, *osteoporosis* is common. In addition, skin is thin and more vulnerable to injury, and wound healing is poor. Hyperglycemia is present in Cushing's syndrome, and development of insulin-resistant diabetes is common in predisposed individuals. Body fat collects in the abdominal wall, face, and upper back, producing a characteristic "buffalo hump." Extremities, however, remain thin because of loss of muscle mass. Since glucocorticoids are similar in structure to mineralocorticoids, large amounts of these hormones can produce sodium and water retention characteristic of excess mineralocorticoid secretion. (See "Mineralocorticoids," below.) Fluid retention and facial fat accumulation account for the moon-faced appearance commonly seen. The majority of individuals with Cushing's syndrome are hypertensive, probably because of fluid retention plus excessive responsiveness of vascular smooth muscle to norepinephrine. Central nervous system effects include insomnia, euphoria or depression, and even psychosis.

Mineralocorticoids

Although there are small amounts of others, *aldosterone* is the primary mineralocorticoid secreted by the adrenal cortex. It is a vital hormone in that it serves to maintain adequate ECF volume through its action of promoting sodium resorption from the urine and, to a lesser extent, sweat, saliva, and gastric secretions. Its primary site of action is the renal tubular network where it directs exchange of sodium ions in the tubular lumen for either potassium or hydrogen ions from the tubular cells. Aldosterone-mediated reabsorption of sodium is therefore associated with moderate urinary loss of potassium and hydrogen.

Three types of regulation are involved in aldosterone secretion. ACTH from the anterior pituitary does play a role, although the amount of ACTH necessary to increase aldosterone secretion is considerably larger than that required to produce maximal glucocorticoid secretion. In addition, the effect of ACTH is transient, and even in the presence of prolonged increases, aldosterone secretion declines after about 2 days.

Another regulatory mechanism in the secretion of aldosterone involves direct stimulation of the adrenal cortex. A rise in serum potassium, a fall in serum sodium, or an increase in the ratio of serum potassium to serum sodium (which is normally very low) also increase aldosterone secretion.

However, the primary regulatory mechanism for aldosterone secretion involves the *renin-angiotensin mechanism*. Renin is secreted from renal juxtaglomerular cells in response to a decrease in ECF or intra-arterial volume as perceived by stretch receptors in renal afferent arterioles. This secretion results in catalytic formation of angiotensin I, which is then rapidly converted to angiotensin II by an enzyme circulating in the blood. Angiotensin II directly stimulates adrenal cortical cells to produce aldosterone. The ECF volume expansion that is produced as a result of aldosterone secretion inhibits further renin secretion by shutting off the stimulus that initiated its increased secretion.

Clinical syndromes involving excess secretion of aldosterone fall into two categories: (1) *primary hyperaldosteronism*, as in the presence of adrenal pathology such as aldosterone-secreting tumors; and (2) *secondary hyperaldosteronism*, as a complication of other pathologies such as congestive heart failure, nephrosis, and cirrhosis. Hypertension is a common feature in both categories as a result of ECF volume expansion and a minimal vasoconstrictive effect produced by high levels of circulating aldosterone.

Characteristic of Conn's syndrome is a marked potassium and hydrogen excretion which can lead to the development of metabolic alkalosis and hypokalemia. Serum hypernatremia may be present but does not always occur because aldosterone-mediated sodium reabsorption is generally accompanied by osmotic, proportionate free water reabsorption. When elevated serum sodium levels do occur in Conn's syndrome they are due at least in part to the effect of hypokalemia upon renal tubular cells. Renal tubular cells are unable to respond to antidiuretic hormone (ADH) in the presence of severely depleted potassium, thus, excessive loss of free water in the urine is likely. Although this *hypokalemic nephropathy* is usually reversible when potassium is replaced, it does produce a hemoconcentration phenomena when it occurs. Thus, serum hypernatremia in Conn's syndrome not only represents a real sodium excess but a relative water deficit as well.

Secondary hyperaldosteronism is associated with increased circulating levels of renin. The basic mechanism of increased renin secretion is, in part, interpretation by the stretch receptors of poor perfusion through the renal arterioles as a need for increased ECF volume. In actuality, the decreased renal perfusion in these states occurs because of poor cardiac function or ECF fluid shifts into the interstitium and peritoneal spaces. While intra-arterial volume may be reduced, increased aldosterone secretion and consequently expansion of overall ECF volume only increases cardiac compromise and furthers fluid shifting; in effect, it increases the pathology. Another pathological mechanism in secondary hyperaldosteronism due to congestive heart failure and cirrhosis is the prolongation of the half-life of aldosterone, which occurs because hepatic inactivation is decreased.

Conditions involving isolated aldosterone deficiency may occur but are relatively rare and occur most frequently in conjunction with renal disease and subsequent decreased renin secretion. Much more commonly, aldosterone deficiency occurs in combination with glucocorticoid insufficiency as a function of overall insufficiency of the adrenal cortex. Deficiency of adrenal sex hormones does occur in this situation but usually is reflected by minor, if any, symptoms in the presence of normal testes and ovaries, the primary sources of these hormones.

Adrenocortical insufficiency which occurs in idiopathic adrenocortical atrophy or damage to the adrenal glands by diseases such as tuberculosis and cancer is called *Addison's disease*. Manifestations of glucocorticoid insufficiency include water retention, significantly depressed to absent ability to maintain blood glucose levels when caloric intake does not occur regularly (e.g., in fasting), and failure to respond

to norepinephrine from adrenergic nerve endings, producing vulnerability to vascular dilatation and collapse in the presence of hypovolemia. All these manifestations reflect lack of glucocorticoid-permissive actions. Exposure to stress does not produce the burst in glucocorticoid secretion that usually occurs. Even when maintenance levels of glucocorticoids are present, seemingly minor stresses can produce physiologic collapse, or *addisonian crisis*. Mineralocorticoid deficiency compounds the picture by allowing excessive sodium loss and therefore ECF depletion with potassium retention. Hyperkalemia and fatal shock occur without aggressive fluid replacement and administration of glucocorticoids.

Adrenal Androgens

Several steroids with sex hormone activity are secreted by the adrenal cortex; however, only one, the androgen *dehydroepiandrosterone,* is produced in significant physiologic amounts. Like other androgens, it exerts a masculinizing effect and promotes protein anabolism and growth. The adrenal androgen has about one-fifth the potency of the most active androgen, testosterone, produced by the testes. Another adrenal androgen, androstenedione, is converted to estrogen in the circulation. The adrenal gland may also secrete small amounts of some estrogens.

Secretion of adrenal androgens is controlled by ACTH, not the gonadotropins. When they are produced in abnormally high quantities, as occurs with adrenal tumors or in the presence of deficiencies in catalytic enzymes necessary for conversion of androgens to other structures, alteration in sexual characteristics results. Prepubertal males display precocious pseudopuberty, while adult males experience accentuation of existing sexual characteristics. In both prepubertal and adult females, excess adrenal androgens result in masculinization (adrenogenital syndrome). Genetically, female fetuses under 12 weeks' gestation develop male-type external genitalia (pseudohermaphroditism) in the presence of excess adrenal androgens.

Adrenal Medulla

The adrenal medulla located in the interior aspect of the adrenal gland secretes two catecholamines, epinephrine and norepinephrine, although proportionately more epinephrine. It is perhaps most appropriately viewed as an extension of the sympathetic nervous system, because norepinephrine is the transmitter of all adrenergic nerve endings and epinephrine is capable of producing adrenergic effects in all tissues with adrenergic receptors. In addition, both catecholamines function as neurotransmitters in the central nervous system.

Secretion of adrenal medullary catecholamines is predominantly under the control of the sympathetic nervous system. Increased secretion of these substances plays a critical role in the physiologic preparation to meet or cope with emergency situations in that they reinforce the sympathetic response. Stimuli known to evoke sympatho-adrenal discharge include hypoxemia, hypoglycemia, cold, hemorrhage, and emotional stresses provoked by situations of a frightening or unfamiliar nature. A schematic depiction of factors producing sympatho-adrenal catecholamine secretion can be seen in Fig. 7-7.

Epinephrine relaxes bronchiolar smooth muscle, producing bronchodilatation and facilitation of maximum ventilation. Both catecholamines increase the force and rate of myocardial contraction, i.e., exert positive ionotropic and chronotropic effects. They also increase myocardial impulse conduction velocity and overall excitability. Norepinephrine produces vasoconstriction (in the presence of glucocorticoids) in most if not all organs, but epinephrine counteracts this effect, producing vasodilatation in skeletal muscles, the central nervous system, the myocardium, and the liver. In the presence of both, total peripheral resistance to blood flow is decreased, but many "nonvital" organs experience decreased oxygen delivery because of decreased perfusion.

Metabolic effects of the catecholamines are profound. Both of these hormones exert a marked calorigenic effect and greatly increase metabolic rate. The mechanisms basic to this increased metabolic rate are not precisely known but are thought to involve increased glycogenolysis in skeletal muscle (producing hyperglycemia) and increased hepatic oxidation of lactic acid. Lactic acid production is a function of norepinephrine-induced vasoconstriction and decreased oxygen delivery to "nonvital" cells, with their subsequent dependence upon anaerobic metabolism. Epinephrine is more potent than norepinephrine, with regard to metabolic effects.

Another metabolic effect of catecholamines is free fatty acid mobilization from adipose tissue, physiologically appropriate in that overall elevation in metabolic rate requires increased availability of energy sources. Free fatty acids are necessary despite hyperglycemia because norepinephrine inhibits insulin secretion and therefore limits glucose uptake by many body cells. (See "Insulin," below.)

Finally, epinephrine and norepinephrine act as central nervous system activators. Both alertness and attentiveness are increased by the presence of catecholamines. In addition, epinephrine is thought to be responsible for production of anxiety and fear.

Excessive and inappropriate catecholamine secretion can occur in the presence of secreting tumors of the adrenal medulla. Such tumors are known as *pheochromocytomas*. Characteristically, they secrete catecholamines not only in conjunction with sympathetic activation, but autonomously as well. Because adrenal medullary catecholamine output consists of proportionately more epinephrine than norepinephrine, hyperglycemia and hypermetabolism are prominent features. Excessive myocardial stimulation also occurs, and development of a *catecholamine myocardiopathy* is fairly common. Paroxysmal and severe hypertension occurs probably because bursts of epinephrine decrease peripheral resistance (and blood pressure), leading to activation of the sympathetic nervous system (SNS). The subsequent release of norepinephrine at vascular adrenergic nerve endings then produces vasoconstriction and hypertension. The bursts of epinephrine probably deplete epinephrine content in tumor and other adrenal medullary cells, and despite adrenal medullary stimulation with SNS activation, norepinephrine-mediated vasoconstriction dominates while synthesis of more epinephrine is occurring.

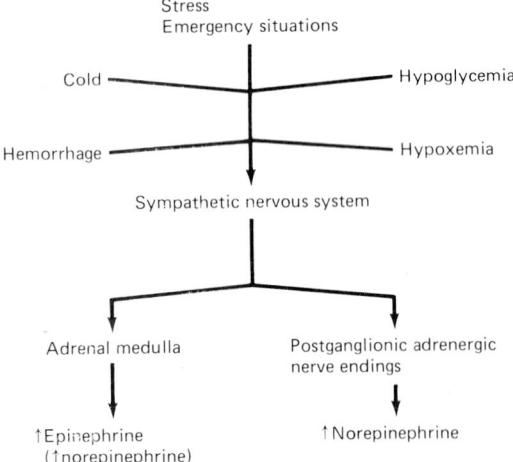

FIGURE 7-7

Control of catecholamine secretion.

ENDOCRINE PANCREAS

The endocrine component of the pancreas is small but mighty. It constitutes about 2 percent of the total pancreatic mass and is composed of clusters of endocrine cells called *islets of Langerhans* or pancreatic islets. The types of cells in the islets are classified into three categories based upon their granulation and staining properties: A (alpha), B (beta), and D. *A* or *alpha* cells compose about one-fifth of the islets and secrete glucagon. *B* or *beta* cells compose the majority of the islets, about 75 percent, and secrete insulin. The D cells compose the remainder of the islets and secrete a polypeptide substance known as *somatostatin*. The precise physiologic role of somatostatin is not known, but it does inhibit secretion of both insulin and glucagon from beta cells and alpha cells, respectively.

Insulin and glucagon play important roles in the regulation of carbohydrates, protein, and fat metabolism. Insulin is anabolic in that it increases storage of glucose, fatty acids, and amino acids. Glucagon is catabolic in that it mobilizes glucose and breaks down or converts stored fat and protein into utilizable energy sources. These two hormones are therefore antagonists, and appropriately, their secretion patterns are generally reciprocal.

The overall status of energy stores at any given time is reflected by the ratio of insulin to glucagon. In normal states, where a balanced diet is being consumed, the *insulin/glucagon ratio* (*I/G*) is quantitatively valued at 2.3:1, indicative of a net storage tendency, establishment of a positive nitrogen balance, and anabolism. In fed (or overfed) states, an increase in insulin results in elevation of the I/G ratio, anabolism, and weight gain. In contrast, fasting produces an increase in glucagon and consequently a decreased I/G ratio, catabolism, and weight loss.

Insulin

Insulin increases glucose uptake in all body tissues except the pancreatic beta islets, brain, renal tubules, intestinal mucosa, and red blood cells. The mechanism involves facilitation of glucose transport across cellular membranes. It also produces increases in free fatty acid and protein synthesis, an action which is accomplished by preventing the action of enzymes necessary for their breakdown and also increasing amino acid transport into cells. Finally, it decreases hepatic glucose output and stimulates glycogenesis in the liver and skeletal muscle.

Regulation of insulin secretion is primarily a function of a feedback mechanism exerted by blood glucose concentration directly upon the pancreas. Glucose entry into beta islet cells is not affected by insulin; thus changes in glucose levels are rapidly sensed by these cells. When blood glucose levels are low, so is insulin secretion. When blood glucose levels increase, insulin secretion by the beta cells also increases. The subsequent decrease in blood glucose thus removes the stimulus that initiated increased insulin secretion. This feedback mechanism normally operates with great precision and results in a close parallel between the blood glucose and insulin levels.

By a mechanism yet to be defined, the presence in the serum of some amino and keto acids also increases insulin secretion. That these substances increase insulin secretion is physiologically appropriate in that insulin increases synthesis of both protein and fat and thus serves to "protect" amino acids from being used as cellular energy sources. When keto acids are present in the serum, free fatty acids have alreay been burned, reflecting fat breakdown and catabolism, both of which are reversed by insulin.

The degree of insulin secretion in response to intravenously infused glucose and amino acids is less than that produced by oral ingestion of the same substances. This occurs as a result of the action of a hormone secreted by the intestinal mucosa known as *gastric inhibitory peptide* (*GIP*). In the presence of glucose or fat in the gastrointestinal tract, secretion of this hormone is increased. GIP then affects beta-cell stimulation and results in increased insulin secretion. Other substances secreted by the gastrointestinal tract produce similar effects and include cholecystokinin (CCK), secretin, gastrin, and mucosal glucagon, although GIP is thought to be the primary "gut factor" normally involved. Glucagon is discussed in detail in the section that immediately follows.

Free catecholamines (primarily epinephrine) as well as sympathetic stimulation prevent insulin secretion. Other inhibitory effects on insulin secretion are produced by thiazide diuretics, diazoxide, and somatostatin. Several hormones, as discussed in other sections, impair insulin effect. Such hormones include glucocorticoids and growth hormone.

Insufficient insulin secretion results in numerous abnormalities that characterize the disease *diabetes mellitus*. The fundamental physiologic defects in diabetes involve reduced entry of glucose into most body tissues and increased hepatic glucose output (hepatic glucogenesis). While the former is totally attributable to insufficient insulin, the latter is not. Increased hepatic glucogenesis is a function, at least in part, of either a relative or absolute increase in glucagon secretion, e.g., depression of the normal I/G ratio. Therefore, diabetes is a disease both of insulin deficiency and glucagon excess.

The fundamental defects in diabetes result in pronounced hyperglycemia. Blood osmolarity is increased, as is the level of glucose in the renal tubules. The renal threshold for glucose reabsorption is exceeded, and as a result, osmotic diuresis occurs. The water and sodium lost in the urine in this situation result in large urine volumes (*polyuria*). ECF volume depletion and hyperosmolarity produce thirst and ingestion of large amounts of liquids (*polydipsia*). Despite serum glucose elevations, intracellular glucose content is low. Increased appetite (*polyphagia*) and cellular reliance upon energy sources other than glucose result. Fat and protein breakdown are uninhibited in the absence of insulin and are in fact accelerated by glucagon. Catabolism, negative nitrogen balance, and weight loss occur.

If untreated, fat catabolism in diabetes eventually overloads the metabolic pathways. Inability of the body to utilize the various by-products of fat catabolism at a rate equal to that of their production leads to accumulation of *ketones*. Because ketones are organic acids, *diabetic ketoacidosis* (*DKA*) ensues. Hyperglycemia-induced hyperosmolarity and ECF volume depletion are thus compounded by progressive acidosis. At this point the I/G ratio is drastically reduced. This triad of physiologic events inevitably produces central nervous system depression and shock. Coma and death result if treatment is not rapidly initiated.

Another dangerous effect of insufficient insulin is *nonketotic hyperosmolar coma* (*NKC*). The most vulnerable population for its development are diabetics who have residual but inadequate beta-cell function. The precipitating event is commonly serious illness or injury that provokes a physiologic stress response. Increased catecholamine and glucocorticoid secretion produce hyperglycemia through the initiation of catabolic processes concomitantly with inhibition of the secretion or effectiveness of insulin. While dietary efforts and/or oral hypoglycemic agents may be adequate to control blood glucose levels in normal circumstances, they are totally inadequate in the stress response. Some insulin secretion occurs, but it is incapable of preventing hyperglycemia. However, insulin is much more potent in its prevention of lipolysis than it is in controlling blood glucose, and

thus ketosis is prevented. While the I/G ratio is decreased in NKC, it is not depressed to the extent seen in DKA. Hyperosmolarity becomes marked, as it does in ketoacidosis, because hyperglycemia still leads to excessive osmotic diuresis and ECF volume depletion, and shock and coma ensue. If shock is severe, acidosis does develop but involves production of lactic acid as a result of insufficient tissue perfusion and subsequent anaerobic metabolism.

Excess insulin produces many clinical manifestations, all of which are directly attributable to *hypoglycemia*. The central nervous system almost exclusively uses glucose as fuel. It is relatively unable to store glucose as glycogen and is dependent upon a continuous glucose supply. When blood glucose falls, the metabolic rate of the brain is rapidly affected and the result is confusion, weakness, dizziness, and hunger. Hypoglycemia is also a potent stimulus to the sympathetic nervous system, and manifestations of that activation include the commonly described tremors, palpitations, and nervousness.

It is sympathetic activation that physiologically promotes reversal of hypoglycemia. Catecholamines and glucocorticoids both elevate blood glucose levels, and the sympathetic nervous system also directly stimulates glucagon secretion. In the presence of normal pancreatic function, severe hypoglycemia is rare and effectively reversed by the mechanisms just described.

Hypoglycemia in diabetics usually occurs in conjunction with excessive administration of insulin or hypoglycemic agents and/or increased energy utilization such as vigorous exercise, because skeletal muscle can pick up glucose without insulin in this situation. It generally occurs more rapidly in diabetics than in those with normal pancreatic function and is more likely to result in serious depression of blood glucose. Convulsions and coma can occur and progress to irreversible cerebral damage if hypoglycemia is prolonged or severe.

Glucagon

The majority of glucagon is secreted by the alpha islets, although as noted, it also is released by mucosal cells of the gastrointestinal tract. It is a catabolic hormone that exerts its influence by increasing hepatic glycogenolysis and gluconeogenesis and promoting fat breakdown. Blood glucose is elevated in its presence, and because it involves alpha-cell cAMP activation, this effect is rapid. When secreted, glucagon also produces an increase in insulin secretion. Although seemingly inappropriate, this effect is physiologically logical because insulin facilitates tissue uptake of the released energy sources. Glucagon in large quantities also exerts an inotropic effect on the myocardium, but this effect is minor in comparison to its role in metabolism.

A variety of stimuli affect alpha-cell glucagon secretion. Sympathetic nervous system activation, glucocorticoids, and exercise are some of these. Large amounts of amino acids also stimulate glucagon secretion. Because amino acids also stimulate insulin, glucagon secretion is necessary in this situation to assure blood glucose adequacy while these substances are used in tissue synthesis. In this way, glucagon facilitates the protein-sparing or storage effect of insulin.

Glucagon secretion in response to orally ingested amino acids is similar to insulin in that it is greater than that produced by intravenous administration of the same substances. Presence of protein in the gastrointestinal tract stimulates the secretion of cholecystokinin (CCK) and gastrin from mucosal cells, and both of these substances increase glucagon secretion from the alpha cells as well as from the intestinal mucosal cells.

Glucagon secretion is inhibited by hyperglycemia; however, this inhibition is dependent upon insulin. Apparently, alpha cells are unable to react to elevated blood glucose levels unless insulin first promotes alpha-cell pickup of glucose. When blood glucose levels are low, increased secretion of glucagon occurs and produces increased blood glucose simultaneously with increased insulin. The subsequent presence of both hormones produces a negative feedback action on further alpha-cell secretion. Glucagon secretion is also decreased by somatostatin.

The effects of elevated glucagon secretion have been discussed in the preceding discussion of diabetes. Increased glucagon may occur in conjunction with glucagon-secreting alpha-cell tumors. Situations in which glucagon secretion is insufficient are rare, because even in the presence of alpha-cell destruction, intestinal mucosal cells are capable of glucagon secretion. A schematic representation of the bihormonal endocrine pancreas control of energy metabolism is presented in Fig. 7-8.

GONADS

In both sexes the gonads, testes in males and ovaries in females, have dual functions. They effect production of reproductive cells (gametogenesis) as well as secrete androgens, or masculinizing hormones, and

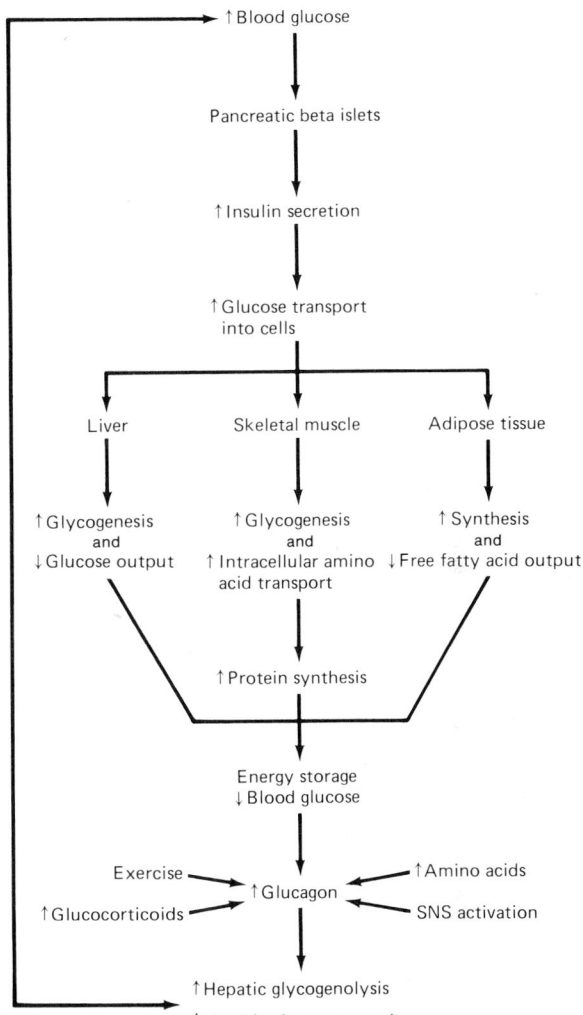

FIGURE 7-8

Bihormonal control of energy metabolism by the endocrine pancreas.

estrogens, or feminizing hormones. Their actions assure reproductive capability (see Chap. 12). The sex hormones also play a role in development and maintenance of interest in the opposite sex and libido, although psychosocial influences are almost impossible to distinguish from those of hormonal origin.

Testes

The Leydig cells in the testes secrete large amounts of androgens, principally *testosterone,* in addition to small amounts of estrogens. The testicular secretion of testosterone and other androgens is under the control of the gonadotropin LH (luteinizing hormone) and accounts for development and maintenance of male secondary sex characteristics, including a muscular, broad-shouldered body configuration, widespread hair growth in a characteristic distribution, increased genital size, and laryngeal growth with a deepening of the voice. All these characteristics occur at puberty, the onset of which is directly controlled by a hypothalamic time clock and effected through release of luteinizing hormone releasing hormone (LRH) and subsequent release of LH from the anterior pituitary. In adult males, negative feedback is exerted upon the hypothalamus by high circulating levels of testosterone. Why increased testosterone levels can occur at puberty is unknown, but is thought to involve a period of hypothalamic nonresponsiveness to the hormone with regard to negative feedback. The cessation of puberty is associated with return of the effectiveness of the negative feedback mechanism. A schematic representation of the hypothalamic–anterior pituitary–testicular relationship with regard to testosterone secretion is presented in Fig. 7-9.

Testosterone is also anabolic. It and other androgens increase synthesis and decrease breakdown of protein. High secretion rates of these substances are responsible for the increased growth rate ("growth spurt") associated with puberty. These substances are also responsible for fusion of epiphyseal growth plates in long bones, thus eventually stopping linear growth. (See "Growth Hormone," above.)

The clinical picture presented by insufficient testosterone depends upon whether deficiency occurs

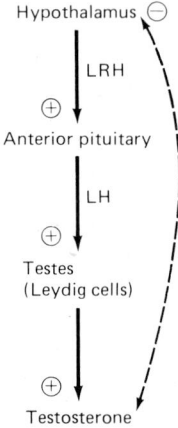

FIGURE 7-9
Control of testosterone secretion.

before or after puberty. Pathology of either the hypothalamus or pituitary glands may produce such a deficiency. If it develops in adulthood, slight regression of sexual characteristics occurs, but these effects are minor because their maintenance requires only miniscule amounts of androgens. Prepubertal deficiency of testosterone results in *eunuchoidism*. Manifestations of this syndrome include tall stature, narrow shoulders, small muscles and genitalia, and a high-pitched voice. The increased stature common to this syndrome occurs despite the lack of testosterone-based anabolic effects because epiphyseal growth plates fail to fuse and other hormones, primarily growth hormone, result in growth beyond the normal time period.

Excess testosterone most commonly occurs as a result of testicular hyperfunction due to the presence of androgen-secreting tumors. However, these tumors are rare and produce symptoms only in prepubertal males. Early development of secondary sex characteristics without reproductive capability is the basis for classification of this syndrome as precocious pseudopuberty (early "false" puberty).

Ovaries

There are two ovaries, each of which is composed of many capsular structures known as primordial follicles. Under the influence of pituitary gonadotropins, primarily follicle-stimulating hormone (FSH), cyclic maturation of one of these follicles occurs, roughly once a month. Theca cells in these matured ovarian follicles are the source of ovarian estrogens. Estrogens may also be produced by other ovarian cells, but if so, they are secreted in physiologically insignificant amounts. Since biosynthesis of estrogens involves their formation from androgens, the latter are present in ovarian tissue and are probably also secreted in small amounts.

The secretion pattern of various estrogens is cyclic and correlates with the development and maturation of ovarian follicles, under the influence of FSH. It is therefore dependent upon hypothalamic influence via release of follicle-stimulating hormone releasing hormone (FRH). Discussion of the dynamics of this cyclic secretion pattern is beyond the scope of this chapter. The reader is referred to the discussion of the reproductive systems presented in Chap. 12.

Estrogens, like androgens, are anabolic, but to a somewhat lesser degree. They facilitate growth and maturation of the breasts, uterus, and vagina. They also play a role in the development of body changes associated with puberty, although also involved is the fact that testicular androgens are absent. Estrogen-based pubertal changes include increased width of the hips and characteristic fat accumulation in the buttocks and breasts.

Secretion of estrogens exerts negative feedback upon the hypothalamus and therefore anterior pituitary secretion of FSH. Thus, in the presence of excessive levels of estrogens, ovarian atrophy and sterility may occur. A similar effect may be produced by primary pituitary hypofunction, which in addition to sterility also produces dwarfism as a result of insufficient release of FSH and other anterior pituitary hormones such as TSH and GH. In contrast, pituitary hyperfunction with excess secretion of FSH as well as estrogen-secreting ovarian tumors produces early development of secondary sex characteristics and reproductive capability (precocious puberty) in prepubertal females. In adults, estrogen-secreting tumors are rare.

PINEAL

The pineal gland (epiphysis) is located midline in the cranial cavity just under the third ventricle. It is primarily composed of nervous system tissue, although some secretory cells are present. During infancy the pineal is large, but by the time puberty occurs, it has undergone involution and has a size approximately equal to that of a small grape.

Melatonin

In humans the function of the pineal is not understood. It produces *melatonin,* a hormone that inhibits the effect of gonadotropins and in rodents produces changes in pigmentation of the skin. Some believe that melatonin secretion does occur prior to puberty when the gland is large, and the gonadotropin inhibition produced plays a role in delaying the onset of puberty until the time deemed appropriate by the hypothalamus. It is *not* thought to be related to skin pigmentation in humans; however, its effect upon skin has not been precisely defined. Some pituitary tumors do produce hyperpigmentation, but this is thought to be because of excess levels of melanocyte-stimulating hormone (MSH) or other chemically similar tropins from the intermediate and anterior lobes. (See "Intermediate Pituitary," above.) Increased melatonin secretion is not known to be an effect of MSH. Rather, secretion of melatonin in humans is directly a function of the nervous system and occurs in a diurnal pattern associated with light and dark. Light receptors in the retina initiate nervous system impulse generation and transmission to the pineal gland. As a result, plasma concentrations of melatonin are consistently high in dark environments and dramatically decreased in those with an abundance of light.

Clinically, the pineal gland does serve a purpose. Since involution is associated with calcification, radiographic opacity is produced. Lateral pineal displacement on skull x-rays is therefore useful in detecting space-occupying intracranial lesions.

THYMUS

The thymus is located in the mediastinum and is the primary central organ of the lymphatic system. It is a single structure composed of two lobes. Its largest dimensions are seen at puberty. From then on it begins to involute and may be essentially absent in old age, having been replaced by fat.

The function of the thymus is still in the process of being defined. It is known to be vital in the development of the immune defense mechanism, a function that is essentially completed early in life and thus unaffected by later involution. Soon after birth it affects maturation of fetal lymphocytes. After their maturation, these lymphocytes leave the thymus and accumulate in the spleen, lymph nodes, and other lymphatic tissue.

Thymosin

The thymus is considered an endocrine gland because soon after birth it secretes a hormone known as *thymosin.* This hormone results in development and maturation of plasma immune cells, *T cells,* or *T lymphocytes* from nonspecific lymphocytes. T cells play a vital role in cellular immunity throughout the body. They are present in just about all body cells, and when they encounter foreign antigens (proteins) on cells such as those from another individual or associated with viruses, they become "activated" and produce *lymphokins,* which are capable of protein destruction and thus foreign cell destruction. It is T-cell activation that produces rejection of transplanted tissue and provides the major defense against viral invasion.

Thymosin administration has been known to increase immune defenses, presumably by increasing the number or activity of T cells. Its use in immunosuppressed individuals such as those undergoing chemotherapy or radiation therapy for malignant disease may provide a means of increasing resistance to systemic infections. It may also prove to be helpful in the body's defense against malignant processes in that tumor cells are known to contain some foreign antigens. Theoretically, if T cells could be sufficiently activated, they could effect destruction of these cells.

REFERENCES

Adlard, J., and J. George: Hyponatremia, *Heart Lung* 7(4):587–593, 1978.

Anthony, C., and G. Thibodeau: *Textbook of Anatomy and Physiology,* St. Louis: Mosby, 1979.

Arieff, A., and H. Carroll: Nonketotic hyperosmolar coma with hyperglycemia: Clinical features, pathophysiology, renal function, acid-base balance, plasma-cerebrospinal fluid equilibria and the effects of therapy in 37 cases, *Crit Care Med* 51(2):73–94, 1972.

Ballinger, W., et al. (ed.): *Manual of Surgical Nutrition,* Philadelphia: Saunders, 1976.

Benson, E.: Acute adrenal failure, *Hospital Medicine* 15(8):64–72, 1979.

Dingman, J., and G. Thorn: Diseases of the neurohypophysis, in M. Wintrobe et al. (eds.), *Harrison's Principles of Internal Medicine,* 7th ed., New York: McGraw-Hill, 1974.

Fitzpatrick, T., and H. Haynes: Pigmentation of the skin and disorders of melanin metabolism, in M. Wintrobe et al. (eds.), *Harrison's Principles of Internal Medicine,* 7th ed., New York: McGraw-Hill, 1974.

Friesen, S.: *Surgical Endocrinology: Clinical Syndromes,* Philadelphia: Lippincott, 1978.

Ganong, W.: *Review of Medical Physiology,* 8th ed., Los Altos, Calif.: Lange, 1977.

Gerich, J., M. Martin, and L. Recant: Clinical and metabolic characteristics of hyperosmolar nonketotic coma, *Diabetes* 20(3):228–238, 1971.

Guthrie, D., and R. Guthrie: *Nursing management of diabetes mellitus,* St. Louis: Mosby, 1977.

Hershman, J. (ed.): *Endocrine Pathophysiology: A Patient Oriented Approach,* Philadelphia: Lea & Febiger, 1977.

Ingbar, S., and K. Woeber: Diseases of the thyroid, in M. Wintrobe et al. (ed.), *Harrison's Principles of Internal Medicine,* 7th ed., New York: McGraw-Hill, 1974.

Katz, M.: Hyperglycemia-induced hyponatremia-calculation of expected serum sodium depression, *N Engl J Med* 289:843–845, 1973.

Kubo, W., M. Grant, and B. Walike: Fluid and electrolyte problems of tube fed patients, *Am J Nurs* 76(6):912–916, 1976.

Myers, F., Jawetz, E., and A. Goldfien: *Review of Medical Pharmacology,* 6th ed., Los Altos, Calif.: Lange, 1978.

Nelson, D.: Diseases of the anterior lobe of the pituitary gland, in M. Wintrobe et al. (eds.), *Harrison's Principles of Internal Medicine,* 7th ed., New York: McGraw-Hill, 1974.

Netter, F. (ed.): Endocrine system and selected metabolic disorders, *The CIBA collection of medical illustrations,* vol. 4. Summit, N.J.: CIBA Pharmaceutical Co., 1974.

Pike, J: Prostaglandins, *Scientific American* 225:84–91, 1971.

Scott, H., J. Oates, A. Nies, H. Burko, D. Page, and R. Rhamy: Pheochromocytoma: Present diagnosis and management, *Ann Surg* 183:587–593, 1976.

Skillman, T.: Diabetic ketoacidosis, *Heart Lung* 7(4):594–602, 1978.

Steinke, J., and G. Thorn: Diabetes mellitus, in M. Wintrobe et al. (eds.), *Harrison's Principles of Internal Medicine,* 7th ed., New York: McGraw-Hill, 1974.

Vander, A., J. Sherman, and D. Luciano: *Human Physiology,* 2d ed., New York: McGraw-Hill, 1975.

Williams, G., R. Dluhy, and G. Thorn: Diseases of the adrenal cortex, in M. Wintrobe et al. (eds.), *Harrison's Principles of Internal Medicine,* 7th ed., New York: McGraw-Hill, 1974.

Williams, R.: *Textbook of Endrocrinology,* 5th ed., Philadelphia: Saunders, 1974.

Wurtman, R.: Diseases of the pineal gland, in M. Wintrobe et al. (eds.), *Harrison's Principles of Internal Medicine,* 7th ed., New York: McGraw-Hill, 1974.

INTRODUCTION

The kidneys are clearly major excretory organs, but they do much more than merely dispose of waste products. In addition, the kidneys play a vital role in acid-base balance and in maintaining normal fluid and electrolyte levels. Endocrine function further extends the scope of renal responsibility for homeostasis. Partly because of its multiple functions and partly because it needs a dependable blood flow for these functions, renal tissue is susceptible to a variety of chemical, bacterial, immunological, and hemodynamic insults.

For critically ill patients the monitoring of renal function by changes in body weight, blood constituents, and urine volume is routine practice. However, before clinical problems affecting renal function and the rationale of nursing and medical interventions designed to minimize them can be appreciated, the normal function of the kidneys must be understood.

BASIC PRINCIPLES

Overview of Renal Anatomy

The kidneys lie behind the peritoneum (retroperitoneal) with the upper border at approximately the level of the twelfth thoracic vertebra and the lower border at about the third lumbar vertebra. When the kidney is divided longitudinally, two major sections, an outer cortex and an inner medulla, can be identified (Fig. 8-1). In the medulla of each kidney there are usually eight to ten *pyramids*. At the apical (papillary) end of each pyramid are a number of small apertures through which fluid from the collecting ducts drains into a *minor calyx*. Urine from the minor calyces drains into a *major calyx*, then into the renal pelvis, and finally into the *ureter*. Striations (*medullary rays*) seen in the pyramids are due to the generally parallel arrangement of long nephron loops and blood vessels in this region of the kidney. In contrast, the cortex appear uniformly granular because of the random arrangement of proximal and distal tubules in many intersecting planes.

Each kidney receives its blood supply through a *renal artery* that branches from the abdominal aorta (Fig. 8-1). Within the kidney, the renal artery divides into *interlobar arteries* that pass between the pyramids. At the base of each pyramid, arterial branches called *arcuate* or *arciform arteries* form an archway of vessels between the medulla and the cortex. *Interlobular arteries* pass at right angles from the arcuate arteries into the cortex. *Afferent arterioles* supplying

8

THE RENAL SYSTEM
LaNelle E. Geddes

INTRODUCTION

BASIC PRINCIPLES
Overview of Renal Anatomy
Transfer of Materials

URINE FORMATION
Glomerular Filtration
Tubular Reabsorption
Tubular Secretion
Renal Concentrating and
Diluting Mechanisms

RENAL CONTRIBUTIONS TO HOMEOSTASIS
Fluid Balance
Electrolyte Balance
Acid-Base Balance

HORMONES OF THE KIDNEY
Renin
Erythropoietin
Renal Conversion of Vitamin D
Prostaglandins

REFERENCES

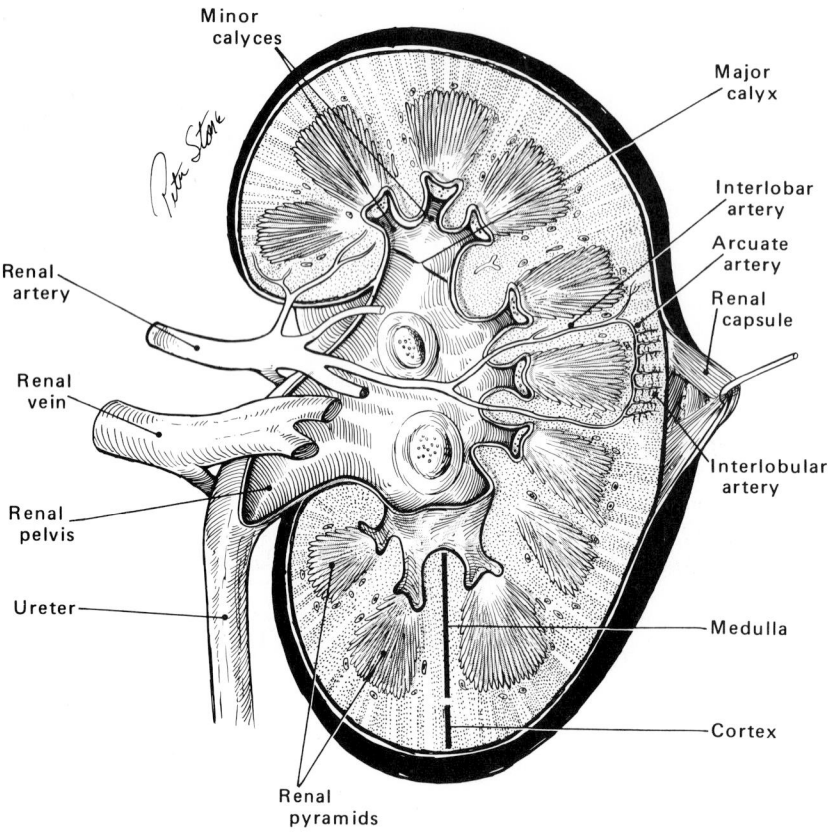

FIGURE 8-1

A longitudinal section of the kidney showing a portion of the major arterial branches of the renal vasculature. (*From L. L. Langley, I. Telford, and J. Christensen, Dynamic Anatomy and Physiology, 5th ed., McGraw-Hill, New York, 1980.*)

each glomerular capillary tuft are branches of the interlobular arteries. After passing through the glomerular capillaries, blood enters *efferent arterioles*. Notice that this part of the renal circulation is a portal system because blood passes through a capillary bed from one arteriole (afferent) to another arteriole (efferent) without going through the heart. The efferent arterioles branch extensively into a peritubular vascular network that entwines each renal tubule and gives rise to the *vasa recta* of the juxtamedullary class of nephrons. Vasa recta are long, thin vascular loops that extend into the renal medulla and lie in close association with the *loops of Henle*. The peritubular vessels coalesce into venules that empty into the interlobular veins. Blood in the interlobular veins next enters arcuate veins, then interlobar veins, and finally leaves the kidney through the renal vein, which empties into the inferior vena cava.

Anatomy of the nephron   The nephron, consisting of a vascular *glomerulus* and a tubular portion, is the functional renal unit, and each kidney contains about 1 million nephrons. Renal function represents the composite function of many nephrons. A brief description of nephron anatomy provides the structural basis for later discussion of renal function.

Each nephron is composed of a glomerulus and a tubular portion. The glomerulus (Fig. 8-2), a capillary plexus, is almost completely surrounded by *Bowman's capsule* (glomerular capsule), a cuplike structure at the origin of the tubular portion of the nephron. The glomerular capillaries branch from the afferent arter-

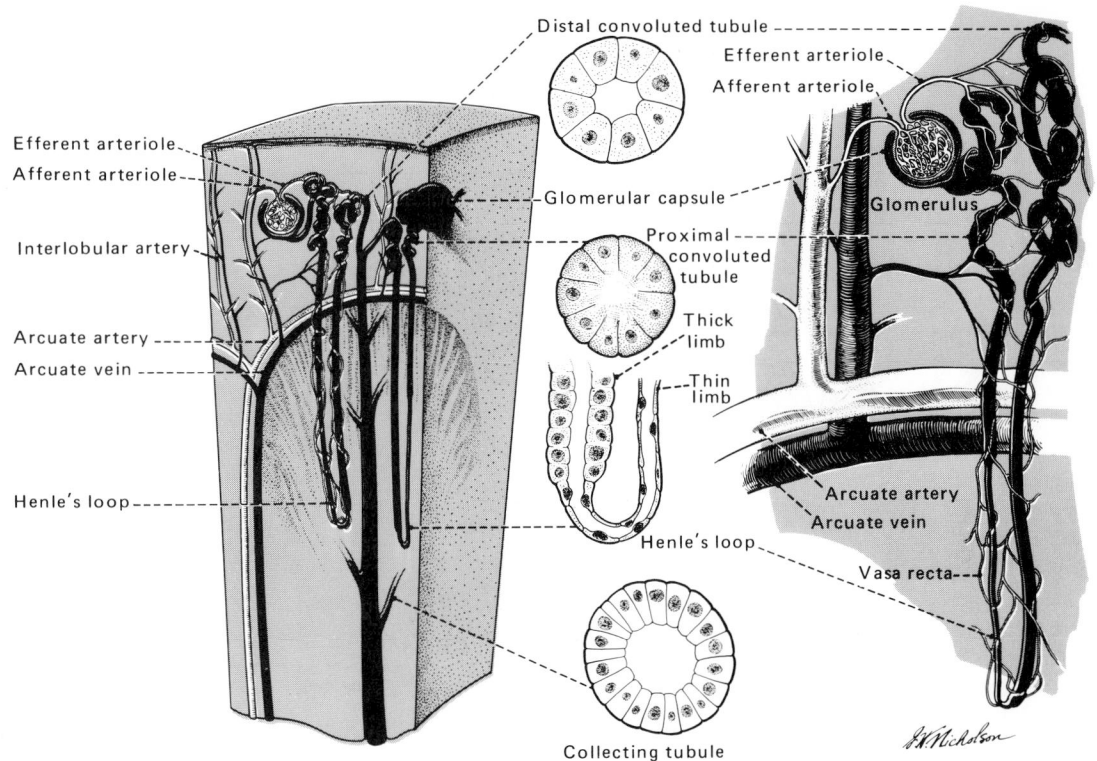

FIGURE 8-2
The nephron and its blood supply are shown at the sides of the figure. Sections of different portions of the tubule are shown in the center. (*From L. L. Langley, I. Telford, and J. Christensen, Dynamic Anatomy and Physiology, 5th ed., McGraw-Hill, New York, 1980.*)

iole and reform into the efferent arteriole. At one point along the course of the nephron, the distal tubule contacts both the afferent and efferent arterioles (Fig. 8-3). Certain cells in the walls of the afferent arteriole and the tubule are structurally and functionally modified. Modified tubular cells form the *macula densa*; modified cells in the afferent arteriolar walls are called *juxtaglomerular cells* and are considered a major source of *renin*. Taken together, the macula densa and the juxtaglomerular cells are considered a functional unit and are called the *juxtaglomerular apparatus*.

Just beyond Bowman's capsule, the *proximal convoluted tubule* begins. Cells of this region are covered with a brush border on their luminal side. The brush border increases the surface area in this portion of the tubule where the majority of reabsorption occurs.

Below the proximal convoluted portion, the renal tubule straightens and passes deeper into the cortex or, further yet, into the medulla, makes a turn, and ascends back in the opposite direction. After forming a relatively straight U-shaped loop (the loop of Henle), the tubule is again convoluted in its distal region. The renal tubule terminates at its point of connection with a collecting tubule that drains a number of nephrons.

Two classes of nephrons, cortical and juxtamedullary, have been identified. The majority of nephrons (about 90 percent) in the human kidney are cortical. Cortical and juxtamedullary nephrons differ in several ways. First is location. As the names imply, cortical nephrons are located in the renal cortex and juxtamedullary nephrons are located near the corticomedullary border and lie partly in the cortex and partly in the medulla. A second difference is in the length and

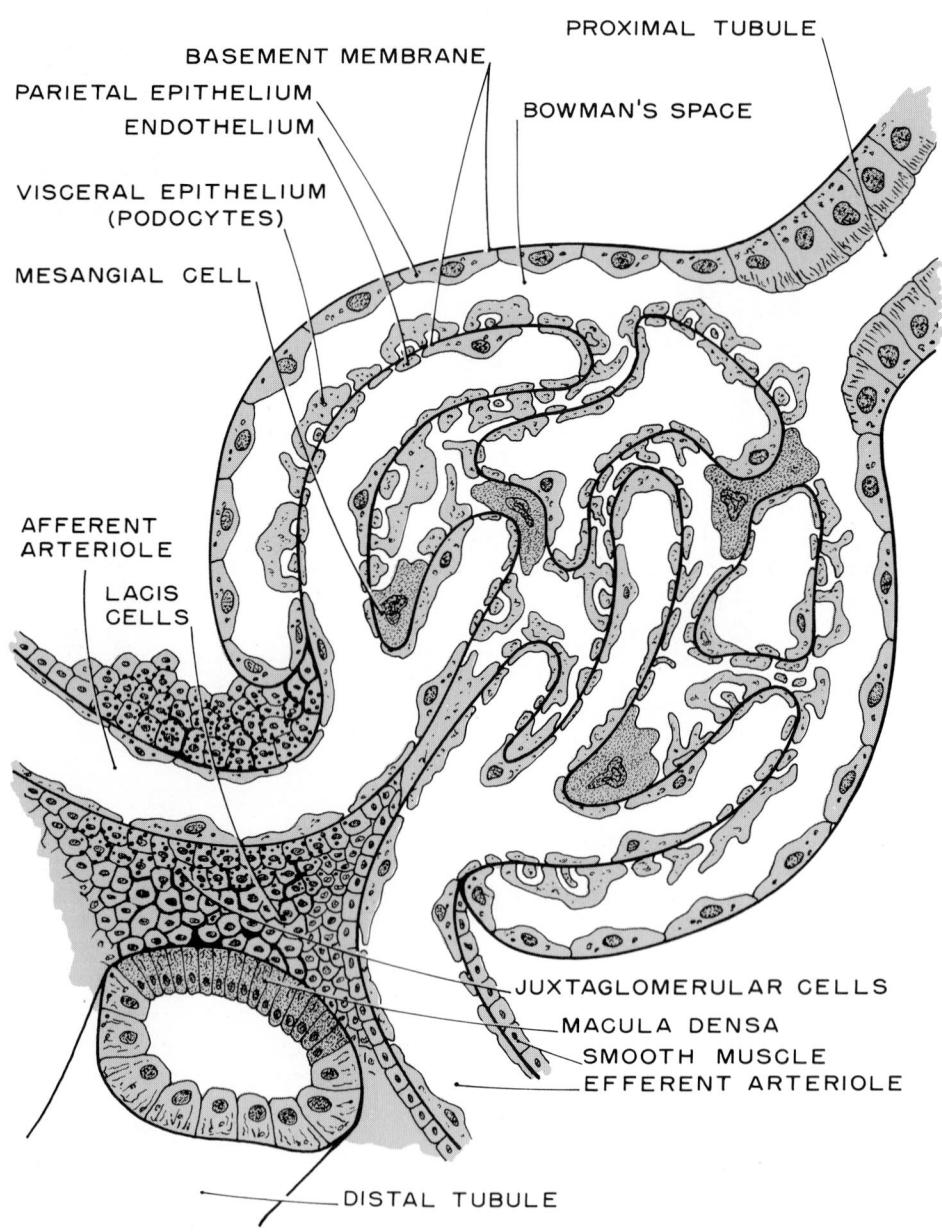

PROXIMAL TUBULE

BASEMENT MEMBRANE

PARIETAL EPITHELIUM

ENDOTHELIUM

BOWMAN'S SPACE

VISCERAL EPITHELIUM
(PODOCYTES)

MESANGIAL CELL

AFFERENT
ARTERIOLE

LACIS
CELLS

JUXTAGLOMERULAR CELLS

MACULA DENSA

SMOOTH MUSCLE

EFFERENT ARTERIOLE

DISTAL TUBULE

FIGURE 8-3

The renal corpuscle and the juxtaglomerular apparatus. The juxtaglomerular apparatus is composed of the macula densa, modified cells in the wall of the distal convoluted tubule, and the juxtaglomerular cells of the afferent arteriole near its entry point into the glomerulus. *(From S. A. Price and L. M. Wilson, Pathophysiology, McGraw-Hill, New York, 1978.)*

diameter of the tubular loop. Cortical nephrons have shorter loops than the juxtamedullary nephrons, and the loops have a relatively smaller proportion of their length occupied by a thin segment. Juxtamedullary nephrons have long loops of Henle that dip deeply into the medulla and are thin throughout most of the descending limb as well as about half of the ascending limb. A third difference is arrangement of the peritubular capillary network. The entire tubule of cortical nephrons is enmeshed by a network of capillaries, whereas only the proximal and distal portions of the juxtamedullary nephrons are entwined within a capillary web. The long loops of Henle are relatively unentangled by capillaries, but long vascular segments, the *vasa recta*, run parallel and in close proximity to this part of the juxtamedullary nephrons. The structural differences between the two types of nephrons are the probable basis for the functional differences between them. A major functional difference is that the juxtamedullary nephrons are much more important to the renal concentrating ability than cortical nephrons.

All nephrons empty into a collecting tubule (duct of Bellini) that serves many individual nephrons. The collecting ducts pass through the entire length of the renal medulla to finally deliver urine to the renal pelvis.

Transfer of Materials

Materials move in two directions across the renal epithelial cells, from the tubular fluid to blood and from blood and extracellular fluid into the tubules. Movement of materials occurs by osmosis, passive diffusion, and active processes.

Osmosis

Osmosis is the passive movement of water (through a membrane permeable to water but not to solutes) from a dilute solution (where the activity, or "concentration," of water is high) to a concentrated one (where the activity of water is lower). The osmotic movement of water across the walls of renal tubules results from prior transfer of solutes and the resulting establishment of an osmotic gradient. No active transport of water is known to occur in the kidney.

The rate of water transfer across the tubular epithelium depends on the permeability of the tubule to water and the magnitude of the osmotic gradient. With the exception of the ascending limb of the loop of Henle, the renal tubule is permeable to water throughout its length. However, the degree of water permeability of the distal tubules and collecting ducts varies according to the level of *antidiuretic hormone* (ADH) in the blood. ADH is a hormone synthesized by specialized hypothalamic neurosecretory cells and then stored in and released from the posterior pituitary gland, or *neurohypophysis*. This hormone increases the permeability of the distal and collecting tubules to water. When the blood levels of ADH are normal or elevated, the permeability of the distal portions of the nephron increases, water moves from tubular to interstitial fluid, the urine is concentrated, and additional water is returned to the body. When the level of ADH is low, permeability is also low and much of the water contained in tubular fluid is excreted in the urine. While ADH exerts an important effect upon the distal portion of the nephron, the permeability of the proximal tubule and the loop of Henle appears to be independent of this hormone.

Osmotic forces can also act to hold increased quantities of water in the tubules and produce a diuresis. For example, when large amounts of solutes such as mannitol, glucose, or any other osmotically active species remain in tubular fluid, water is held in the tubules by these solutes, and an increased volume of urine is produced.

Passive Diffusion

A few substances other than water passively diffuse from tubular fluid into the interstitial spaces of the renal parenchyma and then into the circulation. Passive diffusion occurs without the expenditure of metabolic energy because, in this type of material transfer, substances move along a concentration and/or electrical gradient. Substances that carry no net electric charge, such as glucose, move through a freely permeable membrane along a concentration gradient from a solution where they are highly concentrated to one in which the concentration is less. "Freely permeable" are key words in this context, and, as will be discussed later, biological membranes, including the epithelial renal tubular cells, are not freely permeable to all substances and additional factors must be considered. Nevertheless, from a strictly physical perspective, neutral molecules are moved from one area to another only by concentration gradients, barring any physical barrier to their movement such as a poorly permeable membrane.

When considering the transfer of ions (charged particles), both concentration and electrical gradients must be taken into account. As is the case for neutral molecules, ions diffuse from a region of high concentration to one of lower concentration. In addition, they move along an electrical gradient. Positive ions such as sodium passively migrate from a positively charged compartment to a more negative one. Likewise, negative chloride ions move along an electrical gradient from negative to positive. When both a concentration and an electrical gradient exist and are oriented in opposite directions to each other, net ionic movement will be in the direction of the larger gradient. If, however, both gradients are similarly oriented, the net gradient reflects the sum of the forces.

Urea is the major nonaqueous substance that is reabsorbed primarily by passive diffusion. Urea, a product of protein metabolism, is a small neutral molecule normally present in blood and freely filtered at the renal glomerulus. As water is reabsorbed from tubular fluid, the concentration of urea in the tubules increases above its concentration in the peritubular fluid. Therefore, a concentration gradient for urea directed from tubular to peritubular fluid is established. Since the tubular epithelium is permeable to urea, it passively diffuses out of the tubules. When increased amounts of water are reabsorbed (and urine flow is consequently low), urea in the tubules is highly concentrated, a large gradient for passive diffusion develops, a large fraction of the filtered urea is reabsorbed, and the rate of urinary urea excretion is low. Conversely, when urine flow is high because of decreased water reabsorption, urea reabsorption decreases and its excretion increases. Although urea reabsorption is primarily passive, a small amount may be actively transported.

Active Transport

Active transport implies movement of a material against concentration and/or electrical gradients requiring the expenditure of energy derived from cellular metabolism. Sodium is the most important substance actively transported by the kidney. Quantitatively, more sodium is actively transported (about 20,000 meq/day) than any other ionic species. Consequently, much of the energy expended by cells of the kidneys is for sodium transport. Active transport of sodium produces important secondary results as well. Certain substances such as chloride ions, water, and urea that are said to be passively transported actually owe their transfer to active transport of sodium. As sodium ions are transferred from tubular fluid, the interstitial fluid becomes increasingly positive as these ions accumulate on the peritubular side of the nephron.

This electrical gradient then favors passive reabsorption of negative chloride ions. The transfer of sodium chloride out of tubular fluid creates an osmotic gradient directed from tubular to interstitial fluid which decrees the passive reabsorption of water. As water is reabsorbed, the tubular concentration of urea increases and establishes a concentration gradient for the passive reabsorption of this material. Therefore, sodium transport has consequences that extend beyond the conservation of this important ion.

The energy currency spent on active transport is apparently high-energy phosphate bonds in adenosine triphosphate (ATP) and similar compounds. Energy for active transport is released when the terminal phosphate is split from ATP to form inorganic phosphate and the lower energy compound adenosine diphosphate (ADP). New stores of ATP are generated by the metabolic processes of glycolysis and oxidative phosphorylation. Oxidative phosphorylation, a more rewarding process in terms of energy yield, requires oxygen and can be inhibited by a number of metabolic inhibitors such as cyanide and dinitrophenol. Since so much of the kidneys' metabolic energy is expended on active sodium transport, it follows that the renal oxygen consumption is proportional to sodium reabsorption. When renal perfusion decreases and less sodium than normal is filtered and presented to the tubular cells for reabsorption, renal oxygen consumption also decreases.

Many cells (notably nerve and muscle) other than those of the kidney actively transport materials. While many cells actively extrude sodium ions across the entire surface of the cell membrane and are, therefore, *nondirectional* or *radial* in their transport characteristics, renal epithelial cells are *directional* or *polar*. This means that the mechanism for active transport is located on only one side of the cell. Recall that the task of renal cells is to reabsorb most (about 99 percent) of the sodium ions filtered from the blood. Therefore, the flow of sodium is from tubular fluid that bathes one side of the epithelial cellular layer of the tubules to the opposite, or interstitial, side.

Physically, there are two forces, electrical and concentration, favoring movement of sodium ions from tubular to intracellular fluid. The inside of the tubular cells is electrically negative to the tubular surface. Therefore, positive sodium ions are electrically attracted to the negative cellular interior. Furthermore, the intracellular sodium concentration is much lower than the tubular concentration of sodium. A concentration gradient in addition to an electrical gradient, therefore, aids in passively transferring sodium ions into the epithelial cells. To remove sodium from a negative intracellular interior to a positive interstitial extracellular fluid, and against a concentration gradient as well, requires expenditure of metabolic energy.

The mechanism for providing this energy and extruding sodium ions against an electrochemical gradient appears to be located on the peritubular side of the renal epithelial cells. Thus, renal tubular cells are unidirectional in the sense that active extrusion of sodium does not occur over the entire surface of the cells, but rather is localized to the interstitial side. Obviously, if renal cells extruded sodium back into the tubular fluid as fast as it entered the cells, net sodium reabsorption could never be accomplished and the body's sodium supply would be excreted into the urine in very short order.

Carrier-Mediated Transport

The transport of some substances is attributed to what is described as *carrier-mediated transport*. A hypothetical scheme for this type of transport is diagrammed in Fig. 8-4. The "carrier," although not yet identified, is thought to be located in the membrane of epithelial cells. The mechanism can be functional on either the tubular or the peritubular side. The material, M (molecule or ion), to be transported combines with the carrier, C. The material-carrier complex, M-C, then moves across the membrane. At the cytoplasmic surface of the membrane the complex dissociates and the released material diffuses across the cell and then into the peritubular fluid. As a result of combining with, transporting, and releasing the material, the carrier itself is modified into an inactive form, I. Conversion of the inactive carrier back into a functional form apparently requires energy, and this step probably represents the energy-consuming aspect of carrier-mediated transport. Carrier mediation apparently overcomes some impediment to reabsorption of filtered materials such as concentration or electrical gradients or permeability barriers. Without such a transport mechanism the kidney would be unable to retrieve many of the filtered materials necessary to the body's metabolic economy.

A number of observations, including saturation kinetics (or transport maximum, Tm), competitive inhibition, and vulnerability to metabolic inhibition, are consistent with a carrier-mediated system. Saturation kinetics can be conceptualized by picturing a finite number of carriers (or seats on an airplane). As long as carriers (or seats) are available, the materials

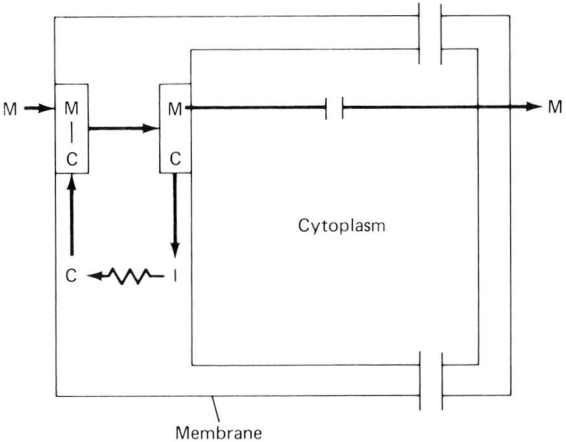

FIGURE 8-4

Schematic representation of carrier-mediated transport. M—the molecule or ion to be transported; C—the carrier; M-C—the material-carrier complex; I—the inactive form of the carrier.

(or passengers) served can be accommodated. However, when the amount of material (or passengers) to be transported increases, the carrier becomes saturated and transport levels off at a maximum value. An example of the consequences of a saturated carrier is the glycosuria associated with elevated blood sugar. As blood glucose increases, the quantity filtered at the glomerulus also increases. All the filtered glucose is reabsorbed—up to a point. As blood glucose, and the amount filtered, increases even further, the glucose carrier system becomes saturated and the excess filtered glucose spills into the urine.

Since carrier molecules apparently have some structural feature that enables them to combine with the materials they transport, e.g., like a lock and key, they are also able to combine with other materials that are structurally similar to the transported molecules of major importance. The presence in tubular fluid of two or more materials that can combine with a common carrier results in *competitive inhibition* of the transport of one material by the presence of the others. Because the reabsorption of many materials requires availability of carrier molecules, the rate of reabsorption of a material is decreased by other materials competing for the same carrier. Many amino acids appear to share a common carrier and, therefore, compete with each other; certain sugars, such as fructose, compete with glucose for reabsorption.

Carrier-mediated transport systems are vulnerable to metabolic inhibitors (oxygen deprivation and certain metabolic poisons such as cyanide) because at least one step in the process requires energy. A steady supply of energy for reabsorption of materials against a concentration gradient depends on intact cellular metabolism, and any factor that reduces the energy supply diminishes the rate of reabsorption.

URINE FORMATION

Urine volume and composition represent the result of four renal processes: filtration, reabsorption, secretion, and concentration. Particular regions of the kidney participate in one or more of these four functions. For example, filtration occurs only at the glomerulus, while reabsorption of various materials occurs throughout the entire length of the nephron. Certain aspects of the activities involved in urine formation are the result of physical forces, such as pressure gradients, while others require cellular integrity and metabolic participation. The various types of structural and functional damage that can occur within the kidney can interfere with normal renal function and are recognized by changes in the volume and composition of urine and the loss from or accumulation of certain substances within the blood.

Glomerular Filtration

The initial step in urine formation is glomerular filtration. While filtration is a passive process that requires no metabolic energy per se, it is dependent on physiologic processes such as adequate renal blood flow and normal permeability of glomerular membranes. The glomerulus is a tuft of capillaries that rests in an enlarged invagination (Bowman's capsule) of the proximal portion of the renal tubule. Blood enters the glomerular capillaries through an afferent arteriole and leaves through an efferent arteriole. As blood flows through the channels of the glomerular capillaries, water and low molecular weight materials in the plasma are filtered from the blood and pass into Bowman's capsule. The filtered fluid is called the *glomerular filtrate* and represents an ultrafiltrate of plasma. An ultrafiltrate results from passing a solution through an ultrafilter with extremely minute pores. The glomerular filtrate is of the same composition as plasma except for the absence of large plasma proteins.

The glomerular filtration membrane is a complex structure with several cellular and noncellular layers. It is more complex than the endothelial layer that is found in most other capillaries of the body. Detailed

structure of the renal filtration surface has only been appreciated since the availability of electron microscopy. It has been estimated that the size of the pores in the glomerular ultrafilter is such that materials in the plasma with a molecular mass of less than about 70,000 daltons are able to pass through. Materials larger than this are physically barred from passing into the glomerular filtrate. Therefore, the glomerular filtrate produced by healthy kidneys contains sugars, salts, amino acids, and metabolic waste products in the same concentration as that found in plasma, but little plasma protein and no formed blood elements such as erythrocytes, white cells, or platelets. However, when the filtration membrane is damaged, large particles enter the tubules and the urine may contain abnormal constituents such as protein and blood cells. On the other hand, the glomerular capillaries may be damaged by pathologic processes, such as sclerosis, that impede filtration.

Two classes of physical forces, namely osmotic pressure and hydrostatic pressure, influence the rate of glomerular filtration. Capillary hydrostatic pressure, or blood pressure, within the glomerular vessels, favors filtration. Oncotic pressure due to the proteins remaining in plasma tends to hold water within the capillaries and acts as a retarding force on filtration. Within Bowman's capsule, the hydrostatic pressure of filtrate already in that structure tends to oppose filtration, while a small oncotic pressure (if there are proteins within the filtrate) tends to encourage it. The net effect of these four forces (plasma hydrostatic pressure, plasma oncotic pressure, filtrate hydrostatic, and filtrate oncotic pressures) on the formation of glomerular filtrate is called the *net filtration pressure* and can be expressed as follows:

$$NFP = (P_c + p_{BC}) - (p_c + P_{BC}) \qquad (1)$$

where NFP is the net filtration pressure, P_c is the capillary blood (hydrostatic) pressure, p_{BC} is the oncotic pressure in Bowman's capsule, p_c is the oncotic pressure of blood, and P_{BC} is the hydrostatic pressure within Bowman's capsule. Characteristic values for these pressures are P_c, 80 mmHg; p_{BC}, 0 mmHg, or a very small value; p_c, 30 mmHg; and P_{BC}, 15 mmHg. When these values are inserted into Eq. (1), the net filtration pressure is calculated as

$$NFP = (80 + 0) - (30 + 15) = 35 \, mmHg \qquad (2)$$

A number of conditions can alter the net filtration pressure by changing one or more of the contributing pressures. For example, a drop in mean arterial pressure reduces P_c and, therefore, net filtration pressure. It is well known that decreased urinary output commonly accompanies hypotension. One reason for the drop in urine formation is a decrease in net filtration pressure. When P_{BC} increases, as can occur with an obstruction within the urinary tract, one force opposing filtration increases and net filtration pressure decreases even though there has been no change in renal perfusion pressure. Other pathologies affect other factors influencing filtration pressure and alter it accordingly.

The *glomerular filtration rate* (GFR) is the rate at which glomerular filtrate is formed and equals about 125 mL/min in a healthy, hydrated adult. The GFR is proportional to net filtration pressure and can be expressed as

$$GFR = K(NFP) \qquad (3)$$

where K is the permeability coefficient of the ultrafiltration membrane and has the units of volume of filtrate formed per minute per millimeter of mercury of driving pressure. If GFR is 125 mL/min and net filtration pressure is 35 mmHg, the permeability coefficient is

$$K = 125/35 = (3.6 \, mL/min)/mmHg \qquad (4)$$

If K decreases, the GFR also decreases even though the net filtration pressure remains within normal limits. Such a decrease in GFR due to a reduction in the permeability coefficient occurs in certain diseases in which there is deposition of material within the glomeruli that interferes with the normal transfer of materials from blood to renal tubules. On the other hand, pathologic changes may result in an abnormally "leaky" membrane and an increased GFR with no increase in net filtration pressure. Abnormally increased permeability also permits filtration of plasma constituents that are normally retained within the blood. Most notable of these is albumin, the smallest of the major plasma proteins. When albumin and other larger proteins escape into the filtrate, the capacity of the kidney to reabsorb them is exceeded, the proteins appear in the urine, and the characteristic proteinuria of serious renal disease is manifested.

Changes in hydrostatic and oncotic pressures on the glomerular and capsular sides, as well as changes in the permeability coefficient, can change GFR. Under physiologic conditions, most of the regulation of GFR is mediated through changes in the relative diameters (and therefore, resistances) of the afferent and efferent arterioles. Adrenergic (sympathetic) constriction of afferent arterioles increases both the resistance to flow in these vessels and the drop in blood

pressure along their length. As a result, hydrostatic pressure in the glomerular capillaries is lowered resulting in decreased net filtration pressure and GFR. Dilation of the afferent arterioles lowers their resistance and allows a greater proportion of the arterial pressure to be realized as glomerular hydrostatic pressure and increased GFR. Modification of efferent arteriolar resistance can also influence GFR. Efferent arteriolar constriction slows blood flow from the glomerular capillaries, increases the pressure within them, and augments GFR. Dilation of the efferent arterioles has the opposite effect. Changes in diameter of intrarenal vessels and the regulation of blood flow through glomerular capillaries, pressures, and GFR are mediated by both intrinsic and extrinsic factors.

Intrinsic regulation of renal blood flow is termed *autoregulation*. Autoregulation is characterized by a relatively constant renal blood flow regardless of extrinsic factors such as mean arterial pressure (perfusion pressure) between the values of about 90 and 250 mmHg. Below and above these limits renal blood flow is proportional to perfusion pressure. In other words, renal blood flow increases proportionately as mean arterial pressure increases up to about 90 mmHg (mean). From 90 to 250 mmHg there is little change (because of autoregulation) in renal blood flow despite the increasing arterial pressure. This observation suggests that there is an intrinsically mediated increase in renal resistance to prevent an increase in blood flow despite an increased arterial pressure. Above 250 mmHg, renal blood flow again becomes proportional to perfusion pressure, suggesting that the ability of the kidney to limit its own blood flow is overwhelmed by the high arterial pressure.

Filtration fraction is the ratio of GFR to renal plasma flow (GFR/RPF) and is approximately 0.2 in humans. This means that about 20 percent of the plasma flowing through the kidneys is filtered into the tubules. Obviously, not all plasma flowing through the glomeruli is filtered, because an immovable, viscous "sludge" of plasma proteins and formed blood elements would be left behind. Factors that increase glomerular hydrostatic pressure or decrease the rate at which blood moves from glomerular capillaries into efferent arterioles increase the filtration fraction, while factors operating in the opposite direction decrease it. Therefore, by adjusting intrarenal blood flow and vessel resistance, the kidneys are able to maintain GFR relatively constant despite fluctuations in extrarenal hemodynamic influences such as mean systemic arterial pressure.

Realizing that GFR represents the composite filtration of about 2 million nephrons, each of which does not necessarily have the same rate of filtrate formation, it becomes apparent that determination of GFR is not a direct measurement. Glomerular filtration rate, as well as other parameters of renal function, is based upon a general indirect approach called *plasma clearance*.

The Concept of Clearance

Most students of physiology initially have difficulty with the concept of clearance. This is because they misinterpret the very precise definition of clearance. Be forewarned that the problem lies not with ambiguity of the definition, but rather in the almost universal tendency toward misinterpretation. Clearance is defined as the *volume* (usually milliliters) *of plasma completely cleared of a material per unit time* (usually a minute). In order to avoid an initial and difficult to dislodge misconception of clearance, a close examination of the concept is in order. First of all, notice that clearance has the units of volume per time, e.g., milliliters per minute. Clearance is *not* the amount of material cleared from the plasma per unit time. This is the excretion rate and is expressed in terms of mass per time, e.g., milligrams per minute. Instead, clearance is concerned with the volume of *plasma* that has been completely cleared, or cleansed, of a substance. For example, if a substance X has a clearance of 1000 mL/min, it means that in 1 min the *equivalent* of 1000 mL of plasma is completely cleared of X.

Inulin clearance, or the volume of blood completely cleared of inulin each minute, is the classical method of determining GFR. Inulin is a fructose polysaccharide with a molecular mass of approximately 5000 daltons and is, therefore, freely filterable at the glomerulus. In addition, inulin is neither reabsorbed nor secreted by renal tubules. Since all inulin excreted in the urine gained access to the tubular system by filtration, and because there is neither removal of any of the filtered inulin nor secretion of additional inulin into the tubules, all inulin excreted in the urine each minute *must* have come from the volume of filtrate produced during that minute. Since glomerular filtrate is derived from plasma passing through the glomerular capillaries, calculation of inulin clearance implies that the volume of plasma cleared of inulin must have passed into the tubules as glomerular filtrate and left its load of inulin in the tubular fluid as the majority of the other filtered substances were reabsorbed. Cal-

culating the inulin clearance in milliliters per minute reveals the volume of glomerular filtrate produced each minute, or the GFR.

During the actual procedure of measuring inulin clearance, inulin is infused into blood at a rate that maintains a constant plasma concentration; i.e., inulin is infused as fast as it is removed by glomerular filtration. After a steady state is realized, plasma inulin concentration, P_{In}, is determined. During inulin infusion, the rate of urine formation, V, in milliliters per minute is also monitored. Finally, the concentration of inulin in the timed urine specimen, U_{In}, in milligrams per milliliter is also determined. Inulin clearance and GFR are then calculated as follows:

$$GFR = C_{In} = \frac{U_{In} \times V}{P_{In}} \tag{5}$$

If, for example, U_{In} is 12.5 mg/mL, V is 1 mL/min, and P_{In} is 0.1 mg/mL, inulin clearance and GFR would be

$$GFR = C_{In} = \frac{(12.5\,mg/mL) \times (1\,mL/min)}{0.1\,mg/mL} \tag{5a}$$

$$= 125\,mL/min$$

It may not always be possible or desirable to administer intravenous inulin to assess GFR. Therefore, creatinine clearance, C_{Cr}, is often used instead for the determination of GFR in the clinical setting. Creatinine is an endogenous substance whose plasma concentration remains relatively constant. Like inulin, creatinine is freely filtered at the glomerulus and is not reabsorbed by the tubules. Unlike inulin, however, a small amount of creatinine is secreted by the human kidney. Therefore, creatinine is cleared from plasma by both filtration and secretion, and its clearance would be expected to be slightly higher than GFR. Fortunately, this imposed error is offset by a proportionate error in the usual means of laboratory determination of plasma creatinine concentration, with the end result that creatinine clearance is an adequate means of calculating GFR.

Tubular Reabsorption

If a person has a total blood volume of 5600 mL and a hematocrit of 45 percent, plasma volume would be 3080 mL [5600 × (1 − 0.45) = 3080]. At a GFR of 125 mL/min the total plasma volume would (theoretically) be completely exhausted in just about 25 min if there were no means for the kidneys to recover the majority of filtrate. Fortunately, the kidneys are quite adept at reabsorbing almost all the filtrate. The normal daily volume of filtrate is about 180 L, yet only about 1.5 L of urine are formed each day. Thus, about 99 percent of the glomerular filtrate is reabsorbed into the blood. The kidneys accomplish this remarkable feat in several ways.

Most of the reabsorption (about 65 to 80 percent) occurs in the proximal tubule. This portion of the tubule has a large reabsorptive surface due to a brush border on the luminal side of the tubular cells that greatly increases the reabsorptive surface of these cells. In general, reabsorption of water is the result of previous reabsorption of solutes.

Reabsorption of Inorganic Ions

Sodium reabsorption The concentration of inorganic salts (especially sodium salts) is the same in the glomerular filtrate of Bowman's capsule as in plasma. Therefore, the osmotic pressure of filtrate in the proximal tubule is isosmotic with plasma. However, as is true for all other cells of the body, sodium is much more concentrated in extracellular than in intracellular fluid. Also, the interior of tubular cells is electrically negative to extracellular fluid (as is true for all cells). Thus, sodium moves from tubular fluid into tubular cells (passively) along an electrochemical gradient. The cells of the renal tubule then actively extrude sodium (against an electrochemical gradient) into the peritubular, or contraluminal, interstitial fluid where it is picked up by the blood flowing through the peritubular capillaries. Removal of positive sodium ions from the filtrate leaves that fluid with an excess of unbalanced negative ions (mainly chloride). The negative ions then passively follow the actively transported sodium ions and are reabsorbed with them. As sodium salts are reabsorbed from the tubular fluid, the osmotic pressure decreases and the filtrate becomes more dilute. Water is consequently reabsorbed passively along an osmotic gradient originally established by the prior active reabsorption of sodium which then electrically attracts negative ions and finally water.

There appear to be two major types of active sodium "pumps" on the interstitial sides of renal tubular cells. In the first type, sodium is transported out of the cells against an electrochemical gradient and chloride ions follow passively to maintain electrical neutrality. As sodium and chloride are continuously moved from tubular to interstitial fluid, reabsorption of salt and water occurs at a normal rate. This type of sodium transport is subject to inhibition by ethacrynic acid. In the presence of this drug,

transport of salt and water slows and a greater than normal amount of these filtered substances remain in the tubular fluid and are ultimately excreted in urine. This action of ethacrynic acid accounts for its utility as a potent diuretic.

The second type of sodium transport out of tubular cells is coupled to inward transfer of potassium ions from interstitial fluid. In this scheme, electrical neutrality is maintained by replacing an extruded sodium ion with the uptake of positive potassium ions. In order for this means of sodium uptake to remain functional, an adequate supply of extracellular potassium in the interstitial fluid is required. When potassium is not available, this pump ceases to function. Furthermore, this sodium-potassium-linked pump is inhibited by cardiac glycosides such as ouabain. Therefore, at least two functional sodium reabsorption mechanisms are operative in the kidney. The first is potassium-independent and is inhibited by ethacrynic acid, and the second is potassium-dependent and ouabain-sensitive.

Throughout the proximal tubule, where the majority of reabsorption occurs, water and salt are reabsorbed proportionately; therefore, although the volume of the filtrate is steadily reduced, there is no change in its solute concentration or osmotic pressure. Although the tubular fluid in the proximal tubule remains isosmotic with plasma, its composition relative to plasma can change. A notable difference in ionic concentrations between plasma and filtrate is that the chloride concentration of tubular fluid may be higher than that of plasma. This is because some of the filtered sodium ions are reabsorbed with bicarbonate ions rather than chloride ions. The difference in chloride concentrations between plasma and tubular fluid is not static and depends in large part upon pH and the kidneys' drive to conserve or lose bicarbonate to maintain acid-base balance of the body fluids.

The ascending limb of the loops of Henle is impermeable to water although salts continue to be reabsorbed. As a result, the filtrate becomes more dilute and its osmotic pressure, relative to interstitial fluid, falls in this tubular segment. Depending on the level of ADH, the walls of the distal portion of the nephron are more or less permeable to water that then moves out of the tubules along an osmotic gradient.

Sodium continues to be reabsorbed in the distal parts of the nephron. However, in this region, its reabsorption is greatly influenced by the adrenal cortical hormone, *aldosterone*. Aldosterone stimulates sodium reabsorption. As sodium is reabsorbed, the tubular fluid becomes less positive. Instead of reabsorbing negative ions, the cells secrete positive ions such as potassium and hydrogen to maintain electrical neutrality. Therefore, the overall effect of aldosterone is to stimulate sodium reabsorption and promote excretion of potassium and hydrogen ions. Since most diuretics inhibit sodium reabsorption in more proximal regions of the tubule, more sodium than usual is presented to the distal reabsorption site. Because this is the kidneys' last chance at sodium reabsorption, they "work overtime" to save sodium at this point. The well-known potassium-wasting action of many diuretics is based on this concept. Because potassium is exchanged for sodium in the distal nephron, potassium excretion increases and depletion can occur. Only those diuretics that antagonize aldosterone, such as spironolactone, counter excess potassium loss.

Potassium Potassium appears to be engaged in a renal revolving door. A great deal of experimental evidence supports proximal reabsorption of potassium. In the distal tubule, circumstances dictate its excretory fate. When intake of potassium is low or extrarenal excretion is high, this ion is reabsorbed in the distal, as well as in the proximal, tubule. When intake is high or the amount of sodium presented to the distal tubule is greater than normal or other circumstances supervene, potassium is secreted into distal tubular fluid in greater quantities than it is reabsorbed.

Other ions Renal reabsorption of calcium ions is greatly influenced by parathyroid hormone (PTH). This hormone stimulates calcium reabsorption and decreases phosphate reabsorption. The serious bone lesions that accompany certain types of renal disease are due, in part, to the fact that diseased kidneys reabsorb less calcium than normal. As a result, serum calcium levels fall and the parathyroid glands secrete increased quantities of PTH. This hormone then mobilizes calcium from bone and diminishes skeletal mass. Little is gained, however, because of the decreased ability of diseased kidneys to reabsorb calcium despite the intensified PTH drive. Therefore, despite continuous infusion of calcium into the blood from bone stores, it is rapidly excreted.

Phosphate reabsorption is decreased by PTH. Therefore, hypophosphatemia is not an unexpected consequence of renal diseases that secondarily increase parathyroid activity. Normally, the proximal tubules reabsorb a certain fraction of the filtered phosphorus compounds. Renal handling of phosphate is also influenced by the body's acid-base balance.

Following chloride, bicarbonate ions are the most frequent anionic partners of reabsorbed sodium ions. When the amount of filtered chloride is decreased, more bicarbonate ions than usual are reabsorbed with sodium (and lead to hypochloremic alkalosis). Increased amounts of bicarbonate are also reabsorbed as the filtered load of this ion increases, up to a point. When bicarbonate concentration exceeds about 2.5 meq/100 mL of filtrate, the bicarbonate reabsorptive capacity appears to be exceeded. Renal cells have the enzymatic capability of producing bicarbonate, and this aspect will be discussed in the section on renal contribution to acid-base balance.

Reabsorption of Organic Materials

Organic materials such as glucose, amino acids, urea, creatine, and other substances are also reabsorbed from the tubular fluid.

Glucose The glucose concentration of glomerular filtrate is the same as plasma because glucose is freely filtered. If plasma glucose is 100 mg/100 mL and the GFR is 125 mL/min, the amount of glucose filtered each minute is the product of these two terms, or 125 mg/min. Obviously, there is almost complete renal reabsorption of glucose because normally only a few milligrams are excreted into the urine each day. While the kidneys normally reabsorb all the glucose filtered, there is a limit to the reabsorptive ability. The upper limit of renal glucose reabsorption is called the *transport* (or tubular) *maximum for glucose*, the Tm_G. An upper limit to glucose transport is attributed to its carrier mechanism. Only a finite amount of glucose can be handled by this mechanism per unit time, and when more glucose is filtered than can be reabsorbed, the excess spills into the urine. The Tm_G is about 375 mg/min for males and somewhat less for the average female.

It is well known that glucose can be detected in the urine of individuals with an elevated blood sugar. Urinary glucose represents that fraction of filtered glucose that was unable to be accommodated by the renal reabsorptive mechanism. The level of blood (arterial) sugar at which greater than normal amounts of glucose appear in urine is termed the *renal threshold*. Theoretically, the renal threshold for glucose should be 3 mg/mL, or 300 mg/dL when the GFR is 125 mL/min (Tm_G/GFR = 375/125 = 3 mg/mL). Actually, the renal threshold is closer to 200 mg/dL. The discrepancy between theoretical and actual levels of blood sugar at which glucose spills into urine can be due to different nephrons having different transport maxima. As soon as the amount of glucose filtered exceeds the Tm_G of the "weakest" reabsorptive nephron, some glucose appears in the urine—despite the fact that other nephrons are still reabsorbing all the filtered glucose presented to them. Finally, as blood glucose increases even further, the reabsorptive capabilities of all the nephrons are exceeded.

The consequence of limitations on renal glucose reabsorption is that as more glucose is filtered per unit time, the amount reabsorbed increases, up to a point. When the rate of glucose filtration exceeds glucose reabsorption, glycosuria develops. As more and more glucose is filtered, more appears in the urine. The familiar glycosuria of diabetes mellitus is the result of elevated blood sugar (and increased glucose filtration) rather than decreased Tm_G, which appears to be normal in uncomplicated diabetes. Notice that the appearance of excessive sugar in the urine depends on *both* the plasma level of glucose and the GFR. Therefore, it is possible for an individual with an elevated blood sugar to exhibit no glycosuria if the GFR is severely depressed.

Amino acids The size of blood-borne amino acids renders them freely filtrable. There are apparently three separate transport mechanisms in the kidney for the reabsorption of amino acids. Not all these mechanisms have the same Tm, and some amino acids are reabsorbed more efficiently than others. Nevertheless, excessive loss of these important substances from the body is prevented; however, there are several known inborn errors of renal amino acid transport that result in clinically identifiable syndromes.

Urea Urea reabsorption depends on the prior reabsorption of salts and water and on the rate of urine flow. At high rates of urine flow, less time is available for urea diffusion out of tubular fluid, and urea reabsorption is proportionately decreased.

Tubular Secretion

Tubular secretion implies the movement of materials from blood to tubular fluid at nonglomerular sites. Secreted materials, while often filtered as well as secreted, are moved across tubular epithelial cells similarly to reabsorbed substances, with the exception that the direction of transport is opposite. Like tubular reabsorption, secretion may be either active or passive. Also like reabsorption, some substances are secreted by mechanisms that exhibit a transport maximum, some are secreted only until a limiting gradient is reached against which secretion can no longer prevail, and some are secreted passively along an electrochemical gradient.

Tm-Limited Secretion

Many, but not all, substances secreted by Tm-limited mechanisms are foreign to the body, such as drugs and dyes. Small amounts of the endogenous substance creatinine also appear to be secreted by this type of mechanism. Like Tm-limited reabsorptive mechanisms, secretion depends on formation of a carrier-substrate complex in the renal tubular cells, and competition between materials sharing a common secretory mechanism is known to occur. It is of historical interest that at one time the secretory competition between substances was clinically utilized to great advantage, illustrating the value of applying physiological principles to clinical practice. During the 1940s, when penicillin was a rare and expensive drug highly valued for its ability to control infections in traumatized war casualities, its renal secretion was slowed by administering another drug, such as probenecid, which competes with penicillin for the same renal secretory mechanism. Thus, administration of a competing agent delayed excretion and permitted higher plasma levels of penicillin. Some of the materials secreted by Tm-limited mechanisms include Diodrast, phenol red or phenolsulfonphthalein (PSP), ethylenediaminetetraacetic acid (EDTA), chlorothiazide, and para-aminohippurate (PAH), in addition to penicillin and creatinine.

The clearance of PAH is very useful in determining the *effective renal plasma flow* (ERPF). The ERPF is the volume of plasma exposed to the filtering and secreting portions of the kidney each minute. When the plasma level of PAH is low, almost all the blood flowing through nondiseased kidneys is cleared of this material. PAH is both filtered and secreted by the kidneys. Therefore, urinary PAH is of two fractions, a filtered and a secreted fraction. The PAH that escapes filtration within the glomerular capillaries (recall that the filtration fraction is only about 0.2) is secreted into the tubules from blood in the peritubular capillaries, provided the secretory mechanism is not saturated. Since filtered PAH is not reabsorbed and since almost all the plasma flowing through the kidneys is cleared of PAH during one pass through renal tissue, the volume of plasma cleared of PAH each minute must have flowed through the kidneys. Therefore, PAH clearance can be used to calculate ERPF (through nondiseased kidneys) as follows:

$$ERPF = C_{PAH} = \frac{U_{PAH} \times V}{P_{PAH}} \qquad (6)$$

If, for example, U_{PAH} is 15 mg/mL, V is 1 mL/min, and P_{PAH} is 0.025 mg/mL, the ERPF would be

$$ERPF = C_{PAH} = \frac{15\,mg/mL \times 1\,mL/min}{0.025\,mg/mL}$$
$$= 600\,mL/min \qquad (6a)$$

About 10 percent of actual renal plasma flow (RPF) bypasses the glomeruli and peritubular capillaries, and only about 90 percent (the *extraction ratio*) of the actual renal plasma flow is cleared of PAH. To calculate RPF, the ERPF is divided by the extraction ratio as follows:

$$RPF = \frac{ERPF}{Extraction\ ratio} = \frac{600\,mL/min}{0.9}$$
$$= 667\,mL/min \qquad (7)$$

Renal blood flow (RBF) is calculated by dividing the RPF by (1 − hematocrit). At a hematocrit of 45 percent, the RBF is

$$RBF = \frac{RPF}{(1 - Hct)} = \frac{667\,mL/min}{(1 - 0.45)}$$
$$= 1213\,mL/min \qquad (8)$$

or about 20 percent of the total cardiac output.

When kidneys are diseased, PAH clearance decreases along with the decrease in functional renal mass. Under these conditions, means other than plasma clearance are used to calculate renal plasma flow. Also, when plasma PAH is elevated to levels above those that saturate the secretory mechanism, not all the plasma is cleared of PAH during one passage through the kidneys, and an increasingly larger fraction of PAH excreted in the urine is the filtered fraction. In other words, above the PAH plasma level that saturates the carrier-mediated mechanism, the secreted fraction maintains a constant maximum level, while the filtered fraction increases proportionately to the plasma concentration. Thus, at plasma levels above saturation, urinary excretion of PAH (and other materials that are filtered, secreted, and not reabsorbed) can be expressed as

$$U_{PAH} \times V = (GFR \times P_{PAH}) + Tm_{PAH} \qquad (9)$$

| Urinary Excretion | Filtered Fraction | Secreted Fraction |

The secreted fraction is equal to the difference between total urinary excretion and the filtered fraction.

Active Secretion Limited by Time or Gradients

The prototype of substances actively secreted by mechanisms with time or gradient limitations is the hydrogen ion. Hydrogen ions are secreted throughout the length of the renal nephron, but the exact mechanism may differ in various tubular segments. The proximal segments transport large numbers of hydrogen ions per unit time but are unable to establish a concentration gradient much in excess of about one-half a pH unit. In other words, proximal tubular hydrogen secretion is gradient-limited but not time-limited. On the other hand, the distal segments, while transporting relatively fewer hydrogen ions per unit time, are able to secrete hydrogen ions against a much larger concentration gradient. In distal tubules, the pH of tubular fluid can be lowered to about 4.4, which represents a "urine"-to-blood concentration gradient of 1000:1. Two types of renal tubular acidosis are representative clinical manifestations of disturbances in these two hydrogen secretion moieties. In classical (type 1) distal renal tubular acidosis, the defect appears to lie with an inability of the kidney to establish the normally high gradient for hydrogen ions, and urinary pH remains inappropriately elevated despite marked systemic acidosis. In proximal (type 2) renal tubular acidosis, the proximal hydrogen secretory mechanism appears to be the one affected.

The time-honored reciprocity between distal secretion of hydrogen and potassium ions has been rendered less secure, quantitatively, by recent evidence, although qualitatively it must still be considered operative. Classically, hydrogen and potassium ions were thought to share a common secretory mechanism and, hence, to compete with one another for exchange with sodium reabsorbed at distal sites. According to this view, the relative intracellular abundance of potassium ions was viewed as displacing hydrogen ions from the distal secretory mechanism, resulting in decreased hydrogen secretion and the well-known hyperkalemic acidosis. Conversely, in hypokalemia, hydrogen ions would be preferentially exchanged for sodium ions and would produce the equally familiar hypokalemic alkalosis. Although a strict hydrogen-potassium reciprocity is in question, there are situations in which secretion of one species of ion is preferentially increased over secretion of the other.

Passive Tubular Secretion

Passive secretion indicates movement of materials from blood to tubular fluid along an electrical and/or concentration gradient without the necessity for expenditure of metabolic energy. Passive secretion of a material does not, however, necessarily preclude the utilization of energy for prior establishment of the gradient that ultimately directs secretion. Weak acids and bases, as well as the important ion potassium, are known to be secreted by passive means.

Secretion of weak bases and weak acids Many exogenous and some endogenous substances are classified as weak acids or bases. Weak bases include administered substances such as neutral red, quinine, and procaine and the endogenous substance, ammonia. In the secretion of these substances, which can be described as "diffusion trapping," uncharged molecules of weak bases cross the tubular membranes with greater ease than charged species. When the blood or tubular cellular level of weak bases is higher than that of tubular fluid, these materials pass into the tubular lumen along a concentration gradient. When the tubular fluid is acid (and its pH is low), the concentration of free hydrogen ions is high and they combine with the secreted weak bases. The bases thereby acquire free hydrogen ions and a net charge. Thus charged, they encounter more difficulty in moving back into blood across tubular membranes and are thus "trapped" in tubular fluid and excreted in urine. Since a greater proportion of the passively secreted bases will combine with hydrogen ions and remain in tubular fluid when the pH of tubular fluid is low, it follows that weak base excretion is enhanced by an acid urine. The urine can be acidified by administering a number of substances such as ammonium chloride and cranberry juice. Notice that while the secretion of weak bases may be passive, maintaining the concentration gradient of hydrogen ions which attracts them requires hydrogen secretion.

Like weak bases, weak acids such as salicylate and phenobarbital may also be subject to diffusion trapping. Therefore, an alkaline urine attracts and holds acids within it. This principle has clinical application in that urine alkalinization by administration of acetazolamide (Diamox) or sodium bicarbonate or by inducing hyperventilation may speed excretion of an overdose of salicylic acid or phenobarbital.

Potassium secretion Under normal conditions, most of the potassium filtered at the glomerulus is reabsorbed in the proximal tubules, and the potassium excreted in the urine reaches it mainly by subsequent distal secretion of these ions. The secretory rate of potassium is not constant and depends on a number of factors. If there is a single determinant of potassium secretion, it is probably the need of the body to conserve sodium. When the kidney is avidly conserving sodium, potassium secretion increases as sodium reabsorption in the distal parts of the nephron increases. For example, if renal perfusion (and glomerular filtration) is reduced by aortic or renal artery stenosis, the kidney is stimulated to avidly save sodium (and water) in an apparent attempt to increase its own blood flow. Therefore, throughout the tubule sodium is reabsorbed, and in the distal tubule this sodium reabsorption is partly at the expense of increased potassium secretion—a positive ion secreted (potassium) for one reabsorbed (sodium). Also, infusing sodium salts with a poorly reabsorbed anion, such as sulfate, reduces proximal sodium reabsorption and delivers more sodium than normal to the distal reabsorptive sites. Since the kidneys' "last chance" to save sodium occurs in the distal tubule where sodium reabsorption occurs in exchange for another positive ion such as potassium, infusion of sodium salts as sulfate results in net potassium excretion. Notice that as sodium is reabsorbed, the negative sulfate (or other nonreabsorbable anion) remains in the tubular fluid and provides an electrical gradient that passively attracts potassium.

Other conditions, such as potassium loading, also increase net potassium secretion. Therefore, the amount of potassium in the urine, while variable, depends on a number of factors. Nevertheless, much of the potassium excreted in urine gains access to the tubular fluid in the distal nephron and its secretion appears to be primarily passive.

Renal Concentrating and Diluting Mechanisms

Daily urine volume can range from a low of 400 mL to a high of between 15 and 20 L, and the osmolality may range from 50 to 1200 mosmol/L. Obviously, the kidney has means of regulating both volume and concentration of the urine it produces. While a number of factors contribute to the final urinary volume and concentration, a major determinant is ADH. Despite the central role of ADH, which is operative in the distal parts of the nephron and in the collecting tubules, the stage for ultimate urine concentration is set in more proximal regions of the nephron, mainly the loops of Henle.

Antidiuretic hormone is elaborated in neurosecretory cells of the hypothalamus and released into the blood from the neurohypophysis (posterior pituitary gland). Under the influence of ADH, responsive areas of the renal system are rendered increasingly permeable to water within the tubular fluid, and water moves from the filtrate to the renal interstitium and then into blood vessels draining the kidney.

Before examining details of the renal concentrating mechanism, let us look first at the overall picture. Filtrate leaving the ascending limb of the loop of Henle and entering the distal convoluted tubule is hypotonic with respect to blood and renal interstitial fluid. Therefore, there exists an osmotic gradient for water directed from tubular to interstitial fluid. When the walls of the distal tubules and collecting ducts are water-permeable, water readily moves from dilute tubular fluid to the more concentrated interstitial fluid and blood. In this way, additional water is recovered from the filtrate under the influence of ADH. This process reduces the volume of the final urine and increases its concentration. In the absence of adequate ADH, tubular water remains within the filtrate and is finally excreted in a dilute urine of large volume. Notice that ultimate movement of water from filtrate to body fluid requires an interstitial fluid with a higher concentration of osmotically active particles than tubular fluid. How this necessary osmotic gradient is established will be discussed first. Although all the fine details have not been resolved completely, it is known that the permeability characteristics for water and solutes are heterogeneous in different regions of the nephron.

Movements of Solutes and Water

It was explained earlier in this chapter that the majority of water and solute reabsorption occurs in the proximal tubule and that solute reabsorption in this part of the nephron is isosmotic, i.e., solute and solvent are reabsorbed proportionately with the result that, although large amounts of matrials are removed, there is no change in the osmolality of the filtrate. Therefore, fluid moving from the proximal tubule into the descending limb of the loop of Henle has an osmolality of about 300 mosmol/L. As the filtrate moves down the descending limb of the loop of Henle, it osmotically equilibrates with the hypertonic interstitial fluid of the renal medulla and is concentrated. In the ascending limb, solute, but not water, leaves the tubule, and the filtrate becomes more dilute than interstitial fluid.

When the level of ADH is high, water moves out of the relatively dilute fluid in the distal tubules and collecting ducts, water is reabsorbed from the filtrate, and urine is concentrated. Notice that two factors are operative in urine concentration—an increasingly hypertonic interstitium from cortex to papilla and the level of ADH. Let us now turn our attention to how the elevated osmotic concentration of the renal tissue surrounding the loops of Henle and collecting tubules is established and maintained.

The counter-current mechanism   The renal counter-current mechanism is composed of two elements, a *counter-current multiplier* and a *counter-current exchanger*. A counter-current system is one in which the inflow and outflow tracts lie adjacent to each other, i.e., in a U-shaped configuration, and transfer of material or energy (such as heat) between the two limbs occurs. A counter-current multiplier is one that increases, or multiplies, the gradient (osmotic, in the case of the kidney) between the top and bottom of the system to a greater extent than can be realized between the points of entry and exit, i.e., across the adjacent limbs of the system.

An osmotic counter-current multiplier is illustrated in Fig. 8-5. This representation assumes that a maximum osmotic gradient of 200 mosmol/L can be established between the limbs of the multiplier by transferring solute from the outflow to the inflow side. The establishment of this translimb gradient of 200 mosmol is called the *single-effect*. The counter-current multiplier increases the magnitude of the single-effect *along* the length of the loops of Henle, although it does not increase the gradient above 200 *across* them at any given horizontal position. When the counter-current multiplier is filled with fluid having an osmolality of 300, the situation is as pictured in frame 1 of Fig. 8-5. A maximum gradient of 200 mosmol/L is generated by transferring solute from the outflow to the inflow limb as shown in frame 2. As fresh fluid at an osmolality of 300 enters the system, the situation is as shown in frame 3. Notice that incoming fluid causes some fluid to move out. Once again, a maximum gradient of 200 is established across the inflow and outflow tracts (frame 4). In frame 5, more new fluid enters the system, and frame 6 illustrates the situation as the single-effect is once again developed. Frames 7 and 8 illustrate development of an even greater difference between the osmolality of fluid at the tip of the multiplier system and the outflow point.

Two important aspects of such a counter-current mechanism need emphasis. First, the gradient developed across the two limbs of the loop is limited,

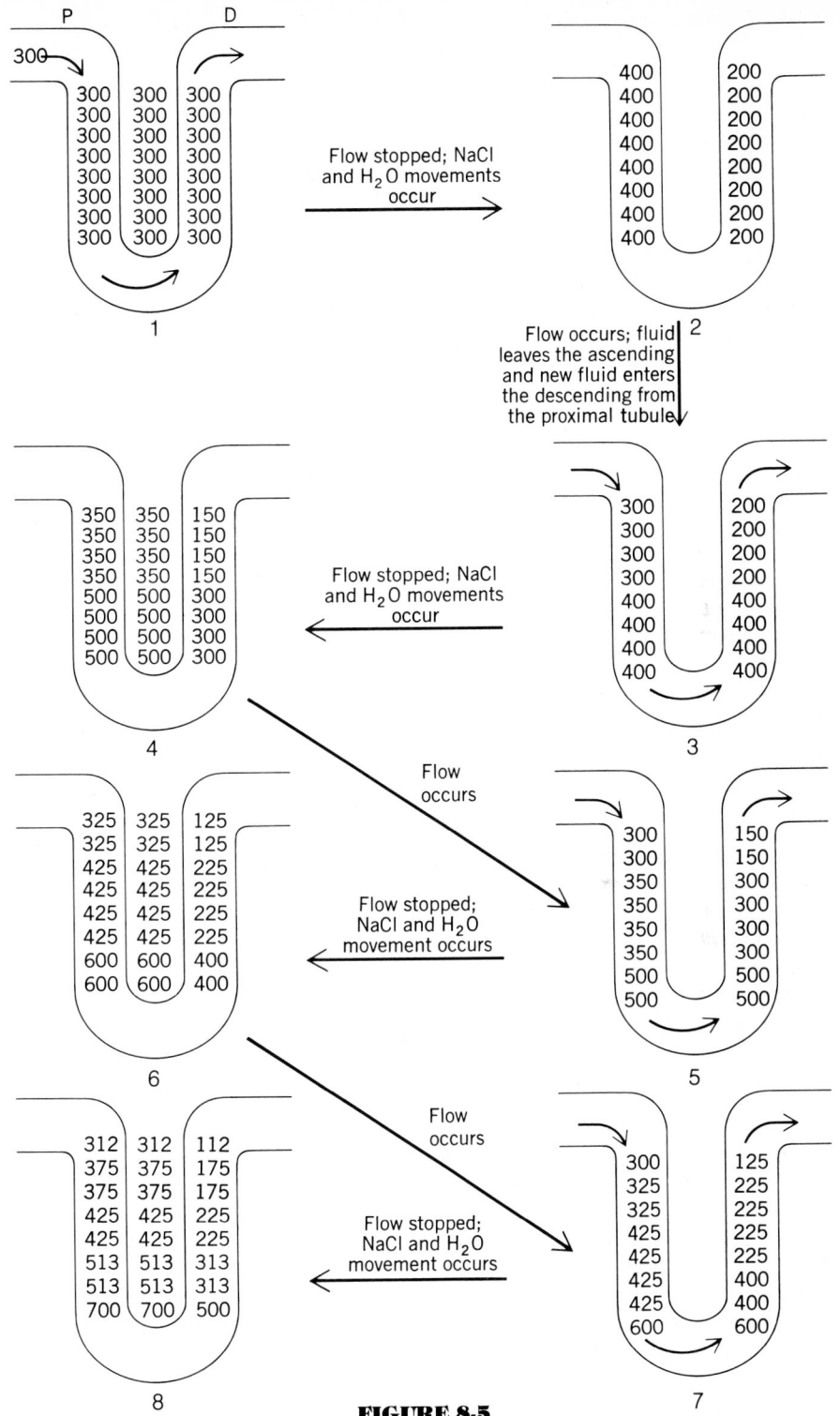

FIGURE 8-5

A counter-current multiplier. The numbered frames referred to in the text follow the direction of the arrows shown in the figure. (*From A. J. Vander, J. H. Sherman, and D. Luciano, Human Physiology, 2d ed., McGraw-Hill, New York, 1975.*)

and second, the gradient between the tip of the loop and the outflow is greater than can be realized by the single-effect alone. Hence, the single-effect is multiplied as fluid flows in this system.

In the human kidney, filtrate enters the loop of Henle (the counter-current multiplier) with an osmolality of approximately 300 mosmol/L and leaves with an osmolality of about 100; however, the osmolality at the tip is about 1200. The longer the loop of Henle, the greater the top-to-bottom osmotic gradient. The loops of cortical nephrons (about 90 percent of all human nephrons) are much shorter than those of juxtamedullary nephrons and consequently produce a less concentrated product. The juxtamedullary nephrons with long loops are, therefore, the ones primarily responsible for hypertonicity of the renal medulla which provides the attraction for water from the collecting ducts that carry filtrate from all nephrons of the kidney. The upper limit of urine concentration is dictated by the osmolality of interstitial fluid at the tip of the loops of Henle and is, therefore, proportional to the length of these loops. For example, mammals living in arid environments have very long loops and the ability to concentrate their urine to a much greater degree than humans.

Tubular filtrate in the descending limb of the loop of Henle can be concentrated either by water moving out of the tubule or solutes moving in. Which mechanism is of primary importance is not known. As filtrate moves up the ascending limb, solutes, but not water, leave the tubular fluid, and its osmolality decreases. A still unresolved question is whether it is sodium or some other solute that is actively reabsorbed against a concentration gradient in this region. Whatever the exact nature of the transported solute, the fact is that filtrate is diluted in this segment.

Since distal tubular fluid is more dilute than the surrounding interstitial fluid, water passively moves from the filtrate along an osmotic gradient when ADH renders the tubular walls water-permeable. The walls of the collecting tubule are also sensitive to ADH, and in the presence of this hormone, water is also reabsorbed from these structures. Notice that the collecting tubules pass back through the increasingly hypertonic inner medulla before delivering their contents to the renal pelvis. The loops of Henle, by virtue of transporting more solute than water out of their ascending limbs, create a hypertonic medullary interstitium that attracts water from the collecting ducts as the filtrate passes back through this region. In the absence of ADH, little water is reabsorbed from the hypotonic distal fluid, and a large volume of dilute urine is

produced. By regulating the ADH level, either a dilute urine of high volume or a concentrated urine of low volume is produced according to the body's fluid requirements.

The renal counter-current exchanger is composed of blood vessels in contrast to the counter-current multiplier, which is the long loops of Henle of the juxtamedullary nephrons. Other notable differences between the counter-current multiplier and exchange systems include the facts that multiplication requires active transport of solute while exchange depends only on passive processes, and that fluid leaving the multiplier is more dilute than fluid entering it while the concentration of plasma leaving the vessels of the exchange system is slightly more concentrated than that of plasma entering them.

The inner reaches of the renal medulla (with its hypertonic interstitial fluid) require a blood supply. If blood were delivered by vessels coursing straight through the medullary region, the interstitial hyperosmolality would soon be dissipated as incoming blood delivered water to and removed solute from interstitial fluid during osmotic equilibration. The arrangement of vessels into U-shaped loops (the *rete mirabile*, or "miracle net") minimizes, but does not completely prevent, removal of solutes from the medullary interstitium.

The counter-current exchange vessels run generally parallel to the long loops of the juxtamedullary nephrons, and the descending and ascending straight limbs (vasa recta) of the individual capillary loops are adjacent to each other. Blood enters the descending vasa recta with an osmolality of about 300 mosmol/L. As it flows toward the papilla, solutes from the interstitium enter and water leaves, thus increasing the plasma osmolality. After rounding the bend, blood moves through an interstitium of decreasing solute concentration. In the ascending vasa recta, water moves along an osmotic gradient into the concentrated blood plasma and solutes are returned to the interstitial fluid. With this pattern of medullary microcirculation, dissipation of the osmotic gradient created by counter-current multiplication is greatly reduced while still allowing blood flow for delivery of nutrients and removal of waste products and the water reabsorbed from the collecting tubules. Without removal of reabsorbed water, the kidney would very soon swell to dangerous dimensions.

Not all details of counter-current exchange have yet been elucidated, but continuing research is providing additional insight into its characteristics. Certain differences seem to exist between the two limbs of the capillary loops. For example, the flow rate in the ascending limb appears to exceed that in the descending limb, a not surprising observation when it is considered that one of the major functions of these vessels is removal of reabsorbed water from the medulla. The sodium permeability coefficient of the ascending vasa recta also seems to be greater than that of the descending limb. Plasma osmolality in the two limbs also varies with the plasma at the top of the ascending limb being somewhat greater than plasma at the beginning of the descending limb. There is experimental evidence that the oncotic pressure and protein concentration of plasma in the ascending limb is less than in the descending limb. Since water and solutes, but not plasma proteins, cross the vessel walls, dilution of the protein concentration and a decrease in oncotic pressure argue for a net removal of water from the renal medulla by the counter-current exchange system.

Role of urea Urea contributes to hyperosmolality of the renal medulla and the concentrating ability of the kidney, especially during periods of antidiuresis. When, under the infuence of ADH, the kidneys save increased amounts of water, urea excretion is low. It has already been pointed out that ADH increases water permeability of the distal tubules and collecting ducts. In addition to increasing the water permeability of these parts of the kidney, ADH also increases the urea permeability of the parts of the collecting tubules that lie deep within the medulla. As filtrate passes through the upper parts of the collecting tubules, water is reabsorbed and the urea is concentrated. Upon reaching the distal part of the collecting tubule rendered permeable to urea by ADH, the elevated urea concentration of the filtrate directs passive reabsorption of this material into the medullary interstitium. Some of the urea then reenters the loops of Henle and contributes to the increasing osmolality of filtrate in the descending limb. Consequently, urea is recycled through the papillary portions of the kidney from collecting tubules to interstitium to loops of Henle to collecting tubules. In the concentrating kidney nearly one-half of the solutes in the interstitium surrounding the collecting tubules and the long loops of Henle is urea. On the other hand, when the kidney is producing a dilute urine of large volume, larger amounts of urea are excreted and little is reabsorbed.

In summary, the counter-current multiplier establishes a large osmotic gradient from outer to inner medulla by the active transport of solute out of the ascending limb of the loops of Henle. The counter-current exchange system both minimizes dissipation of the osmotic gradient established by counter-current multiplication and removes water reabsorbed from the collecting tubules into the hypertonic interstitium. The extent of water (and urea) reabsorption from the collecting tubules along the previously established osmotic gradient and the production of a concentrated or dilute urine is mainly dictated by the level of ADH in the blood.

RENAL CONTRIBUTIONS TO HOMEOSTASIS

Renal contributions to homeostasis include fluid, electrolyte, and acid-base balances. The kidneys are not the sole contributor to any of these but play a major part in all of them. Conservation of water and electrolytes has been discussed earlier in this chapter but will be revisited briefly in this section, while the renal responsibility for acid-base balance will be emphasized.

Fluid Balance

Fluid balance implies just that—a balance between fluid intake and output to the extent that total body water remains constant and appropriately distributed between intracellular and extracellular compartments. A healthy adult male of appropriate weight for his height has a total complement of body water equal to approximately 60 percent of body weight, while a normal female has about 50 percent of her body weight represented by water. For example, a 70-kg (154-lb) male has approximately 42 kg (or liters) of water. Of this amount, two-thirds, or about 28 L, is confined to the cells as intracellular water and the remainder is extracellular, mainly in the interstitial fluid (10.5 L) and blood plasma (3.5 L). From a homeostatic viewpoint, the distribution of body water, i.e., two-thirds intracellular and one-third extracellular, is just as important as the total amount of body water. The distribution of water is determined by solute content of the intracellular and extracellular compartments. This ratio can only be upset by altering the solute concentration of one or the other major compartments; therefore, solute (or electrolyte) and water balance are intimately entwined.

To remain in fluid balance, daily intake must equal daily output. In addition to the obvious source of ingested liquids, water is derived from solid plant and animal food in the diet, which, like our own bodies, is mainly water. Added to water consumed directly with solid food is the water derived from metabolism of carbohydrates, fats, and proteins as they are degraded for energy. Taken together, water from food (both direct and metabolically derived) amounts to about 800 mL/day. Intravenous fluids also are a source of fluids to those receiving them. Fluid output includes urinary water, insensible losses through the moist mucous membranes of the upper respiratory tract and the skin (about 1000 mL/day), sensible perspiration, and a small amount from the gastrointestinal tract. The latter two routes are significant only in a hot, dry climate and in cases of severe vomiting and/or diarrhea. On the average, urinary output is approximately 500 mL less than oral fluid intake, with the balance being accounted for by extrarenal routes of water excretion.

Urinary volume depends on several factors including ADH, the level of renal perfusion, and the solute load to be excreted. The major stimulus for ADH release is increased osmolality of extracellular fluid; however, decreased volume of this compartment may also stimulate its release. Hypothalamic osmoreceptors (which may be the same cells that elaborate ADH) are sensitive to the solute concentration of extracellular fluid. Increased serum osmolality triggers release of ADH, which in turn promotes renal reabsorption of solute-free water to dilute the extracellular fluids and return osmolality to normal. In the face of increased ADH, a small volume of concentrated urine is produced. When serum osmolality is low, ADH release is inhibited, the distal portions of the renal tubules and collecting ducts are rendered relatively water-impermeable, excess water is excreted as a large volume of dilute urine, and serum osmolality increases.

Receptors in vessel walls of the central circulation are sensitive to changes in circulating blood volume. A decrease in blood volume, as well as an increase in osmolality, appears to stimulate ADH release. As water is reabsorbed and blood volume increases, further ADH release decreases. Therefore, ADH appears to be a mechanism for protecting both the volume and the osmolality of extracellular fluid. It appears that preservation of adequate volume takes precedence over maintaining normal osmolality, since, in the face of diminished circulating blood volume in the central pool, water continues to be reabsorbed despite a hypotonic serum.

Decreased renal perfusion is another stimulus to increased renal reabsorption of salts and water; however, this mechanism seems to center on the renal hormone renin and the adrenal cortical hormone aldosterone. Renin is elaborated in and released from juxtaglomerular cells in the walls of the afferent arterioles near the junction with the glomerular capillaries. These cells are also postulated to be receptors sensitive to the magnitude of renal blood flow. With decreased renal perfusion, renin is released by the juxtaglomerular cells into blood flowing through the afferent arterioles. Renin cleaves angiotensinogen, a circulating polypeptide of hepatic origin, into angiotensin I. Angiotensin I is converted into angiotensin II, a potent vasoconstrictor and stimulus to aldosterone release. Under the influence of aldosterone, the kidneys (and the gut) increase sodium and, hence, water reabsorption; urinary volume decreases, water and sodium reabsorption increases, and barring other circulatory abnormalities, blood volume and renal perfusion increase. The kidneys are not favored organs (compared to the heart and the brain) for perfusion during real or relative hypovolemia. This is evidenced by the oliguria so characteristic of hypovolemic shock. Therefore, the compensatory splanchnic vasoconstriction that occurs with low blood volume not only lowers renal perfusion, but through activation of the renin-angiotensin system, stimulates renal reabsorptive mechanisms that benefit not only the kidneys but the body as a whole.

A certain amount of water is "obligated" to excretion by the solute load. Recall that the human kidney cannot concentrate urine in excess of about 1200 mosmol/L. When the solute load presented to the nephrons exceeds their reabsorptive capacity, more water is obligated to excreting that load. This fact is utilized clinically in the administration of osmotic diuretics such as mannitol, a substance not normally present in serum. Mannitol is freely filtered but not reabsorbed by the kidneys. Thus, when mannitol is infused, its renal excretion obligates increased amounts of water, a diuresis ensues, and excess water is excreted. Naturally occurring solutes, when present in excess, also obligate water.

Filtered glucose in excess of what the kidneys can reabsorb constitutes an osmotic diuretic and underlies the familiar polyuria of diabetes mellitus. A large urea load derived from a high protein intake likewise increases obligatory water excretion. These situations do not really represent normal homeostatic mechanisms since they are examples of unusual circumstances; nevertheless, they are indicative of how the kidneys function under less strenuous circumstances to maintain the osmolality of body fluids within normal limits and to excrete waste products.

Electrolyte Balance

Enormous quantities of electrolytes are filtered (amount filtered = GFR × plasma concentration of an electrolyte) each day; yet only a minute fraction is actually excreted into the urine, and even that small fraction, especially in the case of sodium, is negotiable. In an equilibrium condition, the amount of electrolyte excreted through all excretion routes each day equals the amount acquired. For example, if the losses of sodium in sweat and by the intestinal route are not elevated, most of the daily intake is excreted in the urine; however, if the extrarenal losses of this ion are increased through excessive perspiration or diarrhea, renal excretion is proportionately reduced. Thus, the renal system plays a crucial role in electrolyte balance of the body fluids.

The kidneys seem best adapted for sodium regulation. Several factors, including renal perfusion, aldosterone level, and a purported natriuretic, or third, factor are physiologic determinants of renal sodium excretion. Iatrogenic or pathophysiologic influences such as diuretics, nonreabsorbable anions in the filtrate, and intrinsic renal abnormalities also determine the balance between sodium intake and excretion. Potassium balance is also influenced by renal mechanisms, but the kidneys do not seem to be as "teleologically tuned" to potassium balance as they are to sodium equilibrium.

Under normal conditions, renal perfusion and aldosterone levels are closely allied as influences on sodium reabsorption and excretion. Decreased renal perfusion diminishes GFR. As a result, several factors support increased sodium reabsorption. First, a lowered flow rate through the tubules allows for more complete reabsorption of sodium by the active mechanisms of the renal epithelial cells. Second, decreased renal blood flow results in an increased filtration fraction (GFR/RPF = filtration fraction). Since a greater than normal fraction of the plasma perfusing the kidneys is filtered, the protein concentration of plasma leaving the glomerular capillaries and entering the postglomerular peritubular vessels is increased. The elevated oncotic pressure of peritubular plasma increases the attraction for water from tubular to peritubular fluid. Increased water reabsorption contributes to increasing tubular sodium concentration and the concentration gradient promoting its recovery. Third, decreased renal perfusion stimulates renin release from the juxtaglomerular cells of the afferent arteriole. Through the vehicle of the renin-angiotensin system, aldosterone secretion increases (page 161). Elevated aldosterone levels not only increase renal reabsorption of sodium, especially in the distal portion of the nephron, but also stimulate intestinal reabsorption of this ion. Thus, the effects of increased aldosterone secretion, initiated in the kidney, extend beyond the renal realm.

A natriuretic factor has yet to be isolated, but empiric evidence for such a factor and its influence on renal sodium reabsorption (or excretion) is strong. This "third factor" is invoked to explain the observation that increased plasma volume (and hence renal perfusion) stimulates sodium excretion, regardless of plasma sodium concentration. When plasma volume is low, the level of this factor is also low, and sodium excretion diminishes. Such a mechanism would seem beneficial in that as sodium reabsorption increases, so does water reabsorption, and plasma volume is replenished. On the other hand, extracellular volume overload increases sodium excretion and decreases plasma volume. The natriuretic factor appears to subserve maintenance of plasma volume rather than plasma osmolality.

Potassium conservation, or balance, seems to be more capricious than and subservient to sodium considerations. The kidneys are just not as well adapted to maintaining potassium balance as they are to maintaining sodium balance. In fact, potassium excretion may be inappropriately stimulated when sodium conservation is demanded. The major excretory route for potassium is a renal one, and in the face of renal failure, the threat of potassium intoxication looms large. However, when potassium conservation would be appropriate, the renal mechanisms do not always rise to the challenge.

Acid-Base Balance

The kidneys share major responsibility for acid-base balance with the lungs. From a quantitative point of view, the lungs predominate in excreting acid metabolites, but this in no way diminishes the importance of the renal contribution. Approximately 15,000 mmol of carbon dioxide (the acid equivalent of about 1 L of hydrochloric acid) is added to the body each day by cellular processes. Carbon dioxide is a unique acid in that it is volatile, i.e., a gas amenable to excretion through the lungs. While carbon dioxide does not contain hydrogen, it is converted to an acid when hydrated, or combined with water, under the influence of carbonic anhydrase as follows:

$$CO_2 + H_2O \rightleftarrows H_2CO_3 \rightleftarrows H^+ + HCO_3^- \qquad (10)$$

Carbonic
acid

Not all the acidic products of cellular metabolism are volatile and acceptable for pulmonary excretion. Some are *fixed acids* that can only be excreted in solution, and this is where the kidneys contribute to acid-base balance. Fixed acids are exemplified by sulfuric acid (H_2SO_4) derived from protein catabolism and phosphoric acid (H_3PO_4) from phospholipids, purines, and nucleic acids. These and other fixed acids amount to about 0.5 to 1 meq per kg of body weight per day and can only be excreted through the kidneys. While quantitatively minor when compared with carbon dioxide, fixed acids, nevertheless, represent an important consideration in acid-base balance: if they were not excreted at the same rate at which they are produced, the body would soon be flooded with acid. Thus, there exists a cooperative effort between the lungs and the kidneys in maintaining acid-base balance.

As fixed acids dissociate, the various body buffers combine with the released hydrogen ions and prevent their concentration from increasing to dangerous levels. The body's many enzyme systems can tolerate only very small fluctuations in the hydrogen ion concentration (or pH) of body fluids. The pH values compatible with life range between about 6.8 and 7.8 (comparable to a hydrogen ion concentration of from 160 to 16 nmol/L; notice that hydrogen ion concentration and pH are inversely related). Normal arterial pH extends from 7.35 to 7.45 pH units.

The hydrogen ions released from fixed acids combine with body buffers, and an excessive increase in their concentration is prevented. Conversely, when the pH of body fluids increases, hydrogen ions are released from buffer acids to replenish the depleted supply. Buffers, therefore, come in pairs and are composed of a weak acid and a salt, or conjugate base, of that acid. One of the most important buffer pairs in the body is carbonic acid (H_2CO_3) and bicarbonate ions (HCO_3^-), the conjugate base of carbonic acid. As production of fixed acids increases, the hydrogen ions released from them are buffered by the bicarbonate ions in body fluids as follows:

$$H^+ + HCO_3^- \rightarrow H_2CO_3 \qquad (11)$$

Most of the carbonic acid thus formed dissociates into water and carbon dioxide, as shown in Eq. (10); it is then excreted through the lungs. Thus, the hydrogen ion concentration in the body is prevented from rising unduly. On the other hand, when the body loses large amounts of hydrogen ions, e.g., by vomiting or gastric suction, carbonic acid (and other buffer acids) dissociate and release "replacement" hydrogen ions.

The various body buffers represent the "front-line" troops in the protection of pH, while the kidneys are the "reserves." Acid-base balance and a normal pH depend on the *ratio* of the base to acid. When base concentration (and hence pH) increases, as in metabolic alkalosis, renal bicarbonate excretion also increases and rids the body of the excess. When the acid load increases, the kidneys counter on two fronts. First, they increase acid excretion; and second, they generate increased amounts of bicarbonate ions to act as buffers for hydrogen ions.

There are three main renal mechanisms by which the bicarbonate concentration of the body is protected: (1) "direct" reabsorption of bicarbonate; (2) production of titratable acidity; and (3) ammonia production. In the first mechanism, bicarbonate ions associated with a cation (mainly sodium) are filtered at the glomerulus and reabsorbed by the renal tubules. As will become evident, the reabsorbed bicarbonate ions are not the same ones that are filtered, and hence bicarbonate reabsorption is not as direct as it would appear. Within renal tubular cells, carbon dioxide is hydrated (under the influence of the enzyme, carbonic anhydrase) to carbonic acid which then dissociates into hydrogen and bicarbonate ions (Fig. 8-6). As positive sodium ions are reabsorbed from tubular fluid, positive hydrogen ions are excreted. Hydrogen secretion results in intracellular accumulation of bicarbonate ions which then accompany sodium ions into peritubular fluid and capillary blood. The net result is that for each sodium bicarbonate molecule filtered, one is reabsorbed. The sodium ions reabsorbed are the same ones filtered; the bicarbonate ions are not the ones filtered but, rather, those generated within renal tubular cells. Meanwhile, the secreted hydrogen ions combine with filtered bicarbonate in the tubular fluid to form carbonic acid. Under the influence of carbonic anhydrase located on the tubular surface of the brush border, the acid dissociates into carbon dioxide and water. Carbon dioxide can diffuse back into renal tubular cells where it is used again in the reactions described above. This particular scheme of bicarbonate reabsorption results in salvaging filtered bicarbonate ions but does not increase the body's concentration of this ion.

Anions of fixed acids, like bicarbonate ions, are filtered at the glomerulus in association with a cation. Most of the filtered anions of phosphoric acid are in the form of HPO_4^{2-} (Na_2HPO_4). As the cation is reabsorbed and hydrogen is excreted, the phosphoric acid anions are converted to $H_2PO_4^-$ (NaH_2PO_4), as shown in Fig. 8-7. Free bicarbonate ions produced in the renal tubular cells from the dissociation of carbonic acid pass into interstitial fluid and capillary blood. In this particular scheme the body gains additional bicarbonate ions over the quantity filtered. The renal generation of "new" bicarbonate ions replaces those consumed by buffering the hydrogen ions released from phosphoric acid (H_3PO_4) when it was originally added to the body fluids by cellular metabolism. The quantity of hydrogen ions excreted in the urine as $H_2PO_4^-$ is called the *titratable acidity* and can be determined by the amount of strong base that must be added to the urine to bring its pH to 7.4 (the pH of the filtrate in Bowman's capsule).

A third way in which the kidneys excrete hydrogen and return bicarbonate to the body fluids is ammonia generation. Renal tubular cells contain enzymes to deaminate amino acids (particularly glutamine) and generate free ammonia molecules (Fig. 8-8). The ammonia is lipid-soluble and easily crosses renal tubular membranes. The ammonia that enters tubular fluid combines with secreted hydrogen ions to form ammonium cations (NH_4^+). Cellular membranes are much less permeable to the ionized form (NH_4^+) than to the molecular form (NH_3). Once an ammonium ion is formed in tubular fluid, it is "trapped" there. In tubular fluid, ammonium ions combine with negative ions such as Cl^- and SO_4^{2-} and are excreted as a neutral salt. Once again, bicarbonate ions resulting from the intracellular dissociation of carbonic acid return to the blood. The bicarbonate ions generated in this way are, like those associated with the formation of titratable acidity, "new" or "replacement" bicarbonate ions. Because the human kidney can produce a urine with a pH no lower than about 4.4, the renal ability to excrete hydrogen is greatly increased by its ammonia-generating capability. The hydrogen ions excreted in ammonium ions do not dissociate and do not, therefore, contribute to lowering urine pH. In acidosis, the rate of urinary ammonium excretion is greatly increased, since the kidneys utilize this mechanism for ridding the body of excess hydrogen ions.

The three methods by which the renal tubular cells excrete hydrogen ions and return bicarbonate ions to body fluids are all dependent on carbonic anhydrase and its role in the important intracellular and tubular reactions. When this enzyme is inhibited by acetazolamide, a carbonic anhydrase inhibitor, renal excretion of hydrogen and generation of bicarbonate

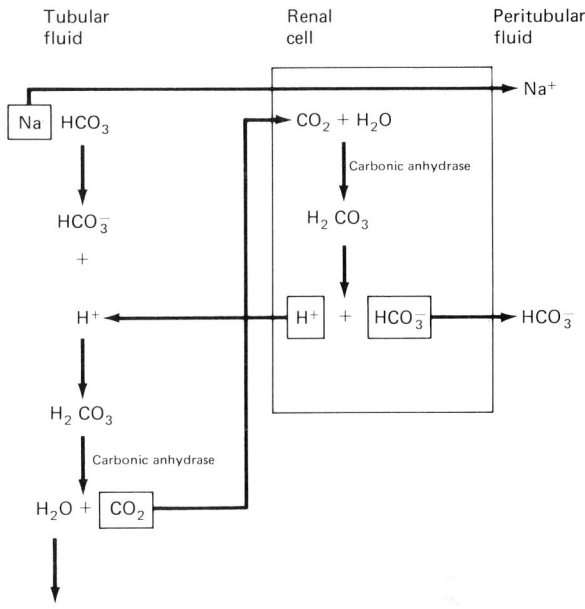

FIGURE 8-6

Bicarbonate reabsorption.

ions decrease, the pH of urine rises, and the pH of body fluids falls. When alkalosis affects acid-base balance, the renal mechanisms for bicarbonate reabsorption are muted and increased urinary excretion and decreased regeneration of bicarbonate com-

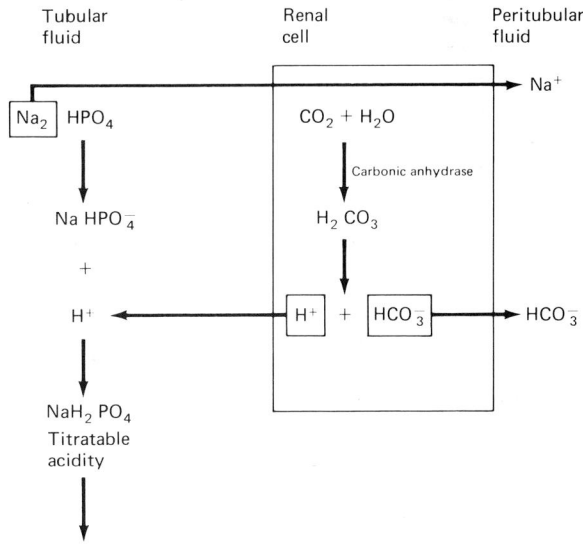

FIGURE 8-7

Formation of titratable acidity.

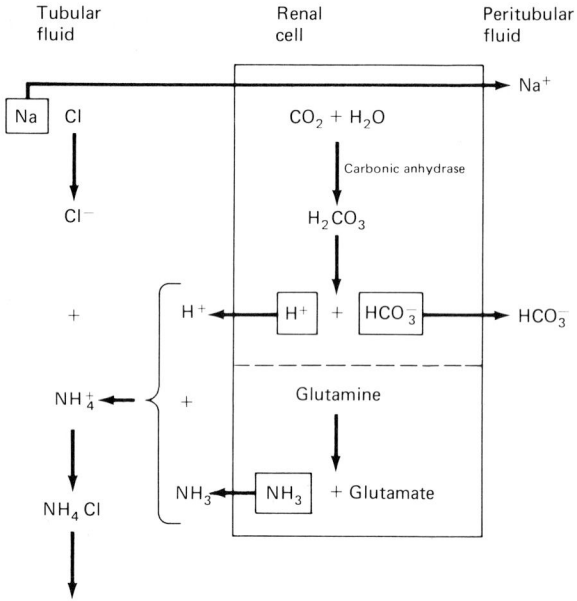

FIGURE 8-8

Ammonia generation in the kidney.

bine to reduce the pH of body fluids toward normal. Because reclamation of filtered bicarbonate and restoration of this important buffer anion to body fluids depends so heavily on renal cellular integrity, it is not surprising that metabolic acidosis is common in renal failure.

HORMONES OF THE KIDNEY

The kidneys are not usually considered endocrine organs, but they do produce several important hormones. A hormone is defined as a substance produced by one tissue that acts upon another tissue or organ of the body. Renal tissue is not the sole source of some of the hormones it produces, but this in no way diminishes the importance of its endocrine contributions. The kidneys are credited with producing at least four hormones—renin, erythropoietin, activated vitamin D, and prostaglandins—and there may be others that remain to be identified.

Renin

Renin has a molecular mass of about 40,000 daltons and is produced in specialized *juxtaglomerular cells* of the afferent arteriole. Juxtaglomerular cells are located in the walls of the afferent arteriole near the

junction of this vessel with the glomerular capillary tuft. The action of renin is proteolytic cleavage of *angiotensinogen*, a plasma-borne substrate that is synthesized by the liver. The product of angiotensinogen cleavage by renin is a decapeptide (10 amino acids) called *angiotensin I*. Angiotensin I, a substance with little intrinsic activity, is converted to *angiotensin II*, a potent vasoconstrictor, by *converting enzyme*. Lung tissue is especially rich in converting enzyme and is apparently where most of the conversion of angiotensin I occurs. Renal tissue apparently has little or no converting enzyme activity. A major function of angiotensin II is regulation of aldosterone release from the adrenal cortex. In addition to its role in aldosterone control and as a vasopressor, angiotensin II exerts some direct influence on renal tissue.

Angiotensin II stimulates the adrenal cortex to release aldosterone. Aldosterone, in turn, influences the kidney, especially the distal nephron, to reabsorb increased amounts of sodium (and secondarily, water) in exchange for potassium. Thus, aldosterone stimulates sodium and water reabsorption and promotes potassium excretion.

Within the kidney itself, angiotensin II stimulates vasoconstriction of both afferent and efferent arterioles. In view of its vasoconstrictive property, angiotensin II has been invoked as a possible influence in renal autoregulation. Low doses of angiotensin II decrease renal blood flow, GFR, and sodium excretion, while high doses amplify the vasoconstrictive effect but are of relatively short duration. High doses also produce a natriuresis.

Renin release is regulated by more than one factor, but not all details of its regulation have been identified. The sympathetic nervous system is one prominent factor in the regulation of renin secretion. Sympathetic nervous stimulation, as well as infusions of catecholamines, result in increased renin release. Renal denervation results in decreased renin release as does administration of propranolol. Blockade by propranolol suggests that renin release is mediated by beta-adrenergic cells.

The baroreceptor theory of renin regulation holds that baroreceptors, that is, pressure receptors, in the afferent arterioles modulate renin release. When afferent arteriolar hydrostatic pressure is high, renin release is inhibited; when it is low, renin release is stimulated. Teleologically, increased renin release in the face of low blood pressure may serve to increase formation of angiotensin II and its vasoactive influence. Experimentally, increased renin release is noted to follow aortic constriction above the origin of the renal arteries. Such a manipulation does decrease hydrostatic pressure at the level of the renal barore-ceptors.

Another theory of renin regulation involves the *macula densa*, a specialized group of cells in the distal convoluted tubule at its point of contact with the afferent and efferent arterioles. According to this theory, renin release is inversely proportional to the sodium load in tubular fluid bathing the cells of the macula densa. While the experimental conclusions are not unanimous, it appears that, in general, any-thing that increases the sodium concentration of distal tubular fluid (such as diuretics or release of ureteral obstruction) decreases renin secretion. Renin release also appears to be inversely related to both serum sodium concentration and blood volume; however, blood volume appears to take precedence. Volume precedence is suggested by the observation that when sodium concentration is low (which should increase renin release) while blood volume is elevated (which should decrease renin release), renin release decreases despite the hyponatremia.

Of clinical interest are two fairly recent pharma-cologic principles that affect the physiologic results of activation of the renin-angiotensin system. First, certain synthetic materials seem to have the ability to block the action of converting enzyme; and second, antagonists of angiotensin II have been described. Both of these manipulations of the physiologic renin-angiotensin system have attracted most attention for their possible therapeutic role in the control of hy-pertension.

Erythropoietin

Erythropoietin is an important hormonal stimulus to production of new erythrocytes by bone marrow. A major source of erythropoietic factor is the kidney. The exact renal cellular source of this hormone has not been identified, but it is believed to be in the glomerular region. Some investigators have sug-gested the juxtaglomerular cells as the source. Many of the details of erythropoietin synthesis and release are not known. For example, it has not been completely determined whether the kidneys synthesize and re-lease the active substance or whether they release some precursory material. Evidence against a renal source of the active material includes the fact that erythropoietin has not been detected in renal extracts. Alternative explanations of the kidneys' role in eryth-ropoiesis have, therefore, been proposed.

One alternative explanation to renal production of an active erythropoietin is that the kidneys produce *erythrogenin* or *renal erythropoietic factor* (REF) that acts upon an inactive precursor, *erythropoietinogen*, to form active erythropoietin. This scheme is analo-gous to the one in which renin acts upon angioten-sinogen to produce angiotensin.

Another alternative that has been proposed to explain the inability to detect active erythropoietin in renal tissue is that the kidneys produce an inhibitor to erythropoietin. Support for this suggestion is pro-vided by reports that certain extracts of renal tissue can inactivate erythropoietin.

Evidence that the kidneys are a major source of erythropoietic activity is that chronic anemia is as-sociated with serious renal failure and uremia. Neph-rectomy also results in decreased production of eryth-ropoietin. Kidneys removed from animals exposed to hypoxic conditions and perfused following removal continued to release material with erythropoietic activity.

Renal hypoxia is the most potent stimulus for release of an erythropoietic factor from the kidneys. The hypoxia may be generalized as occurs with right-to-left shunts, anemia, and residence at high altitudes, or it may be localized to the kidney by splanchnic vasoconstriction or renal artery compression. The end organ for erythropoietin is bone marrow, which is stimulated by this hormone to increase production and release of red blood cells. Relief of renal hypoxia either by increasing the number of oxygen carriers or by relieving a mechanical obstruction to renal blood flow constitutes the negative feedback of this self-regulating loop and decreases erythropoietin produc-tion and release.

Renal Conversion of Vitamin D

The antirachitic properties of vitamin D are well known and have been recognized for many years, but certain characteristics of its biochemical transformation into an active form have been identified more recently. Vitamin D is a sterol found in plants and animals. The relatively inactive product of plants is *ergosterol* and that of animal tissue is *7-dehydrocholesterol*. Under the influence of ultraviolet radiation, ergosterol is converted to *calciferol* (vitamin D_2) and 7-dehydro-cholesterol is converted to *cholecalciferol* (vitamin D_3). Within the microsomes of liver cells, vitamin D_3 is converted to the major active metabolite *25-hy-droxycholecalciferol* (25-OH-D_3). Some of the 25-OH-D_3 circulating in blood is taken up by the kidneys and hydroxylated to *1,25-dihydroxycholecaliferol*, or 1,25-

(OH)$_2$-D$_3$, a very active form of the vitamin. The kidneys secrete 1,25-(OH)$_2$-D$_3$ into the blood, and it is carried to the intestine where it stimulates calcium absorption and to the bones where it promotes calcium mobilization. Direct effects of vitamin D metabolites on calcium and phosphate handling by the kidney have been described, but not all the details are available yet.

The role of the kidneys in producing 1,25-(OH)$_2$-D$_3$ has been compared to the endocrine role of the adrenal cortex. Both organs modify a blood-borne steroid into active hormones. The adrenal cortex extracts cholesterol from the plasma, transforms it into the various corticosteroids, and releases these active products back into the blood to be carried to their various target organs. The kidneys extract the steroid vitamin 25-OH-D$_3$, convert it to 1,25-(OH)$_2$-D$_3$, and release the product into the blood. Within intestinal mucosal cells, 1,25-(OH)$_2$-D$_3$ stimulates production of a calcium-binding protein that has been implicated in calcium reabsorption.

The role of vitamin D metabolites in mineral metabolism of the body is complex and shared by other factors such as parathyroid hormone. There are still unanswered questions about mineral metabolism and all aspects of vitamin D metabolites on this homeostatic process, but the action of the kidneys in producing a hormone that participates in regulating calcium levels of the body is clear.

Prostaglandins

Prostaglandins are a structurally related group of unsaturated lipid acids with a 5-carbon ring. In general, the prostaglandins do not appear to be stored in tissues to any great extent, but rather seem to be synthesized in response to appropriate stimuli. They are synthesized from arachidonic acid by the action of the enzyme *prostaglandin synthetase*, which is widely distributed within body tissues, including the kidneys. Since prostaglandin synthetase is present in many tissues, prostaglandins are found in many parts of the body. They are among the most active of biological substances, but once formed, they are rapidly broken down, especially by the lungs. Because of their relatively short half-life and proclivity to degradation, the prostaglandins are not well suited to production and release by one organ and transport to distant target organs; in that sense they do not fit the classic description of a hormone. Rather they seem to be "local hormones," exerting their influence on the cells or nearby tissue in which they are

synthesized. Although the chemical structure of various prostaglandins is similar, actions of the different compounds of this class of materials are varied.

Within the kidneys most of the prostaglandin synthetic capability appears to reside in the medullary interstitial cells; the collecting ducts may also be a site of synthesis. While synthesis appears to take place primarily in the medulla, degradation may occur mainly in the renal cortex.

The major actions of prostaglandins within the kidney appear to be on renal blood flow and sodium excretion. Two of the prostaglandins, prostaglandin E (PGE) and prostaglandin A (PGA), increase renal blood flow and sodium excretion. These effects are exerted independently of any marked alteration in GFR. The renal vasoconstriction produced by circulating catecholamines and by direct renal adrenergic stimulation is reversed by PGE, whereas it is supported by another prostaglandin of the PGF class. Both PGE and PGF compounds are rapidly inactivated in the lungs, but PGA is not. Therefore, PGA may exist in an active form long enough for it to exert some systemic effects.

The kidneys have long been implicated as an etiologic factor in hypertension. The renal etiologic factors range from the production of vasopressor substances, viz. renin, to loss of renal vasodepressor factors in so-called renoprival hypertension. Renoprival hypertension is the term applied to the elevated blood pressure in individuals with massive renal parenchymal destruction or following nephrectomy. It is explained on the basis of the loss of some vasodepressor factor of renal origin. Such a vasodepressor factor may be one of the prostaglandins. It has been shown that PGE increases renal blood flow and promotes sodium excretion. These actions may provide enough of a local renal effect to keep systemic blood pressure within normal limits. Another possibility is that PGA from the kidneys may exert some influence on systemic vasodilation. Still another hypothesis centers on a neutral lipid from the renal medulla that has experimental evidence to support its role as a vasodepressor. The massive loss of renal tissue either by disease or surgery would remove all these putative renal vasodepressor factors and permit blood pressure to rise.

There are many unanswered questions about the function and fate of the prostaglandins. But despite the incomplete information on them, they have become one of the most widely studied and provocative physiologic substances since cyclic adenosine 5'-monophosphate.

REFERENCES

Brenner, B. M., and F. C. Rector, Jr. (eds.): *The Kidney*, vol. 1, Philadelphia: Saunders, 1976.

Bricker, N. S., and R. G. Schultze: Renal function: General concepts, in Morton H. Maxwell and Charles R. Kleeman, *Clinical Disorders of Fluid and Electrolyte Metabolism,* 2d ed., New York: McGraw-Hill, 1972.

Haussler, M. R., and T. A. McCain: Basic and clinical concepts related to vitamin D metabolism and action, *N Engl J Med* 297(18):974–983, 1977.

Leaf, A., and R. S. Cotran: *Renal Pathophysiology,* New York: Oxford University Press, 1976.

Papper, S.: *Clinical Nephrology,* Boston: Little, Brown, 1971.

Rose, B. D.: *Clinical Physiology of Acid-Base and Electrolyte Disorders,* New York: McGraw-Hill, 1977.

Valtin, H.: *Renal Function: Mechanisms Preserving Fluid and Solute Balance in Health,* Boston: Little, Brown, 1973.

INTRODUCTION

From its earliest embryologic days, the gastrointestinal tract emerged as a simple system. By a natural, yet dramatic, sequence of embryologic foldings, the primitive foregut, midgut, and hindgut evolved into a continuous muscular tube modified along its length by diverse secretory glands. Each segment of the basic tube—be it esophagus, stomach, small intestine, or colon—is anatomically specialized for a unique physiologic role.

The alimentary tract holds a unique position among body systems. Food and water are taken in, processed, absorbed, and delivered in an orderly, efficient sequence of physical and biochemical events. In a coordinated response, the digestive secretions of the salivary glands, the pancreas, the liver, and the gallbladder contribute to the conversion of food and water into metabolic energy and substrates.

This chapter is designed to follow an orderly anatomic course down the alimentary tract (Fig. 9-1). Beginning at the mouth and terminating at the colon, each organ is discussed for its unique contribution to gastrointestinal physiology. Structure and function are critically reviewed.

The extrinsic glands are discussed as they are encountered along the digestive tract. The liver and the pancreas are each presented in two parts. The exocrine pancreas and the biliary system are discussed in the context of their digestive functions. The endocrine pancreas and the remainder of hepatic functions are presented at the end of the chapter.

REGULATION OF HUNGER AND THIRST

Hunger

The desire or need for food is called *hunger*. It is a complex sensation involving many variables. Though much still remains to be learned about hunger, there are several important concepts that research has demonstrated and time has supported.

Two nuclei or groups of cells within the hypothalamus have been shown to mediate hunger and satiety. The ventromedial group, referred to as the *appetite center*, causes increased food intake when stimulated. The ventrolateral cell group, or *satiety center*, will inhibit food ingestion when stimulated.

Normally, these two centers interact. When a person is satiated, the ventrolateral nucleus inhibits the ventromedial nucleus. In a hunger state the reverse occurs. Experimentally, destruction of the satiety center leads to severe obesity if available food is not

9
THE GASTROINTESTINAL TRACT AND THE LIVER
Gail L. Bongiovanni

INTRODUCTION

REGULATION OF HUNGER AND THIRST
Hunger
Thirst

GASTROINTESTINAL HISTOLOGY: AN OVERVIEW
Mucosa
Submucosa
Muscularis Externa
Serosa or Adventitia

THE MOUTH AND THE OROPHARYNX
The Tongue
The Salivary Glands
Mastication and Deglutition

THE ESOPHAGUS
Introduction
Gross Anatomy
Histology
Esophageal Motility
Regulation of Esophageal Function

THE STOMACH
Introduction
Gross Anatomy
Histology
Gastric Secretions
Regulation of Gastric Secretions
Gastric Motility
Regulation of Gastric Motility
The Vomiting Reflex

THE EXOCRINE PANCREAS AND THE BILIARY SYSTEM
Introduction
Exocrine Pancreas
Exocrine Secretions
Regulation of Pancreatic Secretions
The Biliary System

THE SMALL INTESTINE
Introduction
Gross Anatomy
Histology
Intestinal Secretions
Intestinal Motility
Intestinal Absorption

THE LARGE INTESTINE
Introduction
Gross Anatomy
Histology
Colonic Motility
Colonic Secretion and Absorption
Colonic Flora

THE LIVER AND THE ENDOCRINE PANCREAS
The Endocrine Pancreas
The Liver

179

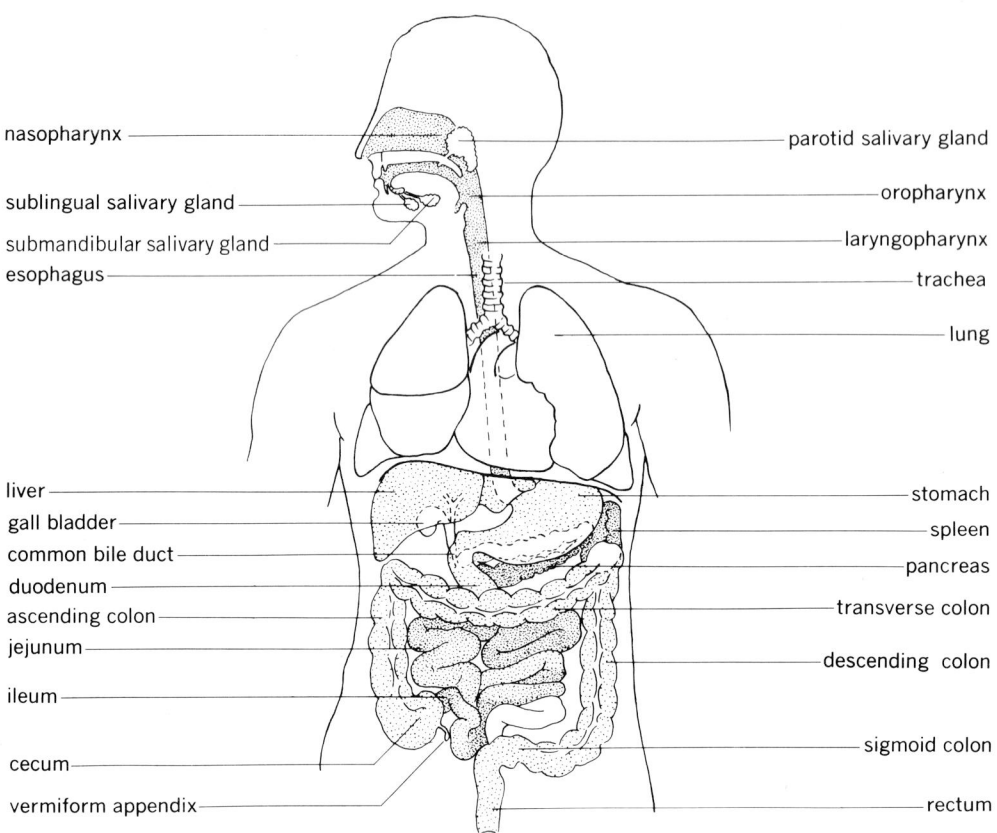

nasopharynx — parotid salivary gland

sublingual salivary gland — oropharynx

submandibular salivary gland — laryngopharynx

esophagus — trachea

— lung

liver — stomach

gall bladder — spleen

common bile duct — pancreas

duodenum

ascending colon — transverse colon

jejunum — descending colon

ileum

— sigmoid colon

cecum

vermiform appendix — rectum

FIGURE 9-1

General topography of the digestive tract. (*From R. M. DeCoursey, The Human Organism, McGraw-Hill, New York, 1974. Reproduced with permission of the publisher.*)

restricted. Likewise, destruction of the appetite center produces marked anorexia and weight loss if corrective intervention is not initiated.

Attempts to explain the careful balance between these regulatory nuclei are varied. Though the theories range from blood glucose concentrations to hypothalamic temperature levels, no satisfactory explanation has been found. The reader is referred to a more detailed source for added information.

Thirst

Analogous to hunger, thirst can be defined as a need or desire for liquid. Interestingly, the sensation of thirst can be satisfied simply by moistening mucous membranes, even if no net change in body fluids occurs.

The kidney is intimately involved in the regulation of body water. Via volume and osmoreceptors throughout the body, the kidney receives its appropriate signals. The role of antidiuretic hormone secreted by the hypothalamus adds yet another fine control to the renal circuit.

Like its solid counterpart, the mechanism of thirst is incompletely understood. Here, too, specialized centers in the hypothalamus seem to be part of a neural circuit that stimulates or inhibits drinking. Again, the reader is referred to a more in-depth text for continued presentation.

GASTROINTESTINAL HISTOLOGY: AN OVERVIEW

Before beginning the anatomic descent down the alimentary tract, a review of basic gastrointestinal histology will be helpful. With very few exceptions, the tubular portion of the alimentary canal has the same histologic structure (Fig. 9-2). Note will be made where significant alterations exist.

The following outline gives the histologic layers of the digestive tube from the inside out.

  I. Mucosa

    A. Epithelium

    B. Lamina propria

    C. Muscularis mucosae

  II. Submucosa

  III. Muscularis externa

    A. Inner circular fibers

    B. Outer longitudinal fibers

  IV. Serosa or adventitia

The Mucosa

The mucosa is composed of three sublayers. From the inside out they are the epithelial layer, the lamina propria, and the muscularis mucosae.

The *epithelium* varies throughout the tube. Squamous epithelium lines the mouth and the anus, while columnar epithelium is found everywhere else. The common columnar epithelium is often modified to better meet the needs of the individual organs.

The *lamina propria* is loosely arranged connective tissue support, often rich in capillaries. The *muscularis mucosae* is smooth muscle only. It receives sympathetic innervation and is responsible for local mucosal foldings.

The Submucosa

This second major layer of the gut wall contains dense connective tissue fibers, blood vessels, and nerve fibers. Meissner's plexus is a collection of parasympathetic nerves found in this layer. Fibers from this plexus stimulate secretion of mucosal glands.

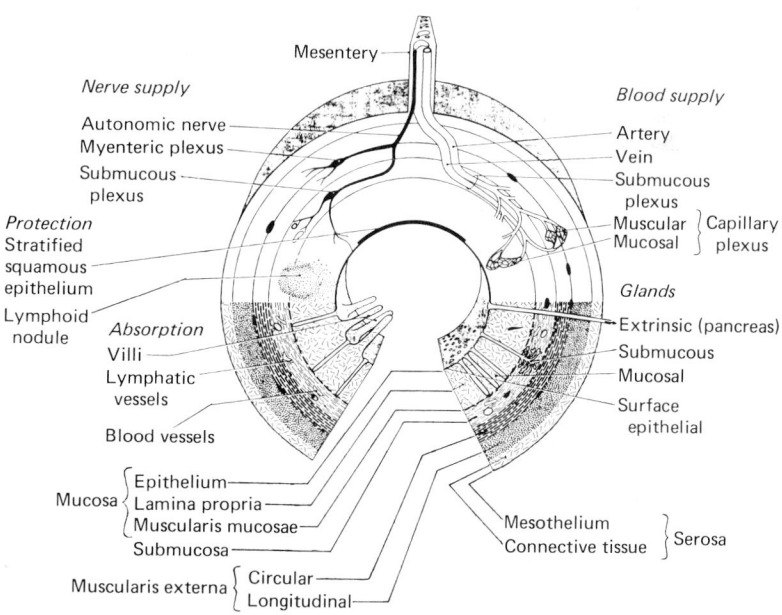

FIGURE 9-2

Histology of the gastrointestinal tract. (*Adapted from R. Passmore and J. S. Robson, A Companion to Medical Studies, vol. 1, Blackwell, Oxford, 1971. Reproduced with permission of the publisher.*)

The Muscularis Externa

This is the major muscular layer of the wall. Normally it is composed of smooth muscle, arranged as an inner circular layer and an outer longitudinal layer. The myenteric nerve plexus (Auerbach's plexus) is located between these two layers. It is responsible for muscular contractions of the wall. The esophagus, stomach, and colon have significant variations of the muscularis externa. They will be discussed later.

The Serosa or Adventitia

This is the outermost layer of the gut wall. It may be continuous with the surrounding connective tissue as the adventitia, or it may be completely separate. If separate, it is named the *serosa*.

THE MOUTH AND THE OROPHARYNX

The alimentary tract begins at the mouth. This cavity houses the tongue, the teeth, and the salivary glands. Each in its own way is needed for effective mastication (chewing) and deglutition (swallowing).

The Tongue

The tongue is a highly muscular organ. It is important for normal speech and for initiation of mastication and deglutition.

The lingual surface is covered with a specialized, durable squamous epithelium. This is further modified by visible clusters of cells called *papillae*. Within these papillae, specialized sensory cells, or taste buds, are found. The circumvallate, the foliate, and the fungiform papillae are mentioned by name because they contain the majority of the taste buds. Branches of the vagus nerve, along with two other cranial nerves, innervate the taste buds and mediate taste sensation.

The Salivary Glands

A person secretes between 1 and 2 L of saliva per day. The composition is mostly water, and a remaining 1 percent contains various salts and a glycoprotein called *mucin*.

Salivary secretion is regulated by nervous innervation alone. There are pressure receptors as well as chemoreceptors which stimulate salivary secretion. Both the parasympathetic and sympathetic nervous systems are involved, mainly via the afferent fibers of the vagus nerve.

There are three major pairs of salivary glands in the mouth: the parotid, the submaxillary, and the sublingual (see Fig. 9-1). Though histologically distinct, each pair of glands produces the substance saliva. This aqueous secretion facilitates the mixing of food early in the digestive process.

In addition, these glands synthesize an α-amylase. This enzymatic protein causes the breakdown of polysaccharides to disaccharides. Thus, even before reaching the stomach or small intestine, the digestion of carbohydrates has begun.

Normally, saliva has an alkaline pH of about 7.0. This keeps the saliva saturated with calcium and prevents loss of calcium from the teeth. In addition, saliva is rich in the secretory immunoglobulin IgA, which plays an important role in control of oral bacterial growth and again promotes healthy dentition.

Mastication and Deglutition

The mechanics of mastication involve biting off and chewing with the teeth; mixing the food bolus with mucins, amylase, and other glandular secretions mainly by the actions of the tongue; and finally the backward propulsion of the bolus toward the oropharynx as deglutition or swallowing is initiated.

The reflex of deglutition begins as the food bolus reaches the oropharynx. The process can be thought of as an organized cascade of steps, each giving rise to the next (Fig. 9-3):

Step 1: The backward propulsion of the food bolus stimulates pressure receptors in the wall of the oropharynx. These afferent signals go to the "swallowing center" in the medulla of the brain.

↓

Step 2: The soft palate elevates to seal off the nasal cavity. This protects it from the reflux of food and liquids.

↓

Step 3: The central "swallowing center" inhibits respiration while the larynx elevates and the glottis closes.

↓

Step 4: The central nervous system signals contraction of the upper esophageal sphincter, causing opening of the esophageal orifice. The food bolus then passes into the esophagus.

↓

Step 5: Once in the esophagus, food passes into the stomach by peristaltic contractions.

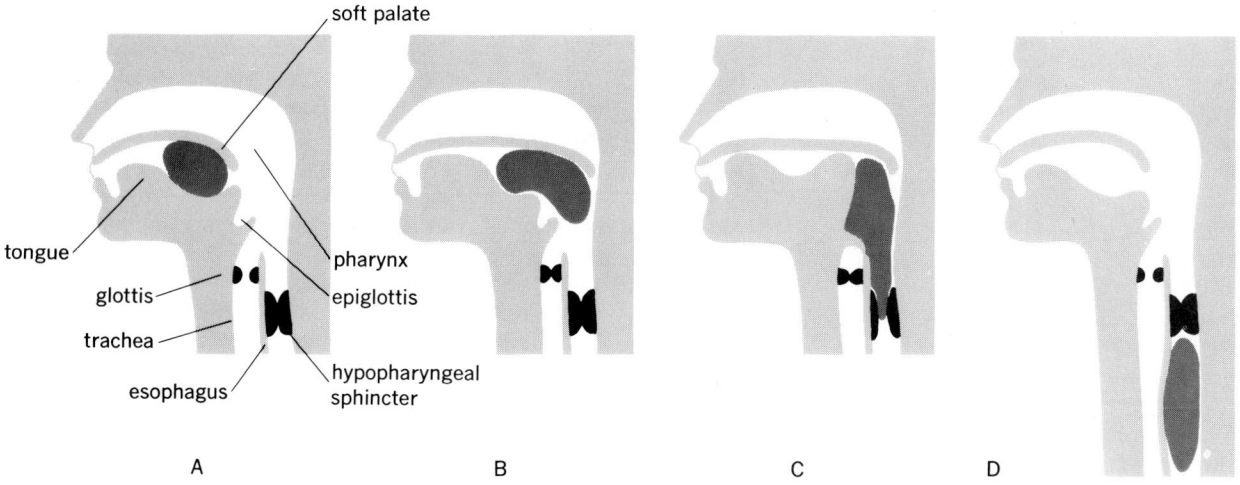

FIGURE 9-3
Movement of a bolus of food through the pharynx and upper esophagus during swallowing. (*From A. J. Vander, J. H. Sherman, and D. Luciano, Human Physiology, McGraw-Hill, New York, 1975. Reproduced with permission of the publisher.*)

THE ESOPHAGUS

Introduction

The primary role of the esophagus is to act as a conduit for the passage of food and liquid from the mouth to the stomach. For the 25-cm length of the esophagus, no absorption takes place and only residual carbohydrate digestion from salivary amylase occurs. It becomes clear early on that the unique role of the esophagus depends upon the mechanics of wall motility and the competence of its upper and lower sphincters.

Gross Anatomy

Anatomically, the esophagus is primarily located within the thoracic cavity. It is crossed anteriorly by the left bronchus. At this same level, it is also in close proximity to the aortic arch.

The arterial supply to the esophagus delivers separate vessels to each section of the organ. Thus the upper third, the middle third, and the lower third are independent.

Another outstanding anatomic feature of the esophagus is the venous drainage. There are two major sets of vessels; one, a large plexus on the surface; and the other, deeper within the esophageal wall. These two vascular groups come together below the diaphragm and merge with veins draining the stomach. Since the venous system of the stomach ultimately drains into the liver, the veins of the stomach, and therefore of the esophagus, are subject to increased pressure and flow if normal hepatic circulation is obstructed. Thus, if a patient develops portal hypertension (elevation of pressure in portal vein secondary to obstructed flow) from whatever cause (e.g., cirrhosis), blood flow will be shunted to the esophageal veins, causing massive dilatation of these vessels. These veins, known as *esophageal varices,* carry tremendous quantities of blood under very elevated pressures. They are easily prone to rupture. Massive hemorrhage from ruptured esophageal varices is a major complication and a potential cause of death for patients with portal hypertension.

Histology

Histologically, the mucosa of the esophageal lumen contains squamous epithelium. It is poorly modified for food absorption and has only rare mucous-producing glands throughout its wall. No major digestive enzymes are secreted by the esophagus.

Unlike the other gastrointestinal organs, the upper quarter of the esophagus contains only skeletal muscle in the muscularis externa. The middle quarter has mixed skeletal and smooth fibers, while the lower half has only smooth muscle. This evolutionary change facilitates the voluntary aspect of swallowing.

Esophageal Motility

Along the esophagus, a series of rhythmic contractions called *peristaltic waves* propel the food bolus downward. A wave consists of a contracting and a relaxing phase. Each peristaltic movement lasts some 5 s and travels toward the stomach at about 3 cm/s. Normal transit time from the top of the esophagus to the stomach is 9 to 10 s.

The role of the upper esophageal sphincter or hypopharyngeal sphincter has been discussed. It is this specialized muscular area of the esophagus which contracts when stimulated by the central nervous system and permits relaxation of the esophageal opening. The food bolus thus passes into the esophagus and down toward the stomach.

The lower esophageal sphincter (LES), also called the gastroesophageal sphincter, helps to maintain the correct direction of flow as digested materials pass into the stomach.

This sphincter, unlike the upper esophageal sphincter, is not identifiable by gross or histologic inspection. It is only through manometric (pressure) studies that the role of a sphincter was assigned to this distal part of the esophagus.

Normally the lower esophageal sphincter is closed when swallowing does not occur. Once the sphincter opens, food passes into the stomach and the sphincter again contracts and closes. In this fashion, the esophageal mucosa is protected from the acid environment of the stomach. Esophageal reflux of food and liquids is also discouraged.

Though anatomically the majority of the esophagus is in the thoracic cavity above the diaphragm, there is a small 3-cm portion below the diaphragm. This special anatomic arrangement utilizes the pressure gradient between the thoracic cavity and the abdominal cavity to further discourage gastric reflux.

Under normal circumstances, intra-abdominal pressure exceeds intrathoracic pressure. The thoracic esophagus and the abdominal esophagus maintain the level of pressure within their respective anatomic cavity. Since the pressure at the gastroesophageal sphincter can and does increase with increases in intra-abdominal pressure, sufficient tone can be generated at the LES to prevent reflux into the esophagus.

If, however, the LES is anatomically displaced by massive ascites or a growing fetus, then the distal esophagus, indeed the entire esophagus, is within the thoracic cavity. Corresponding increases in intra-abdominal pressure are not transmitted to the lower esophagus. The LES is unable to generate sufficient pressure and gastric reflux may occur.

Apparently, then, there is at least a double safeguard against acid reflux: first, the sphincter quality of the LES and its ability to contract and relax; and second, the pressure gradient between the thoracic and the abdominal cavities. While the gastroesophageal junction is below the diaphragm, in the cavity of higher pressure, and the sphincter is competent, reflux back into the esophagus should be adequately controlled.

Regulation of Esophageal Function

The controls regulating the esophageal sphincters are varied. The upper sphincter opens and closes principally by signals from the central nervous system. Once the trachea is protected by closure of the glottis, the brain signals the upper sphincter to contract and thus permits entrance of food into the esophagus. Note that for the upper sphincter, contraction opens the entrance while relaxation closes it.

Unlike its upper counterpart, the lower esophageal sphincter is influenced by an enormous number of factors. The list continues to grow, and the actual mechanism for many of these controls is still speculative. Two basic groups of controls are known. One is hormone-mediated, and the other depends on nervous innervation. A few of the more common ones will be presented.

The vagus nerve is the primary nerve regulating lower esophageal sphincter tone and pressure. Though it is responsible, in part, for creating the normal resting tone of the sphincter, its major function is to relax the sphincter during swallowing. Governed by the myenteric plexus, vagal mediation helps propagate esophageal peristalsis and therefore passage of food into the stomach.

Certain circulating hormones are intricately involved in maintaining the baseline sphincter tone. Though there is still some question about their exact mechanism of action, much progress has already been made in this field.

Gastrin, a hormone secreted by the pyloric glands in the stomach, has many functions. For the discussion here, it is enough to know that gastrin stimulates the secretion of hydrochloric acid (HCl) by the stomach. In so doing, the stomach contents become acidic and digestion is enhanced.

In order to prevent reflux into the esophagus, and therefore possible mucosal damage from the acidity, lower esophageal sphincter tone must increase and narrow the opening. What causes the sphincter tone to increase is not completely understood. Early experiments suggested that LES tone increased because of direct stimulation by gastrin. Teleologically, it seemed reasonable that as gastrin caused secretion of HCl for food digestion in the stomach, it also caused increased lower esophageal sphincter pressure which prevented reflux and damage to the esophagus. However, more current research refutes this role of gastrin and proposes that in physiologic doses gastrin may play only a small role in LES pressure (Sleisenger and Fordtran, 1978).

Two other hormones, secretin and cholecystokinin (CCK), secreted by the duodenum, oppose the action of gastrin and in pharmacologic, but not physiologic, doses decrease lower esophageal sphincter pressure. In addition, they both retard the actual secretion of gastrin itself.

Secretin and CCK are secreted by the small intestine just after the chyme (partially digested food) leaves the stomach. By that time, the partially digested food is farther from the gastroesophageal opening and is therefore less likely to reflux. In addition, stomach acidity has been buffered by pancreatic and duodenal bicarbonate, again making damage to the esophagus less likely. Since at this stage in digestion the esophagus is less vulnerable to harmful reflux, the lower sphincter does not need to be as tightly closed as before.

Lower esophageal sphincter tone is also affected by certain food types. Since fats, proteins, and starches stimulate the secretion of certain hormones, their method of intervention can be considered hormonal. Fats, for example, decrease lower esophageal sphincter tone. The speculative mechanism involves secretion of CCK, which in turn retards the production of gastrin. The proposed, but not proven, direct effect of CCK to reduce lower esophageal sphincter pressure, as well as its indirect effect to lower gastrin and thereby alter sphincter pressure, is potentially responsible for the net change in sphincter tone.

Cigarette smoke and alcohol lower sphincter pressure, whereas caffeine raises it. It has even been shown that some of the prostaglandin compounds affect tone and pressure.

Lastly, a look at the role of antacids in regulating the lower esophageal sphincter. Antacids buffer stomach acidity and raise the pH (make more alkaline). High pH stimulates the secretion of gastrin, and as before, gastrin seems to be related to increased sphincter tone. Perhaps patients with symptomatic esophageal reflux receive a dual benefit from treatment with antacids: the acid is neutralized and sphincter tone is increased.

THE STOMACH

Introduction

Unlike the esophagus, the stomach provides several major digestive functions in addition to mechanical mixing and transport of food. This organ produces important digestive secretions. It has a small but recognizable role in selected absorptive activities and provides a reservoir for partially digested food. Chyme is retained in the stomach until it is sufficiently altered, both physically and chemically, to permit further digestion in the first part of the small intestine, the duodenum.

The stomach has a much greater secretory capacity than the esophagus. The hormones, acid, mucous, water, and electrolytes secreted by the stomach mix and interact while chyme is retained in the stomach.

In the stomach itself, little absorption of foodstuffs occurs. Most of the particles are large and ionically charged, making their diffusion across the cell mem-

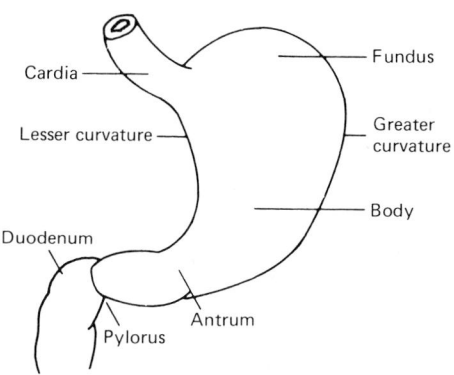

FIGURE 9-4

Gross anatomy of the stomach. (*Adapted from W. F. Ganong, Review of Medical Physiology, 8th ed., Lange, Los Altos, Calif., 1977. Reproduced with permission of the publisher.*)

brane difficult. Because of the stomach's acid environment, substances which are weak acids convert to their noncharged, nonionic form. Under these conditions, they are easily absorbed. Thus a weak acid, such as acetylsalicylic acid (aspirin), is rapidly absorbed in the stomach. Though the majority of alcohol absorption occurs in the small intestine, it can be absorbed to a certain extent in the stomach as well.

Beyond its role in digestion, the stomach also has some antibacterial function. The acidity of the stomach is partially responsible for this phenomenon, but certain aspects remain to be explained. This mild antibacterial control helps to keep the environment of the small intestine sterile.

Gross Anatomy

The stomach is located at the distal end of the esophagus. It is divided into five regions (Fig. 9-4):

1. The *cardia* is the part adjacent to the esophagus.

2. The *fundus* rises above the cardia and merges with the main part of the stomach.

3. The major portion of the stomach is called the *body*.

4. That area of the stomach immediately before reaching the pylorus is the *antrum*.

5. Finally, the *pylorus* is the muscular sphincter between the stomach and the duodenum.

On gross inspection of the stomach, one finds muscular walls thrown into multiple folds, or *rugae*. These folds increase the actual surface area of the organ, and together with the muscular nature of the organ, allow for greater expansion of the stomach. The usual capacity is 1 to 1.5 L.

The major arterial blood supply of the stomach arises from the celiac artery directly off the aorta. Sympathetic nerve fibers from the celiac plexus and parasympathetic fibers, principally from the vagus nerve, innervate the stomach. Parasympathetic tone predominates.

Histology

Histologically, the mucosal surface of the stomach is lined with columnar epithelium. Most importantly, this surface itself is a continuous flow of involutions and convolutions forming deep gastric pits. The gastric pits are important because they increase the overall surface area and because they house the many secretory glands of the stomach. Note also that the muscularis externa of the stomach differs from other gastrointestinal organs. It has an additional layer of muscle. This third layer is arranged in an oblique fashion and forms the innermost fibers of the muscularis externa.

Gastric Secretions

Taking into account all the glandular structures in the stomach wall, there are some 15 million glands present. Grouped by location and function, they are the *cardiac,* the *gastric* (or *fundic*), and the *pyloric* glands.

The *cardiac glands,* as their name suggests, are located near the cardia of the stomach. They are responsible for mucous secretion only.

At the distal end of the stomach, the *pyloric glands* are found, just before the pyloric sphincter. Like their counterpart in the cardia, these glands are mucous secretors as well. However, the pyloric glands also synthesize the hormone gastrin.

The *gastric* or *fundic glands* located in the body of the stomach secrete many different substances (Fig. 9-5). Their ability to produce more diversified products is a result of a more varied cell type in their epithelial layer. The *neck mucous cell* is found in the uppermost part of the gastric gland. It secretes mucus. The *parietal cell* is found in the middle of the gland. This cell secretes HCl and intrinsic factor, a substance necessary for the oral absorption of vitamin B_{12}. The final cell type, located deepest within the gastric gland, is the *chief cell*. The specialization of this cell allows it to secrete other enzymes. The most well known of these is pepsinogen.

The secretory function of the stomach can be conceptualized as two fundamental groups: the acid and the nonacid secretions.

Acid Secretion

The parietal cell, located in the pit of the gastric gland, is solely responsible for secretion of HCl. The amount of HCl secreted is directly proportional to the parietal cell mass. Normally, almost 2 L of HCl are secreted per day.

The internal environment of the parietal cell is composed of normal cellular matrix and the various electrolytes—Na^+, K^+, Cl^-, and so on. Each cell is rich with large adenosine 5-triphosphate (ATP)-producing mitochondria, which supply the needed energy for HCl synthesis.

The secretion of the HCl requires active ionic transport rather than passive diffusion of H^+ and Cl^-. As a consequence, large amounts of energy in the form of ATP are required. Appropriately, the parietal cell contains many large mitochondria.

Why active transport rather than passive diffusion? Since H^+ and Cl^- are pumped against an unfavorable concentration and pH gradient, a specialized transport system must be used. Both H^+ and Cl^- are actively transported, and separate ion pumps are believed to be responsible. Note that the hydrogen ion concentration in the stomach lumen is almost 3 million times greater than the concentration in the blood.

Despite years of study, many of the details surrounding HCl secretion are unclear. There are several simultaneous reactions occurring within the parietal cell which generate and replenish the needed stores of ionic substrates.

The source of hydrogen ions (H^+) is believed to come from the ionization of water (H_2O).

$$H_2O \rightleftarrows H^+ + OH^-$$

Coincidental with this in the parietal cell, an enzyme, carbonic anhydrase, catalyzes the reaction of carbon dioxide (CO_2) and water (H_2O) to make carbonic acid (H_2CO_3).

$$CO_2 + H_2O \rightleftarrows H_2CO_3$$

The carbonic acid is further broken down into a bicarbonate ion (HCO_3^-) and a hydrogen ion (H^+).

$$H_2CO_3 \rightleftarrows H^+ + HCO_3^-$$

For each H^+ that is actively transported across the cell membrane into the stomach lumen, one HCO_3^- ion diffuses (not actively transported) back into the bloodstream. Since this is a 1:1 exchange, as the stomach contents become more acidic, the venous blood leaving the stomach after a meal becomes more alkalotic.

Normally, there are no significant changes in body pH with meals because the pancreas and duodenum secrete HCO_3^- into the intestinal lumen and neutralize the pH. An important point to keep in mind, however, is that measurable pH shifts can occur in patients with large amounts of vomiting. With prolonged vomiting, and therefore loss of H^+ greater than loss of HCO_3^-, patients may become alkalotic.

In summary, H^+ ions are derived from the ionization of H_2O. Both H^+ and Cl^- are actively transported

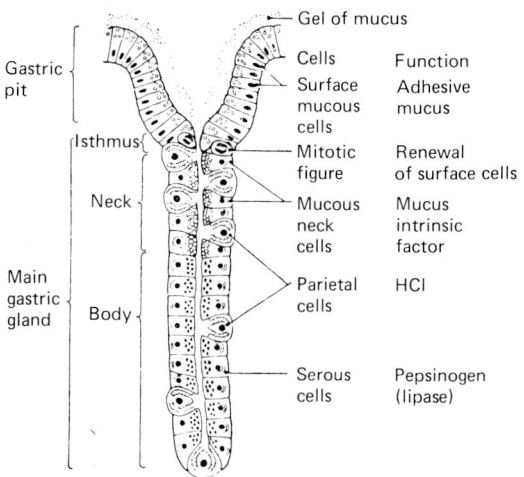

FIGURE 9-5

Histology of the gastric glands. (*Adapted from R. Passmore and J. S. Robson, A Companion to Medical Studies, vol. 1, Blackwell, Oxford, 1971. Reproduced with permission of the publisher.*)

across the cell membrane into the stomach lumen. For each H^+ that is transported into the lumen, one HCO_3^- diffuses back into the blood (Fig. 9-6).

Nonacid Secretion

Intrinsic factor   To finish discussing the secretions of the parietal cell, mention should be made of the nonacid substances that are secreted. *Intrinsic factor* is a glycoprotein necessary for the oral absorption of vitamin B_{12}. Though the mechanism is incompletely understood, it is believed that cyanocobalamin (vitamin B_{12}) binds to intrinsic factor. This complex travels to the distal ileum (third part of the small intestine) and binds to another receptor on the surface of the ileal mucosa. Once attached, the vitamin B_{12}, through an as yet unknown mechanism, is absorbed.

A person without intrinsic factor cannot absorb oral vitamin B_{12}. With gastrectomy (removal of the stomach), a patient will loose parietal cells; therefore, the patient will not produce intrinsic factor. Vitamin B_{12} must be replaced parenterally.

The example of gastrectomy causing absent intrinsic factor is quite obvious. More subtle cases are seen with atrophic gastritis, a condition that reduces parietal cell mass. Decreased and finally inadequate amounts of intrinsic factor are synthesized.

Pernicious anemia, a not uncommon disease is idiopathic gastric atrophy with absence of intrinsic factor, resulting in B_{12} deficiency and anemia.

Other causes of decreased vitamin B_{12} absorption, not strictly related to the absence of intrinsic factor, exist. However, they will not be discussed here.

Pepsinogen *Pepsinogen,* a nonacid substance, is secreted by the chief cells of the gastric glands. In its initial form, this proteolytic enzyme is inactive. It is activated only when the stomach pH becomes sufficiently acidic. In this acid environment, part of the original molecule is hydrolyzed, and the remaining active form, known as *pepsin,* cleaves amino acid bonds within protein chains. Maximal activity of pepsin occurs in a pH range between 1 and 3. Once the intestinal contents are neutralized by pancreatic and duodenal bicarbonate, pepsin loses its enzymatic activity.

Pepsin initiates the first major step in protein digestion. Whole proteins are broken down into small polypeptide fragments. As the digestive process continues, these newly formed fragments will play a role in regulating gastric motility and secretion.

Gastrin The other major nonacid compound to consider is *gastrin*. In recent years, this hormone has been intensively studied and is believed to be one of the major controlling factors in gastric acid secretion. Gastrin is secreted primarily by the cells of the pyloric glands in the antrum of the stomach. However, small amounts have also been found in the upper part of the duodenum and in certain cells of the pancreas. Structurally, gastrin is a peptide of 17 amino acids. The four amino acids at the carboxyl terminal end are believed to be the active agents regulating acid control.

The role of gastrin in the overall functioning of the gastrointestinal tract is growing by leaps and bounds. Here the discussion will cover only the major functions of this versatile hormone.

Gastrin's principal role is to stimulate secretion of HCl by parietal cells. Gastrin actually comes into physical contact with a receptor on the parietal cell surface. In an as yet unknown way, this contact propagates the secretion of HCl. Beyond its role as regulator of gastric acid, gastrin, in pharmacological doses, increases lower esophageal sphincter tone and also enhances gastric motility.

Below is a partial list of the other varied responses which are, at least in part, thought to be related to the

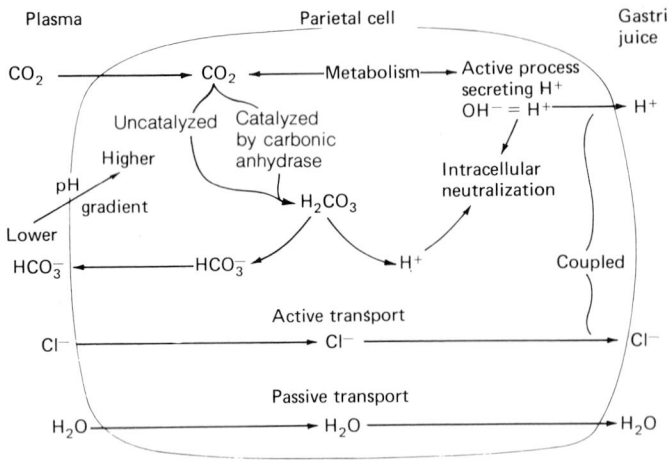

FIGURE 9-6

Proposed mechanism of HCO_3 secretion within the parietal cell of the stomach. (*Adapted from H. W. Davenport, Physiology of the Digestive Tract, 4th ed., Year Book, Chicago, 1977. Reproduced with permission of the publisher.*)

effects of gastrin. Definitive proof of gastrin mediation is forthcoming.

Gastrin is believed to increase:

Secretion of pepsinogen

Secretion of pancreatic bicarbonate and pancreatic digestive enzymes

Secretion of bicarbonate from Brunner's glands in the duodenum

Hepatic secretion of biliary bicarbonate

Intestinal motility

Gastrin is believed to decrease:

Secretion of secretin

Secretion of cholecystokinin (CCK)

Regulation of Gastric Secretions

Hydrochloric Acid

The regulation of gastric acid is as complex as the intricate molecular reactions responsible for HCl secretion. Like the control mechanisms for the lower esophageal sphincter, the regulation of acid secretion is both nerve- and hormone-mediated. In vivo, the humoral and the neural mechanisms are so intermingled that it would be difficult to explore them separately. This discussion will treat them simultaneously. Regulation of pepsinogen secretion virtually parallels HCl output and is included here as well.

The cephalic phase   The first phase of acid secretion, the *cephalic phase,* begins when one sees, smells, tastes, or even thinks about an appetizing meal. Thus, HCl is secreted even before food reaches the stomach. This phase of acid control is via parasympathetic input delivered by the vagus nerve. In part, the vagus directly stimulates acid secretion by the gastric glands. In addition, the vagus increases gastrin production by the pyloric glands in the antrum. This added gastrin augments acid output. Note that antrectomy (removal of the antrum) does not totally obliterate acid secretion. This supports the evidence that the vagus directly stimulates the gastric glands themselves. Acid secretion is not simply mediated by gastrin alone.

Vagal impulses are increased by hunger, hypoglycemia, and anger, as well as by pleasant gustatory stimulation. Measurable reduction in vagal tone is found with hyperglycemia, an overdistended stomach, and certain drugs, especially the anticholinergic agents.

The gastric phase   The second phase of acid secretion, the *gastric phase,* occurs, as its name implies, when food reaches the stomach. Though vagal input is still present, the predominant regulatory factors during the gastric phase are humoral. Alcohol and caffeine have also been shown to increase HCl secretion during this phase.

The hormone of note in acid regulation is gastrin. Though gastrin increases pepsinogen secretion as well, it does so to a lesser degree. Remember that during the cephalic phase, some gastrin is secreted. However, the gastric phase is responsible for the major outflow of this hormone. The secretion of gastrin is stimulated by antral distention, polypeptide fragments in the antrum, and by an alkaline pH in the stomach. Simultaneous secretion of pepsinogen increases the amount of polypeptide fragments, thus adding indirectly to the stimulus for gastrin secretion.

Gastrin secretion employs a feedback mechanism on itself. As gastrin is secreted, HCl is poured out, lowering the pH of the gastric contents. When the pH becomes sufficiently low, and therefore the H^+ ion concentration sufficiently high, gastrin secretion decreases.

The intestinal phase   The final step of acid control, the *intestinal phase,* begins as chyme enters the duodenum. When polypeptide fragments reach the antrum, gastric acid secretion increases. Though it is not well understood why, this mechanism continues to work even when the vagus nerve is not intact.

The intestinal phase has more inhibitory influence on gastric acid secretion than either of the earlier phases. If the pH within the duodenum is 2.5 or less, acid output markedly drops off. Likewise, fat in the duodenum also decreases acid production. CCK and secretin, two duodenal hormones, exert an inhibitory effect on gastrin and thereby decrease acid output. Since CCK is stimulated by fat in the duodenum, there is some question as to the exact mechanism causing the acid reduction. Does fat directly inhibit acid? Or does CCK, stimulated by the presence of fat, inhibit acid? Or both?

In summary, control of gastric acid secretion has three major components: the cephalic phase, mediated principally by the vagus nerve; the gastric phase, influenced primarily by the hormonal effects of gastrin; and finally, the intestinal phase, mainly an inhibitory stage which reduces acid output as chyme leaves the stomach and enters the small intestine.

Gastric Motility

In the stomach, food continues its physical and chemical breakdown. The partially digested food must be physically degraded into particles small enough to pass through the pyloric canal into the duodenum. Similarly, at the molecular level, gastric contents must be adequately mixed to ensure optimal enzyme exposure. Clearly, then, motility plays a central role in the stomach's contribution to digestion.

The movement of the stomach is both active and passive. Initially, as food enters the stomach, the passive phase of gastric motility occurs. This is *receptive relaxation*. It is a reflex initiated by earlier movements of the pharynx and the esophagus. As noted before, the usual reservoir capacity of the stomach is between 1 and 1.5 L. During receptive relaxation, volumes as high as 6 L have been recorded!

The true activity of the stomach, that which mixes and forces food through the pylorus, combines peristaltic contractions across the body of the stomach with strong contractions of the terminal antral segment.

The stomach has an intrinsic electrical pacemaker. These trigger cells are responsible for initiating electrical depolarization and subsequent muscular peristalsis. Initially, the electrical and muscular activity travel in the outer muscle layer. Soon they spread to the inner muscle layer and sweep across the body of the stomach toward the antrum. Normally, the frequency of contractions is three per minute. The initial rate of speed is only about 1 cm/s. However, as the antrum is approached, the peristaltic waves travel faster. They may reach speeds in the range of 3 to 4 cm/s.

Slow, weak muscular contractions are the rule early in digestion. It is only after about 1 h of digestive activity that the speed and the intensity of the waves increase. When contractions reach the antrum, they have enough force to push small amounts of chyme ahead of them. Digested food accumulates in the antrum, and antral pressure rises and actually overcomes the pressure in the open pyloric canal. Small amounts of viscous chyme are able to squeeze through into the duodenum.

However, like the antrum, the pylorus contracts as well. While contracted, the pyloric canal is closed. Chyme is not able to pass through. The antrum, contracting against a closed pylorus, can not generate enough pressure to push food into the duodenum. Instead, the chyme is forced backward into the stomach. It is this retropulsion of chyme into the stomach,

when the pylorus is closed, that accounts for the active mixing quality of gastric motion.

Regulation of Gastric Motility

Several factors control gastric motility. All the influences, whether mechanical, chemical, or neural, interact to produce optimal mixing of food in the stomach before it is passed along to the small intestine for absorption.

Significant abnormalities of gastric motility often lead to malabsorptive states. Though food may reach its destined site of absorption in the small intestine, if it has been improperly or incompletely processed in the stomach, normal absorption will not occur.

Spiro calls the stomach the "handmaiden" of the small intestine. If one considers the stomach as such, perhaps it is easier to understand the control mechanisms of gastric emptying.

Basically the stomach alters partially digested food for absorption within the small intestine. If chyme is adequately prepared, gastric motility increases and chyme passes through the pylorus. On the other hand, the stomach attempts to detain gastric contents by decreasing gastric motility and gastric emptying when chyme is incompletely processed. Similarly, if the duodenum is incapable of accepting more chyme, the stomach will attempt to delay further emptying.

Gastric Influences

The principal gastric factors affecting motility are tension within the stomach wall and gastrin. Tension builds within the stomach walls as the volume of food increases. In an attempt to decrease wall tension, gastric emptying speeds up.

Gastrin, the hormone which causes increased secretion of hydrochloric acid, also enhances antral motility. Acid is for digestion, and mixing promotes digestion. Reasonably, gastrin affects them both in a complementary manner. Remember also that gastrin is related to increased LES pressure. Thus during peak gastric motility, esophageal reflux is discouraged.

Intestinal influences Duodenal distention signals the stomach to slow gastric unloading. If the duodenum is unable to keep pace with the rate of emptying, incomplete interaction of hormones results, and chyme is inadequately prepared for transit further along in the small intestine. Similarly, if chyme reaching the duodenum is too acidic or too hypertonic, gastric emptying is inhibited. This checkpoint, called the *enterogastric reflex*, is partially mediated by the vagus nerve.

Fat in the duodenum stimulates the secretion of cholecystokinin, which in itself directly delays gastric motility. Fats leave the stomach more slowly than proteins and proteins more slowly than carbohydrates.

Hypothetical receptors to HCl, fatty acids, and osmotic stimuli have been postulated to exist in the duodenum and jejunum. By unknown mechanisms, perhaps humoral or neural, these receptors affect gastric emptying. The controls regulating gastric motility seem designed to maximize the unique role of each organ along the gastrointestinal tract. Each checkpoint optimally provides a most economical and a most practical method for food ingestion, digestion, and absorption.

The Vomiting Reflex

Before leaving the stomach, the mechanisms involved in the vomiting reflex will be discussed. Vomiting is initiated in the medulla of the brain. Mechanically, the partially digested food material in the stomach is forced back up through the esophagus into the mouth. Often the process is associated with common signs and symptoms of sympathetic nervous discharge, e.g., tachycardia and sweating.

Incoming signals to the medulla arise from various body sensory receptors. The more common emetic stimulants involve mechanical stimulation of the posterior oropharynx, increased intracranial pressure, overdistention of the stomach or duodenum, pain, or ingestion of certain chemical compounds.

Mechanically there are five steps involved:

1. A deep inspiration is followed by closure of the glottis.
2. The soft palate then rises.
3. The abdominal muscles contract and increase intra-abdominal and intragastric pressure.
4. The gastroesophageal sphincter (LES) relaxes.
5. Elevated intragastric pressure forces the food back through the esophagus, opens the upper esophageal sphincter, and forces food into the mouth.

As was mentioned earlier, prolonged vomiting may lead to severe electrolyte and pH imbalances, and of course, dehydration.

THE EXOCRINE PANCREAS AND THE BILIARY SYSTEM

Introduction

In order to facilitate the study of intestinal digestion and absorption, a short anatomic digression is helpful. Rather than descending the alimentary tract in its strict anatomic outline, the discussion will focus on the structure and function of the exocrine pancreas[1] and the biliary system. Understanding the contributions of these two auxiliary systems is critical to subsequent discussion of gastrointestinal physiology.

Remember, only that part of the pancreas and the liver relevant to digestion are presented here. Further along in the chapter, the other diversified functions of the liver and pancreas will be outlined and discussed.

The Exocrine Pancreas

Gross Anatomy

The pancreas is a large gland, with both endocrine and exocrine activity. It is located retroperitoneally (posterior to the peritoneum) within the abdominal cavity. It is divided into a head, a body, and a tail. The head lies within the C-shaped portion of the duodenum. The body or main portion of the gland is posterior to the stomach. The tail extends to the spleen. Unlike the liver and the other abdominal organs, the pancreas has no defined external capsule.

The arterial blood supply of the pancreas is rich and comes principally from the celiac and superior mesenteric arteries. Sympathetic nerves from the celiac plexus and parasympathetic fibers from the vagus nerve innervate the organ.

Histology

The overall microscopic structure of the whole gland is complex (Fig. 9-7). The principal component is a system of lobules separated by connective tissue septa. Within this multilobulated structure, small grapelike glands called *acinar glands* are found. They are accompanied by a partner system of collecting ducts. These ducts branch into an almost endless array of small ductules. The ductules, in turn, merge to form larger ducts which eventually coalesce and

---

[1] Glands are considered *endocrine* if the hormones they synthesize are secreted directly into the blood. They are called *exocrine* if they secrete hormones into a nonvascular system of ducts.

form the major pancreatic duct of Wirsung. The duct of Wirsung then empties into the duodenum.

Keep in mind that this combined system of acinar glands and connecting ducts belongs only to the exocrine pancreas. The microscopic anatomy of the endocrine pancreas is completely separate and has no connection with the exocrine duct-gland system.

Exocrine Secretions

There are two major products secreted by the exocrine pancreas: digestive enzymes and bicarbonate fluid. The acinar glands produce enzymes while the lining cells of the ducts secrete the bicarbonate-rich pancreatic juice. The combined output of enzymatic and bicarbonate secretions approaches 2 L/day. The actual proportion of the two components is determined by the nature of the food ingested.

Bicarbonate Secretion

In addition to providing the service of carrier conduit for the glandular secretions, the ductal epithelium or lining cells produce a bicarbonate-rich fluid. Unlike the glandular cells, these duct cells have few of the intracellular organelles needed for synthetic functions. Instead they are rich in the enzyme carbonic anhydrase. Like the parietal cells of the stomach, also rich in carbonic anhydrase, the pancreatic duct cells secrete bicarbonate.

Within the duct lumen, the alkaline secretion of the duct cells mixes with the enzymatic secretion of the acinar cells. What eventually reaches the major pancreatic duct, and therefore the small intestine, is a pancreatic juice rich in HCO_3^- and enzymes.

The mechanism of HCO_3^- secretion by the exocrine pancreas is analogous to the secretion of HCl by the stomach. However, in the case of the pancreas, it is HCO_3^- and not H^+ that is pumped into the intestinal lumen. Here, as in the stomach, and for similar reasons of unfavorable osmotic gradients, the process requires active transport, not simple diffusion. Just as the stomach alkalinized venous blood during secretion of HCl, so the pancreas acidifies it because of HCO_3^- secretion.

Pancreatic Enzymes

The acinus, or gland part, of the exocrine pancreas contains many secretory cells. These cells, rich with specialized intracellular organelles, are responsible for enzyme synthesis and packaging. *Zymogen gran-*

ules, large microscopic droplets within each cell, are storage particles laden with digestive enzymes.

The acinar cells secrete their enzymatic products into the duct system. Eventually, after many orders of ductules and ducts merge, the resulting major pancreatic duct empties into the duodenum.

The secretions of the acinar glands are a composite of enzymes, water, and salts. The successful digestion of fat, carbohydrate, and protein depends on the presence of these products. If the gland is unable to produce sufficient enzymes because of disease, or if the enzymes are unable to enter the small intestine because of anatomic obstruction, malabsorption of varying degrees may result. However, the pancreas has a tremendous reserve. Normal digestion can occur even if enzymatic secretion has been reduced to 10 percent of normal.

Pancreatic juice contains three basic groups of enzymes: lipolytic (fat breakdown), proteolytic (protein breakdown), and amylytic (carbohydrate breakdown).

Amylytic Of the amylytic group, *α-amylase* is the principal component. This enzyme, like salivary α-amylase, is responsible for hydrolysis of carbohydrates. The principal end products are glucose and maltose, a disaccharide of two glucose molecules. Pancreatic amylase is active in its original form and, unlike salivary amylase, is able to digest raw as well as cooked starches.

Proteolytic Trypsinogen, chymotrypsinogen, and *procarboxypeptidase* are the major proteolytic enzymes, or rather proenzymes. Each of these three must be altered before it is biochemically active.

Trypsinogen is converted to trypsin by the action of secretin. In addition, the trypsin thus formed acts as a self-catalyst so that trypsin activates trypsinogen. Trypsin cleaves amino acid bonds in the interior of protein chains.

Chymotrypsinogen is activated to chymotrypsin by trypsin. Its biochemical function, similar to that of trypsin, cleaves only interior amino acid bonds and thus adds to the growing pool of small polypeptides and single amino acids in the intestine.

Procarboxypeptidase, unlike the other two proteolytic enzymes, cleaves terminal amino acids and produces amino acids with free carboxyl ends. Procarboxypeptidase is converted to its active form by secretin and probably by trypsin.

Lipolytic The lipolytic enzymes, principally *pancreatic lipase* and *phospholipase A*, are important in early stages of fat digestion.

Lipase degrades triglycerides to free fatty acids and monoglycerides. Active in its original form, it requires the presence of bile salts to stabilize the fat-water interface of the intestinal contents. Phospholipase A is responsible for the hydrolysis of lecithin, a complex lipid, to lysolecithin.

Two additional pancreatic enzymes, *nuclease* and *deoxyribonuclease*, do not fall into any of the groups described. However, they deserve mention. As their names suggest, these enzymes are involved in the degradation of nucleotides within DNA and RNA molecules.

Regulation of Pancreatic Secretion

The secretory mechanisms of the exocrine pancreas are controlled by humoral and neural factors. Not unlike the stomach, the regulatory aspects of exocrine secretion have a cephalic, a gastric, and an intestinal phase.

The cephalic phase, as before, is stimulated by pleasant olfactory, visual, and gustatory aspects of a meal. Mediation is principally through the vagus nerve. Pancreatic juice secreted during the cephalic phase is rich in enzymes and contains only small amounts of HCO_3^-.

The gastric and intestinal phases of control are closely interwoven. The composition of gastric contents delivered to the duodenum decides whether secretin or cholecystokinin will be secreted by the duodenum. These two hormones then dictate how much and what kind (enzyme-rich or HCO_3^--rich) of pancreatic juice will be secreted. When high concentrations of amino acids and/or free fatty acids reach the duodenum, CCK is stimulated. CCK fosters secretion of pancreatic juice rich in digestive enzymes and poor in HCO_3^-.

This design is a reasonable one to serve the ends of digestion. When chyme rich in undigested proteins and fats is the stimulus, further digestion must occur. The pancreas, via stimulation by CCK, causes secretion of an enzyme-rich pancreatic juice. (Although carbohydrates are a stimulant to pancreatic secretion, they are far less potent than either proteins or fats.)

Acid is one of the most important influences during the gastric phase of regulation. High acidity (low pH) in the duodenum stimulates production of secretin. Secretin, in turn, stimulates the output of HCO_3^- and water from the pancreas. Thus pancreatic juice, re-

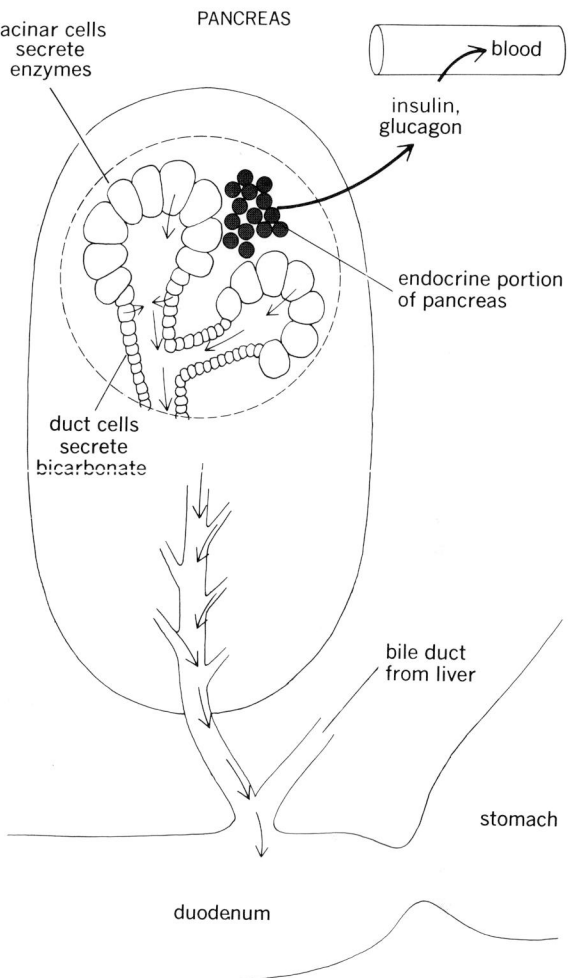

FIGURE 9-7

Endocrine and exocrine structure of the pancreas. (*From A. J. Vander, J. H. Sherman, and D. Luciano, Human Physiology, McGraw-Hill, New York, 1975. Reproduced with permission of the publisher.*)

sulting from acid stimulus and secretin mediation, is rich in HCO_3^- and low in enzyme content. Once again, these actions and reactions are coordinated to serve digestion.

The Biliary System

Introduction

For the purpose of understanding fat digestion and absorption in the intestine, the discussion now focuses on the biliary system. This vast network of connecting channels and ducts involves the gallbladder as well as the biliary passages of the liver. Among its many functions, the liver synthesizes and transports bile salts and bile pigments needed for fat digestion.

From both an anatomic and a functional level, the liver is extremely complex. However, for the purposes of the present discussion, only the biliary component of the liver will be included here. Again remember, this is only a small part of a complex organ. Further along in the chapter, liver structure and function will be presented.

Bile is synthesized by the liver cell, or *hepatocyte*. Then it is secreted into *bile canaliculi* or ductules which lie adjacent to the liver cells. The bile canaliculi have many orders of branching and eventually merge to form the right and left hepatic ducts within the liver. After exiting from the liver, these two ducts join and become the common hepatic duct. The cystic duct, carrying bile from the gallbladder, joins the common hepatic duct and becomes the common bile duct. As discussed earlier, the common bile duct and the major pancreatic duct merge at the ampulla of Vater and enter the small intestine through the duodenal papilla (Fig. 9-8).

The Gallbladder

The gallbladder is responsible for the storage and concentration of bile. Located on the undersurface of the right lobe of the liver, the adult gallbladder has a capacity of 30 to 50 mL. Between meals, bile reaches the gallbladder from the liver by way of the interconnecting duct system.

The cystic duct is a continuation of the gallbladder. Normally about 4 cm long, the cystic duct joins the common hepatic duct and forms the common bile duct. Like the duodenal papilla, the common bile duct also has a muscular sphincter surrounding its orifice. As the sphincter opens and closes, it determines the amount of bile that will pass through from the gallbladder and liver. Note that unlike the common bile duct, the pancreatic duct has no separate muscular sphincter. Hypothetically, this anatomic difference may make the pancreas more suceptible to bile reflux under certain circumstances. As a result, subsequent development of inflammation and pancreatitis may occur.

The arterial blood supply of the gallbladder comes from the cystic artery. Most frequently this is a branch off the right hepatic artery. Venous drainage occurs via the cystic vein into the portal vein.

Histologically, the gallbladder mucosa is remarkable for the many invaginations which characterize its surface. The crypts or pockets formed are of variable depths and, during disease states, are favored spots for bacterial retention and multiplication. Normally bile is sterile.

In addition to the storage facility of the gallbladder, rapid absorption of water and certain electrolytes occurs there as well. Consequently, the bile found in the gallbladder is more concentrated than that found within the bile ducts of the liver. Occasionally these shifts in bile concentration, coupled with other incompletely understood mechanisms, cause precipitation of bile components with resultant formation of gallstones.

Bile Metabolism and Function

Bile production occurs continuously within the hepatocyte. After synthesis, bile is secreted into the canaliculi. The rate of synthesis approaches 0.6 mL/min in an average adult, with a total of 15 mL of bile being secreted for every kilogram of body weight. The rate of synthesis and secretion are controlled primarily by the amount of blood flow reaching the liver.

The major constituents of bile include bile acids and bile salts (principally sodium cholate and chenodeoxycholate) and pigments (most notably bilirubin), cholesterol, phospholipids (especially lecithin), alkaline phosphatase, electrolytes, and water.

Bile salts Bile salts are cholesterol derivatives. Together with lecithin they prevent the precipitation of cholesterol as cholesterol stones in the gallbladder. Bile salts are bipolar compounds, that is, they have a water-soluble and a fat-soluble end. Cholesterol and lecithin are fat-soluble molecules. In the gallbladder, bile salts interact with the water phase of the bile, leaving their fat-soluble end free to mix with cholesterol and/or lecithin. The particles thus formed are called *micelles*. Eventually the micelles become saturated with cholesterol. At this point of supersaturation, cholesterol precipitates out in the bile and cholesterol stones are formed. The ratio of bile salts and lecithin to cholesterol is the basis of stone formation in the gallbladder. If the proportion of cholesterol in the bile increases (without a concurrent increase in bile salts or lecithin), stone formation is favored. Likewise, if the bile concentration of salts and lecithin decreases, stones will also form.

Bile salts are also important because of their role in fat digestion and absorption. Once in the small intestine, bile salts mix with fat to form micelles. As will be explained later, these water-stable complexes facilitate lipid (fat) absorption. In addition, bile salts

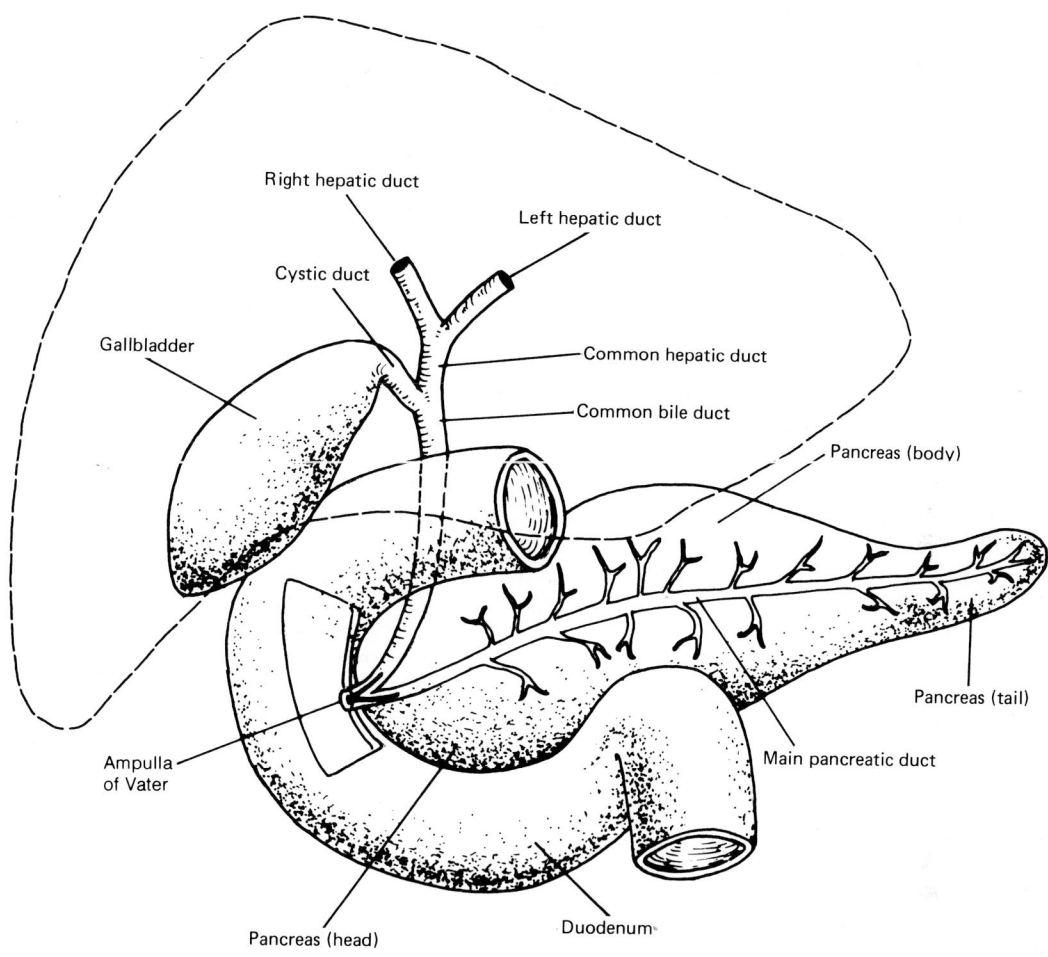

FIGURE 9-8

Connecting ducts of the liver, gallbladder, and pancreas.

are needed to activate pancreatic lipase, an enzyme needed for breakdown of triglycerides.

In short, normal fat digestion and absorption is not possible without bile salts. If obstruction prevents the entrance of bile salts into the intestine, fat malabsorption and steatorrhea (fatty stools) will result.

Normally, bile salts are not lost in the stools. Instead they are reabsorbed in the terminal part of the ilium (third part of the small intestine) and returned, via the venous sytem, to the liver where they are taken up by the liver cell and used again. All but some 2 to 3 percent of bile salts are reutilized in this way.

Bile salts are recycled via the enterohepatic circulation. This vascular circuit, unique to the gastrointestinal tract, drains venous blood from all the alimentary organs and returns it to the liver. In passing through the liver, the venous blood meets a second set of capillaries. At the level of these specialized capillaries, the liver sequesters what it needs for synthetic and detoxifying functions and returns the blood to the heart. This type of anatomic percolator is found only in the liver and in the vascular circuit of the anterior lobe of the pituitary gland.

Bile pigments   Bilirubin and other bile pigments are products of hemoglobin degradation. Plasma bilirubin is bound to the protein albumin as it is delivered to the hepatocyte. However, only free bilirubin is able to enter the liver cell. Inside it binds to a hepatic protein carrier, thereby preventing escape back into the circulation. Bilirubin then reacts with two molecules of glucuronic acid via the enzyme glucuronyl transferase. The new water-soluble compound, bilirubin glucuronide, is then actively secreted into the bile canaliculus.

Once bile pigments are mixed in the bile and delivered to the small intestine, they are degraded by normal bowel flora. Subsequent pigments derived from the continued degradation are responsible for the normal color of stool. Therefore, with extrahepatic biliary obstruction, and consequently absence of bile within the small intestine, stool color will turn from brown to grey. The absence of the usual pigments results in the acholic (without bile) stool.

In normal concentration, bile pigments do not form pigment stones. However, in disease states such as the hemolytic anemias, where there is an increased amount of bilirubin reaching the liver, the concentration of bile pigments increases, and the so-called pigment or bilirubinate stones precipitate out in the gallbladder. Cholesterol stones make up 90 percent of gallstones. The remaining 10 percent are pigment stones.

Regulation of Bile Metabolism

The regulation of bile secretion into the small intestine is a function of the neural and hormonal effects influencing the muscular sphincters of the biliary system and the contractility of the gallbladder.

In what might be called the cephalic phase of bile secretion, vagal stimulation received by the hepatocytes stimulates increased bile secretion and subsequent bile outflow. The sphincter of Oddi is normally in a partially opened state betwen meals. As a result, there is a constant trickle of bile into the small intestine.

When food reaches the duodenum, a more active phase of bile regulation begins. As mentioned previously, fats and polypeptides are strong stimulants for secretion of cholecystokinin. CCK, in turn, is the major hormonal stimulus for gallbladder contraction. With food present within the stomach or duodenum, the sphincter of Oddi relaxes. As the gallbladder contracts, increased bile passes through the relaxed sphincter into the intestine. Between meals, when the stimulus for CCK decreases, the gallbladder does not contract. The sphincter adopts a contracted pose, and the bile, always in continuous flow, travels from the liver to the gallbladder. There it is stored and concentrated until the gallbladder is stimulated to empty.

Since there are no absolute stop valves on hepatic bile production, there is always a flow of hepatic bile arriving directly at the intestine. Hepatic bile contains more water and HCO_3^- than bile from the gallbladder. It is more alkaline and therefore important to the small intestine if a large acid load arrives at the duodenum. Precisely because of these differences, secretin (stimulated by increased acid) causes preferential stimulation of hepatic bile flow rather than contraction of the gallbladder. Likewise, gastrin, a strong stimulant of gastric acid, indirectly increases hepatic bile flow by enhancing the production of secretin. Furthermore, gastrin has its own direct effect on the liver and increases hepatic outflow of HCO_3^--rich bile.

In summary, cholecystokinin is secreted in response to fat and protein in the duodenum. Fats need bile salts for digestion. Fat and protein need enzymes for digestion. CCK causes release of pancreatic digestive enzymes. CCK causes contraction of the gallbladder with resultant release of concentrated bile.

Secretin is stimulated by an acid load reaching the duodenum. The acid contents need a diluting buffer to prevent duodenal mucosal damage and to protect pH-sensitive digestive enzymes. Secretin causes outflow of pancreatic bicarbonate. In addition, secretin provides preferential flow of dilute alkaline, hepatic bile into the small intestine. In the case of both CCK and secretin, the response is an appropriate answer to the stimulus.

THE SMALL INTESTINE

Introduction

With a clear understanding of the contributions made by the hepatic biliary system and by the exocrine pancreas, a discussion of the small intestine, its structure, and its functions will follow.

The small intestine comprises some 3 m of tubing coiled within the abdominal cavity. It extends from the stomach to the ileocecal valve where the colon or large intestine begins.

Together the three parts of the small intestine—the duodenum, the jejunum, and the ileum—are responsible for the majority of digestion and absorption. Almost all food types, as well as water and vitamins, are processed and absorbed before they reach the large intestine.

Mechanical transit of intestinal material, though less important than in other gastrointestinal organs, is still a specialized function of the small intestine. A mixing action predominates as the most important motor activity.

Like other GI organs, the small intestine has a secretory role. But again, its unique contribution to gastrointestinal function is digestion and absorption, not secretion.

Gross Anatomy

The first and the shortest segment of the small intestine is the duodenum. Normally about 20 cm long, the duodenum is critical because of its hormonal secretions; because of its anatomic proximity to the connecting ducts of the liver, gallbladder, and pancreas; and because of its unfortunate predisposition to ulcer disease.

Continuing after the duodenum is the jejunum. Anatomically the jejunum is defined as beginning at the ligament of Trietz.

The remainder of the small intestine, the ileum, terminates at the ileocecal valve. In addition to its role in routine nutrient absorption, the ileum also absorbs vitamin B_{12} and bile salts. Together the jejunum and the ileum usually measure 2 to 3 m in length.

Because of the important absorptive capacity of the small bowel, adequate blood supply to this organ is critical. As a result, even at rest, the small bowel has a blood flow of 1 L/min or one-fifth of the total resting cardiac output.

The sole arterial blood supply of the ileum and jejunum is the superior mesenteric artery. The duodenum is supplied by several different vessels. Because of this anatomic difference, occlusion of the superior mesenteric artery may lead to infarction and death of the entire ileum and jejunum. However, the duodenum, with multiple blood sources, is less likely to suffer the same catastrophic event if part of its arterial supply is cut off.

The venous drainage of the small intestine is noteworthy because, as mentioned before, it is part of the enterohepatic circulation. All venous blood leaving the intestine, rich in absorbed food and vitamin nutrients, passes through the liver before reaching the heart. In the liver the hepatocytes extract what they need and detoxify noxious products. Venous blood then continues to the heart.

Both branches of the autonomic nervous system innervate the small intestine. Extrinsic fibers meet in the various plexuses within the intestinal wall. Reflex pathways also contribute to overall functioning.

The lymphatic system of the small bowel is important because of its central role in fat absorption. In the ileum large collections of lymph nodules, called *Peyer's patches*, are grouped together within the intestine wall.

Histology

The microanatomy of the small bowel is specifically designed to maximize the absorptive functions of this organ. The inner surface of the entire intestine is folded, thus increasing the absorptive surface area for the first time.

Each fingerlike projection thus formed has its own surface covered with multiple small invaginations and projections called *villi*. The surface area has increased for the second time.

Finally, each villus consists of epithelial cells, each of which is covered with thousands of hairlike projections called *microvilli*. The absorbing surface has been increased for a third time.

The net result of this multiplication system provides the small intestine with a surface area that is almost 30 times greater than that defined by the original luminal surface alone (Fig. 9-9).

The villus is the main structural unit of the small bowel. It is constantly in motion, following rhythmic contractions within the muscle layer of the wall. The contractions alter the length, and therefore the surface area, of the villus. Thousands of microvilli, anchored in the surface epithelial cells, cover the surface of each villus. The microvilli themselves contain certain enzymes needed for further nutrient digestion. In the center of the villus, the artery, vein, nerve, and lymph vessel, or lacteal, are found (see Fig. 9-9).

The intestinal lining cells have one of the most rapid turnover rates in the body. New cells from the base of the villus migrate up to the top and replace old, worn cells that are sloughed off into the intestinal lumen. The entire intestinal epithelium is replaced every 36 h. Mechanisms controlling this enormous mitotic and migratory activity are complex and as yet incompletely understood (Williamson and Chir, 1978).

Intestinal Secretions

The role of the small intestine as a secretory organ has only recently come under extensive study. The future may well reveal a more lengthy complement of intestinal products. The lining epithelium of the small intestine is modified with numerous goblet or mucus-producing cells. This mucous secretion, together with CCK and secretin, synthesized by the duodenal mucosa, are the major secretory contributions of the small bowel. Note that CCK and secretin are synthesized by the duodenal mucosa, but they are secreted directly into the blood, not into the intestinal lumen.

One other important component should also be mentioned. Within the duodenal wall there is a collection of glands, *Brunner's glands*, which secrete a

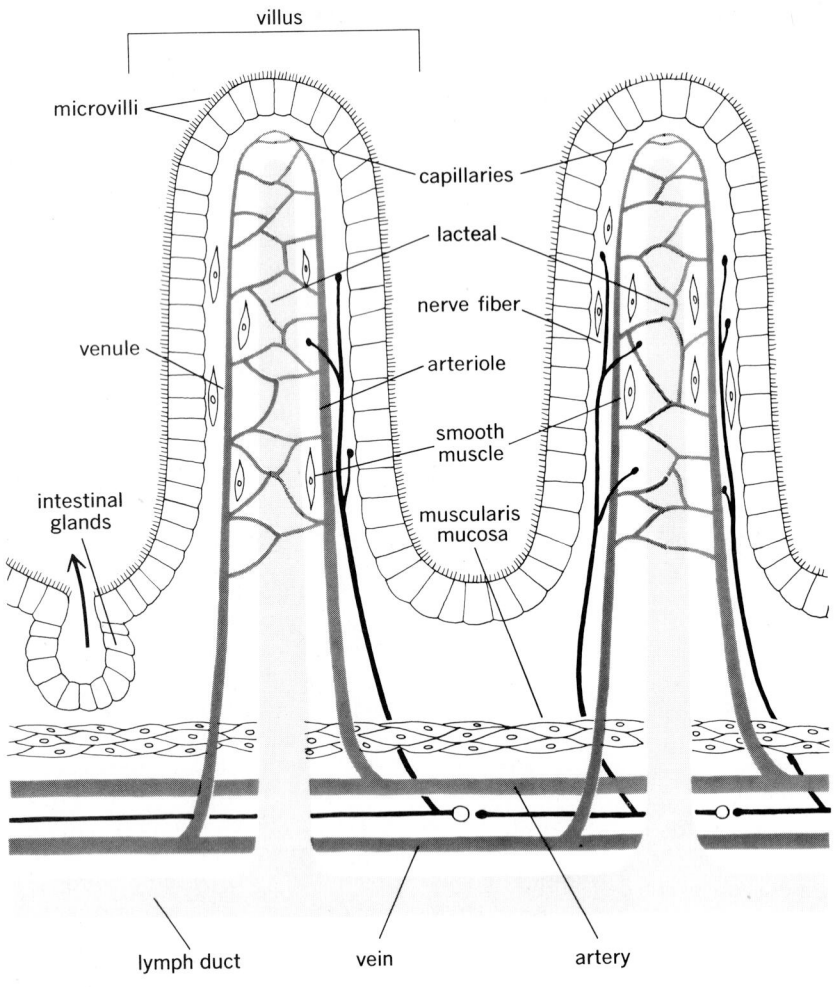

FIGURE 9-9

Structure of the small intestinal villus. (*From A. J. Vander, J. H. Sherman, and D. Luciano, Human Physiology, McGraw-Hill, New York, 1975. Reproduced with permission of the publisher.*)

HCO_3^--rich fluid. Like pancreatic HCO_3^-, the secretion of Brunner's glands helps to neutralize the acid gastric contents and protect the duodenal mucosa. Again like pancreatic HCO_3^-, Brunner's glands are stimulated by acid in the duodenum, by secretin, and by gastrin.

Intestinal Motility

Like each of the organs before it, the small intestine has is own specialized type of motility. Since this organ is designed to digest and absorb chyme, it follows that the principal form of movement should promote mixing and facilitate contact with the absorbing surface. *Segmentation*, the unique motion of the small intestine, achieves precisely these two objectives. However, since the small bowel must deliver the intestinal contents to the colon, a propulsive motion must exist as well. Weak peristaltic waves can be demonstrated throughout the small bowel. Each one contributes to the forward propulsion of chyme toward the colon.

In the duodenum, near the entrance of the common bile duct, an intrinsic electrical pacemaker is found in the longitudinal muscle of the wall. The impulse travels from duodenum to ileum. Importantly, the strength, the frequency, and the speed of the impulse decrease as they get farther from the duodenum. This temporal prolongation allows increased time for digestion and absorption.

Segmentation contractions follow the intrinsic pacemaker rhythm but involve only rings of muscle around the small intestine. As one area relaxes, another contracts all along the intestine, thus creating a "sausage links" effect. This action mixes; it does not propel intestinal contents.

Weak peristaltic waves of contraction, preceded by relaxation, slowly propel chyme toward the colon. Usually they are short waves and do not involve the entire length of the small bowel. Distention of the bowel at any point triggers this sequence of events. It is called the *myenteric reflex*.

As chyme approaches the large intestine, ileal contractions increase. The ileocecal valve, normally in a closed position, relaxes and allows chyme to flow into the colon. This *gastroileal reflex* regulates passage of chyme from the small intestine to the large intestine.

Both segmentation and peristalsis require intact intrinsic (that is, within the intestinal wall) neural structures. For segmentation to occur, the duodenal pacemaker discharges its impulse.

With peristalsis the pressure receptors in the bowel wall respond to the sense of increased distention. The myenteric reflex is stimulated. For the reflex to complete itself, the nerve plexus in the intestinal wall must be intact. Generally, sympathetic stimulation causes decreased intestinal motility, while parasympathetic input increases activity. CCK promotes enhanced motility, but glucagon and secretin slow intestinal action.

Intestinal Absorption

Having traveled from the mouth down the esophagus and through the stomach, and having collected pancreatic and hepatic digestive secretions at the ampulla of Vater, the discussion now turns directly to the major issues of digestion and absorption within the small intestine.

Before reaching the ileum, most foodstuffs, with certain notable exceptions, have been absorbed. Because of the small bowel's tremendous absorbing surface, almost 50 percent of the bowel may be removed without producing clinical malabsorption. In addition to the fats, carbohydrates, and proteins absorbed in the small intestine, significant absorption of water and electrolytes occurs here as well (Fig. 9-10).

Carbohydrate Absorption

Carbohydrates or starches constitute a substantial part of the average North American diet. Consumption varies from 200 to 800 g per day. The majority of carbohydrates are ingested as polysaccharides. Only small amounts of the common disaccharides, lactose and sucrose, are consumed daily.

In the mouth, salivary amylase begins to digest carbohydrates. Some 50 percent of starches, mostly in the form of polysaccharides, are hydrolyzed to disaccharides. This continues to a lesser degree as the food bolus moves down the esophagus. In the stomach, no significant starch digestion occurs, since the acid environment inactivates amylase (optimal pH 6.7).

Once in the small intestine, pancreatic amylase continues the process. The most common disaccharide formed is maltose. Absorption of disaccharides is not feasible because of their size. Therefore, in order for carbohydrate absorption to occur, monosaccharides must be generated. The microvilli of the small intestine contain special enzymes—lactase, maltase, sucrase, and so on—which split the specific disaccharides into monosaccharides. Lactose intolerance is a disease resulting from absence of the enzyme lactase. Consequently, patients with this disorder are unable to absorb lactose, and they suffer from diarrhea and abdominal complaints if lactose is not removed from their diets.

Once formed, the simple sugars—glucose, galactose, and fructose—are absorbed relatively easily because of their smaller size. Most sugars are absorbed before reaching the last portion of the ileum. Both glucose and galactose require active transport across the intestinal membrane into the blood. Their absorption is therefore coupled to Na^+ transport and is directly proportional to the Na^+ concentration in the intestinal lumen. Fructose, however, passively diffuses through the membrane into the blood.

Now in the venous blood, the absorbed sugars are transported to the liver. In the specialized hepatic capillaries, the hepatocytes utilize the sugars either for immediate energy, for storage as glycogen, or as metabolic intermediates in other hepatic biochemical pathways.

In summary, ingested polysaccharides are hydrolyzed to disaccharides by *salivary α-amylase* by the time they reach the stomach. In the stomach no significant change occurs. Within the small intestine *pancreatic α-amylase* continues the generation of disaccharides. *Sugar-splitting enzymes* of the intestinal microvilli cleave disaccharides to monosaccharides. These simple sugars are absorbed across the intestinal membrane into the venous blood either by active transport (glucose and galactose) or by passive diffusion (fructose). Venous blood, rich in absorbed carbohydrate, returns to the liver for appropriate utilization and storage.

Protein Absorption

A daily protein intake of 50 g, under normal healthy conditions, is considered adequate for the average adult. This quantity provides the needed essential amino acids and meets the demands of ordinary protein synthesis and degradation. Most adults in the United States average about 200 g of protein per day in their diets.

Unlike the carbohydrate group, protein is not altered until reaching the stomach. There the acid pH hydrolyzes certain amino acid bonds, and gastric pepsin, activated by the acid, cleaves internal peptide bonds forming amino acid fragments or polypeptides.

In the duodenum, pepsin is inactivated because of the increased alkalinity. However, the pancreatic proteolytic enzymes, trypsin and chymotrypsin (optimal pH 7.8), continue to cleave internal bonds. Carboxypeptidase, also from the pancreas, initiates removal of terminal amino acids. The protein pool is composed of peptide fragments and rare free amino acids.

In a fashion similar to the disaccharides of carbohydrate digestion, the polypeptide fragments are too large to be absorbed across the mucosal surface. Again the intestinal microvilli supply specialized enzymes—dipeptidases, aminopeptidases, and so on—which split polypeptides into free amino acid components. Single amino acids, like single sugars, can be absorbed. Most recently, investigative studies indicate that dipeptides with short side chains may also be absorbed intact and are hydrolyzed to free amino acids within the cell.

Amino acid absorption is highly specific with unique mechanisms for neutral, acidic, and basic amino acids. The molecular structure of the compound determines, in part, whether active transport and Na^+ coupling or passive diffusion are needed for absorption. Most amino acid absorption occurs in the duodenum and the jejunum.

Like the products of starch metabolism, protein building blocks are also returned to the liver. Once there, the liver degrades amino acids into their two organic parts, carbon and nitrogen (ammonia). Free ammonia is toxic to the human body in abnormal amounts. Therefore, the liver uses the free ammonia to form the waste product urea. This urea then travels to the kidney and is excreted in the urine, thus disposing of a toxic product. If, however, because of significant hepatic damage, the liver is unable to synthesize urea, free ammonia will accumulate and reach toxic levels. This phenomena, the liver's inability to handle a nitrogen (ammonia) load, is in part the basis for hepatic encephalopathy, a condition seen not infrequently with severe liver disease.

The above series of metabolic events is the rationale for a protein-restricted diet in patients with hepatic encephalopathy or in those patients where it is likely to develop. Likewise, gastrointestinal bleeding, with resultant blood (composed of protein and therefore amino acids) in the gut lumen, also predisposes selected patients with liver disease to hepatic encephalopathy. With an increased amino acid load presented to the small intestine, increased amino acid absorption occurs. The liver receives an increased load of free ammonia. Since its synthetic ability to make urea is subnormal, the concentration of free ammonia in the blood rises and clinical encephalopathy may result.

Fat Absorption

The fat content of the daily adult diet varies greatly. The biochemical form most commonly ingested is the triglyceride or neutral fat. Cholesterol and the complex phospholipids also add significantly to the daily lipid intake. Normally, stool content is only 5 percent of the daily dietary fat intake. But even this small proportion comes from bacterial metabolism rather than from dietary fats alone.

The overall digestion and absorption of lipids is slightly more complex than the mechanisms involved in carbohydrate and protein metabolism. The additional steps required arise chiefly from the size and solubility characteristics of the lipids.

No fat digestion occurs before reaching the duodenum. Fat arrives at the duodenum mainly as triglycerides, cholesterol, and phospholipids. Pancreatic lipase is the enzyme responsible for the first step of fat digestion.

Triglycerides are fat-soluble. Enzymatic lipase is water-soluble. Therefore, in an aqueous solution such as intestinal fluid, triglycerides will lump together, forming large droplets. Because of their water insolubility, they will not mix with the water milieu. Lipase,

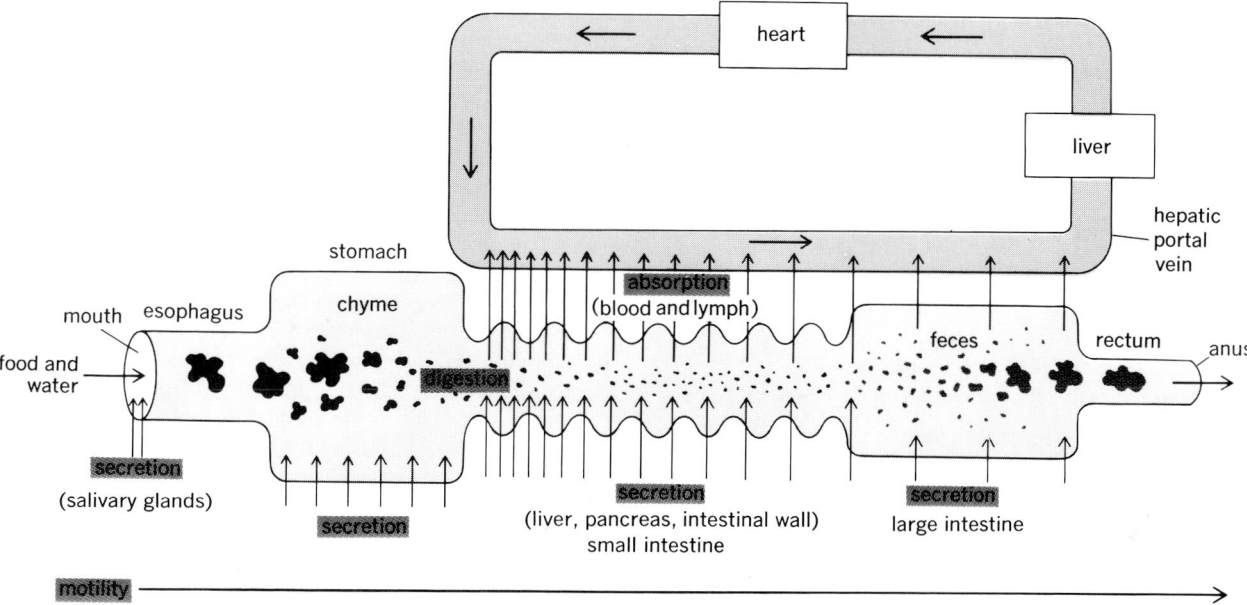

FIGURE 9-10

Summary of gastrointestinal activity involving motility, secretion, digestion, and absorption. (*From A. J. Vander, J. H. Sherman, and D. Luciano, Human Physiology, McGraw-Hill, New York, 1975. Reproduced with permission of the publisher.*)

being water-soluble, will mix with the water phase. How, then, to bring water-soluble lipase in contact with fat-soluble triglycerides?

Bile salts, coming from the liver and primarily the gallbladder, enter the duodenum when a fatty stimulus is present. These salts contain both a water-soluble and a fat-soluble portion. As a result, they can bring together, in a sense bridge, the two otherwise opposing elements.

The large lipid droplets, having been stabilized by the bile salts, now come in contact with lipase. The action of this enzyme, together with normal intestinal motility, causes much mixing and breaking apart of the large fat droplets. This process, called *emulsification,* provides increased numbers of small fat particles and thereby increases the overall surface area where lipase can act. Lipase is responsible for degrading triglycerides (TG) primarily to monoglycerides (MG) and free fatty acids (FFA) (Fig. 9-11).

Step 1: Emulsification

$$\text{Triglycerides as large fat droplets} \xrightarrow[\text{Lipase}]{\text{Bile salts}}$$

$$\text{Smaller droplets} \xrightarrow[\text{Lipase}]{\text{Bile salts}} \text{FFA} + \text{Monoglycerides}$$

The FFA and monoglycerides thus formed combine with varying proportions of cholesterol and phospholipid. This new combination of fatty molecule is again acted upon by bile salts. The new particle, now stabilized and water-soluble, is called a *micelle.* It is from the micellar form that FFA and monoglycerides are absorbed across the intestinal mucosa.

Step 2: Micelle formation

FFA + MG + Cholesterol

$$+ \text{Phospholipid} \xrightarrow{\text{Bile salts}} \text{Micelle}$$

When the micelle is in close proximity to the mucosal surface, passive absorption of the FFA occurs. Depending on the length of the FFA, absorption will take place directly into the blood (for FFA less than 10 to 12 carbons long), or as is more often the case, the FFA (longer than 12 carbons) will be resynthesized to a triglyceride within the intestinal cell (Fig. 9-12).

Once resynthesized, the triglyceride is coated with cholesterol and phospholipid. This new complex, called a *chylomicron,* is then picked up by the lacteal or lymph vessel of the intestinal villus and carried to sites of fat storage (adipose tissue) throughout the

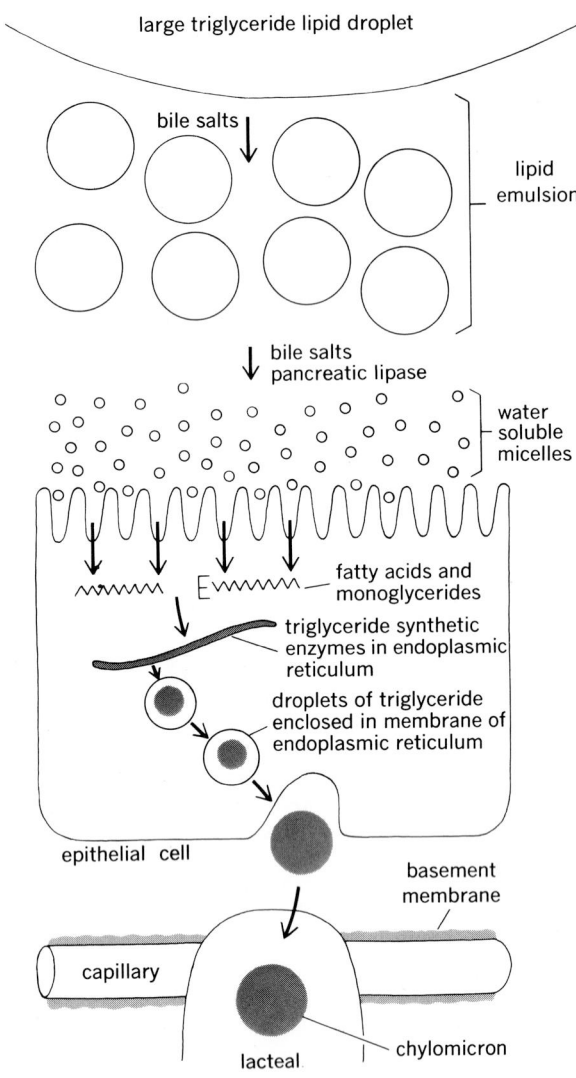

FIGURE 9-11

Summary of fat absorption across the walls of the small intestine. (*From A. J. Vander, J. H. Sherman, and D. Luciano, Human Physiology, McGraw-Hill, New York, 1975. Reproduced with permission of the publisher.*)

body. Thus most free fatty acids travel as triglycerides in chylomicrons via the lymph, not via the blood.

Note that bile salts remain behind within the intestinal lumen when the free fatty acid diffuses into the intestinal cell. Reabsorption of these salts takes place in the terminal ileum. They are reabsorbed directly into the blood and are then recycled in the enterohepatic circulation. The majority of the triglyceride

absorption via lacteals takes place in the jejunum, not in the terminal ileum.

Water, Electrolyte, and Vitamin Absorption

As much as 10 L of fluid enters the gastrointestinal tract each day. Usually, only about 2 L is exogenous. Amazingly, the remaining 7 L comes from gastrointestinal secretions! Contributions from the stomach, pancreas, liver, gallbladder, and small and large intestines accumulate to an impressive sum.

The usual fluid volume lost in stool is only 100 to 200 mL/day. Consequently, the remaining volume must be reabsorbed by the gastrointestinal tract.

From the stomach to the colon, the mucosal surface is adapted for water reabsorption. Though the stomach really contributes relatively little to volume control, it still attempts to achieve isotonicity with the plasma.

The duodenum, on the other hand, is the place of great fluid shifts. All contents leaving the duodenum are isotonic as they pass on to the jejunum. That implies absorption of osmotically active particles (sugars, amino acids) and/or secretion of buffering fluids to dilute the intestinal contents.

The colon is another major site of water absorption. It will be discussed more thoroughly further along in this section.

Electrolyte shifts within the gastrointestinal tract are important to overall function. Having just reviewed the role of the Na^+ ion in carbohydrate and protein metabolism, it is evident that significant electrolyte imbalances may pose serious limitations on the normal absorptive functions of the bowel.

Normally, Na^+ is actively reabsorbed in the small intestine and water passively follows. Chloride is absorbed in the ileum, while HCO_3^- is secreted into the lumen. K^+ is absorbed as well as secreted by colonic mucosa.

Vitamins, with the exception of B_{12}, are absorbed in the upper part of the small bowel. The B_{12}–intrinsic factor complex, as mentioned earlier, is absorbed in the terminal ileum. Water-soluble vitamins do not require any special enzymes or mechanisms for absorption.

Fat-soluble vitamins A, D, E, and K require that normal enzymes and bile salts for routine fat absorption be present. If fat malabsorption occurs, the fat-soluble vitamins are not absorbed.

Iron, though not a vitamin, is important to the balance of hemoglobin synthesis and degradation. Iron is normally easily absorbed in the upper small intestine. It does, however, require active transport.

THE LARGE INTESTINE

Introduction

Just as the mouth gave entrance to the gastrointestinal tract, the colon provides an exit. When digested materials reach the colon and are expelled, the completed circuit between the environment–gastrointestinal tract–environment is realized.

The colon, some 150 cm long, carries intestinal contents to the end of the gastrointestinal tract. Together with its terminal portions, the rectum and the anus, the colon is responsible for mucous secretion and water and electrolyte absorption. The colon houses the natural bowel flora that are important to particular metabolic pathways and that under certain conditions can lead to life-threatening infections.

The final result of all colonic function produces an economic and utilizable end product: stool. Normally, stool is one-quarter solid and three-quarters liquid. Its brownish color is attributed to the products of hemoglobin degradation. The characteristic odor results from certain bacterial metabolites, especially the amine compounds. The bulk of the stool is provided by cellulose and indigestible fibers, bacteria, degenerated cellular debris, fat, and inorganic material.

Gross Anatomy

The large intestine begins just distal to the iliocecal valve. The cecum is the blind pouch which begins the colon (Fig. 9-13). The vermiform appendix is a small outpouching off the cecum. The major part of the colon is divided anatomically into four divisions: the ascending, the transverse, the descending, and the sigmoid, or S-shaped, colon. Following the sigmoid colon are the rectum and the anus.

The muscular iliocecal valve separates the small and large bowel. At the distal end of the large bowel there are two other regulating sphincters, the internal and the external anal sphincters. They play an important role in regulating defecation.

Grossly, the colon is a wider-diameter tube than the small intestine. Inspection of the colon reveals an outer longitudinal muscle layer separated into three fiber tracks. The three muscular bundles eventually fan out at the rectum and form a complete muscle coat. These longitudinal bands, called *teniae coli,* are shorter than the colon itself. This difference in length, coupled with the contractions of the inner muscle layer, causes outpouchings of the colonic wall. They are called *haustra.* The haustra and the

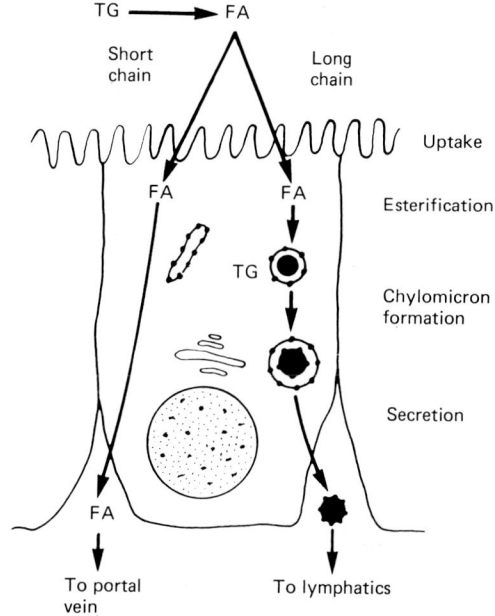

FIGURE 9-12

Differential absorption of short- and long-chain fatty acids across the small intestinal wall. (*Adapted from W. F. Ganong, Review of Medical Physiology, 8th ed., Lange, Los Altos, Calif., 1977. Reproduced with permission of the publisher.*)

teniae give the colon its unique gross appearance (see Fig. 9-13).

The internal anal sphincter is a continuation of the inner muscle layer. It is under involuntary control. The external sphincter is a separate skeletal muscle. Unlike the internal sphincter, it is not an extension of the smooth muscle in the colonic wall. It extends the entire length of the anus and is under voluntary control.

The colonic blood supply originates from the superior and inferior mesenteric arteries. The venous system parallels the arterial system and is noteworthy because of the plexus of veins formed around the anus. This plexus, like the one at the base of the esophagus, may become tortuous and dilated. The resulting hemorrhoids are a frequent development in many people. They are of special interest and concern in patients with portal hypertension. Just as esophageal varices are prone to rupture when blood is shunted away from the liver, so too are the varices of the rectal plexus. The incidence of life-threatening

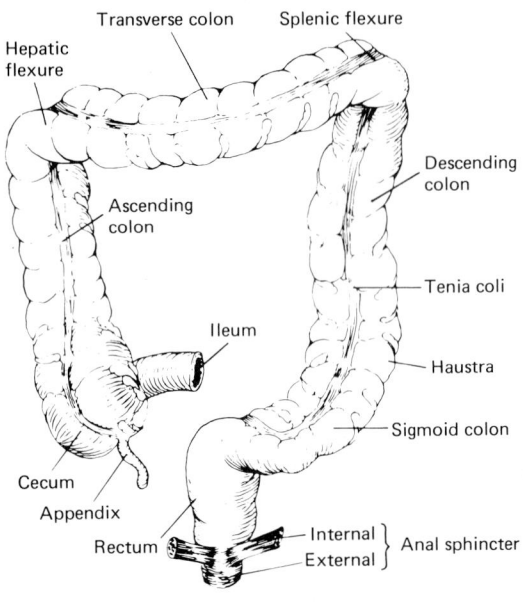

FIGURE 9-13

The human colon. (*Adapted from W. F. Ganong, Review of Medical Physiology, 8th ed., Lange, Los Altos, Calif., 1977, p. 379. Reproduced with permission of the publisher.*)

hemorrhage from rectal varices is significantly lower than with esophageal varices, however.

Nervous innervation of the colon, like the other gastrointestinal organs, contains both parasympathetic and sympathetic fibers. Parasympathetic input has variable consequences, and the overall impact is not clearly worked out. Sympathetic fibers apparently have more effect on colonic vasculature than on colonic muscle tone. Again, the exact role of this adrenergic stimulus is not clear.

Histology

The microscopic anatomy of the colon is less specialized than the details seen in the small intestine. There are relatively fewer foldings of the mucosa, and there are no villi or microvilli in the colon.

Columnar cells line the colonic mucosa, but as one approaches the anus, a more rugged stratified squamous epithelium covers the surface. Mucus-producing glands are found throughout the colon. Their viscous secretions are important lubricants for passage of fecal material.

Colonic Motility

The colon, unlike the small intestine, does not move intestinal contents along rapidly. Instead, the colonic motions permit mixing and molding of stool followed by slow exit from the anus. Since the colon has a relatively small absorptive surface area, slowed transit along its course permits the needed absorption of water and electrolytes.

Chyme reaching the colon is in liquid form. The large intestine must be able to absorb sufficient amounts of water to produce solid stools. Remember, some 9 L of fluid enter the gastrointestinal tract each day. Of that total volume, 1 L reaches the colon. Since only 150 mL of fluid are lost in the stools each day, the colon must absorb between 800 and 900 mL of liquid a day.

The motion accountable for mixing and molding is segmentation. Similar to segmentation in the small intestine, colonic segmentation corresponds to contraction of the inner muscle layer and changes in the haustral configurations. Segmentation occurs simultaneously in various parts of the bowel in a rather uncoordinated pattern. Again, this lack of coordination slows colonic motility and facilitates absorption.

Propulsive motions of the colon are supplied by weak peristaltic contractions occurring along its length. However, this relaxation and contraction of relatively short segments of bowel provides only minimal forward motion. Indeed, there is even some evidence that antiperistaltic waves exist and cancel out the forward distance gained! This is yet another mechanism by which colonic transit is slowed and absorption enhanced.

These short peristaltic waves would be inadequate as the sole source of forward propulsion in the colon. As a consequence, another more assertive type of movement takes place. Normally, during a 24-h period, the colon experiences three or four stronger, more extensive peristaltic contractions. These peristaltic rushes cause what is known as *mass movements* down the colon. As much as one-third of the bowel may be traversed with one of these rushes. Interestingly, man is not aware of their presence.

Little definitive information is known about the control mechanisms of colonic motility. The outcome of autonomic input is not straightforward, and laboratory experiments report variable responses. More recently, suggestion of hormonal control via prostaglandins, 5-hydroxytryptamine, and/or CCK has been proposed. The *gastrocolonic reflex* is a central neural circuit which signals colonic activity as chyme distends the stomach.

Defecation is a reflex initiated by increased tension in the rectal wall. If this pressor stimulus is not inhibited, the normal act of defecation occurs.

The underlying mechanism of defecation involves contraction of the distal colon and rectum, causing increased rectal pressure and shortening of the rectum. As pressure mounts within the rectum, the involuntary internal anal sphincter and the voluntary external anal sphincter relax. Stool is able to pass through.

If one ignores the urge to defecate, the walls of the rectum eventually relax and intralumenal pressure decreases and obliterates the desire to defecate. When another mass movement delivers additional stool to the rectum, pressure again increases and the urge to defecate returns.

Man is able to assist the basic mechanisms involved in evacuation. With deep inspiration, descent of the diaphragm and closure of the glottis increase both intra-abdominal and intrathoracic pressure. This greater pressure is transmitted into the intestine and aids in evacuation.

Note that while straining facilitates defecation, it has potentially dangerous consequences for cardio-respiratory function. As intrathoracic pressure increases, there is an initial abrupt rise in arterial blood pressure and peripheral venous pressure. Immediately following that, a marked decrease in cardiac output develops because of poor venous return to the heart. The decreased output causes a marked reduction in arterial blood pressure. Consequently, many patients, but especially those with cerebral vascular disease and/or coronary artery disease, are at greater risk for life-threatening events if allowed to strain during defecation.

Diarrhea is abnormal evacuation from the colon, usually excessive in frequency and predominantly more liquid than solid. Diseases which induce diarrhea are plentiful and varied. However, despite the commonplace nature of this disturbance, the underlying causative mechanism (or mechanisms) are not obvious.

Many potential theories have been offered. Some focus on abnormal colonic irritability and increased motility; others support defects of water reabsorption and inability to reabsorb nutrients along the bowel. More recently, excessive gut secretions mediated via cyclic adenosine 5-monophosphate have been implicated as the primary abnormality.

Indeed, the answer is not readily apparent. Nevertheless, diarrhea, from whatever cause, is important to clinical medicine. It poses a vivid and annoying threat to body hydration, pH stability, and electrolyte balance.

At the other end of the spectrum, constipation, or abnormally infrequent bowel movements, does not instigate the wide range of metabolic instability that is produced by diarrhea. Its major clinical significance is as a presenting symptom for possible underlying bowel disease, e.g., colonic carcinoma.

Colonic Secretion and Absorption

Unlike the stomach and small intestine, the colon does not produce an abundance of diversified secretions. The major secretory product in the large bowel is mucus. The goblet cells along the mucosal surface are responsible for secreting a viscous fluid which mixes with the forming stool and assists its mechanical passage toward the anus.

The colon is also responsible for secretion of K^+ and HCO_3^- into the intestinal lumen. Potassium is secreted into a favorable electrochemical gradient, and active transport is not required. Both K^+ and HCO_3^- can suffer dangerous shifts if normal colonic activity is hampered. Adequate K^+ replacement and careful management of pH changes are central to the eventual well-being of patients with chronic or acute diarrheal diseases.

The major absorptive processes occurring in the colon are active Na^+ reabsorption accompanied by passive flow of water and active Cl^- absorption coupled to HCO_3^- secretion. Close to 900 mL of fluid must be reabsorbed if body fluid balance is to be maintained. Anything which alters the normal colonic motility or the mucosal surface threatens to alter the sodium-water regulation in the colon. Likewise, if chyme reaches the colon poorly processed because of abnormalities of the upper tract, the colon may be unable to handle the increased load. Thus even a normal large intestine, if associated with diseased small bowel or stomach, or gastrointestinal surgery, may give abnormal results.

Colonic Flora

The colon distinguishes itself as a storehouse for various types of bacteria. The sluggish motility of the colon makes it a lush, pacific breeding ground for multiplying organisms. The enteric (relating to intestine) bacteria, especially *Escherichia coli,* are found in abundance throughout the colon. Other gram-negative rods, anaerobic species, and certain gas-producing organisms are present as well.

Certain of the colonic flora are responsible for

vitamin production. Vitamin K, essential to hepatic synthesis of blood clotting factors II, VII, IX, and X, is produced by certain flora of the large bowel. In addition, several B vitamins and folic acid are derived from bacterial metabolism.

Bacterial organisms are partially responsible for gas found in the intestine. Though 60 to 70 percent of the flatus passed comes from swallowed air, the remaining portion is contributed by bacterial fermentation. At any given time, the normal colon contains as much as 100 cm³ of gas.

THE LIVER AND THE ENDOCRINE PANCREAS

The Endocrine Pancreas

Earlier in this chapter, the structure and function of the exocrine pancreas were presented. To complete the discussion about the pancreas, brief mention will be made about the endocrine portion.

Microscopic inspection of pancreatic tissue reveals an intricate network of acinar glands and their connecting duct system. This is pertinent to the exocrine function of the gland and eventually connects with the small intestinal lumen.

The endocrine pancreas does not participate in this system. Instead, a separate collection of small islands of endocrine tissue are scattered throughout the gland (see Fig. 9-7). These islands are called *islets of Langerhans.* The endocrine pancreas constitutes 1 to 2 percent of total pancreatic weight. Normally the adult pancreas has 1 to 2 million islets. Though found throughout the gland, the tail of the pancreas has a higher concentration of islets than the body or head.

The islet has three main cell types, each responsible for secretion of specific products. The α-cell produces glucagon. The polypeptide insulin is secreted by the β-cells. The third cell type is the δ-cell. Its secretory contributions are controversial and still under investigation. Unlike the exocrine pancreas, the hormones of the endocrine pancreas, by definition, are secreted directly into the blood and not into a system of ducts.

Entire books have been written describing the detailed roles of insulin and glucagon. Since the primary concern here is basic gastrointestinal structure and function, discussion of the intricate biochemical workings of these two hormones will be left for another section. For the purposes here, it is sufficient to remember that insulin and glucagon are essential to the biochemical fate of fats, proteins, and especially of carbohydrates.

The Liver

Introduction

The liver, the largest gland in the human body, occupies an esteemed and essential role in body physiology. To even begin to understand hepatic structure and function, one must concentrate and focus on the detailed microscopic anatomy, the unique vascular circuits, and the endless, always interconnecting channels found throughout the hepatic parenchyma.

As an introductory text, the goal here will be to present certain salient features of the liver as they relate to unique hepatic functions. For the reader who wishes more detailed and specialized discussions, the medical literature is replete with books devoted solely to the liver.

The liver represents $\frac{1}{50}$ of total body weight in the adult. Functionally, this organ has five interrelated and yet anatomically definable components.

The *parenchymal liver cell,* or hepatocyte, is responsible for the major synthetic and storage functions of the organ.

A well-developed and extensive *reticuloendothelial system* throughout the liver provides an effective body-defense barrier against foreign intrusion. In fact, the defense system of the liver comprises some 60 percent of the total body reticuloendothelial system.

The *hepatic biliary system* is responsible for the synthesis and transport of bile salts and pigments to the gallbladder. The details of hepatic bile metabolism have already been presented in the context of fat digestion and absorption.

A vast *circulatory system* pervades the liver. One of the few organs with a dual blood supply, the liver must care for its own well-being and simultaneously deal with the metabolic end products of almost the entire gastrointestinal system and spleen.

Finally, the *connective tissue reticulum* of the liver provides the structural support for all the other components. A healthy hepatic reticulum promotes an environment for hepatocyte regeneration in cases of disease and injury. With absent or damaged connective tissue stroma, the normal liver architecture cannot be sustained and hepatic function becomes deranged.

Having already discussed the biliary system, four

remaining areas of hepatic function remain for discussion: the vascular system, the hepatocyte, the reticuloendothelial system, and the connective tissue stroma.

Before detailing the individual hepatic components, the gross and microscopic anatomy of the liver will be constructed. From that foundation, the remainder of the chapter will discuss each element with emphasis on important structural and functional relationships.

The liver is located in the right upper quadrant of the abdomen. Gross inspection reveals four incompletely separated lobes. The largest is the right lobe, followed in size by the left lobe. Two additional smaller lobes, the caudate and the quadrate, are also discernible. The entire organ is encapsulated by a thin connective tissue covering, Glisson's capsule.

The liver is attached to, and therefore moves with, the diaphragm. The porta hepatis is that area of the liver where the hepatic artery, the portal vein, and the common bile duct emerge from the liver.

Histology

Historically, several different, but not mutually exclusive, models have been offered to describe the microscopic anatomy of the liver. Each of the models stresses different hepatic structures as the focal point of a functional unit. All the models are correct; they merely present a varying perspective on the same question. Remembering that these various models exist, the *classic model* of microscopic liver anatomy will be presented here.

The classic lobule theory describes the functional units of the liver as hexagonal areas poorly demarcated by connective tissue septae (Fig. 9-14). The hexagon is more reproducibly outlined by a triad of structures at each of its six corners. The three structures, collectively referred to as a *portal triad,* are terminal branches of the hepatic artery, the portal vein, and the common bile duct. The center of the hexagon, or lobule, is marked by the central vein, the smallest division of the hepatic veins. Radiating from the central vein out to the portal area are rows of hepatocytes.

The Vascular System

The overall circulatory anatomy provides a dual blood supply to the liver. The hepatic artery, a vessel directly off the celiac trunk, carries fully oxygenated blood to the liver. The portal vein, carrying approximately 80 percent of the hepatic blood supply, is formed by the union of the splenic vein and the superior mesenteric vein. Portal blood is venous blood from the gastroin-

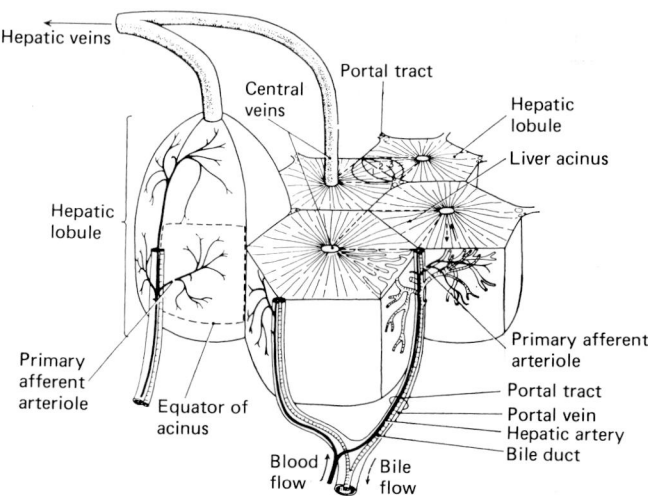

FIGURE 9-14

The classic hepatic lobule. (*Adapted from R. Passmore and J. S. Robson, A Companion to Medical Studies, vol. 1, Blackwell, Oxford, 1971. Reproduced with permission of the publisher.*)

testinal tract, spleen, and pancreas. Though less well oxygenated than blood in the hepatic artery, it is rich in absorbed nutrients and metabolic products from the alimentary tract.

After entering the liver at the porta hepatis, the hepatic artery and portal vein branch out into increasingly smaller tributaries which pervade the entire liver parenchyma (Fig. 9-15).

Anatomically, these vessels travel together and at one level of branching actually mingle their blood in the specialized hepatic capillary, or *sinusoid.*

At the sinusoid hepatocytes absorb what they need. The sinusoids then begin a reverse order of branching. The smallest and first order of branching is the central vein. From the central vein, branching continuously gets larger until finally the right and left hepatic veins emerge from the liver and empty into the inferior vena cava.

In summary, oxygenated blood in the hepatic artery and nutrient-rich venous blood in the portal vein enter the liver through the porta hepatis. Traveling together, this artery and vein arborize into successively smaller branches. Within the specialized hepatic capillary or sinusoid, mixing of arterial and venous blood occurs. The hepatocytes extract needed substrates. The central veins begin to reconstitute the venous system and eventually develop into the hepatic veins. Blood then returns directly to the inferior vena cava.

The tremendous number of vascular structures in the liver and the almost 1.5 L of blood flow per minute that it receives make the liver an unlikely place for tissue destruction from infarction. Contrary to this, trauma and/or lacerations involving the liver may cause massive blood loss, shock, and death.

Portal hypertension can be defined as an elevated pressure in the portal vein. It may result from any number of causes. The common denominator for all these conditions, however, demands that there be pre- or postsinusoidal obstruction to blood flow. Ascites will more commonly develop with postsinusoidal obstruction, however.

In the case of cirrhosis of the liver, the hepatic parenchyma is replaced by fibrous nodules of scar tissue. These areas of abnormal architecture disrupt the normal blood flow and, in essence, cause obstruction to flow. As the obstruction occurs, pressure in the portal vein increases. In an attempt to decrease pressure, blood flow is shunted back to the right heart by way of developing systemic collaterals. Increased vascular marking may be seen on the abdominal wall when collaterals involving the periumbilical veins develop. The collaterals involving the venous plexuses of the esophagus and the rectum cause esophageal varices and hemorrhoids, respectively. Rupture of these delicate and massively distended varices can cause death by exsanguination.

Another distinguishing feature of hepatic blood flow is the specialized capillary bed encountered in

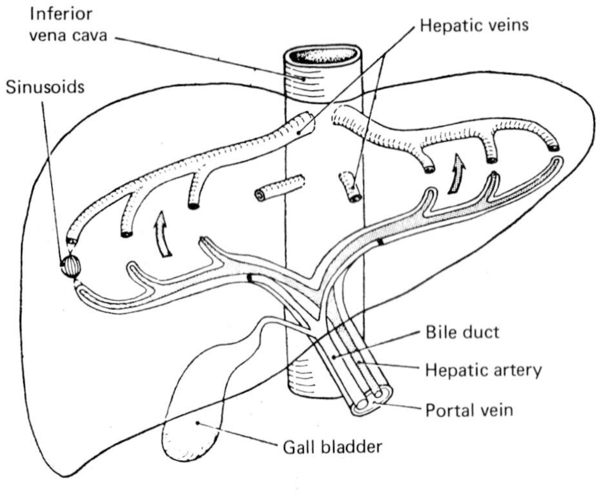

FIGURE 9-15

Hepatic circulation. (*Adapted from R. Passmore and J. S. Robson, A Companion to Medical Studies, vol. 1, Blackwell, Oxford, 1971. Reproduced with permission of the publisher.*)

the liver. Venous blood from the gastrointestinal tract, having already passed through one capillary network, is then filtered through the sinusoidal bed of the liver. Here at this second "capillary stop" the liver extracts needed substances from the rich venous blood. Likewise, products may be removed and detoxified, or newly synthesized compounds may be given up by the liver to the blood. It is an economical and efficient means of maximizing the various metabolic functions offered by the liver.

The Hepatocyte

The liver cell itself is polyhedral in shape. Hepatocytes comprise almost 80 percent of the total cell population within the human liver. Each hepatocyte is rich in intracellular organelles and enzymes. The span of diversified biochemical interactions occurring in the liver is extensive. Present space prevents an adequate discussion here.

The liver is responsible for the synthesis of clotting factors II, V, VII, IX, and X. It is needed for the conversion and inactivation of certain steroidal hormones and many medications. It is critical for carbohydrate synthesis and storage. Hepatic synthesis of plasma proteins such as albumin is fundamental to successful maintenance of body fluid balance.

Simply stated, the liver, or more specifically, the hepatocyte, is responsible for a host of anabolic and catabolic processes that are essential to life.

The hepatocytes are arranged as spokes radiating out from the central vein to the portal triads. They are organized as rows of cells supported by a meshwork of fine connective tissue. Two important anatomic relationships deserve emphasis.

First is the close proximity of the hepatocyte to the bile ductules. Every hepatocyte, on at least one of its sides, lies adjacent to a bile ductule (Fig. 9-16). The liver cell synthesizes bile and secretes it into the bile canaliculus. Communal surface area is therefore critical to an effective system of synthesis and transport.

The second point to note is the physical relationship of the hepatocyte to the sinusoid. Here again, every hepatocyte is in direct apposition to a sinusoid on at least one of its surfaces. As the bile ductule is the conduit for bile transport from the hepatocyte, the sinusoid is the transport vessel for all other hepatic metabolites. Maximal areas of contact are essential to the survival of the system.

The Reticuloendothelial System

The hepatic sinusoid is important not only for its role in the transport of metabolites, but also for its part in the reticuloendothelial system of the liver. The sinusoids are distinct from other capillaries in several ways. Most noticeable is the presence of phagocytic cells along the lining of the vessel. These specialized cells, called *Kupffer cells,* are active phagocytes rich in lysosomes (see Fig. 9-16). They ingest foreign matter, degenerated red blood cells, bacteria, and other metabolic degradation products. Remember, these Kupffer cells make up 60 percent of the total body reticuloendothelial system.

The Connective Tissue Framework

Covering the surface of the liver and throughout the organ, a vast network of connective tissue exists.

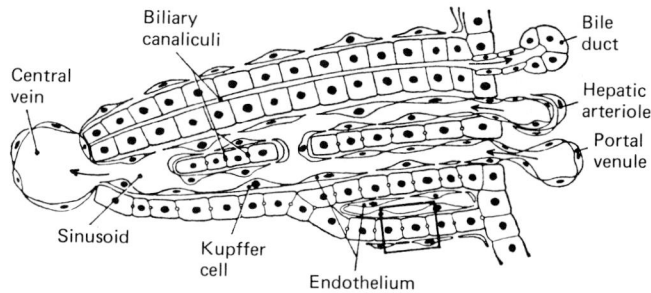

FIGURE 9-16

The anatomic relationship between hepatocytes, sinusoids, and biliary canaliculi. (*Adapted from R. Passmore and J. S. Robson, A Companion to Medical Studies, vol. 1, Blackwell, Oxford, 1971. Reproduced with permission of the publisher.*)

Though difficult to physically delineate, the resulting framework is essential to normal hepatic activity. Glisson's capsule envelopes the entire liver. Major areas of reticulum support are found around the structures of the portal triads and between rows of parenchymal cells.

The connective tissue component of the liver is important for another reason as well. The liver parenchyme has no pain fibers of its own. When a patient is found to have tenderness involving the liver, the pain actually results from stimulated pain-stretch receptors triggered by distention of the hepatic capsule.

In addition to providing structure for normal activity, the connective tissue elements take on a new importance when the liver is diseased. If the injury has been so extensive as to destroy the underlying framework, regeneration of parenchymal cells is retarded. The newly generated cells are arranged haphazardly and do not follow the original carefully built hepatic architecture. Hepatocytes may lose their proximity to sinusoids and bile canaliculi, thus decreasing the effectiveness of the liver's activities. Furthermore, normal vascular connections may be interrupted by injury-induced proliferation of connective tissue, e.g., cirrhosis. Postsinusoidal obstruction and portal hypertension may result.

Even from this brief outline and discussion of hepatic function one can see why so many investigators have dedicated years of study to the liver. Its intricate histologic and physiologic characteristics require full concentration if one is to understand them. Even to the pathologist, free to examine and inspect the minute intricacies of this organ, the liver remains a mystery. As Stanley Robbins has written: "Beneath the deceptively bland glistening capsule of Glisson that envelopes the liver lurks a bewildering host of functional and structural details."

The author acknowledges the assistance of Roger May, M.D., Department of Gastroenterology, Massachusetts General Hospital, in reviewing the manuscript of this section.

REFERENCES

Davenport, H. W.: *Physiology of the Digestive Tract,* 4th ed., Chicago: Year Book, 1977.

Guyton, A. C.: *Textbook of Medical Physiology,* 5th ed., Philadelphia: Saunders, 1976.

Robbins, S. L.: *Pathologic Basis of Disease,* Philadelphia: Saunders, 1974.

Schiff, L.: *Diseases of the Liver,* 5th ed., Philadelphia: Lippincott, 1975.

Sleisenger, M., and J. Fordtran: *Gastrointestinal Disease,* Philadelphia: Saunders, 1978.

Spiro, H. M.: *Clinical Gastroenterology,* New York: Macmillan, 1977.

Williamson, R., and M. Chir: "Intestinal Adaptation. I," *N Engl J Med* 298:1398–1402, 1978.

———— "Intestinal Adaptation. II," *N Engl J Med* 298:1444–1450, 1978.

The skin provides one of our major means of communication with the environment. Through it we experience some of our most pleasurable and most painful sensations. It can be a thing of beauty but also the focus of hours of anguished attention.

Nevertheless, among body organs it is the one most often overlooked and unobserved by health personnel. This is unfortunate because many subtle, yet significant, pathological changes within the body manifest themselves first in the skin. Personnel working with the critically ill patient will seldom care for a patient with a primary skin disorder but will frequently encounter one with skin disorders secondary to another disease or condition. They must be prepared to notice the subtle changes in the skin that reveal serious disease elsewhere. Scientific theoretical knowledge of the structure and function of the skin will provide a sound base for intelligent observations and decisions.

The skin has many functions. One of the most important is protection against infection by maintaining a physical barrier to keep out bacteria and other organisms. The structure of the skin also prevents loss of body fluids, a function essential to avoiding dehydration and maintaining the delicate fluid balance required by the body.

Body temperature is controlled by the increasing or decreasing evaporation of water from the sweat glands. The sweat glands excrete excess water and small amounts of sodium chloride, cholesterol, albumin, and urea.

The skin is an extensive sensory organ. Nerve endings located within the dermis convey impulses which indicate whether a stimulus is light touch, pressure, pain, heat, or cold, thus allowing us to modify our immediate environment to avoid damage or destruction.

The sebaceous glands protect the skin by secretion of oils which soften and lubricate. Vitamin D is made within the skin when sunlight reacts with cholesterol compounds.

The cosmetic effect of the skin varies from individual to individual and serves not only to identify by color but also by the various individual textures of skin, such as the whorls and patterns of fingerprints.

PHYSIOLOGY OF SKIN STRUCTURES

Although a fairly simple-appearing organ on the surface, the skin is very complex and comprises many components (see Fig. 10-1), all of which contribute

10
THE INTEGUMENTARY SYSTEM
Vera M. Harmon

PHYSIOLOGY OF SKIN STRUCTURES
The Epidermis
The Dermis
Subcutaneous Tissue
Appendages

SKIN FLORA

WOUND HEALING

REFERENCES

BIBLIOGRAPHY

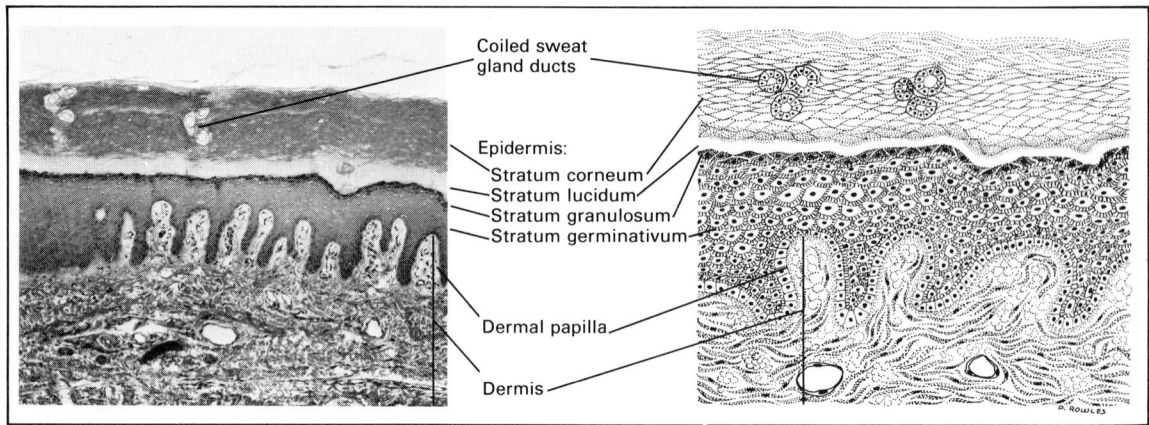

FIGURE 10-1

Cross section of the skin. (*From L. L. Langley, I. Telford, and J. Christensen, Dynamic Anatomy and Physiology, 5th ed., McGraw-Hill, New York, 1980. Used by permission of the publisher.*)

to its functioning. In this section each of these components will be addressed in some detail.

The Epidermis

The most superficial skin layer, the epidermis, is the one clearly visible to the naked eye (see Fig. 10-1). It is made up of four separate layers. The outermost layer, the *stratum corneum*, consists of stratified squamous epithelial cells which are constantly being shed by the body. When dry, the stratum corneum is hard and brittle; when wet, it is soft and pliable. It varies in thickness throughout the body, appearing noticeably thicker on the soles of the feet, the palms of the hands, and in areas exposed to friction and pressure.

The cells of the stratum corneum, as well as the entire epidermis, are primarily keratinocytes. Of the four layers of the epidermis, the only one capable of mitotic cell division, and thus production of keratinocytes, is the basal layer, or *stratum germinativum*. Here the daughter cells divide, providing a continuous source of cells. The cells then migrate through the prickle cell layer (*stratum spinosum*) and granular cell layer (*stratum granulosum*), where increased specialization and maturation occur. Once through these layers, the cells are packed into the stratum corneum and later shed. This process takes approximately 2 weeks from cell division to shedding. It is responsible for production of keratin and is referred to as *keratinization*. Keratin formation appears to be stimulated by shedding of the superficial layer (*desquamation*).

Keratin is the protein which gives the skin its special protective ability. It allows the body to retain fluids and prevents invasion from noxious agents in the environment. It also provides a barrier to electromagnetic waves (except ionizing radiation), microorganisms, parasites, and chemical agents.

Located in the basal layer of the epidermis are special cells called *melanocytes*. These cells produce *melanin*, the brown-black pigment of the skin. The melanin is taken up by the keratinocytes and thus migrates through the skin layers. While the number of melanocytes does not vary from race to race, the activity of the melanocytes does. Melanin formation is under the control of the pituitary gland and melanocyte-stimulating hormone (MSH). Melanocyte-stimulating hormone controls the clumping or dispersion of the melanin granules. The greater the dispersion of melanin, the darker the skin pigmentation.

The importance of melanin is related to its ability to screen out ultraviolet rays of the sun and prevent damage to the deeper structures of the skin. However, when exposed to ultraviolet rays in large quantities, melanin cannot absorb it all and a sunburn results. Ultraviolet light stimulates melanin production and darkening of already present melanin granules, producing a *tan*. Tanning then protects from further sunburn.

There are two more important points to keep in mind. First, although there are four identifiable layers in the epidermis, it is only the thickness of a sheet of paper on most parts of the body. Second, the epidermis has no blood supply or lymph channels of its own and is therefore dependent upon the underlying dermis for nourishment.

The Dermis

The *dermis* lies immediately adjacent to the basal layer of the epidermis (see Fig. 10-1). It varies in thickness from 1 to 4 mm, depending upon the site; it is thickest on the back, thighs, and abdomen. In contrast to the epidermis, the dermis is a semisolid connective tissue of fibers, cells, water, and ground substance.

There are three major types of fibers in the dermis. By far the most abundant and the one that gives the skin its mechanical strength is *collagen*. Production of collagen in the presence of vitamin C is essential to proper wound healing. Second are the *reticulum fibers*. These are probably precollagenous material since they are sparse in normal adults but plentiful in disease states and in the presence of wounds. Third, *elastin fibers* as their name indicates possess the property of elasticity. Although it has not been demonstrated that there is any direct connection between elastin fibers and collagen fibers, it may be that elastin fibers act to draw back stretched collagen fibers to their resting state. Thus it appears that the collagen fibers give the skin its strength, while elastin fibers allow it to return to a resting condition after deforming loads.

The *ground substance* of the dermis is a gelatinous, elastic material that provides an enclosure for the fiber network of the skin. The major components of the ground substance are mucopolysaccharides, which help the skin to resist compression and its fibers to regain their shape after extension.

Three types of cells are found in the dermis. The *histiocyte*, which is phagocytic and part of the reticuloendothelial system, stands ready to attack foreign substances. The *fibroblast* or *fibrocyte* is the master cell of the dermis, since it forms the reticulum and collagen fibers and the ground substance. It is also thought to have a phagocytic property. The third type of cell is the *mast cell*, which is rather specialized in nature. It is predominant around blood vessels and synthesizes and releases heparin. The mast cell also releases histamine when damaged and is present in large numbers when diseases that produce urticaria are present.

The dermis can be divided into two layers although there is no clear line of demarcation between the two. The top layer, or the one adjacent to the epidermis, is called the *papillary layer* because of the papillae that project from it into the epidermis. Beneath this layer lies the *reticular layer*.

One of the major functions of the dermis appears to be that of providing the nutrients and maintenance of the epidermis. It also plays a major role in wound healing and in the immune response. It protects the body from external injury and acts as a barrier to infection and as a water storage organ.

Vascular Network of the Skin

An important feature of the dermis is its vascular network. This network not only provides nourishment for and removes waste products from the cells, it plays a major role in regulating the temperature of the body as well.

The dermal vasculature is primarily composed of two plexuses: (1) the superficial plexus, located just beneath the papillary dermis; and (2) the deep plexus, located in the reticular dermis. These two plexuses are connected by communicating blood vessels (Fig. 10-2). Capillaries branch upward into the papillary dermis from the superficial plexus as well as into the tissue between the two plexuses. These plexuses are capable of holding large quantities of blood, which aids in the regulation of body temperature. In certain locations, *arteriovenous anastomoses* connect arterial vessels with the plexuses. These connecting vessels have muscular walls innervated by sympathetic vasoconstrictor nerve fibers. This arrangement allows direct regulation of the flow of blood from the arteries to the plexuses. Arteriovenous anastomoses are specific to the ears, nose, lips, hands, and feet, where extremes of temperature are most likely to be experienced.

The vasculature of the skin participates in thermoregulation by acting as a buffer between the external and internal environment of the body. The sympathetic nervous system controls the blood flow to the skin in response to core body temperature. This is accomplished by either vasoconstriction (i.e., decreasing the blood flow to the plexuses) or vasodilation (i.e., increasing the blood flow to the plexuses). Therefore, one would expect that as core temperature rises, vasodilation will occur and heat will be lost primarily through radiation as long as the ambient room temperature is lower than the body surface temperature. Heat loss will also occur because of conduction and convection under most normal circumstances, but these mechanisms are limited with the critically ill patient lying in bed. Heat loss by conduction, however, can be expected and

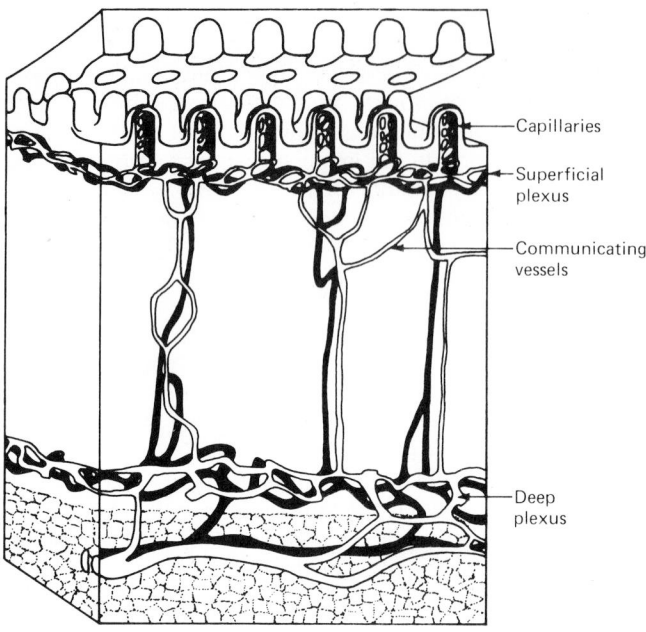

Capillaries

Superficial plexus

Communicating vessels

Deep plexus

FIGURE 10-2

Vascular network of the skin. (*From S. L. Moschella, D. M. Pillsbury, and H. J. Hurley, Dermatology, vol. 1, Saunders, Philadelphia, 1975. Used by permission of the publisher.*)

frequently takes place through the use of the cooling blanket or ice mattress. Heat loss by convection can be affected by creating air movement such as with a fan.

A secondary mechanism in the thermoregulatory function of the skin in terms of blood flow is related to the release of bradykinin from activated sweat glands. Bradykinin acts as a vasodilator when it diffuses into surrounding tissue.

The color of the skin is related to the state of blood in the superficial plexuses. Evidence of pathology is demonstrated by cyanosis, pallor, or flushing. Skin color will vary depending upon the rate of flow of the blood through the cutaneous vessels as well as the degree of oxygenation of the blood.

Cutaneous Innervation

The dermis possesses nerves and nerve end organs which are responsible for the variety of sensations that we experience when we interact with the environment. The dermis has a supply of both autonomic (efferent) nerves and sensory (afferent) nerve endings.

The autonomic nerves are nonmyelinated, while the sensory nerves are myelinated except for their termination point. Sympathetic fibers of the autonomic nerves supply the blood vessels, arrectores pilorum, and the sweat glands, both eccrine and apocrine. (See Fig. 10-3.)

An interesting point about sensory afferent nerves is that the same type of receptors are responsible for the sensations of touch, pressure, and vibration. Which sensation is felt depends on which tissue is stimulated, that is, the skin or deeper tissue such as muscle. Nevertheless, it is the sensory nerve network that gives us sensations of temperature, pressure, touch, vibration, and pain.

For a clearer presentation of the sensory innervation of the skin, it will be helpful to divide the content into three categories. These are (1) mechano-receptive-somatic senses, i.e., the tactile receptors, which provide us with sensation of touch, pressure, and vibration; (2) thermoreceptive senses, which detect heat and cold; and (3) the pain receptors.

There are at least four, or depending upon how you classify them, six, different types of tactile receptors in the skin. Free nerve endings or dermal nerve

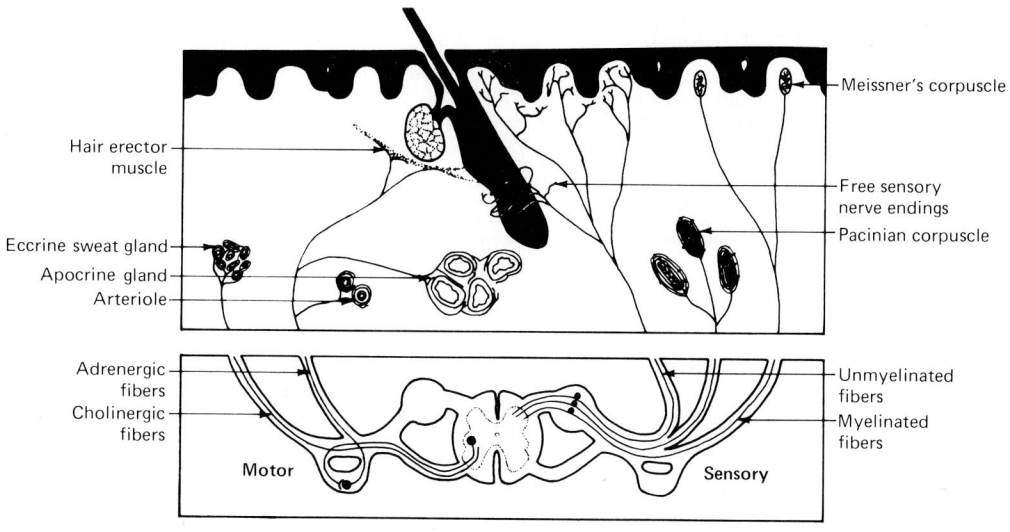

FIGURE 10-3

Innervation of the skin. (*From S. L. Moschella, D. M. Pillsbury, and H. J. Hurley, Dermatology, vol. I, Saunders, Philadelphia, 1975. Used by permission of the publisher.*)

networks are found everywhere in the skin as well as in many other tissues. These free nerve endings detect both touch and pressure. A second type of tactile receptor is *Meissner's corpuscle.* This is an encapsulated nerve ending which allows individuals spatial discrimination of touch. These endings are most abundant on the hands and feet and particularly the tips of the fingers and toes. They are also abundant on the lips. These receptors adapt rapidly and hence they are very sensitive to extremely light touch.

The same skin surfaces that contain large numbers of Meissner's corpuscles also possess expanded tip tactile receptors, one type of which is *Merkel's disks.* It is the combination of Meissner's corpuscles and Merkel's disks that is undoubtedly responsible for our ability to know textures of objects touched as well as where we are being touched. Merkel's disks adapt slowly and therefore allow a continuing perception of touch. Meissner's corpuscles are almost nonexistent on the hairy parts of the body, but there are a few expanded tip receptors located on these parts.

Hair end organs are a fourth type of tactile receptor. These receptors are located at the base of each hair and, when stimulated, allow detection of movement of the hair. They also are rapidly adapting. Located deeper in the skin as well as in deeper tissues are *Ruffini's end organs.* These receptors do not adapt rapidly and are therefore probably responsible for

providing information related to continuous states of alteration of deeper tissues.

The sixth and last type of tactile receptor to be discussed is the *pacinian corpuscle.* These are the largest end organs of the body and they are also located not only in the skin but in deeper tissues. They respond only by very rapid movement of the tissues because they discharge very rapidly and adapt in microseconds. They provide us with sensations of vibration and other rapidly changing mechanical states of the tissues. However, all tactile receptors provide some vibratory information.

Adaptation has been referred to several times in the preceding paragraphs. Perhaps a word of explanation about the word is warranted. When a receptor adapts, it ceases to become responsive to a stimulus, even when that stimulus continues. If a receptor is one that adapts rapidly, the response will cease almost immediately. A slowly adapting receptor will carry out a prolonged response.

Thermal sensations are mediated through cold receptors and warm receptors. Sensations of both extreme hot and cold are undoubtedly felt by the pain receptors as well as warm and cold receptors. However, the range of sensations from cool to cold are perceived only by cold receptors, and warm to hot are perceived only by warm receptors. Temperature gradations are perceived depending upon the receptors stimulated. A very cold temperature, for instance, is perceived through stimulation of pain receptors, while a neutral temperature would be perceived through stimulation of both warm and cold receptors.

Thermal receptors respond both to changes in temperature and to steady states of temperature. This explains why people feel much colder or warmer when a rapid change occurs than they would if it were that same constant temperature. An example of this is when you go from the cold outdoors to the warm inside. Initially you feel much warmer than you will after the thermal receptors have adapted.

Many authors are of the opinion that all free nerve endings are pain receptors and that when these nerve endings are sufficiently stimulated, pain as opposed to touch or pressure is sensed. Others are of the opinion that there are specialized pain receptors but

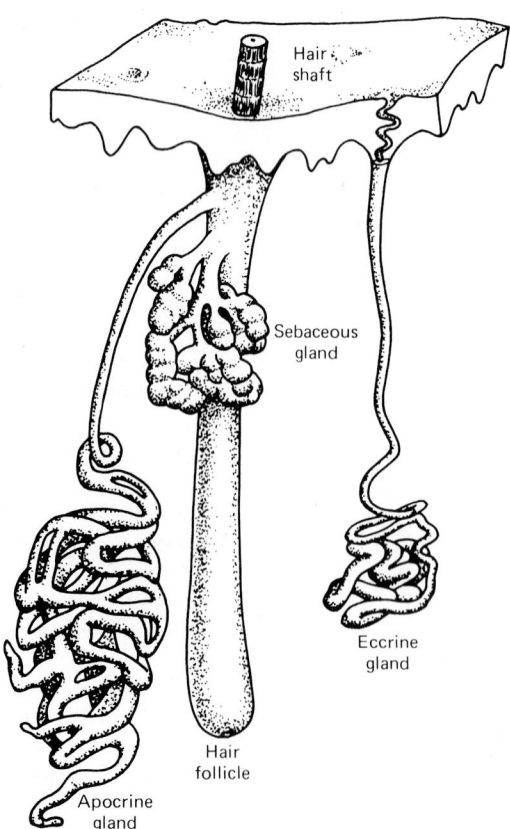

FIGURE 10-4

Sebaceous and sweat glands. (*From W. Montagna, The skin, Scientific American, vol. 212, February 1965. Used by permission of the publisher.*)

they have not as yet been identified. It is postulated that pain nerve receptors respond indiscriminately to any type of stimulus as long as it is sufficiently intense.

Sebaceous Glands

Sebaceous glands are found in the dermis and subcutaneous layers of the skin with their ducts opening onto the surface of the skin by way of the pilosebaceous canal (see Fig. 10-4). For this reason, they can be considered appendages of the hair follicle. The sebaceous glands are most numerous on the scalp, forehead, face, and chin, but are present over the entire body except for the soles and palms. They secrete sebum, which consists primarily of fatty acids, sterols, and lipids.

Sebum production varies with age, with highest secretions prior to birth and during adolescence. After menopause, sebum production is low, thus giving rise to the frequent complaint of dry skin in the older adult. For this reason, it is believed that there is some hormonal control to sebaceous gland activity.

In addition to the function of lubricating the skin, sebum is thought to be bactericidal in nature, therefore aiding in prevention of infection. Provitamin D is also found in sebum, and when exposed to ultraviolet light, it is transformed into vitamin D and absorbed by the body. Montagna and Parakkal (1974) speculate that the only real function of sebum is that of a pheromone (odor producer), thus aiding and abetting the apocrine sweat glands in producing body odors.

Subcutaneous Tissue

There is controversy about whether discussion of subcutaneous tissue or adipose tissue should be presented with a discussion of the skin. However, since it has some important functions that might be of interest to the critical-care nurse, it is included here.

The subcutaneous layer is located beneath the dermis. Lipocytes, or fat cells, arise from mesenchymal cells, which are the primary cells in the subcutaneous layer. The role of fat cells is to produce and store fat. The more cells that are present, the greater the potential for storing fat. A layer of subcutaneous fat is distributed over the entire surface of the body but varies in thickness between the sexes and at varying stages of the life cycle. Located in this layer are the tubules of the eccrine and apocrine sweat glands and the bulbs of hair follicles.

Functionally, the subcutaneous layer serves as a heat insulator, provides a cushioning effect to the body, and acts as a calorie reserve depot. The total effect of any of these functions is obviously directly related to the amount of adipose tissue present.

Sweat Glands

Sweat glands are found both in the dermis and in the subcutaneous layer. There are two types: the apocrine glands and the eccrine glands (see Fig. 10-4).

Eccrine sweat glands are present over the entire body with the exception of the mucocutaneous junctions and the ears. Areas such as the palms and soles, forehead, and axilla have higher numbers of glands than areas such as the legs and arms. All eccrine glands are present at birth, thus leading to decreased density as growth increases.

Production of eccrine sweat is precipitated by both thermal and/or psychic stimuli. However, the intensity of the stimulus plays a significant role in which areas of the body respond by sweating. For example, if the stimulus is thermal in nature, the forehead, neck, and dorsal and ventral aspects of the trunk are the first to respond. If the stimulus is intense, sweating of the palms and soles may occur. On the other hand, psychic stimulation, such as fear, will produce sweating of the palms, soles, axillae, and forehead. With extreme fear there may be stimulation of the trunk and neck.

The composition of eccrine sweat is 99 to 99.5 percent water and 0.5 to 1.0 percent solids, half of which are organic and the other half inorganic. The inorganic portion is primarily sodium chloride, and the organic portion is primarily lactic acid and urea. The pH of eccrine sweat is slightly acid—4.0 to 6.0.

Eccrine sweat glands have at least three functions in man, with the primary one being thermoregulation. When the *core* body temperature rises, a thermal stimulus is present and the body responds by sweating. Sweating allows the body to cool by evaporation. An unfortunate by-product of sweating is loss of sodium chloride, urea, lactic acid, and potassium ions. When the rate of sweating is low, the eccrine glands can accommodate and reabsorb most of the sodium chloride, urea, lactic acid, and potassium, thus causing minimal loss in the sweat. However, at rapid rates of sweating, large quantities of these substances are lost because the eccrine glands cannot reabsorb them quickly enough. Consequently, patients with high temperatures who are sweating profusely can be reducing body temperature and at the same time creating fluid and electrolyte problems.

Another function of eccrine sweat glands is related to its bacterial action either as an aid to the flow of sebum across the surface of the skin or directly as an antibacterial agent. Eccrine glands also function as excretory organs by helping to discharge waste products.

Apocrine glands, the larger of the two sweat glands, are located primarily in the urogenital areas, axillae, and breasts. They arise from and remain associated with hair follicles, opening into the hair follicle close to the skin surface. Apocrine glands do not respond to thermal stimulation but rather to psychic and emotional stimuli alone. Once mature, in adolescence, apocrine glands produce and store their secretions and under conditions of stress pour sweat out from storage. Once stimulated, a gland cannot respond again for 24 to 48 h.

Apocrine sweat is a milkish white fluid which is hypotonic and slightly alkaline in nature. It contains protein, reducing sugars, ferric iron, and ammonia. Secretions from these glands are responsible for the characteristic body odor resulting from sweating. The fluid is odorless as it is secreted, but when bacteria act upon the fat that it contains, it becomes odoriferous. The function of the apocrine gland in man is unknown (see Fig. 10-4).

Appendages

Hair

Hair in man is less functional than it is in lower animals, since it serves as protection in only limited areas of the body. However, it does participate in tactile sensation in all areas of the body where hair is present, regardless of kind.

Hair follicles are invaginations of the epidermis with a dermal papilla at the base. Each hair consists of an outer cuticle layer and an inner layer or cortex of keratinized cells. Melanin is present in pigmented hair, and terminal hair generally has a medulla. All hair follicles are present at birth, and this accounts for a decreased density as body growth occurs. There are estimated to be about 5 million hair follicles in an adult man.

There are three types of hair that have been identified. The first type is *lanugo,* which is a fine, soft, downy hair present only in fetal life. In postnatal life *vellus* hair, which replaces lanugo, is relatively uniformly distributed over the body. At specific times and sites *terminal* hair replaces vellus hair. Such sites are the eyebrows, eyelashes, and head. Terminal hair is often classified as sexual or asexual. Sexual hair is pubic, axillary, and body hair, while asexual hair is the hair around the eyes, the head, the arms, and legs. Sexual hair growth is clearly dependent upon sex hormones, since one sees the greatest increase in this hair growth during adolescence and the diminishing of hair in these areas after menopause.

Hair growth occurs in three phases in a cycle. Active hair growth is termed *anagen,* followed by a short transitional phase, or *categen. Telegen* is the resting phase. In man, hair follicles can be found in all phases of growth. Sources vary on how long each phase is, with some authorities stating that active growth occurs for 6 months followed by a period of rest and others suggesting that anagen lasts for 2 to 3 years followed by a 3- to 4-month rest period. The important thing to remember, however, is that the hair is most easily removed from its follicle during the rest period.

As noted earlier, hair in man does perform a protective function in some areas of the body. Hair on the head protects from trauma as well as from ultraviolet light radiation. The eyebrows provide physical protection for the delicate area around the eyes as well as divert sweat and water. Pubic and axillary hair serve to protect these areas by preventing direct skin contact. Sensation related to hair follicles was discussed earlier in the section on cutaneous innervation.

The Nails

The nails, more so than the hair, are an appendage of the skin which is of some import to the critical-care nurse. A number of internal diseases affect the nails, but perhaps more importantly, the nails reflect circulatory deficits.

The nail, like the hair follicle, arises from an invagination of the epidermis located on the dorsum of the terminal phalanx. Nails consist primarily of keratin but also have water, lipids, and minerals in small amounts. The nail consists of four parts: the nail matrix, nail plate, nail bed, and periungual tissue.

The nail matrix is the root of the nail and produces the nail plate or nail itself. The nail plate or nail is a horny, semiconvex, and semitransparent structure lying on the dorsal surface of the terminal phalanx. It is made up of two parts—the root, which cannot be seen, and the body, which can be seen. The nail plate varies in thickness and attains its maximum thickness on the distal or free end. The nail plate is situated on the nail bed to which it adheres. The nail bed's

primary function is in providing nutrition to the nail plate. Periungual tissue is composed of the eponychium and hyponychium. The eponychium is an extension of the roof of the nail fold proximally and covers a portion of the lanula (half-moon at base of nail) often referred to as the *cuticle.* Under the free margin of the nail lies the hyponychium.

The nail bed and nail matrix have a rich blood supply originating from branches of the digital arteries. Also present is a capillary loop system similar to that of the skin which supplies the nail fold. An abundant supply of glomus bodies are also present which regulate blood supply and skin temperature of the fingertips. These are the origins of splinter hemorrhages.

Unlike the hair, nail growth occurs continuously and uniformly. Variation in rate, however, is related to factors such as menses, biorhythms, nutrition, age, and activity of the concerned limb.

Protection of the delicate terminal phalanx is the primary function of nails in man. However, the nail does aid in picking up objects and is a great asset when one has an itch. When the nails are injured or diseased, however, the major complaint is related to appearance and not function.

SKIN FLORA

One of the greatest efforts of critical-care nurses is directed toward prevention of infection. Since the skin harbors many bacteria, some pathogenic and some not, a discussion of the skin would not be complete if consideration was not given this topic.

In a recent article, Kligman, Leyden, and McGinley (1976) proposed that skin flora could be divided into two categories. *Resident organisms* are those that are commonly found on the skin of most individuals and are able to multiply as well as survive on the skin. However, it is important to remember that resident flora are not necessarily the same for all individuals or all populations. The organisms in the second category can be classified as *contaminants*. Their numbers and kinds are directly related to the numbers occurring in the environment. The skin provides an excellent haven, albeit temporary, for numerous kinds of organisms, because it produces an abundance of substances that can be utilized as nutrients by microorganisms.

Microorganisms are located over virtually every millimeter of the skin. However, one can find certain varieties in one area which will be nonexistent in another area. Also, larger colonizations of some bacteria may be found in certain areas, although they may be present over most of the skin surface in some quantity. Sites which usually carry the highest colonizations are the perineum, scalp, face, hands, axilla, and intertriginous areas.

Resident flora can be primarily divided into gram-positive and gram-negative organisms. However, there is evidence that fungi, yeasts, and perhaps viruses colonize the skin. An example of these is the tinea microsporum, the fungus responsible for athlete's foot.

The most common of the resident flora of the skin are the gram-positive bacteria. *Staphylococcus albus* and *S. epidermidis,* which can be found in almost every region of the body, are representative of these. Their abundance leads to the speculation that their inhabitation prevents less desirable bacteria from taking up residence on the skin. *S. aureus,* a pathogenic gram-positive bacteria, is prevalent on the skin of some individuals. However, its presence to any degree is usually related to its abundance in the nasal passage or some focal lesion such as a carbuncle.

Other common gram-positive bacteria found on the skin are diphtheroids or corynebacteria, which are probably equal in number to the *S. albus* and *S. epidermidis* and are located on most areas of the body. However, *Corynebacteria acnes,* as its name implies, is implicated in acne following rupture of the comedones. It is located primarily in the acne areas, specifically in the sebaceous follicles.

Because the skin is relatively dry, gram-negative bacilli do not find it a particularly good place to set up residence and are therefore found only in small numbers which are probably directly related to their presence in the internal or external environment. A curious question arises here, though, and that is why they do not abound in the moist intertriginous areas. However, as suggested earlier, the abundance of the gram-positive inhabitants keeps the gram-negative in check.

Most of the resident flora do not cause disease, but they can and do under the appropriate circumstances. As indicated earlier, wiping out the normal flora can lead to inhabitance by pathogenic organisms. Also, since many pathogenic organisms are harbored elsewhere in the body in large quantities, such as the nose, throat, mouth, and bowel, any break in the integrity of the skin provides an opportunity for these organisms to multiply. Therefore, it becomes imperative that proper techniques be utilized when caring for any kind of skin wound.

WOUND HEALING

Since most patients being cared for by critical-care nurses have either traumatic or surgical skin wounds, it seems appropriate to include a discussion of wound healing at this time.

There is an orderly progression of a sequence of events that ultimately leads to healing of a wound. However, although there seems to be agreement upon what events occur during wound healing, there seems to be little agreement upon assigning names or identifying the different phases. Therefore, for purposes of this presentation, only the sequence of events will be described.

Initially, the process of hemostasis is set into action when a wound is first received. In this process, constriction and retraction of blood vessels occurs; hence bleeding of smaller vessels is controlled. Also set into motion is the aggregation of platelets to form clots in small arterioles and capillaries. Finally, as a result of a variety of enzymes being released, a cycle of increased permeability, more platelets, increased adhesion, and further local stasis is set up.

Quickly following hemostasis is a cellular response classically referred to as an *inflammatory response.* The first cells to arrive on the scene are leukocytes, which are phagocytic and bactericidal in nature. Their invasion causes an increase in hydrogen ions, which cause the death of the leukocytes and trigger the release of proteolytic enzymes. Monocytes and histiocytes appear at approximately the same time as the leukocytes, but they are able to survive in high concentrations of hydrogen ions. These cells act as reserve units and also set up a line of defense against infection. They have a role in the actual reconstruction process as well. When the inflammatory process begins to abort, fibroblasts and endothelial cells enter the wound area. These cells are responsible for the production of the granulation tissue, which is the foundation for the eventual scar tissue formation. Lymphocytes and mast cells are the last to arrive on the scene and serve very important functions. They are functional in the early phase of inflammation and also serve as the storage area for substances that will be used later on in the early stage of wound healing.

After approximately 3 to 4 days, new collagen fibrils are laid down which in several months will become mature connective tissue. Lastly, the process of epithelization of the wound provides a surface covering of the open wound. This results from the joining of a membrane that has formed on either side of the wound. Much time, upward to months or years, is needed for complete healing to occur.

There are several factors that can retard the process of wound healing. Besides the most obvious one of infection, rough handling and removal of surgical dressings as well as too frequent changing of dressings can cause actual physical removal of the new epithelial cells and thus retard the healing process.

Wound healing is dependent upon physiologic processes in the body. Although it would seem that wound healing would in some way depend upon circulating plasma proteins, this does not seem to be the case. If the protein level is low enough to cause a decrease in colloidal osmotic pressure, however, wound healing can be delayed. It has been found that low levels of the essential amino acid methionine, lack of vitamin C, and administration of high dosages of corticosterone and adrenocorticotropic hormone cause delayed and poor wound healing. Severe anemic anoxia of the cells due to decreased P_{O_2} of the erythrocytes may also cause delayed wound healing.

Wound healing may be classified in three different ways. The type that is most commonly used is healing by primary intention. This healing process is accomplished by approximating and holding together the two edges of the wound. Sutures are frequently used but need not be in all cases. Asepsis is of utmost importance, however. Another type is healing by secondary intention. These wounds heal without mechanical closure. The wound is simply dressed and granulation tissue is allowed to fill the space; this occurs from the bottom of the wound upward. Healing by tertiary intention is the last type of wound healing. This can be accomplished either by applying a skin graft or by waiting several days for granulation tissue to begin to form and then suturing the wound edges together. Obviously, healing by primary intention leaves a much smaller and smoother scar than either of the other two.

REFERENCES

Guyton, A. C.: *Textbook of Medical Physiology,* 5th ed., Philadelphia: Saunders, 1976.

Kligman, A. M., J. J. Leyden, and K. J. McGinley: Bacteriology, *J Invest Dermatol* 67:160–168, 1976.

Montagna, W., and P. F. Parakkal; *The Structure and Function of the Skin,* New York: Academic, 1974.

Moschella, S. L., D. M. Pillsbury, and H. J. Hurley: *Dermatology,* vol. I, Philadelphia: Saunders, 1975.

Nicola, P. D., M. Morsiani, and G. Zavogli: *Nail Diseases in Internal Medicine,* Springfield, Ill.: Charles C Thomas, 1974.

Odland, G. F., and J. M. Short: Structure of the skin, in T. B. Fitzpatrick, K. A. Arndt, W. H. Clarke, A. Z. Eisen, E. J. Van Scott, and J. H. Vaughan, (eds.), *Dermatology and General Medicine,* New York: McGraw-Hill, 1971, pp. 39–48.

BIBLIOGRAPHY

Dunphy, J. E. (ed.): *Wound Healing,* New York: MedCom Press, 1974.

Ferriman, D.: *Human Hair Growth in Health and Disease,* Springfield, Ill.: Charles C Thomas, 1971.

Menaker, L. (ed): *Biologic Basis of Wound Healing,* Hagerstown, Md.: Harper & Row, 1975.

Parrish, J. A.: *Dermatology and Skin Care,* New York: McGraw-Hill, 1975.

Stewart, W. D., J. L. Danto, and S. Maddin: *Dermatology: Diagnoses and Treatment of Cutaneous Disorders,* St. Louis: Mosby, 1974.

INTRODUCTION

As a unit, the human body's skeletal structure and muscular system give it the support and mobility required for an upright biped. Movement requires the presence of contractile elements that attach to the skeleton, cross joints, and coordinate skeletal parts to make purposive action possible. Mobility also relies upon supple joints and an intact nerve supply for voluntary control of musculoskeletal behavior.

In this chapter, the normal structure and function of the musculoskeletal system is presented. The importance of this system, both as an organ and as a structure, is emphasized because disorders of other body systems are often reflected in problems involving the musculoskeletal system as well.

THE SKELETAL SYSTEM

The skeletal system of the human body can be divided into two broad classifications: structure and organ.

Structure

As a structure, bone provides a rigid framework for the body; protects the viscera including the heart, lungs, brain, and spinal cord; and serves as a lever of skeletal muscle. Anatomically, bones are classified as *long, short,* and *flat*. Long bones are divided into a diaphysis (shaft) and two epiphyses (ends). Grossly, bone consists of a dense cortex externally and a spongelike interior. The medullary canal is located in the hollow shaft of long bones and contains marrow. Short bones are irregular in shape and have a spongy interior that houses the marrow. Short bones are found in the hands and feet. Vertebral bones are also examples of irregular short bones. The upper part of the skull is an example of a flat bone. Fig. 11-1 illustrates the different types of bone.

There is a fundamental difference between children and adults in terms of the outer membrane covering the cortex, the *periosteum*. In children, this covering is thick and loosely attached to the bony cortex and produces new bone readily; in the adult, the periosteum is thinner and more adherent to the cortex and produces new bone far less readily. This in part explains why fractures heal less rapidly in adults than in young children (Salter, 1970).

The histological structure of bone is categorized as immature and mature, both of which are different in content of collagen, cells, and mucopolysaccharides. Immature bone is very cellular and contains less

11
PHYSIOLOGY OF THE MUSCULOSKELETAL SYSTEM
Helen F. Ptak

INTRODUCTION

THE SKELETAL SYSTEM
Structure
Bone as an Organ
Bone Growth
Remodeling of Bone

JOINTS
Immovable Joints
Slightly Movable Joints
Freely Movable Joints

BURSAE

SKELETAL MUSCLE
Anatomy and Histology
Muscular Contraction
Types of Muscular Contraction

TENDONS AND LIGAMENTS

REACTIONS OF THE MUSCULOSKELETAL TISSUES TO ACUTE DISORDERS AND INJURIES
Reaction of Bone
Reaction of Epiphyseal Plates
Reaction of Synovial Joints
Reaction of Synovial Membrane
Reaction of Joint Capsule and Ligaments
Reaction of Skeletal Muscle

DEFORMITIES OF THE MUSCULOSKELETAL SYSTEM

REFERENCES

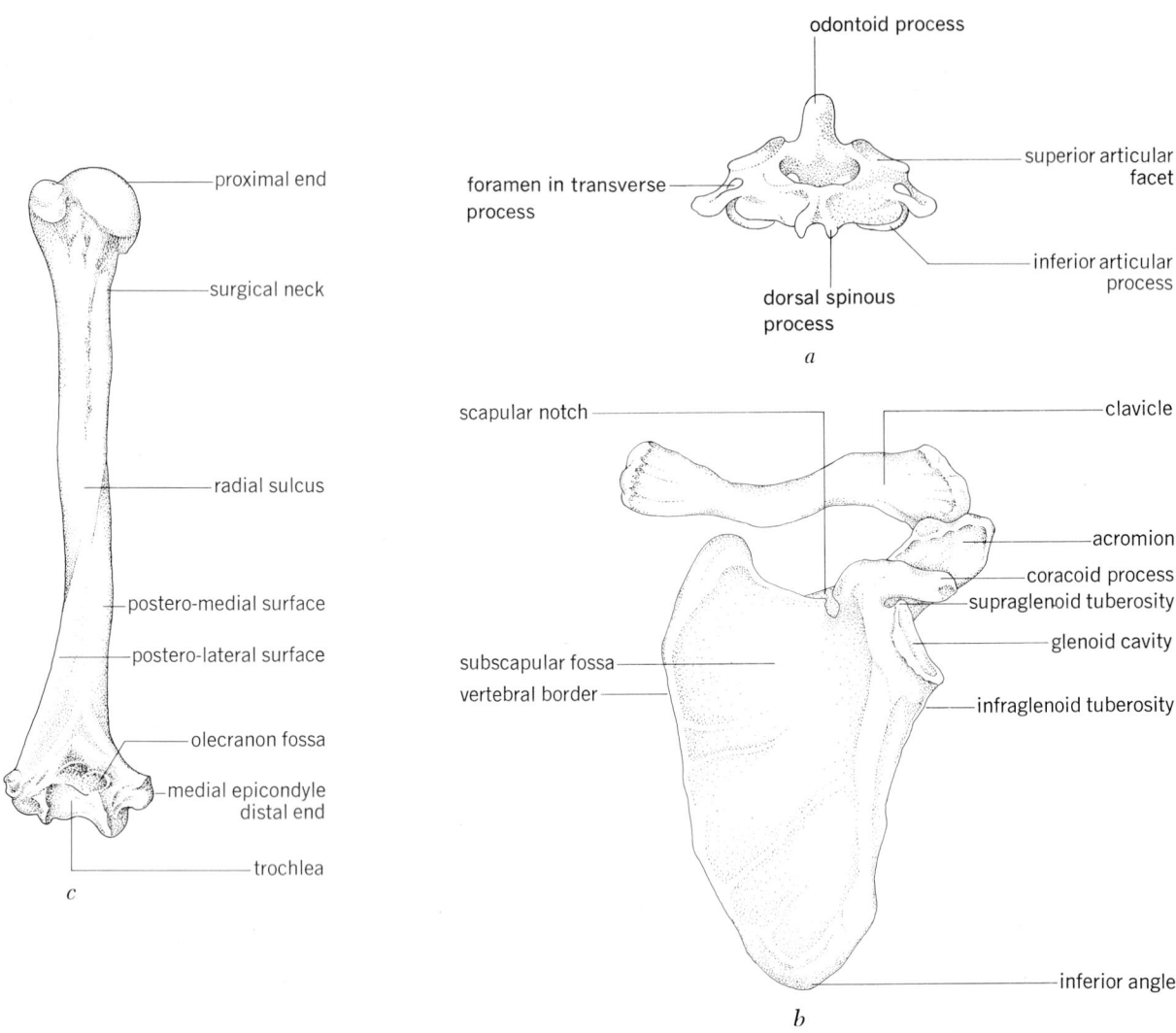

FIGURE 11-1

Types of bones: (*a*) an irregular, short bone (a vertebra); (*b*) a flat bone
(the left scapula, anterior view); and (*c*) a long bone (the left humerus,
posterior view). (*From R. M. DeCoursey, The Human Organism, 4th ed.,
McGraw-Hill, New York, 1974.*)

cement substance as well as less mineral than mature
bone. The first bone formed during embryonic development is of the immature type. It is gradually replaced
by mature bone during the first year of life. However,
under any abnormal condition in which new bone is
formed rapidly, such as in the healing process of a
fracture, the first bone formed is of the immature type
and is subsequently replaced by mature bone.

Mature bone is less cellular than immature bone.
Its dense cortex is characterized by an arrangement
of layers called *lamellae* and by the presence of
haversian systems, which consist of minute channels
penetrating the dense outer cortex. It is through this
unique system that the bony tissue comes in contact
with the blood vessels and nerves which traverse the
channels. This arrangement makes it possible for

blood circulation to exist within the mass of cortical bone. In bones in which marrow exists, blood vessels within the haversian channels offer access to it. In mature cancellous bone, the arrangement of the bony layers is less complex and bone is nourished by surrounding blood vessels in the marrow space.

Bone as an Organ

As an organ, bone functions as a storage area for specific inorganic substances and contains hemopoietic tissue responsible for the production of erythrocytes, granular leukocytes, and platelets. Structural bone changes take place relatively slowly, while microscopic changes take place within bone rapidly because of the active functioning of bone as an organ. The biochemical composition of bone consists of 45 percent *inorganic* substances, 35 percent *organic* substances, and 20 percent *water*.

Inorganic Substances

The inorganic substances of bone include *calcium, phosphorus, magnesium, sodium, fluoride, hydroxyl,* and *carbonate*. Collectively, these minerals form a calcium salt, which in turn forms crystals which become the noncellular building material of bone. Bone crystal is generally considered to be a *hydroxyapatite*.

Calcium and phosphorus are the two most important inorganic substances of bone. The body of a 70-kg man contains about 1100 g of calcium of which more than 99 percent is found within the body skeleton. The remaining relatively small amount of calcium is carried in the plasma. About 40 percent of this amount is carried in combination with plasma albumin, while the remaining 60 percent is carried in solution in free ionized form. It is this ionized form which is essential to specific physiologic processes of bone formation, blood coagulation, neuromuscular transmission, muscular irritability or exitability, acid-base balance, cell membrane permeability, and adhesiveness between cells. The concentration of total calcium in the plasma is normally maintained within narrow limits (9 to 11 mg per 100 mL), and it is the total plasma calcium which is measured by generally available biochemical techniques (Kelman, 1975).

On a normal diet, an individual's intake of calcium is approximately 1000 mg per day. Of this intake, about 100 mg is actively absorbed from the jejunum and duodenum in the presence of *vitamin D* and then either retained in the body or excreted in the urine,

depending on whether or not the body is in calcium balance. The remainder of the ingested calcium is excreted in the feces. When the body is in calcium balance, urinary loss is equal to the net rate of calcium absorption from the intestinal tract. When the body is in negative balance, urinary calcium excretion exceeds net intestinal absorption. During periods of rapid growth, positive calcium balance exists and urinary excretion is less than net intestinal absorption.

The absorption of calcium from the intestinal tract is dependent upon the activity of vitamin D, normal gastric acidity, and the presence of *lipase*, a pancreatic enzyme necessary for the digestion of fatty acids. This latter factor decreases the possibility of fatty acid combination with calcium in the small intestine, resulting in an insoluble calcium soap (Salter, 1970).

In the absence of vitamin D, very little calcium absorption takes place. In the presence of adequate amounts of this vitamin, it is virtually impossible to cause calcium deficiency *by dietary means alone*. In patients with calcium-deficient bone, vitamin D promotes calcium deposit and skeletal recalcification, but in a normal person, the administration of excess amounts of this vitamin may cause skeletal *demineralization* with *hypercalcinuria* and *metastatic deposition* of calcium in soft tissues.

Recently it has been found that vitamin D metabolism is much more complex than was formerly thought (Kelman, 1975). *Cholecalciferol* is first converted in the liver into *25-hydroxycholecalciferol,* and then this substance is further hydroxylated into the active metabolite *1,25-dihydroxycholecalciferol*, by the kidneys. The rate of renal conversion into this metabolite is under the control of a variety of factors, particularly the level of *parathyroid hormone* in the peripheral blood. A decrease in the level of circulating calcium causes release of parathyroid hormone, enhancing renal production of 1,25-dihydroxycholecalciferol; this in turn causes an increase in the absorption of calcium from the small intestine, restoring plasma calcium levels. The plasma calcium concentration is normally maintained within its narrow limits by the activity of the parathyroid hormone and *calcitonin*. Generally, these two hormones have opposing actions relative to bone. Parathyroid hormone not only influences the rate of 1,25-dihydroxycholecalciferol, as discussed, but is also responsible for promoting calcium resorption from bones in the presence of vitamin D, thereby raising plasma calcium concentration. This hormone is not secreted when the plasma calcium concentration *exceeds* 12 mg per 100 mL.

Parathyroid hormone also increases renal phosphate excretion by decreasing tubular reabsorption of this mineral and at the same time increases renal calcium reabsorption. It should be noted, however, that because of increased plasma calcium levels, renal calcium excretion is usually increased rather than decreased.

Excess secretion of parathyroid hormone can produce *hypercalcemia* and *hypophosphatemia* along with a marked increase in urinary excretion of both calcium and phosphate, resulting in a negative calcium balance. Extensive skeletal demineralization and soft tissue calcium deposition are results of this problem.

Calcitonin, like parathormone, is a polypeptide which is produced in the thyroid gland. Its release is stimulated in response to an increased plasma calcium concentration and inhibited by a lowered plasma calcium level. It acts by inhibiting bone calcium resorption by lowering the plasma calcium level. Calcitonin also inhibits tubular calcium reabsorption to some extent.

Organic Substances

The organic substances of bone include the bone cells—namely, the *osteoblasts, osteocytes,* and the *osteoclasts*—which are responsible for the process of bone formation and resorption referred to as *remodeling*. Other components include the *matrix* or organic intercellular substance. Collagen fibrils constitute about 97 percent of the organic matrix. The remaining 3 percent consists of a homogenous medium referred to as *ground substance*. This latter material is composed of extracellular fluid plus mucoproteins, hyaluronic acid, and chondroitin sulfuric acid. The precise function of this substance is unknown, but it is theorized that it assists in providing a medium for deposition of calcium salts.

Bone Growth

Bones grow in *length* and *width* by two different processes: *endochondral ossification* and *intramembranous ossification*. Bone can grow in length only by the process of interstitial growth within the cartilage followed by the endochondral ossification process. The two sites in which such growth occurs are the *articular cartilage* and *epiphyseal plate cartilage* (see Fig. 11-2).

In short bones, the articular cartilage is the only growth plate for the entire bone, while in long bones,

this cartilage provides the growth plate for the growth of its epiphysis. Growth in length of the metaphysis and diaphysis of the long bone is provided by the epiphyseal plate cartilage. Here a constant balance is maintained between the interstitial growth of the cartilage cells of the plate and calcification, death, and replacement of cartilage on the metaphyseal surface through the endochondral ossification process. This interstitial growth makes the bone thicker and thus moves the epiphysis further away from the metaphysis (Salter, 1970).

Bone grows in width by the process of intermembranous ossification in which there is additive growth due to the osteoblasts in the deep layers of the periosteum. The clavicle and most of the skull develop bone directly by this process without going through the cartilaginous phase. At the same time, osteoclastic resorption of bone occurs on the inner surface of the bony cortex, which is lined by endosteum, producing an enlargement of the medullary canal.

Remodeling of Bone

Normally, bone is in a state of dynamic equilibrium undergoing constant formation and resorption. The formation of bone begins as a gelatinous, protein, latticelike matrix called *osteoid*, which is produced by the active bone-forming cell, the osteoblast. The osteoblasts secrete the enzyme *alkaline phosphatase*, which is concerned with the calcification of the matrix. This enzyme functions by liberating inorganic phosphate ions from organic phosphate compounds present in the circulation, causing a high concentration of phosphate ions to accumulate at the site of bone formation. Calcium phosphate salts are deposited when local concentrations of calcium and phosphate ions become so high that the ions can no longer remain in solution, causing calcium phosphate precipitation into the matrix, resulting in calcification. Once calcification occurs, the osteoid becomes *bone*.

It should be noted that only ionized mineral elements, which compose only a portion of plasma calcium and phosphorus, can be utilized for ossification. The ionized calcium in the plasma rises in acidosis and decreases with a rise in blood protein. The acidotic condition will increase solubility of calcium carbonate and cause bone demineralization.

As bone matrix is formed and calcified, some of the osteoblasts become surrounded by organic intercellular substances and are incorporated into bone cells called *osteocytes*. The osteoblasts that remain

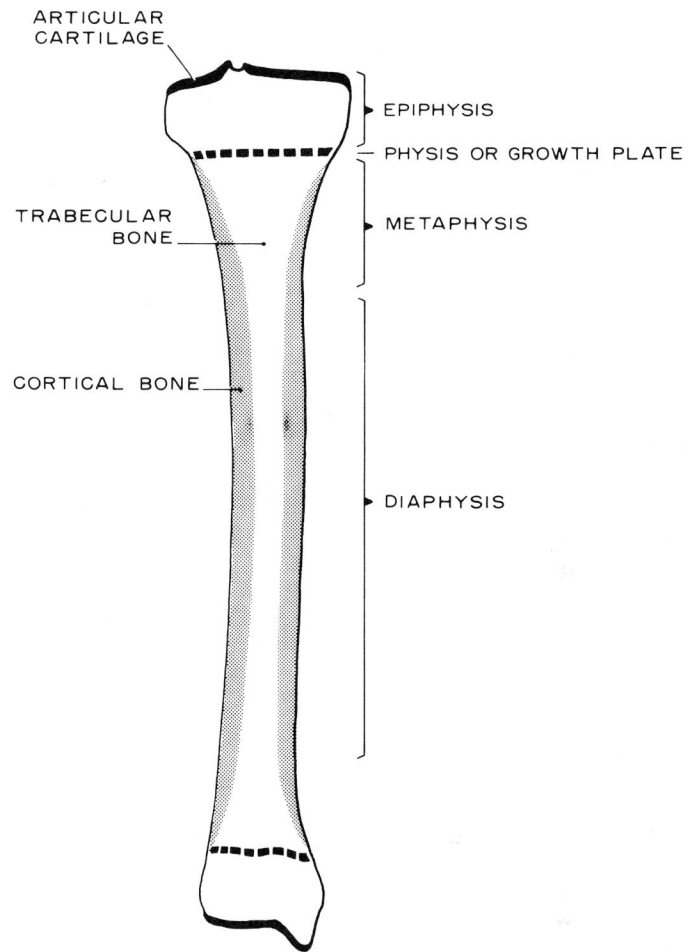

ARTICULAR CARTILAGE

EPIPHYSIS

PHYSIS OR GROWTH PLATE

TRABECULAR BONE

METAPHYSIS

CORTICAL BONE

DIAPHYSIS

FIGURE 11-2

Structure of a long bone. (*From S. Price and L. Wilson, Pathophysiology, McGraw-Hill, New York, 1978.*)

on the surface after their period of collagen synthesis is completed become the lining cells.

The osteocytes are located in the lacunar spaces and have long cytoplasmic process exposed to the fluid bathing the bone surfaces. These cells play a role in the cellular response to hormones involved in calcium homeostasis.

Osteoclasts are large, multinucleated cells which lie on the uncovered bone surface and are concerned with bone resorption or removing bone. These cells remove the organic matrix and the calcium simultaneously by phagocytosis. The bone salts are dissolved, releasing calcium and phosphate ions into the circulation for excretion or for other uses. Bone tends to remain healthy when there is a balance between these two antagonistic cell types.

Bone remains in relative proportions through remodeling. In this way, the general relationship of the medullary cavity to the entire bone diameter remains fairly constant in infant or adult. The process of remodeling includes the shaping of both the interior and exterior of the bone. This is accomplished by a constant interplay of bone absorption and bone formation.

As bone grows in length, the metaphyseal regions are continually being remodeled as the epiphysis moves farther away from the shaft. Simultaneously, there is an accompanying osteoclastic resorption on the opposite surface.

Remodeling continues throughout the life span, since some haversian systems are being continually eroded through the death of cells as well as through the removal of calcium from bone. Bone deposition also continues in order to maintain bone balance. During the rapid growth in children, bone deposition exceeds bone resorption and the child is in a state of positive bone balance. As old age approaches, however, bone deposition no longer keeps pace with bone resorption and elderly individuals are in a state of negative bone balance.

The *presence* or *absence* of *physical stress* also is responsible for the remodeling process. Bone is deposited in sites subjected to stress and is resorbed from sites where there is relatively little stress.

JOINTS

A joint is the place where bones articulate with each other. Joints are classified according to the amount of movement allowed, namely, *immovable, slightly movable,* and *freely movable.*

Immovable Joints

Immovable joints do not allow movement because the ends of the bones are bound together by fibrous tissue, cartilage, or bone tissue. Bones bound together by fibrous tissue alone are referred to as *syndesmosis* joints. An example of this type of joint is the suture joint between skull bones which affords protection to the underlying brain tissue. Bones bound together by cartilage are called *synchondrosis* joints. A typical example of such a joint is the epiphyseal plate which binds the epiphysis to the metaphysis in long bones thereby permitting growth in bone length. A third type of immovable joint is referred to as *synostosis*. This type of joint is bound together by bone tissue in that at some stage it has become obliterated by bony union. *Some* syndesmoses and *all* synchondroses eventually fuse.

Slightly Movable Joints

A type of slightly movable joint is the *symphysis*, in which two opposing surfaces are covered by hyaline cartilage and joined by fibrocartilage and strong fibrous tissue. An example of this type of joint is the intervertebral disk located between each vertebra of the spinal column. Another example is the fibrocartilaginous disk located in the joint between the pubis bones of the pelvic girdle called the *symphysis pubis*.

Freely Movable Joints

Freely movable joints permit a great amount of movement because of their structure. This type of joint is referred to as *synovial*. A cavity, present between the ends of bones, is lined with a synovial membrane. Synovial fluid is secreted by this membrane. The various anatomical structures of a typical synovial joint are shown in Fig. 11-3. One joint surface is always convex and is larger than the opposing joint, which is concave. This structure allows the joint to glide. Articular cartilage, which is resilient like rubber, lines each joint surface. The synovial membrane not only secretes fluid but also has the ability to absorb. The outer fibrous capsule becomes thickened in some areas and forms strong ligaments which assist in providing a degree of joint stability. Most of the joints in the body are of the synovial type and are divided into five subgroups. These subgroups are listed below along with examples of each.

1. Saddle joint—the thumb joint
2. Hinge joint—the knee, elbow, and ankle
3. Pivot joint—the atlas vertebra
4. Gliding joint—the carpal bones of the wrist
5. Ball-and-socket—hip and shoulder joints

Myelinated and nonmyelinated nerve fibers traverse the synovial joints and terminate in the fibrous capsule. The myelinated fibers are particularly sensitive to twisting and stretching of the capsule and to increased fluid pressure within the joints.

Synovial Fluid

Synovial fluid not only lubricates joint surfaces but also nourishes articular cartilage lining each joint surface. A normal joint, like the knee, contains relatively little fluid, and thus the true joint space is virtually a potential space.

Synovial fluid contains a mucin, *hyaluronic acid,* which is produced by cells of the synovial membrane and is responsible for the viscosity of the fluid. Cells within the fluid are predominantly monocytic macrophages and lymphocytes with a small percentage of polymorphonuclear leukocytes. Particulate matter, such as *hemosiderin* from a joint hemorrhage, is removed from the synovial cavity through the phagocytosis of macrophages, but such matter may remain in the synovial membrane and tissues for a relatively long period of time. Synovial fluid does not contain fibrinogen, which may explain why normal synovial fluid does not clot. Blood mixed with synovial fluid also does not clot.

BURSAE

A bursa is a small sac filled with synovial fluid and lined with synovial membrane. The bursae are found between structures that rub against each other. Examples include the *prepatellar bursa*, located between the skin and the kneecap, and the *subdeltoid bursa*, located between the deltoid muscle and the head of the humerus. These structures act as cushions to reduce friction between two moving parts.

SKELETAL MUSCLE

One of the most important effector systems in mammalian organisms is the skeletal musculature. The primary function of this system is reaction to changes in the external environment that will affect the rapid contraction of these muscles indirectly via the central nervous system, producing a movement of the whole or part of the body.

Most skeletal muscle is attached to bone, and the contraction of this skeletal muscle is responsible for movements of parts of the skeleton. Skeletal muscle movement is also involved in other activities of the body such as voluntary release of urine and feces.

There are over 600 skeletal muscles in the human body which are responsible for the active movement of the skeleton as well as for the maintenance of body posture. The basic property of skeletal muscle is *contractility*, which enables the muscle to shorten and thereby provide movement (isotonic contraction) or to resist lengthening without allowing movement (isometric contraction).

Each skeletal muscle has three functional parts: *origin, insertion,* and *action*. Generally, the origin end remains motionless while the insertion end moves a bone.

Anatomy and Histology

A typical skeletal muscle is composed of many multinucleated cells referred to as *muscle fibers*. These cells contain structures similar to those found in many other body cells, but also some specific to skeletal muscle (Fig. 11-4). Among the familiar struc-

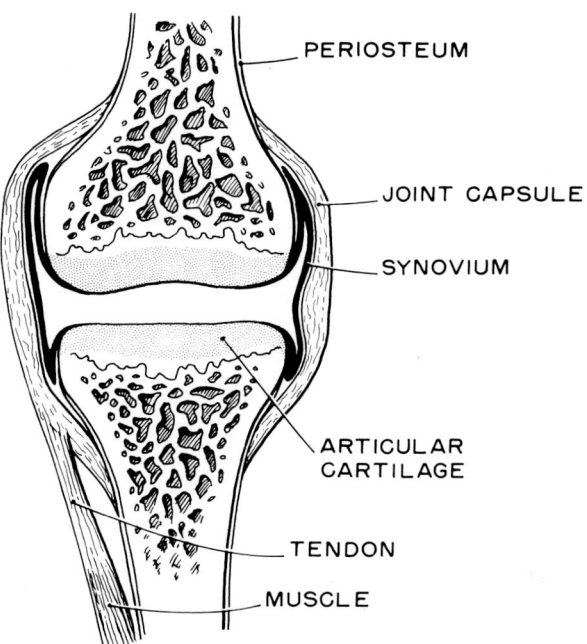

FIGURE 11-3

Anatomical structure of a typical synovial joint. (*From S. Price and L. Wilson, Pathophysiology, McGraw-Hill, New York, 1978.*)

tures are a cell membrane, which in muscle cells is called the *sarcolemma*. The cytoplasm is known as the *sarcoplasm* in the muscle cell. The endoplasmic reticulum is called *sarcoplasmic reticulum* in the muscle cell.

The sarcoplasm of the skeletal muscle cell contains approximately 20 percent protein. *Actin* and *myosin* are the major proteins. They interact to form *actomyosin* during muscular contraction. About 5 percent of the sarcoplasm consists of glucose, glycogen, lipids, inorganic salts, adenosine triphosphate (ATP), phosphocreatine, and small amounts of other substances. The remainder of the sarcoplasm is water.

The sarcoplasmic reticulum is a system of membranes that, among other things, stores and releases calcium ions necessary for the initiation of muscular contraction.

Myofibrils are a special feature of skeletal (and cardiac) muscle cells. These elongated structures, composed of actin and myosin filaments, give the muscle cell its striped (striated) appearance. The darker regions of the cell are called *A bands* and represent a great many thick myosin filaments in precise alignment along with the thinner actin fila-

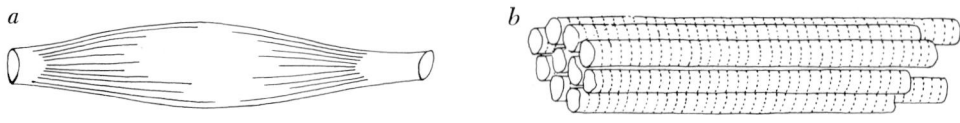

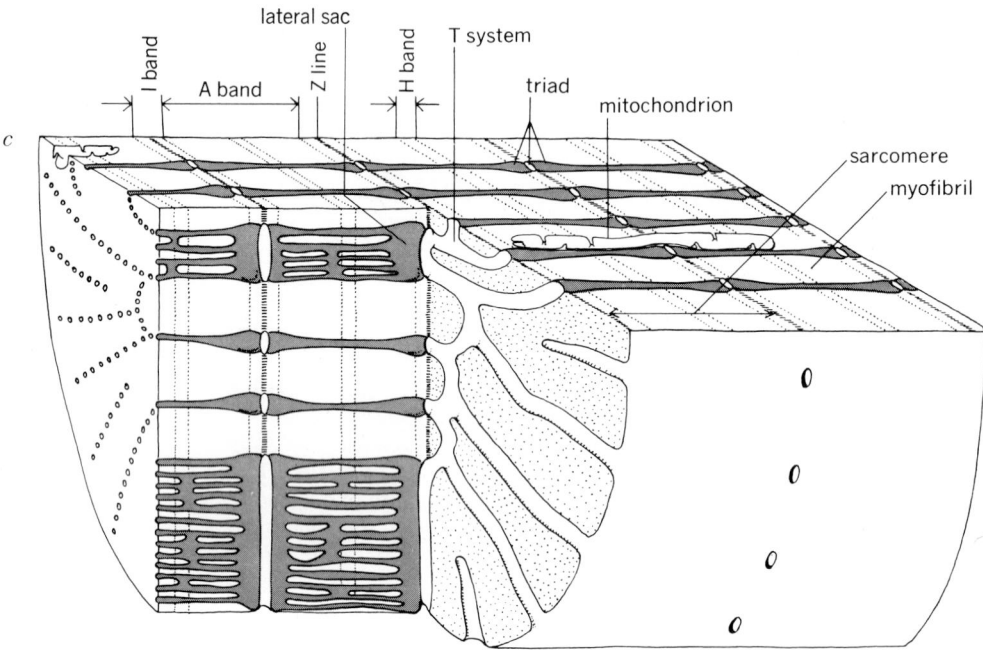

FIGURE 11-4

Structural components of skeletal muscle. (*From R. M. DeCoursey, The Human Organism, 4th ed., McGraw-Hill, New York, 1974.*)

ments. The lighter regions, called *I bands*, consist only of aligned actin filaments. One end of each actin filament inserts into a boundary structure known as the *Z line*. Each Z line gives rise to actin filaments on both of its faces. The actins extend partway across to the neighboring Z line. The portion of the myofibril from Z line to Z line is known as the *sarcomere* and is the basic contractile unit.

The actin filaments are interspersed with the myosin filaments in a regular way. If a sarcomere is looked at in cross section, it can be seen that each large myosin is surrounded by six thin actin filaments in a hexagonal arrangement.

Muscular Contraction

A muscle cell is stimulated to contract by a nerve impulse, which arrives along the axon of a motor neuron. The axon distributes branches among the fibers of the skeletal muscle it serves. The ending of each branch is separated from the sarcolemma by a small gap, the *synaptic cleft*. With the ending are numerous small vesicles that contain the neurotransmitter *acetylcholine*. When a nerve impulse arrives at the ending, some of the acetylcholine is released and diffuses across the synaptic cleft. Reaching the sarcolemma, it combines with receptor sites there. This causes changes in the sarcolemma's permeability to sodium and potassium and triggers an impulse which spreads through the sarcolemma.

The nerve impulse reaches the sarcomeres through *T tubules*. These are infoldings of the sarcolemma that tunnel entirely through the muscle cell. The final ingredient, calcium ions, is supplied by the sarcoplasmic reticulum, which is wrapped like a sleeve around each sarcomere.

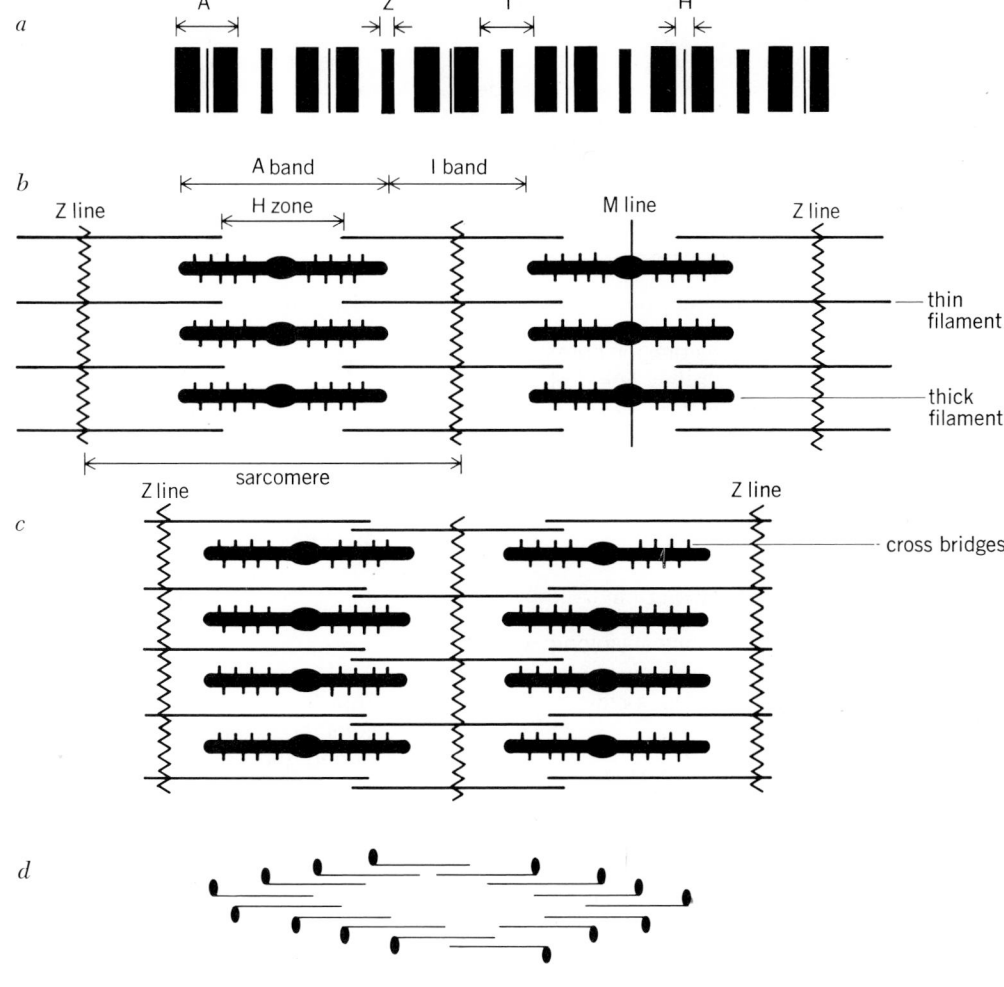

FIGURE 11-5

Sliding filament theory of muscle contraction. (*From R. M. DeCoursey, The Human Organism, 4th ed., McGraw-Hill, New York, 1974.*)

When the nerve impulse reaches the sarcomeres, there is a release of calcium ions. This stimulates the breakdown of ATP molecules. Splitting of ATP brings about the release of energy needed for the reaction between myosin and actin filaments. The myosins break free from the actins, then reattach themselves, repeating the sequence in rapid-fire order. In this way, the actin filaments are brought sliding past the myosin filaments and the Z lines are drawn toward each other. This is the *sliding filament hypothesis* of muscle contraction (Fig. 11-5).

As its sarcomeres contract, the muscle cell contracts. When this occurs in many muscle cells contraction of the entire skeletal muscle takes place.

Each cell (fiber) obeys the "all or none" law in that it either contracts fully or not at all. However, not all fibers necessarily contract at once. Increasing degrees of muscular effort enlist larger numbers of fibers.

Energy Sources for Muscular Contraction

The immediate source of energy utilized for muscular contraction is the breakdown of high-energy bonds of the ATP molecule into adenosine diphosphate (ADP), phosphate, and energy. A portion of the resultant energy is used to contract the sarcomere of the muscle as described. The remainder of the energy is dissipated as heat.

In order for muscular contraction to continue, ATP needs to be replenished. The entire cycle is made up of three phases in which ATP, phosphocreatine, and glycogen are broken down and resynthesized. Figure 11-6 illustrates this cycle. Glycogen is the ultimate source of energy for *convulsions* and *spasms*.

Types of Muscular Contraction

Tonic Contraction

Tonic contraction is responsible for normal muscle tone and occurs when only a few fibers of a muscle contract. This type of contraction keeps the muscle firm but does not stimulate movement. Muscle tone decreases when individuals use their muscles less, as in long-term incapacitation due to illness, injury, or advanced age.

Isotonic Contraction

Normal body movement involves isotonic contractions. The muscle tension remains unchanged, but the muscle shortens and produces movement.

Isometric Contraction

Muscle tension increases in isometric contractions, but muscle length does *not* shorten. This type of contraction is present in muscle that maintains posture or when one pushes against a rigid structure. A tremendous amount of heat energy is given off in this latter example, but none is converted to the mechanical energy needed for movement since the rigid structure cannot move.

Twitch Contraction

A twitch contraction is made up of three phases—namely, the *latent, contraction,* and *relaxation* phases—and is a response to a *single stimulus*.

The latent period consists of the time between stimulus reception and muscle contraction. The contraction phase is the time required for muscle contraction to take place, and the relaxation phase is the time it takes for the muscle to relax. Normal body movements do not include twitch contractions.

Summation Contraction

This type of contraction is the result of added, or summed, stimuli. If a muscle receives a stimulus during the relaxation period, the strength of each succeeding stimulus is added to the first, resulting in a stronger contraction. The stronger contractions result from stimulation of more motor units.

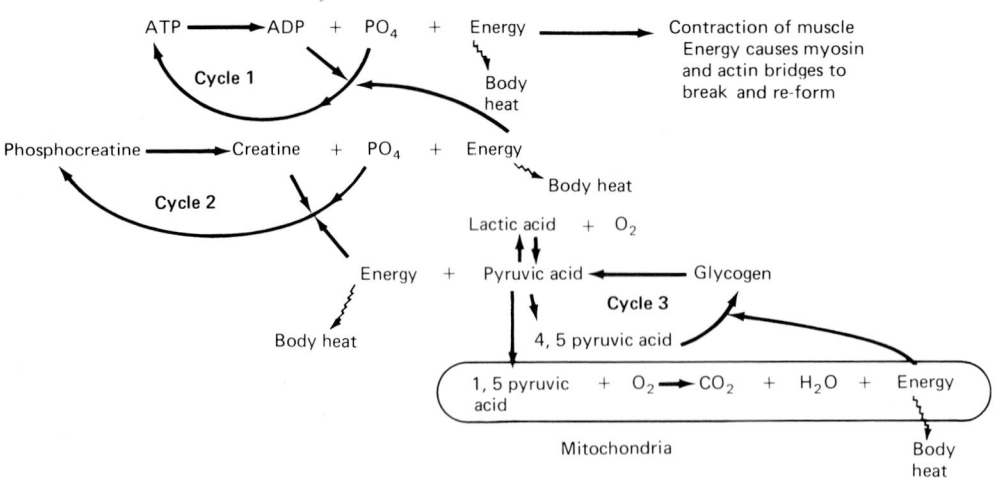

FIGURE 11-6

Three cycles in the chemistry of muscle contraction. (*From T. Randall Lankford, Integrated Science for Health Students, Reston Publishing Company, Reston, Virginia, 1976. Used by permission of the publisher.*)

Tetanic Contraction

Tetanic contractions occur when a muscle receives a series of stimuli so rapidly that the muscle cannot start the period of relaxation. The muscle therefore remains in the period of contraction until the stimuli stop or the muscle fatigues. Normal body movements result from tetanic contractions and not from twitch contractions, since tetanic contractions produce smooth, sustained movement while twitch contractions produce jerky, unsustained contractions.

Fibrillation

This type of contraction is an abnormal one where individual muscle fibers contract in an uncoordinated manner. The muscle appears to quiver, resulting in ineffective movement.

Convulsion

This type of contraction is also an abnormal contraction of groups of muscles. This is similar to fibrillation, but involves groups of muscles rather than a single muscle.

Spasm

This type of contraction is a sudden, involuntary contraction. If the spasms are prolonged, the condition is referred to as a *cramp*.

TENDONS AND LIGAMENTS

Tendons and ligaments are composed chiefly of inert intercellular substance in the form of collagen fibers aligned with rows of flattened fibroblasts scattered between them. In adults, this intercellular substance requires no nutrition and the blood supply is minimal. At sites of friction, a tendon is enveloped by a synovial sheath which consists of a visceral and a parietal layer and contains synovial fluid. Both tendons and ligaments are firmly attached to bone at their sites of insertion via their collagen fibers, which penetrate into the solid substance of cortical bone.

REACTIONS OF THE MUSCULOSKELETAL TISSUES TO ACUTE DISORDERS AND INJURIES

Reaction of Bone

Bone is capable of only a very limited number of reactions to a large number of abnormal conditions.

The results of these reactions may be manifested by marked changes in the gross structure of a bone or bones; however, the basic nature of the reaction rests at the microscopic or cellular level.

Salter states that three basic ways in which bone reacts to abnormal conditions are *local death, alteration of bone deposition,* and an *alteration of bone resorption*.

When an area of bone is completely deprived of blood supply, its reaction is local death. The dead bone then becomes an abnormal condition of itself and incites further reactions from the surrounding living tissue. Bone that remains alive can react to abnormal conditions either by an alteration of deposition or by an alteration of resorption or both.

Bone deposition involves a combination of two major processes: osteoblastic formation of organic matrix *osteoid*, and calcification of this matrix to form bone, in which calcification of matrix may be less than normal (hypocalcification) but is seldom more than normal.

Salter outlined reactions of living bone as:

1. Altered deposition of bone

   a. Increased deposition (increased formation matrix with normal calcification)

   b. Decreased deposition (either decreased formation of matrix or hypocalcification)

2. Altered resorption of bone

   a. Increased resorption

   b. Decreased resorption

3. Combinations of altered deposition and altered resorption

The abnormal condition may incite one or more reactions in an individual bone or part of a bone (localized reaction), or it may incite one or more reactions of all bones (systemic reaction). Reactions in bone cause changes in bone density and can be seen and studied by ordinary x-ray examination. Thus increased radiographic density is evidence of increased deposition or decreased resorption or a combination of these phenemena. Decreased deposition or increased resorption, on the other hand, result in less bone or decreased density.

Examples of Bone Reactions

A wide variety of disorders and injuries may cause reactions in living bone. Some of these disorders and/or injuries arise within the musculoskeletal system itself, and some arise within other systems of the body. Examples of these abnormal conditions relate to alterations in the normal equilibrium or balance between bone deposition and bone resorption.

Osteopetrosis is an example of a condition in which bone deposition is greater than bone resorption, resulting in a generalized increase in bone. It is thought that bone deposition is probably normal, but bone resorption is defective.

Osteoporosis is an example of a condition in which bone deposition is less than that of bone resorption, resulting in a generalized decrease in bone. The decrease in bone deposition is due to a decrease in osteoblastic formation of matrix along with an increase in bone resorption, resulting in a marked decrease in the total amount of bone tissue.

Examples of localized reactions of bone include such disorders as *work hypertrophy, degenerative osteoarthritis, osteosclerotic neoplasms,* and *fractures*. These types of disorders or injuries result in bone deposition greater than bone resorption, leading to a localized increase in bone. Of these examples, only *fractures* relative to their repair process will be discussed.

Repair of Bone Fractures

A break in the continuity of a bone is termed a *fracture*. Fractures can be partial or complete and are classified as simple, compound, comminuted, greenstick, or a combination of compound comminuted. Under certain circumstances, the diagnosis of a fracture may not be apparent. There is a need for careful examination, especially when a communication problem exists, such as a language barrier, or when a patient is unconscious or mentally confused. It is also important to examine for soft tissue injury around the fracture site, as well as for visceral injury, coexisting dislocation, or a possible second fracture.

The repair of a fracture involves the processes of inflammation and wound healing. The process of healing taking place in dense cortical bone, such as that found in shafts of long bones, differs from the process of healing in spongy cancellous bone, such as that composing the metaphyses of long bones and bodies of short bones.

When a fracture of the shaft of a long bone occurs, the minute blood vessels traversing through the haversian system are torn where they cross the fracture site. Following a short period of local bleeding, a blood clot forms between the broken ends of the bones and tissues. Osteocytes in their lacunae near the fracture site die from ischemia because of the destruction of the small arteries, leaving necrotic bone at the fracture surfaces. These "dead" bones are replaced through the process of resorption and deposition of bone.

If the fracture site is severely displaced with disruption of the periosteal sleeve, the large arteries in the surrounding muscle and adipose tissue are also usually torn, resulting in a massive hematoma involving the surrounding tissue.

The repair cells responsible for fracture healing in the shafts of long bones are osteogenic cells supplied by the torn ends of both the periosteum and the endosteum. The clot, osteoblasts, and cartilage-forming cells (chondroblasts) form a *procallus* between the fractured bone segments. At this initial stage, the procallus does not contain bone and is radiolucent. The time needed for organization of the hematoma and its replacement by granulation tissue is variable depending largely on its size. The initial process of blood clot formation takes approximately 6 to 8 h. The organization of the procallus may be complete as early as the end of the first week, but may require from 30 to 60 days (Grollman, 1978; Salter, 1970).

During the second stage of repair, there is a gradual formation of young fibrous connective tissue which hardens to form a *fibrocartilaginous callus*. This callus acts as a model for *ossification* and *calcification*. The callus becomes progressively firmer, and the fracture site becomes less mobile. Histologically, at this point, the callus is characterized by new bone formation beginning at a site distal to the fracture where the periosteum still has a good blood supply. The osteogenic cells differentiate into osteoblasts and primary bone is formed. Closer to the fracture site, where the blood supply is not as adequate and where more mobility exists, osteogenic cells differentiate into chrondroblasts, which form cartilage.

The third stage is characterized by a replacement of the fibrocartilaginous tissue with hard bony tissue. Large numbers of osteoblasts are supplied by the deep layers of the periosteum which secrete new bone tissue from the outside of the callus inward. Calcification follows this process, as discussed earlier in this chapter under *bone growth*. Finally, a hard bony callus is formed connecting the ends of the fractured bone with an excess of bony tissue formation to further protect the site of injury. Once the fracture site becomes firm enough so that immobilization occurs, the fracture site is said to be "clinically" united. At this point, the site of the fracture has not yet regained its original strength. Radiologic examination at this time will show evidence of bone in the callus, but the fracture line will still be apparent.

The fourth and last stage of fracture repair of dense cortical bone is referred to as the stage of *consolidation*. It is at this stage that *mature* bone replaces the callus and the excess callus is gradually resorbed by osteoclastic activity. The bone finally returns to almost its normal diameter as a result of the remodeling process.

The healing of a fracture in cancellous bone occurs principally through the formation of an internal or endosteal callus, although the external callus, especially in children, plays an important role. Since the cancellous bone has a rich blood supply, little necrosis of bone occurs at the fracture site, and a large area of bony contact at the fracture site results in a more rapid healing process than that found in the dense cortical bone of shafts of long bones. The internal callus rapidly fills the open spaces of the spongy bone and spreads across the fracture site. Once union is established, the fracture is clinically united and the union spreads across the entire width of the bone. The fracture becomes consolidated when lamellar bone replaces the united bone formation.

Spongy bone is particularly susceptible to compression forces which result in crush-type fractures. Impaction of the cancellous fragments provides a broad surface contact for fracture healing: however, when a fracture is reduced, thus pulling crushed surfaces apart, a space is created which delays healing. This can result in a possible collapse at the fracture site before bony union is consolidated.

Time Required for Uncomplicated Fracture Healing

Healing time of each bone in the body is predetermined and related to the regional condition. In order to estimate the healing time for any given individual, the type of fracture and bone must be evaluated. Such factors as the age of the patient, site and configuration of the fracture, initial displacement, and blood supply to the fracture fragments need to be assessed.

Age

The rate of healing varies with age. This is especially true during childhood. Healing of a fracture is markedly rapid at birth and tapers off with each year of childhood. There is a relative consistent rate of healing from early adult life to old age. It is theorized that the rate of healing is closely related to osteogenic activity of the periosteum and the endosteum. Fractures of the shaft of femurs will unite in 3 weeks when they occur at birth, while it takes approximately 12 weeks for such union to occur by the age of 8 years. From the age of 20 to old age, such union occurs in approximately 20 weeks.

Fracture Site and Configuration

Fracture of bones surrounded by muscle heal faster than do fractured bones located more subcutaneously or within joints. Cancellous bone fractures heal more rapidly than do fractures involving dense cortical bone; long, oblique fractures and spiral fractures of the shaft of long bones with a large fracture surface heal more rapidly than transverse fractures.

Initial Displacement

Undisplaced fractures with an intact periosteal sleeve have approximately twice the healing rate as displaced fractures. If the initial displacement of the fracture is very extensive, the tearing and trauma of the periosteal sleeve will also be more extensive. Consequently, the healing time of the fracture will be correspondingly longer.

Blood Supply to the Fracture Fragments

If both fracture fragments have a sufficient blood supply, the fracture will heal; if, however, one fragment becomes ischemic because of the loss of its blood supply and the other fragment retains its blood supply, the union will be slow and rigid immobilization of the fracture site is necessary. If both fragments lack adequate blood supply, revascularization of the sites must occur before union can occur, even when rigid immobilization is instituted.

Unsatisfactory Healing of Fractures

A fracture may heal by *malunion* with residual bony deformity. This type of union occurs in the estimated time frame, but the alignment is unsatisfactory. Fractures may also heal by *delayed union,* taking considerably longer than the normally expected time. Finally, fractures may fail to heal by bone formation; instead a fibrous union occurs or a false joint is formed (pseudoarthrosis). This type of abnormality is referred to as *nonunion.*

Examples of *localized decrease* in bone tissue due to bone deposition being less than that of bone resorption include *disuse atrophy, rheumatoid arthritis, osteolytic neoplasms,* and *infection.*

Disuse atrophy is often referred to as *disuse osteoporosis* and is a result of bone reaction to decreased stress and strain of decreased function. This situation results in a decreased bone deposition with bone resorption continuing unchanged. For example, prolonged immobilization, prolonged loss of weight bearing, and severe paralysis over a period of time can cause disuse atrophy of the affected bone(s).

Rheumatoid arthritis is a condition in which there is periarticular soft tissue inflammation. This inflammatory process results in a decreased bone deposition and a possible increase in bone resorption as well. Along with this process, disuse atrophy may also result because of the decrease in function of the involved joint.

Osteolytic neoplasms are the result of localized destruction of existing bone due to increased resorption.

Reaction of Epiphyseal Plates

Epiphyseal plates can react in one of three basic ways to disorders and injuries. These are *increased growth, decreased growth,* and *torsional growth.* Normal growth in the epiphyseal plate requires an intact structure of the plate along with an adequate blood supply and intermittent pressures associated with normal physical activity. An injury to the plate can result in partial or complete lack of growth. Salter states that prolonged hyperemia stimulates growth, while relative ischemia retards it. It is important to note that excessive intermittent pressure retards growth; however, a decrease in normal intermittent pressure also retards growth.

Examples of reactions of epiphyseal plates are divided into *generalized reactions of all epiphyseal plates* and *localized reactions of an epiphyseal plate.*

Generalized reactions include such conditions as *arachnodactyly,* in which there is excessive cartilaginous growth of all epiphyseal plates due to an inborn error of development, and *pituitary gigantism,* in which excessive growth hormone from the anterior pituitary gland during childhood stimulates growth in all plates. Examples of other generalized reactions include *dwarfism,* due to an inborn error of development or to a deficient growth hormone from the anterior pituitary gland during childhood. *Rickets* is another

example of a generalized reaction resulting in a decrease in growth.

Localized reactions of an epiphyseal plate are characterized by either a localized increase or decrease in growth. Examples of the former include *chronic inflammation, displaced fracture of the shaft of a long bone,* and *congenital arteriovenous malformations.* Examples of localized decrease in growth disorders include *disuse retardation,* as when a limb is not used normally for a period of time; *physical injury,* as when a fracture crosses the epiphyseal plate or crushes it; *thermal injury,* when the cartilage of the epiphyseal plate is destroyed by frostbite or burns; *ischemia,* due to blockage or destruction of epiphyseal vessels; and *infection,* where the infection results in cartilage destruction of a part of the epiphyseal plate, usually resulting in uneven growth.

Localized torsional growth occurs when a growing long bone is subjected to continual or intermittent twisting forces. The result of such force is a gradual twisting or torsion of the affected bone.

Reaction of Synovial Joints

Any damage or irregularity of the *articular* surfaces of *synovial joints* results in a progressive *degenerative* change in the joint with limitations of movement and pain. Articular cartilage contains no blood vessels, lymphatics, or nerves; this tissue reacts to abnormal conditions in one of three ways: namely, *destruction, degeneration,* and *peripheral proliferation.* Since power of regeneration of this cartilage is limited, destruction is usually irreparable. It is destroyed by any condition which interferes with the nutrition it receives from the synovial fluid, and it is also destroyed by the chondrolytic enzymes present in certain types of purulent material. Examples of conditions that create destruction of the articular cartilage include *rheumatoid arthritis, infection, ankylosing spondylitis,* and *continuous compression.*

The *normal aging process* results in a slowly progressive type of degeneration of the articular cartilage. In this process, the cartilage becomes thinner and less cellular as well as less resilient and more susceptible to injury. Obese individuals place excessive loads on the joint surfaces, causing aggravation of the degenerative process. A decrease in viscosity of synovial fluid as well as local damage also aggravates the process.

Conditions that cause degeneration of the articular cartilage include *premature aging of cartilage, previous destruction,* and *irregularity of joint surfaces.*

The peripheral articular cartilage of a synovial joint is covered by a type of perichondrium which is continuous with the synovial membrane. When the central area of the cartilage is degenerated, there is proliferation of the peripheral perichondrium with a gradual production of thickened cartilage.

Reaction of Synovial Membrane

The synovial membrane reacts to abnormal conditions by producing an excessive amount of synovial fluid (effusion), by becoming thicker (hypertrophy), and by forming adhesions between itself and articular cartilage. A joint effusion may be *serous*, an *inflammatory exudate, grossly purulent,* or *hemorrhagic*, depending upon the underlying cause. The synovial membranes of tendon sheaths and bursae are capable of the same reactions to abnormal conditions.

Reaction of Joint Capsule and Ligaments

These structures react to abnormal conditions by either becoming very stretched, resulting in instability of the joint, or by becoming unduly tight and shortened. This latter reaction results in a *joint contracture*.

Reaction of Skeletal Muscle

There is a limited number of ways in which skeletal muscles react to abnormal conditions. These include *atrophy, hypertrophy, necrosis, contracture,* and *regeneration*.

DEFORMITIES OF THE MUSCULOSKELETAL SYSTEM

Salter indicates that many disorders and injuries of the musculoskeletal system are characterized by a deformity which may be very obvious, subtle, or completely hidden from the naked eye. When an assessment is being carried out on such a patient, the deformed structure is carefully examined in terms of *significance* of the deformity and its present or future effect on *function*. A deformity may be congenital or acquired. The types of bony deformity include loss of alignment, abnormal length, and bony overgrowth. Causes of bony deformity include congenital abnormalities of bony development, fractures, disturbances of epiphyseal plate growth, bending of abnormally soft bone, and overgrowth of adult bone. Types of joint deformity include displacement of the joint, excessive mobility of the joint, and restricted mobility of the joint.

REFERENCES

Bell, G. H., D. Emslie-Smith, and C. R. Patterson: *Textbook of Physiology and Biochemistry*, 9th ed., Edinburgh: Churchill Livingstone, 1976, chap. 32.

DeCoursey, R. M.: *The Human Organism*, 4th ed., New York: McGraw-Hill, 1974.

Grollman, S.: *The Human Body: Its Structure and Physiology*, 4th ed., New York: Macmillan, 1978, chap. 2.

Kelman, G. R.: *Physiology: A Clinical Approach*, 2d ed., Edinburgh: Churchill Livingstone, 1975, chap. 21.

Lankford, T. R.: *Integrated Science for Health Students*, Reston, Va.: Reston, 1976.

Salter, R. B.: *Textbook of Disorders and Injuries of the Musculoskeletal System*, Baltimore: Williams & Wilkins, 1970, chaps. 2, 3, 15.

Selkurt, E. (ed.): *Basic Physiology for the Health Sciences*, Boston: Little, Brown, 1976, chaps. 8 and 14.

Shepro, D., F. Belamarich, and C. Levy: *Human Anatomy and Physiology: A Cellular Approach*, New York: Holt, 1974.

Wilson, F. C. (ed.): *The Musculoskeletal System*, Philadelphia: Lippincott, 1975, pp. 100–113, 238.

INTRODUCTION

The following chapter addresses the physiology of the adult female and male reproductive systems. Though descriptions of anatomy are presented, the focus is physiologic and does not deal with the period of gestation itself. The list of references at the end of the chapter can be utilized by the reader to study particular areas in greater depth.

THE FEMALE REPRODUCTIVE SYSTEM

The female reproductive system is composed of the vulva, vagina, uterus (cervix and fundus), fallopian tubes, and ovaries. The reproductive organs are frequently referred to as the *external* (vulva and vagina) and *internal* (uterus, fallopian tubes, and ovaries) *genitalia*. Refer to Figs. 12-1 and 12-2.

Internal Genitalia

Ovaries

The ovaries are the genital glands of the female. They are placed on each side of the pelvis just below the fallopian tubes, the outer ends of which are curved over them in an archlike fashion. They measure about $3\frac{1}{2}$ cm by 2 cm by $1\frac{1}{2}$ cm, although there is considerable variation. Anteriorly, the ovaries are set in the posterior surface of the broad ligaments. At the line of attachment is the hilum through which blood vessels and nerves enter and leave the ovary.

The external surface of the ovary has a dull, whitish, opaque appearance. In the young child the ovaries are smooth, in the adult woman they are pitted from previous ovulations, and in the menopausal woman they are shrunken and corrugated. Each ovary is attached to the uterus by a well-developed ovarian ligament, while the upper outer pole is suspended from the side of the pelvis by that portion of the broad ligament beyond the fallopian tube (infundibulopelvic ligament or suspensory ligament of the ovary).

On cross section, the ovary is seen to be divisible into an outer cortex and a central portion, or medulla. Covering the cortex is the germinal epithelium made up of a single layer of cuboidal cells. The ovarian stroma, which is just beneath the germinal epithelium, is made of compactly placed cells in which are to be seen the follicular elements and their derivatives.

In the ovary of the newborn the primary (primordial) follicles are numerous, being estimated at about 1 million functional units, each containing an immature ovum. No new ova formation occurs after birth. Only

12
THE REPRODUCTIVE SYSTEMS

Ann Daly

INTRODUCTION

THE FEMALE REPRODUCTIVE SYSTEM
Internal Genitalia
External Genitalia
Endocrine Summary

THE MALE REPRODUCTIVE SYSTEM
External Genitalia
Internal Genitalia

REFERENCES

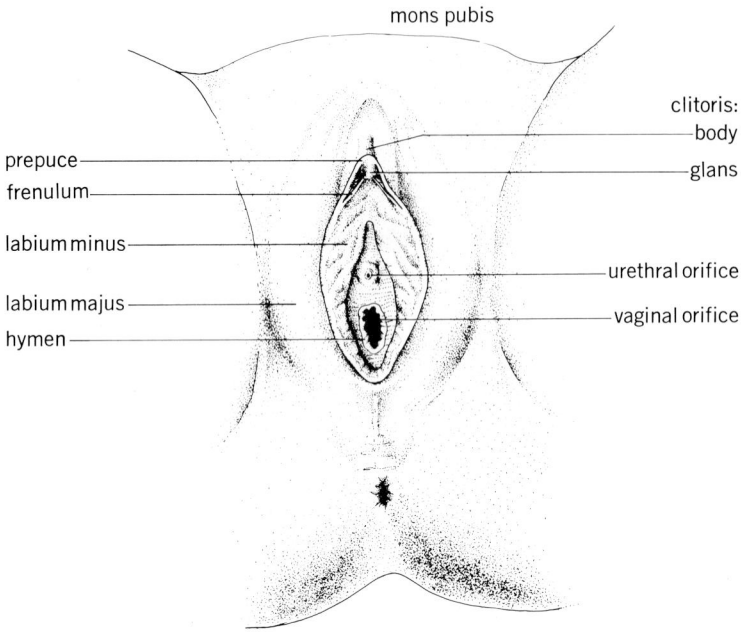

mons pubis

clitoris:
body

prepuce

glans

frenulum

labium minus

labium majus

urethral orifice

hymen

vaginal orifice

FIGURE 12-1

The vulva. (*From R. M. DeCoursey, The Human Organism, 4th ed., McGraw-Hill, New York, 1974. Used by permission of the publisher.*)

a small proportion of follicles, about 500, are stimulated to maturity in the female's reproductive years.

Follicular growth   The cyclic variations in reproductive activity occur as a result of hormonal interactions between the ovaries, the pituitary, and the hypothalamus. The normal cycle is characterized by maturation of primary follicles (Fig. 12-3), ovulation, and preparation of the reproductive tract for implantation of a fertilized ovum.

The anterior pituitary, under control of the hypothalamic luteinizing hormone–releasing hormone (LRH), secretes follicle-stimulating hormone (FSH), which promotes early follicular enlargement. Several follicles are stimulated to enlarge at the beginning, and the ova are surrounded by cavities called *antra*. Though the mechanics are not understood, on about the 6th day, one follicle rapidly outgrows the rest. The remaining follicles degenerate and become atretic. The FSH influences the maturation of the growing (graafian) follicles and stimulates the production of estrogens from the surrounding theca interna cell layer and the secretion of follicular fluid high in estrogens from the granulosa cell layer. The production of FSH is then inhibited by high levels of estrogen. Another gonadotropic hormone, luteinizing hormone

(LH), is necessary. This hormone acts synergistically with FSH for further follicular maturation and eventual ovulation.

Ovulation occurs when, under the influence of the pituitary gonadotropins, the graafian follicle reaches the point where a blisterlike bulge appears on the surface of the ovary just before ovulation. The follicle steadily increases in size so that the thin, bulging wall becomes distended, translucent, and at one area, almost avascular. This area, called the *stigma,* will be the site of rupture. Just prior to rupture, the ovum (at this stage called an *oocyte*) with its surrounding cumulus detaches and floats free in the follicular fluid and migrates upward toward the stigma. At the moment of rupture of the follicle midcycle (about the 14th day), the oocyte and the follicular fluid cascade; the oocyte is released into the abdominal cavity. The follicle immediately fills with blood, becoming the corpus hemorrhagicum. It is at this time that many women experience *mittelschmerz*, or brief abdominal pain, when bleeding into the abdominal cavity may cause peritoneal irritation. The LH, analogous to the interstitial-cell stimulating hormone (ICSH) in the male, acts to promote full estrogen production and luteinization of the theca and granulosa cell layers of the follicle. Thus, the corpus luteum is formed.

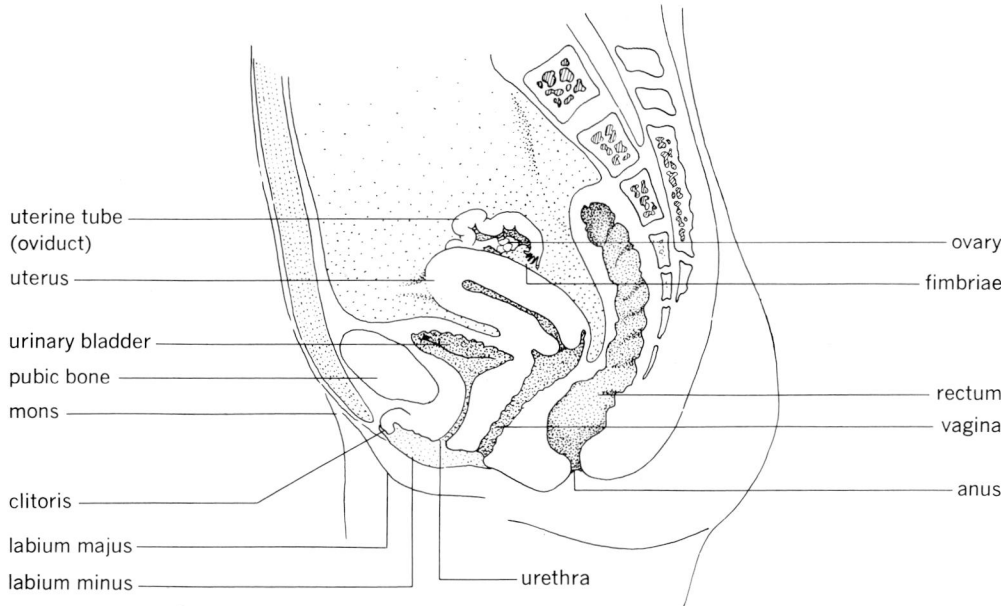

uterine tube (oviduct)
uterus
urinary bladder
pubic bone
mons
clitoris
labium majus
labium minus
urethra
ovary
fimbriae
rectum
vagina
anus

FIGURE 12-2

The female reproductive system. (*From R. M. DeCoursey, The Human Organism, 4th ed., McGraw-Hill, New York, 1974. Used by permission of the publisher.*)

At the point of ovulation, the fimbriated end of the fallopian tubes approximates itself to the ruptured follicle so that the oocyte, aided by the ciliary movement of the tubal epithelium, can be propelled down the tubal lumen. Usually the oocyte is fertilized during a 24- to 48-h period, and fertilization most frequently occurs in the middle third of the tube. If pregnancy occurs, the estrogen- and progesterone-secreting corpus luteum prevails; without fertilization, degeneration takes place, leaving the corpus albicans, or scar tissue. What precisely causes regression of the corpus luteum (luteolysis) is not understood.

Fallopian Tubes

The fallopian tubes are two musculomembranous canals which transport the ova from the ovaries to the uterus. They are about 11 or 12 cm long and are divisible for purposes of description into four parts. The *interstitial portion* is narrow and contained in the muscular wall of the uterus. The *isthmus* is the narrow portion of the tube close to its insertion into the uterine cornu; the *ampulla* is a wider, baggier middle portion. The *distal segment* is a fimbriated extremity which is rather funnel-shaped and has a small orifice surrounded by fimbria. Like the uterine epithelium, that of the tube undergoes definite cyclical changes,

though these are much less conspicuous than in the uterus. During the menstrual period the epithelium of the fallopian tubes is sparse. While under the influence of estrogen in the proliferative phase, the ciliated and secretory cells become abundant. After ovulation the secretory cells of the tube are prominent and glycogen content increases. The columnar cells of the fallopian tubes flatten as their secretion is influenced by progesterone action on the estrogen-prepared lining.

After the oocyte has been discharged from the ovary, it is conducted to the cavity of the uterus via the fallopian tube more than 3 in away. Though unusual, if one fallopian tube has been removed, the oocyte may migrate to the opposite side and enter the remaining tube. It has no primary means of locomotion. However, fluid that bathes the lining of the tube transports it, as do peristaltic contractions of the tubular musculature. The currents in the fluid are created by the cilia lining the tube.

Uterus

The uterus is a hollow, thick-walled, muscular organ which is situated in the pelvis between the bladder anteriorly and the rectum posteriorly. It is placed almost at right angles to the vagina with the bladder below and in front of it (Fig. 12-2). It is somewhat

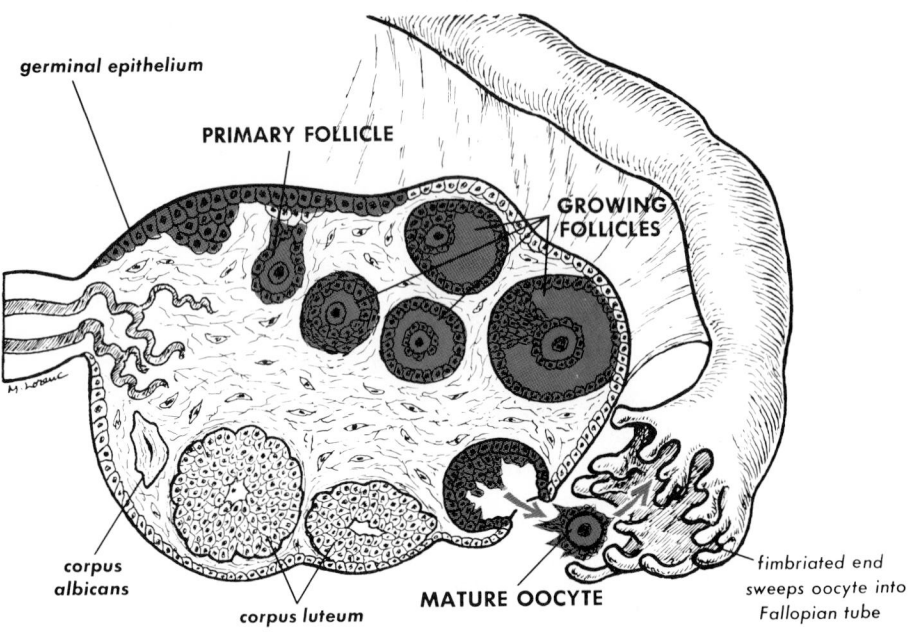

FIGURE 12-3

Stages of follicular development. (*From E. J. Reith, B. Breidenbach, and M. Lorenc, Textbook of Anatomy and Physiology, 2d ed., McGraw-Hill, New York, 1978. Used by permission of the publisher.*)

pear-shaped and measures in the nulliparous woman about 8 to 9 cm in length, 6 cm at its widest portion, and about 4 cm in thickness. It is divisible into the cervix, or fibrous neck, and a corpus, or muscular body.

Cervix   The cervix functions actively during childbirth by dilating and providing a segment of the birth canal; it functions passively otherwise by providing an exit for menstrual discharge. Its primary physiological function, however, is the secretion of mucus which facilitates the survival and transport of spermatozoa and subsequently acts as a plug to seal off the impregnated uterine cavity from the external environment.

The endocervical epithelium is responsive to hormonal stimulation, but the histologic changes in the cycle are not as dramatic or as well-documented as those of the endometrium. The cervical mucus does, however, change dramatically in the course of the cycle. Estrogens cause the cervix to grow in size and vascularity, to develop glands, and to secrete cervical mucus. Physical behavior characteristics of estrogen stimulation are brought about at the same time. Under estrogen stimulation the flow of mucus increases and becomes clear and less viscous. On a glass slide the

mucus dries in a fernlike manner because of its electrolyte content which is typical of an estrogen effect. In the secretory phase of the cycle, under the influence of progesterone, the electrolyte content and the physical-chemical characteristics of the mucus change and "ferning" is no longer observed.

In normal women of reproductive age there are numerous mucous secretory units in the cervical canal. The daily mucus production varies from 600 mg during midcycle to 2 to 20 mg during other periods of the cycle. Cervical mucus contains approximately 90 percent water. At midcycle the water content increases to more than 95 percent. Other component parts of the mucus are primarily glucose, amino acids, and soluble proteins. There are also high levels of lipids and carbohydrates. The sugars, amino acids, lipids, and electrolytes play an important role in providing a suitable medium in which sperm might be nurtured. At midcycle the levels of the components change, causing cervical mucus to become favorable for sperm penetration and fertilization.

Corpus   The corpus, or body, of the uterus is divided into the *fundus,* which is the upper domelike portion, and the *cornua,* which are the angles marking the attachment of the tube at each side. Seen from the front, the corpus takes on a somewhat triangular shape, with the base of the fundus and the two corners extending toward the orifices of the oviducts; it then becomes narrowed as it approaches the cervix. This constricted area separating the corpus from the cervix is known as the *isthmus*. The cavity of the corpus is continuous with that of the endocervix and vagina and has an average depth of about 6 cm and a capacity of 3 to 8 mL.

The uterus is composed of three separate and distinct layers: (1) the *perimetrium,* an outer peritoneal covering; (2) the *myometrium,* an inner layer of smooth muscle; and (3) the *endometrium,* the mucous membrane lining the cavity. The perimetrium is continued laterally as the leaves of the broad ligament and is continued anteriorly and posteriorly as bladder and rectal reflections. The myometrium is composed of three rather indistinct layers of smooth muscle fibers. In each layer there is an interlacing mixture of the nonstriated muscle cells, which are held in position by a connective tissue rich in elastic fibers. The outer muscular layer is chiefly longitudinal and is continuous with fibers entering the broad and round ligaments, whereas the middle layer is thicker and presents fibers in circular arrangement. The middle layer makes up the major portion of the myometrium and contains many blood vessels located between muscle bands. The inner layer represents an exaggerated muscularis mucosa and is composed of thin muscle strands arranged obliquely and longitudinally. The endometrium is a soft inner layer of variable thickness made of simple tubular glands, a stroma of resting cells in a fine connective tissue mesh, and a sensitive vasculature. The physiologic variations of this layer will be discussed later in the chapter.

The significance of menstruation itself and the reasons for its occurrence have been veiled in mystery and superstition through the years. Whatever the explanation for the cause of menstruation, the advent of the menarche has also heralded the young girl's entrance into maturity and the beginning of the reproductive era. The age of onset is usually between 12 and 15 years, with variations depending upon the general health and development of the individual, the family history, and the climatic conditions of her particular country. It is not unusual to find girls in tropical climates starting to menstruate at the age of 9, 10, or 11 years of age, whereas in the more northern climates, onset at age 13 or 14 is more common.

When menses has begun, it is usually unpredictable for a year or so because the early menstrual flow often occurs without ovulation. The actual flow in an anovulatory cycle does not differ in appearance from that of the ovulatory cycle, except for the absence of fragments of secretory endometrium.

Menses normally occurs at intervals of 27 to 32 days, when calculated from the first day of one cycle to the first day of the next, though variations of 20 to 45 days can occur in normal women. The flow will last for approximately 5 days, with the greatest volume in the first or second day. Menstrual fluid is about 50 to 75 percent blood with a mixture of mucus, endometrial tissue fragments, and desquamated vaginal epithelial cells. It is dark in color, is primarily arterial, does not clot, and has a characteristic odor. In the usual menstrual period, an average of 30 mL of blood will be lost (with ranges to 250 mL) and the female may experience a hemoglobin loss of 0.25 to 0.5 g.

In the normal adult female, menstruation occurs through a complex series of events mediated through hormonal interrelationships and reflected by changes in the endometrium and its vascular system. As the hormones fluctuate throughout the menstrual cycle, changes occur in the endometrium. Immediately after a menstrual slough has been completed, the process of regeneration begins with the formation of a new surface from the epithelium of the basal portion of the glands. Under the stimulation of increasing amounts of estrogen from a developing graafian follicle, endometrial growth begins. In this *proliferative phase,* approximately the 5th through the 14th day of the cycle, the uterine glands and stroma grow at about an equal pace. Vessels follow a slightly spiraling course and are of small caliber.

At about the time of ovulation, the uterine glands become somewhat larger in caliber and begin to show a convoluted pattern. The most superficial layer of the stroma becomes more compact, and the vessels show a greater degree of coiling. Under the influence of estrogen and progesterone from the corpus luteum, the *secretory phase* begins. This is characterized by more and more elaborate convolution of the glands, with infolding of the glandular epithelium giving a saw-toothed appearance. The stroma becomes quite edematous. Two or three days before the onset of menstruation, an increasingly heavy infiltration of leukocytes occurs, producing an almost inflammatory picture. The vessels become more and more tightly coiled and appear dilated.

With the regression of the corpus luteum and subsequent withdrawal of progesterone and estrogen, menstruation occurs. Degeneration of epithelial cells produces a granular appearance. Hemorrhage occurs into the stroma. At the same time, large fragments of the more compact upper layer and included glands may be shed intact. The sloughing process, facilitated by endometrial prostaglandins, continues until the basal layer with its straight arteries, compact stroma, and simple veins are all that remain. The bulk of the shedding process occurs in the first or second day of the menstrual cycle.

Hormone withdrawal leads to abrupt shrinkage of the endometrium, as a result of progressive decrease in the volume of blood delivered to this area, paralleled by a decrease in the volume of extravascular fluid. This lack of support leads to buckling of the superficial spiral arterioles, which in turn favors stasis within these vessels. This is then followed by vasoconstriction, necrosis, tissue fragmentation, diapedesis, and finally, frank bleeding. Of paramount importance is the fact that withdrawal of either estrogen or progesterone results in the same sequence of events.

Menopause comes about when ovarian regression occurs. This results in a pronounced decrease of estrogen. Menstrual function also typically decreases with less flow at each period and with longer intervals between menses until complete cessation occurs. Atrophy of the external genitalia results from loss of subcutaneous fat within the labial folds. The vaginal mucosa becomes extremely thin, being only one or two cell layers thick, and the vagina shrinks in size. The uterus and endometrium, along with breast tissue, atrophy proportionately due to a lack of estrogen stimulation.

External Genitalia

Vagina

The vagina is a musculomembranous canal which connects the vulva with the uterus. It is about 9 or 10 cm in length, and in the erect position of the female, its direction is generally upward and backward from the vulva to the uterus. Its upper end expands into the cup-shaped fornix, into which the uterine cervix is fitted. Anterior to the vagina is the fundus of the uterus, the base of the bladder, and the urethra. Posteriorly, the upper portion of the vagina is separated from the rectum by a deep fold of peritoneum which forms the cul-de-sac of Douglas.

The wall of the vagina is made up of three principal layers: (1) mucous membrane, (2) muscularis, and (3) adventitial connective tissue. The mucous membrane is the inner layer and is made up of thick, stratified squamous epithelium beneath which is a thin layer of connective tissue permeated by a network of blood vessels. The muscularis, the middle coat, is composed of external longitudinal and internal circular layers of smooth muscle fibers. The adventitial coat is an outer layer of dense connective tissue in which are numerous blood vessels and nodes. This sheath of connective tissue serves to unite the vagina with surrounding structures.

The vagina has a multilayered epithelial covering consisting of a basal germinal cell row lying upon the basement membrane, with three additional zones of cells that are desquamated cyclically under the hormonal influence. The innermost layer next to the germinal cells consists of parabasal cells with thick, rounded cytoplasms and a centrally placed vesicular nucleus. The next most superficial cell type is the precornified squamous cell, which is thin and platelike and has a rounded vesicular nucleus. The most superficial cells are the cornified squamous cells with the small pyknotic nucleus. The cells that are desquamated into the vaginal fluid may be evaluated by several methods and may vary according to the menstrual cycle.

Estrogens cause thickening of the vaginal epithelial cell layer and an increase in the cornified cells. This is seen in the proliferative phase of the cycle. Progesterone, following estrogen stimulation, results in more precornified cells, clumping of the desquamated cells, and a background of leukocytes and cellular debris. This pattern is seen in the secretory phase of the cycle.

Estrogens are concerned with growth, progesterones with differentiation. The actions of progesterone are, for the most part, not normally displayed until after estrogen has accomplished its growth effect on the reproductive tract and associated structures. In the vagina, most of the evidence suggests that the peak of vaginal cornification occurs at the time of ovulation. Cervical mucus "ferning," a measure of estrogen effect, is negated by the action of progesterone.

Cellular changes are reflected in a cyclic variation in the shedding of squamous cells from the vagina. This fact is useful in the evaluation of the hormonal status of women and is reflected in the vaginal cytogram. Immediately prior to ovulation, when the output of estrogen is at its peak, superficial cells are predominant in the vaginal smear. Following ovulation, and throughout pregnancy, the intermediate cells predominate. As the menopause is approached and the output of hormones from the ovaries decreases, the vaginal epithelial cells undergo less maturation, as indicated by a shedding of the cells largely from the deeper layers of the epithelium.

Muscle support of the vagina and the perineum

consists of the coccygeus and the levator ani muscles. These structures provide support to the vagina and the perineal floor. They carry a heavy work load during labor and delivery. Additionally, the vaginal muscles help provide satisfaction during the act of sexual intercourse. With the birth of children and the natural relaxation of muscles as a woman gets older, the vaginal muscles, no longer firm or strong, often sag. The result is a vagina which may be too large to allow the partner's fullest satisfaction from coitus. At the other extreme, a woman under emotional stress can have contractural spasms of the vaginal muscles during which forced penetration becomes extremely painful or even impossible.

The normal flora of the vagina may include many types of organisms, e.g., streptococcus, staphylococcus, Döderlein's bacillus, diphtheroid organisms (including some of the pathogenic type), and not infrequently, fungi of various sorts. Although bacteriology of the vagina is still very confusing, it does seem clear that the bacillus of Döderlein, a normal inhabitant, plays an important role in maintaining the acidity which characterizes the normal vaginal secretion. This acidity is due to the presence of lactic acid formed from the splitting of the glycogen present in the vaginal epithelial cells. The pH of the normal vaginal secretion ranges from 4.5 to 5.

Vulva

The vulva is the part of the genitalia which is visible externally. It consists of a number of component parts as follows: the labia majora (labium majus), the labia minora (labium minus), mons pubis, clitoris, vestibule, urinary meatus (urethral orifice), vaginal orifice, and hymen. These are demonstrated in Fig. 12-1. Not depicted, but to be reviewed, are Bartholin's glands and Skene's ducts.

The labia majora are two longitudinal raised folds of adipose tissue covered by skin which is heavily pigmented. The external surface of the labia contains many sebaceous and sweat glands, as well as numerous hair follicles usually demonstrating a heavy growth of hair, whereas the hair on the introitus (the entrance to the vagina) is much more sparse and is covered by a moist mucous membrane.

Anteriorly the labia majora are continuous with the mons pubis where they receive the insertion of the round ligaments. Posteriorly they merge with the perineal body, forming a slightly raised ridge between them called the *fourchette*. In nulliparous women the labia majora are usually in close apposition, con-cealing the underlying parts; after childbirth, however, they become and remain separate. The labia themselves are looked upon as corresponding to the scrotum of the male.

Medial to the labia majora are two triangular cutaneous folds, the labia minora, which correspond to the skin on the undersurface of the penis in the male. These folds enclose the vestibule and are much thinner and shorter than the labia majora. The labia minora subdivide anteriorly around the clitoris to form its prepuce and frenulum. Posteriorly, the labia minora merge into the substance of the labia majora. The skin of the labia minora is devoid of hair follicles but is very rich in sebaceous glands. The substance of the labia minora is described as being the erectile type due to the abundant nerve endings and blood vessels.

Anterior to the labia is the mons pubis. This is a mound of fat covered by hair that is situated just above the level of the symphysis pubis, the lower portion of the abdominal wall.

The clitoris is a small organ corresponding to the male penis. It is a structure lying at the anterior region of the vulva and consisting of a glans, a corpus or body, and a crura. Only the glans of the clitoris is visible externally between the two folds into which the labia minora bifurcate anteriorly. The body extends upward toward the pubis beneath the skin and divides into two crura which are attached to the pubic bone. The clitoris is made up of erectile tissue with many venous channels surrounded by large amounts of involuntary muscle tissue.

The vestibule is a boat-shaped fossa which is bounded laterally by the labia minora and becomes visible on separation of the labia. Within it, the vaginal orifice and urinary meatus are located, as are Bartholin's glands, Skene's ducts, and the vestibulovaginal bulb.

The urinary meatus is the small, slitlike or triangular external orifice of the urethra. It is visible in the vestibule at about two-thirds of the distance from the glans of the clitoris to the vaginal orifice. The female urethra is surrounded by paraurethral glands, which are considered to be homologous to the male prostate. Some of these glands enter into the urethra and some into Skene's ducts, which open just below the outer part of the urethral meatus.

Skene's ducts are not to be confused with Bartholin's glands, commonly known as the *greater glands* or the *vulvovaginal glands*. Both Skene's and Bartholin's are accessory sex glands in the female and function by secreting mucus for lubrication of the vaginal orifice and canal. Both glands receive their primary clinical importance from the fact that they are very subject to infection.

The vaginal orifice can be visualized within the vestibule, lying posterior to the urinary meatus. The opening to the vagina varies in size and appearance depending upon the condition of the hymen and the perineal tissues. The hymen is a rather rigid membrane of firm connective tissue which partially occludes the vaginal orifice. When the hymen is ruptured with the initial sexual intercourse or trauma, it tends to lacerate in several areas.

The blood supply of the labia majora, labia minora, and clitoris is derived from the internal pudendal artery through the posterior labial branch, the dorsal artery, and also from a small branch of the obturator artery. The veins have approximately the same source but also communicate with the vesicovaginal plexus and the inferior hemorrhoidal veins. The clitoris is particularly well endowed with blood vessels. Sexual stimulation of the clitoris causes vascular engorgement and enlargement, thereby playing an active role in the process of orgasm.

The lymphatics of the labia, the vestibule, and the clitoris correspond in arrangement and drainage to those of the homologous parts in the male. The mucocutaneous covering of the vulva (vestibule, labia minora, and medial surfaces of the labia majora) contains a copious and intricate network of lymphatic channels. These channels lead laterally and upwardly through the coarser meshwork of the lateral surfaces of the labia majora and the mons pubis to the superficial inguinal nodes. They are accompanied in the genitofemoral sulcus by coarse lymphatic channels from the anal and buttock region. The lymphatics of the clitoris correspond to those of the penis. The drainage of the greater vestibular glands is also to the superficial inguinal lymph nodes.

Since the vulva is covered externally by skin, it takes on most of the characteristics of skin elsewhere in the body. As a result of the excretions of the skin glands, as well as the vaginal secretions, the vulva is kept almost constantly moist.

The apocrine glands of the vulva are sweat glands, identical with those in the axilla. As a result, they are prone to react to stress situations in a similar manner by producing more secretions and odor.

Endocrine Summary

Ovarian Hormones

The ovarian hormones include estrogen and progesterone. It is well established that the steroid hormones, regardless of their site of origin, are derived from cholesterol. The three ovarian estrogens, of which estradiol is the most potent, are secreted into the bloodstream. Approximately one-third of the circulating estrogen remains in a free form, and 70 percent combines with plasma protein. Large amounts of conjugated estrogens are secreted in the bile, are reabsorbed into the bloodstream, and are inactivated by the liver. Multiple metabolites of estradiol are excreted in the urine. The effect of estrogen on the pituitary may be stimulating or inhibiting depending on its blood level. Thus, low levels will stimulate while high levels will inhibit FSH production with stimulation and release of LH. Though not exclusive, Table 12-1 summarizes many of the effects of estrogens in the female.

In addition to estrogens, progesterone is produced in and secreted by the luteinized theca and granulosa cells of the corpus luteum and the placenta. The circulating level of progesterone, like that of estrogens, is very low. It is rapidly metabolized in the liver to pregnanediol. Only a small amount (less than 10 percent) of administered progesterone can be recovered in the urine. Progesterone is believed to inhibit the anterior pituitary release of LH and potentiate the inhibitory effect of estrogens. As mentioned earlier, progesterone is responsible for the endometrial changes during the secretory (or progestational) phase and vaginal and cervical cyclic changes. Along with being a stimulant to respiration and naturiuresis,

---

TABLE 12-1
Estrogen Effects in the Human Female

1. Facilitate growth of the ovarian follicle
2. Increase fallopian motility
3. Promote vaginal epithelial cornification
4. Increase uterine blood flow
5. Increase uterine muscle and contractility
6. Inhibit FSH and LH secretion during early part of follicular phase and later in luteal (negative feedback) phase
7. Promote the abrupt LH secretion (positive feedback)
8. Increase pituitary size
9. Increase libido
10. Stimulate duct growth in the breasts and breast enlargement at puberty
11. Coupled with absence of testicular androgens, promote female body habitus: narrow shoulders, broad hips, convergent thighs and arms that diverge, fat distribution, hair distribution, and retention of prepuberty larynx dimensions
12. Promote salt and water retention

it is thought to be responsible for the rise in body temperature at the time of ovulation.

Ovarian-Pituitary-Hypothalamic Relationships

Though the interrelationship of endocrine changes during the menstrual cycle is not completely understood, several factors discussed earlier are worthy of reiteration and focus. Also refer to Chapter 7.

The pituitary gonadotropin FSH is responsible for the early follicular maturation; FSH and LH are jointly responsible for the final maturation of the ovarian follicle; and the burst of LH secretion results in ovulation and initial corpus luteum development. Prolactin, a third gonadotropin, is not as clearly understood. Though once thought to be luteotropic, it does cause milk secretion after stimulation from estrogens and progesterone. Possibly, along with LH, prolactin is a stimulant to progesterone secretion.

Hypothalamic influence is exerted by the secretion of LRH into the portal hypophyseal vessels, which in turn stimulates FSH and LH secretion. The release of LRH [and possibly an as yet to be determined follicle-stimulating hormone-releasing hormone (FRH)] is cyclical and pulsatile, rather than steady.

The feedback is created by estrogen's inhibitory effect on FSH and LH secretion during the early follicular phase of the cycle, and is coupled with progesterone levels during the luteal phase. Whereas steady, low levels of estrogens result in negative feedback on LH secretion, elevated levels of estrogen stimulate LH secretion (positive feedback). The answer may lie in whether the estrogen effect is exerted at the ventral hypothalamus or the anterior pituitary or both (the negative feedback effect), versus the anterior hypothalamic area (the positive feedback effect). Figure 12-4 summarizes the endocrine relationships discussed above.

THE MALE REPRODUCTIVE SYSTEM

The male reproductive system is composed of external and internal organs, the former being the penis and scrotum and the latter consisting of the testicles, genital ducts, and associated glands (see Fig. 12-5).

External Genitalia

Penis

The penis consists of three cylindrical masses of erectile tissue. There are two corpora cavernosa penises, both of which diverge laterally as the crura of the penis and attach to the pubic arch. The third

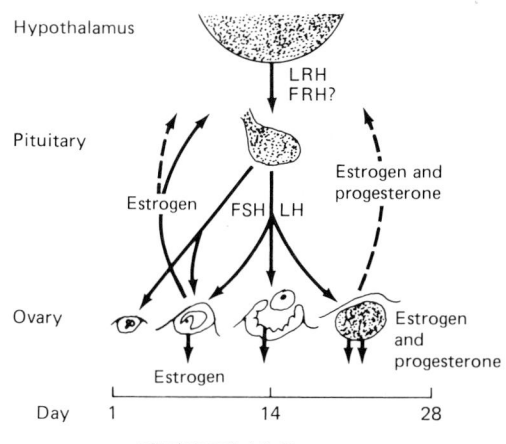

FIGURE 12-4
Known and suspected events in the menstrual cycle. (*From W. F. Ganong, Review of Medical Physiology, 9th ed., Lange, Los Altos, Calif., 1979. Used by permission of the publisher.*)

mass of erectile tissue is the unpaired corpus spongiosum (corpus cavernosum urethrae). The corpus spongiosum is the ventral portion of erectile tissue and through it passes the urethra. The corpus spongiosum stands at its distal end to form the glans of the penis; the proximal end is the bulb of the penis. Each of the three corpora (the erectile tissue) is surrounded by a dense, fibrous coat, the tunica albuginea. All three are enclosed by a layer of fairly dense fascia. The corpora cavernosa penises are partially covered by a sheet of skeletal muscle called the *bulbocavernosus muscle*. These skeletal muscles participate in micturition and aid in expulsion of semen from the urethra.

The glans is formed by the free end of the corpus spongiosum, which expands to shelter the tip of the cavernous body. The glans penis is important for sexual function and is richly endowed with nerves. Most tactile stimulation of the penis is transmitted through the glans.

The erectile tissue receives arterial blood by way of terminal branches of the internal pudendal arteries. These include the dorsal arteries, which are paired and lay on the dorsal surface of the tunica albuginea, as well as the deep arteries which run longitudinally in each corpus cavernosum penis. There is also a pair of bulbourethral arteries, which run longitudinally in the corpus spongiosum. Some of these arteries enter directly into the cavernous spaces or form terminal branches called *helicine arteries*, which end in small capillaries opening directly into the cavern-

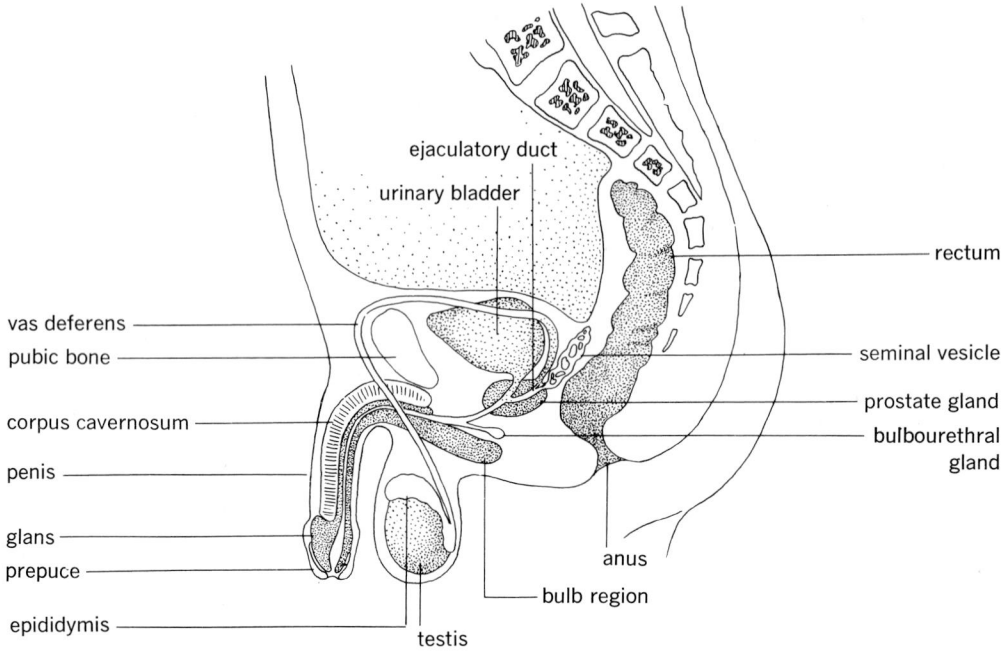

FIGURE 12-5

The male reproductive system. (*From R. M. DeCoursey, The Human Organism, 4th ed., McGraw-Hill, New York, 1974. Used by permission of the publisher.*)

ous spaces. Venous blood leaves the penis by way of the superficial dorsal vein and the deep dorsal vein.

The principal nerve supply to the urogenital region is the pudendal nerve derived from sacral roots 2, 3, and 4 with some normal variations, though primarily from S3.

The parasympathetic nerves to the erectile tissue of the penis are termed the *nervi erigentes.* Parasympathetic stimulation causes basal dilatation of the blood vessels which leads to erection. With dilatation of the arteries serving the penis, there is increase in blood flow to the penis and the vascular spaces of the erectile tissue become filled with blood. This vascular engorgement results in erection. Distention of the vascular spaces presses the veins against the tunica albuginea and thus passively restricts escape of blood from the erectile tissue. Stimulation of the sympathetic nerve supply to the penis results in restriction of its arteries and subsequent loss of erection (detumescence).

The two components of ejaculation are *emission* and *ejaculation,* or the expulsion of semen from the urethra. Emission is produced by the contraction of smooth muscle of the internal genital organs that

deliver semen into the urethra. The entire process is basically a reflex phenomenon. Afferent impulses arise chiefly in the sex organs of the glans of the penis and are transmitted by the internal pudendal nerves to the spinal cord and central nervous system. Efferent impulses for emission are sympathetic and come from the upper lumbar segments via the hypogastric nerves through the hypogastric plexus to the internal male genital organs. Sympathetic stimulation causes contraction of smooth muscle from the tail of the epididymis all the way through the vas deferens and the accessory glands. The latter contract in the following order: Cowper's gland, the prostate, the ampulla, and finally, the seminal vesicles. Secretions from each of these portions of the genital glands are emitted in that order. During the emission phase, seminal fluid collects in the prostatic urethra and the urethral bulb expands two- to threefold. At the onset of emission, the internal sphincter of the bladder closes because of sympathetic stimulation, preventing retrograde ejaculation of semen into the bladder. Closure of the internal sphincter of the bladder and emission of seminal fluid into the prostatic urethra create a pressure chamber in the prostatic urethra.

Ejaculation then proceeds with relaxation of the

external sphincter of the bladder, located at the beginning of the membranous portion of the urethra; this relaxation allows seminal fluid to flow into the distal bulb and penile urethra. The ejaculate is then propelled from the prostatic urethra along the penile urethra by contraction of the perineal musculature (bulbospongiosus and ischiocavernosus muscles and also the sphincter urethra). The urethral bulb contracts regularly and is an aid in the propulsive mechanism.

The skin covering of the glans of the penis is firmly fused to the tunica albuginea and is, therefore, not movable. Otherwise, the skin on the penis is very thin and freely movable. At the base of the penis the skin blends with that covering the pubis and scrotum. Distally on the glans of the penis the skin forms the prepuce, a fold of skin which overlaps the glans. Excision of the prepuce constitutes circumcision.

Scrotum

The scrotum consists of two layers: the skin and the dartos. The dartos is primarily smooth muscle which contracts in response to cold and sexual stimuli.

Each testis resides in a separate scrotal compartment, the scrotum being divided by a muscular (dartos muscle) septum.

While testicular hormone production is unaffected by normal body temperature, effective spermatogenesis requires a lower temperature. The scrotal sac allows the testes such an environment, the temperature being about 2.2° C less than the core temperature.

Internal Genitalia

Testicles

The testes migrate into the scrotal swelling during the latter phases of fetal development. A tunica albuginea covers each testis, giving rise to septa which divide the testis into various lobules. Within each of the lobules are numerous convoluted seminiferous tubules which form loops connected to a straight tubule, in turn communicating with the rete testis. The seminiferous tubules are lined by stratified epithelium composed of two major cell types, the supporting cells (Sertoli cells) and the spermatogenic cells. The latter consists of spermatogonia, the primary spermatocytes, the secondary spermatocytes, the spermatids, and finally, the mature spermatozoa. All these germ cells (the spermatogenic cells) are successive stages in the continuous process of differentiation of male germ cells. The Sertoli cells are large columnar cells which rest on the basement membrane of the

seminiferous tubules and extend upward throughout most of the seminiferous tubule toward the lumen. Sertoli cells provide mechanical support and protection for the developing germ cells and probably participate in their maturation. Sertoli cells do not appear to divide. They are very resistant to heat and ionizing radiation and other toxic agents which tend to destroy the spermatogenic cells. The spermatogonia are the most primitive type of germ cells in the seminiferous tubules. They also rest on the basement membrane. Spermatogonia continually divide throughout the life of the male, one daughter cell producing a primary spermatocyte and the other remaining as a spermatogonia, or stem cell, which will subsequently repeat the process. Primary spermatocytes proceed to secondary spermatocytes, then spermatids, and finally to spermatozoa. Each of these cell stages is at a higher level in the seminiferous tubule as they migrate toward the lumen of the tubule. Spermatogenesis begins at puberty and continues throughout the life of a male. This is due to continual renewal of stem cells for sperm production in males. Since sperm production takes about 74 days within the testis and the sperm is then stored in the epididymis for another 23 days, total sperm production from the initial phase to ejaculation occurs over a period of approximately 3 months.

Also within the testes, between the seminiferous tubules, are the Leydig cells, or interstitial cells which produce the male hormone testosterone.

The pituitary gland secretes two gonadotropins which are necessary for sperm production and hormone synthesis and secretion. The first of these is follicle-stimulating hormone (FSH), which is necessary for sperm production. FSH secretion from the pituitary is controlled by the negative feedback of a substance designated *inhibin,* which is thought to be produced by the seminiferous tubules, perhaps from the Sertoli cells. In addition, FSH is controlled by the central nervous system with a hypothalamic neurohumoral transmitter, luteotropin-releasing hormone (LRH), which causes the release of FSH. This same hypothalamic releasing factor causes LH secretion. (See Fig. 12-6.) In physiological amounts, testosterone has no feedback effects on FSH secretion; but in large amounts, testosterone can have negative feedback effects on FSH secretion.

The second of the pituitary gonadotropins is luteinizing hormone (LH), sometimes referred to as *interstitial-cell stimulating hormone* (ICSH). LH in males causes the synthesis and secretion of the male hormone testosterone. LH is controlled again by a

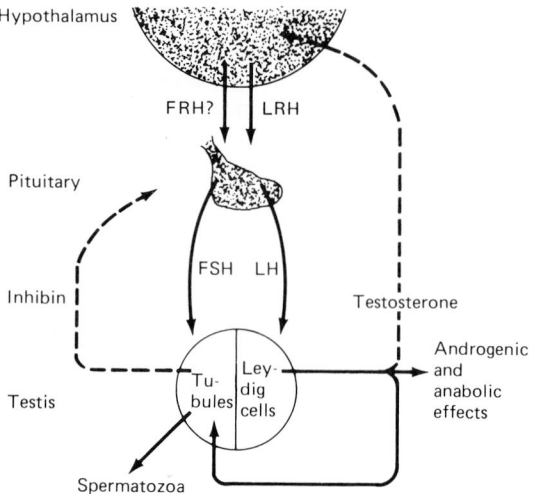

FIGURE 12-6

Proposed hypothalamic, anterior pituitary, and testicular interrelationship. (*From W. F. Ganong, Review of Medical Physiology, 9th ed., Lange, Los Altos, Calif., 1979. Used by permission of the publisher.*)

combination of central nervous system influence and negative feedback mechanisms related to the level of testosterone present. The central nervous system influence is from LRH, the hypothalamic neurohumor which causes LH release. Testosterone is the principal androgen secreted by the testes and is a steroid formed primarily from cholesterol. In some of the male accessory glands, particularly the prostate and epididymis, testosterone is converted to dihydrotestosterone (DHT). This is a more potent form of testosterone and appears to be a form in which testosterone acts on tissue which is sensitive to testosterone actions. Testosterone actions include feedback on pituitary LH and the development and maintenance of the morphological and functional activity of accessory male reproductive organs.

Both testosterone and FSH are required for spermatogenesis. Testosterone is required for development and maintenance of secondary sexual characteristics of the male, including the distribution of pubic hair, as well as axillary, facial, and scalp hair with recession of the hairline. Baldness is genetically determined but does not occur if testosterone or androgens are lacking. Another secondary sex characteristic relates to pubertal changes in the vocal cords. They become thickened and lengthened under the influence of testosterone which results in lowering of the voice. Testosterone also influences body ha-

bitus and muscle mass. Its metabolic effects include its anabolic influences for positive nitrogen balance and bone growth, even though it closes the epiphyses.

Genital Ducts or Accessory Reproductive Ducts

The genital ducts transport sperm from the testes to the outside. Sperm are conducted from the testes to the epididyma via ductules. In the epididymis the sperm mature and become mobile. At the tail of the epididymis the duct gradually assumes a thicker wall and becomes the ductus deferens or vas deferens.

The vas deferens can be considered the excretory duct of the testis, extending from the tail of the epididymis to the neck of the seminal vesicle. The vas deferens is the largest portion of the spermatic cord, which also includes the nerves and vascular supply of the testis. The spermatic cord is covered by the cremasteric muscle. After joining the spermatic cord, the vas deferens enters the pelvic cavity and fuses with the neck of the seminal vesicle to form the ejaculatory duct. The dilated terminal portion of the vas deferens is known as the *ampulla*. It is in the ampulla that sperm are stored prior to ejaculation.

Associated Glands

The associated glands, or male reproductive glands, include the seminal vesicle, the prostate, and Cowper's glands. At the lower extremity of each seminal vesicle there is an area where the tube becomes constricted into a narrow straight duct which joins the corresponding vas deferens to form the ejaculatory duct, which then pierces the prostate and empties into the prostatic urethra. The seminal vesicle is dependent upon testosterone for its development and morphologic and functional integrity. It secretes fluid which is part of the semen. This seminal fluid is alkaline and is ejaculated last and provides the bulk of the ejaculate, generally somewhere between 2 and $2\frac{1}{2}$ mL.

The prostate is a firm, partly glandular, partly fibromuscular body. It is a single structure surrounding the beginning of the urethra. It is traversed by the urethra and the ejaculatory ducts. The prostate is an aggregation of many branched glands with a wide duct which empties into the urethra as many small ducts. The prostate is also completely dependent upon androgens for its development and secretory activity and secretes prostatic fluid which is necessary for sperm motility. There is some secretion from the prostate throughout ejaculation so that there is some prostatic fluid in all fractions of the semen. The volume of prostatic fluid generally ranges between ½ and 1 mL. It is slightly acid with a pH of about 6.5. Prostatic fluid is necessary for liquification of ejaculated semen.

Cowper's glands are two small glands which contribute a small volume to the semen. This secretion is thought to have a lubricating function.

The three accessory reproductive organs mentioned, i.e., Cowper's glands, seminal vesicle, and prostate, secrete the semen in which the sperm are transported. Semen provides nourishment to the sperm and acts as a buffering agent to protect the sperm from the acid secretions of the vagina. Shortly after ejaculation, semen coagulates. This coagulated semen is then acted upon by an enzyme from the prostate which causes liquification. Within 5 to 20 min, liquification of semen occurs; this process is necessary for proper sperm motility and migration.

The author wishes to express appreciation to William J. Schindler, M.D., Ph.D. for assistance with the section on the male reproductive system.

REFERENCES

Behrman, S. J., and R. G. Gosling: *Fundamentals of Gynecology*, 2d ed., New York: Oxford University Press, 1966.

———— and R. W. Kistner: *Progress in Infertility*, Boston: Little, Brown, 1975.

Carey, H. M.: *Clinical Uses of Female Sex Steroids*, Sidney: Butterworth, 1978.

DeCoursey, R. M.: *The Human Organism*, New York: McGraw-Hill, 1974.

Dunbar, R. E., and I. M. Bush: *A Man's Sexual Health*, Chicago: Budlong Press Company, 1976.

Fitzpatrick, E., and S. R. Reeder: *Maternity Nursing*, New York: Lippincott, 1976.

Ganong, W. F.: *Review of Medical Physiology*, 9th ed., Los Altos, Calif.: Lange, 1979.

Gardner, H. L., and R. H. Kaufman: *Benign Diseases of the Vulva and Vagina*, St. Louis: Mosby, 1969.

Jordan, J. A., and A. Singer: *The Cervix*, Philadelphia: Saunders, 1976.

Kistner, R. W.: *Gynecology Principles and Practices*, Chicago: Year Book, 1971.

McCary, J. L.: *Human Sexuality*, Princeton, N.J.: Van Nostrand, 1978.

Novak, E. R., G. S. Jones, and H. W. Jones, Jr.: *Gynecology*, Baltimore: Williams & Wilkins, 1975.

Odell, W. D., and D. L. Moyer: *Physiology of Reproduction*, St. Louis: Mosby, 1971.

Pritchard, J. A., and P. C. MacDonald: *Williams Obstetrics*, New York: Appleton-Century-Crofts, 1976.

Reid, D. E., K. J. Ryan, and K. Benirschke: *Principles and Management of Human Reproduction*, Philadelphia: Saunders, 1972.

Richardson, G. S.: *Ovarian Physiology*, Boston: Little, Brown, 1967.

Vander, A. J., J. H. Sherman, and D. S. Luciano: *Human Physiology–The Mechanisms of Body Function*, New York: McGraw-Hill, 1975.

PART 3

PHYSICAL ASSESSMENT

INTRODUCTION

Assessment is an organized and systematized process of data collection which serves as a basis for identifying patient problems and medical and nursing diagnoses, planning patient care, implementing the plan of care, and evaluating the progress of problem resolution. The three components of assessment are history taking, physical examination, and laboratory assessment. Although the focus of this chapter is on physical assessment, it is very important to recognize the significance and relationships of each assessment component. Therefore, this introduction will consist of a statement of the significance of physical assessment in nursing management, a brief overview of the health history, and a discussion of the relationship of laboratory assessment to history taking and physical examination.

Physical Assessment in Nursing Care Management

Physical assessment has been validated as a significant part of nursing care for many years. In the early days the nurse used only the senses of sight, touch, hearing, and smell to obtain information regarding the status of bodily functions. Today these sensory perceptions are amplified by the use of equipment such as the stethoscope, otoscope, ophthalmoscope, and hemodynamic monitors.

The nurse in the critical-care setting has a particular responsibility to be skillful in the techniques of physical assessment because patients in this setting usually have serious physiologic problems that require continual monitoring. Additionally, the reader is to note throughout that *patient status will always dictate priorities of and depth of history taking and assessment.*

Health History

The health history is the most important part of assessment. It provides information about three important areas: the patient as a person, the past and present health status, and symptomatology, which is the subjective aspect of problem identification.

The critical-care nurse usually has neither the time nor the opportunity to do the traditional comprehensive history; however, the nurse should be knowledgeable about the content of the history in order to contribute to the data collection process. The comprehensive health history usually includes a statement of the chief complaint, patient profile, history of present illness,

13

CONCEPTS OF PHYSICAL ASSESSMENT IN CRITICAL-CARE NURSING

Betty Henderson
Gayle T. Ferguson

INTRODUCTION
Physical Assessment in Nursing Care Management
Health History
Relationship of Physical Assessment, Health History, and Laboratory Assessment
Physical Assessment—A Systematic Approach
Guidelines for Physical Assessment
Basic Techniques and Equipment

THE EXAMINATION
Position of Patient   General Appearance   Vital Signs

SKIN
Color Changes   Moisture   Turgor   Texture
Temperature   Integrity   Hair Changes   Nail Changes
Thermal Injuries

HEAD, NECK, AND FACE
Skull and Face   Ears
Nose, Sinuses, Mouth, and Pharynx   Neck

EYE
External Structures
Visual Acuity and Visual Fields
Ocular Movements
Ophthalmoscopic Examination
Intraocular Pressure

LUNGS
Inspection   Palpation   Percussion   Auscultation
Breath Sounds   Voice Sounds   Adventitious Sounds

HEART
Inspection   Palpation   Percussion   Auscultation
Heart Rate and Rhythm   Normal Heart Sounds
Extra Heart Sounds   Murmurs

NEUROMUSCULAR
Cerebral Function   Cranial Nerves   Motor System
Sensory System   Reflexes

ABDOMEN AND RECTUM
Abdomen   Rectum

MALE AND FEMALE GENITOURINARY SYSTEMS
Examination of Male and Female Genitalia
Assessment of the Urinary Tract

REFERENCES

past medical history, family history, and review of systems.

When a patient is admitted to a critical-care unit, a comprehensive history may or may not be done depending upon: (1) the type of critical-care setting; (2) the condition of the patient when admitted; (3) whether or not the patient had a history taken sometime prior to the onset of the illness which resulted in admission to the critical-care unit; or (4) a combination of these circumstances. For example, if the patient is admitted to the emergency room unconscious, a history cannot be obtained unless family and friends are available. Also, the emergency room, in most instances, is a very busy, fast-moving area which allows for obtaining· only selective information. An-

other example would be that of a patient transferred to the coronary-care unit with a diagnosis of acute myocardial infarction, after being admitted to the hospital for peptic ulcer disease. This patient may have had a comprehensive history taken, but additional historical information may be warranted.

In all the above instances, the nurse needs certain information about the patient to logically plan and implement a plan of care. If a comprehensive history is not available, it is imperative that data be obtained from the patient or significant other(s) to serve as a basis for planning, implementing, and evaluating nursing care and patient status. A defined nursing assessment format for that purpose *may entail* the information in Fig. 13-1.

DEFINED NURSING HISTORY FOR CRITICAL-CARE PATIENTS

Date_____ Time of admission_____AM PM Patient's age_____ Sex: M F Race_____

Patient's name_____ Address _____

Religion _____ Education level _____

Occupation _____ Marital status _____

Home situation _____ Family availability _____

Financial situation _____ Habits_____

Hobbies _____ Handedness: right left_____

Usual daily activities_____

Current medications _____

Information received from_____ Phone_____

GENERAL APPEARANCE

What is the patient's understanding of the illness?

CHIEF COMPLAINT AND/OR REASON ADMITTED

What are the patient's feelings about the illness?

HISTORY OF PRESENT ILLNESS

What is the patient's family feeling about the illness?

ALLERGIES

Medication_____

PAST MEDICAL HISTORY

Foods_____

Environmental _____

Describe the patient's normal coping mechanisms under stress.

_____

(e.g., dust, tape, lotion, wool)

FIGURE 13-1
Defined nursing history for critical-care patients.

TEMPERATURE

If appropriate

Onset _____

Degrees _____

How measured _____

Treatment _____

_____

SKIN

Allergies _____

Bathing and care routines _____

_____

Origin of any wounds _____

_____

Lesions _____

_____

_____

SENSORY

Vision intact: yes no

Glasses: yes no

Contact lenses: yes no

  With patient: yes no

Hearing intact: yes no

Hearing aid: yes no

  With patient: yes no

Taste intact: yes no

  If no, describe _____

  _____

Smell intact: yes no

  If no, describe _____

  _____

Sinus problems: yes no

  If yes, describe _____

  _____

ABDOMEN

Abdominal and/or gastric pain: yes no

  If yes:

  Where _____

  When _____

  Intensity _____

  Precipitated by _____

  Relieved by _____

NUTRITIONAL AND FLUID STATUS

Nausea and/or vomiting: yes no

  If yes:

  Frequency _____

  Type _____

  Relieved by _____

  Color _____

Food preferences _____

_____

Dislikes _____

_____

Intolerances and/or restrictions _____

_____

_____

Fluid intake average

_____ per 24-h period

Dentures: yes no

  If yes, with patient _____

Weight loss _____ amount _____

Weight gain _____ amount _____

ELIMINATION

Urinary: Urethra/stoma, Frequency, Urgency, Hesitancy, Burning, Hematuria, Pain, Polyuria, Nocturia

_____

Bowel: Anal/stoma

  Time of day _____

  Times per day _____ per week _____

  Hard, Soft, Loose, Liquid, Black, Brown, Pale, Frothy, Foul, Melena

Recent change in bowel habits: yes no

  Describe _____

  _____

Any medications: yes no

  Describe _____

  _____

  _____

RESPIRATORY

Pleuritic pain: yes no

  If yes:

  When _____

  Duration _____

  Precipitated by _____

FIGURE 13-1 (*Continued*)

Aggravated by _____

Relieved by _____

Cough: yes no

How long _____

Productive or dry _____

Sputum:

Thick, Thin, White, Clear, Yellow, Green, Brownish, Bloody

Amount per day _____

Smokes _____ p.p.d.

How long? _____ years

Dyspnea: yes no

If yes, describe _____

_____

Shortness of breath: yes no

If yes:

Describe _____

_____

CARDIOVASCULAR

Chest pain: yes no

If yes:

Where _____

When _____

Quality _____

Frequency _____

Duration _____

Precipitated by _____

Relieved by _____

Extremity pain: yes no

If yes:

Where _____

When _____

Onset _____

Quality _____

Duration _____

Relieved by _____

Orthopnea: yes no

Palpitations: yes no

Dyspnea on exertion: yes no

Paroxysmal nocturnal dyspnea: yes no

NEUROMUSCULAR AND SKELETAL

Headaches: yes no

Describe _____

_____

_____

Dizziness: yes no

Describe _____

_____

_____

History of:

Convulsions, Seizures, Syncope, Double vision, Numbness, Tingling, Walking difficulty, Weakness

Describe _____

_____

REPRODUCTIVE

Pelvic pain: yes no

Describe: Sharp, Dull, Steady, Intermittent

Onset _____

Menstrual cycle:

Menarche _____

Cycles _____

Length _____

Last menstrual period _____

Gravida _____

Para _____

Stillborn _____

Abortions _____

Any historical gentalia or reproductive problems _____

Surgeries _____

_____

Contraception _____

_____

_____

REST AND COMFORT

Usual sleep patterns:

Day or night

Hours _____

Room temperature:

Warm or cool

FIGURE 13-1 *(Continued)*

Windows:

  Open or closed

Aids to sleep: yes no

Describe _____

_____

_____

FIGURE 13-1 *(Continued)*

Relationship of Physical Assessment, Health History, and Laboratory Assessment

The primary purpose of physical and laboratory assessment is to obtain objective data which give evidence of the physiologic state of bodily systems and structural integrity. The findings on physical examination and laboratory assessment are most useful in confirming diagnoses, supporting historical data, and evaluating the progress of a patient's condition. Without historical information, however, physical findings and laboratory data are often helpful in determining the presence of significant problems, such as an S_3, which may be evidence of impending congestive heart failure, and a low hematocrit and hemoglobin, which might suggest bleeding. Although the focus of this chapter is on physical assessment, it is very important to recognize the interrelationships of physical, historical, and laboratory assessment and to understand that comprehensive data collection requires all three modes of assessment.

Physical Assessment— A Systematic Process

The patient admitted to a critical-care unit may be unable to undergo an initial complete physical examination. The patient's condition may warrant immediate intervention based upon initial assessment findings; hence the completion of the *classical* initial examination may be prevented. The completion of the examination would depend upon when the patient's condition stabilizes and the importance of the unavailable information to patient care management.

A systematic approach to the complete examination or examination of one or more systems is important. It is also important to remember that repeated observation of salient findings is imperative in the management of acute problems to avert complications.

Being systematic and organized allows for efficiency and thoroughness. In performing the complete physical examination, the examiner may choose the regional or systems approach. The regional approach is based upon an examination of an entire area of the body before progressing to the next region; for instance, when the chest is being examined, the lungs, heart, rib cage, breasts, axillary nodes, and great vessels should be included. The systems approach indicates a progression from one body system to another, such as integumentary, eye, ears, nose and throat, respiratory, cardiovascular, and so on. There are individual preferences, although the regional approach seems more efficient for the practitioner and patient.

Guidelines for Physical Assessment

In performing a physical examination, there are some basic guidelines which should be remembered.

1. The examination should be conducted in a warm, well-lighted room or area.

2. Privacy should be provided.

3. The patient should be draped appropriately.

4. The examined area should be exposed.

5. The practitioner's hands should be washed before and after examination.

6. Consider the patient's physical and psychological comfort during the examination. Observe facial expressions and body language for signs of pain, distress, exertion, mood change, etc.

7. Explain all procedures and maneuvers.

8. Be aware of sensitive areas of the body.

9. Be organized and thorough, and perform the examination in such a manner that the most information is obtained in the least amount of time.

10. Record findings by the systems approach outlined on your physical examination form. This is not necessarily the manner in which the examination is conducted.

11. Physical assessment findings should be written in objective and measurable terminology.

12. Some basic observations should include:

    a. Size, shape, and contour of organs and structures

    b. Rate, rhythm, and intensity of sound

    c. Recognition of close symmetry of all organs and structures which are paired—with the exception of portions of the thoracic and abdominal areas where the liver, spleen, and stomach are located

    d. Consistency of tissue

    e. Sensitivity of organs and structures

    f. Functional ability of a body part or the body as a whole

    g. Existence of abnormalities

    h. Relationship of one or more parts to another and the parts to the whole

Basic Techniques and Equipment

Before an initial examination begins, the equipment to be used should be assembled in an organized way at the patient's bedside. Equipment that is used for determining a patient's progress at intervals (minute to minute, hour to hour, or daily) should also remain at the bedside. The equipment in both instances should include a stethoscope with diaphragm and bell, sphygmomanometer, ophthalmoscope with attachable otoscope, pocket flashlight or penlight, reflex hammer, tuning fork, centimeter ruler or tape measure, wooden tongue depressor, two large straight pins or safety pins, a wisp of cotton, tissues, and thermometer.

The four basic techniques used for physical assessment are inspection, palpation, percussion, and auscultation. These techniques will be described separately. The sequential use of these techniques in examining body regions is as stated when all four techniques are employed. The one exception is in the assessment of the abdomen, when auscultation follows inspection.

Inspection is the deliberate and purposeful observation of phenomena—not just looking or seeing. Inspection also includes the technique of smell. It entails observing the whole person, recognizing specific anatomic structures and physiologic functions, and knowing the relationship of the specific parts to the whole and the whole to the parts. Generally, next to the patient's history, inspection provides the most significant information that leads to the identification of problems.

Palpation is the deliberate use of the hand to feel and touch in physical assessment. The hand has different tactile senses. The fingertips are generally more sensitive to touch and are useful in determining such things as the texture or consistency of skin, size of a nodule or lymph node, and the position of the thyroid. Temperature is best sensed by use of the dorsum of your hands and fingers. Vibration is detected with the palm and lateral aspect of the hand.

The amount of pressure applied when palpating varies depending upon where one is palpating and for what purpose palpation is being done. Generally, light palpation is preferred. Better discrimination occurs with repeated pressure rather than dulling sensation by continuous pressure.

Deep palpation involves exerting more pressure, and it is used primarily in the abdominal area. One hand or two hands may be used. When using the one-hand method, the palmar surface of the right hand is pressed against the abdomen with the fingers slanted inward 4 to 5 cm. Pressure greater than for light palpation is applied as the hand slides over the abdominal wall. In the two-hand method, the right hand is positioned as in single-handed palpation with the fingers of the left hand used to exert pressure on the right hand. The left hand exerts the pressure, and the fingertips of the right hand feel sensations of underlying organs and structures (Fig. 13-2).

Ballottement is another technique used to examine the abdomen. This term applies to two somewhat different techniques. In single-handed ballottement, the approximated fingers may be used to gently and lightly palpate the eyeball to detect tension. Also, by abruptly plunging the fingers into the abdomen and holding them there, one may detect a freely movable mass which will rebound upward and be felt on the fingertips. This is most commonly used to feel an enlarged liver obscured by the presence of free fluid in the abdomen. Bimanual ballottement is used essentially in the abdomen to determine the size of a large mass. The right hand is used to push the anterior abdominal wall while the left hand palpates the flank to obtain an estimate of the thickness of the mass (De Gowin and De Gowin, 1976, p. 497).

Percussion is the act of striking a portion of the body to elicit a sound which reflects the density of an organ and structure. The sound is helpful in identifying and delimiting certain organs and structures and contributing to the assessment of organ function.

Percussion sounds (notes) are produced by vibrating the underlying structure which has been struck. The degree of vibration and the tone of the sound are determined by the ratio of air or fluid to mass. The more solid the organ or structure, the less vibration. The presence of more air to mass, the more vibration. Also, consideration should be given to the depth of the organ or structure and to the size. Sherman and Fields (1978) state that percussion will not produce vibration of deep structures (more than 4 to 5 cm) or structures smaller than 4 to 5 cm.

The indirect act of percussion is performed by placing the middle finger of one hand (pleximeter) firmly against the area to be percussed. The tip of the middle finger of the other hand (plexor) is used to strike or tap the distal third of the pleximeter. The plexor, using flexible wrist motion, taps or strikes the pleximeter with a very short, brisk blow.

The sound produced by percussion depends upon the density of the tissue underneath the pleximeter. The percussion notes which reflect the density of organs and structures should be understood in relation to the characteristics of the sound. Sound is characterized by:

1. Pitch—the vibration frequency of sound

2. Intensity—the measurement of loudness

3. Quality—the distinctiveness of the overtone

4. Duration—the length of time the sound is heard

Thus, to aid in the understanding of the meaning of sounds of percussion, a description of the characteristics of sound, density of tissue, and examples of location are presented in Table 13-1.

Auscultation is the use of a stethoscope to enhance the perception of sound created in organs and structures. The most important aspect of auscultation is using a stethoscope that meets the criteria for adequate transmission of sound, remembering that all parts of the instrument influence the perception of sound.

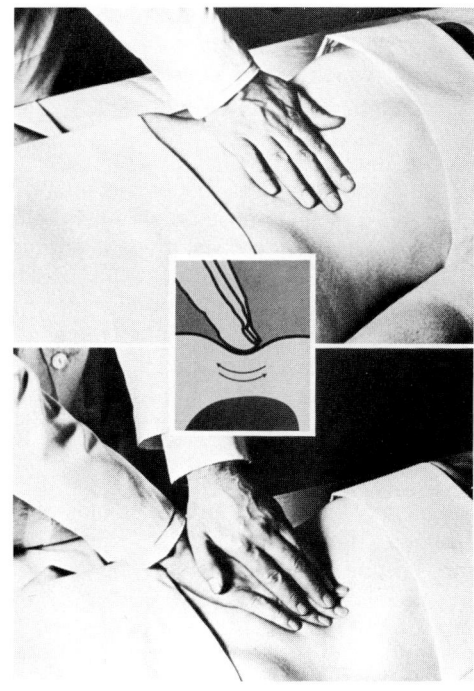

FIGURE 13-2
One-hand and two-hand methods of palpation. (*From A. H. Robins, G.I. Series of the Abdomen. Physical Examination of the Abdomen, part 2, A. H. Robins, Richmond, Va., 1969. Used by permission of the publisher.*)

The stethoscope used for purposes other than blood pressure measurement should have a bell and diaphragm. The bell is normally no more than 1 in in

			TABLE 13-1			
			Percussion Sounds			
Note	Pitch	Intensity	Quality	Duration	Density	Examples of location
Tympany	Very high	High	Musical	Long	More air than solid tissue	Gastric air bubble
Hyper-resonance	Low	Moderately high	Slightly musical	Moderately long	More air than solid tissue	Emphysematous lung
Resonance	Moderately low	Moderate	Nonmusical	Moderate	Normal air to tissue ratio for lung	Normal lung
Dull	Moderately high	Low	Nonmusical, muffled	Short	Fluid plus solid tissue	Liver, heart
Flat	High	Low	Soft thud	Short	Solid tissue	Bone, thigh

diameter. It is used for low-pitched sounds (i.e., some gallops, S_3, S_4) and small or bony areas. The diaphragm, which is the chest piece most frequently used, picks up high-pitched sounds (i.e., S_1, S_2, systolic murmurs).

The length of the tubing should be as short as possible because the shorter the tubing, the more efficient the sound transmission. A length of about 10 to 14 in from yoke to chest piece is suggested.

The tubing should be thick, stiff, and heavy, with an internal diameter of approximately $\frac{1}{8}$ in. Two tubes from chest piece to binaural are said to provide better conduction than one; if they are rubbed together, however, distracting noises can be made during auscultation, possibly giving the impression of an abnormal sound.

Of unquestionable importance are the snug yet gentle fit of the ear tips and the comfort of the binaural headset. The binaural headset should be light, and the ear tips should be large enough to occlude the ear canals around the central opening and prevent intrusion of room noises.

When using the stethoscope for auscultation of heart sounds, lung sounds, bowel sounds, and so on, the practitioner should learn to tune in sounds being assessed and tune out unwanted sounds. The art of tuning in and out simply requires concentration and practice.

THE EXAMINATION

In performing a physical examination, one of the most important things to remember is that you are dealing with a human being who responds not only to intrapersonal and extrapersonal or environmental factors but also to interpersonal factors such as the response of the patient (examinee) to the practitioner (examiner). The practitioner should maintain an awareness of this interpersonal process regardless of the patient's state of consciousness.

A humanistic and individualized approach to the patient helps to promote cooperation and decrease anxiety, which are important to a successful examination. The patient who is able to relax during the physical examination allows for more certainty and less doubt regarding physical findings; for example, a tense abdomen may give the impression of abdominal rigidity or may make it difficult for the examiner to palpate the edge of the liver.

Position of Patient

In the critical-care setting, positioning of the patient for a physical examination in many instances requires a modification of the classical approach. The patient most frequently is on bedrest, which prevents the standing position; frequently, the patient has tubes, is connected to a respirator, or is so critically ill that free movement (mobility) is difficult or impossible. Therefore, these general rules might be followed: (1) Consider the classical position for the regional or systems examination. (2) If the classical position is contraindicated, position the patient in the next best way which allows for the application of assessment techniques to a particular region of the body or the system. (3) If an alternate position is not possible, defer that portion of the examination until a more appropriate time. For example, when auscultating for lung sounds, if sitting is contraindicated, have the patient turn to the left lateral position and then the right lateral position to listen to the lungs; it should be remembered that the lying position does not allow for as much chest expansion as the sitting position, and this influences the quality of lung sounds. For a patient on bedrest, standing may be contraindicated, and therefore the gait and station examination should be deferred.

General Appearance

Just as a person gets a general feeling or impression about another's personality when they first meet, the practitioner also develops an impression of the patient's general state of wellness or illness. This impression, in many instances, helps to determine the seriousness of the patient's condition (i.e., the patient is in severe respiratory distress and has severe chest pain or abdominal pain).

The impression entails observations of the whole individual and represents a gross overview of the patient's appearance. The impression is stated in objective terminology and should include comments relative to the following areas.

Age and development—Noting the chronological age and body build of an individual in comparison to appearance gives an idea of the possible wear and tear on the body or the effects of chronic disease; heredity is also recognized as a basic factor.

Sex and race—The recognition of sex and race are important since certain disease entities are found more frequently or exclusively in the male and female and different races of people.

Level of consciousness—The patient's state of consciousness should be described as alert, lethargic, obtunded, stuporous, semicomatose, or comatose. This is further assessed in the neurological examination.

Speech—The speech is described as clear, slurred, or unintelligible. This is also further assessed in the neurological examination.

Cooperation—The cooperativeness of the patient is described as cooperative, uncooperative, or combative.

Appearance of physical health and comfort—A description of the patient's physical state or disability and the presence or absence of physical pain or discomfort should be noted. This may be stated as "no gross abnormalities" and "in no acute physical distress."

Appearance of psychological health and comfort—A statement of the degree of observable emotional stress is also important. The patient may be described as "a tense man" or "a very anxious young woman."

Nutritional status—This may be noted as obese, malnourished, well-nourished or cachectic. The patient's stated height and weight helps to support this statement, although it is not necessarily stated here. An example of a description of general impression would be "an alert, well-developed, well-nourished, cooperative young man who appears of stated age, is in moderate physical pain, and appears anxious."

Vital Signs

The patient's temperature, pulse, respiration, and blood pressure are taken upon admission and monitored at intervals or continuously, depending upon the patient's condition. Determination of vital signs has been included in the assessment process by nurses for many years. As nurses learn more techniques of physical assessment, it should not be forgotten that vital signs are still key elements in determining the progress of a patient's condition.

The *temperature* may be axillary or may be taken orally or rectally. The normal range for oral temperature in a resting patient is 97.7 to 99.5°F (36.5 to 37.5°C). Rectal temperatures register 1°F higher.

Temperature variation occurs for many reasons. Hyperthermia or fever may be due to infection, inflammation from surgical or accidental trauma, destruction of tissue such as a myocardial infarction, or disease of the central nervous system, which directly affects the thermostat in the hypothalamus. Hypothermia occurs in shock and with infusions of large amounts of cold blood. It is purposefully induced in such

instances as cardiovascular surgery, neurosurgery, gastrointestinal hemorrhage, or high fever.

The *arterial pulse* reflects the patient's heart rate and stroke volume. All pulses should be assessed upon admission to establish a baseline for further evaluation. These pulses include the radial, brachial carotid, femoral, popliteal, dorsalis pedis, and posterior tibial. They should be palpated bilaterally and described in terms of rate, rhythm, contour, and quality.

The *rate* of the pulse is normally 60 to 100 beats per minute. Irregularities of pulse rate range from tachycardia (a pulse greater than 100 beats per minute) to bradycardia (a pulse less than 60 beats per minute). Count the rate for 30 s and multiply by 2. If an abnormality is detected, count the pulse for one full minute.

Rhythm is normally regular. Palpable variations from normal include such irregularities as premature beats, erratic beats, and pauses. Irregular patterns of peripheral pulsation do not always represent true ventricular rate and rhythm since there may be insufficient volume or pressure generated by the ventricle to consistently open the aortic valve to produce a pulse. Therefore, such findings as premature or erratic beats and pauses may be representative of such arrhythmias as premature ventricular or atrial contraction, premature nodal contraction, bigeminy, or ventricular fibrillation. If an abnormality in the radial pulse is suspected, the apical pulse should be taken at the same time as the radial to determine the existence of a pulse deficit. Confirmation of the presence of arrhythmias is best determined by auscultation and electrocardiogram.

The *contour* of the normal arterial pulse consists of a primary wave and a dicrotic wave. The primary wave is smooth and round and starts with a swift upstroke to the peak of systolic pressure followed by a gradual decline. Toward the end of systole, a secondary and normally smaller upstroke occurs. Though not palpable, this upstroke is represented graphically by a notch, dicrotic wave, which is set up by a rebound against the closing aortic valve. Variations of the pulse wave contour include small weak pulse, large bounding pulse, pulsus alternans, bigeminal pulse, and pulsus paradoxus (Fig. 13-3).

The *quality* of the pulse is characterized by its strength and forcefulness. It is described using a four-point scale: 0 is absent, 1+ is thready, 2+ is decreased, 3+ is normal, and 4+ is hyperactive.

Respirations are assessed in terms of quality, rate, depth, and pattern. The quality of normal respiration

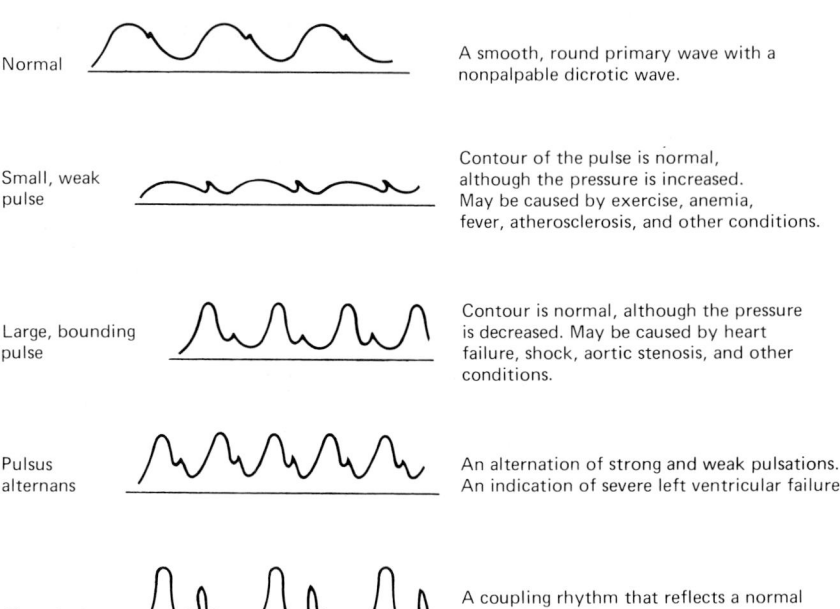

Normal — A smooth, round primary wave with a nonpalpable dicrotic wave.

Small, weak pulse — Contour of the pulse is normal, although the pressure is increased. May be caused by exercise, anemia, fever, atherosclerosis, and other conditions.

Large, bounding pulse — Contour is normal, although the pressure is decreased. May be caused by heart failure, shock, aortic stenosis, and other conditions.

Pulsus alternans — An alternation of strong and weak pulsations. An indication of severe left ventricular failure.

Bigeminal pulse — A coupling rhythm that reflects a normal beat quickly followed by a premature ventricular contraction. May resemble a pulsus alternans.

FIGURE 13-3
Arterial pulse waves.

is effortless, quiet, and regular except for pauses or sighs. Quality is assessed by inspecting the movement of the thorax during breathing. It is noted if the patient is using primarily the diaphragm or costal muscles of respiration, since men and children are primarily abdominal breathers and women generally are thoracic breathers. A change in muscular use may suggest respiratory difficulty.

The patient is further evaluated for abnormal chest movement or difficulty in breathing such as infrasternal, suprasternal, or intercostal retraction; use of neck and back muscles; excessively long expiratory phases as in emphysema; or en bloc movement, where the entire chest moves as a whole unit as seen in emphysema or chronic asthma.

The normal respiratory rate and depth is described as *eupneic* breathing. The normal rate for an adult at rest is 12 to 18 breaths per minute. Determine the rate by counting the breaths for a full minute. If a patient is aware of you observing his or her breathing, it may vary from the normal pattern and rate; therefore, you may wish to check the respiratory rate while pretending to palpate the radial pulse.

The depth of respiration is the volume of air moved in and out of the lung with each breath. It is normally 500 cm³ in the adult. Variations from normal consist of changes such as *tachypnea* (increased rate), seen in patients with pneumonia, respiratory insufficiency, or brainstem lesions. *Hyperpnea* is increased rate and depth of respiration as seen in anxiety states. *Bradypnea* is a decrease in rate as seen in cases of respiratory depression caused by narcotics or a brain tumor (Fig. 13-4).

The normal pattern of respiration is a 6:5 ratio for expiration to inspiration when timed; however, the audible range for vesicular (normal) breath sounds is an inspiratory/expiratory ratio of 3:1. Abnormal respiratory patterns commonly seen are Cheyne-Stokes', Biots', and Kussmaul's respirations (Fig. 13-4).

Cheyne-Stokes' respirations are periods of abnormal breathing which alternate with periods of apnea. The periods of abnormal breathing are characterized by breaths which get progressively deeper, peak, and then get progressively shallow, finally ceasing. Each cycle lasts from 30 to 45 s, with the apneic period lasting up to 20 s. This is seen in increased intracranial pressure, renal and heart failure, meningitis, or drug overdose.

Biots' respiration is similar to Cheyne-Stokes except that during the breathing period, there is no progressive change in the depth of respiration (the depth of each breath remains basically the same). This is evident in central nervous system disorders such as brainstem compression. Kussmaul's respirations are characterized by deep regular breaths which may or may not increase in rate. This is classically seen in diabetic ketoacidosis.

Blood pressure is defined as the pressure exerted against the walls of the arteries. The indirect measurement (blood pressure cuff method) will be discussed here as a technique for physical examination. The blood pressure is taken in both arms of the patient in a lying, sitting, and standing position, if possible. The average normal blood pressure in a young adult is approximately 120 mmHg systolic/80 mmHg diastolic. The American Heart Association defines hypertension as a persistent elevation of blood pressure above 140/90 for an adult under age 40. For an adult age 40 or over, a blood pressure of 160/90 is considered hypertensive. It is seen in such conditions as kidney disease, adrenal hyperfunction, brain tumors, or unknown causes labeled "essential hypertension."

Hypotension is defined as a blood pressure of 95/60. Hypotension may be found in a healthy adult where no other symptoms are manifested. Disease states where hypotension is seen include shock, adrenal hypofunction, myocardial infarction, cardiac tamponade, and hypovolemia.

The arm blood pressure is measured by positioning the arm at heart level and wrapping a cuff evenly over the midportion of the upper arm (brachial artery). The lower edge should be about 2.5 cm above the antecubital fossa. Palpate the radial pulse, inflate the cuff rapidly until the pulse is nonpalpable, and then pump for an extra 20 to 30 mmHg beyond the palpable pulse. Place the diaphragm of the stethoscope over the brachial artery and then slowly release the pressure while listening to the presence and absence of the Korotkoff sounds. The systolic pressure is read as the presence of the first Korotkoff sound. The diastolic pressure is read as the Korotkoff sound, which is heard as the abrupt muffled sound which occurs following the last distinct sound. It is also recommended that the very last sound be recorded to present a clear picture of the blood pressure reading (i.e., 120/80/76).

The thigh blood pressure for an adult is measured by using a cuff and bag 18 to 20 cm wide. The cuff is placed on the midthigh, and the diaphragm of the stethoscope is placed at the popliteal fossa. A normal leg systolic blood pressure is 10 to 40 mmHg higher

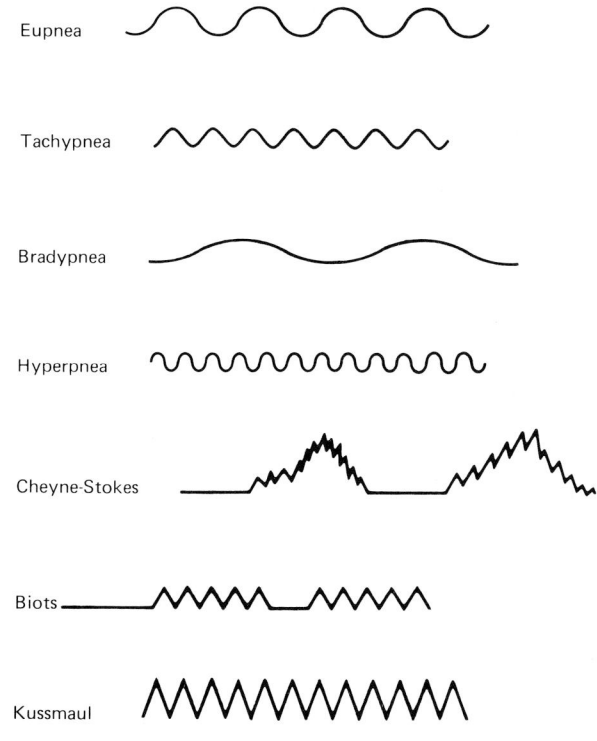

FIGURE 13-4
Abnormalities in rate and pattern of respiration.

than the arm systolic pressure (Schroeder and Daily, 1976, p. 38).

Three additional factors to observe when taking the blood pressure include the pulse pressure, the auscultatory gap, and the presence or absence of pulsus paradoxus or alternans. Pulse pressure is the difference between the systolic and diastolic arterial pressure, normally 30 to 40 mmHg. A narrowing pulse pressure is found in patients with low cardiac output syndromes and hypovolemic states. A widening pulse pressure is seen in normal pregnancy, as well as in neurosurgical patients with head trauma, possibly signaling an increased intracranial pressure. It is also found in patients with aortic valve regurgitation and arteriovenous communications (such as patent ductus arteriosus) and in the elderly patient with sclerotic arteries.

An auscultatory gap is sometimes found in patients who are hypertensive. This is a silent interval or apparent absence of Korotkoff sounds partway between systolic and diastolic pressures. Preliminary determination of systolic pressure by palpation can prevent underestimation of systolic pressure and over-estimation of the diastolic pressure.

Pulsus paradoxus referred originally to collapse of the palpated pulse on inspiration; this can also be detected during blood pressure measurement. Pulsus paradoxus now refers to an exaggeration of the normal respiratory variation of peak systolic pressure. Normally, at end expiration the systolic pressure is 8 mmHg or less higher than at end inspiration. Variations in excess of 14 mmHg may indicate the presence of cardiac tamponade, constrictive pericarditis, or severe obstructive lung disease, each of which interferes with normal left ventricular filling, resulting in variation of stroke volume through the respiratory cycle.

Pulsus alternans refers to alternating strength of pulse as on palpation. This may be observed on a direct blood pressure monitor or noted on auscultation of the blood pressure. Pulsus alternans typically indicates severely compromised left ventricular contractility.

SKIN

Just as the monitoring of other systems is important in critical care, so is the continual assessment of the skin. The skin literally covers a span from head to toe and is the first organ seen on contact with the patient. It protects the patient from disease entry, mirrors disease, and if traumatized, can complicate recovery from an ill state. The physical examination techniques utilized in skin assessment are inspection and palpation.

The examination of the skin, hair, and nails begins with inspection. Palpation is incorporated into the examination to provide further objectivity for physical findings such as demarcating lesions and for assessing skin integrity and temperature of skin.

To adequately assess the skin, proper lighting is imperative. Most critical-care settings do not have windows which allow for daylight, the best type of illumination. Therefore, a stand light or overhead light with at least a 60-W bulb is recommended. Flashlights and soft illuminations of many lights over hospital beds are frequently inadequate for detecting subtle skin color changes. The examination of the skin may be incorporated into the regional approach; however, the bedside nurse should devote a portion of time to assessing the skin as a whole, which can be viewed as a protecting and nurturing aspect of nursing care. The elements included in this assessment process are observing for abnormalities and changes in skin color, texture, turgor, moisture, temperature, and in-tegrity, and recognizing hair and nail changes or abnormalities.

Color Changes

Erythema is an increase in the reddish or bluish red tint of the skin. It may be a result of increased blood flow and dilation of blood vessels (i.e., fever, localized inflammation); decreased oxygen utilization in the skin (i.e., cold exposure, pressure areas cause reactive hyperemia); and a combination of increase in total amounts of hemoglobin, increase in reduced hemoglobin, and capillary stasis (i.e., polycythemia).

Cyanosis is a bluish discoloration of the skin and mucous membrane due to an increased amount of reduced hemoglobin in the small vessels. Cyanosis may be observed peripherally or centrally and is found in patients with pneumonia, severe chronic bronchitis, or heart disease.

Pallor is the whitish tint or absence of the reddish coloration of the skin. It is due to a marked decrease in the hemoglobin level of the blood. Pallor is usually seen in shock and anemia.

Jaundice is the yellowish discoloration of the skin due to increased bilirubin in skin or sclera. This is usually present in liver disease, biliary tract obstruction, and hemolysis of red blood cells.

Observations of skin color changes are best made in areas where the stratum corneum is thin or absent, such as the lips and the mucous membranes. Other areas to observe for color changes are nail beds and palms of the hand. In the light-skinned person, generalized pallor, jaundice, or peripheral cyanosis is not difficult for the practitioner to observe. But the dark-skinned person requires the observations of a practitioner who has good color sensitivity and knowledge of skin color variations. For example, pallor in brown skin appears yellowish brown; in black skin, it appears ashen gray.

Moisture

Increased moisture when abnormalities are not present is perspiration, a normal process; however, excessive perspiration is also associated with fever or thyrotoxicosis. Excessive dryness may be found in the elderly, dehydrated person, or patients with myxedema. Touching the skin is the best way to detect such changes.

Turgor

The turgor of the skin is examined by grasping a small section between the fingers and pulling upward. A delay in the return of the skin to its normal contour denotes dryness or loss of skin elasticity.

Texture

Skin texture refers to depth or quality of the skin. It may be thin or velvety smooth as in hyperthyroidism, puffy as in edema, or thick as in myxedema. The use of palpation is also necessary to determine the texture of the skin.

Temperature

Temperature changes are detected by placing the dorsal portion of the hand against the skin. Increased warmth is due to increased blood flow as a response to a generalized or localized inflammation. Increased coolness is due to reduced blood flow such as in occlusive peripheral vascular disease or therapeutic hypothermia for gastrointestinal hemorrhage or open-heart surgery.

Integrity

Changes in the integrity can best be described in terms of lesions and vascular and purpuric skin changes. Lesions are defined as a circumscribed area of pathological altered tissue, an injury or wound or an infected patch in the skin. Lesions will be categorized as primary, secondary, vascular, and purpuric.

Primary lesions are those occurring initially which result from traumatic stimuli, such as bullae secondary to burns (Table 13-2). Secondary lesions result from

TABLE 13-2
Primary Lesions of the Skin

Types	Definition	Example	Diagram
Macule	A flat, circumscribed area of color change in the skin without surface elevation Size: 1 mm to 2 cm	Freckles, vitiligo, purpura, petechia, flat moles, ecchymosis	
Papule	Circumscribed solid and elevated lesion Size: 1 mm to 1 cm	Ringworms, acne, psoriasis	
Nodule	Solid, elevated lesion extending deeper in the dermis Size: 1 to 2 cm	Erythema nodosum	
Tumor	Solid mass larger than a nodule Size: over 2 cm	Basal cell epithelioma	

TABLE 13-2 (Continued)
Primary Lesions of the Skin

Types	Definition	Example	Diagram
Cyst	A papule or nodule containing fluid or viscous material Size: 1 mm or over	Sebaceous and epidermal cysts	
Wheal	A clustering of papular-type lesions creating an edematous plaque Size: 1 mm to several cm	Mosquito bites, urticaria, and hives	
Vesicle	A bulging, small, sharply defined lesion filled with serous fluid or blood Size: less than 1 cm	Herpes simplex, herpes zoster	
Bulla	Larger than a vesicle Size: over 1 cm	Pemphigus, second degree burns	
Pustule	Vesicle or bulla filled with pus Size: 1 mm to 1 cm	Impetigo, acne vulgaris	

TABLE 13-3
Secondary Lesions of the Skin

Types	Definition	Example	Diagram
Crust	Dried serum, blood, pus, or sebum which forms on the surface of any vesicle or pustule lesion when it ruptures	Infectious dermatitis, eczema, impetigo	
Scale	Dried fragments of sloughed, dead epidermis	Exfoliative dermatitis, seborrheic dermatitis	

TABLE 13-3 (Continued)
Secondary Lesions of the Skin

Types	Definition	Example	Diagram
Excoriation	Scratch or scrape of original lesion		
Fissure	A crack in the skin, usually through the dermis	Chapping, eczema	
Ulcer	A depressed lesion resulting from loss of epidermis and the papillary layer of the dermis	Traumatic ulcers, burns, stasis, ulcer, chancre	
Scar	Replacement of destroyed tissue by fibrous tissue or excessive collagen	Surgical scar, keloid	

TABLE 13-4
Vascular and Bleeding Lesions

Types	Definition	Example	Diagram
Spider telangiectasia	A vascular configuration that is a circular or stellate, bright red, faintly pulsatile, highly branched arterial lesion of the subcutaneous and dermal layers Size: 0.5 to 2 cm	Liver disorders, pregnancy, vitamin B deficiency	

TABLE 13-4 (Continued)
Vascular and Bleeding Lesions

Types	Definition	Example	Diagram
Petechia	Tiny red or red-brown capillary hemorrhages located within the skin papillae; a small macule Size: 0.5 mm or less	Vitamin deficiency, blood dyscrasias, severe infection	
Ecchymosis	Large hemorrhages under the skin; a large macule Size: several mm to several cm	Trauma, blood dyscrasias	

some alteration, usually traumatic, to the primary lesion, for example, scarring of healed burn areas (Table 13-3). Vascular lesions are changes in the superficial vasculature of the skin (i.e., spider telangiectasia) and bleeding lesions, such as purpura, which occur when there is hemorrhage into the skin (Table 13-4). Lesions are described according to their location, distribution, size, contour, and consistency.

Hair Changes

Observe and feel the hair on the head, arms, and hands to determine the quantity, distribution, color, and texture. The quantity of hair may vary. Excessive hair growth is termed *hypertrichosis,* or *hirsutism.* This may be seen in Cushing's syndrome, testicular tumors, and acromegaly. Less hair than normal is known as *hypotrichosis. Alopecia,* the loss of hair, is seen in hypothyroidism, chemotherapy, and scleroderma.

Premature graying is worth noting in a young person but may also be found in pernicious anemia. Hair texture may vary from coarse and brittle (i.e., hypothyroidism) to fine and thin (hyperthyroidism).

Nail Changes

Clubbing of the nails should be assessed by inspection and palpation. There are three ways to determine

if clubbing is present. First, see if the angle of the nail bed is increased from the normal 160° to 180°. Second, check to see if the distal phalangeal depth (middle area of the fingernail) is greater than the interphalangeal depth (area right above the proximal nail fold). Finally, palpate the nail bed for a spongy sensation.

Beau's lines are transverse depressions in the nail bed which appear during the time of an acute illness. The nail grows out with this depression and is related to a decrease in the size of the matrix. (See Fig. 13-5.)

Splinter hemorrhages occur following trauma to the nail bed. In the past, it was thought to be a characteristic sign of subacute bacterial endocarditis; however, they are seen in normal nails as well as disease states, such as subacute bacterial endocarditis, mitral stenosis, and cirrhosis (Fig. 13-6).

Thermal Injuries

The patient admitted to the critical-care unit because of thermal injuries presents a very special problem in terms of assessment and management. Physical assessment of the skin of the patient with thermal injury includes determining the extent of total body surface area burned and assessing the depth of the tissue burned. See Chap. 30 for an indepth discussion.

HEAD, NECK, AND FACE

Assessment of the head, neck, and face region includes examining the skull, face, ears, eyes, nose, mouth, pharynx, and neck; however, in this chapter, the eye examination is discussed separately. In the critical-care patient, assessment of this region is primarily useful in obtaining information reflective of systemic, neurological, and cardiopulmonary functioning and emotional reaction to dysfunction and therapy.

Primary problems of the head, face, and neck do occur; however, these problems seldom require admission to the critical-care setting unless they result in obstruction to breathing, serious neurological problems, or life-threatening complications which require close continuous monitoring. Therefore, discussion of head, neck, and face assessment is directed toward deriving data relevant to emotional reactions and neurologic and cardiopulmonary functioning.

The examination techniques primarily used are inspection and palpation. Auscultation is used when listening to areas of vascular pulsation is needed, such as over the carotid arteries where bruits (vascular murmurs) are frequently heard.

Skull and Face

The *skull* is inspected and palpated for bulges, erythema, tenderness, pulsations, and irregularity of contour and size. This is of particular importance in patients who have fallen or have been in accidents. Temporal pulses are palpated bilaterally and described in terms of rate, rhythm, contour, and quality. If pulsations are noted in the skull, they should be evaluated by auscultation to determine if bruits exist.

The *facies* should be noted for expressions such as anxiety, apprehension, pain, or depression; however, it should not be forgotten that certain diseases have characteristic facies (i.e., the pale edematous facies of the nephrotic syndrome and the round moon face of Cushing's syndrome). The face is also assessed for scars, weakness, asymmetry, moisture, dryness, superficial vascularity, and cranial nerve functioning. Examination of cranial nerves V (trigeminal) and VII (facial) are discussed in the neurological examination.

Ears

The external ear is inspected and palpated for patency and structural integrity, swelling, and pain. The otoscope is then utilized to inspect the ear canal and

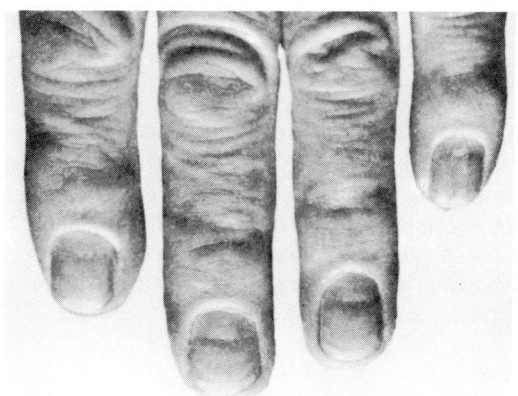

FIGURE 13-5
Beau's lines. (*From T. B. Fitzpatrick, K. A. Arndt, and W. H. Clark, Dermatology in General Medicine, 3d ed., McGraw-Hill, New York, 1979. Used by permission of the publisher.*)

tympanic membrane for the presence of serum, pus, blood, fibrosis, bulging, retraction, and/or congestion.

The acoustic nerve (VIII cranial) is assessed by the use of screening hearing tests such as the watch test, whispered voice test, Weber's test, and Rinne's test. These tests are performed to determine whether the patient has normal hearing perception and conduction. These tests are described as part of the neurological examination.

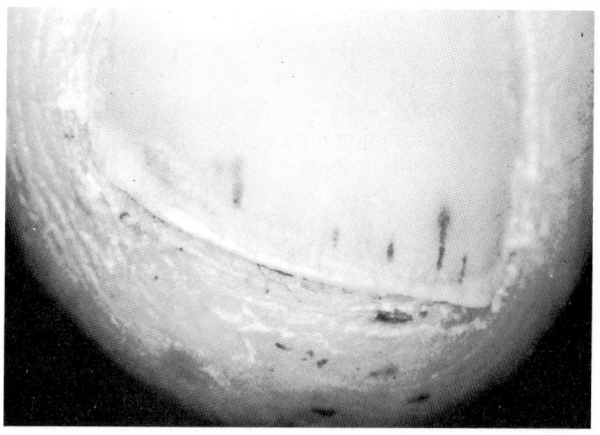

FIGURE 13-6
Splinter hemorrhages. (*From T. B. Fitzpatrick, K. A. Arndt, and W. H. Clark, Dermatology in General Medicine, 3d ed., McGraw-Hill, New York, 1979. Used by permission of the publisher.*)

Nose, Sinuses, Mouth, and Pharynx

The contour of the nose is inspected for asymmetry and abnormalities of profile. It is then palpated for loss of structure or support. Determining the patency of the nares is important because patients are frequently intubated via the nasopharynx. This is done by looking into each naris and digitally compressing each nostril while the patient inhales and exhales with the mouth closed. The soft nasal tip is then pushed upward and the orifices are inspected. Observations of the color of the mucous membrane and color and consistency of the secretions is enhanced by the use of a penlight or the large speculum of the otoscope.

The nasal septum should be transilluminated and examined for deviation, perforation, and masses. This is done by shining the light through one nostril and viewing the septum through the other.

Tenderness over the maxillary and frontal sinuses is detected by applying light pressure over the area medial to the cheekbone bilaterally and over each of the supraorbital ridges.

The *mouth* and *pharynx* are examined by inspection and palpation. The lips are observed for harelip or other congenital or acquired defects, and the alert patient may be asked to whistle or puff the cheeks to assess the facial (VII) cranial nerve. The lips are further assessed for color and for evidence of ulcers, granulomas, neoplasms, or angular stomatitis. The inner surface should always be retracted to observe for foreign particles, especially in the comatose patient.

The mouth is also inspected for foreign particles and symmetry and for the condition of the teeth, gums, buccal mucosa, tonsils, and pharynx.

The absence of teeth and the presence of caries, discoloration, and fillings are noted. The presence of a bridge or dentures should also be recorded. The gums are examined for retraction, inflammation sponginess, or bleeding. The buccal mucosa should be retracted with a tongue blade and examined for melanin deposits, vesicles, ulcers, or neoplasms. Generally, the mucous membrane of the mouth reveals the hydration status of the patient. The tonsils and pharynx should be observed for redness, ulcers, or masses. Hyperplasia of the tonsils should be noted. The patient's breath may have a foul odor indicative of infection or poor oral hygiene, a smell of acetone as in diabetic ketoacidoses, or an ammonia odor as detected in uremic patients.

The patient's tongue is assessed for size, color, mobility, and midline positioning. When asking the patient to extend the tongue for examination, you may also test for vagal (X) nerve paralysis by noting whether the uvula is drawn upward in the midline position when the patient says "eee." It is also suggested that the tongue and sublingual area be palpated with clean or gloved hand to evaluate for deep masses, especially when pain or restricted motion is detected.

Neck

The neck is examined by inspection, palpation, and auscultation. It is first examined as a whole unit with emphasis on color and turgor, size, shape, symmetry, deformity, and pulsation.

The curvature of the cervical spine is assessed by palpating each cervical vertebra and noting alignment. It may be helpful to mark each vertebra with a skin pencil, which makes alignment more noticeable.

The practitioner determines neck movement by flexing, rotating, and laterally bending the neck actively (movement of neck without assistance), passively (practitioner moves neck without assistance from patient), and against hand resistance.

The thyroid gland is checked for bilateral symmetrical enlargement, presence of nodules, and mobility. Adequate exposure of the gland is necessary for examination. One or both of the following techniques may be utilized to examine the thyroid gland. The practitioner stands behind the patient and places the ends of the fingers on each side of the lower half of the neck right below the cricoid cartilage. The patient's chin is slightly lowered in a downward relaxed position to release the tension on the neck muscles. Each side of the thyroid gland is pushed gently to the opposite side, displacing the larynx and trachea and exposing one of the thyroid lobes. The patient is asked to swallow while the lobe is gently palpated by the other hand for nodules. This technique is repeated on the opposite side. A similar technique may also be utilized standing in front of the patient. The patient again is asked to lower the chin, and each lobe area is palpated; the practitioner must remember to displace the larynx and trachea to one side and work around the sternocleidomastoid muscles. The thyroid gland is usually not palpable; therefore, when one or both lobes are easily palpated or nodules are felt, the thyroid gland should be auscultated for bruits.

The position of the trachea is assessed by inspection and palpation to determine if it is in a midline position. Ask the patient to flex the head and insert the index finger into the suprasternal notch on each side of the trachea. The amount of space on each side of the trachea should be approximately the same. Unevenness indicates tracheal and mediastinal shifting.

The lymph nodes of the head and neck are inspected and palpated for enlargement, tenderness, and mobility. Findings may be indicative of infection or inflammation from a variety of causes or malignancy. The following is a listing of the names and locations:

1. Occipital nodes—occipital region of the cranium
2. Posterior auricular nodes—behind the ear
3. Parotid nodes—front of the ear
    a. Preauricular nodes—medial to the ear
    b. Infra-auricular nodes—medial to the ear lobe
4. Submaxillary node—under the mandible along the lateral aspect
5. Submental node—under the chin
6. Posterior cervical nodes—along the posterior angle in front of the trapezius muscle
7. Superficial cervical—along the posterior angle behind the sternocleidomastoid muscle
8. Supraclavicular nodes—in the supraclavicular fossa
9. Deep cervical nodes
    a. Superior deep cervical nodes—in the uppermost part of the anterior angle
    b. Middle deep cervical nodes—in the middle area of the anterior angle
    c. Inferior deep cervical nodes—in the lower part of the anterior angle
10. Tonsillar node—in the area of the carotid plexus or at the posterior mandibular angle

The carotid pulses are palpated for rate, rhythm, quality, and contour and are auscultated for bruits. Jugular venous positioning and filling are assessed in a supine flat position and at a 45° angle. This gives information relative to cardiac compensation.

With the patient in a supine, flat position, inspect the oscillating column of blood in the internal or external jugular vein bilaterally. If it is difficult to detect the height of the column, raise the head of the bed to a 45° angle. Engorgement of the veins is usually only present in the flat position; therefore, if fullness and pulsation are present at the 45° angle, increased venous pressure should be suspected. Notation should be made of the vertical distance between the height of the column of jugular venous distention and the angle of Louis (sternal angle) and this information recorded in the following manner: "The jugular venous distention is 3 cm above the angle of Louis at a 45° elevation."

EYE

Examination of the eye is very useful in determining the status of a patient. Evidence of systemic or local problems or disease is often reflected in the condition of the eyes. A complete eye examination includes inspection of the external structures, testing of visual acuity and visual fields, assessment of extraocular pressure testing, and examination of the fundus.

Examination

The techniques of inspection and palpation are the most useful when examining the eye. In order to perform these techniques, an ophthalmoscope, cotton-tipped applicator, tongue blade, a newspaper or magazine, and a penlight will be needed.

External Structures

The physical examination of the eye begins with examination of the external structures. Observe the general appearance of the face, expression, eyebrows, blinking, alignment of the eyes, and prominence of the eye globes. A few moments spent just looking at a patient's face can reveal a number of clues to the physical and emotional condition of the patient.

The *external lids* are inspected for color abnormalities, lesions, edema, and excessive vascularity. Observe the palpebral fissures (the eye slits) for symmetry and observe the closure of the lids, since incomplete closure can lead to corneal drying with the possibility of permanent damage resulting.

Evaluation of the *eyelashes* will reveal if there is any abnormality in the direction of the lashes. This is important because lashes which are inverted or everted can lead to corneal irritation. The lacrimal ducts are inspected for patency, excessive tearing, and the presence of any infection.

The *conjunctiva* is divided into two portions, palpebral and bulbar (see Fig. 13-7). The palpebral conjunctiva lines the posterior lid surface; the bulbar conjunctiva covers the eye to the limbus. The limbus is the junction of the cornea and the sclera. The bulbar conjunctiva can be examined by having the patient look up, down, and to the side while you hold open

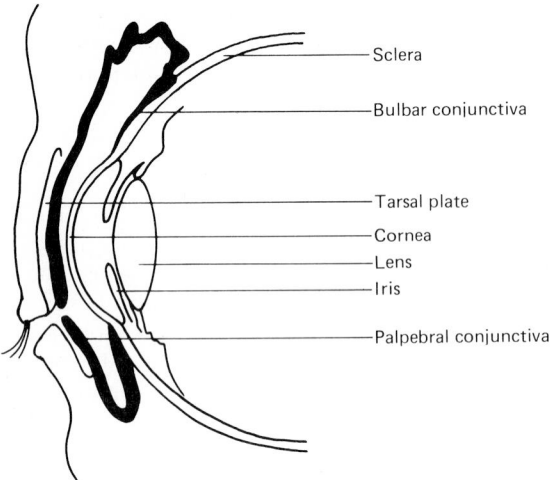

Sclera

Bulbar conjunctiva

Tarsal plate

Cornea

Lens

Iris

Palpebral conjunctiva

FIGURE 13-7
Schematic representation of the eyeball
and related structures.

the lids. The palpebral portion can be examined on the upper lid by everting the lid with an applicator stick. The conjunctiva of the lower lid can be visualized by sliding the skin of the lower lid over the lower orbital rim. Conjunctiva are evaluated for color and vascularity. Frequently, a pale conjunctiva is indicative of anemia, while a dusky color may indicate hypoxia.

Evaluation of the *sclera* can be done at this time and any changes in the color should be carefully noted. The sclera is usually white. A yellow tinge is indicative of jaundice.

In order to assess the conjunctiva and the sclera, manipulation of the eye is necessary. This examination must be done with extreme care and is usually deferred if eye damage exists. Certain of the above observations, however, are necessary to determine the extent of any damage. An example would be the badly bruised, swollen eye of the accident victim. Examination is necessary, but pressure should not be applied to the globe or the orbital rim.

The *cornea* and *lens* are examined with oblique lighting for detection of opacities. Corneal opacities which may be observed are arcus senilis (a circle of gray material just within the limbus, which is common in older persons), corneal scars from old injuries, and possibly pterygium (a triangular thickening of the bulbar conjunctiva which grows slowly across the eye). The pterygium is not a true opacity but can interfere with vision. Cataracts, another type of opac-

ity, may be visualized on examination with oblique lighting and can be seen with the ophthalmoscope as grey or black against the red reflex. In addition, the iris is inspected and any abnormal markings are noted.

The *pupils* are evaluated for size, equality, and the pupillary light reflex. Shine a light directly into one pupil and observe for constriction. This is called the *direct light response*. Again shine a light in one pupil and observe the response in the other pupil. This is called the *consensual light response*. Failure of pupillary response to light is an important sign of possible oculomotor lesions. Test accommodation and convergence by having the patient focus at a distance and then follow your finger as you bring it in toward the patient's nose. Note convergence of the eyes and the pupillary constriction as the pupil accommodates. Loss of the accommodation-convergence reflex may result from a lesion of cranial nerve III (oculomotor).

Visual Acuity and Visual Fields

Since cranial nerves II, III, IV, and VI are principally concerned with the actions of the eye, they will be discussed in depth in this section. The optic nerve (cranial nerve II) carries impulses from the retina to the optic chiasm. From here the impulses go to areas in the cerebral cortex where visual images are recognized and interpreted. Lesions causing disorders can occur anywhere from the eyeball to the occipital cortex. Two aspects of vision are commonly tested: visual acuity and visual fields. In addition, an ophthalmoscope is used to examine the retina, optic disk, vessels, and macula.

Visual acuity is easily tested in the critical-care unit with a newspaper or magazine. The patient is asked to read with one eye at a time, covering the other with a patch. The patient who normally wears glasses is asked to do so. It is important to determine a patient's ability or lack of ability to read, since it may interfere with the ability to fully participate in the program of treatment. For example, instructions regarding activities or consent forms for procedures may be given to the patient to read. Also, certain cerebral disorders may have altered the ability to read and/or to interpret written items. An example would be a stroke.

Visual field testing is done using the confrontation method. Each eye is evaluated separately as the examiner stands an arm's length from the patient. Have the patient close (cover with the hand) the right eye and look with the left eye into the examiner's right eye. Steadily bring a wiggling finger in from the periphery until the patient sees it. The finger should be equal distance between the examiner and the patient except temporally when you must start behind the patient. Perform this maneuver for all quadrants and then repeat with the other eye. If a defect is found, determine the configuration by retesting and sketching the defect. Normally, the patient will see an object 60° nasally, 50° upward, 90° temporally, and 70° downward.

Ocular Movements

The oculomotor (cranial nerve III), trochlear (cranial nerve IV), and the abducens (cranial nerve VI) have similar functions and are usually examined together. These three cranial nerves act together in controlling the ocular muscles to ensure that the eyes remain parallel through all movements. In addition, the oculomotor nerve controls the muscle that elevates the upper lid and innervates the constrictor muscle of the pupil. A lesion of these nerves might produce diplopia because of weakness of ocular muscles and deviation of the eyeball from a parallel position. Ptosis of the eyelid and sustained pupillary dilation indicate possible oculomotor problems. Before testing, inspect the position of the upper eyelids with the patient gazing directly at you. Observe for ptosis and for any lower lid sagging which may indicate weakness of the obiculares oculi muscle.

Extraocular movements are evaluated by asking the patient to follow your finger through the six cardinal positions of gaze (see Fig. 13-8). Pause during lateral and upward gaze to observe for nystagmus. Also observe for any deviation from normal conjugate movements and for the relationship of the upper lid to the eye globe. The upper lid normally overlaps the iris slightly as the gaze moves upward from downward position. This overlapping may not occur with hyperthyroidism.

Ophthalmoscopic Examination

The ophthalmoscopic examination is not an easy task, but it is undertaken to add to the store of knowledge about the critical-care patient. This examination should be conducted in a darkened room. The technique of using the examiner's right hand and right eye to test the patient's right eye and the examiner's left hand and left eye for the patient's left eye should be observed. The ophthalmoscope should be set at the diopter setting best suited to your needs. Zero diopters is neutral (it does not converge or diverge light rays). A plus diopter (black numbers) setting is used for a farsighted patient, and a minus diopter (red numbers) setting is used for the nearsighted patient. Place your thumb on the patient's brow and have the patient focus on a spot at a distance somewhere over your shoulder. Approach gradually from a distance of about 15 in and a position of 15° lateral to the patient's direct line of vision. Shine the light on the pupil, noting the red reflex and any lens opacities. Move in until you are touching your thumb of the opposite hand (which is on the patient's brow) with the ophthalmoscope. You should now be viewing the optic disk which is a red-orange, smooth, round or vertically oval structure. If the disk is not yet in view, follow a blood vessel until you locate the disk. Observe the disk for color, shape, margin clarity, and the physiological cup (a bright area in the center of the disk). Note the disk/physiological cup ratio. Also observe any pigmented rings or crescents around the

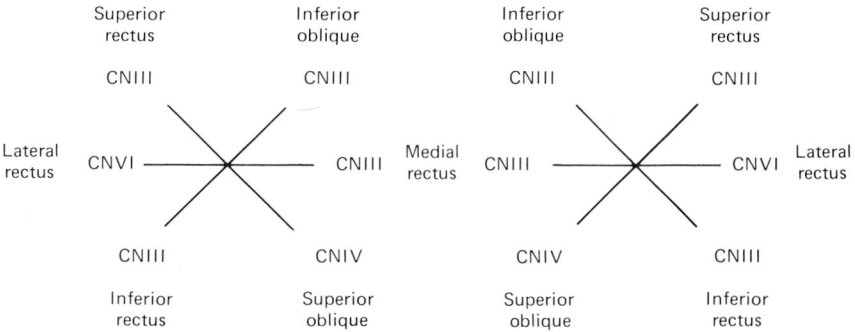

FIGURE 13-8

Cardinal positions of gaze with corresponding cranial nerves and muscles.

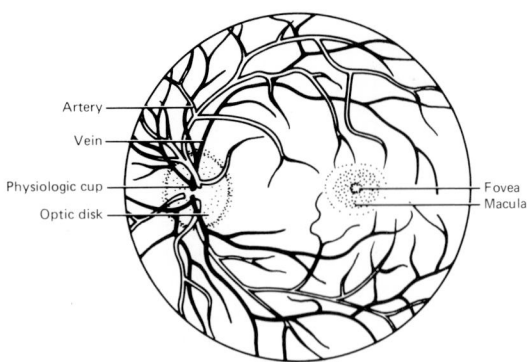

FIGURE 13-9

Illustration of the optic disk, macula, and retinal vessels as viewed through an ophthalmoscope. (*From P. Mayfield et al.: Physical Assessment: A Programmed Approach, McGraw-Hill, New York, 1980. Used by permission of the publisher.*)

disk. Observe the vessels for distribution in all four quadrants. Follow the vessels from the disk to the margin of the fundus, observing for occlusion, arteriole/venous nicking, and abnormal size. (Veins are normally larger, darker, and pulsate; arterioles are smaller, brighter, and do not pulsate.)(See Fig. 13-9.) Examine the general background, noting pig-

mentation appropriate to individual coloring (the darker the skin, the darker the fundus).

Observe also for hemorrhages, cotton wool patches, exudates, and retinal edema. (See Fig. 13-10.) Now have the patient look directly into the light and evaluate the macula and the fovea. The macula is 2 to 3 disk diameters temporally from the disk, and the fovea is in the center of the macula. (See Fig. 13-9).

The most important abnormalities which are found on fundoscopic examination are a disk which is hyperemic (pinker), disk atrophy (pale with blurred edges), or papilledema (choked or swollen disk). The very first signs of papilledema may be the absence of retinal vein pulsation or enlargement and increase in the size of retinal veins as compared to the arterioles. The arteries may be thickened and pulsating which is abnormal. Optic atrophy may be the result of diseases which affect the optic nerve, such as syphilis. Papilledema, which is secondary to increased intracranial pressure, may also result in optic atrophy. The changes which can occur in arteries and veins are seen in Fig. 13-10.

Intraocular Pressure

Intraocular pressure is evaluated manually by placing both index fingers gently on the closed eye. Press with one finger and estimate with the other finger the

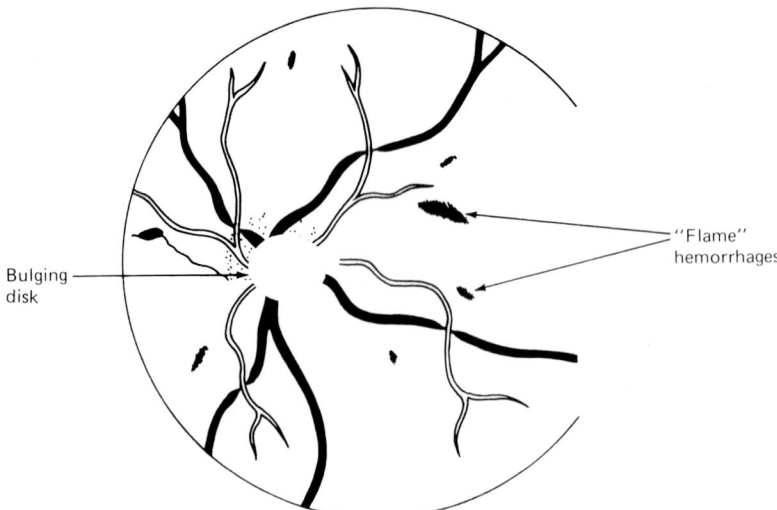

FIGURE 13-10

Ocular fundus illustrating severe hypertensive changes. Note extremely narrowed and tortuous arteries, venous compression, flame-shaped hemorrhages, and bulging optic disk.

amount of pressure needed to move the eyeball. The eyeball is evaluated for hardness or softness. Softened globes are indicative of dehydration, while hardened globes indicate increased ocular tension as in glaucoma. A tonometer is required to most efficiently evaluate ocular tension.

LUNGS

A basic understanding of the topography of the chest is essential in assessing lung function. A working knowledge of the location of organs within the chest and structures of the thorax is important in distinguishing between normal and abnormal findings. It is also important to remember that there are normal variations in structure among individuals.

The bony thorax consists of the sternum, ribs, and vertebral column. The sternum forms the anterior medial connection for the rib cage, and the vertebral column forms the posterior connection. The sternum consists of the manubrium, body, and xiphoid process. The area where the manubrium connects to the body is called the *angle of Louis,* a reference point for locating the 2d costal cartilage and for measuring central venous pressure. There are 12 pairs of ribs. The first seven are connected to the sternum. The 8th, 9th, and 10th ribs are joined together by a common cartilage and attached to the sternum. The 11th and 12th ribs are not connected to the sternum and are called *floating ribs* (Fig. 13-11).

The lungs in midinspiration are located from the first (1st) rib anteriorly to approximately the seventh (7th) rib and from the first (1st) rib posteriorly to approximately the tenth (10th) vertebra or tenth (10th) intercostal space. This is demonstrated in Fig. 13-12 by the lung diagram area with the vertical lines. The lung in deep inspiration (represented in the same figure by the dotted inferior lung area) descends

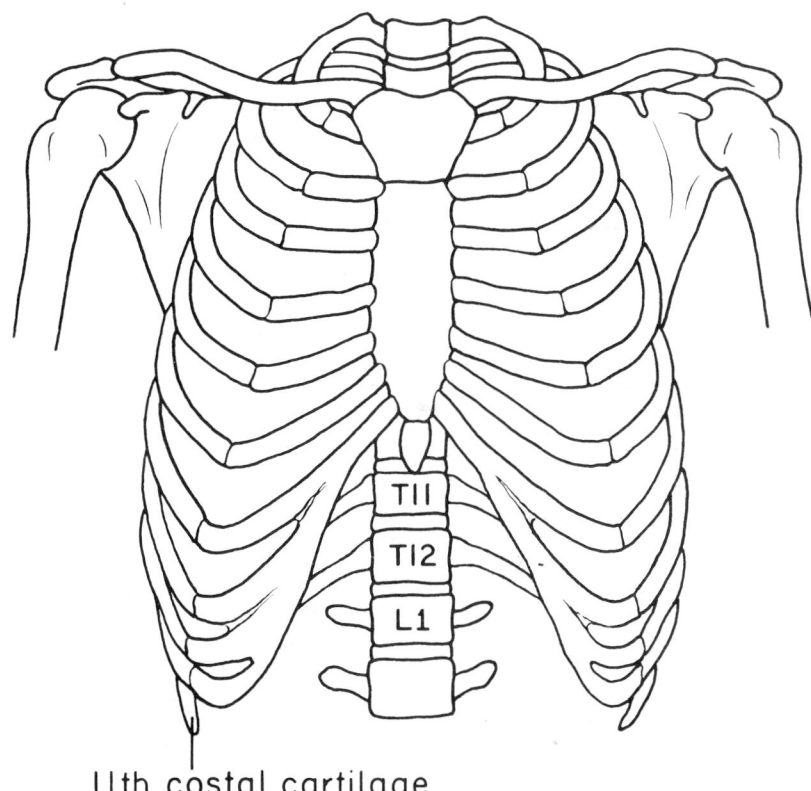

11th costal cartilage

FIGURE 13-11

Bony thorax. (*From E. Hochstein and A. L. Rubin, Physical Diagnosis, McGraw-Hill, New York, 1964. Used by permission of the publisher.*)

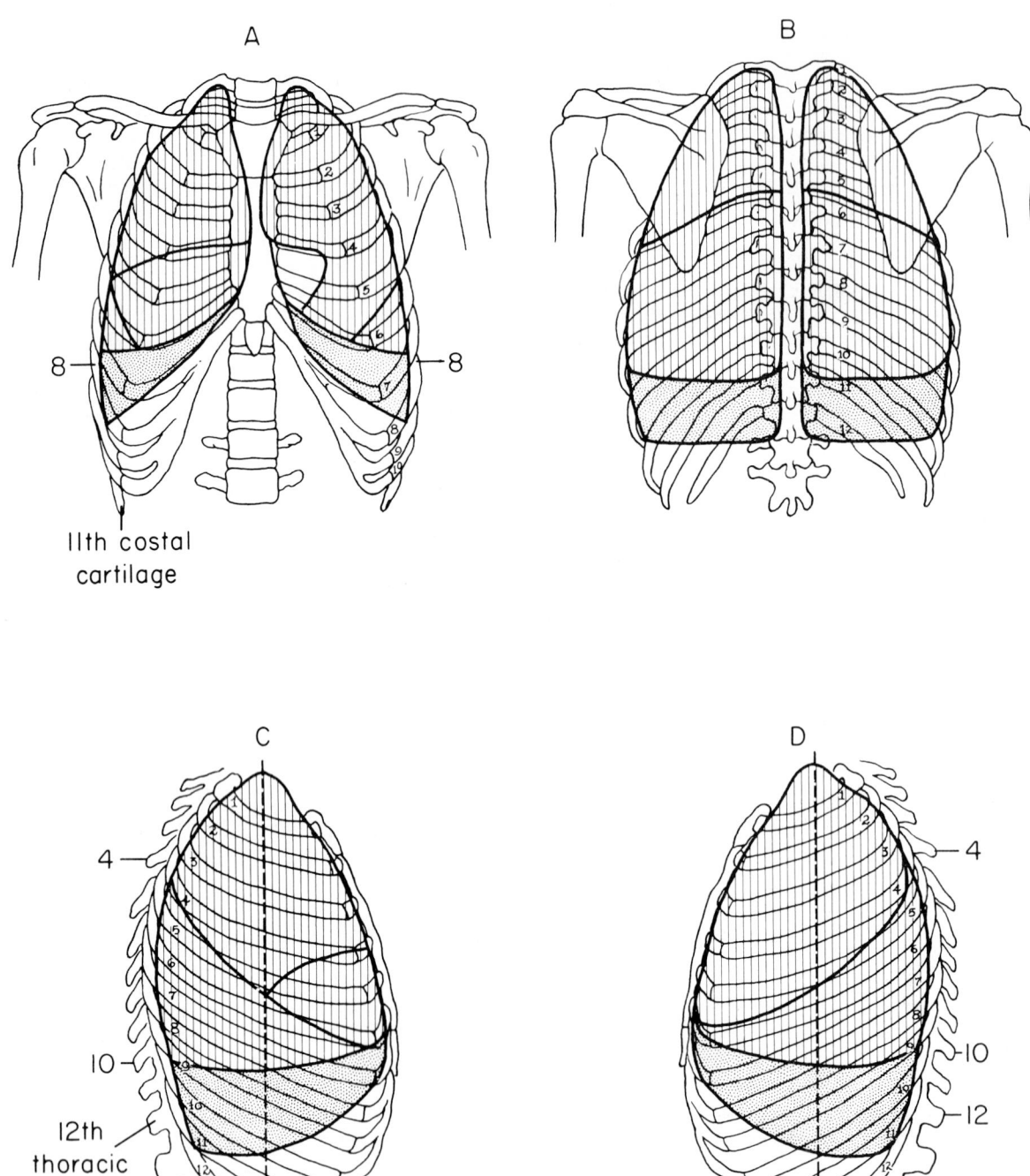

FIGURE 13-12
Surface projections of the fissures of the lung, borders of the lung, and pleura. (*From E. Hochstein and A. L. Rubin, Physical Diagnosis, McGraw-Hill, New York, 1964. Used by permission of the publisher.*)

approximately 2.5 cm anteriorly, 5 cm posteriorly, and 7.5 cm laterally to fill the pleural cavity and part of the costophrenic sinus.

The lungs are relatively symmetrical. The right lung has three lobes: upper, middle, and lower. The left lung has two lobes: the upper and lower. However, the lingular segment of the upper lobe corresponds with the middle lobe of the right lung. Each lobe is separated from the others by a natural division of the lung called *lobar fissures*. The major or oblique fissure separates the upper and lower lobes bilaterally. The fissure is located posteriorly at approximately the 3d or 4th thoracic vertebra, extends to the 5th rib laterally at the midaxillary line, and around to the 6th intercostal space anteriorly. The minor or transverse fissure divides the middle and upper lobes of the right lung and is located at the 4th intercostal space anteriorly to the midaxillary line at the 5th rib (refer to Fig. 13-12).

Each lung is further divided into segments. See Fig. 13-13 for the distribution of the lobar bronchi, their segmental branches, and the pulmonary segments. The *mediastinum* contains such structures as the heart, trachea, major bronchi, lymphatic struc-

tures, great vessels, thymus, and esophagus. Figure 13-14 shows the surface projection of the heart and large vessels. The right border of the heart is normally located 1 cm lateral to the right sternal border edge. It extends from the 3d rib superiorly down to the 5th intercostal space inferiorly. The left border begins superiorly at the 3d rib or 3d intercostal space approximately 1 cm lateral to the left sternal edge. It continues down diagonally to the 6th rib, approximately 5 cm from the left sternal border or 7 to 9 cm from the midsternal line.

Other areas of note anatomically are the diaphragm, liver, stomach, and spleen, as shown in Fig. 13-15. The diaphragm is a dome-shaped projection in the lower thoracic cage and is located (on mid-expiration) at the 5th intercostal space on the right hemithorax and the 6th rib on the left hemithorax. The liver lies beneath the right diaphragm with the superior border located at about the 5th rib and extends downward to the 11th rib.

The stomach normally contains an air bubble of variable size that yields a percussion sound of tympany in an area known as *Traube's semilunar space*. The tympanic sound is usually heard in the upper

RIGHT LUNG AND BRONCHI   LEFT LUNG AND BRONCHI

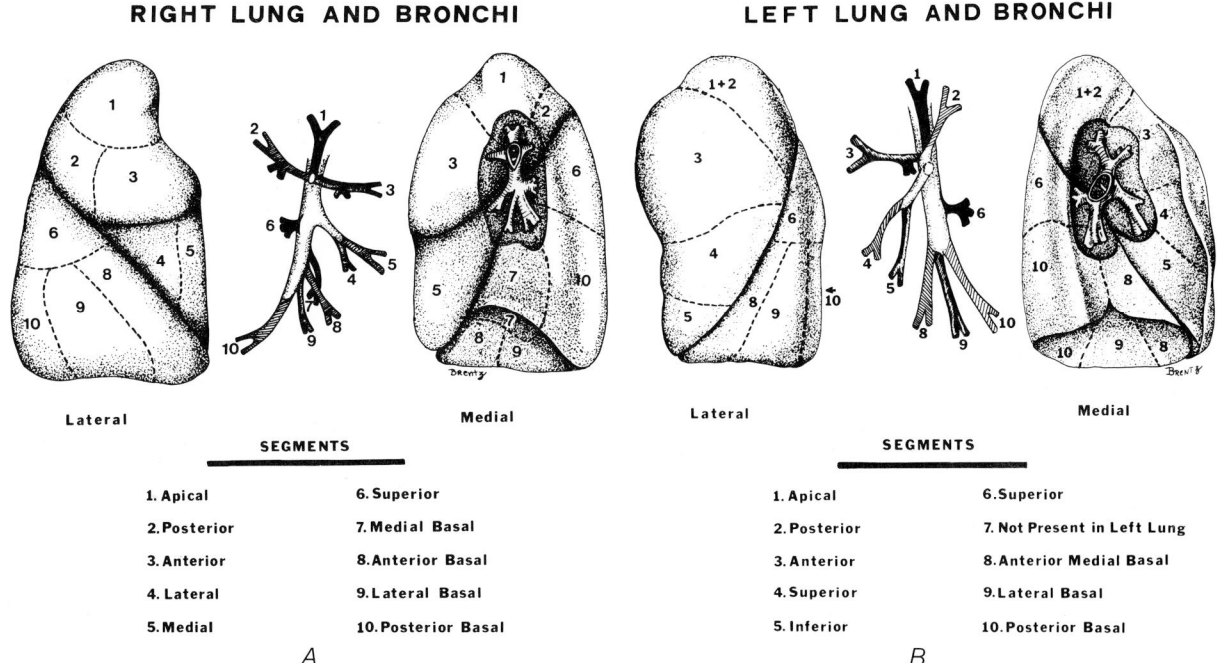

Lateral   Medial   Lateral   Medial

SEGMENTS		SEGMENTS	
1. Apical	6. Superior	1. Apical	6. Superior
2. Posterior	7. Medial Basal	2. Posterior	7. Not Present in Left Lung
3. Anterior	8. Anterior Basal	3. Anterior	8. Anterior Medial Basal
4. Lateral	9. Lateral Basal	4. Superior	9. Lateral Basal
5. Medial	10. Posterior Basal	5. Inferior	10. Posterior Basal

A   *B*

FIGURE 13-13

Lobar bronchi, their segmental branches, and the pulmonary segments. [*From S. Schwartz et al. (eds.), Principles of Surgery, 3d ed., McGraw-Hill, New York, 1978. Used by permission of the publisher.*]

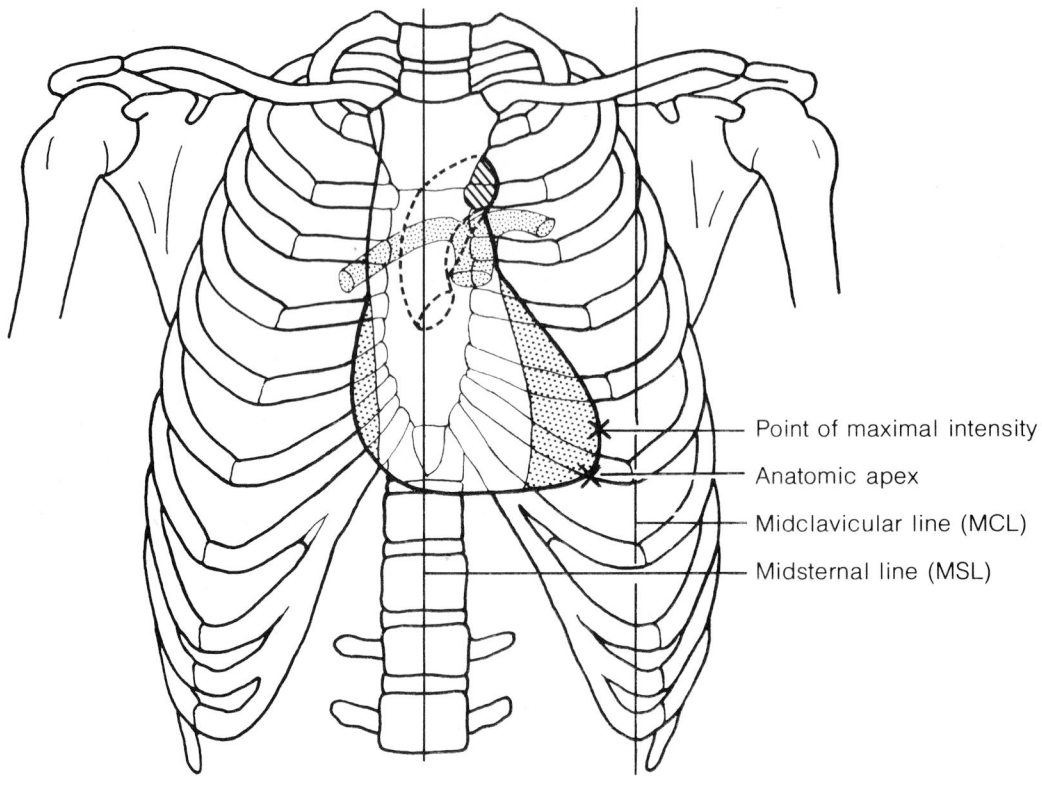

Point of maximal intensity
Anatomic apex
Midclavicular line (MCL)
Midsternal line (MSL)

FIGURE 13-14

Surface projection of the heart and large vessels. (*A modification from Hochstein and Rubin, Physical Diagnosis, McGraw-Hill, New York, 1964. Used by permission of the publisher.*)

portion of the stomach under the left diaphragm and behind the 6th, 7th, or 8th intercostal space.

The left spleen is located under the left lateral thoracic wall and extends down from the 9th to the 11th ribs.

Examination

The techniques utilized in assessing lung function are inspection, palpation, percussion, and auscultation. In the critical-care setting, each technique should be used appropriately to obtain information about lung function, since the presence of respiratory embarrassment in a patient can mean the difference between life and death. Adequate examination of the thorax and lungs can best be achieved with the patient in a sitting position and unclothed from waist up, if possible.

Inspection

The quality, rate, depth, and pattern of respiration were discussed under vital signs. Therefore, inspection specifically related to the size and contour of the chest and findings relative to other organs which reflect lung functioning will be discussed in this area.

The thoracic cage is normally shaped like a truncated cone with the transverse diameter larger than the anterior to posterior (A-P) diameter. In addition, the thoracic spine is slightly convex and makes a perpendicular line with the floor. Abnormalities of size and contour are referred to as barrel chest, kyphosis, scoliosis, kyphoscoliosis, pigeon breast, and funnel breast. These deformities have the potential of interfering with thoracic expansion; therefore, the existence of such deformities should be noted.

Barrel chest is characteristically seen in patients with chronic emphysema. The A-P and transverse

A

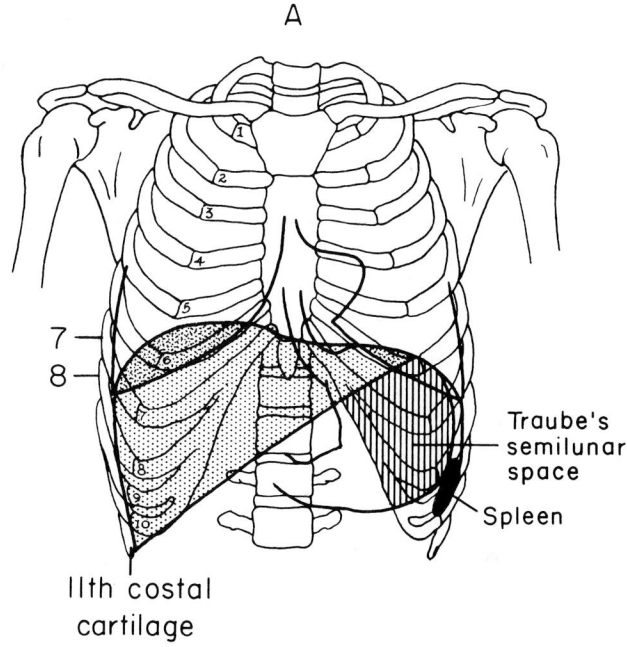

Traube's
semilunar
space

Spleen

11th costal
cartilage

FIGURE 13-15

Surface projections of the diaphragm, liver, spleen, and stomach. (*From E. Hochstein and A. L. Rubin, Physical Diagnosis, McGraw-Hill, New York, 1964. Used by permission of the publisher.*)

diameters increase in size, giving a circular appearance to the cross section of the thorax. The constantly increased lung volume in emphysema is believed to cause the chest to become barreled; thus, little motion of the chest appears evident during the respiratory cycle.

Kyphosis is an exaggeration of the normal posterior convexity of the thoracic spine. The condition may be caused by senile osteoporosis, ankylosing spondylitis, Paget's disease, and acromegaly.

Scoliosis is a lateral curvature of the thoracic spine resulting in an S-shaped formation. This abnormality causes one shoulder to be raised and the hip to be lowered. This deformity may result from polio, congenital deformities, thoracoplasty, or muscular disorders.

Kyphoscoliosis is a deformity in which both kyphosis and scoliosis are present. The significance of this clinical entity is that the thoracic cavity may be so reduced that there is a decreased lung volume which may cause severe respiratory and cardiac compromise.

Pigeon breast, or pectus carinatum, is an abnormality of the thorax usually caused by rickets in childhood. During the active process of rickets, the upper ribs soften and bend inward. This forces the sternum forward, increasing the A-P diameter and diminishing the transverse diameter. The term *keel breast* has also been used to refer to this abnormality, since the sternum protrudes from the narrowed thorax like the keel of a ship.

Funnel breast, or pectus excavatum, is the opposite of pigeon breast. This abnormality is usually congenital and results when the softened ribs of the lower part of the sternum retract inward toward the spine and create a depressed area near the infrasternal notch. This decreases the A-P diameter. Funnel breast has been occasionally observed in members of the cobbler trade; a depressed area is created where shoes have been continually pressed against the sternum. This has resulted in funnel breast being called *cobbler's chest.*

In addition to observing the size and contour of the chest, other abnormalities should be kept in mind, such as pulsations indicative of an aortic aneurysm, precordial lift due to cardiac enlargement, or nodules or masses of the thoracic cage. This also includes examining the axillary area for inflammation of hair follicles and enlarged lymph nodes.

Palpation

Palpation of the chest can be done in conjunction with inspection; however, it will be discussed separately here. Palpation usually begins with assessing observed abnormalities of the chest with particular reference to symmetrical expansion of the thoracic cage during respiration. The chest is palpated using the palmar surface of the fingers for sensitive or painful areas, subcutaneous crepitus (air bubbles under the skin), and tactile fremitus.

To assess *respiratory excursion,* have the patient sit upright. Stand facing the patient's posterior chest wall and grasp the patient's lateral rib cage, placing your thumbs at approximately the level of and parallel to the 10th ribs. Both hands are then drawn medially, pulling the underlying skin with them to position loose skin folds between the thumbs and spine. The patient is asked to inhale deeply. Observe the outward movement of your thumbs for range and symmetry of thoracic expansion.

Tactile fremitus is the palpable vibration transmitted through the bronchopulmonary system to the chest wall when the patient makes a deep vocal sound. Using one hand over symmetrical areas or both hands over corresponding areas, place the palmar aspects of the fingers or the ulnar aspect of the hand on the chest and ask the patient to say in a deep voice, "Ninety-nine" or "one-two-three." A vibratory sensation should normally be felt over lung fields.

The sensation of tactile fremitus is usually uniform over most areas of the lung. Where the right main stem bronchus is closer to the chest wall, however, fremitus is increased. Fremitus is also increased in conditions of consolidated lung such as pneumonia. Decreased fremitus occurs when the bronchus is obstructed or the pleural space is occupied by fluid, air, or solid tissue, such as in pleural effusion, pneumothorax, or fibrosis.

Confirming observations of abnormalities of the spine by palpation is important. If it is difficult to determine the contour by observation and touch, it may be necessary to outline the spinous processes with a skin pencil.

Two other areas are important in palpation as related to lung function: determining the alignment of the trachea, since it denotes the presence of a shifted mediastinum, and detecting the presence of palpable lymph nodes in the axillary and supraclavicular areas, which indicate localized or generalized inflammation or malignancy.

To palpate for tracheal alignment, ask the patient to bend the head in a relaxed position. Locate the trachea in the suprasternal notch. Normally, it should be midline, with the space on each side of the trachea equal distance. Tracheal deviations usually result from masses in the neck or mediastinum or from pleural or pulmonary anomalies.

Percussion

Percussion of the chest provides further information regarding the status of lung functioning. The technique of percussion was outlined earlier, as were the characteristic percussion sounds.

In the thoracic area, a practitioner may normally elicit a variety of sounds due to the presence of different structures making up the bony thorax and various organs located within the thoracic cage (refer to Table 13-1). Normal lung tissue, however, only produces a resonant percussion sound.

The procedure for percussion may start with the apices and progress to the posterior and lateral chest, moving from top to bottom in a systematic manner. If percussion of the anterior chest seems warranted, keep in mind the location of the heart, mediastinum, and liver.

To percuss the apices, the patient should be in a sitting position facing you. Place the pleximeter along one of the supraclavicular areas and percuss approximately a 5-cm span. Then move the arm of the same pleximeter around the patient's shoulder over the trapezius, placing the pleximeter along the other supraclavicular area, and continue percussing. Note whether the areas are symmetrical.

Percussion of the posterior thorax begins with positioning the patient with arms folded over the chest; the shoulders are bent forward in a sitting position if possible. A patient who cannot sit is placed in a left then right lateral decubitus position (remember that the lying position produces dullness in some areas because of the compression of the thorax against the mattress and body weight itself).

The procedure, regardless of position, begins at the top of each shoulder, an area overlying each lung apex. Progress downward and percuss about a 5-cm area at a time, moving to symmetrical areas of each side of the chest posteriorly and laterally. Avoid the scapular areas and spinal column. The lateral chest is percussed with the patient's arm positioned over the head.

To measure diaphragmatic excursion, ask the patient to inspire fully and hold his breath. Percuss along the midscapular line bilaterally from top to bottom until the percussion note changes from resonant to dull. Mark the point of transition bilaterally. Then have the patient exhale fully and hold his breath. Percuss upward from the transition line to a resonant percussion note and mark the point. Measure the excursion distance between the two lines. The normal diaphragm will move bilaterally from 3 to 5 cm. A 1-cm difference in bilateral movement may indicate an abnormality.

Auscultation

Auscultation of the lung is a means by which the practitioner can determine the effectiveness of airflow through the airways of the lungs. The origin of breath sounds is still being debated; however, it is generally felt that breath sounds or *respiratory murmurs* are produced by air moving over the larynx and into the larger airways, creating turbulence of airflow. This turbulence or vibration is transmitted through the smaller airways to the chest wall.

Auscultation of the lungs requires a quiet environment. The patient should be seated upright in a relaxed position; however, this is often difficult in a critical-care setting. Therefore, assistance may be needed to support the patient in a sitting position, or the patient may have to remain in a recumbent position and be turned to the left and right lateral positions. Regardless of the position, the lungs are auscultated over each segment from top to bottom, anteriorly, posteriorly, and laterally. Instruct the patient to breath with the mouth open. Breathing should be normal but deep enough to move secretions, if any are present. Using the diaphragm of the stethoscope (the bell should be used for thin-chested persons), listen over symmetrical areas of the chest. There are three types of sounds to listen for when auscultating the lungs: breath sounds, voice sounds, and adventitious or extra sounds.

Breath Sounds

There are basically three types of breath sounds heard over the normal lung, considering the area that is being auscultated. These three types of breath sounds are vesicular, bronchial or tubular, and bronchove-

sicular. Breath sounds can be described diagramatically, as shown in Figs. 13-16 and 13-17. The upstroke denotes inspiration and the downstroke denotes expiration. The thickness of the line represents the intensity of the sound, and the height of the angle represents the pitch.

Vesicular breath sounds are soft, low-pitched sounds heard over most of the lung; however, vesicular breath sounds are heard best over the lower posterior and axillary region of the chest. Vesicular sounds may vary in intensity and duration from diminished vesicular to harsh vesicular breath sounds. Diminished sounds are found in obese or muscular patients, and harsh sounds are heard in children. The characteristics of the sounds are a result of the intervening air and lung tissue. The inspiratory phase is most easily heard because of the increased inspiratory flow with resulting turbulence. The expiratory phase is short (approximately one-third of the inspiratory phase) and faint because the expiratory flow is initially great; however, the flow diminishes markedly with decreasing turbulence (see Fig. 13-16).

Bronchial or *tubular* breath sounds are usually coarse, high-pitched sounds heard normally over the trachea. The expiratory phase is longer in duration than the inspiratory phase, and they are separated by a silent interval or gap. This type of sound heard elsewhere over lung tissue is indicative of extensive disease which has caused considerable loss of air-containing alveoli. The bronchioles are patent and are surrounded by consolidated lung tissue (Fig. 13-16*b*).

Bronchovesicular breath sounds are a combination of bronchial and vesicular breath sounds. Bronchovesicular sounds are normally of moderate pitch and intensity. The inspiratory and expiratory phases are of equal duration and normally heard near the major bronchi, below the clavicles and between the scapulae, especially on the right. If bronchovesicular sounds are normally present, early pulmonary disease should be suspected (Fig. 13-16*c*).

Voice Sounds

The types of voice sounds which are useful in diagnosing lung disease, primarily consolidation of lung tissue, are bronchophony, whispering pectoriloquy, and egophony.

Bronchophony is the transmission of louder and clearer voice sounds than one normally hears when auscultating the lungs. Listen with the stethoscope while the patient says "one, two, three" or "ninety-

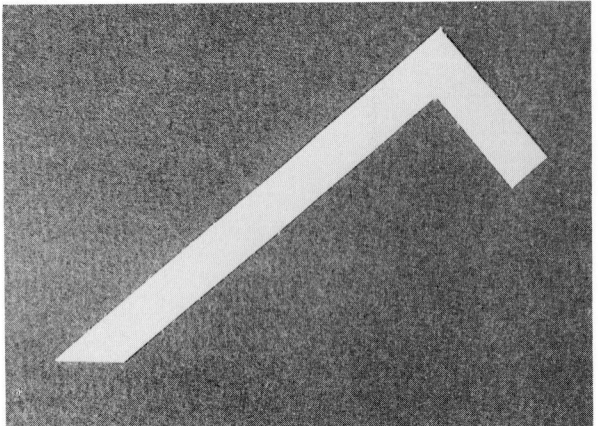

a

b

c

FIGURE 13-16

(*a*) Vesicular breath sounds. (*b*) Bronchial breath sounds. (*c*) Bronchovesicular breath sounds.

nine." The presence of bronchophony is indicative of consolidation.

Whispering pectoriloquy is tested for by having the patient whisper a combination of words such as "one, two, three." If there is consolidation, the whisper is clearly heard with the use of a stethoscope. If there is no consolidation, the whisper is not heard.

Egophony is performed by having the patient say aloud "eee." If the sound of the spoken *E* takes on a nasal quality and sounds like *A* (*E* to *A* change), consolidation is usually present.

Adventitious Sounds

Adventitious sounds are extra sounds heard in addition to breath sounds. There are basically four types of adventitious sounds: wheezes, rhonchi, rales, and pleural friction rubs (Fig. 13-17).

Wheezes are high-pitched, whistling sounds produced by airflow through narrowed tubes, resulting in severe turbulence. Wheezes occur primarily on expiration; however, with severe bronchial constriction, they may be heard on inspiration.

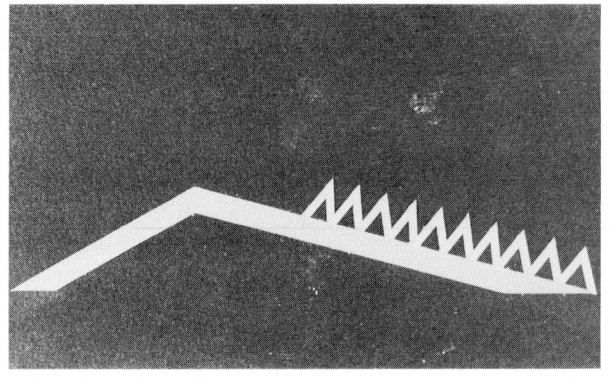

a

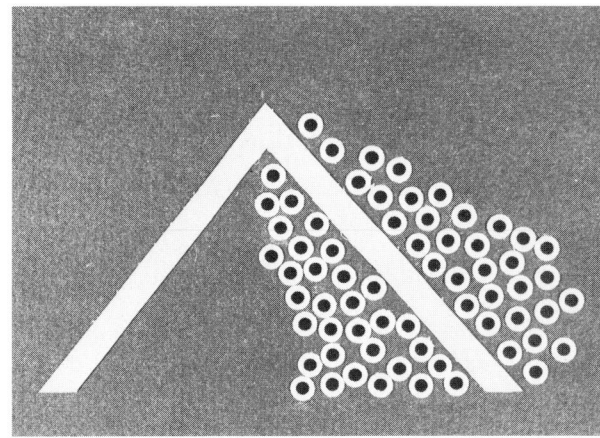

b

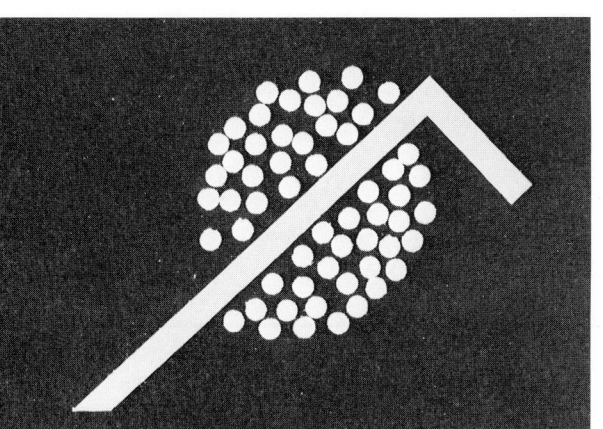

c

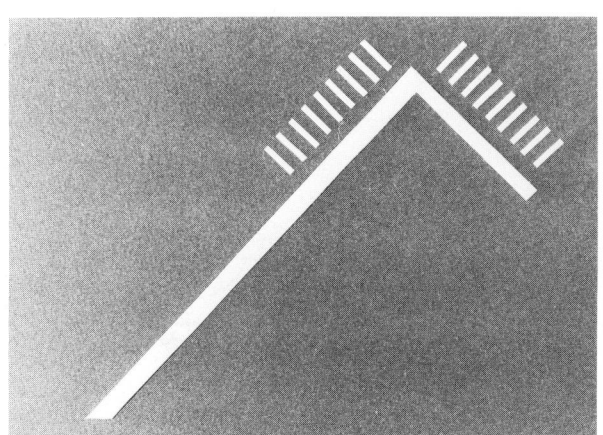

d

FIGURE 13-17
(*a*) Wheezes. (*b*) Rhonchi. (*c*) Rales. (*d*) Pleural friction rub.

Rhonchi are coarse, rumbling, low-pitched sounds produced by airflow over secretions in the larger airways. Rhonchi are heard on expiration and may be cleared by coughing.

Rales are short, discrete, popping or crackling sounds produced by fluid in the small airways or alveoli.

Pleural friction rubs are creaking, leathery, loud, dry, coarse sounds indicative of pleural irritation. They are produced by the rubbing of the inflamed surfaces of two pleural layers against one another during respiration. Pleural friction rubs are heard at the end of inspiration and the beginning of expiration.

HEART

The heart is a wedge-shaped muscle located at the center of the chest, under the sternum, and projected to the left of the midsternal line. The normal heart size is about the size of a fist. The upper part of the heart is called the *base* and is formed by the right and left atria. The lower part of the heart is called the *apex* and is formed by the left ventricle. In addition, the left heart border is posteriorly and laterally positioned. The right ventricle forms the right heart border and makes up most of the anterior surface of the heart lying underneath the sternum.

The heart is enclosed in a tough, fibrous, protective sac called the *pericardium,* which suspends the heart from the great vessels and anchors it to the diaphragm.

Examination

Examination of the heart basically includes inspecting and palpating the *precordium* (the area of the chest overlying the heart and great vessels) and auscultating the heart for normal heart sounds and for extracardiac sounds. Percussing the heart has clinical value in estimating the size and shape of the heart; however, since this technique requires a great deal of skill and practice for accuracy and is not a highly reliable method of examination, it will not be discussed here in depth.

The examination is performed with the patient in a supine position, a left lateral position (to accentuate a palpable apical impulse and auscultate abnormal heart sounds), a sitting position with the patient leaning forward (to bring the heart closer to the anterior chest wall), and standing, if necessary and possible. The examiner develops a systematic approach to assessing the heart. Practitioners should develop their own methods, but traditionally the examination begins at the apical area and progresses upward to all the other areas, or begins at the aortic area and moves across and downward to other areas. As long as the entire precordium is fully examined in all positions, the order is only important to the practitioner for whom the system works. Figure 13-18 shows the significant areas for examination.

Inspection

Inspection and palpation are usually performed simultaneously; however, for the purpose of a clearer discussion, each will be presented separately. Inspection of the precordium primarily focuses on the functioning of the left and right ventricles. To examine

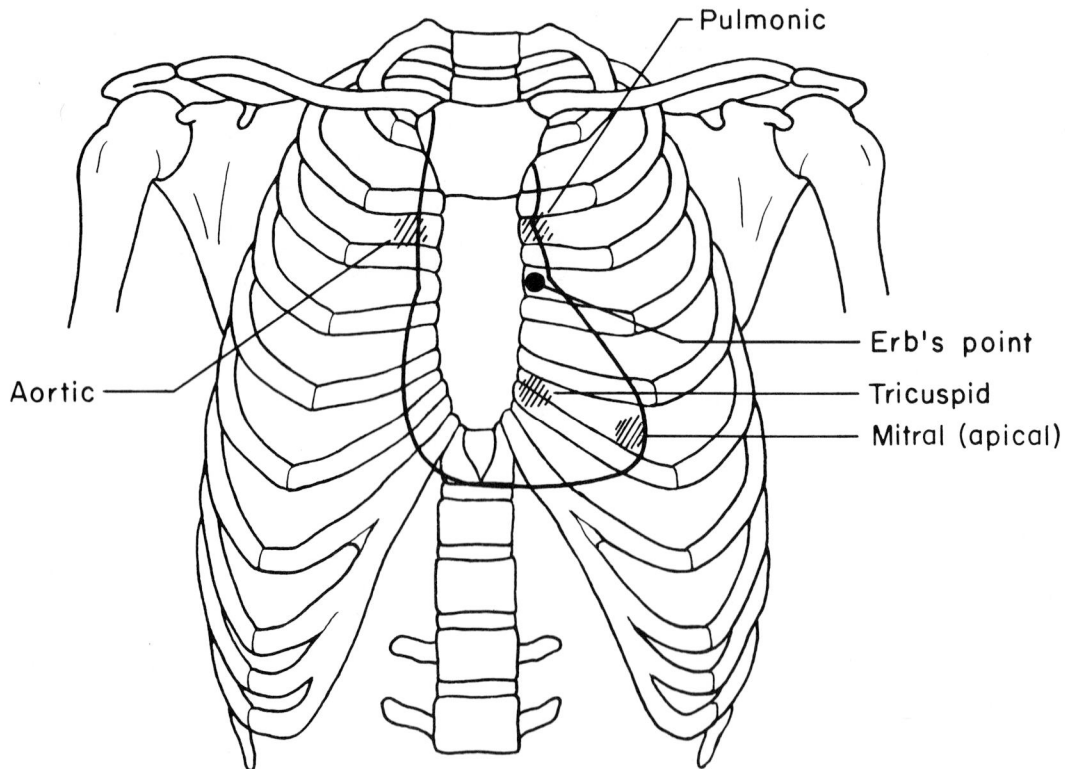

FIGURE 13-18

Cardinal areas for inspection, palpation, and auscultation. (*From E. Hochstein and A. L. Rubin, Physical Diagnosis, McGraw-Hill, New York, 1964. Used by permission of the publisher.*)

the precordium, the practitioner should stand at the patient's right side with a good light source coming from the side so that rays are tangential to the skin; this procedure makes precordial movements more distinguishable.

Begin the examination by observing for an apical impulse; then align your vision with the chest and look for lifting or heaving of the precordium and the presence of epigastric pulsations. Any observations should be confirmed by palpation. The apical impulse is produced when the heart moves forward and to the right, bringing the apex against the chest wall at the onset of ventricular systole. The impulse is visible in about one-fifth of the normal population. It is usually seen in the left 5th intercostal space 7 to 9 cm from the midsternal line or 1 to 2 cm medial to the midclavicular line.

An impulse in the right ventricular area (lower half of the sternum and parasternal area, particularly the area medial to the apex) is usually abnormal except in some thin-chested adults or in patients with increased cardiac output for reasons other than heart disease (i.e., anemia, fever, pregnancy). Lifting or heaving of the right ventricle usually results from right ventricular hypertrophy and should be reported. An epigastric pulsation may be a normal abdominal aortic pulse; however, it may also indicate the presence of an aortic aneurysm or right ventricular hypertrophy.

Palpation

Precordial palpation is done to confirm and qualify visible findings and detect the presence of other normal and abnormal pulsations or vibrations. Palpation begins by placing the palmar surface of the fingers and hand over visible areas of pulsation and then moving over the entire precordium, palpating in a systematic manner. When areas of pulsation or vibration are felt with the palmar surface of the hand, follow up with the use of the fingertips to denote the rate, rhythm, and intensity of the pulsation.

You may begin palpation at the base of the heart and observe for any pulsation, thrill, or vibration. Palpate over the aortic area and then move across the sternum to the pulmonic area. Erb's point, located in the 3d intercostal space, should be palpated since murmurs of aortic and pulmonic origin can be detected. Gradually move the hand down the chest, palpating over the parasternal area until you reach the right ventricular area. Note whether a lift, heave, or thrill is present. Proceed to the epigastric region

to detect the presence of pulsations, and then palpate over the apical area to determine the strength of the *point of maximal impulse* (PMI). The PMI is the palpable apical impulse about the size of a quarter, normally felt in about half of the population. Therefore, the absence of the PMI is not considered abnormal. If it is not palpable in a supine position, sometimes the seated position with the patient leaning forward makes the PMI palpable.

Abnormalities that may be detected by inspection and palpation are shown in Table 13-5.

Percussion

Percussion is usually limited to outlining the left and right borders of cardiac dullness, although the findings may not be as reliable as palpation. The PMI (normally located in the 5th intercostal space 7 to 9 cm from the midsternal line) denotes the farthest point of cardiac dullness from the sternum. To find the left border of cardiac dullness, percuss the 3d, 4th, and 5th intercostal spaces sequentially, moving from the anterior axillary line medially until the percussion note changes from resonance (indicative of normal lung) to dullness. The normal distance of the 3d, 4th, and 5th intercostal spaces from the midsternal line should not exceed 4, 6, and 10 cm, respectively.

The right border of cardiac dullness should not extend beyond the right edge of the sternum; therefore, percussing an area 1 cm to the right of the sternum should produce a more resonant than dull sound. It is normally difficult to distinguish a change from resonant lung to dull. In the same manner as percussing the left border of cardiac dullness, progress from the right hemithorax, moving lateral to medial to denote a change from resonance to dull. A clearly distinguishable change in percussion from resonant to dull beyond the right edge of the sternum may suggest cardiac enlargement.

Auscultation

Auscultation of the heart includes listening to the rate and rhythm of the heartbeat, evaluating normal heart sounds, and determining the presence or absence of extra heart sounds, murmurs, and pericardial friction rubs.

Examining the heart by auscultation begins with a warm, well-lighted, and particularly quiet room. The patient is placed in the same positions for auscultation as palpation: lying, left lateral, sitting, and leaning

TABLE 13-5
Abnormalities of the Heart Detected by Inspection and Palpation

Precordium	Abnormality	Examples of possible cause
Aortic area 2d and 3d interspaces to right of sternum	Forceful pulsation Thrill	Rheumatic heart disease Systemic hypertension Ascending thoracic aortic aneurysm Aortic stenosis
Pulmonary area 2d and 3d interspaces to left of sternum	Forceful pulsation Thrill	Essential pulmonary hypertension Left-to-right intracardiac shunt Mitral stenosis, pulmonary embolism, diffuse pneumonia Obstruction of right ventricular outflow tract
Right ventricular area Lower sternal border to the immediate right and left of sternum	Thrill Lift or heave	Ventricular septal defect Obstructions of right ventricular outflow tract Mitral stenosis Left to right intracardiac shunts Skeletal deformities
Left ventricular area 4th to 6th interspaces Left midclavicular line or beyond	Strong apical impulse or abnormally large PMI Dyskinetic apical impulse Thrill Gallop	Left ventricular hypertrophy Aortic valve diseases Left ventricular aneurysm Mitral valve disease Myocardial dysfunction, mitral or aortic valve disease, HCVD
Epigastric area	Strong pulsation of abdominal aorta Pulsation of liver	Abdominal aortic aneurysm Congestive heart failure

forward. The diaphragm and bell of the stethoscope are both used.

The entire precordium and areas of radiation (axillae and carotid arteries) are auscultated; however, particular attention is given to the areas where valve closure sounds are best heard. These areas are pictured in Fig. 13-19 and include: the aortic area at the 2d right intercostal space adjacent to the sternal border; the pulmonic area in the 2d left intercostal space; the tricuspid area situated at the 5th left intercostal space near the sternal edge; and the mitral or apical area located at the 5th left intercostal space medial to the midclavicular line.

The examiner may begin with the diaphragm of the stethoscope at the aortic area where the second heart sound is loudest, move to the pulmonic area, and inch the stethoscope down the left sternal border to the mitral or apical area. Another approach is to begin at the apical area where the first heart sound

(S_1) is loudest and move upward to the left sternal border and across the sternum to the aortic area. Either beginning at the aortic area or apical area first, listen to and assess the rate and rhythm of the heart to establish a baseline for comparison in each area examined. The course of auscultation is then reversed using the bell of the stethoscope.

In each area auscultated, the following components of the cardiac cycle are assessed:

The characteristics of S_1 (intensity, splitting, effects of respiration)

The characteristics of S_2 (intensity, splitting, effects of respiration)

The presence or absence of extra sounds in systole and diastole

The presence or absence of murmurs in systole and diastole

The presence or absence of pericardial friction rubs

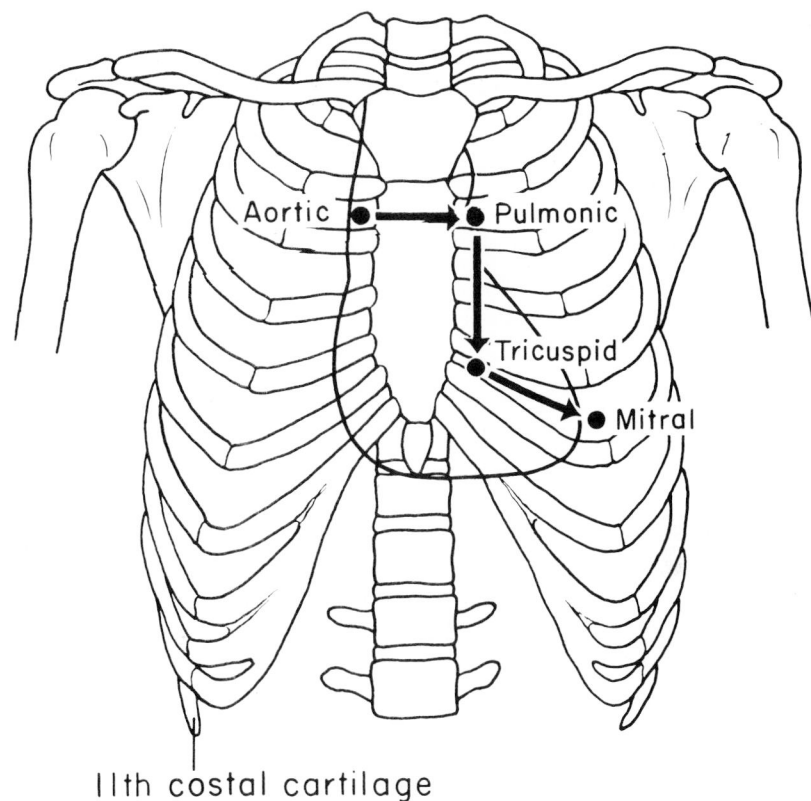

IIth costal cartilage

FIGURE 13-19

Areas for auscultation. (*From E. Hochstein and A. L. Rubin, Physical Diagnosis, McGraw-Hill, New York, 1964. Used by permission of the publisher.*)

Heart Rate and Rhythm

The normal rate and rhythm of the heart is the responsibility of the conduction system of the heart. In the normal heart, a small bundle of fibers called the sinoatrial (SA) node, located in the wall of the right atrium at the vena cava entrance, normally initiates the cardiac impulse. The SA node is known as the *cardiac pacemaker* and automatically discharges an impulse which is conducted throughout the atria to the atrioventricular (AV) node, another small bundle of cardiac fibers located in the posterior lower right atrium near the septum. After a slight delay which allows for completion of atrial systole, the impulse is conducted through specialized conducting tissue called the *bundle of His*. The bundle divides into right and left branches, each passing down the corresponding side of the interventricular septum and spreading into a fine network of Purkinje fibers. These fibers

spread into all portions of the ventricular myocardium. The impulse reaches the ventricles almost simultaneously and excites the muscles, causing ventricular contraction.

Variations in the rate and rhythm of the heart are classified as arrhythmias and are caused by (1) variation in the rate of discharge of the SA node, (2) ectopic impulses which compete with the SA node, or (3) abnormal conduction of impulses from the SA node through the heart. Table 13-6 presents a description of commonly assessed arrhythmias.

Normal Heart Sounds

Normal heart sounds are vibrations produced by the closure of valves and by the turbulence of blood flow through the heart. The first heart sound is a high-pitched sound but is slightly lower in frequency and

TABLE 13-6
Commonly Observed Rhythms

Type	Regularity of rhythm	Origin of beat	Conduction	Typical ventricular rate (beats per minute)
Sinus tachycardia	Regular	SA node	Normal	>100
Sinus bradycardia	Regular	SA node	Normal	<60
Premature contraction	Irregular	Atrial or ventricular extrasystole	Normal to variable	Normal (60–100) unless tachycardia is superimposed
Paroxysmal atrial tachycardia	Regular	Ectopic atrial focus	Normal	130–230
Atrial flutter	Regular	Atrial circus motion	Partial block at AV node; commonly 2:1	140–160
Atrial fibrillation	Irregular	Multiple atrial foci	Dependent on AV nodal refractory time	100–200
Ventricular tachycardia	Regular	Ectopic ventricular focus	Ventricular focus usurps pacemaker function	100–200
Second-degree heart block	Regularly recurring groups of beats	SA node	Block at AV node or His bundle (second degree)	60–100
Third-degree heart block	Regular	Junctional or ventricular focus	AV node incapable of conduction	20–80

longer in duration than the second heart sound. It occurs as a result of closure of the atrioventricular (mitral and tricuspid) valves and can be heard over the entire precordium but is heard best at the apex. S_1 is louder than S_2 at the apex. If any difficulty arises in differentiating between S_1 and S_2, the timing of S_1 correlates with that of the carotid pulse and is usually heard as one sound.

Certain physiologic and pathologic changes can cause the first heart sound to change in character. The loudness of S_1 may be *accentuated* with more forceful closure of the valve leaflets as in mitral stenosis or during increased muscular activity, which increases heart rate (i.e., fever, exercise, hyperthyroidism). S_1 may be *diminished* because of poor sound transmission through the chest wall as in pulmonary emphysema. Weak ventricular contraction will also diminish the first heart sound whether because of muscular damage as in myocardial infarction or delayed conduction as in first degree heart block. The *intensity* of S_1 may vary with any completely

irregular rhythm such as atrial fibrillation or with complete heart block, which results in two separate pacemakers with independent rhythm.

The second heart sound is high-pitched and slightly shorter in duration than S_1. S_2 occurs upon closure of the semilunar (aortic and pulmonic) valves and may be heard most audibly at the base of the heart. It may vary in character when related to loudness as does S_1; however, particular attention should be given to the "splitting" phenomenon of S_2 which explains why two sounds are heard when listening to the second heard sound. Other variations of S_2 will be presented following this discussion.

Since the pressure gradients are greater and valve closure slightly earlier on the left side of the heart than the right side, S_1 and S_2 may produce two sounds, each referred to as *splitting*. The term *splitting* is primarily used in reference to the second heart sound or S_2; however, the asynchronous contraction of the left and right ventricles may produce a normal splitting of the first heart sound (heard best at the tricuspid area). Abnormalities to be ruled out before noting that S_1 is split are the presence of an S_4 and an early systolic ejection sound or a presystolic murmur.

Splitting of the second heart sound may be physiologic or pathologic. Physiologic splitting is normally most audible on inspiration at the pulmonic area when the aortic valve (A_2) closes before the pulmonic valve (P_2); this accentuated asynchronous closure of A_2 and P_2 on inspiration is due to an increased venous return to the right ventricle during inspiration. The prolongation of right ventricular systole delays closure of the pulmonic valve, increasing the time interval between closure of A_2 and P_2.

Pathological splitting of S_2 indicates the presence of disease (Fig. 13-20). When the split does not vary with inspiration or expiration, this is referred to as *fixed splitting*. This occurs in such conditions as pulmonic stenosis and atrial septal defect. Wide splitting refers to an increase in the normal splitting time of S_2 on inspiration along with an S_1 split. This occurs in right bundle branch block where electrical conduction delays right ventricular contraction and pulmonic valve closure. *Paradoxical splitting* refers to a reverse phenomenon in which splitting of S_2 occurs on expiration rather than inspiration. In left bundle branch block, a delay in left ventricular contraction may cause the aortic valve to close after the pulmonic valve, producing a single sound on inspiration and a split sound on expiration.

In further assessing S_2, attention should be given to the intensity of the aortic and pulmonic second heart sound. An *accentuated aortic second heart sound,* as heard in arterial hypertension and aortic regurgitation, results when increased arterial pressure forces the aortic valve to close. A *diminished* aortic second sound occurs when the arterial pressure is low, as in shock, and aortic valve closure is soft. Aortic stenosis also produces a diminished second sound since the valve leaflets are relatively immobile.

An *accentuated pulmonic second heart sound* occurs when the back pressure in the pulmonary artery increases and forces the pulmonary valve closed as with pulmonary hypertension. Other conditions in which an accentuated P_2 is heard and may cause pulmonary hypertension are mitral stenosis, left ventricular failure, and atrial septal defect. A diminished pulmonic second heart sound is heard in pulmonic stenosis when the pressure against the pulmonic valve is less than normal.

Extra Heart Sounds

Extra heart sounds can basically be classified in relation to where they are located in the cardiac cycle and are named and described accordingly. The sounds are either heard in systole or diastole, except for pericardial friction rubs, which are heard in both systole and diastole.

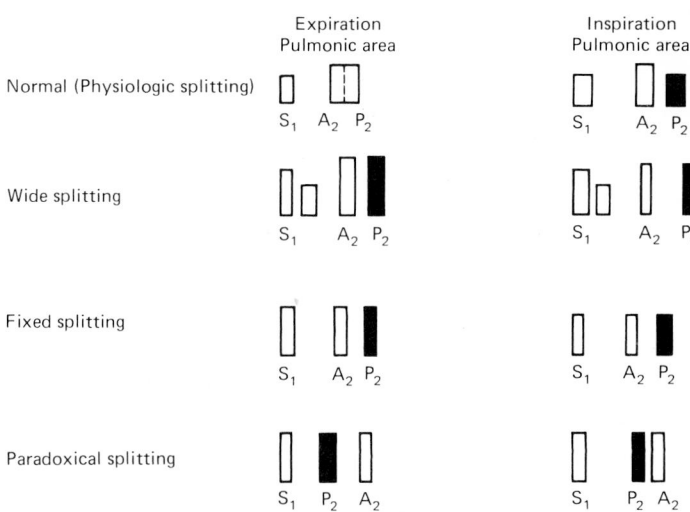

FIGURE 13-20
Splitting of second heart sound.

Systole

Ejection clicks may be heard in the early, middle, or late phase of cardiac systole. Early *systolic ejection clicks* are either aortic or pulmonic in origin and occur immediately after S_1. *Aortic ejection* clicks are heard at the base and apex of the heart and occur in diseases of the aortic valve and aortic aneurysm. The click does not change with respiration.

Pulmonic ejection clicks are heard in the pulmonic area, diminish with inspiration, and occur in pulmonic stenosis. Middle and late systolic clicks are not as well defined as early systolic clicks, but are frequently associated with systolic murmurs of mitral regurgitation.

Diastole

The *opening snap* of mitral stenosis is a high-pitched, short, snappy sound heard in the early phase of diastole. It is best heard along the left sternal border medial to the apex; however, it does radiate widely. It can be differentiated from a third heart sound (S_3) because it occurs earlier in the cycle.

The third heart sound can be physiologic or pathologic. It is a common and usually normal finding in children and young adults. In the older person, however, it is considered abnormal and indicative of myocardial failure. It is a low-pitched sound which occurs early in diastole during rapid ventricular filling, resulting in vibrations. The specific mechanism responsible for the vibrations is not agreed on by all authors. Hochstein and Rubin (1964, p. 199) state that one viewpoint supports the opinion that the vibration is set up in the ventricular myocardium by rapid ventricular filling, while others attribute the vibrations to a temporary reclosure of the atrioventricular valves. S_3 can be heard best at the apex with the bell of the stethoscope.

The fourth heart sound (S_4) may also be physiologic or pathologic. It may be occasionally heard normally in young children, but not as often as S_3. It is usually an abnormal sound which is believed to be a late ventricular filling sound resulting from the accelerated flow of blood into the ventricles produced by atrial contraction. It is a low-pitched sound which occurs late in diastole just before the first heart sound, and it is heard best at the apex with the bell of the stethoscope. A pathologic S_4 is usually associated with hypertensive cardiovascular disease, coronary artery disease, or aortic stenosis.

A *pericardial friction* rub is usually described as a scratching, grating, or squeaking high-pitched sound indicative of pericarditis. It is heard best with the diaphragm of the stethoscope in the region between the apex and left sternal border. The timing of the pericardial friction rub is associated with cardiac movement and consists of three short components: atrial systole, ventricular systole, and ventricular diastole. Usually two components are heard; however, all three components are diagnostic and help to differentiate a pericardial rub from a pleural friction rub, which has two components.

Gallop Rhythm

Gallop rhythm is a term used to describe the rhythm of the heart when an S_3, S_4, or both are perceived by auscultation and possibly palpation. The presence of a S_3 is referred to as a *protodiastolic gallop*. When a S_4 is heard, the term *presystolic* or *atrial gallop* is used. The term *summation gallop* is used when presystolic and protodiastolic gallops combine to form a single, loud, evenly spaced sound in diastole. Gallop rhythms are heard best with the bell of the stethoscope.

Murmurs

Heart murmurs are audible vibrations which originate within the heart and great vessels. These sounds represent turbulence of blood flow caused by (1) an increased rate of blood flow through normal structures (i.e., exercise); (2) the forward flow of blood across a partially obstructed or irregular valve (i.e., valvular stenosis); (3) blood flow into a dilated chamber; or (4) the backward flow of blood across an incompetent valve or defect (i.e., valvular insufficiency).

Murmurs are usually classified as systolic, diastolic, or continuous because of where they occur in the cardiac cycle. To determine the significance of a murmur, certain factors must be identified and described in the process of cardiac assessment. These factors include:

1. The timing of the murmur within the cardiac cycle (early, middle, late, or holosystolic)

2. Characteristics

   a. Intensity (graded on a scale from 1 to 6)
      1 = difficult to hear; barely audible, very faint
      2 = very soft, but can be heard without straining
      3 = moderately loud
      4 = loud
      5 = very loud, but requires stethoscope chestpiece to be placed on chest

6 = extremely loud; heard with chestpiece off chest

b. Pattern (crescendo, decrescendo, or diamond-shaped)

c. Pitch (high, medium, low)

d. Quality (harsh, musical, blowing, or rumbling)

3. Location on the precordium (area where intensity is greatest, i.e., apex, tricuspid, aortic, or pulmonic areas)

4. Radiation (area where murmur is less audible, but still perceptible)

5. Posture and exercise (the body position or activity under which murmur is heard)

6. Stethoscope chestpiece used to hear the murmur (bell or diaphragm)

Systolic Murmurs

Systolic murmurs may be physiologic or pathologic and occur between S_1 and S_2. They may be further described as early systolic or midsystolic because of their relationship or proximity to S_1 and S_2.

There are basically two types of systolic murmurs: ejection and regurgitant. Systolic ejection murmurs occur when ventricular contraction forces blood, under high pressure, forward through the aortic valve, pulmonic valve, or septal defect into normal or dilated vessels which are of lower pressure.

Systolic ejection murmurs occur with such conditions as aortic and pulmonic stenosis. Aortic and pulmonic stenosis produce midsystolic ejection murmurs. The aortic stenosis murmur is heard best at the aortic area and radiates into the neck and down the left sternal border to the apex. The murmur of pulmonic stenosis by contrast is heard best at the pulmonic area and radiates up the left neck. They are both, however, diamond-shaped, medium-pitched, harsh murmurs heard with either bell or diaphragm chestpiece.

Regurgitant murmurs occur in systole when the mitral or tricuspid valves do not close sufficiently to prevent the backflow of blood into the atria during ventricular contraction as seen in mitral and tricuspid insufficiency. These murmurs are holosystolic and heard over their respective valvular areas. They are both high-pitched and blowing, with the intensity remaining relatively the same. Mitral and tricuspid regurgitant murmurs differ characteristically in the effect of respiration and manner of radiation. The intensity of the murmur of tricuspid regurgitation increases with inspiration and may radiate to the left midclavicular line and stop. The murmur of mitral regurgitation does not change with inspiration and radiates into the left axilla. They are best heard with the diaphragm chestpiece.

Diastolic Murmurs

Diastolic murmurs occur after S_2 and before S_1. They are also further classified as early, mid, late, or holosystolic murmurs and are usually pathological. Diastolic murmurs may be ejection, filling, or regurgitant.

The ejection or filling murmur of mitral stenosis may range from a very faint to a loud rumble with a crescendo and/or decrescendo pattern. It is low-pitched, heard best with the bell chestpiece, and usually localized at the apex. The murmur may be heard in a supine and left lateral position.

Regurgitant murmurs as in aortic insufficiency occur when blood flows back into the ventricle at the beginning of diastole, continuing throughout the diastolic phase in a decrescendo pattern. The intensity varies from very faint to loud, depending on the degree of valvular insufficiency. It is a very high pitched, blowing murmur which is heard best with the diaphragm chestpiece at the aortic area. The sound may radiate down the left and right sternal borders and to the apical area. Having the patient lean forward in an upright seated position with the breath held in expiration accentuates the sound.

Continuous murmurs are less common and represent the presence of both systolic and diastolic murmurs. These are evident in conditions where arteriovenous communication exists, such as patent ductus arteriosus.

NEUROMUSCULAR

During the history-taking portion of the examination, the examiner may have already determined the areas where problems will likely be detected. It is also important to realize that a large part of a screening neurological examination will have been accomplished during the other components of the physical examination. The examination presented here is to organize the neurological assessment in a complete form so no part will be omitted. Remember, however, there is no need to repeat previous tests and observations unless reassessment is indicated.

The components to be covered in this area include examination of the general cerebral functioning, cranial nerves, cerebellar functioning, motor and sensory systems, and the reflexes. The area of cerebral function is usually covered in the history-taking part of the examination; however, attention to these functions at the time of the physical examination gives important information regarding the total state of the patient. Musculoskeletal assessment is an integral part of the examination of the motor system.

Examination

The techniques of examination used in other systems are utilized in the neurological examination, but the order of the examination is approached in a different fashion to most effectively present the findings. Equipment necessary for the examination includes a safety pin, cotton balls, reflex hammer, penlight, tongue blades, tuning fork, newspaper or magazine, and items to test smell and taste, if deemed necessary.

Cerebral Function

General cerebral function is assessed in the categories of general behavior, level of consciousness, intellectual performance, emotional status, thought content, and cerebral integration. The components of each of these areas are presented in the following discussion.

The examiner assesses *general behavior* by determining the appropriateness of gestures, facial expressions, attitudes toward self and others, ability to relax, the quality and organization of speech, openness, and receptivity to people. Suspect findings in any of these activities should be recorded and considered in more depth if the abnormalities persist. Often, inappropriate responses may be due to the intensive care setting, anxiety, and medication.

The *level of consciousness* is determined by assessing the functional level of consciousness. Describe your findings according to the following classifications:

Alert: This patient responds fully, immediately, and appropriately to verbal stimuli.

Lethargic: This patient is drowsy, slow, and responds incompletely or inappropriately. She is not asleep and her eyes may be open. She may even appear to be alert; however, when addressed verbally, she responds as one does who is just waking.

Obtunded: This patient is difficult to arouse, but it can be accomplished with strong verbal or touch stimuli. Once awake, this patient is usually confused and lapses back into sleep very easily.

Stuporous: This patient can be aroused only with strong stimuli such as sternal or supraorbital pressure and does not remain responsive when stimuli ceases.

Semicomatose: This patient cannot be aroused, but deep tendon reflex activity is present.

Comatose: This patient cannot be aroused and there is no reflex activity.

Intellectual performance is assessed by determining orientation to time, place, and person. Asking the patient to tell you the time of day, the month, day, year, and length of hospitalization will assess orientation to *time*. Orientation to place can be determined by asking the patient "Where are you? In what city and state?" and "Where do you live?" Assessment of the patient's orientation to person is accomplished by asking for the patient's name, the names of family or friends, and the name of the physician.

Memory, recent and remote, is also tested to aid in determining cognitive functions. Remote memory is assessed by asking for the dates of birthdays, anniversaries, and former places of residence. Testing of recent memory may be accomplished by asking for recall of the events of the day, names of nursing personnel, and names of recent visitors. Another test is to tell the patient a short story and have it repeated to you in 5 min. The examiner must be aware of the tendency to confabulate (the fabrication of ready answers and fluent recital of fictitious events) in order to cover up the inability to remember.

The testing of vocabulary and abstract reasoning are two more ways of assessing cognition. The vocabulary test gives the patient words such as diamond, tint, recede, microscope, horse, orange, and chicken and asks that the words be defined and used in sentences. Abstract reasoning may be evaluated by asking the patient to interpret the meaning of proverbs such as "A rolling stone gathers no moss" or "A stitch in time saves nine." Another way is to ask for descriptions of similiarities between orange and apple, dog and cat, and trees and wood. The appropriateness of the answer is evaluated to determine the intactness of the patient's abstract reasoning.

Emotional status is assessed by determining the presence of euphoria, tension, depression, and apathy. Using the patient's own statements and comments to evaluate these conditions is usually the most effective way. For example, if patients say they are depressed, you might ask why or what are they feeling that they describe as depression. Any severe deviations should receive special attention. Utilization of the patient's own words, ideas, or questions is also a way of assessing thought content. Asking questions or making comments such as "What do you think about at night?" or "Sometimes in a hospital it is easy to feel like people are talking about you," can elicit valuable information about illusions, phobias, delusions, doubts, and anxieties.

Cerebral integration is assessed by determining the ability to recognize objects by touch and sight and to understand and communicate through speech and writing or reading.

The critical-care nurse needs to be cognizant of the effect the critical-care unit can have on patients. Inappropriate responses in the above areas may give insight into a patient's inability to cope with the environment or with the impact of an illness. Identification of altered mental status is a significant factor in the critical-care patient. Disorders such as paranoia, schizophrenia, acute depression, and anxiety do not only occur in patients on psychiatric units but are frequently found in patients in critical-care units, where alterations of sleep patterns, sensory stimulation and/or metabolic balance may be standard.

Cranial Nerves

There are 12 pairs of nerves commonly referred to as *cranial nerves*. Strictly speaking, I and II are not true nerves but rather fiber tracts of the brain; however, we consider them cranial nerves. The 10 other nerves or caudal nerves arise in the brainstem. The motor portion arises deep in the brainstem in motor nuclei analogous to the anterior horn cells of the spinal cord. The sensory portion arises outside the brainstem, usually in ganglia, which are analogous to the dorsal root ganglia of the spinal nerves.

Olfactory I: Sense of Smell

Anosmia is the absence of smell and *hyposmia* is a decrease in the sensitivity of smell. Decreased smell is usually associated with nasal disorders, not neurogenic problems. However, a tumor, meningitis, subarachnoid hemorrhage, or head injury could impair smell. Hallucinations of smell may indicate lesions in the temporal lobes, where the appreciation of smell is interpreted.

Testing is accomplished by having the patient close the eyes and occlude first one nostril, and then the other, while you pass mild aromatic scents under the nose and ask the patient to identify the smell. Commonly used scents include coffee, cinnamon, and vanilla.

Optic Nerve II: Vision

Determining the visual acuity and visual fields and performing the fundoscopic examination are all components of the testing of cranial nerve II and were presented earlier in the examination of the eye.

Oculomotor III, Trochlear IV, Abducens VI: Ocular Movements

These three nerves operate in conjugate fashion and are tested together. The components of this examination were presented earlier in the examination of the eye.

Trigeminal V

This nerve mediates general sensation, including perception of pain, temperature, and touch for the entire face and scalp to the vertex, paranasal sinuses, and the nasal and oral cavities. It carries the efferent arc of the corneal reflex and afferent and efferent arcs of the jaw reflex and supplies motor innervation to all muscles of mastication. The three major divisions of the trigeminal nerve are the ophthalmic, the maxillary, and the mandibular.

Testing of the trigeminal is accomplished by determining the patient's ability to perceive pain (pinprick) and touch (cotton wisp) over all of the face and anterior scalp. The oral and nasal cavities are also tested with pinprick. The corneal reflex is tested by having the patient look up and straight ahead while you approach from her side with a fine wisp of cotton and lightly touch the cornea, avoiding the eyelashes. Testing of the motor portion is accomplished by having the patient clench her teeth while you palpate the temporal and masseter muscles. Muscle strength may also be judged by having the patient move her mandible from side to side against your hand.

The tumor which most commonly affects this nerve is an acoustic neuroma in the pontocerebellar angle. Jaw musculature may also be affected by myasthenia gravis, amyotrophic lateral sclerosis (ALS), tetanus, and trigeminal neuralgia (tic douloureux).

Facial VII

The motor portion of the facial nerve innervates all muscles of facial expression, while the sensory portion mediates taste from the anterior two-thirds of the tongue and carries fibers that innervate the lacrimal, submaxillary, and sublingual glands.

Testing of the motor portion is accomplished by having the patient look up and wrinkle his forehead (frontalis muscle); close his eyes tight and resist the examiner's efforts to open them (obicularis oculi muscle); and smile, whistle, and show his teeth (lower face muscles). During the examination, observe any obvious defects and note any facial asymmetry.

The sensory portion of the facial nerve is tested by having the patient protrude his tongue while you touch each side with a moist applicator dipped in one of the test substances (sugar, lemon, salt). The patient should not withdraw his tongue until the substance is identified. Test each substance separately.

Facial paralysis may be due to lesions of any part of the nerve or the lower motor neurons. An example is *Bell's palsy*, a peripheral facial paralysis where the eyeball on the affected side turns up when an attempt is made to close the lid.

Acoustic VIII

The acoustic nerve has two divisions: the *cochlear,* which mediates hearing, and the *vestibular,* which controls balance, position, and spatial orientation.

Testing for the cochlear portion is done in the following manner. Whisper in each ear alternately with the other ear covered. Assess the patient's ability to repeat your whisper. A second method of testing hearing is Weber's test. This consists of placing a vibrating tuning fork on the vertex of the skull and asking the patient how the sound is heard or perceived. Equal perception in both ears is normal. If there is a sensorineural loss in one ear and the other is normal, the sound is perceived in the better ear. If there is a middle ear disorder in one ear (conductive hearing loss) and normal hearing in the other ear, perception will be best in the poorer ear. The third method of assessment of the acoustic nerve is via Rinne's test. This test is performed on both ears. This test is performed if hearing loss is detected in either of the above tests in order to determine the origin of the deficit. Testing is accomplished by holding a vibrating tuning fork (cycle 512 to 1024 per minute is recommended) on the mastoid process behind one ear. When the patient no longer hears it, then hold the fork beside the ear. The patient should hear approximately 15 s longer beside the ear or have an air/bone conduction ratio of 2:1. The Rinne test is positive when the patient hears longer by air conduction than by bone. With sensorineural loss, the normal ratio is maintained but hearing is reduced both by air and bone conduction. The Rinne test is negative when

hearing is longer by bone than by air. This usually indicates air conductive loss.

Testing for the vestibular portion of the acoustic nerve is done if the patient has a history of vertigo or ataxia. Unless these conditions are present, vestibular testing is not done. Testing is accomplished, if indicated, by doing the cold caloric test in the following manner. Place the patient in a supine position with the head tilted forward 30°. The examiner inspects the ear with an otoscope to be sure no infection or perforation of the eardrum is present. Ice water (5 to 10 mL) is then introduced into the canal. The normal reaction is nystagmus to the opposite side, vertigo, and possible nausea and vomiting. This test is not routinely performed, and physician consultation and presence is desirable.

Glossopharyngeal IX and Vagus X

These nerves are usually considered together. The glossopharyngeal conveys taste from the posterior one-third of the tongue, innervates the carotid sinus and the carotid body, and supplies general sensation to tonsillar and pharyngeal mucous membranes. The vagus nerve innervates all thoracic and abdominal visceral organs, larynx, pharnyx, and palate and conveys numerous sensory impulses from walls of the digestive tract, heart, and lungs.

Determination of the functions of these two nerves proceeds in the following manner. Inspect the soft palate and uvula when the patient says "aaah." The palate should rise promptly and symmetrically. Check the gag reflex by touching the posterior wall of the oropharynx. Test the swallowing by having the patient swallow a sip of water and note any difficulty. If any hoarseness is present, check the vocal cords with a laryngeal mirror. This is called *indirect laryngoscopy*. Test for taste on the posterior part of the tongue in the same manner as with the facial nerve.

Spinal Accessory XI

This nerve supplies the sternocleidomastoid muscle and the upper part of the trapezius muscle. Testing is accomplished by examining the muscles for atrophy and by evaluating strength in the following ways. Have the patient turn her head to one side and then the other while you resist the movement and have the patient shrug her shoulders against your resistance. The most frequent cause of weakness of the sternocleidomastoid muscle is trauma to the neck.

Hypoglossal XII

This nerve innervates the tongue musculature. Testing is accomplished by inspecting the tongue for tremors or wasting and lack of power or mobility. Ask the patient to protrude the tongue and observe for deviation. Press down on the tongue with a tongue blade and estimate the amount of force the patient can exert against your effort. Bilateral weakness of the tongue (or paralysis) can occur in ALS or myasthenia gravis. Unilateral weakness can be associated with neck injury.

Motor System

The motor system includes those components of the nervous system concerned with the initiation, maintenance, and control of movements of the body. Throughout the assessment of the motor system, be aware of any skeletal abnormalities, joint swelling or pain, decrease in range of motion, or disturbances of posture and balance.

In examining the motor system, it is extremely important to be able to distinguish between upper and lower motor neuron problems in relation to clinical signs and symptoms. The commonly used synonyms for upper motor neuron are corticobulbar (ends in the brainstem), corticospinal (crosses in the lower medulla and descends the spinal cord), and pyramidal tract. Common synonyms for lower motor neuron are anterior horn cell, ventral horn cell, or final common pathway. Table 13-7 illustrates selected physical findings which are indicative of upper and lower motor neuron weakness.

Examination of motor function includes determination of muscle strength and mass, including equality or unequality of sides of the body, tonus, presence of involuntary movements, coordination, gait, and balance. The techniques of inspection and palpation are the ones most useful in this examination.

Assessment of *muscle strength* and *mass* begins with inspection of the muscle groups of the arms, legs, and trunk for any differences in size. If differences are seen or suspected, you should measure the limbs. The reduced size of one limb may indicate a lower motor neuron problem. Always evaluate age, sex, and physical condition in judging strength.

Upper Extremities and Trunk

Examination of the upper extremities (Fig. 13-21) proceeds in the following manner. Have the patient

TABLE 13-7
Differentiation of Upper and Lower Motor Neuron Weakness According to Physical Findings

Parameter	Upper motor neuron	Lower motor neuron
Tone	Spasticity which is more pronounced in the upper extremity flexors and the lower extremity extensors	Flaccidity
Mass	Disuse atrophy only	Definite atrophy
Reflexes	Hyperreflexic with a positive Babinski	Decreased or absent
Fasciculations	Absent	Present
Clonus	May be present	Absent

squeeze the examiner's first two fingers, both hands at the same time. You estimate the power of the grip by the force required to remove your fingers. You should have difficulty in doing so. Weakness of the forearm muscle can affect the patient's grip.

Have the patient clench a fist and fix the wrist with the elbow bent and oppose your pressure. You exert downward pressure on the wrist to test the biceps and the brachioradialis. When you exert upward pressure, you are testing the triceps. Any problem affecting these muscle groups may affect the strength of the response.

Test the strength of the fingers and thumbs in the same manner by having the patient spread his fingers and resist your attempts to close them. Inability to resist your pressure is indicative of ulnar nerve disorder.

Have the patient close his eyes and hold both arms in front of him with his palms up. Observe for drift or pronation. Both the tendency to pronate or a downward drift with elbow flexion are suggestive of a mild hemiparesis.

Test for abduction strength in the shoulder by having the patient push out his upper arm against your resistance.

The trunk strength is assessed by having the patient sit up from a lying position. In truncal ataxia due to cerebellar disease, this will be difficult and balance cannot be maintained.

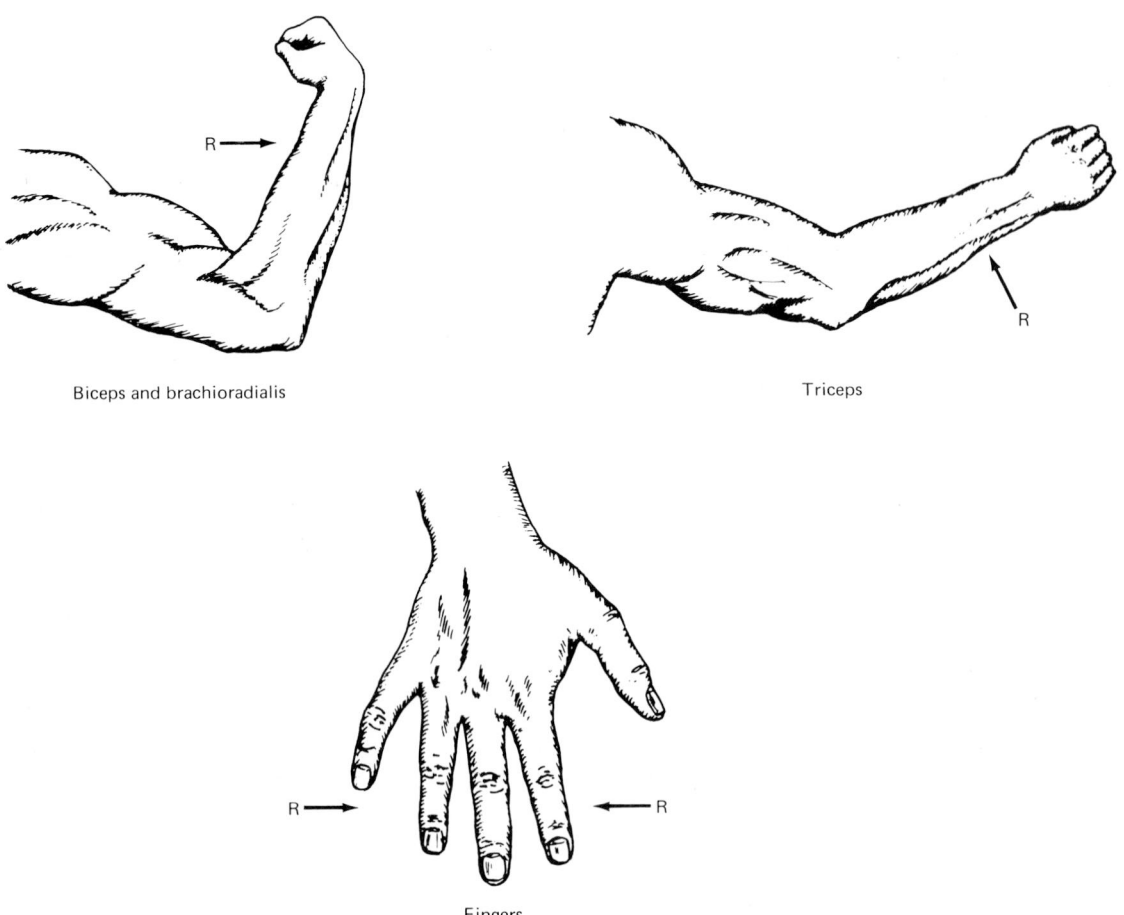

Biceps and brachioradialis

Triceps

Fingers

FIGURE 13-21

Examination of the upper extremities. The patient is instructed to attempt to overcome resistance (R), which is the direction of force applied by the examiner.

Lower Extremities

The lower extremities (Fig. 13-22) are evaluated in the following manner. While the patient is in a supine position, have her raise first one knee and then the other and resist your attempts to push her knee to her chest. This action tests the iliopsoas muscle.

Have the patient hold the knees tightly together while you attempt to open them. This tests the thigh abductor muscles. Have the patient hold the knees apart while you attempt to push them together. This tests the gluteus minimus and medius muscles.

Have the patient stand on his toes while you push down on his shoulders. This tests the gastrocnemius muscle.

Have the patient extend his legs and resist your attempts to flex his knee. This tests the quadriceps. Have the patient flex his knee and resist your attempts to extend the knee. This tests the hamstring muscles.

Have the patient dorsiflex her foot and resist your attempts to overcome the flexion. This tests the tibialis anterior muscle.

Muscle Tone

Muscle tonus is tested by passively putting a limb through full range of motion. Tone refers to the resistance detected by the examiner. Reduced tone may be caused by diseases of the cerebellum and by

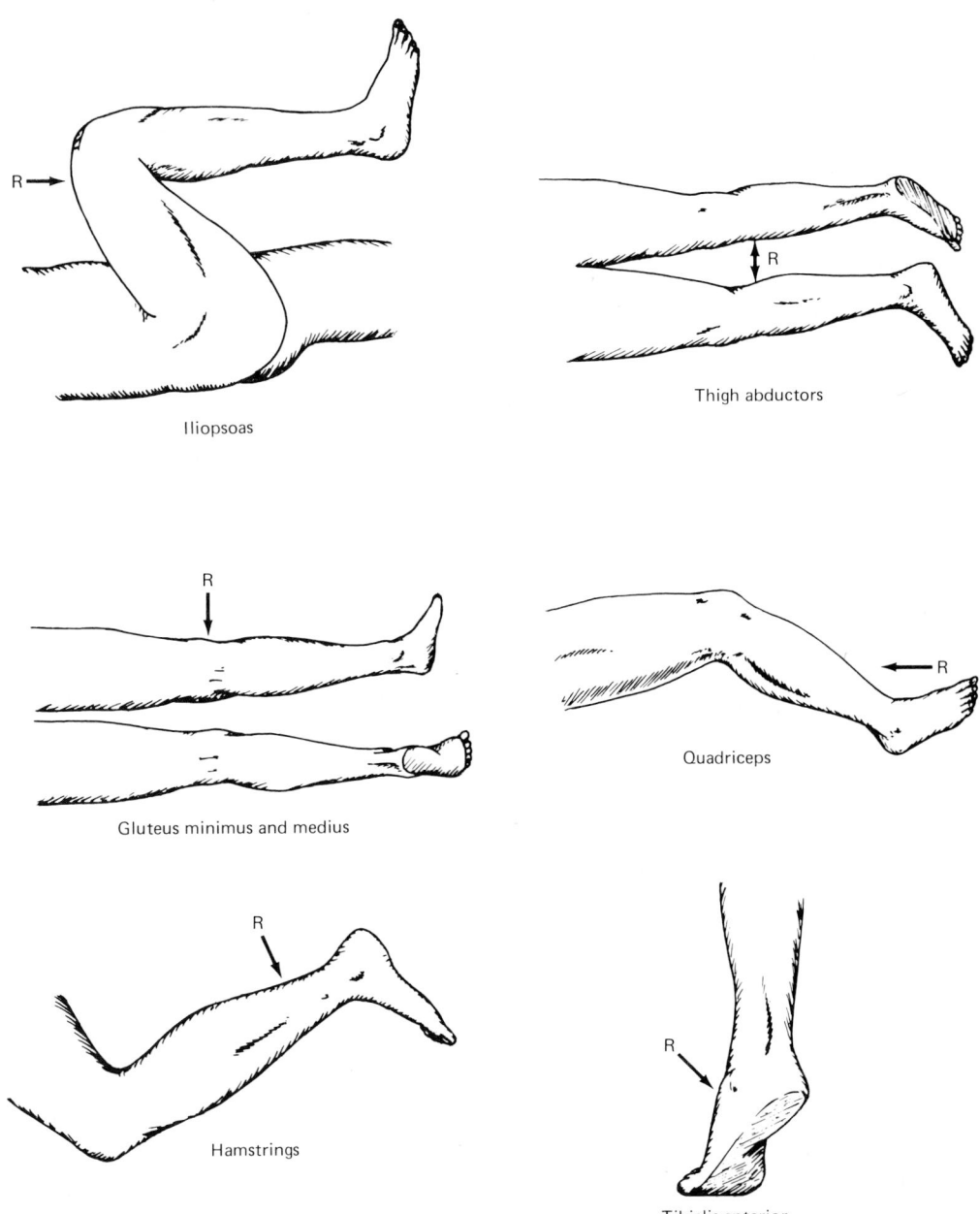

FIGURE 13-22

Examination of the lower extremities. The patient is instructed to attempt to overcome resistance (R), which is the direction of force applied by the examiner.

lower motor neuron diseases; since resistance is slight when normal, it may be difficult to detect.

Increased tone is much easier to detect and is classified as *spastic*, resulting from upper motor neuron lesions, or *rigid*, as in lesions of the basal ganglia. *Spasticity* affects certain muscle groups differently. For example, with upper motor neuron lesions, the flexors in the arms and extensors in the legs are most affected. These are the antigravity muscles where most muscle spindles are located. *Rigidity*, as in Parkinson's disease, is demonstrated in the heightened tone of all flexor muscles, resulting in flexed posture.

A certain type of spasticity is the "clasp knife" phenomenon. This is pyramidal spasticity where resistance to a passive movement rapidly increases to a point and then suddenly gives way. An example is having the patient flex her elbow while the examiner attempts to overcome the flexion. The phenomenon occurs when the flexion suddenly gives way and the patient may hit her chin.

At this point in the examination, if it has not been done before, palpate for lax muscles, tenderness, and pain. Lax muscles may indicate lower motor neuron lesions, while pain and tenderness may signify polyneuritis or polymyositis.

The most common involuntary movement is the rhythmic movement known as the *tremor*. Tremors resulting from diseases affecting the basal ganglia, as in Parkinson's, exist during relaxation and are called *rest tremors*. Tremors associated with cerebellar diseases are characteristically seen when the patient attempts to perform an activity.

Choreas are another type of involuntary movement and are characterized by rapid, jerky, irregular, and purposeless contractions of random muscle groups followed by immediate relaxation. The basal ganglia is affected. The best-known choreas are Huntington's and Sydenham's.

Coordination and Gait

Disturbances in *coordination* can be indicative of cerebellar disorders and of hemiplegia caused by corticospinal tract interruption. The following activities are useful in detecting a lack of coordination and in determining the possible cause.

Have the patient pat his knee rapidly, alternating the back of the hand with the palm. Have him rapidly pat one hand against the palm of the other hand. Have the patient rhythmically touch the tip of his nose with his index finger with his eyes open, then closed. In cerebellar disease, the movements in the above tests are slowed, nonrhythmic, and may "hang." With hemiplegia, movements are just slow and stiff.

Have the patient quickly and consecutively touch the tip of his thumb to each finger of the same hand. These movements are slowed and inaccurate in cerebellar disease, whereas in hemiplegia, the fingers tend to act in unison and the oppositional movement of the thumb is impaired.

Have the patient quickly and smoothly move his finger back and forth between his nose and the examiner's finger. With cerebellar disease, the hand deviates and may miss the target; with hemiplegia, spasticity and jerky, clonic movements may occur.

Ask the patient to wiggle his big toe rapidly up and down. Hemiplegia will greatly reduce the speed. Have the patient run the heel of one foot down the shin of the other leg in a straight line, not looking. Cerebellar disease will cause irregular deviations of the heel to either side.

Since standing and walking properly require adequate muscle strength, coordination, proprioception, vestibular function, and vision, the evaluation of gait and stance may well have already occurred. The observation of simple walking reveals a lot; for example, in hemiparesis the normal rhythmic arm swinging is reduced.

If any difficulty has been noted, the Romberg test should be performed. This is accomplished by having the patient stand with his feet close together with his eyes opened, then closed. Increased swaying and unsteadiness occurs with closed eyes in persons with an impairment of proprioception. Cerebellar disease makes normal stance difficult with the eyes open; and in vestibular disorders of a unilateral type, the patient tends to fall to the ipsilateral side.

Gait is evaluated by having the patient walk heel to toe down a straight line and walk briskly around a chair. Cerebellar disorders cause the patient to walk with a wide base and to stagger or reel laterally. Hemiplegia causes circumduction of the leg with a stiff knee and extended ankle, while a bilateral spastic paresis of the leg produces scissoring of the knees.

The tests for stance and gait may have to be deferred or even omitted in the patient who is quite ill or unable to ambulate. However, the critical-care nurse may have the opportunity to perform these tests and gain valuable information.

Sensory System

The sensory system conveys information to the central nervous system about the status of the body surface and its surrounding environment, about the position of the body and its extremities in relation to space, and about the status of the internal organs. When evaluating the sensory system, great care must be taken to listen carefully and record accurately the patient's reporting because sensory interpretation is extremely subjective. The patient's responses to touch, pain, temperature sensation, proprioceptive (motion and position) sense, vibratory sense, and cortical sensory functions are elicited on the examination. Specific patterns of sensory loss result from specific lesions; therefore, the sensory loss demonstrated may be highly diagnostic.

Superficial pain is tested by lightly pinpricking over the body in a symmetrical fashion. Particular attention should be paid to any suspected or stated area of sensory loss or deficit such as numbness or tingling. When in doubt about the reliability of the response, alternate the sharp point with the dull end of the pin. The dull end acts as a control; it does not test pain perception. If decreased sensation is found, determine the margins of the suspect area. When making a survey of the body in the absence of problems, be sure to compare each side with the other.

Deep pain is tested by squeezing the Achilles tendon, squeezing the calf muscles, and/or applying firm pressure on the sternum. Deep and superficial pain are carried in the same central pathways and therefore lesions affecting one response will usually affect the other.

Temperature perception pathways are very closely related to those for pain and usually do not need testing if pain perception is normal. Always test the temperature response if there is any impairment of pain perception. This is accomplished by using test tubes filled with hot and cold water and applying them alternately over the body and asking the patient to distinguish between them.

Touch is evaluated by using a cotton wisp or a soft brush and stroking corresponding parts of the entire body. Ask the patient to respond when touch is perceived. Touch is usually intact, even with severe involvement of sensory areas, because of the many multiple pathways. If defects are found, however, determine the area of loss by defining margins. Drag the cotton wisp over the area of decreased sensation until margins of sensation can be defined; then record your findings.

Proprioception, or *motion and position sense*, is tested in every extremity by using passive motion and asking the patient to identify the position with eyes shut. Have the patient state when the movement begins and if the extremity is up or down or how it is pointed. Position sense is best tested on the thumbs, fingers, and toes. Position sense is always lost distally first in organic lesions; so if perception is intact in the distal extremities, there is generally no need to test the more proximal portions.

Vibratory sense is tested by placing a vibrating tuning fork against any bony prominence of each extremity—ankle, toe, thumb, or wrist—and asking the patient to tell you when the vibration stops. As with position sense, vibratory perception is initially lost distally.

Cortical sensory perception can occur only if the higher cerebral centers of integration, those beyond the thalamus, are intact. You must evaluate primary sensory modalities first in order to be sure they are intact. For example, a peripheral nerve injury affecting the hand would alter perception of objects placed in the hand but not necessarily indicate a cortical deficit.

Cortical sensory perception is tested in the following ways. *Stereognosis* is the perception of objects through touch. Test each hand with the eyes closed by placing a button, key, coin, or other familiar object in the hand and asking for identification. Two-point discrimination is determined by using a calibrated compass on the fingertip and asking the patient to tell you when one and two points are felt. Normally, two points can be distinguished when the points are 0.3 to 0.6 cm apart. The number of centimeters of separation required to distinguish two points is important. The average distance on the palms and soles is 1.5 cm; on the dorsum of the hand, 3 cm is average; and on the shin, 4 cm is usually necessary. Double simultaneous stimulation is the appreciation of two simultaneous touches on symmetrically opposite sides of the body. This requires normal cortical function. All the above responses are designed to test cortical sensory perception and will be affected by lesions of the sensory cortex.

Reflexes

Deep tendon reflexes are best elicited by having the patient relax. The examiner should then position the limb in a manner which slightly stretches the muscle and strike a brisk blow with a reflex hammer over the tendon insertion of the muscle. Both sides of the body should always be compared for equality of response. Reflexes are usually grades on a 0 to 4+ scale.

4+ = very brisk, hyperactive, and may indicate disease

3+ = more brisk than average, but may well be normal

2+ = average or normal response

1+ = low normal

0 = no response

In addition to the deep tendon reflexes, two superficial reflexes are usually tested: the abdominal and the cremasteric responses. Reflexes, generally speaking, tend to be increased in upper motor neuron disease

TABLE 13-8
Spinal Segment, Stimulus Site, and Expected Response
of Deep Tendon and Superficial Reflexes

Reflex	Spinal segment	Stimulus site	Expected response	
			Observed	Palpated
Biceps	C5, C6	Biceps tendon	Flexion at the elbow	Contraction of biceps
Triceps	C7, C8	Triceps tendon above elbow	Extension at elbow	Contraction of triceps
Brachioradialis or supinator	C5, C6	Radius, 1–2 in above the wrist	Flexion and supination of forearm	
Abdominal	T8, T9, T10 (above umbilicus) T10, T11, T12 (below umbilicus)	Stroke the four abdominal quadrants toward the umbilicus	Contraction of abdominal muscle and umbilicus deviates toward stimulus	
Cremasteric	L1, L2	Scratch inner aspect of upper thigh	Testicle elevates on stimulated side; absence of response suggests corticospinal tract lesion at or below L1-L2	
Patellar or knee	L2, L3, L4	Patellar tendon	Extension of knee	Contraction of quadriceps
Achilles or ankle	S1, S2	Achilles tendon	Plantar flexion at the ankle	
Plantar	L4, L5, S1, S2	Lateral aspect of the sole of the foot from heel to ball and curving across the ball	Plantar flexion of toes and foot (dorsiflexion of the big toe with fanning of the other toes is the *Babinski response*)	

and decreased in lower motor neuron disease. Table 13-8 provides the expected response, site of stimulus, and corresponding spinal segments of commonly tested deep tendon and superficial reflexes.

ABDOMEN AND RECTUM

Examination of the abdomen should be performed with the comfort of the patient foremost in the mind of the examiner. If the patient has any abdominal pain or is apprehensive about the examination, or if the examiner does not carefully explain what is to be done, the examination may not yield full information regarding the state of the abdomen. Prerequisite to the examination is knowledge of the anatomy of the abdomen and an awareness of the proper techniques of examination. Figure 13-23 demonstrates the division of the abdomen into nine areas to show the underlying anatomy.

The nine areas and their representative organs are as follows:

1, *epigastric*: duodenum, pancreas, aorta
2, *umbilical*: omentum, mesentery, jejunum, and ileum
3, *pubic* or *hypogastric*: ileum, bladder, pregnant uterus
4, *right hypochondriac*: gallbladder, right lobe of liver, part of right kidney, adrenal
5, *left hypochondriac*: stomach, spleen, upper pole of left kidney, adrenal
6, *right lumbar*: ascending colon, lower half of right kidney
7, *left lumbar*: descending colon, lower half of left kidney
8, *right inguinal*: cecum, appendix, right ureter, right ovary or spermatic cord
9, *left inguinal*: sigmoid colon, left ovary or spermatic cord

Figure 13-24 shows the more common division into four quadrants:

RUQ (right upper quadrant): liver and gallbladder, duodenum, portion of right kidney, adrenal, portions of ascending and transverse colon

LUQ (left upper quadrant): left lobe of liver, spleen, stomach, portion of left kidney, adrenal, portions of transverse and descending colon

RLQ (right lower quadrant): lower pole of right kidney, cecum and appendix, ovary or right spermatic cord, uterus (if enlarged)

LLQ (left lower quadrant): lower pole of left kidney, sigmoid colon, portion of descending colon, ovary or left spermatic cord, uterus (if enlarged)

Examination

The order of examination of the abdomen differs from that of other systems in that auscultation follows inspection. This alteration in the examination sequence is justified because palpation and percussion may alter the frequency and quality of bowel sounds. The patient should have an empty bladder and be in a comfortable supine position draped from the nipples up and from the pubis down. The knees may be flexed over a pillow for comfort and increased abdominal muscle relaxation. The arms should be placed at the side or over the chest. Be sure you have warm hands and a warm stethoscope. Approach the patient slowly, explain your intent, and be constantly aware of your patient's reactions and facial expressions. The examiner will need a stethoscope and tangential lighting.

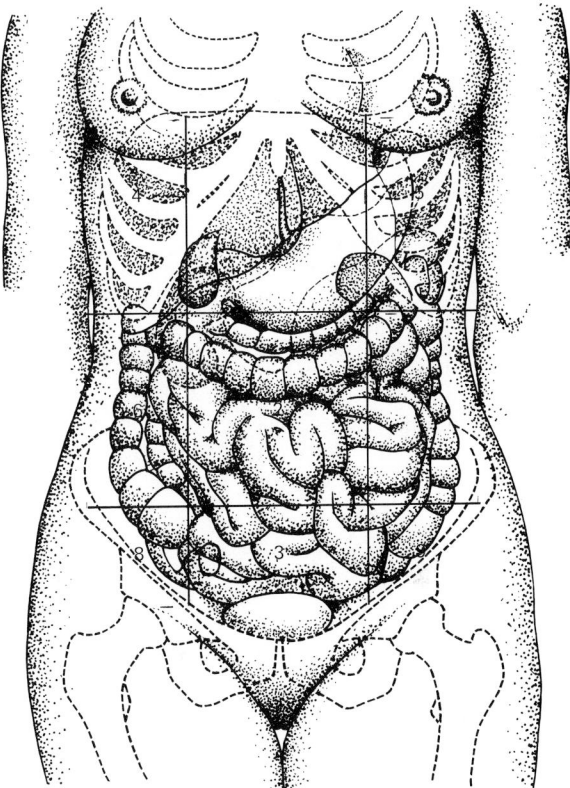

FIGURE 13-23

The nine regions. (*From A. H. Robins, G. I. Series of the Abdomen. Physical Examination of the Abdomen, part 1, A. H. Robins, Richmond, Va., 1969. Used by permission of the publisher.*)

Abdomen

During inspection of the abdomen, the skin is observed for scars, rashes, and lesions. These are recorded as to appearance, location, size, and shape. The presence of dilated veins could be indicative of inferior vena cava obstruction. Striae, or stretch marks, result from prolonged stretching of the skin. New striae are pink or blue in color, while older ones will be silvery. The abdominal contour is usually flat, rounded, protuberant (as in obesity), or scaphoid (as in the emaciated patient). The umbilicus is usually located in the center of the abdomen. Any obvious asymmetry of the abdomen may be an important finding and should be assessed in greater detail. All observations should be made from above as well as from the side. If supraumbilical fullness is noted, it may indicate a mass in the stomach, upper colon, liver, or pancreas, while fullness below the umbilicus could indicate pregnancy, a full bladder, or masses

in the colon, uterus, or ovaries. Careful note should be made of any such findings as to size, shape, location, and so on. Peristalsis may be observed by using tangential lighting and viewing the abdomen from the side. It is usually possible to detect peristalsis in thin people but not in persons with obese abdomens. Peristaltic movements may also be observed with intestinal obstruction. The pulsations which are usually visible in the epigastric area are normal aortic pulsations.

Auscultation of the abdomen is performed using the diaphragm of the stethoscope and placing it lightly over each of the four abdominal quadrants. The bowel sounds will be heard normally at a frequency of 5 to 34 clicks and gurgles per minute. Bowel sounds may be very loud (borborygmi) when one is hungry. This is the familiar stomach growling. In-

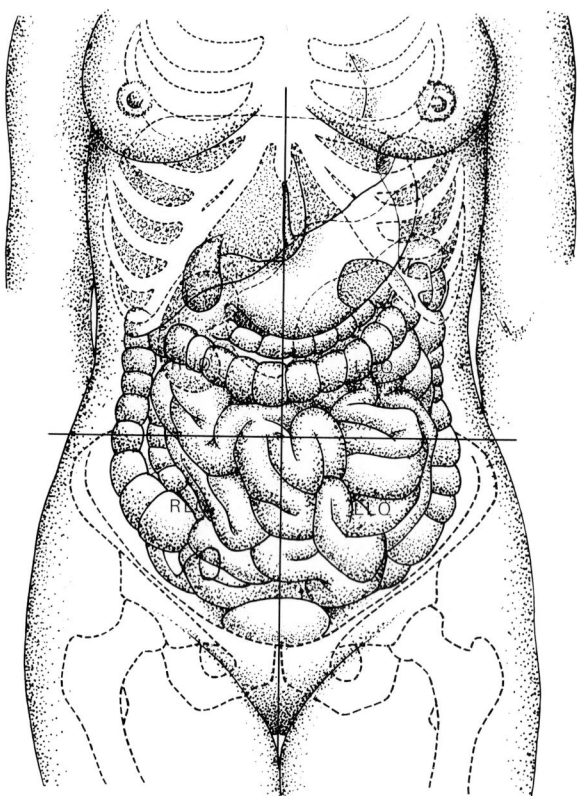

FIGURE 13-24

The four quadrants of the abdomen. (*From A. H. Robins,
G. I. Series of the Abdomen. Physical Examination of the
Abdomen, part 1, A. H. Robins, Richmond, Va., 1969. Used
by permission of the publisher.*)

creased sounds may be heard in diarrhea or early
intestinal obstruction, while absence of sound is
indicative of paralytic ileus, peritonitis, or postabdom-
inal surgery.

The examiner also auscultates for vascular sounds
such as systolic bruits, venous hums, and rubs. The
stethoscope is placed over the renal artery, abdominal
aorta, and the iliac arteries to listen for systolic bruits.
A bruit is the sound of turbulence from partially
obstructed arterial blood flow. Friction rubs are rare,
but when present, they sound like rubbing sandpaper
and are indicative of peritoneal irritation. Venous
hums are also rare, but when heard, they present as
a continous humming sound. Figure 13-25 indicates
sources of diagnostic noises which may be heard
during abdominal auscultation.

Percussion is a useful technique for general orientation to the abdomen for identification of gas, air,

and fluid in the abdominal cavity and/or organs; and
for measurement of the liver. This part of the examination begins with a general orientation to the abdomen by lightly percussing all quadrants and determining the areas of tympany and dullness. Tympany
is usually found over the stomach, gut, and any other
air-filled viscera. Percussion in the left lower anterior
rib cage area will reveal the gastric air bubble.
Dullness is heard over the liver, spleen, a full bladder,
pregnant uterus, and so on. Dullness is also heard
over fluid, and therefore, the technique of percussion
is quite useful in determining the amount of free fluid
present in the abdominal cavity. Percussion for shifting dullness is the technique used for detecting free
fluid. To accomplish this, the patient initially is supine.
The examiner percusses from midline to first one side
then the other. The point where dullness begins is
marked on each side. The patient then is rolled to
one side, then the other, and percussion is used in
the same manner. Mark the line of dullness. The area
between the two lines indicates the amount of free
fluid (see Fig. 13-26).

Liver size is determined through percussion also.
To accomplish this, percuss upward along the right
midclavicular line from a point just below the umbilicus to determine the lower border of liver dullness.
Next, percuss downward on the midclavicular line
from lung resonance to liver dullness. This identifies
the upper border of the liver. The normal liver size is
6 to 12 cm. There are, however, normal livers which
extend as low as the right lower quadrant.

Often the spleen cannot be identified by percussion, but it is located near the 10th rib just posterior
to the midaxillary line (refer to Fig. 13-23). If the
spleen is enlarged, it may be detected by percussing
the lowest interspace in the left anterior axillary line.
The normal sound in this area is tympanic. Have the
patient take a deep breath before you percuss. If the
spleen is of normal size, the percussion sound will
remain tympanic. If the spleen is enlarged, a dull note
will be elicited.

Light and deep palpation are utilized in examining
the abdomen. Before attempting deep palpation, the
examiner should employ light palpation. This is performed by using light, firm pressure and moving
smoothly to feel all quadrants. Areas of tenderness
and increased resistance can be identified during
light palpation. The technique (of light palpation)
involves placing the entire palm and extended closed
fingers of the hand on the surface of the abdomen
and pressing gently with the fingertips to a depth of
about 1 cm (Fig. 13-27). If a patient is ticklish, having

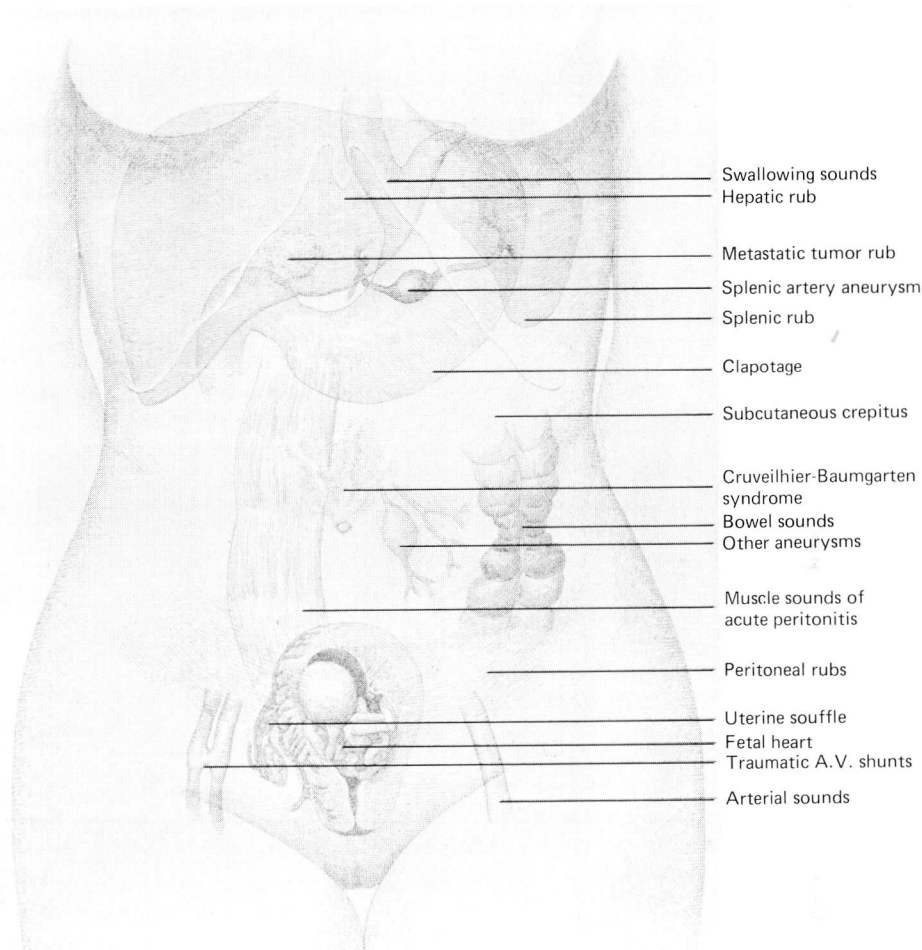

Swallowing sounds
Hepatic rub

Metastatic tumor rub
Splenic artery aneurysm
Splenic rub

Clapotage

Subcutaneous crepitus

Cruveilhier-Baumgarten syndrome
Bowel sounds
Other aneurysms

Muscle sounds of acute peritonitis

Peritoneal rubs

Uterine souffle
Fetal heart
Traumatic A.V. shunts

Arterial sounds

FIGURE 13-25
Sources of diagnostic noises to be considered during a routine abdominal auscultation. (*From A. H. Robins, G. I. Series of the Abdomen. Physical Examination of the Abdomen, part 4, A. H. Robins, Richmond, Va., 1971. Used by permission of the publisher.*)

him place his hand over yours as you examine him will generally decrease the feeling of ticklishness by allowing him to participate. To determine areas of tenderness, press the tips of the fingers gently into the abdomen and then withdraw them suddenly (Fig. 13-28). The transient pain which results is called *rebound tenderness.* This pressure is always applied in an area remote from the suspected area of tenderness.

Deep palpation is usually required to delineate abdominal organs or masses and should be performed very carefully, especially if abdominal disease or injury is present or suspected. Deep palpation is accomplished by pressing the entire palmar surface of the hand with approximated fingers into the abdomen to a depth of 4 to 5 cm. This may be done with only one hand or with the fingertips of the other hand pressing on the distal joint of the examining hand for increased tactile awareness of the examining fingers, as demonstrated in Fig. 13-2. If on the initial deep palpation a mass is felt, it should be determined if it is an intra-abdominal mass or an intramural mass. Having the supine patient raise her head while you palpate will give you this information. The intra-ab-

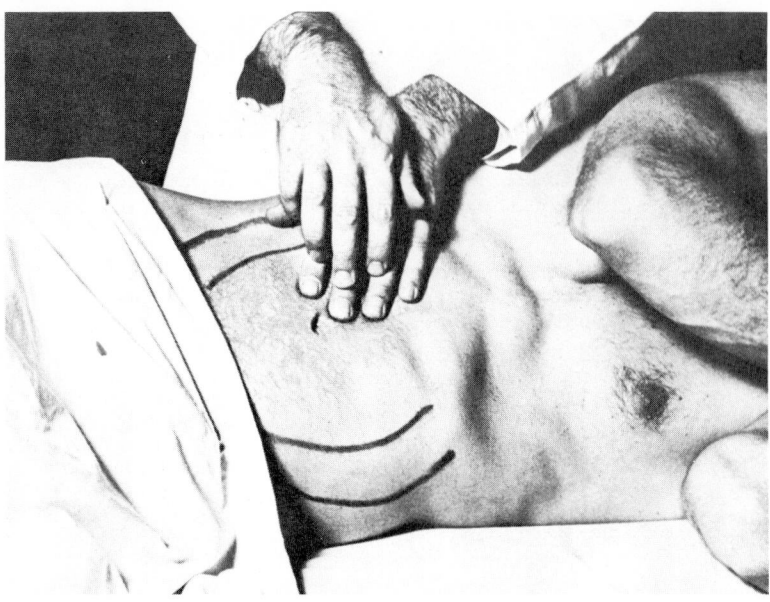

FIGURE 13-26

Technique for percussing for shifting dullness. (*From A. H. Robins, G. I. Series of the Abdomen. Physical Examination of the Abdomen, part 3, A. H. Robins, Richmond, Va., 1970. Used by permission of the publisher.*)

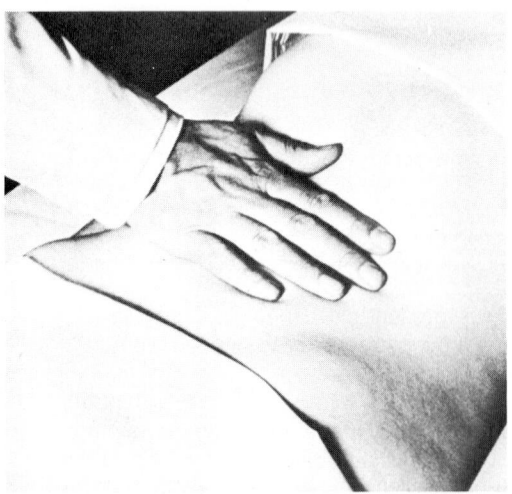

FIGURE 13-27

Light palpation. (*From A. H. Robins, G. I. Series of the Abdomen. Physical Examination of the Abdomen, part 2, A. H. Robins, Richmond, Va., 1969. Used by permission of the publisher.*)

dominal mass will move away from your hand, while the intramural mass will be more readily palpable (Fig. 13-29).

Next palpate the femoral arteries. Diminished or absent femoral pulses could indicate common iliac artery thrombosis or dissecting aortic aneurysm. Now move to the left upper quadrant. Palpation is accomplished in this area by standing on the patient's right side and reaching across the abdomen. Pull the left lower rib cage up with your left hand and press deeply toward the spleen with your right hand (Fig. 13-30). The spleen is not palpable unless enlarged; however, splenomegaly can be slight, moderate, or large. Slight enlargement may result from lupus, rheumatoid arthritis, or subacute bacterial endocarditis. Moderate enlargement may indicate cirrhosis, hepatitis, or infectious mononucleosis. A large spleen may suggest chronic malaria, congenital syphilis, or portal vein obstruction.

Palpation of the kidney is accomplished by supporting the flank with your free hand and pressing deeply into the lower left or right quadrant with your examining hand (depending on which kidney you are examining). You may feel the lower pole of the kidney come to your fingertips during deep inspirations.

Kidneys are most easily palpable in very thin, relaxed persons; the right kidney is more easily felt because of the lowered position. An enlarged kidney could be secondary to hydronephrosis, cysts, or neoplasm.

The liver is located in the right upper quadrant. Palpation of the liver is performed by pushing up from the back with the left hand under the 11th to 12th rib. Place your right hand on the patient's right abdomen with fingertips parallel to the right costal margin where the liver edge is anticipated and press gently up and in under the thorax as the patient inspires. The liver should be felt on deep inspiration. A normal liver edge is smooth and firm. A hard or lumpy liver could indicate carcinoma, whereas tenderness may suggest hepatitis.

The aorta is palpated by pressing firmly deep into the upper abdomen and slightly left of the midline to identify aortic pulsation. You may be able to feel the aorta between the thumb and fingers. Enlargement of the aorta may be indicative of an aneurysm. This component of the examination is another area where great caution is indicated, especially if problems (e.g. aneurysm) are suspected.

Rectum

The examination of the *rectum* is effectively accomplished with the patient in the left lateral position. This is the position usually used on persons in bed. The examiner uses a gloved examining hand and spreads the buttocks apart with the other hand. The index finger of the examining hand is lubricated. The peri-

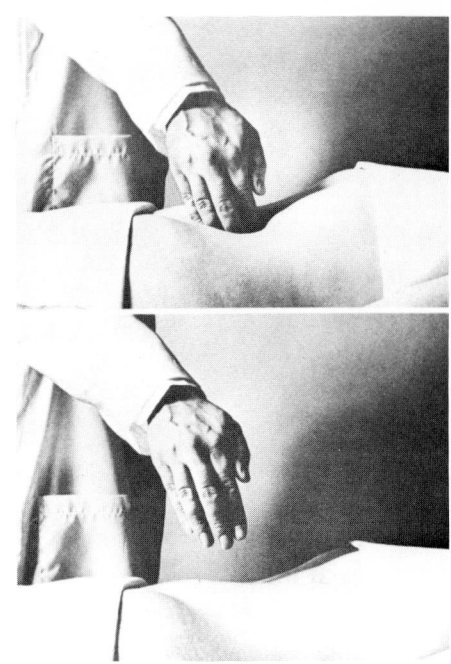

FIGURE 13-28

Testing for rebound tenderness. (*From A. H. Robins, G. I. Series of the Abdomen. Physical Examination of the Abdomen, part 2, A. H. Robins, Richmond, Va., 1969. Used by permission of the publisher.*)

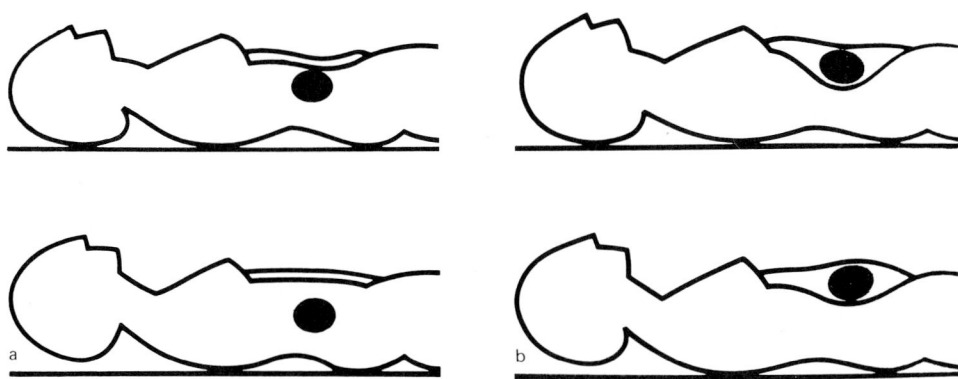

FIGURE 13-29

Distinction between intramural and intra-abdominal masses: (*a*) indicates an intra-abdominal mass. (*b*) indicates an intramural mass. (*From A. H. Robins, G. I. Series of the Abdomen. Physical Examination of the Abdomen, part 2, A. H. Robins, Richmond, Va., 1969. Used by permission of the publisher.*)

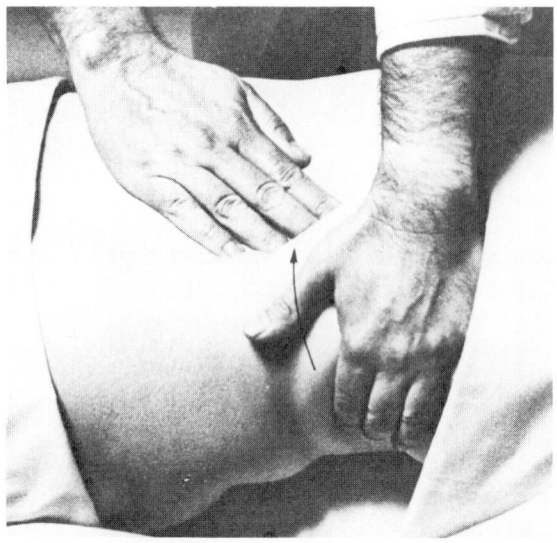

FIGURE 13-30

Bimanual palpation of the spleen. (*From A. H. Robins, G. I. Series of the Abdomen. Physical Examination of the Abdomen, part 2, A. H. Robins, Richmond, Va., 1969. Used by permission of the publisher.*)

anal and sacrococcygeal areas are inspected for inflammation, lumps, lesions, and excoriations. Ask the patient to bear down while you are inspecting the anus. Protruding tags of tissue are usually hemorrhoids. In order to palpate the anus, first have the patient relax and then slip the lubricated finger into the anal canal pointing toward the umbilicus. Note sphincter tone of the anus, and tenderness, and irregularities. Internal hemorrhoids may be felt at this time if they are inflamed. In the male, the prostate will be palpable on the anterior wall; in the female, the cervix is palpable on the anterior wall. Continue to consistently and smoothly examine the entire rectum and inspect any material which adheres to the examining glove when it is withdrawn. Inspection and palpation of the anus and rectum will most probably be accomplished by the critical-care nurse in the course of daily care routine or when impaction is suspected. It may also occur when rectal temperatures are taken.

Examination of the rectum may need to be deferred if the patient is critically ill or has had a coronary, stroke, or injury to the area of the rectum. This is to avoid compounding existing damage or eliciting responses (i.e., Valsalva maneuver) which could endanger the patient.

MALE AND FEMALE GENITOURINARY SYSTEMS

Review of the patient's history is of special importance in this area. It is in the history that problems which may affect or influence patient care may first be revealed. Certain conditions such as urinary retention, dribbling, hesitancy, urgency, or frequency could be significant problems for a patient confined to bed. Any tendency toward urinary tract infections should be noted because drugs and catheterizations may precipitate such infections. Additional consideration for female patients are those of contraceptives and susceptibility to vaginal infections.

Examination of Male and Female Genitalia

The physical examination of the *male genitalia* in the critical-care unit can be accomplished during routine physical care. Inspection for structural abnormalities, lesions, engorged vessels, and discharges can be done while inserting a catheter or giving catheter care. Palpation for masses can occur during perineal care.

As time and opportunity permit, assessment of the male genitalia can continue by determining the presence of testicular tenderness or pain. Phimosis (restriction of the opening of the prepuce) is a common condition that occurs in uncircumcised males. A collection of smegma beneath the foreskin may become infected; therefore, the foreskin should be retracted during examination. The shaft of the penis is inspected for size, shape, skin color, edema, and the size and placement of the urethral meatus. Palpation for tenderness, edema, and nodules of the penis and of the scrotum can occur at the same time. The scrotum should also be palpated for equal distribution of contents. If any abnormal swelling is present, the scrotum should be transilluminated with a penlight. If the swelling is due to an accumulation of serous fluid, the light will be transmitted as red. Blood and solid tissue do not transmit any light.

When the patient's condition permits, the groin may be inspected for the presence of hernias or other abnormalities. The patient stands in front of the examiner who is seated. The inguinal and femoral regions are inspected for lesions, enlarged lymph nodes, and hernia bulges. The inguinal canal is then palpated. To accomplish palpation, the loose skin of the scrotal sac is invaginated as the examiner directs the index finger up into the external inguinal ring. The patient is asked to bear down and cough. If an indirect hernia is present, it will be felt against the fingertip. A direct hernia is sensed through the posterior inguinal canal wall as the fingertip continues to examine.

The *female genitalia* can also be examined externally during daily care. The mons pubis, labia majora, and perineum are inspected for swelling, inflammation, lesions, growths, and scars. The vestibule is inspected for discharge, inflammation, swelling, and odor. The labia minora, clitoris, urethral opening, and the vaginal introitus are also inspected and note made of any obvious disorders or problems.

If an existing condition warrants and the examiner is skilled in the technique, then internal inspection may be conducted. Excessive discharges and abnormal bleeding may be sufficient justification; however, this will need to be very carefully evaluated.

The procedure involves selecting a speculum of the correct size and dipping it in warm water, which acts as a lubricant. The patient can be positioned on her back with thighs spread apart. The examiner should press down on the perineum just under the vaginal introitus and slide the closed speculum over the fingers into the vagina. Turn the blades into a horizontal position and open the blades to visualize the cervix for shape and color and for the presence of any erosions, lesions, or discharges. Also observe the vagina as the speculum is withdrawn. A specimen should be obtained of any discharge and notation made of any bleeding, lesion, or other disorders.

Assessment of the Urinary Tract

Careful questioning, although a part of the history rather then part of the physical examination, can reveal problems of the urinary tract which might not be picked up in any other way, thus yielding information necessary to determine if further investigation is warranted. Symptoms which can be referred to the urinary tract include frequency, nocturia, urgency, hesitancy, oliguria, dysuria, dribbling, hematuria, pyuria, incontinence, pain, and edema.

Frequency may be attended by *polyuria,* which is the passage of only minute amounts of urine at each voiding. Frequency may also be nocturnal in occurrence and is then referred to as *nocturia.* Diurnal frequency may result from acute prostatitis, urinary bladder tumors, renal calculi with renal colic, gonorrhea, diverticulitis, and uterine leiomyoma. Nocturia

commonly occurs with congestive heart failure and nephroangiosclerosis. Frequency and nocturia are often found simultaneously in benign prostatic hypertrophy, prostatic malignancy, renal tuberculosis, and urinary tract infections.

Urgency, an intense desire to urinate, often accompanies frequency and is usually a result of prostatic disease or bladder infection. *Hesitancy,* or difficulty in initiating the urinary stream, is usually secondary to prostatic disease. *Incontinence* may result from infections, mechanical impairment of function, and/or neurological disorders.

Oliguria indicates a substantial decrease in urinary output. The etiology is decreased urine production and occurs in such urinary tract conditions as acute glomerulonephritis and in shock and dehydration. *Dysuria* is pain and burning or discomfort on urination. This is usually indicative of kidney, bladder, or urethral disease. *Dribbling,* or the passage of frequently interrupted small amounts of urine with little or no force, usually indicates an urethral stricture or prostate obstruction.

Hematuria, which occurs at the onset of urination, often indicates an urethral lesion; *terminal hematuria,* or bleeding which occurs at the end of urination, usually signifies disease in the trigone of the bladder or in the prostatic urethra. When bleeding is present throughout urination, the cause may arise from the kidneys, ureters, or the bladder. Hematuria may or may not be accompanied by pain, depending on the site and nature of the disease process. For example, cancer of the bladder could cause intermittent, painless hematuria, while hemorrhagic cystitis may result in profuse hematuria with pain or discomfort in suprapubic region.

Pyuria, pus in the urine, is usually signified by cloudy urine. This may result from infection at any point along the urinary tract. The *edema* which may occur in renal disease is often localized in the hands and periorbital regions or may be generalized. *Pain* which is referrable to the urinary tract may be characterized as mild, moderate, or severe and be classified as dull, sharp, or colicky. In renal colic (resulting from a stone in the ureter), the pain is usually severe, originating in the costovertebral area and radiating toward the groin, testes, or vulva. This may occur on either side of the body. Pain in the suprapubic area may occur in cystitis or simply be the result of an overdistended bladder.

REFERENCES

Bates, B.: *A Guide to Physical Examination,* Philadelphia: Lippincott, 1974.

Beyers, M., and S. Dudas: Patients with integumentary system dysfunction, in *The Clinical Practice of Medical-Surgical Nursing,* Boston: Little, Brown, 1977, pp.1093–1133.

Burrell, Z. L., and L. O. Burrell: *Critical Care,* 3d ed., St. Louis: Mosby, 1977.

De Gowin, E. L., and R. L. De Gowin: *Bedside Diagnostic Examination,* New York: MacMillan, 1976.

Druger, G.: *The Chest: Its Signs and Sounds,* Los Angeles: Humetrics Corporation, 1973.

Fitzpatrick, T. B., K. A. Arndt, W. H. Clark, A. Z. Eisen, E. Van Scott, and J. H. Vaughan: *Dermatology in General Medicine,* 3d ed., New York: McGraw-Hill, 1979.

Harvey, A. M., J. J. Richard, A. H. Owens, and S. R. Richard (eds.): *The Principles and Practice of Medicine,* New York: Appleton-Century-Crofts, 1976.

Hochstein, E., and A. L. Rubin: *Physical Diagnosis,* New York: McGraw-Hill 1964.

Jarvis, C. V.: Vital signs: A preview of problems, in Nursing 77 Books Series, B. McVan (ed.), *Assessing Vital Functions Accurately,* Horsham, Pennsylvania: Intermed Communications, 1977.

Littman, D.: Stethoscopes and auscultation, *Am J Nurs* 72(7):1238–1246, 1972.

Mayfield, P., et al.: *Physical Assessment: A Programmed Approach,* New York: McGraw-Hill, 1980.

Prior, J. A., and J. S. Silberstein: *Physical Diagnosis,* 5th ed., St. Louis: Mosby, 1977.

Programmed instruction, patient assessment: Abnormalities of the heartbeat, *Am J Nurs* 77(4): 647–648, 1977.

Programmed instruction, patient assessment: Examination of the heart and great vessels, part I, *Am J Nurs.* 76(11):1807–1830, 1976.

Programmed instruction, patient assessment: Auscultation of the heart, part II, *Am J Nurs* 77(2):275–298, 1977.

Roach, L. B.: Color changes in dark skin, *Nursing 77* 7(1):48–51, 1977.

Robins, A. H.: *G. I. Series of the Abdomen. Physical Examination of the Abdomen,* parts I-VI, Richmond, Va.: A. H. Robins, 1969–1972.

Schroeder, J. S., and E. K. Daily: *Techniques in Bedside Hemodynamic Monitoring,* St. Louis: Mosby, 1976.

Schwartz, S. I., G. T. Shires, F. C. Spencer, and E. H. Storer (eds.): *Principles of Surgery,* 3d ed., New York: McGraw-Hill, 1978.

Sherman, J. L., and S. K. Fields: *Guide to Patient Evaluation,* New York: Medical Examination, 1978.

The following chapter is divided into two parts. The first part is designed to illustrate the application of physical assessment techniques. Patient examples within the categories of critical-unstable, stable, and comatose will be presented. Each of these examples will include a brief case history and discussion of physical findings within selected assessment parameters. The second part of this chapter will present a number of conditions and related physical findings relevant to patients in critical-care settings.

SELECTED CASES

Case One: Critical-Unstable

Case History

On admission this patient was complaining of upper abdominal pain. The history of the present episode revealed the patient's awareness of black, tarry stools for several days and an increasing feeling of fatigue accompanied by intensifying gastric pain. The patient had been diagnosed several months earlier as having a gastric ulcer for which treatment was prescribed. The patient had not been adhering to the prescribed regimen. Immediately after admission, copious hematemesis occurred. Continual, careful, and thorough assessment of this patient is imperative because the onset of hemorrhagic shock secondary to gastrointestinal bleeding can occur insidiously and the condition of the patient can deteriorate rapidly. Utilization of physical assessment techniques can be of particular value in assisting the critical-care nurse's detection of shock in its earlier stages.

Shock may be defined as a serious reduction of tissue perfusion which, when prolonged, leads to widespread impairment of cellular function. Shock may be classified as (1) nonprogressive or compensated, (2) progressive, or (3) irreversible. The early phase of shock can be incorporated into the nonprogressive stage and the early part of the progressive stage, while the late phase of shock refers to the latter part of the progressive stage. Irreversible shock is that point where, regardless of therapy, the patient cannot be saved. Exactly what constitutes that critical point beyond which death is inevitable has not been fully determined; however, factors including a badly compromised cardiac status, accumulation of destructive enzymes, and acidosis have been proposed as key elements.

14
APPLICATION OF PHYSICAL ASSESSMENT TECHNIQUES APPROPRIATE TO PATIENT STATUS

Betty Henderson
Gayle T. Ferguson

SELECTED CASES
Case One: Critical-Unstable
Case Two: Stable
Case Three: Comatose

SELECTED PROBLEMS
Problems of the Eye
Problems of the Skin
Problems of the Lungs
Problems of the Abdomen and Rectum
Problems of the Nervous System

REFERENCES

Observations

As shock progresses from the early into the late stages, certain physical findings, symptomatology, and laboratory values will be evidenced. These are listed in Table 14-1.

Some of the significant parameters in the assessment of the patient in shock will be discussed. The areas include evaluation of blood pressure, cardiac function, peripheral perfusion, respiration, sensorium, and renal and abdominal status.

Blood Pressure

During the early stages of compensated shock, adaptive mechanisms are operating to maintain adequate cardiac output. Blood pressure measurement at this time may very well be normal. For this reason, the blood pressure may not be a useful indicator. Additionally, pronounced peripheral vasoconstriction during early shock may render the use of a blood pressure cuff ineffective. For this reason, the use of an arterial line is recommended. Serial readings of blood pressure are significant in order to identify trends as they occur.

When the blood pressure begins to fall, the patient is no longer in early shock, and regardless of the previous normal pressure, a systolic pressure below 80 mmHg should be regarded as a danger signal. When the systolic pressure drops to 70 mmHg, a serious degree of perfusion failure exists; a systolic pressure of 60 mmHg is critical and demands precise resuscitative measures.

A decrease in pulse pressure will also occur as the systolic pressure decreases, since the diastolic pressure generally drops less rapidly. The pulse pressure is significant in that it tends to parallel cardiac stroke volume.

Heart Rate, Rhythm, and Quality

Early in shock the pulse rate is increased and the quality may be described as weak and thready. Often the peripheral vascular constriction which occurs during the compensatory phase of shock can be detected through palpation of diminishing peripheral pulses. If peripheral pulses become essentially non-palpable, the carotid and femoral pulses can be utilized.

TABLE 14-1
Physical Findings Related to Stages of Shock

	Stages of shock	
	Early	Late
Physical findings	↓ Pulse pressure ↑ Diastolic pressure Restlessness Hyperventilation Pulse: rapid and thready Skin: cold, clammy and pale Ascending cooling of the extremities Mucous membranes: dry and pale Nail beds cyanotic upon pressure, with slow capillary refill	↓ Systolic pressure ↓ Urine volume Drowsiness Hypothermia Diaphoresis Pronounced tachypnea
Symptoms	Anxiety Apprehension Nervousness Thirst Perceived feeling of cold Nausea Perceived feeling of weakness	Pronounced confusion and lethargy
Laboratory findings	↓ Urine sodium concentration ↑ Urine osmolarity Respiratory alkalosis	Metabolic acidosis

When the radial pulse is palpated, auscultation of the apex of the heart yields information regarding the presence or absence of a pulse deficit. If there is a deficit, further auscultation is used to determine if a precipitating arrhythmia such as atrial fibrillation is present.

Peripheral Perfusion

In the early stages of shock, increased sympathetic activity causes constriction of the blood vessels in the skin. On inspection, the patient will have a cool, pale, moist skin. There is ascending cooling of the extremities. The alteration in peripheral perfusion is evidenced by marked peripheral vasoconstriction. There will be a decreased ability to determine peripheral pulses on palpation and palpating veins will be more difficult.

Respiration

Respiratory assessment focuses on inspection of the rate and pattern of respirations and auscultation of the breath sounds. These parameters are assessed frequently to detect changes. An increasing respiratory rate can occur as the decrease in red blood cells (RBC) and hemoglobin leads to a decrease in oxygen-carrying power. This in turn leads to cellular hypoxia, which increases as blood loss continues. The hyperventilation observed early in shock may reflect increasing hypoxia and respiratory alkalosis; however, only arterial blood gas analysis can determine the precise degree of acid-base imbalance.

Auscultation of the lung fields will reveal alterations in the normal breath sounds if they are present. For example, secretions accumulating in the bronchi could alter the normal vesicular sounds. The removal of these secretions is essential to ensure adequate ventilation.

Sensorium

The amount of blood available to the brain of the patient in the late stage of shock may be insufficient to support cerebral oxygen and glucose needs. In that event, there will be a decrease in the level of consciousness and normal mental functioning. The patient may become apathetic and confused and unable to respond appropriately to questions and instructions.

This decrease in mental acuity will usually begin with restlessness and apprehension in early shock and progress to confusion as the shock state advances. Assessment of the patient for a decreasing level of consciousness and increasing clouding of the sensorium should be accomplished at regular intervals along with assessment of all other parameters.

Renal Function

As decreased perfusion to the kidney occurs, there will be a decline in urine volume. In the early stages of shock, however, this decline usually is nondramatic and can go unnoticed. A decreased urine volume (below 30 mL/h) is a late sign of kidney failure. Since urinary output is a very important parameter in the assessment of a bleeding patient, the insertion of an indwelling catheter, if not already present, is necessary in order to accurately monitor the urine quantitatively and qualitatively.

Abdomen

Since this case speaks to the impending or existent state of hemorrhagic shock due to a gastrointestinal lesion, it is significant to look at certain components of the abdominal physical examination.

Auscultation should be carried out to determine the presence or absence of bowel sounds and to determine if any unusual vascular sounds are present. Inspection of the abdomen may reveal distention or bulging, which could indicate an accumulation of blood or fluid in abdominal organs or cavity. Percussion can be utilized to further determine the presence of such fluids. The percussion sound elicited over fluid is dull as opposed to the normal tympanic sound of gas-filled viscera. Also, percussion of the abdomen may identify areas of exquisite tenderness in one or more areas which require further evaluation. Palpation of the abdomen of a patient with gastrointestinal pathology should be executed with great care, and deep palpation is generally contraindicated. For details of the abdominal examination, refer to Chap. 13.

The inclusion of physical assessment parameters in determining the hemodynamic status of the critically ill patient who is bleeding can assist in predicting and possibly preventing many of the complications of extensive blood loss.

Case Two: Stable

Case History

The patient was an adult male admitted 2 days earlier with severe "indigestion," which was subsequently diagnosed as an anteroseptal myocardial infarction. The complications which may occur following the initial infarction can be very severe; therefore, the patient usually remains in an area where specialized care and monitoring necessary for continued recovery are available. The physical assessment techniques utilized by the critical-care nurse are constantly employed on the patient's behalf to detect impending problems and to facilitate the initiation of appropriate interventions.

Common and potentially deadly complications which can occur following a myocardial infarction are severe arrhythmias, hypoxia, congestive failure, thromboembolism, and cardiogenic shock. The following discussion is focused on these complications and the physical assessment techniques employed in detecting their presence.

Arrhythmias

The cardiac monitor is recognized for the efficacy with which it detects cardiac arrhythmias. Concomitantly, the use of observational and assessment skills by the critical-care nurse provides another source of information to be used in the effective management of the cardiac patient.

For example, palpation of arterial pulses may reveal the presence of tachycardia or bradycardia. In addition, variations from normal rhythm which may be palpated include such irregularities as premature beats, pauses, and erratic beats. Auscultation of the apex of the heart while palpating the radial pulse can reveal the presence or absence of a pulse deficit. An electrocardiogram will confirm the presence of arrhythmias which may be suspected after palpation of pulses and auscultation of the heart.

An awareness of factors which can precipitate arrhythmic activity is crucial in the management of a patient who has suffered myocardial infarction. Examples of such factors are pain, anxiety, and activities which increase the work load of the heart. Therefore, when any of these events are noted, further assessment should take place to determine the extent of the problem and the needs of the patient. Pain and anxiety often produce sweating, restlessness, increased pulse rate, and disturbed facial expressions and posturing. These signs are readily observable and should be followed by auscultation and monitor reading to detect arrhythmia development. Excessive restlessness, coughing, pushing up in bed, and straining when having a bowel movement are signs that the patient may be increasing the work load of the heart, and appropriate intervention is required. The two abnormal rhythms in Table 14-2 are life-threatening arrhythmias which have been selected for discussion to illustrate how the critical-care nurse uses observational and assessment skills in their detection.

Congestive Heart Failure

Congestive heart failure refers to a condition or syndrome which occurs when cardiac output becomes insufficient to meet the body's metabolic demands. Following a myocardial infarction, signs and symptoms of left heart failure, then right heart failure, often appear. Left-sided failure occurs when the left ventricle is involved in a pathological process which ultimately produces a pulmonary capillary pressure that exceeds the intravascular osmotic pressure. This produces an elevation of pulmonary artery pressures, increasing the work load of the right heart, and precipitates right heart failure. Finally, the renal retention of sodium and water prompted by the decreased cardiac output increases the plasma volume and increases the work load of an already compromised heart. The symptoms of left heart failure are dyspnea on exertion (DOE), orthopnea, paroxysmal nocturnal dyspnea (PND), coughing, wheezing, and fatigue. Right-sided heart failure produces anorexia, nausea, right upper quadrant pain, and peripheral edema.

In the patient with left heart failure, pulmonary edema may appear suddenly, but there are usually prodromal signs such as shortness of breath, rales in the lung bases, restlessness, gallop rhythms, tachycardia, and distended neck veins. It is essential that the nurse in the critical-care area be skilled at recognizing heart failure in its earliest stages in order that remedial therapy can begin as soon as possible.

Table 14-3 presents the expected findings in congestive heart failure in order to clarify the assessment process. Pulmonary edema as a manifestation of congestive heart failure is also reviewed because acute left heart failure can occur quite easily following myocardial infarction. Nursing assessment in these areas can be quite crucial to patient survival.

TABLE 14-2
Selected Arrhythmias and Related Clinical Findings

| Abnormality | Ausculation | | | Electrocardiogram | | | |
	Rate	Rhythm	Heart sounds	P wave	P-R interval	QRS complex	Significance of findings
3° or complete AV block	Atrial: normal rate (84 beats per minute) Ventricular: slow rate (45 beats per minute or less)	Regular	Variable S₁, occasional faint atrial contractions	Normal	Completely variable	Normal to bizarre	Circulation may be decreased below level of effective perfusion; angina, congestive heart failure, and Stokes-Adams attacks
Ventricular tachycardia	100–200 beats per minute	Slightly irregular		Usually lost in QRS	Cannot be measured	Deformed	Markedly reduces cardiac output; may deteriorate to ventricular fibrillation and sudden death

TABLE 14-3

Physical Assessment Findings in Congestive Heart Failure and Pulmonary Edema

Problem	Inspection	Percussion	Palpation	Ausculation
Congestive heart failure	Possibly some degree of cyanosis	Dullness over lung base indicative of pleural effusion	Tachycardia	Moist, basilar rales
	Shortness of breath, engorged veins with pulsations of the jugular veins	Enlarged liver	Enlarged and tender liver, apical impulse probably large and displaced to left	Wheezes, decreased breath sounds over bases if pleural effusion is present
	Dependent edema Possible distended abdomen	Free fluid in abdomen if ascites is present	A positive hepatojugular reflex; edema may involve ankle regions of both legs, sacrum, flanks, and genitalia	Gallop rhythm S_3 and/or S_4
Pulmonary edema	Restless; cyanotic; coughing up frothy, possibly blood-tinged sputum		Cool and perspiring profusely, distended neck veins, tachycardia	Audible rales and wheezing, often accompanying blood pressure elevation

Cardiogenic Shock

The precipitating factor in cardiogenic shock is an abrupt and acute reduction in cardiac output. This occurs as a result of either a failure in ventricular filling or ventricular ejection. The result is similar to hypovolemic shock in that peripheral resistance increases as cardiac output decreases.

The manifestations of cardiogenic shock that the critical-care nurse must assess by observation are restlessness, disturbed sensorium, lethargy progressing to coma, and reduced urine output; central venous pressure measurements are of little value. Palpation will reveal a cold, clammy skin and tachycardia. Auscultation will demonstrate diminished heart sounds and a low blood pressure, which may be unattainable by arm cuff.

Thromboembolism

Multiple factors precipitate the formation of thromboemboli. Some of these are atrial fibrillation, venous stasis, bedrest with immobility, and fever. Unfortunately, the development of thrombi often cannot be detected. This is understandable when one considers the generally critical state of the postmyocardial infarction patient. However, a dislodged thrombi embolizing to another area of the body merits attention since it can lead to unnecessary morbidity and mortality.

An awareness of the precipitating factors discussed above is the first step in assessing a patient for thromboembolic formation. In addition, an awareness of the clinical picture presented when an embolus does lodge in some part of the body is necessary. An example of a thromboembolic disorder is a pulmonary embolus.

On inspection, the patient will appear apprehensive and acutely dyspneic. Cyanosis may develop. The patient may describe a knifelike chest pain. Auscultation will reveal hypotension and tachycardia.

The preceding case discussion has focused on the assessment parameters and physical findings which the critical-care nurse must consider in the management of a patient who has suffered a myocardial infarction. Utilization of physical assessment techniques in addition to the use of historical and laboratory data will enable the critical-care nurse to assess patient status in a more comprehensive and accurate manner.

Case Three: Comatose

Case History

The third case presents a young man admitted following a motorcycle accident. He presented with multiple bruises and extremity lacerations and was comatose. His most significant problem was a closed head injury.

Because of the rapidity with which serious problems such as subdural hematomas can occur, frequent, thorough, and organized assessment of the comatose patient is essential. Findings should be systematically recorded in serial fashion in order that changing trends can be readily recognized.

Assessment of the comatose patient is a special challenge since we tend to rely so heavily on the verbal communication that usually occurs with our patients. It is a sad commentary on nursing if we do not exhaust all efforts in the interest of the patient unable to respond to our requests. Physical assessment of the comatose patient includes all those areas which are potentially predictive of changing status. Therefore, the initial examination is essential in establishing baseline data. The areas of special significance in this assessment include the level of consciousness, pulse, respirations, blood pressure, pupillary signs (size, equality, reaction to light), eye movements, strength and tone of the extremities, posturing response to stimuli, and urinary output.

There are several questions the nurse can remember to use as guides to an appropriately thorough and relevant examination of the comatose patient, with particular emphasis on closed head injury. These questions direct the examiner to seek out the assessment information that will provide the most comprehensive set of data to be used in decision making.

1. *What is the level of consciousness of the patient?* The level of consciousness is classified differently by various authorities, but in this instance we shall use the following: alert, lethargic, obtunded, stuporous, semicomatose, and comatose (see Chapter 13 for definitions). Since the level of consciousness is one of the most sensitive indicators of changing status, it is important not only to assess it frequently but also to describe the findings in terminology clearly understood by all persons attending the patient. The change that is impending may be an increase in intracranial pressure, which can have life-threatening implications.

2. *How is the patient breathing?* This second question guides the nurse to inspect critically the rate and pattern of the patient's respiration. Once again, in order to effectively incorporate the findings into the management of the patient, certain respiratory patterns that are seen commonly are presented. (See Chapter 13, Fig. 13-4, for illustrations of these patterns.)

   a. *Cheyne-Stokes* respiration is suggestive of lesions deep in the cerebral hemispheres and basal ganglia that cause damage to the internal capsule. This is a type of periodic breathing that occurs in response to increase of P_{CO_2}. The pattern is one of hyperventilation when the high levels of P_{CO_2} are detected, which will wax and wane and be interrupted by periods of apnea which occur when subnormal levels of P_{CO_2} exist.

   b. *Biot's,* or ataxic, respiration is generally associated with damage to the brainstem, which is the location of the respiratory center (medulla, pons). This type of breathing does not wax and wane and does not respond to the carbon dioxide stimulus that Cheyne-Stokes does. The pattern of breathing in Biot's is one or more respiratory efforts alternating with unequal periods of apnea.

   c. *Eupnea* (normal respirations) with yawning or very deep respirations or sighs could be the very early signs of increasing intracranial pressure or pressure on the diencephalon.

3. *What is the size and reactivity of the pupils?* Normally, pupils are equal or within 1 mm of each other in size and react briskly to light. Pupillary abnormalities in comatose patients are common, and time and attention to observation of their size and shape is critical. The reactions of constriction and dilation are controlled by the sympathetic and parasympathetic nervous system. Brainstem areas controlling consciousness are very close to those controlling pupils; therefore, pupillary changes are valuable in detecting and locating problems of the brainstem that might cause coma. The following are some important pupillary abnormalities that can occur in comatose patients.

   a. *Horner's syndrome* is caused by hypothalamic damage. The presenting signs are ipsilateral pupillary constriction, usually associated with anhidrosis and ptosis. A unilateral Horner's syndrome is often the first sign of impending transtentorial herniation.

   b. *Small reactive pupils* are indicative of diencephalic disturbances.

   c. Pupils which are *midposition,* fixed to light, and often irregular in shape but which may fluctuate in size and show hippus (the spasmodic pupillary movement independent of the action of light) are indicators of midbrain damage.

   d. Pinpoint pupils, independent of drugs taken or instilled in the eye, indicate damage to the pons.

   e. A unilaterally dilated, fixed pupil is evidence of third nerve encroachment. This usually indicates impending uncal herniation, and the affected pupil is usually ipsilateral to the impending herniation.

f. The Argyll Robertson pupil is small, light-fixed, irregular, and without oculomotor paralysis. This abnormality is seen in central nervous system syphilis and sometimes in diabetes.

When evaluating pupillary reactions, it is very important to be aware that, with few exceptions, the pupillary light reflex is preserved until terminal phases of metabolic brain disease which has produced coma. Destructive lesions of the midbrain will abolish the light reflex. Therefore, metabolic disorder should be considered if the light reflex is present yet other signs of midbrain depression are apparent.

4. *How do the eyes move?* Structural causes of coma usually produce asymmetrical oculomotor dysfunction. Therefore, careful evaluation of ocular movements is most helpful in evaluation of the comatose patient.

   Several factors are indicators of diffuse or bilateral hemisphere damage without damage to the neural pathways that influence ocular pathways:

   a. Eyes directed straight ahead or only slightly divergent

   b. No involuntary movements except occasional roving eye movement

   c. Brisk response to oculocephalic movements

   d. Sustained eye deviation held after caloric stimulation

5. *What is the posture of the patient and how does the patient move the limbs?* When a patient is comatose, the most important information that can be obtained from a motor examination is assistance in localizing neurological dysfunction. Motor response is affected in distinct patterns according to the level of the injury in the nervous system. There are three principal responses seen in the patient who is brain-injured which are worthy of considerable attention by the critical-care nurse.

   a. *Decorticate rigidity*—This response is elicited by noxious stimuli. This consists of flexion of the arm, wrist, and fingers with adduction of the upper extremity and extension, internal rotation, and plantar flexion of the lower extremity. Decorticate rigidity is indicative of damage to the internal capsule and rostral cerebral peduncle, which may involve the basal ganglia and the thalamus. It is important to remember that even a simple action such as applying the blood pressure cuff may elicit this response.

   b. *Decerebrate rigidity*—This response will occur in patients with destruction of all brainstem responses above the midpons and also in patients with large cerebral hemorrhage which causes pressure or destruction of the lower thalamus and midbrain. Decerebrate rigidity will usually be seen clinically in one of the following circumstances: (1) during the progression of deterioration from the diencephalon into the midbrain; (2) with midbrain and upper pons damage from expanding posterior fossa lesions; and (3) with such metabolic disorders as hypoglycemia, hepatic coma, anoxia, or any other cause that depresses the upper brainstem functions.

   The motor response in decerebrate rigidity is one of stiff extension, hyperpronation, and adduction of the arms; stiffly extended legs and plantar flexed feet; and usually opisthotonos with teeth clenched. It is possible to see decerebrate responses on one side of the body (usually contralateral to the lesion) and ipsilateral decorticate responses. This tends to occur most often in deep hemispheric conditions with encroachment on the upper brainstem. Decerebrate posturing in the upper extremities and flaccid or weak flexor responses in the lower extremities will be found in patients who have extensive brainstem damage.

Consideration of the preceding information emphasizes the tremendous responsibility the critical-care nurse has in observing the comatose patient. The nurse's assessments and actions can be all that stands between a patient surviving or expiring.

SELECTED PROBLEMS

The patient in a critical-care unit may develop a number of problems which are not necessarily associated with the condition for which he or she is being primarily managed. The problems could be minor yet annoying to the patient, or they could be of a potentially serious nature.

The following tables present certain of these conditions and the related physical findings. Problem areas addressed are related to the eyes, skin, lungs, abdomen, rectum, and nervous system.

Problems of the Eye

Patients may have eye problems prior to their admission to a critical-care area, for example, cataracts, glaucoma, or difficulties requiring visual correction. These difficulties are usually revealed in the patient history. There are a few commonly occurring problems, however, which can be prevented or efficiently treated if the nurse uses good assessment skills (see Table 14-4).

Problems of the Skin

The skin problems described in Tables 14-5 and 14-6 usually do not result in a patient's admission to a critical-care unit, but they are commonly seen in patients admitted for other reasons.

Problems of the Lungs

Many of the problems that patients develop while in critical-care units are respiratory in nature. Table 14-7 presents some of these problems.

TABLE 14-4
Eye Problems Related to Critical-Care Patients

Problem	Physical findings
Corneal drying	Lid does not close fully Lack of tearing Absence of corneal reflex
Conjunctivitis	Reddening and irritation of conjunctival vessels, often accompanied by discharge or increased lacrimation
Scleral icterus	Evenly distributed yellowing of the sclera (due to jaundice)

TABLE 14-5
Skin Problems Related to Critical-Care Patients

Problem	Physical findings	Anatomic location
Cellulitis	Erythema, edema, tenderness of area. Regional lymphangitis or lymphadenopathy may be present. Occasionally vesicle and bullae formation	Any area of skin
Herpes simplex (Type 1)	Circumscribed grouped vesicles surrounded by erythema; forms crusts on rupture	Face and neck
Herpes zoster (shingles)	Crops of clear vesicles along course of a cutaneous nerve; tender, regional lymph nodes	Cervical and thoracic regions
Decubitis ulcer	Pallor followed by reactive hyperemia of skin when pressure removed; dry skin will crack, peel, or itch; wet skin will macerate. Induration of tissue, excavation, and blistering or superficial necrosis and ulcer formation	Any pressure points. There is variation with position: supine (heels, sacrum, elbows, scapulae, back of head); side lying (malleolus, medial and lateral condyles, greater trochanter, ribs, acromion process, ear); prone (toes, knees, genitalia on men, breast on women, acromion process, cheek, and ear)
Skin cancers 1. Basal cell carcinoma *a.* Nodulo-ulcerative epithelioma	Lesions are first pale, nodular, and waxy with telangiectatic vessels on surface; forms into a raised lesion with a shiny edge which further develops into an ulcerative area with a pearly-colored, rounded edge	Head and neck
b. Pigmented basal cell	Similar to nodulo-ulcerative, except lesions are pigmented and dark in color	
c. Superficial basal cell epithelioma	Similar to nodulo-ulcerative, except plaque formation with crusting	

TABLE 14-5 (Continued)
Skin Problems Related to Critical-Care Patients

Problem	Physical findings	Anatomic location
2. Squamous cell carcinoma	Initially appears as ulcerative area with wide borders; crusting of ulcerative tissue	Any area of body; face and hands most frequently
3. Pigmented nevi	Vary in size and may be flat, nodular, or warty in appearance. Color varies from blue to brown to black	Anywhere on body
4. Malignant melanoma	Early stages: if developed from nevi, ulceration follows; if originates from normal skin, irregular shaped, bluish black pigmented area followed by ulceration	Head, neck, and lower extremities
Drug reactions	Sudden onset, symmetrical, frequently generalized distribution, bright red color; may be macules, papules, vesicles, bullae, or pustules; always erythematous	Any area of body

Problems of the Abdomen and Rectum

Problems of the abdomen and rectum may develop as a result of infections acquired prior to or during hospitalization. Preexisting conditions may become more acute or noticeable, and the alteration in activity and dietary patterns may precipitate additional problems. Table 14-8 presents examples of these problems.

Problems of the Nervous System

Problems of the nervous system may occur in any critically ill patient. The patient need not have a primary neurological disorder in order to develop neurological pathology. Table 14-9 presents a few of these problems.

TABLE 14-6
Skin Lesions in Connective Tissue Disorders
Related to Critical-Care Patients

Problem	Physical findings	Location
Sarcoidosis	Purple or flesh-colored plaques, papules, or nodules. Old atrophic scars become elevated and reddened	Face, neck, trunk
Discoid lupus erythematosus	Erythematous raised lesions with irregular borders; telangiectasia, atrophy, and changes in pigmentation; scars from healed lesions, butterfly lesion of nose and cheek	Face, neck, trunk
Scleroderma	Hardened, leathery skin; occasional erythematous, edematous plaques which become waxy, shiny, and surrounded by an erythematous ring	Any area of body

TABLE 14-7
Common Respiratory Problems of Critical-Care Patients

Disease	Tactile fremitus	Percussion	Auscultation
Consolidation (i.e., pneumonia)	Increased	Dull	Bronchial breath sounds, rales, bronchophony, egophony, whispered pectoriloquy
Bronchitis	Normal	Resonant	Normal to decreased breath sounds, wheezes, and rhonchi
Emphysema	Decreased	Hyperresonant	Decreased intensity of breath sounds, usually with prolonged expiration
Asthma (severe attack)	Normal to decreased	Resonant to hyperresonant	Wheezes and rhonchi
Pulmonary edema	Normal	Resonant	Rales at lung bases, possibly wheezes
Pleural effusion	Absent	Dull to flat	Decreased to absent breath sounds; bronchial breath sounds and bronchophony, egophony, and whispering pectoriloquy above the effusion over the area of compressed lung
Pneumothorax	Decreased	Hyperresonant	Absent breath sounds
Atelectasis	Absent	Flat	Decreased to absent breath sounds

TABLE 14-8
Problems of the Abdomen and Rectum Related to the Critical-Care Patient

Problem	Physical findings			
	Inspection	Percussion	Palpation	Auscultation
Acute abdomen peritonitis	Body posturing and facial expression evidencing pain		Rebound tenderness; boardlike, rigid abdomen; guards against palpation	
Ascites	Distended abdomen; bulging flanks in supine position	Shifting dullness; possible area of tympany at top of abdominal curve (due to air-filled gut rising above fluid)		
Ileus	Abdominal distention; possible vomiting		Generalized tenderness, possibly localizing	Bowel sounds are diminished or absent; when present, may be high-pitched
Impaction	Absence of bowel movements for several days, possible slight abdominal distention	May reveal increased dullness in lower colon	Hard fecal mass	
Hemorrhoids	Bright red rectal bleeding; visible "tags" around anal sphincter (external)		If thrombosed, internal hemorrhoids may be palpated	

TABLE 14-9
Problems of the Nervous System Related to Critical-Care Patients

Problems	Inspection/palpation	Auscultation
Increasing intra-cranial pressure	Decreasing levels of consciousness; vomiting; pupillary changes; hemiparesis or hemiplegia	Increasing blood pressure; widening pulse pressure; possible bradycardia
Cerebral vascular accident (stroke)	Development of hemiparesis or flaccid paralysis; sensorial clouding; confusion; coma	Hypertension (if hemorrhagic stroke); possible cardiac murmur or arrhythmias (if embolic stroke)
Meningitis	Photophobia evidenced by squinting; decreased suppleness of neck with nuchal rigidity; hyperthermia; possible vomiting; clouding of sensorium; convulsions	

REFERENCES

American Association of Critical Care Nurses: *Core Curriculum for Critical Care Nursing,* 1975.

Andreoli, K. G., et al.: *Comprehensive Cardiac Care,* 3d ed., St. Louis: Mosby, 1975.

Burrell, Z. L., Jr., and L. O. Burrell: *Critical Care,* 3d ed., St. Louis: Mosby, 1977.

Chusid, J. G.: *Correlative Neuroanatomy and Functional Neurology,* 16th ed., Los Altos, Calif.: Lange, 1976.

De Gowin, E. L., and R. L. De Gowin: *Bedside Diagnostic Examination,* New York: Macmillan, 1976.

Goldman, M. J.: Medical aspects, in R. G. Sanderson (ed.), *The Cardiac Patient,* Philadelphia: Saunders, 1972.

Guyton, A. C.: *Textbook of Medical Physiology,* 5th ed., Philadelphia: Saunders, 1976.

Isselbacher, K. J. et al.: *Harrison's Principles of Internal Medicine,* 9th ed., New York: McGraw-Hill, 1980.

Plum, F., and J. B. Posner: *The Diagnosis of Stupor and Coma,* 2d ed., Philadelphia: Davis, 1972.

Virgilio, R. W., and D. E. Smith: Assessment and therapy of the shock syndrome, in C. W. Sproul and P. J. Mullanney (eds.), *Emergency Care,* St. Louis: Mosby, 1974.

PART 4

THE PSYCHOSOCIAL BASIS OF CRITICAL-CARE NURSING

The purpose of this chapter is to describe the basic concepts of anxiety, stress, and crisis. The concepts are not universally defined and hence their meanings are often conflicting and ambiguous. This chapter describes one method of operationally defining these terms, drawing primarily on the work of one theorist for each concept. Other relevant literature regarding the concepts has been noted but has been kept minimal.

The second purpose of this chapter is to relate these concepts into a working pattern from which nursing action has been suggested. Protocols for intervening in physiological distress of patients have been developed and tested. In many cases, they are accepted as standard practice. In contrast, tested procedures for psychological intervention are in an embryonic stage of development. One reason for this is that nurses and other health care providers may be experiencing varying degrees of psychological distress conceptually similar to that which patients experience. Therefore, actions in regard to anxiety, stress, and crisis have been suggested for staff, families, and patients. This order is purposeful in conserving and allocating energy efficiently. If a nurse's own distress is minimized, family energies can be harnessed on behalf of the patient.

This chapter will not focus on the myriad emotional experiences such as loss, grief, and anger, which also affect each of us, particularly the critically ill. Some concepts will be named in relationship to anxiety, stress, and crisis. This is done in recognition of the hazards of attempting to separate any one part of the human experience from the total human experience. All behavior is contextual; that is, behavior is in part a function of the context in which it occurs. Focusing on specific concepts is done in the belief that illuminating a segment of experience can lead to fuller illumination of future experiences.

ANXIETY

The concept of anxiety was basic to the work of Sullivan (1953) in developing the constructs of interpersonal theory, which serves as the base for our definition of anxiety. *Anxiety* is a state of tension within a person which arises when an interpersonal need for security and/or freedom from tension is not being met. Anxiety is communicable, that is, it is experienced empathically with significant others.

Anxiety is without direction; that is, by its very nature it is a barrier to foresight, or seeing beyond the anxiety to future states of being. The higher the level

ANXIETY, STRESS, AND CRISIS

Doris S. Greiner

ANXIETY
Acute Anxiety
Management of Anxiety: The Triangle

STRESS
Anatomy of Stress
Stress Theory Beyond Selye

CRISIS
The Crisis Process

GUIDES FOR NURSING ACTION
Anxiety and Its Uses
Stress: Learn the Stressors
The Nurse in Crisis
The Patient's Family in Crisis
The Patient in Crisis

SUMMARY

REFERENCES

of anxiety, the less the person experiencing the anxiety can see beyond it. Anxiety is a basic human reaction, resulting specifically in a felt need to change one's current state of being. Anxiety is an automatic response to a decrease in security which triggers automatic relief behaviors, i.e., ways of increasing the comfort of the organism.

Although acute anxiety is the focus of this discussion, chronic anxiety must be considered briefly. It differs from acute anxiety in that it continues over time in all primary relationships, especially family relationships. Chronic anxiety becomes a stressor and increases the potential for development of crisis for many individuals and families.

Anxiety is not fear, though its observable manifestations may be identical. Fear may evoke an acute anxious reaction. Fear, however, is directed. What one fears can be identified, named, and usually managed. What cannot be named evokes the anxious response.

Acute Anxiety

The following steps or operations describe an experience of acute anxiety.

1. A person has needs for interpersonal security.

2. These needs are not met.

3. Tension increases.

4. The person behaves automatically in learned ways to decrease the tension.

   a. Emotional reactions such as anger, or

   b. Physical reactions such as pain, or

   c. Problem-solving reactions such as decreasing activity and increasing thinking.

5. a. The tension decreases, or

   b. The behavior evokes increased tension in the person and in the interpersonal environment.

The last step takes the person back to stage one with the probable triggering of additional behaviors at stage four.

Management of Anxiety: The Triangle

The ways each person has learned to manage anxiety are *numerous* and specific to that person's early family experiences. Some persons, as adults, have made considerable effort to manage anxiety in more productive ways than those developed earlier. In times of acute distress, the chances of reverting to

behavior patterns developed in early life are greatly increased and may serve as a stimulus to increased anxiety as one sees oneself losing this hold on mature development and on the decision-making ability so painstakingly acquired.

Bowen (1978), in observing emotional reactivity in families, observed that when anxiety went up between any two people, a third would be triangled to relieve the anxiety between the two. For example, rather than speaking directly to each other about personal concerns, two people might talk about a third. Or, one person talks to another about the third rather than talking to the third directly. In both cases triangles are in motion. Bowen suggests that a *dyad,* that is, two individuals, is never stable, the smallest stable emotional unit being a triangle. When the anxiety between two cannot be contained by triangling a third, a fourth person may be triangled, starting the formation of a series of interlocking triangles. This concept extends the interpersonal definition of anxiety, suggesting patterns of relief behavior that to the informed observer become increasingly clear and provide a base on which to plan intervention. Nurses are frequent candidates for becoming part of anxious triangles with patients and family members. Often nurses have many ongoing emotional triangles in which they participate within the work system. A very frequent one involves *talking about* rather than *talking to.*

The usefulness of the anxiety concept is threefold. First, it is useful in recognizing anxiety as a possible basis for one's own or another's observed behavior. Second, it is useful in identifying triggers of the anxiety with the anxious person. Third, the concept is helpful in suggesting, when possible, changes in the interpersonal environment conducive to tension decrease and security increase.

STRESS

Stress may be the most elusive of the three concepts considered. It may also be the most crucial to describe if one seeks to establish a common usable language. Selye's experimental work on stress has served as a cornerstone for a burgeoning literature on stress. Much of the literature on stress, however, leads to confusion between what is action and what is reaction. Starting with the basic concept as Selye (1976) described it, stress is the state manifested by a specific syndrome which consists of all the nonspecifically induced changes within a biological system.

Thus, stress is the physiological reaction of the

body to an increase of demands made upon it. These demands come from many sources. Confusion increases when stress is assumed to be a negative experience and the environmental stimuli which evoke it are assumed to be negative. As long as the body functions to meet the demands placed upon it and to signal necessary change prior to permanent injury to the body, the experience of environmental stress can be stimulating, motivating, and satisfying. Critical care as a work situation could be considered a setting that meets those criteria. However, when the body functions to meet the demands placed upon it and the demands increase, a change may be needed. If signals are ignored, stress becomes distress, usually emotional as well as physiological.

Anatomy of Stress

The following steps or operations describe an experience of stress:

1. A person is exposed to demanding agents, conditions, and/or experiences.
2. The demand is met by resistance within the organism.
3. The demand increases and continues.
4. The *general adaptation syndrome* is activated characterized by:
   a. Alarm reaction
   b. State of resistance
   c. Stage of exhaustion

The physiological processes concurrent with each of these phases have been detailed repeatedly and are beyond the scope of this discussion. They necessarily relate to observing and treating all physiological changes a patient experiences.

Stress Theory Beyond Selye

Criticism of the stress concept as formulated by Selye has been abundant. Some researchers and clinicians find it is so nonspecific as to be useless. At the same time, the term has become so much part of the public vocabulary that it can scarcely be ignored. Just as some researchers have approached stress primarily as a physiological reaction to stimuli, others have taken the view that cumulative stressors within a given time span precipitate physiological reaction. According to Rahe and Arthur (1978), sufficient epidemiological studies to substantiate this viewpoint have been reported. At this time, theoretic formulations and

research directions with particular promise for accounting for the noxious effect of psychological stimuli have been suggested by Cassel (1974). First, the level of abstraction of our concepts must be reconsidered if they do not lead to definitive answers. If stressors act indirectly by virtue of their capacity to act as signals or symbols, we must work toward identifying the characteristics or properties of those signs and symbols which evoke the neuroendocrine changes in the recipient. This could lead to identification of classes of stressors even if particular circumstances differ for different people. One of the theories already named for organizing information about people's emotional experience is *family systems theory,* a possible framework for ordering information about these particular circumstances.

Second, Cassel suggests that stressors be consistently considered not only from the dimension of stimuli for producing a reaction but also in the context of identifying the presence or absence of protective elements concurrently experienced by the individual. Again, family theory provides additional direction for this idea. For example, the more open the family emotional system is to a variety of ways of handling emotional demands, the less likely it is that stressful stimuli result in any form of dysfunction, including the general adaptation syndrome as described by Selye.

The usefulness of understanding the stress concept within the context of anxiety and crisis is to identify stressors and to decrease their potency and/or increase the protective aspects of the emotional environment, if they are resulting in distress.

CRISIS

There is an abundance of literature which is directed toward the elucidation of the concept of crisis. The formulations of Caplan (1964) regarding crisis remain a clear, firm foundation for description and discussion. He defines a problem as an upset in equilibrium in an organism being faced with a force or situation which alters previous functioning. An essential factor in the development of a crisis is the imbalance between the difficulty and/or importance of the problem and the resources available to deal with it.

The Crisis Process

The phases or stages in crisis development can be described as follows:

1. In the face of a problem, tension increases, triggering habitual problem-solving behaviors.

2. If these behaviors are not successful, the problem continues and tension increases, triggering the experience of upset and ineffectuality.

3. As tension increases further, one of the following is triggered:

   a. Reserves of strength and novel problem-solving behaviors

   b. A redefinition of the problem and decrease in tension

   c. Negation, resignation, and giving up

   d. Trial and error in both thought and action

   If a solution occurs in this phase, crisis is averted. If the problem continues:

4. Tension mounts, leading to major disorganization (crisis).

For some critically ill patients, the illness constitutes a crisis; that is, the illness itself is the form that the major disorganization has taken. For other patients, crisis does not exist. For these patients the problem-solving behaviors of earlier phases have averted crisis. For a third group of patients, no crisis exists at the time of admission to a critical-care setting; however, during the course of the illness, events may occur which trigger an increase in tension which results in major disorganization.

The crisis concept as outlined by Caplan has served as the basis for crisis intervention models used by nurses in many settings. The usefulness of this concept is in assessing the current problem-solving or coping behaviors and capabilities of individuals and families, recognizing major alterations in organization of coping behaviors, and assisting individuals and families to regain focus and systematically draw on resources available to them through resolution of the crisis aspect of their situation.

GUIDES FOR NURSING ACTION

Three assumptions are suggested to direct nursing action:

1. Assume anxiety in interpersonal contexts and recognize its conversion into relief behaviors.

2. Assume stress and take measures to decrease the negative impact of stressors based on assessment of the nature and usefulness of the stressor.

3. Assume crisis *only if* evidence of major disorganization of coping behaviors is identified.

Each of these assumptions is discussed in terms of suggested nursing action related to self and staff, patient, and family.

Anxiety and Its Uses

Anxiety exists in varying degrees in staff, in family members, and in patients. It can be a useful source of energy to a point, after which it takes energy from the tasks at hand. It is an automatic response which may or may not be subjectively recognized. We often recognize it in ourselves as the relief behavior to which it has been converted. A headache or an angry outburst at a cleaning crew member or head nurse may be the first clue to previously unrecognized anxiety. Using this clue as information to determine possible triggers for the anxiety can lead productively to harnessing the energy of anxiety rather than increasing the necessity for further relief behaviors. Relief behaviors tend to become stressors for others in the interpersonal environment, decreasing the probability of interpersonal security and increasing the experience of anxiety.

Anxiety is communicable, that is, it is emphatically transmitted in the interpersonal environment in patterned ways. The nurse in the critical-care unit is inextricably involved with other staff members. While the common pursuit of staff may ideally be care of patients, the enduring work-related relationships are with fellow staff members. The first place for the nurse to look for triggers to anxiety are in these complex relationship systems, specifically in the areas of control and decision making. Anxiety increases when each staff member's control over practice (and particularly over decisions related to self in the work setting and then to practice) remains unclear. In settings in which nurses have clarified control and responsibility regarding practice, a variety of creative ways have been found for dealing with the anxiety that is inevitably evoked when facing the extreme life-and-death issues with critically ill patients. For example, reported as useful have been staffing patterns that allow for periodic rotation to tasks that do not involve direct care, personal days off rather than sick time for vitally needed rest, and group sessions that focus on understanding anxiety-laden issues with the help of an objective outsider who can assist the group to keep to the task.

Suggested Action   Clarify personally and with one's work group questions regarding control and responsibility, both nursing and interdisciplinary responsibility.

The anxiety of families often triggers staff anxiety. Too frequently the family has been dismissed as a supposed source of distress to the patient. Doing this may increase family anxiety and in turn trigger staff anxiety, setting in motion a series of anxious triangles as described above.

Sources of anxiety for the family members which may be worked with are the same as for the nurse: control and decision making. Control of the patient's care is usually no longer theirs. This might be a considerable relief, but at the cost of loss of control and decision making within the family unit. In both cases, information is a key element to restoring equilibrium.

Information about family systems suggests that each family is likely to have a member who functions as the responsible person for the family. Identifying the responsible family member is the first step in establishing clarity regarding control issues. Asking that family member to identify with the family the issues and concerns about which they need information and/or would like input into decision making sets the stage for brief negotiation sessions between family members and staff rather than anxious attacking encounters.

Suggested Action Identify with the family a responsible family member, and make plans with that person for regular communication with the family.

A great deal is usually written about anxiety experienced by patients, usually with prescriptions for the nurse regarding the ideal ways to relieve anxiety. The demands on the patient in critical care evoke anxiety. Relief behaviors will be employed. An angry outburst or self-protective withdrawal as relief behaviors are useful.

Suggested Action Monitor signs of patient anxiety and assess their effectiveness in maintaining personal integrity.

This monitoring for most nurses necessitates attention to personal reactivity to the patient's anxiety. If the personal reactivity can be kept out of the patient's way, the chances are increased for the patient to employ personally effective ways of managing his or her own anxiety.

For the patient, control and decision making may also be potent issues which relate to the degree of interpersonal security experienced. A brief family history, ideally with information from family members, will make it possible to locate each patient on a continuum between independence and dependence in usual life-style. The person who ranks on the former half is likely to function as an only or oldest child, is likely to assume responsibility and control in decision making, and is likely to want input into as many

decisions as possible as soon as possible. The person who ranks on the dependent end of the continuum is likely to function as a younger child of an older sibling(s), has more life experience being taken care of, and will be much less anxious if few or no decisions are required of him or her in the critical phases of illness.

Suggested Action Gather basic family information, including sibling position of the patient and the responsible family member and usual or known methods of coping with difficulties employed by both patient and family. Use this information to assess the necessity for intervening in anxiety of patients and families.

Stress: Learn the Stressors

Assume that all people involved in the critical-care setting are experiencing stress. Take measures to increase or decrease stressors based on assessment of their nature and usefulness, first for staff. The assumption that stress is endemic in the critical-care setting leads to the question, "Why work there?" Cassem and Hackett (1975) have said that the source of greatest difficulty and the source of greatest satisfaction is the same: Caring for desperately ill patients. They go on to suggest that the intensity may be a cheap way of buying experience to meet needs. This is a serious statement and it warrants careful consideration. It is not possible, or advisable, to remove all stressors. Thankfully, nurses do choose to work in the critical-care setting.

Suggested Action Differentiate between the necessary and useful stressors and those which impede constructive action.

If each individual thought through which elements of the work environment are most distressing, individually and jointly, efforts could be made to share such information, put in order of priority changes needed to decrease stressors, and establish plans of action for making these changes. Cassem and Hackett's list of stresses identified by the group of nurses they studied could be used as a guide to elicit further ideas specific to each setting.

For most families, having a family member in a critical-care unit is a continuing stressor. A brief replication of the process used by staff to identify stressors could be most enlightening. It is vital in this process to try to listen to the family express distress. If staff members can continue to listen in spite of strong negative reactions, ideas from family members which may prove very helpful in decreasing family distress are likely to then be heard. For example, some families may be highly distressed by the limit on time with their family member in the critical-care unit. In most units, visiting rules are based on sound principles, and the natural reaction is to explain the rules. In the face of high anxiety, a power struggle is likely to ensue between staff members and family members regarding visiting rules, each attempting to convince the other of the rightness of their position. When the complaints about limited visiting are heard out, what follows from many family members are expressions of concern about how to behave when visiting. They wonder what behaviors will be helpful or harmful to the patient and encouraged or tolerated by staff. As the potency of visiting rules as a stressor is decreased, the possibility of open and useful communication with the patient is increased.

> **Suggested Action** Expect emotional reactions from families to critical-care conditions, and listen for expression of questions and concerns beyond the reactive statements. Attempt to stay out of the family emotions and think with family members about ways of decreasing what is particularly stressful to each of them.

In approaching the stress assumption from the patient's point of view, numerous ideas about structuring the physical environment of the critical-care unit, with consideration to lighting, privacy, and more control, have been discussed in the literature. Ideally, implementing these ideas would decrease stress for the patient. Basically, stressors are everywhere present for the patient . Managing the physiological manifestation of stress is an imperative staff function. In most instances, by the time the patient is ready for cognitive identification of stressors and planning in regard to these stressors, a transfer to a less intense level of care in the hospital is also in order. The staff of that unit has a great deal of responsibility for working with anxiety- and stress-related patient issues once the critical physiological condition has stabilized.

The Nurse in Crisis

Critical-care nurses are by definition *copers*. The ability to cope, that is, to function more or less effectively in the face of highly complex situations, is a trademark of the critical-care nurse. Nurses who do not cope in highly complex situations do not continue to work in the critical-care setting. The crisis as-

sumption stated earlier was to assume crisis *only if* major disorganization of coping behavior is identified.

Beginning with the experience of crisis in a staff member, by definition that person would be unlikely to be the first to know that he or she was in crisis. Clues that a crisis has been reached are immobilization in an immedite situation, repetitive ineffective behavior, and unexpected removal of self from a problem situation which demands attention. Failure to appear for work without making substitute arrangements, inability to eat or sleep, and continuous restlessness are clues to a crisis which has been developing over time.

Anticipatory planning on the part of a critical-care staff can do much to avert staff crises and to avert disaster in the face of a staff member's experience of crisis. One method is to temporarily remove the nurse from the immediate situation. As soon as possible, one other staff member should talk with the nurse in an effort to name the problem.

In reviewing the stages of crisis development, immediately preceding major disorganization is the stage in which one of four alternatives may be experienced. It is often in this stage that clarity about the problem is lost completely. When failure to cope is observed in the work situation, the effort needed to regain focus on the problem may be minimal. With the problem more clearly in focus, alternative approaches to solving problems may become more readily apparent.

> **Suggested Action** Attempt to identify the particular problem that is distressing the staff member who is no longer coping.

If the nurse's behavior suggests crisis developing over time, as in failure to appear for work, restlessness, and sleeplessness, the likelihood is that the issues and problems precipitating the crisis are not chiefly specific aspects of the work situation. It is still wise to help the nurse regain a focus on the nature of the problem or event.

In addition, working with the assumption that the crisis is based in the life of the nurse and is not necessarily work-related, the usual support system of the nurse should be identified. It is probable that the nurse has lost contact with one or more people in the support system. Either an assist to reestablish contact or an assist to establish contact with another support person is suggested as an immediate step in decreasing tension to previous levels of coping.

Ideally, a crisis or impending crisis provides each of us with the possibility of learning a great deal in a short period of time. The chances of emerging from a crisis situation with new understanding and new problem-solving skills are great and to be valued. A word of caution: Nurses, in their effort to be helpful and in control, may attempt to take on the problems of co-workers and provide the total support for each other. This is a serious occupational hazard.

Establishing important relationships with people who are not also daily putting enormous amounts of energy into critical care increases the probability that one will maintain an objectivity in regard to the frequent potential crisis-evoking events. Once the emotional reactivity has escalated, the chances of it maintaining itself in the triangle pattern described earlier are enormous.

Suggested Action Identify at least one objective person outside the work setting with whom to discuss personal and professional concerns.

The Patient's Family in Crisis

With the family of the critical-care patient, the same framework applies. First, do not assume crisis for family members, but identify which members, if any, are in crisis.

It may be that for the family the fact of the illness of one member has averted a major disorganization for many family members. This idea parallels what will be said about crisis for the patient. For example, in a family that has been facing the prospect of a move to another state, possible work loss, or unexpected school failure of one of the children, a sudden threatening illness of one of the family members may serve as the unifying force around which all action and thinking now center. During the acute phase of the illness, it is not uncommon for the family members to become relatively calm and goal-directed, often surprisingly so to staff and friends in the community. These same family members are likely to take direction from staff and be exceptionally compliant. This response would be particularly true in families in which physical illness is seen as an inevitable part of the human condition, essentially to be expected.

The opposite situation would likely be true for the family who values health at all costs and places a high premium on physical fitness and coping with stressors effectively. The critical illness of one of this family's members precipitates frantic efforts to regain control. The family members will evidence shortsightedness, extreme concern over the sick member, and inability to order their own action. Family members

no longer have a clear idea of the nature of the problem with which they are faced. They have lost sight of their usual support people. The coping behaviors of each family member are ineffective and in the process exhausting to other family members who may be the usual support of each other.

Suggested Action When major family disorganization is identified, focus on the event which precipitated crisis.

The easy assumption that the illness and the event or problem are synonymous may be misleading. For family members to name the event as precisely as possible is an essential step in reordering perceptions around that event and effectively solving the problem. The naming of the event may best be assisted by the usual support system of the family; therefore, efforts to help family members establish contacts in the community are highly recommended.

The Patient in Crisis

The patient may be considered to be experiencing a crisis at one of several levels. First, the illness may be a way of coping and therefore in some ways serve as a mechanism for decreasing tension. The patient who has effective coping mechanisms for managing illness, irritating as they may be to nursing staff, is less likely to be experiencing crisis even when seriously ill than in many other seemingly less extreme circumstances, e.g., getting married, changing jobs, and so on.

If the patient is observed to be experiencing major disorganization, consider that a crisis may exist and again begin by naming the focal event. For the critically ill patient, numerous difficult procedures may have been endured effectively before this disorganization becomes apparent. Thus, the focal event is likely to be obscure and may be surprising even to the patient. Generally, for the patient who has been coping, disorganization occurs when the patient actually becomes aware of the impact of his or her current status on his or her own future life. This may be stimulated by a casual statement, a dream, or a fantasy. Identifying the awareness as the focal point would be a crucial first step in assisting the patient in crisis resolution. The incidence of crisis experience will be less for patients who maintain contact with a supporting person(s) throughout the conscious critical-care experience than for those who do not maintain contact with a supportive person.

Suggested Action   As the patient's level of consciousness allows, assist the patient to name and be in contact with support people.

The process of naming supports or lack of them may be helpful in itself. Contact with people the patient names as a support will probably be even better, though they may not necessarily be sources of support for the family. The value of making that contact for the patient would be wisely assessed with the family in mind.

SUMMARY

The challenges to critical-care nurses are many. Critical-care nurses consistently meet challenges amazingly well. When the nurse can decrease reactivity and increase thinking in regard to any of the concepts discussed in this chapter, chances are increased for keeping one's own anxious issues and concerns out of the way of existing problem-solving methods of others. The chances are also increased for creative professional nursing care.

REFERENCES

Bowen, M.: *Family Therapy in Clinical Practice,* New York: Jason Aronson, 1978.

Caplan, G.: *Principles of Preventive Psychiatry,* New York: Basic Books, 1964.

Cassel, J.: Psychosocial processes and "stress": Theoretical formulation, *Int Journal Health Serv* 4:471–482, 1974.

Cassem, N. H., and T. P. Hackett: Stress on the nurse and therapist in the intensive-care unit and the coronary-care unit, *Heart Lung* 4(2):252–259, 1975.

Garfield, C.: *Stress & Survival,* St. Louis: Mosby, 1979.

Mason, J.: A historical review of the stress field, *J Hum Stress* 1(2):22–36, 1975.

Rahe, A., and R. Arthur: Life change and illness studies: Past history and future directions, *J Hum Stress* 4(1):3–15, 1978.

Selye, H.: *Stress Without Distress,* New York: Lippincott, 1974.

———: *The Stress of Life,* New York: McGraw-Hill, 1976.

Sullivan, H. S.: *The Interpersonal Theory of Psychiatry,* New York: Norton, 1953.

An individual in a critical-care unit attempts to maintain a holistic self-image in which the many facets of physical, social, or psychological being are of equal significance. Individuals take for granted their physical, social, or psychological being until they are in disequilibrium. When one of the body's subsystems loses equilibrium, all other subsystems subsequently become involved. Normally, the individual mobilizes patterns of defense to reestablish or maintain equilibrium. In this respect, "... man is conceptualized as a complex adaptive system comprised of behavioral subsystems that work together to achieve behavioral stability. These behavioral subsystems are regulated by true feedback loops that not only maintain structure according to preestablished limits but also elaborate structure according to environmental demands imposed on the system" (Wu, 1973).

Individuals, including critical-care patients, mobilize patterns of behavior to either protect themselves or reestablish normalcy. Behavioral responses indicate to the critical-care health team the way in which the individual is maintaining psychological equilibrium. According to Auger (1976), "the process of isolating behavior as a quality separate from all other qualities of the individual is intended to develop an abstract formulation of behavior in order to identify the areas of commonality and uniqueness. Behavior can be viewed as a complex system with a surrounding environment that operates according to certain rules that can be specified."

The individual's behavioral response to various situations, including illness, indicates that person's ability to assess the significance of those situations to his or her own self. The individual's altered physical or psychological being has more significance to that person than do the alterations of the person lying in the bed or room nearby. One has more ego involvement with one's own body and the many biological threats it encounters than with those confronting other patients in the environment. Illness and the necessity for hospitalization in critical care represent a severe threat and can reduce an individual's ability to psychologically cope in a positive direction. What may result is psychological disequilibrium and behavioral responses to that disequilibrium. The behavior becomes the system rather than the individual being the system. The behavior as a system involves complex, overt actions or responses to a variety of internal and external stimuli. Such responses can be anger, hostility, depression, or avoidance. Internal stimuli originate from the illness, disease, or injury and the self. External stimuli which are both purposeful and func-

16
PSYCHOLOGICAL EQUILIBRIUM
Sharon L. Roberts

DEFINITION OF TERMS
Intake and Output
Feedback
Stability
Regulation

PSYCHOLOGICAL DISEQUILIBRIUM IN CRITICAL-CARE PATIENTS
Internal Psychological Disequilibrium
Illness: Organ Image
Self-Conflict
External Psychological Disequilibrium
Environmental Factors

NURSING INTERVENTION: FACILITATE EQUILIBRIUM
Internal Psychological Equilibrium
Illness: Organ Image
Self-Conflict
External Psychological Equilibrium
Environmental Factors

REFERENCES

BIBLIOGRAPHY

tional are present in the environment. They may not always be viewed as such when the individual is in psychological disequilibrium.

Behavior as a system is a complex of elements in dynamic interaction. Therefore, a system becomes a group of related structures or substances that together perform certain functions and attempt to maintain some type of balance. The purpose of behavior is "to maximize a potential or desired outcome for the individual or group. It may involve the acquisition of environmental objects or resources, or the avoidance of objects and situations that could result in the potential injury or death of the individual" (Auger, 1976). Psychological disequilibrium and the resulting behavioral response may be a temporary or permanent event. Temporary psychological disequilibrium can be a normal behavioral response found in the avoidance-denial aspect of illness. Once critical-care patients acknowledge their illness and accept its implications, they can move from psychological disequilibrium to equilibrium. Permanent psychological disequilibrium, on the other hand, which may result from an inability to behaviorally cope with illness or a chosen position in relation to the illness, makes the individual a psychological cripple.

The critical-care team attempts through behavioral design to delineate appropriate and inappropriate behavioral responses.

DEFINITION OF TERMS

Psychological equilibrium involves the use of systems theory as an adaptative model. The application of systems theory makes possible the understanding of the origin of a behavioral response, factors which influence stability of behavior, and internal-external variables which contribute to psychological disequilibrium. Behavior is defined as the observable responses and actions which the individual manifests in direct response to external and/or internal stimuli. The behavioral system is significant in the discussion of psychological equilibrium. "A behavioral system is the organized interrelated complex of subsystems each with behavioral patterns which determine and limit how the person interacts with his environment. To operate efficiently and effectively toward accomplishing this end, behavioral patterns develop over time and are influenced by such outside variables as physical, biologic and social factors" (Grubbs, 1974). There are four components of psychological equilibrium which need to be defined. The components can also be found in definitions of systems theory. The

four components consist of intake and output, feedback, stability, and regulation.

Intake and Output

Intake or *input* is any external stimulus from the environment. All open systems, such as patients in critical care, receive input in the form of communication or physical energy from the environment. Matter, which is anything that has mass and occupies space, supplies the input. Input or intake of external stimuli allow the system to function in a congruent fashion with its environment and to detect any incongruity between the existing level of the system and the ideal. The system receives energy from the environment, uses it, and transforms it as needed; then it loses the energy in output to the environment, at which point it is again changed. The body as a system continually utilizes psychological, behavioral, and emotional energy as it strives toward behavioral equilibrium.

Output becomes the observable release of energy in materials into external stimuli. The release of energy is manifested as appropriate or inappropriate behavior. Therefore the system achieves two goals. First, the system takes in information and energy from the surrounding environment. Second, it provides output to the environment in similar forms as communication or energy. The energy output creates the process of feedback which facilitates system stability.

Feedback

Systems will strive toward equilibrium in order to reduce internal and external tension. In order for a system to survive, it must achieve a steady state where input, feedback, and output processes utilize a greater amount of energy. Applied to critical-care patients, the feedback scheme is called *homeostasis,* or *steady state.* Homeostasis is the ensemble of regulations that maintain variables constant and direct the organism toward a goal. They are performed by feedback mechanisms; that is, the result of the reaction is monitored back to the "receptor" side so that the system is held stable or led toward a target or goal.

Feedback that increases movement of the output from a steady state creates positive feedback. On the other hand, feedback that decreases movement of output from the steady state results in negative feedback. A closer look at both negative and positive feedback reveals that positive feedback alters variables and destroys their steady state. Negative feedback can also initiate system change.

Stability

Systems theory, as it applies to critical-care patients, attempts to maintain a degree of stability. Normally, the individual seeks to avoid instability. However, illness and the need for hospitalization may alter the individual's behavioral balance. As defined by Grubbs (1974), "behavioral balance is a dynamic state of interaction between the individual and his environment which allows for a range of input without resulting in disruption. Through the processes of adjustment and adaptation, the individual changes or grows to meet the external demands and constraints." The critical-care patient receives external input and evaluates the appropriateness or usefulness of the output response. The messages received by means of a behavioral feedback mechanism provide a framework for the quality and quantity of the individual's activities and responses.

Therefore the system tends to foster a state of equilibrium or stability. This state represents a balanced relationship between the system as a whole and its energy distribution. Any disruption of stability such as illness, threat to self, role disturbance, or the influence of environmental factors results in stress to the behavioral system. The individual must make an adjustment in order to reestablish behavioral stability or psychological equilibrium. According to Wu (1973), "behavioral stability refers to the continuity and consistency of behavior over time. With maturation and experience, the human system develops preferred ways of behaving that keep interference and conflicts to a minimum and preserve the balance of the organism. With the passage of time these behavioral responses become automatic and increasingly resistant to change."

Individuals, including critical-care patients, are motivated to achieve behavioral stability and psychological equilibrium. Equilibrium is more than mere balance. It represents a dynamic state of fluctuation between equilibrium and disequilibrium. The critical-care patient, because of biological alterations and threats to self, will experience disequilibrium. Equilibrium is more than freedom from tension or the establishment of an optimal state. Total relaxation and freedom from tension in which some tension is normal may lead to psychological disequilibrium in the form of psychosis-type maladaptive responses.

Regulation

One of the unique characteristics of an open system such as a critical-care patient is that the system is capable of self-regulation. Regulation and control mechanisms become the means by which the individual evaluates and determines a desired behavior. Ultimately, the individual will adapt his or her actual behavior to match the desired behavior. Critical-care patients learn the behavioral patterns and ways which maintain efficient behavior. Open systems are able to regulate the existing potential or tension in spontaneous activity or in response to stimuli. In this respect, they maintain a steady state. Through regulation and control, the individual is able to advance toward a higher order and organization of behavioral responses reflecting positive adaptation.

When the individual is unable to recognize potential threats in the external environment, disequilibrium results. According to Auger (1976), "major regulatory mechanisms of the aggressive-protective subsystems are the coping responses of denial or avoidance, vigilance, and nonspecific defenses. Individuals who deny the presence of a potential threat are less able to respond in an effective manner to the actual threat when it occurs in the environment. This is a consequence of the reduced input from the psychological regulatory system which has essentially blocked perception of the source of danger." The system, through self-regulation, must be able to detect any variation between a disturbed state and a normal state.

The behavioral system is continually involved in the process of input, feedback, and output. In this respect it is in a constant state of disorganization and disequilibrium. Psychological disequilibrium exists when the critical-care patient is sufficiently stable to return to a previous occupation or social life-style; however, fears or negative attitudes contribute to the individual becoming an emotional cripple. Psychological disequilibrium reduces the quantity and quality of sensory information available to the organism and reduces the ability of the individual to interact with the environment.

The critical-care patient who feels a loss of personal worth or dignity may experience psychological disequilibrium. If the patient's illness has altered a biological system internally or externally through loss, injury, or disfigurement, the patient may feel less than whole. Depending upon the degree of loss due to illness or disease, the critical-care patient may give up, or the patient may reach a steady state of psychological disequilibrium.

Psychological disequilibrium can arise as a result of physical immobility necessitating supportive devices, loss of a body part because of illness, separation from familiar surroundings, or separation from meaningful people such as family and friends. The critical-care patient is forced to submit to the domination or one or more biological systems in disequilibrium. Some patients in critical care can cope with various threats caused by illness in an adaptive manner. Other patients are unable to cope with illness. The inability to cope may be the result of a psychological response to the illness itself or to new changes in roles imposed by the illness. In either situation, the critical-care patient copes, especially if the situation or future outcome is threatening, by achieving a state of disequilibrium.

PSYCHOLOGICAL DISEQUILIBRIUM IN CRITICAL-CARE PATIENTS

Antecedent events become cues that indicate to the individual which behaviors are appropriate in a given situation. Antecedent events predict the consequences of various adaptive and maladaptive responses in which an individual might engage. Behavioral designing to facilitate psychological equilibrium involves arranging an environment which will produce and maintain specified behaviors in particular situations. This may not always be possible or realistic in critical care. The environment may not always be arranged to accommodate the patient. Biological crisis necessitates immediate action directed toward restoring biological equilibrium.

Illness which leads to hospitalization in a critical-care unit creates feelings of fear which may dominate positive coping mechanisms. Positive coping indicates to both the patient and health team that adaptation to the illness is possible. There are times when psychological disequilibrium occurs in crisis situations in which the stress far exceeds the individual's ability to reduce the tension caused by stress. The critical-care patient may experience psychological disequilibrium because acute illness is viewed as a threat to life.

Behavior is an integrated response to internal and external stimuli which are modified by three factors. Internal psychological disequilibrium consists of two factors, namely, illness and self or role disturbance. Illness which threatens the biological being can cause disequilibrium or behavioral instability. Critical-care patients may refuse to participate in their own care because they think their biological integrity will not tolerate the physical activity. All their energy in this situation is directed toward protecting the damaged body part. In this respect, the patient becomes organ-oriented. The second internal variable is self or role disturbance resulting from the need to adapt to new changes or roles. External psychological disequilibrium involves environmental variables which may be so intense that they intimidate the critical-care patient.

Internal Psychological Disequilibrium

Internal psychological disequilibrium takes into account organ image as it relates to illness, and self or role disturbance. It should be pointed out that the things an individual senses affect what he or she does. Likewise, the individual's actions in turn affect what he or she senses. The method by which the patient senses biological and role changes will affect behavioral responses. The resulting behavioral response attempts to alter internal stimuli and stimulation.

Illness: Organ Image

Organ image is the mental picture the patient assigns to his or her specific biological problem. For example, critical-care patients view themselves as a heart, kidney, or lung. The patient's organ images are reinforced when members of the health team focus on their altered biological systems rather than on the individuals by name. Therefore, patients see themselves from an organ image point of view rather than as a whole. Behavior that is not stressed because of illness is organized and patterned. The result is that patients utilize their energy in a stable and consistent manner. Behavioral responses are flexible and appropriate to the problem-free environment. This reflects a dynamic process of equilibrium or adaptation among the various subsystems. Physical stress such as illness can produce disorganization or instability of ongoing behavioral response patterns.

Psychological disequilibrium begins when the patient arrives in critical care and receives a diagnosis. Depending upon the illness or disease, the patient may have vast or limited previous illness experience. The familiarity of the illness situation and past hospital experience with the contingencies associated with the stressor will influence the degree of instability experienced by the individual. During stress periods associated with illness, the system is in disequilibrium. In its state of disequilibrium, increased amounts of energy will be needed in the system in order to restore balance and stability.

The critical illness can bring about two psychological responses. A critical-care patient could simply freeze, out of fright, or become preoccupied with the diagnosis, disease, or injured organ. This latter response involves organ image. There are times during the initial crisis of illness when the patient's intake system is limited. Organ image, whether it be of myocardial infarction, renal failure, ketoacidosis, chronic obstructive pulmonary disease, or a serious burn, reduces the individual's receptiveness to environmental stimuli. Illness, or organ image, is a stressor that reduces environmental intake and contributes to instability and disorganization. Disorganized behavioral responses can be observed when the critical-care patient encounters a biological or psychological stressor or an unknown complication for which the individual has no previous experiential responses.

According to Coombs, any physical disturbance that severely reduces the energy resources of the organism has effects upon the scope of perception. When an individual is sick enough to be confined to bed, alertness may be restricted by immobility. Whatever decreases alertness has inevitable effects upon perceptive efficency (Coombs and Snygg, 1959). Illness or disease restricts the critical-care patient to bed and thereby eliminates environmental exploration. Unexplained and unfamiliar input such as alarms, beeps, or cycling sounds from a volume respirator may stimulate an internal alarm when the patient cannot identify the noise. The resulting tension increase associated with instability or disequilibrium is experienced as anxiety. The increasing tension alerts the patient to initiate coping mechanisms which attempt to avert imbalance and restore steady state. According to Wu (1973), "between the state of stability and instability there is a state, at least conceptually, that is neither stable nor instable called precarious stability. When the individual experiences a potential threat, such as the deprivation of one or more of his basic needs or the loss of some valued thing, he will appear precariously stable. He will mobilize his energies in an effort to thwart realization of such threats and thereby avert an imbalance" (Wu, 1973).

Illness is a hazardous event and may lead to psychological disequilibrium. According to Rapaport, "the hazardous event creates for the individual a problem in his current life situation. The problem can be conceived of as a threat, a loss, or a challenge. The threat may be to fundamental instinctual needs

or to the person's sense of integrity. A threat to need and integrity is met with anxiety" (Rapaport, 1965). Illness involves loss of function of all or part of an organ. The individual, who had previously taken for granted a particular organ or system, becomes preoccupied with that organ or system. Patients in critical care become preoccupied with their diseased or surgically altered organ. Some patients become preoccupied to the point of physically and psychologically immobilizing themselves. They are fearful of carrying out necessary rehabilitative maneuvers for fear of overtaxing the sick organ. Other critical-care patients have improved biologically to the point of attaining greater mobility, but their psychological condition has reached a steady state of disequilibrium. The psychological disequilibrium prevents greater physical mobility.

The degree of psychological disequilibrium depends not only upon the critical-care patient's previous coping ability but also upon the severity of the illness. Loss of function associated with myocardial ischemia, acute tubular necrosis, or adult respiratory distress syndrome may be temporary. When function does not return to the sick organ, the critical-care patient experiences loss of a part. The loss of a part, for example, may be loss of one kidney due to pathology or injury, loss of myocardial tissue as a result of several infarctions leading to cardiogenic shock, loss of lung tissue due to emphysema or lobectomy, hepatic failure due to cancer, or right-sided hemiplegia due to cerebrovascular accident. In some instances, loss of a part may result in loss of a whole organ, such as in pneumonectomy, bilateral nephrectomy, quadraplegia, or skin loss due to burns.

An organ lost entirely or in part usually has ego value to the critical-care patient. Its loss can cause psychological disequilibrium, thereby preventing the individual from progressing beyond the condition at the time of the initial loss. Even if a sick organ regains part of its function or strength, or if an artificial substitute for the organ is used, such as a pacemaker, respirator, or hemodialysis machine, many critical-care patients cannot bring themselves to recognize biological improvements or substitutes. The patient only sees a future of limitations, controls, and restrictive regulations.

A critical-care patient's biological condition may stabilize so that self-care is permissible. The health team may observe that the patient withdraws from any physical involvement. The patient's attention focuses on the sick organ to the point of giving it a name or simply calling the involved part "it." The critically ill patient's attitude toward the sick organ may change so greatly that the organ itself becomes anthropomorphized; the patient thinks of it as something independent or something that needs special care. The patient's attitude toward the organ (and thus toward herself or himself) may become that of an overanxious mother who is always worrying and overprotecting a child.

Some critical-care patients become organ image-conscious. The cardiac patient views his heart in a revered capacity. The burn patient views her skin as something which protects her body integrity. The hemodialysis patient attributes a new image to the sick or surgically removed organ. Patients who need rehabilitation in order to breathe, walk, or move may refuse to participate in the rehabilitative process because of psychological disequilibrium or behavioral instability. Critical-care patients may fear that rehabilitation will impair the biological process, and they fear the sick organ is not ready for such activity. Or the individual may be content in not challenging the sick organ. Such a patient may reach a steady state of psychological disequilibrium; one may refer to these patients as cardiac, renal, or respiratory cripples.

After a physiological crisis or altered biological state has occurred and stabilized, the critical-care patient has one of three choices. First, the critically ill patient can adapt by reaching a steady state of dependency in which the boundaries of the illness are never exceeded. Such patients move toward behavioral instability and disequilibrium by giving power over themselves to others. Secondly, a patient may adapt by denying that a physiological crisis has taken place and attempt to return to previous behavior. The behavioral response may be maladaptive and may include activities such as eating the wrong foods, working too hard, or sleeping too little. The maladaptive behavioral response can be hazardous. However, in this situation the individual chooses not to force the possibility of physical limitations and thus ignores the severity of the entire experience. The third choice is positive adaptation whereby the patient's behavior is to achieve stability and equilibrium. The patient may choose to establish a new steady state in which the past crisis and future limitations are realistically integrated into a new life. Such a patient has learned new ways of coping from the illness experience.

Critical-care patients who make the first two choices are often physiologically capable of achieving much more than they are psychologically willing to attempt. This is the area in which the health team

may play a vital role. Realizing that the patient may become preoccupied with the organ involved, the nurse should provide subtle support for the sick organ rather than intently focusing upon it through supportive devices and treatment procedures. Much of what the critical-care health team does during a crisis focuses intently on the diseased system, to the exclusion of all else. It is quite understandable that the patient focuses on a sick organ. Critical-care patients may reorganize their futures around their current feelings toward their organs. The critical-care health team can assist patients to develop positive feelings about their altered biological subsystems. As the patients focus on positive aspects of their current illness and hospitalization, they are less likely to overprotect the altered organ and more likely to see positive aspects of their futures.

The loss of an entire organ, or of its function, may result from severe pathology or surgical intervention. The burn patient's skin may be replaced with grafts. The cardiac patient may have various alterations. If conductive tissue is lost, a pacemaker is implanted. Diseased valves and coronary arteries may be replaced. The renal patient might have a kidney transplant. If transplantation is unrealistic, the patient might be hemodialyzed. The pulmonary patient may be maintained on a volume respirator.

The critical-care nurse should be realistic in mobilizing the patient toward a positive outcome. The critical-care patient's psychological acceptance of the sick organ or surgical procedure is "directly related to his concept of illness. When the patient is given a diagnosis, he has to absorb the information in terms of the knowledge he has of it, and in terms of the knowledge the doctor gives him" (Bellak, 1952).

The critical-care nurse keeps in mind that illness has a different connotation for each patient, but each patient may experience a period of psychological disequilibrium. In some cases, the disequilibrium or instability is only temporary; in other situations, it becomes a permanent way of life. The individual may reach either a steady state or psychological death. The critical-care patients may eventually give up and accept roles others have given them, or they may manufacture their own, for example, the invalidism-cripple role.

Self-Conflict

As discussed earlier, critical illness may lead to fear of a loss in function of either a part or whole. The fear may become the focus of the patient's psychological disequilibrium or behavioral instability. While the anxiety which reduces the critical-care patient's intake system may be conscious, the growing fear that the use of an organ or the organ itself may be lost may remain unconscious. This is because the possibility of organ loss constitutes an overwhelming threat to a patient's sense of self. The self can reach disequilibrium and instability when confronted with forced role alterations. The forced role disturbances necessitate that one's behavior be altered to fit the new situation. Therefore two types of role disturbance may occur in critical care: sick role disturbance and social role disturbance. Each role change may lead to self-conflict whereby the individual feels insecure with his or her own body and its real or artificial boundaries. Secord and Backman (1961) state that persons must regulate their systems of interaction so that a balance is maintained between three components of their interpretation matrix: the aspect of the person's self-concept, the person's interpretation of those behaviors that are related to that aspect, and the person's perception of another's behavior toward that aspect.

Self-conflict resulting from sick role disturbance may affect a critical-care patient who has been healthy until forced by a major illness or injury to assume a new role. The restorative events which occur immediately after arrival in a critical-care unit are vague, foreign, and frightening. The illness, together with intrusive diagnostic or treatment procedures, has thrust the patient into disequilibrium. The patient may not have experiential knowledge of sick role behaviors and therefore does not know what to expect. Such a patient fails to comprehend all the technical supportive devices in the environment which are connected to various parts of the body. Since the patient is connected to various supportive devices, thereby confirming the presence of a biological crisis, the patient loses the connection with the supportive assistance of family. All that is familiar has been replaced with strange people, technical language, and foreign objects. Patients at this point find themselves relocated in a new area of hemodialysis, respiratory care, or coronary care or a burn unit. The overall result is a feeling of psychological disequilibrium.

The critical-care patient discovers that previous restorative behaviors no longer seem applicable. According to Grubbs (1974), "when a person is unable to act within the range of his usual behavioral pattern, or when the environmental pressures call for behaviors with which he is not prepared to respond, the behavioral system may become unstable. If the individual can alter his behavior to fit the situations, the instability

is temporary." The patient may act out and utilize behavioral responses such as anger, hostility, denial, defensiveness, or withdrawal. Patient's who are experiencing their first bouts with illness may become preoccupied with certain aspects of it and be unable to verbalize their concerns. Therefore they become annoyed or angry over events that may or may not relate to their immediate biological problem. For example, "the first coronary attack with its overwhelming pain and the accompanying feeling of possible death, is a severe trauma for the patient. Once the acute situation is passed, the patient starts to realize the nature of his affliction within the framework of his established reaction pattern to danger situations. He may feel that he is doomed and his attitude towards life will change" (Bellak, 1952). The critical-care nurse realizes that whatever behavioral response the patient uses, it is an energy output mechanism. Furthermore, the nurse understands that critical-care patients focus their concentration upon their own problems to the exclusion of whatever is happening around them.

Social role disturbance may manifest itself after the biological crisis has subsided. At this time, patients begin thinking about their futures and the futures of their families. This is especially significant if the illness or disease has imposed future limitations, such as dependency on others or supportive devices, or possible changes in role responsibility or life-style. The patient may have difficulty responding to the internal changes and external stresses. Auger (1976) points out that "a system that is in relative equilibrium responds to external stress by resisting the influence of the disturbance, unless it is of sufficient intensity to disrupt system balance. Resistance to a disturbance may take the form of not acknowledging its existence; of activating homeostatic forces that immediately restore or recreate a balanced state; or of reaching a new point of equilibrium. It is necessary to identify those forces that promote change and those that resist change in order to describe the process of resistance to stress."

A critical-care patient who is forced to reduce or change a work schedule may feel less productive and ineffective or useless. For many individuals prior to critical illness, work is a mechanism for achieving personal and financial goals. Illness, disease, or injury which necessitates a change in one's social or work style causes a loss in self-esteem and dignity. An individual who experiences prolonged self-conflict may become depressed and withdraw further into the world of psychological disequilibrium. The patient needs help in realistically evaluating social role changes resulting from illness. The critical-care nurse validates the patient's interpretation of past, current, and future events in an attempt to facilitate a smooth hospital-to-home transition. The patient needs verbal input regarding what behaviors will be expected in the home environment.

Self-conflict also occurs when the sick individual experiences role reversal. Role reversal is a component of social role disturbance. The cardiac or pulmonary patient with limited physiological or energy reserve must assume a less active and more passive role within the family. The physiologically disabled patient may need to assume duties previously performed by the spouse. In addition, financial responsibilities may become the new concern of the partner who does not normally deal with these matters. Neither are prepared to assume the other's responsibilities. A patient feels guilty about the physical inability to assume responsibility for the family, the spouse's sudden need to work, and the creation of a financial burden for the entire family. It is not uncommon for the patient to give up and thus fail to utilize the potential that remains.

External Psychological Disequilibrium

External psychological disequilibrium results when the critical-care patient is in conflict with factors in the environment. The patient's behavioral system has boundaries which are flexible and adjust to the amount of input received from the immediate environment. Therefore, external physiological disequilibrium will be discussed according to environmental factors.

Environmental Factors

The critical-care patient as a behavioral system is dependent upon the external critical-care environment. The system may achieve instability by excess or deficits within the external environment. Stresses within the environment consist of the critical-care unit itself, the use of supportive devices, and the critical-care health team.

The critical-care environment may facilitate feelings of psychological disequilibrium and behavioral instability. It was previously mentioned that behavior is a response which becomes a communicative link between the critical-care patient and the patient's immediate environment. There are times when the immediate environment contributes to behavioral instability as manifested by the output of observable actions. Input from the stressful and threatening en-

vironment reinforces the individual's personal feelings of insecurity and inadequacy within his or her body. The patient sees events which reinforce internal fears. The patient is uncertain as to the purpose or direction of the surrounding numerous activities upon arrival in the critical-care unit. The critical-care patient is forced to absorb a variety of external environmental stimuli. The critical-care health team performs diagnostic procedures while life-support devices tick, hum, beep, or buzz. The boundaries of the individual's behavioral system limit the impact of meaningful stimuli available to the patient. The critical-care patient's boundary system is significant because "if the system is in danger of experiencing overload and the consequent disorganization of behavioral functions, then the boundary will tighten and exclude all but the critical input required for continued function. The function of the boundary is similar to that of sensory threshold; in sensory poor environment the input threshold will be lower than in complex sensory rich environment" (Auger, 1976). The critical-care patient is exposed to a tremendous variety of external environmental stimuli. It is impossible for the individual to behaviorally respond to all potential stimuli. The individual is incapable of processing all the stimuli so that a purposeful response can be made. The critical-care nurse may become the human mechanism which regulates the processing of incoming stimuli so that significant messages may be separated from insignificant ones. The patient then derives personal meaning from the significant stimuli. This is an attempt to maintain psychological equilibrium. The manner by which the patient is physically processed into critical care may be a deterrent or facilitator of internal security.

Supportive devices within the environment also contribute to psychological disequilibrium. The degree of physical immobilization caused by various supportive devices depends upon the type and severity of disease, illness, or injury. A patient in a coronary-care unit, burn unit, intensive-care unit, or respiratory-care unit may need multiple wires and tubes. The more wires and tubes needed, the less physical and psychological mobility the patient has. The patient may move in bed only to have a machine buzz. This causes a sense of frustration, since others who must respond to the alarm are inconvenienced. Ultimately, the patient may choose to remain physically immobile. Physical immobility enhances the critical-care patient's psychological disequilibrium.

The ability to move through the environment facilitates behavioral stability. Physical movement enables emotional contact with people and objects within the environment. The emotional contacts become a source of stimulation and motivation. Normally, while an individual lies in bed, psychological contact is made with the environment. In critical care, the patient's biological problems and subsequent need for supportive devices may limit mobility such as seeking alternative positions while remaining in bed. Patients in other settings are able to freely move in bed, thereby gaining a new awareness of various sounds or visual images. A sudden unfamiliar noise creates both physical and psychological mobilization of energies. This mobilization is not always possible in critical care, since the patient does not have complete physical mobility. If the patient physically turns in an attempt to make visual and auditory contact with the environment, the supportive device buzzes. The patient who chooses to remain physically immobile depends upon visual contact with the immediate environment, which may also be greatly curtailed. When possible, auditory and visual contact with the external environment should be facilitated.

Lastly, the critical-care health team may contribute to psychological disequilibrium. It is not the conscious intention of the health team to contribute to disequilibrium and behavioral instability. Nevertheless, there are times when restorative treatments designed to be supportive are carried out in a hurried manner. The hurried activity pushes the health team into a goal-directed rather than patient-directed framework. Therefore a hurried nurse may unintentionally convey to the patient a feeling of anxiety or sense of urgency, since the nurse knows the consequences of the illness and the potentially life-threatening problems that it might cause. The patient's body boundaries have been violated and simultaneously extended via supportive devices including wires and tubes into the external environment. It is no wonder the patient experences disequilibrium!

NURSING INTERVENTION: FACILITATE EQUILIBRIUM

The critical-care nurse realizes that disease, illness, and injury create instability and disequilibrium. The nurse, together with other members of the health team, witnesses situations in which some loss of function, part, or whole has created imperfection in the patient's input system. The imperfection affects the patient's ability to gain, transmit, or utilize environmental information. The goal of the critical-care health team is

to reduce instability or disorganized energy caused by psychological disequilibrium.

Internal Psychological Equilibrium

The nurse attempts to include the patient's internal stabilizing processes through assessment of the meaning illness has for the individual and degree of self-conflict due to role disturbance. The stabilizing force is a self-regulating one. The critical-care patient as an open system attempts to maintain a steady state among the many illness and self-conflict variables. This implies a dynamic behavioral response—one that seeks positive ways of adapting to biological crisis. Positive adaptation involves accepting the illness and adjusting to any limitations it has imposed upon the patient or the patient's family.

Illness: Organ Image

The critical-care nurse fosters psychological equilibrium by assessing the significance of the illness on the patient. There are times when some critically ill patients enjoy the sick role and the attention focused on the sick organ. The patient may find security in the dependency role whereby others attend to the patient's various needs. The notion of being placed in the center of the health-care stage makes some patients feel significant. For some patients, illness coupled with the immediate need to be hospitalized implies the threat of death. Therefore these patients actively seek to achieve a level of biological and psychological stability so that they may return to the familiar territory called home. The goal-directed behavioral response is viewed by the nurse as desirable and appropriate. The critical-care patient is motivated to avoid further disease or illness which can limit present and future activities. According to Bellak (1952) "Gradually the meaning to the patient of his illness undergoes certain changes. His initial diffuse anxiety is replaced by a more personalized concept. The nature of the pathology and how the illness looks and feels to him take on special meaning to the patient on conscious, preconscious, and unconscious levels. . . . He learns to live with his illness and achieve some degree of acceptance of it." The critical-care nurse must be open to the anxieties, frustrations, and threats of existence experienced by the critically ill patient. The burn patient is anxious when confronted with a whirlpool treatment including debridement and dressing change. The pulmonmary patient is anxious when weaned from a volume respirator. Likewise, the hemodialysis patient may become fearful about dependency on a machine and its future financial cost. The energies of each patient are directed toward a feared event or process. Hopefully, nurses can channel the patient's energy toward deriving some meaning from the disease, illness, or injury. The nurse also attempts to make the patient feel less intimidated by the illness.

A critically ill patient who continues to feel intimidated by illness cannot find meaning in it. Instead, the patient may retreat to invalidism or become a psychological cripple. To avoid disequilibrium and facilitate psychological equilibrium, the nurse actively helps the patient identify accomplishments and assets. Organ image may have caused patients to focus their entire attention upon the sick organ to the exclusion of other variables. Therefore the critical-care nurse assists patients in broadening their vision to include other internal and external stimuli. The stimuli can be support systems in the patient's immediate environment. Furthermore, some patients are forced to expand in areas which they fear might place the sick organ in jeopardy. For example, the pulmonary patient may be afraid to increase physical mobility and therefore distance from the main support system, namely the volume respirator. Furthermore, the patient fears transfer out of the respiratory-care unit and into an intermediate- or general-care unit. Rather than viewing the transfer as a positive statement regarding the state of the sick organ, the patient looks upon it with a degree of fear. To patients, transfer implies learning what is expected of them in a different setting and meeting strangers who are unfamilar with their personal care. The cardiac patient may be afraid to ambulate for fear of experiencing angina or extending the current infarction. The burn patient may experience psychological disequilibrium if there are complications, if grafts are rejected, if overwhelming pain is experienced, if family or friends fail to be supportive, or if body image is so altered that people relate to the patient as if he or she were a different person. In each instance, critical-care patients must sense their own biological and psychological readiness for mobility. Such readiness implies that the patients have achieved psychological equilibrium and behavioral stability.

Self-Conflict

Self-conflict is the most difficult area in which the critical-care nurse intervenes. Hopefully, the patient's self-concept prior to illness and hospitalization was well developed in a positive direction. If not, the patient has difficulty coping with the psychological threat attached to illness and the need to be connected to multiple-support systems. Self-conflict can diminish the patient's already reduced energy system. The critical-care patient must direct energies toward the physiological source of crisis or toward the feared object (e.g., intrusive procedures). As a result, the patient must conserve the energy that remains. The critical-care nurse, on the other hand, represents a stable force with high energy resources. Nurses can contribute some of their energy to the patient by temporarily assuming certain responsibilities and making certain decisions for the patient. The patient with chronic disorders such as emphysema, renal failure, or congestive heart failure may be unable to independently perform the activities of daily living. For the once independent patient, this can cause self-conflict. Consequently, the nurse conserves the patient's energy reserve by performing the activities of daily living for the patient.

Crisis can strip away conventional roles. If the individual has not developed an internal sense of identity or self, any loss of conventional roles may contribute to a feeling of loss of self. Such a loss further contributes to the patient's feelings of nonexistence or nothingness. On the other hand, the biological crisis may facilitate the individual in developing a more enduring sense of identity. At this time the critical-care nurse's role is mainly supportive and facilitative. The nurse's long-term goal is to make the patient as self-sufficient as is realistic considering the biological problem. What happens outside the hospital environment between the patient and the patient's family is out of the nurse's jurisdiction. Nevertheless, while the patient remains in the critical-care unit, the nurse becomes involved with the family. The nurse realizes that family members draw energy from the patient by seeking explanations for the patient's depression or withdrawal behavior and that the family dissipates its energy to the patient by becoming anxious. The energy received may not be constructive and only make the patient more anxious. The nurse's role is to give the family feedback regarding the patient's behavior.

External Psychological Equilibrium

The primary stabilizing force in the patient's immediate environment is the critical-care nurse. The nurse can make the patient's transition from home into the critical-care area with its technology a smooth one.

The nurse should assess those factors in the environment that may create psychological disequilibrium, including the atmosphere of critical care, the supportive devices, and the nursing care itself.

Environmental Factors

A critical-care nurse may influence the patient's environment by minimizing unfamiliar noises, creating a familiar environment, and explaining or removing supportive devices as soon as possible. Unfamiliar noises and supportive devices are a normal part of critical care, but whenever possible the nurse should remove supportive devices and minimize noise in the patient's immediate environment. Removal of unused pieces of supportive devices makes the patient feel that his or her biological system is moving toward stability and wellness. This tends to increase psychological equilibrium. Therefore, the nurse can create a critical-care environment unclouded by continual impending crisis. The nurse accomplishes this goal by creating a facilitating environment in which the patient feels secure and confident that the biological crisis will be resolved.

The nurse provides familiarity when possible. Familiarity with one's environment leads to behavioral stability and psychological equilibrium. Familiarity may be accomplished by placing some of the patient's personal possessions in the nightstand beside the bed. Cards, pictures of family members, and personal items can be placed within physical and visual contact.

In summary, the critical-care patient may experience psychological disequilibrium and behavioral instability when confronted with an acute illness or injury. Once in critical care, the patient draws upon the stabilizing force of the nurse to provide psychological equilibrium. The nurse intervenes to eliminate or reduce internal variables such as organ image and self-conflict, together with the external variable of environmental factors. The overall goal of the critical-care nurse and health team is to facilitate the patient's attainment of psychological equilibrium.

REFERENCES

Auger, J.: *Behavioral Systems and Nursing,* Englewood Cliffs, N.J.: Prentice-Hall, 1976.

Bellak, L.: *The Psychology of Physical Illness,* New York: Grune & Stratton, 1952.

————: Psychological aspects of cardiac illness and rehabilitation, *Social Casework* 37: 488–489, 1956.

Coombs, A., and D. Snygg: *Individual Behavior,* New York: Harper and Row, 1959.

Grubbs, J .: An interpretation of the Johnson behavioral system model for nursing practice, in Callista Roy (ed.), *Conceptual Models for Nursing Practice,* New York: Appleton-Century-Crofts, 1974.

Rapaport, L.: The state of crisis: Some theoretical considerations, in H. Parad (ed.), *Crisis Intervention,* New York: Family Service Association of America, 1965.

Secord, P., and C. Backman: Personality theory and problem of stability and change in individual behavior, *Psychol Rev* 68(No. 1) 1961. (Cited in Wu, p. 98)

Wu, R.: *Behavior and Illness,* Englewood Cliffs, N.J.: Prentice-Hall, 1973.

BIBLIOGRAPHY

Hein, E. C.: Emotional support, *Critical Care Update* November 1978, pp. 13–19.

Putt, A. M.: *General Systems Theory Applied to Nursing,* Boston: Little, Brown, 1978.

Smith, D.: Survivors of serious illness, *Am J Nurs* March 79(3): 441–446, 1979.

Milieu is the French term for "setting" or "environment." A *therapeutic* milieu refers to a health-promoting environment in which staff interventions are based on objective reasoning and problem solving, rather than on personal prejudice and emotion. Objectivity in a milieu serves to increase the quality of patient care by facilitating direct lines of communication. The integrity of communication is a major factor in distinguishing a therapeutic from a nontherapeutic milieu.

An important aspect of critical care involves the management of the environment of a patient experiencing serious illness. This task is best accomplished by a unified, multidisciplinary approach which emphasizes clear communication between the staff, patient, and family. The need for effective communication is increased by the fact that life-and-death situations are encountered frequently in the critical-care area. Individual responses to stress are transmitted verbally and nonverbally within the system. Indecisiveness during an emergency situation is perceived by the team and can evoke responses based on extreme anxiety and emotionality. The result may be a reduction in the efficiency of care administered to the patient. Inefficient patient care can intensify the anxiety and perpetuate a cycle of tension and distorted interaction.

The patient and family also are involved in the communication process of the critical-care milieu. They are often entangled when there is a conflict between nurses and physicians. This conflict may be manifested subtly in the behaviors of the patient or family. An illustration of this principle occurs when there is staff conflict regarding the management of a patient. Unless this issue is discussed, the patient will receive inconsistent messages. In response to this distorted communication, the patient may exhibit a marked rise in anxiety. The family can sense the patient's anxiety and reflect it to the staff in numerous ways. One such way is to suddenly demand extended visiting privileges in an attempt to calm the patient. The incessant requests of the family may soon anger the staff, and thus a cycle of tension will be created and maintained in the system. Unless objective problem solving is instituted, the labeling of the patient or family member as a "psychiatric case" is a possible outcome. In this same manner, a conflict within the family can be projected to the staff.

Communication in a milieu involves the *shifting* of messages throughout an interdependent system. A tendency to resort to *scapegoating* may ensue if interactions are appraised as cause-effect phenom-

17
THE CRITICAL-CARE MILIEU
Susan B. Biddle

THE STAFF
Function of the Nursing Staff
Supporting the Staff
Managing the Environment
Giving Emotional Support

THE PATIENT
Problems of Patient Communication
Overcoming Sensory and Perceptual Disorganization

THE FAMILY

REFERENCES

BIBLIOGRAPHY

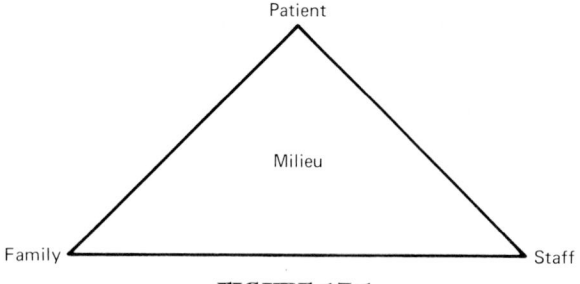

FIGURE 17-1
Pattern of interactions in a milieu.

ena. Scapegoating is a major deterrent in establishing the direct communication techniques essential in a therapeutic setting. A therapeutic milieu will provide a framework for identifying barriers to cohesiveness and will facilitate communication, maturity, efficiency, and personal growth through education and objectivity.

Guidelines for establishing a therapeutic milieu will be discussed according to the special contributions and problems of the staff, patient, and family. The nurses' role will be emphasized since they are the ones most intimately involved in the environment.

THE STAFF

There seems to be general agreement that a multidisciplinary approach is most effective in treating the critically ill. This approach may be coordinated in various ways according to the needs and resources of the hospital and community. One method is to have one physician in charge of treatment. When necessary, this physician may call for the assistance of other specialists. Another method is to have a primary team representative of several specialties committed to the critical-care area. Regardless of the approach, the goals of treatment can be clearly formulated and shared with the staff, patient, and family.

One physician may assume the responsibility for coordinating and communicating the medical treatment plan. A comprehensive plan will include input from other staff, the patient, and the family. An open discussion of choices and alternatives will enhance objectivity. Whenever possible, decisions can be mutually shared. It is essential to clarify lines of responsibility and to outline a procedure for handling ultimate decisions. The medical staff and nursing staff need to be in frequent contact in order to alter treatment as necessary.

Function of the Nursing Staff

According to Hymovich (1979), "Nursing care is a system of interdependent relationships that cannot be altered without affecting the function and viablity of the whole system." The nursing staff provides the continuity of care essential to the milieu. In addition to providing a 24-h service, the nurse contributes technical and observational skills. As Hudak (1973) says, "the essence of the concept of critical-care nursing lies not in special environments, but rather in the decision-making process of the nurse." The nurse's ability to apply the nursing process in making objective decisions establishes the nurse as a key member of the team.

How do nurses in a critical-care milieu know if their decisions and interventions are objective? Complete objectivity is unattainable and undesirable. Objectivity in a milieu is concerned with a balanced integration of feelings and thoughts. It allows the nurse to make evaluations based on factual information rather than personal feelings. A patient may refuse medication. The nurse may sense a rise in anxiety and tell the patient that there is no choice in the matter. In this example, the nurse's personal need for control has interfered with obtaining valuable information about the patient's concern over medication.

It is important for nurses to realize that they will experience both positive and negative feelings about patients. The expectation of nurses to maintain a nonjudgmental attitude in all situations is unrealistic. Gaining self-awareness of one's thoughts and feelings is a prerequisite for dealing directly and objectively with these difficult situations. Objectivity involves (1) recognizing and becoming aware of feelings, (2) discussing feelings, and (3) evaluating the effect of feelings on personal and professional interactions. A nurse who can identify the feelings of helplessness evoked by a patient who refuses medication can gain a more realistic understanding of nursing responsibilities.

Regular staff meetings can be utilized for an open discussion of the positive and negative effects of the environment. In addition, they can include a sharing of feelings engendered by the patient or family. Objectivity is increased if the meetings are structured to include a *balanced* discussion of feelings and problem solving. Occasionally, staff conferences deteriorate into a venting of feelings without consideration of alternatives to problems. This approach will tend to reinforce a powerless position. A goal-directed approach will facilitate objectivity.

Staff meetings can also allow for the direct expression of staff conflict. This does not suggest a stalemate of angry confrontation of right and wrong, but rather a verbalization of disagreement with the goal of seeking alternatives through negotiation. The staff will not always agree. The important factor is the acknowledgement of conflict in order to avoid burdening the patient with displaced staff anxiety.

Clarification of roles will serve to decrease frustration and promote objectivity. A staff which maintains responsibility and accountability will convey a clear message to others in the milieu. Periodic evaluation of the following items can be included in staff meetings in order to examine role differentiation:

1. What are the lines of responsibility?

2. How is responsibility obtained?

3. How does the individual assess his or her responsibility?

4. What effect does assuming responsibility have on the milieu?

5. How can responsibility be delegated more effectively to decrease environmental stress?

Critical-care nurses are generally assertive, confident, and self-directed. These attributes can result in isolation within the milieu and therefore interfere with communication if they are channeled in the direction of exaggerated competitiveness. Nurses can be encouraged to view their contributions as unique in an interdependent system. Assuming responsibility for members of the team who do not share the work load can have a deleterious effect. A persistent feeling of being victimized by the system perpetuates helplessness. Actively seeking alternatives to problems will augment the nursing role.

Supporting the Staff

Nurses in critical-care areas are reminded frequently of their helplessness by a repetition of emergency situations often resulting in the death of a patient. A sense of discouragement may be projected to the system if nurses receive only negative feedback. It is beneficial to handle criticism in the milieu in a constructive manner. This is accomplished by an objective approach which includes an evaluation of strengths and weaknesses. Regular staff evaluations with supervisory personnel will provide the nurse with a consistent appraisal of performance. It is important to allow for validation between the nurse and supervisor. This involves a mutual appraisal in which

supervisors also may be informed of ways they are or aren't helpful. Constructive criticism is a goal-directed process which serves to enhance personal and professional growth.

The nurse is usually the first person to identify a disruptive influence in the milieu. The communication techniques used to relay this information will make a definite impact on the system. The manner in which a nurse communicates information is often a direct reflection of the leadership and organization of the unit. A nurse dealing with the frustrations of understaffing, inadequate space, faulty equipment, unrealistic expectations, and lack of support cannot be expected to have much energy left for developing interpersonal communication. Administrative personnel can assist in decreasing barriers to communication by structuring and organizing an efficient unit. Staff complaints and suggestions are to be taken seriously. It may seem impossible to institute some environmental changes, but the staff can be encouraged to view their role as important contributors in seeking realistic alternatives.

Managing the Environment

A common problem in critical care is managing the environment of a patient who refuses to cooperate. Misinterpretation of the word *management* is often the source of this difficulty. Managing a patient's environment is not synonymous with *controlling* the patient's behavior. Many patients feel they are rendered helpless by the overwhelming environment of critical care. Many patients are able to participate to some extent in the decision-making process of their care. Whenever possible, they can be encouraged to suggest adjustments in the environment in order to promote a sense of personal space and identity. This process of allowing choices (no matter how basic) will help the patient maintain a sense of independence and control over unfamiliar surroundings.

Frequently, power struggles ensue when there is an attempt to enforce medical or nursing care. Coercion reinforces the patient's sense of helplessness. An untenable situation may be created and the patient may try to assert control in destructive and self-defeating ways. Given a therapeutic milieu, the nurse will approach this problem by attempting to understand the meaning of the patient's behavior and instituting measures of negotiation. This approach requires that the staff maintain an awareness and accountability for their own responses to the situation.

Giving Emotional Support

The emotional well-being of the patient is of concern to the nurse. Some critical-care nurses experience a lack of time and expertise to deal adequately with the psychological aspects of care. The nurse can be instrumental in providing support by validating with the patient and family their perceptions of the environment. For example, a nurse may accurately assess the patient's condition as stable. However, there may be increased anxiety in the patient or family because their perception of the critical-care milieu is as anything but stable! The nurse can intervene by clarifying these perceptions and providing the knowledge and support necessary to alleviate the anxiety.

Emotional support is provided in ways which are seldom acknowledged. The fact that nurses are available and consistent in meeting physical needs provides the basis for a trusting relationship. A critically ill patient needs physical contact and reassurance. These needs are routinely met by the nurse's daily work with the patient. The nurse is usually the first person to identify the need for additional psychological support. The fact that the nurse has already established a relationship with the patient can expedite a smooth transition in obtaining psychiatric assistance.

It is important to examine objectively the decision to introduce a psychiatrist or counselor into the milieu. This decision can ultimately affect the entire system. The patient will be required to become acquainted with another unfamiliar person. The family and staff may experience a sense of failure in their attempts to meet the patient's emotional needs. In many cases, the nurses can receive the additional knowledge necessary to handle the emotional needs by working directly with a psychiatrist or psychiatric nurse specialist.

THE PATIENT

The patient enters the critical-care milieu undergoing crisis. The patient's adaptive mechanisms are being stressed maximally in an attempt to regain physiological and psychological homeostasis. Adjustment to the unfamiliar environment of critical care poses yet another problem. Reichle (1973) characterizes the patient's predicament as follows:

> The patient finds himself captive among a large group of unfamiliar people and unfamiliar equipment. His perceptive ability is diminished, his interpretive mechanism is disrupted, and his defensive mechanism is destroyed.

Problems of Patient Communication

Each patient will perceive the milieu in a unique way. Some may view the environment as extremely frightening, while others may experience a sense of relief that they are being carefully monitored. The staff is dependent on patients in order to assess accurately their perception of the milieu. Therefore, a priority in admitting the patient to the critical-care unit is to establish an effective means of communication.

The condition of the patient will influence communication technique. Time must be taken to identify the most satisfactory means of expression. Intubated patients can be assisted to write or use head movements to validate needs. Severely debilitated patients may relate most effectively with family members available to interpret some of their needs. Ensuring a means of communication will serve to enhance the patient's participation in the environment. It will allow for choices and reduce helplessness. The staff will gain invaluable information regarding the patient's perception of his or her illness.

Resistance to facilitate independence through communication may indicate a problem with the patient or staff. Kahn (1975) describes a problem of hospital-induced biphasism which de-emphasizes the holistic approach to care. This may result if the staff feels inept to handle the patient's communication. It represents a form of denial in which an overemphasis on technical proficiency precludes psychosocial needs. A preoccupation with physical needs will greatly diminish the patient-staff interaction. The patient can conceivably participate in this process by consistently questioning the staff about equipment and machinery. Focusing on technical aspects may serve to protect patients from gaining information they are not yet ready to hear.

Overcoming Sensory and Perceptual Disorganization

Two environmental problems of the critical-care patient include sensory deprivation and sensory overload. Sensory deprivation refers to a marked reduction in the quality and quantity of sensory input, with or without a change in pattern. Sensory overload occurs when external stimuli remain excessive and monotonous. An alteration in the variety and degree of sensory input can produce symptoms similar to an acute psychosis (loss of reality testing, restlessness, withdrawal, hallucinations, and delusions). Both phenomena represent a distortion and disruption of the normal communication process. DeMeyer (1967) suggests that critical-care patients generally receive physical overstimulation and emotional deprivation. To minimize the problems of sensory and perceptual disorganization, the following recommendations have been formulated by several authorities:

1. Maintain the normal day-awake, night-sleep cycle whenever possible.

2. When feasible modify treatments and procedures to allow for uninterrupted sleep.

3. Provide individual rooms with an outside window.

4. Allow the patient to have personal belongings brought in from home. Respect the patient's personal space.

5. Provide a variety of stimuli such as radio and TV.

6. Orient the patient frequently. Provide clocks and calendars in the rooms.

7. Eliminate constant, monotonous sounds. Restrict the use of equipment.

8. Allow the patient as much freedom of movement as possible. Remove immediately any unnecessary wiring and tubes.

9. Allow the family to visit frequently.

THE FAMILY

Successful treatment of an acute illness requires an intense focus on the patient. Within the technically complex environment of the critical-care area, the role of the family may seem obscure. However, the family may have a profound effect on the recovery of the patient. Most families and patients exert significant influences on one another. Nurses often err in assuming that they need to be all things to all people. A knowledge of family systems, which utilizes a family assessment, assists the nurse in incorporating the family into the patient's care.

A common feeling experienced by families is a sense of helplessness to participate in caring for a loved person. This problem is compounded by a technical environment which tends to reinforce physical distance between the family and patient. The family may refrain from touching the patient for fear of disturbing important equipment. They may be so preoccupied with their own responses to the environment, that their attempts to comfort the patient may be awkward and unwieldy.

An effective way to assist the family in coping with the critical-care milieu is to assess their response to the environment. By validating the family's percep-

tions, the staff can intervene to provide knowledge and support when necessary. Verbalizing to the family that they are an important part of the milieu will reinforce their sense of worth. The information the family provides about the patient can prove to be invaluable to the staff. When given explicit instructions, the family can participate in some aspects of physical care.

A recent study by Motler (1979) revealed that families of critically ill patients have the need to feel that there is hope and to have questions answered honestly. An honest appraisal by the staff which conveys that the family members are important contributors in patient care will initiate a meaningful relationship. Working with families need not be time-consuming or burdensome. Simple validations and instructions by the staff will enhance family participation. One nurse can effectively deal with families in short-term groups where common questions and concerns can be addressed.

Occasionally a family may become inappropriately angry and critical of the staff. This happens often when the family experiences an unusual amount of guilt about the patient's illness. They may manifest this anxiety by seeking someone to blame. If the staff has doubts about the care they are administering, they may become defensive and defer from sharing information with the family. This can initiate the cycle of interpersonal distortion described previously. If the staff is clear about their responsibilities, the family can gradually deal with their own feelings of doubt with a decreased need to project them to the system.

Once the family has adapted to the environment, they can often function to allay the patient's anxiety more expediently than the staff. The family has the potential of greatly diminishing the hazards of emotional and sensory deprivation. They provide the patient with the innate quality of humanness which develops over years of familiarity and understanding. This contribution of the family is unique.

In summary, a therapeutic milieu is built on a framework of integrated communication between the staff, patient, and family. An awareness of the dynamics of interaction within the system can assist the staff to coordinate care based on knowledge and objective reasoning. Objectivity can greatly minimize the time and energy involved in clarifying recurrent distortions in communication. The nursing role is crucial and can be outlined as follows:

1. Clarify, define, assess, and implement nursing responsibilities.

2. Maintain awareness of personal responses and their effect on the milieu.

3. Validate personal perceptions with others involved in the milieu.

4. Actively seek alternatives to environmental problems.

5. Maintain an organized unit.

6. Participate in conferences utilizing problem-solving techniques.

REFERENCES

DeMeyer, J.: The environment of the intensive care unit, *Nurs Forum* 6:262, 1967.

Hudak, C., B. Gallo, and T. Lohr: *Critical Care in Nursing,* Philadelphia: Lippincott, 1973, p. 1.

Hymovich, D.: *Family Health Care,* New York: McGraw-Hill, 1979, p. 262.

Kahn, A.: Stranger in the world of the I.C.U., *Am J Nurs* 75:2022, 1975.

Motler, N.: Needs of relatives of critically ill patients: A descriptive study, *Heart Lung* 8(2): 332–338, 1979.

Reichle, M.: Psychologic aspects of the acutely stressed in an intensive care unit, in *Respiratory Intensive Care Nursing,* Boston: Little, Brown, 1973, p. 222.

BIBLIOGRAPHY

Berk, J.: *Handbook of Critical Care,* Boston: Little, Brown, 1976.

Bowen, M.: *Family Therapy in Clinical Practice,* New York: Jason Aronson, Inc., 1978.

Geary, M.: Supporting family coping, *Supervisor Nurse* 10(3):52–59, 1979.

Gowan, N.: The perceptual world of the intensive care unit: An overview of some environmental considerations in the helping relationship, *Heart Lung* 8(2):340–344, 1979.

Hofling, C., M. Leininger, and E. Bregg: *Basic Psychiatric Concepts in Nursing,* Philadelphia: Lippincott, 1967, p. 81.

Jones, E. S.: *Essential Intensive Care,* Philadelphia: Lippincott, 1978.

Kornfield, D.: Psychiatric view of intensive care, *Brit Med J* 50:108, 1969.

Ledingham, I. (ed.): *Recent Advances in Intensive Care,* London: Churchill Livingston, 1977, p. 5

Roberts, S.: *Behavioral Concepts and the Critically Ill Patient,* Englewood Cliffs, N.J.: Prentice-Hall, 1976.

Worrell, J.: Nursing intervention in the care of the patient experiencing sensory deprivation, in *Advanced Concepts in Clinical Nursing,* Philadelphia: Lippincott, 1971, p. 133.

INTRODUCTION

The title of this chapter should not obscure the central concept that the authors wish to convey—that the client is the family. While the focus of the technical skills of the nurse in a critical-care setting is directed toward the identified patient, the significance of the family as a system must be recognized by the nurse in order to accomplish an assessment which is both practical and relevant to the life of the family. The major purpose of this chapter is to demonstrate the family as the primary unit of focus in assessment and the corresponding implications for intervention. It is hoped that the reader will begin to question whether a focus dealing with the patient and family as separate components is viable. This chapter will lay the groundwork for a major shift in perspective which will foster nurse-clinicians looking at process and outcomes in critical care in a comprehensive manner fruitful both for family adaptation and future clinical nursing research.

While a great deal has been written about psychological responses of patients and family members, the tendency has been to examine these responses as individual and unidirectional phenomena. In the focus on the individual in relation to phenonema of emotions and stress there has been a failure, until recently, to note that emotions and stress, believed to be important components of illness, depend greatly on communicative interaction (Weakland, 1977). The interactional approach, on the other hand, looks at human events and/or problems as behavior occurring among persons in a system of social relationships. Weakland (1977) decribes this new approach as follows:

> It assumes that the nature of difficulties often is not self-evident and focuses inquiry rather on the "what" and "how" of the situation in question. Such inquiry is less concerned with the ultimate origins or ends than with the present situation, how that is being maintained and how it might be altered for the better, though no solution will ever be final or perfect. Viewing of problems in relation to interaction also puts them on a human scale and in terms of *joint* responsibility: "All in it together" rather than "all or none" or "either you or me" responsibility of specific parties.

Weakland also suggests three ways in which interactional patterns might be important to illness: (1) A pattern of interaction forms the condition for the beginning of a particular disease, (2) a certain kind of interaction comprises a requisite but not sufficient condition for the onset of a particular disease, and (3) certain kinds of interaction are predisposing influ-

18
Psychosocial Assessment of the Patient and Family

Carol J. Dashiff
Susan B. Biddle

INTRODUCTION

PSYCHOSOCIODYNAMICS OF THE SICK ROLE
Anxiety
Issues
Developmental Experiences

COMMUNICATION

FAMILY ADJUSTMENT
Life Events
Emotional Shock Wave
Openness of Systems
Family Roles and Developmental Levels
Family Coping

CASE STUDY
Observation and Investigation
Genogram
Assessment and Validation
Plan and Rationale for Expected Outcome
Summary

REFERENCES

ences for diseases (Weakland, 1977). An example from the literature demonstrates the need for an interactional approach. Various components of the psychological state "Type A behavior" may be linked differentially to angina and myocardial infarction (Jenkins et al., 1978). These "psychological" components (strong temper, eating hurriedly under stress, conscientious effort) are, in fact, descriptors of interactive behavior in that they are patterns which occur in interpersonal contexts—one of the earliest and most significant being the family. The ways in which these interactive components influence illness are not known specifically, but according to Weakland (1977), they may be prerequisite, requisite in combination with other factors, or predisposing to particular diseases.

This chapter will elaborate on various psychosocial factors identified in the literature as significant to assessment of the family with a critically ill member. The literature included is occasionally oriented to an individualistic and unidirectional perspective, but the interpretation is expanded to a broader interactional systems approach. No individual can be understood or related to in isolation.

PSYCHOSOCIODYNAMICS OF THE SICK ROLE

The adoption and/or assignment of the sick role is an important aspect of the psychosociodynamics of behavior. The sick role implies an arrangement between an individual designated as sick (by self and/or others) and significant others. This arrangement may be implicit and informally contracted, and/or explicit and formally contracted, as in the relationship with the health professional. The purpose of the sick role is then to achieve the attention and active assistance of others from whom one is seeking help. The necessity of seeking help indicates an increase in anxiety in the system.

Anxiety

Anxiety in the system will correspond with (1) the degree of physical disorder or the degree to which discomfort affects the system and (2) the degree to which the helper is responsive to the system or subsystem seeking help (Linn, 1977). The approaching of an external system is in itself an acknowledgement of the helplessness and/or nonresponsiveness of the family unit. When, how, and by whom the first contact is made with the health care

system gives important assessment data. The patient who presents may be emotionally cut off from certain significant others. Those who accompany the patient may feel too helpless to respond effectively. According to Roberts (1976), "The sick member feels guilty for becoming ill. The family feels guilty for not being more aware of the other's biological well-being. Both systems temporarily rationalize the stressor event, so that neither one feels totally responsible for the problem."

Bowen (1978) views the emotional cutoff as an important consideration in understanding the phenomenon of illness. Emotional distance may be achieved through internal mechanisms of illness by a family member who is present during periods of emotional tension. The shift in focus to physical symptoms relieves anxiety in the family temporarily by diverting the focus away from the conflict and distancing the members from important family issues. The dysfunction in an individual through physical illness can then be viewed by the health professional as a signal of anxiety in the emotional system of the family. This anxiety operates at a highly contagious level, since the issues which it revolves around are neither in awareness nor confronted directly.

Issues

At least two issues are important in the dynamics of the family antecedent to illness and in response to the additional impact of illness. These issues are disability (or dysfunction) and responsibility. "The factors which determine the degree of disability are numerous, complex, and open to a degree of deception which makes the issue of disability a most crucial one in terms of the manipulative value of an illness" (Alger, 1978). In understanding the issue of disability it is important to ascertain how and if family members are able to ask directly for help and how help-seeking transactions occur in terms of sequence. What part does the extended family play when the nuclear family is in need of help? Is illness the only mechanism available for obtaining help and/or making emotional contact with significant others? The family members' view of illness will give an indication of the operation of responsibility issues. Is illness viewed as something over which a person has no control or as something which one asked for by not taking precautions? The former view results in nonassignment and nonacceptance of responsibility, whereas the latter leads to blame-counterblaming and guilt, since illness is viewed as punishment. Concern over control of self is central to both of these perspectives by family members. According to Alger (1978), "It is also true that sick persons are frequently accused of not wanting to get better and of using their afflictions in the games they play with others. These truths, not withstanding, the ill person usually holds a very powerful card in the dynamics of family manipulations precisely for the reason that he can assume the posture that the illness is happening to him."

An exploration of the previous illness experiences of each member of the nuclear family in their family of origin and then in the nuclear family will give the nurse an idea regarding the function of illness in the family and the transactions and events which precede, surround, and follow it. This endeavor will facilitate identification of the degree of dysfunction and responsiveness to the illness as a symptom of family anxiety. This is probably the most neglected aspect of assessment of physical illness in a variety of settings.

Developmental Experiences

The way in which a person's own developmental experiences with illness influence the assumption of the sick role is discussed by Koupernik, who views opposing wishes of wanting to be sick versus wanting to keep well as aspects of the functioning of each person. A passive-regressive illness which is experienced early in childhood may color an individual's perception of self and the world so that this person is ready to "relapse" when conditions in the outside world are perceived as stressful. Writes Koupernik (1973): "Loss of mothering at a critical period may force the child to mother itself, worry about itself, and cater to its own special needs. Identification with a sick parent or sick sibling and the need to draw attention away from the sick family member may force the child to develop somatic symptoms and thus to become the recipient of loving physical ministrations."

The developmental progress of the nuclear family members from a cared-after to a caring-for-self person will give the nurse an indication of the prognosis for family adjustment and anxiety. When the first experience is accomplished, yet not overdone, the caring-for-self in times of illness is less likely to evoke high levels of anxiety in self and significant others. When it is not accomplished, illness will be accompanied by inordinate amounts of self-concern, and certainly, life-threatening illness will evoke extreme and sustained anxiety in self and others.

COMMUNICATION

Family interactional patterns in both the extended and nuclear families and between these are important aspects in assessing prehospitalization, hospitalization, and posthospitalization family adjustment. While much of the initial data gathering may be from observational skills, the nurse should very quickly move into utilization of verbal skills as a method of both data gathering for self and for the family members as well. If the nurse is able to encourage family members to describe their experiences in the presence of significant others without interruption, an orderly, thoughtful style of communication can take place at a time when usually implicit, confused communications are generated by anxiety. The method of data gathering, then, as an interaction process with the family, becomes an intervention with the potential for lowering anxiety and facilitating rational thinking. In addition, data collection by way of interviews soon after admission opens up the systems by bringing to discussion meaningful information at a time when family members are motivated. The avoidance of family interaction at this time only confirms family anxiety and reinforces that it is dangerous for each person to talk of his or her own thoughts and feelings. Dlin (1977), speaking of his study of coronary patients, relates the usefulness of interviewing during acute stages of illness because "the acutely ill patient was less defensive and more open, and more likely to give meaningful psychological information than he would in a similar interview taking place weeks or months after his heart attack."

FAMILY ADJUSTMENTS

In assessing family adjustment it is important to focus singularly and in totality on various aspects. This portion of the chapter will be devoted to the elucidation of these aspects.

Life Events

Consideration of the life events prior to onset of the illness or during its intensification or exacerbation will assist the nurse to understand the interplay among the various developmental levels of family members, extended and nuclear. Rather than conclude that life events cause illness, the nurse should seek to gather data which might indicate how illness behavior is a means of coping with life stress (Minter, 1977). In addition, awareness of the significance of various life events will cue the nurse to factors which will influence or modify the course of disease (Holmes, 1978).

A glance at the Holmes Social Readjustment Rating Scale will familiarize the nurse with the variety of life changes which may precede illness. However, verbal exchange with the family members is necessary in order to ascertain the relative importance of various changes and events, the emotions associated with the event, and the meaning of the event for each family member (Holmes, 1978). Dlin notes significant troubling events occurring in the life of an individual 2 to 3 years prior to a coronary attack. The event was marked by emotional distress and involved at least one other person with whom there was an emotional involvement. The significant events were related to loss, separation, death, or serious illness. According to Dlin (1977), this individual's "failure to adapt usually resulted in gradually mounting tension, which showed itself in increased smoking, eating, and drinking: irritability, anger, insomnia, indecisiveness, social withdrawal, and increased dependence on spouse; obsessive thinking, preoccupation with body symptoms, inability to concentrate, disturbance in memory, impotence, depression, and fear." A cluster of somatic symptoms were noted a year prior to the coronary episode; these included aches, pains, headaches, gastrointestinal distress, sexual difficulties, fatigue, and insomnia. In the month, weeks, or days prior to the attack, there was an increase in significant events including accidents, losses, or plans for a trip. Fischer (1977) suggests that the identification of a deadline or anniversary reaction as connected with a coronary occlusion in the diagnostic phase is an assessment factor related to a recommendation for psychotherapy. An anniversary reaction is the occurrence of an episode on the anniversary of a significant event in the life of the identified patient; e.g., a patient whose own father died of a heart attack on the patient's fourth birthday has a heart attack when his child is 4 years old. The patient may also set a deadline date in connection with the age of death of significant others.

Emotional Shock Wave

Bowen, in examining these processes from a family perspective, refers to the processes as the "emotional shock wave." The emotional shock wave is a network of symptoms which are reactions to serious life events in a family. The symptoms may occur anywhere in the extended family in the months and years following the emotional event and can include an entire range of physical illness, e.g., increased incidence of respiratory infections, the first appearance of chronic conditions such as diabetes or allergies, and acute medical or surgical illnesses. Emotional symptoms and social dysfunctions may also occur. The emotional shock wave "occurs most often after the death or the threatened death of a significant family member, but it can occur following losses of other types" (Bowen, 1978). Accordingly, knowledge of the presence of the shock wave provides the nurse with important knowledge in treatment. Awareness and knowledge of the shock wave is important in interacting with families in relation to death issues. By knowing of the possibility of a shock wave occurring in the extended family in response to the threatened or actual loss of the critically ill person, the nurse can take steps in prevention by opening up the family system in discussion using direct words. From this perspective, physical illness in a family member may be viewed both as part of the extended family's reaction to an antecedent significant and serious family emotional event and/or as a precipitant of a subsequent emotional shock wave.

Openness of Systems

Bowen (1978) points out that at least three closed systems operate around a terminally ill individual. The same can be said for the critically ill person. These systems are within the patient, in the family, and in the health care providers. Patients may have an extensive amount of private information they do not share with anyone.

The family has information received from the health care providers, which is combined with bits of information from other sources and is then magnified, distorted, and reinterpreted in the family system. Based on these inputs, the family edits its own communication to take place with the ill person and adjusts this to avoid what they interpret as the patients reactiveness to anxiety. As Bowen (1978) points out, "The closed communication system is an automatic emotional reflex to protect self from the anxiety in the other person, though most people say they avoid the taboo subjects to keep from upsetting the other person." Geary describes four coping behaviors of family members in response to the critically ill patient. The first three of these are related to Bowen's ideas regarding a closed system. She describes the most prevalent coping mechanism as minimization, which is characterized by reducing or attempting to ignore the significance of an event. Intellectualization, or the adoption of an overly rational attitude accompanied by de-emphasis or lack of awareness of feelings, is demonstrated by over-concern with technical aspects of care. Acting strong by a family member is a coping behavior that decreases tension in others by taking care of them, yet maintaining the emotional distance among members. The strong one will become increasingly burdened in assuming this role, which decreases his own anxiety, while the rest of the family becomes increasingly dysfunctional and dependent. The family which demonstrates coping behavior by remaining near the patient is probably more exemplary of a well-integrated family, since this family shows "more overt reactiveness at the moment of change but adapt[s] to it rather quickly" (Bowen, 1978). A family's remaining near the patient not only openly acknowledges that they are too upset to function normally, it also indicates the presence of hope. According to Geary (1979), "No matter how serious the prognosis, being near the patient signifies that the family has not given up the patient as a part of their family. Active hoping, demonstrated by remaining near the patient, may be one of the few positive options open to a family during a medical crisis in which they feel frustrated at not being able to do anything to help." The nurse, then, has not only the responsibility to assess the issues and factors contributing to the family's current status but also the responsibility for assessing the impact of the current event. The assessment of these components will give an indication and prediction of overall family functioning.

The third closed system is the health care providers. There is obviously even greater potential for closing the systems of patient and family when the nurse and other health care providers are also functioning as closed systems. A nurse who is very reactive is more likely to respond with the extremes of communicating with medical jargon or oversimplification or overgeneralization. A nurse who becomes anxious is more likely to give too much information at a level which the family cannot understand and is more likely to do too much talking and too little listening. The result will be that the family receives input which it cannot decode and which contributes to further family misperception. The nurse who is unaware of misperceptions will be unable to make an accurate assessment of the family. The best assessment will be accomplished by an unbiased listener who does not aim to correct the family's way of thinking by making tense, emotional speeches. In addition, a data-gathering approach which focuses

on the family has potential for opening up the system by discouraging scapegoating processes in which *all* the family tension and anxiety is focused upon the person manifesting the physical symptoms (Taggert, 1977). An individual approach may be the beginning of a chronic pattern of dysfunctioning (Alger, 1978). A useful tool appropriate for family assessment is the genogram, which depicts the historical development of the family over time and gives the care-giver significant insights into family events, roles, emotional issues, and coping (Fig. 18-1).

Family Roles and Developmental Levels

In assessing family adaptation, it is important to assess the reallocation of roles in the family as the stress of critical illness continues. Awareness of the developmental progress of individual members in addition to their previous illness experiences will assist the nurse in anticipating the nature of stresses. A critical illness occurring in the midst of other changes which may necessitate family restructuring will impose additional stress and anxiety on an already stressed system. An expanding family with the oldest child entering the first year of school will be faced with a possible developmental crisis in at least one member at the same time as a situational crisis in a parent. A contracting family (i.e., one that is growing smaller due to members dying and children leaving) that is planning for retirement within 3 years may have a developmental crisis precipitated by the critical illness of the prospective retiree.

A significant consideration in assessment is the effect of the event of critical illness upon the children in the family. This will vary according to the developmental level of the child, the amount of disruption of daily routine, and the availability of a familiar support system. All too often, children are cut off from direct communication with parents at this time of high emotionality. Distortion and misperceptions which operate in times of high anxiety are likely to be absorbed by children. The nurse, then, has the important role of opening up the system by assessing the children's response through questions in parental interviews. Bowen (1978) states that children are not hurt by exposure to death. So, then, children are also not hurt by exposure to critical illness in parents or by exposure to critical-care settings. In fact, it is the anxiety generated by the closed system which is likely to impede the progress of growth and devel-

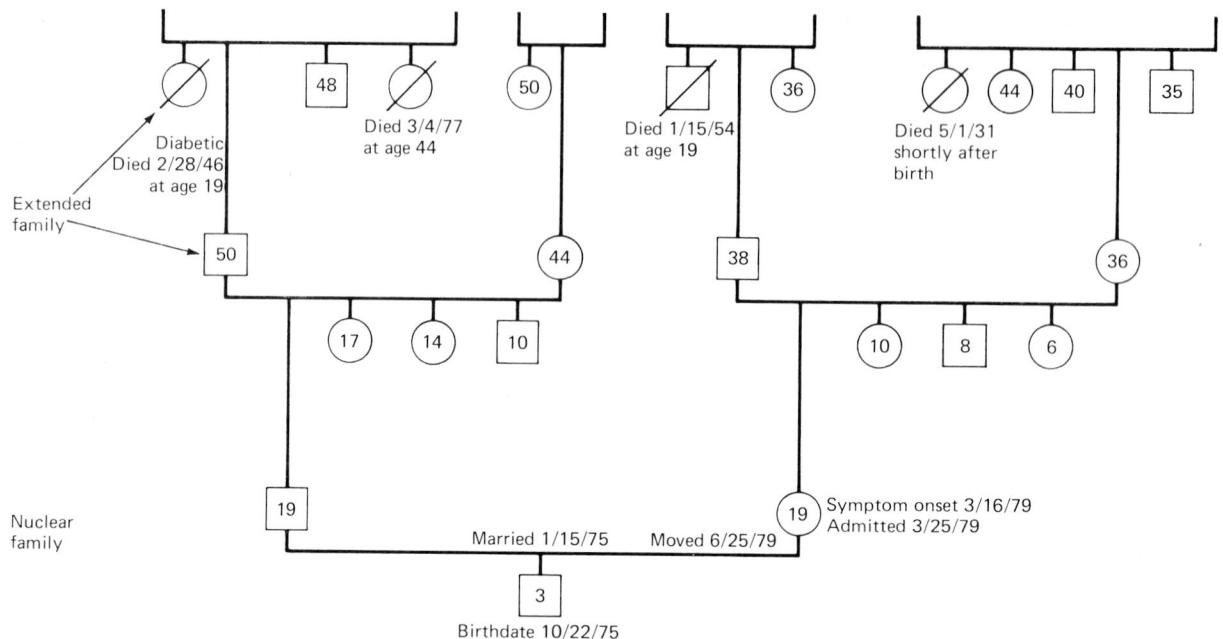

FIGURE 18-1

A genogram is a useful tool for family assessment. The circles represent females, and the squares represent males. Numbers within the symbols represent the current age of that individual. A slash through a symbol represents the death of an individual; the date of death, age at death, and significant contributing factors are listed below an indication of death. Siblings are listed in descending order of age from the eldest at the left. Chronological notes should be made on significant events, including specific dates.

opment. An accurate assessment of developmental levels of family members will facilitate the nurse's objectivity in imparting information to the family. In particular, family members can be helped to understand the reactions that occur.

> Two sets of crisis regarding death may often occur during childhood in sensitive children living in a family in which free emotional expression is accepted and even encouraged. The first crisis, based on separation anxiety and fear of abandonment, occurs between four and six years of age, and the second crisis, an existential crisis at an age between nine and eleven years, is brought about by the realization of the irreversibility of death, in relation to both self and loved ones. (Anthony, 1973)

Awareness of developmental levels will also alert the nurse to the stresses of social loss in the family. These losses include financial loss and temporary or permanent dismemberment. "A family that depends on the sick member instead of having a system of mutual interdependence will have difficulty restructuring and adjusting to new responsibilities" (Roberts, 1976).

Family Coping

The style and content of coping by individual family members yields important assessment data on emotional well-being. Generally speaking, the greater the scope and variety of the coping repertoire, the greater protection will be afforded. However, the same coping mechanisms are not equally effective in different areas of role functioning. To assess coping the nurse will need to consider the coping repertoire in each of the roles assumed by the individual. According to Pearlin and Schooler (1978):

> With relatively impersonal strains, such as those stemming from economic or occupational experience, the most effective forms of coping involve the manipulation of goals and values in a way which psychologically increases the distance of the individual from the problem. On the other hand, problems arising from the relatively close interpersonal relations of parental and marital roles are best handled by coping mechanisms in which the individual remains committed to and engaged with the relevant others.

The behavior and coping of the critically ill person

is likely to be influenced by a variety of family-related characteristics. The literature suggests that male off-springs with better educated mothers and higher socioeconomic status fathers are more likely to reject the sick role (Campbell, 1978). Although the study related to children in the sick role, interpretation of the study results have important parallels in adulthood. The stoical attitude toward illness progressed with age in both sexes but was more pronounced for males. This attitude is demonstrated by an inclination to act well on first feeling sick, to continue in activities, and to demonstrate reluctance to see a doctor and the desire to resume play right away when on the road to recovery. Assessment of parental education and socioeconomic status, then, gives clues to the development of a stoical attitude in the patient and family which are important in both illness onset and resolution. The ability to accept a dependent role in illness is clearly influenced by socioeconomic status. A study by Arluke, Kennedy, and Kessler (1979) indicates that while it is generally accepted that persons who are ill are not responsible for either onset or continuation of illness, members of the lower class are more likely to accept these views. Rosenblatt and Suchman (1964) also found that lower class individuals/families are more likely to become dependent in response to illness.

The ability to become dependent is also related to the nature and extent of group support in occupying a dependent role. People who live alone expect that a sick person has a duty to get well and move out of the sick role. The need to resume well roles is greatest when the immediate family network is absent (Arluke et al., 1979). While individuals living alone may agree to their right to be relieved of normal role responsibilities, their limited physical and emotional resources may interfere with the assumption of a dependent role. In contrast, a household comprising more members especially when several members are adolescent age and older, facilitates the sick person's being relieved of normal role responsibilities.

The age of the critically ill person has an important bearing on expectations of the individual and others regarding the sick role. Older people are less inclined to view the sick role as a temporary state which one has some responsibility for ending. Increasing age seems to be related to the idea that one has a duty to seek professional help, suggesting that aged individuals are more likely to seek help but less likely to relinquish a dependent role (Arluke et al., 1979). This may be a reflection of a societal attitude which equates aging with illness. "Furthermore," states Ar-luke, "the sick role may itself provide a sense of legitimacy to an otherwise dependent state for some elderly, thus making them unwilling to give it up."

A CASE STUDY

Jane, a 19-year-old mother of a young son, was admitted to County Hospital with a diagnosis of acute hemorrhagic pancreatitis. Despite intensive medical and surgical treatment, Jane's condition progressively deteriorated. Six weeks after admission, she experienced a respiratory and cardiac arrest. She became comatose and responded only with decerebrate posturing. A neurological examination revealed a very poor prognosis.

Jane's illness occurred only 9 months after she and her husband, Ed, had moved from a small town in West Virginia to Maryland. The couple had married when they were both 16 years old. They had spent the early part of their marriage living 80 miles from both their families. The contact with their families had been quite limited since their marriage. Both families had been dubious about the marriage. In the early phase of hospitalization Jane said she had married to escape conflict in her own family. She had felt increasing responsibility to care for her siblings, and she felt inadequate and angry in handling this burden. Ed felt the need to care for someone to prove his own worth to his own family.

Ed decided to move to Maryland to work with a close friend. This job was to provide an increase in money and security. When this job did not materialize, Ed found a job with a trucking firm. Jane worked part-time in a supermarket and cared for the couple's 3-year-old son, Eric.

An interactional assessment of this family was constructed according to the following guidelines:

    I. Observation and investigation of:

        A. The interaction of the nuclear and extended families

        B. The system interaction of the staff, families, and patient

    II. Collection of family genogram, including answers to the following questions:

        A. Is there a past history of illness, crisis, and death in this family?

        B. How has this family responded to illness, crisis, and death in the past?

        C. What coping mechanisms has the family utilized to deal with stress in the past?

D. How does illness, crisis, and death affect the family interactional patterns?

III. Assessment and validation of the meaning and response of the current illness to the family.

A. Do they indicate need and motivation to alter their coping and communication techniques?

B. How are their needs being communicated?

IV. Plan and rationale for expected outcomes.

Observation and Investigation

The nursing staff observed that Jane and Ed seemed quite tense when they were together. Ed frequently would summon the nurses to the room and ask many technical questions. Jane responded by increasing her requests of the staff when her husband was visiting. Ed became quite critical of the staff and consistently repeated, "How can someone so young be dying? Somebody must have done something wrong."

Upon investigation it was learned that the nuclear family of Jane, Ed, and Eric was undergoing stress prior to the illness. One week before moving to Maryland (9 months prior to hospitalization), Jane experienced epigastric pain, nausea, and vomiting. The couple discounted these symptoms, attributing them to "nerves." Upon their arrival in Maryland, Ed learned that he could not work with his friend as previously planned. Jane and Ed began having increasing marital difficulties focused on issues of responsibility for child care and finances. They were thinking of returning to West Virginia when Jane's current illness occurred. Both were ambivalent about returning home. An emotional cutoff from their extended families had severely diminished their sense of security and esteem and had impaired their sense of objective problem solving. Jane's response to anxiety had been to assume a somewhat dysfunctional role (being taken care of), and Ed's response was to assume an overfunctional role (taking care of). The basis of their marriage had been an escape from responsibility (Jane) and assuming undue responsibility to prove authority and manliness (Ed).

When Jane was hospitalized, the extended families quickly traveled to Maryland. Jane remained critically ill during the course of the family visits, but she was alert and responsive to their presence. As the course of the illness lengthened, the families returned to West Virginia and maintained frequent contact. The exception was Jane's mother, who refused to leave her daughter's side. Eric, the 3-year-old son, returned to West Virginia with Ed's parents. The child began to "play that he was sick" so he could go to the doctor where his mother was. He had not seen his mother since her hospitalization.

Initially, Ed and Jane's mother, Mrs. T., were mutually supportive. Gradually a power struggle ensued, with each one desiring control over obtaining information from physicians and making decisions regarding Jane's care. At times they blamed each other for Jane's illness, and other times they blamed the staff.

The staff had worked hard to save Jane's life. As their efforts failed, they became increasingly emotionally reactive to the situation. Feelings of guilt were quickly engendered in response to Ed's assault of "someone must have done something wrong." They began to question their competence and they responded by withholding information from the family. The staff had become fond of Jane and they were also experiencing a sense of loss. The staff assessed the situation and requested the assistance of a counselor.

Genogram

Obtaining a genogram can be anxiety-provoking if there are many unresolved family issues. However, in this case it served an important function for the family. The counselor found that the threat of loss seemed to encourage the family to look into their past and also to focus on "all we still have." It also served to facilitate the grieving process as the family began to use the words "death" and "funeral" openly. They wept and expressed guilt and frustration. Ed blamed himself for discounting Jane's early symptoms, and her parents felt they had failed her in her early development. The family consistently maintained hope, but they began to discuss what they might do if Jane died.

The genogram revealed that both Jane and Ed were the oldest of brothers and sisters. They maintained important family functions as the oldest child—dominance, control, and responsibility. Some of their marital difficulties seemed to stem from an inability to resolve these issues. It was also learned that there had been an emotional shock wave which affected both families since the death of Jane's aunt 2 years ago. This aunt was loved by both families, and she had served as a cohesive force. She became even more important when Jane and Ed married. She communicated important information and helped prevent a total emotional cutoff between the families after the marriage.

The family reported that the funeral for the aunt was "strained." No one talked much about her death. The families felt "forced" at the funeral since they still harbored resentment regarding Jane and Ed's earlier marriage. The families had had very limited physical contact, communicating mainly through this aunt. The 2 years following the aunt's death were difficult ones. The children in both families experienced a marked increase in illness—respiratory and flu symptoms, broken bones, and numerous accidents. During this time, the family felt they were losing control and everything was against them. They were extremely religious and sensed that they were being punished for something they had done wrong. They responded by attempting to place blame.

An evaluation of the genogram revealed that Jane's family had a questionable history of metabolic diseases including diabetes mellitus. The family was greatly lacking in health education. Both families had a history of deaths of oldest siblings at a young age. Their characteristic way of dealing with life events was to mutually support one another superficially, avoiding discussion of any conflict. They felt discussion of death, crisis, and illness would make things worse. They viewed these life events as punishment for sins. The women in the family would assume a vigil at the bedside as a demonstration of persistent faith and hope. To abandon this responsibility was an indication of "giving up."

Assessment and Validation

The family stated that Jane's current illness had "brought them all together after a long absence." They had all been contemplating contacting one another, but they were hesitant. They validated a pattern of indirect communication techniques. The families had rarely asked directly for support and caring, and illness served as a means to obtain these needs. It was important that the family members be "strong" and "independent." They perceived that they had very little control over illness and avoided talking about it except to place blame. Both families evidenced some degree of marital conflict, dysfunctional-over-functional patterns, and projective process. Jane's mother expressed fear that if she left the bedside and her daughter died, it would be her fault. She also hesitated to return home because of conflict with her husband.

At the time of Jane's illness, the anxiety in the family was high. This seemed to be one motivating

factor for them to begin to investigate familial patterns. Another motivating force was the medical and nursing staff. They openly communicated their observations to the family, e.g., that the family seemed to be indicating a need for additional support in handling this crisis. The family agreed and the staff obtained a counselor for the family. In collecting data for the genogram, the counselor learned that the medical and nursing staff had already obtained much of this information through observation and conversation with the family. The counselor then assumed a role of working with the family directly as well as assisting the medical and nursing staff to coordinate their care. In many cases, the counselor (psychiatric nurse specialist, psychiatrist, etc.) will need only to offer suggestions and support to the staff who can be quite effective in managing family problems.

Other indicators of the families' interest in altering coping mechanisms included (1) an open questioning of "what is happening to us," (2) active involvement of staff in an attempt to reduce their own anxiety (blaming, anger), (3) physical presence at the hospital and counseling sessions, and (4) agreement that they needed extra support.

Plan and Rationale for Expected Outcome

The following plan was implemented:

1. Decrease the staff's emotional reactivity to the situation by encouraging them to express their own thoughts and feelings about death, illness, crisis, and loss. Suggest staff identify and investigate their own family issues with use of genogram. This will serve to decrease the anxiety in the hospital system and allow the staff to give objective counsel to the family. If the staff can realistically deal with their own anger, guilt, and anxiety, they can avoid the pitfall of withholding information from the family. This withholding serves to reinforce the family's technique of blaming and increases the family's concern that a mistake is being hidden.

2. Assist the family to begin to deal with their own issues. Once the anxiety in the staff is decreased, the family will initially experience a rise in tension as they are confronted with some of their own issues. This can be handled by offering support and caring to the family, emphasizing the positive elements at work in the family system.

3. Once the anxiety in the family is somewhat diminished, obtain a genogram and help them begin to investigate interactional patterns. Offer them alternatives to handling crisis, always allowing for choice.

4. Provide health education for the family to assist

them to decrease their sense of powerlessness over illness.

5. When possible, role model for the family by communicating directly and point out the consequences of such techniques. Allow the son, Eric, to visit his mother in the hospital, and help the family to deal with the son's response. Educate the family to the factors which served to decrease the son's anxiety by being able to see his mother and ask questions about her condition.

Summary

In summary, the utilization of a family perspective in assessment in critical-care settings fosters a comprehensive, relevant, and practical intervention. The family perspective leads to the identification of a variety of interactive factors and patterns that influences the family's adaptation and movement toward health. The authors have explored important areas of family assessment in illness situations with particular attention to critical illness. Psychosocial assessment of the family should include the following vital aspects: psychosociodynamics of the sick role, communication patterns, life events, emotional shock waves, family roles and developmental levels, and family coping. An understanding of family interaction in these areas through the utilization of communication skills which decrease emotionality in various systems provides the care-giver(s) with a dynamic and comprehensive framework for intervention.

REFERENCES

Alger, I.: Family therapeutic approaches of the medically ill patient, in Toksoz B. Korosu and Robert I. Steinmuller (eds.), *Psychotherapeutics in Medicine,* New York: Grune & Stratton, 1978, p. 205.

Anthony, E. J.: A working model for family studies, in E. James Anthony and Cyrille Koupernik (eds.), *The Child in His Family,* New York: Wiley, 1973, pp. 3–11.

Arluke, A., L. Kennedy, and R. Kessler: Reexamining the sick-role concept: An empirical assessment, *J Health Hum Behav* 20:30–36, 1979.

Bowen, M.: *Family Therapy in Clinical Practice,* New York: Jason Aronson, 1978, p. 536.

Campbell, J. D.: The child in the sick role: Contributions of age, sex, parental status, and parental values, *J Health Soc Behav* 19:35–51, 1978.

Dlin, B. M.: Risk factors, life style, and the emotions in coronary disease, *Psychosomatics* 18: 28–31, 1977.

Fischer, H. K.: Management of emotional factors in coronary disease, *Psychosomatics* 18: 10–13, 1977.

Geary, M. C.: Supporting family coping, *Supervisor Nurse* 52:52–59, 1979.

Holmes, T. H.: Life situations, emotions, and disease, *Psychosomatics* 19:747–754, 1978.

Jenkins, C. D., S. J. Zyzanski, and R. Roseman: Coronary-prone behavior: One pattern or several? *Psychosom Med* 40:25–43, 1978.

Koupernik, C.: The roots of hypochondriasis, in E. James Anthony and Cyrille Koupernik (eds.), *The Child in His Family,* vol. II, New York: Wiley, 1973, p. 87.

Linn, L.: Basic principles of management in psychosomatic medicine, in Eric Wittkower and Hector Warner (eds.), *Psychosomatic Medicine: Its Clinical Applications,* New York: Harper & Row, 1977, p. 3.

Minter, R. E., and C. P. Kimball: Life events and illness onset: A review, *Psychosomatics* 18: 334–339, 1977.

Pearlin, L. I., and C. Schooler: The structure of coping, *J Health Soc Behav* 19:2–21, 1978.

Roberts, S. L.: *Behavioral Concepts and the Critically Ill Patient,* Englewood Cliffs, N.J.: Prentice-Hall, 1976, p. 363.

Rosenblatt, D., and E. A. Suchman: Blue collar attitudes and information toward health and illness, in A. B. Shostak and W. Gomberg (eds.), *Blue Collar World,* Englewood Cliffs, N.J.: Prentice-Hall, 1964, pp. 324–332.

Taggert, M.: Medical aspects of marital conflict, in Robert F. Stahmann and William J. Hiebert (eds.), *Klemer's Counseling in Marital and Sexual Problems: A Clinicians Handbook,* 2d ed., Baltimore: Williams & Wilkins, 1977, p. 164.

Weakland, J. H.: "Family somatics": A neglected edge, *Family Process* 16:263–272, 1977.

PART 5

THE DYNAMIC INTERRELATIONSHIP OF SYSTEMS:

PRIORITIES IN PROBLEM SOLVING

INTRODUCTION

The life of every individual depends on the maintenance of a stable internal environment. That internal environment is composed of water, electrolytes, and metabolic end products. In a normal, healthy individual, the internal environment is regulated and maintained by a variety of physiologic functions. However, when an individual suffers a critical illness due to acute or chronic pathology, the normal homeostatic mechanisms of the body are often not sufficient to maintain a stable internal environment. As a result, alterations in the internal environment occur and directly affect the individual's physiologic functioning, physical appearance, and behavior. Indeed, these alterations may be severe enough to precipitate the individual's demise. Therefore, it is essential that the individual receive support from the health care team during this period of instability.

While it is true that all health care team members play an important supportive role in the care of the individual during this time, a majority of the responsibility resides with the nurse because of proximity and the amount of time spent with the individual. Because the nurse has the most frequent, consistent, and extensive contact with the individual, he or she can easily detect changes in patterns of function or behavior. The nurse's responsibilities in relation to alterations in the individual's internal environment include (1) monitoring, (2) interpreting, (3) reporting-recording, (4) intervening, and (5) evaluating. Figure 20-1 illustrates this relationship.

As depicted in Fig. 20-1, the nurse's responsibilities are implemented in response to the external manifestations exhibited by the individual because of the alterations in the internal environment. The nurse works in a systematic manner that begins with monitoring. This includes observing the patient as well as assessing all laboratory and technological data. Monitoring is followed by interpreting, which involves using one's knowledge of the individual's history, physiology, and pathophysiology to determine if the information gained from monitoring is normal or abnormal for the individual and to what degree. Then the information is reported and recorded.

In order to provide quality care, periodic assessments of the individual must be documented as well as conveyed to the physician. The next responsibility of the nurse is intervening. Intervening is the essence of health care, whether it is based on nursing orders or on orders from physician colleagues. Intervening means *action,* and it is action that makes the impact

20

REGULATION AND ASSESSMENT OF WATER AND ELECTROLYTE BALANCE

Charold Lee Baer

INTRODUCTION

AMOUNT AND DISTRIBUTION OF BODY FLUIDS
Total Body Water   Amounts and Distribution

ELECTROLYTE COMPOSITION OF BODY FLUIDS

OSMOLALITY, OSMOLARITY, AND TONICITY
Definitions   Regulation   Calculating Osmolality Values

FLUID AND ELECTROLYTE TRANSPORT
Osmosis   Diffusion   Active Transport
Filtration   Pinocytosis and Phagocytosis

FLUID AND ELECTROLYTE REQUIREMENTS
Average Daily Fluid Intake and Output
Composition of Specific Body Fluids
Alterations in Fluid and Electrolyte Requirements

WATER
Functions   Regulation   Hypervolemia   Edema   Hypovolemia

SODIUM
Functions   Regulation   Hypernatremia   Hyponatremia

POTASSIUM
Functions   Regulation   Hyperkalemia   Hypokalemia

CALCIUM
Functions   Regulation   Hypercalcemia   Hypocalcemia

MAGNESIUM
Functions   Regulation   Hypermagnesemia   Hypomagnesemia

CHLORIDE
Functions   Regulation   Hyperchloremia   Hypochloremia

PHOSPHATE
Functions   Regulation   Hyperphosphatemia   Hypophosphatemia

SULFATE
Functions   Regulation   Variances

PROTEIN
Functions   Regulation   Hypoproteinemia

ORGANIC ACIDS

ACID-BASE
Functions   Regulation   Metabolic Acidosis   Metabolic
Alkalosis   Respiratory Acidosis   Respiratory Alkalosis

SUMMARY

REFERENCES

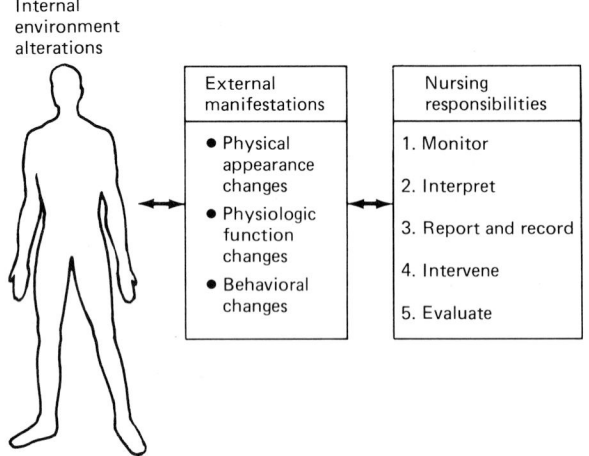

Internal environment alterations

FIGURE 20-1
Nursing responsibilities related to alterations in an individual's internal environment.

on the individual's health state. A nurse could monitor, interpret, report, and record forever, but unless there is action taken based on those functions, the individual's condition may still deteriorate. All action, however, must be based on sufficient data because to intervene inappropriately would also threaten the individual's stability.

The final responsibility of the nurse is to evaluate the results of the intervention based on the desired patient outcomes, or in other words, to find out if the actions taken changed the individual's health state. These five responsibilities or functions, performed at periodic intervals as determined by the health state of the individual, provide the framework for delivering nursing care.

The implementation of these nursing responsibilities makes a significant impact on the care of the individual with an altered internal environment. To perform these responsibilities, the nurse must have a basic comprehension of the components of the internal environment. This discussion is designed to provide information prerequisite to that understanding.

AMOUNT AND DISTRIBUTION OF BODY FLUIDS

Total Body Water

The total body water of an individual is approximately 60 percent of the total body weight in kilograms. This percentage varies according to the muscle mass, amount of body fat, and age of the individual. Since

muscles contain a high proportion of water, an individual with a large muscle mass would have a higher percentage of total body water than someone with less muscle mass. Fat contains less water than lean tissues, so individuals with more body fat tend to have a lower percentage of total body water. These two facts explain why females have lower percentages of total body water than males. Age also affects the percent of total body water. As an individual ages, the percent of total body water decreases. Therefore, a lean, young adult male would theoretically have the highest percentage of total body water, while an obese, elderly female would have the lowest.

Amounts and Distribution

The total body water of an individual is distributed into several different compartments. The two primary compartments are the intracellular and extracellular fluid spaces. The intracellular fluid space includes all the water contained within the cells, including the red blood cells, which are also designated as part of the intravascular fluid. The extracellular fluid space includes the water contained in several smaller fluid compartments. Among these compartments are the interstitial, plasma, transcellular, bone, and connective tissue spaces. Of these fluid spaces, the interstitial and plasma spaces contain functional extracellular fluid, while the transcellular (pleural, peritoneal, joint, and cerebrospinal fluid spaces), bone, and connective tissues spaces contain nonfunctional extracellular fluid. Each of these fluid compartments or spaces contains a percentage of the individual's total body water. Figure 20-2 illustrates the distribution of the total body water throughout the compartments by percent of body weight for a normal healthy adult male. It also indicates that there is an additional fluid compartment, the intravascular space, that contains both extracellular and intracellular fluid. The percentages of body water shown in Fig. 20-2 are translated into liter volumes for a normal, healthy 70-kg male and 60-kg female in Table 20-1.

ELECTROLYTE COMPOSITION OF BODY FLUIDS

The internal environment of an individual does not consist merely of water; it also has numerous electrolytes. These electrolytes are essential to a variety of physiologic functions. The specific physiologic functions that each electrolyte participates in will be enumerated later in this chapter. The electrolytes

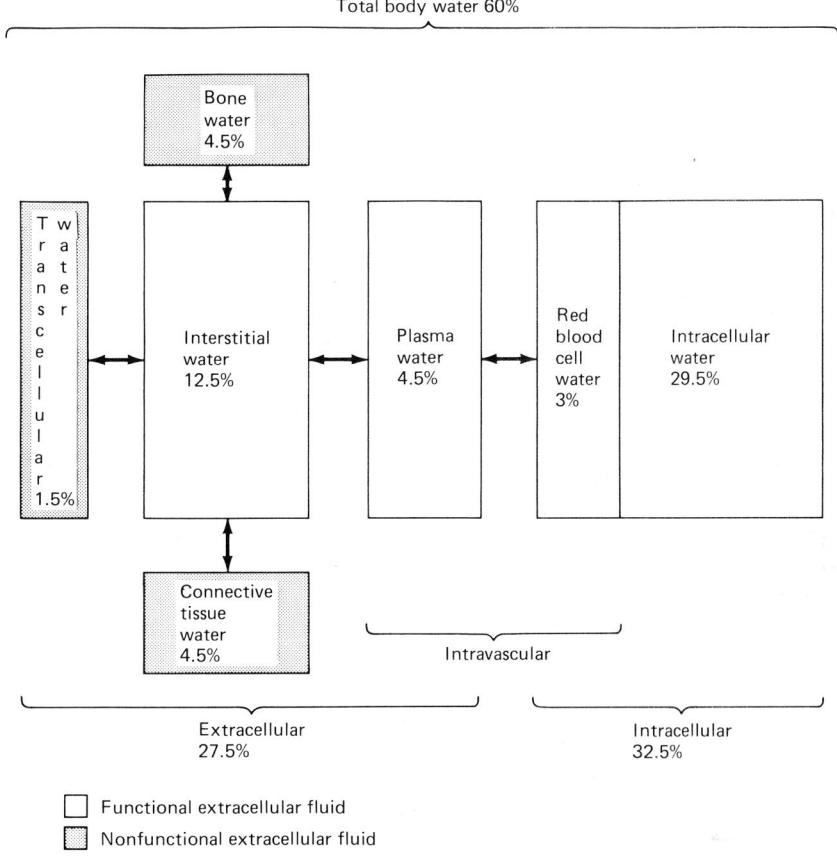

Total body water 60%

Bone water 4.5%

Transcellular water 1.5%

Interstitial water 12.5%

Plasma water 4.5%

Red blood cell water 3%

Intracellular water 29.5%

Connective tissue water 4.5%

Intravascular

Extracellular 27.5%

Intracellular 32.5%

☐ Functional extracellular fluid
▨ Nonfunctional extracellular fluid

FIGURE 20-2

The distribution of total body water by compartment according to the percent of body weight for a normal healthy adult male.

occur in different amounts in the major fluid compartments of the body. Table 20-2 presents the approximate amounts of electrolytes in the various major fluid compartments.

OSMOLALITY, OSMOLARITY, AND TONICITY

The distribution of body fluids in the various compartments depends primarily on the osmotic pressure that exists in those spaces. This osmotic pressure is referred to as the osmolality, osmolarity, or tonicity of the fluid in the space.

Definitions

Osmolality is the concentration of solute, expressed in terms of the number of particles per liter of *solvent.*

Osmolarity is the concentration of solute, expressed in terms of the number of particles per liter of *solution.* *Tonicity* describes the comparison of the osmolality or osmolarity of one solution to another. If solution A had a higher osmolality than solution B, solution A would be described as being hypertonic to solution B. Solution B, on the other hand, would be hypotonic to solution A, because solution B had a lower osmolality. If both solutions were of equal osmolality, they would be described as being isotonic to each other. Such is the case with the body fluids of the normal individual.

Osmolality and osmolarity concentration measurements are so similar in dilute solutions such as the body fluids, that they are often used interchangeably. However, the two measurements are not obtained by the same method, and the laboratory should specify which measurement is being reported. In most cases,

TABLE 20-1
Distribution of Total Body Water
per Compartment in Percent of Body Weight
and Liter Volume for a Normal, Healthy Adult
Male and Female

Compartment	70-kg male		60-kg female	
	% body weight	Volume, L	% body weight	Volume, L
Intracellular	32.5	23	27.5	17
Red blood cells	3	2	3	2
Other cells	29.5	21	24.5	15
Extracellular	27.5	19	27.5	17
Interstitial	12.5	9	12.5	7
Plasma	4.5	3	4.5	3
Transcellular	1.5	1	1.5	1
Bone	4.5	3	4.5	3
Connective tissue	4.5	3	4.5	3
Intravascular*	7.5	5	7.5	5
Red blood cells	3	2	3	2
Plasma	4.5	3	4.5	3

* Combination of intracellular and extracellular fluid.

the laboratories use a freezing-point method of determining concentration that measures osmolality. Hence the term *osmolality* tends to be used more frequently when discussing the concentration of body fluids.

TABLE 20-2
Approximate Electrolyte Composition
of the Major Fluid Compartments of the
Body in Millequivalents per Liter

Ions	Plasma	Interstitial Fluid	Intra-cellular Fluid
Cations			
Na	142	145	10
K	4.5	4	135
Ca	5	3	10
Mg	2.5	2	25
Totals	154	154	180
Anions			
Cl	104	115	5
HCO_3	24	27	10
HPO_4	2	2	100
SO_4	1	1	5
Organic acid	6	7	10
Protein	17	2	50
Totals	154	154	180

Osmolality and osmolarity are both measured in milliosmoles. A milliosmole is $\frac{1}{1000}$ of an osmole. An osmole, the unit for measuring osmotic pressure, is equal to the number of particles in 1 g molecular weight of a dissolved nondiffusible, nonionizable substance. The normal osmolality of extracellular and intracellular body fluids is approximately 275 to 295 mosmol/L.

Regulation

The osmolality of the body fluids is regulated by the osmoreceptor–antidiuretic hormone system and thirst. The osmoreceptor–antidiuretic hormone system involves the functions of the hypothalamus, neurohypophysis, antidiuretic hormone, and renal tubules, while thirst is primarily associated with the hypothalamus.

The Osmoreceptor–Antidiuretic Hormone System

The osmoreceptor–antidiuretic hormone system responds to alterations in the osmolality of the body fluids of as little as 1 to 2 percent. The response begins with the osmoreceptors that regulate the release of antidiuretic hormone. The osmoreceptors are specialized neurons located in or near the supraoptic nuclei of the anterior hypothalamus. These neurons contain fluid chambers filled with intracellular fluid that continuously emit nerve impulses. The fluid chambers respond specifically to changes in the extracellular fluid concentration, with sodium being the most effective stimulant. When the osmolality of the extracellular fluid decreases, making it hypotonic to the fluid in the chambers, water enters the fluid chambers in an attempt to establish equilibrium between the two fluids. The influx of water forces the fluid chambers to swell, which results in a decreased rate of impulse discharge. This means that fewer impulses are transmitted from the osmoreceptors in the supraoptic nuclei through the pituitary stalk to the neurohypophysis to promote the release of antidiuretic hormone. Thus, as illustrated in Fig. 20-3, less antidiuretic hormone is secreted.

When the extracellular fluid osmolality increases, the reverse of the process occurs. The increase in osmolality creates extracellular fluid that is hypertonic to the fluid in the chambers. Water then leaves the fluid chambers and flows into the extracellular fluid, shifting the system toward equilibrium. This outflow of water results in a shrinking of the fluid chambers and an increase in the rate of impulse discharge to the neurohypophysis. The net effect, as shown in Fig. 20-4, is an increased secretion of antidiuretic hormone.

Antidiuretic hormone is synthesized in the supraoptic and paraventricular nuclei of the hypothalamus and stored as granules in the posterior pituitary. It is secreted into the blood according to the rate of impulses transmitted from the osmoreceptors to the

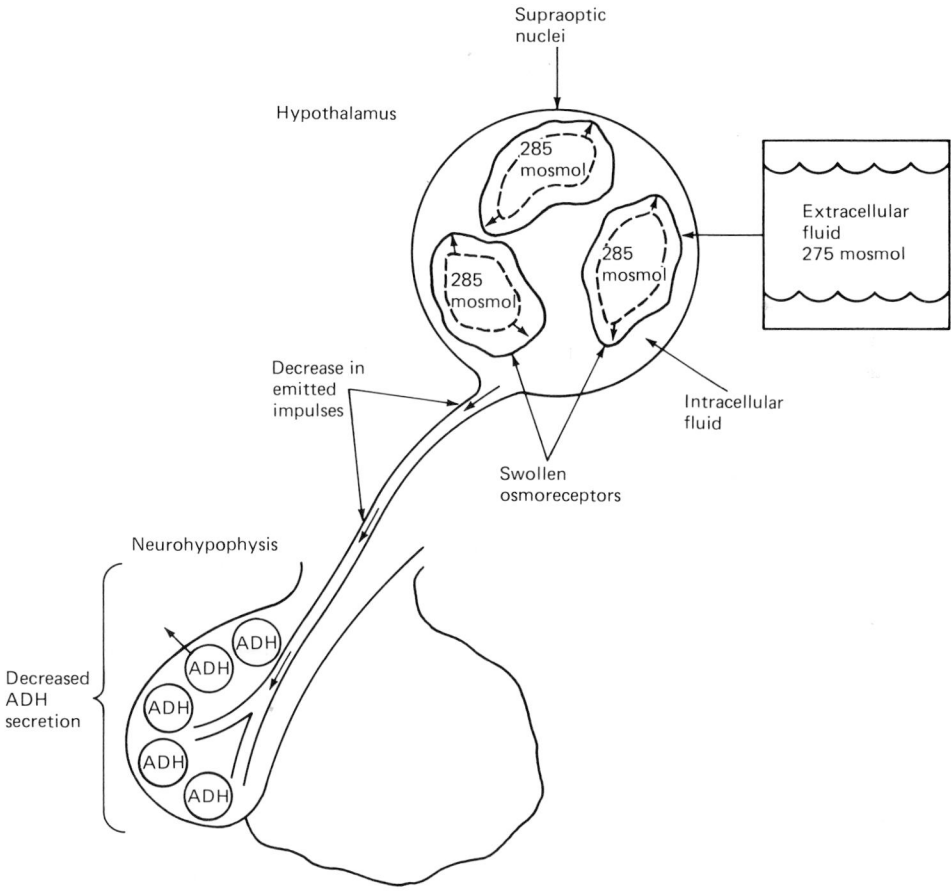

FIGURE 20-3
The osmoreceptor–antidiuretic hormone system response to decreased extracellular fluid osmolality.

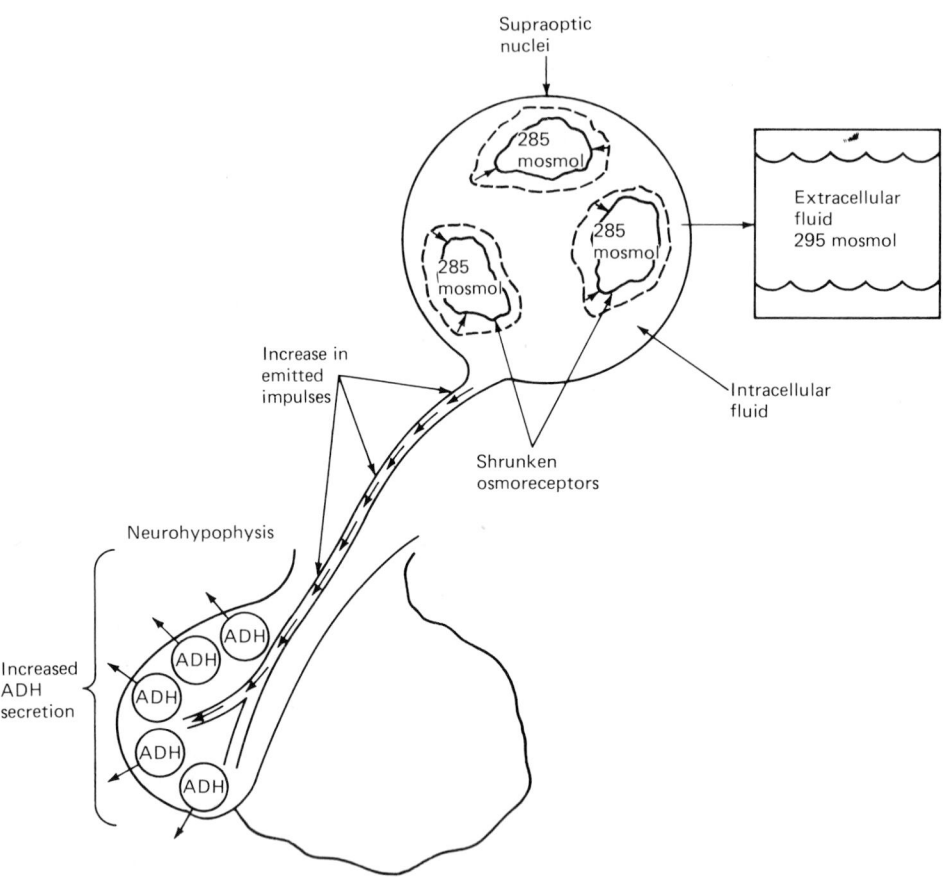

FIGURE 20-4

The osmoreceptor–antidiuretic hormone system response to increased extracellular fluid osmolality.

neurohypophysis. Once it is in the blood, it circulates to the kidneys and acts on the distal tubules and collecting ducts to increase water reabsorption. Thus, the more antidiuretic hormone secreted, the more water reabsorbed.

In summary, the osmoreceptor–antidiuretic hormone system responds to a decrease in extracellular fluid osmolality by decreasing the secretion of antidiuretic hormone, resulting in less water reabsorption, more water excretion, and a return of the osmolality to normal. Conversely, the system reacts to an increase in extracellular fluid osmolality by increasing the secretion of antidiuretic hormone, resulting in

more water reabsorption, less water excretion, and a return of the osmolality to normal.

Thirst

Thirst is also an important mechanism in regulating the osmolality of body fluids, because it is the primary regulator of water intake. There is a thirst center located in the hypothalamus that slightly overlaps the osmoreceptor area. Thirst is stimulated by the effect of intracellular dehydration on the neurons in the thirst center. It is inhibited by the act of drinking and the fullness of the gastrointestinal tract. These two states excite peripheral sensory receptors that transmit impulses to the thirst center to decrease the thirst. Thus, the thirst mechanism is actually inhibited *before* the intracellular dehydration is alleviated. This is a protective feedback mechanism to prevent voluntary water intoxication.

Calculating Osmolality Values

The most accurate method for determining osmolality is to measure it directly. Plasma osmolality can be quickly and accurately measured by determining its freezing point, since the freezing point of a solution decreases in direct proportion to its osmolality. If the plasma osmolality has not been measured, however, it can still be calculated or estimated using other serum laboratory values. It has been found that in normal plasma, the osmotic coefficients and other solute concentrations cancel each other in such a manner that the sodium concentration multiplied by two equals the plasma osmolality. The plasma osmolality, however, is also significantly influenced by glucose and urea, so they must be included in the calculation. In order to include glucose and urea in a formula for determining plasma osmolality, their values must be converted to milliosmoles. A simplified formula for including sodium, glucose, and urea in the calculation of plasma osmolality is:

$$2\,Na\,(meq/L) + \frac{glucose\,(mg\,per\,100\,mL)}{18}$$
$$+ \frac{BUN\,(mg\,per\,100\,mL)}{3}$$
$$= serum\,osmolality\,(mosmol/L)$$

The formula would be applied in the following manner:

Individual's serum lab values:
Na = 140 meq/L
Glucose = 90 mg per 100 mL
BUN = 18 mg per 100 mL

$$2(140) + \frac{90}{18} + \frac{18}{3} = serum\,osmolality\,(mosmol/L)$$
$$280 + 5 + 6 = 291\,mosmol/L$$

This calculated value would provide a close approximation of the actual serum osmolality.

FLUID AND ELECTROLYTE TRANSPORT

The processes involved in the transport of fluids and electrolytes include osmosis, diffusion, active transport, filtration, pinocytosis, and phagocytosis. Each

of these processes affects the movement of fluids and electrolytes in a specific way.

Osmosis

Osmosis is a process that results from the kinetic motion of molecules in solution on either side of a semipermeable membrane. The motion of the molecules is such that water will pass through the membrane to the side that has the greater concentration of nondiffusible substances. This process results in a movement toward establishing equilibrium between the concentration of the solutions on either side of the membrane.

Osmosis can be negated by applying a pressure gradient across the semipermeable membrane in a direction opposite to that of the water flow. The amount of pressure that is required to negate osmosis is called the *osmotic pressure* of the solution.

Diffusion

Diffusion is the net movement of a given substance from one point to another due to the random kinetic motions of its molecules. Molecules diffuse from areas of higher concentration to areas of lower concentration. The net effect of this continuous kinetic movement is the establishment of an equal concentration of the substance throughout the medium, be it liquid, solid, or gas.

The rate at which diffusion occurs is determined by (1) the concentration gradient, (2) the cross-sectional area of the container or chamber, (3) the temperature of the solution, (4) the molecular weight of the molecules, and (5) the distance the molecules have to travel. The greater the concentration gradient, cross-sectional area, and temperature, the greater the diffusion rate. The greater the molecular weight and distance, the less the diffusion rate.

Active Transport

The process of moving a substance against a concentration, electrical, or pressure gradient is called *active transport*. In active transport, energy must be expended to move the substance against the gradient across the cell membrane. The energy that is expended probably comes from adenosine triphosphate that is available in large quantities just inside the cell membrane.

Filtration

Filtration is the process of moving water and dissolved substances through a permeable membrane from an area of higher pressure to an area of lower pressure. Filtration occurs because of the hydrostatic pressure produced by the pumping action of the heart. Filtration is opposed by the oncotic pressure created by proteins in the solution.

Pinocytosis and Phagocytosis

Pinocytosis and phagocytosis are transport processes that move substances across cell membranes by invagination and ingestion. Pinocytosis is the process of transporting primarily proteins and strong electrolyte solutions by invagination. Invagination functions in the following manner: (1) Molecules in the extracellular fluid approach the surface of a cell. (2) Absorption adheres the molecules to the cell surface. (3) The molecules alter the surface tension of the cell membrane. (4) The cell membrane folds inward, pulling the adhered molecules with it. (5) The outer edges of the cell membrane then rejoin to form a continuous cell wall. (6) The result is a cell with a pinocytic vesicle incorporated within its walls. Pinocytosis seems to be the only way of transporting proteins through the cell membrane.

Phagocytosis is the process of transporting large particles of selected matter by cell ingestion. Ingestion occurs in the same sequence of steps as invagination. The only difference is that a phagocytic vesicle is formed rather than a pinocytic vesicle. Phagocytosis is an efficient method of eradicating selected matter such as bacteria, other cells, and species of degenerating tissue. In order for matter to be selected for phagocytosis, it must have the following characteristics: (1) a rough, irregular surface; (2) an electropositive surface charge; and (3) the ability to adhere to the phagocytic cell. This third characteristic is enhanced by antibodies called *opsonins* that combine with the particles.

FLUID AND ELECTROLYTE REQUIREMENTS

In discussing the daily fluid and electrolyte requirements for the normal adult, the following must be considered: (1) the average daily fluid intake and output, and (2) the composition of specific body fluids.

Average Daily Fluid Intake and Output

The average daily fluid intake and output volumes are reflections of the net fluid gains and losses of the body from all sources. Table 20-3 provides a list of the sources and ranges of the volumes for those gains and losses. It is significant to note that in the healthy adult who is in a state of dynamic equilibrium, the volumes of the gains and losses are equal.

Composition of Specific Body Fluids

Each of the specific fluids in the body has its own composition. Table 20-4 presents an analysis of the various body fluids in terms of their major cations, anions, and water composition.

TABLE 20-3
Average Adult Daily Fluid Intake and Output

Intake		Output	
Source	Volume, mL	Source	Volume, mL
Water from fluids	500–1700	Urine	800–1600
Water from food	800–1000	Vapor from lungs and skin	600–1200
Water from oxidation	200–300	Feces	100–200
Total	1500–3000	Total	1500–3000

TABLE 20-4
Water and Electrolyte Composition
of Various Body Fluids

Body fluid	Na, meq/L	K, meq/L	Cl, meq/L	HCO_3, meq/L	Water, mL/day
Cerebrospinal fluid	140	3.3	130	24	500
Sweat	45	5	60	—	500
Saliva	40	20	30	30	1500
Gastric juice	60	10	85	—	2500
Bile	150	5	100	40	500
Pancreatic juice	140	5	75	120	700
Small bowel fluid	110	5	105	30	3000
Normal feces	10	10	15	—	100
Loose feces	80	30	60	—	3000+
Urine	90	80	90	—	1500

Alterations in Fluid and Electrolyte Requirements

Healthy adults deal with alterations in the water and electrolyte composition of their body fluids by the normal process of ingestion. They eat and drink the appropriate foods and fluids to maintain the equilibrium of their internal environment. However, when adults suffer dysfunction, they often cannot cope with the alterations in their internal environment and require professional assistance. In the process of receiving this assistance, they often develop additional changes in the water and electrolyte composition of their body fluids. As a result, they may experience a variety of undesirable physiologic, psychologic, and behavioral changes due to the alterations.

The alterations individuals experience are due to varying levels of the following substances in the body: water, sodium, potassium, calcium, magnesium, chloride, phosphates, sulfates, proteins, organic acids, bicarbonate, and carbonic acid. The remainder of this chapter will discuss the functions, regulations, and variances of each of these substances. The variances for most of the substances will be presented in terms of the following: definition, etiology, clinical assessment parameters, laboratory assessment data, clinical and nursing implications, and treatment.

WATER

Functions

The functions of water in the body are (1) to provide the internal medium for cell metabolism; (2) to transport nutrients and waste products, (3) to participate in chemical and metabolic processes, (4) to provide a lubricant for moving parts, and (5) to participate in the regulation of body heat.

Regulation

The regulation of body water is accomplished by the complex action and interaction of the following: renal concentration and dilution of urine, circulating angiotensin II, antidiuretic hormone, and thirst.

Renal Concentration of Urine

The kidneys produce a concentrated urine by conserving body water while excreting solute. The concentration process occurs primarily as a result of the countercurrent mechanism which takes place within the renal medullary interstitium. It is composed of two processes: countercurrent multiplication and countercurrent exchange.

The countercurrent multiplication process occurs in the loop of Henle and is the mechanism that enables the body to excrete urine that has an osmolality higher than that of serum. The process facilitates this phenomenon by creating hypertonic medullary interstitial fluid from the generation of multiplying osmotic gradients through the active transport of sodium chloride from the impermeable ascending limb of the loop of Henle.

The countercurrent exchange process is the maintenance component of the countercurrent mechanism. This process involves the vasa recta or blood vessels that are looped around the tubules in the renal medullary interstitium. The vasa recta minimize the loss of solute from the interstitium by passive diffusion, thus maintaining the osmotic gradients necessary for the countercurrent multiplication process.

Both of these processes involved in the countercurrent mechanism are significantly affected by the secretion of antidiuretic hormone. Antidiuretic hormone increases the permeability of the renal collecting ducts to water, which assists in producing an osmotically concentrated urine. Antidiuretic hormone also assists in maintaining the hypertonic medullary interstitium by decreasing the rate of blood flow through the vasa recta of the medulla.

Renal Dilution of Urine

The ability of the kidney to affect body water by excreting excessive water in a dilute urine is dependent upon two mechanisms. The first mechanism is the active transport of sodium chloride from the impermeable ascending limb of the loop of Henle. This mechanism results in a glomerular filtrate that is hypotonic to the plasma. The second mechanism is the decreased reabsorption of water that occurs at the collecting ducts due to their low permeability. The result of this mechanism is that the filtrate remains hypotonic and a dilute urine is excreted.

Circulating Angiotensin II

Circulating angiotensin II affects body water by increasing the passive reabsorption of water to increase the total volume. Angiotensin II is the potent vasoconstrictor agent produced via the renin-angiotensin system in response to a real or perceived decrease in arterial pressure or extracellular fluid volume, or an alteration in the renal intratubular sodium load. Angiotensin II not only promotes vasoconstriction but also stimulates the suprarenal cortex to secrete aldosterone. Aldosterone facilitates the active reabsorption of sodium, passive reabsorption of water, and active secretion of potassium at the renal tubules. The net effect of these processes is an increase in body water.

Antidiuretic Hormone and Thirst

The effects of antidiuretic hormone and thirst on body water are to conserve and replace it. The mechanisms by which antidiuretic hormone and thirst achieve their results were outlined previously in the discussion of osmolality.

Variances

The variances or imbalances associated with body water are hypervolemia and hypovolemia. While these labels indicate expansion and contraction of body water, they do not indicate what type of expansion or contraction has occurred. In order to provide that information, the expansion or contraction would need to be further categorized as isosmotic, hyperosmotic, or hyposmotic in relation to normal plasma. This additional categorization would assist the health care personnel in understanding the imbalance more completely. For example, an isosmotic contraction would indicate that the individual had lost equal amounts of solute and water. A hyposmotic expansion would indicate that the individual had gained more water than solute in the process of achieving the imbalance. Obviously, applying this additional classification to the individual's health state necessitates understanding the etiology of the existing imbalance.

Hypervolemia

Definition

Hypervolemia is an excess in extracellular fluid volume.

Etiology

Excessive extracellular fluid volume can have many specific causes. However, the following three general factors seem to be common to all: (1) increased sodium and water amounts due to retention and/or excessive intake, (2) decreased renal excretion of water and sodium, and (3) decreased mobilization of fluid within the intravascular space.

Some specific causes of an excess in extracellular fluid volume are excessive ingestion or intravenous infusion of sodium chloride, renal dysfunction, inappropriate secretion of antidiuretic hormone, excessive use of adrenal cortical hormone therapy, hyperaldosteronism, hypoproteinemia, cirrhosis, and cardiac dysfunction.

Clinical Assessment Parameters

Clinically, an individual experiencing hypervolemia might exhibit any combination of the following signs and symptoms: acute weight gain, usually in excess of 5 percent of the total body weight; systemic, peripheral edema that may be pitting in nature; puffy eyelids; ascites; increased central venous pressure;

hypertension; bounding pulse; dyspnea; and moist rales in the lungs.

Based on the above signs and symptoms, the nurse would focus on the following clinical parameters in order to assess an individual for the presence of hypervolemia: body weight, skin turgor and elasticity, central venous pressure, blood pressure, pulses, respiratory patterns, lung auscultation, cardiac auscultation, and in some cases abdominal girth and neck vein distention.

Laboratory Assessment Data

Data obtained from laboratory testing of blood and urine samples can provide the nurse with valuable information in assessing an individual's internal environment. In order to interpret the data reported, the nurse must know the normal values for those items tested. While it is true that each institution has its own set of standardized normal values that have been calibrated and calculated according to the specific equipment used, in most cases the normal values tend to be very similar. Table 20-5 presents the normal values for selected substances commonly tested from the blood, and Table 20-6 presents those values for selected substances commonly tested from the urine.

Laboratory assessment data may be of dubious assistance in determining the presence of excessive extracellular fluid volume, particularly if it is an isotonic imbalance. However, the following changes are often present: decreased serum values for hematocrit, hemoglobin, and red blood cell counts; and decreased urine values for sodium and specific gravity. Depending upon what causes the imbalance, there may also be an increase or decrease in the serum sodium and an increase in the serum blood-urea-nitrogen and creatinine values.

Clinical and Nursing Implications

The primary clinical implication of hypervolemia for the individual is that it could result in pulmonary edema, a life-threatening complication.

The nursing implications of hypervolemia include performing both monitoring functions and therapeutic interventions. The monitoring functions are (1) to measure all intake and output precisely; (2) to maintain accurate records of all intake and output; (3) to obtain accurate daily weights; (4) to monitor all vital signs closely; and (5) to observe for peripheral dependent, systemic, and pulmonary edema.

The therapeutic interventions include (1) providing only those fluids and foods that are consistent with the restrictions; (2) administering prescribed diuretics appropriately; and (3) infusing intravenous fluids (if prescribed) at a constant, appropriate rate.

Treatment

Excessive extracellular fluid volume is usually treated by eradicating or dealing therapeutically with the causative factors and decreasing the excess volume. Decreasing the excess volume often involves using diuretics, fluid and sodium restrictions, and in some cases, dialysis therapy.

Edema

Edema is often associated with hypervolemia. However, edema can, and does, accompany other im-

TABLE 20-5
Normal Values for Common Blood Laboratory Tests

Item	Normal values*
Sodium	136–146 meq/L
Potassium	3.5–5.5 meq/L
Chloride	96–106 meq/L
BUN	9–20 mg per 100 mL
Creatinine	0.7–1.5 mg per 100 mL
Calcium	8.5–10.5 mg per 100 mL
Phosphorus	2.0–4.5 mg per 100 mL
Carbon dioxide combining power	24–28 meq/L
Magnesium	1.6–2.2 meq/L
Osmolality	280–295 mosmol per kg H_2O
Hematocrit	40–50%
Hemoglobin	12–16 g per 100 mL

*Values given are eclectic and for adults.

TABLE 20-6
Normal Values for Common Urine Laboratory Tests

Item	Normal values*
Amount	1200–1500 mL
Specific gravity	1.003–1.030
pH	5.0–8.0
Creatinine	1.0–1.6 g per 24-h period
Osmolality	50–1200 mosmol per kg H_2O
Sodium	50–130 meq/L
Potassium	20–70 meq/L
Chloride	50–130 meq/L
Calcium	5–12 meq/L
Phosphorus	1 g per 24-h period
Magnesium	2–18 meq/L

* Values given are eclectic and for adults.

balances as well as many pathological conditions. Indeed, edema is such a common occurrence that it warrants further discussion.

Definition

Edema is an excessive accumulation of interstitial fluid. It may be either localized or generalized in nature. Localized edema results from either the activation of the inflammatory process or decreased physiologic ability to remove interstitial fluid from a specific area of the body. Generalized edema results from clinical dysfunction in a primary body system responsible for transporting and/or regulating fluids and electrolytes. Such body systems include the cardiovascular, renal, lymphatic, endocrine, and hepatic systems.

Etiology

Edema can result from a variety of causes. However, each seems to have its origin in one of six common influencing factors (Table 20-7).

Clinical Assessment Parameters

Clinically, the assessment of an edematous individual focuses on the following parameters: (1) presence and degree of edema; (2) location and distribution of edema; (3) color, integrity, turgor, elasticity, sensitiv-

ity, and temperature of the skin; (4) presence and degree of neck vein distention; (5) body weight; (6) vital signs; and (7) presence and degree of discomfort (particularly in dependent body parts).

Laboratory Assessment Data

The laboratory data most helpful in assessing an individual in terms of edema are serum and urine protein and sodium values. The amounts of these substances vary according to the cause of the edema, but the common pattern seen is that of hypoproteinemia, hypoalbuminemia, proteinuria, albuminuria, and hyponaturia. The serum sodium level varies so greatly depending on the cause that it is difficult to identify any common pattern in edema. It is accurate to say, however, that in some cases of edema, the serum sodium is altered significantly enough to require close monitoring.

Clinical and Nursing Implications

Edema can have several clinical implications for an individual, some of which are very hazardous to well-being. The significance of edema is dependent upon its location, severity, and mobility. Certainly severe, painful edema of dependent extremities is significant, but not as significant as mild or moderate cerebral or pulmonary edema. Generalized edema can pose problems, but those problems can be vastly intensified if the edema is mobilized and large shifts of fluid from the interstitial to the intravascular space occur.

Many of the nursing implications associated with edema are similar to those previously discussed in relation to hypervolemia, especially the monitoring functions. Included in those monitoring functions are (1) monitoring and recording intake and output accurately, (2) assessing the status of edematous tissues, (3) obtaining precise measurements of daily weights, (4) monitoring vital signs and laboratory data periodically, and (5) assessing for changes in venous pressure.

Therapeutic nursing interventions that might be used with an individual with edema include (1) providing only fluids and foods that are consistent with the prescribed restrictions; (2) administering diuretics and other medications as prescribed; (3) providing meticulous skin care to prevent breakdown of edematous tissues; (4) maintaining bedrest or a decreased level of activity appropriate to the degree of edema; and (5) promoting comfort in edematous extremities

TABLE 20-7	
Factors Influencing Edema Formation	
Factor	**Clinical examples**
Sustained increase in capillary pressure	Dependent venous stasis Thrombophlebitis
Decreased plasma oncotic pressure	Starvation-catabolic states Nephrotic syndrome
Decreased tissue pressure	Malnutrition Glucocorticosteroid therapy
Increased capillary permeability	Burns Infection
Lymphatic obstruction	Neoplasms Burns
Dilation of precapillary sphincters	Insect toxins Inflammation

by elevating them, by repositioning them carefully and frequently, and by ensuring the appropriate use of constrictive and nonconstrictive clothing, coverings, or bandages on them.

Treatment

The treatment of edema is based on four general principles. Those principles are (1) to treat the underlying primary disease or pathology responsible for the edema, (2) to restrict the amount of salt and water taken in based on the needs of the individual, (3) to promote the mobilization of edema fluid, and (4) to promote the excretion of edema fluid. Adherence to these treatment principles usually results in a decrease in the edema, if not total resolution.

Hypovolemia

Definition

Hypovolemia is a deficit in extracellular fluid volume.

Etiology

Extracellular fluid volume deficit occurs as a result of any one of the following three abnormal physiologic processes: (1) excessive loss of fluids and electrolytes, (2) decreased intake of fluids and electrolytes, and (3) shifts of fluids and electrolytes into nonaccessible areas such as third spaces.

The process of losing excessive amounts of fluids and electrolytes seems to be the underlying mechanism in most etiologies of hypovolemia. The most common reasons for such losses are vomiting, gastrointestinal suction, diarrhea, draining fistulas or wounds, systemic infection, profuse diaphoresis, burns, and the excessive use of diuretics.

The two causes of hypovolemia due to a decreased intake of fluids and electrolytes are (1) coma, inability to swallow, or any other state in which it is physically impossible for the individual to ingest substances; and (2) the absence or unavailability of fluids and electrolytes.

The process of "third spacing," or the shifting of extracellular fluid into cavities where it accumulates and is physiologically inaccessible for use by the body, is another underlying mechanism for hypovolemia. Examples of third spacing are seen in ascites, peritonitis, intestinal obstruction, burns, and pancreatitis.

Clinical Assessment Parameters

An individual with an extracellular fluid deficit will exhibit any number of the following clinical signs and symptoms: acute weight loss, usually in excess of 5 percent of the total body weight; dry skin and mucous membranes; decreased skin turgor and elasticity; longitudinal wrinkling or furrows of the tongue; subnormal body temperature; lassitude or fatigue; oliguria or in a few cases anuria; thirst; decreased postural systolic blood pressure; decreased tension or turgor of the eyeball; decreased venous pressure; increased pulse rate; and decreased perspiration. Of all these parameters, body weight is considered by many to be the most important indicator of an individual's fluid balance. In fact, body weight has been used to roughly categorize degrees of extracellular fluid volume deficit. Table 20-8 presents one such categorization.

Laboratory Assessment Data

The laboratory data that are the most useful in assessing an individual for hypovolemia include serum hemoglobin, hematocrit, red blood cell count, and BUN levels; and urine sodium, chloride, and specific gravity values. The urine-to-serum osmolality ratio also provides valuable assessment data, as can the serum sodium if the cause of the imbalance is considered. The pattern of these values exhibited by an individual experiencing hypovolemia includes increased serum values for hematocrit, hemoglobin, red blood cell count, and blood-urea-nitrogen; decreased urine values for sodium and chloride; increased urinary specific gravity; increased urine-to-serum osmolality ratio; and variable serum sodium values depending on the etiology of the imbalance.

The importance of including the urine values in an assessment of an individual for hypovolemia should be emphasized. Many clinicians feel that the urine

TABLE 20-8
Degrees of Extracellular Fluid Volume Deficit According to Percent Loss of Total Body Weight

Degree of extracellular fluid volume deficit	Loss of total body weight, percent
Mild	2– 6
Moderate	6–10
Severe	10–15
Fatal	> 15

values may provide the earliest signs of hypovolemia. The parameters most frequently cited as guidelines for determining if the specific urine values are indicative of hypovolemia are a sodium content less than 20 meq/L, a specific gravity greater than 1.026, and a urine-to-serum osmolality ratio greater than 2.

Clinical and Nursing Implications

The clinical significance of hypovolemia for an individual is that there are insufficient body fluids to carry out the normal physiologic and metabolic processes necessary to sustain life. Of course, the more severe the imbalance the greater the threat to the individual's well-being.

The nursing monitoring functions related to hypovolemia include (1) obtaining accurate daily weights; (2) measuring and recording *all* intake and output accurately; (3) assessing vital signs, venous pressure, and laboratory data periodically; (4) measuring expanded third-space areas, such as the abdomen, frequently; (5) assessing the status of the skin and mucous membranes periodically; and (6) continuously evaluating the individual's overall energy level.

The nursing interventions used with an individual with hypovolemia are (1) to administer intravenous replacement fluids precisely at a constant rate; (2) to ensure that all fluids administered to the individual, including irrigation solutions, are of the appropriate electrolyte balance; (3) to provide frequent oral hygiene to maintain the integrity and hydration state of the mucous membranes; and (4) to provide skin care to decrease breakdown and promote integrity.

Treatment

The treatment of hypovolemia has two components. The first component is to treat or correct the primary cause of the imbalance. The second component is to replace the lost fluids and electrolytes.

Replacement therapy is usually instituted according to a tri-level approach. The first level is based on an assessment of the individual's renal status. If there is a question as to the adequacy of the individual's renal function, a hydrating solution is given to challenge the renal system and promote function. This hydrating solution is usually composed of water, carbohydrate (in the form of 5% dextrose), sodium, and chloride. Once adequate renal function has been established, replacement therapy moves to the second level.

The second level of replacement therapy can be initiated as soon as it has been determined that renal function is adequate. Thus, in some cases, the first-level replacement can be deleted and replacement therapy actually begins with second-level solutions. Second-level solutions are balanced solutions designed to supply water, calories, and electrolytes in sufficient quantities to meet the maintenance needs of the body as well as to correct existing deficits. These solutions are composed of physiologic proportionate amounts of water, carbohydrate, sodium, potassium, magnesium, chloride, phosphate, and lactate. These balanced solutions are often called *all-purpose* solutions and are utilized frequently in fluid replacement therapy.

Third-level replacement therapy is aimed at replacing specific, concurrent, or ongoing water and electrolyte losses. This level of therapy involves using solutions individually mixed to replace specific fluid and electrolyte losses, such as those created by gastrointestinal suction or fistula drainage. These solutions are composed of water, carbohydrate, and varying amounts of specific electrolytes selected to meet the needs of the individual. It is not uncommon in replacement therapy to see both balanced solutions and specifically created solutions used simultaneously to achieve and maintain proper balance.

SODIUM

Functions

Sodium, the major cation of the extracellular fluid, has four general functions in the body. Those functions are (1) to promote the normal distribution and volume of fluids in the body by creating and maintaining the normal osmolality of those fluids; (2) to enhance the transcellular movement of substances by altering cell permeability; (3) to promote normal neuromuscular irritability by enhancing the conduction and transmission of electrochemical impulses; and (4) to contribute to the regulation of acid-base balance by exchanging with selected cations such as potassium and hydrogen, and combining with certain anions such as chloride and bicarbonate.

Regulation

The renal system, in concert with other mechanisms, has primary responsibility for regulating the reabsorption and excretion of sodium. Approximately 99 percent of the total filtered load of sodium is reabsorbed by various parts of the nephron, leaving only about 1 percent to be excreted in the urine. Of the 99 percent that is reabsorbed, about 70 percent is actively reabsorbed in the proximal tubule, 20 percent is passively reabsorbed in the loop of Henle, 8 percent is actively reabsorbed in the distal tubule, and about 1 percent is actively reabsorbed in the collecting duct. This reabsorption and excretion of sodium is influenced by several factors, many of which are related to maintaining an effective arterial blood volume. Those influencing factors include glomerulotubular balance, aldosterone, third factor, redistribution of renal blood flow, peritubular capillary oncotic pressure, serum sodium concentration, catecholamines, and prostaglandins.

Glomerulotubular Balance

Glomerulotubular balance is the phenomenon of having the rate of tubular sodium reabsorption change in the same direction as the filtered load of sodium because of alterations in the glomerular filtration rate. This mechanism prevents the loss of large amounts of sodium that would result from increases in the glomerular filtration rate.

Aldosterone

Aldosterone is a mineralocorticoid hormone that is secreted in response to a real or perceived decrease in effective arterial volume through the activation of the renin-angiotensin system. Aldosterone acts on the distal renal tubule to promote increased sodium and water reabsorption and potassium excretion.

Third Factor

Third factor is thought to be a natriuretic regulatory mechanism that increases the renal excretion of sodium in the presence of saline volume expansion. The factor is thought to function independently of aldosterone and glomerular filtration rate in regulating sodium excretion. Research continues to be conducted on third factor to determine its precise physiologic nature and composition.

Redistribution of Renal Blood Flow

The redistribution of renal blood flow occurs as a result of a reduction in effective arterial volume sufficient enough to decrease the total blood flow to the kidneys. In such a situation, blood is shunted from the cortical nephrons to the juxtamedullary nephrons. The juxtamedullary nephrons, with their long loops of Henle, tend to retain more sodium for reabsorption than do the cortical nephrons. Thus, this selective perfusion of the juxtamedullary nephrons promotes the increased reabsorption of sodium.

Peritubular Capillary Oncotic Pressure

The peritubular capillaries regulate sodium reabsorption and excretion according to the amount of oncotic pressure in them. An increased protein concentration, usually resulting from a volume and/or sodium deficit, promotes the reabsorption of sodium and water from the nephron. This process assists in returning the peritubular capillary oncotic pressure to normal.

Serum Sodium Concentration

Serum sodium levels seem to have an influence on sodium reabsorption and excretion, but the exact mechanism for this influence is not known. However, it is known that hyponatremia promotes and hypernatremia inhibits sodium reabsorption in the renal tubules.

Catecholamines

Catecholamines are thought to enhance sodium reabsorption, but again, the mechanism for this action is not clearly understood. There seem to be differing opinions as to whether the effect of the catecholamines is direct or indirect in relation to sodium reabsorption.

Prostaglandins

The role of prostaglandins in the regulation of sodium is controversial at this time. It seems that certain prostaglandins may have a natriuretic effect, but the mechanism for that effect is not at all clear. Further research is required on prostaglandins, as well as other factors, before all the mechanisms involved in sodium regulation are precisely comprehended.

Variances

The variances or imbalances related to sodium are hypernatremia and hyponatremia. It should be noted, however, that the serum sodium levels cannot be assessed in isolation. For when serum sodium levels are assessed, it is sodium concentration that is being assessed and concentration should not be evaluated without considering fluid volume. Thus, serum sodium and fluid volume should be assessed concurrently.

It is then possible to determine if an increased serum sodium level is actually due to hypernatremia, or if it is merely a reflection of hypovolemia. In the latter instance, the serum sodium level is not indicative of total body sodium, which might be normal. Rather, it is indicative of having the same amount of sodium present in less fluid volume. With this note in mind, the discussion concerning hypernatremia and hyponatremia can proceed.

Hypernatremia

Definition

Hypernatremia is an excess of sodium in the extracellular fluid in the presence of a normal extracellular fluid volume.

Etiology

Hypernatremia can result from causes of two kinds: (1) those that promote either the loss of water in excess of sodium loss or the inadequate replacement of water; (2) those that foster sodium retention or excess. Examples of the first type are decreased water intake, inability to swallow, unconsciousness, unavailability of fluids, vomiting, diarrhea, diabetes insipidus, osmotic diuresis, fever, heat stroke, high environmental temperatures, hyperventilation, and dialysis therapy. Examples of the second type are excessive ingestion or infusion of sodium chloride, ingestion of seawater, acidosis, renal dysfunction, primary hyperaldosteronism, excessive use of corticosteroid therapy, and neurological lesions.

Clinical Assessment Parameters

The hypernatremic individual usually exhibits many of the following signs and symptoms: dry, sticky mucous membranes; a rough, dry tongue; flushed, dry skin; increased tissue turgor; thirst; decreased lacrimation, elevated body temperature; tachycardia; oliguria; lethargy; central nervous system irritability; muscular rigidity; tremors; seizures; and coma.

Laboratory Assessment Data

The laboratory values that provide the most data for assessing an individual in relation to hypernatremia are serum sodium and chloride, and urine sodium, chloride, osmolality, and specific gravity. The levels of those values that are consistent with hypernatremia are the following: a serum sodium greater than 146 meq/L, a serum chloride greater than 106 meq/L, a urine sodium less than 50 meq/L, a urine chloride less than 50 meq/L, a urine osmolality of greater than 800 mosmol/L, and a urine specific gravity greater than 1.030.

Clinical and Nursing Implications

Hypernatremia can result in serious clinical difficulties for an individual. Probably the most significant problems are those related to the central nervous system and neuromuscular function. Certainly it is easy to visualize the effects of muscular hyperirritability, seizures, and coma on one's health state. Such problems are definitely a threat to well-being and necessitate appropriate nursing support.

The nursing support related to hypernatremia includes the following monitoring functions: (1) assessing the skin turgor, temperature, color, and moisture; (2) assessing the moisture of the tongue and mucous membranes; (3) obtaining precise daily weights; (4) measuring and recording intake and output accurately; (5) monitoring vital signs and laboratory values periodically; (6) assessing muscle movement; and probably the most important function, (7) assessing the neurological status and level of consciousness frequently.

Nursing interventions that provide support for the hypernatremic individual are (1) to provide fluids and foods consistent with prescribed restrictions; (2) to maintain skin integrity through the use of meticulous hygienic measures, moisturizing agents, and frequent repositioning; (3) to maintain the integrity of the oral cavity with frequent oral care employing a variety of nondehydrating agents; (4) to promote comfort by decreasing thirst using a variety of creative measures; (5) to institute seizure precautions; and (6) to provide for the general, overall environmental safety of the individual.

Treatment

The treatment for hypernatremia revolves around treating the cause and correcting the imbalance. The ideal form of treatment is to treat the primary disorder that perpetuates the imbalance, and whenever possible, this is done. The second part of the treatment, correcting the imbalance, is based on the nature of the etiology. If the imbalance is due to a loss of extracellular fluid, intravenous isotonic saline solution will probably be administered to correct the imbalance. If the imbalance is due to a sodium excess, the individual's daily sodium intake will be restricted to anywhere from 0.5 g, to 2 g, and intravenous 5% dextrose and water will be given to replace the intracellular fluid deficit created by the hypernatremia.

Hyponatremia

Definition

Hyponatremia is a deficit of sodium in the extracellular fluid in the presence of a normal extracellular fluid volume.

Etiology

Hyponatremia has two types of causes: (1) those that produce dilutional extracellular fluid expansion; and (2) those that result in a deficit of sodium. The causes of dilutional hyponatremia are excessive ingestion or infusion of electrolyte-free solutions; excessive use of tap water enemas; irrigation of gastrointestinal tubes with electrolyte-free solutions; renal dysfunction; inappropriate secretion of antidiuretic hormone; cirrhosis; congestive heart failure; and hyperglycemia. (In the case of hyperglycemia, it has been estimated that each 100 mg per 100 mL increase in the glucose concentration above normal results in sufficient extracellular fluid volume expansion to decrease the serum sodium concentration by about 2 meq/L.)

A deficit of sodium is caused by inadequate ingestion of dietary sodium, infusions of solutions that are sodium-deficient; salt-wasting renal dysfunctions; potent diuretic therapy, adrenal insufficiency, severe vomiting, severe diarrhea, excessive perspiration, gastrointestinal suction, potassium depletion, and severe malnutrition.

Clinical Assessment Parameters

An individual experiencing hyponatremia may exhibit any combination of the following signs and symptoms: fatigue, muscle weakness, lethargy, confusion, headache, tremors, hyperreflexia, convulsions, coma, apprehension, anorexia, nausea, vomiting, abdominal cramps, diarrhea, and oliguria. As with hypernatremia, the neurological signs and symptoms of hyponatremia seem to be the most significant clinically. However, because the neurological signs and symptoms are so similar in the two conditions, they offer little help in differentiating between the two states. Therefore, the gastrointestinal signs and symptoms may be more discriminating, even if clinically less significant, in identifying hyponatremia.

Laboratory Assessment Data

Hyponatremia can be identified from an assessment of the following laboratory data: serum sodium and chloride, and urine sodium, chloride, osmolality, and specific gravity. The pattern characteristic of hyponatremia is a serum sodium less than 136 meq/L, a serum chloride less than 96 meq/L, a urine sodium less than 20 meq/L, a urine osmolality less than 100 mosmol/L, and a urine specific gravity less than 1.010.

Clinical and Nursing Implications

Clinically, hyponatremia can be a life-threatening imbalance, depending on its severity. The hazards to the individual stem from the effects of the imbalance on the central nervous system. Those effects, ranging anywhere from mere confusion to convulsions and coma, certainly represent a menace to the individual's health state.

Nursing monitoring functions that are performed in relation to hyponatremia include (1) assessing levels of consciousness and central nervous system functioning frequently, (2) assessing muscle strength and energy levels periodically, (3) obtaining precise daily weights, (4) measuring and recording intake and output accurately, and (5) monitoring vital signs and laboratory data at intervals.

Nursing interventions that would be performed with an individual with hyponatremia are (1) giving foods and fluids high in sodium content as prescribed; (2) maintaining fluid restrictions as prescribed (interventions 1 and 2 are *not* done in concert, since the first aims at replacement therapy and the second at returning a diluted expanded extracellular fluid volume to normal); (3) instituting seizure precautions; (4) promoting the conservation of energy by limiting activity; (5) establishing a physical environment conducive to maintaining the individual's safety and orientation; and (6) promoting overall comfort by using creative pain-relieving methods and administering medications as prescribed.

Treatment

The treatment of hyponatremia depends, of course, on its etiology. The first goal of therapy is to treat the causes or primary disorder responsible for producing the imbalance. The second goal is to treat the imbalance. If the imbalance is the result of a dilutional expansion of the extracellular fluid, treatment will consist of restricting the fluid intake (and in some cases administering diuretics). If the imbalance is due to sodium loss, replacement therapy in the form of oral preparations, dietary provisions, or hypertonic or isotonic saline infusions will be instituted.

POTASSIUM

Functions

Potassium, the major cation of the intracellular fluid, has several important physiologic functions that it performs in the body. Those functions include (1) creating and maintaining the osmotic pressure of the intracellular fluid; (2) maintaining the transmembrane electrical potential difference between the extracellular and intracellular spaces that regulates neuromuscular excitability and is necessary for muscle contraction; (3) participating in the maintenance of acid-base balance; (4) enhancing the synthesis of protein; and (5) participating in the metabolism of carbohydrates and synthesis of glycogen.

Regulation

Potassium is regulated primarily by the renal system. Although some potassium is lost in perspiration and the feces, the kidneys remain the foremost organs for the excretion and reabsorption of potassium. The renal handling of potassium begins at the glomerulus where it is filtered. Of that filtered load of potassium, about 70 percent is actively reabsorbed in the proximal tubule, 20 percent is passively reabsorbed in the loop of Henle, and the remaining 10 percent is delivered to the distal tubule. Further active reabsorption can occur in the distal tubule and collecting duct, depending on the level of potassium in the body. The *principal* activity of the distal tubule, however, is the active or passive secretion of potassium. This distal tubular secretion, the main regulator of renal potassium excretion, is influenced by the following factors: aldosterone, sodium delivery to the distal tubule, hydrogen ion secretion, nonreabsorbable anions, urine flow rates, potassium intake, and diuretic therapy.

Aldosterone

Aldosterone, a mineralocorticoid hormone, increases potassium excretion through two very interrelated mechanisms. The first mechanism is related to the increased permeability of the distal tubular luminal membrane to potassium and sodium that is produced by aldosterone. This change in permeability enhances the diffusion of potassium out of the tubular cell into the lumen where it can be excreted. It also enhances the entry of sodium from the lumen into the tubular cell which facilitates active sodium reabsorption. The increase in sodium reabsorption increases the transmembrane potential difference in the distal tubule, which facilitates the passive diffusion of potassium into the lumen for excretion.

The second mechanism is related to the increased concentration of potassium in the tubular cell that is produced by aldosterone. Aldosterone stimulates the peritubular uptake of potassium, thus increasing the concentration in the tubular cell. This increase in concentration enhances the passive diffusion of potassium into the lumen where it can be excreted.

Sodium Delivery to the Distal Tubule

The effect of the concentration of distal tubular sodium on potassium excretion has been mentioned in the previous discussion on aldosterone. When increased concentrations of sodium are delivered to the distal tubule, the amount of sodium that is reabsorbed is increased. The increased reabsorption of sodium creates an increase in the transmembrane potential difference which facilitates the passive diffusion of potassium into the tubular lumen where it can be excreted. Thus, the end result is an increase in urinary potassium excretion.

Hydrogen Ion Secretion

The secretion of distal tubular potassium is influenced by the rate of hydrogen ion secretion. In acute acidotic conditions, there is an extracellular to intracellular shift of hydrogen ions and an intracellular to extracellular shift of potassium. The lower intracellular concentration of potassium in the distal tubular cells decreases the electrical and chemical gradients that enhance the passive secretion of potassium into the lumen. This results in a decreased renal secretion and excretion of potassium, accompanied by a preferential obligatory secretion of hydrogen ions that is facilitated by the increase in the intracellular concentration of hydrogen ions. Of course, the reverse of this process occurs in alkalotic states, and there is an increased urinary excretion of potassium.

Nonreabsorbable Anions

Nonreabsorbable anions, such as phosphate, sulfate, and bicarbonate, are those anions that cannot accompany reabsorbed sodium as easily as chloride does. When there are increased amounts of these anions in the distal tubular fluid, the negative transmembrane electrical gradient is increased as sodium is reabsorbed, resulting in an increased diffusion of potassium into the lumen. Thus, this mechanism increases urinary excretion of potassium.

Urine Flow Rates

Urine flow rates seem to have some correlation with urinary potassium secretion and excretion rates. When urine flow increases, so does potassium secretion and excretion. Likewise, when urine flow decreases, there is also a decrease in the urinary secretion and excretion of potassium. The mechanisms responsible for these variations seem to be the increased sodium concentration that accompanies the urine flow to the distal tubule and the decreased reabsorption of potassium that results from the low potassium concentration of the luminal fluid. Both of these factors contribute to the increased urinary excretion rates of potassium in the presence of high urine flow rates.

Potassium Intake

An increase in the extracellular concentration of potassium due to increased intake increases the urinary secretion and excretion rate of potassium. The effect of an increased extracellular potassium concentration on the rate of urinary secretion and excretion of potassium results from its participation in the following processes: (1) the production of a higher tubular luminal concentration of potassium, (2) the stimulation of increased aldosterone secretion, (3) the production of an increased transmembrane potential difference at the distal tubular cell, and (4) the stimulation of sodium-potassium-adenosine triphosphatase which increases the rate of potassium flow across the peritubular cell membranes.

Diuretic Therapy

Most of the pharmacological agents that produce diuresis are kaliuretic in nature and result in increased urinary losses of potassium. The mechanisms by which they produce this effect vary according to the specific diuretic employed. However, most of them function by either increasing urinary flow rate, decreasing potassium reabsorption, increasing sodium delivery to the distal tubule, or altering the transmembrane potential.

Variances

The variances associated with potassium are hyperkalemia ahd hypokalemia.

Hyperkalemia

Definition

Hyperkalemia is an excess of potassium in the extracellular fluid.

Etiology

The etiologies of hyperkalemia can be classified into three general categories based on the mechanism by which they produce the excess in potassium. Those categories are decreased renal excretion, translocation from the cells, and increased intake. Those etiologies that result in hyperkalemia because of a decreased renal excretion include renal dysfunction, adrenocortical insufficiencies such as Addison's disease and hyporeninemic hypoaldosteronism, and the use of potassium-sparing diuretics such as spironolactone or triamterene.

Those etiologies that result in hyperkalemia because of the translocation of potassium from the intracellular to the extracellular fluid space include severe catabolism, burns, rhabdomyolysis, acute acidosis, intravascular hemolysis, and hyperkalemic familial periodic paralysis.

Hyperkalemia can also be caused by the excessive intake of potassium, usually in the form of intravenous infusions or the oral ingestion of medications or food substances that are high in potassium. This etiology, however, is rarely the cause of hyperkalemia if the individual has normal renal function. This is because in most circumstances it is difficult to exceed the renal capacity for excreting potassium, so even additional loads of potassium are easily excreted. The renal excretion capacity can be exceeded, however, by large bolus intravenous infusions of potassium.

In addition to all the above causes of hyperkalemia, there are other changes that occur in the body that produce a false hyperkalemia. Pseudohyperkalemia can result from the following: increased leukocyte or thrombocyte counts, the hemolysis of drawn blood samples, and using a tourniquet to assist in drawing blood samples.

Clinical Assessment Parameters

Most of the clinical signs and symptoms of hyperkalemia are related to the neuromuscular, cardiac, and gastrointestinal systems. Those signs and symptoms as exhibited by the hyperkalemic individual include mental confusion, neuromuscular hyperexcitability, weakness, paresthesia, ascending flaccid paralysis, cardiac dysfunction (as described below), cardiac arrest, abdominal distension, diarrhea, intestinal colic, and oliguria (which is more a reflection of the etiology than an effect of the imbalance).

The cardiac dysfunction that occurs in response to hyperkalemia seems to follow a distinct pattern. The earliest signs of dysfunction are seen on the electrocardiogram in the form of tall, peaked, tented T waves and a depressed ST segment. As the imbalance progresses, the P waves decrease in amplitude and the P-R interval is prolonged. Then atrial asystole occurs with a widened QRS complex that eventually merges with the T wave forming the sine wave characteristic of hyperkalemia. Dysrhythmia, fibrillation, and cardiac arrest can occur at any time during the above sequence of events, depending on the severity and rate of progression of the hyperkalemia.

Laboratory Assessment Data

The laboratory value that provides the most data in assessing an individual for hyperkalemia is the serum potassium. A serum potassium level greater than 5.5 meq/L is indicative of hyperkalemia.

The urinary potassium value may provide additional data. However, this value will vary depending on the etiology of the imbalance and thus may be more reflective of the specific etiology than of the existence or magnitude of the imbalance.

Clinical and Nursing Implications

The clinical significance of hyperkalemia is based on its profound effect on the neuromuscular and cardiac systems. Certainly nothing could be worse for an individual than paralysis or cardiac arrest.

The nursing implications associated with hyperkalemia include monitoring or assessing the following: (1) rate, rhythm, and characteristics of the pulse (with or without a cardiac monitor); (2) level of consciousness and orientation; (3) muscle strength, sensation, and movement; (4) characteristics of the abdomen; (5) characteristics of the feces; (6) laboratory values; and (7) urinary output.

Also included in the nursing implications of hyperkalemia are the following interventions: (1) provid-

ing only those foods and fluids that are consistent with the prescribed potassium restriction; (2) administering medications as prescribed; (3) establishing a safe physical environment for the individual; (4) providing stimuli appropriate for enhancing orientation; (5) instituting limited active or passive range of motion exercises; (6) assisting with the normal activities of daily living; and (7) providing meticulous skin care at the rectal orifice.

Treatment

The treatment of hyperkalemia focuses on eliminating the primary cause and correcting the imbalance. Measures for correcting the imbalance are aimed at (1) reducing potassium intake, (2) antagonizing the membrane effect of hyperkalemia, (3) shifting the potassium intracellularly, and (4) increasing the excretion of potassium.

Reducing the potassium intake is accomplished by restricting the amounts of potassium ingested in dietary substances or medications and/or infused in intravenous solutions. The usual daily restriction of potassium is about 40 meq, but this amount can vary according to the specific needs of the individual.

The agents most frequently used to antagonize the effect of hyperkalemia on the cell membrane are calcium salts, such as calcium chloride, or hypertonic sodium salts, such as sodium chloride or sodium bicarbonate. While these agents may be very successful in treating severe cases of hyperkalemia quickly (because they are effective within 1 to 5 min after administration), they are also therapeutically very transient and last only 30 min. Furthermore, they have no effect on either serum or total body potassium levels.

Infusions of glucose and insulin or sodium bicarbonate will correct hyperkalemia by facilitating the shift of potassium into the cell. The glucose and insulin therapy becomes effective about 10 to 15 min after infusion, but the sodium bicarbonate requires about an hour. Both agents produce only a temporary correction of the imbalance that is perhaps 2 to 4 h in duration. Both agents will decrease the serum potassium level but have no effect on total body potassium.

The increased excretion of potassium is effected through the use of sodium chloride infusions, cation exchange resins, diuretics, and dialysis. Sodium chloride infusions are effective within 1 h but do not last very long. The infusions are effective in reducing the serum potassium level but have only a slight effect on the total body potassium. Cation exchange resins, diuretics, and dialysis are effective within minutes to hours and last longer than the other types of therapies mentioned. All these methods are effective in decreasing both the serum and total body potassium levels.

Hypokalemia

Definition

Hypokalemia is a deficit of potassium in the extracellular fluid.

Etiology

Hypokalemia results from the following five categories of causes: (1) increased intracellular shift of potassium, (2) decreased potassium intake, (3) increased gastrointestinal potassium loss, (4) excessive renal potassium loss, and (5) excessive integumentary potassium loss.

Specific etiologies that cause hypokalemia by enhancing the intracellular shift of potassium are acute alkalosis, the intravenous infusion of glucose and insulin, and familial hypokalemic periodic paralysis.

The etiologies that produce hypokalemia as a result of decreased intake are the inability to physically ingest fluids or foods, the unavailability of food or fluids, the infusion of large quantities of potassium-free intravenous solutions, and the prolonged ingestion of diets that are deficient in potassium.

Increasing the gastrointestinal loss of potassium is the mechanism by which the following etiologies cause hypokalemia: vomiting, fistulas, malabsorption, diarrhea, inflammatory bowel disease, laxative abuse, and ureterosigmoidostomies.

Etiologies that produce hypokalemia by increasing the renal excretion of potassium include diuretic therapy, renal tubular acidosis, chronic interstitial nephritis, primary and secondary hyperaldosteronism, Cushing's syndrome, adrenal steroid therapy, the excessive ingestion of mineralocorticoid-like substances such as licorice, and diabetic ketoacidosis.

The loss of potassium through the integument in the form of excessive perspiration also causes hypokalemia. This etiology is most frequently observed in individuals who exercise or work intensely in hot climates.

Clinical Assessment Parameters

The clinical manifestations of hypokalemia are evident in almost every system of the body. This imbalance seems to produce signs and symptoms in the neuromuscular, cardiovascular, respiratory, gastrointestinal, endocrine, and renal systems. Table 20-9 summarizes the signs and symptoms of hypokalemia that are observed in those body systems.

Laboratory Assessment Data

The most significant laboratory values used in assessing an individual for hypokalemia are the serum values for potassium, bicarbonate, and pH. A serum potassium of less than 3.5 meq/L and an increased plasma bicarbonate and pH are indicative of hypokalemia.

Other laboratory values that provide additional information in assessing for hypokalemia are the following: urine osmolality, pH, potassium, and phosphate. The levels of those urine values that are consistent with hypokalemia are a decreased osmo-

TABLE 20-9
Signs and Symptoms of Hypokalemia According to Body Systems

System	Signs and symptoms
Neuromuscular	Drowsiness, confusion, apathy, irritability, coma, muscle weakness, paresthesia, muscle pain, muscle cramps, muscle tenderness, hyporeflexia, tetany, paralysis
Cardiovascular	Weak pulse; bradycardia; ECG changes, including a depressed ST segment; flattened, inverted T waves; and U waves
Respiratory	Muscle weakness, hypoventilation
Gastrointestinal	Nausea, vomiting, anorexia, abdominal distention, abdominal cramps, paralytic ileus
Endocrine	Polydipsia, hyperglycemia, and in some cases negative nitrogen balance
Renal	Polyuria, nocturia

lality, a decreased pH, a normal potassium (within the first 3 weeks of the imbalance, then it decreases), and an increased phosphate.

Clinical and Nursing Implications

Hypokalemia represents many clinical problems for the individual. The most significant of those problems are the apnea, cardiac dysrhythmias, muscle paralysis, and paralytic ileus that may develop as hypokalemia progresses in severity. With the possibility of such severe alterations occurring, the implications for nursing support are crucial.

The nursing support includes the following monitoring functions: (1) assessing the rate, rhythm, and characteristics of the respirations and the pulse (with or without a cardiac monitor); (2) monitoring all other vital signs; (3) assessing the level of consciousness frequently; (4) evaluating muscle strength, movement, and sensation; (5) assessing the characteristics of the abdomen; (6) monitoring bowel sounds; (7) measuring and recording intake and output accurately; and (8) monitoring the appropriate laboratory values.

The nursing support for the individual with hypokalemia also includes the following interventions: (1) administering oral or intravenous potassium preparations carefully and as prescribed; (2) positioning the individual to facilitate adequate respirations; (3) providing appropriate stimuli to promote orientation; (4) establishing a safe physical environment for the individual; (5) providing creative comfort measures; and (6) assisting the individual with the normal activities of daily living.

Treatment

The treatment of hypokalemia involves eliminating the cause, if possible, and correcting the imbalance. The preferred method for correcting hypokalemia is to replace the deficit orally with high-potassium foods or potassium supplements. (When liquid potassium preparations are given, they should be well diluted to decrease the gastrointestinal irritation.) Using this method of replacement therapy decreases the likelihood of creating a rebound hyperkalemia.

Intravenous potassium chloride is usually used to replace acute potassium deficits. The potassium chloride is generally infused into a peripheral vein at a rate of 10 to 20 meq/h using a concentration of 40 meq/L. This rate and concentration ensures that the deficit will be slowly but adequately corrected with the minimum of risk to the individual.

CALCIUM

Functions

Calcium, an important, abundant cation in the body, is involved in a variety of physiologic functions. Included among those functions are the following: (1) participating in bone formation and metabolism; (2) influencing neural transmission and function; (3) initiating muscle contraction; (4) participating as a coenzyme in blood coagulation and activation of the complement system; (5) influencing cardiac action potential; (6) participating in the regulation of many enzyme systems; (7) influencing the secretion of blood exocrine and endocrine glands; and (8) preserving the functional integrity of cellular membranes.

Regulation

Serum calcium is regulated primarily by exchange between the extracellular fluid and the intestines, bones, and kidneys. Figure 20-5 illustrates these regulatory relationships and indicates their relative importance by the size of the arrows. These exchanges, or relationships, are influenced by a variety of hormonal and other factors as summarized in Table 20-10.

Intestines

The intestines absorb from 25 to 70 percent of the dietary calcium ingested. The efficiency of this absorption seems to vary inversely with the amount of calcium ingested. The absorption process is enhanced by vitamin D, parathyroid hormone, and growth hormone. It is inhibited by thyrocalcitonin and glucocorticoid hormones.

In addition to supplying the body with essential calcium by the absorption process, the intestines also secrete calcium, which is excreted (along with the unabsorbed calcium) in the feces. The intestinal secretion of calcium seems to be constant in terms of amount and is not dependent upon the quantity ingested.

Bones

The movement of calcium to and from the bones contributes significantly to maintaining a normal extracellular ionized calcium concentration. While it seems that the rates of bone formation (calcium deposition) and bone reabsorption (calcium release) participate in the exchange process equally, that is not the case. Bone reabsorption appears to be the principal process involved in the exchange and thus compensates for lowered serum calcium levels. Bone reabsorption is stimulated by vitamin D, parathyroid hormone, thyroid hormone, prostaglandin, and acidosis. It is inhibited by thyrocalcitonin, glucocorticoid hormone, androgen, estrogen, hyperphosphatemia, and alkalosis.

Kidneys

The renal system regulates calcium by maintaining a balance between intake and output. The renal regulation of calcium is mainly excretory in nature and varies according to dietary intake. Of the filtered calcium load, about 55 percent is reabsorbed in the proximal tubule, about 30 percent is reabsorbed in the loop of Henle, and about 12 percent is reabsorbed in the distal tubule. The remaining 3 percent is excreted by the kidneys. The renal excretion of calcium is increased by the following: increased effective arterial pressure, most diuretics, hypercalcemia, hypophosphatemia, thyrocalcitonin, growth hormone, thyroid hormone, glucocorticoids, and acidosis. Those factors that decrease the renal excretion of calcium include decreased effective arterial volume, thiazide diuretics, hypocalcemia, hyperphosphatemia, vitamin D, parathyroid hormone, and alkalosis.

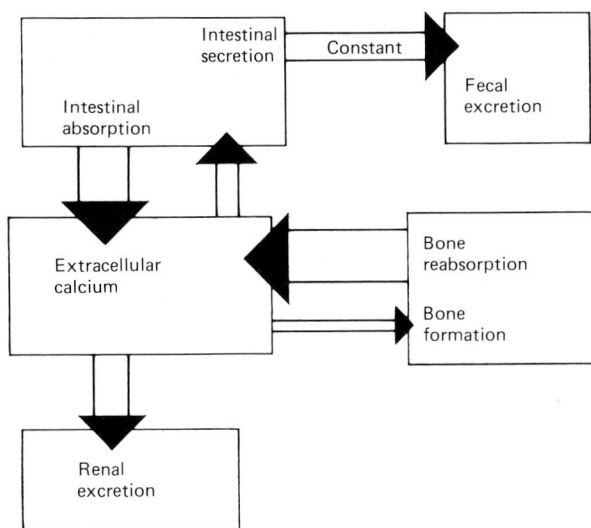

FIGURE 20-5

Mechanisms for regulating extracellular calcium. (Arrow size indicates relative importance.)

TABLE 20-10
Factors Influencing Calcium Regulation

Regulating system	Stimulating Factor	Inhibiting factor
Intestinal (absorption)	Vitamin D Parathyroid hormone Growth hormone	Thyrocalcitonin Glucocorticoid hormone
Skeletal (bone reabsorption)	Vitamin D Parathyroid hormone Thyroid hormone Prostaglandin Acidosis	Thyrocalcitonin Glucocorticoid hormone Androgen Estrogen Hyperphosphatemia Alkalosis
Renal (excretion)	Increased arterial pressure Most diuretics Hypercalcemia Hypophosphatemia Thyrocalcitonin Growth hormone Thyroid hormone Glucocorticoid hormone Acidosis	Decreased arterial pressure Thiazide diuretics Hypocalcemia Hyperphosphatemia Vitamin D Parathyroid hormone Alkalosis

Variances

The variances associated with calcium are hypercalcemia and hypocalcemia.

Hypercalcemia

Definition

Hypercalcemia is an excess of calcium in the extracellular fluid.

Etiology

Hypercalcemia can be caused by a variety of etiologies, the most common of which is malignant tumors. Other causes are vitamin D intoxication, hyperparathyroidism, hypophosphatasia, hyperproteinemia, hyperthyroidism, adrenal insufficiency, renal dysfunction, immobilization, thiazide diuretics, milk-alkali syndrome, sarcoidosis, tuberculosis, idiopathic infantile hypercalcemia, and vitamin A intoxication.

Clinical Assessment Parameters

The clinical signs and symptoms that may accompany hypercalcemia include fatigue, muscle weakness, muscle hypotonicity, drowsiness, lethargy, disorientation, loss of memory, depression, stupor, coma, deep bone pain, anorexia, nausea, vomiting, constipation, thirst, polyuria, renal stones, and cardiac dysrhythmia, which can progress to cardiac arrest. (Hypercalcemia is evidenced on the electrocardiogram by a shortened Q-T interval.)

Laboratory Assessment Data

In assessing an individual for hypercalcemia, the following values provide important data: serum calcium, urine calcium, urine osmolality, and urine specific gravity. The pattern characteristic of hypercalcemia is a serum calcium greater than 10.5 mg per 100 mL, an increased urine calcium, a decreased urine osmolality, and a decreased urine specific gravity.

Clinical and Nursing Implications

The clinical implications of hypercalcemia are very significant for the individual. Not only can this imbalance cause cardiac arrest, but it can also lead to renal dysfunction, central nervous system depression, pain, and pathological fractures.

The implications for nursing include performing the following monitoring functions: (1) assessing the rate, rhythm, and characteristics of the pulse; (2) evaluating the level of consciousness frequently; (3) monitoring muscle movement, strength, and tone; (4) assessing bowel sounds; (5) measuring and recording intake and output accurately; (6) obtaining a daily weight; (7) straining and monitoring the urine for stones; and (8) monitoring all appropriate laboratory data.

The nursing interventions that are performed with a hypercalcemic individual are (1) to encourage frequent ambulation whenever appropriate; (2) to institute active and passive range of motion exercises; (3) to provide appropriate stimuli to increase the individual's level of orientation; (4) to provide a safe physical environment for the individual; (5) to encourage acid-ash fluids such as cranberry or prune juice; (6) to encourage an increased oral intake of fluids; (7) to administer medications as prescribed; (8) to provide foods and fluids that are consistent with the dietary restrictions, if any are prescribed; and (9) to institute extra safety precautions and provide for gentle movement of the individual.

Treatment

As with all other types of imbalances, the treatment of hypercalcemia involves treating the underlying cause and correcting the imbalance. Thus, whenever possible, an attempt is made to deal with the etiology as soon as it is feasible.

Hypercalcemia can be corrected by a variety of therapeutic methods. One of the first methods employed is the administration of saline infusions. These infusions not only hydrate the individual but also dilute the extracellular calcium concentration and increase the renal excretion of calcium through the sodium diuresis. Diuretics are also given to increase the renal excretion of calcium. Other forms of treatment include administering the following: sodium bicarbonate to induce alkalosis and reduce the ionized calcium fraction; phosphate to inhibit the reabsorption of bone; glucocorticoids to inhibit calcium absorption and shift the extracellular calcium intracellularly; mithramycin to decrease bone reabsorption; ethylenediaminetetraacetic acid (EDTA) to lower the serum calcium by chelation; and dialysis therapy to deplete the serum calcium.

Hypocalcemia

Definition

Hypocalcemia is a deficit of calcium in the extracellular fluid.

Etiology

Hypocalcemia is caused by the following: hypoproteinemia; idiopathic, surgical, or pseudohypoparathyroidism; renal dysfunction; hyperphosphatemia; vitamin D deficiency; magnesium deficiency; acute pancreatitis; inadequate dietary intake; intestinal malabsorption; alkalosis; excessive administration of citrated blood; massive subcutaneous infections; osteomalacia; and malignant neoplasms, especially those with bone metastases.

Clinical Assessment Parameters

The individual experiencing hypocalcemia exhibits a variety of signs and symptoms, the majority of which are neuromuscular in nature. The clinical signs and symptoms of hypocalcemia include numbness and tingling of the extremities; circumoral tingling, muscle cramps, tetany, positive Chvostek's and Trousseau's signs, epileptiform seizures; laryngeal stridor; carpopedal spasms; hyperreflexia, mental depression, psychoses, cardiac arrest, abdominal cramps, nausea and vomiting, diarrhea, cataracts, keratitis, dry skin, brittle nails, alopecia, coagulation dysfunction (rarely occurs), and pathologic fractures. If the individual is being assessed using a cardiac monitor, the electrocardiogram will show a prolonged Q-T interval, which is characteristic of hypocalcemia.

Laboratory Assessment Data

The serum calcium is the most helpful piece of laboratory data for determining hypocalcemia. A serum calcium value less than 8.5 mg per 100 mL is indicative of hypocalcemia.

Clinical and Nursing Implications

Clinically, hypocalcemia presents many hazards to the individual's health state and normal ability to function. The neuromuscular effects of hypocalcemia alone constitute major problems for the individual. Add to those effects the cardiovascular and gastrointestinal effects and the individual, indeed, becomes severely compromised and in need of supportive care from the nurse.

The supportive nursing care for an individual experiencing hypocalcemia includes performing the following monitoring functions: (1) assessing neuromuscular function frequently; (2) monitoring the rate, rhythm, and characteristics of the pulse; (3) evaluating the rate, pattern, and characteristics of the respirations; (4) checking Chvostek's sign periodically (This involves percussing the facial nerve in the area of the face just anterior to the ear. If this percussion elicits a unilateral twitching of the facial muscles, including the eyelid and lips, it indicates hypocalcemia.); (5) testing Trousseau's sign periodically (This involves occluding the blood supply to an extremity to produce ischemia. Usually this sign is tested by applying a tourniquet, or inflating a blood pressure cuff around the upper extremity for 3 or 4 min. If the induced ischemia precipitates carpopedal spasms, it indicates hypocalcemia.); (6) assessing the individual's mental status; (7) monitoring the characteristics of the feces; (8) assessing visual acuity and the characteristics of the eyeballs; (9) evaluating the intactness of the skeletal system; (10) assessing the characteristics of the skin, nails, and hair; and (11) monitoring the serum calcium values and the electrocardiograms.

The intervening functions that are performed with the hypocalcemic individual are (1) providing a safe physical environment for the individual; (2) instituting seizure precautions; (3) providing an environment with decreased, but appropriate amounts of stimuli; (4) administering prescribed medications appropriately; (5) providing foods that are high in calcium and low in phosphorus, if prescribed; (6) providing meticulous hygienic care for the skin, nails, and hair; and (7) implementing a variety of nursing comfort measures to deal with the gastrointestinal effects.

Treatment

Hypocalcemia is treated by dealing with the underlying cause, if possible, and correcting the imbalance. The therapy used to correct the imbalance differs depending on whether it is an acute or chronic imbalance. Acute hypocalcemic imbalances are usually treated with intravenous infusions of calcium chloride, calcium gluconate, or calcium gluceptate. (The digitalized individual is monitored extremely closely during these infusions because calcium increases the sensitivity of the heart to digitalis and thus may precipitate digitalis toxicity.)

Chronic calcium depletion is effectively treated by

the following methods: administering daily doses of oral calcium preparations, such as calcium lactate, calcium gluconate, or calcium carbonate; administering daily doses of oral vitamin D preparations; increasing the dietary intake of calcium through the use of foods high in calcium content; and restricting the dietary intake of foods high in phosphorus content.

MAGNESIUM

Functions

The functions of magnesium in the physiologic processes of the body include the following: participating as a coenzyme in transphosphorylation reactions that result in a release of energy; activating other enzyme systems and thus influencing carbohydrate metabolism, protein synthesis, and nucleic acid synthesis and metabolism; acting as a mediator at the myoneural junction; activating adenosine triphosphatase; acting as a mediator of neural transmission in the central nervous system; influencing the transport of sodium and potassium across cell membranes; acting as a structural element of the bone; and influencing the secretion of parathyroid hormone.

Regulation

The extracellular concentration of magnesium is regulated by intestinal absorption and secretion, exchange between bone and the extracellular fluid, and renal excretion.

Intestinal Absorption and Secretion

Approximately 30 to 40 percent of the magnesium ingested is absorbed by the intestines, primarily the small intestines. The efficiency of this absorption varies inversely with the amount of dietary magnesium ingested. The absorption process seems to be enhanced by parathyroid hormone and vitamin D and inhibited by thyrocalcitonin.

There appears to be some intestinal secretion of magnesium, but it is minimal.

Exchange Between Bone and Extracellular Fluid

The exchange of magnesium between bone and the extracellular fluid seems to contribute minimally to the regulation of extracellular magnesium concentration. The factors that govern this exchange process are elusive and have yet to be defined.

Renal Excretion

The renal excretion of magnesium is the primary determinant of magnesium balance in the body. Reabsorption of magnesium occurs in all parts of the tubule but probably more so in the distal portion. This reabsorption is regulated by the tubular maximal capacity which seems to be equal to the filtered load of magnesium that is present at normal plasma concentrations of magnesium. Therefore even small increases in extracellular magnesium surpass the tubular maximal reabsorption capacity and increase the renal excretion of magnesium. Factors other than hypermagnesemia that increase the renal excretion of magnesium include extracellular fluid volume expansion, especially with saline solutions; diuretic agents including osmotic diuretics, renal vasodilatation; hypercalcemia and hypercalciuria; thyrocalcitonin; alcohol ingestion; thyroid hormone; growth hormone; increased sodium intake; acute metabolic acidosis; chronic mineralocorticoid effect; and phosphate depletion. Factors that decrease the renal excretion of magnesium are hypomagnesemia; parathyroid hormone and decreased extracellular fluid volume.

Variances

The variances associated with magnesium balance are hypermagnesemia and hypomagnesemia.

Hypermagnesemia

Definition

Hypermagnesemia is an excess of magnesium in the extracellular fluid.

Etiology

Hypermagnesemia occurs rather infrequently because of the renal system's capacity to excrete large quantities in excess of normal. Therefore, the primary etiology of hypermagnesemia is renal failure. Other factors that can also result in hypermagnesemia include adrenal insufficiency, shock, hypothermia, and an increased intake of magnesium. An increased intake of magnesium may result from excesses in any of the following: infusions of intravenous solutions containing magnesium, intramuscular injections of magnesium, oral laxatives containing magnesium, and enemas containing magnesium.

Clinical Assessment Parameters

The clinical signs and symptoms of hypermagnesemia are exhibited by the individual based on the severity of the imbalance. The individual seems to tolerate instances of mild hypermagnesemia without displaying clinically observable signs and symptoms. As the hypermagnesemia increases, however, the individual exhibits many signs and symptoms. These signs and symptoms increase in severity in accordance with the increased serum magnesium levels. Table 20-11 presents a correlation of the serum magnesium level with the signs and symptoms exhibited by the individual according to body system.

Laboratory Assessment Data

The serum magnesium level is the most significant laboratory value used in assessing an individual for hypermagnesemia. A serum magnesium value greater than 2.2 meq/L indicates hypermagnesemia.

Clinical and Nursing Implications

Clinically, the effects of hypermagnesemia are not hazardous to the individual until the serum magnesium level is increased to 4 or 5 times its normal value. At that point, the increase in serum magnesium not only threatens the individual's ability to function, but even the ability to survive.

The nursing care of the individual experiencing hypermagnesemia includes the following monitoring functions: (1) assessing the rate, rhythm or pattern, and characteristics of all vital signs; (2) assessing the level of consciousness frequently; (3) evaluating muscular strength and function periodically; (4) monitoring neurological responses; (5) monitoring renal output frequently; (6) assessing gastrointestinal function; and (7) monitoring serum magnesium values and the electrocardiogram.

The nursing interventions performed with the hypermagnesemic individual are (1) administering the prescribed medications appropriately; (2) providing a safe physical environment for the individual; (3) providing appropriate stimuli for maintaining orientation; (4) positioning the individual appropriately to facilitate adequate respirations; (5) maintaining bedrest and a decreased activity level as appropriate; (6) instituting active and passive range of motion exercises; and (7) providing nursing comfort measures appropriate for dealing with the gastrointestinal signs and symptoms.

TABLE 20-11

Signs and Symptoms of Varying Levels of Hypermagnesemia According to Body System

Serum magnesium level, meq/L	Body system	Signs and symptoms
2.2–3.0	None	None
3.1–5.0	Vascular	Hypotension
	Gastrointestinal	Nausea
		Vomiting
	Nervous	Depressed deep tendon reflexes
5.1–7.0	Nervous	Drowsiness
		Depression
7.1–10.0	Nervous	Loss of deep tendon reflexes
	Muscular	Weakness
	Cardiac	Sinus bradycardia
		Prolonged P-R interval
		Prolonged Q-T interval
10.1–15.0	Respiratory	Hypoventilation
	Muscular	Paralysis
	Nervous	Coma
15.1–20.0	Cardiac	Arrest
	Respiratory	Apnea

Treatment

The goals for the treatment of hypermagnesemia are to treat the underlying disorder, counteract the harmful effects, and increase the renal excretion. Treating the underlying disorder is easy if the hypermagnesemia is due to excessive intake. However, it may be impossible to treat or stop the underlying cause if it is due to renal failure.

The harmful effects of hypermagnesemia can be effectively counteracted by infusing intravenous calcium preparations because the calcium ion antagonizes the action of the magnesium ion.

Increasing the renal excretion of magnesium can be accomplished in the presence of normal renal function, mainly by expanding the extracellular fluid volume with saline and/or administering diuretics. If renal dysfunction is present, dialysis therapy will effectively remove the increased serum levels of magnesium.

Hypomagnesemia

Definition

Hypomagnesemia is a deficit of magnesium in the extracellular fluid.

Etiology

The etiologies of hypomagnesemia can be classified according to the following five catagories: (1) decreased intake, (2) decreased intestinal absorption, (3) excessive loss of body fluids, (4) excessive loss in the urine, and (5) miscellaneous factors.

Those etiologies of hypomagnesemia that are included in the category of decreased intake are prolonged intravenous therapy and magnesium-free solutions, protein-calorie malnutrition, and starvation.

The category of etiologies that result in hypomagnesemia due to decreased intestinal absorption include malabsorption syndrome such as nontropical sprue, surgical resection of the small bowel, and hereditary intestinal defects in magnesium absorption.

The etiologies of hypomagnesemia that are classified in the category of excessive loss of body fluids are intestinal and biliary fistulas, enema and non-magnesium laxative abuse, prolonged use of nasogastric suctioning, and severe diarrhea, especially as in ulcerative colitis.

The category of etiologies that produce hypomagnesemia due to excessive magnesium loss in the urine include chronic alcoholism; diuretic therapy; primary hyperaldosteronism; the diuretic phase of acute renal failure; hypercalcemia, particularly in association with primary hyperparathyroidism, malignancies, and vitamin D intoxication; hyperthyroidism; renal tubular acidosis; diabetic ketoacidosis; chronic renal failure with magnesium wasting; idiopathic renal magnesium wasting; and gentamycin toxicity.

The last category of etiologies of hypomagnesemia is the group of miscellaneous causes that include acute pancreatitis, hypoparathyroidism, idiopathic hypomagnesemia, inappropriate secretion of antidiuretic hormone, and multiple transfusions with citrated blood.

Clinical Assessment Parameters

The clinical signs and symptoms of hypomagnesemia are very similar to those seen with hypocalcemia. The hypomagnesemic individual will exhibit any combination of the following signs and symptoms: muscle fasciculation; muscle weakness; coarse, flapping tremors; ataxia; vertigo; positive Chvostek's and Trousseau's signs; generalized tetany; generalized muscle spasticity; spontaneous carpopedal spasms; seizures; apathy; confusion; irritability; psychoses; depression, nystagmus; hypertension; cardiac dysfunction; anorexia; and nausea.

If the individual is being assessed using a cardiac monitor, the electrocardiogram will show the following changes: a prolonged Q-T interval, broadened T waves of decreased amplitude; and an occasional shortened ST segment.

Laboratory Assessment Data

The laboratory values used to assess an individual for hypomagnesemia are the serum magnesium, calcium, and potassium, and the urine magnesium and calcium. The levels of these values that are characteristic of hypomagnesemia are a serum magnesium of less than 1.6 meq/L, a decreased serum calcium and potassium; and a decreased urine magnesium and calcium.

Clinical and Nursing Implications

The clinical implications of hypomagnesemia are significant because of the extensive involvement of the neuromuscular system. Having that particular body system so compromised certainly places the individual's well-being at risk.

The implications of hypomagnesemia on the nursing care of the individual require that the following monitoring functions be performed: (1) assess neurologic function frequently; (2) monitor the level of consciousness periodically; (3) assess muscle strength and movement; (4) check Chvostek's and Trousseau's signs; (5) assess gastrointestinal function; (6) monitor the rate, rhythm, and characteristics of the pulse; (7) monitor all other vital signs; and (8) assess the appropriate laboratory values periodically.

The nursing interventions that are performed with the hypomagnesemic individual include (1) instituting seizure precautions, (2) providing a safe physical environment for the individual, (3) maintaining bedrest or limited activity as appropriate, (4) instituting active and passive range of motion exercises as appropriate, (5) providing appropriate stimuli for maintaining orientation, and (6) providing nursing comfort measures to deal with the gastrointestinal effects.

Treatment

As with all the other imbalances, the treatment of hypomagnesemia is aimed at halting the primary cause and correcting the imbalance. The imbalance is usually corrected by administering either intravenous infusions of magnesium sulfate or magnesium chloride, or intramuscular injections of magnesium sulfate. The replacement therapy usually consists of administering 10 to 40 meq of magnesium daily until the serum magnesium level returns to normal.

CHLORIDE

Functions

The functions of chloride in the body are to assist in maintaining the osmotic pressure of the extracellular fluid, to participate in maintaining water balance, to participate in normal gastric digestion by providing an acid medium through the production of hydrochloric acid, and to assist in maintaining acid-base balance.

Regulation

Extracellular chloride concentration is regulated primarily by the renal system. This regulation is dependent upon the acid-base balance of the body fluids and aldosterone secretion.

In general, the renal handling of chloride is very similar to that of sodium, primarily because the two ions are coupled in many of the reabsorption, secretion, and transport processes, thus maintaining electrical neutrality. In most instances, then, chloride ion movement is passive and depends on active sodium transport. There are, however, two sites in the tubular system where this dependent relationship does not exist. The first site is the proximal tubule, where chloride reabsorption and excretion are dependent upon hydrogen ion secretion rather than on sodium transport. Thus, the degree of proximal tubular acidification determines the amount of chloride that is reabsorbed and excreted. The nature of this relationship is such that an increase in hydrogen ion secretion in the proximal tubule results in a compensatory increase in chloride excretion in response to an increase in bicarbonate reabsorption.

The second site is in the loop of Henle where chloride ion transport may be more active than passive. Consequently, chloride movement is less dependent on sodium transport in this portion of the tubule.

The influence of aldosterone in the regulation of chloride is secondary to its effect on sodium and water reabsorption. As was previously discussed, aldosterone acts on the distal tubule and collecting duct to increase the reabsorption of sodium. As the sodium is actively reabsorbed, water and chloride are passively reabsorbed along with it. Thus there is increased reabsorption of sodium, chloride, and water.

Variances

The variances in the balance of extracellular chloride are hyperchloremia and hypochloremia.

Hyperchloremia

Definition

Hyperchloremia is an excess of chloride in the extracellular fluid.

Etiology

Hyperchloremia is caused by the following: excessive intake of chloride, usually in the form of medications; renal tubular acidosis; ureterosigmoidostomy; and increased sodium intake, especially if there is an associated decrease in the extracellular fluid volume.

If the chloride increase is not accompanied by a proportional increase in sodium, hyperchloremic acidosis can result because of decreased hydrogen ion secretion in the proximal tubule.

Clinical Assessment Parameters

The individual experiencing hyperchloremia that is disproportionate to the hypernatremia exhibits the following signs and symptoms: muscle weakness, decreased level of consciousness, and deep rapid respirations. The individual experiencing hyperchloremia that is proportionate to the hypernatremia will exhibit signs and symptoms that are reflective of either the increased sodium concentration or the decreased fluid volume. (The signs and symptoms of both of those imbalances have been previously delineated.)

Laboratory Assessment Data

The laboratory values that provide the most data for assessing an individual in terms of hyperchloremia include the following: serum chloride, sodium, bicarbonate, and pH; and urine pH and specific gravity. The pattern of these values that is consistent with hyperchloremia is a serum chloride greater than 106 meq/L, an increased serum sodium, a decreased serum bicarbonate and pH, an increased urine pH, and a decreased urine specific gravity. The changes in serum pH and bicarbonate and urine pH are reflective, of course, of the hyperchloremic acidosis rather than hyperchloremia accompanied by a proportionate hypernatremia.

Clinical and Nursing Implications

The clinical implications of hyperchloremia are related to the acidotic, hypernatremic, and hypovolemic conditions that may accompany it. This array of imbalances will significantly interfere wtih the internal physiologic processes of the individual and will create threats to his well-being.

The implications of hyperchloremia for providing nursing care for the individual include monitoring and intervening functions related to all the mentioned imbalances. Since the nursing behaviors related to the hypovolemic and hypernatremic individual have been previously delineated, they will not be repeated. This discussion instead focuses on caring for the hyperchloremic individual.

The monitoring functions performed with individuals experiencing hyperchloremia include (1) assessing the level of consciousness frequently; (2) monitoring the rate, rhythm, and characteristics of the respirations; (3) evaluating muscle strength; (4) monitoring appropriate laboratory values; and (5) monitoring all other vital signs.

The intervening nursing functions performed with hyperchloremic individuals are (1) to provide a safe physical environment for the individual; (2) to position the individual appropriately to facilitate adequate respirations; (3) to provide adequate, appropriate stimuli to promote orientation; (4) to maintain an activity level consistent with the individual's muscle strength; (5) to administer fluids and/or medications as prescribed by the physician; and (6) to restrict chloride intake if consistent with the medical plan of care.

Treatment

The treatment of hyperchloremia usually involves a combination of the following therapies: treating the primary underlying cause; administering or encouraging fluids to dilute the chloride; administering sodium bicarbonate; and in some cases, administering diuretics.

Hypochloremia

Definition

Hypochloremia is a deficit of chloride in the extracellular fluid.

Etiology

Hypochloremia is caused by the following: excessive loss of gastric secretions, usually due to vomiting or nasogastric suctioning; excessive secretion or administration of adrenocorticoid hormones; decreased intake, usually seen with severely salt-restricted diets; and in some cases, rigorous use of diuretic therapy.

Hypochloremia is usually associated with hyponatremia, and if the loss of the two ions is proportional, the serum pH will remain virtually unchanged. However, if the chloride loss is disproportionately higher than the sodium loss, a hypochloremic alkalosis may result.

Clinical Assessment Parameters

The hypochloremic individual with a chloride loss that is disproportionate to the sodium loss exhibits the following signs and symptoms: muscle weakness; tetany; agitation; irritability; and slow, shallow respirations. An individual with hypochloremia that has resulted from proportionate losses of chloride and sodium exhibits the signs and symptoms characteristic of hyponatremia and/or hypervolemia. Those signs and symptoms have been previously discussed.

Laboratory Assessment Data

The laboratory values that provide the most data in determining hypochloremia in the individual are the following: serum chloride, sodium, bicarbonate, and pH. The pattern characteristic of hypochloremia is a serum chloride less than 96 meq/L, a decreased serum sodium, and increased serum bicarbonate and pH values.

Clinical and Nursing Implications

The clinical implications for the hypochloremic individual are definitely related to the alkalosis, hyponatremia, and hypervolemia that may accompany the hypochloremia. The interrelationship of those imbalances in an individual indeed jeopardize well-being and require supportive nursing measures.

The monitoring and intervening nursing behaviors that are implemented with individuals experiencing hyponatremia and hypervolemia have been previously discussed. Therefore, only those nursing behaviors that directly relate to the care of the hypochloremic individual are discussed at this time.

The monitoring functions that are performed in caring for an individual experiencing hypochloremia include (1) assessing the level of consciousness; (2) monitoring the rate, rhythm, and characteristics of the respirations; (3) evaluating all other vital signs; (4) assessing muscle strength and movement; (5) measuring and recording intake and output accurately; and (6) monitoring appropriate laboratory values.

The intervening functions that are performed with the hypochloremic individual are (1) to provide a safe physical environment for the individual; (2) to provide a quiet environment with decreased stimuli to minimize agitation; (3) to limit activity in accordance with muscle strength; (4) to provide foods and fluids high in chloride if appropriate; and (5) to administer prescribed medications correctly.

Treatment

The treatment of hypochloremia includes treating the primary underlying cause and correcting the imbalance. The imbalance is usually corrected by replacing the lost chloride with sodium chloride, potassium chloride, or ammonium chloride. Replacement therapy usually involves replacing three-fourths of the imbalance with sodium chloride and one-fourth with potassium chloride. The ammonium chloride is used in place of the potassium chloride if the serum potassium concentration is already elevated.

PHOSPHATE

Functions

The functions of the anion phosphate in the body are (1) participating as a structural element of the bone; (2) influencing the production of energy sources by the red blood cells that are necessary for oxygen delivery; (3) participating in the metabolism of carbohydrates, lipids, and nucleic acids; (4) acting as the major urinary buffer in the formation of titratable acid; (5) participating in oxidative phosphorylation; (6) influencing the absorption of glucose and glycerol in the intestines; and (7) maintaining the structural integrity of the cell wall.

Regulation

The extracellular concentration of phosphate is regulated by the following four mechanisms: intestinal absorption, exchange between the bone and extracellular fluid, exchange between the intracellular and extracellular fluid, and renal excretion.

Intestinal Absorption

Of all the dietary phosphate ingested, approximately 70 percent is absorbed in the jejunum and the remaining 30 percent is excreted in the feces. The intestinal absorption of phosphate is increased by parathyroid hormone and vitamin D and decreased by thyrocalcitonin and binding by calcium or antacids.

Bone and Extracellular Fluid Exchange

The regulation of extracellular phosphate by exchange between the bone and extracellular fluid depends primarily upon a similar exchange process that occurs as part of calcium homeostasis. When calcium is reabsorbed or released from the bone, phosphate accompanies it. Likewise, when calcium is deposited in the bone, phosphate is also deposited. The more active of the two exchange processes in regulating extracellular phosphate concentration is bone reabsorption. Bone reabsorption is increased by parathyroid hormone and vitamin D and decreased by thyrocalcitonin.

Intracellular and Extracellular Fluid Exchange

The concentration of phosphate in the extracellular fluid is also influenced by the exchange of phosphate ions between the intracellular and extracellular fluids. The rate of this exchange is dependent upon the rate of glycolysis that occurs in the cell. When glycolysis occurs, phosphate shifts into the cell. Thus, an increase in glycolysis would increase the phosphate shift into the cell, and a decrease in glycolysis would increase the shift of phosphate out of the cell. Those factors which would facilitate a phosphate shift into the cell include acute alkalosis and the administration of glucose, insulin, or epinephrine. Acute acidosis is one factor that would increase the shift of phosphate out of the cell.

Renal Excretion

The renal regulation of phosphate is excretory in nature. The renal excretion of phosphate is dependent primarily upon the serum phosphate concentration and parathyroid hormone. These two factors affect renal excretion by determining the amount and rate at which phosphate can be reabsorbed by the kidney.

Seventy percent of the filtered phosphate is reabsorbed in the proximal tubule and 25 percent in the distal tubule. This reabsorption is dependent on the tubular maximal reabsorptive capacity that is established by parathyroid hormone.

The renal excretion of phosphate is increased by the following factors: parathyroid hormone, acute fluid volume expansion, hyperphosphatemia, thyrocalcitonin, metabolic acidosis, hypokalemia, and diuretics that function by acting on the proximal tubule. The renal excretion of phosphate is decreased by vitamin D, growth hormone, hypophosphatemia, and a decrease in fluid volume.

Variances

The variances or imbalances that occur in relation to phosphate are hyperphosphatemia and hypophosphatemia.

Hyperphosphatemia

Definition

Hyperphosphatemia is an excess of phosphate in the extracellular fluid.

Etiology

Hyperphosphatemia is caused by the following: renal dysfunction (probably the most common cause), hypoparathyroidism, pseudohypoparathyroidism, excessive ingestion or infusion of phosphate salts, catabolic states, neoplastic diseases, and overingestion of vitamin D metabolites.

Clinical Assessment Parameters

An inverse relationship exists between phosphate and calcium in the extracellular fluid. Therefore, a hyperphosphatemic condition also results in hypocalcemia. This relationship accounts for the fact that the clinical signs and symptoms of the hyperphosphatemic individual are indeed the same as those seen in the hypocalcemic individual. Those signs and symptoms have been previously delineated and will not be repeated. It should be noted, however, that the primary effect of hypocalcemia on the individual was in relation to the neuromuscular system.

Laboratory Assessment Data

The laboratory values used to assess the individual in relation to hyperphosphatemia are the serum phosphorus and calcium values. The pattern characteristic of hyperphosphatemia is a serum phosphorus greater than 4.5 mg per 100 mL and a decreased serum calcium.

Clincial and Nursing Implications

Since the clinical manifestations of hyperphosphatemia are the same as hypocalcemia, it is logical that the clinical implications and nursing behaviors are also the same. Those implications and behaviors have been previously discussed in relation to hypocalcemia.

Treatment

The treatment of hyperphosphatemia is aimed at eliminating the cause and correcting the imbalance. Correcting the imbalance can be accomplished by the following methods: restricting the intake of phosphate; administering intestinal phosphate-binding agents, such as aluminum-hydroxide gel; administering diuretics, if renal function is present; and implementing dialysis therapy if renal dysfunction is present.

Hypophosphatemia

Definition

Hypophosphatemia is a deficit of phosphate in the extracellular fluid.

Etiology

The following are causes of hypophosphatemia: primary and secondary hyperparathyroidism; primary renal tubular defects in phosphate reabsorption; states of chronic metabolic acidosis, as are seen with renal tubular acidosis and ureterosigmoidostomies; hypokalemia; extracellular fluid volume expansion; administration of phosphate binders; malabsorption; starvation; prolonged use of phosphate-free intravenous solutions; abnormalities in vitamin D metabolism, as in vitamin D associated rickets; alcohol withdrawal; recovery phase of diabetic ketoacidosis; administration of agents designed to increase glycolysis; and the recovery phase of malnutrition.

Clinical Assessment Parameters

The hypophosphatemic individual exhibits the following signs and symptoms: lethargy, muscle weakness, anorexia, and mild bone pain. (If the imbalance is prolonged, there may also be signs of platelet dysfunction and decreased phagocytic activity by the white blood cells.)

Laboratory Assessment Data

The most significant laboratory value used in assessing an individual for hypophosphatemia is the serum phosphorus. A serum phosphorus less than 2 mg per 100 mL is consistent with hypophosphatemia. The urine calcium may provide additional assessment data because hypophosphatemia seems to result in hypercalciuria.

Clinical and Nursing Implications

The clinical implications of hypophosphatemia for the individual are not as hazardous as those related to some of the other imbalances. The most significant implication of hypophosphatemia for the individual seems to be the decrease in general muscle strength. This effect decreases the individual's ability to carry out the activities of daily living, as well as to participate in health care. Thus, even though it is not as life-threatening an imbalance, it still requires that the individual receive nursing support.

The monitoring functions that are a part of nursing support include (1) assessing muscle strength, (2) evaluating the individual's level of consciousness, (3) monitoring for signs of associated hypercalcemia, (4) assessing the individual's comfort level, (5) observing for signs of decreased clotting or decreased inflammatory response, (6) monitoring intake, and (7) monitoring appropriate laboratory values.

The following intervening functions are performed with the hypophosphatemic individual: (1) assisting with the activities of daily living; (2) providing activity in accordance with muscle strength; (3) instituting active and passive range of motion exercises; (4) providing stimuli appropriate for maintaining orientation; (5) establishing a safe physical environment for the individual; (6) providing food and fluids high in phosphate, if appropriate; (7) presenting small amounts of food and fluids at intervals in an appetizing manner; (8) providing nursing comfort measures; and (9) administering medications as prescribed.

Treatment

Hypophosphatemia is usually treated by dealing with the primary underlying cause or replacing the lost phosphate. The replacement therapy may be implemented using either oral or intravenous phosphate preparations.

SULFATE

Functions

The functions of sulfate in the body are to participate in the synthesis of sulfated mucopolysaccharides for the cartilage and bone matrix, to influence the synthesis of heparin and the mucoprotein secretions of the gastrointestinal tract, and to detoxify drugs and foreign compounds in the liver.

Regulation

The concentration of sulfate in the extracellular fluid seems to be regulated by intake, the rate of release by metabolic degradation, and renal excretion. The exact mechanisms for these regulating processes are not known.

Variances

The variances in sulfate balance in the body seem to be clinically insignificant.

PROTEIN

Functions

The primary functions of protein in the body are (1) to provide colloid osmotic pressure for regulating fluid volume, (2) to participate in enzyme processes,

(3) to influence the development of natural and acquired immunity, (4) to participate in the regulation of acid-base balance, (5) to participate in blood coagulation, and (6) to influence the production of hormones and some vitamins.

Regulation

The concentration of extracellular protein is regulated by the following factors: dietary intake, the rate of formation by the liver, and the rate of use by the tissues.

Variance

The variance in protein balance that has clinical significance for the individual is hypoproteinemia.

Hypoproteinemia

Definition

Hypoproteinemia is a deficit of protein in the extracellular fluid.

Etiology

Hypoproteinemia is caused by the following: inadequate dietary intake; hemorrhage; severe prolonged infection; gastrointestinal pathology that inhibits absorption, such as obstruction or fistulas; fractures; medical pathology and surgical procedures that produce catabolic states; hypokalemia; and prolonged illness, especially when accompanied by fluid imbalances.

Clinical Assessment Parameters

The individual experiencing hypoproteinemia exhibits the following signs and symptoms: weight loss, muscle wasting, decreased muscle tone, fatigue, mental and emotional depression, anorexia, nausea, vomiting, decreased wound healing, decreased immunity or resistance to infection, and edema.

Laboratory Assessment Data

The laboratory value that provides the most significant data for assessing an individual in relation to hypoproteinemia is the serum albumin. A serum albumin value of less than 4 g per 100 mL is consistent with hypoproteinemia. Other laboratory values that may provide additional data, if iron intake has been ade-

quate, are hemoglobin, hematocrit, and red blood cell count. Decreased values for these three items, in the presence of adequate iron intake, are consistent with hypoproteinemia.

Clinical and Nursing Implications

The clinical implications of hypoproteinemia for the individual are very significant. Without adequate protein, the individual does not heal well, nor is he able to resist infection. Thus, he is predisposed to developing life-threatening complications such as septicemia.

The implications of hypoproteinemia for providing nursing care for the individual indicate that the following monitoring behaviors be performed: (1) monitoring protein intake closely; (2) obtaining precise daily weights; (3) assessing muscle strength and movement; (4) assessing level of consciousness periodically; (5) monitoring gastrointestinal functioning; (6) assessing skin integrity, texture, and turgor; (7) monitoring vital signs; and (8) monitoring appropriate laboratory values.

The intervening behaviors that are performed with a hypoproteinemic individual are (1) providing a physical environment that decreases exposure to bacterial contamination; (2) maintaining a limited activity level consistent with the individual's muscle strength; (3) instituting active and passive range of motion exercises; (4) assisting with the activities of daily living; (5) providing stimuli appropriate to maintaining orientation; (6) providing meticulous skin care; (7) instituting nursing comfort measures to deal with the gastrointestinal effects; (8) using creative nursing measures to decrease mental depression; and (9) providing high-protein foods and fluids as prescribed.

Treatment

Hypoproteinemia is treated by dealing with the underlying cause and correcting the imbalance. The imbalance is usually corrected by providing a high-protein diet that is balanced with adequate calories, vitamins, and minerals; using high-protein oral supplements; or infusing proteins and amino acids parenterally. In some cases, the high-protein oral intake is given via a nasogastric tube if the individual has difficulty taking nourishment.

ORGANIC ACIDS

Organic acids, such as pyruvic acid and lactic acid, which are produced as a result of carbohydrate metabolism, are present in small amounts in the extracellular fluid. Normally, these fixed, nonvolatile acids are clinically not significant for the individual because they are buffered and excreted by the kidneys. When they are produced in abnormal quantities, they result in a change in the acid-base balance of the body. Thus, the clinical significance of having abnormal quantities of organic acids in the extracellular fluid will be discussed in the next section on acid-base.

ACID-BASE

Functions

Acids and bases function in the body not only by participating in the physiologic processes, but also by maintaining a stable environment to facilitate those processes. The physiologic processes and associated chemical reactions of the body occur in a stable, slightly alkaline environment. When the normal balance of that environment is disturbed, through an increase or decrease in hydrogen ions, those processes and reactions may be accelerated, deterred, or totally inhibited. Thus, a change in the pH of the internal environment can affect the entire body. The pH or hydrogen ion concentration of the internal environment is maintained within narrow limits by the buffering actions of acids and bases present in the body.

Regulation

The hydrogen ion concentration, or pH, of the body fluids is maintained and regulated by the following three mechanisms: the body fluid buffers, the respiratory system, and the renal system. These mechanisms act by buffering hydrogen ions to prevent not only increases in hydrogen ion concentration which would result in acidosis, but also decreases in hydrogen ion concentration which would result in alkalosis.

Body Fluid Buffer System

The body fluid buffer system is composed of buffer pairs consisting of a weak acid and its conjugate base, a salt of that weak acid. Table 20-12 presents the composition and approximate amounts of those buffer pairs in the body. As is depicted in Table 20-12, the carbonic acid–sodium bicarbonate pair is the primary constituent of the body fluid buffer system. Figure 20-6 uses the carbonic acid–bicarbonate buffer pair to illustrate how the body fluid buffer system functions.

The body fluid buffer system reacts within a fraction of a second to prevent changes in hydrogen ion concentration in the body fluids. Because of its fast action, it is often called the first line of defense against acid-base imbalances.

Respiratory System

The respiratory system regulates hydrogen ion concentration in the body fluids by altering the amount of carbon dioxide available for forming carbonic acid. This alteration in the amount of available carbon dioxide is governed by the respiratory control center in the medulla which varies the rate and depth of

TABLE 20-12
Composition of the Body Fluid Buffer System

Buffer pairs		Percent contributed to total buffering
Weak acid	Conjugate base	
Carbonic acid (H_2CO_3)	Sodium bicarbonate ($NaHCO_3$)	53
Hemoglobin (Hb)	Potassium hemoglobinate (KHb)	35
Oxyhemoglobin ($HHbO_2$)	Potassium oxyhemoglobinate ($KHbO_2$)	
Plasma protein (HPr)	Proteinate (NaPr)	7
Acid organic phosphate ($NaRHPO_4$)	Alkaline organic phosphate (Na_2RPO_4)	3
Acid inorganic phosphate (NaH_2PO_4)	Alkaline inorganic phosphate (Na_2HPO_4)	2

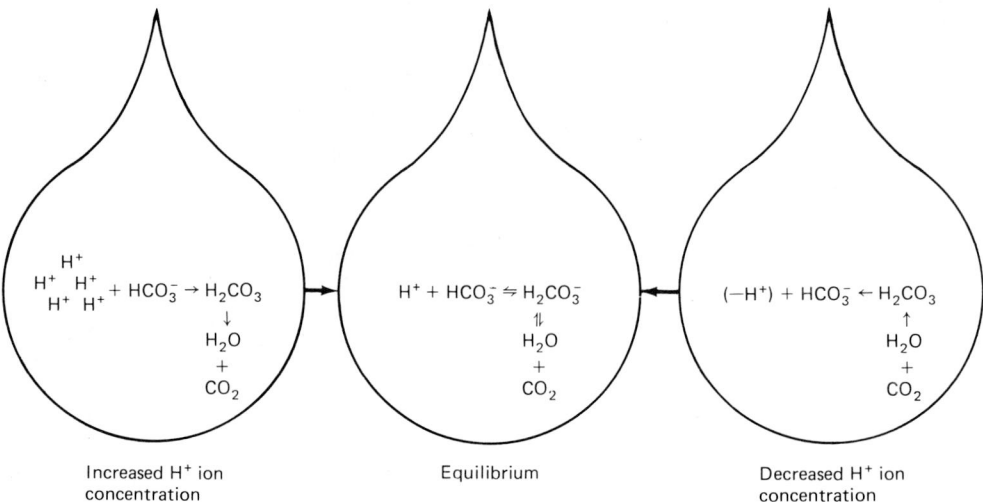

Increased H^+ ion concentration

Equilibrium

Decreased H^+ ion concentration

FIGURE 20-6

Regulation of hydrogen ion concentration by the body fluid buffer system using the carbonic acid–bicarbonate pair.

ventilation according to the carbon dioxide concentration. An increase in carbon dioxide concentration is responded to by an increase in the rate and depth of ventilation. Thus, the carbon dioxide concentration in the alveoli is decreased and less is available for forming carbonic acid. The reciprocal of this process occurs when there is a decrease in carbon dioxide concentration in the alveoli. Figure 20-7 illustrates these respiratory processes for regulating hydrogen ion concentration in the body fluids.

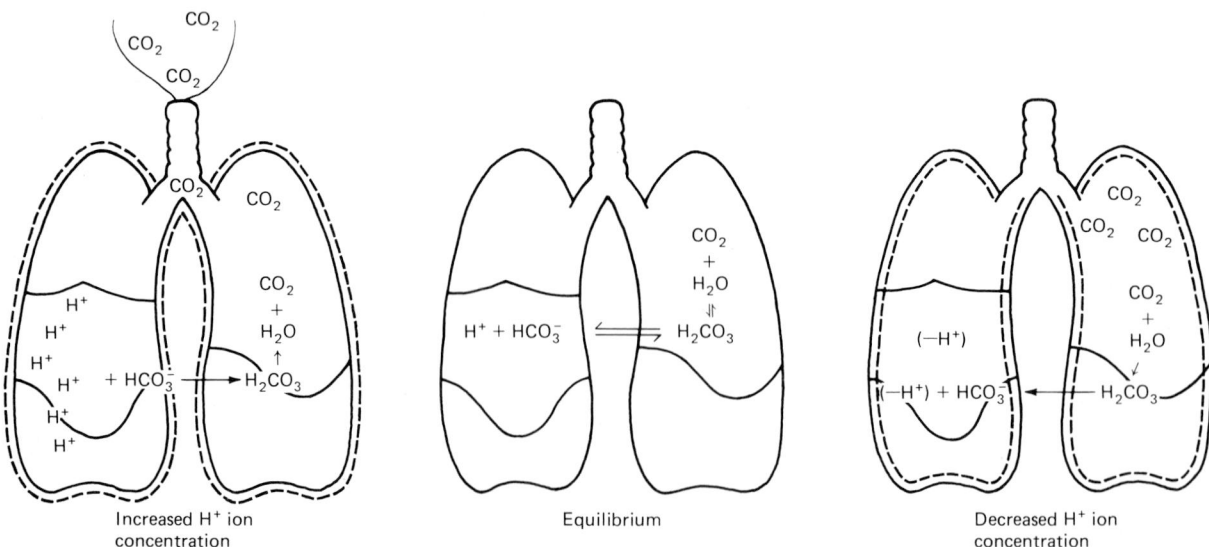

Increased H^+ ion concentration

Equilibrium

Decreased H^+ ion concentration

FIGURE 20-7

Regulation of hydrogen ion concentration by the respiratory system.

The respiratory system usually responds to changes in hydrogen ion concentration within 1 to 3 min to prevent imbalances from occurring.

Renal System

The renal system regulates hydrogen ion concentration in the body fluids through the following five processes: (1) hydrogen ion secretion; (2) sodium reabsorption; (3) bicarbonate reabsorption;(4) excretion of titratable acids, or acidification of phosphate salts; and (5) ammonia synthesis. Figure 20-8 depicts these processes.

The renal system requires hours to days to respond to changes in hydrogen ion concentration and thus is the slowest, but most effective, regulatory method.

Variances

The variances or imbalances associated with acid-base are metabolic acidosis, metabolic alkalosis, respiratory acidosis, and respiratory alkalosis.

Metabolic Acidosis

Definition

Metabolic acidosis is a deficit of bicarbonate in the extracellular fluid.

Etiology

Metabolic acidosis results from two categories of etiologies. It occurs either from causes that produce a loss of bicarbonate from the body, or from causes that produce increased amounts of nonvolatile acids in the body. Those etiologies that produce a loss of bicarbonate from the body, creating a hyperchloremic acidosis, include renal tubular acidosis; use of carbonic anhydrase inhibitors; extracellular fluid volume expansion; hyperalimentation; administration of chloride containing acids, such as hydrochloric acid or ammonium chloride; diarrhea; pancreatic or small bowel draining fistulas; ureterosigmoidostomy; ileal conduit; and the use of anion exchange resins, such as cholestyramine.

Those etiologies that produce metabolic acidosis by increasing the amount of acid in the body, creating a normochloremic acidosis, are renal failure, diabetic ketoacidosis, starvation, ethanol intoxication, tissue hypoxia, paraldehyde intoxication, salicylate intoxication, methanol intoxication, and high-fat diets.

Clinical Assessment Parameters

The individual experiencing metabolic acidosis exhibits a combination of the following signs and symptoms: headache, fatigue, drowsiness, decreased mental function, confusion, coma, seizures, hypotension, tissue hypoxia, cardiac dysrhythmia, Kussmaul respirations, anorexia, nausea, and vomiting.

Laboratory Assessment Data

The laboratory values that provide the most significant data for assessing the acid-base balance of an individual are the blood gas values. Table 20-13 presents the normal values for both arterial and mixed venous blood gas samples. In addition to the blood gas values, selected serum and urine values also provide significant assessment data.

The pattern of laboratory values that is characteristic of metabolic acidosis is a pH less than 7.37, a bicarbonate less than 22 meq/L, a base excess less than -2, a decreased P_{CO_2}, an increased serum potassium; and usually a decreased urine pH that may vary depending on the etiology.

Clinical and Nursing Implications

The clinical implications of metabolic acidosis for the individual are significant because the body does not tolerate changes in hydrogen ion concentration in the internal environment very well. Such changes will accelerate, deter, or inhibit various metabolic processes creating greater hazards to the individual's health state. However, the most threatening change that occurs with severe acidosis is cardiovascular collapse due to arteriolar dilation and decreased cardiac contractility. This change obviously can result in death for the individual.

The nursing monitoring functions performed with the individual experiencing metabolic acidosis include (1) assessing the level of consciousness periodically; (2) evaluating overall muscle strength; (3) assessing the rate, rhythm, pattern, and characteristics of all vital signs, especially the pulse and respirations; (4) monitoring the color and temperature of the skin as a means of determining tissue perfusion status; (5) assessing the gastrointestinal functioning; (6) measuring and recording intake and output meticulously; (7) obtaining accurate daily weights; (8) assessing the comfort level frequently; (9) assessing for signs of hyperkalemia; and (10) monitoring appropriate laboratory values periodically.

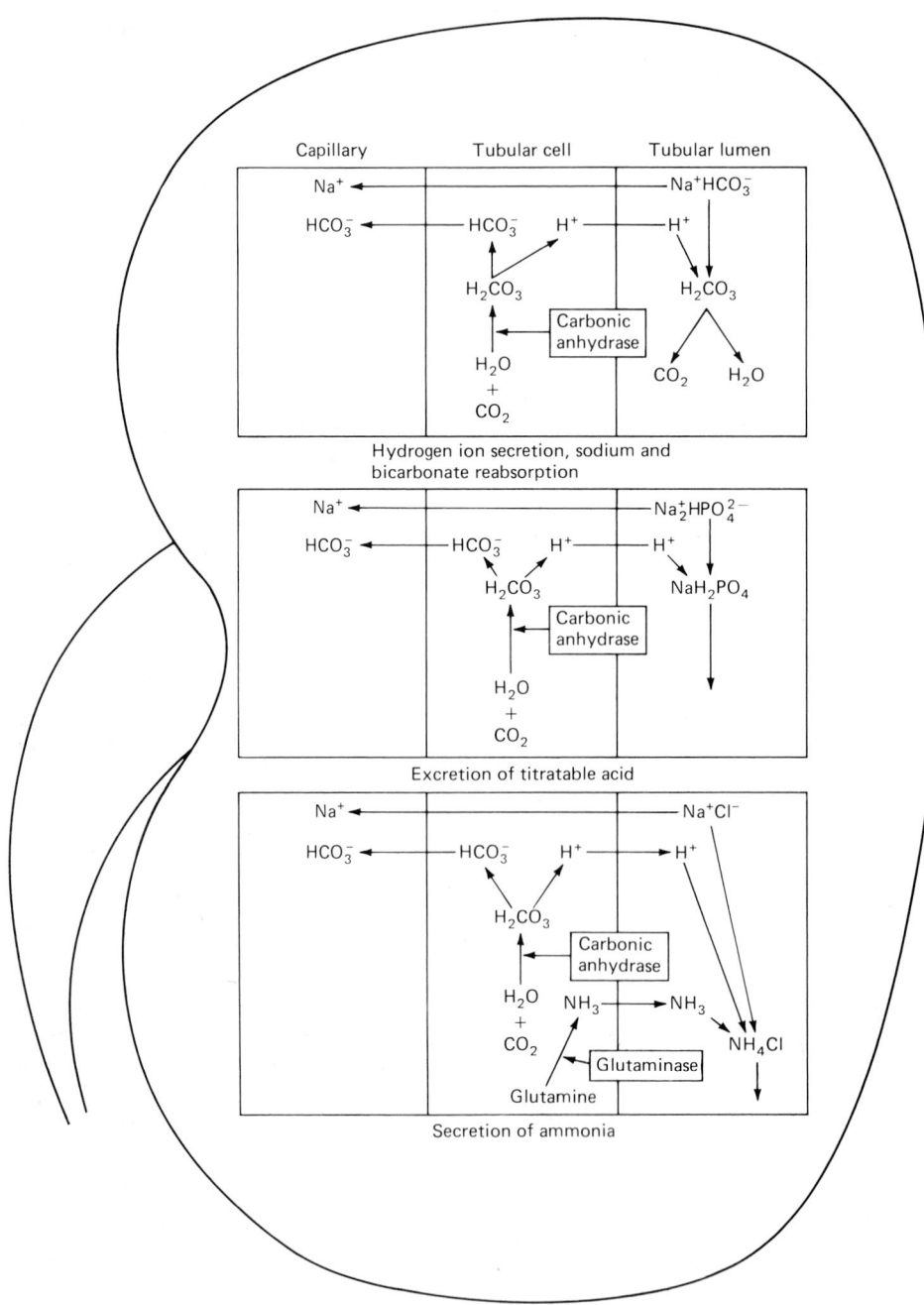

FIGURE 20-8

Regulation of hydrogen ion concentration by the renal system.

TABLE 20-13
Normal Blood Gas Values

Substance measured	Arterial blood	Mixed venous blood
pH	7.37–7.43 (7.35–7.45)*	7.33–7.39 (7.31–7.41)*
P_{O_2}	80–100 mmHg	35–40 mmHg
O_2 saturation	95–97%	70–75%
P_{CO_2}	37–43 mmHg (35–45 mmHg)*	41–51 mmHg
HCO_3	22–26 meq/L	22–26 meq/L
BE (base excess)	+2 to −2	+2 to −2

* The more liberal range is gaining wider acceptance as being the norm.

Nursing interventions that are performed with the individual with metabolic acidosis are (1) administering fluids and medications as prescribed; (2) instituting seizure precautions; (3) maintaining bedrest and instituting active and passive range of motion exercises; (4) assisting the individual in assuming a position to facilitate respirations; (5) providing stimuli appropriate to maintaining orientation; (6) providing nursing comfort measures to deal with the gastrointestinal effects; (7) providing frequent oral hygiene using nondrying agents; and (8) establishing a safe physical environment for the individual.

Treatment

The treatment of metabolic acidosis is aimed at dealing with the underlying cause. Thus, the therapy used will vary according to the etiology. However, if the acidosis is severe, it is important to replace the lost bicarbonate simultaneously with treating the underlying cause. The general rule is to replace the bicarbonate loss slowly with an appropriate alkali over several hours. It is also suggested in this case that a slight undercorrection be achieved in order to prevent a rebound metabolic alkalosis from occurring.

Metabolic Alkalosis

Definition

Metabolic alkalosis is an excess of bicarbonate in the extracellular fluid.

Etiology

Metabolic alkalosis is caused by the following: vomiting; gastrointestinal suctioning; diarrhea (if it has a high chloride content); diuretic therapy; laxative abuse; cystic fibrosis; primary and secondary hyperaldosteronism; Cushing's syndrome; licorice abuse; excessive ingestion of bicarbonate, or other alkalinizing salts; hypokalemia; and hypercalcemia.

Clinical Assessment Parameters

Metabolic alkalosis is exhibited clinically in the individual by a combination of the following signs and symptoms: increased neuromuscular irritability; tetany; seizures; belligerence; confusion; stupor; coma; hypoventilation; cardiac dysrhythmia; nausea; vomiting; and diarrhea.

Laboratory Assessment Data

The laboratory data used to assess an individual for metabolic alkalosis is provided primarily by the blood gas values, but selected serum and urine values can also be of assistance. The pattern of laboratory values that is characteristic of metabolic alkalosis is a pH greater than 7.43; a bicarbonate greater than 26 meq/L; a base excess greater than +2; an increased P_{CO_2}; a decreased serum chloride; a decreased serum potassium; a decreased serum calcium; and a decreased urine chloride, the degree of which depends on the etiology. If the etiology of the metabolic alkalosis is associated with extracellular fluid volume depletion, the individual exhibits a urinary chloride of less than 10 meq/L. If the etiology is related to extracellular fluid volume expansion, the urinary chloride is greater than 20 meq/L.

Clinical and Nursing Implications

The clinical significance of metabolic alkalosis for the individual is related to the neuromuscular and respiratory effects of the imbalance. The hyperirritability of the central nervous system and the compensatory hypoventilation represent definite risks to an individual's well-being.

The nursing monitoring functions that are performed with the individual experiencing metabolic alkalosis include (1) assessing the level of consciousness; (2) evaluating neuromuscular function periodically; (3) monitoring muscle strength and movement; (4) assessing the rate, rhythm, pattern, and characteristics of all vital signs, especially the respirations; (5) measuring and recording intake and output accurately; (6) obtaining precise measurement of daily weights; (7) assessing the characteristics of the feces; (8) monitoring Chvostek's and Trousseau's signs for hypocalcemia; and (9) monitoring appropriate laboratory values periodically.

The intervening functions that are part of the nursing care performed with individuals with metabolic alkalosis are (1) establishing a safe physical environment; (2) instituting seizure precautions; (3) providing stimuli appropriate to maintaining orientation; (4) assisting the individual with the activities of daily living; (5) providing nursing comfort measures to deal with the gastrointestinal effects of the imbalance; and (6) administering fluids and medications as prescribed.

Treatment

The treatment of metabolic alkalosis involves eliminating the primary cause and correcting the imbalance. Correcting the imbalance is accomplished by a four-level therapeutic approach. This therapeutic approach includes (1) replacing any extracellular fluid volume deficit with saline; (2) administering chloride (in the form of ammonium chloride or arginine hydrochloride if the sodium chloride in the saline is not sufficient to replace the lost anion); (3) correcting the potassium depletion with potassium chloride; and (4) increasing the excretion of bicarbonate by using carbonic anhydrase inhibiting diuretics, or in instances of renal dysfunction, dialysis therapy.

Respiratory Acidosis

Definition

Respiratory acidosis is an excess of carbonic acid in the extracellular fluid.

Etiology

Respiratory acidosis is caused by etiologies that create hypoventilation, which result in the retention of carbon dioxide in the body. Those etiologies are categorized according to the mechanisms responsible for creating the hypoventilation. There are five categories of etiologies that result in respiratory acidosis: (1) airway obstructions, (2) depressants of the respiratory center, (3) defects in the nerves and muscles of respiration, (4) lung diseases, and (5) thoracic cage disorders. Table 20-14 presents specific examples for each of the categories of etiologies of respiratory acidosis.

Clinical Assessment Parameters

The individual experiencing respiratory acidosis exhibits many of the following signs and symptoms: dull, slow mental responses; apprehension; restlessness; headache; drowsiness; disorientation; coma; tachycardia; hypoventilation; dyspnea; fatigue; weakness; flapping tremors; uncoordination; and decreased reflexes. Cyanosis due to hypoxia is also present as a *very late* sign of respiratory acidosis.

Laboratory Assessment Data

The blood gas values provide the most significant laboratory data for assessing an individual for respiratory acidosis. However, there are some serum and urine values that can provide additional assessment data. The characteristic pattern of values exhibited by individuals experiencing respiratory acidosis is a pH less than 7.37, a P_{CO_2} greater than 43 to 45 mmHg, a normal to increased bicarbonate; a normal to decreased P_{O_2}, a normal to increased serum potassium, and a decreased urine pH.

Clinical and Nursing Implications

The clinical significance of respiratory acidosis for the individual is related not only to the effects of the acidosis on the body, but also to the effects of the accompanying hypoxia. Without sufficient oxygen, the human organism cannot survive. Thus this imbalance indeed represents a crisis for the individual and requires nursing support in the form of monitoring and intervening functions.

The monitoring functions performed with the individual experiencing respiratory acidosis include (1) assessing skin color, temperature, and moistness for signs of hypoxia; (2) monitoring the rate, rhythm, pattern, and characteristics of all vital signs; (3) assessing the level of consciousness frequently; (4) evaluating muscle strength, coordination, and movement; (5) assessing the individual's comfort level; and (6) monitoring all appropriate laboratory values at intervals.

The intervening functions that are performed with the individual with respiratory acidosis are (1) providing a safe physical environment for the individual; (2) maintaining a decreased activity level consistent with the level of hypoxia; (3) assisting the individual with all activities of daily living; (4) providing a quiet environment with just enough stimuli to maintain orientation; (5) providing emotional support and reassurance; (6) assisting the individual to assume a position that facilitates adequate respirations; (7) instituting preventive pulmonary maintenance therapies to increase the removal of carbon dioxide by the lungs (turning, coughing, deep breathing, suctioning, resistance breathing); (8) administering oxygen when appropriate and as prescribed; and (9) administering fluids and medications if prescribed.

Treatment

The goal for treating respiratory acidosis is to reestablish effective ventilation for the individual. In some instances this may require creating an artificial airway, and/or using mechanical ventilation until the primary cause can be treated. Bicarbonate and oxygen may be administered simultaneous to the efforts to treat the cause in an attempt to correct or lessen the immediate effects of the imbalance.

Respiratory Alkalosis

Definition

Respiratory alkalosis is a deficit of carbonic acid in the extracellular fluid.

Etiology

Respiratory alkalosis is caused by etiologies that produce hyperventilation and a decrease of carbon

TABLE 20-14
Specific Etiologies of Respiratory Acidosis

Category	Examples
Airway obstructions	Aspiration Foreign bodies Pulmonary embolus Severe bronchospasms Pulmonary edema Laryngeal edema
Depressants of the respiratory center	Sedatives Chronic narcotic abuse Metabolic alkalosis General anesthesia Increased intracranial pressure Medullary tumors Meningitis Vertebral artery embolism or thrombosis
Defects in the nerves and muscles of respiration	Myasthenia gravis Guillain-Barré syndrome Poliomyelitis Botulism Spinal cord injury Paralysis associated with hypo- or hyperkalemia
Lung diseases	Chronic obstructive pulmonary disease Smoke inhalation Pneumonia Atelectasis Asthma Interstitial lung disease Bronchitis Bronchiectasis
Thoracic cage disorders	Flail chest Pneumothorax Pickwickian syndrome Ankylosing spondylitis

dioxide in the body. Those etiologies include alcoholic intoxication, anemia, gram-negative sepsis, meningitis, encephalitis, head trauma, brain lesions, congestive heart failure, exercise, fever, cirrhosis, paraldehyde intoxication, pulmonary fibrosis, hypoxia, thyrotoxicosis, mechanical hyperventilation, salicylate intoxication, anxiety, hysteria, and voluntary hyperpnea.

Clinical Assessment Parameters

The individual experiencing respiratory alkalosis exhibits a combination of the following signs and symptoms: breathlessness, vertigo, syncope, nervousness, paresthesias of the extremities, perioral paresthesia, muscle cramps and tetany, seizures, decreased mentation, confusion, decreased psychomotor performance, anxiety, hyperventilation, cardiac dysrhythmia, and hypotension.

Laboratory Assessment Data

The blood gas values are the most significant laboratory data used in assessing an individual for respiratory alkalosis. The characteristic pattern is a pH greater than 7.43, a P_{CO_2} less than 37 mmHg; and a decreased bicarbonate.

Clinical and Nursing Implications

The clinical significance of respiratory alkalosis for an individual is related to the neuromuscular effects it produces. Those effects make it impossible for the individual to function and carry out the normal activities of daily living. The individual may also develop life-threatening seizures as a result of the respiratory alkalosis.

The nursing monitoring functions that are performed with an individual experiencing respiratory alkalosis include (1) assessing the level of consciousness frequently; (2) monitoring the rate, rhythm, pattern, and characteristics of all vital signs; (3) monitoring sensation in the extremities and perioral area; (4) assessing muscle movement and strength; and (5) monitoring all appropriate laboratory data.

The intervening functions that are performed with an individual experiencing respiratory alkalosis are (1) establishing a safe physical environment for the individual; (2) maintaining an activity level appropriate to the degree of weakness, vertigo, and syncope; (3) instituting seizure precautions; (4) providing sufficient stimuli to maintain orientation; (5) assisting the individual in performing the activities of daily living; (6) providing emotional support and reassurance; (7) instituting nursing measures to assist in decreasing the hyperventilation and in increasing the carbon dioxide (such as teaching breathing exercises or having the individual breathe in and out of a paper bag, thus rebreathing carbon dioxide); and (8) administering medications as prescribed.

Treatment

The treatment of respiratory alkalosis is aimed at dealing with the underlying cause. However, when it is not possible to eradicate the cause, sedation, administration of 3 to 5 percent carbon dioxide and breathing exercises are used to correct the imbalance. (See Chap. 19 for further discussion of acid-base balance.)

SUMMARY

This chapter has discussed the regulation and assessment of fluid and electrolyte and acid-base balance. The critical-care nurse is constantly making decisions about patient care based on the utilization of this information. In conducting an assessment of an individual, the critical-care nurse proceeds by beginning with the highest priority substance for the individual. In general, the critical-care nurse would assess the individual in the following manner: fluid volume, acid-base balance, potassium, calcium, sodium, chloride, magnesium, and phosphate. Certainly this order might change depending on the specific history and presenting behaviors of the individual, but all areas would be included in the assessment. In order to assist the critical-care nurse in performing this assessment, the signs and symptoms of each of the imbalances have been summarized according to body systems in Table 20-15.

TABLE 20-15

Summary of the Signs and Symptoms of Fluid and Electrolyte and Acid-Base Imbalances According to Body Systems

Imbalance	Body system							
	Central nervous	Neuro-muscular	Cardio-vascular	Respiratory	Gastro-intestinal	Integu-mentary	Skeletal	Renal
Hypervolemia			Weight gain Systemic edema Ascites ↑CVP Hypertension Bounding pulse	Dyspnea Moist rales		Puffy eyelids		
Hypovolemia	Lassitude	Fatigue	Weight loss ↓Postural BP ↑Pulse ↓Venous pressure		Thirst	Dry skin Dry mucous membranes ↓Skin turgor ↓Elasticity Furrowed tongue ↑Temperature ↓Eyeball turgor ↓Perspiration		Oliguria
Metabolic acidosis	Headache Drowsiness ↓Mentation Confusion Coma Seizures	Fatigue	Hypotension Hypoxia Dysrhythmia	Kussmaul respirations	Anorexia Nausea Vomiting	Tissue hypoxia		
Metabolic alkalosis	Seizures Belligerence a1Confusion Stupor Coma	Irritability Tetany	Dysrhythmia	Hypoventilation	Nausea Vomiting Diarrhea			
Respiratory acidosis	↓Mentation Apprehension Restlessness Headache Drowsiness Disorientation Coma	Fatigue Muscle weakness Flapping tremors Uncoordination ↓Reflexes	Tachycardia	Hypoventilation Dyspnea		Cyanosis		

TABLE 20-15 (*Continued*)

Summary of the Signs and Symptoms of Fluid and Electrolyte and Acid-Base Imbalances According to Body Systems

Imbalance	Body system							
	Central nervous	Neuro-muscular	Cardio-vascular	Respiratory	Gastro-intestinal	Integu-mentary	Skeletal	Renal
Respiratory alkalosis	Vertigo Syncope Nervousness Seizures ↓Mentation Confusion Anxiety	Paresthesia Muscle cramps Tetany ↓Psychomotor function	Dysrhythmia Hypotension	Dyspnea Hyperventilation		Perioral paresthesia		
Hyperkalemia	Confusion	Hyperexcitability Muscle weakness Paresthesia Flaccid paralysis	Dysfunction Arrest		Distention Diarrhea Intestinal colic			
Hypokalemia	Drowsiness Confusion Apathy Coma	Irritability Muscle weakness Paresthesia Muscle pain Muscle cramps Muscle tenderness Hyporeflexia Tetany Paralysis	Weak pulse Bradycardia	Weakness Hypoventilation	Nausea Vomiting Anorexia Distention Cramps Paralytic ileus Polydipsia Hyperglycemia Negative nitrogen balance			Polyuria Nocturia
Hypercalcemia	Drowsiness Lethargy Disorientation Loss of memory Depression Stupor Coma	Fatigue Muscle weakness Hypotonicity	Dysrhythmia Arrest		Anorexia Nausea Vomiting Constipation Thirst		Deep bone pain	Polyuria Calculi
Hypocalcemia	Seizures Depression Psychoses	Paresthesia Muscle cramps Tetany Positive Chvostek's Positive Trousseau's Carpopedal spasms Hyperreflexia	Arrest	Laryngeal stridor	Cramps Nausea Vomiting Diarrhea	Circumoral Paresthesia Cataracts Keratitis Dry skin Brittle nails Alopecia	Pathologic fractures	

TABLE 20-15 (Continued)

Summary of the Signs and Symptoms of Fluid and Electrolyte and Acid-Base Imbalances According to Body Systems

Imbalance	Body system							
	Central nervous	Neuro-muscular	Cardio-vascular	Respiratory	Gastro-intestinal	Integu-mentary	Skeletal	Renal
Hypernatremia	Lethargy Irritability Seizures Coma	Muscular rigidity Tremors	Tachycardia		Thirst	Dry, sticky mucous membranes Rough, dry tongue Flushed, dry skin ↑Turgor ↓Lacrimation ↑Temperature		Oliguria
Hyponatremia	Lethargy Confusion Headache Seizures Coma Apprehension	Fatigue Muscle weakness Tremors Hyperreflexia			Anorexia Nausea Vomiting Cramps Diarrhea			Oliguria
Hyperchloremia	↓Level of consciousness	Muscle weakness		Deep and rapid respirations				
Hypochloremia	Agitation Irritability	Muscle weakness Tetany		Slow and shallow respirations				
Hypermagnese-mia	Drowsiness Depression Coma	↓Deep reflexes Loss of deep reflexes Muscle weakness Paralysis	Hypotension Bradycardia Arrest	Hypoventilation Apnea	Nausea Vomiting			
Hypomagnese-mia	Seizures Apathy Confusion Irritability Psychoses Depression	Muscle fasciculation Muscle weakness Flapping tremors Positive Chvostek's Positive Trousseau's Tetany Muscle spasticity Carpopedal spasms Nystagmus	Hypertension Dysfunction		Anorexia Nausea			

TABLE 20-15 (*Continued*)

Summary of the Signs and Symptoms of Fluid and Electrolyte and Acid-Base Imbalances According to Body Systems

Imbalance	Body system							
	Central nervous	Neuro-muscular	Cardio-vascular	Respiratory	Gastro-intestinal	Integu-mentary	Skeletal	Renal
Hyperphospha-temia	Seizures Depression Psychoses	Paresthesia Muscle cramps Tetany Positive Chvostek's Positive Trousseau's Carpopedal spasms Hyperreflexia	Arrest	Laryngeal stridor	Cramps Nausea Vomiting Diarrhea	Circumoral paresthesia Cataracts Keratitis Dry skin Brittle nails Alopecia	Pathologic fractures	
Hypophospha-temia	Lethargy	Muscle weakness			Anorexia		Mild bone pain	

REFERENCES

Anderson R. J., and R. W. Schrier: Physiology of renal water excretion, *Contrib Nephrol* 14: 50–63, 1978.

Andersson B.: Regulation of body fluids, *Annu Rev Physiol* 39:185–200, 1977.

———: Regulation of water intake, *Physiol Rev* 58:582–602, 1978.

Burgess A.: *The Nurse's Guide to Fluid and Electrolyte Balance,* 2d ed., New York: McGraw-Hill, 1979.

Burke, S. R.: *The Composition and Function of Body Fluids,* St. Louis: Mosby, 1972.

Carroll, H. J., and M. S. Oh: *Water, Electrolyte and Acid-Base Metabolism: Diagnosis and Management,* Philadelphia: Lippincott, 1978.

Chusid, L. E., J. F. Kestner, and T. R. Rogers: Put blood gas analysis to everyday use, *Patient Care,* November, 1976, pp. 18–23, 26–28+.

Cohen, S.: Blood gas and acid-base concepts in respiratory care—programmed instruction, *Am J Nurs* 76:1–30, 1976.

———: Metabolic acid-base disorders. Pt. I. Chemistry and physiology—programmed instruction, *Am J Nurs* 77:1–32, 1977.

———: Metabolic acid-base disorders. Pt. II. Physiological abnormalities and nursing actions—programmed instruction, *Am J Nurs* 78:1–20, 1978.

Deane, N.: *Kidney and Electrolytes—Foundations of Clinical Diagnosis and Physiologic Therapy,* Englewood Cliffs, N.J.: Prentice-Hall, 1966.

del Bueno, D.: Electrolyte imbalance: How to recognize and respond to it, *RN* 38:52–56, 1975.

De Luca, H. F.: Regulation of the vitamin D endocrine system located in the kidney, *Contrib Nephrol* 13:81–95, 1978.

Elbaum, N.: Detecting and correcting magnesium imbalance, *Nursing '77* 7:34–35, 1977.

Feig, P. U., and D. K. McCurdy: The hypertonic state, *N Engl J Med* 297(26):1444–1454, 1977.

The Fundamentals of Body Water and Electrolytes, Morton Grove, Ill.: Baxter Laboratories, 1969.

Guide to Fluid Therapy, Deerfield, Ill.: Baxter Laboratories, 1973.

Guyton, A. C.: *Textbook of Medical Physiology,* 3d ed., Philadelphia: Saunders, 1966.

Hays, R. M.: Principles of ion and water transport in the kidney, *Hosp Practice* 13(9):79–88, 1978.

Hulter, H. N., L. P. Ilnicki, J. A. Harbottle, and A. Sebastian: Correction of metabolic acidosis by the kidney during isometric expansion of extracellular fluid volume, *J Lab Clin Med* 92(4):602–612, 1978.

Josephson, B.: *Chemistry and Therapy of Electrolyte Disorders,* Springfield, Ill.: Charles C Thomas, 1961.

Kee, J. L.: Clinical implications of laboratory studies in critical care, *Crit Care Quart* 2(3): 1–17, 1979.

Keyes, J. L.: Basic mechanisms involved in acid-base homeostasis, *Heart Lung* 5(2):239–246, 1976.

———: Blood-gas analysis and the assessment of acid-base status, *Heart Lung* 5(2):247–255, 1976.

Klahr, S.: *Differential Diagnosis: Renal and Electrolyte Disorders,* New York: Arco, 1978.

Klein, W. J.: Critical electrolyte problems, *Emergency Med* 5:79–83, 89–90, 1973.

Kurtzman, N. A., J. A. R. Arruda, and C. Westenfelder: Renal regulation of acid-base homeostasis, *Contrib Nephrol* 14:1–13, 1978.

Lee, C., V. Stroot, and C. A. Schaper: Extracellular volume imbalance, *Am J Nurs* 74: 888–891, 1974.

Massry, S. G.: The clinical pathophysiology of magnesium, *Contrib Nephrol* 14:64–73, 1978.

Maxwell, M. H., and C. R. Kleeman: *Clinical Disorders of Fluid and Electrolyte Metabolism,* 3d ed., New York: McGraw-Hill, 1980.

Metheny, N., and W. D. Snively: Perioperative fluids and electrolytes, *Am J Nurs* 78:840–845, 1978.

——— and ———: *Nurse's Handbook of Fluid Balance,* 3d ed., Philadelphia: Lippincott, 1979.

Moore, V. B.: Analyzing the ABG analysis, *Nursing '79* 9(9):28–33, 1979.

Ramsay, D. J., and W. F. Ganong: CNS regulation of salt and water intake, *Hosp Practice* 12:63–69, 1977.

Randall, H. T.: Fluid, electrolyte, and acid-base balance, *Surg Clin North Am* 56(5):1019–1058, 1976.

Reed, G.: Confused about potassium? Here's a clear concise guide, *Nursing '74* 4(3):20–27, 1974.

Schrier, R.: *Renal and Electrolyte Disorders,* Boston: Little, Brown, 1976.

Scribner, B. H.: *Teaching Syllabus for the Course on Fluid and Electrolyte Balance,* 7th rev. ed., Seattle: University of Washington, 1969.

Shapiro, B. A.: *Clinical Application of Blood Gases,* Chicago: Year Book, 1973.

Shoemaker, W. C., and W. F. Walker: *Fluid-Electrolyte Therapy in Acute Illness,* Chicago: Year Book, 1970.

Shrake, K.: The ABC's of ABG's, *Nursing '79* 9(9):26–33, 1979.

Snively, W. D., and K. T. Roberts: The clinical picture as an aid to understanding body fluid disturbances, *Nurs Forum* 12(2):132–159, 1973.

Stein, J. H., and H. J. Reineck: Regulation of sodium balance in normal and edematous states, *Contrib Nephrol* 14:25–49, 1978.

Stroot, V., C. Lee, and C. A. Schaper: *Fluids and Electrolytes: A Practical Approach,* Philadelphia: Davis, 1974.

Taylor, W. H.: *Fluid Therapy and Disorders of Electrolyte Balance,* 2d ed., Philadelphia: Davis, 1970.

Tripp, A.: Hyper- and hypocalcemia, *Am J Nurs* 76:1142–1145, 1976.

Trunkey, D. D.: Review of current concepts in fluid and electrolyte management, *Heart Lung* 4:115–121, 1975.

Valtin, H.: *Renal Dysfunction: Mechanisms Involved in Fluid and Solute Imbalance,* Boston: Little, Brown, 1979.

Vander, A. J.: *Renal Physiology,* New York: McGraw-Hill, 1975.

Wilson, R. F.: *Principles and Techniques of Critical Care,* sections k and l, Kalamazoo, Mich.: The Upjohn Company, 1976.

———: Tips on managing fluid and electrolyte problems, *Consultant* 17:31–37, 1977.

Winters, R. W., K. Engel, and R. B. Dell: *Acid-Base Physiology in Medicine,* Cleveland: The London Company, 1969.

Zeluff, G. W., W. N. Suki, and D. Jackson: Hypokalemia—cause and treatment, *Heart Lung* 7(5):854–860, 1978.

INTRODUCTION

The purpose of any human defense is survival. This defense can be as subtle as the destruction of an invading microorganism or as overt as a protective reflex. The body has to protect against exogenous (external) as well as endogenous (internal) threats to its integrity. Historically these defense mechanisms were called *vis medicatrix naturae* (the healing force of nature). They are normally efficient in protecting and maintaining the body's integrity against foreign substances as well as restoring it when damage occurs.

The body employs not only natural defenses but acquired, adaptive defenses as well. *Natural defenses* are nonspecific mechanisms either present at birth or developing in the course of natural maturation. Among the natural defenses are anatomical and chemical barriers that keep potentially harmful substances out of the body. If these should fail, inflammation and nonspecific phagocytosis quickly remove the substances from the body periphery by effectively diluting, neutralizing, or destroying them. Natural defenses also include genetic differences in susceptibility or sensitivity, the effect of age, interferon, natural antibodies, body pH, and body temperature.

If natural defenses allow a foreign substance to invade and subsist in the body, an *acquired, adaptive mechanism* is called into action. This is the *immune response,* which recognizes the foreign substance, as natural defenses cannot do and specifically destroys it (Fig. 21-1). The *reticuloendothelial* (RE) (or lymphoreticular) *system* is responsible for this specific reaction and for preventing repeated challenge by the same type of substance through immunologic memory. The maintenance of these defenses is the topic of this chapter. A homeostatic equilibrium is needed between natural and acquired host responses. If this equilibrium is lost, interventions are needed to enhance or depress the response as necessary. They must be based on knowledge of the processes involved.

Recognition of Nursing's Role

At present nursing textbooks are scant in their documentation of ways to maintain human defense systems. Reasons for this are multiple. First, immunology has only recently become a medical science, and its importance in nursing practice is now being recognized. Immunopathologic mechanisms have been clinically defined within the past 15 to 20 years, but

21

MAINTENANCE OF NONSPECIFIC AND IMMUNOLOGIC DEFENSES

Sister Mary Rebecca Fidler

INTRODUCTION
Recognition of Nursing's Role
Infections and the Compromised Host

EPITHELIAL SURFACES—FIRST LINE OF DEFENSE
Skin and Its Appendages
Respiratory Epithelium
Gastrointestinal Mucosa
Genitourinary Mucosa
Epithelium as a Barrier—A Summary

INFLAMMATION AND NONSPECIFIC PHAGOCYTOSIS—SECOND LINE OF DEFENSE
Inflammation
Phagocytosis
Additional Nonspecific Defenses
Inflammation, Phagocytosis, and Other Nonspecific Defenses—A Summary

ACQUIRED HOST DEFENSES
Immune Defenses and the Biologic Self
Antigen-Antibody
Reticuloendothelial System
Lymphocyte Circulation Patterns
Antigen Recognition and Processing
T-Cell Subsets
B Lymphocytes and B-Cell Subsets
Identification of T and B Cells
The Immune Response
Role of Complement
Physiology of Immunity
Immune Response and Genetics

HYPERIMMUNE RESPONSE PATHOLOGY
Type I: Anaphylactic Reactions
Type II: Cytotoxic Reactions
Type III Complex-Mediated Hypersensitivity
Type IV: Delayed-Type Hypersensitivity
Iatrogenic Conditions
Autoimmune Disease

HYPOIMMUNE RESPONSE PATHOLOGY
Congenital Hypoimmune Conditions
Acquired Hypoimmune Conditions
Stress and Immunity

NURSING AND DEFENSE MECHANISMS

REFERENCES

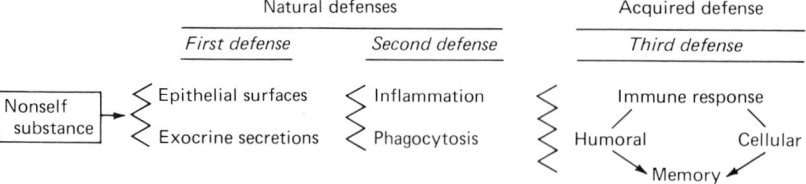

FIGURE 21-1
The concept of human defense.

therapy to enhance or suppress immune mechanisms is only now becoming common. Second, while skin care has always been part of nursing, care to maintain other epithelial surfaces may or may not have been given adequate concern in the clinical setting. For instance, the role of urethral secretions in prevention of ascending bladder and kidney infections has been documented in the past decade. Observations about the importance of proper breathing and humidity in prevention of alveolar mucous plugs have been given new meaning by what is known about immune defenses. The same can be said for the consequences of loss of air conditioning or ciliary action in the patient who has a tracheostomy or is on a respirator.

Sterile techniques have a long history in nursing but were instituted to prevent infection when the first line of defense had been compromised by injury, such as surgery, or trauma. While these are still important, nursing activities have been placed in a broader context of transplantation, congenital and acquired immune deficiencies, autoimmunity, cancer, and immunosuppression. This requires an expanded knowledge base upon which the nurse can practice.

Infections and the Compromised Host

Very soon after birth a human comes in contact with many microorganisms which colonize the epithelial surfaces and are ultimately referred to as normal flora or endogenous microbes. Most infections which have gained prominence in the past were exogenous microbes not normally found surviving on the human body surfaces. For many years only exogenous organisms were considered a threat to human existence, and fear of these organisms enabled scientists to find ways to conquer them through vaccine, antibiotics, and other means. Indeed immunology as a medical science has its origin in efforts to deliberately establish resistance to pathogenic microbes. Technologic and pharmacologic advances have largely solved the problem of exogenous pathogenic organisms and in so doing helped create a milieu conducive to super-

infections from endogenous organisms. These organisms easily colonize epithelial surfaces and are so adaptable that they have become resistant to modern drugs. Thus antibiotics and vaccines have shifted the balance of power in favor of adapted endogenous organisms, a situation which has little effect on the healthy individual but may be devastating and lethal to the compromised host.

A compromised host is an individual who, due to disease, age, therapy, or stress, has inadequate defense mechanisms against normally harmless microorganisms. An infectious disease is a complex interaction of the host with an infecting organism. Though a few infections occur as a direct result of the microorganism or its by-products, most infections occur as a result of variation in the defenses of the host. An environment most conducive to infection is one in which virulent antibiotic-resistant populations of endogenous microorganisms colonize the surfaces of a compromised host. This best describes the situation found in hospitals, and since the patient in a critical-care unit is often a compromised host, the interventions chosen must be aimed at not allowing the defenses to become further compromised.

New knowledge of how surgical techniques, anesthetics, medications, emotional state, and so on, affect the immune response will change attitudes toward maintaining defense mechanisms in the critically ill as well as in healthy persons. Nursing is currently producing scholars with an adequate knowledge base in immunology who are able to discuss the significant relationships between nursing and the maintenance of defense systems. Therefore the role of nursing in maintaining defense mechanisms will rapidly expand.

EPITHELIAL SURFACES—FIRST LINE OF DEFENSE

The first concern in defense is to maintain the integrity of the body surfaces. This includes the skin; oral, anal, vaginal, gastrointestinal, respiratory, and urinary epithelium; and the lining of the external ear as well as the conjunctiva and cornea of the eye. These surfaces are epithelial in nature and prevent penetration by both anatomical structure and chemical secretion. Although all these surfaces are epithelial, they vary from region to region as to their type and function. Recently it has been recognized that epithelial cells have receptors for attachment of certain antigenic determinants. These receptors are very important in maintaining normal flora and also help to explain preferential attachments of certain microbes or chemicals to particular areas.

The antibody known as *secretory IgA* is produced by local submucosal plasma cells and is probably one of our most important defense mechanisms. IgA function has not been fully appreciated because of its role in prevention rather than response. Secretory IgA has been found in most secretions of the human body and may be critical in preventing the attachment of potential pathogens to epithelial cells.

For many pathogens the first step in initiation of infection is attachment to a receptor on an epithelial cell. The virulence of a particular organism may be determined by its ability to attach to such a receptor. The host defense against the attachment is apparently accomplished nonspecifically by pH, motility, flow of mucus and other secretions, cilia, desquamation, and receptor sites being preferentially covered by normal endogenous flora. IgA enhances these natural defense mechanisms by binding to antigens and preventing their attachment to epithelial surfaces. Thus these potential invaders are eliminated from the body.

Skin and Its Appendages

The epidermal layer of skin is a stratified squamous epithelium with a pH of about 5. It is dry and constantly exfoliates its outer surface and regenerates its basal cell layer. Exfoliation will ultimately slough any bacteria or chemicals which penetrate the outer layers of intact integument. The normal flora which can exist in this acidic, dry lipid environment are mainly staphylococci, corynebacteria, and propionibacteria. These particular organisms make survival of other microbes difficult by splitting the lipids of epidermis into bactericidal unsaturated fatty acids (oleic acid). Mechanisms such as these keep the inoculum size of invading agents at a low level, allowing other body defenses to destroy alien agents promptly when injury or a break in the epithelium occurs. Sweat, sebaceous, and mammary glands produce secretions whose flow, osmolality, pH, cellular components, and IgA militate against infection.

Mammary secretions after childbirth contain many chemical and cellular components which not only defend the infant against infections and allergic reactions, but also contribute to the maturation of the infant's intestinal mucosa and the immune system. This is a host defense maturation mechanism.

Respiratory Epithelium

The respiratory tract is usually sterile below the larynx. Ciliated simple columnar epithelia line this area. As one progresses toward the interior of the lung, the epithelium changes gradually to cuboidal and finally to squamous in the alveoli. Mucus is not secreted below the bronchioles. Cilia progressively decrease in number from the trachea to bronchioles and are not found in the alveolar areas. Mucociliary transportation of inhaled particles toward the oropharynx, together with coughing and sneezing, helps eliminate organisms from these areas. Deep breathing and proper coughing help prevent infection in a similar manner. Small quantities of microorganisms are usually aspirated during sleep but are readily phagocytosed by alveolar macrophages or physically removed by ciliary action.

Gastrointestinal Mucosa

The oropharynx is lined with a nonkeratinized squamous stratified epithelium. This is very similar anatomically to skin, but keratin is not produced. Epithelial glands, which include the parotid, sublingual, and submandibular, produce saliva. This secretion contains water, lysozyme, mucus, secretory IgA, enzymes, and cells. These collectively keep bacterial quantity in the mouth to a minimum and create a fluid flow which makes it difficult for chemicals and foreign agents to be absorbed. The lining changes from squamous to cuboidal to columnar as it descends from the oral cavity to the pharynx to the esophagus.

The gastric mucosa produces hydrochloric acid, gastric juice, and mucus. The low pH of the gastric contents does not permit survival of most microorganisms. The intestinal mucosa is lined with a simple columnar epithelium and produces many intestinal juices, secretory IgA, mucus, and various other products. Specific regional features, together with the epithelial receptor attachment of normal flora, peristaltic motility, and exfoliation, help eliminate millions of foreign agents daily by defecation.

The intestine is heavily inhabited by symbiotic-type bacteria which benefit the host in vital digestive assimilative functions, and these microbes compete with pathogenic organisms for epithelial receptors.

Genitourinary Mucosa

Anatomical differences in male and female exemplify the role of structure in infection. The male urethra is long and serves both the urinary and reproductive systems. Seminal fluid and urine maintain adequate flow through the system as well as add secretions which are nonconducive to survival of foreign substances. Prostatic secretions are antibacterial in much the same way as other glandular secretions. Infections of the bladder are rare in the male, even when the system is partially obstructed—unless catheterization has occurred.

The female, on the other hand, has a short urethra, which serves only the urinary system. Bladder infections are more common in women than in men. The urinary tracts of both sexes are lined with transitional epithelium which is capable of secreting mucus, the enzyme lysozyme, secretory IgA, and other antimicrobial and antiviral substances. The peristaltic motility of the ureters, acidity of the urine, and reflexes of the bladder create a unidirectional flow which eliminates many microorganisms daily in the urine. The reproductive system of the female is defended by acidity of its epithelial barrier, as well as by its secretions.

Epithelium as a Barrier—A Summary

Epithelium is an effective barrier between the body's internal and external environments. When epithelium is healthy, very few microorganisms are able to attach and/or penetrate the internal environment. Only when this first line of defense fails is there a need for others (Fig. 21-1).

In summary, healthy epithelial surfaces are extremely difficult to penetrate:

1. Because of their structure and pH.

2. Because the inoculum is kept small by continual elimination.

3. Because both bacterial attachment to epithelial receptors and secretory IgA prevent attachment of pathogenic organisms.

4. Because of local production of chemical antimicrobial and antiviral agents.

INFLAMMATION AND NONSPECIFIC PHAGOCYTOSIS—SECOND LINE OF DEFENSE

If the first line of defense fails and foreign substances penetrate body tissues, an inflammatory response is evoked. This reaction to cellular injury is a local vascular response characterized by increased blood flow, the release of chemotactic chemicals, immigration of cells, and exudation. All these are detrimental to the viability of injurious agents.

Inflammation

Inflammation is nonspecific and is initiated by any cellular injury. Presumably it is a vascular response, but phlogistic (inflammatory) substances arise from various sources, even the autonomic nervous system. Enzymes released from damaged cells and clotting factors also initiate inflammation.

The signs and symptoms of inflammation are well known and universally experienced. The five classical signs (heat, pain, redness, swelling, and loss of function) are the result of functional changes in blood flow through the injured area. The cause of these vascular changes is unclear. Histamine release is known to initiate the process and is followed by a sequential change in the physiology of the localized area.

Inflammation helps in the destruction of injurious agents but also prepares the area for and must precede the healing process.

Inflammation, then, is important to the maintenance of life, but it may also be destructive. Loss of homeostatic control of this process may lead to serious illness and even death.

Phagocytosis

Nonspecific phagocytosis ("cell eating") is the process by which injured cells and antigens are removed from an area. Two general cell types, neutrophils and macrophages, are capable of nonspecific phagocytosis.

Neutrophil Phagocytosis

Phagocytic cells are particularly important in preventing infectious disease at this particular phase of the host response. *Polymorphonuclear neutrophils* are principally concerned with phagocytosis of bacteria. Once phagocytosed the bacteria are usually killed and digested by lysosomal enzymes. The process involves chemotaxis, opsonization, phagocytosis, and killing. *Chemotaxis* is the chemical attraction of phagocytes to the injured area. The chemotactic chemical is thought to be activated by the inflammatory response. An *opsonin* is an antibody which attaches to receptors on phagocytic cells. It causes the organism to adhere to the surface of the phagocyte and thus

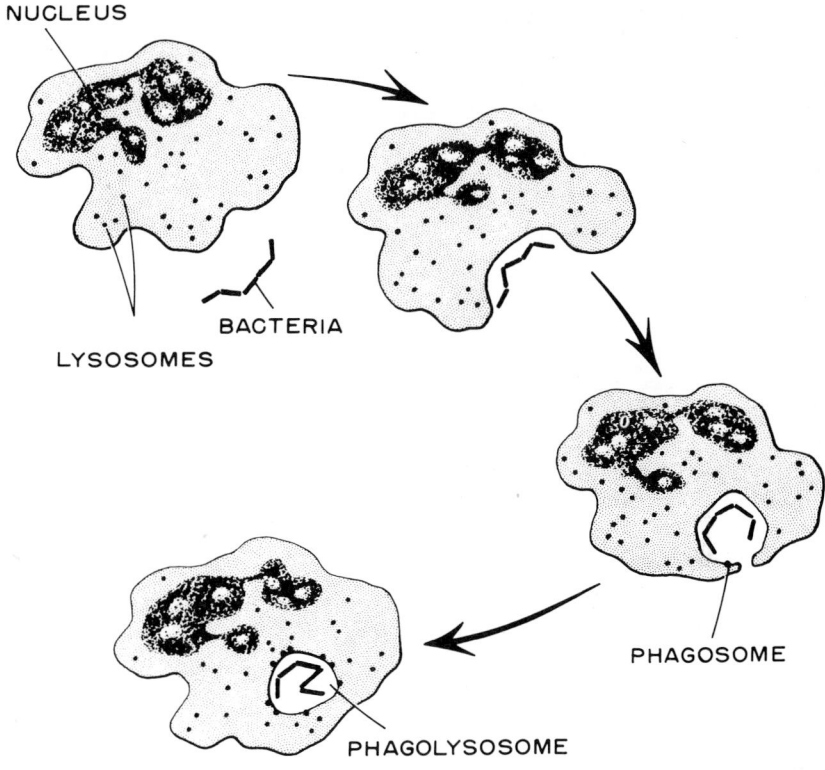

NUCLEUS

BACTERIA

LYSOSOMES

PHAGOSOME

PHAGOLYSOSOME

FIGURE 21-2

Phagocytosis. Neutrophils and monocytes ingest particles by causing cytoplasm to flow around them and then bring them in within an envelop of cell membrane, the phagosome. The digestive enzymes of the lysosomes are then released into the phagolysosome. [*From S. A. Price and L. M. Wilson (eds.), Pathophysiology, Clinical Concepts of Disease Processes, McGraw-Hill, New York, 1978. Used by permission of the publisher.*]

increases the possibility of phagocytosis. Phagocytosis may occur in the absence of opsonins when a microbe is trapped between the surface of two cells, one of which must be a phagocyte (Fig. 21-2). Once the organism is inside the phagocyte, the particle becomes membrane-bound and is called a *phagosome*. The lysosomal hydrolytic enzymes are then released into the phagosome with subsequent death and degradation of the ingested organism. Neutrophil phagocytosis is very rapid and is initiated within minutes after microbial penetration or injury has occurred. The neutrophil usually dies in the process and forms a significant portion of purulent exudates.

The main contribution of neutrophils to the defense of the host is against bacterial infections. Neutropenia places one at high risk of developing bacterial infections. However, neutrophil counts may be normal despite the inability of host cells to kill the bacteria after phagocytosis. Acute infections have a tendency to impair the bactericidal capacity of neutrophils because immature forms (juvenile, stab, etc.) are present in increased numbers. Patients with burns also show similar symptoms. Defects in neutrophil chemotaxis are also commonly seen in diabetes mellitus, cirrhosis, and rheumatoid arthritis. Drugs may affect the killing of bacteria by diminishing the numbers or functioning of neutrophils. In certain conditions this may render the individual susceptible to recurrent pyogenic infections.

Macrophage Phagocytosis

Macrophages are large mononuclear phagocytic cells. They represent a separate cell line differentiating from the bone marrow stem cell. They are characterized by an ability to ingest debris and foreign

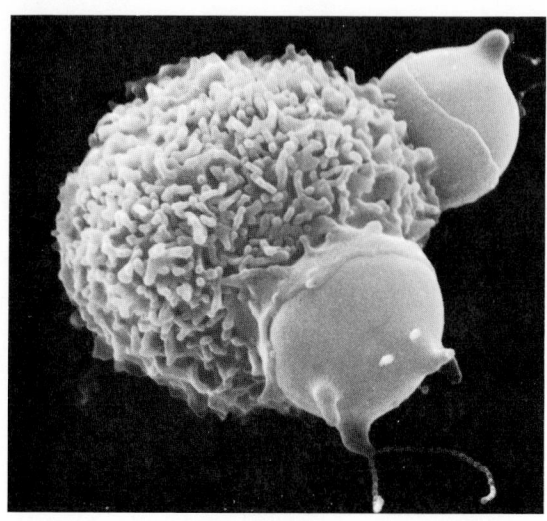

FIGURE 21-3

Mouse macrophage ingesting erythrocytes. The macrophage periphery extends as a collar over the erythrocytes. [*Courtesy of J. P. Revel, M. Rabinovitch, and M. J. DeStefano. From L. Weiss and R. Greep* (eds.), *Histology, 4th ed., McGraw-Hill, New York, 1977. Used by permission of the publisher.*]

materials. Neutrophils are also phagocytes, but they are unable to ingest large particles, and their contribution, though important, is limited to phagocytosis of invading bacteria.

As monocytes leave the vascular system, they mature into macrophages. In tissues they are termed *alveolar macrophages* (lung), or *Kupffer cells* (liver), and in spleen, lymph node, peritoneum, mammary secretions, and other areas, they are termed *macrophages*. Chemotaxis is less apparent for these cells than it is for neutrophils. Macrophages arrive at the locally injured area later in the sequence than neutrophils and have a longer life span and are slower, larger, and more adaptable. They secrete large quantities of *lysozyme*, a protein enzyme liberated from lysosomes of phagocytic cells that lyses bacterial cell walls. It is found in tears and saliva and in nasal, mammary, and other secretions. Bacteria, viruses, cells, debris, and other particles are phagocytosed by macrophages (see Fig. 21-3). Macrophages also play an important role in immune responses, which will be described.

Phagocytosis may occur prior to or simultaneously with the inflammatory process. It is important to note that phagocytosis, while not dependent upon, is increased by the inflammatory response and greatly enhanced by the immune response.

Additional Nonspecific Defenses

Pyrogen

Fever is the body's response to trauma or infection. It is caused by the release from host cells of a substance called *pyrogen.*

Neutrophils produce 5 times as much pyrogen as do macrophages and are thus important in febrile conditions. However, the importance of macrophages in the febrile response, as shown in a study of fever in agranulocytosis, is quite significant.

Pyrogen and subsequent increase in temperature is a nonspecific response which may have an inhibitory effect on bacterial multiplication as well as may change enzyme reactivities and diffusion, which are at least partly temperature-dependent.

Interferon

Interferon is a group of large glycoproteins produced by any human cell when appropriately stimulated. It was first recognized as a nonspecific mechanism to protect host cells from viral infections prior to the start of a specific immune response. Once it is synthesized, it diffuses to other cells and binds on their surface receptors. This attachment triggers production of proteins within the cells which act to prevent use of the cells' synthesizing machinery for viral reproduction. These protein inhibitors remain inactive until the cell is infected by a virus particle.

It now appears that interferon can be stimulated not only by virus but also by microorganisms with an intracellular phase in their growth cycle, bacterial endotoxins, nonspecific mitogens, complex polysaccharides, double-stranded RNA, and other substances. It also has become clear that interferon is capable of more than inhibiting viral infection. Interferon also inhibits division of both normal and malignant cells, enhances the cytotoxic ability of macrophages, and stimulates activities of cytotoxic T lymphocytes.

These actions make logical the use of interferon in treatment of malignancies. It has been shown that interferon is capable of preventing the spread of osteogenic sarcoma and inhibiting multiple myeloma, breast cancer, melanoma, and certain types of leukemia and lymphoma. All persons treated with interferon have been in advanced stages of disease, and thus its effect in early stages would seem even more promising. Even when interferon fails to produce regression of cancer, it may be beneficial to the cancer patient, who is likely to have immune mechanisms in a suppressed state, by inhibiting otherwise fatal viral infections.

Interferon may also be effective therapy in neonatal and adult pericarditis and myocarditis caused by coxsackie B virus, as well as in transplant recipients.

Harmful effects have also been documented, such as bone marrow suppression, altered liver function, fever, chills, and loss of appetite. These effects reverse when therapy ends, however.

Inflammation, Phagocytosis and Other Nonspecific Defenses—A Summary

When epithelial surfaces fail to prevent penetration of foreign substances, the inflammatory process is initiated. Inflammation, a nonspecific process, is necessary before repair can begin. However, it can also be troublesome if uncontrolled. Neutrophils are most effective in phagocytosis of bacteria. Macrophages however, are required for effective phagocytosis of cells and debris.

In a serious inflammation, pyrogens are released by host cells into the blood. This may aid the body by raising its temperature and so inhibiting bacterial multiplication.

Interferon, released by host cells, appears to play a variety of roles, ranging from blockade of viral reproduction to enhancement of the immune response.

ACQUIRED HOST DEFENSES

Immune Defenses and the Biologic Self

Immune defenses are acquired defenses. They are set in motion when natural defenses fail. Immune defenses are based on the precept that self-molecules are to be protected and nonself-molecules destroyed. (Fig. 21-4). When nonself substances are recognized by the reticuloendothelial system, the immune response is evoked. Molecules of the self fail to produce immune reactions because of a natural tolerance produced during fetal development.

Differences between individuals within a species, as well as those between species, start at the level of molecular structure. An individual's particular structure of proteins and other body materials is specified during genetic transcription of DNA. Although the proteins of any one body are similar in structure to those of another, there are small differences in composition and shape which give uniqueness to each individual. This uniqueness is what is meant by the "biologic self." Thus *self* is anything synthesized according to instructions of our own genetic code.

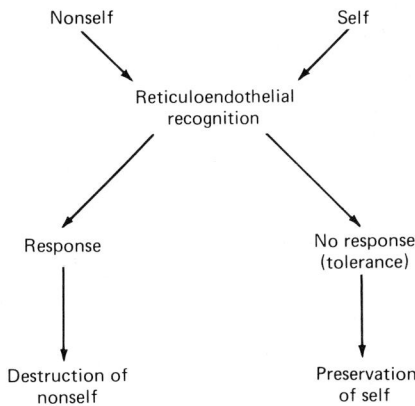

FIGURE 21-4
Preservation of the self by the reticulo-endothelial system.

Nonself is that specified by a different set of chromosomes. Constituents of the self may be called *native;* nonself substances are called *foreign* or *alien,* or *antigenic.* Both self and nonself substances may carry macromolecules known as antigen on their surface, but only nonself material (above a certain size) will be *antigenic,* that is, will evoke an immune response.

Exogenous material such as microorganisms, transplanted cells or tissues is given its structure by an alien genetic code. Endogenous material becomes antigenic more subtly. It may do so through an error in the genetic code, that is, a mutation, or by physical change of its structure. Another way is through attachment of native protein (carrier molecule) to an introduced molecule too small by itself to be antigenic. The carrier molecule together with the *hapten,* as the small molecule is called, is foreign-appearing to the reticuloendothelial system.

Still another source of nonself endogenous substances is native material that has become situated in an abnormal (ectopic) location. The body includes various inviolable compartments. Materials inside cells do not mix indiscriminately with those outside cells. Neither do certain molecules from various organs. The body, therefore, may treat materials or molecules that are out of place just as it does foreign material.

It would seem, therefore, that to be recognized as part of the biological self, a substance must be specified by one's genome in an unmutated form, be unchanged in structure, and be in normal position within the body.

One of the main mysteries of immunity is how the

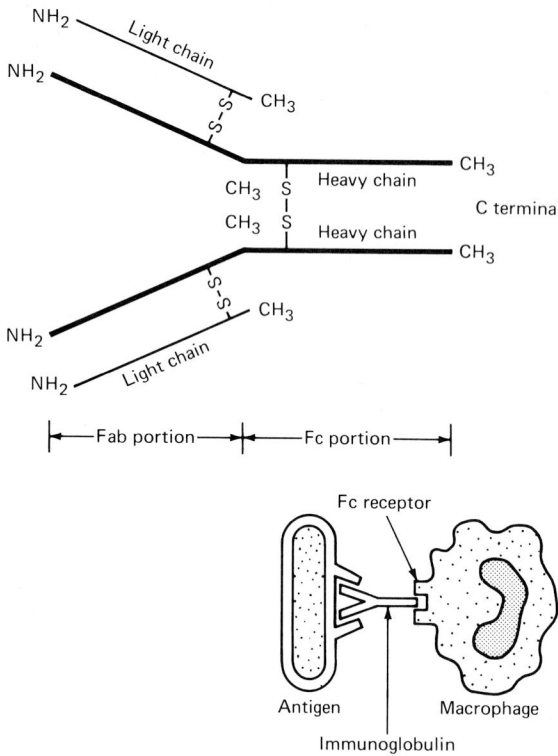

FIGURE 21-5

Structure of immunoglobulin. The Fab portion is variable and confers specificity for antigen attachment. The Fc portion is invariable and will attach to any cell with an Fc receptor (see inset).

body distinguishes between nonself and the antigen of its own cells. When antigenic challenge produces a depressed or no response, a state of *tolerance* is said to exist. The natural tolerance enjoyed by cells of the body is theorized to be a condition in which responsive cell clones have been eliminated or inactivated by antigens present during fetal development. (A *clone* is a group of cells descendant from a single parent cell.) Presentation of antigen to an animal at a time when its immune system is immature often results in an artificially induced tolerance toward the antigen when challenged after maturity.

The most active time for immune mechanisms seems to be shortly after birth when the infant is exposed to a new environment and receives the greatest antigenic stimulation of his or her life. A substantial amount of immunity is acquired during childhood as a consequence of experience with small doses of the same organism or with cross-reacting antigens (antigens on harmless substances that closely match antigens or pathogens). Opsonizing antibody develops within a few weeks as a result of exposure to an effective natural resistance. The newborn infant depends on passive immunity obtained from the mother's milk for prevention of allergies and also assistance in the development of immunocompetence. After about 6 or 7 years the child has a mature immune system.

A normal individual never seems too old or too young to develop resistance mechanisms against nonself antigens, but the ability to respond appropriately is quantitatively less efficient in the very young and in old age and is altered by one's level of wellness.

Specificity is essential to immune defenses. An immune response after exposure to antigen confers immunity for that agent alone, because it produces antibodies and sensitized cells able to recognize, react with, and neutralize only the offending antigen.

The first encounter with nonself antigen stimulates a *primary response*. A second exposure, months or even years later, will elicit a much more intense *secondary response*. This ability of certain reticuloendothelial cells to recall prior experience with the antigen is called *immunologic memory* and is a characteristic of the immune response.

Immune system defenses are said to be either active or passive. *Active defense* occurs when the body participates by manufacturing cells and mediators which destroy the agent. *Passive defense* occurs when the cells or mediators are merely transferred from someone already immune to the antigen to a person lacking such immunity.

Antigen-Antibody

The concept of antigen-antibody must be understood in order to grasp the meaning of immune defense mechanisms. Antigens are macromolecules (large molecules) that provoke an immune response. They are on the surface of substances of all kinds, including cells of the host. Antigens usually have a molecular weight of 10,000 or more. Smaller molecules are not ordinarily antigenic. However, as described earlier, haptens (half-antigens) are able to attach themselves to human body proteins, making a larger complex that will provoke an immune response:

Hapten + native protein = hapten protein complex
(carrier)   (a complete antigen)

Many drugs are haptogenic and, in certain individuals, may bring about drug allergies. Genetic differences ensure that the proteins of each individual are different, and thus only certain protein structures are capable of or will allow combination with a particular hapten. When this happens, sensitivity to drugs will exist.

Antibodies are proteins secreted by *plasma cells* in response to a particular antigen. These antibodies react specifically with the antigen against which they were produced. An antibody consists of two light chains (about 220 amino acids long) and two heavy chains (about 430 amino acids long). The N-terminal end of both chains is quite variable which allows for antigen identification; the rest of the chain (C-terminal) is of a constant pattern. The four chains are held together by disulfide bridges (Fig. 21-5). Experimentally it has been shown that the variable (Fab) portion attaches specifically to antigen, forming an *antigen-antibody complex,* and that the constant (Fc) portion is nonspecific and attaches to any cell which bears an Fc receptor, such as macrophages. Antibody is properly called *immunoglobulin,* since it is found in the globulin fraction of the serum. There are five classes of human immunoglobulin. They are abbreviated as IgG, IgM, IgE, IgD, and IgA. The specific characteristics and differences are indicated in Table 21-1.

Antibodies may be natural or acquired. *Natural antibodies* are usually of the IgM type and are present in the sera of normal individuals who have had no known contact with the particular antigen against which they are directed. Their formation is most likely due to contact with cross-reacting antigens of normal flora, killed organisms in food, and other normally available environmental agents. *Acquired antibodies* arise as part of the humoral response of active immunity.

Reticuloendothelial System

The reticuloendothelial system includes all the cells and structures associated with recognition of, response to, and memory of antigen. Included are primary and secondary lymphoid tissue, lymphatic cells, and a network of phagocytic cells within lymphatic as well as other organs that engulf and process nonself materials.

TABLE 21-1
Five Major Classes of Human Immunoglobulins

Properties	IgG	IgA	IgM	IgD	IgE
Antibody activity	Major antibody in serum	External secretions	Formed to new antigens	Unknown	Histamine release
	Antibacterial Antitoxins Antiviral	Body surface protection	Important in primary response		Subsurface protection
	Important in secondary response	Prevents surface attachment of organisms	Natural antibodies		Responsible for type I anaphylactic reactions
Complement fixing	All but 1 of 4 subclasses	No	Yes	?	No
Placental transfer	Yes	No	No	No	No
Location	Serum and intercellular fluids	Serum Exocrine secretions Intestinal secretions Milk	Serum	Serum	Intercellular fluids and serum

This system grew out of an earlier concept that all macrophages of the body could be considered part of a functional system. In its present-day meaning lymphoid tissue is included as well.

T and B Cells

In the embryo the primitive bone marrow reticular cell is thought to be the common precursor of all cells in the mature immune system. Lymphoid stem cells which differentiate from reticular cells develop along one of two maturational lines leading to a dual-component immune system.

One of these lines leads to the *T lymphocyte*. "T" stands for *thymus-dependent* and suggests a vital role for the thymus gland in making this type of cell competent to participate in the immune response. Thymic hormone (*thymosin*) has been implicated in T-cell function. Whether this hormone acts on stem cells or on mature T cells is not known. In either case, the isolation of thymosin and its use in thymic-deficient animals improved T-cell function. The importance of thymosin in the human awaits clinical trials. Experimentally it has been shown to remodel the surface receptors of lymphocytes during their maturation process in the thymus.

The other line of development leads to the *B lymphocyte*. "B" refers to *bursa-dependent*. This cell line was discovered in animal experiments with chickens, where a lymphoid structure known as the *bursa of Fabricius* plays the same role as the thymus does with the T cell in humans. However, humans do not have a bursa and the equivalent organ for human B cells is not confirmed. After T and B cells attain immunocompetence in development, they migrate and reside in secondary lymphoid structures.

The two principal lymphoid cells are held responsible for the two broad types of immune response. The T cell is the principal actor in *cell-mediated immunity* (CMI). It can be defined as that immunity which can be transferred from one animal to another only by cells. It involves the direct participation of cells at the antigenic site. The B cell initiates what is known as *humoral immunity*, that is, an immunity transferable by serum. The immune factors in the serum include antibody, which is manufactured in a series of reactions dependent on B cells. Humoral immunity is therefore antibody mediated (see Fig. 21-6).

Lymphoid Structures

Central lymphoid tissue is essential for the maturation (ontogeny) of a competently functional RE system. The thymus is necessary for maturation of the cellular immune T lymphocytes. The bone marrow, liver, or spleen is required for full humoral (B lymphocyte) development, although which organ confers immunocompetence is unknown.

Secondary (peripheral) lymphoid structures have been identified as lymph node, spleen, Peyer's patches, and the lamina propria of gut, trachea, vaginal mucosa, and so forth. Any particular lymph structure differs histologically, and while both T and B cells are found in all secondary lymphoid structures, they have definite areas of residence (homing) and circulation patterns within any given organ. In the lymph node the cortex is the location of resident B cells and the medulla (medullary cords) contain many B cells and plasma (antibody-producing) cells, while the paracortical area is the thymus-dependent area where the T cells reside. The spleen also has definite thymus- and bursa-dependent areas.

Lymphocyte Circulation Patterns

Bone marrow is the origin of all lymphoid cells. They differentiate and mature under the influence of primary (central) lymphoid organs and thus must circulate from their place of origin to the thymus and human bursal-equivalent areas. After maturing to immunocompetent cells under thymic and bursal influence, these naive or antigen-unprimed T and B lymphocytes circulate by blood and lymphatics to the secondary (peripheral) lymphoid organs (see Fig. 21-7).

Most bone marrow small lymphocytes are recent postmitotic cells showing different stages of maturation. After division about 30 percent of these cells become B cells. These unprimed B cells migrate preferentially to the spleen rather than to the lymph node.

FIGURE 21-6

Summary of immune responses. [*From D. Jones, C. F. Dunbar, and M. M. Jirovec (eds.), Medical Surgical Nursing, a Conceptual Approach, McGraw-Hill, New York, 1978. Adapted from H. Eisen and J. O. Nysather et al. Used by permission of the publisher.*]

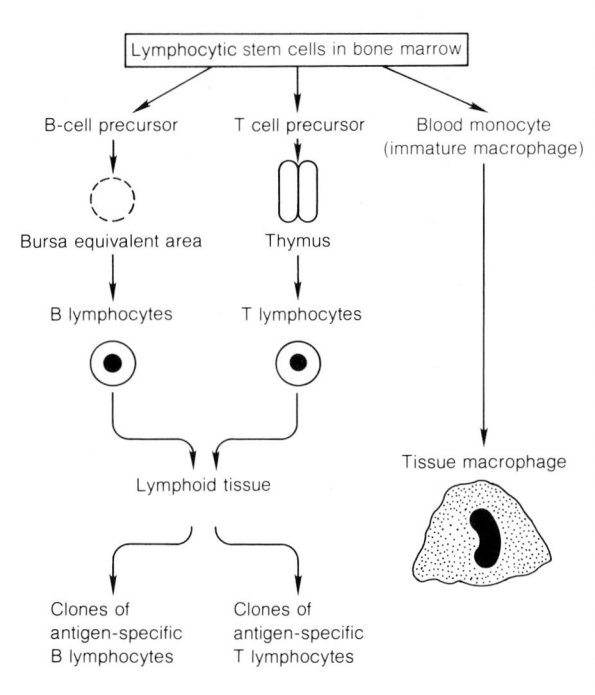

I. Maturation pathways for antibodies, sensitized lymphocytes and macrophages

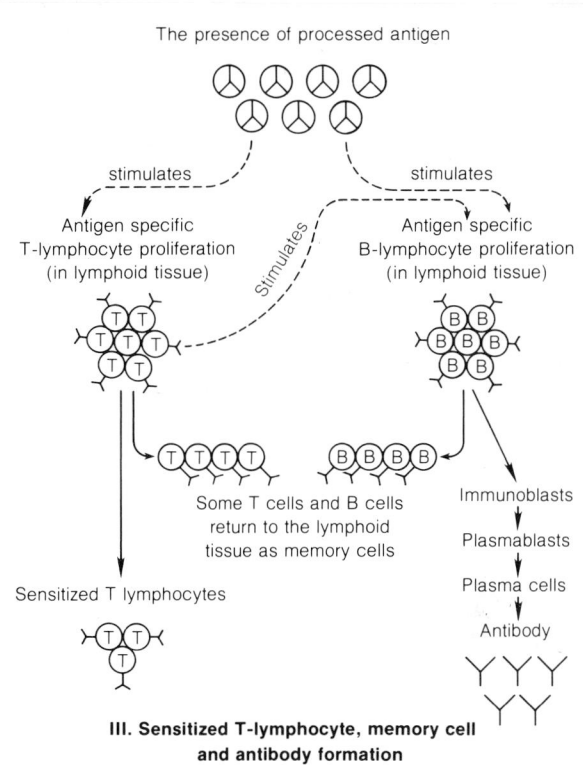

III. Sensitized T-lymphocyte, memory cell and antibody formation

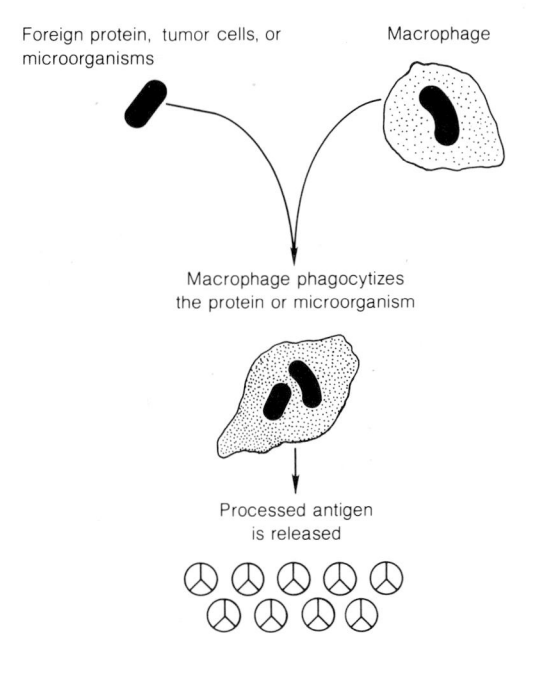

II. Role of the macrophage in stimulating the immune response

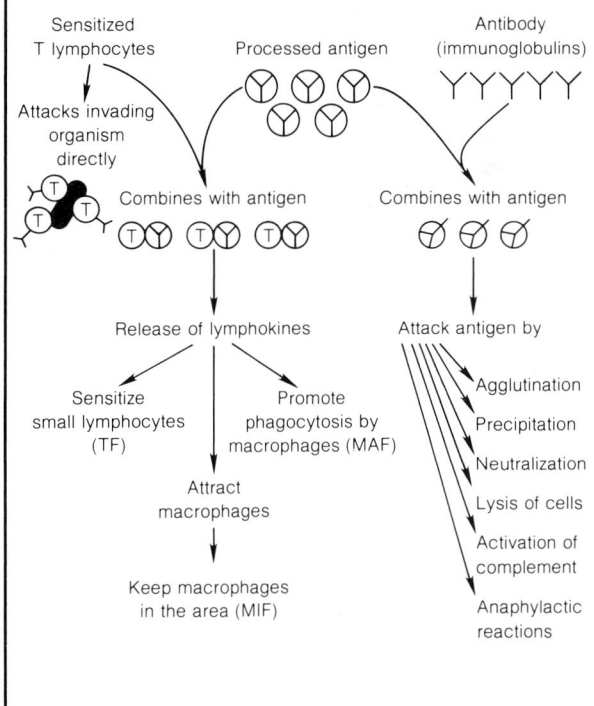

IV. Cellular (cell-mediated) and humoral (antibody) immunity

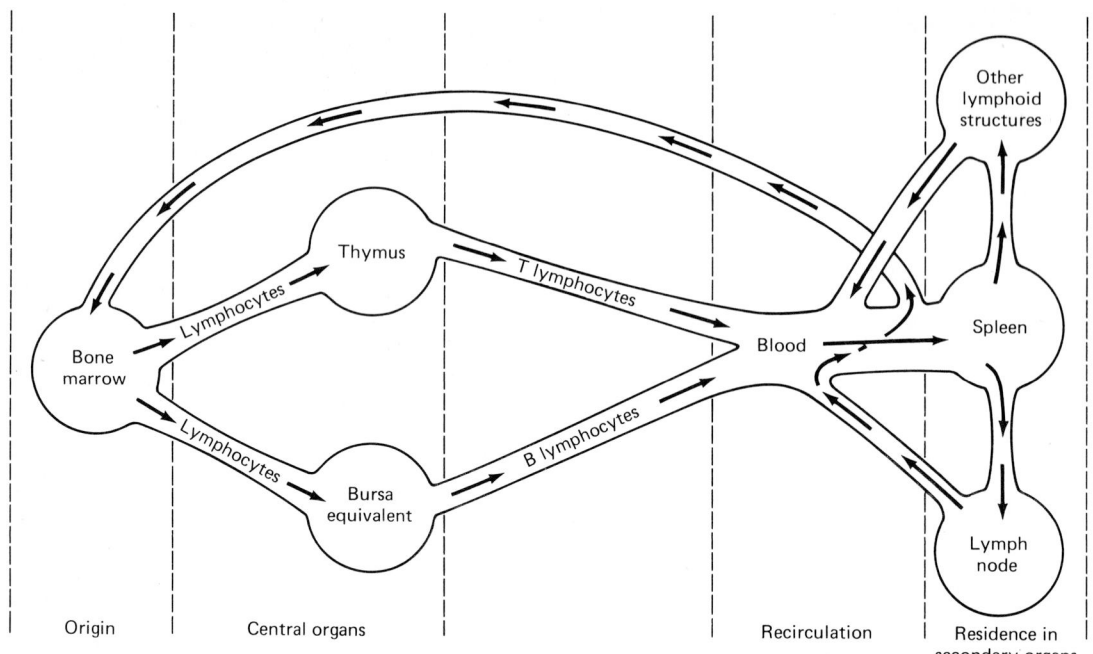

FIGURE 21-7
Lymphocyte circulation patterns.

The precursor T lymphocytes also arise in the bone marrow and circulate in the blood to the thymus. It should be noted that the bone marrow contains stem cells and precursor T and B lymphocytes as well as mature recirculating immunocompetent lymphocytes.

Immunocompetent unprimed T cells then migrate from the thymus to the spleen to provide a population of nonrecirculating "short-lived" T cells. They are short-lived unless primed by encounter with an antigen, which then converts them to a long-lived antigen-specific recirculating pool of T memory cells.

The recirculating lymphocyte pool travels from the blood to the lymph nodes to lymphatic vessels back to the blood. The transit time for recirculating T and B cells is 18 to 30 h with B cells requiring a little longer than T cells.

Both T and B cells enter the spleen through the marginal zone of the white pulp and migrate to the splenic red pulp where they reenter the blood via the splenic vein. This circuit requires about 5 to 6 h to be completed.

Antigen, Recognition and Processing

The RE system plays a major role in the uptake of antigen. Liver, lung, and splenic macrophages screen the blood and remove large amounts of antigen.

Lymph nodes filter or screen the intercellular fluid via afferent lymphatics and capillaries, which convey antigen to the lymph node. Where afferent lymphatics are absent (immunologic privileged sites), the immune response is slow to occur or absent.

On reaching the lymph node, antigen is recognized, taken up by macrophages, processed, and activated; it then becomes localized on the surface of RE cells. This localization occurs within the lymphoid follicle (B-dependent area) and persists for several weeks.

Antigen in the lymph node will within a few hours cause a shutdown of lymphocyte circulation from the node. Lymph and blood flow to the node, however, is increased; thus the node enlarges or swells. Antigen-specific lymphocytes (those able to respond to a particular antigen) are selectively recruited from the recirculating pool ("sensitized"), but just how antigen selects these lymphocytes is not known.

Lymphocyte blastogenesis with subsequent proliferation occurs, increasing the numbers of sensitized lymphocytes within the node.

Effector cells do not seem to recirculate but prefer to migrate to lymphatic tissue in the wall of the gastrointestinal system. Memory cells, however, do recirculate to give a lasting acquired immunity for that particular antigen.

T-Cell Subsets

T lymphocytes through subset T cells participate in many phases of the immune response. One group is responsible for cell-mediated immunity by directly reacting with target cells and/or production of lymphokines to bring about destruction of recognized antigen. They are termed *killer cells,* or *cytotoxic T cells.* These sensitized T cells emerge from the proliferation of selected antigen-specific T lymphocytes once antigen has been recognized and processed. This class of T lymphocytes is known as *effector T cells.*

Two other T-cell subsets influence B cells in bringing about antibody production. T-helper cells facilitate this process and T-suppressor cells diminish antibody production. The two kinds thereby achieve homeostatic control of antibody production. Such T cells are termed *regulatory T lymphocytes.*

A third subset is the *memory T cell.* It circulates throughout life and responds to a challenge by antigen previously encountered by the RE system. Memory cells, then, are responsible for immunity.

B Lymphocytes and B-Cell Subsets

All B cells are thought to be functional, since none appear to have any regulatory function. B lymphocytes have readily detectable surface immunoglobulin, while T cells either do not have it or it is not detectable. B cells are precursors of the antibody-secreting cell, *the plasma cell.* Following antigenic stimulation B cells enlarge, proliferate rapidly into B-cell clones, and differentiate into antibody-secreting plasma cells and B-memory cells. Plasma cells are found in lymphoid organs and bone marrow, but they do not circulate in either normal lymph or blood. They are only seen in the circulation when a person suffers from multiple myeloma.

B cells, in addition to the immunoglobulin, have receptors for the Fc portion of the immunoglobulin molecule and a receptor for C3 (third component of complement) which enable them to bind both antibody and complement in both specific and nonspecific ways.

K cells have been identified by their ability to kill in a nonspecific fashion target cells which have been coated with antibody. They are supposedly able to do this through an Fc receptor system, but the nature of the *K* cell type is not agreed upon. Since B lymphocytes, macrophages, and neutrophils also possess C3 and Fc receptors, all are potential candidates. However, the morphology and receptor analysis of the K cell seems to indicate that they are either B cells or macrophages. Azathioprine seems to preferentially suppress the K-cell population.

Identification of T and B Cells

Receptors on the surface of lymphocytes allow identification and characterization of T, B, K, and other lymphocytes such as the null cell.

T cells can be identified by receptors which form rosettes in the presence of sheep red blood cells (E rosettes). The surfaces of B cells have three different determinants which may be used to identify them. These markers are C3, immunoglobulin, and Fc receptors. Activated T cells also seem to synthesize Fc receptors. Macrophages and neutrophils are known to possess C3 and Fc receptors. It is through receptors that cells can communicate and control immune response.

Null cells are lymphocytes which at present can be identified only by their failure to demonstrate E rosettes or surface immunoglobulin. Their quantity is measured by subtracting B- and T-cell counts from the total lymphocyte count.

There are quantitative and qualitative differences in surface receptors during maturation and activation of lymphocytes. The list of T- and B-lymphocyte receptors is ever-growing, as is their functional significance (Table 21-2). At this time, all lymphoid-type abnormalities, such as lymphomas, leukemias, and Hodgkin's disease, are being classified on the basis of T- or B-cell types. Receptor analysis is being used to discover the predominate cell type. Drugs and therapies are then directed toward the cell type. For instance, chronic lymphatic leukemia is predominately B cell, while acute lymphoblastic leukemia is chiefly T-cell leukemia.

Receptor analysis is also being used to detect and treat immune cell deficiencies.

The Immune Response

Essential elements of the immune response are recognition and processing of antigen, specific destruction of the antigen, and protection against repeated challenge by it through immunologic memory.

Cooperation among T cells, B cells, and macrophages controls the immune response. The precise mechanisms involved are complex and not fully understood, but the process begins with nonspecific phagocytosis, processing, and activation of nonself antigens by macrophages. Antigens processed in this manner are molecularly changed for recognition as

TABLE 21-2
Surface Receptor of Common Cell Types

	SRBC	Fc	Ig	C3b	Viral	HLA
T lymphocyte	+	− (unless activated)	?	−	+ − (Measles)	+
B lymphocyte	−	+	+	+	+ Epstein-Barr	+
Macrophage	−	+	−	+	−	+
Neutrophil	−	+	−	+	−	+

Note: + = receptor present; − = receptor absent; ± = receptor variable; ? = disputed by researchers.

foreign by the lymphocyte populations. Thus macrophages play a crucial role in immune responses.

Lymphocyte recognition of activiated antigen on the surface of macrophages causes them to bind the activated antigen to their surface via receptors and subsequently enlarge and proliferate into distinct clones of cells with specific information about that particular antigen. This ensures specificity.

Macrophages, T lymphocytes and B lymphocytes cooperate to control the immune response. Most antigens evoke the proliferation and sensitization of both T and B cells. However, in any given situation one or the other (humoral or cellular) type of destruction will dominate as determined by the antigenic receptors on the specific T- or B-cell class. In addition to the production of antibody-forming plasma cells and cytotoxic killer T cells, longer-lived T- and B-memory lymphocytes are produced in response to some but not all antigens.

Humoral Immune Response

After recognition and binding of activated antigen, the B cells enlarge, begin to proliferate, and mature into a clone of plasma cells which produce antibodies with specificity for the activated antigen. T lymphocytes play a cooperative (helper) role in this process. The response is humoral in the sense that plasma cells located in secondary lymphoid structures remain there and only the antibody they produce circulates in the blood and body fluids. Hence this type of immunity can be passively transferred in serum. Upon coming in contact with the antigen, the antibody combines specifically to it to form an antigen-antibody complex. The complex is subsequently selectively destroyed by either lysis or precipitation of the com-

plex, followed by nonspecific phagocytosis and degradation by macrophages.

Defects in B lymphocytes render an individual particularly susceptible to bacterial infections such as those caused by *Hemophilus,* pneumococcus, *Staphylococcus,* and *Streptococcus.* While antibodies provide one of the main mechanisms for defense against viruses present in the blood, cell-mediated immunity is more important in the eradication of established viral infections.

Cell-Mediated Immunity

The mediator here is the T cell, which functions at the site of the reaction. This type of immunity can be passively transferred from one animal to another by cells. The T lymphocyte recognizes a foreign antigen on the surface of macrophages and responds by binding it, enlarging, and then proliferating a clone of sensitized T lymphocytes which migrate through the body to the actual location of the antigen. The cells destroy the alien macromolecule by direct participation of the cytotoxic T cell as well as by secretion of soluble mediators known as *lymphokines.* Lymphokines have many different functions and act on different kinds of cells, including macrophages, lymphocytes, neutrophils, eosinophils, and tissue cells. Lymphotoxin (LT) and macrophage inhibition factor (MiF) are two of the better known lymphokines. Others are listed in Table 21-3.

Cell-mediated immunity dominates in most cases of intracellular infections as well as in graft rejection, graft-versus-host disease, and immune defense against neoplasia.

Defects in T lymphocytes are suggested by recurrent infections of fungal, viral, and intracellular or-

TABLE 21-3
Lymphokines Produced by Activated Lymphocytes

Lymphokine released	Cell affected	Effect
Transfer factor (TF)	Lymphocyte	Induces delayed type hypersensitivity
Mitogenic factor	Lymphocytes	Initiation of cell division
Lymphotoxin	Target cells (antigen)	Destruction of target cells
Migration inhibitory factor	Macrophages	Inhibits migration of human macrophages
Chemotaxic factors	Macrophages and/or granulocytes	Attracts cells to area of immune response
Macrophage activation factor (MAF)	Macrophages	Enhances function of macrophages in immune responses
Interferon	Viruses	Inhibition of viral growth
Skin reactive factor	Skin	Causes local inflammatory reaction

ganisms. Serum antibody levels are usually low. Skin grafts are not rejected, neoplasia may be present, and delayed hypersensitivity reactions are absent or diminished in T-cell deficiencies. Many viruses cause a lymphopenia in humans, and this often leads to severe, fatal bacterial and fungal infections.

Role of Complement

Complement[1] is a term applied to a group of nonspecific proteins that circulate in an inactive form in the blood of all warm-blooded animals. Although they are found in the globulin fraction of serum, they are not immunoglobulins and therefore are not increased during immunization. Complement proteins are in-

volved in nonimmune reactions as well as in the immune response, and they function in a nonspecific way in both cases. The complement lyses cells by fixing to any cell to which IgM or IgG has become attached. The antibody thus guides the attack to specific targets, sparing other cells.

Complement Activation

The fraction known as C1 is primarily synthesized by intestinal epithelium, while C2 and C4 are produced by macrophages; C3, C6, and C9 by the liver; and C5 and C8 by the spleen. The usual cascade of complement reactions is usually set off by an encounter of complement with IgG or IgM linked to antigen-antibody complex. This encounter and resultant binding of complement to such a complex is called *complement fixation*. Basically the complement sequence occurs in three major phases (Fig. 21-8). First is the production of C3 splitting enzyme, known as *C3 convertase*; second is the actual activation of

---

[1] The nomenclature for the classic components of complement uses numbers preceded by C (e.g., C1, C2). The subsequent small letters (e.g., C1q, C2a) denote subunits. Complexes are denoted by sequential numbers separated by commas (e.g., C5,6,7).

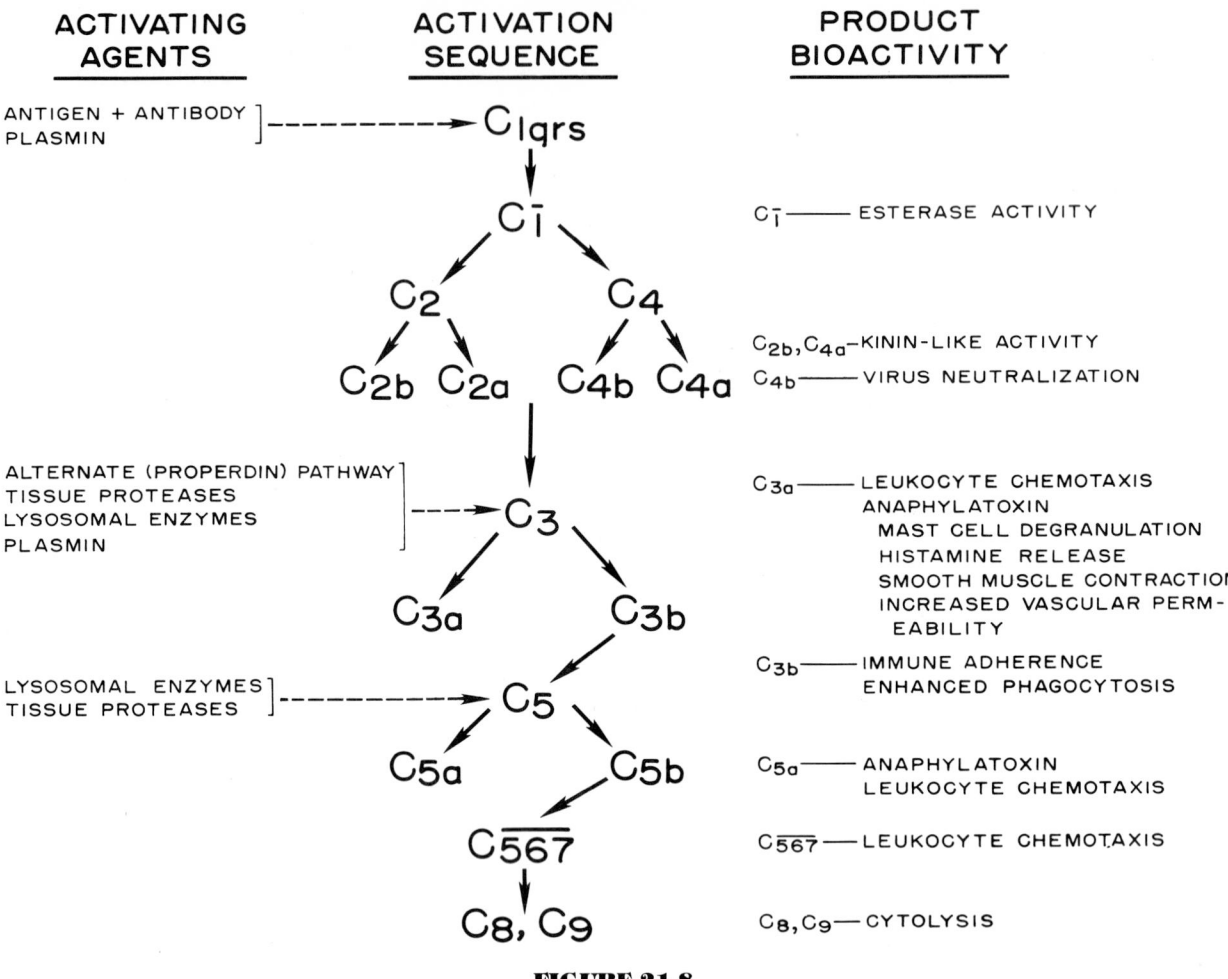

FIGURE 21-8

The complement system. [*From S. A. Price and L. M. Wilson (eds.), Pathophysiology, Clinical Concepts of Disease Processes, McGraw-Hill, New York, 1978. Used by permission of the publisher.*]

C3. The third phase is the activation of the remaining complement proteins (terminal component) in what is called the *terminal sequence.*

C1q fixes to the antigen-antibody complex, which starts a series of reactions leading to the production of C3 convertase (C1,4b,2a) and three inactive fragments C2b, C2b, and C4a.

C3 is thus activated by the convertase to produce biologically significant components C3b and C3a. One function of C3b is to attach itself to phagocytes, facilitating phagocytosis like an opsonin. C3a works as a blood vessel dilator and as a chemotactic agent for neutrophils. An additional C3 fraction (C1,4b, 2a,3b) subsequently activates C5; this marks the third stage in complement activation. The rest of the components, C6 to C9, combine to form a complex C1,2,3,4,5,6,7,8,9, which initiates membrane lesions leading to cell lysis. Two C5 fragments are active in the inflammatory response. C5a, like C3a, acts as a vasodilator and a chemotactic substance. Another chemotactic substance is formed by a second C5,6 fragment which combines with C6 and C7, becoming C5,6,7.

The complement system is capable of being activated by other than antigen-antibody complexes (Fig. 21-8). This alternative pathway is especially important in the body's defense against bacteria of the gastrointestinal tract, since it is set into motion by endotoxin, a polysaccharide released by some enteric organisms. This alternative pathway involves a serum factor *properdin,* certain cofactors, and C3b; the net result is a C3 convertase. "Classical" C3 convertase (C14b2a) and this "alternate" convertase (C3b,Bb) both require Mg^{2+}. The properdin pathway is given positive feedback by C3b. Obviously this feedback must be homeostatically controlled or massive complement activation through amplification would occur every time C3 were split or fixed. A C3b inactivator known as KAF exists as an enzyme in normal serum. KAF can interrupt the feedback cycle essential to the alternative pathway.

Complement Disorders

Complement is involved not only in immunologic defenses but also in immunologic injury (Table 21-4). In man C3 is found at the site of many immunologic lesions and helps to form pathologic immune antigen-antibody-complement complexes. Under favorable conditions these complexes are removed from the circulation by cells with C3 receptors, particularly those of the liver and spleen. When they are not promptly and adequately removed, they tend to filter into the glomeruli of the kidney or are deposited in very small capillaries. This outcome will be discussed in greater detail under complex-mediated hypersensitivity.

Deficiencies of certain complement and complement inactivators cause serious clinical problems because of their influence in controlling the complement cascade (Table 21-5). Decrease in C1 inactivator produces hereditary angioedema (HAE) and is also associated with systemic lupus erythematosus (SLE) and glomerulonephritis, while a deficiency of C3b inactivates or produces a secondary lowering of C3 and thus an immune deficiency. Such persons are usually young and suffer from repeated serious pyogenic infections. C3b inactivator deficiencies are also associated with a high incidence of SLE, but this may be due to an increased susceptibility to viral infections. Terminal component deficiencies produce no apparent clinical problems but are often associated with SLE. Deficiencies of the alternate pathway have not been described.

C1 esterase inhibitory deficiency (HAE) is usually hereditary, and the family history will often reveal a death from asphyxia. When C1 inhibitor is absent, C1

TABLE 21-4
Principal Inflammatory Activities of Activated Complement Proteins or Their Fragments

Biologic activity	Complement component responsible
Cytoadherence (enhances immune response)	C3b
Chemotaxis (attraction of neutrophils and macrophages)	C3b, C5a, and $\overline{C567}$
Anaphylatoxin (acts on mast cells, releasing histamine which dilates blood vessels and initiates exudation)	C3a and C5a
Opsonization (promotes phagocytosis)	C3b and C4a
Kinins (?)	C2b and C4a
Membrane lesions	C1–8
Cell lysis	C1–9

is activated to a greater extent than usual, and this causes increased vascular permeability leading to local edema. The attacks are unpredictable and may involve respiratory edema, abdominal pain, and intestinal obstruction as a result of mucosal wall edema. Fresh plasma containing the C1 inhibitor or anti-inflammatory drugs may be helpful.

Most clinical problems associated with complement have been the result of deficiencies rather than excesses, but cancer patients may exhibit increased complement levels. The significance of this is not known.

Physiology of Immunity

The immune system can be physiologically divided into three sequentially dependent limbs. First, the *afferent limb* includes all processes which are necessary for recognition of foreign antigen within the human body. Cells involved in the afferent limb are macrophage and antigen-sensitive T and B lymphocytes. Recognition and antigen processing are prime attributes of the afferent limb.

The second or *central limb* includes all those events which are necessary for preparation of an effective immune response to antigens and includes

TABLE 21-5
Human Complement Deficiences

Serum complement proteins	Enzyme	Function	Clinical manifestation in deficient state
Functional components			
C1r	+	Activates C1s	Renal and skin disease
C1s	+	Acts on C4 and then C2 to produce C4b2a (Convertase)	
C1q	−	Recognition unit for classical pathway	
C3	−	Split by convertase to produce C3b, C3a biological components Activates C5	Immune deficiency
C4	−	Activates C2; helps to produce convertase	Skin disease
C5	−	Produces C5a, C5b, and activates C6	Skin disease
Regulators of complement			
C3b inactivator (endopeptidase) also called KAF	+	Cleaves and inactivates C3b and C4b	Immune deficiency pyogenic infections
C1 esterase inhibitor (C1INH)	−	Blocks activity of C1r and C1s by chemically combining	Glomerulonephritis, hereditary angioedema and SLE

cell cooperation, cloning, and production of effectors and memory cells.

The *efferent limb* is the third limb; in it sensitized T and B cells and their products act on the antigens. The efferent limb is divided into a dual system of cell-mediated and humoral-(antibody-) mediated destruction of specific antigen.

This classification into three functional phases has practical application in diagnosis and treatment. When we assess the immune response, we often test for defects in the afferent, central, or efferent limb of the response. Likewise, many drugs and therapies are directed primarily at a particular activity or cell type within a particular limb.

Immune Response and Genetics

Several investigators have demonstrated that three families of genes exercise genetic control over the immune response. First are the genes responsible for directing syntheses of immunoglobulin molecules. These are crucial for B-cell function. This *Ig gene system* involves participation of two discrete structural genes in the production of a single polypeptide chain.

One is for the variable (Fab) region and one for the constant (Fc) region of the immunoglobulin molecule.

The second gene family is the *histocompatibility* (HLA) *system,* which consists of several distinct chromosome regions responsible for specifying antigens on tissue cells. Thus HLA genes control transplantation immune response. Siblings identical for this region can exchange grafts more easily than nonidentical siblings.

Because humans are an outbred species, HLA complexes are quite varied, with a large number of alleles at each locus with low gene frequencies. HLA antigens are given numbers, but the different loci are designated as A, B, C, and so forth. In Caucasian populations certain antigen combinations seem to occur more frequently than others. These combined forms are often associated with predispositions to certain pathologies. HLA-B27 is associated with ankylosing spondylitis. B12-A2 occurs in individuals with acute lymphatic leukemia. HLA-BW15 is found with systemic lupus erythematosus. This may indicate that the way in which HLA antigens are linked, aside from their importance in transplantations, may also determine disease susceptibility.

The third family of genes controls an individual's capacity to respond or not respond to various antigens and thus helps determine susceptibility or resistance to a given antigen. These are termed *immune response genes* (Ir genes). They seem completely unrelated to Ig genes. Immune response genes are thought to encode T-cell antigen receptors. T-cell receptors appear to recognize mutated native antigens, as foreign, as well as viruses and intracellular microbes.

The relationship of Ir genes to the HLA complex remains to be determined in humans. In rodents, however, genes of the major histocompatibility complex (MHC complex) control immune responses to antigenic determinants. The function of T cells in graft rejection, recognition of mutant native cells, and graft-versus-host disease seem to support a connection between Ir genes and HLA genes.

HYPERIMMUNE RESPONSE PATHOLOGY

The efferent limb of the immune response presents itself as either cell- or antibody-mediated. So, too, immunopathologic states may be conveniently divided into cell-mediated and humoral pathologic states. Imbalance of homeostatic mechanisms modulating immune responses results in hypo- or hyperimmune states (Fig. 21-9).

Symptoms of hyperimmune states are recognized by the presence of allergies and other immunologic injury. Conversely, hypoimmune individuals demonstrate anergy, increased susceptibility to common infections, increased severity and difficulty in controlling infections, and a lack of response to both new and recall antigens.

When the immune response and its corresponding inflammation is exaggerated beyond a purely protective effect or is directed inappropriately toward a material that is not potentially harmful, we say a person is *hypersensitive. Allergy* is defined as ˙an altered state of immune reactivity. Hypersensitivity and allergy are now used interchangeably by most health workers.

A classification of hyperimmune immunopathologic mechanisms was proposed by Coombs and Gell (1975) based on humoral and cell types of immunity. Immune injuries of type I, II, and III are antibody-mediated, and type IV is mediated by sensitized lymphocytes and their products in the absence of antibodies or complement. Since this categorization is for convenience and understanding, clinical manifestations of loss in immune regulation may express one or more types of reactions. Table 21-6 contrasts and compares these four immunopathologic types. They differ significantly in time sequence, location,

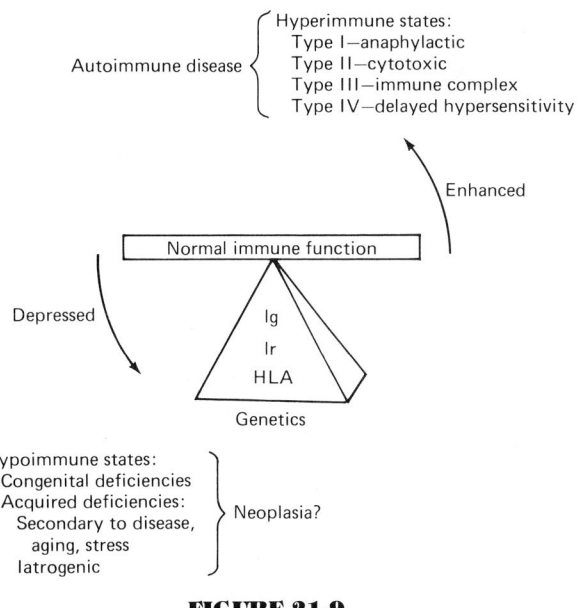

FIGURE 21-9
Concept of immunopathology.

TABLE 21-6
Comparison of Four Hypersensitivity Reactions

Type of reaction	Where occurs	Time after antigen exposure	Observable signs	Mechanism of or effect of injury	Antibody type involved	Complement involved	Other
Type I Anaphylactic (systemic)	Vascular system Mucous membranes Smooth muscle	5–15 min	Respiratory distress and obstruction Cardiovascular shock	Mast cell release of histamine, SRS-A, and other pharmacologic agents	IgE		Strong familial predisposition
Atopy (chronic)	Skin Mucous membranes	5–15 min	Skin eruptions Bronchospasm Airway obstruction Abdominal pain Nausea Diarrhea Edema			None	May be related to IgA deficiency
Type II Cytotoxic	Any tissue but usually vascular system or kidney	Minutes	Deficiency of target cell type, i.e., anemia, thrombocytopenia leukopenia, and vascular purpura	Lysis of target cells due to haptens being absorbed on native cells	IgG or IgM	C1–9 (C fixing)	Associated with autoimmune disease K-cell antibody-dependent cytotoxicity may be involved

456

TABLE 21-6 (Continued)
Comparison of Four Hypersensitivity Reactions

Type of reaction	Where occurs	Time after antigen exposure	Observable signs	Mechanism of or effect of injury	Antibody type involved	Complement involved	Other
Type III Complex-mediated hypersensitivity	Systemic type Vascular system Local type (arthus) occurs Extravascular, i.e., skin, mucous membrane, joint	Minutes 2–5 h	Glomerulo-nephritis Arthritis Polyarteritis nodosa	Anaphylatoxins and neutrophil release of necrotizing lysosomal enzymes which produce local ischemic necrosis at location of antigen-antibody complex	IgG	C3, C5 C567 C8, C9 Anaphylatoxins	Associated with autoimmune disease
Type IV Delayed hypersensitivity	In any tissue	Maximum 24–48 h delayed	Contact dermatitis Poison ivy Tuberculin reaction Graft rejection Allergic reactions to infection Graft-versus host disease	Lymphokine release and subsequent lymphocyte-mediated cytolysis Cell-mediated via lymphocytes and macrophages	None	None	Associated with autoimmune disease K-cell cytotoxicity may be involved

Source: Adapted from Coombs, R. R. A., and P. G. H. Gell, in P. G. H. Gell, R. R. A. Coombs, and P. J. Lackman (eds): *Clinical Aspects of Immunology*, Oxford: Blackwell, 1975, p. 761.

antibody type, and mediators. Classifications listing other types have been proposed but will not be included in this discussion.

Type I: Anaphylactic Reactions

Type I reactions occur immediately after exposure as a result of interactions between mast cells, IgE antibody, and a specific antigen. This interaction results in the release of mast cell granules. IgE is nonspecifically fixed to the surface of mast cells via Fc receptors, leaving the variable portion for specific antigen attachment. When the specific allergen does attach to the IgE, the mast cell degranulates and releases histamine, slow-reacting substance of anaphylaxis (SRS-A), and other vasoactive products which mediate a hyperimmune type of reaction. IgE circulates in the body fluids, but it is also found fixed to mast cells in the subcutaneous tissues of the body. This is usually a local protective response to environmental antigens, but some individuals seem to possess certain HLA combinations or Ir genes which predispose them to hyperimmune sensitivity and result in an overt expression of the anaphylactic type reaction. Recently it has been suggested, but not confirmed, that, since during early development environmental antigens induce IgA synthesis that have no binding for mast cells, perhaps persons hypersensitive to these allergies have a primary IgA deficiency state and produce IgE-mediated responses to these antigens as an adaptive response.

Mast cells are found surrounding small veins in submucosal and subcutaneous areas of the body which most frequently encounter environmental antigens. Known as *basophils* when circulating in the blood, their morphology is not easily discernible because of large basophilic staining granules within the cytoplasm. These granules contain histamine, serotonin, SRS-A, and other vasoactive amines capable of producing anaphylactic type responses.

The type of anaphylaxis expressed clinically depends on the route of antigen access, the target organ, and the person's genetics. *Systemic anaphylaxis* usually occurs when the antigen dose is large and given rapidly by intravenous, intramuscular, or subcutaneous injection. It is a generalized reaction causing contraction of smooth muscle, increased vascular permeability, hypotension, incoagulability of blood, and decreased heart rate and complement levels. Hypersensitive individuals develop circulatory shock and respiratory difficulties within minutes after injection of drugs or insect venom. In extremely sensitive persons, small amounts of antigen on the skin or in the air may cause severe systemic anaphylaxis. To summarize, systemic anaphylaxis involves the entire body, may lead to cardiovascular shock, and may be rapidly fatal.

Cutaneous anaphylaxis has the same mechanism as systemic anaphylaxis but is a localized reaction due to skin-fixing IgE and is manifested in the skin or mucous membranes. The symptoms include many lesions occurring in the skin, gastrointestinal tract, or nasal mucosa, reaching a maximum within 15 to 20 min after exposure to the antigen.

In either type of anaphylaxis, mast cells can release their mediators through lytic or nonlytic means. The *nonlytic* type involves IgE, antigen, and mast cells as previously described, with subsequent degranulation. *Lytic* reactions are mediated by IgG or IgM, and these combine on the surface of mast cells along with complement. Complement involvement results in membrane lesions and finally cell lysis with the release of mast cell granules.

An association of certain HLA-type individuals with allergic sensitivity, elevated titer of IgE, and decreased suppressor T cells has been made. The precise role of genetics in allergy, however, is still to be explained.

Atopic allergy refers to human allergies to natural environmental antigens. The mechanism is essentially the same as systemic and cutaneous anaphylaxis. Sometimes type I reactions are categorized under the general heading of *atopy*. Atopic allergies include hay fever, allergic rhinitis, asthma, hives, serous otitis media, nasal polyps, dermatitis, eczema, food allergies, and so forth. Atopy is controlled by Ir genes, the degree of environmental exposure to potential allergens, and autonomic physiologic mechanisms of a nonimmune nature.

A fact which complicates the diagnosis of type I reactions is that any stimulus which releases histamine will mimic this type of immune injury. This nonimmune release of histamine is called an *anaphylactoid reaction*. Morphine, polymixin B, iodinated contrast materials, and curare, among others, are examples of nonimmune agents which release histamine from mast cells and produce anaphylactoid reactions. In urticaria pigmentosa, which presents a large mast cell population, these drugs could be fatal because of massive histamine release. Clinically, however, it is difficult to distinguish anaphylaxis from anaphylactoid-type reactions.

Environmental conditions such as temperature, humidity, presence of infections, or the emotional state of a person may alter anaphylactic reactions. Treatment for allergy of this type is aimed at artificially producing a state of tolerance to the particular offending allergen. *Desensitization* is the process of injecting small amounts of antigen and gradually increasing the amount over a period of time. This is effective in desensitizing some individuals by producing immunologic competition between IgG and IgE, since both are able to bind the antigen and thus reduce allergic symptoms. *Hyposensitization* is using a specific antibody to block the release of mast cell granules and thus reduce symptoms. Sometimes an effective response to small doses of antigen fails to demonstrate either desensitization or hyposensitization, yet a tolerance has been induced.

Anaphylactic hypersensitivity is usually frightening and disturbing to the individual. Dyspnea associated with asthma certainly elicits fear, but the drippy nose, itching and changes in body image due to urticaria or dermatitis are also stressful. Empathy for these individuals and conveyance of understanding for their problems and feelings is likely to affect the outcome of any therapy.

Smoke, fumes, dust, and aerosols should be avoided in the environment of persons with atopic respiratory problems. Animal danders, feathers, molds, and house dust are also troublesome to these and other atopic individuals. Dry skin promotes itching associated with atopic dermatitis; thus proper skin care and topical lubricants are required to keep the person from scratching. Secondary infections may be reduced by eliminating irritating fabrics, by bathing frequently in mild soaps, and by keeping the hands and fingernails particularly clean. The nurse should observe for any secondary contact dermatitis, which commonly occurs in hypersentitive individuals, due to topical antibiotics or antihistamines. Cataracts also frequently develop in allergic persons, but the cause is unknown.

Asthmatics should avoid dehydration, since this condition will enhance formation of mucus plugs and further impair alveolar ventilation. Sedatives should be avoided despite the anxiety of the individual because they tend to depress respiration. Anxiety then must be reduced by other means.

Long-term antihistamine use frequently produces dryness of oral mucous membranes, nausea, dizziness, and blurred vision. Persons on continual antihistamine therapy will need to be alerted to the possible occurrence of these symptoms.

Aspirin and isoproterenol abuse, as well as electrostatic air filter ozone production, has recently been shown to act as asthmatic stimulants. Many other common habits and environmental agents are probably likewise troublesome and controllable but as yet undetected. Observational skills of the nurse are extremely important in determining significant relationships between environment, emotions, therapies, and the quality of an individual's allergic symptoms. Clinical nursing research must confirm significant observations in order to verify appropriate nursing interventions.

Teaching and learning processes should be used in helping the allergic person, since the environment and the emotional state of the individual will influence the degree of symptoms and the effect of treatment. Control of these in the clinical setting, as well as teaching the patient methods of controlling them in the home setting, is essential. Environmental control and stress modulation are primary nursing activities for the hypersensitive individual.

Type II: Cytotoxic Reactions

Cytotoxic hypersensitivity involves the Fab portion of antibody combining with antigenic receptors on membranes of cells. Haptens combined or absorbed on the surface of native cells to which the antibody combines gives the same net effect. Complement is usually but not always required for cytotoxic reactions; thus cell lysis occurs. If a cell is the antigen and IgG the antibody, removal occurs by phagocytosis, and a deficiency of the cell type will result. Cytotoxic reactions occur most frequently in the vascular system, and thus the target cells for this type II hypersensitivity are usually red blood cells (anemia), white blood cells (leukopenia), platelets (thrombocytopenia), or endothelium (vascular purpura). Cytotoxic reactions may, however, involve any particular cell type in a specific tissue. The immunoglobulin involved in the vascular reaction is either the IgG or IgM type; however, the tissue cytotoxicity necessarily would require IgG because of the small size and ability of this antibody to cross membrane barriers.

Tissue cytotoxicity may occur in almost any tissue, but the kidneys, because of their blood-filtering function, are quite vulnerable to type II as well as type III reactions. Many haptogenic drugs and substances are excreted via the kidney; this adds to their risk of being absorbed on the glomerular cell membrane. The glomerular basement membrane (GBM) seems particularly vulnerable. The introduction of heterologous antiserum can induce nephrotoxic serum nephritis. This type of injury is seen in renal transplant recipients receiving antilymphocyte serum (ALS). Goodpasture's syndrome and many other autoimmune diseases such as scleroderma, systemic lupus erythematosus (SLE), polyarteritis nodosa, and so on, all exhibit some cytotoxic phenomena. The presence of antiglomerular basement membrane (GBA) antibody is diagnostic of renal-type cytotoxic injury.

Cytotoxic injury can affect transplanted kidneys in patients with GBA already present in their serum. Potential transplant recipients should be evaluated for the presence of GBA before transplantation occurs. In Goodpasture's syndrome the GBA are able to attack not only glomeruli but lung basement membranes with subsequent life-threatening pulmonary hemorrhage. Lung and kidney basement membranes seem to share like or similar antigens.

To summarize, cytotoxic injury usually occurs in the vascular system, causing a lysis of specific target cells because of IgG or IgM combining with antigenic determinants or haptens absorbed on the surface of these cells. Complement is fixed to the IgM complex and the target cells are selectively destroyed, producing a cell deficiency. IgG-mediated toxic reactions cause them to be phagocytized by macrophages and subsequently degraded, thus producing a deficiency. Examples of cytotoxic injury include erythroblastosis fetalis, transfusion incompatibility reactions, hemolytic anemia, thrombocytopenia, leukopenia, drug reactions, and certain autoimmune disorders.

Large-volume plasmapheresis has recently been used in conjunction with immunosuppression to treat type II cytotoxic injury. This tends to decrease circulating target cell antibody and prevent further cell lysis similar to the theory behind exchange transfusion mechanisms for the erythroblastotic infants. Immunosuppression, when used alone, has had little effect. Glomerular basement membrane antibodies persist from a few weeks to 2 years, with the titer gradually diminishing with time. Nephrectomy has sometimes been performed to treat Goodpasture's syndrome and prevent pulmonary hemorrhage, but it is a harsh treatment with little effect. In cases of cytotoxic deficiencies of blood components, replacement therapy is used to eliminate the symptoms.

Type III: Complex-Mediated Hypersensitivity

Immunologic injury in immune complex disease is secondary to precipitation and localization of antigen-antibody complexes which, when soluble antigen combines with specific antibody, form insoluble complexes localizing around small blood vessels. In the vascular system they tend to become trapped in blood vessel walls. The antigen-antibody complexes fix and activate the complement cascade. Activated complement subsequently releases phlogistic fragments C3a, C3b, C5a, C567, etc. (Table 21-4) which chemotaxically attract neutrophils and mediate an inflammatory reaction. Release of lysosomal enzymes from accumulated neutrophils causes destruction of the elastic lamina of arteries, the basement membrane of the kidney, and the walls of small vessels. The usual lesion is an ischemic necrosis of the area in which the toxin is deposited. It is important to note that there is usually no specificity for the tissue in which the complex localizes; rather they are shed from the areas of the original infection or pathology, are complexed with the antibody in the circulating fluids, and are physically deposited in an area as they circulate, the complex is trapped in these areas and elicits an inflammatory reaction in that particular location.

Immune complexes precipitate in the kidney as random irregular deposits of inflammation and may be distinguished from the cytotoxic-type nephritis in which the presence of GBA reacts in a smooth linear pattern along the basement membranes.

Ordinarily the reticuloendothelial system should clear immune complexes from the body fluids. When this does not occur, toxic complex disease occurs. Lack of proper clearance may be due to excessive amounts of complex or defects existing in immune phagocytosis.

There are basically two types of immune complex disease which need consideration: an extravascular reaction (arthus) and an intravascular type (serum sickness).

Arthus reaction was originally described as a result of placing antigen-antibody complexes in the skin, which caused edema, erythema and hemorrhage to occur within a few hours. The lesion was characterized by time (2 to 5 h), accumulation of neutrophils, and changes in vascular permeability which culminate in a localized ischemic thrombosis. Typical arthus reactions, which are distributed in vessels throughout the body of man, describe the pathogenesis of polyarteritis nodosa. Similar lesions in articulating joints of the body (arthritis) or kidney (glomerulonephritis) have been confirmed.

Serum sickness is the formation of immune complexes in the bloodstream. It consists of vasculitis, arthritis, and glomerulonephritis and has the same mechanism as the arthus reaction. It is usually associated with drug reactions and transplant recipients receiving ALS. Serum sickness may be caused by immune antibody production to either an exogenous or endogenous antigen, passive transfer of antibody or antigen, or the injection of preformed antigen-antibody complexes. Arthus reactions most often occur when there is an excess of antibody, whereas serum sickness is more often associated with an excess of antigen. Regardless of which is in excess, both form toxic complexes which produce necrotic injury.

Many diseases in their latent form have been associated with immune complex formation. Infections (bacterial, viral, and parasitic), disseminated malignancy, autoimmune disorders, drug reactions, and many other diseases have lesions caused from deposition of toxic complexes. Whether the complexes are primary or secondary to the condition varies and is not always discernible. Most immune complex disorders, however, are associated with an immune response with an excess of either antibody or soluble antigens.

Several factors seem to influence the deposition of immune complexes. The size of the complex, which is determined by the relative antigen-antibody ratio, is important. Avidity of antibody may affect the size and stability of the complex. Vasoactive amines, clearing of complexes by phagocytic cells, hemodynamic factors, blood flow, constrictions, and bifurcation all conceivably contribute or influence the localization process.

In humans the antigen in the immune complex is usually not known, but the result of its presence is quite consistent. IgG and IgM are the usual types of antibody involved. Complement fixation with activation of the complement cascade and release of anaphylatoxins is essential. The pathologic lesions, however, are a result of neutrophil release of necrotizing lysosomal enzymes which produce a local ischemic thrombosis. When this involves organs or organ systems, the damage can be life-threatening.

Type IV: Delayed-Type Hypersensitivity

Types I, II, and III immune injuries have all been *immediate humoral*-type reactions. The final type IV to be considered is *cell-mediated* and is called *delayed hypersensitivity*.

Cell-mediated immune responses (CMI) are, as we have seen, carried out chiefly by sensitized T lymphocytes. These cells destroy antigen by direct or indirect means in the absence of either antibody or complement. Direct destruction requires actual physical contact of T lymphocytes with antigen and may be cytolytic or cytostable in nature.

Indirect toxicity is produced via mediators (lym-phokines) which are released from lymphocytes which induce local lesions characterized by infiltration with macrophages, lymphocytes, and a chronic inflammatory exudate. In either type, direct or indirect or both, the response is maximal in 48 to 72 h after antigen exposure.

Cell-mediate immunity involves a cooperation between T lymphocytes and macrophages. Macrophages as well as T lymphocytes are capable of direct cytotoxicity. Macrophages contain numerous cytoplasmic lysosomes containing a variety of hydrolytic enzymes capable of degrading proteins, lipids, and nucleic acids. From a functional point of view, macrophages are of prime importance in all limbs of the immune response, are radio-resistant, and are able to survive in an adverse environment. When one talks of host defense, the macrophage is always a prime mover, yet its function often is overlooked because of the popularity of lymphocytes.

The exact mechanism of delayed hypersensitivity is still uncertain. It is characterized by infiltration of mononuclear cells 24 to 72 h after antigen exposure at the antigen site. Most of the infiltrating cells are not sensitized by the antigen but recruited into the area by a small number of sensitized T lymphocytes. These few sensitized cells may release lymphokines, which influence cell migration and patterns of non-sensitized mononuclear cells. The most common example of delayed hypersensitivity is the tuberculin skin test. Intradermal injection of old tuberculin will produce erythema, enduration, and possible necrosis of the area in approximately 24 to 48 h in persons previously sensitized by the tuberculin antigen. This differs from the arthus reaction in both time (2 to 5 h) and cellular infiltration (neutrophils). Neither antibody nor complement are required in type IV reactions.

Contact Allergies

Many *contact allergies* are of the type IV delayed hypersensitivity reaction. Poison ivy sensitivity is a classical example; however, many cosmetics, clothing, tapes, jewelry, soaps, and chemicals normally in contact with the skin often produce injury in the predisposed individual. These haptogenic substances need to be lipid-soluble in order to penetrate the skin and then must be chemically capable of combining with body proteins in order to be antigenic. When these situations occur in a previously exposed, sensitive individual, contact dermatitis of delayed hypersensitivity can occur. These must be differentiated from arthus-type reactions, which is readily done since this reaction requires 48 to 72 h to develop (delayed) and mononuclear cells instead of neutrophils infiltrate. Symptoms are redness, enduration, vesiculation, and discomfort, all reaching a maximum in 48 to 72 h after exposure. Rupture of the vesicles may spread the antigen to new areas of skin and prolong the reaction.

Transplants

Transplants of foreign tissue have promoted an intense study of cellular immune responses. Genetic control of transplants via HLA antigens has been readily determined. If an individual has a skin graft from a specific donor with genetic disparity, vascularization and acceptance of the graft will usually occur within 6 to 7 days. After about 1 week, signs of graft rejection begin to appear, with mononuclear cells infiltrating and the graft becoming blanched, white, and edematous (9 to 10 days). Gradually the graft turns brownish, indicating thrombosis of vessels, and finally it dries and/or sloughs off 11 to 14 days after grafting. This is called primary or *first set rejection.*

If a second skin flap from the same donor is again grafted to the same recipient, the graft fails to become vascularized and a more rapid and vigorous rejection ensues. The secondary or *second set rejection* then occurs within 4 to 5 days. Extreme care should therefore be taken to avoid sensitizing the transplant recipient with any kind of donor cells. Antibodies may also affect transplanted tissue toward either acceptance or rejection.

Sometimes antibodies produced against the graft will in fact enhance the "take" by blocking the actions of sensitized T cells. The mechanism of *immunologic enhancement* is not fully agreed upon but appears to be cytolytic or the phagocytic removal of sensitized lymphocytes. Conversely, specific antibody directed against the graft, if injected into the grafting site, will cause an ischemic necrosis and rejection of the graft. Enhancement was first observed and described in trying to destroy tumors via injection of antiserum prepared against tumor antigens. Such therapy disappointingly resulted in enhanced tumor growth.

Infection

Infection is related to delayed hypersensitivity. Although antibodies provide the main mechanism for defense against viral penetration, cell-mediated immunity is required for dealing with established viral infections. IgA seems particularly important in preventing viral attachment to epithelial cells, which is the first step in the infectious process. Failure of these mechanisms or lack of them could cause an individual to become a chronic viral carrier. This is particularly true in polio and hepatitis A virus.

When one looks at cell-mediated defects with respect to viral agents, it becomes clear that a lack of T lymphocytes will allow frequent recurring viral infections. Viral-infected cells may change the surface antigens of the cell; this renders them recognizable as nonself and destroys them by T-cell cytotoxicity. Activated macrophages are also important in removing viral-infected body cells. Certain chronic human viral infections are associated with lymphopenia, though the precise manner in which lymphocytes disappear is unclear. Lack of lymphocytes renders these individuals susceptible to opportunistic and antibiotic-resistant-type infections.

Certain viruses such as polio are released from an infected cell and will be destroyed by a specific antibody. Most, however, spread from cell to cell and will persist despite a high titer of the specific antibody. A cell-mediated response is required to destroy established viral infections, but antibody and interferon are important in preventing the penetration and spread of viral infections.

Bacterial infections are resisted by many mechanisms. Those bacteria which attach to epithelial cells but do not penetrate do not usually provoke an immune response. Preventing entrance of bacteria is effectively accomplished by epithelial structures and their functional activities. If these fail, extracellular-type bacteria are usually nonspecifically phagocytosed by neutrophils and the intracellular types are phagocytosed by macrophages. Both cells have the capability of destroying phagocytosed material, and this is a way of eliminating bacteria which obtain entrance into the mucosa or subcutaneous areas of the body. If bacteria are too numerous or are allowed to multiply faster than phagocytosis can remove them, the bacteria tend to release antigens into the body fluids and this provokes the immune response. The majority of the antigens to which humans are exposed seem to be those of exogenous infective organisms. Natural antibodies support this statement, since they commonly are directed toward microorganisms. It has long been recognized that extracellular-type bacteria are usually defensed by humoral antibodies, while intracellular types require destruction via sensitized T lymphocytes. Fungal organisms are defensed in a manner similar to that of other organisms. Competition between normal flora and other organisms is quite important in preventing fungal disease. The environmental conditions of moisture, warmth, and pH also are helpful.

Most *fungal* diseases are countered by cell-mediated immunity and they often render the individual anergic. *Candida albicans* (a yeast) is commonly found in T lymphocyte–deficient persons. Candida infection in such individuals is difficult to prevent and control and is a prime example of the ability of a fungus to induce immune suppression.

Chronic *parasitic disease* likewise induces immune injury. Many worm infestations are characterized by eosinophilia and IgE antibody formation and an atopic response. Diarrhea in *Ascaris* infestation has an allergic basis.

Immune pathology may occur secondary to infections. The release of a soluble bacterial antigen into the blood in which a specific circulating antibody already exists may produce an immune complex disease. Gram-negative bacteria produce endotoxins which may activate the "alternate" complement pathway which may be one cause of septic shock. Disseminated intravascular coagulation (DIC) may also be caused in some cases by these immune complex lesions. Chronic bacterial infections may also cause a localized immune complex disease.

Iatrogenic Conditions

Iatrogenic drug-induced hyperimmunologic injury is commonly seen in the clinical area. Stopping the drug will usually stop the symptoms. Most drugs function as haptens, which combine with body proteins on the surface of cells. Genetic factors and combining affinity help determine the outcome of drug-induced injury. What is apparent, however, is that an immune response to a drug does not necessarily determine that an allergic reaction will occur.

Many factors homeostatically controlling the balance between defense and immune disease are still unidentified. Many blood dyscrasias are iatrogenically induced and many present themselves as type II cytotoxic, type III complex, or type IV delayed hypersensitivity reactions.

Autoimmune Disease

Inappropriate immune responses often, but not always, result in injury. *Autoimmunity* (auto-self) may fit best into this category, for the immune response is misdirected toward self-antigens. It is felt that autoallergic mechanisms could underlie most chronic disease processes from rheumatoid arthritis to pernicious anemia. Autoantibodies usually arise in response to intracellular antigens which are not normally exposed to the RE system, such as inner layers of cell membranes, nuclear membranes, nucleoprotein, nucleic acids, and cytoplasmic structures such as mitochondria, or they arise in response to haptens, viruses, and so forth. Autoimmune diseases present an odd combination of decreased suppressor T cells and complement with an excess of autoantibody. Most autoimmune lesions are infiltrated with lymphocytes, plasma cells, and macrophages. This describes type IV reactions, but because of the excess immunoglobulin and their known involvement in certain cytotoxic and immune complex diseases, the autoimmune diseases are considered humoral reactions. Experimental studies with the New Zealand Black mice (NZB) seem to indicate that a defect in suppressor T cells exists and that a viral etiology is more than speculation. New Zealand Black mice spontaneously develop antoimmune disease and are an important animal model for study of these conditions. Neither suppressor T-cell deficiency nor viral etiology has been confirmed in human autoimmunity.

Two basic types of autoimmune disease are seen clinically: those which involve a single organ (as in Hashimoto's thyroiditis) or those which involve multiple organs (as in SLE). Controlled cooperation between T cells, B cells and macrophages must occur to give an appropriate immune response. The summation of suppressor and helper T-cell activity results in appropriate types and quantities of antibodies produced by the B-cell progeny. If suppressor T lymphocytes are lacking, then helper T cells would dominate B-cell differentiation and function and could give an overproduction of autoantibodies. This imbalance is characterized by an excessive activity on the part of B-cell progeny and a deficiency of suppressor T-cell activity.

A genetic basis for autoimmunity is of increased interest since a relationship between certain HLA types and the propensity to develop autoimmune disease has been shown. Whether these controlled genes are actually HLA or the nearby Ir region is yet to be determined. It appears, then, that genetics, probably the Ir genes, lymphocyte surface antigens, and viral receptors could all be involved separately or in concert to develop autoimmune reactions.

Theoretically the loss of homeostatic equilibrium between suppressor and helper T cells exists where

B-cell activity is allowed to dominate or is enhanced and suppressor T-cell activity is decreased, resulting in an autoimmune disease. This imbalance may occur as a consequence of Ir genes, in which viral and environmental mechanisms are acting together or independently. The influence of thymic hormones may be important since in animal models they seem to be diminished in autoimmunity, and when therapeutically administered to the affected animal, they improve its condition.

HYPOIMMUNE RESPONSE PATHOLOGY

Functional deficiency of the immune response can be either congenital or acquired. Congenital immune deficiencies are those conditions which are associated with a genetic malfunction or defect. Acquired immunodeficiency is due to an environmental rather than a genetic defect. Deficiencies are generally named according to the component which is decreased; thus stem-cell, T-lymphocyte, B-lymphocyte, immunoglobulin, and complement component deficiencies have been designated. More recently, functional deficiencies have been described, such as functional deficiency of antigen processing (afferent limb defect), lack of lymphocyte communication (central limb defect), and effector cell deficiency (efferent limb defect). Most hypoimmune states are still designated at T-cell, B-cell, or stem-cell deficiencies, but in the clinical situation a functional defect is usually observed and treated accordingly.

Congenital Hypoimmune Conditions

These conditions, since they are congenital, appear early in life. Correct diagnosis is imperative. Improper treatment can be fatal, while proper treatment may sometimes correct the defect. While bone marrow transplants and live vaccines may save a life, they may also initiate graft-versus-host disease (GVH) or lead to a serious or lethal infectious disease in the child.

T-Cell Defects

When primary lymphoid organs fail to develop, defects in T cells, B cells, or both may occur. In thymic aplasia (Di George's syndrome) the thymus fails to develop, along with other third and fourth pharyngeal pouch derivatives. Immunologically the individual expresses a slight decrease in lymphocytes, but T lymphocytes are selectively absent, with the majority of the lymphocytes being of the B type. Clinically

these individuals have recurrent infections of the intracellular type since they have lost their cellular immune mechanisms and have a crippled humoral response due to absence of helper T cells. Individuals who have been successfully diagnosed may sometimes be restored to normal by fetal thymic transplants.

B-Cell Defects

Conversely, X-linked immunoglobulin deficiency due to a defective gene results in the loss of the B-lymphocyte population or a loss of the ability to produce immunoglobulin. Cellular immunity is preserved and recurrent infections due to *Streptococcus,* Staphylococcus, pneumococcus, and *Hemophilus* occur in 9- to 24-month-old children.

Combined Defects

Combined immunodeficiency has been described as stem-cell defects. These children may vary from having few if any type of blood cells and no lymphoid tissue, to having a simple depression of T- and B-cell function. Individuals suffering from combined deficiencies are deprived of both humoral and cell-mediated immunity. Their life expectancy is very short. Passive immunity from the mother may prolong life to the fourth or sixth month, but they may develop graft-versus-host disease as a result of placental transfer of maternal lymphocytes during gestation or via the mother's milk during breast feeding. A normal child may react to these foreign maternal lymphocytes and destroy them; however, in immune deficient infants the foreign lymphocytes are competent, recognize the host as foreign, proliferate, and thus attack and attempt to destroy the infant, i.e., graft-versus-host disease. Symptoms of GVH are a skin rash and exfoliation, slow growth rate, hypothermia, increased production of bile, inflammation of the liver, diarrhea, enteritis, and finally runting and death.

The above examples are the three major types of primary immunodeficiency disease: those of cellular immune defects, humoral defects, and stem-cell or combined deficiency. There are several well-defined congenital immunodeficiencies in each category, and the list is progressively lengthened as new knowledge of immune responses and immune assessment occur.

Acquired Hypoimmune Conditions

Acquired hypoimmune conditions occur when a person who once had a normal immune function progressively or suddenly loses the ability to recognize and respond to foreignness. Acquired immune deficiency is associated with aging, stress, and iatrogenic therapy, and is also observed secondary to certain disease states. Many therapeutic iatrogenic agents such as x-ray, drugs, surgery, and antisera are likely to produce a hypoimmune state. Cancer and infections also reduce the person's immunologic responsiveness. This anergy is sometimes transient and sometimes persistent.

Aging and the Hypoimmune State

The age of a person affects the ability to respond immunologically. The very young and the old are in an immunodepressed condition and thus are more susceptible to injurious agents. The immunocompetence of young children is not fully developed. In the elderly the gradual loss of immune memory, unprimed T and B cells, immune reserve, and perhaps the influence of primary lymphoid organs depresses immune capability and renders them more susceptible to health problems. A readily observable increase in infections, autoimmunity, and malignancy occurs with age. The very young, however, are immunologically immature and receive their initial resistance from passive immunity via placental transfer of maternal IgG and the mother's milk which is rich in IgA, competent lymphocytes, and macrophages.

Malnutrition

Malnutrition is also an important cause of hypoimmune states, particularly where protein deficiency exists. T-lymphocyte deficiencies and their responses are the primary defect in malnutrition. Immunoglobulin levels appear high. Thymus and lymph node atrophy and lymphopenia and diminished CMI reactions all are present in the malnourished. Complement components are also absent with subsequently reduced opsonic activity. Thus the malnourished person is more susceptible to fungal, viral, and intracellular bacterial infections. Hyperalimentation, however, may itself produce a transient period of anergy and may be a complicating problem for the already immune deficient person.

Irradiation

Lymphocytes are radiosensitive, and thus x-ray may destroy T and B lymphocytes. Recirculating T cells seem more sensitive than B cells, while macrophages, plasma cells, and B memory cells are somewhat radio-resistant. Radiation therapy for cancer may reduce peripheral blood T lymphocytes for periods of up to 1 year. This, of course, varies with dose, type, and area of irradiation. Patients in this situation should be made aware of their decreased resistance because they are susceptible to sudden devastating infections; mild infections of any sort should be treated early in their course.

Drugs

Cytotoxic drugs may suppress the immune response of an individual; indeed, they are often given to accomplish that end. Immunosuppression and/or chemotherapy affect immune competence of individuals, but it is often difficult to determine just how it affects a person who already has existing reduction in immune responsiveness. Lymphopenia usually becomes greater in the presence of chemotherapy. If a person is already deficient in T lymphocytes prior to chemotherapy, little effect is seen in either T or B cells. However, with prolonged chemotherapy (4 to 6 months), T lymphocyte levels begin to drop and B cells tend to increase. Some persons receiving chemotherapy have significant changes in T- and B-cell counts or T/B cell ratios. After chemotherapeutically induced T-cell deficiency occurs, it takes approximately 3 months to return to normal T-cell levels and functioning. Chemotherapy seems to have little effect, if any, on humoral immune functions.

In transplantation, immunosuppression is specifically aimed at producing anergy so that a foreign graft may be accepted and tolerated. Therapies which suppress T-cell function without affecting the B-cell function would be ideal since graft rejection is primarily the responsibility of T cells and macrophage therapies aimed only at cell-mediated components of the efferent limb of the immune response. That kind of controlled specificity in chemotherapy does not currently exist. Heterologous antilymphocyte serum (ALS) selectively removes lymphocytes and suppresses immune function. Serum can be produced and has been used in clinical transplant recipients, but its efficiency and safety have not been confirmed. Lack of understanding of precisely how it works does not permit indiscriminate use as a therapeutic agent to prolong grafts.

Stress and Immunity

Important relationships of corticosteroids, personality, and stress to the immune responses has recently been emphasized. All three of these have a definite effect on host defenses. They have in common a high level of plasma adrenal hormones which reduce the inflammatory response, cause a lymphopenia by depleting B lymphocytes, and cause T lymphocytes to sequester in the bone morrow. Neutrophils and monocytes are altered in their circulating patterns and chemotaxic responses are decreased. These events have occurred in animals that are handled in a rough manner, given ether, or have undergone surgery. In human bereavement, tuberculosis, myocardial infarction, leukemia, and diabetes and in individuals with high social readjustment rating scores there are increased levels of endogenously produced steroids. The stress of cold may cause an increase in plasma corticosteroids at 3 times the normal level (Chap. 27).

Stress, with its release of endogenous steroids, is apparently an important factor in the development of infections. This not only applies to healthy individuals but is particularly important for those persons in a clinical setting in which stress levels are usually high. The compromised host as a result of disease, therapies, and age has long been a concern of health professionals. Nurses have recently become aware that stress modulation may be a way of promoting host defenses and preventing infection. The nurse, therefore, has the obligation of promoting factors and initiating interventions to reduce stress in order to enhance human resistance to infectious agents.

NURSING AND DEFENSE MECHANISMS

If the human body can largely protect itself from external and internal threats, what then is the use of health care intervention? To answer this question, the limits of human adaptation must be considered. Clinical experience supports the observation that self-regulation and self-repair has definite limitations. An individual cannot be expected to adapt to self-regulation when the capacity to respond has not developed or was lost or dissipated after initially having such a capability. The overwhelming response of hyperimmune responses has to be countered to achieve a level of wellness consistent with individual independence. Conversely, in hypoimmune situations, enhancement of the body's immune response is necessary and/or the individual must be protected from real and potential injurious agents during this incompetent period. In the face of these interventions it is most important to allow self-mechanisms to function at their highest capability. Time alone may provide this chance of self-regulation, and we must be careful to choose proper timing and sequencing of interventions to maximize the self-defense mechanisms. To vaccinate a child before the child is able to respond immunologically will not achieve immunity and may cause harm. To prevent inflammation may prevent repair and increase scarring. It seems then that interventions by health care professionals which support defense mechanisms in a timed sequence is often important, for the wrong timing may prohibit self-regulation restoration. Sometimes therapeutic agents replace rather than support the physiological self-protective process. The human body has ample reserve for adapting and restoring health. Human capacity for modification of structure and function is quite liberal and far exceeds our expectations at times.

Only a portion of the liver cells function at a given time and the other cells are in a resting reserve. The same can be said of the kidney when it is filtering, or of the cells of the immune system when challenged by antigens. However, if the kidney or liver cells are injured, this tends to reduce the resting reserve as well as the resting time for single healthy cells. If this process of cellular injury is allowed to continue, gradually all reserve is lost and a state of continuous fatigue may result in cells which are unable to divide. With kinetically mitotic cells such as epithelium and lymphocytes, replacement of reserve is probable, but the ability to restore lost cells seems to dissipate with age and experience as well as increase the chances of creating inappropriate responses. Thus we often see increasing cases of neoplasia, autoimmune diseases, and susceptibility to common organisms in elderly or unhealthy individuals.

A new and different homeostatic level is achieved in an ill person as compared to the healthy state. A particular mode of treatment used in the ill state produces more potent and varied results than in the well state. Elevated temperatures may be lowered by application of cold and/or aspirin, but these have no overt effect on a normal temperature. Vitamins will correct a vitamin deficiency but generally have no overt effect on the normal individual.

The cells of the human body exist in a mutual interdependence despite generous provisions of reserve. The integrity of the organism as a whole rests on the integrity of its individual elements, and the elements in turn are useless except as parts of an organized whole.

The nurse must find ways to support and maintain defense mechanisms. Ways to preserve the immune reserve and reduce injury and stress to all lines of defense are helpful to the individual.

Presently the critical-care nurse is involved in maintaining defense systems which have been altered by a critical primary problem. The reason for an individual's presence in the critical-care area is usually trauma, infarction, respiratory distress, neurological injury or disease, poisoning, or shock. These tend to secondarily alter the normal defense mechanisms. The overt expression of an altered defense will be hypersensitivity or a more susceptible situation for the critically ill. Since each situation is unique, it is impossible to include particular means of maintaining defense in all critical-care situations. However, general ways to support human defense mechanisms are appropriate.

In conclusion, the critical-care nurse is responsible for initiating interventions which will accomplish the following:

1. Maintain the physical environment of the critically ill (such as proper temperature, humidity, lighting, bed linens, soaps, and cleanliness) and eliminate fumes, dust, and smells.

2. Show and convey understanding of the individual's condition and concerns through communication with the person and the family.

3. Convey confidence and hope as appropriate realistically to the patient since the nurse has knowledge and prior experience with similar conditions in other individuals. A well-informed nurse can understand and explain to the patient in ways which will reduce fear about the unknown. The nurse can be a means of encouragement for the person who is looking for counsel, and the nurse can help the individual to gain cognitive control over the situation.

4. Enhance defense mechanisms by modulating and reducing stress. This may be done through communication and management of the emotional environment. Fear and its internal preparations for struggle which occur with injury may be the reason for disturbance in vitally important functions.

5. Assess and maintain an adequate comfort level for the critically ill person in order to reduce anxiety, stress, scratching, pain, and contamination and/or removal of tubes.

6. Maintain healthy epithelial surfaces through proper skin care, proper fluid intake and output, and promotion of activity necessary to prevent insult to or impingement on the body's first line of defense.

7. Provide a balanced diet and proper protein to prevent further depression of the immune state, and ensure enough energy to support immune mechanisms such as antibody production, cellular proliferation, and phagocytosis.

8. Time and sequence interventions in a manner that will support a self-regulating defense system. Most infections occur as a result of variation in the defenses of the host, and support here will assist in determining the time and sequence of interventions which will aid in self-regulation of defenses. The laboratory profile will assist in detecitng changes in cells and serum components which would suggest altered immune function.

Planning a therapeutic and a pharmacological regimen in a timed and sequential manner is consistent with allowing self-regulations of the defense mechanisms. Observation is necessary to identify occurrence of adverse reactions to medications and therapies as they are instituted and applied. The logic, then, for health care professionals' interventions in maintaining defense mechanisms in the critically ill is to secure a homeostatic control of defense mechanisms secondarily altered by a critical illness or injury in an individual with limited adaptation for self-regulation and self-repair.

REFERENCES

Allen, J. C. (ed.): *Infection and the Compromised Host,* Baltimore: Williams & Wilkins, 1976.

Austen, K. F.: The chemical mediators of immediate hypersensitivity reactions, in M. Samter (ed.), *Immunological Disease,* 3d ed., Boston: Little, Brown, 1978.

Bach, F. H., and J. J. VanRood: The major histocompatibility complex, *N Eng J Med* 295: 806–813, 872–878, and 927–936, 1976.

Bach, J. F.: *The Mode of Action of Immunosuppressive Agents,* Amsterdam: North-Holland, 1975.

Barker, H. R. C.: *Immunobiology for the Clinician,* New York: Wiley, 1977.

Barrett, J. T.: *Basic Immunology and Its Medical Application,* St. Louis: Mosby, 1976.

Beckley, Harmon Co.: *Practical Concepts in Human Disease,* Baltimore: Williams & Wilkins, 1974.

Benacerraf, B., and **D. H. Katz**: The nature and function of histocompatibility-linked immune response genes, in B. Benacerraf (ed.), *Immunogenetics and Immunodeficiency,* London: London Medical and Technical Publishing Co., 1975.

Bierman, C. W.: New drugs for asthma: A scientific basis for therapy, *Chest 72:689–691, 1977.*

Biglow, N.J.: *Immunologic Fundamentals,* Chicago: Yearbook, 1975.

Blake, P. J., and **R. C. Percy**: *Applied Immunological Concepts,* New York: Appleton-Century-Crofts, 1978.

Cannon, W. B.: *The Wisdom of the Body,* 2d ed., New York: Norton, 1939.

Castro, J. E. (ed.): *Immunology for Surgeons,* Baltimore University Park Press, 1976.

Cohen, J.: "Immunologic effects of Corticosteroids, Personality and Stress". Paper presented at Fifteenth National Meeting of The Reticuloendothelial Society, Charleston, S.C., 1978.

Colton, H. R.: Biosynthesis of complement, *Adv Immuno 22:67–118, 1976.*

Coombs, R. A., and **P. G. H. Gell**: Classification of allergic reactions responsible for clinical hypersensitivity and diseases, in P. G. H. Gell, R. R. A. Coombs, and P. J. Lackman (eds.), *Clinical Aspects of Immunology,* 3d ed., Oxford: Blackwell, 1975, pp. 761–781.

Cooper, M., and **A. Lawton**: The development of the immune system, *Scientific American* November 1974, pp. 59–72.

Cunningham, A. J.: *Understanding Immunology,* New York: Academic, 1978.

Cunningham-Rundels, U. F.: The reticuloendothelial system, in F. H. Bach and R. A. Good (eds.), *Clinical Immunobiology,* vol 2, New York: Academic, 1976, pp. 289–303.

Freedman, S. O., and **P. Gold** (eds.): *Clinical Immunology,* 2d ed., Hagerstown, Md.: Harper & Row, 1976.

Fu, S. M., H. G. Kunkel, H. P. Brissman, F. H. Allen, and **M. Fatino**: Evidence for linkage between HLA histocompability genes and those involved in the synthesis of the second component of complement, *J. Exp. Med.* 140:1108, 1974.

Gell, P. G. H., R. R. A. Coombs, and **P. J. Lachmann**: *Clinical Aspects of Immunology,* 3d ed., Oxford: Blackwell, 1975.

Halbarow, E. J., and **W. G. Reeves**: *Immunology in Medicine,* New York: Grune & Stratton, 1977.

Hobart, M. J., and **I. McConnell** (eds.): *The Immune System: A Course on the Molecular and Cellular Basis of Immunity,* Oxford: Blackwell, 1975.

Ishizaka, I.: Structure and biologic activity of immunoglobulin E, *Hosp Pract* 12(1):57–67, 1977.

————: Experimental anaphylaxis and reaginic hypersensitivity, in M. Samter (ed.), *Immunological Diseases,* 3d ed., Boston: Little, Brown, 1978.

Katz, D. H., and **B. Benacerraf**: The regulatory influence of activated T cells on B cell responses to antigen, *Adv Immunol* 15:1, 1972.

————: and ————: Hypothesis, the function and interrelationship of T cell receptors, in gene and other histocompatibility gene products, *Transplant Rev* 22:175, 1975.

Katz, D. M.: *Lymphocyte Differentiation, Recognition and Regulation,* New York: Academic, 1977.

————: T-lymphocyte receptors and cell interactions in the immune system, in B. Brinkley and K. Porter (eds.), *International Cell Biology, 1976–77,* New York: Rockefeller University Press, 1977, pp. 112–118.

LaVia, M. F., and R. B. Hill, Jr. (eds.): *Principles of Pathobiology, 2d ed.,* New York: Oxford University Press, 1975.

Lichtenstein, L. M.: An evaluation of the role of immunotherapy in asthma, *Am Rev Resp Dis* 117:191–197, 1978.

Middleton, E., C. E. Reed, and E. F. Ellis: *Allergy: Principles and Practice,* St. Louis: Mosby, 1978.

Mieschner, P. A., and H. J. Muller-Eberhard (eds.): *A Textbook of Immunopathology,* vol 1, 2d ed., New York: Grune & Stratton, 1976.

Muller-Eberhard, H. J.: Chemistry and function of the complement system, *Hosp Pract* 120: 33–43, 1977.

Munster, A. M. (ed.): *Surgical Immunology,* New York: Grune & Stratton, 1976.

Nelson, D. S. (ed.): *Immunobiology of the Macrophage,* New York: Academic, 1976.

Nisonoff, A., J. E. Hopper, and S. B. Spring: *The Antibody Molecule,* New York: Academic, 1975.

Perlmann, P.: Cellular immunity: Antibody-dependent cytotoxicity (K-cell activity), *Clin Immunobiol* 3:107–132, 1976.

Rocklin, R. E.: Products of activated lymphocytes, *Clin Immunobiol* 3:195–220, 1976.

Roesel, C. E.: *Immunology: A Self Instructional Approach,* New York: McGraw-Hill, 1978.

Roitt, I.: *Essential Immunology,* 3d ed., Oxford: Blackwell, 1977.

Schreiber, A. D.: Clinical immunology of cortocosteroids, *Prog Clin Immuno* 3:103–114, 1977.

Scoggin, C. H., S. A. Sahn, and T. L. Petty: Status asthmaticus, a nine-year experience, *JAMA* 238:1158–1162, 1977.

Scribner, D. J., and D. Fabrney: Neutrophil receptors for IgG and complement: Their roles in the attachment and ingestion phases of phagocytosis, *J Immunol* 116:892–897, 1976.

Sell, S.: *Immunology Immunopathology and Immunity,* 2d ed., Hagerstown, Md.: Harper & Row, 1975.

Talal, N.: Antibodies to nucleic acids, *Clin Immunobiol* 3:375–385, 1976.

Thaler, M. S., R. D. Klausner, and H. J. Cohen: *Medical Immunology,* Philadelphia: Lippincott, 1977.

VanRood, J. J., A. Van Leeuwen, A. Termijtelen, and J. J. Keuning: The genetics of the major histocompatibility complex in man, HLA, in D. H. Katz and B. Benacerraf (eds.), *The Role of Products of the Histocompatibility Gene Complex in Immune Responses,* New York: Academic, 1976.

Vitetta, E. S., and J. W. Uhr: Immunoglobulin-receptors revisited, *Science* 189:964, 1975.

Waldemann, T. A., and S. Broder: Suppressor cells in the regulation of the immune response, *Prog Clin Immunol* 3:155–199, 1977.

———, M. Durn, M. Blackman, and B. Meade: Suppressor T cells in immunodeficiency, in G. E. Siskind, C. L. Christian, and S. E. Litwin (eds.), *Immune Depression and Cancer,* New York: Grune & Stratton, 1975.

Weigle, W. O.: Immunologic tolerance and immunopathology, *Hosp Pract* 12(6):71–80, 1977.

Yunis, E. J., G. Fernandes, and L. J. Greenberg: Immune deficiency, autoimmunity and aging, *Birth Defects* Orig. Artic. Ser. XI, pp. 185–192, 1975.

The interpersonal relationship between the health team, patient, and family is a significant component of critical care. Failure to accurately assess the dynamics of one component can lead to problems within the others. In critical care, the patient becomes the primary focus of attention by members of the critical-care team. It is the patient, not the family, who enters critical care in acute biological crisis which requires immediate and sometimes continuous intervention. During this time, the family may need to be temporarily removed from the critical-care environment so that the health team is not distracted from effectively intervening. While the patient begins a restorative vigil in critical care, the family members begin a similar vigil within a boundary labeled "Family Room."

Depending upon the severity of the biological crisis, the patient's family may choose to remain in their new territory. Such families only venture out of their territory to receive medical bulletins, eat, or make phone calls to other family members. Therefore the family room may become as active as the critical-care unit. Initially, the family remains on vigil for fear their absence would be viewed as neglect or as a noncaring attitude. The critical-care nurse realizes that he or she is providing care for more than the patient. "However," according to Craven (1972), "if the nurse expands her concept of the patient from that of an individual in a bed to that of a participating member of a family, then she will expand her role to assist relatives to cope with the patient's illness while simultaneously maintaining the family function." Therefore, there are times when the nurse becomes the interpersonal link between the patient and the patient's family. The interpersonal relationship established between the nurse-patient-family triad permits the meeting of basic needs of support and attention.

Through the establishment of a close interpersonal relationship, the critical-care nurse assesses how each is coping with the crisis situation. If the family is not informed regarding the patient's biological status, including any changes, they may overreact to the illness situation. Likewise a patient with a reduced internal coping mechanism may also have a tendency to overreact to biological crisis. The critical-care nurse acts as an intervening variable to resolve the overreactive conflict. The nurse, together with other members of the health team, can only accomplish this goal when they have established a meaningful interpersonal relationship, that is, one based on mutual trust and respect for the other's sense of dignity. Therefore, interpersonal relationships involve the nurse working with both the patient and the family.

22
DYNAMICS OF INTERPERSONAL RELATIONSHIPS
Sharon L. Roberts

ASPECTS OF INTERPERSONAL RELATIONSHIPS AND FAMILY FUNCTIONS
Interrole Relationships
Interpersonal Relationships
The Family—an Elusive Entity

INTERPERSONAL FRAMEWORK
Interpersonal Competence
Interpersonal Needs

NURSING IMPLICATIONS
Foster Patient-Family Support
Facilitate Patient-Family Education
Foster Patient-Family Acceptance

REFERENCES

ASPECTS OF INTERPERSONAL RELATIONSHIPS AND FAMILY FUNCTIONS

Relationships involving people can be divided into two categories: interrole relationships and interpersonal relationships.

Interrole Relationships

In interrole relationships two people enact certain roles such as nurse and patient, mother and father, or child and parent. The list is endless and even includes professional roles. The participants can interact with each other and not really become acquainted on a knowing or feeling level. This has significance for the nurse-patient-family triad. One might expect that the longevity of a relationship means intimate knowledge and sensitivity among the participants. Therefore, the patient and the family, because of their long association with each other, would have a well-established interrole relationship set. The nurse may actually assess the opposite, that both participants have little meaningful knowledge of the other in terms of needs or internal coping ability. Likewise the participants in a role relationship such as nurse and patient may *relate to* each other without *interrelating with* each other. In health care interrole relationships, the critical-care patient and nurse are concerned that each person does his or her part in the relationship. This implies an impersonal attitude in which neither participant may care about the other's subjective side. Such an attitude can only deter meaningful input and exchange between the participants. The critical-care nurse actively seeks to avoid impersonal interrole relationships and instead attempts to establish meaningful interpersonal relationships with both the patient and the family.

Interpersonal Relationships

The second category consists of interpersonal relationships. In contrast to interrole relationships, interpersonal relationships are characterized by a genuine concern and interest with all aspects of the other individual, including the subjective side. To be interested in the patient implies that the critical-care nurse also needs an interest in the family, their previous health problems, their psychological well-being, their social roles, and their intrinsic motivation for recovery. Jourard (1963) has identified seven characteristics of interpersonal relationships which can be adapted to critical-care relationships. Success at each level is dependent upon the participants themselves, the nature and severity of the biological crisis, and the critial-care environment. The seven characteristics consist of the following:

1. The participants know each other as distinct individuals.
2. The participants like more traits in one another than they dislike.
3. Each participant feels concern for the happiness and growth of the other.
4. Each participant seeks to behave in ways which will promote happiness and growth in the other.
5. Each participant can communicate effectively with the other and make himself or herself known and understood.
6. Each participant imposes reasonable demands on the other.
7. Each participant values and respects the autonomy and individuality of the other.

The seven characteristics of interpersonal relationships have significance when the nurse assesses basic needs of the critical-care patient and the patient's family. The critical-care patient is an active participant in the nurse-patient relationship. The family also plays a vital role in the relationship as well as having some unique functions.

The Family—an Elusive Entity

The family functions as an interacting and transacting organization. It is described thusly by Ackerman (1958):

> The family is a designation for an institution as old as the human species itself. The family is a paradoxical and elusive entity. It assumes many guises. It is the same everywhere; yet it is not the same anywhere. Throughout time, it has remained the same; yet it has never remained the same. On the contemporary scene, the family is changing its pattern at a remarkably rapid rate; it is accommodating in a striking way to the social crisis which is the mark of our period in history. There is nothing fixed or immutable about family, except that it is always with us.

A family functions in the capacity of supporting and protecting its members, both individually and collectively. Illness, disease, or injury to one member of the family places other members in a state of readiness. The family system concentrates its energy on supporting each other and the critically ill family member. This relationship implies a complementary coexistence with the critical-care environment and the people therein. The family system is a system of relationships functioning as a unified whole. Such a family is patterned and organized. The pattern and organization may vary depending upon changes in the biological status of their critically ill family member. The critical-care nurse realizes that the potential for fluctuations in the pattern and organization of behavior may change just as frequently as the critical-care patient's condition. Therefore, the critical-care nurse must adapt interactions accordingly in order to maintain a continuous interpersonal relationship.

Families may be described in terms of their functions as a small group or an open system. Many family functions involve interrole relationships. According to Hill (1949), "Family sociologists have come to view the family as a small group, intricately organized internally into paired positions of husband-father, wife-mother, son-brother, and daughter-sister. Norms prescribing the appropriate role behavior for each of these positions specify how reciprocal relations are to be maintained as well as how role behaviors may change with changing ages of the occupants of these positions." When the family functions as an open system, it is capable of intake and output from the environment, which may be the family room or critical-care unit. Furthermore, like the patient, the family maintains control through self-regulation. There are times when the family is unable to function in a steady state. Acute illness or injury to a family member causes stress, and the stress creates an imbalance. The critical-care nurse, having established a meaningful interpersonal relationship with the family, assesses their imbalance and attempts to facilitate return to a more stable level.

> The critical-care nurse then assesses any interrole relationships which may be developed on a personal level, whether or not the characteristics of interpersonal relationships are in operation, and how the family as a whole is performing its functions.

INTERPERSONAL FRAMEWORK

A biological illness, disease, or injury creates a crisis situation which causes the individual to become insecure with himself or herself and the immediate environment. Feelings of insecurity may block normal patterns of interpersonal action, necessitating alternative ways of relating to others and self. According to Parad (1965), crisis is a "period of disequilibrium overpowering the individual's homeostatic mechanism. During a crisis, a person is faced by a problem which, on the one hand, is of basic importance to him because it is linked with his fundamental instinctual

needs and, on the other hand, cannot be solved quickly by means of his normal range of problem-solving mechanisms."

The interpersonal framework consists of two components: interpersonal competence and interpersonal needs. Each will be discussed and applied to the critical-care patient and critical-care family.

Interpersonal Competence

Knowledge of interpersonal behavior helps the critical-care health team with their behavioral interventions. Interpersonal behavior is the personality characteristics of the people involved in the relationship. The critical-care patient's behavior may be strongly influenced by the people who provide care and by the family. The hospitalized patient may have to conform behavior to the rules and customs of the critical-care unit in which he or she is hospitalized. Likewise, the critical-care patient may feel compelled to conform to the expectations of others even when they diverge from his or her own expectations. Patients capable of positive and productive interpersonal encounters are able to conform their behavior to the limits prescribed by their sick-role position. To be hospitalized in critical care necessitates that the patient temporarily abandon some roles while adapting to new roles. Interpersonal competence implies that the patient can assume a variety of roles in transactions with others. In addition, the patient is able to abandon formal roles and be spontaneous in personal relations.

Interpersonal competence also applies to the critical-care health team. Like the patient, the team also performs a variety of roles; some are formal, whereas others may be more spontaneous. Interpersonal competence is a characteristic of healthy interpersonal behavior. Jourard (1963) has identified two aspects of interpersonal competence, namely, role versatility and role adequacy.

Role versatility means that the critical-care patient is able to fulfill a variety of roles. The nurse realizes that an individual will carry out several roles in interpersonal relations with others. Prior to hospitalization in critical care, the patient played the role of husband, son, brother, employee, boss, wife, mother, daughter, and so on. While acute illness, disease, or injury does not necessitate total abandonment of the above social roles, the patient in critical care may need to suppress behavior which is not relevant or compatible to the current sick role. For example, the aggressive business executive who sustains an acute myocardial infarction may need to seek ways in which to lessen the stressors associated with that profession. It may be difficult for such individuals to suppress their controlling behavior. Therefore, the nurse may assess that the above patient or similar ones have difficulty relinquishing control over people and events in the immediate environment. In other words, the patient maintains the previous work behavior.

Normally, individuals choose roles other than those which are ascribed by birth or society. The individual may seek out a particular role such as spouse, leader, or even enthusiastic follower because these roles require participation in interpersonal behavior, which leads to satisfaction and self-esteem. Illness, injury, or disease forces the individual to be versatile in roles not chosen. The sick role may be a new experience for this patient and family. Both may have difficulty adapting to dependency, threat of future biological illness, and possible death. An assessment of the patient and the family's interpersonal behavior helps the critical-care nurse diagnose potential behavioral problems which might impede progress. The critical-care nurse realizes that illness, injury, or disease have an effect on family configuration.

According to Hill (1949), illness, injury, or disease do not result in "dismemberment in the sense of a change in the plurality pattern of the family, but do bring marked changes in the family configuration. Those family situations where roles are involuntarily vacated through illness are examples. Families experience significant strains when members become ill. A critical illness requires a reallocation of a patient's role to others in the family." As family members realize the void created by temporary loss of the sick member, their ability to cope with the stress decreases. The family and sick member may no longer be able to maintain the steady state. While initially caught up in the impact of illness and socialization processes, each subsystem attempts to continue in its respective role. The healthy spouse continues to make both household and business decisions. The other spouse, if hospitalized, gives instruction regarding the household responsibilities, location of various items, schedule of children's activities, and general care of the children. Neither subsystem wants to admit illness and relinquish his or her role. However, as the stresses increase, the steady state of patient and family becomes imbalanced. Consequently, the healthy family member assumes the sick member's role.

Role adequacy means that the individual is able to fulfill a role in socially acceptable ways. Role adequacy implies that the role assumed by the critical-care patient be an effective one. An effective sick role behavior is initial compliance to various diagnostic and treatment procedures. However, the threat of illness and the alteration of a valued body part can force the critical-care patient to be ineffective in the role of patient and in patient interpersonal behavior.

Previous experience with acute illness requiring hospitalization in critical care may sometimes lead to irrational anxiety and the inability to interrelate with those providing acute care. Regardless of prior experiences, the patient's anticipatory anxiety limits the ability to comprehend events beyond the threat of severe complications, loss of body part, loss of financial security, and threat of life. These are very real threats, and unlike the specificity involved in fears, the above concerns maintain a more diffuse quality. The critical-care patient is not sure if, when, or how complications, loss, or financial changes will occur. Nevertheless, the patient establishes an expectancy of failure. Therefore, if a biological change should occur, the self-fulfilling prophecy occurs. In other words, the critical-care patient expects a threat, and no matter how biologically insignificant the threat is to the total picture, the patient perceives major failure and behaves accordingly. This behavior reflects greater anxiety which reinforces the cyclic events associated with the self-fulfilling prophecy. Critical-care patients also become involved in a cyclic self-fulfilling prophecy in their interpersonal relations with others.

Critical-care patients vary in their interpersonal behavior towards members of the critical-care team. Many patients, because of their prior interpersonal competence in establishing effective relationships, behave in a meaningful way with the critical-care team. The patient's role behavior is both adequate and effective. In this respect, the critical-care patient and the nurse can work together to ensure positive progress. Role adequacy and effectiveness is an example of the self-fulfilling prophecy in a positive direction. The patient behaves effectively toward and with the critical-care nurse so that together they establish the expectancy of interpersonal success. On the other hand, there are critical-care patients who respond in a less adequate and effective manner.

As previously mentioned, a critical-care patient may attempt to behaviorally control the nurse. Controlling or manipulating the behavior of others is perceived by the patient to be an effective approach. However, the nurse perceives the same behavior as inappropriate. The nurse realizes that the patient whose interpersonal behavior is manipulative is actively suppressing the real self, leading to further alienation and internalization of fears. Therefore, the critical-care patient is unable to share concerns and fears because of the feeling that sharing necessitates loss of control. The nurse realizes the meaning of manipulative behavior and remains a positive force in the patient's environment. The nurse accomplishes this by establishing limits when the patient is unable to do so and by communicating his or her own accepting behavior.

Interpersonal Needs

Interpersonal needs as they apply to the interpersonal framework involve two components: critical-care nurse-patient and critical-care nurse-family. Critical-care nurse-patient interpersonal needs consist of two phases: the initial encounter phase and the working phase.

During the *initial encounter phase,* the critical-care nurse and patient each obtain knowledge of the other. The "other" concept refers to assessment of someone else's behavior or personality. The nurse-patient component begins the interpersonal relationship by making observations of each other. The initial observations permit each to perceive the other in an organized and meaningful way. The patient classifies the nurse, for example, as supportive, knowledgeable, or abrupt. Likewise, the nurse classifies the patient as manipulative, controlling, gentle, obnoxious, combative, or jovial. Observation, perception, and classification of others establishes a set which influences or determines later encounters. The critical-care nurse learns what the set is for the patient, for example, distance, closeness, formality, spontaneity, or informality. If the patient's interpersonal behavioral set is distance, the critical-care nurse may spend greater time establishing a trustful and meaningful relationship. A trustful relationship provides the foundation so that the patient's set can shift from distance to closeness. Because of the various intrusive diagnostic and treatment procedures, the nurse becomes physically close to the critical-care patient. The critical-care nurse's respect for the patient's sense of dignity at this time facilitates interpersonal closeness. Interpersonal closeness fosters the second phase, namely, the working phase.

The cardiac, pulmonary, or renal patient enters into the working phase with the critical-care nurse. During the working phase, the entire critical-care health team actively seeks to stabilize the patient's biological crisis; perform restorative measures; assist the patient to expand the perception of self in relating to the biological illness, injury, or disease; and actively include the family into all aspects of the patient's care.

This latter aspect of the working phase is the second major component of interpersonal needs. The second aspect is the critical-care nurse-family. In this situation the critical-care nurse assesses events which impinge on the family.

Each family reacts in its own particular way to crisis situations. Hill (1949) believes that

> No crisis-precipitating event is the same for any given family; its impact ranges according to the several hardships that may accompany it. Since no stress or event is uniformly the same for all families, but varies in striking power by the hardships that accompany it, the concept of hardship itself requires some additional attention. Hardships may be defined as those complications in a crisis-precipitating event which demand competencies from the family which the event itself may have temporarily paralyzed or made unavailable.

The sick member represents a subsystem within the whole system called family. As the stress resulting from illness increases, all subsystems within the family become involved. The immediate family may try to keep the crisis contained within its own boundaries. The interpersonal needs involving the critical-care nurse-family component include two aspects: stress of illness and stress of social loss.

Stresses surrounding the family originate from a biological illness, injury, or disease which affects one of its members, necessitating hospitalization in a critical-care unit. The crisis begins for the patient the moment the illness, injury, or disfigurement is understood by the patient. The family experiences a similar state of crisis. The major difference is that the patient or sick member is intimately involved in the crisis; the family, though equally involved, must remain on the periphery. While remaining on the periphery, the family quietly experiences its own special stress, the sources of which have to do with the illness itself and the threats it implies. The threats include the critical-care environment, with all its strange machines, smells, and sounds, and the frustration of being forced to remain outside the unit in a small territory designated for critical-care families.

A family member may learn of the illness, injury, or disfigurement of a husband, wife, mother, or father by telephone. For example, an individual who might have been playing golf, conducting a business conference, or driving a car suddenly becomes ill or injured. The partner at home, receiving the phone call, and being told of the spouse's coronary, quickly makes plans for someone to watch the children and rushes desperately to the hospital. Meanwhile, the hospitalized partner has been transferred from the emergency room into the appropriate critical-care unit. There are times when the family has been instructed to meet a family member in the emergency room only to discover that the individual has been moved. Depending upon the type and severity of the patient's illness, the family member may not be allowed direct admission into the unit, and is instead greeted by the unit clerk or a nurse, who gives a skeletal overview of the patient's status. The family member then retreats into the lonely family room to wait for further progress reports of the patient's condition. If all the admission papers have not been filled out, the family member may be directed to the admission office to expedite this process. Family members may spend their first hour in the hospital locating the sick member, filling out numerous papers, and finally waiting to gain admission into the critical-care unit.

The next source of crisis for the family occurs when the diagnosis is learned. The doctor enters the family's territory and informs them that the patient suffers from an acute myocardial infarction with multifocal premature ectopic beats, acute tubular necrosis necessitating peritoneal dialysis, or some other strange-sounding and frightening ailment. Even if the nurse or doctor translates the problem into a language understood by the family members, they still may not comprehend the significance. To them, the fact that the patient needs critical care is overwhelming enough. In their attempt to maintain a steady state, family members may not be ready to hear these explanations. All they want to do is see the sick member and be reassured that the patient will survive the biological crisis.

Finally, family members are allowed to enter the critical-care unit to see the sick member. It is not unusual for families to react to the critical-care environment, because critical illness may be a new experience for the family and they may not know what to expect. The last time the family members saw their ailing relative was as he or she was leaving the house for work. At that point, the individual appeared healthy and free from injury. Now they see strange-looking supportive devices. They may be so preoccupied with not disturbing the various wires and tubes that they remain at the foot of the bed. If they are brave enough to approach the side of this bed, they remain at arm's

length. In this uncomfortable setting, the family and the patient may make superficial conversation. Each is afraid of frightening the other. Both subsystems are attempting to maintain some type of steady state.

In time, the stability will decrease as the stresses increase. The family members and sick member will then become aware of the effects illness has on them. But until then, the patient is encouraged to rest. Each critical illness has its own effects on the family. The situation may be more crucial when the sick member is severely burned: the family must confront not only various supportive devices but also the sight of the disfigured spouse and similarly disfigured colleagues in the burn unit. Before entering the critical-care unit, the family should be prepared for what it will see and hear.

The stress of illness causes a temporary cessation of all extrafamilial activities. All energies are directed toward the sick member and toward intrafamily restructuring. Even though the family is an open system, it sometimes gives the appearance of a closed system. This is especially true when the family is trying to reorganize and restructure itself.

The critical-care nurse-family interpersonal relationship involves two general types of families. These two types are the *expanding family,* which is a young family with small children, and the *contracting family,* an older family whose nest is emptying or is already empty. Regardless of the type of family, expanding or contracting, the critical-care nurse provides each with supportive understanding. The expanding family may have concern regarding future financial commitment, role changes, or recurring illness which may necessitate expensive hospitalization. Likewise, the contracting family experiences the potential threat of loneliness due to the loss of a vital member. Both families require closeness in their interpersonal behavioral relationship while they are simultaneously experiencing physical distance from the loved one. The critical-care nurse bridges the gap between both spaces of distance-closeness. Because they must wait in a room outside the critical-care unit, family members sometimes experience the previously discussed ineffective behavior of irrational anxiety. If left alone in a room away from the center of care, the family member speculates and fantasizes the worst outcome for the sick member. In other words, without someone to clarify misconceptions, the family develops a distorted image of events surrounding the critically ill person. The family's behavioral response is to ask many members of the critical-care team the same question or to become demanding in their need to participate in the patient's care. At this time the critical-care nurse needs to be consistent in both answers and reassurances. Nurses realize that "the acute anxiety the family experiences often is manifested by the family's short attention span, difficulty with listening, jumping to conclusions, and running from staff member to staff member with the same questions" (Davidson, 1973). The nurse also realizes that expanding and contracting families have made future plans. They each have the expectancy of fulfilling specific goals and dreams. Illness, injury, and diseases necessitating hospitalization in critical care threatens goal attainment. This may have a greater effect on the contracting family who has a limited support system of immediate or extended family members. According to Croog (1968), "in the typically small family, there is high level of emotional intensity and, consequently the illness of a single member produces a higher degree of shock than a larger family system."

Like the critically ill patient, the family also needs meaningful input from the environment. Family members, while giving the appearance of strength, eventually have difficulty independently coping with the stress of illness. There are times when the critically ill patient appears to cope with the stress of illness better than a family member. Since the patient is experiencing the crisis, he or she is adapting to the required changes. Regardless of what appears on the surface, the nurse recognizes that varying degrees of stress may be tolerated by one family member more or less than by another. To the patient, the crisis is only temporary. Furthermore, the patient is able to experience the internal biological changes which indicate progress. The family does not share this personal experiential knowledge, and therefore, until the sick patient is transferred out of critical care and returned home, the family continues to relate to the sick member in a delicate or highly protective manner. The nurse actively seeks to reconcile the difference between the patient and family perceptions of the other.

Regardless of the type, degree, or severity of illness, the family experiences their own unique stress. The stress of illness has its effect upon family configuration. No matter which critical-care unit contains their sick member, families react in similar ways to the threat of serious illness. Because they are under tremendous stress, families do not always hear explanations. If they do hear the diagnosis, or if they see the sick member in the critical-care environment, they do not understand its meaning. It is quite un-

derstandable for family members to run from nurse to nurse asking the same questions and receiving the same answers. Family members may run from nurse to nurse in order to obtain the information they want to hear. Like the sick member, the family initially denies the threats or implications of illness. To them, a biological threat has occurred but the illness can be cured. This may be an attempt on the family's part to relieve their stress. The sick member feels guilty for becoming ill. The family feels guilty for not being more aware of the other's biological well-being. Both subsystems temporarily rationalize the stressor event so that neither one feels totally responsible for the problem.

Regardless of the reason for someone being in a critical-care unit, the famly has tremendous influence over the sick member's immediate and long-term recovery. If the family system has been a strong, supportive one, the members can survive the crisis. The sick member who survives the first hurdle, the biological crisis, looks forward to his next hurdle, long-term recovery. The family plays a major role in helping the sick member make appropriate adjustments. It is understandable that this phase, called *stress of social loss,* may be most difficult. All subsystems have virtually depleted their energy systems. The family has had to assume more than their normal share of responsibilities. For some, the responsibility is assumed by the only surviving member. In other families the role changes will be permanent. Nevertheless, the family of any critically ill patient must restructure or reorganize their ranks and assign new roles to the sick member.

Stress of social loss is the second component of critical-care nurse-family interpersonal need framework. The stress of social loss, or reorganization, affects all families. The larger immediate family has more members to assume additional responsibilities and from which to draw strength. The remaining subsystem must assume all the responsibility. In such cases, dismemberment through illness or injury is immediately felt. Hill (1949) has identified types of stressor events, which include categories such as sudden changes in family status and conflict between members in the conception of their roles.

Changes in family status imply financial alteration or loss. The degree of loss may depend upon the amount of financial status enjoyed by the family. Illness, injury, or disfigurement affect all people, no matter what their financial status. It is understandable that the more wealthy patients and families can afford costly care and specialists. The majority of critical-care patients and their families have moderate incomes. To them, illness necessitating critical care or long-term therapy, such as dialysis, can be catastrophic. Unfortunately, there are patients in critical-care units, who do not have health insurance. One illness can totally wipe out the family's savings. Even if the family has insurance, hospitalization in a critical-care unit can deplete at least a portion of their savings. If the primary provider is ill, injured, or disfigured, the family may experience financial hardships. The financial hardship may affect the critical-care patient's recovery process. "The impact of medical care costs upon families, and the ways in which these affect long-term planning of individual members, may possibly relate to the kinds of adjustments made by patients," according to Croog (1968.) Families of critical-care patients are no exception. Their medical costs can be overwhelming. The family of a hemodialysis patient, for example, will experience tremendous financial hardships. The cardiac patient may no longer be able to work in a management or business position in which stress, deadlines, and pressures are everyday occurrences. Furthermore, the cardiac patient who sustains a massive myocardial infarction may no longer be able to work at physically demanding jobs such as construction. The patient with respiratory problems will be discouraged from future work that might further damage debilitated lungs. Regardless of the biological crisis, the patient and the family experience social loss in terms of their financial status. Financial problems are not the only ones created by illness. The family also experiences conflict among themselves as they assume new roles.

Illness creates either temporary or permanent dismemberment. Both involve role changes within the intrafamily structure. If temporary dismemberment occurs, the sick member returns to the family. The member's illness may have been severe enough to warrant restructuring of family roles. The sick member who experienced biological loss through illness itself, injury, or disfigurement may not be able to assume the previous role. Therefore, this member returns home to a reorganized and restructured family. The transition between hospital and home may greatly influence the sick member's recovery process. Family members who are unsure of their new roles unintentionally create confusion. According to Hill (1949), "most crisis of crippling illness, sooner or later, involve demoralization since the family's role patterns are always sharply disturbed. It may involve a situation in which the patient's roles must be reallocated, and a period of confusion-delay ensues while the members of the family cast learn their new lines." The strength

of the family system as a whole determines how well the independent subsystems do in the adjustment period. Also, according to Hill.

> Adjustment to a crisis that threatens the family depends upon the adequacy of role performance of family members. The family consists of a number of members interacting with one another, and each member is ascribed roles to play within the family. The individual functions as a member of the family largely in terms of the expectations that other members place upon him. The family succeeds as a family largely in terms of the adequacy of role performance of its members. One major effect of crisis is to cause changes in these role patterns. Expectations shift, and the family finds it necessary to work out different patterns.

Hopefully, the family members will be capable of substituting for or assuming the role of the sick member.

A family that depends on the sick member instead of having a system of mutual interdependence will have difficulty restructuring and adjusting to new responsibilities. Furthermore, the degree of role changes depends on which family member is ill. In addition, the nurse realizes that a small family is not always able to assimilate all the new changes and roles. Here is where extrafamily members such as parents, grandparents, aunts, uncles, or close friends can be of assistance. A family system that has been basically dependent upon its own members to accomplish the tasks of daily living has difficulty adjusting to role changes and integrating extrafamily strangers.

Serious illness does bring about stresses of social loss both in financial matters and in role changes. Emotionally and financially, members are bound together by their mutual interdependence for satisfaction or provision of mutual needs. The critical-care nurse's responsibility extends beyond caring for the sick member; the nurse must provide supportive care for the family as well. The nurse becomes the only constant informative individual directly accessible to the family. Therefore, this individual sometimes becomes the family's sounding board against which anxieties such as anger can be expressed. Understanding their behavior, the critical-care nurse can better support them in coping with the individual illness crisis and early recovery process.

NURSING IMPLICATIONS

The critical-care nurse is a primary force in establishing and fostering meaningful interpersonal behavior. The nurse accomplishes this goal by encouraging interpersonal competent behavior and meeting the interpersonal needs of both the critically ill patient and the family. The critical-care nurse is the primary provider of health care in the patient and family's world. It is the nurse who provides a set for interpersonal behavior and future relationships. Both the patient and family turn to the nurse for support and answers to their numerous questions. The critical-care nurse attempts to utilize aspects of the interpersonal framework in order to facilitate patient-family involvement. The nurse therefore attempts to accomplish three goals: foster patient-family support, facilitate patient-family education, and foster acceptance of the temporarily altered patient-family system.

Foster Patient-Family Support

Fostering patient-family support is one of the most important initial nursing interventions. Crisis or stress on both the patient and family make them feel suddenly lonely and alone. Through supportive interpersonal behavior, the critical-care nurse establishes the foundation upon which both individuals can express their fears, anxieties, and concerns. To the family, a significant member is ill, injured, or disfigured and hospitalized in a highly technical environment. The critical-care environment is one that makes the patient inaccessible. To the patient, a primary support system has been removed from the immediate environment and has been placed in an area designated as the family room. At a time when the patient and family need each other's emotional support, the hospital restricts the length of time one may spend with the patient. Therefore, the amount and degree of support is limited. The critical-care nurse must provide support for both the family and the sick family member. The nature, degree, and severity of the illness necessitates that the nurse's primary care be directed toward the patient. Nevertheless, the nurse finds quality time to communicate with the family regarding the patient's progress, change, or general care. When providing supportive care for the family, "the obvious facet for the nurse to recognize is that illness is a stress or crisis to the family. However, what we may lose sight of, is that illness is only one of probably many stresses on this family at any given time" (Craven, 1972).

Unlike the patient who enters the hospital for a diagnostic procedure or elective surgery, the critical-care patient enters in acute biological crisis. Therefore, the patient is not prepared to see what is happening to other patients; the noisy, technical-appearing environment; or events that he or she alone must experience. Various supportive devices may need to be applied or inserted quickly without lengthy explanations. As the initial crisis subsides or stabilizes, the patient can be informed as to the purpose of the supportive devices. Likewise, the nurse also supports the family by preparing them for what they will see in the critical-care unit. According to Wallace (1971), "there is a need to prepare relatives of patients in the intensive care unit beforehand for what they will encounter. As most people have never before set foot in such a specialized and mechanized area of the hospital, the equipment alone overwhelms them." It is not unusual for family members to cry at the sight of their loved one. This is especially true if the individual sustained injuries in an automobile accident or fire. The sight of physical disfigurement may be overwhelming. In addition, the patient's immediate environment may be filled with various supportive devices. Each device has its own unique flashing light and buzzing alarm. It is a foreign environment to the family members. Initially, they feel as though they have entered forbidden territory. The critical-care nurse should attempt to make the family feel comfortable in the strange territory. The family should know that the treatment plan, including various pieces of equipment, is normal for the particular problems of the patient. The nurse should give brief explanations regarding their normalcy. The nurse must realize that the family is experiencing tremendous stress and will hear only fragments of explanations. But family members will hear the word *normal*. A supportive critical-care nurse should remain with the family throughout their initial visits. The family feels secure in the presence of a nurse. Should one of the machine's alarms buzz in their presence, the nurse will know what to do. In addition, the nurse's presence communicates caring.

The family must be prepared for what it is to see in the patient's environment, and it should be prepared for unusual behavior manifested by the sick member. During the impact phase of illness, the sick member may not be aware of his or her own behavior. The family may wrongfully assume the patient has sustained neurological damage or some other problem. According to Davidson (1973), "as families see the symptoms of regression in their loved one, they often become embarrassed by his childish, demanding behavior. Or, they are frightened when he becomes verbally threatening with them. Families need a great deal of support from the staff. One of the most effective means is to teach them about the situation." Just as the nurse explained equipment in terms of its normalcy, the patient's behavior should be explained in the same manner. Any negative behavior expressed by the patient and directed toward the family needs to be explained.

As previously mentioned, the critical-care nurse becomes a communication link between the family and the patient. Such communication can extend beyond the walls of the hospital. It is not unusual to give the unit's phone number to intrafamily members and encourage them to call the unit before retiring or upon rising. Such an intervention personalizes the family's care. The phone call has two purposes: The nurse can give the family members a current report of the sick member's progress and at the same time can give the sick member the latest report regarding the family. In time, the sick member can make phone calls. The nurse fosters communication between family and sick members by increasing the visiting time. A family member can be permitted to remain quietly at the patient's bedside for periods longer than the alloted 5 min. This exception is not applicable to all patients. Some family members' continual presence only serves to make the sick member more anxious. The exception applies to those sick members whose biological status is terminal and to those families who demonstrate supportive strength. In this case, the nurse can perceive a type of mutual interdependence between family and sick member. Flexibility in visiting hours facilitates the family as the primary adjustment support system in the sick member's life. Naturally, the critical-care nurse wants to continue to keep the support system functioning. According to Craven (1972), to "recognize the importance of the patient and family interrelationship as well as energetic encouragements to stimulate the family members' active involvement whenever possible are concrete actions that can be taken by the nurse to assist the family in keeping close and strong ties during an illness."

Facilitate Patient-Family Education

The second goal of the critical-care nurse is to facilitate patient-family education. Both the patient and family need a knowledge base upon which to judge their progress, make necessary changes, and plan for the future. Baden (1972) is of the opinion that "the patient has a right to information that will enable him to return to a normal way of living and the professional nurse has an obligation to provide this information. Patients and their families can live better lives through education. Teaching should begin in the acute phase and be continued throughout convalescence, and families must be included in teaching

programs." Such programs revolve around teaching families of cardiac and other critically ill patients. A family that lacks knowledge regarding the patient's problem is unable to provide support. This is especially true for cardiac and hemodialysis patients. The nurse should educate the family by starting with the illness. Teaching should begin in the acute phase, and the nurse should remember to keep things simple. Like the sick member, the family also has a tendency to hear and learn selectively. Once the critical phase has subsided, the family can begin a more detailed educational program. Such a program includes both family and patient. Each needs to learn expectations of the other. The critical-care nurse constantly keeps in mind that a necessary part of a patient's care and rehabilitation is the education of the family so that they can be a help rather than a detriment to the patient. The family plays a significant role in whether or not the patient accepts the problems that will be encountered. In addition, the family assists in modifying the life-style of the critically ill patient. Patient-family-centered care and teaching involve assisting the patient in a personal education program while involving the family in group education.

The nurse will begin to educate the cardiac patient and family in the critical-care unit and will continue in the intermediate-care unit. If the unit has a clinical specialist, this individual can conduct the program. Group education includes the total family and other cardiac patients and their families. Hemodialysis patients and their families may be educated in the hemodialysis unit. Hopefully, both spouses participate in the educational program. There are instances in which the husband or wife cannot accompany the sick member to the hemodialysis unit. The healthy member is often forced to assume financial responsibility for the entire family; therefore, group teaching is not always possible.

Educational programs may be initiated in any critical-care unit. The nurse must first take time to assess the patient and family's readiness for learning. The learning program should contain terminal behavioral objectives; objectives specific to critical care, intermediate care, and predischarge; media designed to stimulate auditory-visual modalities; and ways to measure learning. In situations where the illness becomes chronic, such as hemodialysis and respiratory care, the family may use group conference to verbalize their feelings and frustrations. According to Craven (1972), "by giving family members the opportunity to express their feelings, the nurse can contribute to the therapeutic role while providing the same function for the patient who, aware of the additional pressures on his family, does not want to further burden them.''

Foster Patient-Family Acceptance

The third and last major role of the critical-care nurse is to foster acceptance of the altered body part, changed life goal, and temporary sick family member as a contributing individual. This seems like a simple task, but it may be an equally trying time for the entire family. The nurse keeps in mind that both the family and sick member have experienced many stresses. These stresses do not cease the minute a sick member is discharged from the hospital. Instead, new stresses may inhibit the sick member's recovery process and the family adjustment as a whole.

When the once critically ill, injured, or diseased patient returns home, a newly organized family structure is waiting there. Members within the family system have assumed the roles that the patient once assumed. The sick member may already feel a social loss in terms of finances. The new roles at home further enhance this feeling. The degree of loss experienced by the sick member depends on the severity of the illness. Watching the family assume new roles, the sick member feels guilty. This may be particularly the case when the spouse is forced to seek employment; the patient may feel a sense of personal failure. The strong family system supports and assists the sick member to accept current limitations; new roles are found. These include roles that are significant within the intrafamily structure. Having established a meaningful interpersonal relationship, the nurse works to-gether with the patient and the family in anticipating potential changes in roles that might lead to early adjustment conflicts. In this respect, the entire family is prepared for these problems experienced by other families in similar situations. If the nurse has maintained a close interpersonal relationship with the family and patient, the family may be encouraged to call the unit with questions and concerns.

Although working primarily with the sick member, the critical-care nurse often comes in contact with the anxious family members who have many questions and concerns. The nurse's time with the family should be utilized to make it a meaningful session of support and education. The family can only become involved in what it understands. All else becomes meaningless and frightening. Therefore, the nurse has the responsibility of educating not only the patient but the family as well. Consequently, the family has a better understanding of the patient's care, treatment program, and future restrictions.

In summary, the critical-care nurse attempts to establish a meaningful interpersonal relationship with both the patient and the family. This goal is accomplished by assessing interpersonal behaviors as they relate to interpersonal competence and needs. The critical-care nurse realizes that the patient and the family are capable of performing many roles in an adequate and effective manner. As members of the nurse-patient-family triad become dynamically involved with each other, the foundation for a positive, helping relationship is established. Such a relationship permits the critical-care nurse to foster support, facilitate an educational program, and foster acceptance of a difficult illness and future changes in life goals.

REFERENCES

Ackerman, N.: *The Psychodynamics of Family Life,* New York: Basic Books, 1958.

Almore, M. G.: Dyadic communication, *Am J Nurs* 79(6):1076–1078, 1979.

Baden, C.: Teaching the coronary patient with his family, *Nurs Clin North Am,* 7:570–571, 1972.

Craven, R.: The effects of illness on family functions, *Nurs Forum* 11:188–191, 1972.

Croog, S.: The heart patient and the recovery process, *Soc Sci Med* 2:135–140, 1968.

D'Addio, D.: Reach out and touch, *Am J Nurs* 79(6):1081, 1979.

Davidson, S. B.: Nursing management of emotional reactions of severely burned patients during acute phase, *Heart Lung* 2:374, 1973.

Fawcett, J.: The family as a living open system: An emerging conceptual framework for nursing, *Int Nurs Rev* 22(4):113–116, 1975.

Gardner, D., and N. Stewart: Staff involvement with families of patients in critical care units, *Heart Lung* 7:105–110, 1978.

Hill, R.: *Families under Stress,* New York: Harper & Row, 1949.

Jourard, S.: *Personal Adjustment,* New York: Macmillan, 1963.

Jungman, L. B.: When your feelings get in the way, *Am J Nurs* 79(6):1074–1075, 1979.

McEver, D. H.: Ode to patient care, *Am J Nurs* 79(6):1083, 1979.

Murphy, J. C.: Communicating with the dying patient, *Am J Nurs* 79(6):1084, 1979.

Parad, H.: A framework for studying families in crisis, in *Crisis Intervention,* New York: Family Service Association, 1965.

Ramaekers, M. J.: Communication blocks revisited, *Am J Nurs* 79(6):1079–1080, 1979.

Schiedman, J. M.: Problem patients do not exist, *Am J Nurs* 79(6):1082–1084, 1979.

Wallace, P.: Relatives should be told about intensive care but how much and by whom? *Can Nurse* 67:33, 1971.

PART 6

PATIENT CARE MANAGEMENT:

SELECTED PROBLEMS

DISORDERS AFFECTING ALVEOLAR PERMEABILITY

Adult Respiratory Distress Syndrome (ARDS)

Catastrophic respiratory failure of sudden onset may occur in patients with previously normal or healthy lungs who sustain any one of a variety of pulmonary or systemic insults that cause diffuse injury to the lung. The initial insult may be any one of a very diverse group of injuries, yet the histological response of the lung, regardless of the insult, is virtually identical. The fact that the lung has a characteristic clinical, physiological, and pathological response to acute injury, regardless of etiology, allows the critical-care practitioner to group a variety of illnesses which have one or more common phases under the singular heading of ARDS.

The lack of a single causative event and the absence of any specific diagnostic test for ARDS necessitates the use of a descriptive definition for this syndrome. The following constellation of pulmonary responses characterize the ARDS:

1. Clinical: dyspnea, tachypnea

2. Radiological: diffuse, bilateral pulmonary infiltrates (an "alveolar pattern")

3. Physiological: decreased pulmonary compliance (i.e., increased "stiffness" of the lungs), impaired oxygen diffusion across alveolar capillary membrane (i.e., decreasing arterial oxygen tension non-responsive to "standard" oxygen therapy)

4. Pathological: interstitial edema, intra-alveolar exudation, hemorrhage, microemboli, and hyaline membrane formation

The clinical hallmarks of this variety of respiratory failure include an initial insult, such as massive hemorrhage and hypovolemic shock, a latent period during which pulmonary function appears normal, followed by respiratory decompensation. Initially the patient will be tachypneic and dyspneic; the arterial oxygen tension will decrease in spite of standard oxygen therapy. The arterial carbon dioxide tension will be low initially (Pa_{CO_2} below 40 torr) but will rise rapidly in spite of the tachypnea as the respiratory insufficiency progresses.

The use of the term *ARDS* should not obscure the fact that the initial insult and mechanism of pulmonary injury vary widely. Therapy should be focused in two areas: supportive therapy to treat the secondary alterations in pulmonary function and maintain the patient, and treatment of the initiating or causal insult.

23
RESPIRATORY DISORDERS

Sheila A. Glennon
Vickie White Matus
Christopher W. Bryan-Brown

DISORDERS AFFECTING ALVEOLAR PERMEABILITY
Adult Respiratory Distress Syndrome (ARDS)
Viral Pneumonia
Aspiration Pneumonia
Radiation Pneumonitis
Cardiogenic Pulmonary Edema
Oxygen Toxicity
Near Drowning
Extracorporeal Membrane Oxygenation

RESTRICTIVE LUNG DISORDERS
Lung Abscess
Pleural Effusion
Kyphoscoliosis

OBSTRUCTIVE LUNG DISORDERS
Asthma
Chronic Bronchitis
Emphysema

PERFUSION DISORDERS
Pulmonary Thromboembolism
Air Embolus
Fat Embolus

CHEST TRAUMA
Pulmonary Contusion
Flail Chest
Pneumothorax
Hemothorax

SELECTED DISORDERS
Atelectasis
Bacterial Pneumonia
Drug Overdose and Head Injury

REFERENCES

Some of the causal factors seen in medical and surgical settings that are related to the development of ARDS are listed in Table 23-1.

The prevalence of ARDS is unknown, although in 1972 an estimated 150,000 such cases were treated, and it appears that this number is increasing (National Heart and Lung Institute, 1972).

Historical Background

This form of respiratory failure has been recognized for a long time. Posttraumatic pulmonary insufficiency had been described by World War I. Most of the victims of respiratory processes during this war died of pneumonia or massive atelectasis. Fulminant respiratory failure and death occurred in young patients with no underlying cardiac or pulmonary disease during the *influenza* pandemics of 1918–1919 and 1957–1958. Military surgeons in World War II used the term *wet lung* to describe casualties with or without direct chest trauma, usually with severe blood loss, who presented with dyspnea, *rales,* and *rhonchi* and with chest roentgenograms ranging from minimal atelectasis to severe pulmonary edema. Moon, in 1948, reported that pulmonary congestion, edema, and hemorrhage were pathologic findings seen frequently in patients who died after a period of hypotension caused by a variety of disorders.

Wet lung became known as "Da Nang lung" during the Vietnam war (Table 23-2). Advances in emergency medical care during this period allowed for prolonged survival of trauma victims who previously would have died on the battleground. Two of the most notable advances were (1) rapid treatment and recovery from initial shock and trauma, and (2) rapid evacuation *within* 15 to 20 min to sophisticated treatment centers. Observations made during World War II were confirmed and *extended* to include development of respiratory failure after a posttraumatic latent period of 12 to 48 h. One reason for the apparently increasing incidence of ARDS over the years has been improvements in medical therapy and technology that facilitate the victim's survival of severe initial insults that lead to ARDS.

Pathology

Although there are a variety of etiologies of ARDS, the pathologic changes are remarkably consistent. On gross examination at autopsy the lungs are heavy, congested, and hemorrhagic and have the appearance of liver. Such lungs sink when placed in water. Generally there is not a significant amount of secretions in the large airways nor is there a visible obstruction of the major vessels.

Frequently cited findings in ARDS include thickened alveolar walls, interstitial edema, intra-alveolar edema, and hemorrhage. Focal atelectasis is present. Congestion of capillaries, occasional plugging of small arterioles with fibrin and debris, and intravascular engorgement with platelets and red cells including migration of the cellular material into the alveoli may be noted. There may be localized areas of alveolar wall necrosis and increased numbers of pulmonary macrophages.

Hyaline membranes are also noted on microscopic examination. They are probably formed from transudated plasma proteins and can increase the alveolar capillary membrane 50 to 100 times its normal thickness. These membranes form a formidable barrier to gas diffusion.

Etiology

The support and management of all ARDS patients is similar, yet it varies somewhat depending on the etiology. A successful outcome depends upon recognition and treatment of all contributing factors. For example, the critically ill multisystem trauma patient may have ARDS, fat embolism, sepsis, and posttraumatic pancreatitis as active problems. It is important to consider all possible contributing problems to facilitate proper management.

The lung exhibits a limited number of responses

TABLE 23-1
Causal Factors Related to ARDS

Aspiration of gastric contents
Drug ingestion and overdose
Hydrocarbon *ingestion*
Trauma and hemorrhagic shock
Near drowning
Smoke and gas inhalation
Disseminated intravascular coagulation
Septic shock
Fat and air embolism
Severe pneumonitis (*viral* and other)
Oxygen toxicity
Postperfusion (cardiopulmonary bypass)
Anaphylaxis
Uremia
Hemorrhagic pancreatitis
Head injury
Homologous blood transfusion

to injury. The picture of ARDS is one type of response to a very severe insult. Knowledge of the mechanisms of pulmonary injury is largely inferred rather than directly observed, with the exception of direct trauma and aspiration. It can also be assumed that some protective mechanisms exist, since not all patients having similar insults develop ARDS. The source of this protection is as yet poorly understood.

It is generally accepted that a period of pulmonary hypoperfusion is the probable origin of most cases of ARDS. The precise mechanism by which this hypoperfusion develops into ARDS is not entirely clear, but it probably involves intravascular coagulation with subsequent thromboembolism within the pulmonary microvasculature (Fig. 23-1).

TABLE 23-2 Synonyms For ARDS
White lung
Shock lung
Da Nang lung
Respirator lung
Wet lung
Pump lung
Congestive atelectasis
Progressive pulmonary consolidation
Acute pulmonary insufficiency
Acute ventilatory insufficiency
Posttraumatic pulmonary insufficiency
Adult hyaline membrane disease
Noncardiogenic pulmonary edema

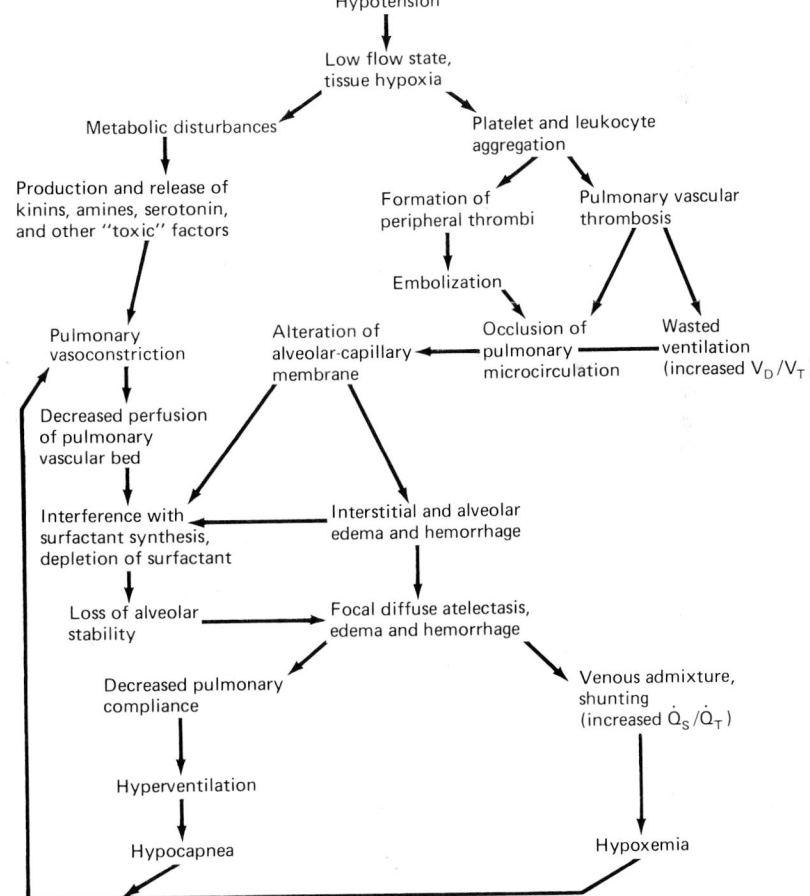

FIGURE 23-1

Pathogenesis and pathophysiology of ARDS. [*Reprinted with permission from K. Lake and J. Rumsfeld, The adult respiratory distress syndrome (shock lung), in G. G. Burton, G. N. Gee, and J. E. Hodgkins (eds.), Respiratory Care: A Guide to Clinical Practice, Lippincott, Philadelphia, 1977, p. 768.*]

Intravascular coagulation can develop from a variety of causes. Transfusion with mismatched blood with resulting hemolysis is a significant cause. Old blood itself is a source of microemboli, and the dead cells produce differing degrees of intravascular clotting. Other complications of shock states that lead to intravascular coagulation are tissue trauma mobilizing tissue thromboplastin, bacterial toxins through platelet aggregation with the release of thromboplastin, ischemia from endothelial cell damage, the release of tissue thromboplastin, and acidosis. Systemic microvascular obstruction with microemboli results in decreased tissue perfusion, progressive metabolic acidosis, and a secondary increase in coagulability.

Following resuscitation of the patient in a shock state, flow in the microcirculation is reestablished and the products of peripheral intravascular coagulation are flushed into the systemic circulation and carried to the vascular bed of the lungs. The filtering action of the pulmonary vascular bed removes gross and microscopic clots. Unstable circulating clots fragment until the microcirculation of the lung is reached. Stasis here in the microcirculation invites further thrombosis because of endothelial cell damage distal to the emboli.

Thromboemboli cause pulmonary damage via at least two mechanisms: (1) by causing the release of potent bronchoconstrictors and venoconstrictors, and (2) by mechanical obstruction of blood flow. Vasoactive amines such as serotonin and histamine are released from platelet microemboli and produce constriction of the postcapillary venules. Other agents including bradykinin and catecholamines are also released from white blood cell–platelet microaggregates and result in vasoconstriction, bronchoconstriction, and alterations in alveolar-capillary membrane permeability.

The primary target for all these forces is the alveolar-capillary membrane. Initially there is extreme vasoconstriction on both the arterial and venous side of the pulmonary capillary. Gradually the precapillary (arterial) end relaxes while the postcapillary venule remains constricted. Stagnation of blood flow in the pulmonary circulation then occurs because of the following:

1. Postcapillary constriction with precapillary relaxation

2. Mechanical obstruction due to microemboli

3. Release of vasoactive substances

There is hypoxia, lactic acidosis, and intravascular clotting due to subsequent stagnation. Hypoxemia and acidemia themselves increase pulmonary artery pressure and pulmonary vascular resistance. The capillary membranes are damaged by these insults and their permeability is increased, allowing extravasation of fluids into the interstitial space. Initially the fluid is a transudate, but as the leak increases, larger molecules such as proteins and formed blood elements leak out. Lymph channels which would normally remove this material are compressed by the extravasated fluid, further favoring interstitial fluid collection and retention (see Fig. 23-2).

Perivascular edema and decreased capillary perfusion damage the alveolar type II pneumocyte, and the production of surfactant decreases. The alveoli become increasingly unstable and tend to collapse unless filled with fluid from the interstitium. These alveoli, in either case, cannot participate in effective gas exchange, and this area becomes a mass of interstitial and alveolar edema with hemorrhage and atelectasis.

Pathophysiology

Pulmonary function abnormalities in patients with ARDS have been well described in several review articles. A reduction in functional residual capacity is a hallmark of this syndrome. Localization of edema fluid in the peribronchovascular interstitial space increases the normally subatmospheric pressure of the interstitial space. This reduces the transmural pressure gradient that helps to maintain patent airways. If these small airways close and remain closed, distal atelectasis and loss of lung volume occur. Lung volume also decreases as accumulating edema fluid begins to flood alveoli or as the alveoli become smaller in size due to the increasing surface forces.

Decreasing pulmonary compliance is another characteristic finding in ARDS. This means that greater than normal inspiratory pressure is needed to deliver the same tidal volume. This loss of compliance is directly due to increasing tissue elasticity or recoil caused by pulmonary congestion and the increasing alveolar surface forces resulting from loss or inactivation of surfactant. The decreasing compliance is indirectly a result of the overall decreasing lung volume. As compliance decreases, there is a progressive reduction in the volume of gas present in the involved lung units at functional residual capacity (FRC). If the process is severe, the volume of gas may be so small and the surface forces so great that the alveoli and/or terminal bronchioles collapse completely on deflation. When this occurs, the unit cannot reopen until a "critical opening pressure" has been exceeded during inspiration.

Hypoxia is an invariable feature of ARDS. A large number of gas exchange units do not contribute fully to the uptake of oxygen and elimination of carbon dioxide because of the processes described above. Alveoli that receive blood flow but no ventilation are sites of intrapulmonary shunting ($\dot{Q}s/\dot{Q}T$). In other areas where there is vasoconstriction and microembolization, "wasted" ventilation (VD/VT) exists. The net result over the entire pulmonary bed is $\dot{V}/\dot{Q}$ mismatching and hypoxemia.

A reflex increase in cardiac output and alveolar minute ventilation occurs in an attempt to compensate for the hypoxia and resultant acidosis. However, the lowered Pa_{CO_2} from hyperventilation increases both airway resistance and oxygen consumption and decreases dynamic compliance. All these effects contribute to additional pulmonary dysfunction. Increased inspiratory effort is needed to open previously closed alveoli. The increased inspiratory effort increases venous return to the right heart, yet the total volume of the pulmonary circulatory bed is decreased because of coagulopathy and increased resistance. This causes further extravasation of fluid and formed elements into the interstitial space. As osmotically active particles leak through the damaged endothelial membrane and into the interstitial space, more water is drawn to them and the lungs become stiffer. The increased oxygen consumption required by the increased work of breathing is far too costly in the face of progressive hypoxemia.

The role of the central nervous system in ARDS deserves special consideration. Neurosurgeons have long recognized an unusually severe form of pulmonary edema following certain types of head injury. Moss and his colleagues have described a model in which cerebral hypoxia initiates the sequence. Shock, aspiration, airway occlusion, or any other cause of hypoxia to the brainstem interferes with hypothalamic cellular metabolism. Descending sympathetic fibers are activated which pass through the cervical spinal cord and on to the vessels of the lung. They exert a constrictor effect on the postcapillary venules, causing congestion of the arterioles and transudation of fluid into the interstitium and alveoli. An intact cervical spinal cord is necessary for these events to occur. (See Fig. 23-3.)

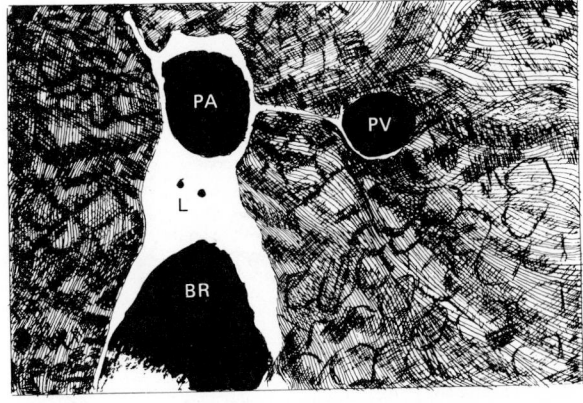

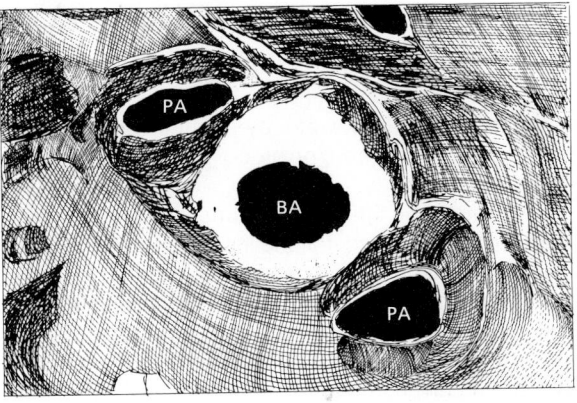

FIGURE 23-2

(a) Normal lung showing bronchus (BR), pulmonary artery (PA), and pulmonary venule (PV). The only visible interstitial space (L) is between the airway and artery in which lymph vessels are located. (b) Massive fluid expansion of loose interstitial perivascular and peribronchial space. Note "halo" effect surrounding the pulmonary artery (PA) and the bronchus (BA). (Illustrations courtesy of E. F. Lenihan.)

Diagnostic Findings

Recognition of ARDS in the late stages is relatively easy, yet diagnosis in the early, subtle stages is difficult unless members of the health care team are alert to its development in susceptible patients. Early diagnosis helps to avoid compounding the problem by mishandling oxygen, mechanical ventilation, and other therapeutic tools.

During the initial shock phase, therapeutic interventions are directed toward converting the low-flow

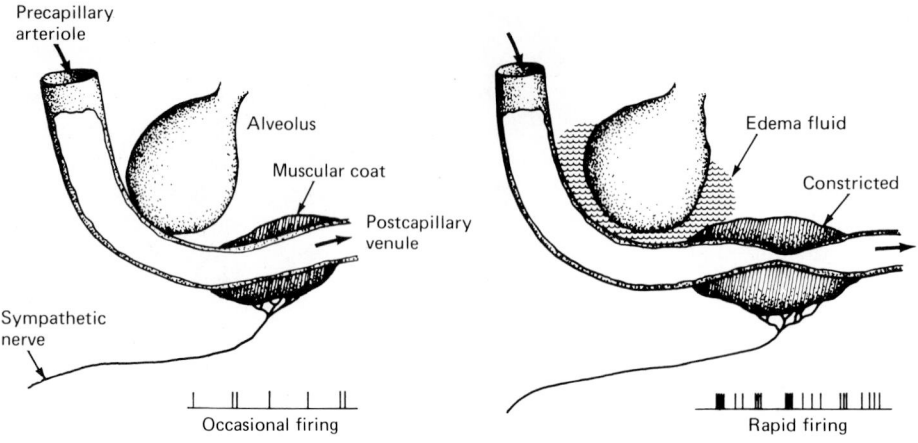

FIGURE 23-3

Constrictor effect can be seen on postcapillary venules producing congestion and interstitial edema.

state to a high-flow state by administration of the appropriate fluids and/or blood products to reverse the hypotension.

There may be little or no pulmonary symptomatology at this time and for the next 12 to 48 h. Early symptoms include dyspnea, restlessness, and/or cough. Dyspnea, however, may not appear early in the young, healthy individual who can double or triple minute ventilation with ease. The initial finding in ventilator patients may be an increased peak inspiratory pressure necessary to deliver a given tidal volume (evidence of decreasing pulmonary compliance).

Abnormal findings on physical examination indicate that the disease process has already progressed beyond the early stages. Evidence of increased work of breathing such as hyperpnea, noisy respirations of a rapid rate, and intercostal and supracostal retraction may be noted. Cyanosis will be present if there is adequate capillary perfusion and greater than 5 g of reduced hemoglobin. Pallor will be seen if perfusion is poor. Tachycardia, diaphoresis, and decreased mentation are seen frequently once the syndrome has progressed. Initially, chest auscultation will be normal, but rales, rhonchi, and bronchial breath sounds may be heard as the syndrome progresses to the later stages. Physical findings related to the underlying etiology, such as skin, conjunctival, and retinal changes in fat embolism and singed nasal hairs in pulmonary burns, should be sought.

Tests of gas exchange and pulmonary mechanics are useful in evaluating and managing ARDS. The hallmark of this syndrome remains a lowered arterial oxygen tension which is poorly responsive to increased concentrations of inspired oxygen. A more exact method of evaluating this is by calculating the alveolar-arterial oxygen gradient, $D(A-a)O_2$. This measure reflects the difficulty with which oxygen crosses the alveolar-capillary membrane (see Chap. 19). Normally the $D(A-a)O_2$ should be less than 15 to 20 torr[1] on room air, but in severe cases of ARDS, values of 200 to 500 have been recorded. This test relates more information about the transfer of oxygen than the Pa_{O_2} alone, especially when followed serially. It is important to remember, however, that the A-a difference does not take into account changes in inspired oxygen concentration, cardiac output, or metabolic rate. Thus, when following the alveolar-arterial oxygen difference clinically, these variables must be continually assessed.

It is also useful to measure shunt fraction ($\dot{Q}s/\dot{Q}T$) in these patients (see Chap. 19). Normal individuals spontaneously breathing have shunt fractions of less than 6 percent, while shunt fractions of less than 10 percent on a mechanical ventilator reflect a normal cardiopulmonary system. Until recently an FI_{O_2} of 100 percent has been used to calculate "true shunt." Recent evidence in critically ill patients has shown that "physiologic shunt" (which includes areas of low $\dot{V}/\dot{Q}$) is more clinically meaningful when calculated at an FI_{O_2} of 50 to 60 percent. In either case, the

---

* A torr is a unit of pressure that is equivalent to 1 mmHg under standard conditions.

following guidelines are useful for evaluation of shunt fractions on ventilator patients:

1. A calculated shunt greater than 30 percent is generally considered incompatible with prolonged spontaneous ventilation.

2. Calculated shunts between 20 and 30 percent are considered compatible with spontaneous ventilation as long as the cardiovascular reserves are adequate and the status of the central nervous system and hepatorenal system are acceptable.

3. Calculated shunts less than 20 percent are considered completely compatible with prolonged spontaneous ventilation (Shapiro et al., 1977).

Alveolar ventilation remains high until late in the course of ARDS. A Pa_{CO_2} of 35 to 45 torr in a very dyspneic, hypoxemic patient is not "normal," and when it does occur, it suggests that the seriously compromised lungs are no longer able to increase alveolar ventilation in response to hypoxemia and other stimuli.

The pH normally rises as Pa_{CO_2} falls (respiratory alkalemia). Failure to do so indicates that a metabolic acidemia is present. In the presence of shock and hypoxemia, this is most commonly the result of lactic acidosis. This can be confirmed by directly measuring serum lactate levels.

Tests of pulmonary mechanics show decreasing static and dynamic compliance. There is also a decrease in lung volumes, particularly FRC.

There is a real need for a sensitive test that can detect ARDS in an early phase when fluid is beginning to collect in the lung. Tests that measure lung water directly would obviously be desirable and might prove a means for early diagnosis. A number of techniques have been used, but at this time none have been sufficiently tested to establish their applicability to the clinical diagnosis of ARDS.

The radiologic picture of this syndrome is the result of movement of fluid out of the injured alveolar capillary into the interstitium and later into the alveolus. There must be a large increase in lung water before the chest roentgenogram becomes abnormal. They frequently appear normal in the early stages of ARDS, although a considerable degree of microatelectasis may be present. Subtle findings such as thickened or blurred margins of bronchi or vessels may be seen first. Except for the absence of a large left ventricle, the roentgenogram of ARDS may be difficult to distinguish from that of cardiogenic pulmonary edema. Proper resolution demands films of good quality with sufficient contrast and good detail.

The first changes of fine reticulation progress to give the lung a ground glass appearance. A typical air-space alveolar pattern may be seen as fluid leaks into the alveoli. Terminally, when consolidation is seen, there may be few recognizable air spaces; at this point the term *white lung* is applicable.

There are no sensitive practical means for early detection of ARDS. Detectable changes are most likely the result of significant water accumulation in the lung. Therefore, relatively minor alteration in tests of pulmonary function of patients who are at risk of ARDS should receive special attention. Early endotracheal intubation and mechanical ventilation should be considered as soon as abnormalities occur.

Figure 23-4 shows by means of x-rays the progress of a 35-year-old man who was admitted with a gunshot wound through the right lobe of the liver. The bullet tract involved the base of the right lung. After admission to the hospital (a), the patient appeared well and breathed room air spontaneously. Blood gases were Pa_{O_2} 67 and Pa_{CO_2} 34; pH was 7.42.

Three days later, after developing severe respiratory failure (b), the patient was transferred to another institution for possible extracorporeal membrane oxygenation. He had been given massive doses of diuretics and concentrated albumin solution and was on controlled mechanical ventilation (CMV) with 10 cmH$_2$O positive end-expiratory pressure (PEEP). Dopamine was needed to maintain blood pressure, and pancuronium was given because ventilation could not be synchronized with CMV. Blood gases were Pa_{O_2} 48 and Pa_{CO_2} 42; pH was 7.12 on F$_{I_{O_2}}$ 1.0. Lactate level was 5.6 mmol/L, and the patient was oliguric.

The final x-ray (c) was made 8 h after the patient was admitted to the second institution. He had received 2 U of whole blood and 4 L of crystalloid and was now on 26 cmH$_2$O PEEP; IMV was 6 breaths per minute; F$_{I_{O_2}}$ was 0.5. Blood gases were Pa_{O_2} 92 and Pa_{CO_2} 43; the pH was 7.37; the lactate level was 2 mmol/L. The patient was producing copious pink frothy sputum from the endotracheal tube and was nursed face down so that pulmonary edema fluid could be allowed to drain. He was not suctioned during the first 36 h of admission, because secretions were being washed out by the pulmonary edema fluid. Circulatory integrity returned in 36 h when the patient had normal renal function. He required some ventilatory support for another 5 days. By then he had returned to his admission weight, having voided the extra fluid given during resuscitation.

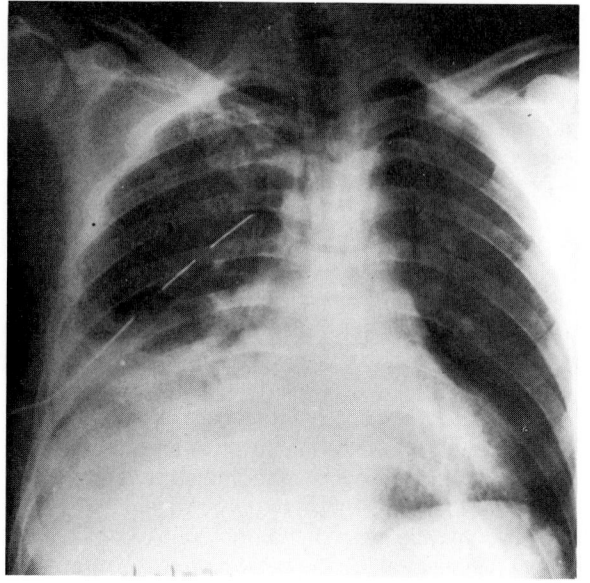

a

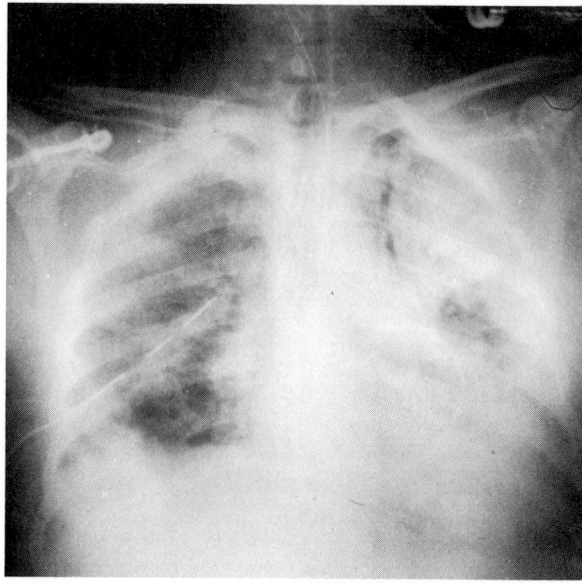

b

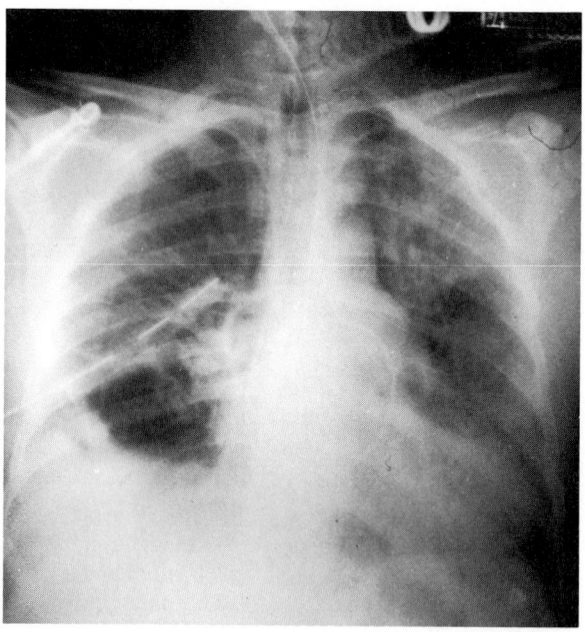

c

FIGURE 23-4

Chest x-rays taken of a 35-year-old man with a gunshot wound through the right lobe of the liver. The bullet tract involved the base of the right lung. (*a*) After admission to the hospital, patient was breathing spontaneously on room air and appeared well. (*b*) Three days later, after developing severe respiratory failure, the patient was transferred to another institution. (*c*) Patient 8 h after admission having received 2 U of whole blood and 4 L of crystalloid. PEEP and IMV had begun.

Management

Fluid replacement in ARDS is an extremely controversial topic. The question focuses on the choice of colloids or crystalloids for fluid volume replacement. It has been proposed that intravascular volume should be replaced with colloids, since the major intravascular force keeping fluid within the capillaries is the protein osmotic pressure. Administration of colloids, then, would keep the protein osmotic pressure within the vascular space from diminishing. However, there is undoubtedly rapid equilibration of protein concentrations between vascular and interstitial spaces in the presence of a very leaky capillary endothelium. There would be a loss of the oncotic pressure gradient across the capillary wall. The administration of colloids and the rapid exudation of protein into the interstitium may actually make the situation worse, since protein-rich fluid is cleared slowly from the interstitium and alveoli. Holcroft and Trunkey found that resuscitation with colloids may increase lung water more than that performed with crystalloids. There is no clear-cut experimental evidence favoring either crystalloids or colloids for fluid replacement.

Crystalloid solutions have several very real advantages in terms of present practicality. They are effective, readily available, and inexpensive. Colloids, on the other hand, are expensive and limited in supply. It would seem that in the absence of documented therapeutic benefits, crystalloid solutions are preferable since they can adequately replenish intravascular volume and restore functional extracellular fluid volumes. It seems reasonable to consider crystalloids early in the course of ARDS when the increase in permeability is greatest. Later, if the serum protein concentration is low, colloid solutions may be used.

It is difficult to say anything more conclusive based on current research. Many related areas merit further study. Recommendations for fluid therapy in situations increasing the risk of development of ARDS should be carefully considered. Carefully defined goals for fluid therapy must be sought and the systemic and pulmonary effects carefully evaluated. Some future promise may exist with the use of synthetic starches (i.e., McGaw Laboratories' Hexastarch); however, few data are presently available. It is crucial for the clinician to select a replacement based on logic and reason. Excessive fluid accumulation increases total lung water. However, appropriate fluids must be used to maintain optimal cardiac output while instituting the treatment of choice—PEEP.

Patients with fully developed ARDS invariably require mechanical ventilation. The decision of when to intervene with ventilatory support in patients with minor pulmonary function abnormalities suggesting ARDS might be difficult. Early intubation and ventilation are recommended because of the previously described cycle of edema, decreasing lung volume, and the appearance of hypoxia leading to more edema and more volume loss, contributing to further hypoxia.

Endotracheal intubation should be performed initially. The widespread use of high-volume, low-pressure cuffs on endotracheal tubes has sufficiently decreased the rate of tracheal complications from these tubes so that today tracheostomy is not normally required unless mechanical ventilation is anticipated for a period of greater than several weeks.

When mechanical ventilation is initiated in ARDS, tidal volumes of 10 to 15 mL per kg of body weight should be used. Volumes in this range are more effective in reducing or preventing atelectasis. When large tidal volumes are used with continous positive pressure ventilation (CPPV), alveolar hyperventilation may be seen. Since a low Pa_{CO_2} has been shown to decrease cardiac output and increase oxygen consumption as well as airway resistance, it is important to keep the Pa_{CO_2} in the range of 35 to 45 torr. Additional mechanical dead space may be added to the ventilator circuit to achieve this, or the respiratory rate may be decreased, providing the patient can be assisted to breathe synchronously with the machine. One would not want to decrease tidal volume in order to relieve the hyperventilation in these patients because of the atelectatic nature of the syndrome.

Many patients with ARDS are restless and tachypneic, which causes them to be overventilated on CPPV and breathe out of phase with the ventilator. Sedation should be used to avoid these problems, usually with intermittent small intravenous doses of morphine (3 to 5 mg given every hour) being sufficient. When larger doses of morphine are required to achieve adequate sedation, adverse effects from peripheral vasodilation may become a problem. A neuromuscular blocking agent such as curare or pancuronium (Pavulon) is helpful to completely paralyze and control a restless patient. Patients who are on such agents are paralyzed but fully awake and aware of their surroundings. Small doses of opiates should be given in conjunction with these drugs.

If continuous positive pressure ventilation is the mode selected for a patient, periodic hyperinflations of the chest may help to reexpand atelectatic areas, particularly when administered by a manually operated bag ventilator (i.e., ambu). The machine selected must have sufficiently rapid inspiratory flow rates to allow delivery of an adequate volume of inspired gas when lung compliance is severely reduced. Inadequate flow rates would lengthen inspiratory time, shorten the period available for exhalation, and increase the possibility of impeding venous return and cardiac output. As compliance decreases and airway resistance increases, tidal volume will be altered when any form of CPPV is used. Pressure-controlled ventilators will reach their preset limit more frequently and expel the tidal volume into the room air. Volume-controlled ventilators lose this tidal volume "internally" as the ventilator tubing expands more at higher pressures and holds a larger volume of gas. This gas is then not available to the patient.

The use of continuous positive pressure ventilation with positive end-expiratory pressure (PEEP) has a well-documented role in the management of patients with ARDS. Initially PEEP was added only in the late stages of the disease, and even then the primary effect sought was the ability of PEEP to increase arterial oxygenation without the use of potentially toxic exposure to oxygen. PEEP was also recognized secondarily for its ability to increase FRC. PEEP augments the reduced lung volumes seen in ARDS by producing a constantly positive distending pressure in the airways and alveoli. This keeps small airways open throughout the entire ventilatory cycle, reestablishes a greater FRC largely by increasing residual volume, and removes the need to achieve a critical pressure during inspiration to reopen closed alveoli, since their patency has been maintained. Intrapulmonary shunt is reduced because alveoli remain open and gases are available for diffusion throughout the respiratory cycle. The improved ventilation to gas exchange units that were previous sites of shunting or marked $\dot{V}/\dot{Q}$ abnormalities increases arterial P_{O_2} and reduces the alveolar-arterial P_{O_2} difference. PEEP also physically expands alveoli and exerts gas pressure against the transudating fluid in the alveoli so that the volume of fluid that previously filled the lumen forms a layer on the alveolar surface wall through which gas diffusion can occur.

The increase in lung volumes achieved with the use of PEEP also improves pulmonary compliance. Experimental evidence suggests that PEEP may conserve surfactant, preventing an increase in surface-active forces within the alveoli. This role may also enhance pulmonary compliance and suggests the use of PEEP prophylactically in patients at risk of developing ARDS.

The use of PEEP with CPPV has certain limitations due to hazards associated with combining these two therapies. PEEP adds more pressure to the already high mean intrathoracic pressures needed to mechanically inflate stiff lungs with positive pressure. This high pressure is transmitted, in part, to the pleural space and great veins of the chest. Added pressure can compress these vessels, reduce venous return to the right heart, and thereby reduce cardiac output. This can lead to poor tissue perfusion and lactic acidosis. Pulmonary vascular resistance is also increased, which increases the work of the right heart to pump blood into the normally low resistance pulmonary bed. High mean intrathoracic pressures also increase the risk of barotrauma (pneumothorax). PEEP in excess of 15 cmH$_2$O has seldom been successful with CPPV.

For PEEP to be effective with CPPV, the patient also should not be allowed to assist or "fight" the ventilator, since either would lower the end-expiratory pressure and could produce a subambient intrapleural pressure. This would again lead to closure of alveoli and a decrease in FRC. Sedation or paralyzation as previously described is routinely required. Extremely close nursing supervision is required on a 24-h basis, since the patient's ability to breathe alone in the event of a disconnection or loss of power is compromised or obliterated completely.

In the early 1970s three changes occurred which, when integrated, led to a new method of treating ARDS. Intermittent mandatory ventilation (IMV) began to be employed as a mode of ventilation. This technique of mechanical ventilation allows patients to breathe spontaneously from a gas reservoir, yet receive periodic mechanical hyperinflations. In this manner the patient's own spontaneous minute ventilation is augmented to a desired level by machine-delivered breaths. The sum of mechanical and spontaneous ventilation provides adequate alveolar minute ventilation.

The second change was the beginning use of PEEP as a therapeutic tool to treat the disease process itself when Downs introduced the concept of incremental PEEP in 1974. Combining the use of PEEP with IMV allowed development of the concept that PEEP reverses the pathophysiologic changes of decreasing lung volumes and compliance, whereas mechanical ventilation should be provided only to help normalize CO_2 removal.

The third change permitting the evolution of this

therapeutic regimen was the development of the Swan-Ganz thermodilution catheter and cardiac output computer. This allowed direct measurement of mixed venous and systemic arterial blood gases, central venous pressure, and pulmonary artery wedge pressure for monitoring cardiovascular compromise and provided information necessary to determine the relationship between PEEP, intrapulmonary shunt, and cardiac output.

The availability of inexpensive programmable calculators allows long and tedious mathematical calculations to be done accurately, rapidly, and inexpensively. Cardiac function can be evaluated by preload, the degree to which the myocardium is stretched before contraction; contractility; and afterload, the resistance against which the blood is expelled. Preload is reflected by the pulmonary artery wedge pressure and central venous pressure. Contractility is evaluated in terms of the measured cardiac output and heart rate as well as the calculated left ventricular stroke work index and stroke volume. Afterload is obtained from calculations of pulmonary and systemic vascular resistance. The effects of ventilatory support can be evaluated along with their effects on the cardiovascular circuit and appropriate interventions instituted to support the cardiovascular system during ventilatory therapy.

In 1978 Gallagher et al. introduced the concept of *optimal PEEP* in which end-expiratory pressure is added in small increments in an attempt to reduce the intrapulmonary shunt to the 15 to 20 percent range. This end point is arbitrary but represents pulmonary function compatible with spontaneous, unassisted ventilation. A reduction in cardiac output representing circulatory embarrassment was no longer the end point for PEEP application. Selective cardiovascular interventions to optimize preload, contractility, and afterload are appropriately instituted so that the desired reduction in intrapulmonary shunt can be achieved. In this manner the hallmarks of ARDS, decreased FRC and increased shunt, are treated aggressively and functional blood gas abnormalities are reversed early in the disease process. The patient's progress is then gauged by the ability to gradually remove ventilatory support while adequate, consistent blood gas values are maintained.

There are numerous advantages to this approach to therapy. The inclusion of IMV avoids the necessity for sedation and paralysis. As mechanical ventilation is terminated, the weaning process is facilitated. The patient has been spontaneously breathing during the entire course of therapy and gradually assumes the total responsibility for ventilation. Relearning of breathing is not necessary and the patient's anxiety level is lower. Nursing time and assessment during the weaning process is reduced to a more realistic level, since continual observation of the patient for weaning "withdrawal" is no longer required. As a result, nursing time can now be spent more advantageously.

Continuous positive airway pressure (CPAP) is positive end-expiratory pressure applied to a patient who is breathing spontaneously. It has the same physiologic effect of increasing functional residual capacity as PEEP. It was originally used for treatment of respiratory distress syndrome in premature infants and has recently been adapted for use with adults. It can be helpful if a patient can maintain a normal Pa_{CO_2} without mechanical ventilatory support but cannot maintain adequate arterial oxygenation at an FI_{O_2} less than 0.5 without positive end-expiratory pressure.

The alkalemia seen in patients on CPPV is diminished in patients on IMV, since these individuals breathe spontaneously most of the time and mechanical ventilation is supplied only as needed. This spares the patient from the increased oxygen consumption and difficulty of unloading oxygen from hemoglobin to the tissues which accompanies alkalemia.

Mechanically supplied breaths under positive pressure increase dead space (V_D/V_T), worsening ventilation perfusion relationships in patients whose primary disease process is characterized by $\dot{V}/\dot{Q}$ mismatching. The use of fewer machine-delivered breaths by employing IMV minimizes this effect.

Mean minute intrathoracic pressures are lower when an IMV-PEEP circuit is employed, since the high-pressure mechanically delivered breaths come less frequently and mean intrathoracic pressure is lower during spontaneous breathing. This means that higher levels of PEEP may be added if indicated to improve FRC and decrease shunt and that fewer interventions will be necessary to maintain cardiovascular status. Decreasing the frequency of high peak inspiratory pressures also decreases the risk of barotrauma.

The principles of this therapeutic regimen are relatively simple:

1. Use of large tidal volumes (12 to 15 mL/kg) for ventilator-delivered breaths.

2. Increase of PEEP in 2- to 3-cm increments until shunt approximates 15 to 20 percent. Pa_{O_2} should be kept at a level greater than 70 torr.

3. IMV rate is determined by patient need based on three criteria:

    a. Pa_{CO_2} normal for the patient.

    b. pH greater than 7.35.

    c. Spontaneous respiratory rate of 30 or less.

Regardless of blood gas values, should the patient exhibit signs of labored breathing, anxiety, or unexplained restlessness, inadequacy in the amount of mechanical ventilatory support being supplied should be considered.

An important determinant of the success of this regimen is the adequacy of the cardiovascular functioning. Invasive cardiovascular monitoring should be instituted whenever potential cardiovascular compromise is anticipated or when levels of PEEP greater than 15 cm of water are applied (Civetta, in press). Pulmonary wedge pressure which reflects left ventricular filling pressure can be "optimized" to a range of 13 to 17 torr in patients with documented cardiovascular dysfunction (Crexells et al., 1973). This is achieved by giving red cells or fluids as bolus intravenous infusions in a "dose" sufficient to maintain a reasonable cardiac output for a particular patient. Support of the cardiovascular function with fluid infusions or pharmacologic agents is only necessary if the ventilatory support needed to achieve adequate pulmonary function actually decreases the pumping ability of the heart.

Successful employment of any regimen utilizing mechanical ventilation is dependent upon a knowledgeable and highly skilled nursing staff. This includes knowledge of principles of mechanical ventilation, interpretation of arterial blood gases, and a level of expertise in physical assessment, techniques of pulmonary toilet, and proper maintenance of cuffed endotracheal tubes. The nurse must also know how to assist in emergency procedures when indicated (i.e., development of bradycardia, emergency insertion of chest tube). Nurses are encouraged to read Chap. 38 to review this information. If monitoring of the patient with a Swan-Ganz catheter is employed, the nurse must be familiar with care of the catheter and insertion site, visual recognition of the various pressure waveforms, and basic interpretation of numerical values associated with pulmonary artery and wedge pressures.

When perfusion to a particular lung is a major concern in addition to ventilation, the Roto bed, originally designed for orthopedic and neurosurgical patients, can be used with IMV and PEEP (Schimmel and Civetta, 1977). When the electrically driven motor is running, this bed rocks slowly from side to side. However, the bed can be stopped in any position, and a patient with unilateral pulmonary disease can be positioned so that the diseased lung is elevated and the unaffected lung is in the dependent position. Both ventilation and perfusion will be preferentially delivered to the unaffected lung, resulting in less perfusion of nonventilated areas in the diseased lung, producing a decreased intrapulmonary shunt and decreased microvascular pressure in that lung, all of which favor the egress of fluid.

The role of oxygen in producing or contributing to ARDS has been well established. The lowest possible FI_{O_2} capable of producing adequate oxygenation should be provided to the patient; levels less than 0.50 seem to be usable for long periods of time without evidence of oxygen toxicity.

Several indices are available for the determination of adequate tissue oxygenation, although no single value is useful unless taken into consideration with others. Arterial P_{O_2} is accessible but provides little useful information since it reflects oxygenation of blood that has not yet reached the peripheral tissues. A more precise estimate of tissue oxygenation is calculation of the mixed venous P_{O_2}. Most tissues compensate for inadequate oxygen delivery by increasing their extraction of the gas from arterial blood, thus widening the difference in oxygen content between arterial and venous blood and decreasing mixed venous P_{O_2} (drawn slowly from the distal lumen of the Swan-Ganz catheter) below the normal 40 torr. Serum lactate levels (also measurable in the laboratory) will also rise as a result of the metabolic acidosis produced by poor oxygenation.

If poor tissue oxygenation exists, its cause must then be determined and the following considered: decreased arterial P_{O_2}, decreased cardiac output, decreased hemoglobin concentration, or increased affinity of hemoglobin for oxygen. Assessment of adequate tissue oxygenation provides crucial information needed for decisions regarding blood or other fluid administration, inotropic drugs, vasopressors, PEEP, and diuretics.

Indications for use and beneficial effects of corticosteroids in ARDS are extremely controversial. There are several theoretically beneficial effects of steroids which could reduce the amount of edema resulting from injury: They may stabilize lysosomal membranes, preventing pulmonary damage from enzymes liberated from white blood cells, and they may reduce the amount of fibrosis following the acute phase of illness. There is, unfortunately, no clear experimental evidence to substantiate or refute these effects.

The role of microembolization in the development of ARDS was postulated earlier in this chapter. These microemboli form either from generalized or localized slowing of blood flow. It may seem to some, then, that heparin therapy would be a logical consideration in these low flow states. However, the degree to which microembolization occurs has not yet been determined, and the magnitude of its role in the pathogenesis of ARDS remains to be proved. Heparin therapy seems hazardous in the absence of documented evidence of the benefits of anticoagulation in the population at risk of developing ARDS, since the effects of heparin therapy are still being studied. In certain situations, such as fat embolism and lung contusion, heparin may actually worsen the situation.

Infection may produce or complicate the picture of ARDS. When infection is suspected, aggressive efforts should be made to identify the specific etiologic agent. This can usually be accomplished by Gram's stain and culture with sensitivity determinations of aspirated tracheal secretions. If more vigorous effort is needed, fiber-optic bronchoscopy can fairly easily be performed in mechanically ventilated patients. Using the fiber-optic bronchoscope makes available the use of a brush biopsy and bronchial lavage of localized areas. Needle aspiration and, rarely, open-lung biopsy may be required. Once an organism has been identified, appropriate therapy can be initiated utilizing the usual principles of antibiotic therapy. Cultures should be obtained if there is a change in the Gram smear, or they may be obtained on a routine basis (i.e., twice weekly) on severely ill patients at higher risk for development of infection.

Viral Pneumonia

Early descriptions of viral pneumonia were often confused by the presence of secondary bacterial pneumonias. Since bacterial pneumonias can be controlled with antibiotic therapy, the pathologic changes of viral penumonia within the lung are now being identified. In fulminating cases the alveoli are filled with fibrin, fluid, red blood cells, and macrophages. These patients have profound hypoxemias, often relatively unimproved by oxygen administration, and should be treated as ARDS. Prognosis is grave,

and fortunately, these cases are rare. Far more common are cases of patchy areas of viral pneumonitis, occurring during an influenzal infection and not extensive enough to cause severe arterial desaturation. In fact, presenting signs and symptoms are less severe than the roentgenogram would seem to indicate.

Although a "viral" pneumonia may be suspected clinically, the diagnosis is usually made retrospectively using serological studies. Pneumonia complicating viral influenza is commonly bacterial, although in the 1957 pandemic, fatal cases were recorded as resulting from purely viral penumonia.

Pneumonia due to varicella virus may complicate severe chicken pox in adults. The attack rate among adults is 38 percent of the varicella cases (Pek and Gekas, 1965). Predisposing factors include chronic illness, steroid treatment, or treatment with antimetabolic drugs. The mortality from varicella pneumonia may be as high as 20 percent (Harper et al., 1969). Pulmonary symptoms begin 2 to 5 days after vesicle eruption. Severe respiratory distress, cough, chest pain, and frequently hypoxemia and hemoptysis are typical, although milder cases do occur. Pleural friction rub, pleural effusion, and radiologic shadows have been described on the ipsilateral side in patients with intercostal herpes zoster, also thought to be caused by the varicella virus.

In addition to influenza and varicella viruses, measles and cytomegalovirus are the most commonly involved organisms in viral pneumonia. Whenever the viral pneumonia is severe, it rapidly progresses to a clinical picture of ARDS and should be treated as previously described.

Aspiration Pneumonia

Aspiration of large amounts of acid gastric contents often results in a widespread, severe chemical pneumonitis with diffuse alveolar filling. Aspiration pneumonia actually occurs in three different forms: acute aspiration pneumonia (septic pneumonitis or Mendelson's syndrome), chronic aspiration pneumonia, and lipoid pneumonia.

Acute aspiration pneumonia results from the aspiration of gastric contents, primarily hydrochloric acid. It is extremely severe and can be fatal. Predisposing conditions include trauma, burns, general anesthesia, comatose states, and the presence of nasogastric or endotracheal tubes. There is characteristically a latent period between aspiration and the onset of respiratory distress. Diagnostic findings are similar to those described previously with ARDS. The chest roentgenogram initially shows bilateral patchy pulmonary edema. Treatment is the same as previously described for ARDS. The use of steroids in acute aspiration pneumonia is also very controversial.

Chronic aspiration pneumonia is a localized consolidation of dependent portions of the lungs or bilaterally in the midzones due to repeated aspirations of small quantities of infected pharyngeal secretions. It is particularly common in chronic alcoholics and drug abusers and those patients who are obtunded. Nasogastric and endotracheal tubes as well as swallowing defects and hiatus hernias are common predisposing factors. Infecting organisms are usually anaerobes or gram-negative bacilli; necrosis and abscess formation are common.

Lipoid pneumonia (oil granuloma) results from aspiration of milk, mineral oil, oily nose drops, etc. It presents radiologically as a chronic consolidation resembling carcinoma.

Radiation Pneumonitis

Radiation therapy in or near the lungs may result in acute radiation pneumonitis and/or radiation fibrosis. The reaction is limited to the area which has been irradiated, and therefore the condition is usually only severe when the irradiation is bilateral. The effect varies with the size of the radiation dose, the amount of lung that has been irradiated, and the rate of administration. It is more likely to occur in thin individuals. It usually appears within a month or two after the initiation of therapy and appears on the roentgenogram as a soft, fluffy alveolar infiltrate. There is an associated loss of lung volume and the characteristic picture of an "air bronchogram." Radiation fibrosis is a chronic restrictive abnormality that usually follows but may develop independently of radiation pneumonitis. The affected area of lung becomes small and firm, and the mediastinum may be shifted to the involved side with elevation of the hemidiaphragm. Cor pulmonale occurs if the process is sufficiently extensive.

Cardiogenic Pulmonary Edema

It is beyond the scope of this discussion to consider cardiogenic pulmonary edema in any depth. Like ARDS ("noncardiac pulmonary edema"), it is the result of excessive accumulation of lung water. In this case the cause is a failing left ventricle or excessive administration of intravenous fluids. Increased left atrial pressure increases hydrostatic pressure in the pulmonary capillary bed. The lung's lymphatics, which can normally handle moderately increased fluid loads with minimal increases in interstitial fluid accumulation, now become overwhelmed. The increased intravascular hydrostatic pressure causes an increase in net filtration pressure. The capillary endothelium remains intact, but fluid transudates from the capillary into the interstitium and eventually into the alveolus. One major difference between ARDS and cardiogenic pulmonary edema is the loss of capillary endothelial integrity in ARDS. If the capillary endothelium remains intact in cardiogenic pulmonary edema, one would expect the fluid migrating into the alveoli to remain a transudate without the proteinaceous material seen in ARDS. In fact, when pulmonary edema fluid is due to high filtration pressures, the protein concentration of tracheal fluid is usually less than one-half that in plasma. In noncardiac pulmonary edema the alveolar fluid protein composition is much higher and similar to that of circulating plasma.

Severe cardiogenic pulmonary edema may be treated as previously described with ARDS, but with particular attention to cardiovascular functioning continually optimizing preload, contractility, and afterload. The reader is encouraged to refer to Chap. 24 for detailed reading.

Oxygen Toxicity

The advent of outer space and underwater exploration has necessitated the development of new perspectives on oxygen exposure. As long as man was confined to living at or near sea level, the term $F_{I_{O_2}}$ was adequate to quantify oxygen exposure. This term reflects the fraction of total inspired gas that is pure oxygen. However, when humans become exposed to oxygen under hyperbaric conditions (increased barometric pressures), they develop oxygen toxicity at a lower $F_{I_{O_2}}$. Alternately, under hypobaric conditions (lowered barometric pressures), oxygen toxicity does not develop even at a very high $F_{I_{O_2}}$. The term $P_{I_{O_2}}$ was developed to give a better index of exposure. It represents the partial pressure of inspired oxygen and is calculated using a formula that takes atmospheric pressure into consideration:

$$PI_{O_2} = (P_B - 47) \times FI_{O_2}$$

P_B is barometric pressure, and 47 represents the partial pressure of water vapor at body temperature. The PI_{O_2} is used to determine oxygen toxicity.

The term *atmosphere of oxygen* was developed to allow PI_{O_2} to be expressed in terms of atmospheric pressure. This term is calculated:

$$\text{Atmosphere of oxygen} = \frac{PI_{O_2}}{760}$$

where 760 represents atmospheric pressure at sea level.

The following examples may help to conceptualize these terms:

1. An astronaut is exposed to a barometric pressure of 258 torr (one-third atmospheric pressure) with an FI_{O_2} of 1.0. The effective dose of oxygen equals $PI_{O_2} = (258 - 47) \times 1 = 211$ torr. Exposure is equal to 0.28 atmosphere (atm), or $211/760 = $ atm O_2. Because of the hypobaric environmental conditions, the astronaut will not develop oxygen toxicity in spite of the high FI_{O_2}.

2. An underwater sea diver descends to a depth of 165 ft (6 atm of pressure with a barometric pressure of 4560 torr), breathing compressed air with an FI_{O_2} of 0.21. The effective dose of oxygen is 948 torr PI_{O_2} ($4560 - 47 \times 0.21 = 948$). The diver has an exposure to 1.25 atm O_2 ($948/760 = 1.25$). The diver is subject to oxygen toxicity, although the FI_{O_2} is the same as room air. Under hyperbaric conditions, the FI_{O_2} must be decreased to extremely low levels if protection from oxygen toxicity is a priority.

Oxygen is a drug, and like any other drug, toxicity is determined by host tolerance, effective dose, and duration of exposure. Host tolerance is very difficult to assess. There is tremendous species variation in response to oxygen. There is a great deal of variation between individual humans and, at times, within the same individual. See Table 23-3 for some strongly suspected modifying factors (Clark, 1974).

Most of this information is the result of study on animals, and one should be somewhat cautious in generalizing results of animal research to humans because of species variation in response. The fact that steroids, hypercarbia, and hyperthermia may facilitate the development of oxygen toxicity could have some clinical significance, since most critical-care patients experience at least one if not all of these conditions in the critical-care unit. It also seems to contraindicate the use of steroids to treat the proliferative phase of oxygen toxicity, a common practice in some areas, and is a serious consideration against the use of steroids in ARDS.

While host tolerance is not able to be manipulated, both dose and duration can be. The relationship between dose and duration is seen in Fig. 23-5. The shape of this curve resembles that of other toxic agents; high doses produce toxicity after brief intervals, and low levels do so with prolonged exposure. Most current evidence suggests that clinically detectable oxygen toxicity does not develop within the first 24 h at an FI_{O_2} of 1.0 and at 1 atm (Clark and Lambertsen, 1971). However, undetectable toxic effects may be occurring at the cellular level. For example, mucociliary clearance has been shown to decrease after 3 h of exposure at an FI_{O_2} of 1.0 and at 1 atm. A safe level for prolonged exposure is generally considered to be an FI_{O_2} of 0.40 to 0.50, since men have been shown to tolerate 40% O_2 for periods of up to 30 days with no serious difficulties.

Intermittent exposure seems to be the strongest minimizing factor for development of oxygen toxicity. This is an excellent area for future research. However, at present, critical-care practitioners are already using PEEP and CPAP to keep oxygen exposure as low as possible while maintaining adequate tissue oxygenation. It would be a gross error in judgment to jeopardize tissue oxygenation intermittently for the purpose of minimizing oxygen toxicity.

The clinical stages of oxygen toxicity can be divided into two phases. The early phase primarily involves the larger airways and the late phase affects the alveoli.

The most consistent physiological finding in oxygen toxicity is a gradual decrease in vital capacity

TABLE 23-3 Factors That Modify Host Susceptibility to Oxygen Toxicity	
Increase Toxicity	Decrease Toxicity
Corticosteriods	Intermittent exposure
Hypercarbia	Adrenergic blocking drugs
Seizures	Anesthesia
Epinephrine	Antioxidants
Norepinephrine	Chlorpromazine
Hyperthermia	Hypothermia
Insulin	Hypothyroidism
X-irradiation	Reserpine

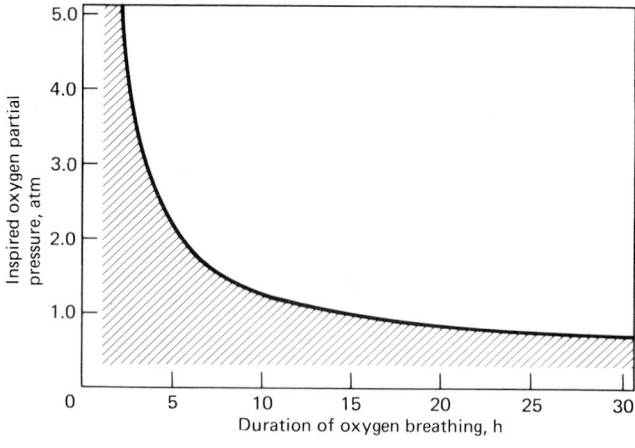

FIGURE 23-5

Pulmonary oxygen tolerance curve in normal men, based on a 4 percent decrease in vital capacity. A plot of the inspired oxygen partial pressure vs. duration of oxygen breathing. Safe dose-duration combinations are within the hatched area. [*From S. J. Menn and G. M. Tisi, in G. G. Burton, G. N. Gee, and J. E. Hodgkin (eds.), Respiratory Care: A Guide to Clinical Practice, Lippincott, Philadelphia, 1977.*]

that begins after 5 h of exposure to 100% O_2 at 1 atm. Clinical symptoms of early oxygen toxicity include tracheobronchitis beginning in the area of the carina, cough, and inspiratory pain. In the late stages of this phase, dyspnea may develop.

The late phase of oxygen toxicity affects the alveolar unit. It has been reported to develop after 4 days exposure to 91% O_2 at 1 atm (Hyde and Rawson, 1969). During this phase, development of noncardiogenic interstitial and later alveolar pulmonary edema occurs. The clinical picture is the same as that previously described for ARDS.

The end stage of oxygen toxicity is one of progressive consolidation and fibrosis of the lung. If the patient's total dose exposure to oxygen is within the toxic range and a compatible clinical picture is present, the diagnosis of oxygen toxicity can be made. Detection of this condition is valuable because, while it is potentially lethal, the chance for complete recovery exists once O_2 levels are reduced below toxicity.

The pathologic picture of oxygen toxicity is the same as that previously described for ARDS. The earliest changes are an exudative phase including capillary endothelial cell damage and loss of membrane integrity, interstitial edema, alveolar hemorrhage, and destruction of type I pneumocytes. Following the death of the type I alveolar cells, the basement membrane is exposed and covered with fibrin and cellular debris, leading to the formation of a hyaline membrane.

The proliferative phase which follows includes hyperplasia of type II pneumocytes. The alveoli become lined with these abnormal cells, and fibroblasts proliferate in the interstitium. Once this stage occurs, recovery is unlikely and permanent fibrosis of the interstitium is probable.

Hypoxemia is a frequent occurrence in critically ill patients and its damage is usually rapid, often irreversible, and sometimes fatal. Pulmonary oxygen toxicity is uncommon, variable in onset, and slow developing. As previously stated, a patient should never be subjected to tissue hypoxia for the purpose of preventing oxygen toxicity. The best approach seems to be the judicious use of oxygen therapy to treat hypoxemia and tissue hypoxia without overtreating the problem and needlessly exposing the patient to excessive amounts of the drug. PEEP and CPAP should be utilized to the extent possible to avoid subjecting the patient to an $F_{I_{O_2}}$ greater than 0.40 to 0.50.

Near Drowning

Drowning is the cause of over 8000 deaths each year in the United States, 40 percent of whom are children under 4 years of age (Giammona, 1971). The statistics are actually misleading because they do not include victims who survive but cannot return to a productive life because of brain damage.

Submersion injuries are classified as drowning or near drowning. The drowning victim is one who dies within 24 h, while near-drowning victims survive for greater than 24 h. Both can be further divided as *wet,* when aspiration has occurred, or *dry,* when damage was caused by asphyxiation without aspiration. In the dry group, intact laryngeal reflexes probably cause laryngospasm, thus preventing aspiration. The wet group are more likely to have been obtunded and experienced aspiration.

The type of injury seen in near-drowning victims depends on the toxicity of fluid aspirated, the temperature, the nature of contaminants in the water (i.e., bacteria, protozoa, algae, sand, etc., which may have been aspirated), and the duration of hypoxia. In animal studies, major differences were found between aspiration of seawater (3.5% NaCl) and hypotonic fresh water. In humans, however, the clinical picture is similar for both. Every near drowning is a response to a unique set of contaminants and environmental circumstances. Many submersion injuries are preceded or accompanied by other primary events such as myocardial infarction, seizures, and spinal cord or head injuries due to a dive into shallow water. Near-drowning victims brought in for resuscitation should be carefully studied for other primary pathologies.

Hypothermia also has a dramatic impact in the near-drowning victim. Body temperature falls rapidly following submersion, since the thermal conduction properties of water are 32 times greater than those of air. Death before drowning may occur in healthy individuals swimming in cold water. Cold water immersion causes hyperventilation, which may result in hypocapnia, disorientation, and possible loss of consciousness, leading to drowning.

Hypothermia also increases blood viscosity, slowing flow through the coronary arteries and other vessels. Shifting of the oxyhemoglobin dissociation curve to the left results in an increased affinity of hemoglobin for oxygen and decreased oxygen unloading.

The hypoxemia after human submersion is caused by a combination of interstitial and alveolar pulmonary edema similar to that previously described for ARDS. There is damage to pulmonary capillaries, decreased surfactant, and a hyaline membrane type of formation by proteinaceous material. There is a decrease in pulmonary compliance, increased dead space, and increased intrapulmonary shunt. Ventilation and perfusion are mismatched, and there is an increased alveolar-arterial oxygen difference.

When first seen, victims of submersion injury may present with a variety of symptoms ranging from rales, rhonchi, and wheezes to cardiac arrest. A few may be relatively asymptomatic but proceed to develop ARDS within the next 24 h. All patients with a history of significant submersion should have medical observation for at least 24 h.

Therapeutic efforts for the pulmonary manifestations of near drowning are the same as those previously described in ARDS. The objectives of increasing lung volumes and matching ventilation with perfusion can be accomplished with the use of mechanical support with IMV ventilation, PEEP, and circulatory support when needed. Mask CPAP may prove very beneficial in patients who are hypoxemic but can maintain a normal Pa_{CO_2}. Mask CPAP should not be used in patients who are obtunded or unconscious because of the hazard of vomiting and aspiration.

There are reports of survival after prolonged submersion and cardiac arrest in very cold water. One report describes a submersion and cardiac arrest lasting approximately 40 min that was followed by survival without significant residual neurological deficits (Siebke et al., 1975). In such cases the decrease in metabolic rate, cellular metabolism, and oxygen consumption in the central nervous system and heart may have prevented damage from hypoxia. Resuscitation should be attempted in the hypothermic drowning victim even though prolonged submersion may have occurred.

Families and friends of near-drowning victims require a great deal of psychological support from critical-care unit personnel. Near drowning represents the extremely sudden onset of critical illness for which family members are totally unprepared. They have not had time to develop any coping mechanisms and certainly will be in the very earliest stages of the grieving process. ICU personnel should also be sensitive to the possibility of extreme guilt plaguing the family members of these patients. If the victim is a small child, the parents may carry unrealistic amounts of guilt regarding supervision of the child. Regardless of the known circumstances surrounding the submersion incident, if family members or friends of the patient exhibit behavior indicating that they are having difficulty coping with the situation, an appropriate referral to a chaplain, psychiatric social worker, or psychologist should be initiated.

Extracorporeal Membrane Oxygenation

For over a decade the use of extracorporeal membrane oxygenation (ECMO) has been researched as an alternate method in the treatment of ARDS. ECMO is the term given to extracorporeal pulmonary bypass life-support system. The concept is basic. Blood, unable to be oxygenated by the lungs, is removed from the body, passed through a membrane oxygenator where it undergoes gas exchange, and is returned to the circulation. It is a similar principle to kidney dialysis or the cardiopulmonary bypass employed during open-heart surgery. Initial research was directed to the possibility that, if patients with severe unresponsive respiratory failure could maintain oxygenation by artificial means, the lung could heal and mortality be reduced.

Technique

Removal of blood from the body is performed by direct cannulation. Since blood flows of over 5 L/min are often used, large-bore cannulas are needed. These can be inserted under local anesthesia by a team experienced in cannulation. Five perfusion routes have been documented (Table 23-4). Since venous drainage is facilitated by gravity, the bed is usually placed on shock blocks to elevate the entire frame off the floor.

Once the selected sites have been cannulated, blood is drained into a membrane lung. This drainage may or may not be facilitated by a pump. At this time, there are a number of commercially made "lungs" available. Each has specified surface areas, volumes needed for priming, areas for diffusion, and blood flow resistance. Membranes are made from a multitude of materials including ultrathin silicone rubber, filler-free silicone, porous Teflon, and a variety of polymers. Many of these are still under investigation. The ultimate goal in selection of a membrane is the capability of high oxygen and high carbon dioxide exchange and low perfusion pressures. This must be

TABLE 23-4
Cannulation Sites for ECMO

Perfusion route	Placement of cannula		Blood flow		Comments
	Drainage	Return	Deoxygenated drainage	Oxygenated return	
Venovenous (VV)	Femoral vein	Internal jugular vein	Inferior vena cava	Superior vena cava	Adapted for children by cannulation in right atrium via right jugular and femoral vein
Venoarterial (VA)	Femoral vein	Femoral artery	Inferior vena cava	Aorta	Indicated with increased pulmonary artery pressure since route decreases pulmonary blood flow
Mixed venovenous and veno-arterial (VVA)	Femoral vein	Internal jugular and femoral artery	Inferior vena cava	Superior vena cava and aorta	Disadvantage of two incision sites and need for flowmeter to determine return to arterial and venous systems
Venoarterial with aortic arch return (VA-arch)	Femoral vein	Femoral artery to aortic arch or axillary artery	Inferior vena cava	Aortic arch	Better distribution of oxygenated blood to brain and coronary arteries
Arterio-venous (AV)	Femoral or brachial artery	Femoral vein	Aorta	Inferior vena cava	Requires increased cardiac output, but can be used without pump

achieved with minimal damage to blood components. The blood flow past the membrane is usually 2 to 5 L/min and is determined by body weight. Once the blood has been oxygenated, it is propelled back into the circulation of the body by a standardized roller pump.

Selection of Patients

The selection of patients for ECMO is a widely debated topic. In 1974 a national study was undertaken by the National Heart and Lung Institute to determine whether ECMO had any advantages over conventional methods. The entry criteria to the study were as follows:

1. With maximal therapy: Pa_{O_2} less than 50 mmHg for greater than 2 h when measured at FI_{O_2} 1.0 and PEEP greater than 5 cmH$_2$O

2. After maximal medical therapy for 48 h:

   a. Pa_{O_2} less than 50 mmHg for greater than 12 h when measured at FI_{O_2} 0.6 and PEEP greater than 5 cmH$_2$O

   b. Qs/QT (shunt) greater than 30 percent cardiac output when measured at FI_{O_2} 1.0 and PEEP greater than 5 cmH$_2$O

Excluded from the study were the following patients: those under 12 or over 65 years of age; those with a duration of pulmonary injury more than 21 days; those with chronic systemic disease (COPD; heart, liver, renal failure or irreversible brain damage); and those with severe body burns.

Once patients met the entry criteria they were assigned to the control group or the experimental group. The controls were managed with optimal mechanical ventilation therapy, while the experimental group were started on ECMO. The descrepancies and results of this study and subsequents reports of ECMO will be discussed later.

Management

Once the decision is made to start ECMO, a total team approach is necessary. The care of the patient requires the presence of a physician, a critical-care nurse, and a pump technician. The enormous workload usually necessitates the presence of two qualified RNs. All members of the team must be trained to evaluate, manage, and troubleshoot the problems of the patient on ECMO. A protocol for starting and maintaining ECMO is a must. A "Who does what, where, and when?" approach saves time and avoids confusion. A sample of such a protocol is seen in Table 23-5.

The patient is sufficiently heparinized to prevent clotting problems, usually by continuous heparin infusion. The pump is also "primed" with heparinized whole blood. Bovine lung heparin has been used

TABLE 23-5 Initiation of ECMO for Respiratory Failure	
Job title	Job responsibility
Physician	Notifies team of decision
	Notifies family and obtains consent
	Supervises priming of the pump by pump technician
	Coordinates all activities of team
	Analyzes baseline data to maximize therapy
	Orders ventilator settings and pharmacologic agents
Registered nurse	Sends blood specimen for type and cross match and 10 U of whole blood
	Obtains complete set of vital signs (temperature, pulse, blood pressure, pulmonary artery pressure, wedge pressure, cardiac output)
	Obtains specimen for arterial blood gases, hemoglobin/hematocrit, coagulation profile, activated clotting time, SMA 6, SMA 12, CBC, and platelet count
	Shaves and prepares area for cannulation
	Ensures adequate sedation and psychological support for patient during cannulation
Nursing assistant and unit secretary	Clears bedside area designated for cannulation and perfusion
	Assembles equipment needed by team at bedside
	Handles all paperwork and directs calls to appropriate personnel
Pump technician	Assembles and primes pump with physician

because of a belief that it may be more stable. Activated clotting times are useful hourly measurements to maintain anticoagulation. A baseline measurement should be obtained before starting ECMO; a clotting time above 120 s is recommended for maintenance of anticoagulation. Whole blood, fresh-frozen plasma, and platelets are given to maintain the patient and help prevent bleeding problems.

Nursing the patient requires strict anticoagulant precautions. No skin punctures, shaves, or vigorous toothbrushing are allowed. Stools and nasogastric drainage should be checked for blood routinely. Nasogastric feeding is preferred to antiacid for the added nutritional benefit. Abdominal girths should be measured every 4 h. Inspection of the cannulation sites is necessary every hour. Minimal oozing is expected, but any more than that should be reported. Topical thrombin should be available at the bedside in case of hemorrhage. There should also be a minimum of 4 U of whole blood available immediately, if needed, and an additional 6 U within 10 min. This requires coordination with the blood bank, which should be apprised of the likely requirement for blood and blood products.

Ventilatory management is continued in order to maintain lung mechanical function. Controlled ventilation or intermittent mandatory ventilation is required. The maintenance of PEEP is useful to prevent further consolidation and fibrosis of lung tissue. Muscle relaxation with curare and pancuronium and sedation with morphine sulfate are usually recommended, although personal experience has shown that these patients may be managed with morphine alone. Lowering the patient's body temperature to 32 to 35°C may be helpful to reduce the metabolic rate and thus decrease oxygen consumption.

The main nursing responsibility is that of improving lung function by facilitating the drainage of secretions with chest physiotherapy. ECMO alone cannot do this. Position changes every 2 h (more frequently, if possible) and tracheobronchial suctioning are used as in other ARDS patients. (See Fig. 23-6.) Positioning on either side or semiprone is difficult with the presence of the perfusion lines, but all efforts must be made to do so. The patient must be observed for signs of tension pneumothorax, a frequent complication with such severe lung disease. Daily chest x-rays monitor progress.

The following are used for hemodynamic monitoring: pulmonary arterial pressure (PAP), pulmonary capillary wedge pressure (PCWP), cardiac output, and systemic arterial pressures. The drainage of large volumes of blood and the eventual return to the circulation have variable effects on the cardiovascular system. Accurate intake and output records and daily weights are needed to monitor fluid loss or accumulation. Other studies performed include SMA 6 and SMA 12, complete blood count with platelet count, coagulation profiles, arterial and venous blood gases, oxygen saturation, and hemoglobin/hematocrit. High lactate levels may indicate inadequate tissue perfusion.

The need for psychological support for this patient and family is more acute. The severity of the disease and the amount of "machinery" necessary may have devastating effects on the family.

Results

It is well known that although acute respiratory failure has a high mortality, it is also a reversible disease. The results of the national study did not show a significant decrease in mortality with the use of ECMO. Results of the national study and subsequent studies have shown equal survival rates in both the experimental and control groups, which remains a small 10 percent. The question arises as to the application of ECMO as a standard mode of therapy. The enormous cost and personnel time required is a major factor and limits its use to those institutions with sufficient funds.

The use of "optimal PEEP" has been suggested as an alternate means of management. Since the national study, high levels of PEEP (up to 60 cmH$_2$O) have been used. One must look carefully, therefore, at the validity of the entry criteria under the national study. 5 cmH$_2$O is really not considered an exhaustive ventilatory method. Most will agree that further studies concerning the use of ECMO are warranted. The types of patients who will benefit from ECMO, appropriate disease entities, and standard entry criteria are all areas for further research. So far, success has been achieved with severe infant respiratory distress syndrome (IRDS) and with the use of ECMO as a cardiopulmonary assist following cardiac surgery.

RESTRICTIVE LUNG DISORDERS

Lung Abscess

Lung abscess is a pyogenic lesion of the lung parenchyma giving rise to a cavity. Most often it is attributed to the aspiration of foreign material into the respiratory tract. It may also arise systemically by hematogenous spread or following a lung infarct.

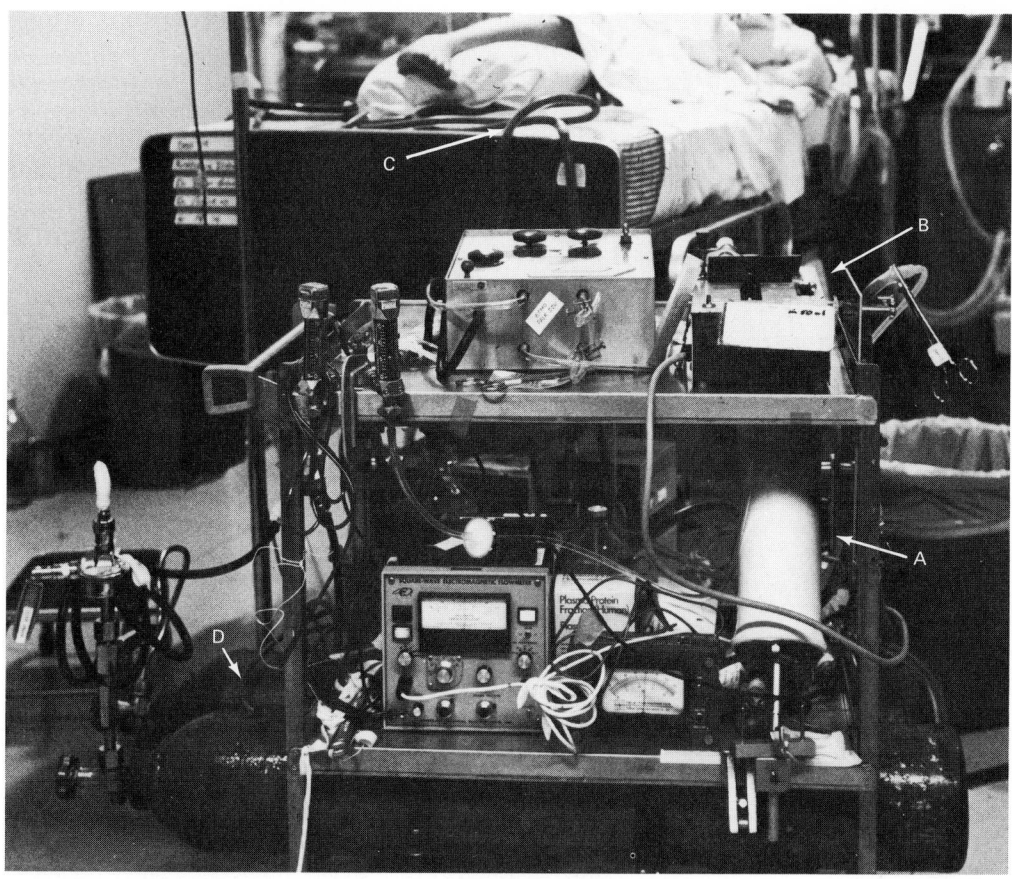

FIGURE 23-6

Extracorporeal membrane oxygenator. (A) Membrane lung. (B) Continuous heparin infusion. (C) Drainage and return catheters. (D) Oxygen tanks for gas delivery to membrane lung. Note frame of the bed is approximately 12 in off the floor and the patient is positioned on left side, despite cannulation in the femoral artery and vein. (*Photograph courtesy of Christopher Bryan-Brown, M.D.*)

Obstruction of the bronchioles and stasis of secretions may contribute to the infection.

An aspiration abscess may be seen in any condition leading to a suppression of the cough reflex. This includes anesthesia, head injury, diabetic coma, drug overdose, epileptic or alcoholic coma, and near drowning. A detailed history should be sought from patients suspected of lung abscess, since any of the above conditions can be found in up to 70 percent of the cases, alcoholic coma being the most common. (See Table 23-6.) Oral infections such as pyorrhea or infected tonsils may be unrecognized causes of abscess formation if the debris is aspirated.

Tumors that cause abscess formation are usually malignant, the most common being bronchial carcinoma (squamous cell type). These tumors are likely to become infected. They cause obstruction of lung segments by acting like a foreign body, causing stasis of secretions. Any patient with a diagnosis of lung abscess and no history of aspiration should undergo diagnostic testing for carcinoma. Very often chest therapy and antibiotics clear the abscess while the tumor remains undetected.

Necrosis of consolidated areas seen in bacterial pneumonia predisposes abscesses. These cyst-like sacs distend with inspired air and can easily burst into the pleura, causing collapse of the lung tissue. This mechanism is seen more frequently in children than adults because of the thin, less tough wall of the pleura in children.

TABLE 23-6
Common Causes of Lung Abscess

Type of abscess	Cause

Aspiration abscess	Alcoholism
	Post anesthesia
	Oversedation
	Coma (diabetic, epileptic,
	  drug overdose,
	  cerebrovascular
	  accident)
	Oral infection
	Food or foreign body
	Laryngeal palsy
	Carcinoma of esophagus
	  ("spill over" aspiration)

Malignant abscess	Necrotic bronchial
	  carcinoma
	Secondary to bronchial
	  obstruction and stasis of
	  secretions
	Head and neck
	  malignancies

Pulmonary embolus	Pulmonary infarct
	  infection
	Septic emboli
	Fragments from bacterial
	  endarteritis

Infection	Pneumonia
	Pyogenic bacteria
	  (notably staphylococcus
	  aureus)
	Defective ciliary action
	Inefficient expectoration
	Infected cysts
	Necrotic lesions
	Subdiaphragmatic
	  infections (usually liver)
	Open chest wounds

Pathophysiology

The site of the abscess is determined by the position of the body during aspiration. The aspirant will travel to the most dependent region of the lung. Thus, in a supine position, the foreign material will move into the right lung (recall the anatomic angle of the right main stem bronchus). From the right bronchus, material usually moves into the posterior segment of the upper lobe or superior segment of the lower lobe.

Fibrous granulation tissue usually forms around most of the abscess while it becomes embedded in the parenchyma. The abscess may extend toward the pleural cavity but rarely ruptures into it. Pleuritic pain and pleural effusion due to irritation of the pleural space by the granulation tissue may be seen. The abscess fills with pus and the now granulated portion often erodes into a bronchus, resulting in the drainage of foul-smelling pus into the trachea. When the pleuritic pain is not significant, often the aspiration of pus is the first sign of abscess formation. The expectoration of the pus may lead to partial healing and cavity formation. However, inadequate drainage and chest therapy can lead to multiple small abscesses within the lung.

Clinical Features

The onset of symptoms may be insidious or acute. Typically, general malaise and fever with or without pleuritic pain is seen. Over a number of days, fever with temperature spikes persists, pleuritic pain is evident, and there may be dyspnea, depending on the size of the abscess and its effect on lung tissue. The presence of foul-smelling pus in tracheal aspirant or expectoration clarifies the diagnosis. There may be blood-tinged purulent drainage due to bronchial erosion. Unfortunately, the symptoms are like those of pneumonia, and often the initial diagnosis is incorrect. For this reason the history is most important.

Physical examination shows a dullness to percussion and decreased or absent breath sounds with intermittent pleural friction rub depending on the extent of abscess formation and its proximity to the pleural space. Rales may be present. Chest x-ray shows areas of consolidation which may indicate other disease entities. It is not until a fluid level is evident, usually indicating communication with the bronchus, that the diagnosis can be narrowed down to either empyema with bronchopleural fistula or a lung abscess.

Treatment

The initial evaluation of the patient must determine the presence of anaerobic or aerobic pyogenic organisms. Antibiotic therapy is desirable and should include drugs effective against anaerobic organisms. The use of large-dose penicillin for 4 to 6 weeks is recommended. Although the culture report should be followed closely to determine sensitivity, flora is usually mixed. In general, however, the antibiotic therapy should be changed on a clinical basis when deterioration of the patient is noted and not on the basis of bacterial culture changes.

Chest physiotherapy and postural drainage are extremely helpful in draining an abscess that has communicated with a bronchus. Proper positioning according to the segment to be drained is essential.

Vigorous percussion will help loosen secretions and thereby enhance removal. The patient is encouraged to sleep in this position if possible. Frequent and vigorous mouth care (at least every 3 h) is essential. Since the purulent drainage is foul-smelling and bad-tasting, all attempts at patient comfort should be made. A mixture of one-half 3% hydrogen peroxide and water followed by mouthwash is often effective.

The use of therapeutic bronchoscopy for drainage is somewhat controversial. Diagnostically, bronchoscopy can be used to rule out carcinoma or foreign body. It can also be useful in locating the site of the draining bronchus, thereby aiding positioning to facilitate drainage. Some clinicians believe that bronchoscopy should be reserved for those cases that do not respond to other treatment. It can be used to aspirate the abscess and to obtain specimens for diagnostic purposes. The fear of spreading infection to other parts of the lung often deters clinicians from performing bronchoscopy.

The need for surgical treatment is rare but has been reported. Complications such as bronchopleural fistula, massive hemorrhage from erosion, and suspicion of carcinoma justify surgery, although each case must receive individual evaluation. The overall condition of the patient plus the response to therapy, even if prolonged, must be taken into account. Transpleural aspiration should not be attempted because of the possibility of empyema.

Pleural Effusion

The potential space between the visceral and parietal pleura is lined with a thin layer of fluid which constantly changes with the motion of the lungs. There are two types of fluid passage, classified on the presence or absence of protein. Protein usually enters the pleural space by leaking from the pleural capillaries and is drained by the lymphatic system. Protein-free fluid flows from the parietal pleura via systemic capillaries into the pleural space and is absorbed into the visceral pleura by the pulmonary capillaries. This mechanism is dependent upon hydrostatic and colloid osmotic pressures across the space.

Systemic capillary hydrostatic pressure (parietal pleura) is higher than the pulmonary capillary pressure (visceral pleura), with colloid osmotic pressure the same in both systems. The pleural space has an osmotic pressure below that of the two capillary systems it separates. Thus the hydrostatic pressure in the systemic capillaries, coupled with negative pleural pressure, forces the movement of fluid from the parietal pleura into the pleural space. Conversely, the lower hydrostatic pressure in the pulmonary capillaries and the higher colloid osmotic pressure in the systemic capillaries results in a shift of fluid into the visceral pleura. (See Fig. 23-7.) Since this movement of fluid is dependent on the various pressures, any hemodynamic changes in the cardiopulmonary sys-

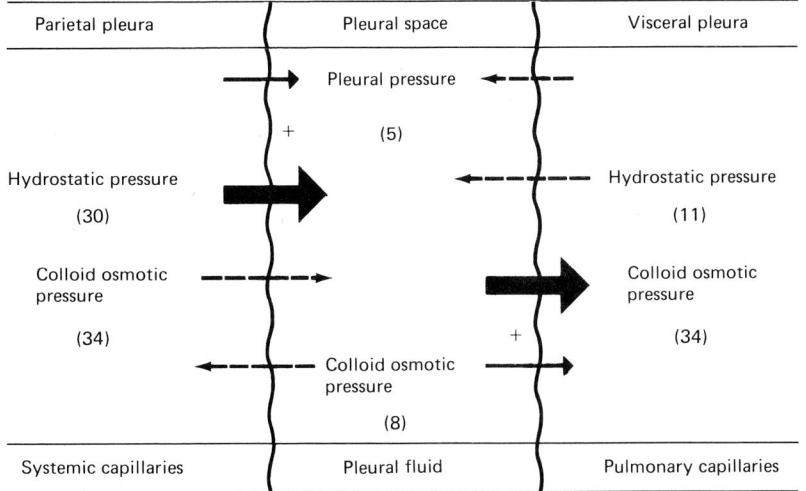

FIGURE 23-7

Process of pleural fluid formation and absorption in the pleural space. Fluid follows the direction of the black arrows because of pressure gradients. (*Adapted from R. W. Light, Pleural effusions,* Med Clin North Am *61:1341 1977.*)

tem will be reflected in the formation and absorption of fluid in the pleural space.

Pathophysiology

A pleural effusion is excess fluid in the pleural space. It is usually thought of as a sign of disease, not a disease entity in itself. Effusions are classified as transudate or exudate, with the distinction between them based on protein content.

Transudates are usually produced when there is a disturbance in the flow of protein-free fluid in the pleural space. Thus the protein content in transudates remains normal or less than 3 g per 100 mL. Pleural transudates are usually clear or pale yellow with a specific gravity of less than 1.015 and are usually bilateral. They are very often termed *hydrothorax*.

Exudates usually result from disease of the pleural surface, due to either increased permeability of capillaries with resultant leak of proteins or an obstruction in the lymphatic system inhibiting drainage of proteins. Therefore, the protein content in exudates is high, usually more than 3 g per 100 mL. The specific gravity is increased (more than 1.016) because of the increased protein. The exudate fluid is often dark yellow or amber in color and usually unilateral.

A partial listing of the causes of pleural effusion categorized as exudate or transudate is shown in Table 23-7. It is necessary to differentiate the type of effusion in order to determine the etiology. Transudates, since they are not caused by pleural disease,

do not usually require the extensive diagnostic follow-up that is often needed for exudates.

A number of tests for pleural fluid are available to differentiate exudates from transudates and to diagnose the cause of exudates. Beside the color, the amount of protein, and the specific gravity, other tests are the differentiation of serum and pleural lactic acid dehydrogenase (LDH) and protein levels, red cell count, white cell count with differential, pleural fluid cytology (for malignant cells), glucose, amylase, pH, and culture with bacteriologic stains.

Clinical Features

Pleural effusions usually show a restriction of chest wall expansion on the affected side if the effusion is large. Dullness to percussion and absent or decreased breath sounds over the area are noted. If the effusion is infected or purulent, temperature elevation may be present. Dyspnea in a rapidly accumulating effusion is common, while chronic or slow accumulation may show no respiratory distress.

Chest x-ray abnormalities may be undetectable if the effusion is small (less than 100 mL). Larger effusions are seen as dense opacities. A level of fluid may be observed in a gravity-dependent position; thus, if the patient lies on the affected side prior to x-ray, fluid may be seen in the lateral chest wall.

Management

Any pleural effusion should be subjected to a diagnostic tap (thoracentesis). Chemical, cytological, and bacteriological analyses may yield valuable information to determine cause.

The position of the patient during the procedure is important to prevent the occurrence of pneumothorax or hemothorax. The patient sitting on the edge of the bed and leaning forward onto an over-bed table is a good position for a lateral or posterior tap. The skin is cleaned with iodophor or iodine solution and anesthesized with local anesthesia. A tap requires inserting the needle into the intercostal space along the upper surface of the lower rib. The presence of fluid confirms entrance into the pleural space. Usually no more than 1000 mL of fluid should be drained rapidly, and even less if the patient exhibits signs of respiratory distress. A pleural biopsy is also recommended at this time.

Recurrent pleural effusions present a management problem. Effusion from bronchial carcinoma and metastatic tumors from extrathoracic sources fall into this category. Very often a malignant effusion reaccumu-

TABLE 23-7
Causes of Pleural Effusions

Transudates	Exudates
Congestive heart failure	Metastatic disease
Hypoproteinemia	Tuberculosis
Cirrhosis	Viral infections
Myxedema	Bacterial infections
Sarcoidosis	Pulmonary infarction
Meigs's syndrome	Systemic lupus
Constrictive pericarditis	erythematosus
Nephrotic syndrome	Pancreatitis
Peritoneal dialysis	Subphrenic abscess
	Trauma
	Whipple's disease
	Hepatic abscess
	Acute rheumatic fever
	Uremia
	Postmyocardial infarction
	syndrome

lates shortly after it is aspirated. Attempts are made to eliminate or reduce the number of recurrent effusions. The use of nitrogen mustard instilled in the pleural space has been reported to slow down the rate of effusion. Pleurodesis using iodized talc in an aerosol produces similar results.

The nurse must be aware of the conditions which precipitate effusions. Since malignancy carries a high incidence of fluid accumulation, those patients being diagnostically worked up for lung cancer should have frequent chest auscultation. Any decreased or absent sounds, as well as signs of dyspnea, should be reported at once.

Kyphoscoliosis

Kyphoscoliosis is not only an orthopedic problem, but may severely impair respiratory and cardiovascular function. Scoliosis is curvature of the spine laterally (twisted); kyphosis is curvature forward. This spinal deformity usually starts in adolescence as scoliosis and later becomes kyphotic. The condition may rarely be due to Pott's disease (tuberculosis of the spine), where the kyphosis is more pronounced, poliomyelitis, rickets, or osteoporosis in the aged. Unfortunately, the majority of cases are designated idiopathic.

Pathophysiology

The impairment of respiratory function results from distortions in the shape of the lung and the rib cage, which prevent normal expansion. If there is a cone-shape effect, compression of the lung by the chest wall is usually more severe at the bases, with atelectasis and bronchopneumonia common findings. Overexpansion of the upper lobes may be evident. Rigidity of the chest wall is common with advancing age.

This rigidity of the chest wall and compression of the lung decrease the vital capacity, tidal volume, and alveolar ventilation, and increase the work of breathing. The atelectasis occurring alters the ventilation-perfusion ratio ($\dot{V}/\dot{Q}$) to increase shunting. The resultant hypoxemia and hypercapnia are pronounced in severe cases.

Constriction of the pulmonary vessels, primarily due to the compression of the chest cavity, may lead to pulmonary hypertension. The vascular resistance may be elevated from the effects of hypoxia, and the right ventricle may fail from continually forcing blood through the compromised pulmonary vasculature. The resultant right-sided failure and the ventilatory compromise is the usual cause of fatality.

Clinical Features

The main clinical signs of a patient with severe kyphoscoliosis are similar to those of cor pulmonale. Severe dyspnea and rhonchi are often present in the late stages of the disease. Lung volumes reveal decreased tidal volume, minute volume, vital capacity, functional residual capacity, and expiratory reserve volume. Arterial blood gas analysis reveals decreased Pa_{O_2}, increased Pa_{CO_2}, and decreased pH due to effects of progressive respiratory failure.

Pitting edema of the extremities is noted if the patient is in failure. Chest x-ray interpretation is often difficult because of poor positioning. The radiologic findings consistent with pneumonia and atelectasis are present.

Management

Initial management of the deformed chest wall in children is correction of the chest wall by body casts. Some increase in vital capacity has been achieved. Operative procedures may be effective.

Ventilatory support is necessary to maintain those with added acute respiratory failure from infection. High peak inspiratory pressure may be useful in improving the compliance of the chest wall, thereby improving lung compliance. The relationship between lung compliance and the amount of peak inspiratory pressure is still under investigation.

Treatment of kyphoscoliosis is purely symptomatic. Management of congestive heart failure and respiratory failure are described elsewhere in this book. Chronic therapy is similar to that of bronchitis. Recurrent infections, a common complication, are treated with antibiotics.

OBSTRUCTIVE LUNG DISORDERS

Asthma

Asthma is a term used to describe a recurrent, reversible airways obstruction with prolonged expiratory length, air trapping during attacks, ventilation perfusion mismatching, increased intrapulmonary shunt, cough, and tenacious sputum. The obstruction may be so mild that the patient experiences dyspnea only on exertion or so severe and prolonged that it results in respiratory failure and even death by asphyxia. Symptoms may be intermittent with normal pulmonary function between attacks or may cause chronic debilitation from compromised pulmonary function.

The acute obstruction of asthma is a reversible process involving spasm of the smooth muscle in the bronchial walls. As the episode progresses, mucus from the lumina of the bronchi, together with edematous inflammation of the mucosa, further narrows the airways. The resultant ventilation perfusion mismatch produces arterial hypoxemia.

Preventive care has decreased the morbidity associated with asthma in recent years, while more appropriate use of medications and respiratory therapy has improved the mortality associated with severe attacks.

Clinical Features

The signs and symptoms of asthma reflect the distal airway obstruction and interference with gas exchange. The primary symptom is that of dyspnea, or breathlessness. The patient has difficulty forcing air out of the lungs and frequently wheezes in the attempt. Prolongation of expiration is audible on auscultation.

Cough is another symptom of bronchospasm in asthma. As the attack progresses, the cough becomes productive, dyspnea and wheezing increase, and the patient may speak only in short phrases. Preferential body position is seated, forward tilt of the upper torso, arms braced, shoulders held high, and chest distended with little movement. There are retractions of the suprasternal notch and intercostal spaces.

In a very severe attack there may be so little air movement in the chest that a wheeze is not audible. Coughing is virtually impossible. The chest is hyperresonant and breath sounds are diminished. Heart tones are distant.

The pulse is rapid and thready. In very severe episodes the pulse may be paradoxical with diminished volume on inspiration. This is from decreased filling of the right atrium due to decreased lung compliance, itself a result of pulmonary overdistention and high intra-alveolar pressures. The patient becomes hypoxemic and cyanotic and lethargic or unresponsive. Asphyxia is imminent unless the symptoms are reversed. The term *status asthmaticus* denotes the point in the course of asthma at which the bronchospasm can no longer be relieved by bronchodilators.

The duration of asthma attacks is variable. It may be terminated by the use of medication, lasting 30 min to 1 h, or it may last for days or weeks. The frequency of attacks is even more variable. Some patients have a single attack once or twice a year, while others will be in a chronic respiratory distress with frequent acute exacerbations.

The exact point at which patients in acute asthmatic attack will tire, become severely hypoxemic, and lose consciousness is unpredictable. Some patients are in *status asthmaticus* almost as soon as symptoms begin. More commonly this occurs when there is a delay between the onset of symptoms and administration of medication. Patients on continuous high-dose therapy are more likely to present in *status* in the emergency room than those on seasonal or no medications at all.

The main abnormality in asthma is airways obstruction. Pulmonary function tests measuring timed expiratory gas flow are decreased. This includes the forced expiratory volume in 1, 2, and 3 s (FEV_{1-3}) and forced vital capacity (FVC). Functional residual capacity (FRC) is increased because of air trapping behind the bronchioles that have spasmed during expiration. Pulmonary function usually improves after inhalation of a bronchodilator, indicating reversibility of the obstruction. During a symptom-free period the pulmonary function studies might be completely normal. Drugs with bronchoconstrictor effects may be used in conjunction with pulmonary function testing to assess the degree of bronchial reactivity or diagnose asthma in a symptom-free period. The asthmatic patient usually develops frank bronchospasm in response to a dose of methacholine, which produces no discernible response in normal individuals.

Radiology is not extremely valuable in asthma. During an asthma attack the chest film may show hyperinflation, identified by a low diaphragm. The heart may be long and narrow and the peripheral vessels poorly visualized. The film is more beneficial if taken during expiration, since the lowered diaphragm is more obvious. The main object in chest radiographs is to exclude the presence of other conditions or complications, especially pneumothorax. Secondary infections may sometimes be detected, and impacted mucus may be suspected from segmental collapse.

Pathophysiology

Asthma reflects a hyperactive state of the bronchial airways to a variety of factors including extrinsic allergens. It is manifested by widespread airway narrowing that changes in severity either spontaneously or with treatment (American Thoracic Society, 1965). It has long been known that immediate hypersensitivity, mediated by immune globulin E (IgE), plays an important role in this syndrome.

Some clinicians divide asthmatics into an additional group referred to as *intrinsic* cases, or those with asthmatic bronchitis. This type of asthma is not mediated by IgE. Emotions and their impact on the sympathetic and parasympathetic nervous systems play a role in this process. Also, most individuals with chronic obstructive pulmonary disease (COPD) have some bronchospastic component to their disease which can be considered intrinsic asthma.

A theory called *beta blockade* suggests that an imbalance exists in the normal sympathetic-/parasympathetic nervous innervation of the airways. Beta-adrenergic receptors in the airways are responsible for bronchial smooth muscle relaxation when stimulated by cyclic adenosine monophosphate (cAMP). When there is no β_2 stimulation, cAMP is lower and bronchoconstriction occurs.

Cardiopulmonary blood vessels are also supplied with β_1 receptors. Stimulation of these receptors produces vasoconstriction and undesirable side effects including tachycardia, possibly arrhythmias, and blood pressure alteration. Without β stimulation, bronchoconstriction occurs in response to a variety of stimuli including hyperventilation, extreme temperature and humidity changes, emotional disturbances, infection, and the classic "allergic" response to extrinsic allergens.

In some individuals, upper airway irritation may cause bronchoconstriction by stimulation of the vagus nerve. This parasympathetic stimulation may also ennance mucus secretion and be responsible for the cough and hyperventilation that accompany bronchospasm. Parasympathetic blockade using atropine might initially appear to be advantageous because of the drying of bronchial secretions that it produces, but it is contraindicated because of the increased risk of bronchial plugging. Parasympathetic and sympathetic forces create two opposing systems, then, with parasympathetic stimulation encouraging bronchospasm while sympathetic stimulation of both alpha- and beta-receptors favors bronchial relaxation.

Chemical mediator substances also exist that influence the degree of bronchoconstriction. These mediators are released by mast cells in the pulmonary submucosa. Mast cell stimulation causes a release of these mediators, producing bronchoconstriction and/or vasodilation. These include histamine, slow-reacting substance of anaphylaxis (SRS-A), prostaglandins, serotonin, and bradykinin. These mediators are inhibited by cAMP. Another mechanism in addition to its direct effect on smooth muscle that β_2 stimulation produces is bronchial relaxation, since such stimulation increases cAMP. Figure 23-8 shows the effects of alterations in sympathetic and parasympathetic

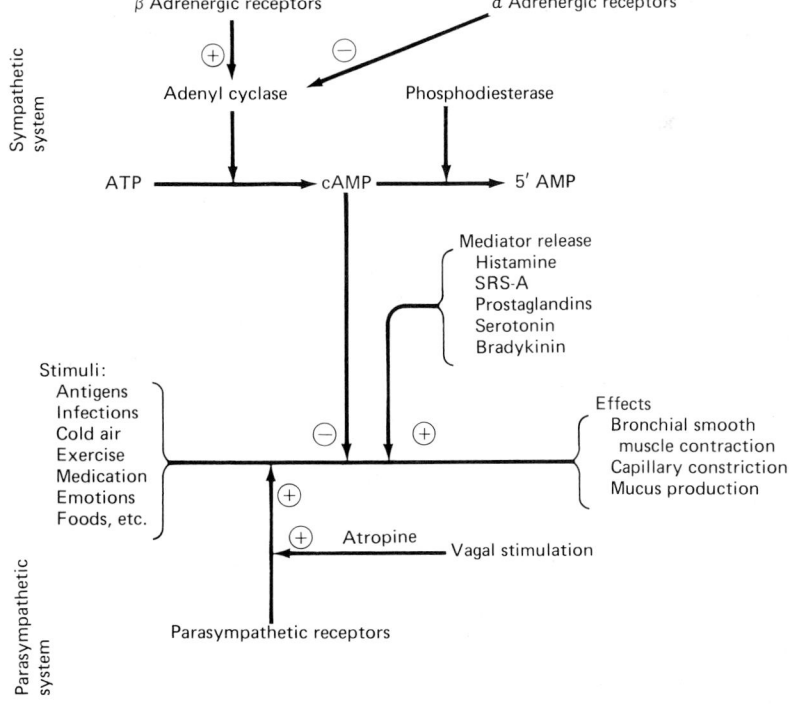

FIGURE 23-8

Sympathetic and parasympathetic influence on the development of bronchospasm.

influence on the development of bronchospasm, as well as the effects of mast cell mediator substances.

It is important to remember that severe bronchospasm involves more than just bronchoconstriction. Bronchial wall edema and mucus hypersecretion are also important contributors to pathophysiologic changes during asthmatic crisis.

Once bronchospasm has developed, a variety of events follow, as shown in Fig. 23-9. Marked pulmonary hyperinflation may result. Total lung capacity may increase by up to 30 percent, and residual volume is markedly increased. An overinflated lung is stiff and compliance is low, and this increases the work of breathing. The patient then begins to perceive dyspnea, a hallmark of asthma attack. This process is aggravated by anxiety and a reflex hyperventilation.

As a result of hyperventilation, Pa_{CO_2} is usually low during an attack. If severe bronchospasm persists, however, the patient tires and cannot maintain hyperventilation. Pa_{CO_2} will rise to normal and finally become elevated. Excessive sedation or narcotic administration decreases ventilatory drive and can hasten decompensation during an asthma attack. Decreasing overall ventilation combined with venti-lation-perfusion mismatching leads to hypercapnia, and mechanical ventilation is needed to maintain the patient.

Accumulation of secretions in airways leads to cough, which may stimulate more bronchospasm. Bronchial hygiene and maintenance of adequate hydration are important in controlling the problems associated with accumulation of secretions.

Hypercapnia is a late sign noted only in severe and prolonged asthma attacks. Hypoxemia is the common blood gas abnormality and results from the shunt created by uneven ventilation and perfusion. Oxygen therapy is needed to treat the hypoxemia, but assisted ventilation is necessary if the Pa_{CO_2} starts to rise.

In status asthmaticus the patient is severely distressed from the dyspnea and exhaustion. The patient is often unable to maintain adequate oxygenation and becomes cyanotic. Severely elevated intrathoracic pressures may interfere with venous return to the right heart, in which case cardiac output falls and vascular collapse may ensue. Dehydration due to fluid loss from hyperventilation may also contribute to impaired venous return. Cor pulmonale only occurs late, when

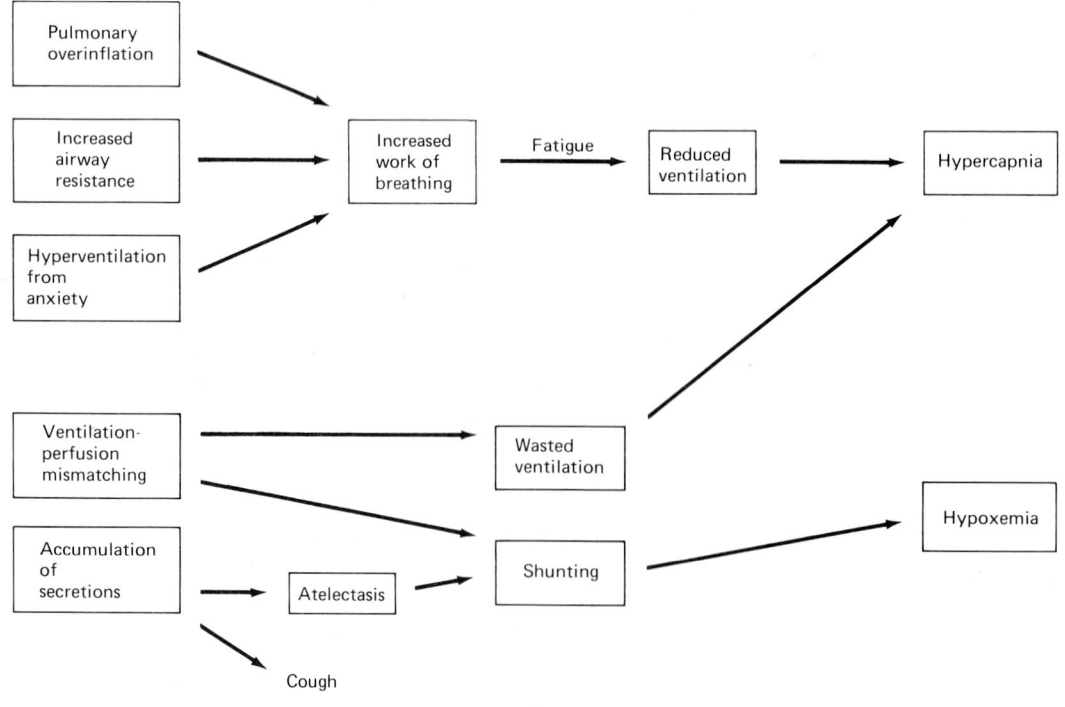

FIGURE 23-9
Consequences of bronchospasm.

the situation is desperate. Tachycardia indicates the stress placed on the cardiovascular system. A pulse rate greater than 120 in a patient who has not taken alpha-adrenergic stimulating drugs (i.e., epinephrine) signifies the need for urgent measures to be taken.

Therapy

Precipitating factors in asthma attacks are identifiable by careful history taking, and many are readily avoidable. Asthmatics should avoid known bronchial irritants, promptly treat respiratory infections, and avoid drugs capable of inducing bronchospastic reactions, such as propranolol.

When a few specific allergens cause a large fraction of asthmatic episodes, hyposensitization injections may be helpful. This therapy induces the formation of IgG antibodies, which block antigen binding with IgE, although this is probably not the sole mechanism. In an unknown manner, hyposensitization also reduces IgE levels, at least in some cases. Unfortunately, hyposensitization is prolonged, expensive, and only partially effective. There may also be some risk in inducing large quantities of IgE, the type of antibody implicated in autoimmune disease.

Cromolyn sodium is an effective preventive agent in about 50 percent of asthmatics. This drug is not a bronchodilator but apparently blocks the release of chemical mediators of bronchospasm from the bronchial mucosa. (See Fig. 23-10.) It is administered as a propelled powder from a hand-held inhaler, and occasionally causes bronchial irritation on contact. Cromolyn sodium should not be given once bronchospasm has begun.

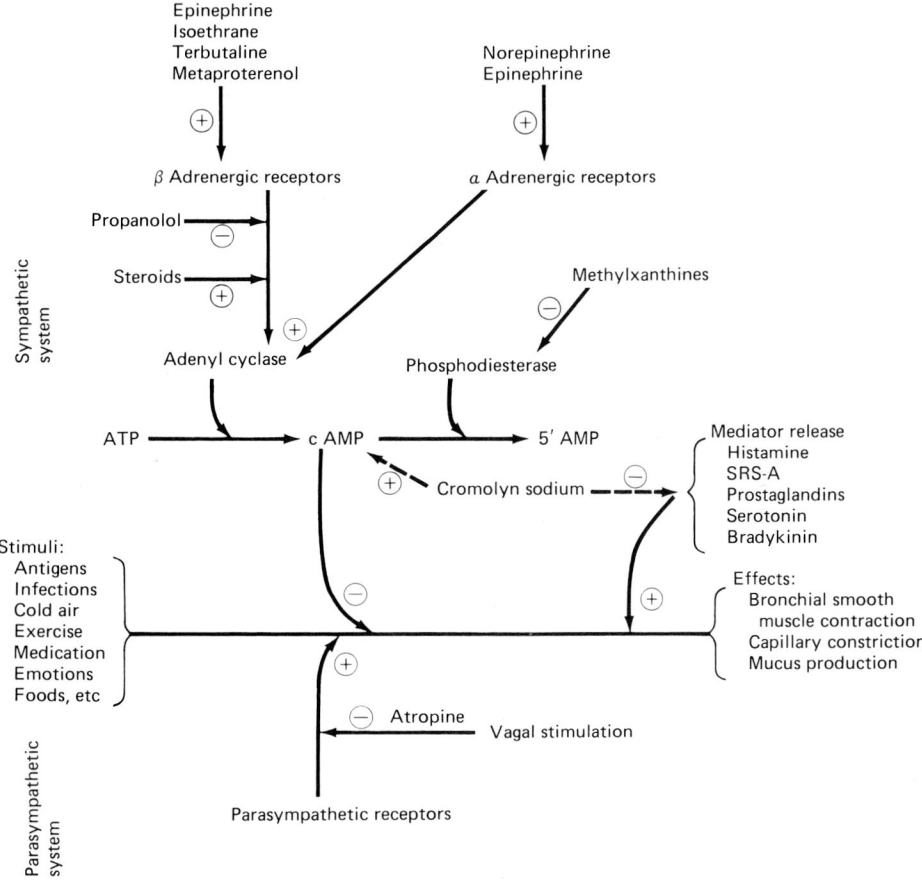

FIGURE 23-10

Interaction of pharmacologic agents with mechanism of asthmatic bronchosapsm.

Vigorous bronchial hygiene is essential during periods of asthmatic exacerbation to keep airways clear and minimize ventilation-perfusion mismatching. Adequate fluid intake is necessary to prevent dehydration from hyperventilation and to liquefy secretions.

Inhaled bronchodilators should be used but not abused. Isoetharine combined with phenylephrine is useful as a metered preparation (Bronkosol) as well as by nebulization. It is a relatively selective β_2 agent and is particularly useful in bronchospastic patients who are hypoxemic and who have tachycardia or underlying coronary artery disease. Metaproterenol (Alupent, Metaprel) is claimed to have fewer cardiac stimulatory side effects than drugs like isoproterenol, but this requires further investigation. β_1 side effects of metaproterenol are probably as common as those of isoproterenol. Terbutaline (Breathine) has a higher β_2/β_1 ratio than either isoproterenol or metaproterenol and possesses negligible alpha activity. Oral administration of this drug has a marked tendency to produce muscular tremor and nervousness. Beclomethasone (Vanceril) is a metered inhaled steroid preparation which delivers 50 μg per puff. Investigations suggest use of up to 2 mg per day without significant steroid absorption (Gaddie et al., 1973). Most asthmatics do well on smaller doses, and many steroid-dependent patients have been transferred from oral preparations, which cause Cushing's syndrome, to safer aerosol therapy.

The beneficial actions of steroids in asthma are not fully understood, but the following actions are believed to be of significant benefit: (1) prevention of antibody-antigen reaction by inhibition of antibody formation; (2) inhibition of formation or storage of mediators such as histamine; and (3) inhibition of nonspecific inflammatory processes. Steroids potentiate sympathomimetic drugs, probably by acting on β_2 receptors, producing smooth muscle relaxation and increasing circulating levels of cAMP. The anti-inflammatory steroids (glucocorticoids) are beneficial in status asthmaticus of any cause.

Prednisone and prednisolone are oral steroid agents suitable for maintenance use. They are similar to hydrocortisone but more potent. During acute exacerbations they may be given in large doses of 40 to 70 mg per day for 5 to 7 days, titrated down to a maintenance dose of 5 to 20 mg per day. Cushing's syndrome can develop with prolonged use. Many asthmatics do well on alternate-day dosage schedules, which decrease the incidence of unwanted side effects. In cases of status asthmaticus in the critical-care unit, intravenous hydrocortisone (Solu-Cortef) can be given as 250 to 500 mg initially followed by 100 to 250 mg every 3 h.

Patients with bronchospasm benefit greatly from any drug with bronchodilator capability. Epinephrine, 0.2 to 0.5 mL of 1:1000 solution by subcutaneous injection, was formerly used extensively, though now its use has been largely supplanted by methylxanthines (aminophylline) and inhaled drugs. Epinephrine has α, β_1, β_2 effects, and thus, in addition to being a potent bronchodilator, it has unwanted cardiovascular and nervous system side effects. It is dangerous to use in individuals with underlying cardiac disease, especially the elderly.

Isoproterenol was once the most popular bronchodilator and is one of the most potent β_2 stimulators. It does carry the risk of dangerous inotropic and chronotropic cardiac stimulation. Also, the unopposed β_2 effect causes vasodilation in the pulmonary vasculature which may produce mucosal congestion.

Methylxanthines are the most popular drug used to treat bronchospasm today. They inhibit phosphodiesterase activity, thereby preventing breakdown of cAMP and favoring bronchial relaxation. Theophylline has many additional beneficial effects including an increase in cardiac output, decrease in venous pressure, dilatation of pulmonary vascular bed, and improved renal circulation and cerebral stimulation.

The most serious common side effect of theophylline and its derivatives is increased gastric secretion, peptic irritation, and gastric bleeding. This is more common in oral preparations but is also a function of the blood level of the drug. Optimal therapeutic blood levels are close to toxic levels, and intermittent dosage may result in serum peak levels in the toxic range. Hepatic metabolism and renal excretion of the drug are often impaired, and for all these reasons, periodic serum drug levels should be monitored (preferably daily) in the critical-care unit. Gastric pH should be monitored whenever possible, and the use of antacids is recommended to minimize gastric complications.

Aminophylline is a synthetic theophylline derivative which is 20 times more soluble in water and can therefore be administered intravenously whereas theophylline cannot. A loading dose of 375 to 500 mg in an average adult who has not had recent administration of aminophylline is recommended. This is followed by 50 mg/h via slow intravenous drip.

Treatment priorities for the patient in status asthmaticus with hypoxemia and increasing Pa_{CO_2} are as follows: (1) oxygen inhalation via mask with patient breathing spontaneously or with manually or mechanically assisted ventilation; (2) normalization of pH when necessary (pH less than 7.35) with IV bicarbonate, preferably in an intravenous drip titrated to maintain a desired arterial pH; (3) pharmacologic management of bronchospasm as described above; (4) supportive measures such as bronchial hygiene and fluid therapy; and (5) as a last resort (in stupor, coma, or inability to clear airway secretions), tracheal intubation, curarization, and sedation, used with controlled ventilation. If mechanical ventilation becomes unavoidable, the patient must be sedated and probably paralyzed to avoid "fighting" the ventilator because of the high risk of pneumothorax and cardiac arrest. A pleural chest drainage apparatus should be readily available on "standby." The use of PEEP can be dangerous if large areas of the lung are already atelectatic because of overdistention of already open lung units. The use of expiratory retard achieves the effect of optimizing gas distribution but allows intrapulmonary pressures to reach atmospheric pressure at the end of expiration. Expiratory retard can also be added to a ball-valve mask apparatus for bag ventilation if mechanical ventilation can be avoided.

Chronic Bronchitis

Chronic bronchitis is a syndrome arbitrarily defined as cough with sputum production during at least 3 consecutive months and for at least 2 consecutive years.

Pathophysiology

The primary abnormality in this process is mucosal swelling, inflammation, and hypertrophy with excess production of thick, tenacious secretions in the airways. There is an increase in the size and number of mucus-secreting glands, which are overflowing with mucus. In the smaller bronchi and bronchioles, excessive numbers of mucus-producing goblet cells are found in the epithelial lining layer. Along the epithelial surface there is denuding of cilia in random fashion. Several inhalants have been implicated as causative agents in the development of chronic bronchitis, the most common of which is cigarette smoking. Other pollutants, such as oxides of nitrogen and sulfur dioxide, have been shown to diminish ciliary activity and stimulate hypersecretion of mucus. Patients with chronic bronchitis should be encouraged to stop their cigarette habit and examine their work environment for possible pollutants. Chronic bronchitis is primarily a reversible disease, since unlike emphysema, permanent structural damage does not occur until late in the course of the disease.

Diagnostic Findings

Expiratory prolongation is notable on physical exam, as in the emphysematous patient. During acute exacerbations, inspiration may also be prolonged because of occlusion of airway lumens by secretions. Percussion is usually normal, and auscultation will reveal rales, rhonchi, and wheezes. The sounds are usually loud and are caused by secretions in the airways. Peripheral edema, hepatomegaly, and cyanosis are present in the patient with severe bronchitis and pulmonary hypertension (cor pulmonale).

On pulmonary function testing, flow rates during both expiration and inspiration may be reduced, although this is more pronounced on expiration. These patients have normal elastic recoil (in contrast to emphysema) and relatively normal diffusing capacities. Air trapping is consistent and depends on the severity of airways obstruction (see Table 23-8).

Patients with chronic bronchitis are sometimes called "blue bloaters" because they are cyanotic, hypercapneic, and have right-heart failure with peripheral edema. They are cyanotic and edematous because of the secondary cor pulmonale. All these changes are related to the severity of the disease process and the amount of ventilation-perfusion mismatch (primarily intrapulmonary shunt).

Treatment

Treatment for chronic bronchitis is aimed at airway clearance. Bronchodilator therapy to control any bronchospasm present (previously described) and adequate hydration are essential. Expectorants such as glyceryl guaiacolate (Robitussin TG) may be helpful but irritating to the stomach. Supersaturated solution of potassium iodine (SSKI) is frequently used but should be used with caution because of the side effects of parotid swelling, skin rash, hypothyroidism, and gastric irritation. When sputum becomes infected, appropriate antibiotic therapy should be used. Patients often have renewable prescriptions at local pharmacies and begin themselves on ampicillin or tetracycline whenever they note a change in sputum color or tenacity. There is controversy over whether the use of continuous antibiotic therapy for prophylaxis is of any value. Steroids and hyposensitization therapy are of no value. Chest physiotherapy is helpful for airway clearance.

TABLE 23-8
Pulmonary Function Profiles of Obstructive Pulmonary Diseases

Disease	Elastic recoil	Static compliance	Airway resistance	Residual volume/ total lung capacity	Bronchodilator response
Bronchitis	Normal	Normal	↑	Normal to ↑	+
Asthma	Normal (↓ in acute attack)	Normal (↑ in acute attack)	↑		++
Emphysema	Normal	Normal	Normal	↑	0

Emphysema

Pulmonary emphysema involves the enlargement of the distal terminal bronchioles with alveolar fragmentation and destruction of the alveolar septa. Lung elasticity (elastic recoil) is lost. Airway support is lost in emphysema because of the loss of parenchymal tissue, which normally gives structural support to the bronchioles and alveolar ducts. The terminal airways collapse during expiration. These patients also tend to retain secretions and develop repeated infections easily.

Approximately 80 percent of patients with chronic obstructive pulmonary disease have centrilobular emphysema in addition to chronic bronchitis. The major areas of destruction are the respiratory bronchioles. Another form of emphysema, *panlobular* or *panacinar,* is primarily caused by alveolar fragmentation. The most common cause of this emphysema is cigarette smoking. Also implicated are certain atmospheric pollutants such as oxidants, certain dusts, and cadmium vapors. One form of panlobular emphysema results from a genetic deficiency of the enzyme α_1 antitrypsin. This enzyme inactivates proteases from white blood cells which, when not inactivated, destroy lung parenchyma.

Pathophysiology

Ventilation, diffusion, and perfusion are all altered in emphysema. Ventilation is regionally decreased because of loss of elastic recoil, poor support of terminal airways, gas trapping, and poor alveolar gas mixing in the involved areas.

Pulmonary diffusion is reduced because of a loss of alveolar surface area and pulmonary vasoconstriction. Hypoxemia and pressure from adjacent distended alveoli may decrease perfusion to normal alveoli, further reducing capillary blood volume and decreasing diffusing capacity.

The perfusion abnormality is one in which hypoxemia causes generalized pulmonary artery constriction shunting blood away from even relatively normal areas of lung.

Cor pulmonale usually occurs during exacerbations of the disease, late in its course. This is probably due to hypoxia producing pulmonary hypertension against which the right heart must pump. The right ventricle, which normally pumps against low resistance, dilates.

Diagnostic Findings

A barrel chest deformity is characteristic of advanced emphysema. There is kyphosis, increased anterior-posterior diameter, horizontal ribs, wide subcostal angles, and flat, immobile diaphragms. Hyperresonance to percussion, decreased breath sounds, and restricted chest wall movement are present. If crepitant rales are present, they will be heard bilaterally at the bases, particularly in those with cyanosis. Cor pulmonale, hepatomegaly, and peripheral edema may be present in severe cases. Prolongation of expiration is pronounced, and accessory muscles of respiration are used. The patient will elect to sit upright with arms braced in the "emphysematous habitus." Heart sounds may be difficult to hear.

The chest roentgenogram will show typically low-lying diaphragms, overexpansion, and a long, narrow heart. The lung fields will be hyperlucent with pronounced vessels and diminished peripheral vascular markings. The lateral view may show flattened diaphragms and an increased retrosternal air space. Sometimes bullae can be identified by fine, hairlike margins and lack of vascular supply.

Pulmonary function testing shows the increased residual volume (RV). The increased ratio of RV to total lung capacity (TLC) reflects expiratory airway collapse and airway trapping. Expiratory flow rates (i.e., FEV_{1-3}) will be significantly decreased because of loss of elastic recoil.

Arterial blood gas analysis will usually show hypoxemia. CO_2 retention may or may not be present. Patients who maintain good ventilation-perfusion matching (the "pink puffers") can maintain blood gases fairly well until late in the disease.

Treatment

Emphysema is an irreversible disease for which care is only supportive. Improved activity performance and decreased morbidity have been demonstrated in patients who participate in pulmonary rehabilitation programs. Pursed-lip breathing adds a form of expiratory retard to the patient's spontaneous respiration and may improve gas distribution. Most patients find that it eases their dyspnea.

Home oxygen is useful for patients who cannot maintain a Pa_{O_2} greater than 55 torr when breathing room air. Low-flow (1 to 2 L/min) oxygen at night is currently used to relieve pulmonary hypertension from hypoxemia and prevent secondary polycythemia.

Chronic obstructive pulmonary disease is a combination of emphysema and chronic bronchitis with a varied component of bronchospasm. Emphysema, like chronic bronchitis, can usually be managed with controlled oxygen therapy, chest physiotherapy to clear airways, bronchial hygiene, antibiotics to treat infection, and cardiovascular support. Low-flow oxygen by nasal cannula is usually used to treat these patients. When Pa_{CO_2} is chronically elevated, breathing drive is regulated by hypoxemia. Oxygen should be carefully monitored to avoid excessive exposure of the patient which might result in respiratory depression. Flow rates of 2 to 4 L/min are usually appropriate. Intrapulmonary FI_{O_2} will vary since it is determined by the tidal volume of room air the patient also inhales. Oxygen by Venturi principle face mask allows more precise administration of oxygen where necessary. Endotracheal intubation and mechanical ventilation are avoided if at all possible because of the high risk of complications and additional morbidity.

Criteria for endotracheal intubation and mechanical ventilation vary, but most agree that if Pa_{CO_2} increases above normal levels for that patient, and if acidemia and hypoxemia with mental obtundation are present, a need exists for more aggressive pulmonary support.

Continuous mechanical ventilation may impede venous return to the right heart and therefore cardiac output. This is more common in patients with COPD, since their highly compliant lung tissue conducts the increased mean intrapulmonary pressure to the heart and great vessels with ease. Downs et al. (1974) have shown that IMV can be successfully used in these patients. IMV offers the advantages of less influence on venous return as well as avoidance of the alkalemia, hypokalemia, and cardiac arrhythmias seen upon rapid reduction of Pa_{CO_2} on CMV. IMV allows the patient to breathe spontaneously with the exact amount of additional minute ventilation required to be delivered by the machine.

Weaning presents little or no difficulty with IMV, since it essentially begins with the onset of mechanical ventilation. The patient does not need to "relearn" breathing and retrain respiratory muscles, because they have been continually used. It eliminates the fear and anxiety experienced by these patients with abrupt removal of the ventilator during conventional weaning. This is particularly significant for this group of patients, since anxiety increases their dyspnea and may increase bronchospasm, making weaning more difficult and very traumatic.

Psychosocial Aspects of COPD

The relationship between the psychological and physical is closer, perhaps, in COPD than in most other chronic diseases. Many patients deal with their disease in one of two ways, and both are maladaptive. Some patients, when experiencing excitement, anxiety, or emotions like anger, become more active and hyperventilate. This adds more strain to their already maximally functioning cardiopulmonary systems and they become dyspneic. This dyspnea creates more anxiety, and a vicious circle ensues.

A second group of patients, possibly those who observed the relationship between their emotions and dyspnea, begin to fear emotion. They use mental defense mechanisms of isolation, denial, and depression to accomplish this. Nurses need to actively assess patients looking for these mechanisms and adjust the plan of care accordingly.

The patient's family also needs special support. With this disease complex the best they can hope for is extension of life and maximization of present level of function. They live from stage to stage of the disease with no hope for cure. They frequently have feelings of helplessness, fear, guilt, and anger. They usually feel so guilty about their feelings of anger that they frequently overprotect the patient. This definitely deters the patient from maximizing his or her own level of functioning. The family of the COPD patient needs and deserves support from the medical and nursing staff. Referral to the psychiatric social worker or staff psychologist may be indicated.

PERFUSION DISORDERS

Pulmonary Thromboembolism

Pulmonary thromboembolism (PTE) is probably the most frequently encountered diagnosis in a hospital today. The term is used to describe a blockage of a portion of the pulmonary arterial system by a blood clot arising from the systemic veins. Three factors concerning PTE should be considered. First, its incidence can be reduced if awareness of the high-risk factors predisposing PTE lead to prophylactic treatment. Second, misdiagnosis is a frequent occurrence because of the nonspecific signs and symptoms. Third, PTE may be grossly overdiagnosed and treated and used as a catchall to explain away symptoms.

Though pulmonary thromboembolism is tragically misdiagnosed, the pressure to overdiagnose needs understanding. "Spurious pulmonary embolus, a non-disease," can be defined as the diagnosis and treatment of a patient who does not have the disease (Stevens et al., 1979). This premise is based on two observations. One is that most statistics on the incidence of PTE have been gathered at postmortem examinations. The patients subjected to autopsy have been in a state of deterioration (a very high risk factor) prior to their death. Thus they are different from the rest of the hospital population. The other is that the incidence of positive diagnosis of PTE following pulmonary angiography has been cited as low as 20 to 30 percent (Stevens et al., 1979; Bell and Simon, 1976). This is a serious problem, since over half the patients who are thought to have the disease sufficiently severe enough to warrant pulmonary angiography have been misdiagnosed.

The fact still remains, however, that there is a high incidence of mortality from PTE, and it is well worth understanding the etiology of this condition. The most common type of embolus is that arising in a peripheral vein. It is usually a result of deep vein thrombosis in the lower part of the body, notably the soleal and pelvic veins.

Virchow, in 1846, described three contributing factors which predispose thrombus formation: stasis or reduction of blood flow, intercurrent illness, and vessel wall damage. Venostasis still remains a leading cause of deep vein thrombosis (DVT). Prolonged bed-rest, immobility due to old age or muscular weakness, and obesity may decrease blood flow. Long intra-operative procedures in which cardiac output is reduced, such as neurosurgery, decrease limb perfusion. Myocardial infarction and congestive heart failure also decrease cardiac output. A history of any of these factors should alert those managing critically ill patients to the increased possibility of PTE.

Changes in coagulation factors as a cause of thrombus formation are still under investigation. Studies have shown that there is an increased incidence of venous thrombosis and PTE during pregnancy and in women taking oral contraceptives. Estrogens are known to promote coagulation and increase platelet aggregation. It is also believed that coagulation changes may precipitate thrombus formation in the postoperative period and after abrupt discontinuation of anticoagulation therapy. Damage to the endothelial wall of a vessel may be precipitated by venostasis, trauma, or sepsis. Thrombus formation is enhanced by platelet adhesiveness and the release of serotonin. Both hypercoagulability and vessel wall injury are factors in thrombus formation, although they are usually seen in conjunction with venostasis. It is still uncertain whether they may cause thrombosis without accompanying stasis.

Pathophysiology

The formed thrombus can dislodge and travel through the circulation of the heart to rest in the pulmonary artery. Although the thrombus may dislodge spontaneously, the more common mechanism is the jarring of the clot from the vessel wall by mechanical forces. These forces include sudden standing, usually during initial ambulation, or changes in the rate of blood flow due to a Valsalva maneuver.

Smaller emboli tend to lodge in the distal branches of the pulmonary artery at the periphery of the lung. The severity of emboli is greater when a large number of small emboli travel to the lungs simultaneously or one large embolus blocks a larger vessel. The subsequent obstruction of blood flow in the pulmonary circuit has both respiratory and hemodynamic consequences.

Initially the number of perfused alveoli decrease, thereby increasing dead space or "wasted ventilation." Recall the property of ventilatory dead space as that of ventilated alveoli that are not perfused. This yields a ventilation-perfusion ($\dot{V}/\dot{Q}$) mismatch. Because no gas exchange can take place, bronchoalveolar hypocarbia results (decreased alveolar CO_2). Hypocarbia contracts the bronchial smooth muscle, causing bronchoconstriction and alveolar shrinking. This constriction leads to maldistribution of ventilation and increased airway resistance and thus increases the work of breathing. The constrictive response may be viewed as a protective measure, since the amount of wasted ventilation is reduced. The inspired air is propelled into functioning alveolar units, rather than the alveoli where diffusion cannot take place. This mechanism is not enough, however, to normalize the $\dot{V}/\dot{Q}$ ratio.

Another mechanism that leads to alveolar collapse is the reduction of surfactant. Cessation of blood flow probably leads to reduced surfactant levels. This reduction may be due to the anoxic effects on the mitochondria of alveolar type II cells, which produce it. Atelectasis as an end result of bronchoalveolar constriction and decreased surfactant levels usually occurs 24 to 48 h after obstruction to blood flow.

Hemodynamic consequences seem to depend on the extent of pulmonary blood flow obstruction and the cardiopulmonary status prior to the episode. The primary consequence of obstruction is the increase in pulmonary vascular resistance. The right ventricle must maintain enough pressure to propel blood through this resistance; thus an increase in pulmonary artery pressure (PAP) is seen. If this pulmonary hypertension is severe enough, the right ventricle will fail. Tachycardia and decreased cardiac output are frequently seen at this stage. Frequently PTE is not totally obstructive and the cardiopulmonary responses may only be slight.

There is evidence that humoral responses (e.g., release of serotonin from platelets surrounding the PTE) may be involved in the constrictive response of the bronchioles and terminal lung units. This is not necessarily in the areas affected by the embolus, and often involves functioning alveoli. Thus one sees perfusion with little or no ventilation because of the constriction of the alveoli. This may lead to areas of atelectasis and shunting, possibly explaining the arterial hypoxemia frequently seen in PTE. Another factor contributing to increased shunting is pulmonary hypertension. The responses to this hypertension have been described in the section dealing with adult respiratory distress syndrome (ARDS). The main response is the decrease in diffusion of gases in the lung. Thus, three main factors lead to ventilation-perfusion mismatching in PTE. One is the dead space effect of alveoli ventilated but not perfused because of the obstruction of blood flow from the thrombus.

Another is the shunting of blood past nonventilated alveoli that have collapsed from atelectasis. A third response is no ventilation and no perfusion seen in silent units. Refer to Chap. 19 for a more detailed description of ventilation-perfusion mismatch.

Pulmonary infarction as an end result of PTE is relatively uncommon. In most instances where infarct develops, there is the presence of underlying pulmonary disease which has already impaired pulmonary circulation or increased pulmonary congestion, as seen in cardiac failure. It is characterized by marked consolidation, usually from hemorrhage, and is frequently associated with pleuritic pain from pleurisy or effusion. Necrosis of the infarct can occur and become infected, forming a lung abscess. Healing of involved lung usually results in some degree of pulmonary fibrosis.

Clinical Features

One of the factors contributing to the misdiagnosis of PTE is the vagueness of the signs and symptoms. In general, sudden onset of dyspnea is the most common complaint. Unless the embolus is severe, this may be the only symptom. Massive PTE may produce symptoms of chest pain, the origin of which is unclear. Tachycardia and increased intensity of pulmonary S_2 can be seen when there is pulmonary hypertension. Other less frequent findings include nonspecific rales, mild temperature elevation, gallop rhythm, and possibly signs of phlebitis. Hypotension from peripheral vasoconstriction with accompanying cyanosis may be evident.

When pulmonary infarct has occurred, the symptoms are usually more specific. Cough, hemoptysis (usually seen as blood-tinged sputum), and pleuritic pain are relatively common. Signs of consolidation, pleural effusion, and infection of the infarct may be seen. Bronchial breathing, pleural friction rub, and high fever are classic signs. It must be remembered that pulmonary infarct is *not* a common complication of PTE; therefore, the presence of these symptoms is rare.

Diagnosis

Laboratory tests are usually not specific for PTE but are useful adjuncts to rule out other pulmonary disease. Leukocytosis is rare except in cases of infarction, but may differentiate a diagnosis of pneumonia. Analysis of arterial blood gases is frequently useful, particularly in cases of massive PTE. Hypoxemia, hypocarbia, and respiratory alkalosis are common changes. Alveolar-arterial P_{CO_2} difference is widened because of increased dead space. However, the presence of underlying pulmonary disease may make the blood gases hard to interpret. The main point to keep in mind is that arterial blood gas changes may help to confirm the diagnosis of PTE; however, normal arterial blood gases do not rule it out.

Chest x-ray and electrocardiogram (ECG) findings are also vague. Normal chest x-ray, frequently seen, does not exclude the diagnosis of PTE. The changes, if any, are subtle, but the following may be seen (Moser, 1977):

1. Differences in the diameter of normally equal size vessels, due to the fact that if one vessel is blocked the other might have to accommodate pulmonary blood flow

2. Abrupt cessation of a vessel due to obstruction

3. Shadow from a clot with no blood flow distally

4. Abnormal radiolucency due to absent or decreased blood flow (Westermark's sign)

5. Diaphragmatic elevation

ECG changes usually do not occur unless there is extensive embolization. A tall peak T wave, S-T changes from right ventricular strain, and tachycardia may be present.

The development of lung scanning has added a useful tool to the diagnosis of PTE. Once there is a suspicion of an embolus based on a history of risk factors and any of the laboratory tests, a lung perfusion scan is usually done. Perfusion scan is performed by the injection of aggregates of serum albumin which are labeled with a radioactive substance, usually iodine 131 or technetium 99. The indicator is mixed in the heart and distributed with blood flow to the lungs (Fig. 23-11). Thus scanning the anterior, posterior, and lateral views of the lung can exhibit the overall distribution of blood. A normal perfusion scan can rule out PTE. However, abnormal scans are seen in a multitude of pulmonary and cardiac diseases and do not establish the presence of PTE with absolute certainty. An abnormal perfusion scan which conforms to a lobe or segment increases the probability of embolism.

Ventilation lung scan determines the distribution of gas in the alveoli by detection of inhaled xenon 133. A defect in the ventilation lung scan that matches the perfusion scan is usually not seen in PTE unless infarction has occurred, and this can be demonstrated

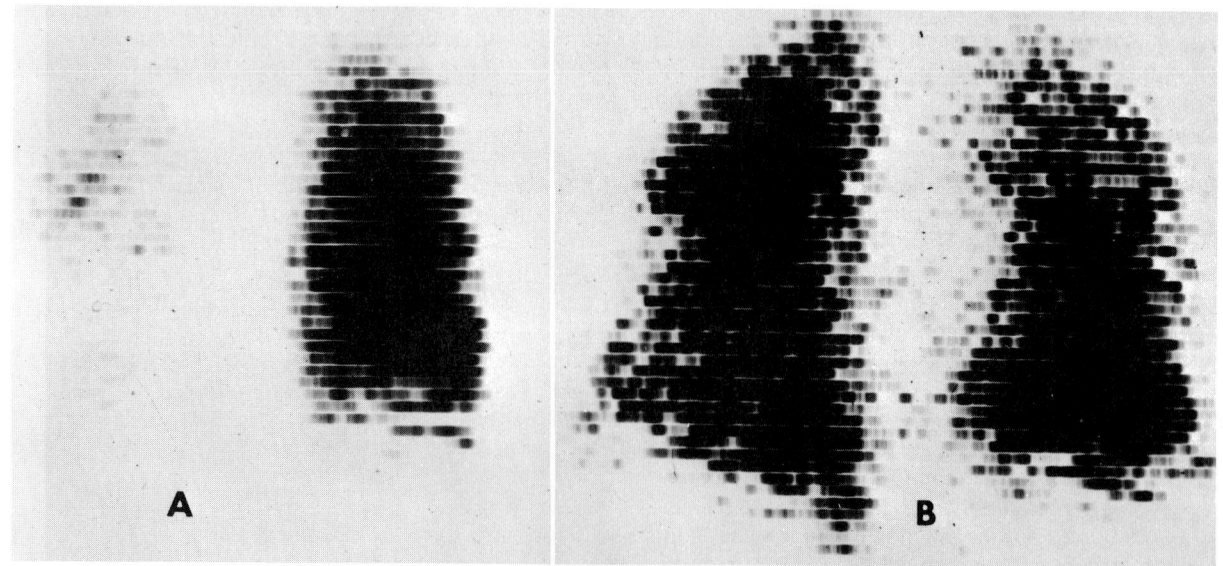

FIGURE 23-11

Radioisotope scans following intravenous injection of macroaggregated albumin tagged with iodine 131. (A) Massive pulmonary embolus to right lung. (B) Small bilateral emboli evidenced by crescent-shaped defects. [*From S. Schwartz et al. (eds.): Principles of Surgery, McGraw-Hill, New York, 1979, p. 994 Reprinted by permission of the publisher.*]

on chest x-ray. If there is no ventilation defect in the nonperfused area. the likelihood of PTE increases. However, if doubt persists, pulmonary angiogram should be performed if operative intervention is contemplated.

Pulmonary angiography is considered the standard definitive test for diagnosis of PTE. The technique involves the injection of radiopaque dye into the pulmonary artery. The presence of a filling defect or "cutoff" of an artery confirms the diagnosis (Fig. 23-12). It should be noted that small peripheral emboli might not be seen by angiography, but these rarely cause symptoms of breathlessness or the usual consequences of embolism.

From this discussion it is easily concluded that the diagnosis of PTE is not a simple task. Anyone presenting with breathlessness warrants a detailed history specifically designed to ferret out risk factors. Prolonged bedrest, obesity, and cardiac failure are all significant findings. A history of recent hip fracture, malignancy, pregnancy, use of oral contraceptives, burns, trauma, respiratory failure, and surgery should all raise the question of possible pulmonary embolism. Although some of the reasons why these conditions precipitate PTE are still unknown, they still merit consideration.

Management

Treatment should include two main objectives: anticoagulation to prevent further thrombosis, and cardiopulmonary supportive therapy. Heparin remains the drug of choice for anticoagulant therapy. This can be administered by any route, but because of the unpredictability of intramuscular or subcutaneous injections, the intravenous (IV) route is preferred. Some clinicians recommend an initial IV bolus of 10,000 to 15,000 U of heparin followed by IV doses of 5000 to 7500 every 4 h. A coagulation profile should be drawn before heparin is administered.

Another method presently being employed is continuous heparin infusion. An initial loading dose of 2000 to 3000 U of heparin can be given. Usually 800 to 1200 U/h is adequate to maintain proper anticoagulation. Periodic determinations of anticoagulation are necessary. With the intermittent mode of heparin administration, the determination is performed $\frac{1}{2}$ to 1 h before the next dose is due. With continuous heparin infusion, twice per day initially and then once per day is sufficient. Lee-White clotting time should remain at 25 to 35 min (about 2 to $2\frac{1}{2}$ times normal). Partial thromboplastin time (PTT)

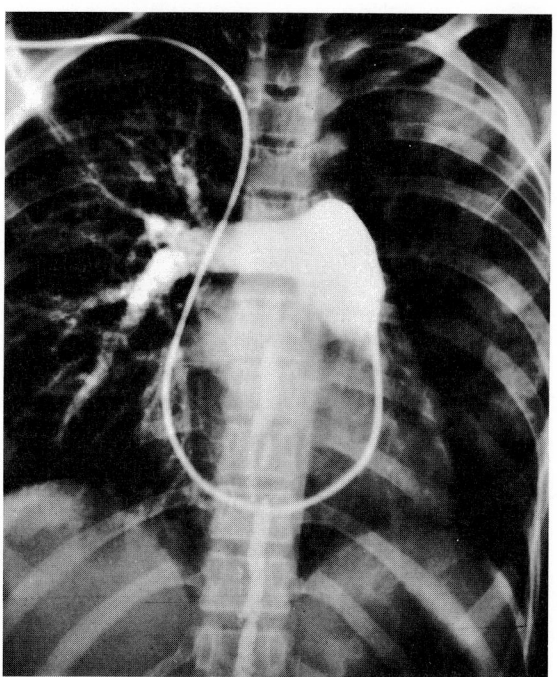

FIGURE 23-12

Pulmonary angiogram demonstrating absence of filling of left pulmonary arterial branches, indicative of large embolus obstructing left main pulmonary. [*From S. Schwartz et al.* (eds.), *Principles of Surgery, McGraw-Hill, New York, 1979, p. 993 Reprinted by permission of the publisher.*]

should also be elevated 2 to $2\frac{1}{2}$ times normal [(50 to 80 s)/(29 to 35 s)].

There is currently much controversy concerning the method of heparin administration and the clotting tests used to monitor response. There seem to be definite advantages to the use of continuous heparin infusion. Studies have shown a significant decrease in the amount of heparin needed over a 24-h period. Major bleeding is seen more frequently with intermittent doses than with continuous doses. This can possibly be explained by the avoidance of high peaks seen with intermittent doses, or by the overall low dose of heparin needed in continuous infusion.

Heparin therapy should be continued for approximately 7 to 10 days. However, this depends on a number of factors. When ambulation can be started, the extent of the venostasis and the preexisting condition of the patient should be considered before it is discontinued. As long as the patient remains on prolonged bedrest with a severe risk factor, he or she should remain on heparin therapy. For example, the patient with acute respiratory failure and sepsis may require bedrest for longer periods, thus predisposing him or her to more thrombus formations. The transition from heparin to oral anticoagulants can be made as soon as the patient is up and about. Prothrombin time (PT) is used to determine the dosage of warfarin needed to maintain anticoagulation. The length of time needed for anticoagulants is dependent upon the existence of factors which predispose the patient to thrombosis.

Nursing care of the patient on anticoagulant therapy should be geared toward the prevention of bleeding. Intramuscular injections should be limited, if not totally barred. If venipuncture is necessary, the puncture site should be compressed for 10 min to prevent hematoma formation. Routine screening of stools for occult blood and observation of urine for red cells should be established. Nasogastric drainage should be tested for blood every 4 h and an antacid administered. If the patient is a candidate for stress ulceration, abdominal girths should be measured every 4 h. Mouth care should not entail vigorous brushing of teeth and gums.

Supportive therapy is required to maintain cardiopulmonary function. The administration of oxygen by nasal cannula or endotracheal tube may be needed to maintain adequate oxygenation. The use of inotropes and pressors to maintain cardiac output have proved effective. One case report shows the effects of volume loading with dextran 40 to increase pulmonary blood flow to previously unperfused segments. The increased and more evenly distributed flow has implications for increased arterial saturation. The use of dextran may be helpful for its anticoagulation properties.

The patient who requires supportive care to maintain adequate oxygenation also requires skilled nursing care. Coughing and deep breathing exercises are necessary to open atelectatic areas, facilitating better diffusion of gases. The administration of pain medication is necessary if the patient is splinting and inhibiting an effective cough. The ventilated, immobile patient requires more intense therapy. The use of heparin should not prevent the turning and positioning of a patient every 2 h. The prevention of more atelectasis, as well as the promotion of adequate peripheral circulation, is needed to correct hypoxemia and prevent further emboli.

Recent studies concerning the treatment of PTE have been directed toward the use of streptokinase and urokinase. Both share thrombolytic properties.

There is evidence to suggest these drugs can achieve lysis of a thrombus formation in 24 to 48 h. Studies by the National Heart and Lung Institute found streptokinase and urokinase to have earlier reduction of the degree of obstruction and a more rapid restoration of hemodynamic properties than heparin administration. There is, however, no documented evidence of reduction of mortality or morbidity from PTE in either mode of therapy, though the incidence of bleeding increased when both were used.

Streptokinase is a secretory protein of hemolytic streptococci which is thought to activate plasminogen, a fibrinolytic enzyme precursor. Adverse reactions cited are bleeding and a low-grade fever. Urokinase, also an activator of plasminogen, is an enzyme found in human urine. It is postulated that these substances can be used in massive PTE or for those patients for whom surgical therapy is contraindicated.

Surgical therapy is reserved for those patients with massive pulmonary embolus (usually 50 percent or more obstruction) who do not respond to conventional therapy and exhibit life-threatening cardiopulmonary compromise. Pulmonary embolectomy for these patients requires documentation by pulmonary angiography and the use of a cardiopulmonary bypass apparatus. Patients who have recurrent embolization despite anticoagulants or those for whom anticoagulants are contraindicated may undergo vena caval ligation. There seems to be an increasing number of patients who may reembolize following this procedure. Because of some of the dangers of increasing venostasis below the ligation, partial obstruction is being sought whenever possible.

The intracaval "umbrella" is being used more frequently. This method causes progressive obstruction of the vena cava, allowing the body to adjust to the subsequent venostasis. The umbrella may be placed under local anesthesia and is associated with a reduced mortality rate.

Another possibility for future study is the use of extracorporeal membrane oxygenation (ECMO) in massive PTE. The use of ECMO may provide sufficient ventilatory and cardiac support to give the lung time to accomplish natural resolution of the PTE.

Many clinicians believe that the main emphasis in the treatment of PTE should be prevention of deep vein thrombosis. Low-dose heparin therapy appears to be the most promising prophylactic measure. Doses of 5000 U subcutaneously every 12 h has shown reduction in the incidence of thrombosis. Studies have also been conducted using warfarin, aspirin, and dextran 70. Mini-dose heparin therapy has shown few bleeding problems and no significant rise in clotting times or PTT.

Nonpharmacologic methods used to prevent thrombus formation are early ambulation, elastic stockings, leg elevation, and various exercise machines. It has not been proved that these methods result in any significant amount of success in reducing deep vein thrombosis, particularly in the high-risk patient. Intraoperative passive range of motion and the use of intermittent compression of the leg seem to retard venostasis and show promising results.

Clearly, the clinical suspicion and identification of high-risk factors of PTE are necessary for prevention. Once the predisposing factors are identified, prophylactic therapy may be instituted. The nurse must be aware of the subtle changes in patient status that might indicate PTE or deep vein thrombosis. Any slight change in heart rate and breathing pattern in a high-risk patient should initiate an investigation for PTE. Preoperative teaching of range of motion exercises and their rationale should be instituted on all patients. Postoperative exercises and early ambulation should be carried out routinely. The dangers of prolonged sitting and crossed legs should be explained, particularly to the patient prone to thrombosis. The key to management of these patients is prevention and early detection.

Air Embolus

Access of air into the circulatory system under appropriate conditions can result in the identical pathological changes found in solid particle emboli. Pathological conditions leading to symptomatic air embolus include intravenous infusion, tubal insufflation, pneumoperitoneum, uterine douches, surgical treatment of the neck, neurosurgical procedures, open-heart surgery, retroperitoneal air injection, irrigation of nasal sinuses, chest trauma, and rapid decompression. It has been estimated that 100 mL of air can be lethal and lesser amounts can lead to frothing in the circulatory system. Symptomatology is as much a function of rate of air entry into the circulation as the absolute amount of air.

The ingress of air into the blood occurs mainly into the venous system. This is accounted for by the fact that venous pressure can reach levels below atmospheric pressure. Under such circumstances, if the venous system is open to the atmosphere, air enters the circulation. This accounts for air embolus occurring during neurosurgical procedures in the sitting position, surgery of the neck, and venous catheterization. Any portion of the venous system positioned above the level of the heart reaches a subatmospheric pressure and poses a potential threat of air embolus if the venous system is opened.

Use of the sitting position in neurosurgery risks air entering the venous system when a vein is perforated. An added risk is encountered during surgery near the major venous sinuses of the brain because their rigid walls fail to collapse when opened and large amounts of air can rush in.

Postcardiac surgery air embolus may develop if air has been trapped in the right or left side of the heart during surgery. The air in the left side poses a more serious problem, not only of myocardial ischemia, but of the possibility of passage through the aorta to the cerebral circulation. Air should be vented out of the heart before cardiopulmonary bypass is discontinued.

When air embolism follows CVP insertion, air has been found to enter via an opening in the catheter system. The catheter tip placed in the superior vena cava or right atrium resides in a venous system that is subatmospheric during inspiration. Therefore, any part of the catheter system open to the atmosphere presents an opening for inrush of air during inspiration. Similarly, catheters placed in veins of the neck may also give rise to air embolus because of negative venous pressure when the head is in the upright position.

The preceding paragraphs emphasized the role of subatmospheric venous pressure in the etiology of air embolism; however, instances of increased air pressure as a cause has been reported. Chest trauma, tubal insufflation, and pneumoperitoneum may result in air entering the venous system because of the increase in air pressure relative to venous pressure. In chest trauma, lung damage may result when communication is established between the venous system and bronchus. Forced expiration or mechanical ventilation force air into the open venous system, resulting in air embolus. Tension pneumothorax can produce similar results.

Similar to air embolus is gas embolus, known as *caisson disease*. This occurs frequently in underwater divers and individuals exposed to increased atmospheric pressure. Under high atmospheric pressure, increased amounts of hydrogen, oxygen, and nitrogen are dissolved in the bloodstream. If the person ascends too quickly to lesser atmospheric pressure, the three gases come out of solution. The hydrogen and oxygen become reabsorbed, but the nitrogen remains out of solution, coalesces, possibly resulting in large nitrogen bubbles that may obstruct the vascular tree. Clotting of small blood vessels may occur because of activation of a clotting cascade downstream of the bubbles and loss of plasma volume with hemoconcentration due to transcapillary leakage of plasma water.

Clinical Features

Air may enter the venous system at a slow infusion rate or as a large bolus. A small, slow infusion during normal respiration has been shown to initiate a gasp reflex, causing a large amount of air to be sucked into the veins. Signs and symptoms usually vary with the amount of air pulled into the venous system. It is believed that slow infusion of air results in decreased peripheral resistance and the physiologic changes seen are due to pulmonary vasculature changes.

ECG changes include a peaking of P waves and, later on, S-T depression. When cardiovascular deterioration has been established, a churning noise ("mill wheel murmur") may be heard on auscultation. Central venous pressure (CVP) gradually rises during slow infusion of air, while pulmonary artery pressure (PAP) increases early. At low infusion rates, blood pressure decreases and pulse increases. Signs of shock may be seen as peripheral resistance decreases.

With a bolus of air, cardiovascular collapse occurs because of an air lock in the heart. The rise in PAP is not seen, probably because the circulatory collapse can occur within seconds and the air is not pumped into the pulmonary artery. Heart failure was demonstrated in dogs to be precipitated by supraventricular tachycardia with 100 mL of air and ventricular tachycardia with 200 mL of air.

Management

Since the effect of air embolus can be fatal within minutes, complete resuscitative methods should be initiated immediately. The patient can be placed on the left side, head-down position (Durant's maneuver). This allows the air bubbles to float to the right atrium and away from the pulmonary artery. This may not prove effective alone or in cases of large air embolism, since inflow to the right heart would also be obstructed. Intracardiac aspiration of air may be achieved through a subclavian or central line positioned in the right atrium. Success, however, depends on early detection and rapid aspiration. It has been demonstrated that large amounts of air can remain in the right heart once clotting of blood has begun.

Air can also be removed from the right heart by external cardiac massage. This is probably effective because air is forced out of the heart into the pulmonary circulation, fragmenting into smaller air bubbles.

Whenever the possibility of air embolus is present, measures should be taken to prevent or detect its occurrence. During insertion of a central venous catheter, the patient should be placed in the head-down position. This will increase venous pressure and prevent the sucking in of air. This technique also applies when treating patients with penetrating lung wounds. Positioning the patient with the laceration below the level of the right atrium may decrease the incidence of air entering the system.

The use of an ultrasonic Doppler has been advocated during neurosurgical procedures to detect the presence of air embolus. With a clear patent system and the transducer at the level of the right atrium, even minute bubbles of air can be detected. The Gardner antigravity suit (a circumferential pneumatic pressure suit) has been used to decrease postural hypotension, thereby increasing venous pressure and preventing air embolus. Its use, however, remains controversial.

Clincans should be aware of the potentially lethal effects of air embolus whenever penetration of the venous system is contemplated. Proper positioning and the use of detection devices may aid in reducing overall mortality.

Fat Embolus

A complex and highly debated entity is that of fat embolization. This is a condition characterized by microembolization (usually 10 to 40 μm) of fat, resulting in obstruction of blood flow and in inflammatory reactions around the vessels affected. Long bone fractures and major soft tissue trauma are the leading causes of fat embolus syndrome (FES)—thus, the high incidence of the syndrome in the young and vigorous and the elderly. Occasionally, embolization follows osteomyelitis, cardiopulmonary bypass, burns, poisoning, pancreatitis, and renal transplantation. Characteristically, larger emboli lodge in the pulmonary vasculature, while the smaller globules travel through the circulation to other parts of the body.

The incidence of pathological fat emboli is far greater than its clinical appearance. Embolization may not be heralded by clinical symptoms, but is an incidental pathological finding in trauma patients dying of other causes.

The origin of fat emboli is controversial, with both mechanical and biochemical theories. The classical theory suggests that the emboli arise from the marrow of the injured bone where fat globules enter the venous circulation through ruptured veins. This is probably due to a difference in pressure in the damaged marrow and the venous system, causing the fat to be drawn into the veins. After the initial injury, the release of fat globules may continue intermittently, depending on the amount of patient manipulation. This theory is supported by the high incidence of fat emboli following long bone fracture and the fact that experiments have shown that fat found in the lungs resembles marrow fat.

The chemical theory suggests that emboli are formed from fat emulsions in the plasma. It is theorized that plasma lipids, under a hypercoagulable state, form with platelets and embolize. This process is probably triggered by the leakage of a small amount of fat from the marrow. The fact that other causes of fat emboli besides fractures have been described tends to support this theory.

Pathophysiology

The majority of emboli rest in the pulmonary vasculature. However, a small portion pass through the lungs and enter the circulation. The mechanism for the passage is still controversial. One theory suggests that a large number of emboli reach the lungs simultaneously and the lung is unable to filter all of them. Another cites local alveolar capillary dilation, or the effects of shunting, which allow emboli to pass through into the circulation. These emboli can travel to the brain, heart, kidney, skin, posterior pituitary, and the eye.

The obstruction of pulmonary blood flow accounts for the number of alveoli ventilated but not perfused (alveolar dead space). However, the effects on the pulmonary vasculature and alveoli are probably similar to those described in ARDS. Intra-alveolar hemorrhagic edema may be associated with rupture of the capillaries. Parenchymal damage is frequently seen and is probably a result of local lipolysis and decreased surfactant production, which are in turn a result of edema and cessation of blood flow. The hypoxemia frequently seen in fat emboli is primarily due to shunting. This may be a result of three factors: considerable atelectasis from the intra-alveolar hemorrhage or inflammatory edema; precapillary shunting; and alveolar capillary dilatation, which allows an accelerated blood flow, inhibiting oxygenation of hemoglobin molecules.

Systemic fat emboli are usually liquid-deformable and most likely result in partial or temporary obstruction of vessels. As emboli penetrate the capillaries, they break into smaller globules, probably explaining why systemic emboli are smaller than those found in the lung. Frequent passage through the circulation and the lungs make the emboli small enough to be eventually removed by phagocytosis. As the fat is broken down by lipases in plasma and macrophages, fatty acids are released which cause an inflammatory reaction.

Although there may be petechial eruption in the white matter of the brain, the main effects are from obstruction of smaller arteries in the gray matter. These cause infarcts which may or may not be hemorrhagic. In the heart there may be areas of fatty degeneration, although symptoms are mild, if they exist at all, and the condition is reversible. Petechiae can also appear in the kidneys but have not been proved to cause tubular necrosis or renal failure. Fat emboli can cause blind spots in the eyes which resolve with no ill effects. Microemboli may be visualized in the retinal vessels. Skin rash, usually seen on the anterior chest, shoulders, and axilla, is probably the result of embolization of the capillaries in the dermis. It has been suggested that thrombocytopenia may induce this petechial eruption, but this has not been definitely proved. Petechiae very often appear in the conjunctiva of the eyelids.

Clinical Features

Although severe fat emboli may develop rapidly and progress to coma and death, most clinical cases are asymptomatic and remain undiagnosed. Emboli reach the lung within minutes, and early signs of hypoxemia may be evident. Most patients have a Pa_{O_2} 60 to 70 torr on admission following a long bone fracture. However, a more fulminant respiratory picture may develop, with Pa_{O_2} levels below 60 torr, along with the clinical signs of systemic emboli phenomena.

Classic symptoms can develop from hours to 4 days post injury. Besides mild hypoxemia, subtle mental changes may appear in the first 24 h. Changes in patient behavior, slight disorientation, and increases in pulse and temperature may be early warning signs. If the embolization is a partial syndrome, any of the cerebral, pulmonary, or skin rash effects may be absent. These symptoms usually disappear in about a week with adequate treatment.

More severe cases exhibit severe respiratory compromise similar to ARDS. Petechial rash usually appears within 24 h. Cerebral effects culminate in coma and death, probably because of brainstem infarction.

Other findings include fat in sputum due to leaking into the alveoli, lipuria, decreased hematocrit related to trapping of red cells, thrombocytopenia, and ECG changes. Elevated serum lipase levels appear about the third day post injury and may be a guide to prognosis.

Management

Prevention of fat emboli following trauma and long bone fracture should be of prime concern when handling these patients initially. Care should be taken to splint the fracture as soon as possible and to avoid overmanipulation.

The use of oxygen is clearly beneficial. Besides correcting the hypoxemia, it is thought that oxygen administration might inhibit passage of emboli through the lungs. Mechanical ventilation and the use of PEEP are required with severe respiratory compromise.

Other therapies designed either to treat or prevent the syndrome remain controversial. The use of alcohol was advocated, but there has been little evidence to support its use. One study recently reported showed a decrease in the incidence of fat embolus in intoxicated patients with leg fractures presenting in the emergency room. However, this method of treatment clearly needs further research.

Heparin, Trasysol, dextran, and steroids have all been advocated. However, the number of conflicting reports concerning the efficacy of these therapies indicates the need for further study. The possibility of dissolving larger fat globules into smaller ones and thus increasing the incidence of passage through the lungs into the circulation is a major deterrent to various lipolytic drugs. Lipolysis may also be harmful because of the local inflammatory reaction. The use of glucose and insulin to slow down this response has been suggested.

Nursing care of any patient following long bone fracture or trauma involves the recognition of the subtle changes seen with fat emboli. The baseline admission data should include a good neurological assessment and arterial blood gases. Any slight change in these parameters may indicate the beginning of a fat embolus syndrome.

CHEST TRAUMA

Pulmonary Contusion

Pulmonary contusion is most usually characterized by damage to the lung parenchyma that results in localized edema and hemorrhage. It is often associated with more acute trauma (e.g., pneumothorax or hemothorax) and may go unnoticed until the hypoxic effects cause severe respiratory distress. Pulmonary contusion was widely recognized during World War II as "blast injury," caused by underwater detonation of high explosives or other forms of shock wave compression on the chest wall.

High-speed automobile accidents are presently a leading cause of lung contusion, resulting from the deceleration of the chest wall striking the steering wheel. The contusion may be the result of direct force (the anterior portion of the lung striking the steering wheel), or a contrecoup effect of the posterior lung bouncing back against the rib cage. Blunt chest trauma, shotgun, and high-velocity missiles often give rise to the same parenchymal damage. Because of the large number of automobile accidents and occasional incidence of bomb explosions, clinicians should be kept aware of this possibility.

Pathophysiology

The rapid compression and decompression by a high-pressure wave results in parenchymal damage, hemorrhage, and edema. It is thought that the initial injury compresses the thoracic cavity and diminishes its size. The increase in intrathoracic pressure compresses the lung, resulting in parenchymal damage. When decompression occurs, the lung springs back, causing rupture of the capillaries and the subsequent hemorrhage.

The degree of pathological changes varies with the severity of the contusion. Less severe trauma usually produces focal areas of hemorrhage, while more severe injury can cause a firm purple lesion. The initial blow produces capillary damage and hemorrhage. The results of this hemorrhage and the vicious cycle effects are summarized in Fig. 23-13. The vascular pathology from cellular debris is similar to the mechanism described in the section dealing with ARDS. In pulmonary contusion, the cellular debris from cell damage also contributes to the collapse of the alveoli. If the patient has multiple trauma, fat embolism is a likely additional cause of pulmonary failure. The reader is advised to review ARDS for a

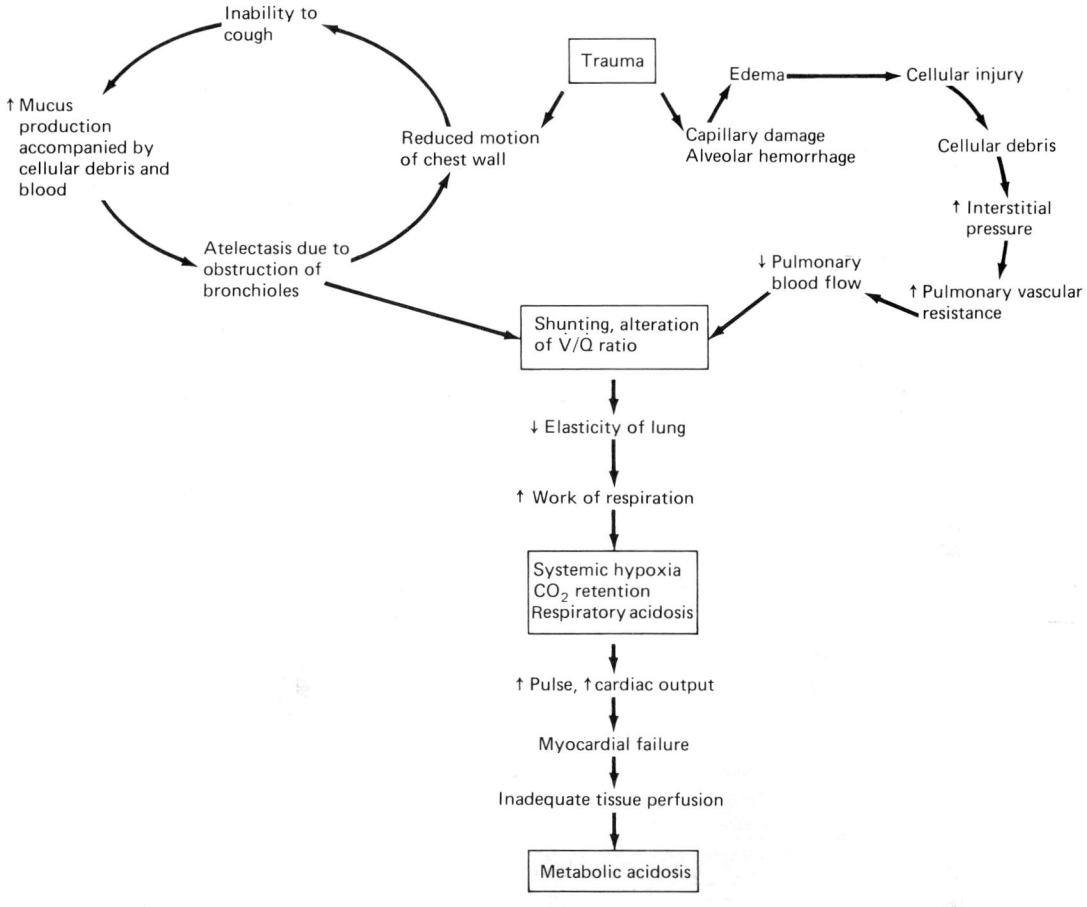

FIGURE 23-13

Pathophysiology of pulmonary contusion.

more complete description of the pathophysiological changes.

Diagnosis

Problems are presented with the recognition of pulmonary contusion. Very often contusion is sustained without penetrating trauma to the chest. Alfano and Hale observed that the more severe contusions are found in cases with no associated rib fractures. They believe that there is a temporary deformity of the rib cage which compresses the lung, or that the acceleration-deceleration effect causes the lung to strike the rib cage.

On the other hand, contusions associated with fractured ribs and flail chest often go unnoticed. It is

probable that the hypoxic effects seen in flailing are not primarily due to the free-floating ribs but rather to the underlying contusion. This is discussed further in the section dealing with flail chest.

Another problem with the diagnosis of pulmonary contusion is the poor correlation of the initial signs and symptoms, the initial chest x-ray, and the extent of the injury. A number of reports have shown that contusion may not appear clinically for 2 to 24 h after chest injury, with a lag of 4 to 6 h frequently found between the time of injury and an abnormal chest x-ray. The appearance of an abnormal roentgenographic pattern also does not correlate well with the extent of the injury. The less severe contusion may reveal patchy areas of ill-defined infiltrates which can progress to well-defined opacities. In its severest form the classic *white lung* may be seen.

Clinical Features

Pulmonary contusion can be classified as mild, moderate, or very severe. Symptoms vary accordingly. Mild contusions usually present with tachypnea, tachycardia, and blood-tinged secretions. There is an inability to cough effectively, probably because of the chest pain associated with the initial trauma. Rales may be heard on chest examination. Arterial blood gas measurements may reveal a slightly decreased Pa_{O_2} on room air and a decreased Pa_{CO_2} due to tachypnea.

If the contusion is more severe, the tachypnea, tachycardia, and rales persist. Secretions become more copious and frank blood may become evident. The patient is unable to clear the secretions. Severe hypoxemia and CO_2 retention with a progressively widening alveolar-arterial gradient, $D(A-a)O_2$, indicate severe respiratory failure. Chest x-rays usually exhibit some abnormal findings at this stage, but they often do not correlate with the extensive damage. The white lung can appear hours later.

Management

The primary goals in treatment of pulmonary contusion are early diagnosis, maintenance of a patent airway, and adequate oxygenation by maintenance of lung function. Because of the frequent lack of symptoms and confirmation of the extent of injury, the suspicion of contusion should be entertained in any chest trauma. Close observation of the patient for 24 to 48 h is highly desirable to detect signs of increased respiratory insufficiency. Once flailing, pneumothorax, and/or hemothorax are corrected, the Pa_{O_2} and $D(A-a)O_2$ should improve. Any subsequent signs of hypoxemia most likely indicate the presence of a contusion.

Mild contusion may be treated without ventilatory support. Oxygen by mask with good humidification may be all that is needed until signs of adequate oxygenation are seen. Using the $D(A-a)O_2$ is a preferable method of assessing oxygenation, since the level of inspired oxygen is taken into account. Vigorous chest physiotherapy and nasotracheal suctioning may be beneficial in helping to clear secretions. If these methods are not sufficient, therapeutic bronchoscopy may be used. Adequate relief of pain is needed to facilitate coughing and deep breathing.

Bacterial culture and sensitivity of sputum should be obtained periodically, since the lung damage may be susceptible to infection. Broad spectrum antibiotics have not proved useful prophylatically, so coverage should be adjusted according to culture reports.

The patient with a mild contusion may be expected to have rapid resolution of the damage (3 to 4 days). However, there is a danger in diagnosing a mild contusion and treating without ventilatory support. A misdiagnosis of mild contusion is a distinct possibility when based on initial chest x-ray findings and presenting symptoms. The patient must be closely observed for signs of increasing hypoxemia as the extent of the disease becomes more apparent.

The more severe contusions require ventilatory support. Since many clinicians consider lung contusions in their severest form a disorder similar to ARDS, the ventilatory management is based on similar principles. Controlled mandatory ventilation or intermittent mandatory ventilation is necessary. The use of positive end-expiratory pressure is adjusted according to the criteria previously described in ARDS.

The use of fluid and steroids remains a debatable topic. Steroid administration in pharmacologic doses has been shown to reduce the size of the lesions and the weight of the lung in dogs. The theory generated is one suggesting decreased capillary permeability, lysosome preservation, and the anti-inflammatory effect. No definitive human studies have proved that steroids are beneficial. Fulton et al. reported a group of patients in which the use of steroids made no significant difference in the clinical course of these patients. The cell structure stabilization theory does warrant more investigation.

The crystalloid versus colloid controversy of fluid administration also affects the management of pulmonary contusions. There are documented advantages and disadvantages for the administration of either fluid as described in the section on ARDS. The current debate on contusion, however, concerns the *quantity* of fluid to be given. Experimental studies using dogs show increased water content of the contused lung and increased weight of the lung following rapid saline administration. Histological evidence of atelectasis has also been produced. Thus, some clinicians recommend fluid restriction and diuretics. When looking at the problem of increased lung water, however, one physiologic principle should be remembered. Lung water will preferentially accumulate in the thick portion of the alveolar septum where it is taken up by collagen fibers. Fluids can be accommodated here without affecting gas exchange at the alveolar-capillary level.

There are certain factors regarding fluid therapy which must be considered. The lungs are not separate from other body systems. The overall homeostasis of the patient must be maintained. Many of the patients seen with chest trauma have multisystem problems. Very often fluid adminsitration is needed to resuscitate the patient in shock. If PEEP is needed to maintain adequate oxygenation, fluid is also necessary to prevent the cardiovascular compromise often seen.

The art of managing a patient with severe pulmonary contusion is to balance *all* the effects of different therapies to maintain all the vital systems. If fluid administration is needed to improve cardiac output and tissue perfusion, it should not be withheld because of its damaging effects to the lungs. The complication of increased pulmonary water content is a treatable side effect through the use of optimal PEEP. The game plan of therapy in the trauma patient is to prevent the complications that cannot be reversed (e.g., cerebral anoxia from decreased perfusion) while tolerating complications that can be dealt with (e.g., water content in the lungs).

Flail Chest

The paradoxical movement of the chest wall during respiration is known as *flail chest*. It is observed when the ribs are broken in two or more places, leaving them free floating in the chest cavity. Flailing is frequently seen following blunt chest trauma and iatrogenically during overzealous cardiopulmonary resuscitation. In the latter case the anterior rib fracture is often associated with costochondral separation.

Pathophysiology

The multiple rib fractures incurred during crushing injuries cause the chest wall to lose its continuity. During inspiration, atmospheric pressure exceeds intrathoracic pressure on the affected side, causing the chest wall to move inward. Conversely, on expiration, intrathoracic pressure exceeds atmospheric pressure, causing the outward motion of the chest wall until the thorax contracts, resulting in reduced pulmonary ventilation. The patient experiences pain and an inability to cough effectively. The increased work of breathing, associated with noncompliant lungs, along with the lack of ventilated alveoli beneath the affected ribs, leads to atelectasis and hypoxemia. It should be noted that since flail chest from crushing injury is often associated with other pulmonary complications including pulmonary contusion, pneumothorax, and hemothorax, the diagnosis of flailing should include a search for these other disorders.

Clinical Features

The most apparent sign of flail chest is the parodoxical movement of part of the chest wall, although tissue swelling, chest wall hematoma, or the poor inspiratory effort by the patient may mask this sign. Pain may be severe and increase with movement. The patient is usually short of breath, tachypneic, or tachycardic. If related to other pulmonary injury or myocardial contusion, hypotension and cyanosis may be evident. Chest x-ray is useful in diagnosing rib fractures and the presence of underlying pulmonary trauma but *not* the presence or absence of flailing.

Management

The main emphasis in treatment of flail chest is stabilization of the chest wall. Formerly this was accomplished by sandbagging the flail segment, chest wall traction with towel clips, or manual pressure during exhalation. The possibility of increased atelectasis due to pressure on the chest wall has led many clinicians away from this type of management. Generally, if adequate oxygenation can be maintained with a manual inflation bag until ventilatory support can be established, mechanical stabilization is not necessary.

The concept of using controlled mechanical ventilation for treatment of flailing was introduced by Avery in 1956. Other modes of support have included intermittent positive pressure breathing (IPPB), control ventilation with PEEP, and more recently, intermittent mandatory ventilation (IMV) with PEEP, or even PEEP alone. These techniques maintain chest wall expansion and prevent the rib cage from becoming permanently smaller when the fractures set, reducing the risk of permanent restriction of ventilatory function.

Allowing the patient to breathe spontaneously with some ventilator support (IMV) and positive pressure has some advantages. The patient on controlled ventilation may build up a subatmospheric intrathoracic pressure trying to breathe spontaneously, thus increasing pain and the potential for dislodging ribs. With the use of IMV and PEEP, the patient does not "fight" the ventilator and the pressure needed to generate a breath is minimized. It has also been demonstrated that the use of IMV has reduced the time needed for mechanical ventilation.

The shorter ventilation period seen with IMV supports a theory that the effects of flail chest may not be due to the orthopedic problem but rather one of tissue damage. It was originally thought that PEEP improved oxygenation by reducing flailing. However, a number of clinicians believe that the hypoxemia is due to underlying pulmonary contusion, atelectasis, and the increased work of breathing. The fractured ribs and flailing may initiate the problem, but the contusion is probably responsible for the continued hypoxic effects.

The administration of pain medication should be according to patient need. Controlled ventilation usually requires large amounts of sedation to keep the patient "in phase" with the ventilator. The use of IMV should not rule out pain medication but can reduce the amount needed. Pain, tachypnea, and tachycardia may increase oxygen consumption and defeat the purpose of ventilation. Morphine sulfate, 1 to 2 mg IV every hour, is enough to control pain without depressing respiration.

Pneumothorax

The entry of air into the pleural space with partial or complete collapse of the lung is defined as *pneumothorax*. Pneumothorax can be classified as closed or noncommunicating (simple); tension; and open or communicating (sucking wound). Since the severity, pathophysiology, and management of these conditions are different, they will be discussed separately. Normally the pleural space is potential rather than actual, occupied by only a thin film of fluid. Any disruption in this "traction" on the lung can cause serious effects on ventilation.

Simple or Closed Pneumothorax

The incidence of pneumothorax in patients sustaining blunt chest trauma has been reported to be as high as 50 percent. Automobile accidents, high falls, blows to the chest, and blast injuries are leading causes. Frequently the pneumothorax is a result of fractured ribs lacerating the lung. When there are no associated fractures, it is a result of compression at the height of inspiration when alveolar pressure is high. A blow to the chest increases the pressure, causing rupture of the alveoli, escape of air, and collapse of lung tissue.

Spontaneous pneumothorax can be due to the rupture of an emphysematous bleb, cystic lung disease, pulmonary carcinoma, and tuberculosis. Iatrogenic causes include subclavian venous catheter insertion, intracardiac injections, thoracentesis, and positive pressure ventilation. Simple or closed pneumothorax has been so classified because of its self-

sealing effect. Once the air has entered the pleural space, the lung seals and prevents further leak. Pneumothorax may be small (<15 percent), moderate (15 to 60 percent), or large (>60 percent).

Although most pneumothoraces produce symptoms, there are those that are totally asymptomatic. In general, the larger the collapse, the more pronounced the symptoms. The presence of underlying pulmonary disease, however, may produce severe symptoms with a small pneumothorax. Chest x-ray is helpful in establishing the presence of a small collapse or the extent of a larger one.

Shortness of breath and restlessness are classic signs. Chest pain radiating to the back, face, abdomen, and shoulders may be caused by stretching of the parietal pleura. The larger the collapse, the more apt one is to see signs of increasing hypoxemia and the inability to maintain adequate ventilation.

Inspection reveals a decreased or absent motion of the chest wall and a tracheal shift toward the unaffected side. Subcutaneous emphysema is often present, particularly in the larger pneumothorax. Absent or decreased breath sounds and hyperresonance to percussion are common.

The treatment of closed pneumothorax is dependent upon the severity of the lung collapse and respiratory compromise. Individuals with a small collapse may be followed by daily chest x-rays. One can expect the lung to reexpand at a rate of approximately 1.25 percent of the area per day. If the size continues to increase, the insertion of a chest tube is the treatment of choice.

Symptomatic pneumothoraces mandate the release of air. A chest tube is inserted into the second or third intercostal space at the midclavicular line. If at all possible, the patient should be in the upright or semi-upright position. This helps to ensure that the underlying lung falls away from the chest wall. The skin should be cleansed with iodine or betadine, and sterile gloves used. After a 1- to 2-cm skin incision, the chest tube is inserted using a trocar or hemostat. When the chest tube is connected to underwater seal drainage, the presence of bubbling confirms the escape of air. The tube should be sutured into place and all tubing connections tightened or taped to prevent disconnection. A chest x-ray is taken after the procedure and repeated daily to monitor the reexpansion of the lung.

In caring for the patient with chest tubes connected to underwater seal drainage, one golden rule should be observed. Chest tubes should *never* be clamped. The effects of tension pneumothorax from pressure build-up are far greater than those from an open pneumothorax from disconnection. In the event of a bottle break or crack, the chest tube may be submerged in a bottle of water until new equipment can be made available.

Pneumothorax is often associated with underlying pulmonary disease. Chest physiotherapy may still be done with the patient in a modified postural drainage position (flat) as long as the underwater seal remains intact and the water seal below the level of the heart. Pain may inhibit vigorous physiotherapy, and therefore this patient should be premedicated and percussed for shorter periods, more frequently. Once the chest tube is inserted, the patient may be turned from side to side. Caution must be taken to prevent kinking of the tubing when turning the patient toward the affected side.

Recurrent or chronic pneumothorax may require additional therapy. One method involves the introduction of a chemical into the pleural space to induce pleural adhesions. Silver nitrate, iodized talc, and camphor in oil have all been used, although the merits of each or any of these are controversial. Recurrence of the pneumothorax is common.

Pleurectomy is reserved for those who have had three or more pneumothoraces on the same side despite repeated treatment. The procedure involves stripping of the parietal pleura from the apex of the lung to allow the visceral pleura to adhere to the chest wall. The mediastinal and diaphragmatic pleura are left intact. The leak in the lung may be repaired or resected during the procedure. Recurrence is relatively rare.

Tension Pneumothorax

Blunt chest trauma may also precipitate a tension pneumothorax. Although controlled mechanical ventilation, when used with positive end-expiratory pressure, has been associated with tension pneumothorax, the use of intermittent mandatory ventilation has reduced this occurrence. It is possible that the incidence of tension pneumothorax in severe pulmonary disease is related to the frequency of high peak pressures during lung inflation.

As air increases in the pleural space, tension increases. If the tear does not seal, a one-way valve effect is produced, allowing air to enter during inspiration but not escape during exhalation. The intrapleural pressure, if not relieved, compresses the vena cava, causing decreased diastolic filling of the right ventricle with a fall in cardiac output. The cardiovascular collapse is coupled with the compression of the unaffected lung because of intrathoracic pressure. The combination of decreased cardiac output and decreased ventilation is soon fatal unless immediate action is taken.

The patient with a tension pneumothorax is usually in marked respiratory distress. Tachypnea, cyanosis, tachycardia, and hypotension accompanied by restlessness and agitation are immediate danger signs. Subcutaneous emphysema is almost always present. If the patient is intubated, there is usually difficulty in ventilating manually because of high intrathoracic pressure. The trachea and mediastinal shift to the opposite side is acute, and absent breath sounds are evident. Very often the affected side of the chest wall will expand because of intrathoracic pressure.

Tension pneumothorax is an emergency situation, and treatment must not be delayed for any reason. Cardiopulmonary resuscitation is often ineffective for cardiovascular collapse until the tension inside the chest cavity is relieved. Insertion of a chest tube is the treatment of choice. If equipment for thoracotomy is not immediately available, a large-bore needle and syringe may be inserted into the second intercostal space to temporarily relieve the pressure. Because of the incidence of lung perforation from needle aspiration, this method should be used carefully. A device currently being tested is a spring-loaded needle (Wung et al., 1978). This needle has a sharp edge for insertion which springs back, leaving a blunt-end needle for escaping air. The use of this device, over a 3-year period, produced no evidence of lung perforation. These techniques, however, are only temporary measures; chest tubes should be inserted as soon as available.

Routine management is the same as that for simple pneumothorax. A functioning chest tube does not preclude the use of PEEP. If positive pressure ventilation is required for respiratory failure, it should be maintained once the chest tube is inserted and functioning, even if the lung collapse was caused by the PEEP. The persistent air leak will be relieved by the chest tube until the mechanical ventilation is no longer needed.

Open or Communicating Pneumothorax

Penetrating trauma to the chest wall causes the atmospheric air to have direct access to the pleural cavity, causing an open sucking wound. Common causes are gunshot and stab wounds, although any defect of the chest wall can cause the open communication. Surgical intervention of the chest may also precipitate an open pneumothorax.

This injury involves the bulging inward of the affected lung during inspiration and an outward motion during exhalation. The affected lung's air is soon depleted, and it is unable to expand because of free air movement from outside into the pleural space. The unaffected lung receives air from the trachea *and* from the affected lung during inspiration. During expiration, air is exhaled into the trachea and into the unaffected lung. Thus this lung is moving deoxygenated air in and out, increasing functional dead space and causing carbon dioxide retention.

The most obvious sign of an open pneumothorax is the chest wall defect. The patient is usually in respiratory distress, tachycardic, and dyspneic. Subcutaneous emphysema is often present and expanding. Immediate action is needed to close the defect. A sterile gauze can be used until a petroleum gauze can be secured with adhesive over the wound. Chest tube insertion is necessary to expand the affected lung once the open air port has been sealed. When the patient is stabilized, surgical intervention may be necessary to explore and debride the wound. Irriga-

tion with saline and broad spectrum antibiotics have been recommended.

This patient requires close observation both pre- and postoperatively. Besides the pneumothorax, the possibility of a hemothorax from a penetrating wound is likely. Infection from the instrument used to inflict the wound may precipitate empyema or pyopneumothorax (collapse of lung from pus). Both of these complications may present 24 to 48 h after trauma.

Hemothorax

Hemothorax is the collapse of the lung from the accumulation of blood in the pleural space. (See Fig. 23-14.) Blunt and penetrating chest trauma, as well as the iatrogenic causes previously stated, may give rise to bleeding. The heart, lungs, great vessels, or any of the chest wall vessels are common sources of rupture. Usually this bleeding is self-limiting because of low pulmonary arterial pressure, thromboplastin in the lungs, and compression of the site of bleeding by the pool of blood already accumulated.

Hemothorax has two main debilitating effects. First, the pool of blood causes the collapse of alveoli; second, the amount of blood loss can lead to hypovolemia. Severity of the condition depends upon the amount of lung tissue displacement and the amount and rate of blood loss.

Less than 400 mL of blood may cause little or no change in the patient's condition. Chest x-ray may show a loss of the acute costophrenic angle and a hazy appearance over the lower chest. Larger losses usually exhibit the classic signs of shock: pallor, tachycardia, hypotension, and restlessness, together with dyspnea and a tightness in the chest. Breath sounds range from diminished to absent, and there is dullness on percussion. Chest x-ray is useful in diagnosing the extent of fluid loss but may often be eliminated because of the severity of the shock.

Treatment of choice for self-limiting hemothorax is chest tube insertion. The patient should be in the upright or semi-upright position when the chest tube is inserted in the fifth or sixth intercostal space at the midaxillary line. This helps to alleviate the risk of puncturing a high-lying diaphragm, spleen, liver, or colon. The catheter is connected to underwater seal drainage with 20 to 30 cmH$_2$O suction. The chest tubes should be "milked" every hour to avoid obstruction by clots.

Massive hemothorax necessitates fluid administration for resuscitation. If the bleeding is not self-limiting, thoracotomy for repair of the site is necessary.

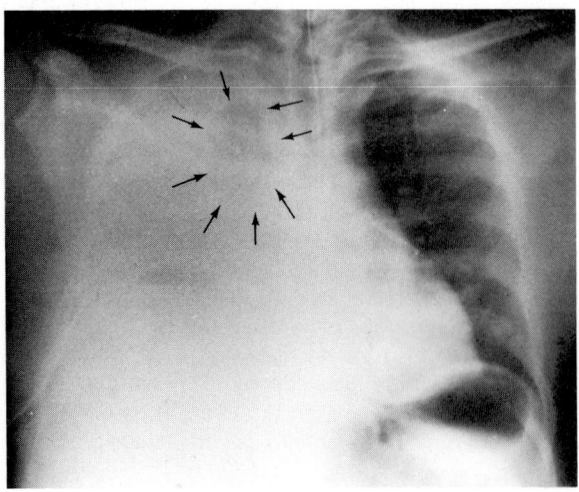

FIGURE 23-14

Chest x-ray of 32-year-old male following attempted right subclavian catheterization. Opacification of the right chest is seen with some mediastinal shift to the left. Arrows indicate collapsed right lung. At thoracotomy to control hemorrhage, 3 L of clotted blood were removed from the right pleural cavity and no bleeding point was found. The patient made a full recovery.

All attempts at stabilization should be made prior to surgery, because of increased mortality when operating on a patient in shock.

SELECTED DISORDERS

Atelectasis

By far one of the most common respiratory disorders in the critically ill patient is that of atelectasis. It may also be one of the most preventable complications of any hospitalized patient. By definition, *atelectasis* is collapse of alveoli or diminution of volume of lung units. Although it is a frequent complication of upper abdominal surgery, atelectasis may be caused by compression of lung tissue such as tumors, effusions, pneumothorax, hemothorax, and empyema as well as any condition which decreases the inspiratory effort of the patient. This collapse may be lobar or segmental but is most often randomly spread throughout the lung (patchy atelectasis).

Pathophysiology

Three factors have been implicated in the collapse of alveoli: airway obstruction (resorptive atelectasis), ineffective ventilation, and decreased surfactant levels. Resorptive atelectasis results when gas is unable to reach alveoli because of obstruction. Mucous plug, foreign body, aspiration, and tumor material can all be causes of decreased ventilation to the alveoli. Once obstruction occurs, the gas distal to it is absorbed into the circulation. The absorption occurs because oxygen tension in the pulmonary arteries is lower than that in the alveoli. Thus, oxygen diffuses from the area of greater concentration. The higher the concentration of oxygen in the alveoli, the faster the absorption rate; thus the higher the Fl_{O_2} of inspired gas at the time of the obstruction, the faster the alveolar collapse.

Obstruction of the larger lobar and segmental branches most certainly leads to collapse of lung tissue distal to it. However, atelectasis beyond this level is probably not caused by obstruction. Collateral ventilation usually permits passage of gas into the obstructed alveoli. Thus, resorptive atelectasis does not occur even with complete obstruction of peripheral airways unless underlying disease has prevented collateral ventilation.

Compression by space-occupying lesions of the chest decreases the number of ventilated alveoli.

Ineffective ventilation is probably the main factor in postoperative atelectasis. Studies have shown that constant tidal values result in decreased lung volume, decreased compliance, and increased shunting. This collapse of alveoli is reversible by hyperinflation of the lung. Upper abdominal surgery may cause "splinting" during breathing, thereby lowering tidal volumes. Stasis of secretions due to ineffective cough further reduces the amount of gas available for gas exchange.

Surfactant, which has the property of lowering surface tension to prevent collapse, may be a significant factor in atelectasis. Decreased surfactant levels are thought to be a factor in promoting collapse of lung units. It has yet to be established whether these low levels are the cause or the result of atelectasis. It seems highly probable, however, that decreased blood flows decrease surfactant levels.

Clinical Features

Frequently, mild atelectasis is asymptomatic. With inadequate treatment, the atelectatic areas may increase and begin to exhibit symptoms of hypoxemia. Acute onset of obstruction is marked with dyspnea, restlessness, and tachycardia. With extensive involvement, cyanosis may be evident. Structures in the mediastinum may shift toward the affected side when a collapse of a major portion of the lung occurs.

Generally, rales are heard on auscultation unless major collapse causes diminished or absent sounds. Characteristically, the blood gases show a decreased Pa_{O_2} and normal or decreased Pa_{CO_2}; the levels are dependent on the extent of shunting and the respiratory rate. Patchy atelectasis may be exhibited on chest x-ray as radiopaque areas bilaterally. Massive involvement may be demonstrated roentgenographically by increased density at the hilus and extending peripherally. The hemidiaphragm may be elevated on the affected side.

With persistent atelectasis, signs of pneumonia may be seen. Increased temperature, dyspnea, tachycardia, and cyanosis are generally evident. The stasis of secretions are a good medium for growth of bacteria, and this type of pneumonia is a frequent occurrence if therapeutic measures are not taken to open atelectatic areas to drain secretions.

Management

Compression atelectasis is usually relieved once the precipitating cause is removed (e.g., drainage of effusion, removal of tumor), while hyperinflation of the lung will aid in opening atelectases of other etiologies. It has been suggested that deep breathing may stimulate surfactant mobilization.

Once atelectasis is present, removal of secretions should be accomplished by coughing, endotracheal suctioning, or therapeutic bronchoscopy, if necessary. The best method of treatment is prevention. This task rests with the nurse or respiratory therapist and should never be overlooked. Preoperative teaching of coughing and deep breathing is essential to maintain efficient postoperative performance.

Frequent position changes, early ambulation, and vigorous chest physiotherapy are mandatory with any patient prone to atelectasis (see Fig. 23-15). Humidification and adequate hydration will keep secretions loose and enhance expectoration. Good nutrition is a vital part of therapy to prevent muscle atrophy which can reduce inspiratory effort. The more chronic the atelectasis, the more vigorous these measures should be.

In the intubated patient, the use of high tidal volumes and/or PEEP can help to maintain open alveoli. Instillation of saline for irrigation during suctioning may loosen secretions and enhance removal.

The use of bronchodilators and mucolytic agents may also prove useful.

Prophylactic measures should be instituted on all critically ill patients to prevent atelectasis. Position changes and chest physiotherapy are required on any patient for which bedrest is prescribed. Coughing and deep breathing is to be encouraged at routine intervals, since they are considered the first line of defense in prevention and treatment of atelectasis.

Bacterial Pneumonia

Bacterial pneumonia is a consolidative inflammation resulting from pathogenic microorganisms. It is a major source of additional morbidity and mortality in the critical patient. Gram-negative pneumonia is reported to carry a 50 to 70 percent mortality (Cushing, 1976).

The most common route of pulmonary infection is through inhalation. A less frequent source is bacteremia secondary to a distant focus of infection. Primary bacterial pneumonia due to streptococcus, klebsiella, and staphylococcus is usually distributed throughout the lung in a lobar or segmental pattern. A single

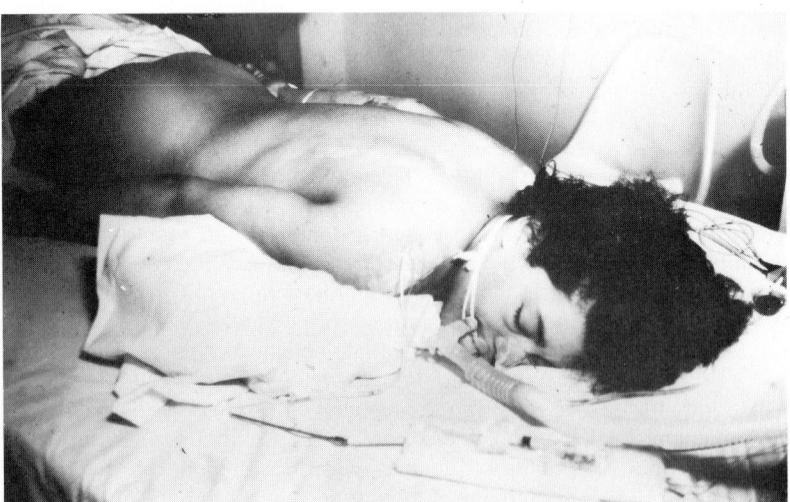

FIGURE 23-15

The semiprone position is one of the best to facilitate drainage of secretions with chest physiotherapy. Even though this patient has a Swan-Ganz catheter, arterial line and hyperalimentation line, the position can be maintained with a towel under the shoulder to keep the anterior chest wall off the bed. Frequent position changes should include right and left semiprone, right and left 45° angle, and out of bed, if possible.

lobe or segment is usually affected, although multiple areas of disease may occur simultaneously, especially with staphylococcus.

The radiographic picture is one of an alveolar-filling pattern, that is, soft, fluffy, and poorly demarcated. If an entire lobe is involved, an air bronchogram may be the most outstanding marker. Lobular bacterial pneumonias are usually primary processes and not a complication of preexisting disease. They present with an acute onset of fever, cough, dyspnea, chest pain, and hypoxemia.

Bacterial pneumonias due to other pathogenic organisms present radiographically as a bronchopneumonia. This includes multiple poorly defined areas of alveolar consolidation involving one or both lungs. Organisms presenting in this fashion include streptococcus, hemophilus influenzae, pseudomonas, serratia, proteus, *Escherichia coli,* and the anaerobes. Staphylococcus may produce a pattern of bronchopneumonia, particularly if the route of infection is bacteremia. Bronchopneumonias are often secondary to other predisposing conditions such as immunosuppressive therapy.

Nosocomial pulmonary infections are commonly bronchopneumonias. Most critically ill patients with pneumonia are septic with fever and leukocytosis, although the most severely ill may be leukopenic and hypothermic.

Several therapeutic tools as well as environmental factors in the critical-care unit contribute to the development of nosocomial pneumonia. Endotracheal intubation inhibits normal cough mechanisms as well as decreases ciliary clearance and humidification. Inhalation therapy equipment may become contaminated unless rigid cleaning and maintenance protocols are followed. The widespread use of antibiotic therapy in critically ill patients suppresses the normal flora of the upper airways and favors colonization with drug-resistant organisms.

Initial therapy of bacterial pneumonia is determined by gram stain of the sputum and later by culture. Antibiotic coverage may be started on the basis of gram stain and modified later when the culture results with antibiotic sensitivities are obtained. Dosage should be calculated as indicated on the package insert for *serious* infection and should be adjusted using pre- and postdrug administration serum levels.

Prevention, not treatment, should be the primary approach to nosocomial bacterial pneumonias in the critical-care unit. Scrupulously sterile technique when using respiratory therapy equipment and during suc-

tioning of patients is necessary. A program of infection control surveillance is essential in the modern critical-care unit.

Drug Overdose and Head Injury

Drug overdose and head injury produce, on rare occasions, a most devastating form of acute hemorrhagic pneumonitis. The effect of some agents, e.g., barbiturates, is to depress other system functions. Indirect effects on the lung may give rise to management problems in the recovery period.

Pathogenesis

Cerebral hypoxia has been indicated as a possible major cause for acute respiratory failure. This would account for the condition arising in head injury and the apnea or hypoventilation of drug overdose. The confirmatory work has been done on beagles. The extent to which it applies to man is uncertain. A possible anatomical mechanism for mediating the effect is the neuroepithelial body. This structure appears to be a sensory receptor found in the mucosa of the bronchioli of mammalian lung. It is juxtaposed to a pulmonary arteriole and a smooth muscle bundle around the bronchiolus. It is innervated and rich in serotonin. It is postulated that it may release serotonin, causing increased bronchial and arteriolar tone, in response to local hypoxia or with central nervous system stimulus.

Acute hypoxia at the time of injury or with the intravenous injection of an excessive dose of heroin (*mainlining*) has been suggested as a possible cause of pulmonary failure by Severinghaus (1977). If a patient has a respiratory arrest, the resulting hypoxia gives rise to a massive sympathetic discharge, with a very marked augmentation of cardiac output. At the same time, the pulmonary vascular resistance is much increased by hypoxia and possible acidemia. Consequently, there is an extremely high pulmonary artery pressure. This hypertension can be demonstrated to damage the pulmonary arterioles enough to allow considerable extravasation of blood. When the patient has airway and ventilation restored, the circulation returns to normal but the lungs have been severely damaged. By the time the patient is being cared for and life-saving maneuvers have been started, the noxious effects of hypoxia have seemingly vanished and the subsequent respiratory distress has been labeled as due to an idiosyncratic reaction to heroin or pulmonary edema due to head injury.

Aspiration pneumonitis is another possible cause of failure in comatose patients who are not properly positioned and whose airways are not secured. Frequently it goes unrecognized, because gastric juice with low pH often is clear, watery, and free from bile.

Myocardial depression is not infrequent with overdosage with sedative drugs, such as barbiturates. When attempts to wash these out of the patient with alkaline diuresis were fashionable, pulmonary edema occurred frequently because of the high filling pressures that developed in the pulmonary veins. Volume loading needs specific monitoring of cardiac filling pressures (or pulmonary capillary wedge pressure) if the lungs are to be kept dry.

Specific Management Problems

Head injury provides a special set of difficulties. The balance of adequate hydration of the body to maintain the circulation, without causing cerebral edema, makes the combination with acute respiratory failure particularly dangerous. High pressures from mechanical support of the lung can increase intracranial pressure. There does not appear to be a universally acceptable answer. Mild hyperventilation, which reduces cerebral edema, in combination with sufficient mechanical support of the lungs to maintain an arterial oxygen tension above 70 torr, with an inspired oxygen fraction of 40 to 45 percent, would seem a reasonable compromise. The use of IMV to minimize intrathoracic pressure that might be transmitted as venous pressure would also seem desirable. Monitoring cardiovascular and intracranial pressures may be helpful in determining the balance of therapy to reduce cerebral edema, but so far the published experience is too sketchy to provide clear guidance.

Drug overdose provides a lesser problem, in that volume loading and standard therapy for acute respiratory failure can be more easily managed without damaging the patient. Hydration should be just sufficient to maintain cardiac and renal function. If a low-output low-pressure state develops, inotropic support is permissible but is associated with a higher mortality.

In general, the basic principles of mechanical support of the lungs in both head injury and overdose patients are not invalid because of the patient's primary condition.

REFERENCES

Disorders Affecting Alveolar Permeability

Asbaugh, D. G. et al.: Continuous positive-pressure breathing (CPPB) in adult respiratory distress syndrome, *J Thorac Cardiovas Surg* 57:31, 1969.

Bartlett, J. G., S. L. Gorgach, and S. M. Feingold: The bacteriology of aspiration pneumonia, *Am Jour Med* 56:202, 1974.

Blake, L. H.: Goals and progress of the National Heart and Lung Institute collaborative extracorporeal membrane oxygenation study, in W. M. Zapol and J. Qvist (eds.), *Artificial Lungs for Acute Respiratory Failure, Theory and Practice,* Washington: Hemisphere Publishing Corp., 1976, p. 517.

Brewer, L. A., III et al.: The "wet lung" in war casualties, *Ann Surg* 123:343–362, 1946.

Burford, T. H., and B. Burbank: Traumatic wet lung: Observations on certain physiologic fundamentals of thoracic trauma, *J Thorac Cardiovasc Surg* 14:415–424, 1945.

Civetta, J. M.: IMV and PEEP in AVI, in R. Kirby (ed.), *Intermittent Mandatory Ventilation,* Boston: Little, Brown, in press.

Civetta, J. M., T. A. Barnes, and L. O. Smith: Optimal PEEP and intermittent mandatory ventilation in the treatment of acute respiratory failure, *Resp Care* 2:551, 1975.

Clark, J.: The toxicity of oxygen, *Am Rev Resp Dis* 110:40, 1974.

Clark, J. M. and C. J. Lambertsen: Development of pulmonary O_2 toxicity in man during O_2 breathing at 2 atmospheres, *J Appl Physiol* 30:739, 1971.

Clements, J. A., and D. F. Tierney: Alveolar instability associated with altered surface tension, in W. O. Fenn and H. Rahn (eds.), *Handbook of Physiology,* vol. 2, sec. 3, Washington, D. C.: American Physiological Society, 1965, pp. 1565–1583.

Crexells, C. et al.: Optimal filling pressure in the left side of the heart in acute myocardial infarction, *N Engl Med* 289:1263, 1973.

Dines, D. E., T. L. Titus, and A. D. Sessler: Aspiration pneumonitis, *Mayo Clin Proc* 45:347, 1970.

Dominquez de Villotta, E., G. Barat, and P. Peral: Recovery from profound hypothermia with cardiac arrest after immersion, *Brit Med J* 4:394, 1973.

Downs, J. B., E. F. Klein, and J. H. Modell: The effect of incremental PEEP on Pa_{O_2} in patients with respiratory failure, *Anesth Anal* 52:210, 1973.

Downs, J. B., H. M. Perkins, and J. H. Modell: Intermittent mandatory ventilation: An evaluation, *Arch Surg* 109:519, 1974.

Fisher, A. B. et al.: Effects of oxygen at 2 atmospheres on the pulmonary mechanics of normal man, *J Appl Physiol* 24:529, 1968.

Froese, A. D., and A. C. Bryan: Effects of anesthesia and paralysis on diaphragmatic mechanisms in man, *Anesthesiology* 41:242, 1974.

Gallagher, T. J. et al.: Terminology update: Optimal PEEP, *Crit Care Med* 6:323–326, 1978.

Ganz, W. et al.: A new technique for measurement cardiac output by thermodilution in man, *Am J Cardiol* 27:392, 1971.

Giammona, S. T.: Drowning: Pathophysiology and management, *Curr Probl Pediatr* 1:1, 1971.

Greenbaum, D. M. et al.: Continuous positive airway pressure without tracheal intubation in spontaneously breathing patients, *Chest* 69:615, 1976.

Harper, J. R. et al.: Intermittent positive pressure ventilation in chickenpox pneumonia, *Brit Med J* 3:637, 1969.

Hattersley, P. G.: Activated coagulation time in whole blood, *JAMA* 196:436, 1966.

Herlocher, J. E.: Physiologic response to increased oxygen partial pressure, *Aerospace Med* 35:449, 1964.

Hers, J. F. P. et al.: Bacteriology and histopathology of the respiratory tract and lungs in fatal Asian Influenza, *Lancet* 2:1141, 1958.

Hoff, B.: Multisystem failure: A review with special reference to drowning, *Crit Care Med* 7: 310, 1979.

Holcroft, J. W. et al.: Extravascular lung water following hemorrhagic shock in the baboon: Comparison between resuscitation with Ringer's lactate and plasmanate, *Ann Surg* 180: 408–417, 1974.

Hyde, R. W., and A. J. Rawson: Unintentional iatrogenic oxygen pneumonitis: Response to therapy, *Ann Intern Med* 71:517, 1969.

Katz, S. et al.: Heroin pulmonary edema: Evidence for increased capillary permeability, *Am Rev Resp Dis* 106:472, 1972.

Keatinge, W. R.: *Survival in Cold Water: The Physiology and Treatment of Immersion Hypothermia and of Drowning,* Philadelphia: Lippincott, 1969.

Kirby, R. R.: Membrane oxygenators: What role (if any) in acute ventilatory insufficiency? *Crit Care Med* 6:19–23, 1978.

Kravitz, M., and N. L. Pace: Management of the mechanically ventilated patient receiving pancuronium bromide, *Heart Lung* 8:81–86, 1979.

Kvittingen, T. D., and A. Naess: Recovery from drowning in fresh water, *Brit Med J* 1:1315, 1963.

Louria, D. B. et al.: Studies on influenza in the pandemic of 1957–1958, II Pulmonary complications of influenza, *J Clin Invest* 38:213–265, 1959.

McCredie, M.: Measurement of pulmonary edema in valvular heart disease, *Circulation* 36: 381, 1967.

Modell, J. H. et al.: Clinical course of 91 consecutive near drowning victims, *Chest* 70:231, 1976.

Moss, C.: The role of the central nervous system in shock: The centroneurogenic etiology of the respiratory distress syndrome, *Crit Care Med* 2:181, 1974.

National Heart and Lung Institute: Task force report on problems, research approaches and needs: The lung program, U.S. Department of Health, Education, and Welfare Publication No. (NIH) 73:432, 1972, p. 243.

Pasteur, W.: Massive collapse of the lung, *Brit J Surg* 1:587–601, 1914.

Pek, S., and P. W. Gekas: Pneumonia due to Herpes Zoster. Report of a case and review of the literature, *Ann Intern Med* 62:350, 1965.

Pontoppidian, H. et al.: Acute respiratory failure in the adult, *N Engl J Med* 287:690–698, 743–752, 799–806, 1972.

Powers, S. R., Jr., et al.: Physiologic consequences of positive end expiratory pressure (PEEP) ventilation, *Ann Surg* 178:265. 1973.

Reines, H. D., and J. M. Civetta: The inaccuracy of using 100% oxygen to determine intrapulmonary shunts in spite of PEEP, *Crit Care Med* 7:301, 1979.

Robin, E. D. et al.: Pulmonary edema, *N Engl J Med* 288:239–246, 292–304, 1973.

Sackner, M. A. et al.: Pulmonary effects of oxygen breathing, *Ann Intern Med* 82:40, 1975.

Schimmel, L., and J. M. Civetta: A new mechanical method to influence pulmonary perfusion in critically ill patients, *Crit Care Med* 5:277, 1977.

Schmidt, G. B. et al.: Continuous positive airway pressure in the prophylaxis of the adult respiratory distress syndrome, *Surg Gynecol Obstet* 143:613, 1976.

Schuman, S. H. et al.: The iceberg phenomenon of near drowning, *Crit Care Med* 4:127, 1976.

Shapiro, B. A. et al.: *Clinical Application of Respiratory Care,* Chicago: Year Book, 1975, p. 342.

Shapiro, B. A. et al: *Clinical Application of Blood Gases,* Chicago: Year Book, 1977, p. 217.

Siebke, H. et al.: Survival after 40 minutes submersion without cerebral sequelae, *Lancet* 1: 1275, 1975.

Skillman, J. J. et al.: Pulmonary arteriovenous admixture: Improvement with albumin and diuresis, *Am J Surg* 119:440–447, 1970.

Starling, E. H.: On the absorption of fluids from the connective tissue spaces, *J Physiol* (Lond) 19:312–326, 1896.

Staub, N. C.: State of the art review. Pathogenesis of pulmonary edema, *Am Rev Resp Dis* 109:358, 1974.

Stuart-Harris, C. H.: Clinical characteristics: Twenty years of influenza epidemics, *Am Rev Resp Dis* 83(suppl.):54, 1961.

Swan, H. J. C. et al.: Catheterization of the heart in man with the use of a flow directed balloon-tipped catheter, *N Engl J Med* 283:477, 1970.

Taylor, G. J. et al.: Severe viral pneumonia in young adults: Therapy with continuous positive airway pressure, *Chest* 69:722, 1976.

West, J. B.: Pulmonary gas exchange in the critically ill patient, *Crit Care Med* 2:171–180, 1974.

Wetmore, N. E. et al.: Extracorporeal membrane oxygenation (ECMO): A team approach in critical care and life-support research, *Heart Lung,* 8:288–295, 1979.

Wilson, R. S. et al.: Acute respiratory failure: Diagnostic and therapeutic criteria, *Crit Care Med* 2:293–304, 1974.

Zapol, W.: Clinical application of the membrane oxygenator in refractory acute respiratory failure, in J. Berk, J. Sampliner, and J. S. Artz (eds.), *Handbook of Critical Care,* Boston: Little, Brown, 1976, p. 496.

Zapol, W. M. et al.: Extracorporeal perfusion for acute respiratory failure: Recent experience with the spiral coil membrane lung, *J Thorac Cardiovasc Surg* 69:439–449, 1975.

Restrictive Lung Disorders

Berte, J.: *Pulmonary Emergencies,* Philadelphia: Lippincott, 1977, p. 147.

Crofton, J., and A. Douglas: *Respiratory Diseases,* 2d ed., London: Blackwell, 1975, pp. 178, 283, 286, 673.

Flavell, G.: Lung abscess, *Brit Med J* 1:1032–1037, 1966.

Gucker, T.: Changes in vital capacity in scoliosis: Pulmonary report on effects of treatment, *J Bone Joint Surg (Am)* 44A:469, 1962.

Jones, G. R.: Treatment of recurrent malignant pleural effusion by iodized talc pleurodesis, *Thorax* 24:69, 1969.

Light, R. W.: Pleural effusion in Symposium on Pulmonary Disease, *Med Clin North Am* 6: 1339–1352, 1977.

Perlman, L. V. et al.: Clinical classifications and analysis of 97 cases of lung abscess, *Am Rev Resp Dis* 99:390–398, 1969.

Suter, P. M. et al.: Optimum end-expiratory airway pressure in patients with acute pulmonary failure, *N Engl J Med* 292:284–289, 1975.

Weiss, W., and H. F. Flippin: Treatment of acute nonspecific lung abscess, *Arch Intern Med* 120:8, 1967.

Obstructive Lung Disorders

American Thoracic Society: Chronic bronchitis, asthma, and pulmonary emphysema: A statement by a committee on diagnostic standards for nontuberculous respiratory disease, *Am Rev Resp Dis* 85:762, 1965.

Crofton, J., and A. Douglas: *Respiratory Diseases,* London: Blackwell, 1975.

Downs, J. B., A. J. Block, and K. B. Vennum: Intermittent mandatory ventilation in the treatment of patients with chronic obstructive pulmonary disease, *Anes Anal* (Cleveland) 53:437, 1974.

Gaddie, J., I. W. Ried, and C. Skinner: Aerosol beclamethosone diproprionate in chronic bronchial asthma, *Lancet* 1:691, 1973.

Pepys, J., and B. J. Hutchcroft: Bronchial provocation tests in etiologic diagnosis and analysis of asthma, *Am Rev Resp Dis* 112:829, 1975.

Rebuck, A. S., and L. D. Pengelly: Development of pulsus paradoxus in the presence of airways obstruction, *N Engl J Med* 288:66, 1973.

Sackner, M. A. et al: Bronchodilator effects of Terbutaline and epinephrine in obstructive lung disease, *Clin Pharmacol* 16:499, 1974.

Perfusion Disorders

Adornato, D. C. et al.: Pathophysiology of intravenous air embolism in dogs, *Anesthesiology* 49:120–127, 1978.

Alvaran, S. B. et al.: Venous air embolism: Comparative merits of external cardiac massage, intracardiac aspiration, and left lateral decubitus position, *Anesth Analg* 57:166–170, 1978.

Bell, W. R., and T. L. Simon: A comparative analysis of pulmonary perfusion scans with pulmonary angiograms. From a national cooperative study, *Am Heart J* 92:700, 1976.

Burton, G. G., G. N. Gee, and J. E. Hodgkin: *Respiratory Care: A Guide to Clinical Practice,* Philadelphia: Lippincott, 1977, p. 744.

Cotton, L. T., S. Sabri, and V. C. Roberts: The dynamics of venous blood flow and the prevention of deep vein thrombosis, in V. V. Kakkar and A. J. Jouhar (eds.), *Thromboembolism: Diagnosis and Treatment,* London: Churchill Livingston, 1972, p. 61.

Crofton, J., and A. Douglas: *Respiratory Diseases,* 2d ed., London: Blackwell, 1975, p. 491.

Cudkowicz, L., and S. Sherry: Current status of thrombolytic therapy, *Heart Lung* 7:97–100, 1978.

Denman, E. F., C. S. Cairnes, and C. M. Holmes: Case of severe fat embolism treated by intermittent positive pressure respiration, *Brit Med J* 2:101–102, 1964.

Durant, T. M. et al.: Body position in relation to venous air embolism: Roentgenologic study (using biplane sterioscopic angiography), *Am J Med Sci* 227:509–520, 1954.

Elliott, D. H., and J. M. Hallenbeck: The pathophysiology of decompression sickness, in P. B. Bennet and D. H. Elliott, (eds.), *The Physiology and Medicine of Diving,* Baltimore: Williams & Wilkins, 1975, pp. 422–444.

Fisher, J. E. et al.: Massive steroid therapy in severe fat embolism, *Surg Gynecol Obstet* 132: 667–672, 1971.

Fitzmaurice, J. B., and A. A. Sasahara: Current concepts of pulmonary embolism: Implications for nursing practice, *Heart Lung,* 3:209–218, 1974.

Genton, E.: Guidelines for heparin therapy, *Ann Intern Med* 80:77–82, 1974.

Gossling, H. R., L. H. Ellison, and A. C. DeGraff: Fat embolism: The role of respiratory failure and its treatment, *J Bone Joint Surg* 56:1327–1337, 1974.

Gurd, A. R., and A. M. Connell: The origin of fat emboli after injury, *Brit J Surg* 56:614, 1969.

Hattersley, P. G.: Activated coagulation time of whole blood, *JAMA* 196:436–440, 1966.

Hauser, C. J., and W. C. Shoemaker: Volume loading in massive pulmonary embolus, *Crit Care Med* 7:304–306, 1979.

Hermann, L. G.: Discussion, *AMA Arch Surg* 65:556, 1952.

Kakkar, V. V. et al.: Low dose of heparin in prevention of deep vein thrombosis, *Lancet* 2: 669–671, 1971.

Kaminski, D.: Air embolism during surgery in the sitting position: Its prevention, detection, and treatment, *J Neurosurg Nurs* 7:65–71, 1975.

Krellenstein, D. J. et al.: Extracorporeal membrane oxygenation for massive pulmonary thromboembolism, *Ann Thorac Surg* 23:421, 1977.

Lambie, J. M. et al.: Dextran-70 in prophylaxis of postoperative venous thrombosis: A controlled trial, *Brit Med J* 2:144–145, 1970.

McFarland, M. B.: Fat embolism syndrome, *Am J Nurs* 76:1942–1944, 1976.

Martyn, D. T., and J. M. Janes: Continuous intravenous administration of heparin, *Mayo Clin Proc* 46:347–351, 1971.

Michenfelder, J. D., R. H. Miller, and G. Gronert: Evaluation of an ultrasonic device (Doppler) for the diagnosis of venous air embolism, *Anesthesiology* 36:164–167, 1972.

Mobin-Uddin, K., H. Bolooke, and J. R. Jude: Intravenous caval interruption for pulmonary embolism in cardiac disease, *Circulation* 41:II, 152–157, 1970.

Moser, K. M.: Pulmonary thromboembolism, in G. W. Thorn (ed.), *Harrison's Principles of Internal Medicine,* 8th ed., New York: McGraw-Hill, 1977, pp. 1403, 1404.

Myers, R., and J. J. F. Taljaard: Blood alcohol and fat embolism syndrome, *J Bone Joint Surg* 59:878–880, 1977.

Nicolaides, A. N. et al.: Soleal veins, stasis and prevention of deep vein thrombosis, in V. V. Kakkar and A. J. Jouhar (eds.) *Thromboembolism: Diagnosis and Treatment,* London: Churchill Livingston, 1972, p. 69.

Pitney, W. R., J. E. Pettit, and L. Armstrong: Control of heparin therapy, *Brit Med J* 4:139–141, 1970.

Pollak, R., and R. A. M. Myers: Early diagnosis of the fat embolism syndrome, *J Trauma* 18: 121–122, 1978.

Ponn, R. B. et al.: Systemic air embolism in experimental penetrating lung injuries, *J Thorac Cardiovasc Surg* 74:766–773, 1977.

Salzman, E. W. et al.: Management of heparin therapy: Controlled prospective trial, *N Engl J Med* 292:1046–1050, 1975.

Salzman, E. W., W. H. Harris, and R. W. DeSanctis: Reduction in venous thromboembolism by agents affecting platelet function, *N Engl J Med* 284:1287–1291, 1971.

Sevitt, S.: The significance and pathology of fat embolism, *Ann Clin Res* 9:173–180, 1977.

Sherry, S.: Therapy for thromboembolic occlusive vascular disease, *Ann Intern Med* 74: 437–440, 1971.

Stein, M., and S. E. Levy: Reflex and humoral responses to pulmonary embolism, *Prog Cardiovasc Dis* 17:167–174, 1974.

Stevens, P.M., E. M. Robin, and D. Jackson: Spurious pulmonary embolism—A nondisease, *Heart Lung* 8:141–147, 1979.

Urokinase-streptokinase embolism trial phase 2 results: A cooperative study, *JAMA* 229: 1606–1613, 1974.

Wessler, S.: Heparin as an antithrombic agent, low dose prophylaxis, *JAMA* 236:389–391, 1976.

Chest Trauma

Alfano, G. S., and H. W. Hale: Pulmonary contusion, *J Trauma* 5:647–658, 1965.

Ashbaugh, D. G. et al.: Continuous positive-pressure breathing (CPPB) in adult respiratory distress syndrome, *J Thorac Cardiovasc Surg* 57:31–41, 1969.

Avery, A. E., E. T. Morch, and D. W. Benson: Critically crushed chests: A new method of treatment with continuous hyperventilation to produce alkalotic apnea and internal pneumatic stabilization, *J Thorac Surg* 32:291–311, 1956.

Bates, D. V., P. T. Macklem, and R. V. Christie: *Respiratory Function in Disease,* Philadelphia: Saunders, 1971, p. 254.

Berte, J.: *Pulmonary Emergencies,* Philadelphia: Lippincott, 1977, p. 122.

Crofton, J., and A. Douglas: *Respiratory Diseases,* 2d ed., London: Blackwell, 1975, p. 483.

Cullen, P. et al.: Treatment of flail chest: Use of intermittent mandatory ventilation, and positive end-expiratory pressure, *Arch Surg* 110:1099–1103, 1975.

Franz, J. L. et al.: Effect of methylprednisolone sodium succinate on experimental pulmonary contusion, *J Thorac Cardiovasc Surg* 68:842–844, 1974.

Fulton, R. L. et al.: The pathophysiology and treatment of pulmonary contusions, *J Trauma* 10:719–730, 1970.

Fulton, R. L., and E. T. Peter: Compositional and histologic effects of fluid therapy following pulmonary contusion, *J Trauma* 14:783–788, 1974.

Jenson, N. K.: Recovery of pulmonary function after crushing injuries of the chest, *Dis Chest* 12:319–346, 1952.

Keen, G.: *Chest Injuries: A Guide for the Accident Department,* Bristol: John Wright and Sons, 1975, p. 59.

Kirsh, M. M., and H. Sloan: *Blunt Chest Trauma: General Principles of Management,* Boston: Little, Brown, 1977, pp. 24, 27, 36, 49, 50.

Richardson, J. D. et al.: Pulmonary contusion and hemorrhage, crystalloid versus colloid replacement, *J Surg Res* 16:330–336, 1974.

Welch, J., and S. C. Lennox: Treatment of spontaneous pneumothorax, *Nurs Times* 75: 324–326, 1979.

Williams, J. R. and V. Stembridge: Pulmonary contusion secondary to nonpenetrating chest trauma, *Am J Roentgenol Radium Ther Nucl Med* 91:284–289, 1964.

Wise, A. J. et al.: The importance of serial blood gas determinations in blunt chest trauma, *J Thorac Cardiovasc Surg* 56:520–529, 1968.

Wung, J. T. et al.: A springloaded needle for emergency evacuation of pneumothorax, *Crit Care Med* 6:378–379, 1978.

Zuckerman, S.: Experimental study of blast injuries to the lungs, *Lancet* 2:219–224, 1940.

Selected Disorders

Bryan-Brown, C. W., and D. C. Adler: Aspiration pneumonia in the intensive care unit, *Int Anesthesiol Clin* 15(No. 1):71–84, 1977.

Cushing, R.: Pulmonary infections, *Heart Lung* 5:611–613, 1976.

Finley, T. N. et al.: Pulmonary surface tension in experimental atelectasis, *Am Rev Resp Dis* 89:372–378, 1964.

Goodman, L. S., and A. Gilman: *The Pharmacologic Basis of Therapeutics,* 5th ed., New York: Macmillan, 1975, pp. 119–121.

Laweryns, J. M. et al.: Neuroepithelial bodies in mammalian respiratory mucosa, *Chest* 65: 22S–29S, 1974.

Moss, G.: The role of the central nervous system in shock: The centroneurogenic etiology of the respiratory distress syndrome, *Crit Care Med* 2:181–185, 1974.

Scarpelli, E. M.: *The Surfactant System of the Lung,* Philadelphia: Lea & Febiger, 1968, p. 215.

Severinghaus, J. W.: Pulmonary vascular function, *Am Rev Resp Dis* 115(Part 2):149–158, 1977.

Shubin, H., and M. H. Weil: Shock associated with barbiturate intoxication, *JAMA* 215: 263–268, 1971.

INTRODUCTION

During the last decade significant progress has been made in the bedside evaluation and acute management of the unstable cardiac patient. Using current techniques, the patient's cardiovascular subsystem can be objectively evaluated, the determinants of ventricular performance can be assessed, and the response to therapeutic interventions can be monitored (See Table 24-1). In the clinical evaluation of cardiac performance, it is important to consider the effects of cardiac rate, rhythm and conduction, myocardial metabolism, and the extent of left ventricular injury in addition to the three basic determinants of muscle performance— the preload, afterload, and contractility. Recent advances in therapy including the use of vasodilators, more specific inotropic agents, intra-aortic counterpulsation, newer antiarrhythmic agents, cardiac pacing, and metabolic interventions have significantly improved the care of patients with unstable cardiovascular problems. This chapter will discuss the approach to bedside diagnosis, the use of physiologic monitoring, and the planning of optimal cardiac care. Emphasis will be placed on the physiologic basis for the disturbances in cardiac function and the application of the newer diagnostic techniques and therapeutic interventions.

DIFFERENTIAL DIAGNOSIS

The working differential diagnosis plays a major role in the evaluation and management of the patient's signs and symptoms. Based on the initial clinical evaluation, the differential diagnosis defines the priorities for the diagnostic evaluation and directs the therapeutic interventions. The following four common clinical problems illustrate the importance of establishing the correct diagnosis in order to develop an optimal therapeutic plan.

Clinical Problems

Chest Pain

A history of chest pain can result from a wide range of causes including acute myocardial infarction, angina pectoris, Barlow's syndrome, pericarditis, aortic dissection, pleuritis, esophagitis, musculoskeletal disorders, referred abdominal pain, psychogenic problems, and so on. As should be apparent from this list, the therapeutic approach will be very different depending on the diagnosis. The clinical approach to a patient with chest pain, therefore, must begin with

24
CARDIOVASCULAR EVALUATION AND THERAPY OF UNSTABLE PATIENTS

John A. Mantle
William J. Rogers
Silvio Papapietro
Richard O. Russell, Jr.
Charles E. Rackley

INTRODUCTION
DIFFERENTIAL DIAGNOSIS
Clinical Problems
DIAGNOSTIC AND MONITORING TECHNIQUES
Routine Assessment
Special Techniques
APPROACH TO THERAPY
Preload
Afterload
Contractility
Cardiac Rate, Rhythm, and Conduction
Metabolic
Extent of Myocardial Injury
SUMMARY
REFERENCES

TABLE 24-1
Major Determinants of Left Ventricular Function

Preload
Afterload
Contractility
Rate, rhythm, conduction
Metabolic state
Extent of injury

efforts to stabilize potential life-threatening problems while proceeding with the diagnostic evaluation. Care must be taken not to embark on a program of therapy directed at one diagnosis that would be contraindicated by an alternative diagnosis that has not been adequately ruled out. As an example, the administration of heparin for a presumed pulmonary embolus in a patient who really had an acute aortic dissection could result in fatal hemorrhage.

Shortness of Breath

A patient can have the signs and symptoms of breathlessness from many different problems including left-sided heart failure, intrinsic lung disease, pleural effusions, metastatic tumor infiltrating the lung, congenital heart disease with right-to-left shunt, Barlow's syndrome, anemia, noncardiac pulmonary edema, pulmonary infections, tracheal obstruction, marked obesity, psychogenic hyperventilation, and so on. Again, the therapeutic approach will be very different depending on the diagnosis. The clinical approach requires support of the ventilatory system as required to maintain adequate gas exchange while proceeding with the diagnostic evaluation. Special care must be taken not to volume deplete patients with diuretic therapy who present with noncardiac rales and dyspnea.

Cardiac Arrhythmias

An endless list of factors can contribute to changes in cardiac rate, rhythm, and conduction. In the critical care unit setting, it is especially important to identify and correct reversible causes such as myocardial ischemic, hypoxia, electrolyte disturbances, drug toxicity, infection, metabolic disturbances, and psychogenic stresses. The successful control of cardiac electrical instability is frequently dependent on correcting the underlying cause and not merely suppressing the manifestations with antiarrhythmic

agents. Because of the vital role that cardiac rate and rhythm play in maintaining cardiovascular homeostasis, however, the initial approach to management must be directed at achieving a satisfactory rate and rhythm while proceeding with the investigation for underlying causes.

Shock

The development of shock is a life-threatening problem which requires prompt supportive therapy to restore an adequate blood pressure. The possible etiologies that must be considered in the differential diagnosis include extensive cardiac injury, hemorrhage, hypovolemia, sepsis, vasomotor center injury, massive pulmonary embolism, cardiac tamponade, extreme bradycardias or tachycardias, severe valve malfunction, drug toxicity, hypersensitivity reaction, vasovagal reaction, and so on. In some of these shock syndromes, the cause is apparent from the clinical presentation, such as gram-negative sepsis or acute hemorrhage. In patients with multiple problems, however, the differential diagnosis can be very difficult and requires the aid of sophisticated bedside diagnostic techniques.

DIAGNOSTIC AND MONITORING TECHNIQUES

Routine Assessment

The standard clinical evaluation of the cardiovascular subsystem consists of a medical history, physical examination, electrocardiogram, chest x-ray, and blood tests including cardiac enzymes. This routine evaluation of patients admitted to a critical-care unit with signs and symptoms of cardiovascular dysfunction provides the initial data base for establishing the working differential diagnosis and for planning further evaluation and therapy. The medical history provides important information about the nature, duration, severity, and etiology of the cardiac problem. The physical examination permits a rapid assessment of the cardiovascular and pulmonary subsystems and is a convenient method for monitoring the patient's clinical course. The electrocardiogram is a convenient and safe bedside technique that can provide valuable information about the cardiac rhythm as well as a wide range of cardiac disorders. The chest x-ray provides a unique visualization of the heart, great vessels, lungs, and airways. The routine blood tests permit the detection of electrolyte disturbances, renal or prerenal insufficiency, abnormal hepatic metabolism, and myocardial necrosis.

History

The clinical evaluation begins with the medical history. Even if the patient is unable to give a history, any available information from family, ambulance drivers, or old records is important to obtain. When no medical history is available, the evaluation of a patient can be very difficult. In addition to the admission evaluation, the patient's ongoing, changing, or new symptoms provide an important and frequently sensitive means for following the clinical course.

The differential diagnosis of chest pain is heavily influenced by the location, character, duration, and severity of the pain; the risk factor profile for coronary artery disease; and a past history of cardiovascular disease. Within the first few minutes to hours of an acute myocardial infarction, the patient's symptoms are frequently the most sensitive and specific for establishing the diagnosis. Important clues that help to differentiate ischemic cardiac pain from pleuretic, pericardial, musculoskeletal, gastrointestinal, nonischemic cardiac, and psychogenic causes of pain can generally be obtained from the history.

Physical Assessment

The physical examination is a fundamental part of the routine clinical evaluation of patients with suspected cardiac disease. Inspection, palpation, percussion, and auscultation are all important in the evaluation of the cardiac and pulmonary subsystems. Even though many of the classic physical findings have been found to be neither sensitive nor specific, the simplicity of the physical assessment makes it useful both for the initial evaluation and the daily follow-up of unstable patients. The discussion of the physical assessment in this section will be limited to a review of several of the more common findings in patients with unstable cardiac disease.

A simple inspection will identify cyanosis, anxiety, coma, respiratory distress, shock, and peripheral edema. The jugular veins reflect the combination of venous tone, blood volume, and right atrial pressures. Distended neck veins can result from right heart failure, tricuspid regurgitation, volume overload, cardiac tamponade, pericardial constriction, A-V dissociation, or superior vena cava obstruction. The absence of neck vein distension, however, does not rule out heart failure and may indicate a state of hypovo-

lemia in patients with low output heart failure. The production of frothy bloody sputum is a sign of advanced pulmonary edema, while frank hemoptysis results from pulmonary emboli, bronchial tumor, severe pulmonary venous hypertension, and so on. A rocking precordial motion suggests the presence of severe valvular regurgitation or a large intracardiac shunt.

Palpation of the carotid arteries permits an indirect assessment of stroke volume, left ventricle outflow tract obstruction, and aortic incompetence. The development of carotid arteriosclerosis will accentuate the pulse pressure, while local carotid stenosis will reduce the pulse amplitude. A carotid bruit can mimic the transmitted murmur of aortic stenosis and vice versa. The location and intensity of the point of maximal intensity (PMI) can be used to estimate the heart size and extent of hypertrophy. A palpable P_2 and parasternal impulse are signs of pulmonary hypertension and right ventricular hypertrophy, respectively. A palpable precordial thrill indicates the presence of significant turbulence across a severely stenotic valve or an intracardiac shunt. The presence of an increased anterior-posterior chest diameter, however, will significantly reduce the sensitivity of these findings.

The auscultation of heart sounds, murmurs, gallops, clicks, rubs, rales, rhonchi, wheezes, egophony, and bronchial breath sounds provides valuable information about the cardiopulmonary subsystems. The location, quality, timing and intensity of the cardiac sounds and murmurs are useful to detect and monitor valvular dysfunction, ventricular failure, and intracardiac shunts. The presence of a ventricular gallop is a useful sign of advanced ventricular dysfunction, either left or right, but its absence does not exclude significant heart failure. Although a ventricular gallop is generally associated with an elevated left ventricular diastolic pressure, it is not invariably present in patients with pulmonary venous hypertension, and conversely, the gallop can persist after the filling pressures have returned to normal. The presence of a ventricular gallop, therefore, indicates significant left ventricular dysfunction which may or may not be associated with an elevated filling pressure. A ventricular gallop is best heard with the patient in the left lateral decubitus position. Mild exercise will often bring out a ventricular gallop which was not present at rest in patients with advanced ventricular dysfunction.

The examination of the lungs is helpful in the differentiation between cardiac and pulmonary subsystem dysfunction. Patients who develop pulmonary venous hypertension will typically develop bibasilar "wet" rales in mild failure which become more diffuse with advanced failure. The finding of wet rales, however, cannot be equated to the presence of pulmonary venous hypertension for the following reasons: (1) Fluid which has extravasated into the alveolar space can persist as wet rales for many hours after the pulmonary venous pressure has been reduced to the nonpulmonary edema range. The finding of wet rales in a patient with acute myocardial infarction, therefore, can be a misleading sign of pulmonary venous hypertension since the acute elevation of the left ventricular diastolic pressure may have already resolved with the administration of nitrates and morphine and the relief of pain. (2) An injury to the capillary membrane can result in wet rales with normal or low pulmonary venous pressures. This clinical picture is commonly seen in patients with an acute respiratory distress syndrome (ARDS), especially following prolonged cardiopulmonary resuscitation, excessive smoke and hot gas inhalation, heroin intoxication, and infection. (3) An abnormally low oncotic pressure can also produce wet rales with normal pulmonary pressures. Low albumin states can develop from cirrhosis, the nephrotic syndrome, and excessive crystalloid administration for volume replacement.

Electrocardiogram

The recording of an electrocardiogram (ECG) is a simple noninvasive technique for assessing the electrical activity of the heart. In addition to the diagnosis of arrhythmias and heart block, the standard 12-lead ECG is valuable in the evaluation of patients with suspected ischemic heart disease. The recording of an ECG both during an attack of chest pain and after the pain has been relieved is an important method for documenting the occurrence of transient ECG changes. The demonstration of reversible T-wave inversion or ST-segment depression or elevation during episodic chest pain is highly suggestive although not specific for underlying coronary artery disease. Patients who have entirely normal coronary arteries can have similar changes because of coronary spasm (Prinzmetal's angina), mitral valve prolapse (Barlow's syndrome), or even hyperventilation. The diagnostic value of the ECG in the evaluation of patients with suspected acute myocardial infarction is significantly improved by recording serial ECGs during the initial 3 to 4 days. The availability of prior ECGs for comparison is also helpful. The electrocardiographic changes that occur during the initial hours of an acute myocardial infarction include nonspecific peaked T waves, T-wave inversion, ST-segment depression or elevation, conduction disturbances, and arrhythmias. Patients who suffer a "transmural" myocardial infarction will typically develop new diagnostic pathologic Q waves. The electrocardiographic changes that occur in patients who have a subendocardial infarction, however, will be limited to transient T-wave changes. The standard 12-lead ECG is also useful for the detection of prior myocardial infarction, bundle branch block, axis deviation, right or left ventricular hypertrophy, and electrolyte disturbances.

Chest X-Ray

A routine admission chest x-ray is a convenient, inexpensive, noninvasive method for evaluating the anatomical features of the cardiac and pulmonary subsystems. Cardiac enlargement, valvular calcification, aortic dilatation, thoracic tumor, pulmonary infiltration, pleural effusion, and pneumothorax are the more common diagnoses that can be readily established with the standard posterior-anterior and lateral views. The radiographic findings of pulmonary edema, pulmonary hypertension, left-to-right cardiac shunts, and various types of congenital heart disease are also reasonably specific. When patients are confined to a critical-care unit, however, the quality of the x-rays obtained by the portable technique is significantly reduced and thus the clinical usefulness is also reduced. The estimation of heart size from a portable x-ray is unreliable because of the nonstandard magnification effects. The assessment of left ventricular function and pulmonary venous pressures from a chest x-ray lacks both sensitivity and specificity. A cardiothorax ratio of greater than 1:2 is a late sign of left ventricular failure and may also occur from right ventricular dilatation and pericardial effusions. The estimation of pulmonary vein engorgement is subjective, and an x-ray pattern of pulmonary edema can be present when the pulmonary venous pressure is normal. Fluid that leaks into the alveolar space can persist for up to 18 to 24 h after the pulmonary venous hypertension has been reversed, and noncardiac causes of pulmonary edema will produce an x-ray picture of pulmonary edema with normal pulmonary venous pressures.

Blood Tests

Routine measurements of the electrolytes, blood urea nitrogen (BUN), creatinine, glucose, liver function tests, and cardiac enzymes permit the early detection of abnormalities before an overt clinical problem develops. Since many commonly used cardiac drugs are primarily cleared by either the kidneys or the liver or both, it is important to assess the function of these organs before administering the drugs. This is especially true in patients with a low cardiac output, since both the renal and hepatic clearances will be affected. The failure to adjust the drug dosage in patients with impaired renal or hepatic function can rapidly result in serious drug toxicity. A common example is the development of central nervous system toxicity in a patient with severe low cardiac output failure who was given lidocaine at the standard rate of 40 μg per kilogram of body weight per minute.

Since most patients admitted to a critical-care unit will receive parenteral fluids and will have electrolyte loss from drainage of the gastrointestinal tract or from diuretic therapy, electrolyte disturbances are likely to occur unless care is taken to maintain a normal balance. It is important, therefore, to measure the electrolytes on admission and to monitor the values during the clinical course in order to detect and correct abnormalities before a clinical complication develops.

The BUN and creatinine and their ratio provide valuable information regarding both renal and cardiac function. Intrinsic renal disease will result in an elevation of both the blood urea nitrogen and the creatinine while maintaining a normal ratio of approximately 10:1. An abnormally low cardiac output from either hypovolemia or advanced left ventricular dysfunction will produce a prerenal azotemia pattern with an elevation of the blood urea nitrogen/creatinine ratio. The development of prerenal azotemia secondary to severe left ventricular dysfunction will generally improve with effective treatment of the heart failure. Likewise, the prerenal azotemia that results from hypovolemia will improve when an adequate blood volume is restored. In the management of patients with advanced heart failure and prerenal azotemia, the blood urea nitrogen is a useful parameter to monitor as an indirect measurement of the response to therapy. A rising blood urea nitrogen/creatinine ratio in response to diuretic therapy is an important clinical sign of excessive diuresis (or too rapid a diuresis) and can be used to help define the optimal "dry" weight of the patient. Patients with end-stage cardiac failure will generally develop refractory prerenal azotemia and are also likely to become hyponatremic unless free water intake is carefully regulated.

A characteristic rise and fall in the serum levels of enzymes released from necrotic myocardium is a valuable aid in establishing the clinical diagnosis of an acute myocardial infarction. Until recently, the serum levels of the three enzymes, creatine phosphokinase (CPK), glutamicoxaloacetic transaminase (SGOT), and lactate dehydrogenase (LDH), have been used as a set in order to more easily recognize a false elevation in one of the enzymes from a noncardiac source. Skeletal muscle trauma, including injections and running, will elevate the CPK. Liver damage will elevate the SGOT and LDH. The development of techniques for isolating the myocardial specific isoenzyme of CPK, the MB-CPK fraction (M-band creatine phosphokinase), therefore, has been a significant advance in the clinical evaluation of patients with a suspected acute myocardial infarction. The MB-CPK is normally only present in the serum in very low levels, usually less than 7 percent of the total CPK level. Six to twelve hours following the onset of an acute myocardial infarction, the MB-CPK level rises, peaks at approximately 18 to 24 h, and then returns to normal by 36 to 40 h (see Fig. 24-1). By measuring the MB-CPK values at frequent intervals, a curve can be plotted and the total amount of enzyme released can be estimated. The total amount of MB-CPK that is released and the peak MB-CPK value have been shown to be proportional to the extent of infarcted myocardium. Release of MB-CPK, however, can also occur as a result of direct current (dC) cardioversions, supraventricular tachycardias, myocarditis, cardiac trauma including surgery, and infarction of the right ventricle. A simultaneous inferior left ventricular and

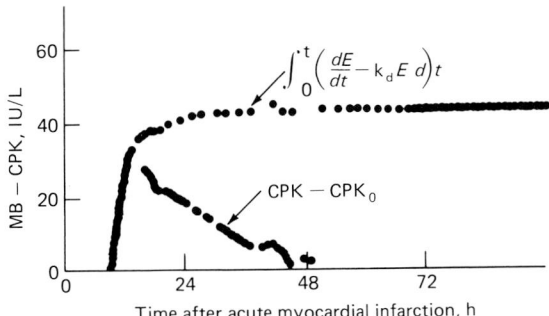

FIGURE 24-1

Plot of the M-band isoenzyme of creatine phosphokinase (MB-CPK) versus time following the acute myocardial infarction. Time 0 was the onset of the chest pain. The CPK-CPK$_0$ curve is the difference between the baseline value and the measured value. The total amount of MB-CPK released is estimated by the model plotted in the upper curve.

right ventricular infarction resulting from a proximal right coronary occlusion will release a large amount of MB-CPK into the blood even though the extent of the left ventricular injury is small. An elevation of the MB-CPK isoenzyme, therefore, must be considered within the clinical context and cannot be used as an isolated test for the diagnosis of acute myocardial infarction. Serial blood samples should be obtained at least every 8 to 12 h throughout the initial 3 days to ensure an adequate documentation of the myocardial necrosis. Extending the sampling over several days will also detect any progression or extension of the infarction that may occur. A repeat series of blood samples for MB-CPK is indicated whenever a patient has a prolonged attack of chest pain that is suggestive of myocardial ischemia. Since the MB-CPK values are only elevated between 6 and 40 h following the onset of infarction pain, this technique is not useful for the evaluation of patients either within the first 6 h or in the subacute phase after the second day.

Special Techniques

The diagnostic evaluation and monitoring of patients with unstable, complex cardiac problems require the use of special techniques to supplement the routine assessment. The need for special techniques arises whenever additional clinical information is required to resolve the differential diagnosis or when physiologic monitoring is required for the optimal clinical management of the patient's problems. The discussion of the diagnostic and monitoring techniques in this section will be limited to their role in the evaluation and management of patients with unstable cardiac problems.

Electrophysiologic Monitoring

Monitoring of the ECG has become a standard practice in critical-care units and has significantly reduced the mortality from ventricular arrhythmias, especially in patients with acute myocardial infarction. The early and reliable detection of cardiac arrhythmias requires continuous monitoring by a specially trained nurse or technician. An optimal unit design places the central monitoring station in an isolated area, removed from the distraction and confusion of the main nursing station. Memory loops, automatic recorders, freeze displays, and more recently, computerized rhythm analysis systems have significantly enhanced the detection, documentation, and diagnosis of cardiac arrhythmias. Computerized systems will detect a high percentage of the ventricular arrhythmic events and will provide trend displays of the data but become unreliable when the electrocardiographic signal is noisy. The ECG diagnosis of arrhythmias is discussed in detail in App. A of this book.

In addition to monitoring the ECG, the recording of atrial electrograms (AEG) can significantly facilitate the bedside diagnosis of complex rhythm and conduction disturbances. The surface ECG will generally permit an accurate identification of the QRS complexes and an assessment of the ventricular activation sequence. The recognition of the low-amplitude P wave, however, can be unreliable, especially in patients with ECG baseline artifacts, tachyarrhythmias, and conduction disturbances. The atrial electrogram overcomes this problem by recording the atrial activity as a large amplitude A wave that can be readily identified. Atrial electrograms can be recorded as either unipolar or bipolar signals (see Fig. 24-2). The unipolar atrial electrogram is a recording of the

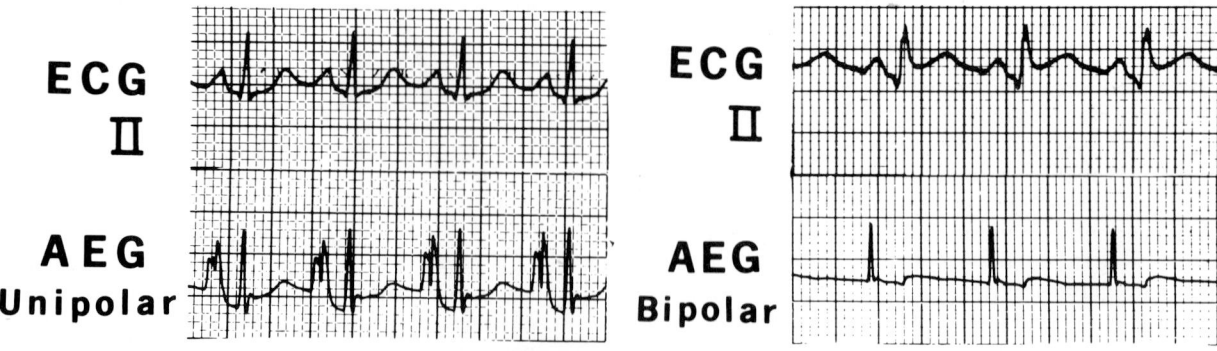

FIGURE 24-2
Simultaneous recording of lead II electrocardiogram (ECG) and unipolar atrial electrogram (AEG) or bipolar atrial electrogram. See text for definition and recording techniques.

electrical difference between the atrial wall and the skin and has the appearance of a conventional ECG with amplification of the P wave. A standard electrocardiographic amplifier can be used to record unipolar atrial electrogram by connecting the left arm lead to an atrial electrode and the right arm lead to a skin electrode with the lead select in the I position. Most electrocardiographic amplifiers also require an additional skin electrode as an indifferent reference lead (generally the right leg). Recording the atrial electrogram as a unipolar signal has the advantages of requiring only a single atrial electrode and of providing information about both the atrial and ventricular rhythm on a single data channel. The disadvantages include baseline noise introduced via the skin electrode and superimposition of the atrial and ventricular signals. The bipolar atrial electrogram is a recording of the atrial electrical behavior recorded from two atrial electrodes and consists of isolated A waves. A standard electrocardiographic amplifier can be used to record a bipolar atrial electrogram by connecting one atrial electrode to each arm lead and recording with the lead select in the I position. As discussed above, an indifferent reference (skin electrode) will be required by most electrocardiographic amplifiers. The use of a high pass filter (12 Hz) will eliminate baseline drift. Since the bipolar atrial electrogram records only information about the atrial rhythm, a simultaneous ECG is required to evaluate the relationship between the atrial and ventricular rhythms. The advantages of recording the atrial electrogram as a bipolar signal include a high signal/noise ratio and an isolated atrial signal without interference from the ventricular activity. The disadvantages are the requirement for two atrial electrodes and the need for a second data channel to display the simultaneous ECG. The polarity of the atrial electrogram can be reversed by interchanging the lead connections.

Atrial electrograms can be recorded from epicardial electrode wires, electrode catheters, and esophageal electrodes. Patients undergoing cardiac surgery can have electrode wires sutured to the atrial epicardium and brought out through the chest wall for temporary postoperative atrial electrogram recording and pacing. The routine placement of two epicardial atrial wires and one ventricular wire has proved to be extremely valuable in the management of these patients. Prior to discharge, the wires are pulled free and removed. Transvenous electrode catheters can be used to record atrial electrograms and to pace the atrium in patients who do not have indwelling epicardial wires. By mounting a pair of electrodes on the shaft of a pulmonary arterial catheter, atrial electrogram recording and atrial pacing can be combined with hemodynamic monitoring via a single right heart catheter (see Fig. 24-3). With the electrodes positioned high in the right atrium near the junction with the superior vena cava, stable high-quality atrial electrograms can be recorded and the atrium can be paced for several days as indicated. In addition to direct fluoroscopic visualization, the electrode position can be determined by monitoring the appearance of the bipolar atrial electrogram (see Fig. 24-4). At the beginning of the recording (left side), when the electrode pair was positioned at the tricuspid valve, the electrogram consisted of an A wave corresponding to the P wave on the ECG and a V wave corresponding to the QRS complex on the ECG. When the electrode pair was withdrawn into the lower right atrium, the electrogram changed to a predominant large negative A wave and a very low amplitude V wave. As the electrodes were withdrawn through the mid right atrium into the high right atrium, the atrial electrogram changed to a biphasic and then to a positive A wave. When the electrode pair was withdrawn completely from the right atrium into the superior vena cava, an atrial electrogram could no longer be recorded. Atrial electrograms can also be recorded by passing an electrode catheter down the esophagus and positioning the electrodes at the level of the atrium. This approach has the advantage of being noninvasive but cannot be used for atrial pacing. A new esophageal "pill electrode" with fine connecting wires can be more easily swallowed and left comfortably indwelling for many hours for electrogram monitoring even while eating. Since the pill electrode is well tolerated by patients and can provide a high-quality atrial electrogram, this noninvasive technique makes the use of atrial electrograms practical for a much larger patient population with complex arrhythmias.

Independent of the technique used for recording the atrial electrogram, great care must be exercised to protect the patient from electric shock. All recording equipment must be electrically isolated from a current leakage of less than 10 μA. Precautions must be used to avoid additional sources of current leakage from electric beds, televisions, radios, razors, or hair dryers. To prevent accidental contact with potential sources of current, the electrode terminal connectors should never be left uncovered. Frequent periodic checks of the recording equipment for ground faults and current leakage are mandatory.

Atrial electrograms are useful in the evaluation of patients with tachyarrhythmias, atrioventricular dis-

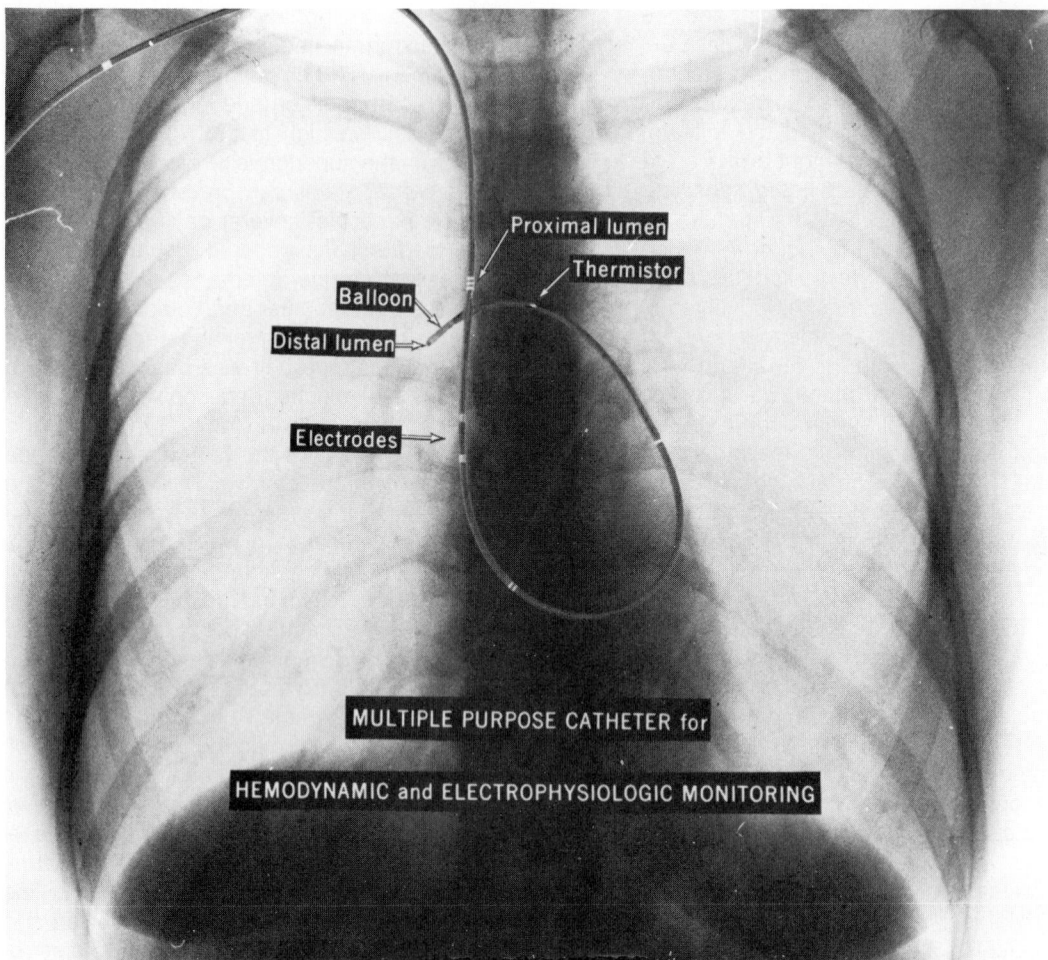

FIGURE 24-3

The multiple-purpose pulmonary triple-lumen catheter with atrial electrodes is shown superimposed on a chest x-ray. The distal lumen records the pulmonary arterial or wedge pressure and is a useful site for withdrawing blood samples. The balloon can be inflated to facilitate passage through the right heart. The thermistor permits measurement of the cardiac output by the thermal dilution technique. The electrodes record the atrial electrogram and can be used for atrial pacing. The proximal lumen records the central venous pressure and is a useful site for infusing fluids and medications. The catheter tip should be kept in the proximal pulmonary artery except when a wedge pressure is being recorded. (*From J. A. Mantle et al.: A multipurpose catheter for electrophysiologic and hemodynamic monitoring plus atrial pacing, Chest 72:285–290, 1977. Reproduced by permission.*)

sociation, heart block, and premature beats. Specific examples where an atrial electrogram may be necessary to establish the correct diagnoses include the differentiation of ventricular tachycardia versus supraventricular tachycardia with bundle branch block; atrial tachycardia (or flutter) with 2 to 1 conduction versus sinus tachycardia; premature ventricular contractions (PVCs) versus aberrantly conducted premature atrial contractions (PACs); nonconducted PACs resulting in isorhythmic dissociation versus sinus pause; and junctional tachycardia versus atrial or sinus tachycardia. The ability to accurately identify both the atrial and ventricular complexes simplifies these electrocardiographic dilemmas into a straightforward rhythm analysis and diagnosis, as illustrated in the following two examples.

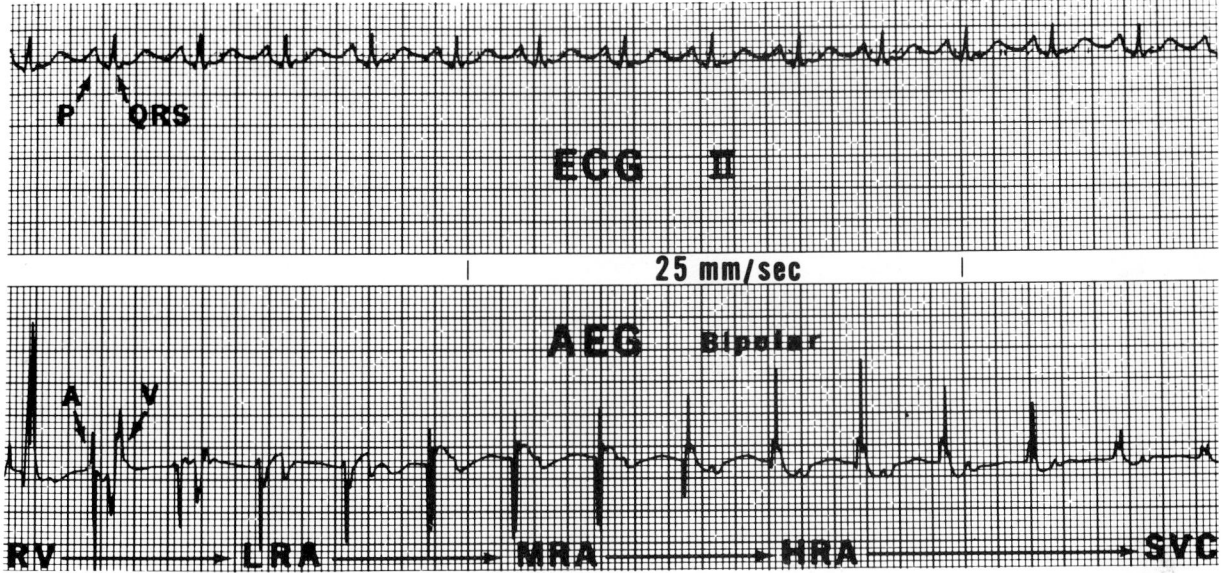

FIGURE 24-4

Simultaneous recording of a lead II electrocardiogram (ECG) and an atrial electrogram (AEG). The P and QRS waves are shown by the arrows in the ECG and the corresponding A and V waves are indicated in the AEG. The electrode pair was withdrawn from the right ventricle (RV) to the low right atrium (LRA), to the mid right atrium (MRA), to the high right atrial (HRA), and to the superior vena cava (SVC).

The tracings shown in Fig. 24-5 were recorded from an elderly patient with known ischemic heart disease and bundle branch block who was admitted because of recurrent palpitations. An example of the admission electrocardiographic monitoring strip is shown in the upper left panel. The rate of 151 beats per minute and the apparent P waves 0.12 ms before each QRS complex suggested a sinus tachycardia, or a supraventricular tachycardia, possibly atrial flutter with 2 to 1 conduction. The bipolar atrial electrogram, however, clearly documented that there was complete atrioventricular dissociation with an atrial rate of 98 beats per minute. The diagnosis, therefore, was a ventricular (or junctional) tachycardia. Following successful dC cardioversion, the patient had a normal sinus rhythm, as illustrated in the right-hand panel.

The tracings shown in Fig. 24-6 illustrate the advantage of monitoring both the ECG and the bipolar atrial electrogram in patients with unstable rhythms. The second beat on the ECG is premature but normally conducted. The third and fourth beats have no preceding P waves, have a wide QRS complex, and are late. The fifth, sixth, and seventh beats are normally conducted but have varying R-R intervals. Did this patient have a transient sinus arrest? Why was there no junctional escape rhythm? The atrial electrogram provides the needed additional information about the atrial activity to answer these questions. The first A wave was a normal sinus beat. The second A wave was a premature atrial beat which was normally conducted to the ventricles. The third A wave was a second premature atrial beat which was blocked within the conduction system. The second premature atrial beat, however, delayed the next sinus beat and suppressed the junctional area which allowed a lower pacemaker to escape. Since the lower pacemaker rate was only slightly slower than the sinus rate and the junctional region was again suppressed from the nonconducted sinus beat (the fourth A wave), the lower pacemaker escaped again before the next sinus beat (the fifth A wave) could conduct to the ventricles. The sixth A wave was a premature atrial beat which interrupted this isorhythmic dissociation and captured the ventricles; the last two A waves are normal sinus beats. With the aid of the atrial electrogram, therefore, the correct diagnosis was shown to be a blocked premature atrial beat with isorhythmic dissociation.

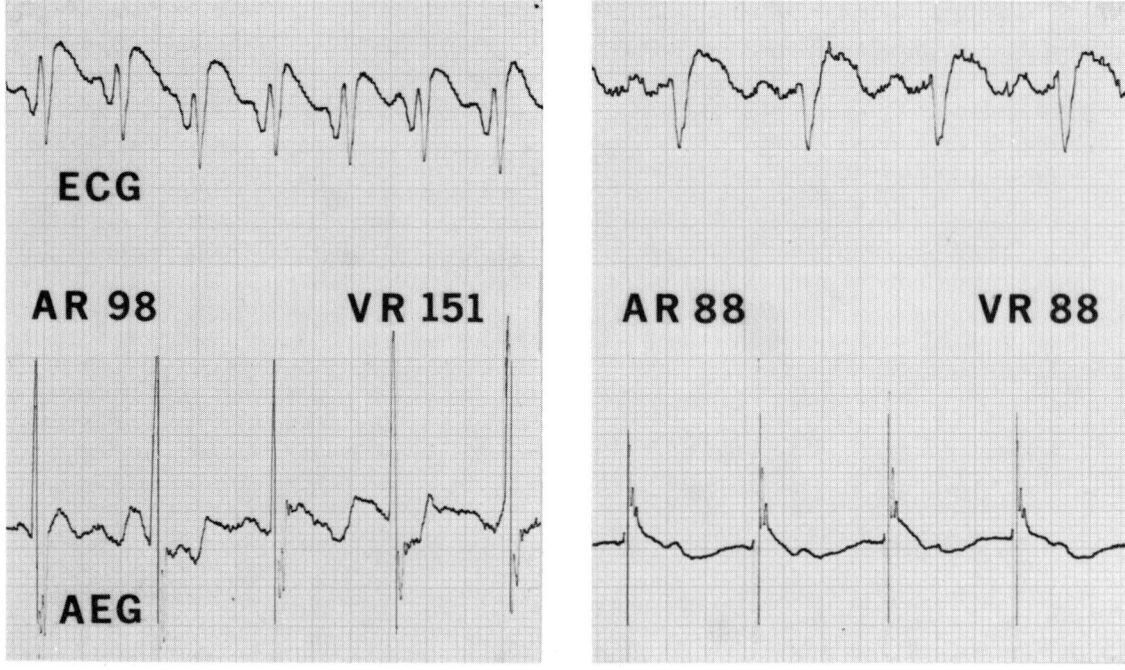

FIGURE 24-5

Simultaneous recording of electrocardiogram (ECG) and bipolar atrial electrogram (AEG). Atrial rate (RA) and ventricular rate (VR) are listed before (left) and after (right) cardioversion of ventricular tachycardia. (*From J. A. Mantle et al.: A multipurpose catheter for electrophysiologic and hemodynamic monitoring plus atrial pacing, Chest 72:285–290, 1977. Reproduced by permission.*)

Hemodynamic Monitoring

Following arrhythmia monitoring, the next major advancement in the evaluation and management of patients with unstable cardiac problems was the development of safe, convenient bedside techniques for hemodynamic monitoring. Patients undergoing cardiac surgery can have small cannulae placed in the right and left atria as well as a peripheral artery for monitoring of the right and left ventricular filling pressures and the arterial pressure during the early postoperative recovery. With the development of a flow-directed pulmonary arterial catheter (Swan-Ganz), it is now practical to perform a bedside right heart catheterization in order to monitor the left ventricular filling pressure and cardiac output in unstable cardiac patients (see Fig. 24-3). In patients with low cardiac output, dilated right heart chambers, tricuspid regurgitation or tortuous vessels, fluoroscopy may be required for successful advancement of the catheter tip into the pulmonary artery. A portable fluoroscopic unit and radiolucent beds, therefore, should be available for bedside right heart catheterization procedures in critically ill patients. The catheter can be introduced via the antecubital, jugular, subclavian, or femoral veins. The antecubital approach has the lowest risk but is limited by previous venous cutdowns and venous spasm. The jugular approach done by the Seldinger technique can be performed easily with a minimum risk of damaging the carotid artery. Although the subclavian vein has been used extensively for central venous lines, it has a potential risk of producing a pneumothorax and further compromising the cardiopulmonary function in an already unstable patient. An indwelling catheter in the femoral vein has a significant risk of producing venous thromboses and should be avoided especially in those patients who are at high risk for developing pulmonary emboli.

Multiple lumen catheters (see Fig. 24-3) permit monitoring of the pulmonary arterial or pulmonary wedge pressures via the distal port, the central venous or right atrial pressure via the proximal port, and the cardiac output via the thermister. The use of a special

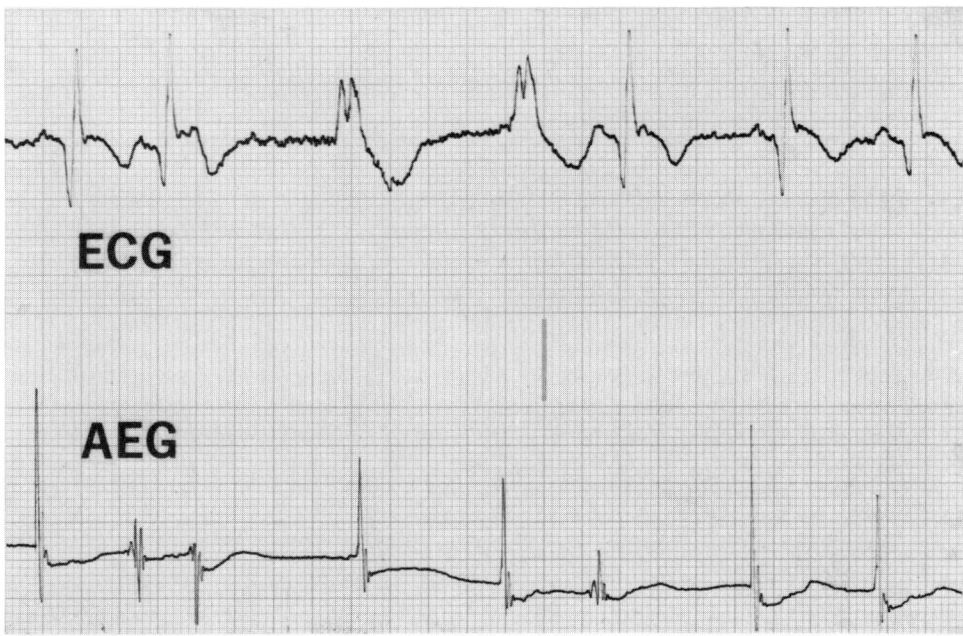

FIGURE 24-6

Simultaneous recording of electrocardiogram (ECG) and bipolar atrial electrogram (AEG) from a patient with frequent and blocked premature atrial beats with periods of atrioventricular isorhythmic dissociation. (*From J. A. Mantle et al.: A multipurpose catheter for electrophysiologic and hemodynamic monitoring plus atrial pacing, Chest 72:285–290, 1977. Reproduced by permission.*)

valve permits a constant perfusion of the catheter lumens with flush while simultaneously monitoring the pressures. Prepackaged and disposable monitoring component kits have simplified the application of these techniques and have also reduced the costs.

The pressure traces in Fig. 24-7 illustrate recordings from the pulmonary wedge, pulmonary artery, right ventricle, and right atrium recorded via this catheter. The pulmonary wedge pressure can be recorded by inflating the balloon and allowing the catheter to advance until it obstructs a pulmonary arterial branch. The distal port will then record the pressure that is transmitted backward through the capillary bed from the left atrium and is thus a useful measure of the left ventricular filling pressure. The presence of a large V wave in the wedge tracing indicates the presence of acute mitral valve incompetence. A major disadvantage of monitoring the pulmonary wedge pressure is the need to reinflate the balloon for each measurement. If the balloon is inflated when the catheter tip is in a small arterial branch, the vessel wall may rupture, resulting in a

significant pulmonary hemorrhage. Careful adherence to the recommended procedures for inflation of the balloon should minimize this risk. With repeated inflations of the balloon, the catheter tip will usually migrate out into a distal branch and become wedged. If the catheter is allowed to remain in the wedged position, a pulmonary infarction will occur in the distribution of the occluded vessel. When the catheter tip is withdrawn from the wedged position, however, it will frequently recoil into the right ventricle or atrium.

As illustrated in Figs. 24-7 and 24-8, the pulmonary arterial end diastolic pressure can be used as an alternative measure of the left ventricular filling pressure in most patients even in the presence of pulmonary venous hypertension. At the time of the right heart catheterization, the pulmonary arterial end diastolic pressure can be compared to the pulmonary wedge pressure. If the pulmonary arterial end diastolic pressure is significantly higher than the pulmonary wedge pressure (> 5 mmHg), a treatable cause of pulmonary hypertension, such as pulmonary emboli, should be carefully considered. With the use of a

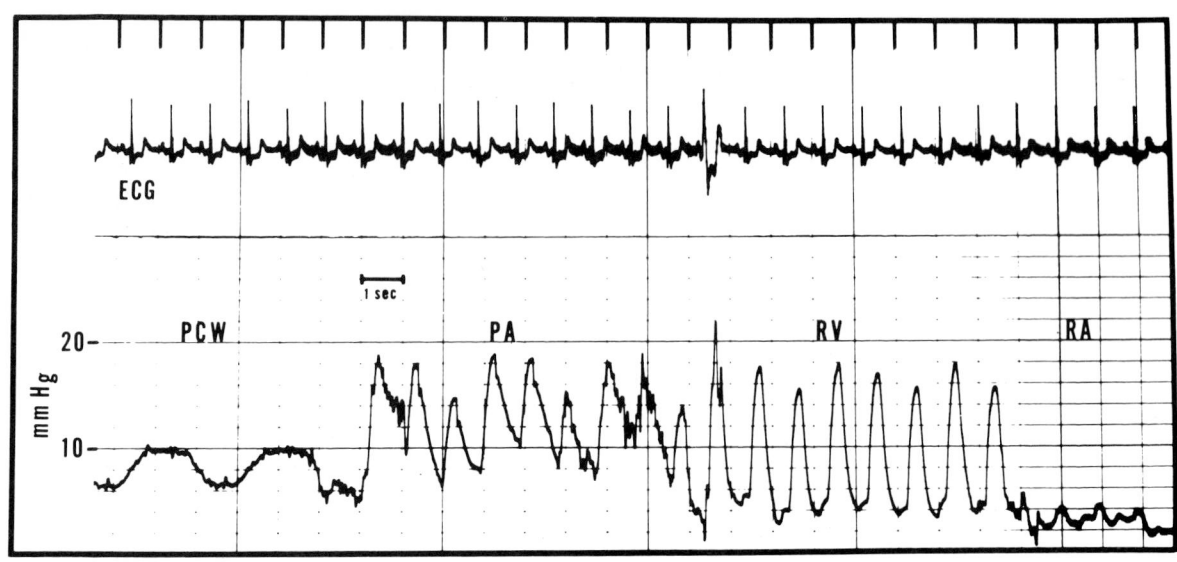

FIGURE 24-7

Simultaneous recording of electrocardiogram (ECG) and pulmonary capillary wedge (PCW), pulmonary arterial (PA), right ventricular (RV), and right atrial (RA) pressures. The pulmonary arterial catheter was initially in a wedged position with the balloon inflated. The balloon was then deflated and the catheter was slowly withdrawn through the right heart chambers. Note the cyclic respiratory effects in the pressure signals. The PCW and PA end diastolic pressures are equal. (*From J. A. Mantle et al.: Advances in the treatment of heart failure, to be published as a chapter in Critical Care Cardiology, Cardiovascular Clinics, Philadelphia, Davis. Reproduced by permission.*)

constant infusion valve, the pulmonary arterial end diastolic pressure can be continuously monitored at the central station (and by a computerized system) for the early detection of a change in the patient's hemodynamic status, wedging of the catheter tip, recoil of the catheter into the right ventricle, and so on. A disadvantage of monitoring the pulmonary arterial end diastolic pressure is the problem of eliminating the catheter whip artifact from the signal. The standard bedside diastolic pressure readout will underestimate the true diastolic pressure since it measures the minimum (valley) of the whip artifact. Until more reliable bedside readouts are developed, the end diastolic pressure should be measured at the midpoint of the oscillations just prior to systole using a calibrated strip chart recorder.

Both the pulmonary wedge and pulmonary arterial end diastolic pressure signals have a significant cyclic respiratory effect, as illustrated in Fig. 24-7. During inspiration the pressure falls as a result of the negative intrathoracic pressure, while during expiration the pressure rises as a result of the positive intrathoracic pressure. Since the external zero reference level is at atmospheric pressure and not at the

intrathoracic pressure, neither the inspiratory nor the expiratory pulmonary venous pressure is an accurate measure of the true left ventricular diastolic pressure. It is necessary, therefore, to record the pressure over several respiratory cycles and use the average value as the estimate of the left ventricular filling pressure. If the patient is having premature beats or is in atrial fibrillation, the pressure may need to be recorded for even longer periods to ensure a reliable value. The problem is more complex in patients with pulmonary disease since a reduction in the lung compliance will increase the inspiratory effect while obstructive lung disease will increase the expiratory effect. The estimation of the left ventricular diastolic pressure is further complicated by the changes in intrathoracic pressure produced by a ventilator. During inspiration the intrathoracic pressure becomes positive, while during expiration the pressure gradually falls to atmospheric pressure. If positive end expiratory pressure (PEEP) is used, the expiratory pressure will remain above the atmospheric reference pressure. The pulmonary wedge and arterial diastolic pressures, therefore, must be adjusted for the pressure difference between the intrathoracic pressure and the atmos-

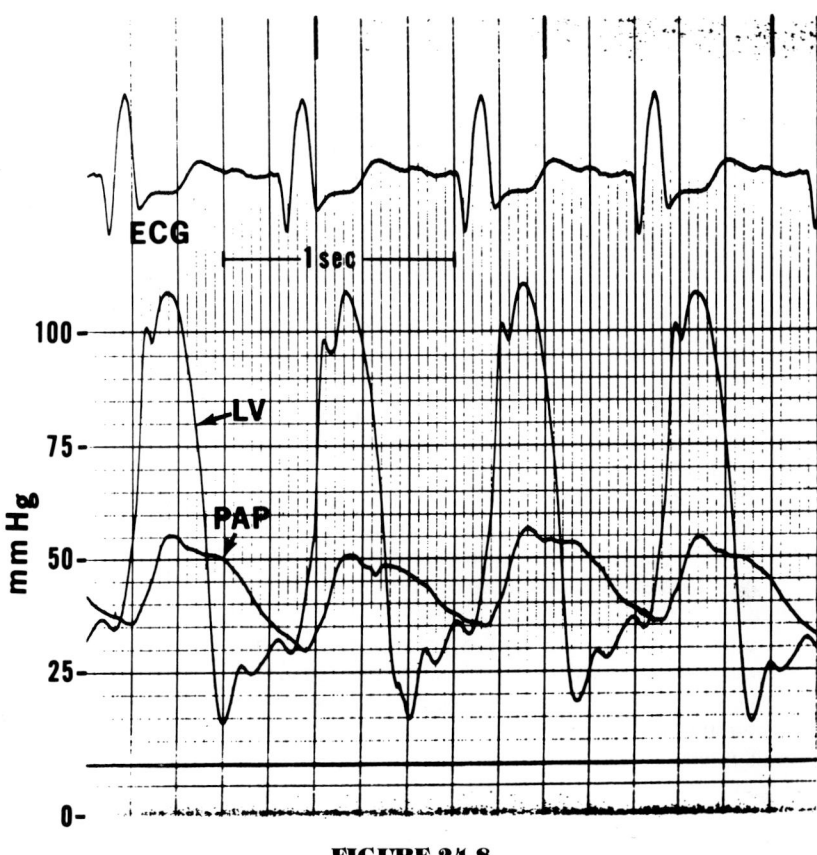

FIGURE 24-8

Simultaneous recording of electrocardiogram (ECG) and left ventricular (LV) and pulmonary arterial pressures (PAP) in a patient with LV failure and pulmonary venous hypertension. Note that the PA end diastolic pressure is equivalent to the LV end diastolic pressure.

pheric pressure. This can be done objectively by directly monitoring the esophageal pressure as a measure of the intrathoracic pressure; otherwise an estimated correction must be made. Recording the wedge pressure with the ventilator off will overestimate the left ventricular filling pressure during ventilator support since the venous return will be reduced during ventilatory support.

A right ventricular pressure is recorded during the initial advancement of the catheter tip, when the tip recoils back into the right ventricle and when the catheter is withdrawn. The systolic pressure will be equal to the pulmonary systolic pressure unless the patient has significant pulmonic stenosis. The end diastolic pressure reflects right ventricular function and will be equal to the right atrial pressure unless the patient has significant tricuspid valve dysfunction. A prominent V wave in the right atrial pressure signal

indicates significant tricuspid insufficiency. Patients with tricuspid stenosis or atrioventricular (AV) dissociation will have a prominent A wave resulting from the atrial contraction against the stenotic or closed tricuspid valve.

It is important to compare the right atrial pressure to the pulmonary arterial end diastolic or wedge pressure. Acute left ventricular dysfunction will abnormally elevate the left ventricular filling pressure without producing a significant change in the right atrial pressure. Patients who are hypovolemic will have a low right atrial filling pressure as well as a low left ventricular filling pressure. Cardiac tamponade, pericardial construction, right ventricular infarction, septal defects, restrictive cardiomyopathy, or severe biventricular congestive failure should be considered in the differential diagnosis whenever the right-sided filling pressure is approximately equal to the left-sided filling pressure. The pressure tracings in Fig. 24-9 demonstrate the equalization of right and left heart diastolic pressures in a patient with combined acute left ventricular inferior wall infarction and right ventricular infarction. The pulmonary wedge, pulmonary arterial end diastolic, right ventricular diastolic, and mean right atrial pressures are all equal. The early diastolic dip and plateau pattern seen in the right ventricular and right atrial pressures is also seen in patients with pericardial constriction and restrictive cardiomyopathy. Care must be taken to avoid making the erroneous diagnosis of cardiac tamponade in patients who develop low cardiac output and equalization of the left and right ventricular filling pressures from combined acute left and right ventricular infarction or advanced biventricular congestive failure. Whenever possible, the presence of a significant pericardial effusion should be demonstrated by the echocardiographic technique in patients suspected of having cardiac tamponade before proceeding with pericardiocentesis or surgical drainage.

The thermistor mounted in the distal portion of the catheter permits the cardiac output to be measured in critically ill patients by the convenient, reliable, and safe thermal dilution technique. Thermal cardiac output measurements are reproducible to within 10 percent and agree closely with the values obtained by the Fick technique from very low to high normal cardiac outputs. Cardiac arrhythmias, left to right intracardiac shunts, and poor technique will all introduce error into the thermal cardiac output measurements. The combined measurements of cardiac output and left ventricular filling pressure permit an objective classification of ventricular function (see Fig. 24-10). Patients with a cardiac index below 2.5 L/min per m² will experience progressive signs and symptoms of low output failure. When the pulmonary venous pressure is elevated above 20 to 24 mmHg, patients will generally develop pulmonary congestion, although patients with chronic heart failure may be able to tolerate pressures greater than 24 mmHg. Patients with a "leaky" pulmonary capillary membrane or a low oncotic pressure will develop pulmonary edema at pulmonary venous pressures below 24 mmHg. The three function curves plotted in Fig. 24-10 illustrate the normal ascending (A), depressed (B), and descending (C) curves from three patients with normal function, moderate left ventricular dysfunction, and cardiogenic shock, respectively. The construction of left ventricular function curves is a useful bedside method for assessing the performance of the left ventricle in unstable patients. Following the baseline measurements, low molecular weight dextran (or other colloid) is rapidly infused in 50-mL increments while monitoring the left ventricular filling pressure. After increasing the left ventricular filling pressure by at

RIGHT HEART PULLBACK — LV & RV INFARCTION

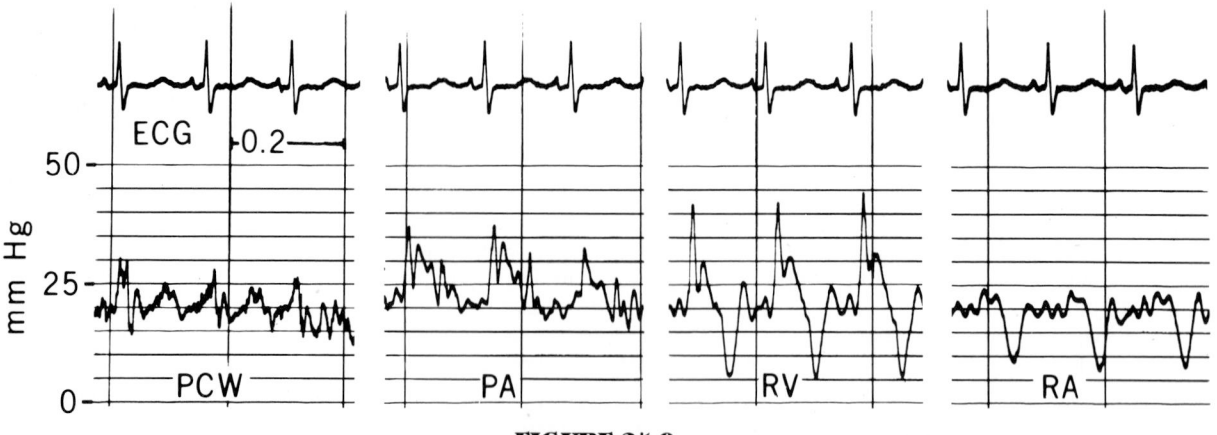

FIGURE 24-9

Simultaneous recording of electrocardiogram (ECG) and right heart pullback pressures in a patient with left ventricular (LV) inferior wall and diffuse right ventricular (RV) infarction secondary to a total occlusion of the proximal right coronary artery. Note that the left and right filling pressures are equal. PCW = pulmonary capillary wedge, PA = pulmonary artery, RV = right ventricle, and RA = right atrium. The RV and RA signals have an early diastolic dip and plateau pattern. (*From J. A. Mantle et al.: Advances in the treatment of heart failure, to be published as a chapter in Critical Care Cardiology, Cardiovascular Clinics, Philadelphia, Davis. Reproduced by permission.*)

least 4 to 5 mmHg, the cardiac output measurements are repeated to construct the function curve.

In addition to assessing and monitoring the cardiac hemodynamics, a pulmonary arterial catheter is also useful for withdrawing serial blood samples, for infusing fluids, and for administering medications. Pharmacologic agents or hyperosmotic solutions should be administered only via the central venous or proximal port and not through the pulmonary or distal port, since a selective infusion into a small pulmonary segment can produce an adverse vascular reaction. The ability to measure both the mixed venous and pulmonary arterial oxygen saturations by sampling from the proximal and distal ports of the indwelling catheter provides a convenient method for documenting left-to-right shunts in patients with ruptured ventricular septum, artrial septal defects, or an intracardiac fistula.

Direct monitoring of the arterial pressure via an indwelling cannula is useful in the management of patients undergoing cardiac surgery, unstable cardiac patients undergoing noncardiac surgery, patients in shock, patients having a hypertensive crisis, patients receiving nitroprusside, and patients requiring aortic counterpulsation. An arterial line is also convenient for obtaining serial arterial blood gas samples from patients with pulmonary failure, especially when ventilatory support is required. The most common site for introducing an indwelling arterial line is the radial artery. A short cannula can be introduced percutaneously with minimal risk. An alternative approach that is useful for patients in shock with peripheral vasoconstriction is to advance a long cannula into the subclavian artery via the brachial artery using the Seldinger technique.

Echocardiography

Echocardiography is a noninvasive bedside technique that utilizes ultrasound waves to visualize cardiac structures. Mitral stenosis, mitral prolapse, aortic stenosis, cardiomyopathy, atrial myxomas, and idiopathic hypertrophic subaortic stenosis can all be readily demonstrated with bedside echocardiography. In the critical-care unit the echocardiogram is especially valuable for identifying and estimating the amount of pericardial effusions in patients suspected of having cardiac tamponade (see Fig. 24-11). The posterior echo-free space (white arrow) indicates a large volume of fluid in the pericardial space in this patient with cardiac tamponade. The slow cyclic motion of the interventricular septum (black arrow)

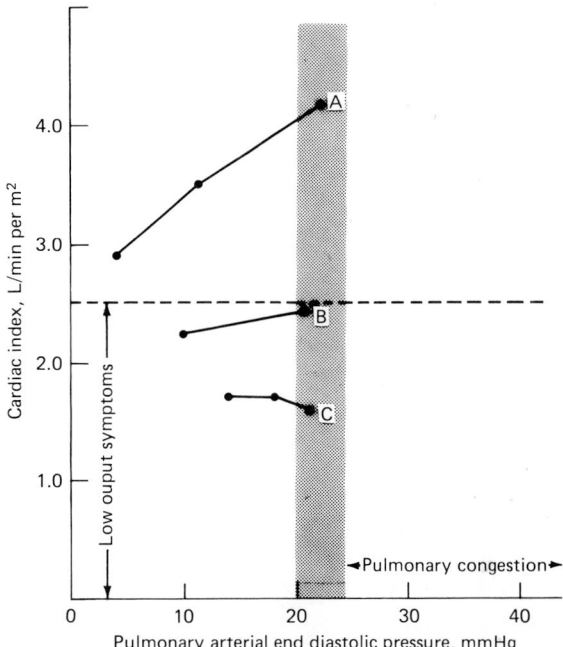

FIGURE 24-10

Left ventricular function curves produced by the rapid infusion of low molecular weight dextran. Curve A has a normal ascending slope. Curve B was depressed as a result of moderate left ventricular dysfunction. Curve C illustrates the descending limb in a patient with severe heart failure. The ranges for symptomatic low cardiac output and pulmonary congestion are indicated by the arrows. The shaded range of 20 to 24 mmHg is the upper limit of the optimal left ventricular filling pressure. (*From J. A. Mantle, et al.: Advances in the treatment of heart failure, to be published as a chapter in Critical Care Cardiology, Cardiovascular Clinics, Philadelphia, Davis. Reproduced by permission.*)

results from the accentuated effects of respiration on venous filling of the heart in cardiac tamponade and is the echocardiographic equivalent of a paradoxical pulse. The two-dimensional echocardiogram is useful for assessing ventricular function, visualizing segmental wall motion abnormalities, demonstrating ventricular aneurysms, and detecting mural thrombi.

Fluoroscopy

Bedside portable fluoroscopy is a valuable aid in the initial placement and follow-up of pulmonary arterial, right ventricular, and atrial catheters. Fluoroscopy is frequently necessary for the successful right heart

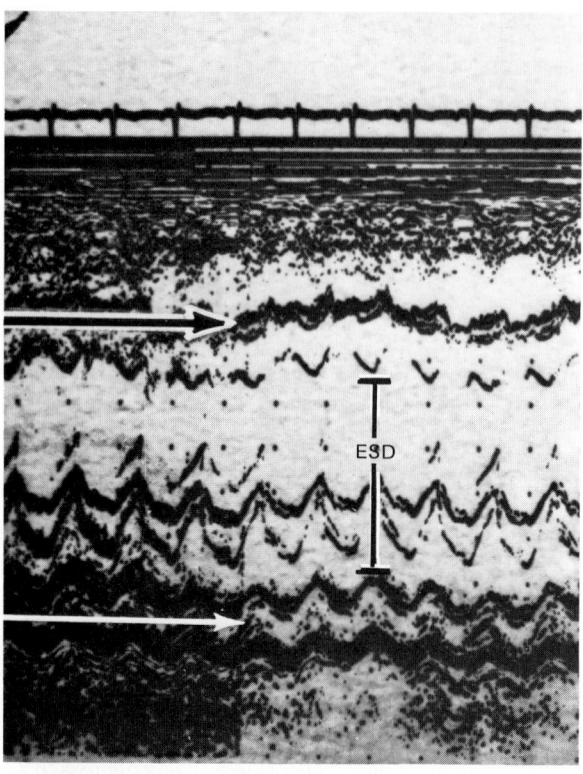

FIGURE 24-11

Echocardiogram (M mode) of a patient with cardiac tamponade. The left ventricular end systolic diameter (ESD) is shown. The white arrow points to an abnormal posterior echo-free space which indicates a significant pericardial effusion. The septal wall (black arrow) has an accentuated cyclic respiratory motion which reduces the left ventricular volume during inspiration and produces pulsus parodoxus.

catheterization of patients with tortuous veins, low cardiac output, tricuspid regurgitation, or markedly dilated right heart chambers. Visualization of the electrode position is important when (1) the pacing threshhold is high, (2) capture is unreliable, or (3) rapid atrial pacing is planned. Other applications of bedside fluoroscopy in unstable cardiac patients include (1) visualization of the needle during pericardiocentesis, (2) identification of calcium in the coronary arteries or cardiac valves, and (3) assessment of prosthetic valves by measuring both the valve ring movement and the excursion of the disk or ball. The routine use of radiolucent beds permits fluoroscopy to be easily and safely performed without the need for moving the patient.

Scintigraphy

As a result of major advances in radionuclide imaging, cardiac scintigraphy has become an important technique in the evaluation of unstable cardiac patients. Cardiac scanning techniques can be subdivided into three types. The first produces a "hot spot" image of acute myocardial infarction by the selective bonding of a labeled substrate to the necrotic myocardium. The most commonly used hot spot scanning agent is pyrophosphate labeled with technetium-99 particles (^{99m}Tc). With hot spot imaging, the area of infarction can be localized and the extent of necrosis can be semiquantitated. Patients who have a large anterior wall myocardial infarction will have a doughnut-shaped image, resulting from the inability of the substrate to penetrate deeply into the necrotic tissue (see Fig. 24-12). The doughnut image is associated with a poor prognosis because of the extensive myocardial damage. Infarcted myocardium will bind pyrophosphate from approximately 18 h after the acute event until the fifth or sixth day. In the subset of patients with continuing ischemia, the hot spot scan may remain persistently positive for an indefinite period. False positive scans can result from persistent blood pool activity, recent dC cardioversions, and myocarditis.

The second type of scintigram uses labeled metabolic substrates or their analogs to produce "cold spot" images in the zones of ischemia or scar. Thallium 201 (^{201}Tl), an analog of potassium, is the most commonly used cold spot scanning agent (see Fig. 24-13). In the critical-care unit setting, thallium scans are useful to detect, localize, and quantitate infarcted myocardium. A thallium defect is not specific for acute myocardial infarction, however, since a transient ischemic attack or a healed scar will also produce a cold spot. A thallium defect resulting from a transient ischemic attack will disappear as the ischemic zone is reperfused, while a defect resulting from an acute myocardial infarction or a healed scar will persist. Cold spot imaging is especially useful in the evaluation of patients who are in the subacute phase of their myocardial infarction since the enzymes will have returned to normal and the infarcted myocardium will no longer bind the hot spot agents. The combination of thallium imaging with limited exercise testing or rapid pacing can be used to detect transient reversible ischemic areas in the more stable patients.

The third type of radionuclide studies assess wall motion and ventricular function by two different methods. The first pass method consists of recording the

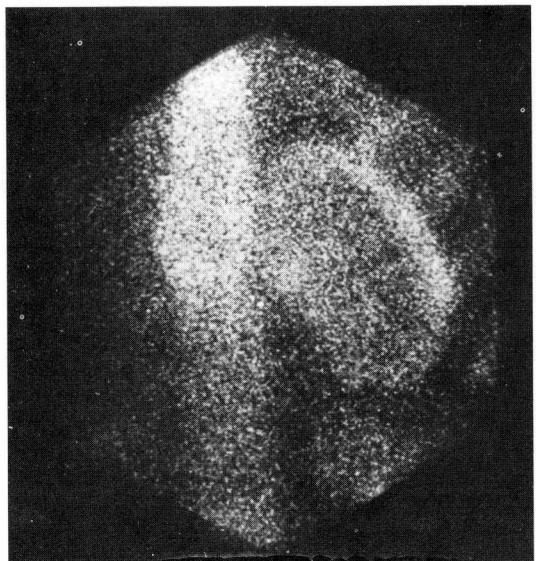 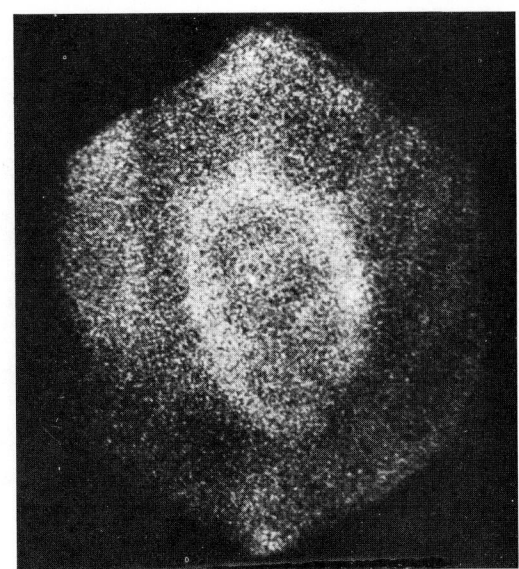

FIGURE 24-12

Myocardial scintigram using technetium-labeled pyrophosphate (^{99m}Tc-PYP) of an acute anterior wall myocardial infarction in the (*a*) anterior and (*b*) left anterior oblique views. The ^{99m}Tc-PYP is taken up by the bones and by the recently infarcted myocardium (hot spot). The doughnut shape indicates a very large infarction and carries a poor prognosis. (*Courtesy of Dr. J. Logic.*)

radioactivity in the heart as a "bolus" of isotope is pumped through the circulation. With the aid of computer processing, the ventricular ejection fraction and regional wall motion can be measured. The first pass method can be used to assess both the right and left ventricle in the right anterior oblique (RAO) projection. The gated blood pool method is performed by counting the cardiac blood pool activity over several minutes (2 to 6 min) into multiple "electrocardiographic gated images." The R wave of the electrocardiogram is used as a reference point to subdivide the cardiac cycle into windows or gates. The counts collected within each gate are used to construct the image for that segment of the cardiac cycle. Because of the simultaneous activity in both the right and left ventricles, the gated images must be obtained in the left anterior oblique (LAO) projection in order to separate the two chambers. With a 20° cranial angulation of the camera, the ventricles can be imaged in a long axial view for a clearer visualization of the septal, apical, and free wall segments (see Fig. 24-14). Serial gated studies are useful to

monitor the acute clinical course, the response to therapeutic interventions, and the effects of exercise.

Arterial Blood Gases

Measurement of the arterial oxygen, carbon dioxide, and pH is a useful method for assessing disturbances in cardiac, pulmonary, and metabolic function. Clinical problems that alter ventilatory gas exchange, cardiac output, pulmonary venous pressures, alveolar membrane properties, systemic metabolism, or respiratory center function will produce disturbances in the normal balance between these three parameters. Although arterial hypoxia is a nonspecific finding that can result from intrinsic lung disease, pulmonary infection, congestive heart failure, noncardiac pulmonary edema, right-to-left cardiac shunts, airway obstruction, pulmonary emboli, and asphyxiation, the arterial oxygen level is a useful parameter in assessing the severity of the problem and monitoring the clinical course. Patients who hyperventilate will develop a pattern of respiratory alkalosis with paresthesias and

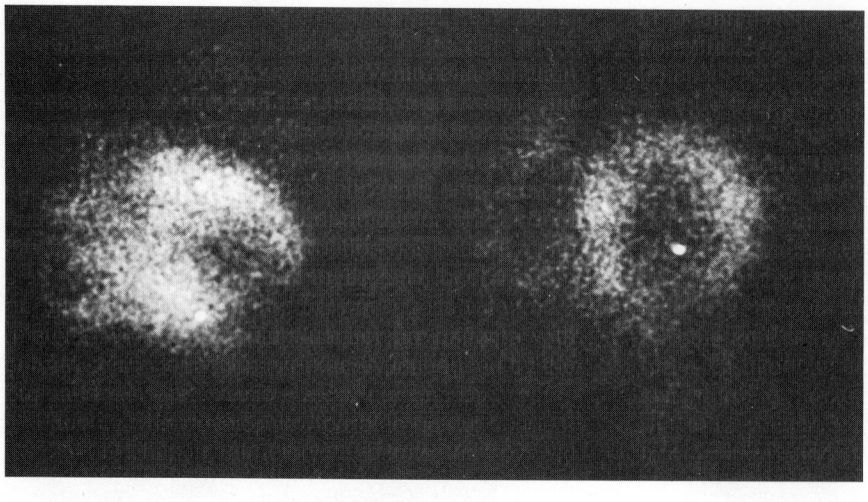

a   *b*

FIGURE 24-13

Myocardial scintigram (using thallium 201) of an apical infarction in the (*a*) anterior and (*b*) left anterior oblique views. The thallium, a potassium analog, is taken up by the normal myocardium and thus a defect (cold spot) occurs in the infarcted apical area. (*Courtesy of Dr. J. Logic.*)

near syncope. In selected cases it is useful to reproduce these symptoms by voluntary hyperventilation in order to demonstrate the nature of the problem to the patient and family. Respiratory acidosis results from respiratory failure, while metabolic acidosis can result from lactic acidosis, ketoacidosis, drug intoxications, and renal failure. Lactic acidosis is a complication of inadequate peripheral perfusion generally from low cardiac output shock. The development of acute metabolic acidosis is a serious complication of a cardiac arrest and must be corrected in order to resuscitate the patient.

Angiography

As a result of the continuing improvement in cardiac surgical and anesthesia techniques and results, the indications for diagnostic angiography have been significantly expanded. Angiographic studies provide a detailed visualization of the coronary arteries, a demonstration of the cardiac anatomy, a documentation of valvular and perivalvular regurgitation, a localization of intracardiac shunts, and an assessment of ventricular function and regional wall motion. Although angiography is an invasive procedure that utilizes a contrast agent which transiently depresses cardiac function, the procedure can be performed

with low risk in both stable and unstable patients. Even patients with low cardiac output shock can undergo angiographic studies with the support of intra-aortic counterpulsation. The specific indications and optimal timing for proceeding with angiographic studies are continually changing. Unstable patients with a diagnosis of unstable angina pectoris, aortic dissection, ventricular septal rupture, acute mitral regurgitation, or prosthetic valve dysfunction are candidates for urgent or emergency angiographic studies as indicated by the clinical course. The evaluation of suspected pulmonary emboli may also require angiography in selected patients when the pulmonary scan is nondiagnostic or when vena caval plication or embolectomy is a consideration. The angiographic evaluation of patients with acute myocardial infarction should generally be postponed until the convalescent phase unless one of the above indications is present. The more routine use of angiographic studies in the evaluation of patients 2 to 3 weeks following acute myocardial infarction has been shown to be a safe and useful method for identifying high-risk patients and establishing the long-term treatment plan and prognosis.

A special laboratory is necessary for cardiac angiographic studies. The selective injection of contrast dye directly into the coronary arteries and coronary

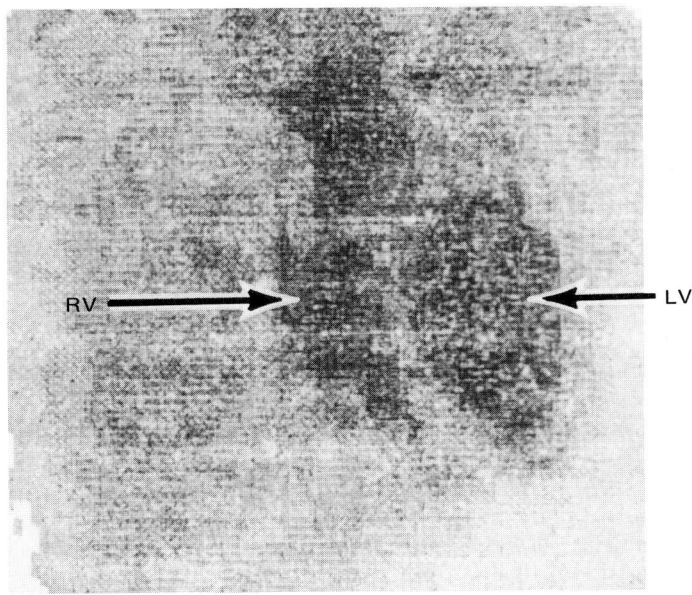

RV ◄———— ————► LV

FIGURE 24-14

Gated scintigram of right ventricle (RV) and left ventricle (LV) in diastole. The 20° cranial 60° left anterior oblique (LAO) view is used to separate the two ventricular blood pools and visualize the chambers in a long axial projection. This image is the summation over 6 min of all the counts obtained during the end diastolic gate or window.

grafts permits the anatomy, stenotic segments, and collateral flow to be defined. In addition to demonstrating the location and severity of coronary stenoses, the distal segments can be examined with reference to the placement of bypass grafts. Left ventriculography provides information on both the anatomy and function of the ventricle as well as the mitral and aortic valves. As a result of recent advances in the equipment design, the conventional anterior/lateral or LAO/RAO views have been replaced with long axial 20° cranial 60° LAO and 45° RAO projections for better visualization of the septal, posterior, and apical wall segments (see Fig. 24-15). In addition to improving the assessment of the segmental wall motion, the cranial LAO projection is useful for the localization of septal defects, the detection of mitral valve abnormalities, and the demonstration of left ventricular outflow tract obstruction. The calculation of the end systolic and diastolic volumes and ejection fraction is a valuable method for quantitating global ventricular function (see Fig. 24-15). It is important to note that since the stroke volume is directly related to the

product of the end diastolic volume and ejection fraction, the patient shown in Fig. 24-15 has been able to maintain a normal stroke volume of 55 mL despite an abnormally low ejection fraction of 0.32 (normal >0.55) because of the ventricular dilatation.

The evaluation of patients with ischemic heart disease requires an assessment of the regional wall motion abnormalities in addition to the measurement of the global function. Biplane ventriculography permits an evaluation of the septal, anterior, lateral, inferior, posterior, apical, and basilar wall segments. Wall motion is characterized as being normal, hypokinetic (reduced systolic motion), akinetic (no systolic motion), or dyskinetic (paradoxical systolic motion). In addition to a subjective visual assessment, the segmental wall motion can be objectively evaluated by calculating both the size of the abnormally contracting segment and the regional ejection fractions (see Fig. 24-15). The left ventriculogram shown in this illustration was obtained 3 weeks following an acute myocardial infarction in a patient with an isolated obstruction of the left anterior descending cor-

EDV = 172 ml   EF = .32   - - - Diastole
ESV = 117 ml   %ACS = 43   —— Systole

45° RAO

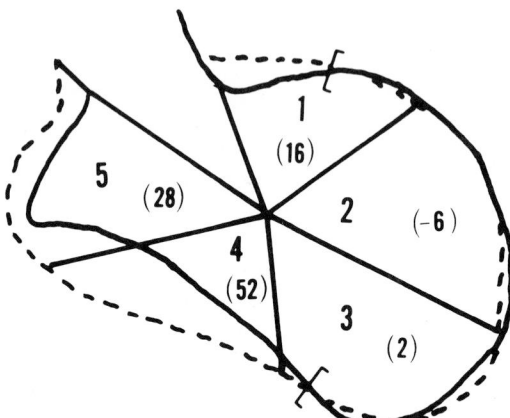

20° Cranial 60° LAO

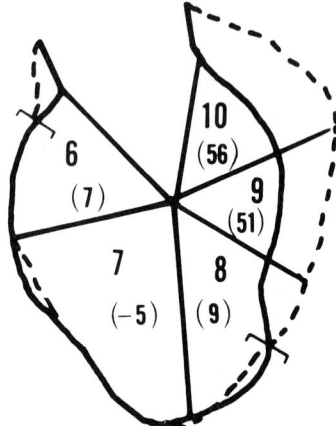

FIGURE 24-15

Angiographic analysis of left ventricular function in a patient 3 weeks postmyocardial infarction with an isolated left anterior descending occlusion and a large anterior septal and apical scar. The left ventricular end diastolic and systolic silhouettes were recorded in the 45° right anterior oblique (RAO) and 20° cranial 60° left anterior oblique (LAO) projections. The [ ] indicate the akinetic or dyskinetic segments. The 10 segments are useful to analyze the regional wall motion. The numbers in the parentheses ( ) are the segmental area ejection fractions defined as the (diastolic area—systolic area)/diastolic area. EDV = end diastolic volume, ESV = end systolic volume, EF = global ejection fraction defined as (EDV − ESV)/EDV, %ACS = percent abnormal contracting segment defined as akinetic and dyskinetic segments/diastolic circumference.

onary artery. The serial electrocardiograms showed the typical evolutionary changes of an anteroseptal myocardial infarction corresponding to the abnormally contracting anterior, septal, and apical location wall segments.

APPROACH TO THERAPY

With the support of the special techniques described in the previous section for assessing the etiology and extent of the cardiovascular problem, a rational physiologic approach can be developed for restoring and stabilizing cardiac function. Since the optimal management of a cardiac problem is dependent on an accurate assessment of the cardiac pathophysiology, the design and supporting facilities of the critical-care unit should be compatible with the needs of the patients who are admitted to that unit. The following

sections describe the clinical assessment of the six determinants of left ventricular function and the therapeutic management of the more common clinical cardiac problems.

Preload

Clinical Assessment

Preload is a term borrowed from the muscle laboratory and is defined as the "diastolic" stretch on the muscle fiber prior to contraction. For isolated cardiac muscle, it is known that the extent of stretch placed on the fibers prior to contraction (within the normal physiologic limits) will result in a progressively stronger contraction. The principle was demonstrated for the intact animal heart by Frank and Starling who both demonstrated that the diastolic volume (preload) was an important determinant of systolic performance.

Sarnoff further defined the role of preload in the animal model by constructing a family of function curves. The slope of the curve relating the systolic cardiac performance to the preload was shown to be directly related to the underlying left ventricular function. Interventions that interfered with normal muscle contraction, such as hypoxia, depressed the slope, while interventions that enhanced the strength of muscle contraction, such as catecholamines, increased the function curve slope.

In the clinical setting, preload can be estimated by measuring the left ventricular filling pressures, as illustrated in Fig. 24-10. The ascending curve A demonstrates a normal improvement in cardiac index in response to the increase in preload produced by the rapid infusion of low-molecular-weight dextran. Curve B was recorded from a patient with moderate left ventricular dysfunction following myocardial infarction. The abnormally low resting cardiac index and depressed slope both indicate significant left ventricular dysfunction. Since the left ventricular filling pressure is only an indirect measure of the diastolic stretch on the myocardial fibers, a depressed slope can result from a loss of either normal function or compliance or both. In the spectrum of cardiac disorders, the relative importance of these two factors ranges from mostly muscle dysfunction (dilated failing heart) to mostly altered compliance (hypertrophied heart). Curve C was recorded from a patient in cardiogenic shock secondary to extensive myocardial infarction. The baseline cardiac index was significantly reduced, the initial segment of the function curve was flat, and the terminal segment demonstrates the descending limb. The range of 20 to 24 mmHg indicated by the shaded zone has been shown to be the upper limit of the optimal left ventricular filling pressure. Above this range, ventricular function may deteriorate, as shown by Curve C, and most patients will develop pulmonary congestion.

In addition to measuring the left ventricular filling pressure at the time of right heart catheterization, it is important to monitor the changes that occur during the clinical course and in response to therapeutic interventions. The serial measurements plotted in Fig. 24-16 demonstrate the use of extended hemodynamic monitoring in an unstable patient with an acute myocardial infarction. The initial pulmonary arterial end diastolic pressure was normal at 8 mmHg. Several hours after admission the patient developed severe prolonged pain, and despite the administration of nitrates and morphine sulfate, the left ventricular filling pressure progressively rose to greater than 20 mmHg. By the second day after treatment with nitrates and diuretics, the pulmonary venous pressure had returned to normal. During the fourth day the patient had two severe but transient episodes of ischemic pain. With each attack, there was an abrupt elevation in the pulmonary venous pressure which responded promptly to sublingual nitrates. On the fifth and sixth days the patient was given a trial infusion of dextran to assess left ventricular function. On each occasion the patient had a marked elevation in the left ventricular filling pressure with no change in the cardiac output, resulting in a flat function curve. Subsequent

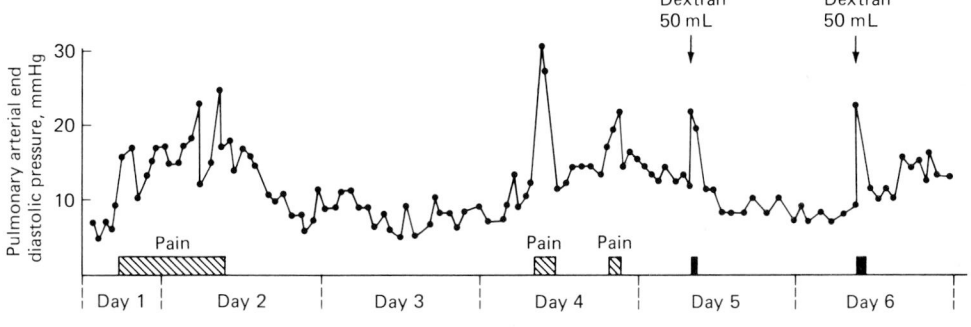

FIGURE 24-16

Plot of pulmonary arterial end diastolic pressure over acute 6-day course of patient with an acute myocardial infarction, recurrent pain, and significant left ventricular failure. Dextran was infused to construct left ventricular function curves. (*From C. E. Rackley et al.: Hemodynamic measurements of heart failure in patients with myocardial infarction, in Hemodynamic Monitoring in a Coronary Intensive Care Unit, chap. 9, Mt. Kisco, N.Y., Futura, 1974, p. 213. Reproduced by permission.*)

angiographic studies documented extensive coronary artery disease as well as severe left ventricular dysfunction.

Hypovolemia

The recognition and identification of patients with low cardiac output secondary to a low preload is critically important, since the prognosis can be significantly improved with volume replacement. Patients admitted to a critical-care unit may have many causes of hypovolemia including diuretic therapy, vomiting, bleeding, dialysis, bowel obstruction, trauma, sepsis, restricted intake, nasogastric suction, and diarrhea.

Although patients with normal ventricular function may be able to compensate for an abnormally low preload, patients with impaired ventricular function and reduced ventricular compliance will develop low cardiac output and even shock from an inadequate left ventricular filling pressure. Patients with advanced heart failure will frequently require a ventricular filling pressure above normal to maintain an adequate preload.

The diagnosis of hypovolemia should be considered in the differential diagnosis of any patient with signs or symptoms of low cardiac output. The combination of orthostatic hypotension, flat neck veins, tachycardia, and oliguria all strongly suggest hypovolemia. A right heart catheterization is useful to detect and demonstrate the presence of hypovolemia and to monitor the response during fluid replacement. If no objective measurements of the ventricular filling pressure are available, a trial expansion of the blood volume with a colloid (low-molecular-weight dextran, albumin, or blood) is a useful therapeutic test for hypovolemia.

The administration of diuretics for the finding of rales is a common iatrogenic cause of hypovolemia. Patients with acute myocardial infarction will frequently develop transient elevations in the pulmonary venous pressures and rales during the acute pain. With the relief of pain, however, the pulmonary venous pressure will generally return to normal, but the rales will persist since the fluid in the alveolar space cannot be cleared immediately. The administration of a diuretic, therefore, can reduce the preload to a critically low value and result in the development of hypovolemia despite the auscultatory findings of rales.

The clinical picture of a relative hypovolemia will be present in patients with large right ventricular infarctions, cardiac tamponade, pericardial constriction, and restrictive cardiomyopathy. In all these cases, the left ventricular filling pressure will overestimate the true preload or diastolic stretch on the myocardium. The diagnosis of right ventricular infarction should be suspected in patients with inferior wall infarction and low cardiac output. The right and left heart filling pressures will be equal and the diastolic dip and plateau pattern will be present in the more severe cases (see Fig. 24-9).

A rapid accumulation of fluid within the pericardial space will abnormally elevate the pericardial pressure and reduce the diastolic filling of the left ventricle. The diagnosis of cardiac tamponade should be considered in the differential diagnosis of hypotension and low cardiac output in patients with chest trauma, recent cardiac surgery, pericarditis, uremia, and metastatic cancer. In addition to the physical signs of pulsus paradoxus and distended neck veins, the echocardiographic demonstration of a significant amount of pericardial fluid and the equalization of right- and left-sided pressures are important clinical findings for establishing the diagnosis of cardiac tamponade. Pericardial constriction and restrictive cardiomyopathy are less common and usually present as subacute problems. Both of these conditions restrict the normal diastolic filling of the left ventricle and thus produce a clinical picture of low cardiac output. The diagnosis of pericardial constriction can occasionally be made from the chest x-ray finding of a calcified pericardial shell. The diagnosis of restrictive cardiomyopathy is made by exclusion and requires a full diagnostic evaluation.

Independent of which of these four conditions is present, the initial approach to therapy is similar. The right-sided filling pressures must be kept abnormally high with colloid expansion of the blood volume. Supplement catecholamines may be required to maintain an adequate blood pressure in patients with acute right ventricular infarction or cardiac tamponade. The patient with acute right ventricular infarction will generally stabilize and improve over a 2- to 4-day period as the pericardium enlarges and relieves the left ventricular compression. Once the diagnosis of cardiac tamponade is made, pericardiocentesis or direct surgical drainage is indicated. Repeated pericardiocentesis should be avoided whenever possible by early surgery. Frequently the pericardial fluid will be loculated which precludes adequate drainage via a needle. Pericardial constriction requires surgical removal. Restrictive cardiomyopathy does not lend itself to a direct form of therapy.

Pulmonary Venous Hypertension

The optimal management of pulmonary congestion is dependent on identifying the underlying pathophysiology. Pulmonary edema will generally develop when the pulmonary venous pressure is acutely elevated above 24 mmHg. As discussed in the section on the diagnostic evaluation of the patient, alveolar fluid may persist for up to 18 h or more after the pulmonary venous pressure has been reduced below 20 mmHg. Patients may also develop pulmonary edema from a wide variety of noncardiac causes with normal pulmonary pressures. It is important, therefore, when planning therapy, to carefully consider both the differential diagnosis between cardiac and noncardiac pulmonary edema and the phase lag that can occur between the clinical signs and the pulmonary venous pressures. Great care must be taken to avoid making a patient hypovolemic as a result of diuretic therapy which was based on misleading clinical findings.

In addition to the conventional management of pulmonary congestion with bedrest, sodium restriction, digitalis, and diuretics, vasodilators can be used to reduce the pulmonary venous hypertension. Vasodilator therapy is actually a more physiologic approach to the management of acute pulmonary venous hypertension that results from a loss of the normal cardiac compliance and an increase in venous tone and not from excessive sodium retention. Although the discussion in this section is focused on the venous vasodilating effects, it is important to remember that most vasodilator drugs will affect both the preload and afterload of the left ventricle.

There are many drugs available for clinical use with vasodilator properties. The most commonly used vasodilators for the management of pulmonary venous hypertension include the nitrates, nitroprusside, prazosin, and aminophylline. Morphine is also a useful agent in the management of acute pulmonary edema. The nitrates, which can be given in sublingual, intravenous and cutaneous forms, have a predominant venous vasodilator effect. The responses to sublingual nitroglycerine and sublingual isosorbide dinitrate in patients with severe cardiac congestive failure are shown in Fig. 24-17. These patients had severe congestive failure following myocardial infarction with elevated filling pressures above the 20- to 24-mmHg range and were refractory to conventional treatment with digitalis, diuretics, sodium restriction, and bedrest. The nitroglycerine successfully lowered the pulmonary venous pressure, with its peak effect occurring at 5 min; its duration, however, was limited to less

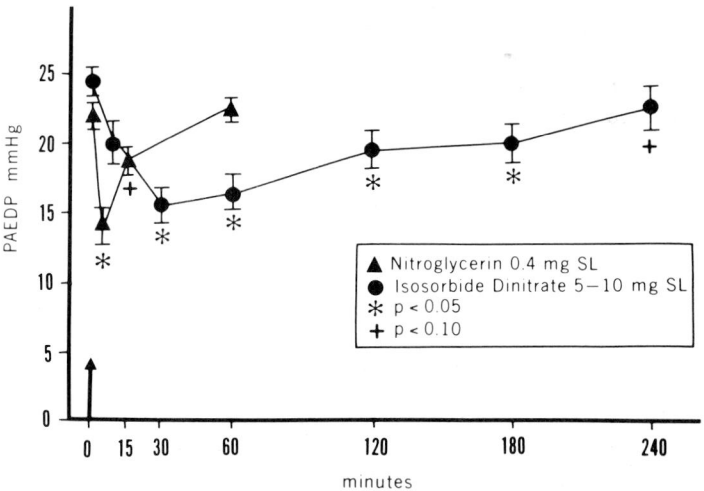

FIGURE 24-17

Effects of nitroglycerine and isosorbide dinitrate on the pulmonary venous hypertension in patients with acute congestive heart failure (CHF) secondary to myocardial infarction (MI). The sublingual (SL) dose was given at time 0. PAEDP = pulmonary arterial end diastolic pressure. *(From J. A. Mantle et al.: Isosorbide dinitrate for the relief of severe heart failure after myocardial infarction, Am J Cardiol 37: 263–268, 1976. Reproduced by permission.)*

than 30 min. The response to sublingual isosorbide dinitrate was similar in magnitude. Although the onset of action was slower, with the peak response occurring at 30 min, the duration was more prolonged, with a reduction in the pulmonary venous hypertension persisting for up to 3 to 4 h. This reduction in the pulmonary arterial end diastolic pressure was associated with a relief of the pulmonary congestion. Nitroprusside and prazosin have more balanced venous and arterial vasodilator properties. Nitroprusside must be given intravenously, can produce severe hypotension, and is generally not required for the management of pulmonary congestion. As will be discussed in the next section on afterload, nitroprusside is most useful in the management of hypertension or severe low cardiac output. Prazosin is an oral agent which is useful in the management of patients with congestive heart failure, especially in those patients who are refractory to nitrate therapy. The prazosin dose must be carefully titrated to prevent orthostatic hypertension. With chronic administration, a tolerance to the hemodynamic effects of both isosorbide dini-

trate and prazosin may develop, especially if the patient has been permitted to expand blood volume by the retention of excessive sodium.

Vasodilator agents can potentiate the renal response to diuretic agents as shown in Fig. 24-18. This patient had an acute myocardial infarction and developed low cardiac output congestive heart failure with a pulmonary arterial end diastolic pressure of 32 mmHg and a cardiac index of 2.2 L/min per m². During the initial 24 h, the 8-h input-output balances were positive and the patient was oliguric with a urine flow of less than 30 mL/h despite intravenous furosemide. With the addition of 2.5 mg sublingual isosorbide dinitrate, the patient had a diuretic response of 1200 mL to a repeat intravenous bolus of furosemide. There was no change in the cardiac output, but the pulmonary arterial end diastolic pressure fell to 18 mmHg. At the higher dose of 7.5 mg every 3 h, the spontaneous urine flow was increased to > 50 mL/h. This patient continued to require supplemental diuretic therapy, however, to prevent edema formation. The improvement in the renal function and the syn-

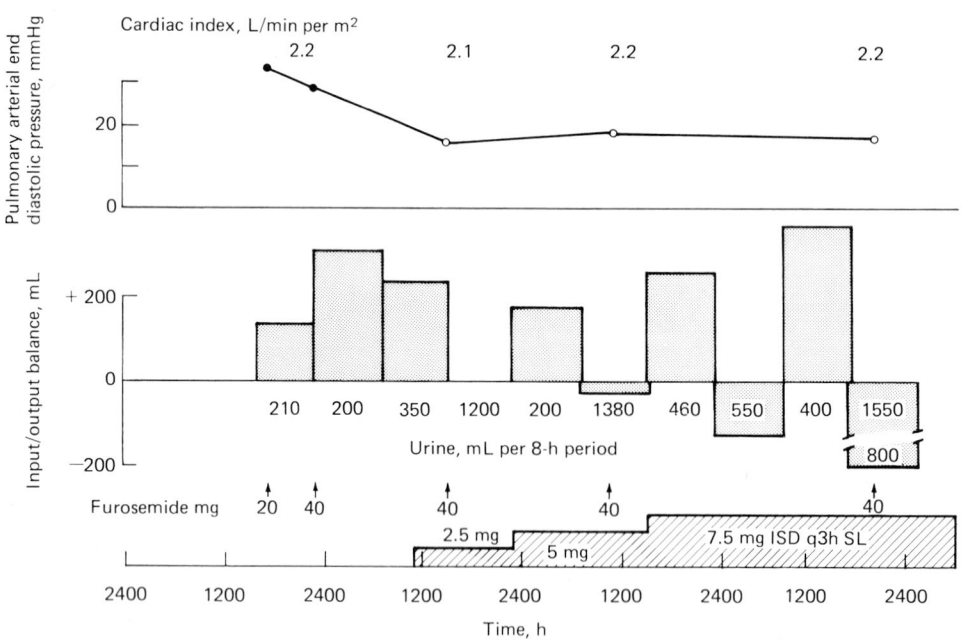

FIGURE 24-18

Case example of acute low cardiac output congestive heart failure with oliguria that improved with isosorbide dinitrate (ISD). See text for discussion. (*From J. A. Mantle et al.: Advances in the treatment of heart failure, to be published as a chapter in Critical Care Cardiology, Cardiovascular Clinics, Philadelphia, Davis. Reproduced by permission.*)

ergistic response to the furosemide results from an increase in the renal plasma flow that was produced by the vasodilator effects on the abnormally vasoconstricted renal vascular bed. Clinical studies in our laboratory have shown that the renal response and the cardiac response are not directly related as illustrated by the data in Fig. 24-18. Despite this improvement in renal function, the subgroup of patients with severe low output failure and arterial hypotension are inclined to develop refractory edema during chronic vasodilator and furosemide therapy. This clinical picture of tolerance can generally be reversed and prevented by the addition of spironalactone or triamterene. This response to the addition of spironalactone indicates that these patients develop a significant secondary hyperaldosteronism. In severe low cardiac output failure, the addition of a diuretic with a more proximal site of action, such as hydrochlorothiazide or metolazone, may also become necessary. When a vasodilator agent is added to a management program which already includes diuretics, it is important to carefully monitor the diuretic response in order to avoid producing hypovolemia. With the addition of vasodilators, the dose of furosemide will generally need to be reduced and a combination of proximal and distal tubular diuretics added. The prerenal azotemia that develops in patients with severe low cardiac output failure will generally reverse with the addition of vasodilators in response to the increase in renal blood flow. If the patient is overdiuresed, however, the cardiac output and renal blood flow will fall and the prerenal azotemia will recur. This pattern of a fall in the blood urea nitrogen in response to therapy followed by a subsequent rise is a useful clinical method for determining the patient's optimal preload or dry weight.

Afterload

Clinical Assessment

Afterload is defined from the papillary muscle laboratory as that force which resists shortening and is inversely related to the rate and extent of muscle contraction. As the afterload is increased, the rate and extent of contraction of the muscle decreases. For the intact heart, afterload can be best approximated by calculating the systolic wall stress (the force per cross-sectional area that resists shortening). The circumferential wall stress (σ) of the left ventricle is directly proportional to the product of the left ventric-

ular pressure (p) and radius of curvature (r) divided by the wall thickness (h):

$$\sigma \approx \frac{pr}{h}$$

The systolic wall stress is near maximal at the time of aortic valve opening, remains fairly constant during ejection, and then rapidly falls during diastolic relaxation. The aortic impedance (the instantaneous relationship between aortic flow and pressure) is directly proportional to the ventricular afterload since the aortic impedance affects both the pressure and volume during ejection. When systolic performance fails, the stroke volume falls and the aortic impedance increases to maintain the systolic pressure. The increased systolic impedance, however, further impairs ventricular ejection and results in even higher systolic wall stresses which further reduces the stroke volume. The major task in the management of low output failure, therefore, is to interrupt this cycle of progressive increase in afterload and decrease in ventricular performance. Since the left ventricular afterload is also a major determinant of oxygen consumption, a major goal in the medical management of angina pectoris is to also reduce the systolic wall stress.

Low Cardiac Output

Patients who develop low cardiac output failure as a result of pressure overload will usually respond promptly to a reduction in the systolic pressure. This can be achieved in patients with hypertension by the use of antihypertension medications and in the case of aortic stenosis, with replacement of the valve. Patients with mild to moderate aortic or mitral valve regurgitation will generally increase their cardiac output with arterial vasodilatation. With severe valve regurgitation, ruptured ventricular septum, or intracardiac fistula, urgent surgical correction should be considered in the management plan. The subgroup of patients who develop low cardiac output failure as a result of muscle damage are generally more difficult to manage. Although the systolic pressure in these patients is typically low at 100 mmHg or less, vasodilators can generally be used to lower the left ventricular afterload and improve the systolic performance as shown in Fig. 24-19. In response to the effects of isosorbide dinitrate, the patients with normal ventricular function moved down the ascending limb of their function curve, while the patients with severe congestive heart failure shifted to an improved func-

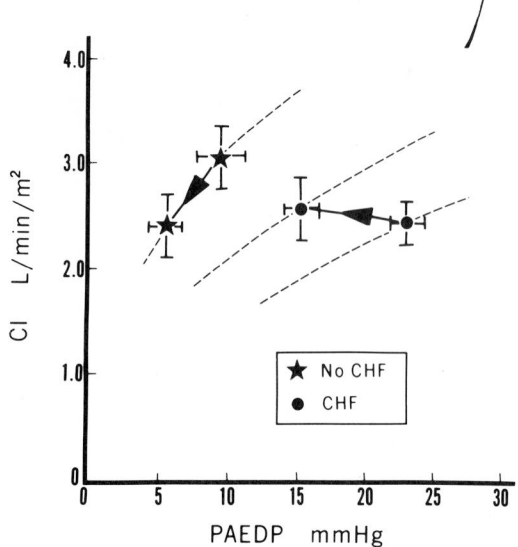

FIGURE 24-19

The effects of isosorbide dinitrate on left ventricular overload. The mean values ± the standard errors are plotted before and after isosorbide dinitrate for patients with normal resting cardiac function and for patients with severe heart failure. The arrowhead indicates the direction of change. The hatched curves are the family of theoretical left ventricular function curves. The patients with normal left ventricular function moved down the ascending limb in response to the drop in preload. The patients with severe heart failure, in contrast, shifted to a better function curve in response to the combined venous and arterial vasodilation. CHF = congestive heart failure. (*From J. A. Mantle et al.: Advances in the treatment of heart failure, to be published as a chapter in Critical Care Cardiology, Cardiovascular Clinics, Philadelphia, Davis. Reproduced by permission.*)

tion curve. This improvement in ventricular function resulted from a significant reduction in the ventricular afterload. The administration of vasodilator agents which have a stronger arterial vasodilating effect, such as nitroprusside, will usually shift patients with heart failure to an even steeper curve. These data illustrate that ventricular function in patients with congestive failure is limited by the afterload and can be improved by reducing the wall stress with vasodilators, while ventricular function in patients with normal cardiac function is primarily influenced by the preload.

Patients who develop low cardiac output congestive failure that is refractory to nitrate therapy will generally respond to the use of a stronger agent such as nitroprusside, prazosin, or hydralazine. Nitroprusside is a potent intravenous vasodilator agent that is useful in the management of patients with severe hypertension or refractory low cardiac output failure. In shock patients nitroprusside can be used in conjunction with intra-aortic balloon counterpulsation and supplemental catecholamines. The use of nitroprusside is limited to a critical-care unit setting, and hemodynamic monitoring is generally indicated to titrate the dose for an optimal response. Prazosin is an oral vasodilator that can be used for both the acute and chronic treatment of heart failure. Since prazosin has a unique first-dose response, the initial dose should be small and the subsequent doses increased as indicated to prevent orthostatic hypotension. Hydralazine has a predominant arterial vasodilating effect with little or no venous vasodilator properties. The management of low cardiac output congestive heart failure with hydralazine, therefore, requires the supplemental administration of diuretics and long-acting nitrates.

The physiologic advantages of using vasodilators in the management of low cardiac output failure include a reduction in the oxygen demands of the left ventricle, a reduction in extent of regurgitation across incompetent mitral and aortic valves, interruption of the cyclic deterioration of cardiac function, and improving peripheral perfusion. The potential risks of using vasodilator therapy reside primarily in misdiagnoses and overtreatment. As shown in Fig. 24-19, patients who are not in heart failure will generally drop their cardiac output and blood pressure in response to vasodilators. The combined venous and arterial vasodilator effects plus the associated diuresis can also produce hypotension and even shock in patients with abnormal ventricular function and compliance.

Intra-Aortic Counterpulsation

The intra-aortic balloon technique for augmenting the diastolic pressure is useful in the management of selected patients with low output cardiac failure and shock. The intra-aortic balloon is introduced via the femoral artery by either a direct cutdown or percutaneous technique and advanced to the level of the mid-thoracic aorta. The electrocardiogram or electrogram is used to time the pulsations. The tracings shown in Fig. 24-20 illustrate the augmentation of the diastolic pressure produced by the inflation of the intra-aortic balloon. This patient had a papillary mus-

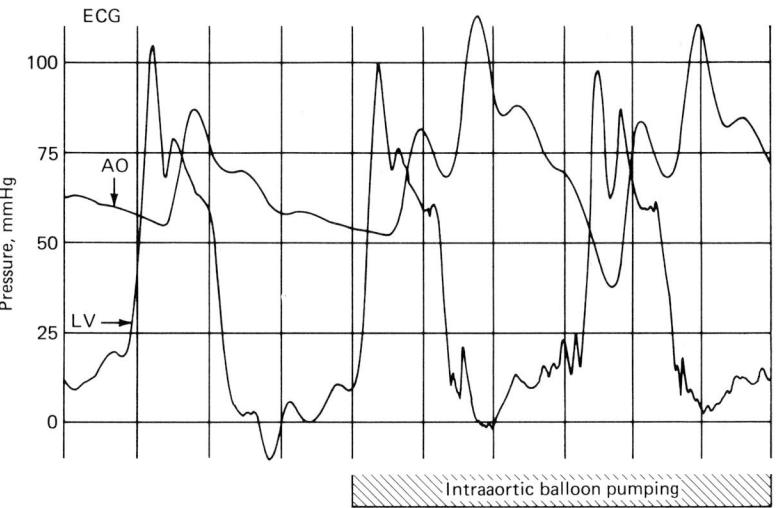

FIGURE 24-20

Aortic (AO) and left ventricular (LV) pressures in a patient before and during intra-aortic balloon pumping (IABP). The patient was in shock with acute mitral regurgitation secondary to myocardial infarction involving the papillary muscle. Note the increase in the middiastolic pressure and the drop in the preejection pressure during IABP. (*From J. A. Mantle et al.: Advances in the treatment of heart failure, to be published as a chapter in Critical Care Cardiology, Cardiovascular Clinics, Philadelphia, Davis. Reproduced by permission.*)

cle dysfunction complicating myocardial infarction and was in shock with an aortic pressure of 85/55 mmHg and a left ventricular filling pressure of 15 to 20 mmHg. During intra-aortic counterpulsation, the systolic pressure remained unchanged but the peak diastolic pressure was elevated to approximately 120 mmHg. During the late diastolic phase, when the balloon collapsed, the diastolic pressure dropped to approximately 37 mmHg. Since this drop in diastolic pressure occurs just before aortic valve opening, it does not interfere with coronary infusion but does allow the ventricle to eject blood at a much lower pressure. Since the ejection of blood at the lower pressure will reduce the systolic wall stress, the stroke volume will increase which will further improve the peripheral perfusion. The intra-aortic balloon is most useful in the support of patients with advanced cardiac failure during the preoperative and postoperative periods. Patients with intractable heart failure and shock from a ruptured ventricular septum, valvular dysfunction, acute papillary muscle rupture, and so on, can be supported with the intra-aortic balloon during diagnostic evaluation and surgery. Unfortunately, the use of intra-aortic balloon counterpulsation

in patients with cardiogenic shock who do not have a reversible cause has been unrewarding. Although an occasional patient may survive, the extensive underlying myocardial injury results in a very poor prognosis. Complications associated with the use of intra-aortic balloon counterpulsation include bleeding at the site of insertion, thrombosis of the distal femoral artery, aortic dissection, rupture of the balloon, and sepsis associated with the indwelling catheter.

Reduction of Myocardial Ischemia

Since the left ventricular systolic wall stress is a major determinant of myocardial oxygen consumption, the reduction in afterload is an important part of the medical management of patients with unstable ischemic heart disease. Patients with unstable angina will frequently have transient elevations of their blood pressure during periods of activity or stress, resulting in anginal attacks which can be prevented with the use of vasodilators and β-adrenergic blocking agents. Recent studies using intracoronary nitroglycerine have demonstrated that the predominant mechanism responsible for the relief of angina is secondary to the peripheral effects on afterload and not any direct effects on the coronary vascular bed. The β-adrenergic blocking agents, such as propranolol, prevent the development of tachycardia and further limit the increases in cardiac output and blood pressure that normally occur in response to exercise, anxiety, and stress. With the frequent administration of long-acting nitrates on a dose schedule of every 3 to 4 h and the initiation of effective beta blockade, patients who present with unstable angina or preinfarctional angina can generally be stabilized while diagnostic studies including coronary angiography are performed. Based on the results of the patient's evaluation, medical or surgical therapy will be indicated.

Patients presenting with an acute myocardial infarction will frequently have transient hypertension which rapidly responds to sublingual nitrates and morphine. Patients with underlying hypertension will require additional hypertensive medications for control. Since a reflex tachycardia will increase the oxygen consumption and a drop in the coronary blood flow will reduce the oxygen delivery, it is important in patients with unstable ischemic heart disease to avoid overtreatment and the development of hypotension. Patients with combined ischemic heart disease and aortic stenosis present a special problem since the use of vasodilators and β-adrenergic blocking agents will generally drop the arterial pressure and further compromise the coronary profusion without significantly lowering the oxygen demand of the left ventricle. Surgical relief of the obstructing aortic valve is the optimal therapy.

Contractility

Clinical Assessment

The term *contractility,* also borrowed from the muscle laboratory, is defined as the (systolic) muscle function that is independent of the preload and afterload but is influenced by inotropic agents. In experimental studies the infusion of digoxin, catecholamines, and calcium will improve the vigor of contraction, while hypoxia, β-adrenergic blocking agents, and calcium blocking agents will depress the performance of the muscle. In the clinical setting it is impossible to directly measure the patient's ventricular contractility independently of the preload and afterload. The construction of a left ventricular function curve and the calculation of the left ventricular ejection fraction are two methods for assessing the relative contractile state of the left ventricle (see Figs. 24-10 and 24-15).

Any disease process that affects the ventricular myocardium will also effect the contractility. Myocardial ischemia is a common problem that impairs the left ventricular contractility, as illustrated in Fig. 24-21. This patient's resting hemodynamic function was normal with a filling pressure of 7 mmHg and a cardiac index of 3.6 L/min per m². As the patient moved up the function curve in response to the higher filling pressures, the blood pressure and afterload increased to the anginal threshold. With the development of myocardial ischemia, the ventricular performance was rapidly shifted to the depressed function curve indicated by the dashed line. With the administration of sublingual nitroglycerine, the pain was promptly relieved and the ventricular function was restored to the baseline level.

Positive Inotropic Agents

Although the direct effects of increasing the contractility will increase the ventricular afterload and oxygen consumption, the indirect effects that result from the improvement in ventricular function can lower the ventricular afterload and myocardial oxygen consumption in patients with heart failure. In addition to the normal adrenergic influence of the autonomic nervous system on the cardiovascular subsystem, the administration of positive inotropic agents can be used to improve the performance of the failing heart. Digitalis has been the traditional positive inotropic agent used in the management of heart failure. In the management of patients with hypertension heart disease, cardiomyopathy, and chronic valvular heart disease, the positive inotropic effects of digitalis complement the use of diuretics and vasodilators in the management of low cardiac output failure. Because of the potential for producing or exacerbating ventricular arrhythmias, digitalis is not recommended in the management of acute heart failure in patients with unstable ischemic heart disease. Since most sympathomimetic agents will increase myocardial oxygen consumption, they also have a very limited role in the management of unstable ischemic heart disease except in patients with cardiogenic shock. The newer agents, dopamine and dobutamine, have the advantage of a more selective inotropic effect and are the agents of choice in patients with low cardiac output secondary to ischemic myocardium. Dopamine has a unique property in the low dose range ($< 10\ \mu$g per kilogram of body weight per minute) of stimulating renal function through specific dopamine adrenergic receptors in the kidney. Dopamine has the disadvantage that its mechanism of action requires the endogenous release of catecholamines. Dobutamine has a direct positive inotropic action. Preliminary results from clinical trials of a new positive inotropic agent, aminone, have been encouraging and indicate that better inotropic agents may become available in the future for the management of chronic congestive failure.

Negative Inotropic Agents

Negative inotropic agents are useful in the management of patients with angina pectoris, idiopathic hypertrophic subaortic stenosis, and thyrotoxicosis heart disease. The β-adrenergic blocking drug propranolol is commonly used in the control of anginal symptoms in patients with obstructive coronary artery disease since its combined negative inotropic and chronotropic actions will lower the left ventricular oxygen consumption. Patients with coexisting left ventricular failure, obstructive lung disease, or brittle diabetes mellitus are not good candidates for propranolol therapy since the beta blockade will worsen the heart failure, exacerbate the bronchospasm, and potentiate the insulin reactions. The administration of propranolol requires a titration of the dose based on the patient's response. The heart rate, blood pressure, attacks of chest pain, and side effects are all important clinical parameters to monitor. An average dose in the range of 40 mg four times a day will usually lower the resting heart rate to 50 to 60 beats per minute.

The antiarrhythmic agents lidocaine, quinidine, and pronestyl all have negative inotropic side effects. Although a stabilization of the cardiac rate and rhythm will generally improve the cardiac output, the use of antiarrhythmic drugs in patients with severe low output heart failure is limited by the negative side effects on ventricular performance. The experimental calcium blocking drugs verapamil and nifedipine also have negative inotropic properties in addition to the electrophysiologic and vasodilator effects. The role of these agents in the clinical management of cardiac patients is currently under intense investigation.

Cardiac Rate, Rhythm, and Conduction

Clinical Assessment

The various techniques available for monitoring and detecting cardiac arrhythmias and conduction disturbances are discussed in the section in this chapter on electrophysiologic monitoring. Disturbances in the cardiac rate, rhythm, and conduction can interfere

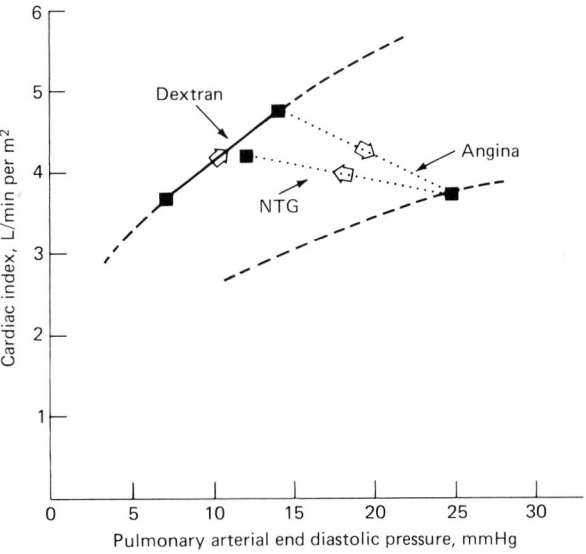

FIGURE 24-21

Effects of ischemia on left ventricular function. In response to the dextran infusion, this patient with normal hemodynamics and ischemic heart disease moved up the ascending limb of his left ventricular function curve. The increase in wall stress and oxygen consumption, however, precipitated an anginal attack which depressed the contractility and shifted the patient to a depressed curve. With nitroglycerine (NTG) the preload and afterload were reduced, the ischemia was relieved, and the ventricular function was restored to the baseline state. (*From J. A. Mantle et al.: Advances in the treatment of heart failure, to be published as a chapter in Critical Care Cardiology, Cardiovascular Clinics, Philadelphia, Davis. Reproduced by permission.*)

with cardiac output, produce cardiac ischemia, worsen congestive heart failure, and result in sudden death. The potential risks of premature ventricular beats, ventricular tachycardia, and ventricular fibrillation are well known to the clinical staffs of critical-care units. The importance of supraventricular arrhythmias in unstable patients, however, is less widely appreciated. In addition to shortening the diastolic filling period and reducing the preload of the left ventricle, supraventricular tachycardias will significantly increase the oxygen consumption of the left ventricle and can produce ischemia in patients with ischemic heart disease. The causes of supraventricular tachycardias in patients admitted to critical-care units include fever, hypoxia, heart failure, hypovolemia, sympathomimetic drugs, supraventricular tachyarrhythmias, and anxiety.

The example shown in Fig. 24-22 demonstrates the effects of a supraventricular arrhythmia on the pulmonary arterial pulse pressure. When the patient had a 2:3 conduction pattern, the pulse pressure alternated between a large pulse and a small pulse corresponding to the long interval and short intervals, respectively. When the patient had a 3:4 conduction pattern, the pulse pressure corresponding to the long interval was accentuated while the pulse pressures corresponding to the short intervals were significantly reduced and ineffective. When the patient had a 1:1 conduction with a ventricular rate of over 200 beats per minute, the pulse pressure was significantly reduced. The effect of a short diastolic filling period on the stroke volume is more pronounced in patients with myocardial disease and a reduced compliance of the left ventricle. The adverse effects of a tachyarrhythmia in patients with unstable ischemic heart disease is illustrated by the example shown in Fig. 24-23. One week after having an anterior myocardial infarction this patient developed a tachycardia of 127 beats per minute, ST-segment elevation, chest pain, hypotension, and pulmonary congestion. The initial clinical diagnosis was an extension of the myocardial infarction with a secondary sinus tachycardia. The atrial electrogram (in the lower tract), however, demonstrated that this patient had developed a sustained atrial tachyarrhythmia of 254 beats per minute with 2:1 conduction for a ventricular rate of 127 beats per minute.

Management

The management of patients with disturbances in the cardiac rate, rhythm, or conduction should include the correction of any underlying causes whenever

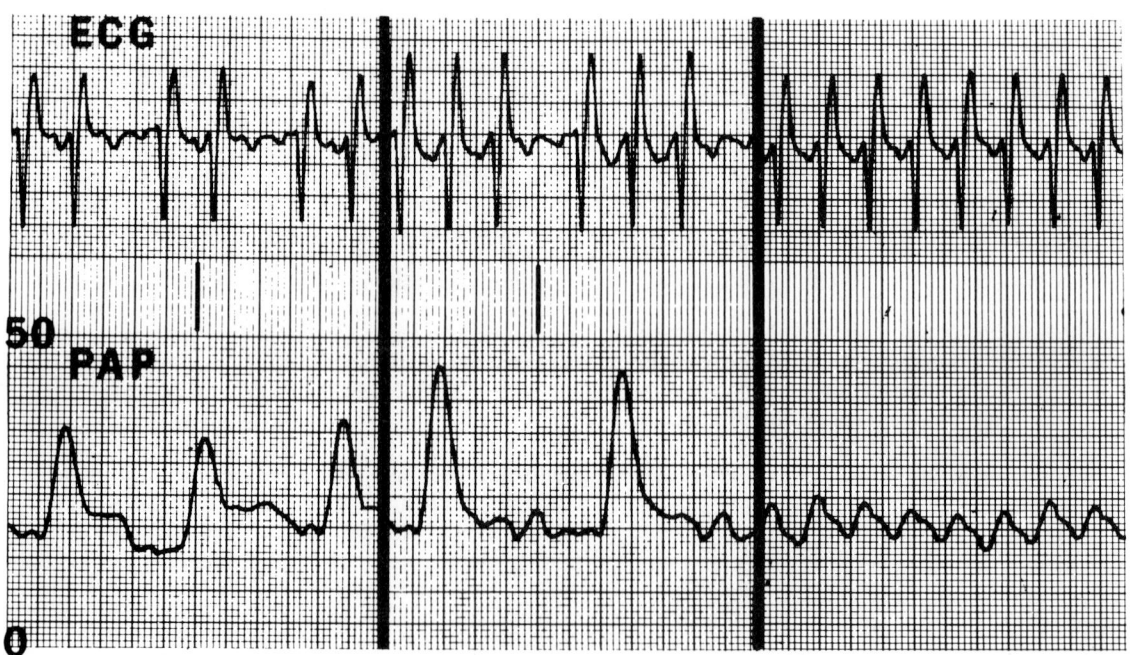

FIGURE 24-22

Simultaneous recordings of electrocardiogram (ECG) and pulmonary arterial pressure (PAP) from a patient with a supraventricular tachycardia (200 beats per minute). In the first panel, every third atrial impulse was nonconducted resulting in alternating long and short diastolic filling periods. The pulse pressure following the short interval was markedly reduced as a result of the incomplete diastolic filling and inadequate preload. The difference in the pulse pressure between the short and normal diastolic filling periods is more marked in the center panel where every fourth atrial impulse was blocked. In the last panel, the patient was conducting 1:1 and had a markedly reduced pulse pressure. (*From J. A. Mantle et al.: Advances in the treatment of heart failure, to be published as a chapter in Critical Care Cardiology, Cardiovascular Clinics, Philadelphia, Davis. Reproduced by permission.*)

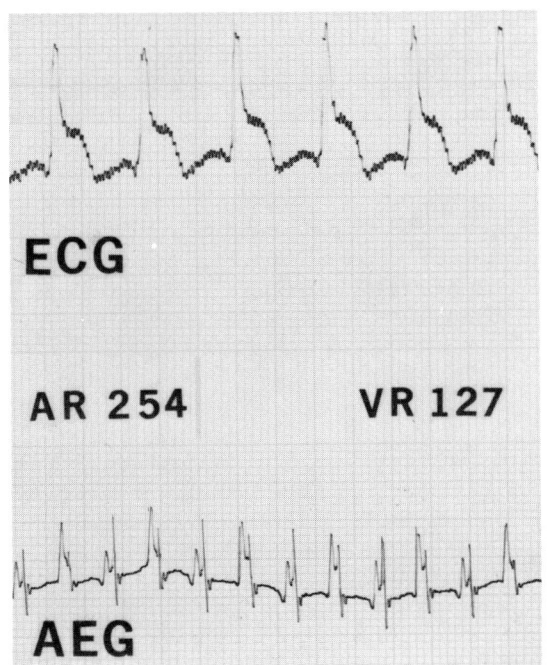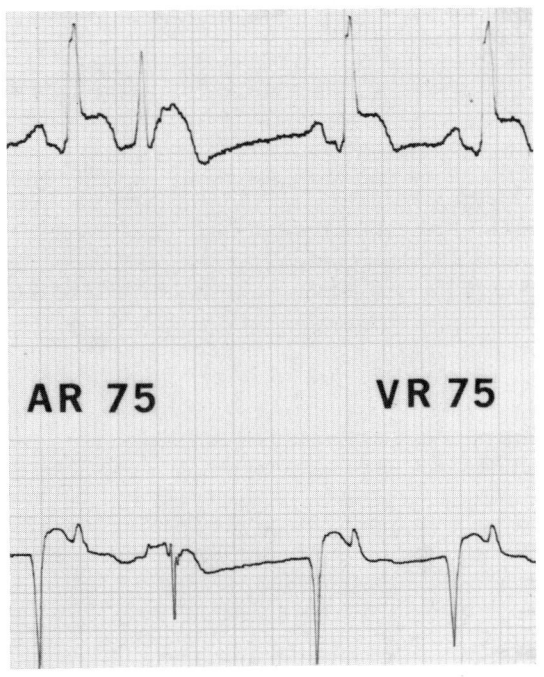

FIGURE 24-23

Simultaneous recording of electrocardiogram (ECG) and bipolar atrial electrogram (AEG). In the left panel the patient had an atrial tachycardia with 2:1 conduction. In the right panel the patient was in sinus rhythm with an isolated premature junctional beat. AR = atrial rate, VR = ventricular rate. (*From J. A. Mantle et al.: A multipurpose catheter for electrophysiologic and hemodynamic monitoring plus atrial pacing. Chest 72:285–290, 1977. Reproduced by permission.*)

possible. In the setting of the critical-care unit, the management of contributing factors will generally include sedation, relief of pain, adequate ventilation, treatment of heart failure, reversal of ischemia, and removal of toxic drugs. The pharmacologic management of cardiac arrhythmias is discussed elsewhere in this book and will not be reviewed here (see App. B).

The use of atrial and ventricular pacing also plays an important role in the management of patients with unstable cardiac rhythm and heart block. The routine placement of epicardial wires at cardiac surgery or the insertion of a transvenous electrode catheter permit the use of atrial, ventricular, or sequential AV pacing at the bedside in unstable patients. Atrial pacing is useful for cardioverting supraventricular tachycardias, for maintaining an adequate rate in sinus bradycardia, and for overdriving ventricular premature beats. The patient example shown in Fig. 24-23 was paced via the pair of atrial electrodes mounted on the shaft of the pulmonary arterial catheter

at a rate of 300 per minute to interrupt the supraventricular tachycardia. When the pacing was stopped, the patient had a spontaneous sinus rhythm as shown in the right-hand panel with an atrial rate of 75 beats per minute and 1:1 conduction.

Atrial pacing is a convenient and safe technique for cardioverting patients with supraventricular tachyarrhythmias. In occasional patients with refractory supraventricular tachyarrhythmias, the production of atrial fibrillation will permit a more satisfactory regulation of the ventricular rate. The example shown in Fig. 24-24 illustrates the use of atrial pacing in the management of a patient with digitalis intoxication. This patient was referred for the management of heart failure and the digitalis toxic arrhythmias shown in panels A and B. The electrocardiogram in panel A shows a ventricular rate of 105 with an irregular irregular rhythm, and the atrial electrogram shows coarse fibrillation. The rhythm in panel B is an atrial tachycardia of 208 with 2:1 conduction to the ventricle. Since the ventricular response was within tolerable

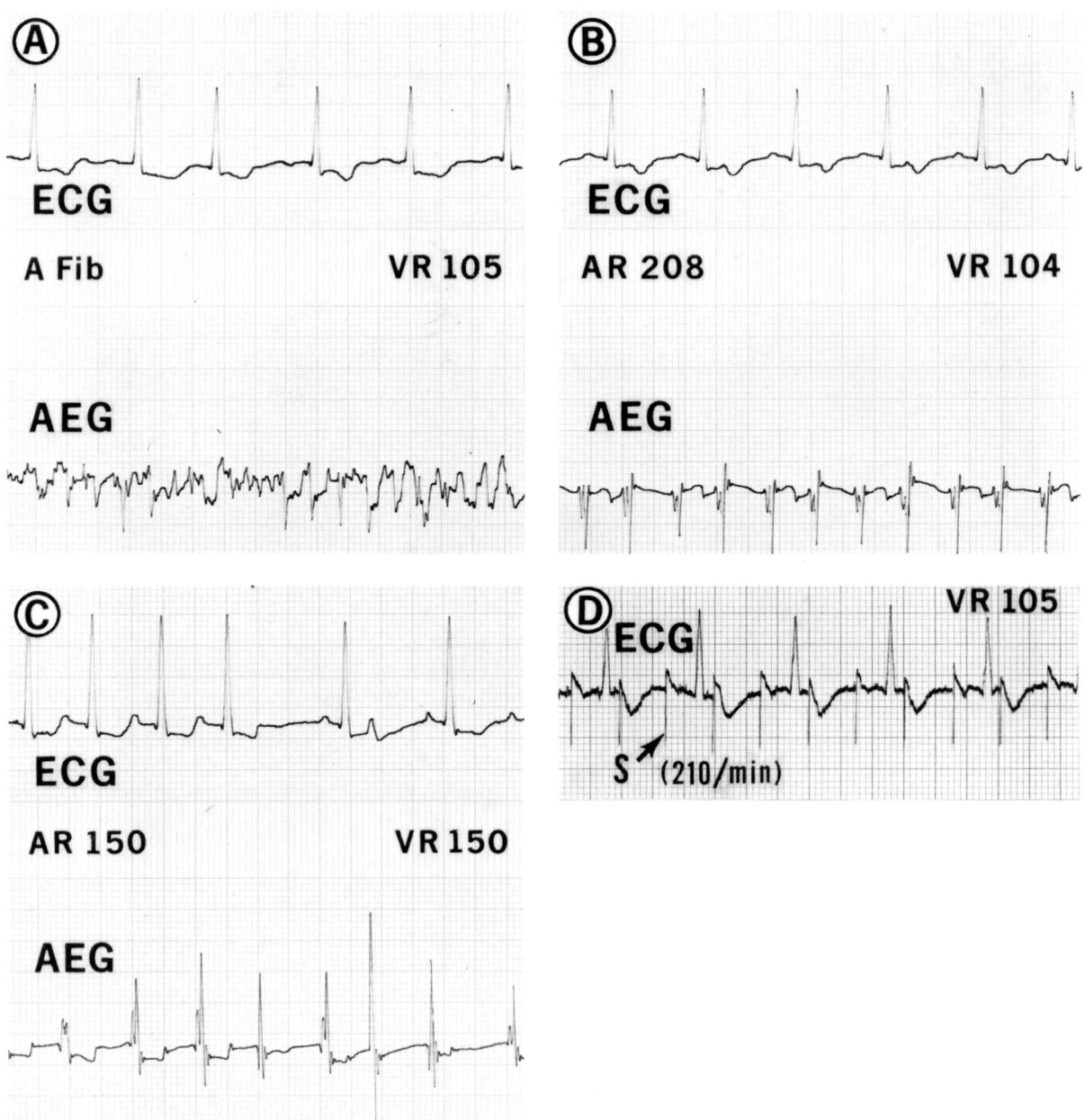

FIGURE 24-24

Simultaneous recording of electrocardiogram (ECG) and atrial electrogram (AEG). A Fib = atrial fibrillation, AR = atrial rate, VR = ventricular rate, S = stimulus artifact. See text for discussion. (*From J. A. Mantle et al.: A multipurpose catheter for electrophysiologic and hemodynamic monitoring plus atrial pacing, Chest 72:285–290, 1977. Reproduced by permission.*)

limits for both arrhythmias, the initial management was to hold the digitalis and treat the underlying congestive failure. The rhythm on the following day is shown in panel C. The atrial rate had slowed to 150 beats per minute, but the patient was now conducting 1:1 for a rate of 150 beats per minute which further compromised the ventricular function. The patient's ventricular rate was slowed by pacing the atrium at 210 beats per minute to produce AV block as shown in panel D. The next morning, when the pacing was stopped, the patient had a spontaneous sinus rhythm at a rate of 95 beats per minute.

Ventricular pacing is indicated for the management of patients with symptomatic heart block which can occur as a temporary complication of acute myocardial infarction, cardiac surgery, electrolyte disturbances, drug toxicity, and other metabolic disturbances, or it may be a permanent problem. When the loss of the atrial contraction produces a significant drop in cardiac output, the use of AV sequential pacing can be used to restore an adequate diastolic filling.

Metabolic

Clinical Assessment

Although disturbances in cardiac metabolism play a major role in depressing the contractility of the myocardium and producing ventricular arrhythmias, it is useful in the clinical setting to separate those factors which lend themselves to measurement, monitoring, and correction. Hypoxia, electrolyte disturbances, acidosis, and alkalosis are systemic metabolic problems that affect the performance of the heart. In recent years attention has been directed toward the role of disturbances in the cardiac metabolism. Insulin deficiency has been shown to interfere with normal cardiac function and can be very important in patients with advanced diabetes and congestive heart failure. Elevated free fatty acids have been shown in experimental studies to be detrimental to the performance of the ischemic heart. Free fatty acids are released by catecholamines and reach levels severalfold above the baseline values in patients with acute myocardial infarction (see Fig. 24-25). In these five patients with acute myocardial infarction, the initial free fatty acid values ranged from 800 to over 1600 meq/L (normal range of 400 to 600 meq/L).

Glucose-Insulin-Potassium

The role of hyperalimentation in the management of patients with malnutrition has been well established

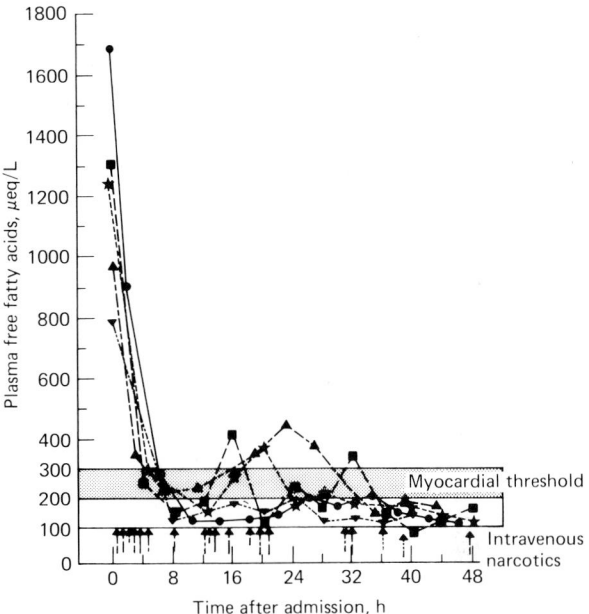

FIGURE 24-25

Plot of free fatty acids versus time in patients with acute myocardial infarction who were treated with glucose-insulin-potassium at an infusion rate of 500 mg glucose per minute. The initial free fatty acids were markedly elevated. During the GIK, the FFA were suppressed to the myocardial threshold for free fatty acids utilization despite recurrent chest pain (arrows). [*From R. O. Russell, Jr., et al.: Glucose-insulin-potassium, free fatty acids and acute myocardial infarction, Circulation 53(suppl. 1): 207–209, 1976. Reproduced by permission of the American Heart Association, Inc.*]

for the management of both surgical and medical patients. Restoring normal myocardial metabolism has been shown in the experimental model to suppress ventricular arrhythmias, improve mechanical function, and limit the extent of infarction. With the infusion of a glucose-insulin-potassium solution, the free fatty acid levels can be suppressed to the myocardial threshold range (see Fig. 24-25). The data in Fig. 24-26 from our randomized trial of the infusion of a glucose-insulin-potassium solution in patients with acute myocardial infarction demonstrate that the incidence of ventricular arrhythmias can be significantly suppressed with the infusion of a glucose-insulin-potassium solution compared to the patients who received controlled therapy. In addition to suppressing the incidence of ventricular premature beats, the incidence of ventricular tachycardia and ventricular fibrillation was also reduced. The patients given

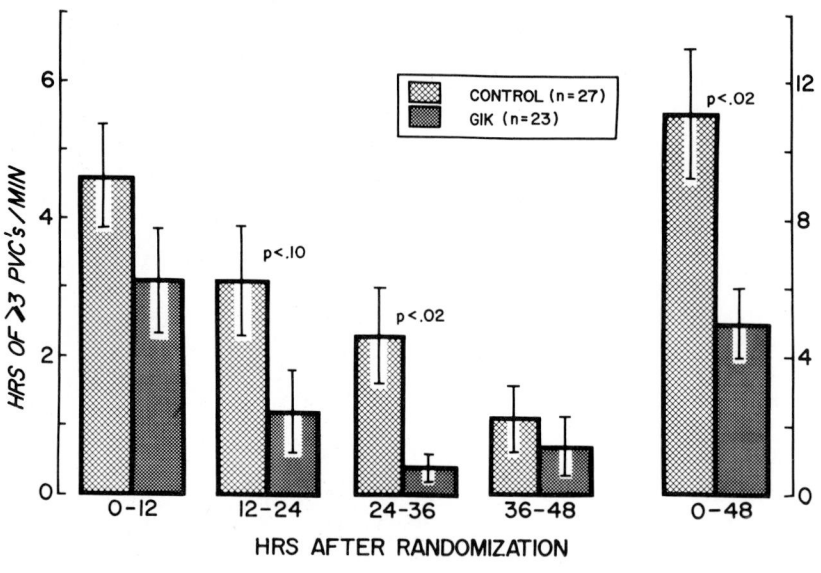

FIGURE 24-26

Comparison of ventricular arrhythmias in patients randomized to control or glucose-insulin-potassium (GIK) treatment groups. HRS = hours, PVC = premature ventricular contractions. Bars represent mean values with standard error of mean indicated. (*From W. J. Rogers et al.: Prospective randomized trial of glucose-insulin-potassium in acute myocardial infarction, Am J Cardiol 43:801–809, 1979. Reproduced by permission.*)

glucose-insulin-potassium solution have also had a significant improvement in their hemodynamics, better ventricular function, and a lower mortality than the control patients. Additional clinical studies are needed to determine the optimal timing, duration, and nature of the metabolic intervention for patients with acute myocardial infarction, but our initial results indicate that the correction of metabolic disturbances has an important role in the management of acute myocardial infarction.

Extent of Myocardial Injury

The size of the myocardial infarction is a major determinant of both ventricular function and long-term prognosis. The techniques available for assessing the extent of injury in patients with acute myocardial infarction have been discussed in the section on diagnostic and monitoring techniques. The indirect methods include the clinical evaluation, electrocardiogram, MB-CPK isoenzyme (see Fig. 24-1), and hemodynamics (see Fig. 24-10). The more direct methods are the scintigraphic (see Fig. 24-14) and angiographic (see Fig. 24-15) demonstration of wall motion abnormalities, the hot spot and cold spot scintigrams (see Figs. 24-12 and 24-13) and the autopsy examination. In the clinical evaluation of patients, it is important to know the limitations of the techniques since the results may have an important influence on the patient's course. A major goal in the clinical investigation of ischemic heart disease is to identify a safe and convenient method to limit and reduce the size of acute myocardial infarctions. Current proposals include the use of β-adrenergic blocking agents, vasodilator agents, hyaluronidose, glucose-insulin-potassium solutions, intra-aortic counterpulsation, and emergency revascularization surgery. All these techniques are unproven and remain the subject of clinical investigations. In addition to acute myocardial infarction, cardiac injury can result from cardiac surgery, myocarditis, chronic pressure or volume overload, amyloidosis, trauma, and cardiotoxic drugs, such as Adriamycin.

SUMMARY

Bedside techniques permit an objective assessment and continuous monitoring of patients with unstable cardiac problems. In addition to establishing the correct diagnosis, the six major determinants of ventricular function can be assessed and a therapeutic plan developed for optimizing ventricular performance. A scheme for the hemodynamic management of patients with unstable cardiac problems is shown in Fig. 24-27. When the filling pressure is less than or equal to 20 to 24 mmHg and the cardiac index is greater than or equal to 2.5 L/min per m² in a stable patient, no active hemodynamic intervention is indicated. Patients who are having recurrent angina or significant hypertension should have their left ventricular afterload reduced with the use of vasodilator and β-adrenergic blocking drugs. Patients who have unstable angina, which is refractory to medical therapy, are candidates for urgent catheterization and surgery. The patients who respond to the medical therapy may also benefit from angiographic study and surgery, but this can be done on an elective basis. When the cardiac index is less than 2.5 L/min

per m² (or the stroke volume is low) and the left ventricular filling pressure is less than 20 to 24 mmHg, the clinical diagnosis of hypovolemia should be considered and the patient should have a trial expansion of the blood volume. The use of catecholamines may also be required initially to support the blood pressure in patients with severe hypovolemia or extensive myocardial injury. When the filling pressure is greater than 20 to 24 mmHg and the cardiac index is less than 2.5 L/min per m², the patients will have the clinical syndrome of low cardiac output congestive heart failure. The therapeutic goal for these patients is to lower the pulmonary venous hypertension to the optimal range while increasing the stroke volume with the use of vasodilator drugs in combination with diuretics. Patients in shock will require the additional support of catecholamines and, when indicated, the intra-aortic balloon. Patients with evidence of valvular dysfunction, intracardiac shunts, or left ventricular aneurysms are candidates for an-

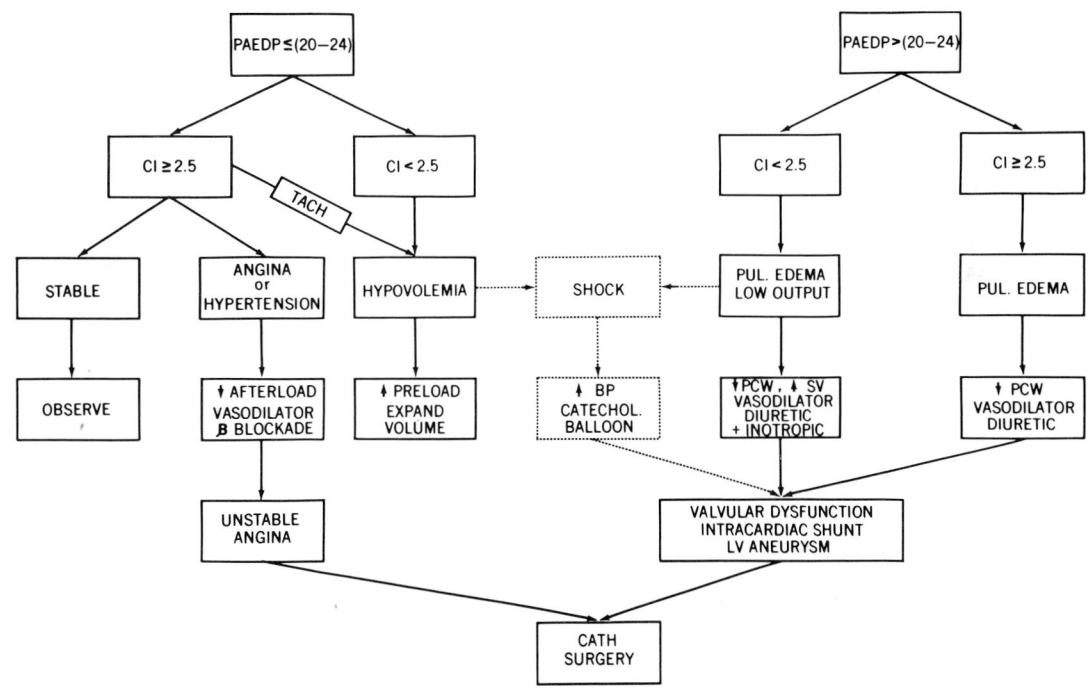

FIGURE 24-27

Schema for the hemodynamic management of patients with unstable cardiac subsystem. The pulmonary arterial end diastolic pressure (PAEDP) of 20 to 24 mmHg is the upper limit of the optimal left ventricular filling pressure. Above this range pulmonary congestion will usually develop. The lower limit of the normal cardiac index (CI) is 2.5 L/min per m². The role of digitalis in the acute management of heart failure is controversial, especially in patients with acute myocardial infarction. Intra-aortic balloon counterpulsation is most useful in the preoperative evaluation and postoperative management of patients with reversible low cardiac output shock.

giography and possibly surgical correction. This can be done on an emergency, urgent, or elective basis depending on the clinical status. Digitalis may be useful in the long-term management of patients with low cardiac output cardiomyopathy. When the cardiac index is greater than 2.5, the therapeutic effort is directed at reducing the pulmonary capillary wedge pressure. The optimal approach is to use a combination of vasodilator and diuretic agents and correct any underlying surgical problems. In addition to optimizing the preload, afterload, and contractility, efforts must be directed toward correcting cardiac arrhythmias and restoring normal cardiac metabolism.

The major goal of the management of the patient with unstable ischemic disease is to prevent, or at least to limit, the extent of left ventricular injury. Once the patient has been stabilized and is ready for discharge from the critical-care unit, the clinical challenge is to develop a long-term management plan that will provide the greatest clinical benefit.

This work was supported in part by the National Heart and Lung Institute (Specialized Center of Research for Ischemic Heart Disease, Grant 5P50HL17667-05)

REFERENCES

Braunwald, E.: *The Myocardium: Failure and Infarction,* New York: Hospital Practice Publishing, 1974.

Cohn, P. F.: *Diagnosis and Therapy of Coronary Artery Disease,* Boston: Little, Brown, 1979.

Forrester, James S., George Diamond, Kanu Chatterjee, and H. J. C. Swan: Medical therapy of acute myocardial infarction by application of hemodynamic subsets, *N Engl J Med* 295: 1356–1362, 1404–1413, 1976.

Hillis, L. D., and E. Braunwald E. : Myocardial ischemia, *N Engl J Med* 296:971–978, 1034–1041, 1093–1096, 1977.

Mason, D. T.: *Congestive Heart Failure,* New York: Dun-Donnelley, 1976.

Rackley, C. E., and R. O. Russell, Jr.: *Coronary Artery Disease: Recognition and Management,* Mount Kisco, N.Y.: Futura, 1979.

Russell, R. O., Jr., and C. E. Rackley: *Hemodynamic Monitoring in a Coronary Care Unit,* Mount Kisco, N.Y.: Futura, 1974.

Waldo, Albert L., and William A. H. MacLean: *Diagnosis and Treatment of Cardiac Arrhythmias following Open Heart Surgery,* Mt. Kisco, New York: Futura (in press).

Willerson, J. T.: *Nuclear Cardiology,* Philadelphia: Davis, 1979.

INTRODUCTION

This chapter will review selected hematopoietic disorders seen by practitioners in critical-care environments, namely, hyperviscosity syndrome, anemia, acute leukemic crisis, and coagulopathies. The etiology of the pathophysiologic process will be discussed, along with clinical assessment parameters, treatment approaches, and nursing implications.

Although the *nurse* and the *physician* may be referred to periodically, the authors wish to stress the importance of the *team approach* in management of a patient with hematologic dysfunction. Roles, activities, and capabilities of individual team members vary from institution to institution; however, the ongoing and dynamic needs of the patient necessitate highly perceptive and knowledgeable assessment. In the course of the complex care given, the critical-care nurse may well be in the ideal position to detect subtle, though potentially significant, changes in patient status.

General Approach to the Patient

With the possible exception of an emergency room, in the setting of a critical-care unit, an initial history has usually already been recorded; however, it is crucial to remember that the history and physical examination are dynamic situations. Therefore, the history taking is always extended and redone depending upon the various new developments in the critical-care unit as well as integrating this with the patient's past medical history and family history.

Primary hematologic diseases are uncommon, but hematologic manifestations secondary to other diseases are quite common. A significant variety of diseases produce signs and symptoms of a hematologic illness. Though Chapter 13 provides a format for a complete history, several points are worthy of mention regarding the hematopoietic system.

Review of the patient's medications should be a part of the *daily history*. Even commonly used drugs such as acetylsalicylic acid (aspirin) have pronounced hematologic ramifications. The patient in the critical-care unit is typically on a variety of antibiotics, and antibiotics have a varied effect on the hematologic system. Additionally, quinine ingestion can be determined via knowledge of the patient's drinking habits, and occupational exposure to toxic chemicals needs to be determined. A family history of bleeding disorders or the patient's past surgical stresses must be elicited. For instance, a tooth extraction should be

25

Hematopoietic Disorders

Jerome B. Bart
Cynthia Boyd Dear

INTRODUCTION
General Approach to the Patient
HYPERVISCOSITY SYNDROME
Etiology of Pathophysiologic Process
Clinical Assessment
Treatment of Hyperviscosity Syndrome
Nursing Implications

ANEMIA

APLASTIC ANEMIA
Etiology of Pathophysiologic Process
Clinical Assessment
Treatment of Aplastic Anemia
Nursing Implications

HEMOLYTIC ANEMIA
Etiology of Pathophysiologic Process
Clinical Assessment
Treatment of Hemolytic Anemia
Nursing Implications

ACUTE LEUKEMIC CRISES
Etiology of Pathophysiologic Process
Clinical Assessment
Treatment of Acute Leukemic Crises
Nursing Implications

COAGULOPATHIES

VITAMIN K–DEPENDENT COAGULATION DISORDERS
Hemorrhagic Liver Disease
Availability and Absorption of Vitamin K

DISSEMINATED INTRAVASCULAR COAGULATION
Etiology of Pathophysiologic Process
Clinical Assessment
Treatment of Disseminated Intravascular Coagulation
Nursing Implications

REFERENCES

considered a major hematologic stress on the clotting system.

A *complete examination* needs to be done on every patient in the critical-care setting and repeated daily with special attention to certain areas. Examination begins with the vital signs. In persons with basic hematologic disorders, fever may be a manifestation of the disease, such as lymphoma or leukemia, and may be very difficult to distinguish from an infectious process.

The skin reveals important clues in the dynamic situation. Pallor is a useful guideline in evaluating anemic conditions. However, since color is determined by not only the influence of pigment but the blood flowing through the capillaries, careful attention to the conjunctival blood vessel pattern and color may be a more reliable index of anemia. The color of the nail beds, mucous membranes, and palmar creases are perhaps more useful guides to hemoglobin level. The pinkness of the palmar creases usually disappears at a hemoglobin of less than 7 g per 100 mL. Plethora can indicate too much hemoglobin or the polycythemic state. Cyanosis can be noted with a reduced hemoglobin (5 g per 100 mL), methemoglobin (1.5 to 2.0 g per 100 mL), or sulfhemoglobin (0.5 g per 100 mL). The patient's conjunctiva and skin should be examined by daylight for evaluation of jaundice. The bilirubin must be from 2 to 3 mg per 100 mL before jaundice is clinically detected.

The presence of petechiae usually indicates thrombocytopenic (decreased platelets) states or capillary fragility. They are usually found in dependent areas, generally in the legs, but in the bedridden patient may be more readily found on the lower back or buttocks. These lesions do not blanch with pressure. The presence of ecchymoses is also important, and one should look for prolonged oozing of blood at or around venipuncture sites.

In addition to the color of the mucous membranes, evaluation of the mouth may show changes in the surface of the tongue and/or ulceration and bleeding due to either lack of granulocytes, monilia superinfection, gingival hypertrophy due to various types of leukemia, and glossitis due to pernicious anemia and iron deficiency.

Ophthalmoscopic examination is important in hematologic diseases to evaluate the condition of the vessels and presence of hemorrhages and exudates.

Palpation for lymphadenopathy is important to evaluate changes in disease status, especially the lymphomas, indicating either progression of disease or response to therapy. Mediastinal lymph nodes can only rarely be found by percussion, and chest x-ray examination is mandatory for their evaluation. Evaluation for splenomegaly has similar significance. Radioisotope imaging of the liver may be necessary where indicated, since palpation and percussion yield inconclusive results. Bone pain should be determined by palpating superficial surfaces with the fingertips.

Neurologic functions should be thoroughly assessed. A variety of hematologic abnormalities can be reflected by neurologic signs and symptoms, ranging from vitamin B_{12} deficiency to leukemias and lymphomas.

Certain basic laboratory parameters are essential in evaluating hematologic problems. The complete blood count (CBC) includes a white blood cell count (WBC), 100-cell differential count, hemoglobin, hematocrit, and usually other indices if automated methods are available. Platelet count and reticulocyte count should be performed where indicated. A biochemical profile including blood urea nitrogen (BUN) and uric acid are important in any hematologic problem. Coagulation studies frequently ordered are prothrombin time (PT), partial thromboplastin time (PTT), quantitative fibrinogen, bleeding time, test for fibrin split products (FSP), and the Lee-White clotting time. The PT evaluates the so-called "extrinsic" clotting system and is usually found to be abnormal in various liver diseases as well as disseminated intravascular coagulation. The PTT evaluates almost the entire intrinsic cascade of blood coagulation. When the PT is known to be normal, an irregular PTT finding indicates an abnormality of factors XII, XI, and VIII, or IX. Fibrin split products are used to evaluate the presence of fibrinolysis, either primary but usually secondary, to disseminated intravascular coagulation. Bleeding time is used to assess quantitative or qualitative abnormalities of platelets. The whole blood clotting time, or Lee-White time, is still a useful way to monitor heparin therapy, but it is considered a rather gross test to define coagulation abnormalities. Refer to Table 25-1 for ranges of normal for the frequently utilized laboratory examinations.

Finally, no laboratory evaluation of the patient is complete without a review of the blood smear and bone marrow, when indicated. Sites most frequently used for obtaining marrow specimens in the adult include the sternum and the anterior or posterior aspects of the iliac crests. As with any procedure, when bone marrow is to be obtained by aspiration or biopsy, the patient needs to have the procedure explained, including the rationale for the procedure and that discomfort might occur with anesthetizing

TABLE 25-1
Normal Laboratory Values

Exam	Ranges	
Blood cell values	**Males**	**Females**
Hemoglobin (g/100 mL)	16 ± 2	14 ± 2
Hematocrit (mL/100 mL)	47 ± 5	42 ± 5
Red cell count ($\times 10^6$/μL blood)	5.11 ± 0.8	4.51 ± 0.6
White cell count (no./mm³)	5000–10,000	5000–10,000
Hematologic and coagulation		
Reticulocyte count	0.5–1.5% of erythrocytes	
Platelet count	140,000–340,000/mm³	
Prothrombin time	Same as control (should be 11–16 s)	
Partial thromboplastin time	60–85 s	
Activated partial thromboplastin time	27–35 s (automated)	
	35–52 s (manual)	
Lee-White coagulation time	6–17 min (glass tube)	
	19–60 min (siliconized tube)	
Bleeding time	Ivy, less than 4 min	
	Duke, 1–4 min	
	Mielke, 1–9 min	
Fibrinogen	200–400 mg/100 mL	
Fibrin degradation products	0–10 μg/mL	
Blood chemistry		
Urea nitrogen (BUN)	10–20 mg/100 mL	
Creatinine	0.7–1.5 mg/100 mL	
Bilirubin	Direct, 0.1–0.4 mg/100 mL	
	Indirect, 0.1–0.5 mg/100 mL	
	Total, 0.2–0.9 mg/mL	
Uric acid	3.0–8.5 mg/100 mL	
Leukocyte differential	**%**	**no./mm³**
Segmented neutrophils	51 ± 15	3800
Band neutrophils	8.0 ± 3	620
Eosinophils	2.7	200
Basophils	0.5	40
Lymphocytes	34 ± 10	2500
Monocytes	4.0	300

the area and later when aspiration occurs, both of which should be brief. A permission form may need to be signed. To ensure cooperation, the extremely anxious patient may be given an analgesic and/or sedative prior to the procedure. At the termination, firm pressure need be applied to the aspiration site for 10 to 15 min to ensure hemostasis.

In summary, all assessment parameters need to be followed for an indication of flow. Stated another way, the absolute values of the parameters (which can vary between institutions) are less significant than the direction of changes within the patient, as an index of progression of disease, versus response to treatment.

HYPERVISCOSITY SYNDROME

Etiology of Pathophysiologic Process

Viscosity is a property of fluid to resist flow. Hyperviscosity of the blood may be due to an elevated plasma or serum viscosity or to an elevated number of cells (polycythemia or leukemia). This section will discuss altered viscosity of the serum due to abnormalities of immunoglobulins or proteins.

The most common clinical setting in which this is found is Waldenström's macroglobulinemia, although it may rarely be found in multiple myeloma. The origin of this neoplastic disease is plasma cell and lymphoid cell populations. These cells, which are responsible for immunoglobulin synthesis, produce only abnormal proteins, IgM macroglobulins.

Though tumors are rarely encountered, the cellular infiltrates seem to proliferate in lymphoid tissue. When the blood is hyperviscous, flow is inefficient to various vascular beds; this occurrence may produce an acute medical situation termed the *hyperviscosity syndrome*.

Clinical Assessment

The age of patients at the time of diagnosis is approximately 60, with a range from 32 to 92 years of age; two-thirds of patients are male. Though the patient may be asymptomatic, the hyperviscosity syndrome tends to produce symptoms in certain organ systems as its primary manifestation (Williams et al., 1977).

The patient may present with complaints of fatigue, weakness, weight loss, and a variety of bleeding problems ranging from bruising to epistaxis, or mucous membrane and gastrointestinal bleeding. The bleeding diathesis associated with the hyperviscosity syndrome is usually in the absence of thrombocytopenia. The hemoglobin level frequently is 12 g per 100 mL or less and the patient's anemia is normochromic and normocytic. The mechanism by which hyperviscous blood disrupts the microcirculation is not totally clear. Platelet function is known to be altered, and platelet interaction with other coagulation proteins has been reported.

Ocular changes may be prominent, from minor disturbances to blindness. The patient may complain of blurred vision or reduced acuity. Ophthalmoscopically, the most consistent features are distention and tortuosity of the retinal veins, local areas of beading and dilatation creating a "string of sausage" appearance, and flame-shaped hemorrhages. Retinal vein thrombosis may occur. The conjunctival tissues are also dilated and tortuous with marked sludging of the red cells.

Neurologic manifestations are quite prominent and frequently abrupt in onset. They include headache, which may progress to confusion, coma, and seizures. The nature of the presentation may resemble a severe intracerebral hemorrhage. The patient may also have true vertigo, nystagmus, transient paresis, and in the presence of serum cryoglobulins may report Raynaud's phenomenon, cold urticaria, or purpura.

Since the hyperviscosity syndrome is associated with a hypervolemic state, cardiovascular symptoms are important. The higher the viscosity, the higher the plasma volume. The hyperviscosity and hypervolemia result in distention of peripheral blood vessels, increased peripheral resistance, and congestive cardiac failure.

The kidneys can be affected by the hyperviscosity syndrome, with patients evidencing degrees of renal insufficiency. However, it is much less common in Waldenström's macroglobulinemia than in multiple myeloma, in that the latter may itself cause renal insufficiency and failure in addition to the hyperviscous state.

The viscosity of serum is measured usually by an Ostwald viscometer. The time required for a constant volume of liquid at a given pressure and temperature to flow through a capillary tube is determined. The normal serum viscosity is 1.4:1.8 as compared with water as a reference. The relationship between viscosity and clinical symptoms differ from individual to individual. Patients with relative viscosity levels between 2 and 4 are rarely symptomatic, whereas most patients with relative viscosity between 5 and 8 have symptoms and nearly all at levels between 8 and 10 are symptomatic.

Treatment of the Hyperviscosity Syndrome

The course of Waldenström's macroglobulinemia is highly variable, and in asymptomatic patients no treatment may be required for years, with the exception of regular examinations and determination of IgM concentrations. The hyperviscosity syndrome is considered a medical emergency, however. Simple removal of the plasma proteins by plasmapheresis is a very rapid and effective way of treating the hyperviscosity syndrome. This treatment has been shown repeatedly to improve the congestive heart failure, the retinopathy, the bleeding diathesis, and central nervous symptoms related to the hyperviscosity syndrome.

In macroglobulinemia this may need to be done on a chronic outpatient basis. Essentially, plasmapheresis consists of removal of 500 mL of blood from the patient, centrifugation to remove the plasma, and return of the patient's packed red blood cells. In the acute situation, 3000 to 4000 mL of blood may have to be processed over 1 to 2 days. This mode of treatment is much more effective in Waldenström's macroglobulinemia than in multiple myeloma, because in the former the abnormal proteins are confined to the intravascular space. The serum viscosity may be lowered rapidly by this method and subsequently the patient maintained by removal of a few units of plasma weekly. Since plasmapheresis does not affect the basic disease process, chemotherapy for the underlying neoplasm may be indicated. Chlorambucil or cyclophosphamide in combination with prednisone is recommended by many clinicians.

The viscosity increments in macroglobulinemia are progressively greater with each unit increase in IgM concentration. For this reason, at higher macroglobulin levels, relatively small reductions in serum macroglobulin concentrations may reduce the serum viscosity dramatically. Removal of 1000 mL of plasma (equivalent to 3 or 4 units of blood) effectively reduces the total IgM by 15 to 20 percent while reducing relative viscosity by 50 to 100 percent.

Plasmapheresis has been proven to be a safe procedure; however, immediate complications include hypotension and bradycardia. For these reasons, it has been suggested that patients with a hemoglobin level of 9 g per 100 mL be transfused prior to plasmapheresis. Intensive plasmapheresis at a rate of 1 L of plasma per day can lead to a significant fall in albumin as well as platelets. The serum albumin may have to be replaced at the beginning of treatment in order to prevent or treat edema. The platelets usually recover rapidly, although platelet packs may be needed.

Nursing Implications

Care of the patient who presents with hyperviscosity syndrome, as with most disorders, centers around the particular organ systems involved and the degree of compromise: for example, careful monitoring of the patient's fluid intake and urinary output by indwelling catheter, if necessary, to evaluate renal involvement. A thorough physical exam and history will dictate the patient's care needs and serve as a basis for serial evaluation of the patient's condition and the effectiveness of plasmapheresis.

The patient who is conscious will most probably be extremely weak, and nursing activities should be carefully planned in order to conserve the patient's energy and provide frequent rest periods. Optimal nutrition need be encouraged. Whether this is the first critical-care admission or one of many for the patient, apprehension and anxiety can be reduced by carefully explaining all procedures and tests, being available to and answering questions for both the patient and family, and encouraging the verbalization of feelings. Promoting the patient's sense of well-being is impor-

tant since the less anxious patient tends to be more cooperative.

Reorientation and possibly soft restraints may be required for the patient who is confused. Because a bleeding diathesis may be present, the patient needs to be protected from injury; small-gauge needles should be utilized for injections; and adequate pressure should be applied to injection, venipuncture, and arterial puncture sites to ensure hemostasis.

The patient who is comatose upon admission will require the most comprehensive attention. Frequent turning, positioning, and skin care are essential along with hourly neurological vital sign assessment. As was indicated earlier, plasmapheresis will most frequently reverse the signs and symptoms present, and the patient need not later contend with the additional problems that are secondary to immobilization.

In most institutions, a specially trained pheresis team will perform the procedure. However, there are several points that the staff nurses need to be alert to before, during, and after the process. Though the rationale for the procedure and potential adverse effects most probably will be explained to the patient and family by the physician, the nurses need to be available to answer any questions or receive any concerns expressed. Vital signs are to be monitored frequently, hourly or more often, since hypocalcemia and hypovolemia can develop during continuous-flow centrifuge.

Hypocalcemia can occur because a great deal of calcium is lost in the plasma which is removed, and additional amounts are inactivated by the acid-citrate-dextrose (ACD) solutions used for anticoagulation. The nurse needs to carefully assess the patient for signs of tetany and prolongation of the Q-T interval electrocardiographically as indices of hypocalcemia. Early clinical symptoms include tingling in the fingers and circumoral region and muscular cramps. If calcium gluconate replacement is administered, the team must be alert to ventricular arrhythmias and possible cardiac arrest caused by hypercalcemia.

Hypovolemia will result if the amounts of plasma removed are not carefully balanced with fluid replacement therapy, usually in the form of Ringer's lactate solution. The monitoring of a decreasing blood pressure and an increased heart rate should alert personnel to reduce the rate of plasma removal and increase fluid replacement. This action will also serve to decrease the rate of calcium loss.

Emotional and supportive care during the crisis and therapy periods are central. Pain is usually only experienced by the patient when the needles (usually

14 to 16 gauge) are inserted; however, the tedium and immobilization for such long periods of time can be quite discomforting. The staff and the pheresis team should coordinate efforts to encourage the patient and provide frequent repositioning and diversion. Nutritional requirements and excretory needs of the patient should not be overlooked; in fact, all efforts should be made to provide continuity of care. Whether or not it is the policy of a particular unit, attempts to allow frequent family visits will generally serve to decrease the anxiety of all involved.

Following the treatment, the pressure dressings in each antecubital space need to be assessed for bleeding and decreased perfusion distally. Cardiovascular and cerebrovascular assessment are ongoing, since one treatment frequently is not adequate. Monitoring heart sounds, ECG, chest x-ray, adventitious sounds, jugular venous pressure, and mental status, in addition to routine vital signs, will reflect the patient's response to therapeutic intervention.

ANEMIA

Anemia, the most common condition resulting from hematopoietic disease, is defined by a reduction below normal in the amount of hemoglobin and/or erythrocytes. Although the general effects of anemia can be attributed to a reduction in oxygen-carrying capacity, certain clinical manifestations may be related to the specific etiology and pathogenesis. Two types of anemia, aplastic and hemolytic, will be presented following a discussion of the general clinical manifestations.

Tissue hypoxia occurs when oxygen is not available or is insufficient on the cellular level for the required metabolic activity. Many of the signs and symptoms of anemia are also related to the compensatory mechanisms called into action to prevent destructive tissue hypoxia. On the cellular level, in the face of anemia, there is an increased synthesis of 2,3-diphosphoglycerate (2,3-DPG) which shifts the oxygen dissociation curve so that more oxygen is released to the tissues at a higher oxygen tension. Compensation also occurs by the use of all potential capillary channels to increase tissue perfusion to vital areas at the expense of nonvital donor areas. The major donor areas for redistribution of the blood are the skin and kidneys. Vasoconstriction occurs with the clinical finding of pallor. There is also a shift away from the kidneys. Though certainly a vital organ, under normal conditions the oxygen supply to the kidneys is in excess of its demand, so that even in severe anemia with renal blood flow reduced by almost 50 percent, reduction in renal function may only be mildly or moderately curtailed. The benefits derived from this redistribution are obvious in terms of supplying the more pressing needs of the myocardium, brain, and muscles.

A high cardiac output is another excellent compensatory mechanism, but it may increase metabolic needs. Cardiac output does not measurably increase in chronic anemia until the hemoglobin level reaches about 7 g per 100 mL. The signs of compensatory cardiac activity include tachycardia, flow murmurs (usually systolic), and orthostatic hypotension. The normal heart will sustain hyperactivity for prolonged periods; however, angina pectoris and high-output heart failure may occur if coronary oxygen demands are not filled or if there is preexisting coronary disease. It is important to note that in chronic anemia the blood volume is normal because of the increased plasma volume. An increased respiratory rate occurs also in an attempt to increase oxygenation. This accounts for symptoms of exertional dyspnea and orthopnea in the anemic patient.

Lastly, and perhaps most reasonably, there is an increase in the rate of erythrocyte (RBC) production in the anemic patient, as determined by increases in the reticulocyte count. There is increased production of erythropoietin as a physiologic response to renal hypoxia, and when the bone marrow is functionally responsive, the patient's clinical complaints may be generalized aches and pains or sternal tenderness.

When these compensatory mechanisms are unable to correct the tissue hypoxia, symptoms on this basis alone occur. The patient may present with angina pectoris, intermittent claudication, and night cramps due to muscle tissue hypoxia. Neurologically, the patient may complain of headache, lightheadedness, roaring in the ears, faintness, irritability, and/or depression.

APLASTIC ANEMIA

Etiology of Pathophysiologic Process

The bone marrow is responsible for the production of granulocytes, platelets, and erythrocytes (see Chap. 5). Aplastic anemia refers to *pancytopenia,* depression of all three cellular elements due to fatty replacement of the bone marrow. The cause of this is related to bone marrow injury from chemical toxins (industrial agents or drugs) or radiation. A remaining 50 percent of the cases are from unknown etiologies (idiopathic).

A list of agents and drugs that have been implicated in aplastic anemia is quite exhausting, ranging from antibiotics, analgesics, and anticonvulsants to chemotherapeutic agents; probably almost any drug could be an etiologic factor.

Clinical Assessment

Aplastic anemia is *usually* insidious, but it can be fulminating in nature. The symptoms may be related to anemia as outlined in the general discussion, or may be fever and infection secondary to neutropenia (a reduced number of neutrophils), or may be bleeding related to thrombocytopenia (reduced number of platelets). Physical examination is usually not remarkable except for pallor and petechiae. Splenomegaly is not usually found in the early stages. Because of the lack of specificity of symptoms, patients are frequently treated symptomatically until advanced marrow depression with frank purpura demands hematologic evaluation.

The diagnosis of aplastic anemia or fatty bone marrow is made primarily on the basis of bone marrow biopsy and may show impaired function in the range from hypoplasia to total aplasia.

From laboratory data, reduction in both erythrocytes, leukocytes, and platelets is an invariable finding. The anemia is usually normocytic (RBCs are normal in size) and normochromic (normal cellular content of hemoglobin), and the reticulocyte count is subnormal. When the granulocyte count (more accurate than the total white blood cell count) is below an absolute number of 200 per mm^3, imminent danger of infection is present. Coagulation defects other than thrombocytopenia are not present.

Treatment of Aplastic Anemia

A serious attempt to determine the etiologic agent and removal of the patient from the agent is mandatory. Efforts are then directed toward support of the patient to provide the chance for spontaneous recovery of the bone marrow.

In chronic uncomplicated anemia, a patient may tolerate hemoglobin levels of 6 to 7 g per 100 mL without any subjective discomfort. When transfusion is required, it should be given not by the numerical hemoglobin reading, but on the basis of demonstration (either subjective or objective) of tissue hypoxia. Transfusion should be given with packed red blood cells or frozen blood, if it is available. Frozen blood has the advantage of less serum hepatitis risk and decreased incidence of transfusion reaction. The blood should be administered over a 2-h period so as not to induce heart failure; it is to be reemphasized that total blood volume is normal and the plasma volume increased.

A platelet count of greater than 20,000 per mm^3 will usually prevent any major spontaneous hemorrhage. In the absence of adequate means of platelet typing, it can be anticipated that the beneficial effects of platelet transfusion will be diminished by the emergence of antibodies. Platelet transfusion efficacy will also be impaired by fever and infection. Because of these problems, platelet transfusions must be used judiciously, since the course of aplastic anemia may span months to years.

Granulocyte transfusion in infection is efficacious and now is available in many centers. Chronic transfusion of white cell concentrates is not realistic because of the short life span of the granulocytes. Continuous-flow centrifugation or filtered leukapheresis appear promising (Williams et al., 1977, p. 270). It should be pointed out that for half the patients with aplastic anemia, death occurs within the first 2 years from hemorrhage or infection. Granulocyte transfusions can greatly reduce the morbidity and mortality from serious bacterial infections.

When infection is suspected, antibiotic therapy should be prompt and aggressive. Cultures should be obtained from the blood, throat, urine, and all suspected inflammatory sites, and the patient should be started on bactericidal, broad spectrum antibiotics before the cultures and sensitivity studies are returned. Though the therapy may have to be modified, in the face of neutropenia, the infection can be so overwhelming that one cannot wait for the culture and sensitivity reports. Additionally, patients with neutropenia cannot make pus, and therefore localization is frequently difficult. Initial broad spectrum therapy should include at least two drugs in the categories of cephalothin, gentamycin, and aminoglycoside drugs, such as carbenicillin. Though adequate studies are not available, prophylactic antibiotics are not considered efficacious and have been thought to be hazardous because of the tendency for resistant organism emergence.

In the face of severe granulocytopenia (< 200 per mm^3), an attempt at reverse isolation is in order; however, complete reverse isolation is not practical unless one has a facility such as a laminar flow room. The *strict* use of gowns and gloves is probably not effective unless life islands are available, and the advantages are questionable if they result in a reduction of optimal nursing care. *Reasonable* reverse isolation would consist of a reduction in exposure to visitors, proper handwashing technique with an antiseptic soap, and the use of face masks to prevent infection from the respiratory tracts of the personnel and visitors.

Therapeutically, adrenal steroids have been used for many years, and a therapeutic trial of 1 to 2 months is usually justified. The true benefit of steroids inducing remission in the patient with aplastic anemia remains controversial, and there are many potential dangers from the side effects of long-term steroid use. When more than the equivalent of 20 mg of prednisone is being administered daily and little or no effect is noted on cellular production, careful study should be given to discontinuation of steroid therapy.

Splenectomy will not improve bone marrow function, but it can, at times, effectively improve the life span of circulating red blood cells, particularly in those patients who, because of inflammation or chronic transfusion, have an element of hypersplenism. Androgens have also been used alone or in combination with adrenal steroids. Beneficial effects have been seen in children, but the results in adults have been less encouraging and certainly controversial.

Lastly, bone marrow transplantation has been found to be an efficacious therapy in aplastic anemia. Problems exist currently, in that it is only being done in certain centers. The decision must be made early before multiple blood and platelet transfusions are administered; a HLA-compatible sibling must be available for donor grafts; and the posttransplantation phase involves intense immunosuppressive therapy in a specialized unit. Even though the mortality rate remains very high, many feel it is the single most effective therapy for aplastic anemia.

The prognosis is highly variable, though patients whose aplastic anemia develops in conjunction with bone marrow toxin exposure seem to respond more favorably to treatment. Approximately one-third of the patients will spontaneously remit, and therefore all attempts should be made to support the patient until remission occurs.

Nursing Implications

Many aspects of care to be given the patient with aplastic anemia have already been discussed in the section above on principles of treatment. Specific nursing activities will be addressed relative to assessment, anemia, infections, and bleeding events.

Once the diagnosis has been established, the nurse may be able to elicit from the patient clues to previous exposure to toxic chemicals. Rapport developed, for example, may allow an individual to reveal an involvement with glue-sniffing, where toluene is the etiologic agent. A nonjudgmental attitude on the part of the staff may encourage the patient to express anger not only about the disease, but about the excessive puncturing required secondary to frequent laboratory examinations. Scheduling of lab work to decrease the number of venipunctures, in addition to decreasing the patient's discomfort, reduces the number of sites for pathogen entry. A central versus a peripheral intravenous catheter, which may need replacement frequently, is desirable, and as with all sites, strict asepsis and care must be the routine daily.

The patient with pancytopenia may be severely hypoxic and weak. Nursing activities should be directed at conserving energy, keeping the patient warm and adequately oxygenated, and providing protection from injury and infection. A danger of burns from hot water bottles or heating pads exists, since the patient with anemia may have neurologic disturbances that decrease sensory perception. Regular assessment of neurologic status provides information regarding cerebral oxygenation, allowing nursing care to be planned accordingly.

Mouth care should be given with soft cotton applicators or one of the commercially available sponge sticks, because the patient with aplastic anemia is highly susceptible to infections (due to leukopenia) which cause ulcerative and necrotic lesions of the mouth and pharynx. Mouth care must be frequent and include mild, cool mouth rinses, lubrication to the lips, and avoidance of irritating foods and beverages. Popsicles may offer some relief and vasoconstriction to the patient with mild oral bleeding.

Though transfusion of packed red blood cells still carries a risk of infection and incompatibility reaction, the ability to raise the hematocrit rapidly without great risk of circulatory overload is very important in the patient with aplastic anemia. The advantage of frozen red cells has already been cited. Filters should always be used in accordance with manufacturer's guidelines and hospital policy, and a Y connection to the IV should be used for saline flush.

Whole blood or packed red cell units "piggybacked" to dextrose in water solutions lacking electrolytes, and medications injected into IV tubing during blood administration can cause hemolysis and clotting. Mixing the cells to prevent settling during administration can be accomplished by squeezing the bag every 20 to 30 min. All basic medical-surgical textbooks contain the signs and symptoms of transfusion reactions. It is mandatory for *any practicing nurse* to commit them to memory.

HEMOLYTIC ANEMIA

Etiology of Pathophysiologic Process

Hemolytic anemia, in general, refers to a shortening of the red blood cell life span, which normally is approximately 120 days, by an increased rate of destruction of the patient's erythrocytes. There are a multitude of both congenital and acquired hemolytic anemias, but this section will be limited to the autoimmune hemolytic anemias.

Evidence of autoimmunity against red cells is usually demonstrated by a positive direct immunoglobulin test, that is, evidence of antibody coating of the red cells as shown by a positive Coombs' test. There should also be evidence of increased red blood cell destruction or shortened life span, and in patients whose bone marrows are capable of responding, an increased production. The antibodies found may be the warm antibody type with maximal activity at 37°C, or the so-called "cold antibody" with maximal activity at 2 to 4°C. Autoimmune hemolytic anemias may be idiopathic or may be secondary to lymphoproliferative disorders, other neoplastic diseases, more generalized autoimmune disorders such as lupus erythematosus, and the other collagen vascular diseases, or to drugs such as methyldopa.

Though the etiology is not completely understood, two basic theories have been proposed. The first suggests that the pathogenesis occurs in the red cell membrane and that the normal immune response is stimulated to react to this new antigen. The second theory proposes that a defect occurs within the immune system, wherein the ability to recognize self is lost or impaired. Many factors remain to be determined about the etiology and pathogenesis of autoimmune hemolytic disorders.

Clinical Assessment

The presentation can be highly variable in that the patient may have a mild anemia or a severe fulminating hemolytic process. Initial complaints may be a fever of unexplained origin or thrombophlebitis. A significant number of patients are only initially recognized when they cannot be cross matched for transfusion. The autoimmune hemolytic anemia may,

of course, be overshadowed by the underlying disease, such as lymphoma or chonic lymphocytic leukemia.

Clinically, a patient with a mild autoimmune hemolytic anemia may become severely anemic when bone marrow function is suppressed by a mild infection. Any stressful situation may aggravate or accelerate the hemolytic anemia. Surgery, trauma, pregnancy, and psychological stress are particularly noteworthy. The patient with hyperacute hemolysis may show jaundice as well as pallor with symptoms of air hunger and cardiovascular failure. Splenomegaly is found frequently and hepatomegaly in approximately a third or more of the patients.

The blood smear of the patient with autoimmune hemolytic anemia shows polychromasia, indicating an increase of reticulocytes (reticulocytosis) and frequently the finding of spherocytes, or sphere-shaped erythrocytes, and red cell fragmentation. In severe anemia, nucleated red cells may be found, additionally megaloblastic forms, as a result of folic acid deficiency. The chronic hemolytic process requires increased red cell production, which exhausts folic acid stores and exceeds dietary replenishment. There is frequently an associated leukocytosis. Bone marrow examination reveals erythroid hyperplasia. Hemoglobinuria may be seen with acute intravascular hemolysis, along with hemosideronuria.

The diagnosis of an autoimmune etiology is established by a positive Coombs' test, indicating immunoglobulin coating of the red blood cells. The most common immunoglobulin is IgG, and complement fixation is frequently found on the red cells.

Treatment of Hemolytic Anemia

As with any anemia, supportive measures should be maintained in terms of trying to increase tissue oxygenation and support cardiovascular function. Transfusions should be avoided when possible because of the difficulties which exist in proper cross matching. The hemolytic transfusion reaction may be severe.

However, in acute cases where circulatory failure or severe anemic anoxia threatens, transfusion may be lifesaving. In that event, units for transfusion should be utilized which show the *least reactivity* with the patient's serum. This is evidenced by the degree of agglutination in cross-match reaction and by tests of the donor's red cells with titrations of the patient's serum. Transfusion of the sedimented red cells should be administered slowly and monitored very carefully with periodic examination of the patient's plasma for the presence of free hemoglobin or for any signs and symptoms of transfusion reaction. In the event of either, the unit should be stopped. The purpose of transfusion is only to provide sufficient oxygen-carrying capacity for a long enough period for other modes of therapy to be utilized.

Administration of corticosteroids in a dose equivalent to 50 to 100 mg of prednisone is efficacious in this disorder. Potassium levels should be monitored regularly. Antacids should be administered with prednisone along with supplemental folic acid. After the patient has been stabilized and the maximum hemoglobin level has been reached, an attempt at tapering the adrenal steroids over several months can be initiated.

Splenectomy is also an effective procedure for autoimmune hemolytic anemia, when the patient continues to deteriorate despite corticosteroid therapy, or when the patient has to be maintained on continued high dosage to effect remission. Postoperative thrombophlebitis is a frequent complication and the patient should be examined carefully for this. In both splenectomy and steroid therapy patients, other immunosuppressive drugs may be utilized to induce immunoparalysis. Though some trials have been effective, this approach is generally only considered in refractory states.

Nursing Implications

Adequate oxygenation and tissue perfusion and maintenance of cardiovascular function are the goals of supportive therapy for the patient with autoimmune hemolytic anemia. The index of skin color can be misleading when jaundice is profound. Evidence of air hunger, restlessness, and tachycardia require further investigation and intervention. The use of an indwelling catheter for blood pressure recordings and arterial blood gas determination is desirable. Serum evaluation for free hemoglobin needs to be done at regular intervals.

In most patients a hemolytic transfusion reaction will occur within the first 15 min of administration; however, the patient with autoimmune hemolytic anemia who is receiving packed red blood cells requires frequent periodic assessment for reactive signs and symptoms. Chills, fever, chest pain, low back pain, increased jugular venous pressure, and/or nausea and vomiting *obligate cessation of the transfusion immediately.* Tachypnea, tachycardia, cyanosis, and hypotension may have been present pretransfusion but can be used as baseline indices for changes.

The use of steroids and antacids has been cited;

however, the nurse should remain cognizant of the secondary problems arising from corticosteroid therapy. If the patient is postoperative, wound healing will be delayed and propensity to infection exists.

Pruritus secondary to jaundice can be a distressing problem to the patient. Soap should be avoided in bathing, and the use of antipruritic lotions such as calamine may provide some degree of relief.

Muscle aches, stiffness, and soreness in the calf may be patient complaints of early thrombophlebitis. Whether or not the patient is verbalizing discomfort, in the course of the critical-care nurse's assessment daily, warmth of the extremities, edema, and a positive Homans' sign should be evaluated. Repositioning the patient, elevation, application of moist heat, and elastic stockings, along with the earliest possible ambulation postsplenectomy, are important.

Prognosis is generally poor for the patient with *idiopathic* autoimmune hemolytic anemia, and survival is limited from months to a few years. However, about one-half of individuals suffering from autoimmune hemolytic anemia will experience years of relapses and remissions. Aggressive supportive therapy and patient encouragement are imperative.

ACUTE LEUKEMIC CRISES

Etiology of Pathophysiologic Process

Acute leukemia is a progressive malignant disease of the bone marrow that is characterized by large numbers of immature malfunctioning cells and abnormal leukocytes of the peripheral blood and the bone marrow. With progression of the disease, these abnormal cells replace the normal hematopoietic elements of the marrow and infiltrate other organs such as the lymph nodes, spleen, and particularly the central nervous system. Modern multidrug chemotherapy that is used to induce remissions of acute leukemia almost universally produces a phase of bone marrow destruction or hypocellularity. Theoretically, then, the bone marrow repopulates with normal cells. It is during the phase of marrow acellularity secondary to chemotherapy, compounded by the initial abnormalities, that most of the problems will be seen in the acute setting.

Clinical Assessment

The clinical features and complications of acute leukemia are basically the same. The central problem responsible is accumulation and proliferation of the leukemic cells in the bone marrow and other organs.

For instance, replacement of the marrow, the most important tissue involved, by leukemic blasts accounts for most of the common manifestations of the disease, i.e., infection associated with granulocytopenia and bleeding due to thrombocytopenia and anemia. Clinical abnormalities related to organ infiltration most frequently occur in the lymph nodes, liver, spleen, kidneys, skeletal system, and central nervous system. As noted above, manifestations or complications of the disease may be directly related to the disorder or to therapeutic attempts at remission.

Infection is a frequent complication of leukemia, as well as being the most serious. Although fever is a common symptom of leukemia alone, infection is the more common cause and *always* needs to be thoroughly assessed. This is especially true as the disease progresses. Increased susceptibility to infection is due to decreased absolute numbers of effective circulating granulocytes and the immunosuppression caused by antileukemic therapy. Infections become more frequent as the quantitative granulocyte count falls below 1000 per mm³ and is very common when below 500 per mm³. Sites most frequently invaded include the skin, throat, gums, and respiratory and urinary tracts.

Anemia has been covered as a separate entity earlier in this chapter. Anemia is universal in acute leukemia because of the bone marrow replacement of leukemic blasts and secondary marrow failure, as well as the hypoplasia produced by chemotherapy. Patient complaints of fatigue and weakness are common, and pallor and lethargy will be evidenced. Weight loss, as with most all neoplastic disorders, is secondary to increased metabolism and reduced appetite.

Bleeding, ranging from purpura, gum oozing, or hypertrophy to hematuria, melena, and frank hemorrhage, is due to thrombocytopenia. When the platelet count falls to 20,000 per mm³ in the presence of either infection, fever, or intravascular coagulation, the patient is considered to be an extreme risk for hemorrhage. It must be kept in mind that there is not only a quantitative, but a qualitative platelet defect in patients with acute leukemia; that is, the platelets present do not function normally. Disseminated intravascular coagulation (DIC) may also be a complication, and it is more prone to develop in acute promyelocytic leukemia. Large confluent ecchymoses or brisk, prolonged bleeding from bone marrow aspiration or venipuncture sites should alert the team to the possibility of DIC. When hemorrhage from DIC is suspected, early diagnosis and treatment should begin prior to the initiation of antileukemic therapy,

since cytostatic drugs will exacerbate the bleeding diathesis. The syndrome of DIC is reviewed later in this chapter, but it is worthy to note that though typically most clotting factors are reduced in DIC, for reasons poorly understood, fibrinogen levels are usually elevated in patients with acute leukemia, making diagnosis of the coagulopathy difficult. Cerebral hemorrhage is a disastrous complication which may not only be associated with thrombocytopenia but, occurring secondary to leukostasis, associated with very high leukocyte counts. The risk of intracerebral bleeding increases in patients whose total white count is above 100,000 per mm³, even when the platelet count is normal.

Organ infiltration varies with different types of acute leukemia, and as was mentioned earlier, the bone marrow is consistently the most significant. Bone pain and tenderness is frequently present and is caused by local leukemic infiltration. Patients' complaints of abdominal fullness, anorexia, and obstipation may indicate hepatosplenomegaly, infiltration of the abdominal viscera, and local infiltration leading to obstruction. Enlarged lymph nodes may be found (especially in children) along with tumor masses in the nodes, skin, breasts, and testes. Hemorrhage and cerebral infarction due to both thrombocytopenia and leukostasis have been mentioned, but clinical signs suggesting central nervous system infiltration can be variable and there may be marked leukemic infiltration without any abnormal signs and symptoms. Vomiting, headache, papilledema, cranial and spinal nerve palsies, lethargy, confusion, and irritability are all suggestive of central nervous system (CNS) infiltration when no obvious alternate explanations exist. A demonstration of leukemic cells in the cerebrospinal fluid will confirm the diagnosis, and more than 10 mononuclear cells present should be regarded as highly suspicious.

Lastly, patients with acute leukemia (untreated or in relapse) are quite prone to renal failure because of increased uric acid excretion. As a breakdown product of nucleic acid degradation, the uric acid can normally be cleared without difficulty; in leukemia, urate increases dramatically and can precipitate in the renal tubules, especially in the presence of dehydration. The patient may evidence oliguria, concentrated urine, and an elevated BUN and uric acid.

Treatment of Acute Leukemic Crises

Infection is probably the most common cause of death in acute leukemia. It is important when one suspects infection to do appropriate cultures of any indwelling catheters, blood cultures, urine, and sputum; to perform a chest x-ray; and to initiate therapy with broad spectrum, bactericidal antibiotics while awaiting the culture results. As a rule, patients with acute leukemia live longer, and as more and newer antibiotics arise, the types of organisms are changing. The predominant organisms encountered now are *Pseudomonas aeroginosa* and other gram-negative organisms, although gram-positive organisms such as *Staphylococcus aureus* are quite prevalent. There is also an increased incidence of opportunistic infections such as fungus, *Pneumocystis carinii,* and *Candida.* Prophylactic antibiotics are not indicated unless the patient is in a life island support system and the attempt is being made to have a totally sterile environment. Granulocyte transfusions, as noted earlier, are now available in many centers and have shown a decreased mortality associated with infection; however, they have not improved the overall survival in acute leukemia.

Anemia can be usually managed well through blood replacement therapy, and when thrombocytopenia is severe, platelet support is essential and effective. This is especially true during the phase of remission induction. Fresh platelets from ABO, HLA-compatible donors represent ideal therapy, but on a short-term basis, random donor platelets are satisfactory. Remission will usually take place before significant isoantibodies develop.

Treatment for DIC includes heparin, platelet, and possibly factor replacements before cytostatic therapy induction is begun. Epsilon aminocaproic acid (EACA) has questionable use with patients in acute leukemic crises who have developed DIC. This therapy will be discussed later in this chapter.

Since patients with acute leukemia survive longer, leukemic meningitis is being increasingly recognized. In acute lymphocytic leukemia of childhood, it is now recommended that prophylactic treatment with craniospinal irradiation and/or intrathecal methotrexate be given routinely. For patients whose white counts are 100,000 per mm³ or greater, leukaphoresis must be rapidly instituted in order to lower the white count and prevent intracerebral hemorrhage and infarction.

Bone marrow transplantation is as yet very experimental. In one study of 100 patients with acute leukemia, 13 percent were surviving with their graft, required no maintenance cytostatic therapy, and had no recurrence of leukemia at stages up to 4½ years posttransplantation (Zimmerman et al., 1977, p. 1313). As with aplastic anemia, although problems exist in this mode of treatment, it also offers much hope.

The prognosis for patients with acute leukemia has improved greatly in the past 20 years. Survival has been increased by the development of more effective chemotherapy regimens, availability of blood component support, improved antibiotics, and better understanding and treatment of the complications that occur. Though prognosis among individuals varies greatly and is dependent upon several factors, the most important of these being cell type and age of onset, a challenge exists for the team treating the patients in crisis and supporting their ability to tolerate the aggressive regimens.

Nursing Implications

Management and treatment of infection is probably the most challenging activity for the critical-care nurse who has a patient in acute leukemic crisis. Nosocomial organisms can be fatal to the patient who is immunosuppressed and granulocytopenic. Though life islands are ideal, relatively few hospitals are so equipped. Antibiotics ordered topically and/or by mouth should be given religiously and ongoing assessment of new areas of invasion treated. The patients themselves present with a great reservoir for infections of autochthonous bacteria from oral, nasal, and gastrointestinal regions.

Pneumocystis carinii, a protozoal infection, frequently is difficult to diagnose because it cannot be detected by culture or serologic study (Williams et al., 1977, p. 823). Fever, malaise, and a nonproductive cough may be the only symptoms, even when chest x-ray demonstrates extensive infiltration. A frequently irreversible respiratory insufficiency can develop in a few days or weeks.

Rigid asepsis to be followed on all patients is imperative in acute leukemia. The multiple invasive tests and treatments, such as venipunctures, finger sticks, bone marrow studies, intravenous therapy, and injections, all provide a portal for potentially fatal pathogens. Site preparation should be carried out meticulously with an antiseptic solution such as betadine, and firm pressure and then dressings should be applied. Laboratory studies, when possible, should be coordinated by the nurse to reduce excessive puncturing. Fever must not be dismissed lightly, and when fever is over 38.5°C., cultures should be obtained and antibiotic therapy begun.

All patient activities should be directed at conserving energy, and high-calorie, high-vitamin meals should be encouraged, perhaps at frequent intervals. Dehydration represents a significant problem, and whether through intravenous fluid therapy and/or oral intake, the patient with acute leukemia needs to maintain a urinary output of 100 mL/h to guard against uric acid nephropathy. Allopurinol will additionally be part of the patient's medical regimen.

Since no cure for acute leukemia exists at this time, the outcome of care is directed toward helping the patient live as normal and as long a life as possible. Ongoing support of the patient and encouragement to verbalize feelings about the disease and therapy are essential.

COAGULOPATHIES

Abnormal or defective hemostasis may be due to abnormalities of platelets, plasma coagulation factors, and/or blood vessels. Of all the hematologic defects discussed thus far in this chapter, the coagulopathies are probably the most frequently encountered in the critical-care environment. Following a general discussion, this section will review coagulation disorders related to vitamin K deficiency and liver disease and disseminated intravascular coagulation.

The primary responsibility of *platelets* in hemostasis occurs in the control of bleeding in the *small vessels.* Whether the platelet abnormality is quantitative or qualitative, the clinical picture is different from bleeding caused by factor abnormality. The predominant findings are petechiae in the skin and mucous membranes (though it may occur on a widespread basis in the internal organs) and bleeding which stops rapidly with local pressure and fails to recur when pressure is withdrawn. Bleeding secondary to *coagulation factor deficiency* usually does not give rise to petechiae, but rather hemorrhage deeper in the body, such as subcutaneous or intramuscular hematomas. When external, these sites respond slowly to applied pressure and tend to recur.

It must be kept in mind that although the preceding are generally clinically directive, platelet and coagulation factors are interdependent mechanisms in the control of bleeding and thus both may be culprits in some coagulation disorders. Von Willebrand's disease, a mendelian dominant inherited trait, and hemorrhage following transfusion replacement with banked blood are two examples.

There is only a rough correlation between the platelet count and degree of bleeding, but generally patients who have platelet counts greater than 50,000 per mm³ are safe for even major surgical procedures. Studies in patients with acute leukemia have shown that major hemorrhage is unusual with a platelet count in excess of 20,000 per mm³. Vascular function may

may be a determinant when petechiae are found in patients with adequate platelet counts. Drugs that affect platelet function, such as aspirin, may also cause bleeding at higher platelet counts.

As stressed at the outset, history and physical examination are extremely important in evaluating patients with bleeding disorders, and precise questioning may reveal a lifelong pattern. Bleeding from a circumcision or history of relatives with bleeding problems may be indicative of an inherited factor defect. The most common inherited defects relate to deficiencies of factors VIII and IX, which are sex-linked in nature and may skip generations. Spontaneous bleeding, most commonly caused by trauma, may be secondary to platelet deficiency or a combination of abnormalities. The petechiae and bruising (< 6 cm) of platelet disorders are usually found in the dependent parts of the body. Excessive bleeding following trauma, such as dental extraction or surgery, may be difficult to assess without a medical record, but it is desirable to err on the side of the patient's possible exaggeration in terms of follow-up evaluation.

It is customary to perform certain screening tests before proceeding to more specific and sensitive studies. Refer to Table 25-1. It is also well known that the screening tests have a certain degree of insensitivity and therefore may miss mild bleeding disorders. For instance, in classic hemophilia, whole blood clotting time will not become abnormal until the factor VIII level has dropped to 1 percent of normal. The kaolin-activated partial thromboplastin time (PTT) is more sensitive and will show abnormalities of factors VIII and IX at 30 to 40 percent levels. The usual screening tests for platelet function are the bleeding time, clot retraction, and platelet count. More specific tests are available, e.g., platelet aggregation, to determine the functional integrity of the platelets. The routine screening tests for plasma coagulation factors are the whole blood clotting time, active partial thromboplastin time, prothrombin time (PT), and quantitative fibrinogen. From there, one may do specific factor assays and substitution studies with serum and barium-absorbed plasma.

The end point of the coagulation sequence is the generation of thrombin which converts fibrinogen to fibrin monomers, which then make the fibrin polymer or clot. The PTT is used to assess the integrity of the *intrinsic coagulation system,* which basically tests factors XII, XI, IX, VIII, X, and V, prothrombin, and fibrinogen. The *extrinsic coagulation system,* which is assessed by the protime (PT), measures factors VII,

X, and V, prothrombin, and fibrinogen. Notice in the simplified coagulation scheme in Fig. 25-1, that there is a final common pathway between the prothrombin time and the partial thromboplastin time where factors X and V, prothrombin, and fibrinogen are common to both tests.

VITAMIN K–DEPENDENT COAGULATION DISORDERS

The vitamin K–dependent coagulation factors are prothrombin (factor II) and factors VII, IX, and X. Disorders among this group are due to liver disease, malabsorption of vitamin K from the intestinal tract, or the use of oral anticoagulant drugs, either therapeutically or surreptitiously. In the newborn, this problem may develop because of immaturity of the liver synthetic apparatus and the absence of vitamin K–synthesizing flora in the intestinal tract, which may produce a hemorrhagic diathesis.

Hemorrhagic Liver Disease

Vitamin K–dependent coagulation factors are synthesized in the liver; therefore, deficiencies are found in patients with cirrhosis or severe hepatitis. The depression of these factors will not be corrected by the

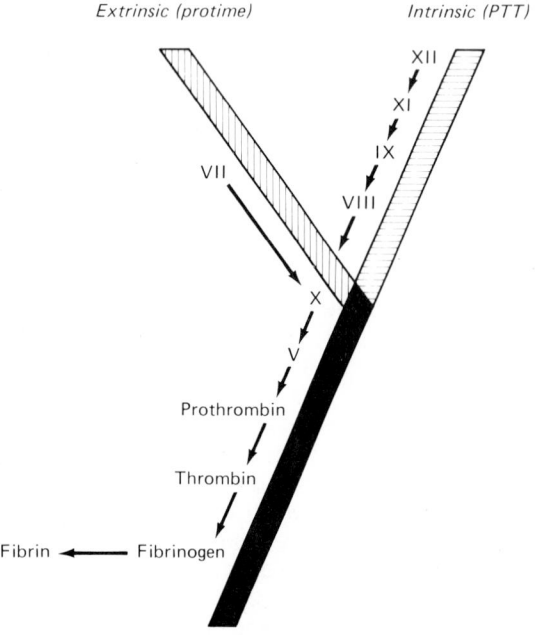

Extrinsic (protime)   *Intrinsic (PTT)*

XII
XI
IX
VIII
VII
X
V
Prothrombin
Thrombin
Fibrin ← Fibrinogen

FIGURE 25-1

Simplified coagulation scheme showing factors tested by prothrombin and partial thromboplastin times.

administration of vitamin K, and this, indeed, is a useful test to differentiate hepatocellular disease from obstructive jaundice. Ten milligrams of vitamin K given parenterally will correct the one-stage prothrombin time in 24 to 48 h if the cause *is not* due to hepatocellular or parenchymal disease. Liver disease is usually fairly far advanced before the prothrombin time will become abnormal. Since parenchymal disease can be secondary to biliary obstruction, which causes the absence of bile salts and an impedance of vitamin K absorption, interpretation of the prothrombin time is not always definitive. Poor prognosis is related to prothrombin times greater than 1.5 times normal which have not responded to vitamin K (Williams et al., 1977, p. 1442).

Other hemostatic defects and factor deficiencies also exist with liver disorder. Factor V levels may be decreased, and in patients having cirrhosis with portal hypertension, platelets can be affected. Additionally, as the reticuloendothelial cells of the liver are responsible for synthesizing certain fibrinolytic inhibitors, as well as the clearance of the components (fibrin split or degradation products) of the fibrinolytic system (see Chap. 5), increased fibrinolytic activity is commonly seen.

Treatment should be based upon the clinical situation such as hemorrhagic symptoms or in preparation for surgery, and not only on the basis of abnormal coagulation tests. When the system is compromised, this coagulopathy is very complex and the survival of the patient with hemorrhagic liver disease is frequently poor. Fresh-frozen plasma will temporarily cover all deficiencies except platelets, which can be given in the form of platelet packs. Concentrates of vitamin K–dependent factors are available, but at present there is an extremely high risk of hepatitis.

The coagulation defects in liver disease can be extremely difficult to differentiate from disseminated intravascular coagulation; indeed, the hypermetabolism of fibrinogen in these disorders may be related to DIC. It is important to attempt to do this, as heparin has produced very disastrous results in the coagulopathy of liver disease, even when DIC has been found to be present. If intense fibrinolysis is a dominant aspect of the hepatic coagulopathy, the use of antifibrinolytic agents such as EACA can be used, especially at the time of surgery.

Availability and Absorption of Vitamin K

Vitamin K is made available by diet and the synthetic activity of the intestinal flora. Absorption is then promoted by a competent biliary tree. Several vitamin K–dependent factor deficiencies can be related to patient therapies within the critical-care environment.

Severe vitamin K deficiency is increasingly being recognized in patients who have been on prolonged nasogastric suction and long-term antibiotics. This can develop in as brief a time as 2 to 3 weeks. All else being equal, this disorder responds promptly to parenteral vitamin K with a rapid increase in prothrombin and factors VII, IX, and X. This disorder needs to be suspected and assessed more carefully in the setting of the critical-care unit because it is such an easily treatable coagulation defect.

Drugs frequently ordered for patients in the critical-care unit can also be responsible for vitamin K deficiency. The action of coumarin anticoagulants is to interfere with the vitamin K–mediated hepatic synthesis of prothrombin and factors VII, IX, and X. Clinical response to these orally administered drugs depends upon functional intestinal absorption, the body stores of vitamin K, the degree of albumin binding, and the rate of anticoagulant detoxification in the liver. This being the case, wide variations of plasma level can exist among patients who receive the same dose. It is important to note that many drugs (only a few of which are noted here) interfere with the effect of Coumadin, making the patient either more or less sensitive to the drug. Phenobarbital, oral contraceptives, and Valium decrease the effect of Coumadin, while phenylbutazone, phenytoin (Dilantin), and reserpine potentiate its effect. Salicylates in high doses may also depress vitamin K–dependent factors, thereby enhancing the effect of Coumadin. It has already been noted that aspirin inhibits platelet function. Clinical evidence of abnormally high anticoagulation includes bleeding gums, hemoptysis, melena, hematuria, and ecchymoses.

The depression of the vitamin K–dependent factors in response to coumarin drugs follows their biologic half-life. Factor VII has the shortest half-life and is depressed first, accounting for the initial prolongation of the one-stage prothrombin time. Factor IX, which is not measured in the prothrombin time, is also affected. Factor X and prothrombin generally reach their lowest level in 5 to 10 days. If reversal is necessary because of bleeding due to overdosage or drug interaction, parenteral vitamin K_1 can be administered. Usually 10 mg of vitamin K_1 intravenously will suffice to correct the anticoagulation effect of the coumarin drugs in 24 to 48 h, though doses up to 50 mg IV can be administered for more rapid reversal (6 to 12 h).

In assessing any patient's response (or lack of response) to Coumadin-like drugs, a careful drug history must be elicited and each medication checked to determine if it has been interfering with the anticoagulant's effect. The team must never rule out the possibility, even in medically trained patients, that the problems with response can arise secondary to intentional overdosage in order to receive medical attention. Education of the patient on anticoagulants cannot be overemphasized. The need for the patient to have regular laboratory evaluation of response is essential, along with orientation to the vast group of drugs that can interact with the coumarins.

DISSEMINATED INTRAVASCULAR COAGULATION

The hemorrhagic state associated with disseminated intravascular coagulation has received extensive and oftentimes controversial attention in recent years, especially in the setting of the critical-care facility. This syndrome *does not* occur as a primary disorder, but *always* as a complication of some other disease or procedure. A decade ago, Peck (1970) compiled statistics from various studies that cited the incidence as follows: 85 percent of cases of renal disease, 67 percent of cases of malignant hypertension, 25 percent of patients with septicemia who were normotensive, and 100 percent of patients with septicemia who were hypotensive. Robbins (1974, p. 746) indicates that of all patients demonstrating DIC, about 50 percent occur with complications of pregnancy and 33 percent with carcinomatosis.

Etiology of Pathophysioligic Process

DIC is due to the presence of thrombin in the systemic circulation which results in fibrin deposition in small vessels, consumption of plasma coagulation factors, aggregation and consumption of platelets, and activation of the fibrinolytic system.

When the vascular endothelium is damaged and collagen is exposed, factor XII (the Hageman factor) is activated, beginning coagulation. Platelets adhere to the exposed collagen surface and release platelet factors which in the presence of six plasma proteins (factors V, VIII, IX, X, XI, and XII) initiate the *intrinsic coagulation system*. The *extrinsic coagulation system* is activated by release of tissue thromboplastin from injured tissue. This also leads to the ultimate conversion of prothrombin to thrombin. Both systems are triggering mechanisms that liberate free thrombin into the circulation and hence produce clotting. The formation of the fibrin clot then activates the *fibrinolytic system.* Plasmin, or fibrinolysin, is produced to dissolve or lyse the clot. Plasmin is a proteolytic enzyme that digests fibrin, fibrinogen, factor V, factor VIII, prothrombin, and factor XII. The fibrin split products or fibrin degradation factors resulting from this are removed from the circulation by the reticuloendothelial system. These fibrin split products are, themselves, anticoagulants; and if the reticuloendothelial system is impaired, they may potentiate a state of anticoagulation.

One can see from this simplified discussion of normal hemostasis that there is a delicate balance between coagulation, fibrinolysis, and the function of the reticuloendothelial system in maintaining hemostasis within the intravascular compartment. Conceptually, DIC occurs when the coagulation mechanism is abnormally stimulated. Pathophysiologically, procoagulant potency, duration of exposure, and route of entry into the circulation determine the severity of the coagulopathy.

There are multiple mechanisms that may initiate disseminated intravascular coagulation. *Endothelial cell damage* exposes large areas of collagen surface, which activates the intrinsic coagulation system. This type of damage is commonly caused by anoxia, but viral and bacterial infections, cyanotic heart disease, acute respiratory distress syndrome (ARDS), shock, and cardiopulmonary resuscitation can also be factors.

Another mechanism is *tissue injury,* which releases large amounts of thromboplastin into the circulation to activate the extrinsic clotting system. Examples of this are abruptio placenta, when placental and decidual fragments enter the maternal circulation; retained dead fetus; crush injuries; and surgical procedures, especially thoracic. Certain tumors may also contain thromboplastic material, which may be liberated into the circulation causing consumption of coagulation factors.

The third area for elucidating DIC is *red cell* or *platelet injury* which releases certain phospholipids that accelerate coagulation. A classic example of this is mismatched blood transfusions. Sickle-cell disease and some hemolytic anemias may result in DIC, mediated in part by ruptured erythrocytes. Platelet damage can be caused by bacterial endotoxins, septicemia, or antigen-antibody reactions. It may also cause endothelial damage.

The last problem area that has already been alluded to is the *reticuloendothelial system,* which can predispose the patient to and potentiate DIC.

Normally this system is protective by removing fibrin and activated coagulation factors, endotoxin, and fibrin split products from the vascular system. Reticuloendothelial system dysfunction may result in an increase of these substances, which may lead to a hypercoagulable state and disseminated intravascular coagulation. Clinically, liver disease, as noted earlier, and steroid therapy can impair the reticuloendothelial system.

Therefore, there are four main pathways (endothelial damage, tissue injury, red cell and/or platelet damage, and reticuloendothelial failure) that are probably common, though not always coexisting, mechanisms in the initiation of a consumption coagulopathy. The end point of all these mechanisms is the production of thrombin, which is a proteolytic enzyme accounting for the clinical and laboratory manifestations of DIC. During thrombin generation, prothrombin and other procoagulants, especially factors V and VIII, are depleted as the hallmarks of DIC. The end point of this is fibrin production. These fibrin strands may be disseminated in the microcirculation, especially in areas of stasis, which encourages thrombus formation. Other fibrin monomers may remain in the circulation as fibrin-forming complexes with fibrinogen and fibrin. These fibrin split or degradation products are, themselves, anticoagulants by interfering with fibrin monomer polymerization.

Thrombin, in addition to converting fibrinogen to fibrin and causing platelet aggregation, which is the thrombotic component of DIC which may lead to organ impairment, then produces a hemorrhagic tendency by depletion of fibrinogen, platelets, and clotting factors, especially II, V, and VIII.

Clinical Assessment

Disseminated intravascular coagulation, therefore, demonstrates a paradoxical thrombosis and hemorrhage and has been termed *consumption coagulopathy.* It begins as a hypercoagulable state, but excessive platelet aggregation and thrombin activation leads to depletion of platelets, plasma coagulation factors, activation of the fibrinolytic system, and a hemorrhagic state. Clinically, one usually sees a hemorrhagic diathesis associated with sepsis, hypotension, crush injuries, neoplasia, or major thoracic surgery procedures. An early clinical clue is bleeding from venipuncture site. Organ failure, such as renal insufficiency, the sudden onset of heart failure, stroke-like symptoms, or convulsions are frequently encountered. Shock from any etiology may be a sign of DIC as well as predisposing cause. When one is faced with the paradox of both thrombosis and hemorrhage, DIC must be ruled out.

Colman (1974, pp. 790–791) described three situations in which a hemorrhagic diathesis is frequently delayed in the critical-care environment:

> First, the critically ill patient often has multiple catheters, venipuncture sites, and surgical wounds. Oozing of blood can occur at these sites but the presence of bleeding diathesis goes unrecognized because the hemorrhage is attributed to the wounds and catheters alone. Similarly, thrombosis of vessels is often attributed solely to the mechanical effects of catheters. Second, when the patient suffers a major hemorrhage from a local site such as a gastrointestinal tract ulcer, other sites of concomitant bleeding such as purpura or hematomas are often overlooked since they lack the drama of the local site hemorrhage. A third situation that can be misleading is occurrence of acral cyanosis which can be mistakenly attributed to hypoxia or hypotension alone. . . . When hypoxemia has been corrected, large vessels are intact and the blood pressure is adequate, the persistence of acral cyanosis or the development of a gangrenous digit is highly suggestive of DIC.

Laboratory studies will usually show a decreased platelet count, prolonged prothrombin time, prolonged activated partial thromboplastin time, decreased quantitative fibrinogen level, and evidence of fibrinolysis in the form of fibrin split products. Diffuse fibrin deposition may cause fragmentation of red cells, or microangiopathic hemolytic anemia. The diagnosis of disseminated intravascular coagulation can be quite difficult. For instance, multiple transfusions may dilute plasma coagulation factors as well as the platelets. Thrombocytopenia from chemotherapy, x-ray therapy, diseases of the bone marrow, and cyanotic heart disease can yield abnormally low platelet counts, and microangiopathic hemolytic anemia occurs with artificial valve replacement. Liver disease with portal hypertension can cause decreased plasma coagulation factors in thrombocytopenia as well as activation of the fibrinolytic system. The quantitative fibrinogen and platelet counts are particularly helpful in that the prothrombin time and partial thromboplastin time measure multiple factors, whereas these tests measure single factors.

As increased fibrinolysis is a secondary phenomenon in DIC, differentiation between a reactive process and primary fibrinolysis can be difficult, but crucial, in the patient who presents with an emergency hemorrhagic syndrome. The keys to distinction are the following: (1) Primary fibrinolysis is a *very rare* phenomenon which, when present with DIC, occurs in prostatic cancer, amniotic fluid embolism, and heat stroke. (2) Platelet counts in primary fibrinolysis are usually normal. (3) The plasma paracoagulation test, which can show evidence of circulating fibrin monomers, is negative in primary fibrinolysis. The medical therapy differs in terms of which phase of coagulation is to be interrupted. Epsilon aminocaproic acid (Amicar), while clotting is still active, can render the body unable to clear thrombi from the microcirculation and can result in problems such as acute renal failure.

Treatment of Disseminated Intravascular Coagulation

Once a diagnosis of DIC is established, treatment may be instituted. The prime treatment of DIC, which is always a secondary syndrome, is to treat the underlying disease. As in obstetrical problems, such as abruptio placentae, correction of the underlying disease will correct the DIC. Other underlying problems that need attention and correction are septicemia, hypovolemia, hypotension, hypoxia, and acidosis. At times, the underlying disease such as neoplasia cannot be corrected, but supportive therapy can be lifesaving during crisis.

Although controversy still exists in many circles, heparin generally has been the treatment recommended for consumption coagulopathy. The major action of heparin is to prevent thrombin from acting, thereby blocking the intravascular clotting or fibrin formation. Fibrinolysis ceases, and the bleeding will subside. Most recently, a trend away from immediate use of herapin has developed; once DIC is diagnosed, many clinicians direct principal attention to correction of the underlying disease, supportive replacement therapy, and observation. However, if obvious end organ failure due to presumed thrombosis (defined by laboratory findings) is found, then heparin is indicated. An additional finding is serious or multi-portal hemorrhage. In the rare patient with DIC *and* extensive secondary fibrinolysis, EACA can be administered *in addition to* heparin.

As with its use, the exact dosage of heparin to be administered is controversial, since the precise amount necessary to break the intravascular clotting syndrome remains unclear. An initial dose of 5000 to 10,000 IU of heparin IV has been recommended, followed by 1000 to 1500 IU hourly by continuous infusion. Serial coagulation studies should be performed to evaluate the effectiveness of the anticoagulation. Fibrinogen, fibrin split products, and plasma paracoagulation tests may provide the most accurate visualization of trends. All should respond within 2 to 3 days when treatment is successful.

If it is necessary to use replacement therapy, such as cryoprecipitate for replacement of factor VIII and fibrinogen or platelets, heparin probably should be instituted beforehand to prevent further prorogational thrombosis. Use of a pooled fibrinogen has a very high risk of hepatitis and is to be avoided when possible. Multiple coagulation factors can be replaced by the use of fresh-frozen plasma and platelets given in the form of platelet packs.

Nursing Implications

The care of a patient with severe DIC in the critical-care unit, in this author's opinion, represents one of the greatest challenges to knowledge base and proficiency in nursing practice. Assessment, timely intervention, and reassessment are crucial. Nursing activities can center around the three major modes of presentation: hemorrhage, organ failure, and shock.

Examination of the total skin surface, easily accomplished during the myriad of treatments given the critically ill patient, may show petechiae, purpura, hemorrhagic bullae, acral cyanosis, gangrene, and unusual wound and venipuncture bleeding. Subcutaneous hematomas following intramuscular injections cannot be overlooked. Careful inspection for hematuria, mucous membrane bleeding, and bloody gastric contents that cannot be explained by direct trauma or lesion, may mark the onset of DIC.

The most frequent organs involved, in the order of occurrence, are the kidneys, skin, and lungs. Renal insufficiency progressing to shutdown may be manifested by oliguria or anuria, with or without the usual chemical abnormalities of renal failure. Pulmonary failure with the sudden onset of rales, dyspnea, cyanosis, hemoptysis, and a "shock lung"-appearing chest x-ray may be other signs of the presence of intravascular clotting. Careful neurological examination is mandatory to detect CNS involvement and may warrant further, more extensive tests. Abdominal pain and sudden diarrhea with or without bleeding may be indicative of DIC. It is readily apparent that DIC is not the only cause of the signs and symptoms just re-viewed, but it should be thought of as part of the differential diagnosis in the presence of appropriate etiologies.

As noted earlier, shock may be both a cause and an effect of disseminated intravascular coagulation. As fibrin is rampantly deposited in the microcirculation, return of blood to the right heart is decreased and cardiac output concomitantly reduced. Obviously this establishes a vicious cyclic phenomenon. The presence of shock in the face of high central venous pressure and little or no pulmonary edema may occur as a result of intravascular coagulation localized in the lungs.

Once diagnosed, the nursing care includes many aspects of intervention previously discussed with other hematologic disorders. Continued careful observation and assessment of response to medical treatment, emotional support, and comfort activities are indicated. Anxiety on the part of the patient and family is a reaction not only to the symptoms presented, but to the staff's reaction to this life-threatening condition. Stress has been implicated in the activation of the fibrinolytic system, and the relief thereof is significant. Protection of the patient from injury and conservation of energy are in order, along with gentle oral hygiene and care in the administration of injections and initiation of intravenous catheters. Organ support should be aggressive.

When heparin infusion is being administered continuously, the staff should regularly and frequently monitor the equipment being utilized and the site in order to ensure proper flow. Laboratory studies done serially should be promptly obtained and reported. Heparinization, when effective, should be continued as long as the acute underlying disease is active, usually between 3 and 7 days; the serial coagulation studies should be continued through and beyond this period to note continued improvement or possible reactivation.

The mortality rate of patients with DIC is high, most frequently because the underlying disease (not the DIC) cannot be corrected. The diagnosis of DIC is difficult. The alert critical-care nurse has the opportunity to detect its early, reversible manifestations and thus avoid disastrous delays in recognition.

REFERENCES

Beyers, M., and S. Dudas: Hematopoietic and lymphatic system dysfunction, in *The Clinical Practice of Medical-Surgical Nursing,* Boston: Little, Brown, 1977, pp. 415–465.

Brunner, L. S., and D. S. Suddarth: Blood disorders, in *The Lippincott Manual of Nursing Practice,* Philadelphia: Lippincott, 1974, pp. 190–230.

Burrell, Z. L., and L. O. Burrell: *Critical Care,* 3d ed., St. Louis: Mosby, 1977.

Colman, R. W., J. D. Minna, and S. J. Robboy: Disseminated intravascular coagulation: A problem in critical-care medicine, *Heart Lung* 3(5):789–796, 1974.

Deykin, D.: The clinical challenge of disseminated intravascular coagulation, *N Eng J Med* 283:636–644, 1970.

French, R. M.: *Guide to Diagnostic Procedures,* 4th ed., New York: McGraw-Hill, 1975.

Luckmann, J., and K. C. Sorensen: *Medical-Surgical Nursing: A Psychophysiologic Approach,* Philadelphia: Saunders, 1974.

Peck, S. D.: Disseminated intravascular coagulation: How often have you missed it?, *Rocky M Med J* 67:25–31, 1970.

Robbins, S. L.: *Pathologic Basis of Disease,* Philadelphia: Saunders, 1974.

Rossman, M., R. Slavin, and E. G. Taft: Pheresis therapy: Patient care, *Am J Nurs* 77(7):1135–1141, 1977.

Scarlato, M. (Consultant): Blood transfusions today: What you should know and should do, *Nursing 78* 8(2):68–72, 1978.

Thorn, G. W., R. D. Adams, E. Braunwald, K. J. Isselbacher, and R. G. Petersdorf (eds.): *Harrison's Principles of Internal Medicine,* 8th ed., New York: McGraw-Hill, 1977.

Williams, W. J., E. Beutler, A. J. Erslev, and R. W. Rundles (eds.): *Hematology,* 2d ed., New York: McGraw-Hill, 1977.

Zimmerman, S., T. Cohen, R. Dickman, C. L. Calvo, and M. Hangsterfer: Bone marrow transplantation, *Am J Nurs* 1977(8):1311–1317, 1977.

Neurological-neurosurgical disorders often present a bewildering array of disease entities to the practicing nurse. For the critical-care nurse, the patient presents an ever-present potential for rapid deterioration in neurological condition. Finally, because the central nervous system regulates all other body systems, neurological disease and trauma can frequently complicate and initiate multisystem problems. How, then, can order be brought to the confusion and mystery which so often surrounds "neuro" in the minds of most nurses and physicians?

Although the disorders which can affect nervous system functioning are numerous, the mechanisms by which they threaten life, their effects on human functioning, and their effects on a person's ability to care for self are reasonably circumscribed. Thus, the concepts which critical-care clinicians must understand to provide informed care for critically ill persons with neurological dysfunction are relatively few in number.

This chapter is organized around these common concepts, with tables indicating the disorders commonly producing the problems identified. The pathophysiology of each subcategory is discussed; disorders commonly causing dysfunction are listed and relevant differences among them in pathophysiology are discussed. Medical therapies are related to both general and specific pathophysiology and to supportive nursing care.

Of the numerous disorders which affect the central and peripheral nervous systems, a relatively small number are acutely life-threatening. There are two major ways in which these disorders act to threaten life: *disruption of consciousness* and thereby self-care, and *disruption of respiration* secondary to loss of movement but not consciousness. The problem areas identified for this chapter which disrupt consciousness are brain herniation syndromes. increased intracranial pressure, and status epilepticus. Severe motor and sensory dysfunctions that affect respiration but not consciousness are usually caused by extracerebral disorders which affect the spinal cord, peripheral nerves, or the motor unit. Examples of such disorders include spinal cord injury, myasthenia gravis, and Guillain-Barré syndrome.

The categories of disruption in consciousness and disruption in respiration are related more to functional neuroanatomy than to specific diseases. However, establishing these categories is useful for predicting

Preparation of this manuscript was supported in part by a grant from the United States Public Health Service, Health Resources Administration, Division of Nursing, NU00081-03.

26
NEUROLOGIC DISORDERS
Pamela H. Mitchell

DISORDERS THAT DISRUPT CONSCIOUSNESS
Brain Herniation Syndromes
Increased Intracranial Pressure
Seizures

DISORDERS THAT DISRUPT RESPIRATION BUT NOT CONSCIOUSNESS
Extracerebral Motor Pathways
Segmental Organization
Life-Threatening Effects of Extracerebral Motor Loss
First-Level Nursing Management of Extracerebral Motor Problems
Third-Level Nursing Management of Extracerebral Motor Disorders

SUMMARY

REFERENCES

which kinds of disorders may produce life-threatening problems such as brain herniation or respiratory insufficiency. Finally, the categories are helpful to the clinician confronted with a patient whose disorder is unfamiliar.

DISORDERS THAT DISRUPT CONSCIOUSNESS

Brain Herniation Syndromes

Observation for brain herniation syndromes is undoubtedly the most commonly taught neurological assessment procedure in nursing. Yet the pathophysiology and nature of what the nurse is attempting to prevent are often left unclear. Brain herniation is usually discussed under increased intracranial pressure, without a clear distinction between the two. Syndromes of central and uncal herniation are addressed as if they are one, and cerebellar herniation is rarely described at all. The following is presented in an attempt to clarify the situation. The Plum and Posner classification of herniation syndromes is widely accepted and will be used to place syndromes in categories by functional anatomy.

Herniation refers to the protrusion of an organ

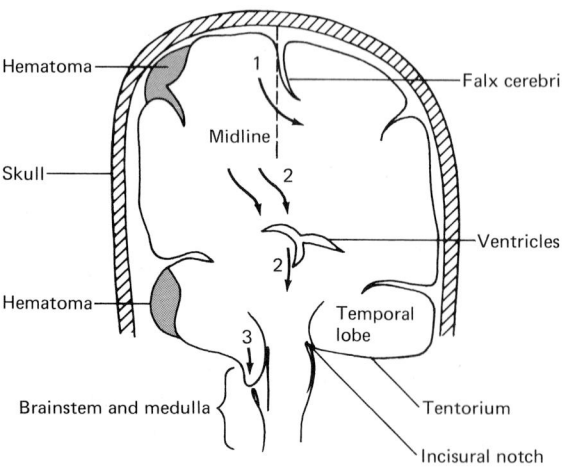

FIGURE 26-1

Three types of supratentorial herniation. Cingulate herniation (1) occurs when the falx cerebri is displaced. Central herniation (2) is the downward movement of the brain, displacing the ventricles. Uncal herniation (3) involves compression of the midbrain and brainstem by the herniating tip of the temporal lobe. [*After H. Moidel et al., (eds.), Nursing Care of the Patient with Medical-Surgical Disorders, 2d ed., McGraw-Hill, New York, 1976, p. 866.*]

through a natural or accidental opening in the wall of its cavity. In the brain, herniation is the protrusion of a portion of the brain through the openings or linings of the cranial cavity. Although the incisure or notch of the tentorium (Fig. 26-1) is the best known of these "natural openings," herniation can also occur under the falx cerebri and through the foramen magnum. Three distinctive syndromes result: (1) that of cingulate lobe herniation, which involves movement laterally under the falx cerebri; (2) the syndrome of central or uncal transtentorial herniation (through the incisure); and (3) the syndrome of cerebellar herniation, which takes place either upward through the incisure or downward through the foramen magnum.

Each of these involves displacement of brain through or around openings in the lining of the cranial cavity. Each produces a distinctive syndrome by virtue of displacement, distortion, or necrosis of specific brain tissue.

Transtentorial Herniation

For all practical purposes, cingulate herniation can be considered with transtentorial syndromes since any condition which creates cingulation herniation is also likely to produce transtentorial herniation. The unifying and essential feature of cingulate/tentorial syndromes is the rostral-caudal, or literally "head-to-tail" nature, of their progression. They are caused by any of a variety of expanding *mass lesions* above the tentorium. Anything which acts as a mass in the relatively closed cranial cavity, and which is growing, will eventually push aside and distort brain tissue. Some compensation can occur as cerebrospinal fluid (CSF) production slows and vascular volume constricts somewhat. Eventually, the expanding brain will seek a relief valve by herniating through the few openings available—around the falx, through the tentorium, or through the foramen magnum. The numerous conditions which can lead to mass effect and brain herniation are listed in Table 26-1. The most obvious is a brain tumor, which is truly a forcing mass. Similarly, the clot from an intracerebral hemorrhage acts as a mass, and as an expanding one if hemorrhage continues. General or local brain edema also increases the mass of the brain. Trauma, contusions, and thrombotic and embolic stroke can create focal and general cerebral edema. Hypoxia and metabolic and infectious processes can create areas of focal or general edema.

It must be emphasized that mass effect and herniation are not inevitable with each condition but must be watched for and detected early if the patient is not

TABLE 26-1
Symptoms of Brainstem Compression Caused by Brain Herniation

Symptoms	Cause of brain herniation
Diminished consciousness; coma (with inability to communicate and to protect airway)	Head injury, e.g., contusion leading to subdural or epidural hematoma; intracranial hemorrhage
Respiratory alkalosis/acidosis from impaired breathing patterns	Cerebral edema from head trauma, tumor, metabolic or fluid-electrolyte disturbance (e.g., Reye's syndrome)
Decerebrate/decorticate rigidity	
Intracranial hypertension (may coexist)	

to die from herniation. While many of the conditions listed in Table 26-1 can lead to increased intracranial pressure, it is important to remember that intracranial hypertension in itself does not inevitably lead to herniation unless the cause of elevated pressure is also a cause of mass effect (for example, massive brain edema). Herniation can also occur secondary to intracranial hypertension if pressure is rising very rapidly or if there are pressure differentials between supratentorial and infratentorial compartments. These points will be discussed in more detail in the section on intracranial hypertension.

Astute observation of changing neurological function not only can aid in early detection of progressing herniation but can help the experienced clinician point to the area of brain still functioning. This last is crucial to detecting further deterioration once consciousness has been lost. It is also central to protecting the patient against complications resulting from absent defenses, such as gag and corneal reflexes.

The purposes of assessment in conditions which are at high risk for brain herniation are three: (1) to detect progressing brain herniation, (2) to determine the level of brain functioning, and (3) to determine the extent of protective care required. Although Chap. 6 provides a review of general neuroanatomy-physiology, pertinent functional neuroanatomy is presented here to aid understanding how signs and symptoms relate to the brain function impaired. Although all nurses know the general signs of herniation ("neurocheck"), there is frequently an overreliance on signs of brainstem dysfunction (pupils) through failure to appreciate the rostal-caudal nature of herniation.

Because of the widespread influence of the ascending reticular activating system, changes in the level of consciousness are the earliest and often most subtle signs of progressing brain dysfunction. In central and transtentorial herniation, changes in respiratory pattern and motor function closely follow alterations in level of consciousness. Conjugate eye movements, equal pupil size, and pupil reactivity change when brain function is disrupted at the level of the midbrain. Recall that the midbrain is at approximately the same level as the tentorial incisure.

Categories of brain function The rostral-caudal pattern of brain herniation generally progresses through five categories of brain function. Inspection of Fig. 26-2 shows that these functions correspond roughly to descending anatomical levels of the brain. In order to determine if the patient is getting better or worse and at what level the brain is functioning, the practitioner must routinely evaluate all five categories. The categories of brain function, in descending order of change, are level of consciousness, motor function, respiratory patterns, eye function (movements and pupillary reaction), and vital signs.

Level of consciousness Consciousness, arousability, and orientation to self and environment are governed by the reticular activating system (RAS). This system originates in the brainstem and ascends to influence the cerebral cortex. It is a physiological rather than an anatomical system; one cannot dissect out a structure called the RAS. It acts neurochemically to arouse or activate the processes of consciousness. Because it is widespread, disturbances at many levels affect consciousness. Although changes in level of consciousness clearly indicate that brain function is disrupted, knowing the level of disruption requires information from the other assessment parameters, particularly motor function and eye movements.

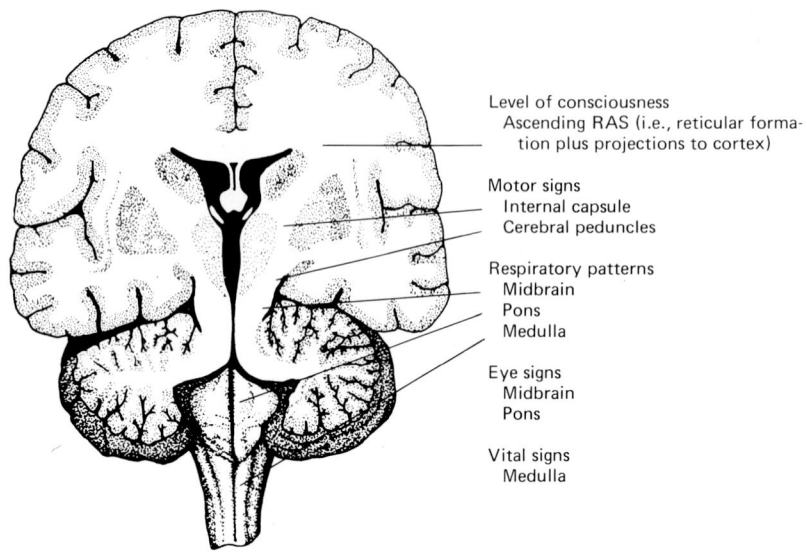

Level of consciousness
Ascending RAS (i.e., reticular formation plus projections to cortex)

Motor signs
Internal capsule
Cerebral peduncles

Respiratory patterns
Midbrain
Pons
Medulla

Eye signs
Midbrain
Pons

Vital signs
Medulla

FIGURE 26-2

The listed functions may be affected by brain herniation as it
reaches the levels shown. (*After George McNeil.*)

Nevertheless, a change in consciousness is clear indication that brain function is further disrupted.

Many schemes have been proposed to quantitate consciousness and to construct terminology consistent among medical centers. Probably the most useful measure is a very simple one, the *Glasgow coma scale.* It was devised to systematically record neurological function in a multi-institutional study of the outcomes of head injury. In the coma scale, consciousness is evaluated with respect to three kinds of response to stimuli: eye opening, verbal response, and motor response (Table 26-2). A sample assessment record is shown in Fig. 26-3.

The kind of stimulus required and response obtained are rough measures of arousability. If a verbal stimulus does not produce measureable response (eye opening, verbal, obeying command), a painful stimulus is employed. Points can be assigned to each level of response and a "coma score" obtained. Provided that instruction is given, a high degree of interrater reliability can be achieved by multiple levels of staff assessing the same patient. Any change of two points or more on the total coma score is likely to represent a real improvement or deterioration (Teasdale et al., 1978). A number of publications listed as references are available for instructing staff on use of the scale.

When recorded in conjunction with data regarding respiratory pattern, symmetry and type of motor response, pupillary response, and eye movements, the coma scale allows one to see graphically any progression toward brain herniation and to judge the level at which the brain is functioning. This last not only allows the physician to better diagnose the nature of the disorder causing progressive brain dysfunction, but it allows the nurse and physician to recognize early the need to protect functions dependent upon brainstem reflexes, such as coughing, gag, and swallowing.

Motor function Evaluation of motor response brought the most consistent ratings in testing the reliability of the Glasgow coma scale. However, best motor response to stimulation is only one aspect of motor function which must be considered in determining whether brain function is worsening.

Motor function needs to be evaluated serially and systematically in relation to the following areas: type of response to verbal or painful stimuli, tone and strength, symmetry of response, and presence of pathological reflexes.

The ability to obey a command to perform a motor act is one measure of how well consciousness and voluntary movement are integrated. Impairment of consciousness (operationally defined as inability to follow a motor command) requires use of a painful stimulus. While a variety of painful stimuli are often employed to elicit motor response, the Glasgow group found pressure applied to the proximal nail bed to provide the most reproducible motor response.

A number of terms have evolved to describe motor response, some related to the "appropriateness" of response to pain, others to the presumed anatomical deficit causing abnormal reflex response (for example, *decerebrate* and *decorticate*). Such terms are open to a range of subjective interpretation and are not as helpful in identifying a rostral-caudal pattern of deterioration as are the operationally defined re-

---

TABLE 26-2
Glasgow Coma Scale

Category of response	Appropriate stimulus	Response	Score
Eyes open	Approach to the bedside	*Spontaneously*	4
	Verbal command	*To speech.* Eyes open to name or to command	3
	Pain (pressure on the proximal nail bed)*	*To pain.* Does not open eyes to previous stimuli, but does to pain	2
		None. Does not open eyes to any stimulus	1
Best verbal response	Score best response patient makes with maximum arousal. Painful stimulus may be needed	*Oriented.* Converses; knows who he or she is; where he or she is; year and month	5
		Confused. Converses but disoriented in one or more spheres	4
		Inappropriate words. Without sustained conversation; words disorganized or inappropriate (for example, cursing)	3
		Incomprehensible. Makes sounds (moaning, for example) but no recognizable words	2
		None. No sound even with painful stimuli	1

*Produces least interrater variability.

TABLE 26-2 (Continued)
Glasgow Coma Scale

Category of response	Appropriate stimulus	Response	Score
Best motor response	Verbal command (for example: "raise your arm; hold up two fingers")	*Obeys command.*	6
	Pain (pressure on proximal nail bed)	*Localizes pain.* Does not obey, but "finds" offending stimulus and attempts to remove it.	5
		Flexion-withdrawal.† Flexes arm in response to pain, without abnormal flexion posture	4
		Abnormal flexion. Flexes arm at elbow and pronates, making a fist	3
		Abnormal extension. Extends arm at elbow, usually adducts and internally rotates arm at shoulder	2
		None	1

†Added to the original scale by many centers.

sponses of the Glasgow coma scale. The coma scale defines "best" motor response in relation to consciousness per se. One must also compare response on both sides of the body, symmetry of response.

In both instances one notes the type of stimulus applied (verbal, then painful if there is no response to verbal) and the nature of the response. At the highest level of integration, the patient follows a verbal command, for example, "Hold out both arms." With some impairment of consciousness, a painful stimulus may need to be applied. If there are reasonably functioning motor tracts (corticospinal and corticobulbar), the patient will attempt to remove the painful stimulus. Pathological motor responses are evident in flexion and extension at the elbow in response to painful stimuli. These responses imply functional disconnection of the inhibiting influences of cerebral cortex on motor tract synapses deep in the hemisphere and midbrain. Appearance of these abnormal postural reflexes spontaneously or in response to pain indicate that transtentorial herniation is impending or may already have occurred. Decerebrate and decorticate posture, or simply "posturing," are terms commonly used in reference to these pathological postural reflexes.

The appearance of an extensor plantar reflex (Babinski's sign) implies dysfunction of the corticospinal tract anywhere from the cortex to the anterior horn cell in the spinal cord. While the appearance of this abnormal reflex does not help localize the dysfunction, it does indicate deterioration of brain function in the patient at risk for herniation.

Neurological Assessment Record

Coma scale																				
		DATE ➤																		EYES CLOSED • BY SWELLING = C
		TIME ➤																		
	EYES OPEN	SPONTANEOUSLY																		
		TO SPEECH																		
		TO PAIN																		
		NONE																		
	BEST VERBAL RESPONSE	ORIENTED																		• ENDOTRACHEAL TUBE OR TRACHEOSTOMY = T
		CONFUSED																		
		INAPPROPRIATE																		
		INCOMPREHENSIBLE																		
		NONE																		
	BEST MOTOR RESPONSE	OBEY COMMANDS																		• USUALLY RECORD THE BEST ARM RESPONSE • AGITATED = A
		LOCALIZE PAIN																		
		FLEXION TO PAIN																		
		EXTENSION TO PAIN																		
		NONE																		
	VITAL SIGNS	BLOOD PRESSURE																		
		PULSE																		
		RESPIRATION																		
		TEMPERATURE																		
	PUPILS REACT = + NO REACTION = − EYE CLOSED = C	R SIZE																		
		REACTION																		
		L SIZE																		
		REACTION																		
	LIMB MOVEMENT	RIGHT UPPER																		
		RIGHT LOWER																		
		LEFT UPPER																		
		LEFT LOWER																		
		INTAKE																		
		OUTPUT																		

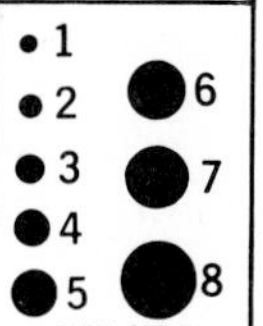

• 1 • 2 ● 6 • 3 ● 7 ● 4 ● 5 ● 8
PUPIL SCALE (mm)

0. No evidence of muscle contraction.
1. Palpable muscle movement—no joint motion.
2. Complete motion without gravity.
3. Barely complete motion against gravity.
4. Complete motion against gravity with some resistance.
5. Complete motion against gravity with full resistance.
F = abnormal flexion
E = abnormal extension

FIGURE 26-3

Neurological assessment record employing the Glasgow coma scale (reduced from original size). According to Teasdale and Jennett (1974), an operational definition of coma is a score of 7 or less (no eye opening, no comprehensible verbal response, no motor response to command). Dysphasic patients cannot be scored on the verbal section; a note is made on the observation record of dysphasia or mechanical impediment to speech, such as endotracheal tube or tracheostomy.

Strength and tone of muscles must be evaluated in conjunction with type of motor response. Motor fibers are fairly widely distributed at the cortex but converge into a relatively tight bundle deep in the hemisphere. Because fibers from the upper extremities are lateral in the corticospinal bundle until they reach the internal capsule, pressure from an expanding hemispheric lesion may cause subtle weakness before consciousness is markedly impaired. Such weakness tends to be of the proximal rather than distal muscles of the upper extremity. Thus simply testing strength of hand grip may not detect early onset of weakness. *Pronator drift* is a subtle early sign of proximal weakness. It can be noted by asking the patient to hold out both arms with palms up (thus simultaneously testing ability to obey commands). If drift (and therefore proximal weakness) is present, the affected arm drifts downward slightly, with the wrist and hand pronating. Such a finding implies dysfunction of motor tracts in the opposite hemisphere. If the patient cannot follow commands, both arms can be lifted simultaneously and then dropped. The weaker one will fall to the bed more rapidly. Absence of spontaneous movement on one side of the body also implies disruption of motor tracts in the opposite hemisphere.

Weakness or paralysis may become bilateral when herniation has progressed to the midbrain level for the following reason. The cerebral peduncles, which carry corticospinal tract fibers, join the brainstem at the midbrain. The fibers course downward in the lateral aspects of the brainstem before they cross in the pyramid of the medulla and continue down the spinal cord to innervate the side of the body contralateral to the hemisphere in which they arose.

An expanding mass which has distorted tissue sufficiently may push the midbrain across the midline, compressing structures between the midbrain and the tentorium on the side opposite the expanding mass. This will be disclosed by the appearance of bilateral decerebrate posturing and ocular abnormalities in a patient who has had unilateral signs. If herniation cannot be reversed at this point in adults, it is likely to be irreversible.

Abnormal postural and cutaneous reflexes may become bilateral with distortion of the brain higher in the hemispheres. Identification of level of brain function and subsequent estimates of irreversibility of herniations cannot be done with signs of a single system alone. Table 26-3 summarizes the constellation of findings at three levels of brain function and the implications for reversibility.

Respiratory patterns Plum and Posner carefully documented the correlations between patterns of respiration and level of brain function. These are

---

TABLE 26-3
Transentorial Herniation Syndromes at Various Brain Levels

Cortex, hemisphere: Signs of early brain shift*	Diencephalon: Signs of later brain shift†	Midbrain: Signs of herniation‡

1. Subtle changes in consciousness
  a. Increased stimulus required to elicit eye opening, verbal response
  b. Ability to follow commands usually intact
	1. Decreased consciousness
	  a. Painful stimulus required for arousal
	  b. Does not follow commands
		1. Unresponsive to verbal stimuli
		  a. Abnormal posturing to painful stimuli

2. Motor changes
  a. Unilateral pronator drift
  b. Gegenhalten (increased tone) may be present
	2. Motor changes (usually unilateral)
	  a. Increased tone
	  b. May be hemiplegic; may show motor change ipsilateral to lesion if brain has shifted across midline
		2. Abnormal motor posturing
		  a. Flexor/extensor posturing
		  b. May show motor change

3. Eye signs
  a. Pupils equal, reactive to light, and accommodation (PERLA) intact; extraocular movements (EOM) intact
	3. Eye signs
	  a. PERLA and EOM intact to "doll's eye" maneuver
	  b. Spontaneous "roving" disconjugate gaze may occur
		3. Eye signs
		  a. Pupils unequal, unresponsive to light unilaterally or bilaterally
		  b. Loss of oculocephalic reflex unilaterally or bilaterally

4. Respirations unremarkable	4. Respirations may be Cheyne-Stokes or hyperventilatory	4. Respirations hyperventilatory

*Reversible if mass lesion can be treated.

† Reversible.

‡May be reversible if herniation does not proceed to pons.

useful in detecting decrease in level of brain function with brain herniation (Fig. 26-4).

Cheyne-Stokes respirations are characterized by a pattern of crescendo-decrescendo breathing, followed by apnea. This pattern represents disturbance of deep-hemispheric function bilaterally and is differentiated from periodic apnea of brainstem origin by the regularity of the hyperpneic-apneic pattern. Cheyne-Stokes breathing occurs physiologically because of abnormally increased central ventilatory response to carbon dioxide (hyperpneic phase). The hyperventilation reduces arterial carbon dioxide to the point where breathing is no longer stimulated and apnea results. Arterial partial pressure of carbon dioxide, building during apnea, finally exceeds the respiratory stimulation threshold and restarts the oscillating cycle (Phillipson, 1978). The overreaction of this control of breathing has been compared to the overcompensation of the drunk driver to the normal variations of movement of the car.

Metabolic disorders usually affect all parts of the nervous system equally and are the most common cause of the bilateral hemisphere dysfunction manifested by Cheyne-Stokes respiration. However, such respirations are also seen in patients with bilateral cerebral infarct, hypertensive encephalopathy (implying bilateral lesions), and during non-REM sleep in some individuals with chronic respiratory disease and some with prolonged circulation time (cardiac failure). However, the appearance of Cheyne-Stokes respirations in a patient at risk for transtentorial herniation signals deteriorating brain function and imminent herniation. Because the appearance of this pattern seems to require bilateral dysfunction of the internal capsules, one would expect simultaneous changes in motor functions.

The manner in which a focal mass lesion can cause bilateral deep hemisphere dysfunction leading to Cheyne-Stokes respiration can be inferred from inspection of Fig. 26-1. Expansion of the right hemisphere lesion and surrounding edema may initially compress structures in that hemisphere and produce focal findings on the opposite side of the body. Further expansion leads to further swelling and eventually movement of brain tissue from one hemisphere across the midline with subsequent downward displacement of structures in both hemispheres.

Other abnormal breathing patterns occur with brainstem and medullary dysfunction. These patterns are useful in determining if neurological status is deteriorating or improving once consciousness is lost. They must be used along with other signs of midbrain and brainstem functioning.

Central neurogenic hyperventilation is a pattern of deep, regular, and rapid hyperpnea. It occurs with dysfunction of the *tegmentum,* or central portion of

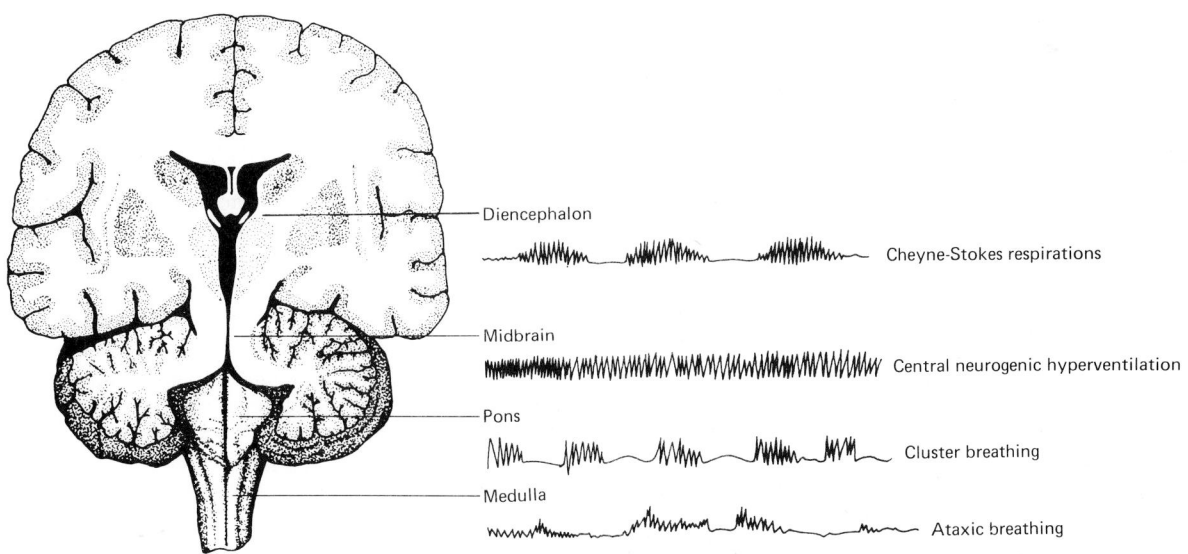

FIGURE 26-4

Respiratory patterns correlated with brain function level. As the influence of higher areas is removed through ischemia or compression, characteristic breathing patterns are found. (*After F. Plum and J. Posner.*)

the brainstem, usually between the lower midbrain and pons. Since arterial oxygen tension is normal in patients with "true" central neurogenic hyperventilation, the physiologic explanation must be an abnormally low threshold for stimulation by carbon dioxide (Plum and Posner, 1972). While metabolic abnormalities or structural lesions of the midbrain-pontine area can cause central neurogenic hyperventilation on a primary basis, the appearance of such a pattern in the patient at risk for brain herniation suggests that tentorial herniation is imminent, if not already present. Recall that the midbrain occupies the anterior portion of the tentorial incisure through which the brainstem passes.

Pontine-medullary breathing patterns include *ataxic* breathing (sometimes called *Biot's respirations*) and *cluster* breathing (see Fig. 26-4). Both are forms of periodic breathing, with frequent periods of apnea. Reciprocal firing of inspiratory and expiratory neurons in the medulla is impaired. Since the medulla is well below the tentorium, such patterns would occur only in well-established herniation and portend very poor prognosis. Posterior fossa lesions which create herniation of brainstem and posterior fossa contents *upward* through the tentorium may produce ataxic breathing. Rapidly expanding posterior fossa lesions leading to herniation of cerebellar tonsils into the foramen magnum are more likely to produce respiratory arrest. Posterior fossa lesions include those of the cerebellum, fourth ventricle, and the area where cerebellar fibers join the pons.

Eye signs *Pupillary reaction* and *ocular motility* are important clues to the state of brain structures at the level of the tentorium. The third cranial nerve controls pupillary reactivity and elevation of the eyelid. Its nucleus is in the midbrain. The nerve itself courses between the posterior cerebral and superior cerebellar arteries and passes out of the brainstem through the incisure. Consequently, pressure from a herniating temporal lobe can produce unilateral pupillary dilation and/or ptosis before the midbrain is compressed sufficiently to alter ocular motility. The parasympathetic fibers of cranial nerve III are in the outermost portion of the nerve bundle. Paralysis of these parasympathetically mediated functions (pupillary constriction and eyelid elevation) follows compression of the nerve against the incisure or the posterior cerebral artery. The appearance of unilateral pupillary dilation in a patient with head trauma or suspected mass lesion is a definitive sign that herniation is occurring and constitutes a neurosurgical emergency.

The pupillary light reflex is mediated by parasympathetic fibers which constrict the pupil when light stimulates the optic nerve. The reflex can be interrupted by structural damage at several points. The points include the optic nerve, diencephalic nuclei (pretectal), midbrain nuclei (Edinger-Westphal), the third nerve itself, and the ciliary ganglion (just dorsal to the eye). In tentorial herniation, damage to the third cranial nerve at the incisure or compression of the midbrain are the most likely reasons pupils lose their reactivity to light. Preservation of the light reflex in coma is an important clue that the cause is metabolic (for example, drug overdose or uremia) rather than structural. A strong light and magnifying glass may be necessary to determine with certainty that the pupillary light reflex is or is not present.

Ocular motility is controlled by brainstem structures. Thus eye movements provide important clues to the level at which the brain is functioning. When consciousness is depressed, changes in eye movements may provide the only clues that brain function is deteriorating due to transtentorial herniation. One evaluates (1) symmetry of eye movements and (2) presence or absence of oculocephalic reflexes. These eye movements not only provide clues as to the level of brain functioning but also yield information regarding the patient's ability to protect vital functions such as respiration and airway.

Eye movement is controlled by cranial nerves III, IV, and VI. Even in the unconscious patient, where voluntary control of eye movement cannot be tested, there may be spontaneous roving eye movement. In general, if brainstem function is intact, these eye movements will be conjugate and full, indicating that all three of the cranial nerves are functioning. Cranial nerve III controls all eye movement except lateral movement and downward movement when the orbit is rotated internally. (In patients lacking voluntary control the function of the fourth cranial nerve can rarely be observed.) Although the third cranial nerve is the same nerve which controls pupillary constriction and eyelid elevation, changes involving movement of the eye are apt to occur later than those controlling pupils and eyelid elevation. Consequently, one may observe changes in pupil size before the onset of disconjugate gaze. Although disconjugate gaze is evidence of abnormally functioning brainstem structures, in the comatose patient it cannot help localize damage. Instead the oculocephalic reflex is employed.

The oculocephalic reflex, commonly referred to as "doll's eye maneuver," is mediated afferently by the eighth cranial nerve and efferently by the third and sixth cranial nerves. This reflex may be tested by rapidly rotating the head to one side and observing the eye movements (Fig. 26-5). If the reflex is intact, when the head is rotated, the eyes appear to remain in the initial position and then will slowly turn to the direction in which the head is rotated. If the reflex is not intact, the eyes will move with the head as though fixed in place.

The term *doll's-eye* refers to old-fashioned dolls that had eyes mounted on a swivel. When the head of such a doll is rotated, the eyes do not rotate immediately with the head, hence the term *doll's eyes present*. In modern dolls the eyes are not mounted on a swivel, hence the eyes rotate as the doll's head is turned. This eye movement is equivalent to what clinicians mean by *doll's eyes absent*.

The oculocephalic reflex is elicited by head movement that moves fluid in a semicircular canal, stimulating the vestibular portion of the eighth cranial nerve. The vestibular impulses pass through the brainstem to the nuclei of the third and sixth cranial nerves, thus eliciting the eye movement seen. The neural connections are shown in Fig. 26-6. The reflex is present in all persons with intact brainstems during sleep. In an awake person the reflex cannot be elicited because the eyes will be fixed upon objects and the reflex overcome. In altered states of consciousness the presence of the reflex indicates that the brainstem function is intact between cranial nerves VIII and III.

The *oculovestibular reflex* is mediated by the same set of cranial nerves. It is stimulated directly by irrigation of the ear with either hot or cold fluid. The method of eliciting this reflex is commonly called "caloric" stimulation. Although the two reflexes utilize the same afferent and efferent pathways, the oculovestibular reflex is preserved somewhat longer in brain dysfunction than the oculocephalic reflex. Thus when the oculocephalic reflex is absent, the physician may wish to perform caloric stimulation to determine if the reflex pathway has indeed been lost.

Testing oculocephalic and oculovestibular reflexes appears to have prognostic value for comatose patients who have suffered structural brain damage and for patients who have suffered metabolic brain damage other than barbiturate overdosage. In two large studies of brain-injured patients and patients in metabolic coma, investigators found that the absence of oculovestibular reflexes for periods greater than 24 h correlates strongly with either death or vegetative existence (Jennett and Teasdale, 1976; Bates et al.,

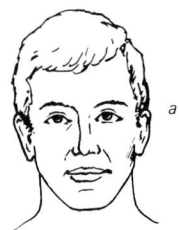

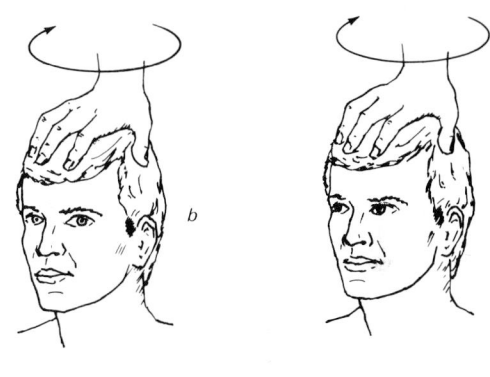

FIGURE 26-5

Oculocephalic reflex. (*a*) Moving the unconscious patient's head to the right (*b*) moves eyes initially to the left if the reflex is present. If the reflex is absent (*c*), eyes will move to the right along with the head.

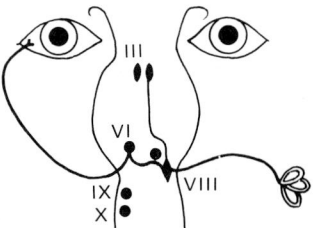

FIGURE 26-6

Protective reflexes: anatomical relationship of ocular motility (cranial nerves III and VI) to swallow, gag, and cough (cranial nerves IX and X). Cranial nerve VIII is the afferent limb of the oculocephalic reflex.

1977). It must be emphasized that this correlation does not apply to patients with drug overdosage, particularly barbiturate overdose. Such substances depress the entire central nervous system but do not appear to cause irreversible metabolic damage. Thus the absence of oculovestibular reflexes in these patients does not itself imply a poor prognosis.

Tests of eye movement symmetry and oculocephalic reflexes have two major uses by critical-care nurses: (1) to detect further rostral-caudal deterioration in patients who have lost consciousness and (2) to determine the need for protective care of the airway.

In the patient who is already unresponsive to verbal and painful stimuli, the appearance of disconjugate eye movements or the change from present to absent oculocephalic reflexes indicates that the brain is functioning at a lower anatomical level than before. Remember that cranial nerves III and VI are at the level of the tentorium, and VIII is nearly at the level of the medulla. Consequently, disappearance of oculocephalic reflexes or a sudden asymmetry of eye movement in response to head rotation indicates that brainstem function is seriously compromised and that tentorial herniation is occurring. Furthermore, it warns that the airway is in imminent danger. As shown in Fig. 26-6, cranial nerves IX and X are innervated just caudal to cranial nerve VIII. These cranial nerves are important in cough and gag reflexes. Thus impairment of intrinsic airway protection is predicted by loss of brain function just rostral to the pons. The absence of oculocephalic reflexes or change in their function thus indicates the need for endotracheal intubation and for particular attention to suctioning and pooling of secretions in the patient's airway.

Vital signs   Vital signs—blood pressure, pulse, respiratory rate—are frequently listed among high-priority observations in the critically ill neurological patient. However, inspection of Fig. 26-2 clearly indicates that the structures which mediate these functions are very low in the brainstem and the medulla. Consequently, sustained major change in these functions occurs very late in the process of transtentorial herniation. Reliance upon changes in vital signs to *detect* impending herniation is unwise because these changes will occur too late to protect the patient and prevent herniation. Fluctuating vital signs may well reflect fluctuating levels of intracranial pressure, as will be discussed in following sections of this chapter.

Blood pressure is mediated at a reflex level in the medulla. Although the classic *Cushing triad* is often

referred to as a sign of increasing intracranial pressure and/or impending transtentorial herniation, it really is a sign of imminent death. The classic triad consists of increasing systolic blood pressure, decreasing diastolic blood pressure, and bradycardia. The mechanism for this triad of symptoms appears to be ischemia and pressure upon medullary brain structures. Although there may well be gradual increases in systolic blood pressure in patients who are herniating and fluctuating periods of bradycardia, the presence of the triad is the terminal event in both experimental and clinical studies of the phenomenon. Waiting for the triad to appear before doing anything is waiting much too long! Respiratory rate in and of itself is not a particularly helpful clue to the level at which the brain is functioning. As described earlier in this chapter, respiratory patterns can provide clues to the level of brain still functioning, but absolute respiratory rate is both notoriously inaccurate and not particularly helpful.

Uncal Herniation

Herniation of the *uncus,* or medial portion of the temporal lobe, can occur in connection with central herniation or by itself with intracranial or epidural lesions of the temporal lobe (Fig. 26-1). Epidural hematoma from a lacerated middle meningeal artery often produces classic uncal herniation, whereas a unilateral intracerebral hematoma might produce a combined central-uncal herniation as the expanding hemisphere pushed the uncus over the tentorial incisure.

The major difference in clinical presentation of central and uncal syndromes is the point at which pupillary changes occur relative to change in consciousness and movement. Because the uncus is at the level of the tentorium, pure uncal herniation may present with rapid changes in motor function and pupillary equality nearly simultaneous with deterioration of consciousness. Although differentiating the type of syndrome is not critical to evaluating impending herniation, the nurse should be aware of patients particularly at risk for the uncal syndrome and be prepared to mobilize neurosurgical help immediately upon change in neurological status. Such patients include those with linear skull fractures of the temporal bone (high risk of lacerating the middle meningeal artery) and those postcraniotomy from temporal lobe surgery, with subsequent risk of postoperative localized edema.

Cerebellar Herniation

The brain not only can be displaced downward through the tentorial incisure; as mentioned already, the contents of the posterior fossa can also herniate upward through the incisure. The posterior fossa contains largely the cerebellum, the nerve trunks connecting the cerebellum to the pons, and the cranial nerves which exit the brainstem at the pons. Downward displacement drives the structures toward the foramen magnum. Abrupt herniation into the foramen magnum impinges upon the medulla and is fatal.

Because the cerebellum lies just posterior to pontine-medullary structures mediating respiration, expansion of posterior fossa contents may be heralded by ataxic respirations or apnea. Upward herniation of posterior fossa contents can compress the brainstem at the midbrain, thus impairing consciousness, pupillary reflexes, and eye movements. Pupils are likely to be constricted and nonreactive due to compression of ocular sympathetic pathways as they pass through the pons, as well as compression of parasympathetic fibers of the third cranial nerve itself. The upward-herniating subtentorial brain accounts for direct compression of the third cranial nerve.

Patients at high risk for acute upward herniation are those with potentially *rapidly* expanding lesions: cerebellar hemorrhage and occipital skull fracture with attendent risk of epidural or subdural bleeding. Patients with cerebellar abscesses and tumors are ultimately at risk for herniation if the disease process is not arrested. However, such lesions are usually slowly expanding, and the brain compensates for the relative compression ischemia for a remarkably long time. In contrast, acutely expanding lesions occur too rapidly for the brain to compensate for the attendant ischemia and compression.

Treatment of Brain Herniation

All types of therapy may be divided into four levels of nursing care as defined by Jones et al. (1978). First-level nursing care consists of those activities which detect persons at risk and prevent disease and dysfunction from occurring altogether. Second-level care consists of those measures which provide for early detection of disease and dysfunction; third-level care consists of care provided for an acute, existing disorder, but which prevents further complications and dysfunction which are not an inevitable outcome of the pathology. Fourth-level nursing care focuses on rehabilitation. Although the preceding discussion has clearly been focused on *third-level care*—detecting incipient brain herniation—it behooves all critical-care personnel to take an active part in community education aimed at *primary prevention*. Head trauma, sustained in motorcycle, bicycle, automobile, and home accidents, accounts for a substantial portion of the patients in any intensive or trauma unit who are at risk for brain herniation. Uncontrolled hypertension is the primary cause of intracerebral and cerebellar hemorrhage. All health personnel have a role in educating the public regarding proper use of helmets on bicycles and motorcycles and seat belts in automobiles. The National High Blood Pressure Education Program has identified a major role for nurses in both education and early detection of hypertension (Robinson, 1976; Giblin, 1978; Report of the Task Force . . ., 1976).

Preventive aspects of third-level nursing care is the level at which the majority of the preceding discussion has been aimed. If herniation can be detected before it has become irreversible, the opportunity for effective medical therapy is greatly enhanced. Computerized axial tomography (CAT scan, CT scan, EMI scan) is frequently used upon admission or upon appearance of focal or diffuse brain damage signs to determine if a mass lesion exists. In institutions which do not have a computerized scanner available, angiography may be used. In some cases echoencephalography may be performed at the bedside to detect brain shift. However, the CAT scan is the definitive, noninvasive diagnostic device currently available. Its use has revolutionized neurodiagnostic radiography.

If a mass lesion is found to be the cause of deteriorating neurologic function, removal of the mass becomes the major aim of medical care. For example, evacuation of a subdural hematoma or evacuation and ligation of the bleeding artery in epidural hematoma removes the expanding mass lesion and allows the brain to assume its normal relationships. Hypertonic agents such as mannitol and urea may be given prior to emergency craniotomy in the hope of shrinking a swollen brain and "buying time" to get the patient to the operating room. If herniation is secondary to focal or general cerebral edema, removal of the cause becomes more difficult. In such cases, symptomatic treatment of the edema and resultant increased intracranial pressure may be pursued until the brain's healing processes have reversed the edema. It must be emphasized that the use of such agents as mannitol, urea, glycerol, corticosteroids, and barbiturates is aimed at controlling intracranial pressure secondary to edema and is not primary therapy of the diffuse brain injury per se. Controversy surrounds the use of corticosteriods and high-dose barbiturates in particular in the treatment of head injury. The evidence for and against their efficacy is reviewed in the section on intracranial pressure.

In severe brain edema surgical decompression may be used in the hope that herniation will be reversed or averted long enough for reparative processes to shrink the swollen brain. A flap of bone is removed to allow the expanding brain a place to expand other than through the tentorium. Needless to say, great care must be taken not to place external pressure on the surgical dressing over the exposed dura matter.

Basic third-level nursing care of the patient at risk for herniation and of the patient with irreversible brain damage consists of the standard protective measures for care of the immobilized, unresponsive patient. Modification of these standard care procedures for the patient with potentially increased intracranial pressure will be discussed in the section on intracranial hypertension.

Increased Intracranial Pressure

Most textbooks describe signs of transtentorial herniation as if they were also signs of increased intracranial pressure. While rapidly increasing intracranial pressure can cause transtentorial herniation, it need not do so and furthermore cannot do so by itself. The purpose of this section is to separate what is known about increased intracranial pressure from its potentially life-threatening outcome in transtentorial herniation.

Pathophysiology of Intracranial Pressure

The brain consists of three basic substances—brain, blood, and cerebrospinal fluid—within a nearly inexpandable cranial cavity. Expansion of the volume of any one of these three elements requires adjustment of the volumes of the other two in order to maintain intracranial pressure at a steady level. This principle is known as the Monro-Kellie doctrine. Experimental work with nonhuman primates has demonstrated that there is considerably more compensatory reserve in the intracranial cavity than was previously believed.

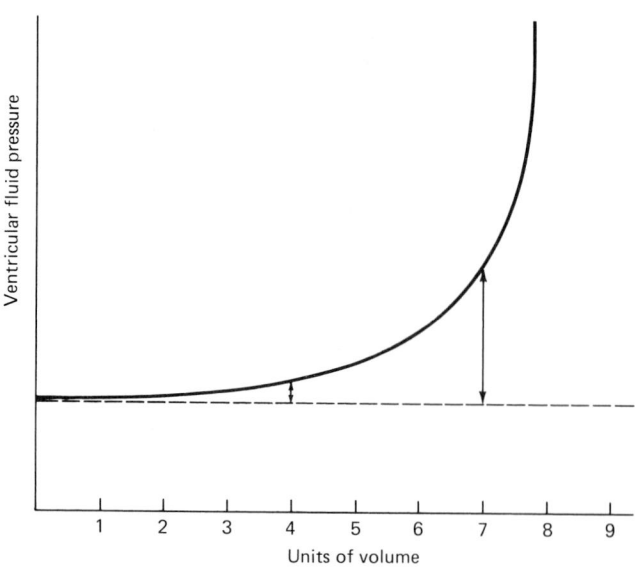

FIGURE 26-7

Intracranial volume-pressure curve. Note that for the addition of any given unit of volume (abscissa) a markedly different rise in pressure occurs, depending whether one is on the flat or steep portion of the curve. Thus adding 1 unit of volume at the second arrow results in nearly 4 times the increase in pressure which occurs from the same volume at the first arrow.

Up to a point, expansion of any of the three elements can be compensated for by contraction of the other two components of the intracranial space.

When an intracranial mass expands or when CSF flow is blocked and fluid accumulates, some CSF will be expressed from the cranial cavity to accommodate the expanded volume. Intracranial pressure (ICP) remains nearly constant as long as the volume of CSF or intravascular blood displaced is nearly equal to the volume of tissue or fluid added to the cranial compartment. This effect is illustrated in the flat portion of the volume-pressure curve shown in Fig. 26-7. In this flat portion, each addition to intracranial volume does not result in an appreciable change in pressure.

Displacement of intracranial fluid volume can occur in three ways: decrease in rate of formation of CSF, slight increase in rate of CSF reabsorption, and displacement of CSF into the spinal sac. In slowly growing brain masses, these compensatory mechanisms may be sufficient to maintain nearly normal ICP for some time.

Eventually, however, the limits of volume displacement are reached; volume is added at a rate greater than displacement, and ICP rises. Note on the steep portion of the volume-pressure curve that continued additions to volume result in disproportionately greater rises in pressure. This relationship of change in pressure with change in volume ($\Delta P/\Delta V$) is termed *elastance*. Elastance is the inverse of *compliance* ($\Delta V/\Delta P$), a term used to describe pressure-volume relationships in the lung. In the case of intracranial pressure, high elastance (synonymous with low compliance) implies a large change in pressure with a small change in volume.

Causes of Increased Intracranial Pressure

Any disorder which increases brain mass, decreases absorption of CSF, or blocks the flow of CSF increases intracranial pressure (ICP). Common examples of these disorders are summarized in Table 26-4.

Increase in brain mass The most obvious example of an increase in brain mass is an intracranial tumor. Most tumors are relatively slowly growing and thus increase ICP at relatively slow rates. Generally it is only late in the course of tumor growth that cranial contents are so displaced that ICP rises rapidly. Tumor growth or brain displacement may obstruct CSF pathways and thus create more rapid rise in ICP.

Hemorrhage, either into the brain substance or subdurally and epidurally, acts as a mass lesion. Although the hemorrhage is not brain tissue, the effect is the same as the expansion of brain tissue itself. The growing mass of blood acts as a rapidly expanding lesion, creating volume-pressure curves like the classic one shown in Fig. 26-7.

Subdural hematomas are of two types, acute and chronic. Acute subdural hematomas may result from head trauma, bleed relatively rapidly from dural-cortical bridging veins, and result in acute brain herniation. In contrast, chronic subdural hematoma is more often associated with lesser or even unremarkable blows to the head, bleeds at a slower rate, and grows more from the coalescence of fibrous membranes and

TABLE 26-4
Intracranial Hypertension

Functional problems: Acute phase	Causes of intracranial hypertension
Headache	Increase in brain mass from tumor, cerebral edema, or hemorrhage
Neuronal ischemia if perfusion pressure is less than 50–60 mmHg	Decrease in CSF reabsorption because of subarachnoid hemorrhage or meningeal infection
Transtentorial brain herniation if ICP increases rapidly, a sudden obstruction occurs in CSF pathways, or the pressure difference between infra- and supratentorial compartments rises	Blocked CSF circulation due to pathway obstruction by tumor, blood clot, herniation, chronic hydrocephalus, or normal pressure hydrocephalus
Permanent brain damage if raised pressure leads to "water hammer" effect	

breakdown products of blood. It acts more like a slowly growing tumor in terms of ICP changes.

Head injury per se does not always cause increased ICP. If the trauma results in hematoma, intracranial hemorrhage, significant brain edema, or alterations in CSF pathways, the result may be increased intracranial pressure. However, a reasonable percentage of patients with head injury have diffuse brain injury with or without intracranial hypertension. This percentage may be as high as 60 to 70 percent of patients in highly specialized neurosurgical critical-care units. The number of patients with nonoperative, diffuse brain injury who do not have increased intracranial pressure varies from 30 to 50 percent, depending upon the level of ICP accepted as upper limit of normal and the specialized nature of the critical-care unit from which the study comes. Many of these patients are comatose and exhibit signs of brainstem dysfunction attributable to their injury on initial impact, rather than to increased intracranial pressure (Adams, et al., 1977).

Another cause of increasing brain volume with effect on ICP is brain edema. If the whole brain or a portion of the brain (for example around a tumor, infarct, or contusion) is swelling rapidly, compensatory volume displacement may be insufficient to maintain normal ICP. Reye's syndrome, a metabolic disorder of children, is a classic example of massive brain swelling with concomitant intracranial hypertension.

Alteration in CSF absorption and flow   Volume of CSF can increase by three means: increase in production, decrease in absorption, or blockage of flow. Increase in production can occur with tumors of the choroid plexus, a relatively rare occurrence. In the populations seen in critical care, decrease in absorption and blockage of flow are the most common CSF volume change factors.

Cerebrospinal fluid is produced in the choroid plexus of the lateral ventricles, flows downward through the third and fourth ventricles, exits the ventricles through the foramen of Magendie, is collected in the cisterns at the base of the brain, and then circulates upward to be reabsorbed over the convexities of the brain. Cerebrospinal fluid also circulates through the subarachnoid space of the spinal cord, passing to and from the basal cisterns. This movement of CSF is shown in Fig. 26-8.

Any disorder which affects the meninges can alter

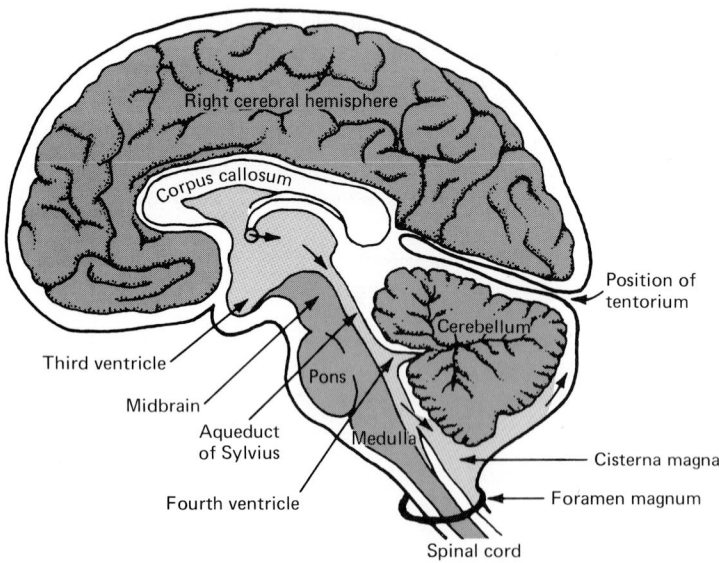

FIGURE 26-8

Normal flow of cerebrospinal fluid. Cerebrospinal fluid is formed in the choroid plexus and flows caudally through the lateral to fourth ventricles. It exits the ventricular system at the cisterna magna and flows up over the surface of the brain, to be reabsorbed over the convexities. A large portion of the CSF is held in the spinal dural sac as well.

reabsorption. Infections such as meningitis can alter CSF reabsorption by covering the meninges with exudate. More commonly, the breakdown of fibrin and blood products after subarachnoid hemorrhage "coats" the meninges and prevents reabsorption. Since the CSF can still circulate (i.e., the pathways are not blocked) but cannot be reabsorbed, increasing cranial volumes of CSF secondary to malabsorption is called *communicating hydrocephalus*. Up to 20 percent of patients with subarachnoid hemorrhage have communicating hydrocephalus at least temporarily. Only about 10 percent require permanent shunt procedures to control ICP.

Blockage of CSF pathways produces *noncommunicating hydrocephalus*. The most common block of CSF pathways related to brain herniation, occurs at the aqueduct of Sylvius (see Fig. 26-8). As the brain herniates over the tentorium, the outflow from the third to fourth ventricle is blocked. Herniation of cerebellar tonsils into the foramen magnum can block the basal cisterns. When elastance is high (when the patient is on the steep part of the volume-pressure curve), even temporary obstruction to CSF flow at the basal cisterns or at the entry to spinal subarachnoid space may leave sufficient CSF in the cranial cavity to precipitate an increase in ICP.

Increase in cerebral blood volume The volume of blood in the normal brain is regulated such that it is relatively constant despite changes in arterial blood pressure through a fairly wide range (mean arterial pressures from 50 to 170 mmHg). Consequently, in normal circumstances, cerebral blood volume contributes little to ICP. However, in the injured brain, and in the brain in which tissue or CSF volumes are already increased, small changes in cerebral blood volume may lead to large changes in ICP.

Causes of altered cerebral blood volume may be (1) vasodilatation, (2) passive transmission of arterial blood pressure if autoregulation is lost, and (3) decrease in venous outflow.

Dilatation of cerebral resistance vessels occurs markedly with hypercapnia (almost on a millimeter by millimeter basis) and hypoxemia (Pa_{O_2} less than 50 mmHg), and if the patient is exposed to volatile anesthetics, such as halothane or nitrous oxide. Arterial pulsations are transmitted to the cerebral cavity most forcibly when mean arterial pressure exceeds 170 mmHg. Such pressures may be achieved in normal persons during straining at stool and in the afterphase of the Valsalva maneuver. When intracranial pressure exceeds about 30 mmHg, autoregulation

of cerebral blood volume is lost. Then arterial pressure is passively transmitted to the cerebral circulation. With continuous ICP monitoring at such times, one sees greater amplitude of ICP pulse pressure and more marked arterial waveforms (dicrotic notch). There is evidence that such arterial pulsations produce a "water hammer" effect on brain cells, which may account for the permanent brain damage seen in such conditions as chronic hydrocephalus.

Finally, cerebral blood volume will be increased if venous return is obstructed. This can happen with increases in intrathoracic pressure as during the Valsalva maneuver or during positive end-expiratory pressure (PEEP) in respiratory therapy. Flexion of the neck and extreme head rotation have been demonstrated to obstruct the internal jugular vein, as well as potentially compress basal CSF cisterns.

Measurement of Intracranial Pressure

Intracranial pressure monitoring research has demonstrated repeatedly that the presence of increased ICP cannot be reliably inferred from clinical signs and symptoms. In a patient at risk for intracranial hypertension, the only reliable means to determine if such exists is to actually measure the ICP continuously.

Many means for measuring ICP exist. The oldest and least reliable is single measurement of CSF pressure in the spinal sac during lumbar or cisternal puncture. Not only are single measurements useless in determining ongoing intracranial dynamics, any pathology which blocks free flow of CSF from cranial to spinal cavity invalidates the spinal pressure as a reliable estimate of intracranial pressure.

Since Lundberg's pioneering work in the 1960s monitoring intraventricular pressure continuously in over 100 patients with space-occupying lesions, such ICP monitoring has become commonplace in many critical-care units throughout the world. ICP may be measured by direct cannulation of a cerebral ventricle (usually a lateral ventricle), by pulsations in the subarachnoid space (via a "screw" or "bolt" threaded into the skull), or by pulsations of the dura (epidural transducer). Pulsations of the CSF or of the meninges are then converted to electrical signals and displayed in graph, computer, or digital format. All three of these most common methods of ICP measurement (ventricular, subarachnoid, epidural) are highly correlated linearly, although the actual values obtained tend to be lower with epidural recording.

In addition to continuous electronic monitoring, some institutions utilize external ventriculostomy shunts as indices of ICP. An intraventricular cannula is connected to a pressure reservoir external to the patient, and CSF is continuously drained against positive pressure. For example, if the surgeon wishes to maintain ICP at about 10 cmH$_2$O (about 8 mmHg), the pressure reservoir is set 10 cm above the zero ICP reference point (usually taken at the external auditory meatus). Whenever pressure inside the ventricle reaches or exceeds 10 cmH$_2$O, CSF drains into the reservoir. A manometer can be set up in such a system for intermittent measurement of ventricular fluid pressure. It must be emphasized that any manometer system can be considered only as an indication of ICP. Manometers dampen the rapid oscillations of ICP which are normally seen with heart rate and respiration. At rapid oscillation the pressure measured in a manometer is likely to be falsely low by an undefined amount.

Ideally, ICP is expressed in millimeters of mercury to facilitate calculation of perfusion pressure. Recall that cerebral perfusion pressure (CPP) reflects the mean arterial blood pressure (MABP) minus the mean intracranial pressure (MICP):

$$CPP = MABP - MICP$$

where CPP = cerebral perfusion pressure
MABP = mean arterial blood pressure
MICP = mean intracranial pressure
[diastolic + $\frac{1}{3}$ (systolic-diastolic)]

Normal ICP is generally accepted to be 0 to 10 mmHg. Miller and his group (1977) make a strong case for using 10 mmHg as the upper limit of normal. They cite numbers of patients with high elastance whose resting ICP was between 10 and 15 mmHg. In other words, though the resting ICP remained relatively "normal," addition of a small volume of fluid precipitated a marked rise in ICP. ICP values of 20 mmHg and over are uniformly regarded as elevated. Values greater than 40 mmHg are considered markedly elevated. Note that with an ICP of 40 mmHg and a MABP of 90 mmHg, CPP would be only 50 mmHg, barely adequate to sustain neuronal perfusion. Ranges of ICP are shown in Table 26-5.

Medical Therapy of Intracranial Hypertension

There is no single therapy for intracranial hypertension. As with brain herniation syndromes, the ideal medical therapy is to remove the cause of the increased ICP. When this cause is a mass lesion or a tumor blocking CSF flow, such surgical therapy is definitive. Unfortunately, the majority of patients with intracranial hypertension in critical-care settings do not have surgical lesions. Recent large series of head injury cases from specialized critical-care settings indicate that patients with surgically treatable lesions range from 25 to 50 percent of all head-injured patients studied (Miller et al., 1977; Gudeman et al., 1979; Marshall et al., 1979a). The largest series is multinational and multi-institutional. Of 700 patients with head injury in three institutions, 27 to 58 percent had surgically treatable lesions (Jennett et al., 1977).

For those patients who do not have surgically remedial lesions, the aim of medical therapy is to control intracranial hypertension in order to protect neuronal function. The pharmacologic and mechanical measures used to control ICP have multisystem effects. Consequently, careful attention must be paid to the fluid-electrolyte status, respiratory status, and cardiac status of the patient.

Assisted ventilation, with *hyperventilation* to maintain Pa_{CO_2} around 20 to 25 mmHg, is commonly used to control ICP. Recall that an increase in Pa_{CO_2} is a potent vasodilator and thus increases cerebral blood volume. Conversely, a decrease in arterial carbon dioxide acts to constrict cerebral vessels.

Hyperosmotic agents, such as mannitol and glycerol, act to draw fluid out of brain cells by increasing the osmolarity of the blood. Such agents depend upon an intact blood-brain barrier to prevent diffusion of the large molecules into the brain itself. In the past, hypertonic glucose and urea were used as hyperosmolar agents. Both of these agents can cross the blood-brain barrier, equilibrate with brain fluid, and thus cause a "rebound" increase in ICP some hours after administration. The inability of mannitol to diffuse across membranes is the factor behind the absence of rebound effect in its use. Usual dose is 0.5 to 1.0 g/kg, given as a bolus. Repeated use of mannitol can

TABLE 26-5 Ranges of Intracranial Pressure (Supratentorial Cavity)		
	mmHg	mmH$_2$O
Normal	0–10	0–136
Possibly elevated	11–15	150–204
Elevated	>15	>200
Moderately elevated	>20	>270
Markedly elevated	>40	>550

lead to continually elevated serum osmolality, with attendant risk of seizures and serious fluid-electrolyte imbalance. Consequently, urine output, serum electrolytes, and osmolality must be monitored frequently in patients receiving repeated mannitol. Serum osmolality should be maintained below 320 mosmol.

Corticosteroids, particularly dexamethasone (Decadron) and methylprednisolone (Solumedrol), are frequently given to control ICP. While the efficacy of corticosteroids on the edema surrounding tumors is well established, similar evidence does not yet exist for the value of corticosteroids in brain edema secondary to head trauma. Recent prospective double-blind studies have not shown any difference in patients treated with placebo, low-dose steroids, or high-dose steroids in terms of ICP or long-term outcome (Cooper et al., 1979; Pitts and Kaktis, 1980).

Although steroids are often implicated as the cause of gastrointestinal bleeding in head trauma patients, the incidence of gastrointestinal bleeding, hyperglycemia, and infection was not demonstrated to be different between steroid and placebo groups by Cooper et al.

Barbiturate coma has come into increasing use for intracranial hypertension unresponsive to other therapies. A considerably decreased mortality has been shown in patients with uncontrollable ICP who were subsequently treated with pentobarbital (3 to 5 mg/kg, with serum levels maintained at 2.5 to 3.5 mg per 100 mL). The mechanism of effect is not clear. Current hypotheses include a direct vasoconstrictive effect on cerebral vessels, reduction of cerebral blood flow secondary to decreased cerebral metabolism, and amelioration of cerebral edema.

Barbiturate coma requires complete supportive care of the comatose, ventilated patient. In addition, barbiturates have systemic effects on cardiac output and blood pressure, requiring monitoring of arterial blood pressure and often monitoring of cardiac output and pulmonary wedge pressure.

Continuous or intermittent drainage of CSF is particularly indicated when the cause of intracranial hypertension is increased production or blocked circulation of CSF. It is of little value in brain edema. Indeed, in such cases, drainage of CSF may lead to ventricular collapse and loss of any capability of monitoring ventricular fluid pressure. CSF drainage does not change the shape of the volume-pressure curve, i.e., does not alter elastance (Miller, 1975). Absolute pressure can be reduced, thus improving cerebral perfusion pressure. Drainage is most safely accomplished against positive pressure so that ventricles are not allowed to collapse. Rapid removal of CSF and ventricular collapse can cause the brain to pull away from the dura, rupture bridging veins, and add subdural hematoma to the patient's problems.

Modifications of Routine Nursing Care

Nursing care of the patient at risk for intracranial hypertension is greatly facilitated by continuous electronic monitoring of ICP. Although ICP monitoring in no way substitutes for careful evaluation of neurologic function, one can detect increasing ICP long before clinical signs of brainstem dysfunction (and thus of herniation) are present. If ICP is increasing or is markedly unstable, routine nursing care procedures may need to be modified to prevent further additions of volume to the patient's already "tight" brain.

Recall from Fig. 26-7 that the patient with high elastance is one in whom very small additions of intracranial volume can result in disproportionately large increases in ICP. These volume additions can stem from increased cerebral blood volume, decreased venous outflow, or obstruction to CSF flow. Of the factors increasing intracranial volume listed in Table 26-4, those which alter cerebral blood volume and which obstruct CSF flow are most influenced by nursing care.

In any given patient, one cannot know the state of intracranial elastance without actually testing the volume-pressure relationship (VPR). VPR can be tested at the bedside by injecting into the intraventricular catheter a 1-mL bolus of saline in 1 s and measuring the ICP response (Miller and Leech, 1975). For obvious reasons, this procedure requires physician supervision and the ability to rapidly remove CSF if necessary. A rough test of elastance which is rapidly reversible is to compress briefly the jugular veins and observe ICP response. Elastance is also correlated with mean ICP value, with higher ICP generally having higher elastance. Another clue to the presence of high elastance is the amplitude of the intracranial pulse. Both high ICP and high elastance occur with wide pulse tracings.

The reality of the clinical world is that most head-injured patients and others at risk for intracranial hypertension are not monitored for ICP. Thus the attending nurse has little to guide a decision to modify nursing care to prevent increases in cerebral blood volume and obstruction of CSF flow. In such cases, one must act conservatively, as if each patient had high elastance.

Nursing activities which may increase ICP It is common knowledge that noise and such nursing care activities as turning the patient and suctioning often precipitate increases in ICP. However, there is little systematic data behind this knowledge. Similarly, there is little data regarding which nursing care activities rarely affect ICP. Activities which have been systematically identified to influence ICP include prone position; turning in bed; suctioning; use of bedpan; rapid shift in position; head rotation; conversation about prognosis, pain, and condition; and cumulative nursing care activity, regardless of nature (Nornes and Magnaes, 1971; Shapiro, 1976; Magnaes, 1978; Mitchell and Mauss, 1978; Shalit and Umansky, 1978; Mitchell et al., 1980). From the mechanisms influencing ICP, one might infer modi-fications of nursing care relevant to patients at risk for high elastance (Table 26-6).

Activities which increase cerebral blood volume Any activity which increases systemic arterial pressure can increase cerebral blood volume by direct transmission of pressure to the brain. In the injured brain, this failure of autoregulation can occur far below the usual limits in the normal brain. Activities known to increase MABP include coughing, Valsalva maneuver, and isometric muscle contractions. Frequent decerebrate posturing is particularly problematic in this regard. Since any tactile stimulus in the course of care can stimulate such posturing, pancuronium (Pavulon) or phenothiazines (Thorazine) may be necessary to reduce the posturing.

TABLE 26-6
Mechanisms by Which Patient Activities Increase ICP

Mechanism	Activity or condition	Nursing intervention
Increase in cerebral blood volume secondary to:		
1. Rise in blood pressure a. Isometric muscle contractions	Turning, moving up and down in bed, pushing self in bed Decerebrate/ decorticate posturing	Turn sheet, encourage patient to allow passive movement Avoid stimuli that cause posturing, if possible; phenothiazines, pancuronium (Pavulon) may help
b. Rebound phase of Valsalva maneuver	Straining at stool	Prevent constipation; use stool softeners, suppositories as dictated by state of consciousness
	Pushing self, moving in bed	Encourage patient to exhale while turning, pushing
c. Emotional stimuli	Family visits, conversation about fears, concerns	Weigh risk vs. benefit for each person; avoid conversations held "over" patient about condition
2. Decreased venous outflow a. Transient mechanical obstruction to jugular, vertebral, and intrathoracic venous systems	Head and body position which obstructs flow: rotated head; flexed, extended neck; extreme hip flexion	Keep head in neutral position when possible, avoid neck flexion and extension both in resting posture and during procedures Slight head up position promotes venous drainage

TABLE 26-6 (Continued) Mechanisms by Which Patient Activities Increase ICP		
Mechanism	Activity or condition	Nursing intervention
b. Increased in- trathoracic and intra-ab- dominal pres- sure	Any activity which causes a Valsalva maneuver Body positions which increase pressure: prone, extreme hip flexion Positive end-expiratory pressure ventilation (PEEP) in some pa- tients	See previous interven- tion re: Valsalva Avoid such positions Head up position may help some; avoid multiple activities in patients who increase ICP with PEEP
3. Cerebral vasodi- latation second- ary to hypercap- nia or marked hypoxia (Pa_{O_2} < 50–60 mmHg)	Occluded airway	Keep airway patent; if suctioning necessary, use intermittent, brief (15 s or less) pe- riods; may help to preoxygenate patient
Increase in CSF volume		
Transient increase in intracranial CSF due to obstruction of basal cisterns	Head position which temporarily occludes CSF outflow to spinal sac: head rotation, neck extension	Avoid head rotation whenever possible; side-lying position may be helpful to pa- tients with decreased CSF absorption (such as postsubarachnoid hemorrhage)

Cerebral blood volume can also be increased by obstruction to venous outflow. Head rotation obstructs jugular venous return, as does the Valsalva maneuver. Moderate elevation of the head (15 to 30°) improves venous outflow and can be shown to decrease ICP. When patients are turned, special care should be paid to the position of the head to avoid neck flexion and head rotation. The combination of head rotation (to reach mainstem bronchi) and suctioning is particularly risky in view of the effect of both coughing and head rotation on venous return.

Prone position probably increases ICP by a combination of both abdominal compression and jugular compression from head rotation. Fortunately, with assisted ventilation and mechanical aids to prevent skin breakdown, the use of prone position is not crucial for the critically ill patient.

Suctioning can produce hypoxemia, leading to vasodilatation, and increased blood pressure related to coughing. Although suctioning is often noted to increase ICP, careful attention to minimizing the suction period (10 to 15 s) and use of intermittent suction can prevent many of the increases seen with longer periods of suction.

Obstruction of CSF flow   While CSF flow obstruction due to pathology is beyond the control of the nurse, body position of the patient can create transient obstruction to CSF flow. Head rotation and neck flexion and extension not only obstruct venous outflow but probably briefly obstruct free communication of CSF between cranial and spinal dural sacs. In the patient with high elastance, even small amounts of CSF trapped in the cranial cavity can potentially increase ICP. The supine position is most likely to create forward neck flexion, whereas the lateral positions with the head in neutral position can allow free flow of CSF in the spinal sac.

The mechanisms underlying both increases and decreases in ICP seen with turning the patient in bed are not clear. Obstruction of CSF flow between cranial and spinal sacs, blood pressure waves secondary to rapid movement, and stimulation of decerebrate posturing are among the possibilities. Not all patients increase ICP with turning; however, Mitchell et al. (1980) did show consistency in the direction of ICP change in any individual patient. In other words, a patient's pressure that increases after turning is likely to continue to do so.

The cumulative effects of nursing activity on ICP require careful planning of necessary care. In a patient with unstable ICP, suctioning, turning, and head rotation occurring within 15 min of each other could be predicted to compound the effects on ICP.

Seizures

By definition, generalized seizures and focal seizures that become general affect the functioning of the whole brain and thereby disrupt consciousness. The only aspect of generalized seizures which will be addressed in detail in this chapter is *status epilepticus,* or uncontrolled, continual major motor (grand mal) seizures. There are several excellent reviews of current classification of seizures and overall problems of persons with seizure disorders in the bibliography.

Generalized Seizures

A generalized seizure is the result of uncontrolled neuronal discharge in the brain. In a seizure, neurons begin to discharge uninhibitedly, recruit other nearby neurons, and thus excite a "storm" of electrical activity in the brain. Discharge may arise from deep in the central core of the brain, immediately disrupting consciousness through excess activity in the reticular activating system. Other generalized seizures may arise from focal areas of hyperactive neurons, whose uncontrolled discharge spreads to central structures and becomes general. Both the typical *grand mal,* or major motor seizure, and *petit mal,* or "absence attacks" of children, are generalized seizures. Electroencephalography during such a seizure shows excessive electrical activity over the entire brain. Clinically, consciousness is disrupted in both types of seizure, but excess motor activity is characteristic of grand mal episodes, while arrest of motor activity (but not loss of tone) is characteristic of the typical petit mal of childhood. In addition, the typical EEG pattern, although general in both, is quite different in petit mal and grand mal.

Most seizures are idiopathic, that is, without identifiable cause. However, in a critical-care setting, they are likely to stem directly from an identifiable pathology which primarily or secondarily affects the patient's brain. Metabolic disorders, by virtue of al-

tering acid-base and fluid environment of the brain, effectively lower membrane potential and thus threshold for seizures. Both hypertonicity and hypotonicity of brain fluid can lead to seizures by altering the normal electrochemical balance on each side of the cell. Trauma can predispose the patient to seizures. The underlying cause is not so likely to be cortical scar formation in the early stages, for healing and thus scar formation has not yet taken place. More likely, the lactic acidosis and respiratory alkalosis secondary to neurogenic hyperventilation alter the electrochemical balance of brain cells. Tumors and subdural hematomas directly irritate the brain tissue, leading to increased cell firing. Correction by the physician of the underlying structural, metabolic, or respiratory problems is the most effective treatment for such seizures. However, particularly in an injured brain, seizures beget seizures. Thus, most clinicians elect to control seizures with anticonvulsants while pursuing the underlying causes in the critically ill patient.

Status epilepticus The final category of seizures which may be encountered in a critical-care unit is that of the person with epilepsy who develops status epilepticus. Any patient who is having seizures from any acute or chronic cause may develop status epilepticus, but it is more common in those whose brain cells have become regulated by anticonvulsants. The sudden withdrawal, either deliberately or by forgetting medication, then renders all the brain cells hyperexcitable, thus leading to seizure activity among epileptic foci cells. Neurochemical changes in the cellular fluid around these cells then render neighboring cells more excitable and lead to generalized seizures.

Grand mal status epilepticus is an absolute emergency! Continual seizures prevent brain cells from restoring metabolic processes between firing. Patients in grand mal status epilepticus whose seizures cannot be controlled die of brain exhaustion with definite evidence of metabolic and structural neuronal death. Meldrum (1978) and others demonstrated that prevention of muscular activity during continual seizures in baboons neither protected the brain nor prevented death. Electroencephalography demonstrated that continual seizure activity occurred even though the motor manifestations were prevented by curare, and even though respirations and blood pressure were supported. In both baboons and rats, neuronal damage was greatest in neocortex and hippocampus.

Critical-care nurses should be prepared to institute anticonvulsant therapy for a patient in status epilepticus. The time necessary for a physician to arrive, evaluate the situation, and initiate therapy may be sufficient for large numbers of brain cells to be irreparably damaged. Therefore, the nurse should be able to (1) recognize status epilepticus and (2) initiate a standard protocol determined in advance by the critical-care staff. A typical protocol is shown in Table 26-7.

A generalized tonic-clonic seizure (grand mal) lasting longer than 30 min or failure of the patient to regain consciousness between a series of generalized seizures are the criteria for diagnosing generalized status epilepticus. Recall that a typical generalized seizure (grand mal) lasts 20 to 40 s, with recovery of consciousness within 30 min.

Treatment of generalized status epilepticus follows the same steps involved in any emergency: attention to airway and breathing, steps to diagnose the underlying cause, protective care while the seizures persist, and definitive treatment. Establishment of an adequate airway is, as always, of prime importance. At the same time, one should administer oxygen by prongs or mask. Most patients who go into status in a critical-care unit already have injured brains. Sustained hypoxia from blocked airway and multiple seizures can superimpose hypoxic brain damage on that sustained from continual seizures. If the patient does not have an artificial airway already in place, one should position the patient on his or her side and insert an oral airway. An endotracheal tube may ultimately be required if the seizures prove difficult to control.

Because most status epilepticus seen in a critical-care unit is a symptom of an underlying structural or metabolic pathology, determination of the primary cause is crucial in long-term therapy. If an intravenous line is not already established in the patient, one should be established as soon as airway patency is attended to. At this time, blood should be drawn for laboratory tests, including blood glucose, serum osmolality, and serum electrolytes. It is often the case that correction of the underlying metabolic deficit (for example, hypoglycemia or hyperosmolality) will end the seizures.

During continuous major motor seizures the patient needs protective care. Such care includes protection from airway blockage and aspiration, and protection from injury to bones and soft tissues. Airway protective care includes lateral position, oral airway or endotracheal tube, and oropharyngeal suctioning to keep the

| **TABLE 26-7** |
| Protocol for Management of Generalized Status Epilepticus |

1. Obtain adequate airway.
2. Establish diagnosis. 30 min of generalized major motor seizure *or* 30 min of a series of seizures without regaining consciousness.
3. Establish intravenous line.
4. Draw blood for laboratory studies.
5. Anticonvulsant therapy
   a. Diazepam (Valium) 10 mg IV "push" or drip at rate of 5 mg/min. Repeat until seizures stop or to maximum of 120 mg/24 h. *Caution:* Danger of respiratory depression; be prepared to intubate and hand ventilate.
   b. Phenytoin (Dilantin; formerly called *diphenylhydantoin*)
   Initial dose: 500 mg IV at 50 mg/min. If seizures are not stopped with diazepam, repeat at 500-mg doses at 50 mg/min until seizures stop or to 1000 mg/24 h. Maintenance dose: 250 mg IV q4h to total of 1000 mg in first 24 h. *Caution:* Monitor ECG. Stop drug if S-T segment widens.
6. If seizures are not ended with one-two initial drugs, general anesthesia may be considered.

mouth free of secretions which can be aspirated. Pillows taped to the side rails or thick commercially made pads are important in preventing injury to bones and soft tissues in the clonic phase of major motor seizures. Blankets are not sufficiently thick to prevent injury. In addition, equipment for respiratory support (hand ventilating bag and oxygen) and electrocardiogram monitoring should be at the bedside during definitive anticonvulsant therapy.

Should seizures persist without return of consciousness for 30 min, the following drugs can be used to control the seizures. The initial drug of choice is *diazepam* (Valium), given intravenously. Diazepam may be given in doses of 10 mg every 20 to 30 min, at a rate of 5 mg/min, until seizures stop or to a maximum of 120 mg in 24 h. Alternatively, 5 mg/min may be administered by intravenous drip. Diazepam is a very short-acting anticonvulsant, but has an equally rapid onset of action. Large doses of diazepam can depress or even arrest respirations. Therefore, it should be given slowly (5 mg/min) and equipment to hand-ventilate the patient should be readily available if needed.

Following the initial use of diazepam, phenytoin (Dilantin) is given for longer-term control of the seizures. It is preferable to phenobarbital in persons being observed for central nervous system disorders because it has much less sedating effect in large doses than does phenobarbital. Phenytoin is given at a rate of 50 mg/min *intravenously*. It may be repeated at the rate of 150 mg every 30 min until seizures stop or to a maximum of 1 g in 24 h. Phenytoin tends to crystallize when standing in solution; therefore it should be given in a bolus intravenously and not mixed in hanging solutions. It is never appropriate to give phenytoin intramuscularly. Tissue absorption and therefore serum levels are unpredictable by this route and crystallization in tissues has been demonstrated (Wilensky and Lowden, 1973).

Phenytoin has potentially dangerous effects on cardiac rhythm, particularly in elderly patients and those with cardiac disease. When it is given in status epilepticus, the ECG should be monitored continuously, in addition to blood pressure and respiratory rate. Criteria for immediate discontinuation of the drug are hypotension, widening of the QRS complex, prolongation of the P-R or Q-T intervals, and depression of T waves.

Beyond giving initial diazepam and a loading dose of phenytoin, consistency in regional practice disappears. If diazepam is not effective, amobarbital or phenobarbital are the next most commonly used drugs, followed by paraldehyde rectally or intravenously. (Be prepared for pulmonary edema if this route is used!) General anesthesia is used as a last resort. Respiratory assistance will be required if the patient does not respond to the initial repeated doses of diazepam, because of the sedating effect of the drugs. If general anesthesia is used to depress the function of the entire central nervous system, continuous electroencephalography (EEG) is imperative. General anesthesia will stop the motor activity; only the EEG can show if the brain seizure activity has ceased as well.

DISORDERS THAT DISRUPT RESPIRATION BUT NOT CONSCIOUSNESS

The disorders commonly seen that may produce respiratory problems include high cervical spinal cord injury, polyneuropathies (such as Guillain-Barré syndrome), and motor unit disorders, such as myasthenia gravis, botulism, and tetanus. In these the respiratory problem is secondary to loss of motor function, rather than to loss of consciousness and ability voluntarily to protect the airway.

These three disorders disrupt human functioning in all basic aspects of self-care except mentation and consciousness. Survival and the quality of life after recovery are vitally dependent upon skilled and knowledgeable nursing care.

Extracerebral Motor Pathways

Voluntary movement is dependent upon the integration of cortical and spinal motor signals and upon the integrity of spinal pathways, peripheral nerves carrying motor fibers, and muscle fibers themselves. The relationships of these components of the motor system are shown schematically in Fig. 26-9. Movement can be disrupted by pathology causing physiological imbalance at any of these junctures or pathways. For example, a cerebral infarct (stroke) damaging the motor cortex (posterior frontal lobe) can prevent voluntary movement of a limb, even though the remainder of the motor pathways are intact. Reflex movement will remain because it is integrated at the spinal, rather than cortical level. Any cerebral lesion which interferes with motor fibers will have similar effects and may interfere with consciousness and mentation, as well as movement, depending upon the extent and location of the lesion.

Movement may also be disrupted by interference with the spinal motor pathways, the peripheral nerves, or the muscle-nerve interface (myoneural junction). Consciousness and mentation will not be affected by these extracerebral lesions, unless breathing is so decreased that hypoxia results.

The major descending motor tract is the *corticospinal*. The *lateral corticospinal tract* is composed of fibers from the cerebral hemisphere, which decussates (crosses) in the medullary pyramid and travels downward in the mediolateral white matter of the cord. Final synapse of this tract is with the anterior horn cell of the ventral spinal cord gray matter. The *anterior corticospinal tract* contains fibers which do not cross the cord until a few spinal segments above their termination. The anterior corticospinal is found on both sides of the anteromedian fissure. The majority of the anterior corticospinal tract terminates in the cervical and thoracic cord. *Corticobulbar* fibers serve the same motor functions as corticospinal axons, but begin in the motor cortex and terminate in the brainstem structures. Their functions are to mediate voluntary control of motor cranial nerves.

Rubrospinal and *vestibulospinal* pathways carry motor impulses to and from the cerebellum and vestibular nuclei. The reticulospinal fibers descend from the pons and medulla, regulating alpha and gamma motor neurons of extensor reflexes.

The major sensory pathways of the spinal cord are

the *anterolateral columns,* carrying fibers for pain, temperature, and proprioception, and the posterior or *dorsal columns,* mediating vibration, position sense, some touch sensation, and some sensory discrimination.

Segmental Organization

The spinal cord and brainstem are organized in *segments.* A segment consists of a core of gray matter (cell bodies) surrounded by white matter (myelinated axons). The white matter is composed of the ascending and descending motor and sensory tracts of the spinal cord and brainstem.

The *ventral horn* of gray matter gives rise to the axons of motor fibers. The *dorsal horn* receives sensory fibers from the periphery.

A short distance from the cord the two kinds of fibers join to form a *spinal nerve.* Each spinal nerve later divides to form several *peripheral nerves.* The area of skin supplied by each segment is called a *sensory dermatome.* In addition, the divisions of each peripheral nerve serve motor and sensory function for specific peripheral nerve fields.

The brainstem segments are the *midbrain, pons,* and *medulla.* In each segment are nuclei (collections of cell bodies) and tracts of myelinated axons. Just as in the spinal cord, sensory fibers enter and leave in the posterior or dorsal brainstem, and motor fibers synapse and exit in the anterior portions. Cranial nerve nuclei are analogous to the central gray of the spinal cord. The cranial nerves themselves consist of motor and/or sensory axons and are peripheral nerves.

As summarized in Table 26-8, neurologic disorders can interfere with functions mediated by the brainstem or spinal cord above the specific segment (*suprasegmentally*), at the segment (*segmentally*), or at the junction between the nerve and muscle (*myoneural junction*). The term *suprasegmental* will be used instead of *upper motor neuron* and *segmental* instead of *lower motor neuron.*

Neurologic disorders can interrupt motor pathways suprasegmentally from the voluntary motor cortex to either brainstem and/or spinal cord segments (see Fig. 26-9). Clinically, such suprasegmental lesions result in weakness or paralysis of voluntary movement, increased or hyperactive reflexes, and mild muscle atrophy secondary to disuse. Corticospinal and corticobulbar motor tracts serve to inhibit the tone of the gamma motor fibers involved in the muscle stretch reflex. Therefore, destruction or depression of the

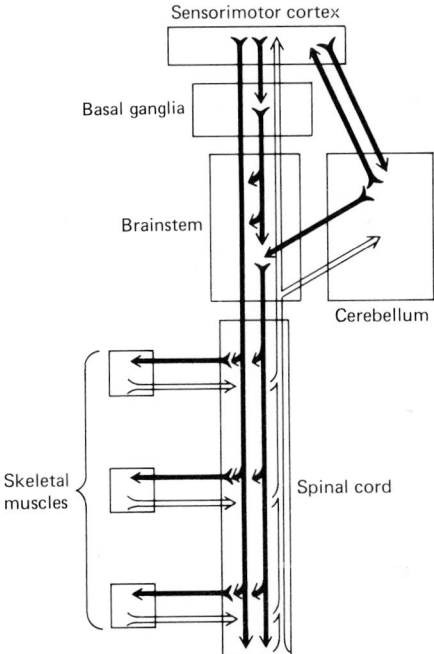

FIGURE 26-9

Schematic representation of the motor systems. Suprasegmental influences are represented by the arrows connecting motor cortex, brainstem, and spinal cord. Segmental pathways are shown by the arrows between spinal cord and skeletal muscles. The cerebellum has no direct segmental or suprasegmental connections, but serves to coordinate the entire system. [*From E. Henneman, in V. Mountcastle, (ed.), Medical Physiology, 13th ed., Mosby, St. Louis, 1974.*]

corticospinal/corticobulbar tract releases this inhibition and leads to the hyperactive reflexes seen with suprasegmental lesions. In traumatic lesions of the corticospinal tract, such as in stroke and spinal cord injury, there is often a period of "cerebral" or "spinal shock," in which reflexes are absent or depressed. It is only after this period (lasting anywhere from hours to months) that the heightened and pathologic muscle stretch reflexes are seen. Because the reflex arc is intact, changes in the electromyogram (EMG) are not seen.

At the segments, neurologic disorders can disrupt sensorimotor function in two ways: (1) destruction or depression of cranial nerve nuclei (brainstem segments) or anterior horn cells (spinal cord segments),

---

TABLE 26-8
Clinical Signs of Disrupted Motor Function at Three Levels of the Nervous System

Level	Clinical signs	Examples of causative disorders
Suprasegmental	Weakness or paralysis of voluntary movement Increased muscle stretch reflexes; reflex arc is intact (after "spinal shock") Some muscle atrophy secondary to disuse EMG normal	Spinal cord lesions such as trauma, infarct, tumor, and hemorrhage
Segmental	Weakness or paralysis of voluntary movement Decreased or absent muscle stretch reflexes (reflex arc disrupted) Marked muscle atrophy secondary to denervation (↓ trophic factors) EMG changes: fibrillation, giant polyphasic action potentials (denervation supersensitivity)	Brainstem lesions affecting cranial nuclei: tumors, infarct, hemorrhage Cerebellopontine angle tumors compressing cranial nerves Polyneuropathies such as Guillain-Barré syndrome, alcoholic polyneuropathy, diphtheric polyneuropathy, and toxic chemical polyneuropathy
Myoneural junction	Weakness or paralysis of voluntary movement Muscle stretch reflexes intact No muscle atrophy EMG diminished: muscle able to contract when directly stimulated. Pattern of ↓ contraction varies with disorder	Chronic: myasthenia gravis (may have acute episodes of life-threatening myasthenic or cholinergic crisis); Eaton-Lambert syndrome (myasthenic symptoms associated with carcinoma) Acute: botulism, curare, succinylcholine, "nerve gas," organophosphate insecticides

---

and (2) interruption of the cranial or peripheral nerve after it exits the segment. Discrete segmental lesions may interfere only with sensory input or with association neurons between sensory and motor cells. Such lesions will affect movement by interfering with sensory feedback; however, for the purposes of this chapter, such discrete lesions are irrelevant because the kinds of disorders seen in critical care produce more widespread damage.

Segmental lesions produce a clinical pattern of decreased or absent voluntary movement, decreased or absent muscle stretch reflexes, and muscular atrophy. Movement is decreased, not from absence of impulses from the voluntary motor cortex, but because such input cannot fire the motor neuron (in cranial nerve nuclei or anterior horn of spinal cord). With destruction of motor neurons, the cell body and axons eventually die, depriving the muscle thus innervated of *trophic* or nourishing influence. Consequently, marked muscle wasting or atrophy occurs.

This atrophy is considerably greater than that seen from disuse.

Segmental lesions that damage the peripheral nerve prevent an intact motor neuron's impulse from reaching the target muscle. If the lesion is close enough to the motor neuron, or severe enough to cause complete destruction of the nerve bundle, the nerve can degenerate antidromically (toward the motor neuron) and destroy the motor neuron itself. However, if the motor neuron cell body remains intact, recovery is possible when the nerve regenerates. Such recovery is the case in most instances of Guillain-Barré syndrome. In contrast, peripheral neuropathies caused by chronic degenerative processes, such as diabetes, may leave permanent nerve damage.

Finally, in segmental damage, muscle stretch reflexes are diminished or absent. The reflex arc has been interrupted either within the gray matter or by interruption of the peripheral nerve. In suprasegmental lesions, the reflex arc remains intact; therefore reflex but not volitional movement remains. In the segmental lesion, neither volitional nor reflex movement is possible. Obviously, one-sided or incomplete lesions allow gradations of the classical segmental clinical effect.

The last point at which movement can be disrupted is at the *myoneural junction.* The nerve terminal of the motor axon releases *quanta,* or packets, of acetylcholine. These quanta of acetylcholine bind to receptors on the membrane of the muscle fiber and create miniature end-plate potentials. These potentials summate and eventually produce an action potential, thus causing the muscle fiber to contract. Deficits in firing can occur because too little acetylcholine is available, because it is cleared too rapidly by acetylcholinesterase present in the synaptic cleft, or because the receptor sites are too few or are bound by another neurochemical. Botulism is a disorder thought to result in too little acetylcholine being released. Organophosphates (nerve gas, some insecticides) inhibit the clearance of acetylcholine by acetylcholinesterase. The drugs curare and succinylcholine compete with acetylcholine for receptor sites. The disorder myasthenia gravis is thought to occur because of autoimmune responses which decrease and inactivate receptor sites. The end result of these differing pathophysiological processes is the same: muscular weakness or paralysis, which becomes worse with repetitive stimulation, and depression of

autonomic nervous system functions mediated by acetylcholine (mostly parasympathetic processes). Unless total paralysis occurs, muscle stretch reflexes are normal unless repetitively stimulated. Afferent and efferent paths of the reflex arc are intact, but repetitive release, binding, or clearing of acetylcholine is impaired at the myoneural junction. Table 26-8 summarizes clinical signs associated with neural dysfunction at each of these three levels.

Life-Threatening Effects of Extracerebral Motor Loss

Extracerebral motor loss can threaten life if it involves sensory and motor reflexes which protect the airway, or if innervation to respiratory musculature is depressed or lost. In addition, extracerebral motor loss can ultimately threaten life through the multisystem involvement characteristic of the disorders which cause widespread motor loss.

Loss of Airway Protection

As discussed earlier in this chapter, the gag, swallowing, and cough reflexes which protect the airway are integrated in the brainstem, at the medullary segment. Cranial nerves IX, X, and XII are the peripheral nerves carrying motor and sensory fibers to and from the structures involved in these functions. Table 26-9 summarizes the anatomical structures involved.

TABLE 26-9
Nerve Fibers and Skeletal Muscles Involved in Protecting the Airway

Function	Afferent fibers	Efferent fibers	Muscle(s)
Gag	Cranial nerve IX (glossopharyngeal)	Cranial nerve IX Cranial nerve X (vagus)	Stylopharyngeus Soft palate, pharynx
Swallow	Cranial nerve IX (posterior $\frac{1}{3}$ of tongue; pharynx, larynx)	Cranial nerve X	Pharynx, soft palate
	Cranial nerve X (epiglottal taste buds)	Cranial nerve XII (hypoglossal)	Tongue
Cough	Cranial nerve X (pharynx, larynx, trachea, bronchial tree)	Cranial nerve X Efferents to respiratory center (medulla) and then to periphery via: (1) Phrenic nerve (C4–C5) (2) Intercostal nerves (T1–T11)	Soft palate, larynx, glottis Diaphragm Intercostal muscles

Nervous system disease or trauma can interfere with airway protection as already described. Voluntary motor pathways can be interrupted by decreased level of consciousness or by lesions of the corticobulbar pathways such as stroke or cerebral hemorrhage. Such suprasegmental lesions remove *voluntary control* of gag, swallow, and cough but leave the reflexes intact, if brainstem structures are intact. However, if hemorrhage, infarct, or herniating brain pressure on the medulla damages cranial nerve nuclei (segmental damage), protective reflexes will be depressed or absent. Infarcts of the posterior inferior cerebellar artery or medullary arteries (*lateral* and *medial medullary syndromes*) are examples of brainstem lesions which may jeopardize the airway without impairing consciousness.

Because lesions of peripheral nerves can also produce segmental symptoms, polyneuropathies which affect the lower cranial nerves will also jeopardize airway protection. Guillain-Barré syndrome and diphtheric polyneuritis are examples of polyneuropathies in which loss of airway protective reflexes is highly likely. Finally, generalized myasthenia gravis and botulism can produce loss of airway protection through interruption of the myoneural junction of the muscles involved. Such deficit is different from both segmental and suprasegmental lesions in that reflexes remain normal and muscular atrophy does not occur.

Evaluation of airway protection Since airway protection is dependent upon those reflexes which serve gag, cough, and swallowing, assessment of adequacy of these functions is important. In contrast to the patient with cerebral involvement who is at risk for inadequate airway protection, the patient with extracerebral motor problems is usually conscious. Consequently, the nurse can utilize evaluation of speech, facial movement, and head and shoulder movement to evaluate closely related cranial nerve function. Finally, one needs to be aware which patients are at risk for loss of airway protection and evaluate potential loss of protection in light of general motor functioning of the patient.

Patients who are at risk for airway problems and who may be seen in critical care include those with myasthenia gravis (particularly postoperative thymectomy, during intercurrent illness, or in myasthenic or cholinergic crisis), those with polyneuropathy involving upper extremities and/or cranial nerves, those with poliomyelitis (involving brainstem motor neurons), and those with brainstem stroke or contusion. The last group of patients may be unconscious if the reticular activating system is involved. Cranial nerves IX, X, and XII are most crucially involved in protecting the airway. Evaluation of function of adjacent cranial nerves helps detect potential problems before aspiration has occurred. Table 26-9 describes cranial nerves in relation to the functions served.

Important questions to consider in evaluating lower cranial nerve function are the following: (1) Is the quality of speech changing or becoming nasal, slurred, or "thick-tongued"? (2) Is the volume of speech decreasing? In regard to swallowing: (1) Is food or fluid coming back through the nose (indicating palatal weakness)? (2) Is there choking on nonviscous substances such as water? (3) Can the patient swallow his own saliva? (4) Is there pooling of secretions in the mouth of the conscious person? Remember in testing swallowing that water is the most difficult substance to swallow, more so than saliva. Therefore, if the nurse is concerned that the patient may aspirate the test substance, use ice chips rather than water.

In ascending polyneuropathies, upper extremity function and movment of head and neck may be affected before cranial nerves serving airway protection. Therefore changes in strength and symmetry of head turning, neck flexion, and extension would be important cues to evaluate swallow, gag, and cough more frequently in such patients. These evaluations of cranial nerve function are not relevant to the patient with cervical spine injury (unless there is associated head injury) because any spinal cord injury compatible with life is below the cranial nerves.

In myasthenia gravis, changes in muscular function may occur very rapidly, within minutes. Therefore, for these patients airway protection and respiratory status must be evaluated frequently. Any slurring or nasality of speech or increased ptosis of eyelids serves as a cue to evaluate swallowing and cough and vital capacity as often as every 5 min if changes are occurring rapidly. Such variables are summarized in Table 26-10.

Of the disorders used as examples in this section, only brainstem stroke and contusion are stable lesions. Once the initial damage has occurred, symptoms tend to remain the same or diminish. The other disorders (polyneuropathies and disorders of neuromuscular transmission) may become progressively worse, and often involve respiratory musculature as well. In these disorders, airway protection and respiratory capacity must be evaluated together. They should be evaluated as frequently as are the vital signs. Any deterioration occurring in any of the functions is an important cue to increase the frequency of

<table>
<tr><td colspan="2" align="center">**TABLE 26-10**
Critical Evaluation in Myasthenia Gravis</td></tr>
<tr><td>Vital capacity</td><td>Maximum expiratory volume following maximum inspiration, measured in liters by spirometer</td></tr>
<tr><td>Swallowing</td><td>Measured subjectively by asking the patient to identify the type of substance/diet thought possible to swallow at the time:
0—nothing   3—pureed soft
1—saliva   4—soft diet
2—liquids   5—regular diet</td></tr>
<tr><td>Ptosis</td><td>Documented according to the following scale (with the patient looking straight ahead)
1—unable to open eye, none of iris visible
2—lids open, some of lowermost iris visible
3—lower half of pupil visible
4—all of pupil visible, none of uppermost iris visible
5—all of pupil visible, some of uppermost iris visible</td></tr>
<tr><td>Diplopia</td><td>Measured subjectively by asking the patient to move eyes through their extreme range of motion and identify positions in which diplopia is experienced.</td></tr>
</table>

Source: Blount, M., A. Kinney, and M. Stone: *Nurs Clin North Am* 14:186, 1979.

evaluation. The nurse *must intervene* if the patient cannot swallow saliva, if gag and/or cough reflex is markedly diminished or lost, if food and fluid regurgitates through the nose, or if vital capacity is less than one-third predicted (about 600 cm³ in the "average" adult). The combination of bulbar dysfunction and decreased vital capacity puts the patient at particular risk of both aspiration and respiratory failure.

Intervention consists of placement of cuffed endotracheal or tracheostomy tube (depending upon anticipated length of dysfunction) to prevent aspiration of saliva and nasogastric, esophageal, or gastric feeding tube. Management of the problems of bulbar dysfunction will be discussed later in the chapter in the context of total management of the patient with severe extracerebral motor loss.

Dysfunction of Respiratory Musculature

Decreased respiration due to disordered respiratory musculature may be life-threatening. Muscles important to respiration are the diaphragm and the intercostal muscles. In health, the diaphragm is the primary muscle of inspiration. The internal and external inter-costal muscles assist in deep inspiration. Expiration is a passive process. The motor neurons of the diaphragm receive impulses from the phrenic nerve, which emerges from spinal nerve C_4, with some input from C_3 and C_5. Spinal nerves T_1–T_{11} innervate the intercostal muscles.

Thus, spinal cord lesions at C_5 and above will affect both diaphragmatic and intercostal musculature. Lesions below C_5 will allow diaphragmatic movement but paralyze the intercostals. During the period of spinal shock, a patient with a lesion of the midthoracic region would be able to voluntarily depress the diaphragm and thus take a breath. The ability to inspire maximally would be lost because of paralysis of the intercostal muscles. When reflexes return, spasticity of the intercostal muscles will aid in maximal chest expansion.

Respiratory musculature can also be affected by peripheral polyneuropathies, which impair both voluntary and reflex movement by demyelination of the motor component of the reflex arc. Myasthenia gravis and other disorders of neuromuscular transmission interfere with respiratory movement by blocking transmission at the myoneural junction. The intense muscular spasms and tetanus can also interfere with respiration by preventing full expansion of the chest.

Evaluation of respiratory function In patients at risk for respiratory musculature failure secondary to extracerebral motor disorders, function can be evaluated by measuring vital capacity serially, measuring blood gas values, and observing respiratory effort. Secondary clues to impending respiratory distress are increasing anxiety and fear of going to sleep. Patients at risk include those with spinal cord lesions above T_6, those with polyneuropathies with trunk and upper extremity weakness, and persons with generalized myasthenia gravis, particularly those who are postoperative or have intercurrent illness.

Since spinal cord sensory roots follow skin dermatomes, and since most traumatic lesions of the cord involve both motor and sensory pathways, one can make a rough estimate of the level of cord injury by mapping sensory dermatome levels. Figure 26-10 depicts schematically important dermatome levels in quadruped man. The figure is shown in the quadruped fashion to aid in appreciation of the extension of sacral and thoracic dermatomes along arms and legs.

Critical dermatomes in terms of functional outcome are shown. T_1 extends from about the level of the scapula along the arm and is the upper limit of the

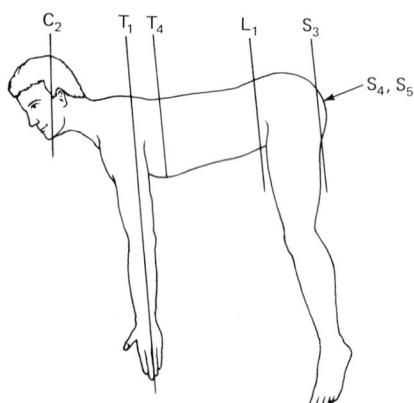

FIGURE 26-10

Representation of demarcating sensory dermatomes in quadruped man. The figure is shown in quadruped fashion to illustrate that the dermatomes dividing thoracic and lumbar spine travel along the arm and leg. Knowledge of dermatome levels in mapping the extent of sensory loss can help predict the functional deficits and abilities of the patient. [*Redrawn from H. Patton, et al., (eds.), Introduction to Basic Neurology, Saunders, Philadelphia, 1977, p. 176.*]

intercostal nerves. T_4 is approximately at the nipple line. Patients with lesions slightly below T_4 will probably have adequate voluntary respiratory function, while those at T_4 and above require frequent evaluation of respiratory function and may need ventilatory assistance. The functional significance of other dermatomes will be discussed later under multisystem problems. Although most of the severe polyneuropathies have greater motor than sensory loss, sensory dermatomes may be of some value in determining the level of peripheral nerve loss in symmetric polyneuropathy. Sensory dermatome evaluation is of no value in disorders of neuromuscular transmission since the pathology is entirely at the neuromotor junction.

Although there are much more sophisticated measures of pulmonary function available, bedside evaluation of vital capacity remains an important tool in serially evaluating respiratory status in neurological disorders. The bedside spirometer is easily used with the conscious patient and provides immediate measurement, without the time lag inherent in blood gas measures. A single measure of vital capacity is not so useful as a series, compared with predicted normal for a person that size. Continually decreasing vital capacity indicates a patient who is losing respiratory muscle function and may need respiratory assistance. As a rule of thumb, vital capacities below one-third of predicted (or below 600 cm³) require assisted ventilation. Decreasing tidal volumes or vital capacity in a patient with spinal cord injury indicates extension of the injury (due to edema or bleeding into the cord). Such decreases may be expected in a patient with ascending polyneuropathy or worsening myasthenia gravis.

Measurement of partial pressures of dissolved gases in the blood is important in evaluating the overall respiratory status of patients with severe motor disorders, but is not to be relied upon in determining the need for assisted ventilation in disorders characterized by rapid worsening. For example, in myasthenia gravis, a patient can move from intact respiratory status to complete loss of voluntary respiratory effort in 20 min. Although polyneuropathies such as Guillain-Barré syndrome have a somewhat slower time course, waiting for results of arterial blood gases may delay respiratory assistance unnecessarily. Blood gas values may be more appropriately used to guide decisions regarding respiratory assistance in more stable lesions such as spinal cord injury. Secondary evaluative clues may be helpful. The nurse may observe respiratory effort or a patient's anxiety about going to sleep. Such secondary cues should initiate measurement of vital capacity and blood gases and an increase in the frequency of evaluation.

In addition to the direct effect of motor loss on respiratory musculature, patients immobilized from motor disorders are at increased risk for pulmonary embolism from deep vein thrombosis. Although there is disagreement in the literature regarding the incidence of deep vein thrombosis and pulmonary embolism in spinal cord–injured patients and others with neurological immobility, studies which report a low incidence rely on clinical signs rather than the more accurate I-fibrinogen studies to detect thrombosis. Clinical signs have been shown to miss both thrombosis and pulmonary embolism in the most widely studied postoperative and postmyocardial infarction groups (Nicolaides and Hobbs, 1978). In addition, patients with spinal cord injury are even less apt to display the typical clinical signs of thrombosis and embolism (pain, temperature increase) because of disordered transmission of such signals past the spinal cord lesion. The few studies published which use appropriate techniques to detect thrombosis show an incidence equivalent to that in other immobilized populations—about 30 to 50 percent.

Multisystem Dysfunctions

Although the effects of severe motor loss on airway protection and respiratory musculature are the most immediately life-threatening, most of the prototypic disorders affect the function of most body systems. These dysfunctions also require management in the critical stages of illness and may ultimately prove life-threatening if not well managed early. The long-term consequence may be increased disability or even death if early management is not effective (Tribe, 1963). Table 26-11 shows the interrelationships of muscle groups, spinal level of innervation, sensory dermatomes, functional abilities, and potential problems at given levels of spinal cord injury during the acute phase of care.

The following discussion of multisystem problems is most pertinent to acute spinal cord injury. Since polyneuropathies can also have an autonomic neuropathy component, it is applicable to patients with polyneuropathies as well. Special considerations in disorders of neuromuscular transmission will be discussed following this section.

Systems which can be compromised by acute spinal cord injury and polyneuropathy include cardiovascular reflexes, temperature control, gastrointestinal motility, elimination, and integument. The effects on the respiratory system have already been discussed.

The *cardiovascular effects* result primarily from loss of sympathetic outflow below the level of injury. Recall that a period of spinal shock occurs for some time after injury, in which somatic and autonomic reflex activity is lost. Although autonomic demyelination is not the rule in polyneuropathy, it can occur and present similar systemic problems.

The majority of visceral innervation is from the sympathetic outflow. These efferents leave the spinal cord in the thoracolumbar spine, between T_1 and L_{1-2}. Heart, lungs, tracheobronchial tree, viscera, peripheral blood vessels, bowel, and bladder all receive their sympathetic innervation from the thoracolumbar sympathetic ganglia. Parasympathetic innervation of these organs is from the vagus (medulla) and from the pelvic plexus (sacral spinal nerves), in the case of bladder, rectum, and penis. Consequently, any lesion of the thoracic or cervical cord will interrupt cardiovascular function and the function of most of the viscera. The higher the lesion, the more autonomic function is disrupted.

The viscera will not cease function entirely because they also receive parasympathetic input. However, the parasympathetic input is unbalanced and will tend toward quiescence. For example, paralytic ileus occurs because motility depends upon the balance of sympathetic and parasympathetic activity. Cardiac and lung function do not cease because of intrinsic rhythmicity in the heart and because vagal input is still intact. However, bradycardia and arrhythmias can occur because the vagal influence is unopposed. In addition, with a cervical lesion, hypotension may occur because there is no sympathetic outflow to maintain peripheral vascular resistance. Cardiovascular reflexes which adjust blood pressure to postural changes are impaired in such cases, and hypotension may manifest itself whenever the patient's position is changed, even side to side. Finally, added to the risk of deep vein thrombosis due to immobility is that from decreased peripheral vascular tone and thus increased tendency for stasis of blood. Absence of muscle tone impairs venous return and contributes to both hypotension and venous thrombosis.

Monitoring of cardiac rate and rhythm should be instituted in patients with cervical cord injury to detect serious arrhythmias or bradycardia that would impair cardiac output. Hypotension is usually time-limited and self-regulating. However, if associated injuries are causing bleeding or sequestering of fluid in third

TABLE 26-11
Relationship of Brainstem and Spinal Segments to Critical Functions
in Acute and Long-Term Spinal Disorders

Muscles	Brainstem or spinal segment	Dermatome reference points	Acute dysfunctions	Functional ability if lesion persists
Soft palate, pharyngeal, tongue	Medulla (CN 9,-10,12)	—	↓ gag, swallow leading to choking, aspiration	Swallowing with retraining if reflex returns; may need permanent esophagostomy
All below trapezius, sternocleidomastoid	C_2	Back of head	Total loss of respiration and movement from shoulder down (such patients now survive with speedy prehospital care)	Requires permanent respirator; can shrug shoulders, turn head (CN11), and use all cranial nerves
Diaphragm	$C_{3,4,5}$	Ear, neckline from clavicle to wrist	↓ or absent diaphragmatic as well as intercostal respiratory effort, high risk of hypotension, hypothermia, ileus, atonic bladder, skin breakdown	Move head, shrug shoulders, breathe with intercostals (after reflexes return); experimental use of phrenic nerve stimulation
Deltoid, biceps	C_6	Lateral third of arm, shoulder to thumb	↓ respiratory function, (diaphragm intact, without intercostals); risk for hypotension, hypothermia, ileus, atonic bladder, skin breakdown	Move head, shoulders; breathe independently but with ↓ reserve; flex elbow, feed self with prosthesis; use electric wheelchair
Latissimus, serratus, pectoralis, radial wrist extensors	C_7	Dorsal mid-arm to 1st/2d digits (dorsal and palmar)	↓ respiratory function (without intercostals); risk for hypotension, hypothermia, atonic bladder, ileus, skin breakdown	Some rolling over; flex elbow, feed self with hand devices; sit up; self propel adapted wheelchair

spaces, cautious volumetric replacement and colloid may be used. Care must be exercised not to put the patient into pulmonary edema through overzealous fluid replacement.

Difficulties with *temperature regulation* are related to loss of peripheral vascular vasodilatation and constriction. Again, the higher the lesion, the less ability the patient has to regulate temperature by constriction and dilatation of skin vessels. The patient becomes *poikilothermic*, taking on the temperature of the environment. Instead of being able to regulate the core temperature through vasodilatation to lose heat through the skin or vasoconstriction to conserve heat, the patient in spinal shock remains with dilated vessels. Most commonly, the functional result is that body temperature drops, particularly in air-conditioned units. However, in extremely warm weather,

hyperthermia may result because the patient can neither sweat below the level of the lesion nor further dilate skin vessels. The patient's environment must be regulated to maintain core temperature. If hypothermia is serious, tympanic membrane or esophageal temperatures may be needed to monitor core temperature. Usually, rectal or oral electronic measurements are sufficient, however, to note trends in temperature. In no case should touch or skin temperatures be relied upon to monitor the patient's temperature status. Warming may be accomplished by blankets, increasing the room temperature, or by electrical heating or cooling devices. It is imperative to remember that the patient cannot feel the latter devices and cannot sense when there is danger of thermal or cold injury.

Loss of gastrointestinal motility may manifest itself

TABLE 26-11 (Continued)
Relationship of Brainstem and Spinal Segments to Critical Functions
in Acute and Long-Term Spinal Disorders

Muscles	Brainstem or spinal segment	Dermatome reference points	Acute dysfunctions	Functional ability if lesion persists
Triceps, finger extensors and flexors	C_8	Medial third of arm to include digits 3 and 4	↓ respiratory function; risk of hypotension, hypothermia, ileus, atonic bladder, skin breakdown	Feed self with devices; roll over, sit up; transfer; dress; toilet; move in bed unassisted
Hand intrinsics, ulnar wrist and fingers	T_1	Midpectoral (T_4 is at nipple line)	↓ respiratory function; risk of hypotension, hypothermia, ileus, atonic bladder, skin breakdown	Independent eating, moving in bed, toilet, use of wheelchair, respiratory reserve
Upper intercostals, upper back	T_6	Two segments below nipple, three segments above umbilicus (T_{10})	Ileus, atonic bladder, skin breakdown; low risk of hypotension and hypothermia	Normal respiratory reserve; independent in all of above; stand with bracing
Abdominals, thoracic extensors	T_{12}	Between umbilicus (T_{10}) and inguinal fold (L_1)	Atonic bladder, fecal retention	Ambulate with bracing; reflex bowel and bladder (true of all lesions above sacral cord)

Note: All lesions above T_6 have high risk for hypotension and hypothermia/hyperthermia due to interruption in sympathetic outflow. These same persons are at increased risk for autonomic hyperreflexia in the rehabilitation period. All lesions above the lumbar level carry high potential of paralytic ileus; all lesions above sacral cord will have atonic bladder and anal sphincter during the acute phase. Lesions above the sacrum convert to reflex, and uninhibited bladder and bowel when reflexes return. Sacral lesions are most apt to retain atonic bladder and bowel secondary to absent reflexes.

in paralytic ileus. One should not wait for distension and vomiting before assessing gastrointestinal function. Any patient with a sensory level above T_8 (output to the splanchnic plexus) is at risk for decreased gastric motility. Note in Fig. 26-10 that L_1 is just above the inguinal crease. Thus patients with lesions between the inguinal fold and umbilicus (and above) should be evaluated for ileus.

Bowel sounds should be assessed regularly and low nasogastric suction begun if they are decreased or absent.

Bowel and bladder elimination will be impaired by a variety of lesions above the sacral cord. The majority of both sympathetic and parasympathetic input is from the lumbar and sacral plexuses. Therefore almost any cord injury or polyneuropathy affecting the lower extremities can be expected to have bowel and bladder involvement. Until reflexes return, the bladder will fill and distend just as does the bowel.

Periodic release of urine with intermittent or continuous catheterization will be necessary. Nasogastric suction and intravenous feeding will be required until bowel sounds return. If feces are present in the rectum, manual removal or gentle enemas may be needed until rectal reflexes return. The presence of rectal reflexes can be determined by inserting a gloved finger in the rectum. The rectal sphincter will contract on the finger if the reflex is present.

Finally, the *integument* is at high risk for breakdown in the paralyzed patient. Loss of sympathetic tone, diminished trophic influence of motor nerves, and paralysis combine in a paralyzed limb or body to create a more rapid breakdown of skin under pressure. Studies in both animals and humans have demonstrated histological evidence of tissue destruction within 1 to 2 h of sustained pressure in normal tissue; this time is shortened by as much as half in paralyzed tissue. In the person with either segmental or suprasegmental motor loss, mechanical devices which vary pressure over body surfaces and frequent change of position are imperative from the moment of admission. Skin breakdown can occur in the severely immobilized myasthenia gravis patient as well, but is not so rapid as in the disorders of central or peripheral nerves. Death from sepsis secondary to pressure sores was the major cause of death in spinal cord injury prior to the development of modern spinal cord injury centers. It remains one of the major sources of disability and hospitalization.

Special Considerations in Myasthenia Gravis

Of the disorders used as examples of disturbance in motor function at various levels of the nervous system, myasthenia gravis is the most unpredictable and unstable. While patients suffering from ascending polyneuropathy may increasingly lose function over a period of days, the patient in myasthenic or cholinergic crisis may lose ability to protect the airway in less than an hour. Furthermore, it is often difficult to determine if increasing weakness is secondary to too little medication (myasthenic state) or too much medication (cholinergic state).

This distinction is of no small importance to the nurse, who must make critical decisions regarding the timing of medication and the institution of supportive respiratory care. Consequently, the characteristics of crisis in myasthenia and of drug therapy will be discussed in more detail than in the other disorders used as examples.

Myasthenia gravis is a disorder of the neuromuscular junction felt to be autoimmune in nature. In ways not clearly understood, antibodies to muscle receptor protein are produced, bind with acetylcholine receptor sites on the muscle, and destroy at least some receptors (Drachman, 1978). The number of acetylcholine receptors is markedly reduced from normal, thus reducing the "margin of safety" in neuromuscular transmission. Normal quantities of acetylcholine are released from the presynaptic nerve terminal, but with repeated stimulation of the nerve, there are not enough receptor sites available; the amplitude of action potentials decreases rapidly and then levels off. With rest, the ability of the muscle to contract returns. Clinically, the patient experiences increasing weakness with continued effort and weakness of specific muscle groups. Some patients have only weakness of the extraocular muscles, with continual or intermittent diplopia and ptosis. Others may have primarily head and upper extremity weakness, and others may

have involvement of all extremities as well as head and neck.

Onset is bimodal, with women more often affected between 20 and 30 years and men between 50 and 60 years. Spontaneous remissions do occur, although remission is more likely following thymectomy in young women. The critical-care nurse is most likely to care for a person with myasthenia who has lost or is at high risk for losing the ability to protect the airway for one of the following reasons: myasthenic crisis (severe weakness with decreasing response to medication), cholinergic crisis (severe weakness plus cholinergic signs due to overdosage with medication), and post-thymectomy. Myasthenic crisis may be directly related to increased demands upon the patient's system, such as severe illness or surgical procedures unrelated to the myasthenia, or may be of unknown causes.

Anticholinesterase drugs are the mostly commonly used treatment for myasthenia. Pyridostigmine bromide (Mestinon) is the most widely used. Neostigmine (prostigmine) is shorter acting and less used for maintenance. However, it can be given parenterally and may be used more often in acute situations. Edrophonium chloride (Tensilon) is an extremely short-acting anticholinesterase, used diagnostically. All anticholinesterase agents act to prevent acetylcholinesterse from chemically breaking acetylcholine in the synaptic cleft into acetate and choline. Such chemical breakdown of the acetylcholine ends depolarization of the muscle membrane and allows the muscle to repolarize and thus be ready for another action potential. Since the number of receptor sites is reduced in myasthenia, prolongation of depolarization allows somewhat longer firing of fewer fibers and thus increased muscle contraction. Obviously, excessive prolongation of depolarization can result in *increased* weakness if further nerve impulses are unable to initiate further action potentials. Consequently, muscle weakness can result from too much anticholinesterase medication as well as from too little. While the drug treatment of myasthenia can dramatically improve the patient's ability to carry on daily tasks, it does not alter the basic pathology.

While patients on neurology units of a hospital may be well enough to administer their own anticholinesterase drugs, those in critical care most often must rely upon the nurse to do so. It cannot be overemphasized that timing is crucial. A delay of 15 to 20 min can make the difference between a patient who has sufficient strength to swallow the medication and one who does not. Any patient at risk for or in crisis has the potential for rapid changes in condition and rapid changes in strength. Since excess medication is one cause of increasing weakness, the nurse is frequently in the position to have to decide whether increasing weakness is from too little or too much medication. If it is from too much, the next dose must be omitted. Unfortunately, the clinical presentation of myasthenic and cholinergic crisis are so similar, even the most experienced clinicians may have difficulty making this differentiation.

While both situations produce increasing weakness in the patient, the timing of such weakness is one clue to the cause. Weakness due to myasthenia is apt to come about the time of onset of the medication, whereas weakness due to excess medication usually occurs within the time of onset of action of the drug. Comparison of these times is given in Table 26-12. The presence of abdominal cramps, salivation, diarrhea, and muscle fasciculations accompanied by increased weakness are also highly suggestive of cholinergic (drug excess) rather than myasthenic state. If the increasing weakness is clearly drug-related, the next dose must be omitted to prevent precipitation of life-threatening cholinergic crisis. However, it is often difficult to tell if the weakness is related to too much or too little anticholinesterase drug. In such cases, the physician will often elect to perform a *Tensilon test* (edrophonium chloride). Tensilon is a rapid-acting, short-duration drug. If weakness is due to excess drug, the weakness will become even worse and often be associated with cramping with the addition of Tensilon. The patient's clinical condition will improve with Tensilon if weakness is secondary to too little anticholinesterase. Because the drug lasts only minutes, both worsening and improvement in condition are transient. The nurse must be prepared to administer atropine sulfate to reverse the anticholinesterase effect and to suction or even ventilate the patient if the Tensilon test precipitates a cholinergic crisis. However, used judiciously, the Tensilon test can often prevent crisis by distinguishing between the two states before dysphagia and bulbar weakness is pronounced.

First-Level Nursing Management of Extracerebral Motor Problems

Management of respiratory and multisystem problems secondary to extracerebral motor dysfunction can be considered in the context of first, second, third, and fourth levels of nursing care, as was management of intracerebral dysfunction (Jones et al., 1978). Of the disorders, which may cause severe extracerebral motor dysfunction, a few are amenable to prevention, or *first-level care*. These disorders may be classed as (1) traumatic (spinal cord injury), (2) toxic (diphtheric polyneuropathy, tetanus, botulism), or (3) chemical (organophosphates). Although plausible theories regarding causation of disorders such as Guillain-Barré syndrome and myasthenia gravis have been advanced, knowledge is insufficient at present to prescribe preventive measures.

Prevention of Trauma

Motor vehicle accidents are the primary cause of both head and spinal cord trauma, with accidents related to such activities as diving, skiing, and skateboarding close behind. The use of such safety devices as seat belts and helmets and proper training in the use of

---

TABLE 26-12
Time of Action for Selected Drugs for Myasthenia Gravis

Drug	Onset	Peak	Duration
Edrophonium (Tensilon: used diagnostically only)	30 s	30–60 s	4–5 min
Neostigmine (Prostigmine)	30 min	1–2 h	2–3 h
Pyridostigmine (Mestinon)	30 min	1–2 h	2–4 h
Parenteral neostigmine	10–15 min	30 min	2–3 h

the vehicle or the technique of the sport are likely to be the most effective preventive measures. The message of an excellent film, "Consequences of Spinal Cord Injury,"[1] is train properly, know your limitations, and use protective equipment. Unfortunately, over 70 percent of head injuries are still caused by the greater than 2 million automobile accidents in the United States each year. An additional 5000 to 6000 accident-related spinal cord injuries occur yearly (Smart and Saunders, 1976), with the preponderance of those injured being male and in the 16 to 25 year age group. The long-term consequences of spinal cord injury are staggering if paraplegia or quadriplegia result. In 1974, of 5000 persons with spinal cord injuries, 2000 were dead on arrival at the hospital. Of the 3000 who survived, 1700 were left paraplegic and 1200 were quadriplegic. In 1974 dollars, the average cost to the patient for the injury care and the first year after was $46,000 ($144,470 for quadriplegics and $72,640 for paraplegics). Lost earnings, hypothetically, from age 20 onward were $187,000 for quadriplegics and $102,000 for paraplegics. The average cost to maintain an independent life for a quadriplegic in 1974 was in excess of $20,000. This cost included such one-time items as adaptive equipment, medical costs, and salary for part-time or full-time attendants (Smart and Saunders, 1976). Social, personal, and economic costs of spinal cord injury are high, and it behooves all health personnel to become involved in efforts to prevent such accidents.

Prevention of Toxic Disorders

The life-threatening motor problems caused by tetanus, botulism, and diphtheric neuropathy are totally preventable by prevention of the basic disorders. Table 26-13 summarizes the sites of action, critical-care problems, and management of these disorders in relation to the endotoxins which attack the nervous system. It is evident that once the endotoxin has been made in the body, there is little in the way of definitive treatment. Expert nursing care is the key to the survival of such persons until the endotoxin is no longer formed and the body can heal itself. How much better to have been appropriately immunized or to have prepared food properly in the first place! Both diphtheria and tetanus are completely preventable by

appropriate immunization in childhood, with booster doses for tetanus at 10-year intervals. Toxoid boosters can be given to persons previously immunized and exposed to diphtheria or who sustain a contaminated injury (tetanus).

Botulism most commonly occurs following the ingestion of food containing botulinus toxin. Improperly cooked home-canned foods are the most common source. The best prevention for botulism then is to follow canning directions carefully, especially for nonacid foods. Many recommend boiling home-canned nonacid foods prior to eating as an additional precaution.

Prevention of Chemically Related Motor Dysfunction

The only chemically related preventable disorder is the severe anticholinesterase effect seen with organophosphates. While most organophosphates are not seen in civilian use, they are the active ingredient of some insecticides commercially available. Severe organophosphate poisoning can cause death by preventing repolarization of muscle membrane.

Third-Level Nursing Management of Extracerebral Motor Disorders

Critical-care nurses may be involved as citizens in general efforts to prevent the above motor disorders. However, in the workaday world, the majority of professional effort and skill is involved in *third-level nursing care*—measures which deal with an existing disorder and which prevent further complications not an inevitable part of the pathological process (Jones et al., 1978). Detection of incipient airway, respiratory, and swallowing problems, management of multisystem involvement, and special considerations in drug therapy of myasthenia gravis have been considered earlier in the chapter. In this section, the emphasis will be on minimizing the extent of spinal cord trauma and helping the patient manage bulbar dysfunction and the psychosocial problems of an alert, immobilized patient.

Minimizing the Extent of Spinal Cord Trauma

Although critical-care nurses are not often the first to receive the newly spinal-injured patient, the principles of movement and transfer of such patients from the moment of injury are crucial to prevention of further damage to spine or cord. Nothing is more tragic than

---

[1]Regional Spinal Cord Injury Center, Department of Rehabilitation Medicine, University of Washington, Seattle, Wash. 98195.

TABLE 26-13

Comparison of Sites of Action, Critical Problems, and Management of Movement Problems Caused by Endotoxins

Endotoxin	Site of action	Effect	Management
Tetanus—tetanospasmin made by *Clostridium tetani*	Local effect on muscle. Major effect is to interfere with spinal inhibitory neurons	Sustained muscle contraction: rigidity, stiffness progressing to paroxysmal spasms without loss of consciousness. Death can occur from apnea, suffocation, 2° spasm of glottal muscles and respiratory muscles. May have circulatory collapse	Single-dose antitoxin (no effect on established symptoms but prevents further endotoxin). Tracheostomy if having spasms; minimal manipulation; sedation; minimal stimulation; nursing care crucial in maintaining quiet environment. Constant monitoring. May use curare if spasms uncontrollable; requires total life support
Diphtheric neuropathy— endotoxin from *Corynbacterium diphtheriae*	Membrane of Schwann cell of proximal peripheral nerve and dorsal root ganglion. Demyelination occurs	Weakness, paralysis of muscles: affects cranial nerves 1–2 weeks after infection; spinal peripheral nerves about 7–10 weeks after infection. Usually descending weakness; bulbar muscles, arms, legs	Symptomatic; antitoxin ineffective once neuropathy established (affects about 20% of patients). Expert nursing care: detection of bulbar symptoms early; tracheostomy if necessary. Prognosis good for recovery if well supported in acute phase.
Botulism—botulinus toxin from *Clostridium botulinum*	Neuromuscular junction; interferes with release of acetylcholine	Weakness, paralysis of bulbar, systemic, and smooth muscles	Expert supportive nursing care; may require complete respiratory, alimental support; symptoms may fluctuate, requiring frequent evaluation

the patient who comes to the hospital with a fractured spine and with moving extremities, but who leaves paraplegic or quadriplegic after inexpert transfer from bed to x-ray to bed.

At the scene of the accident or at the first contact with the patient, one must always keep the possibility of a spinal injury in mind. *Patients with head injury, particularly if unconscious, must be presumed to have cervical spine injury until proven otherwise by x-ray which visualizes all eight cervical vertebrae.* Approximately 10 to 15 percent of head-injured patients have associated cervical spine injuries. In the conscious patient, reported pain over any portion of the spine, parathesias, or decreased sensation in the trunk or extremities or difficulty moving extremities is presumptive evidence of spinal injury. The patient should be transported as if spinal injury were present until this is definitively ruled out by x-ray. Until x-rays have been taken and read, the patient should remain on the emergency vehicle stretcher. Each additional transfer of the patient with an unstable fracture increases the chances of cord compression.

Any patient with a suspected spinal injury must be transported supine on a hard, flat surface. The hard surface is sufficient in itself to immobilize the thoracic or lumbar spine. In suspected cervical spine injury, the head must be in neutral position with the lateral immobilization by sandbags, and preferably a stiff cervical collar. Wide tape or cloth over the forehead and to the spine board will serve to prevent forward flexion. The major objective of neck immobilization is to *prevent flexion, extension, and rotation of the cervical spine.* Figure 26-11 shows one method to manually immobilize the neck while producing maximum visualization of all cervical vertebrae during x-ray.

Transfer of the patient from one surface to another should not be started until a person skilled and trained in such transfers is present to act as team leader. A patient with an unstable fracture will never be harmed by remaining on an emergency vehicle stretcher, but may be permanently paralyzed by improper transfer from it to an emergency room or nursing unit bed. Transfer of the patient with cervical spine injury requires at least four persons: three to support the body and maintain perfect alignment with the head, which is immobilized by the fourth person. The best method of stabilizing the head is to use a cervical traction halter. One hand exerts a gentle cephalad

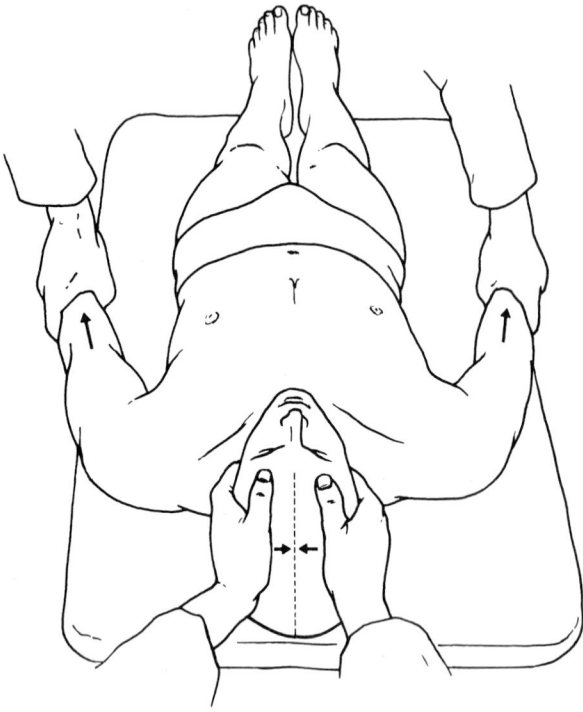

FIGURE 26-11

A method of immobilizing the head and exerting gentle manual traction during x-ray of a patient with suspected cervical spine injury. [*Drawing by Ms. Shirley Baty in Emergency Medicine, 9(12):100, 1977.*]

pull on the ties of the halter and the other is used under the occiput to support the head and neck in neutral alignment. Transfer of the patient with thoracic or lumbar injury is similar, but does not require traction and immobilization of the neck.

If there is an unstable fracture or fracture dislocation, the neurosurgeon or orthopedic surgeon usually applies skeletal traction in the form of skull tongs. The patient in skeletal traction is then maintained on the nursing unit either in a standard bed, Stryker frame, or Roto Rest bed. Cleansing of the insertion sites daily or twice daily and application of antibiotic ointment is useful in preventing local infection around the tongs.

Steroids It is the policy of many institutions to give a bolus of dexamethasone (Decadron) 10 to 20 mg as soon after injury as possible on the grounds that it may reduce cord damage secondary to swelling. While there is evidence of reduced swelling in experimental animal models, there are no controlled studies demonstrating that the use of steroids ultimately alters the outcome of spinal cord injury in man. A number of other experimental techniques such as perfusion of the cord with hypothermic solutions and myelotomy and pharmacologic agents (intended to prevent accumulation of norepinephrine at the injury site) are being studied intensively in animal models. Local cooling has been attempted in man at several centers, but definitive controlled studies remain to be done.

Nursing management Table 26-11 summarizes the major clinical problems faced by the spinal cord–injured patient related to level of injury. Knowledge of the level of spine injury from the x-ray findings plus mapping of sensory dermatomes will enable the nurse to focus observation on those problems most likely to occur for each patient. *Sensory level* can be mapped best by beginning in areas which are known to be anesthetic and moving upward, asking the patient to tell when the pin feels sharper. This level should be marked on the skin to note a baseline and aid in determining if the level of injury is extending. Swelling and intracord hemorrhage in the first hours after injury can extend the level of damage both up and down the cord.

The first days or weeks following cord injury are characterized by a state of *spinal shock* in which all connections below the level of the lesion appear to be afunctional. All skeletal muscle and autonomic reflexes are absent for all segments below the lesion, and often for several segments above, presumably due to edema. It is during this time that the patient is most apt to develop respiratory insufficiency, hypotension (due to inability to vasoconstrict), paralytic ileus, atonic bladder with retention, constipation, and skin breakdown. Management of these problems was discussed under multisystem involvement.

Management of Bulbar Dysfunction

The bulbar muscles are those innervated by cranial nerves located in the brainstem, or "bulb." Although bulbar dysfunction in disorders such as myasthenia gravis is not caused by cranial nerve dysfunction, the functional outcome is the same: potential aspiration and upper airway obstruction. Most crucial in managing bulbar dysfunction is *early detection of failing function*. Whether the disorder is diphtheric neuropathy, Guillain-Barré syndrome, or myasthenia gravis, signs of impending bulbar insufficiency are similar: increasing apprehension, pooling of secretions in the mouth and pharynx, increased nasality of speech, dysarthria, and possibly dysfunction of eye movements, facial expression, gag reflex, and cough. Ability to swallow can be tested using the myasthenic check in Table 26-10 for all "bulbar" disorders. The most difficult substance to swallow is water; therefore swallowing should be tested with crushed ice chips if there is any question of aspiration. If the patient cannot swallow saliva, tracheostomy with a cuffed tube is mandatory to prevent aspiration. In the prototypic disorders of cranial nerve musculature used in this chapter, bulbar dysfunction is likely to be associated with respiratory insufficiency as well, necessitating assisted ventilation. Evaluation of respiratory status is described earlier in this chapter.

Drug therapy of myasthenia gravis was described earlier. Corticosteroids (usually prednisone) are used adjunctively in many patients with myasthenia, particularly those refractory to anticholinesterase drugs. Plasmapheresis is being tested in some centers but is still experimental (Blount et al., 1979). The patient who is begun on steroids may become temporarily more weak and must thus be observed even more closely for bulbar dysfunction. Steroids are also used by many physicians in treating Guillain-Barré syndrome, although there is no clear evidence of efficacy. Based on the theory that the disorder is an autoimmune phenomenon, plasmapheresis has been tried experimentally on polyneuropathy (Brettle et al., 1978).

Psychological Care of the Alert, Immobilized Patient

Although the pathological processes which create extracranial life-threatening motor dysfunction are quite different, they all have the potential to create a severely immobilized person who is fully alert and aware of what is happening. The patient with Guillain-Barré syndrome lives with paralysis creeping upward rather rapidly; the patient with tetanus experiences growing stiffness, culminating in suffocating muscular spasm; the person with myasthenia never knows if the next dose of medication can be swallowed, or worse, if breath will come the next hour. Finally, the patient with a cervical spine injury is transformed suddenly from a healthy active young adult to a person who cannot even breathe alone. Coupled with these devastating changes in body image and function are the frightening sights and sounds of critical care. Many of these patients have only the ceiling or floor to look at and can only imagine the worst about what is happening.

The reactions of most persons with acute, life-threatening illnesses follow a similar pattern: fear, denial, anger, depression, and resolution. In the critical-care setting one is most likely to see alternating fear, anger, and denial. While few patients deny that they cannot move at the moment, most deny that this situation will be permanent. Such denial probably has both physiological and psychological protective value in the critical-care stage. It is appropriate to support the patient's hope for complete recovery in such disorders as Guillain-Barré syndrome and diphtheric polyneuropathy, as this is consistent with the natural history of the disorders. False hope should not be offered the patient with an apparent complete spinal cord injury; neither should the patient be forced to abandon denial of severity of injury. With modern rehabilitative techniques, most persons with spinal cord injuries can expect to lead an independent life. A recent study of the attitudes of nurses toward spinal cord–injured patients suggests that critical-care nurses were the most pessimistic compared to intermediate care and rehabilitation nurses (Leinart, 1979). This pessimism probably reflects exposure to these patients during their bleakest time, and may make it difficult for critical-care unit nurses to offer sincere hope to these patients.

Coupled with the abrupt change in life-style and the reasonable fears which the patient has regarding survival is the difficulty of communicating inherent in tracheostomy and assisted ventilation. It is crucial to invent some means of communication which allows more than "yes" and "no" answers whenever possible. If the patient has any strength in the mouth, a letter board and mouthstick can be used to point out phrases and individual letters. Some patients have been able to use Morse code through eye blinks or small finger taps.

Fear can express itself in both anger and incessant requests for nurse attention. Firm limits regarding what the nurse can and cannot do and when may help provide a sense of security for the patient, *provided* the nurse is consistent in letting the patient know what to expect and consistently follows through. It is important to remember that increased anxiety can reflect respiratory insufficiency as well as psychological response to injury.

Patients with severe extracranial motor dysfunction may spend long periods in critical care if ventilatory assistance is required. Consequently, the axiom that rehabilitation begins in critical care is certainly true with these patients. Skin care to prevent pressure sores, passive range of motion to prevent contractures, and attention to psychological needs are second only to measures to preserve life.

SUMMARY

Neurological disorders can threaten life in two ways: disruption of consciousness with attendant disruption in voluntary self care, and disruption of motor function sufficient to create respiratory insufficiency. Detection of incipient brain herniation is the focus of assessment and intervention in critical disorders which disrupt consciousness. Assessment of respiratory function, airway protection, and potential for aspiration is crucial in extracerebral motor disorders which do not impair consciousness. Interaction of body systems innervated by the central nervous system necessitates evaluation of circulatory, temperature, gastrointestinal urinary, and integumentary function, as well as individualized psychosocial interventions.

REFERENCES

Adams, R., and M. Victor: *Principles of Neurology,* New York: McGraw-Hill, 1977.

Allen, M. B., et al.: *A Manual of Neurosurgery,* Baltimore: University Park Press, 1978.

Bartol, G.: Psychological needs of the spinal cord injured person, *J Neurosurg Nurs* 10: 171–175, 1978.

Bates, D., et al.: A prospective study of non-traumatic coma: Methods and results in 310 patients, *Ann Neurol* 2:211–220, 1977.

Blount, A. B., A. B. Kinney, and M. Stone: Plasma exchange in the management of myasthenia gravis, *Nurs Clin North Am* 14(1):173–190, 1979.

Brettle, R. R., et al.: Treatment of acute polyneuropathy by plasma exchange, *Lancet* 2:1100, 1978.

Bucy, P. C., and P. L. Perot: Injury to the spinal cord, in D. B. Tower (ed.), *The Nervous System,* vol. 2, *The Clinical Neurosciences,* New York: Raven Press, 1975, pp. 421–431.

Celesia, G. G.: Modern concepts of status epilepticus, *JAMA* 235:1571–1574, 1976.

Cerrato, D., C. Ariano, and F. Fiacchino: Deep vein thrombosis and low-dose heparin prophylaxis in neurosurgical patients, *J Neurosurgery* 49:378–381, 1978.

Claggett, G. P., and E. W. Salzman: Prevention of venous thrombosis in surgical patients, *N Engl J Med* 290:93–96, 1978.

Conomy, J. P., and J. O. McNamara: Emergency management of the patient with seizures, II. Generalized status epilepticus, *Postgrad Med* 55(2):71–81, 1974.

Cooper, P. R., et al.: Dexamethasone and severe head injury: A prospective double-blind study, *J Neurosurg* 51:307–316, 1979.

Crill, W. E.: Suprasegmental control of movement, in H. Patton, et al. (eds.), *Introduction to Basic Neurology,* Philadelphia: Saunders, 1977, pp. 269–280.

Drachman, D.: Myasthenia gravis, *N Engl J Med* (Part 1) 298:136–142; (Part 2) 298:186–193, 1978.

Giblin, E.: Controlling high blood pressure, *Am J Nurs* 78:824, 1978.

Gudeman, S. K., J. D. Miller, and D. P. Becker: Failure of high dose steroids to influence intracranial pressure in patients with severe head injury, *J Neurosurg* 51:301–306, 1979.

Guttman, L.: *Spinal Cord Injuries: Comprehensive Management and Research,* Oxford: Blackwell Scientific Publications, 1973.

Hughes, R., et al.: Controlled trial of prednisolone in acute polyneuropathy, *Lancet* 2:700–703, 1978.

Jennett, B., and G. Teasdale: Predicting outcome in individual patients after severe head injury, *Lancet* 1:1031–1034, 1976.

Jennett, B., et al.: Severe head injury in three countries, *J Neurol Neurosurg Psychiat* 40: 291–298, 1977.

Joffe, S. M.: Incidence of postoperative deep vein thrombosis in neurosurgical patients, *J Neurosurg* 42:201–203, 1975.

Johns, T. R.: Treatment of myasthenia gravis; long term administration of corticosteroids with remarks on thymectomy, *Advan Neurol* 17:99–122, 1977.

Jones, C.: Glasgow coma scale, *Am J Nurs* 79:1551–1553, 1979.

Jones, D. A., C. F. Dunbar, and M. M. Jirovec: *Medical-Surgical Nursing: A Conceptual Approach,* New York: McGraw-Hill, 1978, pp. 16–17.

Kealy, S.: Respiratory care in Guillain-Barré syndrome, *Am J Nurs* 77:58–60, 1977.

Kinney, A. B., and M. Blount: Systems approach to myasthenia gravis, *Nurs Clin North Am* 6(3):435–453, 1971.

Larrabee, J. H.: The person with spinal cord injury: Physical care during early recovery, *Am J Nurs* 77:1320–1329, 1977.

Leinart, B.: Attitudes of nurses toward spinal cord injury patients, *ARN* (Journal of the Association of Rehabilitation Nurses) 4(1):7–9, 1979.

Magnaes, B.: Body position and cerebrospinal fluid pressure, Part 1: Clinical studies on the effect of rapid postural changes, *J Neurosurg* 44:687–697, 1976.

Marshall, L. F., R. W. Smith, and H. M. Shapiro: The outcome with aggressive treatment in severe head injuries, Part 1: The significance of intracranial pressure monitoring, *J Neurosurg* 50:20–25, 1979a.

Marshall, L. F., R. W. Smith, and H. M. Shapiro: The outcome with aggressive treatment in severe head injuries, Part 2: Acute and chronic barbiturate administration in the management of head injury, *J Neurosurg* 50:26–30, 1979b.

Maynard, F. M., et al.: Neurological prognosis after traumatic quadriplegia, *J Neurosurg* 50: 611–616, 1970.

Meldrum, B.: Physiological changes during prolonged seizures and epileptic brain dramage, *Neuropadiatrie* 9:203–212, 1978.

Meldrum, B., R. A. Vigoureux, and J. B. Brierly: Systemic factors and epileptic brain damage; prolonged seizures in paralysed artificially ventilated baboons, *Arch Neurol* 29: 82–87, 1973.

Miller, J. D.: Volume and pressure in the craniospinal axis, *Clin Neurosurg* 22:76–105, 1975.

Miller, J. D., and P. Leech: Effects of mannitol and steroid therapy on intracranial volume-pressure relationships in patients, *J Neurosurg* 42:274–281, 1975.

Miller, J. D., et al.: Significance of intracranial hypertension in severe head injury, *J Neurosurg* 47:503–516, 1977.

Mitchell, P. H., and N. K. Mauss: Relationship of patient-nurse activity to intracranial pressure variations: A pilot study, *Nurs Res* 27:4–10, 1978.

Mitchell, P. H., N. K. Mauss, H. Lipe, and J. Ozuna: Effects of patient-nurse activity on ICP, in K. Shulman et al. (eds.), *Intracranial Pressure IV,* Berlin: Springer, 1980, pp. 565–568.

Nicolaides, A. N., and J. T. Hobbs: Diagnosis of venous thrombosis by the ^{125}I-fibrinogen test, in J. Bergen and S. T. Yao (eds.), *Venous Problems,* Chicago: Yearbook, 1978, pp. 213–226.

Nornes, H., and B. Magnaes: Supratentorial epidural pressure recorded during posterior fossa surgery, *J Neurosurg* 35:541–549, 1971.

Pepper, G. A.: A person with spinal cord injury: Psychological care, *Am J Nurs* 77:1330–1336, 1977.

Phillipson, E. A.: Control of breathing during sleep, *Am Rev* 118:909–939, 1978.

Pitts, L. H., and J. Kaktis: The effect of megadose steroids on ICP in traumatic coma, in K. Shulman et al. (eds.), *Intracranial Pressure IV,* Berlin: Springer, 1980, pp. 638–642.

Plum, F., and J. Posner: *Diagnosis of Stupor and Coma,* 2d ed., Philadelphia: F. A. Davis, 1972.

Report of the Task Force on the Role of Nursing in High Blood Pressure Control: *Guidelines for Educating Nursing in High Blood Pressure,* DHEW Publication #77-1241, U.S. Government Printing Office, 1976.

Rimel, R. W., and G. W. Tyson: The neurologic examination in patients with central nervous system trauma, *J Neurosurg Nurs* 11:148–155, 1979.

Robinson, A.: Detection and control of hypertension: Challenge to all nurses, *Am J Nurs* 76:778–780, 1976.

Roglitz, C.: Team approach in the acute phase of spinal injury, *J Neurosurg Nurs* 10:117–120, 1978.

Shalit, M. N., and R. Umansky: Effect of bedside procedures on intracranial pressure, *Israeli J Med Sci* 13:881–886, 1977.

Shapiro, H. M.: Intracranial hypertension, *Anesthesiology* 43:443–469, 1975.

Silver, J. R.: The prophylactic use of anticoagulant therapy in the prevention of pulmonary emboli in 100 consecutive spinal cord injury patients, *Paraplegia* 12:188–196, 1974.

Smart, C. N., and C. R. Saunders: *The Cost of Motor Vehicle-Related Spinal Cord Injury,* Wash., D.C.: Insurance Institute for Highway Safety, 1976.

Teasdale, G.: Acute impairment of brain function. 1. Assessing "conscious level," *Nurs Times* 71:914–917, 1975.

Teasdale, G., and S. Galbraith: Acute impairment of brain function. 2. Observation record chart, *Nurs Times* 71:972–973, 1975.

Teasdale, G., and B. Jennett: Assessment of coma and impaired consciousness. A practical scale, *Lancet* 2:81–84, 1974.

Teasdale, G., R. Knill-Jones, and J. Van der Sande: Observer variability in assessing impaired consciousness and coma, *J Neurol Neurosurg Psychiat* 41(7):603–610, 1978.

Tribe, C. R.: Causes of death in the early and late stages of paraplegia, *Paraplegia* 1:19–46, 1963.

Watson, N.: Venous thrombosis and pulmonary embolism in spinal cord injury, *Paraplegia,* 6:113–121, 1968.

Watson, N.: Anticoagulant therapy in the treatment of venous thrombosis and pulmonary embolism in acute spinal injury. *Paraplegia,* 12:197–201, 1974.

Weller, D. J., and P. M. Miller: Emotional reactions of patient, family and staff in the acute period of spinal cord injury, *Social Work Health Care* 3(1):7–17, 1977.

Wilensky, A. J., and J. A. Lowden: Inadequate serum levels of after intramuscular administration of diphenylhydantoin, *Neurology (Minneap)* 23:318–324, 1973.

The scope of this chapter will extend beyond diagnosed endocrine disorders to include those endocrine abnormalities which result from or exist in critical illness. Some of the endocrine disorders which require critical care are diabetic comas, thyroid storm, myxedema coma, adrenal crisis, and hypercalcemic crises. Management of endocrine crises alone, however, does not constitute endocrine critical care.

In a sense, every critically ill patient has endocrine abnormalities. Hormonal variations from normal are caused by the stress of critical illness, by changes in the sleep-wake cycle, and by various drugs and anesthesias. Lab values show these variations. For example, an elevated blood glucose is abnormal but expected in the patient with an acute myocardial infarction. This is because catecholamine inhibits insulin release and stress increases the secretion of adrenalin, cortisol, and other hormones which elevate blood sugar. The critical patient with adrenocortical competence will show high normal or elevated serum cortisol level, since stress increases cortisol secretion.

Critical illness creates many problems for patients with chronic endocrine disorders. Persons with diabetes or Addison's disease, for instance, require more than routine care for myocardial infarction or other critical illness. Standardized care protocol must be supplemented with nursing interventions based upon understanding of endocrine physiology and a given pathological process. The next section of this chapter will address the nursing care required by any critically ill patient who has diabetes. A discussion of diabetic crises, diabetic ketoacidosis, hyperglycemic hyperosmolar nonketotic coma, and hypoglycemia follows. Critical-care aspects of long-term complications of diabetes are described. Finally, there is information on nondiabetic endocrine crises, thyroid storm, myxedema coma, adrenal crisis, and hypercalcemia.

DIABETIC ENDOCRINE CRISES

Managment of the Critically Ill Diabetic Patient

Management of the critically ill diabetic patient involves giving special attention to monitoring and controlling blood glucose levels and to preventing infection and thromboembolic phenomena. Monitoring diabetes includes blood sugar testing and urine testing. Control of blood glucose focuses on insulin, caloric intake, and drugs which cause hyperglycemia.

27

ENDOCRINE DISORDERS

Madeline Musante Wake

DIABETIC ENDOCRINE CRISES
Management of the Critically Ill Diabetic Patient
Hyperglycemic Crises
Hyperosmolar Hyperglycemic Nonketotic Coma
Hypoglycemia
Long-Term Complications
NONDIABETIC ENDOCRINE CRISES
Thyroid Crises
Adrenal Crisis
Hypercalcemic Crises

REFERENCES

Blood Glucose Determinations

As previously stated, critical illness often causes an elevation of blood glucose. Except in extreme cases such as diabetic ketoacidosis in an undiagnosed diabetic, the diagnosis of diabetes is not made during critical illness. The glucose tolerance test is used to diagnose diabetes after the resolution of the critical illness when results are not skewed by the stress state.

The blood glucose can change rapidly in the critically ill person. Laboratory determinations are insufficient for monitoring rapid changes in blood glucose. In addition to periodic laboratory tests for blood sugar, the critical-care nurse should have access to a product like Dextrostix. This product is an enzyme strip test which changes color according to glucose content of blood from a finger-stick sample. Comparison of the strip to a color chart gives range values of 25, 45, 90, 130, 175, and 250, while use of the Eyetone reflectance colorimeter registers a definite blood sugar level. (See Fig. 27-1.)

Urine testing is a legitimate monitoring tool in the critically ill. It should supplement, not replace, blood sugar determinations as a guide for therapy. The various urine tests for sugar have peculiarities which should be known by the nurse. Urine tests differ in the way their plus values equate with milligrams of glucose per 100 mL, as illustrated in Table 27-1. For example, there is a large discrepancy between a 3+ Tes-Tape ($\frac{1}{2}$%) and a 3+ Clinitest (1%). The American Diabetes Association (ADA) has stated in a recent position paper (Kohler, 1978) that urine tests for sugar should be reported by milligrams of sugar per 100 mL.

Clinitest is a copper reduction test which can be performed by using 5 or 2 drops of urine. The ADA states that the 2-drop Clinitest method is the most quantitatively accurate of all urine tests. However, being less specific for glucose than enzyme tests, Clinitest can be affected by aspirin, cephalosporins, penicillin, barbiturates, and other drugs.

Diastix, an enzyme dipstick test, is a convenient test since it is available with an acetone test as Keto-Diastix. This test has limited use in diabetic ketoacidosis, since a high urine acetone inhibits the sugar test. A patient in my experience who tested $\frac{1}{2}$% (1+) sugar and large acetone had a concurrent blood sugar of 750 mg per 100 mL. Negative or low positive sugar test results with a positive acetone should be rechecked with Clinitest or Tes-Tape.

Tes-Tape, an enzyme test, offers the advantages of low cost and an ability to detect false negatives caused by high doses of aspirin or of vitamin C. When vitamin C or aspirin interferes with the sugar test, the glucose migrates up the strip leaving a stripe of green above a yellow area. The nurse should take the reading from the green stripe.

Any urine test is of more value if the individual patient's renal threshold has been estimated by determining blood glucose levels concurrently with urine sugar levels. The relationship between blood glucose and urine sugar varies from patient to patient. A patient with kidney disease may not spill sugar in the urine with a blood glucose of 300 mg per 100 mL. In this case, control is monitored by blood sugars alone.

Insulin

Insulin requirements may change when a diabetic is critically ill. Need for insulin is calculated on the precrisis requirement and results of blood glucose and urine sugar determinations. Often patients who take intermediate or long-acting insulin are changed to multiple doses of regular insulin to allow for faster response to condition changes. One-fourth of the usual daily insulin dose may be given every 6 h and supplemented as necessary. Decreased peripheral circulation may delay uptake of subcutaneous insulin. Diabetics usually controlled with diet and oral hypoglycemic agents may require insulin during the stress of critical illness. All the oral hypoglycemic agents except chlorpropamide (Diabinese) have exhausted their hypoglycemic effect after 24 h unless hepatic function is impaired. Impaired liver function prolongs their effects. Chlorpropamide, which has a duration of 72 h, can be prolonged by renal impairment.

Caloric Intake

Caloric intake affects blood sugar control in the critically ill whether the intake is oral, parenteral, or by feeding tube. Critical illness increases nutritional needs. Protein-calorie malnutrition has been found in one-fourth to one-half of medical-surgical patients hospitalized for 2 weeks or more (Butterworth and Blackburn, 1975). This statistic is no doubt higher for those with prolonged critical illness. Deficient carbohydrate intake can produce starvation ketosis in the critically ill patient. The nurse can consult with the dietitian to determine the patient's nutritional

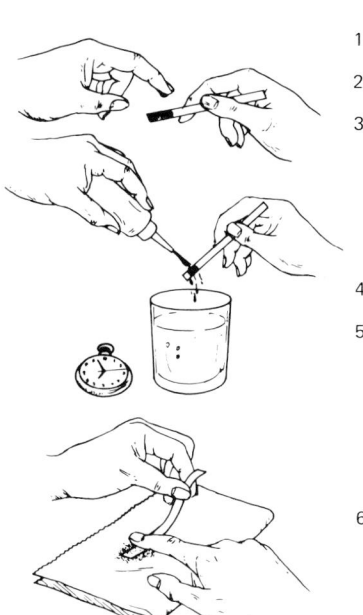

1. Perform daily calibration check, standardization, and control procedures.
2. Place a *large drop* of whole blood on the *entire* reagent area of a Dextrostix reagent strip.
3. (Use capillary [i.e., finger puncture] or venous sample; use only whole blood at room temperature; do not use blood containing fluoride as a preservative.)

4. Wait *exactly* 60 s (use a sweep second hand or timer). Keep the Dextrostix horizontal to avoid blood runoff.
5. Quickly wash off the blood (in 1 or 2 s) with a *sharp stream of water* from an Ames wash bottle. (Do *not* wash under a water faucet.)

6. Blot reagent area of the strip on lint-free absorbent tissue (i.e., heavy paper towel).

7. Insert reacted strip into Eyetone strip guide with reagent area facing meter scale. Push strip in until it stops—*do not force.*
8. Press lid firmly in center. Observe meter needle and record the blood glucose level in blood glucose testing log.

FIGURE 27-1

Eyetone/Dextrostix test procedure. (*Used with permission of Ames Division, Miles Laboratories, Elkhart, Indiana.*)

needs and to assess how those needs are being met. Nutritional intake should be closely monitored on the diabetic patient with prolonged critical illness. Insulin requirements must be altered for the insulin-dependent diabetic receiving parenteral or enteral hyperalimentation.

Drugs Inducing Hyperglycemia

Drugs which increase blood sugar affect the critically ill diabetic. Corticosteroids, diazoxide (Hyperstat, Proglycem), phenytoin (Dilantin), epinephrine, oral contraceptives, and diuretics, especially thiazide di-

TABLE 27-1

Urine Tests for Sugar—Comparison of Plus Values

Test	Grams of glucose per 100 mL								
	0	$\frac{1}{10}$	$\frac{1}{4}$	$\frac{1}{2}$	$\frac{3}{4}$	1	2	3	5
Tes-Tape	N	+	+ +	+ + +			+ + + +		
Diastix	N	Tr	+	+ +		+ + +	+ + + +		
Clinitest 5-drop	N		Tr	+	+ +	+ + +	+ + + +		
Clinitest 2-drop	N		Tr	$\frac{1}{2}$%		1%	2%	3%	5%

uretics, may cause hyperglycemia, which may aggravate existing diabetes or precipitate diabetes in a susceptible individual. Table 27-2 illustrates the mechanisms considered responsible for drug-induced hyperglycemia.

Infection and Thromboembolic Phenomena

Special care is required to prevent infection and thromboembolic phenomena in the critically ill diabetic. Phagocytosis is impaired in uncontrolled diabetes. This fact explains the high incidence of pneumonia, urinary tract infections, and skin infections seen in diabetics. Strategies to prevent infections include judicious use of Foley catheters, diligent care of intravenous and arterial lines, and promotion of effective ventilation.

In uncontrolled diabetes there are abnormalities of platelets and of certain clotting factors which cause hypercoagulation. Incidence of thromboembolic problems can be reduced by measures which prevent stasis of blood. Such measures include adequate hydration, antiembolism stockings, and leg exercises. In assessing any critically ill diabetic, the nurse should be alert to factors which precipitate or indicate infection or thrombus.

Hyperglycemic Crises

The endocrine diagnoses most often seen in critical care are diabetic ketoacidosis (DKA) and hyperosmolar hyperglycemic nonketotic coma (HHNK)—both hyperglycemic crises. Many cases of coma seen in diabetics are due to these entities. However, one cannot assume that coma in a diabetic patient is hyperglycemic coma. Assessment efforts must consider the full spectrum of causes of coma, including lactic acidosis, hypoglycemia, and cerebral vascular accident. Any comatose patient admitted to a critical-care unit should be evaluated for hyperglycemia.

Diabetic Ketoacidosis Pathophysiology

A review of the pathophysiology of diabetes explains the pathogenesis of diabetic ketoacidosis. The primary defect in diabetes is an abnormality of insulin secretion in response to glucose stimulation. This deficiency results in disordered metabolism of carbohydrate, fat, and protein, and has damaging effects on many body tissues. Figure 27-2 illustrates the consequences of insulin deficiency.

The actions of insulin not only include facilitation of glucose transport and promotion of glucose storage. Insulin also enhances free fatty acid uptake, prevents breakdown of the fat depot, and stimulates protein synthesis. All these actions are geared toward storage of nutrients. Stress hormones involved in nutrient regulation—namely, glucagon, cortisol, epinephrine, and growth hormone—are geared to release of nutrients.

In ketosis-prone diabetes, deficiency of insulin and excess of stress hormones cause overproduction of glucose as well as breakdown of fat stores to free fatty acids. Free fatty acids are converted to ketones and glucose in the liver. Conversion of fat and protein stores further raises blood glucose. Hyperglycemia and ketonemia cause osmotic diuresis, leading to dehydration and volume depletion. Excess hydrogen ions dissociated from ketones cause metabolic acidosis. Acidosis is aggravated by poor perfusion.

Precipitating events of DKA include inadequate secretion of endogenous insulin, severe stress, infections, and absence of exogenous insulin. Many cases of DKA are caused by infection, most commonly respiratory, urinary tract, or skin infections. Severe physical or emotional stress can precipitate DKA.

Recognition of DKA

The clinical picture of DKA shows multisystem abnormalities. The hydration status is altered. Osmotic diuresis resulting from hyperglycemia causes as much as a 15 percent loss of total body water. Signs

---

TABLE 27-2
Drugs Inducing Hyperglycemia

Drug*	Mechanism
Corticosteroids	↑gluconeogenesis Antagonize insulin ↓glucose utilization
Diazoxide Hyperstat IV Proglycem (o)	↓insulin secretion Inhibits peripheral glucose utilization
Phenytoin Dilantin	Blocks insulin release
Epinephrine	Stimulates glycogenolysis Blocks insulin release
Diuretics, especially thiazides	K+ loss decreases insulin's effectiveness Toxic to pancreas ? Inhibits insulin release

* Drugs may aggravate existing diabetes or precipitate diabetes in a susceptible person.

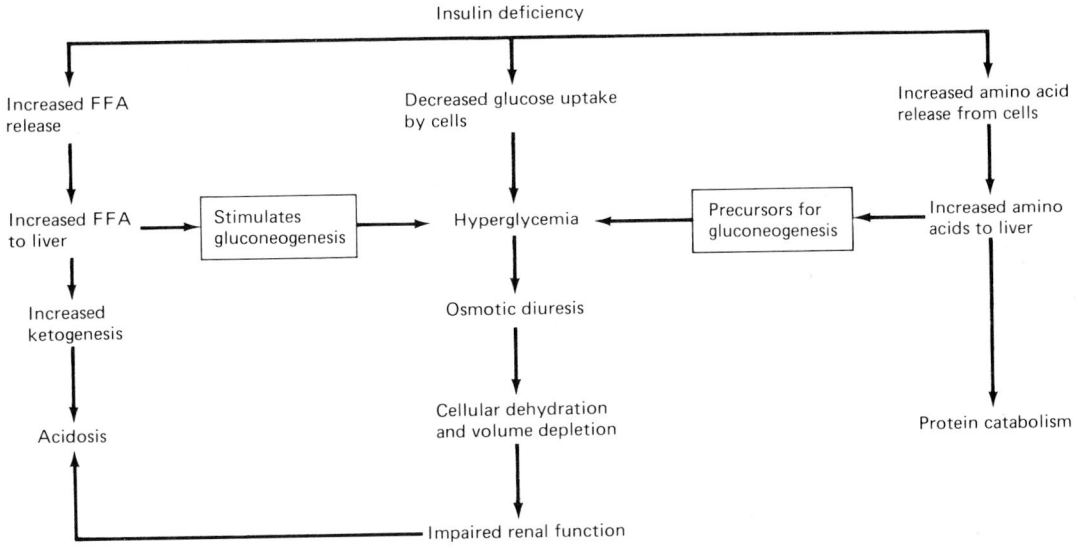

FIGURE 27-2

Metabolic consequences of insulin deficiency. FFA = free fatty acids. (*From Thomas G. Skillman, Diabetic ketoacidosis, Heart & Lung 7:594–602, 1978.*)

and symptoms associated with changing fluid status include polydipsia and polyuria, subsequently changing to oliguria, and warm, dry skin with poor turgor. Cardiovascular evidence of volume depletion may be tachycardia, postural hypotension, hypotension, and decreased pulse pressure. Fluid loss may be accompanied by loss of electrolytes, significantly potassium.

Respirations are characteristically Kussmaul. The increased rate and depth indicate respiratory compensation for metabolic acidosis. However, a pH under 7.0 disrupts this compensatory action, resulting in slow respirations. Acetone excreted by the lungs gives the breath a fruity odor. Lungs are generally clear upon auscultation, even in severe pneumonia, because of the dehydration. Dehydration also accounts for absence of x-ray evidence of pneumonia. As the patient is rehydrated, rales may become present and infiltrates appear on x-ray. Dehydration can cause pleuritic pain and friction rubs which disappear upon rehydration (Matz, 1970).

The state of consciousness is altered from drowsiness to coma. The level of consciousness correlates with the degree of hyperglycemia and hyperosmolarity.

Nausea is often an early sign of DKA. It can warn of ketosis even before the urine acetone is positive. As DKA progresses, vomiting can become a problem since it intensifies the fluid loss. Another gastrointestinal symptom is pain. Abdominal pain with rigidity can be severe, and because it is often accompanied by an elevated white blood cell (WBC) count, it causes physicians to consider the diagnosis of "acute abdomen." The pain of DKA is related to dehydration and/or ketosis and disappears with fluid restoration.

Monitoring in DKA

Monitoring the patient with DKA includes use of blood tests and urine tests. Initial tests for the patient with suspected DKA include blood glucose, serum acetone, blood gases, electrolytes, serum osmolality, urea nitrogen, and hematocrit, as well as urine sugar, acetone, and specific gravity. The blood urea nitrogen, hematocrit, and specific gravity reflect the hydration status. Continuous assessment of hydration is done by hourly checks of specific gravity as well as accurate recording of intake and output. Response to rehydration is assessed clinically, often with the aid of central venous pressure monitoring.

Glucose, pH, and potassium can change rapidly and significantly and are monitored closely in the first hours of treatment. Urine is tested for sugar and acetone hourly. Blood sugar determinations are done every 1 to 2 h. Yet, even hourly determinations do not assure prompt recognition of a falling sugar. Immediate testing with a Dextrostix should be used when an abrupt fall is suspected.

As treatment of DKA corrects the altered metabolism, the body shifts back to use of carbohydrate as a substrate for energy production. Blood glucose falls, acidosis corrects, and potassium falls. Potassium levels are assessed by laboratory tests, ECG monitoring, and clinical signs. Since in acidosis hydrogen ions migrate into cells and force potassium ions out, the initial potassium level in DKA is usually deceptively high. As the pH of urine reaches its limit of acidity, potassium ions are excreted, causing a total body potassium deficit. The potassium shift into the cell with correction of acidosis can cause a dangerous hypokalemia. The lower the pH, the more the potassium will fall when acidosis is corrected. The change from Kussmaul to normal respirations is a clinical indicator of correction of acidosis and suggests a falling potassium. Potassium level should be checked and supplements instituted.

Management of DKA

The medical goals in the treatment of DKA are to restore fluid volume, replace electrolytes, correct the metabolic crisis, treat the underlying condition, and avoid complications. To achieve these ends, the medical therapy for DKA has changed much in the last few years.

Shock is the most common cause of death from DKA. This statistic accounts for the recent changes in treatment emphasis. Instead of reduction of blood sugar, the chief therapy priority is now replacement of fluids. Isotonic saline is given 500 to 1000 mL per hour for the first 2 to 3 h to replace fluid and sodium. In severe cases, plasma and other volume expanders may be used. If the bicarbonate is very low (under 5 meq/L), 0.45% saline with 44 meq sodium bicarbonate may be given.

Bicarbonate is no longer given routinely in DKA, because rapid correction of acidosis alters the oxyhemoglobin dissociation curve, precipitates hypokalemia, and causes paradoxical cerebral spinal fluid acidosis. Potassium is added to initial intravenous solutions when admission potassium values are low or normal. Generally, the initial potassium is above 5 meq/L but falls markedly within the first 2 h of treatment. When potassium enters the normal range and good urinary output is established, potassium is added to the intravenous solution. Potassium given as potassium phosphate (KPO_4) has an added advantage of supplying phosphate which is thought to be deficient in DKA. Phosphate has an essential role in cerebral oxygenation and myocardial function (Zipf et al., 1979).

The objectives of insulin therapy in DKA are to decrease hepatic gluconeogenesis, to inhibit lipolysis, and to promote uptake in glucose by cells. Traditionally, DKA has been treated with repeated high doses of intravenous or subcutaneous regular insulin. A trend toward use of low-dose, physiologic insulin therapy has been growing since the early 1970s. The low-dose method has been proved to be effective in correcting DKA with fewer complications such as hypoglycemia and hypokalemia. Starting with a small bolus of regular insulin, insulin therapy is maintained by intravenous infusion or repeated intramuscular administration. Many specific regimens exist. Daniels' protocol offers a specific example, either of the following:

1. Continuous IV infusion, 40–50 U regular insulin in 500 mL 0.9% saline at 100 mL/h (8–10 U/h)

2. Intramuscular injection, 15–20 U regular insulin initially, 10 U/h subsequently

The use of large amounts of insulin in an intravenous infusion has important nursing implications. Insulin moves toward the bottom of the IV solution container. Hourly rotation of the container is necessary to prevent administration of high doses of insulin. Albumin is sometimes added to the IV solution to keep insulin from adhering to the container and tubing. However, this is not strictly necessary, since the exact dosage of insulin delivered is secondary to the effectiveness of that insulin.

With the use of intravenous insulin, onset, duration, and peak of action differs from that of regular insulin given subcutaneously. The nurse must realize that effects of *intravenous* regular insulin occur within minutes, peak at 20 min, and last approximately 1 h. Regardless of the method used for insulin administration, insulin reduces blood sugar. When the blood sugar falls to 250 mg per 100 mL, the intravenous solution should be changed to one containing glucose. At this point, the continuous infusion and other emergency insulin protocols are changed to maintenance protocols.

Complications of DKA and Its Treatment

Although the prognosis for any given case of diabetic ketoacidosis is good, overall mortality rates vary from less than 2 percent to over 15 percent in medical centers nationwide. Death from DKA can be due to the illness precipitating the crisis, factors complicating the process of DKA, or complications arising from treatment of DKA. Nursing assessment of the patient in DKA should be geared to prevention and early recognition of complications.

These complications include shock, vascular thromboses, hypoglycemia, hypokalemia, renal failure, cerebral edema, paradoxical cerebral spinal fluid acidosis, infections, and aspiration. Shock is a danger initially because of volume depletion. It is also a problem within the first few hours or days of treatment because of fluid shifts and hypoxia. Fluid shifts occur following rehydration. Hypoxia results when correction of acidosis causes a left shift of the oxyhemoglobin dissociation curve. Because of the possibility of delayed onset of shock, monitoring of blood pressure and renal function should continue beyond the initial treatment period.

Vascular thrombosis in DKA can affect any muscle artery. Clotting problems resulting from the hypercoagulation characteristic of uncontrolled diabetes are aggravated by the dehydration and reduced cardiac output present in DKA. The patient with DKA is at risk for vascular thromboses during initial treatment and for the first few days following treatment. The nurse should keep this in mind when doing peripheral vascular assessment and should consider the possibility of mesenteric artery occlusion when patients complain of abdominal pain.

Hypoglycemia and hypokalemia can be prevented by measures described previously. Paradoxical cerebral spinal fluid acidosis resulting from disequilibrium between the pH of the blood and cerebral spinal fluid can be prevented by slow correction of acidosis. Cerebral edema, which occurs more often in younger patients, can be recognized early if level of consciousness and fundi are checked hourly. A patient who lapses into somnolence after having regained alertness during therapy should be suspected of developing cerebral edema; prompt treatment is required. Aspiration can be prevented by nasogastric intubation of the unconscious patient. Risk of iatrogenic infection limits use of Foley catheters, except when essential for obtaining urine samples.

The nursing report given when transferring the patient with DKA from the critical-care unit has many implications. The admission data can become the foundation for a teaching plan, since it reveals the duration and management of diabetes, any concurrent illnesses, and the history of the crisis event and how it was recognized and handled. The critical-care nurse should also comment on the degree of dehydration experienced by the patient. Concentration and learning are impaired from severe dehydration, and patient teaching must wait for recovery of mental status. The long-term goal for care of the DKA patient is not discharge but prevention of repeated admission.

Hyperosmolar Hyperglycemic Nonketotic Coma

In ketosis-resistant or undiagnosed diabetes, a factor which markedly raises blood sugar can start a chain of events leading to hyperglycemic hyperosmolar nonketotic coma (HHNK). This condition is characterized by a very high blood glucose and absence of ketonemia. Precipitating factors of HHNK include (1) stressful events, such as gram-negative bacterial infection, catastrophic illness, or burns; (2) drugs which induce hyperglycemia, such as thiazide diuretics or cortisone; (3) peritoneal dialysis; and (4) hyperalimentation. As outlined in Fig. 27-3, these factors cause hyperglycemia resulting in osmotic diuresis. The patient replaces fluid by drinking until altered sensorium impairs the thirst response. At this point, osmolality of the blood increases rapidly. Volume loss reduces the glomerular filtration rate causing azotemia and more glucose retention. Severe dehydration with as much as a 25 percent loss of total body water ensues.

Lack of ketosis is thought to be due to the fact that

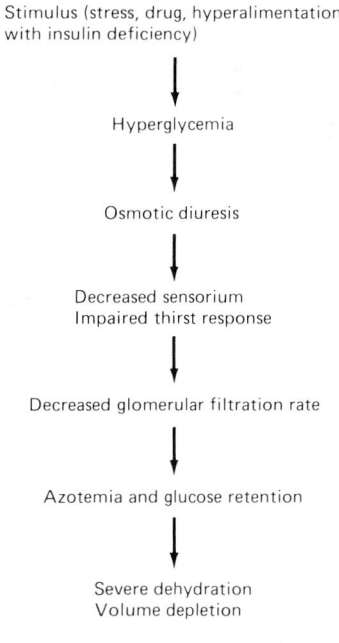

FIGURE 27-3
Pathogenesis of HHNK.

exogenous insulin is sufficient to prevent lipolysis. Acidosis, if present, is caused by shock or renal problems and occurs without significant ketonemia.

HHNK usually occurs in adults over 50 years of age and carries a mortality rate of over 50 percent. Many of its victims have already compromised cardiovascular systems. HHNK occurs gradually, so patients do not seek medical help until they are in crisis. Over a third of those with HHNK are undiagnosed diabetics.

Recognition of HHNK

The person with HHNK presents with severe dehydration with a 15 to 25 percent loss of total body water (TBW). Related clinical signs include fever, dry mucous membranes, poor skin turgor, and soft eyeballs. Other signs and symptoms include tachycardia, shallow respirations, profound depression of sensorium, and possibly focal seizures. The effect of severe dehyration on the nervous system causes the seizures and can cause a positive Babinski response, which disappears after hydration. Some clinical signs are similar to those of a cerebral vascular accident. Any comatose patient admitted to the critical-care unit should have a blood glucose test.

Daniels' criteria for diagnosis of HHNK include a blood sugar of 650 mg per 100 mL or more, serum osmolality of 350 mosmol/L or more, and acetone of 4+ or less in undiluted serum. When HHNK is suspected, initial laboratory tests include blood glucose, serum osmolality, serum acetone, blood gases, and electrolytes.

Management of HHNK

Management of HHNK centers around gradual correction of hyperglycemia and hyperosmolality. Rapid reduction of blood glucose can result in hypotension, shock, and renal failure. Rapid correction of hyperosmolality may lead to cerebral edema. Fluid replacement and insulin therapy are accompanied by administration of deficient electrolytes.

The fluid deficit averaging 8 to 12 L is corrected with isotonic or hypotonic saline intravenously. If the patient is hypotensive, plasma expanders may also be used. One-half of the estimated deficit is replaced in the first 12 h of care, the remaining half in the next 24 h. Since many HHNK patients have cardiovascular disease, it is important to assess cardiac competence at the initiation of fluid therapy. Fluid challenge tests using central venous pressure measurements can be employed for this purpose. Glucose solution is added when the blood glucose falls to 250 or 300 mg per 100 mL or the osmolality to 310 mosmol/L. The HHNK patient often has a severe potassium deficit requiring potassium added to the intravenous solution as soon as sufficient urinary output is established. Severe acidosis is treated with sodium bicarbonate.

Insulin therapy is used cautiously in HHNK, since these patients have some endogenous insulin production and may be quite sensitive to exogenous insulin. Following a crisis of HHNK, many patients control their blood glucose with diet alone. The low-dose insulin protocols described for DKA are not used as widely for HHNK. Traditional regimens of 50 to 100 U of regular insulin intravenously or intravenously and subcutaneously every 1 to 2 h must be accompanied with diligent observation on the part of the nurse. Hypoglycemia can be catastrophic for one of the population affected by HHNK.

Table 27-3 compares diabetic ketoacidosis and hyperglycemic hyperosmolar nonketotic coma. Despite the attempt to clearly differentiate these conditions, at times they coexist. Both entities call for multisystem assessment; knowledgeable use of fluids, insulin, and electrolytes; and patient teaching to avoid repeated crisis episodes.

Hypoglycemia

Hypoglycemia is seen most frequently but not exclusively in the diabetic. Factors contributing to hypoglycemia include exogenous insulin, change of insulin injection site, oral hypoglycemic agents, lack of caloric intake, strenuous exercise, alcohol intake, depletion of liver glycogen, adrenal insufficiency, renal failure, and insulinoma. Oral hypoglycemic agents can cause a severe and prolonged hypoglycemia. Heavy alcohol intake can inhibit hepatic release of glucose for up to 48 h, contributing to hypoglycemia. Failure of the kidney to normally excrete insulin can account for hypoglycemia.

Recognition of Hypoglycemia

Glucose is an obligatory fuel for the brain. The brain does not tolerate glucose lack for long without cerebral symptoms and adrenergic stimulation. Cerebral signs and symptoms include a feeling of vagueness, slow cerebration, headache, irritability, mental confusion, visual disorders, personality change, speech and gait disorders, convulsions, and coma. Adrenergic signs

TABLE 27-3
Comparison of Diabetic Ketoacidosis and Hyperosmolar Hyperglycemic Nonketotic Diabetic Coma

	DKA	HHNK
Age	All ages	Usually over 50 years
Duration of diabetes	Variable	Recent onset
Precipitating events	Infection, stress	Stress, steroids, diuretics
Mortality	5%	50%
Blood sugar	400–800	Over 900
Dehydration	Variable (TBW loss 5–15%)	Severe (TBW loss 15–25%)
pH	Low	Normal
Breathing	Kussmaul	Normal
Serum acetone	Present	Absent

and symptoms are the same as those caused by severe pain, fright, or hemorrhage, and include perspiration, pallor, anxiety, weakness, nausea and vomiting, tachycardia, and palpations. The vasoconstriction of this process can lead to myocardial ischemia and premature ventricular contractions in the patient with coronary artery disease. Hypoglycemia may be involved when a diabetic patient has episodes of tachycardia and premature ventricular contractions. If this is the case, the patient needs a bolus of glucose as well as an antiarrhythmic agent.

Two other considerations are worthy of note when discussing hypoglycemia in critical illness. The first concerns propranolol (Inderal), a commonly used pharmacologic agent. Since propranolol is a beta-receptor blocker, it prevents the adrenergic response to hypoglycemia. The nurse must be more alert to cerebral signs and symptoms of hypoglycemia in patients treated with propranolol. Another thing to consider concerning hypoglycemia in critical illness also involves the adrenergic response. Events other than hypoglycemia can evoke an adrenergic response. For example, the physical response to hemorrhage causes the signs of tachycardia, pallor, and perspiration. It is essential that the nurse search for the cause of signs of adrenergic response instead of assuming that these signs in a diabetic indicate hypoglycemia. A Dextrostix blood sugar rapidly confirms hypoglycemia.

Nighttime symptoms of hypoglycemia include restlessness, tachycardia, nightmares, and morning headache. The patient might not wake up but will report sleep disturbance if asked. The fasting blood sugar the morning following nighttime hypoglycemia might be quite elevated, e.g., 300 mg per 100 mL, because of the Somogyi effect. This effect is a compensatory response of the body to hypoglycemia illustrated in Fig. 27-4. Severe hypoglycemia stimulates release of cortisol, adrenalin, growth hormone, and glucagon all of which raise blood sugar. Several hours after a hypoglycemic event, hyperglycemia exists. If this hyperglycemia is treated with increased insulin, hypoglycemia and rebound hyperglycemia result. Hyperglycemia due to the Somogyi effect is treated by decreasing the insulin dosage.

The key to management of hypoglycemia is knowledgeable monitoring. The veteran diabetic knows the first symptoms experienced as well as effective treatment and should be the nurse's ally in care. The nurse should monitor blood sugar test results, clinical signs, and caloric intake. Replacement of calories not taken at meals is important. When the nurse suspects hypoglycemia in a critically ill patient, a Dextrostix blood sugar should be done. Recurrent hypoglycemia mandates exact records be kept of hypoglycemic events and potential contributing factors. A pattern often emerges from such records which suggests the cause of these events and guides treatment.

Treatment of Hypoglycemia

If the patient can take food orally, 10 to 20 g of carbohydrate (4 to 8 oz orange juice, sugar-sweetened soda, or Glutose) should be given at the first sign of

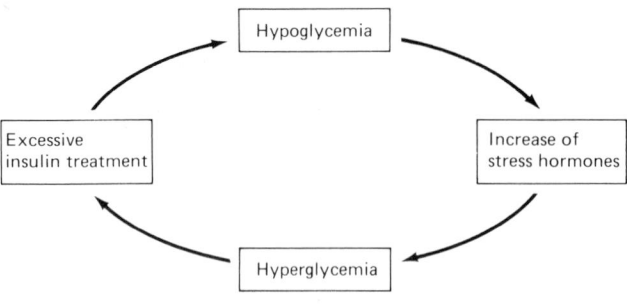

FIGURE 27-4

The Somogyi phenomenon. Hypoglycemia triggers release of stress hormones (epinephrine, glucagon, cortisol, and growth hormone). These hormones increase blood glucose, causing hyperglycemia. If hyperglycemia brings about an increase in insulin, the result again is hypoglycemia.

hypoglycemia. In severe hypoglycemia, intravenous push glucose (50 mL of $D_{50}W$) is given. Hypoglycemia due to insulinoma may be treated with oral diazoxide (Proglycem). The factors which caused the hypoglycemic event must be manipulated if recurrence is to be prevented.

Long-Term Complications

Macroangiopathy and microangiopathy in the diabetic can cause cardiac and renal problems which challenge the critical-care nurse. The following section presents some nursing implications. Since it is not intended to be a comprehensive discussion, additional sources are listed in the bibliography.

The relationship between diabetes and coronary artery disease has several nursing implications. Coronary artery disease occurs more frequently and at an earlier age in diabetics than in nondiabetics. Diabetics have higher mortality following a myocardial infarction, partially because of poor collateral circulation. Silent myocardial infarctions are more common in diabetics. The absence of symptoms is due to diabetic neuropathy blocking the pain. These factors should motivate the nurse to assess any diabetic patient for coronary artery disease.

When caring for a diabetic with myocardial infarction, the nurse should be aware that such tremendous stress is expected to elevate the blood glucose. Attempts to strictly control blood glucose during the crisis period can precipitate hypoglycemia which can extend the infarct or cause another infarct.

The patient with diabetes of over 20 to 30 years' duration should be assessed for associated renal impairment. An abnormal creatinine clearance test should cause the nurse to question the validity of urine sugar tests. Patients with diabetic nephropathy, such as Kimmelstiel-Wilson disease, are very sensitive to insulin. Since insulin is not excreted by the kidney, its half-life is extended. A history of significant decreases in insulin requirement calls for assessment of renal status.

The diabetic patient with end-stage kidney disease can be treated with dialysis or renal transplantation. Dialysis presents problems of labile blood glucose, infection, and clotting of the shunt. The transplanted patient controls blood glucose more easily. The multisystem effects of diabetes complicate the care of the critically ill diabetic and the work of the critical-care nurse.

NONDIABETIC ENDOCRINE CRISES

Nondiabetic endocrine crises are seen less often in critical-care units than diabetic crises are. However, when they do appear in a newly admitted patient or develop during another critical illness, patient welfare depends on rapid recognition and knowledgeable management. Four conditions will be discussed: thyroid storm, myxedema coma, adrenal crisis, and hypercalcemic crisis.

Understanding the pathogenesis and process of these endocrine crises is dependent upon knowledge of physiology. Although some physiology is integrated in this chapter, it is discussed in more detail in Chap. 7.

Thyroid Crises

Normal thyroid function involves the hypothalamus and pituitary as well as the thyroid. The hypothalamic-pituitary-thyroid axis is illustrated in Fig. 27-5. The hypothalamus secretes TRH (thyrotropin releasing hormone), which stimulates the release of thyrotropin (TSH, thyroid-stimulating hormone) from the pituitary. The pituitary secretes TSH, which stimulates the release of T_3 (triiodothyronine) and T_4 (thyroxin) from the thyroid. When thyroid hormone (T_3 and T_4) levels are low, the negative feedback to the pituitary triggers release of TSH which in turn causes secretion of more thyroid hormone. Stress and cold temperatures trigger TRH, which releases TSH, which stimulates thyroid hormone. When thyroid dysfunction exists, the problem can be at any level of this complex system.

Thyroid hormone is responsible for the metabolic rate of the entire body. Its main actions are (1) to increase the body's essential metabolic activities, (2) to increase the rate of nutrient use for energy production, (3) to increase the rate of growth, and (4) to increase activities of other endocrine glands. As one would expect, with these actions affecting all body tissues, extremes of hypo- and hyperthyroidism are dramatic clinical conditions.

Thyrotoxic Crisis

Thyrotoxic crisis, or thyroid storm, occurs in individuals with untreated or inadequately treated hyperthyroidism and is precipitated by infection, especially respiratory infection; stress, such as diabetic ketoacidosis or toxemia of pregnancy; and trauma, either severe psychological trauma or physical trauma, such as surgery. Thyroid surgery no longer is a frequent cause of thyroid storm due to preoperative care routines which prevent excessive release of thyroid hormone during surgery by blocking its production and release.

The most severe thyrotoxic crisis in my experience occurred in a young diabetic woman with diagnosed hyperthyroidism. She developed an upper respiratory infection which led to diabetic ketoacidosis and precipitated thyroid storm lasting over a week.

The pathogenesis of thyrotoxic crisis is poorly understood. Possible explanations for the shift from a hyperthyroid state (thyrotoxicosis) to crisis include (1) a sudden rise in circulating thyroid hormone, (2) adrenergic hyperactivity, and (3) decompensation of peripheral tissues (Urbonic and Mazzaferri, 1978). Although an extreme rise in circulating thyroid hormone would cause thyroid storm, laboratory data do not show a significant difference in thyroid hormone levels of hyperthyroid and thyrotoxic crises patients. T_4 does potentiate catecholamines, and hyperactivity of the sympathetic nervous system characterizes thy-

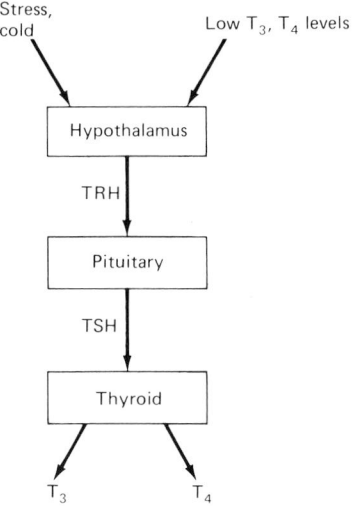

FIGURE 27-5

Hypothalamus-pituitary-thyroid axis. Stress, cold, and low levels of circulating thyroid hormone trigger the hypothalamus to secrete TRH, which stimulates release of TSH from the pituitary. This in turn causes secretion of T_3 and T_4 from the thyroid.

roid storm. Adrenergic hyperactivity may be associated with decompensation of peripheral tissues. The decompensation theory states that at some point, tissues which have been responding to elevated thyroid hormone can no longer do so; cardiac reserve is exhausted, and the body is unable to dissipate heat. For this reason thyrotoxic crisis is sometimes called *decompensated thyrotoxicosis*.

As mentioned earlier, laboratory tests do not differentiate hyperthyroidism from thyrotoxic crisis. For this reason, diagnosis is largely clinical. The patient with a history of hyperthyroidism who is critically ill could be at risk for thyrotoxic crisis.

Signs and symptoms of hyperthyroidism include heat intolerance, weakness, good appetite with weight loss, muscle wasting, tremor, goiter, exophthalmos, stare, pretibial myxedema, dyspnea, tachycardia, atrial fibrillation, emotional instability, and insomnia.

In thyroid crisis these signs are greatly exaggerated. The increased metabolic rate results in fever of 100 to 106°. Minor infections can trigger high fevers. Cardiac and gastrointestinal decompensation is seen. Tachycardia is marked, possibly accompanied by congestive heart failure and/or angina. Gastrointestinal symptoms of diarrhea and vomiting can occur.

The central nervous system can exhibit signs of either extreme agitation, restlessness, and delirium, or apathy, myopathy, and coma. Older patients may have less severe symptoms.

Treatment of thyroid storm focuses on thyroid hormone and its effects and on general supportive care. Supportive care includes hydration, nutrition with vitamin B and glucose, and fever reduction. Hypothermia blankets, tepid bath, and acetaminophen are used for fever reduction.

Physiological support is enhanced by cortisone acetate since endogenous corticosteroids are metabolized faster in the hypermetabolic state. Cardiac problems are treated with appropriate drugs.

Therapy aimed specifically at thyroid hormone includes use of agents to block its synthesis, release, and peripheral effects. Propylthiouracil (PTU) and methimazole block thyroid hormone synthesis. When given after the initiation of PTU, iodides are not utilized to synthesize new hormone. Instead they act to block release of existing hormone. Since T_4 has a half-life of 7 days, blocking new hormone synthesis and release is not enough. It is also necessary to lessen the effects of circulating hormone. The sympatholytics, chiefly propranolol (Inderal) but also reserpine and guanethidine, are used to block peripheral effects of thyroid hormone.

Nursing actions in thyroid storm include promoting a restful environment by restriction of stimuli, providing supportive care, and monitoring closely, especially the cardiovascular status. Since patients in thyroid storm are hypermetabolic, nutrients and drugs are metabolized faster. Higher-than-normal doses of digoxin and other agents may be required to achieve desired effects. Hypermetabolism of bone may cause hypercalcemia.

Myxedema Coma

Myxedema coma is the extreme of hypothyroidism. Hypothyroidism is characterized by cold intolerance, facial edema, thick tongue, hoarse voice, weakness, mental slowing, and hypotension or hypertension.

Precipitating factors for myxedema coma include stressful events such as respiratory infection and exposure to cold in a hypothyroid person. In over 50 percent of cases of myxedema coma, the patient went into coma after admission to the hospital. The severely hypothyroid patient is unable to adequately metabolize sedatives, analgesics, and anesthetics. These agents may precipitate a coma. Thorough nursing assessment can reduce the incidence of myxedema coma.

The nurse doing initial assessment should be alert to history of hypothyroidism or of treatment for hyperthyroidism by radiation or surgery. Radiation with ^{131}I accounts for much of myxedema seen today. A scar on the neck should prompt the nurse to ask if the patient has had thyroid surgery.

Recognition of myxedema coma includes the signs of hypothyroidism plus coma, delayed relaxation phase in deep tendon reflexes, hypothermia (e.g., 90°F), bradycardia, hypotension, hypoglycemia, hyponatremia, and hypoventilation. Early recognition improves the prognosis of myxedema coma, which currently has a mortality rate of 50 to 75 percent. When recognized early, this crisis can be effectively treated with thyroid hormone and support. Blood gas monitoring and avoidance of sedatives in care of the hypothyroid critically ill patient can prevent the crisis state. Hypothyroid patients have decreased response to respiratory stimuli such as hypoxia and carbon dioxide. Ongoing assessment of ventilation and respiration is a nursing responsibility. The hypometabolic state can result in hypoventilation. Respiration can be impaired by changes resulting from myxedema, especially by the interstitial accumulation of mucopolysaccharides. Respiratory failure in myxedema coma is treated by assisted ventilation.

Intervention is geared to other clinical problems also. Temperature regulation is critical. Generally, the lower the temperature, the worse the prognosis. Warming should be gradual, since rapid warming causes increased oxygen requirements and decreased peripheral vascular tone. Hypotension is treated by thyroid hormone, corticosteroids, and volume expanders. Because of the risk of arrhythmias, pressor agents are avoided. Hypoglycemia is treated by intravenous glucose. Hyponatremia is caused by impaired free water clearance and calls for limited use of fluids. The possibility of impaired cardiac function also restricts use of fluids.

As part of ongoing assessment, the nurse must be aware of the hypothyroid patient's inability to normally metabolize drugs. This hypometabolism potentiates action of drugs given.

In both thyroid crises, thyrotoxic crisis and myxedema coma, prognosis depends largely upon prompt recognition and diligent monitoring and support through the critical period. The critical-care nurse has an essential role in prevention, recognition, and management of these disorders.

Adrenal Crisis

The adrenal cortex secretes glucocorticoids, mineralocorticoids, and sex steroids. The glucocorticoid cortisol is essential for life. Its actions include (1) stimulating gluconeogenesis, (2) increasing protein breakdown and free fatty acid mobilization, (3) suppressing the immune response, and (4) enabling an adequate stress response. Cortisol secretion is controlled by a feedback system involving the hypothalamus, pituitary, and adrenal cortex. The most potent mineralocorticoid, aldosterone, conserves sodium and thus affects fluid balance. The pituitary has little control of aldosterone secretion.

Adrenocortical insufficiency may result through disease, injury, or surgery of the adrenals or through suppression of the hypothalamic-pituitary-adrenal (HPA) axis. An estimated 5 million people in the United States receive steroids in doses sufficient to suppress the HPA axis; i.e., the equivalent of over 50 mg of cortisone acetate daily for 10 days or more. Taking cortisone disrupts the feedback loop and suppresses adrenal output of cortisol. It takes 6 to 12 months for the system to recover enough to produce sufficient cortisol for acute stress (Levin, 1977).

Individuals taking steroid replacement therapy must increase the dosage during stress. Normally the output of cortisol is 15 to 20 mg per day, while during major stress it rises to 200 to 300 mg per day. Failure to increase steroids during stress results in adrenal insufficiency.

Patients with known Addison's disease, chronic adrenal insufficiency, can easily develop adrenal crisis during critical illness. Also, many individuals have marginal adrenal insufficiency and can function adequately except during stress. If one of these individuals becomes critically ill, stress results and the person cannot respond adequately. Another source of problems is the stress of critical illness resulting in increased secretion of CRF (corticotropin releasing factor) and ACTH (adrenocorticotropic hormone), which overstimulates the adrenal cortex. Due to hemorrhage caused by overstimulation and/or anticoagulant therapy, critically ill patients can develop adrenal insufficiency. Another cause of adrenal insufficiency is adrenalectomy, a common treatment for metastatic breast cancer. Adrenalectomy is performed to eliminate the sex steroid produced by the adrenals in an effort to retard the metastatic process.

The nurse should identify any patient who is at risk for adrenal crisis. Patients who are cortisone-dependent, such as those with Addison's disease, adrenalectomy, or adrenal suppression, should wear medical identification jewelry and carry an identification card with essential information. The nurse admitting a patient to the critical-care unit should look for such identification. While obtaining the history from the patient or family, the nurse should ask specifically about steroids when their use is suspected. Besides scars indicating mastectomy and adrenalectomy, other factors which may raise such suspicions are history of ulcerative colitis, collagen disease, or other conditions treated with cortisone preparations.

Adrenal insufficiency can be recognized by physical evidence of the chronic or acute condition. Signs and symptoms of chronic adrenal insufficiency include weakness, weight loss, orthostatic hypotension, anorexia, salt craving, hypoglycemia, syncope, vitiligo, and areas of increased pigmentation. Signs of acute adrenal insufficiency and adrenal crisis are hypotension, hyponatremia, hypovolemia, hyperkalemia, hypoglycemia, vascular collapse, lassitude and confusion, and fever, sometimes followed by hypothermia.

Laboratory confirmation of a diagnosis of adrenal insufficiency is necessary since Addison's disease requires lifelong therapy. A "normal" plasma cortisol (10 to 15 μg/mL) in a stressed patient is an abnormally low response. The diurnal nature of cortisol secretion causes a higher level in the morning than at night. Measurement of the response of plasma cortisol to exogenous ACTH stimulation can pinpoint whether the cause of adrenal insufficiency is in the adrenal gland or the pituitary. Electrolyte abnormalities in adrenal insufficiency are hyponatremia and hyperkalemia.

Adrenal crisis is treated with intravenous fluids and sodium and steroid replacement. Because of the lack of mineralocorticoids, fluid and electrolyte status is a major problem. Intravenous fluid orders generally include 5% dextrose in saline. The first liter is given in 30 to 60 min, followed by 1 to 2 L over the next 6 to 8 h. The nurse monitors hydration status with accurate intake and output and daily weights. Initially, corticosteroids are given as an intravenous bolus of 100 mg of hydrocortisone or 2 to 4 mg of dexamethasone. This is followed by 75 mg of cortisone acetate every 6 h to supply the maximum stress level of 300 mg in 24 h. Mineralocorticoid is given as desoxycorticosterone (Doca). Long-term therapy includes cortisone acetate 20 to 35 mg per day (or equivalent) to be taken two-thirds in the morning and one-third in the late afternoon and fludrocortisone acetate (Florinef) 0.05 to 2 mg per day.

Once identified, adrenal crisis can be effectively treated. The nurse who is alert for patients at risk for adrenal insufficiency and for early signs such as hypoglycemia or orthostatic hypotension can prevent the crisis. Postcrisis care includes patient teaching for the cortisone-dependent patient. The nurse teaches the critical necessity of daily cortisone therapy, that cortisol requirements increase in times of stress, and that medical identification should be worn.

Hypercalcemic Crises

Hypercalcemia has proved to be more common than previously thought by its frequent occurrence on multiphasic screening laboratory tests, such as the SMA-12. Severely high serum calcium levels require prompt recognition and management for patient survival. Since causes of hypercalcemia are many, the population at risk is broad.

Pathogenesis

Serum calcium can be elevated by increased calcium absorption, increased bone resorption, and decreased calcium excretion. Any patient who is immobilized and dehydrated, as are many critical-care patients, is at risk for hypercalcemia. Immobilization increases the resorption of calcium from bone. Dehydration decreases renal excretion of calcium. When hypercalcemia is mild to moderate (11 to 14 mg/mL), rehydration and mobilization may be adequate to correct the calcium level. However, when other factors favoring hypercalcemia are added to immobility and dehydration, severe hypercalcemia might occur.

Calcium is regulated by parathormone and calcitonin. Calcitonin from the thyroid retards calcium resorption from bone. Parathormone (PTH) resorbs calcium and phosphate from bone, increases calcium reabsorption and phosphate excretion at the kidney, and acts with vitamin D to absorb calcium and phosphate from the intestines. Increased serum calcium feeds back to the parathyroid to stop PTH secretion. Low serum calcium stimulates PTH secretion. Hyperparathyroidism causes hypercalcemia. The leading cause of hypercalcemia, however, is malignancy. Cancer with metastasis to bone, multiple myeloma, lymphoma, leukemia, and reticulum cell sarcoma cause hypercalcemia by increasing bone turnover. In addition to this, certain tumors such as bronchogenic carcinoma and hypernephromas can produce a parathormone-like substance. This ectopic hormone production can drastically elevate serum calcium. Other causes of hypercalcemia include Paget's disease, vitamin D intoxication, sarcoidosis, thyrotoxicosis, milk-alkali syndrome, and use of thiazide diuretics. Knowing the high incidence of hypercalcemia related to cancer, the critical-care nurse should assess oncologic patients for physical signs and laboratory data indicating this problem.

Hypercalcemia is demonstrated by high serum calcium levels. The normal serum calcium is 8.8 to 10.4 mg per 100 mL. A serum calcium of 13 to 16 mg per 100 mL is serious, and a level of over 16 mg per 100 mL is an emergency. Since almost half of circulating calcium is bound to serum proteins, a normal calcium in the presence of hypoalbuminemia may indicate early hypercalcemia. Misleading serum calcium levels can result from prolonged use of the tourniquet prior to drawing the blood sample. Normal 24-h urinary excretion of calcium is 80 to 200 mg.

Signs and Symptoms

Most of the physical evidence of hypercalcemia is nonspecific to this condition. Signs and symptoms include general malaise, lethargy, muscle weakness, confusion, and coma; polydipsia, polyuria, and renal calculi; and anorexia, abdominal pain, nausea, and vomiting. A shortened Q-T interval on the electrocardiogram may be the first indication of hypercalcemia. Chronic hypercalcemia from hyperparathyroidism causes osteoporosis and other skeletal abnormalities found on x-ray. Manifestation of acute hypercalcemia may include hypertension and cardiac dysrhythmias.

Hypercalcemic crisis is characterized by mental obtundation and coma, absence of deep tendon reflexes, oliguria and mild azotemia, intractable nausea and vomiting, abdominal pain, and circulatory collapse from volume depletion. In severe hypercalcemia, calcium phosphate microthrombi may develop through the body causing pancreatitis, pulmonary thromboses, and focal neuropathies.

Management

Emergency treatment for hypercalcemic crisis is focused upon rapidly reducing the life-threatening level of serum calcium and expanding the circulating volume. Rapid administration of intravenous saline is regulated according to the patient's renal status and central venous pressure. Usually 3 L of saline is alternated with 1 L of 5% glucose. This therapy replaces fluid and sodium and causes urinary excretion of calcium. A forced diuresis with furosemide (Lasix) increases the urinary excretion of calcium. Sodium and potassium are also excreted. Serum and urine electrolytes are determined at intervals. Hypokalemia may exist prior to treatment. Potassium chloride should be added to the intravenous solution as necessary. Patients with impaired renal function may require peritoneal dialysis or hemodialysis to reduce the serum calcium.

Drug therapy of hypercalcemia depends on the severity and cause of the condition. If hydration and forced diuresis fail to lower the serum calcium fast enough, phosphate therapy may be used to promote disposition of calcium into bone and soft tissue. Phosphate can be given orally or intravenously. Intravenous phosphate (Inphos) is given in a liter of solution over 8 to 12 h. 100 mmol of Inphos contains 162 meq of potassium as well as 3.1 g of phosphate. The nurse should be aware of complications of intravenous phosphate therapy which include phlebitis, vascular calcification, heart failure resulting from decreased myocardial contractility, hypotension, acute renal failure, and severe hypocalcemia.

Other drugs are used less frequently. The chelating agent ethylenediaminetetraacetate (EDTA) is a potent hypocalcemic agent but is rarely used because of its nephrotoxicity. Mithramycin, an antineoplastic agent, is used to lower calcium in patients with malignancy. Its side effects include thrombocytopenia and renal and hepatic damage. Calcitonin can reduce calcium levels but is not considered reliable alone in hypercalcemic crises. Glucocorticoids lower calcium in malignancy-caused hypercalcemia, but response rate is slow. For long-term conditions, hypercalcemia is treated with oral phosphate and, if indicated, parathyroidectomy. It is also important to remember that the patient with hypercalcemia is very sensitive to digitalis and that care must be taken to prevent and recognize digitalis toxicity.

Nursing assessment and care is critical in hypercalcemic crisis. The nurse can recognize early indications of hypercalcemia and report abnormal laboratory data promptly to prevent crisis. Monitoring of the patient during treatment of hypercalcemic crisis includes hourly intake and output, vital signs, and central venous pressure as well as attention to results of electrolyte tests.

The critical-care nurse has an essential role in monitoring and managing endocrine alterations in the critically ill. Patients with chronic endocrine disorders such as diabetes have special care needs which must be integrated with critical-care needs. The process of critical illness can precipitate additional problems. The nurse must be watching for patients at risk and for early signs of various endocrine disorders as well as establishing assessment and management regimens once these disorders are identified.

Thanks are due to Pamela Gotch, endocrine clinical nurse specialist, for her many valuable suggestions on content, and to Sandra Senger and Mary Jane Kreidler for their assistance in the preparation of this manuscript.

REFERENCES

Bern, M. M.: Platelet functions in diabetes mellitus, *Diabetes* 27:342–352, 1978.

Butterworth, C. E., and G. L. Blackburn: Hospital malnutrition, *Nutrition Today,* March/April 1975, pp. 8–18.

Cryer, P. E.: *Diagnostic Endocrinology,* New York: Oxford University Press, 1976.

Daniels, G.: Metabolic and endocrine emergencies, in E. Wilkins, J. Dineen, and A. Moncure (eds.), *MGH Textbook of Emergency Medicine,* Baltimore: Williams & Wilkins, 1978, pp. 226–269.

Dumlao, J. S.: Thyroid storm, *Postgrad Med* 56:57–63, 1974.

Eaton, R. P.: Lipids and diabetes: The case for treatment of macrovascular disease, *Diabetes Care* 2:46–49, 1979.

Felig, P.: Combating diabetic ketoacidosis, *Postgrad Med* 56:150–153, 1976.

Hallal, J. C.: Thyroid disorders, *Am J Nurs* 77:418–432, 1977.

Keen, H., and J. Jarret: *Complications of Diabetes,* London: Edward Arnold Ltd., 1975.

Kohler, E.: On materials for testing glucose in the urine, *Diabetes Care* 1:64–67, 1978.

Krueger, J., and J. Ray: *Endocrine Problems in Nursing,* St. Louis: Mosby, 1976.

Levin, R. M.: Diagnosis and mangement of endocrine emergencies, in Allan S. Cohen (ed.), *Medical Emergencies at Boston City Hospital,* Waltham, Mass.: Little, Brown, 1977, pp. 149–161.

Matz, R.: Diabetic coma: A multi-faceted problem, *Medical Counterpoint* 11:21–25, 1970.

O'Dorisio, Thomas M.: Hypercalcemic crisis, *Heart Lung* 7:425–434, 1978.

Rosenberg, J. M.: Antidiabetics: As always, the problem is maintaining control, *Current Prescribing,* March 1977, pp. 57–60.

Skillman, T. G.: Diabetic ketoacidosis, *Heart Lung* 7:594–602, 1978.

Sussman, K. E., and R. J. S. Metz: *Diabetes Mellitus,* 4th ed., New York: American Diabetes Association, 1975.

Tzagournis, M.: Acute adrenal insufficiency, *Heart Lung* 7:603–609, 1978.

Urbonic, R. C., and E. L. Mazzaferri: Thyrotoxic crisis and myxedema coma, *Heart Lung* 7: 435–447, 1978

Witt, K.: HHNK: A newly recognized syndrome to watch for, *Nursing '76* 6:66–70, 1976.

Zipf, W. B., G. E. Bacon, M. L. Spencer, R. P. Kelch, N. J. Hopwood, and C. D. Hawker: Hypocalcemia, hypomagnesemia, and transient hypoparathyroidism during therapy with potassium phosphate in diabetic ketoacidosis, *Diabetes Care* 2:265–268, 1979.

Management of patients with critical renal and genitourinary disorders is complex. To understand these complexities, the nurse needs to appreciate the pathophysiology involved with a variety of disease processes. The purpose of this chapter is to provide a detailed discussion of these processes for the nurse working in a critical-care setting. The chapter is divided into two sections. The first section discusses nephrology and the second section genitourinary disorders. The bibliographies are arranged similarly, and the reader is referred to these references for a more extensive discussion on any topic in the chapter.

Understanding pathophysiology provides the rationale for patient management and nursing interventions, including patient education. Although this chapter does not emphasize patient education, it is assumed the nurse will incorporate it into daily patient care. Hopefully, after reading this chapter, the critical-care nurse will be able to think logically and critically analyze problems related to the care of these patients.

RENAL DISORDERS
Cleo J. Richard[1]

Introduction to Renal Pathophysiology

With diminished renal reserve, kidney function is only mildly or modestly reduced, and the patient is asymptomatic because excretory and regulatory functions are sufficiently intact to maintain a normal internal environment. *Renal insufficiency* can develop over months to years and is characterized by an impaired capability to maintain an internal environment. The abnormalities, for instance an impaired concentrating ability, or mild azotemia, are minimal until the organism is stressed, e.g., by dehydration, infection, or cardiac failure. *Azotemia* is an accumulation of nitrogenous products in the blood. When renal function has deteriorated to the point that there are persistent abnormalities in the internal environment (azotemia, metabolic acidosis, electrolyte imbalances) and the patient is symptomatic, *renal failure* (RF) exists.

Acute Renal Failure

Acute renal failure (ARF) is characterized by a brusque reduction in renal function and usually, but not always, oliguria (400 mL or less of urine in 24 h). The major

[1] The author acknowledges the assistance of Edward J. Lupie; Laura Sophie, RN, MSN; and Kathlyn Phillips, RN, MS, in reviewing this section on renal disease; and Anna Marie Stasi for her clerical assistance.

28
MANAGEMENT OF PATIENTS WITH CRITICAL RENAL AND GENITOURINARY DISORDERS

RENAL DISORDERS
Introduction to Renal Pathophysiology
Pathogenesis of Renal Diseases
Effects of Renal Disease on Body Systems
Treatment Modalities for Renal Failure
Dialysis
Renal Transplantation

REFERENCES

GENITOURINARY DISORDERS
Catheters
Urologic Emergencies
Temporary Urinary Diversion
Permanent Urinary Diversion
Urologic Endoscopic Surgery
Open Urologic Surgery
Spinal Cord Injury and Disease
Genitourinary Trauma
Urinary Incontinence

REFERENCES

causes of ARF are categorized into prerenal, intrarenal, and postrenal. Prerenal causes such as hypovolemia (dehydration, blood loss) and circulatory insufficiency (shock, congestive heart failure) result in diminished renal perfusion. Nephrotoxins, ischemia, intravascular coagulation processes, acute glomerular diseases, acute interstitial diseases, crush injuries, hepatorenal syndrome, and pregnancy are examples of intrarenal causes that lead to renal parenchymal damage. Postrenal failure is related to circumstances that obstruct the flow of urine (calculi, tumors, or surgical accidents). Of all cases of ARF, 75 percent are due to acute tubular necrosis (ATN). The major etiologies of ATN are exposure to nephrotoxic agents or ischemia. Although the pathophysiology of ARF is not clearly understood, a number of explanations have been proposed. Oliguria may result from decreased glomerular filtration rate; redistribution of blood within the kidney; tubular obstruction due to fibrin, necrotic cells, pigments, etc.; or back leak of filtrate into the interstitium and/or vasculature. ARF associated with nonoliguria (1000 mL of urine per day) may be due to an inability of the tubules to reabsorb glomerular filtrate.

There are three phases of acute renal failure. During the *oliguric phase,* hyperkalemia, acidosis, hypocalcemia, and edema occur. Plasma creatinine usually rises 0.5 mg per 100 mL per day and blood urea nitrogen rises 10 to 20 mg per 100 mL per day. If the catabolic rate is high, such as with burns or trauma, the blood urea nitrogen can rise more rapidly. Anemia may occur, and the patient is very susceptible to infection. Random as well as 24-h urine collections should be analyzed. With ATN the urine appears dark and dirty. Oliguria usually begins within hours or a day of the insult and lasts an average of 1 to 2 weeks. The *diuretic phase* is characterized by a steadily rising urinary volume, indicating tubular regeneration. Typically, the urine volume doubles for several days then stabilizes. Some possible causes for the polyuria are that the accumulated urea acts as an osmotic diuretic, the increased extracellular fluid volume is excreted, and/or a defect in the concentrating mechanism exists. Renal function is still poor as evidenced by the elevated creatinine and blood urea nitrogen levels. During the *recovery phase,* urine is concentrated because of returning tubular function. Renal function continues to improve for 3 to 12 months after the onset of ARF. The great majority of patients recover, with only a few who have subtle functional defects but remain asymptomatic. The young and less severe oliguric cases seem to recover better than the elderly and oliguric cases. The principal causes of death are infection and the primary illness that precipitated the renal failure. On the battlefield ARF is still the cause of too many casualties.

Chronic Renal Failure

Chronic renal failure (CRF) is a syndrome resulting from a multitude of pathologic processes which lead to derangements of renal excretory and regulatory functions. The kidney is no longer able to maintain the integrity of the internal environment because there is diffuse, irreversible renal parenchymal disease. It is often difficult to pinpoint the exact cause for the renal failure. The renal deterioration develops over months to years and progresses to *end-stage renal disease* (ESRD) and uremia. The life of a patient with end-stage renal failure would be ended unless the individual were supported by artificial means (dialysis) or renal transplantation.

Uremia

Uremia literally means "urine in the blood." Its current usage, however, refers to a syndrome or symptom complex associated with severe renal failure. The symptoms are related to not only the direct consequences of the renal failure but also the impact on all body systems. Uremia may develop acutely or chronically, and its severity varies from patient to patient. The search for a specific uremic toxin continues. Dialysis seems to lessen the severity of some of the symptoms, so perhaps a toxin exists that is dialyzable. The manifestations of renal failure on body systems and their treatment are discussed later in the chapter.

Nephron Loss

The kidney is susceptible to the destructive effects of a large number of different disease entities. Although the pathogenesis of each disease entity begins uniquely, the end result of those processes that cause CRF is the gradual destruction of nephrons. The consequence of nephron destruction is the eventual loss of the dynamic excretory function of the kidney. Although it is clear that the residual nephrons undergo a series of adaptations, further knowledge about this process is still evolving.

With the loss of even one nephron, the rate of solute and water excretion is reduced and a finite alteration in both volume and composition of extracellular fluid occurs. Therefore, the remaining nephrons increase their individual rates of excretion to compensate for the lost nephron and to restore fluid and solute homeostasis. With each succeeding wave of nephrons lost, each remaining nephron does the excretory work of up to 100 nephrons. The adaptation is so unique that life is maintained in spite of a destruction of 80 to 90 percent of the original 2 million nephrons.

Even though nephron adaptation occurs with CRF, blood urea nitrogen and creatinine concentrations rise, plasma urate and phosphate rise slightly, plasma calcium falls, and sodium, potassium, magnesium, and extracellular fluid volume remain relatively normal until the disease progress is far advanced. Recent investigations have discovered there is a price to pay for the marvelous nephron adaptation: for instance, the elevated levels of parathyroid hormone that are required to maintain phosphate balance, and the high sodium concentration found in a variety of tissues (muscle, red blood cells). These trade-off abnormalities have therapeutic implications and require further investigation.

Classification of Renal Diseases

Renal diseases have been classified in a variety of ways. The following discussion, however, will focus on etiological, morphological, and patient description classification systems. The major etiologies of renal diseases are hereditary disorders, inborn errors of metabolism, congenital disorders, trauma, infections, biochemical or chemical injury, metabolic disorders, circulatory disturbances, immunologic disorders, and neoplasms.

A morphological classification of renal diseases identifies the primary structure that is affected by the disease. The primary categories are congenital anomalies, anatomic anomalies, and glomerular, tubular, interstitial, arterial, and venous diseases. The Council on the Kidney in Cardiovascular Disease (American Heart Association, 1972) developed a three-part classification system related to the patient and renal disease. The first part describes the patient's signs and symptoms through five classes, with class 5 being the most severe. The second part defines renal functional impairment based on glomerular filtration rate and serum creatinine concentration. The third part is a patient performance classification based on what the patient feels he or she can do. The list of renal diseases is too exhaustive to include here; however, the following section will discuss several disease entities with different etiologies, pathological processes, prognoses, and treatments.

Pathogenesis of Renal Diseases

Renal Artery Stenosis

Hypertension can cause renal damage, and conversely, renal damage can cause hypertension. An example of the latter is renal artery stenosis resulting in renovascular hypertension. Although infrequent in occurrence and responsible for only 2 to 5 percent of all cases of hypertension, it is one of the more curable forms of hypertension. Constriction of a main or branch renal artery results from congenital fibromuscular dysplasia or atherosclerotic changes. The former etiology has a greater incidence with women under the age of 50, while the latter etiology affects males older than 50. A family history of hypertension is usually absent with both groups.

The fibrotic lesions, several centimeters in length, cause thickening of the intima, media, or adventitia areas of the renal artery. The atherosclerotic plaques are frequently located at the origin of the renal artery. With a 50 percent reduction in luminal diameter, renal blood flow is significantly diminished. This stimulates the renin-angiotensin-aldosterone system, which causes increased reabsorption of sodium and water from the distal tubule and hypertension. Because of the ischemia, the compromised kidney develops infarcted areas and diminishes in size, but shows minimal vascular changes. In contrast, the nonischemic kidney is affected by the hypertension and develops arteriolar sclerosis and necrotic lesions, which can result in glomerular death and tubular dysfunction.

During physical examination, an abdominal bruit is present and the diastolic blood pressure is above 90 mmHg. An intravenous pyelogram identifies a disparity in kidney sizes and a delay in the appearance of the dye, and/or a hyperconcentration of the dye in the ischemic kidney. An arteriogram of the vessels shows the thickening and the thinning caused by the lesions. A renogram monitors the transit time of an intravenously injected radioisotope as it passes through the arterial system and tubules. In renal artery stenosis, the renal transit time is prolonged.

In addition, split renal function studies, by separate ureter catheterization, help to confirm the diagnosis by identifying the functional differences between kidneys. A high renin concentration in the renal vein of the ischemic kidney, usually 1 to 2 times greater than the contralateral kidney, is a significant finding. If the hypertension does not respond to antihypertensive therapy, surgical treatment is considered. The arterial lesion can be resected or bypassed with a synthetic graft or autograft, or a bilateral nephrectomy can be performed if revascularization fails. Surgical treatment is successful in 70 to 80 percent of most cases in which the nonischemic kidney has been spared from multiple arterial lesions. Occasionally, the pathology progresses to chronic renal failure.

Glomerulopathies

The glomerulopathies contribute significantly as a major etiology category of renal failure. Because of the vast number of glomerular diseases, it has been difficult to develop a satisfactory classification system of the diseases. There are, however, universally accepted terms that describe the histology and pathology of these diseases. *Segmental* refers to involvement of segments of the individual glomerulus, *focal* involves a few glomeruli, and *diffuse* involves many or all glomeruli. The pathology can be *progressive,* with changes occurring gradually over months or years, or *rapidly progressive,* with daily to weekly changes. A closed or open renal biopsy accomplishes the following: it obtains primarily cortical tissue; it examines the tissue under light, electron, and fluorescent microscopy; and it differentiates the specific glomerular pathology, subsequent treatment, and prognosis. Of the glomerulopathies, 75 percent are caused by an immunological process. In 95 percent of these cases, a deposition of exogenous (foreign protein) or endogenous (derived from own tissue) circulating antigens occur in the glomeruli, e.g., acute poststreptococcal glomerulonephritis (GN). The other 5 percent are due to the action of antibodies directed at the glomeruli, e.g., Goodpasture's syndrome.

Acute Poststreptococcal Glomerulonephritis

In acute poststreptococcal GN, a history reveals a recent (1 to 2 weeks old) beta-hemolytic streptococcal infection of the throat or skin, edema, and hematuria. The antigen-complement-antibody complexes aggregate on the epithelial side of the glomerular basement membrane. The immune process begins and lesions develop. Why these complexes are deposited on the glomeruli is unknown. The lesions are diffuse and result in glomerular swelling that fills Bowman's capsule and hypercellularity due to endothelial and mesangial cell proliferation and an increased number of leukocytes; red cell casts and fibrin are present.

Gradually, the pathology extends beyond the glomeruli, causing interstitial edema and tubular destruction. Proteinuria and hematuria result from leakage due to glomerular wall damage. A decreased glomerular filtration rate and tubular damage cause oliguria, and fibrin-split products are the result of the immune process. Serologically, the antistreptolysin titer is elevated, indicating an increase in antibodies; serum complement is decreased because of the active immune process in the glomeruli. Under immunofluorescence microscopy, granular deposits (immune complexes) are seen on the glomeruli. Many adult patients with acute streptococcal GN may temporarily recover adequate renal function. Of these, however, 50 percent develop progressive renal failure that requires supportive treatment.

Goodpasture's Syndrome

In Goodpasture's syndrome antibodies attack an antigen found in the glomerular basement membrane and alveoli of the lung. Why this occurs is still a mystery. Pulmonary hemorrhage is evident from hemoptysis and dyspnea. The glomerular lesions result from the immune process and are focal and segmental at first, progressing to diffuse. Finally, there is necrosis and total degeneration of the glomeruli. Urinary findings are similar to those in acute streptococcal GN. Biopsy findings, however, are different because they contain linear deposits. This is a rapidly progressive form of renal failure which is usually fatal because of pulmonary and renal manifestations. Plasmaphoresis and immunosuppression have done little to alter the disease process.

Diabetic Nephropathy

Among adults with diabetes mellitus (DM), approximately 30 percent will have pathological evidence of diabetic nephropathy. DM can affect the kidney in several different ways. A characteristic nodula lesion, first described by P. Kimmelstiel and C. Wilson in 1936, involves the glomeruli. The basement membrane thickens, and a hyaline mass composed of mucopolysaccharides originates in a peripheral glomerular tuft, grows, and eventually obliterates all glomeruli, causing ischemia and proteinuria. Another hyaline lesion, composed of eosinophilic material, develops in Bowman's capsule; this lesion and the Kimmelstiel-Wilson lesion grow together and seal off the glomeruli. Atherosclerosis develops in the renal arteries or main branches, eventually causing the formation of scar tissue. The incidence of papillary necrosis and pyelonephritis is markedly increased in DM. The nephrotic syndrome is common in 50 percent of the patients with diabetic nephropathy. Retinopathy, frequently resulting in blindness, parallels the development of renal lesions.

A urinalysis demonstrates an increase in protein, glucose, bacteria, and papillae (if sloughed). A renal biopsy will identify the presence of renal lesions; however, no treatment is available that halts their progression. Hypertension and edema are frequent findings during a physical examination. No other clinical or laboratory parameters are consistently abnormal in patients with diabetic nephropathy. A decline in renal function usually occurs between 6 and 30 years, with an average of 20 years, after the onset of adult DM. When proteinuria is present and/or the diabetes is poorly controlled, loss of renal function occurs within a shorter time, usually 6 years, and results in ESRD requiring dialysis or renal transplantation.

Polycystic Renal Disease

Polycystic renal disease exists in two forms, infantile and adult. The infantile form is inherited as an autosomal recessive trait and frequently results in death during the perinatal period. The adult form, usually inherited as an autosomal dominant trait, affects both kidneys and is one of the four major disease categories that results in ESRD. The patient's offspring have a 50 percent chance of inheriting the disease. During the first stage, from birth to the fourth or fifth decade, although the patient rarely manifests symptoms, renomegaly may be seen on an abdominal x-ray. During the second stage, the kidneys become bumpy pal-

pable masses because of large numbers of variable-sized fluid-filled cysts.

Three types of cysts *closed, secretory,* and *excretory,* appear in the adult kidney; they are involved with all segments of the nephron (Fig. 28-1). In the collecting duct the cysts cause hypertrophy and obstruction, are secretory, and communicate with the renal pelvis. The tubules develop secretory and excretory cysts, and closed cysts are located near Bowman's capsule. Although the cysts compress and destroy renal tissue, some nephrons are still able to form urine. Because of the medullary pathology, the decreased ability to concentrate urine is one of the earliest clinical findings. Hematuria results from bleeding into the cysts and is occasionally accompanied by pain. Pain may also be caused by ureteral obstruction due to clots or stones; ruptured, pus-filled cysts; and/or very large kidneys. Fifty percent of the cases have urinary tract infection, 1 percent have stones, and 75 percent have proteinuria less than 0.5 g/day.

An infusion nephrotomogram, a radiological technique, visualizes vertical planes through the kidney, blocking out overlying tissues to demarcate cysts and tumors from renal parenchyma. Cysts appear as translucent, paper-thin-walled structures. Ultrasound scanning, a noninvasive test, uses sound vibrations to identify whether a mass is solid (tumor) or fluid-filled (cyst). In addition, a urinalysis helps to confirm the diagnosis. Hypertension occurs in half the cases and often precedes azotemia. There is a high incidence of cerebral artery aneurysm and cysts in the bile ducts and lungs. Anemia is mild or absent, or polycythemia exists. Skeletal and vascular changes are minimal, which is in contrast to most patients with CRF who have these extrarenal complications. Treat-

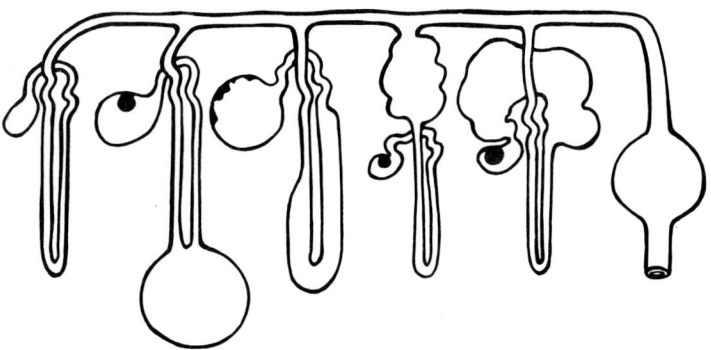

FIGURE 28-1
Locations of cysts in the nephron. The nephron to the far left is normal.

ment includes antihypertensive therapy, urinary infection control, genetic counseling, and eventually dialysis or renal transplantation.

Analgesic Nephropathy

Analgesic nephropathy is a worldwide problem. Its incidence is greater among women who complain of chronic headache and muscle pain. Although different analgesics cause damage, phenacetin seems to be the most toxic. A history reveals daily ingestion of a large amount of analgesics (6 to 8 pills) for several years. A minimum requirement to induce renal damage is daily ingestion of 0.9 to 1.0 g of phenacetin for 1 to 3 years. The metabolites concentrate in the renal medulla causing diminished blood flow at the vasa recta level and subsequent ischemia. Papillary necrosis is a distinctive feature and one which leads to scarring and fibrosa in the medulla (interstitial nephritis), which diminishes the urine concentrating ability of the kidney. Renal, colicky pain results from passing sloughed necrotic papillae through the ureter. Gradually, the pathology ascends the tubules because of ischemia and obstruction from necrotic papillae, impairing renal acidification and sodium conservation and predisposing the kidney to infection. Usually the glomeruli are spared or demonstrate minimal hyalinization. Dehydration accentuates the pathological changes.

The most helpful diagnostic tools are a history, urinalysis, and intravenous pyelography (IVP). A urinalysis reveals leukocytes, bacteria (one-third of cases), increased sodium chloride, red blood cells, entire tips of necrotic papillae, and little to no protein. An IVP demonstrates reduced kidney size, papillary calcification, and dilated calyces. Treatment includes stopping analgesic ingestion, increasing fluid intake, supplementing the diet with sodium chloride to compensate for the renal losses, administering antibiotics if infection is present, and giving supportive therapy for extrarenal manifestations, e.g., hypertension, anemia, and dyspepsia. If analgesic ingestion ceases before permanent renal damage occurs, the prognosis for renal recovery is good. There are cases, however, that have progressed to chronic renal failure and require dialysis or renal transplantation.

Diabetes Insipidus and Nephrogenic Diabetes Insipidus

Diabetes insipidus (DI) and nephrogenic diabetes insipidus are clinical disorders of water metabolism.

Antidiuretic hormone (ADH) or vasopressin originates in the hypothalamus and is secreted from the posterior pituitary gland in response to an increased serum osmolality that is detected by hypothalamic osmoreceptors. Vasopressin alters the luminal cell membrane of the distal tubule and collecting duct, thereby increasing these structures' permeability to water. Subsequently, water is conserved by reabsorption into the hypertonic medulla. In DI, inadequate levels of vasopressin are secreted; in nephrogenic DI, the distal tubule and collecting duct fail to respond to the hormone. In either case, the patient has polyuria, occasionally exceeding 5 to 10 L/day, and hypernatremia, both of which lead to polydipsia.

Posterior pituitary or hypothalamic diseases such as tumors, infections, trauma, or surgery are main causes for DI; however, DI can lack underlying pathological conditions (idiopathic). Onset is frequently abrupt, occurs during the teens or middle twenties, and is equally distributed in both sexes. Nephrogenic DI is rarer than DI and has several etiologies. Intrinsic renal disease that affects the structure or function of the distal tubule and collecting duct, such as hypercalcemia, hypokalemia, amyloidosis, sarcoidosis, cysts, pyelonephritis, hydronephrosis, and drug toxicities, are more common causes. In addition, the disease can be transmitted to males by a sex-linked gene. This form is rarer, occurs in infants, and is frequently fatal.

Urine concentrating tests will differentiate DI from other forms of polyuria. During periods of dehydration, urine osmolality will not increase in DI nor nephrogenic DI, and vasopressin plasma levels will be suppressed in the former and elevated in the latter. It is essential that these tests be conducted under close observation and terminated if a patient loses 3 percent of body weight. Therapy is aimed at preventing dehydration. Fortunately, several pharmaceutical agents are available that produce an antidiuresis in patients with DI. Treating nephrogenic DI, however, is a bit more challenging. An intact thirst mechanism, free access to water, and careful monitoring of fluid balance are essential to prevent dehydration. Occasionally a low-sodium diet or use of thiazide diuretics helps to decrease the polyuria. Correction of any underlying metabolic or renal disease is beneficial.

Nephrolithiasis

One of every thousand persons in the United States has a urinary tract calculi, and one-third of these cases will eventually lose a kidney. Nephroliths are composed of two types of material: a matrix, largely mucoprotein with some sugars that make up 5 percent of the stone; and a crystalloid such as calcium or cystine that accounts for 95 percent of the stone. Although there are several theories of stone formation, each includes a urinary state of supersaturation with the crystalloid component of the stone. Other factors that influence stone formation are urine pH, stasis, concentration, and infection. Clinically, nephrolithiasis may be asymptomatic and discovered during radiography for other reasons. Pain, urinary tract infection, and gross hematuria are, however, associated with nephrolithiasis, and their severity is dependent on the location and activity of the stone. Renal calculi are classified by their crystalloid composition: cystine, struvite, uric acid, and calcium.

One to two percent of nephroliths are composed of *cystine,* an amino acid. An inborn error of metabolism, an autosomal recessive trait, prevents the renal reabsorption of cystine, resulting in cystinuria. Cystine is insoluble at normal urinary pH (4.5 to 7), and subsequently a high urinary concentration of cystine stimulates stone formation. These stones are radiopaque because of their high sulfur content. Administering sodium bicarbonate alkalinizes the urine, taking penicillamine to prevent cystine precipitation, and drinking at least 5 L of fluid daily solubilizes the crystals. If these measures fail to dissolve the stone, surgery is performed.

Struvite stones, composed of ammonium-magnesium-phosphate, account for 15 percent of renal calculi. They are associated with infection by organisms (proteus, pseudomonas) that split urea into ammonia and carbon dioxide, and an alkaline urine. Frequently these stones are staghorn (fill renal pelvis) and require surgical removal. Other treatment would include controlling urinary tract infection, acidifying urine with the administration of ascorbic acid, and maintaining a high fluid intake.

Uric acid calculi account for 5 to 8 percent of renal stones. They are associated with hyperuricemia states such as primary gout, myeloproliferative syndromes, leukemia, acidic urine, chronic dehydration, and hyperuricosuria. However, many patients with uric acid calculi do not have hyperuricemia or hyperuricosuria. These stones are radiolucent and cannot be seen on plain abdominal x-ray unless calcuim is a component of the stone. Treatment includes alkalinizing the urine, increasing fluid intake to 3 L daily, and administering allopurinol. The largest portion of renal stones (80 percent) are composed of calcium and are therefore radiopaque. The exact pathogenesis of *calcium stones* is unclear; however, 50 percent of the cases have an increased urinary excretion of calcium or oxalate, and 20 percent have hyperuricosuria. Several mechanisms contribute to hypercalciuria: (1) increased gastrointestinal absorption of calcium, e.g., sacoidosis or idiopathic; (2) leaching of bone calcium, e.g., hyperparathyroidism or immobilization; and (3) a defect in renal reabsorption of calcium. Treatment is mainly concerned with reducing the concentration of calcium in the urine and increasing the urine volume through adequate hydration. In addition, possible treatment for any underlying causes, e.g., hyperparathyroidism, should be instituted. Indications for surgical removal are pain, infection, and renal deterioration due to obstruction.

Effects of Renal Disease on Body Systems

The kidney is the major organ responsible for maintaining a balanced environment within the organism that houses it. The kidney achieves a steady state by adjusting the sum of the intake of a substance and its endogenous production over a period of time to equal the substance's output during the same time period. For instance, a person consumes water as a liquid and in food and produces it through metabolic processes. Water is excreted in stool and urine and through insensible losses. It is the kidney, however, that must alter its volume of water excretion so a steady state is maintained in spite of alterations in water intake or other losses. With renal failure, the kidney slowly loses its ability to monitor the excretion of substances in relationship to the substance's intake and production. In addition, other regulatory functions of the kidney are altered, such as production of renin or erythropoietin. Subsequently, the ramifications of renal failure on the steady state are detrimental to the organism.

Electrolyte and Metabolic Changes

The major electrolytes that are effected by RF are potassium, sodium, phosphate, calcium, and chloride. Serum sodium may be increased or depleted in different renal diseases and during different stages of RF. *Hyponatremia* accompanies renal salt wasting, water excesses, and polyuria, resulting in decreased extracellular fluid volume that decreases glomerular filtration rate. Possible mechanisms are reduced medullary blood flow (polycystic disease, analgesic nephropathy) and natriuresis secondary to diuresis from high solute concentrations (urea). *Hypernatremia* is associated with ESRD and oliguria, resulting in edema. Typically, renal failure patients retain water because of decreased filtration, inability to dilute urine, and hypernatremia. This results in an expanded extracellular fluid volume, edema, and circulatory overload. In some renal diseases (diabetes insipidus) large amounts of dilute urine are excreted and circulatory insufficiency and dehydration result. The other electrolytes affected by RF are discussed under the specific body systems they affect.

Metabolic acidosis frequently accompanies renal failure because the kidney is unable to excrete hydrogen ions, reabsorb bicarbonate, and produce ammonia and titratable acids. Usually the body adjusts to a lower pH; however, those patients who become symptomatic should be treated.

Although normal quantities of insulin are produced in renal failure, its subsequent pathways are altered and mild *glucose intolerance* results. At the cellular level, the action of insulin on the phosphorylation of glucose is impaired. Perhaps this is due to the interference of some dialyzable substance. Insulin's half-life is prolonged because of slowed degradation secondary to decreased renal mass, malnutrition, and diminished metabolic rate. Subsequently, the circulating amount of insulin increases. Patients with DM and renal failure experience a decrease in insulin requirements. *Hypertriglyceridemia* is associated with elevated insulin in renal failure. The genesis for this abnormality is not completely understood; however, the following has been proposed. The high insulin levels enhance hepatic production of triglycerides and interfere with lipoprotein lipase that mediates the removal of triglycerides from plasma into adipose tissue. *Hypertriglyceridemia* changes minimally with dialysis and hence predisposes renal failure patients to atherosclerosis.

Essential amino acids are decreased in renal failure, whereas nonessential amino acids are usually normal. Guanidine compounds, urea, uric acid, and creatinine are elevated in renal failure because they are primarily excreted by the kidney. They seem to be toxic by interfering with biochemical and physiological processes. Although the significance of these substances and their role in the pathogenesis of renal failure warrants further investigation, a great deal of information indicates that these end products of protein metabolism are responsible for the underlying pathology of uremia.

Hypothermia commonly occurs in RF and may be associated with toxic inhibition of sodium transport,

hypothyroidism, diminished insensible water loss, anemia, decreased basal energy production, nephrectomy, and increased blood urea nitrogen. The temperature may be as low as 33.3°C and rises slightly after dialysis.

Cardiovascular System

The cardiovascular system suffers multiple consequences of RF. Normally erythropoietin is secreted from the kidney in response to hypoxia and stimulates the production and maturation of red blood cells in the bone marrow. In RF, erythropoietin is no longer released from the kidney and/or inhibited, and a normochromic, normocytic *anemia* results. The anemia is mild in the early stages of RF and worsens as the disease progresses, but does not correlate with the severity of uremia. Characteristics of the anemia are a 50 percent reduction in hemoglobin and hematocrit, slow maturation of red blood cells due to poor utilization of iron and a folic acid deficiency, and a red blood cell survival rate of one-third to two-thirds as long as normal because of hemolysis. Patients fatigue easily, are listless, have a general lack of well-being, and are pale. With severe anemia, patients complain of headaches, dyspnea on exertion, palpitations, and angina. Other factors that contribute to anemia are gastrointestinal bleeding and blood losses associated with dialysis. The administration of red blood cells (only to relieve severe symptoms of anemia), folic acid, ferrous sulfate, and androgens are supportive measures along with a nonfatiguing exercise program. Dialysis improves the anemia slightly by removing uremic toxins that may effect the survival rate of red blood cells.

Altered hemostasis develops gradually in renal failure and is characterized by capillary fragility due to uremic toxins, thrombocytopenia, significantly reduced platelet survival (9 days), decreased platelet adhesiveness, and inadequate production of platelet factor III. The results are prolonged bleeding times, spontaneous ecchymoses, and internal bleeding (e.g., pericardium, intracranium). For some unknown reason, T cells are suppressed and leukocyte function is altered, resulting in enhanced patient susceptibility to infection and delayed hypersensitivity reactions. Hypersplenism occasionally occurs and may contribute to the dysfunction of the hematopoietic system, especially the leukopenia.

The most common cardiovascular complication of CRF is *hypertension*. Many factors contribute to the genesis of the hypertension: fluid and sodium retention; overstimulation of the renin-angiotensin-aldosterone system; accumulation of certain vasopressor substances that are normally metabolized and excreted by the kidney; lack of certain vasodilator substances such as prostaglandins and kinins; increased sympathetic nervous system activity; and increased peripheral resistance due to atherosclerosis or calcifications. The majority of hypertensive cases are volume-dependent and respond to antihypertensive therapy, medications, diet control, and dialysis. Only 10 percent of the cases can be contributed to high renin levels and respond best to bilateral nephrectomy. An even smaller minority of cases are related to the other factors.

Fibrinous pericarditis occurs in approximately 30 to 50 percent of CRF cases. The etiology is probably related to uremic toxins and/or an infectious process. Signs and symptoms are anxiety, cardiomegaly, dyspnea, fever, hiccups, chest pain, and pericardial friction rub. The chest pain is precordial; may radiate to the neck and left shoulder; is aggravated by breathing, coughing, and swallowing; and is relieved by sitting up and leaning forward. The pericardial friction rub is best heard over the precordium when the patient sits up and leans forward. Although many of these cases respond to frequent dialysis, 40 percent progress to *pericardial effusion,* an accumulation of hemorrhagic fluid in the pericardial sac. The friction rub disappears, venous pressure increases, chest pain intensifies, the pulse is rapid and weak, systolic blood pressure falls, and blood supply is diminished to most organs. If the pericardial sac continues to fill with fluid, cardiac movement is severely restricted and *cardiac tamponade* results. This is an emergency situation that requires pericardiocentesis. Cardiac tamponade still occurs in a small but significant number of CRF patients.

Pulmonary System

In chronic renal failure the major pulmonary problems include pulmonary edema, fibrinous pleuritis, uremic lung or uremic pneumonitis, and an increased susceptibility to infection. Pulmonary edema results from severe volume overload, altered pulmonary capillary permeability, heart failure, and decreased oncotic pressure. Signs and symptoms are dyspnea, cough, restlessness, anxiousness, orthopnea, and rales. The etiology of *fibrinous pleuritis* is probably similiar to the etiology of pericarditis. Pleuritic pain and a pleural rub may accompany the pleuritis. If it progresses to an effusion, it is usually hemorrhagic. Uremic lung is

purported to be a specific type of pulmonary edema with perihilar vascular congestion and clear peripheral lung fields. It appears radiographically as butterfly wings, and its significance is questionable. Occasionally patients with CRF have Kussmaul's respirations due to metabolic acidosis. These abnormalities are treated with frequent dialysis; however, the response is slow. Because of a compromised immune system and reduced pulmonary macrophage activity, pneumonia, with thick, tenacious sputum, is a chronic problem. Clinically the infectious process is not readily apparent because of hypothermia and normal white blood cell counts. If a specific organism is cultured, an appropriate antibiotic is administered. In addition, preventive measures such as providing rest, avoiding exposure to respiratory irritants and microbes, and maintaining adequate nutrition and hydration are instituted.

Gastrointestinal System

Of all the deaths associated with RF, 4 percent are attributed to gastrointestinal problems. The entire gastrointestinal tract is affected by the consequences of RF. High concentrations of urea in the saliva are hydrolyzed to ammonia by urease. This predisposes the patient to oral lesions, infections (including parotitis), bleeding, and an ammoniacal breath odor (uremic fetor). A metallic taste on the posterior tongue is associated with uremia and marked hyperkalemia. Hydration changes and mouth breathing, which occurs in metabolic acidosis, potentiate oral lesions and a dry tongue. Frequent oral hygiene throughout the day helps to alleviate these problems and prevent anorexia. Some helpful measures are using a soft toothbrush with gentle action, using mouthwashes, applying petroleum jelly or mineral oil to dry lips and mucous membranes, visiting the dentist and eating sour balls or lemon juice and soft, bland food.

Factors that contribute to the development of lesions in the stomach and intestine are increased ammonia concentration due to degradation of urea; mucosal irritation from ammonia and other uremic toxins; decreased histamine secretion that stimulates gastric acid secretion; prominent gastric folds; decreased peristalsis due to uremic neuropathy; generalized vascular abnormalities that cause ischemia and bacterial invasion; and the physiological stress imposed by the chronic illness. Duodenal ulcers are more frequent than gastric ulcers. Signs and symptoms are anorexia, nausea, vomiting, hiccups, heartburn, bleeding, dehydration, pain, and diarrhea.

All emesis and stool should be examined for gross or occult blood, since anemia is a confirmed problem in RF. Although dialysis frequently diminishes the severity of the abnormalities, nausea and vomiting are still distressing symptoms, especially in the morning. A low-protein diet, not eating until several hours after awakening, administration of zinc, and nocturnal hydration to dilute the urea accumulation that occurs during the night, help to control these symptoms and maintain adequate nutrition. If diarrhea is severe, antidiarrheals may help. Constipation is a frequent side effect of phosphate binders, and the administration of bulk-forming laxative and stool softener helps to restore normal bowel activity. Colonic diverticulitis and pancreatitis, associated with increased serum amylase, are less frequent complications.

Calcium, Phosphorus, Vitamin D, Parathyroid Gland, and Skeletal System

There is a complex relationship between calcium, phosphorus, vitamin D, parathyroid gland, bones, and kidneys. Precursors of vitamin D are converted to active forms in the kidney. The active form promotes bone mineralization and enhances intestinal absorption of calcium. Approximately one-third of the calcium is excreted by the kidney and the remaining two-thirds by the bowel. Phosphate is also absorbed from the gastrointestinal tract and excreted by the kidney. Parathyroid hormone (PTH) is secreted from the parathyroid gland in response to hypocalcemia and enhances renal calcium reabsorption and phosphate excretion. In addition, PTH increases the number of osteoclasts and raises serum calcium by activating bone resorption. Both calcium and phosphate are necessary for normal bone growth and maintenance. In RF, the kidneys are unable to respond to PTH, and vitamin D is inadequately converted to its active form. The subsequent pathophysiology is illustrated in Fig. 28-2.

Most patients with RF have some skeletal abnormality; however, many are asymptomatic clinically. Osteitis fibrosa seems to be the earliest and most common bone lesion found in these patients. Osteomalacia and osteosclerosis are more dependent on the chronicity of the renal failure. Alkaline phosphatase is usually elevated with bone lesions. Bone pain and muscle weakness are the two most common clinical symptoms. Bone pain is usually a vague, deep ache aggravated by pressure or sudden movement and commonly associated with osteomalacia, osteitis fibrosa, and fractures. Muscle weakness re-

sults in a waddling gait and difficulty climbing stairs. In addition to increased serum concentrations of calcium, magnesium, and phosphate, local tissue injury and changes in pH are factors that predispose renal failure patients to soft tissue calcifications. Depending on the size and location of the calcifications, they may or may not become symptomatic.

Treatment for bone lesions and soft tissue calcifications include lowering serum phosphate, maintaining normal serum calcium, suppressing parathyroid hyperplasia, and healing bone lesions. Pharmaceutical agents such as phosphate binders, vitamin D supplements, and occasionally calcium are administered. Subtotal parathyroidectomy is performed if the bone lesions become severe. This also seems to lessen the severity of pruritus that is associated with secondary hyperparathyroidism.

Nervous System

A major portion of the clinical abnormalities associated with CRF are related to the nervous system. Peripheral neuropathy affects 80 to 90 percent of the RF cases and begins in the lower extremities. The pathology begins in the distal portion of peripheral nerves, involving sensory pathways first because of acid-base or electrolyte imbalances, and is manifested by peculiar creeping, crawling, pricking, itchy sensations. The abnormality is called the *restless leg syndrome* because the sensations are alleviated by movement of the legs. When the sensory defect worsens, the patient experiences paresthesias with pricking, burning, painful sensations and vibratory and position loss in the soles of the feet with abnormal deep tendon reflexes. These symptoms can be so severe that they cause insomnia and curtail ambulation.

As the peripheral neuropathy worsens, motor pathways are involved. Nerve conduction is diminished because of high creatinine concentrations and because of severe demyelination that causes defective transportation of essential substances from nerve cells and the spinal cord to distal portions of nerves. Signs and symptoms are weakness, difficulty climbing stairs, foot drop, paraplegia, incomplete emptying of the bladder, decreased peristalsis, and lowered two-point discrimination. Dialysis, when instituted early, usually helps to control these symptoms and to decrease motor involvement.

Muscle cramps and twitching, usually in the lower extremities, are associated with electrolyte imbalances particularly, sodium depletion, hypocalcemia,

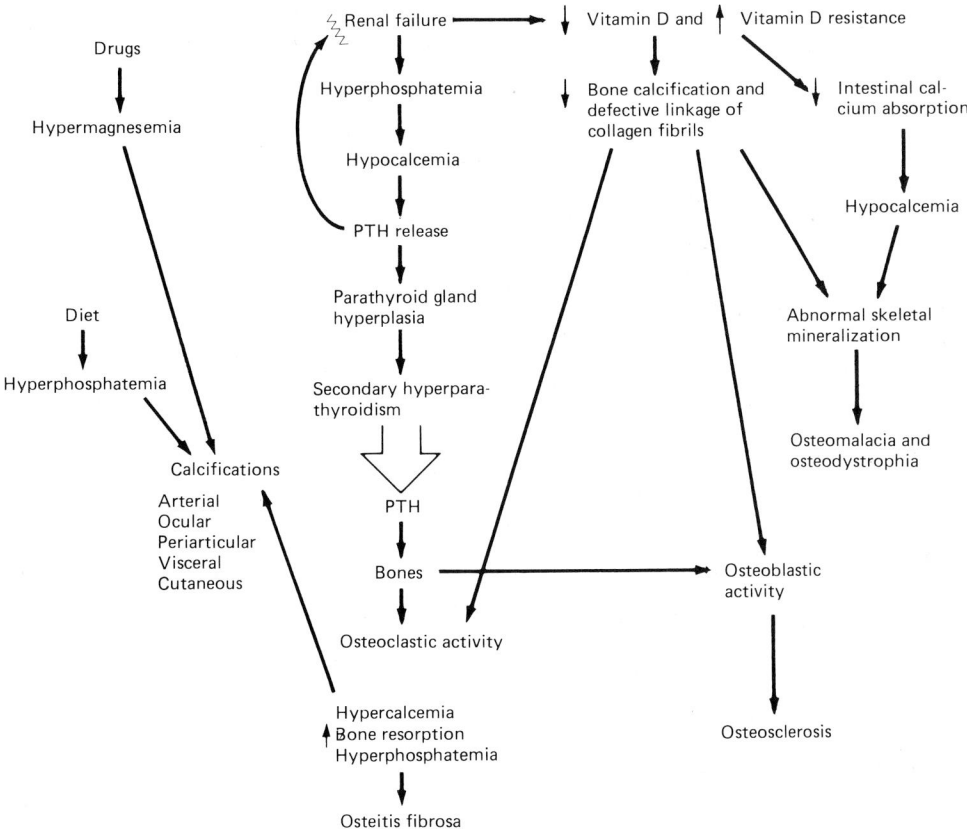

FIGURE 28-2

Pathophysiology of bone disease associated with renal failure.

and hyperkalemia. Asterixis affects the upper limbs because muscular contractions are periodically inhibited. Fasciculations and hiccuping due to neuromuscular irritability annoy patients.

Although most cerebral changes are functional rather than structural, cerebral edema and hypertension contribute to the signs and symptoms: for instance, loss of cognitive functions, concentration, ability to deal with stress, depression, apathy, drowsiness, and fatigue. In severe cases, there is frank psychosis, convulsions, and coma. Proper management of uremia usually prevents these severe symptoms. *Uremic amaurosis* is a severe loss of vision that develops rapidly because of the involvement of the second cranial nerve (optic nerve). Recovery is usually complete in several days with adequate treatment. Other ocular effects of RF are blurred vision caused by retinal lesions due to anemia and hypertension, and red eye syndrome that causes irritation and

increased vascularity due to hypercalcemia, which enhances calcium deposits on the conjunctiva. Corneal calcifications are associated with secondary and tertiary hyperparathyroidism. Rare abnormalities are ophthalmoplegia, paralysis of ocular muscles, nystagmus, and asymmetrical miosis.

Integument

The dermatological manifestations associated with CRF alter body image and present the patient with some of the most frustrating symptoms. The skin appears a pale, dull, yellowish brown because of anemia, hyperpigmentation from melanin stimulation, and retention of urochromes and other pigments ordinarily excreted by the kidney. Reduced size and activity of oil and sweat glands causes diminished perspiration that leads to dry, scaly skin (in spite of the presence of edema). The etiology for pruritus is unknown; however, it is associated with accumulation of metabolites, hyperparathyroidism, and neuropathy. The persistent scratching causes lesions which heal poorly because of chronic infection and a suppressed immune system. Ecchymoses appear frequently because of platelet defects and increased capillary permeability. Occasionally, subdermal calcifications are present, especially in the hands and around joints. Although dialysis diminishes the severity of these abnormalities, daily skin care with oil-based soaps and lanolin creams helps to maintain skin integrity and patient comfort. Nails and hair are similarly affected, and alopecia may occur.

Endocrine System

Although there is much controversial information about endocrine dysfunction associated with renal failure, the major glands that seem to be affected are the pituitary, thyroid, parathyroid, testes, and ovaries. Growth, parathyroid, follicle-stimulating, and luteinizing hormones and prolactin are elevated. Because of decreased Leydig-cell function, testosterone is reduced; there is also a reduction in thyroxine. Although decreased libido, impotence, and amenorrhea are problems, patients with RF have parented offspring. In addition to physiological changes, the psychological stress from the renal failure contributes to the sexual dysfunction.

Genitourinary System

The effects of renal failure on the genitourinary system are discussed under the section on preparing of the recipient for transplantation.

Treatment Modalities for Renal Failure

The management of renal failure is somewhat dependent on the pathophysiology of the disease process. The renal functions that are compromised are the guides to the treatment modalities chosen. A previous section described specific renal disease entities and treatments specific to those renal losses. Another aspect of RF management includes treatment of the abnormalities created in other body systems as a result of the renal failure. These abnormalities and some specific treatments were presented in the section on ramifications of renal disease on body systems. Therefore this section will consider a more general approach to the treatment of ARF and CRF. First,

medical interventions will be discussed, secondly, the use of dialysis, and thirdly, renal transplantation.

Medical Management

Acute renal failure   The underlying cause for ARF should be established to prevent further renal damage. The next goal of treatment is to reestablish normal urine flow. Diuretics such as mannitol, furosemide, or ethacrynic acid are administered in single doses only. Once diuresis begins it can be maintained with intravenous administration of hypertonic solutions or normal saline. Although the mechanism of the diuresis is uncertain, it has been proposed that intrarenal circulation improves or that tubular debris are washed out. If the attempt to restore urine flow fails, the patient may be oliguric or anuric for a few days to several weeks.

Whether or not urine flow is achieved, maintaining fluid balance is the next challenging aspect of treatment. The use of a flowchart is beneficial to monitor fluid balance on a day-to-day basis. The chart should quantify all sources of fluid intake and output. Fluid sources include medications, food, liquids, intravenous sources, and approximately 300 mL for endogenous production. Fluid is lost through urine, stool, drainage from wounds, nasogastric suction, sputum, and emesis, and approximately 900 mL is lost through insensible losses. Insensible losses increase significantly with fever.

In addition to quantification of fluid intake and losses, the patient must be weighed daily, at the same time each day, with similiar clothing, and on the same scale. A very important technical aspect of accurate weight is that the scale be balanced daily and more frequently if used often. Together the daily weight and fluid intake-output records accurately assess fluid balance and double-check each other. For instance, if the patient has gained 1 kg, the quantitative record should indicate an intake excess, or output deficit, of 1 L. Daily fluid management is based on these assessment parameters. The type of fluid replacement is dependent on the needs of the patient.

It is important to maintain the composition of body fluid compartments. Assessment of daily serum and urine electrolytes is essential. In addition, one must consider electrolyte intake, internal shifts, and losses. Electrolytes are in food, medications, intravenous fluids, and so on, and are lost through all body excreta. Hypernatremia and hyperkalemia can be major problems in ARF, especially when oliguria persists. Hypernatremia enhances an expanded extracellular fluid volume that precipitates heart failure. Frequently the dietary sodium is markedly reduced and other sources very closely monitored (medications or intravenous fluids). These measures usually maintain sodium balance.

Potassium balance, however, is more difficult to achieve. Reducing intake alone does not prevent hyperkalemia and serious cardiac arrhythmias. Intracellular compartments have a high concentration of potassium, and with any cellular breakdown, potassium is released into the circulation. A few circumstances in which there is tissue breakdown with associated ARF are severe burns, trauma, and major surgery. Therefore some efforts to control hyperkalemia are the following: limiting all potential sources of intake; decreasing dietary protein; increasing carbohydrates and essential amino acids; and administering ion-exchange resins and/or insulin plus glucose. This type of diet also helps to control metabolic acidosis, which results from an inability of the kidney to excrete hydrogen ions.

Hypertension and anemia are additional problems associated with ARF that require treatment. Hypertension is often associated with volume expansion, and when that is controlled, hypertension decreases. If not, antihypertensive medications are administered. Anemia is treated with packed red blood cells when the patient becomes symptomatic. In addition, nursing interventions are included to conserve the patient's energy.

With some patients, the best medical management cannot control the fluid, electrolyte, and acid-base imbalances and a more vigorous treatment, dialysis, is required. Dialysis as a treatment for ARF and CRF is discussed later in the chapter.

Drug therapy is often helpful in treating different aspects of renal failure as previously discussed. Any drug, however, that is utilized with RF must be carefully chosen, because so many drugs are excreted by the kidney. Frequently the dose of the drug is reduced and the time interval between doses is lengthened. This helps to reduce toxic effects. Many RF patients receiving drugs are also on dialysis. It is beneficial to know which of these drugs are dialyzable so they will be appropriately administered after dialysis and not prior to dialysis.

Chronic renal failure   Management of CRF is based on principles similar to those of the management of ARF. The time frame, however, is different. In CRF the excretory and regulatory losses occur over a longer time period, and the body makes compensatory ad-

justments. Therefore treatment gradually imposes restrictions on the patient's life-style. For instance, with many CRF patients, their only restriction for years may be limited sodium intake. As renal failure worsens, additional therapies are added to treat the abnormalities. When and to what degree these therapies are instituted is dependent on the progression of the renal disease. Therefore, no cut-and-dry management regimen exists for treating CRF. One thing all CRF patients have in common is that they eventually need supportive therapy to sustain life, that is, either dialysis or renal transplantation.

Dialysis

As diffusion and osmosis occur between two solutions that are separated by a semipermeable membrane, the composition of each solution gradually changes. This dynamic process, dialysis, has been employed as a treatment for acute and chronic renal failure. The two forms of dialysis most commonly used to treat renal failure are peritoneal dialysis and hemodialysis. Although each type yields similiar outcomes, the processes are slightly different and are influenced by separate variables.

Peritoneal Dialysis

Kinetics   A catheter is inserted into the peritoneal cavity and a specially prepared solution, dialysate, is infused. Diffusion and osmosis occur across the peritoneum between the dialysate and blood in the peritoneal vessels. The peritoneum, a semipermeable living membrane, is a closed sac that lines the inner surface of the abdominal wall (parietal portion) and invests most of the abdominal organs (visceral portion). The peritoneum approximates body surface area and/or glomerular capillary surface area. Blood flow through the splanchnic area, although variable, is approximately 1800 mL/min (excluding parietal peritoneum).

Dialysate, warmed to core temperature, is infused, usually by gravity, into the peritoneal cavity and dwells for a few moments or up to 15 min. During this dwell time, osmosis occurs between the plasma and dialysate because the tonicity of the dialysate is greater than the plasma. Dialysate is hypertonic to plasma primarily because of the greater concentration of dextrose in the dialysate. After the dwell time lapses, the dialysate and extra fluid removed by osmosis are gravity-drained from the peritoneal cavity. Therefore, if osmosis occurred from plasma to dialysate, the amount of fluid drained from the peritoneal cavity should be greater than the amount infused. Fluid movement occurs intercellularly and transcellularly across the peritoneum from the vascular spaces. Subsequently, the fluid moves from interstitial and intracellular compartments into the vascular spaces. In addition to dialysate hypertonicity, other factors that influence osmosis are length of dwell time, peritoneal permeability, and peritoneal surface area.

During peritoneal dialysis, although solutes are removed primarily by diffusion, a small amount may accompany fluid movement because of solvent drag (solutes are dragged along with water movement). Diffusion occurs through peritoneum intercellular pathways between the plasma and dialysate because solute concentrations of plasma and dialysate vary. Solutes move from an area of higher concentration to an area of lower concentration. Therefore, to remove solutes from the plasma, the dialysate composition is adjusted so that the solute concentration is less than that of plasma. Other factors that influence solute removal are the characteristics of the solute, dialysate, and peritoneum. Solute characteristics include size, protein binding tendency, concentration, and body distribution. In addition to chemical composition, dialysate characteristics include pH, flow rate, temperature, and volume. Peritoneal characteristics include area, pore size, permeability, and blood flow. Small solutes, such as urea, are more sensitive to blood flow and surface area, whereas large solutes that diffuse slower are sensitive to the area and size of their diffusion pathways. An efficiency index of solute removal is peritoneal clearance that is calculated similarily to renal clearance.

Usually the goal of peritoneal dialysis is to remove fluid and solutes ordinarily excreted by the kidney. It is possible, however, to maintain or replace fluid and/or solutes, depending on how the previously discussed characteristics that influence osmosis and diffusion are manipulated (e.g., dialysate, peritoneum, and solute).

Peritoneal access Several devices are available that provide a means to instill and drain dialysate from the peritoneal cavity: temporary, permanent, and subcutaneous catheters, or the Deane and subcutaneous protheses. Prior to implantation of any device, an abdominal assessment should be made for organomegaly, profound obesity, peritonitis, and history of surgery, suggesting adhesions. A temporary catheter is only used when dialysis is urgently and/or infrequently required, because the catheter is inserted

and removed with each dialysis, and this predisposes the patient to peritonitis. The other peritoneal devices remain in situ until a complication such as infection necessitates their removal or dialysis is no longer required.

Methods and schedules Presently several systems, manual or automated, are available to administer peritoneal dialysis. The manual method involves hanging 1 or 2 L of dialysate in bottles or plastic bags, allowing the dialysate to infuse, monitoring the dwell time, and draining, measuring, and discarding the effluent. This manual method can be used with a dwell time (the intermittent method) or without a dwell time (the continuous method). A dialysis schedule using either manual method usually lasts 20 to 48 h, three times a week, and is flexible depending on the patient's needs. Although this system is the simplest of all the methods and can be done anywhere in the hospital, it requires a great deal of nursing time, and sterility is frequently broken to hang dialysate and discard effluent.

A contemporary form of the manual method is continuous ambulatory peritoneal dialysis (CAPD). CAPD is used to treat chronic renal failure and is done 24 h a day, 7 days a week. Dialysate dwells in the peritoneal cavity for 4 h during the day and 8 h during the night.

The multiple cycler and reverse osmosis (RO) machines are two automated methods of peritoneal dialysis. The cycler connects eight 2-L bottles or bags of dialysate in a series, warms them, regulates infusion and dwell time, and drains and weighs the effluent. The large collection bags must be manually emptied. This method saves nursing time; however, sterility is still frequently broken. It can be used anywhere in the hospital to treat acute or chronic renal failure by any dialysis schedule that meets the patient's needs. The RO system involves the most complicated equipment of all the peritoneal dialysis delivery systems. The operator requires instruction about machine operation, maintenance, and repair. Advantages are that seven different dextrose concentrations are available, sterility is maintained throughout the dialysis treatment, and less nursing time is required. Usually this method is used to treat chronic renal failure.

Patient care during peritoneal dialysis The management of a patient receiving peritoneal dialysis is primarily a nursing responsibility. The registered nurse assesses the patient prior to dialysis, conducts the procedure, observes for changes and complications, records and reports these observations, instructs the patient about peritoneal dialysis, and evaluates the outcome of the treatment. Some parameters to assess are fluid, electrolyte, acid-base, and nonelectrolyte balance, peritoneal access, and medications the patient is receiving.

The most important nursing intervention implemented throughout peritoneal dialysis is the use of aseptic technique, because peritonitis is the most serious complication. The following are some preventive measures:

1. The equipment is assembled using aseptic technique.

2. Dialysate, whether in glass bottles or plastic bags, should always be warmed by a dry method.

3. Sterile technique, including a mask, is used whenever the peritoneal access is manipulated and medications are added to the dialysate (e.g., potassium, heparin, or insulin).

4. Gloves are worn when handling effluent.

5. Dialysis tubing is changed daily.

6. A 0.22-μm filter is placed on the inflow tubing.

7. A sample of peritoneal fluid should be sent for culture and sensitivity before each dialysis.

8. The patient should receive instruction on aseptic technique and peritonitis.

During dialysis the nurse monitors and evaluates the parameters assessed before dialysis and observes for and treats complications. Dialysate is a medication and is treated thusly. Fluid balance is calculated at the end of each exchange, except when using the RO system. To do this accurately follow these steps:

1. Measure the exact amount of dialysate to be infused. (Although dialysate manufacturers identify the liter volume of each container, the label does not include the extra 40 mL to 90 mL of dialysate that must be added due to Federal Drug and Administration regulations.)

2. Measure the effluent in a graduated cylinder.

3. Calculate the difference between the two volumes.

Depending on the patient's condition and type of equipment used, he or she may dialyze in a bed or chair or may ambulate. A final evaluation of the patient's response to the treatment is made and documented when dialysis is completed.

Complications Complications associated with peritoneal dialysis are categorized into access problems, physiological reactions, and mechanical problems.

The most serious access problems are infection and perforation of the bowel, major vessel, bladder, or enlarged kidney. Abdominal pain is associated with peritonitis, perforations, pneumoperitoneum, a misplaced catheter, peritoneum irritation due to hypertonic dialysate and low pH, infusion of cold dialysate, and retained dialysate. Poor dialysate drainage is the result of a kinked catheter, omentum wrapped around or aspirated into the catheter, preperitoneal catheter placement, catheter plugged with fibrin, pneumoperitoneum, peritonitis, constipation, and bowel obstruction. Poor dialysate drainage can quickly lead to an undesired positive fluid balance and circulatory overload. Metabolic and electrolyte changes include protein loss, hyperkalemia, hypokalemia, hyponatremia, hypernatremia, hyperglycemia, and metabolic alkalosis. Patients receiving digitalis preparations should have potassium added to the dialysate. Hypotension can occur if fluid is removed too quickly or in too great a volume. Rarely is the dysequilibrium syndrome or death associated with peritoneal dialysis. Mechanical problems are unique to the type of machinery used and will not be discussed.

Hemodialysis

The goal of hemodialysis in treating acute and chronic renal failure is to correct fluid, electrolyte, and acid-base imbalances and to remove uremic toxins. The treatment is administered by specially trained personnel in a unit designed for hemodialysis, or at the patients bedside if the patient's condition is very guarded. When a patient requires hemodialysis and cannot be transported to a hemodialysis unit, the treatment should always be conducted by a registered nurse. The following discussion includes principles and theories of hemodialysis but not all the technical information required to conduct the procedures.

Kinetics In hemodialysis, blood is circulated outside the body, pumped through a man-made dialyzer, and returned to the vascular system. Presently, three types of dialyzers are available: hollow fiber, parallel flow plate, and coil. Inside the dialyzer, a semipermeable membrane (cellophane or cuprophan) separates the blood compartment from the dialysate compartment. The flow pattern of blood and dialysate is countercurrent. The size of the pores in the semipermeable membrane allow water, electrolytes, and small nonelectrolytes to pass, but inhibit the passage of larger solutes such as protein and bacteria.

Movement of fluid occurs from blood to dialysate

because of osmotic and hydrostatic pressures. Glucose, sodium chloride, or urea are added to the dialysate to create an osmotic gradient between the blood and dialysate. Consequently, fluid moves into the more highly concentrated dialysate. There are two hydrostatic pressures within the dialyzer. In the blood compartment, a positive hydrostatic pressure pushes fluid across the semipermeable membrane. A negative hydrostatic pressure in the dialysate compartment pulls fluid from the blood side. Together these pressures are referred to as the *transmembrane hydrostatic pressure* (TMP). The higher the TMP, the greater the fluid removal or ultrafiltration.

A relatively new method that removes fluid is isolated ultrafiltration or dry suction. Dialysate is not required, and as blood flows through the dialyzer, a negative pressure or vacuum is created on the dialysate side by suction. Fluid is pulled from the blood and collects in a bottle. Although this method can remove several liters per hour and patients tolerate it fairly well, solute clearance is minimal and long-term side effects have not been identified.

Solute movement or diffusion in the dialyzer is due primarily to solute concentration gradients between blood and dialysate. Therefore the dialysate composition is adjusted so that selected solutes in the blood are removed, retained, or replaced. Usually dialysate has a pH and electrolyte concentration similar to that of blood. Glucose is frequently added to dialysate when used for a patient with diabetes mellitus to prevent hypoglycemia. Because the dialysate does not come in direct contact with the blood, the dialysate is not sterile. It is, however, warmed to body temperature to prevent vasoconstriction. Other factors that influence diffusion are solute size; membrane pore size, surface area, and thickness; blood flow; and the width of fluid film layers that form on the blood and dialysate sides of the membrane.

Care of vascular accesses To conduct hemodialysis, an access to the circulatory system that permits blood flow rates of 200 to 300 mL/min is required. Presently several methods are utilized. An internal arteriovenous (A-V) fistula is surgically created by anastomosing an artery and vein. The vein becomes arterialized (matures) and can then tolerate high blood flow rates. Approximately 4 to 6 weeks are required for the fistula to mature, and then it can be used for hemodialysis. During this time, arm exercises are encouraged to enhance maturation. The fistula is assessed frequently for signs of infection, and for patency by either listening for a bruit or feeling a thrill. In addition, circulation above and below the fistula

should be assessed. If there is a question about fistula patency, a surgeon should be notified *immediately*. Precautionary measures are posted at the bedside and noted on the nursing care plan. These include avoiding venipuncture, blood pressure, and other forms of external pressure on the extremity with the fistula. A patient with a fistula who requires soft restraints could present a rather challenging situation.

An alternate vascular access for patients with inadequate vessels is a graft arteriovenous fistula. A straight or looped graft which is synthetic material or an autograft or xenograft is implanted between an artery and a vein. The placement sites are similar to those of the internal A-V fistula. The graft may be used for hemodialysis several weeks after surgery. Assessment and precautionary measures are similar to those of the internal A-V fistula.

When either access is used for hemodialysis, frequently two venipunctures are made with large-gauge needles (14 to 16 gauge). Blood travels to the dialyzer from the arterial site and is returned to the patient through the venous site. Occasionally a single-needle devise is preferred. The needles are removed postdialysis, and pressure is applied to the venipuncture sites for a few minutes until bleeding stops. Sterile dressings are applied and should not be removed for 10 to 12 h. The same access is used over and over again until an unconquerable complication inhibits its use and/or the patient no longer requires dialysis. Complications associated with fistula are thrombosis, infection, aneurysm, ischemia, venous hypertension, and high-output cardiac failure.

A less popular but still important vascular access is the external cannula. A cannula is sutured into a vein and an artery. The cannulas extend to the skin surface and are connected together so that blood flow is continuous from the artery through the cannulas and into the vein. This access can be used for hemodialysis immediately after its implantation. The external cannulas are separated and connected directly to the blood lines. Needles are not required. In contrast to the fistula, a cannula can be visually inspected for patency. If patent, the cannula should feel warm. In addition to the precautionary measures discussed for fistulas, a patient with a cannula must *always* have two clamps readily available. If the cannulas disconnect, the clamps are quickly placed on each cannula to prevent exsanguination. Preferably the clamps should be attached to the dressing that protects the cannula. Other complications associated with cannulas are infection, thrombosis, skin erosion, and dislodgment.

It cannot be overemphasized how important it is

to *maintain* the vascular access. During dialysis it is the responsibility of the nurse who performs the venipuncture (or disconnects the cannula) and conducts the dialysis. Between dialysis treatments it is the responsibility of the nurse who cares for the patient to protect the access and report abnormalities *immediately*. In addition, it is the responsibility of the patient.

When hemodialysis is urgently required and/or other vascular accesses are unavailable or not feasible, the femoral or subclavian vessels may be used. Usually this is done with a single needle that is removed immediately following the dialysis treatment. Pressure is applied to the venipuncture site for approximately 10 to 15 min to stop the bleeding. Although a pressure dressing is applied, the site is assessed for bleeding and formation of a hematoma. Peripheral pulses should also be evaluated if the femoral vessels were used.

Patient care during hemodialysis and complications   After the equipment is assembled, all blood pathways primed with normal saline to prevent air embolus, the contents and temperature of the dialysate bath double-checked, and heparin administered, institution can commence. If water is accidently used as dialysate, hemolysis will occur. The patient complains of severe pain, and the dialysis must be stopped immediately. Cold dialysate causes vasoconstriction and possible cardiac arrest. A loading dose of heparin, 2000 to 4000 units, is given to provide anticoagulation to the extracorporeal system. Heparin continues to be administered throughout the dialysis treatment to prevent clotting in the blood lines and dialyzer. Bleeding postdialysis is a potential problem.

The predialysis patient assessment is completed and documented. Some parameters to assess are the following:

1. General appearance: gait, posture, facial expression
2. Hydration status: weight, vital signs, presence of edema, neck veins
3. Electrolyte, acid-base, and nonelectrolyte balance: blood analysis, subjective symptoms
4. Vascular access functioning: patency, infection
5. Medications being administered: antihypertensives, digoxin

After the assessment is completed, the goals for the hemodialysis treatment are identified, e.g., remove fluid, correct acidosis, etc. If the patient is being dialyzed at the bedside, information is shared between the primary nurse and the nurse conducting the dialysis.

During dialysis these parameters are constantly reevaluated, especially weight and vital signs. Fluid and electrolyte shifts occur rapidly during dialysis, and hypotension is a common problem. The ultrafiltration process can be mechanically slowed down, the patient placed in Trendelenburg's position, and fluid replacement or volume expanders administered if necessary. Hypotension can lead to nausea, vomiting, dizziness, diaphoresis, and angina pectoris. Careful patient monitoring, e.g., frequent blood pressures and maybe withholding antihypertensives before dialysis, can avoid a moderate amount of hypotensive episodes. Cramping during and after dialysis is associated with hypotension and electrolyte shifts, especially sodium. Patients receiving digitalis preparations should *always* dialyze with extra potassium in the dialysate. Cardiac monitoring during dialysis can be helpful with these patients and others who have cardiac abnormalities and complain of chest pain.

Air embolism, although rare, is a serious complication of hemodialysis. Patient signs and symptoms are chest pain, dyspnea, coughing, visual problems, confusion, and ringing in the ears. If this occurs, the patient is positioned on the left side with the head lower than the feet and is administered oxygen. Aspiration of air from the right ventricle may be necessary. Cardiac or respiratory arrest and the disequilibrium syndrome are rare but very serious complications and require supportive services. Mechanical problems are significant and somewhat related to the equipment used, but will not be discussed here.

Postdialysis the patient's response to the treatment is evaluated and documented. It is important to obtain a postdialysis weight because this is the primary method that corresponds to the amount of fluid removed. In addition, postdialysis blood chemistries are compared with predialysis blood chemistries. If the patient is dialyzed at the bedside, the nurse who is conducting the dialysis is responsible for that portion of the patient's care. If an emergency arises, the primary nurse and nurse conducting the dialysis work cooperatively to treat the patient.

Renal Transplantation

Kidney transplantation is a treatment for end-stage renal disease. Its purposes are to improve the quality of life for the patient with ESRD by decreasing the restrictions imposed by dialysis, diet, and medications, and to decrease the psychosocial problems created by dialysis and the systemic complications that occur because of renal failure. Transplantation also replaces functions of the kidney that dialysis cannot. Kidney transplantation should be considered early in chronic renal failure because at this time the physiological status of the patient is bound to be more stable since he or she will have experienced fewer side effects from dialysis and prolonged renal failure.

Selection and Preparation of Transplant Recipient

Although different transplant centers have varying criteria for patient selection, essentially any patient who has ESRD, and is between the ages of 5 and 50 is a candidate for renal transplantation if he or she has the following: a functional bladder, freedom from chronic active infections and major extrarenal complications (e.g., uncontrolled hypertension, malignancies, and psychosis), and the willingness to undergo the preparation for surgery. The purpose of the pretransplant workup is to identify those factors that would enhance rejection, renal failure, and risks of major surgery.

The overall state of health and systems review is assessed by a complete history and physical including hematological and chemical analysis of the blood. Sites of infection, e.g., dialysis access, lungs, urinary tract, integument, oral cavity, and so on, are identified and treated because immunosuppressants are required posttransplant. In addition, because immunosuppressants predispose the patient to formation of gastrointestinal lesions, a thorough assessment of the gastrointestinal tract is usually conducted and abnormalities corrected before transplantation. Liver function studies are undertaken to identify whether or not the patient has an Australian antigen, which is not a contraindication to transplantation, and to evaluate hepatic function because some immunosuppressants enhance liver damage.

Because of decreased urine production and uremia, the bladder becomes atonic and is unable to completely empty, which enhances urine stasis and infection. It is therefore essential to assess the urinary tract for infection, patency, and absence of ureterovesical reflux. Usually urine cultures and a voiding cystogram suffice. More extensive studies and corrective surgery may be indicated to correct any abnormalities such as urethral stricture, bladder neck obstruction, or prostatic obstruction. Throughout the preparatory period, immunological studies will be performed to identify the blood type (ABO), human leukocyte antigens (HLA), and antiglomerular basement antibodies. Tissue typing refers to the determination of the HLA. This is important for both the recipient and donor, because it has been proposed that this antigen system is the primary mediator for rejection. It is still controversial how many antigens should match between the donor and recipient and which antigens cause rejection. However, it is known that identical twins who are immunologically perfectly matched experience the best transplant survival.

Bilateral nephrectomy is indicated with severe, poorly controlled hypertension, recurrent urinary tract infection, symptomatic polycystic disease, protein- or salt-losing nephropathy, and with ureter vesical reflux. Splenectomy is controversial but may be indicated with severe leukopenia and/or thrombocytopenia and hypersplenism. It is beneficial to perform any preparatory surgery prior to transplantation rather than with transplantation so that blood pressure is controlled and surgical stress is minimized. The endocrine system is assessed for hyperparathyroidism that may require surgical intervention. Diabetes mellitus is not a contraindication for renal transplantation. Once the pretransplant workup studies are completed, the final preparation before transplant surgery is dialysis. Preferably, dialysis should be done 2 consecutive days prior to the transplant operation to correct fluid, acid-base, and electrolyte imbalances. Throughout the entire preparatory stages, the recipient and family receive instruction about the entire transplantation process.

Organ Procurement and Preservation

Kidneys for transplantation are available from two sources: donation from an immediate family member or from a cadaver. By generally accepted criteria, a suitable cadaver donor has these characteristics:

1. Between the ages of 5 and 50
2. Compatible in blood type with recipient (Rh factor is not important)
3. Free of transmissible infection and malignancy, except brain tumors
4. Normotensive for a while before death
5. Adequate renal function
6. Brain death
7. Free of disease that could affect the kidney
8. Compatible in tissue typing, if possible
9. Death in hospital after a few hours of observation

Ideally, the transplant team obtains the family's consent after brain death is confirmed and then performs the bilateral nephrectomy. It is imperative to maintain adequate renal perfusion even if cardiac massage or artificial devices are required. The kidneys are removed quickly but gently to minimize ischemia. Usually they are removed en bloc. They can be removed separately, but that takes longer. Immediately the kidneys are flushed with cooled solution and transported by one of the preservation methods.

The pulsatile perfusion hypothermia method utilizes a machine that intermittently perfuses the kidneys with a 4°C solution that decreases the kidneys' oxygen and nutrient requirements while removing wastes. Kidneys are viable with this method for 48 to 72 h. With the static storage hypothermic method, kidneys are submerged in a cool, sterile solution and packed in ice. This method preserves kidneys for approximately 12 to 24 h.

Donor Selection and Preparation

An immediate family member is either a sibling or parent and preferably between the ages of 18 and 50. The blood antigens (ABO) are identified for all possible candidates. Those who are compatible with the recipient and express a willingness to donate undergo an extensive evaluation, including a thorough explanation of the risks and donation process. Preferably, the donor should be in excellent health to minimize any inherent risks from the operation. While waiting for tissues typing results, the donor is prepared similarly to anyone anticipating major surgery. History, physical, and hematology studies, blood chemistries, chest x-ray, and electrocardiogram are all completed. If these studies and tissue typing results are favorable, extensive renal examination is undertaken, e.g., urinalysis, urine culture and sensitivity, creatinine clearance, intravenous pyelogram, renogram, and renal arteriogram. Once normal renal function has been confirmed, the donor continues to consent freely, and the recipient is prepared, the nephrectomy and transplant can proceed.

Although both surgeries are performed simultaneously in adjourning suites, the nephrectomy begins first. The donor is well hydrated the night prior to and during the operation. Usually the left donor kidney is preferred because the right renal vein is short and quite friable. A bladder catheter is inserted to closely observe urine output. Ideally the urine volume should remain copious (100 mL per 15 min) throughout the operation. A flank incision is made and the tip of the 12th rib resected. The ureter is transected first (near the bladder) so that urinary output from the donated kidney and contralateral kidney can be separately observed. A diuretic is administered after the renal vein, renal artery, lymphatics, and nerves are dissected. When urine output is liberal, the vessels and nerves are clamped and divided; then the kidney is removed, placed in a cool solution, and carefully escorted to the recipient. After this operation is completed, the donor is transported to a surgical unit.

Transplantation Surgery

The recipient is brought to surgery shortly after the living related donor's operation commences or as soon as possible after a suitable cadaver donor kidney is available. An anesthetic should be chosen that is not exclusively eliminated by the kidney. The renal graft can be placed into the right or left iliac fossa. The right, however, is usually preferred because the iliac vessels are more superficial (Fig. 28-3). In the iliac fossa, the kidney is easier to observe, palpate, biopsy, and remove, if necessary, than if it were placed in the normal anatomical position. A bladder catheter is inserted.

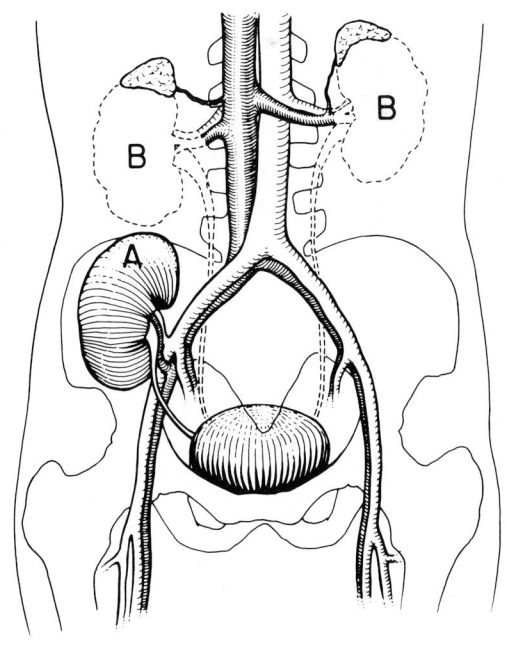

FIGURE 28-3
Placement of a transplanted kidney (A) in relation to the normal anatomical position of the kidneys (B).

The incision is made from the os pubis to the 12th rib. The donated kidney is flushed with cooled Ringer's lactate to clear it of blood. The renal vein is anastomosed to the side of the iliac vein, and the renal artery is anastomosed to the end of the internal iliac artery. Before the final sutures are tied and clamps released, the vessels are flushed with heparinized normal saline to prevent air embolism. Multiple renal vessels must be anastomosed separately. Urine flow commences within minutes if perfusion is adequate. A submucosal tunnel is created in the bladder; the ureter is pulled through the tunnel and sutured to the mucosa with the ends of the ureter rolled back so the opening is wide. The submucosal tunnel acts as a one-way valve to prevent reflux of urine into the graft, predisposing it to infection. The bladder is closed and lymphatics are ligated to prevent the formation of a lymphocele. The operation requires approximately 4 to 6 h. The recipient is then transported to a critical-care unit.

Care of Donor

Postoperatively the donor's fluid balance is carefully monitored because of the preoperative and operative hydration. The bladder catheter should be removed the first postoperative day to decrease susceptibility to infection. Although the donor experiences incisional pain that requires analgesics, ambulation and pulmonary hygiene are encouraged. Psychological support is important because the donor is grieving the loss of a body part and is no longer the focus of attention. Renal function is evaluated daily, and occasionally, transient hypertension, a rise in serum creatinine, and blood urea nitrogen occur. The remaining kidney quickly compensates for the lost kidney, and the patient has 70 percent of the normal renal function he or she had prior to surgery. The donor is discharged approximately 1 week postnephrectomy and continues to have renal function evaluated for 1 year.

Care of Recipient

The postoperative care of the recipient is similiar, regardless of the source of the kidney, to any patient who has undergone major surgery with general anesthesia. Upon arrival in the critical-care unit, the recipient will probably have an endotracheal tube, a nasogastric tube, central venous pressure catheter, hemovac at the surgical site, abdominal dressing, and bladder catheter. Patient assessment is done frequently, at least every 30 to 60 min. This includes vital signs, breath sounds, measurement of intake (e.g., intravenous fluids, blood, volume expanders, etc.), central venous pressure readings, measurement of output (e.g., urinary, nasogastric, stool, hemovac, etc.), weight (if on bed with scale), wound changes, and functioning of dialysis access, if present. Interventions would include:

1. Maintaining a patent airway
2. Calculating and administering fluid and electrolyte replacement
3. Using stool and needle precautions if positive for hepatitis surface antigen
4. Posting precautionary notices for hepatitis and vascular access care
5. Collecting and saving all urine
6. Obtaining urinary and blood samples for laboratory tests
7. Testing stool for occult or microscopic blood
8. Making frequent position changes, but not to unoperated side
9. Gently irrigating bladder catheter only if clots obstruct urine flow
10. Administering immunosuppresants and other ordered medications
11. Changing abdominal dressings
12. Observing for signs and symptoms of diminished renal function, rejection, and complications of surgery

During all procedures, aseptic technique or clean technique, whichever is appropriate, is utilized to prevent introducing microbes that could easily cause infection in the immunosuppressed transplant recipient.

The first postoperative day, the recipient is usually stable and the endotracheal tube, nasogastric tube, and bladder catheter are removed. The recipient ambulates, begins eating, is encouraged to deep breathe and cough, and is instructed to void every half hour. Close monitoring of renal function, fluid-electrolyte balance, possibility of infection (especially pulmonary and urinary), and signs and symptoms of rejection continues. The hemovac and intravenous catheter are removed as soon as possible to eliminate a possible site of infection. Usually a chest x-ray and renogram are done. By the second postoperative day, the patient is typically stable enough to be transferred to a private room on a surgical or transplant unit. Weights and blood analysis, especially for creatinine and electrolytes, are done daily; vital signs and intake and output are recorded every 4 h; frequent voiding, pulmonary toilet, and ambulation are encouraged; assessment of dialysis access, abdominal wound, and peripheral circulation of the leg on the operated side continues.

Although transplant centers have different immunosuppressant protocols, most use a combination of different immunosuppressant agents. Sensitivity to immunosuppressants is tested during the pretransplant workup. Prednisone, which inactivates the macrophage inhibitory factor that minimizes macrophagic infiltration in the transplanted kidney, is administered before the surgery, during the surgery, and daily thereafter. Daily administration of azathioprine or cyclophosphamide is started posttransplant. These agents interfere with sensitized lymphocyte RNA and DNA synthesis. Some centers also administer antilymphocyte globulin intramuscularly or intravenously during the early postoperative period. It inactivates and decreases the number of lymphocytes. Transplant recipients remain on immunosuppressants indefinitely to prevent an otherwise inevitable rejection of the allograft. Nycostatin is administered to minimize oral fungal infections, and antacids are used for gastrointestinal lesions. Other medications are prescribed based on individual needs, e.g., antihypertensives.

Complications of Renal Transplantation

Rejection is a serious complication and can cause loss of the graft. Infection is more serious because it is generally detrimental to the patient and enhances rejection. The administration of immunosuppressant agents predisposes all transplant recipients to infection. Although infection can occur anywhere, the primary sites are the urinary tract, respiratory tract, integument, and blood. Preventive measures such as patient teaching and early detection are the best therapies for infection. Surgical complications include lymphocele, ureteral leaks, bladder leaks, ureteral obstruction, thrombi, vascular leaks, and renal artery stenosis. Although there are many serious and annoying complications related to immunosuppressant therapy, they will not be discussed.

Rejection occurs in approximately 80 percent of renal transplantation cases. The course of the rejection crisis depends on when it is detected and the body's response to treatment. There are three types of rejection: hyperacute, acute, and chronic. Hyperacute rejection occurs during surgery and up to the first 48 h after surgery. Fibrin thrombi are present in small renal arteries and arterioles with extensive cortical necrosis that requires graft nephrectomy. Acute rejection occurs within 1 week to 2 years of transplantation. The kidney is grossly enlarged and edematous, with dilated peritubular capillaries, and fibrin deposits are found in these vessels and the interstitium. The majority of these cases recover with increased immunosuppressant therapy and irradiation. Chronic rejection occurs over months to years. Its course mimics chronic renal failure with gradual loss of graft function. Glomerular damage leads to proteinuria, tubules demonstrate varying degrees of atrophy, and lesions are present in the arcuate and interlobular arterial vessels. No specific treatment is available. Generally, the signs and symptoms of rejection are characteristic of two processes: severe infection (fever, malaise, etc.) and renal failure (increased serum creatinine, diminished urinary output, weight gain, etc.). The transplant team and patient must be cognizant of these signs and symptoms to prevent unnecessary loss of a transplantal kidney.

The transplanted kidney begins excreting urine even before the ureter is sutured into the bladder. The urine volume at first may be copious because of slight ischemia and/or to remove extracellular fluid retained even in the best dialyzed patient. Occasionally a cadaver-donated kidney experiences acute tubular necrosis because of ischemia or for some unexplained reason, and the recipient requires dialysis. The kidney usually recovers within a month. Hopefully the recipient has been psychologically prepared for the possibility of temporary dialysis posttransplant to treat acute renal failure or a rejection crisis. If not, the patient may become severely depressed thinking that the kidney has totally failed. In addition to acute renal failure, the kidney simultaneously can experience rejection, which is both psychologically and physiologically draining on the recipient.

REFERENCES

Brenner, B. M., and F. C. Rector: *The Kidney,* Philadelphia: Saunders, 1976.

David, D. S.: *Calcium Metabolism in Renal Failure and Nephrolithiasis,* New York: Wiley, 1977.

Dunhill, M. S.: *Pathological Basis of Renal Disease,* Philadelphia: Saunders, 1976.

Kochar, M. S., and L. M. Daniels: *Hypertension Control for Nurses and Other Health Professionals,* St. Louis: Mosby, 1978.

Lancaster, L. E.: *The Patient with End Stage Renal Disease,* New York: Wiley, 1979.

Leaf, A., and R. Cotran: *Renal Pathophysiology,* New York: Oxford University Press, 1976.

Metheny, N. L., and W. D. Snively, Jr.: *Nurse's Handbook of Fluid Balance,* New York: Lippincott, 1979.

Papper, S.: *Clinical Nephrology,* Boston: Little, Brown, 1978.

Schrier, R. W.: *Renal and Electrolyte Disorders,* Boston: Little, Brown, 1976.

Valtin, H.: *Renal Dysfunction,* Boston: Little, Brown, 1979.

Vldall, R.: *Renal Nursing,* London: Blackwell, 1977.

GENITOURINARY DISORDERS
Michael J. Moran

Closely related to nephrology, but at the same time distinctly separate from it, is the study of genitourinary disease, or *urology*. Although both of these disciplines deal with the kidney, urology also encompasses the entire genitourinary tract of the male and the urinary tract of the female. It is concerned with the surgical diseases of the genitourinary tract as well as urologic problems which can be managed medically.

Catheters

One of the most basic items used in urology is the indwelling Foley catheter. It is seen on just about any floor in any hospital on any given day. However, its inherent dangers as well as its usefulness are never to be underestimated. Also used a great deal with the male patient is the external or condom catheter. This section of the chapter will deal with catheters in general as well as with specific problems associated with them.

Foley Catheters

A question that commonly arises is concerned with who should be allowed to insert a Foley catheter. Any nurse or doctor who knows the proper sterile technique of inserting a Foley catheter should be allowed to insert a Foley catheter in any male or female patient. If the nurse has difficulty inserting a catheter, a doctor should be asked to do it. Likewise, a doctor who is unable to pass a catheter should call a urologist. One should not subject the patient to repeated traumatic catheterization attempts, which can only cause further discomfort and possible complications for the patient.

A basic point on inserting a catheter is to always wait until one gets a return of urine from the catheter before inflating the balloon. This prevents one from inflating the balloon in the urethra. Applying pressure to the suprapubic area after insertion will often help to get a urine return in a bladder that is only partially full. Lubricant may also obstruct the lumen of the catheter, so irrigating the catheter may help to bring the expected return of urine.

Situations requiring bladder drainage with a Foley catheter are varied. Many surgical patients will have a Foley catheter inserted at the time of surgery, thus preventing urinary retention on the night of surgery. The catheter will be removed when the patient is stable and ambulating. Many surgical patients do not have Foley catheters inserted and should be checked to make sure that they are able to void on the night of surgery. Patients who have undergone abdominal, perineal, or perirectal procedures are especially prone to urinary retention, as are hernia repair patients and postpartum mothers. Any critically ill medical or surgical patient requiring close monitoring of intake and output will also need one.

No matter what the patient care situation, the important point is not to let the bladder become overdistended. The bladder is an organ which can be seriously damaged when its fine vasculature, musculature, and innervation are overstretched.

External Condom Catheters

External condom catheters, sometimes called "Texas catheters," are often helpful in the older male patient who is incontinent or in the patient in whom a long-term Foley catheter is not practical because of infection. However, it is again important to be sure that a patient with an external catheter does not become overdistended. These patients can have overflow incontinence with a large residual urine in a greatly overdistended bladder, and a Foley catheter is required at least until the etiology of the problem is determined and corrected.

A serious complication from external condom catheters is gangrene and necrosis of the penile skin from the catheter being applied too tightly at the base of the penis. The typical patient with an external condom catheter is an elderly male who is often incontinent, disoriented, and generally not aware that the catheter may be too tight. In only a matter of hours the venous return and subsequently the arterial supply of the skin and superficial layers of the penis may be permanently compromised.

The worst case this author has seen was that of an alert, oriented, paraplegic male who had an external condom catheter applied too tightly. Even though the problem was discovered on the same day, the patient subsequently developed gangrene and necrosis of the penile skin with secondary pseudomonas sepsis. A urethrocutaneous fistula also developed at the base of the penis because of pressure necrosis from the constricting catheter. The patient required massive antibiotic coverage and extensive surgical debridement of the penis for the sepsis, as well as numerous skin graft procedures to the denuded penis and for closure of the fistula. Had the catheter been applied correctly in the first place, none of this would have occurred.

Dermatitis and maceration of the penile skin are common problems encountered with the use of the external condom catheter. They usually occur as a result of the penis lying in urine and constantly being wet, oftentimes because the catheter has twisted on itself, thus preventing adequate drainage and causing the catheter to balloon up with urine. This is easily prevented by frequently checking that the catheter has not twisted on itself and that it is draining properly.

Catheter Care and Irrigation

Routine catheter care requires preserving sterility, both at the time of insertion and while the catheter is in place. Ideally, the connection between the end of the catheter and the drainage bag tubing should not be broken while the catheter is in the bladder.

It may happen that a Foley catheter will not function properly because of blood clot, sediment, or stones in the bladder. Gentle manual irrigation of the catheter is indicated in these situations, but it is of the utmost importance to do it with proper sterile technique so as not to introduce bacteria into the bladder. If irrigation of the catheter does not relieve the problem, the catheter should be removed, with moderate suction being applied to the lumen with a piston-type irrigation syringe. Hopefully, this maneuver will pull out the offending blood clot, stones, or sediment, and a new Foley catheter can then be inserted.

If a Foley catheter is to be left in a patient for any length of time, taping of the catheter is important. In the male patient the Foley catheter is taped in a gentle curve back up to the lower abdomen, as shown in Fig. 28-4. This prevents pressure necrosis and abscess or fistula formation by straightening the urethra. In the female patient the catheter should be taped to the medial thigh such that it has enough length to allow mobility of the lower extremities without pulling the catheter's balloon down on the bladder neck.

In order to help prevent bacteria from following a retrograde course along the catheter into the bladder, antibiotic ointment should be applied at the urethral meatus around the catheter twice a day. The drainage bag and tubing should never be raised above the patient's bladder, because this allows for the passage of contaminated urine back into the bladder.

Foley catheters are the leading cause of hospital-acquired urinary tract infections and are the most common predisposing factor in fatal gram-negative sepsis in the hospital. For this reason, good sterile technique and proper catheter care cannot be overemphasized.

Except to obtain a urine culture specimen, a Foley catheter should never be clamped. Clamping a catheter to "train the bladder" does nothing but run the risk of overdistending the bladder if the clamp is left on too long.

Catheter Drainage Systems

The use of drainage systems for urinary catheters is an important topic. The two basic systems are closed drainage and open drainage. A closed system is that of a Foley catheter connected to a sterile drainage tube and bag with no open connections or direct exposure to the air. An example of open drainage would be an external condom catheter and its tubing draining directly into a nonsterile bag, which is merely tightened around the tube with a drawstring. This type of system is not airtight and can only serve to enhance bacterial growth and further contaminate the system. Despite the fact that an external catheter is not sterile, it is the opinion of this author that only closed, sterile

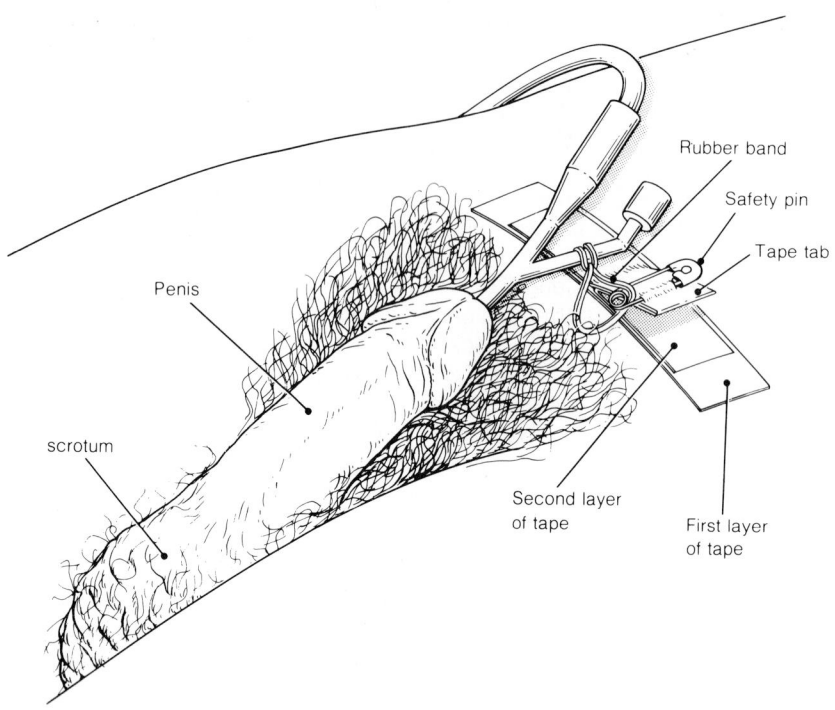

FIGURE 28-4

Taping a Foley catheter (male patient). The objective is to straighten the urethral curve at the penoscrotal area in order to reduce the chance of pressure necrosis within the urethra and to prevent additional force on the catheter and urethra in the event of erection. Positioning the Foley catheter against the thigh would frustrate this objective; therefore, the catheter is anchored on the abdomen instead. (*From Dorothy A. Jones, C. F. Dunbar, and M. M. Jirovec, Medical-Surgical Nursing, A Conceptual Approach, McGraw-Hill, New York, 1978. Used by permission of the publisher.*)

drainage systems should be used with any sort of urinary catheter, whether it be a Foley catheter or external condom catheter.

Other Urinary Catheter

Other types of catheters are commonly employed in various urologic situations. Figure 28-5 illustrates these catheters. Pezzer and Malecot catheters are used most often in patients with suprapubic urinary diversion, either after suprapubic prostatectomy or other procedures where the bladder has been opened and good drainage with a large-gauge catheter is required. These catheters have the advantage of large eyes or openings at the ends of the catheters so that they can more easily accommodate large blood clots or sediment. The care of these catheters and their use in patients with urinary diversion will be discussed later in the chapter.

A variation of the Foley catheter is the three-way Foley catheter which is used for continuous bladder irrigation. Continuous irrigation is very helpful in the patient who has had transurethral resection of the prostate. By providing a continuous flow of irrigation into and out of the bladder, it prevents stasis of bloody urine and formation of blood clots which could obstruct the catheter. Continuous bladder irrigation with an antibiotic solution (neomycin and polymixin) can be used for short 2- to 3-day periods in order to treat a severe cystitis. It must not be used for longer periods, however, because it will select out resistant organisms and lead to more serious infections.

Problems with the Uncircumcised Male

Problems peculiar to the male patient who is uncircumcised deserve special attention. Good hygiene of the foreskin is important in preventing local infection and local malignancy. (Squamous cell carcinoma of the penis is rarely seen in the circumcised male or in the uncircumcised male who maintains good foreskin hygiene.)

Phimosis is simply a fibrosis of the distal foreskin due to chronic infection underneath the foreskin. If severe, phimosis makes retraction of the foreskin impossible, thus preventing good hygiene and making insertion of a Foley catheter very difficult. Circumcision is the only definitive treatment for phimosis. If the patient has a severe inflammation of the foreskin and glans, a dorsal slit circumcision will open up the area so that it can be treated before formal circumcision. This simply involves incising and suturing the dorsal foreskin.

Paraphimosis, seen only in the uncircumcised male, is a condition in which the foreskin becomes irreversibly retracted behind the glans penis. It is due to inflammation of the foreskin and may occur with or without a Foley catheter in place, although it seems to be potentiated by the presence of a catheter. It is an extremely dangerous condition and occurs most commonly after a Foley catheter has been inserted in an uncircumcised male, with the foreskin being left in the retracted position.

The earliest physical sign of paraphimosis is edema of the retracted foreskin and the glans penis secondary to obstruction of its venous return. If not corrected soon by replacing the foreskin to its normal position, the condition may progress to gangrene and necrosis of the glans, because the retracted foreskin constricts down on the shaft of the penis and the increasing edema results in occlusion of the arterial supply to the glans. This is shown in Fig. 28-6.

Treatment of paraphimosis consists of pulling the foreskin back to its anatomical position. If the edema is too great to pull it down, firmly squeezing the glans for about 5 min will sometimes decrease the edema enough to restore the foreskin to its normal position. If this fails, then an emergency dorsal slit circumcision of the constricting foreskin is the only solution, and even this will sometimes be too late if the arterial blood supply has been compromised for too long a period.

Needless to say, prevention is the best solution to paraphimosis. Too many doctors and nurses are not aware of this potentially disastrous condition, so education of house staff physicians and new nurses cannot be overemphasized.

Problems Inserting Catheters

Inserting a Foley catheter in a patient is not always easy. Most difficulties encountered can be explained on an anatomical basis.

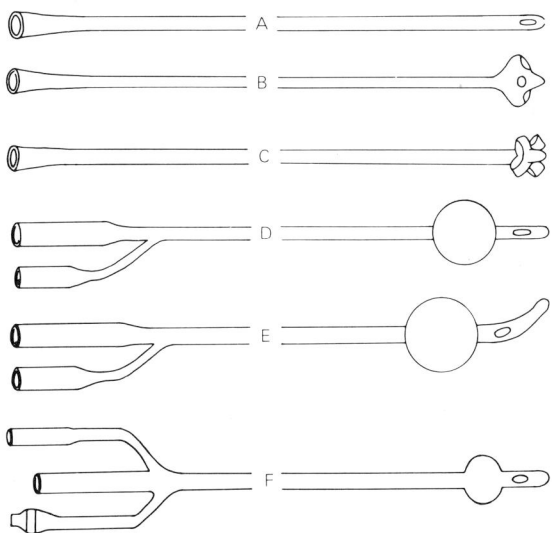

FIGURE 28-5
Different types of commonly used catheters. (A) Simple urethral catheter; (B) mushroom or de Pezzar; (C) winged-tip or Malecot; (D) Foley with inflated bag; (E) Foley with Coudé tip; (F) three-way Foley catheter (the third lumen is used for irrigation of the bladder). (*From H. C. Moidel, E. C. Giblin, and B. M. Wagner, Nursing Care of the Patient with Medical-Surgical Disorders, McGraw-Hill, New York, 1976. Used by permission of the publisher.*)

A large prostate gland and urethral strictures are the problems most commonly observed with catheterizing the male patient. In most patients with a large obstructing prostate, a Coudé-Foley catheter (see Fig. 28-5), with its gently curved tip, will negotiate its way through the narrowed prostatic urethra and into the bladder quite easily. Another technique which is sometimes helpful is to inject about 10 mL of lubricant directly down the urethra before inserting the catheter. If neither the Coudé nor the lubricant in the urethra are successful, a urologist should be called.

Most urethral strictures in the male can be handled simply with dilatation alone. This is usually performed on a regular basis, the frequency of which is determined by the severity of the stricture.

The most commonly used instruments for dilating urethral strictures include van Buren sounds and filiforms and followers. van Buren sounds are tapered metal instruments with a curved end. They are very effective in dilating strictures that are at least 20 French in diameter, and they come in sizes up to 32 French. For tighter strictures, the filiforms and followers are the instruments of choice. The filiform is a pliable rubber instrument with a metal threaded fe-

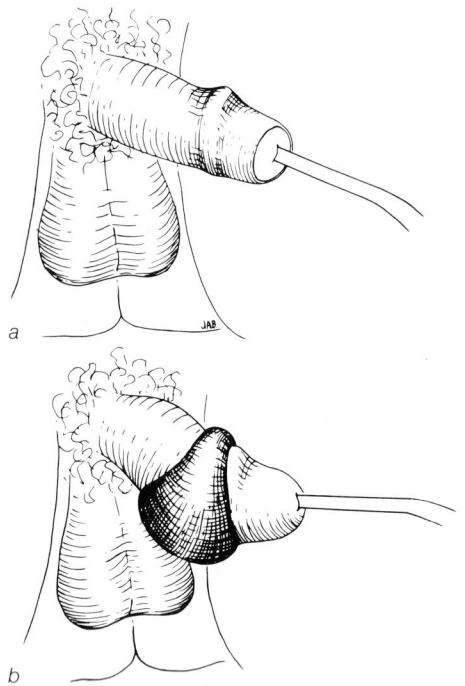

FIGURE 28-6

Foley catheter in the uncircumcised male. (*a*) This shows the proper anatomical position of the foreskin after insertion of the catheter. (*b*) Paraphimosis resulting from leaving the foreskin retracted after insertion of the Foley catheter. Note the marked edema of the retracted foreskin.

male adaptor at the end: it comes in sizes from 3 to 6 French with straight, corkscrew, and Coudé tips.

Once the filiform has been passed gently through the stricture and into the bladder, a pliable tapered follower with its metal threaded male adaptor tip is screwed into the metal end of the filiform. Then the follower is passed into the bladder, simply following the filiform and thus dilating the stricture. Progressively larger followers can then be used to dilate the stricture up to a maximum of 32 French, depending on the severity of the stricture.

Dilatation of urethral strictures should only be performed by a urologist, because the urethra is a very delicate structure which can easily be perforated. Refer to the discussion on perforation and urinary extravasation later in this chapter.

An uncommon problem is inserting a Foley catheter in the male patient with massive edema of the genitalia caused by burns or anasarca from liver or heart disease. This is discussed under penile and scrotal trauma later in the chapter.

Inserting a Foley catheter in the female patient is not always as easy as it may appear. The urethral meatus is often far from obvious and requires wide spreading of the labia with the opposite hand. If this does not reveal the meatus, gentle traction downward and slightly anteriorly on the labia minora just behind the clitoris will usually help to identify it. In preparing the meatus, each sponge should be used only once and should be used from front to back so as not to risk spreading fecal organisms into the bladder. The female urethral meatus is very sensitive, and every effort should be made not to traumatize it.

Urologic Emergencies

Although there are few emergencies in urology, certain situations arise that do require immediate attention. Emergencies such as paraphimosis have already been discussed, and a later section on genitourinary trauma will cover those related emergencies.

Acute Urinary Retention

A common situation both in the emergency room and on the wards is that of acute urinary retention. Whether secondary to mechanical obstruction (e.g., benign prostatic hypertrophy) or postoperatively (e.g., hernia repair, anorectal surgery, etc.), the important thing is to not let the bladder become overdistended.

In cases of urinary retention where a urethral catheter is unable to be inserted, a good temporizing measure is a percutaneous suprapubic cystostomy. This is a catheter that is very similar to an indwelling venous cannula used for intravenous infusion. It has a hollow trocar-type needle which is used to puncture through the skin and abdominal wall into the distended bladder. The flexible Teflon catheter is then advanced over the trocar into the bladder, and then the trocar is removed. The cystostomy catheter is then connected to a sterile drainage system. This temporary suprapubic tube should be sutured to the skin, the puncture site at the skin covered with antibiotic ointment, and a sterile dressing applied with the tubing securely taped to the abdomen. The catheters may be left in the bladder indefinitely if sterility is maintained at the insertion site and the catheter is not accidentally pulled out.

Another method to decompress a greatly overdistended bladder that will not accept a urethral catheter is to insert a fine-gauge spinal needle percutaneously into the suprapubic midline where the bladder is palpable. This will adequately drain the bladder for a matter of hours in a situation where urologic consultation is not immediately available.

An etiologic factor associated with acute urinary retention is the effect of pharmacologic agents upon the bladder. The anticholinergic and antihistamine properties of many drugs can cause varying degrees of bladder dysfunction, with the worst being complete retention. The alert nurse or physician may save a patient a costly and unnecessary urologic evaluation by simply thinking of a possible pharmacologic etiology for the patient's unexpected urinary retention.

Blood Clot Retention

Hematuria with a bladder full of clots presents an acute problem, since the patient will be in great discomfort from a rapidly distending bladder. Whether the hematuria is postoperative (e.g., transurethral resection of the prostate) or secondary to a renal or bladder carcinoma, the clots in the bladder need to be evacuated as quickly as possible.

If the clots are not too large or numerous, they can sometimes be manually irrigated out through a large-gauge Foley catheter (i.e., 24 French). If a catheter is already in place and cannot be irrigated, it should be removed with suction applied at the same time to pull out as many clots as possible. Then a new catheter can be inserted and hopefully will drain.

If none of the above methods are effective in irrigating the bladder free of clots, then a urologist should be called in to insert either a large hollow metal catheter or a cystoscope sheath in order to manually irrigate out the bladder.

Once the bladder is free of clot, a three-way Foley catheter with continuous irrigation should be inserted and kept running at a rate fast enough to prevent formation of blood clots. If bleeding is from the prostate, firm traction may be applied on the inflated 30-mL catheter balloon for a period of 4 to 8 h. Care should be taken not to apply too much traction or to leave it on traction for too long a period, since this may result in ischemia to the area and damage the nerves supplying the external sphincter. If this were to happen, incontinence could be the result.

Catheter Trauma

Catheter trauma is a topic with which critical-care unit and regular ward staffs should be familiar. It is not an uncommon occurrence for a confused patient to pull out a Foley catheter with the balloon still inflated. This often results in trauma to the urethra with resulting hemorrhage. The main objective in these patients, whether they be male of female, is to gently reinsert a Foley catheter in order to splint the urethra and to keep urine from coming into contact with the injured segment of urethra. There is usually no difficulty in reinserting another Foley catheter, but if there is, a urologist should be consulted.

Another form of catheter trauma is injury to the urethra from traumatic attempts at catheterization. These usually occur in the male patient in the form of urethral perforation and false passages caused by forcing a catheter when it meets with resistance. Since a urethral perforation may result in urinary extravasation with subsequent abscess formation and sepsis, a catheter should never be forced when resistance is encountered.

Inability to Deflate the Catheter Balloon

A curious problem seldom seen with Foley catheters, but a difficult one when it does occur, is that of the catheter balloon which will not deflate. This occurs because of obstruction in balloon lumen. If attempts at deflating it with a syringe or by cutting the balloon lumen do not work, several other techniques are available.

One method is to insert a fine-gauge wire such as the guide wire from a central venous pressure catheter or a radiologic angiocatheter into the balloon lumen and pass it out to the balloon in order to puncture it. Another way to deflate the balloon is to inject 5 to 10 mL of mineral oil into the balloon channel lumen. The mineral oil will chemically interact with and dissolve the latex rubber from which the catheter and balloon are made. One should allow at least 10 to 15 min for this to occur.

A method important *not* to try is that of overinflating the balloon in order to burst it. The capacity of even the 5-mL balloons is usually in the proximity of at least 200 mL, so it is next to impossible to overinflate these balloons in hopes of bursting them.

Temporary Urinary Diversion

Urinary diversion is a general term which simply implies a form of urinary drainage different from the normal anatomy of the urinary tract. It encompasses a variety of urologic procedures and deserves special mention in the nursing care of this special group of urologic patients (Fig. 28-7).

Suprapubic Cystostomy

The simplest form of urinary diversion and probably one of the most common is the suprapubic cystostomy.

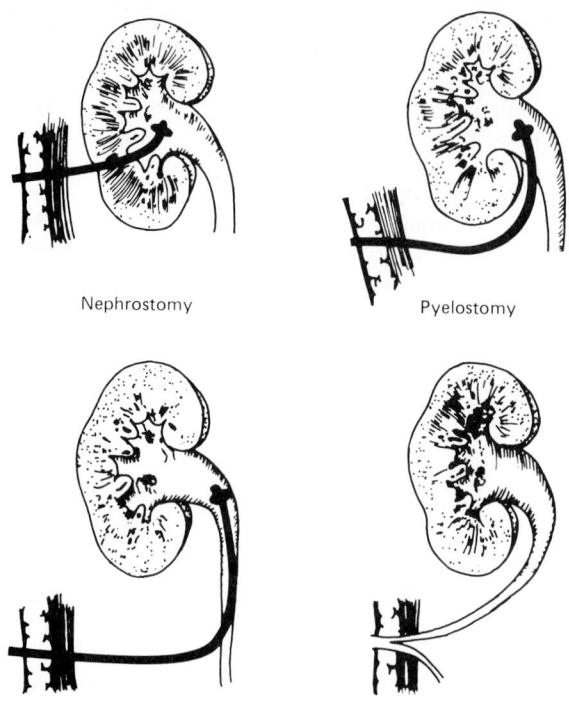

Nephrostomy

Pyelostomy

Temporary ureterostomy

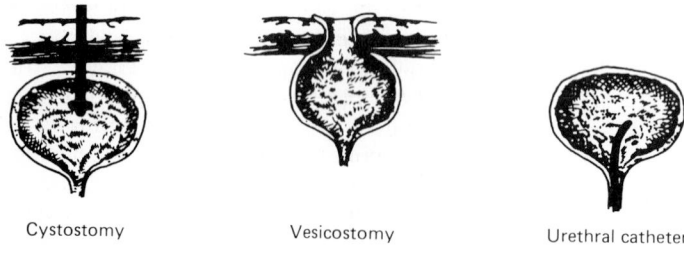

Cystostomy

Vesicostomy

Urethral catheter

FIGURE 28-7

Representative methods of achieving temporary diversion at various sites in the urinary tract. (*From David C. Sabiston, Jr., Davis-Christopher Textbook of Surgery, Saunders, Philadelphia, 1977. Used by permission of the publisher and the author.*)

This is performed simply by placing a large-gauge Foley catheter or a Pezzer or Malecot catheter in the bladder after having performed the cystostomy through a transverse suprapubic incision. The cystostomy tube itself is usually brought out through a separate stab wound above the incision.

Permanent suprapubic cystostomies are frequently used in patients with severely neurogenic bladders and in those patients with inoperable bladder outlet obstruction. (Temporary percutaneous suprapubic cystostomies were discussed earlier in this chapter.) The former category includes mainly spinal cord patients in whom neither chronic Foley drainage or external condom catheter drainage are practical because of catheter-related complications such as fistulas and periurethral abscess formation. The latter category of inoperable bladder outlet obstruction comprises those patients with either severely obstructing carcinoma or benign prostatic hypertrophy of the prostate. Either very advanced age or poor surgical risk factors make these patients good candidates for a simple suprapubic cystostomy rather than difficult prostatic surgery. Occasionally a patient with severe and diffuse urethral strictures is considered for suprapubic cystostomy, because the chances for successful urethroplasty are very poor.

Vesicostomy

Vesicostomy is occasionally used in the neonate male with posterior urethral valves. It is performed by bringing an opening in the bladder out to the skin as a stoma; a urostomy bag is then used for drainage. These are usually taken down later in life after the anatomic problem requiring the diversion has been corrected. Most urologic surgeons today prefer other forms of diversion, since this method often results in a small contracted bladder which is difficult to reconstruct later.

Ureterostomies

Cutaneous ureterostomies are employed in patients with some form of obstruction at either the bladder–urethral vesical junction or in the bladder itself. The ureters are brought out to the skin in each flank as either loop or end ureterostomies, and urostomy bags are applied over them.

When used in the pediatric patient, these are again usually temporary, being taken down within the first few years of life.

Nephrostomies

Nephrostomies can be unilateral or bilateral and often are used in cancer patients when metastatic disease from the genitourinary or gastrointestinal tracts has caused enlarged periaortic lymph nodes to obstruct one or both ureters. With a nephrostomy tube draining the pelvis of the kidney and being then brought out through the renal parenchyma, the kidney drains directly and is protected from obstruction. Pyelostomy is similar to a nephrostomy, but the tube does not actually pass directly through renal parenchyma.

Permanent Urinary Diversion

Although the methods of urinary diversion just discussed are very effective, a more permanent form of urinary diversion provides greater convenience for the patient as well as greater protection for the kidneys. Ileal and sigmoid conduits are the main forms of permanent diversion.

Ileal and Sigmoid Conduits

Urinary diversion by means of an ileal or sigmoid conduit employs a short, isolated segment of either terminal ileum or sigmoid colon as a conduit between the ureters and a cutaneous stoma. The distal end of the conduit is oversewn, and the ureters are anastomosed to the bowel so that the urine will drain freely out to the cutaneous stoma. This acts simply as a constant low-pressure drainage system without the reservoir function of the bladder. With this form of urinary diversion, i.e., by means of a urostomy bag, the patient can keep dry and maintain a very close-to-normal life-style.

Neither type of conduit is without its problems. Early postoperative complications may include hemorrhage, infection, or bowel obstruction, while long-term problems include stone formation and chonic infection, mild electrolyte imbalance, and obstruction to one or both of the kidneys. Stenosis of the stoma is also a common long-term problem with these patients. If recognized early, it can often be treated with dilation, but occasionally this condition requires revision of the stoma.

Because of the high incidence of stone formation in the long-term ileal conduit patient, the current trend in pediatric urology is to employ the sigmoid conduit in the pediatric patient requiring urinary diversion. For adult patients undergoing diversion for cancer of the bladder, this is not as much of a problem, since their normal life expectancy is not as long as that of a child.

Ureterosigmoidostomy

An older form of urinary diversion which is regaining some popularity is the ureterosigmoidostomy, in which the ureters are anastomosed into the sigmoid colon in a nonrefluxing fashion. The rectum then serves as a reservoir for urine as well as stool, and these patients normally are able to achieve continence by means of their anal sphincter. This form of diversion has the advantage of not having a cutaneous urostomy, but its disadvantages are significant.

Patients with ureterosigmoidostomies have a higher incidence of hydronephrosis and infection in the kidneys; they are also prone to hyperchloremic acidosis because of the absorptive qualities of the rectum. In the long term, there is also a higher incidence of carcinoma of the colon.

These patients should empty their rectum every 2 to 3 h while awake, so as not to let too much urine be reabsorbed through the rectum. Management with oral sodium bicarbonate can help avoid the acidosis problems.

Postoperative Care of Urinary Diversion Patients

In the immediate postoperative care of any patient with urinary diversion, the matter of drainage tubes is not to be regarded lightly. It is very important to keep a suprapubic cystostomy or nephrostomy tube securely in place at least for the first few weeks after the surgery until the tract forms around the tube, enabling one to change the tube easily.

If these tubes are inadvertently removed in the immediate postoperative period, it may well be impossible to reinsert them, thus defeating the entire purpose of the surgery. Usually the urologist will have sutured these tubes to the skin, but it provides more security also to tape them to the skin, which has been prepared with an adhesive such as benzoin. This will help prevent undue traction and possible accidental removal of the tube.

Once a good tract has formed for the suprapubic tube or nephrostomy tube, it is still important never to let a tube be removed for more than a short time. Even within a matter of several hours, a permanent tract may close over enough that it is impossible to reinsert the tube.

Depending on the individual preference of the urologic surgeon performing the procedure, ileal and sigmoid conduits may or may not have a Foley catheter in the stoma as well as ureteral stents through the ureteral-bowel anastomoses. If Foley catheter or stents are present, they are only temporary and are normally removed in the first several days following surgery. The most important thing to watch for in the conduit patient is that the conduit drains freely. If there is any indication that the conduit is not draining well (i.e., distention, fever, or decreased urine output), then the surgeon should be called immediately. Since a small or large bowel anastomosis has been performed where the conduit segment was isolated from, these patients will routinely require nasogastric suction for roughly 3 to 5 days postoperatively. As in any patient undergoing bowel surgery, the importance of a properly functioning nasogastric tube cannot be overemphasized. Undue tension on a small or large bowel anastomosis can result in an abdominal catastrophe.

Urologic Endoscopic Surgery

Urologic surgery and cystoscopic procedures make up a unique area in the field of surgery. While at first glance one may think that the urologic surgeon is rather limited in this surgical specialty, this is not the case at all. The open surgery of the genitourinary tract in the male and urinary tract in the female includes a large number of surgical procedures covering a variety of surgical diseases and problems.

Cystoscopy and transurethral surgery, however, are what make the urologic surgeon truly unique among surgeons. While these two areas are often not well understood by the layperson, they are by no means to be regarded lightly. For nursing and medical personnel, a basic understanding and working knowledge of cystoscopy, transurethral surgery, and open urologic surgery are prerequisite to the optimal care of the urologic patient.

Cystoscopy

Cystoscopy in male and female patients, from the pediatric age group to the elderly, is primarily a diagnostic tool performed with the 30° foroblique lens used to inspect the urethra and prostate, and the 70° right-angle lens used to visualize the bladder. These cystoscope lenses have excellent fiber optic light sources, and with their magnification, they provide for very close inspection of the urethra and bladder.

Cystoscopy can be performed under local, general, or spinal anesthesia, depending upon the patient. In conjunction with the physical examination, laboratory studies, and intravenous pyelogram, cystoscopy completes the standard urologic workup in most patients with lower urinary tract complaints.

In the patient with a known allergy to the iodine-containing IVP dye, or in a patient in whom one needs better visualization of the ureters, retrograde ureterograms and pyelograms can be performed with the cystoscope. This is accomplished by injecting contrast through ureteral catheters into the ureteral orifices to the kidneys, followed by an abdominal x-ray.

A number of other diagnostic as well as therapeutic measures can be performed using the cystoscope. Biopsies can be taken through it. Stones can be removed or crushed (lithotripsy) using cystoscopic attachments. Ureteral catheters, both temporary and permanent types, may be passed up the ureters and left in place when ureteral obstruction has occurred because of stones, tumors, or retroperitoneal fibrosis. This procedure will often achieve adequate urinary drainage from the kidneys, thus avoiding open surgery or at least allowing time for it to be done on an elective rather than emergency basis.

Temporary ureteral catheters inserted via the cystoscope may be left in the ureters and brought out through the urethra alongside the Foley catheter and connected to either separate drainage systems or to the end of the Foley catheter where it connects to the drainage tubing. Ureteral catheters may be irrigated if obstructed, but since the normal renal pelvis holds about 5 mL, care should be taken to gently irrigate the catheters with only 3 to 4 mL of saline or sterile water.

Renacidin is a chemical that can be used to irrigate the bladder in order to dissolve calcium and magnesium ammonium phosphate calculi. It may require weeks of irrigation before a stone dissolves completely. Although not approved by the Federal Drug Administration for use above the bladder, it has been successfully used to dissolve stones in the kidneys by irrigating the pelvis of the kidney.

Two ureteral catheters are employed, one for inflow of the Renacidin and the other for outflow. If a stone in the pelvis of the kidney is being irrigated, the patient must be closely monitored on a daily basis for any flank pain, fever, increased white blood cell count, or elevated serum magnesium. If any of these factors become evident, the Renacidin should be stopped immediately

Transurethral Surgery

Transurethral surgery includes transurethral resection of the prostate, resection bladder tumors, and also sphincterotomies. It should be done under general or spinal anesthesia.

Transurethral resection of the prostate (TUR-P) is a unique operative procedure in that it is performed without a cutaneous incision and yet allows for a very adequate resection of the prostate by means of the resectoscope. The resectoscope is a cystoscopic lens fitted into a sheath which has a loop equipped with electro-cutting and coagulating abilities.

During a TUR-P, the prostate tissue obstructing the prostatic urethra is trimmed out with the loop. Bleeding is also controlled, using the coagulating current to touch the bleeders. It is important to understand that only the inner core of prostatic tissue which is obstructing the urethra is removed with TUR-P. The outer surgical capsule of the prostate is left in place.

Once the resection is completed and satisfactory hemostatis is achieved, a large-gauge (24 or 26

French) three-way Foley catheter is inserted into the bladder and about 40 mL of fluid is injected into the 30-mL balloon. The inflated balloon exerts mechanical pressure on the prostatic fossa and bladder neck to tamponade any venous sinus bleeding that is not controlled with the cautery. The three-way Foley catheter is connected to continuous irrigation with glycine, mannitol, or saline. Most urologists will leave the Foley catheter in place for about 3 days following the surgery, assuming that the urine is clear by the third day. If bleeding persists, the Foley should be kept in place for as long as needed.

Care of the TUR-P Patient

In caring for the patient who has just had a TUR-P, it is important to keep the catheter working well and to prevent it from becoming obstructed with blood clots. This is easily avoided by keeping the continuous irrigation running at a rate fast enough to prevent clot formation in the bladder. The safest and easiest type of manual irrigation for this type of patient is that obtained with the drainage system that has an irrigating bulb built into the tubing. Thus, one can irrigate easily and without breaking the sterility of the system. Sometimes manual irrigation with a piston-type syringe is the only solution, however. Small clips of resected prostatic tissue may still be lying in the bladder, and these, too, can obstruct a Foley catheter.

If the Foley catheter cannot be irrigated and will not drain, it may need to be replaced. Only a urologist should be allowed to replace a Foley catheter in the patient who has just had a TUR-P.

In the immediate postoperative period and for 1 or 2 days following a TUR-P, close attention should be directed toward the patient's mental status and electrolyte balance. Because a great deal of irrigating fluid may be absorbed through the open venous sinuses in the prostate during the resection, dilutional hyponatremia and water intoxication can become a problem in this patient. If the patient seems inordinately confused or lethargic postoperatively, electrolytes should be checked immediately. Since most patients undergoing TUR-P are elderly, one has to differentiate this potential problem from the confused mental status seen not infrequently in the postoperative elderly.

General patient care considerations in the patient who is status post-TUR-P are also very important. Antispasmodic drugs such as oral propanthelene or belladonna and opium suppositories will give relief from bladder spasms which are common anytime a large catheter is in the bladder.

Because the raw cut edge of the prostate contains many blood vessels, it is imperative that these patients avoid any straining, whether while lifting objects or having a bowel movement. Bleeding from the prostate may occur and become a serious problem. To avoid this problem, the patient should be warned not to strain in any way and to drink plenty of fluids in order to urinate out any small residual clots or pieces of tissue in the bladder. Stool softners and mild laxatives are also of assistance.

Enemas should never be given to the patient who has just had prostatic surgery, whether it be TUR-P or open prostate surgery. Since the prostate sits just anterior to the rectum, the mechanical irritation from an enema can easily initiate postoperative bleeding. When a TUR-P patient has had his Foley catheter removed, he should be observed closely to make sure that he voids adequately within 4 to 6 h after removal.

TUR-Bladder Tumors

Transurethral resection of small, single bladder tumors is easily accomplished with the resectoscope. In tumors of low-grade malignancy, this is the treatment of choice. After the tumor is resected, a staging bite into the muscle below the tumor is usually taken to determine if there is invasion of the tumor into the muscle. Should perforation of the bladder occur with the staging bite, the Foley catheter must remain in place for at least 5 days until the perforation has sealed itself.

Sphincterotomy

Sphincterotomy is a procedure performed transurethrally to cut the external sphincter and thus make the patient incontinent. This procedure is not done commonly and is reserved for certain male spinal cord patients in whom incontinence treated with an external condom catheter is preferable to an indwelling Foley catheter.

Complications of Cystoscopy and Transurethral Surgery

Cystoscopy and transurethral surgery, like any other area in surgery, are not without their complications. Though careful technique will keep complications to a minimum, occasional problems are inevitable, especially in older, debilitated patients. Since nursing personnel spend the largest percentage of time in direct patient care, it is very important that they be alert to possible complications.

Urinary sepsis Urinary sepsis is always a potential hazard with any instrumentation of the urinary tract, but especially so when blood vessels have been opened, as in a TUR-P. Bacteria may be present anywhere in the urinary tract or prostate, even though the patient is clinically asymptomatic and has grossly clear urine.

A urine sample for culture and sensitivity should always be taken as the bladder is first entered with the cystoscope. If one suspects that the urine is infected, that patient should be covered with antibiotics. Following any cystoscopic procedure or transurethral surgery, the patient's temperature and vital signs should be closely monitored. Any fever, chills, or mental confusion should make one suspect sepsis, and the appropriate diagnostic and therapeutic measures should be taken. If cystoscopy is being performed on an outpatient basis under local anesthesia, the patient should be warned to be alert for any fever or chills in the first 24 to 36 h following the procedure.

Perforation and urinary extravasation Another dreaded complication of any cystoscopic or transurethral surgical procedure is perforation of the urinary tract with subsequent urinary extravasation. Perforation can occur just about anywhere along the urinary tract from the pelvis of the kidney to the distal urethra. It usually results from being too vigorous with a ureteral catheter, stone basket, cystoscope, or resectoscope when some form of obstruction is encountered. If perforation does occur and urine extravasates outside the urinary tract, abscess formation and necrosis of tissue may soon occur.

If the perforation is discovered at the time it occurs, treatment is relatively simple and usually no extravasation will occur. One or more ureteral catheters placed up to the pelvis of the kidney will normally drain the pelvis and ureter adequately, allowing a pelvic or ureteral perforation to heal. Any bladder, prostatic, or urethral perforation without extravasation is easily treated by leaving a Foley catheter in the bladder for 5 to 7 days.

If extravasation has occurred and goes unrecognized, the sequelae may be disastrous. Abscess formation with dissection along fascial planes may occur in the retroperitoneum, up the anterior abdominal wall, and down into the perineum. Extensive necrosis may occur, and wide surgical debridement will often be required on an emergency basis.

If the medical and nursing staffs are alert to any unusual swelling, tenderness, or redness in the flank, lower abdomen, perineum, or in the penis, the insidious perforation and urinary extravasation may be caught early or before the condition becomes too serious.

Urinary retention   Urinary retention after cystoscopy is not unusual. In a male patient with a partially obstructing prostate or in a female patient, just the edema at the bladder neck caused by the cystoscope may be enough to put the patient into retention. If urinary retention occurs, either a Foley catheter or intermittent catheterization should be used until the patient is voiding normally again.

Long-Term TUR-P Complications

Regarding complications following TUR-P, problems associated with hemorrhage and electrolyte imbalance have already been discussed. Long-term complications include those of stricture formation and incontinence.

The most common site in the urethra for stenosis or stricture formation is at the meatus. This results from the constant back and forth motion of the resectoscope during the resection. It is treated with simple dilatation of the meatus.

Another common place for stricture formation is at the bladder neck where bladder neck contracture may occur. This usually does not become a problem until approximately 1 year after the surgery. It can be treated either with dilatation or with transurethral resection of the scar tissue. With either dilatation or resection of the bladder neck, the result is usually only temporary, and the patient may have a chronic problem with stricture formation.

Incontinence following transurethral resection of the prostate is fortunately quite rare. If care is taken during the procedure not to damage the external sphincter, which is distal to the prostate, continence should be unchanged. Most patients will have a certain amount of stress incontinence or dribbling after voiding for the first few days after their catheter is removed, but this usually resolves itself.

It is important to inform the patient that he may not have perfect control over his urinary stream during this period. Patients who persist with incontinence problems after transurethral prostatectomy, in spite of intact external sphincters, may have a neurogenic or decompensated bladder, which has resulted from years of obstruction and back pressure.

Impotence as a complication   In the properly performed cystoscopic examination, impotence is never a complication. Proper transurethral prostatectomy confined to tissue within the surgical capsule of the prostate preserves potency as well.

Open Urologic Surgery

Open urologic surgery is an exhaustive subject on which volumes have been written. Discussion here will be limited to general categories of surgery as they relate to each organ within the genitourinary system. Nursing implications will also be stressed.

The Kidney and Ureter

The kidneys and ureters are located in the retroperitoneum and are subject to a number of surgical diseases. These include congenital anomalies, stone disease, and cancer. Trauma to the kidney is another category that may or may not require surgical intervention, and it will be discussed in a later section.

Congenital anomalies of the kidney and ureter
Congenital anomalies of the kidneys include agenesis, hypoplasia, dysplasia (i.e., multicystic kidney), polycystic kidneys, renal fusion (i.e., horseshoe or pelvic kidney), ectopic kidney, and ureteropelvic junction obstruction. Even though these are congenital, it is often not until adult life that they cause symptoms or are even diagnosed.

With the exception of the unilateral multicystic kidney, these conditions usually do not require surgical management. However, when there is a question of a possible malignancy, as with a multicystic kidney or with a suspicious solitary renal cyst, surgical exploration is indicated.

As a rule, congenital anomalies of the kidneys are more prone to develop obstruction because of their unusual anatomy. A good example of this is the higher than normal incidence of hydronephrosis (dilatation of the pelvis and calyces of the kidney) and stone disease in a horseshoe kidney. This is because the ureters take a looping course anteriorly over the renal parenchyma in this type of kidney and also because of an increased incidence of aberrant renal vessels, which can also obstruct the flow of urine. Any obstruction results in stasis of urine, which increases the potential for stone formation or infection.

Duplication of the ureters is a common urologic anomaly which may be complete or incomplete as well as unilateral or bilateral. There is some tendency toward familial inheritance of these duplications. The only clinical significance of duplication is in the patient with obstruction in one of the duplicated ureters or with vesicoureteral reflux. If one or both of these conditions exists, then surgical correction should be performed.

Vesicoureteral reflux is an abnormal condition most commonly observed in little girls. Since urine should normally not ascend back up the ureter from the bladder, this condition often progresses to infected urine and chronic pyelonephritis. These patients may be asymptomatic or may be quite ill.

The etiology of reflux is felt by most to be a short intramural distance as the ureter passes obliquely through the bladder wall. Fortunately, most of these children stop refluxing as they mature and their intramural ureter lengthens. However, patients who suffer from recurrent infection or who are showing evidence of progressive renal damage should have their ureters reimplanted into the bladder to stop the reflux.

Pelvic and ureteral malignancies Malignancies of the pelvis and ureter are most commonly transitional cell carcinoma and normally present with microscopic hematuria. Treatment consists of nephroureterectomy, with local ureteral resection and primary reanastomosis being reserved for the isolated, low-grade ureteral carcinoma. If the patient has a solitary kidney, an attempt at local resection only is more easily justified. Intrarenal malignancies will be discussed in the section on nephrectomy.

Kidney and ureteral stones Kidney stones (nephrolithiasis) are a common entity, occurring more frequently in males than in females. Please refer to the first half of the chapter for a discussion of the etiology and composition of urinary stones. The smaller stones (less than 1 cm in their greatest diameter) will usually pass from the kidney down the ureter into the bladder and be spontaneously voided from the bladder. These can be extremely painful, and if they obstruct the flow of urine, they may also render serious damage to the kidney. Fortunately, most patients pass these stones spontaneously without requiring intervention.

Surgical management of stone disease is reserved for those stones which are obstructing urinary flow or are just too large to pass spontaneously. If the patient's urine is infected and the obstructing stone is causing generalized sepsis in spite of antibiotic coverage, then surgical or cystoscopic removal should be performed immediately. The most common places for stones to obstruct are at the ureteropelvic junction in the pelvis of the kidney, at the mid-ureter where it crosses the iliac vessels, and at the ureterovesical junction.

Nephrolithotomy and ureterolithotomy are general terms covering a number of surgical approaches to extirpate stones from the kidneys and ureters. The most important consideration in the postoperative nursing care of any patient who has had a stone-removal procedure is good wound drainage.

Almost without exception, these patients have a penrose drain left in the area where the ureter or kidney was opened to remove the stone. Temporary drainage of urine via these penrose drains is to be expected, and many will continue for a week, if not longer. This is in sharp contrast to most other surgical patients in whom drainage stops sooner, thus eliminating the need for prolonged penrose drainage. It is most important that the penrose drain(s) not be removed too soon in the patient who has had urinary tract surgery for stone disease. If the urine drainage from the penrose site is heavy, a good technique to simplify patient care and to minimize the chances for infection is to place a urostomy bag over the penrose drains rather than just dressings.

Nephrectomy and Other Surgical Procedures of the Kidney

Nephrectomy is the complete removal of the kidney, performed for a variety of reasons, ranging from a nonfunctional kidney secondary to obstructive stone disease to cancer of the kidney. Radical nephrectomy, performed for malignant tumors of the kidney, involves taking Gerota's fascia out en bloc with the kidney. Partial nephrectomies of the kidney are done for certain benign conditions involving usually either the lower or upper pole of the kidney.

The most common tumor seen in the kidney is a metastatic one from a primary elsewhere in the body. The most common primary tumor of the kidney is adenocarcinoma (also termed *hypernephroma, renal cell carcinoma,* or *Grawitz' tumor*). In children, Wilms' tumor (nephroblastoma) is the most common form of renal malignancy.

Renal artery surgery and renal transplant surgery are performed by certain urologists, but as a rule, these fall within the realms of the peripheral vascular and transplant surgeons. They were discussed in the first half of this chapter.

Adrenal Gland Surgery

Surgery of the adrenal gland can be accomplished through a variety of incisions and approaches (i.e., midline abdominal, flank, or back lumbar incisions). The indications may be for malignant tumors of the adrenal such as neuroblastomas or adenocarcinoma as well as for benign tumors such as pheochromocytoma and adenomas. These tumors are usually unilateral, and in both malignant and benign cases, the symptoms are usually those of endocrinologic dysfunction. Certain metastatic carcinomas of the breast which are endocrinologically sensitive are indications for bilateral adrenalectomy. Some of these tumors are improved or at least retarded by removing the adrenals. In adrenal surgery, penrose drains are usually not used unless there is a question of adequate hemostasis at the end of the case.

Nursing implications include normal postoperative care in addition to watching for signs of adrenal insufficiency (i.e., sudden diarrhea, vomiting, fever, circulatory collapse, and pulmonary edema). If any of these symptoms are noted, the surgeon should be notified at once.

Carcinoma of the Bladder

Most carcinomas of the bladder are transitional cell carcinoma and are graded I to IV. Solitary low-grade (I or II) lesions are treated easily by transurethral resection and fulguration of the base. The grade III and IV lesions are more malignant and are more adequately treated with cystectomy and urinary diversion because of their aggressive nature.

In the male patient, prostatectomy is performed along with the cystectomy, and total urethrectomy is also commonly done. In the female patient having a cystectomy, hysterectomy and sometimes vaginectomy are indicated. This is because of the tendency for local invasion of the tumor into these organs. Partial or segmental cystectomy for bladder cancer is rarely used because of the possibility of spreading the tumor when opening the bladder. In a regular cystectomy, the bladder is removed without opening it. However, in a high-risk patient who may not be able to withstand a cystectomy and urinary diversion, partial cystectomy is sometimes used.

Surgery of the Urethra

Urethral malignancies are exceedingly rare and are more common in women. Depending on the cell type, local or complete urethrectomy may be performed. In the male this may require radical penectomy. The overall results are not good and survival rate is low.

Urethroplasty performed for urethral strictures in the male is often completed in two- or three-stage operations, each being separated by 6 months to 1 year. It is oftentimes very difficult surgery and may require that the patient have a suprabubic cystostomy or perineal urethrostomy between stages.

Open Surgery of the Prostate

Open surgery of the prostate is required in prostate glands which are felt to be too large for transurethral resection. The suprapubic approach involves opening the bladder in order to enucleate the prostate. Retropubic and perineal approaches achieve the same result, but without opening the bladder.

Radical prostatectomy is a curative procedure involving removal of the outer surgical capsule as well as inner core of the gland. It is reserved for adenocarcinoma which is felt to be confined to the prostate. More advanced cancers of the prostate are best treated with radiation, chemotherapy, bilateral orchiectomy, hormonal estrogen therapy, or a combination of these modalities.

In open prostatic surgery performed either for cancer or benign prostatic hypertrophy, postoperative care is essentially the same. Since the prostate is a very vascular organ, penrose drains are left for drainage of blood as well as urine. Most bleeding stops within the first day or two after surgery. In order to prevent clot retention, a large suprapubic catheter is left temporarily in the bladder along with a urethral catheter.

Most urologists employ continuous bladder irrigation with inflow through the urethral catheter and outflow through the suprapubic catheter. This system prevents clot retention very effectively as long as the irrigation is not allowed to run dry. Large 2- to 3-L bags of urologic irrigant (glycine or mannitol) set up with two bags on a Y-connector are the easiest to manage. The irrigation should be run fast enough that the outflow of irrigation fluid and urine is pink without clots. As with continuous irrigation following TUR-P, urinary output may be difficult to calculate. However, if one keeps a close record of the exact amount of irrigant used and subtracts it from the total amount of fluid in the drainage system, a fairly accurate urine output should be obtained.

Testicular Surgery

Surgery of the testicle includes procedures for cryptorchidism (undescended testis), torsion of the testicle, trauma, and cancer.

The male with a cryptorchid testis should have it brought down into the scrotum before 2 years of age, since changes in the spermatogenic cells are seen microscopically by 2 years of age. There is also an increased incidence of testicular malignancy in cryptorchid testes which are not brought down into the scrotum.

Torsion of the testicle or of the appendices of the testis presents as a spontaneous and extremely painful condition in which the testicle becomes very swollen and tender due to a twisting of the spermatic cord or the appendix of the testis. It is most commonly seen in males in their second and third decades and occurs because of a congenital defect in the attachment of the testis to the scrotum. Surgical exploration is mandatory within hours if the testicle is to remain viable, because if the cord is not untwisted, the testicle will become gangrenous and die. No danger is present for the testicle if it is only an appendix that has twisted, but the only way to differentiate between the two is at surgery. Differential diagnosis includes acute epididymitis and trauma. Epididymitis is not a surgical condition, but trauma requires surgery if there is evidence for rupture of the testis.

In any scrotal or testicular surgery, hemostasis is most important and a supportive pressure dressing should be left on the scrotum at least until the morning following surgery. It is common practice to leave a small penrose drain in the scrotum for adequate drainage. A scrotal support will also ease the discomfort in the postoperative course.

Testicular cancer is the leading cause of death from cancer among males in the 25- to 34-year-old age group. The primary cell types are seminoma, teratocarcinoma, embryonal cell carcinoma, and choriocarcinoma, but any combination of these may also be present.

Any testicular mass should be suspect and explored through an inguinal incision with the spermatic cord being clamped before the testicle is handled. Biopsies of suspected tumors should never be performed, and if there is any doubt, the cord and testis should be removed. In a pure seminoma, the only treatment besides orchiectomy is radiation to the periaortic lymph nodes. Retroperitoneal lymphadenectomy should be performed in the other three cell types both as a staging and therapeutic measure. This is an extensive surgical procedure requiring postoperative nasogastric suction for at least 4 to 5 days.

If the patient has metastatic disease in the lymph nodes or lungs, triple drug chemotherapy with *cis*-platinum, vincristine, and bleomycin may be given. With the recent advent of *cis*-platinum, dramatic advances have been made with metastatic testicular malignancies, many of which were considered incurable just a few years ago.

Since most of the patients with testicular cancer are young, healthy men, they usually tolerate this radical surgery and chemotherapy very well. Psychologically, however, this can be a devastating disease, and it requires a great deal of understanding and compassion on the part of the nursing and medical staffs.

In hopes of detecting these testicular tumors as early as possible, patient education by nurses and physicians is of utmost importance. All young males should be taught in their early teens to perform bimanual examination of their testes on a monthly basis just as females examine their breasts.

Surgery of the Penis

Surgery of the penis other than circumcision is concerned primarily with cancer. Squamous cell carcinoma of the penis is seen almost exclusively in uncircumcised males, and fortunately, it is a very infrequent occurrence. If the lesion is small, partial penectomy can be curative; if the lesion is more advanced, radical penectomy and bilateral inguinal lymph node dissection is the recommended treatment. If only partial penectomy is performed, the patient will still be capable of urinating normally and having erections. However, with a radical penectomy, the patient voids through a perineal urethrostomy and obviously has no capability for sex. Good hygiene of the foreskin and penis is essential in preventing carcinoma of the penis.

Another new and promising area of penile surgery is that of surgical treatment for organic impotence secondary to such diseases as diabetes mellitus and severe peripheral vascular disease. The two basic types of penile prostheses are the permanently erect rod type and the inflatable type. These are placed in the corpora cavernosa of the penis, with the inflatable type also having a pump in the scrotum and a fluid reservoir in the lower abdomen. The inflatable type simulates erections more naturally, but because of its complexity, it also more prone to mechanical difficulties.

Spinal Cord Injury and Disease

One of the most difficult patients with urologic problems to care for is the spinal cord injury patient or the patient with devastating neurologic disease (e.g., the multiple sclerosis patient). The leading cause of death among spinal cord injury patients is renal failure due usually to a combination of stone disease and chronic infection.

The bladder has parasympathetic, sympathetic, and somatic nerve supplies. These nerves have both sensory and motor function, and the S2 to S4 portion of the spinal cord, which corresponds to the T12 to L1 vertebral bodies, is the area controlling voiding. Thus, spinal cord injuries in the T12 to L1 vertebral area result in a flaccid neurogenic bladder (lower motor neuron lesion), and injuries above this region cause a spastic neurogenic bladder. There are also all variations and combinations of these two basic types of neurogenic bladder, depending on the nature and location of the spinal cord injury or neurologic disease.

The spastic bladder is characterized by its small capacity, high pressure, and marked trabeculation with spasm and is seen with high-level cord injuries, multiple sclerosis, and tumor involving the spinal cord. The flaccid or atonic bladder is also seen with trauma to the cord, tumor, and myelomeningocele patients. Typically, it has a large capacity with low intravesical pressure and no involuntary detrusor contractions. The danger from neurogenic bladders of either type is damage to the kidneys. With obstruction, these patients are very susceptible to chronic infection, stone disease, and progressive renal deterioration.

The main objective in caring for these patients is to protect the kidneys from the problems listed above. Depending upon the individual case, intermittent catheterization, Foley catheter, or urinary diversion (i.e., ileal conduit) may be the treatment of choice. Since many of these patients will always have gram-negative bacteria in their urine, it is best to avoid long-term antibiotics in the hospital setting so as not to select out resistant organisms. However, if the patient becomes symptomatic or septic from the urinary tract, aggressive parenteral antibiotic treatment is indicated.

Autonomic hyperreflexia is a dangerous condition which may be encountered in any quadriplegic patient with a cord lesion or injury above T6. It consists of paroxysmal severe hypertension, throbbing headache, sweating, and bradycardia and is the result of uncontrolled sympathetic activity arising from the spinal cord below the level of the cord injury. Stimulation from bladder or rectal distention causes the sympathetic discharge. Overdistention of the bladder can occur quickly and unexpectedly at cystoscopy or with an obstructed Foley catheter on the ward.

Any nurse or physician caring for a quadriplegic patient should be aware of this condition. If it should arise, treatment consists of relieving the bladder distention and getting the blood pressure back down to within normal limits quickly. Simply emptying the bladder might lower the blood pressure, but rapidly acting antihypertensive agents such as diazoxide may be needed. If not lowered, the severe hypertension may cause cerebral hemorrhage or left ventricular failure with pulmonary edema.

Genitourinary Trauma

Genitourinary trauma is a subject that has been alluded to earlier in the chapter. It will be discussed here as it concerns each organ in the genitourinary system. As with any trauma victim, total evaluation of the patient is essential. More often than not, the patient with genitourinary trauma has other associated injuries which may include orthopedic, vascular, intra-abdominal, or neurologic problems. Triage is very important, and a decision should be made quickly on which injury requires the most immediate attention.

Renal Trauma

Trauma to the kidney basically includes penetrating injuries and blunt renal trauma. The former would include stab wounds and gunshot wounds, while the latter would cover deceleration injuries (i.e., auto accidents), crush injuries, or any injury in which the kidney may have been indirectly injured or compressed. In addition to gross and microscopic inspection of the urine, IVP (intravenous pyelogram) and renal arteriogram, if indicated, should be the first diagnostic studies obtained.

All penetrating injuries of the kidney should be surgically explored, preferably through a transabdominal approach so that any possible intraperitoneal injuries may also be evaluated. If any question of injury to the renal pedicle (i.e., renal vein or artery) exists, preoperative arteriograms should be performed if the patient is stable. Unfortunately, with penetrating injuries to the kidney, nephrectomy is often required, since this type of injury often leads to severe vascular damage or a "shattered" kidney. When feasible, vascular or parenchymal repair should be performed. If a severe injury is confined to one pole of the kidney, a partial or heminephrectomy should be attempted.

A key point in any renal surgery, and especially so with trauma to the kidney, is to make sure that the patient has two kidneys before removing the injured kidney. The best way to do this is with IVP or arteriogram, which will also give one a good idea of the function of the opposite kidney as well as its presence. Agenesis of one kidney is not common, but cases have been reported of a solitary kidney being removed during emergency surgery. If radiographic studies are not able to be performed before surgery, a midline incision should be used so that both kidneys may be evaluated.

Treatment for blunt renal trauma is a controversial subject for which surgical exploration as well as nonoperative management have been successfully used. If the patient is stable and blood loss is not great, nonoperative management may be the treatment of choice. These patients are followed by long-term monitoring with IVP, serum blood urea nitrogen, creatinine, and blood pressure. Complications of nonoperative therapy may include urinary extravasation and abscess formation, as well as hypertension from an avascular area of the injured kidney. If any of these problems were to develop, the kidney should be explored and even removed if it is not felt to be salvageable.

A good case can also be made for early surgical intervention in cases of blunt renal trauma. The aim here is to avoid later complications which might lead to subsequent nephrectomy.

Care of the patient with renal trauma who undergoes surgical exploration is no different than any other patient who has had renal surgery. Penrose drains are frequently used and should be attended carefully, since they provide for egress of blood and urine until the kidney has healed sufficiently for their removal. As mentioned earlier in the chapter, these drains may be left in place indefinitely and should not be removed until urine drainage has almost completely stopped.

Ureteral trauma

Ureteral trauma is almost always due to gunshot wounds, with stab wounds rarely injuring the ureters. The only significant form of blunt trauma to the ureter occurs mainly in children. This is a deceleration-type injury which causes tearing of the ureter at the ureteropelvic junction. This type of injury would probably necessitate surgery.

Iatrogenic causes of ureteral injury include transection, ligation, or perforation of the ureter during surgery or cystoscopic procedures involving retrograde passage of ureteral catheters or instruments (i.e., manipulation of a ureteral stone with a Dormia stone basket). Any surgery in the retroperitoneum or pelvis as performed by general surgeons, gynecologists, or urologists carries with it the risk of ureteral injury. Of importance here is that the surgeon recognize at the time of surgery that there has been an injury to the ureter. It is much easier to repair a ureteral injury just after it has happened than later when complications have arisen.

Treatment for ureteral injury may be as simple as placing a ureteral catheter or stent up to the pelvis of the kidney at cystoscopy and leaving it in place for 10 to 14 days. However, with more serious ureteral injuries, more extensive surgical procedures are required. The most straightforward procedure is simple end-to-end reanastomosis of the ureter after the injured segment has been debrided. More complex procedures such as transureteroureterostomy (anastomosing one ureter into the other normal ureter) or autotransplantation of the kidney into the patient's pelvis may be needed if there has been extensive loss of the ureter.

The most important nursing consideration in any patient who has had surgery for ureteral injury is again to take great care not to let the penrose drains come out prematurely.

Bladder Trauma

A significant number of patients with a fractured pelvis will also have a ruptured bladder. These ruptures are usually extraperitoneal, and the diagnosis is made by cystogram which shows extravasation of contrast outside of the bladder.

Penetrating injuries to the bladder are infrequent but require surgical exploration when present. There may well be other associated pelvic or abdominal injuries. Both surgical and nonoperative methods (i.e., Foley catheter drainage) of management have been used successfully with nonpenetrating trauma which results in a ruptured bladder. Perforation of the bladder during transurethral resection of a bladder tumor has been discussed previously.

With either surgical or nonoperative management of the ruptured bladder, the main concern is again to let the bladder remain decompressed with either a suprapubic tube inserted at surgery or with a Foley catheter. These should remain for 7 to 14 days. If the rupture was surgically explored, penrose drains will likely be used to drain the perivesical spaces.

Urethral Trauma

Urethral injuries are a great problem since the initial management may be very difficult and the long-term complications, such as urethral stricture, most distressing.

Because of its greater length and more vulnerable anatomy, the male urethra is more frequently injured than the female urethra. Injuries to the urethra may be seen with a fractured pelvis or with straddle injuries to the perineum. Iatrogenic injuries from catheters and cystoscopic procedures are discussed earlier in the chapter.

Principles of diagnosis and treatment are most important in urethral injuries. In any fracture of the pelvis, concomitant urethral injury should always be suspected along with possible rupture of the bladder. Straddle injuries to the perineum should also raise the question of possible urethral injury. If any resistance is encountered while attempting to pass a Foley catheter or if gross blood is seen coming from the urethra, all efforts to insert a catheter should be abandoned and a urologist called. IVP and retrograde urethrogram should then be performed to rule out a urethral injury or rupture.

Surgical repair of urethral rupture in the posterior urethra of the male is a difficult procedure for which numerous techniques have been described. In many cases, the patient will be left with a urethral Foley catheter as well as a suprapubic catheter and penrose drains in the perineum.

Penile and Scrotal Trauma

Penile and scrotal injuries, including those to the testes, can be penetrating injuries, avulsion injuries, and blunt trauma. Treatment consists of good wound care with surgical debridement and reconstruction when indicated. Although pressure dressings are often used in the first 24 to 48 h postoperatively, fluffs and a scrotal support work very nicely later in the hospital course.

Circumferential dressings around the penis should be avoided when possible for fear of causing ischemia and necrosis. If used, great care should be taken not to wrap the penis too tightly, so as to allow for erection and for edema of the tissue.

Burn injuries and avulsion of the skin of the penis and scrotum (de-gloving injuries) present difficult problems that eventually may require skin grafting to the denuded genital areas. In male patients with extensive burns to parts of their bodies other than the genitalia, tremendous fluid replacement often results in massive edema of the penis and scrotum. This edema will almost always resolve on its own after the patient has stabilized and his body mobilizes excess fluids by means of diuresis. Though unrelated to burns, anasarca from liver disease or congestive heart failure can cause this same type of massive edema of the genitalia.

Inserting a Foley catheter in a patient with massive genital edema can be a formidable task because of edematous foreskin or penile skin covering the meatus in the male and edematous labia doing the same in the female. In the male patient, sustained firm pressure may be safely applied with one's hand to the distal foreskin and penile skin in order to squeeze the edema proximally out of the distal penis. This will hopefully help to find the urethral meatus so that a catheter may be inserted. This technique does not work nearly as well in the female with massive genital edema, because the urethra is not in an extremity type position. However, firm pressure in the area may temporarily lessen the edema. This maneuver causes little or no discomfort to most patients with this affliction.

Urinary Incontinence

Urinary incontinence is a problem that affects both males and females of all age groups, and it can be most distressing. Its etiologies are many as are its therapies, both pharmacologic and surgical. Unfortunately, the success rates for neither of these modalities is as high as one would hope them to be.

On the brighter side, advances have been made in recent years with incontinence. Urodynamics has gone beyond the old cystometrogram, used to measure bladder capacity and function, to include evaluation of the neuromuscular components of voiding. This has been most helpful in investigating such diverse problems as the child with enuresis to the older man with an obstructive uropathy. Artificial sphincters and surgically implanted incontinence devices are also being perfected, and some of the newer pharmacologic agents have shown promise.

REFERENCES

Fraley, E. (ed.): Testicular tumors, in *The Urologic Clinics of North America,* Philadelphia: Saunders, 1977.

Glenn, J. F.: *Urologic Surgery,* 2d ed., New York: Harper & Row, 1975.

Harrison, J. H., R. F. Gittes, A. D. Perlmutter, T. A. Stamey, and P. C. Walsh: *Campbell's Urology,* 4th ed., Philadelphia: Saunders, 1978.

Jones, D. A., C. F. Dunbar, and M. M. Jirovec: *Medical-Surgical Nursing, A Conceptual Approach,* New York: McGraw-Hill, 1978.

Morel, A., and G. Wise: *Urologic Endoscopic Procedures,* 2d ed., St. Louis: Mosby, 1977.

Pearman, J. W., and E. J. England: *The Urological Management of the Patient Following Spinal Cord Injury,* Springfield, Ill.: Charles C Thomas, 1973.

Smith, D. R.: *General Urology,* 9th ed., Los Altos, Calif.: Lange, 1978.

Thompson, I. M., and C. E. Carlton, Jr. (eds.): Genitourinary trauma, in *The Urologic Clinics of North America,* Philadelphia: Saunders, 1977.

Winter, C. C., and A. Morel: *Nursing Care of Patients with Urologic Diseases,* 4th ed., St. Louis: Mosby, 1977.

MANAGEMENT OF ACUTE UPPER GASTROINTESTINAL DISORDERS

Gastrointestinal Hemorrhage

Acute Gastrointestinal Hemorrhage (Hemorrhagic Shock)

Massive upper gastrointestinal hemorrhage may occur as a complication of peptic ulcer disease, esophageal varices, esophagitis, gastritis, alcohol ingestion, and various drug ingestions. The first stage of management is treatment of shock and the second is control of the source of bleeding. A sudden loss of blood volume (hemorrhage) decreases venous return to the heart with a corresponding decrease in cardiac output. The lowered cardiac output results in inadequate tissue perfusion. This cycle of events, along with the compensatory mechanisms that come into action, must be understood to adequately assess and intervene in hypovolemic shock secondary to massive gastrointestinal bleeding (Fig. 29-1).

Vasoconstriction, a vascular response to the decreased cardiac output and decreased right arterial pressure, shunts blood flow toward the cerebral and cardiopulmonary system. If the vasoconstriction continues, the decreased blood flow to the kidneys may result in medullary tubular dysfunction or acute tubular necrosis (ATN). The urinary output is a good index of kidney perfusion and effectiveness of treatment.

The vasoconstriction phase causing decreased tissue perfusion results in cellular dysfunction. The cells attempt to extract oxygen from the available blood, but as shock progresses, this mechanism is not adequate. The cells then shift to anaerobic metabolism. Energy production is decreased, and large quantities of lactic acid are formed. The depressed blood flow to the hepatic and renal systems impairs the function of these systems in breaking down the lactic acid or removing it from the blood. As the lactic acid accumulates, a metabolic acidotic state develops.

If the blood loss continues, cerebral flow becomes compromised. The patient may become confused, and mental changes continue to worsen unless blood flow is increased. The occurrence of brain damage depends upon the duration of lowered tissue perfusion.

Coronary blood flow may be evaluated by electrocardiography (ECG). A flattening of the T wave or a depression of the ST segment denotes coronary blood flow insufficiency.

The body has two compensatory mechanisms that

29
GASTROINTESTINAL DISORDERS

Debra C. Broadwell
William C. McGarity

MANAGEMENT OF ACUTE UPPER GASTROINTESTINAL DISORDERS
Gastrointestinal Hemorrhage
Intestinal Ischemic Disorders
Intestinal Obstructions
Peritonitis
Cutaneous Fistulas

SPECIFIC GASTROINTESTINAL PATHOLOGIES
Zollinger-Ellison Syndrome
Inflammatory Bowel Disease:
Crohn's Disease and Ulcerative Colitis
Sclerosing Cholangitis
Pancreatitis
Obesity

NUTRITION
Parenteral Hyperalimentation
Peripheral Alimentation
Elemental Diets

REFERENCES

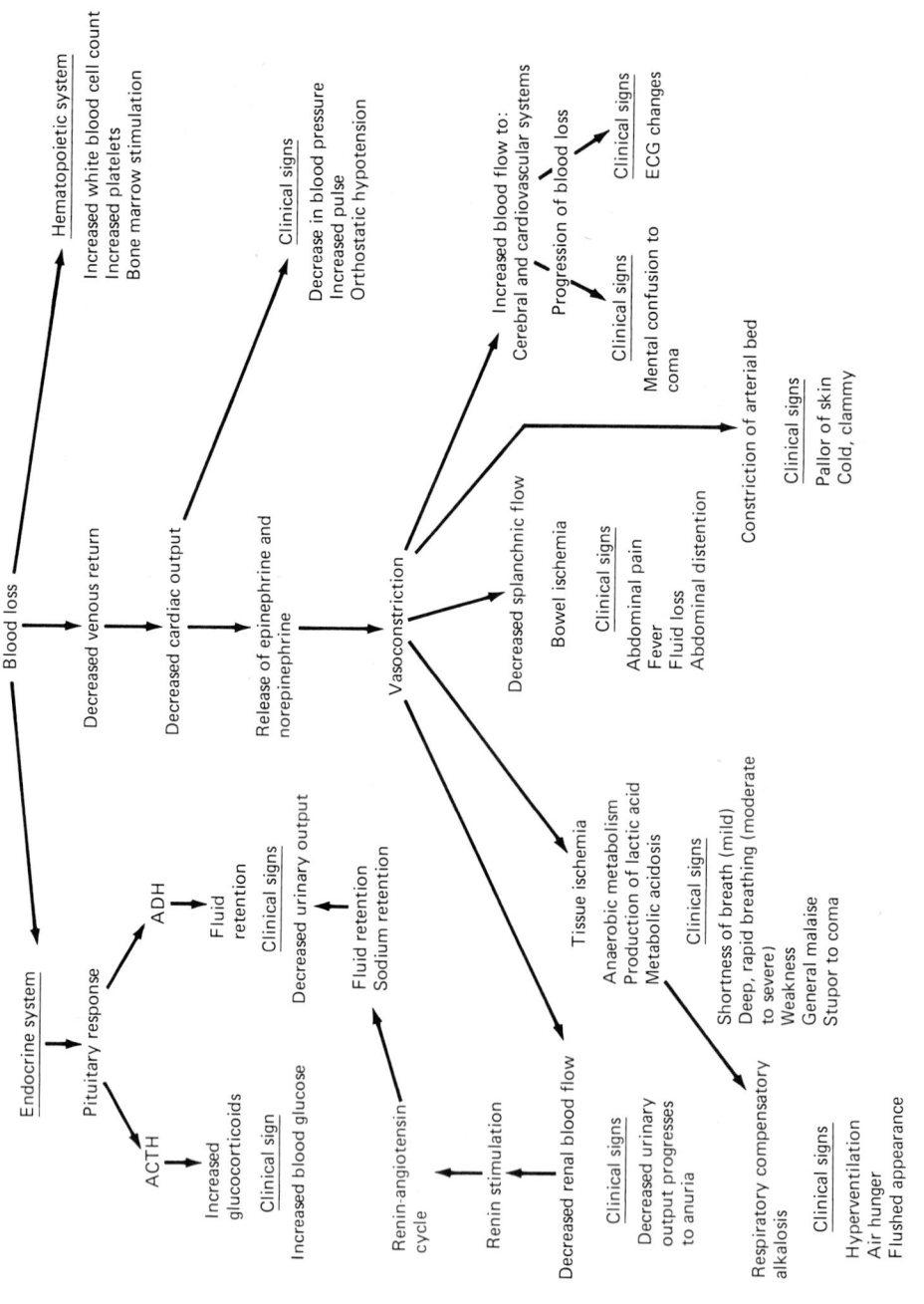

FIGURE 29-1

Hypovolemic hemorrhagic shock.

occur more gradually. First, aldosterone and antidiuretic hormone (ADH) are released in response to blood loss. In response to ADH and aldosterone stimulation, fluid shifts from extravascular spaces to intravascular spaces. Second, in the hematopoietic system, an increase in white blood cells and platelets occurs. The bone marrow is stimulated, with resultant increased red cell production and peripheral reticulocytosis. Correction of hemoglobin occurs over a period of weeks following the hemorrhage.

The first signs of upper gastrointestinal bleeding may include hematemesis or melena. A drop in blood pressure with an increased pulse rate is considered classic of shock. A patient may have a 20 percent loss of fluid volume (1000 mL in a 70-kg person) before these vital signs change. Orthostatic hypotension and syncope may also be indicative of blood loss. A change of blood pressure equal to or greater than 10 mmHg and a corresponding pulse rate increase of 20 beats per minute in a sitting or standing position corresponds to an additional blood loss in excess of 1000 mL. The patient's response to the blood loss depends on the rate of loss, the amount of blood loss, age, preexisting conditions, and the rapidity of treatment.

Treatment of Hemorrhagic Shock

The patient in hemorrhagic shock requires the following immediate treatment: replacement of fluid volume deficit and control of the bleeding. An intravenous (IV) line is inserted with a large-bore needle. When the IV line is started, enough blood should be withdrawn for type and cross, hemoglobin, hematocrit, blood urea nitrogen, electrolytes, and prothrombin time. Fluid replacement should then begin immediately with Ringer's lactate, normal saline, or D₅W until whole blood arrives. The replacement of losses with whole blood or packed red cells is the only method of reestablishing and maintaining oxygen-carrying capacity. A Foley catheter is inserted for accurate evaluation of urinary output.

Hemoglobin and hematocrit values are often difficult to interpret during an episode of acute gastrointestinal bleeding. The hematocrit is a ratio of cell volume to plasma volume, and in acute bleeding, cells and fluids are changed proportionally.

A central venous pressure (CVP) line or a Swan-Ganz catheter is a significant additive in management of a patient in shock. The Swan-Ganz catheter measures the pulmonary arterial wedge pressure (PAWP). The CVP readings are not as dependable as the PAWP measurements. However, the CVP and/or PAWP readings are important in examining the effects of the fluid challenge in patients being treated with massive fluid replacement. The patient should be assessed for fluid balance by checking color, skin temperature, mental status, urinary output, and vital signs.

Blood pressure readings with a cuff are often inaccurate. A change in blood pressure is more important than the accurate reading when the change is related to clinical signs and the treatment. Doppler flowmeters are a more accurate method of measuring blood pressure when a patient is in shock. Intraarterial monitoring is accurate because it records all changes, no matter how minute. When an intra-arterial monitor is used, the patient must be examined frequently for color, pulses, and warmth of the extremity used for insertion of the line (Table 29-1).

Large-lumen nasogastric tubes are inserted and the stomach contents are aspirated. If bright red blood is returned, the site of bleeding is above the ligament of Treitz. However, the failure to return blood does not dismiss the possibility of a lesion above the ligament of Treitz, such as bleeding from a duodenal ulcer. Iced saline lavages are sometimes used to manage bleeding from peptic ulcer disease. The lavage with iced saline is initiated and continued until the returns are clear or only faintly colored. The cold fluid induces vasoconstriction in the splanchnic bed and decreases fibrinolysis, allowing the bleeding vessel to clot. If decompression of the stomach or iced lavages do not control the bleeding, selective intra-arterial infusion of vasopressors may control the bleeding.

In acute hemorrhagic shock, replacement of blood is more effective than intravenous vasopressors. Sodium bicarbonate may be required to relieve lacticemia secondary to shock and the citrate load from the whole blood transfusions.

The late complications of an acute shock syndrome are the wet lung syndrome and ATN. Molyneux-Luick and Knecht (1977) describe the wet lung syndrome, or adult respiratory distress syndrome (ARDS), as the major complication of shock. ARDS manifests clinically as hyperventilation, air hunger, and flushed appearance. Overaggressive fluid therapy (fluid overload), microemboli, and superimposed pulmonary infections increase the risk of pulmonary complications.

Prevention of pulmonary complications may be maximized by the use of the Swan-Ganz catheter to measure PAWP for regulation of fluid replacement. Filters on all IVs will decrease the possibility of

TABLE 29-1

Clinical Evaluation
of a Patient with Hemorrhagic Shock

Evaluation item	Observation	Discussion
1. Pulse	Weak, thready, rapid	Progression of shock
2. Blood pressure	Doppler flowmeter and intra-arterial monitoring are more accurate than cuff blood pressure readings	Blood pressure fluctuations may not be significant unless examined in conjunction with urinary output and respiratory function
3. ECG	Flattening of Twaves; depression of ST segments	Continued loss of blood, with resultant decreased coronary blood flow
4. CVP	Less than 6 cmH$_2$O denotes fluid deficit	
PAWP (Swan-Ganz catheter)	Less than 10 mmH$_2$O leads to hypovolemia. More than 20 mmH$_2$O leads to pulmonary edema	CVP and PAWP readings must be evaluated in light of a fluid challenge and not considered separately from other data
5. Respiratory	Patent airway and blood gases. Decreased Pa_{O_2} leads to respiratory alkalosis, hyperventilation, air hunger, flushed appearance. Check patient's nail beds and lips for cyanosis	A complication of shock is ARDS (wet lung syndrome) from overhydration
6. Fluid balance	Check patient's color, mental status, temperature, skin (color, temperature), pulse, urinary output, daily weights, neck veins	Tissue perfusion. *Note:* The most important indicator of blood flow and tissue perfusion is urinary output. Hourly urine output should be greater than or equal to 30 mL
7. Metabolic acidosis	Shortness of breath (mild); deep, rapid breathing (moderate to severe); weakness, general malaise; stupor, progressing to coma	A result of anaerobic metabolism
8. Laboratory data:		
BUN	240 mg per 100 mL with normal serum creatinine	Blood loss reflected in BUN levels due to absorption of blood products in upper intestinal tract
Blood glucose	Elevated	ACTH secretion
Hct/Hgb	Lowered	Should not be used singularly for evaluating loss
Clotting factors	Prothrombin time; platelet count	If patient has lengthened prothrombin time (associated with liver disease), vitamin K is given parenterally

microemboli. Steroids may be used to minimize ARDS by stabilizing cell permeability. Prevention of ATN is accomplished by increasing circulating fluid volume, which increases renal perfusion.

Diagnosis

Once the hemorrhagic shock is under control, more definitive diagnostic procedures may be instituted. The endoscopy examination (using a fiberoptic gastroscope) is used to locate bleeding lesions in the esophagus, stomach, and duodenum. The endoscopy is preferred over barium studies in most instances. Barium studies are not conclusive when there are clots in the stomach. Many bleeding lesions are superficial and may not be seen with barium studies. If a lesion is detected with the barium examination, there is no indication that it is the lesion that bled. The clearing time of the contrast material also delays further endoscopy or arteriography procedures.

The endoscopy should be done within the first 12 to 24 h after the hemorrhage. Antacids should be held until endoscopy is done. No other bowel preparation is required. The patient is sedated with diazepam (Valium) and meperidine (Demerol) unless there is a contraindication due to the patient's condition at the time of the procedure. In most cases, the source of bleeding can be visualized. Electrocautery probes through the endoscope are sometimes used to control the bleeding.

Arteriography (angiography) is done when the patient continues to bleed at a rate of 0.5 mL/min. The arteriography permits injection and visualization of the various arterial systems, e.g., superior mesenteric artery, celiac axis, and so on. Selective arteriography permits the use of intra-arterial infusion of vasopressors for controlling hemorrhage. The continuous intra-arterial infusion of vasopressin may cause dilutional hyponatremia and a decreased urinary output, which is treated with furosemide (Lasix) administered intravenously and volume replacement. Various means for using arteriography and endoscopy in gastrointestinal bleeding are being explored. Laser treatments and electrocautery probes are two of these.

Esophageal Varices

The patient presenting with a massive gastrointestinal bleed secondary to esophageal varices will require additional nursing care and management to the general care previously presented. The patient is not only hypovolemic, but has a dysfunctioning liver which cannot adequately metabolize, synthesize, or detoxify. Esophageal varices develop when there is an increase in the portal vein pressure. Occlusion of the portal vein, liver parenchymal disease, or occlusion of the hepatic vein may lead to an increased portal pressure. The collateral blood flow, specifically to the stomach and esophagus, and enlargement of the spleen develop in relation to the portal vein pressure increase. A patient with liver disease may also present with ascites, encephalopathy, splenomegaly, spider nevi, palmar muscle atrophy, and anemia. A limited history and physical examination during the acute phase of bleeding will lead one to suspect esophageal varices. However, not all patients with esophageal varices bleed from the varices. There is a high incidence of bleeding gastric lesions associated in patients with portal hypertension. Supportive therapy in patients with compromised liver function includes vitamin K, fresh blood, fresh-frozen plasma, and diuretics.

A triple-lumen nasogastric tube may be inserted for use as a tamponade to control the bleeding. The Sengstaken-Blakemore triple-lumen tube has two balloons and one lumen for gastric aspiration. The Sengstaken-Blakemore tube is frequently used for control of esophageal varices hemorrhage. There are four major complications arising from use of the Sengstaken-Blakemore tube. These include pulmonary problems secondary to aspiration, ruptured esophagus, asphyxia, and erosion of the esophageal or gastric wall. The Linton tube has two aspiration lumens and a gastric balloon. The gastric balloon has a capacity of 800 cm³ and when filled, it applies pressure on the intragastric veins. The two lumens of the Linton tube provide for gastric and esophageal aspiration. The advantage of the Linton tube is the capacity for esophageal aspiration and the large gastric balloon which alleviates the need for intraesophageal tamponade.

The procedure for insertion of the Sengstaken-Blakemore tube (Table 29-2) is similar to that of any nasogastric tube. The balloons are checked prior to insertion, and tracheal suction is available during the actual insertion to prevent aspiration of emesis. A football helmet is worn by the patient. The gastric balloon is inflated and fitted snugly against the cardia of the stomach. Traction is then applied to the tube, and the tube is taped to the football helmet. The excessive pressure created by the traction on the tube would cause pressure necrosis of the nose if the tube were taped to the patient's skin.

If the gastric aspirations are bloody, then the bleeding is from a gastric lesion. Additional air is

TABLE 29-2
Nursing Responsibility with
Sengstaken-Blakemore Tube

Insertion

Activity	Rationale
Inflate both balloons of the Sengstaken-Blakemore tube and hold them under water to observe for minute leaks.	Any escaping air can be detected in the water.
Label all lumens carefully with a waterproof marker.	Prevents inflation and deflation of the gastric balloon for the esophageal balloon and vice versa.
Tracheal suctioning should be available in the room.	Vomiting often occurs during insertion, and aspiration is a hazard.
Rubber-shod hemostats should be available.	Each balloon lumen should be double-clamped.
Cotton disk, football helmet.	The cotton disk should be placed around the tube at the patient's nares, and then the football helmet applied. The traction applied to the Sengstaken-Blakemore tube will create pressure necrosis if the tube is taped to the skin. Tape the tube securely to the chin guard.

Care of a Patient with a Sengstaken-Blakemore Tube

Possible complications	Nursing measures and observations	Rationale
Erosion and perforation of the esophagus and/or gastric mucosa	Careful monitoring of vital signs, particularly blood pressure and respirations	Evaluation of the response of the bleeding to the tamponade, complications, etc.
	Frequent (every 15–30 min) checks of the mmHg pressure of the esophageal balloon. Release the pressure at intervals	Onset of back pain, upper abdominal pain, shock, and fluid in the chest are signs of perforation
		Releasing the pressure at intervals decreases the incidence of tissue necrosis. The tube is removed after 48 h, because the incidence of necrosis increases after this
Aspirate pneumonia	Mouth care; suctioning of naso-esophageal areas	A patient with an inflated esophageal balloon is unable to swallow. Frequent mouth-esophageal suctioning is necessary to prevent aspiration. An option is the insertion of a nasogastric tube above the esophageal balloon
	Irrigation of gastric tube; observe color, consistency, and odor of the output	Patency of the gastric tube. Note any changes in the output, particularly a color change (bleeding) and increased amount (fluid will need to be replaced)
	Keep nostrils clean and well-lubricated; keep cotton disk in place between the skin and the Sengstaken-Blakemore tube	Patient comfort and prevention of pressure necrosis from traction

TABLE 29-2 (*Continued*)

Care of a Patient with a Sengstaken-Blakemore Tube		
Possible complications	Nursing measures and observations	Rationale
Pharyngeal obstruction (asphyxia)	Scissors and an extra S-B tube are readily available. Frequent observation of vital signs—particularly respiratory status. If patient becomes cyanotic, cut through the three lumens simultaneously and remove the tube	The patient begins gasping for air. The most likely cause is a leaking or ruptured gastric balloon. Under traction, when the balloon ruptures, the tube is raised through the esophagus and the esophageal balloon obstructs the airway. By cutting the tube, both balloons are immediately deflated and the tube can be removed without further trauma to the mucosa. Also, by cutting the tube, it can be removed without undoing tape

inserted into the gastric balloon and traction is continued. If the bleeding is from the esophageal varices, the esophageal balloon is inflated to a pressure of 20 to 25 mmHg. The patient should be observed closely while the Sengstaken-Blakemore tube is in place. Because swallowing is impossible with an inflated esophageal balloon, the patient will require frequent nasoesophageal suctioning to control saliva production. Insertion of a Levin tube connected to intermittent suctioning, above the esophageal balloon, is recommended to prevent aspiration. If the gastric balloon ruptures, the entire tube will move upward and obstruct the patient's airway. Immediately cut the tube across all three lumens and remove it. A second Sengstaken-Blakemore tube should be available in the patient's room should this occur.

Endoscopy and arteriography procedures are done to locate and treat the varices which continue to bleed with tamponade. Intra-arterial vasopressin by continuous pump infusion may be given through the superior mesenteric artery. The vasopressin decreases mesenteric blood flow, which decreases portal hypertension and decompresses the bleeding varices, thus allowing for thrombosis of the bleeding lesion.

When the patient has been stabilized from the hemorrhagic shock and the bleeding is controlled, long-range plans for lowering portal hypertension must be considered. Surgical procedures which shunt the blood away from the portal system will decrease portal hypertension.

Peptic Ulcer Disease

Peptic ulcer disease refers to duodenal, gastric, and stomal (gastrojejunostomy junction) ulcerations. Upper gastrointestinal hemorrhage is related to peptic ulcer disease in 50 to 70 percent of upper gastrointestinal bleeding. Peptic ulcer bleeding can sometimes be controlled by 30 to 60 min of iced saline lavages. Antacids are then instilled through the Levin tube every 15 min for 3 to 6 h. If no further bleeding develops, the nasogastric tube is removed and antacids are given orally every 30 min. Cimetidine may be used orally or intravenously to decrease hyperacidity, thus eliminating the need for antacids.

Differential diagnosis of the peptic ulcer is made by endoscopy and barium studies. If medical management fails, surgery is necessary. Many surgical techniques are available, and the decision is based on the location and severity of the ulcer disease.

Gastritis

Gastritis is a superficial erosion of the gastric mucosal and submucosal layers of the stomach. A diagnosis is made by the redness and oozing of blood seen during an endoscopy procedure. Twenty-five percent of severe upper gastrointestinal hemorrhage may be due to gastritis.

The pathophysiology of some types of gastritis involves the alteration of the gastric mucosal barrier.

The functioning gastric mucosal barrier restricts the diffusion of hydrogen ions from the gastric lumen into the mucosa. Ingested drugs, particularly aspirin (acetylsalicylic acid) and alcohol, affect the gastric mucosal barrier, producing a back diffusion of hydrogen ions. Aspirin is also linked to a decreased platelet adhesiveness, which leads to abnormal local hemostasis.

The erosion of the mucosa may appear normal 48 h after cessation of the bleeding. If the offending agent is known, it should be removed to prevent recurrence. The nursing interview should include pertinent questions related to drug ingestion, alcohol usage, previous history of hematemesis or melena, history of ulcer disease, and recent traumas. The patient's response will guide the nurse toward the causative factors of the gastritis.

Stress Ulcers (Acute Peptic Ulcer Associated with Stress)

Acute superficial erosion of the gastric and duodenal mucosa after stressful events are referred to as *stress ulcers*. Stress ulcers are associated with severe burns, neurological procedures, surgery, renal or respiratory failure, hypotension, multiple trauma, and emotional stress. The proposed possible mechanisms by which stress ulcers develop include an increased acid secretion, a defect in the normal mucosal barrier, and a decreased blood supply or ischemia of the mucosa. The lesion may develop within hours after the stressful event, and the first indication may be a severe gastrointestinal bleed. The symptoms and immediate treatment protocol are the same used in hemorrhagic shock. Diagnosis may be made by endoscopy, since the lesions are too superficial to be demonstrated with barium studies.

Mallory-Weiss Syndrome

The Mallory-Weiss syndrome is a linear, nonperforating tear of the gastric mucosa near or at the gastroesophageal junction. The patient presents with a history of hematemesis preceded by a severe vomiting episode of the stomach contents without blood. A massive gastrointestinal hemorrhage may follow. The tear is the result of pressure changes in the stomach during vomiting. The advent of endoscopy has made early diagnosis and treatment possible. When a diagnosis is confirmed, the nasogastric tube is removed and antacids are begun. The bleeding may stop spontaneously. The surgical procedure is to oversew the lesion. Alcohol abuse, hiatal hernias, gastritis, and esophagitis are associated with the Mallory-Weiss syndrome.

Intestinal Ischemic Disorders

Intestinal ischemia develops from a decrease in blood flow or decrease in tissue perfusion, producing an inadequate oxygen concentration to meet the requirements of the splanchnic bed. Three major arterial trunks—the celiac axis, the superior mesenteric artery, and the inferior mesenteric artery—originate from the ventral aspect of the abdominal aorta and branch to form the vascular bed referred to as the *splanchnic circulation*. The splanchnic area receives approximately 20 percent of the cardiac output. Adequate splanchnic perfusion depends upon the patency of the major arteries, arteriolar resistance, perfusion pressure, arterial oxygen saturation, and the oxygen needs of the splanchnic bed. There are three broad categories of intestinal ischemia: acute occlusive mesenteric ischemia, chronic occlusive mesenteric ischemia, and nonocclusive mesenteric ischemia.

Table 29-3 summarizes factors which will influence the splanchnic blood flow. Autoregulation, a physiological process by which changes in systemic arterial pressure are compensated for by a corresponding change in arterial tone, maintains a relatively stable capillary flow. The distribution of splanchnic blood flow within the intestinal wall and within the mucosa may be adjusted through the autoregulation process without altering the total splanchnic flow. Splanchnic blood flow is increased by the presence of food in the gastrointestinal tract. The process of digestion increases the oxygen requirement of the gastrointestinal organs, and the blood flow increases to meet the increased oxygen demand. Gastrin, secretin, and cholecystokinin are digestive hormones which increase the splanchnic flow when secreted during digestion. Beta-stimulating sympathomimetic amines (isoproterenol) have a vasodilation effect on the splanchnic blood flow.

Splanchnic blood flow is decreased when the cardiac output is decreased so that blood is shunted to the vital organs. Physical exercise, marked intralumen pressure (abdominal distention), angiotensin II, alpha-stimulating sympathomimetic amines (epinephrine and norepinephrine), and cardiac glycosides (digitalis) result in arterial vasoconstriction, which decreases splanchnic flow.

The mucosal lining of the intestine is more sensitive to oxygen deprivation than the muscular and serosal

TABLE 29-3	
Splanchnic Blood Flow	
Factors increasing splanchnic blood flow	Factors decreasing splanchnic blood flow
Presence of food	Physical activity
Digestive hormones:	Abdominal distention (marked increase in intra-lumen pressure)
Gastrin	Angiotensin II
Secretin	
Cholecystokinin	Alpha-stimulating sympathomimetic amines (epinephrine, norepinephrine)
Metabolites produced during muscle activity	Cardiac glycosides (digitalis)
Beta-stimulating sympathomimetic amines (isoproterenol)	

layers. Changes occur in the absorptive cells within 5 to 10 min after occlusion of the blood flow. Necrosis, ulceration, and inflammatory cell infiltrate follow. Inflammatory cell infiltrate is a response to the necrosis and the secondary bacterial invasion following ischemic episodes. The bacterial invasion occurs more commonly when the large colon (inferior mesenteric artery) is involved.

Clinically, if the ischemic disorder is sudden or acute, the patient presents with an abrupt onset of severe abdominal pain. Fluid loss, fever, and gastrointestinal bleeding may follow. Clinical signs of peritonitis and perforation are indications of the progression of the ischemia and the involvement of the muscular and serosal bowel layers.

Acute Occlusive Mesenteric Ischemia

Acute occlusive mesenteric ischemia may be related to a thrombosis or an embolus. The acute mesenteric arterial thrombosis may be secondary to atherosclerosis, a dissecting aortic aneurysm, thromboangiitis obliterans, or systemic vasculitis. The acute mesenteric arterial embolus is commonly seen in patients with a history of rheumatic heart disease, atherosclerotic heart disease with a mural thrombosis in the heart, or previous embolic episodes. Occlusion by thrombus or embolus is generally seen in the superior mesenteric artery. Occlusion of the superior mesenteric artery results in an intense spasm of the small intestine which is experienced by the patient as severe griping or colicky pain in the periumbilical area. The spasm relaxes, but the bowel is immobile. The immobility of the bowel results in a paralytic ileus. The patient becomes distended, and vomiting

occurs. The abdominal distention and increased intraluminal pressure further decrease blood flow to the splanchnic bed.

The ischemic bowel loses protein, electrolytes, and fluid into the lumen and wall of the bowel. The third-space extracellular fluid loss decreases the circulating blood volume. This decreases cardiac output, decreases arterial blood pressure, and increases blood viscosity. Clinically, these reactions are manifested by a general increase in vasoconstriction, tachycardia, and respiratory distress. Gastrointestinal bleeding may be seen as the ischemia progresses. The changes in blood volume can be evaluated by observing the urinary output. The bacterial action of tissue destruction produces vasoconstricting agents, further complicating the inadequate perfusion of the splanchnic area.

The progression of ischemia results in a constant, generalized abdominal pain. As the abdominal pain and distention increase, normal respiratory movements are decreased. This further complicates the respiratory problems associated with increased blood viscosity (hemoconcentration), resulting in impairment of perfusion at the capillary level. Perforation and peritonitis denote extensive ischemia and transmural necrosis.

Laboratory findings in a patient presenting with an acute occlusive mesenteric ischemia include leukocytosis, increased hematocrit, and electrolyte imbalances. The patient has an elevated temperature, tachycardia, and hypotension. Hematemesis and bloody diarrhea may occur. Arteriograms are sometimes done to help in the diagnosis and to evaluate the extent of disease.

The medical treatment is to establish stable hemodynamics and prevent further ischemic changes. Nasogastric suctioning is used to prevent bowel distention and vomiting. Fluid replacements with saline, colloids, and electrolytes are monitored by CVP lines or Swan-Ganz catheters, hematocrit levels, blood pressure readings, and urinary output. Antibiotics are given to treat sepsis. Sodium bicarbonate is used to treat the metabolic acidosis. Blood measurements of base excess, P_{CO_2}, and pH are guidelines for determining the amounts of sodium bicarbonate needed. Cardiac monitoring (ECG) and supportive cardiac care are provided as necessary. Isoproterenol is frequently given to increase splanchnic collateral circulation, as well as to achieve the inotropic effect on the heart muscle itself.

The surgical intervention will be based on the results of the arteriogram. An occlusion secondary to thrombosis is treated by surgical bypass of the lesion or an endarterectomy. An embolectomy is performed for an embolic occlusion of a mesenteric artery. A second-look operation sometimes follows both of the primary surgeries 6 to 12 h after the first operation. The serosa of the bowel does not always appear ischemic at the time of surgery. After the patient is hemodynamically stabilized, the viability of the bowel can be determined. If one does not remove all the necrotic tissue, a breakdown of the anastomosis with peritonitis may occur.

The patient with an acute, occlusive, mesenteric ischemia secondary to thrombosis is generally elderly and has other cardiac, pulmonary, renal, or cerebral atherosclerotic changes. The mortality rate for this population is 60 to 70 percent. The increased mortality rate is probably due to the age group and its related health problems, the nonspecific symptomatology of acute occlusive mesenteric ischemia, and the complications associated with successive surgeries. Patients with a history of rheumatic heart disease and previous embolic disorders, presenting with an abrupt onset of severe abdominal pain, are more easily diagnosed. The age group is younger than that with thrombotic lesions. The age factor, along with early diagnosis and treatment, improves the prognosis.

Chronic Occlusive Mesenteric Ischemia

The atherosclerotic changes in two of three of the major splanchnic vessels occurring over a period of time is accompanied by the development of collateral blood flow. Under normal physiological functioning the collateral flow minimizes and occasionally prevents intestinal ischemia. As the atherosclerosis pro-

gresses, the patient may develop intermittent, transitory ischemia. After the ingestion of food, oxygen requirements of the intestines increase. If the blood flow is unable to increase correspondingly with the increased need, intestinal ischemia occurs. The presenting symptom of chronic occlusive mesenteric ischemia is intestinal angina (intermittent mid-abdominal pain following eating). The intestinal angina may be compared to angina pectoris or coronary ischemia.

The syndrome of chronic occlusive mesenteric ischemia is seen in the elderly patient with atherosclerotic changes. The chief complaint is crampy, periumbilical pain which lasts for a few hours after eating. The complaint is nonspecific and often the diagnosis is not made. The patient continues to have postprandial pain, and a fear of eating develops. Weight loss and malnutrition develop as the patient limits oral foods. It is common for the patient to undergo diagnostic evaluation for carcinoma. If the cause of the weight loss is not cancer, the diagnosis of intestinal ischemia is then considered. Additional symptoms which may occur in chronic intestinal ischemia include steatorrhea (fatty stools), diarrhea, constipation, nausea, vomiting, and abdominal bloating. An abdominal bruit may be present.

Arteriography studies may demonstrate partial occlusion of the mesenteric arteries and a development of collateral flow. The surgical procedures which have been successful include bypass of the occlusion, endarterectomy (removal of the thickness in the artery), and reimplantation of the occluded vessels. Surgical intervention is recommended for relief of pain and correction of malnutrition.

Nonocclusive Mesenteric Ischemia

Nonocclusive mesenteric ischemia is secondary to low blood flow to the mesenteric arteries without occlusion. Splanchnic vasoconstriction and a degree of atherosclerotic changes are predisposing factors. In the presence of lowered cardiac output and poor tissue perfusion, blood flow is redistributed to the vital organs. If vasoconstrictive drugs are given to improve arterial pressure and cardiac output, the splanchnic blood flow is further decreased. If the ischemia continues because of atherosclerotic partial occlusions or the self-sustaining cycle of the temporary ischemia (Fig. 29-2), transmural necrosis and frank infarction of the bowel can occur. The progression of ischemia has been previously described. (See the section on acute occlusive mesenteric ischemia.)

An early diagnosis of nonocclusive mesenteric

ischemia is important in order to prevent the multi-systemic complications that may develop from prolonged vasoconstriction, perforation, and peritonitis. The clues to diagnosing nonocclusive mesenteric ischemia include: (1) history of atherosclerosis; (2) predisposing events of redistribution of blood flow, blood loss, and/or hypovolemia; and (3) abdominal pain of abrupt onset. The abdominal complaints may be severe, cramping periumbilical pain, or more commonly, diffuse, nonspecific abdominal pain. Dehydration, fever, increased white blood cell counts, and increased hematocrit may be observed.

Diagnostic studies include angiograms to exclude occlusive diseases. Abdominal films and barium studies may be included in early stages of the disease process. Surgery is not usually recommended in nonocclusive mesenteric ischemia. Treatment is geared toward the correction of the hemodynamic status of the patient with volume support, promotion of cardiac function, and control of sepsis.

Ischemic Colitis

The reduction of blood flow to the inferior mesenteric artery is usually due to atherosclerotic disease, to low flow states (hypovolemia), or to interruption of the inferior mesenteric artery during abdominal surgery. The inferior mesenteric artery supplies the left colon and rectum. The patient's symptoms include an abrupt onset of nonspecific abdominal pain and rectal bleeding. Barium studies demonstrate the submucosal edema and hemorrhage of small ulcerations (thumbprinting).

Ischemic colitis may not be acute. With the cessation of oral feeding and the start of intravenous therapy and antibiotic therapy, the ischemia may be resolved. As the mucosa heals, fibrous formation occurs. A patient undergoes barium studies after the ischemic episode for evaluation of stricture formation from scar tissue.

If the ischemia of the large colon progresses, surgical intervention is recommended to avoid perforation and peritonitis from a gangrenous bowel. The involved bowel is resected and a temporary colostomy is created, with eventual reanastomosis.

Nursing Responsibilities

The nursing responsibility revolves around fluid volume replacement and observations for progression of the ischemia. Fluid replacement is monitored by urinary output, blood pressure, and CVP or Swan-Ganz readings. Abdominal distention is relieved by

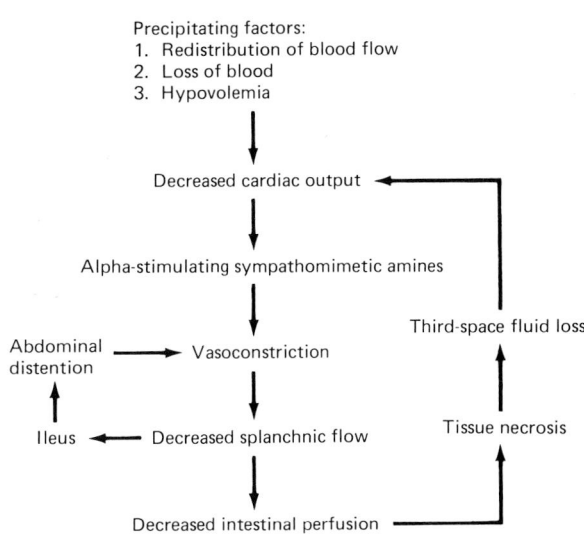

Precipitating factors:
1. Redistribution of blood flow
2. Loss of blood
3. Hypovolemia

FIGURE 29-2

The self-sustaining cycle of nonocclusive mesenteric ischemia.

a nasogastric tube. Large quantities of intestinal output can be expected because of the third-space volume loss secondary to the mucosal changes. Careful intake and output records are mandatory.

Cardiac function will be observed by ECG monitoring. Massive fluid replacement is required to increase circulating volume. This in turn increases cardiac output and splanchnic blood flow. Sepsis further complicates the patient's cardiac function. Signs of systemic sepsis include elevated temperature, tachycardia, and hypotension. If the condition is not improved by fluid replacements and improved cardiac function, transmural necrosis may occur. When the entire thickness of the intestinal wall is involved (transmural), perforation and peritonitis follow. Abdominal tenderness and rigidity are signs of impending perforation.

The patients are usually elderly, with peripheral vasoconstriction and malnutrition. Pressure necrosis (decubitus ulcer) is preventable. Frequent turning and repositioning are important in this group of patients. Existing pulmonary problems and abdominal distention must also be considered in positioning. The head of the bed should be raised to facilitate respiratory movements. Mouth and nose care assist in providing comfort. The patient is usually on nothing by mouth (NPO), and a nasogastric tube is in place. Cleanse the nostrils with cotton-tipped applicators, and apply lubricant where the tube enters the nostril.

If the patient undergoes the surgical corrective procedures, pulmonary therapy will be very instrumental in the patient's recovery. Elderly patients with atherosclerotic changes and a history of thrombosis or embolus must be carefully observed postoperatively for the development of thrombophlebitis. Patients in this age bracket also require range of motion exercises to prevent contractures. Limitation of motion occurs in a short period of time but is avoidable if range of motion exercises are done during the bath.

Intestinal Obstructions

Intestinal obstructions may be divided into two categories: mechanical and functional. Mechanical obstructions involve a physical blockage of the bowel lumen. Lesions outside of the bowel which produce mechanical obstructions include adhesions, hernias, volvuli, and tumors. Tumors, large gallstones, barium impactions, bezoars, and fecalomas may obstruct the intestinal lumen. Intussusception (a telescoping of a portion of the bowel lumen into a second segment with peristalsis) and stricture formation may lead to a mechanical obstruction.

Functional obstructions are more commonly referred to as *paralytic ileus*. A paralytic ileus develops when there is loss of propulsive peristalsis. Conditions that decrease or inhibit intestinal motility are abdominal surgery, hypokalemia, intestinal distention, peritonitis, intestinal ischemia, severe traumas, spinal fractures, and ureteral distention.

Mechanical Obstruction of the Small Intestine

A mechanical obstruction of the small bowel results in an accumulation of intestinal secretions, ingested fluids, and gas proximal to the obstruction. In a 24-h period the gastrointestinal tract secretes approximately 8 L of fluid for digestion and absorption of nutrients. This fluid is reabsorbed in the small intestine. An accumulation of gas and fluid proximal to an obstruction distends the bowel. Intestinal distention increases secretions without increasing the reabsorption capacity and decreases the motility of the small bowel through an intestinointestinal inhibitory reflex.

The increased intestinal secretions accumulating in the small bowel deplete the extracellular fluid volume. Protein may also be lost from the cells and is found in the bowel wall, creating the edematous appearance. The third-space fluid deficit may be sufficient to produce hypovolemic shock. The blood pressure, pulse, and urinary output are indicators of circulatory volume. (Refer to the section on hemorrhagic hypovolemic shock.)

The loss of electrolytes varies with the site of the obstruction. In proximal (pyloric, high jejunum) obstructions, vomiting is frequent and often profuse. This results in a loss of sodium, chloride, potassium, and hydrogen. The patient may present with hypochloremia, hypokalemia, and metabolic alkalosis. In distal (ileum, low jejunum) obstructions, there is less vomiting and more distention. Third-space fluid loss is greater, and the symptoms include dehydration, oliguria, azotemia, and hemoconcentration.

The decreased motility associated with intestinal distention leads to stasis of the accumulated fluid in the bowel lumen. The small intestine has a low bacteria count; however, when a mechanical obstruction occurs, there is a rapid proliferation of bacteria. The overgrowth of bacteria is responsible for the feculent odor of the vomitus from the small bowel.

Strangulation

Strangulation of the bowel occurs when the circulation to an obstructed segment is impaired. Strangulation may progress to gangrene and peritonitis, and for this reason early detection and treatment is imperative. A closed-loop obstruction refers to an intestinal segment which is obstructed proximally and distally. The closed-loop obstruction leads to strangulation by isolating the intestinal segment and impairing the circulation to that segment. As distention increases, there is an increased intraluminal pressure which compromises the circulation to the bowel layers. Volvulus and intussusception impair the mesenteric circulation. Adhesions and hernias produce a pressure necrosis of the intestinal segment and can also lead to impaired blood flow and strangulation.

A strangulated bowel segment seeps blood and plasma into the bowel lumen. In a patient dehydrated from an obstruction, the loss of blood and plasma augments the progression to hypovolemic shock. In addition to the fluid loss, the toxins produced by the proliferation of bacteria cross the damaged intestinal membranes into the peritoneal cavity. The toxins are absorbed from the peritoneal cavity, and septicemia may occur.

Colonic Obstructions

Colonic obstructions are most commonly related to neoplasms and volvulus of the sigmoid colon. The fluid and electrolyte loss is not as profound as in small bowel obstructions. The large bowel distends with gas and waste material and may perforate. When the ileocecal valve is competent, a colonic obstruction behaves as a closed-loop obstruction. Strangulation of the large colon with the resulting sequelae may occur.

Diagnosis of Intestinal Obstructions

The presenting symptoms of intestinal obstructions include abdominal pain, vomiting, abdominal distention, obstipation, and failure to pass flatus. The abdominal pain is crampy and subsides as the intestinal motility decreases. Strangulation and peritonitis are suspected when the crampy abdominal pain is followed by continuous, severe abdominal pain and fever. Vomiting is related to the location of the obstruction. Proximal obstructions are associated with profuse vomiting and minimal abdominal distention. In distal obstructions, abdominal distention is more pronounced. The vomitus in distal obstructions has a feculent odor, secondary to the bacteria proliferation. Vomiting is not common in colonic obstruction when the ileocecal valve is competent.

Auscultation of the abdomen will reveal high-pitched, frequent bowel sounds in proximal obstructions. The bowel sounds are slightly lower in pitch and last longer in the presence of distal obstructions. The changes in bowel sounds are related to the increased peristaltic contractions associated with intestinal obstructions.

Abdominal examinations are done to check for possible hernias, abdominal masses, and rebound tenderness. To examine a patient for rebound tenderness, one hand is slowly pressed into the abdomen and quickly withdrawn. Rebound tenderness is present if the pain is greater when the hand is withdrawn. Rebound tenderness indicates a peritoneal irritation. Laboratory studies include serum electrolyte levels, creatinine, hematocrit, and white blood cell count. Blood studies are done serially to assess the adequacy of the treatment.

A preliminary diagnosis of intestinal obstruction may be documented by abdominal x-rays. Abnormally large amounts of gas, along with other findings, demonstrated on the abdominal films will confirm the presence of the obstruction. In the presence of a paralytic ileus, the gaseous distention is more evenly distributed in the stomach, small bowel, and colon with gas-fluid levels.

Treatment

Surgery is the treatment of choice in most instances of intestinal obstruction. The timing of the operation is important and depends upon the severity of the fluid and electrolyte changes, the duration of the obstruction, the risk of strangulation, and changes in the vital organ functioning. Treatment is initiated to prevent shock and restore fluid and electrolyte losses prior to surgery. Supportive therapy includes intravenous normal saline and nasogastric suctioning. A Foley catheter is inserted for accurate measurement of the urinary output. The normal saline is continued until the urine output depicts an adequate renal blood flow (output $\geq$ 30 mL/h). Potassium is withheld until the renal function is adequately assessed, since the kidney is responsible for excreting excess potassium. Potassium excess is as dangerous as potassium deficit in cardiac functioning.

A central venous pressure (CVP) monitor is used to monitor fluid replacement. The CVP is maintained between 5 and 10 cm of saline to assure adequate circulating volume. If the patient presents with hypovolemic shock (see the section on gastrointestinal hemorrhage, which begins this chapter) or strangulation, blood and plasma are used with the saline to increase the fluid volume.

The nasogastric tube is used to empty the stomach of contents and minimize further abdominal distention from swallowed air. Intestinal suctioning with a Miller-Abbott tube or other long intestinal tubes may be used for intestinal decompression. The Miller-Abbott tube is placed in position at the pyloric antrum with the patient lying on the right side. The tube then moves on its own into the duodenum. Peristalsis and gravity facilitate the movement of the intestinal tube through the small intestine. The placement of the intestinal tube is checked by fluoroscopic examination.

The operative procedures recommended for mechanical small bowel obstructions vary according to the etiology of the obstruction. Various procedures include lysis of adhesions, reduction of hernias, bypass of obstructions, and excision of obstructions or proximal enterocutaneous fistulae. Left colonic obstructions are generally treated in three stages: (1) Initially, a proximal colostomy is done to relieve the distention and provide a fecal outlet. (2) The diseased segment is removed from the colon distal to the colostomy with an anastomosis of the distal segment. (3) When the anastomosis has healed, the colostomy is closed. The rationale for the three-stage procedure is the hazard of operating on a distended colon. An impending perforation may be walled off by the omentum, and manipulation of the bowel may cause a perforation. The surgical anastomosis of a distended colon is not a safe procedure, since the anastomosis of an edematous bowel wall may not be competent.

A paralytic ileus which develops after abdominal surgery generally persists for 2 to 3 days. The treatment includes intravenous fluids and nasogastric suctioning. Replacement and maintenance of normal electrolyte values, particularly potassium, is important.

If the bowel becomes strangulated, an operation is performed to prevent the development of gangrene and peritonitis. The viability of the bowel at the time of the operation is determined by the color, arterial pulsations, and motility of the segment. If the bowel is viable, resection may not be necessary. The operative findings will determine the surgical procedure.

Nursing Implications

The nursing observations made postoperatively are important for early detection of intestinal obstruction. Following abdominal surgery, the bowel is adynamic. A nasograstric tube is necessary to prevent bowel distention, and the patient receives intravenous fluids. The patient is started on oral fluids after bowel sounds return. Occasionally, an ileus or intestinal obstruction will develop after oral fluids have been initiated. The early symptoms of intestinal obstruction include abdominal cramping pain with nausea and vomiting. If a bowel obstruction is suspected, nursing intervention should include restriction of patient's oral intake, examination of the abdomen for distention and bowel sounds, evaluation of the vital signs, and notification of the physician of the findings. If the patient has developed an intestinal obstruction, the nasogastric tube should be reinserted. Fluid replacement will be monitored according to the vital signs, urinary output, and nasogastric output. The patient and the family need emotional support at this time. The development of an intestinal obstruction is a physical setback for the postoperative patient, and further surgery may be necessary.

Long gastrointestinal (Miller-Abbott, Cantor) tubes are occasionally utilized for intestinal decompression. The gastrointestinal tube is inserted mechanically into the stomach. The balloon is filled with mercury. An x-ray is done to determine proper placement of the tube. The tube passes by means of peristalsis through the pylorus into the duodenum. After the balloon enters the duodenum, air or water is inserted into the balloon of the Miller-Abbott. Once through the pylorus, the tube is advanced 2 to 4 in at regular intervals by the nurse. Advancement of longer segments may lead to kinking of the intestinal tube. Decompression of the intestine is accomplished by suction. The patency of the tube is maintained by saline irrigations. The balloon side of the Miller-Abbot tube should be labeled so that irrigation fluid is not inserted in the balloon. Accurate intake and output records of nasogastric or gastrointestinal output through suctioning is mandatory. A patient may lose 3000 mL or more in 24 h with intestinal obstructions. Adequate fluid replacement is based on the intestinal output as well as vital signs, CVP, and urinary output.

Additional gastrointestinal losses include saliva and gastric secretions. Saliva production is increased by nausea, chewing gum, thoughts of foods, and smooth objects in the mouth (for example, cotton mouth swabs and candy mints). Avoiding the above stimuli decreases saliva production but leads to dryness of the mouth. Patient comfort may be facilitated by brushing the teeth frequently. Gastric production is stimulated by thoughts of foods, smelling foods, watching someone eat, and in some patients, increased anxiety levels. Therefore, the patient's environment may be altered to reduce the gastric secretions.

Peritonitis

Peritonitis, inflammation of the peritoneum, may be divided into primary and secondary categories. Approximately 1 percent of the cases of peritonitis result from primary infections of the peritoneum. Primary peritonitis may be idiopathic or tuberculous in origin. Secondary peritonitis results from the contamination of the peritoneal cavity from an altered visceral wall or a defect in the visceral wall. Perforated peptic ulcer, ruptured appendix, ischemic bowel disease, intestinal obstruction, trauma, pancreatitis, and perforated colon may progress to generalized peritonitis.

Pathophysiology

The peritoneum is a semipermeable membrane which encloses the abdominal viscera and mesentery in a sac-like structure open, only in the female, at the fallopian tubes. A small amount of serous fluid is secreted by the peritoneum to prevent friction between the viscera during peristalsis. The surface area of the peritoneum and the skin are comparable. This large amount of absorption area and the bidirectional transfer of fluid, electrolytes, and other material play a role in the process of peritonitis.

The attempt of the peritoneum to localize or wall off any contamination and prevent diffuse peritonitis is the peritoneal defense mechanism. The local reaction of the peritoneum to contamination involves vascular dilatation and increased capillary permeability. Large numbers of polymorphonuclear leukocytes pour into the peritoneal cavity. Phagocytosis of bacteria and any foreign material in the area is carried out by the polymorphonuclear leukocytes. Fibroplastic exudate is deposited on the peritoneum and plasters the adjacent bowel, mesentery, and omentum to the inflamed area, forming a watertight seal. This process is referred to as localization or walling-off of the inflammation, preventing diffuse peritonitis. The localization process is not successful if the contamination is continuous or the original contamination is massive. In these instances, the peritoneal defense mechanism is overwhelmed.

The mechanism of peritoneal irritation in contamination from the stomach, pancreas, and upper small bowel is initially a chemical reaction from the spillage of potent digestive enzymes. Lower small bowel and colonic spillage result in peritoneal inflammation from the bacterial content entering the peritoneal cavity. Vascular dilation, hyperemia, and a fluid shift are reactions stimulated by peritoneal irritation. The vascular dilation and hyperemia lead to an increased number of polymorphonuclear leukocytes in the inflamed area. The absorption capacity of the peritoneum is also increased, facilitating the absorption of toxins and bacteria into the bloodstream and leading to septicemia and bacteremia. A fluid shift occurs from the extracellular fluid compartment into the free peritoneal space, into the loose connective tissue (as edema), and into the lumen of the atonic gastrointestinal tract. The translocation of water, electrolytes, and protein into this third-space compartment depletes the circulating blood volume. The rate of fluid loss from the circulating volume into the third-space compartment is proportional to the degree of peritoneal involvement.

Prior to the institution of treatment, the cardiovascular system response is based on the inadequate circulatory volume, or hypovolemia secondary to the fluid shift. In hypovolemic shock there is a decreased cardiac output, low filling pressure, and decreased tissue perfusion with resultant tissue ischemia. If septicemia is associated with peritonitis, peripheral pooling with a decreased venous return occurs, followed by a further decrease in cardiac output and a lower filling pressure. A failure of cardiac output and central venous pressure (CVP) to be sustained with volume replacement may be seen in septic shock.

Cathecholamines (epinephrine and norepinephrine) are released in response to the acute decrease in circulating volume, resulting in vasoconstriction, increased pulse rate, and diaphoresis (see Fig. 29-1). Adrenocorticotropic hormone (ACTH) and aldosterone are released through a pituitary-adrenal axis response. This results in water and sodium retention and a potassium loss, since the body attempts to conserve fluid. When the circulatory system is unable to maintain adequate tissue perfusion, metabolic acidosis develops secondary to anaerobic metabolism.

Presenting symptoms of peritonitis include pain with any movement, including respirations. The pain experienced with respirations results in compensatory shallow, rapid respirations. The respiratory system increases its effort to oxygenate the circulating blood to compensate for the metabolic acidosis. The increased respiratory activity creates an increase in the oxygen requirement of the muscles of respiration. Thus there is an increased demand on the respiratory system at a time when painful respiratory movements limit the respiratory function. When the required workload exceeds the ability of the respiratory system, respiratory decompensation occurs with resultant respiratory acidosis.

The workload of the kidneys is increased by the presence of circulating toxins, pigments, and necrotic tissue products in the bloodstream. A decreased cardiac output, vasoconstriction, and decreased renal perfusion affect the ability of the kidneys to excrete the metabolic waste products and toxins. Acute renal insufficiency is monitored by hourly observation of urine output and specific gravity measurements of the urine.

Early detection of peritonitis and immediate fluid replacement may inhibit this vicious, life-threatening cycle. The treatment of peritonitis will be discussed in more detail with relation to specific etiology.

Primary Peritonitis: Clinical Signs, Diagnostic Studies, and Treatment

In primary idiopathic peritonitis the bacterial agent is thought to gain contact with the peritoneum through the vascular system or through the fallopian tubes. The peritonitis is manifested by a severe, generalized, steady, burning abdominal pain, fever and chills, irritability, and diarrhea. The bowel sounds are either hypoactive or absent. Primary idiopathic peritonitis is seen more often in children than in adults and is associated with an infection by the same organism elsewhere in the body.

Diagnostic studies include white blood cell counts in which there is an elevated number of leukocytes, primarily polymorphonuclear. A peritoneal aspiration is done to distinguish between primary idiopathic peritonitis and a ruptured viscus. The aspirated fluid is evaluated by culture and sensitivity and electrolyte studies.

The treatment of primary idiopathic peritonitis is conservative, supportive therapy. Intravenous fluid replacement is monitored by CVP, blood pressure, and urinary output. Broad spectrum intravenous antibiotics are begun immediately and may be altered after the causative organism is isolated. Nasogastric suctioning is instituted to prevent abdominal distention secondary to fluid and gas accumulation in the atonic bowel.

Tuberculous peritonitis is associated with tubercular invasion elsewhere in the body. There are two types of tuberculous peritonitis: wet and dry. Wet tuberculous peritonitis is associated with the presence of copious abdominal ascites. In dry tuberculous peritonitis, fibrinous adhesions are present and result in a matting effect of the intestines and omentum. The onset of tuberculous peritonitis is insidious with the development of a dull, steady, generalized abdominal pain of varying intensity. Abdominal distention is seen in approximately half of the subjects. General malaise, weakness, weight loss, low-grade temperature, tachycardia, and a doughy abdomen are symptoms seen in tuberculous peritonitis. The slow onset of vague symptoms makes the diagnosis difficult. The diagnosis is based on evaluations of peritoneal fluid aspiration for specific gravity, albumin level, and white blood cell count. Less than half the cases have positive tubercular cultures from the peritoneum. The drug treatment is isoniazid alone. Para-aminosalicylic acid and antibiotics are given if active tuberculosis is found elsewhere in the patient.

Secondary Peritonitis: Clinical Signs, Diagnosis, and Treatment

Secondary acute peritonitis is the result of peritoneal contamination from various etiologies. Perforated peptic ulcer is the most common cause of peritonitis, followed by a ruptured appendix; gangrene of the bowel from strangulation, obstruction, or mesenteric ischemia; gonorrheal salpingitis (pelvic peritonitis); acute gangrenous cholecystitis; ruptured diverticulum; trauma; and surgery. In gangrene of the bowel, the rapid absorption of spilled toxins increases the severity of the process. Penetrating trauma, which ruptures a hollow viscus, will result in a spillage contamination. Peritonitis may develop in the patient with a penetrating abdominal trauma without visceral perforation because of the entry of foreign material into the peritoneal cavity, i.e., clothing or bullet, as well as the infection from the abdomen being open to the environment. Severe blunt trauma may lead to peritonitis by disrupting the abdominal viscera or separating the viscus from its blood supply. Peritonitis from surgery may occur if bile leakage develops, a localized infection spreads, or an anastomosis breaks down.

The clinical manifestations of acute peritonitis include a moderately severe abdominal pain which is aggravated by movement, including respirations. The pain is most intense at the site of advancing inflammation. If there is a decreased intensity or decreased extent of pain, localization of the peritonitis is considered. The patient is very ill and may be found lying quietly in bed in the supine position, with knees flexed. Since respiratory movements increase the pain, the patient's breathing is usually limited to shallow, rapid, respirations. The pulse is rapid, weak, and thready, representing the cardiovascular changes which may be occurring, i.e., decreased cardiac output and decreased tissue perfusion. Rebound tenderness and muscle rigidity with voluntary guarding are also present in peritonitis. Additional clinical signs associated with acute secondary peritonitis include anorexia, nausea, vomiting, fever with chills, decreased urinary output, abdominal distention, and absence of bowel sounds. Rectal and vaginal examinations are done to diagnose pelvic peritonitis.

Diagnostic studies include white blood cell counts which demonstrate an elevated leukocyte level, especially polymorphonuclear cells. Serial white blood cell counts are done to evaluate the progress of the peritonitis. If the diagnosis is not clear-cut, a peritoneal aspiration may be done. Abdominal x-rays demonstrate the amount of abdominal distention and inflammation and edema of the intestinal wall. Free air will be present on abdominal films in the event of a perforation.

The treatment is timely surgical intervention after supportive therapy has stabilized the patient's cardiac and pulmonary status. The supportive therapy includes the insertion of a venous catheter to begin immediate fluid replacement, central venous pressure monitoring, nasogastric tube for decompression, and an indwelling Foley catheter for urinary monitoring. The volume of fluid replacement is monitored by the CVP and hourly urinary output. Plasma, albumin, Ringer's lactate, and D_5W may be given for fluid replacement. Antibiotics are started intravenously, and oxygen is used to augment the respiratory exchange. Patients with a history of heavy cigarette smoking, obesity, or debilitation may require mechanical respiratory assistance. Blood gas levels are determined to assess the patient's respiratory status. Early signs of respiratory decompensation include an increased arterial-venous differentiation and a decreased arterial carbon dioxide from hyperventilation. The pulse rate continues to be elevated with a slight increase in blood pressure despite the restoration of blood volume. Clinically, the patient is flushed, restless, and anxious, with rapid, shallow, labored breathing.

Operating approach includes control of contamination, removal of any foreign material, and drainage of any collected fluid. The control of contamination may be done by simple closure, excision, or exteriorization. Peritoneal irrigation during the surgical procedure decreases the mortality and morbidity of acute diffuse peritonitis. Peritoneal catheters may be inserted into the abdominal cavity for continuous irrigations after surgery. The type of contaminate and the age and general health status of the patient will influence the patient's prognosis.

Nursing Intervention

The early detection of peritonitis is dependent upon knowledge of conditions and situations which predispose a patient to secondary peritonitis. The symptoms are generalized and vague, and differential diagnosis must be made. Clinical signs of peritonitis include an increased temperature and elevated pulse rate with diffuse abdominal tenderness, rebound tenderness, nausea, and vomiting.

Intravenous fluids and broad spectrum antibiotics are started immediately. A Foley catheter is inserted for evaluation of renal perfusion, and thereby evaluation of the overall cardiac output and tissue perfusion. A nasogastric tube is inserted and assists in the decompression of the bowel if an ileus develops. The total fluid output (urinary, nasogastric, and wound) is assessed and utilized in planning fluid and electrolyte replacement.

After surgical intervention, some patients will have an open wound. Intensive wound care is necessary. Continuous irrigations of the peritoneal cavity may be instituted. Two to four peritoneal dialysis catheters may be placed in the peritoneal cavity during surgery. One to three catheters are used to instill antibiotic solution; one catheter is used for drainage. Accurate recording of the intake and output is essential.

The life-threatening condition of the patient is recognized by the patient and the family. An important area of nursing intervention involves assessment of the emotional responses, planning intervention, and implementing steps to assist the patient and family in coping with the severity of the situation. The emotional needs are great when the patient is in an acute state, requiring many technical nursing skills, physical assessments, and implementation of life-sustaining measures. The nurse must permit patients to express their fears. The greatest comfort measure a nurse can utilize is active listening, in other words, hearing the meaning and perceiving the significance of a casual remark.

The etiology of the peritonitis will determine the surgical procedure. Peritonitis secondary to perforations of the colon often results in diversion of the fecal stream by a colostomy. The care of the colostomy differs according to location of the stoma in the large bowel. Briefly, the purpose of the large colon includes water reabsorption and storage of waste products (Fig. 29-3). The contents of the small bowel entering

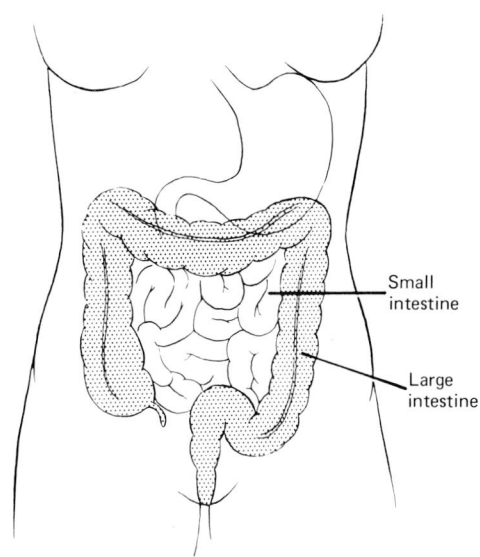

Small intestine

Large intestine

FIGURE 29-3
Anatomy of the gastrointestinal tract.

the ascending colon are liquid in consistency. The contents of the transverse colon are soft stool containing varying amounts of unabsorbed water. As the contents of the large colon move through the descending and sigmoid colon, the water has been absorbed and the stool is firm. A general rule when caring for a new postoperative colostomy patient is to use a skin barrier and an open-end, drainable, odor-proof pouch. Two skin barriers, karaya washers and Stomahesive (Squibb) wafers, may be used to protect the skin. The skin barrier is placed on clean, dry skin at the base of the stoma. It is important that the barrier hug the stoma but not ride up onto the stoma. The opening cut in the pouch must be $\frac{1}{8}$ in larger than the stoma. The edema of the stoma decreases in the early postoperative days, and the opening in the pouch and the skin barrier are adjusted to these changes.

If a loop colostomy is done, a rod is placed under a loop of bowel to support the bowel until adhesions with the abdominal wall occur (Fig. 29-4). The pouching procedure for a loop colostomy with a rod can be made easier by keeping some simple hints in mind. It is almost impossible to place a skin barrier or pouch over a large stoma and not get mucus from the stoma onto the materials. Any mucus trapped under the skin barrier can irritate the skin and create a leakage in the pouch system. A washer can be cut through one side and placed under the rod (Fig. 29-5). The adhesive backing of the pouch can be removed and cut into sections, then replaced over the adhesive. The adhesive is then protected as the pouch is placed

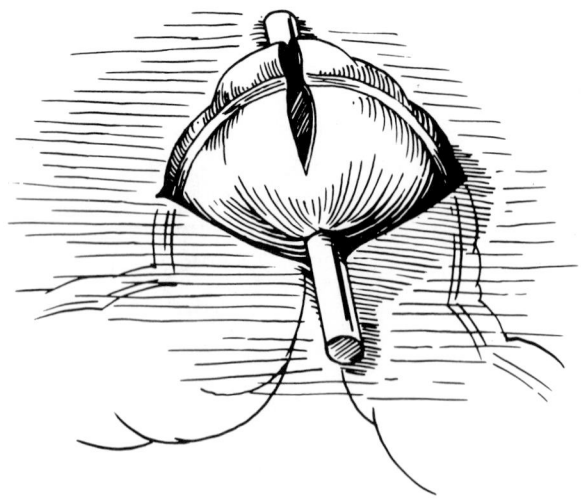

FIGURE 29-4
Loop ostomy stoma procedure with rod.

on the patient. A pouch which is directed straight to the patient's side is often pulled off by the weight of the stool when the patient is up. Angle the pouch toward the lateral aspect of the thigh as the patient's activities change (Fig. 29-6). The pouch seal is often broken by the weight of the stool in an unemptied pouch or the tension from flatus trapped in the pouch. Pinholes for flatus work well for the staff, but the patient suffers. Every time the covers are lifted or adjusted, the odor is present. This does not encourage a patient to accept the change in his or her body image. If patients are aware of their own odors, the family, visitors, and staff must be also. A fear of rejection because of the stoma and the odor is associated with colostomies. Emptying a pouch of flatus from the closed end means that the rest of the time the odor is contained in an odor-proof pouch. Do not ignore the odor. Discuss the colostomy and lack of sphincter control, and use commercial products to remove the odor in the room.

A colostomy following peritonitis is often temporary. However, the duration of the need for the colostomy varies from patient to patient. Learning self-care and returning to presurgical activities are encouraged. The colostomy will not limit a person's activity. However, the reactions of patients to colostomies vary. Acceptance of the changed body image takes a long time. When a person feels the problem of coping with a colostomy is "temporary," the patient may adapt more easily and participate in all aspects of care more readily. Each patient is an individual and has special needs related to the adaptation to the ostomy and related pouching needs. If your institution has a nurse enterostomal therapist (ET), contact this person when the patient returns from surgery. The ET can assist in setting up criteria for pouching the colostomy, in establishing rapport with the patient and family, and in teaching self-care when appropriate.

Cutaneous Fistulas

A cutaneous fistula is a communication between an organ and the abdominal wall and is referred to as an external fistula. Most cutaneous fistulas are associated with surgical complications following intestinal, biliary, and pancreatic procedures. Externalization of drainage may occur through the surgical incisions, drain sites, or separate abdominal wall defects. Intestinal, biliary, and pancreatic fistulas require intensive medical and nursing care.

Enterocutaneous (intestinal) fistulas may develop from anastomotic leaks, prolapse of the bowel into an abdominal or perineal wound, injury to the bowel when dividing adhesions, injury to the bowel by wire mesh or retention sutures, or errors in surgical techniques. Intestinal fistulas are more prone to develop in the presence of inflammatory lesions, neoplasms, or ischemic lesions. Postoperative external biliary fistulas may indicate operative injury to the bile duct or stricture of the common bile duct. Proximal pancreatic resections involve anastomosis of the upper jejunum to the common bile duct, the stomach, and the remaining portion of the pancreas. Leakage may occur from any one of the anastomoses.

Diagnosis

Diagnosis of external fistulization may be established by fistulograms (the injection of dye through the fistula). Small bowel studies and intravenous cholangiograms may also be utilized in diagnosing fistular tracts involving these structures. The etiology of the fistula will determine the management: surgical or medical. Conservative management of external fistulas involves fluid and electrolyte replacement, nutritional support, control of sepsis, drainage of associated abscess formations, and skin protection from digestive enzymes. Surgical intervention may be necessary if the fistula does not close with conservative management. Conditions which adversely affect spontaneous closure include a complete breakdown of an anastomosis, distal obstructions, and necrotic segments of intestine.

The location of an intestinal fistula influences the amount and the contents of the drainage. The higher in the small bowel that a fistular tract forms, the greater the fluid loss through the external communication. Intestinal fistula output contains digestive enzymes, sodium, chloride, and potassium. A patient may lose up to 3 L (3000 mL) in a 24-h period with a high-output jejunal fistula. Management of fluid and electrolytes lost from enterocutaneous fistulas is of crucial importance. The fluid replacement is based on the patient's total output (milliliter for milliliter): fistula, urinary, and insensible. Electrolyte replacements are calculated according to the contents of the fistula drainage and laboratory blood chemistry levels. Biliary fistula electrolyte losses are predominantly sodium chloride, and pancreatic losses are proteolytic enzymes and bicarbonate. Metabolic acidosis occurs when the patient with a fistula does not maintain electrolyte and fluid equilibrium.

Malnutrition is associated with external fistulas. The segment of intestine proximal to the fistula may

FIGURE 29-5

Application of a skin barrier with a rod.

be too short to ensure adequate nutritional support. The food substances and digestive secretions may be excreted through the fistula before absorption can occur. Therefore, fluid and electrolyte loss may increase with oral feedings when an enterocutaneous fistula is present.

Bile is an emulsifying agent which facilitates the absorption of fats and fat-soluble vitamins. When bile is lost through an external biliary fistula, fats are not digested properly and malnutrition develops. In addition, fat-soluble vitamins are not available for absorption. Vitamin K loss is a potential threat, and prothrombin studies are done to evaluate the status of vitamin K. In addition, diarrhea may develop from the bile salts present in the large colon.

Hyperalimentation is recommended for the maintenance of a positive nitrogen balance. Adequate

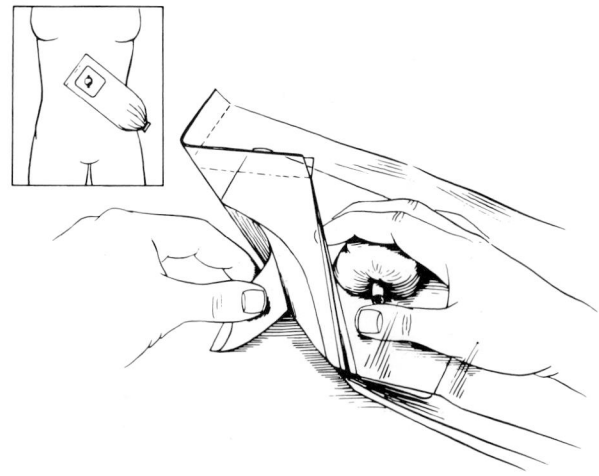

FIGURE 29-6

Application of a pouch on a stoma with a rod.

calories, amino acids, electrolytes and minerals are supplied to meet the patient's daily requirement. Wound healing improves with positive nitrogen balance. Hyperalimentation also places the bowel at complete mechanical rest and decreases the digestive secretions, thus lowering fluid loss via the fistula. Studies have demonstrated that hyperalimentation results in an increase in the number of spontaneous

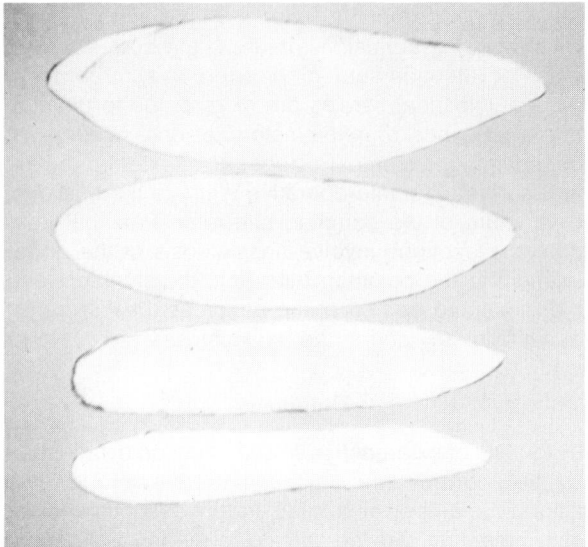

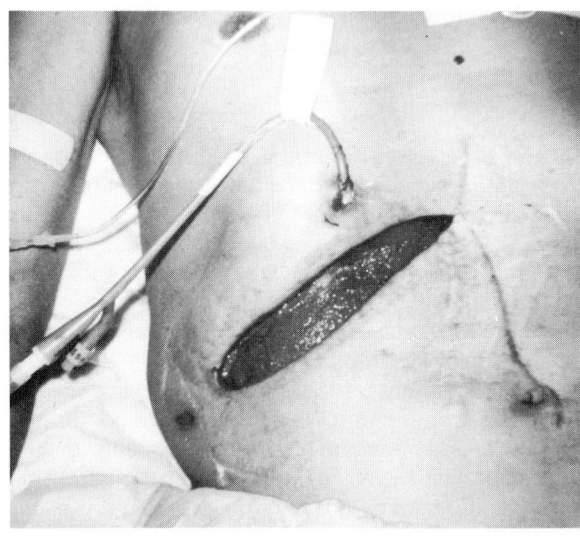

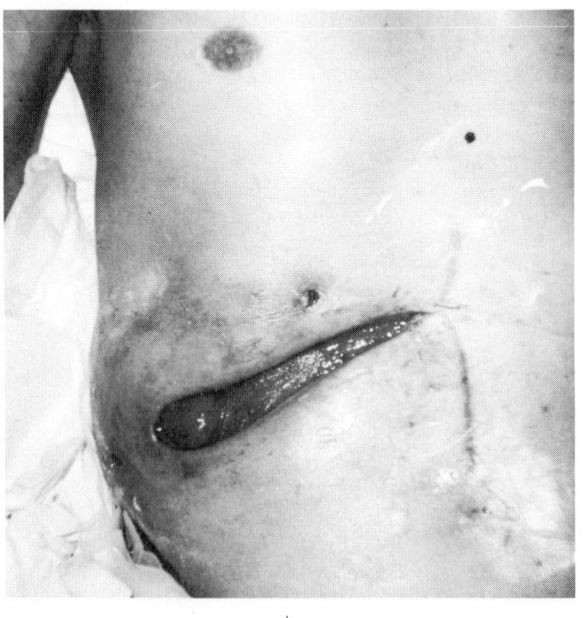

FIGURE 29-7

Effects of hyperalimentation on fistula healing. (*a*) Fistula. (*b*) Fistula after 3 weeks. (*c*) Patterns demonstrating wound size decrease.

closures of fistulas and improved prognoses of those cases requiring operative closure.

The patient in Fig. 29-7 demonstrates the change in an abdominal wall defect with multiple fistulas in 3 weeks. The patient received hyperalimentation, replacement fluids, and antibiotics. The skin was protected from digestive enzymes by the use of ostomy equipment. The advent of progressive pouches and skin barriers for ileostomy patients in the past decade has proven beneficial for fistula management.

Nursing Intervention

The patient with an external fistula requires close observation of vital signs to assess systemic effects of fluid loss, accurate measurement of output, careful monitoring of hyperalimentation and intravenous fluid replacement, and protection of the patient's skin from the fistula drainage.

Fistula drainage may be managed in three ways: dressings, continuous suctioning, or pouching procedures. The location of the fistula and the amount and type of drainage should be considered when choosing an appropriate method. The low output, nonirritating drainage may be effectively managed with dressings. Continuous sump drainage may be preferred with high-output fistulas. However, pouching a fistula or a draining wound offers the greatest number of advantages. The cost of pouching a moderate to high-volume fistula is less than the cost of dressings necessary in a 24-h period. Skin can be protected from the caustic drainage which contains digestive enzymes. Many times a small amount of drainage will seep out around the sump tube and erode the skin. A pouch may be used in combination with a sump catheter. The sump catheter may be open in the pouch or come out through the bottom and connect to suction or to straight drainage. If the tube is left open in the pouch, connect the pouch to a bedside drainage bag or empty it for accurate measurements of the fistula output.

The patient is usually more comfortable using a pouch to collect the fistula drainage. The patient is dry, odor-free, and ambulatory when wearing a pouch. Patients or families may be taught the technique for pouching the fistula and discharged when stabilized with the fistula care.

There are many types of pouches available, and choosing the appropriate equipment for a particular patient is essential. The first issue to examine is the need for sterility. Sterile pouches are available from companies, or pouches may be sterilized with ethylene oxide. External biliary fistulas are generally managed with sterile urinary equipment. Bile does not usually demonstrate a bacteria growth, and prevention of reflux of bile back to the fistula and facilitation of drainage into a collecting device (bedside drainage) is used. Urinary pouches used for control of liquid output are more effective than open-end ileostomy pouches. The urinary pouch can be disconnected from the bedside collecting device and the spout closed for ambulation of the patient. In addition to biliary fistulas, surgically created drainage sites (i.e., penrose drains) are managed with aseptic techniques.

Jejunal and ileal (enterocutaneous) fistulas may develop through an operative incision. When a wound dehiscence occurs, a fistula tract may develop within the open wound. A clean, but not sterile, management of the drainage is indicated. An open-end drainable pouch is used for enterocutaneous fistulas. There are various sizes of pouches, each having different adhesive areas (faceplates). The shape and size of the wound or fistula to be contained will determine the pouch chosen. If the wound has multiple fistulas present, the faceplate on the maxi-pouches (largest pouches available) may be too small. The pouch faceplate must be large enough to accommodate the wound with enough adhesive area retained to attach the pouch to the skin. If the faceplate is not large enough, there are three alternatives: (1) add a maxi-adhesive disk or double-faced adhesive disk to the pouch to increase the size of the faceplate; (2) add skin cement that was developed for ostomy appliances to the pouch, extending the adhesive area; (3) put two pouches together. Preparing a pattern of the enterocutaneous fistula will assist in identifying the size of the pouch faceplate required. A pattern is cut and laid against the skin to assess the adequacy of the template prepared. The opening must be cut to avoid deep crevices, retention sutures, and fine wrinkles. In most cases, $\frac{1}{8}$ to $\frac{1}{4}$ in of skin will be exposed between the fistula and pouch adhesive. This places the pouch seal on smooth skin away from the freely movable wound edges. If a pouch comes directly to the edge of the wound, patient activities including respirations, turning, and ambulation may lift up the inner edge of the pouch and create a leakage. The pattern should be labeled to indicate the patient's right and left sides, head and feet, and the side of the pattern against the skin. When drawing the pattern on the pouch or the skin barrier, it is important that the correct side be against the pouch; otherwise the pattern will be cut in reverse.

The pouch may be adhered directly to the skin; however, a skin barrier is recommended when pouching enterocutaneous fistulas. Skin barriers include Stomahesive, karaya paste, karaya washers, Reliaseals, Crixilene, Colly-seels, or HolliHesive wafers. Sealant products are available to coat the skin and prevent irritation from pouch adhesives. The sealant products are available in the form of sprays, gels, wipes, and liquids. The pattern is used to cut the opening in the skin barrier, unless a silicone product is used. The pouch may then be attached to the skin barrier and applied to the patient's skin at one time, or applied separately to the patient. Skin around a fistula can be protected and remain clear and intact by maintaining a pouch seal. At the first indication of a leakage, the pouch should be removed and a fresh pouching system applied. Prior to applying the skin barrier, the skin is cleansed with warm water and patted dry. If the skin is irritated, care must be taken to improve the skin. Wet, weepy skin must be dried before a skin barrier will adhere. One method for drying the skin is a heat lamp (60 W bulb) 1 ft away from the skin and a hair dryer set on cool. Skin barriers recommended for use on irritated skin include Stomahesive, karaya products, and Colly-seels. Irritated skin is painful for the patient, and karaya products and sealant sprays will sting when applied.

After the skin barrier and the pouch are applied, the exposed skin around the wound edges must be protected to prevent irritation and corrosion by the potent digestive enzymes present in pancreatic and small bowel drainage. One method of protecting the skin is through the use of karaya paste. Karaya paste may be purchased or prepared by mixing karaya powder and glycerine. There is no magic recipe, as humidity and temperature affect the consistency of the paste. A rule of thumb is that the karaya paste, when mixed to the desired consistency, looks like peanut butter cookie dough. The desired consistency enhances the setting time of the paste, and within 10 to 15 min the paste is firm. The patient's body temperature affects the karaya paste by melting the paste and this increases the setting time. If the fistula output is high (800 to 1000 mL per 8 h), the karaya paste may need to be regularly replaced to provide continuous skin protection. When the paste is firm, close the end of the pouch with a rubber band, or attach to a bedside drainage bag. Paper tape may be applied to the pouch edges for extra support.

A careful explanation to the patient prior to initiating the procedure is important. The pouching of a fistula may take 30 to 60 min, depending on the condition of the skin, the size and number of fistulas present, and the amount of drainage. The patient should be positioned comfortably before starting. Intermittent suction or dressings may be used to collect or absorb the drainage throughout the procedure. As the fistula becomes smaller, the patient should be informed. The appearance of healing is encouraging for the patient and the family.

SPECIFIC GASTROINTESTINAL PATHOLOGIES

Zollinger-Ellison Syndrome

Zollinger-Ellison syndrome is characterized by a non-insulin-secreting tumor of the pancreas, hypergastremia, and multiple peptic ulcers. The non-beta cell adenoma (ulcerogenic tumor) of the pancreas increases the serum levels of the hormone gastrin, resulting in hypersecretion of gastric acids. The pancreatic lesion may be malignant, single, or multiple, or a general hyperplasia of the pancreas. When malignant, metastasis to the liver and regional lymph nodes may occur. A relationship between the ulcerogenic tumor of the pancreas and abnormalities in other endocrine organs has been reported.

The first indication of the Zollinger-Ellison syndrome may be a recurrence of ulcer disease following surgical removal of a peptic ulcer. The presenting symptoms include abdominal pain, diarrhea, vomiting, melena, and hematemesis. The ulcer activity in Zollinger-Ellison syndrome is more virulent than the usual peptic ulcer displays. Multiple ulcers, located atypically in the postbulbar or the proximal jejunum, are seen in Zollinger-Ellison syndrome.

The high gastric acid secretions in Zollinger-Ellison syndrome result in a massive amount of acids pouring into the upper small bowel, causing alteration of the pH of the duodenum, damage to the mucosa of the duodenum, increased intestinal motility, and a shift of fluid from extracellular volume into the bowel lumen. Activation of pancreatic enzymes (particularly lipase) requires an alkaline pH in the duodenum. Without active pancreatic enzymes, the fats in the diet remain undigested and steatorrhea (fatty stools) occurs. Steatorrhea, increased fluids, and increased gastrointestinal motility result in diarrhea. Dehydration, hypokalemia, and metabolic acidosis may be seen, depending on the severity and duration of the diarrhea. Severe diarrhea, with or without the absence of ulcers, may be an indication to rule out Zollinger-Ellison syndrome.

Hyperparathyroid adenomas are sometimes related with the Zollinger-Ellison syndrome. Hypercalcemia has been demonstrated to be associated with a subsequent increase in gastric acid levels. The multiple endocrine adenomatosis type I (MEA-I) refers to the multiglandular lesions which may be associated with the pancreatic tumor of Zollinger-Ellison syndrome.

Diagnosis

Gastric analysis, augmented histamine tests, radioimmunoassays, and radiography are used in diagnosing Zollinger-Ellison syndrome. Gastric analysis involves a 12-h overnight collection of gastric secretions through a nasogastric tube. The patient remains NPO throughout the procedure. High levels of gastric acid (Table 29-4) will be demonstrated in the presence of Zollinger-Ellison syndrome.

The augmented histamine test is begun after an overnight fast. A nasogastric tube is inserted and the residual gastric contents are removed. The patient is instructed to expectorate saliva during the procedure. Following removal of the gastric contents, the basal secretions are collected for 1 h. Histalog is then injected subcutaneously, and gastric contents are collected every 15 min for 2 h. The presence of a non-beta cell adenoma will be documented by the lack of gastric response to the Histalog. When the parietal cells are functioning at maximum levels in response to serum gastrin, Histalog does not increase cell response.

Radioimmunoassay methods measure the serum gastrin levels. The upper limit of serum gastrin is 200 pg/mL of serum. In Zollinger-Ellison syndrome the serum gastrin level is greater than 1000 pg/mL.

Radiographic studies document the unusual locations of the multiple ulcers found in Zollinger-Ellison syndrome. The stomach appears enlarged because of the increased parietal cell mass and the edematous mucosal lining. The margins of the ulcers appear jagged and irregular. When barium studies are done, the high gastric acid content dilutes the barium.

Selective abdominal angiography may demonstrate the pancreatic lesion in a select number of patients. The neoplasm may appear as a tumor blush which depicts the vascularity of the lesion.

Treatment

Symptoms of intractable ulcer disease are commonly seen in Zollinger-Ellison syndrome. Hemorrhage, perforation, obstruction, and internal fistulization are possible complications of Zollinger-Ellison syndrome. The recommended operative intervention is total gastrectomy with esophagojejunostomy. Any remaining gastric mucosa is capable of secreting large quantities of gastric acid which will then result in recurrent ulceration and possible complications of intractable ulcer disease (hemorrhage, perforation, etc.). The pancreatic tumor is removed when possible. The location of the non-beta cell adenoma is often difficult. Occasionally the pancreatic involvement is a generalized hyperplasia. Following total gastrectomy, remission of pancreatic lesions and liver metastasis has improved. The prognosis following early total gastrectomy for Zollinger-Ellison syndrome is favorable.

Nursing Intervention

Initial nursing assessments of Zollinger-Ellison syndrome may include a history of abdominal pain, diarrhea, melena, or hematemesis. The presence of high levels of gastric acid result in increased duration of abdominal pain unrelieved by medications. The severity of diarrhea may be assessed clinically. Dehydration, hypokalemia, and metabolic acidosis are

TABLE 29-4	
Gastric Analysis: 12-h Nocturnal Results	
Condition	Amount of HCl
Ulcer-free	18 meq
Duodenal ulcer	60 meq
Gastric ulcer	12 meq
Zollinger-Ellison syndrome	>100 meq

secondary to the fluid and electrolytes lost through diarrhea. Dry mucous membranes, decreased skin turgor, and low urinary output are indicative of dehydration. The dehydrated patient may complain of thirst and fatique. A weak, irregular pulse and flabby muscles are observed clinically in hypokalemia. The patient may complain of a gaseous, bloated feeling in the abdomen, muscular weakness when ambulating, and a tingling sensation in the extremities. Clinical signs of metabolic acidosis include shortness of breath (mild), deep rapid breathing (moderate to severe), weakness, general malaise, and stupor progressing to coma.

Complications of intractable peptic ulcer in Zollinger-Ellison syndrome are gastrointestinal hemorrhage, perforation, obstruction, and internal fistula formation. Gastrointestinal hemorrhage may be first noted as hematemesis or melena. In an acute upper gastrointestinal hemorrhage, the first response of the medical team is replacement of fluid volume deficit and control of the bleeding. An intravenous line is inserted to begin replacement, and a Foley catheter is inserted to monitor urinary output. The urinary output is an index of fluid balance. Gastric perforations result in a chemical peritonitis from the spillage of potent digestive enzymes into the peritoneal cavity. Peritoneal irritation stimulates vascular dilation, hyperemia, and fluid shifts. Clinical manifestations of perforation and acute peritonitis include severe abdominal pain increased by movement; shallow, rapid respirations; rapid, weak pulse; rebound tenderness, muscle rigidity and guarding; nausea; fever with chills; decreased urinary output; and abdominal distention. Obstruction in Zollinger-Ellison syndrome may be first indicated by nausea and vomiting with abdominal cramping. Internal fistulization is documented by radiographic studies.

The treatment for Zollinger-Ellison syndrome is

total gastrectomy. Postoperative nursing intervention revolves around fluid maintenance, electrolyte balance, respiratory adequacy, and protection of the esophagojejunostomy suture line. Careful monitoring of intravenous fluids, urinary output, and daily weights, along with laboratory studies of electrolytes, hemoglobin, and hematocrit, are used to assess the fluid replacement pattern. The high abdominal location of the incision makes coughing and deep breathing extremely painful. The nurse must encourage the patient by providing measures designed to decrease discomfort associated with deep breathing and coughing. Providing adequate pain medication and splinting the abdomen with a pillow while coughing may assist the patient in these efforts.

A nasogastric tube is inserted during surgery to prevent distention of the esophagojejunostomy incision by an accumulation of gases, secretions, and drainage. The patency of the nasogastric tube is maintained by careful irrigations of the tube. Pressure should not be used with irrigations because of the incision line. The normal saline is inserted into the Levin tube with an ascepto syringe and is allowed to return by gravity drainage. Careful measurement of the returns is noted. If the tube is obstructed and gentle irrigations do not clear the obstruction and the irrigating saline does not return, do not continue the irrigation. Do not remove the nasogastric tube. Consult with the attending physician.

The loss of the stomach results in an absence of gastric storage, loss of the intrinsic factor necessary for vitamin B_{12} absorption, and interference with iron absorption. The dumping syndrome, characterized by weakness, profuse perspiration, nausea, faintness, flushing, epigastric discomfort, vomiting, and palpitation, may occur within 15 min after a meal. The syndrome is related to the sudden dilation of the small intestine after eating and hypertonic solution in the proximal small bowel. The dilation of the small intestine and hypertonic solution results in a shift of extracellular fluid into the bowel lumen, creating the symptoms of volume loss. Postgastrectomy hypoglycemia reactions (late dumping syndrome) are related to high intakes of carbohydrates in the diet. The increased digestion and absorption of carbohydrates causes a response of insulin release in excess of need and results in hypoglycemic symptoms (rebound hypoglycemia).

If eating becomes painful, the patient may omit meals or greatly decrease the intake per meal. Weight loss may be encountered after total gastrectomy from a poor nutritional intake. Pernicious anemia may be prevented by vitamin B_{12} supplements following surgery.

When the pancreas is involved in the surgical treatment of the Zollinger-Ellison syndrome, the observations of endocrine and exocrine functions of the pancreas are made. The pancreas is responsible for the release of insulin and glucagon in addition to the pancreatic enzymes secreted into the small bowel. Pancreatic fistulas are a possible surgical complication, and assessments of the wound for dehiscence or increased drainage should be made. If a cutaneous fistula develops, accurate measurement of drainage and skin protection are important. The use of ostomy appliances facilitates containment and measurement of the fistula output, as well as provides skin protection from the pancreatic enzymes.

Inflammatory Bowel Disease: Crohn's Disease and Ulcerative Colitis

Crohn's Disease

Crohn's disease is an inflammatory disorder of the gastrointestinal tract and may be referred to as regional enteritis, granulomatous colitis, granulomatous ileitis, or transmural disease. Crohn's disease may involve any part of the gastrointestinal tract, although the small bowel, particularly the terminal ileum, and colon are the common sites. Bacterial, viral, allergic, autoimmune, and hereditary factors have been explored as possible causes of Crohn's disease, but the etiology remains unknown. The disease is pathologically different from ulcerative colitis even though the clinical signs are similar (see Table 29-5). In Crohn's disease all layers (transmural) of the bowel are involved. Crohn's disease is a chronic condition with many remissions and exacerbations. There is no known cure for Crohn's disease. The surgical and medical management of Crohn's disease is influenced by the high incidence of exacerbations and recurrences after surgery.

In Crohn's disease the mesentery thickens, the mesenteric lymph nodes enlarge, serositis occurs, and the mesenteric fat envelops the serosal surface of the bowel. Adhesions develop when loops of bowel become matted together by the serositis and mesenteric changes. Internal fistulization between loops of bowel, bladder, and vagina may occur in Crohn's disease. External (cutaneous) fistula formation is not usually seen unless surgical intervention has taken place. Skipped lesions are common. A cobblestone appearance to the mucosa develops as the bowel lumen narrows, the mucosal surface develops fissures, and the submucosal layer becomes edematous.

The initial clinical symptoms include abdominal pain and diarrhea. The narrowing bowel lumen creates a partial intestinal obstruction, which results in an increased intestinal motility and intestinal distention. The increased motility and distention results in pressure on the afferent visceral nervous system which is perceived as abdominal pain. Motility of the bowel is stimulated by the ingestion of food, which enhances the process of abdominal pain. This may progress to a self-inflicted nutritional deficiency when meals are omitted because of the associated abdominal pain.

The increased frequency of watery or unformed stools is related to the partial intestinal obstruction, bacterial proliferation, lactose intolerance, and surgical loss of bowel. The increase of fluid into the bowel lumen and increased bowel motility associated with partial intestinal obstructions result in a decreased absorptive capacity in the diseased bowel and in diarrheal stools. When the bowel contents stagnate behind a partial obstruction or after a surgical bypass of a loop of bowel, bacterial growth may proliferate and alter the pH of the bowel. An altered environment of the bowel may prevent the effective utilization and reabsorption of bile salts. Bile salts in the right colon have a cathartic effect and result in watery, frequent bowel movements. Lactose intolerance is the inability to digest and absorb lactose. The unabsorbed lactose attracts water and sodium chloride into the bowel lumen, and peristalsis increases. The colon's reabsorption is decreased, and the result is watery stools.

Nutritional deficiency may develop in response to the pain associated with eating, the effects of the chronic water and electrolyte loss, or the decreased absorptive ability of the bowel. The patient may present with weight loss, vitamin deficiencies, and anemia. Perianal fissures and fistulas may be observed in Crohn's disease. In addition to the intestinal manifestations, extracolonic conditions such as erythema nodosum and arthritis may be present.

The initial involvement of Crohn's disease is primarily seen in the terminal ileum, and the constant right-sided abdominal pain mimics appendicitis. A careful explanation of terminal ileitis is required by the health team. The word *terminal* is associated with death in our society. Terminal in this instance refers to the end portion of the ileum.

Diagnosis of Crohn's disease is often a process of elimination of other entities, i.e., spastic colon, appendicitis, partial intestinal obstruction, ileocecal tuberculosis, ischemic bowel disease, cancer, and

TABLE 29-5

Comparison of Crohn's Disease and Ulcerative Colitis

Crohn's disease	Ulcerative colitis
Transmural	Mucosal
Segmental	Progressive, starting in the rectum, and continues proximal
Involves entire GI tract	Confined to the colon and rectum
Watery diarrhea	Bloody diarrhea
Partial intestinal obstruction	Hemorrhage
Fistulas, abscesses	Bowel perforation
Recurrence after surgical intervention	Cure with total proctocolectomy and ileostomy

ulcerative colitis. Barium studies demonstrate the stenotic narrowing of the bowel lumen, longitudinal and transverse ulcers (cobblestoning), and fistula tracts. Sigmoidoscopy examinations are generally negative, since rectal sparing (absence of disease in the rectum) is common in Crohn's disease. A rectal biopsy may help in diagnosis.

Medical treatment is symptomatic. However, it is of utmost importance and is geared toward relief of the symptoms of diarrhea and abdominal pain. Analgesics, codeine, Lomotil (diphenoxylate hydrochloride with atropine), steroids, and Azulfidine (salicylazosulfaphridine) are used. Questran (cholestyramine) is given to bind bile salts when necessary, and anemia is treated with iron (intramuscularly), vitamin B_{12}, and folic acid. Steroids may be given intravenously during an acute attack, and then progressed to oral tablets. The potential hazards of steroid treatment include loss of potassium, retention of sodium and water, hypertension, osteoporosis, diabetes, and psychotic behavior disorders.

Dietary restriction of raw fruits and vegetables is recommended to reduce the amount of fiber in the bowel. Elemental diets may be used in acute situations. For the debilitated patient, hyperalimentation is used.

Surgery is palliative and is performed only when the patient does not respond to medical therapy and when the disease process interferes with the patient's activities of daily living (intractable disease). Additional indications for surgery in Crohn's disease include partial or complete intestinal obstruction, internal or external fistulas, or massive hemorrhage.

If the disease involves the distal stomach or duodenum, a bypass procedure (gastrojejunostomy) is sometimes necessary. When the disease involves the small bowel or segments of the colon, a segmental resection is the procedure of choice. A bypass procedure is used only when there is an abscess present, and this is usually a first stage of a two-stage procedure. The second stage consists of resection of the diseased segment. If the entire colon is involved, a total colectomy and ileostomy is necessary.

Possible complications from surgical intervention in Crohn's disease are recurrence of disease, short bowel syndromes, fluid and electrolyte imbalance, and cutaneous fistula formation. Recurrence of Crohn's disease following segmental resection is high, and the progression of the disease increases the potential removal of more and more bowel. Short bowel syndrome occurs when large amounts of small bowel have been resected or bypassed. Absorption of vitamin B_{12}, fats, and reabsorption of fluid and electrolytes may become compromised. Vitamin B_{12} is absorbed in the terminal ileum, and after loss of a large portion of the terminal ileum, vitamin B_{12} is replaced intramuscularly. Fat absorption may be affected by a low pH in the intestines (Zollinger-Ellison syndrome) or by loss of terminal ileum. Loss of terminal ileum results in a decreased capacity for absorption of bile salts in the small intestine. This alters the circulating bile salts and fat absorption. Bile salts in the large colon have a cathartic effect and result in steatorrhea. The motility of the bowel is increased after resection and the transient time is shortened. Fluid and electrolytes may not be reabsorbed adequately. Watery stools are often noted.

Ulcerative Colitis

Ulcerative colitis is a disease in which universal inflammation involves the mucosal lining of the colon and rectum. The etiology is unknown, and as in Crohn's disease, similar areas have been examined for cause and effect. Ulcerative colitis is a disease process of remissions and exacerbations. The patient is generally young (20 to 30 years of age) when first diagnosed. Pathological changes in the colon are usually confined to the mucosal and submucosal layers. The process generally begins in the rectum and progresses proximally in the colon.

The presenting symptom is bloody diarrhea, and a person may have up to 30 stools a day. The rectal involvement creates an urgency sensation when fecal material enters the rectum. The need to defecate is immediate.

Symptoms observed in ulcerative colitis include abdominal pain, weight loss, tenesmus, vomiting, and fever. Extracolonic manifestations associated with ulcerative colitis are arthritis, iritis, skin lesions, and hepatic dysfunction. The extracolonic conditions mirror the disease process. During exacerbation of ulcerative colitis, the extracolonic involvements worsen; with treatment, they improve. The one exception is hepatic dysfunction, which does not necessarily improve with treatment of the ulcerative colitis.

The diagnosis of ulcerative colitis may involve the differentiation between ulcerative colitis and Crohn's disease. A proctosigmoidoscopy is beneficial in diagnosing ulcerative colitis. The mucosa may appear erythematous and friable. Bleeding may occur when the mucosa is gently touched with a cotton applicator. In advanced ulcerative colitis, ulcers and pseudopolyps may be seen on proctosigmoidoscopy. Radiography studies may show crypt abscesses, mucosal ulcerations, and shortening of the colon. Pseudopolyps, irregularities of the colon wall, and loss of haustral markings are also noted on barium studies.

Medical management of ulcerative colitis revolves around the treatment of symptoms. Anti-inflammatory agents (such as ACTH) are used intravenously initially in treating acute ulcerative colitis, followed by oral steroids (prednisone) for maintenance therapy. Azulfidine and prednisone are the medications of choice in managing ulcerative colitis. Fluid and electrolyte replacement is based on the extent and duration of the disease. Weight loss is frequently observed. Dietary therapy is an important aspect of medical management in ulcerative colitis. Low-residue diets and lactose-free diets are used to decrease colon stimulation and roughage in the lumen. In acute situations, the colon may be placed completely at rest with the use of elemental diets and clear liquids. Elemental diets are absorbed in the proximal small bowel, and no residue enters the colon. Hyperalimentation may be used for patients in debilitated states to improve their overall nutritional status.

Diarrhea is treated by altering the contents of the bowel lumen. Metamucil, a bulk-forming laxative, and Gelusil, aluminum hydroxide, are used to thicken the bowel contents. Opiates are not used for antidiarrheal agents since this may precipitate toxic megacolon.

Complications of ulcerative colitis that may indicate the need for surgical intervention include toxic megacolon, perforation, hemorrhage, cancer, and intractable disease. The procedure of choice is total colectomy and ileostomy. Removal of the colon provides a cure for ulcerative colitis.

Toxic megacolon is a massive dilatation of the large colon. The cause is not known. Barium enemas performed during a period of severe diarrhea may precipitate toxic megacolon. Opiates, anticholinergics, and hypokalemia are factors which may play a role in the advent of toxic megacolon. Abdominal distention and absent bowel sounds with a sharp decrease in the number of daily stools is indicative of toxic megacolon. Intestinal decompression, antibiotic therapy, fluid and electrolyte replacement, and intravenous alimentation are initiated. The use of opiates and anticholinergic drugs is discontinued. Careful observations for perforation or impending perforation are made. Operative intervention is indicated for toxic megacolon in the presence of perforation or failure of the clinical status to improve after intensive medical therapy. Free perforation of the bowel may be demonstrated on abdominal films. The clinical manifestations of bowel perforation are abdominal pain aggravated by any movements, including respiration; rapid, shallow breathing; rapid, weak pulse; rebound tenderness; fever and chills; nausea; vomiting; and decreased urinary output.

When ulcerative colitis interferes with the daily living style, the disease process may indicate operative intervention. The quality of life can be improved by having a total proctocolectomy and ileostomy. The patient is cured of ulcerative colitis by having the colon and rectum removed. There are two options for a patient with ulcerative colitis: a conventional ileostomy or a continent, internal pouch (Kock pouch). The surgeon carefully evaluates a patient in determining the appropriate procedure.

The incidence of colon cancer is higher in patients with a history of ulcerative colitis than in the general population. When cancer is suspected or diagnosed, operation for removal of the colon and rectum is done.

The mucosa of the colon is very friable in ulcerative colitis, and massive rectal hemorrhages may occur. The first sign may be bright red blood in the stool. A decrease in the systolic blood pressure on sitting or standing and elevated pulse are measures of blood flow changes. Vital signs, urinary output, and amount of blood loss are factors used to evaluate the status of the patient. An intravenous line should be inserted for fluid and blood replacement. (See Table 29-1.)

Nursing Intervention

The needs of a patient with inflammatory bowel disease are related to the extent and duration of the disease process. The emotional component associated with inflammatory bowel disease has been frequently discussed. The question debated is this: Does the patient's personality affect the disease or the disease the personality? However, if life centers around finding the nearest bathroom and a fear of accidents, it is understandable that a nervous individual is admitted to the hospital. The staff must be supportive of the patient and family as the battery of diagnostic studies is begun. Careful explanations of the diagnostic procedure, the purpose of the procedure, and what is expected of the patient prior to, during, and after the diagnostic study should be given.

In mild cases of ulcerative colitis and Crohn's disease, patient teaching involves the medication plan, nutritional needs with dietary restrictions, antidiarrheal agents, and fluid and electrolyte imbalances associated with chronic diarrhea. Sitz baths or irrigations of perianal lesions may be included in the care. The patient will need instructions in adapting the procedures to the home environment.

A discussion may be initiated by the physician regarding surgical intervention. The patient will need an opportunity to discuss the effects of surgery with the nursing personnel for clarification and redefinition of terms. Patients with ulcerative colitis may require more information about ileostomies. A positive explanation of an ileostomy and the ramifications of having an ileostomy will allay many fears associated with the person's future life-style. The ileostomy and wearing an external pouch is not limiting in itself. A person can bathe with or without a pouch, swim, ski, play tennis, have children, and work full-time. The reactions to a change in the body image, the loss of a body part, and the loss of sphincter control will occur in varying degrees after the operation, not before surgery. If a patient asks to see a pouch, then show that person one pouch used in your institution. If the person does not make such a request, then do not initiate a "show and tell." The person knows how much he or she can handle during an interview. The patient is the best guide for a nurse during an interview. The questions a patient has should be answered first. Then, if there is additional pertinent data the patient should know (return to presurgical activities, for example), further discussion can be initiated. The patient may or may not have surgery after the operational procedures have been discussed. When and if the operation is necessary, the same general information will need to be discussed with the patient and family.

In acute ulcerative colitis the nurse should observe the patient for signs of hemorrhage, perforation, toxic megacolon, fluid and electrolyte imbalances, and nutritional needs. The common complications that occur in Crohn's disease include partial intestinal obstructions and fistulization. After operations for Crohn's disease or ulcerative colitis, the nursing care includes nasogastric suctioning, intravenous fluid therapy, urinary output and vital sign monitoring, respiratory adequacy, frequent turning, and wound care.

Ileostomy

An ileostomy stoma may be created when Crohn's disease involves the entire colon or as a cure for ulcerative colitis (Fig. 29-8). The small bowel (ileum) is brought through the abdominal wall and the stoma is matured, leaving a "bud" above the surface of the skin. Rehabilitation with ostomy surgery begins prior to the surgical procedure and continues posthospitalization. A nurse enterostomal therapist is involved in assessing the patient's needs and planning the

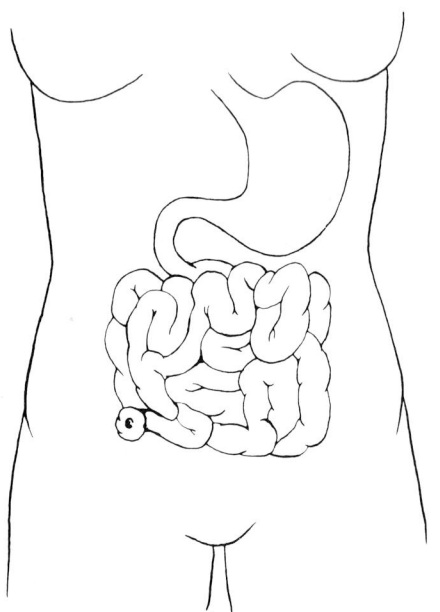

FIGURE 29-8
Ileostomy stoma.

rehabilitation program for each patient. Initial assessments include the patient's (and significant others') knowledge of the disease, the meaning of ileostomy, and family dynamics. A definition of stoma, ileostomy, stool, and pouch is given to the patient. A patient who has no term for the stoma will call the ileostomy stoma "it," or "she," or "Snowball," or "Tom," etc. Internalization of the stoma as part of the body is more difficult if the patient has identified the stoma with a name or separate identity.

Following ileostomy surgery the patient fears rejection from family and friends. The new ileostomate (patient with an ileostomy) will test family, friends, and staff verbally and nonverbally for signs of acceptance. The acceptance as a person, a sexual being, a family member, a friend, and an employee is checked to assure the person that the surgery has not altered previous relationships. The patient has a responsibility to become independent in ostomy care. The nurse's responsibility is to provide the information and techniques necessary for the patient to become self-sufficient.

One of the most confusing aspects of ileostomy care is understanding the differences between a colostomy and an ileostomy, and between an ileal conduit (or ileal loop) and an ileostomy. The ileostomy (small bowel) cannot be regulated by irrigations or diet as the colostomy (large bowel) is managed. A pouch is worn at all times to collect the fecal drainage. The ileostomate cannot take enemas (usually no rectum) or laxatives. A common and severe error is giving a bowel prep for intravenous pyelograms (IVP) and upper bowel series to an ileostomate. The result of the bowel prep is severe fluid and electrolyte loss, and in the presence of Crohn's disease, an exacerbation of the disease may occur. The ileal conduit is a urinary diversion, not a fecal diversion, and the underlying disease, the type of equipment, and the patient needs differ.

The most appropriate time for patient teaching is during a pouch change. The patient and significant other can be given valuable information even though intravenous lines and a nasogastric tube limit the patient's participation. The involvement by a family member is encouraged. The patient and the significant other are made aware of the patient's possible need for assistance when the patient is learning the routine or in case future illness occurs. The preferred results are that ileostomates be responsible for their own care, but have a backup when necessary.

The bright red color of the stoma disturbs the patient and family initially. The red color implies pain, and there is a fear of hurting the patient. The stoma has no nerve endings and touching the stoma for the first time is a strange sensation. The patient should not be forced into touching the stoma. During a pouch change, as the stoma and skin is cleansed, the nurse should demonstrate touching the stoma. The patient should be told that carrying packages or children against the stoma will not create a problem. In addition, an ileostomate can sleep on the abdomen or hold someone closely. This information will decrease many anxieties in the patient and in the family.

Since there is no feeling in the stoma, close observations are necessary during a pouch change for an alteration of the stomal color and/or presence of small ulcers on the stoma. A stomal color change from a bright red to a dusky color may indicate pressure on the vascular supply to the stoma. The presence of small ulcers may indicate a recurrence of Crohn's disease. The physician should be notified. The stoma is mucosal membrane and may bleed when cleansed. The small amount of blood on the washcloth should not alarm the patient. However, bleeding which continues after the stoma has been cleansed or in between pouch changes should be evaluated by the physician.

The new ileostomate remains on a low-residue diet for approximately 6 weeks following surgery. This allows the bowel time to adjust after the operation. Then, one food is added each week from a list of high-fiber foods. The food should be chewed thoroughly and eaten as part of a meal. High-fiber foods such as celery, Chinese food, nuts, corn, coleslaw, coconut, popcorn, dried fruits, and whole vegetables are not digested by the intact gastrointestinal tract. If a large mass of undigested food develops in the small bowel of an ileostomate, it could become lodged at a kink or narrowing in the bowel and create a food blockage (Fig. 29-9). If the blockage of food does not move forward, it results in a complete intestinal obstruction. The cycle which follows intestinal obstructions begins with fluid and electrolyte accumulation in the bowel and progresses to shock.

The patient may recognize early signs of food obstructions (Table 29-6) by correlating changes in the ileostomy output with the diet. A food blockage may be relieved by the patient's getting into a knee-chest position and cupping the hand gently under the stoma. Tense abdominal muscles will prevent a blockage from moving out of the bowel. The ileostomate should relax in a hot tub or hot shower, and then go into the knee-chest position. If the obstruction has been present for over 3 h without relief, the patient is

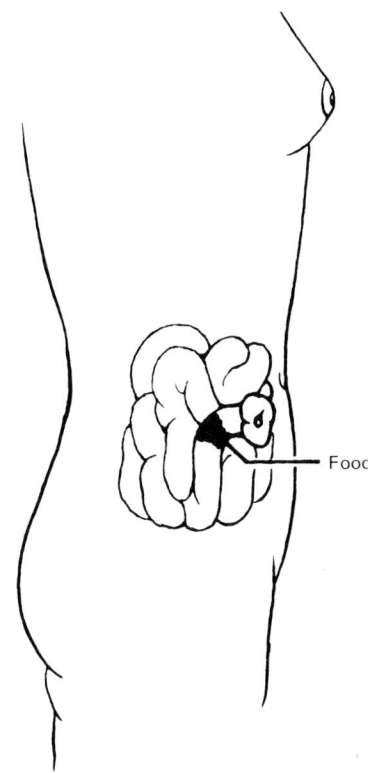

FIGURE 29-9
Food blockage with an ileostomy.

nauseated or vomiting, or no drainage is coming around the blockage, the physician should be seen. The physician may then order a mechanical removal of the blockage by irrigation.

The pouch opening may be too small as the stoma swells when the bowel becomes partially or totally obstructed. A disposable pouch with a larger stoma opening and a skin barrier should be applied. The pouch should be left on during the ileostomy irrigation, since more fluid will return than is inserted. A small rubber catheter is gently inserted into the stomal opening, and 50 mL of normal saline is instilled through an ascepto syringe. It may take several instillations of saline and gentle suction of the ascepto to break up the blockage. Once the blockage is relieved, a large amount of fluid will flow through the bowel. Careful recordings of intake and output are required to provide adequate fluid replacements. The patient may experience diarrhea for several days following an obstruction. The high-fiber foods that may create an obstruction are not omitted from an

---

TABLE 29-6
Intestinal Obstruction from a
Food Blockage with an Ileostomy

Symptom	Cause
Discharge changes from semisolid to liquid	Food is blocked but water passes around it, a partial intestinal obstruction
Total volume of output increases and the ileostomy functions constantly	Water is drawn from the extracellular fluid in an attempt to rid the body of the obstruction, and the intestines become hyperactive
Objectionable odor	Bacterial proliferation occurs at the site of obstruction and causes fermentation of the bowel content
Cramping, followed by an increased watery output	Increased bowel activity to move blockage forward
Distended abdomen	The obstruction traps gas and liquids in the bowel lumen
Vomiting	Reverse peristalsis. The body's attempt to move the increased bowel contents in the direction of least resistance
No ileostomy output	Complete intestinal obstruction

---

ileostomate's diet, but discretion should be used regarding the amount and combinations of high-fiber foods eaten at one meal. Food should be chewed thoroughly.

The small bowel will absorb all the nutrients, fluid, and electrolytes an ileostomate requires. Immediately after surgery, the patient has a high fluid and electrolyte concentration in the ileostomy output. An ileostomy adaptation occurs approximately 3 to 6 months after surgery, and the drainage becomes the consistency of toothpaste and more fluid and electrolytes are reabsorbed. The ileostomate tends to be on a border line between well-hydrated and dehydrated. The patient is told to quench the desire for water and salt, above the eight 8-oz glasses of fluid recommended daily. The problems occur when other medical problems develop, whether it is the flu or a heart attack. The ileostomate can lose more fluid and electrolytes faster than a person with a colon. The ileostomate should be taught to replace fluid losses immediately with products high in needed electrolytes, such as Gatorade, salt water, bouillon, tea, or other products high in electrolyte value. If the ileostomate cannot keep up with the fluid losses, the physician should be contacted.

Diarrhea in an ileostomate can be described as hot, watery stool which requires frequent (every 30 min) emptying of the pouch. Diarrhea may be associated with other medical problems, or stimulated by specific foods in some individuals. Green beans, broccoli, spinach, raw fruits, highly seasoned foods, and beer may increase the ileostomy drainage. Presurgical effects of these foods should be examined with regard to the individual patient. The amounts eaten at a given time also affect the amount of ileostomy output. Bananas, boiled milk, tapioca, and peanut butter are effective in thickening diarrheal stools.

The ileostomate with recurrent Crohn's disease or multiple small bowel resections may have chronic diarrhea associated with the short bowel syndrome. In the short bowel syndrome, the transient time is shortened and absorption of fluid is limited. The result is watery stools. Vitamin B_{12} and fat absorption may be affected if large amounts of terminal ileum have been resected. Steatorrhea may be noted with the ileostomy output.

The ileostomate cannot absorb hard tablets or enteric-coated tablets. These tablets should not be prescribed. Time-released and time-sustained capsules and tablets should also be avoided in patients with an ileostomy. The time-released drugs may not remain in the bowel for 8 or 12 h, and the dosage received by the patient cannot be ascertained. Lomotil tablets should be crushed or Lomotil given in liquid form, because it is not absorbed otherwise. Liquid medication is the best for ileostomates. However, if in doubt about a tablet, drop the medication in a glass of water, without stirring; wait 30 min; if the pill has begun to dissolve, the patient should be able to obtain full benefit from the drug. Medications which promote potassium or sodium excretion (Lanoxin, diuretics) may create more severe problems for an ileostomate because of the fine fluid and electrolyte balance the ileostomy patient maintains. Antibiotics will cause a flora change in the ileum, resulting in diarrhea. Careful maintenance of fluid replacement is necessary.

Sexuality is an important aspect of rehabilitation after ileostomy surgery. The ileostomy should not alter the patient's sexual patterns. The previous sexual patterns are assessed prior to planning nursing intervention. The patient and significant other who have a steady, loving relationship should encounter no sexual difficulties, once their questions have been answered. The acceptance of an altered body image is easier if the loved one demonstrates a continued acceptance. The single ileostomate may encounter new problems. In our society, sex is more open and common among unmarried partners. The single ileostomate may have problems in telling others about the surgery and the pouch, or may question when others should be told. The supportive professional (enterostomal therapist, nurse, social worker, physician) will need to offer counseling and assistance as new obstacles are faced. The single ileostomate may be rejected by a sexual partner. Of course, the same problem may arise with a married ileostomate whose spouse rejects the idea of the pouch or stoma.

The ileostomate and partner can be assisted by being given permission by the professional to be a sexual being, to have sexual concerns, and to ask questions. Not everyone is comfortable discussing sexuality with patients. The responsibility of the nurse who is uncomfortable is to find a resource person who can comfortably discuss sexuality with the couple. The stoma cannot be hurt by the pressure of being held or touched or by sleeping on the abdomen. The spouse must know this to avoid being afraid of hurting the patient. The pouch should be emptied prior to sexual activity and the seal checked. Ileostomates should be reminded that they can have children, and birth control may be desired. An effective nursing measure is to answer the questions of the ileostomate

and significant other as they arise. When specific problems occur, refer the couple for specialized sexual therapy.

If the proper pouching system is not chosen for the patient and stool leaks, the patient is no better off than with thirty stools a day. The stoma opening in the ileostomy pouch should be $\frac{1}{8}$ in larger than the stoma. This allows for peristaltic movements in the stoma. The residual digestive enzymes in ileostomy output are very irritating to the skin. A severe skin denudation can develop in a short period of exposure to ileostomy output. A skin barrier is placed up to the base of the stoma to protect the exposed skin. Effective skin barriers are karaya, Colly-seels, and Stomahesive. A skin barrier does not hold a pouch on; it merely protects exposed skin. The next step is deciding on a pouch (Table 29-7). The pouch should be odor-proof and drainable. The pouch application procedure should be written and left on the nursing care plan. Each person working with a new ostomy patient should use the same procedure. The first step is gathering all the necessary supplies: damp washcloth, towel, toilet paper, skin barrier, pouch, scissors, tape, and rubber band or pouch closure. The patient should sit in a chair and use the bedside table for the supplies. As the patient regains strength, the procedure should be done in the bathroom. The pouch opening is cut in the clean pouch before the soiled pouch is removed from the skin. The pouch the patient is wearing is emptied and removed from the skin. The stoma may have stool on it. If so, wipe the stoma with toilet paper. The skin and stoma are then cleansed with warm water and patted dry. Soaps will leave a film residue on the skin which increases skin breakdown under pouches. The skin barrier is then applied to the skin up to the stoma base leaving no skin exposed. The pouch is then applied and the end secured. The technique for emptying a pouch is facilitated by applying the pouch so that the spout is directed toward the inner aspect of the thigh. The patient can then sit on the toilet and drain the pouch between the legs. Splashing of the water can be decreased by placing toilet paper in the commode prior to draining the pouch. It is not necessary for the patient to rinse the pouch every time it is emptied. Once a day the ileostomate may rinse the pouch using an ascepto syringe and tepid water. Overcleansing may break the pouch seal.

Odor is a major concern of many ileostomates. Odor is controllable by the use of odor-proof pouches, oral preparations, and pouch deodorants. Bismuth subgallate (Devrom) is an oral preparation for odor

TABLE 29-7
Basic Considerations in
Choosing Disposable Pouches

1. Type of ostomy will indicate:
   a. Spout opening: drainable, urinary spout, closed
   b. Material of pouch: odor-proof, odor-resistant
   c. Skin protection: karaya, Stomahesive, Collyseels, HolliHesive

2. Parastomal skin area and stoma:
   a. Stoma size and shape: protruding, flushed, edematous
   b. Where does the stoma drain
   c. Available space for a faceplate
   d. Presence of abdominal folds, dimples, scars
   e. Stomal complications: prolapse, retraction, ulcerations
   f. Presence of a stomal support: rod, catheter, loop-lock

3. Physical abilities of the patient:
   a. Arthritis, paralysis
   b. Poor eyesight, blindness

4. Mental abilities of the patient
   a. Confusion, senility
   b. Emotional aspects: denial

5. Financial situation of the patient

6. Patient sensitivities:
   a. Adhesives, tapes
   b. Plastics, vinyls, rubber

7. Pouches available in the area:
   a. Starter openings are helpful in the hospitals
   b. Pouch material: noise factors, odor-proof
   c. Drainable rather than closed-end for hospital use

control which may be purchased without a prescription. The tablet is chewed before meals and will effectively control odor and thicken the stool. When the patient first starts taking bismuth subgallate, the tongue may turn black and the stool may become black. The discoloration is temporary. Bismuth subgallate is contraindicated in renal disease and with Coumadin therapy. The drug should be omitted for 48 h before radiography studies because it shows opaque areas on the films. Overdosage of bismuth subgallate or long-term misuse may result in metal toxicity. The signs of metal toxicity include myoclonic jerks, tremors, inability to walk, loss of balance, poor power of concentration, depression, insomnia, and confusion.

Dietary control of odors is also possible. Certain foods produce more odor, especially when eaten in large quantities. Fish, asparagus, eggs, onions, garlic, and some spices may be limited when odor is a concern. However, the use of odorproof pouches is an effective method of controlling odor. Odor will be released when the pouch is emptied, but the patient can be reminded that people with rectums have odor with bowel movements. Sprays and deodorizers are available for use when emptying pouches.

Opaque pouches and pouch covers are available for ileostomates. Most patients are relieved to know they do not have to see stool continuously. Another possible reaction is compulsive behavior. Excessive cleansing of the pouch, frequent checking to see if the stoma is functioning, or ritualistic procedures for changing the pouch are examples of compulsive behavior. Opaque pouches can be effective for changing behavior in some individuals.

Prior to discharge, an ostomy visitor from the United Ostomy Association (UOA) may be called. The visitor has one very positive effect—the patient is able to see another person who has an ileostomy. The UOA visitor is a rehabilitated individual, and the patient can identify with the healthy person who happens to wear a pouch. Local UOA groups have monthly educational meetings, bulletins, and a journal full of hints for ostomates.

Continent Internal Pouch

The continent internal pouch is the construction of an internal reservoir with a continent valve and ileostomy stoma. Dr. Kock in Sweden developed and reported the procedure in 1969. The reservoir is constructed from 30 cm of terminal ileum, and since 1969, many revisions have been developed to enhance the continency of the ileal valve. The advantage of the procedure is that an external appliance is not worn by the patient.

Postoperatively, a catheter is left in the pouch and connected to low suction to prevent pressure on the incision line of the internal pouch. Intravenous fluids, nasogastric suctioning, and a Foley catheter are initially in place. The postoperative needs are similar to needs following conventional ileostomy surgery.

After 2 weeks the catheter is disconnected from the low suction but remains in place in the internal pouch and is clamped and released at specific intervals. The next step is removal and insertion of the catheter into the internal pouch by the nursing staff. The time between emptying gradually increases as the volume capacity of the pouch increases. The patient is instructed in emptying the continent internal pouch. Written instructions should be included in the patient teaching.

The following material is needed for emptying a continent pouch: a large-lumen catheter, water-soluble lubricant, catheter-tip syringe, container, gauze, and tape. The patient begins emptying the continent pouch sitting on the side of the bed, and later the patient should empty the internal pouch sitting on the commode. The dressing is removed from the stoma. The tip of the catheter is lubricated and gently inserted into the stoma. After the catheter has entered approximately 2 in, resistance of the valve can be felt. The patient should take a deep breath and apply some pressure, and the catheter will slip into the continent internal pouch. A catheter should never be forced, as the internal pouch can be perforated. The stool will begin draining through the catheter when it enters the pouch. When the pouch is empty, the catheter is removed, the stoma cleansed, and a gauze pad applied to collect any mucus drainage.

The pouch capacity gradually increases, and by the time discharge from the hospital takes place, the patient will empty the internal pouch three to four times a day. Gas may also collect in the pouch and will need to be released by inserting the catheter. There is an outward bulging of the skin as the continent pouch fills.

Two disadvantages of a continent internal pouch are thick fecal consistency and an inability to insert the catheter. If the feces are excessively thick, 30 min may be required to drain the continent pouch. The patient may drink two glasses of water or a glass of prune or grape juice to loosen the stool. The fecal material may be diluted with warm water, or the patient may need to irrigate the internal pouch using water and a syringe. Debris left in the pouch can result in bacterial proliferation. The pouch should be emptied completely and flushed with irrigation solution at least weekly.

Inability to insert the catheter through the nipple valve is frightening for the patient. When the abdominal muscles become tense, the patient should attempt to relax. The patient should lean back and breathe deeply. If this does not permit entry of the catheter, the patient may try relaxing in a warm tub of water. The catheter should be well-lubricated and inserted while the patient is in a supine position. Once the catheter is inserted, the patient should sit or stand to drain the pouch. Squeezing air or water through a syringe may assist the patient in inserting the catheter. If the internal pouch is full and the patient cannot empty the pouch after 3 to 4 h, the surgeon should be notified.

The dietary interests following the development of an internal reservoir include gaseous foods and undigested food products. This is similar to the ileostomate. New foods should be added to the diet slowly in limited amounts, and should be chewed thoroughly. Gas-forming foods may cause distention and abdominal pain the first few months following surgery. Undigested foods may plug the catheter or may need to be rinsed out of the internal pouch. The patient should be given instructions prior to discharge on unplugging the catheter.

The continent internal pouch is a new procedure and is indicated for only a select number of patients at this time. The diagnosis of ulcerative colitis, familial polyposis, or multiple tumors of the large colon imply a cure by surgical removal of the diseased colon. These patients are eligible for consideration for a continent pouch.

The United Ostomy Association (UOA) has developed a group for those individuals with continent stomas. The UOA provides visitors and current information for new and old patients.

Sclerosing Cholangitis

Sclerosing cholangitis is a rare, chronic, inflammation of the extrahepatic biliary ductal system. Sclerosing cholangitis has been associated with ulcerative colitis, Riedel's struma, and retroperitoneal fibrosis. The etiology is unknown. Bacterial, viral, and autoimmune factors were examined as possible etiology, but these theories have not been substantiated.

The lumen of the common bile duct, and occasionally the hepatic duct, is narrowed from inflammation and edema of the mucosa and subserosa. The regional lymph nodes are enlarged. The involvement of the liver is secondary to the chronic obstructive process of sclerosing cholangitis. Bile stasis or biliary cirrhosis may be observed. The gallbladder is generally uninvolved, and gallstones are not associated with sclerosing cholangitis.

Clinical signs of sclerosing cholangitis are similar to clinical manifestations of biliary obstruction from calculi. The obstructive jaundice persists and progressively worsens. Pruritus may be severe, and right upper-quadrant abdominal pain is present. The liver may be palpable and tender, and signs of portal hypertension may be observed. Additional clinical manifestations include intermittent low-grade fever, chills, general malaise, weakness, weight loss, nausea, and vomiting. Diagnostic studies include liver function studies, prothrombin times, and endoscopic retrograde cholangiography or transjugular cholangiography. The liver function studies may demonstrate hyperbilirubinemia and an elevation of the serum alkaline phosphate level. The absence of bile salts in the intestines alters the absorption of vitamin K. Vitamin K deficiency may progress to altered blood clotting factors.

A differential diagnosis between sclerosing cholangitis and biliary duct carcinoma is attempted during exploratory surgery. A biopsy of the liver and common bile duct is obtained during the operation. The laparotomy allows for clear visualization of the narrowed, irregular common bile duct. Sometimes a fine probe is used to dilate the common bile duct for the insertion of a T tube.

In addition to prolonged T-tube drainage, treatment of sclerosing cholangitis includes the administration of steroids, antibiotics, fat-soluble vitamins, and oral bile salts. Bile salts may be given orally to decrease the viscosity of the bile. Oral bile salts are also helpful in treating pruritus. The prognosis of sclerosing cholangitis is guarded. Five asymptomatic years is an indication of a good prognosis. However, the patient may have remissions and exacerbations of sclerosing cholangitis. Secondary biliary cirrhosis may develop.

Complications from sclerosing cholangitis include uncontrollable biliary sepsis with hepatic abscesses, liver failure, or hemorrhage from esophageal varices. The prognosis and prevention of secondary complications is related to the adequacy and continuity of the decompression of the extrahepatic biliary ducts.

When sclerosing cholangitis is associated with chronic ulcerative colitis, a total proctocolectomy with ileostomy may be indicated in an effort to slow down the progression of the disease. The effect of colectomy in sclerosing cholangitis is questionable in terms of slowing down, stopping, or reversing the disease process. In ulcerative colitis the diagnosis of sclerosing cholangitis may need to be differentiated from other hepatic disorders associated with chronic ulcerative colitis.

Nursing Responsibility

Initially the nursing care revolves around preparation of the patient for diagnostic studies, and later for surgery. The patient generally suffers from moderate to severe abdominal pain. The pain must be assessed and eased before patient teaching can be initiated.

The patient should be observed closely for signs of bleeding on admission. Vitamin K deficiency is associated with obstructed common bile ducts or absence of bile salts in the intestines. Prothrombin studies are done prior to surgery, and vitamin K may be administered intramuscularly. The increased portal pressure associated with sclerosing cholangitis is responsible for the development of esophageal varices and ascites. Bleeding esophageal varices is a medical emergency. Treatment centers around replacement of lost fluid and control of bleeding with a Sengstaken-Blakemore tube (Table 29-2). The patient presenting with ascites should have daily measurements of the abdomen, weight, and intake and output recorded on flow sheets.

The patient will require careful instruction and return demonstration of deep breathing and coughing techniques prior to surgery. The location of the incision line intensifies discomfort in deep breathing. The postoperative patient breathes with rapid, shallow respirations. These are contributory factors to pulmonary complications following surgery. Frequent turning, deep breathing, and coughing are part of the nursing plan. The patient can participate more effectively in the breathing exercises following pain medication. A pillow may be used to splint the incision.

A T tube will usually be left in the common bile duct during surgery. A stab wound is made in the skin and the stem portion of the T is brought through the abdomen wall. The T-tube drainage should be observed frequently for amount and color. The average output of bile into the gastrointestinal tract is 500 mL a day. The amount of bile drainage through the T tube varies. Part of the bile will continue through the top portion of the T tube into the duodenum.

In addition to the T tube, a nasogastric tube is sometimes present to allow for decompression by suction. The monitoring of fluid loss through the T tube and the nasogastric tube should be recorded. The sodium content of bile is high, and the patient should be observed for signs of hyponatremia. Lethargy, feelings of apprehension, abdominal cramps, cold skin, fingerprinting on the sternum, and syncope are indications of severe sodium loss. Intravenous fluids are given to replace fluid and electrolyte losses, and for nutritional support while the patient is NPO. Hyperalimentation may be used when the patient's nutritional status is poor.

A possible complication following surgical intervention is bile leakage into the peritoneal cavity. Bile is irritating to the peritoneal lining, and contact of bile with the lining results in a chemical peritonitis. Clinical indications of peritonitis include fever, abdominal pain, distention, and abdominal rigidity.

A biliary (cutaneous) fistula may develop after biliary surgery. The drain tract is a common site of fistulization. The development of a fistula requires the use of skin barriers and pouches to protect the skin from the excoriating bile and for accurate measurement of biliary loss. Stomahesive is an appropriate skin barrier for this purpose. The pouch used for biliary drainage should be sterile if the cultured bile is sterile. A urinary pouch with a drainage spout is most convenient for the patient to manage (see "Cutaneous Fistulas" above).

Prolonged T-tube drainage is maintained following surgery for sclerosing cholangitis. The patient should be instructed in the care of the T tube and the stab wound site. A kink in the T tube or the drainage collector will create a temporary obstruction and pressure will be placed on the biliary ductal system. The patient should check the tubing when changing positions to ensure a patent drainage system. Occasionally, bile will leak around the T tube. If this occurs, a skin barrier (Stomahesive) should be applied around the T tube. Dressings can be applied around the T tube and changed when necessary. The skin barrier will keep the skin dry and protected. If a substantial amount of bile is leaking around the T tube, a sterile pouch should be applied over the skin barrier enclosing the T tube.

When prolonged T-tube drainage is utilized or large amounts of bile are lost through the T tube, the patient may be required to replace the bile orally. The bile should be chilled and diluted with grape or apple juice for oral ingestion. A nasogastric tube may be inserted for bile replacement. Florantyrone (Zamhol) or sodium dehydrocholate (Decholin Sodium) may be given to replace bile salts.

Nutritional support is an important aspect of care. Fat-soluble vitamins may be replaced. The amount of fat in the diet may be limited for a temporary period.

Pancreatitis

Pancreatitis has been classified to reflect the degree of functional damage and frequency of attacks. Acute pancreatitis refers to a single attack of pancreatitis in a previously normal gland. Episodes of acute pancreatitis without functional damage is classified as recurrent acute pancreatitis. Recurrent chronic pancreatitis describes recurring episodes of acute attacks with progressive damage to the pancreas. The intervals between episodes are pain-free. The pancreatic function is permanently altered and the pain is constant in chronic pancreatitis.

The etiology of pancreatitis is unknown. Ductal obstruction and vascular changes occur, and reflux of pancreatic enzymes have been related to pancreatitis. Conditions associated with pancreatitis include chronic alcoholism, biliary tract disease, hyperparathyroidism, allergies, and metal toxicity.

Acute Pancreatitis: Clinical Manifestations and Diagnosis

Signs and symptoms of acute pancreatitis will vary according to the degree of functional alteration of the pancreas. There are two types of pathology in acute pancreatitis: interstitial and hemorrhagic. In interstitial acute pancreatitis, the pancreas is edematous. The pancreas may recover with mild attacks. However, if complications develop, the pancreas may become necrotic. The term *necrotic pancreatitis* is used interchangeably with hemorrhagic pancreatitis. The sudden development of acute pain in the epigastric region which radiates to the back usually follows a heavy meal in patients with gallbladder disease or an episode of excessive alcohol intake (acute alcoholism). The pain may be diminished by maintaining a sitting position, whereas lying down intensifies the pain. Fever and vomiting are observed in acute pancreatitis. The vomiting does not relieve the epigastric pain and may become persistent.

Spillage of pancreatic enzymes into the peritoneal cavity will result in chemical peritonitis. Shock may develop from pooling of fluid and blood into the retroperitoneal area and peritoneal cavity. Diaphoresis, tachycardia, hypotension, and abdominal rigidity may be indicative of shock in acute pancreatitis. Bowel sounds are decreased, and a paralytic ileus, with its sequelae, may occur including abdominal distention and fluid loss into the bowel lumen. The physical examination may reveal upper abdominal tenderness.

Serum and urinary amylase values are elevated in pancreatitis. Serum amylase levels are not used singularly for diagnosing pancreatitis because increased serum amylase is observed in acute cholecystitis, active alcoholism without pancreatitis, perforated peptic ulcer, intestinal obstruction, mesenteric thrombosis, ectopic pregnancy, renal failure, mumps, and after the administration of Demerol (meperidine). Urinary amylase levels tend to reflect the amount of amylase secreted from the pancreas. Amylase values of pleural fluid and paracentesis drainage are used in diagnosing pancreatitis. A lowered serum calcium may be observed in necrotizing pancreatitis. Radiography studies may demonstrate pancreatic or biliary calcification. The presence of a loop of dilated small bowel adjacent to the pancreas may be seen on radiography examination in acute pancreatitis.

Treatment of Acute Pancreatitis

Therapy involves fluid administration and a reduction in pancreatic stimulation. Fluids lost in the retroperitoneal space, in the peritoneal cavity, and in the adynamic bowel may result in hypovolemic shock. Colloids, fluids, blood, and electrolytes are replaced, and in addition, adequate maintenance fluid therapy is supplied. Urinary output, alterations in hematocrit, central venous pressure (CVP), and occult losses in the peritoneum are used in calculating the fluid needs.

The pancreas is stimulated by gastric acid in the duodenum and the vagal nerve. Nasogastric suction is used to decrease the amount of hydrochloric acid (HCl) in the stomach, and thus in the duodenum. This alters the gastric acid–secretin mechanism. Anticholinergics, such as propantheline bromide, are used to lower vagal stimulation of the pancreas. Antibiotics are used in fulminating, necrotic pancreatitis and in the presence of a pancreatic abscess. Meperidine is used for pain control. Acute episodes of pancreatitis are usually resolved within 2 to 3 days unless complications develop.

Complications of acute pancreatitis include pseudocyst, abscess formation, rupture of a major vessel, or thrombosis of a major vessel. The vessels involved in pancreatitis hemorrhage or thrombosis include splenic, mesenteric, or portal blood vessels. Respiratory failure may be observed, and abnormal blood gases are indicative of a poor prognosis. The patient may present with rapid, shallow breathing. Potassium and calcium losses are also seen in pancreatic complications. Cardiac dysfunction associated with the lowered potassium and calcium levels may be observed on ECG or cardiac monitoring systems.

Ultrasound studies may be used to diagnose pseudocyst or abscess formation associated with pancreatitis. Surgery may be indicated when a definitive diagnosis has not been made and the patient's status is not improving. Pancreatic abscesses may be surgically drained.

Chronic Pancreatitis: Clinical Signs and Diagnosis

Permanent functional damage to the pancreas is present in chronic pancreatitis. The pancreas becomes nodular and indurated. Fibrous bands surround the acinar and islet cells. The ductal system has alternating areas of stricture and dilatation. In late stages of pancreatitis, calcification of the ductal system is observed. As in acute pancreatitis, the etiology of chronic pancreatitis is unknown. The association between chronic alcoholism and chronic biliary tract disease is well documented. Clinical manifestations of chronic pancreatitis include weight loss, steatorrhea, and diabetes. Laboratory studies used to evaluate the exocrine and endocrine function of the pancreas include serum amylase and lipase levels, urinary amylase levels, glucose tolerance studies, stool collections for fat content, and secretin stimulation.

The clinical history usually reveals a long duration of alcohol abuse and recurrent attacks of acute pancreatitis. The persistent epigastric pain radiates to the back and is improved by a sitting position.

Radiographic examination may reveal biliary tract disease or ductal calcification. An oral fiberoptic endoscopy with cannulation of the ampulla of Vater may be used for diagnostic evaluation in chronic pancreatitis.

Treatment of Chronic Pancreatitis

Treatment for chronic pancreatitis is based on the underlying disease. Primary biliary tract disease may be evidenced by gallstones or by the inability to visualize the gallbladder. Surgical correction of the ductal obstruction will decrease the number of attacks and control the pain. When chronic alcoholism is the underlying factor, complete abstinence may be helpful in eliminating the progression of the disease.

Various operations have been utilized in the treatment of chronic pancreatitis. Cholecystectomy (removal of the gallbladder), sphincteroplasty (alteration of the sphincter of Oddi), direct pancreatic duct drainage, pancreaticojejunostomy (retrograde drainage of the pancreas), and distal pancreatectomy have been performed in relation to chronic pancreatitis. Total pancreatectomy is not an acceptable solution because of the metabolic complications which would then require medical attention.

Nursing Responsibilities

The nursing history should include the location and duration of pain; the relation of pain to meals and posture; alcohol ingestion; recent weight loss; nausea and vomiting; anorexia; and food intolerances. Urine should be observed for discoloration associated with obstructive jaundice. Characteristics and frequency of bowel movements should be observed. Fatty stools (steatorrhea) are associated with pancreatitis.

Physical assessments that may be present in pancreatitis include abdominal distention, rigidity, or masses. The mucous membranes and sclera may show signs of jaundice associated with compression of the common bile duct. The patient's position may be indicative of pancreatitis. A hunched sitting position is observed as the patient attempts to alleviate the severe pain associated with pancreatitis.

The battery of diagnostic procedures include serum levels of amylase, lipase, calcium, potassium, sodium, alkaline phosphate, and glucose. A glucose tolerance test is done to evaluate the endocrine function of the pancreas. The exocrine pancreatic function is assessed by a secretin stimulation study. Urinary amylase levels are obtained, and 72-h stool samples for quantitative fats are collected.

The secretin stimulation study requires the insertion of a duodenal tube after a 12-h fast. Baseline samples are obtained and then secretin is given intravenously, followed by an injection of pancreozymin. Serial aspirations of the duodenal contents are then or subsequently withdrawn at specified intervals. A blood sample for serum amylase is also drawn as a phase of this procedure. The patient will need instructions regarding the secretin stimulation procedure the evening before the study. The insertion of the duodenal tube may cause additional discomfort in the presence of severe epigastric pain. The patient should be made as comfortable as possible for the procedure.

The medical treatment of pancreatitis revolves around the replacement of fluid loss to prevent shock and reduction of pancreatic stimulation. Careful monitoring of fluid and electrolyte replacement, observations of impending shock, and signs of electrolyte depletion should be assessed frequently. Intravenous fluid administration is based on urinary output, nasogastric drainage, and occult losses. Postural hypotension, decreased urinary output, and tachycardia are signs of decreased circulating volume. Fever may be the first indication of sepsis or pancreatic abscess, particularly fever which persists for more than 10 days.

Shallow, rapid respirations are associated with progressive pancreatitis. Blood gas studies are done, and if abnormal, respiratory support may be initiated. The loss of fluid into the retroperitoneal space elevates the diaphragm, limiting adequate respiratory inspiration.

Pain and anxiety stimulate the vagal nerve which in turn increases pancreatic secretion. Anxiety levels may be decreased by careful and continuous clarification of procedures to the patient. Pain may be reduced by meperidine or pentazocine (Talwin). Anticholinergic drugs may be administered to decrease vagal nerve stimulation. Side effects of the anticholinergic medications are dry mouth, urinary retention, and abdominal distention. These effects may also be indicative of progressive pancreatitis, making the diagnosis more difficult.

After an episode of pancreatitis, the person is placed on a bland, low-fat diet and antacids in an effort to maintain minimal pancreatic stimulation. Patient education should cover a bland, low-fat diet, antacid therapy, and the avoidance of alcohol ingestion.

When surgery is indicated, the patient should be taught to deep breathe and cough prior to surgery. A complication which may develop after surgery is the development of a pancreatic fistula. The protection of the skin from the proteolytic enzymes is most important. A skin barrier and drainable urinary pouch is an effective method of protection for this situation (see "Cutaneous Fistulas" above).

The patient with chronic pancreatitis associated with alcoholism will not improve or stabilize without abstinence from alcohol. A referral to an agency to assist the person in coping with the alcoholism should be initiated prior to discharge from the hospital.

Obesity

Obesity is defined as an excess of adipose tissue. Society has established norms concerning body size and weight, and obesity exceeds the socially accepted levels. Medically, an excess of adipose cells is associated with a variety of pathologies, including heart disease, hypertension, diabetes, psychosocial problems, and osteoarthritis. Morbid obesity is 100 lb over the ideal weight for height and sex, or two to three times greater than the ideal weight. The etiology of obesity is an excess of caloric intake over caloric expenditure. The emotional component of overeating to cope with inner needs and feelings is one aspect of obesity.

The number of adipose cells in the body is determined during childhood. Thereby, no new adipose cells are developed and weight gain occurs by increasing the size of the existing adipose cells. Weight gain is related to changes in the caloric intake and expenditure. Moderate weight gain occurs when the activity level or energy expenditure decreases and the caloric intake remains the same. Activity generally decreases during a depressive state, thus reducing the energy expenditure. Overeating is also related to depression. External cultural and social cues are associated with excessive weight. The clock time, availability of food, and attractiveness of the food are indicators for eating, rather than internal signals of hunger.

The complications of obesity revolve around the increased work load required of the organs, and obesity is associated with a shortened life expectancy. The obesity-hypoventilation syndrome, known as the Pickwickian syndrome, is described as a falling asleep at inappropriate times. There is hypoventilation, somnolence, and carbon dioxide retention. The excess adipose tissue decreases the compliance of the thoracic wall, increasing the work of respiration. A failure to increase the respiratory efforts to move the heavy thoracic wall initiates the process. The person becomes hypoxic, and pulmonary hypertension and polycythemia may develop if left uncorrected. Weight loss will improve the symptoms.

Hemodynamic changes include an increased circulation volume and additional vascular beds to the excess adipose tissue. The increased cardiac output and stroke volume increases the cardiac work load. Left ventricular hypertrophy develops. Hypertension is another complication of obesity and is the result of the increased stroke volume without an increased heart rate. Diabetes mellitus in obese persons is associated with an increased insulin production which may progress to pancreatic exhaustion. Weight loss will improve the diabetes and is observed in a decreased insulin requirement. Thrombophlebitis, chronic cholelithiasis, liver dysfunction, osteoarthritis of the lumbar spine, intertriginous dermatitis, stasis dermatitis, herniated intervertebral discs, and infertility in women are reported complications of obesity.

Social or psychosocial problems are also associated with obesity. The emotional component of the etiology of obesity may limit social interactions. Emotionally, the obese may be unable to relate to others. Continued weight gain may intensify existing emotional components. Employment is another area limited by obesity. The person may be too large to occupy a desk chair or fit onto a workbench, and employers are aware of the high risk of medical problems which increase sick time pay without production. The health risk increases insurance premiums and obtaining coverage is often difficult. Clothing is also expensive, unbecoming, and hard to find. Simple things such as riding in compact cars or sitting in telephone booths are difficult if not impossible for obese individuals.

Diagnosis of obesity is accomplished by the exclusion of endocrine and metabolic syndromes associated with an increased weight gain. Diagnostic studies are done to exclude hypothyroidism, Cushing's disease, Stein-Leventhal syndrome (women), and hyperinsulinism. If there are no disturbances in digestion, absorption, or utilization of food, the obesity is related to an excess of caloric intake or deprivation of activity.

Treatment

Weight loss will improve the health problems associated with excess adipose tissue in the body. The methods used for weight reduction include dietary restrictions, drugs, fasting, psychotherapy, surgical wiring of the jaws, jejunoileal bypass and gastric bypass. The reduction of caloric intake is the preferred mode of therapy for weight reduction. The restriction of calories results in a loss of protein, fat, and glycogen store. In the initial period of dietary restrictions, the negative nitrogen balance encourages loss of protein tissues and fluid losses. Significant weight loss occurs initially. As the dietary restrictions continue, the body compensates for the negative nitrogen balance, and weight loss is then the result of loss of adipose tissue. Protein synthesis is occurring simultaneously with the caloric loss of adipose tissue. The new protein-rich tissue may equal the weight loss in adipose tissue. Fat synthesis from carbohydrates may be stimulated to replace lost adipose tissue. For the person dieting, the initial weight loss is positive and encouraging. When the plateau is reached where tissue loss equals protein synthesis, no weight change is noted and the person often becomes discouraged. Depression, decreased activity levels, hunger, decreased metabolic rate, and weakness are associated with caloric reduction. The combination of these symptoms and the absence of weight loss discourage the individual and self-imposed dietary restrictions end.

Group therapy has become effective in assisting individuals in maintaining the dietary restrictions. Along with the dietary restrictions, exercise programs are encouraged to increase the energy requirements of the body. Psychotherapy is indicated in some situations. The original etiology of the overeating may be successfully dealt with by means of psychotherapy. Clinics are being developed across the nation to treat the problems of obesity. Drugs to decrease the appetite may be used in conjunction with diet and exercise programs. Amphetamines for appetite control have been banned by the Food and Drug Administration. Long-term use of amphetamines leads to tolerance and psychological dependence. The effects of amphetamines include nervousness, insomnia, dry mouth, and tachycardia.

Total fasting for weight loss is done under close medical supervision. The weight loss is rapid in the first 48 to 72 h from salt and water loss. Postural hypotension may occur as the plasma volume decreases. Prolonged fasting may progress to vitamin deficiencies and electrolyte imbalances. The surgical wiring of the jaws has been used successfully for weight loss. The person remains on liquids until the desired weight is reached.

The number of adipose cells is not altered by weight loss; the size of the cells decreases. The person losing weight often regains the weight if the dietary caloric intake increases after the desired weight is obtained. The final phase of weight loss is planning for a caloric intake which equals the caloric requirement.

Jejunoileal Bypass

The jejunoileal bypass may be indicated for morbid obesity. The bypass of a sufficient length of small intestine will progress to weight loss through malabsorption. The body will use fat deposits for energy when the caloric deficit from malabsorption occurs. The process of fat utilization for energy will continue until caloric absorption equals the energy requirement. The individual requesting a jejunoileal bypass must meet a specific list of criteria. The person must be 100 lb over the ideal weight for height and age and must have attempted weight reduction by dietrary restrictions. The patient is examined carefully to rule out causative endocrine or metabolic dysfunction. The patient is provided with a careful and detailed explanation of the operation and the potential complications, and the patient must agree to participate. The mental capacity of the patient to comprehend the explanation of the operation is assessed. The emotional stability of the individual is observed. The patient must demonstrate an ability to tolerate the operation and postoperative sequelae. The patient selected for jejunoileal bypass should have no history of alcoholism and agree to avoid alcoholic beverages for 3 postoperative years. Patients should accept their responsibility in the long-range aspect of the management.

The jejunoileal bypass is not a panacea for obesity. The procedure bypasses all but 14 in of jejunum and 4 in of ileum. The induced malabsorption will lead to diarrrhea, electrolyte imbalances, and impaired vitamin B_{12} absorption. Hair loss, polyarthritis, urinary calculi, and liver dysfunction are complications associated with jejunoileal bypass operations.

Fat absorption after the jejunoileal bypass is impaired, and combined with the decreased fluid absorption, diarrheal stools are common. The rapid transit of food through the small intestine and the presence of gastric enzymes in the large colon enhance the diarrhea. The body will adapt to the change in absorptive surface, and water, calcium, and potassium reabsorption improves with time. Vitamin B_{12} will continue to be required to prevent anemia, and fat content of the diet will need to be restricted indefinitely. Protein stores may be decreased after jejunoileal bypass. The liver complications are related to this protein loss. High-protein diets are required following jejunoileal bypass to prevent hair loss and fatty liver dysfunction. The patient will require close observations by the surgeon.

Positive effects of the jejunoileal bypass, in addition to the weight loss, include decreased serum cholesterol levels, decreased serum triglyceride levels, lowered blood pressure, reversal of cardiovascular changes, and relief of respiratory distress. Osteoarthritic changes and varicosities improve with weight loss. The psychosocial problems of obesity may also improve with weight reduction.

Nursing Care for Jejunoileal Bypass

The patient admitted for a jejunoileal bypass may present a variety of nursing problems in areas of physical care, preventing postoperative complications, patient education, pre- and postoperative electrolytes, and psychosocial needs. The patient may be too large for the hospital bed, chair, or bathroom. Two hospital beds may be wired together for an obese patient. The size of the blood pressure cuffs should be assessed and provisions made for a leg cuff. Assessments of the patient environment and provision for alterations should be accomplished before surgery, not afterward.

The patient's respiratory function will be evaluated by blood gases prior to surgery. The preoperative instruction of deep breathing, coughing, and postural hypertension is of utmost importance. Support stockings are ordered prior to surgery. If the patient's legs are larger than the manufactured hose, ace bandages should be utilized.

Postoperatively, the obese patient may develop pulmonary complications, wound infections, or incisional hernias. The average postoperative patient has compromised pulmonary function from spasms of abdominal muscles, pain, abdominal distention, immobilization, and posture. The obese patient has an additional problem of reduced respiratory efficiency (see "Pickwickian Syndrome" above). The nursing staff attempting to turn the obese patient might encounter problems if the patient is too large for the bed or the patient cannot assist in moving from side to side. A trapeze bar will assist the nursing staff in positioning the patient. A semirecumbent position, early mobilization, and respiratory physiotherapy are recommended for the prevention of pulmonary complications. Bed exercises, antiembolus hose, and early ambulation are encouraged to prevent emboli.

Careful monitoring of fluid and electrolytes is important in the postoperative hospital course. The patient may become fluid-depleted, hypocalcemic, and hypokalemic from the malabsorption process. Signs of hypovolemia include dry skin and mucous membranes, longitudinal wrinkling of the tongue, oliguria, drop in body temperature, exhaustion, and sudden weight loss. Hypocalcemia may be noted by clinical manifestations of tingling of the fingers, muscle cramps, tetany, and convulsions. The decreased potassium levels may be observed by signs of weak irregular pulse, shallow breathing, muscular weakness, flabby muscles, gaseous intestinal distention, and paresthesia of the extremities. The patient should be taught signs of fluid and electrolyte losses prior to discharge. Gatorade is useful in replacing fluid and electrolyte losses. Potassium may be replaced by adding the following to the diet: tea, banana, bouillon, orange juice, and grape juice. Calcium gluconate may be ordered for calcium depletion. In addition to observing and replacing lost fluid and electrolytes, the patient requires instruction for diarrhea. Foods which are helpful during bouts of diarrhea following a jejunoileal bypass include cottage cheese, cheddar cheese, peanut butter, bananas, and tapioca. Fat intake should be limited to prevent steatorrhea. If these measures do not effectively reduce the number of diarrheal stools, liquid Lomotil (diphenoxylate with atropine) or paregoric may be used. A high-protein diet is recommended for avoidance of complications following a jejunoileal bypass. Liver dysfunction is associated with the procedure, and the patient should consult the surgeon if peripheral edema, anorexia, and easy fatigability develops.

NUTRITION

Parenteral Hyperalimentation

The maintenance of normal body composition is the goal of nutritional supplements when metabolic requirements are elevated, when there are disturbances in the function of the gastrointestinal tract, or when the caloric intake is reduced. Metabolic requirements are increased in traumatic injuries and severe burns. Crohn's disease, ulcerative colitis, or pancreatitis interfere with the digestion and absorption of nutrients.

Anorexia, pain, nausea, and vomiting lead to reduced caloric intake regardless of the underlying cause of the symptoms. Inadequate nutrition interferes with wound healing, lengthens convalescence, and predisposes individuals to infection. Nutritional alimentation may be provided in various forms and concentrations. Parenteral hyperalimentation and fluid therapy or oral and tube feedings are available. Initial patient nutritional assessments, overall treatment modality, and the underlying disease entity are considerations in planning alimentation.

Parenteral hyperalimentation or total parenteral nutrition (TPN) provides essential carbohydrates, amino acids, and other nutrients needed for prolonged durations of limited oral intake. Folic acid and vitamin K are added to the solution each day. The quantity of nutrients provided is greater than the basal caloric and nitrogen level required. TPN is designed to achieve a positive nitrogen balance and an anabolic state during conditions associated with a catabolic response. Total parenteral hyperalimentation is recommended in many clinical situations, such as enterocutaneous fistulas, inflammatory bowel disease, short bowel syndrome, burns, and traumatic injury.

The hyperosmolar solution must be rapidly diluted by a high blood flow to prevent complications of hyperosmolar fluid absorption. Therefore, TPN is administered through a catheter inserted through the subclavian vein into the superior vena cava. The rate of administration and concentration of the solution is gradually increased.

Nursing involvement begins prior to the insertion of the catheter. Patient teaching is centered around the explanation of the procedure and an understanding of what is required of the patient. Anxiety and fears are decreased by answering pertinent patient questions.

The area of catheter insertion is shaved, and a surgical prep is used for the skin. Sterile technique is used to prevent contamination during the insertion of the catheter. The patient is put in a supine position with towels under the shoulders to hyperextend the neck. The patient's head is turned in the direction away from the incision. Once the catheter is inserted, a slow drip of normal saline is begun. Radiographic studies are then done to ascertain the location of the catheter. Technical errors in the catheter insertion may result in pneumothorax, hydrothorax, hemothorax, or subclavian artery puncture. Clinical manifestations of complications following the insertion include dyspnea, decreased breath sounds, sharp chest pain, tingling sensation in the fingers, and weakness or pain in the arm.

If the correct catheter position has been obtained, the hyperalimentation solution is infused at a slow rate. An intravenous pump is used to provide a continuous, regulated flow of the fluid. Frequent observations of the hyperalimentation fluid is required to prevent a decrease or increase in the rate of administration. Sudden increases of serum osmolality result in osmotic diuresis, serum and urine electrolyte alterations, dehydration, and abnormal central nervous system function progressing to coma.

The nursing management during the administration of hyperalimentation includes daily weights, accurate intake and output records, urine collections for sugar and acetone every 4 to 6 h, monitoring vital signs, and providing mobilization for the patient. The IV tubing is changed with each liter of solution. Aseptic technique is closely observed when the system is opened and during dressing changes. A mask and gloves are required with the sterile dressing procedure. A membrane filter is used on the tubing to prevent transmission of microorganisms or inert substances in the solution which would contaminate the infusing hyperalimentation solution. Sepsis is the major complication of hyperalimentation therapy. Aseptic technique in caring for the incision site, fluid, and tubing is of utmost importance in preventing infections. The solution alone is an excellent growth medium for bacteria.

The pharmacy prepares the appropriate hyperalimentation solution under laminar flow-filtered air hoods. Unexplained temperature elevations require cultures of the insertion site, catheter tip, solution, and tubing. The site of infusion is changed if any of the above are positive for growth.

The increased glucose delivered may not be tolerated in severely debilitated persons or diabetics. Hyperglycemia may first be observed by glycosuria. Postinfusion hypoglycemia, which develops with a sudden discontinuation of the solution, is a preventable complication of hyperalimentation therapy. Infusion of D_5W solution is utilized to taper the hyperalimentation fluid administration in order to prevent insulin rebound.

Serum levels of electrolytes, glucose, urea nitrogen, protein, calcium, phosphorous, and magnesium are followed closely during the administration of alimentation fluid. These levels are a reflection of the patient's progress and tolerance of the hyperalimentation.

Passive and active exercises are an important area of nursing care. Battery-charged IV pumps allow activity levels to be increased. Footboards are useful in those persons who are confined to bed. Skin care, frequent turning, and range of motion exercises should be included in the physical management during prolonged convalescence.

Medications should not be given through the central line used for the hyperalimentation. A peripheral vein should be utilized for the infusion of additional fluids and/or medications.

Peripheral Alimentation

Intravenous Fluids

Short-term fluid therapy involves the replacement of fluid and electrolytes with carbohydrates. The basal fluid requirement is approximately 2000 mL in a 24-h period, with 800 mL to replace insensible water loss and 1200 mL to maintain adequate urinary output. Potassium and sodium chloride additives are also required. Alterations in the fluid and electrolyte needs are based on preexisting deficits or losses secondary to the disease process.

Carbohydrate replacement is required to provide glucose for caloric (energy) requirements in an effort to avoid depletion of the liver glycogen stores. Glyconeogenesis with protein catabolism is minimized when carbohydrates are supplied in the fluid therapy. This glucose limits the reduction of insulin levels. Decreased insulin levels lead to the development of starvation ketosis. Nitrogen losses are also minimized by the administration of carbohydrates which decreases the amount of protein broken down for energy.

Peripheral Hyperalimentation

Peripheral hyperalimentation is a solution of less osmolar concentration than central hyperalimentation which can be infused through a small-bore needle into a peripheral vein. The modified hyperalimentation solution is referred to as P-900. The P describes the peripheral route of administration, and the 900 reflects the number of milliosmoles in each liter. (Correspondingly, C-1800 refers to central hyperalimentation and P-400 refers to intravenous fluids.) Peripheral hyperalimentation is designed for malnourished patients who are unable to maintain adequate oral intake or patients with prolonged reduction in oral intake.

Intralipids

Soybean fat emulsions (intralipids) are available to complete the nutritional supplements. Intralipids provide essential fatty acids and high caloric values for the patient. Intralipids are not combined with other fluids or additives. The intralipids are infused by means of a Y connector through the same vein as other IV solutions. The two fluids flow concomitantly through the vein. The Y connector should be close to the skin insertion point for the administration of intralipids.

Fat emulsion administration is contraindicated when the ability of the body to clear fats from the blood is compromised. Therefore, intralipids are not indicated in the presence of acute pancreatitis, severe liver disease, coagulopathies, or in the acute phase of trauma.

Elemental Diets

Oral Supplements

Chemically formulated oral diets, or elemental diets, are liquid feedings which contain all essential nutrients, need minimal digestion, and are bulk-free. The elemental diets are used for supplemental, high-protein feedings in patients who can continue oral intake and are unable to consume adequate caloric replacements with the diet ingested. Elemental diets are fat-free and do not stimulate pancreatic or biliary secretions. The volume of the stool decreases, and in inflammatory bowel disease, elemental diets may be used to place the colon at rest. Small bowel function must be adequate to absorb the contents of the solution.

The elemental diet has a strong taste and odor because of the amino acid content. Flavoring packets are available to make the solution more palatable. The feeding should begin with slow sipping of a diluted concentration. If the concentration of the liquid or the rate of ingestion is too high, diarrhea will develop. Gastric retention and vomiting with aspiration may occur. The elevation of the head of the bed is beneficial in preventing aspiration.

Hypertonic dehydration and hyperosmolar nonketotic coma may develop if the solution concentration is too great or if fluid ingestion is inadequate. Hyperglycemia and glycosuria have been associated with elemental diets in severely debilitated states, sepsis, or diabetes.

Tube Feedings

Small-bore pediatric feeding tubes or nasogastric tubes may be used to provide nutritional support when elemental diets are not palatable or when patients are comatose. Gastrostomy or jejunostomy tubes may be inserted for feeding after surgical procedures involving the upper gastrointestinal tract. This allows for nutritional replacements while the incision in the bowel heals.

Elemental diets are commonly used for tube feedings; however, commercial tube feeding products are available. The concentration of the solution and flow rate are carefully controlled to prevent diarrhea and abdominal cramping from the hypertonic liquid. The pattern of slow increments is similiar to the one used for oral alimentation. If the tube feedings are discontinued and reinstituted, the amount and concentration will be increased as if the patient had never received the feedings.

The placement of the tube is checked prior to initiating the feeding. The head of the bed should be elevated and the stomach observed for retention. Medications may be given through the feeding tube.

REFERENCES

Ansley, J. D., B. Gardner, J. Issacs, M. Martin, W. C. McGarity, P. O'Brien, and J. Tebeau: *Total Parenternal Nutrition*, Atlanta: Emory University Hospital, 1977.

Beeson, P. B. and W. McDermott (eds.), *Textbook of Medicine*, 14th ed., Philadelphia: Saunders, 1975.

Clearfield, H. R. and V. P. Dinoso, Jr. (eds.), *Gastrointestinal Emergencies*, New York: Grune & Stratton, 1976.

Greenberger, N. J., and D. H. Winship: *Gastrointestinal Disorders: A Pathophysiologic Approach*, Chicago: Year Book, 1976.

Molyneux-Luick, M., and J. Knecht: The emergency that supercedes all your other duties: Hypovolemic shock, *Am J Nurs* 77(11):32–77, 1977.

Sabiston, D. C. Jr. (ed.), *Davis-Christopher Textbook of Surgery*, Vol. 1, 11th ed., Philadelphia: Saunders, 1977.

Schwartz, S. I. (ed.), *Principles of Surgery,* Vol. 1, New York: McGraw-Hill, 1969.

Sheridan, J. L.: Obstructions of the intestinal tract, *Nurs Clin North Am* 10(1):147–155, 1975.

Sleisenger, M. H. and J. S. Fordtran (eds.), *Gastrointestinal Disease: Pathophysiology, Diagnosis, Management,* Philadelphia: Saunders, 1973.

Spiro, H. M.: *Clinical Gastroenterology,* 2d ed., London: Collier-Macmillan, 1977.

Wentworth, A., and B. Cox: Nursing the patient with a continent ileostomy, *Am J Nurs* 76(9): 1924–1928, 1976.

INTRODUCTION

History and Philosophy

Burn victims differ from other trauma victims only by the size of their wound. Both require similar care. The healthy human body can, with proper support, heal a partial-thickness burn of any size, but a full-thickness burn of greater than 0.5 percent of the total body surface area (TBSA) must be resurfaced with autografts. The essence of care of a major burn is providing systemic support while reducing the size of the wound.

Throughout history burn wound care has been remarkable in its variety but limited in progress—even until today. Ancient formulas attempted to "feed" the wound and then seal it, and it was not until Lister recognized the possibility of infection that physicians' thoughts turned to sepsis and antisepsis. Hippocrates recommended old swine's fat mixed with resin and bitumin, spread on a piece of cloth, warmed in a fire, and applied as a bandage to the burn. Byzantines in the seventh century advocated soaks using bull's gall dissolved in much water with the brine of pickled olives and pounded leeks. This same nutritional approach continued through the Renaissance. Paré, a famous French surgeon in the fifteenth century, upon the recommendation of a country lady, put the burn wound on a diet and advised salted onions; this became accepted in medical literature for three centuries. Once the germ theory was accepted (late 1800s) physicians soaked dressings in 10% silver nitrate to eliminate "beasties" (today a 0.5% solution is used and the objective of topical agents is to control bacteria in the wound).

Throughout this period blood-letting was the most popular form of systemic therapy. David Cleghorn, an English brewer during the Renaissance era, is credited with recognizing that purging was harmful to the burn victim. Cleghorn gained a great deal of clinical experience by treating burns among his employees and became recognized as an authority. Contrary to prevailing antiphlogistic theories, he advocated a supportive regimen. He allowed his employees to drink his brew during their recovery, thus providing them with fluid and nutritional replacement. In 1831, cholera victims were found to benefit from saline solution administration, and a quarter of a century later it was pointed out that persons with severe burns and cholera victims seemed to share a similar fluid depletion, and saline solution was occasionally given to patients with major burns. At about that time, in 1857, Passavant introduced continuous saline baths, using them to treat the survivors of an explosion and

$$30$$

BURN CARE
Claudella Archambeault-Jones
Irving Feller

INTRODUCTION
History and Philosophy
Etiology of Burns: How? Who? Where?
Skin Anatomy and Physiology
Determining Severity of Injury
Planning Burn Care

THE EMERGENT PERIOD
General Principles
The Admission Procedure

ADMINISTRATION OF FLUIDS
Emergent Period
Acute Period
Care of Intravenous Catheter Site
Monitoring Urinary Output

RESPIRATORY CARE
Introduction to the Problem
Immediate Respiratory Complications
Pulmonary Insufficiency

INFECTION CONTROL
Principles of Infection Control
Planning and Maintaining an Infection Control Unit
Wound Infection and Clinical Sepsis

BASIC CARE
Meeting Nutritional Needs
Comfort and Hygiene
Positioning, Contracture Control, Exercise, and Splinting
The Contractual Approach to Nurse-Patient Interaction
Quality Control Measures: Recording and Assessment of Data Collection

WOUND CARE
Basic Wound Care Procedures
Special Area Care
Hydrotherapy and Dressing Change
Skin Grafting

REFERENCES

fire in Frankfurt-am-Main. Twenty-five years later, autopsy studies in Munich revealed that the water content of the blood was reduced in severe burn victims, and in 1905 an article appeared in the *Journal of the American Medical Association* addressing the importance of parenteral saline, as well as early skin grafting, for burn victims. In the past few decades, beginning with the Coconut Grove fire and the work of Cope and Moore (1947) and continuing with the Evans and Brooke formulas, fluid therapy has become something of a science.

Skin grafting, a technique known to ancient Hindus, was the first form of tissue transplant used in human beings. Its role was minor, however, until the late nineteenth century. Reverdin's success with tiny epidermal grafts in 1869 began to put skin grafting on a firm footing. Shortly after, others reported success with larger pieces of skin, then with deep slashes, and finally with full-thickness grafts. In 1939, Padgett invented the dermatome and eliminated the roadblock of freehand slicing. The problem of speeding the closure of the wound continues to spur intensive study. Tangential excision, homografts, fresh-frozen pigskin, plastic skin substitutes, enzymes, and drugs are being used to reduce healing time.

Today, all the skill and knowledge gained through care of other trauma, medical, and surgical patients is being coordinated into a method of care which ensures 100 percent survival for patients with full-thickness burns of up to 20 percent TBSA. Patients with larger burns require meticulous and comprehensive care for survival not only by a physician but, more important, by nurses who are with the patient 24 h a day.

Each nurse who endeavors to care for a critically ill patient must find the time to consider an approach to total coordination of therapy. No one person can provide this care; a team philosophy must be developed, with each member providing his or her particular expertise in harmony with others. A key member in structuring an environment for recovery is the nurse who is at the patient's bedside the major portion of the day. Basic nursing as well as the skills of all other medical specialties are required. If measures or tasks are overlooked because they superficially appear trivial, the resulting problems are soon compounded, often reaching gargantuan proportions.

Becoming a specialist requires competency in nursing essentials as well as in the technicalities of critical care—*not only* treating disease but anticipating and recognizing subtle early warnings and initiating appropriate intervention. The ability to meet these criteria, combined with a knowledge of the specific requirements of the severely burned individual, is the foundation of an environment for recovery. Concentrating treatment on only one of the patient's problems at a given time is an ineffective approach because other physiologic and psychologic derangements soon become additive and may ultimately destroy the patient. Thus, we see patients in whom initial shock has been successfully combated by a meticulous fluid therapy program later die of pneumonia, which might have been controlled had they received vigorous preventive measures.

The routine essentials of nursing care frequently are neglected in the flurry of activity surrounding any critically ill patient. The practitioner may become caught up in intravenous transfusions and medications, invasive monitoring, and respiratory therapy equipment and may overlook the basic ingredients essential to recovery: comfort, rest, hygiene, nutrition, position change, deep breathing exercises, and infection control. These activities have traditionally been the nurse's domain and are seldom included in physician's orders. Medicine has been forced to specialize, and the modern nurse has taken on many new responsibilities. The truly professional nurse must ask, *"If nurses don't provide essential nursing care, who will?"* For it is in providing excellence in basic care that the battle is won.

Etiology of Burns: How? Who? Where?

Burns are the third largest cause of accidental death in the United States, exceeded only by motor vehicle accidents and falls. In the age group 0 to 5 years, fires and burns are the leading cause of death. Nearly 2,200,000 people are burned badly enough to seek medical attention each year; of these, 75,000 are hospitalized, and 9,000 die from their burns.

How?

Burn injuries are caused by heat from flame, hot liquids, or hot surfaces; by electric currents; by chemicals; or by radiation. Extreme cold, producing frostbite or freezing, causes an injury requiring treatment similar to that for the burn injury. Flame (fire) causes two-thirds of all burn injuries. The second largest cause of burn injuries is by scalding or contact with a hot surface. Next are chemical and radiation burns. Note particularly that 85 percent of all flame burns involve ignition of fabrics. If clothing catches fire, the injury, length of hospital stay, and hospital costs increase dramatically.

Who?

Burn victims fall into five categories. In the largest category (70 percent) are those who are victims of their own action, e.g., the child whose clothing ignites while playing with matches. In the next group (20 percent) are innocent bystanders, such as the person burned at home by a furnace explosion. In the third category (4 percent) are persons with a medical condition that predisposes them to the accident; for example, the epileptic person injured during a seizure. Intended victims make up another 4 percent, typified by the child intentionally burned by a parent as punishment. Rescue workers, such as firefighters injured in the line of duty, are in the final category, making up only 1 percent of the total. Even though these workers frequently risk contact with flame and possible burn, few are injured, primarily because of effective safety precautions.

Different types of burn injuries are more common in different age groups. Among toddlers, scalds are more common than flame burns. Industrial burns involving caustic elements or hot liquids are more common in adult males. Flame burns are frequently sustained by children playing with matches who set themselves or the building in which they are playing on fire. Infants and small children are also more susceptible to sunburn.

In the last 10 years an alarming increase in inflicted burns to children has been noted. It is important to recognize and report any suspected neglect or intended injury so that the situation may be adequately evaluated. Failure to recognize a particular living or work situation as hazardous may permit a child or adult to return to a potentially lethal environment.

Where?

About 85 percent of all burn injuries occur in the home, while 15 percent occur either at work or in recreational areas. The kitchen, the bathroom, and the bedroom (in that order) are the rooms most often involved in home accidents.

Skin Anatomy and Physiology

The skin is the largest organ of the body (1.8 m² or about 2 yd² in the adult male). It provides much more than a tough, pliable surface covering. Skin anatomy is reviewed in greater depth in Chap. 10, but it is worth repeating here that it has two anatomic layers called the epidermis and the dermis (Fig. 30-1). The epidermis, the outer nonvascular layer, is very thin and consists of layers of epithelial cells which, as they mature, form a protective covering of dead cells.

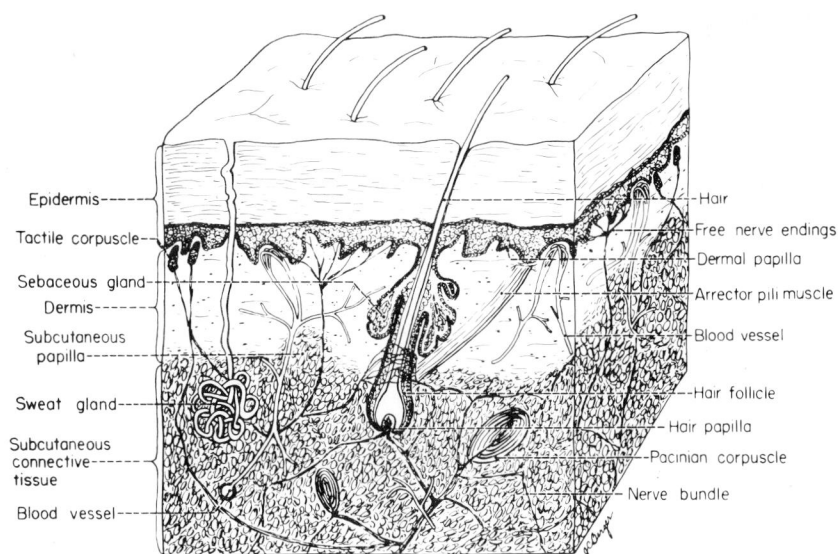

FIGURE 30-1
Anatomy of the skin.

The thickness of the epidermis ranges from 0.02 in on the eyelid to 0.24 in on the back.

The many functions of the skin are summarized in Table 30-1 and reviewed in greater detail in Chap. 10. When the skin is burned, these functions are either diminished (when the burn is partial-thickness) or eliminated (in complete destruction of the skin). Burn severity is determined to a great extent by the amount of skin lost and by the depth of the damage. Trauma results in decreased function or complete loss of the two most important life-preserving functions of the skin: protection against infection and prevention of loss of body fluids. However, once the patient has recovered these functions, the loss of cosmetic appearance and pleasure-pain sensations may complicate the patient's readjustment to society.

Determining Severity of Injury

Not all burns are alike. A first consideration in planning care is determining the severity of injury because treatment is directly related to severity. Five major factors influence severity: (1) extent of burn, (2) depth of injury, (3) age, (4) past medical history, and (5) parts of the body injured.

Extent of Burn

The extent of burn is expressed as a percentage of the total body surface area. There are two commonly used methods of determining extent of burn. The rule of nines, the simplest method, is "quick and dirty," does not require charts or diagrams, and does not take into consideration proportional differences related to age. The body is divided into components of nine. The arms (from shoulder to fingertip) and the head are each given a value of 9 percent. Each leg

---

TABLE 30-1
Functions of the Skin

1. Protects against infection
2. Prevents loss of body fluids
3. Controls body temperature
4. Functions as an excretory organ
5. Functions as a sensory organ
6. Produces vitamin D
7. Determines identity (e.g., cosmetic)

---

is valued at 18 percent, the anterior and posterior trunk are also valued at 18 percent each, and the perineum is given a 1 percent value, yielding a total of 100 percent.

A second method, after Berkow and Lund and Browder, is more exacting and requires the use of tables to calculate the changes in proportion of the head and lower extremities which occur with growth. For example, the head of an infant represents 19 percent of total body surface area, while in an adult the head accounts for only 7 percent. Use of the second method is described in Fig. 30-2.

Depth of Burn

Most difficult to determine is the depth of burn. There are signs and symptoms which indicate the level of tissue damage, but only with demarcation, spontaneous healing, or the appearance of granulation tissue can the exact depth of injury be determined.

Depth of burn is best described in terms of *partial-thickness* or *full-thickness*. These terms are anatomically descriptive and therefore are preferable to the popular references of "first and second degree" (partial-thickness) and "third degree" (full-thickness) burns, which arose from visual impressions. In a partial-thickness burn, the tissue damage and destruction do not include the deeper dermal layers, which may regenerate. All skin layers have been destroyed in a full-thickness burn, and there may be injury of subcutaneous tissues, muscle, and bone as well. Skin grafting is necessary to replace destroyed tissues.

Differential diagnosis of depth of injury Signs and symptoms which are helpful in differentiation of depth of injury immediately after a burn injury are as follows: Erythematous areas which blanch with fingertip pressure and then refill are shallow partial-thickness burns; the erythema indicates tissue damage where viability remains. Vesicles which increase in size immediately usually represent a deeper partial-thickness injury.

Full-thickness burns are characterized by a leathery surface that may be white, tan, brown, red, or black. Because of destruction of the dermis, where pain fibers terminate, there is no pain sensation. (Deep partial-thickness burns may be anesthetic during the first few days, but sensation returns as tissues recover.) Absence of pain response to stimuli such as a pinprick or the pulling out of a hair indicates full-

National Burn Information Exchange

I. Feller, M.D., Director, Ann Arbor, Michigan 48104

Form Completed By: ____________

Name: ____________

Date: ____________ Age: ____________

Past Medical History: ____________

Concurrent Injuries: ____________

Estimation of Size of Burn by Percent

❶ ☐ COLOR IN THE BURN

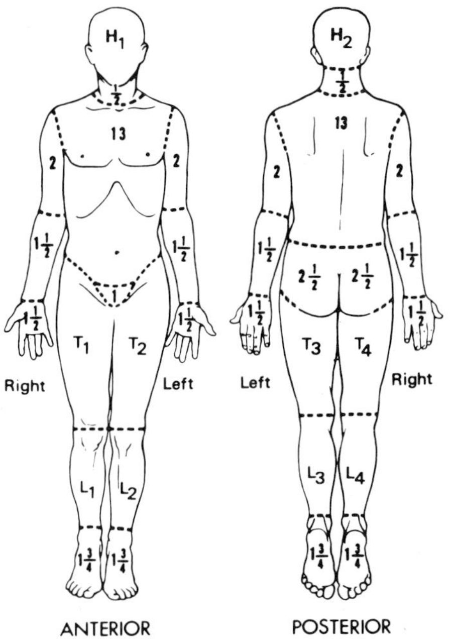
H1
H2
13
13
2
2
2
2
1½
1½
1½
1½
2½
2½
T1
T2
T3
T4
Right
Left
Left
Right
L1
L2
L3
L4
1¾
1¾
1¾
1¾
ANTERIOR
POSTERIOR

❸ CALCULATE EXTENT BURN

	ANTERIOR	POSTERIOR
Head	H1 ____	H2 ____
Neck	____	____
Rt. Arm	____	____
Rt. Forearm	____	____
Rt. Hand	____	____
Lt. Arm	____	____
Lt. Forearm	____	____
Lt. Hand	____	____
Trunk	____	____
Buttock	(R) ____	(L) ____
Perineum	____	____
Rt. Thigh	T1 ____	T4 ____
Rt. Leg	L1 ____	L4 ____
Rt. Foot	____	____
Lt. Thigh	T2 ____	T3 ____
Lt. Leg	L2 ____	L3 ____
Lt. Foot	____	____
SUBTOTAL	____	____
% TOTAL AREA BURNED		____ %

❷ CIRCLE AGE FACTOR

PERCENT OF AREAS AFFECTED BY GROWTH

	AGE 0	1	5	10	15	Adult
H(1 or 2) = ½ of the Head	9½	8½	6½	5½	4½	3½
T(1,2,3 or 4) = ½ of a Thigh	2¾	3¼	4	4¼	4½	4¾
L(1,2,3 or 4) = ½ of a Leg	2½	2½	2¾	3	3¼	3½

FIGURE 30-2
Form for estimating extent of burn by percentage of body surface area.

thickness skin loss. Small vesicles caused by steam may be present in areas where intense heat destroyed all layers of the skin; these vesicles will not increase in size. Following a severe scald, there may be full-thickness skin loss, although the surface appears only red and discolored; however, this area will not blanch with pressure nor refill.

In general, a painful erythematous surface with vesicles indicates a partial-thickness burn. When there is no complaint of pain and the surface is anesthetic, a full-thickness burn usually exists (see Table 30-2 and Fig. 30-3).

Age

Age contributes greatly to severity of injury. Patients less than 4 years old and those over 35 have a lower survival rate than those in other age groups with comparable injuries. Essentially, the problem in the infant and youngster is vulnerability to infection, leading to septicemia, Exacerbation of latent degenerative processes may be fatal to the older patient. This does not mean that these individuals have no chance for recovery—patients can and do beat the odds when excellence in burn care is provided (Fig. 30-4).

Past Medical History

If the patient has a past medical history of some significant illness—for example, diabetes, cirrhosis, or heart disease—this will complicate a burn injury. Exacerbation of that disease process by stress will increase the mortality rate in these patients.

Part of Body Burned

The part of the body injured also contributes to severity. Burns of the head, neck, and chest lead to increased incidence of pulmonary problems. Burns of the perineum are prone to early infection. Concurrent injuries, e.g., fractures, also increase severity.

Planning Burn Care

Based on the derangements which follow an appreciable full-thickness skin loss, burn care can be divided into three definable but overlapping periods, each with well-defined principles on which care is planned. These are the emergent, the acute, and the rehabilitation periods. In the emergent period the traumatic insult to the skin, the largest organ of the body, results in an immediate, dramatic, natural inflammatory response and massive fluid shift of extracellular fluid from the bloodstream into the damaged tissues. The acute period deals with the loss of normal function—primarily protection against infection—and the body's attempt to heal the massive wound, creating a disposition to serious complications. In the rehabilitation period, primary considerations are functional and cosmetic deficits caused by contracture and scar formation.

Emergent Period

The emergent period refers to the first 2 days to 2 weeks after the burn injury, depending on the severity. This is the period when the patient is admitted, the severity of the injury is determined, and first aid and wound care are given. The most important aspects of care involve determining and giving the exact amounts of fluid required, assessing respiratory status, and maintaining pulmonary function. The emergent period usually ends when the initial fluid therapy is completed and the patient starts to lose some of the weight gained when large amounts of fluid were given intravenously.

Acute Period

The acute period of treatment begins at the end of the emergent period and lasts until all of the full-thickness wounds are covered with autografts. If the burn is only a partial-thickness injury, the acute period is over within 10 to 20 days; the healing is spontaneous and grafts are not necessary.

During the acute phase there are two main principles of management; the first is to remove the eschar (dead tissue) as soon as possible and to cover the wound with homografts or autografts. The second major task is to avoid, as far as possible, the complications that are known to occur. The most common

TABLE 30-2 Differential Diagnosis of Depth of Burn		
	Partial-thickness	Full-thickness
Sensation	Normal or increased sensitivity to pain and temperature	Anesthetic to pain and temperature
Blisters	Large, thick-walled; will usually increase in size	None or, if present, thin-walled and will not increase in size
Color	Red, will blanch with pressure and refill	White, brown, black, or red; if red, will not blanch with pressure
Texture	Normal or firm	Firm or leathery

complications are infection leading to septicemia and pneumonia, renal failure, and heart disease. Some complications cannot be avoided, and it is necessary to detect these early and treat them vigorously. It is very important to remember that the seriously burned patient is acutely ill for a long period of time. The patient is not in a chronic state, as this prolonged, difficult period would suggest, but rather is acutely ill and in danger of death from complications.

Because of the severe metabolic strain, the patient may appear to be doing well one day, only to be found with a severe complication the next. *Only when the full-thickness wound is reduced to less than 20 percent of the body surface area are these dangers past.*

Rehabilitation Period

Rehabilitation is concerned with returning the patient to a useful place in society. Fortunately, most patients who survive do very well, having learned to cope through the long and difficult hospitalization. A recent survey of severely burned patients treated in the University of Michigan Burn Center revealed that 85 percent were returned to society as well as or better than prior to the accident. This took into consideration both functional and emotional factors.

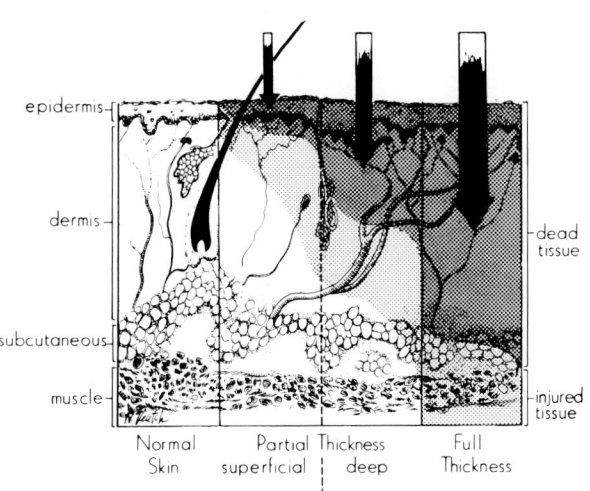

FIGURE 30-3

Depth of burn. The arrows represent degrees of heat or intensity of burning agent and the duration of contact with skin. The darker shaded area represents dead tissue. The lighter shaded area indicates damaged or injured tissues which will heal with good care.

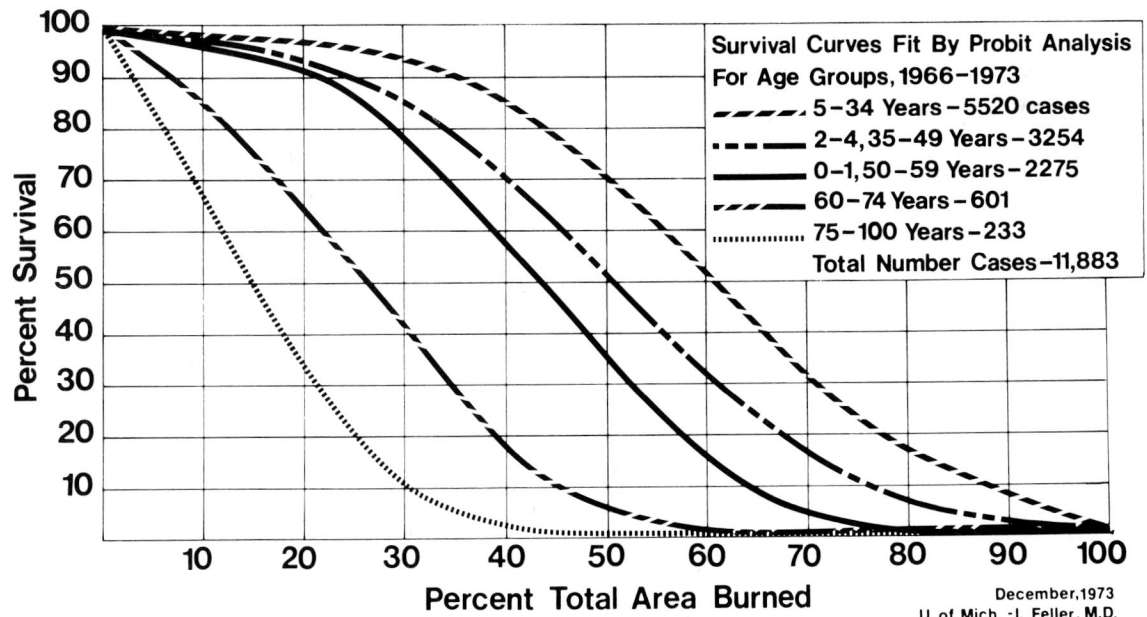

FIGURE 30-4

Burn patient survival by age group. (*From the National Burn Information Exchange.*)

There are two basic considerations during the rehabilitation phase. One is the restoration of function in joint surfaces. The second is concerned with the social and emotional assistance that the patient will need. The rehabilitation of the patient actually begins on admission and is continued throughout care. After the initial discharge, many readmissions may be necessary for reconstructive procedures as well as for emotional assistance and counseling. The rehabilitation period may last 2 to 5 years.

The next part of this chapter discusses the emergent period and admission procedure. Acute period care is not discussed as a separate entity because care is a continuation from the emergent period. Many of the complications seen in burn care are similar to those discussed in other sections of this book. The nurse should be able to apply that information to burn patients.

THE EMERGENT PERIOD

General Principles

Ironically, the most satisfying phase of burn treatment today is often the emergent period. Advances in the knowledge of fluid therapy which have occurred in the past two decades make it possible to successfully resuscitate most severely burned patients; formerly, many deaths occurred during this period of care. Other considerations pertaining to emergent care following trauma, however, are equally important in providing a complete and successful therapeutic program. Arrival of the severely burned patient presents many problems common to other types of injury. The burn is obvious but appropriate therapy for other injuries is essential.

The Admission Procedure

Admitting the severely burned victim demands a protocol which will prepare the patient for excellence in care. Table 30-3 lists these procedures and Table 30-4 suggests admission orders. Through years of experience, we know the problems the burned patient will face during hospitalization. *Each of the tasks outlined in the admission procedure is intended to either eliminate a problem or reduce it to manageable proportions*—to lay a foundation on which care is built. Although some considerations may seem unimportant, none are. *No task may be overlooked.* Attention to detail may mean the difference between life and death. This constant attention continues throughout the emergent and acute periods. Research has shown (through the National Burn Information Exchange, a voluntary data registry for burn patient care) that survival of burn patients differs by as much as 80 percent, depending on the hospital in which the patient is treated as demonstrated by Feller, Flora, and Bawol (1976). An efficient, comprehensive approach to care by skilled, knowledgeable practitioners is a most important variable in the difference in survival.

Any efficient procedure requires a plan of action and the necessary supplies on hand. If these measures are taken, the medical staff will have time to consider the patient's emotional and physical condition on admission rather than their own and will not waste precious time scurrying about gathering supplies and providing inappropriate care. Time spent in preparation is never wasted—it is important to have a protocol planned, supplies and equipment available, and a staff trained. Keep a cart, containing all supplies and equipment needed for an admission, always ready. Store it either in the admission area or with sterile supplies to be brought to the admission area. Clean, restock, and return it to the storage area after use. Supplies to be on this cart are listed in Table 30-5. Although each task is listed separately, in practice they are performed simultaneously by several members of the team. For a single admission, the admission procedure may be completed efficiently within 1 h without undue stress to the patient.

First Aid

When administering first aid to any seriously injured patient, *breathing, bleeding,* and *shock* are paramount considerations, usually in the order presented. Infection control technique is essential to all phases of management. Remove all clothing and dressings for a satisfactory appraisal of the extent of the burn as well as of possible associated injuries.

The airway is more frequently a problem with the burned patient than is bleeding. The history of the accident is a good indicator of imminent respiratory difficulty. If the patient was "burned in an enclosed space"—forced to breathe smoke and other products of combustion—there is a strong likelihood of immediate airway involvement. Blackened oral and nasal mucous membranes, singed nasal hairs, and burn injury including the face and neck indicate *impending* airway obstruction. A later part of this chapter discusses respiratory management.

TABLE 30-3
Admission Procedure

Preadmission Activity

Based on the information obtained from the referring physician and the expected time of arrival, take the following steps a few minutes before the patient arrives in the unit:
  Prepare the area to be used for the admission.
  Assign one RN and a helper (LPN, technician, aide, etc.) to the tasks.
  Obtain the proper size and type of bed for the patient.
  Take the admitting cart to the admission area.
  Place the emergency cart near the area (if indicated).
  Prepare the medication tray (see Table 30-5, item 6).
  Set up cleansing, debriding, and dressing supplies and any invasive catheter and specimen trays which will be used.
  Order supportive equipment as needed (respiratory assistance, suction, etc.).

Admission Procedures

Many of these activities will occur simultaneously:
  Evaluate the patient for respiratory distress, bleeding, and responsiveness.
  Initiate appropriate emergency measures to provide an open airway and to stop bleeding.
  Call for the physician if not present.
  Greet the patient by name and introduce yourself.
  Briefly explain what is happening and send the family to the admission office.
  Call the social worker or take time later to meet with the family.
  Move the patient directly to admission area while giving a brief, simple explanation of what to expect during the admission procedure.
  Obtain a brief history from the patient or a reliable family member.
  Record any allergies, illnesses, medications, etc. and immediately report them to the physician.
  Review records sent with the patient; place on chart.
  If IV in place, note type of solution, amount, and flow rate. Put a strip of tape on bottle and mark time and level of solution.
  Remove all clothing and dressings.
  Cover the patient with a sterile sheet.
  Take and record blood pressure, pulse, respirations, and temperature.
  Conduct brief physical examination; begin definitive treatment for other injuries if critical.
  Start IV fluid therapy: Place large-bore (18 gauge for an adult) subclavian, jugular, or cutdown catheter. Begin 1000 mL of 5% dextrose in lactated Ringer's (D_5LR) solution with 25 g human serum albumin or fresh-frozen plasma at a rate to produce

Admission Procedures (Continued)

30 to 60 mL of urine per hour in an adult (correspondingly less in a child, geriatric patient, or patient with heart or lung problems).
Give IV pain medication as needed.
Obtain blood samples for laboratory tests and cultures when inserting IV catheter.
Insert indwelling urinary catheter and connect to drainage.
Measure output.
If catheter already in place, change catheter tubing and bag if indicated.
If changing IV or urinary catheter, culture tips of catheters for possible pathogens.
Insert nasogastric tube, connect to drainage.
Remove all hair in and around the wound, including scalp hair or whiskers if those areas are involved. Shave a 2-in margin around the wound.
Debride and cleanse wound (in hydrotherapy tub if available).
Cleanse all unburned areas (bathe patient).
Obtain urinary, nasopharyngeal and wound cultures.
Weigh the patient and record weight; obtain the patient's preburn weight from the patient or family.
Estimate extent of burn.
Photograph patient.
Move patient from tub, cover with sterile sheet, and prepare for dressings.
Dress the wound.
Obtain chest x-ray and electrocardiogram.
Place patient in bed and position patient properly.

Postadmission—Emergent Period Care

Assign one nurse to postadmission care of the severely burned patient. Physician's orders dictate care; however, generally the nurse's responsibilities are as follows:
  Explain to the patient what may be expected of the medical staff and what will be expected of the patient.
  Answer any questions and prepare the patient for future care.
  Position the patient to reduce the work load of the heart and lungs and to provide comfort (high Fowler's position with arms above level of heart).
  Instruct the patient to cough and deep breathe every 15 to 20 min while awake.
  Alternate position as frequently as possible (every 1 to 2 h).
  Titrate urinary output with IV intake hourly. (Perform bedside urine tests.)
  Check vital signs hourly and compare with those of the previous hour.
  Observe closely for signs of respiratory distress.
  Instruct the family on isolation technique, burn unit routines, what to expect of the patient and medical staff, and what will be expected of them. Take them to the bedside.
In general, structure an environment for the patient which will promote recovery.

TABLE 30-4
Example of Admission Orders
for Burn Patients*

Respiratory Care

Cold steam continuous with oxygen
Chest x-ray on admission (and prn daily or weekly thereafter)
Blood gas analysis for respiratory involvement as indicated; *always* indicated for patients with indoor flame burns (forced inhalation of products of combustion)
Observe for need for aminophylline, steroids, intubation, or tracheostomy
Cough and deep breathing exercises qh

Vital Signs and Organ Systems

BP, pulse, temperature, respirations, CVP qh
Weight (nude) on admission and qd thereafter
Record preburn weight (ask patient or family)
ECG on admission and weekly prn

IV Intake

Resuscitation fluids for first 48 h after burn (titrate: see output)
Lactated Ringer's solution with 5% dextrose, with 25 g albumin added to each 1000 mL
Or titrate with plasma when
   60% TBSA or greater is burned
   Full-thickness burns are over 40% TBSA
   CVP and output are not responding to lactated Ringer's solution with albumin
Fluid resuscitation after first 48 h
   10% dextrose in an *appropriate salt solution* according to topical agent (e.g., $AgNO_3$) and electrolytes
   To each 1000 mL of 10% dextrose in a salt or water solution add 1000 units *heparin, 10 units regular insulin, appropriate amount KCl, and 25 g serum albumin*
   Mannitol, 12.5 or 25 g, for hemo- or myoglobinuria

Output

Urinary catheter to dependent drainage
Maintain urine output at 30 to 50 mL/h (most adults) or 10 to 30 mL/h for children, geriatric patients, and patients with cardiac or pulmonary problems (this is the output part of *titration*)
Measure and record hourly urine output: volume, specific gravity, glucose, acetone, pH, blood
Collect 24-h urine specimen for creatinine clearance, keto- and hydroxysteroids, Na, K, Ca, Cl for 3 days (begin first specimen on admission and restart at 7 A.M. the following day), then every week

Oral Intake

Admission
   NPO (except for antacid)
   Insert nasogastric tube and connect to low suction for 2 days, continue prn
   Clamp NG tube q2h for 1½ h after antacid (e.g., Maalox); connect to suction ½ h q2h; if distended, clamp ½ h after antacid, suction 1½ h
Day 2
   If bowel sounds are present, milk of magnesia via tube to empty colon before removing tube
   Remove NG tube
Day 3
   Magnesium citrate PO after NG tube removed
   Start liquids, progressing to general diet
   Soapsuds enema if necessary (if no BM by 3d day after tube out)

Infection Control

Cubicle isolation for bedside care and tubbing
Aseptic technique for dressing applications and all procedures that penetrate an anatomical barrier
Penicillin, 5 million units IV piggyback (PB) q6h; if penicillin-sensitive, use erythromycin, 1 g IV PB q6h
Pseudomonas vaccine, 0.5 mL SQ on admission and weekly (after skin test with 0.1 mL)
Hyperimmune (*Pseudomonas*) serum 250 mL IV qd (adult), 125 mL IV qd (child)
Tetanus toxoid, 0.5 mL on admission and weekly
Tetanus immune human globulin (Hyper-Tet) 250 units (IM) on admission
Nystatin USP (Nycostatin), 800,000 U (topical), rinse mouth or swab mouth and swallow qid
Lactinex, 1 g, packet (PO) qid (via tube when NPO)
Gamma globulin 5 mL in *each* buttock weekly (adult), 0.1 mL per lb of body weight for child

Medications

Pain control
   Morphine IV (PB) prn for pain on admission; dose by body weight; alternate weekly with equivalent dose of Demerol
Prevent Curling's ulcer
   Maalox × 60 mL via NG tube q2h (see "Oral intake" above)
Heart action
   Digoxin (Lanoxin) 0.5 mg IV on admission, then 0.25 mg IV PB (q8h × 3); then daily maintenance 0.125 to 0.25 mg IV; pediatric dose, 0.2 mg per kg body weight per 24 h then one-quarter digitalizing dose as daily maintenance
   Regular plasma, 1 unit daily, prn for metabolic control
Vitamin and mineral supplements
   Solu B Forte, 1 amp IV PB daily
   Vitamin B_{12}, 100 μg weekly

Medications (Continued)

Magnesium sulfate, 500 mg IM or IV (adult) give twice daily in large burns (50% TBSA or over)
Folic acid, 1 mg IV daily (adult)
Sedation and sleep
  Pentobarbital sodium (Nembutal) IM, hs, prn
  Chlordiazepoxide (Librium), diazepam (Valium), or meprobamate (Miltown) for sedation prn

Laboratory Work

All tests stat on admission, then
  WBC count qd
  Hematocrit q6h for 2 days and then qd
  Na, K, CO_2, Cl, BUN, creatinine clearance on admission and qd for 4 days, then prn
  Total serum protein, albumin, globulin, Ca and P on admission and weekly thereafter
  Blood gas analysis for suspected respiratory involvement
  Wound, urine, nasopharynx or Leukins cultures on admission and weekly thereafter
  Blood type on admission

Wound Care

Referral to ophthalmology for eye injury: Polysporin eye ung q2h if eye involved in face burns

Wound Care (Continued)

Hand splints for suspected deep partial-thickness or full-thickness burns of dorsal surface
Dressings—0.5% silver nitrate q4h; keep wet; hydrotherapy 1 or 2 times daily (*Note:* if patient is hypernatremic, saturate dressings q1–2h to help remove sodium; obtain serum Na levels q12h)
Face care q4–6h (except 11 P.M. to 6 A.M.) with gentamicin ung. and "thirds"; povidone-iodine (Betadine) and peroxide (1:1) ear dressing q4–6h
Observe for need for escharotomy of neck, chest, and extremities

Positioning

Semi-Fowler's position with foot of bed up, hands and arms elevated to heart level or above (down ½ h q2h for patient comfort) for burns of upper body
Prop side to back to side hourly (do not interfere with breathing)
Out of bed as soon as possible

* Modifications in dosage are necessary for children and patients with preexisting diseases, renal failure, or with other problems or complications.

TABLE 30-5
Suggested Admission Cart Supplies and Equipment

1. Specimen collection sets
   Blood tubes
     1 purple
     2 blue
     1 pink
     1 large red
     1 small red
   Culture tubes
     1 wound culture tube with swabs
     1 nasopharyngeal culture tube
     2 urine specimen bottles
     1 blood culture set (special transport media)
   Requisitions and labels
     6 bacteriology
     2 biochemistry (1 & 2)
     1 hematology
     2 coagulation
     1 blood bank
     1 pulmonary function
     1 urinalysis
   Blood culture supplies
     1 tourniquet
     8 syringes: 4 10-mL, 2 20-mL, 2 50-mL
     Needles, 6 assorted sizes
     Clean gloves

2. Intravenous fluids and tubing
   IV fluids
     3 L Hartmann's solution (Ringer's lactate) in 5% glucose
     500 mL Hartmann's solution in 5% glucose
     250 mL Hartmann's solution in 5% glucose
   Tubing
     4 blood tubing with Y connector
     2 buretrols
     1 peditrol (minidrip)
     1 stopcock
     1 anesthesia extension
3. IV infusion and CVP supplies
     1 subclavian tray
     1 adult cutdown tray
     1 pediatric cutdown tray
     2 armboards, 1 each size
     2 pairs gloves, sterile, sizes 7 and 7½
     2 CVP manometers
     2 tourniquets
     4 sizes subclavian catheters
   Skin preparation set
     Surgical sponges and swabs
     250 mL povidone-iodine (Betadine)
     250 mL alcohol

TABLE 30-5 (Continued)
Suggested Admission Cart Supplies and Equipment

Scalp vein needles (various sizes)
1 tube povidone-iodine (Betadine)
Sutures
    6 2–0 with cutting needle
    6 4–0 with needle
Tape: clear plastic
    3 rolls, $\frac{1}{2}$ in wide
    3 rolls, 1 in wide
4. Respiratory care supplies
    Ambu bag and tubing
    Laryngoscope and various blades and bulbs
    Various sizes endotracheal tubes
    Hemostats and syringes
    Curved and straight adaptors
    Tracheostomy tray
5. Charting supplies
    Pen and pencil
    Complete patient chart
    Daily and monthly flow sheet in holder
    Burn estimation sheet
    ECG and x-ray request
    Referral sheet
6. Medications (stored in medication room or refrigerator
    and placed on cart for admission)
    Morphine sulfate, 10 mg
    Secobarbital, 100 mg
    Tetanus toxoid, 0.5 mL
    Hyper-Tet
    Aqueous penicillin, 5 million units
    1 30-mL vial sodium chloride
    1 vial lidocaine (Xylocaine), 1%, without epinephrine
    Diazepam (Valium), 20 mg
    1 tube Cortisporin ointment
    25 g serum albumin
    25 g mannitol
    Frozen plasma, AB negative, 500 mL
    1 syringe
7. Physical examination equipment
    Otoscope and ophthalmoscope
    Stethoscope

Sphygmomanometer with sterile cuffs
Tongue blades
Safety pins
Percussion hammer
Telethermometer and probe
Flashlight (in working order)
8. Urine collection and measuring equipment
    Urinary catheter insertion trays
    Indwelling catheters, sizes 8 to 12
    Drainage tubing
    Urimeter
    Toomey syringe
    Urine testing equipment
    Irrigation set
    Antibiotic ointment
9. Wound debridement and hair cutting supplies
    Disposable razors
    Electric clipper
    Scissors and forceps
    Sponges, 4 in × 4 in
    Plastic bags
    Ring remover
    Soap
    Shaving cream
    Optional wound cleaning supplies:
        2 large basins
        2 boxes 4 in × 4 in dressings
        3 pairs gloves, assorted sizes
        Cotton applicators
        4 L of sterile saline solution
        1 L of detergent solution
        Plastic bags for debris
10. Nasogastric tubes
    Double-lumen NG tubes, 1 adult and 1 child
    1 Toomey syringe
    1 plastic emesis basin
    1 Sims connector
    1 water-soluble lubricant

Hemorrhage, internal as well as external, may be due to associated trauma at the time of injury and should be carefully evaluated and treated as indicated. Burns cause no external bleeding; however, as much as 10 percent of the red blood cell volume may be destroyed by hemolysis from deep thermal injury. Whole-blood requirements, therefore, are limited to approximately 500 mL later in the emergent period in a severely burned patient who does not have associated injuries.

Shock may be neurogenic at first but later is due to extensive and rapid fluid shift. Fluid therapy is designed to control hypovolemic shock resulting from the loss of serum to the extracellular spaces.

Analgesics may be required if the patient is in pain and are *always given intravenously*. Subcutaneous or intramuscular injections pool locally, because of hypotension, and then are suddenly released when the systemic circulation returns to adequate function, resulting in dangerously high blood levels from accumulated doses

After attending to immediate emergent matters and preliminary evaluation, take time to reassure the patient and explain the problems to the family.

Supportive Treatment

Antimicrobial therapy Tetanus toxoid or antitoxin is administered routinely, the choice being dependent upon previous immunizations. Tetanus immune human globulin (Hyper-Tet) is given as additional passive coverage. Prophylactic antibiotic therapy is started on all patients on admission. The dosage which we are currently advising is 5 million units of penicillin (intravenously) daily. If the patient is allergic to penicillin, erythromycin is used. The prophylactic use of antibiotics in burn patients remains a controversial issue. It is our present belief that early infections can be limited by their use.

Initial clinical measurements A routine chest film is obtained on all patients on admission to rule out pulmonary problems as well as confirm correct placement of the subclavian catheter. Other x-ray examinations are performed as indicated. An electrocardiogram (ECG) is indicated as a baseline for any patient with suspected cardiac involvement.

It is helpful to record all injuries photographically when possible. Obtain anterior and posterior views of the burned areas as soon as conditions permit.

Baseline laboratory determinations are important in evaluating the patient's state of health on admission and as a measure of changes due to therapy. A complete blood count (CBC), hematocrit, blood gas analysis, serum sodium and potassium levels, carbon dioxide concentration, blood urea nitrogen (BUN), serum protein level, and wound cultures are obtained on admission and are repeated each day for the first 3 days and as indicated thereafter.

ADMINISTRATION OF FLUIDS

Emergent Period

Principles

The trauma of a severe burn causes many complex systemic changes. The most significant change, which is seen immediately, is the body's normal inflammatory response in which fluids shift out of the intravascular spaces and into the interstitial spaces. The extent of the wound and local changes are visible on the surface. If severe enough, the depth of the wound and systemic changes may cause hypovolemic shock. The goal of initial fluid therapy is to prevent shock by fluid replacement without overloading the vascular system.

The severe burn results in an outer layer of dead tissue and a deeper band or zone of damaged cells. The dead tissue is not important in immediate fluid treatment, but the zone of damaged tissue below it is extremely important. It is here that plasma leaks from the injured vessels into the interstitial and intracellular spaces, resulting in edema.

The red blood cells stay within the vessel, resulting in a high hematocrit. The loss of fluid through the eschar into the dressings or the air is insignificant during the first few days compared with the volume that passes into the burned area. When the burn is greater than 20 percent of the total body surface area and a large injured tissue space is created, a large plasma loss occurs during the first day and continues at a lesser rate for another day or two. When the fluid replacement has been adequate, the process reverses itself, and much of the fluid returns to the vascular space during the following days. If excessive fluids have been given and large amounts of fluid return to the vascular space suddenly during this period of time, hypervolemia, hypernatremia, congestive heart failure, and pulmonary edema may result. The goal of fluid therapy for severely burned patients is to avoid hypovolemic shock during the first few days of therapy and to prevent hypervolemic complications.

Each patient should be given the quantity and quality of fluid required to compensate for the losses sustained during the first few days. The rate of loss and the depth of burn cannot be predicted or measured and herein lies the weakness of formulas. Formulas attempt to predict a specific volume requirement for each patient.

In order to meet fluid therapy objectives it is important to determine which patients require fluid therapy, the type of fluid to be given, and the amount of fluid that should be given.

Which patients require fluid therapy? Not all burned patients require fluid therapy. If the burn involves less than 20 percent of the total body surface, intravenous therapy may not be necessary. Generally, fluid therapy is indicated when the total area burned is greater than 20 percent of the body surface area, the patient's age is less than 4 years or more than 35 years, or there are individual considerations such as dehydration, past medical problems, or concurrent injuries.

What type of fluid should be given? The type of fluid lost from the bloodstream into tissues is essentially plasma. It is necessary, therefore, to replace this fluid with plasma or a plasmalike substitute. A variety of fluids have been advocated, but a balanced salt solution with plasma or protein added is generally used. Hartmann's (lactated Ringer's) solution is a good solution because it contains electrolytes in concentrations approximating those in the blood. Serum albumin (25 to 50 g) may be added to each liter to supply the protein to make a plasmalike solution. Fresh-frozen, blood-type-specific plasma may also be used.

How much fluid should be given? The amount of fluid required varies, depending on extent and depth of burn and the patient's age and past medical history. Each patient requires individual consideration. The correct amount of fluid is that which achieves maintenance of normal blood pressure and urinary output without overloading the vascular system. The method of monitoring this fluid therapy is termed *titration*.

Titration

Titration is defined in burn care as the amount of intravenous fluid input required to produce a predetermined amount of urinary output. During the emergent period, intravenous fluids are administered in amounts to maintain (titrate) urinary output at 30 to 60 mL/h for adults and 10 to 30 mL/h for children or elderly patients. It is important to note certain special precautions: lesser amounts are necessary for infants, very young children, the aged, and patients with respiratory or renal problems or congestive heart failure. The physician should order the range desired.

This amount of hourly urine output indicates that there is fluid volume replacement adequate to perfuse all organ systems and thereby combat hypovolemia and prevent shock as measured by kidney (renal) function. Maintaining output over these amounts risks fluid overload, increased cardiac output, increased interstitial edema, congestive heart failure, wet-lung syndrome, and renal failure. Too much is as lifethreatening as too little.

Other parameters of titration, in addition to urinary output, are blood pressure, pulse, central venous pressure (CVP) and/or pulmonary artery pressure (PAP); these measurements are taken hourly.

Recording the preburn weight and accurate daily nude weights also serves as a useful parameter. Each liter of fluid retained results in a 2.2-lb weight gain. The total weight gained in the first few days of fluid therapy must not exceed 10 to 15 percent of the patient's total body weight.

Mannitol is used *only* when hematuria or hemoglobinuria (black urine), indicating impending acute tubular necrosis, is evident on catheterization. Usually 6 to 12 g is given intravenously, and it is rarely necessary to repeat the dose of mannitol.

Hematocrit values are utilized to determine hemoconcentration. Determinations are repeated every 6 h during the first day and as often as indicated thereafter. The hematocrit rises immediately after a burn injury, and as the patient responds to fluid therapy, the hemoconcentration dilutes to normal and then falls below normal as a result of hemolysis and anemia.

Procedure for titration The nurse new to burn care may be confused by the titration procedure. There are no hard, fast rules governing the amount of input needed to obtain a desired output. The amount varies with each patient, and you will learn with experience to be comfortable with the procedure. The order may be written as "IV flow rate to maintain urinary output at 30 to 60 mL/h." You can gauge present intake by the amount of intake required to maintain output during the admission procedure and the patient's response from the previous hour (see Fig. 30-5). Frequent, accurate adjustments of IV flow rate are *essential* to maintain the predetermined hourly urine output. An adult with a negative medical history may require as much as 500 to 1000 mL of solution per hour in the early period of therapy to titer output, while severity factors may dictate an intake as low as 150 mL in an infant or geriatric patient. Use the following guidelines for titration.

Maintain constant vigilance.

Make accurate hourly measurements of intake and output—*no "fudging" or guessing*! Put a strip of tape along the increment markings on the IV bottle and write on the hourly amounts. Use an IV measuring chamber (e.g., Buretrol) and a urine measuring chamber (e.g., Urimeter).

Do not record an amount as infused until it actually has been infused.

If urine output increases over that of the previous hour or rises above the desired amount, slow the IV rate.

If urine output decreases from that of the previous hour or falls below the desired amount, speed the IV rate.

Check for a plugged urinary catheter and irrigate (with a small amount of measured fluid) if output falls significantly with seemingly adequate intake.

Evaluate output in light of other parameters: blood pressure, pulse, CVP, PAP, hematocrit, and weight.

DATE	12 Midnite	1am	2am	3am	4am	5am	6am	7am		
TEMPERATURE		98⁶	98⁶	98⁴	98⁴	98⁶	99	99⁶		
PULSE		100	120	120	116	100	96	92		
RESP.		28	28	32	24	24	20	20		
B.P.		110/80	100/70	100/70	110/70	120/80	124/80	124/60		
C.V.P.		0	0	0	0	0	0	1		
HEMATOCRIT		64						60		
INTAKE ORAL		ice chips					ice chips		50 ml.	
DEXTROSE										
SALINE										
HARTMAN'S (+25 Gm. Alb. per L.)		1000	750	700	500	250	200	200	3600	
OTHER										
BLOOD										
PLASMA										
HYPERIMMUNE SERUM										
								8 hrs TOTAL	3650	
OUTPUT URINE		12	30	40	55	40	30	30	237	
EMESIS										
OTHER/STOOL										
								8 hrs TOTAL	237	
SPECIFIC GRAVITY		1.005	1.008	1.015	1.016	1.012	1.008	1.008		
SUGAR/ACETONE		N/N	TR/TR	TR/TR	TR/TR	N/N	N/N	N/N		
PROTEIN/PH		TR/6.5	TR/6.5				→/	N/6.5		

FIGURE 30-5

Titration of fluid therapy; excerpt from a patient's chart. A 50-year-old male was burned on 50 percent of his total body surface area at 10:35 P.M. He was admitted at 12:15 A.M. The chart monitors this patient's satisfactory response to therapy in the first 8 h after admission.

Notify the physician if the output is less than 30 mL/h or over 60 mL/h for adults, is less than 10 mL/h or over 30 mL/h for children, or does not respond to adjustments in flow rate within 1 to 2 h.

Once the patient has been successfully resuscitated and capillary permeability returns to normal, fluids will be returned to the intravascular spaces and a profuse diuresis will occur. This signals the end of the emergent period. At this time, the rate of fluid administration is reduced and fluids are switched to glucose in water to compensate for the fluid and electrolytes, primarily sodium, returning to the vascular spaces.

Acute Period

During the acute period of care, the adult patient with a large ungrafted wound will require an open IV line with an average infusion rate of 1000 to 1500 mL per 24 h. The types and amounts of fluids patients require depend on their metabolic balance. It is the responsibility of the nurse to calculate the amounts the patient is to receive each hour and to regulate the flow rate accordingly.

Blood and blood products are administered as needed. Whole blood, which is approximately 45 percent cellular (hematocrit) and 55 percent plasma, is required to replace losses through bleeding during wound debridement, from hemolysis due to the burn injury or sepsis, or blood loss through coagulopathies and hemorrhage. Burned patients should always receive fresh blood that is not more than 3 days old because (1) the clotting factors are more effective in fresh blood, (2) older blood may contain a higher potassium concentration due to hemolysis, and (3) the oxygen-carrying efficiency is decreased in older blood.

Packed cells obtained through centrifuging whole blood to draw off plasma (plasmapheresis) are given to replace red blood cell loss in anemia, to replace red blood cells lost through marrow depression, or when there is a danger of circulatory overload from whole-blood therapy, e.g., in the patient with present or impending congestive heart failure.

Care of Intravenous Catheter Site

Because the patient's natural immunity is depressed as a result of the burn injury, the site chosen for intravenous infusion (or any percutaneous catheter site) requires special care. A popular site at present is the subclavian vein because it allows insertion of a large-diameter catheter, freedom of the extremities, and the most accurate venous pressure assessment. However, many authorities are returning to peripheral lines because of the multitude of iatrogenic complications, primarily infection, possible with a central line. Preparation of the site is most important to prevent contamination. A burn wound site may be used if necessary.

A skin preparation procedure is given here to emphasize its importance. Shave the area if necessary. Wash the site with surgical soap and rinse thoroughly, using water for a wound, and alcohol for an unburned area. Apply povidone-iodine (Betadine) and allow to dry. Finally, repeat alcohol rinse and Betadine.

If a central line is inserted, the catheter should be sutured to the site to prevent dislodgement, and a chest x-ray is necessary to detect proper placement and rule out pneumothorax. You must also observe respirations and monitor fluids closely until x-ray confirms correct placement. The puncture site requires that a sterile dressing with antibiotic ointment or topical agent be applied over the site, and the site is observed for bleeding.

Daily care of the catheter site is also important to check infection. Examine the site daily for signs of inflammation and bleeding. Change the catheter every

7 days, more frequently if there are signs of systemic infection or local infection at site (alternate sites). Cleanse the site daily with soap and water or Betadine. Apply a sterile dressing over site. Cut a 4-in by 4-in gauze pad (similar to "trach pants"), saturate in Betadine, and apply to (around) catheter site if in wound. Culture the catheter tip on removal. Prepare the skin as noted above before removal if culturing tip.

In addition, daily care of tubing and equipment is also important. Use aseptic technique for all IV procedures and maintain IV tubing as a closed system! Change all IV tubing including manometer and stopcock for CVP every 24 h, more often if there is any contamination. Tape connections on tubing to avoid separation. Discard any IV solution which has been hanging for 24 h or is suspected of being contaminated. Note on all bottles the date and time the solution was mixed and hung.

Monitoring Urinary Output

General Principles

The kidneys perform a major role in regulating the electrolyte and fluid balance and in the excretion of waste products. Accurate measuring and testing of urine is crucial in assessing the patient's overall condition. During the period immediately following the burn injury, urinary output is an effective guide to replacement fluid therapy. Throughout the acute period of care, urinary output reflects the patient's general systemic response to the injury and therapy. An indwelling catheter is inserted when the area involved exceeds 20 percent of the total body surface area (10 percent in children), when the perineum is included in the burn, or when there are complications or problems in the medical history. Keep in mind that an indwelling urinary catheter penetrates an anatomical barrier. Therefore, aseptic technique is essential in any procedure involving a catheter. Also, remember that the catheter drains by gravity. The tubing must be coiled above the collector.

Hourly Urine Testing

Hourly testing of urine helps determine the function of the kidney, the fluid and electrolyte balance of the body, as well as the systemic response to stress and therapy. Monitoring the urine during care provides another parameter to assess the patient's condition.

Volume The amount of urine output varies with intake, condition of the cardiovascular system, kidneys, etc. A daily output of 1200 mL is considered average. Below 400 mL in 24 h indicates oliguria and possible renal failure; over 2000 mL daily (polyuria) may indicate high output failure. Intervention should take place before anuria as this indicates a grave prognosis. Dialysis is of little use to the burn victim unless initiated at the first signs of azotemia.

Specific gravity (SG) Urine is composed of approximately 95 percent water and 5 percent wastes. Measuring the specific gravity indicates the amount of waste in relationship to the water in the urine (the specific gravity of water is 1.000) and helps signal metabolic changes, and may indicate either the need for or an excess of fluid therapy. The normal specific gravity of urine fluctuates between 1.002 and 1.035, depending on the amount of fluid intake, type of food eaten, etc. A fixed specific gravity, e.g., 1.008 to 1.012, in spite of intake, indicates kidney disease and demands treatment.

Protein The amount of protein normally excreted by the kidneys is negligible; therefore, this test should be negative. If the body is burning tissue protein rather than food, e.g., is in negative nitrogen balance as are the majority of severely burned patients, protein will be present in the urine and the test will be positive. Protein in urine may be considered normal when the patient is NPO for long periods of time but keep in mind positive protein is also seen in kidney disease such as glomerulonephritis, and it should be reported when first noted.

pH Testing the pH of the urine helps monitor the acid-base balance of the body. Report anything over 7 or under 6.

Sugar Normally, urine contains no sugar; therefore, this test should be negative. If the test for sugar is positive, it may indicate either that the body is not utilizing ingested glucose, or it may indicate diabetes or pseudodiabetes, which is a symptom of stress seen in burn victims, or both. Report a positive sugar when first read, as daily insulin may be necessary to compensate for the inability of the pancreas to meet the insulin needs of the burn patient during stress.

Acetone Acetone is normally negative in the urine. A positive reading may indicate that the body is burning its own fats and proteins because of starvation (NPO) or lack of proper dietary intake, or that the oxidation of fats is not being carried to completion. Children frequently show acetone during the period of initial stress.

Color or sediment Normal urine is clear and yellow, or straw colored. Discoloring may be due to drugs, and cloudiness is not necessarily abnormal, but both should be recorded and reported. Bright red urine usually indicates lower urinary tract bleeding. When certain topical or systemic drugs are used, however, they may be broken down and excreted by the kidneys, causing a discolored urine. Brown or black urine indicates metabolized blood and possible severe renal damage. When brown urine is seen on admission, massive hemolysis and kidney damage are likely. *Report immediately,* as an osmotic diuretic is indicated stat to flush the tubules. Green to dark green urine may indicate frank *Pseudomonas* infection. Report any abnormal color or sediment on first reading and on continuation.

Blood In addition to the above, red blood cells are not normally present in the urine. A positive reading in the burn patient may indicate hemolysis from initial injury or from septic shock.

Dialysis

The indications for dialysis are oliguria, unrelieved azotemia, and an increase in blood potassium concentrations with ECG changes in the patient with impending or acute renal failure. Hypernatremia and severe acidosis are also indicators. When impending renal failure cannot be reversed by fluid and electrolyte therapy and diuretics, dialysis may be the only hope.

The goals of dialysis are to assist in removing toxic substances and metabolic wastes, to decrease excessive body fluids, and to balance body fluids. Both peritoneal dialysis and hemodialysis penetrate an anatomical barrier and require absolute aseptic technique. Dialysis, however, is useless if not initiated before the kidney is actually damaged!

Peritoneal dialysis is rarely used in extensive burns and certainly only if there is no damage to the skin on or near the abdomen. Hemodialysis is more frequently employed. An artificial kidney may be used to perform the clearance function of the normal kidney. In most situations, a specially trained dialysis team will prepare the dialysis solution, perform the dialysis procedure, and care for the equipment. The burn nurse will be expected to assess the patient's general condition, report any significant changes before and after dialysis, and assist with placement and care of the arteriovenous (AV) shunt.

After dialysis, record vital signs every 2 h until stable. Be alert for signs of complications, such as orthostatic hypotension, fever, chills, fatigue, lethargy, rebound anticoagulation (possible hemorrhage), and adverse psychological reactions. Report these immediately.

RESPIRATORY CARE

Introduction to the Problem

More than 90 percent of severely burned patients require some form of respiratory therapy. Therefore, burn care includes an awareness of the principles and procedures required for effective ventilation; a working knowledge of pulmonary function, of ventilators, and of other equipment; and above all, an ongoing dialogue with the respiratory therapists. In the last few years respiratory therapy has become a science, and the nurse cannot be expected to be knowledgeable in all aspects of this care. However, it is important to remember that new developments do not replace basic nursing.

Pulmonary complications may be grouped into those that occur within the first 24 to 48 h as a result of the accident and those that occur any time after that. Immediate complications include upper airway obstruction secondary to edema of the face, neck, mouth, pharynx, and larynx and primary pulmonary damage from forced inhalation of products of combustion, such as smoke, gases, noxious chemicals, etc. The second group of complications includes pulmonary insufficiency secondary to shock, trauma, and increased lung water due to overhydration or secondary to extensive injury characterized by alveolar collapse. Other complications include pneumonia and pulmonary embolism. These complications may occur any time after a burn injury. Embolism, if seen, is usually a late occurrence.

The treatment of these complications varies widely from basic nursing care measures to maintenance of respirations through an artificial upper airway by a mechanical ventilator. The basic principle of respiratory therapy is to *assist or support the patient's ventilation, without causing additional complications, until the patient has resumed effective spontaneous ventilation.*

Immediate Respiratory Complications

Observations

The respiratory complications resulting directly from the accident are either upper airway obstruction or primary pulmonary damage. Little can be done to prevent immediate respiratory distress. However, merely "observing" the patient for signs and symptoms, or "watchful waiting," can be fatal.

Definitive signs and symptoms may not be apparent during the first several hours after burn or until edema forms. Stridor (a shrill, harsh respiratory sound) is a fairly late symptom of obstruction. Early chest x-rays frequently show no abnormality. *Arterial hypoxemia may be the first sign of pulmonary insufficiency.*

The following signs indicate probable respiratory involvement; the presence of one or more indicates the need for immediate action: a history of forced inhalation of products of combustion (e.g., burned in a house fire or an explosion); burns of the face, especially around the nose and mouth, or of the neck and upper chest; singed nasal hairs; darkened oral and nasal mucous membranes; and coughing up of darkened sputum.

Management

Principles The principles of care are to ensure a patent airway and to maintain adequate ventilation. This may be accomplished by providing humidified oxygen with a face mask, or it may require an artificial airway such as an endotracheal tube for severe upper airway obstruction or a tracheostomy for primary pulmonary damage. If the trauma has affected the alveoli, treatment is difficult. Steroids, antibiotics, and bronchodilators will also be indicated.

Procedure The steps discussed here may be taken to decrease the seriousness of respiratory involvement and to pave the way for proper clinical management. If one or more of the signs of respiratory involvement are present, elevate the patient's head and torso (if systolic BP is not below 100 mmHg) to ensure a patent airway, set up intratracheal suction at the bedside, place a laryngoscope and endotracheal tube and supplies near the bedside, and have a tracheostomy tray and tubes at hand. Start measured humidified oxygen (over 40 percent by Venturimask, as arterial blood gases will be assessed in light of FI_{O_2}) and obtain specimens for arterial blood gas analysis. Instruct the patient to cough and deep breathe every 20 min. Begin an hourly turning schedule from side to back to side. Begin intermittent positive pressure breathing (IPPB) (if indicated). Watch for any signs of cerebral depression and keep narcotics at a minimum to prevent a decrease in cerebral response. Observe for tight chest or neck eschar and perform an escharotomy as soon as indicated. (See discussion of debridement later in this chapter.) Monitor resuscitation fluids, respirations, and other vital signs closely. Begin pulmonary artery pressure monitoring only if absolutely necessary.

Upper airway obstruction will decrease as edema subsides and trauma to tissues of the upper airway is resolved. With proper management, this problem will not require long-term care. Deep lung damage, however, cannot be resolved as quickly and may prove fatal. The symptoms of primary pulmonary damage are similar to those of respiratory distress and failure, and treatment is similar. The principles of care that follow provide a basis for management of all pulmonary complications.

Pulmonary Insufficiency

Pathogenesis

The burned patient is predisposed to the second group of complications (those which may occur other than as a direct result of the accident) by a number of factors which may not immediately appear to be related to pulmonary problems. If these factors are recognized and better controlled, the incidence of pulmonary complications can be reduced. The predisposing factors are as follows:

Hypovolemic shock and fluid therapy. Titration, if not properly managed or if combined with primary pulmonary damage, leads to overhydration and stiff, wet lungs due to pulmonary interstitial edema.

A general lowered resistance to infection due to decreased immunity, nutritional imbalances, protein losses, continuous wound infections, etc.

Stasis of secretions due to prolonged bedrest, infrequent turning and positioning, and to limited activity.

Principles of Respiratory Care

The following general principles of care underlie prevention as well as management of early and late pulmonary complications. These measures alone may not be adequate to maintain oxygenation, ventilation, and acid-base balance; an artificial upper airway and mechanical respiratory support may be required.

Recognize early clinical signs of respiratory distress When assessing the degree of pulmonary involvement and possible insufficiency, keep in mind that the clinical signs and symptoms are also those of many other problems. Do not overlook the subtle changes that may be the first indications of insufficiency. Be especially alert to insidious changes in respiratory rate and volume. Note a change in the rate of breathing to over 20 (tachypnea) or under 8 (bradypnea) respirations per minute, any irregular breathing patterns, difficulty in breathing (dyspnea), or cessation of breathing (apnea). Chest pain or a change in the amount, color, or consistency of sputum may indicate a problem. A change in pulse rate or blood pressure may be significant, and any anxiety and restlessness should be noted. Cyanosis and stridor are a crude guide. By the time cyanosis is detected, oxygenation problems are already well under way. Therefore, authorities agree that frequent blood gas analysis is mandatory at the first suspicion of pulmonary insufficiency.

Monitor blood gases frequently Blood gas analysis is mandatory in assessing pulmonary function. Basically, blood gases are analyzed to determine the effectiveness of gas exchange and arterial oxygen tension (Pa_{O_2}) in the lungs and to evaluate the acid-base status of the patient through measurement of the hydrogen ion concentration (pH) and bicarbonate (HCO_3^-) concentration level. The accepted normal values are shown in Table 30-6.

Blood gas analysis is indicated when there is suspicion of respiratory involvement on admission or any clinical change (e.g., hypotension, unusual cardiac arrhythmias, restlessness, or agitation) in the patient. For patients on artificial ventilation, blood gases are analyzed 20 min following any ventilator setting changes which would alter such measurements as minute ventilation or Pa_{O_2} and during the weaning period. In assessing blood gas values it is important to indicate the inspired oxygen concentration or FI_{O_2} (e.g., room air, 24 percent by Venturimask, nasal prongs 2 L/min) and whether the patient is on assisted ventilation.

If the patient is on a respirator at the time the gases are drawn, record the setting of flow rates, percentage of oxygen, and tidal volume when the gases are drawn to aid in evaluation. Consider arterial blood gas samples as emergency specimens—the results are called to the unit at the completion of the studies. Be sure to use aseptic technique and to compress arterial puncture sites for at least 5 min and longer for patients

TABLE 30-6
Normal Blood Gas Values

	Arterial blood	Mixed venous blood
Respiratory Component		
pH	7.40 (7.35–7.45)	7.36 (7.31–7.41)
Pa_{O_2}	80–100 mmHg	35–40 mmHg
O_2 saturation	95% or greater	70–75%
P_{CO_2}	35–45 mmHg	41–51 mmHg
Metabolic Component		
HCO_3^-	22–26 meq/L	22–26 meq/L
Base excess (BE)	−2 to +2	−2 to +2

with bleeding disorders (thrombocytopenia, disseminated intravascular coagulation, patients on anticoagulants, etc.). Flush arterial lines with heparinized solution if gases are drawn through a catheter.

Keep lung water as close to normal as possible Extravascular water accumulates in the lungs for a variety of reasons. If there has been significant inhalation of noxious gases at the time of injury, there will be pulmonary interstitial edema. Toxins released from injured burn tissue are also thought to contribute to wet lungs. In addition, fluids required for initial resuscitation also increase interstitial edema in the lungs. Overhydration results in stiff, wet lungs. Use of colloids (e.g., salt-poor albumin and plasma) for initial resuscitation, however, tends to decrease lung water extravasation. Ultrasonic nebulization can also contribute to wet lungs and consideration of this factor should dictate use of the device.

Monitor IV fluids carefully. (See the discussion of fluid therapy earlier in this chapter for instruction on careful IV fluid monitoring.) Whenever regulating fluid balance, keep in mind the possibility of circulatory overload and pulmonary insufficiency.

Establish and maintain a turning schedule. Inadequate positioning can also add to lung water. Only one-sixth of the lung capacity is filled with each respiration. If the patient is forced to remain in one position for longer than 1 h, the same area of the lungs is aerated with each breath. If this continues, blood will be shunted through nonaerated lung and will be poorly oxygenated. The result will be a decrease of oxygen to body tissues (hypoxemia) and an increased number of respirations (tachypnea). There will be a decrease of alveolar elasticity, water will accumulate in the lungs, atelectasis (alveolar collapse) takes place, and stiff, wet lungs result. Susceptibility to infection is increased, as is vulnerability to a variety of other complications, including pulmonary edema, congestive heart failure, renal failure, and acid-base imbalances. These factors increase lung water even more.

One nursing measure which can decrease the severity of wet-lung syndrome is *frequent change of position*. No patient, including those on ventilators or IPPB machines, should be forced to remain in the same position for longer than 1 h. Position changes include turning side to back to side, alternating the level of the head of the bed from the highest to a semi-Fowler's position, and turning the patient on their abdomen every 3 to 4 h using the CircOlectric bed. If the patient is on a ventilator, be sure enough tubing is available so that pressure is not put on the IV or tracheostomy tube when turning. During the emergent period keep the patient in a high Fowler's position and elevate the upper extremities above the level of the heart.

Postural drainage is another effective method of providing pulmonary drainage. Figure 30-6 illustrates the basic postural drainage positions. Because of the location of their wounds, many burned patients cannot tolerate all of these positions. However, each can be modified to benefit the patient. Incorporate postural drainage into position changes. Postural drainage is also indicated after extubation.

Encourage the patient to take deep breaths and cough every 15 to 20 min. Tell the patient early in their care why this is important and establish a contract. Soon deep breathing will become a habit.

IPPB enhances, but does not replace, position change and cough and deep breathing exercises. Administer IPPB *before* postural drainage and cough and deep breathing exercises. (See contraindications above, e.g., congestive heart failure.)

Maintain good nutritional balance The diaphragm is a skeletal muscle and is susceptible to wasting as the result of the catabolic processes of the burn and a poor protein intake. Ensure adequate daily intake of a high-calorie, high-protein diet.

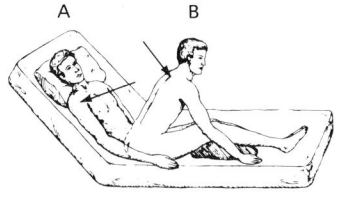

Upper lobes: (A) Apical segment (anterior)
(B) Apical segment (posterior)

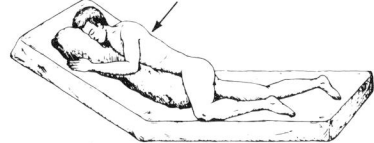

Left upper lobe: Posterior segment

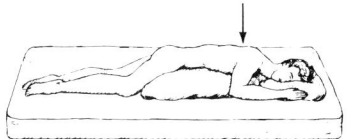

Right upper lobe: Posterior segment

Upper lobes: Anterior segments

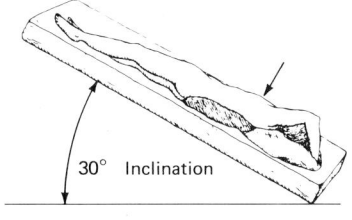

Lingular process (roll to right side)
Right middle lobe (roll to left side)

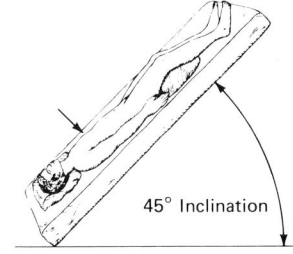

Lower lobes: Anterior basal segment

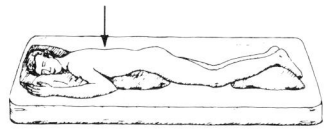

Lower lobes: Apical segments

FIGURE 30-6

Postural drainage. Modifications of postural drainage should be incorporated into hourly position changes. (Check with the physician before applying postural drainage techniques.) Dressings are not removed. Use clean gloved hand for percussion; if gloves cause inefficient cupping, use clean hand. The arrows indicate areas to be percussed in the position shown. The CircOlectric bed may enhance positioning. These positions may also be adapted for children while they are held in the lap.

Limit infection   An entire procedure manual could be devoted to controlling infection. Obviously, once pneumonitis is added to pulmonary problems, therapy becomes much more difficult. Strict aseptic technique is necessary in all procedures that penetrate an anatomical barrier, e.g., insertion of tubes, suctioning, and drawing blood gases. Clean (isolation) technique is necessary for all other procedures. Infection cannot be eliminated, but it can be controlled! The respiratory therapy department is responsible for daily change of equipment and terminal cleaning. However, the nursing staff must accept some responsibility for daily handling of equipment. When equipment (in-line filters, mouthpieces, etc.) is not in use, place it in a clean wrapper or plastic bag rather than draping it over the bedside or stand. A good rule is to dispose of and replace or clean equipment before reuse.

INFECTION CONTROL

Principles of Infection Control

The patient, the medical and nursing staffs, the equipment and supplies, the air conditioning, and the housekeeping methods all interact in both the spread and the control of infection. Traditionally, the responsibility for monitoring and controlling infection has fallen to the nurse. Today, however, this responsibility is multifaceted and must be shared by many. Infection control is one of the primary goals of burn care.

Infection is one of the most devastating complications a burned patient faces. Fifty percent of all burned patients who die, do so from infection. Infection has numerous consequences. It can cause pain and nutritional imbalance. Bacterial invasion may cause partial-thickness wounds to become full-thickness wounds or may result in graft rejection, both of which necessitate additional grafting procedures. Infection can also result in delayed healing, scars, contracture, and prolonged hospitalization. Septicemia and death are even more costly consequences. All infection complications result not only in a drain on the patient's metabolic and emotional resources but also in a greater cost to the patient and family in terms of time, financial strain, and chronic problems after discharge from the hospital. For the medical staff, these complications necessitate long hours of detailed care and follow-up. The tangible effects can be measured in time and money spent in medications, treatments, and procedures. The intangible consequences, such as pain, worry, and apathy, which add to the emotional stress of the patient and all those concerned with patient care, are of even greater relevance in the assessment of the need for a good infection control program.

As important as elimination of infection may be, both to the recovery of the patient and to the preservation of energy among the medical staff, a sterile environment cannot be achieved, nor is it a worthwhile goal, because bacteria play an important role in our existence. The struggle is more precisely defined as a campaign to control infection that demands constant caution and refinement of technique in all aspects of burn care.

The principles of controlling infection are the (1) elimination of reservoirs of infection, (2) suppression of infection transfer channels, (3) support of the patient's natural immunity, and (4) judicious use of antimicrobials.

Elimination of reservoirs of infection Elimination of reservoirs of infection begins with the patient, who is autocontaminated by the bacteria in the gastrointestinal (GI) and upper respiratory tracts, on the unburned skin, and in the hairy areas of the body. In addition, the burn wound provides an ideal medium for bacterial growth; it offers bacteria food, warmth, and moisture. The patient's general environment represents a giant reservoir of potential infection. Other patients, dressings, wounds, linen, trash, equipment, sinks, utensils, etc. are all possible reservoirs, as are personnel and visitors. Excellent wound care, basic hygiene, housekeeping, and personnel cleanliness are indispensible in eliminating reservoirs of infection.

Suppression of infection transfer channels Cross contamination—the transfer of pathogens from an infection source or reservoir to the patient—is probably the greatest threat to the infection control program. Cubicle isolation and aseptic technique are time-tested methods of preventing cross contamination.

Support of the patient's natural immunity Support of the patient's immune mechanisms involves reinforcement of the patient's natural and acquired immunity. This may be accomplished by basic nursing care measures concerning diet, rest, hygiene, positioning, and emotional support and by vaccines, serums, and globulins that may be specific or nonspecific for particular organisms.

Judicious use of antimicrobials Judicious use of topical and systemic antimicrobials (antibiotics and chemotherapeutics) is one of the most important factors in assisting the body's resistance to invasive infection. These agents are effective when properly used because they are harmful in one way or another to microbes but are less harmful to viable tissues. Disinfectants, which may be bacteriostatic or bactericidal, are also toxic to the body. Use of antimicrobials requires consideration of the interactions which will occur between the host, the microbes, and the antibiotic.

Planning and Maintaining an Infection Control Unit

Before discussion of the various procedures for controlling infection, it is worthwhile to consider the environment in which these procedures are to be accomplished. *No effective infection control program can take place in a chaotic or poorly planned environment, nor can apathetic or uneducated personnel be expected to be responsible for the effectiveness of infection control.*

Environment

A detailed plan and the supplies and equipment necessary for its execution are essential before an infection control program can be undertaken. The philosophy of the directors of care will probably dictate the methods to be used. Some use the latest techniques of laminar flow units and a program of patient sterilization, while others use strict or modified, reverse precaution isolation techniques; each depending on the floor plan, methods of care, etc. We make no recommendations other than to urge that a great deal of thought and planning go into choosing a method.

Patient care areas, such as cubicles, wound care areas, and other treatment areas; patient support areas, such as storage rooms, housekeeping areas, handwash sinks, and clean and dirty utility rooms; and personnel areas, such as visitor and personnel changing rooms, lounges, and conference areas, must be planned in detail. Supplies and equipment must be identified, properly stored, and constantly inventoried. *Planning and Designing a Burn Care Facility* (Feller and Crane, National Institute for Burn Medicine, 1973) and *Isolation Technique for Hospitals* (United States Public Health Service, Publication No. 2054) are suggested as resources for planning an environment for infection control. Maintaining this environment once it has been established requires constant vigilance and is the responsibility of all involved in care.

Personnel

The patient's life depends on the actions of all those involved in care; therefore, all personnel coming into contact with the patient or the patient care area are responsible for maintaining and monitoring the principles and practices of infection control. It is the responsibility of the physicians, the nursing staff, and the directors of departments that provide services to acquaint their staff with the infection control program and to enforce this code. Breaks in technique are called to the attention of the person and corrected at the time. No one should feel that corrections are a personal attack. Observing the infection control code is an important part of everyone's obligation to provide the best care to the patient. Frequent or continued disregard for infection control practices are reported to the director of the unit or the head nurse, who will take the necessary steps to correct or discontinue the service of those who disregard these principles.

An initial training program in infection control is essential for all personnel, from janitors to physicians, as well as for visitors. Staff members must be trained in the principles of infection control to the degree needed for their performance before they can be expected to follow these principles. A continuous reinforcement program is also essential.

The nursing staff shoulders the greatest burden of infection control because they provide care 24 h a day. Through education, practice, and example, infection control should become a normal part of the thinking process for all involved. Infection control is one aspect of the burn care philosophy which demands that each person develop a *surgical conscience,* that is, a strong sense of what is correct and necessary to maximize each patient's chance of survival. A table on aseptic technique is included to emphasize its importance (Table 30-7).

Wound Infection and Clinical Sepsis

The battle against invasive infection begins when the severely burned patient is admitted. The burning agent has produced an avascular area made up of nonviable material called *eschar.* The permeability of blood vessels in this area has been altered, and edema forms. Potential pathogens are in the patient's normal flora as well as in the hospital environment. There is a great likelihood that these pathogens will be transferred from their reservoirs to the burn wound, which provides an ideal climate for bacterial growth, the outcomes of which may be wound infection, septicemia, pneumonia, and eventually death. In addition, research has shown that burn patients have a decrease in effectiveness of white blood cells, protein is used for wound healing, and if proper basic supportive care is not provided, the patient is soon further debilitated!

Wound Infection

The burn wound can never be completely sterile; some degree of infection is expected. However, once bacterial growth in the wound exceeds 100,000 organisms per gram of wound tissue, the patient is said to have a wound infection. An infected wound does not look clean—purulence, debris, and odor are present.

Treatment　Prevention of a wound infection is the primary goal. Although these steps to prevent infection are discussed in detail in other parts of this chapter, they are repeated here for emphasis. During admission, the procedures for reducing wound infection are to cleanse the entire wound of all debris, loose tissue, and/or products of combustion; debride all loose tissue; shave all hairy areas in or near the wound, and clip scalp hair on unburned scalp; and bathe the entire body.

TABLE 30-7
Principles and Applications of Aseptic Technique

Principle	Guide to maintaining asepsis	Examples of contamination
1. An article that is sterile remains so until it is contaminated.	Do not use unsterile objects for sterile procedures. Discard any contaminated object and replace as necessary. Do not touch the innermost side of bottle caps on sterile solutions (e.g., eye drops, topical agents) or sterile wrapper. The outer side of a cap or wrapper is unsterile and may be touched with an ungloved hand.	Touching a sterile item to any unsterile object. Dropping an item on the floor. Holes in gowns, gloves, and drapes signify contamination. Touching the inside of a sterile bottle cap or sterile wrapper. Touching eyedropper tip to eye when giving eye drops. Pouring solutions from a bottle held too close to the basin, allowing splashing.
2. Once a sterile item touches a contaminated surface it is unsterile. A sterile item or field can become contaminated as follows:		
a. By becoming *wet* if the underlying area is unsterile.	Use care when pouring solutions into a sterile basin. Place wet fine mesh gauze or Kerlix in basin of same solution if it is to be used again during that dressing. Discard gauze or Kerlix if contaminated other than by that patient.	Splashing solution from a container onto a sterile drape. Returning wet gauze and Kerlix to the table rather than to the basin.
b. By allowing any unsterile objects to drop or touch a sterile field.	Place contaminated items in the proper receptacle. Avoid reaching over a sterile field (1) to drop a sterile object, (2) to pour solutions, or (3) to fix suction, cautery, or drainage tubes.	Placing contaminated items such as basins, bottles, powder, gloves, on a sterile field. Reaching an unsterile arm over a sterile field. Touching a sterile suction catheter to ungloved hand or tracheostomy tube.
c. By infectious or soiled materials from a wound.	Dispose of soiled linens, dressings, instruments, and gloves properly. Place instruments used to debride on a sterile towel. Don't use these instruments for applying dressings. Place soiled gauze, eschar, etc., in waste container.	Placing eschar, gauze, or instruments used to debride wound on the sterile field. Touching the sterile field with gloves worn while removing dressings or debriding.
d. From airborne contaminants transported by air currents.	Close doors to the dressing room. Exclude anyone with a respiratory infection from the tub and dressing room.	Dust, human expirations from the nose and throat, and tossed soiled linens. Flapping sheets or drapes in the air when making beds or opening packs.

During the emergent and acute periods daily wound care is designed to heal the wound and prepare it for grafting. The primary principle of wound care is to prevent infection. Cleanse the wound once or twice daily with soap and water and rinse, preferably in the hydrotherapy tub. Give special care to face, eyes, ears, nose, mouth, perineum muscle, tendon, or bone if included in the wound. Keep all hairy areas shaved until the wound has healed. Bathe unburned areas daily and maintain good hygiene of all unburned areas. Prevent decubiti and pressure areas. Provide adequate rest and nutrition, and maintain a regular turning schedule.

Treatment of an established wound infection is as follows: First, culture the involved areas to identify organisms. To reduce the number of organisms

TABLE 30-7 (Continued)
Principles and Applications of Aseptic Technique

Principle	Guide to maintaining asepsis	Examples of contamination
	Cover the nose and mouth with an effective mask. If clearing throat, coughing, or sneezing, turn the head away from the sterile field. Keep conversation at a minimum. Do not shake or wave linen in the air. Prohibit anyone not involved with that patient's care from contact while the wound is open. Ensure that all persons entering the dressing room are properly attired, including members of other departments. Wet scrub and vacuum-mop floors at the end of each dressing schedule.	Using same mop and bucket for cleaning different areas. Dry mopping floors or dusting horizontal surfaces stirring dust into air.
3. A sterile area (field) remains sterile even when sterile articles are added to it.	A sterile article is moved from one sterile area to another by use of a sterile gloved hand, use of sterile transfer forceps, being dropped from a sterile container to a sterile field, pouring a sterile solution into a sterile basin.	See Principle 1. Tipping sterile transfer forceps up—allowing solution to run to contaminated area then tipping forceps down allowing contaminated solution to run onto sterile transfer tips.
4. Sterile areas are kept in view to prevent accidental contamination. Table — Sterile field	Only the top of a sterile table is considered sterile. Only the gown area above the waist and the anterior face of the sleeves are sterile. Keep sterile *gloved* hands in view. When opening a sterile pack or draping a table for a sterile field, open or drape front to back.	Touching sides and back of sterile drape. Dropping articles over the side of the table. The back, below the gown's waist, and the back of the gown's sleeves are unsterile unless wraparound sterile gowns are worn. Sterile gloved hands dropped below the waist or raised above eye level are unsterile. Draping back to front does not allow you to observe your hands and front of gown—leading to contamination.
5. Sterile persons face sterile objects. Unsterile persons face sterile objects but maintain a distance of 12 in.	Face sterile area. Pass any sterile gowned person back to back.	Turning your back on a sterile field may contaminate it.

cleanse the infected wound areas aggressively, debride the eschar and open subeschar pockets of infection, and change dressings more frequently. Apply an appropriate topical agent as indicated by culture and sensitivity studies. Provide basic nursing care (adequate diet, rest, hygiene, positioning) and encourage the patient to turn, cough, and deep breathe regularly to prevent pneumonia.

Wound Sepsis

If wound infection becomes established and is not controlled, bacteria will begin to seep into the bloodstream via the lymphatic system. This condition is first termed transient and then persistent (or breakthrough) bacteremia. The patient will begin to show signs of an impending sepsis. If the infection is not stopped at this level, the patient will soon develop septicemia, which has a poor prognosis. Treatment is as above.

Septicemia

Once large numbers of microbes are in circulation, the patient is at the last line of defense, the systemic filters. If the pathogens are particularly virulent, the body's defenses are soon taxed, and the patient will succumb to septicemia. Detecting subtle signs and symptoms of impending sepsis allows therapy to be initiated early to possibly prevent or better control a life-threatening septicemia or fungemia.

Clinical signs of impending sepsis are as follows: temperature over 101°F or below 98.6°F rectally, an increase in pulse rate or respiratory rate, an insidious decrease in blood pressure or urinary output, and a white blood cell (WBC) count between 10,000 and 20,000 cells per mL. General signs include: mild confusion, headache, chills, general malaise, cyanosis, and swollen regional lymph nodes.

Late symptoms of sepsis (septic shock), which are seen as septicemia becomes overwhelming, include a drop in temperature to below 98.6°F, a decrease in WBC count to below 10,000 cells per mL, ileus from septic shock, an enlarged liver and spleen, metastatic lesions, necrotic granulation tissue, and pneumonia. If irreversible shock occurs, the patient will die. Be alert! When you find yourself saying, "Something just doesn't seem right about that patient," review all parameters and rule out or treat bacteremia before it becomes septicemia.

Treatment The same principles of treatment apply to sepsis, septicemia, and fungemia. Eliminate the suspected cause; change and culture IV and urinary catheters and cleanse the wound of all exudates and products of infection. Initiate appropriate antimicrobial therapy, and culture the wound, urine, and blood daily. Support pulmonary function by establishing a turning, coughing, and deep breathing schedule and by maintaining adequate suction and postural drainage. Maintain proper fluid and electrolyte balance and monitor vital signs and CVP closely. Cool elevated temperature with antipyretics, cooling dressings, or fanning. (Use of a cooling mattress is a last resort!) Monitor hematocrit frequently and WBC daily; maintain hematocrit at 35 for adults and at 30 for children. Maintain adequate nutrition and rest.

Fungemia

Monilial septicemia, a severe infectious complication usually caused by *Candida albicans,* mimics the clinical response to gram-negative sepsis, except that the course is much more insidious. The temperature and WBC count respond slowly to the invasive organisms, continuing to rise despite broad-spectrum antibiotic coverage. Debilitation and long-term broad spectrum antibiotic therapy set the stage for fungemia.

The diagnosis of systemic moniliasis should be suspected in the debilitated patient who is on antibiotics but not responding to treatment. If this patient also has *C. albicans* organisms in the urine, treatment should be started (see treatment for septicemia).

BASIC CARE

Meeting Nutritional Needs

General Principles

The basic nutrient requirements of a severely burned adult patient are almost double those of the healthy individual. However, most studies show that a child's needs are met if the intake matches the recommended dietary allowance (RDA) for his or her age. Adequate nutritional intake is vital to sustain energy needed for metabolism, healing, fighting infection, and resisting stress. Poor nutrition causes weakness, fatigue, poor healing, protein derangements, wasting of tissue, impaired fat and carbohydrate metabolism, anemia, cardiac and respiratory problems, and death.

No one method can maintain the necessary daily nutritional balance; diet, supplemental feedings, and hyperalimentation may all be utilized. In planning nutrition for the burned patient, the dietitian considers nutritional status, age, sex and body build, severity of burn, medical history, dietary history (including likes, dislikes, and eating patterns), and present general condition. The nurse's role is to recognize the need for increased intake, to maintain adequate intake, and to be aware of the signs of nutritional deficiencies and their consequences.

Emergent Period Care

During the first few days after a burn injury, the severely burned patient is rarely able to tolerate oral intake. Frequently, gastric motility is depressed as a result of hypovolemic shock, increasing the possibility of ileus. In this period the usual procedure for severe injuries is to maintain the patient NPO for 24 to 48 h. Insert and secure a nasogastric (NG) tube and connect to intermittent suction for ½ out of every 2 h. Give antacids prophylactically for Curling's ulcer (a stress ulcer common in severely burned patients) and allow the patient small amounts of ice chips; give frequent mouth care for comfort. Remove the NG tube when bowel sounds return and the patient's fluid balance is stabilized (in 2 to 3 days). *Note:* Limit oral fluid intake for a time after the tube is removed (usually until body weight returns to normal), as thirst may be inappropriate and the patient, if not monitored, may take copious amounts of water and other fluids, resulting in water intoxication. Give a laxative per NG tube before the tube is removed. After the tube is removed, begin a clear liquid diet progressing to a full diet as tolerated. It is important to check for fecal impaction daily and to remove any fecal impaction present.

Acute Period Care

During the period of debridement and grafting, the patient must be provided with a sufficient quantity of carbohydrate, fat, protein, vitamins, salts, minerals, and water to meet energy needs. Changes in the GI tract due to infection (sepsis) and stress must be considered (e.g., alterations in gastric absorption, secretions, and motility). Hyperalimentation with high-calorie tube feedings (1.5 kcal/mL) may act as a hypertonic solution, pulling water into the GI tract which will be lost through diarrhea, and pseudodiabetes may well result from overfeeding. Stress diabetes or pseudodiabetes is not due directly to overfeeding but can occur if combined with stress. Stress diabetes may also occur while the patient is on IV therapy alone, without hyperalimentation, formula, or oral intake. Only in rare cases is it possible to overfeed a severely burned patient; there have been instances of patients who require more than 6000 kcal to maintain their weight.

Recommended diet   The recommended daily diet for an adult burn patient should provide the following:

Calories—50 to 80 kcal per kg of body weight (e.g., for a 70-kg adult male, 3500 to 5500 kcal per day)

Protein—2 to 4 g per kg of body weight (150 to 250 g protein)

Fat and carbohydrate—each should equal 40 percent of calorie intake

Vitamins and minerals:
  Ascorbic acid—1000 to 1500 mg
  Thiamine—10 to 50 mg
  Riboflavin—10 to 50 mg
  Niacin—100 to 500 mg
  Calcium pantothenate (pantothenic acid)—800 mg
  Magnesium—500 mg
  Folic acid—5 mg
  Vitamin B_{12}—200 μg

Total calorie count   Keep an accurate record of all caloric intake. A total calorie count may be calculated by the dietitian. Instruct the patient and family to record on the menu the amount of each item taken for that meal and to return the menu cards to the dietitian. Keep an in-between-meal nourishment sheet at the bedside so that the staff, patient, and family can record all caloric intake (food, drink, and tube feedings) for each 24-h period. When the patient requests a drink, offer a liquid with caloric value rather than water. Record liquid intake on the intake and output part of the 24-h flow sheet as well as on the between-meal nourishment sheet. The dietitian can calculate the patient's total caloric intake for a 24-h period from the menu cards and between-meal nourishment sheets and then record the calorie total on the 24-h flow chart.

Daily weights   Daily weights are also necessary in evaluating nutritional and metabolic balance. These measurements should be viewed by the nurse as being as important as vital signs, not as an irritating task. The patient should not lose more than one-third of the total weight or death follows.

Oral fluid restrictions   The total amount of fluids to be taken in a 24-h period may be restricted during periods of renal and pulmonary problems.

Feeding the patient   No patient should be deprived of nutritional intake because of exhaustion, the inability to eat without assistance, or dislike of food presented. In addition to assessing the patient's nutritional needs, also assess the patient's inability to eat independently and any other associated feeding problems. Consult with the occupational therapist, family, and other team members as necessary to solve feeding problems. Once a method or regimen is established, see that it is maintained.

Tube feedings   Tube feedings are usually given only as a supplement to a regular diet because they tend to dull the appetite and may cause diarrhea. When oral intake is impossible, tube feedings, supplemented by hyperalimentation, may be the only source of food intake. Give tube feeding within $\frac{1}{2}$ h after meals and at bedtime to allow normal rest periods for the stomach and to simulate normal intake. Do not give feedings between 11 P.M. and 6 A.M. During feedings it is important to elevate the head of the bed. Be sure to locate the tube in the lower esophagus, not in the stomach; the correct location of a feeding tube is just above the cardiac sphincter of the stomach.

Comfort and Hygiene

Attention to the basic needs of any patient, particularly the severely burned patient, contributes not only to the return to physical health but also to a feeling of confidence in the nursing staff. Much of the patient's interpretation of injury and possible outcome of hospitalization is based on the respect and interest shown by those carrying out routine duties. Although some of the procedures listed here may seem trivial, the critical-care nurse must keep in mind that the patient is not in a position to be responsible either for meeting these needs or even requesting this care.

Comfort

The patient must be made comfortable, provided with a correct diet, bathed, given mouth care, turned, and assisted, without requesting care. The nurse must anticipate patient needs and be firm in carrying out duties even when the patient does not realize their importance. Patient comfort is as important to recovery as medications and technical procedures. One of the nurse's most important responsibilities is to structure an environment in which the patient can recover. Although this structure may not be immediately obvious to the new nurse, through experience and training nurses learn which conditions set the stage for recovery.

It is difficult for a patient to relax and rest when external stimuli are disturbing. Conditions beyond their control, such as a bright light shining in the eyes, unnecessary noise, excessive warmth or cold, an uncomfortable position, unpleasant odors, or a messy bed will add to discomfort. Be alert to these irritations and eliminate them. Comfort includes proper body positioning, hygiene, and rest, as well as emotional support. When patients look uncomfortable, they probably are, and they are dependent on the nurse to correct the problem. As recovery progresses, patients can assume increasing responsibility for their own comfort.

Rest

Quiet hour   Structuring a quiet hour into all the other activities is especially important on the day shift. Frequently the patient is awakened at 6 A.M. and activities continue until 9 or 10 P.M. After lunch each day, establish a routine of turning off all ward lights, radios, and TVs and pulling the shades for at least 1 h. Allow no visitors and explain to the patient, family, and other personnel that this quiet hour is just as important to the patient as treatments. Vital signs should be checked, IVs regulated, and the patient made comfortable prior to this rest period. Other activities may take place quietly. This period gives the patients and the nursing staff a chance to recharge their batteries. Although at first the staff may argue that there are activities that must be done at this time, with thought and organization this period can become a pleasant time of day for both patients and nurses.

Settling   In the evening, after visiting hours, establish a routine of settling patients before bedtime. The sign "Intensive Care Unit" on the door does not excuse the basic considerations that ensure a good night's rest. Each patient should receive a snack or nourishment, use the bedpan, receive a back rub, have a linen change, and be repositioned. During this time encourage the patient to discuss any concerns. After all these little attentions are given, TVs and radios are turned off and lights are dimmed. Even the most critically ill who cannot receive all aspects of this care will benefit from comfort measures.

Undisturbed sleep   The period from 11 P.M. to 6 A.M. is set aside for undisturbed rest. Only emergency dressings or treatments are done during this period. Vital signs, urine testing, IV regulation, and turning should take place quietly with a genuine concern for the patient's rest. Obviously, there should be no neglect. If the patient is anxious or uncomfortable and cannot rest, the nurse makes a thorough review of all comfort measures, then sedatives and/or pain medications are given.

Hygiene

Daily bath The daily bath will promote the patient's feeling of general comfort and well-being, help control infection, and maintain the unburned skin in optimal condition. Keeping unburned skin healthy helps control infection and preserve skin surfaces to be used as donor sites.

Wash all unburned areas, rinse, dry, and apply lotion at least once daily. Check fingernails and toenails at each bath, clean with a cuticle stick, and trim as needed. Cut the nails straight across and file smooth. In addition to providing a feeling of well-being, this will decrease damage and transfer of infection should the patient scratch burned or healed areas. Shave facial hair (whiskers) once daily, even if the face is included in a partial-thickness burn. Encourage the patient to do so if face is unburned and the patient is capable. Shampoo scalp hair daily in the tub or at least weekly at the bedside. Use a no-rinse shampoo if done at the bedside. Clean inside the nose with applicators. Hygiene can be done in the hydrotherapy tub, but remember to spray rinse the patient thoroughly on the way out of the tub. *Note:* No body area should be allowed to remain dirty or excessively wet.

Mouth care Restrictions on oral fluids, burns around the mouth, and/or mouth breathing soon cause the mouth to become dry and foul. Mouth care not only provides a feeling of well-being but is essential to prevent stomatitis, oral candidiasis, and associated infection of the oral structures.

Elimination care The genitalia and perineum require special care to prevent deposits of urea on the burned areas and reduce the danger of infection with colon bacilli from fecal contamination.

Decubitus prevention The overall response to the trauma of the burn devitalizes body tissues. The continuous loss of body protein, the wasting effect of immobility, and the constant stress of sustained pressure on surface areas all contribute to decubitus formation. Decubiti cause considerable patient discomfort and are an additional source for infection. There is also the added disadvantage and consequence of increasing the size of wound area. Nursing care remains the single most important element in preventing decubitus ulcers!

Positioning, Contracture Control, Exercise, and Splinting

Principles of Positioning

A position the patient considers comfortable is seldom one that will control contracture formation. However, if proper positioning is initiated early in care, explained frequently, and continued, the patient will accept these positions as comforting. Attempting to correct established contractures later in burn care is far more time-consuming and painful. The nurse must make the patient as comfortable as possible while maintaining a position of contracture control. The position desired is generally nonfetal. Remember, it is easier to flex an extended tendon than to extend a tendon fixed in a flexed position.

Position change and proper body alignment are an essential part of nursing any severely ill patient. The objectives of positioning may be any of the following: to reduce the work load of the heart, to prevent or reduce contracture formation (see Table 30-8); to reduce the incidence of phlebitis, thrombi, and emboli; to promote lung expansion and drainage of pulmonary secretions; to reduce the incidence of pneumonia; to prevent decubitus; and to provide patient comfort.

Exercising

Cough and deep breathing exercises All burn patients must be started on a schedule of regular turning, coughing, and deep breathing shortly after admission. Respiratory therapy (IPPB specifically) enhances this procedure but does not replace it. Soon after admission, tell the patient that it is necessary to take deep breaths as often as possible. Explain that this helps prevent fluid accumulation in the lungs; thus, it will help prevent pneumonia and other respiratory complications. Encourage the patient to cough up secretions and deep breathe at least once every hour until it becomes a habit.

Full range of motion exercises Exercises which take the joints (burned or unburned) through the full range of motion are done at least once daily. However, do not take a joint beyond the free range of motion unless so instructed by a physician or therapist. Not only burned joints but all joints should be included. Bedrest, decreased protein, altered fluids and electrolytes, and poor circulation serve to decrease all

TABLE 30-8
Positioning to Prevent Deformity

Area burned	Potential resulting deformity	Position for prevention of deformity
Neck		
Anterior aspect or circumferential	Flexion contracture of neck	No pillow under head
Posterior aspect only	Extension contracture of neck Prone—pillow under upper chest to flex cervical spine Supine—small pillow under neck	
Axilla		
Anterior	Abduction and internal rotation	Shoulder joint in abduction (100 to 130°) and external rotation
Posterior	Abduction and external rotation	Shoulder in forward flexion and 100 to 130° abduction
Pectoral region	Shoulder protraction	No pillow; shoulders abducted and externally rotated
Chest or abdomen	Kyphosis	As above, with hips neutral (*not* flexed)
Lateral trunk	Scoliosis	Supine, affected arm abducted
Elbow—anterior surface or circumferential	Flexion and pronation	Arm extended and supinated
Wrist		
Total or volar surface	Flexion	Splint in 15° extension
Dorsal surface	Extension	Splint in 15° flexion
Hip (includes inguinal and perineal burns)	Internal rotation, flexion and abduction, possible joint subluxation if contracture severe	Neutral rotation and abduction and maintain extension by prone position or *pillow under buttocks*
Knee—popliteal surface or circumferential	Flexion	Maintain extension, using posterior splints or suspend heels with plastic heel protecting boots; *no pillows* under knees while supine or under ankles while prone
Ankle	Plantar flexion if foot dorsiflexor muscles are weak or their tendons are divided	90° dorsiflexion with splint if possible (rather than footboard)

Source: Courtesy of the Department of Physical Medicine, St. Joseph Mercy Hospital, Ann Arbor.

joint function and to encourage heterotopic bone formation as well as contracture. Exercising is best done while the patient is in the hydrotherapy tub. Active and passive range of motion may be combined, depending on the patient's capabilities. The physiatrist and physical therapist (PT) are skilled in providing these exercises; there is no reason, however, why a nurse cannot conduct them. Exercising should not be neglected because of a lack of PT coverage. Active range of motion requires that the patient do the exercising voluntarily. Encourage the full range of motion, as well as increased self-care, for example, brushing teeth, combing hair, and feeding. Many devices may be provided by the occupational or physical therapist to increase or enhance this type of exercise.

Passive range of motion requires that the patient be taken through the range of motion by another individual. The exercises are best done in hydrotherapy or immediately after tubbing. If done at the bedside, a pain medication may be useful prior to exercising. In performing these exercises, stabilize the proximal joint (e.g., the elbow) with one hand and support the distal part of the extremity (e.g., the wrist) with the other hand. Then move the proximal joint through its entire range slowly and gently.

Splinting

Principles The principle of splinting any area of the body is to place the area in a position which will preserve or regain function. Splinting may be employed throughout burn care. If contractures continue after discharge, which may be the case regardless of preventive measures, corrective splinting is necessary. Custom-made splints, those fashioned for a particular area of a particular patient, are ideal. However, custom-made splints are not always available or necessary. Ingenuity may replace the availability of custom-made splints. An elbow or knee joint may be maintained in proper position by use of a padded IV board. Contracture of the Achilles tendon, which causes foot drop, may be prevented by use of sandbags, towels, or pillows. The preservation of function is always the primary guide in the use of splints.

Dorsal and total hand burns The objectives in treating burns of the hand are to prevent deeply damaged tissues from becoming infected and to maintain a position which will preserve function. Because severe consequences result when hand function is damaged or lost, special or custom-made splints are desirable. Because the tendons of the dorsum (back) of the hand have little fatty padding and protection they require special care. If the hand has sustained either a deep partial-thickness or a full-thickness burn, some contractures may be expected. However, much can be done to minimize these contractures, and in some instances they can be avoided.

Many methods may be employed. Exercising or using the hand without splinting is an excellent method; however, use must be constant to prevent contractures. The splinting method we recommend is one which maintains most of the joints of the hand in an extended position (see Fig. 30-7). This splinting method can be very effective, provided that the splints are correctly applied immediately after the burn injury and are checked frequently to see that they are maintained in proper position.

Initially, the extent and depth of burn often cannot be accurately determined, and hand splints may be applied as a precautionary measure; they can be removed later if not required. Hand splints are continued until the major healing process has been completed in a partial-thickness burn or until grafting is completed in a full-thickness injury. After grafting, splints are removed and full use of the hand is encouraged.

Palmar burns Full-thickness burns limited to the palm of the hand may be less deforming than dorsal burns because the flexor tendons are protected by thick palmar fascia and fat. Palmar burns are usually treated by splinting in a position with the fingers extended and the thumb in abduction. Apply one layer of fine mesh gauze and one layer of Kerlix as padding and protection. Anchor the splint at the wrist and hold in place with a continuous Kerlix wrap.

The Contractual Approach to Nurse-Patient Interaction

General Principles

Assisting the patient to cope with the psychological aspects of this often severely disfiguring and physically incapacitating injury is another component of burn care. Recognizing this, nurses are frequently distressed by the demands made upon them. There is no magic formula to relieve this stress; however, we have developed some general guidelines to use in approaching the problem. In brief, the principles of this approach are to accept the patient as an individual and to understand that each individual has developed personal coping mechanisms. By making use of an individual's strengths, the nurse can guide the patient to deal more effectively with this period of life.

The basic method in this approach is to establish on-going contracts between yourself and the patient that help both to *identify short-term, achievable goals*. These contracts establish a respect for each other's integrity and, when consistently used, help reduce frustration for both parties. The ability to recognize situations in which the expertise of other team members such as the social worker, occupational therapist, physical therapist, dietitian, or chaplain can be called upon to assist also relieves stress and improves care.

Developing an Approach to Burn Care

Before you can successfully offer intensive care and support to a severely burned patient, the conflicts that arise from working with this type of patient must be resolved. Constant contact with emotionally distraught, severely disfigured, critically ill patients in life and death situations arouses strong emotions and frequent anxiety. Each nurse must develop a general philosophy and learn to *break down each situation into manageable components*. This search of self cannot be superficial but involves a complete evaluation of your approach to nursing. The desired

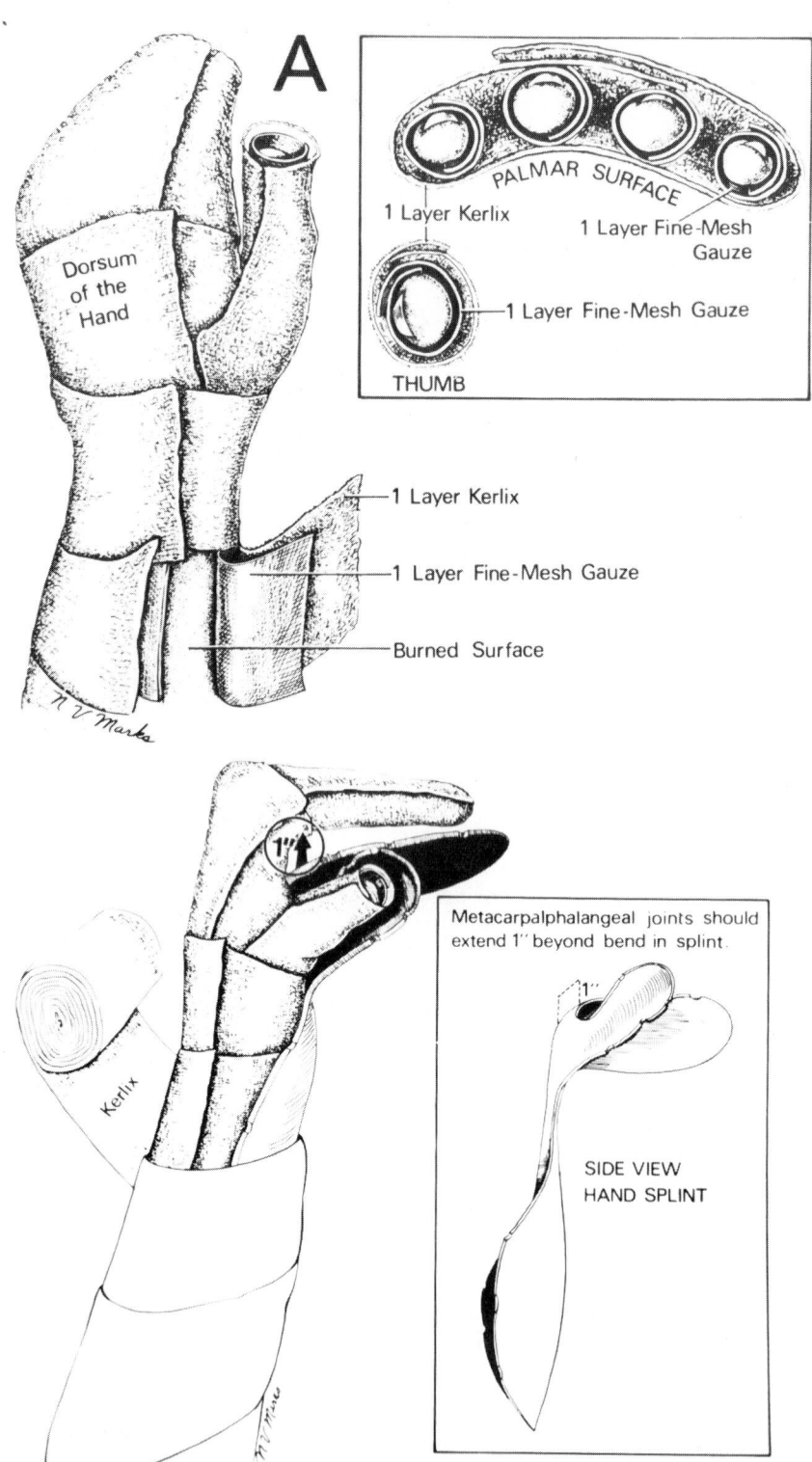

A

Dorsum of the Hand

PALMAR SURFACE

1 Layer Kerlix

1 Layer Fine-Mesh Gauze

1 Layer Fine-Mesh Gauze

THUMB

1 Layer Kerlix

1 Layer Fine-Mesh Gauze

Burned Surface

Kerlix

Metacarpalphalangeal joints should extend 1" beyond bend in splint.

1"

SIDE VIEW
HAND SPLINT

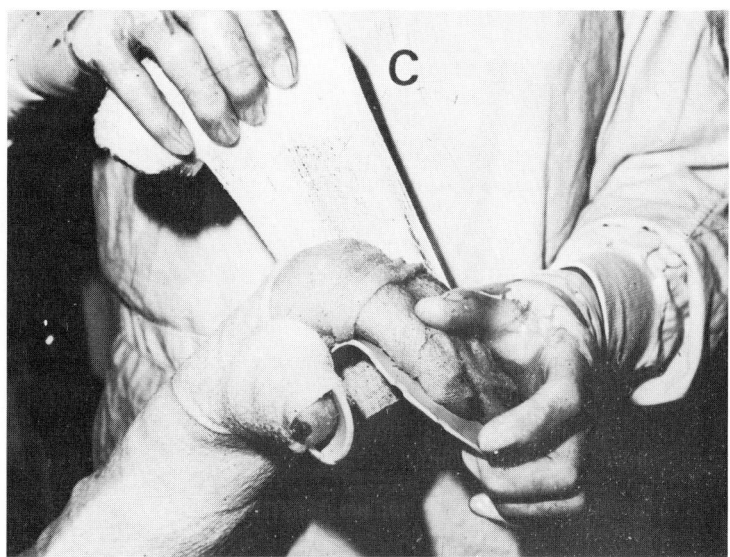

outcomes are (1) an acceptance of the patient as an individual without attaching labels as to good or bad behavior and (2) a patient-oriented approach to nursing. With this acceptance and self-awareness comes the understanding that personal likes and dislikes do not influence reactions. The main concern is to respond to all situations in a manner which will provide the best care for the patient.

Keep in mind that you use many of the same coping mechanisms as the patient; denial, minimization, and avoidance of anxiety. There is a strong tendency to depersonalize—to regard the patient as an object rather than as a person with pain and suffering. There may be a tendency to become procedure-oriented, to be involved in "busy work," and to say, "I've set my priorities—I'm doing all I can to meet the patient's physical needs."

However, once your personal conflicts are resolved, the confidence necessary to help the patient focus on appropriate coping mechanisms will follow. A calm, confident nurse, capable of assessing a situation, can assist the patient to mobilize energy to meet daily demands while teaching the patient to recognize milestones of progress.

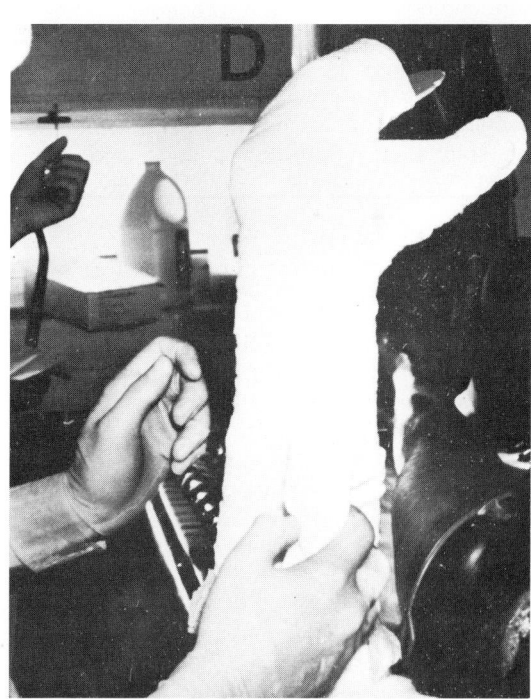

FIGURE 30-7

Splinting palmar hand burns. (*a*) A padding of one layer of fine mesh gauze and Kerlix are applied. (*b*) The splint is placed with the metacarpophalangeal joints extended 1 in above the bend in the splint and is then anchored at the wrist with Kerlix. (*c*) The Kerlix wrap is continued up and around the thumb and then is pulled tightly over the fingers to secure metacarpophalangeal and interphalangeal joints in proper position. (*d*) The Kerlix wrap is returned down the wrist and fastened.

Initial Contact

Remember your first contact with a critical-care unit? Were you overwhelmed by new faces, terms, and equipment? Your own anxiety reflects only some of the anxiety the patient experiences on admission to such a unit. You could have walked away had you wanted to. The patient must handle the memory of the accident and the rush to the hospital, thoughts of guilt or thoughts of how the accident might have been prevented, and the fear of what it all means both personally and to loved ones in addition to fear of the unknown. If you do not meet the patient's emotional needs at this point, there is a strong likelihood that no one will. In addition to physical care, you have a responsibility to sincerely and simply answer questions and to provide calm in the storm of anxiety. The transition from person to patient can be made less traumatic by your efforts.

Introduce yourself to the patient when you first meet. Orient the patient in simple terms to the new surroundings and explain procedures, treatments, and medical terms. Explain the physical and emotional feelings the patient may experience. Offer guidelines which indicate what behavior will be expected of the patient and what behavior to expect of the staff. Remember, your attitude and comments affect the patient's attitude and behavior.

Establishing a Contract

Patient care progresses more smoothly if you establish a contract as each task is begun. This contract is an understanding of what must be done and the expected behavior and responsibilities of both parties. The purpose of the contract is to eliminate inconsistency, inequality, and many of the other unfavorable effects of being a patient. If contracts are established early in care and continued throughout the period of hospitalization, the patient then has a tool to assist in coping with this overwhelming experience. The contract also gives the patient a sense of being included in planning care. Most of all, it helps both parties set *short-term, achievable goals.* Goals which can be, and are, accomplished give both the patient and the nurse a sense of success, pride, and progress.

The contract also recognizes the patient's lack of control over this new situation. Offer the patient choices when possible, *but only if there is a choice.* Don't say, "Do you want your dressing done now?" when you know that, regardless of the answer, you'll do it now anyway.

The steps of establishing a contract are as follows: at the outset of each procedure, state what must be done, why it must be done, and what will be expected of both parties. Request the patient's cooperation. Suggest possible ways of participation and encourage expression of feelings. Alter the contract to comply with patient requests when possible. Whether or not full agreement is reached, both parties should understand the terms under which the task will be carried out.

When establishing the contract, it is also helpful to set short-term achievable goals—e.g., turning without help, sitting, standing, taking a step. Allow the patient choices when possible. Honor patient requests when legitimate. Acknowledge the patient's feelings and encourage discussion of feelings.

Quality Control Measures: Recording and Assessment of Data Collection

Charting—Recording Data

With the great technological advances in medicine, the vital information which may be obtained for each patient has vastly increased. Charting, therefore, has also grown both in complexity and importance, since it is necessary to record all aspects of care in a fashion which will allow efficient data retrieval. We offer here a relatively simple method of data collection that allows both immediate recording and relative ease in reviewing all aspects of the data. The method consists of (1) a daily or 24-h flowchart and (2) a monthly summary sheet. All care for a 24-h period is recorded on one sheet; then a summary is transferred daily to a column on the monthly summary sheet. The monthly one-page summary sheet allows a rapid evaluation of the patient's progress for a 30-day period. This method eliminates the need for flipping back and forth through a conventional chart to gain a comprehensive picture of the course of treatment.

Daily or 24-h flowchart The important data and notes necessary to provide good patient care for a 24-h period are recorded on one 17-in by 11-in page. The chart is printed on NCR paper; one copy is folded and put on the conventional chart as a legal record, and the other is kept in a folder with other 24-h sheets and the monthly summary sheet, which are later used for research purposes (see Fig. 30-8). Included on the 24-h flowchart are:

Vital signs (T, P, R, BP), CVP, blood gases, and hematocrit

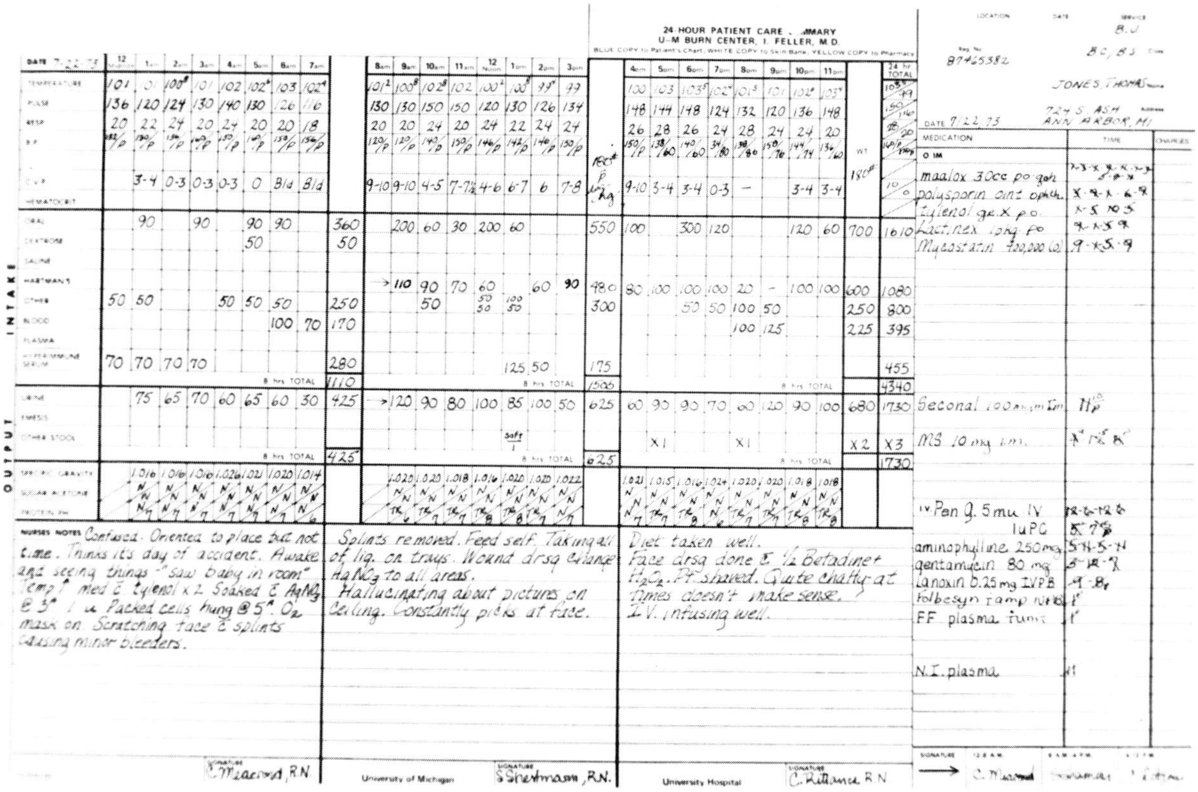

FIGURE 30-8
A 24-h flowchart.

All medications, including intravenous solutions and additives, and their dosages, times given, and routes of administration

Tabulation of fluid intake and output with 8-h subtotals and 24-h total

Parameters for monitoring aspects of renal function and blood sugar

Daily weight

Nurse's notes

Monthly summary sheet The monthly summary sheet includes, on one 23-in by 11-in sheet of paper, a complete summary of the patient's progress for a 30-day period. It allows rapid evaluation of a large amount of data at a glance (see Figs. 30-9 and 30-10). The following are included on the monthly summary sheet:

The high and low of the patient's vital signs for each 24-h period

All laboratory (blood, urine, and culture) determinations

The daily calorie intake and body weight

A complete tabulation of the patient's fluid intake and output as well as amounts of various types of intravenous fluids given

A record of all systemic medications and topical therapy the patient has received since admission, including the dosage as well as the number of days the patient has taken the medication

The number of days since the burn injury occurred

A list of complications and special tests

On the reverse side of this sheet, an estimate of the area burned and the physician's progress notes

Burn Team Conferences

At least once weekly a burn team conference ("chart rounds") should be held to discuss and plan care for

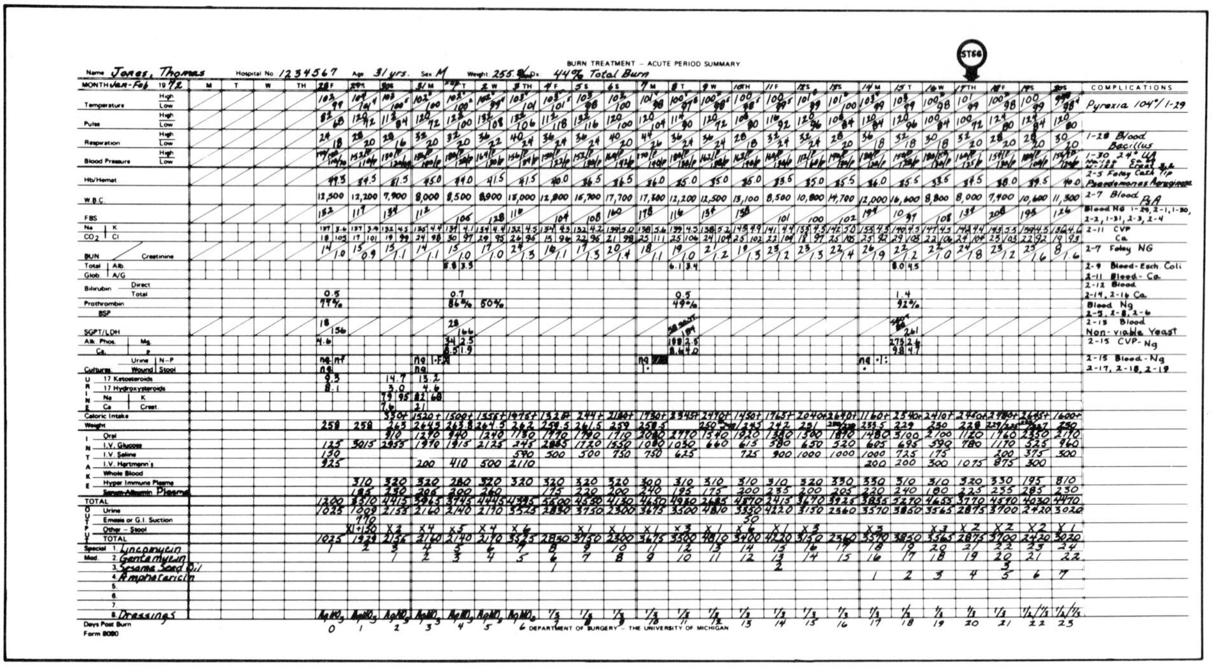

FIGURE 30-9

Example of completed monthly summary sheet (front). This method of record keeping provides on one sheet of paper a summary of the massive amount of data required to plan and evaluate a total care program. The high and low of T, P, R, and BP; daily laboratory values for blood, urine, and cultures; caloric intake; daily weights; fluid intake and output totals; and the systemic and topical medications administered are listed for each 24-h period. Complications are listed at the right. Any surgical procedures or special tests may be indicated in the circle (see arrow at the top). The day postburn is listed across the bottom.

the coming week. The entire burn team including at least one representative from each supporting department should attend. A system for evaluation of the patient's condition and planning nurse coverage is given in Fig. 30-11.

Wound Care Rounds

Once weekly (or more frequently) the directors of the unit, the house officers, and the charge nurse make "rounds" of each patient. Other team members may also attend. Take care to keep the number of people making rounds small enough to avoid undue exposure of the patient to chilling, contaminants, and emotional stress.

These rounds are principally for viewing and discussing the patient's wound with regard to the need for debridement and grafting, status of granulation tissue, changes in topical agents, etc. Photographs are made of the wound, and wound care is planned. Wound care rounds are best held immediately prior

to the weekly planning conference but may be held on any day. Viewing of the wound is best done at the bedside if the patient cannot be tubbed.

Special Rounds and Conferences

Various team members may make individual rounds or hold conferences for specific purposes daily or weekly as needed. Those likely to make individual rounds include the nursing staff, psychiatrist, physical or occupational therapists, dietitian, social worker, psychologist, physiatrist, and respiratory therapists.

These conferences or rounds may be combined with wound care rounds but are usually more effective if held individually. Spot teaching can be done during and after these rounds, depending on the needs and goals of the patient, nurses, and specialists. The charge nurse and other team members should participate as much as possible to foster interdisciplinary cooperation and learning on both sides.

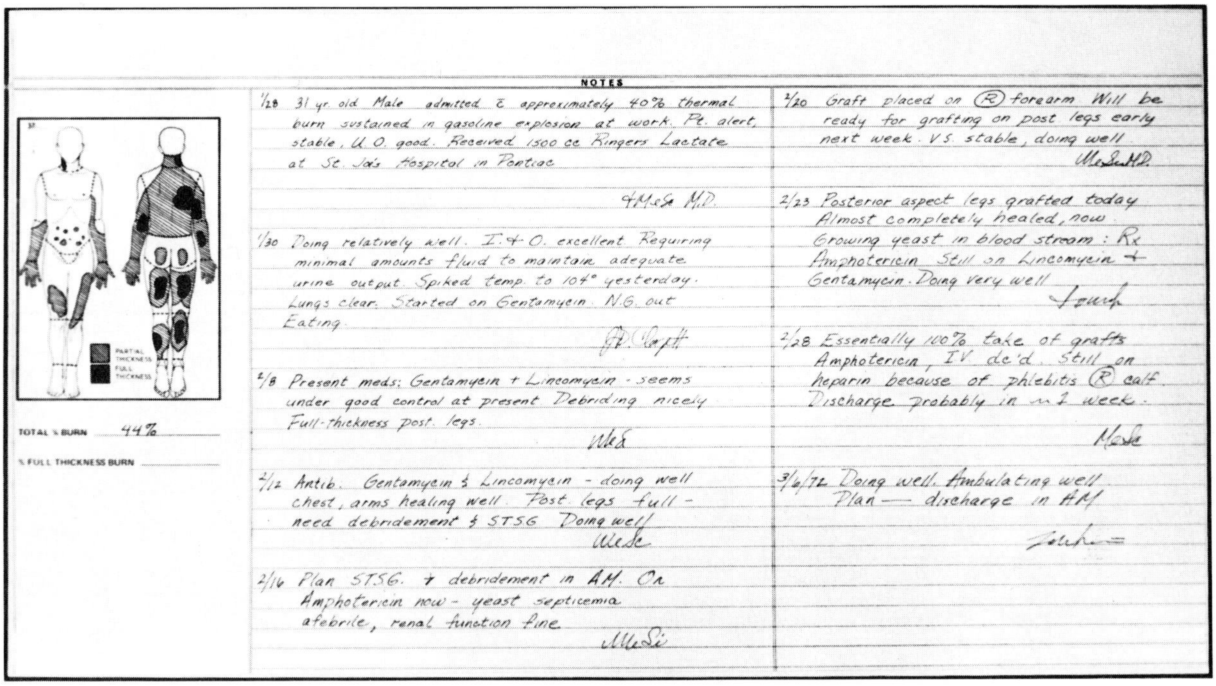

NOTES

1/28 31 yr old Male admitted ē approximately 40% thermal burn sustained in gasoline explosion at work. Pt. alert, stable, U.O. good. Received 1500 cc Ringers Lactate at St. Jo's Hospital in Pontiac

TMcGa M.D.

1/30 Doing relatively well. I. & O. excellent Requiring minimal amounts fluid to maintain adequate urine output Spiked temp. to 104° yesterday. Lungs clear. Started on Gentamycin. N.G. out Eating.

G.R.Clapp

2/8 Present meds: Gentamycin + Lincomycin - seems under good control at present Debriding nicely Full-thickness post. legs.

Wck

2/12 Antib. Gentamycin & Lincomycin - doing well chest, arms healing well Post legs full - need debridement & STSG Doing well

Wck

2/16 Plan STSG + debridement in A.M. On Amphotericin now - yeast septicemia afebrile, renal function fine

McGa

2/20 Graft placed on Ⓡ forearm Will be ready for grafting on post legs early next week. V.S. stable, doing well

McGa M.D.

2/23 Posterior aspect legs grafted today Almost completely healed, now Growing yeast in blood stream; Rx Amphotericin Still on Lincomycin + Gentamycin. Doing very well

Smith

2/28 Essentially 100% take of grafts Amphotericin I.V. dc'd Still on heparin because of phlebitis Ⓡ calf Discharge probably in ~ 2 week.

McGa

3/6/72 Doing well. Ambulating well Plan — discharge in A.M.

Smith

TOTAL % BURN 44%

% FULL THICKNESS BURN

PARTIAL THICKNESS
FULL THICKNESS

FIGURE 30-10

Example of a completed monthly summary sheet (back). This side provides an area for estimate of burn extent and for the physician's progress notes. This sheet is kept in a folder with the daily flow sheets so that the patient may be rapidly evaluated for the recent 24-h period and for total progress.

WOUND CARE

Basic Wound Care Procedures

Principles of Wound Care

Reducing the size of the wound increases the patient's chance for survival. This should be accomplished as rapidly as possible without providing additional stress to the patient. The day-to-day principles of wound care are to eliminate the media for bacterial growth, to prevent conversion of a partial-thickness wound to full-thickness, to prepare the partial-thickness wound for spontaneous healing and the full-thickness wound for autografting, to decrease the incidence of scarring and contractures, and also to provide comfort for the patient.

The essence of wound care is to keep the wound as clean as possible with the least discomfort to the patient. *Daily* cleansing, debridement, and dressing changes, coupled with good basic nursing care, can assure these objectives. Wound care is continued until the wound is healed. The burn patient cannot recover until the wound is healed, and in this case there is no complication which contraindicates wound care.

Routine Orders for Wound Care

Although these orders are routine, each must be a written physician's order. The reasons for each, if not explained, will become apparent as the procedure is discussed.

Change dressings twice daily on all wounds unless ordered otherwise. The times of dressing change are usually 7 A.M. to 12 noon and 6 to 9 P.M., allowing for mealtime, rest periods, and visitors. Dressing times may be altered as necessary to accommodate the patient load. Do not change dressings between 11 P.M. and 6 A.M. No dressings are done after 11 P.M. to allow a relatively undisturbed rest period for the patient.

Apply neomycin (0.5%) solution dressings for 24 h prior to grafting. The last dressing is applied 1 to $\frac{1}{2}$ h prior to grafting. (Neomycin is ototoxic and

CHART FOR EVALUATION OF SEVERITY OF ILLNESS			Edwards	Bathos	Snuck		
Isolation	3	Not Necessary					
	2	Dressings Only	1	2	3		
	1	Complete					
Ambulation	3	Self					
	2	With Assistance	1	3	3		
	1	SCB					
Bathing	3	Self					
	2	Partial Self	1	2	2		
	1	Complete Assistance					
Feeding	3	Self					
	2	Partial Self	1	2	3		
	1	Complete Assistance					
Respiratory	3	No Problem					
	2	Oxygen					
	1	Suction	1	3	2		
	1	Tracheostomy or Endotrach					
Intake and Output	3	Not Necessary					
	2	Foley					
	1 or 2	IV	1	2	3		
	1 or 2	NG Tube					
	1	Combination					
Vital Signs	3	q Shift					
	2	q 2 hr. to 4 hr.	1	1	2		
	1	q 2 hr. or less					
Orientation	3	Oriented					
	2	Confused					
	1	Disoriented	1	3	3		
	1	Unconscious					
Dressing Changes	3	Less than 15 min.					
	2	Less than 30 min.	1	1	2		
	1	30 min. or more					
Complications	3	None					
	2	Incapacitating	1	2	3		
	1	Life Threatening					
Average "Severity" Score:		Add Total Points And Divide by 10	10/1.0	21/2.1	26/2.6		

Patient Classification:
I   1.0 - 1.4 = INTENSIVE CARE
II 1.5 - 2.4 = COMPREHENSIVE CARE
III 2.5 - 3.0 = CONVALESCENT CARE

FIGURE 30-11

Classification of severity of illness sheet. This helps in objective determination of the stage of patient care. Each patient is discussed as to each category and the appropriate point value is given, e.g., total care on isolation is 1 point. The points are then totaled and divided by 10 (the number of categories) to provide a severity score. A score of 1.0 to 1.4 = intensive care, or a class I patient, requiring one-to-one nursing; 1.5 to 2.4 = comprehensive care, a class II patient who is improving and requires less care; 2.5 to 3.0 = convalescent care, or a class III patient, who is on a rehabilitation program and requires only supervisory care.

nephrotoxic and is used only with caution where it will do the greatest good.)

Apply hand splints on admission to all patients with dorsal hand burns (palmar hand burns are evaluated by physiatrist as to need for splinting).

Physicians dress newly grafted areas for the first 24 to 72 h. Experienced nurses also may change these dressings, but neophytes are discouraged because it is difficult to distinguish new grafts and they may be inadvertently removed.

Apply all dressings as indicated in the following procedures unless otherwise directed. Only the topical agent will vary according to physician's choice. Debride eschar at *each* dressing change until the wound is clean. Shave all hairy areas in or near the wound until the wound is healed. Cleanse all wounds before application or reapplication of topical agents. Use fine mesh gauze on all debriding wounds, granulation tissue, and new grafts. Repeat special area care (to burned face, eyes, ears, nose, mouth, perineum, muscle, tendon, and bone) every 4 to 6 h (except between 11 P.M. and 6 A.M.). Keep exposed muscle, tendon, and bone clean and moist at all times. Weigh the patient without dressings at each dressing change, and record weight on the daily and monthly flow sheets. All other orders and any exceptions to the above orders must be specifically written.

Use of Topical Agents

Excellence of wound care is not decided on the merits of a particular topical agent but on the skill and interest of those caring for the patient. The new nurse may be bewildered by the seemingly arbitrary decisions for using different topical agents. Each has advantages and disadvantages. The following discussion considers the agents most frequently used. *Note:* As with any medication, the nurse should read the label before using any solution or ointment.

Balanced salt or normal saline solution may be used on clean granulation tissue or newly grafted areas or to soak dressings. Normal saline has no bactericidal properties and is not used on a debriding or dirty wound. Equal parts (1:1) of normal saline and hydrogen peroxide (3%), termed "halves," may be used to soak dressings before removal and for donor site care. Equal parts (1:1:1) of balanced salt, hydrogen peroxide (3%), and acetic acid (0.25%), termed "thirds," may be used intermittently during the debridement process and on granulating wounds because of its effectiveness in removing secondary eschar and in cleaning a "dirty" wound (removing

crusts, drainage, debris, etc.). *Note:* "Halves" or "thirds" should never be used on new grafts because peroxide may cause trauma.

Neomycin (0.5%) is used only to clean the wound before grafting. Neomycin is nephrotoxic and ototoxic when used in high concentrations or for long periods of time. It is thought that a 1% solution of neomycin will traumatize new autografts. For these reasons, neomycin is used sparingly despite its excellent bacterial action.

Special topical agents such as silver nitrate, silver sulfadiazine, mafenide acetate, gentamicin, furazolium, and cerium nitrate are bacteriostatic or bactericidal solutions or ointments used to decrease the bacterial population of a wound. Use of commercial preparations requires review of the package insert.

Silver nitrate ($AgNO_3$) 0.5% is a common agent which is prepared in the hospital pharmacy. It may be used on admission to penetrate, harden, and sterilize eschar. $AgNO_3$ dressings are usually continued for the first 7 to 10 days after the burn injury. $AgNO_3$ (0.5%) may also be used as a dialysate, i.e., to "pull" sodium chloride from a hypernatremic patient. Potassium may also be affected, and frequent laboratory monitoring of electrolytes is· essential whenever $AgNO_3$ is used. Since $AgNO_3$ must be in solution to be bactericidal, $AgNO_3$ dressings must never be allowed to dry out. That is why multiple (four to six) layers of Kerlix and frequent soakings are necessary. A *dry* sheet or blanket must also be kept over the wet dressings to reduce evaporation.

New drugs may be evaluated as indicated. For *investigational drugs* which do not have FDA approval the law requires that the patient and/or family be informed of this by the physician and that permission be obtained before use.

Whenever topical agents in an *ointment base* are used, *the ointment must be completely removed by washing before reapplication.* A good rule is to always cleanse the wound before applying or reapplying a topical agent.

Dressing Change Procedure

Although there are various methods of wound care, we feel that the multiple dressing change method best fulfills the objective of wound care. Not only does the dressing protect the wound and provide warmth, but removal of the dressing also enhances debridement and wound cleansing. The principles of aseptic technique and cubicle isolation should be incorporated into the dressing change procedure. Removal of dressings is a clean procedure; application of dressings is a sterile procedure.

Preparation   Gather all supplies needed before beginning the procedure, and set up the dressing table using sterile technique (see Fig. 30-12). It is helpful to establish a contract with the patient regarding the dressing change before beginning the procedure. Give a pain medication at least 20 min prior to dressing change if indicated. (If intravenous medication is indicated, it will be given immediately prior to the procedure.) Position the patient, soak the dressings with a warmed "halves" or "thirds" solution, and cover with a sheet. (If hydrotherapy is available, soaking may not be necessary.)

Removal of dressing   First wash both hands thoroughly. Since cubicle isolation technique is used, put on barrier gown, mask, and gloves. Slit outer dressing (Kerlix) up the midline with blunt-end scissors and lay open or unwrap, whichever is best for the patient. Using forceps or gloved hand, lay back fine mesh gauze. Lift extremity or encourage patient to do so and remove soiled dressings, which are then discarded in a waste container. Place a sterile towel or sheet under the exposed wound; lift patient into tub if hydrotherapy included. Debride (as listed in pro-

cedure) if eschar is present and culture any suspicious area. If an ointment base topical agent is present on the wound, and if the patient is not tubbed, wash the wound with a detergent solution on coarse gauze sponges (4 in by 4 in) and rinse well with a balanced salt solution. If not immediately reapplying dressing, cover wound with a sterile sheet. Repeat this procedure for all other wound areas. Remove gloves.

Application of dressing   If removal and application procedure is interrupted, wash hands before resuming. When applying a new dressing, first add topical solution to sterile basin (always check label on container before adding solution). Then expose the area to be dressed. Be sure to put on sterile gown and gloves (the same gloves may be worn to dress all areas if the gloves do not become contaminated) and to use sterile technique throughout the procedure.

When applying a dressing to an *extremity* (Fig. 30-13 *a, b,* and *c*) ask the patient to raise the extremity or have an assistant do so. Pick up the scissors in one hand and hold the fine mesh gauze roll, soaked in topical agent and lightly squeezed out, in the other. Beginning at the distal portion of the extremity, apply fine mesh gauze, wrap around once, slightly overlapping, and cut. A double thickness of fine mesh gauze defeats its effectiveness! Wrap distal to proximal (as

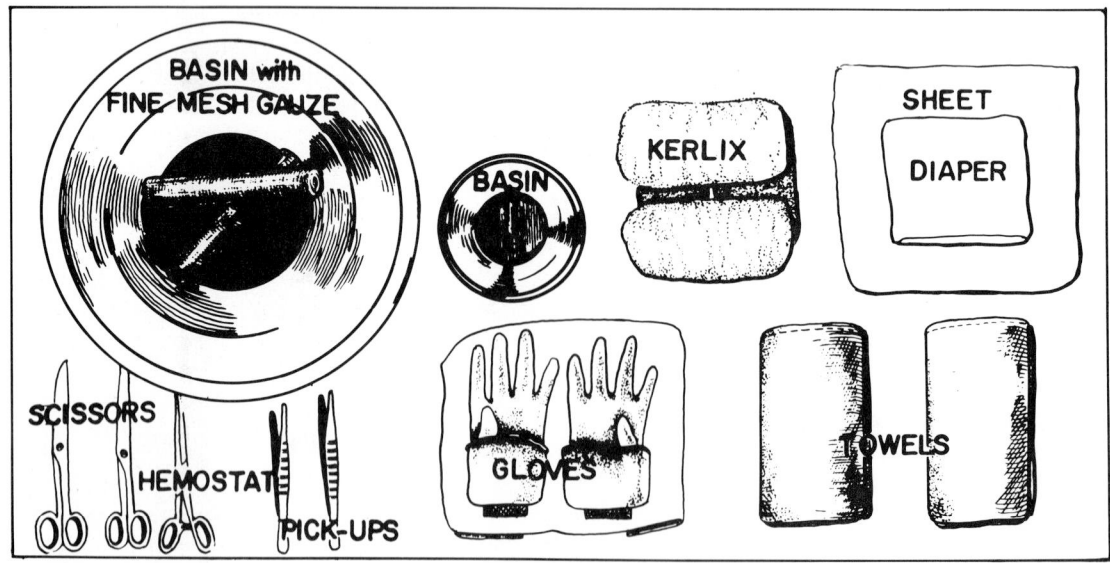

FIGURE 30-12

Layout for dressing tables. The uniformity of this layout permits the nurse to know where to look for each supply. Remember, the dressing table is a sterile field. Basic supplies shown here (additional supplies may be added depending on size of wound) are (1) extra fine mesh gauze or Kerlix, (2) towel gauze for chest or back area, (3) a small basin in case more than one solution is needed, (4) a second pair of scissors for debridement or to remove old dressings, and (5) diapers.

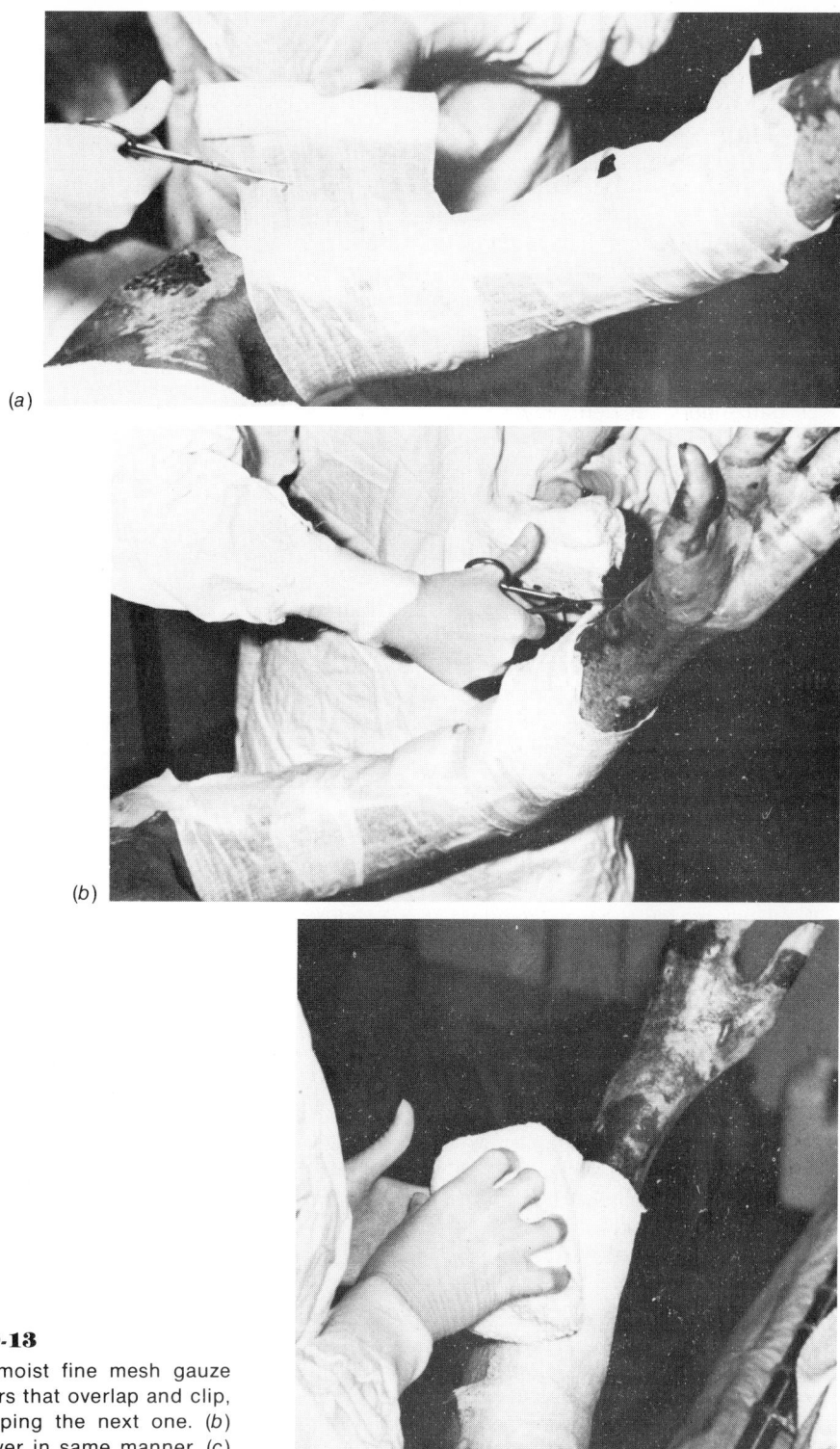

FIGURE 30-13

Dressing application. (*a*) Wrap moist fine mesh gauze (distal to proximal) in single layers that overlap and clip, with each wrap slightly overlapping the next one. (*b*) Apply moist Kerlix as second layer in same manner. (*c*) Apply continuous dry Kerlix (*c*) to hold moist layers in place (third layer).

the blood returns to the heart) to prevent edema and to enhance circulation. Continue to wrap interrupted fine mesh gauze around the extremity so that each wrap slightly overlaps the previous application (clip and repeat) to cover entire burned area. This overlap and clip method is used in preference to continuous wrap to allow expansion, prevent constriction of motion and circulation, and facilitate removal.

Apply the dressing gently and snugly but not tightly—and without wrinkles. Do not tug and pull to rearrange dressings after they have been applied. Apply one layer of saturated Kerlix, also in a fairly snug interrupted wrap, distal to proximal. Next, apply dry Kerlix in a continuous spiral wrap to hold the fine mesh gauze and wet Kerlix layer in place; attach at the proximal end. (If AgNO₃ is used, wet all Kerlix and apply multiple layers.) If ordered by the physician, apply an Ace bandage over the dressing (distal to proximal). This may be done to decrease the incidence of scarring and to enhance venous return. Place a sterile towel or blue incontinence pad folded lengthwise around dressings of the upper thigh to prevent contamination from urine or feces.

To facilitate covering large flat surfaces, such as the *chest, abdomen, thighs,* and *back*, use of a towel gauze—a surgical towel covered with a few layers of coarse gauze and topped with a layer of fine mesh gauze—is recommended. This method eliminates using many small pieces of fine mesh gauze which may slip out of place, become uncomfortable, and possibly traumatize healthy granulation tissue or new grafts.

When using a towel gauze, separate all gauze from the towel and saturate only the gauze in the solution; squeeze out some of the solution before applying. If AgNO₃ is used, also saturate the towel. Apply the gauze to the wound only, not to unburned areas, and clip to fit. Do not excessively rearrange the gauze after it has been applied. Follow the same procedures until all areas are covered; then apply towels over the gauze-covered areas. Secure the towels (front to back) with safety pins to form a vest. Do not wrap the chest tightly or circumferentially with Kerlix. It may constrict breathing or circulation.

If *fingers* or *toes* are burned, wrap each with a separate single thickness of fine mesh gauze to prevent webbing; *no two burn surfaces may touch*. Be sure there are no folds or wrinkles in the fine mesh gauze; then apply Kerlix in the same manner as previously described. If the hands are burned, splinting may be necessary; the method for splinting the hands is described in the preceding section on contracture control.

Ingenuity must be used when wrapping the *axillae, neck,* and *shoulders* because of the difficulties of wrapping neatly and maintaining the dressing in place. Expertise in applying dressings to these areas comes with practice and use of common sense. Speed is not the primary consideration. Fine mesh gauze and Kerlix are applied as described above but so they do *not* constrict. A figure-eight wrap may be indicated.

Patch dressings are used on areas of granulation tissue between healed autografts. To apply a patch dressing, cut strips of fine mesh gauze to fit the unhealed area, soak in "thirds" solution, and apply to the area with slight pressure from a gloved finger. Use no outer dressing; expose the gauze to the air. Soak off patches with next dressing change. *Note*: Do not wrap unburned or healed areas unless absolutely necessary. Capillary action allows organisms from the unburned area to travel to the wound on the moist dressing. Wrapping of unburned areas also tends to decrease function.

After the dressing has been applied remove gloves, cover the patient with a sterile sheet and blanket if needed for warmth, and return the patient to bed. If dressing has been done in bed, change the linen. Make the patient as comfortable as possible. If ambulation is ordered, it may be done at this time, or the patient may wish to rest.

Dismantling the dressing table   The dressing table that was used is now a source of contamination and must be handled as such. Wear a barrier gown and gloves to dismantle the table. First remove nondisposables (basins, instruments, bottles, etc.) from the room to the dirty utility room. Discard wet dressings in the appropriate container and pour used solutions down the drain. Discard disposable gloves and other disposable items and place linen in soiled linen container. Double-bag all items to be removed from the room. If double bagging is not used, rinse items, wrap or autoclave, and return to central service to be reprocessed. Use a germicidal solution to rinse or wipe outer surfaces of containers of solutions to be reused and then store them properly. Check for expiration dates and discard solutions when indicated. Store open solutions no longer than 24 h. Tidy room. When finished, remove barrier gown and gloves.

Debridement

Principles   Debridement is the removal of any nonviable tissue (eschar) from the wound. Because eschar provides the conditions necessary for bacterial growth, it is essential to remove it from the wound as rapidly as possible. Daily debridement of loose eschar and debris with each dressing change is preferred to debridement of large areas under anesthesia in the operating room. Daily debridement (1) eliminates the possibility of hemorrhage from too aggressive or very deep, sharp debridement, (2) decreases excessive bacterial shower due to manipulation of large areas of the wound, and (3) decreases the risk of prolonged anesthesia time.

Debride loosened eschar and shreds of debris with *each* dressing change until the wound is clean. If the wound is inspected and debrided daily, there will be little need for extensive debridement under anesthesia and fewer wound infection complications. To prevent both undue stress to the patient and excessive bacterial shower, debride no longer than 20 min or not more than 4 in² at one time.

Supplies needed for debridement include sterile gloves, pickups, scissors, hemostatic agent (e.g., Oxycel), and coarse gauze sponges (4 in by 4 in).

Procedure Pick up the eschar at a loosened edge and cut away dead tissue. Be sure to *cut next to dead tissue; never cut next to viable tissue.* Leave a $\frac{1}{4}$-in edge on remaining eschar. If bleeding or oozing occurs, apply pressure with a gauze pad and apply a hemostatic agent (e.g., Oxycel). Call a physician if bleeding continues or there is a spurter. Have the following supplies ready to ligate the bleeder: needle holder, hemostat (if indicated for large bleeder), gut suture with needle, gloves, and scissors. Continue to apply pressure until the physician arrives. *Note:* If a large vessel (e.g., the carotid or temporal artery) is apparent in or under a debriding area, have a hemostat available at the bedside at all times in the event of erosion and hemorrhage.

Grid escharotomy Another form of escharotomy, used to facilitate debridement, is the grid escharotomy (Fig. 30-14). The purpose of cutting the eschar into small squares, or a grid, is to allow purulent material to drain from beneath the eschar and to expose more edges of eschar to hasten debridement.

Tangential excision A method of sharp excision of damaged or nonviable tissue down to viable tissue on the third to fifth day after burn is coming into popularity (Fig. 30-15). After excision, hemostasis is obtained, and all areas exposed are covered with split-thickness grafts (autografts or homografts) to prevent necrosis of viable tissue. Dressings are changed daily, and pooled blood and purulent ma-

FIGURE 30-14
Cutting eschar into a grid allows more surface area and enhances the debridement process.

terial beneath grafts are dabbed out. The goal of this method is to reduce the period of hospitalization required for daily debridement of an extensive wound. At present only moderate-size wounds are being treated by tangential excision. The principles, however, may be incorporated into care of any wound.

Special Area Care

Principles

In addition to the basic wound care previously discussed, some areas of the body require special treatment to ensure proper functional and cosmetic healing (Table 30-9). The principles of wound care—keeping the area clean and free of infection—remain the same; however, the frequency of care is increased. Attention to special areas should be given at every dressing change regardless of the rush the nurse feels. If infection is allowed to become established in these special care areas, cosmetic and functional healing is greatly impaired. Sterile technique is required for all procedures. No special care is done between 11 P.M. and 6 A.M.

Face Care (Exposure Method)

Establish a routine of face care as soon as possible after admission and repeat every 4 to 6 h except

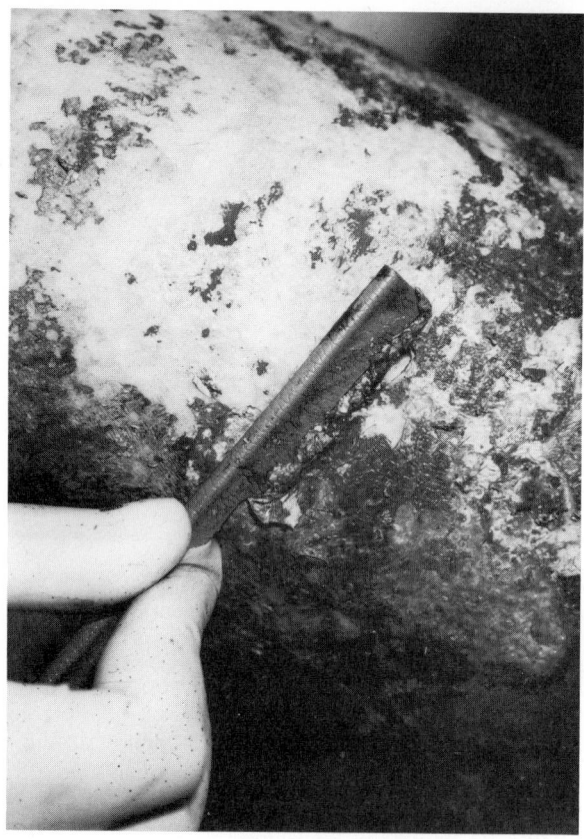

FIGURE 30-15
Tangential excision. Shaving away dead tissue early after burn is an adjunct to debridement.

between 11 P.M. and 6 A.M. Until the face begins to debride, it may be treated either by the open method or with moist dressings. After debridement begins, fine mesh gauze and Kerlix dressings are indicated. The following procedure is used when the face is being treated by the open method (either before debridement or for a partial-thickness wound).

Supplies needed for the procedure are sterile gloves, a small basin, coarse gauze sponges (4 in by 4 in), applicators, solution as ordered by the physician (usually detergent and saline, or "thirds"), and an antibiotic ointment or topical agent of physician's choice. Cleanse the face gently with the gauze sponges and the prescribed solution. If crusts and excessive drainage are evident, soak the face with "thirds" solution for 20 min. (Use fine mesh gauze and Kerlix or coarse gauze sponges for soaks.) Rinse and pat dry. Apply a thin layer of antibiotic ointment and expose to air.

During debridement of full-thickness burns of the face, a fine mesh gauze and Kerlix dressing will be used. The procedure is the same as for other areas of the body, but the frequency of care is increased. *Note:* If major vessels are exposed in the wound, keep a hemostat at the bedside for use in the event of erosion.

Nose care   Because the nose is made of cartilage and soft tissue, which can be easily destroyed by infection, the nose must also receive special attention during face care. After cleansing inside the nares with an applicator soaked in "halves" solution, remove any crusts. Then apply topical antibiotic ointment sparingly inside the nares. *Note:* If a nasogastric tube has been inserted, do not tape tightly to the nose; cleanse around the tube every 4 to 6 h.

Eye care   On admission, if the patient's eyes or eyelids appear to be burned, cover the eyes with saline pads until they can be evaluated by the physician. An ophthalmology referral will probably be made as soon as possible. If the ophthalmologist writes orders, follow them closely. If the eyes do not require an ophthalmology referral, give the following special attention.

Supplies needed for eye care are a balanced salt solution, sterile gloves, a basin, applicators, and eye drops or ointment as ordered by the physician. Gently cleanse the area around the eyes and eyelids with applicators or gauze sponges and a sterile solution to remove crusts and drainage. Repeat this on the same schedule with face care. Use balanced salt soaks to soften or loosen crusts. If eye ointment or drops are ordered, give them at the prescribed times and in an effective manner.

If the patient is unable to close the eyes, inform the physician and possibly suggest a methylcellulose or lubricating drop to protect against corneal abrasion. A tarsorrhaphy (a procedure in which the eyelids are sutured closed) may be done to protect the cornea, but this does *not* eliminate the need for eye care; follow the above cleansing procedure. If eye pads have been ordered, have the patient close the eyes under the pad to prevent corneal abrasion. It is important to explain each procedure and contact to the patient who must wear the eye pads or who has impaired vision due to tarsorrhaphy, medication, or injury.

If the patient normally wears glasses, have the family bring them in and have the patient wear them as soon as possible. Cover grafted or open areas with sterile gauze pads or dressings before putting on the glasses.

Do not apply Cortisporin or any other ointment containing steroids in or near the eyes (unless ordered) because the anti-inflammatory effect of steroids may increase the possibility of a severe infection of the eye (panophthalmitis).

Postoperatively, if stents are placed over a released lid contracture, gently cleanse the area around the stents with a saline solution on an applicator; instill drops or ointment as ordered.

Ear Care

The ears are composed of cartilage and require special attention to prevent chondritis and deterioration or loss of cartilage from infection. Repeat ear care with each dressing change and every 4 to 6 h. Clip all hair and shave a 2-in margin around the immediate wound area. Keep the area shaved until the ears are healed. At the time of tubbing or dressing change, cleanse the external auditory canal with a detergent or "thirds" solution on applicators to remove crusts and debris. Lightly pack a padding of fine mesh gauze or Kerlix, moistened with the topical agent prescribed, in the outer ear and behind the ear, between the ear and scalp, to prevent webbing. Hold this packing in place with a Kerlix dressing (see Fig. 30-16). Report and record any difficulty in hearing or complaints of ringing, buzzing, etc. Have an otoscope available so that the physician may view the inner ear. Do not drape dressings over the ears. Dress all unhealed wounds of the ear because wound contact with linen or the pillow can lead to chondritis.

Burns of the inner ear are rare. However, ear drops or irrigations may be ordered to cleanse the inner ear. The inner ear is a delicate area, requiring gentle treatment and aseptic technique. Treatment is done only under a physician's order.

Scalp

If the scalp is included in the wound, keep all hair shaved to prevent matting and wound infection; cleanse and dress the scalp like other wounds. Change the patient's position frequently so that the pressure of lying on one area of the scalp will not cause a decubitus ulcer.

Perineum

A perineal wound requires special care because the area is both usually moist and in constant danger of

---

TABLE 30-9
Special Area Care*

1. Face, eyes, ears, nares, and mouth
   Cleanse with applicators or coarse gauze pads, using saline (for eyes) or a saline detergent solution to remove crusts and purulence.
   Allow soaks to remain on 10 min for heavy crusts.
   Rinse thoroughly with saline.
   Air-dry.
   Apply topical antibiotic ointment.
   Apply thin film of povidone-iodine (Betadine) or detergent to the ears (only).

2. Perineum
   Frequency: every 4 to 6 h and after each elimination.
   Cleanse with saline and detergent solution on gauze pads.
   Rinse thoroughly with saline.
   Air-dry or apply dressing and topical agent as ordered.

3. Tendon and bone
   Keep area moist and sterile.
   Change dressing every 4 to 6 h.
   Soak with saline prn between dressings.
   Use sterile technique for all procedures.

* To be done every 4 to 6 h except between 11 P.M. and 6 A.M.

---

contamination. Insert an indwelling urinary catheter on admission, and cleanse the catheter at the meatus twice daily. If dressings cannot be maintained, exposure is the best treatment, but be sure to abduct the legs to prevent contractures and maceration. Cleanse the perineum with soap and water and a clean water rinse after each elimination and every 4 h. Pad the area with sterile towels or diapers when the patient uses the bedpan. If the bedpan cannot be used, the patient may eliminate in sterile diapers. Keep moist fine mesh gauze dressings between burned buttocks to enhance debridement and formation of granulation tissue and to prevent webbing. Place a sterile towel or blue incontinency pad around dressings of the upper thighs to prevent fecal contamination. Change the sterile towel when it is soiled, rather than the entire dressing.

Muscle, Tendon, and Bone

The basic principles of wound care apply to burned or exposed muscle, tendon, and bone. In addition, if exposed muscle, tendon, and bone becomes dry,

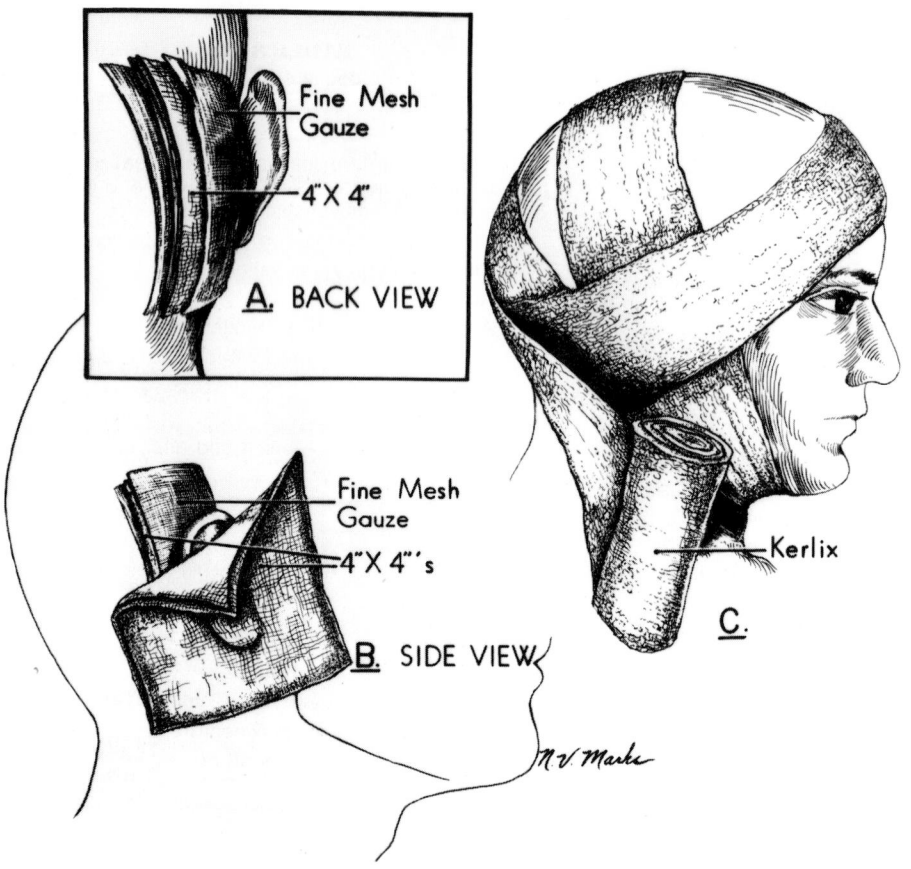

FIGURE 30-16

Dressing the ear. To protect its delicate cartilage, special care is required. After shaving a margin of hair around the ear and removing any crusts and exudate, a layer of fine mesh gauze is placed behind the ear to prevent "webbing." Fine mesh gauze and coarse gauze pads (4 in by 4 in) saturated in the topical agent of choice are placed over the ear and held in place with a Kerlix wrap. The ear should not be exposed until completely healed.

viable tissue will die. *Keep these areas moist* and scrupulously clean to prevent any infection. Using sterile technique, change fine mesh gauze and Kerlix over these areas at least every 4 h. As soon as these areas are debrided they will be homografted for protection until autografts can be applied.

Hairy Areas

Because hair provides a nidus or focus for infection, keep all hair in or near the wound shaved clean to ensure infection control. Hair will grow in a partial-thickness wound. Frequently, nurses are reluctant to shave hair in or near a wound, fearing that this may further traumatize the wound. Keep in mind that the tissue in the wound is firm and that if you are as gentle as you would be in shaving yourself, no damage will be done. It is most important that no hair be allowed in or near the wound. (This also applies to personnel hair falling into the wound.)

Shaving When shaving is accomplished during hydrotherapy, thoroughly rinse the patient on the way out of the tub to remove any debris and loose hair. Before shaving an area, clip any excessively long hair and then wash the area to be shaved with soap and water. Gently shave the area and thoroughly rinse with clean water or saline. Pat dry and apply the dressing to the area.

Shave male facial hair (whiskers) daily whether the face is included in the wound or not. Shave any hairy areas of the body (axilla, perineum, chest, extremities, etc.) in or near the wound on admission and as necessary thereafter.

Scalp hair Clip scalp hair to 2 in on all patients admitted (except reconstructions) to prevent "fall out" into the wound and to ensure infection control. If the face and/or neck are included in the wound area, clip scalp hair to 1 in and shave a 2-in margin around the wound. If the scalp is included in the wound, shave the scalp on admission and afterward as needed until the wound is healed.

Hydrotherapy and Dressing Change

Principles of Hydrotherapy

Hydrotherapy—bathing the patient and/or the wound in water—has become an important part of burn wound care. Traditionally, the hydrotherapy procedure was a part of the physical medicine or rehabilitation program; however, because of the advantages provided the burned patient, a hydrotherapy tub and team are frequently included in a central dressing change area.

The hydrotherapy procedure is relatively simple and does not require the services of a physical therapist. However, the physical therapist should be included, if at all possible, for range of motion exercises. Essential to the procedure is cleaning the tub, the equipment, and the room after every tubbing. The benefit of tubbing is eliminated if infection is spread. There are a variety of tubs available for use. The size and location of the wound and the patient's age, size, and ability to ambulate will determine which tub will be used. Generally, the warm bath provides a feeling of comfort and well-being to the severely burned patient and facilitates dressing removal.

The specific principles of tubbing for wound care are wound cleansing, relatively frictionless exercise of extremities, and total body cleansing. Dilution (and thereby, reduction) of the bacterial population of the wound is accomplished within the first 3 min the patient is in the tub. Gentle scrubbing is required to remove exudate, debris, and previously applied topical agents. This is enhanced by water agitation. Eschar is softened and loosened, although sharp debridement is necessary to remove adherent eschar.

Maintenance of joint motion, possibly decreasing the incidence of contractures, may be accomplished, provided that the patient either is encouraged to exercise or is taken through full range of motion.

Perineal care, shaving, daily bath, shampoo, etc. may be accomplished while the patient is in the tub. Gentle washing is required to clean any area; the agitation will not provide cleansing. Healed grafted areas may also be cleaned. *Note:* Spray-rinse the patient on the way out of the tub to remove the debris from cleaning and shaving.

Indications for Hydrotherapy

Hydrotherapy is begun on admission (as part of the admission procedure) and is continued until grafting is completed unless contraindicated. During the emergent period, the patient is usually tubbed only once daily. Twice-daily tubbing begins as soon as the patient's condition warrants, that is, when debridement begins and the patient's condition is stabilized. The physician must order any changes in the frequency of tubbing. Wound care, however, does *not* stop because of complications.

Contraindications to Hydrotherapy

Tubbing is discontinued where there is *any sudden change in the patient's condition which would signal an impending complication*. Examples of such changes are a sudden sharp rise or fall in blood pressure, pulse, or respiration; a temperature over 103°F or below 98°F; and an electrolyte or fluid imbalance. Hydrotherapy is also contraindicated for *patients with endotracheal tubes or tracheostomies or who require respiratory assistance*. Patients with endotracheal tubes may be taken, on a plinth, to the tub room. Their dressings are removed, and they are sprayed clean over the tub—not immersed in it—and weighed. If respiratory assistance is required, a respiratory therapist should accompany the patient. Patients having tracheostomies for a long period of time may be immersed on physician's orders if their general condition permits.

Tubbing is discontinued on newly grafted areas for 3 to 5 days or until grafts have "taken." Tubbing resumes per the physician's written orders. Patients with fractures cannot be tubbed until the fracture mends.

Solution Used for Tubbing

Water from the tap, warmed to a certain temperature, is the major component of the solution. A variety of chemical additives may be included, depending on the needs of the patient. Salts, detergents, antibacterial agents, antifoam, etc. may be added.

Water A temperature of 98 to 104°F is average, although individual adjustments may be made. Higher temperatures may be more comfortable for some patients, taking into consideration the dissipation of heat. New admissions frequently find lower temperatures (96 to 98°F) more comfortable because of the cooling effect. The volume of water to be used is predetermined, allowing for displacement by the patient, and all other additives are based on this figure.

Salt *Sodium chloride* (NaCl) is added to provide an isotonic (0.9%) solution which will neither irritate the tissues nor dialyze the patient. To provide an isotonic solution, 1.2 oz (34.02 g) of salt is added per gallon of water. For example, approximately 11.25 lb of salt are needed for 150 gal of water, 22.48 lb for 300 gal of water. Sodium chloride may be withheld on physician's orders if the patient is hypernatremic.

Frequently, potassium chloride (KCl) is added to prevent "pulling off" potassium from the patient. Potassium chloride is added at the rate of 0.03 oz (0.85 g) per gallon of water. This provides an isotonic solution. The physician's orders dictate the addition of desired solution of salts.

Detergent A neutral soap or detergent solution may be added to provide a gently abrasive cleansing action. The amount is determined by the tub capacity. If detergent cannot be used because of environmental reasons, such as clogging drains, calcium hypochlorite may be substituted.

Calcium hypochlorite Calcium hypochlorite, $Ca(OCl)_2$, is a bleaching powder used for its disinfectant properties. A 20 ppm solution is desired for tubbing. This requires the addition of 1 tbsp (15 mL) of $Ca(OCl)_2$ to 150 gal of water. Calcium hypochlorite must be stored in covered containers, since moisture causes deterioration (liberation of chlorine).

Antifoam If a detergent is used, then antifoam, a surfactant, is added to decrease the sudsing that results from agitation. Only 2 or 3 drops of antifoam need be added to 150 gal of water. Addition of too much antifoam causes a coating on the patient and the tub, interfering with the desired action of tubbing.

Procedure for Tubbing

Although there are many steps in the hydrotherapy procedure, many may be performed simultaneously, depending on the number of personnel assigned to tubbing. The entire procedure—filling the tub, tubbing, disinfecting, and cleaning—requires about 45 min. Allow 15 to 30 min for treatment of the patient (10 min for dressing removal, weighing the patient, etc. and 15 to 20 min in the tub) and 15 to 20 min for cleaning and filling the tub. If the patient has an extensive burn, this procedure may take an hour.

All tubbing activities are done using cubicle isolation technique. The nurse should establish a contract with the patient and encourage self-help (exercise, removing dressings, etc.).

Remember to talk to the patients during the procedure rather than about them.

The following *safety measures* are important: *Stay with the patient at all times;* do not leave the patient unattended. Do not use the lift control to pull the patient to and from the tub. Always check the hooks holding the plinth to see that they are securely fastened before lifting. Check plinth windings and holes for tears and be sure that the overhead electric cord is not tangled before raising or lowering the plinth. Do not handle the lift control with bare or wet hands. *Do not* turn the agitator on unless it is in the water. It is water-lubricated and will burn out if turned on dry.

Prior to tubbing, be sure the patient has adequate IV solution and respiratory assistance and that vital signs have been checked, etc. Organize all supplies needed for the tubbing procedure. Fill tub with the proper solution for that patient and attach the headrest. Then transport the patient to hydrotherapy on a plinth. Put on gown, gloves, mask, and shoe covers; use clean gloves to remove dressings, and use axilla-length gloves for tubbing. Remove outer dressings and loose inner dressings (place dressings in proper receptacle). Attach the plinth to an overhead carrier and transfer the patient to the tub.

The following may serve as a step-by-step checklist for the tubbing procedure:

Lower the patient into the water.

If the patient has an endotracheal or tracheostomy tube, suspend the plinth just inside the tub or rest it on the bars. Bars may be designed to fit on top of the tub; rest the plinth on them while spraying the patient. Do not lower the patient into tub.

Spray inner dressings and remove.

Spray-rinse the wound.

Debride.

Allow patient to soak; remove remaining inner dressings. (Place dressings in proper receptacle; if allowed to float in the water, they will jam the agitator when it is turned on.)

Turn on the agitator.

Clean unburned areas (Fig. 30-17a and b): wash all unburned skin, shave hairy areas in or near the wound, shave facial hair, shampoo scalp hair, give mouth care (brush teeth, have patient expectorate into emesis basin), give perineal care, and clean inside nose with applicators.

Clean burned areas with coarse gauze pads or sponges.

Do special area care; use applicators to clean folds of ears, eyes, and inside nose.

Exercise extremities or encourage patient to do so.

Turn off the agitator.

Raise the patient out of the water (not out of the tub).

Spray-rinse the patient's entire body (Fig. 30-18).

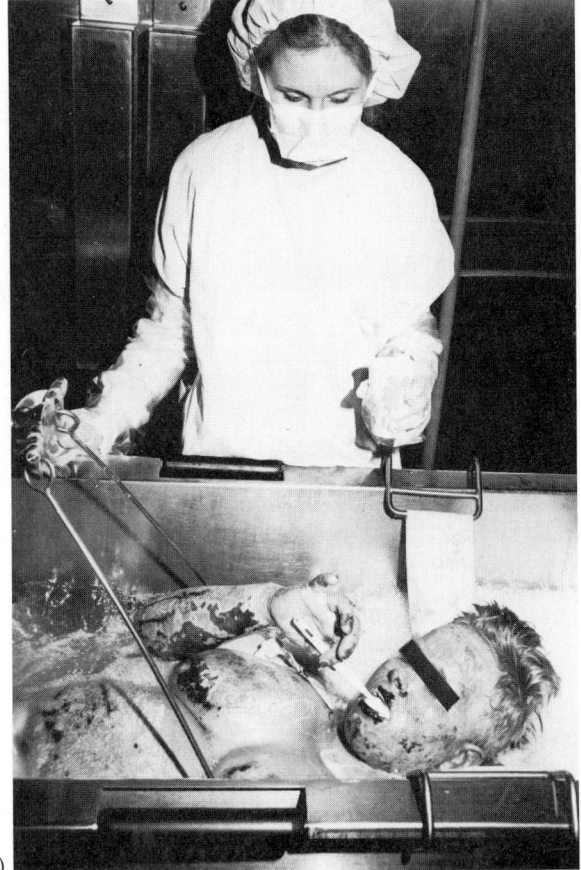

(b)

FIGURE 30-17

(a) Patient may be tubbed with cast for fracture if ingenuity is used. The wound is not cleaned, however, unless gently washed. (b) Hygiene can be done while the patient is in the tub. Wash all unburned skin, shampoo, shave, care for mouth, and total bath.

After tubbing, cover the stretcher with a sterile sheet and folded bath blanket and transfer the patient to the stretcher on a plinth. Cover the patient with the sterile sheet (sterile bath blanket may be added for warmth). Pat unburned areas dry. Then transfer the patient from the plinth to a second stretcher covered with a sterile bath blanket and sheet. Remove gown and gloves and transfer patient to dressing room.

Procedure for Dressing Change

All dressing procedures require sterile technique. Prior to dressing, put on a cover gown and mask. Set

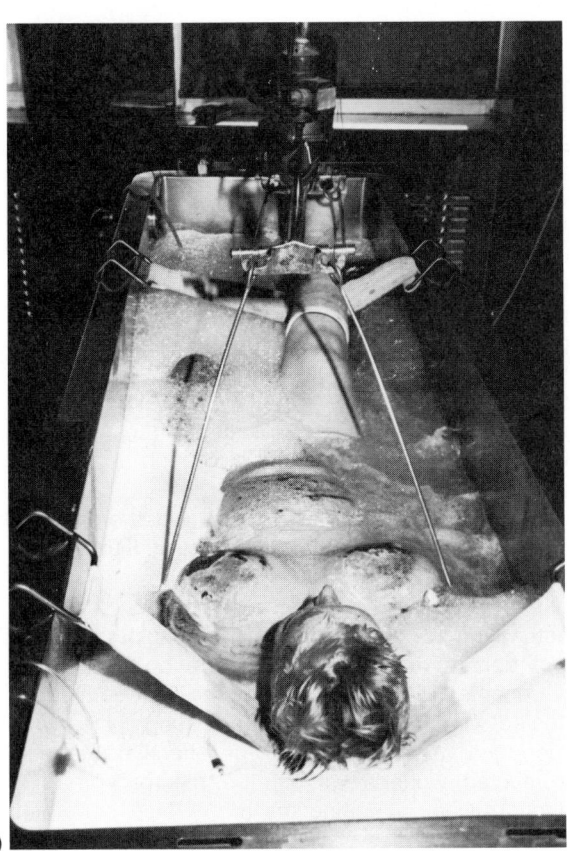

(a)

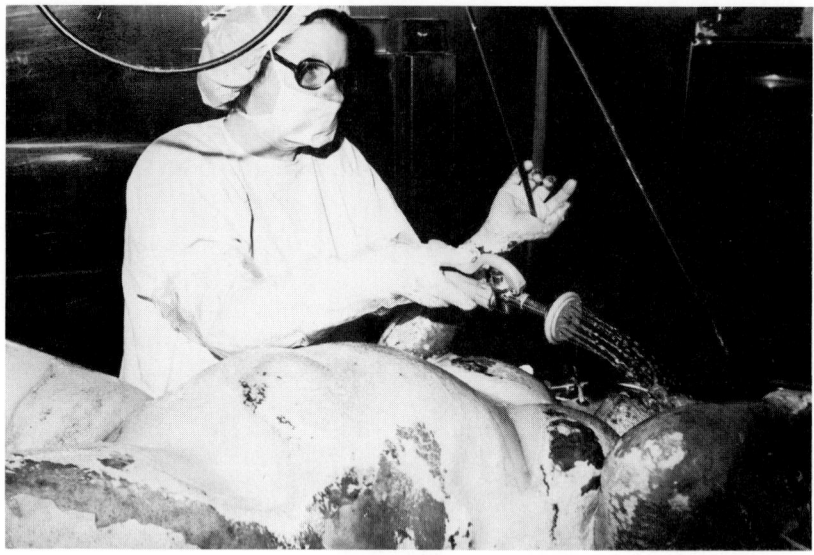

FIGURE 30-18

Spray-rinsing the patient on the way out of the tub removes debris from tubbing
and is most important to the effectiveness of the procedure.

up the dressing table for that patient and then place a sterile cover over it.

The following may serve as a step-by-step checklist for dressing the patient:

Transfer the patient to a stretcher covered with a bath blanket and sterile sheet (if this wasn't done in tub room).

Uncover the dressing table.

Add solutions to the basin.

Put on sterile gown and gloves.

Debride any areas overlooked in tub.

Change gloves after debriding.

Lay grafts.

Exercise extremities (if not done in tub).

Do special area care (if not done in tub).

Apply dressings and splints.

Cover the patient with sterile sheets.

Remove gown and gloves.

Transfer the patient to the cubicle.

After dressing, dismantle the dressing cart and dispose of all linen and trash. Clean all horizontal surfaces with specified cleaning solution, spot wash walls, and clean floors to sight. Remove cover gown, mask, and gloves and replace all equipment and supplies.

Cleanup of Hydrotherapy Room

The entire effectiveness of the hydrotherapy procedure hinges on effective cleaning of equipment between patients to prevent cross-contamination. Hydrotherapy decreases the number of bacteria on the wound by dilution and by washing them away from the wound. In essence, after the first 3 min of immersion, the greatest effectiveness of bacterial cleansing has been reached and the patient is floating in a bath of bacteria and debris.

There is some controversy over whether tubbing spreads infection more than it reduces it. If the patient is not thoroughly rinsed, bacteria will remain on the patient, and if the tub is not thoroughly cleaned, bacteria will be passed on to the next patient. In a study done at the University of Michigan Burn Center on decontamination of the tub during treatment of infected wounds, a simple, but thorough, cleansing procedure was shown to provide effective treatment of infected wounds without the risk of spreading infection. *Note:* Cleaning the tub is also performed using the principles of cubicle isolation.

Skin Grafting

Survival is directly related to the size of the wound. The primary objective of wound care is to reduce the size of the wound as rapidly as possible, thereby increasing the patient's chance for survival (see Fig. 30-19). Once the wound is reduced to less than 20 percent of the total body surface area, the chance for survival approaches 100 percent. Full-thickness wounds require autografting to obtain permanent skin coverage and to achieve the natural immunity of the intact anatomical barrier of the skin destroyed by the burn injury. With good care, the body can reheal a partial-thickness wound.

Types of Grafts

Various grafts may be used to achieve this goal; however, only autografts provide permanent coverage (Table 30-10).

Autografts (isografts) Autografts are grafts of the patient's own skin and are applied to provide permanent coverage for full-thickness injuries.

Homografts (allografts) Homografts are skin grafts taken from another member of the same species. In burn care, homografts (usually cadaver skin) are applied to provide temporary coverage. Homografts are used as a biological cover to decrease infection, protect nerve endings, and to prevent heat and fluid loss. Homografts may be used on partial-thickness wounds to protect them while healing takes place or on full-thickness wounds until the patient can tolerate the autografting procedure or has donor areas available. They may also be used to prepare an area for autografting.

Heterografts (xenografts) Heterografts are skin grafts from another species (e.g., an animal, such as a pig) which are also applied to provide temporary cover.

Synthetic grafts Synthetic grafts (e.g., Epigard) also provide temporary cover.

The Recipient Site

The ideal recipient site is clean, healthy granulation tissue which is ready to accept an autograft. All the previously discussed care of full-thickness wounds is directed toward achieving a healthy recipient site. Autografts either take poorly or are rejected on an unclean or infected recipient site. Homografts or

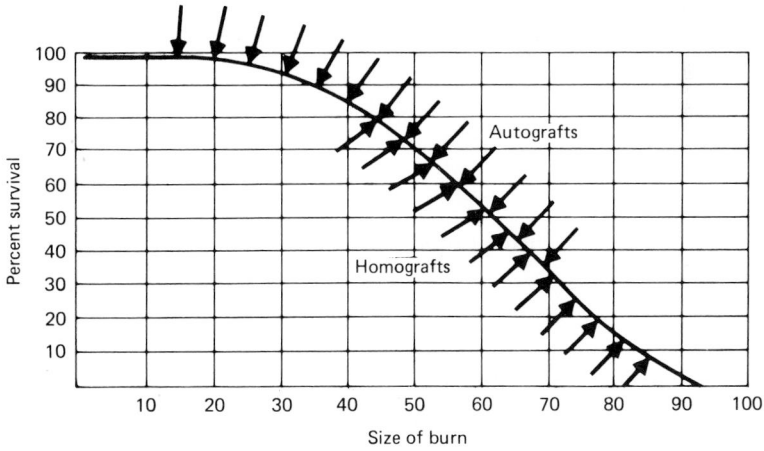

FIGURE 30-19

Survival is related to the size of the wound. This curve describes the recovery of a 32-year-old female admitted with an 85 percent full-thickness wound. The chance for survival on admission was less than 5 percent. However, as the wound was reduced by homografts and then by autografts to less than 20 percent total body area, the patient's chance for survival increased to 100 percent. Her recovery was typical of burn patients in the group of age 5 to 34 years. (*Courtesy of National Institute for Burn Medicine.*)

TABLE 30-10
Types of Grafts

Graft	Source	Coverage
Autograft	The patient's own skin	Permanent
Isograft	Genetically identical source (e.g., twin)	Permanent
Homograft (allograft)	Another of the same species (e.g., cadaver skin)	Temporary
Heterograft (xenograft)	Another species (e.g., pigskin)	Temporary
Synthetic substitute	Artificial material which is skinlike	Temporary

heterografts may be applied to a less than totally clean recipient site to assist in preparing the granulation bed for autografting. With good wound care, some areas of healthy granulation tissue should be available for autografting as soon as 21 days after the burn injury.

Healthy granulation tissue is pinkish red, slightly granular, and only faintly shiny. No eschar, shreds of debris, or products of infection remain on the wound. If a recipient site is in this condition and autografts are not available, or the patient's condition contraindicates a surgical procedure, the healthy granulation tissue should be covered with homografts. If wound tissue is allowed to continue to granulate, the tissue will become very granular, red, and shiny and will not accept a graft.

Preoperative Preparations

Conduct a physical examination 24 h prior to surgery to reevaluate the patient's physical condition and correct any problems. Review vital signs and laboratory studies from the previous 3 days and repeat hematocrit, WBC, creatinine clearance, BUN, and urinalysis to evaluate blood volume, presence of infection, and renal function. Obtain a chest x-ray and ECG to determine cardiopulmonary function, and type and cross-match blood for possible transfusion.

Explain the surgery to the patient and family and answer all questions. Tell the patient what to expect after surgery; explain postoperative positioning and the need for regular coughing and deep breathing. Discuss the expected outcome of the grafting procedure. Arrange a consultation with the anesthesio-

logist to evaluate the patient's physical condition and to determine preoperative medication and the anesthetic agent. The anesthesiologist can also reassure the patient, explain the anesthesia process, and answer questions.

Obtain an operative permit for each procedure performed under general anesthetic. The patient may sign the OR permission sheet if able or may make an X. If an X is used, two witnesses are required. If the patient cannot sign, permission from the next of kin is necessary. This may be telegrammed to the hospital if the person cannot visit. Any difficulties in obtaining an operative permit may be solved by a social worker. The social worker may also be useful in helping the patient work through worry over self, family, finances, etc.

Preoperative physical preparations include the following: Select the donor site and prepare with a soap and water wash twice in the 24-h preoperative period. The final shave and scrub are done in the OR. To decrease the chance of infection from "nicks," a depilatory is used. Prepare the recipient site with at least three dressing changes in the 24-h period prior to grafting. Do the last dressing 1 h prior to laying skin, whether in the OR or at the bedside.

Keep the patient NPO 8 to 12 h prior to general anesthesia. Increase IV fluids correspondingly during the period to avoid dehydration. Ensure adequate rest the night before surgery through ample sedation (either sleep medication and/or narcotics).

On the day of surgery, prepare the donor site with a soap and water wash and rinse 1 h before the surgery. Prepare the recipient site with a tubbing and a dressing change with 0.5% neomycin solution 1 h prior to laying skin or debridement. Remove hairpins, false teeth, contact lenses, and any prostheses. Empty bladder by draining catheter or have patient urinate, and then regulate the IV flow rate. Give preoperative medication as ordered, usually 1 h prior to the procedure and protect the patient after medication is given (e.g., side rails up).

The Grafting Procedure

Skin is taken under anesthesia, but anesthesia is *not* necessary to lay skin. Grafting of skin may be done in the operating room or at the bedside. Either way, the grafting procedure requires sterile technique.

The following are supplies required for laying skin: autografts or homografts, sterile towels, sterile basin, sterile gloves, sterile scissors and pickups, dressing supplies, fine mesh gauze, Kerlix, topical agent, and skin slitter or expander (optional). After you have set up the supplies, put on a sterile gown; then expose the wound. Remove the skin from the storage container and place it in a sterile basin. Put on sterile gloves. It is important to remember to handle the skin as little as possible. Do *not* rinse in saline unless specifically ordered to do so. Apply the skin (shiny side down) to the clean granulation tissue, smoothing out all folds and wrinkles with the handle of a hemostat or pickups. Clip any skin that overlaps onto an unclean wound or unburned area so that it will "fit" the wound. Ater all skin is laid, apply a fine mesh gauze and Kerlix dressing that has been saturated in the topical agent of choice.

Postgraft Care

Principles   The principles of ensuring a successful graft are to use sterile technique to prevent infection, keep the newly grafted area moist if dressings are applied (the graft may also be treated open), prevent tension (pulling on the graft), prevent pressure (e.g., lying on the new graft or use of a BP cuff), and prevent excessive heat (from heat lamp or body heat from lying on the wound). A capillary bed will build within 24 h after a graft, which ensures "take." The graft will usually be "pink" within an hour. Do not disturb the dressing over a new graft for 12 to 24 h unless otherwise ordered. The physician usually does new graft dressings because it is felt the physician will take greater care not to dislodge the new graft; however, an experienced nurse can do as well. The physician continues to change the dressings over newly grafted areas for the first 3 days; then the nurse resumes dressing changes.

Procedure   Remove the Kerlix from the grafted area down to the fine mesh gauze 12 to 24 h after grafting, on the second day, and on the third day. Report on the condition of the grafts. If purulence is present, also remove the gauze and gently cleanse the area. Soak dressings over new grafts (before removal) with saline only. Use of peroxide may traumatize new grafts. Use the handle of the pickups to hold the graft in place and ease the gauze off the graft. Gently cleanse the area with applicators soaked in saline (if necessary). Clip blebs on new grafts and dab out the exudate using a sterile applicator; *do not roll exudate out*. Reapply dressings; place fine mesh gauze saturated with topical agent over the graft, cover with an intermittent layer of Kerlix, and hold in place with continuous Kerlix.

Omit hydrotherapy to the grafted area for at least 3 to 4 days after grafting. (First tubbing is done without agitation.) If patient must remain in one position on abdomen or back to allow grafts to take, change the sheets as often as necessary. Grafted, healed, or unburned areas should not be neglected because of positioning. Prop the patient alternately on one side then the other, using pillows under the abdomen or back. Expose healed grafted areas to air whenever possible. Cleanse healed grafted areas carefully; remove crusts with soap and water, and then apply lanolin cream. Encourage the patient to exercise the area when fully healed. New autografts on the lower extremities require bedrest for at least 10 days after grafting to prevent venous engorgement from standing or dangling. After that time the patient may be up with Ace bandages wrapped to the thighs.

Donor Care

Principles   The donor site (the area of the body from which the autograft is taken), represents a partial-thickness wound that temporarily increases the total wound area. Meticulous care is required to heal the donor site as rapidly as possible and thereby decrease the total size of the wound. The principles of donor care are to (1) keep the area free from infection, (2) dry and heal the area, and (3) provide patient comfort.

Postoperative care   The patient will return from surgery with a dressing over the donor site, which will bleed and ooze until hemostasis is established. A variety of dressings may be used over the donor site as the physician chooses, but the principles of care remain the same. The following is one method used when scarlet red dressings cover the donor site:

Wrap a Kerlix dressing saturated in "halves" solution over the donor area every 6 to 8 h until the dressing on the donor site has dried and oozing has stopped. The peroxide in the "halves" solution aids the drying process. Discontinue moist dressings when the donor site is sufficiently dry, usually in 3 to 5 days. Expose the donor site dressing and trim ragged edges. Peel off and clip the dressing as it dries. When the gauze is totally dry, usually within 10 days, soak with water to aid removal. A dry dressing indicates healing. Remove crusts with soap and water and apply a lanolin cream after the dressing is removed. Do not apply lanolin cream until the dressing is totally dry. If any evidence of infection (purulence and/or inflammation) is noted, soak off the donor site dressing and dress the area with a topical agent ordered by the physician. Do not apply pressure, tension, or heat to donor sites. The only exception to this is profuse bleeding of a fresh donor site; apply Ace wraps over dressing soaked in "halves" solution, and elevate the extremity. Do not apply a blood pressure cuff or heat lamp to a donor site. Apply a lanolin cream daily to completely healed donor sites as well as to healed recipient sites both to keep them pliable and to help remove crusts.

All illustrations in this chapter were obtained from the following references.

REFERENCES

Archambeault-Jones, Claudella, and Irving Feller: *Procedures for Nursing the Burned Patient,* Ann Arbor, Michigan: National Institute for Burn Medicine, 1975.

Feller, Irving: *International Bibliography—Burns,* Ann Arbor, Michigan: American Burn Research Corporation, 1969. *Supplements to International Bibliography on Burns 1970, 1971, 1972, 1973, 1974, 1975, 1976, 1977, 1978, 1979.*

Feller, Irving, and Claudella Archambeault: *Nursing the Burned Patient,* Ann Arbor, Michigan: National Institute for Burn Medicine, 1973.

Feller, Irving, and Claudella Archambeault-Jones: *Teaching Basic Burn Care,* Ann Arbor, Michigan: National Institute for Burn Medicine, 1975.

Feller, Irving, Claudella Archambeault-Jones, and Katherine E. Richards: *Emergent Care of the Burn Victim,* Ann Arbor, Michigan: National Institute for Burn Medicine, 1977.

Feller, Irving, Jairus D. Flora, Jr., and Richard Bawol: Baseline results of therapy for burned patients, *JAMA* 236(17):1943, 1976.

INTRODUCTION

Civilian trauma only recently has been recognized as one of the major afflictions of modern man. It is the third cause of death (behind cardiovascular disease and cancer) for persons of all ages and is the leading cause of death of children and young adults. Approximately 120,000 persons are killed in accidents in the United States each year. Additionally, there are about 400,000 permanently disabled trauma victims. Because of the prevalence of accidents in the young, trauma is the leading cause of disability for all diseases. The tragic death or crippling of the young in the prime of life deserves the attention of all the public and particularly the health professions, who by their exposure to the problem are aware of its magnitude.

The written history of medicine repeatedly has addressed the problem of wound care. The history of trauma surgery has followed, by necessity, the major wars, and from that wartime experience standards of care have been developed and carried over into peacetime. Prior to the nineteenth century, the management of battlefield injuries was disorganized and primitive, and the mortality rate from wounds exceeded 20 percent. Improvement in care in the field, rapid evacuation, and modern surgical management have progressively lowered the mortality rate from 8 percent in World War I and 4.5 percent in World War II to 2.7 percent in the Vietnam war. Although the lessons from the battlefield have been applied to civilian medicine, the overall mortality rate for civilian trauma remains 3 to 5 percent. A number of factors contribute to this. First, civilian trauma affects persons of all ages and mortality can be directly related to age. Second, care at the scene of the accident and evacuation to medical facilities remain primitive in many parts of the country when compared to military standards. And finally, the prevalence of severe blunt trauma, primarily from auto accidents, predicts a high baseline mortality rate. The goal of trauma surgery should be not only to attempt to decrease the mortality rate, but also to decrease morbidity. The morbidity of trauma is not easily measured, but probably represents a major cost to society; moreover, the proper care of trauma victims will probably have its greatest impact in decreasing morbidity.

The key to an improved approach to the trauma patient is to consider trauma itself as a disease which has its own natural history and specialized problems, and one which would benefit from specialized care. Inherent in this concept is that the trauma victim

31

THE MANAGEMENT OF TRAUMA

A. Crane Charters
Nancy Stewart

INTRODUCTION
SCENE OF THE ACCIDENT
Signs to Recognize
INITIAL RESUSCITATION
Priorities
Airway
Hemorrhage
Examination and Diagnostic Approach
Procedures
Logistics of Resuscitation and Equipment
General Principles of Wound Care
MANAGEMENT OF SPECIFIC INJURIES
Head
Spine
Eye and Maxillofacial
Neck
Chest
Abdomen
Genitourinary
Vascular
Orthopedic
ICU CARE OF THE TRAUMA PATIENT
General Considerations
Special Problems in Intensive Care of Trauma Victim
MORBIDITY OF TRAUMA: SPECIAL CONSIDERATION FOR THE CRITICAL-CARE NURSE
Physical Disability
Social and Cultural Disability
Psychological Implications
The Patient's Family
Stress in the Trauma Unit
Mechanisms for Dealing with Stresses
REFERENCES

should be taken out of the mainstream of medicine and surgery in the hospital and treated by a team that has specialized training and interests. The *trauma center* has developed from this type of team approach, and for the most severely injured, it represents a significant advance in care.

The natural history of trauma has not been well defined. The traditional breakdown into blunt and penetrating injuries appears valid. The most common cause of death in patients with penetrating wounds is hemorrhage, followed thereafter by infection or pulmonary failure. Except for patients who have lethal wounds of critical organs (i.e., the brain), most of these deaths can be attributed to errors in treatment or management. With blunt trauma, the primary cause of death is head injury, which accounts for over one-half of the deaths. If the patient survives the head injury, then pulmonary failure and infection represent the greatest risk to life. Hemorrhage follows thereafter, a much less important factor than with penetrating injuries. Although not well proved prospectively, there is little doubt that improper resuscitation of the injured patient initially contributes to subsequent pulmonary failure and infection, and may aggravate the consequence of head and other injuries.

It becomes apparent that there is a great need for enlightened care of trauma victims. Early and late deaths can often be attributed to mismanagement, and the inherent morbidity of any injury is critically influenced by the care given. Care at the scene of the accident, resuscitation, management of specific injuries, intensive care, convalescent care, and rehabilitation must all be considered.

THE SCENE OF THE ACCIDENT

Any trained health professional should offer assistance at the scene of an accident. Tradition as well as Good Samaritan laws have protected individuals who render first aid. It is usually possible to establish continuity of care with ambulance responders, and seldom is it necessary to accompany the victim beyond the immediate scene of the accident. The trauma professional at the scene of an accident often can provide critical help.

Signs to Recognize

The most important sign of significant injury is external evidence of trauma, and except for obvious hemorrhage, it is often overlooked. Abrasions, contusions, and pain on movement can be observed at the accident scene and may lead to early recognition of occult injuries. Back and neck pain may suggest spine injury. Abrasion and contusion of the chest and abdomen may herald occult injuries and are particularly useful signs in the presence of concomitant head injury. Deformity and pain suggest extremity injury. All patients should be managed as though they had sustained serious injury until a thorough examination can be made, usually at a medical facility. If the patient is unresponsive because of head injury, it should be assumed that spine, thoracic, and abdominal visceral injuries are present until proved otherwise.

There are several first aid principles to follow at the scene of accident or injury.

1. Remove patient from hazard only when risk (e.g., fire) outweighs danger of moving patient.

2. Establish airway, usually by elevating jaw.

3. Initiate cardiopulmonary resuscitation if indicated.

4. Control hemorrhage, usually with direct pressure.

5. Splint spine and extremity injuries.

6. Move and transport as soon as possible.

One of the main objectives of care at the accident scene is to prevent further injury. Care in extracting and transporting victims to avoid further damage in spinal injuries cannot be overemphasized. Similarly, attention to limb position and simple splinting will decrease the sequelae of long bone fracture. Avoiding further contamination of open wounds can be accomplished by mere attention to the problem.

In most urban settings there is no way of providing extensive field care of trauma victims, and it should be discouraged, despite television coverage of paramedic services which suggests that field care should be provided in every instance. Ordinarily, the most important axioms of care of trauma victims are (1) avoid further damage and (2) "load and go." It is difficult to argue against intravenous fluid support as long as it does not significantly delay transit. A good rule of thumb is that any in-field procedures should not exceed 3 min. Definitive care of trauma victims requires the hospital setting, and the sooner the patient is in it the better.

A trained health professional at the accident scene can often contribute in addition to providing first aid. The professional is a source of reassurance and strength to the victim and other responders. A series of priorities can be established, such as indicating which victims should be transported first and what first aid need be provided. Frequently, available communication equipment is not utilized, and usually one can communicate directly with the receiving hospital through ambulance or police radio and convey critical information about the victim which will enable the hospital staff to better prepare for the arrival.

One of the most useful functions that can be performed is to be an enlightened observer, recording such facts as time of the accident, the mechanism of injury, neurological status, contributing factors, and knowledge of the victim's family. This information is often only available at the accident scene and can be of considerable importance in the hospital setting when it accompanies the patient in transit.

INITIAL RESUSCITATION

Priorities

The first step in the resuscitation of the severely injured is to establish some priorities which will dictate the subsequent course of events. The margin between survival and death will be significantly influenced by the appropriateness of this initial decision making. It is useful to categorize injuries into (1) injuries which are an immediate threat to life, (2) injuries which need attention but are not an immediate threat to life, and (3) injuries which produce occult damage and the risk is not immediately apparent. The first group of injuries, those that are an immediate threat to life, fortunately are rare but are important because often simple therapeutic measures will be life-saving. Injuries which require attention but are not life-threatening make up the majority of injuries seen. Soft tissue injuries, bony injuries, and many head and visceral injuries can be treated within a reasonable time frame without endangering the patient. Finally, injuries which produce occult damage are infrequent but particularly troublesome diagnostic problems.

The following general outline suggests an overall approach to the resuscitation of a trauma victim upon admission to the emergency room. The three main items are phrased as questions which should always be asked.

1. Are any first-aid measures necessary?

   a. Establish adequate airway and ventilate if necessary.

   b. Stop hemorrhage.

   c. Initiate treatment of shock.

   d. Note neurological status of patient. (The baseline neurological status of the trauma victim is of such a critical nature that it warrants being considered a first-aid procedure and must be done immediately upon admission.)

2. What are the patient's obvious injuries? (This should be a superficial assessment and not a detailed examination.)

3. What is the plan or sequence of the resuscitation? It is important not only to be aware of the categories of injuries outlined above, but also to recognize the most common indications for "urgent operation," that is, those injuries which would require rapid operative intervention and would take precedence over soft tissue or bony injuries. The indications for urgent operation are

   a. Intra-abdominal visceral injuries

   b. Intracerebral injury with expanding hemorrhage

   c. Thoracic injury resulting in uncontrolled hemorrhage or massive air leak (i.e., ruptured bronchus or trachea)

   d. Major vascular injury

The resuscitation should then proceed to include the following items, but not necessarily in the sequence listed. Each resuscitative effort should be individualized based upon an understanding of the principles involved and the specific injuries encountered.

1. Airway and respiratory support

2. Large-bore central IV

3. Blood to laboratory

4. Foley catheter

5. Nasogastric tube

6. Splints

7. Diagnostic studies (peritoneal lavage, x-ray, arteriogram, IVP, cystogram)

8. Assessment of peripheral factors (availability of blood, operating room, special studies; specialty consultation; consent, family, law, press)

9. Repair of superficial injuries

Accident victims with minor injuries do not necessarily need a central line, a Foley catheter, or abdominal paracentesis; however, a major multiple trauma victim might require those procedures plus a great deal more. Standardized resuscitations have the advantage of decreasing decision making and providing a minimum level of care; however, individualizing the response is clearly optimal if the expertise is available.

Airway

Establishing and maintaining an airway and providing respiratory support, if necessary, are the initial steps and cornerstone of any resuscitative effort. Failure to provide adequate oxygenation may seriously aggravate head injuries, further damage ischemic organs such as the kidney and liver, and will markedly interfere with efforts to reverse hypovolemic shock. The majority of trauma victims maintain their own airway and ventilate adequately; however, patients with head and facial injuries, patients with multiple injuries, and patients with thoracic injuries represent a high-risk group and may need an airway. Stridor, retraction, and the other clinical signs of upper airway obstruction or respiratory insufficiency are the prime indications. Often an oral or nasopharyngeal airway will suffice, particularly until a planned intubation with a nasotracheal or oral tracheal tube can be performed. It is important to avoid causing the patient to gag and vomit and incur the risk of aspiration. Under some circumstances, a cuffed endotracheal tube should be inserted primarily to prevent this problem. Patients requiring ventilatory support also require an endotracheal airway. The following airway problems require individual attention.

Fractured Jaw

The unstable fractured jaw presents a potential airway problem in that the tongue lacks the bony support for protrusion. Although sufficiently conscious to attempt to bring the tongue forward and maintain an airway, the patient may not be able to do so. Any patient who has an unstable jaw fracture represents a potentially serious airway problem and requires at least a nasopharyngeal airway and may require intubation.

Neck Trauma

Patients with severe blunt trauma to the neck may present with two particular airway problems. They can have a disruption of the larynx or trachea per se, or there may be sufficient soft tissue swelling to lead to airway obstruction. Often these patients will have an adequate airway on admission and then develop progressive difficulty with soft tissue swelling. They may lose their airway acutely anytime in the early postinjury period.

Cervical Fracture

It is important to avoid extending the neck in patients who have suspected or known cervical fractures. When these patients require intubation, the best choice is a nasotracheal airway. If this is not possible technically, a tracheostomy may be required; however, this is often a difficult operation because of the low-lying position of the trachea in the unextended position. In an emergent situation, an oral tracheal intubation can be performed in many patients by holding the head firmly in axial traction without extension using strong, forward traction on the base of the tongue and jaw to visualize the laryngeal structures.

Blood in the Oral or Nasopharynx

Blood, clots, and other foreign bodies, such as teeth and vomitus, in the oral and nasopharynx present a great risk to the airway in multiple-injured patients. It should be assumed that all patients with significant nasal or facial trauma have blood in their pharynx. Although they are often able to ventilate adequately, they may acutely obstruct, particularly when they are stimulated by an attempt at intubation. It is important to be aware of the risk and keep the mouth and pharynx clear with suction throughout the course of resuscitation.

Emphasis should be placed on the need for preparation and expertise in the intubation of multiple-injured patients. Those patients who arrive at the hospital usually will be able to ventilate sufficiently to allow adequate preparation. Sufficient help, light, suction, appropriate equipment, and expertise (anesthesiologist) should be obtained. It is not a situation for the junior house officer to learn intubation by experience. The multiple-injured patient presents the most challenging airway problem, and the most experienced person should perform the procedure. Acute airway problems in the emergency room area are often precipitated by an attempt at intubation. A planned, systematic approach is the best prophylaxis.

When is an emergency tracheostomy indicated? The answer to this question is almost never. The majority of patients who need airway and respiratory support can be intubated as outlined above. If this is not possible technically, then a tracheostomy should be considered. Again, in the majority of patients, this can be done as a semi-urgent procedure in a controlled operating room setting. In the rare situation where a patient acutely loses his or her airway and intubation is not possible, a cricothyroidotomy should be performed as an emergency procedure, followed by an elective tracheostomy in the operating room when the patient's condition permits. It is important to note the potential difficulty in attempting emergency tracheostomies in children. The thyroid cartilage does not become a permanent structure until puberty, and the loss of this important cervical landmark increases the difficulty in doing emergency tracheostomy in children.

Hemorrhage

The appropriate management of traumatic hemorrhage depends on recognition of blood loss and an estimate of the amount. As blood loss continues, the rate of loss becomes an important additional factor. External losses may not always be appreciated, particularly if a history of blood at the scene of the accident is not available. Patients with scalp lacerations can potentially bleed to shock levels at the scene of the accident and have minimal evidence of bleeding in the emergency room. Hidden blood loss, particularly intra-abdominal and intrathoracic hemorrhage, can only be estimates at best, until some actual evacuation of the blood is performed. It is an axiom that a trauma victim in shock without evidence of blood loss is bleeding into the chest or abdomen, and this should be an important guideline in dictating diagnostic studies.

Trauma victims who present with the clinical signs of hypovolemia already have significant blood volume depletion, and their existing deficit can be estimated by appreciating the body's compensatory mechanisms at each level of volume deficit. Table 31-1 is helpful in estimating blood loss based on these findings.

A knowledge of the time from the accident to arrival in the emergency room and time course of the resuscitation is helpful in estimating the rate of bleeding. This is particularly important in patients with hidden hemorrhage in the visceral cavities. A patient in shock who arrives in the emergency room 20 min after an injury has a much greater potential rate of blood loss and is in a much more precarious situation than the patient who drifts into hypovolemia 3 or 4 h after an injury.

Controlling hemorrhage is second only to airway in providing first aid to the trauma victim. Usually, control of external loss from surface wounds can be obtained by direct compression, and the use of tourniquets is seldom, if ever, indicated. Ultimately, specific control of the bleeding vessel can be obtained in the course of managing the wound per se. Facial wounds, at times, require immediate direct control because of the difficulty in applying compression dressings. Rarely, patients with massive hemorrhage from intrathoracic or intra-abdominal wounds will require immediate operative control as a first-aid maneuver, and this may preclude the usual sequence of resuscitation.

The following principles are useful in understanding the rational approach of the hypovolemic trauma victim:

1. Electrolyte solution is as effective as colloid for volume replacement if appropriate volumes are used.

TABLE 31-1
Estimation of Blood Loss

Volume Deficits	Pathophysiology	Manifestations
Mild shock (20 percent of blood volume)	Decreased perfusion of nonvital organs and tissues (skin, fat, muscle, bones)	Pale, cool skin. Complains of feeling cold, urine is concentrated
Moderate shock (20 to 40 percent of blood volume)	Decreased perfusion of vital organs (liver, gut, kidneys)	Oliguria to anuria, slight drop in blood pressure
Severe shock (40 percent or more of blood volume)	Decreased perfusion of heart and brain	Restlessness, agitation, coma, cardiac irregularities, ECG abnormalities, and cardiac arrest

2. The space of distribution of infused colloid is the intravascular space.

3. The space of distribution of infused electrolyte solution is the extracellular fluid space.

4. Blood is the only solution with oxygen-carrying capacity.

Balanced salt solution is readily available in all emergency rooms and is the best first choice for volume replacement. Initial fluid therapy should be the rapid infusion of up to 2 to 3 L of balanced salt solution. If the patient has not returned to the normal volume state, if blood loss continues, or if the hematocrit falls below 30, then blood should be started at that time. It is important to emphasize that blood should be given when it is indicated based upon the patient's clinical state and not when it is "available" from the blood bank. Usually by the time 2 to 3 L of salt solution has been infused, major group typing will be completed; this markedly reduces the potential of mismatched transfusions, particularly in this group of patients who are often young and have not had previous transfusions. The large experience using uncrossmatched blood in the Vietnam war supports this concept. It is important not to severely hemodilute the patient before starting blood. The initial infusion of 2 to 3 L of saline takes advantage of the beneficial effects of hemodilution and yet will usually maintain a hematocrit of about 30. This maintains an optimal oxygen-carrying capacity and provides some margin of safety in the event of a misjudgment in replacement or in the instance where hemorrhage continues. The argument between the use of electrolyte solutions and nonblood colloid solutions, such as albumin, has been going on for 20 years without resolution. Because there is no great advantage of colloid solutions over electrolyte solution and some potential disadvantages, the simplified approach outlined above has merit. It is important to reemphasize, however, that the space distribution of electrolyte solution is three to four times that for colloid solutions, and therefore, appropriate volumes must be given.

In the event that the shock state does not respond to what appears to be appropriate volume therapy, a number of other factors must be considered. The following are important causes of treatment failure which should be considered:

Continued and/or hidden loss of blood or fluid

Acid-base imbalance

Hypothermia

Hypocalcemia

Previous treatment with antihypertensive drugs

Cardiac contusion or tamponade

Pneumothorax

Anesthesia

Vascular fatigue

Examination and Diagnostic Approach

After the resuscitation has been initiated, it is essential to perform a thorough physical examination including certain routine diagnostic tests. The objective of this exam is to identify all the injuries as well as coexisting medical diseases that may contribute to the patient's outcome. Only then will it be possible to proceed with appropriate special diagnostic studies to assess known or suspected occult injuries. In the course of the examination, it is important to categorize the injuries by priority so that the appropriate sequence of diagnostic and therapeutic procedures can follow. The physical examination should be a planned systematic evaluation of all organ systems. Although portions of that exam frequently are composite, the organization in this chapter will be by organ systems. Injuries to specialized areas such as the eye and hand require detailed examination and diagnostic studies beyond the scope of this text, and only general principles will be alluded to. One of the most important concepts of examining the injured patient is that the same person or team should perform serial examinations to accurately assess changing findings. Occult injuries usually manifest themselves by a developing symptom complex, and this can only be appreciated by serial exam by the same examiner.

Neurological

Direct trauma to the nervous system may be grossly apparent by evidence of injury to the head, spine, or peripheral nerves or the presence of cerebrospinal fluid (CSF) rhinorrhea or hemotympanum. The goal of the neurological exam is to document the extent of the injuries, identify expanding intracranial hemorrhage, and establish a prognosis when that is possible. The most important aspect of the examination is the level of consciousness and mental status. The level of consciousness ranges the spectrum from alert and oriented to a deep unresponsive coma. Altered mental status may be related to the trauma but is often overlooked. Somnolence, confusion, disorientation, inappropriateness, and combativeness may all be manifestations of intracerebral trauma. The picture is often confused by the coexistent presence of drugs, alcohol, and hypovolemic shock.

Changes in pupil size and asymmetry suggest rising intracerebral pressure compressing the third cranial nerve. It is important to distinguish these eye signs from those of direct eye trauma. Anisocoria alone may not be significant, but in conjunction with other neurological findings or their development during the resuscitation period, anisocoria is an important sign of increased intracerebral pressure.

Lateralizing motor and sensory findings are important in the assessment of peripheral nerve injuries and in certain discrete central lesions. It is important to assess these before anesthesia is induced, particularly if there is a known or suspected spine or extremity injury.

The most useful diagnostic study for evaluating expanding intracerebral hemorrhage is the CAT (computerized axial tomography) scan. Skull x-rays are obtained on patients with head injury and abnormal neurological examination but are seldom helpful in identifying mass lesions. At times an arteriogram or a ventriculogram may be the diagnostic technique of choice, particularly if the CAT scan is unavailable.

Head and Neck

The most threatening injuries to the head and neck are to the cervical cord, the larynx, and the trachea. Cervical spine injury may be suggested by an abnormal neurological exam, soft tissue swelling, or tenderness in the region of the cervical spine, or at times, pharyngeal swelling. Frequently, however, there is little evidence of trauma, and recognition of cervical spine injury results only from a high index of suspicion. Pharyngeal and tracheal injury are usually suggested by adjacent soft tissue trauma and signs of upper airway obstruction. Patients with severe cranial facial trauma must be evaluated not only for bony injury but also for damage to the cranial nerves, lacrimal ducts, and parotid ducts. A thorough search of the scalp must always be performed for the presence of unrecognized lacerations. It is a useful axiom that any patient with a head injury has an eye injury until proven otherwise; therefore, it is critical to assess separately visual acuity, visual field, and extraocular eye movements as well as the structural integrity of the globe and its contents. Loose or dislodged teeth must be identified and preserved for fixation or reimplantation. Jaw injuries can be rapidly assessed by noting not only dental occlusion but the ability to bite

a wooden tongue blade. There is little or no value, and in fact some potential hazard, in probing penetrating wounds of the neck. It is important to note the direction of the wound if possible, especially wounds of the thoracic outlet which potentially can injure major vessels in that area.

Chest

Examination of the patient with a chest injury begins with the assessment of the respiratory status as well as the recognition of any external signs of trauma. Examination of the bony thorax should include not only the clavicles, ribs, and scapulae but also an assessment of the stability of the chest wall itself. Auscultation is helpful in assessing the extent of the ventilatory effort and the presence of respirations bilaterally. Detailed auscultation of the chest is seldom rewarding. Early chest x-ray is indicated in all patients with major trauma and is part of the initial resuscitative efforts in patients with penetrating chest injuries. Occasionally, insertion of thoracostomy tube will be required prior to obtaining a chest x-ray, as in an obvious sucking chest wound. However, in the majority of injuries it is possible to obtain chest x-ray first to assess the extent of the pneumothorax and hemothorax. It is important to attempt to distinguish early between the entities of pulmonary contusion, aspiration, and pulmonary or cardiac failure secondary to underlying disease and chest wall injury.

Abdomen

It is useful to divide abdominal injuries into blunt and penetrating and the latter into gunshot wound and stab wound in order to categorize the diagnostic approach to these different injuries.

A careful search should be made for an exit wound in all gunshot injuries; however, it cannot be assumed that it necessarily reflects the trajectory of the wound. Chest and abdominal x-ray should be obtained in all patients with gunshot wounds. Appreciating that the diaphragm can ascend to the fifth intercostal space during full expiration makes any chest wound below the nipples suspect for a concomitant abdominal injury until proven otherwise. Similarly, upper abdominal wounds must be suspect for thoracic injury because of the extent of the posterior sulcus. Unless the gunshot wound is clearly a grazing injury, all wounds require surgical exploration in the operating room and few diagnostic studies are required beyond the presence of a nasogastric tube, rectal exam, and a urinalysis, all looking for blood.

Stab wounds to the abdomen require a selective management, and it is not necessary to explore all wounds. Little is gained by probing the wound. The primary indication for operation is the presence of peritoneal irritation, suggesting visceral injury; therefore, the abdominal exam must be a careful search for those signs, including tenderness, guarding, rebound, and the absence of bowel sounds. Serial examination by the same examiner is an essential feature of this management.

Blunt abdominal injuries present one of the most difficult diagnostic challenges to the examiner. The presence of contusions and abrasions suggests abdominal injury in many instances. If signs of peritoneal irritation are present, then exploration is indicated. However, in the absence of these signs or in patients in whom an adequate examination cannot be obtained (such as intoxicated patients, comatose patients, and combative patients) the technique of peritoneal lavage is useful in distinguishing those patients which require exploration. This is a highly sensitive test with few false negative results; as such it has replaced abdominal paracentesis as a diagnostic study in blunt abdominal trauma. Patients with blunt abdominal trauma and a positive lavage require exploration. When the lavage is clear, serial observation is appropriate. Rarely, when the index of suspicion is high, further diagnostic studies such as isotope scanning, sonography, or arteriogram may be indicated.

Genitourinary Tract

Careful examination of the perineum and a pelvic exam should be performed on all trauma victims to rule out injuries to the external genitalia. In the absence of signs of external injury, hematuria is a hallmark of genitourinary tract injury. If bright red blood issues from the penis, it suggests urethral injury and dictates a urethrogram prior to insertion of a Foley catheter. This should be suspected in patients with pelvic fractures, and they should be encouraged to void spontaneously prior to inserting catheter. All patients with hematuria regardless of the mechanism of injury must have an intravenous pyelogram and cystogram. Usually this can be obtained preoperatively, even in patients with major intra-abdominal injuries, simply by injecting the intravenous pyelogram dye prior to taking an abdominal flat plate. A detailed study may not be possible; however, knowing the functional status of the kidneys is useful infor-

mation in planning the operative approach. If there is failure to visualize one or both kidneys, then an arteriogram is indicated to assess the vascular supply of the kidneys.

Spine

The key to recognition of spinal injuries is to be highly suspicious. Neurologic examination may be positive in those instances where there is cord or nerve root damage. It is important to obtain a baseline neurological exam and note even the most subtle changes, because a changing neurological examination may be an indication for exploration and decompression. Examination of the spinous processes for tenderness, soft tissue swelling, and deformity, particularly in the area of the low thoracic and lumbar spine, often is neglected because patients are resuscitated in the supine position.

Extremities

Extremity injuries are often obvious at the time of admission, and they are frequently noticed because of the associated pain, particularly on movement. The unconscious patient or the patient with overwhelming associated injuries requires special attention. Careful palpation of the extremity for deformity, angulation, soft tissue swelling, and functional deficit may suggest some occult injury. It is important to carefully document sensation, motor function, and vascular supply, particularly in patients with proximal injuries. Peripheral vascular injury should be suspected in both blunt and penetrating trauma to the extremity. Arteriogram is indicated when the wound is approximate to a major vessel, when there is a large or expanding hematoma, in the instance where pulses are absent, or when there is a history of absent pulses. At times, the approach to such injuries may be direct operative intervention rather than an arteriogram, and this should be individualized on the basis of the wound itself.

Routine Laboratory Studies

In general, patients sustaining major injury will have normal baseline laboratory values. However, the rationale for obtaining studies in the acute situation is to recognize underlying disorders such as anemia or diabetes and to obtain a baseline against which subsequent changes can be measured. The list indicates those studies which should be obtained in all patients with major trauma.

1. Hematocrit

2. Type and crossmatch

3. Urinalysis

4. Chest x-ray

5. ECG (chest trauma, patients over 45 years of age, history of heart disease)

6. Arterial blood gases

7. Glucose

8. Creatinine

9. Electrolytes

10. Amylase (abdominal injuries)

11. Liver function studies (liver disease)

12. PT, PTT, platelets (bleeding disorders)

Procedures

The mark of an experienced trauma team is a rapid meticulous technical approach to the procedures which must be performed, frequently in the presence of the apparent turmoil of the resuscitation itself. Unfortunately, all too often sloppy technique, failure to maintain sterile fields, and failed attempts at procedures are testimony to the lack of preparation and knowledge of the trauma team or emergency area staff. It should be reemphasized that the sequence of the procedures should be dictated by the injuries themselves.

Intravenous Lines

Establishing a large-bore intravenous line is the first step in fluid resuscitation. The best first choice for an intravenous line is a large peripheral vein, often in the forearm or antecubital fossa. A no. 14 plastic catheter often can be inserted percutaneously. This should then be connected to tubing which contains a hand pump and filter to allow the rapid administration of fluid and blood. Because trauma frequently strikes young, healthy individuals, the veins in the arm and antecubital fossa are usually accessible. When this is not the case, one should consider a cutdown just proximal to the antecubital area. A subclavian line is seldom the best first choice for an intravenous line in a trauma victim. The incidence of complications is appreciable, particularly when done in less than optimal situations, and the complications themselves are potentially lethal in these seriously injured patients. Central venous lines of the subclavian and supraclavicular route may well be indicated

in the course of the patient's therapy; however, they are seldom the best initial choice as a route of access. Central venous lines provide the knowledge of filling pressure of the right side of the heart and as such are useful in monitoring resuscitation. Although these are important and useful, they are not needed initially to begin resuscitation, and prolonged attempts to establish a central line should not preclude the administration of fluid by other routes. Often the central line can be passed percutaneously with a long line at the initial attempt to establish an IV. Most patients with major trauma will require more than one intravenous line, and lower extremity IVs should be considered in patients with chest trauma, particularly injuries to the thoracic outlet. Lower extremity lines are often used in children because of the accessibility of the saphenous vein. The one technical feature which should be emphasized is the need to adequately immobilize the IV sites with tape and dressings to prevent dislodgement or kinking. As soon as the initial intravenous line has been established, it is usually possible to withdraw blood through that line and submit it to the laboratory. This avoids a second venapuncture and ensures that the blood is sent to the laboratory early in the course of the resuscitation.

The advent of the Swan-Ganz pulmonary artery catheters has been applied rapidly to the field of trauma. If a central venous line is indicated, then a Swan-Ganz catheter should be considered. There are several important advantages of this line over a central venous catheter: (1) access to central venous blood, (2) access to the left atrial filling pressure, and (3) facility for rapid repetitive measures of cardiac output by thermal dilution. A Swan-Ganz catheter is indicated in patients who have traumatic shock and concomitant heart failure, patients who develop pulmonary failure, and patients who fail to respond to appropriate resuscitative measures.

Arterial Lines

An arterial line is a useful adjunct in the management of trauma victims and provides constant arterial pressure monitoring as well as access to the arterial system for blood gas determination. Usually a percutaneous radial artery line can be established; however, at times a more central line or a cutdown may be necessary. One should consider a temporal artery cutdown as an alternative in some patients. Because of the concern for the rare ischemic complications, arterial lines have been reserved primarily for patients with severe trauma and shock and those who require respiratory support.

Foley Catheter

A Foley catheter is indicated in patients with severe trauma and shock. In the presence of pelvic trauma, it is important to rule out urethral injury. If a pelvic fracture is suspected and the patient is unable to void spontaneously or bright red blood issues from the penis, then a urethrogram should be performed prior to an attempt at passing a Foley catheter. Unless a simple stricture can be dilated or a prostatic obstruction is identified, a suprapubic tube would be indicated as an alternative. The need for a meticulous sterile technique in passing the catheter cannot be overemphasized. Urine output should be monitored at 15-min intervals during resuscitation and then at hourly intervals until the patient's hemodynamic status is stable.

Nasogastric Tube

A sump-type nasogastric tube is preferred and should be inserted early in the resuscitation of all major trauma victims, especially those with suspected abdominal trauma. An attempt should be made to empty the stomach, and then the nasogastric tube should be placed on suction during the resuscitation effort. Alkalinization of the gastric content should be considered early in the patient's course and continued until the tube is removed. This will effectively minimize the incidence of stress ulceration and decrease the insult should aspiration of gastric content occur.

Thoracostomy Tube

When closed thoracostomy tube drainage is indicated in trauma patients, a posterior lateral tube is usually preferred. This should be placed in about the fifth intercostal space laterally and never below the sixth or seventh space to avoid injury to the subdiaphragmatic structures. The lateral tube is preferred in anticipation of hemothorax as well as pneumothorax, even though the initial x-ray may not demonstrate it. At times a second chest tube is required to effectively expand the lung and evacuate the chest cavity. It is important to make every effort to remove all the blood initially to minimize the development and sequelae of a pleural peel from an organized clot. All connections from the patient to the water-trapped seal should be taped. It is important to tape the chest tube itself to the patient's side to avoid traction on the tube at the skin suture site. In patients with penetrating chest wounds, it is best not to use the wound as the site of the thoracostomy tube but rather choose a different area so that those wounds can be managed independently. It is important to monitor the chest tube drainage at frequent intervals in the early course of resuscitation to establish that the drainage is decreasing and that urgent thoracotomy is not indicated.

Peritoneal Lavage

Peritoneal lavage is an important diagnostic procedure in patients with blunt abdominal trauma. Two techniques can be used. If the patient is able to tense the rectus muscles, then a small vertical skin incision can be made and the catheter inserted by a gentle dissection using a trocar and direct penetration of the abdominal wall and peritoneum accomplished. If, however, the patient is unable to tense the rectus muscle or is otherwise uncooperative, a small cutdown procedure should be performed to avoid injury to the intra-abdominal viscera. A vertical incision is made and the dissection carried down through the linea alba. Meticulous hemostasis is secured, and the fascia is then held upward on traction and the peritoneum penetrated with the trocar catheter. Then 1 L of balanced salt solution should be run into the abdomen, and it is helpful to gently role or shake the abdominal contents to ensure good mixing. The tubing is then lowered to the floor and the lavage fluid allowed to run out. We have preferred a qualitative examination of the fluid. If the return fluid is sufficiently discolored with blood so that the examiner cannot read newsprint through the tubing, that is considered a positive lavage. Only enough return need be examined to clearly define the results of the tests. If the return is slightly pink initially and then clears, this is considered negative and probably reflects some local bleeding at the puncture site. After the test has been interpreted, the catheter is removed and the wound is closed with steri-strips. The procedure itself should not alter the physical examination of the abdomen except in the immediate area of the puncture site, and patients can be followed with serial exams after a negative lavage. The technical aspects of peritoneal lavage should be emphasized because an equivocal result complicates the management of the patient significantly.

Gardner Wells Tongs

Patients with cervical spine injury require traction in an axial position, and the simplest form of management is the immediate application of Gardner Wells tongs in the course of the resuscitation. This can be accomplished with local anesthesia and markedly simplifies management of those patients, particularly if they require a transfer and other operative procedures. Although cervical collar traction has been advocated, it may at times complicate the airway problem. Direct tong traction is preferred.

Burr Holes

The insertion of burr holes is seldom indicated in the emergency room, since most expanding hematomas can be adequately managed in the acute situation with mannitol, steroids, and hyperventilation. This usually will provide a time interval during which the patient can be taken to the operating room and the craniotomy performed in a controlled setting. Occasionally, however, rapid deterioration of the patient in the emergency room and failure to respond may necessitate performing burr holes immediately. For that eventuality, the emergency room area should be prepared and a sterile tray kept on hand. Bilateral burr holes are usually performed over the frontal temporal regions as a temporizing procedure to enable the patient to be moved to the operating room for definitive therapy.

Thoracotomy

Rarely, a thoracotomy must be performed in the emergency room area. Although infrequent, preparation should be made for that eventuality. Indications for opening the chest in the emergency room are the following:

1. To treat cardiac arrest that is unresponsive to closed-chest massage
2. To cross-clamp the thoracic aorta in uncontrolled abdominal hemorrhage
3. To control the hilum of the lung in uncontrolled pulmonary hemorrhage

It is important to emphasize that the last two indications are only temporizing procedures which should be performed on the way to the operating room. They may provide 10 to 15 min of control until the patient can be moved to the operating room setting. This time interval is critical, and the procedure should not be done and then the resuscitation resumed since this would result in a prolonged interval before definitive operation.

Logistics of Resuscitation and Equipment

Most modern emergency rooms have the basic equipment that is required to resuscitate major trauma. However, it is often poorly organized and not readily available when needed. The design of the emergency room area should identify one specific area for the resuscitation of major trauma, and the equipment and supplies in that area should be chosen specifically with the trauma victim in mind. A number of general principles apply to the selection and arrangement of this equipment.

1. It is essential that the medical personnel have immediate access to the patient and not be encumbered by the location and design of the supporting equipment.
2. Suction, oxygen, and monitoring equipment must be immediately adjacent to the patient's head.
3. Overhead IV tracts and traction setup minimize the congestion of surrounding equipment.
4. Adequate lighting must be provided.
5. There must be room for additional equipment such as respirators, defibrillators, and portable x-ray machines.
6. The basic essentials for repair of lacerations and application of plaster must be available.
7. Prepared sterile trays for the basic procedures must be available.

An ideal trauma center has x-ray facilities as an integral part of the resuscitation room. However, this usually is not available and portable x-ray equipment must be used. Therefore, its location and accessibility must be considered in preparing the room for resuscitation of major injuries. In general, operating room capability in the resuscitation area is not necessary, and the underutilization of such a facility makes it less functional in this instance than the regular operating suite.

Maintaining an accurate inventory of equipment and supplies in the resuscitation room is an essential duty of the nurse in charge, and this should be done every shift for critical items and at least weekly to check all equipment and supplies, especially expiration dates. Calibrating monitoring equipment should be considered part of this inventory process. Many of the procedures that will be performed in resuscitation can be anticipated, and it is important to have certain setups ready and waiting, should a trauma victim arrive. Intravenous lines, suction, and monitoring attachments can all be set up ahead of time. Moreover, as soon as knowledge of the patient's arrival and condition is known, special setups can be made ready for insertion of arterial and central lines, transducers, insertion of a Foley catheter, insertion of thoracostomy tube, peritoneal lavage, and other procedures that might be anticipated.

Effective resuscitation of a trauma victim requires coordination of the personnel involved. The saying "Every patient deserves to have at least one doctor" emphasizes the concept that one physician must assume responsibility for the trauma victim's care and it cannot be divided among many specialists. That physician, sometimes known as the *trauma surgeon,* may have any of several special interests; however, it is essential that this doctor be well versed in the management of shock and be knowledgeable about resuscitation. Other physician specialists function in a consultative role and are able to practice their specialty with the understanding that patients' general needs are being met. Nurse roles must also be clearly defined. In the optimum situation, there are at least two nurses involved in resuscitation. One nurse is directly responsible for patient care, including monitoring the patient, evaluating the injuries, helping in the resuscitation, assisting the physician with procedures, and seeing to the patient's immediate needs. The other nurse, or circulating nurse, is responsible for the logistics of the resuscitation and sees that proper consultations are obtained, monitors the traffic in the resuscitation area, ensures that the blood has gone to the laboratory, obtains supplies and equipment, and in general, troubleshoots so that the patient care nurse is not distracted from primary objectives. Other people, such as the ward clerk and nurses aide, may have important roles in the resuscitation; if these individuals are routinely involved, these roles should be clearly outlined.

Several general principles of nursing care should be emphasized. Most important is that every person on the team should have some idea of the general plan of the resuscitation and know "what's next" in the patient's course. Is the patient going to the operating room? Is the patient going to the critical-care unit? Does the patient require immediate x-ray? What is the plan? It is possible to manage patients with multiple-system injury with a minimum of patient movement when all these factors are considered in advance. Moreover, it is important to attend to the psychosocial needs of the patient during the period of turmoil of the resuscitation. Maintaining the patient's psychological well-being and attending to families are equally important to the resuscitative efforts themselves.

General Principles of Wound Care

Often in the course of resuscitation, superficial wounds are repaired. Several principles of wound care are pertinent.

1. Adequate cleansing of the wound cannot be accomplished without suitable anesthesia; therefore, most wounds should be anesthetized prior to cleansing. The usual sequence of superficially washing the area and draping before administration of anesthesia is painful and seldom results in an adequately cleansed wound.

2. All devitalized tissue and foreign body must be debrided from the wound; however, all viable tissue should be preserved whenever possible. In general, converting ragged injuries to linear scars and complicated plastic revisions have little place in initial wound care.

3. Wounds should be approximated throughout their depth and foreign body avoided if possible. Adequate hemostasis, an appropriate use of subcutaneous sutures, and skin closure without tension will lead to the best cosmetic result.

4. Adequate dressings are an important part of wound care. Sealing of the wound does not occur for 12 to 24 h, and during that period an appropriate dressing will significantly protect the wound from external contamination. Moreover, dressings are important in providing immobilization of injured areas as well as minimizing pain and discomfort to the patient.

Central venous lines, arterial lines, and drains all require specialized wound care. This should be meticulously outlined in the written orders, and every dressing should have written on it the date it was changed and what lies beneath it. Only by meticulous attention to detail can these lines be preserved and complications of their use minimized.

THE MANAGEMENT OF SPECIFIC INJURIES

Head Injuries

The successful treatment of open head wounds depends upon an adequate exposure and meticulous hemostasis. With all head lacerations it is important to diagnose the extent of the underlying bony injury. Depressed fractures require elevation, and the galea and scalp should be closed in layers. Wounds extending into the brain require debridement of foreign body, macerated brain, and loose bone fragments. Prophylactic antibiotics are usually recommended with wounds extending into the cranial vault.

The management of closed head injuries depends

primarily upon the diagnosis and treatment of expanding intracranial lesions, the control of cerebral edema, and the maintenance of optimal circulation and oxygenation of the brain. *Extradural hematomas* usually result from lacerations of the meningeal artery associated with linear fractures. Often there is a history of a blow to the head with loss of consciousness. The patient comes to, only later to lapse into coma. During this so-called lucid interval, the patient may have headache, focal neurological signs, or evidence of increasing intracerebral pressure. A CAT scan or arteriogram often confirms the diagnosis. Early surgical treatment gives the best chance for a cure and return of neurological function. During the acute phase, intravenous mannitol can be used to shrink the brain and allow time to get to the operating room. Occasionally, emergency burr holes may be required. Surgical treatment consists of a formal craniotomy over the hematoma, evacuation of the clot, and control of the bleeding vessel.

Acute subdural and *subarachnoid hemorrhage* may have similar clinical presentations; however, the lucid interval is less characteristic. Often these entities will present with a progressive downhill course and evidence of increasing intracerebral pressure. The operative management is similar: the dura is opened and the hemorrhage controlled. However, these lesions are often associated with severe brain injury and the prognosis is poor. Chronic subdural hematomas related to trauma, where the mass effect is more gradual, have a much better prognosis.

It is important to maintain optimal circulation and oxygenation to the brain with any head injury. The circulation to the brain is a function of not only the systemic arterial pressure but also intracerebral pressure which in head injuries determines vascular resistance. Intracerebral pressure is affected by the central venous pressure as well as the oncotic pressure in the brain. These basic physiologic assumptions suggest the following principles of management of head injuries:

1. *Treat shock adequately*—The goal is to provide a normal arterial pressure for maximum perfusion of the brain.

2. *Maintain a normal central venous pressure*—Avoid fluid overloading, prevent straining, and use PEEP judiciously.

3. *Minimize brain swelling*

   a. Hyperventilation will result in a fall in P_{CO_2}, with resulting cerebral vasoconstriction and a decrease in brain size.

   b. Osmotic diuretics—Mannitol or urea can be used to shrink the brain tissue.

   c. Steroids, hypothermia, and barbiturate coma may have some application in special cases.

4. *Provide optimal oxygenation*

   a. Provide normal P_{O_2}.

   b. Maintain adequate hemoglobin levels (hematocrit 30 percent or greater).

   c. Maintain oxygen-hemoglobin dissociation curve in the normal range.

Spinal Cord Injuries

The most important concept in the treatment of spinal cord injuries is to prevent further damage. With open injuries to the spine, operative intervention is indicated if there is a CSF leak, if x-rays suggest foreign body or a bone fragment compressing the cord, or if there is a changing neurological status suggesting compression. Closed spinal cord injuries can be divided into three groups: (1) those with fixed neurological deficits, (2) those without neurological deficits, and (3) those with changing neurological status. In general, the first two groups are treated with traction and a frame bed to meet the primary objectives of preventing further damage by immobilizing the fracture. Although some neurosurgeons explore spine injuries with fixed neurological deficits, most reserve operation for those with unstable fractures, and in many instances, that treatment can be delayed until the patient's condition is stable. Patients who have spine injury and a progressively worsening neurological deficit usually should undergo exploration and decompression of the cord. It should be emphasized that any patient who presents with a neurological deficit needs special attention to skin care, bowel and bladder care, and psychological support from the very beginning. Successful rehabilitation needs an early start.

Eye and Maxillofacial Injuries

The potential loss of sight demands proper handling of all eye injuries. If any injury to the globe is recognized, the immediate treatment is to immobilize the eyes by placing bilateral eye patches. Any cleansing, examination, or manipulation of the eye must be done in the operating room with good anesthesia and proper equipment. Beyond testing visual acuity and voluntary extraocular eye movements, the remainder of the exam should be performed in a proper setting. In general, prophylactic antibiotics are advocated with major eye injuries. Corneal and scleral lacerations can often be repaired, but more extensive injuries to the globe must be assessed individually. After the initial treatment of major eye injuries, the eye can be observed for up to 2 weeks and the need for enucleation reassessed during that period in an effort to preserve the eye if at all possible. The presence of foreign body must be suspect in any eye injury, particularly if there is a noticeable laceration. An x-ray should be obtained in addition to detailed examination of the globe. Contusion to the eye is a common cause of loss of vision, and hemorrhage into the anterior chamber is an ominous sign. The specific management of the complications of blunt trauma to the eye is beyond the scope of this text.

Maxillofacial injuries are at high risk for the development of upper airway obstruction, and this must be kept in mind not only initially but throughout their management. Although many soft tissue injuries are repaired in the emergency room area, the following injuries deserve to be treated in the operating room setting.

1. Parotid gland or duct injury

2. Facial nerve injuries

3. Nasolacrimal injuries

4. Injuries with moderate soft tissue loss

5. Extensive lacerations

Mandibular fractures are often heralded by malocclusion or pain on biting. Usually the fracture can be palpated intraorally and the diagnosis confirmed by x-ray. Treatment consists of wiring the jaw to the maxilla for stabilization, and if the patient is edentulous, this may require a molded prosthesis for proper alignment. Fractures to the orbital rim, maxilla, and nose can usually be diagnosed by palpation, or there may be entrapment of the extraocular eye muscles with orbital floor fractures. Appropriate x-rays must be obtained; however, it is to be remembered that the bone injury is usually more severe than is indicated on the x-ray. Most surgeons favor early repair with open reduction and fixation of the fractures. Fixation can be accomplished by interosseous wires or pins, interdental wiring, and arch bars. At times, however, it is appropriate to await resolution of some of the soft tissue swelling to obtain optimal cosmetic result. Loosened or fractured teeth present a special problem. Loose teeth should be splinted. Avulsed teeth can be reimplanted in some instances when this can be done shortly after injury. The appropriate management of fractured teeth often results in a stable foundation for subsequent reconstruction. Although a fractured or loose tooth may be the least life-threatening problem to the multiple-trauma victim, it may become a greater concern to the patient as the injuries resolve. The best cosmetic result can usually be obtained by appropriate early management.

Neck Injuries

All *penetrating wounds* to the neck and thoracic outlet require surgical exploration in the operating room. Little can be gained by probing the wound, and the incidence of unrecognized injuries to the major vascular structures, the esophagus, and the trachea indicate the need for exploration. Most penetrating injuries can be repaired directly. If an injury to major vessels is suspected, preparation should be made for significant blood loss and extension of the incision into the chest if necessary to control bleeding. Lacerations of the carotid vessels can usually be repaired and circulation restored. With penetrating wounds to the thoracic outlet, an arteriogram is frequently indicated to define the integrity of the vascular structures in that area.

Occasionally, *blunt trauma* to the neck will result in significant injury to the airway, esophagus, or carotid vessels. With laryngeal disruption, open reduction and internal stenting will usually provide the optimum result. Traumatic occlusion of the carotid arteries due to blunt trauma may be suggested by absent pulses in the neck or in the external carotid arteries and can be defined by arteriography. In general, no attempt is made to restore flow in such injuries, because the potential subsequent neurological deficits resulting from reestablishing flow outweigh the potential advantages.

Chest Injuries

Open-Chest Wounds

Open sucking chest wounds present a life-threatening situation. Not only does the lung collapse, but there is a shift of the mediastinum toward the uninvolved side which compromises the ventilation of the good lung as well. The initial treatment of these injuries is to simply close the wound with a simple occlusive dressing, and this will tend to stabilize the mediastinal shift. The second step is to establish closed thoracostomy tube drainage in order to reexpand the lung and evacuate the thoracic cavity of blood and air.

Major defects in the thoracic wall may require operative closure, and at times a thoracotomy will be indicated to repair the underlying lung damage, particularly if there is a continued air leak or major hemorrhage.

Flail Chest

Severe crushing injuries with multiple rib fractures may result in loss of the structural integrity of the thoracic cage. In this situation, when the patient attempts to breathe, the chest cage itself moves in and out, resulting in the so-called flail chest. The degree of movement of the chest wall or flail chest is dependent upon intrathoracic pressures. The flail may be relatively minimal at the time of admission, but with progressive respiratory difficulty and stiffening of the lung, it will become more pronounced. Therefore, patients who are suspect for this type of injury should be observed for the development of a significant flail even though it may not be present on admission. Treatment of a flail chest is to stabilize the chest cage. Traditionally, this was done by external stabilization using either sandbags or sternal traction. However, current management is by means of internal stabilization. This is achieved by intubation and positive pressure ventilation until the chest becomes sufficiently stable that the patient can breathe without help. With a large flail segment and particularly with respiratory insufficiency, an early tracheostomy is advised. Less severe injuries can often be managed with oral or nasotracheal intubation.

Traumatic Hemopneumothorax

Hemopneumothorax can occur secondary to penetrating injuries or blunt trauma to the chest. The diagnosis is confirmed by chest x-ray. Although the chest x-ray may show only a pneumothorax, it must be assumed that there is blood in the thoracic cavity as well. Emergency chest x-rays often are taken with the patient in the supine position, and a relatively large amount of blood can collect in the posterior gutters without being evident. Treatment of a hemo- and/or pneumothorax initially is closed thoracostomy tube drainage. A large-bore (no. 36 French) thoracostomy tube is inserted in the lateral chest, directed posteriorly, and attached to water seal with 30 cm of water suction. In many instances, this will evacuate the chest and reexpand the lung; however, if this does not occur, a second tube should be placed. The location of this tube is somewhat dependent upon the

segment which fails to reexpand. If air is trapped in the apex, a second intercostal space, anterior tube usually suffices. The amount of blood that is obtained from the chest cavity will give some indication of the existing volume deficit, since this blood has already been lost to the patient. Continuing blood loss must be accurately measured to determine whether it is decreasing or an urgent thoracotomy is indicated. Every effort should be made to completely evacuate the chest to prevent the development of an organized clot. The majority of traumatic hemopneumothoraces can be managed by simple closed thoracostomy tube drainage; however, if a large air leak persists or if the bleeding continues, then a thoracotomy is indicated to repair the injury directly.

Pulmonary Contusion

Direct contusion of the pulmonary parenchyma can occur with either penetrating or blunt injury, and this entity should be distinguished from aspiration or posttraumatic pulmonary insufficiency. X-ray findings show evidence of consolidation of lung tissue which is usually focal and often present on admission and tends to clear during the first week with progressive improvement in pulmonary function. Improvement in the x-ray may lag the improved pulmonary function. Changes secondary to aspiration are usually of a more diffuse nature and are associated with a greater degree of pulmonary insufficiency and evidence of tracheobronchitis. In many instances, the aspiration event can be traced. The pulmonary insufficiency that has been described in association with trauma, shock, and major injuries tends to develop after several days. The x-ray findings lag the pulmonary dysfunction. The findings are diffuse, and the characteristic physiologic dysfunction is arteriovenous shunting and progressive loss of compliance of the lung. The treatment of pulmonary contusion consists of prophylactic antibiotics, respiratory therapy to assist in mobilizing secretion, and ventilatory support if indicated.

Heart

Cardiac contusions secondary to blunt trauma should be suspected in all patients with significant chest injury, and an electrocardiogram is needed for these patients. Cardiac enzyme determinations are not particularly useful because of the frequently associated skeletal muscle injuries. Disruption of the epicardial and pericardial vessels can lead to a traumatic pericardial tamponade. This diagnosis is difficult to make but must be suspected in those patients who fail to respond to appropriate volume therapy and have elevation in central venous pressure. Pericardiocentesis can be diagnostic as well as therapeutic. In the acute situation, a relatively small amount of blood in the pericardial space will produce significant alterations in cardiac output, and removing a small amount of blood often will buy enough time for the patient to be moved to the operating room for thoracotomy and direct control of the bleeding.

Most patients with penetrating wounds of the heart will not survive long enough to reach the hospital. However, those who do are a select group, and successful repair of the injury can usually be accomplished. Pericardial tamponade must be suspected and treated by aspiration if present. Patients should undergo immediate thoracotomy and direct repair of the injury as soon as they can be moved to the operating room area.

Thoracic Aorta

With sudden deceleration injuries, the thoracic aorta may disrupt just distal to the take-off of the left subclavian. This unique injury usually results in a false aneurysm of that portion of the aorta. In those patients who arrive at the hospital alive, the bleeding will be tamponaded by the surrounding hematoma and pleura. The diagnosis is suggested by evidence of widening of the mediastinum on chest x-ray and must be confirmed by arteriography. The definitive treatment consists of controlling systemic arterial pressure and urgent thoracotomy with direct repair of the injury.

Esophagus

Successful treatment of traumatic rupture of the esophagus depends upon prompt recognition of the injury and definitive treatment before the onset of mediastinitis. The injury may be suggested by air in the mediastinum on x-ray or in any patient with a wound that traverses the mediastinal structures. Diagnosis can be made by endoscopy and esophagogram using water-soluble medium. Treatment consists of direct layered closure of the injury and drainage of the mediastinum. In those instances where the injury is not recognized early and mediastinitis occurs, it is often more difficult to effect closure of the injury. The principles of management consist of isolating the esophagus from the gastrointestinal tract by performing an esophagostomy, closing the esophagogastric

junction, performing a gastrostomy, and draining the mediastinum. At a later date, repair of the injury and reestablishment of gastrointestinal continuity can be attempted.

Diaphragm

Injury to the diaphragm can occur as a result of blunt disruption or a penetrating injury. This injury may not always be suspected initially. The presence of bowel in the chest on x-ray is diagnostic. Early direct repair is indicated, and the abdominal approach is usually chosen to rule out associated injuries to the intraabdominal viscera.

Abdominal Injuries

Stomach and Duodenum

Most wounds of the stomach are penetrating in origin, and blunt disruption is rare. Blood is usually present in the nasogastric aspirate, and its presence should increase the suspicion for gastric injury. Defects can be closed in layers and a good result anticipated. Duodenal injuries are more serious than gastric injuries because of the potential for unrecognized retroperitoneal perforation and the development of a duodenal fistula. Penetrating injuries can usually be closed in layers; however, duodenal disruption secondary to crush injuries may involve extensive soft tissue damage, and operative management becomes much more complicated. This is particularly true in the presence of infection related to delay in diagnosis and treatment. Duodenostomy drainage, serosal onlay grafts, and procedures which defunctionalize the duodenum, removing it from the gastrointestinal stream, all have a place in the management of these difficult injuries. Occasionally, intramural hematoma of the duodenum will present as a bowel obstruction in the early postinjury period, and this unique injury often can be managed by simple evacuation and drainage.

Small Intestine

Penetrating wounds of the small intestine usually can be managed by simple layered closure and good results anticipated. It is important to make a meticulous search to identify all the perforations and to be cautious in the repair to avoid interfering with the blood supply or significantly narrowing the lumen. Blunt trauma to the small intestine can result in a spectrum of injuries, from simple contusion to total disruption, as well as injuries to the mesentery which may or may not impair the vascular supply. The most common areas of injury are the ligament of Treitz and ileocecal valve region where the mesentery is short and the intestine relatively fixed and subject to shearing forces. The intestine in the midabdomen is at risk to injury by direct compression against the vertebral column. This type of injury can be caused by seat belts, particularly if improperly worn, and should be suspected in those patients with transverse contusion across the lower abdomen. Repair of the injuries consists of obtaining hemostasis, establishing the viability of the bowel, and resecting areas of major disruption.

Colon Injuries

Injuries to the colon require special attention because of the great potential for infection and the difficulties in obtaining satisfactory healing in that portion of the bowel. It should be emphasized that any intra-abdominal infection in a posttrauma victim is life-threatening, and every effort should be taken to prevent its occurrence. The morbidity and mortality of bowel injuries can be directly related to breakdown in the repair or anastomosis, and usually these are related to errors in judgment or technique on the part of the surgeon. In general, the most conservative management of large bowel injuries is to exteriorize the injured portion of the colon by way of a colostomy when that is possible. Simple injuries may be closed in layers if there is minimal fecal contamination. For those portions of the colon which are not easily exteriorized, resection or primary closure with a proximal colostomy to defunctionalize that segment of the bowel can be employed. The use of antibiotics and extensive irrigation of the abdomen to minimize contamination is advocated. Because of the potential for infection, delayed closure of the skin seems appropriate with most open colon injuries. Impalement of the perineum can result in significant anal and rectal injuries. Treatment of these wounds dictates adequate drainage of the presacral space as well as a proximal diverting colostomy.

Liver and Biliary Tract

The principles of management of hepatic injuries are (1) hemostasis, (2) debridement of devitalized tissue, and (3) drainage. Although conceptually simple, application of these principles requires considerable judgment. The spectrum of injury ranges from small lacerations due to knife wounds to extensive parenchymal disruption due to blunt trauma or shotgun blast. Small wounds without massive parenchymal disruption can usually be managed locally by obtaining adequate exposure, directly controlling hemorrhage from the injured surface, and then draining the area to the exterior. More extensive injuries at times may require resection. Usually this is in the form of a debridement type of resection where the laceration is extended and the injured portion of the liver removed. With massive injuries, however, formal hepatic lobectomy may be required. Control of bleeding can be facilitated at times by selective hepatic artery ligation as an alternative to resectional therapy. Injuries to the hepatic veins and the retrohepatic vena cava present the most challenging technical problem to the trauma surgeon, and the repair of these injuries requires special techniques in exposure and shunting of the vena caval blood to obtain control.

Disruption of the gallbladder or bile ducts can occur secondary to either blunt or penetrating trauma. Gallbladder injuries are managed by cholecystectomy. Injuries to the extrahepatic bile duct should be repaired primarily if possible and adequate drainage established.

Spleen

The spleen is the most commonly injured solid viscus due to blunt abdominal trauma. However, because of its location it is infrequently injured by penetrating trauma. In adults, injury to the spleen is managed by a splenectomy. In children, splenectomy should be reserved for major disruptions, and small injuries should be managed by application of hemostatic agents in an attempt to preserve the spleen. Recent evidence suggests that the asplenic child is at risk for development of infections and the management of splenic injuries in children has evolved to one of preservation of the spleen if possible.

Pancreatic Injuries

The successful management of pancreatic injuries depends upon the surgeon's ability to adequately expose the pancreas and diagnose the extent of the injury. The typical injury from blunt trauma is a fracture across the body of the pancreas directly over the vertebral spine. This usually can be managed by distal pancreatectomy and splenectomy. Major injuries to the head of the pancreas and combined pancreatoduodenal injuries are less common but are more serious. Defunctionalizing procedures which remove the pancreas and duodenum from the gastrointestinal stream and actual pancreaticoduodenal resection have been suggested as methods of management. Penetrating wounds of the pancreas should be managed by careful debridement and hemostasis and ligation of the duct injury. Adequate drainage must be established in all instances because of the potential development of a pancreatic fistula.

Retroperitoneal Hematomas

The management of retroperitoneal hematomas must be individualized. Those hematomas which occur adjacent to the retroperitoneal portions of the bowel, particularly the duodenum, must be explored to rule out injuries to the hollow viscera. Similarly, bile staining of the retroperitoneum or air in the retroperitoneum dictate exploration. Expanding or pulsatile retroperitoneal hematoma must be explored to rule out and manage major vascular injury. Other retroperitoneal hematomas related to blunt trauma should not be explored because of the great difficulty in controlling bleeding from the retroperitoneal veins. This is particularly true of large pelvic hematomas associated with pelvic fractures. Retroperitoneal hematomas associated with penetrating injuries must be explored to the extent that the surgeon is assured that there are no associated injuries to retroperitoneal structures such as the ureters or major vessels.

Genitourinary System

Kidneys

Most penetrating injuries of the kidney are explored because of the high association of injury to the intraperitoneal viscera. Direct repair of the renal injury or partial nephrectomy can frequently be accomplished, and nephrectomy is reserved for massive injuries. Blunt trauma to the kidneys can produce a whole spectrum of injuries from simple contusion to major disruption. Nonoperative management is recommended by many surgeons, based upon the knowledge that the majority of these injuries will heal by themselves. If the intravenous pyelogram shows functioning parenchyma, even though there may be some extravasation, judicious observation is often the treatment of choice. On the other hand, if the arteriogram shows major vascular damage or parenchymal disruption, then direct exposure and operative repair is indicated. In most instances, control of the renal

vascular pedicle should be obtained prior to exposure of the injury.

Injuries to the ureters are usually a result of penetrating trauma, and in most instances, the wound can be debrided and direct primary repair accomplished. Drainage of the injury is important, and some authors advocate internal splinting of the ureters.

Bladder and Urethra

Blunt trauma to the distended bladder can result in simple disruption of the muscular dome. This may be intraperitoneal or retroperitoneal. Direct primary repair and drainage of the bladder by catheter or suprapubic tube is indicated. A more serious injury, often associated with severe pelvic fractures, is a shearing off of the membranous urethra just distal to the prostate. Although some surgeons have recommended primary repair, many advocate delayed reconstruction. The injury is associated with a high incidence of urethral stricture and impotence. Injury to the more distal urethra, which may be suggested by swelling and bright blood issuing from the penis, is diagnosed by urethrogram. Early primary repair gives the best result.

Vascular Injuries

Penetrating wounds can result in lacerations or complete avulsion of major peripheral vessels. Although the injury may be clinically apparent, as evidenced by an expanding pulsatile hematoma or distal ischemia, in many instances the diagnosis depends upon a high index of suspicion. Any penetrating wound that is in the vicinity of a major vessel must be suspect and an arteriogram considered. Blunt injuries to an extremity can result in contusion of vessels, intimal disruption, and thrombosis. Fractures adjacent to major vessels can also cause vascular damage, ranging from simple compression of the vessel to complete disruption.

The principles of treatment of all vascular injuries consist of first achieving vascular control and then exploration and direct repair of the injury. Both proximal and distal vascular control should be obtained prior to exploring the injury whenever possible. When there is an associated venous injury, the vein should be repaired first. Although many venous injuries can be simply ligated, the recent trend is toward direct repair in an effort to provide better drainage of the extremity and improve runoff for the arterial repair. The two most common causes of failure of vascular injury repair are (1) inadequate debridement of damaged tissue and (2) anastomosis performed under tension. It is important to debride the injured vessel back to normal tissue, and at times a graft may be necessary to complete the repair without tension. It is important to reduce and stabilize bony fractures prior to attempting any vascular repairs so that subsequent movement does not endanger the repair, and in general this indicates internal fixation as a preferred method.

Orthopedic Injuries

The general principles of fracture treatment depend upon an understanding of the factors which influence healing of bones. In general, fracture healing depends upon local factors of soft tissue injury, circulation, apposition of the fragments, and immobilization. Systemic factors such as age or associated diseases have a greater influence on the patient's survival than healing of the bone itself. Deficiency states, however, can affect fracture healing. In children, fracture healing is usually rapid and complications are limited primarily to problems with bone growth. In adults, certain particular fractures, especially in areas of relatively ischemic bone, will require special treatment and there is higher incidence of nonunion. Nonunion of fractures can result from distraction of the fragments, infection, or inadequate fixation, and often these factors can be attributed to inappropriate management. It is important to recognize that the disabilities which result from bony injury may be due to associated injuries to nerves, vessels, and soft tissue, and that these can be further influenced by immobilization and bony deformity. The goals of fracture treatment are the following:

1. To reduce the fracture to an anatomical setting

2. To immobilize the fracture in such a manner that the healing process occurs at an optimal rate

3. To rehabilitate the patient during the process of healing and obtain an optimally functioning extremity upon healing of the fracture

An important and at times neglected aspect of fracture management is appropriate splinting at the scene of the accident or in the hospital setting prior to definitive treatment. Upper extremity splints may consist of simple coaptation splints with padded boards; sling or swathe dressings for shoulder, arm, or elbow; or air splints for the wrist and forearm. Lower extremity splints may be of the air splint or board splint type or a traction type such as the Thomas splint, which is particularly useful in femur fractures.

The successful reduction of extremity fractures depends upon the time of the reduction, the anesthesia employed, the displacing forces, and the method of reduction. The earlier the fracture is reduced, the less difficulty will be encountered in obtaining an adequate reduction. Once the soft tissue has become fixed, reduction is more difficult. Similarly, appropriate anesthesia is essential to eliminate pain and obtain muscle relaxation. The interposition of loose bone fragments or soft tissue between the fracture can further interfere with the reduction.

There are four basic methods of fracture reduction:

1. Closed reduction

2. Continuous traction

3. External skeletal fixation

4. Open reduction and internal fixation

Closed reduction is usually chosen when good alignment can be obtained and adequate immobilization achieved in a plaster cast or splint. The disadvantages of this type of treatment are restriction in joint motion and interference with normal neuromuscular function. *Continuous traction* as a means of fracture reduction has the advantages of reducing pain and muscle spasm and restoring and maintaining length; this method has particular application in those areas where there is strong muscular pull, such as femoral fractures. Continuous traction can be applied to a bone by fixing the traction apparatus to the *skin* with adhesive material or by *skeletal* traction, where a pin is placed through bone distal to the fracture and the traction apparatus is attached. Traction is referred to as *balanced traction* when the extremity is suspended in a system of splints and rings attached to counterweights. This kind of traction is particularly helpful in nursing when there are associated systemic injuries. *External skeletal fixation* consists of pins inserted in the bone fragments proximal and distal to the fracture and the projecting pins incorporated into plaster of paris or mechanical devices to hold the fracture immobilized. *Open reduction and internal fixation* has the advantage of good apposition and alignment of the fragments and is particularly useful in repairing fractures through joints. Its disadvantages are infection and failure to maintain fracture reduction.

Open fractures are those where the skin overlying the fracture is broken and the normal barrier to infection has been violated. All fractures that communicate with skin wound must be considered contaminated and at risk to infection. The object of treatment is to prevent infection from occurring. Appropriate wound management includes meticulous cleansing of the skin, debridement of all devitalized tissue and foreign body, meticulous hemostasis, alignment of fracture fragments, lavage cleansing of the wound, and meticulous wound closure. The type of fixation that is chosen must take into consideration the potential for infection, and in general, internal fixation with metallic foreign bodies is avoided.

Several principles of fracture management should be emphasized.

1 Treat every extremity injury as a fracture until proven otherwise.

2. Reduce fractures with a minimum delay to obtain optimal result.

3. The main objective in treating upper extremity fractures is to ensure a proper functioning hand; at times, shortening and misalignment are acceptable.

4. The main objective in treating fractures of the lower extremity is to provide a painless, stable, weight-bearing limb. Misalignment is less acceptable and full length desirable.

5. Rehabilitation of a fracture patient must begin at the time of injury to achieve an optimal result.

ICU CARE OF THE TRAUMA PATIENT

General Considerations

The intensive care of the patient with multiple-system injury requires the skills of a variety of medical and related professional groups. These efforts must be coordinated in such a way as to provide optimal care and to minimize the physiologic and psychologic stress of the injury. It is essential, when a variety of disciplines contribute to the care, that a primary physician and/or nurse coordinate the efforts of the others. Many times physicians from different services are able to communicate plans to one another directly or by progress notes in the chart. However, integrating important information about the patient from other health professionals, such as physical therapist, respiratory therapist, social worker, and nurse, often can be accomplished best in a conference situation. Conferences involving representatives from the various disciplines are helpful and can be arranged most effectively by the nurse in the ICU who has contact with all the potential participants. Trauma patients often have a wide variety of problems, both physical and psychological, and coordinating the efforts of all the health care providers is integral to their management.

Special Problems in Intensive Care of Trauma Victim

Monitoring

The critical-care nurse should assess the trauma patient's changing status through direct observations as well as collection and interpretation of various monitored data. Because of the multiplicity of problems frequently associated with severe trauma, there is a need to monitor and document a variety of data concurrently.

Monitoring physiologic parameters such as pulse, blood pressure, CVP and PA pressures, intracerebral pressure, urine output, and daily weights assists in evaluating the ongoing status of the patient. Pressure readings transduced to a monitor provide continuous numerical readings and a pressure waveform displayed on an oscilloscope. This allows for observation of changes in not only the absolute value but also in the shape of the displayed tracing. It is essential that the nurse integrate and interpret the monitored data with respect to the care given the trauma patient. For example, urine output should be assessed in the light of the pulse, blood pressure, CVP, and/or PA readings. When the intracranial pressure is measured by ventriculostomy, the arterial P_{CO_2} and mean arterial pressure also must be considered. The critical-care nurse must be able to consider and integrate the variety of data representing different organ systems in order to properly assess the status of multiple-trauma patients.

Care of Combined Injuries

The critical-care nurse needs to coordinate the care of various disciplines in such a manner that priorities are met and the nursing plan can be carried out effectively. Because of the high incidence of orthopedic and soft tissue injuries, their care must be integrated with the care of injuries to the head, abdomen, thorax, and other systems. The nurse must determine which aspects of care should have priority. At times, it may be essential to provide lifesaving pulmonary care at the expense of the alignment of a femur fracture in traction. Abdominal wound and drains in the patient with vertebral fracture pose logistic problems for the nurses, especially if the patient is in traction and on a frame. Assessments must be made to determine the type of care which will facilitate wound healing and promote patient comfort.

Care of Injury with Concomitant Organ Failure

The patient with multiple injuries may develop failure of one or more organ systems. This necessitates not only additional monitoring but also further coordination of personnel and treatments. For example, if a patient with abdominal injuries and elevated intracranial pressure develops renal failure, it becomes necessary to monitor concurrently intracranial pressure, electrolytes, and fluid balance and relate these data to renal function, cerebral function, and gastrointestinal output and drainage. One of the most difficult problems is the management of the patient with increased intracranial pressure and pulmonary complications. Cerebral venous pressure and ICP can be elevated by positive end-expiratory pressure; moreover, prolonged suctioning leads to an elevation in P_{CO_2} and mean arterial blood pressure. Therefore, intracranial pressure must be carefully monitored when positive end-expiratory pressure is added to the ventilator. Suctioning must be carefully timed with periods of maximum sedation and accompanied by hyperventilation with an ambu bag to decrease P_{CO_2} levels. In summary, the critical-care team must evaluate each system and assess its relationship and priority in care.

Record Keeping

Critical-care flow sheets are useful in cataloging the various parameters. Figure 31-1 shows an example of a flow sheet which allows for synchronous charting of pulse, blood pressure, respirations, CVP, PA, temperature, and neuro checks. In this way, the members of the team caring for a patient can quickly see trends and determine relationships between values.

Wound Care

Because of their nature of origin, wounds of trauma victims are often initially contaminated, and extra caution must be exercised to prevent extensive infection. Treatment is specific to the type and location of the wound. There are certain important guidelines for the management of the wounds of trauma patients in the ICU. The wound must be handled carefully so as to prevent further contamination. If possible, the area should be elevated to promote venous and lymphatic drainage and decrease edema. Wounds should be carefully observed for signs of inflammation, purulent drainage, and ischemia. Extremity wounds occluded by plaster require particular attention; systemic temperature, local extremity temperature, capillary filling, and signs of swelling are important parameters. Dressing changes should be done with meticulous sterile technique. When there are multiple wounds, care should be taken so as to prevent cross infection. The utmost care should also be taken to prevent cross contamination between patients in the ICU. Proper nutrition and adequate caloric intake are integral to wound healing.

Tubes, Drains, Lines

The large number of tubes, drains, and lines that are often required complicate the management of trauma victims. The management of these may have to be modified because of the injuries or by the patient's clinical course. For example, the patient with facial fractures and lacerations may also require endotracheal and nasogastric tubes. These cannot be taped in the usual fashion but, rather, must be secured by another means, such as with suture or cloth umbilical tape. Special care must be given to prevent infection if a drain or intravenous line is placed near the wound.

The usual care given to management of drains includes knowledge of the origins of the drains and observation of the character and volume of the drainage. If the drain originates in the gastrointestinal tract, the composition of the lost electrolytes can often be estimated. Analysis of drainage contents in addition to the serum electrolyte levels enables a more accurate determination of replacement needs.

Sump drains are used frequently with abdominal surgical procedures. These drains have two lumens: one for drainage and the second as a vent to prevent vacuum occlusion of the drain. It is important that the vent side of the drain remain open to allow the sump to function properly. It should be covered with sterile gauze to prevent gross contamination.

Trauma Victims as Potential Organ Donors

When it becomes evident that the trauma patient may not survive, consideration must be given to possible organ donation. Aside from the legal aspects, there are certain physiologic criteria which are specific to geographic areas and institutions. The trauma patient often is an organ donor candidate by virtue of age and the high incidence of lethal head injury. It is important that the critical-care nurse remember the potential use of certain organs and continue to monitor and protect function accordingly. Renal function is preserved by monitoring fluid and cardiovascular

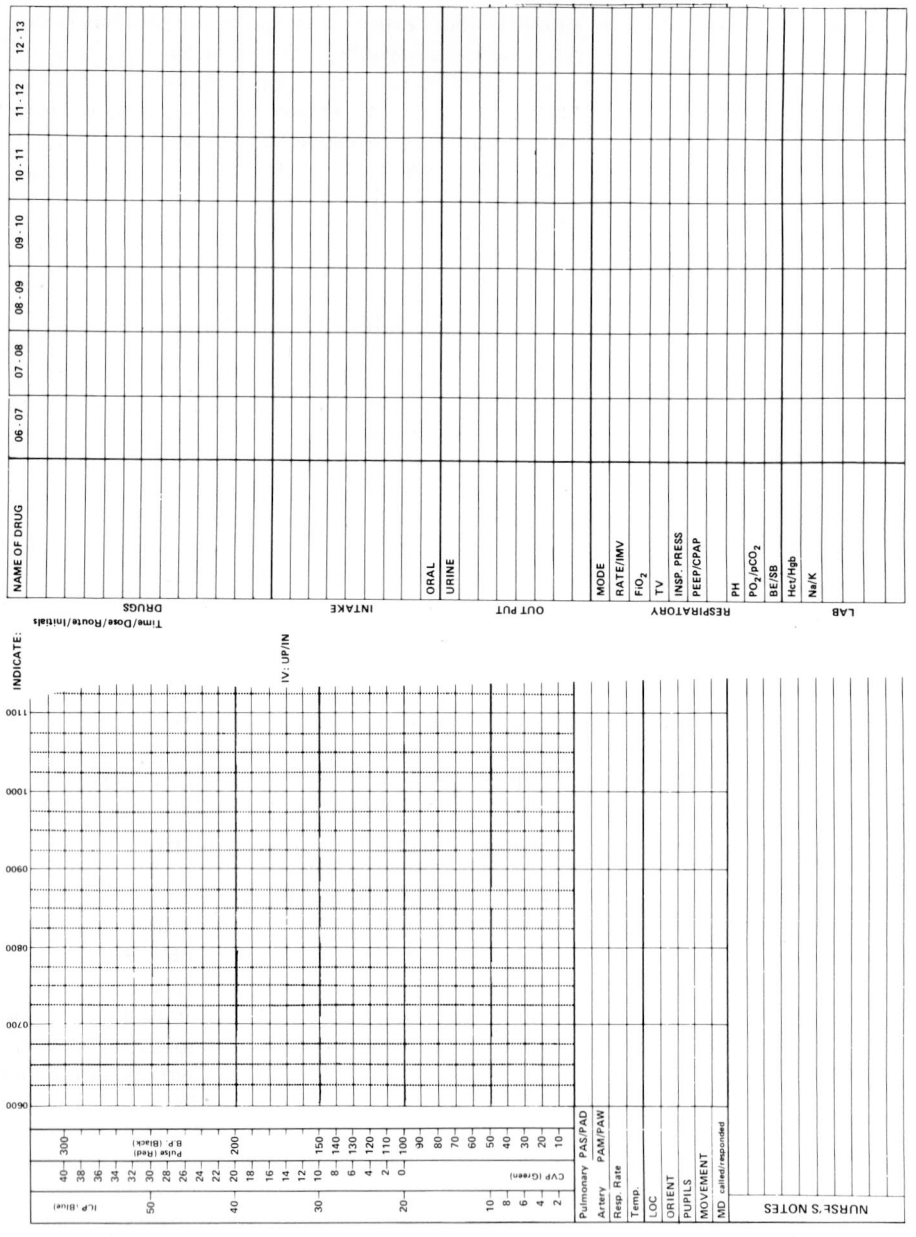

FIGURE 31-1

Critical-care unit flow sheet.

status. Eyes must be kept clear and well-lubricated to prevent corneal abrasion. Appropriate surgical services should be notified of potential organ donation so that they may offer suggestions for pre- and postmortem care.

MORBIDITY OF TRAUMA: SPECIAL CONSIDERATION FOR THE CRITICAL-CARE NURSE

The patient with multiple injuries requiring intensive care is subject to the stresses that accompany any critical-care setting. In addition, the trauma patient may be confronted with physical and sociocultural disabilities that are a result of the injuries themselves. The suddenness of the illness must always be considered. The trauma patient entering a critical-care unit has had little or no time to adjust to such an abrupt change in life-style. In a matter of hours the individual has left a former independent state to enter one of total dependence upon others and their machines. Adaptive mechanisms so often seen in medical and surgical diseases are not available to the trauma patient in the early stages of recovery.

Physical Disability

The trauma victim may become physically disabled as a result of injuries. Moreover, the individual is placed in a dependent state by the restrictions and physical limitations imposed by the care of these injuries. The psychological impact of this should not be underestimated. Physical disability in the critical-care unit may be acute or permanent. The patient with a spinal cord injury or amputation is confronted with an immediate permanent disability in addition to the temporary dependence on the ICU staff and equipment. Physical rehabilitation must begin in the critical-care unit. Remaining function and tone should be preserved with range of motion exercises and splinting. Psychological rehabilitation also should be provided in the critical-care unit. This will assume many forms, from simple emotional support by the staff to formal counseling and therapy.

Social and Cultural Disability

When evaluating the effects and extent of physical disability, certain social and cultural factors must be considered. The patient with multiple injuries faces lengthy hospitalization and potential loss of future income. There is immediate sudden separation from family and friends. The person's role in the family may be altered, either temporarily or permanently. The individual's self-concept and personal identity may be altered. The patient and family may not be aware of these factors. The nurse caring for the patient, therefore, must be aware of these areas of concern and provide resources to help the patient and family deal with them.

Psychological Implications

Physical, social, and cultural disabilities all have psychological implications for the patient with multiple injuries. The nurse must be watchful for clues from the patient and/or family that assistance is needed, and depending upon the nature of the injuries, help the patient in dealing with changes in self-image, depression, guilt, and grief. The goal of care during the acute phase of the illness should be to establish trust through dependability and consistency of nursing care. Approaches to the patient should be constant between the nursing shifts. This will assist the rehabilitation efforts following the critical-care management. It is helpful also to determine the patient's preinjury status as well as previous ways of coping with stress. This can guide the staff in dealing with the patient and family.

The Patient's Family

During the initial stages of treatment, the family's emotional needs are often as great as the patient's physical needs. Consideration must be given for means of meeting them. Family members initially feel shock, fright, and numbness. Guilt feelings are often present. As with any patient in an ICU setting, relatives feel powerless to influence the recovery process, and frustration develops. The critical-care unit must be considered an alien environment not only to the patient but also to the family. Predisposing family situations also may affect the family's response to the patient's hospitalization.

The nursing staff may alleviate the family's stresses by supportive interventions. These interventions include providing information, encouraging appropriate expression of feelings, and creating an optimal environment for interaction. Initial meetings with family members to determine their needs and provide information concerning management are followed with daily contact in which information is given and questions are answered. The staff should attempt to prepare the family members for visits to the patient in the unit.

Explanations of equipment, lines, and tubes should be offered. Based on assessments of the family members, information can be provided to include them in part of the care of the patient. Allied personnel such as social workers and psychiatrists should be involved in meeting the psychosocial needs of the patient and family members.

Stress in the Trauma Unit

The nurses caring for patients with multiple injuries are perhaps the only constant factor in the critical-care unit. These nurses encounter a variety of stresses relative to the ICU environment, patient population, medical personnel, and other staff members. The nursing staff must interface between the patient, the health team members, and the patient's family members and friends. When considering stresses related to working with trauma patients, it is helpful to conceptualize patients, family, and staff as being interrelated. If there is a problem in one of these areas, the staff must deal with it effectively. If they fail to do so, the other areas may be adversely affected. An example is the anxious demanding family member who repeatedly calls the unit requesting the same information. If the staff fails to meet with this relative to determine the cause and extent of anxiety and ways to meet family needs, further anxiety may develop. This can result in a breakdown in communication between the family, patient, and professional staff. Unless recognized, nurses may become frustrated and resentful, and these feelings can carry over to intrastaff and staff-patient relationships.

Environmental factors which stress the critical-care nurse caring for trauma patients are similar to those in other critical-care situations. Lack of space, constant noise, enclosed cubicles, and varieties of equipment are some of these. In addition, the nurse in a trauma unit must deal with often elaborate traction devices, Stryker frames, and other equipment which may make care of the patient on a ventilator, for example, more difficult. The elaborate technology of the critical-care unit for trauma patients may create frustration and stress for the nurses.

The human factors with which the critical-care nurse must deal are significant. Trauma patients on admission are frequently mutilated, and the nurses must learn to deal with the horrors of disfigurement. Trauma victims are often young and may be in the same age range as the nurses caring for them. It is not uncommon to identify with a particular patient, and this can be threatening to the nurse's self-image. Caring for the patient with spinal cord injury during the acute phase is an example of this kind of stress.

In any critical-care situation, there is the anxiety in caring for the acutely ill. Nurses may be anxious about making mistakes which could affect the patient's condition. Like other ICU nurses, those in a trauma unit must make split-second decisions and actions regarding patient care.

Trauma patients with preexisting social pathologies may present significant management problems for the nurse. These patients are often manipulative and cannot be dealt with in the usual manner. Their behavior can tax the patience of the nurses and arouse feelings of hostility. Awareness of these hostile feelings can then lead to a guilt reaction.

Mechanisms for Dealing with Stresses

Suggestions for dealing with stresses of caring for trauma patients are based on the premise that patient, family, and staff are interrelated. The nurses must learn to identify their own feelings and anxieties regarding various aspects of care of these patients. Regular meetings to discuss patient management, problems, and progress are helpful. These meetings should include physicians, the unit psychiatrist, social worker, and others who are able to assist with care problems. Consultation with the psychiatrist regarding specific problems provides the nurses with assistance in dealing with particular patient and family management situations. When the nurses are able to solve problems as a group, they will be able to deal more effectively with problems and thus diffuse some of the stresses.

The cohesiveness of the nursing group within the critical-care unit influences their ability to deal with the frustrations and stresses of working with trauma patients. Trauma patients require a high output of emotional energy, and the nurses will be better able to give this if they understand and are comfortable with their role as part of a specialized team.

REFERENCES

Artz, Curtis P.: *Early Care of the Injured Patient,* Saunders, Philadelphia, 1972.

Ballinger, Walter F., Robert B. Rutherford, and George D. Zuidema: *The Management of Trauma,* 2d edition, Saunders, Philadelphia, 1973.

Gann, Donald S.: "Endocrine and Metabolic Response to Injury," in S. I. Schwartz, et al. (eds.), *Principles of Surgery,* 3d ed., McGraw-Hill, New York, 1979.

Kinney, John M.: *Manual of Surgical Intensive Care,* Saunders, Philadelphia, 1977.

Walt, Alexander J. and Robert F. Wilson: *Management of Trauma: Pitfalls and Practice,* Lea and Febig, Philadelphia, 1975.

INTRODUCTION

Definition

Sepsis is a clinical syndrome characterized by systemic signs and symptoms of severe infection. In many instances, sepsis is due to or associated with septicemia, which refers to infection with rapidly multiplying bacteria in the bloodstream. Septic shock represents the most severe form of sepsis and is usually associated with septicemia. However, live organisms can only be cultured from blood in about 70 to 80 percent of patients with septic shock.

Bacteremia refers only to the presence of bacteria in the bloodstream; these bacteria may be alive or dead, and they may or may not cause any pathophysiologic changes. For example, dental extractions and drilling of dental caries may introduce bacteria to the bloodstream, but unless there is a deformed rheumatic valve, these bacteria almost never cause any adverse effects. Endotoxemia refers to the presence of endotoxin, a component of the cell wall of gram-negative bacteria, in the bloodstream; it is generally associated with severe signs and symptoms of infections, and it is often, but not necessarily, associated with septicemia.

Incidence

The importance of sepsis cannot be overemphasized. Sepsis is probably the most frequent disease or problem which is acquired in the hospital, and its incidence appears to be increasing. It has been estimated that about 7 percent of the 30 million patients admitted to hospitals annually in the United States develop an infection. Of these 2 million patients, about 10 to 15 percent develop a bacteremia, usually with gram-negative organisms. If one also assumes a mortality rate of 20 to 40 percent for patients with gram-negative bacteremia, the annual death rate of 50,000 to 100,000 from these organisms alone equals or exceeds that caused by motor vehicle accidents.

Of the 18 to 20 million surgical procedures performed annually in the United States, it has been estimated that about 7 percent become infected. The resultant medical expenses and value of the time lost from work are staggering. Furthermore, sepsis is a major contributing factor in at least a third of the deaths following surgery. In burns, sepsis is the leading cause of death, particularly if the patient survives for more than 2 days.

The apparent increased incidence of sepsis may

32
SEPSIS

Robert F. Wilson
Jacqueline A. Wilson

INTRODUCTION
Definition
Incidence
Importance of Early Diagnosis and Therapy

HOST DEFENSE
Reticuloendothelial System
Factors Altering Host Resistance

MICROORGANISMS
Virulence
Number of Organisms
Combinations of Organisms
Antibiotic Resistance
Classification

PATHOPHYSIOLOGIC CHANGES WITH SEPSIS
Bacterial Effects
Host Responses

DIAGNOSIS
History
Physical Examination
Laboratory Studies
Monitoring

TREATMENT
Treatment of the Infection
Enhancement of Host Defense Mechanisms
Therapy to Improve Host Defenses
Correction of Pathophysiologic Changes

SUMMARY

REFERENCES

be partially due to improvements in the media used for blood and other cultures and the techniques and instrumentation for growing and identifying anaerobic bacteria. However, the increased number of patients with impaired host defenses is probably a more important factor. Because of advances in critical care, many elderly individuals who in the past succumbed rapidly to heart attacks, strokes, cancer, and other disease now live long enough to develop sepsis. Others who are much more susceptible to infection include cancer patients receiving chemotherapy and transplant patients receiving immunosuppressants. Furthermore, the massive utilization of antimicrobial therapy has resulted in elimination of the normal bacterial flora in many patients and replacement with strains which are resistant to these antimicrobial agents. This is particularly true in hospitals, where resistant strains become concentrated and can rapidly replace the normal flora of patients shortly after they are admitted.

Importance of Early Diagnosis and Therapy

Although hospital-acquired (nosocomial) infections are frequent and can have disastrous consequences, many of them can be prevented. Most of these nosocomial infections occur in predictable settings. This is particularly true with certain types of surgery (e.g., urinary tract instrumentation) and in patients who have altered host resistance because of disease or drugs (such as immunosuppressive agents).

Because the early signs and symptoms of infection in immunosuppressed or critically ill patients are often subtle, it is important to know which patients are likely to become infected so that they can be watched extremely carefully. All too often the diagnosis of sepsis is made late, after organ failure has already developed. The nurse who is at the bedside for prolonged periods of time can contribute significantly to the early diagnosis of sepsis by looking for and noting any changes in the patient's condition.

HOST DEFENSE

Within all of us there is a constant struggle between our defense mechanisms and the microorganisms attempting to invade our bodies. When the host defenses are impaired and/or the virulence of the invading microorganisms is so great that the balance is altered in favor of the microorganisms, infection is apt to result.

Reticuloendothelial System

The most important activities of our host defenses involve the reticuloendothelial system (RES). The cells of the RES act against invading microorganisms primarily by phagocytosing (ingesting) them and/or by forming immune bodies (antibodies) which react with them or their toxins to destroy them, inactivate them, or enhance their removal by the phagocytes.

To facilitate understanding the complex interplay of cellular and humoral components in the RES, this discussion will be divided into descriptions of phagocytic cells, antibodies, complement, and the inflammatory (vascular) response.

Phagocytes

The phagocytes, which engulf bacteria or foreign particles, may be divided into fixed and circulating cells. The fixed (tissue) phagocytes are found primarily in the liver (where they line the hepatic sinusoids and are called *Kupffer cells*), spleen (particularly in the red pulp), and lymph nodes (in the medullary sinuses). The circulating phagocytes are primarily the polymorphonuclear leukocytes (PMNs) in the bloodstream and bone marrow.

When bacteria manage to get into the body, the fixed phagocytic cells of the reticuloendothelial system attempt to isolate and engulf them. If the number of bacteria is very large or if the RES is not functioning well, the task falls back chiefly on the PMNs.

Opsonins refer to a group of substances in serum which attach themselves to the surface of antigens (usually microorganisms or particulate matter) and thereby enhance the ability of phagocytes to recognize and engulf them. Antibodies may function as opsonins. Indeed, IgG and IgM antibodies are two of the most common opsonins.

Recently it has been noted that patients with severe continuing active infections tend to use up or "consume" their important opsonic proteins. This process, referred to as *consumptive opsinopathy,* can be corrected at least partially by administration of fresh frozen plasma.

Functional abnormalities of neutrophils have been found in a variety of hereditary and acquired diseases. This group includes severe burns, trauma, and chemotherapy or immunosuppression to treat malignancies or prevent rejection of transplanted tissues. A direct relationship between the degree of the functional abnormality of circulating neutrophils and the development of life-threatening infections has been well established in burn patients.

Recently it has been noted that malnutrition is associated with acquired abnormalities of neutrophil function and impaired delayed skin reactions to antigens such as mumps, candida, streptokinase, and purified protein derivative (PPD). This impairment of host defenses is particularly apt to be present if the serum albumin levels fall below 2.8 g/dL. It has also been found that resistance to infection may be returned to normal in many of these patients by an increased intake of calories, minerals, and trace elements with intravenous (IV) or oral hyperalimentation.

Antibodies

Antibodies (also called *immune bodies*) are specific proteins which are generally developed in response to a particular antigen, which may be an invading microorganism, or a foreign body, or a foreign substance. These antibodies attempt to destroy or inactivate the antigen and/or enhance its phagocytosis and removal from the body.

Most antibodies are gamma globulins, but a few are beta globulins and a very few are alpha globulins. Almost all antibodies are formed in plasma cells, which are found primarily in lymph nodes, the spleen, and the bone marrow.

Complement

Complement refers to a group of at least 11 proteins in serum which, when activated in a cascade fashion, destroy or assist in the destruction of bacteria and cells which have been sensitized by specific antibodies. Thus, complement acts to enhance the standard antigen-antibody immune reactions.

Inflammatory Response

Inflammation is the tissue response to injury or infection. Several processes appear to be involved, including vasodilation, increased capillary permeability, and chemotaxis (attraction of neutrophils to the inflamed area). The vasodilation results in an increased supply of blood, bringing more PMNs and antibodies to the involved area. The increased capillary permeability allows large quantities of fluid and protein to leak into the tissues. The antibodies and complement that enter the tissue with the fluids can attach to the microorganisms to assist in their destruc-

tion and removal by the phagocytes. The fibrinogen that also enters may coagulate and thereby help isolate the noxious agent or bacteria from the rest of the body. The chemotaxis is first manifested as margination or adherence of neutrophils to the capillaries of the involved tissue, apparently in response to chemicals liberated there from bacteria or involved tissue cells.

The tissue response to infection appears to be mediated to a large extent by substances released during complement activation and by kinins. The kinins involved in inflammation are a group of polypeptides, usually 9 to 11 amino acids in length, which can produce profound hemodynamic effects, including increased capillary permeability and vasodilation or vasoconstriction.

Bradykinin, the best known of the kinins, is extremely potent. Even in nanogram (10^{-9}) quantities, it can cause profound vasodilation and increased capillary permeability. Much of the flushing seen with sepsis, alcoholism, and pancreatitis is probably due to bradykinin.

Impaired vascular responses in sepsis may be caused by hypovolemia or impaired cardiovascular function. However, it is becoming increasingly apparent that excessive activation of complement and the kinins can also be extremely deleterious to the patient. This excess activation of vasoactive substances can cause inappropriate vasoconstriction or vasodilation and increased capillary permeability and loss of fluid into tissues. A vicious downward cycle of increased release of vasoactive substances and progressively impaired cardiovascular activity may then develop. Eradication of the underlying infection is usually the only way to stop this downward spiral, but occasionally, massive steroids may help by reducing the excess activation of complement and kinins.

Factors Altering Host Resistance

Many factors can impair host resistance. Some of the more important factors include loss of skin or mucous membrane integrity, prostheses and foreign bodies, diseases involving the RES, certain types of drug therapy, extremes of age, and impaired metabolic, cardiovascular, and pulmonary function.

Skin and Mucous Membrane Integrity

The anatomic integrity of the skin and mucosal surfaces and their secretions are usually extremely effective obstacles to invasion by pathogenic micro-organisms. Any procedure or condition that disrupts or impairs this integrity is associated with an increased risk of hospital infection. Infection in patients with extensive burns or skin diseases is particularly difficult to prevent and poses a serious risk during hospitalization. Injury to mucous membranes, particularly in the genitourinary tract, is also an important cause of infection, particularly if the urine is infected and/or a foreign body such as a urethral catheter is inserted and/or left in place.

Prostheses and Foreign Bodies

Prostheses and foreign bodies have been noted experimentally and clinically to be associated with an increased risk of infection. Much lower numbers of bacteria must be injected into tissue to cause an infection if a foreign body is present. In addition, it is usually very difficult or sometimes impossible to eradicate the infection until the foreign body is removed. The most common foreign bodies associated with infection appear to be IV plastic catheters, urethral catheters, and tracheostomy tubes. Cardiovascular prostheses and vascular grafts have also been implicated in hospital infections. All too often the foreign body is essential to life, and if it becomes infected, it cannot be removed without great risk to the patient.

Intravenous plastic catheters left in place longer than 2 days are important causes of thrombophlebitis and sepsis in critically ill patients. Prospective studies have demonstrated that bacteremia develops in at least 2 percent of patients with intravenous catheters, and intravenous catheters inserted via a cutdown are associated with an even higher rate of sepsis. If such catheters are inserted in the emergency department, they occasionally must be inserted very rapidly with less than ideal sterile techniques and should be replaced within 12 to 24 h. Any patient who has an IV line and becomes septic should be considered to have an infected IV line until proved otherwise. A blood culture should be drawn through the catheter as it is removed, and the catheter tip should be cultured.

Although metal needles are less apt to cause septic thrombophlebitis, they are more difficult to maintain in the vein, and plastic catheters are often preferred if a secure IV for rapid administration of blood or other fluids is essential. If a plastic IV catheter must be inserted, there appears to be some value in having at least 1 to $1\frac{1}{2}$ in distance between the puncture site or incision in the skin and the point at which the catheter enters the vein.

Urethral catheters and/or instrumentation in patients with infected urine is a frequent source of serious infection, particularly by gram-negative rods such as *Escherichia coli*. Although closed drainage can greatly delay the onset of infection, virtually all long-term indwelling Foley catheters result in infection. Urinary tract infections account for at least one-third of hospital-acquired infections, and the majority of these are associated with or caused by insertion of urethral catheters.

Although some bacteria from the skin may move up into the bladder alongside the urethral catheter, most of the bacteria probably enter the bladder by movement up through the urine in the lumen of the drainage tubing. Consequently, maintenance of a closed drainage system is extremely important. A high rate of urine flow may also be helpful in decreasing the number of organisms ascending the tubing. Nurses need to take special precautions and exercise additional care when dealing with urinary drainage systems in the compromised patient. Careful cleansing of the catheter near the urethral meatus may be particularly helpful.

A large number of critically ill or injured patients require ventilatory assistance for at least a few days. Although an endotracheal tube may be more uncomfortable to the patient, particularly if it is an orotracheal tube, it is less apt and slower to introduce infection into the lungs than a tracheostomy.

Tracheostomies are often routinely performed if an endotracheal tube is required for more than 2 to 5 days. However, a tracheostomy probably does not have to be performed unless (1) the patient tolerates the endotracheal tube poorly, (2) pulmonary secretions cannot be removed adequately through the endotracheal tube, or (3) the endotracheal tube is damaging the vocal cords, nasal septum, or paranasal sinuses.

Diseases Involving the Reticuloendothelial System

The acute leukemias and lymphomas tend to be associated with severe cellular and humoral immunologic defects. Not only malignant processes but also the drugs used for treatment attack the RES. The malnutrition frequently involved with these and other advanced malignancies can also seriously impair host defense and must, therefore, be vigorously prevented or corrected with oral or IV hyperalimentation.

Drug Therapy

The various immunosuppressive and cytoxic drugs, as well as radiation, can profoundly depress the bone marrow and the RES. This may be particularly important in patients with advanced malignancies who already have a reduction of the total mass of phagocyte- and antibody-forming tissues. In addition, cytotoxic drugs tend to injure rapidly growing cells such as those of the intestinal mucosa and can thereby create new portals of entry for opportunistic organisms.

Antibiotic therapy profoundly alters the host microflora and may thereby determine which microorganisms are likely to cause infection. Almost all antibiotics in therapeutic doses will produce changes in the gastrointestinal, oropharyngeal, and skin flora, replacing relatively antibiotic-sensitive microorganisms with others which are much more resistant. Antimicrobial agents can also reduce host resistance by altering tissue pH and inducing vitamin deficiencies.

Prolonged corticosteroid therapy is frequently associated with an increased incidence of infection by opportunistic bacteria, viruses, fungi, and parasites. Glucocorticoids depress the inflammatory response and induce lysis of lymphoid cells, thereby decreasing antibody synthesis. Large doses may reduce fibroblastic proliferation and further impair reticuloendothelial system activity. Adrenocortical hormones in high doses may also suppress the formation and activity of interferon, a factor which may be important in preventing opportunistic viral infections. Nevertheless, patients with severe septic shock who are not responding to aggressive therapy with fluid and other agents may benefit from the ability of pharmacologic doses of corticosteroids to stabilize lysosomal and capillary membranes and reduce the excessive activation of the complement and kinin systems.

Age

Host resistance is most apt to be impaired in the very young or very old, especially those less than 3 months or greater than 70 years of age. The newborn, particularly the premature infant, is compromised by immunological immaturity. Aged patients are apt to have cardiovascular disease, carcinomatosis, diabetes mellitus, neurological problems, and other debilitating diseases. Many gram-negative bacilli, usually not regarded as pathogenic for humans, have been the cause of hospital-acquired infections in such patients.

Metabolic Functions

Patients with impaired metabolic function, particularly when due to diabetes mellitus, renal failure, or hepatic failure, have been noted to have an increased incidence of infection.

Increased blood sugar levels per se probably do not play a major role in increasing the severity of systemic infection in the uncontrolled diabetic patient. However, ketoacidosis causes a delayed and defective inflammatory response because of sluggish polymorphonuclear migration, ineffective phagocytosis, and decreased fibroblast proliferation. In addition, the small blood vessel disease that often complicates diabetes mellitus may interfere with local nutrient tissue blood flow, may reduce absorption of drugs given intramuscularly or subcutaneously, and can cause renal and cardiovascular insufficiency.

Uremic acidosis impairs the early phases of the acute inflammatory response. Uremia also causes suppression of the immune response to antigenic stimuli, impaired delayed cellular hypersensitivity, abnormal production of all types of immunoglobulins, and defective cell division.

Patients with cirrhosis have a greatly reduced resistance to infection, and many of these patients develop septic shock and can die from relatively mild infections. In addition to the impaired metabolism and reduced hepatic RES function, there is shunting of portal venous blood—which may contain enteric bacilli or endotoxin—around the hepatic reticuloendothelial system, directly into the systemic venous circulation.

Cardiovascular Function

Rheumatic heart disease, arteriosclerosis, hypertension, and other cardiovascular diseases are associated with an increase in bacteremia in hospitalized patients. Any impairment of tissue perfusion tends to increase the likelihood that otherwise harmless endogenous bacteria may cause an infection. Patients with shock have a particular tendency to infection, especially if the shock persists for more than 30 min and requires massive transfusions.

Pulmonary Function

The respiratory tract is normally sterile below the glottis. This sterility is mechanically maintained by alveolar macrophages and the mucociliary clearance apparatus. In patients with bronchopulmonary disease, such as emphysema or chronic bronchitis, these mechanisms are impaired; such individuals have an increased risk of developing respiratory infections, particularly in the hospital, because of exposure to antibiotics, inhalation therapy, and nebulizers. Procedures such as tracheostomy or endotracheal intubation further increase the possibility of infection, particularly the necrotizing gram-negative pneumonias caused by *Pseudomonas aeruginosa*, *Serratia marcescens*, and *Klebsiella-Enterobacter*.

MICROORGANISMS

The ability of microorganisms to cause infection varies with their virulence, the number of bacteria present, the presence of other bacteria, and the resistance of these organisms to antimicrobial agents.

Virulence

The virulence or ability of bacteria to invade and cause infection varies tremendously. Some of the factors involved include the various toxins or enzymes that these organisms can release. These substances may either directly damage the host or counteract or neutralize the host defense mechanisms. *Clostridium tetani* organisms produce a powerful exotoxin which can damage neurologic tissue far from the infection, and *Cl. welchii* produce several powerful exotoxins which can cause severe local damage at the infected site.

Bacterial capsules can greatly enhance virulence. The loose, gelatinous covering of mixed polysaccharides can impede phagocytosis. Some gram-negative bacilli, for example, certain klebsiella, have very thick capsules.

Number of Organisms

The incidence and degree of infection developing in any wound correlates directly with the number of contaminating organisms. The number of bacteria necessary to cause infection is often referred to as the *critical inoculum*. The critical inoculum varies considerably with the local environment. Foreign bodies, blood, and dead space in a wound greatly reduce the number of organisms needed to cause infection.

Combinations of Organisms

Another important factor in virulence is the number and types of other bacteria in the area. These other bacteria may be antagonistic and reduce the chance of infection by competing for nutrients, or they may be synergistic and enhance infection. For example, aerobic bacteria in a wound may consume the oxygen that is present, thereby improving the environment for the growth and multiplication of anaerobic bacteria.

Antibiotic Resistance

A bacterial population may become resistant to an antimicrobial agent, either by spontaneous mutation or by transfer of genetic material from resistant bacteria to sensitive bacteria.

The organisms most frequently causing sepsis at the present time are not the classic high-virulence organisms such as streptococci, but rather organisms such as pseudomonas, which, although they are usually of relatively low virulence, have great genetic versatility. Most of these bacteria can replicate by binary fission every 20 min. Therefore, if the proper nutrients and temperature are available, one organism can produce over 10 billion in 10 h. With such large numbers of bacteria, the mutation rate does not have to be very high (for example 1×10^{-7} or 1 in 10 million) in order for mutant organisms to be seen regularly.

If some mechanism occurs whereby the mutant bacteria are given an advantage over the other bacteria present, they profilerate. One way to "select out" such organisms is to administer antibiotics to which the mutant strain is resistant but the others are sensitive. Now the mutant no longer needs to compete since it is the only organism capable of replicating in the presence of the antibiotics. Within a day or so, the microbial population may be replaced by descendants of the antibiotic-resistant mutant organism.

Recently, a great deal of evidence has accumulated which shows that bacteria are able to directly transmit antibiotic resistance to other bacteria. The genetic information controlling antibiotic resistance is frequently contained in extrachromosomal deoxyribonucleic acid (DNA) molecules called *plasmids*. These DNA molecules or resistance (R) factors are self-replicating and may be passed on to or exchanged with adjacent bacteria. This material does not diffuse from one organism to another; actual physical contact is required.

Classification

The most frequent microorganisms causing infection in man may be classified into bacteria, fungi, viruses, and parasites.

Bacteria

Bacteria are generally classified according to their need for oxygen, their gram-stain reaction, and their shape. Strictly speaking, *aerobic* bacteria require oxygen for their metabolism, *facultative* organisms can grow with or without oxygen, and *anaerobic* bacteria can only metabolize properly in the absence of oxygen. For the sake of simplicity, the facultative and aerobic organisms will be combined.

The staphylococci are gram-positive cocci which are divided into two species: *Staphylococcus aureus* (which is coagulase-positive) and *S. epidermidis* (which is coagulase-negative). Both species can be present in normal flora of the skin and mucous membranes. *S. aureus* is the more virulent species and is a major cause of sepsis in all hospitals. *S. aureus* is particularly apt to be found in infections of skin, soft tissue, IV catheters, and bone. It is also a major cause of acute endocarditis, particularly among narcotic addicts. This species often produces a penicillinase, which makes it resistant to aqueous penicillin. They are, however, usually sensitive to cephalothins and many synthetic penicillins such as methicillin and oxacillin.

S. epidermidis can also cause disease and is an increasing problem, particularly in postsurgical infections. However, it is usually sensitive to the penicillins.

The multiple types of streptococcal organisms are usually quite sensitive to penicillin. Classically, these gram-positive organisms are divided into several groups according to their serological typing.

Streptococcus pyogenes, group A, particularly those which are beta-hemolytic, is generally considered to be the most virulent of streptococci, and it causes or participates in most of the throat infections and cellulitis that are seen, particularly outside the hospital.

Streptococcus pyogenes, group B, may cause infections similar to those in group A and is more frequent in many hospitals.

Streptococcus pyogenes, group D, is generally divided into those species which are enterococci (*S. faecalis, S. faecium,* and *S. durans*) and those which are not (*S. bovis* and *S. equinus*). The enterococci tend to be more resistant to antibiotics than are other streptococci, and they are particularly important in patients with wound infections following surgery or trauma to the small bowel or colon.

The viridans streptococci are a group of streptococci which are alpha-hemolytic but do not contain antigens by which they can be serologically typed into one of Lancefield's groups. These organisms were notorious in the past for causing subacute bacterial endocarditis.

Streptococcus pneumoniae, formerly known as *Diplococcus pneumoniae* or the pneumococcus, can be part of the normal flora of the upper respiratory tract, but it is the most frequent cause of lobar pneumonia and is frequently cultured from patients with respiratory infections.

There are many species in the genus *Neisseria,* but only two—the meningococcus and gonococcus—are normally pathogenic to man. These gram-negative cocci often grow in pairs. The meningococci have a capsule, and meningococcemia may have an extremely fulminant course. It can cause acute adrenal insufficiency with disseminated intravascular coagulation, a syndrome known as Waterhouse-Friderichsen syndrome. Gonococcal infections are more common than those caused by *N. meningitidis,* but septicemia with *N. gonorrhoeae* is rather rare.

A number of gram-positive bacilli are pathogenic to humans. *Listeria monocytogenes* usually only infects patients who are very young or compromised, such as those receiving immunosuppressive drugs.

Corynebacterium diphtheriae is virulent, but this organism rarely, if ever, causes septicemia. It usually causes local symptoms in the throat, but the systemic symptoms and signs are due to the exotoxin it elaborates. Proper immunization can prevent disease by these organisms.

Organisms of the genus *Bacillus* are fairly common, but only the organism *B. anthracis* is usually pathogenic. Cutaneous or inhalation types of anthrax are rarely seen except in sheep handlers.

B. subtilus organisms, which are only rarely pathogenic, are large gram-positive bacilli which are not infrequently confused with clostridia on gram stain.

The last 15 years have seen a marked increase in gram-negative bacteria as a major cause of infections. The selection of resistant strains of bacteria, the increased numbers of compromised patients, and better antibiotic control of gram-positive bacteria have all contributed to the increasing incidence of infections by these organisms.

The cell wall of the gram-negative bacilli is extremely important and consists of structured layers of protein and lipopolysaccharides. The polysaccharides, which have a core of common sugars with various side chains, are antigenic and account for the roughness or smoothness of the surface of the various bacteria. The polysaccharide (endotoxin) released from the cell wall after the bacteria die can cause severe pathophysiologic changes and is a major cause of pathogenicity of these organisms.

Escherichia coli is the most frequent gram-negative bacillus causing infection in man both inside and outside the hospital. They are particularly apt to cause urinary tract infections and are involved in most infections secondary to trauma or disease involving the gastrointestinal tract. Fortunately, *E. coli* is susceptible to many antibiotics, particularly the aminoglycosides.

The *Klebsiella-Enterobacter-Serratia* (KES) group seem to be increasing in incidence as causes of nosocomial infections, and they are more resistant in vitro to antibiotics than most of the other genera of this family. *Klebsiella* and *Serratia* species which have become resistant to multiple antibiotics have been particular problems in many nosocomial outbreaks of infection.

Klebsiella is usually susceptible to the cephalosporins, cephalothin and cephaloridine, and resistant to carbenicillin; *Enterobacter,* by contrast, tends to be resistant to cephalosporins but susceptible to carbenicillin.

Organisms of the genus *Proteus* are generally separated into indole-negative and indole-positive groups. *Proteus mirabilis,* which is indole-negative, is responsible for about 80 percent of all *Proteus* infections. This group is fairly sensitive to antibiotics and can usually be successfully treated with ampicillin or cephalothin. The indole-positive strains—*P. rettgeri, P. morganii,* and *P. vulgaris*—on the other hand, are usually resistant to these antibiotics. However, they are usually susceptible to kanamycin, gentamicin, and carbenicillin.

Salmonella bacteremia is unusual except in epidemics of typhoid or paratyphoid fever. This organism is extremely sensitive to chloramphenicol.

The genus *Acinetobacter* includes organisms previously called *Mima, Herellea,* and *Achromobacter.* The organisms are common in nature and are frequently part of the normal flora of the skin and gastrointestinal and upper respiratory tracts. They have a relatively low virulence and cause sepsis primarily in compromised hosts.

Infections due to members of the *Herellea-Mima* group usually originate in the skin from venous catheters or in the tracheobronchial tree as a result of contaminated ventilatory equipment. These organisms may be adequately treated with tetracyclines or aminoglycosides.

Pseudomonas aeruginosa, also known as *Bacillus pyocyaneus, B. aeruginosa,* and *P. pyocyanea,* has long been the most difficult of the gram-negative pathogens to eradicate. This organism tends to infect patients who have been on multiple antibiotics and are debilitated by other infections, burns, or neoplasms, particularly leukemia. Before the wide use of antibiotics, pseudomonas rarely caused human infections. However, this genus not only contains strains which are resistant to most of the antimicrobial drugs but also has the ability to rapidly develop resistance to antibiotics used therapeutically against them. Therefore, pseudomonas often becomes a major part of the flora or even the dominant organism at multiple sites in individuals who have been on antibiotics for more than 7 to 14 days. The urinary tract or surgical wound is often the initial site of infection prior to development of septicemia. Pulmonary infections are particularly common in patients requiring prolonged ventilatory assistance. It is also frequently seen in endocarditis among heroin addicts.

All the mechanisms of pathogenicity of pseudomonas are not understood, but the organism produces both endotoxin and exotoxin; once pseudomonas septicemia develops, multiple organ failure becomes increasingly evident and the patient's prognosis is extremely poor.

Anaerobic bacteria generally cannot cause infection in healthy well-vascularized, well-oxygenated tissue. However, factors which make conditions favorable for anaerobic growth include: (1) coinfection with a facultative organism which utilizes the oxygen present and/or produces toxins which alter the blood supply and/or viability of healthy tissue, and (2) trauma which directly damages tissue and/or interferes with its blood supply.

The peptococci (anaerobic staphylococcus) are anaerobic gram-positive cocci which are usually only seen in mixed infections. Occasionally they are found in pure culture in deep abscesses, but they are an infrequent cause of sepsis. This organism is somewhat difficult to grow in the laboratory, and peptococcal involvement is often missed unless careful anaerobic blood cultures and subcultures are performed.

The peptostreptococci (anaerobic streptococcus) are the most common anaerobic cocci causing sepsis. This genus is quite virulent and is often found in pure culture in tuboovarian abscesses, brain abscesses, deep wound infections, and puerperal sepsis. Usually, however, it is present in mixed infections, particularly with aerobic gram-negative bacilli.

Veillonella are gram-negative cocci which are present in normal flora of the mouth, intestinal tract, upper respiratory tract, and vagina. However, they are frequently recovered in mixed infections from abdominal abscesses and bronchial infections and are occasionally cultured from blood, brain abscesses, and pleural fluid. Very occasionally they are isolated in pure culture from abdominal abscesses. The endotoxin associated with the outer envelope of this cell wall appears to be a lipopolysaccharide similar to that associated with many aerobic gram-negative bacilli.

Clostridia are gram-positive bacilli which produce spores that can help identify individual species. They produce disease primarily by their exotoxins.

C. tetani produces the clinical entity known as tetanus. These bacteria are prevalent in soil and are especially concentrated in manure on farms. They are particularly apt to multiply in deep penetrating dirty wounds. Their virulence is related almost entirely to their exotoxin, which is attracted to nerve tissue. Even a relatively mild, localized peripheral infection can cause central neurologic dysfunction. This disease can be completely prevented by proper immunization against its exotoxin.

Cl. perfringens (*welchii*) is the classic organism causing gas gangrene, but it is only one of several clostridia which can cause this problem. The exotoxins released, particularly a lecithinase, cause a liquefaction necrosis which favors increased growth and multiplication of these bacteria and thereby results in a vicious cycle of increasing exotoxin production, liquefaction necrosis, and bacterial multiplication.

The propionibacteria constitute a major proportion of the normal skin flora and frequently are contaminants in blood culture. However, since the propionibacteria can, and occasionally do, cause sepsis, they cannot always be ignored, particularly if recovered in reported blood cultures.

Eubacteria are non-spore-forming anaerobic bacilli which are part of the normal flora of the intestinal tract. They are frequent isolates from wounds but are a rare cause of sepsis.

Bifidobacteria are bacilli which are almost routinely found in the intestinal tract of infants and adults. They are frequently recovered from mixed infections but are only occasionally seen in pure culture.

Members of the genus *Bacteroides* are gram-negative bacilli which compose up to 90 percent of the bacteria found in the human large intestine. They also are found as normal flora in the oral cavity and upper respiratory tract and in the urogenital tract of women. They have been isolated from infections of most areas of the body, either in pure culture or in mixed infections. There are several species which are frequently isolated, but the two most common species found in wounds and sepsis are *B. fragilis* and *B. melanogenicus.*

B. melanogenicus is generally found in the mouth and is frequently involved in mixed infections of the respiratory tract. It is usually quite sensitive to penicillin.

B. fragilis is the most prevalent and most important anaerobic organism in the distal small bowel and colon. It is likely to be involved in any infection arising secondary to trauma or surgery involving these organs and may be involved in up to 10 percent of lung abscesses. Unlike virtually all the other anaerobic bacteria, it is resistant to penicillin.

Disease due to mycobacteria remains a major problem. Miliary tuberculosis, a fulminant form of the disease which is diffusely spread by the bloodstream, is particularly apt to occur in the elderly, debilitated, or immunosuppressed. Infections by mycobacterium tuberculosis are particularly increased in immunosuppressed patients. Corticosteroid therapy may cause granulomas to break down, resulting in reactivation of the tuberculosis.

Diagnosis in debilitated individuals is often difficult unless special efforts are made to identify the organisms on smears, cultures, or tissue biopsies. Because of the overwhelming nature of the infection, anergy tends to develop and the standard tuberculin skin tests are often negative. In one series, 38 percent of the patients with miliary tuberculosis had negative skin tests. Even older, otherwise healthy patients have had a 10 to 15 percent incidence of false negative skin tests.

Rarely, atypical mycobacteria, which are much less virulent than the typical mycobacteria, are the cause of infection, usually in the lungs of patients with chronic obstructive pulmonary disease. These mycobacteria are differentiated on the bases of their rapid growth and pigment formation in vitro. Differential Mantoux skin testing may be helpful.

Fungi

Fungal infections of the skin are common but seldom pose serious problems. Bloodstream or deep tissue infections are quite rare. However, life-threatening infections with candida, aspergilla, *Torulopsis glabrata,* and histoplasma have emerged in the past few years as major complications of parenteral nutrition, cancer therapy, burns, and broad spectrum antibiotic and steroid therapy. Coccidioidomycosis and cryptococcosis can be severe infections in normal individuals but are particularly apt to be life-threatening in the immunosuppressed. Actinomysin D is the drug of choice for most severe systemic fungal infections. However, it is a very toxic agent which must be given with great care.

Candida albicans is a normal commensal organism of man. The fungus is recovered from the pharynx in 30 percent and stools in 65 percent of normal individuals. These percentages are much greater if the normal bacterial flora are suppressed by antibiotics. Disruption of mucous membranes further increases the likelihood of local infections. Because of its commensal behavior, a diagnosis of parenchymal involvement should be confirmed by demonstration of histologic tissue invasion. When invasive, candida assumes a mycelial-like or pseudohyphae appearance. Evidence of pseudohyphae in unspun urine denotes tissue invasion, usually of the bladder. *Candida* fungemia is an increasing problem, particularly in patients receiving large doses of multiple antibiotics for a period of several weeks. However, recovery of organisms from the bloodstream is difficult, and it is estimated that blood cultures are negative in at least 50 percent of cases.

Invasive aspergillosis is assuming increased importance in patients on immunosuppressive drugs to treat malignancies and prevent rejection of transplanted organs. The lung is the commonest site of tissue invasion. Invasive aspergillus pneumonia is particularly apt to occur in patients with acute granulocytic leukemia. Since aspergillus is found in about 7 percent of sputum smears in patients with chronic chest diseases, diagnosis must be based on demonstration of tissue invasion.

Torulopsis glabrata is a saprophyte similar to and often mistaken for candida. It rarely causes infection except in the debilitated, particularly those with severe burns and/or those receiving parenteral hyperalimentation.

Histoplasma capsulatum frequently causes mild pulmonary infections, particularly in individuals living on farms along the Ohio Valley. Multiple small diffuse calcifications in the lung are often the only evidence, except for serologic tests, that the infection was present. It occasionally causes a generalized infection involving the mouth, lymph nodes, blood, and bone marrow.

Coccidioides immitus produces a frequent pulmonary infection in the San Joaquin Valley in California. This infection is characterized by pulmonary nodules or thin-walled cavities. In its generalized form it may also involve the central nervous system.

Cryptococcus neoformans may involve the skin and lungs, but its infections of the central nervous system are usually the only ones which are serious. This disease is particularly frequent and severe in patients with Hodgkin's disease and other lymphomas.

Viruses

The viruses most likely to be involved in septic-like conditions are Herpes simplex virus (HSV) Types I and II, Varicella-Zoster virus (V-Z), Ebstein-Barr virus (EBV), Cytomegalovirus (CMV), and members of the Papova virus groups. Most of the serious infections caused by these organisms occur in immunosuppressed or severely debilitated individuals. Diagnosis of these agents is made by recovery of the virus in tissue culture and serologic testing.

Herpes simplex viruses Types 1 and 2 characteristically only cause intermittent mild vesicular eruptions (cold sores) on the mucocutaneous margins of the mouth. Occasionally they may involve the male and female genital tracts. Rarely, the cornea is involved and the result can be blindness. Very rarely this virus causes catastrophic illness in the central and peripheral nervous systems of apparently normal people. Between attacks, the virus is in a latent phase in the nerve root ganglia in various parts of the body.

An increasing frequency and severity of herpes simplex virus infections had been noted in renal transplant recipients who are maintained on large doses of immunosuppressive drugs such as steroids, azothioprine, and antilymphocyte globulin. Immediately following birth, while the immunological system is immature, infants are also particularly prone to life-threatening systemic infections with this virus. Treatment with adenine arabinoside may be of value.

Another latent infection that may be activated in patients with altered immunity is herpes zoster. Susceptible children usually acquire the virus by developing chicken pox (varicella). Complete recovery is the rule, but the virus usually persists in a latent form in the nerve tissue. Occasionally the virus reawakens in the skin of the chest wall or face in the distribution of an intercostal nerve or the trigeminal nerve. The resultant vesicular eruption and associated pain are generally referred to as *shingles*.

The incidence of this problem is particularly increased in patients with lymphomas or Hodgkin's disease. In some patients, especially those with lymphomas and particularly those receiving steroid or radiation therapy, the vesicular eruption may spread out past the involved dermatome and become disseminated. Pneumonia or encephalitis in such individuals may result in death. The development of interferon, an antiviral agent in the vesicle fluid, is an important factor in the natural cessation of the cutaneous spread of this disease.

Ebstein-Barr virus has been found in the cell cultures of Burkitt's lymphoma. Antibodies reactive with Ebstein-Barr virus have also been reported in cases of infectious mononucleosis.

The cytomegalovirus causes mild self-limited respiratory infections and a heterophile-negative mononucleosis syndrome in apparently healthy young adults. However, it can cause fatal pneumonia in renal and cardiac transplant recipients. In addition, evidence is accumulating that acquisition or reactivation of the cytomegalovirus may further impair cellular immunity by multiplication in activated lymphocytes.

Members of the Papova virus group have recently been recognized to be the cause of progressive multifocal leukoencephalopathy. This is a "slow" viral demyelinating disease of the central nervous system that usually occurs in immunosuppressed patients.

Parasites

Three of the more frequent parasites in the United States that can cause disease which may resemble bacterial infections include plasmodia (causing malaria), pneumocystis cariniae, and toxoplasma.

Infections with plasmodia are usually only seen in patients who have recently traveled to an area in the tropics in which malaria is prevalent; however, outbreaks have also occurred in addicts sharing contaminated needles.

The four malarias that are important in man are *Plasmodium vivax, P. ovale, P. malariae,* and *P. falciparum.* Fatalities usually only occur with *P. falciparum,* since it parasitizes all red cells. *P. vivax,* which parasitizes only reticulocytes, is much more benign. Death results from cerebral involvement or renal failure.

Pneumocystis carinii forms tiny cysts which can be domonstrated by Giemsa, periodic acid-Schiff, or silver stains but not by ordinary hematoxalin and eosin stains. Diagnosis is suspected in immunodeficient patients who have pulmonary infiltrates on x-ray, fever, and dyspnea, but clear lungs on auscultation.

It is most apt to occur in premature infants, children with acute leukemia, and organ transplant recipients. Diagnosis is usually made on open-lung biopsy. Treatment with pentamidine or trimethoprim-sulfamethoxazole is often successful if begun early.

Toxoplasma gondii is a protozoan of worldwide distribution. The common cat is the definitive host, but man also acquires the infection by ingestion of undercooked meats or by transplacental transfer. Mild infections are frequent, but clinical manifestations are rare. Disseminated toxoplasmosis is unusual except in immunosuppressed patients, particularly those with lymphomas or organ transplants. Central nervous or respiratory symptoms predominate under such circumstances. Treatment includes pyrimethamine with sulfa.

PATHOPHYSIOLOGIC CHANGES WITH SEPSIS

The pathophysiologic changes occurring with sepsis are extremely complex. The bacteria and their toxins in themselves can have profound local and systemic effects. These in turn trigger certain *local* reactions by the host followed by or coincident with *systemic* endocrine, metabolic, and organ changes. The net result is the clinical picture referred to as *sepsis.*

Bacterial Effects

Bacterial invasion results in release of a number of powerful chemicals from the damaged tissue, not only locally but also into the bloodstream. In addition, exotoxins may be released directly from various live microorganisms (especially gram-positive bacteria), and endotoxins may be released from the cell wall of dead microorganisms (especially gram-negative bacilli).

Local Chemical Release

A wide variety of chemicals are released locally from cells which are damaged or destroyed by an infectious process. Some of the more important chemicals released include histamine and a wide variety of lysosomal enzymes which are capable of destroying or altering many compounds and cellular components. The enzymes in turn may cause the release of several vasoactive polypeptides.

Two types of histamine are generally recognized as being released in sepsis. *Preformed histamine,* which is stored in mast cells and which can be inhibited or inactivated by antihistamines, is much less important than the *induced histamine,* which is released. Induced histamine is not stored; it is formed directly in the cell at the time the cell is damaged or stimulated, and it is not altered or affected by antihistamines.

The enzymes present in lysosomes include a wide variety of extremely powerful chemicals including cathepsin D, beta-glucuronidase, acid phosphatase, arylsulfatase, and ribonuclease. These enzymes normally are used to destroy and/or "digest" bacteria and other foreign substances that are taken up into the lysosomes, particularly in macrophages. Consequently, lysosomes have been referred to as "intracellular stomachs."

If the lipoprotein membrane surrounding the lysosome breaks down, the lysosomal enzymes escape into the cell and destroy the cell. If enough lysosomes break down, increased levels of lysosomal enzymes can be detected in the blood. These enzymes may cause not only a great deal of local cellular and tissue damage but also the release or activation of various substances, including vasoactive polypeptides, which can cause even greater and more distant changes.

An increasing number of vasoactive polypeptides are being recognized. Normally these substances exist in an inactive form bound to protein, particularly α_2-globulins. Endotoxin and various proteolytic enzymes from lysosomes or the pancreas can separate the kinin from its protein, thereby activating it. Two of the best-known vasoactive polypeptides are bradykinin and myocardial depressant factor.

Bradykinin is one of the most potent vasodilators known to man. Much of the flushing seen with sepsis, pancreatitis, and alcoholism is due to bradykinin. In addition, bradykinin greatly increases capillary permeability, causing an increasing interstitial edema with a corresponding decrease in blood volume. Much of the increased fluid requirement in sepsis may be due to bradykinin.

Myocardial depressant factor (MDF) is liberated primarily from the ischemic pancreas. This substance, as its name implies, depresses myocardial contractility and, in addition, causes splanchnic vasoconstriction, which may result in even more MDF production.

Host Responses

Vasoactive Substances

As mentioned previously, the local host responses to infection consist of local vascular changes, especially vasodilation and increased capillary permeability, and the release of a number of chemicals, including histamine, anaphylatoxin, and kinins. If the infection is relatively minor and readily controlled, systemic changes may be minimal. However, if the infection becomes widespread, the host response tends to be excessive and may be damaging to the patient. The excessive release of histamine, anaphylatoxin, and kinins can increase capillary permeability. The resultant loss of fluid into the interstitial space may cause hypovolemic shock. These agents may also cause widespread vasodilation, thereby increasing vascular capacity and further exaggerating the discrepancy between intravascular volume and vascular capacity.

Systemic Changes

Some of the systemic responses to sepsis include changes in endocrine function metabolism and the function of various organ systems, particularly the cardiovascular system, lungs, kidneys, liver, and intestinal tract.

Endocrine Changes

Sepsis causes an intense activation of the autonomic nervous system and endocrine system, resulting in increased secretion and release of most hormones. The secretion of insulin and thyrotropin (TSH), however, are usually decreased by sepsis or shock.

Sepsis causes a consistent increase in adrenocorticotropin (ACTH) secretion. The increased growth hormone secretion with infection appears to be an important mechanism for providing the additional substrate, particularly glucose, needed to satisfy the greater metabolic needs of the body.

Increased antidiuretic hormone (ADH) secretion, causing a tendency to water retention and oliguria, occurs with all types of stress, including infection, particularly if hypovolemia develops. By reducing the renal excretion of water, ADH helps to maintain an adequate intravascular volume and tissue perfusion. However, if the oliguria it produces is prolonged or severe, the tendency to renal failure is greatly increased.

Sepsis is characterized by a profound tendency toward a diabetic-like state caused primarily by an increased insulin resistance. Insulin secretion is usually also reduced. However, even when insulin secretion is normal or increased, the insulin/glucagon molar ratio is decreased and hyperglycemia results. Late in sepsis, hypoglycemia may develop. This is an extremely ominous sign and reflects a lack of substrate for proper metabolism.

Glucagon secretion is markedly increased in sepsis. This causes glycogen to be mobilized and converted to glucose, resulting in hyperglycemia, which helps to supply the substrate needed for the increased metabolic demands of sepsis.

Sepsis causes a profound stimulation of the sympathetic nervous system including the adrenal medulla, resulting in increased secretion of catecholamines, particularly epinephrine. These catecholamines have profound cardiovascular effects and can cause an increased pulse rate, blood pressure, and cardiac contractility. They also tend to mobilize triglycerides and fatty acids and increase insulin resistance, thereby increasing the blood levels of glucose and energy substrates from fat.

There is a great increase in secretion of adrenal cortical steroids in sepsis. Cortisol secretion is stimulated largely by ACTH. Cortisol is primarily a glucocorticoid and as such raises blood glucose levels by stimulating gluconeogenesis.

Aldosterone secretion is largely stimulated by the renin-angiotensin system, which in turn is largely stimulated by impaired perfusion of the kidney. Aldosterone acts primarily to increase sodium and water retention and increase potassium excretion. Thus, aldosterone helps to maintain the extracellular fluid volume and tissue perfusion.

Metabolic Changes

In spite of the high fever and restlessness often seen in sepsis, many patients with severe infections do *not* have an increased oxygen consumption. In fact, septic shock is not infrequently associated with an oxygen consumption which is lower than normal. Surprisingly, this reduced oxygen consumption is not necessarily associated with a metabolic acidosis. In fact, many of the most septic patients develop a metabolic alkalosis, at least initially, which cannot readily be explained. Some of these and other data suggest that anaerobic (as well as aerobic) metabolism is impaired in sepsis. Consequently, lactate is not produced in as large a quantity as might be expected from the low oxygen consumption. If an increased lactic acidosis does develop, the prognosis in septic shock is quite poor.

Sepsis, and particularly septic shock, greatly increases glycogenolysis, the process by which glycogen is broken down into glucose. As a consequence, glycogen stores in the liver may disappear rapidly.

If the mobilized glucose is burned or metabolized aerobically, 38 mol of adenosine triphosphate (ATP) is released from each mole of glucose. However, when glucose breakdown (glycolysis) must function anaerobically because of decreased tissue perfusion or altered cell function, energy production is decreased by almost 80 percent and lactic acid is a byproduct, causing an increasing tendency to metabolic acidosis.

Glucose is the only substrate which can supply energy to the brain under acute conditions and to muscle under anaerobic conditions. If adequate glucose is not available from glycogen for these functions, the liver attempts to form new glucose by the process of gluconeogenesis from other substances, particularly protein. The amino acid alanine appears to be a particularly important precursor of glucose by this process. The glucocorticoids strongly stimulate gluconeogenesis, and if the sepsis is severe and persistent, the protein catabolism and resultant tissue and organ breakdown may be so severe that it is lifethreatening in its own regard. On the other hand, if gluconeogenesis is inhibited because of overwhelming sepsis or adrenal insufficiency, hypoglycemia and death may rapidly develop.

Lipolysis, the catabolism of fatty tissue, releases fatty acids and glycerol, which can enter the glycolytic cycle via acetyl coenzyme A, to provide energy. These lipolytic reactions are stimulated primarily by catecholamines and to a certain extent by glucocorticoids and thyroid hormones. This metabolic degradation of fat also results in the formation of ketone bodies (acetone, acetoacetic acid, and beta-hydroxybutyric acid) which may spill over in large quantities into the blood and urine, causing ketoacidosis and ketonuria.

Organ System Changes

Sepsis generally causes a strong beta-adrenergic stimulation of the heart, resulting in tachycardia and occasional tachyarrhythmias. In fact, the first sign of sepsis not infrequently is a tachyarrhythmia. Because of the beta-adrenergic stimulation, cardiac output may be significantly greater than normal, but only if an adequate blood volume is available. This hyperdynamic form of septic shock, often called *warm septic shock*, is present in 30 to 50 percent of patients during early septic shock.. In contrast, if hypovolemia is allowed to develop because of increased capillary permeability or other losses from the extracellular fluid space, cardiac output will fall. This hypodynamic form of septic shock, also referred to as *cold septic shock*, tends to occur relatively late and can often be converted to warm septic shock by providing adequate fluid.

Systemic arteries and veins tend to dilate in sepsis, but if inadequate blood volume is available, they tend to constrict. Because of this tendency to vasodilation, many septic shock patients will have relatively low systolic and diastolic pressures in spite of a normal or high cardiac output and a good pulse pressure.

Capillaries in sepsis tend to dilate and have a greatly increased permeability, particularly in infected areas and in the lungs. This tends to increase the quantity of interstitial fluid at the expense of the blood volume. This increased interstitial fluid makes the patients edematous with congested lungs, producing a clinical picture of fluid overload, even when the blood volume may be much lower than normal.

The fluid needs in septic patients may be truly extraordinary and may exceed 8 to 10 L in the first 24 h after sepsis develops. Whenever a patient begins to require more than 200 mL of fluid per hour to maintain adequate vital signs and urine output, sepsis should be considered present until proved otherwise.

The increased capillary permeability in the lungs in sepsis quickly leads to increasing pulmonary interstitial edema. As a consequence, the lungs become increasingly stiff and oxygen transfer is impaired. In addition, platelet aggregates and pulmonary venous constriction (perhaps due to central neurogenic reflexes initiated by cerebral hypoxemia) cause an increasing congestion in the pulmonary capillaries. Simultaneous with the increasing congestion, there is an increasing tendency to a diffuse atelectasis. This is followed by breakdown of alveolar lining cells and increasing leakage of fluid and protein into the alveoli. This protein, particularly the fibrinogen fraction, tends to inactivate surfactant and cause even more atelectasis.

During sepsis, total renal blood flow tends to rise or fall with the cardiac output. However, even if the cardiac output is high, the "effective" renal blood flow, as determined by para-aminohippurate (PAH) extraction, tends to be greatly reduced. Glomerular filtration rates, as measured by inulin or endogenous creatinine clearance, also tend to be very low.

Interestingly, the total creatinine production and excretion in many septic patients is much lower than normal. As a consequence, the endogenous creatinine clearance is often much lower than would be expected from the serum creatinine values. This may be of particular importance when regulating the dosage and frequency of administration of aminoglycosides. Furthermore, if the creatinine clearance is less than 40 mL/min, the incidence of other organ failure and eventual death is significantly increased.

Hepatocyte and RES function in the liver is impaired during sepsis, particularly if shock is also present. Consequently, important metabolic functions, including release of adequate substrate into the blood, may be greatly reduced. The excretion of bile may also be impaired. As a result, patients with severe sepsis, especially polymicrobial infections of the peritoneal cavity, tend to develop jaundice, often referred to as "septic jaundice." These patients tend to have high white blood cell (WBC) counts and mildly elevated serum glutamic oxaloacetic transaminase (SGOT), moderately elevated alkaline phosphatase, and severely elevated lactic dehydrogenase (LDH) levels.

The impaired function of the RES in the liver is a severe problem because sepsis, and particularly shock, causes mucosal ischemia in the gut. As a consequence, increasing quantities of bacteria and bacterial products penetrate the bowel mucosa and are brought to the liver. If the RES in the liver cannot handle these adequately, they pass through to the systemic circulation and cause increasing havoc.

As mentioned previously, if the liver is already impaired by cirrhosis, the risk of sepsis is very high and very few patients with cirrhosis and septic shock leave the hospital alive.

Sepsis is associated with a tendency to gastrointestinal mucosal ischemia and increased fluid loss into the bowel lumen and ileus. The ischemia, as mentioned previously, increases the absorption of bacterial and bacterial products, particularly in the colon and distal small bowel. In addition, the mucosal ischemia in the stomach greatly increases the tendency to stress gastric bleeding. The association between sepsis and stress gastric bleeding is so high that gastric bleeding following abdominal surgery or trauma should be considered due to sepsis until proved otherwise.

The fluid loss into the bowel lumen, particularly with generalized peritonitis, may result in the loss of 8 or more liters of fluid from the extracellular fluid space, further increasing the tendency to hypovolemia.

Paralytic ileus in sepsis may be severe and may strongly suggest the presence of intraperitoneal disease. This ileus not only interferes with return of gastrointestinal function but may also elevate the diaphragm and interfere with ventilation. If the patient has had recent abdominal surgery, the distended bowel may disrupt the abdominal wall closure. Occasionally this may result in bowel leaks as the distended bowel rubs against the suture material.

DIAGNOSIS

The diagnosis of sepsis may be extremely difficult at times and involves a search not only for the overall systemic effects of severe infection but also for the primary site of the infection. Although it may be a clinical triumph at times to determine that a patient's deterioration is due to sepsis, it is equally important to determine the primary site of the sepsis so that it can be adequately treated.

History

Careful review of the patient's history will usually indicate situations or procedures which are likely to cause infection. Various symptoms may indicate the probable site of the infection. The history may also provide information concerning impairment of the patient's host defense mechanism.

Procedures or Situations Predisposing to Infections

Urinary tract infections should be suspected in patients who have had their bladder catheterized or instrumented, particularly if done in the presence of urinary tract obstruction or trauma.

Intra-abdominal infections should be suspected in any patient who has surgery, trauma, or disease involving the colon, esophagus, biliary tract, or appendix. Intra-abdominal and wound infections should be particularly suspected in patients who have had emergency surgery for a gastrointestinal leak or obstruction, especially if it involves the distal small bowel or colon.

Pulmonary infections should be suspected in patients with chronic obstructive lung disease, chest trauma, vomiting while lethargic or comatose, and endotracheal intubation or tracheostomy for prolonged mechanical ventilation.

Infection involving intravenous plastic catheters should always be suspected, particularly if the catheter is inserted during an emergency situation or if it is in place for more than 48 to 72 h. The presence of any prosthetic device, whether cardiac valve, pacemaker, or vascular graft, should also make one suspicious of an associated infection.

Infections of the genital tract should be suspected after any instrumentation, particularly for abortion.

Ruptured placental membranes for more than 24 to 48 h prior to delivery is likely to be associated with an infection of the contents of the gravid uterus.

Large burns, abrasions, or skin rashes must all be considered prime sources of severe infection.

Symptoms with Various Infections

An awake and alert patient can usually relate symptoms which will localize the site of infection fairly accurately. However, some referral and overlap of symptoms between areas of the body is apt to occur. For example, a stiff neck may be due to meningeal irritation. Jaw pain may be due to an ear problem. Upper abdominal pain may be caused by a lower lobe pneumonia. Lower abdominal pain may be caused by genitourinary or gastrointestinal problems. Nausea and vomiting may be due to a primary gastrointestinal problem or may be due to sepsis completely outside the abdomen.

Impaired Host Defenses

Careful search must be made for any history of immunosuppressive drugs such as steroids or various agents used to treat malignancies or to prevent transplantation rejection. Various malignancies, particularly the leukemias in their advanced stages, even without chemotherapeutic drugs, predispose to infections. Patients with advanced diabetes mellitus or cirrhosis tend to develop infections early and tolerate them poorly. Previous infections and prior treatment with antibiotics are also important factors. Increasing attention has also been directed to patients with a history of poor nutrition and recent weight loss.

Physical Examination

The signs of sepsis, particularly if associated with gram-negative organisms, may be extremely deceptive and may mimic a wide variety of clinical problems. Fever, with or without chills, may be the only manifestation in some patients, and in others only hypothermia may be present. Other nonspecific signs include confusion, tachypnea, and tachycardia.

In spite of the wide variations in the physical appearance of these patients, three characteristic stages or types of clinical presentation may be noted: (1) sepsis without shock, (2) hyperdynamic (warm) septic shock, and (3) hypodynamic (cold) septic shock.

Sepsis without Shock

Septic patients tend to be restless, anxious, and confused. Not infrequently, increasing confusion is the first sign that a patient is becoming septic. In many instances, the increasing confusion and restlessness may be difficult to differentiate from delirium tremens. However, some clinicians have been impressed that patients with gram-negative sepsis are often bright-eyed and alert, even until just prior to death.

The systolic blood pressure tends to be normal, but it may be elevated at the beginning of the sepsis and tends to decrease as the sepsis worsens. The pulse pressure is usually normal or increased and is particularly apt to be increased if the pulse rate is slow or only slightly increased. Tachycardias and occasionally tachyarrhythmias, however, are very characteristic, and the pulse, though fast, is usually full and almost bounding.

The respiratory rate is characteristically rather fast, often greater than double normal with a slightly reduced tidal volume, producing a minute ventilation which is often 1.5 to 2.0 times normal. Even without any pulmonary involvement, rales are often present at the bases.

The abdomen is somewhat distended. These patients often tend to be air swallowers and can develop an ileus rapidly, even without any abdominal sepsis. If any abdominal or renal sepsis is present, the ileus usually becomes quite severe very rapidly.

The skin is often warm and dry with a flushed or pink color unless hypovolemia develops.

Hyperdynamic (Warm) Septic Shock

Characteristically, these patients are vasodilated and have a warm, dry, pink, or flushed skin. It may be extremely difficult to determine when severe sepsis becomes hyperdynamic septic shock. However, shock is generally considered to be present if the systolic blood pressure falls below 80 or 90 mmHg or drops by more than 25 percent, if the urine output falls below 25 mL/h, or if a metabolic acidosis develops. Patients with septic shock usually also tend to become increasingly lethargic, restless, and confused.

Even if hypotension becomes fairly severe, the cardiac output tends to be normal (2.5 to 4.0 L/min per m²) or high and may be as high as twice normal, particularly if the blood volume has been adequately maintained. Any anemia or cirrhosis will tend to increase cardiac output even more. Consequently, arterial pulses tend to remain easily palpable. Hyperventilation tends to increase. The lungs have increasing rales, and the patients may develop what appears to be air hunger in spite of relatively good arterial blood gases.

Hypodynamic (Cold) Septic Shock

This type of shock generally represents an advanced stage of septic shock in which hypovolemia and low cardiac output have been allowed to develop. This results in increasing vasoconstriction, eventually producing a cold, clammy, mottled, or cyanotic skin and severe oliguria. In some instances, the skin is warm and pink except at the tips of the fingers, toes, ears, or nose, which may be cyanotic and/or cool.

As sepsis progresses, capillaries throughout the body, particularly in the lungs and infected areas, develop a greatly increased permeability. Consequently, progressively greater amounts of fluid are lost from the intravascular space into the interstitial space. In a period of 12 to 24 h, 10 or more liters of extra fluid may be required to keep up with this loss. Eventually, fluid also begins to move into cells whose impaired metabolism cannot maintain the large sodium gradient that normally exists between the intracellular and extracellular spaces. Consequently, even though the total body water may be much greater than normal, and the patient clinically appears to be overloaded with fluid, there is an ever-increasing tendency to develop a reduced intravascular volume.

Laboratory Studies

White Blood Cell Count

In most septic patients the WBC count is elevated to 15,000/mm³ or higher, and not infrequently it exceeds 30,000/mm³, usually with a "shift to the left" (i.e., an increased number of band forms). In some instances the total WBC may be normal, and the only evidence of sepsis is a marked shift to the left. In severe advanced sepsis, however, the WBC count may be extremely low, particularly with gram-negative sepsis, and this is often an ominous prognostic sign.

The lymphocyte count may provide some indication of the type of infection present and the status of the patient's host defenses. A relatively high lymphocyte count may be a reflection of a viral, rather than a bacterial, infection. If the absolute lymphocyte count is less than 1500/mm³, however, one should suspect the presence of impaired host defenses; if the absolute lymphocyte count is less than 800/mm³, host defenses are very likely to be impaired.

Blood Chemistries

Blood chemistries may be quite normal until organ failure begins to develop. The LDH tends to rise rather early. The blood urea nitrogen (BUN) and alkaline phosphatase may also begin to rise, and renal and hepatic dysfunctions begin to develop. Albumin levels also tend to fall relatively early because of (1) increased gluconeogenesis, (2) movement of albumin into the interstitial fluid space because of increased capillary permeability, and (3) impaired hepatic function.

A rise in bilirubin without obvious damage or disease of the liver or extrahepatic biliary tract should make one suspect sepsis, particularly sepsis due to peritonitis with anaerobic organisms.

Blood Gases

As the patient progresses into sepsis and then into more and more advanced stages of septic shock, there is a standard progression of acid-base changes from (1) respiratory alkalosis with or without metabolic alkalosis, (2) compensated or partially compensated metabolic acidosis, (3) uncompensated metabolic acidosis, and finally (4) combined metabolic and respiratory acidosis.

Sepsis and shock are extremely powerful stimuli to ventilation. Therefore, the initial blood gas analysis in patients going into sepsis and early septic shock generally reveals a low Pa_{CO_2} (25 to 35 mmHg), a normal bicarbonate (21 to 26 meq/L), and an elevated pH (7.45 to 7.55). Early hyperventilation so frequently accompanies shock and sepsis that, if a patient with known shock or sepsis is not hyperventilating, the incidence of later respiratory failure is increased. If a septic patient is not hyperventilating and does not have a fairly severe metabolic alkalosis (which can depress ventilation somewhat), one must immediately search carefully for a serious abnormality of the central nervous system, airway, lungs, chest wall, or diaphragm and rapidly correct that abnormality.

The initial respiratory alkalosis is generally a nonspecific response and not a compensatory mechanism for hypoxemia or metabolic acidosis. However, if the effects of shock or sepsis are not immediately remedied, lactic acid levels will eventually rise, causing the patient to hyperventilate even more as a compensatory mechanism. If the Pa_{CO_2} is driven below 20 to 25 mmHg, this severe hypocapnia may in itself cause some hemodynamic impairment.

Metabolic alkalosis has been noted in an increasing number of critically ill and injured patients, particularly when severe sepsis is present. The etiology of the increased bicarbonate levels, often developing in spite of a concurrent moderate to severe respiratory alkalosis, is not always clear. Some of the more frequently recognized possible causes of this metabolic alkalosis include excessive administration of bicarbonate, administration of large amounts of antacids into the stomach to reduce gastric acidity, removal of large quantities of highly acidic gastric secretions, hypokalemia due to excessive diuresis and/or the use of corticosteroids, and metabolism of citrate (from stored blood) or lactate (from Ringer's lactate). However, in about half of the severely septic patients with metabolic alkalosis, no cause for the metabolic alkalosis can be found. This phenemenon may in part be due to impairment of anaerobic metabolism and a consequent reduced breakdown of glucose to lactic acid.

When metabolic alkalosis is present, the seriousness of the patient's condition is often underestimated because any tendency to lactic acidosis caused by perfusion and metabolic defects is apt to be masked. Furthermore, as the patient with a metabolic alkalosis goes into shock, the fall in bicarbonate levels to normal may be misinterpreted as an improvement in the patient's condition.

If a combined metabolic and respiratory alkalosis is allowed to progress until the arterial pH rises to 7.55 or higher, the mortality begins to also rise significantly. Relatively few critically ill septic patients who develop an arterial pH of 7.70 survive.

As shock progresses, local changes in cellular metabolism eventually results in the development of acidosis. This first occurs intracellularly in the involved tissues and then at local capillary and venous levels. By the time a significant lactic acidosis and base deficit is present in the arterial blood, the shock process is often quite advanced.

Initially, the patient can maintain a relatively normal pH (7.35 to 7.45) because the fall in bicarbonate is compensated well by the fall in Pa_{CO_2}. Later, however, the bicarbonate may fall so low that the lungs cannot keep pace, and the pH falls below 7.35. The lower the pH falls below 7.35, the poorer the prognosis.

A patient who is in severe progressive shock and lives long enough will usually eventually develop a combined respiratory and metabolic acidosis. In the terminal patient, the number of functional pulmonary capillaries may be so critically reduced and dead space in the lungs so increased that it is impossible for the patient to eliminate carbon dioxide properly. Consequently, in spite of hyperventilation, the Pa_{CO_2} begins to rise above normal levels. Thus, in the final stages of shock, the patient will eventually develop an elevated Pa_{CO_2}, low HCO_3^-, and very low pH. If a combined metabolic and respiratory acidosis is allowed to develop, the chances for ultimate survival are extremely poor.

Smears

Gram-stained smears of various secretions or body fluids may be extremely helpful in making a diagnosis of infection and determining the organism(s) most likely to be involved in the patient's sepsis. However, for a smear to be accurate, it must be performed on a good representative sample of the material available.

Obtaining good, accurate samples of tracheobronchial secretions, except by bronchoscopy or transtracheal suction, may be difficult. Many sputum samples are deceptive because the sample consists largely of mouth and pharyngeal secretions. For a sputum sample to indicate a pulmonary infection, it must contain many polymorphonucleocytes and an abundance of bacteria. If alveolar macrophages (dust cells) can be recognized in the specimen, a relatively good sample of lower respiratory tract material has probably been obtained.

Obtaining a good urine specimen can also be a problem. If the patient is catheterized, the specimen should be obtained by aspirating the Foley catheter tubing with a needle rather than by disconnecting the tube, breaking the closed drainage system. If the patient is not catheterized, a clean midstream catch in a man is usually a fairly good specimen. In women, a suprapubic aspiration or a catheterized specimen should be obtained for greatest accuracy.

Material from a closed-space infection, particularly if it is aspirated rather than swabbed, can provide accurate information when the gram stain is compared with the culture results.

Culture and Sensitivity Studies

As with smears and gram stains, the accuracy of culture and sensitivity studies depends primarily on how representative the material submitted is of the involved fluid or organ. It also depends on how rapidly

and carefully the specimen is handled. For example, great care must be taken to avoid skin contaminants when taking blood cultures.

The cultures taken with swabs should not be allowed to dry out. They should be brought to the laboratory as soon as possible for inoculation on or in the appropriate culture medium. In most instances, both aerobic and anaerobic cultures should be obtained. Anaerobic organisms are particularly fragile, and cultures for these organisms should be drawn with the same precautions as an arterial blood gas sample.

In septic individuals, smears and aerobic and anaerobic cultures of material from all possibly infected sites should be obtained. In addition, separate aerobic and anaerobic blood cultures should be obtained on at least two, and preferably three, separate occasions at least 15 min apart from a direct venous or arterial puncture. If an IV catheter may be infected, blood cultures should also be drawn through that catheter, and the tip of the catheter should be cultured. However, tips are often not cultured because of the high incidence of contamination as the catheter is removed.

All too often the most rapidly growing organism, rather than the organism responsible for the sepsis, is grown out on culture. If the culture result correlates well with what was found on the gram stain, the results are more reliable. If they do not correlate, one must use clinical judgment and/or obtain further cultures and smears.

Cultures should be obtained, whenever possible, before antibiotic therapy is begun. Once antibiotics are started, they can stop growth of all or some of the bacteria in the culture medium unless specific steps are taken to inhibit or dilute out the antibiotic. If the patient is already on antibiotics and not critically ill, it may be helpful to stop the antibiotics for 24 h and then obtain new cultures.

Monitoring

Monitoring of the patient who is septic and may go into shock must be almost continuous. Some of the factors which should be monitored particularly closely include:

1. Blood pressure. Watch pulse pressure changes particularly and use an intra-arterial line if the blood pressure is difficult to obtain or if serial blood gases are indicated.

2. Heart rate and rhythm (cardioscope).

3. Respiratory rate and depth.

4. Urine output (in milliliters per hour).

5. Central venous pressure (also pulmonary wedge pressure in selected cases).

6. Serial blood gases (arteriovenous oxygen differences may be particularly helpful).

7. Blood flow (cardiac output). This may be estimated from arteriovenous oxygen differences, but dye dilution or thermodilution techniques are much more accurate and helpful.

Whenever possible, critically ill patients should be monitored objectively and almost continuously. The observations should be recorded and, whenever possible, graphed. Graphic recordings of vital signs, particularly blood pressure, are extremely helpful in demonstrating trends in the pulse pressure. A fall in venous oxygen saturation or a rise in arteriovenous oxygen content differences is usually good evidence of a fall in cardiac output and tissue perfusion. It must be emphasized repeatedly that responses in critically ill patients are extremely variable. Single or isolated measurements are of much less value than trends or responses; this is particularly true of the central venous pressure.

TREATMENT

The treatment of septic patients can be divided into three main categories: (1) treatment of the infectious process, (2) enhancement of host defense mechanism, and (3) correction of associated pathophysiologic changes.

Treatment of the Infection

In treating patients with sepsis, it is important to delineate the underlying infection as soon as possible. Left uncorrected for more than a few hours, particularly if shock develops, problems such as intra-abdominal abscesses or necrotic bowel carry an extremely high mortality rate, regardless of how well the cardiovascular, respiratory, and metabolic changes are corrected.

Treatment of the infectious process itself primarily involves the use of antimicrobial drugs and surgical removal or drainage of infected or necrotic material.

Antimicrobial Agents

Antibiotics are often misused. No antibiotic, or combination of antibiotics, "covers everything." Therefore,

if antibiotic therapy appears to be needed before culture results are known, the physician must make an educated guess from gram-stain results on the organism most likely to be present in a given situation. In addition, proper cultures should be obtained so that therapy can be changed if the initial guess is wrong.

Table 32-1 provides a few guidelines to initial antimicrobial therapy based on the site of infection and gram stains if material is available for smears.

Although bacteriocidal agents tend to be favored, there is no evidence that bacteriocidal drugs are better than bacteriostatic, except in the therapy of endocarditis. *No* drug kills 100 percent of organisms— the body defenses are needed to do this.

It is important to administer antibiotics in the proper dosage. With some drugs, such as gentamicin, the proper dose approaches toxicity. "Playing it safe" by giving lower doses, however, is useless and tends to promote resistance. Familiarity with standard doses is a must, as is knowledge of signs of toxicity; prompt reporting is necessary if they occur.

In critically ill patients, absorption by the oral route is erratic and often totally inadequate. In addition, even if the gastrointestinal tract were working well, gram-negative organisms often require much higher antibiotic doses than can be achieved or tolerated by oral administration. For example, oral administration of ampicillin and cephalosporins is usually totally inadequate for serious gram-negative infections. Only relatively mild urinary tract or soft tissue infections will usually respond to treatment with these drugs.

For certain drugs, the intramuscular route should *not* be used because of (1) poor absorption and a tendency to form sterile abscesses (tetracycline, chloramphenicol, erythromycin); (2) excessive pain at the injection site (cephalothin, methicillin, aqueous penicillin); or (3) inability to achieve adequate doses (carbenicillin). The intramuscular (IM) route is also inappropriate in shock and, perhaps, in some severely chronic diabetics, because of the impaired microcirculation. However, the dose of IV penicillin or cephalosporin is higher than the IM dose because of rapid urinary excretion of these drugs.

It is necessary to know which drugs require either dosage change or complete avoidance in uremic patients. This is particularly true of aminoglycosides. If such agents must be used, blood levels of the antibiotic and/or creatinine clearance levels must be monitored very closely. Concomitant hepatic failure often requires further reduction in drug dosage in such patients, but guidelines for this situation have not been well established.

TABLE 32-1
Guidelines to Initial Antimicrobial Therapy

Site of infection	Gram stain results	Antibiotic
Lungs	Mixed or unknown	Penicillin
	Gram-positive diplococci	Penicillin
	Gram-positive in clumps	Methicillin
	Gram-negative	Gentamicin
Abdomen		
Hepatobiliary		Ampicillin and gentamicin
Upper GI tract		Penicillin and gentamicin
Lower GI tract		Penicillin, gentamicin, and clindamycin
Urinary tract	Gram-positive	Ampicillin
	Gram-negative mild infection	Ampicillin
	Gram-negative severe infection	Gentamicin
Pelvic (severe)	Mixed	Penicillin, gentamicin, and clindamycin
Central nervous system	Gram-positive diplococci	Penicillin*
	Gram-negative diplococci	Penicillin*
	Gram-negative rods	Penicillin* and gentamicin

*Chloramphenicol if penicillin allergy.

The antimicrobial agents used to treat infections generally act by damaging or interfering with (1) the cell wall, (2) intermediary metabolism, (3) the cell membrane, or (4) ribonucleic acid (protein synthesis) of microorganisms. Examples of each are given in Table 32-2.

Surgery

Surgical control of the primary or underlying infectious process is often far more important than the antimicrobial agents. In fact, most failures of antimicrobial therapy are due to inadequate removal, drainage, or

TABLE 32-2
Mechanisms of Action of Antimicrobial Agents

Agents acting on the cell wall	Agents acting on RNA protein synthesis	Agents acting on the cell membrane	Agents acting on RNA synthesis
Penicillins	Tetracycline	Polymyxin B	Rifampin
Penicillinase-susceptive	Chloramphenicol	Polymyxin E (Colistin)	Amphotericin B
Penicillins (penicillin G)	Aminoglycosides	Clindamycin (Cleocin)	5-Fluorocytosine
Penicillinase-resistant	Streptomycin	Sulfas	
Penicillins (methicillin)	Neomycin		
Broad spectrum penicillins	Kanamycin		
Ampicillin	Gentamicin		
Carbenicillin	Tobramycin		
Cephalosporins	Amikacin		
Vancomycin			

debridement of infected secretions, fluid, or tissue (rather than from the use of improper antibiotic).

Most large collections of pus will cause severe toxicity and will not resolve unless they are drained. Such drainage should be as complete as possible without spreading the infected material and should be dependent, if at all possible, so that gravity can help promote drainage. In situations in which drainage of the abdomen can only be accomplished anteriorly, the nurse must exercise judgement in determining the best balance between position changes to prevent pulmonary complications and those promoting maximal drainage of infected materials. Anterior abdominal drainage in children may be greatly facilitated if the child is encouraged to play on hands and knees with toys that can be pushed along the floor.

Continued leakage of intestinal contents, particularly from the colon or distal small bowel, into the peritoneal cavity is tolerated very poorly. Under such circumstances, the involved bowel should be excised or exteriorized and a proximal colostomy or enterostomy performed. The intestinal rest provided by nasogastric suction only is usually not adequate to prevent continued leakage from diseased or injured bowel.

Deep third-degree burns eventually all become infected. However, if the eschar can be excised relatively early and the underlying tissue successfully covered with skin grafts, infection of the area is unusual. Removal of infected or necrotic tissue is particularly important if an anaerobic infection, such as gas gangrene, is present.

Catheterization of the urinary tract should be avoided if possible. However, if the urine is infected and the urinary tract is even partially obstructed, the infection may be virtually impossible to correct without drainage.

Bronchoscopy is particularly helpful for managing bronchopulmonary infections or atelectasis if the patient cannot or will not cough effectively, even with nasotracheal suction. Bronchoscopic drainage may be particularly helpful in promoting endobronchial drainage of the suppurative material associated with bronchiectasis and lung abscesses.

Enhancement of Host Defense Mechanisms

Enhancement of host mechanisms may be divided into three categories: (1) removal of factors which impair host defenses, (2) protective isolation, and (3) active treatment to directly improve or enhance host defenses.

Some of the more important and more commonly occurring factors which impair host defenses include loss of integrity of skin or mucous membranes, presence of foreign bodies, use of immunosuppressive agents in transplantation patients, use of chemotherapeutic agents in patients wih malignancies, and the presence of metabolic abnormalities such as diabetes mellitus, uremia, and hepatic failure.

Any defect in the skin or mucous membrane may act as a portal of infection. This is particularly important in burns, which eventually all become infected in spite of all preventive efforts. Consequently, efforts should be made to remove the dead skin and cover the area with skin grafts as soon as possible.

Foreign bodies greatly increase the likelihood of infection, and if an infection does involve a foreign body, the infection is often impossible to eradicate until the foreign body is removed. Consequently, foreign bodies which are not essential to the life or function of the patient should be removed as soon as possible if they become infected. Certainly an infected IV catheter should be removed and another IV started at another site as soon as possible. However if vital foreign bodies such as cardiac valves, pacemakers, and large vascular grafts become infected, strong efforts are made to control the infection with local or systemic antibiotics. However, if the antibiotics are not rapidly successful, the infected foreign body usually has to be replaced by another prosthesis, with the hope that recurrent infection can be prevented.

If a patient with a transplanted organ develops a severe infection which does not respond adequately to antimicrobial agents, the immunosuppressive drugs should be reduced as much as possible or discontinued. It is far better to lose a transplanted organ than it is to lose a life trying to save the transplanted organ.

Patients with malignant lesions are often given chemotherapeutic agents in hope of obtaining a remission. In many instances, the response to the chemotherapeutic agent is minimal or infrequent and there is little reluctance to discontinue the drug. However, in some patients with lymphomas or acute leukemia, the chemotherapeutic agent is extremely important, and reduction or discontinuation of the drug requires careful judgment.

Control of diabetes mellitus during sepsis is often extremely difficult but must be obtained. Careful monitoring of blood glucose and acetone levels and carefully controlled infusions of insulin and glucose are essential.

Renal function is generally best improved by providing an optimal cardiac output and blood pressure and by maintaining a high urine output without the use of loop diuretics. Reduction of nitrogenous waste products in the blood by debridement of necrotic tissue is extremely important. Administration of essential amino acids with adequate calories may also be very helpful.

Hepatic failure is best prevented or corrected by providing an optimal cardiac output and oxygenation, by supplying adequate glucose, and by reducing the amount of ammonia reaching the liver from the intestinal tract. Reduction of the ammonia is best obtained by cleaning the bowel with cathartics or enemas and by administration of nonabsorbable antibiotics to reduce the number of bacteria in the bowel.

Protective Isolation

Increasing efforts have been made to isolate severe immunologically depressed patients from all types of microorganisms which might cause infection. Particular efforts have been made in this regard in caring for patients with transplanted hearts and those who are on large doses of powerful chemotherapeutic agents for treatment of various malignancies. The environment of such individuals is kept as sterile as possible and contact of medical and paramedical individuals with such patients is often only through plastic drapes or special plastic windows. Complete isolation for all extrinsic organisms is at least theoretically possible. However, such efforts are often only successful for a few days or weeks, and furthermore, the microorganisms which the patient already has are often the patient's own greatest enemies.

Therapy to Improve Host Defenses

Some of the attempts to improve host defenses have included improved nutrition and administration of fresh-frozen plasma. Experimental efforts have also included use of various phagocytic stimuli, administration of transfer factor, and transfusions of leukocytes.

Improved Nutrition

As mentioned previously, hyperalimentation of malnourished individuals can help restore phagocytosis toward normal levels. This is particularly important if the patient has albumin levels less than 2.8 g/dL. These patients may require more than 3000 to 4000 calories daily to restore immunologic competence. Unfortunately, IV hyperalimentation is difficult to give during severe acute infections and may in itself increase the risk of additional infections.

Fresh-Frozen Plasma

Administration of fresh-frozen plasma may help restore host defenses, particularly complement, in patients with prolonged infections or malnutrition. Unfortunately, relatively large amounts of plasma may be required to restore immunoglobulin and complement levels to normal.

Correction of Pathophysiologic Changes

Correction of the pathophysiologic changes in sepsis is essential not only to maintain optimal organ function but also to maintain adequate host defenses to combat the infective process. No antibiotic or operation can completely eradicate infection. Ultimately, the body's host defense mechanisms must accomplish this. However, if advanced organ failure is allowed to develop, the patient may die even if the infectious process is finally controlled.

Pulmonary System

In any critically ill or injured patient, the first priority of treatment is to ensure adequate ventilation, not only for proper oxygen and carbon dioxide exchange, but also to prevent or combat the tendency toward a progressive congestive atelectasis. It must be emphasized that adequate ventilation in the patient with severe sepsis is often $1\frac{1}{2}$ to 2 times normal or more. In such patients, a "normal" minute ventilation of 6 to 8 L may be totally inadequate. If the patient with severe sepsis is not hyperventilating, one must suspect that a significant ventilatory problem is present and make an orderly search for the most likely causes, which include:

1. Central nervous system depression by disease or drugs
2. Airway damage or obstruction
3. Damage or abnormalities of the chest wall or diaphragm
4. Collections of fluid or air in the pleural space
5. Damage or disease of the lung parenchyma
6. CO_2 narcosis or removal of hypoxic stimulus in patients with chronic lung disease

If the patient's own ventilation cannot be brought to adequate levels rapidly and effectively, ventilatory assistance should generally be begun. The Pa_{CO_2} in patients in early moderate shock averages about 30 to 35 mmHg. If the Pa_{CO_2} is greater than 45 to 50 mmHg in a patient who does not have metabolic alkalosis, ventilator assistance is usually indicated. If oxygenation is inadequate in spite of oxygen administration, if alveolar-arterial oxygen differences $P(A-a)_{O_2}$ are high, or if physiologic shunting (Q_s/Q_t) is excessive, ventilatory assistance should be begun. These indications are summarized in Table 32-3.

Even if ventilation is adequate, patients with sepsis or shock often benefit from the administration of oxygen. Oxygen exchange in the lungs and in the tissues may become impaired very quickly in these patients, particularly if the cardiac output is decreased. Consequently, virtually all patients with sepsis or shock should be given enough oxygen to maintain an arterial P_{O_2} of at least 80 mmHg. After the patient has had adequate fluid and blood replacement, pulmonary function may be further improved by elevating the patient's head and chest, increasing the tidal volume to 12 to 15 mL/kg, and/or adding positive end expiratory pressure (PEEP). Because PEEP tends to reduce venous return and cardiac output, particularly in hypovolemic patients, PEEP should not be added until or unless the blood volume is normal or greater than normal. If more than 10 cmH$_2$O PEEP is used, the cardiac output and oxygen transport (cardiac output multiplied by the arterial oxygen content) should also be monitored.

Fluids

In sepsis it is extremely important to maintain a cardiac output which is normal or preferably greater than normal. However, septic patients tend to become hypovolemic because of increased capillary permeability, with resultant fluid sequestration, particularly at the site of infection. Consequently, early aggressive fluid administration is extremely important in these patients.

In critically ill septic patients who may be seriously hypovolemic, it is important to insert two and preferably three large IV catheters. With three large IV lines, fluid can be administered rapidly, and hypotension due to hypovolemia should be corrected within 20 to 30 min, if at all possible. Administration of fluids at a slower rate may not correct the volume deficit for several hours or longer because of continued leakage of large quantities of fluid into the interstitial space.

In the septic patient who is severely hypovolemic, volume replacement is begun with 2 to 3 L of a balanced electrolyte solution, such as Ringer's lactate solution. However, if the patient is in severe shock or is severely cirrhotic, a buffered electrolyte solution without lactate may be preferable. Such a solution can easily be made by adding one to two ampules of sodium bicarbonate to a liter of normal saline.

The relative amounts of crystalloid, colloid, and blood which should be used in critically ill or injured patients is extremely controversial. Although albumin levels are often very low in septic patients, administration of large quantities of albumin may cause more harm than good. The albumin may move rapidly into the interstitial space, particularly in the lungs, drawing water with it, thereby increasing the tendency to respiratory failure. However, other investigators believe that the amount of colloid used probably has relatively little effect on the lung.

In general, fluid is given rapidly to septic patients,

TABLE 32-3

Indications for Endotracheal Intubation and Ventilatory Assistance in Patients with Sepsis and/or Shock

Respiratory rate greater than 35 inhalations per minute

Excessive ventilatory effort

Minute ventilation less than 5 L/min or greater than 20 L/min

Tidal volume less than 5 mL/kg or more than 50% of the vital capacity

Vital capacity less than 12 mL/kg

P_{CO_2} greater than 45 mmHg if a metabolic acidosis is present or P_{CO_2} greater than 50 mmHg with normal bicarbonate levels

P_{O_2} less than 60 mmHg on 40% O$_2$ or P_{O_2} less than 250 mmHg on 100% O$_2$

$P(A-a)_{O_2}$ on room air of more than 55 mmHg or $P(A-a)_{O_2}$ on 100% oxygen of more than 400 mmHg

Q_s/Q_t of more than 20%, especially if the cardiac output is low

particularly those in shock, until an adequate tissue perfusion is achieved or until the patient shows evidence of fluid overload. To do this properly requires monitoring of multiple factors including blood pressure, pulse rate, urinary output, skin perfusion, and the number and location of any rales that persist in spite of efforts to prevent or correct atelectasis. If the patient is in severe shock or does not respond promptly to fluids, an effort should be made to insert a central venous pressure (CVP) or preferably a pulmonary wedge pressure (PWP) catheter to measure the filling pressure changes in the heart.

Isolated CVP levels have relatively little physiological significance; however, the response of the CVP to a fluid challenge is extremely important. Some physicians feel that if the CVP is above 12 to 16 cmH$_2$O, fluid administration should be stopped because the patient is probably overloaded. However, we have found that the CVP in septic patients is extremely variable. A number of patients, particularly those with sepsis and acute respiratory failure, were found to have a CVP above 20 to 25 cmH$_2$O, in spite of hypovolemia as demonstrated by blood volume determinations or wedge pressures.

In many centers, great care is taken to measure the CVP with the patient flat in bed without ventilator assistance. Such maneuvers increase the accuracy of the CVP reading, but they are often unnecessary because as mentioned previously, the *response* of the CVP to a fluid load is far more important than the absolute *level* of the CVP.

If the CVP rises abruptly (by more than 2 cmH$_2$O) as fluid is given rapidly (200 mL in 10 min), the rate of administration should be decreased or stopped until the CVP falls to within 2 cmH$_2$O of the baseline levels present before each fluid challenge.

In most instances, the function of the right and left ventricles are quite similar; therefore changes in the CVP (which reflect filling pressure in the *right* heart) correlate fairly well with changes in the pulmonary wedge pressure (which reflects *left* ventricular filling pressure). In a number of instances, however, the CVP and PWP may be quite disparate. Hypovolemic patients with severe sepsis tend to have some obstruction to blood flow in the lungs and therefore not infrequently will have a high CVP with a low PWP.

If a PWP catheter is in place, the pulmonary artery pressure is monitored constantly. The diastolic pulmonary artery pressure is usually relatively close to the pulmonary wedge pressure unless there is pulmonary hypertension. However, a true wedge pressure should be obtained periodically (once or twice a shift) by transiently inflating the balloon.

Acid-Base Therapy

Most acid-base problems in shock will improve spontaneously if adequate ventilation and tissue perfusion are provided. However, any serious acid-base abnormality which persists in spite of these measures should be corrected.

A persistently severe respiratory alkalosis with a Pa_{CO_2} less than 20 to 25 mmHg may cause vasoconstriction in cerebral and possibly also coronary vessels. If the blood volume and blood pressure have been restored and the patient can tolerate sedatives, these agents may reduce the respiratory rate, thereby raising the Pa_{CO_2}. If sedatives cannot be used safely or effectively, the addition of dead space in 60-mL increments up to a total of 300 mL between the ventilator and the endotracheal or tracheostomy tube may restore the Pa_{CO_2} to desired levels. We usually reduce the tidal volume below 12 mL/kg only if it is impossible to correct the respiratory alkalosis by slowing the rate and adding dead space.

A moderate metabolic acidosis (pH < 7.30) that persists in spite of fluid loading should be corrected. Some investigators have felt that acidosis need not be corrected unless the arterial pH is less than 7.20. However, we have found that patients tend to do best if they are maintained in acid-base balance with a pH of 7.35 to 7.50, Pa_{CO_2} of 30 to 40 mmHg, and HCO_3^- of 20 to 26 meq/L.

Inotropic Agents

If shock persists in spite of rapid and aggressive fluid loading, attempts should be made to improve the cardiac output by increasing the contractility of the heart. The inotropic agents used most frequently in shock include digoxin, dopamine, isoproterenol and calcium; epinephrine and glucose-insulin-potassium combinations are also used in some centers.

The use of digitalis preparations in shock is becoming more controversial. Dopamine is a much more powerful inotropic agent and its effects can be stopped in a few minutes. In addition, although digitalis may improve myocardial function, it also increases myocardial oxygen demands and may significantly increase the incidence and severity of dysrhythmias. Since single large doses of these agents may also cause splanchnic and systemic vasoconstriction, they are often administered in multiple intravenous increments.

In addition, some patients in shock may be adequately digitalized or may even develop digitalis toxicity with half the usual dosage. Consequently, after an initial dose of 0.5 mg digoxin IV, we usually complete the digitalization with 0.125 to 0.25 mg every 1 to 2 h, running an ECG strip before each dose.

Dopamine, in contrast to classical vasopressors such as norepinephrine or metaraminol, apppears capable of raising both blood pressure and cardiac output in most patients with shock. The response to this agent varies according to the dosage used. At doses of 1 to 3 μg per kg per min, renal blood flow and urine output tend to increase significantly with little or no increase in blood pressure, cardiac output, or stroke volume. At intermediate doses of 5 to 20 μg/kg per min, the blood pressure, cardiac output, stroke volume, and myocardial contractility usually increase rather substantially, and the renal blood flow and urine output may rise even further. Higher doses of dopamine, exceeding 30 μg/kg per min, tend to cause increasing vasoconstriction, and the cardiac output may fall because of the increasing peripheral vascular resistance.

The only problems we have seen with dopamine are a tendency to tachyarrhythmias if the dosage is increased too rapidly and a tendency to hypovolemia. The hypovolemia develops because of the increased urine output, the tendency to vasodilation, and the improved capillary perfusion, which tends to increase fluid loss into the interstitial space. Some difficulty weaning patients from dopamine may be caused by this hypovolemia and/or a tendency for septic patients to develop an ionic hypocalcemia.

If the patient with shock has a slow pulse rate, isoproterenol in doses of 1 to 2 μg/min may raise blood pressure and cardiac output and restore tissue perfusion to normal. If the pulse rate exceeds 120 beats per minute, however, as it usually does in sepsis, it is much less likely to improve cardiac output and has a tendency to cause dangerous tachyarrhythmias. Isoproterenol should also not be given to patients with an acute myocardial infarction, since it tends to increase myocardial oxygen demands more than it increases coronary blood flow.

A normal concentration of ionized calcium (2.1 to 2.4 meq/L) may be extremely important for maintaining optimal cardiovascular function in sepsis and shock. Administration of 1 to 2 g of calcium chloride (10 to 20 mL of 10% $CaCl_2$) IV over a period of 10 to 30 min should be considered in any patient with a persistently low cardiac output.

Administration of calcium is particularly important in patients who require massive transfusions while they are in shock. Under such circumstances, the citrate in the transfused blood may reduce ionized calcium levels to the point of severely impairing cardiovascular function. Consequently, a gram of calcium chloride would be given after every 2 to 4 units of blood in patients with persistent hypotension.

Alkalosis also reduces the ionized calcium levels in the blood and may be an additional indication for giving calcium. Since calcium increases the response of the heart to digitalis, it must be used with great caution in patients who are fully digitalized.

Epinephrine's cardiovascular effects are about 50 percent alpha-adrenergic (causing vasoconstriction) and 50 percent beta-adrenergic (causing an increased heart rate and myocardial contractility). This may be contrasted with isoproterenol, which has essentially only beta-adrenergic effects, and norepinephrine, which has about 90 percent alpha- and 10 percent beta-adrenergic effects.

A few physicians use epinephrine a great deal because they have learned to use its combination of alpha- and beta-adrenergic effects to great benefit. Doses as low as 0.1 to 0.2 μg/min can have significant cardiovascular effects. However, this agent can cause severe tachyarrhythmias if given too abruptly or in too large a dose.

Over the past few years there have been scattered reports of significant improvement in cardiac function following the administration of concentrated solutions of glucose with added potassium and insulin. Such a solution may act by driving increased quantities of glucose into the myocardial cells, thereby providing additional energy substrate to the heart. The usual dosage recommended consists of 100 to 200 g of glucose, 20 to 40 meq of potassium chloride, and 10 to 20 units of regular insulin IV given over a period of 1 to 2 h. We have seen only occasional benefit with such solutions, and it has been difficult to prove that the glucose-insulin-potassium solution rather than other agents given at the same time were the cause of the improvement.

Steroids

It has been estimated that up to 3 percent of the adults in the United States have a subclinical adrenal insufficiency. Such patients may appear to be normal but will go into severe shock which is unresponsive to the usual resuscitative measures with relatively mild sepsis or trauma. In our own limited studies, 15 percent of patients with severe sepsis seemed to have adrenal insufficiency. They did not have the increased plasma cortisol characteristic of severe sepsis, and they did not respond adequately to ACTH. The only survivors among this group were those who were given steroids.

Because of the possibility that subclinical adrenal insufficiency may be present, all patients with sepsis or shock that is unresponsive to fluid loading and inotropic agents should be given at least 200 mg of hydrocortisone by rapid IV injection. If the patient appears to respond to the hydrocortisone or if there is a reasonable suspicion of subclinical adrenal insufficiency, the patient should be given 75 to 100 mg of hydrocortisone IV every 6 h for at least 2 to 3 days or until the patient's condition has stabilized. The dose of steroids should then be tapered over another 4 to 5 days.

Although there is general agreement that "replacement" doses of steroids should be given if there is adrenal insufficiency, the use of massive doses of steroids in shock remains extremely controversial. Although continuing administration of steroids interferes with the inflammatory response and certain host defenses, there is much data to suggest that massive steroids can be valuable in experimental and clinical shock. They can stabilize lysosomal and capillary membranes and improve cardiovascular function and cell metabolism. Oxygen delivery to the tissues may also be improved by shifting the oxyhemoglobin dissociation curve to the right.

Because massive steroids can cause significant vasodilation, they should not be used until hypovolemia is definitely corrected, and they should be given slowly with additional fluid over a period of 15 to 30 min with close observation of the blood pressure. Our present regimen consists of giving a pharmacologic dose intravenously to patients whose condition is deteriorating in spite of aggressive treatment with other modalities. If possible, the decision to give steroids should be made within 2 h of the onset of shock. The massive steroids may be repeated in 4 to 6 h if needed. Whenever possible, objective hemodynamic and respiratory studies are performed before and 30 and 120 min after each dose to determine if there is a beneficial effect which might indicate the value of further doses.

Vasopressors

Vasopressors should be considered potentially lethal drugs which should only be given when there appears to be no other rapidly effective method for restoring an adequate coronary or cerebral blood flow. In general, vasopressors should not be administered until an adequate trial with ventilation, oxygen, fluids, acid-base correction, inotropic agents, and steroids has been given. It is particularly important to avoid vasopressors if hypovolemia is present. Under such circumstances, vasopressors may cause blood flow through some arterioles to cease, and areas of ischemic necrosis may develop. Since small amounts of vasodilator such as phentolamine (Regitine) reduce the excessive vasoconstriction and lethality of norepinephrine in experimental animals, phentolamine is always added to our norepinephrine solutions.

If other therapy (including dopamine) has not been effective in raising the blood pressure, a solution of four ampules of norepinephrine (Levophed) and two ampules of phentolamine (Regitine) in 500 mL of 5% glucose in water will be used. Phentolamine in this dosage may prevent excessive vasoconstriction, but it does not alter the cardiac output or peripheral vascular resistance significantly. Furthermore, if the norepinephrine should extravasate into the tissue around the vein, the phentolamine usually prevents the local necrosis which can be caused by the excessive vasoconstrictor effect of the norepinephrine. In instances when the patient already seems excessively vasoconstricted, the concentration of phentolamine may be increased to two ampules for each ampule of norepinephrine.

It must be emphasized that the minimal acceptable blood pressure in shock is extremely variable. Consequently, close observation of the patient's intravascular volume and tissue perfusion as reflected by the cardiac output, central nervous system (CNS) activity, ECG, and urine output is required to properly regulate the dose of vasopressors.

There is some question as to whether vasopressor drugs are required in young patients. However, in older patients with significant coronary or cerebral arterial stenosis, blood flow to those vital organs may require pressures that are normal or higher than normal. In patients with coronary artery disease, raising the systolic blood pressure to 90 mmHg may increase coronary blood flow more than it increases the myocardial oxygen demands, and the cardiac output may rise. Raising the systolic blood pressure above 90 mmHg in such patients, however, often causes a disproportionate increase in myocardial oxygen needs and a fall in cardiac output.

Vasodilators

If the patient shows evidence of excessive vasoconstriction and poor tissue perfusion in spite of all therapy, and if the patient's blood pressure is normal or high, a vasodilator may occasionally be very helpful. It should be remembered that the best vasodilator in a hypovolemic patient is intravenous fluid. Furthermore, vasodilators should not be used in patients who are hypovolemic because these agents may increase vascular capacity by as much as 2 to 3 L, accentuating the hypovolemia dramatically and causing a sudden severe hypotension. Even in the presence of an adequate intravascular volume, vasodilators will often cause the systolic blood pressure to fall by 10 to 15 mmHg. If the patient is already hypotensive, such a drop in blood pressure may seriously jeopardize coronary and cerebral blood flow, particularly if these vessels have a 70 to 80 percent occlusion, which makes flow through them pressure-dependent.

Diuretics

If a patient does not have an adequate urine output after restoration of blood volume and good tissue perfusion and acid-base balance, diuretics should be administered. However, it must be emphasized that diuretics are rarely needed and may cause great harm. Most oliguria can be corrected by administering adequate fluids; even if renal failure develops, a normal or high urine output is of value. Oliguric renal failure following sepsis which requires dialysis has a mortality rate exceeding 80 percent. Similar patients who develop nonoliguric renal failure have a much better prognosis. Consequently, we strive to maintain a urine output of at least 0.5 mL/kg per h and preferably 1.0 mL/kg per h.

One must, however, also be alert for mechanical occlusion of the catheter, ureters, or the urethra, particularly if the patient is completely anuric. If the urine output is less than 0.5 mL/kg per h in spite of all these efforts, 12.5 to 25.0 g of mannitol may be infused rapidly IV over a period of 10 to 15 min, followed by a slow infusion of 12.5 g of mannitol per hour as needed. If there is still no response, 5 to 10 mg of furosemide (Lasix) IV may be given. The dose of furosemide is then doubled every 15 min until an adequate output is obtained or until a single dose of 500 to 1000 mg furosemide is reached. If there is no response to 80 to 160 mg of furosemide, 100 to 200 mg of ethacrynic acid may be given IV.

Unless the patient is obviously overloaded with fluid, all urine losses should be replaced. If oliguria persists in spite of all these drugs, we assume that the patient is in renal failure; the patient is then treated accordingly. Prophylactic dialysis and proper nutrition may be of value in such individuals.

Heparin

Some degree of intravascular coagulation can be assumed to be present in most patients with severe persistent sepsis or shock. Relatively few, however, show the full-blown clinical syndrome of disseminated intravascular coagulation (DIC) until terminal.

There is increasing controversy regarding the value of heparin for the treatment of DIC. However, if serial coagulation studies in septic patients reveal a progressive reduction in the platelet count and in the concentrations of Factor V, Factor VIII, fibrinogen, and prothrombin, aggressive treatment with heparin should be considered. Heparin therapy should be particularly considered if the fibrin split products are not elevated (indicating lack of increased fibrinolysis). If the full-blown DIC syndrome with bleeding from multiple areas is allowed to develop, reversal of the process is extremely difficult and the patient's chances for survival are markedly decreased.

Treatment of DIC includes: (1) correction of the sepsis and/or shock and (2) replacement of clotting factors if troublesome bleeding is occurring. Whether or not to use heparin may be a difficult decision. Reversal of the primary septic or shock process is the most important part of the therapy of DIC, but it is also the most difficult.

Mechanical Assistance

If shock persists in spite of adequate ventilation, oxygen, fluids, acid-base correction, inotropic agents, steroids, vasopressors or vasodilators, and control of arrhythmias, it can generally be assumed that at least part of the problem is due to inadequate function of the heart.

Although intra-aortic balloon pumping (IABP) has been shown to be of value in cardiogenic shock, its role in septic shock is still being investigated. Nevertheless, it is clear that IABP can reduce the oxygen demands of the heart (by reducing systolic pressure and improving cardiac emptying) and improve coronary blood flow (by raising diastolic aortic pressure). This may be particularly helpful in older patients who are likely to have a cardiac problem in addition to the sepsis.

SUMMARY

Sepsis should be diagnosed and treated as early as possible. Its development should be anticipated in critically ill or injured patients, particularly if they are immunosuppressed.

Trends are far more important than isolated levels in evaluating the patient's condition and response to therapy. Any tendency to reduced tissue perfusion or impaired cellular metabolism should be treated aggressively according to a previously well-designed plan.

Eradication of the sepsis (surgically and with antibiotics as needed), provision of adequate ventilation and oxygen, and early aggressive administration of fluids are the mainstays of therapy. Close monitoring of the response of the patient to the various types of treatment is essential to determine which types of therapy are of most benefit and should be continued.

REFERENCES

Alexander, J. W.: Emerging concepts in the control of surgical infections, *Surgery* 75:934–946, 1974.

Brown, W. J.: A classification of microorganisms frequently causing sepsis, *Heart Lung* 5:397–405, 1976.

Chodak, G. W., and M. E. Plant: Use of systemic antibiotics for prophylaxis in surgery: A critical review, *Arch Surg.* 112:326–334, 1977.

Clowes, G. H. A., Jr., H. Martin, S. Walji, E. Hirsch, R. Gazitua, and R. Goodfellow: Blood insulin responses to blood glucose levels in high output sepsis and septic shock, *Am J Surg* 135:577–583, 1978.

Cushing, R.: Pulmonary infections, *Heart Lung* 5:611–613, 1976.

Duff, J. H.: Cardiovascular and metabolic changes in shock and sepsis. Review of changing concepts, *Eur Surg Res* 9:155–165, 1977.

Finegold, D. S.: Hospital acquired infections, *N Engl J Med* 283:1384–1389, 1970.

Meakins, J. L, J. B. Pietsch, O. Bubenik, R. Kelly, H. Rude, J. Gordon, and L. D. MacLean: Delayed hypersensitivity: Indicator of acquired failure of host defenses in sepsis and trauma, *Ann Surg* 186:241–250, 1977.

Schumer, W.: Metabolism during shock and sepsis, *Heart Lung* 5:416–421, 1976.

———, Steroids in the treatment of clinical septic shock, *Ann Surg* 184:333–341, 1976.

Sibbald, W. J., V. M. Sardesai, A. Short, and R. F. Wilson: Variations in plasma levels of adenosine 3′,5′-monophosphate during clinical sepsis, *Surg Gynecol Obstet* 144:199–206, 1977.

———, A. Short, M. P. Cohen, and R. F. Wilson: Variations in adrenocortical responsiveness during severe bacterial infections, *Ann Surg* 186:29–33, 1977.

Siegel, J. H., M. Greenspan, and L. R. M. Del Guercio: Abnormal vascular tone, defective oxygen transport, and myocardial failure in human septic shock, *Ann Surg* 165:504–511, 1967.

Silva, J., Jr.: Anaerobic infections, *Heart Lung* 5:406–410, 1976.

Swan, H. J. C., and W. Ganz: Use of balloon flotation catheters in critically ill patients, *Surg Clin North Am* 55:501–520, 1975.

Weil, M. H.: Current understanding of mechanisms and treatment of circulatory shock caused by bacterial infections, *Ann Clin Res* 9:141–191, 1977.

Wilson, J. A.: Infection control in intravenous therapy, *Heart Lung* 5:430–436, 1976.

Wilson, R. F.: A brief introduction to sepsis, its importance and some historical notes, *Heart Lung* 5:393–396, 1976.

———: Endocrine changes in sepsis, *Heart Lung* 5:411–415, 1976.

———, C. Christensen, M. Ali, A. Percinel, and L. P. LeBlanc: Oxygen consumption in critically ill surgical patients, *Ann Surg* 176:801–804, 1972.

——— and **R. Cushing:** Sepsis in trauma, in A. J. Walt and R. F. Wilson, *The Management of Trauma: Practice and Pitfalls,* Philadelphia: Lea & Febiger, 1975, pp. 463–484.

——— and **R. R. Fisher:** The hemodynamic effects of massive steroids in clinical shock, *Surg Gynecol Obstet* 127:769–774, 1968.

———, **E. J. Sarver,** and **R. Birks:** Central venous pressure and blood volume determinations in clinical shock, *Surg Gynecol Obstet* 132:631–636, 1971.

———, ———, and **L. P. LeBlanc:** Factors affecting hemodynamics in clinical shock with sepsis, *Ann Surg* 174:939–944, 1971.

———, **W. J. Sibbald,** and **J. L. Jaanimagi:** Hemodynamic effects of dopamine in critically ill septic patients, *J Surg Res* 20:163–1972, 1976.

——— and **J. A. Wilson:** Pulmonary function, pathophysiology, diagnosis and treatment of acute respiratory failure in critically ill and injured patients, *J Am Assoc Nurs Anesth* 44: 25–53, 1976.

——— and ———: Pathophysiology, diagnosis and treatment of shock, *J Emerg Nurs* 3: 11–26, 1977.

INTRODUCTION

Perinatology is a rapidly developing complex area of specialization in health care which incorporates concepts from many disciplines to provide health care to the family, the mother, and the neonate. The multidisciplinary approach to perinatal care considers the biological, psychological, and sociological interactional forces that affect the health of the mother and the neonate. Familial and societal factors affect the mother, neonate, and the family. To maximize the ultimate potential of the neonate and the mother, all factors influencing pregnancy and birth must be considered. Perinatology strives to take into account all events and influences that may ultimately affect the perinatal circuit.

This chapter will focus on perinatal crisis, which is defined as a maternal-fetal-neonatal maladaptation that may lead to death or disability in the mother or the fetus from the time of conception to 1 month after birth. Five to ten million conceptions occur yearly in the United States. Of these, approximately 3.2 million pregnancies reach 20 weeks' gestational age. It is estimated that of these, 320,000 fetuses may be at risk for damage or death. Also, although maternal mortality has decreased drastically over the past 20 years, the rate in 1974 was 20.8 per 100,000 live births.

The evolving trend toward smaller family size has made perinatal loss even more significant than it was at a time when large families were the norm and perinatal loss was expected. The recent technological advances in perinatology have allowed mothers and babies who once might have died to lead productive lives. Aggressive, decisive perinatal care will contribute to higher survival rates and a better quality of life.

The current trend in high-risk perinatology is toward the development of regional perinatal centers that are carefully designed to provide the specialized care needed to reduce maternal and neonatal morbidity and mortality. Mothers or infants identified as high-risk clients will be treated at these regional centers. Those not identified prior to their perinatal crisis will be transported by special teams to the centers for treatment. Regional high-risk centers have significantly lowered mortality rates as a direct result of their sophisticated equipment, procedures, and personnel.

Conditions covered in this chapter are limited to those considered to be life-threatening to the mother or neonate and requiring immediate recognition and action by the nurse. Since other resources are avail-

33
PERINATAL CRISIS

Carole Ann Miller McKenzie
Katherine Wheeler Vestal

INTRODUCTION

THE HIGH-RISK OBSTETRIC PATIENT
Contributory Factors
Recognition and Basic Management
Antepartal and Intrapartal Crises
Postpartal Crises

THE HIGH-RISK NEONATE
Classification and Evaluation
Resuscitation, Stabilization, Thermoregulation, and Transport
Psychosocial Effects on the Family
Respiratory Crisis
Supportive Management for the High-Risk Neonate
Cardiovascular Crisis
Chemical Imbalances
Neurological Crisis
Neonatal Hyperbilirubinemia
Neonatal Sepsis

REFERENCES

able that clearly delineate all complications seen in mothers and neonates, this chapter is intended to serve as an immediate reference for the critical-care nurse who has had limited exposure to concepts of perinatal crisis care.

THE HIGH-RISK OBSTETRIC PATIENT

Any adverse condition affecting the mother has a potential negative effect on the fetus. The extent of this effect, or compromise, depends on the condition itself, the extent to which the condition is allowed to continue, and the vulnerability of the mother and fetus (or their ability to withstand stress).

In most instances, the mother and fetus/neonate would realize a better chance of optimum restoration from compromise if more specialized care were available to them prior to birth. While the mother may be diagnosed as having a problem prior to delivery, too often she is in a setting without specialized care immediately after birth, either for her or for the neonate. The neonate must then be transported and attendant problems may very well worsen. In the meantime, the mother may also exhibit continuing problems but not be in a setting equipped to provide optimum care for her.

If specialized care were made available to provide facilities for care of the maternal-fetal unit prior to delivery, perinatal mortality and morbidity would decrease. In this situation, the mother is hospitalized in a specially equipped unit to provide care for her and to continuously assess her condition as well as the fetal condition.

Application of the above principles can be made with all the complications subsequently discussed. Basic recognition of the patient at risk, preventive measures, and appropriate care will do much toward lowering mortality and morbidity in the maternal-fetal unit.

Contributory Factors

Factors affecting pregnancy may come from a variety of sources—the obstetric history, the medical/surgical history, biologic and marital factors, and paternal factors. The environmental factors, emotional factors, psychosocial factors, economic factors, and factors which develop as a result of the pregnancy itself all have bearing on the course of a pregnancy.

Table 33-1 depicts most of the potential influences on the pregnancy. It is very important to assess the impact of these factors on the mother in order to determine their potential risk to the pregnancy. Also, it should be noted that each of these influences, while affecting pregnancy and its outcome, also affect each other and may overlap.

Recognition and Basic Management

After recognizing that various factors influence pregnancy and its outcome, it is then possible to utilize specific criteria to identify the high-risk pregnancy. Utilizing these criteria in a screening process (prenatal care) prior to the actual development of a crisis may facilitate prevention or amelioration of specific problems. Also, the criteria may be utilized for priority assessment during a crisis to facilitate recognition and emergency care.

In order to properly screen high-risk patients and provide appropriate care, some basic principles of care must be followed. The client should be followed on a regular basis in the prenatal period. She should be seen as early as possible in the pregnancy and should follow a general schedule for visits, such as follows:

Prior to 28 weeks' gestation—once every 4 weeks

28 weeks' gestation to 32 weeks' gestation—once every 3 weeks

32 weeks' gestation to 36 weeks' gestation—once every 2 weeks

36 weeks' gestation to delivery—once every week

The patient should be thoroughly interviewed as early as possible in the pregnancy regarding any of the risk factors, any complaints and problems she is having, and *anything* she wishes to discuss. Thorough discussion of patient-perceived problems and clear, concise, yet thorough patient teaching is effective in inhibiting or diagnosing complications. It is absolutely crucial to *listen carefully* to what the obstetric patient is saying. An undocumented but thoroughly effective diagnostic aid is the patient's perception of well-being ("Something feels wrong") and the nurse's intuitive sense ("I can't pinpoint it, but I have a sensitive 'feeling' that something is wrong").

In addition, an overall physical examination and specific obstetric examination with careful documentation must be completed. Continuous fetal assessment is essential: i.e., fetal heart rate; fundal height; estimation of fetal size; fetal movement; and fetal position, presentation, and lie. If problems occur, specific tests to assess fetal well-being may be performed, including studies resulting from amni-

TABLE 33-1
Potential Influences on Pregnancy and Its Outcome

Obstetric/gynecologic history	Medical/surgical history	Paternal influences	Biologic factors
Grandmultiparity Previous surgical delivery Previous prolonged labor Previous fetal loss or complication Blood Factor immunization Previous pregnancy Recent delivery Infertility Gynecologic complication	Chronic disease Hereditary disorders Psychiatric disease Infectious disease Family history	Family history Age Blood group Chronic disease Hereditary disease	Hormonal insufficiency Weight Height Abnormal laboratory findings Age

Emotional factors	Environment factors	Psychologic, social, and economic factors	Present pregnancy factors
Family relationships Problems with other children Any stress-producing factor	Stressors Smoking Drugs Alcohol Genetic influences High altitude Infection Exposure to environmental hazards	Accidental pregnancy (unwanted) Culture and race Occupation/education Financial status Marital status Housing and environment Support systems Age	Nutrition Complications present Indifference to health needs Lack of progression Gestation Surgery during pregnancy Irradiation

TABLE 33-2
Criteria for Identification of High-Risk Pregnancy

Characteristics of the patient

  Age
    Teenage: under 18 at conception
    Elderly: 35 years and over at conception

  Weight
    Underweight: 100 lb or less
    Overweight: more than 20% over standard weight
    Gain: over 30 lb and under 15

  Height
    Short stature: 60 in or less

Race (specific problems affecting specific races, i.e., Tay-Sachs, sickle-cell anemia, cystic fibrosis)

Marital status
  Single
  Separated/divorced
  Widowed

Culture (specific cultural practices affecting pregnancy, i.e., pica)

Education/occupation
  Less than high school diploma
  Other than skilled or professional workers

Economics (lack of money for pregnancy care, housing and environment)

Available emotional supports (if none, may have emotional and other additional stressors)

Drug addiction or ingestion

Alcoholism

Smoking (two packs plus per day)

Emotionally stressed
  Fear
  Anger
  Hostility
  Anxiety and tension
  Lack of support
  Ambivalence
  Family problems

Patient perceptions ("I know something is wrong")

Characteristics of the father

Age
Elderly: age 40 and over (increased incidence stillborn)
Teenage: under age 18 (lack of support and/or responsibility)

Blood group
Rh positive with Rh negative mother
ABO incompatibilities

Family history
Genetically transferred conditions
Genetically predisposed conditions

Chronic disease
Drug addiction
Alcoholism
Diabetes mellitus

Previous pregnancy history

Parity
Grandmultipara (seven or more pregnancies over 20 weeks or 500 g)
Primigravida

Previous surgical delivery
Caesarian section
Version
Vacuum extraction
Mid to high forceps
Breech extraction

Previous outcomes
"Early" fetal loss (two pregnancies terminated under 28 weeks)
"Late" fetal loss (one or more at 28 weeks plus)
Live prematures (two or more under 2500 g)
"Early" neonatal death (one or more under 7 days)
"Early" fetal loss and live premature [one fetal loss under 28 weeks in last two pregnancies plus one live premature (any pregnancy)]
"Large" infant (one or more greater than 4000 g)
"Damaged" or traumatized infant (one or more, living or not)
Infants small for gestational age

Pregnancy occurrence
Less than 3 months after last delivery
More than 5 years after last delivery

Labor length
Prolonged or dystocia
Precipitate

Medical/surgical history (during nonpregnancy period, previous pregnancy, or present pregnancy)

Hypertensive disease
Renal disease
Diabetes
Cancer in past 5 years
Thyroid disease
Hereditary disorders
Cardiovascular disease
Respiratory disease
Blood factor sensitization
Severe malnutrition
Psychiatric disorder
Neurologic disease
Drug addiction or ingestion
Alcohol addiction or ingestion
Mental retardation
Lupus erythematosus
Infectious disease
Infertility
Gynecologic complication

Additional medical complications (during previous or present pregnancy)

Toxemia

Bleeding

Rubella

Anemia
Hemoglobin 8 g or less
Hematocrit 30% or less
Sickle-cell anemia
Cooley's anemia

Multiple pregnancy

Abnormal positional problems
Abnormal presentation
Abnormal lie
Abnormal position

Indifference to health needs
Missed appointments (three or more)
Failure to follow recommendations consistently

Nutrition
Weight loss and/or crash dieting, fasting
Weight gain (less than 15 lb or more than 30 lb)

Progression
Incompatible fundal height with gestation
SGA (small for gestational age fetus)
LGA (large for gestational age fetus)
Multiple pregnancy
Incorrect calculation of dates
Hydramnios or oligohydramnios

Other
General anesthesia or surgery
Abdominal x-rays
High altitude
Stressors
Decreased fetal movement

ocentesis; oxytocin challenge or stress tests; fetal monitoring; ultrasound; radiography; amnioscopy; amniography; and HCG (human chorionic gonadotrophin), HCS (human chorionic somatotrophin), and estriol testing.

The following laboratory tests should be obtained from the mother early in pregnancy, and the tests marked with an asterisk (*) should be repeated in the second and third trimesters of pregnancy:

1. Complete blood count, including hemoglobin* and hematocrit*

2. Urinalysis (protein and glucose levels checked at each visit)

3. Rubella antibody titer

4. Serologic test for syphillis* (last trimester only)

5. Toxoplasmosis antibody titer

6. Blood grouping and Rh determination

7. Papanicolaou cervical and vaginal smear

8. Cervical culture for *Neisseria gonorrhoeae** (last trimester only)

Other tests such as antibody screening tests,* urine cultures,* glucose level and tolerance testing,* and vaginal culture may be performed according to individual need.

Antepartal and Intrapartal Crises

Once the patient is screened appropriately for potential or actual development of conditions which are contributory to a crisis, it is essential to understand the appropriate disease entities and their medical and nursing management.

Early bleeding disorders Because bleeding disorders comprise one of the three leading causes of maternal and fetal mortality, it is essential that the nurse be aware of the problem and its ramifications. The aims of therapy, in order of priority, are (1) to render emergency care, (2) to control present and prevent future bleeding, (3) to diagnose the problem, (4) to secure the most optimum outcome to the pregnancy, and (5) to minimize the emotional effects on the family.

Abortion is the termination of the pregnancy before the fetus reaches viability. Viability refers to the fetal ability to survive in the extrauterine environment and is usually synonymous with a fetal weight of 500 g or more. If the abortion occurs because of natural causes, it is considered spontaneous. If the pregnancy is

interrupted purposely, it is considered a therapeutic or elective abortion. Therapeutic abortions are performed for medical indications, and elective abortions are performed for social indications.

Although the exact cause of spontaneous abortion is unknown, it is thought that the following are factors:

1. Maternal—15–20%, cervical incompetence, trauma, endocrine disorders, sepsis, uterine malformation and/or disorders, foreign body presence (e.g., intrauterine device)

2. Fetoplacental—50–60%, chromosomal anomalies, abnormal placenta

3. Other—20–25%, nutrition, drug and/or alcohol ingestion, irradiation

The patient undergoing a spontaneous abortion exhibits severe, "cramping" pain with persistent uterine bleeding which becomes more severe as termination nears. A pregnancy test is negative or weakly positive. The blood hemoglobin may be less than 11 g per 100 mL. Temperature and white blood cell count may be elevated indicating sepsis. An elevated sedimentation rate may also be noted. Diagnosis may be difficult unless tissue examination is possible and a prior positive pregnancy test has occurred.

A pregnant patient who threatens abortion (that threat being associated with cramps and/or bleeding) is always placed on bedrest and sedation and is instructed to avoid stress and coitus. Some patients are placed on estrogen and/or progesterone therapy and intravenous alcohol 5% may also be administered. However, there is no conclusive evidence that either hormonal replacement or alcohol is beneficial.

In the case of the inevitable abortion (uterine hemorrhage, pain, and cervical dilatation persist and suggest that an abortion will occur), the mother becomes very vulnerable to hemorrhage, shock, and infection. The amount of bleeding is observed, the number of perineal pads are counted, tissue and clots passed vaginally are saved for later inspection, vital signs are monitored, and the mother is observed for signs of shock. A complete blood count and type and cross match are performed. Ergonovine 0.2 mg PO or IM is given every 4 h for three to four doses to control bleeding *after the uterus is emptied*. Strict aseptic technique is essential to prevent infection.

If the patient has had an incomplete abortion (some of the products of conception are retained and pain and bleeding persist), a dilatation and curettage is performed. If the patient becomes shaky or anemic, a blood transfusion may be required, and broad spectrum antibiotics, such as ampicillin, may be given to prevent infection. (In addition, Trendelenburg's position and ice to the lower abdomen may be used.) Alleviating fear and anxiety and dealing with misconceptions and guilt are also part of the care the patient should receive.

The patient who is diagnosed as having had a missed abortion (fetal death has occurred undetected, with the products of conception retained in the uterus for longer than a month) will have a dilatation and curettage if she is less than 3 months pregnant. If she is more than 3 months pregnant, intrauterine injection or intravaginal suppository of a prostaglandin compound and oxytocin intravenously or hypertonic saline solution may be employed. If the pregnancy persists, a hysterectomy may be necessary. Prostaglandin or saline induction may be lengthy and uncomfortable procedures. The patient should be clean and comfortable and should receive a great deal of emotional support.

Disseminated intravascular coagulation (DIC) and incoagulability of the blood with uncontrolled hemorrhage from all body orifices may occur with fetal death after 12 weeks if the products of conception are retained for longer than 6 weeks. This may occur when thromboplastin-like substances enter the maternal circulation from contaminated amniotic fluid due to the breakdown of products of conception. Plasma fibrinogen levels are measured, and if they are below 100 mg per 100 mL, heparin therapy is initiated to correct the coagulation defect and the evacuation of the uterus is delayed. In an emergency, human fibrinogen may be given. Because of the attendant incidence of hepatitis, however, this is avoided if possible.

With the habitual aborter (three or more spontaneous abortions), the etiology may be related to cervical incompetence. In this case, a circlage of the cervix may be performed employing either the McDonald or Shirodkar procedure.

In all cases of spontaneous abortion, the patient's blood type must be obtained; if it is Rh-negative, anti-D immune globulin (Rhogam) is given within 72 h, to prevent Rh isoimmunization. The patient should also be appropriately sedated. In addition, the patient may want the fetus to be baptized. The nurse is responsible for obtaining the clergy or seeing that the baptism is performed.

An *ectopic pregnancy* is any pregnancy which is implanted outside the endometrium of the uterine cavity. Approximately 1 out of every 200 pregnancies is considered ectopic, and 90% of these are located in the fallopian tube, usually the right. Of all ectopic pregnancies, 75 percent are symptomatic and diagnosed in the first trimester. Causative factors are abnormalities of the fallopian tube, adhesions of the tubes secondary to infections, tumors or previous surgery on or near the tubes, or anything that partially or completely obstructs the tubes. There is increasing evidence that women with infertility problems may have an increased incidence of ectopic pregnancies and that women with intrauterine devices (IUDs) may be more susceptible to ectopic pregnancy. Ectopic pregnancy may also rarely occur after hysterectomy or sterilization.

A patient with an ectopic pregnancy may experience many symptoms associated with pregnancy in the first trimester because of hormonal changes. She may present with amenorrhea, breast changes, and morning sickness, although many patients have some vaginal spotting or bleeding as well. Amenorrhea, adnexal tenderness, and fullness are indicative of an unruptured tubal pregnancy. The three most common symptoms of early ruptured ectopic pregnancy are amenorrhea or an abnormal menstrual period followed by slight uterine bleeding, an adnexal or cul-de-sac mass, and unilateral pelvic pain (colicky) over the mass. Symptoms of chronic ruptured tubal pregnancy are a feeling of pelvic fullness or pressure, slight and dark vaginal bleeding, flatulence, lower abdominal tenderness, and a tense and extremely sensitive palpable cul-de-sac mass. Anemia, fever, elevated white blood cell count, Cullen's sign (ecchymotic blueness of umbilicus), shock, shoulder pain, and acute blood loss may ultimately develop.

The primary objective of treatment is control of hemorrhage as quickly as possible. The patient is at high risk to develop shock. Laparotomy is performed with excision of pregnancy and tube if this is a tubal pregnancy. Hysterectomy may be necessary.

Prior to surgery, the following must be done: patient status is monitored; a complete blood count is measured; blood type and cross match is completed; intravenous infusion is begun (consideration that a blood transfusion may be necessary should be recalled when selecting intravenous equipment); surgical preparations are completed (abdominal preparation, Foley catheter, permits, etc.); oxygen and emergency and preoperative medications are administered; the patient's blood Rh is noted in case she is Rh-negative and Rhogam is required; the patient's religious preference is noted in case she desires baptism for the products of conception or in case a blood transfusion is necessary; significant patient history and allergies are noted; vital signs are monitored; the patient and her family are informed about what is occurring and what will occur and the implications of both; medical explanations are clarified; and emotional support is provided to the patient and her family.

After surgery, routine postoperative care is given. The patient is told what to expect, and both the patient and family are encouraged to express and work through grief and emotional reactions. Rhogam is given within 72 h, if appropriate.

Hydatidiform mole, a developmental placental anomaly, results from a defective fertilized ovum. The embryo usually dies and the chorionic villi change into grapelike masses of clear vesicles. The growth of the vesicles is rampant and takes over the uterine cavity. It occurs in 1 of 100 pregnancies, with the incidence higher in women under age 20 and over age 40. When clomiphene citrate (Clomid) has been taken to induce ovulation, the risk is 1 in 650 pregnancies. The causes are unknown.

The vesicles produce high levels of chorionic gonadotrophin, which may produce excessive and severe nausea and vomiting. Because of the rapid growth of the vesicles, the uterus enlarges so rapidly that a 3-month uterus presents as the size of a 5- to 6-month uterus. The patient may experience vaginal spotting and pass some of the vesicles and may even develop anemia. After 12 weeks, a brownish discharge may be seen. No fetal heart sounds are heard and no fetal parts can be palpated. Ultrasonic radiology reveals no fetal skeleton and can detect molar vesicles. Prior to 20 weeks' gestation, symptoms of preeclampsia may appear. The client may spontaneously abort the mole at or near 18 weeks. If the mole is not aborted spontaneously, hemorrhage and/or uterine rupture may occur with surgery being required.

Evacuation of the uterus is accomplished by carefully induced abortion, followed a few days later by dilatation and curettage. The uterine wall is firmer and less friable at this time. Hysterectomy may be performed with an older client or if the uterus is approaching rupture. Uterine tissue is examined for proliferative or residual trophoblastic tissue. Blood transfusion may often be necessary.

The client must be followed for a 1-year period. She is advised *not* to become pregnant and to have titers checked frequently for levels of rising HCG (human chorionic gonadotrophin). If titers continue to rise or remain high, a dilatation and curettage may be performed. If malignant cells are found in the tissue examination, chemotherapy, usually with dactinomycin or methotrexate, is begun since metastasis to other body systems may occur. If chemotherapy is not effective, the choriocarcinoma tends toward rapid and widespread metastasis. If titers are normal for a year, the couple may elect another pregnancy. Recurrence is unlikely if the patient is under 40 years of age.

Nursing care includes observation of symptoms, provision of physical and emotional support if evacuation is induced, facilitation of the grieving process and provision of emotional support, preparation of the patient for surgery, reinforcement of explanations, and provision of thorough patient teaching related to follow-up and contraception.

Late bleeding disorders *Placenta previa* describes placental implantation in the lower uterine segment near or over the internal cervical os. The placenta is lower in the uterus than the fetus, and if the placenta were to be delivered first, fetal anoxia and death would occur. Placenta previa is seen in 1 of 200 pregnancies. There are three types of placenta previa:

1. Total—The placenta completely covers the internal cervical os and occurs in 10 percent of cases.

2. Partial—The placenta covers only a portion of the internal cervical os.

3. Marginal or low implantation—The placenta approaches the internal cervical os. As cervical dilatation occurs, the placenta may be palpated.

Two predisposing factors may be multiparity and pregnancy in an older patient. Multiparity is the major predisposing factor. Although the true cause is not known, it is thought that the upper uterine lining is incapable of providing proper nourishment and therefore encourages the placenta to implant lower. The placenta is usually 30 percent larger in this position because it spreads over the lower uterine segment to allow better nutrition.

The most important symptom observed with placenta previa is *painless* bleeding. The pregnancy is proceeding normally and suddenly hemorrhage begins, usually after the seventh month. Sometimes the hemorrhage stops and the patient may be without symptoms for a period of time, after which bleeding recurs.

Definite diagnosis is difficult because pelvic examination, which might confirm the diagnosis, is contraindicated. However, a double set-up may allow pelvic examination to be performed. A *double set-up* is a sterile vaginal examination done in the caesarian section room with all facilities and personnel ready to perform a caesarian section if necessary. Vaginal examination is contraindicated because the examining finger could perforate the placenta. The most appropriate diagnostic tool is ultrasonography, which can localize the placenta.

The major objectives of management are to control hemorrhage and provide a viable neonate. The client is hospitalized and placed on strict bedrest. Fetal maturity and welfare are established by previously mentioned diagnostic tools. If the client is close to term, a double set-up vaginal examination is performed. No other vaginal or rectal examinations are performed. If hemorrhage is severe, observations are made regarding blood loss, pallor, and edema; vital signs and fetal heart rate are assessed frequently; blood is typed and cross matched; and clotting times and a complete blood count are determined. The client may be medicated for apprehension; an intravenous infusion may be begun, oxygen therapy initiated, and blood transfusions given as necessary. The patient is also prepared for caesarian section. If the bleeding loss is profuse, the patient is placed on strict bedrest in Trendelenburg's position with bleeding, vital signs, and fetal heart rate observed frequently. A sterile speculum examination may be performed to rule out cervical lesions as a source of bleeding. The patient may also be transfused as necessary, receive intravenous infusions, and be placed on a high-iron, high-protein diet with iron supplements. Signs of labor are carefully monitored. If the placental implantation is marginal, labor may be allowed to begin or may be induced. Otherwise, caesarian section is indicated.

Complications may be hemorrhage, occurring prenatally and especially after examination and postpartally due to uterine atony (the lower uterine segment does not contract as efficiently); stillbirth; prematurity; and postpartal infection due to loss of blood and the proximity of the open placental site to the vagina.

Supportive nursing includes dealing with fear and anxiety, providing reassurance and explanations, and assisting with homemaker and/or babysitter help at home. Financial assistance may also be necessary because of lengthy hospitalization.

Abruptio placentae is premature separation of a normally implanted placenta prior to the third stage of labor. It may occur from after the 20th week of gestation until delivery. The frequency of occurrence is 1 of 150 pregnancies and can be classified as follows:

Total—Separation of the complete placenta.

Partial—Separation of a portion of the placenta. When the placenta separates, maternal bleeding occurs between the uterine wall and the placental surface.

Bleeding which escapes through the cervix is considered an *apparent* hemorrhage. Sometimes bleeding is contained between the uterine wall and the placenta membranes. This is a concealed hemorrhage and occurs more often with total abruptio placentae.

Predisposing factors may be severe preeclampsia or eclampsia, chronic hypertensive vascular disease, endocrine imbalances, vitamin E deficiency, multiparity, trauma, and a short umbilical cord. The major symptoms are blood-tinged amniotic fluid and pain (the uterus contracts so rigidly as to be described as "boardlike"). The uterus is tender and hemorrhage may produce shock. Bleeding may be vaginal with the amount of blood loss being variable. Hypofibrinogenemia may occur with abruptio placentae. If a total abruption occurs without immediate intervention, fetal death follows and shock may lead to maternal death.

The primary objectives of management are to restore maternal equilibrium and optimally to salvage the fetus. Blood loss is replaced, intravenous fluids are given, blood typing and cross matching are performed, and complete blood count and blood clotting times are measured. Fibrinogen may be given as necessary. If the abruption is total, an immediate caesarian section is performed. If partial, the client may be allowed to labor or may be induced, but is usually delivered within 6 h, either vaginally or surgically. Observations are made regarding the patient's general condition, vital signs and fetal heart rate, amount of blood loss, and the state of the abdomen. A Foley catheter is inserted and intake and output are calculated. If there is time, fetal welfare and maturity may be established by previously mentioned tests. Analgesia is administered judiciously.

Supportive nursing care includes support of maternal systems. The nurse may be the first to recognize the signs and symptoms of abruption, and prompt recognition by the nurse may salvage maternal and fetal life. Explanations to the client are important. If the fetal heart rate remains good, the nurse can encourage the patient about fetal welfare. If fetal heart sounds are absent, honest and constant support are essential. The father's presence may provide additional support.

Uterine rupture occurs when the uterine fibers separate and may be classified as follows:

Complete—Uterine contents spill into the abdominal cavity.

Incomplete—Uterine contents are retained by the uterine peritoneum or broad ligament.

Uterine rupture occurs once in every 1000 to 2000 deliveries, and although it is rare, it is life-threatening. Infant mortality occurs in 50 to 75 percent of all cases, and uterine rupture is responsible for 5 percent of all maternal deaths. Rupture which occurs in a patient who has had a previous classical caesarian section (which is rarely done today) is most likely to happen in the latter trimester of pregnancy, while rupture which occurs in a patient who has had a previous lower segment caesarian section is most likely to occur during labor. Causative factors may be previous uterine surgery, multiparity, oxytoxics given during labor, internal version of the fetus, external fundal pressure, difficult forceps delivery, difficult breech delivery, cephalopelvic disproportion, and a difficult and/or obstructed labor. Uterine rupture may occur with a predisposing cause and a long, exhaustive labor.

The primary symptoms of uterine rupture are intense, sharp, shooting pains with the patient feeling something "give way" or "tear" inside. Following this, contractions stop, some slight vaginal bleeding may occur, and abdominal palpation reveals the fetus beside the uterus. Fetal death follows and maternal shock occurs. If the rupture is incomplete, the symptoms may be less dramatic and a delay in diagnosis may occur. This delay is significant for mother and baby in terms of increased mortality. There may be premonitory signs of rupture when there is cephalopelvic disproportion. The nurse can observe a ridge or "ballooning out" of the uterus above the symphysis pubis as the lower uterine segment thins out and a contractile ring moves up toward the body of the uterus. The client may then develop tetanic contractions (over 90 s duration), experience pain in the lower uterine segment, and may vomit.

Management is aimed at restoring maternal systems and optimally salvaging the neonate. Immediate removal of the fetus by laparotomy is necessary, and frequently a hysterectomy is performed. Blood, fluid, and electrolyte replacement is necessary. Monitoring vital signs and close observation of the uterus is important when the patient has a contributing history. Supportive nursing care includes dealing with the grief process and feelings generated by loss of the fetus and hysterectomy, if performed.

Preeclampsia/eclampsia Hypertension found only in pregnancy or 72 h after delivery is termed *preeclampsia/eclampsia*. Pregnant women in North America have a 5 percent chance of developing preeclampsia. This disorder occurs after at least 20 weeks' gestation and usually after 28 weeks' gestation. Preeclampsia/eclampsia is classified as follows:

Mild preeclampsia—Blood pressure above 140/190 mmHg or the systolic pressure has risen 30 mmHg and/or the diastolic pressure has risen 15 mmHg. Weight gain has been 3 lb plus per week in the second trimester or 1 lb plus per week during the third trimester. Slight generalized edema occurs and is defined as fluid accumulation (greater than 1+) after 12 h of bedrest. Proteinuria of 0.3 g/L is also significant (1 to 2+).

Severe preeclampsia—The above symptoms occur with the following additions: blood pressure is above 160/100 mmHg on two separate occasions 6 h apart; proteinuria of 5 g/24 h or greater; oliguria of 400 mL/24 h or less; severe headache; visual problems such as blurred vision, double vision, or other visual changes and/or retinal arteriolar spasm on fundoscopy; epigastric pain; nausea; vomiting; irritability; emotional tension; pulmonary edema; and cyanosis.

The above findings with one or more of the following is evidence of further progression of the disease: tonic and clonic convulsions, coma, hypertensive crisis, and/or shock and is diagnosed as *eclampsia*.

There are numerous theories regarding the cause of preeclampsia, but none have yet gained widespread or complete acceptance. Predisposing factors may be multiple pregnancy, low socioeconomic status, younger or older primigravidity, diabetes, hydatidiform mole, hydramnios, dietary deficiency and poor nutrition, and prior chronic cardiovascular or renal disease. Clinical findings have revealed generalized vascular involvement of the kidney, eyes, heart, brain, and liver.

Aims of management are to prevent or control convulsions, optimally to salvage the fetus, and to restore maternal equilibrium. Constant monitoring after initial symptoms appear is essential. Mild preeclampsia is treated with bedrest and may possibly require hospitalization. The patient is maintained in a restful environment such as a darkened quiet room with comfortable positioning. She may be sedated with phenobarbital, and visitors may be restricted. Vital signs are monitored frequently, weight measured daily, intake and output measured, and protein and specific gravity of urine assessed with each voiding. There is some discrepancy in the literature regarding restriction of sodium in the diet, but additional protein should be added and adequate fluid intake (but not more than 2500 mL fluid) should be maintained. Hyperreflexia is noted and retinas examined. The mother needs bedrest, reassurance, diversional activity, and explanations. She may also need housekeeping, babysitting, and financial assistance.

Management of the patient with severe preeclampsia incorporates principles of critical care. The previously mentioned concepts of management are all incorporated into the total patient care picture. Prevention of convulsions becomes paramount in this phase of care. Magnesium sulfate is used to depress activity at the neuromuscular junctions, increase urinary output, and lower blood pressure. Because of the high dosages, awareness of potential toxicity of the drug is vital. Respiratory depression and cardiac arrest are the primary complications. An eclampsia tray should be in the room and contain calcium gluconate (magnesium sulfate's antidote), padded tongue blades, phenobarbital, and a reflex hammer (reflexes and respiratory rate should *always* be checked prior to administration of magnesium sulfate), as well as other emergency medications. Oxygen, a tracheostomy tray, and suction should be available in the room, and side rails should be kept up because the patient will be drowsy. Magnesium suflate may be given intravenously, intramuscularly, or in combination. Intravenous administration should be carefully monitored via infusion pump. A piggyback solution of D₅W should be provided. Intramuscular administration of magnesium sulfate should be given with xylocaine to decrease discomfort, with halved dosages injected into each hip. Since deep intramuscular administration is desired, long large-bore needles should be utilized and Z technique employed. Jarring of the bed or sudden, loud noises can precipitate convulsion. Therefore, decreased stimulation is important. Blood pressure is monitored frequently (every 15 min), and the fetal heart rate is monitored constantly. Urine output is calculated hourly and an indwelling catheter is inserted for accurate measurement and decreased stimulation. If the patient's urinary output decreases, the levels of magnesium sulfate may accumulate and cause toxicity to occur quickly; the drug should be discontinued. Other medications, such as phenobarbital and Demerol, may potentiate this effect. Signs of labor are monitored. Nursing care is constant—the patient is never left alone.

In eclampsia, all of these measures are important, but the primary objectives are patient safety, fetal well-being, and convulsion control. If convulsions occur, a padded tongue blade is used and the patient is not restrained. Padded side rails should be employed. If breathing difficulty occurs, tracheostomy may be performed. Suctioning and oxygen may be necessary, and additional medication may be administered. The patient is at risk for convulsion up to 72 h after delivery.

In addition, support and explanation to the family are vital, especially since the fetus will be delivered as quickly as possible.

Maladaptive positional disorders   The fetus adapts to existing space in the pelvis and uterus by assuming the best presentation and position for the space available. In this sense these positions are not maladaptive, but rather appropriate for existing circumstances. The following definitions are essential for understanding these disorders:

> Lie—The relationship of the long axis of the fetus to the long axis of the mother: transverse, horizontal, oblique.
>
> Presenting part—The most dependent part of the fetus which lies nearest to the cervix.
>
> Attitude—The relationship of the fetal parts to each other: *flexion,* chin approaches chest; *extension,* occiput approaches back; *military,* head straight up.
>
> Position—The relationship of an arbitrarily chosen point or denominator on the presenting part to the front, back or sides of the maternal pelvis. When the presentation is vertex, the *occiput* usually faces anteriorly. Sometimes the fetal occiput lies posteriorly (sunny-side up).

During labor, with the fetus in the posterior position, the mother usually experiences a large amount of back pressure. Other than usual nursing care during labor, sacral pressure is helpful and Sims's position facilitates rotation. If the posterior position persists, labor may be prolonged, and the mother tires quickly because of back discomfort and the prolongation of labor. Sedation to facilitate rest and relaxation and intravenous fluids are important. The neonate may be delivered posteriorly or may be rotated with forceps (Scanzoni's maneuver). General anesthesia or large amounts of narcotics should not be given because the neonate will be exposed to additional stress and be further depressed.

A *brow presentation* occurs when the fetal head is not flexed, but is partially extended so that the brow of the fetus is closest to the cervix. This is usually seen in small infants and pelvic contracture. The brow is the broadest diameter of the fetal head and the smallest or anteroposterior diameter should enter the pelvis first. The major difference in care is that the patient may require a caesarian section.

When the presenting part is the shoulder, the fetus

assumes a *transverse lie*. Predisposing factors are grand multiparity, placenta previa, and pelvic contracture. Vaginal delivery is impossible except with the second premature twin. When diagnosed by ultrasonography, a caesarian section is scheduled according to fetal maturity and welfare. If the patient is allowed to labor, uterine rupture may occur.

When the fetus assumes a longitudinal lie and the head is extended fully with the chin or mentum as the presenting part, the fetus exhibits a *face presentation*. Predisposing factors are a large fetus and pelvic contracture. A caesarian section may be necessary. If vaginal delivery occurs, labor is prolonged and after delivery the face may be edematous and ecchymotic.

A *breech presentation* is one in which the fetus is in a longitudinal lie and the buttocks and/or feet or knees present closest to the cervix. The classification of breech presentations is as follows:

Frank—The buttocks alone are the presenting part.

Complete—The feet and buttocks together are the presenting part.

Incomplete—The feet, singly or together, or the knees of the fetus are the presenting part (single or double footling breech).

Predisposing causes are prematurity, multiparity, placenta previa, and second twin or multiple births. The denominator is the sacrum. The fetal heart rate is auscultated in the upper quadrants of the mother's abdomen. Complications may be premature rupture of membranes, prolapsed cord, and fetal mortality (the cervix may clamp around the head after the body is delivered). The major objective of management is to ensure an optimum neonatal outcome. Fetal head size is assessed via ultrasound, x-ray pelvimetry is performed, and maternal and fetal monitoring is maintained during labor. If the patient is a primigravida, a caesarean section is almost always performed. When the fetus is in an incomplete breech presentation, often the feet extend from the vagina before the cervix is fully dilated. Warm wet cloths should cover the feet. The presenting part often appears bruised because these soft tissues have acted as a dilator force against the cervix. During labor, meconium-stained amniotic fluid is not necessarily an indication of fetal distress. Since there is pressure on the fetal abdomen when the thighs are flexed, meconium is expelled. If the neonate is delivered vaginally, delivery may occur spontaneously or be assisted via "breech extraction." Because of cord compression, oxygen is limited to the neonate once

delivered up to the waist. General anesthetic must be accessible in the delivery room. If the cervix is not completely dilated or if it contracts after the body is delivered but prior to the head delivery, there is danger of fetal death. General anesthetic relaxes the cervix so that the head can be delivered. After delivery the infant may need resuscitation immediately and may appear to be in shock. The manipulation required to deliver the neonate may cause fracture of the clavicle and humerus, brachial plexus injury, or intracranial hemorrhage. Many families have misunderstanding and fear about breech births. Supportive nursing care includes dealing with these fears and anxieties. The nurse should clarify information, help the mother to relax, provide explanation and support about procedures utilized for the neonate, and provide information regarding the baby's condition.

Prolapsed cord   Prolapsed cord occurs after rupture of membranes when the umbilical cord slips below the presenting part. Compression of the cord occurs because it precedes the presenting part and may be between the presenting part and the cervix, with anoxia resulting. With every contraction or when the presenting part descends, the degree of compression is increased. Prolapsed cord occurs once in every 400 pregnancies. Because oxygen transfer between mother and fetus is impaired, there is immediate threat to fetal well-being. The causes are premature rupture of membranes, rupture of membranes after an enema or vaginal examination, or any condition which creates a positional change for the fetus or disrupts the membrane integrity, especially when the presenting part is at a high station. Predisposing factors may be breech presentation, multiple pregnancy, prematurity, or lack of engagement of the presenting part.

The only possible treatment is caesarian section. Frequently the nurse is the professional with the patient at this time. The following are the priority actions of the nurse:

1. Keep hand in vagina and push the presenting part up and away from the cord. Once the nurse's hand is in the vagina, it remains there until delivery is accomplished. The nurse can also continuously assess fetal welfare by feeling cord pulsation.

2. Call for assistance.

3. Have physician notified and other staff prepare for an immediate caesarian section.

4. Assist patient to knee-chest or Trendelenburg's position.

5. Administer oxygen.

6. Ascertain presentation, cervical dilatation, station, and cord condition. Fetal heart rate is monitored by cord pulsation.

7. Reassure patient.

If cord compression occurs for 5 min or longer, central nervous system damage or death of the fetus will result.

Postpartal Crises

Postpartum hemorrhage Since the fourth stage of labor may be defined in numerous ways (the first hour postpartum, the first 12 h postpartum, or the entire 6-week postpartal period), it is clearer to describe this type of hemorrhage as *early postpartal hemorrhage.* Hemorrhage is considered the leading cause of maternal mortality and morbidity and occurs in 5 percent of obstetric clients. It is defined as blood loss of 500 mL or more for 24 h after delivery. However, the average obstetric client can usually lose up to 1 percent or more of her normal blood volume without consequence. Some of the more recent literature has defined hemorrhage as the loss of 1 percent or more of body weight. One can easily compute this since 1 mL of blood is equivalent in weight to 1 g.

In the first postpartal hour, the patient is most likely to hemorrhage because of uterine atony. Because of the network of blood vessels throughout the uterine musculature, hemorrhage occurs if the uterus is not well-contracted. Normally, as long as the uterus appears contracted and firm, bleeding is minimal. However, blood can collect in the uterus and not become evident for a few hours. The concealed bleeding can be assessed by the nurse by palpating the fundal height regularly. If the fundus rises insidiously, hemorrhage might be suspected.

The primary causes of postpartal hemorrhage are considered to be poor uterine tone, retained placental fragments which do not allow the uterus to contract efficiently, lacerations of the cervix and/or vagina, and perineal tear or extension of the episiotomy. Predisposing factors may be a long or traumatic delivery, an overdistended uterus (multiple births, polyhydramnios, tumors of the cervix or uterus), medical conditions (vitamin K deficiency, hyperthyroidism, defibrination syndrome, endometritis), inversion of the uterus, placenta accreta, and large amounts of analgesia and/or anesthesia. There is also some evidence indicating that red-haired patients lack some intrinsic clotting factor and tend to be postpartal

bleeders. Intervention must occur quickly to prevent maternal death.

Frequent monitoring of vital signs will alert the nurse to signs of shock. If the nurse notices a relaxed uterus, it should be grasped and firmly massaged. Counterpressure must *always* be applied at the symphysis pubis. Failure to apply counterpressure may lead to an inverted uterus. When the uterus becomes firm, massage should be discontinued, but careful assessment must continue. If massage is continued once the uterus is firm, the muscles may become fatigued and relax, thereby yielding additional bleeding. The number of perineal pads utilized must be counted, prescribed oxytoxics administered, the patient placed in Trendelenburg's position, ice applied to the uterus, an intravenous infusion ensured, and blood typed and cross matched for possible transfusion.

It is important to bear in mind that methergine oxytoxic preparations are contraindicated with elevated blood pressure. If bleeding continues and the uterus persists in relaxing, bimanual compression may be employed, *as a last resort,* until medical care arrives. Utilizing sterile gloves, one hand is inserted into the vagina and formed into a fist which is placed against the cervix and pressed upwards. The uterus is grasped by the free hand and held between the internally applied fist and the externally grasping hand. The uterus is massaged and held until firm. Typically, the uterus will relax as soon as pressure is withdrawn, so maintenance of this position may be required until medical assistance arrives. Failure of the uterus to contract with continued bleeding could lead to hysterectomy.

Late postpartal hemorrhage is described as occurring after 24 h postpartum and up to 6 weeks postpartum. A late postpartal hemorrhage usually occurs in days 6 through 10. A sudden, massive loss of blood occurs after normal lochial flow is decreasing. Causes are usually abnormal involution of the placental site and/or retention of placental fragments. The patient is usually at home and may need transportation to the hospital and help with her new baby.

All the emergency measures discussed for early postpartal hemorrhage apply. The patient is examined and a dilatation and curettage is performed. After any hemorrhage, broad spectrum antibiotics are given to prevent infection.

A third type of hemorrhage, which is considerably less easily recognized, is the *hematoma.* Blood may collect in the connective tissue of the vulva, the perineum, or under the vaginal mucosa, because of injury of a blood vessel in these tissues. This may occur during delivery or during episiotomy repair. Although bleeding into the tissues may be slow, it is continuous. The major symptom is severe pain, disproportional to the amount of bleeding even after analgesia has been administered. The hematoma may not be visible and therefore is less easily recognized.

The hematoma must be incised and drained and blood clots removed. The bleeding vessel is ligated. Blood transfusion may be necessary, antibiotics are given prophylactically, intravenous fluids are administered, and ice is applied to the perineum. If the hematoma expands, circulatory shock may occur due to extravasation of blood. Perineal assessment is an integral and all-too-often overlooked aspect of postpartal care.

Postpartal infection Postpartal infection is defined by the Joint Committee on Maternal Welfare as a temperature of 100.4°F (38°C) (taken orally at least four times per day) on two occasions, occurring on days 2 through 5 postpartum (exclusive of the first 24 h). Postpartum infection, known also as puerperal infection, sepsis, or childbed fever, may be any infection of the genital area occurring within 28 days of delivery or abortion. It occurs in approximately 6 percent of obstetric clients and has been cited often in historical literature.

Postpartal infection may be found by the nurse during a simple, yet complete, postpartal assessment of all portals of entry. Unfortunately, obstetric clients are frequently not assessed appropriately in the postpartal period. This should include assessment of breast, abdomen, fundus, costovertebral angle, bladder, perineum, rectum, lochia, and legs.

Predisposing factors of postpartal infection may be trauma during labor and delivery (additional portals of entry), hemorrhage, prolonged labor of 24 h and over, premature rupture of membranes, placental fragment retention, manual removal of the placenta, severe anemia, malnutrition, general debilitation, numerous vaginal examinations during labor, poor hand washing technique, and droplet infection in personnel.

The numerous portals of entry for causative organisms following delivery are as follows: the site of placental attachment, the perineal area with episiotomy and/or lacerations, and the urinary tract. The urinary tract has distended ureters due to pregnancy changes, which predisposes to urine backflow stasis and decreased size and emptying time of the bladder leading to stagnation of urine. There is also poor blood and lymph drainage in the bladder because of

pressure of the fetus which results in less defense in fighting infection, edema, and a more easily traumatized area. Anesthesia also temporarily decreases bladder tone, and frequently clients are catheterized more than once in the intrapartal and postpartal periods. Other portals of entry are the vagina, with its increased pH and increased mucus formation, and the breasts. All these portals of entry may provide an appropriate medium for infectious growth and routes for more extensive infection to the uterine vein and circulatory system (thrombophlebitis and pulmonary embolism), the lymphatics (peritonitis and parametritis), and the fallopian tubes (salpingitis).

When the infection is localized to the perineum, vulva, vagina, or cervix, symptoms may be pain at the site, burning on urination, heat sensation, discoloration of tissues, edema, purulent and foul-smelling discharge, and temperature elevation (above 100.4°F). When the infection is based in the uterus (endometritis, site of placental attachment; metritis, muscle of uterus; parametritis, pelvic connective tissue), symptoms may be elevated temperature (101 to 103°F 48 h or more postpartum), elevated pulse, chills, general malaise, anorexia, and headache. If uterine infection becomes severe, symptoms may be elevated temperature (104 to 105°F); elevated pulse; prolonged and severe afterpains; tender and enlarged uterus; and profuse, dark brown, foul-smelling lochia. Symptoms of peritonitis are elevated temperature (103 to 105°F), chills, tachycardia (140 or higher), severe pain, paralytic ileus, and diarrhea. Symptoms occurring just prior to death are delirium and coma.

General care of the obstetric client with postpartal infection includes proper utilization of aseptic technique, promotion of rest and sleep, replacement of fluids (3000 to 4000 mL per 24 h) and blood loss, adequate nutritional intake (high in calories, vitamins, and protein), isolation from the neonate and other mothers, semi-Fowler's position (to facilitate lochial drainage), assessment of the fundus for firmness and contractions, monitoring of vital signs, assessment for complications, collection and dispatch of appropriate laboratory specimens and promotion of parent-child interaction within the limits imposed by isolation. The nurse can promote parent-child interaction by bringing the neonate to the door of the mother's room, providing a picture of the neonate in the mother's room, frequently reporting the neonate's progress, and encouraging the father's participation in neonatal care.

Mastitis is an inflammatory condition of the mammary glands and/or their tissues which *usually* occurs

1 to 4 weeks postpartum. However, it may occur at any time while breast feeding. Predisposing factors are improper hygiene, erosions or fissures of nipples, engorgement, and breast injuries or bruising. Mastitis may lead to breast abscess. Symptoms of mastitis are elevated temperature (103 to 104°F); elevated pulse; marked engorgement; severe, acute pain and tenderness unilaterally or bilaterally; chills; malaise; and a hard, red, tender irregular mass observed unilaterally or bilaterally. Care includes antibiotics, breast support via binders or bra, application of heat, and analgesics. If the mother is breast feeding, current opinion is that she may continue and, in fact, may obtain some pain relief from emptying her breasts, particularly the affected one. However, this remains controversial and judgment should be based on the individual situation.

Urinary tract infections include cystitis (bladder infection) and nephritis. These are usually due to stagnation of urine postdelivery or to frequent catheterizations. Symptoms of cystitis are pain or burning upon urination, elevated temperature (100 to 101°F), and tenderness over the bladder. Patients with kidney infections may present with elevated temperature (100°F or greater), costovertebral angle tenderness (when the costovertebral angle is palpated over the area of the kidney, pain is felt), urgency to urinate, frequency of urination, and pyuria. Care includes calculation of intake and output, avoidance of bladder distention, attention to aseptic technique, administration of antibiotics (following collection of specimens for culture and sensitivity), promotion of complete emptying of bladder, and forcing of fluids.

Thromboembolic disorders   In thrombophlebitis, a thrombus or vascular clot is formed because of the progression of an inflammatory or infectious process within the venous system. Postpartal thrombophlebitis may result from blood stagnation secondary to vessel overdistension and/or development of thrombi at the placental site, which may become infected. Extension of infection may occur via the circulatory and lymphatic systems. The greatest danger of thrombophlebitis is pulmonary embolism. Predisposing factors may be intrapartal complications, such as placenta previa or caesarian section, or third-stage delivery problems and varicosities. Symptoms may include pain, elevated temperature (to 105°F), heat in calf, chills, bilateral or unilateral positive Homans' sign (dorsiflexion of the foot with light pressure of knee yields pain in the calf), swelling, tenderness, redness along the infected vein, blanched appearance of the leg (arterial circulation constriction), severe pain in groin, and insomnia. Symptoms usually appear in the 10th to 20th postpartal day. Thrombophlebitis may recur with succeeding pregnancy or age and a history of previous thrombus formation.

Symptoms of a pulmonary embolus include cardiac pain, dyspnea, irregular and/or faint pulse, pallor, cyanosis, and increasing feelings of apprehension.

Care may include anticoagulant therapy, antibiotics, strict bedrest, elevation of extremities without restrictive bedcovers, moist heat, elastic stockings, increased fluids, and oxygen therapy as needed. Leg massage is strictly avoided.

A rare but frequently fatal disorder of pregnancy is amniotic fluid embolism. In this condition, amniotic fluid with its particles of vernix caseosa, fetal hair, fetal skin, and possibly meconium is introduced into the maternal circulation. In order for amniotic fluid embolism to occur, a tear in the amnion and chorion is necessary, the maternal venous circulation must be open and accessible (marginal placental separation, laceration of uterus or cervix), and increased pressure must be present to force fluid into the maternal circulation (vigorous labor, particularly with oxytocin induction). If there is meconium in the amniotic fluid (as in fetal distress due to vigorous labor), the effect is more toxic.

Amniotic fluid embolism may occur during labor after rupture of the membranes or during delivery (vaginal or caesarean section), amniocentesis, uterine rupture, abruptio placentae, or placenta previa. A predisposing factor is a precipitant labor with severe contractions in a multipara. Symptoms may be pulmonary distress, dyspnea, pulmonary edema, cyanosis, and shock with intravascular coagulation and hemorrhage. Death usually follows. Treatment is aimed at reversing shock and hemorrhage and assuring adequate ventilation.

The previously discussed conditions have been related to crises which are specific to the maternal-fetal unit. It is now appropriate to deal with those crises which relate to the neonate.

THE HIGH-RISK NEONATE

The high-risk neonate is one whose life or potential quality of life is placed in jeopardy by some degree of maladaptation. In about 60 percent of the cases, the high-risk neonate can be predicted. This prediction is based on the complications of the pregnancy and unfavorable environmental factors that may influence the development of the fetus. Early recognition of the high-risk situation allows time for adequate and appropriate preparation for the birth. Specially trained personnel and equipment can ensure the neonate optimal care at the time of delivery.

The remaining 40 percent of high-risk births are not predictable and may present with a multitude of problems at the time of birth. Being unprepared for delivery of such high-risk neonates may further compromise their chances of survival. Any facility anticipating the possibility of childbirth must anticipate the possibility of perinatal crisis and must have the proper equipment and regimens available to offer supportive care until the high-risk mother or neonate can be transported to a high-risk facility.

The primary evaluation and care of the neonate after delivery is usually the responsibility of the nurse in the delivery room. The physician delivering the baby is preoccupied with the mother and cannot always leave her to attend to the baby. A physician *qualified to treat the neonate* should be close by in order to be quickly summoned. However, because time is crucial to survival, the immediate care of the neonate must be initiated by the nurse. The nurse plays an important role in assessing the condition of the neonate and in initiating life-support measures.

Classification and Evaluation

In the past, many different terms and methods for classification of the neonate have been used. At one time, birth weight alone was considered to be a reliable indication of a neonate's maturity. However, current classification systems recognize that intrauterine growth rates are different for all fetuses and in order to establish a more accurate assessment of maturity, gestational age must be viewed in conjunction with the weight. Neonates born at less than 38 weeks are called *preterm*; those born at 38 to 42 weeks are called *term*; and those born at greater than 42 weeks of gestation are called *postterm*. Neonates above the 90th percentile on the intrauterine growth curves are considered large for gestational age (LGA); those between the 10th and 90th percentile are considered appropriate for gestational age (AGA); and those born at less than the 10th percentile are considered small for gestational age (SGA). Optimal weight for the lowest perinatal mortality is a term neonate between 3500 and 4000 g. Above or below this range the mortality rates increase. Other assessment tools are available which are useful in determining maturity at birth and in assessing progress in development of the neonate.

One valuable tool for the immediate clinical evaluation of the neonate at birth is the scoring system devised by Dr. Virginia Apgar. The Apgar appraisal begins at the birth of the baby and is completed at 1 min; it is repeated at 5 min and later as needed. This scoring method has proved valuable as a rapid practical appraisal of the neonate in determining the need for immediate resuscitation to combat neonatal distress. A total Apgar score at 1 and 5 min after delivery is obtained by adding the values assigned to the observations in Table 33-3.

To be in good condition, neonates should achieve an Apgar score of 7, 8, 9, or 10. Severely depressed neonates score 0, 1, or 2.

The heart rate is the most important of the five Apgar signs. A heart rate above 160 beats per minute or below 100 beats per minute is considered abnormal. Tachycardia may indicate moderate asphyxia, while bradycardia may indicate severe asphyxia with a need for resuscitation. If a heartbeat cannot be heard or if the rate does not increase with lung expansion, closed-chest cardiac massage should be instituted.

Respiratory effort is the second most important sign. Inadequate respiratory effort will lead to respiratory and metabolic acidosis. Prolonged apnea in-

TABLE 33-3
Clinical Appraisal of the Neonate in the Delivery Room by the Apgar Scoring Chart

Sign	0	1	2
Heart rate	Absent	Slow ($\downarrow$100)	$\uparrow$100
Respiratory effort	Absent	Weak cry; hypoventilation	Good; strong cry
Muscle tone	Limp	Some flexion of extremities	Active motion; extremities well flexed
Reflex irritability	No response	Cry; some motion	Cry
Color	Blue, pale	Body pink; extremities blue	Completely pink

Source: V. Apgar: The role of the anesthesiologist in reducing neonatal mortality, *N.Y. State J. Med.* **55**:2365, 1955.

dicates the need to provide appropriate ventilatory support.

Muscle tone is rated according to the degree of flexion and the resistance the neonate offers to the straightening of the extremities.

Reflex irritability is judged by the neonate's response to stimulation. One method is to give several flicks to the soles of the neonate's feet.

Color is the least valuable sign and is directed to evaluating the presence or the absence of pallor and cyanosis. Few infants are completely pink because of the high incidence of acrocyanosis.

The 1- and 5-min Apgar scores have proved to be a valuable predictor of neonatal survival and future neurologic status. There is also a close relationship of the Apgar score to arterial blood pH. As the score decreases, the pH also decreases indicating increasing acidosis. Low-birth-weight infants show a higher incidence of low Apgar scores, while larger babies tend to have higher scores. These relationships indicate that the nurse who conscientiously and accurately utilizes the Apgar scoring chart has a sound basis for initiating appropriate supportive measures for the neonate.

In addition to the immediate evaluation of the neonate with tools such as the Apgar scoring chart, the nurse must carefully inspect the neonate for obvious anomalies that may jeopardize good health. Failure to fully assess the physical state of the neonate may delay treatment for anomalies that should be initiated immediately. A knowledgeable and accurate assessment of the neonate's condition provides the data necessary to proceed with the appropriate care.

Resuscitation, Stabilization, Thermoregulation, and Transport

Resuscitation A poor score on the Apgar rating scale or obvious signs of respiratory distress indicate the need for an immediate resuscitative effort. Placement in a neutral thermal environment (abdominal skin temperature of 97.7°F) will keep the neonate warm during the resuscitation attempt.

Mouth-to-mouth resuscitation has been replaced by positive pressure ventilation as a resuscitative method when the equipment is available. The positive pressure ventilation can be accomplished by use of a tight-fitting face mask or endotracheal tube connected to a ventilation bag or a mechanical ventilator. Resuscitation is directed toward providing oxygen to the neonate and controlling carbon dioxide levels by means of positive pressure ventilation and toward maintaining circulation by the use of external cardiac

massage. In addition, it is occasionally necessary to infuse alkali buffers to combat the metabolic acidosis that occurs.

Equipment needed for resuscitation of the neonate should be readily available in the delivery setting. An anticipated high-risk delivery allows time for a physician to be present and ready to initiate resuscitation if necessary. Unnecessary delays in the resuscitation effort may further compromise the infant's condition and make the resuscitation process more difficult. Equipment that must be readily available includes an oxygen source with tubing, a resuscitation bag (infant size), a laryngoscope with light, a variety of sizes of endotracheal tubes with appropriate adaptors, suction equipment, and the necessary syringes, needles, catheters, fluids, and drugs.

Brief suctioning of the airway, followed by insertion of the endotracheal tube, allows either mouth-to-tube or bag-to-tube inflation of the lungs. The ventilation rate should be approximately 50 times per minute with allowances made for adequate emptying of the lungs between inflations. Success of ventilation can be determined by observing the chest wall rise and fall, and by auscultation of the chest with a stethoscope. Overinflation of the lungs may lead to pneumothorax and/or pneumomediastinum. A neonate failing to respond to positive pressure ventilation is assumed to be in severe acidosis. The administration of $NaHCO_3$ via umbilical catheter is indicated.

If the infant still fails to respond and the Apgar score continues to be low with a poor heart rate, epinephrine may be given and external cardiac massage begun. Closed-chest massage should be performed at a rate of approximately 120 compressions per minute in conjunction with a continued lung inflation every 2 to 3 s. In the neonate, closed-chest cardiac massage is best accomplished by compression of the middle third of the sternum with the fingertips of the index and middle fingers. After the immediate resuscitative effort is accomplished, a nasogastric tube should be passed into the stomach and air and secretions gently removed by suction.

The immediate resuscitative efforts can often prevent or minimize brain damage. Prolonged hypoxia can lead to numerous neurological disorders which may have lifelong results. Every effort should be made to have well-planned and well-executed resuscitative procedures to offer each neonate optimal potential for growth and development.

Stabilization During the resuscitation effort or upon arrival in the neonatal unit, an umbilical vessel catheterization will be performed to aid in evaluation and stabilization of the high-risk neonate. A central catheter can be inserted into the aorta via the umbilical artery. Blood samples for monitoring acid-base status can be withdrawn through such a catheter, and parenteral fluids can be administered through the catheter as needed. Such a procedure is not without risk. The placement of the catheter must be verified by x-ray to ensure proper positioning. Vessel thrombosis, hemorrhage, and occlusion may result. Peripheral infusion is associated with a lower risk factor and is utilized when the umbilical catheter is no longer necessary.

Further assessment of blood gases, x-rays, blood sugar, and hematocrit are necessary for stabilization of the neonate. Adequate stabilization is a necessity before considering transport of the neonate to the high-risk neonatal unit.

Thermoregulation Optimal temperature regulation and maintenance is a critical aspect of the care of the neonate. Cold stress precipitates unfavorable physiologic responses in the neonate and can inhibit resuscitative efforts as well as interfere with stabilization. Regardless of a neonate's efforts to produce heat, heat loss can be excessive and may be a threat to survival. Infants who are small for gestational age or of low birth weight have the greatest capacity for heat loss and are at the greatest risk for thermal stress.

At birth the neonate's core temperature drops rapidly, mainly because of evaporation from a wet body. The neonate's small subcutaneous fat stores and large body surface area to body weight ratio account for the temperature drop when suddenly exposed to the cold air of the delivery room. Both radiant and convective heat loss results. Studies have shown that although a moderate heat loss may play a part in initiating respiration, severe heat loss will result in metabolic acidosis, a decrease in arterial oxygen levels, slow respiration, bradycardia, and hypoglycemia. Such adverse reactions can be prevented by placing the neonate in a neutral thermal environment for recovery.

A neutral thermal environment can be provided through the use of numerous devices. Warmers and isolettes as well as the overhead radiant warmers can be used. Radiant warmers allow for easy visualization of the baby, adequate space for resuscitative efforts, and maintenance of the neonate's temperature by means of a servo-heating probe taped to the skin of the abdomen. Maintaining the skin temperature at 97.7°F (36.5°C) minimizes oxygen consumption. Oxygen delivered to the neonate must also be warmed to prevent heat loss.

Optimal thermal management can be achieved if the neonate is immediately dried and placed under a radiant heater with a servo-temperature control. Frequent temperature checks must be obtained to prevent hypothermia or hyperthermia, because either will affect oxygen consumption and metabolic processes. Continuous vigilance to thermal environmental factors is necessary to maintain thermal stability and provide the optimal setting for the neonate's care.

Transport Transportation of the high-risk neonate is developing as an important area of high-risk care. The establishment of high-risk neonatal critical-care centers has necessitated the organization of personnel and the development of protocols for efficiency and expediency of transport. Special transport incubators have been developed that allow both adequate oxygen maintenance and thermoregulation during transfer. Regional neonatal critical-care facilities are beginning to establish special transport teams to provide the necessary equipment and care needed during the transport. Ideally, the high-risk neonate would go directly to a high-risk neonatal unit in the institution where birth took place. Because it is financially impractical for all institutions to maintain such a unit in terms of both equipment and personnel, neonatal critical-care facilities are being planned regionally that will accept referrals from settings not equipped for intensive neonatal care.

Because all transport, whether intrainstitutional or interinstitutional, involves risk, the complex organization of such an act must be planned and executed to perfection. The transport is initiated by the physician requesting the transfer to a regional center. The physician receiving the referral must collect sufficient data on the infant to allow the transport team to prepare a plan and select the necessary equipment for the transfer. The transport should be done as soon as possible so that early treatment can be instituted. Neonates transported by untrained personnel without adequate support measures are at a disadvantage for optimal recovery.

Conditions such as asphyxia, chemical imbalance, hypoglycemia, and hypovolemia must be evaluated and treated prior to transport. During transport, appropriate equipment must be present for ventilatory assistance, fluid administration, suctioning, thermal regulation, and for pharmacologic support. Backup systems should be included in anticipation of possible mechanical failure of battery-operated equipment.

Informing the parents of the destination and methods of communication with the regional facility will help allay their anxiety over the departure of their child. Frequent communication with the family is a necessity for the duration of the neonate's hospitalization.

Psychosocial Effects on the Family

The psychosocial effect on the family of a high-risk neonate is finally receiving the recognition it deserves. In the past, the mother and father were often relegated into a peripheral role, while nursing and medical personnel assumed the caretaker roles for the neonate. Consequences of such an arrangement have manifested in documented evidence that a disturbed maternal/paternal–child relationship often results and this may ultimately contribute to a high incidence of battered child syndrome among high-risk neonates. Current trends now emphasize the need for maternal/paternal involvement in the care of the neonate to promote optimal parent-child bonding.

The birth of a high-risk neonate is a source of unexpected and severe stress for the family. The expected joy at the birth of a child is suddenly fraught with anxiety and fear over the outcome of the delivery. Some high-risk neonates are the result of a previously diagnosed high-risk pregnancy, so the fear of delivering an unhealthy baby is experienced both before and during delivery. Other high-risk neonates are only identified during labor or after birth when a problem or anomaly becomes evident. In this case, the family has no time to prepare for the birth of an unhealthy baby. The neonate is usually transported immediately after delivery to a neonatal unit, often before either of the parents has seen the baby or been apprised of the baby's condition. Contacts between the medical and nursing personnel and the family from the time of delivery must be planned to keep the family well-informed about the progress and treatment of the baby.

The immediate physical separation of the mother and neonate has been shown in many studies to be detrimental to the mother-child relationship. The mother's need to touch, look at, and become acquainted with her new child is important in the process of developing attachments to her baby. The psychological separation also adversely affects this relationship. The mother's loss of her "normal" baby invokes varied reactions including guilt, anger, shock, denial, depression, and grief. When these reactions are not evident, the absence of anxiety about the welfare of the child may indicate an unfavorable response, and

the future mother-child relationship may be jeopardized. The longer the mother must wait to see her baby, the more opportunity she has to fantasize about the actual appearance or condition of her child. Often other family members are able to have earlier contact with the baby than does the mother, and she is left feeling inadequate and depressed and finding it hard to believe that she has a baby.

Obviously, the need to have the neonate in a specialized setting for care precludes the opportunity to have the baby with its mother. However, there are ways to decrease this separation and lessen the detrimental effects on the neonate and parents. Initially, the parents must establish close communication with both the medical and nursing staff involved in the baby's care. Frequent reports and explanations are needed to allay some of the parents' anxiety. The more critical the neonate's condition, the more often the parents should be given condition reports. Telephone contact between the mother and the nursery staff may establish an initial relationship that can be expanded as contact increases. As soon as the mother is physically able and expresses the desire to visit the baby, she should be brought to the neonatal unit. Prior explanation of the equipment, monitors, and infusions may relieve some of the stress of seeing her baby's complex environment. The nurse's presence at this beginning visit is essential, and an honest and simple explanation of the baby's care is necessary.

The parents should be encouraged to stroke, talk to, and have eye contact with their infant. Calling the baby by name and encouraging the parents to notice the baby's individuality help the parents to begin working through their own feelings about their child. The relationship between the parents and the child develops as the parents are able to cope with the problems at hand and begin to accept the baby in its present condition. Signs that the parents do not seem to be progressing in the development of a healthy relationship should not be overlooked and may require the intervention of other health care workers.

If the neonate's survival is in question, the parents may have increased difficulty in forming a relationship. Parents who are preparing themselves for the infant's death, and at the same time are trying to maintain some hope for survival, may limit their contact with their baby. Frequent progress reports are needed to keep the parents adequately informed, and appropriate supportive measures must be taken when they come to visit the baby.

The concept of maternal-infant bonding has recently received a great deal of attention in the literature. Studies point out the importance of recognizing and supporting the mother's and father's need to develop a healthy relationship with their infant. The neonatal staff can promote such a relationship with knowledgeable and planned intervention and support for the family. A failure to do so from the moment of birth may lead to a faulty development of these critical relationships, ultimately jeopardizing the child. The nurse's continuous presence in the neonatal care setting allows her the opportunity to assist the family in establishing a healthy relationship with the baby.

Respiratory Crisis

Respiratory crisis in the neonate can be the result of many causes, all of which compromise the ability of the neonate to adequately aerate the lungs. Although the most frequently occurring respiratory crisis is the respiratory distress syndrome (RDS), or hyaline membrane disease (HMD), not every neonate with rapid breathing, cyanosis, or respiratory distress has hyaline membrane disease. Hypovolemia, hypoglycemia, congenital heart defects, cerebral hemorrhage, congenital anomalies, and reactions to drugs may all precipitate respiratory symptoms that resemble hyaline membrane disease. Careful assessment and diagnosis is necessary to determine the underlying pathologic process. Diagnostic evaluation tools such as x-ray, blood studies, and systematic assessment of all body systems are needed for a valid diagnosis. Supportive care and treatment of the neonate with respiratory crisis is similar for most pulmonary disorders and will be discussed in detail.

Idiopathic respiratory distress syndrome (IRDS)
The respiratory adaptation of the normal neonate from intrauterine to extrauterine life usually occurs quickly and without complication. A variety of events occur which are thought to contribute to the neonate's first gasp. These events include prior intrauterine fetal breathing movements; asphyxia, which stimulates the respiratory control center in the medulla; and an abrupt drop in the neonate's ambient temperature.

In the aveoli, surface tension opposing the entry of air into the lungs is minimized by the presence of *surfactant,* a lipoprotein substance that serves to maintain alveolar stability once air has entered the alveolus. Recent studies have shown that although most fetuses have some surfactant as early as 24 weeks, there is a surge in surfactant production at 34 to 35 weeks. As a result, before 35 weeks' gestation, the incidence of IRDS is significantly increased.

It is estimated that as many as 2 percent of all live births and up to 35 percent of all premature births are affected by IRDS. The histopathologic correlate of IRDS is hyaline membrane disease. Because IRDS is primarily associated with incomplete maturation of the lungs at the time of birth, preterm infants are at the greatest risk for development of this syndrome. Also infants of mothers who have bleeding, anemia, diabetes, or other IRDS children are at risk. Symptoms include respiratory distress within 6 h after delivery, tachypnea (over 60 per minute), expiratory grunt, nasal flaring, and chest wall retraction during inspiration. Apneic spells and cyanosis may also be present. Breath sounds are diminished with occasional crepitant rales. Thermal instability is often present.

The severity of the disease is best evaluated by the determination of arterial pH and blood gas values. Neonates with IRDS have hypoxemia, hypercapnia, and mixed respiratory and metabolic acidosis caused by *atelectasis,* the incomplete expansion or collapse of the alveoli. This acidosis may precipitate pulmonary vasoconstriction, irregular heartbeat, and dilation of cerebral vessels. Thus a vicious cycle develops in which atelectasis leads to hypoxia, which in turn leads to acidosis. Acidosis intensifies vasoconstriction due to hypoxia and decreases surfactant production, which in turn promotes additional atelectasis. Management of IRDS is directed toward the reduction of acidosis, support of the neonate, and prevention of inhibitors to surfactant production.

Management of the neonate with IRDS is directed toward providing adequate physiologic support until such time as normal surfactant production and stable metabolic processes occur. Such support includes:

1. Administration of oxygen required to maintain an arterial P_{O_2} between 60 and 80 mmHg

2. Ventilatory assistance of respirations as needed

3. Continuous positive airway pressure (CPAP) to prevent alveolar collapse on expiration

4. Maintenance of acid-base balance

5. Hydration and caloric support to meet metabolic needs

6. Thermoregulation

7. Blood replacement as needed to combat anemia or hypotension

8. Prevention of infection

These therapeutic measures will be discussed later in this section. Although these supportive management concepts are included under respiratory crisis, they are applicable to the general management of any high-risk neonate.

Pneumonia   Neonates may develop pneumonia in utero or after birth. Symptoms include tachypnea, retractions, grunting, nasal flaring, lethargy, thermal instability, and apnea. Diagnosis is made by chest x-ray, and sterile tracheal aspirates are obtained for culture and determination of the infectious organism. Treatment includes supportive management and appropriate pharmacologic therapy.

Meconium aspiration   Neonates who have suffered some distress in utero often have meconium present in the amniotic fluid. Aspiration of this fluid may occur before, during, or after birth and may contribute to airway obstruction. Careful suctioning of the posterior pharynx and trachea at delivery may prevent further aspiration. Stomach contents should also be removed by suctioning if meconium aspiration has occurred. Symptoms of meconium aspiration include labored respirations, sternal retraction, hypoxia, and acidosis. Treatment includes supportive management and observation for pneumothorax or pneumomediastinum.

Pneumothorax   The rupture of alveoli with a resultant escape of air into the pleural space creates a pneumothorax. If the air progresses into the mediastinal space, a pneumomediastinum results. A high percentage of neonates developing pneumothorax have aspirated blood or meconium which cause obstruction to the flow of air. Others at risk to develop pneumothorax include neonates with IRDS or those who have required positive pressure ventilation or CPAP. Symptoms include a sudden onset of cyanosis, tachypnea, grunting, nasal flaring, and rapid onset of a tense, distended abdomen. Breath sounds and chest movement on the affected side may be diminished. Diagnosis is made by chest x-ray and treatment is with a needle or tube thoracentesis and supportive care.

Transient tachypnea of the newborn (TTN—RDS Type II)   This syndrome usually occurs in the full-term infant after an uneventful pregnancy. The primary symptom is tachypnea that occurs during the first few hours of life and resolves itself within 48 h. Some blood gas abnormalities may be present, but cyanosis is usually not prominent. Diagnosis is by chest x-ray. Supportive care is indicated.

Congenital respiratory tract malformations   Malformations of the respiratory tract are relatively rare, but when they occur, they may cause respiratory distress in the neonate. There are three types of congenital respiratory tract malformations: *choanal atresia* or *obstruction, diaphragmatic hernia,* and *tracheoesophageal fistula* (TEF).

The choanae are the posterior nares that open into the nasopharynx. Because neonates are nose breathers, obstruction or atresia of one or both apertures may result in serious respiratory distress. Cyanosis and severe retractions develop, and thick mucous secretions fill the nose. Diagnosis of *choanal atresia* is made by the failure of a catheter to pass through the nose to the nasopharynx. An oral airway should be inserted until surgery can be performed.

Diaphragmatic hernia is the result of a congenital incomplete formation of the diaphragm which allows the displacement of abdominal organs into the thoracic cavity. Herniation is more common on the left side and results in severe respiratory distress with absence of breath sounds on the affected side. Resuscitation may be required at birth, and immediate surgery is indicated. Bag-and-mask resuscitation should not be used because swallowed air will further expand the bowel and cause increased respiratory distress. The neonate should be positioned with the head and chest elevated to prevent increased pressure on the lungs.

The three most common types of tracheoesophageal fistulas are (1) esophageal atresia with fistulous connection between the lower esophageal segment and the trachea, (2) esophageal atresia with a normal respiratory tract, and (3) normal esophagus and trachea connected by a fistula. Such malformations are more common in neonates whose history includes maternal polyhydramnios, neonatal respiratory distress, excessive pharyngeal mucus production (bubbling), or gagging and regurgitation with feedings. Often the abdomen is distended and atelectasis and pneumonia develop. Chest x-ray following the attempted passage of radiopaque catheter is used in diagnosis. Management of these neonates includes positioning on the abdomen with head and chest elevated to prevent reflux of stomach contents into the lungs. Surgery is indicated for correction.

Supportive Management for the High-Risk Neonate

Oxygen therapy   An adequate oxygen supply is essential to sustain normal tissue metabolism. If the respiratory crisis requires oxygen therapy, provisions must be made for careful determinations of the arterial oxygen tension. Hazards of inadequate monitoring include oxygen toxicity, especially to the lungs, and retrolental fibroplasia. The amount of oxygen required varies from neonate to neonate, but is usually monitored to maintain a Pa_{O_2} of 60 to 80 mmHg. The Pa_{CO_2} and pH are also determined with each sample of arterial blood. The Pa_{CO_2} is monitored to maintain a level between 35 and 40 mmHg and a pH between 7.35 and 7.44.

Oxygen can be administered to the neonate by hood, isolette, or endotracheal or nasotracheal tube with mechanical ventilation. The oxygen hood and intubation have proved to be the most successful methods of maintaining alveolar distention with continuous positive airway pressure. Thus, the alveoli remain expanded when they normally collapse. This has been shown to be useful in treating neonates with IRDS, pulmonary edema, atelectasis, and other disorders of diminished lung compliance.

To apply CPAP, special adaptors may be attached to the endotracheal tube, nasal piece, or face mask. Newer models of neonatal mechanical ventilators may also be adjusted to provide CPAP. Adverse effects of CPAP may include pneumothorax, pneumomediastinum, and complications of intubation, if required.

Assisted ventilation　Neonates who experience prolonged asphyxia, hypoxia, hypoventilation, or apneic spells may require mechanical ventilatory assistance. The ventilatory assistance is useful support for respiratory insufficiency and hypercarbia. The use of mechanical ventilators requires care from a nurse familiar with the equipment, and protocols are needed to maintain a therapeutic and safe environment for the baby. The endotracheal tube must be maintained in the proper position with frequent assessment of its patency. The ventilators must be adjusted to the proper settings and changed as the neonate's status changes. Proper oxygen administration must be maintained by frequent monitoring of the FI_{O_2} and the blood gases. The types of mechanical ventilators now commonly in use for babies include (1) pressure-limited positive pressure ventilators (Baby Bird, Bournes BP 200, Bennet CR2), (2) volume-limited positive pressure ventilators (Bennet MA-1, Bournes LS-104-150), and (3) negative pressure ventilators.

Acid-base balance　Respiratory distress, which causes varying degrees of hypoxia, precipitates a state of metabolic acidosis. This state in turn causes constriction of the pulmonary arterioles, which further compromises the respiratory status. Measurements of the pH and Pa_{O_2} serve as a guide for the administration of intravenous sodium bicarbonate. Rapid administration of sodium bicarbonate may cause a sudden change in serum osmolality that would increase the risk of intracranial hemorrhage. Administration of sodium bicarbonate is generally limited to less than 10 meq/kg/24 h.

Fluid therapy　An intravenous infusion of fluid is begun for the neonate in respiratory distress as soon after birth as possible. If an umbilical arterial catheter has been inserted to facilitate drawing blood samples for blood gas determinations, fluids may be given through this catheter. If no umbilical catheter is inserted, peripheral veins may be used. The umbilical vein is suitable only for short-term therapy because of the risk of infection, thrombosis, or cirrhosis later in life. Fluid therapy usually involves the administration of $D_{10}W$ at the rate of 100 mL per kg of body weight per 24 h. Insensible fluid loss can be very high in the small infant, and fluid balance must be assessed at frequent intervals. Records of fluid intake, urinary output, urine specific gravity, body weight, Clinitest determinations, and blood electrolyte studies aid in accurate assessment of fluid balance in the neonate.

Temperature support　The necessity of careful thermoregulation has been discussed previously. The neonate in respiratory distress will be further stressed if hypothermia or hyperthermia are experienced as well. A resultant increase in metabolism may further compromise the neonate's ability to adequately oxygenate tissues and will lead to further metabolic acidosis. Both the proper body temperature of the neonate and the temperature of the environment must be constantly maintained.

Physical therapy　The neonate with respiratory complications requires consistent efforts by the nurse to promote optimal oxygenation. Chest physiotherapy is an important aspect of this care. The loosening of secretions is facilitated by providing humidified air or oxygen. Short, intermittent positive pressure breathing treatments (IPPB) may also be useful. Proper body positioning will promote optimal lung expansion. Frequent turning to side-back-side positions, with care not to fold the neonate's arms over the chest, will aid lung inflation. Postural drainage and chest percussion and vibration may be used as tolerated by the neonate. Airway secretions should be suctioned on a regular schedule and as needed to keep the airway clear.

Cardiovascular Crisis

Episodes of cardiovascular crisis seen most often in the neonate include cardiac failure, cyanosis, cyanotic episodes, shock, and congenital heart defects. The symptomatology of cardiovascular crisis closely resembles the symptomatology of respiratory crisis, and the two are often difficult to distinguish.

At birth, the neonate makes several cardiovascular adjustments. The pulmonary blood flow suddenly increases, and the increased blood return to the left atrium from the lungs increases the pressure in the left atrium, resulting in functional closure of the foramen ovale. The ductus arteriosus responds to the increased oxygenation of the blood by constricting and finally becoming obliterated. Failure of the cardiovascular system to make such adaptive changes results in a continued right-to-left shunt, and optimal oxygenation of the blood is not obtained. Such maladaption is more common in the preterm neonate.

The normal heart rate for a neonate is 120 to 160 beats per minute. The heart rate increases when the neonate is restless or crying and decreases when the neonate is hypothermic, acidotic, or hypoxic.

Cyanosis Cyanosis in the neonate is difficult to evaluate. Immediately after birth, some cyanosis is expected, but the normal newborn will usually be relieved of central cyanosis within 30 min after birth. Because mild cyanosis is difficult to see, the visibly cyanotic neonate may have a very low Pa_{O_2} or a high hemoglobin and moderate hypoxemia. Thus the color of the mucous membranes is not an accurate indicator of tissue oxygenation. Cyanosis that persists after the first few hours of life constitutes an urgent problem which must be evaluated immediately. Central cyanosis may result from a variety of causes including central nervous system damage, hypoglycemia, congenital heart disease, shock, sepsis, or heart failure. Administration of 100 percent O_2 to test the resulting Pa_{O_2} levels in the blood helps to distinguish between primary respiratory and cardiovascular disease. If the neonate responds with an appreciable rise in the Pa_{O_2}, it is more likely that primary lung disease rather than primary heart disease is the cause. Additional diagnostic information from a history and physical, radiography, and laboratory studies aid in diagnosis.

Peripheral cyanosis may be present in the neonate for days following birth. It is usually due to a cold thermal environment, a high hematocrit level, ecchymosis, peripheral vasoconstriction, or a local circulatory obstruction.

Blood pressure measurement is a very useful diagnostic tool in the neonate. It can be accomplished with either an intra-arterial line or a cuff measurement. The blood pressure cuff must be carefully chosen for proper fit in order to obtain an accurate reading. The Doppler machine has the added advantage of emitting an auditory response. Normal blood pressure for the neonate is dependent upon gestational age and birth weight. A blood pressure graph in a neonatology book should be consulted to determine the normal blood pressure for each neonate. A systolic reading that is 8 to 10 mmHg below the normal is indicative of hypotension, and treatment is needed.

Cardiac failure Heart failure may also mimic other systemic disorders, and careful clinical evaluation and diagnosis is necessary. The closer to birth the symptoms arise, the more critical the results may be to the neonate. Causes include congenital heart defects, myocarditis, respiratory disease, polycythemia, circulatory overload, anemia, and cardiac arrythmias. The most common symptoms include tachypnea (60 to 100 respirations per minute), tachycardia (over 160 beats per minute), fatigue, poor feeding, enlarged liver, and pulmonary rales or rhonchi. In addition, venous congestion and cardiac enlargement may be present.

Management of the neonate in cardiac failure encompasses all the normal neonatal care such as respiratory support, temperature support, fluid and nutritional support, and monitoring of the respiratory and cardiovascular systems. Frequent laboratory data are needed to assess the results of treatment. Specific treatment consists of digitalizing the neonate with frequent observations for bradycardia (less than 100 beats per minute), arrhythmias, and hypokalemia. A normal digitalizing dose should not exceed 0.07 mg per kg of body weight for children under 2 years of age, and maintenance doses of one-eighth of the digitalizing dose are then given twice daily. Intravenous doses may be lower. Diuretics such as Lasix (1 mg per kg of body weight) may be given to control edema. Further diagnostic studies, such as cardiac catheterization, and angiocardiography, and surgery may be needed.

Shock Shock in the neonate is an emergency requiring immediate intervention and treatment. It is the result of severe circulatory failure which leads to inadequate cardiac output to meet the tissue oxygen requirement. Causes include hypovolemia, sepsis, cardiac failure, asphyxia, respiratory distress, or metabolic crisis. Symptoms include tachycardia, tachypnea, pallor, poor tissue perfusion, metabolic acidosis, decreased urinary output, and hypotension. Treatment focuses on respiratory support including oxygen, if needed; cardiovascular monitoring; monitoring of urinary output; monitoring of blood gases; and maintenance of a neutral thermal environment. Blood volume expanders such as blood or Plasmanate can be given intravenously. Normal saline solution and albumin are sometimes used as alternatives. Metabolic acidosis is corrected by the administration of sodium bicarbonate. Antibiotics or digitalization may also be indicated.

Congenital heart defects Congenital heart defects in the neonate occur in about 8 per 1000 births. Diagnosis and treatment of these defects have rapidly advanced in recent years, and the prognosis for many of these infants is excellent. Although there are numerous heart defects that occur, only the most life-threatening defects of the high-risk neonate will be mentioned here. References for information on other defects are available at the end of the chapter.

Cardiac malformations that most often prove fatal to the neonate include the hypoplastic left ventricle syndrome, complicated coarctation of the aorta, transposition of the great vessels, and severe Tetralogy of Fallot. Symptoms of severe cardiac problems include cyanosis, respiratory distress, systemic venous congestion, and decreased cardiac output. Heart murmurs may be present, but because they are common even in normal newborn infants, they are not always indicative of heart defects. Congenital heart defects of these types lead quickly to respiratory difficulty, and congestive heart failure follows. Supportive care for symptoms is needed until a positive diagnosis can be made. Surgery is usually indicated as soon as the neonate's condition permits it. It may be palliative or corrective, depending on the type of defect present.

Chemical Imbalances

Hypoglycemia Glycogen stores of the neonate are rapidly depleted after birth. A difficult delivery or transition may cause an abnormally rapid depletion of carbohydrate. Stresses such as hypoxia, cold stress, acidosis, or hypermetabolism will further increase metabolic utilization of glycogen, thus precipitating hypoglycemia. Normal blood sugar concentrations range from 20 mg per 100 mL to 100 mg per 100 mL in low birth weight infants, to 30 mg per 100 mL to 100 mg per 100 mL in term babies during the first 3 days after birth. After this period, 40 mg per 100 mL is the diagnostic level for hypoglycemia. Hypoglycemia is diagnosed when a true blood sugar value below the lower limits of normal is established in two consecutive blood samples. Monitoring the blood sugar for low values can be done by the nurse using the Dextrostix. Periodically scheduled checks with a Dextrostix provide a guide for indicating the need for a laboratory determination of the blood sugar. Symptoms of hypoglycemia include apnea, tremors, jitteriness, twitching, seizures, lethargy, and coma.

Management of the hypoglycemic neonate includes the administration of oral or intravenous glucose solutions. Usually solutions of 10 to 15% glucose can be used successfully. The administration of steroids may be indicated if glucose (up to 25% at 120 to 150 mL per kg per day) alone is not effective. Continued periodic monitoring of the blood sugar levels is indicated until the neonate is stabilized.

Hypocalcemia The incidence of hypocalcemia in the preterm infant is high. This condition is frequently seen during the first 48 h and as late as the 10th day of life. Normal blood calcium levels range from 8 to 10.5 mg per 100 mL. A calcium level of under 7 mg per 100 mL is considered to be abnormally low and indicates a need for treatment. Symptoms may include irritability, jitteriness, twitching, seizures, and a high-pitched cry.

Management of the hypocalcemic neonate includes the intravenous administration of 10% calcium gluconate, 1 to 2 mL per kg of body weight. Intravenous injection of calcium gluconate must be given slowly over a period of not less than 5 min with continuous monitoring of the heart rate. Development of bradycardia (<100 beats per minute) may occur suddenly, and treatment should be stopped until the heart rate stabilizes. A continuous infusion of intravenous fluids with calcium gluconate may be indicated. Calcium gluconate can cause local tissue necrosis and sloughing of tissues if it infiltrates. This fact precludes its administration through a scalp vein infusion, and it must be carefully monitored to prevent peripheral tissue damage.

Neurological Crisis

The success of neonatal critical-care units in saving the lives of the critically ill neonate has increased the need for attention in the area of neonatal neurology. Many perinatal events can precipitate a neurologic crisis in the neonate. A careful, ongoing neurologic assessment is necessary to detect changes or problems in the neurological functioning of the baby. Although many critical neurologic states exist, the conditions covered here will include seizures, intracranial hemorrhage, and meningitis. Other sources should be consulted to review neurological assessment of the newborn.

Seizures Seizures are a distinctive symptom of a large number of neurological diseases that affect the neonate. Seizure activity can interfere with other ongoing treatment modalities or may be a source of brain injury. Determination of the etiology of the seizures should be done as soon as possible so that the appropriate treatment can be instituted.

Seizure activity in the neonate can manifest itself in a variety of ways. The most subtle seizure activity is often overlooked. It consists of tonic horizontal deviation of the eyes, repetitive blinking of the eyes, drooling, sucking, "swimming" motions of the arms, "pedaling" motions of the legs, and apnea. One or more of these signs may be observed. Electroencephalography is often needed for confirmation. This subtle seizure activity may occur in both preterm and term neonates.

More striking seizure activity will include generalized tonic extension of the legs. This sometimes is accompanied by eye signs, apnea, and stertorous breathing. These generalized tonic seizures are seen most often in the premature infant. They may indicate the presence of intraventricular hemorrhage.

Other seizure activity can include multifocal clonic seizures which migrate in an ordered manner to the extremities, focal clonic seizures which remain well-localized, and myoclonic seizures which produce single or multiple jerks or flexion of the upper and/or lower extremities.

A state of jitteriness in the neonate is often confused with seizures. Jitteriness involves tremulous movements but does not include abnormalities in eye movement or clonic jerking. Jitteriness may be the result of hypocalcemia, hypoglycemia, or drug withdrawal.

The most frequent causes of neonatal seizures are perinatal asphyxia, intracranial hemorrhage, hypoglycemia, hypocalcemia, intracranial infection, neurological developmental defects, or drug withdrawal. Diagnosis should include careful evaluation of the history, laboratory data, encephalography, and observation. The nurse is in a position to recognize and carefully observe seizure activity and should keep written records to aid in the evaluation process.

Treatment is directed toward the cause. If the seizure activity is not controlled, anticonvulsant drugs such as phenobarbital (5 to 20 mg per kg per day) may be administered. Blood levels of phenobarbital should be monitored.

Intracranial hemorrhage Four major types of intracranial hemorrhage occur in the neonate. Subdural hemorrhage and subarachnoid hemorrhage are most often the result of trauma. The incidence of these disorders is decreasing with improvements in obstetrical care. Periventricular (intraventricular) hemorrhage and intracerebellar hemorrhage are usually the result of hypoxia. Diagnosis of intracranial hemorrhage is improving, and more neonates who have had intracranial hemorrhage are surviving. The survivors have exhibited a high incidence of hydrocephalus. As treatment improves, the long-term sequelae of such events must be considered.

Subdural hemorrhage Subdural hemorrhage, which is relatively uncommon now, is the result of tears in the falx, tentorium, or superficial cortical veins. It is seen most often in full-term babies. A hematoma forms which may be accompanied by a contusion at the trauma site. Symptoms differ depending on the site of the trauma, but they usually include seizures, deviation of the eyes, and changes in pupillary response. Symptoms may not be evident until several days after birth, and they increase in severity as the clot enlarges.

Subarachnoid hemorrhage Subarachnoid hemorrhage that is not secondary to hemorrhagic extension from subdural, intraventricular, or intracerebellar sites is referred to as *primary* subarachnoid hemorrhage. It is the most common type of neonatal intracranial hemorrhage, and it is the result of venous bleeding, usually due to trauma or hypoxia. Premature babies have a higher incidence of this type of hemorrhage than do full-term infants. Seizures often occur on the second day after birth, but the infant may otherwise appear healthy. Premature infants may also exhibit recurrent apneic spells which may or may not coincide with the seizure activity. Rarely, with massive hemorrhage, a catastrophic course develops and the neonate's condition deteriorates rapidly, ending in death. Generally the prognosis is good, and recovery is normal in the majority of cases. Hydrocephalus has been shown to be a sequela in some infants.

Intraventricular hemorrhage Intraventricular hemorrhage occurs almost exclusively in the premature neonate. Bleeding is not generally confined to the ventricular system but is more often periventricular or intracerebral. Hemorrhage generally occurs following a severe hypoxic state, either at the time of birth or as a result of the respiratory distress syndrome. Symptoms include generalized tonic seizures, "decerebrate" posturing, fixed pupils, flaccid extremities, hypoventilation, coma, or respiratory arrest. The neonate may also exhibit hypotension, bradycardia, poor thermal regulation, metabolic acidosis, or hyperglycemia. Symptoms may alternate with periods of relative stability, since bleeding intermittently occurs. The prognosis for neonates with major intraventricular hemorrhage is grave, with survivors often exhibiting hydrocephalus.

Intracerebellar hemorrhage Recent research has shown an increase in this type of intracranial hemorrhage in the small premature neonate. This may occur alone or in conjunction with intraventricular hemorrhage. Intracerebellar hemorrhage usually follows a state of severe hypoxia, either at birth or as a result of severe respiratory distress syndrome. Symptoms include apnea, bradycardia, bloody cerebral spinal fluid, and a falling hematocrit. Onset may occur as early as the first day after birth or as late as several weeks after birth. Prognosis is grave, with survivors exhibiting a high incidence of hydrocephalus.

Treatment of all types of intracranial hemorrhage is primarily symptomatic support. Although many treatment courses have been investigated, none has yet emerged as a predictable successful modality of care. Supportive care, by both physicians and nurses, has resulted in a higher rate of survival for these infants. The long-range sequelae for these survivors will bear investigation.

Bacterial meningitis Bacterial meningitis continues to be responsible for a high morbidity and mortality rate in the neonate. Neonatal bacterial meningitis is most often the result of septicemia and is more common in the premature than in the full-term neonate. Although any pathogenic organisms could produce disease in the neonate, studies have shown that *Escherichia coli,* group B beta-hemolytic streptococci, and *Listeria monocytogenes* are most frequently the cause of neonatal meningitis.

Symptoms include irritability, poor feeding, lethargy, vomiting, poor thermal regulation, tachypnea, apnea, tachycardia, bradycardia, and hypotension. The presentation of symptoms may vary, and the course of the illness may range from mild to rapidly fulminating. Neurological signs such as seizures, abnormal reflexes, abnormal cry, bulging fontanels, and a stiff neck may occur.

Diagnosis is made from observation of the presenting symptoms and analysis of the cerebrospinal fluid and blood cultures. Treatment includes antibiotic therapy and anticonvulsant therapy, if seizures are present, in conjunction with supportive neonatal care. Sequelae may include many permanent neurological deficits such as hemiparesis, quadriparesis, deafness, blindness, seizures, hydrocephalus, or mental retardation.

Neonatal Hyperbilirubinemia

Hyperbilirubinemia in the neonate is a normal physiologic phenomenon. A serum bilirubin in excess of 1 mg per 100 mL of blood usually occurs within a few days following birth and may or may not produce visible jaundice. This state of hyperbilirubinemia may be termed *normal physiologic jaundice.* It occurs largely as a result of the rapid breakdown of red blood cells and the resultant poor bilirubin conjugation in the liver. This leads to deposits of unexcretable unconjugated bilirubin in the extravascular tissue, including the brain. Serum bilirubin levels must exceed 4 to 6 mg per 100 mL before jaundice is visible. In term infants, a peak unconjugated bilirubin level is reached on the third or fourth day after birth. In the premature infant, a peak level is reached on the fifth or seventh day. This normal physiologic jaundice rarely requires therapy and usually resolves itself. However, hyperbilirubinemia which exceeds 12 mg per 100 mL or results in jaundice before 24 h or after the seventh or eighth day usually indicates a pathologic process for which cause and treatment must be determined.

Pathologic neonatal jaundice may be caused by a number of factors including Rh or ABO incompatibility, polycythemia, red blood cell abnormalities, drug toxicity, infection, metabolic disorders (including asphyxia), biliary disorders, familial blood cell disorders, or enclosed hemorrhage. The underlying mechanism of pathologic jaundice is related either to overproduction and/or underexcretion of bilirubin, and determination of the cause establishes the appropriate mode of treatment. Diagnosis includes a detailed family and pregnancy history; blood determinations for "direct," "indirect," and "total" bilirubin levels; blood cellular studies; Coombs' test; blood typing of the mother and baby; and determinations of the presence of sepsis or congenital deficiencies.

The most serious complication of neonatal hyperbilirubinemia is kernicterus. Kernicterus is the result of bilirubin toxicity of the central nervous system which pathologically shows yellow staining of the nuclear areas of the brain. Deposition of both unconjugated and unbound bilirubin in the brain cells results in irreversible damage to the central nervous system (CNS) that may later manifest itself in conditions ranging from minimal brain damage to severe cerebral palsy with other neurological deficiencies. Death may occur in the neonatal period.

Clinical symptoms of kernicterus are usually seen by the third or fourth day of life. They include a diminished Moro's response, hypotonia, and a weak sucking reflex. Central nervous system depression is then followed by irritability and excitation which may include seizures, twitching, hypertonia, opisthotonos, and a high-pitched cry.

No precise bilirubin level has been established as the point at which kernicterus is likely to occur. General standards use 20 mg per 100 mL in a term infant and 15 mg per 100 mL in the preterm infant as a guide for determining the need for an exchange transfusion. However, cases of kernicterus have been reported at levels as low as 10 mg per 100 mL in neonates who were perhaps more vulnerable because of factors such as low birth weight, asphyxia, hypothermia, septicemia, and meningitis.

Current methods of treatment for pathologic neonatal jaundice include phototherapy and exchange transfusion. The use of phototherapy is still a controversial treatment because the scientifically prescribed units of safety of such a treatment have not been definitively established. Phototherapy has been shown to be effective in lowering serum bilirubin, but this effect may also be deceptive to the inexperienced nurse. The exposure of a nude infant to cool white or blue lamps has a tendency to bleach the color from the infant's skin, and the infant may look less jaundiced than actually is the case. Indeed, as the visible jaundice diminishes under the effects of the lights, the serum bilirubin may continue to rise, and unless closely monitored laboratory studies are performed,

the condition of the infant may go unnoticed. In addition, because light may damage the retina of the eyes, eye patches must be in place during the course of phototherapy. It is recommended that the lights and eye patches be periodically removed so that the neonate may be visually stimulated and the eyes inspected for injury. Although phototherapy has gained wide acceptance as a treatment for hyperbilirubinemia, the course of therapy must include careful monitoring of metabolic rate, fluid and electrolyte balance, thermal regulation, skin integrity, and serum bilirubin levels.

The use of exchange transfusion for the treatment of pathologic hyperbilirubinemia is the classic therapeutic procedure. Considerations for performing an exchange transfusion include the rate of rise in the serum bilirubin, the degree of anemia, the condition of the neonate, the cause of the jaundice, signs of CNS deterioration, age of the neonate, and alternative modes of treatment. In the case of erythroblastosis, the offending antibodies and the susceptible cells are removed during the exchange. In cases of drug toxicity, the toxic substances are removed. In the case of hyperbilirubinemia, bilirubin is removed although it tends to accumulate again after the transfusion as the bilirubin moves from the extravascular tissue into the blood. Repeated transfusions may be necessary until the serum bilirubin remains within acceptable levels.

Prior to the transfusion, the blood must be warmed to prevent hypothermia in the neonate. The exchange is best accomplished in a neutral thermal environment such as a radiant warmer where the neonate's temperature can be maintained without compromising accessibility to the patient. Emergency equipment must be readily available. A polyethylene catheter with a three-way stopcock is inserted into the umbilical vein and small amounts (10 to 20 mL at a time) of the newborn's blood are withdrawn and replaced with the same amount of new blood. This process is repeated until approximately 500 mL of blood have been replaced. Vital signs and glucose and calcium levels are carefully monitored throughout the exchange. Possible complications include heart failure, hyperkalemia (especially if old donor blood is used), acidemia, hypoglycemia, hypothermia, or air embolus. Careful observation of the neonate during and after the exchange greatly lowers the potential hazards of the exchange transfusion. Postexchange serum bilirubin determinations aid in further assessment of the neonate's condition.

Neonatal Sepsis

The fetus and neonate are vulnerable to a variety of organisms including bacteria, viruses, fungi, and parasites. Susceptibility to these organisms, combined with the low efficiency of their inflammatory and immune response, puts the neonate at a great risk for both congenitally transmitted and acquired infections. Special precautions for the prevention of infection, as well as prompt recognition and treatment, are necessary for an optimal outcome for the neonate.

Discussion of all possible sources and types of infectious organisms is not within the scope of this text. Many good sources of this information are available and should be consulted for desired details. However, the management of the septic neonate is predictable and will be discussed as it relates to the nurse. During the antepartal or intrapartal periods, pathogenic organisms may be transmitted from the mother to the fetus. Maternal symptoms may never be manifested, and only after birth will the fetal involvement be recognized. Transplacental infections tend to be nonbacterial and frequently include syphilis, rubella, herpes, and cytomegalovirus. Acquired infections from personnel, equipment, or other objects may be readily transmitted to the neonate, whose vulnerability is further complicated by such factors as prematurity, congenital abnormalities, difficult delivery, or difficult transition. Acquired infections can be caused by a variety of organisms but most often involve bacteria such as *E. coli, Pseudomonas aeruginosa*, group B streptococci, staphylococci, and *L. monocytogenes*.

Management of the neonate with sepsis requires constant vigilance and acute awareness of the subtleties of the neonate's behaviors. Symptoms of sepsis in neonates are vague and nonspecific. Often by the time overt symptoms appear the neonate will have sustained permanent damage to body systems. Careful review of the prenatal and intrapartal histories may alert the staff to the increased potential for infection in a neonate. In addition, frequent observations of the neonate by the same nurse enables the most subtle changes to be noticed. Observations such as a slight change in color, tone, or activity may be the earliest indicators that an infection is developing. A neonate who "does not seem to be doing as well" may warrant an aggressive investigation before overt symptoms appear. Symptoms such as apnea, lethargy, irritability, temperature instability, diarrhea or vomiting, jaundice, failure to gain, or shock may be seen. Because such symptoms could also indicate disorders other than septicemia, a positive laboratory diagnosis is attempted.

Cultures of blood, spinal fluid, and urine should be obtained from any neonate suspected of being septic. When sepsis is strongly suspected, treatment is begun immediately after the specimens for culture have been obtained. Drug therapy for the suspected organisms is begun. The most frequently used combinations for septicemia include kanamycin and penicillin or kanamycin and ampicillin. Methicillin, oxacillin, and gentamycin may also be used. The nurse must have a clear understanding of the immature pharmacologic response of the neonate, because the newborn's ability to absorb, metabolize, and excrete drugs is significantly different from that of the older infant or child.

After antibiotic therapy has begun, continuous supportive care such as respiratory support, thermoregulation, and careful observation of the neonate's condition is needed. Special attention should be given to observation of pH, blood glucose, fluid and electrolyte balance, neurologic signs, and jaundice. Protection of other infants in the unit may be accomplished by careful handwashing, proper attire, appropriate isolation techniques, and strict protocols for aseptic techniques and cleanliness within the area of the unit.

Continued care and maintenance of the high-risk neonate may involve hospitalization of a relatively short duration or extended care both in and out of the hospital. Long-range problems usually include not only the primary pathology but also areas such as complex nutritional support, growth and development, stress on the family and neonate, and determination of a plan for continued comprehensive care. The nurse's role in all such management and planning is inherent to a successful outcome for the family and child. The nurse's need for a sound background in perinatal nursing is obvious. Content in this chapter provides a basis for delivering immediate critical care to the mother and neonate. However, for the nurse who anticipates frequent perinatal experiences, this chapter will be insufficient to provide the constantly changing, updated knowledge which is part of perinatal care and the extensive knowledge base required to function in these areas on a regular basis. This chapter, then, is designed to assist nurses who find themselves with occasional or sudden perinatal crises and need reference regarding the appropriate care to be given.

REFERENCES

Abramson, H. (ed): *Resusitation of the Newborn Infant,* 3d ed., St. Louis: Mosby, 1973.

Anderson, B. A., M. E. Comacho, and J. Stark: *Interruptions in Family Health During Pregnancy,* New York: McGraw-Hill, 1979.

Apgar, V.: The role of the anesthesiologist in reducing neonatal mortality, *NY State J Med* 55: 2365, 1955.

————: The newborn (Apgar) scoring system, *Pediat Clin North Am* 13:645, 1966.

Babson, S. G., R. C. Benson, M. I. Pernoll, and G. I. Benda: *Management of High Risk Pregnancy and Intensive Care of the Neonate,* 3d ed., St. Louis: Mosby, 1975.

Clausen, J. P., M. H. Flook, and B. Ford: *Maternity Nursing Today,* 2d ed., New York: McGraw-Hill, 1977.

Conway, B.: *Pediatric Neurologic Nursing,* St. Louis: Mosby, 1977.

Drage, J. S., C. Kennedy, H. Berendes, B. K. Schwartz, and W. Weiss: The Apgar score as an index of infant morbidity, *WW Med Infant Neurol* 8:141, 1965.

Guntheroth, W.: Neonatal and pediatric cardiovascular crisis, *Emergency Med* 8(4):39–51, April 1976.

Jensen, M. D., R. C. Benson, and I. B. Bobak: *Maternity Care: The Nurse and the Family,* St. Louis: Mosby, 1977.

Klaus, M., and A. Fanaroff: *Care of the High-Risk Neonate,* Philadelphia: Saunders, 1973.

————, and J. Kennell: *Maternal-Infant Bonding,* St. Louis: Mosby, 1976.

Korones, S.: High-risk newborn infants, in *The Basis for Intensive Nursing Care,* St. Louis: Mosby, 1976.

Marlow, D.: *Pediatric Nursing,* Philadelphia: Saunders, 1977.

Moller, J.: *Essentials of Pediatric Cardiology,* Philadelphia: Davis, 1973.

Myles, M.: *A Textbook for Midwives,* London: Churchill Livingstone, 1971.

Oxorn, H., and W. R. Foote: *Human Labor and Birth,* 2d ed., New York: Appleton-Century-Crofts, 1968.

Pritchard, J. A., and P. C. MacDonald: *William's Obstetrics,* 15th ed., New York: Appleton-Century-Crofts, 1976.

Romney, S. L., M. J. Gray, A. B. Little, J. A. Merrill, E. G. Quilligan, and R. Stander: *Gynecology and Obstetrics: The Health Care of Women,* New York: McGraw-Hill, 1975.

Ross Laboratories Clinical Education Aid, *Neonatal Respiratory Distress,* Ross Laboratories, 1977.

Volpe, J. (guest ed.): *Clinics in Perinatology,* vol. 4, no. 1, Philadelphia: Saunders, March 1977.

SOME COMMON PEDIATRIC CONSIDERATIONS

The critical-care nurse needs technical skills, theoretical knowledge, and experiential knowledge to deal with the crises common to that setting; for a critical-care nurse working with critically ill children, the family-centered approach and child advocacy also are essential components. The stress experienced by the child and the child's family commands understanding and necessitates the selection of nursing interventions which decrease anxiety, enhance the development of trusting relationships, and facilitate greater understanding of both the complex equipment being utilized and the meaning of rapid changes in the client's status. In order to grasp the intense, yet fragile, nature of working with acutely ill children, several variables need further elaboration.

The most obvious difference in working with pediatric clients is the age and stage of the patient. There are six specific stages of childhood, from birth through adolescence, and each one is characterized by variations in physical, psychosocial, and cognitive development which accentuate those differences. Also, many body systems are at various maturational stages which account for differences in vital signs, laboratory values, and nutritional needs. Since body surface is greater in proportion to body weight, fluid and electrolyte needs, medications, and intake and output determinations are calculated on the basis of weight, measured in square meters (m^2).

As a result of variations in the size of pediatric patients, equipment is not standardized as it is with adults. It is chosen to meet the specific dimensions of the individual child. Therefore, improvisation and creativity are valuable attributes of a nurse who works with acutely ill children. These critical-care nurses face innumerable frustrations and challenges, and while they must know the equipment which is being utilized, they must also be resourceful in adapting available technology to meet the needs of an infant, child, or adolescent. When the child is unable to understand the crucial nature of the apparatus, there is a need either to protect the child from the equipment or the equipment from the child.

Safety is another important pediatric consideration. Whenever a rectal temperature is taken, the thermometer is held in place; when arterial lines or chest tubes are inserted, they are thoroughly secured, and young patients are restrained, as necessary. Children are unpredictable. Since the bodies of children are more sensitive than those of adults, caution is always

34
PEDIATRIC CRISES
Gladys M. Scipien
Susan D. Foster

SOME COMMON PEDIATRIC CONSIDERATIONS
Primary Nursing in Critical-Care Settings

THE FAMILY IN A PEDIATRIC CRITICAL-CARE UNIT

THE NEONATE WITH A SURGICAL EMERGENCY
The Newborn
Tracheoesophageal Fistulas and Esophageal Atresia
Omphalocele and Gastroschisis
Congenital Diaphragmatic Hernia

CHILD ABUSE AND BURNS IN THE TODDLER
The Toddler
Child Abuse
Burns

HEMOLYTIC UREMIC SYNDROME IN THE PRESCHOOLER
Preschoolers
Pathophysiology
Medical Treatment
Nursing Management

NEUROLOGIC DISORDERS IN THE SCHOOL-AGE CHILD
Psychosocial Aspects
CNS Evaluation: Level of Consciousness and Intracranial Pressure
Brain Tumor
Reye's syndrome

THE ADOLESCENT WITH OSTEOGENIC SARCOMA
The Adolescent
Pathophysiology
Medical/Surgical Management
Nursing Management

REFERENCES

exercised in the use of hypothermia or hyperthermia blankets, prepping solutions, or new medications. In a pediatric critical-care unit (ICU), nurses need to think for a majority of their patients and anticipate their needs as well as their responses to the milieu, the procedures, or the equipment.

Verbal communication is the traditional mode of expressing one's needs; however, in pediatrics, clients who may not have achieved that developmental milestone may not be able to convey their desires. In addition, the nurse cannot rely on verbalization alone because, in many instances, children cannot describe what they are experiencing. In pediatrics, nonverbal cues frequently indicate physical and psychosocial changes. The irritable child who becomes placid may not be deteriorating neurologically; however, the patient may be regressing, withdrawing, or suffering from sensory overload. While it is necessary to observe these children in toto in order to be able to interpret their behavior more accurately, this information is useless if it is used in isolation. Such knowledge, combined with data obtained from parents at the initial nursing interview, can be particularly significant. For example, a child who has had major abdominal surgery begins to vomit and has a distended abdomen. However, bowel sounds are present. Albeit an ileus is suspected, an intense search for the cause of these clinical manifestations continues. If the initial data collection is complete, it may reveal that this child typically responds to fear and stress by swallowing air and vomiting. In the proper context, it is a most significant piece of information.

Although an intensive care setting is stressful to clients and their families, it also has an effect upon those nurses who staff these units. Frustration, anger, disappointment, sorrow, and anxiety are commonly experienced. In those situations nurses are vulnerable, for no one can face repeated crises, life-threatening situations, or death without being affected by them. At times, demands made upon them are excessive. In addition, these nurses must possess tremendous amounts of knowledge and skill which can be implemented almost instantly. The stress is constant and such that one must always function at maximum potential. There is little tolerance for a "bad day." Realistically, there is no escape from those variables which contribute to that stressful environment, and nurses, being human, have their own emotional reactions to that which they are experiencing. As primary health care providers in an ICU, nurses interact and deal with the responses of innumerable individuals who interface with that unit. In essence, they make a substantial investment. However, there are satisfactions and gratifications. The rewards for time and effort expended in caring for these children are many, and in spite of the stress they experience daily, these nurses can see the tangible contributions they make when these young patients are able, once again, to enjoy the carefree activities of childhood.

Primary Nursing in Critical-Care Settings

There is so much a nurse needs to know about a critically ill child that it is impossible for that health care provider to be completely informed about all patients found in an intensive care setting. It is realistic, however, for a nurse to have a very thorough knowledge of all aspects of one child's pathophysiologic and psychosocial status, especially in pediatrics, where even the most miniscule changes are significant.

In order to acquire and utilize the information collected, it is important for the nurse to develop meaningful relationships with the child and the child's family. Since the patient is not in a position to develop multiple relationships, and the family is usually in desperate need of such a temporary reciprocal dependency, a most effective mode of clinical practice is found within the concept of primary nursing care. In addition, the multiple needs of these children necessitate interdisciplinary involvement; therefore, it is appropriate for a primary nurse to collaborate with and coordinate the activities of all these health professionals.

Since the primary nurse in a critical-care unit is accountable for providing a high calibre of care to a designated patient, this health care provider is also responsible for recognizing personal educational needs. Primary nursing helps this professional nurse to focus on learning needs which are of an emergent nature, facilitates immediate utilization of knowledge and thereby ensures greater retentivity. With a single nurse accountable for implementing all aspects of the nursing process, it is possible for that nurse to look at patient outcomes and use them as tools for performing self-evaluations, which are integral components of professional growth.

THE FAMILY IN A PEDIATRIC CRITICAL-CARE UNIT

While critical illness is a crisis for the child, it also catapults the family into a crisis situation which disrupts normal activity and possibly contributes to family disorganization. Nurses in critical-care settings need to concern themselves with these social units and their intactness, because their clients will be returning to these family structures and depending on them as prime, supportive resources during their growing years. Also, parents frequently verbalize their needs; realistically, they cannot be ignored.

A child is perceived by a parent as an extension of "the self," and a sudden, devastating illness threatens to destroy the hopes, dreams, the aspirations held for that child. Children are particularly vulnerable human beings who have not had an opportunity to experience that which their parents wish for them or that which they themselves desire.

When one considers the legal aspects of hospitalization, children are not able to sign permission forms, excepting the "emancipated minor"; parents usually assume this responsibility. Being honest and providing information which will allow parents to arrive at decisions are substantial, time-consuming nursing responsibilities.

While recovery and returning to the family at a maximum level of wellness is the most desired outcome for a critically ill child, there are situations in which the quality of life has been seriously compromised by residual sequelae which have sharply curtailed future development. The extent of the limitation or the quality of that child's life is a moral-legal-ethical issue which is much too complex for elaboration in this text. Nevertheless, the critical-care nurse needs to understand all aspects of this dilemma and to respect those difficult decisions parents must make. Since these limitations are long-term, it is important for critical-care nurses to know the community resources that are available and to initiate referrals which will assist the family in meeting the child's changing needs.

THE NEONATE WITH A SURGICAL EMERGENCY

The Newborn

The neonatal period extends from birth through the first 28 days of life. In pediatrics it is the period of greatest mortality and morbidity, and if these figures are to be reduced, health care providers must concentrate on assessing and evaluating these newborns more effectively in order to better manage problems as they are identified. At delivery, the newborn assumes responsibility for initiating function of all body systems. The Apgar score taken at 1 and 5 min evaluates the newborn's overall response to birth, which is a stressful experience. Any neonatal physical examination *must* include the passage of a nasogastric tube to determine patency of the gastrointestinal tract and a digital examination of the rectum. Vital signs, including blood pressure, provide invaluable baseline data regarding the newborn's adaptive ability.

A crucial aspect of the newborn assessment is an evaluation of neuromuscular development. One must remember that the nervous system is not fully developed at birth. Since the results vary with gestational age, the nurse performing this evaluation must know what is normal for a neonate's age in order to be able to identify what is abnormally present. Typically, the normal newborn responds to selective stimuli. Any asymmetrical response to reflexes or poor muscle tonus suggests some type of problem which needs to be further investigated without delay. The following reflexes should be evaluated soon after birth: Babinski, plantar, palmar, rooting, sucking, tonic-neck, and startle (Moro). An active and passive muscle tone examination also supplies valuable information.

In the process of being observed and cared for, a neonate is often left without clothing. While thermoregulation is essential to adaptation, the loss of body heat is a significant stressor to this young client. In order to compensate for this loss, the newborn releases more catecholamine, which stimulates metabolism even more. Since the body tries to conserve heat, blood flow to the skin is decreased, doubling oxygen consumption needs. Therefore, stress from hypothermia can compromise the already sick neonate.

Often these critically ill newborns are transferred to facilities which can better meet their unique needs. However, the subsequent long-term separation of a newborn from its mother can have disastrous effects in regard to its motor, mental, and affective development. Attachment begins during pregnancy, and it is strengthened appreciably after birth when the neonate is totally dependent on the nurturing mother. This mother-infant bond which develops influences and affects all of the newborn's future relationships; therefore, it is a crucial process. Statistical data clearly demonstrate that early separation of a child from the mother can result in subsequent battering and failure to thrive without an organic cause. In view of the research, health care providers must assist in establishing contact between parents and their newly born offspring. Establishment of eye-to-eye contact and attachment are facilitated by liberal visiting hours, during which parents are allowed to touch and hold the baby despite the equipment or monitoring devices. Often parents are frightened by the complex, buzzing apparatus which encompasses their tiny, acutely ill neonate (see Fig. 34-1). Explanations regarding procedures or equipment can decrease parental anxiety and unfamiliarity. Parenting skills can be practiced under the watchful eyes of knowing providers. Considering the ramifications of maternal deprivation, nurses are in a prime position to strengthen the maternal-child bonding process by conscientiously acquainting parents with their newborn; by promoting frequent contact between neonate and parent; and by actively sharing growth and development principles with them. Gradually, responsibility for care can be assumed by parents who are reasonably comfortable in their new roles.

The neonate presents a challenge to the nurse which is different from any other aspect of pediatrics. At birth, systemic changes occur rapidly in order to assist the newborn in adjusting to extrauterine life. Malformations make their presence known at this time, and difficulties may arise hours after delivery. Some of these anomalies are usually visually evident, others are not. The latter are identified initially by a nurse who astutely observes the neonate accommodating to a new environment. Sometimes the changes the neonate demonstrates are dramatic; others are insidious in nature. The newborn must be assessed often in order to identify variations in its apical or respiratory rates, changes in the color of skin or mucous membranes, or behavior, all of which are indicative of an impending problem.

Approximately 250,000 children delivered each year have birth defects, and while some conditions are minor, others are life-threatening malformations which become chronic in nature, costing millions of dollars in hospitalization, hundreds of thousands of days lost from school, and incomprehensible ensuing problems. No statistics can express the emotional cost experienced by those affected or their families at the time of diagnosis and during the lengthy, often uncertain, treatments or procedures they may need to endure. The authors have elected to elaborate on several malformations which are seen in neonatal ICUs or referral centers. The nursing care of newborns with these acquired defects typifies the challenges experienced by those who work in neonatology.

It is important to understand that the causes of these malformations are not always known. The National Foundation-March of Dimes, an organization committed to investigating birth defects, states that 20 percent of malformations occur as a result of environmental influences (viruses, radiation, drugs), and another 20 percent can be traced to the genetic traits of one or both parents. However, the remaining 60 percent appear to be caused by an interaction of environmental and hereditary influences. Therefore, the task of identifying the cause is, more often than not, almost impossible.

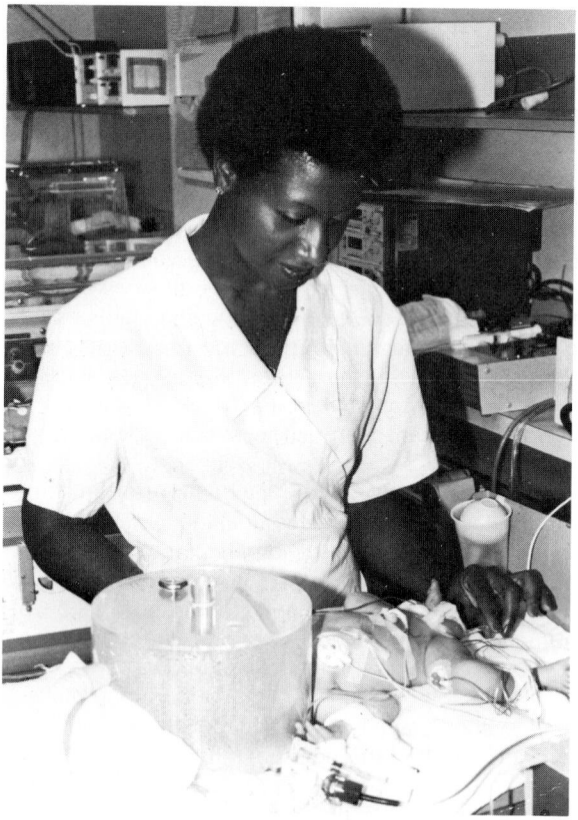

FIGURE 34-1

The equipment that is essential in caring for an acutely ill neonate may be frightening to its parents. (*Photo courtesy of Irwin J. Weinfeld, Toledo Hospital, Toledo, Ohio.*)

Tracheoesophageal Fistulas and Esophageal Atresia

There are six types of tracheoesophageal fistulas (TEF) and/or esophageal atresia (EA) which occur in 1 out of every 4000 live births. Over 80 percent of these newborns have blind proximal esophageal pouches (EA) with distal segments of the esophagus coming from the tracheobronchial tree (TEF). The obstructed, proximal end of the esophagus is responsible for oral secretions gravitating to the trachea, while gastric juices reflux from the distal segment of the esophagus and flow into the pulmonary parenchyma. While aspiration pneumonias are common in these newborns, the gastric fluid consists of powerful, activated enzymes which can have a particularly powerful, necrotizing effect.

Surgical Treatment

The diagnosis of either a tracheoesophageal fistula with an esophageal atresia or a simple esophageal atresia is made when the nasogastric tube which is passed in the physical examination does not go beyond a distance of 9 to 13 cm or fails to aspirate gastric contents. Early detection of either anomaly can prevent aspiration and pneumonitis; therefore, the nasogastric tube is passed soon after birth. Excessive drooling of saliva and abdominal distention are two early signs of esophageal atresia. When the distal pouch of the TEF communicates with the trachea, abdominal percussion is hyperresonant because of the presence of air in the gastrointestinal tract. Some cases of TEF and EA can go undetected until the first feeding when the neonate characteristically chokes, regurgitates, and becomes cyanotic. An upright chest x-ray taken with a radiopaque nasogastric tube in place quickly confirms the diagnosis.

Preoperative management includes sump drainage of the proximal pouch and a gastrostomy to prevent distention, aspiration, and pneumonitis. The surgical repair can be delayed until the neonate's physical condition stabilizes.

Surgical correction depends on the exact nature of the defect. The most common variation of TEF, in which the distal esophagus forms the tracheal fistula and the proximal esophagus exists as a blind pouch, is usually repaired by an extrapleural approach through a right thoracotomy. The fistula is then divided, and an end-to-end anastomosis of the esophagus is completed. The latter step is done occasionally during a second-stage operation if the newborn is either too small or too ill to tolerate prolonged anesthesia. A second stage also is done when there is inadequate esophageal tissue to complete the anastomosis. A tube, then, is placed in the extrapleural space, brought out through a stab wound, and connected to underwater seal drainage to provide for the evacuation of saliva should a leak develop at the newly anastomosed site. The gastrostomy tube remains in place to prevent gastroesophageal reflux. An isolated TEF is usually anatomically high. A division of this type of fistula is performed utilizing a right clavicular approach, and only a gastrostomy tube is left in place at the end of the procedure.

When an esophageal atresia occurs without TEF, often there is an insufficient amount of tissue to perform an initial end-to-end anastomosis; hence, the repair is done in two stages. At birth, a gastrostomy tube is inserted and a pharyngostomy is created by bringing the proximal esophageal pouch to the skin via the suprasternal notch. Both of these procedures control secretions and allow feedings until the second-stage repair is performed at about 6 to 12 months of age. In this instance, esophageal substitution is necessary to accomplish the anastomosis, and most often a section of the colon is used to replace the absent esophageal tissue. It is also possible to construct a tubular insert from the greater curvature of the stomach to facilitate attachment to the proximal esophagus. Although attempts have been made to elongate the proximal esophageal pouch with bougie stretching, these trials have not been particularly successful.

Leakage at the esophageal anastomosis is the most serious complication, which occurs in 10 to 20 percent of the patients on about the seventh to tenth postoperative day. It is a less likely occurrence when the anastomosis is an extrapleural one. A leak into the pleural space leads to empyema and septicemia. A tenuous esophageal blood supply, excessive operative handling of esophageal tissue, local inflammatory reactions, and esophageal irritation caused by gastric reflux can lead to the development of esophageal strictures, necessitating repeated dilatations at later intervals. Neuromuscular abnormalities of the distal esophageal segment can result in dysphagia. Occasionally these newborns exhibit an abnormal catlike or barking cry, but their speech is usually normal.

Nursing Management

Preventing respiratory complications before and after the surgical repairs of tracheoesophageal anomalies is the primary nursing concern. Aspiration and pneumonitis occur easily because of the excessive secretions which tend to collect about the tracheobronchial tube or as a result of gastroesophageal reflux. In addition, these defects are frequently associated with prematures or low birth weight neonates who also have a high incidence of respiratory distress syndrome. Often the presence of cardiovascular anomalies results in the development of congestive heart failure. Aspiration can be critical in either situation. Important nursing measures include: efficient sump drainage of the proximal esophageal pouch preoperatively; elevating the newborn at a 20 to 45° angle; and maintaining a patent gastrostomy tube before and after surgery. Assessing the neonate for early indications of respiratory compromise and vigorous chest physical therapy in the presence of pulmonary infiltrates are certainly critical nursing interventions. *A catheter clearly marked so that it will not pass the esophageal anastomosis site must be used for all nasopharyngeal suctioning.*

Postoperative feeding is accomplished by gastrostomy for about 2 weeks. Once oral feedings are begun, it is important to feed the patient very slowly to eliminate any possibility of choking. The neonate needs to be elevated during and after feedings to decrease the likelihood of gastric reflux. Reoccurrence of a TEF at the anastomosis site or the presence of an esophageal stricture causes a coughing, choking response to swallowing. Also, parents should be encouraged to feed their newborn early. Supervision by a nurse enhances their confidence prior to discharge.

Omphalocele and Gastroschisis

The presence of either omphalocele or gastroschisis is noted at delivery when viscera protrude through and lie out on the abdomen. These anomalies, which affect the anterior abdominal wall, occur as a result of an unknown disturbance involving closure during embryonic development. Omphaloceles, seen in 1: 5000 births, are large, centrally located malformations which include the umbilicus; they are usually covered by an amniotic membrane which encloses the viscera. On rare occasions, this membrane disintegrates in utero. Gastroschisis appears below and separate from the umbilicus. While viscera herniate outside the abdominal cavity, there are no remnants of an amniotic sac. Both defects constitute surgical emergencies which must be corrected without delay.

Surgical Treatment

These defects are obvious at birth, and initial management is designed to protect the exposed abdominal organs and to prevent infection. The exposed amniotic membrane is intact over the anomaly, and it provides the best means of maintaining a moist, sterile environment for the gut it covers. However, it can rupture easily either during labor or on manual examination of the defect. Should it rupture, warm, wet, sterile dressings of normal saline are applied. Extreme precautions are taken not to twist or apply pressure to the protruding mass. A nasogastric tube is inserted to relieve distention of the gut and prevent vomiting and aspiration. Other anomalies associated with omphalocele include intestinal malrotation, Meckel's diverticulum, patent omphalomesenteric duct, intestinal stenosis or atresia, intestinal duplication, meconium ileus, and biliary atresia. Preoperative x-ray examination of the chest and abdomen confirm or rule out the presence of these anomalies.

If the defect is small, the initial operative procedure accomplishes a return of the abdominal contents and closure of the fascia. However, often the abdominal cavity has not grown large enough to accommodate the contents, and surgery is done in several stages. If possible, abdominal skin flaps are mobilized and sutured to protect the viscera. A ventral hernia is created and left to be repaired at a later date when the infant is larger. When even this procedure is not possible, a prosthetic pouch of Silastic sheeting is sutured to the muscle and fascia on opposing sides of the defect then sutured to itself with a minimum amount of tension. The bowel and mesentery lose edema as they are returned slowly to the abdominal cavity. This process and the newborn's growth allow the Silastic pouch to be tightened daily by progressively twisting the pouch closed until all contents are returned to the abdominal cavity. Then fascia and skin are sutured across the defect. The procedure is carefully done to prevent pressure on the abdominal contents, which can lead to respiratory distress. Infection control is critical also, and often antibiotic solutions are irrigated through the prosthetic pouch until closure is realized. A gastrostomy tube is usually inserted to relieve any abdominal distention. When closure has been completed, oral feedings are started.

Nursing Management

In the preoperative period, protecting the amniotic sac and maintaining a moist, sterile environment is absolutely imperative. The neonate is monitored to detect symptoms of respiratory distress, early signs of sepsis, and the possible presence of heretofore unknown anomalies. The patient is handled very gently to decrease the likelihood of rupturing the encompassing sac. Efforts must be taken to prevent tension on the area. In addition to exercising caution when positioning or turning the newborn, arms may need to be gently restrained.

Postoperatively, the nurse must help to evaluate the newborn's tolerance of the closure, whether primary in nature or a staged repair. Observation of the incisional area and monitoring the neonate for early symptoms of respiratory difficulty due to abdominal compression are important nursing activities. The surgical area is managed utilizing sterile technique. An ileus can be present for several weeks, possibly necessitating the use of intralipid and total parenteral nutrition. An assessment of the tolerance of early feedings through measurements of prefeeding gastric residuals and an evaluation of abdominal tenderness can prevent complications from vomiting and aspiration. Parenteral antibiotics also are ordered. Restraints may be necessary and depend on the newborn's activity. Nasopharyngeal suctioning, intravenous fluids, and the use of an incubator (oxygen *and* humidity) are other common interventions early in the postoperative phase. As the neonate stabilizes, the vital signs are determined with less frequency (every 3 to 4 h).

Congenital Diaphragmatic Hernia

This defect is present because of a failure in fusing parts of the diaphragm during embryonic development. This congenital hernia most frequently occurs in the posterior portion of the diaphragm along the foramen of Bochdalek. When present, there is a free, communicating pathway between the thoracic and abdominal cavities. If the malformation is extensive, the stomach, small intestines, right side of the colon, and spleen may be found in the thoracic cavity. The distress a newborn experiences is substantial, quickly compromising its respiratory status.

Surgical Treatment

While the severe aeration and pulmonary circulation disturbances which signify the presence of a congenital diaphragmatic hernia (CDH) may not be obvious at birth, this anomaly represents a most acute emergency. The pulmonary parenchyma have been compromised in utero, and when the displaced intrapleural intestine fills with ingested air and secretions, an acute cardiorespiratory deterioration ensues. The amount of bowel and the extent of internal organs which are displaced into the pleural cavity affect the degrees of mediastinal shifting and collapse of the lungs. Labored respiratory effort pulls more of the gut into the pleural cavity, and the infant exhibits typical clinical manifestations such as cyanosis, tachypnea with rocking respirations and intercostal retractions, scaphoid abdomen, dullness to percussion on the *affected* side, lack of breath sounds, heart sounds which are displaced to the opposite side, and lack of peristalsis in the herniated bowel. Radiologic studies usually confirm the diagnosis of CDH.

An immediate goal of therapy is to maximize existent pulmonary function. The insertion of a nasogastric or sump tube decreases intestinal distention. The neonate must be elevated *on* the affected side, because this position decreases intestinal compression and enhances respiratory effort. Oxygen therapy is instituted for cyanosis or dyspnea. If respiratory assistance is necessary, it must be provided by endotracheal tube, because ventilation by face mask increases gastric distention. In the presence of a limited capacity for expansion, continuous positive airway pressure (CPAP) or positive end expiratory pressure (PEEP) must be maintained below 20 cm of water to prevent a pulmonary rupture. Metabolic and respiratory acidosis can develop; therefore, arterial blood gases are monitored closely, and appropriate treatment (sodium bicarbonate and mechanical ventilation) is instituted when necessary.

The surgical repair is accomplished using a thoracic or abdominal approach. The latter is preferred because it permits the surgeon to explore, identify, and correct the malrotation or volvulus which is frequently associated with CDH. An abdominal approach also permits surgical creation of a ventral hernia which may be necessary, at times, to allow space to replace viscera into the peritoneal cavity. Since the infant is a diaphragmatic breather, care must be taken not to increase the intra-abdominal pressure, which would further restrict ventilatory exchange and prohibit venous return through the inferior vena cava. Diaphragm margins are closed with suture. A silon patch is necessary on rare occasions. A gastrostomy tube is left in place to alleviate any postoperative distention.

Expansion of the ipsilateral lung must be gradual. Compression in utero may have caused this lung to be hypoplastic, and an abrupt expansion can result in rupture of pulmonary alveoli or a tension pneumothorax of this or the opposite lung. Occasionally, bilateral pulmonary hypoplasia exists as a result of the displaced mediastinum and visceral encroachment on both pleural cavities. A pleural catheter, which is positioned posteriorly, allows air to enter the pleural space and facilitates postoperative drainage. This intrapleural chest tube is connected to underwater seal drainage without suction to permit a gradual lung reexpansion, which can take 2 to 4 days. An experimental approach to reexpanding the ipsilateral lung maintains bilateral chest tubes. Air is injected into the ipsilateral tube to maintain a constant pressure until the mediastinum stabilizes in 4 to 5 postoperative days. After surgery, the physiologic changes which result from pulmonary insufficiency pose critical management problems. A delicate balance between pulmonary artery and ductus arteriosus tone and the ability of the right ventricle to sustain an adequate cardiac output must be realized until the ipsilateral lung reexpands. A great deal of research is being done to determine the nature of the pulmonary changes in CDH and to identify the most effective method of preventing and correcting postoperative pulmonary hypertension as well as acidemia. At present, a medication regimen also can be instituted for these purposes. This regimen includes steroids to prevent pulmonary vasoconstriction; chlorpromazine to diminish the workload of the right ventricle, decrease pulmonary vascular resistance, and increase cardiac output; and dopamine and digoxin to enhance myocardial contractility.

Nursing Management

The nurse who monitors the neonate with CDH must observe the patient closely in order to detect the earliest signs of difficulty which are crucial to an initial diagnosis and subsequent treatment as well as the maintenance of adequate pulmonary function. These neonates may demonstrate clinical symptoms of respiratory distress, interstitial pulmonary edema, or pulmonary hemorrhage. They need to be placed in semi-Fowler's position *on* the affected side to facilitate expansion of the unaffected lung. Preoperatively, nursing actions include monitoring the high concentrations of oxygen being administered, facilitating the removal of nasogastric drainage, and regulating positive airway pressure if tracheal intubation is necessary.

Postoperatively, the neonate has a chest tube connected to underwater seal drainage for 2 to 3 days. Vigorous chest physical therapy, along with frequent positioning and nasotracheal suctioning, is essential to reexpansion, and these activities also prevent the development of pneumonia. Serial arterial blood gases are monitored. If ventilatory assistance

(CPAP) (PEEP) is necessary, the neonate's blood pressure must be observed closely. It is important to know that positive pressure in the thoracic cavity may diminish venous return. Likewise, central venous pressures are measured using the superior vena cava rather than the inferior vena cava, which is subjected to intra-abdominal pressure changes.

Abdominal distention can be a major problem after surgery, and it must be minimized to maintain integrity of the wound and prevent pulmonary compromise. A patent gastrostomy tube facilitates drainage of secretions and removal of air. Gastric output is measured at 8-h intervals to calculate fluid and electrolyte replacement. Abdominal girths measured at 8-h intervals also help to document distention. Calculated intravenous fluid therapy meets the neonate's nutritional needs until the presence of peristalsis signals readiness for oral feedings. They are started in very small amounts, and when tolerance for sterile water is demonstrated, the feeding schedule progresses to either breast milk or formula. The young patient needs to be closely observed for any respiratory distress, tiredness, or color changes as diet is resumed.

CHILD ABUSE AND BURNS IN THE TODDLER

The Toddler

The toddler years extend from the beginning of the first year to the beginning of the third year of life. It is a period of increasing independence, autonomy, negativism, ritualistic behavior, limit setting, and temper tantrums which occur as a result of the frustrations experienced between internal impulses and demands exerted by reality.

Motor development is rapid during these 2 years. Walking, running, and climbing are types of gross motor skills which are much more perfected at this stage than are the fine motor skills, which will not be mastered until after the start of school. Language ability has reached a point (2 to $2\frac{1}{2}$ years) at which two- or three-word sentences express the child's wants, needs, and desires. Social development is minimal, primarily because of limited exposure to peers; and although the toddler participates in parallel play, interaction skills have not been learned successfully. Attention spans are short, and these children are easily distracted by innumerable stimuli. They have an intense, insatiable curiosity about the world they are free and mobile to explore.

The most important aspect of this age is play, recognized as a child's "work" because it has endless therapeutic, educational, and physical advantages for the child. Therapeutically, it provides the toddler with an active release for frustrations and tensions. Educationally, it is an enjoyable method of learning colors, sizes, shapes, and textures. Physically, the motor activities, which are vigorous and seemingly endless, further develop the neuromuscular system. Learning is based upon the trial and error struggle of fitting a square block into a round hole or attending a make-believe party with stuffed animals. Such activities are important because the child mimics adults, learns sex roles, and practices language skills during endless monologues both alone and with toys.

Serious illness and subsequent prolonged hospitalization not only disrupts the toddler's potential to continue the normal pattern of development, but it can seriously injure the toddler's emerging sense of self. In the preconceptual, egocentric phase of thought, toddlers believe that everyone knows what they are thinking just because they think it, and that everything that happens is directly related to their thoughts or behavior. The young child distortedly senses that attempts to be independent make parents angry, and illness is perceived as a punishment. The young child experiences the normal developmental conflict between revolting against the dependence of infancy and the desire for autonomy. Therefore, a forced dependence from illness can have a negative effect. It can reinforce feelings of shame and doubt and destroy a child's attempts to exist as an independent person. Nursing care which allows toddlers some control over their environment permits them to make choices, encourages them to do as much for themselves as they are able, and helps to nurture their developing self-esteem.

Bodily injury, whether it is an invasive procedure such as a laboratory test, or is as extensive as a burn, has special meaning for the toddler. The toddler is not yet able to conceptualize the body's structural anatomy and hence believes that damage to the outer integrity allows everything inside to escape. What happens to a balloon if it is punctured? It is little wonder then that great fears emerge within the lively imaginations of these children. The dressing is significant because the child might simply think that "It's holding me together."

While the pain of the injury and procedures is great, to the toddler the pain of being separated from the familiar world, especially parents, is greater. The toddler's sense of security relies on the relationship with mother and father. In their absence, the strange world of the hospital and its people are incredibly frightening. In time the child may be able to develop a trusting relationship with one of these caretakers; and while continuity of care promotes this process, the toddler needs and wants the parents. A 1- or 2-year-old child might have difficulty recalling that its parents exist when they are not present. Later, an object, such as a mother's purse, can be held symbolically until her return. If the child has experienced abuse, the child's ability to form relationships can be even further compromised and may not be possible without psychiatric intervention.

In the midst of stress caused by being physically hurt, torn from the familiar world and separated from parents, the toddler reacts with anger or withdrawal. Regression to a previous developmental level of safety and security may take place. It is then that incontinence and requests for a bottle are evident. Although these responses are normal coping mechanisms, it may be necessary to help the child mobilize other defenses so that learning and growth may result from this experience. Play therapy is especially valuable. This mode of expression allows the toddler to vent frustrations by pounding; helps the toddler to cure "teddy" while recuperation is taking place; and provides a way for the toddler to act out feelings about injections, dressings, or treatments. Also, in reenacting a particularly stressful incident, the child is able to reconstruct the world and regain autonomy.

Child Abuse

The true incidence of child abuse nationally is unknown; however, it is estimated that more than 1 million children or 650 children per million people are neglected or abused in some manner. This major health problem is responsible for at least two reported deaths of children in the United States each day. These statistics are staggering and reflect serious, distorted child-rearing patterns which affect the most vulnerable segment of our population.

The complex situation which produces such violence is rooted in the childhood experiences of the abuser, who is usually the primary caretaker. While the most serious offenses are committed by the mother, others who can be implicated are fathers, boyfriends, and babysitters. Its incidence crosses all social, ethnic, racial, and religious barriers; however, it is intensified in the presence of poverty. Without a health care provider's intervening, about 5 percent of these children can be killed and another 35 percent can be seriously reinjured.

The types of assaults against children vary from

simple malnutrition to injuries so severe as to leave the child in a moribund state. Albeit burns account for 50 percent of the physical abuse, the following are frequently seen: abrasions; ecchymoses; lacerations; hepatic, splenic, or renal damage; severe head injuries, including skull fractures; intraocular and intracranial hemorrhages; and pneumothorax, rib, and limb fractures (in various stages of healing). See Fig. 34-2.

Child abuse is probably the most difficult clinical circumstance with which health care providers must deal. Health professionals who are treating a child who has received these extensive injuries must understand their own emotional responses to the incident because they can interfere with both objectivity and judgment where the abused and abuser are concerned. Interviewing parents to elicit information regarding the injuries may be more difficult for those who have angry feelings toward the abuser.

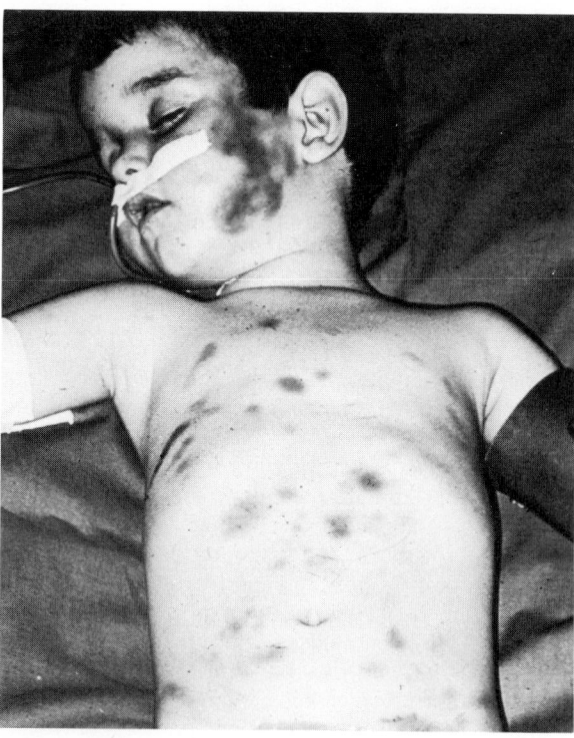

FIGURE 34-2

Bruises on the body of a 3-year-old child who was abused. (*From Andrew M. Margileth, Cutaneous Trauma, in R. A. Hoekelman et al. (eds.), Principles of Pediatrics, McGraw-Hill, New York, 1978, p. 1424.*)

While infants and children may need protection from such destructive abuse, it is important that there is no punitive abuse of the adult involved. Most abusive individuals are lonely, frustrated, and isolated persons who were abused as children. Trust, self-esteem, and confidence were not fostered during their early years, and as parents they look toward their child to provide them with love, security, and a feeling of importance. Unfortunately, the child cannot meet the demands of such a role reversal, because the child needs huge amounts of love, caring, and security which the parents are also seeking so desperately. Unable to meet these parental needs, the child's age-appropriate behaviors are interpreted as evil, destructive, and purposely designed to make life miserable for parents. Incidents in which the child cries to be fed, needs diapers changed, or breaks things while exploring the environment deserve punishment.

The use of punishment as a major form of discipline relates to the lack of a positive role model on which to base appropriate parenting behaviors. The nature of the punitive act is severe because the parent perceives the child as being more mature than the child actually is and thus capable of better self-control. The abusing parent may try to reason with a child, and the failure of the child to respond to this approach is interpreted as purposeful.

These abusing adults also are unable to interact socially, which means that they lead lonely lives with little opportunity to gain any satisfaction apart from their children. The lack of skill and resourcefulness of the parent in dealing with current crises means that minor disruptions are magnified and go unresolved, compounding the emotional stress they are experiencing. When a crisis occurs, striking out at the child seems to be the most obvious outlet. In turn, this action leaves the abusing parent with feelings of guilt, shame, denial, frustration, anger, and most certainly in desperate need of help.

Once the violence has occurred, medical attention is sought; but interestingly enough, with each episode of abuse assistance is sought at a different facility so that tracing the family is a difficult process. Obtaining an accurate history can be a frustrating, arduous task primarily because of the conflicting data being given and the discrepancy between a description of the incident and the physical findings on examining the child's body. Most authorities recommend admission to the hospital whether medical or surgical intervention is necessary because it prevents another incident and it protects the child. Nearly half of all abused children seen in an emergency room have serious injuries, and 10 to 25 percent of those seen die, although the mortality figures vary among different cities. Nurses must give particular attention to the pattern, age (old or new), and distribution of physical evidence found on the body. Photographs of the injuries, an assessment of the child's development, a skeletal survey, and a battery of laboratory tests furnish additional data.

Reporting known or suspected cases of abuse to a protective agency is mandatory nationally, and although the law provides a framework within which to function, each state has its own statutes, especially in regard to who can notify agencies. In 1974 Congress finally passed the Child Abuse Prevention and Treatment Act, Public Law 93-247. It is imperative for all to know that when a case is to be reported to a child protective agency, the parents *must* be so advised.

Trauma-X or child abuse teams have improved the management of these children. Its members come from many disciplines within the hospital and also include child protective personnel. Efforts are made to evaluate the family's functioning, to observe parent-child interactions, to assess the child's physical and psychological development, and to determine parental expectations of the child. These data are essential in deciding whether the child is to be returned home, retained at the hospital, or temporarily placed in a foster home. An interdisciplinary approach is necessary because the members of a single profession are unable to meet the most complex needs of these families. This type of collaborative endeavor can be responsible for taking definitive action, but it also serves as an important support system for the child care providers.

In view of the medical, legal, psychological, and social aspects of abuse, rehabilitation is on a long-term basis with all participants committed to acting as child advocates. Treatment modalities are different, but current theory and practice utilize two approaches: (1) remove the child from the home and work with the parents, or (2) keep the family intact and work with all its members. Other resources which are available include: 24-h "hot lines" for those parents who fear they will batter again; visits from community health nurses; membership in Parents Anonymous or other comparable groups; homemaker services; and crisis nurseries and day-care centers which offer temporary relief.

Since abuse is related to poor parenting skills and parenting is a learned behavior, not an instinct, efforts need to be made toward providing formal didactic input on the topic at the secondary school level.

Federal funds which can be used to sensitize the public to the severity and extent of this maltreatment problem are necessary—if it is to diminish within the next generation.

The violence to which many of these children are subjected often seriously affects their physical, psychosocial, and cognitive development. In addition, they frequently suffer from residual neurologic sequelae. Unfortunately, these victims learn to distrust adults before they are able to develop trusting relationships. It is no wonder that they are frightened, withdrawn, noncommunicating young patients. For the infant or toddler, cuddling and nurturing are the only nursing interventions. Preschoolers need psychiatrically directed play therapy, positive parenting experiences, and attendance at nursery school.

In view of the prevalence of child abuse, there should be a national focus on prevention, since the potential for battering can be identified early. Helfer has developed a questionnaire which is useful in screening for and identifying those capable of committing such acts. Verbal and nonverbal cues in the delivery room correlate with potential mother-child interaction problems. Taking the time to observe a parent feeding a neonate can identify the presence of a problem.

The vicious violence to which these children are subjected all too often results in their admission to ICUs, and nurses there must know the complex nature of neglect and abuse. It has ramifications for future generations. In one longitudinal study of a large group of children who received a variety of soft tissue injuries, after $4\frac{1}{2}$ years these children demonstrated extensive psychological trauma. Learning problems, poor self-concepts, and withdrawal were evident. But the most poignant characteristic noted was the inability of a great majority of these children to laugh, to play, and to simply enjoy themselves in the activities of childhood.

Burns

Pathophysiology

Burns rank second as the cause of accidental death in the first 15 years of life, and they are the leading cause of death at home in the first through fourth years. Thermal injuries account for approximately 10 percent of the physical child abuse seen, and 50 percent of these injuries are caused by scalding water. Abuse is suspected when the burn has an unusual pattern or distribution. For example, the body

TABLE 34-1
Characteristics of a Thermal Injury

Depth	Appearance	Anatomic involvement and depth	Pain sensitivity	Edema	Healing time	Causes
1st degree	Pink to red	Stratum corneum of epidermis Partial thickness	Painful	Slight	3–5 days	Sunburn, flash, explosives
2d degree	Red to pale ivory; moist; may have vesicles and bullae	Dermis Partial thickness	Extremely painful	Very edematous	21–28 days	Scalds, flash, flame, brief contact with hot objects
3d degree	White, cherry red, or black; may have bullae and thrombosed veins; dry; leathery	Subcutaneous adipose tissue, fascia, muscles and bone Full thickness	Painless to touch	Severe edema, may require escharotomies	Requires grafting	Flame, high intensity flash, electrical, chemical, hot objects and scalding

Source: J. A. Marvin and M. C. Caulfield, Integumentary system, in G. M. Scipien et al. (eds.), *Comprehensive Pediatric Nursing*, 2d ed., New York: McGraw-Hill, 1979, p. 968.

part looks as if it had been submerged in hot water. Characteristics of thermal injuries are shown in Table 34-1.

There is a multisystem response to this integumentary insult which is in direct relationship to the severity of the burn. In addition, the physiologic response of one system relates to the response of another, making assessment, treatment, and the complications of a burn extremely complex, urgent, and interdependent.

The cardiovascular response to a severe thermal injury occurs immediately. One result is hypovolemia with a marked decrease in cardiac output which is thought to be due to exaggerated reflex responses and a decreased venous return. Increased vascular permeability at the burn site, which progresses throughout the vascular tree in burns greater than 30 percent, causes significant losses of water, electrolytes, and proteins from the vascular compartment to the interstitial tissues. This phenomenon is the resultant edema which is evident soon after injury. The extent of these losses is difficult to ascertain because the fluids have accumulated deep in tissue; however, they are greater during the first 18 hours, possibly equaling as much as one-third of the total blood volume. The skin barrier normally prevents evapora-

tion; thus disruption of this barrier further augments fluid loss. Insensible water losses are 4 to 15 times greater than normal and especially significant in children where the ratio of body surface to body weight is greater. The loss of electrolytes, particularly potassium, is increased in the second 24 h, and protein loss continues for the first 4 days. During the 3d to the 10th day after a burn, edema begins to mobilize, expanding blood volume, increasing cardiac output, and causing a marked diuresis as well as a subsequent drop in the hemoglobin. Children are most prone to the cardiovascular complications of congestive heart failure and pulmonary edema which occur frequently in the presence of septic shock and renal failure. Blood loss from the burn site is minimal; therefore, early anemia is not usually noted. However, red cells damaged at the site of injury are lysed and blood is lost from granulating tissue which results in a declining hematocrit 4 to 7 days after a burn.

Following an extensive burn, there is an immediate effect on the renal system, when decreased cardiac output causes a reduction in renal blood flow and glomerular filtration rates. Severe oliguria may develop and tubular function may be compromised temporarily. Because of the immaturity of the renal system, this phenomenon is most pronounced in children under 2 years of age. The increased secretion of antidiuretic hormone and aldosterone further decrease urine formation, and the increased reabsorption of sodium as well as increased excretion of potassium yield highly concentrated urine. Renal insufficiency tends to reverse itself during the first 12 to 24 h as the cardiac output increases. However, it may persist in the presence of drug toxicity or renal infection, which stems from either sepsis or a urinary tract infection.

There are early physiologic responses of the gastrointestinal tract, such as acute gastric dilatation and paralytic ileus. These problems may also occur later as a result of sepsis, hypokalemia, or Curling's ulcer. On occasion, these gastric and duodenal ulcers can be life-threatening. Hemorrhagic gastritis develops because the body's vascular responses to the thermal injury causes a congestion in the gastric capillaries.

Caloric expenditures increase sharply after a burn injury. As the rate of water evaporation increases, there is an associated loss in body heat which must be replenished in order to maintain a normal temperature. In response to this need, the basal metabolic rate increases, and as the body mobilizes its energy stores, the catabolic process results in heat and weight loss.

Direct injury to the respiratory system associated with the inhalation of toxic substances or carbon monoxide intoxication can lead to either bronchopneumonia or tracheobronchitis. An actual burn to the lower airway is very rare. When the injured site is located about the neck and chest wall, edema formation may lead to primary airway obstruction very early in the course of the insult. Later, eschar formation over the chest wall can prevent muscular excursion, giving rise to pneumonias and atelectasis.

The risk of infection following burn injury remains a major concern throughout the healing process. Initially, skin loss allows easy entry of bacteria, and the exposed tissue provides an excellent culture medium for growth. Although streptococcal and staphylococcal infections have been brought under control, gram-negative bacteria (*Pseudomonas, Aerobacter, Klebsiella,* and so on) have brought new problems. In addition, nonpathogens (*Serratia, Providencia stuartii*), fungi, and viruses invade the integument. The vascular response to this injury results in an inability to localize invading agents, and a generalized septicemia is a critical danger. In addition, resistance to infection is compromised by (1) low serum immunoglobulin levels because of plasma loss and (2) ab-

normal phagocytosis from trauma to the reticuloendothelial system. After 2 to 3 days, granulation tissue developing below the burn eschar forms scar tissue, which prevents free drainage of the wound and enhances bacterial growth. Not only does infection represent a serious complication in terms of shock, but it may also convert deep dermal burns to full thickness burns. Infection may originate in the urinary and gastrointestinal tracts as well as at the intravenous catheter and the wound itself.

Immobilization, infection, and metabolic changes result in severe disfigurement and painful changes in the neuromuscular system. Contractures, tendon dislocations, dislocation or fusion of joints, and limb amputations are some examples of neuromuscular complications following severe burns. In most instances, a generalized muscular weakness persists during the healing process, and pain related to nerve and tissue regeneration can be extensive.

Nursing Management

In children, burns involving 10 percent of the body need hospitalization. Thermal injuries in excess of 15 to 20 percent are considered to be extensive insults. On admission it may be necessary to assign two nurses to provide care to a child. The task-related activities and procedures which are done at half-hour or hourly intervals necessitate meticulous adherence to a devised nursing care plan.

When the history is taken, it is important to identify prior respiratory problems (asthma, bronchitis, cardiac), because it is possible to identify patients who are predisposed to developing pulmonary complications. Also, it is necessary to determine whether the child has been properly immunized. If the immunizations are up-to-date, the child is given 0.5 mL of tetanus toxoid. If there has been no immunization against tetanus, the child is given human immune globulin. The nurse should anticipate making continuous assessments during the first 72 h after admission. Use of a flowchart to record intravenous fluids, urine output, specific gravity, various laboratory test results, and the child's overall status enables the nurse to know the patient's condition at a glance.

Vital signs change very quickly in children and therefore need to be monitored at half-hour intervals. An adequate airway is a prime concern in the child whose burns extend over the head, neck, and chest, because the rapid formation of edema can result in respiratory distress. The presence of rales, dyspnea, stridor, and an increased respiratory rate are important observations. These patients will need to be encouraged to cough and to breathe deeply.

Fluid and electrolyte imbalance in an extensive injury is a very serious problem which must be corrected as expeditiously as possible. Establishing an infusion site is difficult in the young child who has very small veins which collapse easily. Cutdowns are usually performed because access to a vessel can be obtained easily and the infusion remains functional longer than with a pediatric scalp vein set-up. Patients who are active may need to be restrained to maintain fluid therapy. Once the desired rate of

lished, it should be checked judiciously every half hour for the extent of the acute phase of the illness. The infusion site needs to be observed closely for symptoms of infiltration and the development of phlebitis. Several methods of calculating fluid requirements for burn patients can be found in Table 34-2.

Although body weight is a basic indicator of fluid needs, the percentage of body surface area (BSA) involved is also computed. The Lund and Browder method is particularly helpful in determining pediatric needs because it considers changes in body surface ·cur during various stages of growth.

TABLE 34-2
Formulas for Calculating Fluid Requirements

Evans Formula

Day 1   % BSA* burned × body weight (kg) × 1 = mL colloid
         % BSA burned × body weight (kg) × 1 = mL 5% dextrose in normal saline } one-half given in first 8 h

         Plus maintenance fluids: 2000 mL 5% dextrose in water per day

Day 2   % BSA burned × body weight (kg) × 0.5 = mL colloid
         % BSA burned × body weight (kg) × 0.5 = mL 5% dextrose in normal saline

         Plus maintenance fluids: 2000 mL 5% dextrose in water per day

Day 3   and thereafter—intravenous fluids as indicated (burns over 50% BSA calculated as 50% burn)

Brooke Army Formula

Day 1   % BSA burned × body weight (kg) × 1.5 = mL 5% dextrose in normal saline } one-half given in first 8 h
         % BSA burned × body weight (kg) × 0.5 = mL colloid†

         Plus maintenance fluids: 2000 mL 5% dextrose in water per day

Day 2   % BSA burned × body weight (kg) × 0.75 = mL 5% dextrose in normal saline
         % BSA burned × body weight (kg) × 0.25 = mL colloid

         Plus maintenance fluids: 2000 mL 5% dextrose in water per day

Children's Hospital of Michigan Formula

Day 1   % BSA burned × body weight (kg) × 2 = mL 5% dextrose in lactated Ringer's solution two-thirds in first 8 h

         Plus maintenance fluids: 1500 mL 5% dextrose in lactated Ringer's solution per square meter BSA per day

         For burns of 40–60% BSA, add 50 meq sodium bicarbonate to each liter of fluid and reduce rate by 10%

         For burns over 60% BSA, add { 40 meq sodium bicarbonate to each liter of fluid
                                       50 meq sodium chloride (12.5 mL of 15% saline) to each liter of fluid; slow rate by 20%

Day 2   Same fluids, but for burns over 40% with hyperosmolar solutions in use, monitor electrolytes at 18, 24, 30, and 36 h and q4 h thereafter. Stop hyperosmolar solution when serum sodium rises to or above 150 meq or serum osmolarity exceeds 350 millimoles. Resume 5% dextrose in lactated Ringer's original rate

Day 3   and thereafter—5% dextrose in lactated Ringer's solution at a rate sufficient to maintain urinary output of 40 mL/m² BSA per hour

---

* BSA = body surface area.

† Because colloid is now considered ineffective during the first 24 h after a burn, some authors advocate eliminating colloid from the Brooke formula.

Source: R. Howard and N. Herbold: *Clinical Nutrition,* New York: McGraw-Hill, 1978, p. 534.

The types of fluids that are ordered and the rate at which they are to flow depend on the clinical status of the child, especially vital signs, urinary output, central venous pressure, and hematocrit level. Lactated Ringer's is the solution of choice during the first 24 h. Colloids are used during the second 24-h period. Thereafter, the patient's fluid needs will vary. An accurate ongoing assessment is imperative. Although baseline data were obtained on admission, subsequent electrolytes and serum protein determinations are repeated at 4- to 8-h periods because they provide guidelines to fluid therapy. The nurse carefully records all the types of fluids the child has received, the rate of flow, and the output, which includes urine, vomitus, and aspirate.

The urine output is recorded hourly, and an indwelling Foley catheter ensures collection as well as an accurate measurement. The physician should be notified if the patient excretes less than 10 mL or more than 50 mL in an hour. Infants and toddlers eliminate about 10 to 20 mL/h. A formula which can be used to compute an approximate urinary output for a child is: 2 mL/kg per h. Also, a specific gravity reading should be monitored every 4 h.

Sepsis in burns is common. In fact, it is the leading cause of death among the thermally injured. Without its protective barrier and in the presence of immunosuppression induced by the insult, the skin is easy prey for invasion by bacteria, fungi, and viruses. Burned children are placed in isolation rooms or laminar flow units to minimize the possibility of infection. In addition to the exposed burn area, other points of entry are the respiratory and urinary tracts, as well as the infusion catheter. Strict isolation technique (gown, gloves, mask, shoe covers) and sterile procedures in wound dressings are concerted efforts to decrease contamination. However, these modes of protection necessitate strict adherence by all persons. Such precautions begin at the time of admission and continue through the formation of granulation tissue. Short courses of prophylactic penicillin may be instituted for the first 5 to 7 days of hospitalization. Routine cultures of urine, respiratory secretions, and the wound itself facilitate early diagnosis of an infection, although serial wound biopsy cultures taken every 3 to 4 days are most effective evaluators of isolation technique. The nurse should closely examine the burn when the dressing is changed because its pale appearance or a foul-smelling odor may validate bacterial infiltration.

While there are several topical agents for treating burns, the ultimate selection is the surgeon's preference. Topical Sulfamylon, used on partial or full thickness burns, is applied to the area ($\frac{1}{8}$ in thickness) three times per day and left open to the air. One disadvantage to its use is the pain which patients experience up to 1 h after its application. Gentamycin creme is especially effective in wounds infected with *Pseudomonas*. The most popular ointment in use is silver sulfadiazine (1%), which is applied directly to the burn in much the same manner as Sulfamylon. It has widespread utilization because it is effective with a variety of organisms; it is painless on application; it loosens eschar, making debridement less painful; and it does not cause side effects. Normal saline scrubs are given before the $\frac{1}{8}$-in application. In active children, loose gauze dressings may be necessary to confine the ointment to the burned area. Silver nitrate in hypotonic solution (0.5%) is a "closed" method of treating burns. It is applied to thick layers of gauze dressings which cover the wound. These bulky dressings need to be changed at 8-h intervals. In addition, they are kept saturated at all times. Hence they consume a great deal of nursing time and effort in application and maintenance. Whether applying an ointment or a dressing, it is important that the nurse is gentle and patient.

Children who have extensive burns are kept NPO, and nasogastric tubes are inserted to decrease the likelihood of vomiting and/or aspiration. The tubes are removed when peristalsis is resumed. As fluids are started by mouth, they must be given slowly and in small amounts (30 to 60 mL). Since these patients are dehydrated, they tend to gulp fluids which are offered. Most surgeons order electrolyte solutions orally to decrease the vomiting which can occur when plain water is given. When all types of fluids are tolerated, the patient progresses to a high caloric–high protein diet which is necessary for energy and tissue formation as well as to control weight loss. Protein needs are two to four times normal after a thermal injury. Encouraging a reluctant child to consume a nutritious meal may be a tremendous challenge which forces a nurse to demonstrate creativity. It is a common problem. Small, frequent feedings can be given four or five times a day. If the child cannot state preferences, parents often identify likes and dislikes. A special treat is food "brought from home." Supplementary feedings are necessary and may consist of ice cream or frappes. Consultations with a nutritionist are helpful. Multiple vitamins, including vitamin C and B complex, are started routinely. An iron preparation is ordered if an anemia has been diagnosed.

Although proper positioning is not as dramatic as

attempting to restore fluid and electrolyte balance or control infection, maintaining function of a body part is crucial to rehabilitation. The burned patient must be turned frequently and positioned properly. Joints should be maintained in a neutral position, with the shoulders abducted and knees as well as elbows in extension. Diligent nursing care can prevent severe contractions in the child with a burn. Active and passive exercises, performed frequently by the physical therapist or the nurse, maintain function. Splints can be used to sustain certain desired positions. When skin grafting is necessary, children are often immobilized in plaster casts or bulky dressings for several days postoperatively.

There are several gastrointestinal complications which can occur in the presence of a burn. Ulcerations in the duodenum or stomach, sometimes called Curling's ulcers, continue to occur in about 20 percent of the hospitalized burn patients. However, milk and antacids at 2-h intervals have reduced the incidence. Massive hemorrhages or tarry stools alert the nurse to the presence of ulcerations. Efforts are directed toward treating them conservatively. Gastric dilatation and paralytic ileus should be suspected when the nurse observes that the patient has not had any stools; the abdomen is distended, and the patient complains of nausea and pain. The passing of a nasogastric tube decompresses the stomach. No food or fluids are given to the patient with an ileus until bowel sounds return. The nasogastric tube remains in the stomach of the child with gastric dilatation until fluids are tolerated, at which time it is removed.

These children experience emotional trauma in the course of receiving this injury, whether it was accidental (house fire) or purposeful (child abuse). They must endure constant pain on movement. While age affects any young patient's response, a toddler's adjustment is usually particularly difficult. The toddler kicks, bites, screams, and hits to demonstrate anger. Fearful of losing that recently acquired autonomy, the toddler is hostile and rebellious. The child hurts and has many strange things happening that are beyond her or his understanding. She or he may be frightened by people who wear strange masks and gowns, and may strongly resent restraints, which only contribute to belligerence. It is important that parents stay with the toddler. It is also important that care is provided by a consistent, small number of people.

Play therapy is beneficial to the child who is angry and having difficulty expressing it, if the child has unimpaired dexterity. Moving the bed close to the window permits the child to watch other children participate in a variety of activities. Asking the young patient to tell a story provides an opportunity for verbalizing feelings. The rebellion, withdrawal, anger, and regression which are seen in this age group demonstrate that the child possesses effective coping mechanisms at a crucial time.

Parents are very important to a young child who has sustained such an insult; however, the entire hospitalization can be anxiety-producing for them. Initially, parental concerns focus on survival, and perhaps they are experiencing real or imagined guilt about the events surrounding the accident. Once the parents realize that the child will survive, they are concerned with disfigurement, loss of function, and incapacitation. Nurses need to spend time with these parents who need (1) an opportunity to verbalize their thoughts, (2) an occasion to put things in proper perspective, and (3) a chance to discuss the long-term rehabilitative phase of the illness. These are opportunities to teach them about the child's future development, basic health care, and safety. Getting parents involved in the care of their child relieves the helplessness they frequently experience.

These patients present a tremendous challenge to nurses who work with critically ill patients. They demand care which requires an abundance of theoretical and experiential knowledge and the acquisition of highly refined organizational skills. A great deal of time and effort is expended in the process. Nurses make a substantial investment in these children. And in spite of heroic efforts, children with extensive burns (45%+) seldom survive. This reality can have a devastatingly demoralizing effect on the staff, especially when one stops to consider that thermal-injured patients die weeks or months after admission. Nurses are human beings, too, and they experience frustration, anger, discouragement, disappointment, or failure. Time needs to be set aside, in ward conferences for example, where staff personnel can share their thoughts about a client or a situation. All too often nurses fail to support each other and to relieve their own stress levels in order to provide care to children who have incredible physical and psychosocial needs.

HEMOLYTIC UREMIC SYNDROME IN THE PRESCHOOLER

Preschoolers

This period encompasses the third, fourth, and fifth years of childhood. Great strides are made in certain tasks. The child speaks well, has bowel and bladder control, is able to eat alone, and gets partially dressed and undressed alone. Friends are boys and girls. Parallel play (side-by-side) exists at the third year, but as a child socializes with peers, eventually they will play cooperatively. However, since they are not capable of seeing another person's point of view, disagreements arise among these children.

Although the preschooler is increasingly more comfortable with newly acquired independence, a child this age needs the security, reassurance, and trusting relationships which exist at home. They help the child to master the new experiences to which he or she is exposed. Separation from the family, misconceptions about illness, and the struggle to behave in a socially acceptable manner affect the child's ability to cope successfully with the crisis of illness. During these three years, any confinement in a health care facility is a threatening and confusing event which requires perceptive creativity and patience to resolve.

Hospitalization is abandonment to this child. A preschooler may perceive a critical-care unit as an incredibly frightening place, from which there is no hope of rescue. The situation may be interpreted as punishment for real or fantasized transgressions. In an effort to regain control, the child regresses, withdraws, and sublimates. Often, the child projects frustration and anger by exhibiting negativistic behavior which creates more stress. For example, a child may refuse to eat when hungry or may ignore his or her mother when she visits, despite the fact that the child wants to be held by her. The older preschooler demonstrates tension by whining, nail-biting, or complaining of a stomach ache.

How does a nurse deal with a preschooler? Recognizing those situations which are perceived as threatening enhances the likelihood of successful interventions. Explanations which allay the child's fears should be provided at every opportunity, regardless of how minor the procedure may be. However, they should not be elaborate because too much detail confuses rather than enhances understanding at this age. There is a "best time" for teaching and in this age group, preparation should be just prior to the actual experience.

Body image, with its intactness, is of paramount importance to the preschooler. Intrusive procedures mean much more than being hurt. They threaten the entire sense of self. A child is unable to comprehend that a wound will heal. Constant reassurance and repeated explanations must be given, but accepting that the child's fears exist is essential.

The preschooler, intent on resolving Oedipus/Elec-tra fantasies and developing a sexual role, has critical concerns which focus on the genitalia. Modesty is just beginning. Therefore, a urinary catheterization, peritoneal dialysis, or rectal temperatures pose threats of a nature different from actual pain or discomfort. It is important for the nurse to (1) identify the individual child's developmental level, (2) learn different methodologies which help the child deal with the complexities of hospitalization, and (3) provide interventions which meet intricate psychosocial needs of the child.

Parents of preschoolers can be utilized as historians and as providers of care. They are especially valuable in preserving familiar routines which are important to the child. In order to maximize parental support, nurses need to help them anticipate and understand the reasons for rejection and negativism which are so important to the resiliency children demonstrate.

Pathophysiology

There are many renal and hematologic diseases of childhood which are chronic in nature, and while problems such as nephrotic syndrome or various anemias have acute phases, for the most part treatment occurs on a pediatric unit. However, in acute renal failure or in the presence of bleeding disorders, children may be admitted to critical-care units where they can be managed more effectively. Hemolytic uremic syndrome (HUS) demonstrates a myriad of common renal and hemopoietic problems which can arise.

The following triad of pathologic features characterize HUS; hemolytic anemia with fragmented cells, thrombocytopenia, and acute nephropathy. See Table 34-3 for a thorough review of findings. Its etiology is unknown, albeit endotoxin-induced causes (viral/bacterial organisms), drugs, and other chemical agents as well as genetic factors, especially immunoglobulin deficiencies, are suspected.

Both males and females are affected, and these children are under 5 years of age. The acute illness is abrupt in onset, and it usually follows an episode of gastroenteritis or upper respiratory infection which appears to have been resolved 10 to 14 days earlier. The mortality rate of this disease is about 30 percent.

Initial symptoms include pallor, purpura, and oliguria or anuria, with generalized edema. Neurologic deterioration ranges from hyperirritability and lethargy to seizures, coma, or hemiparesis. On admission, the child is febrile, tachypneic, tachycardic, and hypertensive. Splenohepatomegaly is present and there may be evidence of circulatory congestion (pulmonary edema) as well as congestive heart failure. The child is acutely, critically ill. Blood work reveals a high urea nitrogen, hyperkalemia, hyperphosphatemia, metabolic acidosis, and oliguria.

The severity of the disease varies directly with the degree of renal damage. In its mild form, anuria never exceeds a 24-h period; however, in its life-threatening form there is increasing oliguria, azotemia, a complete renal shutdown, severe hypertension, and congestive heart failure. The former lasts 1 to 2 weeks with a steady improvement over 1 to 2 months. In severe cases, however, there is extensive kidney damage, sustained oliguria, and a persistent hemolysis which leads to a more severe anemia as well as progressive renal failure with hypertension (see Table 34-3).

Medical Treatment

Treating the child with HUS is mainly supportive, and although many approaches to a specific cure have been utilized, none have been successful. The goal is to control renal failure, improve hematologic findings, and resolve the neurologic manifestations. While there is evidence that early peritoneal dialysis is effective, investigators are unable to determine whether a noxious substance is removed or there is spontaneous recovery. Certainly dialysis corrects the electrolyte disturbances, hypertension, and uremia.

Severe anemias are treated with small transfusions which are administered cautiously in view of the oliguria, circulatory congestion, and severe hypertension. Usually these fresh-packed red cells are given in conjunction with dialysis, thereby decreasing the possibility of a circulatory overload. Platelets are given for the thrombocytopenia.

After the acute phase of the illness has passed, a renal biopsy is performed to confirm the diagnosis, identify the extent of kidney impairment, and hence determine the prognosis. In the severe form, children may die from hyperkalemia, the hypertensive encephalopathy, or heart failure. The prognosis is poor when anuria is present for 3 days or more. If the disease progresses significantly, then dialysis becomes a long-term process, and transplantation may eventually be necessary to sustain life.

Nursing Management

While treatment is primarily supportive, the variety of procedures performed on this frightened child, who is irritable as a result of the disease, can have a devastating effect. Explanations are essential and they should be given immediately prior to carrying out the procedure being done. Obtaining a preschooler's cooperation is not an easy task. Parents are encouraged to stay because they can be especially helpful in calming the child; however, they need to be fully informed of each aspect of treatment so that they may be more effective.

Baseline information is collected, electrolytes are monitored closely, and vital signs are recorded hourly, as are levels of consciousness. The patient is observed for any signs of deterioration, i.e., renal shutdown, severe hypertension, or congestive heart failure. These clinical manifestations are demonstrative of a life-threatening situation in which there is an obvious, continual progression of the syndrome.

During dialysis, major nursing responsibilities demand extensive theoretical and technical knowledge, outstanding organizational abilities, and refined observational skills. The patient is first asked to void prior to the procedure to decrease the risk of perforating the bladder; then the patient is medicated with either chlorpromazine (Thorazine) or meperidine (Demerol). The dosage depends on the patient's age, weight, and overall status. Once the skin is prepped, the incision made, and the stylet-catheter inserted, tubing is connected and administration of dialysate is started. It is beneficial to warm the dialysis solution from 20 to 37°C (68 to 98.6°F), because it causes peritoneal blood vessels to dilate, thereby improving urea clearance by 35 percent. The standard solution given is 1.5 g of glucose per 100 mL, and it is usually prescribed to run at about 50 mL per kg per cycle. The dialysate runs into the peritoneal cavity over a 10- to 15-min period, and after it is allowed to equilibrate for 30 to 45 min, it is drained off in 15 to 20 min. Fluid withdrawn from the abdominal cavity should equal or exceed the amount administered. (It is absolutely imperative for the nurse to be *precise* in recording every single aspect of the complete cycle.) Fluid administration sets are changed every five or six cycles, and the dialysis fluid is cultured at 8-h intervals. The patient is constantly assessed to determine the response to the treatment. This procedure continues for 24 to 48 h, and cessation depends on falling urea and creatinine levels as well as restoration of normal sodium, potassium, chloride, and bicarbonate levels.

When dialysis is started, the patient's vital signs are monitored at 15-min intervals for the first 2 h; then they are monitored hourly. The fluid drained off initially

TABLE 34-3
Systemic Responses to HUS

Affected system	Pathologic mechanism	Pathologic/laboratory findings	Clinical symptomatology
Renal	Not known Possible immunologic or endotoxic factors involved	Thickening of capillary walls Often total occlusion of the renal capillaries Glomerular thrombosis often in massive proportions Segmental glomerular necrosis Extraglomerular changes: interstitial inflammation, edema, tubular atrophy Elevated urine levels of protein, red and white blood cells, casts Azotemia Elevated serum levels of blood urea nitrogen, creatinine, uric acid, potassium, phosphorus, hydrogen ion, lipids (triglyceride, cholesterol, phospholipid), amylase Low serum levels of calcium, bicarbonate, albumin	Oliguria, anuria, edema, hypertension, congestive heart failure
Hemopoietic Hemolytic anemia	Not proven Clinical evidence that red blood cells are damaged by fibrin strands of microvessels located in glomerular endothelium. Damaged red cells are then destroyed by liver and spleen	Red cell fragmentation—schizocytes Reticulocytosis Nucleated red cells in peripheral blood Erythroid hyperplasia Thrombocytopenia Disseminated intravascular coagulopathy possible	Clinical bleeding usually limited to the gastrointestinal tract, skin, retina, and occasionally central nervous system bleeding Hepatosplenomegaly
Thrombocytopenia	Same as above May also be due to platelet consumption occurring with disseminated intravascular coagulopathy or platelet aggregation in kidney during a local intravascular coagulopathy or platelet adhesion to damaged glomerular capillary endothelium	Anisocytosis Elevated white blood count Low hemoglobin Low platelets (may remain normal or fluctuate) Coombs' test negative Polymorphonuclear leukocytosis	
Central nervous system	Probably due to hypertension, volume overload, hyponatremia, acid-base changes, and/or hypocalcemia Intracranial bleeding secondary to anticoagulation less common	Hypoxic or ischemic lesions Cerebral edema	Convulsions Lethargy, coma Hemiparesis Aphasia Decerebrate spasms

Source: B. S. Kaplan, P. D. Thompson, and J. P. De Chadarevian, The hemolytic uremia syndrome, *Pediatr Clin North Am* 23:761–777, 1976; and C. F. Piel, and R. H. Phibbs, The hemolytic-uremic syndrome, *Pediatr Clin North Am* 13:295–314, 1966.

may be pink because of trauma to tissue during insertion of a stylet-catheter; however, once outflow is established, it should be clear and straw-colored.

Checking the tubing is a vital nursing action which needs to be done frequently because kinking is an ever-present risk. Fluid is removed from the peritoneal cavity by gravity drainage; therefore, the bed should be at its maximum height. If any difficulty is experienced in outflow, some effective interventions are changing the child's position, elevating the head of the bed, and flexing the patient's knees. Since thrombocytopenia is present, the patient should be handled very gently. The head of the bed may need to be raised slightly to prevent the diaphragmatic discomfort which occurs as a result of increased intra-abdominal pressure.

Routine comfort measures such as positioning and skin and mouth care are performed frequently. Coughing and deep breathing exercises are necessary at 4-h intervals. Since the preschooler may pull out the catheter, hands may need to be restrained. If restraints are used, it is necessary to remove them, one at a time, every 3 to 4 h to exercise the upper extremities.

Heparin (1000 U) is usually added to the first three bottles of solution administered to prevent clot formation at the tip of the catheter. Whether potassium is added or not depends on the preschooler's serum potassium level.

Since hyponatremia can occur in the presence of oliguria and the administration of continuous hypotonic solution, fluids are restricted to enable the sodium to return to a normal level. Ice chips can be offered to the child who understands that they are to be sucked on—not swallowed whole. Lollipops may also be provided.

During dialysis the child may be unable to eat. Even if it is possible, in all probability the child will be unable to consume the amount of protein and calories essential for normal growth. Any sodium restrictions made will depend on the patient's hydration and blood pressure. In essence, the dietary intake is highly individualized and dependent on protein catabolism and fluid and electrolyte balance. Usually these children need to alter their intake of water, protein, potassium, sodium, phosphorus, and calcium. Nutritionists are especially helpful in designing meals which appeal to these children. In discharge planning, parents find these team members extremely valuable resources.

There are some complications of dialysis which always need to be considered during the procedure. Fluid overload is a real problem in view of the circulatory congestion which is characteristic of the syndrome. Therefore, the patient must be observed for signs of pulmonary edema. Also, the rapid loss of body fluids can result in hypovolemia, with the development of tachycardia, hypotension, and ultimately, shock. Punctures of the bowel or bladder can occur with the insertion of the stylet-catheter, so particular attention is given to the color of the fluid being drained from the abdominal cavity. Peritonitis is a persistent threat, and leakage around the catheter, as well as any other indication of an infection, should be investigated immediately.

Once the renal dysfunction stabilizes and hemodialysis becomes a frequent, long-term procedure, there are some effects which take their toll on these children. The side effects of some antihypertensive medications can cause a depression. In addition, children with chronic renal pathology are moody and irritable. Many restrictions of the medical regimen may cause the child to rebel or to refuse to take medications or the diet which has been prescribed.

While these treatments offer survival, the child is affected by a number of other variables. The child must cope with dependence-independence conflicts, the demands of the dialysis itself, multiple losses, and restricted school attendance, and hence inconsistent peer interactions. With a shunt or fistula, the child is not able to participate in those normal childhood activities which enhance development.

Parents may feel guilty about what the child must endure each week in order to live. They also may be emotionally drained by the demands of caring for the child. There are innumerable trips to the dialysis center, arrangements to make for siblings, and work days missed. Realistically, it may be a financial burden which causes additional anxiety. In the presence of these circumstances, it is essential that channels of communication are effective between and among interdisciplinary team members (nephrologist, social worker, nutritionist, play therapist, and nurse). They can then share observations and concerns so that everyone is always informed of the child's/family's overall status.

Although transplantation may be ultimately necessary, the interim period should focus on educating both child and parents about all aspects of this long-term problem. Compliance is critical to the quality of life which is realized. There are no options. Dialysis must be continued, medications must be taken as prescribed, and a highly individualized diet must be rigorously adhered to if renal function is to be maintained and the hypertension is to be controlled.

NEUROLOGIC DISORDERS IN THE SCHOOL-AGE CHILD

Psychosocial Aspects

The school-age period, which begins at the sixth year and continues to the twelfth year, is a stage of rapid change, especially in the areas of physical, psychosocial, and cognitive development. In starting school, the child has many new experiences, is exposed to additional adult role models, and meets many new children, i.e., the peer group, who become increasingly important as these middle childhood years are experienced. According to Erickson, it is the stage of industry versus inferiority. On the one hand, it is a time when the child can enjoy success in mastering certain tasks. On the other hand, the child may become discouraged while attempting to reach certain goals and perceive himself or herself as inadequate or inferior.

At 6 years of age, a child plays with both boys and girls; however, by the eighth year there is an important "best" friend and playmates are children of the same sex only. As the child moves through the ninth and tenth years, the peer group influences psychosocial development by (1) reinforcing appropriate sex role behavior; (2) teaching fair play, cooperation, and compromise; (3) assisting the child in the acquisition of values and attitudes different from those of the family; and (4) aiding in the development of a self-concept and facilitating autonomy. Acceptance by peers is crucial.

The greatest progress during these 6 years is in cognition. Although six-year-olds use language and memory (with an increasing comprehension of the past, present, and future), they are not capable of understanding basic relationships between and among phenomena. They are egocentric and focus on one aspect of the situation, which demonstrates illogical thinking. Between the ages of seven and eleven, the child is better able to understand relationships between events and objects. The child is capable of internalizing, mastering scholastic efforts (math), classifying, and utilizing logic in drawing conclusions. Classroom and peer success and failures affect self-esteem, self-confidence, and the child's outlook on life. These children are better able to deal with a hospitalization than those who are younger, primarily because of advancements made in cognitive development.

In the hospital these children have concerns about modesty and privacy, and therefore six- and seven-year-olds are reluctant to be examined, to discuss their symptoms, or to have rectal temperatures taken. At nine or ten, they are stoic during these procedures, despite the fact they do not like them.

Young school-age children also object to procedures such as having blood drawn or a gastric tube inserted. Losing self-control represents regression and a feeling of inferiority. Nurses need to identify and accept such feelings. Sitting down with the young patient and explaining the reason for these tests usually results in cooperation. Many of the older school-age children have had biology, and they have a basic knowledge of body organs and their functions. Knowing what is to be done and why is significant to them, in view of their cognitive progress.

On occasion, the nurse sees a school-age child who appears to be demonstrating especially "mature" behavior; however, the child may be suppressing the entire experience by being docile in response to what is happening. Procedures are endured without comment, and conversations extend to "yes" or "no." A child perceiving the confinement as punishment may deny symptoms, too. It is crucial to spend time with the child, to explain, to demonstrate, and to anticipate questions the child may be afraid to ask.

In order to cultivate mutual respect, a nurse must be honest with a school-age child. The child needs to know about the discomforts which may be experienced and the limitations which may be imposed as a result of the treatment or the surgery.

Neurologic dysfunction can be devastating to the school-age child who is becoming a more autonomous person and developing rapidly both psychosocially and cognitively. Disorders which affect the nervous system can result in varying degrees of residual damage which may seriously impair the young child's subsequent development. Both brain tumors and Reye's syndrome affect children in middle childhood more so than any other age group; hence they have been selected for discussion.

CNS Evaluation: Level of Consciousness and Intracranial Pressure

The techniques utilized in the neurologic evaluation of a child are similar to those used to assess neurologic status in the adult. However, evidence of CNS dysfunction appears in signs which are markedly different because they depend on the child's physical and developmental stage. A frightened, shy, or angry young child does not comprehend the importance of cooperating during neurologic testing. It is essential to establish a good relationship, to test functioning through game play, and to consider the observations of parents. Such data are vital to a pediatric assessment. In addition, an evaluator must have a theoretical base of developmental knowledge in order to determine the appropriateness of the child's responses. Although each child progresses at his own pace, comparing his performance to established criteria such as those in the Denver Developmental Screening Test substantiates one's observations.

Determining the level of consciousness is one of the most important neurologic vital signs of cerebral function. While it is true that alterations follow an adult pattern and they can be described by the same staging sequence in children as in adults, it is there that similarities end. In evaluating children, a nurse relies more heavily on motor functioning than verbal cues, and hence developmental landmarks are especially significant. Infants who do not recognize their mothers may be disoriented. Lacking the ability to perceive time accurately, preschoolers' orientation to person and place is a significant observation.

A young child is easily overwhelmed by new surroundings and numbers of people, and an evaluation by the same person is especially important because it ensures greater cooperation, provides a consistent basis for comparison, and avoids a mistaken interpretation that a child is confused when in reality this is not the case. Irritability can be attributed to the child's fear in a strange environment. Whether a child is hyperactive can be determined by knowing the usual behavior of that child; this information should have been obtained from the parents. Likewise, the adolescent who appears to be lethargic in an ICU may simply be unable to meet the tremendous sleep requirement in those surroundings.

The physiologic causes and clinical symptoms of increased intracranial pressure (IICP) in the older child parallel those of the adult. However, the infant with an immature nervous system and open cranial sutures does not develop signs of IICP as rapidly. Its presence is demonstrated in different ways. In the infant with IICP, the nurse finds dilated scalp veins; a shrill, high-pitched, or a weak cry; nystagmus; and a tense, bulging anterior fontanel. While projectile vomiting is a manifestation of increasing pressure, one must be cautious not to confuse it with the force vomiting which occurs in severe gastrosophageal reflux or pyloric stenosis. With an IICP, projectile vomiting which occurs in severe gastrolesophageal been taken, especially when the infant is in an upright position.

Direct monitoring of the epidural, subdural, or subarachnoid spaces ensures an accurate and rapid identification of rising pressures. Although the technique used is the same as that used in adults, there is no consensus regarding the pressure readings which require treatment. Usually pressures higher than 15 to 20 mmHg are treated. In infants, noninvasive monitoring can be done by placing a sensor probe over the open anterior fontanel. Normal pressures and the significance of fluctuations in infants have not as yet been determined. Treatment of IICP includes fluid restriction, osmotic diuretics, corticosteroids, and/or removal of the underlying cause.

Brain Tumor

Medical-Surgical Management

Next to leukemia, tumors of the central nervous system (CNS) are the most common types of malignant lesions in childhood. The highest incidence of brain tumors occurs between the fifth and the ninth year of life. Since more than two-thirds of these neoplasms are located in the posterior fossa, increased intracranial pressure develops early.

The clinical manifestations which a child demonstrates typify the growth of an expanding mass within the confines of the cranium. Projectile vomiting, especially after rising and eating breakfast, and complaints of a headache are common. There are a variety of focal neurologic deficits which include impaired vision, nystagmus, ataxia, and seizure activity.

It is impossible to separate the child from age and stage of development. In pediatrics, some of the symptoms are difficult to evaluate because of wide variations in development. It is important to differentiate between symptoms related to underlying pathology and behavior which is generally associated with the child's age group. Increased intracranial pressure is difficult to detect in an infant whose suture lines have not fused. The growing lesion causes an increase in this patient's head circumference. Vomiting in a school-age child can be attributed to a school phobia or some other difficulty in the classroom setting. In the presence of a slow-growing tumor which causes a gait disturbance, the child can automatically compensate, thereby making an identification difficult.

While there are many kinds of brain tumors, five are seen most frequently in children. A *cerebellar astrocytoma* is a slow-growing mass which causes IICP, hypotonia, diminished reflexes, focal disturbances, papilledema, nystagmus, optic atrophy, and blindness. Total removal is possible. The *medulloblastoma*, also located in the cerebellum, is more acute, with cellular proliferation more rapid. These patients demonstrate an unsteady gait, anorexia, vomiting, and early morning headaches. It is difficult to remove this entire lesion, and consequently, survival does not exceed approximately 3 years. A *brainstem glioma* is responsible for multiple nerve palsies and a wide variety of ataxias in children. It is least amenable to any type of therapy. An *ependymoma* is usually found in the first, second, or most often, in the fourth ventricle of the brain. These children complain of nausea, vomiting, headache, and ataxia. While it is not usually possible to remove the entire tumor because of its attachment to the floor of the ventricle, surgery allows the cerebrospinal fluid to circulate without obstruction. *Craniopharyngioma*, whose site is near the pituitary gland, is responsible for a number of hypothalamic or pituitary dysfunctions. While total excision may not be possible, the surgery is effective.

Although many neoplasms can only be treated palliatively, slow-growing lesions that cannot be removed permit a prolonged survival without severe neurologic deficits. Treatment for the described lesions usually includes one or a combination of the following: surgery, irradiation, chemotherapy, and drugs administered to reduce IICP.

Nursing Management

Nursing management of a child after a craniotomy focuses on an accurate assessment of the patient's neurologic status, vital signs, prevention and detection of infection, and close observation for bleeding, as well as signs of shock. Evidence of cerebral edema and IICP is identified by frequent evaluations of deep tendon, Babinski reflex, and pupillary reflex, as well as ascertaining the child's level of consciousness. The patient's serum osmolality is monitored closely. Maintaining it at a level higher than the intracelluar osmolality causes brain cell dehydration. The resultant, precipitous drop in intracranial pressure can be followed by a rebound effect. When the decreased intracranial pressure facilitates entry of urea into the brain cells, there is a sudden rise in the intracranial pressure.

A patient's head is elevated to 30° to decrease the intracranial pressure, operative edema, and pain. Vigorous coughing and suctioning are avoided for the same reason. Restraints should not be used after surgery, because as the child struggles against them, intracranial pressure may rise.

Constipation is a problem which occurs as a result of vagal damage and/or immobility. Since straining causes a rise in intracranial pressure, the cause needs to be treated. When corneal reflexes are absent, a lubricating eye medication, such as methyl cellulose, should be used to prevent ulcerations from developing. The ability of a child to demonstrate the gag and swallow reflexes must be evaluated early because of the possibility of transient cranial nerve palsies. If these reflexes are absent, the nurse may need to suction the oronasopharyngeal areas and position the child so there is no danger of aspiration. Nasogastric feedings may be necessary until these reflexes return.

Neural damage, irritability from surgical manipulation, residual effects of preoperative pressure, and/or the removal of a hemispheric mass often leads to convulsive activity. Seizure precautions are instituted, and anticonvulsive drugs are administered.

Blood loss during or after these neurosurgical procedures may be extensive and sudden. Drainage from the operative site should be observed closely for color, amount, and odor. After simple craniotomies, the drainage becomes serosanguinous quickly. However, after burr holes or the removal of skull plates, bloody drainage is greater and more pronounced. Dressings should be reinforced whenever possible.

Wound hematomas, which occur frequently, are closely associated with the removal of posterior fossa masses. Lumbar or ventricular drainage of cerebrospinal fluid must be performed immediately to prevent compression of the brainstem.

Hemorrhage signifies the development of a Cushing-Rotikansky ulceration of the stomach or duodenum. It is a severe complication which can follow posterior fossa neurosurgery. Constant alkalinization of the upper gastrointestinal tract is routine therapy, along with blood replacement and other supportive measures.

Formation of edema in the head, neck, and intracranial spaces can interfere with both swallowing and respirations. A nurse needs to make astute observations of respiratory compromise, because a tracheostomy may be necessary.

Hyperthermia frequently occurs following surgical procedures which involve the fourth ventricle. However, it can also be associated with an aseptic meningitis or an infection of the operative site. Therefore the patient needs to be observed for any unusual meningeal signs. The hyperthermia, which is of hypothalamic origin, is difficult to correct with the use of antipyretics. Utilizing a hypothermia blanket is a more successful intervention.

A craniopharyngioma, which involves the pituitary gland, can result in the development of diabetes insipidus. Sodium, potassium, chloride, pH, hematocrit, carbon dioxide, and weight must be monitored at least daily. Treatment consists of fluid regulation and administering pitressin tannate or Desamino-8-d-arginine-vasopressin (DDAVP).

Whenever the postcraniotomy patient's position is changed, it is most important to support the head. The patient is not turned to the operative site. Range of motion exercises are performed to maintain and strengthen muscular ability, especially if the child has a prolonged, immobile postoperative course.

Metastatic tumors are treated with chemotherapeutic agents, intravenously, orally, or intrathecally. Radiation is usually started after the acute postoperative phase, when the patient has left the ICU.

The diagnosis is usually difficult for parents to accept. It is imperative that opportunities be provided for them to sit down, unhurriedly, to discuss their thoughts and feelings about a situation which will change the lives of this family unit. They must be included in the nursing care plan which is developed. A nurse should stress the need for fostering independence in the child, as difficult as it might be at times, in order to maximize effective functioning.

Reye's Syndrome

Pathophysiology

Those congenital and acquired encephalopathies which are associated with trauma, infection, or toxic agents often result in such diffuse symptoms that treatments are designed to provide supportive care. Neurologic sequelae are slow or impossible to reverse. One of these neuropathies, Reye's syndrome, was first described in 1963. A greater understanding of the physiologic mechanisms present in this infectious process has facilitated an earlier, more accurate diagnosis. In addition, the aggressive therapy has changed a 50 to 100 percent mortality to 70 to 80 percent survival rate.

Reye's syndrome is a disease which affects six- to eleven-year-old children most frequently. Its etiology is unknown; however, some suggested causes include viral agents such as type B influenza, varicella, coxsackie, adenovirus, and echovirus. Toxic agents, such as halogenated hydrocarbons and isopropyl alcohol, and a genetic predisposition are also possible factors. In some instances this disease is self-limiting, with the patient improving before neurologic deterioration occurs. More often, the course progresses rapidly to its fulminating and devastating potential.

Characteristic findings include severe encepha-lopathy, cerebral edema and a fatty infiltration of the viscera, especially the liver. The child's history reveals a state of generally good health, with the exception of a flu-like illness several days prior to the onset of various symptoms. Invariably there is the onset of protracted vomiting and a sudden alteration in the level of consciousness which includes extreme agitation, delirium, lethargy, stupor, or coma. Upon initial examination, the child is dehydrated and slightly tachycardic; however, both temperature and blood pressure are normal. There are hyperactive reflexes, a lowered sensorium, and possible pupillary changes. While the electroencephalogram (EEG) has a markedly abnormal pattern which is characteristic of Reye's syndrome, it is not diagnostic of the disease. Although the serum oxaloacetic transaminase (SGOT) is elevated, there is no jaundice or hepatomegaly. The prothrombin time is prolonged, and hyperaminoaciduria as well as an elevated blood urea nitrogen is present. High serum ammonia levels are found early in the illness, and a cerebral uptake of ammonia may account for the hyperventilation. The panlobular microvesicular stratosis found on a liver biopsy is the only purely diagnostic confirmation of this disease.

It is thought that the physiologic mechanisms present in Reye's syndrome are the result of a metabolic crisis initiated by a viral or viral-toxin interaction. The immobilization of fatty acids and intracellular accumulation of lipids follows. Enzyme inhibition leads to the failure of the detoxification pathways and the possible release of abnormal metabolites which act as toxins themselves. As a result, the liver and kidneys are seriously affected by the lipid accumulation. Hypoglycemia ensues when the liver becomes depleted of its glycogen stores. Actual liver cell damage causes the elevated SGOT and coagulopathy. Fatty degeneration of renal tubules and glomeruli produce an azotemia which rapidly progresses to renal failure with its severe electrolyte disturbances. Since ammonia excretion is impaired because of hepatic and renal damage, these levels continue to rise. However, once the fulminating course of this pathophysiologic process is halted, visceral damage is reversible. Cerebral edema causing transtentorial, uncal, and tonsillar herniation is the prime factor in the mortality rate associated with Reye's syndrome.

Treatment and Management

Treatment is based on the physiologic changes which occur. It is designed to arrest hepatic failure and prevent neurologic damage. Urine glucose levels are monitored carefully, and hypertonic glucose is given to correct hypoglycemia. Fluids and electrolytes are administered according to the degree of dehydration and the presence of metabolic acidosis. Potassium and sodium retention, caused by the excessive secretion of aldosterone in response to both stress and dehydration, is also monitored. Persistent, low phosphate levels must be treated.

The child must be weighed twice a day. Intake and output recordings must be precise as they are utilized in order to calculate the necessary fluid needs. The coagulopathies and possible hypovolemic shock are treated with vitamin K, fresh frozen plasma, platelets, or whole blood. All outputs are tested for blood, and prolonged oozing after invasive procedures should be noted. Since ammonia is an end product of the bacterial digestion of protein, neomycin may be given in an attempt to sterilize the bowel and hence lower the ammonia level. An exchange transfusion or total body washout is also prescribed to remove the ammonia, provide essential coagulation factors, provide new albumin binding sites for an exogenous toxin, and remove metabolites which may be responsible for the encephalitis.

Controlling the intracranial pressure (ICP) is crucial. Some physicians who believe the encephalopathy to be vascular in origin treat the child with dexamethasone, while others who consider it cytotoxic do not. Fluids are restricted to alleviate the cerebral edema. Direct ICP monitoring is done to determine early rises in ICP, especially when osmotic diuretics are used.

Patients are usually ventilated mechanically so that the PA_{CO_2} can be kept between 20 and 25 mmHg in an effort to decrease the ICP. Positive end expiratory pressure levels and the body temperature must be closely observed. An elevation in either measurement increases blood flow, which increases ICP. Arterial blood pressures are monitored to permit a calculation of the cerebral perfusion pressure (CPP), (mean arterial blood pressure minus intracranial pressure). Cerebral blood flow falls when the CPP falls. A CPP of less than 30 mmHg results in neuronal hypoxia and cell death. A frequent, thorough assessment of the child's neurologic status is critical because neurologic deterioration occurs very rapidly in Reye's syndrome. A patient's level of consciousness, deep tendon and Babinski reflexes, extraocular movements, and pupillary responses are essential inclusions in the ongoing evaluation.

Research is being conducted in a number of medical centers to determine the etiology of Reye's syndrome, to improve treatment modalities, and to prevent this disease. Accurate documentation of a patient's status and responses to the treatment provided are crucial to the research and to individual patients. Observing for the unexpected is an integral component of the nursing care which is provided to children with this critical and puzzling disease.

THE ADOLESCENT WITH OSTEOGENIC SARCOMA

The Adolescent

Adolescence is a most trying stage of development for the teenager and his or her parents. It is a period in which the youth questions his or her identity, strives for independence, and establishes meaningful relationships with peers. A great deal of thought is given to the future, to professional or vocational aspirations, marriage, and so on. Also, it is a time for adjusting to innumerable physical changes which reflect both increased hormonal activity and sexual maturation. These psychosocial and biologic alterations are difficult for the adolescent to comprehend. Certainly all these variables contribute to those unexplained, tearful outbursts, impulsive acts, or outright antagonisms which strain parent-offspring relationships. The teenager tests limits which have been established and demonstrates unacceptable behaviors in an effort to display an ambivalence to approaching maturity and adulthood. The child who had parental attention, love, comfort, and security, as an adolescent, now asks whether that love prevails, in spite of arrogant and infuriating behavior.

Peer group acceptance and approval are important components of a teenager's socialization. By virtue of membership in the group, there is an increased emphasis on conforming, on accomplishing, on physical attractiveness, and on physical activity, all of which are essential to the development of one's self-esteem and one's social worth.

The diagnosis of osteogenic sarcoma takes its toll on the adolescent who must confront it and interpret its meaning to friends. While the amputation of a limb is devastating to anyone, its implications are awesome for the adolescent who is struggling to "become" a mature person. While acceptance by peers is an imperative, the loss of a limb affects those relationships which were established previously. He or she will be "different" from others in the group after the amputation, and this difference is visible. The loss cannot be disguised by clothing, and a prosthesis will not be available immediately. Surgical intervention affects body image, alters self-concept, and influences his or her role within the group. The youth is forced to cope with and adapt to different responses elicited from social contacts. The alteration significantly limits activities; however, the teenager may date or continue with other school-related tasks. Friends so crucial to social existence may withdraw as a result of their own inability to cope with either the disease process and/or the amputation. Hence, these important role relationships are altered and may precipitate additional demonstrations of frustration, anger, and futility in the young client.

At the present time the prognosis for osteosarcoma is poor, and the mortality rate is high. So, in addition to coping with the loss of a limb, the adolescent is asked to face a shortened life, to give up dreams of the future, and to sever relationships with friends who have become so significant. It is reasonable to expect bitterness, anger, and resentment. It is acceptable for this patient to express these feelings to those around— especially to parents and health care providers.

By 9 or 10 years of age, children understand that death is inevitable and permanent. Personally they cannot comprehend it as an event which occurs to individuals close to them. Therefore, a friend's dying can be an overwhelming experience for an adolescent. Withdrawal of strong support systems, such as friends, contributes substantially to the social isolation a client experiences. Both the client and peer group members need to verbalize and explore their feelings about the diagnosis, the amputation, and death, if normalcy is to be maintained.

The course of treatment is a strong one. Depending on the extent of infiltration, chemotherapy is initiated following surgery. There are repeated hospitalizations, with exacerbations and remissions, as well as alopecia, the consequence of using certain drugs. The adolescent and the family live with an uncertain future, an unknown which contributes to the existent anxiety and apprehension. The authors believe that the teenager should be fully informed of the disease and its treatment and should have an opportunity to participate in the decision making that will affect him or her. It is difficult for adults to discuss the disease, its statistics, or the prognosis with the adolescent. On the one hand, parents tend to shield and protect the adolescent from discussing the topic, and on the other hand, health care providers are committed to saving lives.

Certainly, whether adolescents are told of their diagnosis or not depends on parental wishes regarding that disclosure, and these wishes need to be respected. By the same token, honesty regarding future outcomes is essential for the development of realistic goals.

Pathophysiology

Osteogenic sarcoma, also known as osteosarcoma, is the most malignant of primary bone tumors. Arising from osteoblasts, the tumor develops in the metaphyseal region of the bone, an area of rapid growth due to the calcification of bone which occurs in that site. The age group most commonly affected includes individuals from 10 years through 25 years of age, and it occurs twice as often in males as it does in females.

The sites most commonly involved include the lower end of the femur and the upper portion of the tibia in more than 50 percent of the cases. The second most commonly affected regions are the upper ends of the humerus and femur.

As the tumor grows in the medullary cavity of a long bone, the cellular proliferation penetrates the cortex and pushes up on the periosteum. Local pain, intermittent at first, becomes constant and severe within weeks. Some children demonstrate a limp. Trauma, especially in the physically active school-age child or adolescent, may precipitate the pain. As the mass grows, a swelling may be palpated. Some clients sustain a pathologic fracture through the lesion, and a diagnosis is made at that time. Many times, when seen for the first time, the patient does not appear to be ill. In those situations where pulmonary metastasis has occurred, the general health status is poor.

Confirmation is made by radiologic studies and biopsy. Hematologic tests may confirm an anemia, and a serum alkaline phosphatase is elevated in some but not all instances. In performing the biopsy, a coagulation diathermy knife is used to decrease spillage of neoplastic cells into the vascular bed for seeding in other areas of the body.

Amputation is the treatment of choice in most instances, and the level at which the amputation is to occur depends on the site. Most orthopedic surgeons remove the limb at a level proximal to the involved bone. While early detection and treatment is crucial, an important consideration related to the prognosis is the position of the tumor. The closer it is to the trunk, the higher the mortality rate. Another variable which affects both treatment and prognosis is pulmonary infiltration. Albeit limb removal is completed in the presence of lung metastasis, the goal of the surgery is to relieve the severe pain—not to alter the course of the tumor.

Chemotherapy is begun after surgery and continued for 1 to 2 years. The agents most often selected are methotrexate and Adriamycin, vincristine, and cyclophosphamide separately or in combination with the methotrexate. The mortality rate is about 95 percent, and while early detection and vigorous treatment are important, minimal manipulation of the affected limb prior to confirmation of the diagnosis may also affect the eventual outcome.

Medical/Surgical Management

The management of a patient with osteogenic sarcoma is directed toward the multiple goals of cure, palliation, physical and emotional comfort, and research designed to create more positive, curative regimens. At present, medical management of osteogenic sarcoma usually employs a multidisciplinary approach which includes chemotherapy, ablative surgery, and radiotherapy. Diagnosis of the primary lesion is initially made using the tools of nuclear medicine: (1) bone scan and (2) C.T. scan. The extent of the lesion can be further investigated radiologically with tomograms. A biopsy of the lesion confirms the diagnosis. The treatment regimen is highly individualized and varies with the cancer therapy research protocols of the institutions involved. To date no one approach has provided results which would indicate its singular implementation. In addition, osteogenic sarcoma is considered to be a systemic disease. Therefore, a particular patient's symptoms dictate one mode of treatment or a combination of modalities which are most appropriate for that patient.

The use of chemotherapeutic agents certainly has an established role in the management of patients with osteosarcoma. Alone they are not curative; however, they prolong life. In combination with other treatment modalities, they are a part of a regimen aimed at achieving a cure. The primary tumor of osteogenic sarcoma is a continual source of metastases. Chemotherapeutic agent utilization is the major method of destroying cells of this disseminated disease which takes place before the diagnosis and continues to act even after the tumor has been resected. Candidly known as "poisons," these drugs affect healthy systems with a potency similar to the effect they have on cancerous cells. Therefore, medical management must incorporate a method of monitoring and minimizing the toxicity of these drugs while achieving maximum destruction of metastatic disease. High-dose methotrexate therapy is currently showing promise as an adjuvant therapy for osteogenic sarcoma. In combination with Adriamycin and Citrovorum Factor, it is capable of decreasing the size of the tumor, and occasionally it has eradicated small, primary tumors in a period of 12 to 14 months. However, methotrexate is excreted through the kidneys, and in an acidic environment it could precipitate in the renal tubules causing an acute tubular necrosis (ATN). Baseline and serial values of CBC, creatinine, BUN, and liver function studies must be monitored closely in order to alert the physician of the pending, intolerable toxic drug effect. A basic substance, such as sodium bicarbonate, and adequate hydration are prescribed during methotrexate therapy to prevent the necrosis. In addition, methotrexate interferes with surgical healing, and its utilization must be balanced with the patient's wound status. Vincristine, an alkaloid, acts to concentrate the methotrexate within the cell, and therefore it is frequently a part of a chemotherapeutic protocol. Some of its noxious effects are loss of reflexes; pain in the abdomen, chest, and jaw; anemia; and severe local inflammation if extravasated. Citrovorum Factor provides a "rescue" therapy by minimizing the effect of high-dose methotrexate on noncancerous cells, thereby preventing gastrointestinal toxicity, myelosuppression, and to some degree, liver damage. Table 34-4 includes the most common agents.

On the one hand, chemotherapy has been unable to eradicate the primary lesion of osteogenic sarcoma. On the other hand, the osteosarcoma cells are not entirely radiosensitive. Therefore amputation of the limb is a common orthopedic intervention. Amputation alone can cure one in six patients.

At the present time, preservation of the limb is being attempted on a limited, research basis. The patient is given an extensive pre- and postoperative course of chemotherapy. An en bloc resection of the lesion is then performed and an internal prosthesis is inserted. Although the aim of surgery is to achieve a tumor-free margin in the resection, lesions have become reactivated or have recurred within 3 to 14 months despite postoperative chemotherapy.

Radiation therapy in osteogenic sarcoma is primarly aimed at irradiating secondary sites once the primary lesion has metastasized. A majority of patients with osteogenic sarcoma develop pulmonary metastasis 6 to 9 months after ablative surgery. Some aggressive therapy involves the surgical removal of the affected lung.

TABLE 34-4
Some Anticancer Drugs

Drug	Dose/route of administration	Side effects	Toxic symptoms	Precautions to be taken	Indications for utilization
Cyclophosphamide (Cytoxan) Alkylating agent	500–1500 mg/m² as a single dose IV; or 60–120 mg/m² per day PO; if severe leukopenia develops, dose is decreased	Nausea and vomiting	Bone marrow depression, alopecia, cystitis	Maintain an adequate fluid intake to avoid development of cystitis	Hodgkin's disease and other lymphomas; neuroblastoma; multiple myeloma; carcinomas of breast, lungs, and ovaries
Methotrexate (MTX, amethopterin) Antimetabolite	10–30 mg/day PO or IM for 5 days q 2 weeks	None	Bone marrow depression; diarrhea; megaloblastic anemia; alopecia; vomiting; stomatitis. Less common signs: hepatic fibrosis; vasculitis; pulmonary fibrosis	Adequate renal function must be present. Urine output must be maintained	Adjuvant for osteosarcoma; choriocarcinoma; acute leukemia; testicular tumors; carcinoma of the head, neck, and breast
Doxorubicin (Adriamycin) Antibiotic	60–100 mg/m² IV q 3 weeks	Nausea; fever; vomiting; local phlebitis if extravasated; red urine which is not blood	Bone marrow depression; alopecia; stomatitis; cardiac toxicity related to cumulative dose	Should be given through a *running* IV. Avoid giving to patients with heart disease. If administered, watch ECG for abnormalities, evidence of heart failure	Sarcomas; neuroblastomas; acute lymphoblastic leukemia; Ewing's sarcoma; carcinoma of breast, bladder, lungs, and thyroid
Vincristine (Oncovin) Plant alkaloid	0.4–1.4 mg/m² IV weekly in adults, 2 mg/m² weekly in children	Local inflammation if extravasated. Nausea/vomiting are rare	Paresthesias; loss of reflexes and weakness; constipation; marrow toxicity is mild with anemia and reticulocytopenia; alopecia; mental depression; chest, abdominal, and jaw pain	Should be given through a running IV or injected with great care to avoid extravasation; dose should be decreased in the presence of liver disease; patients with neurologic disorders more susceptible to neurotoxicity. Alopecia can be prevented by using a scalp tourniquet for 5 min during and after administration	Acute lymphoblastic leukemia; lymphomas; Wilm's tumors; neuroblastoma; testicular tumors; carcinoma of the breast

Source: J. C. Marsh and M. S. Mitchell, *Chemotherapy of Cancer; Drugs in Current Use*, Adria Laboratories, 1976.

With a high percentage of patients who demonstrate pulmonary metastasis, pneumothorax is a very possible complication. The exact mechanism which causes the collapse is not known; however, two theories have been formulated. One suggestion is that necrotic, neoplastic tissue pouts into the pleural cavity and forms a bronchopleural fistula which creates the pneumothorax. Another theory is that the tumor nodules act as ball valves to produce partial bronchiolar obstruction and hyperinflation of the alveoli. The latter leads to an interstitial emphysema and a subsequent dissection of air along the perivascular routes to the lung's surface. When the pleural blebs rupture, the pneumothorax occurs.

A tremendous amount of coordination is necessary to realize successful treatment for the patient with osteogenic sarcoma. Each aspect of therapy has implications for the other, and it is their synchronization which affects a satisfactory outcome.

Nursing Management

The objective for the care of patients with cancer is to provide treatment which maintains as normal a lifestyle as possible for as long as possible. Despite their need at times for intensive nursing care, these patients are rarely admitted to a critical-care unit. However, the complications of osteogenic sarcoma can require the specialized nursing skills and equipment of an ICU, and admission there becomes a part of the total care program. Nursing management, therefore, must be designed to meet the needs of the immediate emergency and to continue the plan of care previously established by nursing personnel who have been and will continue to be involved with this patient on a long-term basis.

For the adolescent with osteogenic sarcoma, transfer to the ICU represents a crisis of a very special nature. The adolescent has probably been told of the diagnosis, but may be in any one of the many stages of accepting that diagnosis. While the patient is almost certain to understand the seriousnesss of the situation, a complication may unrealistically signify that a hope for remission is now unattainable. In addition, the complication is likely to cause physical discomfort which can further interfere with the patient's ability to cope with the diagnosis and the immediate situation. Skilled actions, knowledge, and honesty of a nurse at this point are essential in establishing a trusting relationship and enhancing the effectiveness of interventions selected.

A nursing assessment begins with the immediate crisis, but it certainly includes the total physical and psychosocial status of the adolescent, which may be evaluated at a later point. Management is rather complex because it includes the disease and its complications as well as the therapy and its complications. In addition, the unique needs of a teenager must be met as each aspect of the care plan is implemented.

A frequent complication of osteogenic sarcoma is pulmonary metastasis, and it is usually its presence which necessitates care in an ICU setting. Once metastasis to the lungs has occurred, the possibility of pneumothorax is substantial. Close monitoring through auscultation and percussion is necessary because many pneumothoraces are "silent" in nature. Even if the patient is asymptomatic, treatment is usually instituted because the lung is already compromised in its diseased state. At times aggressive therapy, such as a lobectomy, is performed. In addition to the routine nursing care given to a patient following thoracotomy and chest tubes, an adolescent with osteogenic sarcoma has special needs. Often immunosuppressed and frequently being treated with chemotherapeutic agents, the client's wounds are slow to heal. The threat of infection is always present, and a careful inspection of incisional areas for signs of infection is necessary if a life-threatening septicemia is to be noted before it fulminates. Platelet counts are usually markedly lowered, and bleeding from arterial lines and punctures is a real danger.

If chemotherapy is in progress, then a knowledge of the actions, interactions, and toxic effects of the drugs used must be incorporated into the care plan. Some of these drugs are experimental and their side effects have not yet been documented. Nursing observations, especially for the unexpected, are essential to patient care and to a contribution to the body of knowledge about the drug. Usually these drugs require preciseness in administration. Serum levels must be monitored by a hematologist, and since one drug affects another, the sequence and timing of administration is vital to their effective utilization. Many chemotherapeutic drugs (especially vesicant drugs) cause necrosis of tissue if extravasated or if they are allowed to remain undiluted in the vein. Careful checking for intravenous infiltration and the use of a flush after administration can save the patient from a painful site or possible entry for infection. Hematologic suppression, caused by the drugs and the disease process, means that measures must be taken to prevent further hemopoietic insult. Platelet-interfering drugs, such as acetylsalicylic acid, should not be administered. Stools, urine, and emesis should be examined for occult blood to detect early signs of bleeding. Intramuscular injections should be avoided. The white count must be closely monitored, and patients with low counts must be kept in an environment which protects them from infection. In order to provide adequate excretion of drugs, hydration and an alkaline urine need to be maintained, and by output and pH testing, urine is monitored carefully. A diet high in foods from the alkaline ash group and low in purine contribute to the essential base balance. The stomatitis which results from the drug therapy is another potential source of infection, especially candidiasis. Thorough mouth care with frequent rinses and a soft toothbrush can minimize the discomfort and decrease opportunities for infection. These chemotherapeutic drugs tend to be constipating, and perirectal abscesses and fissures often occur as a result. Rectal temperatures can further irritate the rectal mucosa and be responsible for severe bleeding. Stool softeners are administered to alleviate straining and to protect the rectum from potential damage. Most of these chemotherapeutic agents do not cross the blood-brain barrier, and yet they can affect the CNS. The patient should be observed for ataxic movements and loss of fine motor control; paresthesia may be present.

The primary lesion of osteogenic sarcoma is most often treated by amputation of the affected limb. Occasionally this step of therapy warrants ICU care. Nursing actions include monitoring the limb stump for an adequate blood supply, maintaining a sterile dressing, and positioning the patient so that both edema and contractures do not occur. These clients need to be observed for signs of infection. It will also be important to medicate the patient for surgical and phantom pain. Blood loss at the time of surgery and a subsequent low platelet count are responsible for causing abnormal amounts of bloody drainage from incisional drains which may further complicate the patient's already anemic status; anticipatory care can prevent shock. On resuming oral nutritional intake, a diet which is high in protein, minerals, and vitamins can speed the healing process. Early rehabilitation efforts are essential, and exercises to maintain and develop muscles needed for ambulation must begin in the unit.

As is so often true, the nurse is the only member of the health care team in a position to observe and evaluate the interactions and effects of all other members of the team. The more disciplines which make up a team, the more complex the therapy; and the more life-threatening the patient's condition, the more the nurse becomes the focal practitioner and the more essential that the role of patient advocate be implemented. Nursing the adolescent with osteogenic sarcoma is a prime example. The hematologist, the orthopedic surgeon, the thoracic surgeon, the radiologist, the pediatrician, the social worker, the psychiatrist, the dietitian, the physical therapist, and the pharmacist all have important input regarding the care of this patient. Uncoordinated, one therapy can adversely affect another (chemotherapy, for example, can prohibit surgical healing if not designed to be modified at the time of operation), and the patient and family can become overwhelmingly confused and discouraged by partial and seemingly contradictory communication. Orchestration of this multifaceted treatment plan and facilitation of communication among the team and to the patient and family is as critical a component of nursing care as is provision of knowledgeable direct treatment.

REFERENCES

Alexander, M. M., and M. S. Brown: Physical examination, Part 17: Neurological examination, *Nursing '76,* June 1976, pp. 38–43.

Ashcraft, K. W., and T. M. Holder: Esophageal atresia and tracheoesophageal fistula malformations, *Surg Clin North Am* 56(2):299–315, 1976.

Campbell, L.: Special behavioral problems of the burned child, *Am J Nurs* 76(2):220–224, 1976.

Derdeyn, A. P.: Child abuse and neglect: The rights of parents and the needs of their children, *Am J Orthopsychiatry* 47(3):377–385, 1977.

Erickson, E.: *Childhood and Society,* New York: W. W. Norton, 1963.

Farrell, J.: *Illustrated Guide to Orthopedic Nursing,* Philadelphia: Lippincott, 1977.

Fraiberg, S. H.: *The Magic Years,* New York: Scribner, 1959.

Gorrell, J. F.: Hemolytic-uremic syndrome: An overview and a pediatric patient report, *Maternal-Child Nursing Journal* 3(4):235–241, July-August 1978.

Gullo, S.: Chemotherapy: What to do about special side effects, *RN*, April 1977, pp. 30–32.

Haller, J. A., and J. L. Talbert: *Surgical Emergencies in the Newborn,* Philadelphia: Lea & Febiger, 1972.

Helfer, R. E., and C. H. Kempe (eds.): *The Battered Child,* Chicago: The University of Chicago Press, 1968.

Helfer, R. E., and C. H. Kempe: *Child Abuse and Neglect,* Cambridge, Mass.: Ballinger Publishing Company, 1976.

Johnson, M., and J. Quinn: The subarachnoid screw, *Am J Nurs* 77(3):248–250, 1977.

Kaplan, B. S., P. D. Thompson, and J. P. de Chadarevian: The hemolytic uremic syndrome, *Pediatr Clin North Am* 23(4):761–777, 1976.

Kempe, C. H., and R. E. Helfer (eds.): *Helping the Battered Child and His Family,* Philadelphia: Lippincott, 1972.

Kunzman, L.: Some factors influencing a young child's mastery of hospitalization, *Nurs Clin North Am* 7(1):13–26, 1972.

Lander, A. J.: Oesophageal atresia with tracheo-oesophageal fistula associated with hydramnios, *Nurs Times* 72(35):1351–1352, 1976.

Maier, H.: *Three Theories of Child Development,* New York: Harper & Row, 1969.

Mussen, P. H., J. J. Conger, and J. Kagan: *Child Development and Personality,* New York: Harper & Row, 1974.

Neill, K., and C. Kauffman: Care of the hospitalized abused child and his family: Nursing implications, *Maternal-Child Nursing Journal*, March-April 1976, pp. 117–123.

Rowe, M. I., and M. B. Marchildon: Physiologic considerations in the newborn surgical patient, *Surg Clin North Am* 56(2):245–261, 1976.

Scipien, G. M., M. U. Bernard, M. A. Chard, J. Howe, and P. Phillips: *Comprehensive Pediatric Nursing,* New York: McGraw-Hill, 1975.

Smith, C. A. (ed.): *The Critically Ill Child, Diagnosis and Management,* Philadelphia: Saunders, 1972.

Schmitt, B. D., and C. H. Kempe: Child abuse and neglect, in David W. Smith (ed.), *Introduction to Clinical Pediatrics,* Philadelphia, London, Toronto: Saunders, 1977, pp. 187–193.

Steele, B. F.: *Working with Abusive Parents from a Psychiatric Point of View,* Washington, D.C.: Department of Health, Education, and Welfare, Office of Human Development/Office of Child Development, Children's Bureau/National Center on Child Abuse and Neglect, Publication No. (OHD)76-30070, 1976.

Surveyer, J. A.: The emotional toll on nurses who care for comatose children, *Maternal-Child Nursing Journal,* July-August 1976, pp. 243–248.

Wadsworth, B. J.: *Piaget's Theory of Cognitive Development,* New York: McKay, 1974.

Wheeler, P.: Care of a patient with a cerebellar tumor, *Am J Nurs* 77(2):266, 1977.

Young, J. F.: Recognition, significance, and recording of the signs of increased intracranial pressure, *Nurs Clin North Am* 4(2):223–236, 1969.

PART 7

PRINCIPLES OF SPECIAL PROCEDURES AND THERAPIES

INTRODUCTION

The goal of advanced life support is to maintain or restore both cardiac and cerebral functions at the optimal level for the individual patient. The American Heart Association and the National Academy of Science–National Research Council sponsored a conference in May 1973 to develop standards for performance and training in basic and advanced cardiac life support. These standards were published in a supplement to the *Journal of the American Medical Association* in February 1974. The proceedings from the conference, the *Journal of the American Medical Association* supplement, and the American Heart Association textbook used in the advanced cardiac life support course have been used extensively in the preparation of this chapter. We would encourage every person involved in critical care to take the advanced cardiac life support course and to include these topics in staff development programs.

The premise that prevention is as valuable as treatment cannot be disregarded when dealing with acute, life-threatening situations. Through the years, the American Heart Association has encouraged lay programs about the symptoms of impending myocardial infarction and actions to take for survival. These programs have resulted in a more sophisticated bystander approach to sudden, unexpected collapse. Often, cardiopulmonary resuscitation (CPR) is started immediately, and the victim is admitted to the hospital in a more salvageable condition. Nurses and physicians are encouraged to help educate the public, as well as being trained themselves to perform correct CPR in or out of the hospital, should they find themselves in a bystander situation.

With the expanded role of the nurse now including diagnostic skills and therapeutic measures not dreamed of two decades ago, the teamwork which can develop between nurse and physician in the critical-care unit not only improves patient care but can be a source of professional pride and satisfaction. It is best fostered by open dialogue and regular conferences focused on improving the management of the patient and his family.

Advanced life support includes management of the prearrest phase of a person who has suffered a myocardial infarction or other cardiopulmonary emergency, as well as the definitive therapy used during and after a cardiac arrest. Other chapters deal with specific precipitating causes of arrest. The following sections deal with each of the elements concerned in advanced life support:

35
ADVANCED LIFE SUPPORT

Shannon Champion
John M. Packard

INTRODUCTION

MANAGEMENT OF THE PRE-ARREST PHASE

BASIC LIFE SUPPORT (CPR)
Unwitnessed Arrest
Monitored Arrest

ADJUNCTS TO VENTILATION
Oxygenation
Airway
Suctioning
Surgical Procedures

ADJUNCTS TO CIRCULATION

ESTABLISHING AND MAINTAINING INTRAVENOUS LIFELINE
Peripheral Veins
Central Veins
Intracardiac Route

MONITORING AND DYSRHYTHMIA RECOGNITION

DEFIBRILLATION AND SYNCHRONIZED CARDIOVERSION
Pathophysiology
The Machine
Skin Resistance
Electrode Placement
Energy Selection
Procedure for Defibrillation
Procedure for Emergency Cardioversion

DEFINITIVE THERAPY
Sinus Bradycardia
Complete Heart Block
Premature Ventricular Contractions
Ventricular Tachycardia
Ventricular Fibrillation
Asystole
Electromechanical Dissociation

STABILIZATION OF PATIENT'S CONDITION FOR TRANSPORTATION

CONCLUSION

REFERENCES

1. Management of the pre-arrest phase
2. Basic life support
3. Use of adjunctive equipment for ventilation
4. Use of adjunctive equipment for circulation
5. Establishing and maintaining an intravenous lifeline
6. Cardiac monitoring for dysrhythmia recognition
7. Defibrillation
8. Definitive therapy, including drug administration to correct acidosis and to establish and maintain effective cardiac rhythm and circulation
9. Stabilization and transportation, if the patient is not in a critical-care unit

MANAGEMENT OF THE PRE-ARREST PHASE

Very often the mechanisms which precipitate arrest seem to occur in a vicious cycle, e.g., dysrhythmia → decreased output → poor tissue perfusion → hypoxia → dysrhythmia, and so on. Interfering with the progression of this pattern is the goal of management during the pre-arrest phase, and appropriate care can often preclude the need for resuscitation.

Patients with suspected myocardial infarction should be immediately worked into an emergency cardiac care system. Cardiac monitoring should be instituted as soon as possible to diagnose rhythm disturbances and to obtain a baseline from which to judge subsequent rhythm patterns.

Ensure adequate oxygenation by proper position to maintain an open airway, and provide supplemental oxygen by mask or nasal prongs. Lessening anxiety also decreases myocardial oxygen consumption.

Start an infusion of D_5W through a peripheral vein for administration of fluids and drugs as necessary to prevent, minimize, or treat life-threatening shock, dysrhythmias, or pump failure.

Medication for the relief of pain may be appropriate at this time. Morphine given in small intravenous doses is the preferred therapy. Monitoring other parameters such as vital signs, arterial blood gases, chest roentgenogram, intake and output, and serum electrolytes enable the health care team to evaluate the therapy being given and to make changes as indicated.

The importance of the physician, nurse, and allied personnel working as a team at this time and throughout the patient's therapeutic and recuperative periods cannot be stressed enough. The team approach enhances continuity of care, facilitates proper treatment, and creates a secure atmosphere for the patient.

BASIC LIFE SUPPORT (CPR)

Basic life support constitutes a holding action only, since it rarely restores cardiac dysrhythmias to normal sinus rhythm. However, without CPR (with the exception of monitored arrest), the delivery of advanced life support is of no value. It must be instituted at once and continued as advanced life support measures are instituted. All critical-care nurses and physicians should maintain current certification in basic life support.

Unwitnessed Arrest

1. *Confirm unconsciousness* by shaking and shouting at the patient; place patient in the supine position on a firm surface; call for help.
2. *Open the airway* using the head-tilt chin-lift method.
3. *Check breathing* by looking, listening, and feeling for respirations, which requires 3 to 5 s. If none,
4. *Give four mouth-to-mouth breaths* in rapid succession, not permitting the patient to exhale completely after each ventilation. Next,
5. *Check carotid pulse,* allowing 5 to 10 s. If absent, call for cardiac arrest team and
6. *Start chest compressions* at a rate of 80 compressions per minute, if alone, with two ventilations after each 15 compressions, or at a rate of 60 compressions per minute with a second rescuer interposing a breath after every fifth compression. Recent evidence confirms the value of a smooth downstroke which occupies at least 50 percent of the entire cycle. Between compressions, the heel of the hand must completely release its pressure but should remain in constant contact with the lower half of the sternum. The rescuer's fingers should not rest on the ribs.

Monitored Arrest

When the monitored patient has sudden ventricular fibrillation, asystole, or ventricular tachycardia without pulse:

1. Give single *precordial thump.*
2. *Check monitor* for rhythm and simultaneously *palpate for carotid pulse.*
3. If there is ventricular fibrillation or ventricular tachycardia without pulse, *countershock* as soon as possible.
4. *Open airway* and give *four quick, full-lung inflations.*
5. *Check carotid pulse again,*
6. If pulse is absent, begin one- or two-rescuer *CPR.*

It must be emphasized strongly that no time be lost in waiting to assess the results of the precordial thump or by delivering repeated precordial thumps.

The monitor should be observed for return of effective cardiac activity and the carotid artery palpated for a pulse before discontinuing basic CPR.

ADJUNCTS TO VENTILATION

Maintenance of adequate ventilation is essential to prevent or reduce the insult produced by hypoxia and subsequent anaerobic metabolism (Fig. 35-1). The nurse should constantly be aware of the patient's ventilatory status and observe for change in any of the parameters that would indicate impending or present hypoxia, e.g., sensorium, color, rate and character of respirations, presence and severity of chest pain, heart rate and rhythm, and arterial blood gases.

Proficiency in the use of airway devices should be maintained through practice and staff education programs. Periodic checks regarding proper function of equipment is necessary, as is rapid access to adjunctive equipment.

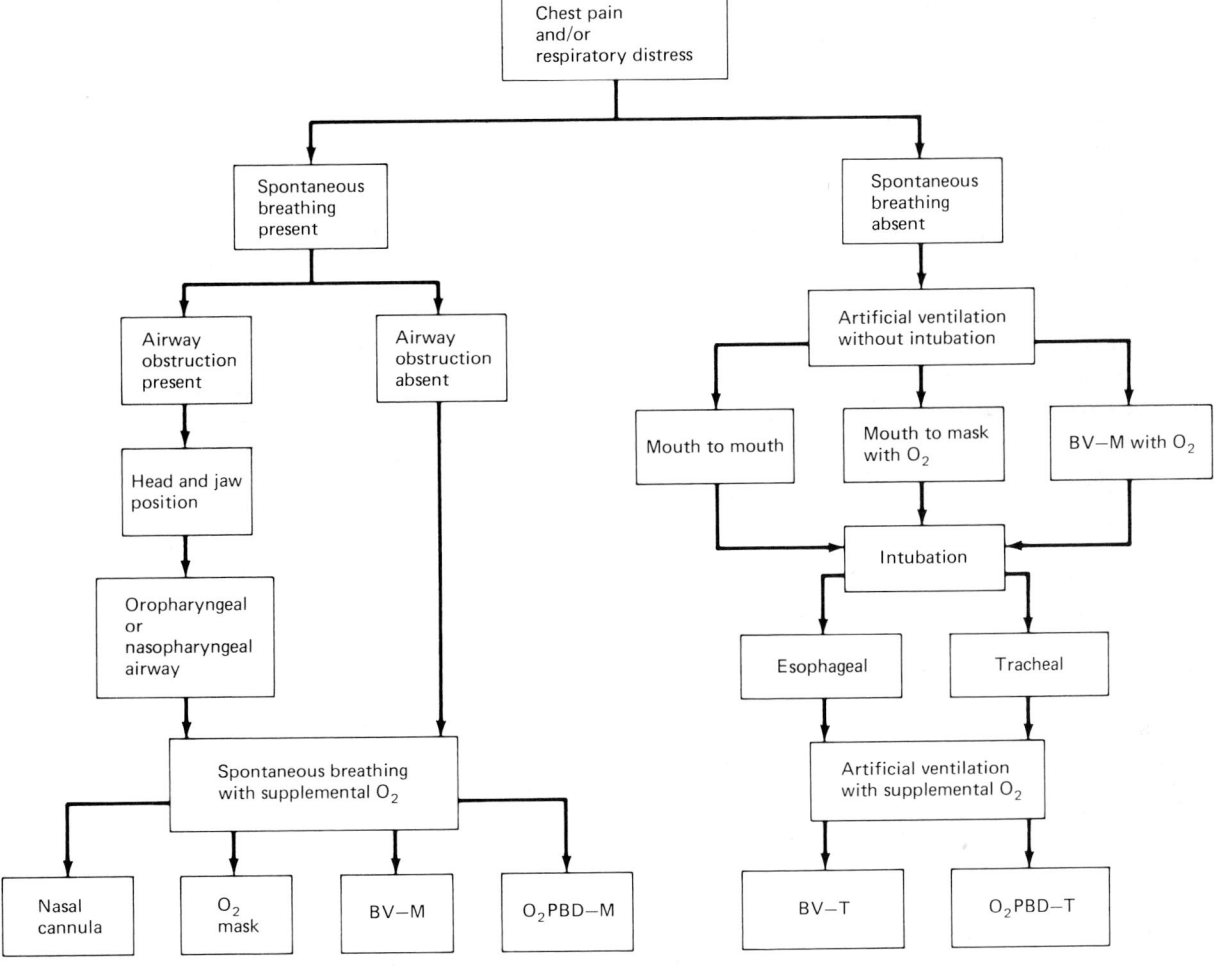

FIGURE 35-1

Overview of adjuncts for airway and breathing (ventilation). BV-M = bag-valve-mask; BV-T = bag-valve-tube; O_2PBD-M = oxygen-powered breathing device-mask; O_2PBD-T = oxygen-powered breathing device-tube. (*From "Advanced Cardiac Life Support," 1975; reprinted with permission of the American Heart Association, Inc.*)

Oxygenation

Mouth-to-mouth breathing delivers approximately 16 percent oxygen to the patient. Ideally, this will produce an alveolar oxygen tension of 80 mmHg. However, intrapulmonary right-to-left shunting and ventilation-perfusion defects reduce arterial oxygen tension. Therefore, supplemental oxygen should be used as soon as possible.

In the hypoxic patient, modest increases in arterial oxygen tension greatly increase hemoglobin saturation and arterial oxygen content and improve tissue oxygenation. In the patient with suspected myocardial infarction, ventilation with oxygen-rich gas may improve myocardial oxygenation. Oxygen should be administered in the presence of suspected hypoxia of any cause and, of course, in all cases of cardiopulmonary arrest. For short-term use, 100% oxygen is recommended. This therapy is not considered hazardous in the resuscitative period, although patients with chronic pulmonary disease may need ventilatory assistance because of respiratory depression.

In the conscious patient, nasal cannulae (prongs) are well tolerated, and with an oxygen flow of 6 L/min they create concentrations of 25 to 40%. The venturi masks provide specific concentrations of oxygen: 24 and 28 percent at oxygen flow rates of 4 L/min, and 35 and 40 percent at 8 L/min.

In the unconscious patient, the pocket mask, when equipped with an oxygen inlet, allows mouth-to-mask ventilation with supplemental oxygen. If a rapid flow of oxygen (50 to 100 L/min) can be achieved, the patient may be ventilated merely by intermittently occluding the mouth opening of the mask.

A bag-valve-mask device with reservoir bag or tube provides delivery of 100% oxygen and permits assisted respiration. A trained individual is necessary to use the various bag-valve-mask devices effectively.

Airway

The unconscious patient should be intubated for complete control of ventilation and prevention of aspiration of gastric contents. Until endotracheal intubation can be accomplished, the upper airway should be kept open by the head-tilt chin-lift method, supplemented by an oropharyngeal or nasopharyngeal airway.

The S tube is not advisable in resuscitation. It does not provide adequate airway seal, poor tidal volumes are obtained, and it tends to promote regurgitation.

The esophageal obturator airway (Fig. 35-2) is a most useful adjunct which provides temporary control of the airway if a person trained in endotracheal intubation is not immediately available. It is a cuffed tube 35 cm in length, open at the upper end and closed at the bottom, which passes through a specially fitted clear plastic face mask. Multiple openings along the upper portion of the tube allow passage of the air into the pharynx. When properly inserted, the blind end of the tube is in the esophagus with the cuff below the bifurcation of the trachea. After the face mask is seated over the mouth and nose, the cuff is inflated and oxygen is blown through openings at the level of the pharynx into the trachea. A recent modification, the esophageal (gastric tube) airway, allows simultaneous gastric suction.

The advantages of the esophageal obturator airway include rapid introduction without the need for visualization, prevention of regurgitation and aspiration, and facilitation of endotracheal intubation. Potential hazards are endotracheal insertion, esophageal rupture, and tracheal occlusion if the cuff is inflated above the carina. The airway should only be used for short-term therapy (2 h maximum) and should be withdrawn when the patient begins spontaneous respiration. As soon as possible after insertion of the airway, an endotracheal tube should be inserted if ventilatory assistance will be required for prolonged periods. The esophageal airway should *not* be removed until after successful endotracheal intubation, since vomiting usually occurs following removal of the esophageal airway. Suction must be available and the patient's head turned to one side for adequate removal of regurgitated stomach contents. Care should be taken to ensure that the esophageal cuff has been deflated prior to removal of the tube. The esophageal obturator airway should not be used in patients under 16 years of age, nor in those patients with preexisting esophageal disease, nor following ingestion of caustic poisons.

Although endotracheal intubation gives complete control of ventilation, it should always be preceded by exhaled air methods or the simpler adjunctive measures described above which provide quick ventilation in the emergency situation. Only those individuals highly skilled in the insertion of endotracheal tubes should be allowed to use this technique to prevent loss of valuable time.

Suctioning

The removal of accumulated secretions is necessary for maintaining the airway. The most common complication involved with suctioning is hypoxia due to

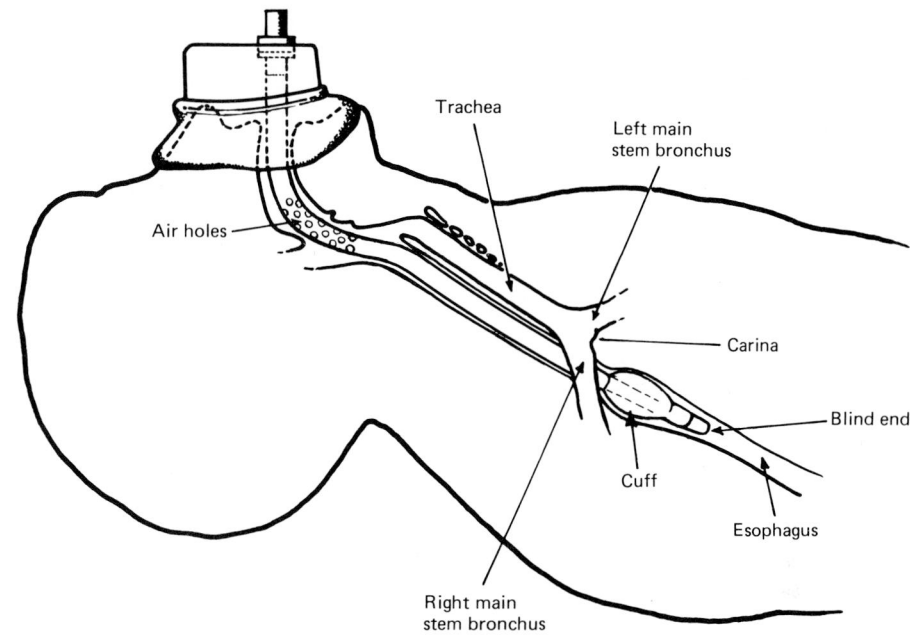

FIGURE 35-2
Final position of esophageal airway and mask.

prolonged application of suction. Suction should be applied intermittently for no longer than 5 s, and supplemental oxygen should be delivered before and after suctioning.

Trauma to the mucous membranes can be avoided by not applying suction as the catheter is inserted and by using a rotating motion as the catheter is withdrawn.

Surgical Procedures

When all other methods for establishing an airway have failed at relieving airway obstruction, surgical procedures may be necessary. Transtracheal catheterization employs a 14-gauge catheter-needle assembly, which is inserted in the cricothyroid membrane. When intermittent high-pressure oxygen is administered by tank or wall oxygen supply (at least 50 lb/in²), the lungs are inflated. A manually controlled valve is used to regulate the rate and depth of ventilations. The retrograde leak of oxygen tends to propel secretions toward the oropharynx where they can be easily removed by suction.

Cricothyrotomy is performed with a knife blade inserted into the cricothyroid membrane. Usually, a small (4.0 mm ID) tube is inserted to maintain patency of the opening. Again, this affords rapid access to the airway.

Either of these procedures allows for rapid ventilation until endotracheal intubation or a tracheotomy can be accomplished.

Complications for either of these procedures include hemorrhage, perforation of the esophagus, subcutaneous emphysema, and later tracheal stenosis.

ADJUNCTS TO CIRCULATION

Optimal closed-chest compression provides a cardiac output of only 25 to 30 percent of normal. Operator fatigue will result in even less output. Mechanical means of providing closed-chest compression are therefore advisable after institution of manual CPR.

The cardiac press is inexpensive, is easily stored and carried to the bedside, provides a firm support to the back, and can be applied to the patient quickly after CPR has been initiated using manual methods. Advantages include ease of operation, elimination of operator's fatigue, and provision of more space about the patient for starting the IV, for auscultation, and for defibrillation.

Precautions during use of the cardiac press include close observation to ensure that the plunger does not shift from the correct position and that the adjustment knob does not loosen and thereby diminish the depression of the sternum from the required 1½ to 2 in. Proper use of this device depends on a well-trained team familiar with its use.

Automatic gas-powered chest compressors are designed to perform closed-chest compression automatically by a plunger mounted on a backboard and powered by compressed gas. Most models are also designed to provide automatic ventilation of the lungs after each fifth chest compression. A well-trained team can apply one of these devices with minimal interruption of manual CPR. Advantages include the reduction in the number of personnel needed and the elimination of operator fatigue that may cause variations in the cardiac output during manual CPR. ECGs can be recorded and the patient defibrillated and, if necessary, transported without stopping the compressor.

Disadvantages include the cost, bulk, and weight of the machine; the continued training (using mannikins) necessary for its use; and the limitation of 80 percent oxygen delivery.

Recent evidence shows that increased cardiac output, especially to the cardiac and cranial circulations, can be obtained during CPR by elevating the legs, using an abdominal binder, or applying anti-shock trousers.

ESTABLISHING AND MAINTAINING AN INTRAVENOUS LIFELINE

Intravenous cannulation gains direct access to the venous circulation and provides a route for intermittent or continuous administration of fluids or drugs. In low cardiac output states, shunting removes blood from skin or muscle and greatly reduces uptake of drugs given subcutaneously or intramuscularly. Drugs administered by the intravenous route will have assured access to the circulation.

Certain complications are common to all types of intravenous techniques. Locally, they are hematoma formation, cellulitis, thrombosis, and phlebitis. Systemic complications are sepsis, pulmonary thromboembolism, catheter fragment embolism, and fiber embolism from contamination of the solution.

Peripheral Veins

The most common areas used for intravenous therapy are the peripheral veins of the arm and hand, the dorsum of the foot, and the greater saphenous vein in the leg. Often disregarded but readily cannulated is the external jugular vein. In cases of circulatory collapse, the external jugular vein may be the only peripheral site that remains visible.

Peripheral cannulation offers certain advantages: effective route for administration of drugs, no interference with CPR, and an easy technique to master. Disadvantages include difficulty in finding veins when circulatory collapse is present, no access to central circulation, inability to administer hypertonic solutions, and a high incidence of phlebitis if the saphenous vein is used.

Central Veins

Sites for central venipuncture are the femoral, the internal jugular, and the subclavian veins. The central route can be used to place catheters for physiologic monitoring and for obtaining blood samples for analysis, as well as for the administration of fluids and drugs. Central venous cannulation requires special training.

The femoral vein can be cannulated without stopping CPR, but it is difficult to locate without a palpable femoral artery pulse. Use of the femoral vein precludes further use of the saphenous vein. Internal jugular or subclavian cannulation does not require visualization of the veins and provides direct access to the central circulation. The internal jugular puncture carries less risk of pleural trauma and is easier to perform during CPR. The subclavian vein has a higher rate of successful puncture, and more neck movement is allowed. The disadvantages present for either site include the need for a high degree of training, possible interference with chest compressions, and a high risk of complications related to close proximity of the veins to major arteries, lymphatics, apical pleura, and various nerves. Cannulation of the internal jugular or subclavian should be followed by chest x-ray to ascertain correct placement and to detect possible hemothorax or pneumothorax.

Except where the catheter must be threaded into the central circulation the cannula-over-needle type is preferred. This eliminates the danger of shearing off the end of the cannula and minimizes hematoma formation, since the cannula left in place is the same size as the original puncture.

Intracardiac Route

Intracardiac administration of drugs is discouraged in most situations because of the need to interrupt

CPR and because of the possibility of pneumothorax, hemopericardium, or intramyocardial injection. Injection of epinephrine into the myocardium produces intractable ventricular fibrillation. It should be remembered that epinephrine and lidocaine may be instilled through the endotracheal tube with prompt absorption if the intravenous route is not immediately available.

MONITORING AND DYSRHYTHMIA RECOGNITION

The recognition of cardiac dysrhythmias is a major element in prearrest, arrest, and postarrest treatment of the critically ill patient. The dysrhythmias are covered in an appendix, which deserves careful study by the critical-care nurse.

Monitor leads are positioned in such a way as to display a prominent P wave if organized atrial activity is present. The QRS complex should be of sufficient amplitude to trigger the rate meter, and it must be upright when cardioverting in order to trigger the

synchronizer circuit. The precordium is best left free for auscultation and for paddle placement should defibrillation be required. The positive electrode should be to the left or below the negative electrode to result in positive deflections. The indifferent, or ground, electrode is generally fixed below the right pectoral muscle.

Artifacts resulting from loose electrodes or patient movements should be recognized, and clinical observation of the patient *must* be correlated with the rhythm strip before emergency measures are instituted.

DEFIBRILLATION AND SYNCHRONIZED CARDIOVERSION

Pathophysiology

Ventricular fibrillation is a disordered rhythm in which each individual myocardial cell contracts as powerfully as ever, but in a totally random, asynchronous fashion. The heart quivers rather than showing coor-

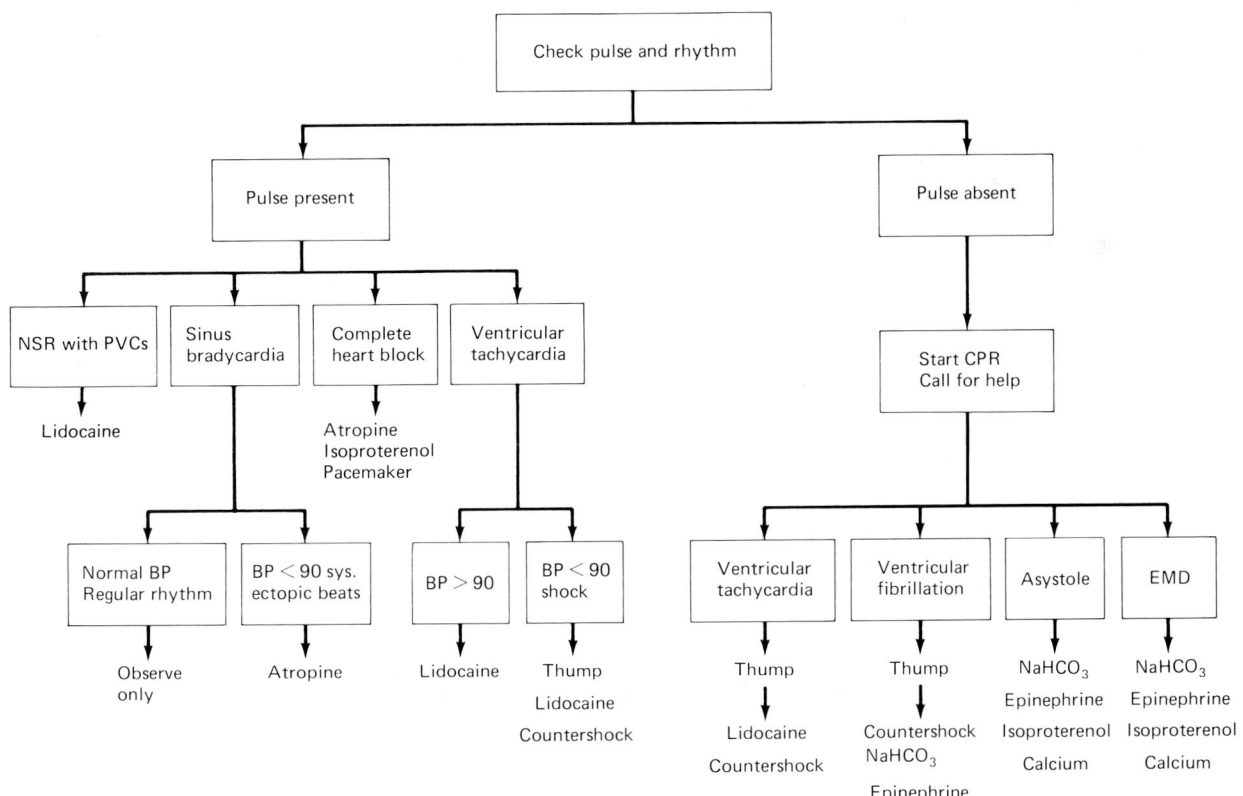

FIGURE 35-3

Decision tree for monitoring life-threatening dysrhythmias.

dinated contraction and relaxation, and therefore no effective pumping action is possible. Unless effective cardiac output can be restored within 4 to 6 min, the patient will die.

Electrical defibrillation results in the simultaneous depolarization (contraction) of all myocardial cells. The subsequent repolarization of all cells at the same time often permits the sinoatrial node to resume its pacemaker function, with resultant coordinated myocardial contraction and resumption of effective cardiac output. The earlier the electric shock is applied after the onset of ventricular fibrillation, the less is the opportunity for the myocardium to become anoxic and acidotic, and the better is the chance for resumption of normal sinus rhythm. Even minute electrical discharges, such as those generated by a precordial thump (0.2 to 0.5 joules), may be effective if performed within seconds of the onset of ventricular fibrillation. Indeed, cases are recorded of self-administered thumps reversing ventricular fibrillation. Likewise, in the catheterization lab a hard cough or series of coughs have been shown to eliminate premature ventricular contractions (PVCs) and to terminate ventricular tachycardia and fibrillation.

The Machine

Defibrillators in common use are capacitor-induced direct-current machines which deliver a monophasic discharge of several thousand volts lasting only a few milliseconds. The brief duration of the shock enables it to be triggered by the R wave with synchronized delivery of the shock into a specific portion of the QRS complex for treating dysrhythmias other than ventricular fibrillation (see section on cardioversion). When defibrillating with machines equipped with such a synchronizer circuit, one must be sure that the machine is switched to the defibrillate mode, since the synchronizer requires an R wave to fire and none are present in ventricular fibrillation.

The energy stored in a defibrillator does not equal the energy delivered to the patient and may decrease over time. It is therefore important to check the output of the machine at regular intervals. Some older machines may deliver as little as 10 to 15 percent of stored energy and should be replaced. Newer machines have meters which display delivered energy, but even they should be tested regularly.

Members of the cardiac arrest team must be thoroughly familiar with the controls on the defibrillators they will be using.

Skin Resistance

To reduce skin resistance and to avoid burns of the chest wall, electrode paste or saline pads are used beneath the paddles. Care must be taken to prevent the electrode paste or saline from spreading from one paddle to the other, since the electrical "bridging" results in surface burns and insufficient energy passing through the body to defibrillate the heart. Saline pads can be prepared in advance and kept with the defibrillator in closed dishes. They also avoid the slippery residue on the chest which is left by electrode paste and which interferes with closed-chest compression after defibrillation. Alcohol-soaked gauze pads *should not be used* since they burst into flames with the passage of the electric current.

Electrode Placement

One paddle is normally positioned over the second interspace to the right of the sternum and the other to the left of the precordium, using 20 to 25 lb (10 kg) of muscular pressure. The operator must take care to avoid contact with the patient and with the surface of the paddles.

For elective cardioversion or when the heart is not defibrillated using the standard electrode placement, the patient may be positioned on the right side and one paddle placed over the precordium and the other just below the left scapula to obtain a front-to-back current through the heart. An alternative method, if the machine is not equipped with a flat paddle, is to slip one end of a 6-in by 12-in stainless steel rectangle, well lubricated with electrode jelly, under the patient's left scapula while the patient is supine, and to place one electrode on the projecting surface with the other over the precordium.

Energy Selection

Despite the fact that electrical defibrillation was developed over 30 years ago, there still exists considerable controversy over the optimal energy required for successful defibrillation, the potential damage to the human heart from high energy levels, and the variables that are the primary determinants of success. Until these controversies are settled, it is recommended that the initial attempt at defibrillation be in the range of 200 J *delivered* energy. Since there is evidence that the transthoracic resistance drops with successive countershocks, it is recommended that if the first shock is unsuccessful, a second countershock of 300 J be delivered as soon as possible. If ventricular fibrillation persists, basic life support should be continued with (1) supplemental oxygen, (2) appropriate doses of sodium bicarbonate and epinephrine given intravenously, and (3) after adequate circulation of these drugs, the maximum output of the defibrillation should be delivered.

For children, the recommended energy level is 2 to 3.5 J per kg of body weight.

Procedure for Defibrillation

1. Institute basic CPR and call for defibrillator.

2. If arrest has continued more than 60 s, give IV bolus of 100 meq $NaHCO_3$ and subsequent bolus of 5 mL epinephrine 1:10,000.

3. Apply saline pads or electrode gel to chest and paddles.

4. Turn on defibrillator, checking to be sure synchronizer circuit is off, and charge to selected output for an adult.

5. Place paddles firmly on chest.

6. Clear area so that no one, including the operator, is touching the bed or patient. Unplug electrode cable if separate electrocardiograph (ECG) machine is being used.

7. Press buttons on both paddles simultaneously.

8. Immediately reinstitute basic CPR while others check monitor and carotid pulse for resumption of effective cardiac action. Basic CPR must be continued until a carotid pulse is detected, even if the monitor shows an apparently regular pattern.

Procedure for Emergency Cardioversion

Emergency cardioversion is indicated for rapid ventricular or supraventricular rhythms with inadequate cardiac output, except for those resulting from digitalis toxicity. If the patient is not already unconscious, the procedure should be delayed until adequate diazepam (Valium) or sodium thiopental (Pentothal) can be injected intravenously to cause anesthesia. The monitor must be adjusted so that the R wave is at least 1 cm high, and the electrode cable must be plugged into the defibrillator-synchronizer unless the machine is equipped with "quick-look" paddles.

The procedure is the same as for defibrillation, except that the synchronizer switch is activated, less energy is needed (25 to 50 J), and the discharge buttons must be held down until the machine fires.

If ventricular fibrillation is accidentally produced by the attempt at cardioversion, turn off the synchronizer switch, recharge to maximum output, and defibrillate.

DEFINITIVE THERAPY

Objectives of drug therapy are to accomplish the following:

1. Correct hypoxia
2. Correct metabolic acidosis
3. Increase perfusion pressure
4. Stimulate spontaneous or more forceful myocardial contractions
5. Accelerate the heart rate
6. Suppress ventricular ectopic activity
7. Relieve pain
8. Treat pulmonary edema

Specific pharmacologic actions of the drugs mentioned will not be repeated in this section. The accepted standard dosages of essential drugs as they are related to the life-threatening dysrhythmias will be given.

Drugs other than those mentioned below may be useful in resuscitative efforts. The many actions, indications, and varied dosages preclude discussion of each drug in this section. The following list of drugs should be considered basic for the nurse's knowledge of emergency cardiac drug therapy. There are many sources the nurse can use for detailed information about essential and useful drugs.

Levarterenol (Levophed)
Metaraminol (Aramine)
Propranolol (Inderal)
Corticosteroids
Dopamine (Intropin)
Furosemide (Lasix)
Ethacrynic acid (Edecrin)
Procainamide (Pronestyl)
Bretylium tosylate (Bretylol)
Dobutamine (Dobutrex)

Sinus Bradycardia

A heart rate below 60 beats per minute usually requires no treatment unless the systolic pressure falls below 90 mmHg or ectopic ventricular contractions occur.

Rx: Atropine 0.5 mg IV as bolus. Repeat every 5 min until rate is greater than 60 beats per minute.

Maximum dose 2.0 mg.

Complete Heart Block

Rx: Atropine as above.

Isoproterenol IV infusion, 4 mg/mL (1 mg in 250 mL D$_5$W)

Cardiac pacemaker

Premature Ventricular Contractions

PVCs require treatment if they are frequent (5 per min), if multifocal, if occur in runs, or if exhibit the R-on-T phenomenon.

Rx: Lidocaine 100 mg IV bolus, followed by lidocaine IV infusion, 1 to 4 mg/min (2000 mg in 1000 mL D$_5$W = 2 mg/mL, or 1000 mg in 250 mL D$_5$W = 4 mg/mL)

Ventricular Tachycardia

Patient conscious with palpable pulse:

Rx: Lidocaine as above.

Patient unconscious and no signs of circulation:

Rx: Emergency cardioversion.

Ventricular Fibrillation

Rule out artifact as cause of chaotic rhythm strip.

Rx: CPR immediately.

Countershock as soon as possible.

Epinephrine 5 mL 1:10,000 IV or endotracheally for converting fine fibrillation to coarse fibrillation.

Sodium bicarbonate, 1 meq/kg IV as bolus. If effective circulation is not restored, a repeat dose may be given. Thereafter one-half dose every 10 min. Arterial blood gas and pH determinations should guide further administration.

Asystole

Rx: Immediate CPR.

Epinephrine and bicarbonate as above.

Isoproterenol as above, titrating flow for desired effect, usually 1 to 10 mL/min.

Calcium chloride, 2.5 to 5.0 mL of 10% solution, slow IV bolus. This is 3.4 to 6.8 meq Ca^{2+}.

Equal doses of Ca^{2+} can be administered with 5 mL (4.5 meq) calcium gluceptate 10% or 10 mL (4.8 meq) calcium gluconate 10%.

Electromechanical Dissociation (EMD)

No pulse or blood pressure are present with apparently normal ECG pattern. Rule out hypovolemia or cardiac tamponade. (See appropriate chapters for treatment.)

Rx: Same as for asystole.

STABILIZATION OF PATIENT'S CONDITION FOR TRANSPORTATION

When cardiac arrest occurs outside the ICU, basic life support must be started at once and advanced life support measures must be instituted as soon as possible. Every effort should be made to restore effective ventilation, a stable cardiac rhythm, and effective circulation before attempting to move the patient. During transportation, the intravenous lifeline must be maintained. When a plastic bag is used for the infusion, the bag may be placed under the patient's back and this weight will cause a flow of about 25 mL/min. Cardiac monitoring should continue, and trained personnel should accompany the patient in case arrest occurs again.

CONCLUSION

Advanced life support is possible only because of the teams of highly skilled nurses, physicians, and allied health personnel capable of using the sophisticated diagnostic and therapeutic measures now available. It is an exciting field and one in which continuous upgrading of knowledge and skills is necessary to keep abreast of new developments such as methods to minimize neurologic damage following cardiac arrest.

As we become more competent to reverse previously fatal disorders, troublesome moral and ethical issues are being raised: What should our response be to the patient admitted to the ICU with orders not to resuscitate? Who decides to terminate life support for the patient who has no evident possibility of being restored to "meaningful" life? What should be the basis for such a decision? Discussion of these matters is outside the scope of this chapter, but the reader is encouraged to read an excellent review article (Cohen, 1977).

REFERENCES

American Heart Association: *Advanced Cardiac Life Support Textbook,* 1975.

American Heart Association: *Proceedings of the National Conference on Standards for Cardiopulmonary Resuscitation (CPR) and Emergency Cardiac Care (ECC): The American Heart Association and the National Academy of Science–National Research Council,* 1975.

Cohen, C. B.: Ethical problems of intensive care, *Anesthesiology* 47:217–227, 1977.

Copley, D. P., J. A. Mantle, W. J. Rogers, R. O. Russell, Jr., and C. E. Rackley: Improved outcome for pre-hospital cardio-pulmonary collapse with resuscitation by bystanders, *Circulation* 56:901–905, 1977.

Standards for cardiopulmonary resuscitation (CPR) and emergency cardiac care (ECC), *JAMA* 227(7)(suppl.):833–868, 1974.

Taylor, G. J., W. M. Tucker, H. L. Greene, M. T. Rudikoff, and M. L. Weisfeldt: Importance of prolonged compression during cardiopulmonary resuscitation, *N Engl J Med* 296: 1515–1517, 1977.

Circulatory assistance devices are designed to support the mechanical function of the heart during periods of depressed myocardial function. The technology underlying the design and development of these devices is rapidly changing. A multitude of devices have been conceived and developed. However, despite differences in design, commonalities exist among all circulatory assistance devices. The key to these commonalities is that the principles of circulatory assistance are derived from the principles of cardiovascular physiology. Consequently, the initial sections of this chapter will be devoted to a discussion of the physiologic principles underlying circulatory support.

The final sections will consider selected devices within a historical framework, with emphasis upon the intra-aortic balloon pump. Since the field of circulatory assistance is still in its infancy, its past, present, and future are intertwined. Therefore, consideration of one period of development without the others would omit considerations necessary to a comprehensive understanding of the current status and future applications of circulatory assistance.

PRINCIPLES OF CIRCULATORY ASSISTANCE

Assist devices are easiest to conceptualize if they are grouped according to their primary physiologic mechanism of support. There are three primary mechanisms: (1) reduction of preload, (2) reduction of afterload with diastolic pressure augmentation, and (3) direct cardiac compression. These categories are based upon three fundamental determinants of myocardial function: preload, afterload, and contractility. Alterations in these determinants bring about the need for circulatory assistance. Reversal of these alterations is the underlying goal of circulatory support. At the start, then, these physiologic variables and alterations shall be examined.

Determinants of Myocardial Function

Preload

Preload is an important determinant of myocardial function because it influences the force of myocardial contraction. *Preload* is defined as the degree of myocardial fiber stretch at the end of diastole, the period of ventricular filling. The degree of fiber stretch is determined by ventricular volumes. Increasing ventricular volumes during ventricular filling increases the stretch of the myocardial fibers. Within

36
CIRCULATORY ASSISTANCE
Penny J. Ford
Mortimer J. Buckley

PRINCIPLES OF CIRCULATORY ASSISTANCE
Determinants of Myocardial Function
Physiology of Myocardial Failure
Effects of Circulatory Assistance Devices

HISTORICAL EVOLUTION OF DEVICES
Preload Reduction Devices
Afterload Reduction Devices
Direct Cardiac Compression Devices

CURRENT DEVICES
Counterpulsation Devices
Left Heart Assist Devices

REFERENCES

925

limits, this increases the force of contraction during systole. An analogous relationship is that of increasing the stretch on a rubber band to increase the force of elastic recoil upon release of the rubber band. However, if a rubber band is overstretched, the force of elastic recoil falls. The same is true of the myocardial fiber; excessive stretch reduces contractile force.

Cardiac output is directly affected by changes in preload. As contractile force increases, cardiac emptying improves and stroke volume (i.e., the volume ejected per beat by each ventricle) rises. This relationship between fiber stretch, determined by ventricular filling, and cardiac output, determined by force of contraction, is referred to as *Starling's law of the heart* (Fig. 36-1). The law states that increased ventricular filling during diastole will increase the force of contraction during systole, elevating cardiac output.

The relationship between myocardial fiber stretch and cardiac output is best illustrated by a graph referred to as the *ventricular function curve*. To illustrate the relationship, the graph utilizes two clinical measures: (1) ventricular end-diastolic volume and (2) stroke volume. The graph shows ventricular volume on the horizontal axis and stroke volume on the vertical axis (Fig. 36-2). As the curve illustrates, increasing ventricular volume initially will increase stroke volume. Subsequently, further increments in ventricular volume will depress stroke volume.

As illustrated, the ventricular function curve demonstrates an ascending limb of improved function and a descending limb of reduced function. The ascending limb represents the cardiac reserve ability to improve function by increasing preload or fiber stretch; the descending limb is cardiac failure precipitated by volume overload excessively stretching the myocardial fibers.

Clinically, the estimation of preload is indirect. Since ventricular volumes and fiber stretch cannot be measured directly at the bedside, ventricular filling pressures are relied upon to determine preload. An optimal filling pressure can be determined at the bedside by plotting a ventricular function curve based upon readily obtainable bedside measurements. For example, the pulmonary capillary wedge pressure, reflecting left ventricular end-diastolic pressure, can be substituted for ventricular volume on the horizontal axis; the cardiac output can be utilized on the vertical axis. If cardiac output measurements are not available, measurements reflecting the adequacy of tissue perfusion, such as arterial pressure and urine output, can be substituted. Correlation of these parameters with pulmonary capillary wedge pressure should permit determination of the optimal filling pressure that maximizes the force of contraction and cardiac output.

In summary, increasing preload or myocardial fiber stretch will increase the force of contraction up to a point, and consequently, the volume of blood ejected from the ventricle. However, excessive preload produces a fall in contractility and cardiac output.

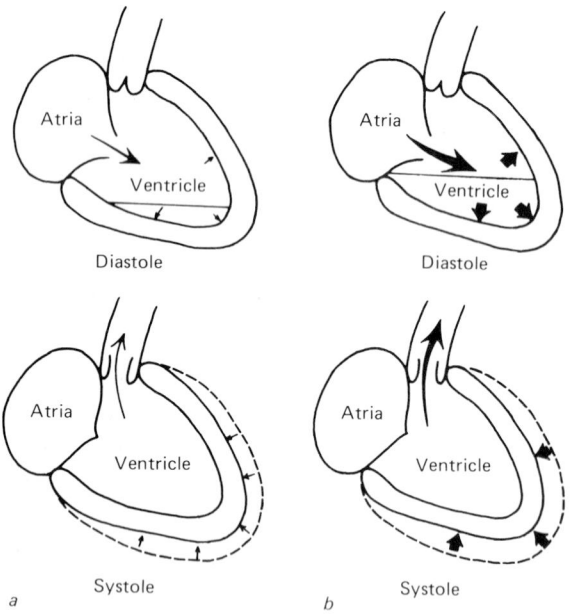

FIGURE 36-1

Starling's law of the heart. (*a*) Normal filling during diastole causes normal fiber stretch, normal contractile force, and normal stroke volume. (*b*) Increased filling during diastole causes increased fiber stretch, increased force of contraction, and increased stroke volume. (*From S. Price and L. Wilson, Pathophysiology: Clinical Concepts of Disease Processes, McGraw-Hill, New York, 1978. Used by permission of the publisher.*)

Afterload

Afterload is the amount of tension the ventricle must develop during contraction to eject blood. This amount depends upon (1) arterial pressure and (2) ventricular size or radius. In the clinical setting, arterial pressure is considered the most significant determinant of afterload, since blood pressure can be altered acutely and controlled precisely with a variety of interventions. Consequently, clinical references to changes in afterload refer to changes in arterial pressure. Physiologically, however, the influence of each variable is significant. The relationship between ventricular tension, arterial pressure, and ventricular size is known as the law of *LaPlace*.

Ventricular tension
= arterial pressure × ventricular radius

As the equation indicates, both hypertension and chamber dilation increase ventricular tension. The rationale for these relationships is straightforward. If arterial pressure is elevated, the ventricle confronts increased resistance to ejection during systole. To overcome the increased resistance, the ventricle must generate more force during ventricular contraction to empty adequately. Similarly, if the ventricular radius is increased, ventricular volumes are elevated. An enlarged, dilated ventricle must generate more force to empty this excess volume than a ventricle of normal size.

Thus, both arterial pressure elevation and ventricular dilation increase afterload, elevating cardiac work and myocardial oxygen demand. Once again, excessive elevation of afterload can impair the ability of the ventricle to empty, thereby reducing cardiac output.

Contractility

Contractility refers to changes in the force of contraction occurring independent of myocardial fiber length or preload. It is a function of the intensity of interactions between myocardial contractile elements at the cellular level. Contractility can be directly affected by substances such as calcium and epinephrine. Increased contractility improves ventricular emptying, elevating stroke volume. Mechanical assist devices cannot directly affect the intrinsic contractile process. However, devices designed to compress the heart can generate external contractile force.

Physiology of Myocardial Failure

Myocardial dysfunction can be self-perpetuating. Progressive myocardial failure is a function of the following disturbances in myocardial function: (1) reduced contractility, (2) increased preload, and (3) increased afterload. -

Reduced contractility impairs the ability of the ventricle to empty. Consequently, residual ventricular volume rises, producing chamber dilation and stretching the myocardial fibers. Initially, this increase in preload is beneficial. The increased ventricular volume augments the force of ventricular contraction, maintaining cardiac output. However, progressive

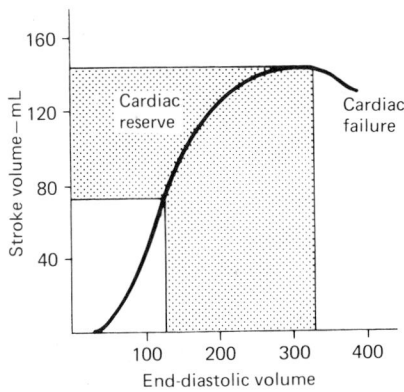

FIGURE 36-2

Ventricular function curve. As the end-diastolic volume increases, so does the force of ventricular contraction. Thus the stroke volume becomes greater up to a critical point, after which stroke volume decreases (cardiac failure). (*From L. L. Langley, Review of Physiology, 3d ed., McGraw-Hill, New York, 1971. Used by permission of the publisher.*)

increases in volume eventually overstretch the myocardium and reduce contractility, thereby compromising ventricular function still further. The descending portion of the ventricular function curve is reached, perpetuating the underlying dysfunction.

The compensatory sympathetic response to myocardial failure produces vasoconstriction, which elevates arterial pressure and thereby increases afterload. In addition, the elevated ventricular volume further increases afterload. The combination of increased afterload and increased preload elevates the pressure work and the volume work of the heart. Since the failing myocardium does not possess the functional reserve to overcome this increased work load, further dysfunction ensues.

Effects of Circulatory Assistance Devices

Mechanical circulatory assistance can reverse the abnormal circulatory dynamics perpetuating myocardial failure. The three primary mechanisms of circulatory assistance are (1) reduction of preload, (2) reduction of afterload with diastolic pressure augmentation, and (3) direct cardiac compression. Assist devices can be categorized in these three groups according to their primary effect. However, it must be remembered that interactions exist between preload, afterload, and contractility. Consequently, secondary changes in another variable may be noted for any given assist device.

Reduction of Preload

To reduce preload, the volume of blood the ventricle must eject must be decreased. This is accomplished by diverting a portion of the blood volume through an artificial circuit, bypassing the left ventricle. Preload reduction lowers the volume work of the heart.

Preload reduction improves the function of the failing ventricle, operating on the descending limb of the ventricular function curve. As ventricular volume and chamber size are reduced, correction of excessive myocardial fiber stretch is achieved and contractile force improves.

Reduction of Afterload with Diastolic Pressure Augmentation

To reduce afterload, the pressure the ventricle must generate to eject blood must be lowered. To accomplish this, the resistance to ventricular emptying must be lowered by reducing arterial pressure. Reduction of afterload is achieved with devices utilizing the principle of *counterpulsation.* Counterpulsation devices alter arterial pressure and resistance to ventricular emptying by changing arterial volume in synchrony with the mechanical phases of the cardiac cycle.

Counterpulsation devices operate in the following manner. During ventricular contraction, or systole, volume is withdrawn from the aorta into the device, and hence arterial pressure is reduced. The fall in arterial pressure lessens the resistance to ventricular ejection. Consequently, the ventricle does not have to generate as much pressure to eject blood into the aorta. This reduction of afterload lowers the pressure work of the heart.

In addition to afterload reduction, counterpulsation devices exert a second effect produced by the reinfusion of the volume withdrawn from the aorta. The volume is replaced during ventricular relaxation, or diastole, and arterial pressure is increased. This diastolic pressure elevation is referred to as *diastolic augmentation.* Since coronary flow occurs primarily during diastole, diastolic augmentation potentially increases myocardial blood flow and oxygen supply. Therefore, counterpulsation improves the oxygenation of the heart by reducing cardiac work and oxygen demand and increasing oxygen supply.

These devices are referred to as counterpulsation devices because the pumping or pulsating action of the ventricle and of the assistance device are synchronized to operate counter to one another. The ventricle pumps volume into the aorta during ventricular contraction, and the device reinfuses aortic volume during ventricular relaxation. Counterpulsation techniques are discussed more extensively in a subsequent section.

Direct Cardiac Compression

Contractile force can be increased mechanically only through the direct compression of the heart by the assist device. Cardiac massage maintains cardiac output in a similar manner.

HISTORICAL EVOLUTION OF DEVICES

Preload Reduction Devices

The design for preload reduction devices evolved from the technique utilized for total cardiopulmonary bypass during cardiac surgery. Gibbon introduced this technique in 1953. During total cardiopulmonary bypass, all the venous blood is shunted away from the right atrium into the circulatory assist device through catheters inserted into the venae cavae. The device oxygenates and pumps the blood into the arterial system through a cannula in the aorta (Fig. 36-3a). This technique, referred to as *veno-arterial bypass,* diverts blood around both the heart and lungs. Consequently, both the work of oxygenation and of tissue perfusion is assumed by the assist device. This complete cardiopulmonary support is utilized during open-heart surgery.

Partial cardiopulmonary bypass has been used for low-output states after myocardial infarction. With this technique, a portion of the venous return to the heart is diverted into the oxygenator pump through a catheter threaded through the femoral vein into the inferior vena cava (Fig. 36-3b). Blood from the oxygenator is pumped into the femoral artery. Partial bypass significantly reduces the volume work of the heart.

The primary disadvantage of partial bypass devices is this. Since the blood volume is returned to the arterial system throughout the entire cardiac cycle, arterial pressure elevation is produced throughout systole and diastole. Consequently, the resistance to ventricular ejection during systole is increased by partial bypass devices. This adverse consequence increases the pressure work of the heart. To overcome

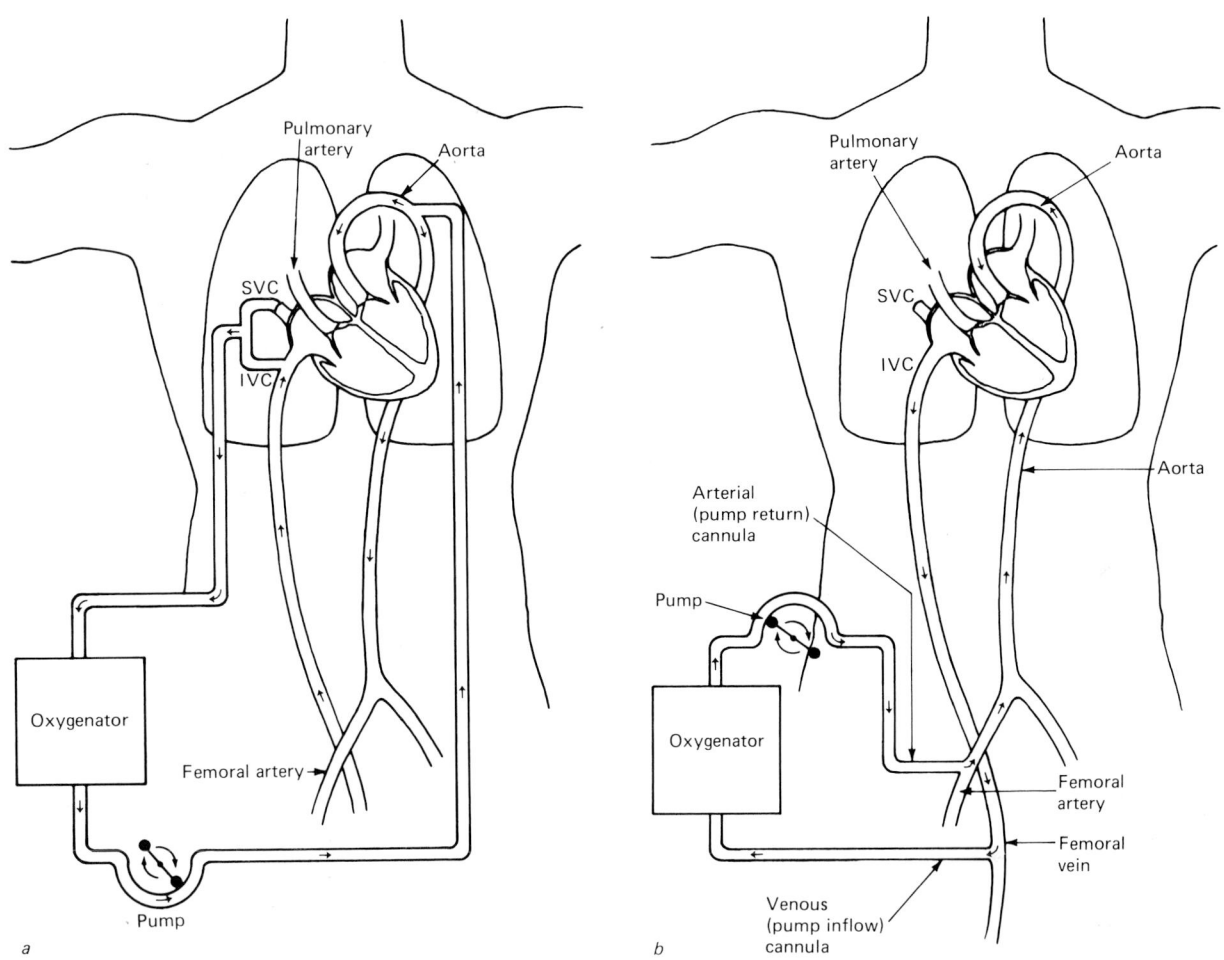

FIGURE 36-3

Cardiopulmonary bypass. (*a*) Total bypass. Venous blood is shunted from right atrium to assist device via catheters inserted into the superior vena cava (SVC) and inferior vena cava (IVC). The blood is oxygenated by the device and returned to the arterial system through a cannula in the aorta. (*b*) Partial bypass. A portion of the venous return is diverted into the assist device via a catheter threaded through the femoral vein into the inferior vena cava. Oxygenated blood is returned to the femoral artery.

this disadvantage, the principle of counterpulsation is being incorporated into the design of partial bypass units. During counterpulsation, volume is pumped into the arterial system only during diastole.

Despite the fact that cardiopulmonary bypass, either total or partial, is capable of great reductions in cardiac work, the clinical application of these devices for myocardial support is limited by many factors. First, blood element destruction during prolonged assistance secondary to mechanical trauma in the artificial circuit can be significant. Second, clotting and systemic embolization can be produced by clotting factor activation, where blood contacts the foreign surface. Third, the nonpulsatile flow of the artificial pump is not ideal for tissue perfusion. Finally, the complexity of operation necessitates the utilization of sophisticated monitoring and adjunctive measures.

Since myocardial disease predominantly compromises left ventricular function, some preload reduction devices bypass only the left heart. These devices permit the lungs to maintain oxygenation while relieving the left ventricle of volume work. During left heart bypass, blood is shunted from either the left atrium or left ventricle into the bypass device and returned to the arterial system. Thus, either left atrial-arterial bypass or left ventricular-arterial bypass is possible.

The following designs have been utilized for left atrial-arterial bypass: (1) direct cannulation of the left atrium with reperfusion of volume into a systemic artery (proposed by many authors); and (2) indirect left atrial cannulation via the internal jugular through the right atrium and interatrial septum with volume replacement into the femoral artery (Senning and Dennis) (Fig. 36-4). Bernhard's concept of left ventricular-arterial bypass has been applied as follows: (1) direct cannulation of the left ventricular apex with arterial return into either the ascending or descending aorta (Fig. 36-5a); and (2) Zwart's retrograde cannulation of the ventricle via the subclavian artery and aortic valve with replacement into the femoral artery

(Fig. 36-5b). Design considerations concerning thrombogenicity, mechanical trauma to blood elements, durability, and ease of application limit the current use of these devices.

Afterload Reduction Devices

In 1953 Kantrowitz and Kantrowitz advanced the concept of counterpulsation. The first experimental application was in 1961 by Clauss, with clinical application in 1964 by Harken. Over the years, many counterpulsation devices have been developed. The common thread among the devices is the reduction in aortic volume and pressure during systole and the elevation of aortic volume and pressure during diastole. The first method utilized to achieve this end was arterio-arterial pumping. A cannula was placed in a major artery, usually the subclavian or femoral artery. A bolus of blood was withdrawn during systole and replaced during diastole.

The form of arterio-arterial pumping known as the *auxiliary ventricle* was developed by Kantrowitz in 1968. This device operates according to the principle of counterpulsation, with blood withdrawal from the ascending aorta and blood replacement into the descending aorta. Problems with blood element destruction and clotting during arterio-arterial pumping led investigators to consider alternative methods to obtain counterpulsation.

Moulopoulos reported experimental results with the intra-aortic balloon pump for counterpulsation in 1962. This technique substitutes gas volume for blood volume as the counterpulsation agent. The balloon, threaded retrograde into the descending thoracic aorta via a femoral arteriotomy, is inflated with gas during diastole and deflated during systole, changing aortic volume and pressure accordingly (Fig. 36-6). The intra-aortic balloon pump gained popularity as a circulatory assistance device in 1967 after Kantrowitz published initial clinical studies of balloon pumping in cardiogenic shock. Subsequently, the clinical application of balloon pumping has been developed at multiple centers.

Counterpulsation can be effected without entering the vasculature by the application of external pressure to the lower extremities. During external counterpulsation, the legs are enclosed in water-filled sleeves (Fig. 36-7). The pressure exerted on the extremities is varied in synchrony with the cardiac cycle, alternatively compressing the legs during diastole and decompressing the legs during systole. Compression reduces the capacity of the peripheral vasculature,

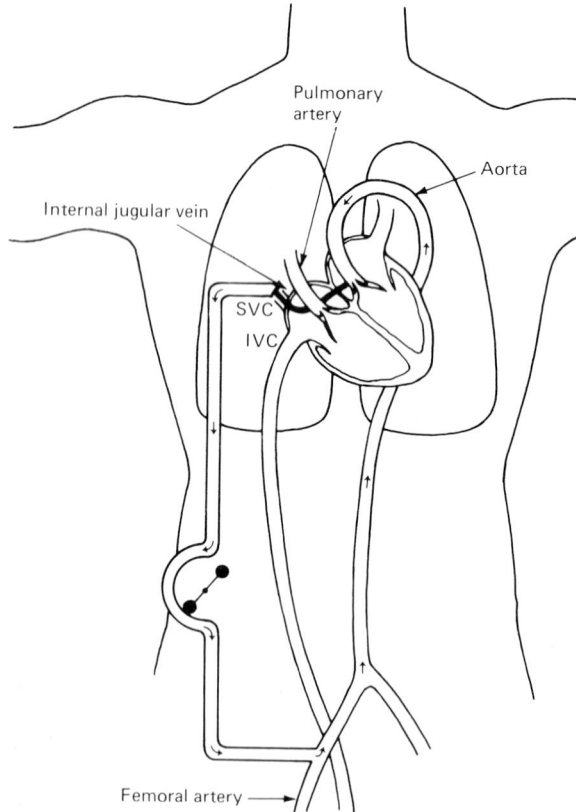

FIGURE 36-4

Left atrial-arterial bypass. Cannulation of the left atrium via catheter inserted into internal jugular through right atrium and atrial septum with return into the femoral artery. Utilized by Senning and Dennis.

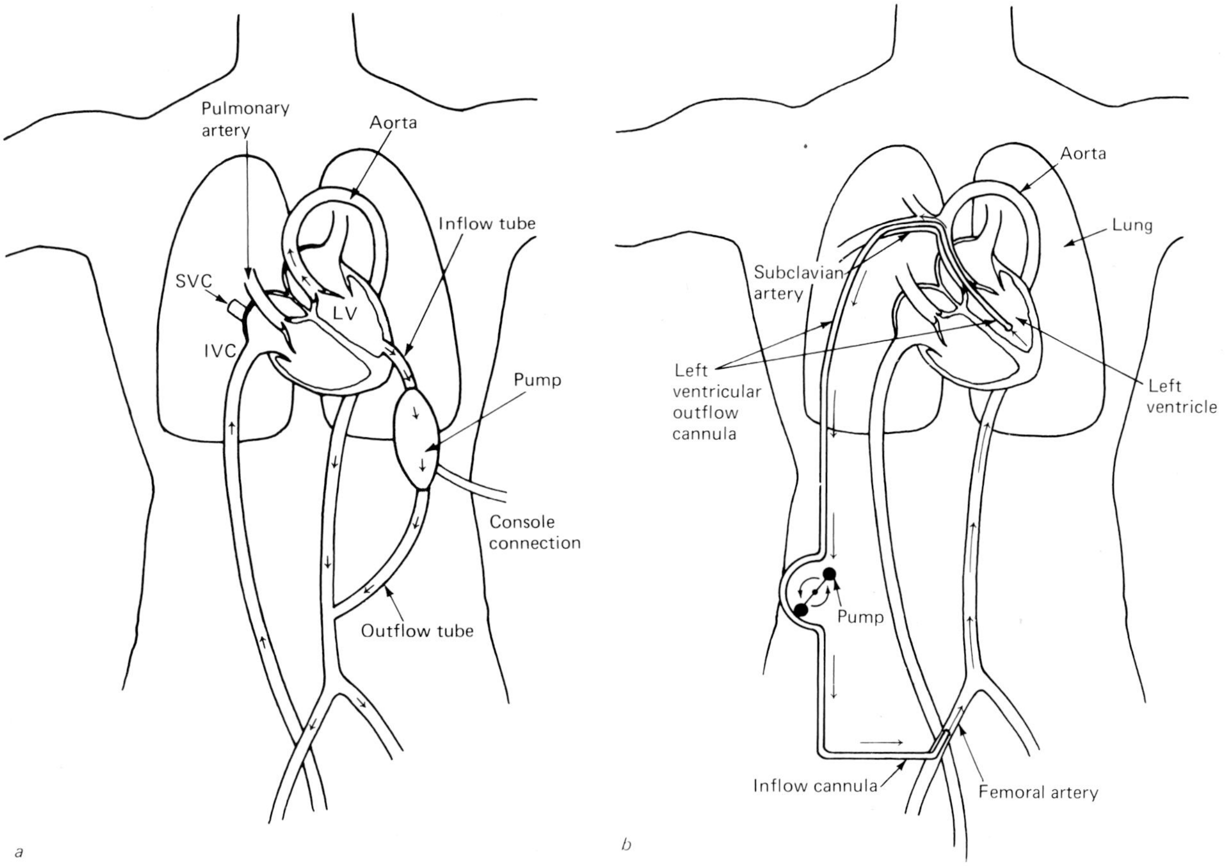

FIGURE 36-5

Left ventricular-arterial bypass. (*a*) Cannulation of left ventricular apex with arterial return into descending thoracic aorta. Utilized by Norman. (*b*) Retrograde ventricular cannulation via subclavian artery through aortic valve with arterial return to femoral artery. Utilized by Zwart.

displacing blood centrally and producing diastolic augmentation. Decompression during systole increases the peripheral vascular capacity, displacing blood into the extremities and lowering central aortic pressure and thereby reducing afterload. Experimental studies of external counterpulsation were first reported by Dennis, Osborne, and Birtwell in 1963, with subsequent clinical application by Ruiz in 1968 and Soroff in 1972.

Direct Cardiac Compression Devices

Direct cardiac compression was utilized as a means of artificially maintaining contractile force in the arrested heart as early as 1881 by Niehaus. Schiff

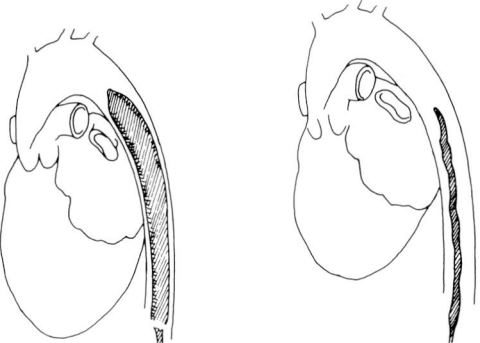

FIGURE 36-6

Intra-aortic balloon pump. The balloon is inflated with gas during diastole and deflated during systole.

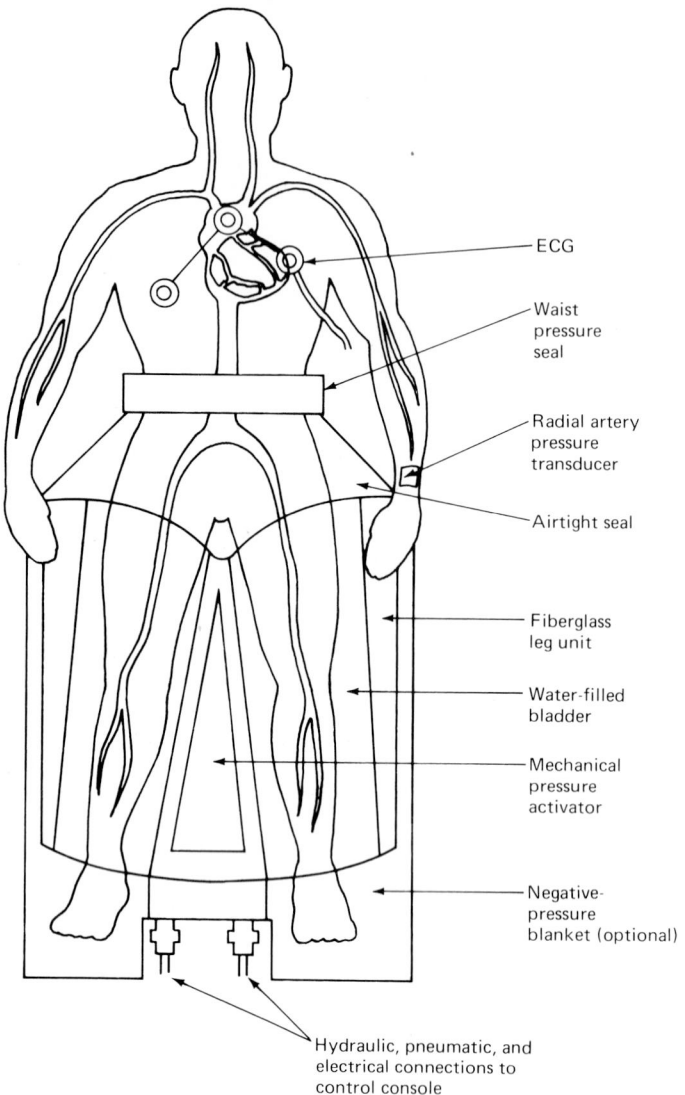

ECG

Waist pressure seal

Radial artery pressure transducer

Airtight seal

Fiberglass leg unit

Water-filled bladder

Mechanical pressure activator

Negative-pressure blanket (optional)

Hydraulic, pneumatic, and electrical connections to control console

FIGURE 36-7

External counterpulsation. Legs are enclosed in water-filled sleeves. Compression is applied during diastole, with decompression during systole. [*Used by permission from W. B. Saunders, Methods in Critical Care: The AACN Manual (in press).*]

developed a method of open-chest cardiac compression that was first used successfully in 1901.

Circulatory assist devices have been developed which utilize this same principle. One approach to direct cardiac compression that has been evaluated extensively is the Anstadt cup. The cup, placed over the ventricles, pneumatically compresses the heart. Potential myocardial trauma and the need for a thoracotomy limits the clinical application. The current application of the Anstadt cup is for preservation of other organs in preparation for transplantation.

CURRENT DEVICES

Two counterpulsation devices are currently available commercially for circulatory assistance in critical-care unit settings: (1) intra-aortic balloon pump (IABP) and (2) external pressure circulatory assist (EPCA).

The intra-aortic balloon pump is an internal, invasive unit; external counterpulsation is noninvasive. The intra-aortic balloon pump is utilized most extensively; consequently, its clinical application will be explored in depth. In addition, two categories of left heart assist devices are undergoing extensive clinical trials: (1) left atrial-arterial bypass units and (2) left ventricular-arterial bypass units. The unique features and current status of each will be discussed.

Counterpulsation Devices

Intra-Aortic Balloon Pump

The intra-aortic balloon is threaded retrograde via the femoral artery into the descending thoracic aorta just distal to the left subclavian artery and proximal to the renal arteries. The balloon is inflated and deflated with gas in synchrony with the mechanical events of the cardiac cycle. Typically, the R wave of the ECG, corresponding to ventricular depolarization, is the triggering signal for balloon synchronization. Alternatively, the arterial pressure waveform may be used as a stimulus.

During left ventricular ejection, or systole, the balloon must be deflated. Conversely, during ventricular relaxation, or diastole, the balloon is inflated. Thus, the timing of balloon activation is opposite that of ventricular activation. Therefore, balloon action is referred to as *counterpulsation*. The effects of counterpulsation are twofold: (1) augmentation of diastolic pressure and (2) reduction of afterload. The first effect occurs just as the aortic valve closes at the end of ventricular ejection, when gas is propelled into the balloon. Balloon inflation raises intra-aortic volume, thereby elevating aortic pressure. The increment in aortic pressure during diastole is referred to as *diastolic augmentation* (Fig. 36-8).

The physiologic effects of diastolic augmentation are significant in terms of coronary flow and tissue perfusion. Coronary flow is phasic because the branches of the coronary arteries are deeply embedded in the myocardium. During systole these intramyocardial branches are compressed, increasing the resistance to flow. During diastole, however, the coronary vascular resistance is minimal; therefore, coronary filling occurs primarily during diasole. The timing of pressure augmentation during balloon pumping is therefore optimal. Elevating diastolic pressure increases coronary perfusion pressure and potentially increases coronary blood flow and oxygen supply.

Diastole:
Augmentation of
diastolic pressure

A. Coronary perfusion
B. Systemic perfusion

Inflation

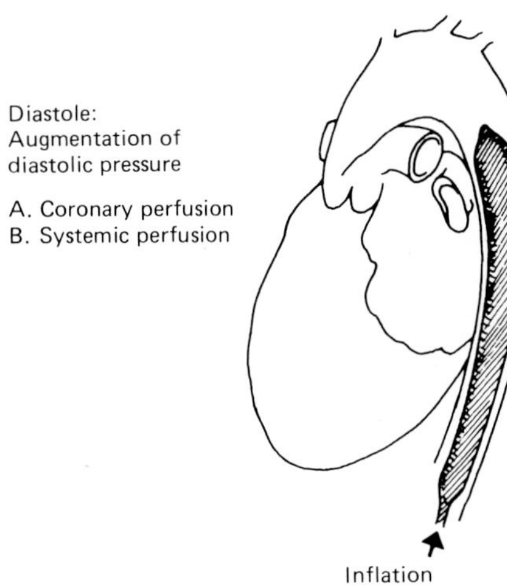

FIGURE 36-8

Effect of intra-aortic balloon inflation. (*From S. Price and L. Wilson, Pathophysiology: Clinical Concepts of Disease Processes, McGraw-Hill, New York, 1978. Used by permission.*)

However, despite the fact that coronary perfusion pressure is elevated by balloon pumping, variable effects on total coronary blood flow have been documented. In some instances, total coronary blood flow is elevated by diastolic augmentation; in others it is unchanged or even reduced. This variability results because the dominant mechanism controlling coronary blood flow is autoregulation within the coronary bed—not coronary perfusion pressure. Autoregulation is an intrinsic mechanism altering coronary blood flow in response to tissue need for oxygen. The process of autoregulation maintains a precise balance between myocardial oxygen supply and demand. Local tissue hypoxia or oxygen lack is the most potent stimulus for increasing coronary blood flow and oxygen supply through coronary vasodilation. Conversely, a reduction in oxygen demand produces a corresponding reduction in coronary blood flow through vasoconstriction. Since counterpulsation reduces myocardial work and oxygen demand, overall coronary blood flow may be reduced during balloon pumping via autoregulated vasoconstriction, despite the elevation of aortic diastolic pressure.

Typically, absolute increases in total coronary blood flow are noted when the myocardium has been underperfused because of hypotension prior to initiation of balloon pumping. In this instance, the myocardium is flow-deprived by the low-pressure state and is maximally dilated by the resultant tissue hypoxia. Consequently, elevation of pressure elevates flow. However, in the absence of hypotension, the balloon essentially supplements the autoregulatory process, offering a reserve in coronary perfusion pressure and oxygen supply.

In contrast to the variable effects on total coronary blood flow, favorable localized effects on flow do occur with diastolic augmentation. Flow to myocardium threatened by significant obstructive lesions is pressure-dependent. The normal autoregulatory ability is impaired by disease. Therefore, flow to these potentially ischemic regions improves with elevation of diastolic pressure. In addition, the balloon may increase coronary collateral development.

Clinical evidence of improved tissue perfusion may be apparent, especially in low-output states with compensatory sympathetic vasoconstriction and high peripheral vascular resistance, in the following parameters: (1) urine output, (2) mentation, (3) peripheral pulses, and (4) skin temperature and color. Circulatory support maintains an adequate mean arterial pressure, typically permitting discontinuation of catecholamine support.

In summary, diastolic augmentation increases the available myocardial oxygen supply, improves the

distribution of coronary blood flow to potentially ischemic regions of the myocardium, and improves peripheral tissue perfusion.

Balloon deflation occurs rapidly, immediately prior to systole just before the aortic valve opens. As gas is removed from the balloon, the intra-aortic volume is diminished and therefore aortic pressure is reduced. This reduction in aortic pressure lowers the resistance to left ventricular ejection during systole. This effect is referred to as *reduction of afterload* (Fig. 36-9).

Since the resistance to left ventricular ejection is reduced, the ventricle can empty more easily and more completely. The balloon therefore facilitates "systolic unloading" or emptying. This effect is manifested by an increase in cardiac output and a reduction in left ventricular end-diastolic pressure, left atrial pressure, and pulmonary capillary wedge pressure.

Afterload reduction produces a number of physiologic alterations. Since the resistance to ventricular ejection is reduced, the systolic pressure the left ventricle must generate to open the aortic valve and eject blood is correspondingly lower. As a result, the ventricle does not have to generate as much pressure during systole, and cardiac work is reduced. Finally, a reduction in cardiac work lowers myocardial oxygen demand and oxygen consumption. In essence, afterload reduction improves myocardial efficiency and reduces cardiac work and oxygen demand.

The cumulative effect of intra-aortic balloon counterpulsation is to elevate diastolic pressure and lower systolic pressure. Cardiac work is reduced, while tissue perfusion is maintained. Myocardial oxygenation is improved with a reduction in oxygen demand and an increment in oxygen supply.

Multiple indications for balloon pumping have been identified. Historically, the first application was cardiogenic shock. The development of cardiogenic shock after myocardial infarction carries an ominous prognosis because of extensive muscle necrosis. Usually, over 40 percent of the left ventricular muscle mass is involved. A self-perpetuating cycle of progressive left ventricular dysfunction characterizes the shock syndrome, with mortality approaching 100 percent (Fig. 36-10). The myocardial dysfunction produces hypotension with resultant systemic and myocardial hypoperfusion, hypoxia, and acidosis. Coronary flow to potentially viable, ischemic myocardium is compromised, extending the size of the infarct and increasing the degree of ventricular dysfunction. The balloon pump, by virtue of its ability to simultaneously improve coronary perfusion and re-

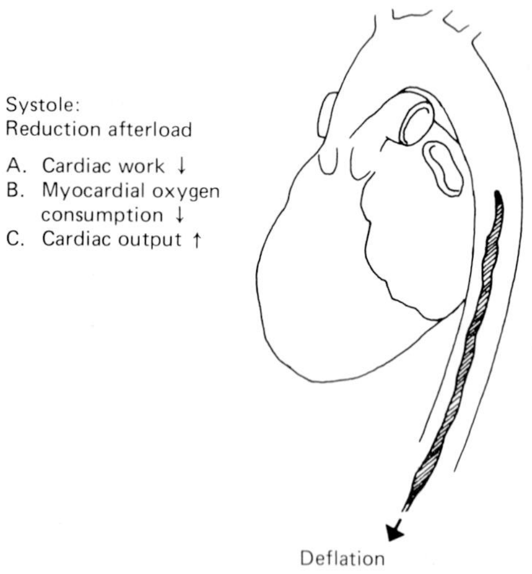

Systole:
Reduction afterload

A. Cardiac work ↓
B. Myocardial oxygen consumption ↓
C. Cardiac output ↑

Deflation

FIGURE 36-9

Effect of intra-aortic balloon deflation. (*From S. Price and L. Wilson, Pathophysiology: Clinical Concepts of Disease Processes, McGraw-Hill, New York, 1978. Used by permission of the publisher.*)

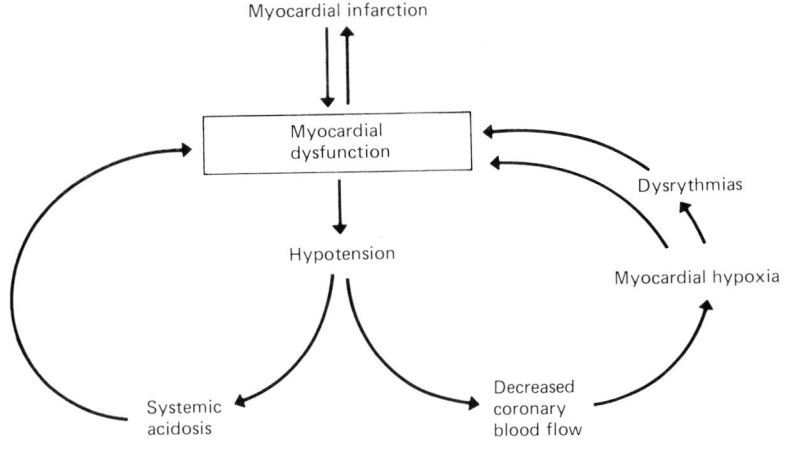

FIGURE 36-10

Self-perpetuating cycle of cardiogenic shock. (*From W. Bruce Dunkman et al., Clinical and hemodynamic results of IABP and surgery for cardiogenic shock, Circulation 46:474, 1972.*)

duce cardiac work, seemed the ideal intervention to interrupt this vicious cycle of deterioration.

The treatment of cardiogenic shock with balloon pumping has evolved in two phases. Beginning in 1968, patients in cardiogenic shock refractory to standard medical therapy were treated with balloon pumping of variable duration. The diagnosis of shock was established by clinical and hemodynamic criteria. Impressive clinical and hemodynamic improvement was noted in approximately 80 percent of the patients, usually within 1 to 2 h. However, the apparent improvement was deceptive, for the balloon effect was transient. Approximately 70 percent of the patients with early improvement showed later deterioration despite adequate counterpulsation. Only about 17 percent of the patient group could become balloon-independent. The mortality rate for established cardiogenic shock was not greatly improved by temporary circulatory assistance with the balloon pump. Apparently, the myocardial dysfunction associated with cardiogenic shock was so extensive that only more aggressive intervention could effect survival.

In 1970 a combined medical-surgical approach was investigated with institution of balloon pumping, followed by emergency angiography and acute revascularization. This combination was associated with a survival rate of approximately 30 to 40 percent. These relatively bleak statistics indicated that extensive, irreversible damage to the left ventricle is incompatible with survival. More recent statistics indicate a survival rate of 50 to 55 percent in patients

carefully selected for surgery. Survival is highest in the setting of associated reversible, ischemic depression of myocardial function. Balloon pumping offers temporary protection for ischemic muscle by reducing oxygen demand and increasing oxygen supply and support for the failing circulation until cardiac catheterization and surgery can be undertaken. Consequently, intervention in the shock state must be early to maximize myocardial salvage. However, even with early intervention, patients falling into two groups still inevitably die: (1) those unresponsive to balloon pumping and (2) those dependent upon the balloon for hemodynamic stability who do not undergo surgery.

The clinical syndrome of shock after myocardial infarction can be produced by mechanical defects other than extensive destruction of left ventricular muscle mass. Two structural defects can produce extensive myocardial dysfunction and rapid clinical deterioration: (1) ventricular septal rupture and (2) acute mitral regurgitation due to papillary muscle rupture or dysfunction.

Both defects produce abnormalities in blood flow by creating a second outflow tract from the left ventricle, either through the ventricular septum or retrograde through the mitral valve. Consequently, during ventricular contraction, there is competitive outflow through the aorta and the defect. Since blood flow will follow the path of least resistance, considerable volumes of blood can be lost through the defects into the relatively low-pressure chambers of either the right ventricle or left atrium (Fig. 36-11). The flow abnormalities produced by both defects can be minimized by balloon pumping. Deflation of the balloon immediately prior to ventricular contraction reduces the resistance to ejection into the aorta and lowers the systolic pressure the ventricle must generate. As a result, forward flow into the aorta increases and backward flow through either the ventricular septal defect or mitral valve decreases.

Maximum stabilization is usually achieved within 24 h. Typically, there is a plateau of improvement

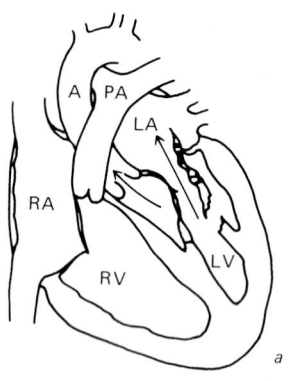

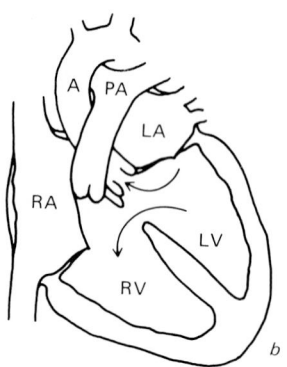

FIGURE 36-11

Structural defects after myocardial infarction. (*a*) Ventricular septal rupture. (*b*) Papillary muscle rupture producing mitral regurgitation. (*From S. Price and L. Wilson, Pathophysiology: Clinical Concepts of Disease Processes, McGraw-Hill, New York, 1978. Used by permission of the publisher.*)

lasting 24 to 48 h, followed by progressive clinical deterioration despite continued balloon pumping. Consequently, angiography and cardiac surgery are usually advisable during the period of peak improvement.

Ventricular aneurysm is the third mechanical defect associated with myocardial infarction that is responsive to balloon assistance. With this defect, the myocardial scar has thinned and balloons outward with each systole. A portion of the stroke volume is lost to passive distention of this noncontractile segment. Ventricular aneurysms can produce significant mechanical dysfunction, but frequently of greater concern is the incidence of malignant ventricular arrhythmias refractory to medical therapy. Insertion of the balloon pump improves the mechanical dysfunction by reducing intracardiac and pulmonary congestion and improving cardiac output. The incidence of malignant arrhythmias initially responds well to balloon pumping with either transient abolition of episodes or a significant reduction in frequency. This stabilization permits safe angiography. As a rule, unless subsequent surgical intervention is feasible, recurrence of arrhythmic episodes with progressive mechanical dysfunction ensues. Surgical intervention may abolish arrhythmias in a large proportion of patients.

The intra-aortic balloon pump has also demonstrated efficacy in the reversal of myocardial ischemia. During balloon pumping, a favorable balance between myocardial oxygen supply and demand can be restored by the simultaneous increase in coronary perfusion pressure and the reduction in cardiac work. Balloon pumping to reverse ischemia and salvage myocardium is a compelling concept because the myocardial dysfunction and clinical sequelae of established muscle necrosis can be irreversible and lethal. To effect a substantive reduction in the mortality and morbidity associated with coronary atherosclerotic disease, efforts must focus upon the protection and salvage of viable ischemic tissue rather than upon end-stage support of nonviable, infarcted muscle.

Intra-aortic balloon pumping is considered as a means of reversing ischemia and protecting the myocardium if all conventional modes of therapy have failed, including bedrest, nitrates, and propranolol. Ischemia must be documented according to clinical, hemodynamic, and electrocardiographic criteria. Persistent refractory ischemia is considered an indication for balloon pumping in certain institutions. Refractory ischemia may occur either in the early recovery phase of myocardial infarction or without evidence of prior myocardial infarction. This latter syndrome of unstable, refractory ischemia without infarction is referred to as *accelerated* or *preinfarction angina*. Typically, patients with postinfarction angina are either threatening infarct extension or infarction of another myocardial region. Progressive loss of functioning myocardium can precipitate cardiogenic shock. Early intervention with balloon pumping can potentially prevent the loss of a critical muscle mass, thereby improving prognosis.

Following insertion of the intra-aortic balloon pump, patients with refractory ischemia undergo coronary and left ventricular angiography to document the extent and location of disease. As a rule, the ischemic episodes are controlled by balloon pumping. Poor control of angina on the balloon is usually associated with high-risk lesions, such as left main or high-grade left anterior descending lesions, or severe multivessel disease. If angina recurs during pumping, balloon support may be supplemented with intravenous nitroglycerin infusion or beta-blockade to further reduce afterload and oxygen demand.

If at catheterization it is determined that surgery is indicated, it is usually performed within 12 to 36 h to avoid unnecessary prolongation of balloon pumping and further myocardial deterioration. However, if angina persists or recurs while a patient is on the balloon, surgery on a more urgent basis is considered. The intraoperative and immediate postoperative course of patients with refractory preinfarction ischemia supported by the balloon pump is remarkably benign. Weaning and removal of the balloon can usually be undertaken within 12 to 24 h. This course is consistent with the fact that the ventricle has not suffered any irreversible damage. The course of postinfarction patients is also stabilized by the ongoing pumping; however, the timing of balloon removal is usually slightly later because of the residual ventricular damage incurred during the acute infarction.

The transient myocardial depression produced during cardiac surgery by such factors as the intraoperative manipulation and the sequelae of total cardiopulmonary bypass is well-recognized. Reversible global or localized ischemia can be induced by prolonged aortic cross-clamp time, inadequate myocardial preservation techniques, or low-flow states. The myocardial depression and ischemia is usually reversed within 24 to 48 h postoperatively as physiologic perfusion is restored. However, myocardial function can be precarious immediately upon termination of cardiopulmonary bypass.

Until recently, postcardiotomy patients with profound myocardial depression immediately following bypass usually died in the operating room despite prolonged resuscitative maneuvers. The intra-aortic balloon pump was introduced to reverse resistant postcardiotomy shock in 1972. Temporary support of these patients with a grave intraoperative prognosis not only permitted termination of total cardiopulmonary bypass but also tided many patients through the transient period of postcardiotomy myocardial depression with eventual functional recovery. At this time, approximately 50 percent of patients who would die intraoperatively secondary to profound myocardial depression can be salvaged through the application of balloon pumping for variable periods of time after bypass.

Preoperative insertion of the balloon may be utilized to protect the myocardium during the induction of anesthesia in the setting of high-risk lesions, such as left main coronary lesions. Intraoperative infarction in this setting may produce massive myocardial necrosis, preventable with appropriate myocardial protection. The balloon pump is also utilized in certain institutions to protect the myocardium during noncardiac surgery on patients with unstable cardiac disease. For example, the mortality rate for general anesthesia performed within the first 6 weeks after an acute myocardial infarction is 34 to 57 percent. Insertion of the balloon pump for myocardial protection during the anesthetic induction of these patients and the subsequent surgery may reduce the associated morbidity and mortality.

The absolute contraindications to intra-aortic balloon pumping are anatomical considerations. For the most part, the relative contraindications involve ethical issues that must be decided at the discretion of the patient, family, and physician.

The absolute contraindications are the following: (1) aortic aneurysm, (2) aortic dissection, (3) aortic valve insufficiency, and (4) severe peripheral vascular disease. Aortic wall damage precludes insertion because of the hazard of progressive damage with potential aortic rupture secondary to the mechanical stress of pumping. Balloon inflation in the setting of aortic valve insufficiency would increase the retrograde flow into the left ventricle during diastole, worsening the underlying dysfunction. Severe peripheral vascular disease significantly increases the incidence of arterial trauma and peripheral embolization. Extensive atherosclerosis in the peripheral arterial vessels may prevent passage of the balloon catheter through the femoral artery. If balloon pumping is required urgently, consideration will be given to an alternative approach intraoperatively through the aorto-iliac system or retrograde via the ascending aorta into the descending aorta.

Nursing care of the patient undergoing balloon pumping does not differ significantly from the care of any critically ill patient. Only those considerations unique to the care of patients on the balloon pump will be considered in this chapter. It is assumed that nurses caring for these patients possess a sound knowledge of hemodynamic monitoring, cardiac pacing, cardiac rhythm analysis, and patient assessment. Expertise in these areas is essential to provide safe and effective patient care during balloon pumping.

The balloon is usually inserted in the intensive-care unit (ICU) under local anesthesia. The conversion of an ICU cubicle into a mini operating room is potentially taxing to even the most experienced critical-care nurse unless careful consideration is given to precise room organization prior to the arrival of the surgical entourage. The absolute necessity of consistently organizing the available space to ensure easy access to all equipment, medication, and the patient cannot be overemphasized. Any medical emergency or complication can be handled readily without unnecessary delay if appropriate precautions are taken. Failure to effectively organize the overabundant equipment can be catastrophic.

It is a nursing responsibility to create an environment that is safe and efficient for patient care and balloon insertion. A room plan should be developed with designated locations for essential equipment and supplies, including defibrillator, pacemaker, intubation equipment, emergency medications, monitor, IV poles with transducers, infusion pumps, bed, balloon console, operating room light, instrument tray, and waste bins. A minimum of two oxygen outlets and two vacuum outlets for endotracheal and operative field suction must be available. An equipment cart containing all miscellaneous supplies required during insertion is an invaluable addition. As a rule, setting up the cubicle according to a predesignated plan can be accomplished within half an hour by one nurse.

Upon arrival of the patient, an initial clinical assessment must be completed during the admission procedure. The following information is critical to the anticipated insertion procedure: (1) Status of peripheral pulses must be determined. Pulses must be checked and the quality recorded. Significant peripheral vascular disease may prevent the passage of the balloon catheter through the ilio-femoral system and increases the risk of arterial trauma during insertion. Also, postinsertion assessment of pulses is meaningless without accurate baseline data for comparison. (2) History of bleeding tendencies or medication sensitivity must be noted. Anticoagulants and antibiotics are routinely administered during the insertion procedure. (3) Patient expectations and preparation for the procedure must be assessed to guide subsequent teaching and support efforts. Depending upon time constraints and the presenting problem, additional information elicited should be tailored accordingly.

Once the admission procedure is completed, the first priority is to establish quality electrocardiographic and hemodynamic monitoring signals. The electrocardiogram is of primary importance during balloon pumping since it provides the triggering signal for balloon action. To effectively coordinate balloon and cardiac action, the balloon console must sense the R wave of the electrocardiogram. To ensure that the console senses only the R wave and not other ECG waves, a lead should be selected that demonstrates maximal R wave amplitude and minimal amplitude of all other ECG components, including pacing artifacts. This is most easily accomplished by recording a 12-lead ECG, reviewing all leads, and identifying the lead with the required ECG configuration. The patient electrodes can then be placed on the chest to duplicate the desired lead. For example, if lead I evidences the desired waveforms, the negative recording electrode would be placed near the right arm with the positive recording electrode near the left arm. If none of the standard 12 leads are adequate, the electrodes can be systematically moved around the precordium until the ideal electrode placement is identified.

Insertion of the arterial line is the next priority. The arterial line is necessary to accurately time balloon action. The arterial tracing represents the mechanical activity of the heart, whereas the ECG reflects the electrical activity. Since the intra-aortic balloon is a mechanical assist device, accurate synchronization can only be obtained utilizing the arterial tracing. On certain consoles, the ECG trace is used as a guide for "initial" timing adjustments prior to initiation of pumping. This is possible since a rough relationship exists between the electrical and mechanical cycle (Fig. 36-12). Ventricular contraction begins approximately at the R wave and continues through the peak of the T wave; consequently, a deflation marker can be placed in the P-R interval with the inflation marker superimposed on the peak of the T wave. Once pumping begins, precision timing is possible only by observing the arterial tracing for waveform alterations indicative of effective balloon pumping.

The arterial line is usually inserted in the radial artery. Although arterial tracings obtained directly from the aortic root would best reflect the balloon effect relative to aortic valve closure and opening, aortic root pressure monitoring is not currently a bedside technique. Radial arterial monitoring is a useful alternative since it has minimal waveform delay and distortion despite the peripheral location. Femoral arterial monitoring can also be used; however, the greater anatomic distance from central aortic events produces more wave transmission delay and waveform distortion. The left radial artery is usually selected rather than the right, since the balloon lies just below the left subclavian artery. If the balloon is displaced slightly upward in the aorta, the waveform obtained via the left radial artery will become damped, providing a valuable diagnostic index of balloon location, particularly useful during insertion.

Insertion of a Swan-Ganz balloon-tipped, flow-directed, thermodilution pulmonary arterial catheter may be indicated to evaluate the effect of the balloon on left heart function. Continual recording of pulmonary arterial pressure with periodic measurement of pulmonary capillary wedge pressure, right atrial pressure, and cardiac output is possible with this catheter. These data are particularly valuable in the management of patients with severely compromised left ventricular function, such as cardiogenic shock. All hemodynamic lines are connected to a continuous or intermittent flush system and pressure transducers.

The insertion of an additional central line and a peripheral line is recommended. The central line is necessary for the infusion of vasopressors, if required during balloon insertion. The right atrial lumen of the Swan-Ganz thermodilution catheter should only be substituted as the route for vasopressor infusion in an emergency, since the lumen is required for cardiac output measurement. Vasopressors, such as Levophed or dopamine, must be mixed and connected on standby to the line, requiring only the release of the infusion clamp for administration. A peripheral line is necessary in the event that volume must be rapidly infused during the procedure. Volume, such as 5% albumin, should be available in the room. Blood must be set up in the blood bank in the event of significant arterial trauma and bleeding. If insertion of a pacing wire is indicated, the wire must be connected to the unit on standby. Unfortunately, these simple preparations can be easily overlooked. Seemingly minor omissions can have grave consequences if a draped, relatively inaccessible patient becomes unstable.

Finally, the balloon console should be prepared for start-up either by the nurse or the responsible

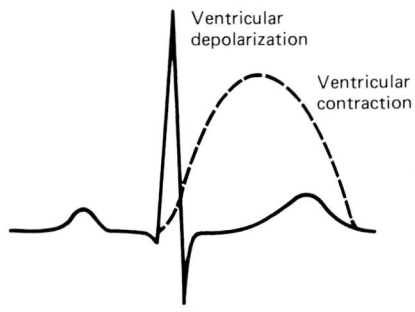

FIGURE 36-12

Correlation between ventricular depolarization and ventricular contraction. (*From S. Price and L. Wilson, Pathophysiology: Clinical Concepts of Disease Processes, McGraw-Hill, New York, 1978. Used by permission of the publisher.*)

balloon technician. If console operation is a nursing responsibility, a second nurse should be responsible for console preparation and operation during insertion. Ideally, the primary nurse should be free of console responsibilities to monitor patient status and provide patient support. In addition, one of the two available nurses should expect to circulate as needed to support the operating room team. The circulating function is not time-consuming if the operating room staff has their equipment organized and centralized on the instrument tray or an independent balloon equipment cart.

Immediately prior to insertion, the operative field is prepped and the patient is draped. The drape should be arranged so that the patient's head is uncovered and access to all lines and pacing wires is maintained. The operating room light or head light is arranged, and the suction is brought into the field. The most common oversight once this operative environment is created is to forget that the patient is not under general anesthesia. The patient must remain the pivotal figure during insertion, and continual attention must be given to patient needs and perceptions. Mild sedation may be advisable during the procedure, if tolerated. However, the most important tranquilizer is ongoing support and interaction with the nurse. The nurse must interpret events for the patient and establish appropriate expectations for the patient, minimizing the opportunity for misperception.

In brief, the insertion procedure consists of the following events. The incision site is infiltrated with local anesthesia, usually xylocaine 1% without epinephrine. The femoral artery is then exposed and tourniquets are placed around the vessel. The vessel is occluded and a femoral arteriotomy is made. The balloon is then guided up the iliofemoral system through the arteriotomy into the descending thoracic aorta just distal to the left subclavian artery. A sidearm graft, previously placed around the balloon, is anastomosed to the arteriotomy. All air is aspirated from the balloon, and the balloon is inserted through the graft into the femoral artery. The balloon must not come in contact with metal objects, since this may disrupt the antithrombogenic surface. The graft is then tourniqueted about the balloon catheter protruding out of the femoral artery (Fig. 36-13). In this fashion, upon completion of the procedure, blood flow through the femoral artery around the catheter is not compromised. The excess graft is then pruned down. The incision is closed and a sterile, all-occlusive dressing is applied.

Balloon location must be confirmed immediately after insertion either by fluoroscopy or a stat chest film. During insertion, the following two techniques are used to facilitate accurate placement: (1) Prior to insertion, the catheter is placed over the chest with the distal tip at the angle of Louis and the proximal end extending over the insertion site. A tie is placed around the catheter at the level of the arteriotomy. The catheter is then inserted into the femoral artery up to the level of the tie. (2) The balloon is inserted into the descending aorta until the surgeon feels the aortic arch with the distal tip of the balloon or notes damping of the left radial trace. The balloon is then withdrawn a few centimeters until the tracing clears.

During the insertion, specific nursing interventions can be anticipated, based upon events encountered during the procedure. Patient comfort is the foremost concern. Adequate local anesthesia should be administered to avoid any sensation of pain at the insertion site. Typically, the greatest patient discomfort is secondary to the immobility required by the procedure. The patient should be instructed not to move, particularly not to flex the leg; and the patient must be assured that the nurse will provide comfort measures. Most patients are able to cooperate and do not require restraint. During the procedure, when the femoral artery must be tourniqueted off for short periods of time, transient leg numbness may be experienced. Patients must be aware that this is normal and will not last long. Any pain must be reported to the nurse to ensure appropriate intervention. Angina may be precipitated and must be controlled with medication during insertion. Back pain, if acute and sudden, may indicate dissection, warranting immediate notification of the physician.

To prevent infection, sterile conditions must be ensured during insertion. Room activity must be minimized. Everyone in the room should be gowned and masked. A broad spectrum antibiotic is administered one-half hour before insertion and every 6 h for at least 24 to 48 h.

Anticoagulation may also be indicated because insertion of a foreign substance into the vasculature can initiate clotting along the blood–foreign substance interface of the balloon. Despite the fact that the balloon is antithrombogenic, many institutions implement anticoagulation during balloon pumping. If anticoagulation is desired, an initial dose of heparin is administered intravenously approximately 3 min prior to the femoral arteriotomy. Heparinization is subsequently maintained either via continuous infusion or divided bolus doses. Low-molecular-weight dextran or Rheomacrodex may be administered at 10 to 20 mL/h, either alone or in conjunction with heparin after the balloon is in place. Rheomacrodex reduces the platelet aggregation precipitated by the balloon.

Once the balloon is in place, peripheral pulses

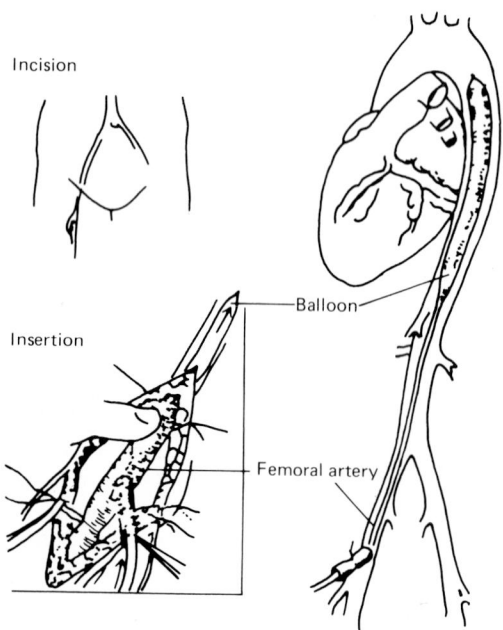

Incision

Insertion

Balloon

Femoral artery

FIGURE 36-13

Insertion and location of intra-aortic balloon. (*From P. J. Ford and R. W. Weintraub, Intra-Aortic Balloon Pumping, Aristocrat Press, Cambridge, 1974. Used by permission of the publisher.*)

must be checked immediately to ensure that blood flow to the extremity distal to the balloon is not compromised. The balloon catheter in the iliofemoral system should not impede blood flow distally to the leg. Diminished peripheral pulsation can be secondary to transient arterial spasm, arterial occlusion by the catheter or a thrombus, or peripheral embolization. Inadequate perfusion of the leg may necessitate balloon removal to preserve limb viability. On occasion, the balloon can then be reinserted on the contralateral side to maintain balloon pumping.

As soon as the balloon is positioned, pumping can begin. The timing is adjusted from the arterial tracing. To accurately adjust the timing of balloon inflation, the dicrotic notch corresponding to aortic valve closure must be identified on the arterial trace. The pressure elevation produced by balloon inflation should begin at the dicrotic notch on the arterial trace, confirming that the balloon is inflating at the end of ventricular ejection just as the aortic value is closing. Minor corrections must be made to adjust timing from a radial or femoral arterial line to account for slight delays in waveform transmission from the aorta to these more peripheral recording sites. The balloon curve of diastolic augmentation should continue from the dicrotic notch until slightly before the next patient systole. Immediately prior to systole, a reduction in arterial pressure to levels approximating end-diastolic pressure without balloon assistance will be noted as the balloon deflates rapidly. This fall in arterial pressure reduces the pressure that the ventricle must generate during systole. Thus, systolic pressure will be lowered during effective balloon pumping. Therefore, the expected waveform alterations evident during balloon pumping are elevated diastolic pressure and reduced systolic pressure (Fig. 36-14). Timing should be adjusted by trained personnel, because inappropriate timing can increase cardiac work and compromise myocardial function.

During balloon pumping in the critical-care unit, selected nursing considerations are most easily summarized according to systems. As would be expected, the cardiovascular system warrants close attention.

The hemodynamic and clinical response to balloon pumping should be evaluated every 15 to 60 min as patient condition dictates. Typically, within 1 to 2 h, even patients in cardiogenic shock with severely compromised ventricular function should evidence signs of improvement, e.g., falling pulmonary capillary wedge pressure and rising cardiac outputs. Catecholamine requirement for support of arterial pressure should diminish. Clinical signs and symptoms of compromised cardiac output, such as oliguria or obtundation, should improve. Failure to respond hemodynamically and clinically to balloon pumping carries a grave prognosis.

Patients requiring pumping for refractory myocardial ischemia usually experience either complete relief from pain or a reduction in the frequency of ischemic episodes. Recurrent angina on the balloon pump should immediately be brought to the attention of the responsible physician, since more aggressive therapy might be required to control the ischemia.

Evaluation of perfusion to the involved extremity should be performed hourly. Peripheral pulses and skin temperature and color should be checked relative to preinsertion status. It is essential that the quality of posterior tibial and dorsalis pedis pulses be assessed and recorded. The Doppler flow technique can be used to locate difficult-to-palpate pulses. When evaluating pulses, the opposite leg can be used for comparison, but it must be remembered that either leg can be the site of embolization from the aorto-iliac tree. Peripheral pulses, when located initially, should be marked to facilitate subsequent localization.

Timing must be evaluated and adjusted as needed. Even if timing adjustments are not the responsibility of nursing, nurses must be able to distinguish between normal and abnormal arterial waveform configurations. Quality hemodynamic signals must be preserved to ensure the accuracy of timing adjustments and to permit valid interpretation of hemodynamic status. In addition, since balloon triggering depends upon the ECG signal, electrode security must be maintained.

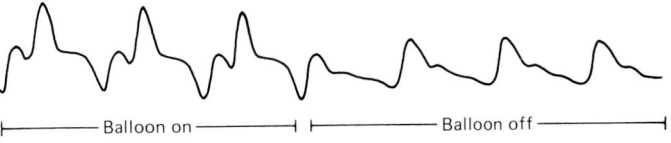

├── Balloon on ──────┤ ├────── Balloon off ──────┤

FIGURE 36-14
Balloon timing from arterial trace.

Hematologic studies must be evaluated closely to detect abnormalities. Platelet counts may fall because of disruption of platelet integrity by the balloon surface and the mechanical trauma. Rheomacrodex infusion at 10 to 20 mL/h minimizes this fall in platelets. Rarely is the administration of platelets required unless active bleeding is noted in the presence of thrombocytopenia. Hematocrits may also fall secondary to the inevitable blood loss during insertion and subsequent blood sampling. All blood losses, including blood sampling, should be recorded. Excessive blood loss or reduction in hematocrit may necessitate infusion of packed cells. At least 1 unit of blood should be on standby in the blood bank at all times. Anticoagulation status should be monitored closely with anticoagulation precautions in effect.

Respiratory considerations during balloon pumping are straightforward. The balloon should not interfere with respiratory care or chest physical therapy. The only modifications are positional. The head of the bed should not be elevated over 45°, nor should the involved leg be flexed at the hip. Either one of these maneuvers could kink and crack the balloon catheter at the site of insertion in the groin, or could displace the catheter proximally into the aortic arch, potentially traumatizing the intima. The patient can be turned from side to side with only mild angulation of the affected extremity. The balloon leg should be restrained if patient cooperation cannot be achieved. During chest physical therapy, avoid inducing artifact in the electrocardiogram, since it is the ECG that provides the triggering stimulus to the balloon.

Renal parameters are significant since renal perfusion is a sensitive index of cardiac output. Persistent oliguria on the balloon can be secondary to an inadequate cardiac output. However, unexplained oliguria should prompt assessment of balloon-related causes. The position of the balloon should be reevaluated on x-ray. Poor perfusion of the kidneys could also indicate renal embolization during insertion.

Similarly, neurological or psychological signs and symptoms can have multiple origins. Disturbances of mentation can be secondary to low cardiac output, embolization, hypoxia, or psychosis. Careful evaluation and documentation is therefore required. Psychological disturbances can be minimized by careful, ongoing attention to emotional support and patient teaching. Efforts to reduce sensory overstimulation and sleep deprivation are essential.

The number of indwelling catheters and the high frequency of invasive procedures predisposes these patients to infection. If surgery is necessary, preoperative infection increases the likelihood of endocarditis and other septic complications postoperatively. Therefore, strict sterile technique must be maintained during line management and dressing changes. Antibiotic coverage must not be overlooked for 24 to 48 h after insertion. Signs and symptoms of infection must be monitored closely.

Ideally, the indication for weaning is evidence of potential hemodynamic independence. However, on occasion, the balloon must be removed because of ischemia to the involved extremity. The contribution of the balloon pump to circulatory support can be progressively reduced over a period of hours. The weaning process can be accomplished either by gradual reduction in the frequency of balloon support or in the volume of balloon inflation. The first method is preferred. Most units have a weaning control to reduce the ratio of patient to balloon cycles. Typically, patients are weaned from 1:1 to 1:8 over a period of hours. The duration of weaning depends upon patient condition and physician preference. The primary nursing responsibility is to evaluate patient tolerance of the weaning process. Specific orders should be obtained prior to initiation of weaning to guide the weaning process. The criteria for resumption of balloon pumping at a higher frequency should be predetermined. Indications for substituting other pharmacologic means of support, such as vasopressors or volume, should be established. Weaning intolerance would be evidenced by rising pulmonary capillary wedge pressure, falling mean arterial pressure, falling cardiac output, oliguria, cardiac arrhythmias, or chest pain.

It must be remembered that despite the fact that patient stability is the usual indication for balloon removal, the procedure should be approached with the same care as balloon insertion. Careful planning is essential to avoid unnecessary complications. The environment must be organized to permit ready access to all equipment and supplies and to maintain sterile operative conditions in the critical-care unit. The patient must be prepared psychologically and physically for the procedure. Antibiotics should be reinstituted one-half hour before removal begins. The patient is draped and the balloon is removed under local anesthesia. During balloon removal, the femoral artery is fogartarized proximally and distally to remove any accumulated clot. Pulses should be evaluated during removal and immediately thereafter. Balloon removal represents the final stage of the weaning process, and patients should be observed closely for tolerance.

The complications of balloon pumping can be

considered in four categories: (1) infectious, (2) hematologic, (3) arterial, and (4) thromboembolic. All currently available units have fail-safe alarm systems with automatic unit shutdown in the event of an unsafe pumping condition. Therefore, complications are rarely related to unit malfunction; rather, they relate to the operative procedure and blood element reaction to the foreign, pulsatile balloon. The overall incidence of complications is less than 4 percent.

Wound sepsis is a potential infectious complication that must be prevented. Administration of a broad spectrum antibiotic one-half hour before balloon insertion and removal and for 24 to 48 h thereafter is common practice. Maintenance of strict aseptic technique during the operative procedures and subsequent dressing changes is obviously essential. Finally, all-occlusive, sterile dressings should be maintained over the groin incision and all long-line insertion sites. The following dressing change procedure has demonstrated efficacy: (1) Swab the area with acetone to defat the skin. (2) Scrub the area for 2 min with iodine. (3) Allow the iodine to dry. (4) Remove the iodine with alcohol. (5) Apply Betadine ointment to the incision. (6) Apply a dry, occlusive dressing. Dressing changes are performed in mask and gloves every 48 h and as needed.

Hematologic complications are secondary to the mechanical trauma of the balloon and potential balloon thrombogenicity. The potential platelet depression and recommended administration of Rheomacrodex has been discussed. The prophylactic anticoagulation to reduce the likelihood of thrombus formation on the balloon surface or catheter necessitates close observation of bleeding studies. Since the balloon surface is designed to be antithrombogenic, discontinuation of anticoagulation in the event of bleeding problems does not constitute an unwarranted risk. Hemolysis, once a problem during prolonged balloon pumping, is no longer a significant problem.

Arterial complications are closely related to the extent of peripheral vascular disease. Aorto-iliac trauma or dissection during insertion can be minimized by careful evaluation of the peripheral vasculature prior to insertion. Suspicion of severe peripheral vascular disease in a balloon candidate can be investigated by injection of contrast material into the aorto-iliac system. Balloon insertion in experienced hands is associated with a low incidence of arterial complications despite arterial disease. If the balloon catheter cannot be easily passed through one femoral artery, the opposite vessel is attempted with gentle catheter manipulation. Difficult insertions may neces-

sitate utilization of a smaller balloon or consideration of insertion directly into the iliac or ascending aorta.

Thromboembolic complications are also usually seen in the setting of peripheral vascular disease. A plaque may be dislodged during the insertion procedure. The potential for embolization of thrombi from the balloon surface is recognized, yet rarely reported. To minimize this potential, anticoagulation is advised and the balloon is never left deflated in the aorta for extended periods of time. Prolonged balloon deflation predisposes to pooling, stagnation of blood flow, and subsequent clot formation. The balloon should not remain deflated over 30 min. Gas embolism has been reported only in conjunction with mishandling of the console or the balloon. For example, perforation of the balloon surface with metal instruments may occur during insertion. No deaths have been reported with the units currently available.

External Pressure Circulatory Assist

External pressure circulatory assist is a noninvasive counterpulsation technique. Each lower extremity is enclosed in a water-filled cylindrical pumping chamber. External pressure applied to the lower extremities alters the volume of blood in the peripheral vasculature, and consequently, aortic pressure is modified.

The application of external pressure is synchronized with the cardiac cycle via the ECG. During diastole, positive pressure, up to +250 mmHg, is applied to the legs, compressing the peripheral vasculature. Compression modifies pressure in the arterial and venous circulation. In the arterial circuit, positive pressure in the periphery is transmitted retrograde into the aorta, elevating aortic diastolic pressure. Thus, diastolic augmentation is produced and coronary and systemic perfusion is enhanced. In the venous bed, external compression propels blood forward through the unidirectional venous valves into the right heart. As right heart filling increases, right heart output rises according to Starling's law.

During systole, the positive pressure is removed and negative pressures up to −50 mmHg may be applied. The relative negativity in the extremities displaces blood forward into the periphery, lowering aortic volume and pressure. Arterial resistance to ventricular ejection is reduced and the pressure work of the heart falls. The magnitude of afterload reduction is not as significant with external counterpulsation as with balloon pumping. Consequently, some centers will infuse vasodilators, such as nitroprusside, simultaneously to increase the effect upon afterload.

Volume displacement from the central venous system to the periphery is prevented by the venous valves.

The most extensive clinical evaluation of external counterpulsation has been undertaken at Tufts-New England Medical Center with Banas, Soroff, and Birtwell. The following indications for external counterpulsation have been considered: (1) cardiogenic shock, (2) severe chronic angina pectoris, and (3) acute, uncomplicated myocardial infarction.

The most intriguing proposed effect of external counterpulsation is that of enhancing the development of coronary collateral vessels. Dormant, interarterial anastomoses exist normally. These arterial channels are potential routes for collateral blood flow. However, for flow to occur via a collateral vessel, there must be a difference in pressure or a pressure gradient along the vessel. In the absence of coronary arterial disease, no difference in pressure exists between arteries. Progressive occlusion in one vessel produces a drop in pressure distal to the lesion. Consequently, dormant collateral channels, connecting the occluded vessel to normal arterial segments, are exposed to a pressure difference and flow can occur. Thus, dormant collaterals open. Counterpulsation may enhance this natural development of collateral flow by augmentation of coronary perfusion pressure during diastole. Diastolic augmentation may increase the pressure gradient across the collateral channel, potentially increasing flow.

The efficacy of external counterpulsation in cardiogenic shock is controversial. However, subjective relief of angina and improvement in exercise tolerance has been observed in a group of patients with chronic angina treated with external counterpulsation for 5 days with 1 h of counterpulsation daily. Apparently, this improvement was due to collateral development. The question arises as to whether external counterpulsation applied early in the course of acute myocardial infarction can salvage the ischemic zone surrounding the infarct, reducing the size of the ultimate infarct. This issue is currently under investigation.

Contraindications to external counterpulsation are aortic valve insufficiency and peripheral arterial or venous disease. The noninvasive nature of the procedure precludes complications associated with invasive counterpulsation. Mild patient discomfort has been noted.

Left Heart Assist Devices

Institution of left heart assist is currently considered for profound intraoperative myocardial depression evidenced by failure to wean from cardiopulmonary bypass. The present goal of left heart assistance is to provide temporary mechanical support until myocardial recovery occurs. During left heart assistance, oxygenated blood is diverted from either the left atrium or the left ventricle into the assist device, thereby decreasing preload and the volume work of the left heart. Concurrent with this reduction in cardiac work, adequate systemic perfusion is maintained by adjustments in the rate of blood flow through the assist device into the arterial circulation.

Left Atrial-Arterial Bypass

The left atrial-arterial bypass unit with the most extensive clinical application is the left heart assist device at Mt. Sinai in New York under the direction of Dr. Robert Litwak. This unit consists of two internal cannulas sutured to the left atrium and the ascending aorta, external extension tubing, and a roller pump (Fig. 36-15). The cannulas traverse the mediastinum and diaphragm and terminate in the subcutaneous tissue of the right upper quadrant of the abdomen. The cannulas are connected to the extension tubing of the roller pump, and the connections are buried in the abdominal subcutaneous tissue. The roller pump is secured to the abdominal wall and connected to the control console.

Candidates for the left atrial-arterial assist must evidence failure to wean from cardiopulmonary bypass after approximately 1 h of resuscitative efforts, including the balloon pump when possible. The following criteria for postcardiotomy depression are utilized at Mt. Sinai: (1) elevated left ventricular filling pressure (i.e., left atrial pressure over 25 mmHg), (2) systemic hypotension (i.e., systolic pressure under 90 mmHg), and (3) visibly compromised left ventricular contractility.

Institution of left atrial-arterial assist typically produces prompt hemodynamic stabilization. Since ventricular preload is reduced as blood volume is diverted from the left atrium into the assist device, left atrial pressure falls and normalizes. Simultaneously, the steady infusion of the diverted volume into the ascending aorta by the roller pump maintains arterial pressure at adequate levels. The rate of blood flow through the assist device is adjusted according to measured left atrial and arterial pressures. The maximum flow capacity of the unit is approximately 5 L/min.

The ability of left atrial-arterial devices to reduce afterload depends upon the design of the specific unit. Blood return to the arterial circuit can be either continuous, i.e., throughout the cardiac cycle, or phasic, i.e., during diastole. Continuous flow can increase afterload and, consequently, the pressure work of the heart, since the ventricle must eject against the resistance produced by a steady infusion of blood into the arterial circuit. Consequently, the design of some units permits synchronization of pump and cardiac action. These synchronized units fill during ventricular systole and infuse volume into the aorta during diastole. Thus, a counterpulsation effect can be achieved with afterload reduction and diastolic augmentation.

Once hemodynamic stabilization is achieved with left heart assist, cardiopulmonary bypass can be discontinued and transfer to the critical-care unit undertaken. Standard hemodynamic, physiologic, and hematologic parameters are measured in the critical-care unit. In addition, the relative contribution of the assist device and of the left ventricle to the total systemic blood flow is calculated. In essence, the assist device supplements the volume of blood ejected by the left ventricle to maintain adequate tissue perfusion. As ventricular recovery occurs, the ventricle is capable of assuming proportionately more volume work. Consequently, the process of weaning involves progressive reduction in the volume of blood diverted into the assist device and a corresponding increase in ventricular volume. When the left ventricle is contributing approximately 90 percent to the total systemic blood flow, termination of left heart assist is instituted.

Discontinuation of the device is performed without reentry of the thorax. Under local anesthesia, a small incision is made in the abdominal subcutaneous tissue; this procedure exposes the connection between the cannulas and pump tubing. The tubing is disconnected and an obturator is inserted into each cannula, completely occluding the lumen. The incision is closed over the occluded cannulas. The cannulas are well tolerated in situ because the material is biocompatible.

Left Ventricular-Arterial Bypass

Three centers are currently involved in the clinical evaluation of left ventricular-arterial bypass units: (1) Children's Hospital in Boston with Dr. William Bernhard, (2) Texas Heart Institute with Dr. John Norman, and (3) Hershey Medical Center in Pennsylvania with Dr. William Pierce. The design of these left heart assist devices must meet criteria established by the National Heart and Lung Institute in 1974 for the

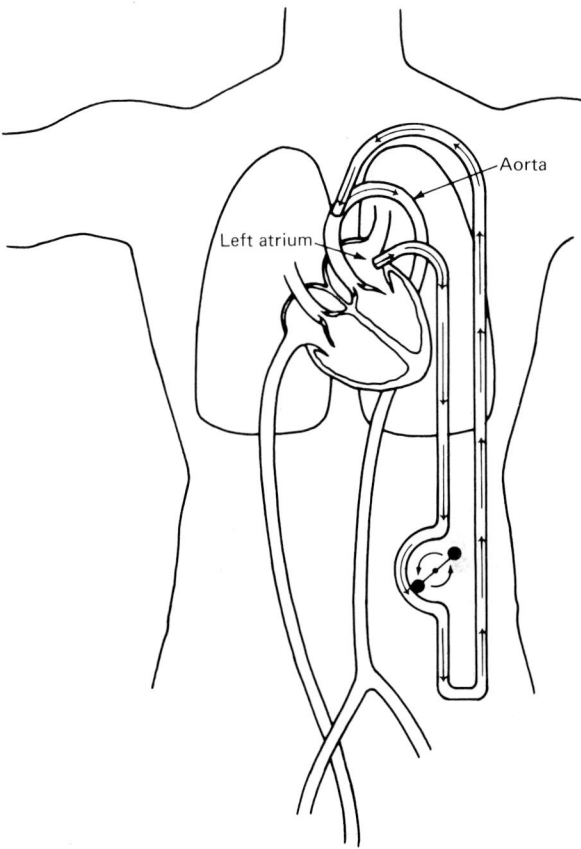

FIGURE 36-15
Left atrial-arterial bypass.

clinical investigative use of left ventricular assist devices.

The device used at Texas Heart Institute is referred to as the *auxiliary left ventricular assist device*. This unit is an implanted blood pump which diverts volume directly from the left ventricle into the descending thoracic aorta. The left ventricular assist device utilized in Boston by Dr. Bernhard is an external unit secured to the right anterolateral chest with an inflow tube attached to the left ventricular apex and an outflow tube anastomosed to the ascending aorta. The inflow tube exits from the chest beneath the xiphoid, and the pump outflow tube reenters the chest through an incision in the third or fourth intercostal space via a small rib resection. The unit designed by Pierce's group in Pennsylvania is also an external pump connected to the left ventricular apex and thoracic aorta.

Left ventricular-arterial assistance may be considered under the following circumstances: (1) dependence upon cardiopulmonary bypass despite 30 to 60 min of maximum pharmacologic and circulatory support, including partial cardiopulmonary bypass and the intra-aortic balloon pump; and (2) persistent low-output state within 24 h postoperatively despite balloon support. The rationale for instituting support is to mechanically rest the left ventricle in order to enable any potentially reversible ventricular depression to subside.

Pumping is initiated at low rates as the patient is weaned from cardiopulmonary bypass. The pumping rate is progressively increased until it equals the patient's heart rate. Synchronized pumping is then instituted to achieve a counterpulsation effect. As with balloon pumping, the ECG is used as the triggering signal to synchronize pump and cardiac action. The incorporation of counterpulsation into the design of left heart assist devices produces a profound reduction of myocardial work, since the pressure work as well as the volume work of the heart is decreased.

The units can assume over 80 percent of total cardiac work. A left ventricular transducer-tipped catheter may be inserted during surgery to permit direct measurement of developed left ventricular pressure. Initial adjustments of the assist device are made to maximize flow through the unit and to minimize the pressure the ventricle must develop to eject the residual cardiac volume. This maximal reduction of preload and of afterload in effect "rests" the heart, permitting clinical evaluation of the ability of the ventricle to recover. Maximal synchronized pumping is maintained for the first 12 to 24 h. Subsequently, the pump can be operated in the synchronous or asynchronous mode, depending upon the ventricular response to pumping. Test periods of reduced flow through the assist device or reduced levels of synchronous counterpulsation (i.e., 1:1, 1:2, · · ·, 1:10) guide weaning decisions. The unit is removed within 14 to 30 days under general anesthesia. The inflow and outflow tubes are oversewn and remain in situ.

REFERENCES

Bernhard, W. F., V. Poirier, C. G. LaFarge, and J. G. Carr: A new method for temporary left ventricular bypass, *J Thorac Cardiovasc Surg* 70:880, 1975.

Birtwell, W. C., R. H. Clauss, C. Dennis, D. E. Harken, and H. S. Soroff: The evolution of counterpulsation techniques, *Medical Instrumentation* 10:1, 1976.

Bregman, D.: Clinical experience with the dual-chambered intra-aortic balloon and System 80, *J Cardiovasc Surg* (*Torino*) 15:193, 1974.

————: *Mechanical Support of the Failing Heart and Lungs,* New York: Appleton-Century-Crofts, 1977.

Buckley, M. J., J. M. Craver, H. K. Gold, E. D. Mundth, W. M. Daggett, and W. G. Austen: Intra-aortic balloon pump assist for cardiogenic shock after cardiopulmonary bypass, *Circulation* 47 and 48 (Suppl III): III–90, 1973.

————, J. D. Laird, P. M. Madras, R. T. Jones, A. R. Kantrowitz, and W. G. Austen: Left heart assist system: Intra-aortic balloon pump, *Surg Clin North Am* 49:505, 1969.

————, R. C. Leinbach, J. A. Kastor, J. D. Laird, A. R. Kantrowitz, P. N. Madras, C. A. Sanders, and W. G. Austen: Hemodynamic evaluation of intra-aortic balloon pumping in man, *Circulation* 41 and 42 (Suppl II):II-130, 1970.

————, E. D. Mundth, W. M. Daggett, H. K. Gold, R. C. Leinbach, and W. G. Austen: Surgical management of ventricular septal defects and mitral regurgitation complications. Acute myocardial infarction, *Ann Thorac Surg* 13:513, 1978.

Chrzanowski, A. L.: Intra-aortic balloon pumping: Concepts and patient care, *Nurs Clin North Am* 13:513, 1978.

Cohen, S. I., and R. M. Weintraub: A new application of counterpulsation; Safer laparotomy after recent myocardial infarction, *Arch Surg* 110:116, 1975.

Concepts of Intra-Aortic Balloon Pumping: An Interdisciplinary Approach, presented by Massachusetts General Hospital Departments of Medicine, Nursing and Surgery, Boston, Mass. 1975.

DeBakey, M. E.: Left ventricular bypass pump for cardiac assistance, *Am J Cardiol* 27:3, 1971.

De Sanctis, R. W., E. D. Mundth, M. J. Buckley, W. M. Daggett, and W. E. Austen: Surgical treatment of ventricular irritability, *J Thorac Cardiovasc Surg* 66:943, 1973.

Dunkman, W. B., R. C. Leinbach, M. J. Buckley, E. D. Mundth, A. R. Kantrowitz, W. G. Austen, and C. A. Sanders; Clinical and hemodynamic results of intra-aortic balloon pumping and surgery for cardiogenic shock, *Circulation* 46:465, 1972.

Ford, P. J., and R. M. Weintraub: *Intra-Aortic Balloon Pumping Manual,* presented by Beth Israel Hospital Departments of Nursing and Surgery, Boston, Mass., 1975.

Gold, H. K., R. C. Leinbach, C. A. Sanders, M. J. Buckley, E. D. Mundth, and W. G. Austen: Intra-aortic balloon pumping for ventricular septal defect or mitral regurgitation complicating acute myocardial infarction, *Circulation* 47:1191, 1973.

———, ———, ———, ———, ———, and ———: Intra-aortic balloon pumping for control of recurrent myocardial ischemia, *Circulation* 47:1191, 1973.

Kantrowitz, A., S. Tjonneland, P. S. Freed, S. J. Phillips, A. N. Butner, and J. L. Sherman, Jr.: Initial clinical experience with intraaortic balloon pumping in cardiogenic shock, *JAMA* 203:135, 1968.

Kolff, W. J.: Artificial organs: Landmarks of the past and prospects for the future, *Trans Am Soc Artif Intern Organs* XXIII:1, 1977.

———, and J. Lawson: Status of the artificial heart and cardiac assist devices in the United States, *Trans Am Soc Artif Intern Organs* XXI:620, 1975.

Leinbach, R. C., M. J. Buckley, W. G. Austen, H. E. Petschek, A. R. Kantrowitz, and C. A. Sanders: Effects of intra-aortic balloon pumping on coronary flow and metabolism in man, *Circulation* 43 and 44 (Suppl I): I-77, 1971.

———, R. E. Dinsmore, E. D. Mundth, M. J. Buckley, W. B. Cunkman, W. G. Austen, and C. A. Sanders: Selective coronary and left ventricular cineangiography during intra-aortic balloon pumping for cardiogenic shock, *Circulation* 45:845, 1972.

———, H. K. Gold, R. E. Dinsmore, E. D. Mundth, M. J. Buckley, W. G. Austen, and C. A. Sanders: The role of angiography in cardiogenic shock, *Circulation* 47 and 48 (Suppl III): III-95, 1973.

Litwak, R. S., R. M. Koffsky, R. A. Jurado, S. B. Lukban, C. K. Saha, M. Vrandecic, B. Mindich, B. Mitchell, P. King, and L. Kaminsky: Support of severely impaired cardiac performance with left-heart assist device following intracardiac operation, *Heart & Lung* 7:622, 1978.

Mondejar, E. S.: The patient with left-heart assist device: Nursing management, *Heart & Lung* 8:296, 1979.

Moulopoulos, S. D., S. Topaz, and W. J. Kolff: Diastolic balloon pumping (with carbon dioxide) in the aorta—A mechanical assistance to the failing circulation, *Am Heart J* 63: 669, 1962.

Mundth, E. D., M. J. Buckley, R. C. Leinbach, H. K. Gold, W. M. Daggett, and W. G. Austen: *Ann Surg* 178:379, 1973.

Norman, J. C.: Intracorporeal partial artificial heart: Initial clinical trials, *Heart & Lung* 7:788, 1978.

Page, D. L., J. B. Caufield, J. A. Kastor, R. W. DeSanctis, and C. A. Sanders: Myocardial changes associated with cardiogenic shock, *N Engl J Med* 285:133, 1971.

Parmley, W. W., K. Chatterjee, Y. Charuzi, and H. J. C. Swan: Hemodynamic effects of noninvasive systolic unloading (nitroprusside) and diastolic augmentation (external counterpulsation) in patients with acute myocardial infarction, *Am J Cardiol* 33:819, 1974.

Pierce, W. S., J. H. Donachy, D. L. Candis, J. A. Brighton, G. Rosenbert, J. J. Migliore, G. A. Prophet, W. J. White, and J. A. Waldhausen: Prolonged mechanical support of the left ventricle, *Circulation* (in press).

Sanders, C. A., M. J. Buckley, R. C. Leinbach, E. D. Mundth, and W. G. Austen: Mechanical circulatory assistance, *Circulation* 45:1292, 1972.

Skinner, O. B.: Experimental and clinical evaluations of mechanical ventricular assistance, *Am J Cardiol* 27:146, 1971.

Soroff, H. S., C. T. Cloutier, W. C. Birtwell, L. A. Begley, and J. V. Messer: External counterpulsation, *JAMA,* 299:1441, 1974.

Weintraub, R. M., P. C. Voukydis, J. M. Aroesty, S. I. Cohen, P. J. Ford, G. S. Kurland, P. J. LaRaia, E. Morkin, and S. Paulin: Treatment of preinfarction angina with intra-aortic balloon counterpulsation and surgery, Am J Cardiol 34:809, 1974.

Whitman, G. Intra-aortic balloon pumping and cardiac mechanics: A programmed lesson, *Heart & Lung* 7:1034, 1978.

INTRODUCTION

The idea of external mechanical life support has been a fantasy of mankind through recorded time. Even before Harvey demonstrated to England's Charles I that blood was a dynamic, circulating nutrient for all human organs, the conviction was widespread that the hands of a miracle worker or even that beliefs could support or restore life.

The French Revolution of the eighteenth century allowed bold attempts at external life support to be made, the guillotine providing an ample supply of subjects. Various methods of infusing solutions were employed to permit life to continue, at least from the neck cephalad. Although these gruesome efforts were at best pseudoscientific, they may have been the first concerted attempts to support life extracorporeally.

Although it was not until the early 1950s that the fruition of his long laborious dream was realized, it was in the mid-1930s that John Gibbon began his research to develop a method for both oxygenation and circulation of blood by mechanical means so that the heart and lungs could be relieved of their primary function, i.e., providing adequate tissue perfusion.

In 1953, Gibbon, employing extracorporeal circulation, was the first to repair an intracardiac defect (atrial septal defect) under direct vision and with the complete exclusion of the patient's heart and lungs for physiologic support. Mention must be made of the incalculable contributions of the IBM Corporation and Dr. John Kirklin in applying engineering, electronics, and basic physiology to the ideas and accomplishments of Gibbon to finally put extracorporeal circulation on a sound metabolic, physiologic, and hemodynamic basis.

Through the years many types of oxygenators have been developed. To a lesser degree different pumping devices have also been utilized. Basically four types of oxygenators have been successful: (1) sheet, or film, (2) bubble, (3) disk, and (4) membrane. All except the membrane oxygenator depend on a blood-gas interface for transfer of oxygen. This process is indeed "unphysiologic" as compared to the membrane system (which, of course, simulates the natural transfer of oxygen in the lungs); however, the practicality and proven good results with present-day bubble oxygenators have established it as the current system used in most open-heart operations. This will be discussed further later in the chapter.

In general the occlusive rotating (roller) pump has been adapted and utilized as the propelling system for the blood. Cylinder pumps have been abandoned,

37
EXTRACORPOREAL CIRCULATION
Billy M. Hightower
Marguerite R. Kinney

INTRODUCTION

CONCEPT OF BYPASSING THE HEART AND LUNGS
Mechanical Anatomy
Physiology of Extracorporeal Circulation
Myocardial Preservation

POSTOPERATIVE COMPLICATIONS
Immediate Postoperative Period
Convalescent Period

REFERENCES

and in general pulsatile systems have not proved to be greatly advantageous, although from the theoretical standpoint, the future may well prove this to be a more physiologic approach.

Whereas in the early days of open-heart surgery utilizing extracorporeal circulation, a few changes and improvements dramatically reduced mortality and morbidity rates, today incalculably large improvements may be necessary to reduce the mortality rate by even 1 percent.

CONCEPT OF BYPASSING THE HEART AND LUNGS

Mechanical Anatomy

The cardiovascular system may be divided into four parts: (1) heart (pump), (2) lungs (oxygenator), (3) arterial (resistance) system, and (4) venous (capacitance) system. In general, at rest, approximately 70 percent of the total blood volume is contained within the venous (capacitance) system. Because of the autonomic neurogenic control within the smooth muscle of both arteries and veins, the shift in volume within the vascular reservoir becomes an automatic regulator of cardiac output.

Obviously, there are several points within the vascular system where blood can be removed from the body, oxygenated outside the body, and returned to the arterial system. Most centers today favor the removal of venous blood from the body by cannulation of the superior and inferior venae cavae, placing separate cannulae through the right atrium into the venae cavae as they enter the right atrium. These cannulae are then connected by tubing to a single vinyl tube which passes to the oxygenator containing a reservoir system in which volume can be controlled either by addition of fluid or blood or by regulation of venous return versus output from the pumping system. Following oxygenation of the venous blood, it passes through a heat exchanger, which is capable of maintaining whatever temperature is desired by means of a controlled water system surrounding the perfusate, which is contained within a closed cylinder. From the heat exchanger, the oxygenated, temperature-controlled perfusate is passed via tubing within a roller pump head to a cannula placed in the arterial system. The roller pump head is capable of pumping whatever volume is desired by increasing or decreasing the speed of the rotating (roller) head (usually double heads). In most cases filters and bubble traps are inserted within the arterial side of the circuit for removal of air, fibrin, fat, and platelet aggregates.

The site of arterial input from the pump varies from center to center, but in general the ascending aorta at or just below the right innominate artery is utilized (Fig. 37-1).

In addition, sucker systems for removal of intracardiac and pericardial perfusate, vent systems to remove blood from specific heart chambers, and separate perfusion systems for direct coronary artery perfusion or introduction of cold cardioplegic solution may easily be combined within the extracorporeal circuit as required.

Physiology of Extracorporeal Circulatioin

The ideal extracorporeal system would be capable of reproducing the normal circulation including cardiac output and normal and adequate perfusion of all organ systems, utilizing gas exchange without blood-gas interface (thus, eliminating traumatic effects on both cells and protein). Such a system has not been designed. Some differences in normal circulation and extracorporeal circulation are listed in Fig. 37-2.

Priming the Pump

The priming volume in the pump should be adequate to provide a venous reservoir volume combined with venous blood from the patient to initiate and maintain adequate blood flow (output) from the pump. Many institutions now use total hemodilution, i.e., no blood within the initial pump prime. Decreased viscosity, hemolysis, and risk of transfusion reaction and hepatitis are listed as advantageous. The maintenance of a bypass hematocrit between 25 and 30 percent is achieved by the addition of 500 to 1000 mL of blood to the pump prime. This, of course, can be achieved, monitored, and maintained by addition of blood to the system during cardiopulmonary bypass. Fresh blood, preferably drawn within 24 h prior to use, is obviously advantageous because of preservation of active blood components.

A "blood prime" commonly employed contains 500 mL of blood, along with heparin, sodium bicarbonate, plasmalyte (pH 7.4), Osmitrol, and calcium to a total volume of approximately 2000 mL for blood flows exceeding 3 L/min. Plasmalyte is added to expand volume when necessary; blood is added when hematocrit decreases to below 25 percent. The addition of microfilters within the extracorporeal circuit has increased confidence in the use of this prime solution; however, it must be stated that excellent studies have

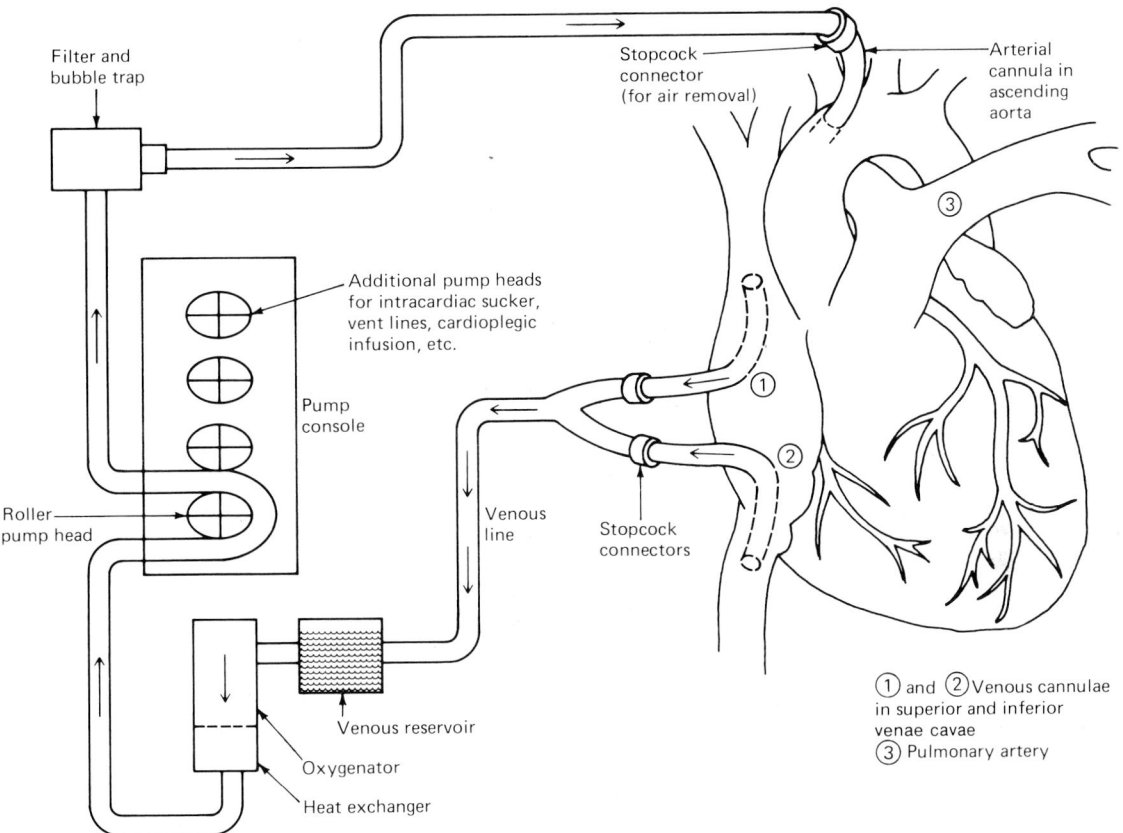

FIGURE 37-1
Cardiopulmonary bypass.

provided unequivocal rationale for the use of "non-blood" prime. Blood gases and electrolytes, particularly potassium, are monitored during cardiopulmonary bypass with necessary chemical adjustment accomplished as indicated. Maintenance of adequate potassium levels is of particular importance.

Blood Flow (Pump Flow Rate)

Normal physiologic cardiac output is generally accepted as approximately 3 L/min per m² of body surface area (cardiac index). Because of mechanical factors such as cannula size, pressure gradients, trauma to blood elements, and particularly the use of some degree of hypothermia this degree of flow is not feasible, desirable, or necessary during extracorporeal circulation.

A flow rate between 2.2 and 2.4 L/min per m² of body surface appears completely adequate to maintain satisfactory perfusion of body tissues. With the current use of deeper hypothermia systemically, this flow rate seems completely adequate for most procedures.

Venous return from the patient to the pump reservoir is, of course, one of the limiting factors in determining arterial flow rate from the pump. As mentioned previously, this can be controlled in two ways: (1) addition of priming volume and (2) maintenance of adequate function of the venous cannulae.

The question of desirability of pulsatile ("physiologic") versus nonpulsatile flow (currently employed in most pump systems) has not been adequately answered. Apparently the greatest demonstrable difference is in the renal system. Pulsatile flow appears to have some advantages in terms of renal performance, but the difference may not be significant.

	Physiologic changes with ECC	Mechanical factors	Pharmacological factors
Blood flow	↓ Total flow Negative venous pressure	Venous cannula size	Steroids
	↑ Adrenergic response		Adrenergic blockers
	↑ Renin-angiotensin	Arterial cannula site	
	Abnormal distribution		Diuretics
	Nonpulsatile flow	Pump characteristics	
	Absence of feedback control		Volume expanders
Gas exchange	↓ Tissue washout		Hypothermia
	↓ Oxygen delivery Acidosis	Heat exchanger	Buffers-tris HCO_3^-
	O_2–CO_2 exchange requires large blood volume	Oxygenator; disk; bubble; membrane	
Blood-endothelial interface	Microbubbles		Defoamer
	Emboli and aggregates	Reservoirs, connectors, tubing	Platelet-active Drugs (?)
	Stagnant zones		
	Anticoagulation	Surface coating	Heparin
RES function	↑ Fibrinolytic activity		Priming solutions
	↓ Platelet function	Coronary suction	
	Blood dilution		Hemodilution
	Tissue hystiocytes loaded	Filters	
	↓ Phagocytosis		

FIGURE 37-2

The physiology and pharmacology of extracorporeal circulation compared to normal circulation and pulmonary function. [*Modified from M. I. Ionescu and G. H. Wooler (eds.), Current Techniques in Extracorporeal Circulation, Butterworth, 1976. Used by permission.*]

Oxygenation of Blood (Prime)

The P_{O_2} of the prime can be controlled by altering the flow of oxygen in a "bubble" oxygenator or increasing the surface area of exposure in either the film (sheet) or membrane oxygenators. Because of the higher P_{O_2} of the oxygenation system compared to the P_{O_2} in venous blood, oxygen diffuses from the liquid phase of the prime solution (serum, hemodilution components, etc.) through the red blood cell membrane and combines with hemoglobin. Diffusion through the cell membranes to tissues is then accomplished depending upon the rate of diffusion through the prime solution. The rate of diffusion of CO_2 is considerably (20 times) greater than that of O_2, so in many systems CO_2 is added to the gas mixture (O_2, anesthetic gases) to prevent alkalosis.

It is interesting to note that not more than 15 years ago considerable research was being done on the use of pressure chambers as "operating rooms" for open-heart surgery. The rationale was that glucose water alone could be used as a total-body fluid for perfusion because, at 3 atm of pressure, adequate oxygenation of the tissues could be achieved. This, of course, is an oversimplification but does point out the efforts to achieve adequate tissue perfusion without dependence on blood. Many factors did not make this approach feasible.

Because of excellent performance, simplicity, and low cost, the bubble oxygenator has become the most popular and useful in most institutions. Much of the improvement in this type of oxygenator has come from the ability to control the size and distribution of gas bubbles and at the same time regulate the rate of gas flow without great complexity.

Advantages of membrane oxygenators are obvious because of the more physiologic transfer of oxygen, negating the possibility of air emboli, protein denaturation, and increased red blood cell fragility and platelet aggregation. Indeed it may be possible to maintain extracorporeal life support for many hours and even days. The membrane oxygenator certainly must be considered the oxygenator of choice in anticipated long periods of extracorporeal circulation (probably for periods exceeding 3 to 4 h).

Temperature Control

The heat exchanger is usually incorporated within the oxygenator although some prefer to use separate heat exchangers. The obvious advantage of reducing total-body temperature by use of the heat exchanger is that the total-body metabolic needs are reduced. The reduction of body temperature by only 1°C may reduce the metabolic need of certain tissues by as much as 10 percent.

The use of mild to moderate hypothermia (30 to 34°C) has been a common practice by many cardiac surgeons from the beginning of open-heart surgery. It is felt that total circulatory arrest (complete cessation of extracorporeal circulation) is safe at 30°C for as long as 10 min. Myocardial preservation is probably adequate (as in cases in which the aorta is cross-clamped) for up to 20 min at this temperature. The authors have had the experience of utilizing deep hypothermia (15°C) with complete circulatory arrest in several infants for more than 60 min without any obvious neurologic deficit.

Myocardial Preservation

Of primary concern in all cases of cardiac surgery, especially in surgery for ischemic heart disease (coronary artery atherosclerosis in particular), is preservation of myocardial tissue. Indeed, the incidence of intraoperative or perioperative myocardial infarction has been reported as high as 30 percent.

Various attempts to reduce myocardial damage have been utilized through the years including external potassium diastolic arrest, external myocardial cooling with iced saline, intermittent aortic cross-clamping using moderate hypothermia, and deep systemic hypothermia and cold cardioplegia. In recent years a clearer understanding of the principles involved in preserving myocardial tissue has come about through the cooperation of cardiac surgeons, physiologists, microbiologists, and pharmacologists.

Cold cardioplegia consists of the infusion of a 4°C solution with 30 meq of K^+ per L into the aortic root for about 2 min immediately after aortic cross-clamp-

ing and again after about 45 min or when myocardial temperatures rise above 19°C. External cardiac cooling is achieved by the constant infusion of 4°C Ringer's solution into the pericardium. The method also includes keeping the whole-body perfusate at 20 to 26°C and systemic flow lowered to 1.6 L/min per m² during the period of aortic cross-clamping.

Several variations of the cold cardioplegia method are now being used around the world. There is no question that some form of cold cardioplegic extracorporeal circulation has a definite advantage in myocardial preservation. This is a most interesting aspect and all-important achievement for present cardiac surgery and affords a continued opportunity for further research and development. The importance of developments in myocardial preservation undoubtedly are mirrored in the improvement in postoperative cardiac output.

POSTOPERATIVE COMPLICATIONS

Immediate Postoperative Period

Cardiovascular Complications

Low cardiac output is indeed the most serious of all postoperative complications because it in itself can lead to many other complications, which will be enumerated. What happens in the operating room, including the ability to correct the cardiac abnormality, most assuredly is the major determinant of cardiac output postoperatively. Monitoring of blood pressure, left atrial and right atrial pressures, urine output, blood gases, and electrolytes is all-important in the manipulation and control of cardiac output, either chemically or by assisting devices.

Hemorrhage must be watched for closely, and one should not be bashful in returning the patient to the operating suite if chest tube drainage continues at an excessive or accelerated rate. In most cases multiple "oozing" points can be controlled by "reopening" the chest.

Tamponade is difficult to diagnose, and a certain "seat-of-the-pants" feeling is often the tip-off that tamponade is the problem. A sudden decrease in chest tube drainage, progressive decrease in cardiac output, increase in right atrial pressure (often a late sign), and decrease in pulse pressure are all significant signs of tamponade. Probably the best index is increase of the mediastinal silhouette (particularly the upper portion); this can be seen on serial x-rays. A significant suspicion often should be followed by immediate reoperation.

Dysrhythmias, both ventricular and atrial, are not uncommon, and of course, the constant monitoring of the ECG is imperative in their recognition and identification. Many institutions now routinely utilize both atrial and ventricular temporary electrode wires so that management of the dysrhythmia may be facilitated by electrical means (pacing). Complete heart block can and does occur. It is also important to manipulate electrolytes, especially potassium, which plays an important role in ventricular irritability and stability. Oxygenation also is most important; thus, ventilator function and pulmonary function are both paramount to myocardial function.

Myocardial infarction may be the cause or effect of low cardiac output. In either case it can be a fatal complication. It has often been said that myocardial infarction postoperatively is the "best kind to have," since it is controlled. Obviously, there is no "best" myocardial infarction. Its management, however, is certainly conducted under more controlled conditions.

Renal Complications

Acute tubular necrosis with resultant renal shutdown is rare at the present time because of the excellence of extracorporeal circulation and ability to control hemodynamics both operatively and postoperatively. Here, again, adequate cardiac output is an all-important prerequisite of adequate renal function. The readily available dialysis units in most institutions should be utilized without hesitation when warranted.

Pulmonary Complications

Preoperative pulmonary disease can have a profound effect on the pulmonary capacity and function postoperatively. Emphysema, restrictive lung disease, and "smoker's lung" can adversely affect one's ability to control respiratory function. Atelectasis and diffuse focal atelectasis are common postoperative findings. Pneumothorax is seldom a problem, although if undetected, it can be a serious complication, especially in children.

Pulmonary emboli are not often a problem and probably occur less frequently in postoperative cardiac patients than in general surgery or medical patients.

With the judicious use of modern ventilators and blood gas monitoring, a close and constant watch with appropriate manipulation can often be lifesaving. Although in the past, tracheostomy in the early postoperative period was not uncommon, it now seems to be rarely indicated.

Neurologic Complications

Complications are most often secondary to air emboli, although fibrin and fat emboli can and do occur. The present use of microfilters seemingly has reduced this by a considerable degree. Vigorous attempts at removal of air when the left side of the heart has been opened (including aortotomy) have also reduced the incidence of cerebral damage from air emboli.

Paresis of the ulnar nerve is not uncommon but is usually transient. It is due in most cases to pressure at the elbow during surgery and in the early postoperative period when the patient is immobile.

Convalescent Period

Most of the immediate postoperative complications can occur or recur after the patient is dismissed from the critical-care unit to the hospital intermediate-care area. Telemetry is often continued for several days, especially if there were problems with dysrhythmias in the critical-care unit.

Early progressive ambulation seems most important in relief of orthopedic soreness of the chest wall including shoulder and back pain.

Median sternotomy disruption is rare but can occur. Immediate closure of the wound dehiscence, including rewiring of the sternum, is important and in most cases successful.

The postpericardiotomy syndrome is of obscure etiology and characterized by fever, chest pain, and pleuropericardial reaction. This delayed reaction may occur in up to 30 percent of patients experiencing open-heart surgery, although the clinical picture may vary in severity. Manifestations of the syndrome include ECG changes, a friction rub, or pericardial effusion. Although the syndrome is generally self-limiting, responding to bedrest and treatment of symptoms, it can result in tamponade.

The so-called "post-pump psychosis" has been well described, and a multitude of demographic and physiologic variables have been implicated in the etiology. This postcardiotomy delirium state typically begins on the second to fifth postoperative days and disappears within a few days without definitive therapy. Perceptual distortions are often accompanied by restlessness, anxiety, and confusion and may progress to hallucinations or gross disorientation. Although studies of the effect of age, sex, severity of heart disease, and length of time on bypass have yielded inconsistent data, several variables that can be controlled have been observed to influence the incidence: windows in the critical-care unit, frequent orientation to time, frequent contact with family members, preoperative information related to the immediate postoperative period, and planned uninterrupted periods of sleep.

REFERENCES

Conti, V. R., et al.: Cold cardioplegia versus hypothermia for myocardial protection: Randomized clinical study, *J Thoracic Cardiovas Surg* 76(5):577, Nov. 1978.

Dubin, W. R., et al.: Postcardiotomy delirium: A critical review, *J Thoracic Cardiovas Surg* 77(4):586, 1979.

Dutton, R. C., and L. H. Edmunds: Measurement of emboli in extracorporeal perfusion systems, *J Thoracic Cardiovas Surg* 65:523, 1973.

Galletti, P. M., and G. A. Brecker: *Heart Lung Bypass: Principle and Techniques of Extracorporeal Circulation,* New York: Grune & Stratton, 1962.

Gibbon, J. H.: Application of a mechanical heart and lung apparatus to cardiac surgery, *Minnesota Med* 37:171, 1954.

Ionescu, M. I., and G. H. Wooler (eds.): *Current Techniques in Extracorporeal Circulation,* London: Butterworths, 1976.

Langou, R. A., et al.: Incidence and mortality of perioperative myocardial infarction in patients undergoing coronary artery bypass grafting, *Circulation* 56:11, 1977.

Long, M., et al.: Cardiopulmonary bypass, *Am J Nurs* 74(5):860, May 1974.

HISTORICAL PERSPECTIVE

Artificial ventilation is not a recent innovation. Biblical scholars will recognize this citation in Genesis 2:7, "And the Lord God formed man of the dust of the ground, and breathed into his nostrils the breath of life; and man became a living soul." Another classical reference indicating the antiquity of artificial ventilation is II Kings 4:34 which states, "And Elisha went up, and lay upon the child, and put his mouth upon his mouth, and his eyes upon his eyes, and his hands upon his hands; and he stretched himself upon the child; and the flesh of the child waxed warm."

It is noteworthy that the evolution of artificial ventilation has been punctuated by several singularly outstanding contributions, between which have passed centuries, remarkable only by their abysmal ignorance and promulgation of misconceptions and false impressions. In the mid-sixteenth century, Andreas Vesalius showed that animals could be kept alive by the rhythmic inflation of the lungs with a bellows as he pumped air through an opening in the windpipe. In the mid-seventeenth century, Robert Hook repeated the work of Vesalius and obtained similar results. One hundred years later, in the 1770s, the bellows was gaining some popularity in the resuscitation of drowning victims. However, over-zealous resuscitation efforts too frequently ruptured alveoli and produced pneumothoraces and the victims died. Artificial ventilation soon fell into disrepute.

About 350 years had elapsed between the first recorded use of endotracheal intubation and the clinical application! In 1896 Northrup reported the use of O'Dwyer's modification of the Fell apparatus. This consisted of a foot-operated pump which blew air into the patient's lungs through a curved metal tube designed to be fitted into the glottal opening. The recovery of three patients with morphine poisoning was attributed to the use of this instrument.

Much of our present knowledge of mechanical ventilation stems from the work of Sauerbruch in Breslau. In 1904 he initiated the use of subatmospheric pressure around the chest wall. This process was subsequently used by the proponents of the cuirass ventilator and later, the tank ventilator.

In 1907 the idea of using positive airway pressure in resuscitation was "rediscovered" by Heinrich Dräger in his famous Pulmotor. Later, Drinker designed and built the tank ventilator in which a poliomyelitis patient was treated in Boston.

In the late 1930s Poulton and Barach independently suggested the use of continuous positive-pressure

38
MECHANICAL SUPPORT OF VENTILATION
Joanne Lagerson

HISTORICAL PERSPECTIVE

CLASSIFICATION OF MECHANICAL VENTILATORS
Volume-Cycled Ventilators
Pressure-Cycled Ventilators
External Body Ventilators

PRINCIPLES OF MECHANICAL VENTILATION
Clinical Goals

INDICATIONS FOR MECHANICAL VENTILATION

MANAGEMENT OF THE PATIENT RECEIVING CONTINUOUS ASSISTED VENTILATION
The Artificial Airway
Humidification of the Airway
Suctioning the Airway
The Ventilatory Pattern
Positioning and Physical Therapy
Psychological Considerations

WEANING FROM MECHANICAL VENTILATION

COMPLICATIONS OF MECHANICAL VENTILATION
Tracheal Tube Complications
Ventilator Malfunctions
Nosocomial Infection
Cardiac Dysrhythmias
Barotrauma
Gastrointestinal Complications
Medication Side Effects
Oxygen Toxicity
Hypotension

ROLES AND RESPONSIBILITIES OF PERSONNEL

REFERENCES

ventilation to treat pulmonary edema. The polio epidemics in Denmark and Sweden in the 1950s gave Engström the opportunity to use his newly designed ventilator. It functioned by predetermined ventilatory volumes instead of pressures.

Today we have a proliferation of sophisticated instrumentation. The last decade has seen remarkable progress in the science and technology of medicine, and illnesses that were once fatal are now amenable to the newer knowledge and skills of a variety of treatment personnel.

CLASSIFICATION OF MECHANICAL VENTILATORS

In recent years a vast number and variety of mechanical ventilators have become available. Because many different capabilities are represented by the various machines, an absolute classification is difficult. For the sake of simplicity, ventilators will be classified according to the mechanism most often employed to terminate the inspiratory phase.

Volume-Cycled Ventilators

The volume-cycled (or volume-preset) ventilators, such as the Emerson, Ohio 560, and Bennett MA-1, terminate inspiration after delivering a preset volume of gas. These ventilators will deliver the desired volume regardless of the pressure required to do so. The volume remains the same unless excessively high peak airway pressures are reached. To prevent potential lung damage due to high peak inspiratory pressures, all volume-preset ventilators have a built-in safety release valve. The safety release pressure is set manually at about 10 cm H_2O above the peak inspiratory pressure.

The inspiratory time is determined by adjusting the flow rate of the gas to be delivered. The more rapid the flow of gas, the shorter the inspiratory time. Conversely, the slower the flow rate, the longer the inspiratory time. Expiratory time is determined by setting a respiratory rate. Thus, if inspiratory time is adjusted and a certain number of breaths are to be given per minute, the remaining time is available for expiration. For example, if the tidal volume is preset for 1000 cm³ and the respiratory rate is 10 per minute, this allows 6 s for each respiratory cycle. If the flow rate is adjusted so that inspiration of the desired tidal volume occurs in 2 s, then 4 s remain for expiration.

Many models of volume-cycled ventilators have a built-in oxygen selector and can be adjusted to deliver any concentration of oxygen from 21 to 100 percent. However, because of their variable accuracy, the concentration should be frequently checked by a reliable oxygen analyzer.

Some volume-cycled ventilators totally control inspiration without any influence from the patient's own inspiratory effort. However, most recent models are capable of controlling and/or assisting the patient's own inspiratory effort by delivering the predetermined volume of gas when the patient's inspiratory effort creates a negative pressure in the system. The amount of negative pressure the patient must generate to trigger a breath from the machine can be manually adjusted.

Generally, the volume-cycled ventilators are more powerful and they are certainly more useful when ventilating those patients with "stiff" lungs, such as in adult respiratory distress syndrome; the ventilator will continue to deliver a constant tidal volume regardless of the changes in airway resistance or in compliance of the lungs and thorax.

Pressure-Cycled Ventilators

The pressure-cycled (or pressure-preset) ventilators, such as the Bennett PR-2 and Bird Mark VII, terminate inspiration upon achieving a preset pressure. Gas flows to the patient until the preset pressure is reached throughout the system—ventilator, tubing, and patient's airways. When this pressure is reached, the gas flow is terminated and the patient passively exhales. Many pressure-cycled ventilators have some means of adjusting the gas flow rate, the sensitivity of the ventilator to respond to the patient's own inspiratory effort, and the respiratory frequency initiated by the machine.

One of the greatest disadvantages of pressure-cycled ventilators is that varying resistance interferes with gas flow, since flow is a function of pressure and resistance. This resistance causes a change in tidal volume since volume is a product of flow and time. Thus, the delivered volume varies as resistance varies. If resistance does not vary appreciably, such as with a young drug-overdosed patient, this ventilator could be used. However, it would be inappropriate for patients with changing pulmonary resistance, such as in acute bronchospasm and in postoperative states. These patients would receive varying amounts of volume with each breath.

The relatively low pressure capability (top effective peak pressure is 30 to 40 cm from a 50 psi source) is another disadvantage of the pressure-cycled ventilators. A patient with very stiff lungs may need a pressure of 80 cm to deliver an adequate tidal volume.

External Body Ventilators

The external body ventilators assist the patient's spontaneous ventilatory effort by applying intermittent subatmospheric ("negative") pressures to the trunk of the body. For example, the body tank ventilator, or iron lung, may be of great value for the patient who has a reduced vital capacity to a value just below that needed for spontaneous ventilation. However, they are very large, noisy, and restrictive.

Another example of this class of ventilators is the cuirass, which functions similarly to the iron lung. This is a rigid shell that covers only the thorax and abdomen. A disadvantage is the difficulty in attaining and maintaining a tight seal.

PRINCIPLES OF MECHANICAL VENTILATION

Mechanical ventilation is a supportive technique; it cannot cure. The ventilator can accomplish no more than maintain cardiopulmonary homeostasis within acceptable physiologic limits for a period of time. This necessitates the presence of potentially reversible pathology. Ventilator commitment is always best avoided when unnecessary; when indicated, it should be initiated early, not waiting for cardiopulmonary collapse and resuscitation to finalize a decision.

When a patient is connected to a mechanical ventilator, the staff must assume responsibility for that patient's life. The patient has been placed in a situation where optimum airway management and human and physiologic needs must be assured.

Clinical Goals

Appropriate rationale on which to base clinical judgment and care is possible only when supportive clinical modalities have clearly delineated goals. The clinical goals of mechanical ventilation are (1) to provide the pulmonary system with the mechanical power to maintain physiologic ventilation; (2) to manipulate the ventilatory pattern and airway pressures for purposes of improving the efficiency of ventilation and/or oxygenation; and (3) to decrease myocardial work by diminishing the work of breathing and improving ventilatory efficiency. These are the physiologic benefits offered by mechanical support of ventilation; it is upon the accomplishment of these goals

that the criteria, indications, and rationale for ventilator care must be based.

INDICATIONS FOR MECHANICAL VENTILATION

Mechanical ventilation must be initiated whenever the ventilatory function of the patient fails to maintain an adequate pulmonary blood gas exchange. It is emphasized that the clinical observation or measurement of pulmonary function does *not* reflect the adequacy of effective ventilation. A blood gas analysis is essential to confirm a suspicion of impending acute ventilatory failure. A specific number is not as important as noting the trend in serial blood gas analysis.

Ventilatory failure can be due to a wide spectrum of clinical problems, including central neurological problems, neuromuscular disorders, chest wall abnormalities, and obstructive airway disease. Many of these conditions are associated with normal lungs, but the common denominator is alveolar hypoventilation and subsequent retention of carbon dioxide. As carbon dioxide accumulates in the body, acidosis and narcosis ensue; in addition, if the patient is not receiving supplemental oxygen, as alveolar carbon dioxide levels increase, oxygen levels decrease. Hypoxemia then potentiates the arrhythmic and depressant effects of hypercapneic acidosis.

Another category of patients, those with primary hypoxemic respiratory failure, have (1) ventilation-perfusion abnormalities, (2) right to left shunting, or (3) impaired diffusion. Patients with severe parenchymal or interstitial pulmonary disease and with low pulmonary compliance may have a combined hypoxemic and hypercapneic picture.

It should be noted that it is *not* the disease entity itself that necessitates ventilator support, but rather the degree of physiologic stress caused by the disease as it compromises the cardiopulmonary reserves. The decision to institute ventilatory support must be based on cardiopulmonary pathophysiologic data.

The adequacy of the patient's ventilatory function is determined by monitoring the arterial P_{CO_2} and the amount of ventilation that does not contribute to pulmonary gas exchange, called wasted ventilation or "dead space" ventilation. Mechanical ventilation should be considered when the P_{CO_2} is greater than 10 mmHg above the patient's normal value or the dead space to tidal volume ratio (VD/VT) is greater than 60 percent.

Oxygenation is the least common of pathophysiologic states requiring mechanical support of ventilation. Oxygenation and ventilation are different entities, and many oxygenation problems can be adequately supported by oxygen therapy (nasal prongs, ventimask), bronchial hygiene, and cardiovascular support. However, mechanical ventilation may be warranted when hypoxemia is due to (1) decreased functional residual capacity (FRC), (2) excessive work of breathing, or (3) an inefficient breathing pattern.

To evaluate oxygenation, the arterial P_{O_2} is compared with the P_{O_2} in the alveolus, which is directly proportional to the pressure of oxygen in the inspired air. This is called the alveolar-arterial difference, or gradient, of oxygen, $D(A-a)O_2$. Mechanical ventilation may be considered when the patient's $D(A-a)O_2$ on 100 percent oxygen is greater than 400 mmHg.

Ventilatory mechanics are also measured to assess the patient's ability to sustain adequate pulmonary gas exchange. Mechanical ventilation may be considered if the vital capacity is less than 15 mL per kg of body weight, or the inspiratory force is less than -25 cmH$_2$O.

There is no specific cookbook recipe to follow when deciding whether or not to intubate. The absolute numbers of the diagnostic studies are not as valuable as the serial measurements and the evaluation of patients' general response to therapeutic intervention over a period of time.

MANAGEMENT OF THE PATIENT RECEIVING CONTINUOUS ASSISTED VENTILATION

The Artificial Airway

The effectiveness of any life support system depends upon the patency of the airway. Endotracheal tubes, including nasotracheal, orotracheal, and tracheostomy tubes, are used to eliminate any soft tissue or laryngeal obstruction. A nasal tube is generally preferred for long-term intubation because: (1) it is easier to stabilize; (2) it is easier to suction (longer catheters may be necessary); and (3) it is better tolerated by the alert patient. One disadvantage of nasotracheal intubation is that the tube diameter is limited by the nostrils and turbinates and meticulous care must be given to prevent pressure necrosis. Also, significant septal deviation may cause encroachment on the lumen of the tube which does not affect ventilation but does not permit the suction catheter to pass readily. Feeding by the oral route is generally poorly

tolerated although the patient can swallow water reasonably well.

Many respiratory problems, particularly those due to retained secretions, can be resolved during the 48 to 72 h of the more conservative endotracheal intubation if given vigorous treatment. However, if prolonged ventilatory support is anticipated, tracheostomy may be performed at any convenient time following initial intubation. There are no specific criteria concerning the appropriateness of endotracheal versus tracheostomy airway management. Endotracheal tubes have been safely left in place for 3 to 10 days (and even longer); however, each clinical encounter must be decided on an individual basis. The primary concern is to prevent laryngeal trauma and granuloma.

Humidification of the Airway

Room air imposed directly on the airways is irritating and drying and inhibits ciliary function. It is imperative that the gas delivered through an artificial airway be 100 percent humidified at body temperature. Effective airway humidification may be accomplished by incorporating a heated humidifier into the ventilator so that the air reaching the patient's airway (37°C) is 100 percent saturated with water vapor. The humidifier must be heated because an air mixture passing through water at room temperature is only 20 to 30 percent saturated when it is heated to body temperature in the tracheobronchial tree.

Humidifying devices and connecting tubing must be inspected at regular intervals. Condensed water within the tubing may either obstruct airflow or empty into the trachea. Condensed water should never be returned retrogradely to the sterile humidifier.

Suctioning the Airway

The intubated patient has an ineffective cough reflex and cannot exert a large intrathoracic pressure against a closed glottis; therefore, secretions must be suctioned from the airway. Tracheal suctioning should never be performed on a routine schedule; "every half-hour" may be too often for one patient and not enough for another. Needless suctioning produces unnecessary tracheal irritation and should be avoided. Since secretions can only be suctioned from the mainstem bronchi, it is essential that they be mobilized from the more distal regions by a regular schedule of patient repositioning.

The patient should be informed of the suctioning procedure and the ventilator tubing disconnected after the inspiratory phase of respiration. How disquieting to have inspiration suddenly halted! When disconnected, the ventilator end of the tubing should be placed so that it does not become contaminated.

High concentrations of oxygen should always be administered for several minutes prior to and immediately following tracheal aspiration so that myocardial hypoxia and cardiac arrhythmias may be prevented. This can be accomplished by turning the oxygen concentration dial on the ventilator to 100 percent (and not forgetting to return it to its preaspiration concentration) or by "ambuing" or "bagging" the patient.

Strict adherence to sterile suctioning techniques is mandatory. These patients are generally debilitated and therefore more susceptible to infection. In addition, the mere placement of a tube in the airway greatly reduces the normal protective and defense mechanisms of the lungs. The catheter, about one-half the diameter of the tube, should be smooth and flexible and should be rotated between the thumb and index finger as it is gently guided, not pushed or shoved, into the trachea. Suction is not applied while the catheter is being inserted. Lung collapse is possible if a vacuum exists. For this reason, suctioning should not be longer than 8 to 12 s and the negative pressure not greater than 150 cm H_2O (for adults). Since each aspiration period lowers the P_{O_2} about 35 mmHg (the level being proportional to the amount and duration of negative pressure applied), it is unwise to make a second attempt at suctioning without first reoxygenating the patient. It is well known that oxygen tensions below 50 mmHg potentiate arrhythmias, and reported cases of cardiac arrest during or following tracheal suctioning are well substantiated in the literature. All ventilator patients must have continuous electrocardiographic monitoring, and it must be observed during the suctioning procedure.

The Ventilatory Pattern

After intubation, the patient's spontaneous inspiratory efforts should initially be augmented by manual ventilation. There are a wide variety of ventilation bags available. Although many can deliver similar minute ventilation, there may be considerable variation in the concentration of inspired oxygen which each device is capable of achieving. In patients with low cardiac outputs or high venous admixtures, atelectasis, and so on, short-term delivery of up to 100 percent inspired

oxygen may be required to adequately oxygenate such a patient. Some ventilation bags can achieve greater than 60 percent inspired oxygen, but this requires a flow of 10 to 15 L/min. Permitting the bag to reinflate slowly by gradually releasing the squeezed hand will further increase the concentration of oxygen in the bag. It is also possible to attach a reservoir bag which would maintain a high inspired oxygen concentration.

The transfer from manual to machine ventilation should entail as little physiologic change as possible. Adjustment of the machine-patient interface is very important. The relationship of inspiration to expiration (I/E ratio) and the frequency of the ventilatory cycle make up the ventilatory pattern. The maintenance of adequate physiologic ventilation with the smallest degree of compromised venous return is accomplished by incorporating large tidal volumes with slow ventilatory rates. By utilizing this type of ventilatory pattern, the incidence of atelectasis is decreased and the large tidal volumes appear to be better-tolerated by the conscious patient.

Frequently, medication is required to relax or sedate the patient so that adequate ventilation will be assured. Due to the sometimes very urgent situation and the stress-producing nature of endotracheal intubation and ventilatory control, it is predictable that the patient, if conscious, will be tense, anxious, and afraid. During the entire procedure someone should hold the patient's hand, if possible, and maintain a continuous monologue (even when the patient appears not to be listening), offering brief, simple statements as to what is being done and what the results will be. The calm and reassuring attitude of all involved are of paramount importance if the patient is indeed to believe that "soon you will be feeling much better" and "everything will be all right." Chances are the patient has never been intubated before and does not understand what it is all about; perhaps to the patient, surviving the crisis may even be doubtful.

A patient who is "fighting" the ventilator is restricting the respiratory cycle by actively "pushing out" while the machine is "pushing in." This dramatically decreases alveolar ventilation and increases intrathoracic pressure, consequently decreasing venous return and cardiac output. When patients fight the ventilator, they usually are hypoxemic, underventilated, or uncomfortable because of an inappropriate filling wave form, or they suffer pain and/or anxiety.

Ventilators are generally set to provide a fairly high tidal volume of approximately 10 cm^3 per kg of body weight at a relatively low respiratory rate of 10 to 14 breaths per minute. If a rapid respiratory drive is present, higher rates may initially be necessary to provide patient comfort and to keep the patient from fighting the ventilator. Final adjustments of the mechanical ventilatory pattern ultimately depend on blood gas analysis.

Each clinical situation determines the frequency and timing of arterial blood gas studies. Since it generally takes about 15 to 20 min to reach a blood gas steady state after a ventilator adjustment, the stability of the clinical situation should be noted before performing the arterial puncture. In patients with chronic airway obstruction, the carbon dioxide tension should be lowered by not more than 10 mmHg/h until the P_{CO_2} is in the fifties and the pH maintained below 7.50. Hourly arterial blood gas determinations are needed to establish a trend in the clinical course. When the P_{CO_2} reaches the desired value, the blood gases are checked every 4 to 6 h thereafter. In stable clinical situations these may be checked less frequently, such as once daily. The important point is that no matter how the patient's "ideal" alveolar ventilation is determined, it must be continuously reevaluated until there is assurance that it is appropriate to maintain an ideal arterial carbon dioxide tension. An arterial blood gas analysis is the only way to assess the adequacy of ventilation. A Wright res-

pirometer may be used for monitoring tidal volume and minute ventilation. (See Fig. 38-1.)

Even though oxygen therapy may be necessary for the intubated patient, the ventilator is basically supporting ventilation. Oxygenation and ventilation are entities to be considered separately. Most oxygenation problems can be adequately treated by oxygen therapy (mask, nasal prongs), along with other therapeutic modalities (bronchial hygiene, cardiovascular support). As mentioned earlier, mechanical ventilation may be warranted even when hypoxemia is not accompanied by hypercapnea.

When arterial hypoxemia results from alveolar hypoventilation alone, such as with drug overdose, mechanical assistance will be sufficient to correct it and room air is used. In patients with chronic airway obstruction who have a chronically low arterial oxygen tension, concentrations of oxygen should be given that would yield a P_{O_2} in the range of 60 to 70 mmHg. In normal individuals a P_{O_2} of 70 to 90 mm Hg is more desirable.

Some patients with severe gas exchange abnormalities require increasingly higher concentrations of inspired oxygen in order to maintain an arterial oxygen tension which will sustain life. The necessary high inspired oxygen tension may be toxic and may contribute further to the deteriorating gas exchange by inducing alterations in the structure and function of

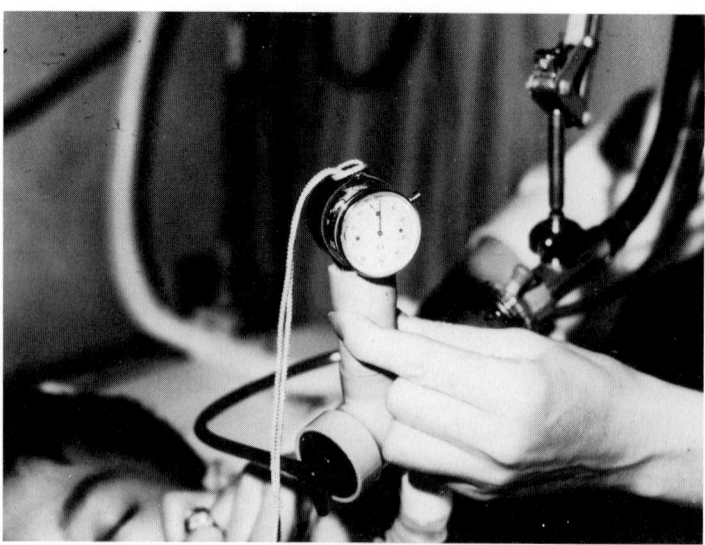

FIGURE 38-1

A Wright respirometer is used to measure expired volume of patient on ventilator.

the lung exposed to it. The concept of positive end expiratory pressure breathing (PEEP) was designed to prevent alveolar collapse, thereby increasing end-tidal lung volume and the FRC. The FRC represents the volume of gas left in the alveoli at the end of a normal expiration, and as the FRC decreases, the potential for further expiratory alveolar collapse increases. This alveolar collapsing results in hypoxemia and decreased compliance. Regardless of the method used to apply PEEP, the end result is the same—an increase in alveolar pressure at the end of expiration because the airway and thoracic pressures are not permitted to return to atmospheric.

The major goal of PEEP is to enhance oxygen transport. Since the amount of oxygen transported is the product of blood oxygen content times blood flow, PEEP will not be beneficial if there is a fall in cardiac output (due to decrease in venous return as a result of increased intrathoracic pressure) disproportionate to the gain in arterial oxygenation. Hypovolemia needs to be corrected before initiating PEEP, and then the patient's arterial blood gases and electrocardiogram must be carefully monitored.

Continuous positive airway pressure (CPAP) is a positive end expiratory pressure applied to a patient who is breathing spontaneously. It is a technique of applying PEEP and has the physiologic effect of increasing FRC.

Positioning and Physical Therapy

The patient's position in bed dictates which portions of the lungs are ventilated and perfused. Stasis of secretions in the bases and periphery of the lungs is enhanced by the all too frequently observed supine semi-Fowler's position. In this upright position, it is difficult, if not impossible (particularly with positive pressure ventilation), for secretions to ascend from the bases of the lungs to the mainstem bronchi where they can then be reached by the aspirating catheter.

Right and left lateral positioning, with the head of the bed gradually lowered, is tolerated by most patients connected to a ventilator. A study in dogs of the physiologic and pathologic effects of a systematic regimen of movement revealed that the immobile animals suffered early loss of oxygenating capability of the dependent lung that developed early atelectasis, hemorrhage, and pulmonary edema. A regimen of movement to alternate lateral positions every 30 min preserved oxygenating ability of both lungs, while hourly changes restored lost function and minimized the extent of pathologic findings in random zones of the lungs. Active regimens of movement were observed to prevent or relieve arteriovenous shunting. The study concluded that immobility, a critical factor in the genesis of hypoxemia, must be replaced by planned, systematic antigravity changes in position to maintain optimal lung mechanics and to prevent wasted work of the heart.

It is sometimes beneficial to compress the patient's lower thorax during exhalation (in rhythm with the cycling of the ventilator) in an attempt to promote the movement of secretions from the peripheral branches to the mainstem bronchi. The maneuver may produce more effective results when it is carried out in conjunction with a larger than tidal volume ventilation. An optimum time to suction is just prior to position change. When turning the patient, the head should be turned at the same time and kept in alignment with the rest of the body. Extreme care must be taken to avoid twisting, hyperextending, or hyperflexing the neck, since these maneuvers traumatize the trachea. Arm and leg exercises are essential to maintain muscle tone and joint range of motion (Fig. 38-2). A program of breathing retraining and strengthening exercises should begin as soon as possible for patients with chronic airway obstruction. Deconditioning may be prevented and exercise tolerance increased by various arm and leg exercises, which should be synchronized with the breathing pattern while the patient is being assisted by the ventilator. Thus "weaning" is easier to accomplish.

As soon as medically stable, the patient should sit in a chair, even if only for brief periods of time, since this produces both physiologic and psychologic improvement. Continuous ventilatory assistance should not interfere with the patient's freedom out of bed (Fig. 38-3). A walker could be equipped with a small ventilator to allow the initiation of early ambulation. Elastic stockings should be worn to prevent thromboembolic complications. Before returning to bed, the patient should stand on the toes and bounce several times (bending slightly at the knees) to prevent the "sea legs syndrome" which is frequently observed following a period of bedrest. It is very discouraging for a patient to discover that following extubation, fatigue is experienced after even the smallest energy expenditure; this is because the hospital staff permitted the patient to become deconditioned while their attention was focused primarily on the pulmonary problem. Another serious consequence of deconditioning is the inability to cough effectively, which could precipitate another bout of respiratory insufficiency.

FIGURE 38-2
Active leg motion while in bed prevents deconditioning.

Psychological Considerations

As the treatment of conditions which once were rapidly fatal has become more successful, the patient requiring ventilatory assistance is exposed to much longer periods of uncertainty, general emotional distress, sensory deprivation, and monotony. The ventilators and monitors with their buzzers and flashing lights surround the patient like sentinels. Flow sheets, chronicling the vicissitudes of numerous physiochemical variables, dangle from the bed and every available hook. But the tears, pain, loneliness, fear, helplessness, and despair cannot be measured or computed. How easy it is to neglect the patient's emotional well-being because of the pressing demands to take care of the more tangible and task-oriented duties.

One of the most frustrating problems the patient experiences is communication. At a time when the patient's ability to breathe has reached a crisis point, a tube is passed between the vocal cords, thereby preventing speech. The needs of the patient to communicate are intensified; the ability to do so is severely compromised. A magic slate or pencil and paper may be used. The intravenous apparatus should be placed, if possible, in the nonwriting arm.

It is ironic that a patient suffering sensory overload may at the same time be deprived of the sensory perceptions needed for orientation. The artificial elimination of the day and night sequence, sleep deprivation, and the almost constant bombardment by strange and obtrusive auditory and visual stimuli could produce severe behavior disturbances. Every effort should be made to organize care in such a way as to permit the patient to have disturbance-free rest periods during the day and quiet nights, interrupted only when absolutely necessary for clinical evaluation or treatment.

Orientation may be enhanced by windows, a visible clock, and a large wall calendar (marking off each day as it passes). Talking about family, the news, and weather will help the patient to keep in touch with reality. Many patients, of course, will not be able to respond, but they *can* hear and use the information to prevent confusion and disorientation. Family members should be encouraged to visit the patient, touch or hold the patient's hand, and participate in routine care whenever or however possible.

A small vase of flowers can do much to brighten the patient's immediate environment. Even in crowded units there is certainly room for a single rose sent daily by a loved one, if the rose is placed in a test

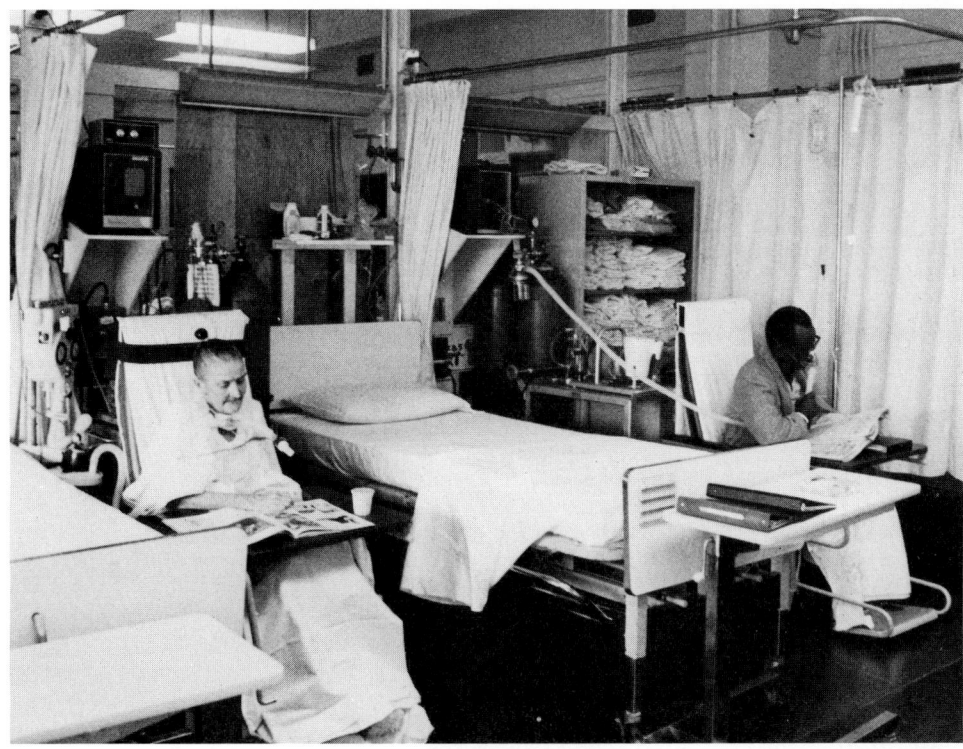

FIGURE 38-3

Patients should be out of bed as much as possible, and reading may occupy leisure hours.

tube and attached to an intravenous pole. The sight of a familiar object may relieve some of the anxiety produced by unfamiliar and frightening surroundings (Fig. 38-4). Background music interrupts the rhythmic monotony of ventilators cycling and monitors beeping and helps to relieve tension in both patients and staff.

Sitting in a chair frequently bolsters patient's morale, and orientation is enhanced if eyeglasses, dentures, and hearing aids are returned to the patient as soon as practical. Combing the hair should not be overlooked. Perhaps the patient would enjoy a game of checkers or the daily newspaper?

WEANING FROM MECHANICAL VENTILATION

Modern respiratory care has demonstrated that the majority of patients appropriately committed and maintained on mechanical ventilation are discontinued from it readily when their disease process has been reversed. The criteria for weaning from me-

chanical ventilation are approximately the reciprocals of the indications for which ventilatory support was initiated. Since ventilatory support is primarily used for patients with profound gas transport abnormalities, its use may be discontinued *only* when therapy has been directed at correcting the pathophysiologic alteration. The ventilator does not cure; it is simply a temporary support system which merely "buys time" for correction of the underlying situation that precipitated its use in the first place. Once it has been established that the patient is physiologically capable of independence from the ventilator, the weaning process should be directed toward the psychological aspects of ventilator weaning.

Several physiologic tests have been established to serve as guidelines for determining the patient's readiness for ventilator discontinuance. These are the vital capacity, the alveolar arterial oxygen tension difference measured breathing 100 percent oxygen, and the maximum inspiratory force.

A patient recovering from an episode of acute respiratory failure should have a vital capacity of at

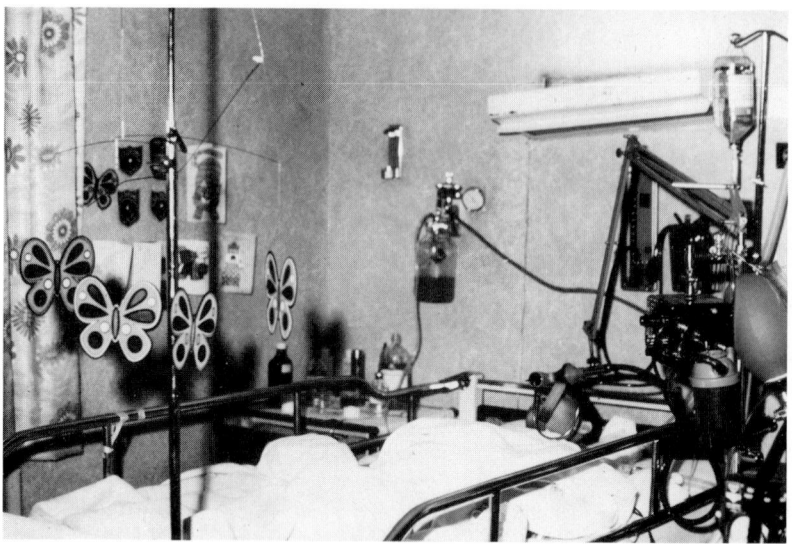

FIGURE 38-4

A familiar object brought from home, such as this child's butterfly mobile, will partially reduce the anxiety resulting from sudden exposure to strange surroundings.

least 10 to 15 mL per kg of body weight before weaning is attempted. Generally, patients who breathe spontaneously with a capacity less than 10 mL per kg of body weight will need to return to controlled ventilation within 24 h. Breathing a low vital capacity prevents the patient from taking a deep breath and coughing effectively.

The alveolar arterial oxygen tension difference should be less than 300 to 350 mmHg prior to discontinuation of mechanical ventilation. If the shunt volume is large enough to cause a $D(A-a)O_2$ greater than 350 mmHg, patients are generally not ready to be weaned. When the $D(A-a)O_2$ is around 350 mmHg, weaning can optimistically be initiated; however, if an inspired oxygen concentration of greater than 60 percent is required to maintain an arterial P_{O_2} of 80 mmHg during the time the patient is breathing spontaneously, the weaning attempt is likely to be unsuccessful.

The maximum inspiratory force which a patient can generate when the tracheal tube is completely occluded should be greater than −20 cmH₂O. This measurement is a good test of muscular strength and is particularly useful in unresponsive and uncooperative patients, since the test does not require patient cooperation.

When the patient is breathing spontaneously, it is possible to predict whether or not normal arterial P_{CO_2} will be maintained by measuring the ratio of dead space ventilation to total ventilation (VD/VT). When dead space ventilation (that which does not participate in gas exchange) is greater than 0.6 (60 percent of each breath), it usually indicates that a patient will be unable to sustain adequate spontaneous ventilation. This test is not performed routinely, but is reserved for the evaluation of patients who repeatedly fail to wean.

For the patient who does not assume ventilator independence readily, the process of intermittent mandatory ventilation (IMV) or intermittent demand ventilation (IDV) may be employed. The purpose of IMV is to allow the patient's own reasonable breathing pattern to be maintained with positive-pressure breaths intermittently delivered by the ventilator; the positive-pressure breath is completely independent of the patient's own breathing pattern. The concept of IDV is to allow the patient to breathe a controlled atmosphere at a reasonable, spontaneous pattern, with intermittent positive augmentation in phase with the patient's breathing pattern (on demand).

Prolonged ventilatory assistance leads to respiratory muscle weakness and markedly interferes with the patient's ability to breathe alone when disconnected from the ventilator. The incorporation of IMV as soon as it is clinically feasible (not when one considers ventilator discontinuance) is certain to decrease the time of ventilator support and the weaning process; and IMV allows a far more gradual transition from completely controlled ventilation to completely spontaneous ventilation.

One of the main advantages of IMV, particularly for patients with chronic airway obstruction, is that patients can adjust their own arterial carbon dioxide tension. Stabilization generally occurs at a higher tension than would have been provided with controlled ventilation.

Premature and unsuccessful attempts at weaning have adverse psychologic effects on the patient; therefore it is of utmost importance that the patient be both physically and psychologically prepared for ventilator discontinuation. When the ventilator is discontinued, the patient should be in a sitting position and humidified 40 percent oxygen should be readily available by mask. An oxygen catheter should never be placed in the tracheostomy or endotracheal tube because it obstructs airflow.

When it is clinically advisable to remove the airway, the oropharynx and trachea should be suctioned, bagging with oxygen between suctioning attempts to prevent hypoxia. As the tracheal cuff is slowly deflated, the patient is given one big breath via the ambu bag. As the tube is gently removed, the patient's automatic response is to either exhale forcibly or to cough up any remaining secretions lodged in the vicinity of the cuff.

Following both ventilator discontinuation and airway removal, the patient should be observed for signs of respiratory insufficiency (increased respiratory rate, increased pulse, diaphoresis); however, the nurse's overt preoccupation with the patient's condition may elicit responses that could be attributed more to emotion than to respiratory insufficiency. A radio, television, or newspaper may assist in minimizing the patient's apprehension.

COMPLICATIONS OF MECHANICAL VENTILATION

Tracheal Tube Complications

Prolonged intubations may promote laryngeal trauma and massive gastric distention. Right mainstem intubation will produce alveolar hyperventilation, atelectasis, and/or pneumothorax. Herniation of the cuff over the distal end of the tube causes airflow obstruction. Tracheal ischemia and necrosis are not as common today with the use of high-volume, low-pressure "floppy" cuffs. The intermittent deflation of

these cuffs has no proved advantage in preventing mucosal necrosis. Any routine of inflation and deflation generally leads to careless reinflation and possibly higher cuff pressures. It is generally agreed that it would be optimal to have a high-volume cuff that could maintain an adequate seal at a resting tracheal mucosal pressure of 15 mmHg. The low-volume, high-pressure cuffs should *not* be used. The intraarterial pressure in blood vessels within the adult tracheal wall is approximately 30 mmHg, and the high-pressure cuffs are capable of exceeding pressures of 300 mmHg.

Ventilator Malfunctions

Some of the potentially serious ventilator malfunctions include mechanical breakdown, overheating of the inspired air, inadequate nebulization, and alarm failure. An extremely common error in the suctioning procedure is neglecting to turn the alarm system back on following suctioning. If a patient's tubing becomes disconnected while the alarm is shut off, the result could be catastrophic. A patient receiving continuous ventilatory support should never be left unattended. When the alarm does sound, it does not identify the nature of the problem, but merely indicates that something is wrong. The patient should be immediately ventilated with a self-inflating bag (always available) until the situation can be corrected. If the patient can readily be ventilated without resistance, the problem is with the ventilator, tubing, or humidifier.

The excessive pressure alarm usually indicates that the patient needs to be suctioned. If the pressure required to deliver a constant volume slowly rises, it may indicate decreasing pulmonary compliance (pulmonary edema due to fluid overload).

Nosocomial Infection

Patients requiring ventilatory support are often debilitated and have a lowered resistance to infection. Endotracheal tubes bypass the normal upper airway defense mechanisms. Aerosol therapy is a great source of nosocomial infection because *Pseudomonas* and other gram-negative bacteria thrive in such hot, wet environments. For this reason, all parts of the ventilatory equipment that come in contact with the patient should be changed at least every 24 h. Meticulous attention to details of good respiratory care techniques, sterile procedures, and frequent hand washing will minimize the incidence of nosocomial infections. Sputum examination should be performed on a routine basis.

The intubated patient is no longer capable of warming and humidifying the inspired gas; therefore, this must be continuously provided to the upper airway. The lack of humidification promotes drying and retention of secretions which may obstruct airways and result in atelectasis and pneumonia.

Cardiac Dysrhythmias

There are multiple reasons for the frequency of cardiac dysrhythmias in the patient receiving controlled ventilation. Severe ventricular and supraventricular dysrhythmias may be produced by inappropriate hyperventilation or hypoventilation. Hypoxemia and hypokalemia also potentiate the risk of cardiac dysrhythmias. Too enthusiastic efforts at lowering the P_{CO_2} causes transient alkalosis, which lowers the serum potassium. Patients receiving controlled support of ventilation must have electrocardiographic monitoring.

Barotrauma

Barotrauma means injury as a result of pressure. Patients receiving continuous ventilatory support are subjected to high positive pressures in the lungs which may produce pneumothorax, pneumomediastinum, or subcutaneous emphysema. A common cause for pneumothorax is "ball-valving." This phenomenon occurs in an area of the lung that can accept air during inspiration but cannot expel it during expiration. This occurs because bronchial tubes are larger on inspiration than expiration and may therefore close with expiration. As this sequence persists, air collects in this particular lung zone, pressure builds up, and rupture occurs. Pneumothorax in a patient on a ventilator can be detected by an abrupt rise in peak inspiratory pressure for the same tidal volume delivered. In patients with chronic airway obstruction, barotrauma frequently results from overdistention. It has been emphasized by some that there is no longer any place for the sigh in modern ventilatory management, except that a single manually activated sigh may be a useful physical therapy adjunct.

Gastrointestinal Complications

Gastrointestinal (GI) bleeding is frequently observed during the treatment of respiratory failure. Among patients requiring respiratory intensive care, 25 to 30 percent suffer mild to massive GI bleeding. "Stress" ulcers are a frequent source; however, even without stress, patients with chronic airway obstruction are known to have an increased incidence of peptic ulceration. Another potentiator of gastrointestinal bleeding is the use of adrenocortical steroids. In addition, patients receiving ventilatory support often swallow quantities of air and may develop marked gastric dilatation or paralytic ileus. This is more common when a small leak around the endotracheal cuff is permitted, since gas under positive pressure insufflates the stomach. Such dilatation can be avoided by using a nasogastric tube.

Although antacid therapy is frequently instituted, the complication of massive upper GI hemorrhage from stress ulcers has emerged as the leading cause of death in patients undergoing treatment for acute respiratory failure. A recent study of immediate blood transfusions and Pitressin infusion into the celiac axis using a constant infusion pump has eliminated the need for surgery in patients with severe GI bleeding.

Medication Side Effects

Certain antibiotics, such as gentamycin and kanamycin, can cause neuromuscular paralysis. If the patient appears to have developed acute myasthenia gravis, antibiotics of this group may be suspect. Severe respiratory depression may develop after "standard" doses of sedatives or narcotics. Isoproterenol may cause hypoxemia, because it dilates pulmonary vessels in poorly ventilated zones of the lung.

Oxygen Toxicity

Oxygen, too, is a drug. It can depress respiration in the hypercapnic patient, but this is generally no problem if the patient is receiving ventilatory support. However, increased oxygen tensions for prolonged periods of time can produce an adult respiratory distress syndrome. The safe use of oxygen dictates that it be used judiciously—only in the concentration required to achieve an appropriate arterial oxygen tension, and only for the period it is required.

Hypotension

Positive-pressure ventilation can reduce cardiac output by decreasing venous return to the heart, particularly if the patient is hypovolemic. This adverse effect on venous return can be minimized if the expiratory phase is long enough to allow venous return during this period to compensate for the decrease that occurs during inspiration. An expiratory time that is 30 percent longer than inspiration will usually stabilize cardiovascular hemodynamics; however, marked hypotension may occur if the patient is hypovolemic or is receiving PEEP therapy.

Obviously, all complications cannot be prevented, but it is interesting to ponder that if a specific complication can be successfully treated, could it be prevented?

ROLES AND RESPONSIBILITIES OF PERSONNEL

The care of the critically ill patient in respiratory failure is a multidisciplinary challenge. In the past decade the field of respiratory intensive care has advanced exponentially, and the proliferation of instruments, tests, procedures, and devices continues to accelerate so that exposure to future shock is almost a daily occurrence.

Respiratory intensive care demands moment-to-moment monitoring, diagnosing, and therapy. The increasing emphasis on knowledgeable intervention in critical care has broadened the scope of health professionals to include decision-making capabilities heretofore delegated only to physicians. Such responsibilities mandate a level of clinical competence in which actions are based upon a comprehensive knowledge of cause and effect; the clinical practitioner must understand abnormal physiological processes, recognize their varied clinical manifestations, and be able to initiate and appropriately alter management modes and assess the outcomes of such therapeutic intervention.

There are many people involved in the critical-care setting—nurses, physicians, physical therapists, respiratory therapists, x-ray technicians, and laboratory technicians to name but a few—and each has an important contribution to make. However, it is important that there be a specific plan of operation so that all activities will be coordinated in the best interests of the patient. The patient in a critical-care unit must be intensively managed 24 h a day. The specific details as to how this is accomplished are not as important as the fact that there *are* details. The plan of action for an ICU in a small community hospital would not be the same as for one in a large medical center. For instance, in one facility the respiratory therapist is "on call" at night and the nurse manages all the technical aspects of the ventilator and blood gas analysis. In the other facility, there are two respiratory therapists working only in the ICU for every 8-h shift.

Careful attention must be given to avoid partitioning responsibilities in respiratory care to one discipline or another. There is a moment when the knowledgeable, capable individual is totally involved in the care of the patient. This is the moment for which all train, through each of the varying disciplines; this is the point at which the discipline in which one is trained is no longer important. Mutual respect and consideration of others' abilities and desires to contribute are essential ingredients in a well-organized critical-care unit.

The critical-care nurse is the patient's guardian and the provider of care. And that which shapes our idealized conception of the nurse is the capacity to respond to patients as complete human beings. This requires intangible skills that go beyond technical expertise, critical though it is. The scientific knowledge and technology must be combined with devotion and the kind of creative versatility that ensures psychological tranquility, as well as physical comfort, for every patient. For when a patient is lost among a welter of transducers and tubings, and when we can no longer feel the despair, hear the silent anguish, or notice the tears of the patient, the critical-care staff is diminished also.

REFERENCES

Caroline, N.: Quo vadis intensive care: More intensive or more care?, *Critical Care Medicine* 5:256, 1977.

Fairley, H. B.: *Management of Respiratory Failure,* S. Hershey (ed.), Philadelphia: Lippincott, 1973.

Fitzgerald, L., and G. Huber: Weaning the patient from mechanical ventilation, *Heart Lung* 5:228, 1976.

Heironimus, T. W.: *Mechanical Artificial Ventilation,* Springfield: Charles C Thomas, 1973.

Lawrence, R. M.: Evaluating mechanical respiratory devices, *Contemp Surg* 11:36–40, 1977.

The critical-care nurse participates in numerous types of special procedures and therapies during the process of delivering health care to acutely or chronically ill individuals. While all these procedures and therapies have the common bond of being necessary to sustain life, they are each unique in how they contribute to that sustenance. Each of the special procedures and therapies imparts its support to the total human being by affecting a specific body system. This intervention usually enhances the function of the body system and, thus, minimizes or corrects the adverse effects on the total individual. Such is the intent of the special therapy called dialysis.

BASIC COMPONENTS

The best approach to use in comprehending the concept of dialysis is to first analyze its basic components. These basic components include a definition, the purposes, the indications for use, the principles involved, and the types of dialysis available for use.

Definition

Dialysis is defined as the separation of solutes by differential diffusion through a porous membrane placed between two solutions. This general definition permits one to distinguish between the various types of dialysis merely by identifying the porous membrane and describing the two solutions that are involved. As such, it will be used later in this context to explain the various types of dialysis.

Purposes

The purposes of dialysis therapy are directly related to the functions of the body system it attempts to imitate—the renal system. The kidneys have a very elaborate and sophisticated mechanism for regulating the fluid and electrolyte balance of the circulating plasma, but when they cease to function, dialysis can act as a substitute for them. The purposes of dialysis in this substitution role are to (1) eliminate excess body fluids, (2) maintain or restore the electrolyte balance of the circulating plasma, and (3) eliminate waste products and dialyzable poisons from the blood. Obviously, the kidneys perform other functions that dialysis cannot imitate, such as secreting erythropoietin or activating the renin-angiotensin system. Therefore, dialysis cannot totally replace the physi-

39
DIALYSIS THERAPY
Charold Lee Baer

BASIC COMPONENTS
Definition
Purposes
Indications for Use
Principles Involved
Types of Dialysis

PERITONEAL DIALYSIS
Definition
Contraindications
Advantages
Disadvantages
Initiating the Therapy
The Dialysis Cycle
Nursing Care Components
Potential Complications

HEMODIALYSIS
Definition
Contraindications
Advantages
Disadvantages
Initiating the Therapy—Vascular Access
Nursing Care Components
Complications

REFERENCES

ologic functions of the renal system, but it can substitute sufficiently to sustain life during a crisis.

Indications for Use

There are five broad categories of conditions for which dialysis would be indicated: (1) acute and chronic renal failure, (2) severe water retention, (3) electrolyte disorders, (4) drug intoxication (assuming the drug is dialyzable), and (5) hepatic coma. Of these five categories, the first one, acute and chronic renal failure, is the most frequently encountered indication for dialysis therapy.

Principles Involved

Dialysis therapy is based on three physical principles that are related to the movement and transport of fluid and electrolytes within the body: osmosis, diffusion, and filtration. *Osmosis* is the movement of fluid, or water molecules, across a semipermeable membrane from an area of lesser solute concentration to an area of greater solute concentration. This movement continues until the concentrations of the solute are equal on both sides of the membrane. *Diffusion* is the movement of solute molecules across a semipermeable membrane from an area of greater solute concentration to an area of lesser solute concentration. Diffusion continues until equilibrium is established

across the membrane. *Filtration* is the movement of fluid across a semipermeable membrane from an area of greater pressure to an area of lesser pressure.

These three principles are affected by many factors that determine the extent of their activity. Among those factors are the size of the pores of the semipermeable membrane; the size of the solute molecules; the osmotic, concentration, and pressure gradients that are established; the temperature of the solution; and in the human body, the rate of blood flow. The size of the pores of the membrane and the size of the solute molecules determine which substances can participate in the transport processes. The gradients that are present determine the extent to which the various transport processes can occur. These gradients are sustained by the high rate of blood flow in the body. As the blood flows through the body it continuously replaces the dialyzed blood with undialyzed blood. The undialyzed blood has very high concentrations of solutes that maintain the established gradients. The temperature of the solution influences the velocity of the molecular movement and thus affects the rate of the transport processes. An increase in the temperature of a solution will increase the rates of the transport processes that occur within the solution.

Figure 39-1 illustrates how osmosis, diffusion, and filtration take place during dialysis therapy. As is depicted, the dialysate solution contains sufficient glucose molecules to make it hypertonic when compared to the blood. This establishes an osmotic gradient that compels water to move from the blood to the dialysate. The dialysate also contains fewer potassium molecules and no urea molecules, while the blood contains many of both molecules. This creates a diffusion or concentration gradient that enables the urea and potassium molecules to cross the semipermeable membrane from the blood to the dialysate. A concentration gradient also exists for glucose, but because of the relatively large size of the molecules, its rate of diffusion from the dialysate to the blood is very slow. In addition to the osmotic and concentration gradients that are present, there is also a pressure gradient, which is due to the weight and force of the water or fluid circulating through the blood vessels. This pressure is referred to as hydrostatic pressure. Because there is more force exerted on the blood to circulate it through the vessels than there is on the static dialysate, a pressure gradient is established from the blood to the dialysate.

The presence of these three gradients—osmotic, concentration, and pressure—in dialysis therapy en-

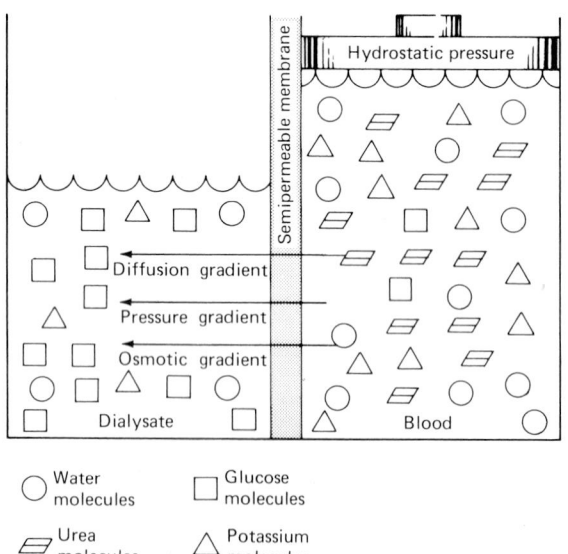

FIGURE 39-1

Osmosis, diffusion, and filtration in dialysis therapy.

ables excess fluid and waste products to be extracted from the blood while the appropriate electrolyte balance is maintained or restored.

Types of Dialysis

The concept of dialysis therapy has undergone experimentation for many years. The purpose for most of these experiments was to determine the most efficient, yet pragmatic and safe, system to use in implementing dialysis. In all these experiments, the blood and a dialysate containing varying constituents were the two solutions used to institute the therapy. The major differences in the experiments concerned the porous membranes that were used to facilitate the transport processes. Among the membranes used were gastric, intestinal, pleural, pulmonary, vaginal, and peritoneal membranes. In addition to these intracorporeal membranes being explored, several extracorporeal systems were devised using animal, as well as synthetic, membranes. The results of this extensive experimentation appeared to indicate that peritoneal dialysis and extracorporeal hemodialysis were the most efficient and practical and the least hazardous methods of implementing the concept of dialysis in human beings. Thus, these are the two types of dialysis that are most frequently encountered by critical-care nurses today.

PERITONEAL DIALYSIS

Peritoneal dialysis necessitates the extensive involvement of the critical-care nurse. The nurse is a vital part of the therapy and, as such, is required to know all the facets of the therapy in order to deliver the highest standard of care. The purposes, indications, and principles of dialysis therapy that were previously discussed also apply to peritoneal dialysis. Therefore, the aspects of peritoneal dialysis that are included in this discussion are the definition, contraindications, advantages, disadvantages, the technique for initiating the therapy, the dialysis cycle, nursing care components, and potential complications.

Definition

Peritoneal dialysis is defined by using the general definition of dialysis and inserting the appropriate identifying terms for the porous membrane and the two solutions that it separates. In that context, *peritoneal dialysis* is the separation of solutes by differential diffusion through the peritoneal membrane which is positioned between an individual's blood and dialysate solution which has been instilled into the peritoneal cavity.

Contraindications

There appear to be conflicting opinions as to what conditions might contraindicate the use of peritoneal dialysis therapy. The more liberal approach asserts that nothing contraindicates using peritoneal dialysis and that any obstacle can be overcome. The conservative approach contends that there are many conditions that would preclude using peritoneal dialysis because of the added risk to the individual's well-being. In response to this conflict, most physicians seem to accept a moderate approach concerning contraindications and tend to function somewhere between the two extremes. The moderate approach suggests that the following conditions at least be considered as contraindications to implementing peritoneal dialysis: (1) acute active peritonitis, (2) recent abdominal surgery, (3) known peritoneal adhesions, (4) severe abdominal trauma or burns, (5) massive intraperitoneal hematoma, and (6) any major abdominally located vascular anastomosis.

Advantages

The advantages of using peritoneal dialysis therapy include the following: (1) the equipment is easily and rapidly assembled; (2) the equipment is relatively inexpensive; (3) very little physical preparation of the patient is needed; (4) there is minimal danger of acute electrolyte imbalances or hemorrhage; (5) the dialysate can easily be individualized for the patient; and (6) no specially trained team of personnel is needed to implement the therapy.

Disadvantages

Using peritoneal dialysis therapy has several disadvantages, including the following: (1) the procedure is time-consuming (usually requiring about 36 h for therapeutic effect); (2) biochemical disturbances are corrected slowly; (3) there is a risk of various complications; (4) the patient will lose approximately 30 to 70 g of protein per dialysis session; and (5) difficulties may occur in relation to gaining or maintaining access to the peritoneal cavity.

Initiating the Therapy

Peritoneal dialysis therapy is initiated either by using an existing peritoneal access device or by inserting a temporary catheter that will be removed at the termination of the dialysis session. Since the critical-care nurse usually participates in peritoneal dialysis that is instituted using the temporary catheter, this discussion will relate to that specific situation. However, one should remember that there are many different types of indwelling peritoneal dialysis catheters and access devices that may be used with both chronically and acutely ill individuals.

In initiating the therapy, the physician first explains the procedure to the patient. The patient is then instructed to empty the bladder, if possible, to minimize the risk of perforation during the catheter insertion. A predialysis weight is obtained; then the patient assumes a supine position in bed. After opening the peritoneal dialysis catheter tray and putting on sterile gloves, the physician prepares the abdomen, using either an antibacterial iodine solution, tincture of benzalkonium chloride (Zephiran Chloride), or some other suitable agent. The physician then uses 1 percent lidocaine (Xylocaine) or a lidocaine and epinephrine mixture to anesthetize an area in the lower abdomen just below the level of the umbilicus.

A scalpel is used to make a small incision at the midline of the abdominal wall in the anesthetized area. Then a large-bore (No. 18), 2½-in needle or Angiocath is inserted into the incision, and 1 L of dialysate solution is infused into the peritoneal cavity. This liter of solution, often called a primer run, acts as a cushion to prevent vital organs from being perforated during the insertion of the dialysis catheter. Once the primer run is infused, the needle or Angiocath is removed and the catheter is prepared for insertion.

The temporary catheter most frequently used is the Weston-Roberts trocar catheter. This catheter is made of stiff Silastic or Teflon, is hollow, and accommodates a metal trocar during insertion. One end of the catheter has numerous small holes in it, while the other end is designed to fit into a connecting tube that will eventually be attached to a set of fluid administration tubing. Prior to the catheter insertion, the physician slides the trocar in and out of the catheter to be sure that it moves easily. The trocar is then pushed into the catheter until its pointed end protrudes through the catheter tip. The catheter-enclosed trocar is introduced through the incision, and gentle, steady pressure is applied to pass it through the peritoneum and downward toward the base of the pelvis.

After the catheter is in place, the trocar is removed and the connecting tube and the fluid administration tubing are attached. The physician inserts a purse-string suture around the catheter to anchor it and deter the leakage of fluid. Then an antibacterial ointment and a dry sterile dressing are applied. The final step in the catheter insertion procedure is the positioning of a paper cup around the catheter to prevent it from kinking. The paper cup is then taped to the abdomen. Once the catheter is in place, the dialysis can proceed.

The Dialysis Cycle

Peritoneal dialysis is performed in cycles, or runs. Each dialysis cycle is composed of three phases and usually lasts an hour or less. The three phases of a dialysis cycle are insertion, equilibration, and drainage.

The Insertion Phase

The insertion phase, the most stable of the three phases in length, is usually 5 to 10 min in duration. It is the period of time that it takes for 2 L of warmed dialysate solution to flow into the peritoneal cavity as fast as gravity will permit. The dialysate solution that is instilled during this phase is usually prepared and sterilized commercially. The solution has a definite electrolyte composition which approximates that of the extracellular body fluid. It is also available in varying dextrose concentrations to provide the degree of hypertonicity appropriate for a specific patient's condition. The dialysate solution is warmed to 37°C, or body temperature, to increase the rate of the transport processes and provide for a more efficient dialysis.

The Equilibration Phase

The equilibration phase can be of variable duration, but it usually lasts 20 to 25 min. This phase is the period of time that the dialysate solution is allowed to remain in the peritoneal cavity so that the transport processes can take place. The length of this phase is important because once equilibrium is achieved between the blood and the dialysate, further exchange is negated. Therefore, prolonging this phase beyond 20 to 30 min is neither therapeutic nor efficient.

The Drainage Phase

The drainage phase is also a variable phase that usually lasts 20 to 25 min. It is the period of time needed for the fluid to drain out of the peritoneal cavity by siphoning. This phase may be varied according to the fluid balance of the patient. If the individual has a large amount of excess fluid, the drainage phase might be lengthened to allow more fluid to return. However, the fluid that is extracted from an individual should be removed at a steady rate throughout the course of the dialysis session, rather than sporadically. Therefore, this phase should not be prolonged beyond 20 to 30 min.

Nursing Care Components

The nursing care of the individual receiving peritoneal dialysis can be divided into three categories: care of the patient during the catheter insertion, performing the mechanics of the dialysis, and care of the patient during the dialysis.

Care During the Catheter Insertion

The nursing care of the patient during insertion of the peritoneal dialysis catheter includes the following functions:

1. Reinforcing an explanation of the procedure to the patient
2. Reassuring the patient and family members about the procedure
3. Assisting the patient in emptying the bladder
4. Obtaining a predialysis weight
5. Monitoring the patient's vital signs in order to establish a baseline for future comparisons
6. Administering analgesics or sedatives as indicated
7. Assembling the appropriate equipment for the catheter insertion
8. Assisting the physician in preparing the abdomen
9. Assisting the physician in inserting the catheter
10. Restraining the patient if necessary
11. Providing emotional support for the patient

Performing the Mechanics of the Dialysis

Performing the mechanics of the dialysis demands that the nurse engage in the following activities at least hourly:

1. Establishing and maintaining a dialysis cart containing the appropriate equipment and types and number of liters of solution; 2 L of solution are used for each cycle, and it is prudent to have obtained sufficient amounts of 1.5 percent and 4.25 percent dialysate to complete the therapy.
2. Warming the dialysate solution by placing the bottles in a warming chamber or a pan of hot water.
3. Adding the appropriate medications to one of the solution bottles of a cycle. The two most frequently added medications are potassium chloride and heparin. The dosages of these medications may vary but usually they are 4 meq of potassium chloride and 500 units of heparin per liter of dialysate.
4. Marking the solution bottle with the name and amount of medications that were added.
5. Marking the solution bottles with the number of the cycle in the dialysis session.
6. Attaching the fluid administration tubing to the solution bottles.
7. Testing the temperature of the solution prior to infusing it. In many instances the insides of the wrists are used to test the temperature, since most other methods would involve the possibility of contaminating the solution.
8. Hanging the solution bottles on an intravenous infusion pole.
9. Flushing all the air out of the fluid administration tubing.
10. Joining the catheter connecting tube and the fluid administration tubing using aseptic technique.
11. Clamping off the tubing with some fluid remaining in it after the solution bottles have infused. This remaining fluid will enhance the siphoning effect during the drainage phase.
12. Lowering the empty bottles to the floor.
13. Dislodging the airways from the bottles.
14. Clamping off the white flow ball in the drip chamber of the fluid administration tubing so that it does not impede the flow of draining fluid.
15. Taping the tubing to the side rail of the bed to stabilize it to prevent kinking.
16. Unclamping the tubing.
17. Measuring the amount of fluid returned in the drainage phase.
18. Recording the measured amount of fluid returned during the drainage phase. This is an extremely vital function of the nurse during peritoneal dialysis therapy. It is important that all calculations and recordings be double-checked, consistent, and accurate because any error could present a false picture of the patient's status and thereby jeopardize the patient's well-being.

Care During the Dialysis

The care of the patient during the dialysis involves the nurse's performance of the following interventions:

1. Positioning the patient in a comfortable posture to facilitate adequate respiration and minimize discomfort
2. Changing the dressing around the catheter whenever necessary, using aseptic technique
3. Monitoring the patient's vital signs and fluid balance
4. Maintaining adequate, accurate records about the patient and the dialysis
5. Attending to the patient's basic physical needs
6. Attending to the patient's basic psychological needs
7. Keeping the family informed and aware of the patient's condition and progress
8. Observing the patient closely for signs of complications

The previously listed components of the nursing care required by patients who are experiencing peritoneal dialysis therapy are general in nature. They do not include the numerous extra little things that a nurse does for a patient to provide individualized care. These additional interventions are as important to the total care of the patient as are the essential procedural tasks.

Potential Complications

There are many complications that can result from the therapeutic use of peritoneal dialysis. Fortunately, most complications occur infrequently. The complications that may result from peritoneal dialysis can be divided into three categories: complications resulting from mechanical problems, complications resulting from metabolic difficulties, and complications resulting from inflammatory reactions.

Complications Resulting from Mechanical Problems

The potential complications resulting from mechanical problems include the following:

1. Perforation of abdominal viscera during insertion of the catheter
2. Hemorrhage from the catheter insertion
3. Preperitoneal placement of the catheter
4. Improper drainage due to blockage of the catheter
5. Leakage of fluid around the catheter
6. Pain during catheter insertion
7. Discomfort due to the pressure of the fluid within the peritoneal cavity
8. Pulmonary complications due to the pressure of the fluid in the peritoneal cavity

Complications Resulting from Metabolic Difficulties

Some of the potential complications that may result from metabolic difficulties are as follows:

1. Hypovolemia due to too rapid removal of fluid
2. Hypervolemia due to impaired drainage of fluid
3. Hypernatremia due to too rapid removal of fluid
4. Hypokalemia due to using potassium-free dialysate
5. Alkalosis from using alkaline dialysate
6. Disequilibrium syndrome due to too rapid removal of fluid and waste products
7. Hyperglycemia due to high glucose concentration of the dialysate

Complications Resulting from Inflammatory Reactions

The potential complications that may result from inflammatory reactions are (1) peritoneal irritation produced by the catheter and (2) peritonitis due to bacterial infection, which is the most common complication encountered in peritoneal dialysis therapy. The incidence of peritonitis appears to be related to the duration of the dialysis session. Some clinicians have found that peritonitis seems to occur more frequently when a session is prolonged beyond 36 h.

HEMODIALYSIS

The critical-care nurse's involvement with hemodialysis is not nearly as encompassing as it is with peritoneal dialysis. This is because the degree of specialization that is required to implement hemodialysis dictates that a separately trained team of personnel be employed to carry out the therapy. Consequently, the critical-care nurse is more concerned with the patient's status prior to dialysis and the effects of the dialysis on that status than on the actual process itself. Therefore, this discussion will present only a cursory view of hemodialysis, covering the definition, contraindications, advantages, disadvantages, initiating the therapy, nursing care components, and complications. The purposes, indications for use, and principles involved are identical to those discussed at the beginning of this chapter under "Basic Components" and will not be repeated. However, a treatment of the subtopic of vascular access will be presented.

Definition

Hemodialysis is defined, using the general definition of dialysis, as the separation of solutes by differential diffusion through a celluloid membrane positioned between an individual's blood and the dialysate solution. An additional dimension of hemodialysis is that it is extracorporeal, meaning that it occurs in a receptacle that is located outside the individual's body.

Contraindications

Insufficient blood volume, or hypovolemia, is the most frequently stated contraindication to hemodialysis. However, there are some dialysis centers that contend that there are no contraindications to using hemodialysis therapy.

Advantages

The two major advantages of hemodialysis are that (1) it requires only 6 to 8 h per session and (2) it is very efficient and corrects biochemical disturbances quickly.

Disadvantages

The disadvantages of hemodialysis include the following: (1) a specially trained team of personnel is required to implement the therapy; (2) acute electrolyte imbalances can occur rapidly; (3) an individual may hemorrhage or exsanguinate easily; (4) there is a risk of hepatitis; (5) the equipment is complex and expensive; and (6) there are not sufficient machines available for those who need them.

Initiating the Therapy—Vascular Access

The major steps in initiating hemodialysis therapy are setting up the dialysis machine and connecting the patient to it. Since the critical-care nurse usually does not participate in either of these procedures, the technical complexities involved will not be enumerated here. The critical-care nurse does intervene indirectly in the initiation process, however, by monitoring and maintaining the individual's vascular access system. Therefore, a discussion of the nurse's role in relation to vascular access methods is indicated and will include the following aspects: types of vascular access, advantages, disadvantages, and nursing care goals.

Types of Vascular Access

There are two arteriovenous systems that may be created to provide easy access to the bloodstream for hemodialysis. The two systems are the arteriovenous fistula and the arteriovenous shunt.

An arteriovenous fistula is a surgically created communication between an artery and a vein. The most common arteriovenous fistula is the Brescia-Cimino fistula, which is created by anastomosing the radial artery and cephalic vein in a side-to-side or end-to-side manner. This anastomosis permits blood to bypass the capillaries and flow directly from the artery into the vein. As a result, the vein is forced to dilate in order to accommodate the increased pressure that accompanies the arterial blood. This produces a vein that is much easier to cannulate for hemodialysis.

The creation of an arteriovenous shunt necessitates the implantation of an extracorporeal apparatus to connect an artery and a vein. Once the apparatus is in place, it can easily be opened or punctured to provide access to the bloodstream. There are several types of shunts in use today, but the most popular is the Quinton-Scribner shunt, which is made of Silastic and Teflon and consists of two lengths of tubing joined by a connector. Each length of tubing has three portions. The first portion is implanted in the vessel and lies beneath the skin. The second portion is a steplike gradation that emerges from the plane of the vessel upward to exit onto the skin through a puncture wound. The third portion is external and lies flush with the skin. Access to the vascular system is obtained by removing the connector and attaching tubing directly to the arterial and venous lines of the shunt.

Advantages and Disadvantages

The major advantages and disadvantages of fistulas and shunts are listed in Table 39-1.

TABLE 39-1
The Advantages and Disadvantages of Arteriovenous Fistulas and Shunts

Fistula	Shunt
Advantages	
Located internally	Can be placed in almost any vessel
Permanent	Available for use immediately
Few complications	No venipunctures required for dialysis
Few limitations to movement	No blood pump required for dialysis
Requires minimal care	Provides easy access to bloodstream
Disadvantages	
Needs to mature before using	Located externally
Requires venipunctures prior to dialysis	Temporary
Requires a blood pump for dialysis	Easily dislodged causing hemorrhage
May lead to circulatory problems in the extremity	Prone to infection and thrombosis
Clotting may occlude it	Movement is restricted
Constrictive clothing cannot be worn	Apparatus parts may erode through the skin
	Requires close monitoring and care

Nursing Care Goals

The critical-care nurse's interventions with arteriovenous fistulas and shunts revolve around three goals: (1) to monitor the patency; (2) to prevent infection; and (3) to promote safety and adequate function.

Monitoring the patency of an arteriovenous fistula begins by palpating the fistula area to determine the presence of the thrill. A *thrill* is the buzzing feeling caused by the pressurized arterial blood striking the walls and valves of the veins as it circulates through the fistula. Next, the diaphragm of a stethoscope is placed over the fistula to detect the presence of a bruit. A *bruit* is the sound that is created as the blood flows from the artery to the vein. Auscultation is also used to monitor the patency of an arteriovenous shunt. With the shunt, however, the bruit is often very faint or totally inaudible. Visual inspection of the shunt tubing for signs of clotting is the second method of monitoring the patency of a shunt.

Preventing infection in a fistula involves meticulous care of the incision. This would include cleansing the incision with an antibacterial solution and hydrogen peroxide, applying an antibacterial ointment, and covering the wound with a dry sterile dressing. Incision care should be performed at least every 8 h or more frequently until the wound is healed. Preventing infection in a shunt also involves meticulous cleansing with the same types of agents. In the case of the shunt, it is important to cleanse not only the puncture wounds or insertion sites but also the shunt tubing and the connector. The antibacterial ointment and dry sterile dressing are then applied to the insertion sites.

Promoting safety and the adequate function of a fistula is done primarily by explaining to the individual the need to wear nonconstrictive clothing, to have no blood pressures taken or blood drawn from the involved extremity, and to be cautious about the types of activities in which that extremity is used. Promoting safety and the adequate function of a shunt includes issuing similar kinds of explanations as well as being concerned with the proper positioning and stabilization of the shunt. The involved extremity should be positioned in proper alignment but in such a manner that the shunt tubing will not become kinked or occluded due to pressure. Stabilizing the shunt is accomplished by using a system of tabs and bridges created with ½-in paper tape. A tab is a piece of tape that is placed around the shunt tubing and then is fastened to the skin. A bridge is the second piece of tape that is used to hold the tab in place. The bridge is placed across the portion of the tab that adheres to the skin. Three tabs and two bridges are used to anchor the shunt tubing in place. One tab is placed on either side of the connector and another tab is placed opposite the connector. Figure 39-2 illustrates a shunt stabilized using this method. After the shunt is stabilized, the extremity may be placed on an armboard for further stabilization, and then it is wrapped with gauze. It is important when wrapping the extremity to leave a small portion of the shunt tubing uncovered so that it can be inspected for patency.

Nursing Care Components

The nurse who is a member of a hemodialysis team participates in the following activities:

1. Setting up the machine
2. Obtaining baseline vital signs
3. Obtaining a predialysis weight
4. Connecting the individual to the machine
5. Monitoring the individual's responses
6. Monitoring the equipment
7. Providing reassurance and emotional support for the individual
8. Discontinuing the dialysis
9. Obtaining a postdialysis weight

Complications

The critical-care nurse becomes very involved in monitoring the individual's status after dialysis. This monitoring includes assessing the individual's response to dialysis as well as observing for potential complications. Some of the potential complications

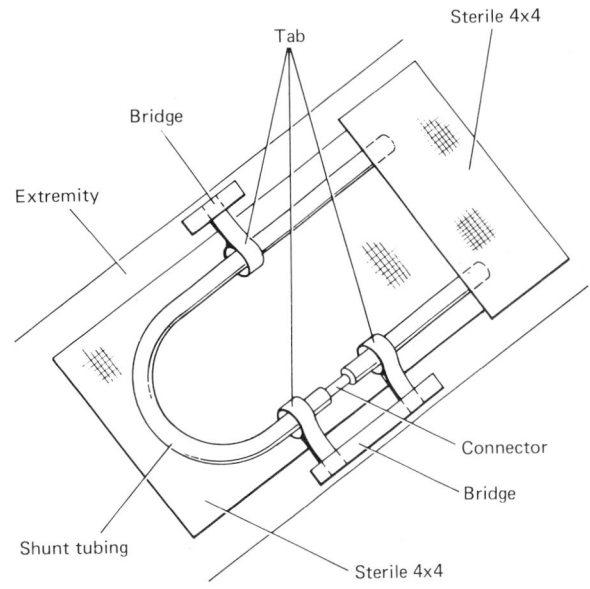

FIGURE 39-2

A stabilized shunt.

of hemodialysis therapy are (1) shunt or fistula sepsis; (2) shunt or fistula clotting; (3) hemorrhage; (4) hypovolemia; (5) acute electrolyte imbalances; and (6) disequilibrium syndrome.

REFERENCES

Baer, Charold: A Description of the Care and Treatment Given to Patients Undergoing Peritoneal Dialysis and the Patients' Responses to That Care and Treatment, unpublished master's thesis, The Ohio State University, Columbus, 1970.

Barry, Kevin, Franklin D. Schwartz, and Frank E. Matthews: Further Experience With the Flexible Peritoneal Cannula in Several Hospital Centers, *Transactions of the American Society For Artificial Internal Organs* 10:400–405 (1964).

Berlyne, G. M., H. A. Lee, A. J. Ralston, and H. A. Woolcock: Pulmonary Complications of Peritoneal Dialysis, *The Lancet* 2:75–78 (July 9, 1966).

Boen, S. T.: Kinetics of Peritoneal Dialysis, *Medicine* 40:243–287 (September 1961).

Boen, S. T.: *Peritoneal Dialysis in Clinical Medicine,* Springfield, Ill.: Charles C Thomas, 1964.

Brundage, Dorothy J.: *Nursing Management of Renal Problems,* St. Louis: Mosby, 1976.

Cangiano, Jose L., Thomas Kuruvila, Biman Kastagir, and Victor Vertes: Intermittent Peritoneal Dialysis, *The Ohio State Medical Journal* 65:681–687 (July 1969).

Cattell, W. R.: Peritoneal Dialysis, *Nursing Mirror* 127:26–28 (1968).

Clark, James E., and Richard R. Soricelli: Indications for Dialysis, *Medical Clinics of North America* 49:1219–1239 (September, 1965).

Dialysis & Transplantation 6:11–90, Feb. 1977.

Dolan, Patricia O'Conner, and Harry L. Greene: Renal failure and peritoneal dialysis, *Nursing '75* 5:40–49, July 1975.

Edelbaum, David N., Albert Sokol, Sanford Gaynor, and Milton E. Rubini: Peritoneal Dialysis in Chronic Renal Failure, *California Medicine* 108:85–89 (February 1968).

Fretter, Colin: Peritoneal Dialysis, *Nursing Times* 62:42–44 (January 14, 1966).

Goldberg, Edward M., Willis Hill, Sherwin Kabins, and Barry Levin: Peritoneal Dialysis, *Dialysis & Transplantation* 4:50, 52, 56 (June–July, 1975).

Graduate Students of the Catholic University of America School of Nursing Education: *Care of the Patient Having Hemodialysis or Peritoneal Dialysis,* New York: National League of Nursing, 1962.

Gross, Melvin, and Harold P, McDonald: Effect of Dialysate Temperature and Flow Rate on Peritoneal Clearance, *Journal of the American Medical Association* 202:363–365 (October 23, 1967).

Gutch, C. F., and Martha H. Stoner: *Review of Hemodialysis for Nurses and Dialysis Personnel,* St. Louis: Mosby, 1971.

Harrington, Joan D., and Etta R. Brener: *Patient Care in Renal Failure,* Philadelphia: Saunders, 1973.

Jennrich, Judith A.: Some aspects of the nursing care for patients on hemodialysis, *Heart and Lung* 4:885–889, Nov.–Dec. 1975.

Lange, Kurt, and Gerhard Treser: Automatic Continuous High Flow Rate Peritoneal Dialysis, *Transactions of the American Society for Artificial Internal Organs,* 13:164–167 (1967).

Light, Jimmy A.: A Review of Vascular Access Management, *Dialysis & Transplantation* 4:20, 22, 27, 28, 30–31 (December–January, 1975).

Malette, W. G., J. J. McPhaul, F. Bledsoe, D, A, McIntosh, and E. Koegel: A Clinically Successful Subcutaneous Peritoneal Access Button for Repeated Peritoneal Dialysis, *Transactions of the American Society for Artificial Internal Organs,* 10:396–399 (1964).

Merrill, Richard H.: Review of vascular access, *Dialysis & Transplantation* 6:22, Dec. 1977.

Miller, Ronald B., and Carl R. Tassistro: Current Concepts—Peritoneal Dialysis, *The New England Journal of Medicine* 281:945–949 (October 23, 1969).

Nose, Yukihiko: *Manual on Artificial Organs: Volume I—The Artificial Kidney,* St. Louis: Mosby, 1969.

O'Neill, Mary: Peritoneal dialysis, *Nurs Clin North Am* 1:309–323, June 1966.

Ribot, Seymour, Martin G. Jacobs, Howard J, Frankel, and Arthur Bernstein: Complications of Peritoneal Dialysis, *The American Journal of the Medical Sciences* 252:505–517 (November, 1966).

Richard, Cleo: Nursing implications in prevention of complications in peritoneal dialysis, *Heart and Lung* 4:890–893, Nov.–Dec. 1975.

Smith, Earl C., and Philip Freedman: Dialysis—Current status and future trends, *Heart and Lung* 4:879–884, Nov.–Dec. 1975.

Solomon, Margot B.: The Care and Maintenance of AV Shunts, *Dialysis & Transplantation* 3:36–37, 41 (June–July, 1974).

Tenckhoff, H.: Catheter Implantation, *Dialysis & Transplantation* 1:18–20 (August–September, 1972).

Twiss, Mary R., and Morton Maxwell: Peritoneal Dialysis, *American Journal of Nursing* 59: 1560–1563 (November, 1958).

INTRODUCTION

The caloric needs of the critically ill person can be markedly elevated by the stress of injury, disease, major organ failure, sepsis, and fever. Without adequate nutritional support, the body will use its lean muscle mass (protein) to meet these high metabolic requirements. If greater than 30 percent of the lean body mass is lost, death may result. This catabolic process can be prevented by the administration of adequate protein (amino acids) and carbohydrate (glucose) by vein. This procedure is known as *total parenteral nutrition* (TPN).

Over the past 10 years, the administration of parenteral nutrition has become a sophisticated, often lifesaving, therapy. Its application has proved beneficial in varied disease settings so that parenteral nutrition has become an integral component of the management of critically ill patients.

Although various methods of administering solutions intravenously (IV) had been attempted since the seventeenth century, it was not until 1952 that Aubaniac described the percutaneous method of catheterizing the subclavian vein to administer volume replacement to France's Vietnam war casualties. This catheterization procedure was adapted in the 1960s for monitoring central venous pressure and administering fluids.

Stanley Dudrick used the method of subclavian cannulation to infuse nutritional solutions. Experimenting with beagle puppies, he and his coworkers were able to demonstrate that normal growth and development could be achieved by a totally intravenous form of nutrition. The first attempt to employ this therapy in treating humans was in the late summer of 1967. Dudrick was asked to treat a critically ill female newborn infant with near-total small bowel atresia. She survived for nearly 22 months with TPN therapy.

Delivering total nutrition by vein is dependent on two factors: (1) the proper type of nutrient solution and (2) safe transcutaneous access. Forms of intravenous nutrient solutions have been available since the late 1930s. However, successful use of these solutions was prevented by the limited techniques of cannulating and safely maintaining a vein of adequate size for the infusion of hypertonic solutions.

[1] Special acknowledgement is given for assistance in the preparation of this manuscript to Jay Bates, RN; Rita Colley, RN; Barbara Curran, LPN; Ronald Malt, MD; and Luc Michel, MD.

40
PARENTERAL NUTRITION[1]

Jeanne M. Wilson
M. Theresa Holland

INTRODUCTION

SOLUTION CONTENTS

CATHETER PLACEMENT

TECHNICAL COMPLICATIONS

AIR EMBOLISM

DRESSING CARE

METABOLIC MANAGEMENT
Glucose
Proteins
Electrolytes
Trace Elements
Fatty Acids

SEPSIS CONTROL
Candida Septicemia

PSYCHOLOGICAL ASPECTS

REFERENCES

SOLUTION CONTENTS

TPN solutions are composed of proteins, carbohydrates, electrolytes, minerals, vitamins, and if indicated, trace elements. Amino acids provide nitrogen essential for tissue growth and repair. Therefore, to achieve or maintain positive nitrogen balance, protein intake that supplies these amino acids is essential.

A form of carbohydrate, usually dextrose, provides calories and prevents gluconeogenesis, the breakdown of protein for energy. Some 150 to 250 nonprotein calories should be provided with each gram of nitrogen in order to achieve positive nitrogen balance. For this reason, hypertonic dextrose is mixed with the amino acids to formulate TPN solutions.

Originally, protein hydrolysate solutions were the source of protein used in the manufacture of TPN solutions. Approximately 40 percent of the nitrogen contained in these solutions was in the form of peptides and was metabolically nonutilizable. A newer version of protein, synthetic crystalline amino acids, provides essential and nonessential amino acids which are readily utilized by the body. Although protein hydrolysate solutions are less expensive, the trend has been to use these synthetic amino acids.

The type and amounts of electrolytes added to the formulations are determined by patient need. Trace element deficiencies appear in patients with long-term dependence on total IV nutritional support. Therefore, trace elements may be added to the TPN regimen to cover daily requirements.

Water- and fat-soluble vitamins are usually added to TPN solutions. However, much research is still needed to determine accurate IV vitamin requirements.

With the advent of synthetic amino acids, the trend has been to tailor the amino acid content, as well as the glucose concentration, to meet the requirements posed by specific disease states. A solution containing only essential amino acids (Nephramine) is presently commercially available. Mixed with hypertonic (40 to 50%) dextrose and vitamins, this solution provides nutritional support specifically required by patients with acute renal failure. This solution provides a higher calorie/nitrogen ratio than found in standard TPN solutions.

Another alternative solution used is a peripheral amino acid formulation. Designed to be infused peripherally, the final concentration is 5 to 10% dextrose. Peripheral solutions may appear to be ideal because they do not require placement of a central venous catheter, but their use should be limited to supplemental therapy because sufficient calories may not be able to be provided peripherally. An IV fat emulsion may be infused in conjunction with these solutions to provide additional calories as well as to supply essential fatty acids (EFA).

CATHETER PLACEMENT

Because TPN solutions are hyperosmolar (15 to 50% dextrose), they are infused into a wide-diameter, high-flow central vein so that the threat of chemical phlebitis is significantly reduced. The ideal central vein is the superior vena cava, where rapid dilution of the infusion may occur. Safe access to this central venous position is achieved by the percutaneous introduction of a catheter into the subclavian or internal jugular vein.

The subclavian vein provides the ideal entry site for long-term catheter maintenance. Because the subclavicular area is relatively flat, immobile, and free of secretions, the care of occlusive dressings is less of a problem for the nursing staff and more comfortable for the patient.

Access via the brachial or femoral vein is contraindicated for long-term TPN therapy because of the extra indwelling catheter length necessary to achieve central venous position. This extra catheter length increases the possibility of thrombophlebitis and clotting. Nursing care of these sites is also a problem, because they are difficult to keep occlusively dressed.

TPN therapy should only be initiated under ideal conditions to decrease the incidence of complications. If the patient is hypovolemic, location of the vein and threading of the catheter may be more difficult. For this reason, IV fluids or blood products may be prescribed to adequately replenish fluid volume before catheterization.

If necessary, it is preferable to shave the proposed site the evening before or at least several hours prior to catheterization, because the prepping solutions used during the procedure may irritate freshly shaven skin.

Before the actual catheterization begins and when the patient's condition allows, the patient should be told about the procedure and allowed ample time for questions. Organizing supplies beforehand ensures that the nurse will be free to psychologically support the patient during the procedure. Narcotics or sedatives may also be helpful in decreasing anxiety and allowing the patient to relax. A calm, relaxed atmosphere during catheter insertion may actually help to reduce the incidence of complications.

The patient should also be forewarned of the towel roll placed along the thoracic vertebral column. Although a source of some discomfort for the patient, this roll helps to ease the shoulders back and elevates the clavicles. The patient is also placed in Trendelenburg's or the head-dependent position. Although this position is uncomfortable, its use is necessary to cause venous engorgement and dilatation, making venous catheterization easier and decreasing the possibility of air embolism.

Insertion of the catheter used for TPN is an aseptic surgical procedure. The physician wears a gown, mask, and sterile gloves, and all in attendance wear a mask. The skin of the patient's infraclavicular area is prepped with surgical scrub solutions. Acetone may be used as a defatting agent to remove cellular debris. This is followed by a 2 min scrub of iodine tincture or povidone-iodine preparation. If iodine tincture is used, 70% isopropyl alcohol should be used as the third prepping agent to thoroughly remove the iodine and for further antisepsis. The area is then surgically draped with sterile towels.

The skin, the subcutaneous tissue, and the area under the clavicle must be well anesthetized with 1% lidocaine to ensure that the patient feels less discomfort during the insertion of the large-bore needle used to insert the catheter. Incidentally, this also decreases sudden patient movement. It might also be wise to use the small-bore needle used for the local anesthetic to locate the vein.

Once the subclavian vein is located, the patient is instructed to perform the Valsalva maneuver (forced exhalation against a closed glottis). This increases central venous pressure and decreases the possibility of air embolism, as the physician removes the syringe from the large-bore needle and quickly but gently threads the catheter through the subclavian vein. The Valsalva maneuver may be achieved on an intubated patient by maintaining positive pressure with an ambu bag or, on a confused, uncooperative patient, by pressing on the abdomen.

The catheter is then secured to the skin with a single suture at the insertion site to prevent accidental dislodgment. A sterile dressing is applied to the site using an antimicrobial ointment and an occlusive dressing cover. Isotonic solution is infused through the catheter at a slow infusion rate (20 mL/h) until the catheter tip position is confirmed by chest roentgenogram. To avoid such complications as myocardial perforation, valvular damage, or cardiac irritability, the catheter should be in the superior vena cava, not the right atrium.

TECHNICAL COMPLICATIONS

The complications of catheter placement have been well described in the literature. Some of the common complications associated with catheter insertion are pneumothorax, hydrothorax, hemothorax, and arterial (subclavian or carotid) laceration. Nerve damage (brachial plexus or phrenic) and thoracic duct injury may also occur. Another noteworthy but rare complication associated with a difficult insertion is that of the catheter embolization. This occurs when a piece of catheter is sheared off by the bevel of the needle and floats into the vascular system.

Although some of these complications are noticeable immediately, others, such as hydrothorax, hemothorax, mediastinal hematoma, and myocardial or valvular damage, might not become apparent for hours. Therefore, it is important during both the immediate and late postcatheterization period that the nurse observe the patient for signs and symptoms of all these complications.

As stated previously, a calm, immobile patient may help to decrease the occurrence of these complications during catheter placement. The routine chest roentgenogram done after catheter placement determines the location of the catheter tip and aids in the early detection of complications.

AIR EMBOLISM

Air embolism is a possibility for any patient with a central venous catheter. It may occur whenever the central venous system is open to air, such as during catheter insertion when the syringe is removed from the large-bore needle to thread the catheter. Or it may occur during the purposeful or accidental disconnection of the IV tubing from the central catheter. Embolism may even occur after catheter removal before the skin tract has healed. According to Ryan (1976), the patient who is hypovolemic, sitting upright, and breathing deeply so that there is negative intrathoracic pressure relative to the pressure at the site of the open catheter is most susceptible to sustaining an air embolism.

To prevent air embolism, the patient should be instructed to perform the Valsalva maneuver when the catheter is threaded during insertion. The patient should be positioned flat in bed and also instructed to perform the Valsalva maneuver when the IV administration system is changed. All IV tubing junctions should be secured with tape to prevent accidental separation. Should accidental separation occur, the catheter hub should immediately be occluded. Patients may also be instructed to place their finger over the hub, preventing the entry of air, even though this is a break in sterile technique. When the catheter is removed, antimicrobial ointment and an air-occlusive dressing should be applied to the site for approximately 24 to 48 h until the site is healed.

DRESSING CARE

After a central venous catheter has been placed for TPN, the catheter must receive scrupulous care to minimize the risk of sepsis. The nurse has a pivotal role in achieving this goal by giving diligent attention to the catheter site. Care of the site should involve a standardized method of dressing change done every 48 h or more often to maintain an occlusive dressing seal. A dressing not totally occlusive should be completely redone, not simply resealed.

The dressing change is an aseptic procedure, and all personnel at the head of the bed should wear a mask. If the patient is unable to wear a mask because of respiratory equipment, the patient's head should be positioned so that this apparatus is angled away from the catheter site. To prevent contamination by aerosol droplet, steps should be taken to protect the site from humidity-producing equipment and respiratory secretions, as illustrated in Fig. 40-1.

Bedside curtains should be drawn to prohibit unnecessary traffic. A clean table should be used for establishing the sterile work area. When all equipment is assembled, the outdated dressing is carefully removed and the insertion site inspected for any evidence of inflammation, crusting, or drainage. If present, this should be reported, documented, and appropriately cultured and treated. Appearance of purulent drainage at the insertion site mandates removal of the catheter. The skin condition should also be inspected, and if excoriation or skin irritation secondary to the prep solutions or dressing tape is evident, an adjustment in the dressing procedure should be made. To promote optimal dressing adhesion and patient comfort, the catheter area should be carefully reshaved when necessary. The stabilizing suture should be checked at this time and replaced if necessary.

With the use of sterile gloves and instruments, the catheter area is prepped in an aseptic manner. Beginning at the insertion site and working outward in larger concentric circles (clean-to-dirty method), the catheter area is first thoroughly cleaned with a defatting agent such as acetone or an acetone-alcohol mixture. This removes cellular debris and adhesive residue from both the skin and catheter which could potentially harbor bacteria and cause skin excoriation.

In a similar manner, the skin is gently prepped for

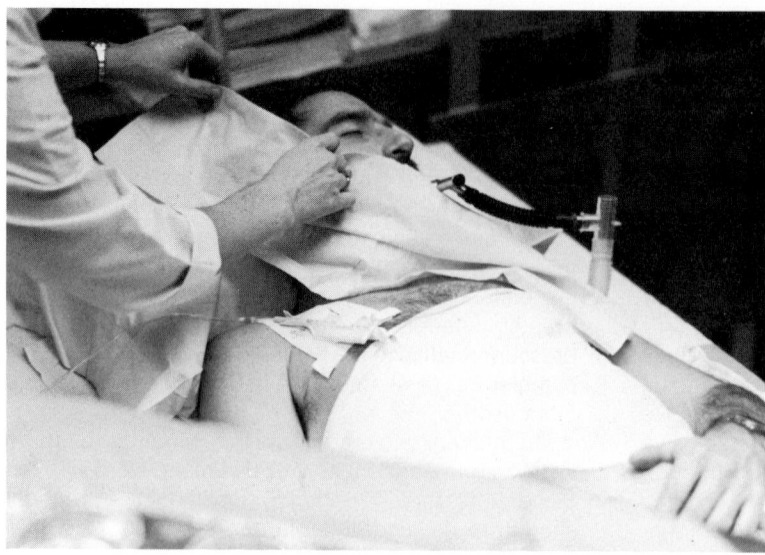

FIGURE 40-1
Protection of catheter site from humidity-producing equipment and respiratory secretions.

2 min with either 1 or 2% iodine tincture and allowed to air dry. The iodine tincture should be thoroughly removed with 70% isopropyl alcohol. Iodine tincture, if allowed to remain on the skin under an occlusive dressing, could burn the skin. If the patient is iodine-sensitive, povidone-iodine solution may serve as a substitute for the iodine tincture. In this case, the povidone-iodine solution should remain on the skin and should not be removed with alcohol.

Alcohol, the final prep solution, should also be allowed to air dry before a topical antibacterial and antifungal ointment is placed at the site. The ointment is covered with a small sterile gauze sponge. The skin area may be lightly sprayed with aerosol tincture of benzoin, then allowed to dry to a tacky state. Benzoin enhances dressing adhesiveness and helps to "toughen" the skin. Other aerosol (ostomy) skin-care products may also be useful for this purpose. An occlusive bandage is applied using a "no-touch" method. While it has been common practice to use an elasticized adhesive bandage, in cases where tape sensitivity is evident or waterproofing indicated, a sterile adhesive-backed plastic drape is useful. Some newer products that are now commercially available offer the added advantage of allowing moisture vaporization which helps prevent skin maceration. It is best not to stretch the dressing cover when applying it to the skin. A tight dressing might cause kinking of the catheter and undesirable tension on the skin during normal range of motion. The dressing cover should be trimmed to a small size, allowing it to extend approximately 1 in beyond the edges of the underneath gauze sponge. The lower border of the dressing should be applied to cover approximately half of the catheter hub. This allows easy access to the hub for tubing change without disrupting the dressing seal.

The dressing cover is edged with 1-in hypoallergenic tape. A slit piece of tape is slid under the catheter hub and over the lower dressing edge to create an occlusive seal around the hub. All tubing junctions should be secured with adhesive tape to prevent accidental separation. The finished dressing is dated and initialed, and notation of the procedure is made in the patient's record.

METABOLIC MANAGEMENT

Metabolic imbalances can occur as a result of TPN therapy. The concentration of glucose, amino acids, electrolytes, vitamins, and trace elements, in addition to the amount of solution infused, can have profound effects. By considering each of the components in TPN solutions, the nurse, will be able to correlate its relationship with the patient's metabolic state.

Glucose

Because of the high glucose concentration in TPN solutions, the infusion is begun at a slow rate, usually 60 to 80 mL/h for the average adult. This allows the pancreas to adjust insulin production to utilize the glucose load. The flow rate is increased daily, depending upon the patient's glucose tolerance, fluid status, and caloric need.

Checking the urinary sugar and acetone content every 6 h is necessary to evaluate glucose tolerance. Glycosuria may occur in the first 2 to 3 days of therapy. If the urinary glucose exceeds 2+, a serum glucose level should be determined. By correlating levels of glycosuria with the serum glucose, the patient's renal threshold may eventually be determined.

In the presence of glycosuria, factors such as serum potassium levels, renal function, and concurrent drug therapy should be considered. Because potassium is needed for glucose utilization by the cell, glycosuria can occur when the patient is hypokalemic. If there is compromised renal function, fractional urine sugar determinations can be inaccurate and serum glucose levels should be measured. Certain drugs such as the cephalosporins or acetylsalicylic acid can yield a false positive result if a sugar test tablet (such as Clinitest) is used. A glucose-specific indicator (Tes-Tape, for example) should be substituted in these instances.

Treating glucose intolerance may be directed toward reducing the initial flow rate or by supplying exogenous insulin. The ability of critically ill patients to respond to large quantities of IV glucose is often compromised. Most notably, sepsis, shock, hepatic or renal dysfunction, diabetes, pancreatic disorders, certain drugs such as steroids and catecholamines, and the patient's age can alter this response. In these settings, exogenous insulin is often necessary.

Insulin can be administered by adding regular crystalline zinc insulin (CZI) directly to the TPN solution. The insulin is bound to the protein component of the solution and will not adhere to the glass bottle or tubing. This method provides a more consistent level of serum insulin than intermittent subcutaneous injections.

In addition to checks of urinary sugar and acetone levels every 6 h, important nursing measures include daily weights whenever possible, accurate intake and output, and the maintenance of the prescribed infusion rate. The flow rate should be checked every 30 min and, if necessary, reset to the prescribed rate. Do not adjust the flow rate to accommodate slowed or rapid infusion rates. Time-taping the bottle serves as a quick reference in monitoring infusion delivery.

Flow rate can be maintained using a gravity drip system or by mechanical device. Although an infusion apparatus may provide more accurate flow, appropriate education of the staff is necessary to ensure safe application. If a gravity drip system is used, a second screw-type clamp should be employed to prevent an inadvertent bolus of solution. A bolus of TPN solution could lead to the severe metabolic complication of hyperosmolar hyperglycemic non-ketotic (HHNK) coma. This condition is also associated with pancreatic exhaustion. The clinical signs include neurologic deterioration, elevated serum glucose levels (1000 mg per 100 mL), 4+ glycosuria without ketonuria, normal serum pH, high serum osmolarity, and osmotic diuresis. Hyperglycemia occurs without acidosis because the low level of insulin present is sufficient to avoid the release of free fatty acids and the development of ketosis. This syndrome may be misdiagnosed as a cerebral vascular accident (CVA) because of the neurologic changes caused by cellular dehydration of the brain. Treatment in this setting includes immediate cessation of the hypertonic TPN solution, rapid repletion of the dehydrated state with a hypotonic solution (0.45% normal saline or 2.5% dextrose in 0.45% normal saline), and frequent serum glucose determinations with subsequent administration of exogenous insulin.

When unexplained hyperglycemia develops in a previously stable patient, it may be a sign of impending sepsis. This hyperglycemia is related to an altered rate of glucose metabolism rather than an alteration in infusion rate. The sepsis often may become evident within 12 to 24 h after glucose intolerance begins.

Hypoglycemia, evidenced by serum glucose levels of 30 to 40 mg per 100 mL, is most commonly associated with abrupt decrease or termination of TPN solution. The infusion rate may be hindered by mechanical problems in the administration system (e.g., kinked tubing or catheter, clogged filter) which should be identified and corrected. In most instances, by gradually weaning the rate of TPN, rebound hypoglycemia can be avoided. During the weaning period, observe the patient for signs of hypoglycemia; these might include a change in level of consciousness, trembling, and diaphoresis. Untreated hypogly-

cemia may rapidly progress to loss of consciousness and convulsions.

Proteins

Administration of the protein component in TPN also has metabolic ramifications. The incorporation of protein into the lean body mass is dependent upon the provision of sufficient calories and is also influenced by the presence of insulin. In certain diseases the patient may have a limited tolerance to the quantity and quality of protein content of standard TPN solutions. As previously mentioned, alterations can be made to suit these conditions.

Electrolytes

Serum electrolyte determinations should be monitored twice weekly or more frequently if necessary. Alterations in the electrolyte content of the TPN solution can be made depending upon the patient's metabolic needs. To prevent incompatibilities, the pharmacy should establish allowable type and amount of electrolyte supplementation.

Trace Elements

Trace elements are usually present in the oral diet in minute amounts. When oral or enteral tube feeding intake is impossible and nutrition is supplied intravenously for extended periods, trace element deficiencies may occur. As stated previously, trace element supplementation may be incorporated into the therapeutic regimen. Zinc deficiency is associated with the development of marked dermatitis involving the nasolabial fold and oral mucosa. If untreated, symptoms may progress to include alopecia and diarrhea. Zinc may have an effect on wound healing. The administration of chromium has been shown to correct glucose intolerance. Copper deficiency has been associated with hematologic abnormalities such as anemia, leukopenia, and neutropenia. At present, little is known of the role of manganese and iodide in man.

Fatty Acids

Essential fatty acid (EFA) deficiency can be manifested by poor wound healing, sparse hair growth, and dry scaly skin. It may occur when the patient's nutritional intake has not included a source of fat for approximately 2 weeks. Intravenous fat emulsions can be administered both to prevent essential fatty acid deficiency and to provide a source of calories (1.1 cal/mL). Examples of such emulsions are Intralipid (Cutter) and Liposyn (Abbott). They are made up of a fat source (soybean or safflower oil), egg yolk phospholipids, glycerin, and water. Because the emulsions are isotonic, they can be infused into a peripheral vein and do not require central venous access.

The IV fat emulsion should be infused slowly (1 mL/min) for the first 15 to 30 min. If no adverse reactions are evident after this initial period, the infusion rate may then be adjusted to the prescribed rate. Usually, one 500-mL bottle may be administered to an adult patient over a 4- to 6-h period. Carefully observe the patient for any adverse reaction during the entire infusion. The reader is encouraged to review the literature accompanying the product. This package insert information will also provide storage instructions.

Before administration, each bottle should be carefully inspected. If the emulsion appears to have oiled out, it should not be used. To preserve the stability of the IV fat emulsion, no additives should be injected directly into the bottle and the emulsion should be administered separately from other infusing IV solutions. It is often used as part of a peripheral amino acids–glucose regimen to supply extra calories. If infused simultaneously with this peripheral regimen, piggybacking should be done via a Y-connector incorporated into the IV administration system near the venous site. This allows minimal interfacing of the infusing solutions before entering the bloodstream.

Although this is not recommended, if it ever becomes necessary to piggyback the fat emulsion into an IV site being used for the infusion of fluid or medications, compatibility of the solutions and the emulsion must be established. An emulsion should never be filtered because the fat particles may become entrapped in the filter.

SEPSIS CONTROL

Sepsis is the most dreaded and potentially serious complication associated with TPN therapy. This is not surprising when one considers that the majority of patients who are candidates for TPN therapy are already compromised hosts. By the very nature of their illness and because they have frequently been treated with drugs (antibiotics, steroids, and immunosuppressants) which may alter the host-defense mechanism, they are susceptible to TPN-related in-

fection. Prevention of infection involves adherence to a highly organized protocol designed to protect the patient from the multiple sources of contamination posed by TPN therapy. For this reason, a unified team approach is essential.

To ensure asepsis, preparation of TPN solutions is most effectively done in the pharmacy in a laminar airflow (LAF) unit. The use of commercially available closed transfer systems further minimizes the risk of contamination. To maintain sterility, solutions should be prepared daily and refrigerated until use. The container should be appropriately marked with the patient's name, hospital identification number, the solution contents, and the solution expiration date and time. Bacteriological sampling and chemical assaying should be done to ensure quality control in the solution preparation and stability.

Before administration, each bottle is carefully checked under a strong light to determine that the container is intact and that the solution is clear and free of precipitates. If a patient develops a sudden fever coincidental with beginning the infusion of a new bottle, the solution and the administration system should be suspect as a potential source of this fever and appropriately cultured and replaced.

An in-line filter may be incorporated into the IV administration system. Although the use of a filter is optional and its cost-effectiveness and efficacy controversial, filtration may prove advantageous in reducing the incidence of phlebitis. Currently available 0.2-μm filters trap particulates, bacteria, and fungi, and some also feature an air-eliminating ability. If filtration is incorporated into the IV administration system to be monitored by infusion apparatus, check the recommendations of the filter manufacturer to ensure that the filter is able to withstand the amount of pressure generated by the pump. Follow the package insert for priming instructions.

Asepsis and air embolism precautions are essential when changing the TPN administration system. The patient should be placed in a supine position, or in some cases in Trendelenburg's position. The cooperative, alert patient should be asked to perform the Valsalva maneuver before the outdated IV tubing is quickly removed from the catheter hub and the new sterile system attached. To avoid inadvertent contamination and to attain better leverage, a clean clamp should be used to gently grasp the catheter hub and elevate it off the skin.

The intubated patient or patient with a tracheostomy should be maintained in prolonged inspiration by an ambu bag while tubing change is done. An extra pair of hands is obviously needed to do this safely. A Leur-locking extension tube, while creating an additional tubing junction and another potential portal for contamination, may be of use when changing the administration system of a comatose, confused or intubated patient. Allowed to remain outside the dressing seal, this extension tubing may be clamped to prevent accidental air embolism when tubing change is performed. If employed, strict protocols should be designed to govern the care and frequency of changing the extension tubing. Obviously, if this extension is accidentally contaminated, it must be changed.

Some institutions have opted to prep all junctions with a povidone-iodine solution before and after tubing change. All junctions should be secured with tape to avoid accidental separation and contamination. The tubing should be coiled and secured to the dressing cover with tape to prevent tension on the catheter.

Intravenous tubing (and filter, if used) should be changed every 24 h. To avoid an additional break in the closed administration system, this should be done at a standardized time when beginning the new day's solution. Some institutions are investigating the practice of changing IV tubing every 48 h. Although this may be cost-effective, the efficacy of this practice must be established by the individual institution.

The TPN administration system and central venous catheter should be inviolate. The catheter is specifically placed and used only for the infusion of nutritional solutions. It should not be used for blood sampling, monitoring central venous pressure, or for the piggyback or bolus administration of medications. To keep the number of tubing junctions to a minimum, extraneous pieces of IV equipment (stopcocks, T-connectors) should not be incorporated into the administration system.

A leading cause of catheter-related infection is the growth of organisms along the percutaneous catheter tract. For this reason, a standardized dressing change procedure (as described previously) should be performed only by specially trained nurses. Strict aseptic technique is essential to significantly reduce the incidence of infection.

A prepackaged kit containing all necessary supplies may help to standardize and organize dressing care. Commercially prepared kits are available, if it is not feasible for the individual institution to prepare them.

During infusion of TPN, the patient's temperature should be checked at least every 6 h. The nurse should be alert to the possible signs of sepsis: fever, shaking chills, and decline in general condition or conscious state. If a patient receiving TPN develops a fever of unknown etiology, an immediate fever workup should be done. This involves a physical examination; complete blood count; cultures of blood, urine, sputum, and wounds; and chest roentgenogram.

If, as a result of this fever workup, the febrile episode seems to be caused by a source other than the nutritional system, appropriate treatment of the septic focus will most probably be instituted. TPN may then be cautiously continued through the same catheter. An indwelling catheter can be colonized during a transient bacteremic episode originating from another remote focus (surgical wounds, pneumonia, urinary tract infection). This colonized catheter can then be the re-seeding focus of bacteremia.

However, if the fever persists and no other obvious source becomes evident, the TPN catheter must be removed and cultured. To culture the catheter tip, aseptic technique is employed. The catheter site should first be prepped with 70% isopropyl alcohol to remove the antimicrobial ointment from the skin. The catheter is withdrawn and the tip is cut off into a dry sterile tube with sterile scissors. The tip of the catheter should be smeared immediately on appropriate culture media.

When the TPN catheter is removed for suspected sepsis, hypoglycemia could occur as a result of abruptly stopping the concentrated glucose infusion. A 10% dextrose solution should be infused peripherally to compensate for this abrupt cessation.

As with any indwelling vascular catheter, venous thrombosis is a potential threat. The patient should be carefully observed for arm and facial swelling on the side of the catheter. If thrombosis is suspected, the catheter should be removed and cultured and anticoagulation therapy instituted.

Candida Septicemia

One type of TPN-related septicemia is the result of the fungus *Candida*, particularly *C. albicans*. Because *Candida* can be found in the normal flora of the skin, respiratory tract, gastrointestinal tract, and vagina, it colonizes tubes, drains, and intravenous catheters. With these portals of entry, actual infection may result because of the patient's altered immune response. In addition, the TPN solution is capable of supporting fungal growth.

However, a fungal septicemia can be difficult both to diagnose and eradicate. It is important to remember that clinically the patient may be asymptomatic, unlike bacterial sepsis. Venous blood cultures may often be negative because of filtering by various organs, especially the kidney. Therefore, arterial blood cultures may be beneficial. A catheter tip positive for *Candida* may be the first indication of sepsis and should be investigated.

Unfortunately, symptoms of deep tissue invasion (candidiasis) may be the first sign of *Candida* sepsis. The retina, heart, and kidneys are most commonly involved. The patient may complain of eye pain, loss of vision, or other visual defects. Fundoscopic examination of the retina will reveal the classic whitish abnormalities. In the presence of candidemia, fundoscopic exam should be done to determine if candidiasis has occurred. Treatment with intravenous antifungal agents may reverse impaired vision.

In treating candidemia, TPN therapy must be stopped and the catheter removed. TPN therapy can not be resumed until the candidemia is resolved. Appropriate cultures and fundoscopic eye exams should be done to follow resolution of the infection.

PSYCHOLOGICAL ASPECTS

Many aspects of TPN therapy can be frightening to the uninformed patient. A full explanation, geared to the patient's clinical condition and medical knowledge, will help to allay various misconceptions about the therapy.

The patient's family should also be informed. It may be comforting to know that among the myriad IV bottles often seen hanging above the bed of critically ill patients, one or more is providing the nourishment so essential to "getting better."

REFERENCES

Abel, R. M. et al.: Amino acid metabolism in acute renal failure: Influence of L-amino acid hyperalimentation therapy, *Ann Surg* 180(3):350–355, 1974.

Alvaran, S. B. et al.: Venous air embolism: Comparative merits of external cardiac massage, intracardiac aspiration, and left lateral decubitus position, *Anesth Anal* 57:166–170, 1978.

AMA Department of Foods and Nutrition: Guidelines for essential trace element preparations for parenteral use: A statement by an expert panel *JAMA* 241(19):2051–2053, 1979.

AMA Department of Foods and Nutrition, 1975: Multivitamin preparations for parenteral use: A statement by the nutrition advisory group, *Parenteral Enteral Nutr* 3(4):258–262, 1979.

Colley, R.: Total parenteral nutrition—Nursing practice, in A. L. Plumer (ed.), *Principles and Practice of Intravenous Therapy,* Boston: Little, Brown, 1975, pp. 185–213.

Colley, R., and J. M. Wilson: Hyperalimentation—A plus for nitrogen balance, in *Monitoring Fluid and Electrolytes Precisely,* Pennsylvania: Intermed Communications, Inc., 1978, pp. 183–188.

Colley, R., and J. M. Wilson: Meeting patients' nutritional needs with hyperalimentation, *Nursing 79,* May–September, 1979.

Dudrick, S. J., and J. E. Rhoads: Total intravenous feeding, *Scientific American* 226(5):73–80, 1972.

Fischer, J. E. (ed.): *Total Parenteral Nutrition,* Boston: Little, Brown, 1976.

Fischer, J. E.: Parenteral and enteral nutrition, in *Disease-A-Month,* Chicago: Yearbook, 1978.

Freund, H. R., S. Atamian, and J. E. Fischer: Chromium deficiency during TPN, *JAMA* 241(5): 496–497, 1979.

Hoshal, V. et al.: Fibrin sleeve formation on indwelling subclavian central venous catheters, *Arch Surg* 102:353–358, 1971.

Jordan, H. A. et al.: Hunger and satiety in humans during parenteral hyperalimentation, *Psychosom Med* 36:144–154, 1974.

Kay, R. G. et al.: A syndrome of acute zinc deficiency during total parenteral alimentation in man, *Ann Surg* 183:331–340, 1976.

Maki, D.G.: Preventing infusion-related infection, *Drug Ther (Hosp)* pp. 37–46, January 1977.

Maki, D.G. et al.: A semiquantitative culture method for identifying intravenous catheter-related infection, *N Engl J Med* 296:1305–1309, 1977.

Massachusetts General Hospital Nursing Procedure Manual, Boston: Little, Brown, 1974.

Paskin, D. L. et al.: A new complication of subclavian vein catheterization, *Ann Surg* 179:266–268, 1974.

Ryan, J.A.: Complications of total parenteral nutrition: Etiology, prevention and treatment, in J. E. Fischer (ed.), *Total Parenteral Nutrition,* Boston: Little, Brown, 1976, pp. 55–100.

Ryan, J. A. et al.: Catheter complications in total parenteral nutrition. A prospective study of 200 consecutive patients, *N Engl J Med* 290:757, 1974.

Sanders, R., and G. Sheldon: Septic complications of T.P.N.—A five year experience, *Am J Surg* 132:214–220, 1976.

Vilter, R.W. et al.: Manifestations of copper deficiency in a patient with systemic sclerosis of intravenous hyperalimentation, *N Engl J Med* 291:188–191, 1974.

Although in the last 125 years, our equipment has become much more expensive and elaborate, the two most important research tools are still the cerebral hemispheres of the investigator (Gollan, 1959).

OVERVIEW

Within critical-care settings, persons may present from a multiplicity of life experiences involving hypothermia. *Accidental hypothermia* often includes victims of drowning, those exposed to cold temperature insult, and recipients of rapid infusions of refrigerated bank blood or intravenous solutions. *Drug-induced hypothermia* may be caused by chlorpromazine, barbiturates, alcohol, or carbon monoxide. *Hypothermia secondary to alterations in health status* may be considered with such disease states as hypoglycemia, adrenal insufficiency, hypopituitarism, and myxedema. *Elective hypothermia,* or cooling therapy, is used frequently in cardiovascular surgery and neurosurgery and is often prescribed for febrile multiple trauma, acute cerebral ischemia, burn insults, thyroid crisis, and graft preservation.

NURSING CONCEPTS

The critical-care nurse's ability to meaningfully monitor all phases of the deliberative nursing process for persons in hypothermia or undergoing hypothermia therapy lies in an appreciation of the subject beyond an isolated protocol. To facilitate the dimensions of this responsibility, a concept approach is offered.

Main Concept

Hypothermia refers to a body temperature below the normal physiologic level of 37°C (98.6°F) and the response of major support systems.

Supporting Concepts

Prescribed hypothermia therapy for selected persons in multimedical crisis offers potential for improving their health status and future quality of life.

Hypothermia slows metabolic processes that can lead to organ distress or an irreversible state.

Varying physiologic effects occur at specific hypothermia levels.

Critical to hypothermia therapy is respect for physiologic parameters that reflect the status of cooling dynamics and the integration of appropriate nursing interventions.

41

HYPOTHERMIA
Sister Maurita Soukup

OVERVIEW
NURSING CONCEPTS
Main Concept
Supporting Concepts
COOLING DYNAMICS AND SELECTED PHYSIOLOGIC EFFECTS
Classification
Thermal Zones
Selected Physiologic Effects
CLINICAL METHODS FOR PRODUCING HYPOTHERMIA
CLINICAL APPLICATION OF SURFACE COOLING FOR ACHIEVING MODERATE HYPOTHERMIA
Induction Phase
Maintenance Phase
Rewarming Phase
SELECTED PATIENT NEEDS AND NURSING INTERVENTIONS DURING MODERATE HYPOTHERMIA
Selected Assessment Secondary to Hypothermia Therapy
Comfort Level
Patient and Family Education
Safety Monitoring

991

Hypothermia monitoring, as with all monitoring, requires observation of *alterations,* rather than absolute levels, and an assessment of the effects of these alterations on the person.

COOLING DYNAMICS AND SELECTED PHYSIOLOGIC EFFECTS

In human beings homeothermic capability is achieved through two feedback mechanisms—physical and hormonal regulation. Inactivating these temperature mechanisms alters a multiplicity of interacting systems and subsystems. Since distinct physiologic effects occur at various temperatures, understanding the significance of certain data can be critical to maintaining optimum cooling without major consequences.

Classification

Hypothermia is classified according to the temperature maintained:

1. Mild hypothermia (32 to 37°C)
2. Moderate hypothermia (28 to 32°C)
3. Deep hypothermia (20 to 28°C)
4. Profound hypothermia (0 to 20°C)

Thermal Zones

Body cooling occurs at one of three levels. Presently recognized thermal zones are as follows:

1. Superficial zone (includes the skin and subcutaneous tissues)
2. Intermediate zone (includes skeletal muscles)
3. Core zone (includes internal organs)

Selected Physiologic Effects

Metabolic System

For each 1°C lowering of body temperature to 28°C, there is a 6.5 percent reduction in metabolic demands. At 30°C, total-body oxygen demand is reduced by 50 percent, and oxygen demand in the brain is reduced by 54 percent. During moderate hypothermia, there is maximal reduction in metabolic demands with minimal risk for complications. The critical physiologic level is 28°C; however, recognition must be given to a critical physiologic range for some individuals.

At 28 to 32°C, metabolic alterations include impairment of the hypothalamus to regulate temperature; increase in lactic acid, potassium, and calcium; reduction in hormonal response; suppression of thyroid activity; and 10 percent reduction of normal adrenocortical activity. Changes in hepatic function occur: detoxification mechanisms are less active, bile becomes more dilute, and secretions slow. Below 28°C or during anesthesia, thermoregulatory centers are totally inactivated.

Neurologic System

Hypothermia depresses higher centers of the brain first to offer greater metabolic protection. During total-body hypothermia, there is a difference in the initial rate of brain and body core cooling, since the brain is normally 1°C colder at normothermia. During moderate hypothermia, however, the brain remains 1 to 2°C warmer than the core zone. During all phases of hypothermia, the systolic blood pressure is recognized as the most important factor in controlling cerebral blood flow.

At 30°C, there is a reduction in brain metabolism by 54 percent (provided that shivering is controlled), cerebral blood flow by 30 percent, cerebrospinal fluid pressure by 38 percent, and brain volume by 20 percent. Also, electrical activity of the brain, inflammatory processes, and brain cell size and permeability are reduced.

Cardiovascular System

The immediate response to hypothermia is peripheral vasoconstriction, thereby reducing blood supply and heat transport to the skin and subcutaneous tissues. In *altered hemodynamics due to a reduced cardiac output,* hypothermia therapy can greatly enhance peripheral vasoconstriction and result in tissue hypoxia, anaerobic metabolism, and metabolic acidosis.

At certain hypothermic levels, cardiac function and electrodynamics are altered. The greatest reduction in heart rate usually occurs with the initial reduction in temperature. At 28 to 32°C, the heart rate may be reduced by 50 percent. Also, diastole is prolonged; contractility is increased. Dysrhythmias include bradycardia, atrial fibrillation, atrioventricular blocks, premature ventricular contractions, and ventricular tachycardia. Below 28°C, there is critical prolongation of ventricular systole, lengthening of all ECG intervals, T-wave inversion, and high risk for ventricular fibrillation.

Additional ECG manifestations associated with hypothermia include muscle tremor artifact, the J wave, and delayed intrinsicoid deflection. *Muscle tremor artifact* often precedes visible shivering. The *J wave,* a humplike wave occurring at the junction of the QRS complex and ST segment and prominent in the left chest leads, is one of the most characteristic ECG signs in hypothermia. Its amplitude is proportional to the degree of hypothermia. The *delayed intrinsicoid deflection* is also a sign of the degree of hypothermia. A delay of over 24 percent is considered to be significant warning of impending ventricular fibrillation.

Generally, cardiovascular alterations during hypothermia therapy are evidenced by decrease in heart rate, increase in blood pressure, and diminished circulation to the hypothermic area. Under controlled hypothermia, circulation to specific organs can be interrupted without risk of permanent damage.

Pulmonary System

Hypothermia therapy initially produces an increase in respiratory rate; then the rate decreases in response to lowered metabolism. At 28 to 32°C, carbon dioxide production is diminished and the oxygen-hemoglobin dissociation curve is shifted to the left. Below 28°C, respirations cease.

Renal System

Generally, renal function is not significantly altered until profound hypothermia is reached. At 28 to 32°C, the rate of glomerular filtration is only moderately reduced. At 32 to 35°C, there is stabilization of the specific gravity.

Gastrointestinal System

At 28 to 32°C, pepsin production continues while digestive activity is reduced. In addition to hypothermia effects, pharmacologic therapy, nasogastric suction, or stress of illness may contribute to such complications as gastric erosions, ileus, or altered elimination patterns.

Musculoskeletal System

Initially, vasodilation of muscle and visceral tissues occurs as a protective activity to threatened core zone cooling. During hypothermia, muscle tone diminishes. Below 28°C, muscle reflexes are absent.

Coarse muscular action of the body, or *shivering,* can be seen before actual changes in body temperature take place. The sequence of muscular action begins with facial muscles, progressing to pectoral muscles, and finally to muscles of the extremities. Shivering must be respected as a critical complication during all phases of hypothermia therapy; metabolic demands can increase 100 to 300 times (equivalent to demands during heavy exercise).

Hematologic System

During hypothermia carbon dioxide concentration is lowered, and the oxygen-hemoglobin dissociation curve is shifted to the left, making it more difficult for red blood cells to release oxygen to the tissues. At 28 to 32°C, hemolysis is decreased. Below 28°C, metabolic acidosis can occur. To avoid intravascular aggregation, cooling rates should be less than 1°C/min.

Psychosocial System

In spite of greater manipulation of life processes and multifarious stressors, psychiatric complications in hypothermia with anesthesia are reportedly lower at 28 to 37°C. Below 28°C, however, psychiatric complications increase.

Figure 41-1 illustrates selected physiologic effects of the various subsystems at specific hypothermia levels.

CLINICAL METHODS FOR PRODUCING HYPOTHERMIA

Elective hypothermia may include one or more of the following clinical methods:

Localized cooling is restricted to a specific body area or organ (e.g., gastroesophageal hypothermia, cardioplegic hypothermic arrest, and cerebral hypothermia).

Extracorporeal cooling is achieved through a direct approach of intravascular cooling during cardiopulmonary bypass or through an indirect approach by cooling inspired air via alveoli.

Surface cooling is accomplished through noninvasive techniques of cold water immersion, air cooling, and use of ice packs and/or hypothermia blankets.

CLINICAL APPLICATION OF SURFACE COOLING FOR ACHIEVING MODERATE HYPOTHERMIA

Surface cooling for achieving moderate hypothermia is a proficiency required of the critical-care nurse. Scientific advances in the electrically controlled hypothermia blanket have enhanced quality and con-

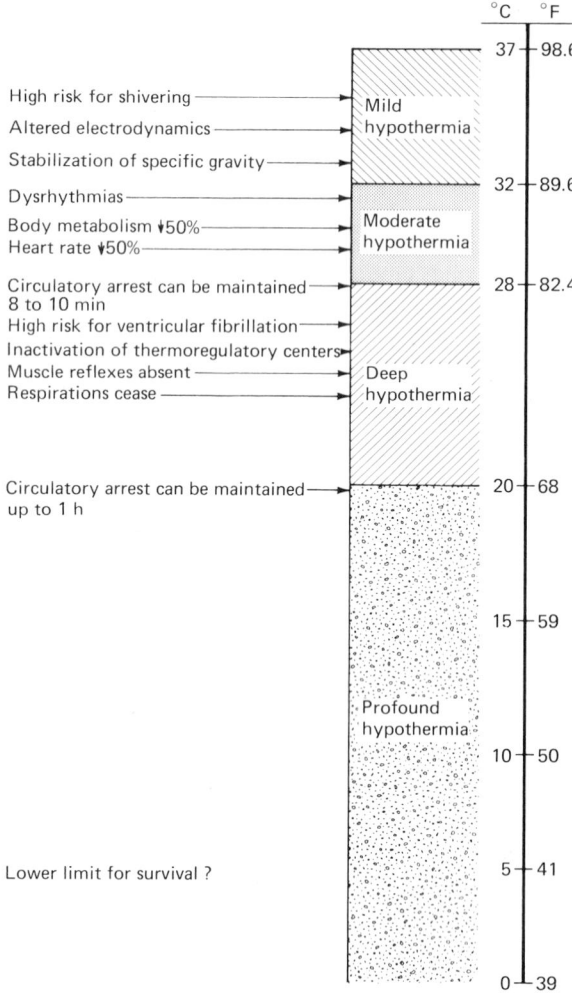

FIGURE 41-1

Hypothermia levels with selected physiological effects.

venience in accomplishing this prescribed therapy. The rapidity with which dramatic clinical alterations can occur for persons in critical illness reaffirms the importance of readiness by the person entrusted with direct patient care.

Throughout all phases of surface cooling, completeness of hypothermia monitoring includes interpretation of the following data: health history, vital signs, ECG, fluid intake and output, laboratory profile, pharmacologic profile, multisystem assessment, and hemodynamic parameters. These data become significantly useful only when meaningful interpretation has been related to the holistic health status of the person.

Surface cooling hypothermia focuses on three phases. Activities to be considered within clinical protocols are offered.

Induction Phase

To facilitate prompt induction, room temperature is reduced to 36°C, lighting is dimmed, and hypothermia blankets are precooled to between 5 and 10°C. A sheet blanket between hypothermia pads enhances induction without insulating against cooling. Ice packs or additional hypothermia pads, placed where major arteries lie close to the skin surface, can supplement cooling blankets. Temperature reduction is monitored closely with a rectal probe or esophageal lead. Hands and feet are protected with mitts. Below 32°C, 2 to 5 percent carbon dioxide is added to ventilations to enhance oxyhemoglobin dissociation by the Bohr effect and cerebral perfusion by vasodilation.

Early in the induction phase, there is a *high risk for shivering*, which demands close assessment and immediate treatment by IV medications or anesthesia. Initial manifestations are ECG muscle tremor artifact, visible facial muscle twitches, hyperventilation, and verbalized comfort level alterations.

Late in the induction phase, there is a *high risk for drifting*, or *afterfall*, which is continued body temperature reduction after the hypothermia blanket is turned off. Factors influencing this phenomenon include body size, muscle tone, age, vascular response, room temperature, and pharmacologic interventions. To prevent or reduce this complication, supplementary cooling supports and the top hypothermia blanket are removed and the lower hypothermia blanket control is reset prior to reaching 2 to 5°C of the prescribed temperature.

Hypothermia induction should be prompt but always controlled. A maximal limit of 1°C lowering per 15 min should be respected. In 40 to 50 min, a 33 to 34°C hypothermia level can be achieved. It is important to reemphasize that the greater the area of body surface in contact with cooling, the faster the desired temperature is reached. The lower the temperature, the higher the risk for entry into the critical range. Finally, the more rapid the induction, the greater the afterfall.

Maintenance Phase

This phase focuses on maintaining the prescribed hypothermia level while minimizing any adverse effects. Activities are individualized, requiring frequent evaluation and refinement. Generally, for every 1°C temperature reduction, the vital signs are taken every 30 min, then every 2 h. The rectal thermistor probe is removed every 4 h, cleansed, and reinserted to ensure accurate readings; automatic controls are checked every 4 h. Eye care to protect corneal reflexes, thigh support stockings to prevent venous stasis, coughing and deep breathing, repositioning every 30 min, massaging pressure points, inspection of total body surface, and skin lubrication every 2 h are examples of necessary preventive health measures. A critical activity, also, during this phase is pharmacologic profile assessment because of possible cumulative drug effects and an additional temperature reduction of 1 to 3°C from tranquilizers or opiates.

Rewarming Phase

Rewarming is done slowly to avoid increasing metabolic demands on a heart in hypothermia. Generally, it should take 6 h for rewarming from 30 to 37°C. Vital signs are monitored closely, usually at 15-min intervals. Active rewarming is not encouraged because of the risk of cutaneous vasodilation and further lowering of peripheral vascular resistance. During this phase, the nurse should be alert for temperature overshoot, edema secondary to increased cell permeability, acidotic shock secondary to shivering, cumulative drug effects, altered ventilation, and fluid imbalance.

SELECTED PATIENT NEEDS AND NURSING INTERVENTIONS DURING MODERATE HYPOTHERMIA

A person in hypothermia or undergoing hypothermia therapy presents with individual needs; these needs can change in importance and even in perspective within a given situation. It is anticipated that the following information will intensify responsibilities for planned individualized care rather than limit patient needs to those selected.

Selected Assessment Secondary to Hypothermia

A person with myocardial trauma or hypokalemia or who is reaching the lower limits of mild hypothermia is at *high risk for altered electrodynamics*. Nursing interventions focus on ECG surveillance, pharmacologic intervention, and readiness for emergency in-

tervention. A person with left ventricular dysfunction, altered electrodynamics, or obesity is at *high risk for altered hemodynamics*. Appropriate nursing actions include meaningful interpretation of hemodynamic data, fluid control, and readiness for pharmacologic interventions. *High risk for altered metabolic response due to shivering* can rapidly lead to hypokalemia, hypoglycemia, or altered neurologic status. Nursing interventions focus on continuous assessment for early manifestations of shivering, immediate administration of prescribed IV medications, and monitoring of laboratory data and neurologic status.

Persons with alterations in temperature control mechanisms, allergies, or autoantigen or vasomotor disturbances are at *potential risk for hypersensitivity to cold*. A history of subnormal body temperature; systemic reactions on the face, ears, hands, and feet; and an abnormal increase in pulse with a decrease in blood pressure are early cues and necessitate the discontinuance of hypothermia therapy.

The elderly, thin, or quadriplegic person is at *high risk for altered skin integrity*. Skin insults may occur from decreased blood flow, pressure points, or actual crystallization of tissue fluids in the subcutaneous tissues. Nursing interventions include assessment for skin discoloration or hardness; reported tingling, numbness, or burning sensations; and protective measures such as total-body repositioning every 30 min, skin lubrication, and massage.

Comfort Level

Verbalized discomfort or verbalized anticipation of cold discomfort during hypothermia, manifestations of shivering, and hyperventilation exemplify alterations in comfort level. Immediate pharmacologic intervention is needed; usually IV chlorpromazine (Thorazine) or promethazine (Phenergan) is prescribed. Additional nursing responsibilities include controlling for negative stressors such as noise stimuli, light intensity, or interruptions during planned 2-h rest-sleep cycles.

Patient and Family Education

Lack of knowledge about hypothermia therapy and anxiety due to anticipated body cooling deserve consideration in the initial teaching situation. Often early, selective teaching with the family regarding their responsibilities in stress control (to minimize metabolic demands on the patient) greatly enhances therapeutic care during hypothermia maintenance.

Safety Monitoring

Hypothermia blankets and instrumentation during actual use should meet all aspects of electrical safety requirements. A person with a temporary pacemaker or an isolated epicardial lead is at *high risk for microshock.* Thermal monitoring includes routine temperature monitoring even if the rectal probe or temperature safety alarms are used. Machine vibrations may cause deviations from prescribed settings; however, more frequently inaccuracy of the electrical temperature display is due to a broken probe or a probe embedded in feces. Infection control necessitates explicit equipment cleaning and protocols. All potential sources for contamination such as grillwork, applicator probes, fluid reservoir, and applicators should be included in routine environmental control cultures. Storage and maintenance safety requires routine maintenance checks and recalibration of hypothermal machines. Build-up of lint or dust on the grillwork or airflow vent, tube kinking, improper connections, or insufficient fluid in the reservoir may prevent cooling.

SUMMARY

A person in hypothermia or undergoing prescribed hypothermia therapy requires deliberative, holistic monitoring. Respect for physiologic parameters that reflect the status of cooling dynamics, clinical proficiency during all phases of surface cooling, and responsibility for assessed patient needs enhance meaningful participation and contributions in multidisciplinary health management.

REFERENCES

Abby, J., et al.: A pilot study: The control of shivering during hypothermia by a clinical nursing measure, *J Neurosurg Nurs* 5:78–88, Dec. 1973.

Emslie-Smith, D., et al.: The significance of changes in the electrocardiogram in hypothermia, *Br Heart J* 21:343, 1959.

Gollan, F.: *Physiology of Cardiac Surgery,* Springfield, Ill.: Charles C Thomas, 1959, p. vi.

Hicks, C. E., et al.: Electrocardiographic changes during hypothermia and circulatory occlusion, *Circulation* 13:21, 1956.

Meltzer, L. E., et al. (eds.): *Concepts and Practices of Intensive Care for Nurse Specialists,* Maryland: The Charles Press, 1976, pp. 282, 473, 502–503, 508–510, 537.

Nealon, T. F., and Gosin, S.: Hypothermia physiologic effects and clinical application, *Med Clin N Am* 49:1181–1194, 1965.

Schamroth, L., and Perlman, M. M.: The electrocardiographic manifestations of hypothermia, *Heart and Lung* 1:233–235, March–April 1972.

Skillman, J. J.: *Intensive Care,* Boston: Little Brown, 1975, pp. 162, 545–558.

Stevens, V. C.: Clinical hypothermia: Some nursing concepts, *J Neurosurg Nurs* 4:33–44, July 1972.

PART 8

THE CRITICAL-CARE ENVIRONMENT

The modern critical-care environment is, in many ways, symbolic of the effect technology has had on our society. The development of modern mechanical, electromechanical, and electronic medical instrumentation has altered and shaped the way medical care is administered to the critically ill. Cardiac surgery as we know it today has been made possible by these developments. Specially designed instruments make possible the continuous monitoring of variables like arterial blood pressure, electrocardiograms (ECG), pulse rate, and so on. The alarm functions contained in these instruments alert the staff to any deviation from a prescribed range. This and other features free the critical-care staff to perform true patient care.

Critical care might be defined as the management of patients with life-threatening physiological alterations. Access to and understanding of multiple physiologic variables are intrinsic to this function. Since instrumentation must be used to acquire data with the frequency and accuracy needed, a basic understanding of the instrumentation is as important to the critical-care nurse as an understanding of the measured physiology.

PARAMETER ACQUISITION INSTRUMENTATION[1]

ECG

The electrocardiogram is probably the most commonly monitored physiologic signal in the critical-care environment. From this signal, information can be derived about cardiac rhythm, atrial-ventricular conduction, ischemia, infarction, and so on. The clinical significance derived from the interpretation of the electrocardiogram will not be discussed in this section but rather a description of the techniques and technology attendant on its acquisition.

As can be seen in Fig. 42-1, a basic ECG monitor consists of four elements:

1. Electrodes

2. Cable

3. Amplifier

4. Display oscilloscope

Electrodes   In critical-care units where reliable monitoring of the electrocardiogram for extended periods

---

[1] The authors acknowledge the assistance of Peter M. Guzy, M.D., Ph.D., in reviewing the manuscript of this section.

42

THE CRITICAL-CARE ENVIRONMENT: INSTRUMENTATION

Richard A. de Asla

Rae Nadine Smith

PARAMETER ACQUISITION INSTRUMENTATION
ECG
Pulse
Temperature
Indirect Pressure Measurement
Direct Pressure Measurement
Cardiac Output
Respiratory Volume
Capnograph
Oximeter
Mass Spectrometer
Respiratory Waveforms
Cerebral Function Monitor

THERAPEUTIC INSTRUMENTATION
Defibrillators
External Pacemakers
Infusion Pumps

RECORDING AND DISPLAY
Oscilloscopes
Numeric Displays
Paper Recorders

GLOSSARY

REFERENCES

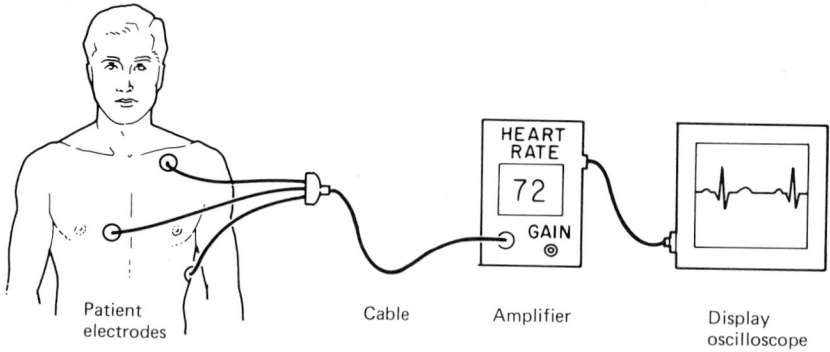

FIGURE 42-1

The elements of a basic ECG monitor.

of time is required, it is particularly important that special attention be given to both the type of electrode used and the site and nature of attachment. Poor quality and/or attachment of electrodes is the single most common cause of a poor-quality signal. Although it is true that properly trained and experienced personnel are usually able to discriminate artifact and thus not be misled by it, the same is not so of the tachycardiographs (heart rate monitors) which are often part of the monitoring system. Artifact-riddled signals will often give false tachycardia alarms, and if a patient-monitoring system is given to frequent alarms, its utility will be discredited.

The electrodes commonly used in the critical-care environment are the pregelled adhesive type. The best-quality recordings are obtained when the electrode skin contact impedance is low and as stable as possible. Contact impedance for the individual electrodes should be as equal as possible; also, any potential difference provided across the electrode-skin interface should also be as small as possible and should differ little from one electrode to the other. To ensure this, the skin should be prepped by mild abrasion. Silver–silver chloride electrodes are considered best for long-term monitoring applications. A chest lead system that approximates leads V_2 and V_6 was suggested by Marriott (Fig. 42-2).

Cable   A discontinuity in the cable which interfaces the patient's electrodes to the amplifier is probably the second most common cause of failure in an ECG monitoring system. At times a cable break may behave in an intermittent fashion, thus making troubleshooting an exasperating experience. Troubleshooting by switching cable sets is the easiest and quickest way to find this problem.

In addition to providing an interface, cables often contain resistance elements for the purpose of limiting current flow when a patient is defibrillated. Since this and other features may be included in the cable by the monitor manufacturer, using cables other than those supplied is not recommended unless the user is informed as to the special features that may or may not be required.

Amplifiers   The type of amplifier used not only in electrocardiography but in the measurement of most bioelectric signals is called a *differential amplifier*. An in-depth description of this device is beyond the intended scope of this chapter. However, an understanding of its principle of operation can be very helpful to clinical personnel in quickly making the diagnosis between an external (i.e., electrode or cable) or an internal (i.e., electronic) malfunction.

A differential amplifier as used in electrocardiography is an electronic device that amplifies the instantaneous difference between the electric signals present and its two inputs. This is one of the features that makes this device suitable for the amplification of electrocardiograms. Since the frontal plane representation of the electrical axis of the heart is a two-dimensional vector, the difference between two of the three basic limb leads yields a time variant signal with the dimensional component of that vector. When augmented or chest leads are monitored, a resistive network is used to sum the signals from two or more limb leads as one input; the second input is then the lead of interest. For example, *AVR* is the differential input between the sum of the left arm and left leg and the right arm. A second useful feature of the differential amplifier is the ability to cancel out signals simultaneously common to both inputs. This feature is commonly referred to as the amplifier's common-mode rejection; i.e., an amplifier with good (the higher the number the better) common-mode rejection will be less affected by 60-cycle interference.

The last feature of an ECG amplifier to be discussed is the gain or degree of amplification of which it is capable. Instruments used for the recording of diagnostic electrocardiograms have fixed gains since the amplitude of the recorded signal has diagnostic significance. In contrast, ECG amplifiers used for monitoring have either an automatic gain control (AGC) or a variable gain control. The requirement for this seemingly nonstandard feature is mandated by the fact that these monitors often are equipped with some kind of rate indicator. Functionally these devices detect the QRS, and then the lengths of the RR intervals are used to calculate the heart rate. Because of the variety of monitoring leads used in addition to the variable effects of pathology, it is necessary for a *tachycardiograph* to have some threshold for QRS detection. The satisfaction of these threshold requirements can be met either automatically with an automatic gain control or manually by operator adjustment. It should be born in mind that the gain needed for QRS detection is independent of, and usually not the same as, the gain required for a diagnostic electrocardiogram.

Display oscilloscopes Oscilloscopes are discussed in this chapter under "Recording and Display."

ECG telemetry The monitoring of ambulatory patients' electrocardiograms can be accomplished with the use of an appropriately designed radio transmitting and receiving system. All the factors discussed in the previous paragraphs relative to the acquisition and display of an electrocardiogram apply to a telemetry system. However, the fact that the ECG signal from the patient's amplifier to the display is now accomplished via a radio link introduces yet another dimension that may deleteriously affect the electrocardiographic signal. Most modern commercially available telemetry systems are designed so that they are unlikely to be affected by, or interfere with, other types of radio frequency. However, they are affected by environmental factors that attenuate the received signal. These factors are:

1. The distance between the transmitter and the receiver
2. The structure within which they must operate

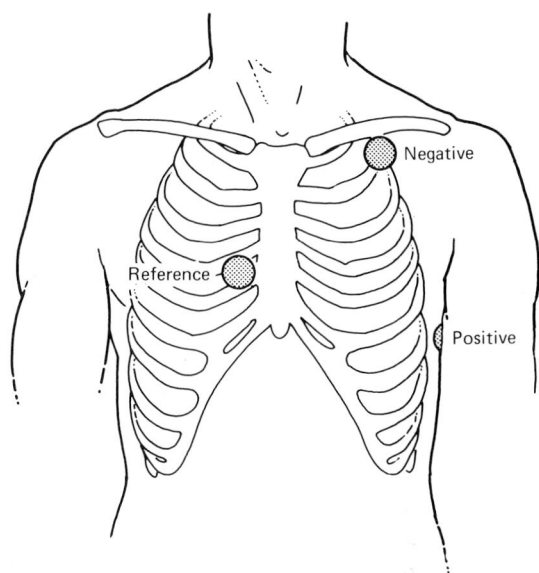

FIGURE 42-2

Chest lead placement (*After Marriott and Fogg, 1970.*)

These factors singularly or in combination can create "dead spots" from which the transmitted signal is too weak to be received properly. The staff of a telemetry-equipped unit should be made aware of any dead spots that may be present in an ambulatory patient's environment.

Pulse

In situations where it is not possible to obtain a clear ECG or when the QRS amplitude is insufficient to trigger a cardiotachometer, monitoring the pulse will provide an indication of heart rate. The device used to obtain the pulse signal from the patient is called a photo-plethysmograph. This instrument contains a light source and photo sensor. When the light source is directed into the skin, the blood flowing through the capillary bed, driven by the pulse pressure, will transiently make the skin more opaque, thus modulating the light received by the photo sensor. This signal, when received by an appropriately designed amplifier, can be used to calculate the heart rate. The major limitation of this method is that it will not function in the presence of vasoconstriction. The usual sites of attachment for photo-plethysmographs are the fingers or ears.

When the intra-arterial pressure waveform is available, some commercially available monitors are able to use this signal to derive and display the heart rate.

Temperature

Continuous temperature monitoring should be, and usually is, the simplest and most trouble-free of measurements. One simply places the thermistor probe in the desired location (skin, esophagus, tympanic membrane, and rectum are the most common sites), plugs the other end into the electronic thermometer, and that's it! Actually, nothing is that simple. There are some pitfalls.

1. The cleaning solutions used on temperature probes may tend to corrode the surface of the plug which goes to the electronic thermometer. The corroded surface (not always obvious) causes an increased resistance at the plug connection. Since the electronic thermometer determines the temperature by measuring the thermistor resistance, and the plug is in series with that resistance, the indicated temperature may be erroneously low (as much as 2°C in the author's experience).

2. Not all temperature probes are interchangeable. Unfortunately, this is most often the case with instruments that use temperature as a control input, i.e., radiant infant warmers, warming and cooling blanket units, and so on. The user must pay careful attention that the probe being used is the one specified by the instrument's manufacturer. To restate, although all or most of the probes seem to have the same size phone plug, the thermistor in the probe may be very different. It must be checked. The normal failure mode of thermistor temperature probes is a short or open wire in the probe cable. Fortunately, this is very easy to diagnose; the temperature reading will be unrealistically high or low if one of these conditions is present. The more sophisticated electronic thermometers usually have a feature that will directly indicate a fault in the probe.

Some pulmonary artery catheters contain thermistors which take the pulmonary artery temperature and display it on a cardiac output computer. Variations in temperature occur according to the technique employed in measurement. Usually, rectal temperatures are approximately 1°F higher than oral temperatures (normal 98.6°F, 37°C); axillary temperatures, 1°F lower. Since pulmonary artery temperatures are core temperatures taken directly from pulmonary artery blood, they may be higher than rectal temperatures. Because skin temperature is a function of peripheral circulation, skin probes (banjo type) are affected by changes in peripheral vascular tone.

A relatively unique method of measuring skin temperature is the use of "liquid crystals." These are commercially available as adhesive strips that change color at different temperatures.

Indirect Pressure Measurement

In the contemporary clinical environment, the arterial pressure is probably one of the most measured and treated of physiological parameters. In spite of the emphasis given the interpretation and management of central arterial pressure, often there is insufficient attention given to the technical details of its acquisition. Since the topic of this chapter is instrumentation, it seems logical to subdivide the topic according to the technique of measurement used, hence indirect versus direct methods. It is certainly accurate to state that virtually all nursing personnel are trained and skilled in the standard method of indirect pressure measurement, i.e., the use of a sphygmomanometer and stethoscope. However, it is probably equally accurate to state that not all the users of these instruments are aware of their limitations and of all the factors that affect their accuracy. Riva-Rocci reported on the first clinically acceptable sphygmomanometer before the Italian Congress of Medicine in 1896. He occluded the upper arm with an inflatable rubber cuff until it obliterated the brachial artery pulse, thus obtaining the systolic pressure. In 1901 von Recklinghausen increased the width of the cuff from 5 to 11 to 13 cm for greater accuracy, and in 1905 Korotkoff introduced the auscultatory method for measuring the systolic and diastolic brachial artery pressures. Since that time many studies have been published regarding the accuracy, instrumentation, and techniques relevant to this method; so it is perhaps better to read Korotkoff's own description of the method, which was translated (by A. S. Badger) as follows:

"On the Subject of Methods of Determining Blood Pressure" (From the clinic of Professor S. P. Federov) Dr. N. S. Korotkoff:
On the basis of his observations, this report has arrived at the conclusion that a completely compressed artery in a normal condition does not produce any sound. Taking advantage of this situation the reporter proposes the sound method for determining the blood pressure in humans. The sleeve (cuff) of Riva-Rocci is placed on the middle $\frac{1}{3}$ of the arm toward the shoulder. The pressure in the sleeve is raised quickly until it stops the circulation of the blood beyond the sleeve. Thereupon, permitting the mercury manometer to drop, a child's stethoscope is used to listen to the artery directly beyond the sleeve. At first no audible sound is heard at all. As the mercury manometer falls to a certain height the first short tones appear; the appearance of which indicates the passage of part of the pulse wave under the sleeve. Consequently, the manometer reading at which the first tones appear corresponds to the maximum pressure. With a further fall of the mercury in the manom-

eter, systolic pressure murmurs are heard, which change again to a sound (secondary). Finally, all sounds disappear. The time at which the sounds disappear indicates a free passage of the pulse wave; in other words, at the moment the sounds disappear, the minimum blood pressure in the artery exceeds the pressure in the sleeve. Consequently the reading of the manometer at this time corresponds to the minimum blood pressure. Experiments on animals gave positive results. The first sound-tones appear (10–12 mm) sooner than the pulse, for the perception of which (r. art. radialis) the breakthrough of a greater part of the pulse wave is required.[2]

With this original description as background, let us now examine what has been learned about the factors that influence the accuracy of the Riva-Rocci–Korotkoff method.

Cuff size One of the most important factors that influence the accuracy of the occlusive cuff method is the length of the arterial segment which is compressed. This is determined by the width of the occluding cuff relative to the size of the limb on which it is applied. If the cuff is too narrow, the indirect pressure will be read higher than actual. Conversely, if the cuff is too wide, the pressure will read lower. From von Recklinghausen (1901) to the present, investigators have studied the relationship of cuff width to limb diameter in terms of its effect on accuracy. The presently accepted recommendation is that the cuff should be 20 percent wider than the diameter of the arm. Because commercially available cuffs are often sized by age range (i.e., adult, child, and so on), it should be remembered that this is intended only as a guide and that the width of the cuff should be appropriate for the size of the limb to which it is applied. Circumference, being easier to measure than diameter, can be used as a determinator by using a cuff width about 40 percent of the limb circumference.

Whether the inflatable bladder within the cuff should be long enough to surround the extremity or half encircle it is not certain. In 1967 the American Heart Association Committee reported: "The inflatable bag should be long enough to go halfway round the limb if care is taken to put it directly over the compressible artery. A bag 30 cm in length which nearly (or completely) encircles the limb obviates any risk of misapplication."[3]

Technique There are four factors attendant to the technique of indirect arterial pressure measurement that influence its accuracy and reproducibility. They are: (1) cuff placement, (2) deflation rate, (3) systolic and diastolic identification points, and (4) the auscultatory apparatus.

1. Cuff placement—The inflatable bladder within the cuff should be placed directly over the artery to be compressed. Failure to do so will cause the measured pressure to be higher than it actually is.

2. Deflation rate—Since the technique of listening to Korotkoff sounds is a time-sampling process, the rate of deflation relative to the heart rate will influence the resolution of the method. For example, a measurement is being made on a patient with a systolic pressure of 100 mmHg and a heart rate of 50 beats per minute. In addition, the cuff is being deflated at a rate of 10 mm/s. Will the measurement error be acceptable? Let us assume that when the cuff pressure is at 101 mmHg, and systole occurs, it will not be recorded. When the next systole occurs, the cuff pressure recorded will be 89 mmHg, an error of more than 10 percent. A deflation rate of 2 to 3 mmHg per heartbeat is recommended to accommodate both slow and fast heart rates and to avoid unnecessary venous congestion in the distal bed.

3. Systolic and diastolic points—The criterion for identifying the systolic pressure has not changed since it was suggested by Korotkoff. Systolic pressure is recorded when the first sound appears during deflation of the cuff. Some have suggested that the systolic pressure be checked by palpation, and if higher, it be reported. The criterion for diastolic pressure has been, and may still be considered to be, controversial. Should the diastolic pressure be recorded when the Korotkoff sounds become dull and muffled or when the sounds disappear? After an extensive review of the literature, Geddes wrote: "In view of all this evidence and in the opinion and experience of the author, the point of muffling should be accepted as the most constant indicator of diastolic pressure. However, this point is known to occur at a cuff pressure above the true diastolic pressure. Nonetheless, its reliability argues in favor of its use because, in the many instances, sounds often persist well below the true diastolic pressure."[4]

4. Auscultatory apparatus—The observer's auditory system and a stethoscope constitute the auscultatory apparatus. Since Korotkoff sounds are low-frequency sounds just above the normal hearing threshold, it is obvious that normal hearing is a prerequisite for the observer. A good quality stethoscope with an intact diaphragm and ear pieces that effect a good seal is equally important in ensuring an accurate measurement.

---

[2] A. S. Badger, trans., *Cardiovasc Res Center Bull* (Houston) 5:57–74, 1967.

[3] Kirkendal, et al., American Heart Association recommendations for human blood pressure determination by sphygmomanometer, *Circulation* 36:980–988, 1967.

[4] L. A. Geddes, *The Direct and Indirect Measurement of Blood Pressure,* Chicago: Year Book, 1970, p. 108.

A discussion of the origin of Korotkoff sounds is beyond the intended scope of this chapter; however, if the reader is interested in doing further research on this subject, Geddes offers an excellent synoptic review.

Goodman and Howell recognized five phases of Korotkoff sounds. Their description has stood the test of time. In their own words, they are as follows:

Phase I—A loud clear-cut snapping tone

Phase II—A succession of murmurs

Phase III—The disappearance of the murmurs and the appearance of a tone resembling to a degree the first phase but less well marked

Phase IV—Becomes less clear in quality or dull

Phase V—The disappearance of all sounds[5]

Automatic indirect pressure measurement There are many automatic or semiautomatic noninvasive arterial pressure measurement instruments available on the market. They all have in common the use of an occlusive cuff; therefore, the previous discussions pertaining to cuff size and applications are relevant to these instruments. The system used to detect the systolic and diastolic points is either acoustic or ultrasonic. The acoustic systems utilize a microphone located under the occlusive cuff to detect the Korotkoff sounds. Specially designed circuitry then determines and displays the measured systolic and diastolic pressures. The ultrasonic systems utilize an acoustic beam to detect the artery wall motion beneath the cuff, and from this information the systolic and diastolic points are determined.

These types of automated noninvasive systems offer the capabiity of making more frequent measurements at regular intervals than would otherwise be practical. They would probably be of most use in situations where invasive monitoring is not indicated or practical. The major disadvantage of these automated systems is that they are sensitive to the patient's motion, and therefore, motion artifact can cause erroneous readings.

Direct Pressure Measurement

Invasive monitoring For selected patients, the precise information needed to assist in diagnosis, to define therapy, and to evaluate the patient's response to the selected therapy is best obtained through continuous invasive monitoring. Invasive monitoring indicates procedures which involve penetration of the skin, such as the placement of an arterial cannula, a pulmonary artery catheter, or an intracranial pressure measurement device. The pressures measured, for example, pulmonary artery (PA), pulmonary capillary wedge (PCW), central venous (CVP), left atrial (LAP), intracranial (ICP), and mean arterial (MAP), are not readily detectable using noninvasive techniques.

The first report of direct arterial measurement was by Lambert and Wood in 1947. Ryder published on ICP monitoring in 1952, and in 1970 Swan and Ganz introduced the flow-directed balloon-tipped pulmonary artery catheter. Invasive procedures have now become widely utilized to complement and supplement noninvasive forms of assessment, such as history taking, physical examination, and ECG monitoring. Invasive techniques provide the quickest, most accurate physiologic data. Eliminating the need for frequent, intermittent manual measurements, such as vital signs and blood gas samplings, permits increased time to be devoted to other aspects of caring for the critically ill patient. In the hands of skilled personnel, the insertion and maintenance of invasive lines to obtain accurate and continuous data provide less risk to the patient than the alternative of intermittent, estimated data. These procedures can be done with a high degree of safety and are well tolerated by the seriously ill patient.

Basic pressure system The basic system for the continuous measurement of physiologic pressure consists of a cannula or catheter connected to a transducer via a system of stopcocks and tubing. The area between the patient's blood or cerebral spinal fluid (CSF) and the diaphragm of the transducer is filled with solution to transmit the pressure from the patient to the monitor (Fig. 42-3).

Cannula → Stopcock → Pressure Tubing →
 Transducer → Monitor

A variety of satisfactory techniques is in use to measure various pressures. An understanding of the basic principles of transducers and amplifiers will facilitate the setting up and use of any type of monitoring equipment for any type of pressure measurement.

Transducers A transducer is a device which converts one form of energy into another. It may be defined as a device used to change a varying pressure into a proportionately varying signal which can be

---

[5] E. H. Goodman, and A. A. Howell, Further clinical studies in the auscultatory method of determining blood pressure, *Am J of Med Sc* 142:334–352, 1911.

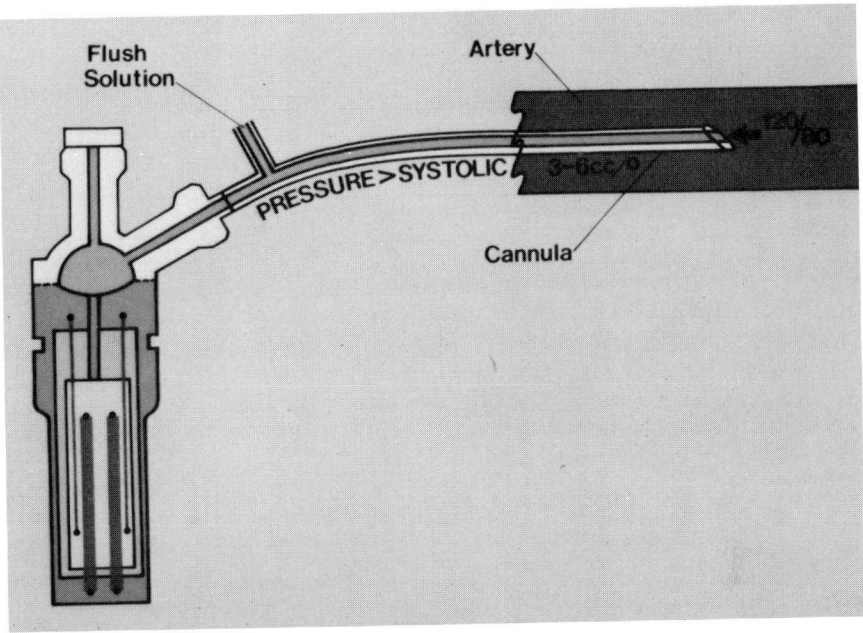

FIGURE 42-3
Basic vascular pressure system.

displayed on a scope, meter, and/or recorder. The type of transducer discussed in this application is one which converts a physiologic pressure to an electric signal.

It is recommended that in a clinical setting only isolated transducers be used. The isolated transducer protects the patient against inadvertent shock and withstands the high voltage generated during electrocautery and defibrillation. If a metal-cased or non-isolated transducer is in use when defibrillation or electrocautery is applied, the internal components of the transducer could be damaged, resulting in failure of the transducer at a usually critical time.

Basically, a transducer consists of the following components:

1. Diaphragm—This is the external sensing element of the transducer.

2. Dome—When the transducer is not in use, the dome protects the diaphragm from damage. When the transducer is in use, the dome holds the solution which transmits the patient's pressure to the diaphragm. Domes are available in a variety of configurations. From the standpoint of electrical safety, only plastic domes should be incorporated in the critical-care area. All accessories such as stopcocks and tubing should also be plastic.

a. Disposable diaphragm domes—These are the most commonly used domes in critical-care areas. They contain a thin membrane or diaphragm which acts as a sterile barrier between the nonsterile transducer and the solution in direct contact with the patient's blood or cerebral spinal fluid. They eliminate the need for sterilization of the transducer in most applications. The disposable diaphragm dome is strictly for one-patient usage. Episodes of sepsis secondary to resterilization of disposable diaphragm domes have been documented. Sterilizing agents react with the thin Lexan diaphragm, causing it to develop small fissures, eliminating the sterile barrier between the diaphragm of the dome and the diaphragm of the transducer (Fig. 42-4).

b. Reusable domes—Like the disposable diaphragm dome, these are usually made of Lexan, a polycarbonate. Before sterilization, Lexan is the strongest commercially available plastic. However, it does react with fluid and gas sterilizing products, eventually leading to cracking and warping of the dome. When the dome leaks, it should be discarded so that a sterile, airtight system is maintained between the patient and the transducer. When this type of dome is used, both the transducer and the dome must be cleaned and then fluid- or gas-sterilized (ETO).

a

b

FIGURE 42-4

(*a*) Luer Lok diaphragm dome. (*b*) Linden diaphragm dome.

c. Linden fittings—When manifolds are used or when there is considerable movement such as in the catheterization lab, the Linden dome provides the most secure and most adaptable fitting (Fig. 42-4*b*).

d. Luer Lok fittings—For routine bedside setups, the Luer Lok dome is most commonly used. In this type of application, it provides a secure fitting (Fig. 42-4*a*).

3. Body—This portion of the transducer houses the electronic components.

4. Cable—The cable contains air vents to facilitate balancing the transducer and wires connecting the transducer itself to resistors in the connector.

5. Connector—The type of connector varies with the type of monitor being used. It usually contains various resistors. In addition to mechanically fastening the transducer to the amplifier via a wall plate, junction box, or directly into the monitor itself, the connector is functional in balancing and calibrating procedures.

A basic understanding of the principles involved in the functioning of the transducer is often of value in preventing major transducer problems, such as breakage, and in certain instances facilitates troubleshooting. Most direct physiologic pressure measurements are made using one of the following three types of transducers:

1. Unbonded strain gauge

2. Semiconductor

3. Differential transformer

Unbonded strain gauge This is the most commonly used transducer today. It employs four strain-sensitive resistance wires, with one end fixed and the other movable, arranged in a Wheatstone bridge configuration (Fig. 42-5). This device measures displacement, with the displacement of the diaphragm being proportional to the pressure being measured. The four strain-sensitive wires are mounted between the frame and the armature. As the diaphragm of the transducer is displaced by the patient's pressure, there is a change in the length and therefore the diameter of the strain wires, two becoming more strained or stretched and two becoming relaxed. As the diameters of the strain wires change, their electrical resistance is altered. This alters the current flow, which is directly proportional to changes in pressure, thereby converting a mechanical or physiological pressure into an electric signal. This type of transducer may be used with ac or dc excitation.

Semiconductor This is also a type of strain gauge utilizing a Wheatstone bridge configuration as the

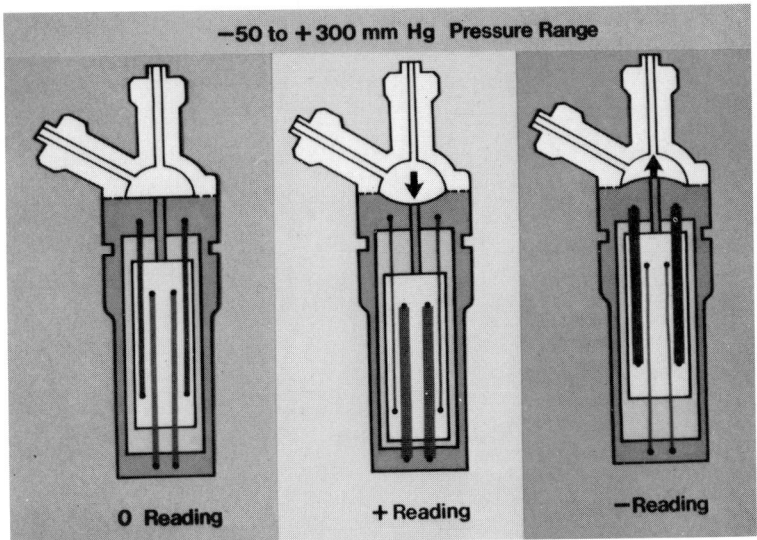

-50 to +300 mm Hg Pressure Range

0 Reading   + Reading   −Reading

FIGURE 42-5
Unbonded strain gauge.

electric circuit. It does not, however, contain strain wires as does the unbonded strain gauge. It contains a semiconductor material, usually silicon-bonded to a beam. It also functions on a displacement principle and clinically is set up, balanced, and calibrated like unbonded strain gauges. They may be used with ac or dc excitation (Fig. 42-6).

Differential transformer transducers   These are also displacement devices. A magnetic core inside a differential transformer is displaced by the applied force. These transducers tend to be considerably larger in size than unbonded strain gauges and semiconductors and they require ac excitation. Setup, balancing, and calibration procedures are the same as for the other two transducers described.

Range   Transducers are designed to measure pressure accurately within a specified range. A commonly used range is −50 to +300 mmHg. They are designed to tolerate pressures at a considerably higher level before transducer damage occurs. This is referred to as *maximum overpressurization*. Transducers designed to measure within a range of −50 to +300 mmHg usually will tolerate overpressurization up to 5000 to 10,000 mmHg.

Overpressurization may occur by direct mechanical pressure on the diaphragm or by syringe pressure. For example, a 1-mL tuberculin syringe exerts approximately 25,000 mmHg; therefore, if directed to-

ward the transducer, it will overpressurize it. Pressures of less than 5000 mmHg are exerted by 12-mL or larger syringes, making them safe to use with most transducers.

Balancing and calibration   All transducers must be balanced (zeroed) before and during pressure measurements. A balanced transducer gives a reading of zero (±1 mmHg). Since physiologic pressures are relative to atmospheric pressures, the transducer must be balanced at atmospheric pressure. This is done by referencing (venting) the diaphragm of the transducer to air while it is balanced via the amplifier. The level of the transducer system which is vented to air (e.g., stopcock port) should be at the patient's mid-axillary (right atrial) level. For every 1 in of discrepancy between heart level and transducer level, there will be an error of approximately 2 mmHg.

Prior to balancing, the transducer should be fluid-filled and attached to the monitor with the power turned on for the time recommended by the manufacturer, usually 5 min. Transducers in use for blood pressure measurement should be balanced approximately every 8 h. Transducers in use for low-range pressures, such as pulmonary artery and intracranial pressure, should be balanced approximately every 2 to 4 h. In addition, they should be rebalanced when they are repositioned, if the pressure reading is in question or if there is a loss of power.

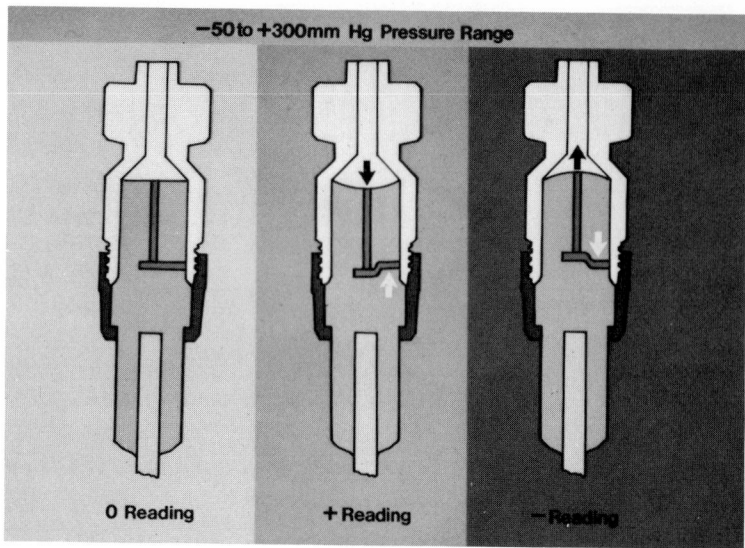

FIGURE 42-6
Semiconductor.

Once the transducer is balanced, most systems require calibration. Calibration refers to adjusting the monitor to display the pressure being exerted on the transducer. The most accurate form of calibration is by mercury sphygmomanometer, and all systems should periodically be checked with this system (Fig. 42-7).

Pressure amplifiers The pressure amplifier or module in the monitor enlarges or amplifies the signal being transmitted from the patient via the transducer. Although widely diverse in appearance, all amplifiers perform the same basic functions. These consist of the following:

1. Display—Digital or analog meters display systolic, diastolic, and/or mean pressures, usually in millimeters of mercury.

2. Alarm controls—A means of selecting the highest and lowest acceptable range for the pressure being monitored.

3. Alarms—Audible and visual alarms indicate when a pressure change is above or below the range set on the meter.

4. Balance (zero) control—A means of adjusting the transducer to a zero reading at atmospheric pressure.

5. Calibration control—A means of adjusting the amplifier, scope, and/or recorder to read the same pressure the transducer is receiving. Some monitors are precalibrated; others incorporate electronic calibration or calibration (cal) factors. Some older model amplifiers require direct pressure on the transducer via a mercury sphygmomanometer for calibration (Fig. 42-7).

6. Gain control (sensitivity)—A means of controlling the accuracy and size of the pressure displayed. For example, since pulmonary artery pressures are considerably lower than systemic arterial pressures, it is necessary to enlarge the waveform so that important waveform variations are easily visualized. This is done by changing the range switch on the amplifier to enlarge the signal being received. Frequently used gains are 0 to 250 to 300 mmHg for arterial blood pressure, 0 to 60 to 90 mmHg for pulmonary artery and intracranial pressures, and −5 to +20 to 30 mmHg for central venous pressures.

7. Selector switch—A means of determining which pressure—systolic, diastolic, mean, or a combination of pressures—is to be displayed.

Arterial blood pressure For the normotensive, non-critically ill patient, the indirect method of blood pressure measurement is usually satisfactory, since the inaccuracies inherent in the indirect or cuff method of measurement are not usually physiologically significant. In the critically ill, hypertensive, or hypotensive patient, however, alterations in cardiac output and peripheral vasoconstriction, combined with the inherent errors of the indirect method, cause meas-

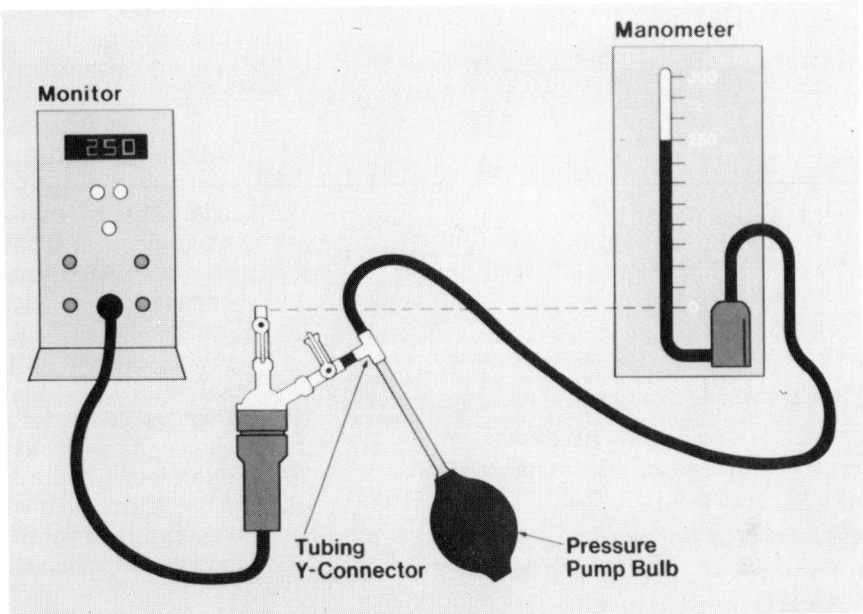

FIGURE 42-7
Mercury sphygmomanometer for calibration of transducer-monitor system.

urement errors that could seriously distort blood pressure data. Such incorrect data could lead to inappropriate diagnosis and management. Indications for direct or invasive blood pressure monitoring include:

1. Hypotension—It is not always possible to obtain cuff or palpated pressures on a patient in shock. Obviously the patient still has a pressure at this critical stage, and it is very important to be able to accurately ascertain the pressure. When the patient has a low stroke volume and a low cardiac output with excessive peripheral vasoconstriction, Korotkoff sounds may not be heard at all.

2. Vasoactive drug therapy—The administration of drugs which markedly lower or raise blood pressure, such as sodium nitroprusside or dopamine, require continual monitoring of pressure for safe, effective regulation.

3. Blood sampling—The need for frequent blood samples for measurement of Pa_{O_2}, Pa_{CO_2}, pH, and other parameters is a major indication for an arterial line. The placement of an arterial cannula leads to fewer complications than repeated needle punctures of an artery.

4. Neurologic conditions—In patients with increased intracranial pressure (IICP), or the potential to develop it, measures are taken to maintain cerebral perfusion pressures (mean arterial pressure—mean intracranial pressure) of at least 50 mmHg. In the stroke patient, maintaining the mean arterial pressure at a level above 60 to 70 mmHg is believed to be helpful in preventing the loss of autoregulation mechanisms in areas of focal cerebral ischemia. Patients with acute cervical cord injuries are often hypotensive. An increase in blood pressure may be a sign that abnormal pressure is being exerted on the spinal cord. For example, a post-op laminectomy patient may develop increased pressure on the cord from bleeding.

Catheter insertion The direct measurement of systolic, diastolic, and mean arterial blood pressure is usually done by cannulating the radial, brachial, or femoral arteries. Ordinarily after suitable preparation of the skin, the cannula is placed percutaneously and sutured in place. Occasionally an arterial cutdown is required. Systemic arterial pressure may also be obtained via catheterization of axillary or superficial temporal arteries or the central aorta.

Although the radial artery is small and anatomically unstable, it usually has good collateral circulation. It is routinely used for short-term (less than 24 h) monitoring of cardiac surgery patients. The patient's palmar arch should be assessed prior to insertion of the radial line. This can be done by using the Allen

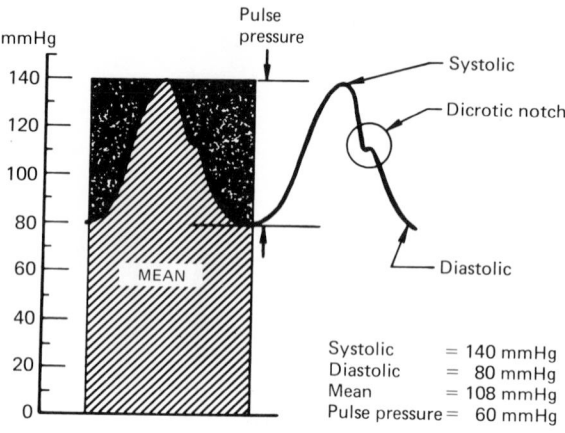

FIGURE 42-8

Typical arterial pressure waveform.

Systolic = 140 mmHg
Diastolic = 80 mmHg
Mean = 108 mmHg
Pulse pressure = 60 mmHg

test[6] and/or a Doppler ultrasound device. Prior to insertion of a radial line, the patient's wrist is restrained in a position of mild hyperextension to avoid kinking the cannula. A kinked cannula interferes with infusion of the continual flush solution.

An alternative insertion site is the brachial artery. This vessel is larger and more anatomically stable than the radial, with less collateral circulation. For patients requiring long-term monitoring or for the restless patient, the femoral artery is frequently used. This is a large, anatomically stable artery with minimal collateral circulation.

Waveform   A normal arterial waveform consists of a sharp ascent during systole with a gradual descent during diastole (Fig. 42-8). The downstroke has a dicrotic notch, indicating closure of the aortic valve. The ascent during systole correlates with electrical depolarization of the ventricles as demonstrated in the ECG by the QRS complex. Delay between the QRS and systolic ascent can be caused by many factors. One of these is the distance between the

---

[6] Allen test. Simultaneously compress both the ulnar and radial arteries and open and close the hand to promote exsanguination. This takes approximately 1 min. Following release of one artery, usually the ulnar, there should be a blushing (reactive hyperemia) of the extended hand within 5 s. This reactive hyperemia due to capillary refilling indicates adequate circulation to the hand. If blanching occurs, it is evidence of inadequate palmar arch circulation. A radial artery cannula placed in such a patient could lead to the complication of ischemia of the hand. A false positive Allen test may occur with hyperextension of the fingers or wrist.

cannulated vessel and the left ventricle. For example, there will be more lag time noted between the QRS and the upstroke of the waveform if the cannula is in the femoral artery rather than in the central aorta. The dicrotic notch correlates with the T wave documenting the end of ventricular repolarization (Fig. 42-9). Cardiac arrhythmias can be reflected in alterations in the arterial pressure waveform (Fig. 42-10). Other causes of waveform variations are the patient's clinical state, cardiac output, and vascular resistance, as well as artificial pacemakers and artifacts in the monitoring system. Infrequently, inspirations and expirations will affect the overall waveform pattern (Fig. 42-11).

Bedside setup for a standard size transducer   A variety of satisfactory systems is available for doing direct blood pressure measurements. The following procedure (and list of items necessary to carry it through) represents a frequently used system incorporating a continuous flush technique (Fig. 42-12).

Transducer

IV 500-mL bag of D_5W, normal saline, or lactated Ringer's solution

IV heparin

Minidrop (microdrop) IV administration set (60 drops/mL)

Pressure tubing, male-female

Continuous flush device

Three-way stopcock (3)

Female cap or deadhead (optional)

Transducer holder

Pressure infusor

IV pole

1. Connect the transducer to the monitor with the power on so that the transducer will have at least 5 min to warm up.

2. Prepare a flush solution such as D_5W, normal saline, or lactated Ringer's solution with 1000 units of aqueous heparin per 500 mL of solution.

3. Insert a minidrop (microdrop) infusion set (60 drops/mL) and place the solution in a pressure infusor bag. A syringe pump or roller pump may also be used.

4. Inflate the pressure infusor bag to 300 mmHg and hang on an IV pole. Fill the IV tubing, making certain it is air-free.

5. Using sterile technique, fasten the continuous flush device to the side port of the transducer.

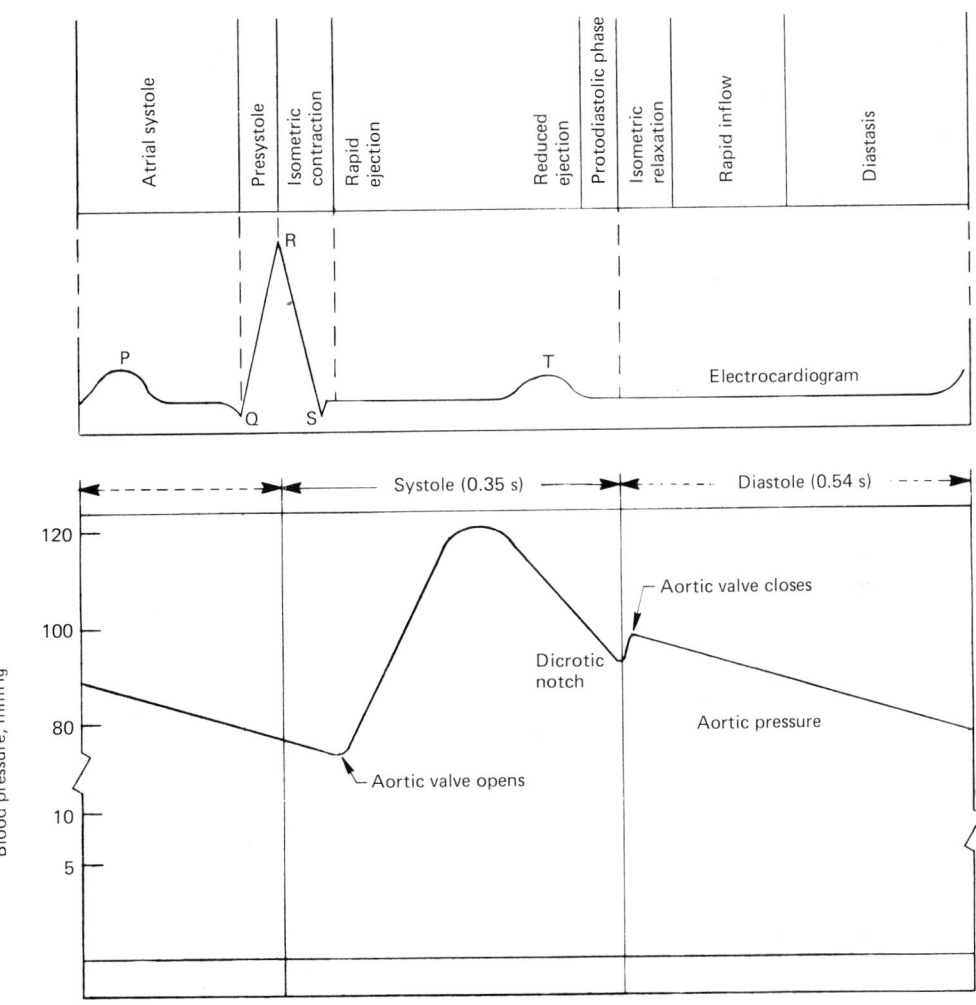

Atrial systole

Presystole

Isometric contraction

Rapid ejection

Reduced ejection

Protodiastolic phase

Isometric relaxation

Rapid inflow

Diastasis

R

P

Q

S

T

Electrocardiogram

Systole (0.35 s)

Diastole (0.54 s)

120

100

80

10

5

Blood pressure, mmHg

Aortic valve closes

Dicrotic notch

Aortic valve opens

Aortic pressure

FIGURE 42-9

Correlation of arterial pressure waveform and ECG.

Keep the cap on the unused port of the continuous flush device.

6. Connect the flush solution to the continuous flush device.

7. Pull back on the rubber valve, filling the continuous flush device and the transducer dome. Make certain the continuous flush device and the area above the transducer diaphragm have no air bubbles.

8. Place a cap or stopcock on the vertical port of the transducer to close the system.

9. Connect a length of pressure tubing to the remaining port of the continuous flush device and fill the tubing with flush solution. A stopcock may

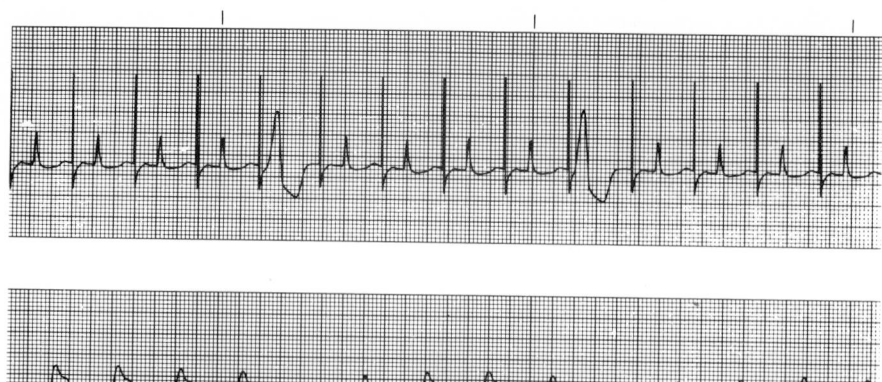

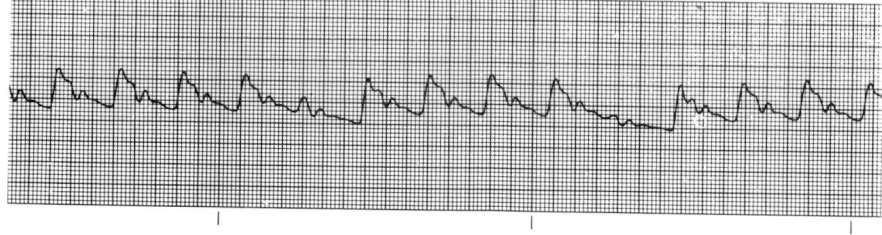

FIGURE 42-10

Effect of PVC on arterial pressure waveform demonstrating decreased stroke volume (paper speed 25 mm/s).

be inserted between the pressure tubing and continuous flush device for the purpose of drawing blood samples.

10. Place the transducer in a holder at the bedside with the tip of the vertical port level with the patient's right atrium (approximately midaxillary).

11. With the vertical port vented to air, balance the transducer to zero, then calibrate as required.

12. Connect pressure tubing to the stopcock attached to the patient's cannula or catheter.

13. Flush by pulling back on the rubber valve, and check the waveform for any signs of damping. Check to be certain the minidrop rate is 3 to 6 drops per minute and the pressure infusor is at 300 mmHg (Fig. 42-12).

Pulmonary artery pressure Pressures within the pulmonary artery reflect left ventricular function. Utilizing the Swan-Ganz technique, pulmonary artery (PA) and mean pulmonary capillary wedge (PCW) pressure may be obtained by the bedside insertion of a flow-directed balloon-tipped catheter through the right side of the heart into a branch of the pulmonary artery.

The PCW pressure obtained when the catheter occludes a branch of the pulmonary artery indicates (1) the presence and degree of pulmonary congestion and (2) the performance of the left ventricle via mean left atrial and mean left ventricular diastolic pressure (in the absence of mitral valve disease).

Prior to 1970, left heart function could be directly measured only in the cardiac catheterization laboratory. Use of the pulmonary artery catheter for diagnosis was supplemented by its use for monitoring as a result of the development of the flow-directed balloon-tipped catheter by Drs. Swan and Ganz. Ordinarily, this procedure is now done without fluoroscopy at the bedside, with the position of the catheter being determined by the pressure waveforms.

PA systolic pressure represents right ventricular contraction. PA diastolic pressure reflects resistance to flow by small arterioles and pulmonary capillaries. When there is no pulmonary vascular obstruction, PA diastolic pressure is approximately the same as PCW pressure. A positive difference of 6 mmHg or more between PCW pressure and pulmonary diastolic pressure indicates the presence of obstructive vascular disease in the lungs, such as pulmonary fibrosis, pulmonary embolus, or cor pulmonale. Therefore, a patient's PCW and PA diastolic pressure need to be correlated before it can be assumed that the PA diastolic pressure is providing an accurate reflection of pulmonary venous pressure, PCW, LAP, or left ventricular end diastolic pressure (LVEDP). A PCW in the normal range (8 to 12 mmHg) with a normal cardiac output indicates satisfactory ventricular performance.

Indications for pulmonary artery pressure measurement include:

1. Cardiac problems

2. Intravascular volume control

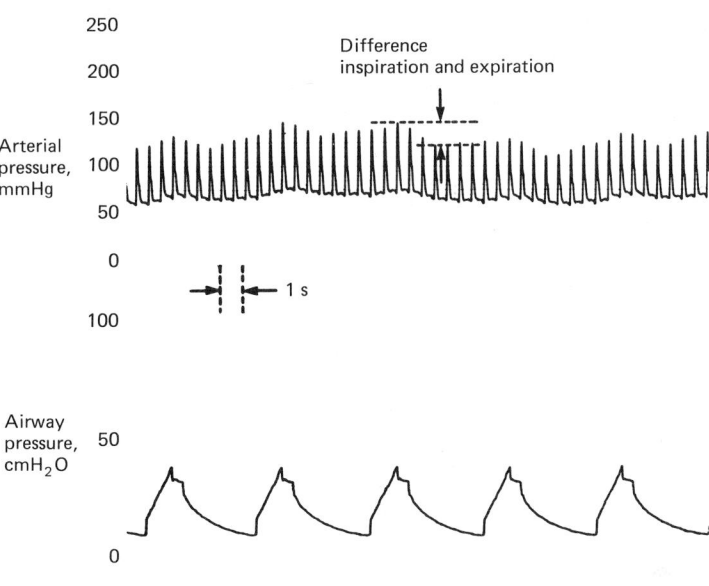

FIGURE 42-11

Effect of airway pressure on arterial pressure (paper speed 5 mm/s)

3. Pulmonary problems

4. Cardiac output determinations

5. Mixed venous blood samples

A variety of flow-directed balloon-tipped catheters is available. The style and size of catheter used depend upon the type of patient being monitored. For the adult patient, the 4-lumen 7 French catheter is most frequently used. This enables the measurement of right atrial (CVP), PA, and PCW pressures with intermittent cardiac output determinations via thermodilution.

Prior to insertion, the transducer system is set up as described under arterial blood pressure. Using sterile technique, fill both the right atrial (proximal) and PA (distal) lumens with flush solution, usually mildly heparinized. The balloon is submerged in solution and inflated to test its integrity. Tiny air bubbles can be detected if the balloon is defective.

The catheter is inserted via the internal or external jugular, subclavian, antecubital (median basilic or lateral cephalic), or femoral vein. The catheter is then advanced through the right atrium. Respiratory fluctuations in the waveform may be detected at this time. A large excursion in the right atrial waveform may be demonstrated by having the patient cough. The balloon may be inflated in the atrium (usually) or immediately after the flow of blood has propelled it through the tricuspid valve into the right ventricle.

Although room air is usually used for balloon inflation, carbon dioxide should be used if a right to left shunt or septal defect is known or suspected. The solubility of carbon dioxide in blood eliminates the risk of air emboli entering the systemic circulation. As soon as the catheter enters the right ventricle, the balloon should be at full inflation to reduce stimulation of the ventricular wall during insertion. The circulation of blood through the heart will then float the catheter through the pulmonary valve into the pulmonary artery, advancing it until the balloon wedges in a distal branch of the pulmonary artery. Once it is determined that the catheter is correctly placed, an x-ray should be taken to confirm catheter-tip location, and the catheter should be sutured into place.

This waveform consists of A and V waves. The A wave indicates left atrial contraction during left ventricular relaxation. The V wave reflects left atrial relaxation during left ventricular contraction. A "giant V" wave can indicate mitral regurgitation. For maintenance of PA lines, it is essential to be able to differentiate between PA and PCW waveforms.

Pulmonary capillary wedge   As with an arterial line, the pulmonary artery line should be continually monitored.

It is very important that the critical-care nurse be very familiar with pulmonary artery pressure waveforms, since these waveforms are used to determine

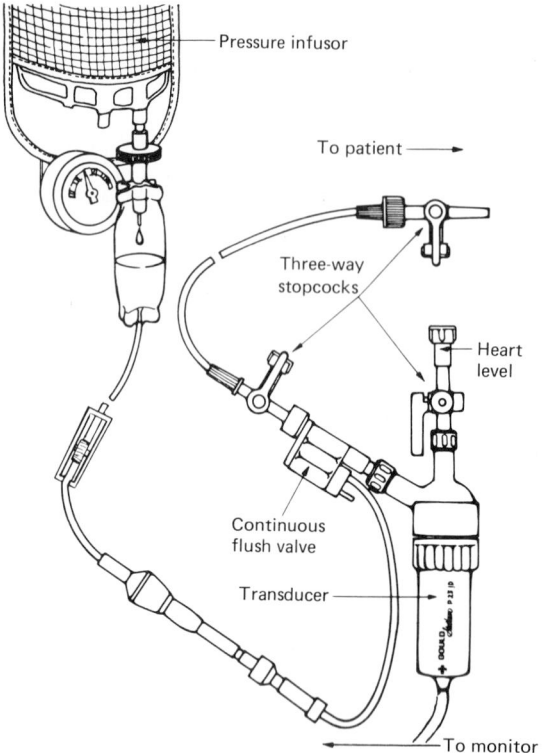

FIGURE 42-12

Bedside setup for a standard size transducer.

the positioning of the catheter in the heart (Fig. 42-13). It should be kept in mind that patients with chronic lung disease or ischemic heart disease often have pressures considerably higher than the normal range.

Right atrial (RA) pressure RA pressure reflects right ventricular (RV) pressure. It consists of three positive and three negative waves, or descents. The positive waves are A, C, and V. The A wave indicates right atrial systole. The C wave is caused by movement of the closed tricuspid valve during atrial diastole; the V wave is caused by atrial diastole. The negative waves are X, X' and Y, with the X indicating atrial relaxation, X' atrioventricular movement, and Y passive right atrial emptying.

Right ventricular (RV) pressure The ventricular waveform is demonstrated by a rapid rise representing isovolumetric contraction, followed by opening of the pulmonary valve with blood ejected from the RV into the pulmonary artery. With closure of the pulmonary valve, right ventricular pressure falls rapidly. The tricuspid valve opens with passive filling of the right ventricle from the right atrium.

Risks Risks associated with pulmonary artery pressure monitoring include thrombosis, emboli, perforation of the pulmonary artery, pulmonary infarction, intracardiac knotting of the catheter, ventricular arrhythmias, sepsis, and balloon rupture. The risk can be minimized by careful insertion and maintenance of the PA line.

Air emboli can result from the direct injection of air into the proximal or distal ports and/or balloon rupture. The latex balloon tends to absorb lipoprotein from the blood, causing it to lose elasticity, thereby increasing the risk of balloon rupture; these events make it impossible to determine PCW pressure. Fragments of the balloon may become emboli. Ideally, the catheter should be removed from the patient and discarded after approximately 48 h. PA catheters tend to be thrombinogenic.

Continuous flushing of a heparinized solution through both distal and proximal lumens will aid in preventing thrombus formation. The development of thrombus at the lumens will be demonstrated as a damped waveform. Syringe flushing of the lumens may cause thrombotic emboli. PA lines should be continuously monitored.

PA catheters may spontaneously advance into a wedge position without the balloon being inflated. If this occurs, it will be demonstrated on the monitor by a change in waveform from PA to wedge, a change in the mean pressure reading, and a drop in PA diastolic pressure. Leaving the balloon inflated for periods any longer than necessary for obtaining wedge readings may lead to pulmonary infarction.

Arrhythmias are often associated with catheter insertion and are resolved by correct placement or removal of the catheter.

Should the catheter fall back into the right ventricle from the PA, ventricular tachycardia may occur. ECG should be monitored during insertion and maintenance of the line to indicate arrhythmias. Pneumothorax and damage to the brachial plexus by direct trauma or bleeding has been reported with catheter insertions via the subclavian or internal jugular veins.

The frequency of wedge measurement should be limited to avoid trauma to the pulmonary artery vessel wall. In addition, care should be taken not to "overwedge" the catheter. During balloon inflation, the scope should be watched. As soon as the waveform converts from a PA to a PCW pattern, inflation should be stopped. This minimizes trauma to the vessel and prevents false high or low pressure reading caused by overinflation of the balloon.

Bedside setup for pulmonary artery catheter The transducer system may be set up exactly the same as

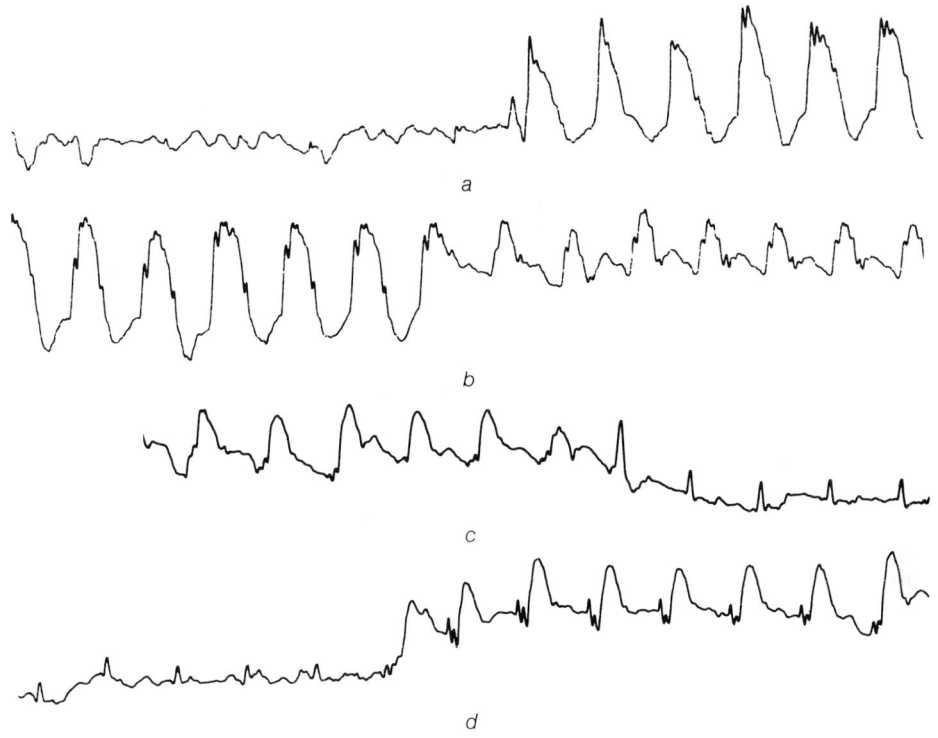

FIGURE 42-13

(*a*) Waveform during insertion of pulmonary artery catheter, right atrium to right ventricle. (*b*) Waveforms during insertion of pulmonary artery catheter, right ventricle to pulmonary artery. (*c*) Waveforms during insertion of pulmonary artery catheter, pulmonary artery to pulmonary capillary wedge. (*d*) Waveforms during insertion of pulmonary artery catheter, pulmonary capillary wedge to pulmonary artery.

in arterial pressure measurement. Frequently, a miniature transducer is used for this application. Because of the length of the PA catheter, however, it is not necessary to use pressure tubing as illustrated (Fig. 42-14).

Left atrial pressure (LAP) This measurement is usually associated with cardiovascular surgery and requires surgical placement of the catheter directly into the left atrium. Left ventricular end diastolic pressure is measured. Although it is important to keep air out of all vascular lines, this requirement is critical with the LAP line. Air on this side of the circulation may interrupt blood flow in the coronary arteries and cerebral vasculature.

The waveform consists of an A wave (atrial systole), a C wave (valvular closure), and a V wave (ventricular systole).

Central venous pressure (CVP) A catheter is placed percutaneously into the jugular, subclavian, or antecubital vein, such as the median basilic, and ad-

vanced into the vena cava or right atrium. Cutdowns are also used for insertion via antecubital veins. This measurement is useful in determining central venous return to the right side of the heart. A low CVP is indicative of inadequate blood return. In patients without heart, lung, or kidney disease, the CVP is satisfactory for volume replacements. Patients with heart or lung problems are monitored by PA lines. Patients with 3- or 4-lumen PA catheters may be monitored simultaneously for PA and central venous pressures.

The waveform consists of A, C, and V waves indicating atrial systole, valve closure, and ventricular systole, respectively. For continuous readings with a closed system, the CVP line may be set up the same as an arterial line.

Risks associated with vascular lines The three major risks associated with invasive vascular pressure monitoring are hemorrhage, thrombosis with emboli, and infection. These complications can be kept to a minimum when the patients are under the care of a

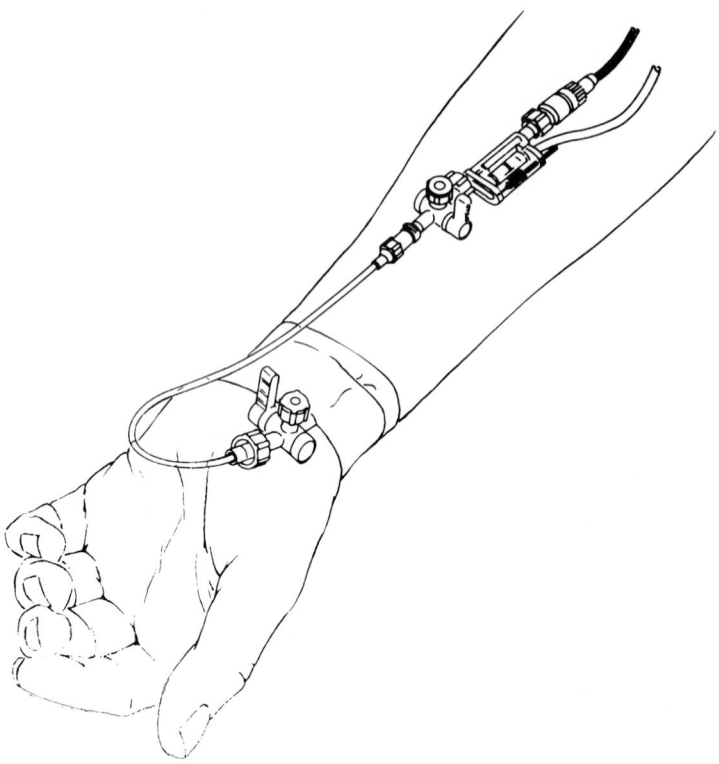

FIGURE 42-14

Bedside setup for a miniature size transducer for a radial arterial line.

skilled critical-care team with adequate instrumentation. Gardner reported the risk to be 0.2% with a total of 4500 direct arterial lines in over 12,000 patient days. Similar statistics have been reported from other hospitals.

1. Bleeding back is the most obvious and most acute problem. The pressure of the systemic arterial system can cause rapid exsanguination through the 18- or 20-gauge cannula commonly used for arterial lines. Bleeding back is controlled by maintaining the flush solution in a closed system at a pressure greater than the patient's systolic pressure. Any leak within the system, such as tubing disconnecting or a stopcock in the wrong position, will cause bleeding back. It is essential that the alarm limits be set correctly and used to notify staff immediately of this complication.

2. Thrombus formation with the risk of emboli can be minimized by continuously flushing the vascular line with a mildly heparinized solution. The development of thrombus will cause damping of the waveform and initiate an alarm condition.

3. To prevent infection, sterile techniques must be utilized for the insertion and maintenance of invasive lines. When a reusable-type dome is used, both the dome and transducer must be sterilized since the flush solution in the dome is in direct contact with both the transducer and the patient. Disposable diaphragm domes are strictly for one-patient use. The resterilization and reuse of these disposable domes has resulted in death secondary to sepsis.

4. Insertion sites should be dressed daily. Evidence of infection at the cannulation site is an indication for cannula removal.

See Table 42-1.

Intracranial pressure Indications for intracranial pressure measurement include:

1. Increased volume of brain

2. Increased volume of blood

3. Increased volume of cerebrospinal fluid (CSF)

4. Lesions

The three major techniques for monitoring intracranial pressure are intraventricular, subarachnoid, and epidural.

TABLE 42-1
Troubleshooting Vascular Lines

Problem	Cause	Solution
Damping of waveform (Usually results in false low systolic and false high diastolic readings) A. Bleeding back	The patient's pressure has become higher than the counteracting pressure of the flush solution	If an Intraflo (continual flush device) is being used, the counteracting pressure (i.e., pressure bag) should be at 300 mmHg
	A loose connection in the system	Make certain the dome is tightened securely on the transducer. Check to see that all connections between the patient and transducer are secure
	Incorrect stopcock position	Check stopcock positions Flush the line and check for a good waveform
B. Air bubbles	A loose connection in the system	Check to be certain all connections are secure
	A cracked stopcock, Intraflo, or pressure tubing	Change the Intraflo, pressure tubing, or stopcock with visible signs of damage
	Pulling too vigorously on the fast flush valve of the Intraflo, thereby pulling air into the system	When using the fast flush valve, watch the drip chamber and control the amount of valve pressure to prevent turbulence in the drip chamber Flush out all air bubbles between the diaphragm of the transducer and the patient
C. Clotting	Inadequate flush solution	Adjust drip rate to 3 to 6 minidrops per minute (3 to 6 mL/h) of a mildly heparinized solution. Flush using the fast flush valve of an Intraflo. (If the waveform remains damped, aspirate with a syringe. Do not reinject any aspirated blood, since it may include clots.)
Transducer will not balance	Damaged transducer	Try another transducer
	Transducer may be connected to the wrong amplifier	Check the amplifier connection
	Broken amplifier	Change amplifiers
Drifting	Insufficient warm-up time	Allow recommended time for transducer warm-up with power on
	The air vents in the cable may be kinked or compressed	Make certain the cable is not compressed

TABLE 42-1 (Continued)
Troubleshooting Vascular Lines

Problem	Cause	Solution
False low reading	Damped waveform	Refer to discussion on damping
	Transducer not balanced correctly	Place transducer at heart level for vascular pressures and level of foramen of Monro for ICP, and re-zero with transducer vented to air
	Calibration incorrect	Repeat calibration procedure
False high reading	Transducer not balanced correctly	Rebalance. For each foot of discrepancy between the transducer and the pressure source, there is an error of approximately 25 mmHg
	Flush solution being administered too rapidly. A maximal continual flush during pressure measurement is 6 to 8 mL/h	Slow continual flush to 3 to 6 mL/h
	Air in the system	Remove all air. At times, air in the system will amplify the pressure signal
Cuff blood pressure different from direct blood pressure	Direct pressure is more accurate, particularly in hypotensive patients. The transducer pressure usually reads higher than the cuff pressure	Direct pressure is a more accurate representation of true systemic blood pressure
	Transducer measures systolic and diastolic from the same heartbeat, whereas with cuff pressures systolic is taken from one beat and diastolic from another	
	Low cardiac output and peripheral vasoconstriction make it difficult to hear the indirect pressure	
No waveform on scope	Transducer connected incorrectly	Make certain transducer is securely connected and the appropriate connector for the amplifier is in use
	Incorrect gain setting	Check to see that amplifier is not set on too low a gain
	Damaged transducer	Try another transducer
	Broken amplifier	Change amplifiers

TABLE 42-1 (Continued)
Troubleshooting Vascular Lines

Problem	Cause	Solution
	Transducer not open to patient's pressure	Check positions of stopcocks
	Broken scope	Replace scope
Loss of ICP waveform	Occlusion of intracranial pressure measurement device	Flush intracranial catheter or SA screw as directed by physician
	Air between the transducer diaphragm and pressure source	Disconnect transducer and eliminate air from the system
Correlation of pressure readings taken with a water manometer to that taken with a transducer	Water manometers measure in cmH_2O, amplifiers usually display in mmHg	Conversion: 1 mmHg = 1.36 cmH_2O
Erratic or noisy traces	If a nonisolated transducer (exposed metal case) is in use, it may be secondary to electrical noise such as electrocautery	Use an isolated transducer
	If an isolated transducer is in use, it may mean that moisture has entered the back of the transducer via the venting tubes in the cable	Use a different transducer on the patient. Check the cable for evidence of cracks. If cracked, have it repaired Moisture may be removed from the transducer by: a. Placing the transducer through the aeration cycle of a gas sterilizing chamber b. Baking for 8 h at 150°F c. Several days at room temperature (not in use)
	Patient movement	Limit patient movement
Leaky domes	All plastic (Lexan, polycarbonate) domes react to various sterilizing agents. After repeated sterilizations, they will become cloudy, warped, and cracked	Discard dome and replace with sterile dome
Frequent damping of waveform	The cannula may have lodged against a vessel wall	A slight alteration in the position of the cannula will sometimes resolve this
	A clot may be forming	This may be indicated by the ability to flush but not aspirate the line
	If a disposable diaphragm dome is in use, there may be air trapped between the transducer diaphragm and dome diaphragm	Follow manufacturer's instructions for dome application

Intraventricular technique The intraventricular technique of ICP measurement was first reported in 1952 and consists of placing a catheter into the lateral ventricle. A twist drill hole is placed lateral to the midline at the level of the coronal suture, usually on the nondominant side. A catheter is placed through the cerebrum into the anterior horn of the lateral ventricle. On occasion, the occipital horn is used. Connected to the ventricular catheter via stopcock and/or pressure tubing is a pressure transducer (Fig. 42-15). Saline or Ringer's lactate solution provides the fluid column between the CSF and diaphragm of the transducer. A continuous flush system is not used.

1. Advantages:

    a. Direct measuring of pressure from the CSF

    b. Access for CSF drainage or sampling

    c. Access for determining volume-pressure responses

2. Disadvantages:

    a. Risk of infection (Sundbarg et al. documented a clinically apparent CNS infection rate of 1.1%.)

    b. Difficulty in locating the lateral ventricle following midline shifting of the ventricle, or collapse of the ventricle as a normal compensatory mechanism for increases in pressure

Subarachnoid technique The measurement of ICP via a subarachnoid screw was first reported in 1973. The screw device is inserted via a twist drill hole and

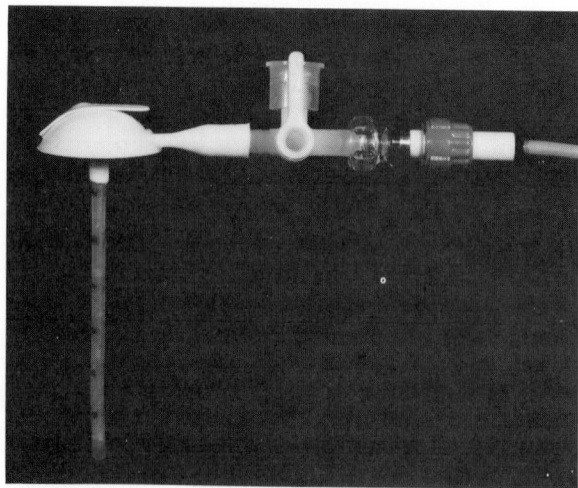

FIGURE 42-15
Intraventricular pressure cannula with miniature transducer.

extends into the subdural or subarachnoid space. Although the cerebrum is not penetrated, pressures are measured directly from the CSF, as with the ventricular technique. A transducer filled with saline or Ringer's lactate solution may be fastened directly to the screw or connected via pressure tubing (Fig. 42-16). Volume-pressure responses have been determined using this technique:

1. Advantages:

    a. Direct pressure measurement from CSF

    b. Does not require penetration of cerebrum to locate ventricle

    c. Access for determining volume-pressure responses

    d. Access for CSF drainage and sampling

2. Disadvantages:

    a. Risk of infection comparable to intraventricular technique

    b. Requires closed skull

Epidural technique This technique involves placing an epidural device such as a balloon with radioisotopes, a radio transmitter, or a fiberoptic transducer between the skull and the dura. Some researchers feel that dural compression and surface tension, as well as thickening of the dura during prolonged monitoring, tend to cause inaccuracies in the pressure readings. Although subarachnoid and intraventricular pressures correlate well with each other, there have been inconsistent correlations between direct CSF pressure and the various epidural techniques.

1. Advantage: less invasive

2. Disadvantages:

    a. Questionable reflection of CSF pressure

    b. No route for CSF drainage and sampling

    c. Volume-pressure responses not feasible

Waveforms The type of pressure measurement technique employed affects the waveform pattern. Hemodynamic and respiratory oscillations can be observed in the intracranial pressure traces. At times, the waveforms closely resemble arterial pressure waveforms; at other times, they resemble CVP waveforms (Fig. 42-17).

Certain patients exhibit a phenomenon known as plateau waves. *Plateau waves*, as defined by Lundberg, are spontaneous rapid increases of pressure to 50 to 115 mmHg, usually occurring in patients with existing elevations of intracranial pressure. They last approximately 15 to 20 min and are usually accompanied by a temporary increase in neurological deficits. Patients who sustain ICPs greater than 50 mmHg for periods longer than 20 min usually have poor prognosis. Although the mechanisms of plateau waves (A waves) are not clear, they have been correlated with certain clinical conditions. A report by Nornes correlates an increased frequency of plateau waves in the patient with an aneurysm who has a tendency to rebleed. Although B and C waves have been described, these do not have the clinical significance of the A (plateau) wave.

Risks associated with intracranial pressure monitoring   The complications associated with ICP monitoring are minimal. The infection rate in short-term monitoring (less than 5 days) using both the subarachnoid screw and intraventricular technique has been reported in the range of 0 to 1.1 percent.

Cardiac Output

Cardiac output, expressed in liters per minute, is the amount of blood pumped by the heart. It is the product of heart rate and stroke volume (the amount of blood ejected with each heartbeat). *Cardiac index* is the cardiac output per square meter of body surface area (height and weight). A small person requires less circulating blood and therefore less cardiac output than a larger person. By calculating the cardiac output and then computing the cardiac index according to the individual's height and weight, a more specific and useful measurement is available.

The intermittent measurement of cardiac output is essential to determine a patient's response to drugs which affect the heart and the blood vessels. With the aid of cardiac output measurements, a patient's poor response to a given therapeutic program can be recognized and alternative methods of therapy selected.

Techniques   A variety of techniques is available for the measurement of cardiac output. These include Fick, dye, thermal, radioisotope, pulse contour, and carbon dioxide rebreathing methods. Fick, dye, and thermodilution techniques are most commonly used. The initial technique for cardiac output determination was introduced by Fick in 1870 and is still utilized widely in cardiac catheterization laboratories. To obtain accurate results with this procedure, the patient must be in a stable condition and be cooperative.

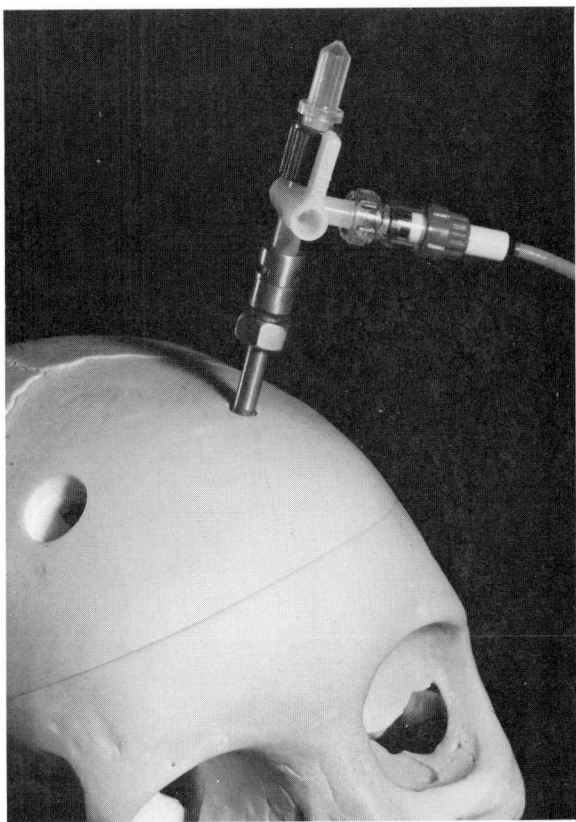

FIGURE 42-16
Subarachnoid screw with miniature transducer.

Samples of expired oxygen and simultaneous venous and arterial blood are used to make the calculation. This procedure is impractical for use on the critically ill patient because of the requirements for moving the patient to the equipment, for the patient to be in a stable condition, for highly trained technicians to perform the procedure, and for drawing arterial and venous blood samples.

The dye dilution technique requires the injection of dye, usually indocyanine green, into the patient's venous circulation. An arterial blood sample is withdrawn and passed through a densitometer to determine the degree to which the dye has been diluted

FIGURE 42-17
Intracranial pressure waveform.

by the blood. This technique has the disadvantage of requiring injecting into the patient a substance which recirculates many times before reabsorption, thereby interfering with repeated studies. Some patients have a serious allergic reaction to the dye. Dye dilution also requires blood withdrawal. For determination of certain types of shunts, however, it is the method of choice.

The most suitable procedure and the one most commonly utilized to determine cardiac output on the critically ill patient is thermodilution (Fig. 42-18). The technique was introduced by Fegler in 1954 but did not become clinically applicable until the development of the balloon-tipped flow-directed catheter by Swan and Ganz in 1970. The procedure is now routinely done at bedside by the critical-care nurse. A 4-lumen balloon-tipped catheter is placed in the patient. A bolus of cool solution, either D_5W or normal saline, is injected into the RA via the proximal port of

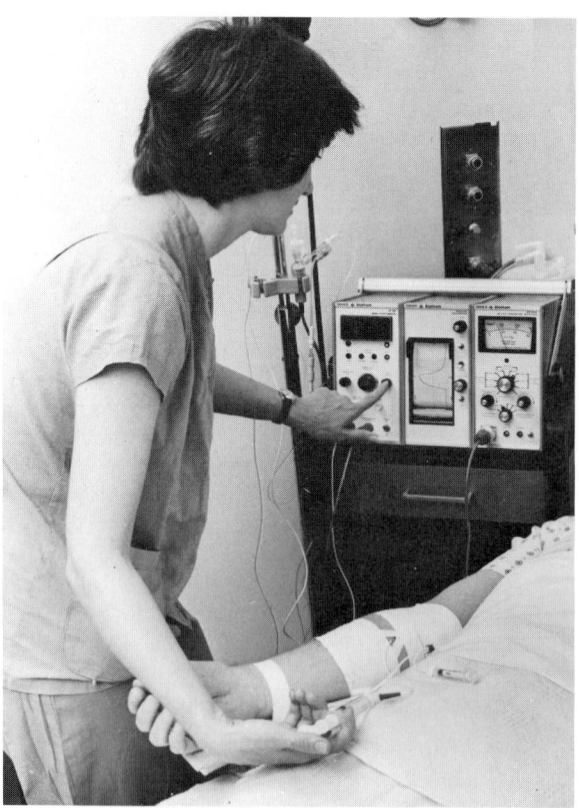

FIGURE 42-18
Bedside determination of cardiac output via thermodilution technique.

the catheter. As venous mixing occurs, primarily in the right ventricle, the temperature of the injectate is altered. A thermistor bead (small thermometer) located near the tip of the catheter, which is in the pulmonary artery, measures the change in the temperature of the blood caused by the injection. A cardiac output computer, using the amount of temperature change that has occurred between the injection into the right atrium and the flow through the pulmonary artery, calculates the cardiac output in liters per minute. Using the patient's height and weight and cardiac output, the cardiac index is determined.

This procedure requires:

1. A flow-directed thermodilution catheter
2. A monitoring system
3. Injectate
4. Thermodilution cardiac output computer, preferably with recorder

A 4-lumen balloon-tipped flow-directed catheter is prepared for insertion. This includes testing the integrity of the balloon under solution, testing the thermistor by attaching it to the cardiac output computer, filling both the proximal (CVP) and distal (PA) lumens with heparinized flush solution, and attaching the catheter to the monitoring system. The catheter must be kept sterile during these procedures (Fig. 42-19).

The minimal requirements for a safe system for the insertion of the catheter into the pulmonary artery includes a two-channel scope, ECG amplifier, and at least one pressure amplifier and transducer. The transducer is set up exactly as for an arterial line. The only difference is that the catheter is attached to the transducer system and filled prior to insertion. In this way the transducer can be used to identify the location of the catheter tip within the heart.

With the later model cardiac output computers, cardiac output can usually be measured with room temperature injectate. Room temperature injectate is preferable to iced injectate since it is more accurate because of less heat absorption during injection and it is easier to prepare. Because of the proximity of the pulmonary artery to the lungs, there are times when more temperature differential between the blood and injectate is necessary. Conditions which usually necessitate the use of iced injectate include cardiac output greater than 10 L/min, patients on respirators, and patients with erratic respiratory patterns such as Cheyne-Stokes.

The following procedure (and list of items neces-

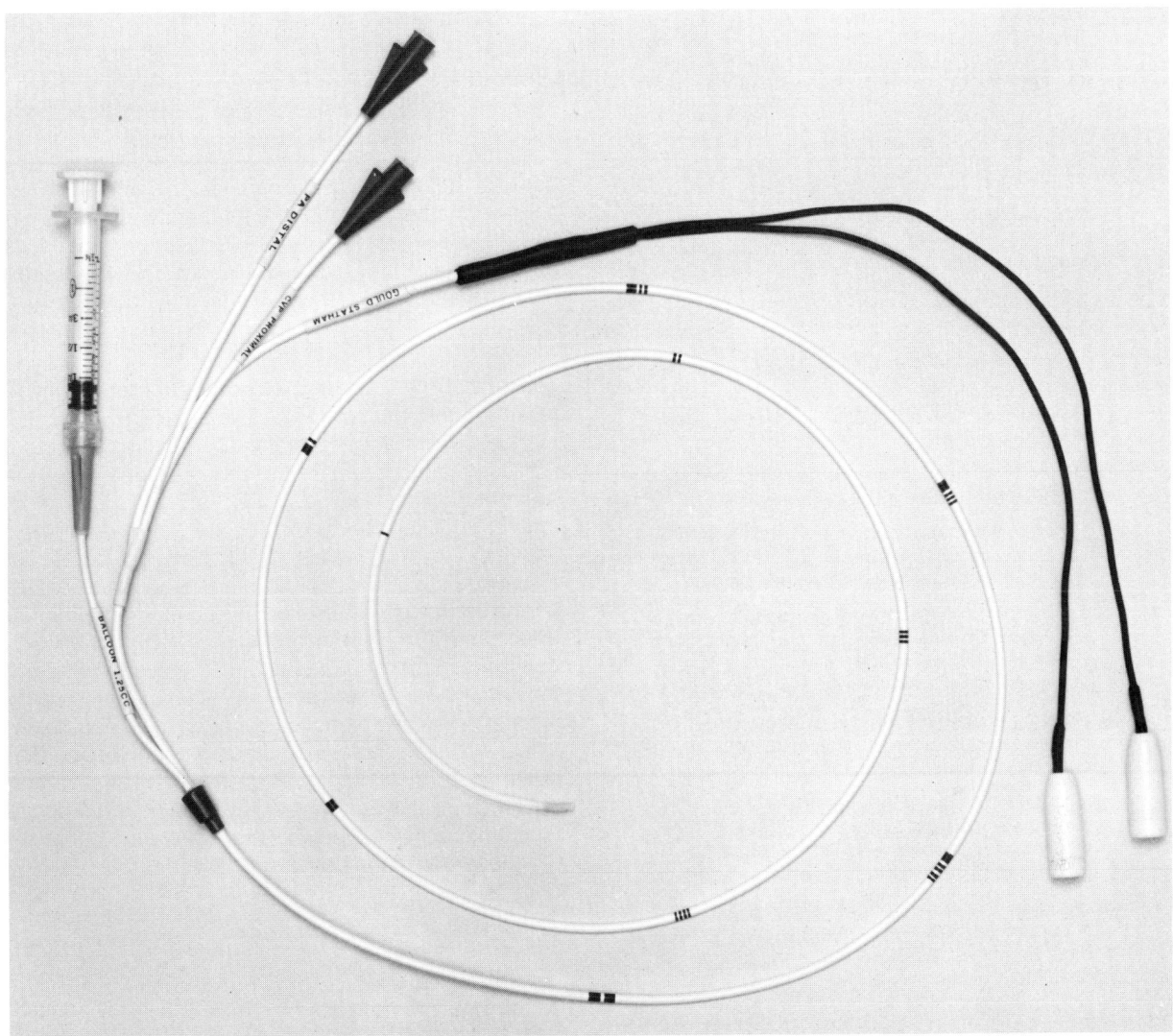

FIGURE 42-19

Four-lumen cardiac output catheter.

sary to carry it through) represents a system of preparing injectate.

1. Room temperature injectate

1 bag IV solution, such as D₅W or normal saline
Stopcock
18-gauge needle
Five 10- to 12-mL syringes
Sterile injectate probe

   a. Insert the sterile injectate probe securely into the port of the IV usually used for IV tubing.

Make certain that at least 3 cm of the probe tip is in the solution.

   b. Connect the injectate probe to the computer connector.

   c. Puncture rubber plug (medication site) of IV solution with an 18-gauge needle. Attach a stopcock to the needle, keeping all ports sterile.

   d. Just prior to injecting the bolus for cardiac output determination, connect a 10- to 12-mL syringe to the needle-stopcock arrangement.

e. Withdraw the exact volume of IV solution to be injected. Make certain there are no air bubbles. Handle the syringe as little as possible between the time the injectate is withdrawn and injected.

f. Repeat this syringe-filling procedure just prior to each cardiac output determination.

2. Iced injectate

1 bag IV solution, such as D_5W or normal saline
Stopcock
18-gauge needle
Five 10- to 12-mL syringes
Sterile injectate probe
Basin and ice

a. Insert the sterile injectate probe securely into the port of the IV usually used for IV tubing. Make certain that at least 3 cm of the probe tip is in the solution.

b. Connect the injectate probe to the computer connector.

c. Puncture the rubber plug (medication site) of IV solution with an 18-gauge needle. Attach stopcock to the needle, keeping all ports sterile.

d. Place the IV into a container and pack it with ice and water (slush). Keep the needle-stopcock connection out of the ice-water mixture to preserve sterility.

e. Determine when the injectate has reached the proper temperature. The injectate should be cooled to between 0 and 15° C.

f. Just prior to injection, prepare a syringe by aspirating iced IV solution into the syringe, working plunger back and forth to equalize the temperatures of the syringe and the ice solution.

g. Withdraw the exact volume required and then inject immediately. The syringe should be handled as little as possible between the time the injectate is withdrawn and injected.

h. Using this procedure, fill each syringe just prior to cardiac output determination.

Cardiac output computer   Numerous computers are available (Fig. 42-20). Current models incorporate catheters with thermistors which can measure the patient's body temperature directly from the pulmonary artery and have probes which measure the injectate temperature. The direct and continuous monitoring of the patient's temperature and the injectate temperature makes cardiac output measurement more accurate and simplifies the procedure. Ideally, the computer should be able to display cardiac output in liters per minute, the patient's body temperature, or the injectate temperature in degrees Celsius.

The computer should have a test cycle so that the accuracy of the instrument can be verified before the procedure is begun on the patient. Alarms may indicate a low battery, faulty catheter, broken interfacing cable, or incorrect injectate temperature or volume.

The computer is corrected for the size of the catheter being used, the number of centimeters inserted, whether iced or room temperature injectate is used, and the warming of the injectate by the patient's body temperature (computation constant). Most companies provide a chart which simplifies computation.

Thermal curve   Usually a 5 mm/s recorder is utilized to record the thermal curve. The curve is very useful in determining the accuracy of the cardiac output measurements. Ordinarily, a series of four injections are done, with the first being discarded. If room temperature injectate is used, the bolus is injected into the proximal (CVP) port at 1-min intervals. For iced injectate, 1½-min intervals are used. Three measurements are made to allow for normal variations in the patient's heart rate and stroke volume (Fig. 42-21). If one cardiac output value is significantly different from the others, the cause may be determined by evaluation of the thermal curve. An inverse correlation exists between the area under the curve and the patient's cardiac output. In other words, the greater the area under the curve, the lower the cardiac output. Fluctuations in the baseline of the curve are the result of respiratory irregularities (Fig. 42-21).

Guidelines

1. Prior to measurement, the position of the catheter in the pulmonary artery should be determined to ensure that the thermistor is not lodged against a vessel wall. This can be done by inflating the balloon and determining exactly the volume required to convert the PA waveform into a PCW. If less than 75 percent of maximum balloon volume is required, the catheter is too far advanced in the pulmonary artery for correct cardiac output determination, although it may be satisfactory for routine monitoring of PA and PCW.

2. Prior to the first measurement, flush the CVP lumen with the same temperature and volume of injectate to be used. Wait 1 min if using room temperature and 1½ min before iced. The maximum injection volume for a 7 French catheter is 10 mL; for a 5 French, 5 mL.

3. Handle the syringes as little as possible so that the injectate temperature is not altered by your body temperature.

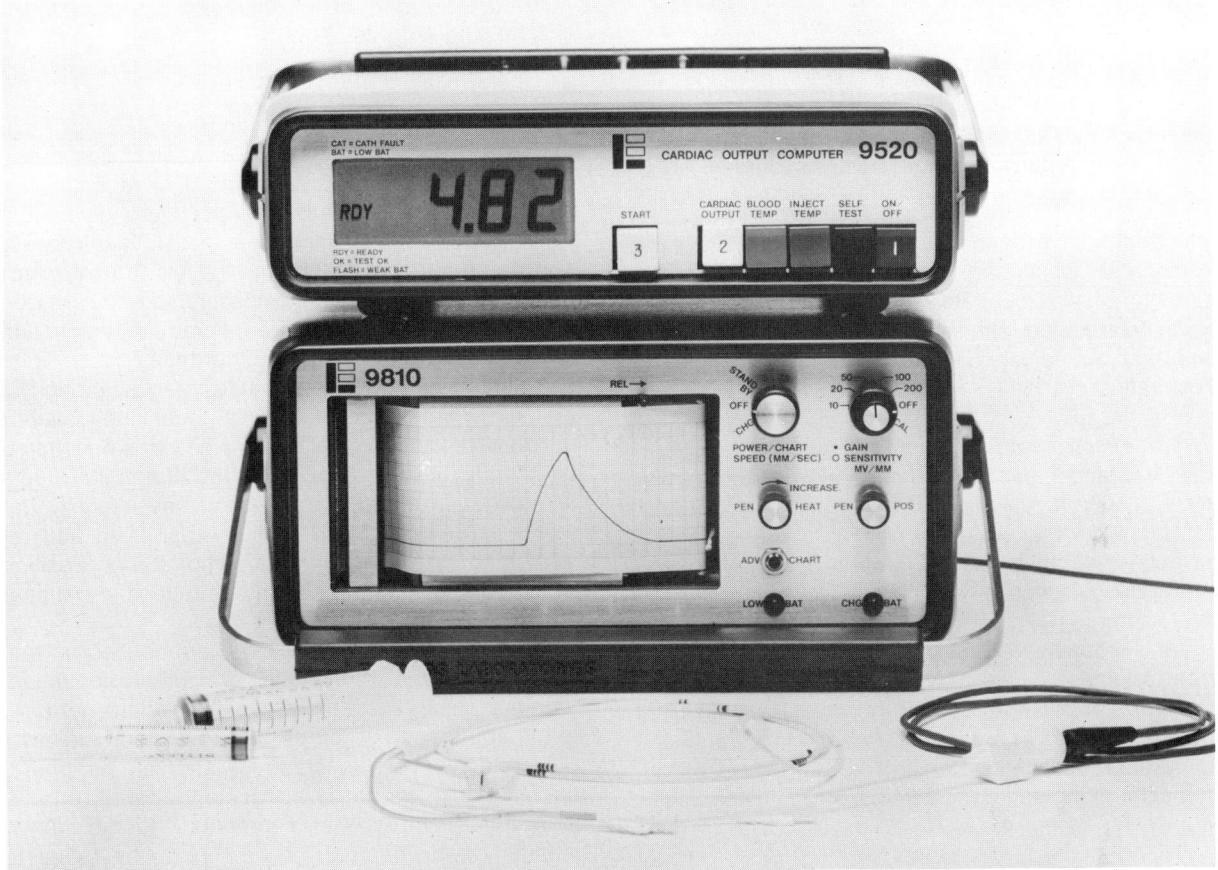

FIGURE 42-20

Cardiac output computer. (*Courtesy of Edwards Laboratories, Division of American Hospital Supply Corporation.*)

4. Make certain the volumes in the syringes are the same and inject as rapidly and smoothly as possible at the 1- or 1½-min intervals for a series of three measurements. Certain types of computers are injection-sensitive and may require the use of an automatic injector.

5. Low or erratic measurements may be due to lodging of the thermistor against a vessel wall or thrombus formation over the thermistor bead.

6. When possible, all IV solution should be reduced to keep open rates for 3 to 5 min prior to and during the cardiac output determinations.

Respiratory Volume

Respiratory rate Respiratory rate may be continuously monitored utilizing the principle of impedance pneumography. Two electrodes are placed on the patient's chest, approximately midaxillary at the level of maximal chest excursion. An ECG signal may also be obtained. A respiratory amplifier displays the respiratory rate, and a respiratory waveform may be displayed on a scope and/or recorder. Amplifiers are available which indicate periods of apnea as well as respiratory rate. Apnea monitors are particularly valuable for infants.

This type of respiratory monitoring is based upon the relationship between the tidal volume and thoracic electrical impedance. As the patient breathes, the changing volume of air in the lungs alters the thoracic impedance (resistance to the electrical signal through the thorax). Thoracic impedance increases during inhalation and decreases during exhalation.

Technique and location of electrode placement are very important. Many monitors indicate if the

FIGURE 42-21
Thermal curve trace (paper speed 5 mm/s).

electrodes have been adequately applied for respiratory rate monitoring. Frequently, when a patient goes on or off a respirator, the level of the electrodes must be changed. The sensitivity of the amplifier may need to be adjusted if the depth of the patient's respirations vary.

Wright respirometer   The Wright respirometer is a low-resistance, mechanical, hand spirometer. It consists of low inertia miniature air tubing responding to airflow in only one direction. The number of liters of gas which have passed through the respirometer between two successive readings is shown on a dial. It is useful in bedside measurements of the patient's tidal and minute volumes. It is also used to monitor tidal volumes delivered by respirators. It underreads low flows and overreads high flows (Hill, 1976). The respirometer may be attached directly to a tracheostomy tube via an adapter and is often used as an indicator of the patient's tolerance to ventilator weaning.

Capnograph

The capnograph is an instrument for determining Pa_{CO_2} with minimal discomfort to the patient. It is a carbon dioxide analyzer used on adults and infants to determine the volume percent CO_2 in expired gases. A range of 0 to 10 volume percent CO_2 can be measured. A pulmonary recorder may be attached.

The capnograph is utilized in detecting chronic hyperventilation, hypoventilation, and other similar ventilatory disorders. The instrument may be used during anesthesia and in the critical-care area for regulating respirators to control the patient's P_{CO_2}. This limits the frequency of arterial blood gas determinations. In the neurosurgical unit, P_{CO_2} measurements are made on patients with increased intracranial pressure (IICP). An increase in Pa_{CO_2} in such patients promotes cerebral vasodilation with further intracranial pressure increases.

The instrument operates on the principle of the absorption of infrared radiation by carbon dioxide. The radiation intensity is relative to the gas concentration. Therefore, the CO_2 content of alveolar gases

may be measured via the intensity decrease of the gas mixture (Fig. 42-22).

Oximeter

Oximetry provides a continuous noninvasive measurement of arterial oxygenation. Until recently, this technique has had limited clinical application because the equipment has been both difficult to use and often inaccurate. Recently developed oximeters appear to provide accurate measurements when used on patients with adequate peripheral circulation, and are less difficult to use than older types.

Continuous in vivo arterial oxygen saturation is obtained by transmitting light through the patient's ear via an earpiece. The pinna of the ear is penetrated by a light pulse passing from one fiberoptic bundle to another to a digital processor. The intensity detected is amplified and digitally displayed and recorded as arterial oxygen saturation (Sa_{O_2}). Position of the earpiece on the ear and variations in pigmentation do not affect the readings.

It is essential that the ear be arterialized so that adequate arterial circulation is available for measurement. This is done initially by rubbing the ear prior to the application of the probe. A perfusion indicator device is available to screen for adequate peripheral circulation. If the ear is adequately arterialized, the heated earpiece (probe) is applied. Arterialization is maintained by heating the ear under the probe to approximately 38 to 39°C.

Oximetry cannot be utilized on patients with peripheral vasoconstriction such as those in shock. It has been found to be a useful technique in determining ventilator adjustments and in ventilator weaning. Oxygenation information is available continuously and immediately. Optimum times for arterial blood gas sampling are indicated, and the frequency of sampling may be reduced. The onset and resolution of hypoxemic episodes can be detected, making it particularly valuable in treating the patient with changes in oxygenation such as chronic obstructive lung disease (Fig. 42-23).

Mass Spectrometer

These instruments are used for the continuous or intermittent monitoring of airway, tissue, and blood gases. In respiratory monitoring, gas is withdrawn from the airway by the instrument's vacuum system. Blood gas monitoring is done via the use of special catheters that have semipermeable membranes. These catheters permit dissolved gases in the plasma

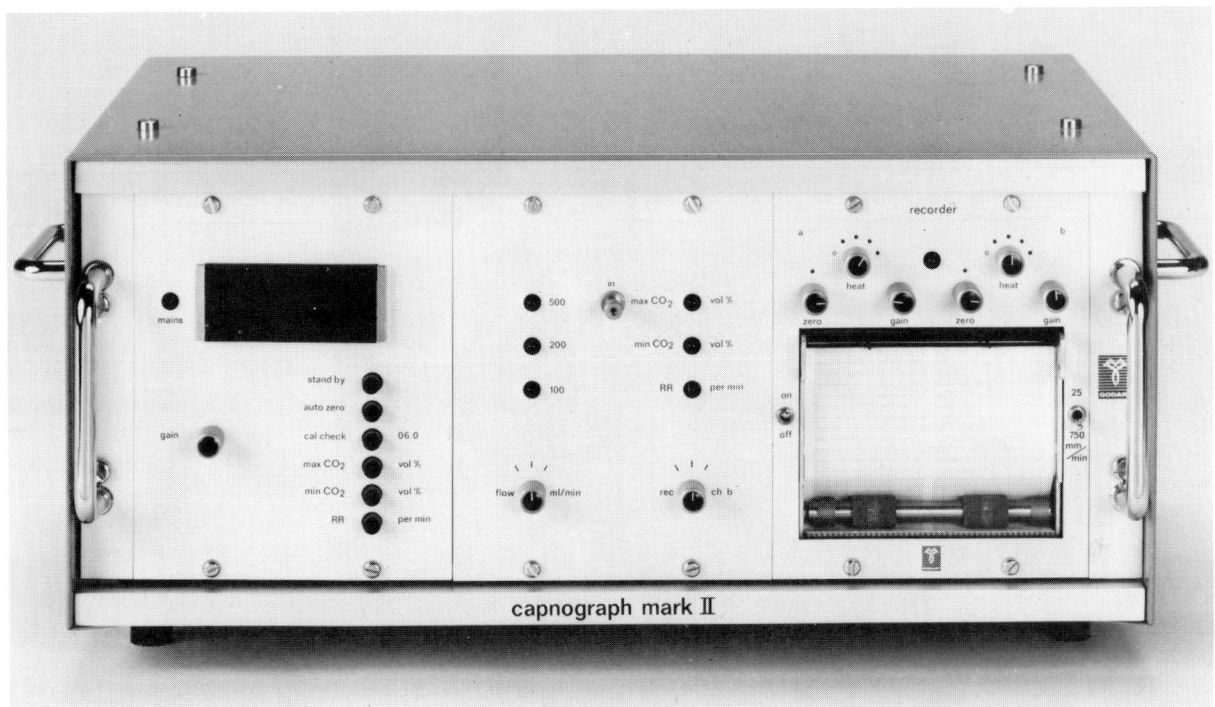

FIGURE 42-22
Capnograph, carbon dioxide analyzer.

to be withdrawn for analysis. Mass spectrometers have rapid response times, which make them suitable for breath by breath respiratory analysis. There are two types of mass spectrometers available. Magnetic mass spectrometers are capable of measuring multiple gases (up to eight); however, installation and/or modification to obtain different gases require internal alterations. The main advantage of the magnetic mass spectrometer is that it requires little operator intervention after the critical set-up. With Quadrapole mass spectrometers, the operator can tune the instrument to sample any gas or gases (up to eight) desired; however, this device requires significant operator intervention and is probably best-suited for use in a pulmonary lab rather than at a patient's bedside.

Respiratory Waveforms

A mechanical ventilator's airway pressure and volume measurement apparatus are, in most institutions, used to monitor respiratory function. The information yielded is mainly quantitative rather then qualitative. The acquisition and monitoring of qualitative parameters require the acquisition of respiratory waveforms.

Figure 42-24 shows the variables acquired by a computerized respiratory monitoring system developed by Dr. John Osborn.[7] From these four variables can be calculated the following parameters: respiration rate, tidal volume in, tidal volume out, minute volume, inspiratory/expiratory ratio, maximum inspiratory pressure, compliance, resistance, work of inspiration, fraction of inspired oxygen, fraction of expired oxygen, end-tidal CO_2, oxygen uptake, CO_2 production, and the respiratory quotient. Although this is an exceptional example, it serves to illustrate how much information can be obtained by having respiratory waveforms available. Several recently introduced volume ventilators generate airway pressure and flow signals internally. These are available for recording and computational purposes. The airway pressure signal shown in Fig. 42-25 can be used to calculate not only the positive end-expiratory pressure (PEEP) level but also system resistance and total chest compliance when the tidal volume is known. The availability of respiratory waveforms offers the

---

[7] J. J. Osborn, et al., Measurement and monitoring of acutely ill patients by digital computer, *Surgery* 64:1057, 1968.

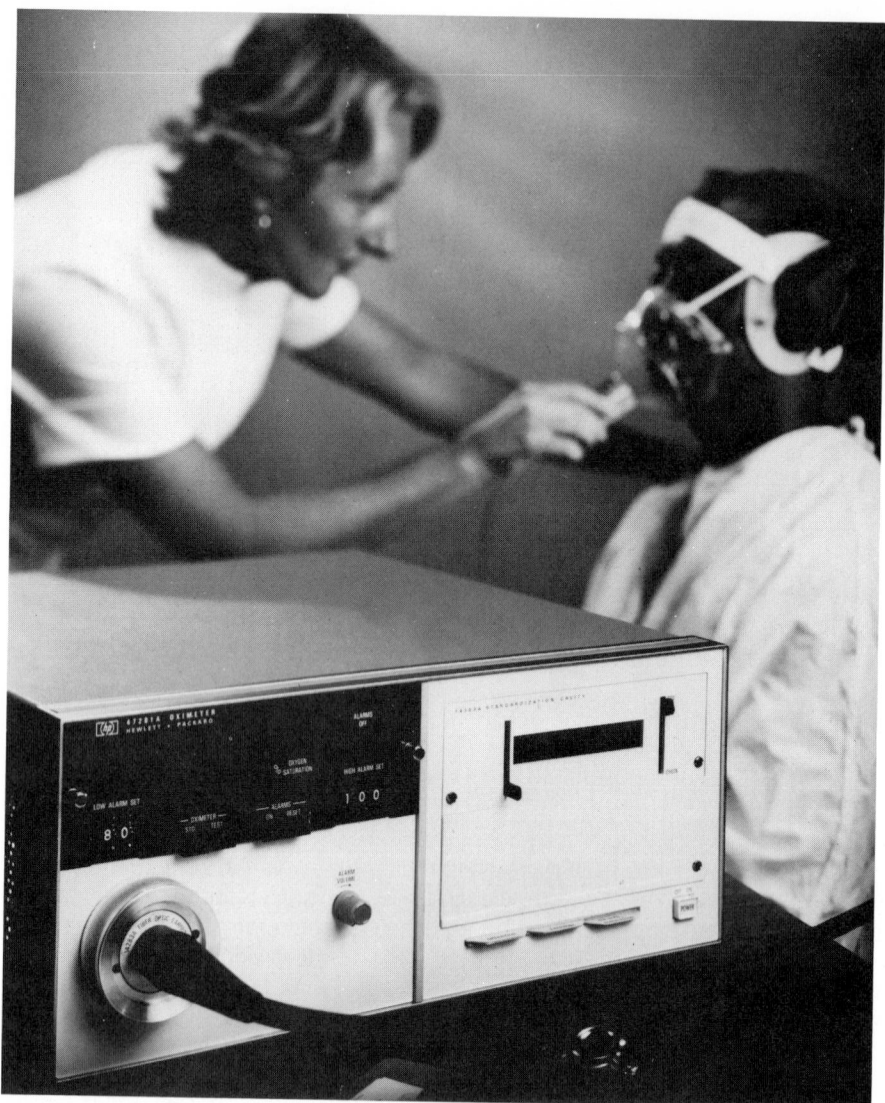

FIGURE 42-23
Oximeter. (*Courtesy of Hewlett-Packard.*)

additional advantage of providing the ability to more rapidly and accurately diagnose subtle ventilator malfunctions.

Cerebral Function Monitor

The cerebral function monitor (CFM) is a portable device which continuously monitors electrical activity of the brain. The electroencephalography (EEG) signal is filtered to minimize electrical interference. Two standard silver–silver chloride electrodes are attached to the scalp in the parietal areas with collodion. Disposable-needle EEG electrodes may also be used. A built-in slow-speed chart recorder (6 and 30 cm/h) documents cerebral activity via gradations in the density and width of the trace. A rise or fall of the tracing corresponds respectively to an increase or decrease of cerebral activity.

The monitor is useful when cerebral activity needs to be followed or insufficiency of cerebral blood flow

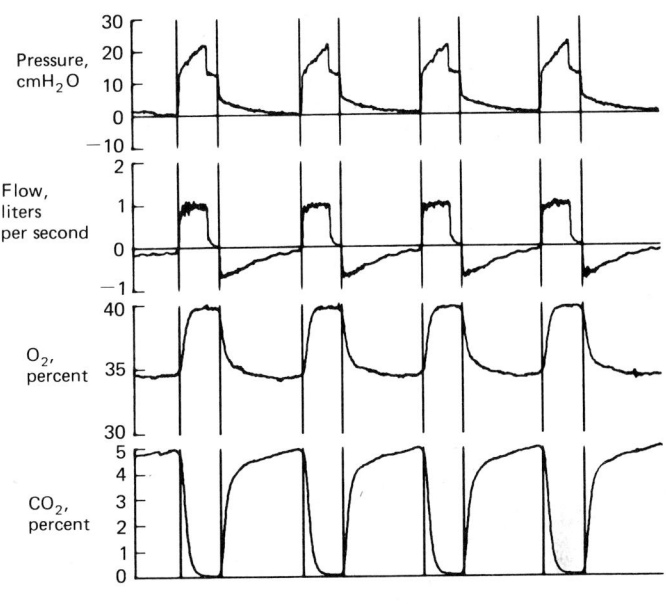

FIGURE 42-24

Computer acquired respiratory waveforms.

is suspected. The monitor is used in surgery to indicate acute changes in cortical activity. The reversal of cerebral depression, such as induced by hypothermia and hypotension, reduces the risk of neurological damage. In the critical-care area, the monitor has proved to be of value in monitoring the frequency and intensity of seizures, in aiding in the assessment of postcardiac arrest anoxic brain damage, and as an aid in guiding therapeutic intervention in the unconscious patient. It provides an indication of recovery from poisoning or drug overdose before clinical signs become evident.

The CFM is not designed to localize and diagnose anomalies of cerebral activity or document the absence of cerebral activity. This must be done by standard electroencephalography (EEG).

THERAPEUTIC INSTRUMENTATION

Defibrillators

After its development in 1962 by Dr. Bernard Lown, the direct current (dc) defibrillator rapidly became a fundamental necessity in the critical-care environment. Defibrillators, relative to most other medical instruments, are internally rather simple. They function by first charging a large capacitor to a high voltage. When triggered by the operator, or if synchronized by the ECG, the capacitor is discharged within a few milliseconds across the patient's chest. An inductor, in series with the capacitor, is used to damp the output waveform and thus eliminate a sharp current spike that would otherwise occur at the beginning of discharge.

In spite of their simplicity, defibrillators, like all other machines, are subject to failure. It is imperative that these instruments undergo frequent functional checks. There are three levels of testing that can be applied to defibrillators. All involve discharging the device into a simulated patient load (50 Ω) and obtaining some indication of its output. The simplest test uses a neon bulb to indicate that some threshold, commonly 75 to 100 W·s, has been met or exceeded. Although these test devices are built into many defibrillators, they provide only minimal information as to the unit's function. The second level requires the use of a calibrated defibrillator tester. This instrument has a readout that records the energy output of the defibrillator in watt-seconds or joules. The third level requires that the discharge voltage waveform be displayed for analysis. It is the only way to recognize certain faults, such as transient spikes, that may occur in an apparently functional unit. The last two tests are best done by qualified electronic personnel.

The preceding functional tests help ensure that the patients will be properly served. Visual inspection of the paddle insulators and cables for cracks and for

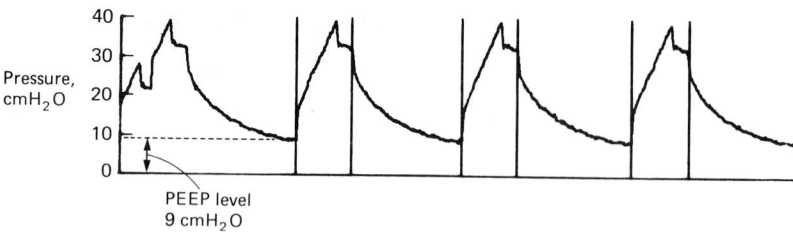

FIGURE 42-25
Airway pressure with PEEP.

fraying is equally necessary to protect the clinical staff.

Successful electroversion requires that sufficient electrical energy to depolarize a critical mass of myocardial cells be passed through the heart. This is a deceptively simple concept in patients with an intact chest. The principal factors that influence how much energy passes through the myocardium are the following:

1. The power stored in the defibrillator at the time of discharge
2. The location of the paddles
3. The size of the paddles
4. The electrical properties of the coupling paste
5. The pressure applied to the paddles

The last three factors determine what the paddles' impedance will be, and this influences how the stored charge will be transferred to the patient.

Current will follow the path of least resistance. To be sure that the heart is a major part of the current path, for anterior placement one paddle electrode should be placed over the cardiac apex, the other at the right upper sternal border. The optimal location for the second paddle, whether anterior or posterior, has not been conclusively determined. However, there does seem to be some advantage in using the large (12.8 cm diameter) posterior paddle because it presents a lower impedance. Despite the defibrillator's universal acceptance, there still remain certain unanswered questions pertaining to its optimal use. For example, we do not know how to calculate the optimal dose for a given patient or what the toxic dose will be for that patient. We do not know whether energy or peak current is clinically the most relevant way to measure dose. Energy is presently used, probably because it is technically easier and cheaper to measure. More research must be done before definitive answers to these questions are found.

External Pacemakers

External pacemakers contain circuitry for generating stimulating pulses at adjustable rates and for controlling their current or voltage intensity. The electrical pulses applied to the heart are generally in the range of 5 to 15 V, or up to 20 mA, and have a duration of 1.5 to 2.5 ms.

Pacemakers are connected by wires that are attached directly to the surface of the heart (surgically implanted) or by catheter electrodes that are introduced transvenously into the right ventricle. There are various types and manufacturers of external pacemakers. These instruments have a wide variety of special features. The most common feature is sensing, i.e., the ability to sense an R wave and inhibit the pacemaker output. Usually the R wave is sensed through the pacing wires or catheter so that no additional connections are required. Other features may include output rates to 800 pulses per minute, used for suppression of atrial arrhythmias, and dual outputs for sequential atrial and ventricular pacing.

It is incumbent on the clinical staff to become familiar with *all* the operating characteristics of pacemakers used on their patients. In the authors' experience, the manufacturers' support literature concerning the operation and clinical use of these instruments is excellent.

Infusion Pumps

There are generally two classes of infusion pumps available today. One class is categorized as volumetric, the other as rate controllers. The volumetric type, as the name implies, functions on the principle of direct volume displacement at a controlled rate. This class of pump is the most accurate, both in terms of volume infused and minimal variation in the rate of infusion. Because of their superior accuracy, it is recommended that volumetric pumps be used to infuse potent pharmacological agents such as sodium nitroprusside and all intravenous medications for infants and neonates. The rate controllers use drops as their measure of volume, and they control the drop rate by either pumping or restricting the flow of fluid to the patient.

The mechanical designs used to implement these classes of infusion pumps are as varied as the number of manufacturers. Choosing a particular make and model is sometimes difficult. The following guidelines may be useful:

1. Choose a pump that will handle a variety of infusion needs, i.e., hyperalimentation, IV medications, blood, etc.

2. Calculate the disposable cost. Since most volumetrics require the use of a disposable appliance, the cost of the pump over a period of time may be insignificant compared with the cost of the disposables.

3. Air emboli detectors are a must for these units.

4. Last and most important, obtain a trial before purchasing.

Due to the wide variety of configurations and features, the setup time and ease of use of these pumps vary.

RECORDING AND DISPLAY

Oscilloscopes

The introduction of the oscilloscope into the clinical environment was the keystone of the modern intensive-care unit (ICU)–critical-care unit (CCU) monitoring system. This device made it possible to continuously monitor a patient's electrocardiogram and thus to implement the basic principle of a CCU. The advantages of having a real-time display of physiologic information, in addition to the electrocardiogram, were soon recognized; techniques such as the measurement of pulmonary capillary wedge pressure and intra-aortic balloon pumping require that the pertinent intravascular pressure be visible in order to make a proper interpretation and/or adjustment.

The "heart" of all oscilloscopes is the cathode-ray tube (CRT). A simple CRT consists of (Fig. 42-26):

1. A glass tube or envelope

2. A screen face made of some appropriate phosphor

3. A cathode and anode (anode not shown in Fig. 42-26)

4. A pair of horizontal deflection plates

5. A pair of vertical deflection plates

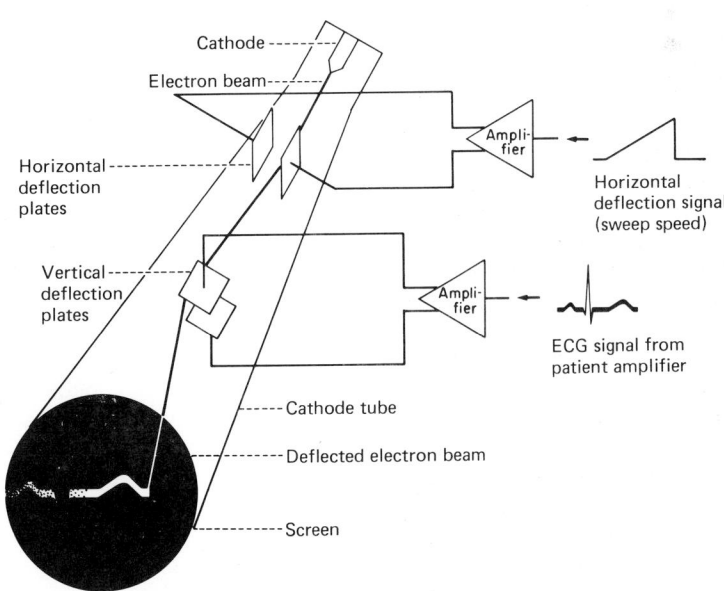

FIGURE 42-26
Cathode-ray tube (CRT) "scope" used for ECG monitoring.

The principle of operation is this. A very large voltage difference is created between the anode and the cathode. (The anode is located near, but not on, the face of the screen.) When the cathode is heated, it emits a stream of electrons in the direction of the anode, i.e., in the general direction of the screen, because of the shape and construction of the CRT. The electron beam emitted from the cathode passes through two sets of deflection plates. When a voltage is applied to these sets of plates, it causes the electron beam to deflect vertically and horizontally, thus striking the phosphor screen. The phosphor deposited on the inside face of the screen has a special property that causes it to emit visible light when excited by an electron beam.

Commercially manufactured oscilloscopes are available in a wide variety of configurations and have a multiplicity of features which include multiple channels, multiple sweep speeds, and a large variety of screen sizes. There are two different technologies used to generate the image, and thus the display, on the CRT. These warrant further discussion because it is important for the user to understand the advantages and disadvantages inherent in each. The two types are (1) the conventional oscilloscope, sometimes referred to as the "bouncing ball," and (2) the refreshed or "nonfade" display.

The conventional type of oscilloscope consists of a cathode-ray tube (CRT) and internal horizontal and vertical amplifiers (Fig. 42-26). The input signal to the horizontal amplifier is the sweep signal which governs how fast the trace will move across the screen. Often the user can select the sweep speed with an external control. Most of the oscilloscopes designed for medical use have sweep speeds calibrated in millimeters per second; for example, the selection of a 25 mm/s sweep will render an image which has the same horizontal proportion as a standard electrocardiogram. The signal to be displayed is applied to the vertical amplifier, thus causing the electron beam to deflect along the vertical axis in direct proportion to the instantaneous voltage change of the electrocardiogram or other input signal. This type of oscilloscope utilizes a high-persistence phosphor which continues to emit light for a short period of time after excitation. Visual result of this system's operation is the writing of a slowly fading trace on the screen.

The refreshed type medical oscilloscope utilizes an electronic memory to store the information displayed. This technique is termed *analogue-to-digital* (A/D) conversion. The digitally stored signal is continually replayed on the oscilloscope screen, the last sample stored being the first to be read out. If the memorized signal were to be replayed exactly as stored, it would appear as a series of dots closely approximating the shape of the original signal (Fig. 42-27). In order to give this reconstructed signal greater fidelity, it is reproduced as a continuous line which connects all the sample points. If the reader has found this explanation somewhat confusing, perhaps the following analogy may be helpful. Picture a clear tube into which a marble is being placed at the rate of one per second. Each marble has a number on it that represents the amplitude of the signal being monitored at the instant the marble is placed into the tube. When the tube is full, the addition of one marble will cause another one to fall out the other end. The tube represents the electronic memory, the marbles represent the digitized sample points. If we could, between each sample interval, plot the value of each marble on the vertical axis of a graph and space them evenly on the horizontal axis in proportion to the sample interval, we would have a graphic representation of the input signal that would be updated each second. Of course, the electronic circuitry is capable of working at much higher speeds, in fact it repeats this process 400 to 500 times per second.

The advantage of this somewhat complicated method of data display may now be appreciated. The trace on the oscilloscope screen does not fade but appears to move as if an ECG strip were being moved continuously behind the screen. Some instruments permit the user to "freeze" the display for further study, an obviously useful feature. The key point that must be remembered is that the displayed trace is a reconstruction from samples of the original, and that the fidelity of the reconstruction is dependent on the frequency with which the samples are taken.

For example, if an oscilloscope has a sample frequency of only 200 samples per second, the interval between samples would be 5 ms (0.005 s). Consider that an external pacemaker has a pulse width of approximately 2 ms (implanted pacemakers often have shorter pulse widths). The pacemaker pulse is of shorter duration than the sample interval and could occur between sample periods; thus if not sampled, it would appear to be absent on the oscilloscope display. A strip chart recorder that receives its input from the display scope memory can reproduce only what has appeared on the screen (Fig. 42-27).

Numeric Displays

There are a variety of ways to display numeric data at the bedside or central station. The two methods most commonly used in medical instrumentation are the analogue meter and the digital display. Each method offers some advantages and disadvantages. The analogue meter consists of an indicator needle mounted over a calibrated scale. Its major advantage is that an observer does not necessarily have to "read" it to obtain the desired information. For example, if we are monitoring a patient's heart rate on an analogue meter whose scale reads from 0 to 200, a quick glance tells us the needle is slightly to the left or below center and the impression is one of normal range. It is not necessary to know that the heart rate is 87 beats per minute to reach that conclusion. Because it is possible to obtain a quick qualitative impression from this device, it is best-suited for central station monitoring where the observer has to monitor data from several patients. The drawbacks of analogue meters are that they are subject to mechanical drift, electrostatic interference, and interpolation error, and they tend to lack fine resolution.

Digital displays offer optimal resolution without risk of interpolation error. In addition, they have excellent readability at moderate distances. They must be "read," however, before an impression can be gained. In the opinion of the author, they are less suitable for central station monitoring but offer a superior choice at the bedside.

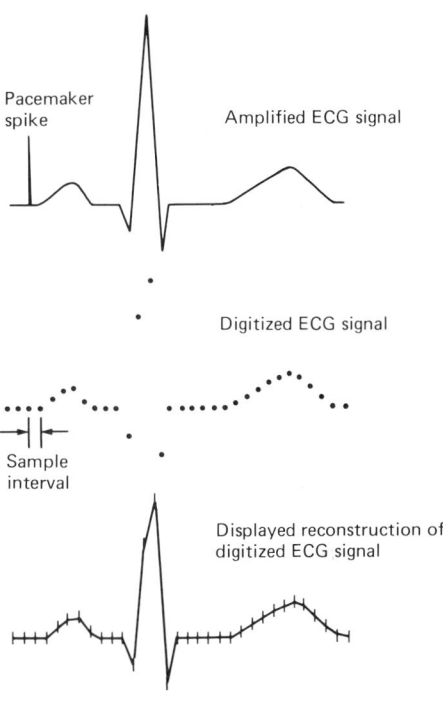

FIGURE 42-27

Graphic representation of signal processing for refreshed display "scopes" (see text for explanation).

Paper Recorders

There are four types of paper recorders made for use in the clinical environment:

1. Photo-optical
2. Ink jet
3. Ink
4. Hot stylus

Optical recorders "write" on special photosensitive paper with a moving light beam. The paper is then either wet- or dry-developed. Their advantages include very fast paper speed (some as high as 4000 mm/s), high-frequency responses (as high as 5000 Hz), and full-trace overlap. This type of recorder is most often used in cardiac catheterization laboratories.

Ink jet recorders write by magnetically deflecting a stream of special ink. They have a frequency response of approximately 800 Hz and partial-trace overlap capability. These recorders are very flexible and thus are useful for many clinical and research applications.

Ink recorders utilize a hollow stylus to deposit ink on the moving paper. Their frequency response is approximately 100 Hz, with maximum paper speeds of approximately 200 mm/s. Some ink recorders, using a special paper, write dry, a useful feature in the patient-care environment. An advantage of ink over heated stylus recorders is that the trace thickness remains uniform regardless of paper speed or stylus motion.

Hot stylus recorders are the oldest and are most commonly used in the patient-care environment. They write with a heated edge on the end of a stylus. This heated edge melts the white coating on the paper, exposing the black underlayer. Newer chemically heat-sensitive papers are available for these machines. The advantage of this paper is that it can be handled and folded without smudging. The paper speed and frequency response of the heated stylus recorders are about the same as ink recorders.

Since recorder tracings are often used to make diagnoses, it is important that they undergo routine testing and calibration by qualified electronics personnel on a scheduled basis. Gain and paper speed errors may lead to false clinical impressions. For example, an ECG trace from a recorder with irregular paper speed may give the impression that an arrhythmia is present.

The commonly used paper speeds in the clinical environment are the following:

1. 0.1 to 1 mm/s for intracranial pressure

2. 5 mm/s for cardiac output recording

3. 25 mm/s for ECG and pressure

4. 50 mm/s for pediatric or adult tachycardia

GLOSSARY

Amplifier   An electronic device which increases the gain (size) of the signal being received, such as blood pressure or ECG.

Analog   A readout of a parameter, such as blood pressure, on a meter as distinguished from a scope or digital readout.

Balancing   Term used to indicate a zero output from a Wheatstone bridge, for example balancing a transducer to read zero at room air.

Bridge   Abbreviation of Wheatstone bridge. An electrical circuit useful in measuring small changes in resistance; for example, the sensitive electrical circuit of a transducer which can be broken by overpressurizing the diaphragm of the transducer.

Calibration   Checking output against a known value.

Cannula, Arterial   A length of Teflon or polyethylene tubing, usually $2\frac{1}{2}$ to 6 in long and 16- or 18-gauge, which is placed in the patient's artery (radial, brachial, femoral) for the purpose of monitoring pressure and/or obtaining blood samples.

Capacitance   That property which permits the storage of electrically separated charges when potential differences exist between conductors. It is measured in farads.

Capacitor   A device that stores electric energy as a result of its capacitance.

Cerebral Perfusion Pressure (CPP)   Mean arterial pressure minus mean intracranial pressure, usually measured in millimeters of mercury.

Current   The movement of electrons through a conductor. It is measured in amperes.

Damping or **Damped**   Distortion of the waveform; e.g., an arterial waveform without a dicrotic notch.

Dome   The disposable plastic (Lexan) or permanent epoxy reservoir that holds the fluid connecting the patient to the transducer.

Drift   A shift in the position of the zero baseline with time.

Frequency Response   The portion of the frequency spectrum which can be reproduced by a device within specified limits of amplitude error.

Gain   An increase in size (power) when a signal is transmitted through an amplifying device.

Gauge   Same as transducer.

Gradicule   Lines applied to the face of a scope to visually indicate levels of pressure waveform, usually in millimeters of mercury. Same as grid.

Hz   Abbreviation for "hertz," cycles per second.

Impedance   The total opposition (i.e., resistance and reactance) a circuit offers to the flow of alternating current. It is measured in ohms.

Inductance   The property which opposes any change in existing current. Inductance is present only when the current is changing.

Inductor   A conductor used for introducing inductance into an electric circuit.

Interpolate   The estimation of a value based between two known values.

Joule   The unit of work and energy in the MKSA system. It is equal to 1 W·s (watt-second).

Line (Arterial, PA, LAP, or Venous)   The system of a cannula in either the artery or vein which is fastened via stopcocks or by some other method to the transducer.

Linearity   Constant gain ratio between input and output through its specified range.

Manifold   A device which contains a series of stopcocks, often used for setting up two or more transducers.

Millisecond   One thousandth of a second.

Module   An individual component, such as an amplifier of a monitoring system; e.g., a blood pressure module.

Noise   An alteration of waveform and readout caused by electrical disturbance or mechanical vibration.

Ohm   The unit of resitance. One ohm is the value of resistance through which a potential difference of 1 V will maintain a current of 1 A.

Overpressurization   Application of pressure in excess of what the transducer is designed to tolerate; results in breaking of bridge of the transducer.

Parameter   Commonly used to mean variables measured; e.g., pulse, blood pressure, central venous pressure, temperature, pulmonary artery pressure, intracranial pressure.

Pulse Pressure   Systolic pressure minus diastolic pressure.

Resistance   The opposition which a material offers to current. It is measured in ohms.

Sensitivity   The function is the same as gain.

Servo   A device that delivers power to move a controller.

Thermistor   A solid-state semiconducting device, the electrical resistance of which varies with temperature; e.g., the thermistor bead in a cardiac output catheter.

Voltage   The force which causes current to flow through an electrical conductor. It is measured in volts.

Watt   Unit of electrical power required to do work. It is the power expended when 1 A of direct current flows through a resistance 0f 1 Ω.

Watt-second   The amount of energy corresponding to 1 W acting for 1 s. It is equal to 1 J.

Zeroing   Same as balancing.

REFERENCES

Badger, A. S., trans: *Cardiovasc Res Center Bull* 5:57–74, 1967.

Cromwell, L., M. Arditti, F. J. Weibell, E. A. Pfeiffer, B. Steele, and J. Labok: *Medical Instrumentation for Health Care,* Englewood Cliffs, N.J.: Prentice-Hall, 1976.

Geddes, L. A.: *The Direct and Indirect Measurement of Blood Pressure,* Chicago: Year Book, 1970.

Hill, D. W., and A. M. Dolan: *Intensive Care Instrumentation,* New York: Grune & Stratton, 1976.

Hudak, C. M., T. Lohr, and B. M. Gallo: *Critical Care Nursing,* 2d ed., Philadelphia: Lippincott, 1977.

INTRODUCTION

The words *critical-care environment* will bring many mental images to mind. What is the critical-care environment? For many it is the large, open surgical critical-care unit with monitors buzzing, ventilators flowing, lights flashing, people shouting, and patients unconscious, tied to many lines, and connected to all varieties of devices. To others, the critical-care environment is the private, quiet area of the coronary care unit. Here the patient is connected to some equipment, but there is a hushed tone to both the technology and the physical environment. Between these two mental images are the many other critical-care units such as the emergency room, recovery room, medical intensive care, and so on, which are combinations of the hushed and highly stimulating extremes found in critical care.

How does the critical-care environment affect patients, families, and personnel? Are there any rules which should define the dimensions, shape, and design of the critical-care environment? What are the hazards associated with the critical-care environment? Are there any guidelines for nursing staff on how to work safely and effectively within the critical-care environment? This chapter will attempt to provide the reader with an appreciation for and at least some preliminary answers to the questions raised above.

The critical-care environment is a complex area where new technology and techniques of patient care abound. Innovation is the rule rather than the exception. Application of electronics and physics to enhancing techniques of patient care have led to improved capabilities of diagnosis and therapy. Along with these benefits have come hazards associated with equipment and the critical-care environment itself.

A hazard is a possible source of danger. It may threaten or involve a patient, nurse, or any other member of the health care team. For a device, support system, or procedure to be labeled hazardous, no actual injury need occur. Even a reasonable probability of injury justifies the label "hazardous."

Nurses and other health professionals frequently participate in developing a hazardous patient care environment by their attitude of acceptance and enthusiasm for all that is "new technology." The lack of critical acceptance of new devices and support systems (e.g., isolated power) contributes to the problems associated with managing patients in a critical-care environment. Institutions frequently buy medical devices or build in specified "necessary" support sys-

43

THE CRITICAL-CARE ENVIRONMENT: SAFETY [1]

Elizabeth A. Trought

INTRODUCTION

ELECTRICAL SAFETY

COMMON SAFETY ISSUES

NOSOCOMIAL INFECTION

PSYCHOLOGICAL HAZARDS
Psychological Responses
Causes
Nursing Interventions

SUMMARY

REFERENCES

[1] Many of the concepts expressed and the examples cited in this chapter were developed and acquired by the author while she was a staff member of the Emergency Care Research Institute, Pennsylvania. The author gratefully acknowledges the assistance and direction of Drs. Joel J. Noble and Herbert Patrick during that time.

tems to critical-care units on the advice of health professionals. Nurses involved in these decisions frequently are speaking not from knowledge, but on the basis of brochures read or a sales representative's statements about safety and performance. Careful medical evaluation and clinical analysis of safety and performance should not be replaced by enthusiasm for new technology. Qualified engineering advice should be sought in environmental design and device selection, either through in-house experts or special consultants. The first step in providing a safe critical-care environment is adequate design and critical purchase of safe and effective technology.

Hazards may be inadvertently designed into health technology or may develop after installation and use. This implies a responsibility to the purchaser to incorporate safety checks prior to use and to evaluate equipment periodically thereafter. Institutions which have designed such safety programs have frequently found support systems and medical devices that simply do not operate according to their specifications upon delivery. They have also found that their ability to pick up problems by periodic checks has prevented some hazardous situations. It is obvious that an institution which is going to offer critical-care services to any group of patients must have not only trained health professionals and quality technology but also adequate engineering service.

Generally, in discussing the critical-care environment two major areas of concern arise. The first concerns the physical well-being of patients and staff. Usually the hazards cited revolve around issues of technology (electrical and mechanical safety) and nosocomial infection. These hazards will be explored in an effort to provide background information and some basic methods of preventing and safely handling these problems.

The second major area of concern focuses on the emotional or psychological well-being of patients and staff. This area will be explored in a later section of the chapter.

ELECTRICAL SAFETY

In considering the issue of electrical safety, it is necessary to first put it into perspective. Electrical hazards in hospitals have received a great deal of publicity in the last few years. The Food and Drug Administration has estimated that more than 1600 injuries and 100 deaths are caused by electrical equipment annually. Other hazards associated with the use of electronics are those of fire and explosion. Sparking and overheating of electrical equipment are

documented causes of hospital accidents. In critical-care units these events become particularly important since the frequent use of oxygen provides an environment which more readily supports fire. Some authorities think this number is exaggerated. Nevertheless, the possibility of electrical hazards must be acknowledged, and prevention of electric shock to both patients and staff must become a realistic goal for every health institution.

To attain the goal of prevention of electrical hazards it is necessary for the health care team at the bedside to participate in an active program of electrical safety. Nurses must understand some basic principles of electricity and acquire new habits of surveying the critical-care environment and handling equipment to participate responsibly in this program.

To understand electricity and how it works in the environment, it is necessary to master a new vocabulary. Many new texts and monographs are available which provide in-depth discussions of electricity for those who would like to pursue this interest. The following discussion reflects the belief that nurses need no more than a cursory knowledge of electricity to perform safely in a critical-care environment.

Electricity is simply a form of energy which has magnitude (force) and travels in a certain direction. Conceptually the world is made of atoms. Each atom consists of a central nucleus and rings of particles called *electrons*. The electrons in the rings farthest from the nucleus have the ability to move to the rings of an adjacent atom. The movement of electrons from atom to atom is the flow of electricity. The directed movement of electrons is electricity and is commonly called *electrical current* (see Fig. 43-1).

Voltage is the pressure needed to force electrons to move from atom to atom. Voltage is necessary for electrons to flow, and therefore, for electric current to flow. A *volt* is simply the unit of measurement for this pressure or electrical potential. Generally, voltage comes through power lines and in the United States is around 110 to 120 V, except for specially wired areas which receive 220 to 240 V to provide electric current for particular appliances such as stoves, air conditioners, x-ray equipment, and so on.

There is also a unit of measurement for how much current is flowing. An ampere (A) reflects the number of electrons passing a given point per second. The materials which carry electricity in homes and hospitals typically have an electrical current capacity of 15 A.

Different materials either enhance or restrict the flow of electrons or flow of electric current. An *ohm* is a unit of measurement which indicates a level of resistance to electrical flow. The factors which serve to influence the amount of resistance in any material are numerous but generally are thought of as (1) the individual components of the material and (2) the diameter of the material. Individual components of material allow their classification as either conductors or insulators. Conductors are materials which permit an easy flow of electricity. All metals are conductors, but some of the best are copper, silver, gold, aluminum, nickel, iron, and zinc. Copper wire is the most widely used conductor of electricity.

The diameter of a material also affects the flow of electricity. The thicker the diameter of a conductor the more current can flow; therefore, large-diameter conductors offer lower resistance than thin, small-diameter conductors.

Insulators are just the opposite of conductors. Insulators are highly resistant to the flow of electrons. That is, they do not allow an electric current to flow through them. Some examples of widely used insulators are rubber, mica, porcelain, glass, plastic, cotton, and ceramics.

A final unit of electrical measurement is the watt. A *watt* (W) is the unit of electrical power and reflects the rate at which energy is used. Different electric devices consume different amounts of power. For example, a small light bulb uses only 10 W of power, while an electric toaster uses approximately 1000 W. This is because more electrons are needed to heat the large heating elements in the toaster as compared to the small filament in a light bulb.

To harness the energy of electricity to perform work, the electric circuit is used. An electric circuit

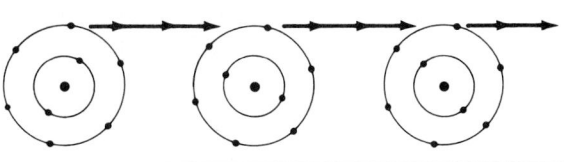

FIGURE 43-1

Electrical current. The arrows indicate the movement of electrons from atom to atom.

always has a certain configuration. It begins with a power source of electrons. A power source may be a battery which supplies electrons because of internal chemical reactions or an electric power generating station which supplies electrons by mechanical means.

The electric current flows on a lead wire (conductor) which is surrounded by a layer of insulation. The insulation restricts the flow of electrons to the conductor. The flow of electric current is initially from the power source, via the lead wire, to the device which uses electricity. From the device, the current then flows along a second wire, the return wire, back to the power source via a connection to physical ground. For any circuit to be complete, it must have all four components intact or no current will flow. Generally the lead wire of the circuit is called the *hot wire* and the return wire is called *neutral* (see Fig. 43-2).

Switches function to control current flow through the circuit. When an electric switch is off, the continuity of the circuit is broken so electric current cannot flow. When the electric switch is on, the continuity of all

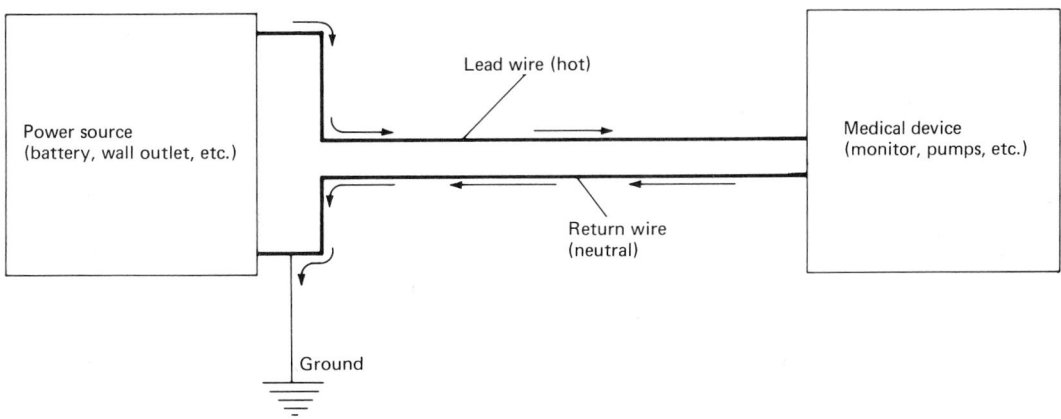

FIGURE 43-2

Electrical circuit. The arrows indicate the movement of electrons through the circuit.

four parts of the circuit is reestablished and the current can flow. Fuses and circuit breakers are only protective switches which will interrupt the continuity of the circuit if the electric current level becomes too high. The only difference between a fuse and a circuit breaker is that a fuse must be replaced to reestablish the circuit, whereas a circuit breaker needs only to be reset.

In summary, electricity can be channeled to do work whenever an electric circuit is intact. In a hospital all that is needed to generate most electric devices is an electrical system which has a lead wire (hot wire) connected to a power source and a return wire (neutral wire) connected to ground. A device is then attached to this electrical system by a plug which connects lead wires and return wires. When the device is switched on, the electric current will flow through the circuit causing the device to become operational.

However, for safety reasons, a third wire has been added to the electrical system in all patient-care areas and in many other areas of institutions as well. This third wire, or ground wire, is a conductive low-resistance connection to the physical ground. It connects to the metal frame or chassis of an electric device and provides a pathway for any stray current which might be on the chassis to return to ground safely.

In trying to understand how a grounding system provides a safer electrical environment, it is important to remember that the return wire (neutral wire) of any electric circuit is merely a means of returning the flowing electrons to the physical earth where they can be returned to a source. Therefore, anything which would function to allow the flow of electrons (electric current) back to the physical ground, when brought into contact with a lead wire, will complete a circuit. People standing on floors in buildings with metal frames which connect to the earth could allow such a flow when brought into contact with a source of electric current. This generally does not happen because electricity follows the path of least resistance, and the human body, though a conductor, is higher in resistance than the return wire. However, if the return wire is somehow broken or if current inadvertently comes into contact with metal not attached to the return wire (a fault), then it is possible for an individual to complete a circuit (see Fig. 43-3). The grounding system serves to prevent this accident from occurring by providing a backup low-resistance pathway for any current to follow which contacts the chassis of a device.

Electrical systems in critical-care environments must be designed not only to protect personnel and patients from the obvious hazards of becoming part of a circuit when a fault develops, but also to protect patients from small amounts of current called *leakage current*, or the loss of minute numbers of electrons into the metal frame or chassis of an electric device. These currents are typically small in comparison to the current which flows through a device in operation and usually present no hazard to a normal person. However these leakage currents are hazardous to patients who have direct connections, or current pathways, to the heart. Pacemakers, pulmonary artery lines, and so on, all effectively bypass the patient's skin and provide direct pathways to the heart. Patients

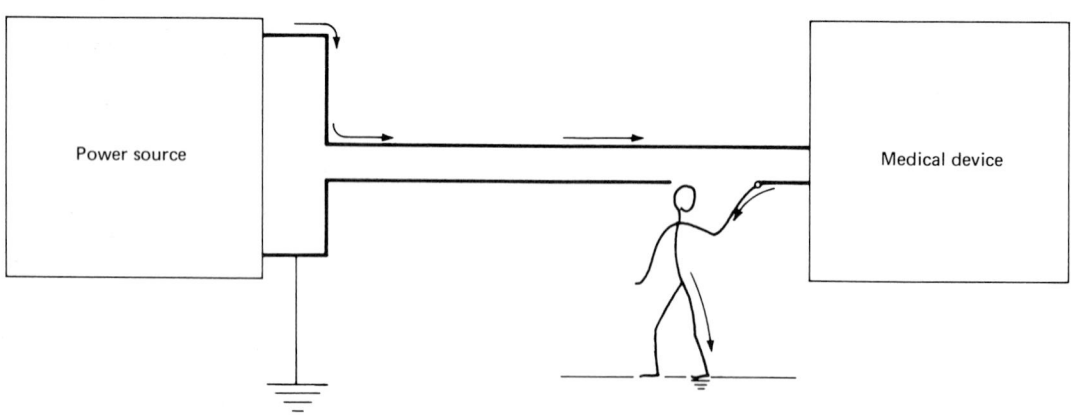

FIGURE 43-3

The stick figure represents a human who is completing a faulty circuit. This hazard can be prevented by properly grounding the electrical circuit.

with such devices in place are termed *electrically sensitive* or *electrically susceptible* because leakage currents, though very small, can disrupt the normal electrical function of the heart when introduced to the heart via a current pathway. The possibility of this occurrence is frequently termed *microshock hazard*. Most critical-care units today are designed to prevent this occurrence by providing effective means of grounding equipment so all leakage current bypasses patients. Also, special electrical isolation systems have been added to most monitoring systems and other devices which prevent patients from inadvertently becoming alternative ground pathways for electric currents if a ground system fails.

Nurses can greatly enhance safe patient care by following the three steps to electrical safety given in Table 43-1. The point of a grounding system most susceptible to damage is the plug and line cord of an electric device; therefore, they must be handled particularly carefully. A routine electrical safety program should be carried out by the hospital engineering department or consultant. This should include checking all new equipment for safety prior to use, outlets for proper wiring, and each electric device for intact grounding on a routine basis.

COMMON SAFETY ISSUES

The recognition of the electrical safety problem in critical-care units has led to a proliferation of information concerning that issue. This has frequently resulted in an overemphasis on the electrical safety problems in critical-care units and has caused practitioners to forget that all devices and support systems have other hazards inherent in their use. It is important to remember that the failure of a device or support system can be just as lethal as an electric shock and is perhaps more likely in a critical-care unit.

The examples of nonelectrical hazards associated with critical-care technology are not uncommon and represent almost every class of equipment used. It was not too many years ago that bag-mask resuscitators were available in critical-care units without nonrebreathing valves or standard 15-mm adaptors. Nurses, respiratory therapists, and physicians used this equipment, accepting without criticism design faults which essentially provided recycled CO_2 to patients rather than oxygen; precious minutes were wasted during crises while staff tried to identify and put into place various-sized adaptors.

Every critical-care nurse can cite examples of devices with manufacturing defects which have se-

---

TABLE 43-1
Three Steps to Electrical Safety

1. Handle equipment with care.

   Do not step on plugs or line cords.

   Do not remove a plug from an outlet by pulling on the line cord itself.

   Do not use any piece of equipment which has a damaged plug or line.
   Inspect all cords for cracked or frayed insulation. Always coil line cords properly to avoid kinks. Keep line cords out of traffic paths and away from sources of heat (radiators). Have the hospital engineering staff replace all damaged plugs and line cords.

2. Be alert to signs of trouble.

   Report all outlets which do not firmly hold a plug. A plug that is loose in an outlet indicates that the outlet must be replaced.

   Report all complaints of shock, even if a slight tingle is felt.
   Realize that a small amount of electric current through your body is not harmful, but may be sufficient to cause fibrillation if it flows through a patient's heart.

   Report anything suspicious immediately. Unplug equipment that is giving off smoke, sparks, or strange noises. Place a prominent warning sign on any faulty equipment that reads, "Do Not Use," and call the hospital engineering department immediately.

3. Follow electrical safety guidelines.

   Never use equipment with two-wire cords and plugs in the vicinity of a patient. Have the hospital engineering staff rewire all two-wire equipment with three-wire cords and plugs.

   Never use a "cheater" adaptor to connect a three-wire plug to a two-wire outlet. Have the hospital engineering staff replace all two-wire outlets with three-wire outlets.

   Never intentionally break off the third prong (ground) of a plug or use a plug with this prong broken off. Have the hospital engineering staff replace all damaged plugs.

   Never use two-wire extension cords to connect electrical equipment. Extension cords should be avoided, but if used, must have three wires and be as heavy duty as the line cord of the equipment.

riously endangered patients. The list of examples could be enormous; a few which should serve to illustrate this point are the following:

The pulmonary artery catheter with a defective balloon which no one discovered prior to insertion, therefore requiring repetition of a serious procedure.

The endotracheal tube whose balloon slips down during inflation, thus obstructing the patient's airway.

The intravenous infusion regulator which allowed excess volume to be flushed into a patient with tenuous cardiac function.

Gas systems are used in all critical-care units to drive ventilators, provide oxygen, and apply suction. There is nothing more frustrating and dangerous than the situation where an unconscious patient vomits and the wall suction is not functioning with high enough flow to remove the vomitus quickly.

Another example of a hazard associated with pneumatic systems is the inadequate functioning of a ventilator in providing respiratory support because of changing pressures in the gas system. The maintenance of gas systems is essential to effectively run supporting equipment. Critical-care nurses should be alert to malfunction of these systems which may directly compromise patients or indirectly cause other equipment to malfunction. Pneumatic systems should be routinely checked to be sure that the correct pressure and flows are in fact being maintained.

All devices have evolved to perform a specific function. A device may be hazardous if it does not perform its function adequately. For example, a defibrillator which delivers substantially less than the indicated voltage may be ineffective in converting ventricular fibrillation. This may directly contribute to the patient's death. A suction machine which does not function to adequately aspirate secretions because of inadequate airflow or other malfunctions may directly contribute to a patient's developing further physiological complications. This category of performance-related hazards has been the least explored in the literature but is perhaps the most dangerous and common in the critical-care environment. Have you ever had an infusion device which delivered powerful intravenous medications at erratic rates?

These examples serve to illustrate that critical-care nurses must be aware not only of the electrical safety issue but also of how equipment and support systems should operate and therefore how they may malfunction. Nurses do not have to understand the internal workings of all equipment, and they should not be required to provide engineering evaluations. How-

ever, it is a professional responsibility to understand the actions of the technology in use and the principles of how it functions, just as one would strive to understand the actions, methods of action, and adverse effects of any drug prescribed for a patient. Understanding increases the practitioner's sensitivity to possible problems so that they can be detected early, thus avoiding harm to patients and personnel.

Common sense is the most important factor in detecting malfunction. When a device is not functioning as anticipated and one has progressed through all the routine troubleshooting maneuvers, the device should be replaced with another which is functioning appropriately. When a support system, e.g., gas, humidity, or temperature, is suspected of not functioning adequately, it should be reported repetitively until measures are instituted to maintain its effectiveness or alternative arrangements are provided for the needed support.

Malfunctioning equipment or support systems should be referred to an engineering support department (e.g., medical electronics) for repair. It is impossible to maintain a safe critical-care environment without adequate engineering support which routinely checks equipment and support systems to determine their ability to function safely and is available for repairs when malfunctions occur.

NOSOCOMIAL INFECTION

A constant hazard to the critically ill patient is nosocomial infection. Infections acquired during a critical illness at least complicate the patient's recovery, and fairly often they contribute to or cause a patient's demise.

Patients cared for in a critical-care environment are most susceptible to pathogens for several reasons. First, their level of illness is associated with a lowering of their normal body defenses. Second, frequently prolonged care, with invasive devices and decreasing nutritional status, contributes to lowered resistance.

There are three possible sources of infection: autogenous, environmental, or cross infection. Frequently the single origin of an infection cannot be identified with certainty or the infection is found to have many sources. It is important to remember that many studies have shown that patients who become infected may do so from organisms found in their own intestinal and/or respiratory tracts (autogenous source).

Common nursing procedures can reduce the problem of autogenous sources of infection by reducing the numbers of organisms and/or preventing them from contaminating a susceptible site for pathogenic growth. Do you remember looking into a patient's mouth, endotracheal tube in place, and being overwhelmed by the odor and sight of oral hygiene (or lack of it)? Later the patient develops pneumonia, and not uncommonly, the source is the oral cavity. Frequent mouth care may have prevented that situation. Another common example which can be thought of here are patients touching invasive devices with hands that have not been cleansed after elimination. Patient hygiene is within the nurse's realm of responsibility and it should be attended to more seriously.

Environmental sources found within critical-care units are multiple. Generally the environmental sources which most support the growth of organisms are those which provide a warm, humid environment. Some examples of frequently encountered sources within the critical-care unit are sinks, ventilators, humidifiers, suction apparatus, tubes of lubricating jelly, and stock bottles of various solutions. It is obvious that the potential sources of infection in a critical-care unit are almost infinite.

Cross infection is another source of infection which occurs when an organism travels from one human source to another. Usually the source of the organism is another patient, with the transporter a nurse or other health professional; however, it is not unknown that an unsuspecting member of the staff may function as a source.

Various methods have been devised to protect patients in critical-care units from nosocomial infection. Some units have tried to protect the patient by refusing admission of any infected patients to the area. This is usually not successful for several reasons: (1) The patient may be admitted prior to detection of the infection and therefore be a source of contamination to other patients, (2) the noninfected patient may become infected while being cared for in the critical-care unit, and (3) patients with borderline sepsis are frequently found in critical-care units because of various political and/or administrative reasons. The reality exists that there may be no other nursing area that can provide the level of care the critically ill infected patient requires. Even if the infected patient could be eliminated from the critical-care environment, a poorly designed facility will frequently serve as a source of contamination to the patients in the critical-care unit.

Generally, infection can be controlled in the critical-care unit by the staff. The first rule should be absolute cleanliness within the unit. The physical environment should be designed to allow periodic cleaning with a liquid germicide. Sinks should be immediately available for personnel to frequently wash hands. Critical-care units should set up systems to monitor the obvious sources of infection. Most units have guidelines requiring respiratory equipment to be sterilized between patients' usage. They also may require bacteriologic testing of respiratory devices several times a week during use on an individual patient. All ventilator, oxygen, and suction tubing should be replaced daily.

Invasive devices and their attachments should be considered sources of infection. Many units change all IV tubings every 24 h, though a study done by the IV team at Duke University Hospital indicates that every 48 h may actually be preferred. Transducers and other devices directly attached to invasive systems should be sterilized on a scheduled basis. It is frequently useful for other common sources of infection within the environment, such as sinks, overflows, and water taps, to have routine bacteriologic monitoring.

The critical-care unit should be air conditioned and its temperature maintained at approximately 75°F, with a relative humidity of close to 50 percent. A slight positive pressure relative to the outside corridor should be maintained to prevent the infiltration of contaminating air. At least 12 air changes per hour are needed, and higher rates of ventilation will reduce the concentration of contaminates. The ventilation system should be independent of other areas of the hospital, preferably with no recirculation. Ideally, each room and cubicle in the critical-care unit should have an independent air inlet and exhaust, with the system balanced for equal pressure in bed areas and elsewhere in the unit.

Nurses can best protect patients from infections by washing their hands between patient contacts. Staffing should be maintained so that nurses may maintain a steady working pace which allows time for frequent hand washing. Remember, not only hands but frequently the tools used at the bedside (e.g., stethoscope) come in contact with a variety of patients, one of whom may be a source of infection. Equipment used on one patient should never be used on another without decontamination.

Programs of comprehensive infection surveillance should be developed in all critical-care units. Assistance in development of specific criteria is available through review of material published by the U.S. Department of Health, Education and Welfare, Public Health Service, Center for Disease Control. Consultation is available through the Center for Disease

Control in Atlanta, Georgia, to obtain answers to specific questions.

PSYCHOLOGICAL HAZARDS

It is apparent that the critical-care environment, which is designed for survival, may actually interfere with the survival or recovery of some patients and contribute to emotional disorders in many others.

A great deal has been written about the psychological effects of the critical-care environment. It has been generally acknowledged that the critical-care unit may in itself adversely affect coping, precipitating psychotic behaviors in patients. Concern is being expressed over the psychologic stress responses associated with these psychological effects. Although most of the psychologic effects appear to be reversible, there is mounting evidence to indicate that some patients may suffer long-term adverse psychological effects from their critical-care experience.

The critical-care environment is made up of the physical structure, devices, and people who come together for one aim—patient survival. It is ironic but true that this environment so designed for survival may actually interfere with the health care of some patients. The core of the problem appears to be that the environment is really designed to treat pathology, not people.

It is essential that the critical-care nurse recognize that the emotional and psychological care of critically ill patients cannot be separated from their physical care and/or the control of their environment. Emotional responses to the critical-care environment and/or treatment modalities, with their somatic expression, may prolong or disrupt the normal road to recovery.

Psychological Responses

Patients' psychological responses to the critical-care environment can generally be thought of as occurring on three levels. The behaviors associated with these responses have been studied and are generally referred to as being symptomatic of ICU syndrome.

The first level is identified by patients displaying minor affective problems while in the critical-care unit. It is generally thought to be due to normal coping and/or initial inadequate or maladaptive coping. Symptoms include those commonly associated with anxiety states such as increased irritability, loss of sense of time, restlessness, withdrawal, and so on. These behaviors, though at times somewhat disruptive to care and taxing on nursing staff, rarely appear to

seriously endanger patients and can usually be relieved fairly simply by methods to be discussed.

The second level, identified as acute brain syndrome, is generally thought to be due to maladaptive coping. At this level the patient can exhibit a broad spectrum of symptoms, all of which classify as psychotic behaviors, e.g., hallucinations, delusions, illusions, and so on. These behaviors frequently produce physiologic effects which, in unstable patients, can be quite life-threatening. The behaviors are also difficult to modify without removing the patient from the critical-care unit. This obviously engenders conflict and setting of priorities which often satisfy no one. Therefore the best method of treatment is prevention by not allowing progression beyond the first level.

The third level of psychological responses is the most complex and frustrating to identify and treat. This level includes long-term affective disorders which may be related to the intensity of the experience. This area has not been explored as frequently in research and literature as the first two levels, but may be seen as more serious in its impact as it so obviously relates to the quality of life the patient may survive to pursue.

Causes

What causes these psychological responses? The causes appear to be multivariate but primarily include the dynamics between the patient's own preexisting psychological/emotional profile and sensory disturbances caused by the environment of the critical-care unit.

Many authors have discussed the syndromes classed under environmental sensory disturbances. It is important to remember that most people receive stimuli through all five of their senses fairly routinely. These stimuli are processed in terms of both quantity and quality with final perceptions varying dramatically with individuals. There are three groups of sensory disturbances most commonly associated with the levels of psychological responses within the critical-care environment.

1. *Sensory deprivation* includes a decrease in the quantity and/or quality of stimuli. Social isolation may relate closely with this decrease in stimuli. In terms of patient care, this may be associated with situations such as those found in attempts to isolate infectious patients or patients deemed more susceptible to infection, or patients who are oxygen-deprived where reduced stimulation is thought necessary to prevent cardiac failure, etc. It should

be remembered that patterning of stimuli, the same levels and types of stimuli constantly being given over time without variance, may also be thought of as a sensory deprivation problem.

2. *Sensory overload* involves the increase in the quantity and frequently the quality of stimuli. Sensory overload often is related to sleep deprivation in a clinical area. Clinical environments which lend themselves to sensory overload are typically open units with high levels of noise and light and aggressive patient monitoring and management modes.

3. *Sensory distortion* usually is associated with the introduction of a patient with a preexisting psychosis into a strange or unfamiliar environment. Here the individual blocks or distorts stimuli thereby producing skewed perceptions. At times this skewing of perceptions may be caused by organic factors such as decreasing perfusion, high levels of sedation, etc.

Regardless of the cause of the sensory disturbance, the results are very similar. Depending on the amount of stimulus change and the individual's own psychological profile, symptoms will begin to appear usually progressing from level one (minor affective problems) to level two (acute brain syndrome) to level three (long-term affective disorders). Occasionally patients will progress from minor affective problems to long-term affective disorders without an acute episode.

Nursing Interventions

"The best defense is a good offense." This saying is particularly true in dealing with the problems associated with patients' psychological responses to a critical-care environment. Aggressive preventive interventions aimed at meeting the patient's needs should begin as early as possible in the patient's hospitalization. If possible, information should be provided prior to transfer to a critical-care unit regarding the physical layout of the unit, devices which will be seen and heard, what the devices will be used for, and procedures which might be encountered. When patient preparation is not possible prior to admission to a critical-care unit, it is imperative that the environment and procedures be explained while caring for the patient. Information is necessary for all individuals to appropriately control anxiety and interpret new sights and sounds accurately. Clear explanations, provided in a compassionate manner, go a long way in assisting the patient to orient to the new surroundings quickly and prevent distortions which can cause sensory disturbances at a later time.

Due to the anxiety surrounding an admission to a critical-care unit and the flood of new information and other stimuli with which a patient must cope, it is not surprising that frequent repetition of information is necessary to assure a clear patient understanding. This repetition also serves to provide an opportunity for reality testing which can assist the patient to maintain more natural ties with the environment. Nurses should develop the habit of explaining all procedures and devices which involve a patient and those which are observed from the patient's particular vantage point.

It is appropriate at this point to deal with the concept of the "unconscious" patient. It is now not really possible to determine true unconsciousness through bedside examination. It is inappropriate for nurses and other health professionals to assume that a bedside evaluation of "unresponsivenss" indicates that the patient cannot still receive stimuli from some, if not all, of the five senses. Many patients have recovered after experiences of unresponsiveness to tell of their ability to feel, hear, smell, taste, and at times see in an environment where the staff assumed this wasn't possible. All measures used to protect a responsive patient's psychological state should also be used when caring for those patients who are exhibiting an inability to respond.

The physical environment of a critical-care unit is often hard to control in terms of the stimuli it provides to patients. The use of technology requires devices which often add to the environmental pollution of a unit; however, some common sense can make a difference in the degree of stimuli the patient must bear. All patients need sleep, and careful organization of a nursing assignment will allow for rest periods where monitors can serve to provide assessment data. Reduction of noise and lights during rest periods will greatly enhance the patient's ability to take advantage of that organization.

Significant reductions in noise levels can occur in a critical-care setting by following some simple rules:

Avoid unnecessary conversation at or near the bedside of patients.

Place monitors so that amplifiers of audible signals are turned away from patients.

Turn ventilators so that the outflow valve faces away from the patient.

Turn off suction between uses.

If you have an opportunity to participate in the design of a new or renovated critical-care unit, consider these additional options as perhaps lowering the noise level:

Insulating the utility room

Using carpeting and draperies to absorb sound

Using private rooms

Using a conference room for discussions during "rounds"

When considering the other five senses needing protection, other common sense answers are available. Think of your own normal needs for a balance of sensory input and periodic rest periods. Try to attain a balanced environment for the patient. Consider each sense separately.

Visual—Protect eyes from glaring lights and dim lighting at night to reduce visual stimulation in a manner which matches most individuals' biorhythms. Windows make a major difference in assisting patients to maintain a somewhat normal day-night cycle.

Tactile—Reduce pain and itching whenever possible through judicious use of medications and other comfort measures. Use back rubs and turning and positioning to provide soothing tactile stimulation.

Olfactory—Control odors through good patient hygiene and prompt, repetitive cleaning of the patient's environment. Avoid the use of strong perfumes which sensitive patients may find offensive.

Gustatory—Provide oral hygiene. Early use of tube feedings may assist in providing a balance of stimuli to the gastrointestinal system when oral feedings must be avoided. When possible, sips of water and/or the use of lozenges can considerably improve the quality of the stimuli being received by a patient who is NPO.

In general, a humanistic approach will decrease the severity of patients' psychological responses. Empathetic communication skills can be used to balance the overall stimuli the patient is receiving and to provide support to the patient's attempts to cope with a very frightening environment. Ignoring the patient's sensitivities and concentrating only on the medical/nursing tasks to be accomplished can be very dehumanizing.

SUMMARY

The critical-care environment is complex and may provide more hazards to patients than initially rec-

ognized. Knowledge of the technology used within this setting provides a base for establishing methods of control which can substantially reduce the potential for adverse effects.

Regardless of the critical-care environment, a nurse functioning within some basic approaches will serve to protect the patient.

1. Be assured of a safe physical environment. If a routine preventive maintenance system does not exist, ask for one. Keep in contact with the engineering department or consultant and use them to assist in acquisition of new equipment and supplies.

2. Follow the three steps to electrical safety. (See Table 43-1.) Vigilance may prevent a needless accident.

3. Treat equipment with care. Know the manufacturers' recommended routines for cleaning and general maintenance of each device in the unit. Follow the guidelines carefully at regular intervals.

4. Be alert to defective equipment and supplies. Even manufacturers with excellent quality control systems make mistakes. Early detection of defects can save time and protect patients.

5. Create a humanistic environment of patient care within the unit. Initiate discussions with nurses and other health care professionals directed toward improving the perceptual experience of patients within the unit.

6. Remember a patient's need for a balance of stimuli for all five senses. Whenever possible, organize patient care in ways which provide opportunities for sleep and which assist patients in maintaining their sense of a day-night cycle.

The physical design of a critical-care unit influences the patient's ability to respond appropriately to treatment modalities. However, alert nursing care can compensate in many ways for almost all design defects and can serve as a mediator between the patient and the environment. The converse is not true. The ideal critical-care environment is yet to be designed and probably cannot be developed due to the varieties of patients and their needs which every unit must serve. Furthermore, it appears that no physical layout will ever be able to compensate for nursing care which dehumanizes the patient and the lack of attentive/preventive maintenance which protects both staff and patients from technology failure.

REFERENCES

Friedlander, G. D.: Electricity in hospitals—elimination of lethal hazards, *IEEE Spectrum* Sept. 1971.

Levenson, S. M., and H. Laufman: Infection hazard of surgical intensive care, in *Manual of Surgical Intensive Care,* Philadelphia: Saunders, 1977, p. 157–160.

Woods, N. F., and S. A. Falk: Noise stimuli in the acute care area, *Nursing Research* 23: 144–150, 1974.

PART 9

ISSUES IN CRITICAL-CARE

THE ROLE OF CONSENT
Marvin S. Fish

Nurses, physicians, coworkers, health care facilities, and patients and their families all have rights, privileges, and responsibilities to each other. Whoever violates the right or privilege of another may be held accountable, liable, or responsible. The number of possible situations is infinite, and space does not permit us to deal with more than a few. Thus, the reader is cautioned not to consider this chapter as all-inclusive. The issues presented herein should be the subject of further study, and an attorney who is licensed in the jurisdiction where a question arises should be consulted on specific matters.

Battery

The rights and privileges of patients may be found in several sources. Among them are statutes, constitutional provisions, regulations of administrative agencies, decisions of courts, and agreements between individuals. One such right is the freedom to refuse to be touched without consent. The intentional touching of another person without consent is considered to be a legal wrong and is called a *battery*. If such a right has been violated, the person who is touched may assert a claim for money damages. Unless the person who committed the act of touching has a valid defense, the result may be an award by a court in favor of the person who is touched. If consent is proved, there will be no liability or responsibility, and therefore no award will be granted by a court. This, however, should be clearly distinguished from any claim based upon negligence or malpractice in reference to the quality of the performance of the professional act. If the claim is that of an intentional touching without appropriate consent, neither the quality of the performance nor the beneficial nature of the outcome is relevant. The mere touching itself may be a wrongful act. It is within the exclusive domain of the court to weigh all the factors in light of the circumstances in each particular case in determining the amount of the financial award to be assessed against the wrongdoer. The law presumes that every one intends the natural and probable consequences of all voluntary actions. The issue in each litigated case is the nature, extent, and scope of the consent which would constitute a valid defense to the claim being asserted by the patient.

$$44$$

Issues in Critical Care: Contemporary Opinions

THE ROLE OF CONSENT
Battery
Express versus Implied Consent
Statutory Consent
Informed Consent
Consent Withdrawn or Refused
Responsibility
Special Problems

SOME MEDICAL, ETHICAL, AND LEGAL ISSUES
Introduction
Quality of Life versus Quantity of Life
Additional Issues

REFERENCES

SPIRITUAL CONCERNS OF THE CRITICALLY ILL
Illness Situations
Traumatic Situations

TWO QUESTIONS ABOUT SHARED RESPONSIBILITY
Is the Nurse Primarily Responsible to the Patient or to the Physician?
What Can Be Done When Doctors and Nurses Disagree?

REFERENCES

Express versus Implied Consent

Consent may be either expressed or implied. Expressed consent may be stated orally or in writing or may be the subject of specific terminology in certain enactments of the legislature in the form of statutes. Consent may be implied from the circumstances relating to the relationship between a nurse and a prospective or current patient. If the patient has been adequately informed, the voluntary submission of the patient would be sufficient to constitute implied consent even if never verbalized, and there would be no wrongful touching and no liability for a battery. As long as these factors are proved to the satisfaction of the court, it would be sufficient. *There is no sanctity to or requirement of a written document.* It may all be communicated orally or by actions or inactions alone. The only issue is whether or not sufficient data was adequately communicated to and received by the patient, as a result of which the patient voluntarily agreed to allow the prescribed treatment to be administered. This determination is based upon the testimony presented by witnesses under oath. If there is a question of credibility, it is resolved by the jury.

When a person signs his or her name to a piece of paper, it appears to have greater probative value than merely the oral statement of a witness or reliance upon implied circumstances. A patient who signs a form becomes subject, at trial, to questions concerning handwriting, date and place of signature, name and presence of witnesses, identification of the form to the court, and perhaps even the reading aloud of the words which appear above the signature. This is all very impressive and helpful to the physician, hospital, and nurse, but it does not dispose of the issue as to whether the patient did in fact consent. Assuming that some form of written consent is utilized, the objectives should be clarity of language and assurance of an understanding on the part of the patient of the scope of the risk which is voluntarily being assumed. The person who procures the consent of the patient must at all times attempt to project himself or herself into the position of the particular patient under the special circumstances then prevailing, and must attempt to prove with reasonable satisfaction that there has been a complete understanding and a total acquiescence without reservation. If there is any doubt or any reservation, it must be resolved. If not, then the contemplated procedure should be canceled.

The words used in a written consent form should accomplish the objectives of clarity and understanding on the part of the patient or the person representing the patient. The personal relationship established when the signature is procured should be used fully to assure the accomplishment of those objectives. Thereafter, in every situation, the person who explained the procedure and the form utilized, should in his or her own handwriting, in narrative form, explain, describe, and certify that this procedure was employed. That statement should conclude with a statement of opinion that those objectives were fulfilled. Many institutions use general consent forms at the time of admission. In many instances the particular purpose of admission is omitted or is rather vague. It is rare to find mention of any care plan, and details are traditionally sparse. In all such cases, if a problem should arise, the court will inquire as to the omitted detail and a complete explanation will be allowed. It would therefore be better for the procedure to tend more in the direction of specificity. The language used should be closer to common parlance at the level of the least common denominator. We must come as close as possible to an absolute assurance that the patient understands that to which the consent is being given and the nature of the inherent risks which were disclosed.

Statutory Consent

Every state has enacted a series of statutes dealing with the issue of consent. One such statute is commonly referred to as the *Good Samaritan law*. This deals with emergency situations and most often does not apply to the events which occur in a health facility. The immunity granted under such statutes is rather limited and should not be considered applicable to the problem being considered in this chapter. Nurses working in an emergency department may be called upon to participate in the taking of certain tests concerning a patient who is believed to be inebriated, the victim of a crime, the perpetrator of a crime, the operator of a motor vehicle, or in some other special category provided for by the law of the state where the hospital is located. There are many varieties of such statutes, and they deal with such subjects as narcotics, alleged rape, and the abused or neglected child or spouse. Each practitioner should inquire from the employer as to the specific provisions of the statute in effect. Those statutes should be understood and complied with since they afford a measure of protection to the nurse whether they take the form of implied consent or statutory privilege.

Informed Consent

When a court of law attempts to reach a decision in a particular case it may rely upon prior decisions or some of the other sources referred to earlier. One such source may be the Patient's Bill of Rights as set forth by the American Hospital Association in 1972. It is significant to note that the third right states that the information to be supplied

> should include but not necessarily be limited to the specific procedure and/or treatment, the medically significant risks involved, and the probable duration of incapacitation. Where medically significant alternatives for care or treatment exist, or when the patient requests information concerning medical alternatives, the patient has the right to such information. The patient also has the right to know the name of the person responsible for the procedures and/or treatment. . . .

This quote, however, is preceded by the opening words which state that "The patient has the right to receive *from his physician* [emphasis supplied] information necessary. . . ." It appears therefore that the American Hospital Association has taken the position that the obligation in this area is that of the physician. The problem arises when the physician does not fulfill that obligation and an aware patient raises a question which is presented to the nurse. Under those circumstances this should be brought to the immediate attention of the responsible physician and the nurse should be aware of the response. If the patient continues to appear to be dissatisfied or uncertain, this should be brought to the attention of the responsible physician. If there is no resolution of the problem at that stage, the matter should be brought to the attention of hospital administration.

Special situations have been dealt with by statute in various ways by each of the states. Consents to the treatment of pregnancy by an unwed minor, the giving of advice concerning birth control or abortion, and the general status of those who have not reached the statutory age of majority are all subjects of special legislation. When dealing with a patient all reasonable efforts should be made on the part of the nurse to determine the applicability of any such statute. If the statute is complied with it will afford protection to the nurse against the charge of battery. However, as stated before, this will in no way protect the nurse against a charge of negligence or malpractice if the quality of the performance on the part of the nurse is below the standard of care required under the law of the jurisdiction where the treatment is being rendered.

Consent Withdrawn or Refused

When dealing with a question of consent the nurse should be aware of the right of the patient to withdraw the consent any time before the procedure in question has begun or has been completed. In such event, when it comes to the attention of the nurse that consent has been withdrawn, this must be communicated to the responsible physician and others, exactly as in the case of a lack of understanding, as referred to earlier. If the situation is one of a refusal on the part of the patient to allow a prescribed treatment or procedure to be carried out, the nurse must recognize that this is also within the realm of the right of the patient. The refusal should not be disregarded, nor should the procedure or treatment be forced upon the patient, since this would constitute a battery. However, merely respecting the refusal is not sufficient, even if it has been communicated to the appropriate authority, as suggested above. The issue is then whether or not the patient understands the consequences of the refusal. It is also the responsibility of the physician to adequately inform the patient. The nurse's role is, once again, to be aware of the effectiveness of the communication and the response of the patient and to take such action as may be indicated and reasonably necessary in order to communicate that response, as in the case of withdrawal of consent or lack of informed consent.

Responsibility

When a nurse participates in the commission of a wrongdoing, the nurse is personally responsible. Although there are times when others, such as the physician or the hospital, may also be responsible, this will never absolve the nurse from individual responsibility to the patient. In such situations the nurse may be held accountable in a court of law, and an award may be entered against the nurse. This is true whenever the rights of a patient have been violated, even when the nurse is acting under the affirmative specific orders of a physician and even if there are others who are simultaneously participating in the commission of such a wrongdoing.

Each state has the right to enact its own legislation governing the practice of nursing, and has done so. This is pursuant to what is commonly referred to as the "police power" which is possessed by each state individually and encompasses the areas of health, safety, morals and general welfare. Such a statute should first define the area of activity or practice which is governed by the many regulatory provisions. Such a statute is referred to by courts for many purposes. One such purpose may be to determine the scope of activities which would be included, even if only implied, when a patient consents to any care to be rendered in a health care facility where nurses are employed. If a nurse acts outside the scope of such practice, a claim may be made by the patient that this was not part of the understanding or scope of consent. Therefore the nurse has committed the intentional wrongdoing called battery. If so, there is no question as to the quality of the nature of the services performed. The only question which would be presented to the court would be whether or not in fact the nurse acted intentionally in the particular situation. If the act was performed intentionally and was outside the scope of practice, the patient would be entitled to a verdict and ultimately a judgment for such amount of money damages as would be awarded by the court. This precise type of situation arose in the state of Washington and became the subject of a case which was decided by the supreme court of that state in 1966. In that case (*Barber v. Reinking*), a practical nurse gave an intramuscular injection to a 2-year-old boy as part of her activities as a doctor's office nurse. When the needle was inserted into the child's buttock, the boy suddenly moved and the needle broke off. The court determined that the giving of an inoculation by a practical nurse was contrary to law. Consequently, the court stated that this raised an inference that the nurse did not possess the required knowledge and skill to administer the inoculation in question. In that case the jury was permitted to consider such violation as evidence of negligence. It could very well have been contended, quite successfully, that the violation of the statute was also evidence of action beyond the scope of consent, and once again, liability could be imposed upon the nurse for the intentional wrongdoing called battery. This hazard can and should be reduced, if not totally eliminated, by a clear definition of the scope of practice of each individual practitioner. That definition and its various classifications and explanations should be the subject of administrative regulations promulgated by agencies which are given that authority by statute. This procedure has begun to be employed in over a dozen states, including Idaho and North Carolina. Unless and until that is clarified, nurses are exposed to the hazard of liability without an adequate source of defense.

If the condition of a patient is such that it requires immediate action from the standpoint of the safety and security of the patient, the court may consider it to be an "emergency." If so, the courts have universally considered an emergency to constitute a privilege to act, and in such situations the consent of the patient is not a prerequisite.

Special Problems

If a hospital uses a standard general form of consent when a patient is admitted and thereafter the patient becomes unconscious, can the nurse rely upon its continued validity? Unless there are some other extenuating circumstances presented to the nurse in the nature of communications from the patient or a representative of the patient, it can be assumed that whatever validity existed at the outset continues.

If a patient is awake, alert, coherent, not sedated, and well oriented and states that the written signed consent previously given is now withdrawn, what is the nurse's obligation? Although it is easy to reiterate the obligations of recording and reporting to the appropriate authorities, there is still an underlying problem. This deals with the evaluation of the competence of the patient to understand the consequences of the withdrawal of consent. The nurse is required to be aware of such a potential problem and respond to those indications of lack of competence which other reasonably prudent professional nurses would have recognized under the same or similar circumstances. The resolution of such a dilemma is a matter of professional opinion. If it cannot be agreed upon, it must be decided by a court of law after weighing the testimony of competing experts. If the assessment is that the patient is competent, the consent should be considered withdrawn. If that assessment is uncertain, the procedure should be deferred and the responsible physician should be notified.

Suppose a patient has consented to a particular treatment or procedure, and it becomes impossible for either the nurse or other personnel to carry it out. What is the nurse's role and responsibility? Although impossibility may be an excuse for nonperformance from a contractual standpoint, the patient is entitled to assume and expect that the treatment or procedure will be carried out. If in fact it becomes impossible, the patient should be notified and the appropriate explanation should be given by the appropriate party. The nature of the explanation and the identity of the person communicating these facts will depend upon the circumstances. It is the role and obligation of the nurse to be aware of the relationship between consent, expectation, impossibility, and impending failure to fulfill. The next step is one of evaluation of the condition and the importance of the delay or failure to the well-being of the patient, and then a determination must be made as to the course of action to be taken. Under those circumstances as long as the evaluation and choice are made reasonably in such fashion as other reasonably prudent competent professional nurses would have made under the same or similar circumstances, there would be no responsibility. Examples of situations in which this may occur deal with inadequate personnel, insufficient equipment, or competing demands for either.

If a physician is required to supervise a nurse under certain circumstances but withdraws before the task has been completed, what is the legal exposure for the nurse? If the requirement is implicitly a part of the terms of the consent of the patient, then the withdrawal of the physician fails to fulfill the necessary prerequisite. Under those circumstances the nurse is acting outside the restricted scope of consent and could be liable for a battery. If the requirement is the result of the state's definition of the practice of medicine, then the withdrawal of the physician may also place the nurse in jeopardy of violating that statute. By implication the scope of the patient's consent is likewise restricted, and the nurse who continues to act under those circumstances might once again be exposed to a claim of the intentional wrongdoing called battery.

State legislatures are beginning to consider statutes defining death, the right to die, the right to life, quality of life, living wills, and other related topics. As those statutes are enacted, one of the provisions will deal with the right of the patient to come to a voluntary decision as to an action to be taken or terminated. Those statutes are sources of authority. They should be read, understood, and complied with by nurses dealing with patients whose conditions relate to the subjects dealt with in those statutes. By complying with those statutes the nurse will achieve a measure of protection against responsibility for harm to a patient. In the absence of such statutory authority defining the scope and circumstances of consent, the nurse acts in a realm of uncertainty. The only certainty is that *a nurse cannot be protected merely because an order from someone else was being complied with.* If either in fact or as a matter of law, the rights of the patient are being violated, then all who participate in such violation will be held accountable. If the doctor orders a "no code" when not legally justified, the nurses who fail to resuscitate

may not rely on that order for protection. If restraints are not ordered but are indicated based on a nursing assessment, the failure to restrain may be a wrongdoing of omission. If so the nurse will be responsible for the patient's foreseeable injury. If the medication order is clearly erroneous, the nurse cannot find legal solace in the fact that it was someone else's order which was being fulfilled. If an unexpected change in the condition of a critically ill patient occurs, and crisis intervention is indicated the absence of a medical order would not justify abstinence. Nursing has independent status as well as individual responsibility.

SOME MEDICAL, ETHICAL, AND LEGAL ISSUES
Mark H. Elovitz*

Introduction

The teacher A. J. Heschel once remarked: "To know that a question is an answer in disguise is a minimum of wisdom." Anyone who is even tangentially involved with critical care is well advised to assimilate the foregoing type of thinking into their daily behavior patterns. My personal, perhaps unorthodox, thrust presupposes that it is the humanist's primary responsibility not to provide dogmatic answers but rather to identify and clarify issues in the biomedical revolution. Answers alone often beg inherent issues. Dogmatically unreflective "standard operating procedures" (SOP) may be less illuminating, less prescriptive, less definitive, less ethical and—in the final analysis— less philosophically and/or medically and legally acceptable than a series of aptly posed questions designed to elicit the broad spectrum of alternative choices for action in the critical-care encounter.

Let me be blunt: Antiseptic scientific rationality and sterilized procedural methodology may resolve a specific critical issue of fact. On the other hand, such an *SOP* approach may, with equal—and often frightening—regularity, tend to yield actions and behavior patterns that obfuscate real issues. SOP behavior may be humanistically offensive, medically questionable, and legally suggestive of the absence of ordinary prudence at best and, regrettably, potentially indicative of gross negligence and reckless disregard of realistic alternatives!

At this writing, the accumulation of biomedical

---

*For the references to this section of Chap. 44, see p. 1059 knowledge and critical-care technology is occurring at such an accelerated pace that it is improbable for any of the medical, legal, or ethical disciplines to assimilate and apply its expertise to the manifold challenges of the new technology. Nonetheless, even this observation leads us to certain postulates that need to be clearly stated at the outset:

1. An inherent problem of coping with the rapidity of current change is *the presumption that the future will resemble the past.* Such thinking is jaundiced at best. Critical care ought to be predicated on the notion that the past deserves a vote, but not a veto, over any future critical-care situation, or any situation for that matter.

2. Norman Cousins (1969) once observed that "people involved in a great crisis or upheaval seldom understand what is happening to them." This notion should operate as a continually disquieting reminder to critical-care personnel amidst their appointed rounds.

3. It is well for each individual in the critical-care process to totally internalize the implications and ramifications of C. S. Lewis's recognition that, "Each power won by man is a power over man as well." As such, the rapidity, awesome power, and inherent ethical and sociolegal challenges in the biomedical explosion pose a central question: While there may be many things that we can do, are there some that we should not do, particularly in the critical-care area?

4. Advances in medical technology do not per se establish criteria for their implementation or restrictions on their utilization. Technology itself cannot be a self-determining or a self-justifying factor in critical-care treatment. Shall a new device be utilized simply because a particular ICU might have one? Shall a new procedure be eschewed because it is experimental or has a high mortality rate or because the ICU staff has qualms with reference to its use? Shall patients be made unequivocally aware of the availability of high-risk and/or experimental techniques which the ICU opts not to employ?

5. In recognition of the *qualitative* life changes held out by the growing technology, is there a continuing obligation for all ICU people to subject their present assumptions concerning law, morality, ethics, and the nature of life itself to critical and remorseless examination and reevaluation? Is it imperative that no previously held assumption be deemed inviolate or sacrosanct simply because it *once* was basic? Is it not true that past and present critical-care assumptions and procedures continue to exist only as glib and potentially gratuitous guidelines to confront and cope with the biomedical and biopsychological revolutions caused by the new technology?

The situation now confronting our legal system may serve as a case in point. Law is not intrinsically good or evil, moral or immoral. Rather, law is a reflection of the mores of the society which proclaims any specific law. Yet, the pace of change may be so great that our basically conservative legal system and its presuppositions may have great difficulty in coping with an entirely new set of standards and an aberrantly altered set of societal facts and mores. Clearly the law and lawyers will no longer be able to rely on Robert Theobald's notion that "almost all of our study, our planning, our actions continue to be based on the assumption that the future will resemble the past." New laws, new morals, and new ethics are continually in the making. Law is not a monolithic system, and contrary to the belief of many, ethics and morals are not static or absolute; they vary with time, place, and situation. The reality of this position must be operative and functional in the critical-care situation.

Among the challenges posed by this essay is the basic question concerning the sanctity of human life which is so vaunted in the Western world. There seems to be little argument that the intrinsic sanctity of life and the unique preciousness of each individual underlies American thinking. It is, furthermore, highly significant that the principles of the dignity of the individual and its related concepts of individual liberty and equality have become central assumptions and values deeply imbedded in the fabric of American society. Granting the pervasive nature of these basic assumptions concerning the sanctity and dignity of human life, the ethicist operating in the critical-care situation must ultimately ask: How does one attain two highly respectable goals—namely, the expansion of medical knowledge and the protection of the dignity and security of the individual within the fabric of the law as it exists? Alternately stated, the biomedical-technological revolution implies a subtle assault on the core concepts of the sanctity of life, individual dignity and equality, and heretofore assumed human rights to life—to procreate normally and to die. Thus, the new technology poses numerous critical questions: What does it mean to create life? Is physiological life, i.e., biologic vitality and vegetative survival, sacrosanct? Must the law always take the position that human life must be held inviolate? Must the humanist always take the position that human life must never be violated? Under what circumstances is the technologist invited or, indeed, encouraged to violate the law and/or theological and so-called ethical positions based on a new technology awaiting implementation? Is it a false humility or subtle determinism that asks us to "leave things in God's hands"?

In short, the questions posed above touch the very nature, substance, worth, and purpose of the human being as a functioning member of society and operating within the confines of a particular legal system that is predicated on past precedent and past technology.

In the course of probing these questions, we would be well advised to also ponder the following: What is really human? What is, or ought to be, normatively human? Will the rights, obligations, and responsibilities of the so-called normal human being be identical to those of the "non-normal" human? Should the critical-care patient be treated in the same legal, theological, and ethical fashion as the non-critical-care patient? If not, why not, and who decides? Should legal standards continue to be identical for comatose and noncomatose ICU patients? What about distinctions between terminal and nonterminal ICU patients? This all leads to the question of what makes a human being? To be a person in the constitutional sense, must there be a minimum of cerebrocortical function? Need there be some levels of self-awareness, self-control, and/or memory? What are the human requirements for a sense of time and the future? Is there any requirement or necessity for a capacity for interpersonal relationship—or love? Can or should a minimum IQ ever be a determining factor? Since human beings are self-interpreting animals, can a comatose critical-care patient ever be dehumanized if that person is never able to interpret his or her own existence? Since Western civilization insists upon the sanctity of every human life, what is the relationship of the concept to the notion of the unique irreplaceability of each individual vis-à-vis the apparent necessity to "terminate" some human beings within the context of critical-care treatment? Based on the foregoing, the following critical-care issues present themselves.

Quality of Life versus Quantity of Life

Can a "dollar value" be placed on human life? If so, are some lives worth more than others? If so, what criteria determine how much each life is worth? Who determines the criteria? Who applies the criteria? Who explains the criteria to the patient and the family? Can the family reject the established criteria? How? What are their rights to "total" treatment regardless of who they are?

If some lives are worth more than others how much are they worth? Who decides? How does one become a certified appraiser of human worth? Is there to become a university graduate degree offered in "human worth appraisal"? Will the various states offer a license to practice as a CHA (certified human-worth appraiser or adjustor)? Is not the placement of dollar value on human lives inherent in the ICU procedure?

What are the implications of human worth appraisal for legal due process and equal protection? Is the suggestion of placing a "dollar value" on human life simply an exercise in sophistry or is it a medical, legal, theological and sociological probability that must be faced with objectivity, if not with equanimity? Does it make a great deal of difference whether a critical-care patient is relatively young and has a possibility of a lengthy and viable life or is relatively old with degenerative diseases? Is there a distinction to be drawn between the good life for an older person with little rehabilitation possibility versus the good life for a younger person with excellent rehabilitation possibilities? Why, how, and when is that distinction to be drawn? By whom?

In discussing the quality of life in relation to one's age, the following anecdote about Justice Oliver Wendell Holmes should be kept in mind. At the ripe old age of approximately 85, Justice Holmes was walking in a corridor of the Supreme Court. He paused as his eyes focused on an attractive, well-endowed young woman who was walking by. Justice Holmes, noting her shapely figure, nudged a nearby colleague and sighed, "Oh, to be 75 again!" Well, now, what about the quality of life of an 85-year-old versus that of an 18-year-old in the context of the critical-care situation? Assume both are comatose. Assume neither is comatose. Alternatively, assume that one is and one is not comatose. Assume there is only one machine available and that only one could survive by use of that machine; who gets it? Who makes the decision? What criteria are used? Assume both are brought into an emergency unit simultaneously, but there is only one team available; to whom does it lend its medical expertise? Why?

If it is determined that society cannot place a dollar value on human life, can a price be placed on human suffering? Is there a bona fide distinction to be made between human life and human suffering? What is it? Is there a distinction to be made between pain and suffering? Is such a distinction illuminating, or is it without value?

Does the critical-care team have an obligation to limit a patient's suffering while preserving a patient's right to pain? Is there a legal right to pain just as there is a Hippocratic duty to do no harm? Is there any legal obligation to suffer? Is pain ennobling, as is suggested by some theologians? Does pain help preserve one's identity? Under what circumstances should identity be preserved or denied? Is suffering dehumanizing? Does suffering vitiate one's identity and sterilize the patient as an identifiable personality? Should this be a concern to ICU personnel? Why?

Additional Issues

There are quite a number of additional critical-care issues that suggest themselves at this point, but space permits only a partial listing. Such issues include: optimal care classification systems; patient confidentiality within the sphere of the ICU; treatment decisions; patient management options; physician and nursing responsibility; experimentation; risk-benefit comparisons; consent procedures to discontinue treatment for terminal ICU patients; the problem of house staff rotations and the potential fragmentation of medical care within the context of the ICU as well as elsewhere in the medical facility; and the heretofore alluded to question of informed consent with the attendant problems of when, why, how, and where such consent is rendered or attained and by whom. To this we might add the general problem of the adoption of guidelines for admission to and discharge from the ICU as well as the problem of the utilization of the always-scarce resources within the ICU. With regard to the above, the reader is referred to the guidelines adopted in the *New England Journal of Medicine* in 1977. Those guidelines elicit the following questions: When should a patient be removed from a respirator? Should a patient on a respirator ever be removed from the ICU? Who should make these decisions? Why? If a patient is removed from the ICU and is presumed to be dying, what type of care is procedurally necessary, medically advised, and legally required? Should such care be rendered by ICU nurses, other staff nurses, physicians, or a combination thereof, and to what extent? Is not every dying person a *critical*-care patient in the true meaning of the term? Should critical care be limited to the ICU?

Perhaps a few case studies themselves will be illuminating for these concerns:

A premature baby (weighing approximately 1600 g) was born to young parents at a large, well-regarded metropolitan hospital. Five days after childbirth, the mother visited the baby for the first time in the neonatal ICU. The resident told the mother that the baby was in satisfactory condition. The mother had previously been quite upset and had been crying, but she

seemed to have quieted down after the reassurances from the resident as to the baby's satisfactory condition. Additional reassurances from the nursing staff helped further calm the mother. A few moments later, shortly after the parents had been peering through the ICU looking at the baby and talking to the nurses, the resident confirmed that the baby had developed pneumonia, obviously a serious complication for such a small infant. The resident was in a quandary as to whether to inform the parents regarding the probabilities implied by the pneumonia. The resident did not inform the parents!

The critical-care issues implicit herein present themselves as follows in the above situation: By not telling the parents, has the resident, in essence, lied to them, shirked responsibility, and allowed the parents to leave the ICU believing that the baby was doing well? What is the nurses' obligation to parents when they have knowledge of such a situation? Should the mother's potential emotional relapse affect the decision concerning whether or not the ICU should advise them as to the premature infant's newly developed dangerous condition? To what extent are the parents of a critically ill infant also critical-care patients? By failing to inform the parents as to the infant's condition, was the resident acting paternalistically, and if such was the case, was it justifiable behavior? Under what circumstances would this behavior be (a) ethically reprehensible, (b) medically unconscionable, (c) legally culpable, (d) ethically neutral, (e) ethically functional, (f) legally responsible, (g) ethically desirable, (h) medically necessary, or (i) legally excusable or justifiable?

A brief discussion of another actual case that occurred at a major hospital might also be suggestive of some ICU critical issues. A child was born to a Chinese father and a Puerto Rican mother. These parents had six children by the previous marriage of the father and three children by the previous marriage of the mother. The new infant is the first child born to this particular marriage. The cited infant was born with numerous problems, including a missing ear and thumb and an anatomical defect involving an obstructed digestive tract which suggested immediate corrective surgery. The staff considered the possibilities of chromosomal abnormalities and mental retardation. Tests were necessary to confirm the presence of the chromosomal defect. The immediate issue was whether or not to perform corrective surgery. A discussion between the surgeon and the father yielded a decision not to proceed with the surgery. The baby was kept alive as comfortably as possible. ICU personnel assumed the infant would expire shortly of pneumonia and its complications. It did.

An appropriate analysis of the above situation would yield the following alternative possibilities which might be acted upon to varying degrees:

1. Operate and discover the actual existence of a chromosomal problem

2. Operate and not discover any additional problems

3. Do not operate and still discover a chromosomal problem

4. Do not operate and not discover any chromosomal problem

In considering these alternatives, the following questions present themselves under option 1: Do competing interests exist (i.e., parent versus child, parent versus parent, parent versus medical opinion, medical opinion versus all of the foregoing)? How are such competing interests to be resolved? What are the values, benefits, and risks implicit in each of the foregoing possibilities? Does such a case admit to "rational decision"? If chromosomal defect is found under option 1, does the infant have the right to live as long as medically possible? Does it matter that the parents' desires play under option 1? What role or veto should the physician take under option 1? What role should the ICU nursing staff play in the decision? This same series of questions and analysis applies to each of the other suggested alternatives.

In addition to the foregoing possibilities, the above case raises additional issues. Should *both* the parents be consulted with reference to this child? In the case at hand, only the father was consulted by the surgeon and pediatric intern. They indicated that surgery was "not medically indicated." Still, the prognosis for corrective surgery was good. What issues are involved in this conflicting presentation to the parents versus medical indications? Does it make any difference if the physician and the father reach an identical conclusion, but on different grounds? Whose clear responsibility is it to consult with the parents in any critical-care situation? Does that person have the right to rely on the decision of only one of two parents in a given situation? Do both parents have a right either ethically, medically, or legally to a full and clear understanding of the medical situation so that they may make a completely informed decision?

The issues raised and the questions posed above strike at the heart of human existence as we know it, not only in the critical-care situation. In a sense, as Rene DuBos indicated: "We must not ask where science and technology are taking us, but rather how we can manage science and technology so that they can help us get where we want to go." (MacLeish, 1968). The direction in which we proceed both in the critical-care area and in the manifold issues raised therein, as well as in the external medical situation, will depend not only on our self-concepts, ethics, mores, and laws but also upon the question of whether we shall, at each particular instance, pose the proper questions at the proper time and in the proper context. The central issues for the critical-care nurse should be not only the basic *how* but also the equally important *why, when,* and *who*? If these questions are absent from the critical-care situation, then it is allowed to operate as a sterile technological monster whose tentacles embrace the *critical* without the requisite *care*!

REFERENCES

Cousins, Norman: Proposal to a foundation: An editorial, *Saturday Review,* 52:26, April 26, 1969.

Lewis, C. S.: *The Abolition of Man,* New York: Collier Books, MacMillan, 1956, p. 71.

MacLeish, Archibald: The great American frustration, *Saturday Review* 51:16, July 13, 1968.

Theobald, Robert: *Dialogue on Technology,* New York: Bobbs-Merrill, 1967, p. 9.

SPIRITUAL CONCERNS OF THE CRITICALLY ILL

Robert D. Wheelock

For the great majority of people, religion plays at least some role in their personal lives. The importance of a supreme being and/or a religious value system is vastly sharpened in the face of serious illness or a life-threatening trauma. At times of crises, when the temporal, mortal nature of a person is endangered, a common reaction is to turn to some supernatural or transcendent source of faith or hope or strength. Thus, regardless of the care giver's belief or lack of it, for patients who have a religious framework that is part of their life, religion becomes a possibly helpful adjunct to total patient treatment.

In this section the focus of interest will be on some of the more commonly seen crisis situations. We will discuss the emotional states surrounding these, and relate them to religious values or concerns that could be crucial in understanding the patient's attitude and needs.

We will look at two general lists of critical situations: (1) illness and (2) trauma. Under illness we will limit ourselves to coronary disease, cerebrovascular accidents, carcinoma, neuromuscular disease, and the phenomena of medical complications that occur following routine, usually uneventful procedures. The discussion of trauma will limit itself to violent accidents, physical attack upon one's person, sexual assault, burns, and finally, dismemberment—whether by trauma or surgical procedure.

The method we will use will be to look at the emotional state of the patient (and loved ones, as appropriate) and then explore what a religious value system might have to offer the therapy by way of explication of the feeling tone or by way of spiritual catharsis.

Illness Situations

Coronary Disease

Undoubtedly, the most common illness treated in critical-care nursing is coronary disease. Every day patients are admitted to coronary-care units. For some patients this is the first of numerous hospitalizations they will have for treatment of their disease. For others it may be a repeat admission. For all it is a shattering experience. Who has not heard of supposedly healthy persons suddenly stricken by a coronary attack only to expire within hours or, if they do survive, to become "coronary cripples" for the rest of their lives. Personal experience, news stories, and many dramatized medical situations on television shows all contribute to the quantity and quality of knowledge each patient has of what the layperson labels a "heart attack."

Concern for their immediate chances of survival is then the primary concern of patient and loved ones in the first hours following the episode. People with even rudimentary religious beliefs will soon also turn to religion for help. Mixed in with prayer for help may be a variety of religious attitudes. The patient may feel anger toward God for permitting this dreaded thing to happen to one who had observed divine laws, lived a good life, etc. For those who may have been more casual in their practice of religion, there is often an attitude of bargaining: "Okay, God, I get your message—just let me live and I'll do better." Yet another group of patients will for some reason feel that God is punishing them for what they perceive as their many sins. There are many other attitudes people will have, but anger, bargaining, and guilt are the most common.

It is obvious that if some coronary patients feel they are in a confrontation with the Almighty, it can affect their attitudes toward those treating them and their medication and may even affect their willingness to help in their own healing process. If a patient expresses any of the above attitudes, it would be entirely appropriate for the attending nurse to probe a bit. Ask why the patient feels that God is responsible. How does the patient conceive of God? As primarily loving? Or as all-just and consequently punishing? Ask the patient to describe a "good life" vis-à-vis living well spiritually. Who does the patient most admire in life? Who would the patient like to be? This line of questioning, if it does not tire or disturb the patient, can be a healthy venting of feelings, forgotten ideals, elusive dreams.

Least helpful to patients expressing feelings of anger or guilt is the too-rapid assurance that they are really good persons or that God does not inflict suffering on people. This simply forces such patients to turn inward with unresolved and very raw feelings.

If the patient agrees to it, the nurse might wish to suggest a referral to the hospital chaplain or the patient's own pastor, if the latter seems to be respected by the patient. If the nurse is comfortable in doing so, he or she may offer to pray with the patient or share a favorite reading from the Bible or some other religious book, or just spend a quiet moment holding the patient's hand.

Roman Catholic, Episcopal, and some other Christian denominations have spiritual sacraments or prayer services especially for the sick. These may be sensitively suggested to the patient as part of the ordinary religious ministration for all patients of their faith in the unit. This suggestion need not be anxiety-provoking, if the staff in the unit understand that these are *not* "last rites" but rather powerful prayers for healing and present them in that manner to the patient.

Carcinoma

Cancer is another disease that presents crises in nursing care. The cancer patient will often have the same feelings as the coronary patient; however, the situation can be compounded by feelings of uncleanness and rejection and a profound feeling of injustice.[1] Even intelligent people still fear "catching" cancer from touching a cancer patient. This is a disease that, for many, has aspects of the biblical leprosy. This only adds to the patient's feeling of hopelessness, which is then further compounded by an experience of loneliness when even loved ones fail to kiss or caress them or even to shake their hand.

Many cancer patients feel that they did not have a fighting chance with cancer. Perhaps they were diagnosed during a routine examination, never felt any pain, had no symptoms, and sometimes did not feel ill after the diagnosis. If they turn these feelings toward the person of God, they will sometimes want to strike back at the god they feel so unfairly allowed this hideous disease to sneak into them. When this is the case, they may be hostile toward religion, the mention of prayer, or a visit by a priest, minister, rabbi, or other religious persons.

Patience is important at this time. If the patient vents to the nurse, this can usually help. Eventually, the idea that God is not responsible for the disease should be brought up. A member of the clergy who is able to take a good deal of verbal abuse and vocalized anger toward God is the only acceptable pastoral person to work with this kind of patient. These patients are often seen in a critical stage after hemorrhaging or radical surgery. At these times they are weakened physically and spiritually. A nursing staff that understands these frustrations, anger, and sense of betrayal can be the best help to them. If a referral to the chaplain or pastor is deemed advisable, a team approach of both clergy and nursing personnel counseling together will usually produce the best results.[2]

Cerebrovascular Accidents and Neuromuscular Diseases

Patients who have suffered cerebrovascular accidents and those diagnosed as having progressive neuromuscular disease suffer some of the same experiences. Both situations often present problems of vastly altered concepts of one's bodily integrity. Suddenly they perceive themselves as only partially a person. The frustration of speech or visual impairment is exacerbated by the fear of permanent impairment, fear for their safety, etc. In the case of neuromuscular disease, the patient often has been told of the prospect of eventually losing the ability to swallow and the danger of aspiration. This is also a constant source of anxiety for the CVA victim whose throat has been affected.

The common feeling in these patients is one of abandonment. They may feel anger or guilt, but the feeling of having been abandoned by God is even more prevalent. The sudden onslaught of symptoms, including the sometimes rather gross disability, all cause a doubt of their value, their personhood. Once the initial shock and anger wear away, these patients need to rebuild their faith in their value as individuals. The religious values of trust in God, divine love for them, their intrinsic value as persons, and a sense of hope and courage are all aids that a good counselor will hope to build. Again, good communication between nurse and clergy is imperative.

Life-Threatening Complications

Especially puzzling are patients who become critically ill during the course of routine treatment. This can be due to an unforeseen allergy to a medication, an untoward reaction to an anesthetic, or a number of other conditions. These situations shock the patient and family and often devastate the health care professional's own feeling of competence. Mistakes and anomalies happen. Often we can explain what happened, but not why. If the nurse is the person responsible for the complication, it will be necessary to work through a grieving process and eventually come to self-forgiveness. If the nurse perceives some-

---

[1] Further discussion of this topic can be found in *Human Values and Cancer: Proceedings of a Conference,* The American Cancer Society, 1971.

[2] Readers are encouraged to see the film "The Clergy and Cancer Management," produced by The American Cancer Society, 1976.

one else to be at fault, it may be necessary to take administrative procedures and then work to rebuild a feeling of confidence in the competence of the staff. Admittedly, this is not always an easy task, but it is necessary to do this if one is to adequately assist the stricken patient and family. They will need to be assured that good care is presently being given. Everyone involved will be confronted with the most difficult of religious truths—mystery. No religion and no religious person has an explanation for every tragedy that occurs. It is necessary at times to stand in the stillness of our being and confront the fact that we have no answer—just faith that somehow there is meaning to what appears meaningless. Religious faith is often taxed at this point, but the experienced nurse has undoubtedly seen people and families rise to the occasion in a magnificent manner.

Any pastoral person working with the nurse and patient will need to be briefed on the present state of the patient's condition and what reasonable expectations can be had. The chaplain or pastor will then have to work to rebuild confidence, faith, and trust and to deal with anger, and desire for vengeance, or any bitter, personal assaults that may have been made against an individual or group of individuals.

In all these instances there is a need to be sensitive to the patient's and family's feelings toward God and religion in the face of crisis. Only then can the nurse be of help or make the proper referral. Anyone who is a person of faith can assist another person of faith in crisis. The nurse who builds a relationship with the patient or family in crisis may be the best person to do the principal counseling needed to correct false religious ideation, build self-confidence, or neutralize debilitating emotional states. The enlightened critical-care nurse who understands the religious component of illness can, when referral is indicated, give the chaplain or pastor the kind of information and continuing cooperation that can lead to a better chance for more complete healing.

In some people, their religious faith is of such depth that they will feel little, if any, of the negative emotions outlined above. In that case, the nurse can affirm this faith and encourage the patient and family to continue to turn to their religion to maintain the atmosphere of serenity that is so helpful in the healing process.

Traumatic Situations

The word *trauma* carries a wide range of emotions. We will not include the many obvious emotions con-

nected with the traumas discussed here but rather will focus only on those of a religious or moral nature.

Violent Accidents

Most accidents in which victims are admitted to emergency rooms could be placed in one of two classes for the sake of our study: (1) those which happen to the victim alone and (2) those involving several people. In the first situation, as when one falls in the home, is injured while operating machinery or equipment, or ingests poison, the religious reactions will be basically the same as those of the coronary patient—anger, guilt, bitterness, and at times a feeling of shame, particularly if the accident occurred because of carelessness or during drug or alcohol intoxication. The nurse can respond successfully to these patients by following the same procedures applied to the coronary patient—permit venting, probe the patient's attitude toward religion, pray, or call a chaplain as appropriate.

When other persons are involved in an accident, additional feelings may be present. Concern over the legal and moral culpability for the accident will be intensified if the patient knows he or she was the cause of the accident and others were seriously harmed or possibly killed. If carelessness or drugs were contributing factors, the sense of guilt and shame is usually deepened. If a child was a victim or if the other victims are permanently harmed, disfigured, or disabled, the sense of guilt and self-hatred can be extreme.

The nurse can help the patient by offering assurance that accidents are just that and by reminding the patient that no amount of guilt can undo it. A direct approach is usually the best in this particular instance. If moral guilt is present, the expression of it to the nurse can be helpful in itself. The patient expressing guilt needs to do so in confidence. Assurance that the patient does not have to face the moral guilt alone or in depth at this moment is important, and the understanding chaplain or pastor who befriends the patient and promises to stand by and provide support is needed. Sometimes even seriously injured patients are nearly unmanageable until they can be convinced that they will not be abandoned in this tragedy. Self-hatred may be neutralized or reduced by an honest statement that the nurse does not know all the facts but will protect the patient from incriminating remarks and official interrogation until the patient is sufficiently well mentally and physically to endure such examination. This may not be possible in every situation, but when it is, it is important and helpful.

Concern for the condition of the other victims shows a genuine moral conscience in the patient. The friendship of the clergy at such moments can be a great help for patient and staff alike.

Physical Attack upon One's Person

This category of attack usually includes knife wounds, gunshot wounds, and beatings. When the attack is perpetrated by someone known to or related to the victim, it often indicates a detrimental milieu. There is often enormous alienation, rage, desire for vengeance, and the feeling that forgiveness is out of the question. All these situations are deep-seated and require in-depth religious counseling, if such is possible. About all the nurse can hope to accomplish is to neutralize the immediate rage by pointing out the consequences of violence and urging calm for the patient's own good. Occasionally it helps to mention that the crime was probably one of passion and that the perpetrator lost all self-control, since otherwise he or she probably would not have attacked the victim.

A direct question as to whether or not the person believes in God is not out of order in this situation. If the person is a believer, a member of the clergy should be contacted to assist in neutralizing the rage. If the person is not a believer, appealing to the victim's best self is about the only moral option open. Since these are criminal cases, the police should be alerted to homicidal threats made by the victim.

Victims who did not know their attackers are usually tremendously fearful of everyone. Sometimes they will need to have their entire attitude toward humankind restored; at other times, they will develop hatred for a particular race or nationality. Ventilation of such feelings is important. A great deal of kindness from the nurse is needed to restore the victim's sense of personhood. If the nurse happens to be of the same nationality or race as the attacker, the nurse may experience some vicarious anger. The care given the patient in these circumstances is both physical and emotional.

The primary religious problem in these situations, once anger at the attacker comes under control, is often one of personal cynicism. The religious and emotional goal of care will be to renew the feeling that people are basically good. The patient is a lovable person, and this unfortunate incident has to be erased by the experience of the love and concern of many people for the victim. Compassionate care by the nurse at the time of crisis already begins the long process of inner healing that is so necessary.

Sexual Assault

The most wrenching attack on a woman is the crime of rape. Raped women feel a terrible sense of violation, guilt, and shame. They need reassurance that not all males are evil. They need to have others understand their sense of shame and violation but at the same time to be assured that they are good, lovable, and precious to their family. Dealing with their need to forgive their attacker sometimes helps them focus away from their sense of shame. Male relatives and friends should be coached as to how to approach the victim and should avoid giving even the slightest hint that she wanted or caused the rape. The sense of shame, as often experienced, is an outgrowth of violation of an innate sense of modesty, not moral guilt!

The religious themes of the value of the person; an acceptance of their feeling of loss of personhood; the need for self-respect; and the promotion and restoration of a self-image as a good and decent person are all appropriate.

Burns and Dismemberment

Disfigurement for many people truly destroys the desire to live. Burns that greatly disfigure the person as well as amputation or radical neck and face surgery that vastly alters the image of one's body also alter the concept of one's lovableness, usefulness, and value.

These patients become severely depressed and angry over their situation. It does no service to these people to act as though they are not terribly disfigured, but it is especially important to point out their value as human beings and to remind them of the potential they still have. There is a need to speak to them of hope and courage and of the people who love, admire, and respect them and who will continue to do so. Nurses in burn units should warn families of what to expect when they see the patient and should explain the patient's need to be reassured of the family's continuing love. The same is true of accident victims who will be greatly scarred or have lost a limb or limbs.

TWO QUESTIONS ABOUT SHARED RESPONSIBILITY
Jeanne Quint-Benoliel*

Is the Nurse Primarily Responsible to the Patient or to the Physician?

Since the end of World War II the expansion of medical technology has radically altered the hospital and its functions. This change was hastened by the federal government's active movement into financial support for medical research which, in turn, led to the creation of many life-sustaining procedures and machines. During the decade between 1960 and 1970 a variety of kinds of critical-care settings appeared in hospitals, all emphasizing the application of new medical technology to lifesaving activity. As Engel (1977) has shown, these settings were manifestations of the expanding power of the biomedical model of disease, and they had in common an emphasis on control over death.

The Nature of Critical-Care Work

Some of these settings offered generalized services to patients with critical medical or surgical conditions. Others were created to provide specialized services— for example, to patients with extensive burns or to premature infants. Regardless of whether they were generalized or specialized in function, however, critical-care settings had in common the primary objective of initiating and maintaining medical curative efforts in their most intensive forms. The term "intensive care" came to be used to describe the tempo, style, and nature of the activity expected of the staff who worked in many of these wards.

Centered on intensive medical treatment of critically ill patients, these settings are typically designed to facilitate rapid action in response to sudden emergency. To achieve this goal, both space and equipment are organized to permit direct and easy observation of all patients. As a consequence, personal privacy for patients is sacrificed to the need for constant attention to their physical signs and symptoms.

As a rule these wards make maximum use of new and innovative medical procedures. Machines of various kinds are utilized for diagnosing, monitoring, and treating the patients; and not infrequently, several pieces of technical equipment are simultaneously in

*For the references to this section of Chap. 44, see p. 000.

operation on a single patient. A good deal of the nurses' time and attention has to be focused on the procedural and mechanical aspects of various medical treatments while concurrently the work requires almost continuous attention to the physical changes occurring in the patients.

The tempo of work is rapid and oriented to the need for quick decisions in case of sudden crisis. The tension of the work is often high owing to the strain of continuing surveillance of patients and machines and the need to set priorities as to the patients most in need of help.

The social structure of a critical-care unit is typically organized to maximize staff control over the work to be done. One manifestation of this control is a tight restriction on patient-family interpersonal contacts and on information given about a patient's condition. It follows, of course, that the patients and their families have minimal control over the situation in which they find themselves. Often they feel powerless to influence what is taking place.

Nurses' Responsibilities for Lifesaving Goals

Although intensive treatment of life-threatening ailments is acknowledged by society as a medical obligation, in critical-care settings it is the nurses who carry the primary responsibility for implementing and supporting the medical lifesaving goal. Often they have received specialized training for the tasks they perform, and many feel a great deal of pride in their work. The rewards and satisfactions accruing to the nursing staff in critical care come mainly from their associations with medical activities.

These reactions of nurses are readily understandable, for they reflect the dominant values of Western society. Stated another way, critical-care units are organized to implement the cure goal of medical practice through attention to the diagnosis and treatment of life-threatening disease. The principal tasks that nurses perform are technical procedures in support of the lifesaving goal. Within the critical-care system, as presently organized, the care goal for patients carries a comparatively low priority.

As used in this discussion, the care goal for patients is concerned with the welfare and well-being of the person, in contrast to the diagnosis and treatment of disease. The care goal provides for the subjective meanings of the disease and treatment experience rather than the objective aspects of the case. Implementation of the care goal in practice depends on a reciprocal patient-nurse relationship in lieu of the nurse as the expert "doing things to" the patient. The success of the care goal in practice is measured by the patient's opportunity for active involvement in decisions affecting his or her living and dying.

The low priority given to implementing the care goal in critical-care settings is not due to nurses' lack of concern. Rather, the situation occurs because the critical-care system is not designed for follow-through on *care* in the same way that it is organized for *cure*. In addition, governing boards and administrators of hospitals have given relatively little attention to the high stress nature of work in critical treatment settings and the problems involved in implementing care as well as cure to patients and their families.

It is increasingly clear that the circumstances of critical-care practice create a context high in stress for the nurses and doctors who work there on a continuing basis. In fact, Hay and Oken (1972) have compared the work required of nurses to that expected of an elite team of soldiers in time of war. Yet hospitals have for the most part failed to recognize the need for social support systems to help the staff in coping with the stresses of their work, and more often the provision of support has come on an ad hoc basis if at all. The relationship between the staff's needs for a socially supporting environment and their capacities to offer personalized services to patients and families has not been given much attention.

Achievement of Balance between Care and Cure

A better balance between the goals of care and cure in critical-care settings could probably be achieved if the nurses working there were willing to accept collective responsibility for the well-being of patients and families. The assumption of such responsibility, in this writer's judgment, requires an ethical orientation toward the goals and means of professional nursing practice. It requires of nurses that they see the need for social mechanisms within the patient care system to protect the human rights of patients as people.

Conversations with many nurses suggest that many are personally committed to the goal of care, and yet they encounter many obstacles in their efforts to achieve its implementation. One factor inhibiting nurses comes from the strength of the lifesaving norms and values of critical-care settings. Going against an ethic of such power is bound to create ripples, if not giant waves, among physicians and other persons committed to the present cure-dominated system. In addition, the traditional doctor-nurse working relationship fosters and perpetuates a superior-subordinate pattern instead of a collegial one for reaching decisions about patients' needs and priorities. Another obstacle preventing many nurses from taking overt action on behalf of care comes in relation to the personal difficulties and stressful reactions they anticipate experiencing as a result of involvement with patients and their families. For some, the principal obstacle is produced by the nonsupporting attitudes of other nurses.

Yet the implementation of care depends on personal involvement, for it is concerned fundamentally with patients' goals and wishes. To be effective, care cannot be offered with an attitude of objectivity and detachment. It requires an environment in which the human concerns of patients and staff alike are recognized as worthy of serious consideration.

The core of this argument is that nurses have a moral obligation to the well-being of patients and families, and the fulfillment of this obligation requires explicit attention to the goals of care. Achievement of the goal will not come easily but requires that explicit plans be made for ensuring that *responsibility and accountability for care* be built into the system. Ultimately, nurses themselves must be willing to carry responsibility for care, and to do so they need a socially supporting network established as part of the system.

It is clear that no one nurse can achieve this goal alone. The implementation of care in critical treatment settings depends on nurses working together in a mutually supporting person-centered environment. It requires social mechanisms that make it possible for human problems to be given attention comparable to that devoted to disease and treatment. That nurses can develop mechanisms which respond to problems of care has been demonstrated by Dracup and Breu (1977), whose leadership promoted the creation of a nursing protocol for assisting the grieving spouses of patients on a critical-care ward in one university hospital.

A Moral Justification for Care

In a persuasive argument, Fried (1974) has noted that the physician's primary function is not so much the prevention of death as the preservation of life capacities toward the goal of a reasonable life plan for the individual. In many ways critical-care settings have evolved as mechanisms for implementing the utilitarian principle of the greatest good for the greatest number based on the value of lifesaving activity, but the organization and social structure have not provided much protection for the basic rights and personal integrity of the human person who happens to be a patient. Recently, physicians have acknowledged the need for criteria and mechanisms for removing hopelessly ill patients from activities that merely postpone the event of death (Report of the Clinical Care Committee of the Massachusetts General Hospital, 1976). It is this writer's belief that critical-care nurses have a moral responsibility to develop related criteria and mechanisms for safeguarding the personal integrity and autonomy of the patients in their charge and thereby to assume leadership in the delivery of personalized care to them and to their families.

What Can Be Done When Doctors and Nurses Disagree?

Conflict-Producing Problems in Critical Care

In many ways nursing in critical-care settings is hazardous work because the context creates a multitude of conflict-producing problems. Among the problems found troublesome for the staff is the case of the patient and/or the family who want active medical treatment discontinued. Another difficulty arises with the situation in which a young patient is diagnosed as having an untreatable problem, and the doctor tells the nurses that the patient is not to know the full extent of the diagnosis and prognosis. A third example of a troublesome situation occurs when a patient is clearly dying and members of the family insist on active medical treatment.

These and similar problems are difficult for the staff because they easily lead to conflicts of various kinds. Interpersonal conflicts between staff and patient, between doctors and nurses, or between staff and family can easily arise because of differences in beliefs about the "proper action" to be taken. Intergroup conflicts between doctors and nurses can readily appear because of differences in perceptions about the primary needs of patients and families. Internal (intrapersonal) conflicts are also easily precipitated when a nurse's or a physician's personal and professional value systems are not in agreement.

The nature of critical-care work is such that the staff have continued exposure to situational stresses that never really go away. The work creates a conflict-producing situation of high intensity, but the structure often does not provide ways and means for coping in positive ways with the various conflicts that are pro-

duced. When the tensions and strains of interpersonal and intergroup conflicts continue unabated, they add further to the stresses of critical-care work and may also interfere with the quality of service that is offered.

Social Mechanisms for Conflict Management

The negative influence of unresolved interpersonal and intergroup conflicts on staff working relationships and ultimately on patient care must be openly acknowledged before change can be started. The value of open communication about differences of opinion must also be recognized as essential for effective problem solving by groups of health care providers working together in the delivery of critical-care services. Only when unresolved conflict is recognized as a barrier to effective communication can social mechanisms be sought for managing the conflict in productive ways for patients and staff alike.

A number of social mechanisms need to be created for preventing and dealing with the problems of interpersonal and intergroup conflict. One of the much-needed mechanisms in many critical-care settings is a *formalized* opportunity for give-and-take discussion among physicians and nurses about the problems and progress of the patients under their care. Ad hoc and informal conversations between nurses and doctors play a valuable part in the network of information exchange, but they should not be viewed as alternatives to regularly scheduled meetings for responding to the ongoing problems of patient care. At the same time, the scheduling of opportunities for nurse-physician dialogue may not be easy, for by tradition the two groups have had limited opportunity to function together in a collegial manner. As Hertzberg (1977) has described, arrangements for regularly scheduled meetings involving nurses, social worker, and physicians on a cancer unit, for example, have been difficult to bring into being.

Scheduled meetings and other methods of making available socially supporting interpersonal contacts are undoubtedly important when the staff on a unit is faced with difficult choices and decisions in patient care. Specifically focused problem-solving work sessions dealing with a particular situation provide a valuable mechanism for assisting the staff members most deeply involved in the decision-making process to grapple with the complexity of the problem and to have access to feedback from their colleagues. Caplan (1974) makes the point that persons whose work brings them into frequent contact with emotional crises and strain are able to function much more effectively when they have regular contact with a social network providing consistent communication, appropriate rewards, and feedback about their performance. Achievement of such a network among the professional providers working together in critical care requires explicit planning if it is to be brought into being, and nurses are often in a position to initiate movement in this direction.

The actual bringing about of a program designed for problem solving and support for all members of a staff working in critical care can be aided by the use of an outside intermediary who can serve as facilitator of discussion among the different parties. Once again, nurses are in a position to exert leadership in identifying suitable people to provide this essential service to them and the other providers with whom they share responsibility.

Nursing Protocols and Conflict Resolution

The relative frequency of conflict-producing situations on critical-care units suggests strongly the need for organized efforts to prevent their occurrence and to find effective methods for resolution of conflict once it has appeared. The same types of conflict-producing situations appear again and again despite a proclaimed insistence by some nurses that "each case is unique." There is a great need for the development of nursing protocols designed explicitly for responding to these common conflict-producing problems.

Each protocol would be concerned with clarification of several necessary steps: definition of the problem, proposals for action, plans and strategies for implementation of action, and means for evaluation of outcomes. Each protocol should provide a framework and methodology for responding to the interpersonal and intergroup conflicts associated with a particular type of conflict-inducing situation. Each protocol should provide the nursing staff with guidelines for action so that nurses themselves can assume leadership in coping with the complexities of social conflict so as to facilitate open communication and the resolution of that conflict in positive ways.

REFERENCES

Benoliel, Jeanne Quint: The realities of work, in Jan Howard and Anselm L. Strauss (eds.), *Humanizing Health Care,* New York: Wiley, 1975, pp. 175–183.

Benoliel, Jeanne Quint: Overview: Care, cure and the challenge of choice, in Ann Earle et al. (eds.), *The Nurse as Caregiver for the Terminal Patient and His Family,* New York: Columbia University Press, 1976, pp. 9–30.

Caplan, Gerald: *Social Systems and Community Mental Health,* New York: Behavioral Publications, 1974.

Dracup, Kathleen A., and Christine S. Breu: Strengthening practice through research utilization, in *Communicating Nursing Research,* vol. 10, Boulder: Western Interstate Commission on Higher Education, 1977, pp. 339–353.

Engel, George L.: The need for a new medical model: A challenge for biomedicine, *Science* 196:129–136, April 8, 1977.

Fried, Charles: *Medical Experimentation: Personal Integrity and Social Policy,* New York: American Elsevier, 1974, pp. 94–104.

Hay, Donald, and Donald Oken: The psychological stresses of intensive care nursing, *Psychosomatic Medicine* 34:109, March–April 1972.

Hertzberg, Leonard J.: Living in a cancer unit, in E. Mansell Pattison (ed.), *The Experience of Dying,* Englewood Cliffs, New Jersey: Prentice-Hall, 1977, pp. 252–261.

Report of the Clinical Care Committee of the Massachusetts General Hospital: Optimum care for hopelessly ill patients, *N Engl J Med* 295(7):362–364, August 12, 1976.

PART 10

PATIENT TEACHING AND REHABILITATION

EFFECTS OF PATIENT AND FAMILY TEACHING

Beneficial Effects

Teaching of hospitalized patients and their families is no longer considered an option in nursing care; it is a necessary component—the patient's right. Research has shown that teaching, if it fosters patient learning, can decrease patients' anxiety, free energy to cope with disease and hospitalization, increase the likelihood of patients' complying with prescribed medical and nursing management, shorten the duration of hospitalization, and decrease the frequency of readmissions due to complications and recurrent health problems. If family members understand the patient's basic pathologic problems, medical and nursing management, and progress, they tend to be less anxious, more supportive of patients during hospitalization and after discharge, and more satisfied with the quality of care provided.

Concern about the rising costs of hospitalization as well as the human rights issue renders these benefits of patient education even more significant. To ensure that the patient and family receive these benefits, organizations throughout the nation are taking a close look at educational opportunities provided for patients in the hospital setting. The Joint Commission of Hospital Accreditation is evaluating institutions' programs of patient education in making its decision as to whether or not to grant them accreditation. The American Hospital Association repeatedly emphasizes in *A Patient's Bill of Rights* that the patient has the right to "know." Nurse practice acts written by state nurses' associations are including statements on the nurse's responsibility for patient teaching, and schools of nursing are designing curriculums to prepare their students for this role.

In hospitals, administrators are hiring patient educators, developing standard patient care plans for teaching, and auditing medical records to determine whether or not these standards are being met. Directors of nursing service are involved in reorganizing systems of nursing care so that each patient will have a primary nurse responsible for all aspects of nursing care, including patient and family teaching. The recognition of the value of teaching and learning even goes beyond the people and organizations concerned with health care delivery. Sources of third-party payment, such as Blue Cross, are recommending that their local plans reimburse hospitals for programs of planned patient teaching.

45
PRINCIPLES OF TEACHING AND LEARNING APPLIED TO CRITICAL CARE
Andrea M. Nassen

EFFECTS OF PATIENT AND FAMILY TEACHING
Beneficial Effects
Detrimental Effects

PATIENT TEACHING PROGRAMS
Need
Development of a Program

REFERENCES

Detrimental Effects

In the midst of all the papers, studies, and discussions concerning the value of teaching, however, it is important to note that not all teaching is effective, yielding positive learning results. If teaching is not well planned and the teachers are not thoroughly prepared, the learners may be at a greater disadvantage than if they had not been taught at all. Patients and their families may receive too much or too little information, inaccurate information, or conflicting information from various members of the nursing staff or health team. As a result, they may learn nothing at all, forget much of that which has been taught, or lose their motivation for future learning experiences. Nurses can become frustrated, too. A series of unsuccessful teaching experiences may cause them to become discouraged in their patient education efforts and to lose confidence in their abilities.

PATIENT TEACHING PROGRAMS

Need

To maximize the beneficial effects of teaching for patients, families, and nurses and to minimize the potential for unnecessary problems and failures, teaching and learning experiences should be well organized and carefully planned. Everyone realizes the importance of an individualized teaching plan which recognizes the learning needs of a particular patient and family, but planning of this scope takes time. If teaching were nurses' sole responsibility, it would not be a problem. Unfortunately, however, after taking care of those patient problems and needs requiring immediate attention, nurses have little time and energy available to plan, implement, and evaluate effective teaching and learning experiences for each patient assigned. As much as they might like to, they do not have the resources to identify the learning experiences each of their patients may have had on a preoperative or medical unit preceding transfer to the critical-care unit as well as the expected experiences following transfer to an intermediate-care, progressive-care, or predischarge unit. Nurses do not have the time to assess which health team members have the expertise and willingness to teach, research effective teaching methods, locate or purchase appropriate teaching tools and devices, learn the teaching preferences or guidelines of various physicians, and accomplish all the other things necessary to design and implement a plan.

As a result, in most institutions individualized teaching plans simply do not get written and teaching does not get done. In other hospitals, only some of the patients get taught only some of the time. Often, there are needless duplications of teaching efforts, wide gaps in learning when the patient is transferred to other units, conflicting information presented by nurses on different shifts or on different units, and altercations between physicians and nurses concerning what the patient should or should not be taught.

How, then, can this dilemma be solved? One solution, which will be reviewed in this chapter, is for nurses to work together to develop a general patient teaching program for a defined group of patients in a given clinical setting. In other words, rather than every nurse having to write and implement a separate teaching plan for each assigned patient with a myocardial infarction, a program would be designed for all patients having this diagnosis in common. Since teaching programs recognize the experiential and learning commonalities of patients and provide nurses with the information and resources necessary to meet basic, patient learning needs, it frees nurses to adapt the general teaching plan and do the additional assessment, planning, implementation, and evaluation required to meet the learning needs of individual patients. Initially, this approach to planned teaching may require a little more time and effort; but in the long run, it will be more efficient in terms of human and material resources and, more important, will provide all patients and families with the opportunity for standard, quality teaching and learning experiences.

Development of a Program

Provided that you have identified a patient population which could benefit from a patient teaching program and are interested in developing one, what are the systematic steps of the process by which it can be accomplished? First, working with other nurses, the head nurse, clinical specialist, or patient educator, documents the need for a program. Identify the problems experienced by patients, families, and nurses because an organized system of patient teaching does not exist. Second, assess the learning needs of patients and families. Third, develop a plan. Given the learning needs, decide who is going to provide the teaching, when, and where. Consider how the nurse will acquire the information necessary to teach, and identify the person(s) whose approval or consent for the teaching program will be needed. Decide when implementation will begin and how it will be documented. Determine how the program will be evaluated and what criteria will be used to discover whether or not the program is effective. Fourth, having assessed and planned, implement the teaching program. Fifth, evaluate. What did the patient and family learn? Did they wish they had learned more—or less? What problems developed after the patient returned home? Might they have been avoided? How? You may discover that additional learning needs exist or that a more efficient means of documentation or alternative teaching methods or tools are required to facilitate learning. Finally, reassess the program, revise the plan, implement the new plan, and evaluate.

To clarify the steps involved in the development of a patient teaching program, each one will be discussed in detail. Concomitantly, experiences in developing a teaching program for cardiovascular surgical patients in a large teaching hospital will be presented to illustrate the implementation of the process in a clinical setting.

Documentation of Need

In documenting the need for a teaching program, it is necessary to use skills of observation, interviewing, and listening to ascertain those problems existing for patients, families, and nurses which could be ameliorated by teaching. Present and past patients and family members, local medical doctors, referring and attending physicians, nursing personnel in outpatient clinics, nursing peers, and other health team members are excellent sources of information. From these persons, you may learn that patients are frightened or fearful of their clinical environment—its sights and sounds. They may not understand their diagnosis, the basic pathophysiology involved, the medical and nursing management required, or the expected results of treatment. Not knowing the facts, patients may fantasize what they believe to be true and harbor harmful misconceptions. As a result, they may be recalcitrant, combative, withdrawn, or passive. Transferring from one unit to another may precipitate fears of not knowing whom they can trust, who will care for them, and what they can expect. Upon discharge, patients may feel unprepared for the home environment. They may not know how to perform the skills or secure the equipment and supplies required for self-care at home, what normal occurrences or complications to expect during recovery, or when to call a doctor to report signs and symptoms. Consequently, serious, but avoidable, complications may develop, necessitating readmission to the hospital.

You may find that significant others make unrealistic demands on patients during and after hospitalization, voice frequent complaints concerning the quality of nursing care and hospital facilities, or threaten legal action against staff members. Other family members or friends who want to be supportive of the patient may lack knowledge of the types of behaviors which would be helpful and thus may avoid the patient. They may also avoid the nursing staff if they do not have a trusting relationship with the personnel or know the place and time to verbalize questions and concerns. Not understanding the patient's clinical course, significant others might interpret any change in the patient's treatment, equipment, or unit location as proof of new complications. Feeling unprepared for care of the patient after discharge, they may ask the physician or nurses for an extension of the patient's hospitalization, request transfer of the patient to an extended-care facility, or refuse to support the patient in care in the home setting.

By talking to and observing nursing personnel on your unit, you may find that they are distressed when patients are readmitted to the unit for recurrent clinical problems, such as congestive heart failure, which may have been prevented by following medication and diet prescriptions. Nurses may become distressed on hearing that former patients died because of omissions in self-care, such as not having prothrombin times drawn or not taking warfarin (Coumadin) to prevent clotting of prosthetic valves. Not understanding the cause of the acting-out or withdrawn behavior of patients and families in the hospital, nurses may feel powerless, unrewarded, or hostile. Tired of dealing with heavy physical and emotional demands, they may exhibit low morale, be unsupportive of each other, or request transfer to other nursing units.

No one of these patient, family, or nursing problems alone would be sufficient to document the need for a teaching program. However, viewed together, a common thread may be isolated—a lack of knowledge, a lack of understanding, a lack of teaching and learning.

Such a thread was identified several years ago when documenting the need for a teaching program for cardiovascular surgical patients. Patients were admitted to a preoperative unit a day or two prior to surgery and received no organized orientation to the unit or preparation for surgery. As a result, some of the patients went to surgery with amazing misconceptions. They believed that the heart was taken out of the body during surgery and replaced afterward, that atrioventricular and semilunar valves were located on the outside of the heart, or that atherosclerotic coronary arteries were removed during bypass surgery and plastic tubes inserted in their place. A few patients thought that they had a 95 percent chance of not surviving the operation rather than of surviving it. Others thought that patients were awake during the operation with only the body paralyzed, that the ventilator in the critical-care unit was an iron lung, or that the subcuticular sutures used to close the incisions were not sutures but a special type of glue. No health team member, of course, had taught these misconceptions to patients and families, but in the course of reading popular magazines, talking with other patients and families, hearing stories in the waiting room, or misinterpreting information they had received during anxious moments from doctors and nurses, this is what some of the patients had learned. Some kind of learning had occurred even though it was not planned. That which was not known was, indeed, fantasized. *Patients needed to know.*

Since patients had not been taught what to expect postoperatively, they were frightened by equipment in the critical-care unit, tried repeatedly to pull out tubes and devices, and were unable to find ways to communicate nonverbally while intubated. They tended to believe that vibropercussion was cruel and unnecessary nursing care. Slight temperature elevations and disruptions of normal sleep, eating, and bowel habits as well as incision redness and swelling, benign arrhythmias, cardiac monitoring, external cardiac pacing, and the presence of keep-open IVs for antibiotic therapy were interpreted as signs of unusually complicated, protracted postoperative courses.

Family members were uncertain about whom to contact if they had questions or concerns, since the patient was transferred to three or four nursing units during hospitalization. Not understanding expected postoperative occurrences and normal routines of care, they tended to work against rather than with health team members. They were often demanding and distrustful of nursing personnel.

Prior to discharge, only some of the patients were taught about home care. Discharge orders were written late, and only a few nurses saw teaching as their responsibility. Having received conflicting pieces of information from residents, dietitians, pharmacists, nurses, and other patients or having received teaching on the morning of discharge, patients were uncertain about how long to stay on low-sodium diets, how to care for their incisions, when to see their local doctor, and what their activity restrictions entailed. Sometimes patients lost their prescriptions, did not get them

refilled, resumed preadmission medications, substituted home remedies, or decided that if one pill was good, two would be even better. Family members, not understanding the improvement in cardiac function resulting from the operation or the importance of activity, put needless restrictions on the patient's activity at home and reinforced the patient's concept of being a "cardiac cripple." Since they did not realize the importance of medications, diet, and clinic appointments, patients were sometimes readmitted with serious cardiovascular or pulmonary problems, dehydration, edema, or other problems that could have been prevented if the patients and their families had understood and the health team members had provided the opportunity for them to learn.

Assessment

What is it, then, that patients need to know in order to eliminate these problems? What knowledge and skills do family members require in order to support the patient? These questions and the answers to them constitute the assessment step of program development.

In identifying and defining learning needs, you will need to use the same skills exercised in the previous step of the program development process—observing, interviewing, and listening. You may also want to use the same sources of information. Observe and interview patients currently on your unit as well as their significant others. If patients in a critical-care unit are too ill to talk, visit with patients on a progressive-care or predischarge unit. Ask them what they remember from their critical-care experience, what they perceived their learning needs to be, and what they wish had been explained to them in greater or less detail at that time. Interview the patients' physicians as well as the pharmacist, dietitian, social worker, physical therapist, and other health team members providing care. Ask them to identify the specific learning experiences which they believe would maximize the patient's and family's understanding of the diagnosis and treatment and their participation in care. Additionally, study the information acquired in documenting the need for a patient teaching program. Work backward from each patient, family, and nursing problem identified to the knowledge deficit responsible for it.

Once you have completed the assessment of learning needs, design a framework to organize the information collected. Develop one framework for patient learning needs and another for the needs of significant others. Select major categories for each framework based either on the phases of hospitalization or on the clinical settings in which patients are located during the usual course of hospitalization. For example, if you choose to base your framework on the phases of hospitalization, major categories might include the admission phase, the diagnostic phase, the therapeutic phase, the convalescent phase, and the discharge phase. If, on the other hand, you prefer to organize learning needs according to clinical settings, major categories might encompass the critical-care unit, the intermediate- or progressive-care unit, and the predischarge unit.

Next, subdivide each major category into the three general types of learning which can occur—cognitive, affective, and psychomotor. *Cognitive learning* would entail facts, principles, and concepts which patients and their significant others need to know, comprehend, apply, analyze, synthesize, or evaluate. *Affective learning* would include the beliefs, attitudes, and values that they might need to develop; and *psychomotor learning* would involve the motor skills which they would need to perform.

Having developed the framework, complete it. Record each learning need identified during assessment in the appropriate category. Starting with the first major category (e.g., admission phase or critical-care unit), list all the learning needs which patients might evidence during that phase or while in that clinical setting. Next, list the affective learning needs and, then, the psychomotor needs. Proceed to the next major category and note the knowledge, values, and skills needed to be learned by patients. Continue recording learning needs in each category until the assessment framework is complete.

Using another framework, specify the learning needs of the patients' significant others. What are their needs during every phase of hospitalization or while patients are being cared for on each nursing unit? After completing the framework, compare it with the framework summarizing the learning needs of patients. You may notice that while some of the needs are quite different, others are very much the same, an important consideration in the planning step of program development.

In assessing the learning needs of patients admitted to the hospital for open intracardiac surgery, it was learned that, in general, patients wanted to know two basic types of information—experiential expectations and personal responsibilities before, during, and after surgery. Upon admission, patients needed information regarding the nursing unit, their room, visiting hours, meal service, mail delivery, and smoking, diet, and activity restrictions. They asked questions concerning the purpose of admission laboratory work and the rationale behind the numerous health histories and physical examinations performed. The functions of various health team members as related to the patient and the means to be used to "call" a nurse or contact a clergyman or social worker were other sources of concern.

Prior to surgery, many learning needs centered on diagnostic procedures such as x-rays, electrocardiograms, echocardiograms, exercise tolerance tests, and cardiac catheterizations. Regardless of the type of procedure, both patients and their significant others wanted to know the purpose of the test, the nature of the procedure itself, changes required in diet or activity before as well as after the procedure, the location of the diagnostic laboratory, and the personnel responsible for performing the procedure.

The day prior to surgery, the need to know seemed to increase or decrease markedly depending on the particular patient. The patients' "need to know" focused more on themselves and less on their surrounding environments. The most frequently asked questions concerned the expected results of surgery, the time and duration of the operation, the type of anesthetic agent, the body shave and preparation, and diet and medication modifications prior to surgery.

The day of surgery, patients usually wanted to know what time they should awaken and shower. Female patients asked whether or not they could wear cosmetics, jewelry, hairpieces, dentures, and personal garments to surgery. Having seen their roommates or talked with other patients prepared for surgery, patients requested information regarding the purpose of premedication, discomfort caused by the injections, mode of transfer to surgery, characteristics of the operating room, time and means of anesthetic induction, location of the postoperative care unit, and expected experiences after operation.

During the days after surgery, patients and their significant others wanted to know about the expected duration of hospitalization and the usual diet and activity progressions. Many questions were related to medications available to minimize pain and discomfort, appearances of incisions, and purposes of epicardial wires, pacemakers, IVs, oxygen, and indwelling urinary catheters. Patients who seemed to recover more slowly than others, developed arrhythmias, experienced "up" and "down" days, or had difficulty sleeping and eating were concerned about the causes and treatment of these problems.

Finally, during the days before discharge, another set of needs became evident. Having become accustomed to their hospital environment, patients were fearful of leaving the unit and apprehensive about their ability to manage at home. They asked questions about medications, diet, incisional care, activity, rest, return to work or school, and medical and surgical follow-up. They wondered how long the incisional discomfort would last, what the signs and symptoms of complications would be, and how to handle emergencies if they developed. Parents of infants or small children sought information regarding discipline, immunizations, and play. Significant others wanted information about the hospital's discharge procedure, billing practices, processing of insurance papers and banked blood requirements, and means of providing care and support to facilitate patients' recovery at home.

These learning needs identified after observing, interviewing, and listening to patients and families were also elicited when interviewing members of the health team. Additionally, other needs were identified. Nurses thought that patients needed to acquire skills of deep breathing and coughing prior to surgery and to recognize the importance of complying with fluid intake and output recordings as well as activity, diet, and rest prescriptions postoperatively. They believed that significant others needed to acquire knowledge and skills related to applying antiembolism stockings prior to discharge, purchasing and preparing low-sodium foods, and assisting the patient with incisional care, if required. Physicians thought it important for patients and their families to understand the basic cardiac pathology, natural history of the disease without surgery, risks and imponderables of surgery, expected and actual results of operative intervention, and its implications for the patients' quality of life subsequent to hospitalization. Health team members concurred that patients needed to be involved in an exercise program during hospitalization and after discharge to decrease muscle and bone discomfort and enable patients to return more quickly to their normal activities of daily living. Dietitians thought patients and families needed to know how to modify favorite menus and recipes and adapt food preferences to satisfy the requirements of a low-sodium diet. Pharmacists believed that patients should know the purpose of each medication prescribed, directions for taking and storing them, precautions to follow, and adverse reactions to report to their medical doctor.

Since patients sometimes developed bacterial endocarditis after discharge, necessitating readmission to the hospital, all health care providers felt patients should know the basics of preventing infection. They agreed that patients should understand the importance of notifying each physician and dentist caring for them of their previous cardiac surgery and reporting immediately any signs and symptoms of infection to their physician. Educating patients with prosthetic valves regarding the risks and benefits of anticoagulant therapy was identified as another teaching priority by all health team members.

Once learning needs of cardiovascular surgical patients and their families had been identified and defined, two frameworks were developed, using clinical settings as their bases. Major categories identified in the frameworks included the admission or preoperative unit, the critical-care unit, the intermediate-care unit, and the postoperative or predischarge unit. Most of the learning needs listed were cognitive in nature, the balance being either affective or psychomotor. Many similarities were noted between patient and family needs, and these similarities served as the starting point for the planning step of program development.

Planning

Not unlike the documentation and assessment steps of program development, planning involves every member of the health team. One of the most efficient planning methods which can be used is to arrange a meeting involving at least one representative from each group providing health care. Meeting as a group has several advantages over talking with each member individually. In a group setting, one member's ideas tend to stimulate anothers, there is an opportunity for immediate feedback and exchange, and group members learn to work with each other toward a common goal.

The goal of your group will be to plan how to meet the existent learning needs of patients and their significant others. Using the assessment frameworks as a guide, the first task will be to determine the general content areas which will be involved in teaching to provide for the cognitive, affective, and psychomotor learning needs identified. Major content areas might include the health care delivery system; hospital environment; diagnostic procedures; anatomy and physiology; medical, surgical, and nursing treatment; diet; medications; activity; and rest. Content in these areas is relevant to teaching of patients and families in almost all clinical settings.

The second task entails writing general objectives

for each major content area identified. General objectives specify the learning outcomes expected of patients and their significant others as a result of teaching efforts in a particular content area. Since objectives are used as a guide in teaching and learning experiences and as a tool in evaluating the patient teaching program, they must be well written. In formulating each objective, begin with a verb such as *know, understand,* or *appreciate* and follow it with a word or phrase identifying the content area. Try to write the objective in terms of learning (not teaching) outcome (not process). Be realistic. Make certain that each objective is potentially attainable for patients and families, given the restraints of their situation, the duration of hospitalization, and the time available for learning. A simple example of a general objective might be "to understand medications prescribed." As you can see, it is general in nature, but that is its purpose—to provide an overall picture of the final learning outcome in a particular content area.

The third task is to write specific objectives for each formulated general objective. Their purpose is to specify the behavior which the patient and family must demonstrate in order to achieve the learning outcome specified in the general objective. Specific objectives clarify what the learner must be able to do when the teaching and learning experiences have been completed; they are the components of the overall picture. Not unlike general objectives, specific objectives must be well written. Each statement should specify only one expected behavior or learning outcome and must be sufficiently precise and clear so that both the teacher and learner understand what is to be accomplished or learned. When writing specific objectives, begin each one with a verb (such as identify, list, recite, write), describing observable, measurable behavior, and follow it with a word or phrase identifying the specific content area. Additionally, if either the quality of performance or the situation and time in which the learners perform the behavior is important, qualifiers may be included in the objective.

Previously the statement "To understand all medications prescribed" was used to illustrate a general objective. Examples of specific objectives defining what learners must do to demonstrate that they "understand" might include: "to describe the purpose of each medication prescribed"; "to state the dosage in milligrams of each drug prescribed"; "to explain the directions for taking each medication prescribed"; "to recite the directions for storing each drug prescribed"; "to list five signs or symptoms of adverse

reactions to each medication prescribed"; and "to name the person to whom adverse reactions should be reported." An example of a specific objective to which qualifiers have been added would be, "Given a cup containing one sample of each medication prescribed, the patient will state, without assistance, the name of every tablet or capsule as it is withdrawn from the container." The phrases, "given a cup containing one sample of each medication prescribed" and "without assistance" specify the conditions under which the patient must perform the tasks, and the word "every" defines the criterion or the minimum standard of acceptable performance. According to this objective, the patient who named only three out of five medications would not achieve either the specific or the general objective, "to understand all medications prescribed." Qualifiers are not a necessary component of specific objectives, however, and may be more appropriate when writing objectives for a teaching plan for a particular patient and family.

Having identified major content areas and written general and specific objectives for each, the fourth task of your group then is to decide which health team member will be responsible for teaching patients and their significant others. The nature of the content to be taught and the expertise and willingness of team members to teach are important factors to be considered in making this decision. Perhaps you will identify the pharmacist as the person primarily responsible for the content concerning medications; the dietitian, for diet; physicians, for pathophysiology and medical or surgical intervention; and nurses, for activity, rest, and nursing care.

The fifth group decision is concerned with additional learning required to enable health team members to teach. Your colleagues may decide that a review is indicated for group members concerning the principles of teaching and learning, teaching methods and tools available, characteristics of an effective teacher, or theory and skills pertaining to particular content areas. Group members may decide to learn the information on their own or arrange for an inservice program. Eventually, information concerning teaching may be incorporated in orientation programs for new personnel.

The sixth task is to decide when patient and family teaching and learning experiences should occur. Significant determinants of this decision are the time and place the learning needs are usually evidenced and the learners are generally receptive to and available for teaching. The complexity of the content to be learned should also be taken into consideration. It is important to stress that, like every other decision regarding the patient teaching program, this decision will serve only as a guideline when teaching a particular patient and family. The decision will be modified as needed in order to meet individual learning needs and abilities.

The seventh decision concerning where teaching will be accomplished is closely related to the previous one. What teaching will occur while the patient is on an admission or preoperative care unit, in the critical-care unit, or on a progressive-care or predischarge unit? Will the health team members meet with each patient individually at the bedside, or will they arrange a class for several patients in a conference room? Factors such as the wellness of the patient, the teaching tools and devices required for the class, the availability of the classroom space, and the perceived benefits of group versus individual instruction must be considered in making this decision.

Based on previous decisions regarding content, the time and location of teaching, and the characteristics of the patient population selected, health team members in your group are ready to make the eighth decision concerning the methods, tools, and devices which they will utilize in teaching. There are many methods which can be used. Lectures, discussions, and demonstrations are the most commonly employed methods and usually are the most effective in teaching adults, while role playing, play therapy, and games are useful learning experiences for young children and adolescents. Some group members may prefer using only one method, while others may find that a combination of methods is required to produce the desired learning milieu.

Next, the members in your group need to decide which of the numerous teaching tools and devices available are most appropriate to the teaching method chosen and the type of teaching and learning experience desired. A partial list of teaching aides available includes chalkboards, transparencies used with overhead projectors, drawing boards, movies, slides, audiovisual tapes, cassette recordings, posters, flannel or magnetic boards, photographs, diagrams, charts, posters, pamphlets, booklets, models, and the actual object. Regardless of the devices selected, one important requirement exists; teachers must know how to operate them. Nothing is more disruptive to a teaching session and more disconcerting to the learner than a teaching device which cannot be operated. If booklets, pamphlets, or movies are used, they should first be reviewed to determine whether or not the information is accurate, facilitates the learner's

meeting of the objectives, and promotes the desired learning. By making an inventory of all teaching aides available in various departments, group members can avoid needless duplication of resources and expenditures for them. If, however, additional tools and devices are needed, consider using unit funds or monies secured from sources of third-party payment to purchase them.

It is neither probable nor necessary to accomplish these eight planning tasks in the course of a single meeting. If several group sessions are held, group members have an opportunity to reflect on the decisions made during the meeting, discuss them with peers in their health care areas, revise objectives, research alternative teaching methods and devices, review theory and skills related to content areas they will be teaching, and return to the next meeting with new suggestions and ideas. During meetings, group members should not hesitate to identify and articulate potential problems and discuss them openly and freely. Not all decisions made during planning sessions are wise. Sometimes during a meeting, away from the pressures and concerns of the clinical setting, a group makes decisions that in practice would be unrealistic and logistically difficult. At subsequent meetings, these decisions can be reconsidered and modified, incorporating the additional suggestions of group members.

Once the plan has been revised, your group is ready to make the last five planning decisions. When will the program be implemented? How will the results of teaching and learning be documented? How and when will the program be evaluated? Whose permission or consent must be obtained prior to implementation of the program?

When will the program be implemented? The answer to this question is dependent on how long it will take members of the group to organize and develop the teaching program and to prepare for teaching. If teaching devices and tools must be obtained or purchased, when will they be available? In order to maximize the success potential of the program, it should not be initiated until each component is complete. Allow enough time after each member is prepared to have one final meeting for group members to share their portion of the program with the others. During this time, group members should check for gaps, overlapping, or conflict in the information in various parts of the teaching program and should make modifications and corrections as indicated.

Having made a decision regarding the date of

implementation, design a means for documenting the teaching and learning which will occur. There are several types of records to use as a model, including problem-oriented charting, checklists, and narrative entries in progress notes. The means of documentation developed should have several characteristics. Most important it must provide a succinct, cogent record identifying the extent to which the patient and significant others have achieved the general objectives, clarifying what has been learned as well as what remains to be learned. It should include information regarding when the teaching and learning occurred and which health team members were responsible for the experience. Completion of the documentation record should be time-efficient. The more laborious and time-consuming the means of documentation, the less likely it will be completed. Finally, the record must meet the standards specified by the medical records committee within the institution.

How and when will the program be evaluated? The record documenting the teaching and learning experiences of patients and their families will be a valuable source of information in the evaluation. Were the learning needs identified in the documentation of need and assessment steps met? If not, were there deficiencies in the planning or implementation of the teaching content, the general and specific objectives, the teaching accomplished by health team members, the preparation of members for their teaching responsibilities, the time and location of teaching and learning experiences, or the types of methods, devices, and tools utilized in these experiences? Health team members responsible for teaching may make their own subjective evaluation of these factors throughout the course of implementation as well as by meeting together as a group for a formal evaluation at the end of 1 month, 2 months, or 6 months. The date specified for structured evaluation should be sooner rather than later to avoid perpetrating a program which may not only let the learning needs identified in the assessment frameworks go unmet but also allow health team members, patients, and families to become discouraged with the patient teaching program.

Finally, having planned means and dates for implementation and evaluation, present the program for approval to persons responsible for care of patients within the organization. Consent is necessary, since being a part of a social system obviates the possibility of proceeding unilaterally with any decision or action, let alone one which affects so many persons in the system. The director of nursing, the patients' physi-cians, and the medical director or chief of service are persons with whom you will most likely need to meet. In presenting the program, review the results of your documentation of need for the patient teaching program, the assessment, and the plan for implementation and evaluation. Ask for their comments concerning the program and their perceptions of potential problems, and incorporate their suggestions into your plan. Undoubtedly, this will not be the first time you have discussed the program with these persons, since their input would have been valuable throughout the previous steps of program development as well. They may also be of significant assistance in finally presenting the program on a hospital-wide basis prior to implementation and providing support throughout this phase of program development.

The director of the division of cardiovascular nursing and the chief of surgery were invaluable sources of counsel and support in the planning step of program development for teaching cardiovascular surgical patients and their families. In developing a plan, members in every area of health care providing care for patients and their families were involved. They included the head nurses and clinical specialists on the preoperative, critical-care, intermediate-care, and predischarge units; supervisors of clinical pharmacy and dietetics; physical conditionists; social workers; anesthesiologists; and surgeons. To provide for the learning needs documented in the assessment frameworks, the following content areas were identified: the health care delivery system, including the roles and functions of health team members; the environment of nursing care units, diagnostic laboratories, and operating rooms; basic anatomy and physiology of the cardiovascular and pulmonary subsystems; medical, surgical, and nursing interventions during hospitalization including diet, activity, rest, and medications; home care; and medical and surgical follow-up.

Goals of learning in each area were defined by general and specific objectives. Since many of the health team members were familiar with the needs and problems experienced by patients and their significant others because an organized program of teaching was not existent, members volunteered to be responsible and accountable for content in their areas of expertise. Health team members in nursing, surgery, pharmacy, and dietetics worked with their representatives in clarifying the objectives of teaching and learning, deciding the most appropriate times and places for teaching to occur during the patients' course of hospitalization, selecting teaching methods, and locating or purchasing tools and devices to be used in teaching.

Once these tasks and decisions had been accomplished, guidelines were written summarizing the teaching content and responsibilities of each health care area. Group members worked together in identifying areas of overlap, deficiency, and conflict and in revising the guidelines as indicated. The purpose of the guidelines was to clarify the teaching content for which each health care area was responsible, to ensure that all health team members in a given area would provide each patient and family the same opportunity for teaching and learning, and to enable members in each health care area to know the content reviewed with patients by those in other areas and therefore to accurately reinforce teaching. To further decrease the probability of patients and their families receiving conflicting information, team members agreed to refer questions not reviewed in the guidelines to members in whose domain the content of the questions fell.

It was decided that upon admission of patients to the preoperative unit, the registered nurse responsible for their care would assess the learning needs of patients and their families and provide teaching concerning the nursing unit, patient room, routines of care, unit system of nursing care delivery, and diet, activity, and medication prescriptions. Prior to diagnostic procedures, the nurse would also meet with the patient and family to discuss the scheduled test. Information reviewed with the patient and family by the attending physician would also be clarified.

During visiting hours the day prior to surgery, it was planned that three health team members would meet with the patient and family for the purpose of preoperative teaching. The surgeon would be responsible for content related to cardiac pathology, natural history of the disease without surgery, expected and actual results of operative intervention, and the risks and imponderables of surgery. The anesthesiologist would explain the basics of anesthetic management and the operative and immediate postoperative care. Patient and family expectations and responsibilities before, during, and after surgery would be content areas reviewed by registered nurses in teaching. They would also demonstrate deep breathing and coughing techniques and guide the patients in their return demonstrations. Additionally, nurses would reinforce and clarify content discussed with patients and families by the surgeon and anesthesiologist and would identify special problems and needs of the learners related to the operative experience.

In the critical-care unit, registered nurses would reinforce teaching accomplished preoperatively concerning the unit environment and the purpose of equipment, lines, and devices. They would also explain the nature and purpose of nursing interventions required by the patient, provide information to the family about the patient's condition, and clarify information regarding the operative procedure explained to family members by the surgeon prior to their first visit to the patient in the critical-care unit. When the patient was transferred from the critical-care to the intermediate-care unit, nurses would again explain the procedure involved to both patients and their significant others.

Concerning teaching of patients during their course of hospitalization on the intermediate-care unit, it was decided that nurses would be responsible for teaching regarding the patient's environment, medications and treatments prescribed, nature and purpose of nursing interventions such as the recording of atrial electrograms and electrocardiograms, purpose of equipment used in patient care, activity and diet progression, expected postoperative occurrences, and complications experienced by the patient. They would, furthermore, reinforce teaching which had occurred previously concerning the operative procedure and the patient's condition.

On the predischarge unit, the physical conditionist would be responsible for teaching two exercise classes, the first being on the fifth postoperative day. During the class, the conditionist would review the "dos," "don'ts," and major precautions of exercise, demonstrate exercises in the program, and guide patients in their performance of the exercises.

During visiting hours several days prior to discharge, the nurse, the surgeon, and if appropriate, the pharmacist and dietitian would provide discharge teaching for the patients and their families. The content areas for which nurses would be responsible included the discharge procedure; discharge prescriptions written for the patient regarding activity, rest, incisional care, prevention of infection, and expected postdischarge, convalescent experiences; special treatments or procedures to be performed by the patient after discharge; and medical and surgical follow-up.

The surgeons would teach patients and families about the implications of the surgery and postoperative course for the patient's quality of life after discharge. They also provided patients on anticoagulant therapy information pertaining to variations in daily warfarin dosage and the necessity of having frequent prothrombin times drawn.

If patients were to continue medications after discharge, the pharmacist would be responsible for teaching patients and their families about the purposes, dosages, and precautions of medications and the directions for taking and storing them. Patients who required alterations in their diet after discharge would be taught by a dietitian. The dietitian reviewed foods allowed and those not allowed on the diet and provided guidelines concerning shopping for special food items and recipes for preparing them.

Most of the health team members planned to use a combination lecture and discussion method of teaching and to rely on models, diagrams, and pamphlets as their major teaching tools. The nurses, surgeons, pharmacists, and dietitians elected to teach on a one-to-one basis at the patient's bedside, while the physical conditionist chose to teach in a group setting in a conference room in the clinical setting.

All health team members planned to document teaching efforts and resultant patient and family learning by means of narrative entries in progress notes in the patient's medical record. To coordinate teaching efforts and to enable health team members to see at a glance what teaching and learning had been accomplished and what remained to be accomplished, a brief patient teaching checklist was developed. The checklist provided a list of content areas to be discussed with the patient and family and spaces for health team members to record their names and the date of the teaching and learning experience.

Next, group members selected a date for implementation and, 6 months later, a date for formal evaluation. It was decided that the program would be evaluated in terms of the extent to which patients and their significant others had achieved the general and specific outcomes. Additionally, problems originally identified in the documentation of need would be reviewed to determine whether or not the patient teaching program had been effective in decreasing them. Sources of information in making these determinations would include patients, families, nurses, physicians, outpatient clinic personnel, local medical doctors, referring physicians, and other members of the health team.

Implementation

In every other step of program development—the documentation of need, the assessment, the planning, and the evaluation—responsibility can be shared by health team members and work can be accomplished as a group. In the implementation step, however, when it comes to teaching a particular content area to a particular patient and family, responsibility rests on the individual health team member. The patient teaching program has specified in general what the member is responsible for teaching, the general and specific learning outcomes desired, the time and place to teach, and the teaching methods and tools to use; but how this information is used in interacting with the patient and family to effect the desired behavior change is the individual's task, the essence of teaching and learning.

The steps you will follow in developing a teaching plan for a particular patient and family are similar to those used in developing the general teaching program: assessment, planning, implementation, and evaluation. Prior to assessing the patient and family as learners, however, make an assessment of yourself as a teacher—your knowledge, skills, personality, beliefs, attitudes, and values. The purpose of this assessment is to identify not only your strengths as a teacher (which will give you confidence in your abilities) but also your weaknesses (which will isolate areas in which growth is needed). To the extent that you are comfortable with yourself as a teacher, you will engender feelings of confidence and trust in patients and their significant others and maximize the potential for successful teaching and learning experiences for both them and yourself.

In making your assessment, use evaluations of previous teaching efforts and your peers as sources of information. In defining your knowledge and skills, decide how well you know the content you will be responsible for teaching. While teaching, will you have to rely on notes or will you know the subject matter well enough to be able to manipulate it, reorder its elements, and answer unanticipated questions? How refined are your nursing skills as well as your skills of observation, communication, and interpersonal relations? How well can you pick up on verbal and nonverbal cues? Are you able to make yourself understood and use language patients can understand? Are you able to relate to people?

In assessing your personality, beliefs, attitudes, and values, you will need to look at your commitment to teaching and learning. How confident are you in your knowledge and skills? Are you responsible as well as persistent so that once a goal is defined, you can be counted on to achieve it? A teacher must also be secure, since not all learners are eager and enthusiastic about learning. Patients who have had previously unsuccessful and unrewarding experiences may be hostile, fearful, and closed. What are your thoughts and feelings about people of various ages, socioeconomic classes, races, nationalities, and cultures and about persons with different value systems, levels of intelligence, abilities, and personalities? Only after making these assessments and understanding yourself can you communicate warmth, genuine interest, and empathic concern to all types of patients and families. How patient are you with yourself as a teacher and learner and with others? Not everyone learns quickly and easily; individuals must learn and grow at their own pace, and an effective teacher will allow them that right. Are you flexible enough to adapt to different learning abilities? Teaching different types of learners necessitates facility in using many kinds of methods and tools, trying alternative teaching styles, and revising teaching plans. Finally, can you be honest with yourself? Can you admit to your feelings and your needs to grow? Are you able to be honest with patients, saying you do not know but will research the answer? Are you willing to evaluate your own teaching performance and to seek supervision and guidance as indicated, ask others for assistance, and listen to their suggestions?

If in asking yourself these questions, you identified areas in which personal growth is needed, how can you foster that growth? Observe effective teachers. Evaluate various teaching styles and identify what methods and tools seem to be successful in teaching people with different kinds of learning abilities. After observing teaching sessions, ask questions. How did the teachers know that the patients were ready for learning? Why did they answer particular questions as they did? Why did they not go into more or less detail in their answers? How did they know when patients or families were ready for teaching and learning experiences to end? Arrange to have your role model observe your teaching and join with you in the evaluation of it. Over time, with continued assessment, growth, performance, and evaluation, you will become a more effective teacher.

Having assessed yourself as a teacher, you can now assess the patient and family as learners. Assessment is necessary, since teaching is an interactive process; and without knowing the person with whom you are dealing, it is difficult to interact. Knowledge about the physical, mental, and emotional characteristics of the learners as well as their socioeconomic environment will enable you to identify the factors which will promote learning and the obstacles which will make learning difficult. Assessment equips you with the knowledge needed to formulate a plan for teaching and to implement it. Without the assessment, you can only make assumptions about the learners—who they are, what they know, and how they learn. If the assumptions are incorrect, the plan will be inappropriate, and the teaching ineffective.

In assessing the patient and family, their abilities, and readiness to learn, your most obvious sources of information are the patient and the family. Your assessment can be formal, as in an admission interview, or informal, as in the course of daily conversation with and observation of the learners. Whether formal or informal, it is important to note not only what is expressed and how but also what is not expressed and why. Often the learners' verbal messages conflict with their nonverbal messages, and this, too, is significant. Since sometimes what patients express when they are interviewed alone differs from what they express when interviewed together with their significant others, it is a good idea to interview the patient and family alone as well as together. Ask patients about themselves as well as about their families and vice versa. Other sources of information for your assessment include records of the patients' medical histories and physical examinations, charts from previous admissions, and physicians, nurses, and social workers familiar with patients and their significant others.

Regardless of the sources used in the assessment, the information to be obtained is the same—the patient's and family's mental status, physical status, emotional status, and socioeconomic status. The mental status assessment is important in planning the manner in which to meet cognitive learning needs. In performing this part of the assessment, you will need to consider the learner's level of consciousness; intelligence; knowledge concerning health, illness, medical and surgical treatment, and teaching and learning; educational background; memory; speed of comprehension; language; problem-solving and analytical skills; perceptions; and judgment. In planning teaching and learning experiences to meet psychomotor learning needs, you will need information about the learner's age, sex, neuromuscular system, strength, balance, reaction time, coordination, health, manual skills, and aptitudes. Since the emotional status of the patient and significant others affects learning, especially affective learning, you will also need to assess their motivation for learning, personality, beliefs, attitudes, values, and emotional stability. The learners' socioeconomic status is important, too. Here, you will consider family structure, major support systems, race, nationality, housing, life-style, religion, occupation, and community health care facilities.

Since the task of assessing learners is so comprehensive, you may find it difficult initially. Remember, however, that the assessment does not need to be completed at any one time. It is a continuous process which, if done well, will save time in the remaining steps of the teaching and learning process, make teaching and learning more effective, and increase the likelihood of enduring behavior change and compliance after the teaching is completed and the patient has been discharged.

Having acquired information about the mental, physical, emotional, and socioeconomic status of the patient and family, you can begin modifying and adapting the plan defined in the general patient teaching program to meet their learning needs. Perhaps you will need to augment the plan by defining ways in which to communicate with a foreign patient or one who is deaf; teach a blind person who lives alone to self-administer daily medication; help a person denying having had a myocardial infarction restrict activity, take medication, alter a highly pressured life-style, and understand risk factors; or encourage family members who do not value health care to bring a patient to the hospital three times a week for hemodialysis.

In developing effective teaching plans, it is important to incorporate several basic principles of teaching and learning. First, begin planning teaching and learning experiences immediately upon the patient's admission to the hospital. This is necessary not only because the patient's learning needs become evident at this time but also because teaching, if it is to result in behavior change, takes time. In the cognitive domain, for example, it generally takes learners 1 to 4 days to begin to know or comprehend facts, principles, and concepts; 5 days to 6 weeks to apply them; and 6 weeks to a year or more to analyze, synthesize, and evaluate them. Affective learning involving the acquisition of new beliefs, attitudes, and values requires even more time since it necessitates changing the ways in which persons view themselves and feel about the world. The time required for psychomotor learning varies, depending on the complexity of the skill to be learned and on the learner's previous knowledge, manual dexterity, level of neuromuscular performance, sensual acuity, and aptitude. Even if teaching and learning experiences are begun immediately, however, because of the time required for various types of learning to occur, it may not be possible to satisfy all the learning needs of a particular patient and family while they are in the acute care setting. You may be able to write the plan and accomplish some of the objectives, but it may be necessary for the remainder of the teaching and learning process to occur after discharge. The public

health nurse, visiting nurse, referring physician, local medical doctor, or significant other will then be responsible for completion of the plan.

The second principle applied to planning is to divide the content to be taught and the objectives to be achieved into separate learning units. The duration and content of each teaching and learning experience will depend on the complexity of the material to be learned, the learner's attention span and speed of comprehension, and the time and energy available for teaching and learning. In the critical-care setting where the patient is acutely ill or in a situation in which the patient is anxious or in pain, the learning units will be extremely brief. As the patient progresses, the units can be longer and the content more complex.

Third, organize the individual learning units into a logical, meaningful sequence. Usually patients learn best if the elements in a teaching and learning experience progress from those which have highest priority (i.e., immediately needed knowledge and skills) to less essential learning (i.e., learning which will be needed at a later time). Learning content should progress from familiar to unfamiliar, known to unknown, general to specific, simple to complex, and concrete to abstract. Begin with what learners want to know and proceed to what they need to know. By sequencing and ordering learning in this way, the patient and family are less likely to feel overwhelmed and needlessly frustrated and will be able to develop a sense of mastery by using the knowledge and skills already possessed as a foundation upon which to build and interpret new information.

Fourth, since the content has been divided into units and will be separated in time and perhaps place, plan for continuity in the teaching and learning experience by developing transitions between parts. This is important not only on a daily basis while teaching the patient and family on a particular unit but also when transferring patients between units or discharging them to the home setting. Documenting your plan and the learner's progress toward the objectives in the progress notes or in a nursing Kardex and sharing this information with persons who will be responsible for the continuation of learning or the completion of the plan are excellent ways to provide for the transition. You may also wish to maintain contact with the learner through office or home visits or telephone calls for a short time to provide an additional opportunity for clarification, reinforcement, and continuity.

Fifth, having defined and organized the content in each teaching and learning experience and provided transitions between them, match teaching methods and tools to be used in each experience with the learning styles and needs of the patient and family as identified in the assessment. The teaching aids selected during the planning step of the development of the patient teaching program will generally be appropriate to all learners; however, the manner in which they are used during individual teaching and learning experiences will be specific to the needs of the learners. For example, since meeting cognitive learning needs relies heavily on verbal skills, the combined lecture and discussion method may have been identified as the best method to use in teaching a patient regarding a particular diet. The language you will use in the lecture discussion, however, will depend on what words the patient and family understand. By listening carefully as they speak, you will learn the words they use to define certain phenomena and what meanings different words hold for them. If the learner has difficulty abstracting, you may plan to use teaching tools like models or the actual object to augment language and promote understanding. The teaching program may specify role modeling as a method to provide for affective learning, but the person you select as a role model will depend on the type of individual with whom the patient or significant other can relate or identify and whose beliefs, attitudes. or values you plan for them to emulate. In order to promote psychomotor learning, the general teaching plan might call for direct experiential learning, but you will define the quality of that experience. To maximize the probability of transfer of learning after discharge, you may use information about the patient's socioeconomic status to design an experience as closely related to the home environment as possible. Allowing the patient and family to practice a skill in a setting similar to their postdischarge setting and using supplies and equipment which will be available to them at that time will promote learning and foster confidence that they will be able to perform the necessary skills after discharge.

Last, realizing that one-half to one-third of all learning acquired is forgotten over time, include opportunities for review in patient teaching. Provide learners with summary sheets, booklets, or pamphlets so that they can retrieve the information as needed. Teaching family members together with the patient maximizes the probability that they will be able to support the patient in remembering the knowledge, attitudes, and skills learned during hospitalization and required for care in the home setting.

In the course of assessing the learners and planning learning experiences to meet their cognitive, affective, and psychomotor learning needs and providing nursing care, you probably have interacted with the patient and family many times. Now that you are ready to begin teaching, however, it is necessary for you to establish a formal relationship. The learners must understand your role and functions as teacher, the nature of your relationship as teacher and learners, the duration of your interaction, and the goal toward which you will be working. Most important, the learners need to trust you and see you as a helping person. Communicating with the patient and family daily even when formal teaching and learning experiences are not being conducted, being available when they have needs, and demonstrating that you are one who can be trusted are ways of fostering the development of that trust.

While establishing your relationship with the patient and family, you can assess their readiness to learn. If you are observant, you will see that the patient and family give many verbal and nonverbal cues indicating that they are ready to learn. For example, patients may ask you a specific question about their diagnosis or an aspect of the medical and nursing management. They may inquire as to your interpretation of what their physician has told them about their condition. You may hear them, in the course of normal conversation, make comments revealing that they are lacking necessary information or are harboring certain misconceptions.

If patients seem to be unable to formulate questions or experience difficulty verbalizing them, you might need to assist them. Asking a simple question such as "What do you understand about the reason for your hospitalization?" sometimes helps both of you learn what the patient knows or does not know about the diagnosis. The question also elicits considerable information regarding how patients feel about their diagnoses and how well they have begun to accept the situation. When this question was posed to patients with whom physicians had just discussed their diagnosis of myocardial infarction, the following responses were obtained: "My doctor told me I had a heart attack but I do not believe it." "The doctor does not really know yet." "The doctor told me my heart burst and I have 3 weeks to live." "My pulmonary artery is plugged up." Other answers to this question revealed that some patients clearly were able to verbalize the cause and treatment of their clinical problem; but, by their refusal to follow diet and activity restrictions, they demonstrated their denial of the diagnosis and their role in convalescence.

In assessing patients' readiness to learn, try to

avoid questions that tend to precipitate monosyllabic answers, such as "yes" or "no." For example, avoid questions which begin with the words "Do you understand. . . ." Even if you receive an affirmative response, you cannot be certain of the extent to which the patient understands. Regardless of the question asked, however, phrase it carefully to avoid implying that the patients ought to know or be able to do something that they do not or cannot or that you do not have confidence in their ability to comprehend or interpret information and events for themselves.

Patients and families also give nonverbal cues which may be as significant as their verbal cues. You may notice that a patient with a colostomy or arteriovenous shunt refuses to look at it during care or that the significant other leaves the patient's room during that time rather than observing or assisting with care. On the other hand, you may be surprised by someone's enthusiasm to learn and eagerness to participate in care. The facial expressions and eye movements of intubated patients can communicate fear, concern, questions, or needs. By validating your observations with the patient or family, you can help them begin to recognize and accept their feelings and begin to learn. It is important to stress here that some patients, such as those with decreased levels of consciousness secondary to serious neurologic defects, are incapable of giving either verbal or nonverbal cues but yet have a need to know and a need for communication. In this instance, you will need to make an assumption concerning what and when the patient needs to learn and intervene appropriately.

Having laid the groundwork for the teacher-learner relationship and assessed the learner's readiness to learn, you are ready to begin interacting formally and informally with the patient and family to provide for their cognitive, affective, and psychomotor learning needs and to effect the desired change in behavior. In interacting with the learners, use the general patient teaching plan and your own individual teaching plan as a guide. As you interact, keep in mind several basic teaching and learning principles. At the beginning of each experience, share with the patient and family your mutual learning goals and the objectives to be achieved during that session. Start at an appropriate level for the patient and family in terms of their knowledge, feelings, and abilities. Use words and patterns of speech they can understand. Define all medical terms used, and if there are several terms which refer to the same phenomena, clarify this, too. Consistently throughout teaching and learning experiences, use examples and analogies and point out

relationships among concepts. Help the patient and family integrate information received from other health team members, learn to solve problems, and consider the implications of learning acquired for their lives after discharge.

A good way to help them consider transfer is to ask them whether or not they think a particular idea will work or whether it would be possible for them to perform an activity or follow prescriptions at home. Additionally, provide opportunities for questions, review, and clarification. Observe and interpret the patient's and family's nonverbal reactions to learning and validate and share your observations with them. Ask frequently if they have questions or comments and convey genuine interest in their responses. When learners give evidence, either by a verbal response or correct behavior, that they have learned, provide positive reinforcement. If on the other hand, learners demonstrate inaccurate or inappropriate learning, point out the error after each incorrect response to discourage repetition, minimize the development of bad habits, and decrease the amount of unlearning which eventually will need to be accomplished. In determining what are meaningful and effective positive or negative reinforcers for the learners, use the information you acquired in your assessment of the patient's or family's emotional status. Identify whether the satisfaction of needs in the area of physiologic drives, safety, love and belonging, esteem, or self-actualization is the most valuable reinforcer for them. Regardless of the source of reinforcement, the most important point is that it be consistent and immediate. So that learners can begin to reinforce their own learning and be less dependent on persons to provide rewards, point out natural positive reinforcers of appropriate learning. For example, if patients need to follow a prescribed low-sodium diet, point out that if they comply they may notice less edema, discomfort, and immobility and will avoid serious complications that may result in readmission to the hospital.

By teaching the family together with the patient, you can develop another source of reinforcement and support for the patient. Significant others may be able to explain information to the patient in a more meaningful way than perhaps you could, help interpret the patient's nonverbal communications, and offer suggestions for care. In between teaching sessions, at times when you are not with the patient, family members may be able to help the patient recall information forgotten or support the patient in going through the various stages of accepting illness or practicing skills learned during the teaching and learning experiences.

By the time of discharge, patients and families will have had experience in communicating and working with each other which may facilitate care in the home setting.

At other times throughout the patient's hospitalization, you may want to teach the family apart from the patient. By meeting with them prior to visiting hours to bring them up to date on the patient's condition and treatment, clarifying and reinforcing communications they have received from physicians, correcting misconceptions, meeting their specific requests and needs, and allowing them to ventilate their thoughts and feelings to someone who cares, you enable the family to use energy formerly tied up in fear and anxiety to support the patient, answer questions, relay confidence, and meet needs. When a patient is unconscious or terminally ill, the significant others may be the persons who most need and can benefit from your teaching and support. With your help, they may be able to learn to accept their feelings of guilt, anger, or fear and eventually resolve their grief.

Finally, in teaching patients and families, watch carefully for cues that the learners are ready for the teaching and learning experience to end. By varying teaching settings, methods, and tools and by alternating between active and passive and talking and listening activities, you may be able to hold the learner's attention for longer periods of time and minimize fatigue and boredom, but there comes a time when the learner is tired. The cues provided may be direct or indirect, verbal or nonverbal. In the middle of a discussion, patients may close their eyes, greet visitors and ask them to stay, answer telephone calls and talk for prolonged periods of time, or go for a walk. Sometimes patients may want to continue learning but their bodies may give cues that it is time to stop. Patients may become diaphoretic or flushed; develop frequent ectopic beats, tachypnea, or tachycardia; or experience angina or dyspnea. Since it is not always easy for acutely ill patients in a critical-care unit to provide either verbal or nonverbal cues, you must be extremely careful not to attempt to teach for long periods of time or discuss information that is either too complex or not of interest to the patient. Teaching in this environment must be done in very short, structured segments, and the verbal communications must be direct, brief, clear, and simple. If you were to overextend teaching and learning experiences in this setting or any other setting in an attempt to complete the scheduled teaching plan, you would be meeting your own needs at the expense of the patient. Fatigue and frustration could result and could lead to blocks in future learning. Once the cue is supplied by the patient or family or you believe that sufficient learning has occurred during a particular teaching experience, you should summarize and bring the session to a close. Before leaving the learners, tell them when you will be seeing them again as well as where they can contact you or one of your peers should questions, needs, or problems related to learning arise. It may be minutes, hours, or days before the patient or family are ready for another learning experience. At times, you may find it frustrating to wait for the cues of readiness to become evident, but remember that learning requires time. Time is needed by patients and significant others to review the information discussed during the experience, go through the stages of acceptance of the diagnosis, and think about the implications of the illness and treatment for their future. When they are ready to learn once again, ask them if they have questions regarding information discussed or skills demonstrated in the previous session, review the major points of that discussion, list the objectives for the present lesson, and proceed.

Evaluation is an ongoing process in which you will be involved both during and after teaching and learning experiences with the patients and families. Regardless of when you accomplish it, however, your primary tasks will be the same: to determine the extent to which the desired behavior changes have occurred in the learners and to judge the effectiveness of your interactions with the patient and family in bringing about the changes. Information obtained as a result of evaluation is valuable both for the patient and family as learners and for you as a teacher. If the information is shared with the patient and family on a daily basis, it serves as a source of encouragement by identifying for them the knowledge, attitudes, and skills acquired in each teaching and learning experience. Second, it tends to motivate them by focusing on the disparity between their current level in learning and the ultimate learning needed. Third, the information enables you to identify particular strengths and weaknesses in your teaching plan and consequently to modify and revise the plan to facilitate future patient and family learning. You may need to include additional content areas, provide opportunities for review, rewrite objectives, or select additional tools and devices. Fourth, at the time of discharge, the results of evaluation allow you to identify those persons who, in spite of teaching and learning, do not have the requisite knowledge and skills to care for themselves adequately and safely in the home setting. As a result, you may need to provide for their continued learning in the home environment by writing referrals to community health care workers. Without the data secured in evaluation, you would have to base these decisions regarding teaching and learning on assumptions which may or may not prove to be correct.

In evaluating patient and family learning, you will use the general objectives identified previously in the patient teaching program plan and your individual teaching plan as a guide. To determine the extent to which the patient and significant others have achieved the desired learning outcome defined in the general objective, you will require the learners to perform the behaviors described in each specific objective. If the learners are able to accomplish them all, you will know that learning or the desired behavior change has occurred. If, on the other hand, they can perform only some of the behaviors, you will know that their learning is not yet complete. By analyzing the results of the evaluation, you can isolate the block to learning and revise your plan to incorporate additional experiences to assist the learners in meeting the objectives.

Asking the patient and family questions and observing their behavior are probably the most useful ways of evaluating learning. In evaluating cognitive learning, you may ask learners, either orally or in writing, to list, state, define, enumerate, identify, or respond in some other way to demonstrate that they know or understand the facts, principles, or concepts in a particular content area.

When determining whether or not the patient and family have acquired desired beliefs, attitudes, or values you may also ask questions. This probably is not the most effective indicator of affective learning, however, since what learners say they believe may not be what they actually believe. Patients and families tend to provide answers which they think the teacher wants to hear or respond in ways they believe sound correct or socially acceptable. The best way to evaluate learners' beliefs, attitudes, and values is to observe their behavior. If, for example, a patient and family preparing for discharge say they believe that it is necessary to perform sterile dressing changes daily and is their responsibility to do so, and yet they never initiate the procedure or notify nursing personnel when it is not accomplished, the probability is high that the desired affective learning has not occurred. The old axiom that actions speak louder than words is especially appropriate when evaluating affective learning.

Observation of behavior is also important in eval-uating psychomotor learning. You may require the patient to self-administer insulin, suction a tracheos-tomy, or perform shunt care. In the evaluation of some skills, all that may be important is the completion of the task; while in the performance of other skills, sequence, technique, and speed may also be signif-icant criteria.

In the course of daily teaching and learning experiences during hospitalization, the focus of your evaluation is on the patient's and family's learning of isolated knowledge, attitudes, and skills. As you prepare them for discharge, however, your emphasis shifts to evaluation of their ability to integrate cognitive, affective, and psychomotor learning acquired from various sources of teaching, to interpret events, and to deal with potential problems after discharge. An excellent way to evaluate their ability to solve problems and determine the extent to which they are able to transfer learning is to present them with situations they might experience in the home setting: "What would you do if you experienced angina while mowing the lawn?" "What would you do if you vomited after taking your daily medications?" "What would you do if your spouse started hemorrhaging in the night?" In order to answer these questions, patients and families will need to recall the specifics of their home and community setting and their resources available, visualize themselves experiencing the problem in a more realistic setting than the hospital, list possible solutions or courses of action to deal with the problem and identify the advantages and disadvantages of each, select the most appropriate or feasible solution, and identify the possible consequences of their decision. By presenting the learners with situations of this type, you help them develop their problem-solving abilities, learn to evaluate their own decisions and behavior, and develop confidence in their ability to manage self-care after discharge.

Even if patients and families perform well in evaluation sessions during hospitalization, however, once discharged they may not be able to retain or operationalize the learning. Having acquired most of their learning in a relatively short period of time when their ability to learn was compromised by physiologic and emotional stress, they may forget many of the facts, principles, attitudes, and skills learned. Additionally, in their socioeconomic setting, patients and families may not be able to comply with prescribed care due to negative social sanctions, fixed economic incomes, recurrent health problems, or situational stresses unrelated to health. For these reasons, you may want to arrange for health care workers in the community to provide support for the patient and family after discharge or consult with medical or nursing personnel in clinics where the patient will be returning for follow-up visits to ensure that the patient and family will have opportunities for continued learning and reinforcement.

In addition to guiding and directing the patient and family in self-care, these community health care members can provide you with information which will enable you to evaluate your effectiveness as a teacher. From them you may learn that the patient and family could have benefited from discussions of additional content areas, a more realistic setting in which to practice skills required after discharge, more opportunities for review and questions, or written materials summarizing essential knowledge and procedures needed for care at home. Other sources of information to assist you in your evaluation include comments from patients and families and telephone calls received from them after discharge, questionnaires sent from the hospital to former patients and families, and records of patient readmissions for complications and recurrent health problems. In reviewing this information, determine your strengths as a teacher, the type of teaching and learning experiences which patients and families found most or least helpful, the problems and needs experienced by patients and families after discharge, and the complications most commonly necessitating readmission to the hospital. Although the information acquired will not enable you to help previous learners, it will guide you in modifying and further developing your skills of assessment, planning, and implementation and in interacting with future patients and families.

Evaluation

By generalizing the information obtained in your evaluation of teaching and learning experiences with specific patients and families and comparing it with that secured by your peers in their teaching efforts, you will have valuable knowledge to share with other health team members when you meet as a group to evaluate the general patient teaching program. The task of your group during this step of program development will be to determine whether or not the cognitive, affective, and psychomotor learning needs of patients and significant others identified in your assessment frameworks were met and to judge the effectiveness of the planning and implementation of the program in facilitating learning. The results of the evaluation are very important, since they determine the future of the patient teaching program and future

learning of patients and families. If group members can show that the program decreases the problems experienced by patients, families, and health team members identified earlier when documenting the need for a program and that it provides for the learning needs of patients and families, then the time, energy, and economic resources expended in patient teaching can be justified. If, on the other hand, it cannot be shown that teaching has made a difference in the quality of health care administered to patients and families in the institution, the teaching program must be revised if it is to accomplish its original purpose.

In accomplishing this task, members of your group may wish to secure the assistance of medical records or audit committee personnel, since the primary source of information for the evaluation will be the documentation of patient and family learning in the patient's medical record. If health team members made appropriate entries in the chart, information will be available concerning the patients' and families' learning in terms of the behavioral objectives, the name of the health team member responsible for the teaching and learning experience, and the date learning was evidenced. Additional sources of objective data include hospital records of patient admissions and accompanying diagnoses, clinic records of patient and family follow-up visits, and documentation of care provided by community health care members. Subjective data can be obtained from local medical doctors, referring physicians, patients and families, and other health team members.

Using information from these sources and from the assessment frameworks, group members should determine whether or not the learning needs identified in the frameworks were met. If learning needs were not met, group members should review the plan for the patient teaching program to identify areas responsible for the learning deficit. Each decision made previously in the planning step of program development should be analyzed. Were the content areas correctly identified? Did the general and specific objectives clearly communicate the terminal learning outcomes as well as the individual learning behaviors? Were the health team members responsible and accountable for patient teaching in assigned content areas? Did the members have sufficient knowledge and skills to teach the patient and family? Were the timing and location of teaching and learning experiences appropriate to the needs of the learner? How well did the teaching methods, tools, and devices facilitate learning? And finally, were the means of documenting teaching and learning adequate?

Having evaluated patient and family learning and

determined the effectiveness of teaching in facilitating learning, group members need to evaluate the extent to which problems identified in the documentation of need have been decreased by teaching efforts. Consistently, when reviewing each problem, the group must decide whether or not teaching made a difference. Are patients and families more knowledgeable about themselves and their environments? At the time of discharge, are they equipped with the knowledge, attitudes, and skills required for home care? Do health team members feel less frustrated and more productive in their work? If the answers to these questions are affirmative, health team members may decide to continue with the teaching program without alteration. Usually, however, in the course of evaluation, group members find additional content areas to be included in the program; behavioral objectives to be written or revised, additional teaching tools to be purchased; or means of documentation to be revised.

Prior to formal evaluation of the patient teaching program for cardiovascular surgical patients, health team members in nursing, surgery, dietetics, pharmacy, and physical conditioning met with their peers to pool the evaluation results of their individual patient teaching efforts. Subsequently, representatives from each care area met to discuss the evaluation. Problems related to teaching and learning experienced by patients, families, and health team members were identified, and recommendations to improve the quality of the program were made.

The first problem identified was that health team members had difficulty retrieving information to use in evaluation because documentation of teaching and learning experiences frequently was incomplete. Sometimes the narrative entries included a clear description of patient and family progress toward behavioral objectives, while at other times they simply noted that teaching and learning had been accomplished. Health team members identified the following reasons for the omissions in documentation: writing narrative entries was time-consuming, recording the teaching and learning both in the progress notes and on the patient teaching checklist required duplication of effort, and patient teaching sometimes was incompletely accomplished because of late notification of patient discharge. Since documentation was incomplete, health team members found it difficult to determine the extent to which teaching and learning had been completed by persons in other health care areas.

The second group of problems identified by group members related to patients and their significant others. Although most of the patients and families participated in teaching and learning experiences during hospitalization and gave evidence of having achieved the desired learning outcome by the time of discharge, after they left the hospital they experienced problems. Some patients could not read the notes they had taken during the learning sessions, lost summary sheets or prescriptions for medications or had difficulty interpreting them, or received conflicting information concerning home care from their local medical doctor.

Other patients experienced additional problems. If health team members received late notification of patient discharge and discharge prescriptions, they did not have time to provide the necessary teaching and learning experiences concerning diet, activity, and medications. Since exercise classes were conducted only twice a week, some patients could not attend. Although they received a pamphlet illustrating the exercises with stick figures, they had difficulty interpreting the figures. Those patients who attended the class sometimes became frustrated because they felt other patients were more intelligent and could perform better than they could. If the class was large, patients did not have time to ask questions, could not view the demonstration, or became uncomfortable because the classroom was crowded and warm. During the course of hospitalization, some patients continued to receive conflicting information. Although nursing personnel knew physicians' preferences regarding activity and diet progression during and after hospitalization, surgical residents who rotated services every 2 months did not. Several patients were readmitted to the hospital with bacterial endocarditis due to lack of antibiotic coverage when having dental work completed, and frequently patients did not receive necessary follow-up care because they could not locate the clinic building.

Although they recognized that as a result of patient teaching efforts, patients and families were experiencing fewer problems and having more of their learning needs met, health team members agreed that several major revisions in the program were needed. First, to solve the problem of inadequate documentation, checklists were developed to record the results of preoperative and discharge teaching and learning experiences. The checklists, which would eventually replace the dual entries in the progress notes and on the previous patient teaching checklist, would be completed by all health team members providing teaching and learning experiences for the patient and family and would become a permanent part of the patient's medical record.

The preoperative checklist contained several columns (Fig. 45-1). The first column provided a section on patient information including the type of operative procedure, date and time of surgery, allergies to medications, mental or physical handicaps, and current, noncardiac medical problems. This information would be important to nurses providing care for patients in the cardiovascular surgical critical care unit. The second section in the first column listed desired learning outcomes to be achieved by patients and families prior to surgery. The third section identified skills to be learned and demonstrated by the patient prior to surgery, and the fourth section listed patient or family preferences, needs, or concerns related to surgery or the critical-care unit. The second,

the University of Alabama in Birmingham
the Medical Center / UNIVERSITY OF ALABAMA HOSPITALS

NURSES' PROGRESS NOTES/PREOPERATIVE TEACHING

Keyplate

	YES	NO	N/A	COMMENTS
1. PATIENT INFORMATION				
a. Operative Procedure				
b. Date and Time of Surgery				
c. Allergies to Medications				
d. Mental or Physical Handicaps				
1) Blindness				
2) Deafness				
3) Fractures				
4) Muscular Weakness				
5) Paralysis				
6) Retardation				
7) Other				
e. Current, Non-cardiac Medical Problems				
1) Arrhythmias				
2) Arthritis				
3) Bleeding Tendency				
4) Cancer				
5) COLD				
6) Convulsions				
7) Diabetes				
8) Glaucoma				
9) Gout				
10) H/O Cardiac Arrest				
11) Hypertension				
12) Migraine Headaches				
13) Prostatic Enlargement				
14) Pulses (Diminished)				
15) Renal Problems				
16) Ulcers				
17) Other				
2. INFORMATION DISCUSSED WITH AND UNDERSTOOD BY PATIENT AND _____ (RELATION):				
a. Basic Cardiac Pathology, Surgical Procedure and Time of Operation				
b. Day Before Surgery				
1) Preoperative Instructions by Surgeon and Anesthesiologist, Purpose and Approximate Times of Completion				
2) Consent to Operation				
3) Body Shave and Prep				
4) Diet				
5) No Smoking				

FIGURE 45-1

Nurses progress notes—preoperative teaching. (*Courtesy of University of Alabama Hospitals.*)

the University of Alabama in Birmingham
the Medical Center / UNIVERSITY OF ALABAMA HOSPITALS

NURSES' PROGRESS NOTES/PREOPERATIVE TEACHING

Page Two

	YES	NO	N/A	COMMENTS
c. Day of Surgery				
1) Visiting Hours				
2) Time of Awakening				
3) Premedications				
4) Transfer to Surgery				
5) Family Responsibilities				
6) Surgery				
7) Notification of Family				
8) Intensive Care				
9) CICU Visiting Hours				
d. Days After Surgery				
1) Transfer from CICU				
2) Notification of Family				
3) Diet				
4) Activity				
5) Normal Postoperative Occurrences				
e. Other				
3. DEEP BREATHING AND COUGHING TECHNIQUE UNDERSTOOD AND DEMONSTRATED BY PATIENT				
4. PATIENT OR FAMILY HAS PREFERENCES, NEEDS OR CONCERNS RELATED TO SURGERY OR CICU				

Signature

Title

Date

FIGURE 45-1 *(Continued)*

third, and fourth columns entitled "Yes," "No," and "N/A" provided spaces for health team members to note whether or not the statement applied to the patient or family or had been accomplished by the learners. And the last column entitled "Comments" provided space for members to record special considerations or additional learning outcomes.

The discharge checklist was also divided into columns (Fig. 45-2). The first section in the first column listed the criteria which the patient must meet prior to discharge. The criteria were based on anatomic and physiologic subsystems. The second section identified the desired learning outcomes for the patient and significant others. The third section listed patient procedures to be completed before discharge. The fourth section specified written information and equipment or supplies required by the patient for care after discharge, and the fifth column covered the various steps of the discharge procedure. As in the preoperative checklist, the second, third, fourth, and fifth columns were entitled "Yes," "No," and "N/A," and "Comments" and the last column provided space for the initials of the health team member providing care or teaching and learning experiences. Space for identification of initials was provided at the bottom of the second page.

The next group task was to identify commonalities in the problems experienced by patients and families and to define solutions to these problems. To solve the problem of late notification of patient discharge and confusion concerning patient discharge orders, group members designed a dismissal order sheet which would be placed in the patient's chart in the same section as the doctor's order sheets (Fig. 45-3). The preprinted dismissal order sheet listed the types of information needed by health team members to teach patients and families prior to discharge. The information included the date of discharge; diet and duration; duration of activity restrictions; duration of wearing antiembolism stockings; dates of clinic appointments and diagnostic procedures to be performed prior to each appointment; name of the patient's referring physician or local medical doctor; and the dosage, frequency, and duration of medications to be self-administered by the patient after discharge. Surgeons agreed to complete the form 48

the University of Alabama in Birmingham
the Medical Center / UNIVERSITY OF ALABAMA HOSPITALS

NURSES' PROGRESS NOTES/PATIENT DISCHARGE

Keyplate

	YES	NO	N/A	COMMENTS	INITIALS
1. PATIENT MEETS THE FOLLOWING DISCHARGE CRITERIA					
a. Neurologic (Oriented to Time, Place, Person)					
b. Pulmonary (No SOB, ↑ WOB, DOE)					
c. Cardiovascular (No Major Arrhythmias, Hypertension)					
d. GI/Renal (Adequate I and O)					
e. Metabolic (Afebrile, Weight $<$ Preoperative Weight)					
f. Integumentary (Incisions Free of Drainage and Thrombosis)					
2. INFORMATION DISCUSSED WITH AND UNDERSTOOD BY PATIENT AND _____ (RELATION):					
a. Discharge Procedure					
b. Diet, _____ , and Duration, _____ Weeks					
c. Directions for Taking and Storing Medications and the Purposes, Dosages and Precautions of the Following Medications:					
d. Incisional Care					
e. Anti-embolism Stockings and Duration of Wear, _____ Weeks					
f. Activity					
g. Rest					
h. Prevention of Infection					
i. Medical and Surgical Followup					
j. Physical Conditioning Program					
k. Other					
3. PATIENT HAS HAD:					
a. Stitches from Catheterization and Surgery Removed					
b. Myocardial Wires Pulled					
c. Other					

FIGURE 45-2

Nurses progress notes—patient discharge. (*Courtesy of University of Alabama Hospitals.*)

the University of Alabama in Birmingham
the Medical Center / UNIVERSITY OF ALABAMA HOSPITALS

NURSES' PROGRESS NOTES/PATIENT DISCHARGE

Page Two

Keyplate

	YES	NO	N/A	COMMENTS	INITIALS
4. PATIENT HAS RECEIVED:					
a. Cardiovascular Surgery Booklet					
1) Clinic Appointments					
2) Diet, General Guidelines and Recipes					
3) Physical Conditioning Program and General Guidelines					
4) Prescribed Medications for _____					
5) Daily Dosage Schedule					
6) Completed Coumadin Dosage Calendar					
7) Descriptions of Medications					
8) Rules for Taking and Storing Medications					
b. Medications and Copies of Prescriptions					
c. Prescriptions for Medications					
d. Identification Card					
e. Bag Lunch					
f. Permission to Fly Form					
g. Personal Clothing					
h. Valuables					
i. Prostheses (Dentures, Glasses)					
j. Pre-admission Medications					
k. Supplies and Equipment for Home Care					
5. PATIENT WAS:					
a. Discharged on _____ (Date) at _____ am/pm as a result of: _____ Routine Discharge _____ Transfer to _____ _____ Death					
b. Transported from Unit by _____ and from Discharge Area by _____					
c. Accompanied by _____					

INITIAL IDENTIFICATION:

INITIAL	SIGNATURE	TITLE	DATE

FIGURE 45-2 *(Continued)*

hours prior to discharge. The advance notice of patient discharge allowed health team members time to complete teaching, and pharmacists were able to supply patients with a month's supply of medication and copies of the prescription for their reference.

The next group task involved writing a handbook, entitled *Cardiovascular Surgery,* which contained a written record of all the information discussed with patients and families by various health team members throughout the patient's course of hospitalization. The

the University of Alabama in Birmingham
Medical Center / UNIVERSITY OF ALABAMA HOSPITALS AND CLINICS

DOCTOR'S ORDER SHEET

DATE & HOUR	ORDERS WRITE LEGIBLY WITH BALL POINT PEN. EACH NEW SET OF ORDERS MUST BE STARTED BELOW HEAVY LINE AND SIGNED BY DOCTOR.	NURSING
	DISMISSAL ORDERS	KEY PLATE
	Date of Discharge	
	Diet Duration	
	Duration of Activity Restriction	
	Anti-embolism Stockings	NOTED BY
	Date(s) of Clinic Appointment(s)	KEY PLATE
	EKG	
	Blood Work	
	Chest X-Ray	
	To Be Followed By	NOTED BY
	Medications to be Dispensed by Pharmacy	KEY PLATE
	(Medication, Dosage, Frequency, and Duration)	
		NOTED BY
		KEY PLATE
		NOTED BY
		KEY PLATE
		NOTED BY

FORM N—20

ATTENTION: Detach white copy at perforation below last section containing orders. Forward all white copy sections to pharmacy whether medication orders appear or not.

FIGURE 45-3

Doctor's order sheet. (*Courtesy of University of Alabama Hospitals.*)

patient handbook would take the place of the individual summary sheets, which had differed in size, quality of print, style of writing, and completeness of content. After the booklet was developed, a copy was given to each patient upon admission. It contained a preface describing the purpose of the booklet; a table of contents; a narrative portion describing experiences and responsibilities of patients and families before, during, and after surgery; summaries of hospitalization and discharge prescriptions; and an index listing questions and the page numbers where answers could be found.

The summary of hospitalization provided spaces for recording the locations of preoperative and postoperative units; the names of head nurses; and the nurse, surgeon, and anesthesiologist providing preoperative instructions; the type of operative procedure performed; labeled diagrams showing internal and external views of the heart; the date of discharge; and

the names of the nurse, dietitian, and pharmacist providing discharge instructions as well as telephone numbers where they could be reached (Fig. 45-4).

The summary of discharge orders contained statements concerning diet, medications, antiembolism stockings, activity, and medical and surgical follow-up (Fig. 45-5). Blanks adjacent to each statement were checked by the nurse during discharge instructions if they applied to the particular patient being taught.

The booklet was bound with metal fasteners so that

SUMMARY OF HOSPITALIZATION

ADMISSION

    DATE   ———————————————

    PHYSICIAN   ———————————————

    UNIT   ———————————————

        HEAD NURSE   ———————————————

OPERATION

    PREOPERATIVE INSTRUCTIONS

        SURGEON   ———————————————

        ANESTHESIOLOGIST ———————————————

        NURSE   ———————————————

    DATE   ———————————————

    OPERATIVE PROCEDURE ———————————————
    (Complete after surgery)

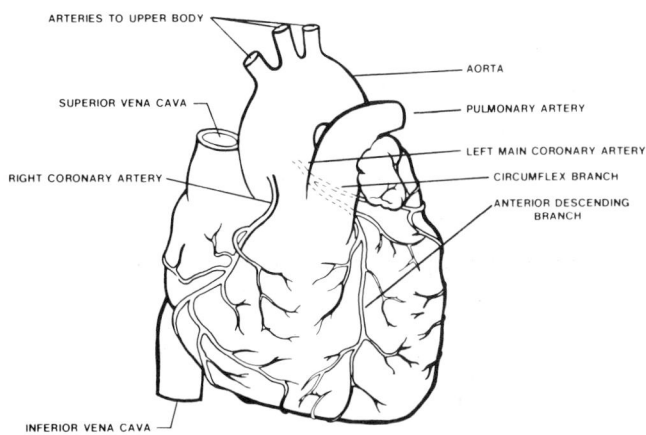

FIGURE 45-4

Summary of hospitalization. (*Courtesy of University of Alabama Hospitals.*)

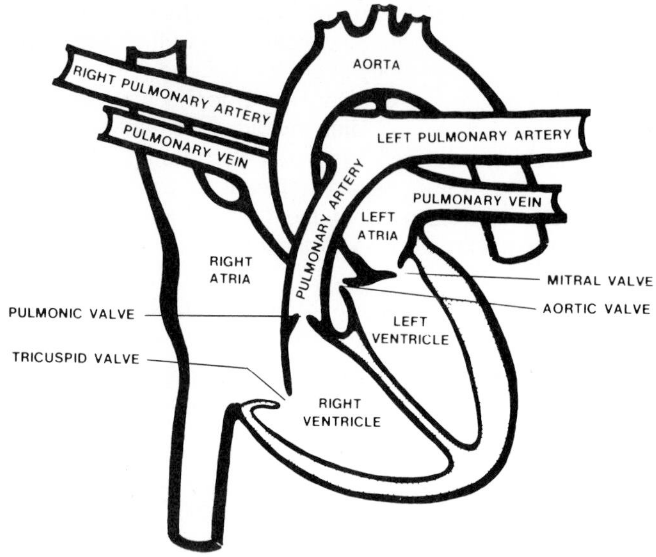

POSTOPERATIVE CARE

UNIT _____

    HEAD NURSE _____

UNIT _____

    HEAD NURSE _____

UNIT _____

    HEAD NURSE _____

DISCHARGE

    DATE _____

DISCHARGE INSTRUCTIONS

    NURSE/UNIT TELEPHONE NUMBER _____ (1-205-934-____)

    DIETITIAN _____

    PHARMACIST/TELEPHONE NUMBER _____ (1-205-934-3606)

FIGURE 45-4 *(Continued)*

prior to discharge, appropriate information concerning clinic appointments and maps, diet, physical conditioning, medications, warfarin dosage calendars, and copies of prescriptions could be added.

The next group project was to develop an identification card for patients in an effort to decrease the incidence of patients readmitted to the hospital with bacterial endocarditis. A card containing the patient's name, surgeon's name, operative procedure, date of operation, and name and address of the hospital was designed for patients to show to all dentists and physicians caring for them after discharge.

Finally, an audiovisual tape of the physical conditioning program was produced to take the place of postoperative classes. The tape made it possible for patients to view and review the material on the tape as frequently as desired and expend minimal energy in acquiring the information. During the first portion

SUMMARY OF DISCHARGE ORDERS

ONLY THE STATEMENTS CHECKED APPLY TO YOU. DISREGARD THOSE STATEMENTS WHICH ARE NOT CHECKED.

DIET

— You will be on a regular diet and may eat any foods you like.

— You will be on a _____ diet for _____ weeks. Eat and drink only those foods and beverages which are allowed or your diet. After _____ (day) _____ (date), you should return to a regular diet and eat any foods you like. A copy of your diet is included in the last portion of this booklet.

MEDICATIONS

— You do not need to take medications after discharge unless your local or referring physician prescribes them for you.

— You need to take medications when you return home. Memorize the names and dosages of the medications. Take your medicine exactly as prescribed. Do not take more or less than ordered. When your supply is running low, see your local doctor so he can write a new prescription and you can have it filled before you run out of medicine. Your local doctor will decide how long you need to continue on the medication.

— You are taking Coumadin, a blood thinner, for an indefinite period of time. You MUST see your local doctor two or three days after discharge and periodically thereafter to have blood tests, called Prothrombin Times, to determine how much Coumadin you need to take. Until you see him, take the dosage specified on your Coumadin Dosage Calendar or on the bottle label. Take this booklet with you when you see your doctor so he can review your "Record of Prothrombin Times and Coumadin Administrations During Hospitalization." At all times, wear an identification bracelet or necklace indicating that you are taking anticoagulants. A hospital pharmacist or nurse will give you an application form for the identification jewelry.

— A pharmacist will discuss your medications with you before discharge and give you a thirty day supply and copies of the prescriptions for your reference. Take the prescriptions with you when you see your local doctor.

— A pharmacist will discuss your medications with you and will give you prescriptions for the medications that you will be taking at home. Have the prescriptions filled in the hospital pharmacy or at a drug store before the next scheduled dose of your medication is due.

ANTI-EMBOLISM STOCKINGS

— You do not need to wear your knee-length stockings at home.

— You need to wear your anti-embolism stockings for _____ weeks, until _____ (day), _____ (date). If swelling of your legs persists after this time, continue to wear your stockings for another week or two until the fullness subsides. You do not need to wear them at night, but do apply them before you stand up and walk around in the morning. Wash them when they become soiled in soapy, lukewarm water; rinse and air dry.

FIGURE 45-5

Summary of discharge orders. (*Courtesy of University of Alabama Hospitals.*)

of the tape, the physical conditionist reviewed the dos, don'ts, and major precautions of exercises, and during the last portion, a former cardiovascular surgical patient demonstrated the exercises at a pace slow enough to allow the hospitalized patient to perform the exercises in concert. Prior to viewing the tape, the patient received the portion of the cardiovascular surgery booklet on exercise. The stick figures were replaced by diagrams of a person performing the exercises to eliminate previous problem of patient interpretation.

Once the preoperative and discharge checklists,

ACTIVITY

— Perform the exercises in your physical conditioning program everyday for at least the first six weeks after discharge.

— For the first _____ weeks after discharge, do not lift, push or pull anything heavier than three to five pounds. After _____ months, you may lift up to twenty pounds and after _____ months, thirty or more pounds.

— Sexual relations are permissible _____ after discharge, provided you are not fatigued. For the first six weeks, refrain from assuming the upper, prone position; rather, assume the supine (lower), side to side or sitting position. Women should check with a doctor about the adequacy of previously used birth control methods and the advisability of pregnancy. Women may notice some delay in the resumption of menstrual periods due to the stress of surgery. This is normal.

— You may drive an automobile _____ weeks after discharge; a truck, after _____ weeks. Riding in a car, plane, bus or train is permissible anytime after discharge provided you flex and extend your legs and feet to promote circulation every hour or so; preferably, you should leave the vehicle and walk around.

— _____ weeks after discharge you may resume moderate activities such as fishing, boating, bicycle riding, sweeping, vacuum cleaning, attending ball games, and mowing the lawn. After _____ months, you may resume heavy activities including raking, hoeing, shoveling, jogging, tennis, contact sports, hunting, shooting a gun and golfing. Really strenuous golfing, hunting and jogging should be delayed until _____ months after discharge.

You may resume the following activities at the specified times:

_____ after _____ weeks/months

_____ after _____ weeks/months

_____ after _____ weeks/months

_____ after _____ weeks/months

_____ after _____ weeks/months

_____ after _____ weeks/months

— You may return to work/school in approximately _____ weeks/months after discharge. Because it is impossible to predict the rate of recovery after your discharge, please check with your local doctor as to the exact date of your return. When you go back to work or school, try to arrange to begin on a part-time basis until you feel ready to assume full-time status.

FIGURE 45-5 *(Continued)*

dismissal order sheet, *Cardiovascular Surgery* handbook, identification card, and audiovisual tape had been developed, they were incorporated into the previous general patient teaching program. These teaching aids were used by health team members as tools and did not replace the one-to-one, teacher-learner interaction so necessary for learning to occur. A formal evaluation of the revised teaching program has not yet been completed, but from the written and oral responses of patients, families, local medical doctors, and the audit committee members, the program seems to have been revised for the better. When the evaluation is complete, the process of assessment, planning, implementation, and evaluation will begin again, for in patient and family teaching, the process never ends.

MEDICAL AND SURGICAL FOLLOW UP

___ After discharge, you need to stay in Birmingham until you see your surgeon, Dr. _____. For information concerning the dates, times and locations of your appointments with him, refer to the page entitled "Clinic Appointments" in the last portion of your booklet. Take the booklet with you to your appointments.

___ See your local doctor, Dr. _____ , on or before _____ (day), _____ (date). Take this booklet with you each time you see your physician.

___ See your referring physician, Dr. _____ , on or before _____ (day), _____ (date). Take your booklet with you when you see your physician.

ADDITIONAL INSTRUCTIONS

___ _____

___ _____

___ _____

___ _____

___ _____

___ _____

FIGURE 45-5 (*Continued*)

REFERENCES

American Hospital Association: *A Patient's Bill of Rights,* Chicago: The American Hospital Association, 1972.

American Nurses' Association: *Standards of Nursing Practice,* Kansas City, Missouri: The American Nurses' Association, 1973.

Bloom, B. S. (ed.): *Taxonomy of Educational Objectives: Cognitive Domain,* New York: McKay, 1956.

Blue Cross Association: *White Paper: Patient Health Education,* Blue Cross Association, 1974.

Gronlund, Norman E.: *Stating Behavioral Objectives for Classroom Instruction,* New York: Macmillan, 1970.

Krathwohl, D. R., B. S. Bloom, and B. B. Masia: *Taxonomy of Educational Objectives: Affective Domain,* New York: McKay, 1964.

Mager, Robert F.: *Preparing Instructional Objectives,* Belmont, California: Fearon Publishers, 1962.

Redman, Barbara K.: *The Process of Patient Teaching in Nursing,* St. Louis: Mosby, 1976.

PART 11

APPENDIXES

APPENDIX A

DYSRHYTHMIAS

Carolyn B. Chalkley

INTRODUCTION

The purpose of this section is to serve as a basic guide for the critical-care nurse in assessing dysrhythmias in an orderly sequence. It is not intended to be all-inclusive, and the reader is directed to the excellent texts listed in the references for more details of these rhythms, more complex rhythms, and less commonly seen rhythms.

The features of ventricular activity are listed first, since no patient will survive without an adequate ventricular rhythm. The setting is intended to call to mind some of the causes of these dysrhythmias and some nursing observations and/or interventions which contribute to the management of these patients.

In the event of a dysrhythmia, the nurse should:

1. Document the dysrhythmia on a rhythm strip including the onset and termination

2. Assess the patient

3. Verify rhythm with 12-lead ECG if necessary

4. Notify physician of significant change

5. Follow standing orders of the institution

NORMAL SINUS RHYTHM

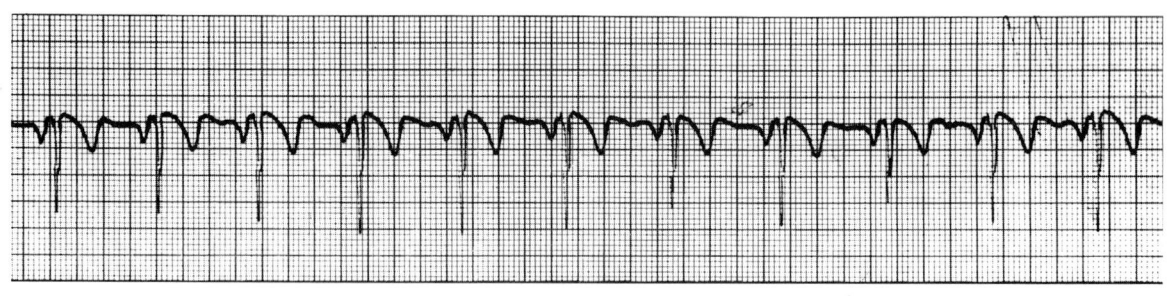

FIGURE A-1
Normal sinus rhythm.

Ventricular:	Rate—60–100 beats per minute Rhythm—Regular or very slightly irregular Contour—Normal
Atrial:	Rate—60–100 beats per minute Rhythm—Regular or very slightly irregular Contour—Normal
PR Interval:	Normal
Sequence:	P wave precedes each QRST complex All beats have same appearance
Significance:	Normal

SINUS BRADYCARDIA

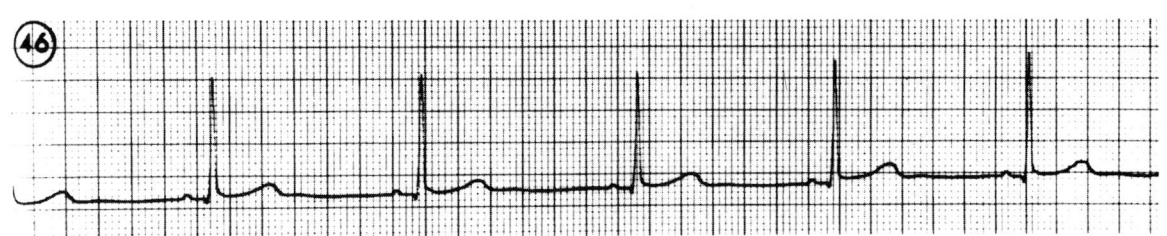

FIGURE A-2

Sinus bradycardia. (*From R. E. Phillips and M. K. Feeney, The Cardiac Rhythms, Saunders, Philadelphia, 1973.*)

Ventricular: Rate—< 60 beats per minute
Rhythm—Regular or very slightly irregular
Contour—Normal

Atrial: Rate—< 60 beats per minute
Rhythm—Regular or slightly irregular
Contour—Normal

PR Interval: Normal

Sequence: P wave precedes each QRST complex
All beats have same appearance

Setting: Normal variant (common in athletes), sleep, digitalis, vagal influence, extreme fright, carotid sinus pressure, myxedema, obstructive jaundice, ocular pressure, increased intracranial pressure, Valsalva maneuvers, hypothermia, propranolol, reflex following vasopressors

Significance: Depends on cause and patient's tolerance of rate

SINUS TACHYCARDIA

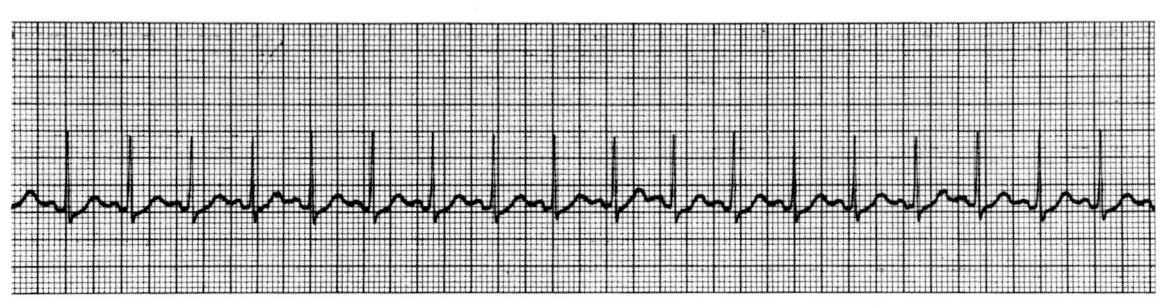

FIGURE A-3
Sinus tachycardia.

Ventricular: Rate—>100 beats per minute
Rhythm—Regular or very slightly irregular
Contour—Normal

Atrial: Rate—>100 beats per minute
Rhythm—Regular or very slightly irregular
Contour—Normal

PR Interval: Normal

Sequence: P wave precedes each QRST complex
All beats have same appearance

Setting: Fever, shock, anxiety, congestive heart failure, pain, hypoxia, thyrotoxicosis, anemia, drugs
(such as epinephrine, atropine, caffeine), exercise, hypovolemia

Significance: Depends on cause and patient's tolerance of rate

SINUS ARRHYTHMIA

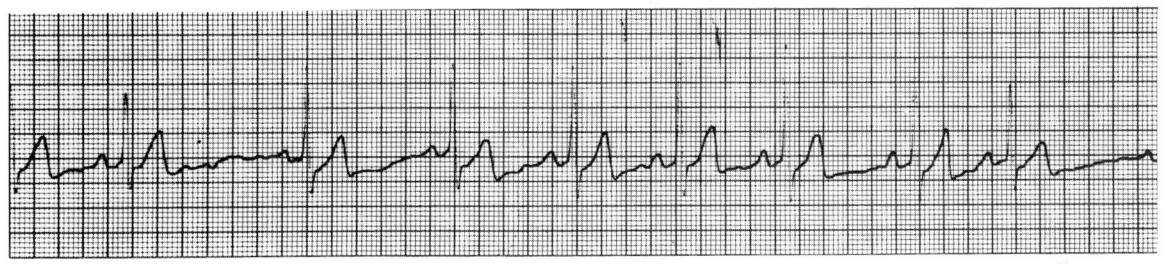

FIGURE A-4
Sinus arrhythmia.

Ventricular:	Rate—Variable Rhythm—Irregular Contour—Normal
Atrial:	Rate—Variable Rhythm—Irregular Contour—Normal
PR Interval:	Normal
Sequence:	P wave precedes each QRST complex All beats have same appearance Rate increases and decreases cyclically; may be related to respiration
Setting:	Common in young people
Significance:	None

SINUS ARREST (PAUSE, BLOCK, EXIT BLOCK, STANDSTILL)

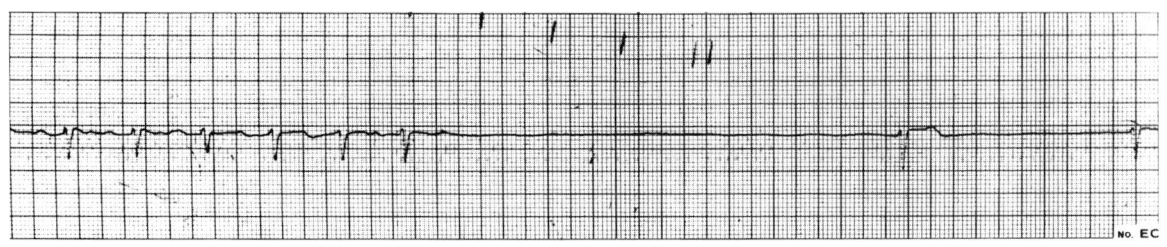

FIGURE A-5
Sinus arrest (first half of ECG). See Fig. A-6 for second half.

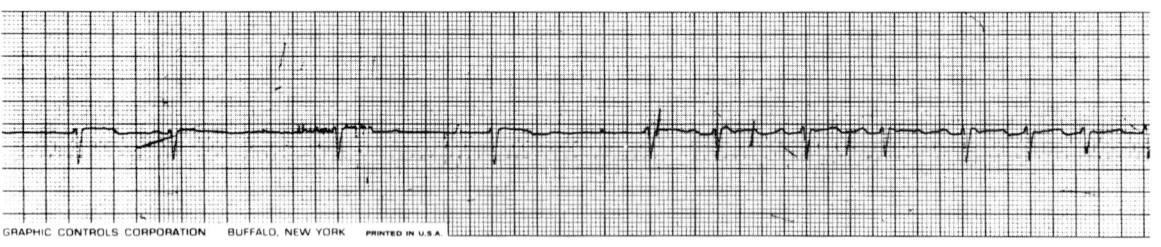

FIGURE A-6
Sinus arrest (second half of ECG). See Fig. A-5 for first half.

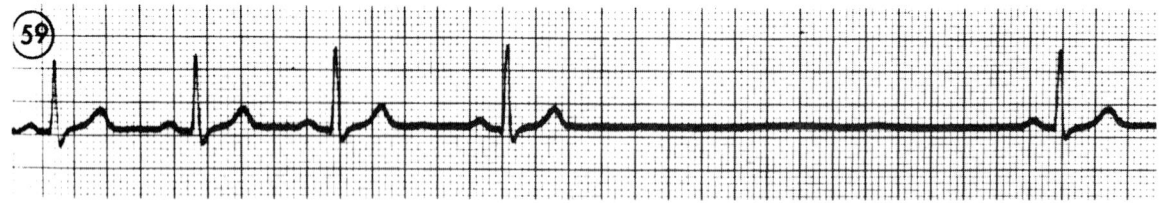

FIGURE A-7
Sinus arrest. (*From R. E. Phillips and M. K. Feeney, The Cardiac Rhythms, Saunders, Philadelphia, 1973.*)

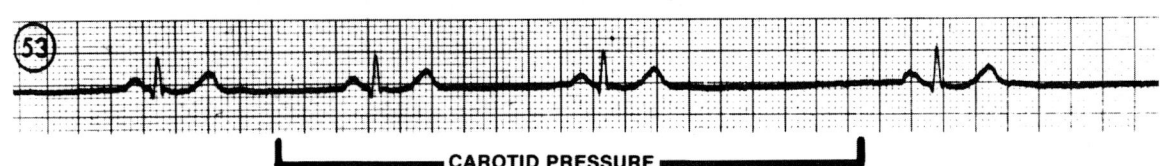

CAROTID PRESSURE

FIGURE A-8

Sinus arrest. (*From R. E. Phillips and M. K. Feeney, The Cardiac Rhythms, Saunders, Philadelphia, 1973.*)

Ventricular: Rate—Depends on underlying rhythm, frequency, and duration of sinus arrest
Rhythm—Irregular
Contour—Normal

Atrial: Rate—Depends on underlying rhythm, frequency, and duration of sinus arrest
Rhythm—Irregular
Contour—Normal

PR Interval: Normal

Sequence: Failure of SA impulse to emerge for one or more beats produces a straight line on the electrocardiogram. This pause may be followed by resumption of the sinus rhythm, an escape rhythm, or death.

Setting: Vagal influence, carotid sinus stimulation, digitalis, propranolol, inflammation or infarction of SA node

Significance: Depends on length of arrest. In any event, the physician should be notified at once since short pauses may forewarn of complete arrest.

WANDERING ATRIAL PACEMAKER (PATHWAY, MECHANISM)

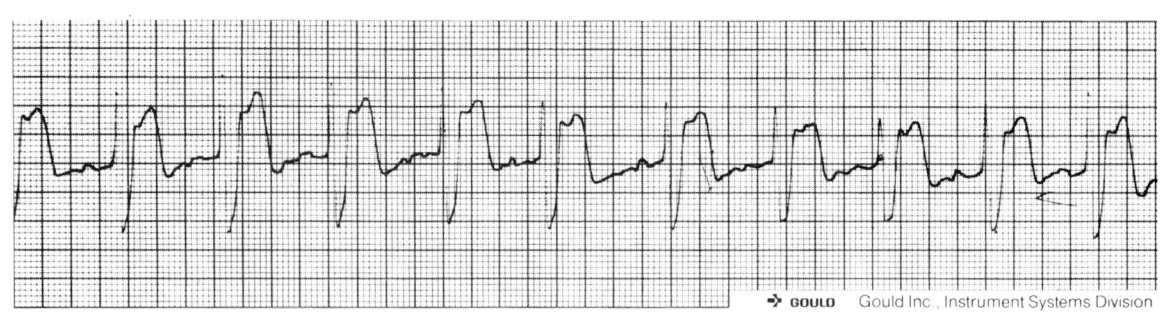

GOULD   Gould Inc., Instrument Systems Division

FIGURE A-9
Wandering pacemaker.

Ventricular:	Rate—Variable Rhythm—Irregular Contour—Normal
Atrial:	Rate—Variable Rhythm—Irregular Contour—Variable
PR Interval:	Variable
Sequence:	P wave precedes each QRST complex P wave contour and PR interval vary from beat to beat
Setting:	Increased vagal tone, disease of sinus node, digitalis, rheumatic heart disease
Significance:	May indicate dysfunction of sinus node

PREMATURE ATRIAL CONTRACTION (BEAT, DEPOLARIZATION, SYSTOLE)

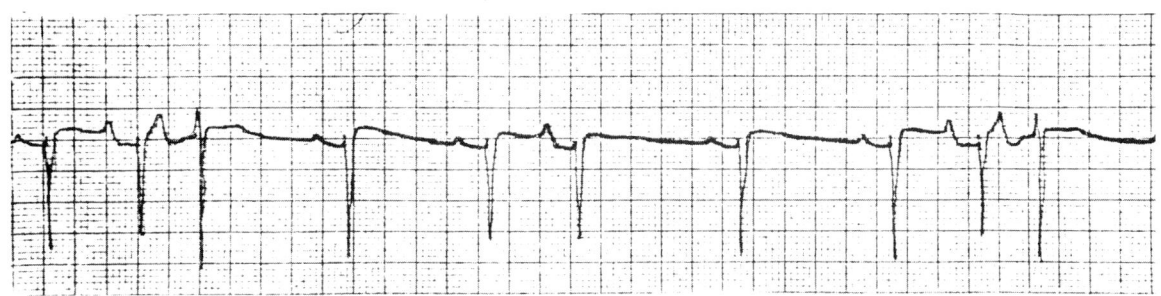

FIGURE A-10
Premature atrial contraction.

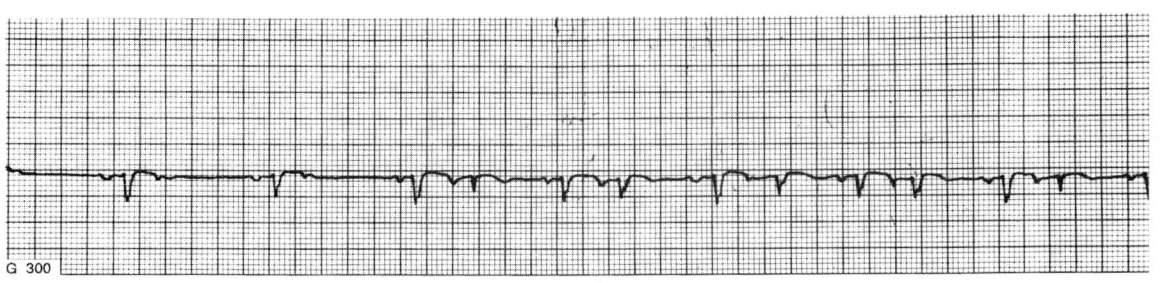

FIGURE A-11
Premature atrial contraction, some nonconducted.

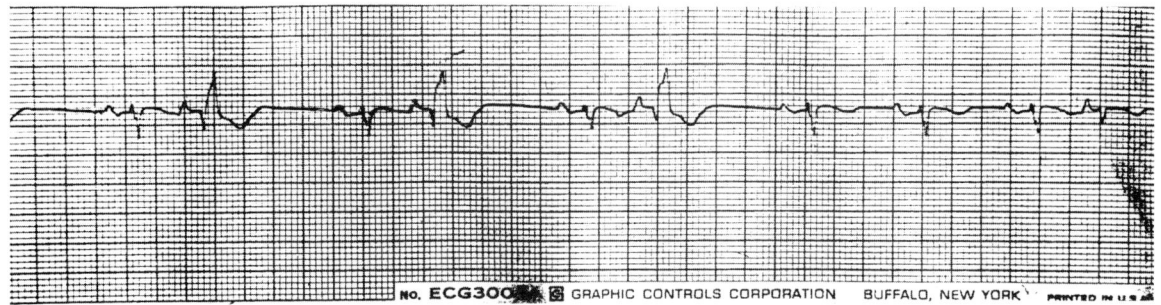

FIGURE A-12
Premature atrial contraction with aberrant conduction.

Ventricular: Rate—Depends on underlying rhythm and frequency of premature beats
Rhythm—Irregular
Contour—Normal, abnormal, or absent on premature beats

Atrial: Rate—Depends on underlying rhythm and frequency of premature beats
Rhythm—Irregular
Contour—Abnormal on premature beats

PR Interval: Normal or prolonged

Sequence: Early abnormal P wave
Conduction to the ventricles may be absent, aberrant, or normal

Setting: Normal hearts, emotional stress, caffeine, rheumatic heart disease, atherosclerotic heart disease, thyrotoxicosis

Significance: May be precursor of atrial tachyarrhythmias

PAROXYSMAL ATRIAL TACHYCARDIA

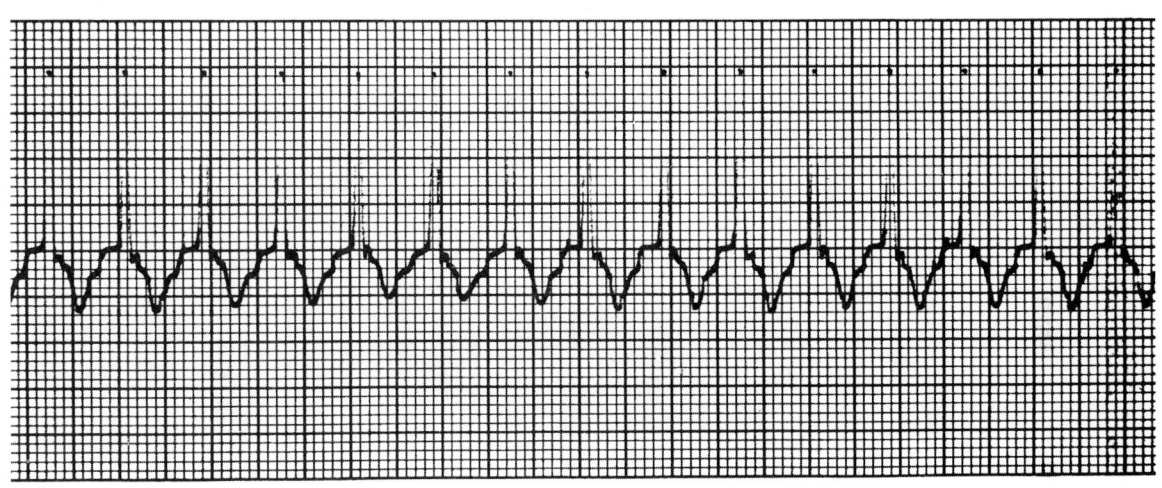

FIGURE A-13
Paroxysmal atrial tachycardia.

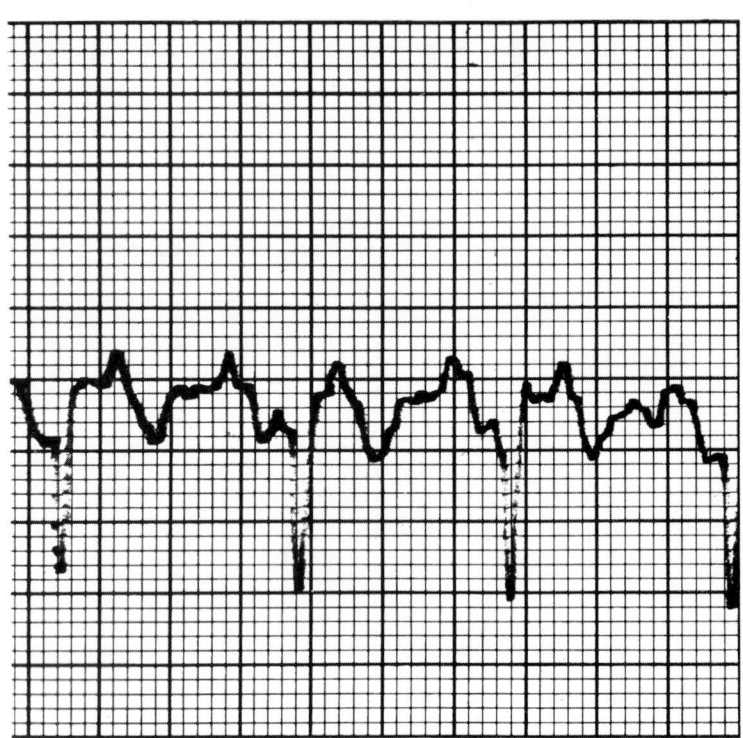

FIGURE A-14
Paroxysmal atrial tachycardia with 2:1 block.

Ventricular: Rate—100–300 (commonly around 200) beats per minute
                  Rhythm—Regular
                  Contour—Normal

Atrial: Rate—100–300 (commonly around 200) beats per minute
                  Rhythm—Regular
                  Contour—Abnormal (different from sinus P waves)

PR Intervals: Normal

Sequence: P wave precedes each QRST complex
                  Tachycardia begins and ends abruptly

Setting: Myocardial infarction, rheumatic heart disease, hypertensive heart disease, thyrocardiac
                  disease, overexertion, emotional factors, hyperventilation, changes in position, swallowing,
                  deep inspiration, heavy meals, pulmonary emboli, coffee, smoking, preexcitation syndrome

Significance: Depends on cause and patient's tolerance

ATRIAL FLUTTER

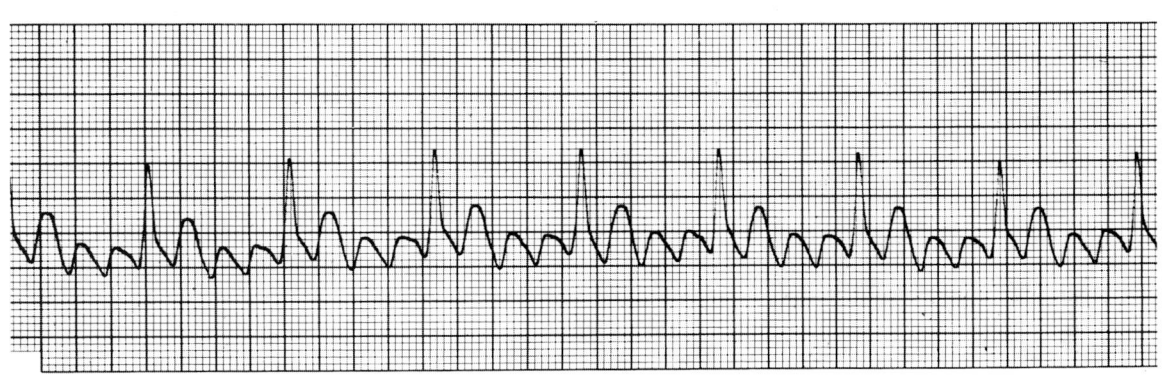

FIGURE A-15
Atrial flutter with 4:1 conduction.

Ventricular:	Rate—Variable Rhythm—Regular or irregular Contour—Normal
Atrial:	Rate—220–375 (commonly 300) beats per minute Rhythm—Regular Contour—Sawtooth
PR Interval:	Variable flutter–R interval depending on ratio of AV conduction
Sequence:	Conduction of flutter waves may be 1:1 or greater—usually 2:1 or 4:1 Some flutter waves may be buried in QRST complex
Setting:	Hypertensive heart disease, atherosclerotic heart disease, rheumatic heart disease, congenital heart disease, constrictive pericarditis, cor pulmonale, trauma, infection, hypoxia, stress, exercise, myocardial infarction, hyperthyroidism, drugs (digitalis, epinephrine, quinidine), preexcitation syndrome
Significance:	Depends on cause, underlying condition, ventricular rate

ATRIAL FIBRILLATION

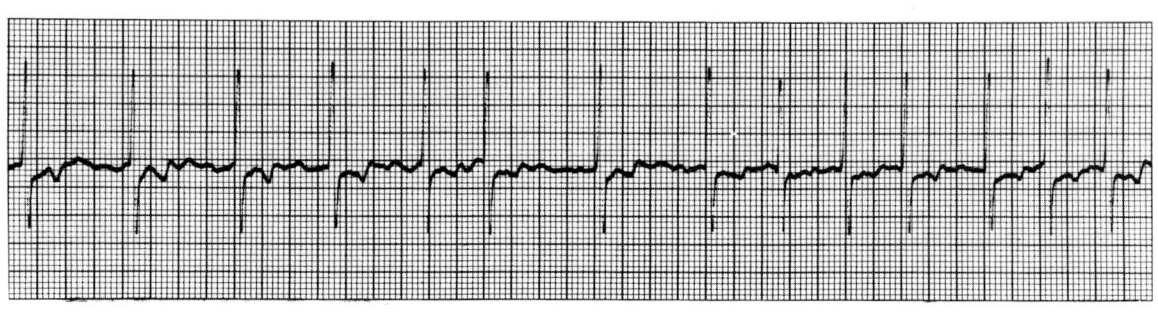

FIGURE A-16
Atrial fibrillation.

Ventricular:	Rate—Variable Rhythm—Irregular Contour—Normal
Atrial:	Rate—350–600 beats per minute Rhythm—Irregular Contour: "Squiggly," undulating, no definite P wave
PR Interval:	Cannot be measured
Sequence:	Irregular R-R interval with no definite P waves
Setting:	Myocardial disease, idiopathic development, familial tendency, stress, nausea, acute gastroenteritis, coughing, heavy ingestion of alcohol, hypoglycemia, pain, infection, exertion, heart or chest trauma, hyperthyroidism, electrolyte disturbances, sympathomimetic drugs
Significance:	Some persons remain in atrial fibrillation for many years; however, an abrupt onset may cause hemodynamic deterioration, depending on the underlying condition

PREMATURE JUNCTIONAL (NODAL OR AV NODAL) CONTRACTION (BEAT, DEPOLARIZATION, SYSTOLE)

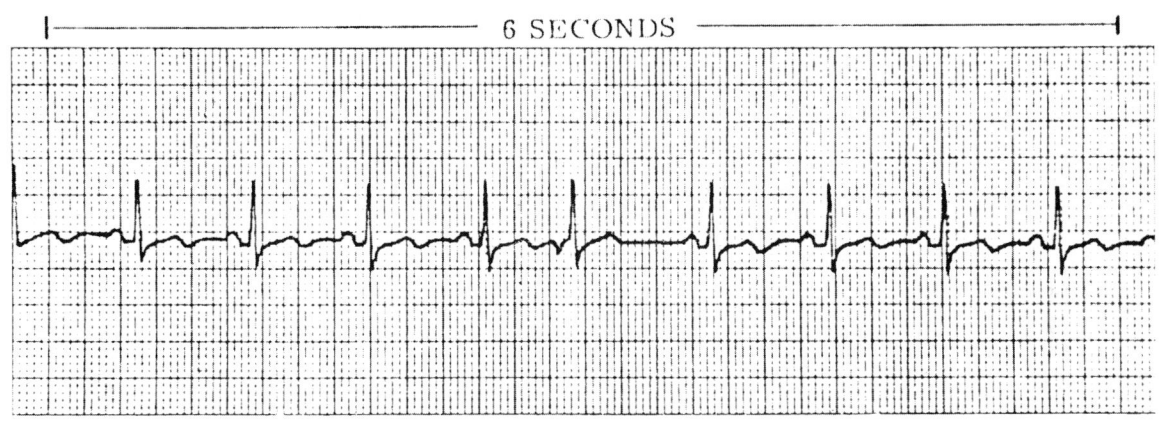

FIGURE A-17
Premature junctional contraction.

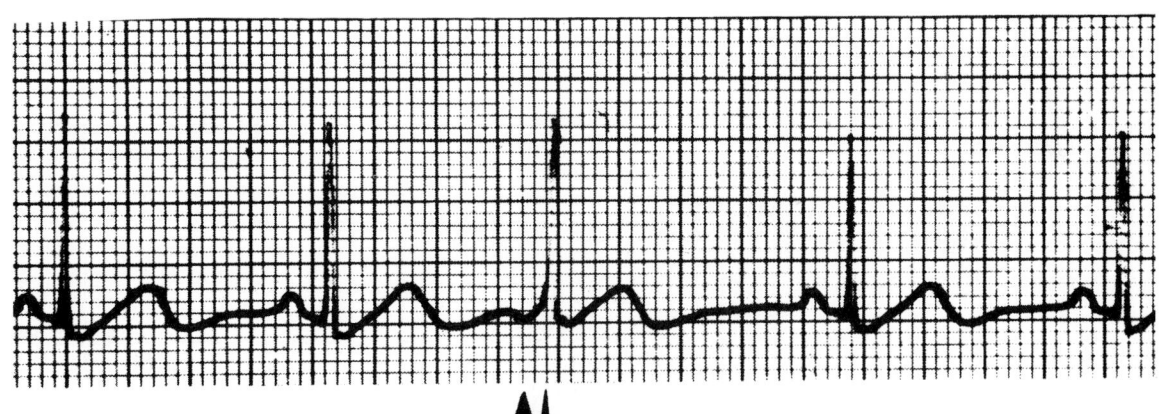

FIGURE A-18
Premature junctional contraction. (*From R. E. Phillips and M. K. Feeney, The Cardiac Rhythms, Saunders, Philadelphia, 1973.*)

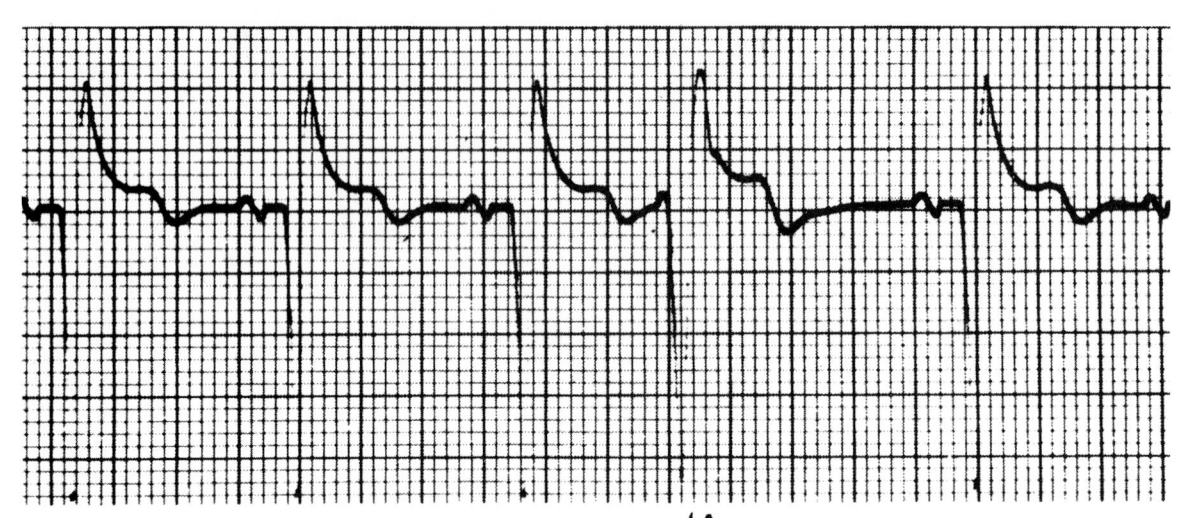

FIGURE A-19
Premature junctional contraction. (*From R. E. Phillips and M. K. Feeney,
The Cardiac Rhythms, Saunders, Philadelphia, 1973.*)

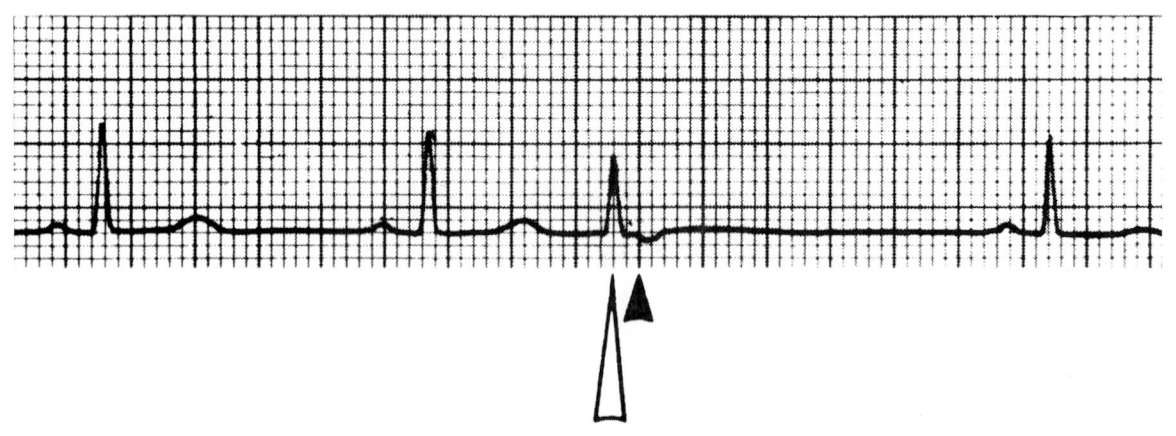

FIGURE A-20
Premature junctional contraction. (*From R. E. Phillips and M. K. Feeney,
The Cardiac Rhythms, Saunders, Philadelphia, 1973.*)

Ventricular: Rate—Depends on underlying rhythm and frequency of premature beats
                Rhythm—Irregular
                Contour—Normal

Atrial: Rate—Depends on underlying rhythm and frequency of premature beats
           Rhythm—Irregular
           Contour—Abnormal on premature beats

PR Interval: <0.12 sec. when P wave precedes QRS complex

Sequence: Premature QRST complex with P wave shortly before, during, or after the QRST complex

Setting: Carotid sinus pressure, digitalis, rheumatic or atherosclerotic heart disease

Significance: May be precursor of junctional tachycardia

JUNCTIONAL (NODAL, OR AV NODAL) RHYTHM

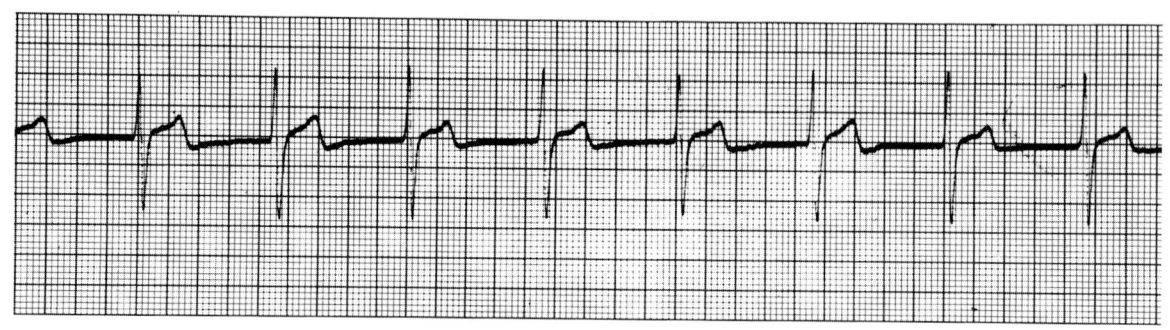

FIGURE A-21
Junctional rhythm.

Ventricular:	Rate—Usually 40–60 beats per minute Rhythm—Regular Contour—Normal
Atrial:	Rate—Usually 40–60 beats per minute Rhythm—Regular Contour—Abnormal
PR Interval:	<0.12 sec. when P wave precedes QRS complex
Sequence:	Usually an escape rhythm characterized by regular QRS complexes with P waves shortly before, during, or after the QRS component
Setting:	Sinus node disease, digitalis, increased vagal tone
Significance:	Cardiac output may decline; may indicate serious dysfunction of SA node
Note:	Junctional rhythms at rates of 60 to 100 beats per minute should be referred to as accelerated junctional rhythms since they are too slow to classify as tachycardia and more rapid than would be expected in an idiojunctional rhythm.

JUNCTIONAL (NODAL OR AV NODAL) TACHYCARDIA

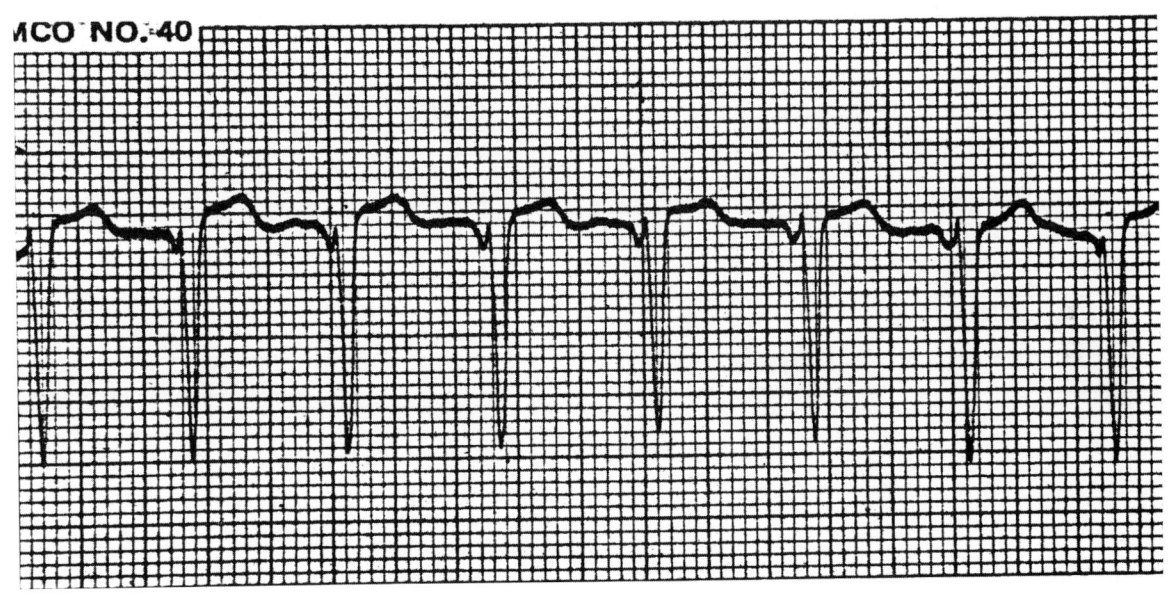

FIGURE A-22
Junctional tachycardia.

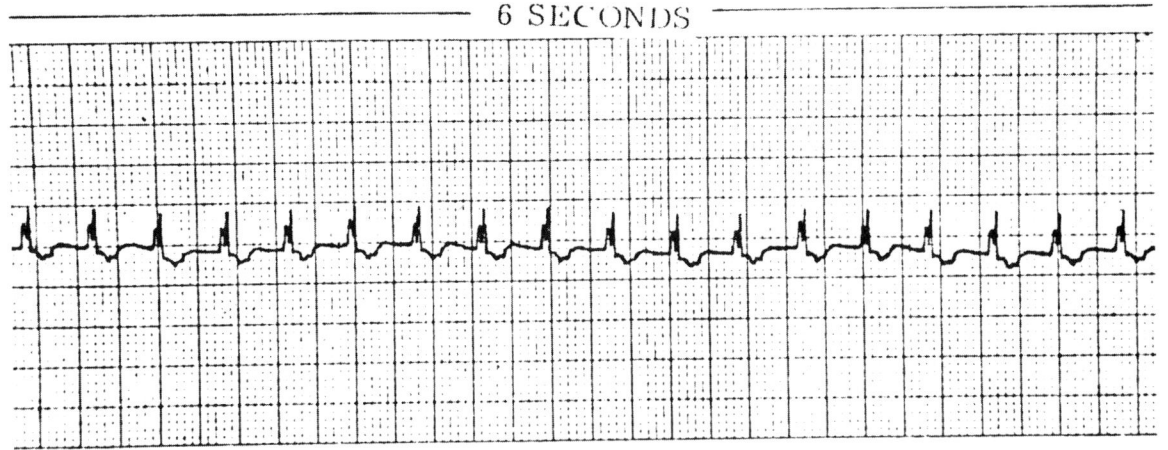

FIGURE A-23
Junctional tachycardia.

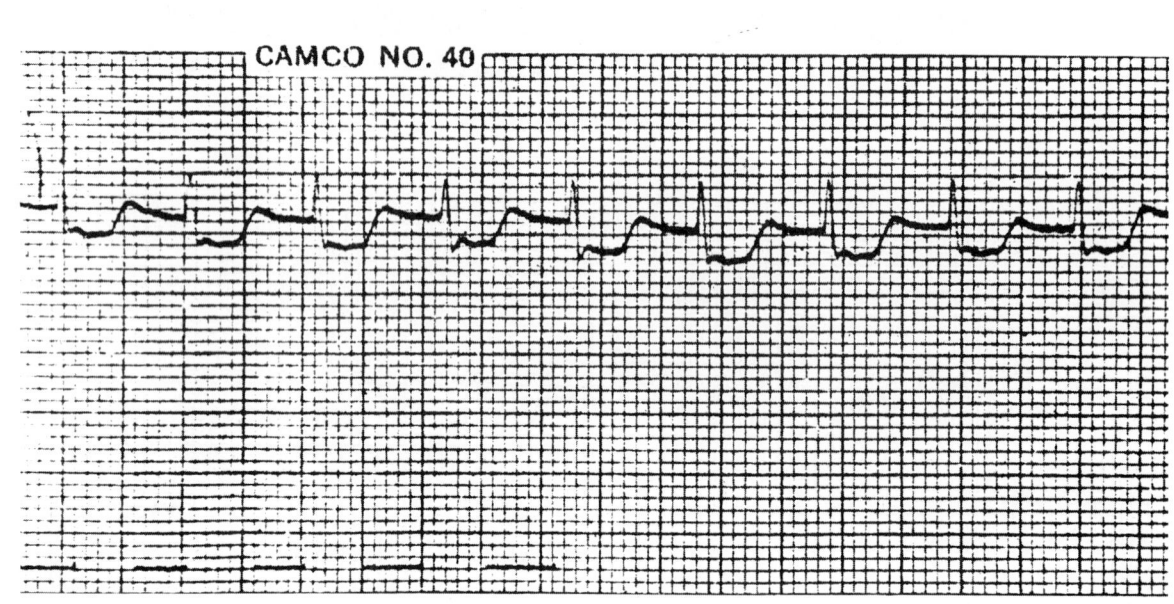

FIGURE A-24
Junctional tachycardia.

Ventricular:	Rate—>100 beats per minute
	Rhythm—Regular
	Contour—Normal
Atrial:	Rate—>100 beats per minute (same as ventricular rate or at sinus rate if dissociated)
	Rhythm—Regular
	Contour—Abnormal if retrograde; normal if sinus
PR Interval:	<0.12 sec. if P wave precedes QRS complex
Sequence:	Rapid regular rhythm with P wave shortly before, during, or after QRS complex
	May be paroxysmal or nonparoxysmal
Setting:	Paroxysmal—same as paroxysmal atrial tachycardia (PAT)
	Nonparoxysmal—inferior wall infarction, acute rheumatic myocarditis, following cardiac surgery, digitalis
Significance:	Same as PAT

PREMATURE VENTRICULAR CONTRACTION (BEAT, DEPOLARIZATION, SYSTOLE)

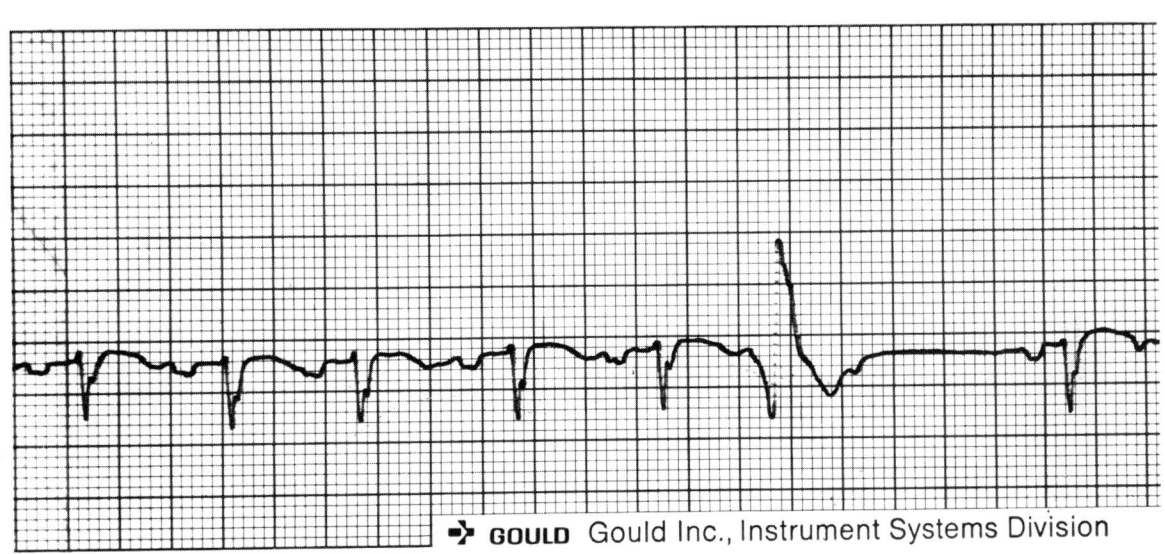

→ GOULD Gould Inc., Instrument Systems Division

FIGURE A-25
Premature ventricular contraction.

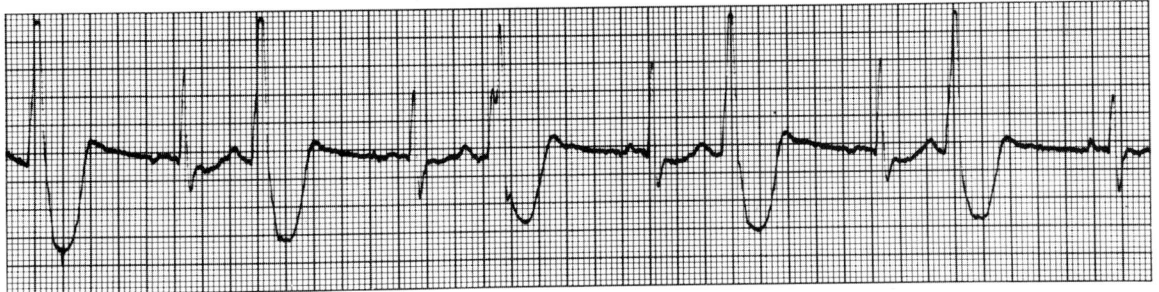

FIGURE A-26
Ventricular bigeminy.

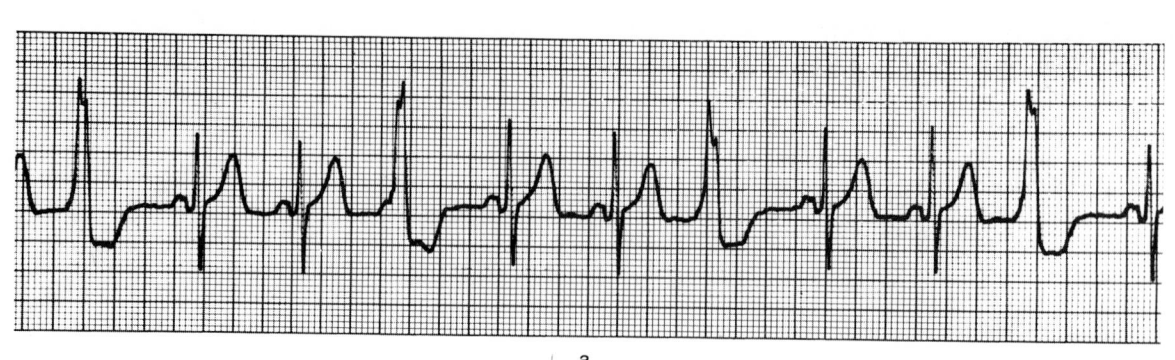

a

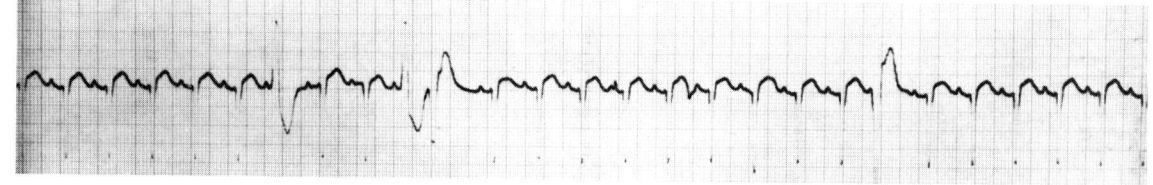

b

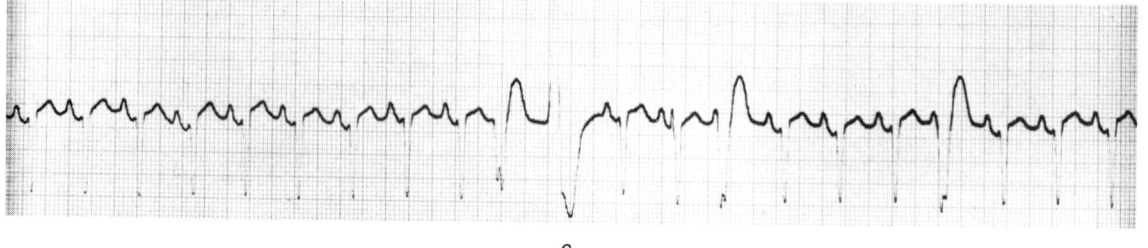

c

FIGURE A-27

(*a*) Ventricular trigeminy. (*b*) Fusion premature ventricular contractions.
(*c*) Multifocal premature ventricular contractions.

Ventricular: Rate—Depends on underlying rhythm and number of premature beats
Rhythm—Irregular
Contour—Abnormal on premature beats

Atrial: Rates—Depends on underlying rhythm and number of premature beats
Rhythm—Irregular
Contour—Abnormal when retrograde; normal if sinus P wave

Sequence: Underlying rhythm is periodically interrupted by early abnormal QRS complexes which may be preceded by a sinus P wave, may have no P wave, or may be followed by a sinus P wave or retrograde P wave.
If premature beats occur after each normal beat, the pattern is *ventricular bigeminy;* if they occur after every two normal beats, the pattern is *ventricular trigeminy.*
Premature abnormal QRS complexes of varying contour are multifocal or multiform PVCs.
Fusion PVCs are late diastolic beats resulting from the sinus node depolarizing the atria and part of the ventricles while the simultaneously occurring PVC depolarizes the remainder of the ventricle.

Setting: Myocardial infarction, other cardiac disease, normal hearts, electrolyte imbalance, digitalis, irritation of ventricles by intracardiac catheters

Significance: May be precursor of ventricular tachycardia or ventricular fibrillation

VENTRICULAR ESCAPE BEATS AND RHYTHMS

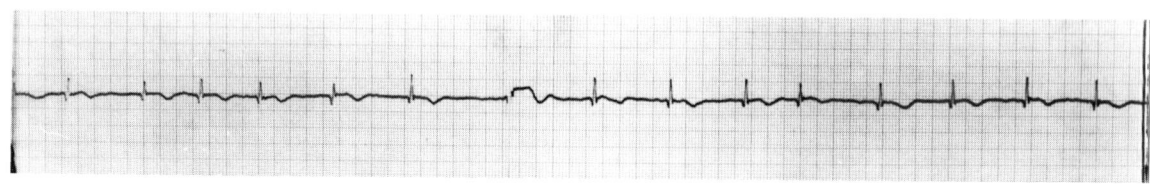

a

b

FIGURE A-28

(*a*) Ventricular escape beat. (*b*) Accelerated idioventricular rhythm.

Ventricular: Rate—Depends on underlying rhythm and frequency of occurrence of escape rhythm or beats
Rhythm—Irregular
Contour—Abnormal on escape beats

Atrial: Rate—Depends on underlying rhythm and presence of retrograde conduction to atria
Rhythm—May be regular or may be difficult to determine if dissociated from escape rhythm
Contour—Abnormal if retrograde; normal if sinus P wave

Sequence: Underlying rhythm slows sufficiently to allow ventricular beats or rhythm to escape from whatever causes the underlying rhythm to slow or cease.
Fusion beats may be seen at the beginning and/or end of the escape rhythm.

Setting: Myocardial infarction, other cardiac disease, digitalis, vagal influence, electrolyte imbalance, and any other cause of sinus arrest, ventricular rhythm in complete heart block

Significance: May be preterminal rhythm; may represent ventricular tachycardia with exit block

VENTRICULAR TACHYCARDIA

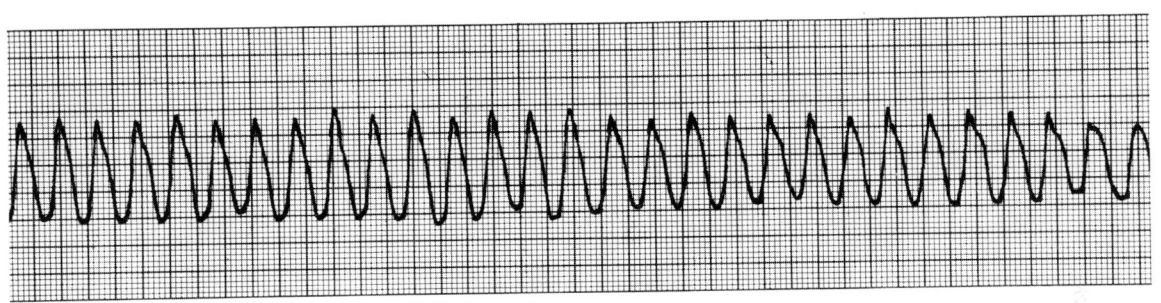

FIGURE A-29
Ventricular tachycardia.

Ventricular: Rate—100–200 beats per minute
Rhythm—Usually regular
Contour—Abnormal

Atrial: Rate—Same as ventricular rate if retrograde or as underlying sinus rate
Rhythm—Regular
Contour—Abnormal if retrograde; normal if sinus

PR Interval: Unmeasurable

Sequence: Rapid abnormal ventricular depolarization with sinus, retrograde, or absent P waves.
Three or more PVCs in a row constitute ventricular tachycardia

Setting: Cardiac disease, electrolyte imbalance, digitalis toxicity, irritation due to intracardiac catheters

Significance: Life-threatening; may progress to ventricular fibrillation

VENTRICULAR FIBRILLATION

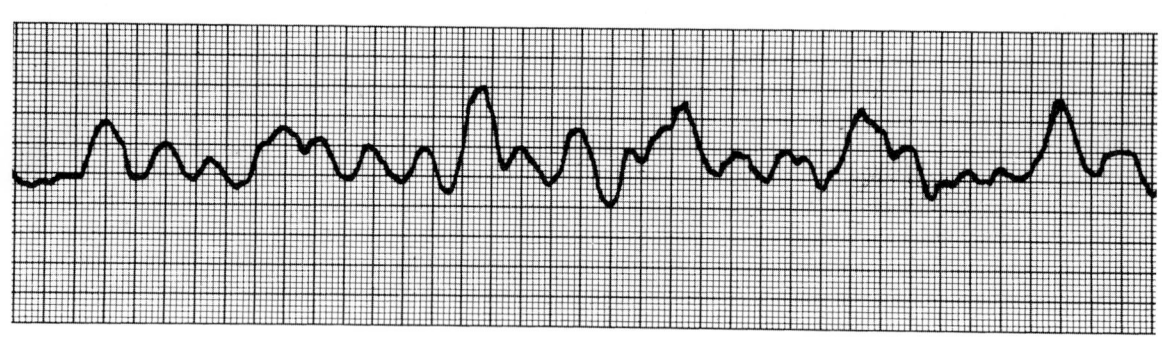

FIGURE A-30
Ventricular fibrillation.

Ventricular: Rate—Unmeasurable
                Rhythm—Chaotic
                Contour—Undulating

Atrial: Rate—Unmeasurable
                Rhythm—Not seen
                Contour—Not seen

PR Interval: Unmeasurable

Sequence: Chaotic, disorganized undulations of varying contour; may occur spontaneously, without prior warning rhythms such as PVCs (*primary ventricular fibrillation*) or following a PVC or run of ventricular tachycardia

Setting: Cardiac disease, electrocution

Significance: Clinical death

FIRST-DEGREE HEART BLOCK

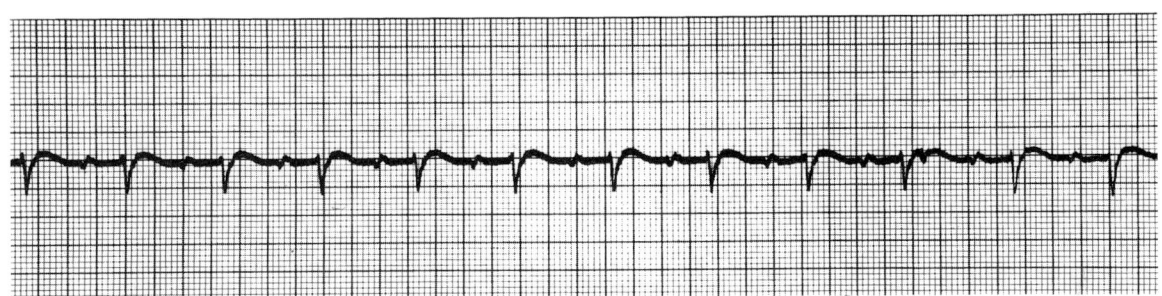

FIGURE A-31
First-degree heart block.

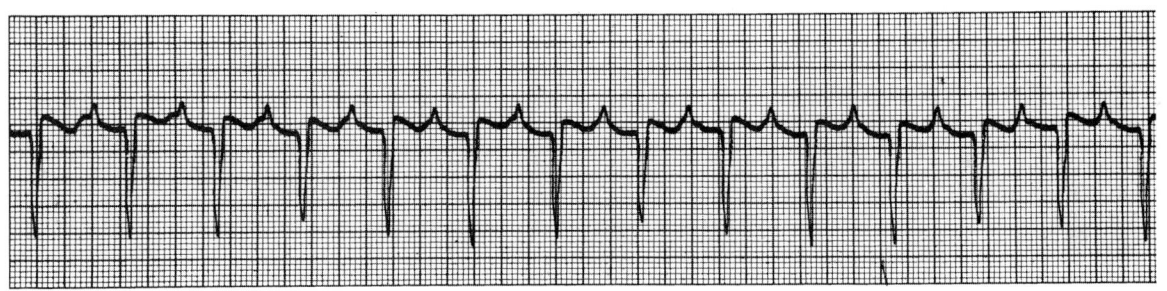

FIGURE A-32
First-degree heart block.

Ventricular: Rate—Variable; depends on sinus rate
Rhythm—Usually regular
Contour—Normal

Atrial: Rate—Same as ventricular
Rhythm—Same as ventricular
Contour—Normal

PR Interval: >0.20 sec.

Sequence: P wave precedes each QRST complex
All beats have same appearance

Settings: Atherosclerotic or rheumatic heart disease, following acute myocardial infarction, digitalis,
propranolol

Significance: May precede higher degrees of heart block

SECOND-DEGREE HEART BLOCK, TYPE I (MOBITZ I, WENCKEBACH)

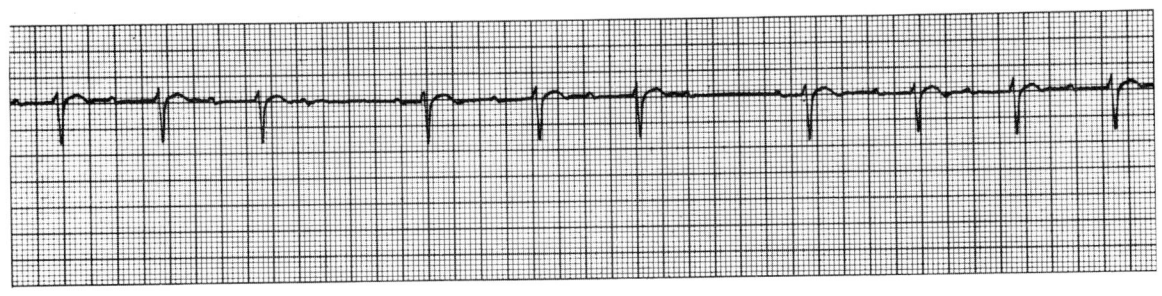

FIGURE A-33
Second-degree heart block, type I.

Ventricular: Rate—Variable; depends on sinus rate and atrial/ventricular ratio (3:2, 4:3, 5:4, etc.)
Rhythm—Irregular; R-R interval shortens before nonconducted P wave
Contour—Normal

Atrial: Rate—Variable
Rhythm—Regular
Contour—Normal

PR Interval: Progressively lengthens

Sequence: P wave precedes each QRS complex; PR interval lengthens on each beat until one P wave is not followed by a QRS complex; then cycle repeats

Setting: Atherosclerotic or rheumatic heart disease, digitalis, propranolol

Significance: May precede higher degrees of heart block; decrease in ventricular rate may compromise cardiac output

SECOND-DEGREE HEART BLOCK, TYPE II (MOBITZ II)

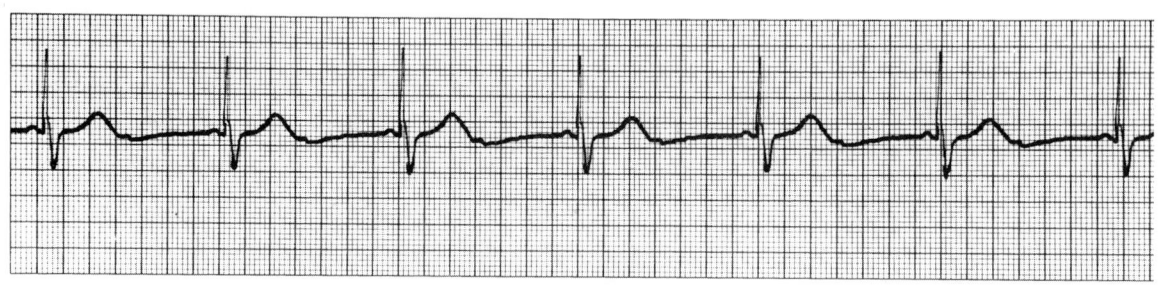

FIGURE A-34
Second-degree heart block, type II.

Ventricular: Rate—Usually <60 beats per minute; depends on sinus rate and degree of heart block
Rhythm—Regular or irregular
Contour—Normal

Atrial: Rate—Depends on sinus rate
Rhythm—Regular
Contour—Normal

PR Interval: Normal or prolonged on conducted beats

Sequence: Two or more P waves precede each QRS complex; PR interval remains constant on conducted beats

Setting: Atherosclerotic or rheumatic heart disease, digitalis toxicity

Significance: Slow rate may compromise cardiac output; ventricular escape rhythms may emerge

THIRD-DEGREE (COMPLETE) HEART BLOCK

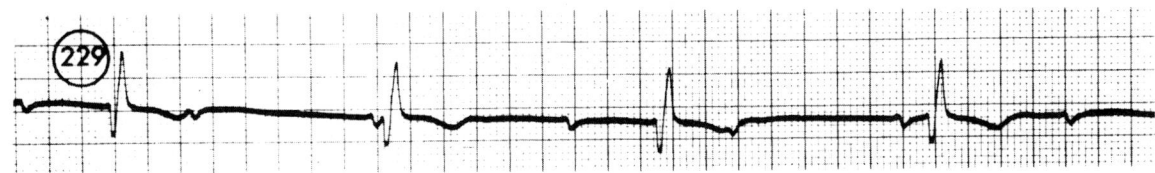

FIGURE A-35

Third-degree heart block. (*From R. E. Phillips and M. K. Feeney, The Cardiac Rhythms, Saunders, Philadelphia, 1973.*)

Ventricular:	Rate—<45 beats per minute Rhythm—Regular Contour—Abnormal
Atrial:	Rate—Depends on sinus rate Rhythm—Regular Contour—Normal
PR Interval:	Variable; no pattern
Sequence:	P waves occur at regular intervals completely unrelated to QRST complexes, which occur at regular intervals
Setting:	Atherosclerotic or rheumatic heart disease
Significance:	Slow rate compromises cardiac output; ventricular escape rhythm may fail and thereby produce asystole

RIGHT BUNDLE BRANCH BLOCK

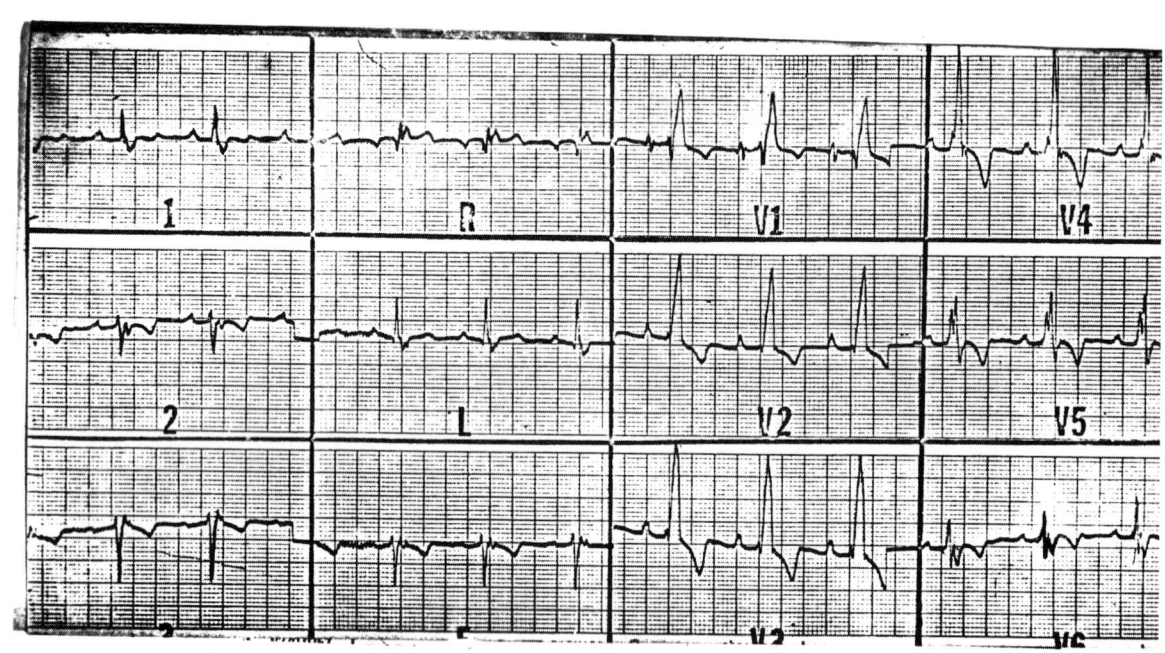

FIGURE A-36
Right bundle branch block.

Ventricular: Rate—Depends on underlying rhythm
Rhythm—Depends on underlying rhythm
Contour—Abnormally wide QRS complex; abnormal T wave; lead V_1 shows delayed R wave; lead V_6 shows wide S wave

Atrial: Rate—Depends on underlying rhythm
Rhythm—Depends on underlying rhythm
Contour—Depends on underlying rhythm

Sequence: Underlying rhythm is conducted slowly through the ventricles giving a QRS complex >0.12 sec. and with abnormal contour.

Setting: Cardiac disease, trauma

Significance: If acute onset following cardiac event, may indicate deterioration of condition and be precursor of complete heart block or cardiac arrest. If chronic, patient may be asymptomatic.

LEFT BUNDLE BRANCH BLOCK

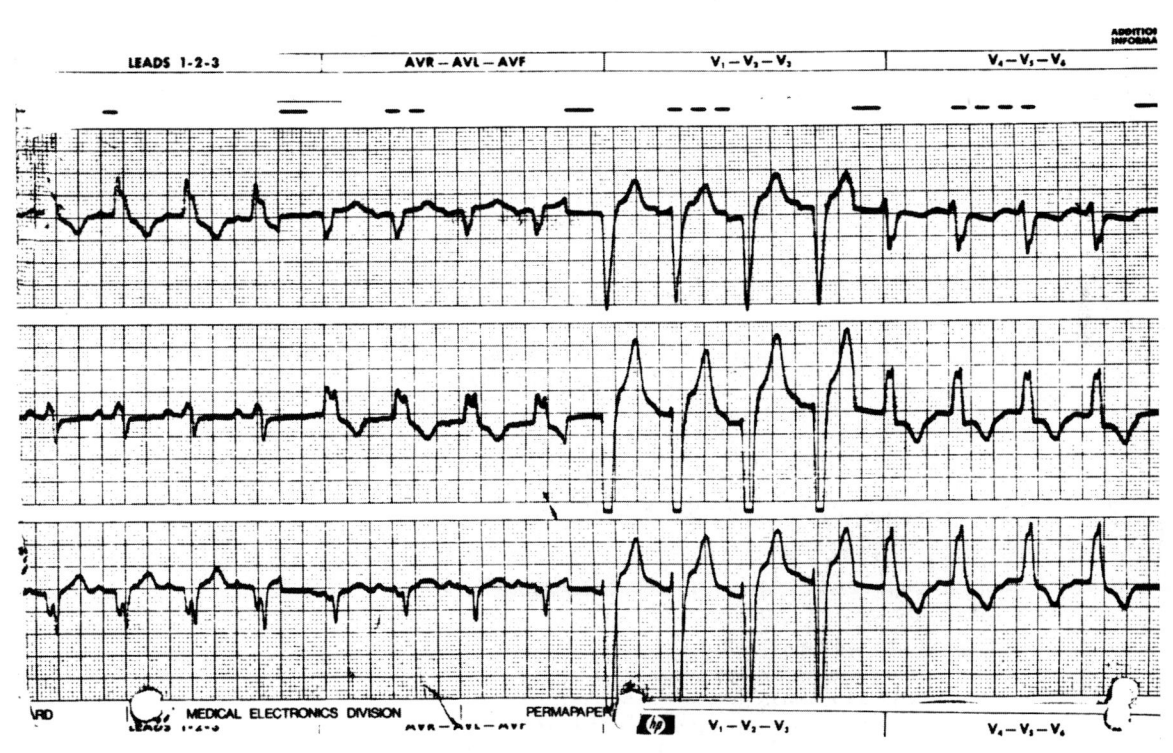

FIGURE A-37
Left bundle branch block.

Ventricular:	Rate—Depends on underlying rhythm Rhythm—Depends on underlying rhythm Contour—Abnormally wide QRS complex; abnormal T wave; lead V_1 shows wide S wave; leads V_6, aV_L, and I show delayed R wave
Atrial:	Rate—Depends on underlying rhythm Rhythm—Depends on underlying rhythm Contour—Depends on underlying rhythm
Sequence:	Underlying rhythm is conducted slowly through the ventricles giving a QRS complex that is >0.12 sec. and with abnormal contour.
Setting:	Cardiac disease, trauma
Significance:	If acute onset following cardiac event, may indicate deterioration of condition and be precursor of complete heart block or cardiac arrest. If chronic, patient may be asymptomatic.

REFERENCES

Andreoli, K. G., et al.: *Comprehensive Cardiac Care,* 4th ed., St. Louis: Mosby, 1979.

Bellet, S.: *Essentials of Cardiac Arrhythmias—Diagnosis and Management,* Philadelphia: Saunders, 1972.

Conover, M. H., and E. G. Zalis: *Understanding Electrocardiography—Physiological and Interpretive Concepts,* 2d ed., St. Louis: Mosby, 1976.

Goldman, M. H.: *Principles of Clinical Electrocardiography,* 9th ed., Los Altos, Calif.: Lange, 1976.

Marriott, H. J. L.: *Practical Electrocardiography,* 5th ed., Baltimore: Williams & Wilkins, 1972.

Shamroth, L.: *An Introduction to Electrocardiography,* 4th ed., Oxford: Blackwell Scientific Publications, 1971.

APPENDIX B

DRUGS

Joseph A. Albanese

ACETAMINOPHEN

Category

Analgesic: antipyretic

Brand Names

Datril (Bristol-Meyers)

Phenaphen (Robins)

Tempra (Mead Johnson)

Tylenol (McNeil)

Valadol (Squibb)

Pharmacological Mechanism

Acetaminophen raises the pain threshold and affects the hypothalamic heat-regulating center. The drug has the same analgesic activity as aspirin but lacks anti-inflammatory and uricosuric activity.

Uses and Doses

Analgesic and antipyretic.

P.O.	
Pediatric	
Under 3 years	Consult with physician.
3–6 years	120 mg, 3–4 times daily. Do not exceed a total daily dose of 480 mg.
7–12 years	162–325 mg, 3–4 times daily. Do not exceed a total daily dose of 1.3 g.
Adults	
General	325–650 mg, 3–4 times daily. Do not exceed a total daily dose of 2.6 g.

Administration

May be administered without regard to meals.

Contraindications

Hypersensitivity or known glucose 6-phosphate dehydrogenase deficiency.

Adverse Effects

Anemia, pancytopenia, leukopenia, urticaria, and rare instances of methemoglobinemia and hemolytic anemia.

Drug Interactions

Use with caution in patients on oral anticoagulants.

ACTINOMYCIN D (DACTINOMYCIN)

Category

Antineoplastic: antibiotic

1137

Brand Names

Cosmegen (Merck Sharp & Dohme)

Pharmacologic Mechanism

Antineoplastic activity probably due to complexation with DNA which results in an inhibition of DNA-dependent RNA synthesis. Actinomycin D also exhibits bacteriostatic activity against both gram-positive and gram-negative bacteria.

Uses and Doses

1. As a sole agent or in combination therapy for Wilms's tumor, rhabdomyosarcoma, testicular tumors, and Ewing's sarcoma.

2. Alternative for choriocarcinoma and other related trophoblastic tumors.

Parenteral (IV Infusion)	
Pediatric	
Over 6 months	15 μg/kg for 5 days or 2.4 mg/m² in divided doses over 1 week. Maximum daily dose is 0.5 mg.
Adult	0.5 mg for 5 days or a single weekly dose of 2 mg for 3 weeks.

Dosage must be individualized and is dependent upon the stage and severity of the neoplasm, type of therapeutic regimen, and patient tolerance to treatment. Repeat courses of treatment usually require a rest period of at least 2 weeks and no signs of residual toxicity.

Administration

1. Reconstitute by using 1.1 mL of sterile water for injection.

2. Reconstituted solution may be added to a running infusion (usually 5% dextrose).

Contraindications

Pregnancy, severe bone marrow depression, liver or renal impairment, and chicken pox.

Adverse Effects

Nausea, vomiting, diarrhea, ulcers, bone marrow depression, alopecia, acne, and skin pigmentation.

Drug Interactions

Use with extreme caution with chlorambucil or methotrexate because of additive bone marrow depression and gastrointestinal toxicity.

AMIKACIN SULFATE

Category

Antibiotic: aminoglycoside antibiotic

Brand Names

Amikin (Bristol)

Pharmacologic Mechanism

Bactericidal activity due to inhibition of ribosomal protein synthesis in susceptible microorganisms.

Uses and Doses

The toxicity of aminoglycoside antibiotics restricts their use to serious gram-negative infections. Amikacin has a spectrum of activity similar to kanamycin.

1. Indicated in the treatment of infections caused by susceptible strains of:
   Enterobacter aerogenes
   Escherichia coli
   Klebsiella pneumoniae
   Mima-Herellea (Acinetobacter)
   Proteus spp.
   Providencia spp.
   Pseudomonas spp.
   Serratia spp.

2. Alternate for penicillin-methicillin–resistant staphylococcus infections.

3. As initial therapy in suspected or confirmed gram-negative infections prior to obtaining sensitivity test results.

4. Alternate for gentamicin-tobramycin–resistant gram-negative infections.

5. In combination with penicillin for treating neonatal sepsis.

Parenteral (IM or IV)	
Neonates	Initial dose of 10 mg/kg, followed by 7.5 mg/kg every 12 h.
Pediatric and adults	Up to 15 mg/kg in 2–3 equally divided doses. Do not exceed 1.5 g per day.

Treatment usually requires 7–10 days. Dosage for patients with impaired renal function must be adjusted. Dosage adjustment should be based on amikacin serum level and serum creatinine clearance rates.

Administration

1. For IV administration, amikacin solution (500 mg) is added to 200 mL of sterile diluent.

2. Do not premix with other drugs.

3. Amikacin may be mixed with 5% dextrose, 5% dextrose in Ringer's, 10% dextrose, etc.

Contraindications, etc.

See GENTAMICIN SULFATE.

AMINOPHYLLINE

Category

Bronchodilator: decongestant

Brand Names

Mini-Lix (Ferndale)

Somophyllin (Fisons)

Pharmacologic Mechanism

Aminophylline relaxes smooth muscle of the respiratory tract, stimulates the CNS, promotes diuresis, produces a positive chronotropic and inotrophic effect on the heart, and increases the release of epinephrine.

Uses and Doses

Indicated for bronchial asthma, cardiac paroxysmal dyspnea, Cheyne-Stokes respiration, congestive heart failure, status asthmaticus, and emphysema, and for promoting diuresis.

P.O.	
Pediatric	7.5 mg/kg for acute asthmatic attack and 5 mg/kg every 6 h for maintenance.
Adult	500 mg for acute asthmatic attack and 200–250 mg every 6–8 h for maintenance.
Parenteral (IV)	
Pediatric	15 mg/kg daily in 3 divided doses.
Adult	250 mg as required.

Administration

Oral administration with meals will help reduce gastric upset.

Contraindications

Hypersensitivity, angina pectoris, or coronary artery disease.

Adverse Effects

Nausea, vomiting, epigastric distress, diarrhea, sinus tachycardia, ventricular tachycardia, hypotension, extrasystole, clonic and tonic generalized convulsions, and albuminuria.

Drug Interactions

Avoid concurrent use with adrenergic drugs.

AMOXICILLIN TRIHYDRATE

Category

Antibiotic: extended spectrum penicillin

Brand Names

Amoxil (Beecham)

Larotid (Roche)

Polymox (Bristol)

Trimox (Squibb)

Pharmacologic Mechanism

Bactericidal activity due to inhibition of mucopeptide cell wall synthesis in susceptible organisms.

Uses and Doses

Extended spectrum penicillins should not be substituted for penicillin G when treating infections caused by penicillin G–sensitive organisms.

1. Indicated in the treatment of infections caused by susceptible strains of
   Escherichia coli
   Hemophilus influenzae
   Neisseria gonorrhoeae
   Proteus mirabilis

2. Treatment of *S. faecalis* and *S. pneumoniae* infections.

P.O.	
Pediatric	
Under 20 kg	20–40 mg/kg in divided doses every 8 h.
Over 20 kg	250–500 mg daily every 8 h.
Adults	
General	250–500 mg daily every 8 h.
Gonorrhea	3 g as a single daily dose.

Administration

The penicillins are best administered on an empty stomach.

Contraindications, etc.

See AMPICILLIN.

AMPHOTERICIN B

Category

Antibiotic: antifungal antibiotic.

Brand Names

Fungizone (Squibb)

Pharmacologic Mechanism

Fungistatic activity due to alteration of cell membrane permeability in susceptible fungi.

Use and Doses

1. Indicated in the treatment of infections caused by susceptible strains of
   Aspergillus fumigatus
   Blastomyces dermatitidis
   Candida spp.
   Coccidioides immitis
   Cryptococcus neoformans
   Histoplasma capsulatum
   Mucor mucido
   Sporotrichum schenckii

2. Treatment of infections caused by susceptible species of the genera *Rhizopus, Absidia, Entomophthora,* and *Basidiobolus.*

Parenteral	
Pediatric and adults	Start with a daily dose of 0.25 mg/kg and gradually increase as tolerance permits. Total daily dosage may range from 1 to 1.5 mg/kg. Do not exceed a total daily dose of 1.5 mg/kg.

Administration

IV infusion should be given over a period of 6 h at a concentration of 0.1 mg/mL.

Contraindications

Hypersensitivity unless required for a life-threatening infection.

Adverse Effects

Headache, nausea, vomiting, malaise, dyspepsia, diarrhea, local phlebitis and thrombophlebitis, hypokalemia, azotemia, hyposthenuria, renal tubular acidosis, and nephrocalinosis.

Drug Interactions

1. Use with caution in patients on concurrent cardiac glycosides or corticosteroids.

2. Amphotericin can enhance the activity of surgical neuromuscular blocking agents.

AMPICILLIN

Category

Antibiotic: extended spectrum penicillin

Brand Names

Alpen (Lederle)

Amcill (Parke-Davis)

Omnipen (Wyeth)

Pen A (Pfipharmecs)

Penbritin (Ayerst)

Pensyn (Upjohn)

Polycillin (Bristol)

Principen (Squibb)

Totacillin (Beecham)

Pharmacologic Mechanism

Bactericidal activity due to inhibition of mucopeptide cell wall synthesis in susceptible bacteria.

Uses and Doses

Extended spectrum penicillins should not be substituted for penicillin G when treating infections caused by penicillin G–sensitive organisms.

1. Indicated in the treatment of infections caused by susceptible strains of
   Escherichia coli
   Hemophilus influenzae
   Neisseria gonorrhoeae
   Neisseria meningitidis
   Proteus mirabilis
   Salmonella spp.
   Shigella spp.

2. Treatment of subacute bacterial endocarditis and enterococcal infections.

3. The drug of choice for treating typhoid fever that is resistant to chloramphenicol.

P.O.	
Pediatric	
Under 20 kg	50–100 mg/kg daily in divided doses every 6/8 h.
Over 20 kg	250–500 mg 4 times daily.
Adults	
General	250–500 mg 4 times daily.
Gonorrhea	3.5 g administered with 1 g of probenecid.

Administration

The penicillins are best administered on an empty stomach.

Contraindications

Hypersensitivity to any of the penicillins.

Adverse Effects

Nausea, vomiting, glossitis, stomatitis, urticaria, fever, edema, arthralgia, laryngeal edema, anaphylaxis, maculopapular skin rash, and black hairy tongue.

Drug Interactions

Avoid concurrent use with bacteriostatic antibiotics, antacid, and antidiarrheal suspensions.

AMPICILLIN SODIUM

Category

Antibiotic: extended spectrum penicillin

Brand Names

Alpen-N (Lederle)

Amcill-S (Parke-Davis)

Omnipen (Wyeth)

Pen A/N (Pfizer)

Penbritin-S (Ayerst)

Polycillin-N (Bristol)

Principen/N (Squibb)

Totacillin-N (Beecham)

Doses

Parenteral (IM or IV)	
Pediatric	
General	25–50 mg/kg daily in equally divided doses 4 times daily.
Meningitis	100–200 mg/kg daily.
Adults	
General	250–500 mg every 6 h.
Meningitis	8–14 g daily.

Pharmacologic Mechanism, etc.

See AMPICILLIN.

ASPIRIN

Category

Analgesic: anti-inflammatory, antipyretic

Brand Names

A.S.A. (Lilly)

Ecotrin (Smith Kline & French)

Pharmacologic Mechanism

Aspirin raises the pain threshold and affects the hypothalamus heat regulatory center. Accordingly, analgesia and antipyresis are produced. Salicylates also exhibit anti-inflammatory and uricosuric activity, inhibition of prothrombin synthesis, inhibition of platelet adhesiveness, and ulcerogenic activity.

Uses and Doses

P.O. or Rectal	
Pediatric	
Analgesic-antipyretic	11–16 mg/kg 4–6 times daily.
Antirheumatic	16 mg/kg 6 times daily. Reduce as soon as possible to 10 mg/kg 6 times daily.
Adults	
Analgesic-antipyretic	650 mg 4–6 times daily.
Antirheumatic	1 g 4–6 times daily. Do not exceed 10 g daily.

Administration

Administration with meals will help reduce gastric upset.

Contraindications

Hypersensitivity or active ulcers.

Adverse Effects

Epigastric distress, nausea, gastrointestinal bleeding, ulcers, tinnitus, hypoprothrombinemia, angioedema, and asthma.

Drug Interactions

1. Avoid concurrent use with ulcerogenic drugs, indomethacin, oral anticoagulants, probenecid, and sulfinpyrazone.

2. Aspirin can increase the activity of the oral hypoglycemic agents and methotrexate.

ATROPINE SULFATE

Category

Anticholinergic: antimuscarinic, parasympathalytic

Pharmacologic Mechanism

Anticholinergic activity due to competition with acetylcholine for muscarinic receptors at the postganglionic fiber of the parasympathetic nervous system.

Uses and Doses

1. To treat, manage, or cause bradycardia, bronchial asthma, cardiospasm, colitis, dilation of pupils, dysmenorrhea relief, enuresis control, gastrointestinal spasm, inhibition of bronchial and gastric secretions, inhibition of salivation and sweating, paralysis of accommodation, paralysis agitans, postencephalitis, parkinsonism, pylorospasm, secretions due to coryza and rhinitis, spastic and rigid states due to CNS injury, ureteral colic, and urinary frequency reduction.

2. Antidote for cholinergic drugs.

Oral	
Pediatric	0.01 mg/kg every 4–6 h. Do not exceed a single dose of 0.4 mg.
Adult	0.1–1.2 mg every 4–6 h.

Parenteral (IM, IV, and SC)		
Pediatric		
Anticholinergic	0.01 mg/kg every 4–6 h.	
Antidote	Initial dose of 1 mg followed by 0.5 mg every 10–15 min until signs of atropine toxicity appear.	
Preoperative	3 kg	0.1 mg
	7–9 kg	0.2 mg
	12–16 mg	0.3 mg
	20–27 mg	0.4 mg
	32 kg	0.5 mg
	41	0.6 mg
Adult		
Anticholinergic	0.4–0.6 mg every 4–6 h.	
Antidote	Initial dose of 2–4 mg followed by 2 mg every 5–10 min until signs of atropine toxicity appear.	
Preoperative	0.4–1 mg.	
Topicals		
Ophthalmic solution, 0.5–4%	0.1 mL 3–4 times daily.	

Administration

1. Tablets are usually administered before meals.

2. In parenteral antidotal therapy, the first administration of atropine is usually by IV injection. Repeated injections are usually by the IM route.

Contraindications

In patients with adhesions between the iris and lens, advanced hepatic and renal impairment, asthma, hiatal hernia associated with reflex esophagitis, hypersensitivity, intestinal atony, myasthenia gravis, narrow-angle glaucoma, obstructive diseases of the gastrointestinal and urinary tract, and severe ulcerative colitis.

Adverse Effects

Blurred vision, cycloplegia, increased ocular tension, constipation, loss of taste, dysphagia, suppression of lactation and body secretions, tachycardia, mental confusion, and urinary retention.

Drug Interactions

Concurrent use with antihistamines, monoamine oxidase inhibitors, phenothiazines, and tricyclic antidepressants will produce enhanced anticholinergic effects.

CARBENICILLIN DISODIUM

Category

Antibiotic: extended spectrum penicillin

Brand Names

Geopen (Roerig)

Pyopen (Beecham)

Pharmacologic Mechanism

Bactericidal activity due to inhibition of mucopeptide cell wall synthesis in susceptible microorganisms.

Uses and Doses

1. Indicated in the treatment of infections due to susceptible strains of
   Escherichia coli
   Pseudomonas aeruginosa
   Proteus spp. (especially indole-positive strains)

2. Treatment of urinary tract infections due to susceptible microorganisms.

Parenteral (IM or IV)	
Neonatal	
Under 2000 g	Initial dose of 100 mg/kg. Subsequent doses during first week 75 mg/kg every 8 h. After 7 days of age, 100 mg/kg every 6 h.
Over 2000 g	Initial dose of 100 mg/kg. Subsequent dose for first 3 days, 75 mg/kg every 6 h. After 3 days of age, 100 mg/kg every 6 h.
Pediatric	50–500 mg/kg daily in divided doses.
Adult	200–500 mg/kg daily in divided doses. Do not exceed 40 g daily.

Administration

1. Administer IM injection in the upper outer quadrant of the buttock or the midlateral thigh in adults. Do not exceed 2 g per injection site. The recommended site for children is the midlateral muscles of the thigh.

2. Administer the IV injection as slowly as possible to avoid vein irritation.

3. For IV infusion, the reconstituted solution may be added to 5% dextrose, 10% invert sugar, normal saline, Ringer's injection, and lactated Ringer's injection.

Contraindications, etc.

See PENICILLIN G POTASSIUM FOR INJECTION, STERILE.

CEPHALOTHIN SODIUM, STERILE

Category

Antibiotic: cephalosporin antibiotic

Brand Names

Keflin (Lilly)

Pharmacologic Activity

Bactericidal activity due to inhibition of mucopeptide cell wall synthesis in susceptible microorganisms.

Uses and Doses

1. Indicated in the treatment of infections caused by susceptible strains of
   Escherichia coli
   Group A beta-hemolytic Streptococci
   Hemophilus influenzae
   Klebsiella spp.
   Proteus mirabilis
   Salmonella spp.
   Shigella spp.
   Staphylococci (including penicillinase-producing strains)
   Streptococcus pneumoniae

2. In patients with hypersensitivity to penicillin (with caution).

3. In treating serious unknown intra-abdominal infections in conjunction with an aminoglycoside antibiotic prior to identifying the causative agent and receiving sensitivity test results.

Parenteral (IM or IV)	
Pediatric	100 mg/kg daily in divided doses. Dose may range from 80 to 180 mg/kg.
Adult	0.5–1 g every 4–6 h. Dose may range from 2 to 12 g daily. Renal impairment requires dosage adjustments. In patients with no essential renal function, the dose should be reduced to 500 mg every 8 h.

Administration

1. IM injection is painful, and a large muscle mass such as the gluteus or lateral aspects of the thigh should be utilized to minimize pain and induration.

2. IV injection should be administered slowly for 3–5 min.

3. For IV infusion, the reconstituted solution may be added to acetated Ringer's injection, 5% dextrose, 5% dextrose in lactated Ringer's injection, Ionosol B in D₅W, Isolyte M with 5% dextrose, lactated Ringer's injection, normal saline, Normosol-M in D₅W, Plasma-Lyte, Plasma-Lyte M in 5% dextrose, and Ringer's injection.

Contraindications

Hypersensitivity to cephalothin or cephalosporin antibiotics.

Adverse Effects

Neutropenia, thrombocytopenia, hemolytic anemia, maculopapular rash, anaphylaxis, hepatic toxicity, and nephrotoxicity.

Drug Interactions

1. Concurrent use of cephalothin with gentamicin or furosemide will enhance nephrotoxicity.

2. Bacteriostatic antibiotics can antagonize the bactericidal activity of the cephalosporins.

3. Broad spectrum antibiotics may enhance the activity of the oral anticoagulants.

CHLORAMPHENICOL

Category

Antibiotic: antirickettsial

Brand Names

Chloromycetin (Parke-Davis)

Pharmacologic Mechanism

Bacteriostatic activity due to inhibition of ribosomal protein synthesis in susceptible microorganisms.

Uses and Doses

The toxicity of chloramphenicol restricts its use to serious infections when less toxic antibiotics are ineffective or patient contraindicated.

1. One of the drugs of choice for *Salmonella typhi.*

2. Treatment of infections caused by susceptible strains of *Hemophilus influenzae, Salmonella spp.,* and *Rickettsia,* and in lymphogranuloma and psittacosis.

3. Other susceptible microorganisms that are resistant to all other appropriate antimicrobial drugs.

4. Cystic fibrosis regimens.

P.O.	
Neonatal	
Under 2 weeks	25 mg/kg daily divided into 4 equal doses.
Over 2 weeks	50 mg/kg daily divided into 4 equal doses.
Pediatric	50 mg/kg daily divided into 4 equal doses.
Adult	50–100 mg/kg daily divided into 4 equal doses.

Dosage for newborn must be adjusted according to serum levels to prevent gray baby syndrome. Infants and children with immature metabolism must receive lower dosages. A dose of 25 mg/kg will usually produce adequate blood levels.

Administration

Oral dosage forms should be administered on an empty stomach.

Contraindications

1. Hypersensitivity or previous toxic reactions to chloramphenicol.

2. In treating minor bacterial or viral infections.

Adverse Effects

1. The most serious is bone marrow depression. Irreversible bone marrow depression leading to fatal aplastic anemia can appear weeks or months after therapy. This risk factor is approximately 1 in 25,000 to 1 in 41,000.

2. Reversible type of bone marrow depression which is dose-related and is characterized by vacuolization of erythroid cells, reduction of reticulocytes, and leukopenia.

3. Gray baby syndrome in premature or newborn babies. Symptoms appear after 3–4 days of treatment and include abdominal distention, progressive pallid cyanosis, vasomotor collapse, and irregular respiration.

Drug Interactions

1. Chloramphenicol is an enzyme inhibitor and can affect the metabolism of oral anticoagulants, sulfonylureas, and phenytoin.

2. Concurrent use with other bone marrow–depressing drugs should be avoided.

3. Chloramphenicol can antagonize the bactericidal effects of the penicillins and cephalosporins.

4. Chloramphenicol may decrease the effects of vitamin B_{12}, folic acid, and iron preparations in anemic patients.

CHLORAMPHENICOL SODIUM SUCCINATE FOR INJECTION

Category

Antibiotic: antirickettsial

Doses

Parenteral (IV)	
Neonatal	
Under 2 weeks	25 mg/kg daily divided into 4 equal doses.
Over 2 weeks	50 mg/kg daily divided into 4 equal doses.
Pediatric and adults	50 mg/kg daily divided into 4 equal doses. Severe infections may require up to 100 mg/kg daily. Reduce to 50 mg/kg daily as soon as possible.

Dosage for newborn must be adjusted according to serum levels to prevent gray baby syndrome. Infants and children with immature metabolism must receive lower dosage. A dose of 25 mg/kg daily will usually produce adequate blood levels.

Administration

1. IV injection should not exceed 100 mg/mL and should be administered over 1–2 min.

2. Reconstituted solution is compatible with most infusion solutions.

3. Patients should be switched to an oral dosage form as soon as possible.

CHLORPROMAZINE HYDROCHLORIDE

Category

Antipsychotic: phenothiazine tranquilizer

Brand Names

Chlor-PZ (USV)

Oramazine (Hauck)

Promapar (Parke-Davis)

Thorazine (Smith Kline & French)

Pharmacologic Mechanism

The phenothiazines block postsynaptic dopamine receptors in the limbic system and basal ganglia, which results in a tranquilizing effect in psychotic patients. The phenothiazines exert strong anti-alpha-adrenergic and weaker peripheral anticholinergic activity and varying degrees of antiemetic activity. They also possess antihistamine, antiserotonin, and ganglionic blocking activity.

Uses and Doses

Neonatal (under 6 months)	Not recommended.
Pediatric	
Psychiatric (outpatient)	
Nausea-vomiting	
Oral	025 mg/lb every 4–6 h.
IM	0.25 mg/lb every 6–8 h.
Rectal	0.5 mg/lb every 6–8 h.
Psychiatric (hospitalized)	
Oral	Start with low doses and increase slowly 50–100 mg daily. Older children may require 200 mg daily or more.
IM	40 mg daily up to 5 years of age. 75 mg daily for 5–12 years of age.
Surgery	
Preoperative	
Oral	0.25 mg/lb, 2–3 h before surgery.
IM	0.25 mg/lb, 1–2 h before surgery.
Postoperative	
Oral	0.25 mg/lb every 6–8 h.
IM	0.25 mg/lb. Repeat in 1 h if no hypotension develops.
During surgery	
IM	0.125 mg/lb. Repeat in 1 h if no hypotension develops.
IV	1 mg per fractional injection at 2-min intervals and not exceeding IM dosage.

Tetanus
IM or IV

0.125 mg/lb every 6–8 h. Do not exceed daily dose of 40 mg in children under 50 lb and 75 mg in children from 50 to 100 lb.

Adults

Anxiety-tension-agitation
Oral

10 mg 3–4 times daily, or 25 mg 2–3 times daily. More severe cases, 25 mg 3 times daily. After 1–2 days, dosage may be increased by 20–50 mg semiweekly until patient improves. Continue optimum dosage for 2 weeks, then gradually reduce to a suitable maintenance level. Dosage of 200–800 mg is not unusual.

IM

25 mg for prompt control. Repeat in 1 h, if necessary. Subsequent dosage should be given orally, 25–50 mg 3 times daily.

Intractable hiccups
Oral

25–50 mg 3–4 times daily. If symptoms persist for 2–3 days, give 25–50 mg IM. Should symptoms persist, use slow IV infusion of 25–50 mg in 500–1000 mL of normal saline with patient flat in bed.

Nausea, vomiting
Oral

10–25 mg every 4–6 h prn. May be increased if necessary.

IM

25 mg. If no hypotension occurs, give 25–50 mg every 3–4 h prn.

Rectal

100 mg every 6–8 h prn.

Mild alcohol withdrawal
IM

25–50 mg. Repeat if necessary. Start subsequent oral dosages of 25–50 mg 3 times daily.

Cancer, severe pain
Oral

10 mg 3–4 times daily, or 25 mg 2–3 times daily.

IM

25 mg 2–3 times daily. Reduce dosage of concomitant narcotics and sedatives to one-quarter or one-half.

Acute intermittent porphyria
Oral

25–50 mg 3–4 times daily.

IM

25 mg 3–4 times daily until patient can take oral therapy.

Surgery
Preoperative
Oral

25–50 mg 2–3 h before surgery.

IM

12.5–25 mg 1–2 h before surgery.

Postoperative
Oral

10–25 mg every 4–6 h prn.

IM

12.5–25 mg. Repeat in 1 h if necessary and if no hypotension occurs.

During surgery
IM

12.5 mg. Repeat in $\frac{1}{2}$ h if necessary and if no hypotension develops.

IV

2 mg per fractional injection at 2-min intervals. Do not exceed 25 mg.

Tetanus
IM or IV

25–50 mg 3–4 times daily.

Psychiatric (outpatient)
Oral

10 mg 3–4 times daily, or 25 mg 2–3 times daily. More severe cases, 25 mg 3 times daily. After 1–2 days, daily dosage may be increased by 20–50 mg semiweekly until patient improves.

IM

25 mg for prompt control. Subsequent doses should be given orally, 25–30 mg 3 times daily.

Psychiatric (hospitalized)
Acutely agitated manic
IM

25 mg. If necessary, 25–50 mg in 1 h. Increase subsequent doses over several days (up to 400 mg every 4–6 h). Substitute oral doses when patient is calm and cooperative (usually within 48 h).

Oral

500 mg daily is usually sufficient. Doses exceeding 1000 mg daily usually do not produce further therapeutic gains.

In general, dosage levels should be lower in the elderly, the emaciated, and the debilitated.

Administration

1. For IM administration inject slowly and deeply into the upper outer quadrant of the buttock. Because of possible hypotensive effects keep patient lying down for at least ½ h after injection.

2. IM injection initiation may be reduced by diluting with sterile normal saline injection.

3. IV route should be limited to surgery and severe hiccups.

4. Recommended IV dilution is 1 mg of drug in 24 mL of sterile normal saline injection.

Contraindications

Hypersensitivity to chlorpromazine or phenothiazines in comatose patients or in comatose states, in the presence of large amounts of CNS depressants, and with bone marrow depression.

Adverse Effects

Mild to moderate drowsiness, photosensitivity, exfoliative dermatitis, lactation and breast enlargement, extrapyramidal symptoms, persistent tardive dyskinesia, postural hypotension, ECG distortions of the Q and T waves, agranulocytosis, hemolytic anemia, thrombocytopenic purpura, skin pigmentation, pigmentary retinopathy, and corneal and lenticular changes.

Drug Interactions

1. Dosage reductions as required for narcotics, barbiturates, and other CNS depressants when used concurrently with phenothiazines.

2. The phenothiazines and the amphetamines are mutually antagonistic to each other.

3. The antihypertensive effects of guanethidine and related drugs will be antagonized by the phenothiazines.

CLINDAMYCIN HYDROCHLORIDE

Category

Antibiotic

Brand Names

Cleocin HCl (Upjohn)

Pharmacologic Mechanism

Bacteriostatic activity due to inhibition of ribosomal protein synthesis in susceptible microorganisms.

Uses and Doses

Clindamycin can produce severe and sometimes fatal colitis and should be reserved for serious infections where less toxic antibiotics (especially the penicillins and erythromycins) are ineffective or patient contraindicated.

1. Indicated in the treatment of susceptible strains of pneumococci, staphylococci, and streptococci.

2. In the treatment of susceptible anaerobic bacteria including intestinal strains of *Bacteroides*.

	P.O.	
Pediatric*	8–12 mg/kg daily divided in 3–4 equal doses. For severe infections, 13–16 mg/kg daily divided into 3–4 equal doses. For more severe infections, 17–25 mg/kg daily divided into 3–4 equal doses.
Adult	150–300 mg every 6 h. More severe infections, 300–450 mg every 6 h.

* Clindamycin palmitate hydrochloride.

Administration

Clindamycin must be given on an empty stomach with a full glass of water 1–2 h before meals, and no food may be eaten for at least 1 h after administration.

Contraindications

Hypersensitivity to clindamycin or lincomycin.

Adverse Effects

Abdominal pain, nausea, vomiting, diarrhea, colitis, maculopapular rash, urticaria, anaphylaxis, erythema multiforma, agranulocytosis, and thrombocytopenia.

Drug Interactions

1. Kaolin and pectin suspensions will greatly reduce the oral absorption of clindamycin.

2. Antibiotic antagonism can exist between clindamycin and chloramphenicol, the erythromycins, the penicillins, and the cephalosporins when used concurrently.

CLINDAMYCIN PHOSPHATE INJECTION

Category

Antibiotic

Brand Names

Cleocin phosphate (Upjohn)

Pharmacologic Mechanism

Bacteriostatic activity due to inhibition of ribosomal protein synthesis in susceptible microorganisms.

Uses and Doses

Indicated in the treatment of infections caused by clindamycin-sensitive organisms.

Parenteral (IM or IV)	
Newborn (under 1 month)	Not recommended.
Pediatric	15–25 mg/kg daily in 3 or 4 equal doses. Severe infections 25–40 mg/kg in 3 or 4 equal doses.
Adult	600–1200 mg/kg daily in 2–4 equal doses. Severe infection may require 1200–1700 mg/kg daily in 2–4 equal doses.

Administration

1. Single IM doses greater than 600 mg are not recommended.

2. Single IV doses greater than 1200 mg in 1-h infusions are not recommended.

3. Sterile solution intended for IV administration should be diluted and administered according to the manufacturer's recommendations.

4. Sterile solution may be mixed with 5% dextrose, 10% dextrose, sodium chloride injection, and Ringer's for IV infusions.

Contraindications, etc.

See CLINDAMYCIN HYDROCHLORIDE.

COLISTIMETHATE SODIUM, STERILE

Category

Antibiotic: polypeptide antibiotic

Brand Names

Coly-Mycin M (Parke-Davis)

Pharmacologic Mechanism

Bactericidal activity due to disorientation of the lipoprotein cell membrane in susceptible microorganisms.

Uses and Doses

Indicated in the treatment of infections caused by susceptible strains of

Enterobacter aerogenes

Escherichia coli

Klebsiella pneumoniae

Pseudomonas aeruginosa

Parenteral (IM or IV)	
Normal kidney function	2.5–5 mg/kg daily in 2–4 divided doses.
Moderate kidney impairment	2.5–3.8 mg/kg daily in 2–4 divided doses.
Considerable kidney impairment	1.5 mg/kg daily in 2–4 divided doses.

Administration

1. During reconstitution, gently swirl the solution to avoid frothing.

2. For direct IV administration, inject one-half of the total of the daily dose over a period of 3–5 min every 12 h.

3. For continuous infusion:
   a. Slowly inject one-half of the total dose directly.
   b. Add the remaining one half dose to 5% dextrose, 5% dextrose–sodium chloride combinations, 10% invert sugar, or lactated Ringer's injection.

4. Start infusion 1–2 h after initial dose and administer at a rate of 5–6 mg/h. Reduce dosage according to recommended dose schedule in patients with renal insufficiency.

Contraindications

Hypersensitivity.

Adverse Effects

Respiratory arrest, increased BUN and serum creatinine, fever, paresthesia, vertigo, urticaria, and slurring of speech.

Drug Interactions

See POLYMIXIN-B.

CORTICOSTEROIDS

Category

Adrenal glucosteroid

Brand Names

Cortisone acetate—Cortone Acetate (Merck Sharp & Dohme)

Dexamethasone—Decadron (Merck Sharp & Dohme)

Dexamethasone acetate—Decadron LA (Merck Sharp & Dohme)

Dexamethasone sodium phosphate—Decadron Phosphate (Merck Sharp & Dohme)

Hydrocortisone—Cortef (Upjohn)
Hydrocortone (Merck Sharp & Dohme)

Hydrocortisone sodium succinate—Solu-Cortef (Upjohn)

Methylprednisolone—Medrol (Upjohn)

Methylprednisolone acetate—Depo-Medrol (Upjohn)

Methylprednisolone sodium succinate—Solu-Medrol (Upjohn)

Prednisone—Deltasone (Upjohn)
Meticorten (Schering)
Paracort (Parke-Davis)

Pharmacologic Mechanism

Glucosteroids cause a wide variety of pharmacologic activity. Their major effects include a potent anti-inflammatory effect, an increase in gluconeogenesis and protein catabolism, inhibition of the immune response, and redistribution of fat to central body areas.

Uses and Doses

Treatment of allergic states, collagen diseases, dermatologic diseases, endocrine disorders, neoplastic diseases, rheumatic diseases, and other assorted conditions.

The dosage for any glucosteroid is extremely variable and must be individualized.

	Oral Range	IM Range	IV Range
Cortisone acetate	25–300 mg	20–300 mg	—
Dexamethasone	750 μg–9 mg	—	—
Dexamethasone acetate	—	8–16 mg	—
Dexamethasone sodium phosphate	—	500 μg–24 mg	500 μg–24 mg
Hydrocortisone	10–320 mg	—	—
Hydrocortisone sodium phosphate	—	15–240 mg	15–240 mg
Methylprednisolone	2–60 mg	—	—
Methylprednisolone acetate	—	40–120 mg	—
Methylprednisolone sodium succinate	—	40–120 mg	10–250 mg
Prednisone	5–250 mg	—	—

The above schedules are only guidelines and can vary depending upon the specific clinical situation. Corticosteroids can also be administered by intra-articular and soft tissue injection as well as intralesional, topical, ophthalmic, and rectal administration.

Contraindications

Hypersensitivity and systemic fungal infections.

Adverse Effects

Peptic ulcer, pancreatitis, ulcerative esophagitis, menstrual irregularities, cushingoid state, secondary adrenocortical and pituitary unresponsiveness, increased insulin requirements in diabetics, sodium and fluid retention, potassium loss, impaired immunity, cataracts, and glaucoma.

Drug Interactions

1. Severe hypokalemia can occur with concurrent use of acetazolamide, chlorthalidone, ethacrynic acid, furosemide, mercaptomerin, metolazone, quinethazone, and thiazides.

2. Concurrent use with indomethacin and other ulcerogenic drugs can produce additive effects.

3. Glucosteroids antagonize the effects of the oral anticoagulants.

4. Concurrent use with antidiabetic agents may require higher doses for the antidiabetic drugs.

DESMOPRESSIN ACETATE

Category

Synthetic posterior pituitary hormone: antidiuretic

Brand Names

DDAVP (Ferring)

Pharmacologic Mechanism

Antidiuretic activity due to an increase in water reabsorption in the nephrons of the kidneys.

Uses and Doses

Indicated for the treatment of polydipsia, polyuria, and dehydration due to neurohypophyseal diabetes insipidus or trauma or surgery in the pituitary region.

Dosage must be individualized according to patient response.

Intranasal	
Pediatric (3–12 years of age)	0.05–0.3 mL daily
Adults	0.1–0.4 mL daily

Administration

According to patient response, may be administered as a single daily dose or in divided doses.

Contraindications

Hypersensitivity.

Adverse Effects

Transient headache, nausea, nasal congestion, rhinitis, and flushing.

Drug Interactions

1. Use with caution in patients receiving lithium carbonate, epinephrine, or heparin.

2. Concurrent use with chlorpropamide may enhance the antidiuretic effect.

DEXTRAN 40

Category

Plasma expander

Brand Names

Gentran 40 (Travenol)

LMD (Abbott)

Rheomacrodex (Pharmacia)

Pharmacologic Mechanism

Dextran administered IV creates hyperoncotic pressure within the circulatory system which results in an immediate expansion of plasma volume. Dextran also retards and reverses cellular aggregation resulting from shock.

Uses and Doses

Parenteral	
Shock	Up to 20 mL/kg during the first 24 h of treatment. Infuse the first 500 mL of solution rapidly and the remaining dose more slowly. Reduce to 10 mL/kg after 24 h and discontinue after 5 days.
Extracorporeal circulation	10–20 mL/kg can be added to the perfusion circuit. Do not exceed 20 mL/kg.
Thrombis prophylaxis	10 mL/kg administered on the day of surgery. After surgery, continue with 500 mL per day for 2–3 days. An additional 500 mL may be given every 2–3 days for up to 2 weeks if the risk of complications still exists.

Contraindications

Hypersensitivity, hemostatic defects, cardiac decompensation, severe oliguria, or anuria.

Adverse Effects

Nausea, vomiting, urticaria, wheezing, and anaphylaxis.

Drug Interactions

Dextran may increase the activity of anticoagulants.

DIAZEPAM

Category

Antianxiety agent

Brand Names

Valium (Roche)

Pharmacologic Mechanism

The antianxiety activity of diazepam appears to be related to depression of the CNS at the brainstem recticular formation and limbic system. Diazepam exerts moderate anticonvulsant and skeletal muscle relaxation activity and possesses a drug-misuse potential and a weak addiction liability.

Uses and Doses

P.O.	
Children over 6 months	1–2.5 mg 3–4 times daily. May be increased slowly if necessary.
Adults	
Anxiety and psychoneurotic states	2–10 mg 2–4 times daily.
Alcoholism	10 mg 3–4 times during the first 24 h. Subsequent doses of 5 mg 3–4 times daily as needed.
Skeletal muscle spasm	2–10 mg 3–4 times daily.
Convulsive disorders	2–10 mg 2–4 times daily.
Geriatric patients	2–2.5 mg 1–2 times daily. May be increased slowly if necessary.
Parenteral (IM or IV)	
Children	
Tetanus	
Neonates over 3 days	1–2 mg repeated every 3–4 h as necessary.
Children over 5 years	5–10 mg repeated every 3–4 h as necessary.
Status epilepticus and severe convulsive seizures	
Neonates over 30 days	0.2–0.5 mg slowly every 2–5 min up to a maximum of 5 mg IV.
Children over 5 years	1 mg every 2–5 min up to a maximum of 10 mg IV. Repeat in 2–4 h as necessary.
Adults	
Moderate psychoneurotic reactions	2–5 mg IM or IV. Repeat in 3–4 h if necessary.
Severe psychoneurotic reactions	5–10 mg IM or IV. Repeat in 3–4 h if necessary.
Alcoholism	10 mg IM or IV followed by 5–10 mg in 3–4 h if necessary.
Endoscopic procedures	10 mg is usually adequate. May give up to 20 mg IV just prior to procedure.
Muscle spasm	5–10 mg IM or IV followed by 5–10 mg in 3–4 h if necessary.
Status epilepticus and severe convulsive seizures	5–10 mg. May be repeated at 10- to 15-min intervals to a maximum dose of 30 mg.
Preoperative	10 mg IM before surgery.
Cardioversion	5–15 mg IV within 5–10 min prior to procedure.

Administration

1. For IM administration, inject deeply and slowly into a large muscle mass.

2. For IV administration, inject slowly, taking 1 min for each 5 mg given. Extreme care should be taken to avoid intra-arterial administration or extravasation.

Contraindications

Hypersensitivity and narrow-angle glaucoma.

Adverse Effects

Drowsiness, fatigue, ataxia, and paradoxical reactions including hyperexcited states, anxiety, and hallucinations.

Drug Interactions

1. Avoid concurrent use with monoamine oxidase inhibitors.

2. Concurrent use with CNS depressants will produce additive depression.

DICUMAROL

Category

Anticoagulant

Pharmacologic Mechanism

Coumadin anticoagulants inhibit prothrombin synthesis (factor II) and also interfere with the production of proconvertin (factor VII) and the Christmas factor (factor IX) in the liver by interfering with the action of vitamin K.

Uses and Doses

1. Adjunct in coronary occlusion
2. Atrial fibrillation with embolization
3. Prophylaxis and treatment of pulmonary thrombosis and venous thrombosis

P.O.	
Adult	Start with a dose of 200–300 mg on the first day. Prothrombin time should determine the maintenance dose, which is usually 25–200 mg daily.

Administration

1. Maintenance dose is usually administered as a single daily dose.
2. Therapy should be discontinued slowly.

Contraindications

Hypersensitivity to coumarin anticoagulants, subacute bacterial endocarditis, any type of bleeding conditions, and with patients who cannot be carefully supervised.

Adverse Effects

Hemorrhage from the gastrointestinal and urinary tracts, nausea, vomiting, diarrhea, hepatitis, jaundice, urticaria, alopecia, agranulocytosis, leukopenia, and anemia.

Drug Interactions

1. Drugs which can cause significant increases in anticoagulant activity include anabolic steroids, broad spectrum antibiotics, clofibrate, dextrothyroxine, disulfiram, oxyphenbutazone, phenylbutazone, and thyroid preparations.
2. Drugs which can cause significant decreases in anticoagulant activity include barbiturates, cholestyramine, estrogens, oral contraceptives, and glutethimide.

DIGITOXIN

Category

Cardiac glycoside

Brand Names

Crystodigin (Lilly)

Purodigin (Wyeth)

Pharmacologic Mechanism

The digitalis glycosides increase the force of myocardial contraction, increase the refractory period of the atrioventricular and sinoatrial nodes, and decrease the conductivity of the bundle of His and heart rate. Digitoxin exhibits good oral absorption, a moderate onset of activity, a long half-life, and slow urinary excretion.

Uses and Doses

Congestive heart failure, atrial fibrillation, atrial flutter, and paroxysmal atrial tachycardia.

Digitalization and maintenance doses must be individualized.

P.O.–Parenteral	
Pediatric	The following digitalizing doses are given in divided doses at 6- to 8-h intervals:
Newborn	0.025 mg/kg.
2 weeks to 1 year	0.04–0.045 mg/kg.
1–2 years	0.04 mg/kg.
2 years or over	0.02–0.03 mg/kg. The usual maintenance dose is approximately $\frac{1}{10}$ of the digitalizing dose.
Adult	Initial dose of 0.8 mg followed by 0.2 mg every 6–8 h. Usual maintenance dose is 0.05–0.2 mg daily.

Administration

1. Maintenance dose is usually administered as a single dose in the morning with breakfast.

2. Parenteral administration should be by IV injection.

Contraindications, etc.

See DIGOXIN.

DIGOXIN

Category

Cardiac glycoside

Brand Names

Lanoxin (Burroughs Wellcome)

SK-Digoxin (Smith Kline & French)

Pharmacologic Mechanism

The digitalis glycosides increase the force of myocardial contraction, increase the refractory period of the atrioventricular and sinoatrial node, and decrease the conductivity of the bundle of His and the heart rate. Digoxin exhibits good oral absorption, a moderate onset of activity, a short half-life, and rapid urinary excretion.

Uses and Doses

Congestive heart failure, atrial fibrillation, atrial flutter, paroxysmal tachycardia, and cardiogenic shock. Digitalization and maintenance doses must be individualized.

P.O.	
Pediatric	The following digitalizing doses are given in divided doses at 6- to 8-h intervals:
Newborn	0.04–0.06 mg/kg.
1 month to 2 years	0.06–0.08 mg/kg.
2 years or over	0.04–0.06 mg/kg. The usual maintenance dose is approximately $\frac{1}{5}$ to $\frac{1}{3}$ of the digitalizing dose.
Adult	Usual digitalizing dose is 0.5–1 mg. Usual maintenance dose is 0.125–0.5 mg daily.

Parenteral (IM and IV)	
Pediatric	The following digitalizing doses are given in divided doses at 6- to 8-h intervals:
Newborn	0.025–0.04 mg/kg.
2 weeks to 2 years	0.035–0.05 mg/kg.
2 years or over	0.025–0.04 mg/kg. The usual daily maintenance dose is approximately $\frac{1}{5}$ to $\frac{1}{3}$ of the digitalizing dose.
Adult	Usual digitalizing dose is 0.5–1 mg. Usual maintenance dose is 0.125–0.5 mg daily.

Administration

1. Maintenance dose is usually administered as a single daily dose in the morning with breakfast.

2. The preferred route for parenteral administration is by IV injection.

Contraindications

Hypersensitivity, toxic effects, and ventricular tachycardia.

Adverse Effects

Anorexia, nausea, vomiting, diarrhea, ventricular premature beats, paroxysmal and nonparoxysmal nodal rhythms, and blurred or yellow vision.

Drug Interactions

1. Use with caution with drugs that induce hypokalemia. Acetazolamide, amphotericin B, chlorthalidone, ethacrynic acid, furosemide, mercaptomerin, and thiazides can induce hypokalemia.

2. Calcium preparations with parenteral administration can produce serious cardiac arrhythmias.

DISOPYRAMIDE PHOSPHATE

Category

Antiarrhythmic

Brand Names

Norpace (Searle)

Pharmacologic Mechanism

Disopyramide is similar to procainamide and quinidine (type I antiarrhythmic drugs). It decreases the rate of diastolic depolarization in cells with augmented automaticity and upstroke velocity while increasing the action potential duration of normal cardiac cells. The drug possesses no alpha- or beta-adrenergic activity but does exhibit anticholinergic activity.

Uses and Doses

1. Unifocal premature (ectopic) ventricular contractions.

2. Premature (ectopic) ventricular contractions of multifocal origin.

3. Episodes of ventricular tachycardia.

P.O.	
Adult	400–800 mg 4 times daily in divided doses. Usual dose is 150 mg every 6 h.

Dosage must be individualized according to patient response and tolerance. Patient renal impairment requires careful dosage adjustments.

Administration

Maintenance is usually administered every 6 h.

Contraindications

Hypersensitivity, cardiogenic shock, and preexisting second- or third-degree AV block if no pacemaker is present.

Adverse Effects

The most frequent are anticholinergic effects, which include dry mouth and throat, urinary hesitancy, constipation, blurred vision, hypotension, congestive heart failure, and hypoglycemia.

Drug Interactions

Concurrent use with procainamide or quinidine should be reserved for life-threatening arrhythmias that do not respond to single-agent therapy.

DOPAMINE HYDROCHLORIDE

Category

Sympathomimetic: vasopressor

Brand Names

Intropin (Arnar-Stone)

Pharmacologic Mechanism

Sympathomimetic effect due to activity with adrenergic and dopaminergic receptors. Dopamine produces direct stimulation of β_1 receptors and dopaminergic receptors, and in higher doses the drug also effects α receptors. The sum total of adrenergic and dopaminergic activity results in a positive inotropic effect and increased renal and mesenteric blood flow. The alpha-adrenergic effects of the drug become more pronounced with high doses, producing vasoconstriction and an elevation of blood pressure.

Uses and Doses

Treatment of the shock syndrome due to chronic cardiac decompensation, endotoxic septicemia, myocardial infarctions, open-heart surgery, renal failure, and trauma.

Parenteral (IV infusion)	
Adults	Start with an infusion rate of 1–5 μg/kg per min. May be increased until the desired response is obtained. For more severe cases, start with a rate of 5 μg/kg per min and increase gradually until the desired response is obtained. Usual satisfactory dose is 20 μg/kg per min, and doses of 50 μg/kg per min have been used safely.

Administration

1. Dilute 1 ampul (200 mg) in 250 or 500 mL of 5% dextrose, 5% dextrose and sodium chloride, dextrose in lactated Ringer's solution, lactated Ringer's solution, sodium lactate, or sodium chloride injection.

2. Do not mix with alkaline substances.

3. Treat extravasation with phentolamine as soon as possible after noted.

Contraindications

Pheochromocytoma, uncorrected tachyarrhthmias.

Adverse Effects

Tachycardia, anginal pain, ectopic beats, hypotension, and vasoconstriction.

Drug Interactions

Avoid concurrent use with cyclopropane and halogenated hydrocarbons.

ERGONOVINE MALEATE

Category

Oxytocic

Brand Names

Ergotrate (Lily)

Pharmacologic Mechanism

Produces tetanic contraction of the postpartum uterus for approximately 90 min which is followed by clonic contractions that persist for another 90 min.

Uses and Doses

Indicated for the prevention and treatment of postpartum and postaborted hemorrhage due to uterine atony.

P.O.	Initial dose of 0.2 mg administered parenterally, followed by 0.2–0.4 mg given orally every 6–12 h until the danger of atony is over.
Parenteral (IM and IV)	0.2 mg which can be repeated for severe uterine hemorrhage.

Administration

Ergonovine maleate may also be administered perlingually and rectally (suspended in water as a retention enema).

Contraindications

Hypersensitivity, threatened spontaneous abortion, or for labor induction.

Adverse Effects

Nausea and vomiting and ergotism with prolonged use.

Drug Interactions

Concurrent or sequential use with vasoconstrictors or oxytocin may produce hypertension.

ERYTHROMYCIN LACTOBIONATE FOR INJECTION

Category

Antibiotic: macrolide antibiotic

Brand Names

Erythrocin Lactobionate-I.V. (Abbott)

Pharmacologic Mechanism

Bacteriostatic activity due to inhibition of ribosomal protein synthesis in susceptible microorganisms.

Doses

Parenteral (IV) Pediatric and adults	15–20 mg/kg daily. Severe infections may require up to 4 g daily.

Administration

1. After reconstitution, the solution may be added to lactated Ringer's, sodium chloride injection, or Normosol-R for IV administration.

2. For slow continuous infusion, a concentration of 1 g/L should be utilized.

3. For intermittent administration, one-quarter of the daily total can be given in 20–60 min by slow administration.

Uses, etc.

See ERYTHROMYCIN STEARATE.

ERYTHROMYCIN STEARATE

Category

Antibiotic: macrolide antibiotic

Brand Names

Bristamycin (Bristol)

Erypar (Parke-Davis)

Erythrocin Stearate (Abbott)

Ethril (Squibb)

Pfizer E (Pfipharmecs)

Pharmacologic Mechanism

Bacteriostatic activity due to inhibition of ribosomal protein synthesis in susceptible microorganisms.

Uses and Doses

1. Indicated in the treatment of infections caused by susceptible strains of
   Alpha-hemolytic streptococci
   Group A beta-hemolytic streptococci
   Entamoeba histolytica
     (intestinal amibiasis only)
   Hemophilus influenzae
   Listeria monocytogenes
   Mycoplasma pneumoniae
   Neisseria gonorrhoeae
   Staphylococci
   Streptococcus pneumoniae
   Treponema pallidum

2. Treatment of erythrasma (*Corynebacterium minutissimun*).

3. As an adjunct to antitoxin therapy in treating *Corynebacterium diphtheriae* infections. Also to prevent the establishment of carriers or to eliminate the organisms in carriers.

P. O.	
Pediatric	30–50 mg/kg daily in 3 or 4 divided doses. Severe infections may require up to 60–100 mg/kg daily.
Adult	250 mg 4 times a day. Severe infections may require 4 g or more daily. Primary syphilis requires 30–40 g in daily divided doses for 10–15 days.

Administration

Administer before meals.

Contraindications

Hypersensitivity.

Adverse Effects

Dose-related abdominal cramps, nausea, vomiting, diarrhea, urticaria, rash, and anaphylaxis.

Drug Interactions

Avoid concurrent use with penicillin and cephalosporin because of antibiotic antagonism.

ETHACRYNATE SODIUM FOR INJECTION

Category

Diuretic

Brand Names

Sodium Edecrin (Merck Sharp & Dohme)

Dose Ranges

Parenteral	
Pediatric	1 mg/kg.
Adult	50 mg or 0.5–1 mg/kg.

Administration

Administer by slow, direct IV injection or by a running infusion.

Pharmacologic Mechanism, etc.

See ETHACRYNIC ACID.

ETHACRYNIC ACID

Category

Diuretic

Brand Names

Edecrin (Merck Sharp & Dohme)

Pharmacologic Mechanism

Ethacrynic acid promotes the excretion of water, sodium, chloride, and other electrolytes by inhibiting tubular reabsorption, especially in the medullary and cortical portions of the ascending limb of the loop of Henle.

Uses and Dosages

1. Edema due to renal dysfunction.

2. Adjunct in treating edema due to congestive heart failure and hepatic cirrhosis.

3. Short-term management of ascites due to malignancy, idiopathic edema, and lymphedema.

4. Short-term management of edema in pediatric congenital heart disease or nephrotic syndrome.

P. O.	
Infants	Dosage not established.
Children	Start with a dose of 25 mg. Subsequent dose increments of 25 mg should be made to achieve effective maintenance.
Adults	50–100 mg. After diuresis has been achieved, the lowest effective dose should be given. Usual maintenance dose range is 50–300 mg.

Administration

1. Usually administered as a single daily dose in the morning.

2. Administration with meals will help reduce gastric upset.

Contraindications

1. Hypersensitivity, patients with anuria, increasing electrolyte imbalance, azotemia, oliguria, or watery diarrhea.

2. Nursing mothers.

Adverse Effects

Nausea, vomiting, diarrhea, anorexia, dysphagia and abdominal pain, agranulocytosis, neutropenia, thrombocytopenia, deafness, tinnitus, skin rash, headache, and blurred vision.

Drug Interactions

1. Avoid concurrent use with potentially neurotoxic drugs. Amikacin, capreomycin, chloroquine, gentamicin, kanamycin, neomycin, phenylbutazone, streptomycin, vancomycin, and viomycin are neurotoxic.

2. Use with caution during digitalis therapy because of possible hypokalemia. Concurrent use with corticosteroids can produce severe hypokalemia.

3. Concurrent use with lithium is best avoided.

4. Patients on anticoagulants may require anticoagulant dosage adjustments.

5. Concurrent use with antihypertensives can produce orthostatic hypotension.

FLUCYTOSINE (5-FLUOROCYTOSINE)

Category

Antifungal: antimonilial

Brand Names

Ancobon (Roche)

Pharmacologic Mechanism

Fungistatic activity due to unknown mechanism. Constant sensitivity tests are required during therapy since resistant strains can emerge quickly.

Uses and Doses

Indicated for the treatment of infections caused by susceptible strains of *Cryptococcus* and *Candida*.

P. O.	
Pediatric and adult	50–150 mg/kg daily divided in 4 doses.

Administration

To reduce nausea, administer the capsules a few at a time over a 15-min period until the correct dose (one-quarter of the daily dose) is attained.

Contraindications

Hypersensitivity.

Adverse Effects

Nausea, vomiting, diarrhea, anemia, leukopenia, and thrombocytopenia.

Drug Interactions

Avoid concurrent use with bone marrow–depressing nephrotoxic and hepatotoxic drugs.

FUROSEMIDE

Category

Diuretic

Brand Names

Lasix (Hoechst-Roussel)

Pharmacological Mechanism

Furosemide promotes the excretion of water, sodium, chloride, and other electrolytes by inhibiting tubular reabsorption, especially in the medullary and cortical portions of the ascending limb of the loop of Henle.

Uses and Doses

1. Edema due to renal dysfunction.

2. Management of hypertension as a sole agent or in combination with other antihypertensives.

3. Adjunct in treating edema due to congestive heart failure and hepatic cirrhosis.

P. O.	
Pediatric	2 mg/kg given as a single dose. Dosage may be increased if needed. Do not exceed a daily dose of 6 mg/kg.
Adult	
Edema	20–80 mg as a single dose. Refractory patients may require 600 mg as a single dose or divided into 2–3 doses.
Hypertension	40 mg 2 times daily.
Parenteral	
Pediatric	1 mg/kg. Doses greater than 6 mg/kg are not recommended.
Adult	20–40 mg. May be followed by a second dose 2 h later.
Acute pulmonary edema	40 mg IV, followed by a second 40-mg dose $1–1\frac{1}{2}$ h later, if needed.

Administration

1. Diuretic dose is usually administered as a single daily dose in the morning.

2. Administration with meals will help reduce gastric upset.

Contraindications

1. Hypersensitivity, patients with anuria, increasing electrolyte balance, azotemia, or oliguria.

2. Use in women of childbearing potential is not recommended unless the expected therapeutic benefits outweight the potential harm.

Adverse Effects

Nausea, vomiting, diarrhea, anemia, leukopenia, aplastic anemia, thrombocytopenia, tinnitus, hearing impairment, urticaria, exfoliative dermatitis, erythema multiforme, paresthesia, and blurred vision.

Drug Interactions

1. Avoid concurrent use with potentially neurotoxic drugs. Amikacin, capreomycin, chloroquine, gentamicin, kanamycin, neomycin, oxyphenbutazone, phenylbutazone, streptomycin, vancomycin, and viomycin are neurotoxic drugs.

2. Use with caution during digitalis therapy because of possible hypokalemia. Concurrent use with corticosteroids can produce severe hypokalemia.

3. Concurrent use with lithium is best avoided.

4. Concurrent use with cephaloridine can produce additive nephrotoxicity.

GENTAMICIN SULFATE

Category

Antibiotic: aminoglycoside antibiotic

Brand Names

Garamycin (Schering)

Pharmacologic Mechanism

Bactericidal activity due to inhibition of ribosomal protein synthesis in susceptible microorganisms.

Uses and Doses

The toxicity of aminoglycoside antibiotics restricts their use to serious gram-negative infections.

1. Indicated in the treatment of infections caused by susceptible strains of

Enterobacter aerogenes
Escherichia coli
Klebsiella pneumoniae
Proteus spp. (both indole-positive and indole-negative)
Pseudomonas aeruginosa
Salmonella spp.
Shigella spp.
Serratia (nonpigmented)

2. Alternate for penicillin-resistant staphylococcus infections.

3. As initial therapy in suspected or confirmed gram-negative infections prior to obtaining sensitivity test results.

4. In treating serious unknown infections in conjunction with a penicillin or cephalosporin prior to identification of the causative agent and obtaining sensitivity test results.

5. In combination with carbenicillin for treating stubborn infections caused by *Pseudomonas aeruginosa*.

6. In combination with a penicillin for treating sepsis or staphylococcal pneumonia in neonates.

Parenteral* (IM or IV)	
Premature or full-term neonates	
1 week of age or less	5 mg/kg daily or 2.5 mg/kg every 12 h.
Neonates and infants	7.5 mg/kg daily in 3 equal doses every 8 h.
Children	6–7 mg/kg daily in 3 equal doses every 8 h.
Adults	3 mg/kg daily in 3 equal doses every 8 h. 5 mg/kg daily in 3–4 equal doses for life-threatening infections. Reduce to 3 mg/kg daily when clinically indicated.

* For patients with normal renal function, treatment usually requires 7–10 days.

Dosage for patients with impaired renal function must be adjusted. Dosage adjustment should be based on gentamicin serum levels, serum creatinine levels, and creatinine clearance rates.

Administration

1. For IV administration, a single dose of gentamicin may be diluted in 50–200 mL of sterile normal saline or 5% dextrose solution and infused over a period of 30 min to 2 h. Pediatric administration should use less diluent.

2. In combined therapy with carbenicillin the two drugs should not be premixed. Administer both drugs separately.

Contraindications

Hypersensitivity, previous serious toxic effects with gentamicin or other aminoglycosides.

Adverse Effects

Ototoxicity involving auditory impairment and vestibular damage, nephrotoxicity, anemia, arthralgia, hypotension, and purpura.

Drug Interactions

Avoid concurrent use with potentially neurotoxic or nephrotoxic drugs. Amikacin, cephaloridine, colistin, ethacrynic acid, furosemide, kanamycin, neomycin, paromomycin, polymixin-B, streptomycin, tobramycin, vancomycin, and viomycin are best avoided.

HEPARIN SODIUM

Category

Anticoagulant

Brand Names

Lipo-Heprin (Upjohn)

Heprinar (Armour)

Liquaemin Sodium (Organon)

Panheprin (Abbott)

Pharmacologic Mechanism

Heparin primarily interferes with the conversion of prothrombin to thrombin. The drug also appears to have an antithrombin action and can decrease the agglutination of platelets.

Uses and Doses

1. Prophylaxis and treatment of pulmonary embolism and venous thrombosis

2. Atrial fibrillation with embolization.

3. Diagnosis and treatment of acute and chronic consumption coagulopathies.

4. Prevention of clotting in arterial and heart surgery.

5. Prophylaxis and treatment of peripheral arterial embolism.

6. Adjunct in treating coronary occlusion with acute myocardial infarction.

7. Anticoagulant for use in blood transfusions, extracorporeal circulation, dialysis procedures, and in blood samples for laboratory purposes.

Parenteral	
Pediatric	By IV infusion, 50 U per kg of body weight followed by 100 U per kg or 3333 U per m² of body surface 6 times a day.
Adult	Initially 10,000 U followed by 5000–10,000 U 4–6 times a day by IV administration. By infusion, 20,000–40,000 U/L at a rate of 51–30 U/min. By subcutaneous injection, 10,000–20,000 U initially, followed by 8000–10,000 U 3 times a day.

Administration

1. Heparin may be administered by deep subcutaneous injection (two-tract or bunch method), intermittent IV injection, or continuous IV infusions.

2. IM administration not recommended because of the dangers of hematoma formation.

Contraindications

Hypersensitivity, any type of bleeding, and with patients who cannot be carefully supervised.

Adverse Effects

Hemorrhage, acute reversible thrombocytopenia, rebound hyperlipemia, osteoporosis and suppression of renal function during long-term therapy, alopecia, priapism, and aldosterone suppression.

Drug Interactions

Avoid concurrent use with aspirin, ethacrynic acid (IV), and oral anticoagulants.

HYDROCHLOROTHIAZIDE

Category

Diuretic: antihypertensive, thiazide diuretic

Brand Names

Diaqua (Hauck)

Esidrix (Ciba)

Hydro-Diuril (Merck Sharp & Dohme)

Oretic (Abbott)

Pharmacological Mechanism

The thiazides promote the excretion of water, sodium, and chloride by inhibiting the reabsorption of sodium ions in the ascending limb of the loop of Henle and in the early distal tubule of the nephron. The thiazides lower peripheral vascular resistance, which results in significant antihypertensive activity.

Uses and Doses

1. Management of hypertension as a sole agent or in combination with other antihypertensives.

2. Treatment of edema due to renal dysfunction.

3. Adjunct in treating edema due to congestive heart failure, hepatic cirrhosis, and corticosteroid or estrogen therapy.

P.O.	
Pediatric	
Under 6 months	1.5 mg/lb daily in 2 doses
Up to 2 years	12.3–37.5 mg daily in 2 doses
2 or more years	37.5–100 mg daily in 2 doses
Adult	50–100 mg daily. Do not exceed 200 mg daily.

Administration

1. Diuretic dose is usually administered once daily in the morning.

2. Administration with meals will help reduce gastric upset.

Contraindications

Hypersensitivity to thiazides and other sulfonamide-derivative drugs and in patients with anuria.

Adverse Effects

Weakness, fatigue, dizziness, urticaria, leg cramps, necrotizing angiitis, photosensitivity, agranulocytosis, thrombocytopenia, aplastic anemia, anorexia, gastric irritation, and transient blurred vision.

Drug Interactions

1. Use with caution during digitalis therapy because of possible hypokalemia. Concurrent use with corticosteroids can produce significant hypokalemia.
2. Diabetic patients may require antidiabetic dosage adjustments.

ISOPROTERENOL HYDROCHLORIDE

Category

Sympathomimetic: beta-adrenergic agent

Brand Names

Isuprel (Breon)

Pharmacologic Mechanism

Isoproterenol produces a sympathomimetic effect by stimulating both β_1, and β_2 receptors. This results in an increased cardiac rate and force of contraction, bronchodilation, gastrointestinal relaxation, and a decrease in peripheral vascular resistance.

Uses and Doses

Inhalation	
Asthma-broncho-spasm	1–5 treatments if needed daily
Parenteral	
Shock	Infusion rate of 0.5–5 μg/min. The dosage should be adjusted according to heart rate, blood pressure, and urine flow. Doses up to 30 μg may be required for advanced shock.
Heart block-arrhythmias	
Intracardiac	0.02 mg.
IM	Initial dose of 0.2 mg with a subsequent dose range of 0.02–1 mg.
IV	Initial dose of 0.02–0.06 mg with a subsequent dose range of 0.01–0.2 mg.
IV infusion	0.5–5 μg/min.
SC	Initial dose of 0.2 mg with a subsequent dose range of 0.15–0.2 mg.
Sublingual	
Bronchospasm	
Pediatric	5–10 mg. Do not exceed 30 mg daily.
Adult	15–20 mg. Do not exceed 60 mg daily.
Heart block	
Pediatric	One-half the initial adult dose.
Adult	10–15 mg 4–6 times daily.

Administration

Injection may be diluted with 5% dextrose or sodium chloride injection.

Contraindications

Digitalis-induced tachycardia and preexisting cardiac arrhythmias.

Adverse Effects

Flushing of the face, headache, tachycardia, anginal-type pain, and weakness.

Drug Interactions

Avoid concurrent use with monoamine oxidase inhibitors, guanethidine, and tricyclic antidepressants.

KANAMYCIN SULFATE

Category

Antibiotic: aminoglycoside antibiotic

Brand Names

Kantrex (Bristol)

Pharmacologic Mechanism

Bactericidal activity due to inhibition of ribosomal protein synthesis in susceptible microorganisms.

Uses and Doses

The toxicity of aminoglycoside antibiotics restricts their use to serious gram-negative infections.

1. Indicated in the treatment of infections caused by susceptible strains of
   Enterobacter aerogenes
   Escherichia coli
   Klebsiella pneumoniae
   Mima-Herellea (*Acinetobacter*)
   Proteus spp.
   Serratia marcescens

2. Alternate for penicillin-resistant staphylococcus infections.

3. In treating mixed staphylococcal gram-negative infections.

4. Preoperative intestinal antisepsis.

5. Reducing the population of nitrogen-producing bacteria in hepatic coma.

P.O.	
Pediatric	12.5 mg/ kg 4 times daily.
Adult	3–12 g daily in divided doses.
Parenteral	
Pediatric-Adult	Do not exceed 1.5 g daily.
IM	7.5 mg/kg every 12 h.
IV	15 mg/kg in 2–3 divided doses.
Inhalation	250 mg 2–4 times daily.

Dosage for patients with impaired renal function must be adjusted. Dosage adjustment should be based on kanamycin serum levels and serum creatinine clearance rates.

Administration

1. For IV administration, dilute 500 mg in 200 mL of sterile normal saline or 5% dextrose and administer 60–80 drops per min. Dilute 1 g in 400 mL.

2. For inhalation administration, dilute 250 mg in 3 mL of normal saline and nebulize.

3. For intraperitoneal instillation, dilute 500 mg in 20 mL of water for injection.

4. Do not mix kanamycin with other drugs.

Contraindications, etc.

See GENTAMICIN SULFATE.

LEVARTERENOL BITARTRATE

Category

Sympathomimetic: vasopressor

Brand Names

Levophed (Breon)

Pharmacologic Mechanism

Levarterenol produces a sympathomimetic effect by activating adrenergic receptors in the body. The drug produces powerful vasoconstriction (α receptors) and stimulation of the heart and dilation of coronary arteries (β receptors).

Uses and Doses

For controlling acute hypotensive states due to:

Blood transfusion

Drug reactions

Myocardial infarction

Pheocromocytomectomy

Poliomyelitis

Septicemia

Spinal anesthesia

Sympathectomy

Parenteral (IV)	
Pediatric	1 mL of a 0.2% solution added to 250 mL of 5% dextrose for continuous infusion.
Adult	2–8 mL of a 0.2% solution added to 500 mL of 5% dextrose for continuous infusion.

Administration

1. Pediatric IV rate of 0.5 mL/min is recommended.

2. Adult IV rate is adjusted to maintain a low normal blood pressure (80 to 100 mmHg systolic).

3. Whole blood or plasma if indicated to increase blood volume should be administered separately.

Contraindications

1. Hypotensive states due to blood volume deficits except as an emergency measure.

2. Mesenteric or peripheral vascular thrombosis unless necessary to save life.

3. During cyclopropane and halothane anesthesia.

Adverse Effects

Occasional bradycardia and headache.

Drug Interactions

Avoid concurrent use with monoamine oxidase (MAO) inhibitors.

MAGNESIUM SULFATE

Category

Anticonvulsant, saline laxative, electrolyte

Pharmacologic Mechanism

Anticonvulsant activity due to inhibition of peripheral neuromuscular transmission. Cathartic activity may be due to hyperosmotic effect of the magnesium ion.

Uses and Doses

1. Anticonvulsant for seizures associated with toxemia of pregnancy, epilepsy, glomerulonephritis, and hypothyroidism.

2. Treatment of magnesium deficiency.

3. Saline laxative.

4. Antidote for barium poisoning.

P.O.	
Pediatric	
Laxative	
2–5 years of age	2.5–5 g.
6–12 years of age	5–10 g.
Adult	
Laxative	10–30 g.
Parenteral	
Pediatric	
Anticonvulsant	20–40 mg/kg in a 20% solution.
Adult	
Anticonvulsant	1–40 g daily.
IM	1–5 g in a 25–50% solution.
IV	1–4 g in a 10–20% solution.
Infusion	4 g in 250 mL of 5% dextrose.
Magnesium deficiency (IM)	1 g every 6 h. For severe deficiencies, up to 250 mg/kg may be given IV over a 4-h period.
Barium poisoning	1–2 g IV.

Administration

1. For IV administration do not exceed a 20% solution or a rate of administration of 150 mg/min.

2. For IM administration do not exceed a 50% solution for adults or a 20% solution for children.

Contraindications

Heart block or myocardial damage (parenteral administration).

Adverse Effects

Primarily due to hypermagnesemia, these include flushing, sweating, hypotension, and respiratory and circulatory collapse.

Drug Interactions

1. Concurrent use with CNS depressants requires dosage adjustments.

2. Use with great caution in digitalized patients.

MEPERIDINE HYDROCHLORIDE

Category

Narcotic: Nonopiate addicting analgesic

Brand Names

Demerol Hydrochloride (Winthrop)

Pharmacologic Mechanism

The narcotic analgesics exhibit a wide range of activity and produce their main pharmacologic effects on the central nervous system and gastrointestinal tract. They are the most effective analgesics available, and they all possess a high addiction liability. Analgesic activity is probably due to interference with pain impulses at the subcortical level of the brain. Other CNS effects include powerful medullary depression of respiration, stimulation of the chemoreceptor trigger zone, constriction of the pupils, and depression of the cough reflex. Gastrointestinal effects include an increase in smooth muscle tone and a decrease in propulsive movements and emptying time.

Uses and Doses

P.O. or Parenteral	
Pediatric	
Analgesic	0.5–0.8 mg/kg every 3–4 h as needed.
Preoperative sedation	0.5–1 mg/lb 30–90 min before anesthesia.
Adult	
Analgesic	50–150 mg every 3–4 h as needed.
Preoperative sedation	50–100 mg 30–90 min before anesthesia.

Support of anesthesia	Repeated IV injections of fractional doses (10 mg) or continuous IV infusion (1 mg/mL). The exact dose should be determined by the needs of the patient.
Obstetrical	50–100 mg when pain becomes regular. May be repeated at 1- to 3-h intervals.

Administration

1. IM route is preferred when repeated doses are required.
2. For IV administration, the injection should be made slowly, using a diluted solution.

Contraindications

Hypersensitivity and with patients currently or recently on monoamine oxidase inhibitors.

Adverse Effects, etc.

See MORPHINE SULFATE.

METARAMINOL BITARTRATE

Category

Sympathomimetic: vasopressor

Brand Names

Aramine (Merck Sharpe & Dohme)

Pharmacologic Mechanism

Sympathomimetic effect due to direct and indirect adrenergic activity. Metaraminol produces direct stimulation of alpha-adrenergic and beta-adrenergic receptors and causes the release of norepinephrine, which results in vasoconstriction and cardiac stimulation.

Uses and Doses

1. Indicated in the prevention or treatment of acute hypotension due to spinal anesthesia
2. As an adjunct in hypotension due to drugs, hemorrhage, and surgical complications
3. In shock associated with brain damage

Parenteral (IM, IV, or SC)	
IM or SC	2–10 mg. Recommended pediatric dose is 100 μg/kg.
IV infusion	15–100 mg in 500 mL of solution and administered at rate to maintain satisfactory blood pressure. Severe shock may require a direct injection of 0.5–5 mg, followed by an infusion.

Administration

Metaraminol may be mixed with sodium chloride, 5% dextrose, Ringer's, lactated Ringer's, and 6% dextran in saline.

Contraindications

Hypersensitivity.

Adverse Effects

Sinus or ventricular tachycardia, tissue necrosis, and possible relapse in patients with a history of malaria.

Drug Interactions

Avoid concurrent use with cyclopropane or halothane, monoamine-oxidase inhibitors, and tricyclic antidepressants.

METHICILLIN SODIUM FOR INJECTION

Category

Antibiotic: penicillinase-resistant penicillin

Brand Names

Azapen (Pfizer)

Celbenin (Beecham)

Staphcillin (Bristol)

Pharmacologic Mechanism

Bactericidal activity due to inhibition of mucopeptide cell wall synthesis in susceptible microorganisms.

Uses and Doses

Indicated in the treatment of infections due to penicillinase-producing staphylococci.

Parenteral		
IM		
Pediatric	25 mg/kg every 6 h.	
Adult	1 g every 4–6 h.	
IV		
Adult	1 g every 6 h.	

Administration

1. Reconstitute powder according to the manufacturer's direction.

2. For direct IV use, dilute each milliliter of reconstituted solution with 25 mL of sodium chloride injection, and administer at a rate of 10 mL/min.

3. For IV drip, the reconstituted solution may be mixed with sodium chloride injection, 5% dextrose, 10% D-fructose, 10% D-fructose in normal saline, 10% invert sugar, and Travert 10% electrolyte #1, #2, or #3.

Contraindications, etc.

See PENICILLIN G POTASSIUM FOR INJECTION, STERILE.

METHOTREXATE

Category

Antineoplastic: antimetabolite, folic acid antagonist

Pharmacologic Mechanism

Antimetabolic activity due to competitive inhibition of dihydrofolate reductase. This results in reduced amounts of tetrahydrofolic acid, and therefore, DNA synthesis and cell reproduction is inhibited, especially in malignant tissue.

Uses and Doses

1. Indicated in the treatment of gestational choriocarcinoma, chorioadenoma destruens, and hydatidiform mole (trophoblastic tumors).

2. Treatment of lymphoblastic leukemias and meningeal leukemia.

3. In combination for the treatment of carcinoma of the breast, lung, testes, neck, and pelvis.

4. Treatment of Burkitt's lymphoma and advanced states (III and IV, Peters Staging system) of lymphosarcoma.

5. Treatment of advanced cases of mycosis fungoides.

6. Control of severe and disabling psoriasis not responsive to other therapy.

P.O.		
Pediatric		
Antineoplastic	120 mg/kg daily.	
Adult		
Antineoplastic	2.5–30 mg daily.	
Mycosis fungoides	2.5–10 mg daily.	
Psoriasis	Single weekly dose of 10–25 mg. Do not exceed a dose of 50 mg per week.	
	Divided dose schedule of 2.5 mg every 12 h for 3 doses or at 8-h intervals for 4 doses each week. Do not exceed a dose of 30 mg per week.	
	Daily dose schedule of 2.5 mg daily for 5 days followed by a rest period of at least 2 days. Do not exceed a dose 6.25 mg per day.	
Parenteral		
Pediatric		
Antineoplastic (IM or IV)	120 μg/kg daily.	
Meningeal leukemia (intrathecal)	200–500 mg/kg.	
Adult		
Antineoplastic (IM or IV)	2.5–30 mg daily.	
Mycosis fungoides (IM)	50 mg once weekly or 25 mg twice a week.	
Psoriasis (IM or IV)	Same as the oral schedule.	

Administration

1. For intrathecal administration the drug must be diluted to 1 mg/mL with sodium chloride injection without preservatives and filtered before using.

2. The 25 mg/mL solution should be used for dilution.

3. Leucovorin calcium may be administered following intrathecal administration to help reduce systemic toxicity.

Contraindications

1. In patients with severe preexisting liver, bone marrow, or kidney impairment.

2. During the first trimester of pregnancy.

Adverse Effects

Ulcerative stomatitis, leukopenia, nausea, alopecia, photosensitivity, erythematous rash, bone marrow depression, periportal fibrosis, hepatic cirrhosis, renal failure, azotemia, teratogenic effects, abortion, aphasia, convulsions, headache, and blurred vision.

Drug Interactions

1. Avoid vitamin preparations containing folic acid and prepartions containing salicylates.
2. Concurrent use with oral hypoglycemics, sulfonamides, and thiazides may increase the effect and toxicity of methotrexate.

MORPHINE SULFATE

Category

Narcotic: opium alkaloid

Pharmacologic Mechanism

The narcotic analgesics exhibit a wide range of activity and produce their main pharmacologic effects on the central nervous system and gastrointestinal tract. They are the most effective analgesics available, and they all possess a high addiction liability.

Analgesic activity is probably due to interference with pain impulses at the subcortical level of the brain. Other CNS effects include powerful medullary depression of respiration, stimulation of the chemoreceptor trigger zone, constriction of the pupils, and depression of the cough reflex. Gastrointestinal effects include an increase in smooth muscle tone and a decrease in propulsive movements and emptying time.

Uses and Doses

Relief of severe pain, preanesthetic sedation, and postoperative analgesia.

P.O.	
Adult	Not recommended. Adult guide dose 5–15 mg every 4 h.
Parenteral	
Pediatric, SC	0.1–0.2 mg/kg per dose. Do not exceed a single maximum dose of 15 mg.
Adult	
SC, IM	10 mg/70 kg of body weight per dose.
IV	2.5–15 mg per dose.

Administration

For IV administration, dilute desired dose in at least 4–5 mL of sterile water for injection and inject slowly over a 5-min period.

Contraindications

Hypersensitivity.

Adverse Effects

Nausea, vomiting, sedation, sweating, dry mouth, constipation, biliary tract spasm, euphoria, hypotension, urinary retention, pruritis, and urticaria.

Drug Interactions

1. Avoid concurrent use with tricyclic antidepressants.
2. Use with caution with antihistamines, barbiturates, benzodiazepines, methotrimeprazine, phenothiazines, and other CNS depressants.

NALOXONE HYDROCHLORIDE

Category

Narcotic antagonist

Brand Names

Narcan (Endo)

Pharmacologic Mechanism

Narcotic antagonism primarily due to competition with narcotics for receptor sites in the central nervous system. Naloxone is a pure narcotic antagonist because it possesses no agonist morphine-like properties.

Uses and Doses

Parenteral (IM, IV, and SC)	
Neonates	
Narcotic-induced depression	Initial dose of 0.01 mg/kg. May be repeated at 2- to 3-min intervals.
Children	
Narcotic over-dose	Initial dose of 0.01 mg/kg. May be repeated at 2- to 3-min intervals.
Adults	
Narcotic over-dose	Initial dose of 0.4 mg. May be repeated at 2- to 3-min intervals.
Postoperative narcotic depression	0.1–0.2 mg at 2- to 3-min intervals to the desired degree of reversal.

Contraindications

Hypersensitivity.

Adverse Effects

Nausea and vomiting in postoperative patients with high doses.

Drug Interactions

None currently reported.

NEOMYCIN SULFATE

Category

Antibiotic: aminoglycoside antibiotic

Brand Names

Mycifradin Sulfate (Upjohn)

Neobiotic (Pfipharmecs)

Pharmacologic Mechanism

Bactericidal activity due to inhibition of ribosomal protein synthesis in susceptible microorganisms.

Uses and Doses

The toxicity of aminoglycoside antibiotics restricts their use to serious gram-negative infections. Furthermore, neomycin has poor oral absorption characteristics and is extremely toxic. Accordingly, the drug is limited to local antibacterial activity in the gastrointestinal tract and topical applications. Systemic parenteral use is extremely hazardous.

P.O.	
Premature and full-term infants	10–50 mg/kg daily in divided doses for 2–3 days for enteropathogenic diarrhea.
Children	50–100 mg/kg daily in divided doses for 2–3 days for enteropathogenic diarrhea.
Adults	3 g daily in divided doses for 2–3 days for enteropathogenic diarrhea. 4–12 g daily in divided doses for hepatic coma. Chronic hepatic insufficiency may require up to 4 g daily for an indefinite period.

Parenteral (IM)	
Adults	15 mg/kg daily in four equally divided and spaced doses. Do not exceed 10 days of therapy.

Administration

1. Administer neomycin with a low-residue diet during preoperative preparation.

2. Administer with protein for treatment of hepatic coma.

Contraindications

Hypersensitivity, previous serious toxic effects with neomycin or other aminoglycosides, and intestinal obstructions.

NITROGLYCERIN IV

Category

Antianginal: coronary vasodilator

Preparations

Commercial preparations not currently available. The IV dosage form must be prepared in the pharmacy.

Pharmacologic Mechanism

Nitrates relax smooth muscle in small blood vessels and dilate arteries and capillaries, especially in coronary circulation, which reduces myocardial ischemia.

Uses and Doses

To relieve myocardial ischemia. Dosage must be individualized for each patient. Usually administered in 5% dextrose at an infusion rate of approximately 32 μg/min. A mean dose of 960 ng/kg per min has been suggested for hypertensive patients during coronary surgery.

Contraindications

Hypersensitivity, severe anemia, or increased intracranial pressure.

Adverse Effects

Hypotension.

Drug Interactions

Concurrent use with tricyclic antidepressants may result in additive hypotension.

PANCURONIUM BROMIDE

Category

Skeletal muscle relaxant: nondepolarizing neuromuscular blocking agent

Brand Names

Pavulon (Organon)

Pharmacologic Mechanism

Pancuronium bromide is a competitive blocking agent which causes skeletal muscle paralysis by combining with cholinergic receptors on the motor end plate. Following a single effective IV dose, the onset of activity is 30–45 s, with a peak effect between 3 and 4½ min. Competitive muscular relaxation produced by nondepolarizing agents can be antagonized by the acetylcholinesterase drugs.

Uses and Doses

Promotes skeletal muscle relaxation and facilitates the management of mechanical respiration.

Parenteral (IV)	
Neonates	Start with a test dose 0.02 mg/kg.
Pediatric–Adults	0.06–0.1 mg/kg for intubation. Subsequent doses start with 0.01 mg/kg for continued muscle relaxation repeated as required.

Dosage must be individualized to each patient.

Administration

Limited to trained individuals familiar with its use.

Contraindications

Hypersensitivity.

Adverse Effects

Respiratory depression, apnea, and a slight increase in pulse rate.

Drug Interactions

1. Lower doses are required for surgical procedures when used with enflurane, ether, halothane, and methoxyflurane.
2. Significant neuromuscular blockage can result from concurrent use with aminoglycoside antibiotics, amphotericin B, colistin, and polymixin B.

PENICILLIN G POTASSIUM FOR INJECTION, STERILE

Category

Antibiotic: penicillin antibiotic

Pharmacologic Mechanism

Bactericidal activity due to inhibition of mucopeptide cell wall synthesis in susceptible microorganisms.

Uses and Doses

Penicillin G is the drug of choice for most strains of

Actinomyces israelii

Alpha hemolytic streptococci

Clostridium perfringens

Clostridium tetani (in conjunction with antitoxin therapy)

Corynebacterium diphtheriae (in conjunction with antitoxin therapy)

Fusobacterium (Vincent's angina)

Group A beta-hemolytic streptococci

Neisseria gonorrhoeae (most strains)

Neisseria meningitidis

Bacillius anthracis

Bacteroides (except *B. fragilis*)

Pasturella multocida

Spirillum minus

Staphylococci (non-penicillinase-producing)

Streptobacillus moniliformis

Streptococci (groups C, G, H, L, and M)

Streptococcus pneumoniae

Treponema pertenus

Treponema pallidum

Parenteral (IM or IV)	
Premature and full-term infants	30,000 U/kg twice a day.
Children	300,000 to 1.2 million U daily. Some infections may require up to 10 million U daily.
Adults	300,000 to 8 million U daily. Some infections may require up to 60 million U daily.

May be administered IM or by continuous IV drip. Daily doses exceeding 10 million U should be administered by IV infusion only.

Administration

1. Depending on the route of administration, reconstitute powder with sterile water for injection, 5% dextrose, or sodium chloride injection.

2. For doses greater than 10 million U daily, dilute reconstituted solution in 1–2 L of infusion solution and administer in a 24-h period.

3. For intermittent IV infusion, one-quarter of the dose should be given over a 1- to 2-h period and repeated every 6 h.

Contraindications

Hypersensitivity.

Adverse Effects

Urticaria, fever, edema, arthralgia, laryngeal edema, anaphylaxis, maculopapular rash, exfoliative dermatitis, hemolytic anemia, leukopenia, and thrombocytopenia.

Drug Interactions

1. Concurrent use of bacteriostatic antibiotic with penicillin can lead to antagonism.

2. Probenecid will increase and prolong the serum levels of penicillin by decreasing urinary excretion.

PENICILLIN G PROCAINE SUSPENSION, STERILE

Category

Antibiotic: penicillin antibiotic

Brand Names

Crysticillin (Squibb)

Duracillin AS (Lilly)

Pfizerpen-AS (Pfizer)

Wycillin (Wyeth)

Pharmacologic Mechanism

Bactericidal activity due to inhibition of mucopeptide cell wall synthesis in susceptible microorganisms.

Uses and Doses

Indicated in the treatment of infections caused by penicillin G–sensitive microorganisms.

Parenteral (IM)	
Newborn	Not recommended.
Pediatric	500,000 to 1 million U/m² once daily.
Adult	Up to 5 million U daily.

Administration

1. Use at least a 22-gauge needle for 300,000-U doses and a 20-gauge needle for doses greater than 300,000 U.

2. Administer into a large muscle mass.

Contraindications, etc.

See PENICILLIN G POTASSIUM FOR INJECTION, STERILE.

PHENTOLAMINE

Category

Antihypertensive: alpha-adrenergic blocking agent

Brand Names

Regitine (Ciba)

Phentolamine hydrochloride—for oral administration (tabs)

Phentolamine mesylate—for parenteral administration

Pharmacologic Mechanism

Antihypertensive effect due to competitive blocking of α receptors which results in reduced peripheral vascular resistance.

Uses and Doses

Diagnosis of pheochromocytoma, hypertensive crisis from clonidine withdrawal or monoamine oxidase inhibitor–sympathomimetic interaction, treatment of dermal necrosis following norepinephrine administration, and control of hypertensive crisis during surgery for pheochromocytoma.

P. O.	
Pediatric	25 mg 4–6 times daily.
Adult	50 mg 4–6 times daily.
Parenteral (IM or IV)	
Pediatric	
Preoperative	1 mg 1–2 h before surgery; repeat if necessary.
Surgery	1 mg as required.
Adult	
Preoperative	5 mg 1–2 h before surgery; repeat is necessary.
Surgery	5 mg as indicated.
Dermal necrosis	
Prevention	10 mg to each liter of norepinephrine.
Treatment	5–10 mg diluted in 10 mL sodium chloride injected into the area of extravasation within 12 h.
Pheochromocytoma diagnosis	5 mg for adults and 1 mg for children. Inject and record blood pressure at 30-s intervals for 3 min and at 60-s intervals for the next 7 min.
Drug-induced hypertensive crisis	5–30 mg.

Contraindications

Hypersensitivity, myocardial infarction, or coronary artery disease.

Adverse Effects

Hypotension, tachycardia and cardiac arrhythmias, nasal stuffiness, nausea, and vomiting.

Drug Interactions

Possible added antidiabetic effect in diabetic pediatric patients.

POLYMYXIN B SULFATE, STERILE

Category

Antibiotic: polypeptide antibiotic

Brand Names

Aerosporin (Burroughs Wellcome)

Pharmacologic Mechanism

Bactericidal activity due to disorientation of the lipoprotein cell membrane in susceptible microorganisms.

Uses and Doses

1. Indicated in the treatment of infections caused by susceptible strains of *Pseudomonas aeruginosa*, especially in the urinary tract, meninges, and bloodstream.

2. Indicated in the treatment of infections caused by susceptible strains of
   Aerobacter aerogenes bacteremia
   Escherichia coli urinary tract infections
   Hemophilus influenzae meningeal infections
   Klebsiella pneumoniae bacteremia

Parenteral (IV)	
Neonatal	40,000 U/kg daily.
Pediatric and adult	
Normal kidney function	15,000–25,000 U/kg daily. Do not exceed 25,000 U/kg daily.
Kidney impairment	15,000 U/kg daily or less.
Intrathecal	
Pediatric, under 2	20,000 U once daily for 3–4 days. Continue with a dose of 25,000 U every other day for at least 2 weeks after cultures of cerebrospinal fluid are negative and sugar content is normal again.
Pediatric and adult	50,000 U once daily for 3–4 days. Continue with a dose of 50,000 U every other day for at least 2 weeks after cultures of cerebrospinal fluid are negative and sugar content is normal again.

Administration

1. Reconstitute powder for injection (one vial) in 300–500 mg of 5% dextrose for continuous IV drip.

2. For intrathecal administration, dissolve one vial in 10 mg of sterile normal saline.

Contraindications

Hypersensitivity.

Adverse Effects

Respiratory arrest, albuminuria, azotemia, drowsiness, ataxia, peripheral paresthesias, fever, and rash and thrombophlebitis at IV injection site.

Drug Interactions

1. Avoid concurrent use with potentially neurotoxic and nephrotoxic drugs. Colistin, colistimethate, gentamicin, kanamycin, streptomycin, and viomycin are best avoided during polymixin B therapy.

2. Respiratory depression and paralysis can result from surgical neuromuscular blocking agents and polymixin B.

PROCAINAMIDE HYDROCHLORIDE

Category

Antiarrhythmic

Brand Names

Pronestyl (Squibb)

Pharmacologic Mechanism

Antiarrhythmic activity due to depression of cardiac automaticity, excitability, and conductivity which results in a widening of the QRS complex. The P-R and Q-T intervals may be prolonged.

Procainamide exhibits anticholinergic activity and produces cardiac effects that are similar to quinidine.

Uses and Doses

Indicated in the treatment of arrhythmias associated with surgery, atrial fibrillation, paroxysmal atrial tachycardia, and premature ventricular contractions and tachycardia.

P.O.	
Pediatric	Suggested dose is 50 mg/kg daily in 4–6 doses for cardiac arrhythmias.
Adult	
Atrial arrhythmias	A loading dose of 1.25 g, followed by 0.75 g in 1 h. Additional doses of 0.5–1 g may be given every 2 h until tolerance limit is reached. Usual maintenance dose is 0.5–1 g every 4–6 h.
Ventricular arrythmias	A loading dose of 1 g, followed by 50 mg/kg daily in divided doses.
Parenteral	
Pediatric	Suggested dose is 3–6 mg/kg over 5 min followed by an infusion of 28–80 μg/kg per min.
Adult	
IM	0.1–0.5 mg.
IV	25–50 mg/min to a maximum of 1 g.
IV infusion	500–600 mg over 30 min. Usual maintenance rates 2–6 mg/min.

Administration

1. Injection may be mixed with 5% dextrose.

2. In switching stabilized patients to the oral dose route, allow 3–4 h to elapse before administering the first oral dose.

Contraindications

Hypersensitivity, complete AV block, myasthenia gravis, and second- and third-degree AV block without an electrical pacemaker.

Adverse Effects

Hypotension, lupus erythematosus–like syndrome, agranulocytosis, angioneurotic edema, maculopapular rash, and a bitter taste.

Drug Interactions

Possible additive effects with concurrent anticholinergic and antihypertensive agents.

PROMETHAZINE HYDROCHLORIDE

Category

Antiemetic: antihistamine

Brand Names

Ganphen (Tutag)

Phenergan (Wyeth)

Provigan (Reid-Provident)

ZiPan (Savage)

Pharmacologic Mechanism

Antihistamines antagonize histamine by occupying histamine H_1 receptors on peripheral effector cells. Promethazine also exhibits anticholinergic, antiemetic, antipruritic, and sedative properties.

Uses and Doses

Parenteral (IM or IV)	
Pediatric	
Allergy	6.25–12.5 mg 3 times a day or 25 mg once a day at bedtime.
Nausea, vomiting	250–500 μg/kg 4–6 times daily.
Sedation	12.5–25 mg at bedtime.
Preoperative	0.5 mg/kg with an equal dose of meperidine and appropriate dose of an atropine-like drug.
Postoperative	12.5–25 mg with a suitable analgesic.
Adult	
Allergy	25 mg; repeat in 2 h if required.
Nausea, vomiting	12.5–50 mg 4–6 times daily.
Sedation	25–50 mg at bedtime.
Obstetrics	
Early labor	50 mg.
Labor	25–75 mg with 25–75 mg of meperidine. Dose may be repeated if needed.
Preoperative	50 mg with an equal dose of meperidine and appropriate dose of an atropine-like drug.
Postoperative	25–50 mg with a suitable analgesic.

Administration

1. Preferred parenteral route is IM.

2. For IV administration do not exceed a concentration of 25 mg/mL and a rate of 25 mg/min.

Contraindications

Hypersensitivity to promethazine or phenothiazines.

Adverse Effects

Drowsiness, dizziness, dry mouth, blurred vision, hypotension, and rare instances of photosensitivity.

Drug Interactions

1. Additive depressant effects with barbiturates and narcotics.

2. Additive anticholinergic effects with tricyclic antidepressants.

PROPRANOLOL HYDROCHLORIDE

Category

Antiarrhythmic: beta-adrenergic blocker, antihypertensive

Brand Names

Inderal (Ayerst)

Pharmacologic Mechanism

Propranolol hydrochloride reduces heart rate, myocardial contractility, and hypertension.

Uses and Doses

P.O.	
Adults	
Hypertension	160–480 mg daily. Doses of 650 mg may be required.
Angina	Up to 160 mg daily. Do not exceed 320 mg daily.
Arrhythmias	10–30 mg 3–4 times daily.
Hypertrophic subaortic stenosis	30–40 mg 3–4 times daily.
Pheochromocytoma	60 mg daily in divided doses for 3 days prior to surgery with concurrent alpha-adrenergic blocking agents.
Parenteral (IV)	
Adults	
Arrhythmias	1–3 mg in life-threatening situations.

Administration

1. Administer tablets before meals.

2. Do not exceed a rate of 1 mg/min during IV administration.

Contraindications

Bronchial asthma; allergic rhinitis; sinus bradycardia and greater than first-degree block; cardiogenic shock; right ventricular failure secondary to pulmonary hypertension; congestive heart failure, unless the failure is secondary to a tachyarrhythmia treatable with propranolol; augmenting psychotropic drugs, including monoamine oxidase inhibitors and during the 2-week withdrawal period.

Adverse Effects

Bradycardia, congestive heart failure, intensification of AV block, atrial insufficiency, nausea, vomiting, and abdominal cramps.

Drug Interactions

Avoid concurrent use with furazolidone, general anesthetics, monoamine oxidase inhibiters, isoproterenol, and levarterenol.

PYRIMETHAMINE

Category

Antimalarial: antitoxoplasmic agent

Brand Names

Daraprim (Burroughs Wellcome)

Pharmacologic Mechanism

Antimalarial activity due to folic acid antagonism.

Uses and Doses

1. Chemoprophylaxis of susceptible strains of malaria (plasmodia).

2. In combination with quinine and sulfonamide (sulfadiazine or sulfisoxazole) for treating chloroquine-resistant strains of malaria (*Plasmodium falciparum*).

3. In combination with a sulfonamide (sulfadiazine or triple sulfa) for treating toxoplasmosis (*Toxoplasma gondii*).

P.O.

Malarial chemoprophylaxis*	
Children under 4 years	6.25 mg once weekly.
Children 4–10 years	12.5 mg once weekly.
Children and adults	25 mg once weekly.
Chloroquine-resistant *P. falciparum*†	
Quinine	600 mg 3 times a day for 14 days.
Pyrimethamine	25 mg twice a day for 3 days.
Sulfonamide	Loading dose of 2 g followed by 500 mg every 6 h for 6 days.
Toxoplasmosis‡	
Pyrimethamine	50–75 mg daily for 1–3 weeks. Reduce by one-half and continue for 4–5 weeks.
Sulfonamide	1–4 g daily for 1–3 weeks. Reduce by one-half and continue for 4–5 weeks.

* Dosage should be initiated 2 weeks before entering and continue for 10 weeks after leaving the endemic malarial area.

† Approximately one-half the adult dose should be used for children under 15 years of age.

‡ Pediatric dose is 1 mg/kg daily divided into 2 equal doses. Reduce by half after 2–4 days and continue treatment for 4–5 weeks.

Administration

Administration with meals will help reduce gastric upset.

Contraindications

Hypersensitivity, severe megaloblastic anemia.

Adverse Effects

Anorexia, vomiting, megaloblastic anemia, leukopenia, thrombocytopenia, pancytopenia, and atrophic glossitis.

Drug Interactions

Folic acid and *p*-aminobenzoic acid can inhibit the activity of pyrimethamine.

Rh_0 (D) IMMUNE HUMAN GLOBULIN

Category

Immunosuppressant biological

Brand Names

D-Imune (Lederle)

Gamulin Rh (Parke-Davis)

$HypRh_0$-D (Cutter Biological)

RhoGAM (Ortho Diagnostics)

Pharmacologic Mechanism

Suppresses the immune response of nonsensitized Rh_0 (D)^u-negative, D^u-negative individuals who receive Rh_0 (D)-positive or D^u-positive blood as a result of fetomaternal hemorrhage or a transfusion accident.

Uses and Doses

Used to suppress antibody formation in

1. Rho (D)-negative, D^u-negative mothers after delivering an Rh_0 (D)-positive or D^u-positive infant.
2. Abortion of an Rh-positive fetus.
3. Transfusion accident where Rh_0 (D)-positive blood is used in a Rh_0 (D)-negative recipient.

Parenteral

IM injection of the total contents of a single-dose vial in nonsensitized individuals within 72 h or less after Rh-incompatible delivery, terminated incomplete pregnancies, or blood transfusions.

Administration

Fill out the special patient form that is provided in the dosage package and attach to patients hospital records after administering IM injection.

Contraindications

In Rh_0 (D)-positive or D^u-positive individuals, in Rh_0 (D)-negative and D^u-negative individuals that have been previously sensitized to Rh_0 (D) or D^u antigen (if in doubt, the preparation may be given).

Adverse Effects

Limited allergic reactions.

RIFAMPIN

Category

Antitubercular: rifamycin antibiotic

Brand Names

Rifadin (Dow)

Rimactane (Ciba)

Pharmacologic Mechanism

Bacteriostatic activity due to inhibition of DNA-dependent RNA polymerase activity in susceptible microorganisms.

Uses and Doses

P.O.	
Pediatric	
Pulmonary tuberculosis	10–20 mg/kg. Do not exceed 600 mg daily.
Meningococcal carriers	
3 months–1 year	5 mg/kg twice a day for 2 days
1–12 years	10 mg/kg twice a day for 2 days.
Adult	
Pulmonary tuberculosis	600 mg daily.
Meningococcal carriers	600 mg twice a day for 2 days.

Administration

Rifampin is usually administered as a single daily dose on an empty stomach with a full glass of water.

Contraindications

Hypersensitivity.

Adverse Effects

Anorexia, nausea, cramps, diarrhea, rash, pemphigus, sore mouth and tongue, exudative conjunctivitis, thrombocytopenia, hemolytic anemia, drowsiness, visual disturbances, and menstrual disturbances.

Drug Interactions

1. Concurrent use may require dosage adjustment for corticosteroids, dapsone, digitalis glycosides, methadone maintenance, oral anticoagulants, and oral hypoglycemics.

2. Oral contraceptives may lose significant activity during rifamycin therapy.

STREPTOMYCIN SULFATE

Category

Antibiotic: aminoglycoside antibiotic

Pharmacologic Mechanism

Bactericidal activity due to inhibition of ribosomal protein synthesis in susceptible microorganisms.

Uses and Doses

The toxicity of streptomycin limits its use to serious gram-negative infections and tuberculosis.

1. Indicated in the treatment of infections caused by susceptible strains of
Calymmatobacterium granulomatis (granuloma inguinale)
Francisella tularensis (tularemia)
Yersinia pestis (plague)

2. In combined therapy for tuberculosis.

3. In combined therapy (with penicillin) for enterococcal endocarditis and alpha-hemolytic and non-hemolytic streptococcal endocarditis.

Parenteral	
Pediatric	
Premature, newborn infants	20–30 mg/kg daily in 2 divided doses.
Children	40 mg/kg daily in 2 divided doses.
Adult	
Tularemia	1–2 g daily in divided doses for 7–10 days until the patient is afebrile for 5–7 days.
Plague	2–4 g daily in divided doses until the patient is afebrile for 3 days.
Tuberculosis	1 g daily with 200–300 mg isoniazid and 5 g *p*-aminosalicylic acid 3 times daily. Dosage of streptomycin should be discontinued or reduced to 1 g 2–3 times weekly.
Enterococcal endocarditis	0.5–1 g twice a day for 4 weeks in combination with penicillin.
Alpha-hemolytic and nonhemolytic steptococcal endocarditis	1 g two times a day for 1 week and 0.5 g twice a day for the second week in combination with penicillin.

Dosage for patients with impaired renal function must be adjusted. Do not exceed a serum concentration of 20–25 mg/kg.

Administration

1. Sterile powder should be dissolved in sterile water for injection or sodium chloride injection according to the manufacturer's directions. Avoid solutions stronger than 500 mg/mL.

2. Streptomycin is usually administered by deep intramuscular injection.

Contraindications, etc.

See GENTAMICIN SULFATE.

TETRACYCLINE HYDROCHLORIDE

Category

Broad spectrum antibiotic: tetracycline antibiotic

Brand Names

Achromycin V (Lederle)

Panmycin (Upjohn)

Tetracyn (Pfipharmecs)

Pharmacologic Mechanism

Bacteriostatic effect due to inhibition of protein synthesis in susceptible microorganisms.

Uses and Doses

1. Indicated in the treatment of
Granuloma inguinale
Lymphogranuloma, psittacosis, and ornithosis
Mycoplasma (PPLO, Eaton agent)
Rickettsial diseases
Spirochetal relapsing fever

2. Alternative in penicillin-sensitive patients (especially for gonorrhea and syphilis) or for infections where bacteriologic testing indicates good pathogen susceptibility.

P.O.	
Pediatric	10–20 mg/lb of body weight divided into 4 doses.
Adults	1–4 g daily.
Parenteral	
Pediatrics	
IM	15–25 mg/lb body weight daily.
IV	12 mg/kg body weight.
Adult	
IM	250–500 mg daily.
IV	250–500 mg daily.

Administration

1. Oral dosage forms must be given before meals or 2 h after meals.

2. Oral dosage forms should not be given with milk or dairy products, antacid suspension, or antidiarrheal suspensions.

3. IV can be mixed with Ringer's injection, lactated Ringer's normal saline injection, dextrose, dextrose and sodium chloride, or 10% invert sugar injections or infusions.

4. Avoid rapid IV administration.

Contraindications

Hypersensitivity.

Adverse Effects

Anorexia, nausea, vomiting, diarrhea, dysphagia, enterocolitis, monilial overgrowth, photosensitivity, increased BUN, maculopapular rash, exacerbation of systemic lupus erythematosus, hemolytic anemia, and thrombocytopenia.

Drug Interactions

1. Tetracycline will antagonize the bactericidal effects of the penicillins and cephalosporins.

2. A reduction in the maintenance dose of the oral anticoagulants may be indicated during long-term tetracycline therapy.

3. Methoxyflurane and tetracycline will produce significant nephrotoxicity.

THIOPENTAL SODIUM FOR INJECTION

Category

Ultrashort barbiturate

Brand Names

Pentothal (Abbott)

Pharmacologic Mechanism

Barbiturates are central nervous system depressants that act primarily on the brainstem reticular formation to produce dose-related sedative and hypnotic effects. Ultrashort-acting barbiturates are used to produce surgical anesthesia.

Uses and Doses

Anesthetic agents for short surgical procedures, anesthesia induction, supplement for regional anesthesia, hypnosis during balanced anesthesia, convulsion control, narcoanalysis and narcosynthesis, and for neurosurgical patients with increased intracranial pressure.

Parenteral (IV)	
Anesthesia	50–75 mg at 20- to 40-s intervals. After anesthesia is obtained, additional doses of 25–50 mg can be given whenever the patient moves.
Convulsions	75–125 mg. Convulsions induced by local anesthetics may require doses of 125–250 mg.
Neurosurgical	1.5–3.5 mg/kg.

Administration

Reconstitute powder with 5% dextrose, sodium chloride injection, or sterile water for injection. Discard unused solution after 24 h.

Contraindications

Hypersensitivity, status asthmaticus, and porphyria.

Adverse Effects

Respiratory depression, cardiac arrhythmias, bronchospasm, and laryngospasm.

Drug Interactions

Concurrent use with phenothiazines may enhance the effect of thiopental.

TOBRAMYCIN SULFATE

Category

Antibiotic: aminoglycoside antibiotic

Brand Names

Nebcin (Lilly)

Pharmacologic Mechanism

Bactericidal activity due to inhibition of ribosomal protein synthesis in susceptible microorganisms.

Uses and Doses

The toxicity of aminoglycoside antibiotics restricts their use to serious gram-negative infections. Tobramycin has a spectrum of activity similar to gentamicin.

1. Indicated in the treatment of infection caused by susceptible strains of
   Citrobacter spp.
   Escherichia coli
   Klebsiella-Enterobacter group
   Proteus spp. (both indol-positive and indole-negative)
   Providencia spp.
   Pseudomonas aeruginosa
   Serratia spp.

2. Alternate for penicillin-resistant staphylococcus infections.

3. As initial therapy in suspected or confirmed gram-negative infections prior to obtaining sensitivity test results.

4. In treating serious unknown infections in conjunction with a penicillin or cephalosporin prior to identifying the causative agent or receiving sensitivity test results.

Parenteral (IM or IV)	
Neonates (1 week of age or less)	4 mg/kg daily in 2 equal doses every 12 h.
Older infants, children, and adults	3 mg/kg daily in 3 equal doses every 8 h. More serious infections may require 5 mg/kg daily in 3 or 4 equal doses. Reduce to 3 mg/kg daily as soon as clinically indicated.

Treatment usually requires 7–10 days. Dosage for patients with impaired renal function must be adjusted. Dosage adjustment should be based on tobramycin serum levels and serum creatinine clearance levels.

Administration

1. For IV administration, a single dose of tobramycin may be diluted in 50–100 mL of normal saline or 5% dextrose solution and infused over a period of 20–60 min. Use less diluent for pediatric administration.

2. In combined therapy do not premix with penicillin or other drugs.

Contraindications, etc.

See GENTAMICIN SULFATE.

TRIMETHOPRIM - SULFAMETHOXAZOLE

Category

Antibacterial combination preparation

Brand Names

Bactrim (Roche)

Septra (Burroughs Wellcome)

Pharmacological Mechanism

Bacteriostatic activity due to the inhibition of folic acid synthesis. Sulfamethoxazole is a competitive antagonist of *p*-aminobenzoic acid, while trimethoprim inhibits the enzyme dihydrofolate reductase. Consequently, two successive steps in the biosynthesis of folic acid are blocked, resulting in enhanced antimicrobial activity in susceptible organisms.

Administration

Administer with large volumes of water to keep the patient well-hydrated.

Uses and Doses

1. Indicated in the treatment of urinary tract infections caused by susceptible strains of
   Enterobacter spp.
   Escherichia coli
   Klebsiella spp.
   Proteus mirabilis
   Proteus morganii
   Proteus vulgaris

2. Alternative for treating otitis media caused by susceptible strains of *Hemophilus influenzae* or *Streptococcus pneumoniae*.

3. Treatment of shigellosis caused by susceptible strains of *Shigella flexneri* and *Shigella sonnei*.

4. Treatment of *Pneumocystis carinii* pneumonitis.

P.O.

Pediatric

Otitis media and urinary tract infections	8 mg/kg trimethoprim and 40 mg/kg sulfamethoxazole divided into 2 doses for 10 days.
22 lb	5 mL or ½ tablet every 12 h.
44 lb	10 mL or 1 tablet every 12 h.
66 lb	15 mL or 1½ tablets every 12 h.
88 lb	20 mL or 2 tablets every 12 h.
Shigellosis	Same dosage schedule for 5 days.
Pneumonitis	20 mg/kg trimethoprim and 100 mg/kg sulfamethoxazole in 24 h given in 4 equally divided doses every 6 h for 14 days.
18 lb	5 mL or ½ tablet every 6 h.
35 lb	10 mL or 1 tablet every 6 h.
53 lb	15 mL or 1½ tablets every 6 h.
70 lb	20 mL or 2 tablets every 6 h.

Adults

Urinary tract infections	2 tablets or 20 mL every 12 h for 10–14 days.
Shigellosis	Same dosage schedule for 5 days.
Pneumonitis	20 mg/kg trimethoprim and 100 mg/kg sulfamethoxazole in 24 h given in 4 equally divided doses every 6 h for 14 days.

Dosage must be reduced for patients with renal impairment. Use one-half the dosage schedule for patients with a creatinine clearance of 15–30 mg/kg of body weight. Do not use if below 15.

Contraindications

Hypersensitivity or severe kidney impairment.

Adverse Effects

Agranulocytosis, aplastic anemia, megaloblastic anemia, hypoprothrombinemia, erythema multiforme, Stevens-Johnson syndrome, epidermal necrolysis, exfoliative dermatitis, photosensitization, hepatitis, pancreatitis, peripheral neuritis, tinnitus, toxic nephrosis, and lupus erythematosus phenomenon.

Drug Interactions

1. Avoid concurrent use with urinary acidifiers and multiple vitamins and other preparations that contain *p*-aminobenzoic acid.

2. Dosage adjustments may be required in patients taking oral anticoagulants, oral hypoglycemic agents, and methotrexate.

VASOPRESSIN TANNATE

Category

Posterior pituitary hormone: antidiuretic

Brand Names

Pitressin Tannate (Parke-Davis)

Pharmacologic Mechanism

Antidiuretic activity due to an increase in water reabsorption in the nephrons of the kidneys.

Uses and Doses

Indicated for the treatment of polydipsia, polyuria, and dehydration due to neurohypophyseal diabetes insipidus.

Parenteral (IM)

Dosage must be individualized according to patient response. 0.3–1 mL, repeated if required.

Administration

Shake vial to produce a homogenous suspension before using.

Contraindications

Hypersensitivity

Adverse Effects

Tremor, sweating, vertigo, circumoral pallor, headache, abdominal gas and cramps, nausea, vomiting, bronchial constriction, and cardiac arrest.

Drug Interactions

1. Use with caution in patients receiving lithium carbonate, epinephrine, or heparin.

2. Concurrent use with chlorpropamide may enhance the antidiuretic effect.

WARFARIN SODIUM

Category

Anticoagulant

Brand Names

Coumadin (Endo)

Panwarfin (Abbott)

Pharmacologic Mechanism

Coumarin anticoagulants inhibit prothrombin synthesis (factor II) and interfere with the production of proconvertin (factor VII) and the Christmas factor (factor IX) in the liver by interfering with the action of vitamin K.

Uses and Doses

1. Adjunct in coronary occlusion.
2. Atrial fibrillation with embolization.
3. Prophylaxis and treatment of pulmonary thrombosis and venous thrombosis.

P.O.

Adult	Start with a dose of 40–60 mg on the first day. Prothrombin time should determine the maintenance dose which is usually 2–10 mg daily.
Geriatric	Start with a dose of 20–30 mg on the first day. Maintenance is 2–10 mg as indicated by prothrombin time evaluations.

Parenteral

Adult	Start with an IM or IV dose of 40–60 mg on the first day. Maintenance dose is usually 2–10 mg daily.

Administration

1. Maintenance dose is usually administered as a single daily dose.
2. Therapy should be discontinued slowly.

Contraindications, etc.

See DICUMAROL.

INDEX

Page numbers in *italic* indicate illustrations or tables.

Abdomen:
  auscultation of, 301–302
    in diagnosis of intestinal obstruction, 709
  distention of, in sepsis, 836
  examination of, 300
    in assessment of shock patient, 311
    in trauma victim, 801–802
  palpation of, 302–305
  percussion of, 302
  physical assessment of, 300–305
  problems of, application of physical assessment techniques to, 318, 319
  traumatic injuries to, management of, 810–812
Abdominal pain in diabetic ketoacidosis, 645
Abducens nerve:
  anatomy of, 111, 112
  assessment of, 293
  type and functions of, 113
Abortion:
  habitual, management of, 856
  incomplete, management of, 855–856
  inevitable, management of, 855
  missed, management of, 856
  spontaneous, 855
Abruptio placentae, management of, 858
Abscess, lung, 504–507
  [See also Lung(s), abscess of]
Absorption:
  in capillary dynamics, 49
  in small intestine, 199–202
    of carbohydrates, 199–200
    of electrolytes, 202
    of fats, 200–202, 203
    of proteins, 200
    of vitamins, 202
    of water, 202
Abuse, child, 887–889
  burns in, 889–890
Ac globulin, 93, 95
Accident:
  cerebrovascular, patient with, spiritual concerns of, 1061
  trauma management at scene of, 796–797

  violent, victims of, spiritual concerns of, 1062–1063
Acclimatization, 377
Acetaminophen, 1137
Acetic acid in burn wound dressings, 779
Acetone in urine, hourly testing of, in fluid therapy for burns, 757
Acetylcholine:
  deficiency of, in myoneural junction lesions, 625
  effect of, on electrical conduction in SA node, 38
  in nerve impulse conduction for muscular contraction, 228
  as neurotransmitter, 115
  in regulation of peripheral regulation, 69
Acid(s):
  fatty, in total parenteral nutrition solution, metabolic significance of, 986–987
  hydrochloric (see Hydrochloric acid)
  organic, in extracellular fluid, 422–423
  in regulation of pancreatic secretion, 193
  weak, tubular secretion of, in urine formation, 165
Acid-base balance, 423–430
  carbon dioxide in, 26
  functions of, 423
  for high-risk neonate, 871
  in homeostasis, 171–174
  regulation of, 423–425
Acid-base therapy in treatment of sepsis, 844
Acid secretions of stomach, 186–187
Acidophils in anterior pituitary, 130
Acidosis:
  cerebral spinal fluid, paradoxical, complicating diabetic ketoacidosis, 647
  metabolic, 425, 427
    in renal disease, 664
    in septic shock, 837–838
    signs and symptoms of, 421
    in unstable cardiac patient, 560
  respiratory, 428–429
    in septic shock, 837–838
    signs and symptoms of, 421

  in unstable cardiac patient, 560
  uremic, altering host resistance to sepsis, 825
Acinar glands in pancreas, 191–192
Acinetobacter in sepsis, 828
Acoustic nerve:
  anatomy of, 111, 112
  assessment of, 269, 294
  type and functions of, 113
Acromegaly from excessive growth hormone, 132
Actin in sarcoplasm of skeletal muscle cell, 227–228
Actinomycin D, 1137–1138
Action potential:
  atrial, 38, 39
  in AV node, 39
  of cardiac cell membrane: generation of, 34–35
    propagation of, 36–38
    refractory period of, 37–38
  in SA node, 38, 39
Active transport:
  of hydrochloric acid, 187
  in renal system, 156–157
Actomyosin in sarcoplasm of skeletal muscle cell, 227
Adaptation in tactile receptors, 215
Addison's disease, 141
  adrenal crisis in, 653
Adenohypophysis, 130–133
  location of, 126
  (See also Pituitary gland, anterior)
Adenosine 3′,5′-monophosphate, cyclic (cAMP), activation of hormones by, 127
Adenosine triphosphate (ATP):
  in active transport in kidneys, 156
  conversion of, to cAMP, 127
  as energy source for muscular contraction, 229–230
Adenyl cyclase in conversion of ATP to cAMP, 127
Adhesion of platelets, 89
Adolescent:
  development of, illness and, 903–904
  with osteogenic sarcoma, 903–908
    medical/surgical management of, 905–907
    nursing management of, 907–908
    pathophysiology in, 904–905

Adrenal androgens, 141
Adrenal cortex, 139–141
  adrenal androgens of, 141
  glucocorticoids of, 139–140
  mineralocorticoids of, 140–141
Adrenal crisis, 652–654
Adrenal glands, 139–142
  location of, *126*
  surgery of, 690–691
Adrenal medulla, 141–142
  innervation of, 115
Adrenalectomy, 691
β-Adrenergic blocking agents for prevention of angina, 569–570
Adrenocortical insufficiency, 141
Adrenocorticotropic hormone (ACTH), 131
Adrenocorticotropin (ACTH), secretion of, increased, in sepsis, 832
Adriamycin:
  as anticancer drug, *906*
  for osteogenic sarcoma in adolescent, 905
Adult respiratory distress syndrome, 485–497
  (*See also* Respiratory distress syndrome, adult)
Adventitia of gastrointestinal tract, 182
Adventitious sounds, auscultation of, 282–283
Aerohypoxia in hypoxemia, 376–377
Afferent fibers of central nervous system, 102
Afterload, 75
  in left ventricular function: clinical assessment of, 567
    intra-aortic counterpulsation and, 568–569
    low cardiac output and, 567–568
    reduction of myocardial ischemia and, 569–570
  in myocardial function, 926–927
  reduction: devices for: counterpulsation, 928, 930–931, 933–944
    (*See also* Counterpulsation devices for afterload reduction)
    historical evolution of, 930–931
    with diastolic pressure augmentation by circulatory assistance devices, 928
Age:
  altering host resistance to sepsis, 825
  burn severity related to, 746, *747*
  time required for bone fracture healing and, 233
Aggregation of platelets, 89
Aging, hypoimmune state in, 465
Air embolism, 523–524

complicating hemodialysis, 673
complicating pulmonary artery pressure monitoring, prevention of, 1014
in total parenteral nutrition, 983–984
Airflow resistance in ventilation, 17–18
Airway:
  as adjunct to ventilation, 916, *917*
  artificial, in management of patient on continuous assisted ventilation, 960
  establishment of, in status epilepticus, 621
  humidification of, in management of patient on continuous assisted ventilation, 960
  in initial resuscitation of trauma victim, 798–799
  maintenance of, in first aid for burns, 748
  obstruction of: in asthma, 510
    atelectasis due to, 533
  protection of: evaluation of, 626–627
    loss of, in extracerebral motor loss, 625–627
  suctioning of, in management of patient on continuous assisted ventilation, 960–961
Airway pressure, effect of, on arterial pressure, 1012
Albumin:
  fall in, in sepsis, 837
  serum, 81–82
Aldosterone, 140–141
  in chloride regulation, 417
  effect of, on sodium reabsorption, 161–162
  in potassium regulation, 406
  in regulation of peripheral regulation, 69
  release of, in gastrointestinal hemorrhage, 699
  secretion of, increased, in sepsis, 833
  in sodium regulation, 403
Alert, definition of, *292*
Alimentary tract (*see* Gastrointestinal tract)
Alimentation, peripheral, 737–738
Alkaline phosphatase in bone formation, 224
Alkalosis:
  metabolic, 427–428
    in sepsis, 837
    signs and symptoms of, *421*
  respiratory, 429–430
    in sepsis, 837
    signs and symptoms of, *432*
Allen test for palmar arch assessment, 1009–1010

Allergic reactions, 455, 456–*457*, 458–464
Allergy(ies), contact, 461–462
Allograft, 791, 792
All-or-nothing law in action potential propagation, 36
Alopecia in physical assessment, 268
Altitude, effect of, on platelet levels, 89
Alveolar-capillary block, increased diffusion in, 385–386
Alveolar dead space, 16, 31
Alveolar gas equation, 364
Alveolar minute ventilation, increase in, reflex, in ARDS, 489
Alveolar ventilation, 16
  in hypoxemia, 377
Alveoli:
  collapse of, 533–534
    (*See also* Atelectasis)
  destruction of, decreased diffusion in, 386
  permeability of, disorders affecting, 485–504
    adult respiratory distress syndrome as, 485–497
    (*See also* Respiratory distress syndrome, adult)
    aspiration pneumonia as, 497–498
    cardiogenic pulmonary edema as, 498
    extracorporeal membrane oxygenation for, 502–504
    near drowning as, 501–502
    oxygen toxicity as, 498–500
    radiation pneumonitis as, 498
    viral pneumonia as, 497
Amaurosis, uremic, in renal disease, 667
Amethopterin as anticancer drug, *906*
Amikacin sulfate, 1138–1139
Amines, 125–126
Amino acids:
  absorption of, 200
  decreased, in renal disease, 664
  reabsorption of, in urine formation, 163
  in total parenteral nutrition solution, 982
Aminophylline, 1139
  in alteration of second messenger mechanism of hormone response, 127
  in asthma therapy, 574
Ammonia generation in kidney, 173, *174*
Amniotic fluid embolism, 864
Amobarbital in status epilepticus treatment, 622
Amoxicillin trihydrate, 1139–1140
Ampere, 1038

Amphotericin B, 1140
Ampicillin, 1140–1141
Ampicillin sodium, 1141
Amplifiers:
    in ECG monitor, 1000–1001
    pressure, in direct blood pressure
        monitoring, 1008
Ampulla in emission, 246
Amputation of limb:
    in adolescent, significance of,
        903–904
    for osteogenic sarcoma in adoles-
        cent, 904–905
Amylase:
    in carbohydrate digestion, 199
    pancreatic, 192
Amylytic enzymes of exocrine pan-
    creas, 192
Anagen, 218
Analgesic nephropathy, pathogenesis
    of, 662
Analgesics in first aid for burns, 752
Anaphylactic reactions, *456*, 458–
    459
Anaphylactoid reactions, 458
Androgens, adrenal, 141
Anemia(s), 584–588
    aplastic, 584–587
        (*See also* Aplastic anemia)
    complicating leukemia, 589
    erythrocyte precursors in, 85
    hemolytic, 587–588
        (*See also* Hemolytic anemia)
    hypoxia in, 373
    treatment of, in acute renal failure
        management, 669
Anemic hypoxia, 373–374, *375*
Anesthesia, general, in status epilepti-
    cus treatment, 622
Aneurysm, ventricular, intra-aortic bal-
    loon pumping for, 936
Angina in myocardial ischemia, pre-
    vention of, 569–570
Angiographic monitoring of unstable
    cardiac patient, 560–562
Angiography:
    in diagnosis of gastrointestinal hem-
        orrhage, 701
    pulmonary, in diagnosis of pulmo-
        nary thromboembolism, 521
Angiotensin:
    in fluid balance, 170
    production of, 174
    in regulation of peripheral regula-
        tion, 69
Angiotensin II, circulating, in regula-
    tion of body water, 398
Angiotensinogen, cleavage of, by
    renin, 174
Angle of Louis, 275

Anions, nonreabsorbable, in potassium
    regulation, 406–407
Anisocoria in evaluating intracerebral
    pressure in trauma victim, 801
Ankylosing spondylitis, destruction of
    articular cartilage due to, 234
Anniversary reaction in psychosocial
    assessment, 352
Anosmia, 293
Anrep effect, 75
Anstadt cup for direct cardiac
    compression, historical evolution
    of, 932
Antacids:
    effect of, on lower esophageal
        sphincter, 185
    for kidney transplant recipient, 677
    for peptic ulcer bleeding, 703
Antagonist, system, in coagulation
    mechanism, 97
Antepartal and intrapartal crises,
    855–862
    late bleeding disorders as, 857–859
    maladaptive positional disorders as,
        860–861
    preeclampsia/eclampsia as,
        859–860
    prolapsed cord as, 861–862
Anterior pituitary gland, 120–133
    (*See also* Pituitary gland, anterior)
Anterolateral columns, 622–623
Antibiotics:
    altering host resistance to sepsis,
        825
    in burn therapy, 753
    for infections in aplastic anemia, 585
    for lung abscess, 506
    for neonatal sepsis, 877
    neuromuscular paralysis due to,
        complicating mechanical venti-
        lation, 968
    in peritonitis treatment, 712, 713
    resistance of, to microorganisms in
        sepsis, 826
    in treatment of infection in sepsis,
        839–840
Antibody(ies):
    in host defense against sepsis, 823
    in immune defense mechanisms,
        445
Anticholinesterase drugs for myas-
    thenia gravis, 632–633
Anticoagulant(s):
    in balloon pumping, 940
    coumarin, vitamin K deficiency due
        to, 593
    in pulmonary thromboembolism ther-
        apy, 521–522
Anticoagulant effects of plasmin activ-
    ity, 99

Anticoagulant forces in coagulation
    mechanism, 98
Antidiuretic hormone (ADH), 134–136
    in autonomic nervous system, 122
    blood level of, in osmosis in kid-
        neys, 155
    in fluid balance, 170
    in regulation of body water, 398
    in regulation of osmolality of body
        fluids, 392–394
    release of, in gastrointestinal hemor-
        rhage, 699
    secretion of, increased, in sepsis, 832
    in urine concentration determination,
        165–166
Antifoam in tubbing solution for burn
    care, 788
Antigen(s):
    in immune defense mechanisms,
        444–445
    regulation and processing of, by re-
        ticuloendothelial system, 448
Antihemophilic factor, *93*, 95–96
Antihemophilic factor B, *93*, 96
Anti-inflammatory effects of glucocorti-
    coids, 139
Antilymphocyte globulin for kidney
    transplant recipient, 677
Antimocrobial(s):
    in burn therapy, 753
    in postburn infection control, 30–32
    in treatment of infection in sepsis,
        839–840
Antrum:
    contraction of, in digestion, 190
    of stomach, 186
Anulus fibrosus of disk, 105
Anxiety, 323–324
    acute, 324
    definition of, 323
    in family of critical-care patient,
        476–477
    guides for nursing action related to,
        326–327
    management of, 324
    in psychosociodynamics of sick role,
        350
Aorta:
    coarctation of, as chronic local auto-
        regulation, 65
    palpation or, 305
    thoracic, traumatic injuries to, man-
        agement of, 810
Aortic bodies as peripheral chemore-
    ceptors, 28
Aortic ejection clicks, 290
Aortic valve, regurgitation through,
    murmur of, 291
Apex of heart, 283
Apgar score for neonate, 865–866

Aplastic anemia, 584–587
  clinical assessment of, 585
  etiology of pathophysiologic process
    of, 584–585
  nursing implications of, 586–587
  treatment of, 585–586
Apneustic center, 27–28
Apocrine sweat glands, 217
Appearance, general, in examination,
    260–261
Appetite center in hypothalamus,
    179–180
Aqueduct of Sylvius, 105, 107
Arachnodactyly, 234
Arachnoid, 105
Arachnoid granulations, 105
Arbenicillin disodium, 1143
ARDS (*see* Respiratory distress syn-
    drome, adult)
Arginine vasopressin, 134–136
Argyll Robertson pupil in assessment
    of comatose patient, 316
Arrest, sinus, 1108–1109
Arrhythmias, 287, *288*
  in assessment of myocardial infarc-
    tion, 312, *313*
  atrial pacing for, 573–575
  clinical assessment of, 571–572
  complicating pulmonary artery pres-
    sure monitoring, prevention of,
    1014
  in differential diagnosis of unstable
    cardiac patient, 544
  management of, 572–575
  monitoring for, in unstable cardiac
    patient, 548–551, *552, 553*
  sinus, 1107
  (*See also* Dysrhythmias)
Arterial blood gases in assessment of
    unstable cardiac patient, 559–560
Arterial blood oxygen tension in hy-
    poxemia, 375–376
Arterial blood pressure, monitoring of,
    indications for, 1008–1009
Arterial lines in trauma victim manage-
    ment, procedure for, 803
Arterial pressure, regulation of, 69–71
Arterial pulse wave, transmission of,
    70–71
Arterio-arterial pumping for afterload
    reduction, historical evolution of,
    930
Arteriography:
  in diagnosis of gastrointestinal hem-
    orrhage, 701
  in location and treatment of esopha-
    geal varices, 703
Arterioles of kidneys, 151–152
Arteriovenous anastomoses in dermis,
    213

Arteriovenous fistula for hemodialysis,
    672, 977, *978*
Arteriovenous malformation, congeni-
    tal, localized increase in growth
    due to, 234
Arteriovenous shunt for hemodialysis,
    977, *978*
Artery(ies):
  of brain, 108–109
  carotid, palpation of, in assessment
    of unstable cardiac patient, 545
  femoral, palpation of, 304
  of kidneys, 151–152
  pulmonary, trauma to, complicating
    pulmonary artery pressure moni-
    toring, prevention of, 1014
  renal, stenosis of, pathogenesis of,
    659–660
  of spinal cord, 109
  supplying colon, 203
  supplying esophagus, 183
  supplying gallbladder, 194
  supplying liver, 207
  supplying penis, 245
  supplying small intestine, 197
  supplying stomach, 186
  supplying vulva, 244
  systemic, in sepsis, 834
  trauma to, complicating balloon
    pumping, 943
Arthritis, rheumatoid, destruction of ar-
    ticular cartilage due to, 234
Arthus reaction, 460–461
Articular cartilage:
  bone growth in, 224
  reaction of, to acute disorders and
    injuries, 234–235
Ascites in critical-care patients, *319*
Aspiration:
  complicating diabetic ketoacidosis,
    647
  of meconium in high-risk neonate,
    870
Aspiration pneumonia, 497–498
Aspiration pneumonitis:
  in drug overdose, 536
  in head injury, 536
Aspirin, 1141–1142
  in alteration of second messenger
    mechanism of hormone re-
    sponse, 127
Assessment:
  of family as learner, 1082–1083
  of patient as learner, 1082–1083
  physical, 251–320
    (*See also* Physical assessment)
  psychosocial, of patient and family,
    349–358
  of self as teacher, 1081–1082
Asterixis in renal disease, 667

Asthma, 509–515
  clinical features of, 510
  in critical-care patients, *319*
  pathophysiology of, 510–513
  therapy of, 513–515
Astrocytoma, cerebellar, in school-age
    child, 900
Asystole, drug therapy for, 922
Ataxic breathing in assessing transten-
    torial herniation, 608
Atelectasis, 533–534
  clinical features of, 533
  complicating surgery with extracor-
    poreal circulation, 954
  in critical-care patients, *319*
  in idiopathic respiratory distress
    syndrome, 869
  in kyphoscoliosis, 509
  management of, 533–534
  pathophysiology of, 533
  prevention of, 534
Atherosclerosis:
  chronic occlusive mesenteric isch-
    emia from, 705
  nonocclusive mesenteric ischemia
    from, 705–706
Atlas, 104
Atopic allergy, 458
Atresia:
  choanal, in high-risk neonate, 870
  esophageal, in neonate, 882–884
Atria:
  functional anatomy of, 53
  impulse conduction through, 38
Atrial baroreceptors in regulation of
    peripheral regulation, 68
Atrial contraction, premature,
    1111–1112
Atrial electrograms in monitoring of
    unstable cardiac patient, 548–551,
    552, 553
Atrial fibrillation, *288*, 1116
Atrial flutter, *288*, 1115
Atrial pacemaker, wandering, 1110
Atrial pressure:
  left, monitoring of, direct, 1015
  right, monitoring of, direct, 1014
Atrial systole, 61
Atrial tachycardia, paroxysmal, *288*,
    1113–1114
Atrioventricular (AV) block in myocar-
    dial infarction, *313*
Atrioventricular (AV) node, 287
  conduction in, 38–40
Atrioventricular valves, functional anat-
    omy of, 53, *54*
Atrium, pacing of, indications for,
    573–575
Atropine sulfate, 1142

Auerbach's plexus of gastrointestinal
tract, 182
Auscultation:
of abdomen, 301–302
in diagnosis of intestinal obstruction, 709
in assessment of unstable cardiac
patient, 545
of heart, 285–286
of lung in physical assessment,
281–283
in physical assessment, 259–260
Auscultatory gap in hypertensive patient, 263
Autograft, 791, *792*
Autoimmune diseases, 463–464
Automatic indirect pressure measurement, 1004
Automaticity:
in control of heart rate, 73
myocardial cells capable of, 35–36
Autonomic hyperreflexia in spinal cord
injury, 693
Autonomic nervous system:
activities of, functional and pharmacological, *122*
anatomy of, 115
physiology of, 121–123
Autoprothrombin, *93, 96*
Autoregulation:
of coronary blood flow, 933
of peripheral circulation, 65
of renal blood flow, 159
of stroke volume, 75–76
Autotransfusion in acute blood loss, 81
Axis, 104
Axons, 101
Azathioprine for kidney transplant recipient, 677
Azotemia:
definition of, 657
in polycystic renal disease, 661

B cell, 88
B-cell subsets in immune response,
449
B lymphocytes:
circulation patterns of, 446, 448
defects of, in congenital hypoimmune conditions, 464
identification of, 449
in immune response, 446, 449
Bachmann's bundle in impulse conduction, 38
Bacillus, Döderlein's, in vagina, 243
Bacillus anthracis in sepsis, 827
Bacillus subtilus in sepsis, 827
Bacteremia:
in burn patient, 765
definition of, 821

Bacteria:
in colon, 205–206
in sepsis, 827–829
on skin, 219
Bacterial effects of sepsis, 831–832
Bacterial infections, delayed hypersensitivity and, 462
Bacterial meningitis in high-risk neonate, 875
Bacterial pneumonia, 534–535
Bacteroides fragilis in sepsis, 829
Bacteroides melanogenicus in sepsis,
829
Bainbridge reflex in control of heart
rate, 74–75
Balloon, intra-aortic, in management of
low-output cardiac failure and
shock, 568–569
Balloon pump, intra-aortic, 930, *931,*
933–943
(*See also* Intra-aortic balloon
pump)
Ballottement in physical assessment,
258
Barbiturate coma in intracranial hypertension management, 617
Barometric pressure, reduced, aerohypoxia due to, 376–377
Baroreceptor(s):
in regulation of arterial pressure, 71
in regulation of peripheral regulation, 68
Baroreceptor reflex in control of heart
rate, 74–75
Baroreceptor theory in renin regulation,
174–175
Barotrauma complicating mechanical
ventilation, 968
Barrel chest, 278–279
in emphysema, 516
Bartholin's glands, 243–244
Basal cell carcinoma in critical-care
patients, *317*
Basal ganglia, 109, 110, *111*
in extrapyramidal system, 119
in motor integration of nervous system, 119–121
Bases, weak, tubular secretion of, in
urine formation, 165
Basophils, 86–87
in anterior pituitary, 130
Bath, daily, in burn care, 769
Battery, role of consent in, 1051
Beau's lines in nails in physical assessment, 268, *269*
Beclomethasone in asthma therapy,
514
Behavior:
manipulative, of critical-care patient,
474–475

as system, 332
Bell's palsy, 294
Beta blockade in asthma, 511
Bicarbonate, secretion of: by colon,
205
by exocrine pancreas, 192
Bicarbonate ions:
concentration of, in body fluids, regulation of, 172–174
reabsorption of, in urine formation,
162
Bifidobacteria in sepsis, 829
Bile:
function of, 194–196
metabolism of, 194–196
regulation of, 196
Bile canaliculi, 194
Bile ductules and hepatocyte, relationship of, 209
Bile pigments, 195–196
Bile salts, 194–195
indigestion of triglycerides, 201–202
Biliary system, 193–196
hepatic, 206
Biliary tract, traumatic injuries to, management of, 811
Bilirubin, 196
rise in, in sepsis, 837
Biot's respiration, 262–263
in assessing transtentorial herniation, 608
in assessment of comatose patient,
315
Birth defects, identification and care
of, 882
Bladder:
carcinoma of, 691
effects of spinal cord injury and
polyneuropathy on, 631
neurogenic, in spinal cord disorders,
693
spastic, in spinal cord disorders,
693
trauma to, 695
traumatic injuries to, management of,
812
tumors of, transurethral resection of,
688
Bleeding:
associated with platelets, 91
gastrointestinal, complicating mechanical ventilation, 968
(*See also* Hemorrhage)
Blink reflexes, 123–124
Block, exit, 1108–1109
Blood:
in burn therapy, 755–756
cells of, 84–91
origin and development of, 82–83
platelets as, 89–91

Blood: (*Cont.*)
cells of: red, 84–85
(*See also* Erythrocytes)
white, 85–89
(*See also* Leukocytes)
clots of, retention of, in bladder, 683
coagulation of (*see* Coagulation)
color of, 80
composition and characteristics of, 79–81
distribution of, 80–81
flow of: cerebral, decreased, in gastrointestinal hemorrhage, 697
coronary, regulation of, 55–57
determinants of, 45–46
in extracorporeal circulation, 951
oxygen delivery and, 371
renal: effects of prostaglandins on, 176
redistribution of, in sodium regulation, 403
resistance to, in pulmonary circulation, 51–52
glucose in, determinations of, in diabetic patient management, 642, 643
hydrogen ion concentration of, 80
loss of, acute, effects of, 81
in mouth, airway problems in, 798–799
osmotic pressure of, 80
oxygen content of, 368
oxygenation of, in extracorporeal circulation, 952–953
perfusion of, pulmonary, 20–23
pH of, 80
in pharynx, airway problems in, 798–799
replacement of: in hemorrhagic shock treatment, 699
in trauma victim, 800
specific gravity of, 80
supply of, to fracture fragments, time required for bone fracture healing and, 233
tests on, in assessment of unstable cardiac patient, 546–548
and tissues, gas exchange between, 371–372
transfusions of: in aplastic anemia treatment, 585
in hemolytic anemia treatment, 587–588
in urine, hourly testing of, in fluid therapy for burns, 757
viscosity of, 80
volume of, 80–81
cerebral, increase in, increased intracranial pressure due to, 615

regulation of, 66
Blood chemistries in diagnosis of sepsis, 837
Blood count in assessment of patient with hematopoietic disorders, 580, *581*
Blood gases:
arterial, in assessment of unstable cardiac patient, 559–560
in diagnosis of sepsis, 837–838
monitoring of, in assessing pulmonary function in burn care, 759–760
nervous system control of, 26–30
Blood pressure:
in assessing transtentorial herniation, 610
in assessment of shock patient, 310
measurement of: direct, monitor for, 1004–1021
(*See also* Monitoring, blood pressure, direct)
indirect, monitor for, 1000–1004
in physical assessment, 263–264
Blood urea nitrogen, levels of, in assessment of unstable cardiac patient, 547
Blood vessels:
anatomy of, *63*
cerebral, control mechanisms of, 66
diameter of, in hemodynamics of circulation, 45
pulmonary, control mechanisms of, 66
renal, control mechanisms of, 66
sepsis, 834
small, coagulation process in, 99–100
smooth muscle of, 63–64
traumatic injuries to, management of, 812–813
Body fluid buffer system in acid-base balance regulation, 423
Body of stomach, 186
Bonding, maternal-infant: in critically ill newborn, 881–882
with high-risk neonate, 868–869
Bone(s):
burns of, care of, 785–786
in calcium regulation, 410–411
death of, local, 231
deposition of, altered, in response to abnormal conditions, 231
effects of growth hormone on, 132
effects of kidney disease on, 666, 667
and extracellular fluid: exchange of magnesium between, in magnesium regulation, 414
exchange of phosphate between, in phosphate regulation, 419

fractures of, 232–234
[*See also* Fracture(s), bone]
growth of, 224
inorganic substances of, 223–224
long, shaft of, displaced fractures of, localized increase in growth due to, 234
as organ, 223–224
organic substances of, 224
reactions of, to acute disorders and injuries, 231–234
remodeling of, 224–226
resorption of, altered, in response to abnormal conditions, 231
structure of, 221
types of, 221, *222*
Bone marrow:
blood cell production in, 82, *83*
erythrocyte production in, 84
specimen of, in assessment of patient with hematopoietic disorders, 580–581
transplantation of: in acute leukemia treatment, 590
in aplastic anemia treatment, 596
Botulism:
acetylcholine deficiency in, 625
motor disorders from, *635*
prevention of, 634
Bowman's capsule, 152
Boyle's law, 15
Brachial vein as entry site for total parenteral nutrition, 982
Bradycardia, sinus, *288*, 1105
drug therapy for, 921
Bradykinin:
in host defense against sepsis, 823
in regulation of peripheral regulation, 69
release of, in sepsis, 832
Bradypnea, 262, *263*
Brain:
anatomy of, gross, 109–111
blood flow to, decreased, in gastrointestinal hemorrhage, 697
blood vessels of, control mechanisms of, 66
blood volume in, increase of, increased intracranial pressure due to, 615
circulation in, 108–109
diseases of, effect of, on ADH secretion, 135
edema of: complicating diabetic ketoacidosis, 647
increased intracranial pressure due to, 614
functions of: categories of, evaluation of, in assessing transtentorial herniation, 601, *602*

Brain: (*Cont.*):
functions of: monitor of, 1028–1029
in hypothermia, 992
mass of, increase in, increased intracranial pressure due to,
613–614
tumor of, in school-age child,
900–902
ventricles of, 105, 107
Brain barrier system, 107
Brain herniation syndromes, 600–612
cerebellar herniation as, 611
transtentorial herniation as, 600–610
treatment of, 611–612
uncal herniation as, 610
Brain syndrome, acute, in patient in
critical-care unit, 1044
Brainstem:
anatomy of, 110–111
compression of, from brain herniation, symptoms of, *601*
contusion of, loss of airway protection in, 626
glioma of, in school-age child, 901
segmental organization of, 623–625
stroke in, loss of airway protection
in, 626
Breast:
funnel, 279
pigeon, 279
Breath sounds, auscultation of, 281,
282
Breathing:
deep, 758–759, 769
(*See also* Respiration)
Breathlessness in differential diagnosis
of unstable cardiac patient, 544
Bronchi, *277*
Bronchial breath sounds, 281, *282*
Bronchitis:
chronic, 515
in critical-care patients, *319*
Bronchodilators:
for chronic bronchitis, 515
inhaled, in asthma therapy, 514
Bronchophony, 281–282
Bronchoscopy for lung abscess, 507
Bronchospasm in asthma, mechanism
of, 511–512
Bronchovesicular breath sounds, 281,
282
Bruit in monitoring patency of arterio-
venous fistula, 978
Brunner's glands, 197–198
Buffer system in regulation of periph-
eral regulation, 68
Bulbar muscles, dysfunction of, man-
agement of, 637
Bulbocavernosus muscle, 245
Bulla, *266*

Bundle branch block:
left, 1135–1136
right, 1134
Bundle of His, 287
Burns, 268
care of, 741–794
acute period of, 746–747
approach to, developing, 771, 773
art of, 5
on bone, 785–786
comfort and hygiene in, 768–769
contractual approach to nurse-patient interaction in, 771,
773–774
determining severity of injury in,
744–746
on ears, 785, *786*
emergent period of, 746, 748–753
admission procedure in,
748–753
first aid in, 748, 752
general principles of, 748
supportive treatment in, 753
etiology of, 742–743
exercise in, 769–770
on eyes, 784–785
on face, 783–785
fluids in, 753–758
[*See also* Fluid(s), in burn ther-
apy]
hairy areas, 786–787
hydrotherapy in, 787–789
infection control in, 761–766
on muscle, 785–786
on nose, 784
nutritional needs in meeting,
766–768
on perineum, 785
planning of, 746–748
positioning in, 769
quality control measures in,
774–776, *777*, *778*
rehabilitation period of, 747–748
respiratory care in, 758–761
on scalp, 785
skin anatomy and physiology in,
743–744
skin grafting in, 791–794
(*See also* Skin, grafting of)
splinting in, 771
on tendon, 785–786
wound care in, *777*, 779–783
wound infection and clinical sepsis in, 763–766
depth of, determination of, 744–746,
747
extent of, determination of, 744
full-thickness, 744–746, *747*
partial-thickness, 744–745, *746*,
747

severity of, determination of,
744–746
in toddler: nursing management of,
891–894
pathophysiology of, 889–891
victims of, spiritual concerns of,
1063
Burr holes in trauma victim management, procedures for, 805
Bursae, 227
Bypass, jejunoileal, for obesity, 735

Cable in ECG monitor, 1000
Caisson disease, 523–524
Calcitonin, 138
for hypercalcemic crisis, 655
in plasma calcium concentration
control, 223, 224
Calcium, *93*, *95*
in bone, 223–224
deficiency of, 413–414
effects of kidney disease on, 666,
667
excess of, 412
functions of, 410
ionized, serum levels of, effects of
parathormone on, 138
metastatic deposition of, in soft tissues from vitamin D excess, 223
regulation of, 410–412
serum levels of, high, crisis from,
654–655
in treatment of sepsis, 845
Calcium hypochlorite in tubbing solution for burn care, 788
Calcium ions, reabsorption of, in urine
formation, 162
Calcium stones, 663
Calculus(i):
kidney, surgery for, 690
ureteral, surgery for, 690
urinary tract, 662–663
Renacidin to dissolve, 687
surgery for, 690
Callus, fibrocartilaginous, in fracture
repair, 232
Caloric intake in diabetic patient management, 642–643
Caloric test for vestibular portion of
acoustic nerve, 294
Calvaria of skull, 102–103
Calyces of kidneys, 151
Canaliculi, bile, 194
Candida albicans:
postburn infection due to, 766
in sepsis, 830
Candida septicemia complicating TPN,
988–989
Cannula, external, for hemodialysis,
672

Capacitance in venous system, 50
Capillary(ies):
　blood flow through, regulation of, 64
　of dermis, 213, *214*
　distention of, in decreasing pulmo-
　　nary vascular resistance, 21
　dynamics of, in systemic circulation,
　　47–49
　of liver, 208–209
　membrane of, exchange across, 49
　peritubular, oncotic pressure in, in
　　sodium regulation, 403
　pulmonary, destruction of, de-
　　creased diffusion in, 386
　in sepsis, 834
　Starling law of, 64
Capnograph, 1026, *1027*
Carbaminohemoglobin in carbon diox-
　ide transport, 26
Carbohydrates:
　absorption of, by small intestine,
　　199–200
　for hypoglycemia, 649–650
　in total parenteral nutrition solution,
　　982
Carbon dioxide:
　arterial levels of, monitoring of, in
　　unstable cardiac patient,
　　559–560
　effect of, on ventilation, 28
　partial pressures of, 19–20
　　alveolar increased, effects of, 20
　　arterial, determination of, capno-
　　　graph for, 1026, *1027*
　transport of, 25–26
Carbon monoxide in anemic hypoxia,
　373–374
Carbonic acid in carbon dioxide trans-
　port, 25–26
Carcinoma:
　adrenal gland, surgery for, 691
　bladder, 691
　colon, complicating ulcerative coli-
　　tis, 723
　lung abscess due to, 505
　patient with, spiritual concerns of,
　　1061
　penile, surgery for, 692
　prostate, surgery for, 691
　skin, in critical-care patients,
　　317–*318*
　testicular, surgery for, 692
　urethral, surgery for, 691
Cardia of stomach, 186
Cardiac arrest:
　monitored, basic life support for,
　　914–915
　prevention of, 914
　unwitnessed, basic life support for,
　　914

Cardiac cycle, 59–61
Cardiac glands, 186
Cardiac index:
　definition of, 1021
　function of, 72
Cardiac output:
　blood flow and, 371
　control of, 71–78
　decreased, in pulmonary throm-
　　boembolism, 519
　definition of, 71–72
　effect of, on blood oxygen tensions,
　　366–367
　factors influencing, 72
　high, in anemia, 584
　increase in, reflex, in ARDS, 489
　low: complicating surgery with extra-
　　corporeal circulation, 953
　　in hypothermia, 992
　　vasodilators for, 567–568
　measurement of, 73, 1021–1025
　　computerized, 1024, 1025
　　guidelines for, 1024–1025
　　thermal curve for, 1024, *1026*
　monitoring of, in unstable cardiac
　　patient, 556
　in sepsis, 833
　techniques for, 1021–1024
Cardiac output computer in ARDS
　management, 495
Cardiac pacemaker, 287
Cardiac patient:
　monitoring technique for, fluoro-
　　scopic, 557–558
　unstable: assessment of, 544–548
　　differential diagnosis of, 543–544
　　evaluation and therapy of, 543–578
　　monitoring techniques for,
　　　548–562
　　　angiographic, 560–562
　　　for arterial blood gases,
　　　　559–560
　　　echocardiographic, 557, *558*
　　　electrophysiologic, 548–551,
　　　　552, 553
　　　hemodynamic, 552–557
　　　scintigraphic, 558–559, *560, 561*
　　　therapy for, approach to, 562–576
Cardiac press in cardiac arrest, 917–918
Cardiac pump, 52–62
　(*See also* Heart)
Cardiac tamponade:
　complicating surgery with extracor-
　　poreal circulation, 953
　hypovolemia in, 564
　in renal disease, 665
Cardiogenic pulmonary edema, 498
Cardiogenic shock:
　in assessment of myocardial infarc-
　　tion, 314

　intra-aortic balloon pumping for,
　　934–936
Cardiomyopathy, restrictive, hypovole-
　mia in, 564
Cardioplegia, cold, for myocardial
　preservation, 953
Cardiopulmonary bypass, 928–930
Cardiopulmonary resuscitation,
　914–915
Cardioregulatory center in control of
　heart rate, 74
Cardiotomy, myocardial depression af-
　ter intra-aortic balloon pumping,
　937
Cardiovascular crisis in high-risk neo-
　nate, 872
Cardiovascular critical care, art of, 3–4
Cardiovascular reflexes, 124
Cardiovascular system:
　action potential propagation in,
　　36–38
　arterial pressure regulation in, 69–
　　71
　cardiac pump in, 52–62
　　(*See also* Heart)
　as circuit, 44–46
　complications of, extracorporeal cir-
　　culation involving, 953–954
　disorders of, patient with, 543–578
　　(*See also* Cardiac patient)
　effects of kidney disease on,
　　664–665
　effects of spinal cord injury and
　　polyneuropathy on, 629–630
　electrical conduction in, normal,
　　38–40
　electrocardiography and, 40–42,
　　43
　electrophysiology of, 33–44
　evaluation of, 543–578
　functions of, altering host resistance
　　to sepsis, 825
　peripheral circulation in, 62–69
　　(*See also* Peripheral circulation)
　physiologic effects of hypothermia
　　on, 992–993
　physiology of, 33–78
　pulmonary circulation in, 50–52
　response of, to burns in child, 890
　systemic, circulation and, 46–50
　transmembrane potential of, 33–35
　vectorcardiography and, 42, 44
Cardioversion:
　emergency, procedure for, 921
　synchronized, in advanced life sup-
　　port, 919–921
Care:
　and cure, achievement of balance
　　between, 1065
　moral justification for, 1065–1066

Carotid arteries, palpation of, in assessment of unstable cardiac patient, 545
Carotid bodies as peripheral chemoreceptors, 28
Carrier-mediated transport in renal system, 157–158
Cartilage:
  articular: bone growth in, 224
    reaction of, to acute disorders and injuries, 234–235
  effects of growth hormone on, 132
  epiphyseal plate, bone growth in, 224
Cascade theory in coagulation mechanism, implications of, 97
Catecholamines:
  effect of, on platelet levels, 89
  metabolic effects of, 142
  secretion of: by adrenal medulla, 141–142
    increased, in sepsis, 833
  in sodium regulation, 403
Categen, 218
Catheter(s):
  altering host resistance to sepsis, 824
  Foley, in trauma victim management, procedures for, 804
  insertion of, for direct blood pressure monitoring, 1009–1010
  for peritoneal dialysis, insertion of, nursing care during, 975
  placement of, for total parenteral nutrition, 982–983
  Swan-Ganz: in hemorrhagic shock treatment, 699
    in trauma victim management, procedures for, 803
  thermodilution, Swan-Ganz, in ARDS management, 495
  urinary, 678–682
    care of, 679
    drainage systems for, 679–680
    external condom, 678–679
    Foley, 678
      balloon of, inability to deflate, 683
    irrigation of, 679
    problems with, in uncircumcised male, 680–681
    problems inserting, 681–682
    trauma from, 683
  Weston-Roberts trocar, in peritoneal dialysis, 974
Catheterization, transtracheal, in cardiac arrest, 917
Cathode-ray tube in oscilloscope, 1031
Cauda equina, 114
Cecum of colon, 203

Cell bodies of neurons, 101
Cell-mediated immunity, 450–451, 461–463
  T cell in, 446, *447*, 461
Cellulitis in critical-care patients, *317*
Central nervous system (CNS):
  in ARDS, 489
  evaluation of, in assessment of neurologic disorders in school-age child, 899–900
  gross anatomy of, 109–115
    brain in, 109–111
    cranial nerves in, 111–113
    spinal cord and spinal nerves in, 113–115
  physiology of, 115–124
    motor integration in, 119–121
    reflex activities in, 123–124
    sensory integration in, 115, 117–118
  support structures of, 102–109
    brain barrier system as, 107
    cerebral circulation as, 108–109
    cerebrospinal fluid as, 107
    meninges as, 105, *106*
    skull as, 102–103
    spinal cord circulation as, 109
    vascular system as, 107–108
    ventricular system as, 105, 107
    vertebral column as, 103–105
Central nervous system ischemic response in regulation of arterial pressure, 71
Central neurogenic hyperventilation in assessing transtentorial herniation, 607–608
Central veins for intravenous lifeline, 918
Central venous pressure:
  line in hemorrhagic shock treatment, 699
  monitoring of, direct, 1015
Cephalic phase of hydrochloric acid secretion, 189
Cephalothin sodium, sterile, 1143–1144
Cerebellar astrocytoma in school-age child, 900
Cerebellar herniation, 611
Cerebellum:
  anatomy of, 111
  in motor integration of nervous system, 119–121
Cerebral blood volume, increase in, increased intracranial pressure due to, 615
Cerebral circulation, 108–109
Cerebral cortex, 109
  in control of heart rate, 74
  in sensory integration, 117, *119*

Cerebral function, assessment of, 292–293
Cerebral function monitor, 1028–1029
Cerebral hemisphere, anatomy of, 109–110
Cerebral hypoxia:
  in drug overdose, 535
  in head injury, 535
Cerebral vascular accident in critical-care patients, *320*
Cerebral vessels, control mechanisms of, 66
Cerebrospinal fluid, 107
Cerebrospinal fluid (CSF):
  absorption and flow of, alteration in, increased intracranial pressure due to, 614–615
  drainage of, in intracranial hypertension management, 617
  flow of, obstruction of, activities causing, 619–620
Cerebrospinal fluid acidosis, paradoxical, complicating diabetic ketoacidosis, 647
Cerebrovascular accident, patient with, spiritual concerns of, 1061
Cervical fractures, airway problems in, 798
Cervix, 240
Charles's law, 15
Chemical imbalances in high-risk neonate, 873
Chemical release, local, in sepsis, 831–832
Chemistry, blood, in assessment of patient with hematopoietic disorders, 580, *581*
Chemoreceptors:
  in control of blood gases, 28–29
  in regulation: of arterial pressure, 71
    of peripheral regulation, 68
Chemotaxins in chemotaxis, 86
Chemotaxis, 440, 442
  in neutrophilia, 86
Chemotherapy for osteogenic sarcoma in adolescent, 905, *906*, 907–908
Chest:
  barrel, 278–279
  cobbler's, 279
  examination of, in trauma victim, 801
  flail, 529–530
    in trauma victim, management of, 809
  trauma to, 526–533
    flail chest from, 529–530
    hemothorax from, 532–533
    pneumothorax from, 530–532
    pulmonary contusion from, 526–529
    [See also Lung(s), contusion of]

Chest (*Cont.*):
traumatic injuries to, management of, 808–810
Chest pain in differential diagnosis of unstable cardiac patient, 543–544
Chest physiotherapy:
in atelectasis management, 534
in closed pneumothorax management, 531
for lung abscess, 506–507
Chest tubes:
in closed pneumothorax management, 530–531
in hemothorax management, 532
in open pneumothorax management, 532
in tension pneumothorax management, 531
Chest x-ray in assessment of unstable cardiac patient, 546
Cheyne-Stokes respiration, 262, 263
in assessment of comatose patient, 315
in assessment of transtentorial herniation, 607
Chicken pox, pneumonia complicating, 497
Chief cells:
in gastric gland, 186
in parathyroid glands, 138
Child abuse, 887–889
burns in, 889–894
(*See also* Burns, in toddler)
Children:
effect of critical illness in family on, 353–354
school-age: development of, illness and, 899
neurologic disorders in, 899–903
(*See also* Neurologic disorders, in school-age child)
Chloramphenicol, 1144–1145
Chloramphenicol sodium succinate, 1145
Chloride:
deficiency of, 418–419
excess of, 417–418
functions of, 417
regulation of, 417
Chloride shift, 26
Chlorpromazine in congenital diaphragmatic hernia management in neonate, 886
Chlorpromazine hydrochloride, 1145–1147
Choanal atresia in high-risk neonate, 870
Cholangitis, sclerosing, 729–731
Cholecalciferol in vitamin D metabolism, 223

Cholecystokinin:
in regulation: of bile metabolism, 196
of lower esophageal sphincter, 185
of pancreatic secretion, 193
secretion of, 145
Cholesterol stones, formation of, in gallbladder, 194
Chondritis, prevention of, in burns of ear, 785
Choreas, 298
Choroid plexus, 107
Christmas factor, *93*, 96
Chromophobes in anterior pituitary, 130
Chronic obstructive pulmonary disease (COPD), psychosocial aspects of, 517–518
Chylomicron in fat digestion, 201–202
Chymotrypsinogen, 192
Cigarette smoking (*see* Smoking)
Cimetidine for peptic ulcer bleeding, 703
Circulation:
adjuncts to, in advanced life support, 917–918
assistance of, 925–946
devices for: current, 932–946
effects of, 923–928
historical evolution of, 928–930
principles of, 925–928
cerebral, 108–109
collateral, as chronic long-term autoregulation, 65
coronary, 55–57
extracorporeal, 949–954
(*See also* Extracorporeal circulation)
hemodynamics of, 45–46
peripheral, 62–69
(*See also* Peripheral circulation)
portal, control mechanisms of, 66
pulmonary, 50–52
requirements for, specific, 64–65
spinal cord, 109
systemic, 46–50
capillary dynamics in, 47–49
functional characteristics of, 46–47
venous system in, 50
Circulatory hypoxia, 374, *375*
Circulatory reflexes:
in regulation of arterial pressure, 71
in regulation of peripheral regulation, 68
Circulatory system of liver, 206–209
Cirrhosis, 208
altering host resistance to sepsis, 825
effect of, on ADH secretion, 135

in sepsis, 834
Cisterna magna, 105
Citrovorum factor for osteogenic sarcoma in adolescent, 905
"Clasp knife" phenomenon, 298
Clearance, concept of, 160
Clindamycin hydrochloride, 1147
Clindamycin phosphate injection, 1148
Clinitest for urine sugar testing, 642, *643*
Clitoris, 243
Clostridium perfringens in sepsis, 829
Clostridium tetani in sepsis, 829
Clubbing of nails in physical assessment, 268
Cluster breathing in assessing transtentorial herniation, 608
Coagulation, 91–100
disorders of: in liver disease, 592
vitamin K-dependent, 592–593
intravascular, disseminated, 593–596
(*See also* Disseminated intravascular coagulation)
intrinsic and extrinsic system of, 92, *94*
mechanism of, 97–100
cascade theory of, implications of, 97
hemostasis in, 99–100
positive feedback in, 97
system antagonists in, 97–99
in small blood vessels, 99–100
studies of, in assessment of patient with hematopoietic disorders, 580, *581*
tests of, *92*
Coagulation factor(s), 92–96
nomenclature of, 91–92
platelet, 91
prothrombin, *93*, 94
I (fibrinogen), 92–93
III (tissue thromboplastin), *93*, 94–95
IV (calcium), *93*, 95
V (labile factor, Ac globulin, proaccelerin), *93*, 95
VII (stable factor, proconvertin), *93*, 95
VIII (antihemophilic factor), *93*, 95–96
IX (plasma thromboplastin component), *93*, 96
X (Stuart-Prower factor), *93*, 96
XI (plasma thromboplastin antecedent), *93*, 96
XII (Hageman factor), *93*, 96
XIII (fibrin stabilizing factor), 91, *93*, 96
Coagulation systems, assessment of, 591–592

Coagulopathy(ies), 591–592
  consumption, 594, 595
Coarctation of aorta as chronic local
    autoregulation, 65
Cobbler's chest, 279
Coccidioides immitus in sepsis, 830
Cold, hypersensitivity to, in hypother-
    mia, 995
Colistimethate sodium, sterile,
    1148–1149
Colitis:
  granulomatous, 720–721
  ischemic, 707
  ulcerative, 722–723
    (*See also* Ulcerative colitis)
Collagen in dermis, 213
Collagen fibrils in bone matrix, 224
Collateral circulation as chronic long-
    term autoregulation, 65
Colon:
  cancer of, complicating ulcerative
      colitis, 723
  flora of, 205–206
  gross anatomy of, 203–204
  histology of, 204
  mass movements in, 204
  motility of, 204–205
  obstruction of, 708–709
  secretion and absorption by, 205
  traumatic injuries to, management of,
      811
  water absorption in, 202
Color:
  in Apgar scoring, *865*, 866
  of blood, 80
  changes in physical assessment of
      skin, 264
  of urine, hourly testing of, in fluid
      therapy for burns, 757
Colostomy in peritonitis therapy, nurs-
    ing care for, 713–714, *715*
Coma:
  barbiturate in intracranial hyperten-
      sion management, 617
  hyperosmolar hyperglycemic nonke-
      totic complicating TPN, 986
  myxedema, 652
  nonketotic hyperosmolar: hypergly-
      cemic, 647–648, *649*
  from insulin insufficiency, 144
Comatose, definition of, 292
Comatose patient, application of phys-
    ical assessment techniques to,
    315–316
Comfort in burn care, 768
Communicating pneumothorax,
    531–532
Communication:
  with patient in critical-care milieu,
      problems of, 346

for patient in mechanical ventilation,
    964
  in pediatric care, 880
  in psychosocial assessment of pa-
      tient and family, 351
Competence, interpersonal, 473–475
Complement:
  in acquired host defense, 451–453
  activation of, 451–453
  disorders of, 453
  in host defense against sepsis,
      823
Complement fixation, 451
Compliance:
  pulmonary, reduced, in ARDS,
      488–489
  ventilatory, 18
Compression:
  cardiac: closed-chest: automatic, in
        cardiac arrest, 918
      manual, in cardiac arrest, 917
    direct: by circulatory assistance
        devices, 928
      historical evolution of, 931–932
  continuous, destruction of articular
      cartilage due to, 234
Computer, cardiac output, 1024, *1025*
  in ARDS management, 495
Computerized axial tomography (CAT):
  in detection of brain lesion, 611
  scan in evaluating intracerebral
      hemorrhage in trauma victim,
      801
Conduction, electrical, normal, in car-
    diovascular system, 38–40
Conductors, electrical, 1039
Conduit:
  ileal, for urinary diversion, 685
  sigmoid, for urinary diversion, 685
Confusion in sepsis, 836
Congenital anomalies, identification
    and care of, 882
Congestive heart failure in assessment
    of myocardial infarction, 312,
    314
Conjunctiva, assessment of, 271–272
Conjunctivitis in critical-care patients,
    317
Connective tissue framework of liver,
    206, 209–210
Conn's syndrome, 140–141
Consciousness:
  levels of, 292
    in assessment of comatose pa-
        tient, 315
    in diabetic ketoacidosis, 645
    evaluation of, in assessing tran-
        stentorial herniation, 601–602
    in neurologic evaluation of child,
        899–900

neurologic disorders disrupting,
    600–622
Consent:
  battery and, 1051
  expressed, 1052
  implied, 1052
  informed, 1053
  responsibility in, 1053–1054
  role of, 1051–1055
  special problems in, 1054–1055
  statutory, 1052
  withdrawn or refused, 1053
Conservation functions in critical-care
    nursing, 11–12
Consolidation stage of fracture repair,
    233
Constipation, 205
  postcraniotomy in child, manage-
      ment of, 901
  in renal disease, 666
Consumption coagulopathy, 594, 595
Consumptive opsinopathy, 822
Contact allergies, 461–462
Continent internal pouch, 718–719
Continuous positive airway pressure
    (CPAP):
  in ARDS management, 495
  for oxygen toxicity, 500
Continuous positive pressure ventila-
    tion (CPPV) in ARDS management,
    493–494
Contractility:
  in myocardial function, 927
  ventricular: clinical assessment of,
      570
    in control of cardiac output, 76–77
    inotropic agents effecting,
        570–571
Contraction(s):
  atrial premature, 1111–1112
  in burned children, prevention of, 894
  junctional, premature, 1117–1119
  muscular, 228–230
    convulsive, 231
    energy sources for, 229–230
    isometric, 230
    isotonic, 230
    spastic, 231
    summation, 230
    tetanic, 231
    tonic, 230
    twitch, 230
    types of, 230–231
  peristaltic, in small intestine, 199
  premature, *288*
  segmentation, in small intestine, 199
  ventricular, premature, 1123–1125
Contracture(s):
  joint, 235
  prevention of, in burn care, 769, *770*

Contusion:
brainstem, loss of airway protection in, 626
cardiac, in trauma victim, management of, 809
pulmonary, 526–529
in trauma victim, management of, 809
[*See also* Lung(s), contusion of]
Conus medullaris, 113
Convulsion, 231
in preeclampsia, prevention of, 860
Coordination in assessment of motor system, 298
Cornea:
assessment of, 272
drying of, in critical-care patients, *317*
Cornua of uterus, 240
Coronary artery disease, diabetes and, 650
Coronary circulation, 55–57
Coronary disease, patient with, spiritual concerns of, 1060–1061
Corpora cavernosa penis, 245
Cor pulmonale in emphysema, 516
Corpus callosum, 110
Corpus hemorrhagicum, 238
Corpus luteum, formation of, 238–239
Corpus spongiosum of penis, 245
Corpus of uterus, 240–242
Cortex:
adrenal, 139–141
transtentorial herniation syndromes at, *606*
Cortical nephrons, 153, 155
Cortical sensory perception in assessment of sensory system, 299
Corticospinal motor tracts, 622
Corticosteroids, 1149
in adrenal crisis management, 653
altering host resistance to sepsis, 825
in ARDS management, 496–497
in hemolytic anemia treatment, 588
in intracranial hypertension management, 617
for myasthenia gravis, 637
Corticosterone, 139
Cortisol, 139
secretion of, increased, in sepsis, 833
Cortisone acetate in adrenal crisis management, 653
Corynebacterium diphtheriae in sepsis, 827
Coudé-Foley catheter for patient with large prostate, 681
Cough in asthma, 510
Cough reflex, suppression of, lung abscess due to, 505

Coughing in burn care, 758–759, 769
Coumarin anticoagulants, vitamin K deficiency due to, 593
Counter-current exchanger, renal, 168–169
Counter-current mechanism, renal, osmotic concentration and, 166–169
Counter-current multiplier, renal, 166–168
Countercurrent exchange process in renal concentration of urine, 397–398
Countercurrent multiplication process in renal concentration of urine, 397
Counterpulsation:
intra-aortic, for low-output cardiac failure and shock, 568–569
in partial bypass units, historical evolution of, 929
Counterpulsation devices for afterload reduction, 928
current, 932–944
external pressure circulatory assist as, 943–944
intra-aortic balloon pump as, 933–943
(*See also* Intra-aortic balloon pump)
external, historical evolution of, 930–931, *932*
historical evolution of, 930–931
Cowper's glands, 249
in emission, 246
Cramp, 231
muscle, in renal disease, 666–667
Cranial nerves:
anatomy of 111–113
assessment of, 293–295
polyneuropathy of, loss of airway protection in, 626
Craniopharyngioma:
in child, management of, 901–902
in school-age child, 901
Craniotomy for brain tumor in child, nursing management following, 901–902
Creatine phosphokinase (CPK), serum levels of, in assessment of unstable cardiac patient, 547–548
Creatinine:
clearance of, in glomerular filtration rate determination, 160
levels of, in assessment of unstable cardiac patient, 547
production and excretion of, reduced, in sepsis, 834
Cretinism, 137
Cricothyrotomy in cardiac arrest, 917
Crisis, 325–326

for family from critical illness, 475–478
in interpersonal framework, 473, 475
nurse in, guides for nursing action related to, 328–329
patient in, guides for nursing action related to, 329–330
patient's family in, guides for nursing action related to, 329
physiological, choice following, 336
Critical care:
issues in, 1051–1067
consent as, 1051–1055
ethical, 1055–1059
legal, 1055–1059
medical, 1055–1059
quality of life versus quantity of life as, 1057–1058
shared responsibility in, questions about, 1064–1067
spiritual, 1060–1063
Critical-care environment, psychological disequilibrium due to, 338
Critical-care milieu, 343–348
communication in, 343–344
family in, 347–348
patient in, 346–347
communication problems of, 346
sensory disorganization in overcoming, 346–347
perceptual disorganization in, overcoming, 346–347
staff in, 344–346
emotional support given by, 346
environmental management by, 345
function of, 344–345
support for, 345
Critical-care nurse:
and family, interpersonal needs of, 475–478
future of, 8
implications of individual subsystems for, 10–11
interpersonal behavior of patient with, 474–475
and patient, interpersonal needs of 475
and physician: disagreement of, management of, 1066–1067
relationship between, 7
responsibilities of, for life-saving goals, 1064–1065
Critical-care nursing:
art of, 3–5
burn, art of, 5
cardiovascular, art of, 3–4
competence in, assessment of, 5–6
concepts of physical assessment in, 253–307

Critical-care nursing (*Cont.*):
  continuing education in, 6
  death by chance or choice and, 7
  defense mechanisms and, 466–467
  educational barrier in, 6
  fragmentation of care and, 7
  future of, 7–8
  image of, 6
  medical-surgical, art of, 5
  nature of, 1064
  neurological-neurosurgical, art of, 4
  newborn, art of, 5
  nurse-physician relationship in, 7
  obstetrical, art of, 5
  pediatric, art of, 5
  psychosocial basis of, 321–359
  pulmonary, art of, 4
  renal, art of, 4–5
  research in, 7–8
  science of, 5–6
  separation of nursing education and practice in, 6
  spirit of, 6–7
  team approach and, 7
  technical versus professional preparation for, 6
  technology and life-saving techniques in, 7
Critical-care unit, conflict-producing problems in, 1066
Critical opening pressure, 21
Critical-unstable patient, application of physical assessment techniques to, 309–311
  abdomen in, 311
  blood pressure in, 310
  case history in, 309
  heart rate in, 310–311
  observation in, 310
  peripheral perfusion in, 311
  renal function in, 311
  respiration in, 311
  sensorium in, 311
Critically ill:
  care of, holistic approach to, 9–12
  spiritual concerns of, 1060–1063
Crohn's disease, 720–722
  continent internal pouch for, 728–729
  ileostomy for, 724–728
  (*See also* Ileostomy)
  nursing intervention in, 723–724
Cromolyn sodium in asthma therapy, 513
Crust, *266*
Cryptococcus neoformans in sepsis, 830
Cryptorchid testis, surgery for, 691–692

Crystalloid solutions in ARDS management, 493
Cuff size in indirect pressure measurement, 1002
Cul-de-sac of Douglas, 242
Cultural disability in trauma victim, 817
Culture in diagnosis of sepsis, 838
Curling's ulcer:
  in burned children, prevention of, 894
  postburn, prevention of, 767
Current, electrical, 1038, *1039*
  leakage, hazards from, 1040–1041
Cushing-Rotikansky ulcer, postcraniotomy, in child, management of, 901
Cushing triad in assessing transtentorial herniation, 610
Cushing's syndrome from glucocorticoid excess, 139–140
Cutaneous anaphylaxis, 458
Cutaneous fistulas, 714–718
  diagnosis of, 715–716
  nursing intervention in, 716–718
  pouching of, 717–718
Cuticle of nail, 218
Cyanide poisoning, histotoxic hypoxia in, 374
Cyanosis:
  in high-risk neonate, 872
  in hypoxemia, 24
  in physical assessment, 264
Cyclophosphamide:
  anticancer drug, *906*
  for kidney transplant recipient, 677
Cyst(s):
  cutaneous, *266*
  in nephron, 661
Cystic duct, 194
Cystine nephroliths, 663
Cystitis, postpartum, 864
Cystoscopy, 686–687
  complications of, 688–689
Cystostomy:
  percutaneous suprapubic, for acute urinary retention, 682
  suprapubic, 683–685
Cytomegalovirus in sepsis, 831
Cytotoxic drugs:
  altering host resistance to sepsis, 825
  hypoimmune state due to, 465
Cytotoxic reactions, *456,* 459–460
Cytotoxic T cells in immune response, 449
Cytoxan as anticancer drug, *906*

Dactinomycin, 1137–1138
Dalton's law of partial pressure, 16, 19, 363

Dartos of scrotum, 247
Dead space:
  alveolar, 16, 31
  anatomical, 16, 31
  physiologic, calculation of, 31
Deadline reaction in psychosocial assessment, 352
Death:
  of bone, local, 231
  by chance or choice in critical-care nursing, 7
Debridement in burn wound care, 782–783
Decadron:
  in intracranial hypertension management, 617
  to minimize extent of spinal cord trauma, 636
Decerebrate rigidity in assessment of comatose patient, 316
Decompression, surgical, in brain herniation management, 612
Decorticate rigidity in assessment of comatose patient, 316
Decubitus ulcer:
  in critical-care patients, *317*
  prevention of, in burn care, 769
Deep pain in assessment of sensory system, 299
Defecation, mechanism of, 205
Defenses:
  host, acquired, 443–455
  natural, 437
  (*See also* Natural defenses)
Defibrillation:
  in advance life support, 919–921
  electrical, 920
  procedure for, 921
Defibrillators, 920, 1029–1030
Defibrination, 93
Deformities of musculoskeletal system, 235
Deglutition, 182, *183*
Dehydration in diabetic ketoacidosis, 644–645
Dehydroepiandrosterone, 141
Demineralization, skeletal, from vitamin D excess, 223
Dendrites, 101
Dentate ligaments, 105
Deoxyribonuclease, 193
Dermatomes, 117
Dermis:
  anatomy of, 213
  functions of, 213
  innervation of, 214–216
  physiology of, 213–216
  sebaceous glands in, 216
  vascular network of, 213–214
Desensitization, 459

Desmopressin acetate, 1150
Desoxycorticosterone in adrenal crisis management, 653
Detergent in tubbing solution for burn care, 788
Developmental experiences in psycho-sociodynamics of sick role, 351
Dexamethasone:
  in adrenal crisis management, 653
  in intracranial hypertension management, 617
  to minimize extent of spinal cord trauma, 636
Dextran in balloon pumping, 940
Dextran 40, 1150–1151
Dextrostix for blood glucose determination, 642, *643*
Diabetes insipidus, 662
  inadequate ADH secretion in, 135–136
  nephrogenic, 662
Diabetes mellitus, 143–144
  altering host resistance to sepsis, 825
  complicating obesity, 734
  long-term complications of, 650
  stress, in burn patient, 767
Diabetic endocrine crises, 641–650
Diabetic ketoacidosis:
  comparison of, with hyperosmolar hyperglycemic nonketotic coma, *649*
  complications of, 646–647
  Kussmaul's respirations in, 263
  management of, 646
  monitoring in, 645–646
  pathophysiology of, 644
  recognition of, 644–645
Diabetic nephropathy, pathogenesis of, 660–661
Diabetic patient, critically ill, management of, 641–644
  blood glucose determinations in, 642, *643*
  caloric intake in, 642–643
  drugs inducing hyperglycemia in, 643–644
  infection and thromboembolic phenomena in, 644
  insulin in, 644
Diabetogenic hormone, growth hormone as, 132
Dialysis, 669–673, 971–979
  basic components of, 971–973
  definition of, 971
  in fluid therapy for burns, 757–758
  indications for, 972
  peritoneal, 669–671, 973–976
    (*See also* Peritoneal dialysis)
  principles involved in, 972–973

purposes of, 971–972
types of, 973
  (*See also* Hemodialysis)
Diaphragm:
  dysfunction of, 627–628
  traumatic injuries to, management of, 810
Diaphragmatic hernia:
  congenital, in neonate, 885–886
  in high-risk neonate, 870
Diaphysis of long bones, 221
Diarrhea, 205
  in Crohn's disease, 721
  in ileostomate, 726
  in renal disease, 666
Diastix for urine sugar testing, 642, *643*
Diastole, extra heart sounds heard in, 290
Diastolic murmurs, 291
Diastolic pressure, 70
  augmentation of: by intra-aortic balloon pump, 933–934
  reduction of afterload with, by circulatory assistance devices, 928
Diathesis, hemorrhagic, in DIC, 594–595
Diazepam, 1151
  in status epilepticus treatment, 621
Diazoxide for hypoglycemia, 650
Dicumarol, 1152
Diencephalon, 110
  transtentorial herniation syndromes at, *606*
Diets, elemental, 738
  in Crohn's disease treatment, 721
  in ulcerative colitis treatment, 722
Diffusion:
  abnormalities of, in hypoxemia, 385–387
  in capillary dynamics, 49
  in dialysis, 972
  in fluid and electrolyte transport, 395
  passive, in renal system, 155–156
Digestive tract (*see* Gastrointestinal tract)
Digitalis:
  effects of, on ventricular contractility, 570
  intoxication from, atrial pacing for, 573–575
  in treatment of sepsis, 844–845
Digitoxin, 1152–1153
Digoxin, 1153
  in congenital diaphragmatic hernia management in neonate, 886
  in treatment of sepsis, 844–845
1,25-Dihydroxycholecalciferol:
  renal production of, effects of parathormone on, 138

in vitamin D metabolism, 223
Dilantin in status epilepticus treatment, 621–622
2,3-Diphosphoglycerate (2,3-DPG):
  effect of, on oxygen-hemoglobin affinity, 25
  in oxygen transport, 85
  synthesis of, increased, in anemia, 584
Diphtheria, motor disorders from, *635*
  prevention of, 634
Direct pressure measurements, monitor for, 1004–1021
Disability in psychosociodynamics of sick role, 350–351
Discoid lupus erythematosus in critical-care patients, *318*
Disk(s):
  intercalated, in myocardium, 57
  intervertebral, 105
Dismemberment, victims of, spiritual concerns of, 1063
Disopyramide phosphate, 1153–1154
Disorientation in patient on mechanical ventilation, 964
Displays:
  instruments for, 1021–1024
  numeric, for medical instrumentation, 1032
Disseminated intravascular coagulation, 593–596
  clinical assessment of, 594–595
  complicating leukemia, 589, 590
  etiology of pathophysiologic process of, 593–594
  in missed abortion, 856
  nursing implications of, 596
  treatment of, 595–596
Diuretic phase of acute renal failure, 658
Diuretics:
  in acute renal failure management, 668
  in potassium regulation, 407
  in treatment of sepsis, 847
Dobutamine, effects of, on ventricular contractility, 571
Doca in adrenal crisis management, 653
Döderlein's bacillus in vagina, 243
Doll's-eye maneuver in assessing transtentorial herniation, 608–609
Donor site for skin graft, care of, 793–794
Donors, organ, potential, trauma victims as, 815–816
Dopamine:
  in congenital diaphragmatic hernia management in neonate, 886

Dopamine (*Cont.*):
  effects of, on ventricular contractility, 570–571
  in treatment of sepsis, 845
Dopamine hydrochloride, 1154–1155
Doppler flowmeter in hemorrhagic shock treatment, 699
Dorsal columns, 623
Douglas, cul-de-sac of, 242
Doxorubicin as anticancer drug, *906*
Drainage:
  of cutaneous fistulas, 716–717
  postural, for lung abscess, 506–507
Drainage phase in peritoneal dialysis cycle, 974–975
Dressings:
  care of, for total parenteral nutrition, 984–985
  change of: in burn care, 789–790
    procedure for, 779–782
Dribbling, urinary, 307
Drowning, near, 501–502
Drug(s), 1137–1179
  overdose of: acute hemorrhagic pneumonitis due to, 535–536
    management problems in, 536
  reactions to, in critical-care patients, *318*
  side effects of, complicating mechanical ventilation, 968
Drug therapy:
  altering host resistance to sepsis, 825
  in cardiac resuscitation, 921–922
Duct(s):
  cystic, 194
  of exocrine pancreas, 191–192
  genital, 248
  Skene's, 243–244
  of Wirsung, 191–192
Dumping syndrome after gastrectomy, 720
Duodenum:
  distention of, effect of, on gastric motility, 190–191
  gross anatomy of, 197
  traumatic injuries to, management of, 810
  ulcers of, in renal disease, 665
  water absorption in, 202
Dura, spinal, 105
Dura mater, 105
Durant's maneuver in air embolus management, 524
Dwarfism, 234
  from insufficient growth hormone, 132
Dye dilution technique for measuring cardiac output, 1021–1022
Dysglobulinemia, 95

Dyspnea:
  in asthma, 510
  in atelectasis, 533
  in closed pneumothorax, 530
  in differential diagnosis of unstable cardiac patient, 544
Dysrhythmias, 1103–1136
  complicating mechanical ventilation, 968
  complicating surgery with extracorporeal circulation, 954
  in hypothermia, 992
  recognition of, in advanced life support, 919
  (*See also* Arrhythmias)
Dysuria, 307

Ear(s):
  assessment of, 269
  burns of, care of, 785, *786*
Ecchumosis, *268*
Eccrine sweat glands, 217
Echocardiographic monitoring of unstable cardiac patient, 557, 558
Eclampsia, management of, 860
Ecology, definition of, 9
Ecosystem, definition of, 10
Edema, 399–401
  brain, increased intracranial pressure due to, 614
  causes of, 49
  cerebral, complicating diabetic ketoacidosis, 647
  in diabetic nephropathy, 661
  postcraniotomy, in child, management of, 901
  pulmonary: cardiogenic, 498
    in critical-care patients, *319*
    in myocardial infarction, physical findings in, *314*
    in renal disease, 665
    in sepsis, 834
  in renal disease, 307
Edrophonium chloride for myasthenia gravis, 632–633
Education:
  continuing, for critical-care nurse, 6
  of family, facilitation of, critical-care nurse in, 480–481
  of patient, facilitation of, critical-care nurse in, 480–481
Effector T cells in immune response, 449
Efferent fibers of central nervous system, 102
Effusion:
  pericardial, in renal disease, 665
  pleural, 507–509
Egophony, 282

Einthoven's triangle in electrocardiography, 42
Ejaculation, 246–247
Ejection clicks, 290
Ejection murmurs, 291
Elastin fibers in dermis, 213
Electrical conduction, normal, in cardiovascular system, 38–40
Electrical defibrillation, 920
Electrical safety, 1038–1041
Electrocardiogram (ECG):
  and arterial pressure waveform, correlation of, *1011*
  in assessment of unstable cardiac patient, 546
  monitor for, 999–1001
Electrocardiogram telemetry in ECG monitor, 1001
Electrocardiography, 40–42
Electrodes:
  in ECG monitor, 999–1000, *1001*
  placement of, in defibrillation, 920
Electrodynamics, altered, in hypothermia, 995
Electrolytes:
  absorption of, by small intestine, 202
  balance of: effects of kidney disease on, 663–664
    in homeostasis, 171
  in body fluids, 390–391, *392*
  imbalance of, effect of, on ventricular contractility, 76
  loss of, in small intestinal obstruction, 708
  measurement of, in assessment of unstable cardiac patient, 547
  replacement of, in cutaneous fistula management, 715
  requirements for, 396–397
  in total parenteral nutrition solution, 982
  metabolic significance of, 986
  transport of, 395–396
Electromechanical dissociation, drug therapy for, 922
Electrons, 1038, 1039
Electrophysiologic monitoring of unstable cardiac patient, 548–551, *552*, *553*
Elemental diets, 738
  in Crohn's disease treatment, 721
  in ulcerative colitis treatment, 722
Elimination, hygiene for, in burn care, 769
Embolectomy, pulmonary, in pulmonary thromboembolism therapy, 522
Embolism:
  air: complicating hemodialysis, 673
    for total parenteral nutrition, 983–984
  amniotic fluid, 864

Embolus(i):
  acute occlusive mesenteric ischemia
      from, 704–705
  air, 523–524
  complicating pulmonary artery pres-
      sure monitoring, prevention of,
      1014
  fat, 524–526
      (*See also* Fat embolus)
  gas, 523–524
  pulmonary, postpartal, 864
Emergency, cardioversion, procedure
    for, 921
Emission, 246
Emotional cutoff in illness, 350
Emotional shock wave in psychosocial
    assessment of family adjustment,
    352
Emotional status, assessment of,
    292–293
Emotional subsystem of individual, 10
  implications of, for critical-care
      nurse, 11
Emotional support given by critical-
    care staff, 346
Emotional trauma in burned toddler,
    894
Emphysema, 516–518
  barrel chest in, 278–279
  in critical-care patients, *319*
  diagnostic findings of, 516–517
  hypoxemia in, 386
  pathophysiology of, 516
  psychosocial aspects of, 517–518
  treatment of, 517
Emulsification in fat digestion, 201
Encephalopathy, hepatic, 200
Endochondral ossification, 224
Endocrine changes in host response to
    sepsis, 832–833
Endocrine crises, nondiabetic,
    650–655
  adrenal crisis as, 652–654
  hypercalcemic crises as, 654–655
  thyroid crises as, 650–652
Endocrine pancreas, 143–145, 206
Endocrine system, 125–148
  disorders of, 641–655
      diabetic, 641–650
  effects of kidney disease on, 668
  [*See also* Hormone(s); *and specific
      glands; e.g.,* Pancreas; Thyroid
      gland]
Endometrium of uterus, 241
Endoscopic surgery, urologic, 686–689
Endoscopy:
  in diagnosis of gastrointestinal hem-
      orrhage, 701
  in location and treatment of esopha-
      geal varices, 703

Endothelial cells:
  damage to, DIC due to, 594
  in wound healing, 219
Endotoxemia, definition of, 821
Endotracheal intubation:
  in ARDS management, 493
  in cardiac arrest, 916
  in emphysema therapy, 517
Energy:
  conservation of, in critical-care nurs-
      ing, 11
  selection of, in defibrillation,
      920–921
  sources of, for muscular contraction,
      229–230
Enteritis, regional, 720–721
Enterobacter in sepsis, 828
Enterocutaneous fistulas, 714–715, 717
Environment:
  critical-care, 343–348
      instrumentation in, 999–1034
          (*See also* Instrumentation)
      psychological hazards in,
          1044–1046
      safety in, 1037–1046
          (*See also* Safety)
      (*See also* Critical-care milieu)
  of infection control unit for burn pa-
      tients, 762–763
  management of, by critical-care
      staff, 345
Environmental factors in external psy-
    chological disequilibrium,
    338–339
  avoidance of, nursing intervention in,
      341
Enzymes:
  intestinal: in digestion of carbohy-
      drates, 199
      in digestion of proteins, 200
  lysosomal, release of, in sepsis, 832
  pancreatic, 192–193
Eosinophils, 86
Ependymoma in school-age child, 901
Epidermis, physiology of, 212–213
Epididymis in sperm transport, 248
Epidural technique for intracranial
    pressure monitoring, 1020
Epinephrine:
  in asthma therapy, 514
  in regulation of peripheral regula-
      tion, 69
  secretion of: by adrenal medulla,
      141–142
      increased, in sepsis, 833
  in treatment of sepsis, 845
Epiphyseal plate cartilage, bone
    growth in, 224
Epiphyseal plates, reaction of, to acute
    disorders and injuries, 234

Epiphysis, 147
  of long bones, 221
Epithelial surfaces in defense system,
    438–440
Epithelium:
  of esophageal mucosa, 183
  of gastrointestinal mucosa, 181
  respiratory, in defense system, 439
  vaginal, 242
Epithelization in wound healing,
    219–220
Epstein-Barr virus in sepsis, 831
Equilibration phase in peritoneal di-
    alysis cycle, 974
Equilibrium, psychological, 331–341
    (*See also* Psychological equilib-
    rium)
Equipment for pediatric patients, 879
Erb's point in palpation of heart, 285
Ergonovine maleate, 1155
Erythema in physical assessment,
    264
Erythrocytes, 84–85
  injury to, DIC due to, 594
  life span and removal of, 85
  maturity of, clinical consideration of,
      85
  production of: increased, in anemia,
      584
  regulation of, 83–84
Erythromycin lactobionate for injection,
    1155
Erythromycin sterate, 1156
Erythropoiesis, 83–84
  control of, 82
Erythropoietin, 175
  in erythrocyte production regulation,
      83–84
Escape beats, ventricular, 1126
Escape rhythms, ventricular, 1126
Eschar, 763
Escharotomy, grid, 783
Escherichia coli:
  in colon, 205
  in sepsis, 828
Esophageal atresia in neonate,
    882–884
Esophageal obturator airway in cardiac
    arrest, 916, *917*
Esophageal varices, 183
  gastrointestinal hemorrhage second-
      ary to, 701–703
Esophagojejunostomy, total gastrec-
    tomy with, for Zollinger-Ellison
    syndrome, 719
Esophagus, 183–185
  function of, regulation of, 184–185
  gross anatomy of, 183
  histology of, 183–184
  motility of, 184

Esophagus (*Cont*):
  traumatic injuries to, management of, 810
Estrogens:
  effects of: on female, *244*
    on vagina, 242
  ovarian, 146–147, 244
Ethacrynate sodium for injection, 1156
Ethacrynic acid, 1156–1157
Ethical issues in critical care, 1055–1059
Ethylenediaminetetraacetate (EDTA) for hypercalcemic crisis management, 655
Eubacteria in sepsis, 829
Eunuchoidism from testosterone deficiency, 147
Eupneic breathing, 262, 263
Examination:
  ophthalmoscopic, 273–274
  physical, in diagnosis of sepsis, 835–836
  in physical assessment, 260–264
    general appearance in, 260–261
    position of patient in, 260
    vital signs in, 261–264
Excision, tangential, in burn wound debridement, 783, *784*
Excitation-contraction coupling in myocardium, 58–59
Excoriation, *267*
Excursion, respiratory, assessment of, 280
Exercise in burn care, 769–770
Exit block, 1108–1109
Exocrine pancreas, 191–193
  enzymes of, 192–193
  gross anatomy of, 191
  histology of, 191, *193*
  secretions of, 192–193
  regulation of, 193
Exophthalmic goiter in Graves' disease, 137
Exophthalmos in Graves' disease, 137
Experiences, developmental, in psychosociodynamics of sick role, 351
Expressed consent, 1052
External body ventilators, 959
External pressure circulatory assist, 943–944
Extracellular fluid:
  and bone: exchange of magnesium between, in magnesium regulation, 414
    exchange of phosphate between, in phosphate regulation, 419
  calcium deficiency in, 413–414
  calcium excess in, 412
  chloride deficiency in, 418–419

chloride excess in, 417–418
  and intracellular fluid, exchange of phosphate between, in phosphate regulation, 419–420
  magnesium deficiency in, 416–417
  magnesium excess in, 414–416
  organic acids in, 422–423
  phosphate deficiency in, 420–421
  phosphate excess in, 420
  potassium deficit in, 409–410
  potassium excess in, 407–409
  protein deficiency in, 422
  sodium deficit in, 405–406
  sodium excess in, 404–405
  volume of: deficient, 401–402
    excessive, 398–399
    regulation of, 66
      antidiuretic hormone secretion, 134
Extracerebral motor loss:
  first-level management of, 633–634
  life-threatening effects of, 625–633
  third-level nursing management in, 634–638
Extracerebral motor pathways, 622–623
Extracorporeal circulation, 949–954
  cold cardioplegic, for myocardial preservation, 953
  concept of bypassing heart and lungs in, 950–953
  history of, 949–950
  mechanical anatomy of, 950, 951
  in myocardial preservation, 953
  pharmacology of, *952*
  physiology of, 950–953
  postoperative complications of, 953–954
  temperature control in, 953
Extracorporeal membrane oxygenation, 502–504
  cannulation sites for, *502*
  management of, 503–504, *505*
  patient selection for, 503
  in pulmonary thromboembolism therapy, 522
  results of, 504
  technique for, 502–503
Extrapyramidal system in motor integration of nervous system, 119
Extremity(ies):
  amputation of: in adolescent, significance of, 903–904
    for osteogenic sarcoma in adolescent, 904–905
  examination of, in trauma victim, 802
  lower, motor system of, assessment of, 296, *297*
  upper: motor system of, assessment of, 295, *296*

polyneuropathy of, loss of airway protection in, 626
Extrinsic coagulation system, 92
  assessment of, 591–592
Exudates, pleural effusions as, 508
Eye(s):
  assessment of, 271–275
  burns of, care of, 784–785
  movements of: assessment of, 273
    in assessment of comatose patient, 316
    in assessment of transtentorial herniation, 608–610
  problems of, application of physical assessment techniques to, 316
  traumatic injuries to, management of, 807–808
Eye signs in assessing transtentorial herniation, 608–610
Eyelashes, assessment of, 271
Eyelids, assessment of, 271

Face:
  assessment of, 269
  burns of, care of, 783–785
Facial nerve (VII):
  anatomy of, 111, *112*
  assessment of, 293–294
  type and functions of, *113*
Failure, expectancy of, in critical-care patient, 474
Fallopian tubes, 239
Falx cerebelli, 105
Falx cerebri, 105
Family:
  acceptance of critical illness by, fostering, critical-care nurse in, 481
  adjustments of, in psychosocial assessment of patient and family, 351–355
  assessment of, as learner, 1082–1083
  coping mechanisms of, in psychosocial assessment of family adjustment, 354–355
  crisis for, from critical illness, 478
  in critical-care milieu, 347–348
  and critical-care nurse, interpersonal needs of, 475–478
  education of: facilitation of, critical-care nurse in, 480–481
    about hypothermia therapy, 995
  as elusive entity, 472–473
  functioning of, 472–473
  functions of, aspects of interpersonal relationships and, 472–473
  learning by, evaluation of, 1086–1088

Family (*Cont.*):
　in pediatric critical-care unit,
　　880–881
　psychosocial assessment of,
　　349–358
　psychosocial effects of high-risk
　　neonate on, 868–869
　readiness of, to learn, assessment
　　of, 1084–1085
　roles and developmental levels of, in
　　psychosocial assessment of
　　family adjustment, 353–354
　roles in, reallocation of, due to criti-
　　cal illness, 474
　support for, fostering of, critical-care
　　nurse in, 479–480
　teaching of: effects of: beneficial,
　　　1071
　　　detrimental, 1072
　　programs for, 1072–1099
　　　(*See also* Teaching of patient
　　　and family, programs for)
　of trauma victim, care of, 817–818
Fasciculations in renal disease, 667
Fat(s):
　absorption of, by small intestine,
　　200–202, *203*
　digestion of, bile salts in, 194–
　　195
　effect of, on lower esophageal
　　sphincter, 185
Fat cells, functions of, 217
Fat embolus, 524–526
　clinical features of, 525–526
　management of, 526
　origin of, 524
　pathophysiology of, 525
Fatty acids:
　free, elevated, in myocardial infarc-
　　tion, 575
　in total parenteral nutrition solution,
　　metabolic significance of,
　　986–987
Feedback:
　positive, in coagulation mechanism,
　　97
　in psychological equilibrium,
　　332–333
Feedings, tube: for burn patient, 768
　elemental diets for, 738
Femoral arteries, palpation of, 304
Femoral vein as entry site for total par-
　enteral nutrition, 982
Fertilization, 239
Fetus:
　lie of, transverse, management of,
　　860–861
　position of: maladaptive, manage-
　　ment of, 860–861
　　posterior, management of, 860

presentation of: breech, manage-
　　ment of, 861
　brow, management of, 860
　face, management of, 861
Fibers, muscle, 229
Fibrillation, 231
　atrial, *288*, 1116
　ventricular, 1128
　　drug therapy for, 922
　　reversing, 919–921
Fibrin stabilizing factor, *93*, 96
Fibrinogen, 92–93
Fibrinogen-activating factor, 91
Fibrinogenopenia, 93
Fibrinolysis, 98
　increased, in DIC, 595
Fibrinolytic forces in coagulation
　mechanism, 98–99
Fibrinous pleuritis in renal disease,
　665
Fibroblast(s):
　in dermis, 213
　in wound healing, 219
Fibrocartilaginous callus in fracture re-
　pair, 232
Fibrocyte in dermis, 213
Fibrosis:
　interstitial, hypoxemia in, 385–386
　radiation, 498
Fick technique for measuring cardiac
　output, 1021
Filiforms, van Buren, for dilating ure-
　thral strictures, 681–682
Filtration:
　in capillary dynamics, 49
　in dialysis, 972
　in fluid and electrolyte transport, 396
　glomerular, in urine formation,
　　158–160
Filtration fraction, 159
Financial implications of critical illness
　for family, 477–478
First aid for severe burns, 748, 752
First-degree heart block, 1129–1130
Fissure(s), *267*
　of cerebral hemispheres, 110
　lobar, *276, 277*
Fistula(s):
　arteriovenous, for hemodialysis, 672,
　　977, *978*
　cutaneous, 714–718
　　(*See also* Cutaneous fistulas)
　tracheoesophageal: in high-risk neo-
　　nate, 870
　　in neonate, 882–884
Fixation, skeletal, for fracture reduc-
　tion, 813
Flail chest, 529–530
　in trauma victim, management of, 809
Floating ribs, 275

Flora:
　colonic, 205–206
　skin, 218–219
Florinef in adrenal crisis management,
　653
Flucytosine, 1157–1158
Fludrocortisone acetate in adrenal cri-
　sis management, 653
Fluid(s):
　in acute pancreatitis therapy, 732,
　　733
　in adrenal crisis management, 653
　balance of: in homeostasis, 169–170
　　maintenance of, in treatment of
　　　sepsis, 843–844
　　skin in, 211
　body: amount and distribution of,
　　390, *392*
　　composition of, 396, *397*
　　electrolyte composition of,
　　　390–391, *392*
　　osmolality of: definition of,
　　　391–392
　　　regulation of, 392–395
　　pH of: functions of, 423
　　　regulation of, 423–425
　　tonicity of, definition of, 391
　in burn therapy, 753–758
　　in acute period, 755–756
　　care of intravenous catheter site
　　　in, 756
　　for children, 892–893
　　in emergent period, 753–755
　　monitoring urinary output in,
　　　756–758
　　titration of, 754–755
　in cutaneous fistula management,
　　715
　daily intake and output of, 396
　in diabetic ketoacidosis manage-
　　ment, 646
　extracellular (*see* Extracellular fluid)
　in hemorrhagic shock treatment, 699
　for high-risk neonate, 871
　in hyperosmolar hyperglycemic non-
　　ketotic coma management, 648
　interstitial, excessive accumulation
　　of, 399–401
　in intestinal obstruction treatment,
　　709
　intracellular, and extracellular, ex-
　　change of phosphate between,
　　in phosphate regulation,
　　419–420
　intravenous, in parenteral alimenta-
　　tion, 737
　need for, in sepsis, 834
　in peritonitis treatment, 711–713
　in pulmonary contusion manage-
　　ment, 528–529

Fluid(s) (*Cont.*):
  reabsorption of, by colon, 205
  regulation of, in acute renal failure
    management, 668
  replacement of, in ARDS manage-
    ment, 493
  requirements for, 396–397
  synovial, of joint, 226–227
  transport of, 395–396
5-Fluorocytosine, 1157–1158
Fluoroscopic monitoring of unstable
  cardiac patient, 557–558
Flutter, atrial, *288*, 1115
Foley catheter(s), 678
  balloon of, inability to deflate, 683
  in trauma victim management, pro-
    cedures for, 804
Follicle-stimulating hormone (FSH),
  131
  in menstrual cycle, 245
  in reproductive activity in female,
    238
  in sperm production, 247, 248
Follicles, ovarian, growth of, 238–239,
  240
Foramen magnum of skull, 103
Foramen of Monro, 105, 107
Foramina of skull, 103
Foreign bodies altering host resistance
  to sepsis, 824
Fourchette, 243
Fracture(s):
  bone: fragments of, blood supply to,
    time required for bone fracture
    healing and, 233
    initial displacement of, time re-
      quired for bone fracture heal-
      ing and, 233
    repair of, 232–233
    uncomplicated, time required
      for, 233
    unsatisfactory, 233–234
    site and configuration of, time re-
      quired for bone fracture heal-
      ing and, 233
  cervical, airway problems in, 798
  of jaw, airway problems in, 798
  mandibular, in trauma victim, man-
    agement of, 808
  in trauma victim, management of,
    813–814
Frank-Starling law of heart in control of
  stroke volume, 75
Frank-Starling phenomenon and myocardial contraction, 59
Free fatty acids, elevated, in myocardial infarction, 575
Fremitus, tactile, in palpation of chest,
  280
Frequency, urinary, 307

Frontal lobe of cerebral cortex, func-
  tions of, 117, *119*
Functional residual capacity, reduced,
  in ARDS, 488
Fundic glands, 186
Fundus:
  of stomach, 186
  of uterus, 240
Fungal infections, delayed hypersensi-
  tivity and, 462–463
Fungal septicemia complicating TPN,
  988–989
Fungemia in burn patient, 766
Fungi in sepsis, 829–830
Funnel breast, 279
Furosemide, 1158
  for hypercalcemic crisis manage-
    ment, 654
  in treatment of sepsis, 847

Gait in assessment of motor system,
  298
Gallbladder, 194
  traumatic injuries to, management of,
    811
Gallop rhythms, 62, 290
  ventricular, in assessment of unsta-
    ble cardiac patient, 545
Gardner Wells tongs in trauma victim
  management, procedures for,
    804–805
Gas(es):
  blood, nervous system control of,
    26–30
  in colon, 206
  concentration of, changes in, effects
    of, on effusion, 20
  distribution of, in ventilation, 18
  respiratory: diffusion of, 18–20
    transportation of, 23–26
Gas embolus, 523–524
Gas exchange, tests of, in evaluating
  ARDS, 490–491
Gas laws, 15–16
Gastrectomy, total, with esophagojejunostomy for Zollinger-Ellison syndrome, 719
Gastric glands, 186
Gastric inhibitory peptide (GIP), 143
Gastric phase of hydrochloric acid secretion, 189
Gastric reflux, control of, 184–185
Gastrin:
  effect of, on gastric motility, 190
  functions of, 188–189
  in regulation of gastric phase of hy-
    drochloric acid secretion, 190
  in regulation of lower esophageal
    sphincter, 184–185

  secretion of, 145
Gastritis, gastrointestinal hemorrhage
  secondary to, 703–704
Gastrocolonic reflex, function of, 204
Gastroesophageal sphincter, 184
Gastroileal reflex, function of, 199
Gastrointestinal tract, 179–207
  complications of mechanical ventila-
    tion involving, 968
  Crohn's disease affecting, 720–729
  disorders of, 697–738
    nutrition during, 736–738
  effects of kidney disease on,
    665–666
  effects of spinal cord injury and
    polyneuropathy on, 630–631
  histology of, 181–182
  mucosa of: in defense system, 439
    ischemia of, in sepsis, 834
  obesity affecting, 733–736
  pancreatitis affecting, 731–733
  physiologic effects of hypothermia
    on, 993
  response of, to burns in child, 891
  sclerosing cholangitis affecting,
    729–731
  topography of, *180*
  upper: disorders of, acute, manage-
    ment of, 697–718
    hemorrhage in, 697–704
      (*See also* Hemorrhage, gastroin-
      testinal)
  Zollinger-Ellison syndrome affecting,
    718–720
  (*See also specific segments; e.g.,*
    Esophagus; Stomach)
Gastroschisis in neonate, 884–885
Gay-Lussac's law, 15
Genetics of immune response,
  454–455
Genital ducts, 248
Genitalia:
  external: of female reproductive sys-
    tem, 242–244
    of male reproductive system,
      245–247
  female, assessment of, 307
  internal: of female reproductive sys-
    tem, 237–242
    of male reproductive system,
      247–249
  male, assessment of, 306–307
Genitourinary reflexes, 124
Genitourinary system(s):
  disorders of, 678–695
    catheters and, 678–682
    [*See also* Catheter(s), urinary]
    genitourinary trauma as, 693–695
    open urologic surgery for,
      689–692

Genitourinary system(s) (*Cont.*):
  disorders of: in spinal cord injury
     and disease, 692–693
    urinary diversion for: permanent,
      685–686
      temporary, 683–685
    urinary incontinence as, 695
    urologic emergencies as, 682–
      683
    urologic endoscopic surgery for,
      686–689
  effects of kidney disease on, 668
  examination of, in trauma victim, 802
  female, assessment of, 306–307
  male, assessment of, 306–307
  mucosa of, in defense system, 440
  trauma to, 693–695
    management of, 812
Genogram in psychosocial assessment
  of family adjustment, 353, *354,*
  356–357
Gentamicin in burn therapy for children, 893
Gentamicin sulfate, 1158–1159
Gibbs-Donnan equilibrium in capillary
  dynamics, 48–49
Gigantism:
  from excessive growth hormone, 132
  pituitary, 234
Gland(s):
  acinar, in pancreas, 191–192
  adrenal, 139–142
    surgery of, 690–691
  Bartholin's, 243–244
  Brunner's, 197–198
  cardiac, 186
  Cowper's, 249
    in emission, 246
  fundic, 186
  gastric, 186
  male reproductive, 248–249
  parathyroid, 138
    effects of kidney disease on, 666,
      667
  pineal, 147
  pituitary, 129–136
    ovaries and hypothalamus, rela-
     tionships between, 245
  prostate (*see* Prostate gland)
  pyloric, 186
  salivary, 182
  sebaceous, 216
  sweat, 217
  thyroid, 136–138
    (*See also* Thyroid gland)
  vulvovaginal, 243–244
Glans penis, 245
Glasgow coma scale, 602, 603–*604,*
  605
Glial cells, 101

Glioma, brainstem, in school-age
  child, 901
Glisson's capsule, 207, 211
Globulin(s):
  Ac, *93,* 95
  antilymphocyte, for kidney transplant
    recipient, 677
  $Rh_0(D)$ immune, 1174
  serum, 82
Glomerular filtration rate, 159–160
Glomerular filtration in urine formation,
  158–160
Glomerulonephritis, poststreptococcal,
  acute pathogenesis of, 660
Glomerulopathies, pathogenesis of,
  660
Glomerulotubular balance in sodium
  regulation, 403
Glomerulus, 152
Glossopharyngeal nerve (IX):
  anatomy of, 111, *112*
  assessment of, 294
  type and functions of, *113*
Glucagon, 144–145
  gastrointestinal functions of, 206
  secretion of, increased, in sepsis,
    833
Glucocorticoids, 139–140
  for hypercalcemic crisis, 655
Gluconeogenesis in sepsis, 833
Glucose:
  in hyperosmolar hyperglycemic non-
    ketotic coma management, 648
  intolerance to, in renal disease,
    664
  intravenous, for hypoglycemia, 650
  with potassium and insulin, in treat-
    ment of sepsis, 845
  reabsorption of, in urine formation,
    162–163
  in total parenteral nutrition solution,
    metabolic significance of,
    985–986
Glucose-insulin-potassium solution in
  myocardial infarction therapy,
  575–576
Glutamic-oxaloacetic transaminase
  (SGOT), serum levels of, in assessment of unstable cardiac patient, 547
Glycerol in intracranial hypertension
  management, 616
Glycogenolysis, increased, in sepsis,
  833
Glycosuria in total parenteral nutrition,
  985
Gonadotropins, 131
Gonads, 145–147
  location of, *126*
Good Samaritan Law, 1052

Goodpasture's syndrome, pathogen-
  esis of, 660
Grafting of skin, 791–794
  (*See also* Skin, grafting of)
Granulocytes:
  polymorphonuclear, 85
  transfusions of, in aplastic anemia
    treatment, 585
Granulocytosis, 87
Granuloma, oil, 498
Granulomatous colitis, 720–721
Granulomatous ileitis, 720–721
Graves' disease, 137
Groin, assessment of, 306–307
Ground substance:
  in bone matrix, 224
  of dermis, 213
Grounding for electrical system, 1040
Growth:
  decreased, due to disorders and in-
    juries of epiphyseal plates, 234
  follicular, 238–239, *240*
  increased, due to disorders and in-
    juries of epiphyseal plates, 234
  torsional, due to disorders and inju-
    ries of epiphyseal plates, 234
Growth hormone (GH), 132–133
  functions of, 132
  secretion of, 132–133
Guillain-Barré syndrome:
  loss of airway protection in, 626
  respiratory musculature dysfunction
    in, 628–629
  steroids for, 637
Gyrus(i):
  of cerebral hemispheres, 110
  hippocampal, functions of, 117

Hageman factor, *93,* 96
Hair, 217–218
  changes in, in physical assessment,
    268
  growth of, 218
  scalp, in burn care, 787
  terminal, 217–218
  vellus, 217
Hair end organs in dermis, functions
  of, 215
Hairy areas, burns of, care of, 786–787
Hand, burns of, splinting for, 771,
  772–773
Hartmann's solution in burn therapy,
  754
Haustra of colon, 203, *204*
Haversian systems of mature bone,
  222–223
Hazard(s):
  definition of, 1037
  electrical, prevention of, 1038–1041
  mechanical, 1041–1042

Hazard(s) (*Cont.*):
  microshock, 1041
  new technology and, 1037–1038
  nosocomial infection as, 1042–1044
  psychological, in critical-care envi-
      ronment, 1044–1046
Head:
  edema of, postcraniotomy, in child,
      management of, 901
  examination of, in trauma victim, 801
  injury to: acute hemorrhagic pneu-
      monitis due to, 535–536
    closed, patient with, application of
        physical assessment tech-
        niques to, 315–316
    increased intracranial pressure
        due to, 614
    management of, 806–807
    problems in, 536
Healing:
  of fractures, unsatisfactory, 233–234
  of wounds, 219–220
Health history:
  in physical assessment, 253–257
  relationship of, to physical assess-
      ment and laboratory assess-
      ment, 257
Heart, 52–62
  apex of, 283
  atria of, 53
  auscultation of, 285–286
  base of, 283
  bypassing, concept of, in extracor-
      poreal circulation, 950–953
  circulation through, 55–57
  compression of: closed-chest: auto-
      matic, in cardiac arrest, 918
      manual, in cardiac chest, 917
    direct: by circulatory assistance de-
        vices, 928
      devices for, historical evolution
          of, 931–932
  conduction in, disturbances of: clini-
      cal assessment of, 571–572
    management of, 572–575
  cycle of, 59–61
  defects of, congenital, in high-risk
      neonate, 873
  disease of, patient with, spiritual
      concerns of, 1060–1061
  examination of, 284
  failure of: congestive: in assessment
      of myocardial infarction, 312,
      314
      effect of, on ADH secretion,
          134–135
    high-output, in thyrotoxicosis, 137
    in high-risk neonate, 872
  functional anatomy of, 53–55
  inspection of, 284–285, *286*

massage of: in air embolus manage-
    ment, 524
  closed-chest, in resuscitation of
      neonate, 866
mechanical, in treatment of sepsis, 847
metabolism in, disturbances of,
    575–576
murmurs in, 290–291
  diastolic, 291
  systolic, 291
output of (*see* Cardiac output)
palpation of, 285, *286*
percussion of, 285
pericardium of, 55
physical assessment of, 283–291
rate of, 287
  in Apgar scoring, 865
  in assessment of shock patient,
      310–311
  control of, 73–76
  disturbances of: clinical assess-
      ment of, 571–572
    management of, 572–575
rhythm of, 287, *288*
  in assessment of shock patient,
      310–311
  gallop, 290
sounds of, 61–62
  extra, 289–291
    diastolic, 290
    systolic, 290
  first, 287–288
  fourth, 290
  normal, 287–289
  second, 288–289
  third, 290
Starling's law of, 926
stimulation of, in sepsis, 833
traumatic injuries to, management of,
    809–810
valves of, 53
ventricles of, 53–55, 283
(*See also* Myocardium)
Heart block:
  atrial pacing for, 573
  complete, complicating surgery with
      extracorporeal circulation, 954
  drug therapy for, 922
  first-degree, 1129–1130
  second-degree, *288*, 1131–1132
  third-degree, *288*, 1133
Helicine arteries of penis, 245–246
Hematemesis in gastrointestinal hem-
    orrhage, 699
Hematocrit, 80
Hematologic system, physiologic ef-
    fects of hypothermia on, 993
Hematoma(s):
  extradural, in trauma victim, man-
      agement of, 807

postpartum, 862–863
retroperitoneal, in trauma victim,
    management of, 812
subdural, increased intracranial
    pressure due to, 613–614
wound, postcraniotomy, in child,
    management of, 901
Hematopoiesis, 82–84
Hematopoietic system, 79–100
  disorders of, 579–596
    patient with: assessment of,
        579–581
      general approach to, 579–581
  functions of, 79
  (*See also* Blood; Coagulation; He-
      matopoiesis; Plasma)
Hematuria, 307
  in trauma victim, evaluation of, 802
Hemispheres:
  cerebellar, 111
  cerebral, anatomy of, 109–110
Hemocytoblast as origin of blood cells,
    82
Hemodialysis, 671–673, 976–979
  advantages of, 977, *978*
  in burn therapy, 757–758
  care of vascular accesses in, 672
  complications of, 673, 979
  contraindications to, 977
  definition of, 977
  disadvantages of, 977, *978*
  initiating, 977–978
  kinetics of, 671–672
  nursing care components of, 979
  patient care during, 673
  (*See also* Dialysis)
Hemodynamic monitoring of unstable
    cardiac patient, 552–557
Hemodynamics, altered, in hypother-
    mia, 995
Hemoglobin:
  affinity of, for oxygen, 368–371
    increased, hypoxia from, 374
  oxygen bound to, transport of,
      23–25
  oxygen-carrying capacity of, 368
  in oxygen transport, 85
  reduced, 24
  transport of, by erythrocytes, 84
Hemoglobin saturation, 23–24
Hemolytic anemia, 587–588
  clinical assessment of, 587
  etiology of pathophysiologic process
      of, 587
  nursing implications of, 588
  treatment of, 587–588
Hemolytic uremic syndrome in pre-
    schooler, 894–898
  medical treatment of, 896
  nursing management of, 896, 898

Hemolytic uremic syndrome in preschooler (*Cont.*):
  pathophysiology of, 895–896, *897*
  systemic responses to, *897*
Hemophilia B, 96
Hemophilia C, 96
Hemopneumothorax, traumatic, in trauma victim, management of, 809
Hemorrhage:
  in abruptio placentae, 858
  complicating surgery with extracorporeal circulation, 953
  evaluation and treatment of, in first aid for burns, 752
  gastrointestinal: diagnosis of, 701
    esophageal varices in, 701–703
    in gastritis, 703–704
    in Mallory-Weiss syndrome, 704
    in peptic ulcer disease, 703
    in stress ulcers, 704
    treatment of, 699–701
    (*See also* Hemorrhagic shock)
  increased intracranial pressure due to, 613
  intracerebellar, in high-risk neonate, 875
  intracranial, in high-risk neonate, 874–875
  intraventricular, in high-risk neonate, 875
  in placenta previa, 857–858
  postcraniotomy, in child, management of, 901
  postpartum, 862–863
  rectal, complicating ulcerative colitis, 723
  splinter, in nails in physical assessment, 268, *269*
  subarachnoid: in high-risk neonate, 874–875
    in trauma victim, management of, 807
  subdural: acute, in trauma victim, management of, 807
    in high-risk neonate, 874
  traumatic, control of, 799–800
Hemorrhagic diathesis in DIC, 594–595
Hemorrhagic liver disease, 592
Hemorrhagic pneumonitis, acute: from drug overdose, 535–536
  from head injury, 535–540
Hemorrhagic shock, 697–701
  clinical evaluation of, *700*
  hypovolemic, 697, *698*
  treatment of, 699–701
Hemorrhoids in critical-care patients, *319*
Hemosiderin in synovial fluid, 226–227
Hemostasis, 99–100

altered, in renal disease, 664
platelets in, 89–90
in wound healing, 219
Hemothorax, 532–533
Henderson-Hasselbach equation in blood pH calculation, 26, *27*
Henle, loops of, 152
  concentration of urine in, 165–169
Henry's law, 16, *17, 23, 24*
Heparin:
  in ARDS management, 497
  in balloon pumping, 940
  in basophils, 87
  for consumption coagulopathy, 595, 596
  in dialysate, 673
  in pulmonary thromboembolism therapy, 501–523
  in treatment of sepsis, 847
Heparin sodium, 1159–1160
Hepatic artery in liver, 208
Hepatic encephalopathy, 200
Hepatocyte, 206, 209
  bile synthesis by, 194
  plasma protein synthesis in, 81
Herellea-Mima in sepsis, 828
Hernia:
  diaphragmatic, congenital: in neonate, 885–886
    in high-risk neonate, 870
  examination for, 306–307
Herniation:
  cerebellar, 611
  definition of, 600
  transtentorial, 600–610
    (*See also* Transtentorial herniation)
  uncal, 610
Herpes simplex in critical-care patients, *317*
Herpes simplex viruses in sepsis, 830–831
Herpes zoster in critical-care patients, *317*
Heterograft, 791, *792*
Hiccupping in renal disease, 667
Hippocampal gyrus, functions of, 117
Hirsutism in physical assessment, 268
His, bundle of, 287
Histamine:
  in basophils, 87
  in regulation of peripheral regulation, 69
  release of, in sepsis, 831–832
Histamine test, augmented, in diagnosis of Zollinger-Ellison syndrome, 718–719
Histiocytes:
  in dermis, 213
  in wound healing, 219
Histoplasma capsulatum in sepsis, 830

History:
  iin diagnosis of sepsis, 835
  medical: burn severity related to, 746
  of unstable cardiac patient, 545
Histotoxic hypoxia, 374–375, *376*
Holes, burr, in trauma victim management, procedures for, 805
Holism, definition of, 9
Holistic approach to care of critically ill, 9–12
Homeostasis:
  as feedback scheme, 332
  renal contributions to, 169–174
    acid-base balance in, 171–174
    electrolyte balance in, 171
    fluid balance in, 169–170
Homograft, 791, *792*
Hormone(s), 125–129
  adrenocorticotropic, 131
  antidiuretic, 134–136
    in autonomic nervous system, 122
    in regulation of body water, 398
    in regulation of osmolality of body fluids, 392–394
  diabetogenic, growth hormone as, 132
  follicle-stimulating, 131
  functional categories of, 127–129
  growth, 132
  inhibiting, 128
  of kidney, 174–176
  luteinizing, 131
  luteotropic, 132
  mechanisms of, action of, 127
  melanocyte-stimulating, 136
  ovarian, 244–245
  parathyroid: in plasma calcium concentration control, 223–224
    in vitamin D metabolism, 223
  peripheral, 128–129
    of anterior pituitary, 132–133
  polypeptide, 126
  in regulation of peripheral regulation, 69
  releasing, 128
  steroid, 126
  structural categories of, 125–127
  thyroid, functions of, 137
  tissue, 126
  tropic, 128
    anterior pituitary, 131–132
Horner's syndrome in assessment of comatose patient, 315
Hospitalization:
  for preschooler, significance of, 885
  for school-age child, significance of, 899
  for toddler, significance of, 887

Host:
  compromised, infections and, 438
  defenses of: acquired, 443–455
    impaired, in diagnosis of sepsis,
      835
    improvement of, therapy for, in
      treatment of sepsis, 842
    mechanisms of, enhancement of,
      in treatment of sepsis,
      841–842
    against sepsis, 822–826
      factors altering, 823–826
      reticuloendothelial system in,
        822–823
    responses of, to sepsis, 832–835
      endocrine, changes in, 832–833
      metabolic changes in, 833
      organ system changes in, 833–835
      systemic changes in, 832
      vasoactive substances in, 832
Humidification of airway in manage-
  ment of patient on continuous as-
  sisted ventilation, 960
Humoral immunity, 450
  B cell in, 446, *447*
Hunger, regulation of, 179–180
Hyaline lesion in diabetic nephropathy,
  660
Hyaluronic acid in synovial fluid, 226
Hydatidiform mole, management of,
  857
Hydralazine for low cardiac output, 568
Hydration, monitoring of, in diabetic
  ketoacidosis, 645
Hydrochloric acid, secretion of,
  186–187
  gastrin in, 188
  regulation of, 189
Hydrochlorothiazide, 1160–1161
Hydrocortisone:
  in adrenal crisis management, 653
  in treatment of sepsis, 846
Hydrogen ions:
  active tubular secretion of, 164
  concentration of: in body fluids:
    functions of, 423
    regulation of, 172–174, 423–425
  effect of, on ventilation, 28
  (*See also* pH)
  secretion of, in potassium regulation,
    406
Hydrogen peroxide in burn wound
  dressings, 779
Hydrostatic pressure:
  in dialysis, 972
  glomerular filtration rate and,
    158–159
  in venous system, 50
Hydrotherapy:
  in burn care, 787–789

  contraindications to, 787
  indications for, 787
  principles of, 787
  room for, cleanup of, 790
  solution used for, 787–788
Hydrothorax, 508
25-Hydroxycholecalciferol in vitamin D
  metabolism, 223
Hygiene in burn care, 769
Hymen, 243, 244
Hyperaldosteronism, 140–141
Hyperalimentation:
  in cutaneous fistula management,
    715–716
  parenteral, hyperosmolarity due to,
    136
  peripheral, 736–737
Hyperbilirubinemia, neonatal, 875–
  876
Hypercalcemia, 412
  effect of, on ventricular contractility,
    76
  in parathormone excess, 138, 224
  signs and symptoms of, *432*
Hypercalcemic crises, 654–655
Hypercalcinuria from vitamin D excess,
  223
Hypercapnia in asthma, 512
Hyperchloremia, 417–418
  signs and symptoms of, *433*
Hyperdynamic septic shock, 833, 836
Hyperemia, reactive, in autoregulation
  of peripheral circulation, 65
Hyperexcitability, neuromuscular, in
  parathormone insufficiency, 138
Hyperfibrinogenemia, 92–93
Hypergastremia in Zollinger-Ellison
  syndrome, 718
Hyperglobulinemia, 95
Hyperglycemia:
  complicating TPN, 986
  in diabetes, 144
  drugs inducing, in diabetic patient
    management, 643–644
Hyperglycemic crises, 644–647
Hyperimmune response pathology,
  455–464
Hyperkalemia, 407–409
  effect of, on ventricular contractility,
    76
  signs and symptoms of, *432*
Hypermagnesemia, 414–416
  signs and symptoms of, *433*
Hypernatremia, 404–405
  signs and symptoms of, *433*
Hyperosmolar hyperglycemic nonketotic coma, 647–648, *649*
  complicating, TPN, 986
  management of, 648
  recognition of, 648

Hyperosmotic agents in intracranial
  hypertension management,
  616–617
Hypernatremia in renal disease, 664
Hyperphosphatemia, 420
  signs and symptoms of, *434*
Hyperpnea, 262, *263*
Hyperreflexia, autonomic, in spinal
  cord injury, 693
Hypersensitivity:
  to cold in hypothermia, 995
  complex-mediated, *457*, 460–461
  cytotoxic, 459–460
  delayed-type, *457*, 461–463
Hypersensitivity reactions, 455,
  456–457, 458–464
Hypertension, 263
  complicating obesity, 734
  in diabetic nephropathy, 661
  intracranial, 612–620
    (*See also* Intracranial pressure, in-
    creased)
  in myocardial infarction, reduction
    of, 570
  in polycystic renal disease, 661
  portal, 208
    esophageal varices, 701
  in pregnancy, 859–860
  pulmonary, in pulmonary throm-
    boembolism, 519
  pulmonary venous, 565–567
  in renal disease, 664–665
  renoprival, 176
  renovascular, 659
  treatment of, in acute renal failure
    management, 669
Hyperthermia:
  postcraniotomy, in child, manage-
    ment of, 901
  in spinal cord injury and poikilother-
    mia, 630
Hyperthyroidism, 137
  thyrotoxic crisis in, 651–652
Hypertonic agents in brain herniation
  management, 611–612
Hypertrichosis in physical assessment,
  268
Hypertriglyceridemia in renal disease,
  664
Hyperuricemia, uric acid calculi in,
  663
Hyperventilation:
  in asthma, 512
  central neurogenic, is assessing
    transtentorial herniation,
    607–608
  in intracranial hypertension manage-
    ment, 616
  in sepsis, 837

Hyperviscosity syndrome, 581–584
  clinical assessment, 582
  etiology of pathophysiologic process of, 581–582
  nursing implications of, 583–584
  treatment of, 582–583
Hypervolemia, 398–399
  signs and symptoms of, *431*
Hypocalcemia, 413–414
  complicating plasmapheresis for hyperviscosity syndrome, 583
  in high-risk neonate, 873
  signs and symptoms of, *432*
Hypochloremia, 418–419
  signs and symptoms of, *433*
Hypodynamic septic shock, 833–834, 836
Hypofibrinogenemia, 93
Hypoglossal nerve (XII):
  anatomy of, 111, *112*
  assessment of, 295
  type and functions of, *113*
Hypoglycemia, 648–650
  complicating diabetic ketoacidosis, 647
  complicating TPN, 986
  in diabetes, 144
  after gastrectomy, 720
  in high-risk neonate, 873
  in insulin excess, 144
  recognition of, 648–649
  treatment of, 649–650
Hypoimmune responses, 464–466
Hypokalemia, 409–410
  complicating diabetic ketoacidosis, 647
  signs and symptoms of, *432*
Hypokalemic nephropathy in Conn's syndrome, 141
Hypomagnesemia, 416–417
  signs and symptoms of, *433*
Hyponatremia, 405–406
  in renal disease, 663–664
  signs and symptoms of, *433*
Hyponychium of nail, 218
Hypoperfusion, pulmonary, in origin of ARDS, 487
Hypopharyngeal sphincter, 184
Hypophosphatemia, 420–421
  from parathyroid hormone excess, 224
  signs and symptoms of, *434*
Hypophysis, 129–136
  (*See also* Pituitary gland)
Hypoproteinemia, 422
Hyposensitization, 459
  in asthma therapy, 513
Hyposmia, 293
Hypotension, 263
  complicating hemodialysis, 673

complicating mechanical ventilation, 968–969
Hypothalamus:
  anatomy of, 115
  and anterior pituitary, hormonal relationships between, *133*
  in autonomic function, 121–122
  ovaries and pituitary gland, relationships between, 245
  and periphery, hormonal relationship between, *129*
  and pituitary, hormonal relationships between, *129*
  in regulation: of antidiuretic hormone secretion, 134
    of growth hormone secretion, 131–133
    of hunger and satiety, 179–180
    of oxytocin secretion, 134
    of thyroid hormone secretion, 137, *138*
Hypothermia, 991–996
  accidental, 991
  classification of, 992
  clinical methods for producing, 993
  cooling dynamics in, 992
  drug-induced, 991
  elective, 991
  with extracorporeal circulation, 953
  moderate: clinical application of surface cooling for achieving, 993–995
    nursing interventions during, 995–996
    patient needs during, 995–996
  in near-drowning victim, 501
  nursing concepts of, 991–992
  overview of, 991
  physiologic effects of, 992–993, *994*
  in renal disease, 664
  secondary to health disorders, 991
  in spinal cord injury and poikilothermia, 630
Hypothyroidism, 137
  myxedema coma in, 652
Hypotrichosis in physical assessment, 268
Hypoventilation in hypoxemia, 377–379
Hypovolemia, 401–402
  complicating plasmapheresis for hyperviscosity syndrome, 583
  in low preload, 564
  signs and symptoms of, *431*
  in trauma victim, management of, 799–800
Hypovolemic hemorrhagic shock, 697, *698*

Hypoxemia, 32
  arterial, in pulmonary thromboembolism, 519
  in asthma, 512
  in atelectasis, 533
  in closed pneumothorax, 530
  definition of, 364
  of fat emboli, 525
  in kyphoscoliosis, 509
  mechanical ventilation for, 960
  in near drowning, 501
  in oxygen toxicity, 500
  pathophysiology of, 375–387
    aerohypoxia in, 376–377
    diffusion abnormalities in, 385–387
    hypoventilation in, 377–379
    shunting in, 382–385
    ventilation/perfusion abnormalities in, 379–382
  in pulmonary contusion, 528
Hypoxemic hypoxia, 372–373, *375*
Hypoxia, 31–32
  acute: in drug overdose, 535
    in head injury, 535
  anemic, 373–374, *375*
  in ARDS, 489
  cerebral: in drug overdose, 535
    in head injury, 535
  circulatory, 374, *375*
  definition of, 364
  effect of, on platelet levels, 89
  histotoxic, 374–375
  hypoxemic, 372–373, *375*
  from increased hemoglobin affinity of oxygen, 374
  pathophysiology of, 372–375
  renal, stimulating release of erythropoietic factor from kidneys, 175
  stagnant, 374, *375*
  tissue, assessment of, *373*

Iatrogenic drug-induced hyperimmunologic injury, 463
Icterus, scleral, in critical-care patients, *317*
Idiopathic respiratory distress syndrome (IRDS), 869–870
IgA, secretory, in defense system, 439
IgE in asthma, 510
Ileal conduit for urinary diversion, 685
Ileitis, granulomatous, 720–721
Ileostomy, 724–728
  in ulcerative colitis therapy, 723
Ileum, gross anatomy of, 197
Ileus:
  in critical-care patients, *319*
  paralytic, 708, 710
    in sepsis, 834

Illness:
in internal psychological disequilibrium, 334–336
avoidance of, nursing intervention in, 339–340
stress of, for family from critical illness, 475–477
Immobilization, psychological disequilibrium due to, 338–339
Immune defenses, 443–444
Immune response, 437, 449–451
genetics of, 454–455
Immunity:
cell-mediated, 450–451, 461–463
T cell in, 446, *447*, 461
humoral, 450
B cell in, 446, *447*
lymphocytes in, 88
natural, support of, in postburn infection control, 762
physiology of, 453–454
stress and, 465–466
Immunocytes, 88
Immunoglobulin in immune defense mechanisms, 445
Immunologic enhancement, 462
Immunologic memory, 444
Immunosuppressive drugs altering host resistance to sepsis, 825
Impaction in critical-care patients, *319*
Impedence pneumography in respiratory rate monitoring, 1025
Implied consent, 1052
Impotence:
complicating transurethral resection of prostate, 689
penile prostheses for, 692
Incontinence:
complicating transurethral resection of prostate, 689
urinary, 307, 695
Indicator dilution technique in measurement of cardiac output, 73
Indirect pressure measurement:
automatic, 1004
monitor for, 1000–1004
Individual, subsystems of, 10
implications of, for critical-care nurse, 10–11
Infant (*see* Neonate)
Infarction(s):
myocardial (*see* Myocardial infarction)
right ventricular, hypovolemia in, 564
Infection(s):
in arteriovenous fistula, prevention of, 978
in burn wound, 763–765
complicating ARDS, 497
complicating balloon pumping, 943

complicating burns in children, 891
complicating diabetic ketoacidosis, 647
complicating leukemia, 589–590
complicating renal transplantation, 677
and compromised host, 438
control of, in burn care, 761–766
antimicrobials in, 762
elimination of reservoirs of infection in, 762
support of patient's natural immunity in, 762
suppression of infection transfer channels in, 762
unit for, planning and maintaining, 762–765
delayed hypersensitivity and, 462–463
destruction of articular cartilage due to, 234
in diabetic patient management, 644
localized decrease in growth due to, 234
nosocomial, 1042–1044
complicating mechanical ventilation, 967–968
postpartal, 863–864
procedures or situations predisposing to, in diagnosis of sepsis, 835
protection against, skin in, 211
pulmonary, control of, in burn patient, 761
symptoms in diagnosis of sepsis, 835
treatment of, in treatment of sepsis, 839–841
(*See also* Sepsis)
Inflammation:
chronic, localized increase in growth due to, 234
in defense system, 440
neutrophilia in, 86
Inflammatory response:
in host defense against sepsis, 823
in wound healing, 219
Informed consent, 1053
Infusion pumps, 1030–1031
Inhibiting hormone, 128
Innervation, cutaneous, 214–216
Inorganic ions, reabsorption of, in urine formation, 161–162
Inorganic substances of bone, 223–224
Inotropic agents:
effect of, on ventricular contractility, 570–571
in treatment of sepsis, 844–845
Inphos for hypercalcemic crisis management, 655

Insertion phase in peritoneal dialysis cycle, 974
Inspection:
in assessment of unstable cardiac patient, 545
of heart, 284–285, *286*
in physical assessment, 258
Instrumentation:
in critical-care environment, 999–1034
parameter acquisition, 999–1029
capnograph in, 1026, *1027*
for cardiac output, 1021–1025
cerebral function monitor in, 1028–1029
for direct pressure measurements, 1004–1021
for electrocardiogram, 999–1001
for indirect pressure measurement, 1002–1004
mass spectrometer in, 1026–1027
oximeter in, 1026, *1028*
for pulse, 1001
for respiratory volume, 1025–1028
respiratory waveforms in, 1027–1028
for temperature, 1002
recording and display, 1031–1034
therapeutic, 1029–1031
Insulators, electrical, 1039
Insulin, 143–144
deficiency of, consequences of, 644, *645*
in diabetic ketoacidosis management, 646
in diabetic patient management, 642
gastrointestinal functions of, 206
for glucose intolerance in total parenteral nutrition, 985
glucose with potassium and, in treatment of sepsis, 845
in hyperosmolar hyperglycemic nonketotic coma management, 648
Integrity of skin in physical assessment, 265–268
Integumentary system, 211–220
(*See also* Skin)
Intellectual performance, assessment of, 292
Intellectual subsystem of individual, 10
implications of, for critical-care nurse, 11
Intensive Care Unit in care of trauma patient, 814–817
(*See also* Trauma, management of, ICU care in)
Interactional approach to patient and family, 349–350
Intercalated disks in myocardium, 57

Intercostal muscles, dysfunction of, 627–628
Interferon in defense system, 442–443
Intermediate pituitary (pars intermedial), 136
Intermittent mandatory ventilation (IMV):
  in ARDS management, 494–496
  in emphysema therapy, 517
  in flail chest management, 529–530
  in waning from mechanical ventilation, 966–967
Intermittent positive pressure breathing in prevention of postburn wet-lung syndrome, 760
Interpersonal competence, 473–475
Interpersonal framework, 473–478
Interpersonal needs, 475–478
Interpersonal relationships, 472
  dynamics of, 471–481
  and family functions, aspects of, 472–473
  nursing implications for, 478–481
Interrole relationships, 472
Interstitial-cell stimulating hormone in testosterone production, 247–248
Interstitial fibrosis, hypoxemia in, 385–386
Interstitial fluids, excessive accumulation of, 399–401
Intervertebral disk, 105
Intestinal phase of hydrochloric acid secretion, 189
Intestines:
  in calcium regulation, 410
  effect of, on gastric motility, 190
  inflammatory disease of, 720–729
    continent internal pouch for, 728–729
    Crohn's disease as, 720–722
      (See also Crohn's disease)
    ileostomy for, 724–728
      (See also Ileostomy)
    nursing intervention in, 723–724
    ulcerative colitis as, 722–723
      (See also Ulcerative colitis)
  ischemia of, 704–708
    mesenteric, 705–706
    nursing responsibilities in, 707–708
  large, 203–206
    flora of, 205–206
    gross anatomy of, 203–204
    histology of, 204
    motility of, 204–205
    secretion and absorption by, 205
      (See also Colon)
  in magnesium regulation, 414
  obstruction of, 708–710
    in Crohn's disease, 721

diagnosis of, 709
nursing implications of, 710
treatment of, 709–710
perforation of, complicating ulcerative colitis, 723
in phosphate regulation, 419
small, 196–202
  absorption in, 199–202
  gross anatomy of, 197
  histology of, 197, *198*
  mechanical obstruction of, 708
  motility of, 198–199
  secretions of, 197–198
  traumatic injuries to, management of, 811
  (See also specific segments; e.g., Duodenum; Ileum; Jejunum)
Intoxication, digitalis, atrial pacing for, 573–575
Intra-aortic balloon, insertion of: preparation for, 938, 939
  procedure for, 938–940
Intra-aortic balloon pump:
  for afterload reduction, historical evolution of, 930, *931*
  complications of, 942–943
  contraindications to, 937
  indications for, 934–937
  nursing care for, 938–943
  physiologic effects of, 933–934
  weaning from, 942
Intra-aortic balloon pumping:
  timing of, 941
  in treatment of sepsis, 847
Intra-aortic counterpulsation for low-output cardiac failure and shock, 568–569
Intracardiac route for intravenous lifeline, 918–919
Intracellular fluid and extracellular fluid, exchange of phosphate between, in phosphate regulation, 419–420
Intracellular mechanism of hormonal action, 127, *128*
Intracerebellar hemorrhage in high-risk neonate, 875
Intracranial hemorrhage in high-risk neonate, 874–875
Intracranial pressure:
  compensatory mechanisms in, 613
  increased, 612–620
    causes of, 613–615
    measurement of, 615–616
    medical therapy of, 616–617
    nursing activities causing, 618
    nursing care modifications for, 617–620
    pathophysiology of, 612–613
    patient activities causing, 618–619

increasing, in critical-care patients, *320*
  monitoring of, 1016, 1020–1021
    epidural technique for, 1020
    indications for, 1016
    intraventricular technique for, 1020
    risks associated with, 1021
    subarachnoid technique for, 1020, *1021*
    waveforms in, 1020–1021
  in neurologic evaluation of child, 899–900
Intracranial spaces, edema of, post-craniotomy, in child, management of, 901
Intralipids in parenteral alimentation, 737–738
Intramembranous ossification, 224
Intraocular pressure, assessment of, 274–275
Intrapartal and antepartal crisis, 855–862
  (See also Antepartal and intrapartal crises)
Intravascular coagulation in ARDS, 488
Intravenous catheter site, care of, in fluid therapy for burns, 756
Intravenous fluids in parenteral alimentation, 737
Intravenous lifeline, establishing and maintaining, 918–919
Intravenous lines in trauma victim management, procedures for, 803
Intraventricular hemorrhage in high-risk neonate, 875
Intraventricular technique for intracranial pressure monitoring, 1020
Intrinsic coagulation system, 92
  assessment of, 591
Intrinsic factor, functions of, 187–188
Intrinsicoid deflection, delayed, in hypothermia, 992, *993*
Intubation, endotracheal: in ARDS management, 493
  in cardiac arrest, 916
  in emphysema therapy, 517
Inulin, clearance of, in glomerular filtration rate determination, 160
Ions:
  bicarbonate, concentration of, in body fluids, regulation of, 172–174
  hydrogen (*see* Hydrogen ions)
  inorganic, reabsorption of, in urine formation, 161–162
  passive diffusion of, 155–156
Irradiation, hypoimmune state due to, 465
Irrigation of catheters, 679
Irritant receptors, 29

Ischemia:
  gastrointestinal mucosal, in sepsis, 834
  localized decrease in growth due to, 234
  mesenteric, 705–706
  myocardial: intra-aortic balloon pumping for, 936–937
    reduction of, 569–570
    ventricular contractility in, 570
  renal, increased erythropoietin levels in, 84
Ischemic colitis, 707
Islets of Langerhans, 143–145
  secretions of, 206
Isoetharine in asthma therapy, 514
Isograft, 791, *792*
Isolation, protective, in treatment of sepsis, 842
Isometric contraction, 230
Isoproterenol:
  in asthma therapy, 514
  hypoxemia due to, complicating mechanical ventilation, 968
  in treatment of sepsis, 845
Isoproterenol hydrochloride, 1161
Isosorbide dinitrate:
  for low cardiac output, 567–568
  for pulmonary venous hypertension, 565, 566
Isotonic contraction, 230
Isovolumetric component of ventricular systole, 60
Isovolumetric relaxation in left ventricular ejection, 61
Isthmus of uterus, 241

J wave in hypothermia, 992, 993
Jaundice:
  neonatal, 875–876
  in physical assessment, 264
  physiologic, normal, in neonate, 875
Jaw, fractured, airway problems in, 798
Jejunoileal bypass for obesity, 735–736
Jejunum, gross anatomy of, 197
Joint(s), 226–227
  freely movable, 226–227
  immovable, 226
  slightly movable, 226
  synchondrosis, 226
  syndremosis, 226
  synostosis, 226
  synovial, 226
    reaction of, to acute disorders and injuries, 234–235
  synovial fluid of, 226–227

Joint capsule, reaction of, to acute disorders and injuries, 235
Junctional contraction, premature, 1117–1119
Junctional rhythm, 1120
Junctional tachycardia, 1121–1122
Juxtacapillary receptors, 29
Juxtaglomerular apparatus, 153, *154*
Juxtaglomerular cells, 153
  renin production in, 174
Juxtamedullary nephrons, 153, 155

K cells in immune response, 449
Kallikrein:
  in coagulation, 97
  in regulation of peripheral regulation, 69
Kanamycin sulfate, 1161–1162
Keratin, functions of, 212
Keratinization, 212
Kernicterus complicating neonatal hyperbilirubinemia, 876
Ketoacidosis, diabetic, 144, 644–647
  (*See also* Diabetic ketoacidosis)
Ketones, accumulation of, in diabetes, 144
Kidney(s):
  in acid-base balance regulation, 425, *426*
  ammonia generation in, 173, *174*
  anatomy: overview of, 151–155
    transfer of materials in, 155–158
  blood flow in: redistribution of, in sodium regulation, 403
    in sepsis, 834
  blood vessels of, control mechanisms of, 66
  in calcium regulation, 411
  in chloride regulation, 417
  complications of, extracorporeal circulation involving, 954
  concentration of urine in, in regulation of body water, 397–398
  congenital anomalies of, surgery for, 689–690
  contributions of, to homeostasis, 169–174
    (*See also* Homeostasis, renal contributions to)
  conversion of vitamin D in, 175–176
  dilution of urine in, in regulation of body water, 398
  disease of: classification of, 659
    in diabetic, 650
    effects of: on body systems, 663–668
      on calcium, phosphorus, vitamin D, parathyroid gland, and skeletal system, 666, *667*

      on cardiovascular system, 664–665
      on electrolyte and metabolic balance, 663–664
      on endocrine system, 668
      on gastrointestinal system, 665–666
      on genitourinary system, 668
      on integument, 667–668
      on nervous system, 666–667
    pathogenesis of, 659–663
      on pulmonary system, 665
    polycystic, pathogenesis of, 661–662
  disorders of, 657–677
  erythrocyte production in, 84
  erythropoietic activity of, 175
  failure of: acute, 657–658
    medical management of, 668–669
      altering host resistance to sepsis, 825
    chronic, 658
      medical management of, 669
    complicating leukemia, 589
    in spinal cord disorders, 693
    treatment modalities for, 668–669
      (*See also* Dialysis; Hemodialysis)
  function of, in assessment of shock patient, 311
  hormones of, 174–176
  in hyperviscosity syndrome, 582
  ischemia of, increased erythropoietin levels in, 84
  in magnesium regulation, 414
  open urologic surgery on, 689–690
  palpation of, 304–305
  pathophysiology of, introduction to, 657–659
  in phosphate regulation, 420
  physiologic effects of hypothermia on, 993
  response of, to burns in child, 890–891
  stones in, surgery for, 690
  transplantation of, 673–677
    care of donor in, 676
    care of recipient in, 676–677
    complications of, 677
    donor selection and preparation for, 675
    organ procurement for and preservation of, 674–675
    selection and preparation of recipient for, 674
    surgical procedure for, 675–676
  trauma to, 693–694
    management of, 812
  tumors of, surgery for, 690

Kimmelstiel-Wilson disease, 650
Kimmelstiel-Wilson lesion in diabetic nephropathy, 660
Kinins:
  in host defense against sepsis, 823
  in regulation of peripheral regulation, 69
Klebsiella in sepsis, 828
Korotkoff sounds in blood pressure measurement, 1002–1004
Kupffer cells:
  in host defense against sepsis, 822
  lining hepatic sinusoids, 209
  in phagocytosis, 442
Kussmaul's respirations, 263
Kyphoscoliosis, 279, 509
Kyphosis, 279

Labia majora, 243
Labia minora, 243
Labile factor, *93*, 95
Laboratory studies:
  in assessment of patient with hematopoietic disorders, 580–581
  in assessment, relationship of, to physical assessment, and health history, 257
  in diagnosis of sepsis, 836–838
  in trauma victim evaluation, 802–803
Lactate dehydrogenase (LDH), serum levels of, in assessment of unstable cardiac patient, 547
Lactated Ringer's solution in burn therapy, 754
Lactose intolerance, 199
Lamellae of mature bone, 222
Lamina propria of gastrointestinal mucosa, 181
Laminar flow in hemodynamics of circulation, 46
Langerhans, islets of, 143–145
  secretions of, 206
Lanugo, 217
Laplace, law of: in left ventricular ejection, 61
  in vascular system, 63
Laplace relationship and myocardial oxygen consumption, 57
Large intestine, 203–206
  [*See also* Intestine(s), large]
Lasix:
  for hypercalcemic crisis management, 654
  in treatment of sepsis, 847
Lavage(s):
  iced saline: in hemorrhagic shock treatment, 699
  for peptic ulcer bleeding, 703

peritoneal, trauma victim management, procedures for, 804
Leakage current, hazards from, 1040–1041
Left atrial-arterial bypass, 944–945
Left atrial pressure, monitoring of, direct, 1015
Left bundle branch block, 1135–1136
Left heart assist devices, 944–946
Left ventricular-arterial bypass, 945–946
Left ventricular filling pressure in assessment of preload, 563
Legal issues in critical care, 1055–1059
Length-tension relationship and myocardial contraction, 59
Lens, assessment of, 272
Leptomeninges, 105
Lethargic, definition of, 292
Leukemic crisis, acute, 588–591
  clinical assessment of, 588–589
  etiology of pathophysiologic process of, 589
  nursing implications of, 590–591
  treatment of, 589–590
Leukocytes, 85–89
  counts of, in diagnosis of sepsis, 836–837
  in wound healing, 219
Leukocytosis, 87
  neutrophilic, 87–88
Leukopoiesis, control of, 82–83
Levarterenol bitartrate, 1162
Levophed in treatment of sepsis, 846
Leydig cells in testes, 247
Lidocaine, effects of, on ventricular contractility, 571
Life:
  quality versus quantity of, issue of, 1057–1058
  sanctity of, 1056–1057
Life events in psychosocial assessment of family adjustment, 351–352
Life support:
  advanced, 913–922
    adjuncts to circulation in, 917–918
    adjuncts to ventilation in, 915–917
    defibrillation and synchronized cardioversion in, 919–921
    definitive therapy in, 921–922
    establishing and maintaining intravenous lifeline in, 918–919
    management of pre-arrest phase in, 914
    monitoring and dysrhythmia recognition in, 919
    stabilization of patient condition for transportation in, 922

basic, 914–915
  mechanical, external, 949–954
    (*See also* Extracorporeal circulation)
Life-threatening complications, patient with spiritual concerns of, 1061–1062
Life-threatening effects of extracerebral motor loss, 625–633
Lifesaving goals, nurses' responsibilities for, 1064–1065
Lifesaving techniques in critical-care nursing, 7
Ligament(s), 231
  dentate, 105
  reaction of, to acute disorders and injuries, 235
  of vertebral column, 105
Light, pupillary responses to, in physical assessment, 272
Limbic structures, functions of, 117
Linton tube for esophageal varices hemorrhage, 701
Lipase, pancreatic, 193
  in fat digestion, 200–201
Lipocytes, functions of, 217
Lipoid pneumonia, 498
Lipolysis in sepsis, 833
Lipolytic enzymes of exocrine pancreas, 193
Listeria monocytogenes in sepsis, 827
Liver, 206–210
  biliary system of, 206
  circulatory system of, 206–209
  cirrhosis of, 208
    effects of, on ADH secretion, 135
  connective tissue framework of, 206, 209–210
  disease of, hemorrhagic, 592
  failure of, altering host resistance to sepsis, 825
  functional anatomy of, 206–207
  gross anatomy of, 207
  hepatocyte of, 206, 209
  histology of, 207
  palpation of, 305
  percussion of, to determine size, 302
  protein degradation in, 200
  reticuloendothelial system of, 206, 209
  traumatic injuries to, management of, 811
Lobar fissures, *276*, *277*
Lobules, hepatic, 207
Loops of Henle, 152
  concentration of urine in, 165–169
Louis, angle of, 275
Lung(s):
  abscess of, 504–507
    clinical features of, 506
    pathophysiology of, 506

Lungs:
abscess of: (*Cont.*):
treatment of, 506–507
assessment of, 275–283
auscultation of, 281–283
adventitious sounds in, 282–283
breath sounds in, 281, *282*
voice sounds in, 281–282
blood vessels of, control mechanisms of, 66
bypassing, concept of, in extracorporeal circulation, 950–953
compliance of, reduced, in ARDS, 488–489
complications of extracorporeal circulation involving, 954
contusion of: clinical features of, 528
diagnosis of, 527
management of, 528–529
pathophysiology of, 526–527
in trauma victim, management of, 809
diseases of: effect of, on ADH secretion, 135
hypoventilation in, 377
disorders of: obstructive, 509–518
asthma as, 509–515
(*See also* Asthma)
chronic bronchitis as, 515
emphysema as, 516–518
restrictive, 504–509
kyposcoliosis as, 509
lung abscess as, 504–507
pleural effusion as, 507–509
edema of: in renal disease, 665
in sepsis, 834
effects of kidney disease on, 665
examination of, 278
functions of, altering host resistance to sepsis, 825–826
inspection of, 278–280
mechanics of, tests of, in evaluating ARDS, 491
metastasis of osteogenic sarcoma in adolescent to, 907
palpation of, 280
pathophysiologic changes in, correction of, in treatment of sepsis, 842–843
percussion of, 280–281
physiologic effects of hypothermia on, 993
pressure variations in, 21–23
problems of, application of physical assessment techniques to, 317, *319*
radiation fibrosis of, 498
secondary receptors in, 29
uremic, in renal disease, 665
wet, 486

postburn, prevention of, 760
(*See also* Respiratory distress syndrome, adult)
white, in pulmonary contusion, 527
Lung perfusion scan in diagnosis of pulmonary thromboembolism, 520
Lupus erythematosus, discoid, in critical-care patients, *318*
Luteinizing hormone (LH), 131
in menstrual cycle, 245
in reproductive activity in female, 238
in testosterone production, 247–248
Luteotropic hormone (LTH), 132
Lymph nodes, assessment of, 271
Lymphadenopathy, palpation for, in assessment of patient with hematopoietic disorders, 580
Lymphatic system in capillary dynamics, 49
Lymphatics:
of small intestine, 197
of vulva, 244
Lymphocytes, 88
B: circulation patterns of, 446, 448
defects of, in congenital hypoimmune conditions, 464
in immune response, 446, 449
count of, in diagnosis of sepsis, 836–837
T, 147–148
in cell-mediated immunity, 461
circulation patterns of, 446, 448
defects of, in congenital hypoimmune conditions, 464
identification of, 449
in immune response, 446, 449
in wound healing, 219
Lymphoid structures in reticuloendothelial system, 446
Lymphokins, 147
Lympholines in cell-mediated immunity, 450
Lymphoreticular system, immune response and, 437
Lysosomes, enzymes in, release of, in sepsis, 832

Macroglobulinemia, Waldenström's hyperviscosity in, 581–584
Macrophage phagocytosis in defense system, 441–442
Macrophages, 87
in cell-mediated immunity, 461
Macula densa, 153
in renin regulation, 175
Macule, *265*
Magnesium:
deficiency of, 416–417

excess of, 414–416
functions of, 414
regulation of, 414
Magnesium sulfate, 1163
to prevent convulsions in preeclampsia, 860
Mallory-Weiss syndrome, gastrointestinal hemorrhage secondary to, 704
Malnutrition:
in chronic occlusive mesenteric ischemia, 705
in cutaneous fistulas, 715
hypoimmune state due to, 465
Male reproductive system, 245–249
(*See also* Reproductive system, male)
Malignant melanoma in critical-care patients, *318*
Mal-union of fractures, 233
Mandible, fractures of, in trauma victim, management of, 808
Mannitol:
in intracranial hypertension management, 616–617
in treatment of sepsis, 847
Marey's law of heart, 74
Masculinization, adrenal androgens causing, 141
Mass spectrometer, 1026–1027
Massage, cardiac, in air embolus management, 524
Mast cells:
in anaphylactic reactions, 458
in dermis, 213
in wound healing, 219
Mastication, 182
Mastitis, management of, 863–864
Matrix of bone, 224
Maxillofacial area, traumatic injuries to, management of, 808
Meatus, urinary, 243
Mechanical assistance of heart in treatment of sepsis, 841
Mechanical safety, 1041–1042
Mechanical ventilation, 957–969
in ARDS management, 493–494
complications of, 967–969
continuous, management of patient receiving, 960–965
artificial airway in, 960
humidification of airway in, 960
physical therapy in, 963, *964, 965*
positioning in, 963
psychological considerations in, 964–965
suctioning of airway in, 960–961
ventilatory pattern in, 961–963
in emphysema therapy, 517

Mechanical ventilation Cont.):
  historical perspective on, 957–958
  indications for, 959–960
  principles of, 959
  roles and responsibilities of personnel in, 969
  weaning from, 965–967
Mechanical ventilators:
  classification of, 958–959
  external body, 959
  malfunctions of, 967
  pressure-cycled, 958–959
  volume-cycled, 958
Meconium aspiration in high-risk neonate, 870
Mediastinum, 277
Medical history:
  burn severity related to, 746
  of unstable cardiac patient, 545
Medical-surgical critical care, art of, 5
Medication for ileostomate, 726–727
Medulla, adrenal, 141–142
Medulla oblongata, 110
Medullary respiratory center, 27
Medulloblastoma in school-age child, 900–901
Megacolon, toxic, complicating ulcerative colitis, 723
Megakaryocytes, platelet formation in, 89
Meissner's corpuscle in dermis, functions of, 215
Meissner's plexus of gastrointestinal submucosa, 181
Melanin:
  function of, 212
  in hair, 217
Melanocyte-stimulating hormone (MSH), 136
Melanocytes, melanin production by, 212
Melanoma, malignant, in critical-care patients, *318*
Melanotropins, 136
Melatonin, 147
Melena in gastrointestinal hemorrhage, 699
Membrane(s):
  capillary, exchange across, 49
  mucous, integrity of, altering host resistance to sepsis, 823–824
  synovial, reactions of, to acute disorders and injuries, 235
Memory, immunologic, 444
Memory T cells in immune response, 449
Mendelson's syndrome, 497–498
Meninges, 105, *106*
Meningitis:
  bacterial, in high-risk neonate, 875

in critical-care patients, *320*
Menopause, 242
Menstrual cycle, ovarian-pituitary-hypothalamic regulation of, 245
Menstruation, 241–242
Meperidine hydrochloride, 1163–1164
Merkel's disks in dermis, functions of, 215
Mesenteric ischemia, 705–706
Mestinon for myasthenia gravis, 632, *633*
Metabolic acidosis, 425, 427
  in renal disease, 664
  in septic shock, 837–838
  signs and symptoms of, *431*
  in unstable cardiac patient, 560
Metabolic alkalosis, 427–428
  in sepsis, 837
  signs and symptoms of, *431*
Metabolic changes in host response to sepsis, 823
Metabolic functions altering host resistance to sepsis, 825
Metabolic management in total parenteral nutrition, 985–987
Metabolic system, physiologic effects of hypothermia on, 992
Metabolism:
  cardiac, disturbances of, 575–576
  effects of kidney disease on, 664
Metaproterenol in asthma therapy, 514
Metaraminol bitartrate, 1164
Methemoglobin, 23
Methicillin sodium for injection, 1164–1165
Methotrexate, 1165–1166
  for osteogenic sarcoma in adolescent, 905, *906*
Methylprednisolone in intracranial hypertension management, 617
Methylxanthines in asthma therapy, 514
Micelles:
  in fat digestion, 201
  formation of, 194
Microorganisms in sepsis, 826–831
  antibiotic resistance of, 826
  classification of, 827–831
  combinations of, 826
  fungi as, 829–830
  number of, 826
  parasites as, 831
  virulence of, 826
  viruses as, 830–831
Microphages, eosinophils as, 86
Microshock hazard, 1041
Midbrain, 110
  transtentorial herniation syndromes at, *606*
Milk ejection, oxytocin in, 134

Miller-Abbott tube in intestinal obstruction treatment, 709
Mineralocorticoids, 140–141
  in adrenal crisis management, 653
Mithramycin for hypercalcemic crisis, 655
Mitochondria in myocardium, 57
Mitral valve:
  functional anatomy of, 53
  regurgitation through: acute, intra-aortic balloon pumping, 935–936
  murmur of, 291
  stenosis of, opening snap of, 290
Mittelschmerz, 238
Mobitz heart block, 1131–1132
Moisture of skin in physical assessment, 264
Moniliasis in burn patient, 766
Monitoring:
  in advanced life support, 919
  blood pressure, direct, 1004–1021
    arterial, 1008–1009
    basic system for, 1004, *1005*
    bedside setup for pulmonary artery catheter in, 1014–1015
    catheter insertion for, 1009–1010
    indications for, 1009
    intracranial pressure in, 1016, 1020–1021
    invasive, 1004
    left atrial pressure in, 1015
    pressure amplifiers in, 1008
    pulmonary artery pressure in, 1012–1013
    pulmonary capillary wedge in, 1013–1014
    right atrial pressure in, 1014
    right ventricular pressure in, 1014
    risks of, 1014
    risks associated with vascular lines in, 1015–*1019*
    transducers in, 1004–1008
      (*See also* Transducers in direct blood pressure monitoring)
    waveform in, 1010, *1011, 1012*
  in diabetic ketoacidosis, 645–646
  in ICU care of trauma patient, 814
  intracranial pressure, 615–617, 1016, 1020–1021
    (*See also* Intracranial pressure, monitoring of)
  safety, for hypothermia, 996
  in sepsis, 838–839
  of unstable cardiac patient, 548–562
    (*See also* Cardiac patient, unstable, monitoring techniques for)

Monocytes, 87
  in wound healing, 219
Monro, foramen of, 105, 107
Monro-Kellie doctrine, 612
Mons pubis, 243
Morbidity of trauma, 817–818
Morphine sulfate, 1166
Mother and infant, bonding between: in
    critically ill newborn, 881–882
  with high-risk neonate, 868–869
Motility:
  gastric, 190–191
    regulation of, 190
  of small intestine, 198–199
Motor function, evaluation of, in as-
    sessing transtentorial herniation,
    602–606
Motor integration in nervous system,
    119–121
Motor system:
  assessment of, 295–298
    coordination in, 298
    gait in, 298
    muscle tone in, 296–298
  of lower extremities, assessment of,
    296, *297*
  of trunk, assessment of, 295
  of upper extremities, assessment of,
    295, *296*
Mouth, 182
  assessment of, 270
  in assessment of patient with hema-
    topoietic disorders, 580
  blood in, ariway problems in,
    798–799
  care of, in burn care, 769
MTX as anticancer drug, *906*
Mucin in saliva, 182
Mucosa:
  esophageal, 183
  gastrointestinal, 181
    in defense system, 439
    ischemia of, in sepsis, 834
  genitourinary, in defense system,
    440
Mucous, secretion of, by colon, 205
Mucous membranes, integrity of, alter-
    ing host resistance to sepsis,
    823–824
Mucus, production of, by cervix, 240
Multiple myeloma, 89
Murmurs, heart, 290–291
Muscle (s):
  bulbar, dysfunction of, management
    of, 637
  bulbocavernosus, 245
  burns of, care of, 785–786
  cramps in, in renal disease, 666–667
  effects of growth hormone on, 132
  intercostal, dysfunction of, 627–628

physiologic effects of hypothermia,
    on, 993
  respiratory, dysfunction of, 627–629
  skeletal, 227–231
    (See also Skeletal muscle)
  smooth (see Smooth muscle)
  strength and tone of, in assessment
    of transtentorial herniation,
    605–606
  supporting vagina, 242–243
  tone of: in Apgar scoring, *865*, 866
    in assessment of motor system,
    296–298
  weakness of, in renal disease, 666
Muscle tremor artifact in hypothermia,
    992–993
Muscularis externa:
  of esophagus, 184
  of gastrointestinal tract, 182
Muscularis mucosae of gastrointestinal
    mucosa, 181
Musculoskeletal system:
  deformities of, 235
  physiology of, 221–235
  tissues of, reactions of, to acute dis-
    orders and injuries, 231–235
  [See also Bone(s); Joint(s); Liga-
    ment(s); Muscle(s); Skeletal sys-
    tem; Tendon(s)]
Myasthenia gravis:
  critical evaluation of, *627*
  loss of airway protection in, 625–626
  respiratory musculature dysfunction
    in, 627–628
  special considerations in, 632–633
  treatment of, 632–633
Mycobacteria in sepsis, 829
Myelin sheath, 101
Myeloma, multiple, 89
Myenteric reflex in stimulation of peri-
    stalsis in small intestine, 199
Myocardial depressant factor, release
    of, in sepsis, 832
Myocardial infarction:
  arrhythmias in, 312, *313*
  assessment of, 312–314
  cardiogenic shock after, intra-aortic
    balloon pumping for, 934–936
  complicating surgery with extracor-
    poreal circulation, 954
  in diabetic, 650
  electrocardiographic changes in,
    546
  extent of injury in, assessment of,
    576
  free fatty acid elevation in, 575
  suspected, management of, 914
  therapy for, glucose-insulin-potas-
    sium solution in, 575–576
Myocardiopathy, catecholamine, 142

Myocardium:
  depression of: in drug overdose, 536
    in head injury, 536
  failure of, physiology of, 927
  function of, determinants of, 925–927
  ischemia of: intra-aortic balloon
    pumping for, 936–937
    reduction of, 569–570
    ventricular contractility in, 570
  preservation of, cold cardioplegic
    extracorporeal circulation in,
    953
  structure of, 57–59
  (See also Heart)
Myofibrils:
  in myocardium, 57–58
  of skeletal muscle cell, 227–228
Myometrium of uterus, 241
Myoneural junction neurologic lesions,
    624, 625
Myosin in sarcoplasm of skeletal mus-
    cle cell, 227
Myxedema, 137
Myxedema coma, 652

Nails, 218
  changes in, in physical assessment,
    268
Naloxone hydrochloride, 1166
Narcotics, side effects of, complicating
    mechanical ventilation, 968
Nasogastric tube:
  in intestinal obstruction treatment,
    709
  in peritonitis treatment, 712, 713
  in trauma victim management, pro-
    cedures for, 804
  triple-lumen, for esophageal varices
    hemorrhage, 701
  in Zollinger-Ellison syndrome treat-
    ment, 720
Nasopharynx, blood in, airway prob-
    lems in, 798–799
Natriuretic factor in renal sodium reab-
    sorption, 171
Natural defenses, 439
  epithelial surfaces in, 438–440
  inflammation in, 440
  phagocytosis in, 440–442
Nausea in diabetic ketoacidosis, 645
Neck:
  assessment of, 270–271
  edema of, postcraniotomy, in child,
    management of, 901
  examination of, in trauma victim, 801
  trauma to: airway problems in, 798
    management of, 808
Neck mucous cell in gastric gland,
    186

Neisseria gonorrhaeae in sepsis, 827
Neisseria meningitidis in sepsis, 807
Neomycin in burn wound dressings, 777, 779
Neomycin sulfate, 1167
Neonate:
  assessment of, 881
  critical care of, art of, 5
  high-risk, 864–877
    cardiovascular crisis in, 872–873
    chemical imbalances in, 873
    classification and evaluation of, 865–866
    hyperbilirubinemia in, 875–876
    neurological crisis in, 874–875
    psychosocial effects of, on family, 868–869
    respiratory crisis in, 869–870
    resuscitation of, 866
    sepsis, 877
    stabilization of, 866–867
    supportive management for, 870–872
    thermoregulation of, 867
    transport of, 867–868
  and mother, bonding between: in critically ill newborn, 881–882
    with high-risk neonate, 868–869
  with a surgical emergency, 881–886
    congenital diaphragmatic hernia, 885–886
    esophageal atresia as, 882–884
    gastroschisis as, 884–885
    omphalocele as, 884–885
    tracheoesophageal fistulas as, 882–884
Neostigmine for myasthenia gravis, 632, *633*
Nephrectomy, 690
Nephritis, postpartum, 864
Nephrogenic diabetes insipidus, 662
Nephrolithiasis, 662–663
  surgery for, 690
Nephrolithotomy, 690
Nephrology nursing, art of, 4–5
Nephron:
  anatomy of, 152–155
  cysts in, 661
  loss of, 658–659
Nephropathy:
  analgesic, pathogenesis of, 662
  diabetic, 650
    pathogenesis of, 660–661
  hypokalemic, in Conn's syndrome, 141
Nephrosis, effect of, on ADH secretion, 135
Nephrostomies, *684*, 685
Nerve(s):
  abducens (VI), assessment of, 293

acoustic (VIII), assessment of, 269, 294
buffer, in regulation of peripheral regulation, 68
cranial: anatomy of, 111–113
  assessment of, 293–295
    polyneuropathy of, loss of airway protection in, 626
facial (VII), assessment of, 293–294
glossopharyngeal (IX), assessment of, 294
hypoglossal (XII), assessment of, 295
oculomotor (III), assessment of, 293
olfactory (I), assessment of, 293
optic (II), assessment of, 293
spinal, anatomy of, 113–115
spinal accessory (XI), assessment of, 294
supplying dermis, 214–216
supplying penis, 246
trigeminal (V), assessment of, 293
trochlear (IV), assessment of, 293
ulnar, paresis of, complicating surgery with extracorporeal circulation, 954
vagus (X): assessment of, 294
  in regulation of cephalic phase of hydrochloric acid secretion, 189
  in regulation of lower esophageal sphincter, 184
  in regulation of pancreatic secretion, 193
Nervi erigentes, 246
Nervous system, 101–124
  anatomical divisions of, 101
  anatomy of, 115
  application of physical assessment techniques to, 318, *320*
  autonomic, physiology of, 121–123
  central (*see* Central nervous system)
  complications of extracorporeal circulation involving, 954
  in control of blood gases, 26–30
  effects of kidney disease on, 666–667
  parasympathetic: in control of ventricular contractility, 76
    effect of, on electrical conduction: in AV node, 39–40
      in SA node, 38
    in regulation of peripheral regulation, 68
  sympathetic: in control of ventricular contractility, 76–77
    effect of, on electrical conduction: in AV node, 39
      in SA node, 38
    on vascular smooth muscle, 63–64

Neuroglial cells, 101
Neurohypophysis, 110, 122, 133–136
  location of, *126*
  in storage and release of ADH, 155
Neurologic crisis in high-risk neonate, 874–875
Neurologic disorders, 599–638
  disrupting consciousness, 600–622
    brain herniation syndromes as, 600–612
    increased intracranial pressure as, 612–620
    seizures as, 620–622
  disrupting respiration, 622–638
    extracerebral motor pathways in, 622–623
    first-level nursing management of, 633–634
    life-threatening effects of, 625–633
    psychological care of alert, immobilized patient with, 637–638
    segmental organization in, 623–625
    third-level nursing management of, 634–638
  in hyperviscosity syndrome, 582
  myoneural junction, *624*, 625
  in school-age child, 899–903
    brain tumor as, 900–902
    central nervous system evaluation of, 899–900
    psychosocial aspects of, 899
    Reye's syndrome as, 902–903
  segmental, 623
  suprasegmental, 623, *624*
Neurologic functions in assessment of patient with hematopoietic disorders, 580
Neurologic-neurosurgical critical care, art of, 4
Neurologic system:
  examination of, in trauma victim, 800–801
  physiologic effects of hypothermia on, 992
Neuromuscular hyperexcitability in parathormone insufficiency, 138
Neuromuscular system:
  disease of, patient with, spiritual concerns of, 1061
  examination of, 292
  physical assessment of, 291–300
Neurons, 101, *102*
  impulse transmission in, 115, *117*
Neuropathy, peripheral, in renal disease, 666
Neurotransmitters, 115
Neutrophil phagocytosis in defense system, 440–441

Neutrophilia, 86
shifts to left and right in, 87–88
Neutrophils, 86
abnormalities of, 822–823
Nevi, pigmented, in critical-care patients, *318*
Newborn (*see* Neonate)
Nifedipine, effects of, on ventricular contractility, 571
Nitrates for pulmonary venous hypertension, 565
Nitrogen, partial pressures of, 19
Nitrogen mustard in pleural effusion management, 509
Nitrogen washout, effects of, on diffusion, 20, *21*
Nitroglycerin for pulmonary venous hypertension, 565–566
Nitroglycerin IV, 1167–1168
Nitroprusside:
for low cardiac output, 568
for pulmonary venous hypertension, 566
Nocturia, 307
Node(s):
atrioventricular (AV), 287
lymph, assessment of, *271*
sinoatrial (SA), 287
Nodule, *265*
Norepinephrine, 125–126
in control of heart rate, 74
effect of, on electrical conduction: in AV node, 39
in SA node, 38
increase in, neutrophilia associated with, 86
as neurotransmitter, 115
in regulation of peripheral regulation, 69
secretion of, by adrenal medulla, 141–142
in treatment of sepsis, 846
Normoblasts in anemias, 85
Nose:
assessment of, 270
burns of, care of, 784
Nosocomial infection, 1042–1044
complicating mechanical ventilation, 967–968
Nuclease, 193
Nucleus pulposus of disk, 105
Null cells, 449
Numeric displays for medical instrumentation, 1032
Nurse:
in crisis, guides for nursing action related to, 328–329
critical-care (*see* Critical-care nurse)
primary responsibility of, 1064

Nursing:
critical-care (*see* Critical-care nursing)
primary, in pediatric critical-care setting, 880
Nursing care:
goal of, 11
modifications of, for intracranial hypertension, 617–620
Nursing care management, physical assessment in, 253–257
Nursing implications for interpersonal relationships, 478–481
Nursing intervention in facilitating psychological equilibrium, 339–341
Nutrition:
in burn therapy, 766–768
for children, 893
in gastrointestinal disorders, 736–738
improved, to improve host defenses in treatment of sepsis, 842
parenteral, 736, 981–989
(*See also* Parenteral nutrition, total)
Nycostatin for kidney transplant recipient, 677

Obesity, 733–736
jejunoileal bypass for, 733–736
treatment of, 734–735
Objectives in planning patient teaching program, 1076–1077
Obstetric critical care, art of, 5
Obstetric patient, high-risk, 852–864
antepartal and intrapartal crises in, 855–862
contribution factors in, 852
postpartal crises in, 862–864
recognition and basic management of, 852–855
Obstructions:
colonic, 708–709
food, in ileostomy, 725–726
intestinal, 708–710
(*See also* Intestines, obstruction of)
Obtunded, definition of, 292
Occipital lobes of cerebral cortex, functions of, 117, *119*
Occlusive mesenteric ischemia, 705–706
Oculocephalic reflex in assessing transtentorial herniation, 608–610
Oculomotor nerve (III):
anatomy of, 111, *112*
assessment of, 293
types and functions of, *113*
Oculovestibular reflex in assessing transtentorial herniation, 609–610

Ohm, 1038–1039
Olfactory nerve (I):
anatomy of, 111, *112*
assessment of, 293
types and functions of, *113*
Oliguria, 307
Oliguric phase of acute renal failure, 658
Omphalocele in neonate, 884–885
Oncotic pressure, glomerular filtration rate and, 158–159
Oncovin as anticancer drug, *906*
Oocyte in reproductive cycle, 238–239
Ophthalmoscopic examination, 273–274
in assessment of patient with hematopoietic disorders, 580
Opsinopathy, consumptive, 822
Opsonins:
in host defense against sepsis, 822
in phagocytosis, 440
Optic nerve (II):
anatomy of, 111, *112*
assessment of, 293
types and functions of, *113*
Organ, bone as, 223–224
Organ image in internal psychological disequilibrium, 334–336
avoidance of, nursing intervention in, 339–340
Organ system changes in host response to sepsis, 833–835
Organic acids in extracellular fluid, 422–423
Organic materials, reabsorption of, in urine formation, 162–163
Organic substances of bone, 224
Orifice:
urethral, 243
vaginal, 243, 244
Oropharynx, 182
Orthopedic injuries, traumatic, management of, 813–814
Oscilloscopes, 1031–1032
Osmolality:
of body fluids, regulation of, 392–395
definition of, 391–392
of plasma, calculation of, 395
Osmolarity, definition of, 391–392
Osmoreceptor-antidiuretic hormone system in regulation of osmolality of body fluids, 392–394
Osmoreceptors in regulation of antidiuretic hormone secretion, 134
Osmosis:
in dialysis, 972
in fluid and electrolyte transport, 395
in renal system, 155
Osmotic pressure of blood, 80

Ossification:
  endochondral, 224
  intramembranous, 224
Osteitis fibrosa in renal disease, 666
Osteoblasts:
  in bone, 224
  in bone remodeling, 224–225
Osteoclasts:
  in bone, 224
  in bone remodeling, 225
Osteocytes:
  in bone, 224
  in bone remodeling, 224–225
Osteogenic cells in fracture repair, 232
Osteogenic sarcoma, adolescent with, 903–908
  (*See also* Adolescent, with osteogenic sarcoma)
Osteoid in bone formation, 224
Osteomalacia in renal disease, 666
Osteopetrosis, 232
Osteoporosis, 232
  in Cushing's syndrome, 140
Osteosclerosis in renal disease, 666
Ovarian hormone, 244–245
Ovary(ies), 146–147, 237–239
  location of, *126*
  pituitary gland and hypothalamus, relationships between, 245
Ovulation, 238–239
Ovum, release of, 238
Oximeter, 1026, *1028*
Oxygen:
  arterial levels of, monitoring of, in unstable cardiac patient, 559–560
  atmosphere of, 499
  in blood, total, measuring, 24
  bound to hemoglobin, transport of, 23–25
  consumption of: measurement of, 73
    myocardial, factors affecting, 57
  delivery of: in internal respiration, 369
    in oxygenation, 369
  dissolved, in plasma, transport of, 23, *24*
  distribution of, in peripheral circulation, 65
  in emphysema therapy, 517
  in fat embolus management, 526
  hemoglobin affinity for, 366–369
    increased, hypoxia from, 372
    measuring of, 24–25
    shifts in, 25
  for hypoxemia: from diffusion abnormalities, 386–387
    from shunting, 384
  partial pressures of, 19–20
  in plasma, 368

in pulmonary contusion management, 528
in pulmonary thromboembolism therapy, 522
therapy with, for high-risk neonate, 870–871
toxicity of, complicating mechanical ventilation, 968
transport of: and delivery of, in oxygenation, 368–371
  hemoglobin in, 85
Oxygen cascade, 362–364
Oxygen content of blood, 366
Oxygenation:
  adequate, 363–389
  as adjunct to ventilation, 916
  in ARDS management, monitoring of, 496
  arterial, measurement of, oximeter for, 1026, *1028*
  of blood in extracorporeal circulation, 952–953
  extracorporeal membrane, 502–504
    in pulmonary thromboembolism therapy, 522
  practical physiology of, 363–372
    external respiration in, 366–367
    internal respiration in, 371–372
    oxygen cascade in, 364–366
    oxygen transport and delivery in, 368–371
    partial pressures in, 363–364
  problems of, mechanical ventilation for, 959–960
Oxygenator:
  bubble, 949, 952
  in extracorporeal circulation, 949
  membrane, 952–953
Oxyhemoglobin dissociation curve, 368–371
Oxytocin, 134

Pacemaker cells of myocardium, 35–36
Pacemakers:
  cardiac, 287
  external, 1030
  wandering atrial, 1110
Pacing:
  atrial, indications for, 573–575
  ventricular, indications for, 575
Pacinian corpuscle in dermis, functions of, 215
Pain:
  abdominal, in diabetic ketoacidosis, 645
  bone, in renal disease, 666
  chest, in differential diagnosis of unstable cardiac patient, 543–544

deep, in assessment of sensory system, 299
postprandial, in chronic occlusive mesenteric ischemia, 705
receptors for, in dermis, 216
superficial, in assessment of sensory system, 299
Pallor in physical assessment, 264
Palpation:
  of abdomen, 302–305
  in assessment of unstable cardiac patient, 545
  of chest in physical assessment, 280
  of heart, 285, *286*
  for lymphadenopathy in assessment of patient with hematopoietic disorders, 580
  in physical assessment, 258, *259*
Panacinar emphysemia, 516
Pancreas:
  endocrine, 143–145, 206
    location of, *126*
  exocrine, 191–193
    enzymes of, 192–193
    gross anatomy of, 191
    histology of, 191, *193*
    secretions of, 192–193
  traumatic injuries to, management of, 811–812
  tumor of, in Zollinger-Ellison syndrome, 718
Pancreatic lipase, 193
Pancreatitis, 731–733
Pancuronium bromide, 1168
Pancytopenia in aplastic anemia, 584
Panlobular emphysema, 516
Paper recorders, 1033–1034
Papillae of tongue, 182
Papillary layer of dermis, 213
Papillary necrosis in analgesic nephropathy, 662
Papilledema, 274
Papova virus in sepsis, 831
Papule, *265*
Para-aminohippurate, clearance of, in effective renal plasma flow determination, 163–164
Paraldehyde in status epilepticus treatment, 622
Paralysis in assessment of transtentorial herniation, 606
Paralytic ileus, 708, 710
  in sepsis, 834
Parameter acquisition instrumentation, 999–1029
  (*See also* Instrumentation, parameter acquisition)
Paraphimosis complicating catheterization, 681, *682*

Parasites in sepsis, 831
Parasitic infections, delayed hypersensitivity and, 463
Parasympathetic nervous system, 115
  in brochospasm of asthma, 511
  in control of heart rate, 74
Parathormone (PTH), 138
Parathyroid glands, 138
  effects of kidney disease on, 666, 667
  location of, 126
Parathyroid hormone:
  in plasma calcium concentration control, 223–224
  in vitamin D metabolism, 223
Parathyroidectomy for hypercalcemic crisis, 655
Parenchymal liver cell, 206
Parenteral hyperalimentation, 736–737
  hyperosmolarity due to, 136
Parenteral nutrition, total, 736, 981–989
  air embolism in, 983–984
  catheter placement for, 982–983
  dressing care in, 984–985
  history of, 981
  metabolic management in, 985–987
  psychological aspects of, 989
  sepsis control in, 987–989
  solution contents for, 982
  technical complications of, 983
Parents of burned child, assisting, 894
Parietal cell in gastric gland, 186
Parietal lobes of cerebral cortex, functions of, 117, 119
Paroxysmal atrial tachycardia, 288, 1113–1114
Pars intermedia, 136
  location of, 126
Partial pressure(s):
  Dalton's law of, 16, 19
  in diffusion of respiratory gases, 19–20
  in oxygenation, 363–364
Passive diffusion in renal system, 155–156
Patient(s):
  acceptance of critical illness by, fostering, critical-care nurse in, 481
  assessment of, as learner, 1082–1083
  in crisis, guides for nursing action related to, 329–330
  in critical-care milieu, 346–347
    communication problems of, 346
    perceptual disorganization of, overcoming, 346–347
    sensory disorganization of, overcoming, 346–347
  and critical-care nurse, interpersonal needs of, 475

education of: facilitation of, critical-care nurse in, 480–481
  about hypothermia therapy, 995
family of, in crisis, guides for nursing action related to, 329
learning by, evaluation of, 1086–1088
position of, in examination, 260
psychosocial assessment of, 349–358
readiness of, to learn, assessment of, 1084–1085
support for, fostering of, critical-care nurse in, 479–480
teaching of, effects of, beneficial, 1071
  detrimental, 1072
  programs for, 1072–1099
  (See also Teaching of patient and family, programs for)
Pectoriloquy, whispering, 282
Pectus carinatum, 279
Pectus excavatum, 279
Pediatric crises, 879–908
  (See also Adolescent; Child(ren); Neonate; Preschooler; Toddler)
Pediatric critical care, art of, 5
Pediatric critical-care unit:
  family in, 880–881
  primary nursing in, 880
  stress in, 880
Pediatric patients, considerations for, 879–880
Pelvis, malignancies of, surgery for, 690
Penicillin for lung abscess, 506
Penicillin G potassium for injection, 1168–1169
Penicillin G procaine suspension, sterile, 1169
Penis, 245–247
  assessment of, 306
  complications of external condom catheter involving, 679
  prosthesis for, 692
  surgery of, 692
  trauma to, 695
Pepsinogen, functions of, 18
Peptic ulcer(s):
  gastrointestinal hemorrhage secondary to, 703
  perforated, peritonitis secondary to, 712
  in Zollinger-Ellison syndrome, 718
Peptococci in sepsis, 828
Peptostreptococci in sepsis, 828–829
Perceptual disorganization of patient in critical-care milieu, overcoming, 346–347

Percussion:
  of abdomen, 302
  of chest in physical assessment, 280–281
  of heart, 285
  in physical assessment, 258–259
Perforation:
  intestinal complicating ulcerative colitis, 723
  and urinary extravasation complicating cystoscopy and transurethral surgery, 688–689
Perfusion, disorders of, 518–526
  air embolus as, 523–524
  fat embolus as, 524–526
  pulmonary thromboembolism as, 518–523
Pericardial constriction, hypovolemia in, 564
Pericardial effusion in renal disease, 665
Pericardial friction rub, 290
Pericardial tamponade in trauma victim, management of, 809–810
Pericarditis, fibrinous, in renal disease, 665
Pericardium, functional anatomy of, 55
Perimetrium of uterus, 241
Perinatal crisis, 851–877
Perineum, burns of, care of, 785
Periosteum in children and adults, 221
Peripheral alimentation, 737–738
Peripheral circulation, 62–69
  in control of cardiac output, 77
  extrinsic regulation of, 66–69
  intrinsic regulation of, 64–65
  vascular tree in, 62–64
Peripheral hormones, 128–129
  of anterior pituitary, 132–133
  and hypothalamic hormones, relationships between, 129
  and pituitary hormones, relationships between, 129
Peripheral hyperalimentation, 737
Peripheral neuropathy in renal disease, 666
Peripheral perfusion in assessment of shock patient, 311
Peripheral veins for intravenous lifeline, 918
Peristalsis:
  in colon, 204
  in esophagus, 184
  in small intestine, 198–199
Peritoneal dialysis, 669–671, 973–976
  advantages of, 973
  complications of, 671
  contraindications to, 973
  cycles in, 974–975
  definition of, 973

Peritoneal dialysis (*Cont.*):
  disadvantages of, 973
  for hemolytic uremic syndrome in
      preschooler, 896, 898
  initiating, 974
  kinetics of, 669–670
  methods for, 670
  nursing care components of,
      975–976
  patient care during, 670–671
  peritoneal access for, 670
  potential complications of, 976
  schedules for, 670
Peritoneal lavage in trauma victim
    management, procedures for, 804
Peritoneum, inflammation of, 710–714
    (*See also* Peritonitis)
Peritonitis, 710–714
  in critical-care patients, *319*
  nursing intervention in, 713–714
  pathophysiology of, 710–711
  primary, 711–712
  secondary, 712–713
  tuberculous, 712
Peritubular capillary oncotic pressure
    in sodium regulation, 403
Personal integrity, conservation of, in
    critical-care nursing, 11–12
Personnel in infection control unit for
    burn patients, 763
Petechia, *268*
  in fat emboli, 525
Peyer's patches, 197
pH:
  arterial, monitoring of, in unstable
      cardiac patient, 559–560
  of blood, 80
    calculation of, *27*
  of body fluids: functions of, 423
    regulation of, 172–174, 423–425
  in sepsis, 837
  of urine, hourly testing of, in fluid
      therapy for burns, 757
Phagocytes in host defense against
    sepsis, 822–823
Phagocytosis:
  in defense system, 440–442
  in fluid and electrolyte transport, 396
Pharynx:
  assessment of, 270
  blood in, airway problems in, 798–799
Phenacetin, nephropathy due to, 662
Phenobarbital:
  for neonatal seizures, 874
  in status epilepticus treatment, 622
Phentolamine, 1169–1170
  in treatment of sepsis, 846
Phenylephrine in asthma therapy, 514
Phenytoin in status epilepticus treat-
    ment, 621–622

Pheochromocytomas, 142
Phimosis, 306
  complicating catheterization, 681
Phosphate:
  deficiency of, 420–421
  excess of, 420
  functions of, 419
  for hypercalcemic crisis manage-
      ment, 655
  reabsorption of, in urine formation,
      162
  regulation of, 419–420
Phospholipase A, 193
Phosphorus:
  in bone, 223–224
  effects of kidney disease on, 666,
      667
Photo-plethysmograph for pulse moni-
    toring, 1001
Phototherapy for pathologic neonatal
    jaundice, 876
Physical assessment, 251–320
  of abdomen, 300–305
  basic techniques and equipment for,
      258–260
  of ears, 269
  examination in, 260–264
    (*See also* Examination, in physical
    assessment)
  of eyes, 271–275
  of face, 269
  of genitourinary system, 306–307
  guidelines for, 257–258
  health history in, 253–257
  of heart, 283–291
  of lungs, 275–283
  of mouth, 270
  of neck, 270–271
  of neuromuscular system, 291–300
  of nose, 270
  in nursing care management,
      253–257
  of pharynx, 270
  of rectum, 305–306
  relationship of, to health history and
      laboratory assessment, 257
  of sinuses, 270
  of skin, 264–268
  of skull, 269
  systematic process of, 257
  techniques of, application of, 309–320
    to abdominal problems, 318,
      319
    to comatose patient, 315–316
    to critical-unstable patient,
      309–311
    to eye problems, 316, *317*
    to lung problems, 317, *319*
    to nervous system problems,
      318, *320*

  to rectal problems, 318, *319*
  to skin problems, 317, *318*
  to stable patient, 312–314
  of unstable cardiac patient, 545–546
Physical attack, victims of, spiritual
    concerns of, 1063
Physical disability in trauma victim,
    817
Physical examination in diagnosis of
    sepsis, 835–836
Physical subsystem of individual, 10
  implications of, for critical-care
      nurse, 10–11
Physical therapy:
  for high-risk neonate, 871–872
  in management of patient on contin-
      uous assisted ventilation, 963,
      964, 965
Physician(s):
  and critical-care nurse, relationship
      between, 7
  and nurses, disagreement of, man-
      agement of, 1066–1067
Physiologic dead space, 31
Physiologic shunt, 30–31
Physiotherapy, chest: in atelectasis
      management, 534
    in closed pneumothorax manage-
      ment, 531
    for high-risk neonate, 870–871
    for lung abscess, 506–507
Pia mater, 105
Pickwickian syndrome in obesity, 734
Pigeon breast, 279
Pigmented nevi in critical-care pa-
    tients, *318*
Pigments, bile, 195–196
Pineal gland, 147
  location of, *126*
Pinocytosis in fluid and electrolyte
    transport, 396
Pitressin in regulation of peripheral
    regulation, 69
Pituitary gigantism, 234
Pituitary gland, 129–136
  anatomy of, 129–130
  anterior, 130–133
    and hypothalamus, hormonal rela-
        tionships between, *133*
    peripheral hormones of, 132–133
    tropic hormones of, 131–132
  and hypothalamus, hormonal rela-
      tionships between, *129*
  intermediate, 136
  location of, *126*
  ovaries and hypothalamus, relation-
      ships between, 245
  and periphery, hormonal relation-
      ships between, *129*
  posterior, 133–136

Placenta previa, management of, 857–858

Plasma, 80–82
  carbon dioxide in, transport of, 26
  fresh-frozen, to improve host defenses in treatment of sepsis, 842
  osmolality of, calculation of, 395
  oxygen in, 366
    transport of, 23, *24*

Plasma cells, 88–89

Plasma proteins, 81–82

Plasma thromboplastin antecedent, *93*, 96

Plasma thromboplastin component, *93*, 96

Plasmapheresis for hyperviscosity syndrome, 582–583

Plasmin:
  activity of, anticoagulant effects of, 99
  in coagulation mechanism, 98–99
  secretion of, eosinophils in, 86

Plasmodium falciparum in sepsis, 831

Plasmodium vivax in sepsis, 831

Plateau waves in intracranial pressure monitoring, 1020–1021

Platelet coagulation factors, 91

Platelets, 89–91
  abnormalities of, in defective hemostasis, 591
  adhesion of, 89
  aggregation of, 89
  bleeding associated with, 91
  characteristics of, 90
  deficiency of, hemorrhagic diathesis due to, 91
  in hemostasis, 89–90
  injury to, DIC due to, 594
  production of, regulation of, 83
  quantity and quality of, variables affecting, 89

Plates, epiphyseal, reaction of, to acute disorders and injuries, 234

Pleural effusion, 507–509
  in critical-care patients, *319*

Pleural friction rubs, 283

Pleurectomy in closed pneumothorax management, 531

Pleuritis, fibrinous, in renal disease, 665

Pleurodesis with iodized talc in pleural effusion management, 509

Plexus(es):
  Auerbach's, of gastrointestinal tract, 182
  dermal, 213, *214*
  Meissner's, of gastrointestinal submucosa, 181
  spinal nerve, 114

Pneumatic systems, hazards in, 1042

Pneumocystis cariniae in sepsis, 831

Pneumography, impedence, in respiratory rate monitoring, 1025

Pneumonia:
  aspiration, 497–498
  bacterial, 534–535
    lung abcess due to, 505
  in critical-care patients, *319*
  in high-risk neonate, 870
  lipoid, 498
  in renal disease, 665
  viral, 497

Pneumonitis:
  aspiration: in drug overdose, 536
    in head injury, 536
  hemorrhagic, acute: from drug overdose, 535–540
    in head injury, 535–536
  radiation, 498
  septic, 497–498

Pneumotaxic center, 28

Pneumothorax, 17, 530–532
  closed, 530–531
  communicating, 531–532
  complicating osteogenic sarcoma in adolescent, 907
  in critical-care patients, *319*
  in high-risk neonate, 870
  open, 531–532
  simple, 530–531
  tension, 531

Poikilothermia in spinal cord injury and polyneuropathy, 630

Poiseuille's law in hemodynamics of circulation, 46

Poliomyelitis, loss of airway protection in, 626

Polycystic renal disease, pathogenesis of, 661–662

Polycythemia, definition of, 83

Polydipsia:
  in diabetes, 144
  in diabetes insipidus, 136

Polymorphonuclear granulocytes, 85

Polymorphonuclear neutrophils in phagocytosis of bacteria, 440

Polymyxin B sulfate, sterile, 1170–1171

Polyneuritis, diphtheric, loss of airway protection in, 626

Polyneuropathy(ies):
  of cranial nerves, loss of airway protection in, 626
  multisystem dysfunction in, 629–632
  peripheral, respiratory musculature dysfunction in, 627–628
  of upper extremities, loss of airway protection in, 626

Polypeptides, 126
  vasoactive, release of, in sepsis, 832

Polyphagia in diabetes, 144

Polyuria, 307
  in diabetes, 144
  in diabetes insipidus, 135–136

Pons, 110

Pontine-medullary breathing patterns in assessing transtentorial herniation, 608

Porta hepatis, 208

Portal circulation, control mechanisms of, 66

Portal hypertension, esophageal varices in, 701

Portal triad, 207

Portal vein in liver, 207–208

Positioning:
  in burn therapy, 769
    for children, 893–894
  in management of patient on continuous assisted ventilation, 963
  in prevention of postburn wet-lung syndrome, 760

Positive end-expiratory pressure (PEEP):
  in ARDS management, 494–496
  in flail chest management, 529–530
  for oxygen toxicity, 500

Posterior pituitary gland, 133–136

Postextrasystolic potentiation, 76

Postpartal crises, 862–864

Poststreptococcal glomerulonephritis, acute, pathogenesis of, 660

Postural drainage:
  for lung abscess, 506–507
  in respiratory care for burn patient, 760, *761*

Postural reflexes, 124

Potassium:
  balance of: in homeostasis, 171
    maintenance of, in acute renal failure management, 669
  deficiency of, 409–410
  in diabetic ketoacidosis management, 646
  excess of, 407–409
  functions of, 406
  glucose with insulin and, in treatment of sepsis, 845
  intake of, in potassium regulation, 407
  reabsorption of, in urine formation, 162
  regulation of, 406–407
  secretion of, by colon, 205
  in transmembrane potential development, 34
  tubular secretion of, in urine formation, 165

Potassium chloride in tubbing solution for burn care, 788

Pott's disease, kyphoscoliosis due to, 509

Pouching of cutaneous fistulas, 717–718

Prazosin:
  for low cardiac output, 568
  for pulmonary venous hypertension, 566

Precocious pseudopuberty:
  from adrenal androgen excess, 141
  from testosterone excess, 147

Precordium in examination of heart, 284

Prednisolone in asthma therapy, 514

Prednisone:
  in asthma therapy, 514
  for kidney transplant recipient, 677
  for myasthenia gravis, 637

Preeclampsia/eclampsia, 859–860

Pregnancy:
  ectopic, 856–857
  high-risk, 852–864
    (*See also* Obstetric patient, high-risk)

Preload:
  in left ventricular function: clinical assessment of, 562–564
    hypovolemia and, 564
    pulmonary venous hypertension and, 565–567
  in myocardial function, 925–926, *927*
  reduction of: by circulatory assistance devices, 928
    devices for, historical evaluation of, 928–930

Premature atrial contraction, 1111–1112

Premature junctional contraction, 1117–1119

Premature ventricular contraction, 1123–1125
  drug therapy for, 922

Prepatellar bursa, 227

Preschooler:
  development of, illness and, 894–895
  hemolytic uremic syndrome in, 894–898
    (*See also* Hemolytic uremic syndrome in preschooler)

Pressure:
  hydrostatic: in dialysis, 972
    in venous system, 50
  intracranial: increased, 612–620
    (*See also* Intracranial pressure, increased)
    in neurologic evaluation of child, 899–900
  intraocular, assessment of, 274–275

Pressure-cycled ventilators, 958–959

Proaccelerin, *93*, 95

Procainamide hydrochloride, 1171

Procallus in fracture repair, 232

Procarboxypeptidase, 192

Proconvertin, *93*, 95

Proerythroblasts in anemias, 85

Progesterone, effects of: on female, 244–245
  on vagina, 242

Proglycem for hypoglycemia, 650

Prolactin, 132

Proliferative phase of menstrual cycle, 241

Promethazine hydrochloride, 1172

Pronator drift in assessment of transtentorial herniation, 605–606

Pronestyl, effects of, on ventricular contractility, 571

Propionibacteria in sepsis, 829

Propranolol:
  effects of, on ventricular contractility, 571
  for prevention of angina, 570

Propranolol hydrochloride, 1172–1173

Proprioception in assessment of sensory system, 299

Prostaglandins, 126–127
  renal, 176
  in sodium regulation, 403

Prostate gland, 248–249
  in emission, 246
  large, complicating catheterization, 681
  open surgery of, 691
  transurethral resection of, 687
    complications of, long-term, 689
    patient care after, 687–688

Prostatectomy, radical, 961

Prostheses altering host resistance to sepsis, 824

Prostigmine for myasthenia gravis, 632, *633*

Protein(s):
  absorption of, by small intestine, 200
  functions, regulation and deficiency of, 421–422
  plasma, 81–82
  in total parenteral nutrition solution, 982
    metabolic significance of, 985–986
  in urine, hourly testing of, in fluid therapy for burns, 757

Proteolytic enzymes of exocrine pancreas, 192

Proteus mirabilis in sepsis, 828

Prothrombin, *93*, 94

Pruritus in renal disease, 667–668

Pseudomonas aeruginosa in sepsis, 828

Pseudopuberty, precocious: from adrenal androgen excess, 141
  from testosterone excess, 147

Psychological aspects of total parenteral nutrition, 989

Psychological care of alert, immobilized patient with neurologic disorders disrupting respiration, 637–638

Psychological considerations in management of patient on continuous assisted ventilation, 964–965

Psychological disequilibrium in critical-care patients, 334–339
  external, 338–339
  internal, 334–338
    illness in, 334–336
    organ image in, 334–336
    self-conflict in, 336–338

Psychological equilibrium, 331–341
  disorders of, 334–339
    (*See also* Psychological disequilibrium in critical-care patients)
  external, facilitating nursing intervention in, 340–341
  facilitating, nursing intervention in, 339–341
  feedback in, 332–333
  intake in, 332
  internal, facilitating, nursing intervention in, 339–340
  output in, 332
  regulation in, 333–334
  stability in, 333

Psychological hazards in critical-care environment, 1044–1046

Psychological implications of trauma, 817

Psychosocial aspects of neurologic disorders in school-age child, 899

Psychosocial assessment of patient and family, 349–358
  case study in, 355–358
  communication in, 351
  family adjustments in, 351–355
  psychosociodynamics of sick role in, 350–351

Psychosocial basis of critical-care nursing, 321–359

Psychosocial effects of hypothermia, 993

Psychosociodynamics of sick role, 350–351

Puberty, early, false: from adrenal androgen excess, 141
  from testosterone excess, 147

Pulmonary arterial pressure, monitoring of, in unstable cardiac patient, 553–554

Pulmonary arterial wedge pressure, measurement of, in hemorrhagic shock treatment, 699

Pulmonary artery, trauma to, complicating pulmonary artery pressure monitoring, prevention of, 1014

Pulmonary artery pressure, monitoring of, direct, 1012–1013

Pulmonary capillary wedge pressure, monitoring of, direct, 1013–1014

Pulmonary circulation, 50–52

Pulmonary critical care, art of, 4

Pulmonary edema:
cardiogenic, 498
in critical-care patients, *319*
in myocardial infarction, physical findings in, *314*

Pulmonary embolus, postpartal, 864

Pulmonary insufficiency in burn patient, 759–761

Pulmonary stretch receptors, 29

Pulmonary system, 15–32
blood perfusion in, 20–23
diffusion of respiratory gases in, 18–20
effects of kidney disease on, 665
nervous system control of blood gases in, 26–30
pathophysiologic changes in, correction of, in treatment of sepsis, 842–843
physiologic effects of hypothermia on, 993
transportation of respiratory gases in, 23–26

Pulmonary thromboembolism:
clinical features of, 519
diagnosis of, 519–520
etiology of, 518
management of, 521–523
misdiagnosis of, 518
pathophysiology of, 518–519

Pulmonary vascular resistance, increased, in pulmonary thromboembolism, 509

Pulmonary venous hypertension, 565–567

Pulmonary vessels, control mechanisms of, 66

Pulmonary wedge pressure, monitoring of, in unstable cardiac patient, 553, *554*

Pulmonic ejection clicks, 290

Pulse:
arterial, in physical assessment, 261
contour of, in physical assessment, 261, *262*
monitor for, 1001
quality of, in physical assessment, 261
rate of, in physical assessment, 261
rhythm of, in physical assessment, 261

Pulse pressure, 70

Pulsus alternans, 264

Pulsus paradoxus, 264

Pump(s):
cardiac, 52–62
(*See also* Heart)
flow rate of, in extracorporeal circulation, 951
infusion, 1030–1031
priming of, for extracorporeal circulation, 950–951

Pumping, balloon, intra-aortic, in treatment of sepsis, 847

Pupil(s):
assessment of, 272
in assessment of comatose patient, 315–316
in evaluating intracerebral pressure in trauma victim, 801

Pupillary light reflex in assessing transtentorial herniation, 608

Pupillary reflexes, 123

Purkinje system, impulse transmission through, 40

Pus, production of, 87

Pustule, *266*

Pyloric glands, 186

Pylorus of stomach, 186
contraction of, in digestion, 190

Pyramidal system in motor integration of nervous system, 119, *120*

Pyridostigmine bromide for myasthenia gravis, 632, *633*

Pyrimethamine, 1173

Pyrogen in defense system, 442

Pyuria, 307

Q wave, 42

QS complex, 42

Quadriplegic, autonomic hyperreflexia in, 693

Quinidine, effects of, on ventricular contractility, 571

R wave, 41

Radiation pneumonitis, 498

Radiation therapy for osteogenic sarcoma in adolescent, 905

Radiography in diagnosis of Zollinger-Ellison syndrome, 719

Radioimmunoassays in diagnosis of Zollinger-Ellison syndrome, 719

Radiologic picture of ARDS, 491, *492*

Rales, 283
in atelectasis, 533
in pulmonary contusion, 528
wet, in assessment of unstable cardiac patient, 546

Rape, victims of, spiritual concerns of, 1063

Reabsorption:
of amino acids in urine formation, 163
of bicarbonate ions in urine formation, 162
of calcium ions in urine formation, 162
of glucose in urine formation, 162–163
of inorganic ions, renal, in urine formation, 161–162
of organic materials in urine formation, 162–163
of phosphate in urine formation, 162
of potassium in urine formation, 162
of sodium: renal, and potassium secretion, 165
in urine formation, 161–162
tubular, in urine formation, 160–163
of urea in urine formation, 163

Recorders, paper, 1033–1034

Recording, instruments for, 1031–1034

Recovery phase of acute renal failure, 658

Recruitment in decreasing pulmonary vascular resistance, 21

Rectal reflexes, 124

Rectum:
hemorrhages in, complicating ulcerative colitis, 723
physical assessment of, 305–306
problems of, application of physical assessment techniques to, 318, *319*

Red blood cells (*see* Erythrocytes)

Red eye syndrome in renal disease, 667

Reduction of fractures, 813

Reflex(es):
assessment of, 299–300
blink, 123–124
cardiovascular, 124
cough, suppression of, lung abscess due to, 505
deep tendon, 123
gastrocolonic, function of, 204
gastroileal, function of, 199
genitourinary, 124
myenteric, in stimulation of peristalsis in small intestine, 199
oculocephalic, in assessing transtentorial herniation, 608–610
oculovestibular, in assessing transtentorial herniation, 609–610
postural, 124

Reflex(es) (*Cont.*):
pupillary, 123
light, in assessing transtentorial herniation, 608
rectal, 124
stretch, 123
superficial, 123
visceral, 123
vomiting, 191
Reflex activities in nervous system, 123–124
Reflex irritability in Apgar scoring, *865,* 866
Regional enteritis, 720–721
Regitine in treatment of sepsis, 846
Regulation in psychological equilibrium, 333–334
Regurgitant murmurs, 291
Regurgitation, mitral, acute, intra-aortic balloon pumping for, 935–936
Rehabilitation:
in burn care, 747–748
psychological disequilibrium interfering with, 336
Rejection:
complicating renal transplantation, 677
of transplants, 462
Relationships:
interpersonal, 472
dynamics of, 471–481
nursing implications for, 478–481
interrole, 472
Releasing hormones, 128
Renacidin to dissolve urinary calculi, 687
Renal artery, stenosis of, pathogenesis of, 659–660
Renal concentrating and diluting mechanisms in urine formation, 165–169
Renal critical care, art of, 4–5
Renal insufficiency, 657
Renal system, 151–176
[*See also* Kidney(s)]
Renal vessels, control mechanisms of, 66
Renin, 174–175
in fluid balance, 170
juxtaglomerular cells as source of, 153
Renin-angiotensin mechanism of aldosterone secretion regulation, 140
Renoprival hypertension, 176
Renovascular hypertension, 659
Repolarization of transmembrane potential of cardiac cells, 35
Reproductive system:
female, 237–245

assessment of, 306–307
fallopian tubes in, 239
internal genitalia in, 237–242
ovaries in, 237–239
uterus in, 239–242
male, 245–249
assessment of, 306–307
external genitalia in, 245–247
internal genitalia in, 247–249
Resistance:
in hemodynamics of circulation, 45, 46, *47*
in pulmonary circulation, 51–52
pulmonary vascular, determinants of, 20–21
Respiration, 15–32
in assessment of comatose patient, 315
in assessment of shock patient, 311
Biot's, in assessment of comatose patient, 315
Cheyne-Stokes, in assessment of comatose patient, 315
definition of, 364
depth of, in physical assessment of, 262
in diabetic ketoacidosis, 645
external, in oxygenation, 366–367
as function of erythrocytes, 85
as function of hematopoietic system, 79
internal, in oxygenation, 371–372
musculature of, dysfunction of, 627–629
neurologic disorders disrupting, 622–638
painful, in peritonitis, 711
patterns of: evaluation of, in assessing transtentorial herniation, 606–608
in physical assessment, 262–263
in physical assessment, 261–263
quality of, in physical assessment, 261–262
rate of: in physical assessment, 262, *263*
in sepsis, 836
Respiratory acidosis, 428–429
in septic shock, 837–838
signs and symptoms of, *421*
in unstable cardiac patient, 560
Respiratory alkalosis, 429–430
in sepsis, 837
signs and symptoms of, *432*
Respiratory care in burn therapy, 758–761
for immediate respiratory complications, 758–759
for pulmonary insufficiency, 759–761
Respiratory complications, immediate, in burn patient, 758–759

Respiratory crisis in high-risk neonate, 869–870
Respiratory distress syndrome (RDS):
adult, 485–497
complicating acute hemorrhagic shock, 699, 701
diagnostic findings in, 489–492
extracorporeal membrane oxygenation for, 502–503
historical background of, 486
infection complicating, 497
management of, 493–497
pathophysiology of, *487,* 488-489
synonyms for, 487
etiology of, 486–488
idiopathic, 869–870
pathology of, 486
Respiratory effort in Apgar scoring, 865–866
Respiratory epithelium in defense system, 439
Respiratory exchange ratio, 364
Respiratory excursion, assessment of, 280
Respiratory function, evaluation of, 628–629
Respiratory gases:
diffusion of, 18–20
transportation of, 23–26
Respiratory rate:
in assessing transtentorial herniation, 610
monitoring of, 1025–1026
Respiratory system:
in acid-base balance regulation, 423–425
disorders of, 485–536
affecting alveolar permeability, 485–504
(*See also* Alveoli, permeability of, disorders affecting)
chest trauma as, 526–533
(*See also* Chest, trauma to)
perfusion, 518–526
(*See also* Perfusion, disorders of)
malformation of, congenital, in high-risk neonate, 870
response of, to burns in child, 891
[*See also* Lung(s)]
Respiratory volume, monitoring of, 1025–1028
Respiratory waveforms, 1027–1028
Respirometer, Wright, in respiratory volume monitoring, 1026
Responsibility in psychosociodynamics of sick role, 350–351
Rest in burn care, 768
Restless leg syndrome in renal disease, 666

Restlessness:
    in atelactasis, 533
    in closed pneumothorax, 530
Resuscitation:
    cardiopulmonary, 914–915
    of high-risk neonate, 866
    initial, in trauma management,
            797–806
        airway in, 798–799
        equipment for, 805–806
        examination and diagnostic ap-
            proach in, 800–803
        hemorrhage control in, 799–800
        logistics of, 805–806
        priorities for, 797
        procedures for, 803–805
        wound care in, 806
Retardation, disuse, localized de-
    crease in growth due to, 234
Rete testis, 247
Retention:
    blood clot, in bladder, 683
    urinary, 682–683
        complicating cystoscopy and
            transurethral surgery, 689
Reticular formation in sensory integra-
    tion, 117
Reticular layer of dermis, 213
Reticuloendothelial system, 445–446
    disease involving, altering host re-
        sistance to sepsis, 824
    dysfunction of, DIC due to, 594
    function of, impaired, in sepsis, 834
    in host defense against sepsis,
        822–823
    immune response and, 437
    of liver, 206, 209
    monocytes in, 87
Reticulum fibers in dermis, 213
Retinopathy in diabetic nephropathy,
    661
Retroperitoneal hematomas in trauma
    victim, management of, 812
Reye's syndrome in school-age child,
    902–903
$Rh_0(D)$ immune human globulin, 1174
Rheomacrodex in balloon pumping,
    940, 941
Rheumatoid arthritis, destruction of ar-
    ticular cartilage due to, 234
Rhonchi, 283
Rhythm of heart, 287, *288*
    in assessment of shock patient,
        310–311
    escape, ventricular, 1126
    gallop, extra heart sounds heard in,
        290
    junctional, 1120
    sinus, normal, 1104
Ribs, 275

Rickets, 234
    pigeon breast due to, 279
Rifampin, 1174–1175
Right atrial pressure, monitoring of: di-
    rect, 1014
    in unstable cardiac patient, *554,*
        555–556
Right bundle branch block, 1134
Right ventricular pressure, monitoring
    of: direct, 1014
Right ventricular pressure, monitoring
    of: direct, 1014
    in unstable cardiac patient, *554,*
        555
Rigidity, 298
    decerebrate, in assessment of coma-
        tose patient, 316
    decorticate, in assessment of coma-
        tose patient, 316
Ringer's solution, lactated, in burn
    therapy, 754
Rinne's test of acoustic nerve function,
    294
Riva-Rocci-Korotkoff method of blood
    pressure measurement, 1002–1004
Rolando, fissure of, 110
Roles:
    changes in, in family due to critical
        illness, 478
    in family, reallocation of, due to criti-
        cal illness, 474
    flexibility in, interpersonal compe-
        tence and, 473–475
    reversal of, of sick individual, self-
        conflict resulting from, 338
Roto bed in ARDS management, 496
RS waveform, 42
Rubrospinal motor tracts, 622
Ruffini's end organs in dermis, func-
    tions of, 215
Rugae of stomach, 186

Safety:
    electrical, 1038–1041
    issues in, common, 1041–1042
    mechanical, 1041–1042
    new technology and, 1037–1038
    from nosocomial infection,
        1042–1044
    in pediatric care, 879–880
Saline:
    in burn wound dressings, 779
    for hypercalcemic crisis manage-
        ment, 654
Salivary glands, 182
Salmonella in sepsis, 828
Salt(s):
    bile, 194–195
        in digestion of triglycerides,
            201–202

    in tubbing solution for burn care,
        788
Salt solution, balanced, for volume re-
    placement in trauma victim, 800
Sarcoidosis in critical-care patients,
    318
Sarcolemma, 227
Sarcoma, osteogenic, adolescent with,
    903–908
    (*See also* Adolescent, with osteo-
        genic sarcoma)
Sarcoplasm of skeletal muscle cell,
    227
Sarcoplasmic reticulum, 227
Satiety center in hypothalamus,
    179–180
Scale, *266*
Scalp:
    burns of, care of, 785
    hair on, in burn care, 787
Scans, lung, in diagnosis of pulmonary
    thromboembolism, 520–521
Scar, *267*
School-age child, neurologic disorders
    in, 899–903
    (*See also* Neurologic disorders, in
        school-age child)
Schwann cells, 101
Scintigraphic monitoring of unstable
    cardiac patient, 558–559, *560, 561*
Sclera, assessment of, 272
Scleral icterus in critical-care patients,
    317
Scleroderma in critical-care patients,
    318
Sclerosing cholangitis, 729–731
Scoliosis, 279
Scrotum, 247
    assessment of, 306
    trauma to, 695
Sebaceous glands, 216
Sebum:
    functions of, 216
    production of, variations in, 216
Second-degree heart block,
    1131–1132
"Second messenger" mechanism of
    hormonal action, 127, *128*
Secretin:
    in regulation of bile metabolism, 196
    in regulation of lower esophageal
        sphincter, 185
    in regulation of pancreatic secretion,
        193
Secretin stimulation study in evaluation
    of pancreatitis, 733
Secretions:
    of exocrine pancreas, 192–193
    gastric, 186–189
        (*See also* Stomach, secretions of)

Secretions (*Cont.*):
of small intestine, 197–198
transport maximum–limited, in urine formation, 163–164
tubular, in urine formation, 163–165
Secretory IgA in defense system, 439
Secretory phase of menstrual cycle, 241
Sedation in ARDS management, 493
Sedatives, side effects of, complicating mechanical ventilation, 968
Sediment in urine, hourly testing of, in fluid therapy for burns, 757
Segmental neurologic lesions, 623–625
Segmentation:
in colon, 204
in small intestine, 198–199
Seizures, 620–622
generalized, 620–622
grand mal, 620
in high-risk neonate, 874
petit mal, 620
Self-conflict in internal psychological disequilibrium, 336–338
avoidance of, nursing intervention in, 340
Selye, stress theory beyond, 325
Semi-comatose, definition of, 292
Semilunar valves, functional anatomy of, 53
Seminal vesicles, 248
in emission, 246
Seminiferous tubules in testes, 247
Sengstaken-Blakemore tube for esophageal varices hemorrhage, 701–703
Sensitivity studies in diagnosis of sepsis, 838
Sensorium in assessment of shock patient, 311
Sensory deprivation, psychological responses in critical-care unit due to, 1044–1045
Sensory disorganization of patient in critical-care milieu, overcoming, 346–347
Sensory distortion, psychological responses in critical-care unit due to, 1045
Sensory integration in nervous system, 115, 117–118
Sensory overload, psychological responses in critical-care unit due to, 1045
Sensory system, assessment of, 298–299
Sepsis, 821–848
in burns, 765–766

in children, 893
complicating balloon pumping, 943
control of, in total parenteral nutrition, 987–989
definition of, 821
diagnosis of, 835–839
history in, 835
laboratory studies in, 836–838
monitoring in, 838–839
physical examination in, 835–836
and therapy of, early, importance of, 822
host defense against, 822–826
(*See also* Host, defenses of, against sepsis)
incidence of, 821–822
microorganisms in, 826–831
(*See also* Microorganisms in sepsis)
neonatal, 877
pathophysiologic changes with, 831–835
without shock, 836
treatment of, 839–847
correction of pathophysiologic changes of, 842–847
enhancement of host defense mechanisms in, 841–842
infection treatment in, 839–841
summary of, 847–848
therapy to improve host defenses in, 842
urinary, complicating cystoscopy and transurethral surgery, 688
Septic shock:
cold, 833–834, 836
hyperdynamic, 833, 836
warm, 833, 836
Septicemia:
in burn patient, 766
Candida, complicating TPN, 988–989
definition of, 821
Serosa of gastrointestinal tract, 182
Serotonin in regulation of peripheral regulation, 69
Serratia in sepsis, 828
Sertoli cells of seminiferous tubules, 247
Serum:
in plasma, 81
sodium concentration in, in sodium regulation, 403
Serum albumin, 81–82
Serum globulins, 82
Serum sickness, 460–461
Sexual assault, victims of, spiritual concerns of, 1063
Sexuality in ileostomate, 727
Shaving in burn care, 786–787

Shingles, 830
Shivering in hypothermia, 993
Shock:
abdomen in, 311
assessment of: blood pressure in, 310
observations in, 310
cardiogenic: in assessment of myocardial infarction, 314
intra-aortic balloon pumping for, 934–936
classification of, 309
control of, in first aid for burns, 752
definition of, 309
in diabetic ketoacidosis, 646, 647
in differential diagnosis of unstable cardiac patient, 544
heart rate, rhythm and quality in, 310–311
hemorrhagic, 697–701
(*See also* Hemorrhagic shock)
in high-risk neonate, 872–873
peripheral perfusion in, 311
physical findings in, *310*
renal function in, 311
respiration in, 311
sensorium in, 311
sepsis without, 836
septic: cold, 833–834, 836
hyperdynamic, 833, 836
warm, 833, 836
spinal, 636–637
Shunt(s):
anatomic, 383
arteriovenous, for hemodialysis, 977, *978*
physiologic, 30–31, 383–384
Shunting in hypoxemia, 382–385
Sick role, psychosociodynamics of, 350–351
Sick role disturbance, self-conflict resulting from, 337
Sigmoid conduit for urinary diversion, 685
Signs, vital, in examination, 261–264
Silastic pouch for omphalocele or gastroschisis in neonate, 884
Silver nitrate:
in burn therapy for children, 893
in burn wound dressings, 779
Silver sulfadiazine in burn therapy for children, 893
Sinoatrial (SA) node, 287
conduction in, 38
Sinus arrest, 1108–1109
Sinus arrhythmia, 1107
Sinus bradycardia, *288*, 1105
drug therapy for, 921
Sinus rhythm, normal, 1104
Sinus tachycardia, *288*, 1106

Sinuses, assessment of, 270
Sinusoids, hepatic, 208
    and hepatocyte, relationship of, 209
Skeletal muscle, 227–231
    anatomy and histology of, 227–228
    contraction of, 228–230
        [*See also* Contraction(s), muscular]
    reaction of, to acute disorders and injuries, 235
Skeletal system, 221–226
    effects of kidney disease on, 666
    structure of, 221–223
    [*See also* Bone(s)]
Skene's ducts, 243–244
Skin, 211–220
    altering host resistance to sepsis, 823–824
    anatomy and physiology of, 743–744
    in assessment of patient with hematopoietic disorders, 580
    cancers of, in critical-care patients, 317–*318*
    color changes in, in physical assessment, 264
    in defense system, 439
    in diabetic ketoacidosis, 645
    effects of kidney disease on, 667–668
    effects of spinal cord injury and polyneuropathy on, 631–632
    flora of, 218–219
    grafting of, 791–794
        care following, 793
        donor site, care of, 793–794
        history of, 742
        procedure for, 792–793
        recipient site for, 791–792
        types of, 791
    innervation of, 214–216
    integrity of: altered, in hypothermia, 995
        in physical assessment, 265–268
    lesions of: bleeding, 267–*268*
        primary, 265–*266*
        secondary, 265, 266–*267*, 268
        vascular, 267–*268*, 268
    moisture of, in physical assessment, 264
    physical assessment of, 264–268
    problems of, application of physical assessment techniques to, 317, *318*
    resistance of, in defibrillation, 920
    structures of, physiology of, 211–218
        appendages of, 217–218
        dermis in, 213–216
        epidermis in, 212–213
        sebaceous glands in, 216

subcutaneous tissue in, 216–217
    temperature of, in physical assessment, 265
    texture of, in physical assessment, 265
    thermal injuries to, 268
    turgor of, in physical assessment, 265
    vascular network of, 213–214
Skull, 102–103
    assessment of, 269
Sliding filament hypothesis of muscle contraction, 229
Small intestine, 196–202
    [*See also* Intestine(s), small]
Smears in diagnosis of sepsis, 838
Smoking:
    carboxyhemoglobin levels and, 373
    chronic bronchitis due to, 515
    effects of, on platelets, 89
Smooth muscle, vascular, 63–64
Social disability in trauma victim, 817
Social integrity, conservation of, in critical-care nursing, 12
Social loss, stress of, for family from critical illness, 477–478
Social role disturbance, self-conflict resulting from, 337–338
Sodium:
    active transport of, by kidney, 156–157
    in adrenal crisis management, 653
    balance of: in homeostasis, 171
        maintenance of, in acute renal failure management, 668–669
    deficiency of, 405–406
    delivery of, to distal tubule, in potassium regulation, 406
    excess of, 404–405
    excretion of, effects of prostaglandins on, 176
    functions of, 402
    reabsorption of: by colon, 205
        renal, and potassium secretion, 165
        in urine formation, 161–162
    regulation of, 402–404
    serum levels of, in renal disease, 663–664
    in transmembrane potential development, 34
Sodium chloride in tubbing solution for burn care, 788
Sodium pumps, 161
Solumedrol in intracranial hypertension management, 617
Solutes, movements of, renal, 166–169
Somatomedin, stimulation of, by growth hormone, 132
Somatostatin, secretion of, 143

Somogyi phenomenon in hypoglycemia, 649, *650*
Spasm, 231
Spasticity, 297–298
Specific gravity:
    of blood, 80
    of urine, hourly testing of, in fluid therapy for burns, 757
Specificity in immune defenses, 444
Spectrometer, mass, 1026–1027
Spermatogenesis, 247
Spermatogenic cells of seminiferous tubules, 247
Spermatozoa, production of, 247
Sphincterotomy, 688
Sphincters, esophageal, 184
    regulation of, 184–185
Sphygmomanometer for indirect blood pressure measurement, 1002–1004
Spider telangiectasia, *267*
Spinal accessory nerve (XI):
    anatomy of, 111, *112*, 113
    assessment of, 294
    types and functions of, *113*
Spinal cord:
    anatomy of, 113–115
    circulation in, 109
    injury to: and disease of, urologic problems in, 692–693
        minimizing extent of, nursing care in, 634–637
        multisystem dysfunctions in, 629–632
        prevention of, 633–634
        segmental organization of, 623–625
        traumatic injuries to, management of, 807
Spinal cord receptors in regulation of peripheral regulation, 68
Spinal dura, 105
Spinal nerves, anatomy of, 113–115
Spine:
    examination of, in trauma victim, 802
    tuberculosis of, kyphoscoliosis due to, 509
Spiritual concerns:
    of critically ill, 1060–1063
    of patient: with carcinoma, 1061
        with cerebrovascular accident, 1061
        with coronary disease, 1060–1061
        with life-threatening complications, 1061–1062
        with neuromuscular diseases, 1061
    of victims: of burns, 1063
        of dismemberment, 1063
        of physical attack, 1063
        of sexual assault, 1063
        of violent accidents, 1062–1063

Spironolactone for pulmonary venous hypertension, 567
Splanchnic blood flow, 704, *705*
decreased, intestinal ischemia in, 704–708
(*See also* Intestines, ischemia of)
Spleen:
palpation of, 304
traumatic injuries to, management of, 811
Splenectomy:
in aplastic anemia treatment, 586
in hemolytic anemia treatment, 588
Splinter hemorrhages in nails in physical assessment, 268, *269*
Splinting in burn care, 771, *772–773*
Splitting of heart sounds, 288–289
Spondylitis, ankylosing, destruction of articular cartilage due to, 234
Sputum, smears of, in diagnosis of sepsis, 838
Squamous cell carcinoma in critical-care patients, *318*
S-T segment, 41–42
Stability in psychological equilibrium, 333
Stabilization:
of chest wall in flail chest management, 529
of high-risk neonate, 866–867
Stable factor, *93*, 95
Stable patient, application of physical assessment techniques to, 312–314
arrhythmias in, 312, *313*
cardiogenic shock in, 314
case history in, 312
congestive heart failure in, 312, *314*
thromboembolism in, 314
Staff in critical-care milieu, 344–346
Stagnant hypoxia, 374, *375*
Standstill, 1108–1109
Staphylococcus aureus:
in sepsis, 827
on skin, 219
Staphylococcus epidermidis:
in sepsis, 827
on skin, 219
Starling equilibrium in capillary dynamics, 47–49
Starling's law:
of capillaries, 64
of heart, 926
Status asthmaticus, 510, 512–513
treatment priorities for, 514–515
Status epilepticus, 620–622
Statutory consent, 1052
Stem-cell defects in congenital hypoimmune conditions, 464

Stem cells as origin of blood cells, 82
Stenosis:
aortic, murmur of, 291
mitral valve, opening snap of, 290
pulmonic, murmur of, 291
renal artery, pathogenesis of, 659–660
Stereognosis in assessment of cortical sensory perception, 299
Steroids, 126
adrenal, 139
in aplastic anemia treatment, 586
in adrenal crisis management, 653
in asthma therapy, 514
in congenital diaphragmatic hernia management in neonate, 886
in Crohn's disease treatment, 721
to minimize extent of spinal cord trauma, 636
in pulmonary contusion management, 528
in treatment of sepsis, 845–846
in ulcerative colitis treatment, 722
Stethoscope in auscultation, 259–260
Stoma, ileostomy, 724–725
Stomach, 185–191
gross anatomy of, 186
histology of, 186
motility of, 190
regulation of, 190–191
secretions of, 186–189
acid, 186–187
nonacid, 187–189
regulation of, 189
traumatic injuries to, management of, 810
wall of, tension in, effect of, on gastric motility, 190
Stones, cholesterol, formation of, in gallbladder, 194
Strangulation, intestinal, 708
Stratum corneum of epidermis, 212
Stratum germinativum of epidermis, 212
Stratum granulosum of epidermis, 212
Stratum spinosum of epidermis, 212
Streamlining in hemodynamics of circulation, 46
Streptococcus pneumoniae in sepsis, 827
Streptococcus pyogenes in sepsis, 827
Streptokinase in pulmonary thromboembolism therapy, 522
Streptomycin sulfate, 1175
Stress, 324–325
anatomy of, 325
glucocorticoid secretion in, 139
guides for nursing action related to, 327–328

immunity and, 465–466
in pediatric critical-care unit, 880
physical, in bone remodeling, 226
theories of, beyond Selye, 325
in trauma unit, 818
Stress ulcers, gastrointestinal hemorrhage secondary to, 704
Stretch receptors in regulation of peripheral regulation, 68
Stretch reflexes, 123
Stroke:
brainstem, loss of airway protection in, 626
in critical-care patients, *320*
Stroke volume:
control of, in control of heart rate, 75–76
definition of, 72
Structural integrity, conservation of, in critical-care nursing, 11
Struvite stones, 663
Stuart-Prower factor, *93*, 96
Stuporous, definition of, 292
Subarachnoid hemorrhage in high-risk neonate, 874–875
Subarachnoid space, 105
Subarachnoid technique for intracranial pressure monitoring, 1020, *1021*
Subclavian vein as entry site for total parenteral nutrition, 982–983
Subcutaneous tissue, 216–217
Subdeltoid bursa, 227
Subdural hemorrhage in high-risk neonate, 874
Subdural space, 105
Submucosa of gastrointestinal tract, 181
Suctioning:
as adjunct to ventilation, 916–917
of airway in management of patient on continuous assisted ventilation, 960–961
Sugar in urine, hourly testing of, in fluid therapy for burns, 757
Sulci of cerebral hemispheres, 110
Sulfamylon in burn therapy for children, 893
Sulfate, functions and regulation of, 421
Summation contraction, 230
Superficial pain in assessment of sensory system, 299
Support devices, psychological disequilibrium due to, 338
Suprapubic cystostomy, 683–685
Suprasegmental neurologic lesions, 623, *624*
Supraventricular arrhythmias, 571–572
Supraventricular tachyarrhythmias, atrial pacing for, 573

Supraventricular tachycardias, atrial pacing for, 573
Surfactant:
  decreased levels of, atelectasis due to, 533
  in gas distribution, 18
  in protection against respiratory distress syndrome in neonate, 869
Swallowing, 182, *183*
Swan-Ganz catheter:
  in hemorrhagic shock treatment, 699
  in trauma victim management, procedures for, 803
Swan-Ganz thermodilution catheter in ARDS management, 495
Sweat glands, 217
Sylvius:
  aqueduct of, 105, 107
  fissure of, 110
Sympathetic nervous system, 115
  in bronchospasm of asthma, 511
  in control of heart rate, 74
Symphysis, 226
Synaptic cleft in nerve impulse conduction for muscular contraction, 228
Synchondrosis joints, 226
Synchronized cardioversion in advanced life support, 919–921
Syndesmosis joints, 226
Synostosis joints, 226
Synovial fluid of joint, 226–227
Synovial joints, 226
  reaction of, to acute disorders and injuries, 234–235
Synovial membrane, reactions of, to acute disorders and injuries, 235
System(s):
  around critical-care patient, openness of, in psychosocial assessment of family adjustment, 352–353
  definition of, 10
System antagonists in coagulation mechanism, 97
Systemic changes in host response to sepsis, 832
Systole:
  atrial, 61
  extra heart sounds heard in, 290
  ventricular, 60
Systolic murmurs, 291
Systolic pressure, 70
Systolic wall stress in approximating afterload, 567

T-cell subsets in immune response, 449
T lymphocytes, 88, 147–148

in cell-mediated immunity, 461
circulation patterns of, 446, 448
defects of, in congenital hypoimmune conditions, 464
identification of, 449
in immune response, 446, 449
T tube drainage after surgery for sclerosing cholangitis, 730–731
T tubules in nerve impulse conduction for muscular contraction, 228
T wave, 42
Tachyarrhythmia(s):
  diagnosis and effects of, 572
  in sepsis, 836
  supraventricular, atrial pacing for, 573
Tachycardia(s):
  in atelectasis, 533
  atrial, paroxysmal, *288*, 1113–1114
  junctional, 1121–1122
  in pulmonary contusion, 528
  in pulmonary thromboembolism, 519
  in sepsis, 836
  sinus, *288*, 1106
  supraventricular, atrial pacing for, 573
  ventricular, *288*, 1127
    drug therapy for, 922
    in myocardial infarction, *313*
Tachypnea, 262, *263*
  of newborn, transient, in high-risk neonate, 870
  in pulmonary contusion, 528
Tactile fremitus in palpation of chest, 280
Tactile receptors in dermis, 214–215
Taeniae coli, 203, *204*
Talc, iodized, pleurodesis with, in pleural effusion management, 509
Tamponade:
  cardiac: complicating surgery with extracorporeal circulation, 953
    in renal disease, 665
  pericardial, in trauma victim, management of, 809–810
Tangential excision in burn wound debridement, 783, *784*
Taste buds, 182
Teaching of patient and family:
  effects of, 1071–1072
  programs for, 1088–1099
    assessment in, 1074–1076
    development of, 1072–1098
    implementation in, 1081–1088
    need for, 1072
      documentation of, 1073–1074
    planning in, 1076–1081
Technology in critical-care nursing, 7
Telangiectasia, spider, *267*
Telegen, 218

Telemetry, electrocardiogram, in ECG monitor, 1001
Temperature:
  body: in physical assessment, 261
    regulation of (*see* Thermoregulation)
  monitor for, 1002
  perception of, in assessment of sensory system, 299
  of skin in physical assessment, 265
Temporal lobes of cerebral cortex, functions of, 117, *119*
Tenderness, rebound, in diagnosis of intestinal obstruction, 709
Tendons, 231
  burns of, care of, 785–786
Tensilon for myasthenia gravis, 632–633
Tension pneumothorax, 531
Tentorium, 105
Terbutaline in asthma therapy, 514
Terminal hair, 271–218
Test-tape for urine sugar testing, 642, *643*
Testis(es), 145–146, 247–248
  cancer of, surgery for, 692
  cryptorchid, surgery for, 691–692
  location of, *126*
  surgery of, 691–692
  torsion of, surgery for, 692
Testosterone, 145–146
  production of, regulation of, 247–248
Tetanic contraction, 231
Tetanus, motor disorders from, *635*
  prevention of, 634
Tetany in parathormone insufficiency, 138
Tetracycline hydrochloride, 1175–1176
Tetraiodothyronine (T$_4$), 136, 137
Texas catheters, 678–679
Texture of skin in physical assessment, 265
Theophylline in asthma therapy, 514
Therapeutic instrumentation, 1029–1031
Thermal injury(ies)
  localized decrease in growth due to, 234
  to skin, 268
Thermal receptors in dermis, 215–216
Thermodilution in measurement of cardiac output, 73, 1022–1024
Thermoregulation:
  in critically ill neonate, attention to, 881
  eccrine sweat glands in, 217
  effects of spinal cord injury and polyneuropathy on, 630
  in high-risk neonate, 867, 871
  in myxedema coma management, 652
  skin vasculature in, 213–214
  sweat glands in, 211

Thiopental sodium for injection, 1176
Third-degree heart block, 1133
Third factor in sodium regulation, 403
Thirst:
    regulation of, 180
    in regulation of body water, 398
    in regulation of osmolality of body
        fluids, 394–395
Thoracentesis in pleural effusion man-
    agement, 508
Thoracic aorta, traumatic injuries to,
    management of, 810
Thoracic cage, inspection of, 278–279
Thoracostomy tube in trauma victim
    management, procedures for, 804
Thoracotomy in trauma victim manage-
    ment, procedures for, 805
Thorel's pathway in impulse conduc-
    tion, 38
Thrill in monitoring patency of arterio-
    venous fistula, 978
Thrombin in coagulation, 97
Thrombocytes (*see* Platelets)
Thrombocytopenia:
    hemorrhagic diatheses due to, 91
    relative and absolute, 90
Thromboembolic phenomena in dia-
    betic patient management, 644
Thromboembolism:
    in assessment of myocardial infarc-
        tion, 314
    complicating balloon pumping, 943
    pulmonary, 518–523
        (*See also* Pulmonary thromboem-
        bolism)
Thromboembolus, pulmonary damage
    from, in ARDS, 488
Thrombophlebitis, postpartal, 864
Thromboplastin, tissue, *93*, 94–95
Thrombopoiesis, control of, 83
Thrombopoietin, effect of, on platelet
    production and levels, 89
Thrombosis:
    acute occlusive mesenteric ischemia
        from, 704–705
    complicating pulmonary artery pres-
        sure monitoring, prevention of,
        1014
    deep vein, prevention of, in pulmo-
        nary thromboembolism therapy,
        522–523
    vascular, complicating diabetic ke-
        toacidosis, 647
Thymosin, 147–148
Thymus, 147–148
    location of, *126*
Thymus-dependent lymphocyte, 88
Thyrocalcitonin, 138
Thyroid crises, 650–652
Thyroid gland, 136–138

assessment of, 270
    location of, *126*
Thyroid-stimulating hormone (TSH),
    131
Thyroid storm, 651–652
Thyrotoxic crises, 651–652
Thyrotoxicosis, 137
Thyroxine (T₄), 136–137
Tidal volume, 16
Tight junction in myocardium, 57
Tissue(s):
    and blood, gas exchange between,
        371–372
    injury to, DIC due to, 594
    metabolic demands of, in internal
        respiration, 371
    musculoskeletal, reactions of, to
        acute disorders and injuries,
        231–235
    subcutaneous, 216–217
Tissue hormones, 126
Tissue thromboplastin, *93*, 94–95
Titratable acidity, formation of, in regu-
    lation of bicarbonate concentra-
    tion, 172–173
Tobramycin sulfate, 1177
Toddler:
    burns in, 889–894
        (*See also* Burns, in toddler)
    development of, illness and,
        886–887
Tomography, axial, computerized, in
    detection of brain lesion, 611
Tongue, 182
    assessment of, 270
Tonic contraction, 230
Tonicity, definition of, 391
Topical agents in burn wound care,
    779
Torulopsis glabrata in sepsis, 830
Touch in assessment of sensory sys-
    tem, 299
Toxic megacolon complicating ulcera-
    tive colitis, 723
Toxoplasma gondii in sepsis, 831
Trace elements in total parenteral nu-
    trition solution, metabolic signifi-
    cance of, 986
Trachea:
    alignment of, palpation for, 280
    assessment of, 270–271
    complications of mechanical ventila-
        tion involving, 967
Tracheoesophageal fistulas:
    in high-risk neonate, 870
    in neonate, 882–884
Tracheostomy:
    altering host resistance to sepsis,
        824
    emergency, indications for, 798–799

Traction, continuous, for fracture re-
    duction, 813
Transducers in direct blood pressure
    monitoring, 1004–1008
    balancing of, 1007–1008
    calibration of, 1007–1008, *1009*
    differential transformer in, 1007
    range of, 1007
    semiconductor in, 1006–1007, *1008*
    standard size, bedside setup for,
        1010–1011, *1013*
    unbounded strain gauge in, 1006, *1007*
Transfusion(s):
    blood: in acute leukemia treatment,
        590
        in aplastic anemia treatment, 585
        exchange, for pathologic neonatal
            jaundice, 876
        in hemolytic anemia treatment,
            587–588
    granulocyte, in aplastic anemia
        treatment, 585
Transient tachypnea of newborn in
    high-risk neonate, 870
Transmembrane hydrostatic pressure,
    672
Transmembrane potential of cardiac
    cells, 33–35
Transmission of nerve impulses, 115, *117*
Transmural disease, 720–721
Transplantation:
    bone marrow: in acute leukemia
        treatment, 590
        in aplastic anemia treatment, 586
    renal, 673–677
        [*See also* Kidney(s), transplanta-
        tion of]
Transplants, delayed hypersensitivity
    and, 462
Transport:
    active, in renal system, 156–157
    carrier-mediated, in renal system,
        157–158
    fluid and electrolyte, 395–396
    following cardiac arrest, stabilization
        of patient condition for, 922
    of high-risk neonate, 867–868
Transport maximum (Tm)-limited se-
    cretion in urine formation, 163–164
Transpulmonary pressure in gas distri-
    bution, 18
Transtentorial herniation, 600–610
    assessment of: brain function cate-
        gories in, 601, *602*
        eye signs in, 608–610
        level of consciousness in,
            601–602
        motor function in, 602–606
        respiratory patterns in, 606–608
        vital signs in, 610

Transtracheal catheterization in cardiac arrest, 917
Transudates, pleural effusions as, 508
Transurethral surgery, 687
  complications of, 688–689
  for resection of bladder tumors, 688
  for resection of prostate, 687
    complications of, long-term, 689
    patient care after, 687–688
Traube's semilunar space, 277, *279*
Trauma:
  management of, 795–818
    ICU care in, 814–817
      care of combined injuries in, 814
      care of injury with concomitant organ failure in, 815
      drains in, 815
      monitoring in, 814
      recordkeeping for, 815, *816*
      tubes in, 815
      wound care in, 815
    initial resuscitation in, 797–806
      (*See also* Resuscitation, initial, in trauma management)
    at scene of accident, 796–797
    for specific injuries, 806–814
      (*See also specific body parts; e.g.,* Chest; Head)
    morbidity of, 817–818
    neck, airway problems in, 798
    victims of, as potential organ donors, 815–816
Traumatic hemopneumothorax in trauma victim, management of, 809
Tremors, 298
Treppe phenomenon, 76
Triamterene for pulmonary venous hypertension, 567
Tricuspid valve:
  functional anatomy of, 53
  regurgitation through, murmur of, 291
Trigeminal nerve (V):
  anatomy of, 111, *112*
  assessment of, 293
  type and functions of, *113*
Triglycerides, digestion and absorption of, 200–202
Triiodothyronine (T_3), 136, 137
Trimethoprim-sulfamethoxazole, 1177–1178
Trochlear nerve (IV):
  anatomy of, 111, *112*
  assessment of, 293
  type and functions of, *113*
Tropic hormones, 128
  anterior pituitary, 131–132
Trypsinogen, 192

Tube feeding:
  for burn patient, 768
  elemental diets for, 738
Tuberculosis of spine, kyphoscoliosis due to, 509
Tuberculous peritonitis, 712
Tubes, fallopian, 239
Tubular breath sounds, 281, *282*
Tubular necrosis, acute, complicating acute hemorrhagic shock, 699, 701
Tubular reabsorption in urine formation, 160–163
Tubular secretion in urine formation, 163–165
Tubule(s):
  distal, sodium delivery to, in potassium regulation, 406
  necrosis of, acute, complicating surgery with extracorporeal circulation, 954
  renal, 153
Tumor(s):
  bladder, transurethral resection of, 688
  brain, neurologic disorders, 900–902
  kidney, surgery for, 690
  pancreatic, in Zollinger-Ellison syndrome, 718
  skin, *265*
Tunica albuginea:
  covering testis, 247
  of penis, 245
Turgor of skin in physical assessment, 265
Twitch contraction, 230

Ulcer(s):
  Curling's, postburn, prevention of, 767
    in children, 894
  Cushing-Rotikansky, postcraniotomy, in child, management of, 901
  decubitis, in critical-care patients, *317*
  duodenal, in renal disease, 665
  peptic: gastrointestinal hemorrhage secondary to, 703
    perforated, peritonitis secondary to, 712
    Zollinger-Ellison syndrome, 718
  skin, *267*
  stress, gastrointestinal hemorrhage secondary to, 704
Ulcerative colitis, 722–723
  continent internal pouch for, 728–729
  ileostomy for, 724–728
    (*See also* Ileostomy)
  nursing intervention in, 723–724

Ulnar nerve, paresis of, complicating surgery with extracorporeal circulation, 954
Umbilical cord, prolapsed, management of, 861–862
Uncal herniation, 610
Unique, definition of, 11
Urea:
  reabsorption of: by passive diffusion, 156
    in urine formation, 163
  role of, in concentration of urine, 169
Uremia, 658
  altering host resistance to sepsis, 825
Uremic amaurosis in renal disease, 667
Uremic lung in renal disease, 665
Ureter(s):
  congenital anomalies of, surgery for, 689–690
  malignancies of, surgery for, 690
  open urologic surgery on, 689–690
  stones in, surgery for, 690
  trauma to, 694
Ureterolithotomy, 690
Ureterosigmoidostomy for urinary diversion, 685–686
Ureterostomies, *684*, 685
Urethra:
  orifice of, 243
  stricture of: complicating catheterization, 681–682
    complicating transurethral resection of prostate, 689
  surgery of, 691
  trauma to, 695
    management of, 812
Urgency, urinary, 307
Uric acid calculi, 663
Urinary diversion:
  patients with, postoperative care of, 686
  permanent, 685–686
  temporary, 683–685
Urinary extravasation, perforation and, complicating cystoscopy and transurethral surgery, 688–689
Urinary incontinence, 695
Urinary meatus, 243
Urinary sepsis complicating cystoscopy and transurethral surgery, 688
Urinary tract:
  assessment of, 307
  infections of, postpartum, 864
  perforation of, and urinary extravasation complicating cystoscopy and transurethral surgery, 688–689

Urine:
  flow rates of, in potassium regulation, 407
  formation of, 158–169
    concept of clearance in, 160
    glomerular filtration in, 158–160
    renal concentrating and diluting mechanisms in, 165–169
    tubular reabsorption in, 160–163
    tubular secretion in, 163–165
  hourly testing of, in fluid therapy for burns, 756–757
  output of, monitoring of, in fluid therapy for burns, 756–758
  renal concentration of, in regulation of body water, 397–398
  renal dilution of, in regulation of body water, 398
  retention: of acute, 682–683
    complicating cystoscopy and transurethral surgery, 689
  smears of, in diagnosis of sepsis, 838
Urokinase in pulmonary thromboembolism therapy, 522
Urologic emergencies, 682–683
Urologic endoscopic surgery, 686–689
Urologic surgery, open, 689–692
Urology, 678–695
Uterus, 239–242
  contraction of, oxytocin in, 134
  rupture of, diagnostic and management of, 858–859

Vagal stimulation of SA node, effects of, 38
Vagina, 242–243
  orifice of, 243, 244
Vagus nerve:
  anatomy of, 111, *112*
  assessment of, 294
  in regulation of cephalic phase of hydrochloric acid secretion, 189
  in regulation of lower esophageal sphincter, 184
  in regulation of pancreatic secretion, 193
  type and functions of, *113*
Valium in status epilepticus treatment, 621
Valsalva, sinuses of, 53
Valsalva maneuver for catheter insertion for TPN, 983
Valve(s):
  aortic, regurgitation through, murmur of, 291
  cardiac, functional anatomy of, 53
  mitral: regurgitation through, murmur of, 291

stenosis of, opening snap of, 290
  triscuspid, regurgitation through, murmur of, 291
van Buren filiforms for dilating urethral strictures, 681–682
van Buren sounds for dilating urethral strictures, 681
Varicella virus, pneumonia due to, 497
Varicella-Zoster virus in sepsis, 830
Varices, esophageal, 183
  gastrointestinal hemorrhage secondary to, 701–703
Vasa recta of kidneys, 152
Vascular (*see* Blood vessels)
Vascular access for hemodialysis, 977
Vascular lines, risks associated with, 1015–*1019*
Vascular network of skin, 213–214
Vascular system, supplying central nervous system, 108
Vascular thrombosis complicating diabetic ketoacidosis, 647
Vascular tree, 62–64
Vas deferens in sperm transport, 248
Vasoactive polypeptides, release of, in sepsis, 832
Vasoactive substances in host response to sepsis, 832
Vasoconstriction:
  in gastrointestinal hemorrhage, 697
  in hypothermia, 992
Vasodilatation, sympathetic, in regulation of peripheral regulation, 67–68
Vasodilators:
  for low cardiac output, 561–568
  for prevention of angina, 569–570
  for pulmonary venous hypertension, 565–567
  in treatment of sepsis, 846–847
Vasomotion in peripheral circulation, 64
Vasomotor system in regulation of peripheral regulation, 67
Vasopressin, 134–136
  deficient, in diabetic insipidus, 662
  in regulation of peripheral regulation, 69
  in treatment of esophageal varices, 703
Vasopressin tannate, 1178
Vasopressors in treatment of sepsis, 846
Vectorcardiogram, 42, 44
Veillonella in sepsis, 829
Vein(s):
  brachial, as entry site for total parenteral nutrition, 982
  of brain, 109
  central, for intravenous lifeline, 918

of colon, 203–204
  of esophagus, 183
  femoral, as entry site for total parenteral nutrition, 982
  of gallbladder, 194
  of penis, 246
  peripheral, for intravenous lifeline, 918
  of small intestine, 197
  of spinal cord, 109
  subclavian, as entry site for total parenteral nutrition, 982–983
  systemic, in sepsis, 834
  in systemic circulation, 50
  vulva, 244
Vellus hair, 217
Veno-arterial bypass, 928–929
Ventilation, 16–18
  adjuncts, to, in advanced life support, 915–917
  alveolar, 16
    in hypoxemia, 377
  alveolar minute, increase in, reflex, in ARDS, 489
  assisted: for high-risk neonate, 871
    in intracranial hypertension management, 616
  definition of, 364
  failure of, mechanical ventilation for, 959
  gas distribution in, 18
  ineffective, atelectasis due to, 533
  intermittent mandatory, in weaning from mechanical ventilation, 966–967
  mechanical, 957–969
    (*See also* Mechanical ventilation)
  positive-pressure, in resuscitation of neonate, 866
  resistance in, sources of, 17–18
  support of, in pulmonary contusion management, 528
Ventilation lung scan in diagnosis of pulmonary thromboembolism, 520-521
Ventilation/perfusion abnormalities in hypoxemia, 379–382
Ventilation/perfusion ratio, abnormalities of, 30–31
Ventilators, mechanical, classification of, 958–959
Ventilatory pattern in management of patient on continuous assisted ventilation, 961–963
Ventricles, cardiac, 283
  aneurysm of, intra-aortic balloon pumping for, 936
  auxiliary, for afterload reduction, historical evolution of, 930

Ventricles, cardiac (*Cont.*):
contractility of, in control of cardiac output, 76–77
distensibility of, in control of cardiac output, 76
excitation of, 42–44
functional anatomy of, 53–55
left, hypertrophy of, complicating obesity, 734
pacing of, indications for, 575
Ventricular contractions, premature, 1123–1125
drug therapy for, 922
Ventricular ejection, 61
Ventricular escape beats, 1126
Ventricular escape rhythms, 1126
Ventricular fibrillation, 1128
drug therapy for, 922
reversing, 919–921
Ventricular gallop in assessment of unstable cardiac patient, 545
Ventricular pressure, right, monitoring of, direct, 1014
Ventricular system, 105, 107
Ventricular systole, 60
Ventricular tachycardia, *288*, 1127
drug therapy for, 922
in myocardial infarction, *313*
Verapamil, effects of, on ventricular contractility, 571
Vermis, 111
Vertebrae, 104
Vertebral column, 103–105
Vesicle, *266*
Vesicostomy, 684, 685
Vesicoureteral reflux, surgery for, 690
Vesicular breath sounds, 281, *282*
Vestibule, 243–244
Vestibulospinal motor tracts, 622
Vibratory sense in assessment of sensory system, 299
Villi of small intestine, 197, *198*
Vincristine as anticancer drug, *906*
Viral infections, delayed hypersensitivity and, 462
Viral pneumonia, 497
Viruses in sepsis, 830–831
Visceral reflexes, 123
Viscosity in hemodynamics of circulation, 45
Viscous resistance in ventilation, 17

Vision:
blurred, in renal disease, 667
problems with, in hyperviscosity syndrome, 582
Visual acuity, assessment of, 272
Visual fields, assessment of, 272–273
Vital capacity, decreased, in oxygen toxicity, 499–500
Vital signs:
in assessing transtentorial herniation, 610
in examination, 261–264
Vitamin(s):
absorption of, by small intestine, 202
B$_{12}$, absorption of, intrinsic factor in, 187–188
D: active renal production of, effects of parathormone on, 138
in calcium absorption, 223
effects of kidney disease on, 667
metabolism of, 223
renal conversion of, 175–176
K: availability and absorption of, 592–593
production of, in colon, 206
in prothrombin synthesis, 94
in total parenteral nutrition solution, 982
Vitamin K-dependent coagulation disorders, 592–593
Voice sounds, auscultation of, 281–282
Voltage, 1038
Volume-cycled ventilators, 958
Vomiting in intestinal obstruction, 709
Vomiting reflex, 191
Vulva, *238*, 243–244
Vulvovaginal glands, 243–244

Waldenström's macroglobulinemia, hyperviscosity in, 581–584
Wandering atrial pacemaker, 1110
Warfarin sodium, 1179
Water:
absorption of, by small intestine, 202
body: functions of, 397
regulation of, 397–398
total, 390
movements of, renal, 166–169
partial pressures of, 19
in tubbing solution for burn care, 788

Watt, 1039
Weakness:
in assessment of transtentorial herniation, 606
in renal disease, 666
Weber's test for cochlear portion of acoustic nerve, 294
Wenckebach heart block, 1131
Wenckebach's tract impulse conduction, 38
Weston-Roberts trocar catheter in peritoneal dialysis, 974
Wet lung syndrome complicating acute hemorrhagic shock, 699
Wheal, *266*
Wheezes, 282, *283*
Wheezing in asthma, 510
Whispering pectorioquy, 282
White blood cell count in diagnosis of sepsis, 836–837
White blood cells (*see* Leukocytes)
Willis, circle of, 108–109
Wirsung, duct of, 191–192
Wound(s):
burn: care of: debridement in, 782–783
dressing change procedure in, 779–782
principles of, 777
routine orders for, 777, 779
topical agents in, 779
infection in, 763–765
sepsis in, 765–766
care of, in trauma victim, 806
in ICU, 815
healing of, 219–220
hematoma of, postcraniotomy, in child, management of, 901
Wright respirometer in respiratory volume monitoring, 1026

Xenograft, 791, 792

Zollinger-Ellison syndrome:
diagnosis of, 718–719
nursing intervention in, 719–720
treatment of, 719
Zymogen granules in acinus of exocrine pancreas, 192

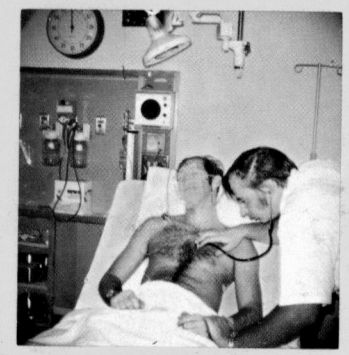
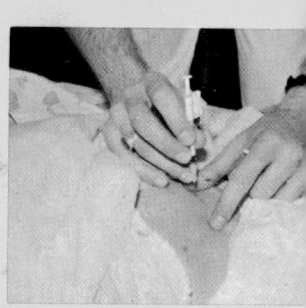
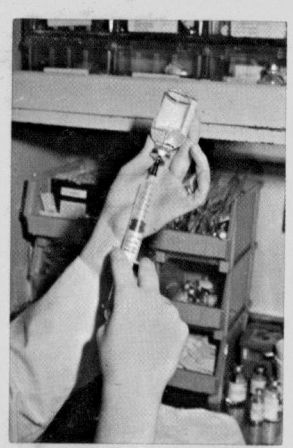
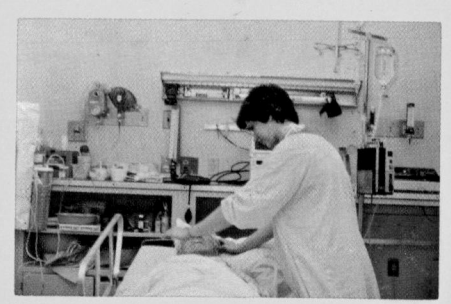
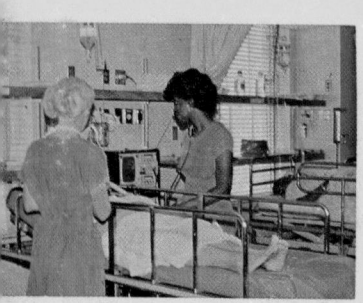
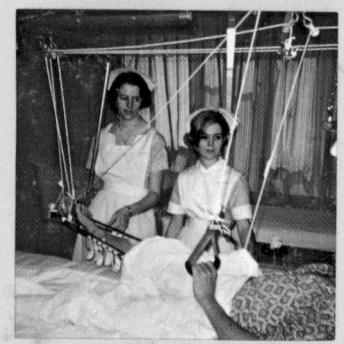

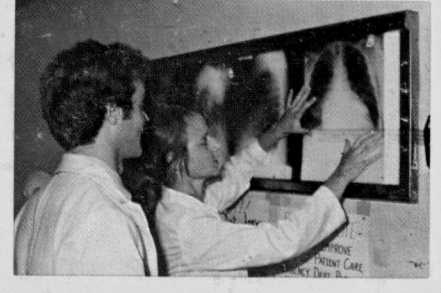
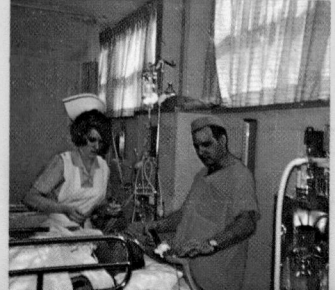